# JONATHAN STRANGE & MR NORRELL

# JONATHAN STRANGE
# &
# MR NORRELL

Susanna Clarke

Illustrations by Portia Rosenberg

BLOOMSBURY

First published in 2004 by Bloomsbury
This paperback edition published 2007



Bloomsbury Publishing Plc, 36 Soho Square, London W1D 3QY

A CIP catalogue record for this book is available from the British Library

ISBN 9780747590057

10 9 8 7 6 5 4 3 2 1

Typeset by Hewer Text UK Ltd, Edinburgh
Printed in Great Britain by Clays Ltd, St Ives plc

Bloomsbury Publishing, London, New York and Berlin

www.bloomsbury.com/susannaclarke
www.jonathanstrange.com

The paper this book is printed on is certified by the © Forest Stewardship Council 1996 A.C. (FSC). It is ancient-forest friendly.
The printer holds FSC chain of custody SGS-COC-2061

# Introduction
## Audrey Niffenegger

Several years ago my family members were passing around the books of a certain British lady novelist who writes about the doings of wizards and such. My father, who is a Civil Engineer and not a Reader of Fiction, was entranced by the books. He had never encountered anything quite like them. At one point he turned to my sister and said, with perplexity and wonder in his voice, 'But – does she really *make it all up*?'

We all assured him that she did, indeed. But we could tell that he didn't exactly believe us, and that the books would have lost some of their lustre if he had been forced to truly think that they were only *made up*.

I feel that way about Susanna Clarke's masterpiece, *Jonathan Strange & Mr Norrell*. Surely something so charming, so authoritative, so heavily footnoted cannot be simply ... invented. The History of English Magic: it must be out there somewhere, along with all those less amusing things we learned at school. Somewhere in an attic stuck between the Treaty of Versailles and a box of used spats there must be a whole steamer trunk filled with the works of Martin Pale and William Pantler and back issues of *The Friends of English Magic*. We take so much on faith, when it comes to History. Surely we should not be unduly surprised to discover an entire discipline such as Theoretical and Practical Magic hiding in plain sight under 'C' on the Fiction shelves of our local bookstore?

Fantasy is simply the branch of literature which contains a very high ratio of invented things to real things. Susanna Clarke straddles the line – her inventions dovetail so perfectly with things we know to be true (though how we know this is another perplexing question) that after spending an afternoon with Jonathan Strange doing magic in the service of Lord Wellington or kibitzing with Lord Byron it is no wonder that some of us yearn for the good old days of English Magic, or start hunting in the *Encyclopaedia Britannica* for the Raven King. (Though what name would he be under? And who would write that article? Perhaps Lord Portishead would oblige.)

But *Jonathan Strange & Mr Norrell* is not only about the Revival of English Magic. English Magic is a fine excuse for the protracted pondering of human nature. The book is about the greed and wonder that scholars feel in the presence of books; the perils of marrying a magician and thus attracting the attention of selfish and amoral fairies; the satisfactions we can only achieve by conversing with other people who are devoted to the same obscure pursuits we ourselves cannot live without. It is, in short, a book about the irrational love of knowledge, the past, the unknown, the beloved. Since the only kind of love worth talking about is irrational, and the irrational is usually dangerous, it may follow that *Jonathan Strange & Mr Norrell* is a demonstration of the perils and pleasures of attempting to master that which one loves but does not understand.

A lack of total comprehension is something many of

Susanna Clarke's characters share. A little knowledge *is* a dangerous thing, as her magicians demonstrate repeatedly at other people's expense. Some of the book's most hilarious and agonising moments come when characters who have spent half the book enchanted attempt to make themselves understood: we, the readers, hear their pleas, but our magic is only strong enough to imagine them; we cannot help them.

*Jonathan Strange & Mr Norrell* is also about nostalgia, the yearning for that period of time when They Really Knew How to Do Things Properly. The irony, of course, is that all the characters in *Jonathan Strange & Mr Norrell* yearn for an earlier, more effective period of English Magic, when all the spells still worked, while those of us in the present day audience would happily settle for one tiny verifiable act of the most minor magic imaginable. We find ourselves in the Non-Existent Era of English Magic, in which none of the spells work and no one is here to Revive Magic, English or otherwise. We live in an era where technology must suffice; we have mobile phones and iPods to fill the gap that Magic (and God) left when they tapered off sometime in the almost imaginary past. But the gap is immense; we want magic. Only magic will do.

Susanna Clarke has invented for us a very beautiful, subtle, and wholly satisfying history, complete with tinctures of madness and Pillars of Darkness, books that become ravens and characters that become so real one cannot bear to leave them at the final chapter. Fortunately for you, you are not yet at page 1006: you are safely at the beginning of this marvellous book, and once you turn this page English Magic will live again. So go ahead; revive it: enjoy, and beware.

In memory of my brother,
Paul Frederick Gunn Clarke, 1961–2000

# CONTENTS

# Volume I

# Mr NORRELL

He hardly ever spoke of magic, and when he did it was like a history lesson and no one could bear to listen to him.

# 1

# The library at Hurtfew

## Autumn 1806–January 1807

SOME YEARS AGO there was in the city of York a society of magicians. They met upon the third Wednesday of every month and read each other long, dull papers upon the history of English magic.

They were gentleman-magicians, which is to say they had never harmed any one by magic – nor ever done any one the slightest good. In fact, to own the truth, not one of these magicians had ever cast the smallest spell, nor by magic caused one leaf to tremble upon a tree, made one mote of dust to alter its course or changed a single hair upon any one's head. But, with this one minor reservation, they enjoyed a reputation as some of the wisest and most magical gentlemen in Yorkshire.

A great magician has said of his profession that its practitioners ". . . must pound and rack their brains to make the least learning go in, but quarrelling always comes very naturally to them,"[1] and the York magicians had proved the truth of this for a number of years.

In the autumn of 1806 they received an addition in a gentleman called John Segundus. At the first meeting that he attended Mr Segundus rose and addressed the society. He began by compli-

[1] *The History and Practice of English Magic*, by Jonathan Strange, vol. I, chap. 2, pub. John Murray, London, 1816.

menting the gentlemen upon their distinguished history; he listed the many celebrated magicians and historians that had at one time or another belonged to the York society. He hinted that it had been no small inducement to him in coming to York to know of the existence of such a society. Northern magicians, he reminded his audience, had always been better respected than southern ones. Mr Segundus said that he had studied magic for many years and knew the histories of all the great magicians of long ago. He read the new publications upon the subject and had even made a modest contribution to their number, but recently he had begun to wonder why the great feats of magic that he read about remained on the pages of his book and were no longer seen in the street or written about in the newspapers. Mr Segundus wished to know, he said, why modern magicians were unable to work the magic they wrote about. In short, he wished to know why there was no more magic done in England.

It was the most commonplace question in the world. It was the question which, sooner or later, every child in the kingdom asks his governess or his schoolmaster or his parent. Yet the learned members of the York society did not at all like hearing it asked and the reason was this: they were no more able to answer it than any one else.

The President of the York society (whose name was Dr Foxcastle) turned to John Segundus and explained that the question was a wrong one. "It presupposes that magicians have some sort of duty to do magic – which is clearly nonsense. You would not, I imagine, suggest that it is the task of botanists to devise more flowers? Or that astronomers should labour to rearrange the stars? Magicians, Mr Segundus, study magic which was done long ago. Why should any one expect more?"

An elderly gentleman with faint blue eyes and faintly-coloured clothes (called either Hart or Hunt – Mr Segundus could never quite catch the name) faintly said that it did not matter in the least whether any body expected it or not. A gentleman could not do magic. Magic was what street sorcerers pretended to do in order to rob children of their pennies. Magic (in the practical sense) was much fallen off. It had low connexions. It was the bosom companion of unshaven faces, gypsies, house-breakers; the frequenter of dingy rooms with dirty yellow curtains. Oh no! A gentleman could not do magic. A gentleman might study the history of magic (nothing could be nobler) but he could not do any. The elderly gentleman looked with faint, fatherly eyes at Mr Segundus and said that he hoped Mr Segundus had not been trying to cast spells.

Mr Segundus blushed.

But the famous magician's maxim held true: two magicians – in this case Dr Foxcastle and Mr Hunt or Hart – could not agree without two more thinking the exact opposite. Several of the gentlemen began to discover that they were entirely of Mr Segundus's opinion and that no question in all of magical scholarship could be so important as this one. Chief among Mr Segundus's supporters was a gentleman called Honeyfoot, a pleasant, friendly sort of man of fifty-five, with a red face and grey hair. As the exchanges became more bitter and Dr Foxcastle grew in sarcasm towards Mr Segundus, Mr Honeyfoot turned to him several times and whispered such comfort as, "Do not mind them, sir. I am entirely of your opinion;" and "You are quite right, sir, do not let them sway you;" and "You have hit upon it! Indeed you have, sir! It was the want of the right question which held us back before. Now that you are come we shall do great things."

Such kind words as these did not fail to find a grateful listener in John Segundus, whose shock shewed clearly in his face. "I fear that I have made myself disagreeable," he whispered to Mr Honeyfoot. "That was not my intention. I had hoped for these gentlemen's good opinion."

At first Mr Segundus was inclined to be downcast but a particularly spiteful outburst from Dr Foxcastle roused him to a little indignation. "That gentleman," said Dr Foxcastle, fixing Mr Segundus with a cold stare, "seems determined that we should share in the unhappy fate of the Society of Manchester Magicians!"

Mr Segundus inclined his head towards Mr Honeyfoot and said, "I had not expected to find the magicians of Yorkshire quite so obstinate. If magic does not have friends in Yorkshire where may we find them?"

Mr Honeyfoot's kindness to Mr Segundus did not end with that evening. He invited Mr Segundus to his house in High-Petergate to eat a good dinner in company with Mrs Honeyfoot and her three pretty daughters, which Mr Segundus, who was a single gentleman and not rich, was glad to do. After dinner Miss Honeyfoot played the pianoforte and Miss Jane sang in Italian. The next day Mrs Honeyfoot told her husband that John Segundus was exactly what a gentleman should be, but she feared he would never profit by it for it was not the fashion to be modest and quiet and kind-hearted.

The intimacy between the two gentlemen advanced very rapidly. Soon Mr Segundus was spending two or three evenings out of every seven at the house in High-Petergate. Once there was quite a crowd of young people present which naturally led to dancing. It was all very delightful but often Mr Honeyfoot and Mr Segundus would slip away to discuss the one thing which really interested both of them – why was there no more magic done in England? But talk as they would (often till two or three in the morning) they came no nearer to an answer; and perhaps this was not so very remarkable, for all sorts of magicians and antiquarians and scholars had been asking the same question for rather more than two hundred years.

Mr Honeyfoot was a tall, cheerful, smiling gentleman with a great deal of energy, who always liked to be doing or planning something, rarely thinking to inquire whether that something were to the purpose. The present task put him very much in mind of the great mediaeval magicians,[2] who, whenever they had some seemingly

---

[2] More properly called *Aureate* or Golden Age magicians.

impossible problem to solve, would ride away for a year and a day with only a fairy-servant or two to guide them and at the end of this time never failed to find the answer. Mr Honeyfoot told Mr Segundus that in his opinion they could not do better than emulate these great men, some of whom had gone to the most retired parts of England and Scotland and Ireland (where magic was strongest) while others had ridden out of this world entirely and no one nowadays was quite clear about where they had gone or what they had done when they got there. Mr Honeyfoot did not propose going quite so far – indeed he did not wish to go far at all because it was winter and the roads were very shocking. Nevertheless he was strongly persuaded that they should go *somewhere* and consult *someone*. He told Mr Segundus that he thought they were both growing stale; the advantage of a fresh opinion would be immense. But no destination, no object presented itself. Mr Honeyfoot was in despair: and then he thought of the other magician.

Some years before, the York society had heard rumours that there was another magician in Yorkshire. This gentleman lived in a very retired part of the country where (it was said) he passed his days and nights studying rare magical texts in his wonderful library. Dr Foxcastle had found out the other magician's name and where he might be found, and had written a polite letter inviting the other magician to become a member of the York society. The other magician had written back, expressing his sense of the honour done him and his deep regret: he was quite unable – the long distance between York and Hurtfew Abbey – the indifferent roads – the work that he could on no account neglect – etc., etc.

The York magicians had all looked over the letter and expressed their doubts that any body with such small handwriting could ever make a tolerable magician. Then – with some slight regret for the wonderful library they would never see – they had dismissed the other magician from their thoughts. But Mr Honeyfoot said to Mr

Segundus that the importance of the question, "Why was there no more magic done in England?" was such that it would be very wrong of them to neglect any opening. Who could say? – the other magician's opinion might be worth having. And so he wrote a letter proposing that he and Mr Segundus give themselves the satisfaction of waiting on the other magician on the third Tuesday after Christmas at half past two. A reply came very promptly; Mr Honeyfoot with his customary good nature and good fellowship immediately sent for Mr Segundus and shewed him the letter. The other magician wrote in his small handwriting that he would be very happy in the acquaintance. This was enough. Mr Honeyfoot was very well pleased and instantly strode off to tell Waters, the coachman, when he would be needed.

Mr Segundus was left alone in the room with the letter in his hand. He read: ". . . I am, I confess, somewhat at a loss to account for the sudden honour done to me. It is scarcely conceivable that the magicians of York with all the happiness of each other's society and the incalculable benefit of each other's wisdom should feel any necessity to consult a solitary scholar such as myself . . ."

There was an air of subtle sarcasm about the letter; the writer seemed to mock Mr Honeyfoot with every word. Mr Segundus was glad to reflect that Mr Honeyfoot could scarcely have noticed or he would not have gone with such elated spirits to speak to Waters. It was such a *very* unfriendly letter that Mr Segundus found that all his desire to look upon the other magician had quite evaporated. Well, no matter, he thought, I must go because Mr Honeyfoot wishes it – and what, after all, is the worst that can happen? We will see him and be disappointed and that will be an end of it.

The day of the visit was preceded by stormy weather; rain had made long ragged pools in the bare, brown fields; wet roofs were like cold stone mirrors; and Mr Honeyfoot's post-chaise travelled through a world that seemed to contain a much higher proportion of chill grey sky and a much smaller one of solid comfortable earth than was usually the case.

Ever since the first evening Mr Segundus had been intending to ask Mr Honeyfoot about the Learned Society of Magicians of Manchester which Dr Foxcastle had mentioned. He did so now.

"It was a society of quite recent foundation," said Mr Honeyfoot, "and its members were clergymen of the poorer sort, respectable ex-tradesmen, apothecaries, lawyers, retired mill owners who had got up a little Latin and so forth, such people as might be termed half-gentlemen. I believe Dr Foxcastle was glad when they disbanded – he does not think that people of that sort have any business becoming magicians. And yet, you know, there were several clever men among them. They began, as you did, with the aim of bringing back practical magic to the world. They were practical men and wished to apply the principles of reason and science to magic as they had done to the manufacturing arts. They called it 'Rational Thaumaturgy'. When it did not work they became discouraged. Well, they cannot be blamed for that. But they let their disillusionment lead them into all sorts of difficulties. They began to think that there was not now nor ever had been magic in the world. They said that the *Aureate* magicians were all deceivers or were themselves deceived. And that the Raven King was an invention of the northern English to keep themselves from the tyranny of the south (being north-country men themselves they had some sympathy with that). Oh, their arguments were very ingenious – I forget how they explained fairies. They disbanded, as I told you, and one of them, whose name was Aubrey I think, meant to write it all down and publish it. But when it came to the point he found that a sort of fixed melancholy had settled on him and he was not able to rouse himself enough to begin."

"Poor gentleman," said Mr Segundus. "Perhaps it is the age. It is not an age for magic or scholarship, is it sir? Tradesmen prosper, sailors, politicians, but not magicians. Our time is past." He thought for a moment. "Three years ago," he said, "I was in London and I met with a street magician, a vagabonding, yellow-curtain sort of fellow with a strange disfiguration. This man persuaded me to part with quite a high sum of money – in return for which he promised to tell me a great secret. When I had paid him the money he told me that one day magic would be restored to England by two magicians. Now I do not at all believe in prophecies, yet it is thinking on what he said that has determined me to discover the truth of our fallen state – is not that strange?"

"You were entirely right – prophecies are great nonsense," said Mr Honeyfoot, laughing. And then, as if struck by a thought, he said, "We are two magicians. Honeyfoot and Segundus," he said trying it out, as if thinking how it would look in the newspapers and history books, "Honeyfoot and Segundus – it sounds very well."

Mr Segundus shook his head. "The fellow knew my profession and it was only to be expected that he should pretend to me that I was one of the two men. But in the end he told me quite plainly that I was not. At first it seemed as if he was not sure of it. There was something about me . . . He made me write down my name and looked at it a good long while."

"I expect he could see there was no more money to be got out of you," said Mr Honeyfoot.

Hurtfew Abbey was some fourteen miles north-west of York. The antiquity was all in the name. There had been an abbey but that was long ago; the present house had been built in the reign of Anne. It was very handsome and square and solid-looking in a fine park full of ghostly-looking wet trees (for the day was becoming rather misty). A river (called the Hurt) ran through the park and a fine classical-looking bridge led across it.

The other magician (whose name was Norrell) was in the hall to receive his guests. He was small, like his handwriting, and his voice when he welcomed them to Hurtfew was rather quiet as if he were not used to speaking his thoughts out loud. Mr Honeyfoot who was a little deaf did not catch what he said; "I get old, sir – a common failing. I hope you will bear with me."

Mr Norrell led his guests to a handsome drawing-room with a

good fire burning in the hearth. No candles had been lit; two fine windows gave plenty of light to see by – although it was a grey sort of light and not at all cheerful. Yet the idea of a second fire, or candles, burning somewhere in the room kept occurring to Mr Segundus, so that he continually turned in his chair and looked about him to discover where they might be. But there never was any thing – only perhaps a mirror or an antique clock.

Mr Norrell said that he had read Mr Segundus's account of the careers of Martin Pale's fairy-servants.[3] "A creditable piece of work, sir, but you left out Master Fallowthought. A very minor spirit certainly, whose usefulness to the great Dr Pale was questionable.[4] Nevertheless your little history was incomplete without him."

There was a pause. "A fairy-spirit called Fallowthought, sir?" said Mr Segundus, "I . . . that is . . . that is to say I never heard of any such creature – in this world or any other."

Mr Norrell smiled for the first time – but it was an inward sort of smile. "Of course," he said, "I am forgetting. It is all in Holgarth and Pickle's history of their own dealings with Master Fallowthought, which you could scarcely have read. I congratulate you – they were an unsavoury pair – more criminal than magical: the less one knows of them the better."

"Ah, sir!" cried Mr Honeyfoot, suspecting that Mr Norrell was speaking of one of his books. "We hear marvellous things of your library. All the magicians in Yorkshire fell into fits of jealousy when they heard of the great number of books you had got!"

"Indeed?" said Mr Norrell coldly. "You surprize me. I had no idea my affairs were so commonly known . . . I expect it is

---

[3] *A Complete Description of Dr Pale's fairy-servants, their Names, Histories, Characters and the Services they performed for Him* by John Segundus, pub. by Thomas Burnham, Bookseller, Northampton, 1799.

[4] Dr Martin Pale (1485–1567) was the son of a Warwick leather-tanner. He was the last of the *Aureate* or Golden Age magicians. Other magicians followed him (c.f. Gregory Absalom) but their reputations are debatable. Pale was certainly the last English magician to venture into Faerie.

Thoroughgood," he said thoughtfully, naming a man who sold books and curiosities in Coffee-yard in York. "Childermass has warned me several times that Thoroughgood is a chatterer."

Mr Honeyfoot did not quite understand this. If *he* had had such quantities of magical books he would have loved to talk of them, be complimented on them, and have them admired; and he could not believe that Mr Norrell was not the same. Meaning therefore to be kind and to set Mr Norrell at his ease (for he had taken it into his head that the gentleman was shy) he persisted: "Might I be permitted to express a wish, sir, that we might see your wonderful library?"

Mr Segundus was certain that Norrell would refuse, but instead Mr Norrell regarded them steadily for some moments (he had small blue eyes and seemed to peep out at them from some secret place inside himself) and then, almost graciously, he granted Mr Honeyfoot's request. Mr Honeyfoot was all gratitude, happy in the belief that he had pleased Mr Norrell as much as himself.

Mr Norrell led the other two gentlemen along a passage – a very ordinary passage, thought Mr Segundus, panelled and floored with well-polished oak, and smelling of beeswax; then there was a staircase, or perhaps only three or four steps; and then another passage where the air was somewhat colder and the floor was good York stone: all entirely unremarkable. (Unless the second passage had come before the staircase or steps? Or had there in truth been a staircase at all?) Mr Segundus was one of those happy gentlemen who can always say whether they face north or south, east or west. It was not a talent he took any particular pride in – it was as natural to him as knowing that his head still stood upon his shoulders – but in Mr Norrell's house his gift deserted him. He could never afterwards picture the sequence of passageways and rooms through which they had passed, nor quite decide how long they had taken to reach the library. And he could not tell the direction; it seemed to him as if Mr Norrell had discovered some fifth point of the compass – not east, nor south, nor west, nor north, but somewhere quite different and this was the direction in which he led them. Mr Honeyfoot, on the other hand, did not appear to notice any thing odd.

The library was perhaps a little smaller than the drawing-room they had just quitted. There was a noble fire in the hearth and all was comfort and quiet. Yet once again the light within the room did not seem to accord with the three tall twelve-paned windows, so that once again Mr Segundus was made uncomfortable by a persistent feeling that there ought to have been other candles in the room, other windows or another fire to account for the light. What windows there were looked out upon a wide expanse of dusky English rain so that Mr Segundus could not make out the view nor guess where in the house they stood.

The room was not empty; there was a man sitting at a table who rose as they entered, and whom Mr Norrell briefly declared to be Childermass, his man of business.

Mr Honeyfoot and Mr Segundus, being magicians themselves, had not needed to be told that the library of Hurtfew Abbey was dearer to its possessor than all his other riches; and they were not surprized to discover that Mr Norrell had constructed a beautiful jewel box to house his heart's treasure. The bookcases which lined the walls of the room were built of English woods and resembled Gothic arches laden with carvings. There were carvings of leaves (dried and twisted leaves, as if the season the artist had intended to represent were autumn), carvings of intertwining roots and branches, carvings of berries and ivy – all wonderfully done. But the wonder of the bookcases was nothing to the wonder of the books.

The first thing a student of magic learns is that there are books *about* magic and books *of* magic. And the second thing he learns is that a perfectly respectable example of the former may be had for two or three guineas at a good bookseller, and that the value of the latter is above rubies.[5] The collection of the York society was reckoned very fine – almost remarkable; among its many volumes were five works written between 1550 and 1700 and which might reasonably be claimed as books of magic (though one was no more than a couple of ragged pages). Books of magic are rare and neither Mr Segundus nor Mr Honeyfoot had ever seen more than two or three in a private library. At Hurtfew all the walls were lined with bookshelves and all the shelves were filled with books. And the books were all, or almost all, old books; books of magic. Oh! to be sure many had clean modern bindings, but clearly these were volumes which Mr Norrell had had rebound (he favoured, it seemed, plain calf with the titles stamped in neat silver capitals). But many had bindings that were old, old, old, with crumbling spines and corners.

Mr Segundus glanced at the spines of the books on a nearby shelf; the first title he read was *How to putte Questiones to the Dark and understand its Answeres.*

---

[5] Magicians, as we know from Jonathan Strange's maxim, will quarrel about any thing and many years and much learning has been applied to the vexed question of whether such and such a volume qualifies as a book of magic. But most laymen find they are served well enough by this simple rule: books written before magic ended in England are books of magic, books written later are books about magic. The principle, from which the layman's rule of thumb derives, is that a book of magic should be written by a practising magician, rather than a theoretical magician or a historian of magic. What could be more reasonable? And yet already we are in difficulties. The great masters of magic, those we term the Golden Age or *Aureate* magicians (Thomas Godbless, Ralph Stokesey, Catherine of Winchester, the Raven King) wrote little, or little has survived. It is probable that Thomas Godbless could not write. Stokesey learnt Latin at a little grammar school in his native Devonshire, but all that we know of him comes from other writers.

Magicians only applied themselves to writing books when magic was already in decline. Darkness was already approaching to quench the glory of English magic; those men we call the Silver Age or *Argentine* magicians (Thomas Lanchester, 1518–90; Jacques Belasis, 1526–1604; Nicholas Goubert, 1535–78; Gregory Absalom, 1507–99) were flickering candles in the twilight; they were scholars first and magicians second. Certainly they claimed to do magic, some even had a fairy-servant or two, but they seem to have accomplished very little in this way and some modern scholars have doubted whether they could do magic at all.

"A foolish work," said Mr Norrell. Mr Segundus started – he had not known his host was so close by. Mr Norrell continued, "I would advise you not to waste a moment's thought upon it."

So Mr Segundus looked at the next book which was Belasis's *Instructions*.

"You know Belasis, I dare say?" asked Mr Norrell.

"Only by reputation, sir," said Mr Segundus, "I have often heard that he held the key to a good many things, but I have also heard – indeed all the authorities agree – that every copy of *The Instructions* was destroyed long ago. Yet now here it is! Why, sir, it is extraordinary! It is wonderful!"

"You expect a great deal of Belasis," remarked Norrell, "and once upon a time I was entirely of your mind. I remember that for many months I devoted eight hours out of every twenty-four to studying his work; a compliment, I may say, that I have never paid any other author. But ultimately he is disappointing. He is mystical where he ought to be intelligible – and intelligible where he ought to be obscure. There are some things which have no business being put into books for all the world to read. For myself I no longer have any very great opinion of Belasis."

"Here is a book I never even heard of, sir," said Mr Segundus, "*The Excellences of Christo-Judaic Magick*. What can you tell me of this?"

"Ha!" cried Mr Norrell. "It dates from the seventeenth century, but I have no great opinion of it. Its author was a liar, a drunkard, an adulterer and a rogue. I am glad he has been so completely forgot."

It seemed that it was not only live magicians which Mr Norrell despised. He had taken the measure of all the dead ones too and found them wanting.

Mr Honeyfoot meanwhile, his hands in the air like a Methodist praising God, was walking rapidly from bookcase to bookcase; he could scarcely stop long enough to read the title of one book before his eye was caught by another on the other side of the room. "Oh, Mr Norrell!" he cried. "Such a quantity of books! Surely we shall find the answers to all our questions here!"

"I doubt it, sir," was Mr Norrell's dry reply.

The man of business gave a short laugh – laughter which was clearly directed at Mr Honeyfoot, yet Mr Norrell did not reprimand him either by look or word, and Mr Segundus wondered what sort of business it could be that Mr Norrell entrusted to this person. With his long hair as ragged as rain and as black as thunder, he would have looked quite at home upon a windswept moor, or lurking in some pitch-black alleyway, or perhaps in a novel by Mrs Radcliffe.

Mr Segundus took down *The Instructions* of Jacques Belasis and, despite Mr Norrell's poor opinion of it, instantly hit upon two extraordinary passages.[6] Then, conscious of time passing and of

[6] The first passage which Mr Segundus read concerned England, Faerie (which magicians sometimes call "the Other Lands") and a strange country that is reputed to lie on the far side of Hell. Mr Segundus had heard something of the symbolic and magical bond which links these three lands, yet never had he read so clear an explanation of it as was put forward here.

The second extract concerned one of England's greatest magicians, Martin Pale. In Gregory Absalom's *The Tree of Learning* there is a famous passage which relates how, while journeying through Faerie, the last of the great *Aureate* magicians, Martin Pale, paid a visit to a fairy-prince. Like most of his race the fairy had a great multitude of names, honorifics, titles and pseudonyms; but usually he was known as Cold Henry. Cold Henry made a long and deferential speech to his guest. The speech was full of metaphors and obscure allusions, but what Cold Henry seemed to be saying was that fairies were naturally wicked creatures who did not always know when they were going wrong. To this Martin Pale briefly and somewhat enigmatically replied that not all Englishmen have the same size feet.

For several centuries no one had the faintest idea what any of this might mean, though several theories were advanced – and John Segundus was familiar with all of them. The most popular was that developed by William Pantler in the early eighteenth century. Pantler said that Cold Henry and Pale were speaking of theology. Fairies (as everybody knows) are beyond the reach of the Church; no Christ has come to them, nor ever will – and what is to become of them on Judgement Day no one knows. According to Pantler Cold Henry meant to enquire of Pale if there was any hope that fairies, like men, might receive Eternal Salvation. Pale's reply – that Englishmen's feet are different sizes – was his way of saying that not all Englishmen will be saved. Based on this Pantler goes on to attribute to Pale a rather odd belief that Heaven is large enough to hold only a finite number of the Blessed; for every Englishmen who is damned, a place opens up in Heaven for a fairy.

the queer, dark eye of the man of business upon him, he opened *The Excellences of Christo-Judaic Magick*. This was not (as he had supposed) a printed book, but a manuscript scribbled down very hurriedly upon the backs of all kinds of bits of paper, most of them old ale-house bills. Here Mr Segundus read of wonderful adventures. The seventeenth-century magician had used his scanty magic to battle against great and powerful enemies: battles which no human magician ought to have attempted. He had scribbled down the history of his patchwork victories just as those enemies were closing around him. The author had known very well that, as he wrote, time was running out for him and death was the best that he could hope for.

The room was becoming darker; the antique scrawl was growing dim on the page. Two footmen came into the room and, watched by the unbusinesslike man of business, lit candles, drew window curtains and heaped fresh coals upon the fire. Mr Segundus thought it best to remind Mr Honeyfoot that they had not yet explained to Mr Norrell the reason for their visit.

As they were leaving the library Mr Segundus noticed something he thought odd. A chair was drawn up to the fire and by the chair stood a little table. Upon the table lay the boards and leather bindings of a very old book, a pair of scissars and a strong, cruel-looking knife, such as a gardener might use for pruning. But the pages of the book were nowhere to be seen. Perhaps, thought Mr

---

[6] *cont'd* Pantler's reputation as a theoretical magician rests entirely on the book he wrote on the subject

In Jacques Belasis's *Instructions* Mr Segundus read a very different explanation. Three centuries before Martin Pale set foot in Cold Henry's castle Cold Henry had had another human visitor, an English magician even greater than Pale – Ralph Stokesey – who had left behind him a pair of boots. The boots, said Belasis, were old, which is probably why Stokesey did not take them with him, but their presence in the castle caused great consternation to all its fairy-inhabitants who held English magicians in great veneration. In particular Cold Henry was in a pickle because he feared that in some devious, incomprehensible way, Christian morality might hold him responsible for the loss of the boots. So he was trying to rid himself of the terrible objects by passing them on to Pale who did not want them.

Segundus, he has sent it away to be bound anew. Yet the old binding still looked strong and why should Mr Norrell trouble himself to remove the pages and risk damaging them? A skilled bookbinder was the proper person to do such work.

When they were seated in the drawing-room again, Mr Honeyfoot addressed Mr Norrell. "What I have seen here today, sir, convinces me that you are the best person to help us. Mr Segundus and I are of the opinion that modern magicians are on the wrong path; they waste their energies upon trifles. Do not you agree, sir?"

"Oh! certainly," said Mr Norrell.

"Our question," continued Mr Honeyfoot, "is why magic has fallen from its once-great state in our great nation. Our question is, sir, why is no more magic done in England?"

Mr Norrell's small blue eyes grew harder and brighter and his lips tightened as if he were seeking to suppress a great and secret delight within him. It was as if, thought Mr Segundus, he had waited a long time for someone to ask him this question and had had his answer ready for years. Mr Norrell said, "I cannot help you with your question, sir, for I do not understand it. It is a wrong question, sir. Magic is not ended in England. I myself am quite a tolerable practical magician."

## 2

# The Old Starre Inn

### January–February 1807

As the carriage passed out of Mr Norrell's sweep-gate Mr Honeyfoot exclaimed; "A practical magician in England! And in Yorkshire too! We have had the most extraordinary good luck! Ah, Mr Segundus, we have you to thank for this. You were awake, when the rest of us had fallen asleep. Had it not been for your encouragement, we might never have discovered Mr Norrell. And I am quite certain that he would never have sought us out; he is a little reserved. He gave us no particulars of his achievements in practical magic, nothing beyond the simple fact of his success. That, I fancy, is the sign of a modest nature. Mr Segundus, I think you will agree that our task is clear. It falls to us, sir, to overcome Norrell's natural timidity and aversion to praise, and lead him triumphantly before a wider public!"

"Perhaps," said Mr Segundus doubtfully.

"I do not say it will be easy," said Mr Honeyfoot. "He is a little reticent and not fond of company. But he must see that such knowledge as he possesses must be shared with others for the Nation's good. He is a gentleman: he knows his duty and will do it, I am sure. Ah, Mr Segundus! You deserve the grateful thanks of every magician in the country for this."

But whatever Mr Segundus deserved, the sad fact is that

magicians in England are a peculiarly ungrateful set of men. Mr Honeyfoot and Mr Segundus might well have made the most significant discovery in magical scholarship for three centuries – what of it? There was scarcely a member of the York society who, when he learnt of it, was not entirely confident that he could have done it much better – and, upon the following Tuesday when an extraordinary meeting of the Learned Society of York Magicians was held, there were very few members who were not prepared to say so.

At seven o'clock upon the Tuesday evening the upper room of the Old Starre Inn in Stonegate was crowded. The news which Mr Honeyfoot and Mr Segundus had brought seemed to have drawn out all the gentlemen in the city who had ever peeped into a book of magic – and York was still, after its own fashion, one of the most magical cities in England; perhaps only the King's city of Newcastle could boast more magicians.

There was such a crush of magicians in the room that, for the present, a great many were obliged to stand, though the waiters were continually bringing more chairs up the stairs. Dr Foxcastle had got himself an excellent chair, tall and black and curiously carved – and this chair (which rather resembled a throne), and the sweep of the red velvet curtains behind him and the way in which he sat with his hands clasped over his large round stomach, all combined to give him a deeply magisterial air.

The servants at the Old Starre Inn had prepared an excellent fire to keep off the chills of a January evening and around it were seated some ancient magicians – apparently from the reign of George II or thereabouts – all wrapped in plaid shawls, with yellowing spider's-web faces, and accompanied by equally ancient footmen with bottles of medicine in their pockets. Mr Honeyfoot greeted them with: "How do you do, Mr Aptree? How do you do, Mr Greyshippe? I hope you are in good health, Mr Tunstall? I am very glad to see you here, gentlemen! I hope you have all come to rejoice with us? All our years in the dusty wilderness are at an end. Ah! no one knows better than you, Mr Aptree and you, Mr Greyshippe what years they have been, for you have lived through a great many of them. But now we shall see magic once more Britain's counsellor and protector! And the French, Mr Tunstall! What will be the feelings of the French when they hear about it? Why! I should not be surprized if it were to bring on an immediate surrender."

Mr Honeyfoot had a great deal more to say of the same sort; he had prepared a speech in which he intended to lay before them all the wonderful advantages that were to accrue to Britain from this discovery. But he was never allowed to deliver more than a few sentences of it, for it seemed that each and every gentleman in the room was bursting with opinions of his own on the subject, all of which required to be communicated urgently to every other gentleman. Dr Foxcastle was the first to interrupt Mr Honeyfoot. From his large, black throne he addressed Mr Honeyfoot thus: "I am very sorry to see you, sir, bringing magic – for which I know you have a genuine regard – into disrepute with impossible tales and wild inventions. Mr Segundus," he said, turning to the gentleman whom he regarded as the source of all the trouble, "I do not know what is customary where you come from, but in Yorkshire we do not care for men who build their reputations at the expence of other men's peace of mind."

This was as far as Dr Foxcastle got before he was drowned by the loud, angry exclamations of Mr Honeyfoot and Mr Segundus's supporters. The next gentleman to make himself heard wondered that Mr Segundus and Mr Honeyfoot should have been so taken in. Clearly Norrell was mad – no different from any stark-eyed madman who stood upon the street corner screaming out that he was the Raven King.

A sandy-haired gentleman in a state of great excitement thought that Mr Honeyfoot and Mr Segundus should have insisted on Mr Norrell leaving his house upon the instant and coming straightway in an open carriage (though it was January) in triumph to York, so that the sandy-haired gentleman might strew ivy leaves in his path;[1] and one of the very old men by the fire was in a great passion about something or other, but being so old his voice was rather weak and no one had leisure just then to discover what he was saying.

There was a tall, sensible man in the room called Thorpe, a gentleman with very little magical learning, but a degree of common sense rare in a magician. He had always thought that Mr Segundus deserved encouragement in his quest to find where practical English magic had disappeared to – though like everyone else Mr Thorpe had not expected Mr Segundus to discover the answer quite so soon. But now that they had an answer Mr Thorpe was of the opinion that they should not simply dismiss it: "Gentlemen, Mr Norrell has said he can do magic. Very well. We know a little of Norrell – we have all heard of the rare texts he is supposed to have and for this reason alone we would be wrong to dismiss his claims without careful consideration. But the stronger arguments in Norrell's favour are these: that two of our own number – sober scholars both – have seen Norrell and come away convinced." He turned to Mr Honeyfoot. "You believe in this man – any one may see by your face that you do. You have seen something that convinced you – will you not tell us what it was?"

Now Mr Honeyfoot's reaction to this question was perhaps a little strange. At first he smiled gratefully at Mr Thorpe as if this was exactly what he could have wished for: a chance to broadcast the excellent reasons he had for believing that Mr Norrell could do magic; and he opened his mouth to begin. Then he stopped; he paused; he looked about him, as if those excellent reasons which had seemed so substantial a moment ago were all turning to mist and nothingness in his mouth, and his tongue and teeth could not catch hold of even one of them to frame it into a rational English sentence. He muttered something of Mr Norrell's honest countenance.

[1] The conquerors of Imperial Rome may have been honoured with wreaths of laurel leaves; lovers and fortune's favourites have, we are told, roses strewn in their paths; but English magicians were always only ever given common ivy.

The York society did not think this very satisfactory (and had they actually been privileged to see Mr Norrell's countenance they might have thought it even less so). So Thorpe turned to Mr Segundus and said, "Mr Segundus, you have seen Norrell too. What is your opinion?"

For the first time the York society noticed how pale Mr Segundus was and it occurred to some of the gentlemen that he had not answered them when they had greeted him, as if he could not quite collect his thoughts to reply. "Are you unwell, sir?" asked Mr Thorpe gently. "No, no," murmured Mr Segundus, "it is nothing. I thank you." But he looked so lost that one gentleman offered him his chair and another went off to fetch a glass of Canary-wine, and the excitable sandy-haired gentleman who had wished to strew ivy leaves in Mr Norrell's path nurtured a secret hope that Mr Segundus might be enchanted and that they might see something extraordinary!

Mr Segundus sighed and said, "I thank you. I am not ill, but this last week I have felt very heavy and stupid. Mrs Pleasance has given me arrowroot and hot concoctions of liquorice root, but they have not helped – which does not surprize me for I think the confusion is in my head. I am not so bad as I was. If you were to ask me now, gentlemen, why it is that I believe that magic has come back to England, I should say it is because I have seen magic done. The impression of having seen magic done is most vivid here and here . . ." (Mr Segundus touched his brow and his heart.) "And yet I know that I have seen none. Norrell did none while we were with him. And so I suppose that I have dreamt it."

Fresh outbreak of the gentlemen of the York society. The faint gentleman smiled faintly and inquired if any one could make any thing of this. Then Mr Thorpe cried, "Good God! It is very nonsensical for us all to sit here and assert that Norrell can or cannot do this or can or cannot do that. We are all rational beings I think, and the answer, surely, is quite simple – we will ask him to do some magic for us in proof of his claims."

This was such good sense that for a moment the magicians were silent – though this is not to say that the proposal was universally popular – not at all. Several of the magicians (Dr Foxcastle was one) did not care for it. If they asked Norrell to do magic, there was always the danger that he might indeed do some. They did not want to see magic done; they only wished to read about it in books. Others were of the opinion that the York society was making itself very ridiculous by doing even so little as this. But in the end most of the magicians agreed with Mr Thorpe that: "As scholars, gentlemen, the least we can do is to offer Mr Norrell the opportunity to convince us." And so it was decided that someone should write another letter to Mr Norrell.

It was quite clear to all the magicians that Mr Honeyfoot and Mr Segundus had handled the thing very ill and upon one subject at least – that of Mr Norrell's wonderful library – they did seem remarkably stupid, for they were not able to give any intelligible report of it. What had they seen? Oh, books, many books. A remarkable number of books? Yes, they believed they had thought it remarkable at the time. Rare books? Ah, probably. Had they been permitted to take them down and look inside them? Oh no! Mr Norrell had not gone so far as to invite them to do that. But they had read the titles? Yes, indeed. Well then, what were the titles of the books they had seen? They did not know; they could not remember. Mr Segundus said that one of the books had a title that began with a 'B', but that was the beginning and end of his information. It was very odd.

Mr Thorpe had always intended to write the letter to Mr Norrell himself, but there were a great many magicians in the room whose chief idea was to give offence to Mr Norrell in return for his impudence and these gentlemen thought quite rightly that their best means of insulting Norrell was to allow Dr Foxcastle to write the letter. And so this was carried. In due time it brought forth an angry letter of reply.

Hurtfew Abbey, Yorkshire,
Feb. 1st, 1807

Sir—

Twice in recent years I have been honoured by a letter from the gentlemen of the Learned Society of York Magicians soliciting my acquaintance. Now comes a third letter informing me of the society's displeasure. The good opinion of the York society seems as easily lost as it is gained and a man may never know how he came to do either. In answer to the particular charge contained in your letter that I have exaggerated my abilities and laid claim to powers I cannot possibly possess I have only this to say: other men may fondly attribute their lack of success to a fault in the world rather than to their own poor scholarship, but the truth is that magic is as achievable in this Age as in any other; as I have proved to my own complete satisfaction any number of times within the last twenty years. But what is my reward for loving my art better than other men have done? – for studying harder to perfect it? – it is now circulated abroad that I am a fabulist; my professional abilities are slighted and my word doubted. You will not, I dare say, be much surprized to learn that under such circumstances as these I do not feel much inclined to oblige the York society in any thing – least of all a request for a display of magic. The Learned Society of York Magicians meets upon Wednesday next and upon that day I shall inform you of my intentions.

Your servant
Gilbert Norrell

This was all rather disagreeably mysterious. The theoretical magicians waited somewhat nervously to see what the practical magician would send them next. What Mr Norrell sent them next was nothing more alarming than an attorney, a smiling, bobbing, bowing attorney, a quite commonplace attorney called Robinson, with neat black clothes and neat kid gloves, with a document, the like of which the gentlemen of the York society had never seen before; a draft of an agreement, drawn up in accordance with England's long-forgotten codes of magical law.

Mr Robinson arrived in the upper room at the Old Starre promptly at eight and seemed to suppose himself expected. He had a place of business and two clerks in Coney-street. His face was well known to many of the gentlemen.

"I will confess to you, sirs," smiled Mr Robinson, "that this paper is largely the work of my principal, Mr Norrell. I am no expert upon thaumaturgic law. Who is nowadays? Still, I dare say that if I go wrong, you will be so kind as to put me right again."

Several of the York magicians nodded wisely.

Mr Robinson was a polished sort of person. He was so clean and healthy and pleased about everything that he positively shone – which is only to be expected in a fairy or an angel, but is somewhat disconcerting in an attorney. He was most deferential to the gentlemen of the York society for he knew nothing of magic, but he thought it must be difficult and require great concentration of mind. But to professional humility and a genuine admiration of the York society Mr Robinson added a happy vanity that these monumental brains must now cease their pondering on esoteric matters for a time and listen to him. He put golden spectacles upon his nose, adding another small glitter to his shining person.

Mr Robinson said that Mr Norrell undertook to do a piece of magic in a certain place at a certain time. "You have no objection I hope, gentlemen, to my principal settling the time and place?"

The gentlemen had none.

"Then it shall be the Cathedral, Friday fortnight."[2]

---

[2] The great church at York is both a *cathedral* (meaning the church where the throne of the bishop or archbishop is housed) and a *minster* (meaning a church founded by a missionary in ancient times). It has borne both these names at different periods. In earlier centuries it was more usually called the *Minster*, but nowadays the people of York prefer the term *Cathedral* as one which elevates their church above those of the nearby towns of Ripon and Beverley. Ripon and Beverley have minsters, but no cathedrals.

Mr Robinson said that if Mr Norrell failed to do the magic then he would publicly withdraw his claims to be a practical magician – indeed to be any sort of magician at all, and he would give his oath never to make any such claims again.

"He need not go so far," said Mr Thorpe. "We have no desire to punish him; we merely wished to put his claims to the test."

Mr Robinson's shining smile dimmed a little, as if he had something rather disagreeable to communicate and was not quite sure how to begin.

"Wait," said Mr Segundus, "we have not heard the other side of the bargain yet. We have not heard what he expects of us."

Mr Robinson nodded. Mr Norrell intended it seemed to exact the same promise from each and every magician of the York society as he made himself. In other words if he succeeded, then they must without further ado disband the Society of York Magicians and none of them claim the title "magician" ever again. And after all, said Mr Robinson, this would be only fair, since Mr Norrell would then have proved himself the only true magician in Yorkshire.

"And shall we have some third person, some independent party to decide if the magic has been accomplished?" asked Mr Thorpe.

This question seemed to puzzle Mr Robinson. He hoped they would excuse him if he had taken up a wrong idea he said, he would not offend for the world, but he had thought that all the gentlemen present were magicians.

Oh, yes, nodded the York society, they were all magicians.

Then surely, said Mr Robinson, they would recognize magic when they saw it? Surely there were none better qualified to do so?

Another gentleman asked what magic Norrell intended to do? Mr Robinson was full of polite apologies and elaborate explanations; he could not enlighten them, he did not know.

It would tire my reader's patience to rehearse the many winding arguments by which the gentlemen of the York society came to sign Mr Norrell's agreement. Many did so out of vanity; they had publicly declared that they did not believe Norrell could do magic, they had publicly challenged Norrell to perform some – under such circumstances as these it would have looked peculiarly foolish to change their minds – or so they thought.

Mr Honeyfoot, on the other hand, signed precisely *because* he believed in Norrell's magic. Mr Honeyfoot hoped that Mr Norrell would gain public recognition by this demonstration of his powers and go on to employ his magic for the good of the nation.

Some of the gentlemen were provoked to sign by the suggestion (originating with Norrell and somehow conveyed by Robinson) that they would not shew themselves true magicians unless they did so.

So one by one and there and then, the magicians of York signed the document that Mr Robinson had brought. The last magician was Mr Segundus.

"I will not sign," he said. "For magic is my life and though Mr Norrell is quite right to say I am a poor scholar, what shall I do when it is taken from me?"

A silence.

"Oh!" said Mr Robinson. "Well, that is . . . Are you quite sure, sir, that you should not like to sign the document? You see how all your friends have done it? You will be quite alone."

"I am quite sure," said Mr Segundus, "thank you."

"Oh!" said Mr Robinson. "Well, in that case I must confess that I do not know quite how to proceed. My principal gave me no instruction what to do if only *some* of the gentlemen signed. I shall consult with my principal in the morning."

Dr Foxcastle was heard to remark to Mr Hart or Hunt that once again it was the newcomer who brought a world of trouble upon everyone's heads.

But two days later Mr Robinson waited upon Dr Foxcastle with a message to say that on this particular occasion Mr Norrell would be happy to overlook Mr Segundus's refusal to sign; he would consider that his contract was with all the members of the York society *except* for Mr Segundus.

The night before Mr Norrell was due to perform the magic, snow fell on York and in the morning the dirt and mud of the city had disappeared, all replaced by flawless white. The sounds of hooves and footsteps were muffled, and the very voices of York's citizens were altered by a white silence that swallowed up every sound. Mr Norrell had named a very early hour in the day. In their separate homes the York magicians breakfasted alone. They watched in silence as a servant poured their coffee, broke their warm white-bread rolls, fetched the butter. The wife, the sister, the daughter, the daughter-in-law, or the niece who usually performed these little offices was still in bed; and the pleasant female domestic chat, which the gentlemen of the York society affected to despise so much, and which was in truth the sweet and mild refrain in the music of their ordinary lives, was absent. And the breakfast rooms where these gentlemen sat were changed from what they had been yesterday. The winter gloom was quite gone and in its place was a fearful light – the winter sun reflected many times over by the snowy earth. There was a dazzle of light upon the white linen tablecloth. The rosebuds that patterned the daughter's pretty coffee-cups seemed almost to dance in it. Sunbeams were struck from the niece's silver coffee-pot, and the daughter-in-law's smiling china shepherdesses were all become shining angels. It was as if the table were laid with fairy silver and crystal.

Mr Segundus, putting his head out of a third-storey window in Lady-Peckitt's-yard, thought that perhaps Norrell had already done the magic and this was it. There was an ominous rumble above him and he drew in his head quickly to avoid a sudden fall of snow from the roof. Mr Segundus had no servant any more than he had a wife, sister, daughter, daughter-in-law, or niece, but Mrs Pleasance, his landlady, was an early riser. Many times in the last fortnight she had heard him sigh over his books and she hoped to cheer him up with a breakfast of two freshly grilled herrings, tea and fresh milk, and white bread and butter on a blue-and-white china plate. With the same generous aim she had sat down to talk to him. On seeing how despondent he looked she cried, "Oh! I have no patience with this old man!"

Mr Segundus had not told Mrs Pleasance that Mr Norrell was old and yet she fancied that he must be. From what Mr Segundus had told her she thought of him as a sort of miser who hoarded magic instead of gold, and as our narrative progresses, I will allow the reader to judge the justice of this portrait of Mr Norrell's character. Like Mrs Pleasance I always fancy that misers are old. I cannot tell why this should be since I am sure that there are as many young misers as old. As to whether or not Mr Norrell was in fact old, he was the sort of man who had been old at seventeen.

Mrs Pleasance continued, "When Mr Pleasance was alive, he used to say that no one in York, man or woman, could bake a loaf to rival mine, and other people as well have been kind enough to say that they never in their lives tasted bread so good. But I have always kept a good table for love of doing a thing well and if one of those queer spirits from the Arabian fables came out of this very teapot now and gave me three wishes I hope I would not be so ill-natured as to try to stop other folk from baking bread – and should their bread be as good as mine then I do not see that it hurts me, but rather is so much the better for them. Come, sir, try a bit," she said, pushing a plateful of the celebrated bread towards her lodger. "I do not like to see you get so thin. People will say that Hettie Pleasance has lost all her skill at housekeeping. I wish you would not be so downcast, sir. You have not signed this perfidious document and when the other gentlemen are forced to give up, you will still continue and I very much hope, Mr Segundus, that you may make great discoveries and perhaps then this Mr Norrell who thinks himself so clever will be glad to take you into partnership and so be brought to regret his foolish pride."

Mr Segundus smiled and thanked her. "But I do not think that will happen. My chief difficulty will be lack of materials. I have very little of my own, and when the society is disbanded, – well I cannot tell what will happen to its books, but I doubt that they will come to me."

Mr Segundus ate his bread (which was just as good as the late Mr Pleasance and his friends had said it was) and his herrings and drank some tea. Their power to soothe a troubled heart must have been greater than he had supposed for he found that he felt a little better and, fortified in this manner, he put on his greatcoat and his hat and his muffler and his gloves and stamped off through the snowy streets to the place that Mr Norrell had appointed for this day's wonders – the Cathedral of York.

And I hope that all my readers are acquainted with an old English Cathedral town or I fear that the significance of Mr Norrell's chusing that particular place will be lost upon them. They must understand that in an old Cathedral town the great old church is not one building among many; it is *the* building – different from all others in scale, beauty and solemnity. Even in modern times when an old Cathedral town may have provided itself with all the elegant appurtenances of civic buildings, assembly and meeting rooms (and York was well-stocked with these) the Cathedral rises above them – a witness to the devotion of our forefathers. It is as if the town contains within itself something larger than itself. When going about one's business in the muddle of narrow streets one is sure to lose sight of the Cathedral, but then the town will open out and suddenly it is there, many times taller and many times larger than any other building, and one realizes that one has reached the heart of the town and that all streets and lanes have in some way led here, to a place of mysteries much deeper than any Mr Norrell knew of. Such were Mr Segundus's thoughts as he entered the Close and stood before the great brooding blue shadow of the Cathedral's west face. Now came Dr Foxcastle, sailing magisterially around the corner like a fat, black ship. Spying Mr Segundus there he steered himself towards that gentleman and bid him good morning.

"Perhaps, sir," said Dr Foxcastle, "you would be so kind as to introduce me to Mr Norrell? He is a gentleman I very much wish to know."

"I shall be only too happy, sir." said Mr Segundus and looked about him. The weather had kept most people within doors and there were only a few dark figures scuttling over the white field that lay before the great grey Church. When scrutinized these were discovered to be gentlemen of the York society, or clergymen and Cathedral attendants – vergers and beadles, sub-choirmasters, provosts, transept-sweepers and such-like persons – who had been sent by their superiors out into the snow to see to the Church's business.

"I should like nothing better, sir," said Mr Segundus, "than to oblige you, but I do not see Mr Norrell."

Yet there was someone.

Someone was standing in the snow alone directly in front of the Minster. He was a dark sort of someone, a not-quite-respectable someone who was regarding Mr Segundus and Dr Foxcastle with an air of great interest. His ragged hair hung about his shoulders like a fall of black water; he had a strong, thin face with something twisted in it, like a tree root; and a long, thin nose; and, though his skin was very pale, something made it seem a dark face – perhaps it was the darkness of his eyes, or the proximity of that long, black greasy hair. After a moment this person walked up to the two magicians, gave them a sketchy bow and said that he hoped they would forgive his intruding upon them but they had been pointed out to him as gentlemen who were there upon the same business as himself. He said that his name was John Childermass, and that he was Mr Norrell's steward in certain matters (though he did not say what these were).

"It seems to me," said Mr Segundus thoughtfully, "that I know your face. I have seen you before, I think?"

Something shifted in Childermass's dark face, but it was gone in a moment and whether it had been a frown or laughter it was impossible to say. "I am often in York upon business for Mr Norrell, sir. Perhaps you have seen me in one of the city bookselling establishments?"

"No," said Mr Segundus, "I have seen you . . . I can picture you . . . Where? . . . Oh! I shall have it in a moment!"

Childermass raised an eyebrow as if to say he very much doubted it.

"But surely Mr Norrell is coming himself?" said Dr Foxcastle.

Childermass begged Dr Foxcastle's pardon, but he did not think Mr Norrell would come; he did not think Mr Norrell saw any reason to come.

"Ah!" cried Dr Foxcastle. "then he concedes, does he? Well, well, well. Poor gentleman. He feels very foolish, I dare say. Well indeed. It was a noble attempt at any rate. We bear him no ill-will for having made the attempt." Dr Foxcastle was much relieved that he would see no magic and it made him generous.

Childermass begged Dr Foxcastle's pardon once more; he feared that Dr Foxcastle had mistaken his meaning. Mr Norrell would certainly do magic; he would do it in Hurtfew Abbey and the results would be seen in York. "Gentlemen," said Childermass to Dr Foxcastle, "do not like to leave their comfortable firesides unless they must. I dare say if you, sir, could have managed the seeing part of the business from your own drawing-room you would not be here in the cold and wet."

Dr Foxcastle drew in his breath sharply and bestowed on John Childermass a look that said that he thought John Childermass very insolent.

Childermass did not seem much dismayed by Dr Foxcastle's opinion of him, indeed he looked rather entertained by it. He said, "It is time, sirs. You should take your stations within the Church. You would be sorry, I am sure, to miss anything when so much hangs upon it."

It was twenty minutes past the hour and gentlemen of the York society were already filing into the Cathedral by the door in the south transept. Several looked about them before going inside, as if taking a last fond farewell of a world they were not quite sure of seeing again.

# 3

# The stones of York

## February 1807

A GREAT OLD CHURCH in the depths of winter is a discouraging place at the best of times; the cold of a hundred winters seems to have been preserved in its stones and to seep out of them. In the cold, dank, twilight interior of the Cathedral the gentlemen of the York society were obliged to stand and wait to be astonished, without any assurance that the surprize when it came would be a pleasant one.

Mr Honeyfoot tried to smile cheerfully at his companions, but for a gentleman so practised in the art of a friendly smile it was a very poor attempt.

Upon the instant bells began to toll. Now these were nothing more than the bells of St Michael-le-Belfrey telling the half hour, but inside the Cathedral they had an odd, far-away sound like the bells of another country. It was not at all a cheerful sound. The gentlemen of the York society knew very well how bells often went with magic and in particular with the magic of those unearthly beings, *fairies*; they knew how, in the old days, silvery bells would often sound just as some Englishman or Englishwoman of particular virtue or beauty was about to be stolen away by fairies to live in strange, ghostly lands for ever. Even the Raven King – who was not a fairy, but an Englishman – had a somewhat regrettable habit of abducting men and women and taking them to live with him in his castle in the Other Lands.[1] Now, had you and I the power to seize by magic any human being that took our fancy and the power to keep that person by our side through all eternity, and had we all the world to chuse from, then I dare say our choice might fall on someone a little more captivating than a member of the Learned Society of York Magicians, but this comforting thought did not occur to the gentlemen inside York Cathedral and several of them began to wonder how angry Dr Foxcastle's letter had made Mr Norrell and they began to be seriously frightened.

As the sounds of the bells died away a voice began to speak from somewhere high up in the gloomy shadows above their heads. The magicians strained their ears to hear it. Many of them were now in such a state of highly-strung nervousness that they imagined that instructions were being given to them as in a fairy-tale. They

[1] The well-known ballad "The Raven King" describes just such an abduction.

Not long, not long my father said
Not long shall you be ours
The Raven King knows all too well
Which are the fairest flowers

The priest was all too worldly
Though he prayed and rang his bell
The Raven King three candles lit
The priest said it was well

Her arms were all too feeble
Though she claimed to love me so
The Raven King stretched out his hand
She sighed and let me go

This land is all too shallow
It is painted on the sky
And trembles like the wind-shook rain
When the Raven King goes by

For always and for always
I pray remember me
Upon the moors, beneath the stars
With the King's wild company

thought that perhaps mysterious prohibitions were being related to them. Such instructions and prohibitions, the magicians knew from the fairy-tales, are usually a little queer, but not very difficult to conform to – or so it seems at first sight. They generally follow the style of: "Do not eat the last candied plum in the blue jar in the corner cupboard," or "Do not beat your wife with a stick made from wormwood." And yet, as all fairy-tales relate, circumstances always conspire against the person who receives the instructions and they find themselves in the middle of doing the very thing that was forbidden to them and a horrible fate is thereby brought upon their heads.

At the very least the magicians supposed that their doom was being slowly recited to them. But it was not at all clear what language the voice was speaking. Once Mr Segundus thought he heard a word that sounded like "*maleficient*" and another time "*interficere*" a Latin word meaning "to kill". The voice itself was not easy to understand; it bore not the slightest resemblance to a human voice – which only served to increase the gentlemen's fear that fairies were about to appear. It was extraordinarily harsh, deep and rasping; it was like two rough stones being scraped together and yet the sounds that were produced were clearly intended to be speech – indeed *were* speech. The gentlemen peered up into the gloom in fearful expectation, but all that could be seen was the small, dim shape of a stone figure that sprang out from one of the shafts of a great pillar and jutted into the gloomy void. As they became accustomed to the queer sound they recognized more and more words; old English words and old Latin words all mixed up together as if the speaker had no conception of these being two distinct languages. Fortunately, this abominable muddle presented few difficulties to the magicians, most of whom were accustomed to unravelling the ramblings and writings of the scholars of long ago. When translated into clear, comprehensible English it was something like this: *Long, long ago*, (said the voice), *five hundred years ago or more, on a winter's day at twilight, a young man entered the Church with a young girl with ivy leaves in her hair. There was no one else there but the stones. No one to see him strangle her but the stones. He let her fall dead upon the stones and no one saw but the stones. He was never punished for his sin because there were no witnesses but the stones. The years went by and whenever the man entered the Church and stood among the congregation the stones cried out that this was the man who had murdered the girl with the ivy leaves wound into her hair, but no one ever heard us. But it is not too late! We know where he is buried! In the corner of the south transept! Quick! Quick! Fetch picks! Fetch shovels! Pull up the paving stones. Dig up his bones! Let them be smashed with the shovel! Dash his skull against the pillars and break it! Let the stones have vengeance too! It is not too late! It is not too late!*

Hardly had the magicians had time to digest this and to wonder some more who it was that spoke, when another stony voice began. This time the voice seemed to issue from the chancel and it spoke only English; yet it was a queer sort of English full of ancient and forgotten words. This voice complained of some soldiers who had entered the Church and broken some windows. A hundred years later they had come again and smashed a rood screen, erased the faces of the saints, carried off plate. Once they had sharpened their arrowheads on the brim of the font; three hundred years later they had fired their pistols in the chapter house. The second voice did not appear to understand that, while a great Church may stand for millennia, men cannot live so long. "They delight in destruction!" it cried. "And they themselves deserve only to be destroyed!" Like the first, this speaker seemed to have stood in the Church for countless years and had, presumably, heard a great many sermons and prayers, yet the sweetest of Christian virtues – mercy, love, meekness – were unknown to him. And all the while the first voice continued to lament the dead girl with ivy leaves in her hair and the two gritty voices clashed together in a manner that was very disagreeable.

Mr Thorpe, who was a valiant gentleman, peeped into the chancel alone, to discover who it was that spoke. "It is a statue," he said.

And then the gentlemen of the York society peered up again into the gloom above their heads in the direction of the first unearthly voice. And this time very few of them had any doubts that it was the little stone figure that spoke, for as they watched they could perceive its stubby stone arms that it waved about in its distress.

Then all the other statues and monuments in the Cathedral began to speak and to say in their stony voices all that they had seen in their stony lives and the noise was, as Mr Segundus later told Mrs Pleasance, beyond description. For York Cathedral had many little carved people and strange animals that flapped their wings.

Many complained of their neighbours and perhaps this is not so surprizing since they had been obliged to stand together for so many hundreds of years. There were fifteen stone kings that stood each upon a stone pedestal in a great stone screen. Their hair was tightly curled as if it had been put into curl papers and never brushed out – and Mrs Honeyfoot could never see them without declaring that she longed to take a hairbrush to each of their royal heads. From the first moment of their being able to speak the kings began quarrelling and scolding each other – for the pedestals were all of a height, and kings – even stone ones – dislike above all things to be made equal to others. There was besides a little group of queer figures with linked arms that looked out with stone eyes from atop an ancient column. As soon as the spell took effect each of these tried to push the others away from him, as if even stone arms begin to ache after a century or so and stone people begin to tire of being shackled to each other.

One statue spoke what seemed to be Italian. No one knew why this should be, though Mr Segundus discovered later that it was a copy of a work by Michael Angel. It seemed to be describing an entirely different church, one where vivid black shadows contrasted sharply with brilliant light. In other words it was describing what the parent-statue in Rome could see.

Mr Segundus was pleased to observe that the magicians, though very frightened, remained within the walls of the Church. Some were so amazed by what they saw that they soon forgot their fear entirely and ran about to discover more and more miracles, making observations, writing down notes with pencils in little memorandum books as if they had forgotten the perfidious document which from today would prevent them studying magic. For a long time the magicians of York (soon, alas, to be magicians no more!) wandered through the aisles and saw marvels. And at every moment their ears were assaulted by the hideous cacophony of a thousand stone voices all speaking together.

In the chapter house there were stone canopies with many little stone heads with strange headgear that all chattered and cackled together. Here were marvellous stone carvings of a hundred English trees: hawthorn, oak, blackthorn, wormwood, cherry and bryony. Mr Segundus found two stone dragons no longer than his forearm, which slipped one after the other, over and under and between stone hawthorn branches, stone hawthorn leaves, stone hawthorn roots and stone hawthorn tendrils. They moved, it seemed, with as much ease as any other creature and yet the sound of so many stone muscles moving together under a stone skin, that scraped stone ribs, that clashed against a heart made of stone – and the sound of stone claws rattling over stone branches – was quite intolerable and Mr Segundus wondered that they could bear it. He observed a little cloud of gritty dust, such as attends the work of a stonecutter, that surrounded them and rose up in the air; and he believed that if the spell allowed them to remain in motion for any length of time they would wear themselves away to a sliver of limestone.

Stone leaves and herbs quivered and shook as if tossed in the breeze and some of them so far emulated their vegetable counterparts as to grow. Later, when the spell had broken, strands of stone ivy and stone rose briars would be discovered wound around chairs and lecterns and prayer-books where no stone ivy or briars had been before.

But it was not only the magicians of the York society who saw wonders that day. Whether he had intended it or not Mr Norrell's magic had spread beyond the Cathedral close and into the city. Three statues from the west front of the Cathedral had been taken to Mr Taylor's workshops to be mended. Centuries of Yorkshire rain had worn down these images and no one knew any longer what great personages they were intended to represent. At half past ten one of Mr Taylor's masons had just raised his chisel to the face of one of these statues intending to fashion it into the likeness of a pretty saintess; at that moment the statue cried out aloud and raised its arm to ward off the chisel, causing the poor workman to fall down in a swoon. The statues were later returned to the exterior of the Cathedral untouched, their faces worn as flat as biscuits and as bland as butter.

Then all at once there seemed a change in the sound and one by one the voices stopped until the magicians heard the bells of St Michael-le-Belfrey ring for the half hour again. The first voice (the voice of the little figure high up in the darkness) continued for some time after the others had fallen silent, upon its old theme of the undiscovered murderer (*It is not too late! It is not too late!*) until it too fell silent.

The world had changed while the magicians had been inside the Church. Magic had returned to England whether the magicians wished it to or not. Other changes of a more prosaic nature had also occurred: the sky had filled with heavy, snow-laden clouds. These were scarcely grey at all, but a queer mixture of slate-blue and sea-green. This curious coloration made a kind of twilight such as one imagines is the usual illumination in fabled kingdoms under the sea.

Mr Segundus felt very tired by his adventure. Other gentlemen had been more frightened than he; he had seen magic and thought it wonderful beyond any thing he had imagined, and yet now that it was over his spirits were greatly agitated and he wished very much to be allowed to go quietly home without speaking to any one. While he was in this susceptible condition he found himself halted and addressed by Mr Norrell's man of business.

"I believe, sir," said Mr Childermass, "that the society must now be broken up. I am sorry for it."

Now it may have been due entirely to Mr Segundus's lowness of spirits, but he suspected that, in spite of Childermass's manner which was very respectful, in some other part of Childermass's person he was laughing at the York magicians. Childermass was one of that uncomfortable class of men whose birth is lowly and who are destined all their lives to serve their betters, but whose clever brains and quick abilities make them wish for recognition and rewards far beyond their reach. Sometimes, by some strange combination of happy circumstances, these men find their own path to greatness, but more often the thought of what might have been turns them sour; they become unwilling servants and perform their tasks no better – or worse – than their less able fellows. They become insolent, lose their places and end badly.

"I beg your pardon, sir," said Childermass, "but I have a question to put to you. I hope you will not think it impertinent, but I would like to know if you ever look into a London paper?"

Mr Segundus replied that he did.

"Indeed? That is most interesting. I myself am fond of a newspaper. But I have little leisure for reading – except such books as come my way in the course of my duties for Mr Norrell. And what sort of thing does one find in a London paper nowadays? – you will excuse my asking, sir, only Mr Norrell, who never looks at a paper of any sort, put the question to me yesterday and I did not think myself qualified to answer it."

"Well," said Mr Segundus, a little puzzled, "there are all sorts of things. What did you wish to know? There are accounts of the actions of His Majesty's Navy against the French; speeches of the Government; reports of scandals and divorces. Is this what you meant?"

"Oh yes!" said Childermass. "You explain it very well, sir. I wonder," he continued, growing thoughtful, "whether provincial news is ever reported in the London papers? – whether (for example) today's remarkable occurrences might merit a paragraph?"

"I do not know," said Mr Segundus. "It seems to me quite possible but then, you know, Yorkshire is so far from London – perhaps the London editors will never get to hear of what has happened."

"Ah," said Mr Childermass; and then was silent.

Snow began to fall; a few flakes at first – then rather more than a few; until a million little flakes were drifting down from a soft, heavy greenish-grey sky. All the buildings of York became a little fainter, a little greyer in the snow; the people all seemed a little smaller; the cries and shouts, the footsteps and hoofsteps, the creaks of carriages and the slammings of doors were all a little more distant. And all these things became somehow less important until all the world contained was the falling snow, the sea-green sky, the dim, grey ghost of York Cathedral – and Childermass.

And all this time Childermass said nothing. Mr Segundus wondered what more he required – all his questions had been answered. But Childermass waited and watched Mr Segundus with his queer black eyes, as if he were waiting for Mr Segundus to say one thing more – as if he fully expected that Mr Segundus would say it – indeed as if nothing in the world were more certain.

"If you wish," said Mr Segundus, shaking the snow from his cape, "I can remove all the uncertainty from the business. I can write a letter to the editor of *The Times* informing him of Mr Norrell's extraordinary feats."

"Ah! That is generous indeed!" said Childermass. "Believe me, sir, I know very well that not every gentleman would be so magnanimous in defeat. But it is no more than I expected. For I told Mr Norrell that I did not think there could be a more obliging gentleman than Mr Segundus."

"Not at all," said Mr Segundus, "it is nothing."

The Learned Society of York Magicians was disbanded and its members were obliged to give up magic (all except Mr Segundus) – and, though some of them were foolish and not all of them were entirely amiable, I do not think that they deserved such a fate. For what is a magician to do who, in accordance with a pernicious agreement, is not allowed to study magic? He idles about his house day after day, disturbs his niece (or wife, or daughter) at her needlework and pesters the servants with questions about matters in which he never took an interest before – all for the sake of having someone to talk to, until the servants complain of him to their mistress. He picks up a book and begins to read, but he is not attending to what he reads and he has got to page 22 before he discovers it is a *novel* – the sort of work which above all others he most despises – and he puts it down in disgust. He asks his niece (or wife, or daughter) ten times a day what o'clock it is, for he cannot believe that time can go so slowly – and he falls out with his pocket watch for the same reason.

Mr Honeyfoot, I am glad to say, fared a little better than the others. He, kind-hearted soul, had been very much affected by the story that the little stone figure high up in the dimness had related. It had carried the knowledge of the horrid murder in its small stone heart for centuries, it remembered the dead girl with the ivy leaves in her hair when no one else did, and Mr Honeyfoot thought that its faithfulness ought to be rewarded. So he wrote to the Dean and to the Canons and to the Archbishop, and he made himself very troublesome until these important personages agreed to allow Mr Honeyfoot to dig up the paving stones of the south transept. And when this was done Mr Honeyfoot and the men he had employed uncovered some bones in a leaden coffin, just as the little stone figure had said they would. But then the Dean said that he could not authorize the removal of the bones from the Cathedral (which was what Mr Honeyfoot wanted) on the evidence of the little stone figure; there was no precedent for such a thing. Ah! said Mr Honeyfoot but there was, you know; and the argument raged for a number of years and, as a consequence, Mr Honeyfoot really had no leisure to repent signing Mr Norrell's document.[2]

The library of the Learned Society of York Magicians was sold to Mr Thoroughgood of Coffee-yard. But somehow no one thought to mention this to Mr Segundus and he only learnt about it in a round-about fashion when Mr Thoroughgood's shopboy told a friend (that was a clerk in Priestley's linen-drapers) and the friend chanced to mention it to Mrs Cockcroft of the George Inn and she told Mrs Pleasance who was Mr Segundus's landlady. As soon as Mr Segundus heard of it he ran down through the snowy streets to Mr Thoroughgood's shop without troubling to put on his hat or his coat or his boots. But the books were already gone. He inquired of Mr Thoroughgood who had bought them. Mr Thoroughgood begged Mr Segundus's pardon but he feared he could not divulge the name of the gentleman; he did not think the

---

[2] The example cited by Mr Honeyfoot was of a murder that had taken place in 1279 in the grim moor town of Alston. The body of a young boy was found in the churchyard hanging from a thorn-tree that stood before the church-door. Above the door was a statue of the Virgin and Child. So the people of Alston sent to Newcastle, to the Castle of the Raven King and the Raven King sent two magicians to make the Virgin and the Jesus-Child speak and say how they had seen a stranger kill the boy, but for what reason they did not know. And after that, whenever a stranger came to the town, the people of Alston would drag him before the church-door and ask "Is this him?" but always the Virgin and Child replied that it was not. Beneath the Virgin's feet were a lion and a dragon who curled around each other in a most puzzling manner and bit each other's necks. These creatures had been carved by someone who had never seen a lion or a dragon, but who had seen a great many dogs and sheep and something of the character of a dog and a sheep had got into his carving. Whenever some poor fellow was brought before the Virgin and Child to be examined the lion and the dragon would cease biting each other and look up like the Virgin's strange watchdogs and the lion would bark and the dragon would bleat angrily.

Years went by and the townspeople who remembered the boy were all dead, and the likelihood was that the murderer was too. But the Virgin and Child had somehow got into the habit of speaking and whenever some unfortunate stranger passed within the compass of their gaze they would still turn their stone heads and say, "It is not him." And Alston acquired the reputation of an eerie place and people would not go there if they could help it.

gentleman wished his name to be generally known. Mr Segundus, hatless and coatless and breathless, with water-logged shoes and mud-splashes on his stockings and the eyes of everybody in the shop upon him, had some satisfaction in telling Mr Thoroughgood that it did not signify whether Mr Thoroughgood told him or not, for he believed he knew the gentleman anyway.

Mr Segundus did not lack curiosity about Mr Norrell. He thought about him a great deal and often talked of him with Mr Honeyfoot.[3] Mr Honeyfoot was certain that everything that had happened could be explained by an earnest wish on Mr Norrell's part to bring back magic to England. Mr Segundus was more doubtful and began to look about him to try if he could discover any acquaintance of Norrell's that might be able to tell him something more.

A gentleman in Mr Norrell's position with a fine house and a large estate will always be of interest to his neighbours and, unless those neighbours are very stupid, they will always contrive to know a little of what he does. Mr Segundus discovered a family in Stonegate who were cousins to some people that had a farm five miles from Hurtfew Abbey – and he befriended the Stonegate-family and persuaded them to hold a dinner-party and to invite their cousins to come to it. (Mr Segundus grew quite shocked at his own skill in thinking up these little stratagems.) The cousins duly arrived and were all most ready to talk about their rich and peculiar neighbour who had bewitched York Cathedral, but the

---

[3] To aid his better understanding of Mr Norrell's character and of Mr Norrell's magical powers Mr Segundus wrote a careful description of the visit to Hurtfew Abbey. Unfortunately he found his memory on this point peculiarly unclear. Whenever he returned to read what he had written he discovered that he now remembered things differently. Each time he began by crossing out words and phrases and putting in new ones, and he ended by re-writing completely. After four or five months he was obliged to admit to himself that he no longer knew what Mr Honeyfoot had said to Mr Norrell, or what Mr Norrell had said in reply, or what he – Mr Segundus – had seen in the house. He concluded that to attempt to write any thing upon the subject was futile, and he threw what he had written into the fire.

beginning and the end of their information was that Mr Norrell was about to leave Yorkshire and go to London.

Mr Segundus was surprized to hear this, but more than that he was surprized at the effect this news had upon his own spirits. He felt oddly discomfited by it – which was very ridiculous, he told himself; Norrell had never shewn any interest in him or done him the least kindness. Yet Norrell was Mr Segundus's only colleague now. When he was gone Mr Segundus would be the only magician, the last magician in Yorkshire.

# 4

# The Friends of English Magic

## Early spring 1807

CONSIDER, IF YOU WILL, a man who sits in his library day after day; a small man of no particular personal attractions. His book is on the table before him. A fresh supply of pens, a knife to cut new nibs, ink, paper, notebooks – all is conveniently to hand. There is always a fire in the room – he cannot do without a fire, he feels the cold. The room changes with the season: he does not. Three tall windows open on a view of English countryside which is tranquil in spring, cheerful in summer, melancholy in autumn and gloomy in winter – just as English landscape should be. But the changing seasons excite no interest in him – he scarcely raises his eyes from the pages of his book. He takes his exercise as all gentlemen do; in dry weather his long walk crosses the park and skirts a little wood; in wet weather there is his short walk in the shrubbery. But he knows very little of shrubbery or park or wood. There is a book waiting for him upon the library table; his eyes fancy they still follow its lines of type, his head still runs upon its argument, his fingers itch to take it up again. He meets his neighbours twice or thrice a quarter – for this is England where a man's neighbours will never suffer him to live entirely bereft of society, let him be as dry and sour-faced as he may. They pay him visits, leave their cards with his servants, invite him to dine or to dance at assembly-balls. Their intentions are largely charitable – they have a notion that it is bad for a man to be always alone – but they also have some curiosity to discover whether he has changed at all since they last saw him. He has not. He has nothing to say to them and is considered the dullest man in Yorkshire.

Yet within Mr Norrell's dry little heart there was as lively an ambition to bring back magic to England as would have satisfied even Mr Honeyfoot, and it was with the intention of bringing that ambition to a long-postponed fulfilment that Mr Norrell now proposed to go to London.

Childermass assured him that the time was propitious and Childermass knew the world. Childermass knew what games the children on street-corners are playing – games that all other grown-ups have long since forgotten. Childermass knew what old people by firesides are thinking of, though no one has asked them in years. Childermass knew what young men hear in the rattling of the drums and the tooting of the pipes that makes them leave their homes and go to be soldiers – and he knew the half-eggcupful of glory and the barrelful of misery that await them. Childermass could look at a smart attorney in the street and tell you what he had in his coat-tail pockets. And all that Childermass knew made him smile; and some of what he knew made him laugh out loud; and none of what he knew wrung from him so much as ha'pennyworth of pity.

So when Childermass told his master, "Go to London. Go now," Mr Norrell believed him.

"The only thing I do not quite like," said Mr Norrell, "is your plan to have Segundus write to one of the London newspapers upon our behalf. He is certain to make errors in what he writes – have you thought of that? I dare say he will try his hand at interpretation. These third-rate scholars can never resist putting in something of themselves. He will make guesses – wrong guesses – at the sorts of magic I employed at York. Surely there is enough confusion surrounding magic without our adding to it. Must we make use of Segundus?"

Childermass bent his dark gaze upon his master and his even darker smile, and replied that he believed they must. "I wonder, sir," he said, "if you have lately heard of a naval gentleman of the name of Baines?"

"I believe I know the man you mean," said Mr Norrell.

"Ah!" said Childermass. "And how did you come to hear of him?"

A short silence.

"Well then," said Mr Norrell reluctantly, "I suppose that I have seen Captain Baines's name in one of the newspapers."

"Lieutenant Hector Baines served on *The King of the North*, a frigate," said Childermass. "At twenty-one years of age he lost a leg and two or three fingers in an action in the West Indies. In the same battle the Captain of *The King of the North* and many of the seamen died. Reports that Lieutenant Baines continued to command the ship and issue orders to his crew while the ship's doctor was actually sawing at his leg are, I dare say, a good deal exaggerated, but he certainly brought a fearfully damaged ship out of the Indies, attacked a Spanish ship full of bounty, gained a fortune and came home a hero. He jilted the young lady to whom he was engaged and married another. This, sir, is the Captain's history as it appeared in *The Morning Post*. And now I shall tell you what followed. Baines is a northerner like you, sir, a man of obscure birth with no great friends to make life easy for him. Shortly after his marriage he and his bride went to London to stay at the house of some friends in Seacoal-lane, and while they were there they were visited by people of all ranks and stations. They ate their dinner at viscountesses' tables, were toasted by Members of Parliament, and all that influence and patronage can do for Captain Baines was promised to him. This success, sir, I attribute to the general approbation and esteem which the report in the newspaper gained for him. But perhaps you have friends in London who will perform the same services for you without troubling the editors of the newspapers?"

"You know very well that I do not," said Mr Norrell impatiently.

In the meantime, Mr Segundus laboured very long over his letter and it grieved him that he could not be more warm in his praise of Mr Norrell. It seemed to him that the readers of the London newspaper would expect him to say something of Mr Norrell's personal virtues and would wonder why he did not.

In due course the letter appeared in *The Times* entitled: "EXTRAORDINARY OCCURRENCES IN YORK: AN APPEAL TO THE FRIENDS OF ENGLISH MAGIC." Mr Segundus ended his description of the magic at York by saying that the Friends of English Magic must surely bless that love of extreme retirement which marked Mr Norrell's character – for it had fostered his studies and had at last borne fruit in the shape of the wonderful magic at York Cathedral – but, said Mr Segundus, he appealed to the Friends of English Magic to join him in begging Mr Norrell not to return to a life of solitary study but to take his place upon the wider stage of the Nation's affairs and so begin a new chapter in the History of English Magic.

AN APPEAL TO THE FRIENDS OF ENGLISH MAGIC had a most sensational effect, particularly in London. The readers of *The Times* were quite thunderstruck by Mr Norrell's achievements. There was a general desire to see Mr Norrell; young ladies pitied the poor old gentlemen of York who had been so frightened by him, and wished very much to be as terrified themselves. Clearly such an opportunity as this was scarcely likely to come again; Mr Norrell determined to establish himself in London with all possible haste. "You must get me a house, Childermass," he said. "Get me a house that says to those that visit it that magic is a respectable profession – no less than Law and a great deal more so than Medicine."

Childermass inquired drily if Mr Norrell wished him to seek out architecture expressive of the proposition that magic was as respectable as the Church?

Mr Norrell (who knew there were such things as jokes in the world or people would not write about them in books, but who had never actually been introduced to a joke or shaken its hand) considered a while before replying at last that no, he did not think they could quite claim that.

So Childermass (perhaps thinking that nothing in the world is so respectable as money) directed his master to a house in Hanover-square among the abodes of the rich and prosperous. Now I do not know what may be your opinion yet to say the truth I do not much care for the south side of Hanover-square; the houses are so tall and thin – four storeys at least – and all the tall, gloomy windows are so regular, and every house so exactly resembles its neighbours that they have something of the appearance of a high wall blocking out the light. Be that as it may, Mr Norrell (a less fanciful person than I) was satisfied with his new house, or at least as satisfied as any gentleman could be who for more than thirty years has lived in a large country-house surrounded by a park of mature timber, which is in its turn surrounded by a good estate of farms and woods – a gentleman, in other words, whose eye has never been offended by the sight of any other man's property whenever he looked out of the window.

"It is certainly a small house, Childermass," he said, "but I do not complain. My own comfort, as you know, I do not regard."

Childermass replied that the house was larger than most.

"Indeed?" said Mr Norrell, much surprized. Mr Norrell was particularly shocked by the smallness of the library, which could not be made to accommodate one third of the books he considered indispensable; he asked Childermass how people in London housed their books? Perhaps they did not read?

Mr Norrell had been in London not above three weeks when he received a letter from a Mrs Godesdone, a lady of whom he had never heard before.

". . . I know it is very *shoking* that I should write to you upon no acquaintance whatsoever & no doubt you say to yourself who is this impertinent creachure? I did not now there was such a person in existence! and consider me shokingly bold etc. etc. but Drawlight is a dear freind of mine and assures me that you are the sweetest-natured creachure in the world and will not mind it. I am most impatient for the pleasure of your acquaintance and would consider it the greatest honour in the world if you would consent to give us the pleasure of your company at an evening-party on Thursday se'night. Do not let the apprehension of meeting with a croud prevent you from coming – I detest a croud of all things and only my most intimate freinds will be invited to meet you . . ."

It was not the sort of letter to make any very favourable impression upon Mr Norrell. He read it through very rapidly, put it aside with an exclamation of disgust and took up his book again. A short while later Childermass arrived to attend to the morning's business. He read Mrs Godesdone's letter and inquired what answer Mr Norrell intended to return to it?

"A refusal," said Mr Norrell.

"Indeed? And shall I say that you have a prior engagement?" asked Childermass.

"Certainly, if you wish," said Mr Norrell.

"And *do* you have a prior engagement?" asked Childermass.

"No," said Mr Norrell.

"Ah!" said Childermass. "Then perhaps it is the overabundance of your engagements on other days that makes you refuse this one? You fear to be too tired?"

"I have no engagements. You know very well that I do not." Mr Norrell read for another minute or two before remarking (apparently to his book), "You are still here."

"I am," said Childermass.

"Well then," said Mr Norrell, "what is it? What is the matter?"

"I had thought you were come to London to shew people what a modern magician looked like. It will be a slow business if you are to stay at home all the time."

Mr Norrell said nothing. He picked up the letter and looked at it. "Drawlight," he said at last. "What does she mean by that? I know no one of that name."

"I do not know what she means," said Childermass, "but I do know this: at present it will not do to be too nice."

At eight o'clock on the evening of Mrs Godesdone's party Mr Norrell in his best grey coat was seated in his carriage, wondering about Mrs Godesdone's dear friend, Drawlight, when he was roused to a realization that the carriage was no longer moving. Looking out of the window he saw a great lamp-lit chaos of people, carriages and horses. Thinking that everyone else must find the London streets as confusing as he did, he naturally fell into the supposition that his coachman and footman had lost their way and, banging on the roof of the carriage with his stick, he cried, "Davey! Lucas! Did not you hear me say Manchester-street? Why did you not make sure of the way before we set off?"

Lucas, on the box-seat, called down that they were already in Manchester-street, but must wait their turn – there was a long line of carriages that were to stop at the house before them.

"Which house?" cried Mr Norrell.

The house they were going to, said Lucas.

"No, no! You are mistaken," said Mr Norrell. "It is to be a small gathering."

But on his arrival at Mrs Godesdone's house Mr Norrell found himself instantly plunged into the midst of a hundred or so of Mrs Godesdone's most intimate friends. The hall and reception rooms were crowded with people and more were arriving at every moment. Mr Norrell was very much astonished, yet what in the world was there to be surprized at? It was a fashionable London party, no different from any other that might be held at any of half a dozen houses across Town every day of the week.

And how to describe a London party? Candles in lustres of cut-glass are placed everywhere about the house in dazzling profusion; elegant mirrors triple and quadruple the light until night outshines day; many-coloured hot-house fruits are piled up in stately pyramids upon white-clothed tables; divine creatures, resplendent with jewels, go about the room in pairs, arm in arm, admired by all who see them. Yet the heat is over-powering, the pressure and noise almost as bad; there is nowhere to sit and scarce anywhere to stand. You may see your dearest friend in another part of the room; you may have a world of things to tell him – but how in the world will you ever reach him? If you are fortunate then perhaps you will discover him later in the crush and shake his hand as you are both hurried past each other. Surrounded by cross, hot strangers, your chance of rational conversation is equal to what it would be in an African desert. Your only wish is to preserve your favourite gown from the worst ravages of the crowd. Every body complains of the heat and the suffocation. Every body declares it to be entirely insufferable. But if it is all misery for the guests, then what of the wretchedness of those who have not been invited? Our sufferings are nothing to theirs! And we may tell each other tomorrow that it was a delightful party.

It so happened that Mr Norrell arrived at the same moment as a very old lady. Though small and disagreeable-looking she was clearly someone of importance (she was all over diamonds). The servants clustered round her and Mr Norrell proceeded into the house, unobserved by any of them. He entered a room full of people where he discovered a cup of punch upon a little table. While he was drinking the punch it occurred to him that he had told no one his name and consequently no one knew he was here. He found himself in some perplexity as to how to proceed. His fellow-guests were occupied in greeting their friends, and as for approaching one of the servants and announcing himself, Mr Norrell felt quite unequal to the task; their proud faces and air of indescribable superiority unnerved him. It was a great pity that one or two of the late members of the Society of York Magicians were not there to see him looking so all forlorn and ill at ease; it might have cheered them up immeasurably. But it is the same with all of us. In familiar surroundings our manners are cheerful and easy, but only transport us to places where we know no one and no one knows us, and Lord! how uncomfortable we become!

Mr Norrell was wandering from room to room, wishing only to go away again, when he was stopped in mid-perambulation by the sound of his own name and the following enigmatic words: ". . . assures me that he is never to be seen without a mystic robe of midnight blue, adorned with otherlandish symbols! But Drawlight – who knows this Norrell very well – says that . . ."

The noise of the room was such that it is to be marvelled at that Mr Norrell heard anything at all. The words had been spoken by a young woman and Mr Norrell looked frantically about him to try and discover her, but without success. He began to wonder what else was being said about him.

He found himself standing near to a lady and a gentleman. *She* was unremarkable enough – a sensible-looking woman of forty or fifty – *he*, however, was a style of man not commonly seen in Yorkshire. He was rather small and was dressed very carefully in a good black coat and linen of a most exquisite whiteness. He had a little pair of silver spectacles that swung from a black velvet ribbon around his neck. His features were very regular and rather good; he had short, dark hair and his skin was very clean and white – except that about his cheeks there was the faintest suggestion of rouge. But it was his eyes that were remarkable: large, well-shaped, dark and so very brilliant as to have an almost liquid appearance. They were fringed with the longest, darkest eyelashes. There were many little feminine touches about him that he had contrived for himself, but his eyes and eyelashes were the only ones which nature had given him.

Mr Norrell paid good attention to their conversation to discover if they were talking about him.

". . . the advice that I gave Lady Duncombe about her own daughter," said the small man. "Lady Duncombe had found a most unexceptional husband for her daughter, a gentleman with nine hundred a year! But the silly girl had set her heart upon a penniless Captain in the Dragoons, and poor Lady Duncombe was almost frantic. 'Oh, your ladyship!' I cried the instant that I heard about it, 'Make yourself easy! Leave everything to me. I do not set up as any very extraordinary genius, as your ladyship knows, but my odd talents are exactly suited to this sort of thing.' Oh, madam! you will laugh when you hear how I contrived matters! I dare say no one else in the world would have thought of such a ridiculous scheme! I took Miss Susan to Gray's in Bond-street where we both spent a very agreeable morning in trying on necklaces and earrings. She has passed most of her life in Derbyshire and has not been accustomed to really *remarkable* jewels. I do not think she had ever thought *seriously* upon such things before. Then Lady Duncombe and I dropt one or two hints that in marrying Captain Hurst she would put it quite out of her power to make such delightful purchases ever again, whereas if she married Mr Watts she might make her choice of the best of them. I next took pains to get acquainted with Captain Hurst and persuaded him to accompany me to Boodle's where – well I will not deceive you, madam – where there is gambling!" The small man giggled. "I lent him a little money to try his luck – it was not my own money you understand. Lady Duncombe had given it to me for the purpose. We went three or four times and in a remarkably short space of time the Captain's debts were – well, madam, *I* cannot see how he will ever get clear of them! Lady Duncombe and I represented to him that it is one thing to expect a young woman to marry upon a small income, but quite another to expect her to take a man encumbered with debts. He was not inclined to listen to us at first. At first he made use of – what shall I say? – some rather *military* expressions. But in the end he was obliged to admit the justice of all we said."

Mr Norrell saw the sensible-looking woman of forty or fifty give the small man a look of some dislike. Then she bowed, very slightly and coldly, and passed without a word away into the crowd; the small man turned in the other direction and immediately hailed a friend.

Mr Norrell's eye was next caught by an excessively pretty young woman in a white-and-silver gown. A tall, handsome-looking man was talking to her and she was laughing very heartily at everything he said.

". . . and what if he should discover two dragons – one red and one white – beneath the foundations of the house, locked in eternal struggle and symbolizing the future destruction of Mr Godesdone? I dare say," said the man slyly, "you would not mind it if he did."

She laughed again, even more merrily than before, and Mr Norrell was surprized to hear in the next instant someone address her as "Mrs Godesdone".

Upon reflection Mr Norrell thought that he ought to have spoken to her but by then she was nowhere to be seen. He was sick of the noise and sight of so many people and determined to go quietly away, but it so happened that just at that moment the crowds about the door were particularly impenetrable; he was caught up in the current of people and carried away to quite another part of the room. Round and round he went like a dry leaf caught up in a drain; in one of these turns around the room he discovered a quiet corner near a window. A tall screen of carved ebony inlaid with mother-of-pearl half-hid – ah! what bliss was this! – a bookcase. Mr Norrell slipped behind the screen, took down John Napier's *A Plaine Discouverie of the Whole Revelation of St John* and began to read.

He had not been there very long when, happening to glance up, he saw the tall, handsome man who had been speaking to Mrs Godesdone and the small, dark man who had gone to such trouble to destroy the matrimonial hopes of Captain Hurst. They were discoursing energetically, but the press and flow of people around them was so great that, without any ceremony, the tall man got hold of the small man's sleeve and pulled him behind the screen and into the corner which Mr Norrell occupied.

"He is not here," said the tall man, giving each word an emphasis with a poke of his finger in the other's shoulder. "Where are the fiercely burning eyes that you promised us? Where the trances that none of us can explain? Has any one been cursed? – I do not think so. You have called him up like a spirit from the vasty deep, and he has not come."

"I was with him only this morning," said the small man defiantly, "to hear of the wonderful magic that he has been doing recently and he said then that he would come."

"It is past midnight. He will not come now." The tall man smiled a very superior smile. "Confess, you do not know him."

Then the small man smiled in rivalry of the other's smile (these two gentlemen positively jousted in smiles) and said, "No one in London knows him better. I shall confess that I am a little – a very little – disappointed."

"Ha!" cried the tall man. "It is the opinion of the room that we have all been most abominably imposed upon. We came here in the expectation of seeing something very extraordinary, and instead we have been obliged to provide our own amusement." His eye happening to light upon Mr Norrell, he said, "*That* gentleman is reading a book."

The small man glanced behind him and in doing so happened to knock his elbow against *A Plaine Discouverie of the Whole Revelation of St John.* He gave Mr Norrell a cool look for filling up so very small a space with so very large a book.

"I have said that I am disappointed," continued the small man, "but I am not at all surprized. You do not know him as I do. Oh! I can assure you he has a pretty shrewd notion of his value. No one can have a better. A man who buys a house in Hanover-square knows the style in which things ought to be done. Oh, yes! He has bought a house in Hanover-square! You had not heard that, I dare say? He is as rich as a Jew. He had an old uncle called Haythornthwaite who died and left him a world of money. He has – among other trifles – a good house and a large estate – that of Hurtfew Abbey in Yorkshire."

"Ha!" said the tall man drily. "He was in high luck. Rich old uncles who die are in shockingly short supply."

"Oh, indeed!" cried the small man. "Some friends of mine, the Griffins, have an amazingly rich old uncle to whom they have paid all sorts of attentions for years and years – but though he was at least a hundred years old when they began, he is not dead yet and it seems he intends to live for ever to spite them, and all the Griffins are growing old themselves and dying one by one in a state of the most bitter disappointment. Yet I am sure that *you*, my dear Lascelles, need not concern yourself with any such vexatious old persons – your fortune is comfortable enough, is it not?"

The tall man chose to disregard this particular piece of impertinence and instead remarked coolly, "I believe that gentleman wishes to speak to you."

The gentleman in question was Mr Norrell who, quite amazed to hear his fortune and property discussed so openly, had been waiting to speak for some minutes past. "I beg your pardon," he said.

"Yes?" said the small man sharply.

"I am Mr Norrell."

The tall man and the small man gave Mr Norrell two very broad stares.

After a silence of some moments the small gentleman, who had begun by looking offended, had passed through a stage of looking blank and was beginning to look puzzled, asked Mr Norrell to repeat his name.

This Mr Norrell did, whereupon the small gentleman said, "I do beg your pardon, but . . . Which is to say . . . I hope you will excuse my asking so impertinent a question, but is there at your house in Hanover-square someone all dressed in black, with a thin face like a twisted hedge-root?"

Mr Norrell thought for a moment and then he said, "Childermass. You mean Childermass."

"Oh, Childermass!" cried the small man, as if all was now perfectly plain. "Yes, of course! How stupid of me! That is Childermass! Oh, Mr Norrell! I can hardly begin to express my delight in making your acquaintance. My name, sir, is Drawlight."

"Do you know Childermass?" asked Mr Norrell, puzzled.

"I . . ." Mr Drawlight paused. "I have seen such a person as I described coming out of your house and I . . . Oh, Mr Norrell! Such a noodle I am upon occasion! I mistook him for you! Pray do not be offended, sir! For now that I behold you, I plainly see that whereas *he* has the wild, romantic looks one associates with magicians, *you* have the meditative air of a scholar. Lascelles, does not Mr Norrell have the grave and sober bearing of a scholar?"

The tall man said, without much enthusiasm, that he supposed so.

"Mr Norrell, my friend, Mr Lascelles," said Drawlight.

Mr Lascelles made the slightest of bows.

"Oh, Mr Norrell!" cried Mr Drawlight. "You cannot imagine the torments I have suffered tonight, in wondering whether or not you would come! At seven o'clock my anxieties upon this point were so acute that I could not help myself! I actually went down to the Glasshouse-street boiling-cellar expressly to inquire of Davey and Lucas to know their opinions! Davey was certain that you would not come, which threw me, as you may imagine, into the utmost despair!"

"Davey and Lucas!" said Mr Norrell in tones of the greatest astonishment. (These, it may be remembered, were the names of Mr Norrell's coachman and footman.)

"Oh, yes!" said Mr Drawlight. "The Glasshouse-street boiling-cellar is where Davey and Lucas occasionally take their mutton, as I dare say you know." Mr Drawlight paused in his flow of chatter, just long enough for Mr Norrell to murmur that he had not known that.

"I have been most industriously talking up your extraordinary powers to all my wide acquaintance," continued Mr Drawlight. "I have been your John the Baptist, sir, preparing the way for you! – and I felt no hesitation in declaring that you and I were great friends for I had a presentiment from the first, my dear Mr Norrell, that we would be; and as you see I was quite right, for now here we are, chatting so comfortably to one another!"

# 5

# Drawlight

## Spring to autumn 1807

EARLY NEXT MORNING Mr Norrell's man of business, Childermass, answered a summons to attend his master in the breakfast-room. He found Mr Norrell pale-faced and in a state of some nervous agitation.

"What is the matter?" asked Childermass.

"Oh!" cried Mr Norrell, looking up. "You dare to ask me that! You, who have so neglected your duties that any scoundrel may put a watch upon my house and question my servants without fear of disturbance! Aye, and get answers to those questions, too! What do I employ you for, I should like to know, if not to protect me from such impertinence as this?"

Childermass shrugged. "You mean Drawlight, I suppose."

A short, astonished silence.

"You knew of it?" cried Mr Norrell. "Good God, man! What were you thinking of? Have you not told me a hundred times that, in order to secure my privacy, the servants must be kept from gossiping?"

"Oh! certainly!" said Childermass. "But I am very much afraid, sir, that you must give up some of your habits of privacy. Retirement and seclusion are all very well in Yorkshire, but we are not in Yorkshire any more."

"Yes, yes!" said Mr Norrell irritably. "I know that we are not.

But that is not the question. The question is: what does this Drawlight want?"

"To have the distinction of being the first gentleman in London to make the acquaintance of a magician. That is all."

But Mr Norrell was not to be reasoned out of his fears. He rubbed his yellow-white hands nervously together, and directed fearful glances into the shadowy corners of the room as though suspecting them of harbouring other Drawlights, all spying upon him. "He did not look like a scholar in those clothes," he said, "but that is no guarantee of any thing. He wore no rings of power or allegiance but still . . ."

"I do not well understand you," said Childermass. "Speak plainly."

"Might he not have some *skill* of his own, do you suppose?" said Mr Norrell. "Or perhaps he has friends who are jealous of my success! Who are his associates? What is his education?"

Childermass smiled a long smile that went all up one side of his face. "Oh! You have talked yourself into a belief that he is the agent of some other magician. Well, sir, he is not. You may depend upon me for that. Far from neglecting your interests, after we received Mrs Godesdone's letter I made some inquiries about the gentleman – as many, I dare say, as he has made about you. It would be an odd sort of magician, I think, that employed such a creature as he is. Besides, if such a magician had existed you would have long since found him out, would not you? – and discovered the means to part him from his books and put an end to his scholarship? You have done it before, you know."

"You know no harm of this Drawlight then?"

Childermass raised an eyebrow and smiled his sideways smile. "Upon the contrary," he said.

"Ah!" cried Mr Norrell, "I knew it! Well then, I shall certainly make a point of avoiding his society."

"Why?" asked Childermass. "I did not say so. Have I not just told you that he is no threat to you? What is it to you that he is a bad man? Take my advice, sir, make use of the tool which is to hand."

Then Childermass related to Mr Norrell what he had discovered about Drawlight: how he belonged to a certain breed of gentlemen, only to be met with in London, whose main occupation is the wearing of expensive and fashionable clothes; how they pass their lives in ostentatious idleness, gambling and drinking to excess and spending months at a time in Brighton and other fashionable watering places; how in recent years this breed seemed to have reached a sort of perfection in Christopher Drawlight. Even his dearest friends would have admitted that he possessed not a single good quality.[1]

Despite Mr Norrell's tuttings and suckings-in of air at every new revelation, there is no doubt that this conversation did him good. When Lucas entered the room ten minutes later with a pot of chocolate, he was composedly eating toast and preserves and appeared entirely different from the anxious, fretful creature he had been earlier that morning.

A loud rap was heard at the door and Lucas went to answer it. A light tread was next heard upon the stairs and Lucas re-appeared to announce, "Mr Drawlight!"

"Ah, Mr Norrell! How do you do, sir?" Mr Drawlight entered the room. He wore a dark blue coat, and carried an ebony stick with a silver knob. He appeared to be in excellent spirits, and bowed and smiled and walked to and fro so much that five minutes later there was scarcely an inch of carpet in the room that he had not stood upon, a table or chair he had not lightly and caressingly

[1] He had once found himself in a room with Lady Bessborough's long-haired white cat. He happened to be dressed in an immaculate black coat and trousers, and was therefore thoroughly alarmed by the cat's stalking round and round and making motions as if it proposed to sit upon him. He waited until he believed himself to be unobserved, then he picked it up, opened a window and tossed it out. Despite falling three storeys to the ground, the cat survived, but one of its legs was never quite right afterwards and it always evinced the greatest dislike to gentlemen in black clothes.

touched, a mirror he had not danced across, a painting that he had not for a moment smiled upon.

Mr Norrell, though confident now that his guest was no great magician or great magician's servant, was still not much inclined to take Childermass's advice. His invitation to Mr Drawlight to sit down at the breakfast-table and take some chocolate was of the coldest sort. But sulky silences and black looks had no effect upon Mr Drawlight whatsoever, since he filled up the silences with his own chatter and was too accustomed to black looks to mind them.

"Do you not agree with me, sir, that the party last night was the most charming in the world? Though, if I may say so, I think you were quite right to leave when you did. I was able to go round afterwards and tell everyone that the gentleman that they had just espied walking out of the room was indeed Mr Norrell! Oh! believe me, sir, your departure was not unobserved. The Honourable Mr Masham was quite certain he had just caught sight of your esteemed shoulder, Lady Barclay thought she had seen a neat grey curl of your venerable wig, and Miss Fiskerton was quite ecstatic to think that her gaze had rested momentarily upon the tip of your scholarly nose! And the little that they have seen of you, sir, has made them desire more. They long to view the complete man!"

"Ah!" said Mr Norrell, with some satisfaction.

Mr Drawlight's repeated assurances that the ladies and gentlemen at Mrs Godesdone's party had been utterly enchanted by Mr Norrell went some way to diminish Mr Norrell's prejudices against his guest. According to Mr Drawlight, Mr Norrell's company was like seasoning: the smallest pinch of it could add a relish to the entire dish. Mr Drawlight made himself so agreeable that Mr Norrell grew by degrees more communicative.

"And to what fortunate circumstance, sir," asked Mr Drawlight, "do we owe the happiness of your society? What brings you to London?"

"I have come to London in order to further the cause of modern magic. I intend, sir, to bring back magic to Britain," answered Mr Norrell gravely. "I have a great deal to communicate to the Great Men of our Age. There are many ways in which I may be of service to them."

Mr Drawlight murmured politely that he was sure of it.

"I may tell you, sir," said Mr Norrell, "that I heartily wish this duty had fallen to the lot of some other magician." Mr Norrell sighed and looked as noble as his small, pinched features would allow. It is an extraordinary thing that a man such as Mr Norrell – a man who had destroyed the careers of so many of his fellow-magicians – should be able to convince himself that he would rather all the glory of his profession belonged to one of them, but there is no doubt that Mr Norrell believed it when he said it.

Mr Drawlight murmured sympathetically. Mr Drawlight was sure that Mr Norrell was too modest. Mr Drawlight could not suppose for a moment that anyone could be better suited to the task of bringing back magic to Britain than Mr Norrell.

"But I labour under a disadvantage, sir," said Mr Norrell.

Mr Drawlight was surprized to hear it.

"I do not know the world, sir. I know that I do not. I have a scholar's love of silence and solitude. To sit and pass hour after hour in idle chatter with a roomful of strangers is to me the worst sort of torment – but I dare say there will be a good deal of that sort of thing. Childermass assures me that there will be." Mr Norrell looked wistfully at Drawlight as if hopeful that Drawlight might contradict him.

"Ah!" Mr Drawlight considered a moment. "And that is exactly why I am so happy that you and I have become friends! I do not pretend to be a scholar, sir; I know next to nothing of magicians or magical history, and I dare say that, from time to time, you may find my society irksome, but you must set any little irritations of that nature against the great good that I may do you in taking you about and shewing you to people. Oh, Mr Norrell, sir! You cannot imagine how useful I may be to you!"

Mr Norrell declined to give his word there and then to accompany Mr Drawlight to all the places that Mr Drawlight said were so delightful and to meet all those people whose friendship, Mr Drawlight said, would add a new sweetness to Mr Norrell's existence, but he did consent to go with Mr Drawlight that evening to a dinner at Lady Rawtenstall's house in Bedford-square.

Mr Norrell got through the dinner with less fatigue than he expected, and so agreed to meet Mr Drawlight upon the morrow at Mr Plumtree's house. With Mr Drawlight as his guide, Mr Norrell entered society with greater confidence than before. His engagements became numerous; he was busy from eleven o'clock in the morning to past midnight. He paid morning-visits; he ate his dinner in dining-parlours all over the Town; he attended evening-parties, balls and concerts of Italian music; he met baronets, viscounts, viscountesses, and honourable thises and thats; he was to be met with walking down Bond-street, arm-in-arm with Mr Drawlight; he was observed taking the air in a carriage in Hyde-park with Mr Drawlight and Mr Drawlight's dear friend, Mr Lascelles.

On days when Mr Norrell did not dine abroad Mr Drawlight took his mutton at Mr Norrell's house in Hanover-square – which Mr Norrell imagined Mr Drawlight must be very glad to do, for Childermass had told him that Mr Drawlight had scarcely any money. Childermass said that Drawlight lived upon his wits and his debts; none of his great friends had ever been invited to visit him at home, because home was a lodging above a shoemaker's in Little Ryder-street.

Like every new house, the house in Hanover-square – which had seemed perfection at first – was soon discovered to be in need of every sort of improvement. Naturally, Mr Norrell was impatient to have it all accomplished as soon as possible, but when he appealed to Drawlight to agree with him that the London workmen were extraordinarily slow, Drawlight took the opportunity to ascertain all Mr Norrell's plans for colours, wallpapers, carpets, furniture and ornaments, and to find fault with all of them. They argued the point for a quarter of an hour and then Mr Drawlight ordered Mr Norrell's carriage to be got ready and directed Davey to take him and Mr Norrell straight to Mr Ackermann's shop in the Strand. There Mr Drawlight shewed Mr Norrell a book which contained a picture by Mr Repton of an empty, old-fashioned parlour, where a stony-faced old person from the time of Queen Elizabeth stared out of a painting on the wall and the empty chairs all gaped at each other like guests at a party who discover they have nothing to say to one another. But on the next page, ah! what changes had been wrought by the noble arts of joinery, paper-hanging and upholstery! Here was a picture of the same parlour, new-furnished and improved beyond all recognition! A dozen or so fashionably-dressed ladies and gentlemen had been enticed into the smart new apartment by the prospect of refreshing their spirits by reclining in elegant postures upon the chairs, or walking in the vine-clad conservatory which had mysteriously appeared on the other side of a pair of French windows. The moral, as Mr Drawlight explained it, was that if Mr Norrell hoped to win friends for the cause of modern magic, he must insert a great many more French windows into his house.

Under Mr Drawlight's tutelage Mr Norrell learnt to prefer picture-gallery reds to the respectable dull greens of his youth. In the interests of modern magic, the honest materials of Mr Norrell's house were dressed up with paint and varnish, and made to represent things they were not – like actors upon a stage. Plaster was painted to resemble wood, and wood was painted to resemble different sorts of wood. By the time it came to select the appointments for the dining-parlour, Mr Norrell's confidence in Drawlight's taste was so complete that Drawlight was commissioned to chuse the dinner-service without reference to any one else.

"You will not regret it, my dear sir!" cried Drawlight, "for three weeks ago I chose a set for the Duchess of B—— and she declared the moment she saw it that she never in her life saw anything half so charming!"

On a bright May morning Mr Norrell was seated in a drawing-room in Wimpole-street at the house of a Mrs Littleworth. Among the people gathered there were Mr Drawlight and Mr Lascelles. Mr Lascelles was exceedingly fond of Mr Norrell's society, indeed he came second only to Mr Drawlight in this respect, but his reasons for courting Mr Norrell's notice were quite different. Mr Lascelles was a clever, cynical man who thought it the most ridiculous thing in the world that a scholarly old gentleman should have talked himself into the belief that he could perform magic. Consequently, Mr Lascelles took great pleasure in asking Mr Norrell questions about magic whenever the opportunity arose so that he might amuse himself with the answers.

"And how do you like London, sir?" he asked.

"Not at all," said Mr Norrell.

"I am sorry to hear it," said Mr Lascelles. "Have you discovered any brother-magicians to talk to?"

Mr Norrell frowned and said he did not believe there were any magicians in London, or if so, then all his researches had not been able to uncover them.

"Ah, sir!" cried Mr Drawlight. "There you are mistaken! You have been most abominably misinformed! We have magicians in London – Oh! forty at least. Lascelles, would not you agree that we have hundreds of magicians in London? One may see them upon practically every street corner. Mr Lascelles and I will be very happy to make you acquainted with them. They have a sort of king whom they call Vinculus – a tall, ragged scarecrow of a man who has a little booth just outside St Christopher Le Stocks, all splashed with mud, with a dirty yellow curtain and, if you give him two pennies, he will prophesy."

"Vinculus's fortunes are nothing but calamities," observed Mr Lascelles, laughing. "Thus far he has promised me drowning, madness, the destruction by fire of all my property and a natural daughter who will do me great injury in my old age by her spitefulness."

"I shall be glad to take you, sir," said Drawlight to Mr Norrell. "I am as fond as any thing of Vinculus."

"Take care if you do go, sir," advised Mrs Littleworth. "Some of these men can put one in a dreadful fright. The Cruickshanks brought a magician – a very dirty fellow – to the house to shew their friends some tricks, but when he got there it seemed he did not know any – and so they would not pay him. In a great rage he swore that he would turn the baby into a coal scuttle; and then they were in great confusion because the baby was nowhere to be found – though no new coal scuttles had appeared, just the old familiar ones. They searched the house from top to bottom and Mrs Cruikshank was half-dead with anxiety and the physician was sent for – until the nursemaid appeared with the baby at the door and it came out that she had taken it to shew her mother in James-street."

Despite such enticements as these, Mr Norrell declined Mr Drawlight's kind offer to take him to see Vinculus in his yellow booth.

"And what is your opinion of the Raven King, Mr Norrell?" asked Mrs Littleworth eagerly.

"I have none. He is a person I never think of."

"Indeed?" remarked Mr Lascelles. "You will excuse my saying so, Mr Norrell, but that is rather an extraordinary statement. I never met a magician yet who did not declare that the Black King was the greatest of them all – the magician *par excellence*! A man who could, had he so desired, have wrested Merlin from the tree, spun the old gentleman on his head and put him back in again."[2]

Mr Norrell said nothing.

"But surely," continued Mr Lascelles, "none of the other *Aureates* could rival his achievements? Kingdoms in all the worlds

[2] Merlin is presumed to have been imprisoned in a hawthorn tree by the sorceress, Nimue.

that ever were.[3] Bands of human knights and fairy knights to carry out his bidding. Magic woods that walked about. To say nothing of his longevity – a three-hundred-year reign – and at the end of it we are told that he was still, in appearance at least, a young man."

Mr Norrell said nothing.

"But perhaps you think that the histories lie? I have frequently heard it suggested that the Raven King never existed – that he was not one magician at all, but a long train of magicians, all looking much the same. Perhaps that is what you think?"

Mr Norrell looked as if he would prefer to remain silent, but the directness of Mr Lascelles's question obliged him to give a reply. "No," he said at last, "I am quite certain that he existed. But I cannot consider his influence upon English magic as any thing other than deplorable. His magic was of a particularly pernicious sort and nothing would please me more than that he should be forgot as completely as he deserves."

"And what of your fairy-servants, sir?" said Mr Lascelles. "Are they visible only to yourself? Or may other people perceive them?"

Mr Norrell sniffed and said he had none.

"What none?" exclaimed a lady in a carnation-pink gown, much surprized.

"You are wise, Mr Norrell," said Mr Lascelles. "Tubbs *versus* Starhouse must stand as a warning to all magicians."[4]

---

[3] Mr Lascelles exaggerates. The Raven King's kingdoms were never more than three in number.

[4] Tubbs *versus* Starhouse: a famous case brought before the Quarter Sessions at Nottingham a few years ago.

A Nottinghamshire man called Tubbs wished very much to see a fairy and, from thinking of fairies day and night, and from reading all sorts of odd books about them, he took it into his head that his coachman was a fairy.

The coachman (whose name was Jack Starhouse) was dark and tall and scarcely ever said a word which discomfited his fellow-servants and made them think him proud. He had only recently entered Mr Tubbs's household, and said that previously he had been coachman to an old man called Browne at a place called Coldmicklehill in the north. He had one great talent: he could make any creature love him. The horses were always very willing when he had the reins and never cross or fidgety at all, and he could command cats

"Mr Tubbs was no magician," said Mr Norrell. "Nor did I ever hear that he claimed to be one. But had he been the greatest magician in Christendom, he would still have been wrong to wish for the company of fairies. A more poisonous race or one more

---

[4] *cont'd* in a way that the people of Nottinghamshire had never seen before. He had a whispering way of talking to them; any cat he spoke to would stay quite still with an expression of faint surprize on its face as if it had never heard such good sense in all its life nor ever expected to again. He could also make them dance. The cats that belonged to Mr Tubbs's household were as grave and mindful of their dignity as any other set of cats, but Jack Starhouse could make them dance wild dances, leaping about upon their hind legs and casting themselves from side to side. This he did by strange sighs and whistlings and hissings.

One of the other servants observed that if only cats had been good for any thing – which they were not – then all this might have had some point to it. But Starhouse's wonderful mastery was not useful, nor did it entertain his fellow-servants; it only made them uncomfortable.

Whether it were this or his handsome face with the eyes a little too wide apart that made Mr Tubbs so certain he was a fairy I do not know, but Mr Tubbs began to make inquiries about the coachman in secret.

One day Mr Tubbs called Starhouse to his study. Mr Tubbs said that he had learnt that Mr Browne was very ill – had been ill for all the time Starhouse had claimed to work for him – and had not gone out for years and years. So Mr Tubbs was curious to know what he had needed a coachman for.

For a little while Jack Starhouse said nothing. Then he admitted that he had not been in Mr Browne's employ. He said he had worked for another family in the neighbourhood. He had worked hard, it had been a good place, he had been happy; but the other servants had not liked him, he did not know why, it had happened to him before. One of the other servants (a woman) had told lies about him and he had been dismissed. He had seen Mr Browne once years ago. He said he was very sorry that he had lied to Mr Tubbs, but he had not known what else to do.

Mr Tubbs explained that there was no need to invent further stories. He knew that Starhouse was a fairy and said he was not to fear; he would not betray him; he only wished to talk to him about his home and people.

At first Starhouse did not at all understand what Mr Tubbs meant, and when finally he did understand, it was in vain that he protested that he was a human being and an Englishman, Mr Tubbs did not believe him.

After this, whatever Starhouse was doing, wherever he went, he would find Mr Tubbs waiting for him with a hundred questions about fairies and Faerie. Starhouse was made so unhappy by this treatment (though Mr Tubbs was always kind and courteous), that he was obliged to give up his place. While yet unemployed, he met with a man in an ale-house in Southwell who persuaded him to bring an action against his former master for defamation of character. In a famous ruling Jack Starhouse became the first man to be declared human under English law.

inimical to England has never existed. There have been far too many magicians too idle or ignorant to pursue a proper course of study, who instead bent all their energies upon acquiring a fairy-servant – and when they had got such a servant they depended upon him to complete all their business for them. English history is full of such men and some, I am glad to say, were punished for it as they deserved. Look at Bloodworth."[5]

[4] *cont'd* But this curious episode ended unhappily for both Tubbs and Starhouse. Tubbs was punished for his harmless ambition to see a fairy by being made an object of ridicule everywhere. Unflattering caricatures of him were printed in the London, Nottingham, Derby and Sheffield papers, and neighbours with whom he had been on terms of the greatest goodwill and intimacy for years declined to know him any more. While Starhouse quickly discovered that no one wished to employ a coachman who had brought an action against his master; he was forced to accept work of a most degrading nature and very soon fell into great poverty.

The case of Tubbs *versus* Starhouse is interesting not least because it serves as an illustration of the widely-held belief that fairies have not left England completely. Many Englishmen and women think that we are surrounded by fairies every day of our lives. Some are invisible and some masquerade as Christians and may in fact be known to us. Scholars have debated the matter for centuries but without reaching any conclusion.

[5] Simon Bloodworth's fairy-servant came to him quite out of the blue offering his services and saying he wished to be known as "Buckler". As every English schoolchild nowadays can tell you, Bloodworth would have done better to have inquired further and to have probed a little deeper into who, precisely, Buckler was, and why, exactly, he had come out of Faerie with no other aim than to become the servant of a third-rate English magician.

Buckler was very quick at all sorts of magic and Bloodworth's business in the little wool-town of Bradford on Avon grew and prospered. Only once did Buckler cause any sort of difficulty when, in a sudden fit of rage, he destroyed a little book belonging to Lord Lovel's chaplain.

The longer Buckler remained with Bloodworth the stronger he became and the first thing that Buckler did when he became stronger was to change his appearance: his dusty rags became a suit of good clothes; a rusty pair of scissars that he had stolen from a locksmith in the town became a sword; his thin, piebald fox-face became a pale and handsome human one; and he grew very suddenly two or three feet taller. This, he was quick to impress on Mrs Bloodworth and her daughters, was his true appearance – the other merely being an enchantment he had been under.

On a fine May morning in 1310 when Bloodworth was away from home Mrs Bloodworth discovered a tall cupboard standing in the corner of her kitchen where no cupboard had ever been before. When she asked Buckler about it, he said immediately that it was a magical cupboard and that he had

Mr Norrell made many new acquaintances, but kindled no pure flame of friendship in the hearts of any. In general, London found him disappointing. He did no magic, cursed no one, foretold nothing. Once at Mrs Godesdone's house he was heard to remark that he thought it might rain, but this, if a prophecy, was a disappointing one, for it did not rain – indeed no rain fell until the

---

[5] *cont'd* brought it there. He said that he had always thought that it was a pity that magic was not more commonly used in England; he said it pained him to see Mrs Bloodworth and her daughters washing and sweeping and cooking and cleaning from dawn to dusk when they ought, in his opinion, to be sitting on cushions in jewel-spangled gowns eating comfits. This, thought Mrs Bloodworth, was very good sense. Buckler said how he had often reproved her husband for his failure to make Mrs Bloodworth's life pleasant and easy, but Bloodworth had not paid him any attention. Mrs Bloodworth said that she was not a bit surprized.

Buckler said that if she stepped inside the cupboard she would find herself in a magical place where she could learn spells that would make any work finished in an instant, make her appear beautiful in the eyes of all who beheld her, make large piles of gold appear whenever she wished it, make her husband obey her in all things, etc., etc.

How many spells were there? asked Mrs Bloodworth.

About three, thought Buckler.

Were they hard to learn?

Oh no! Very easy.

Would it take long?

No, not long, she would be back in time for Mass.

Seventeen people entered Buckler's cupboard that morning and were never seen again in England; among them were Mrs Bloodworth, her two youngest daughters, her two maids and two manservants, Mrs Bloodworth's uncle and six neighbours. Only Margaret Bloodworth, Bloodworth's eldest daughter, refused to go.

The Raven King sent two magicians from Newcastle to investigate the matter and it is from their written accounts that we have this tale. The chief witness was Margaret who told how, on his return, "my poor father went purposely into the cupboard to try if he could rescue them, tho' I begged him not to. He has not come out again."

Two hundred years later Dr Martin Pale was journeying through Faerie. At the castle of John Hollyshoes (an ancient and powerful fairy-prince) he discovered a human child, about seven or eight years old, very pale and starved-looking. She said her name was Anne Bloodworth and she had been in Faerie, she thought, about two weeks. She had been given work to do washing a great pile of dirty pots. She said she had been washing them steadily since she arrived and when she was finished she would go home to see her parents and sisters. She thought she would be finished in a day or two.

following Saturday. He hardly ever spoke of magic, and when he did it was like a history lesson and no one could bear to listen to him. He rarely had a good word to say for any other magician, except once when he praised a magician of the last century, Francis Sutton-Grove.[6]

"But I thought, sir," said Mr Lascelles, "that Sutton-Grove was unreadable. I have always heard that *De Generibus Artium* was entirely unreadable."

"Oh!" said Mr Norrell, "how it fares as an amusement for ladies and gentlemen I do not know, but I do not think that the serious student of magic can value Sutton-Grove too highly. In Sutton-Grove he will find the first attempt to define those areas of magic that the modern magician ought to study, all laid out in lists and tables. To be sure, Sutton-Grove's system of classification is often erroneous – perhaps that is what you mean by 'unreadable'? – nevertheless I know of no more pleasant sight in the world than a dozen or so of his lists; the student may run his eye over them and think 'I know this,' or, 'I have this still to do,' and there before him is work enough for four, perhaps five years."

The tale of the statues in the Cathedral of York grew so stale in

[6] Francis Sutton-Grove (1682–1765), theoretical magician. He wrote two books *De Generibus Artium Magicarum Anglorum*, 1741, and *Prescriptions and Descriptions*, 1749. Even Mr Norrell, Sutton-Grove's greatest (and indeed only) admirer, thought that *Prescriptions and Descriptions* (wherein he attempted to lay down rules for practical magic) was abominably bad, and Mr Norrell's pupil, Jonathan Strange, loathed it so much that he tore his copy into pieces and fed it to a tinker's donkey (see *Life of Jonathan Strange* by John Segundus, 1820, pub. John Murray).

*De Generibus Artium Magicarum Anglorum* was reputed to be the dreariest book in the canon of English magic (which contains many tedious works). It was the first attempt by an Englishman to define the areas of magic that the modern magician ought to study; according to Sutton-Grove these numbered thirty-eight thousand, nine hundred and forty-five and he listed them all under different heads. Sutton-Grove foreshadows the great Mr Norrell in one other way: none of his lists make any mention of the magic traditionally ascribed to birds or wild animals, and Sutton-Grove purposely excludes those kinds of magic for which it is customary to employ fairies, e.g. bringing back the dead.

the retelling that people began to wonder if Mr Norrell had ever done anything else and Mr Drawlight was obliged to invent some new examples.

"But what can this magician do, Drawlight?" asked Mrs Godesdone one evening when Mr Norrell was not present.

"Oh, madam!" cried Drawlight. "What can he not do? Why! It was only a winter or so ago that in York – which as you may know, madam, is Mr Norrell's native city – a great storm came out of the north and blew everybody's washing into the mud and the snow – and so the aldermen, thinking to spare the ladies of the town the labour of washing everything again, applied to Mr Norrell – and he sent a troop of fairies to wash it all anew – and all the holes in people's shirts and nightcaps and petticoats were mended and all the frayed edges were made whole and good again and everybody said that they had never seen such a dazzling whiteness in all their days!"

This particular story became very popular and raised Mr Norrell in everyone's estimation for several weeks that summer, and consequently when Mr Norrell spoke, as he sometimes did, of modern magic, most of his audience supposed that this was the sort of thing he must mean.

But if the ladies and gentlemen whom Mr Norrell met in London's drawing-rooms and dining-parlours were generally disappointed in *him*, then he was becoming equally dissatisfied with *them*. He complained constantly to Mr Drawlight of the frivolous questions that they put to him, and said that the cause of English magic had not been furthered one whit by the hours he had spent in their company.

One dull Wednesday morning at the end of September Mr Norrell and Mr Drawlight were seated together in the library in Hanover-square. Mr Drawlight was in the middle of a long tale of something that Mr F. had said in order to insult Lord S., and what Lady D. had thought about it all, when Mr Norrell suddenly said, "I would be grateful, Mr Drawlight, if you could advise me on the following important point: has any body informed the Duke of Portland of my arrival in London?"[7]

"Ah! sir," cried Drawlight, "only you, with your modest nature, could suppose it possible. I assure you *all* the Ministers have heard of the extraordinary Mr Norrell by now."

"But if that is the case," said Mr Norrell, "then why has his Grace sent me no message? No, I begin to think that they must be entirely ignorant of my existence – and so, Mr Drawlight, I would be grateful if you could inform me of any connexions in Government that you may have to whom I could apply."

"The Government, sir?" replied Mr Drawlight.

"I came here to be useful," said Mr Norrell, plaintively. "I had hoped by now to play some distinguished part in the struggle against the French."

"If you feel yourself neglected, sir, then I am heartily sorry for it!" cried Drawlight. "But there is no need, I do assure you. There are ladies and gentlemen all over Town who would be happy to see any little tricks or illusions you might like to shew us one evening after dinner. You must not be afraid of overwhelming us – our nerves are all pretty strong."

Mr Norrell said nothing.

"Well, sir," said Mr Drawlight, with a smooth smile of his white teeth and a conciliatory look in his dark, liquid eyes, "we must not argue about it. I only wish I were able to oblige you but, as you see, it is entirely out of my power. The Government has its sphere. I have mine."

In fact Mr Drawlight knew several gentlemen in various Government posts who might be very glad to meet Mr Drawlight's friend and to listen to what that friend might have to say, in return for a promise from Mr Drawlight never to tell one or two curious things he knew about them. But the truth was that Mr Drawlight could see no advantage to himself in introducing Mr Norrell to any

[7] Duke of Portland, Prime Minister and First Lord of the Treasury 1807–09.

of these gentlemen; he preferred to keep Mr Norrell in the drawing-rooms and dining-parlours of London where he hoped, in time, to persuade him to perform those little tricks and what-not that Mr Drawlight's acquaintance longed to see.

Mr Norrell began writing urgent letters to gentlemen in Government, which he shewed to Mr Drawlight before giving them to Childermass to deliver, but the gentlemen in Government did not reply. Mr Drawlight had warned Mr Norrell that they would not. Gentlemen in Government are generally kept pretty busy.

A week or so later Mr Drawlight was invited to a house in Soho-square to hear a famous Italian soprano, newly arrived from Rome. Naturally, Mr Norrell was invited too. But on arriving at the house Drawlight could not find the magician among the crowd. Lascelles was leaning upon the mantelpiece in conversation with some other gentlemen. Drawlight went up to him and inquired if he knew where Mr Norrell was.

"Oh!" said Mr Lascelles. "He is gone to pay a visit to Sir Walter Pole. Mr Norrell has important information which he wishes conveyed to the Duke of Portland immediately. And Sir Walter Pole is the man that Mr Norrell intends to honour with the message."

"Portland?" cried another gentleman. "What? Are the Ministers got so desperate as that? Are they consulting magicians?"

"You have run away with a wrong idea," smiled Mr Lascelles. "It is all Norrell's own doing. He intends to offer his services to the Government. It seems he has a plan to defeat the French by magic. But I think it highly improbable that he will persuade the Ministers to listen to him. What with the French at their throats on the Continent, and everybody else at their throats in Parliament – I doubt if a more harassed set of gentlemen is to be found anywhere, or one with less attention to spare for a Yorkshire gentleman's eccentricities."

Like the hero of a fairy-tale Mr Norrell had discovered that the power to do what he wished had been his own all along. Even a magician must have relations, and it so happened that there was a distant connexion of Mr Norrell (on his mother's side) who had once made himself highly disagreeable to Mr Norrell by writing him a letter. To prevent such a thing ever occurring again Mr Norrell had made this man a present of eight hundred pounds (which was what the man wanted), but I am sorry to say that this failed to suppress Mr Norrell's mother's relative, who was steeped in villainy, and he had written a *second* letter to Mr Norrell in which he heaped thanks and praise upon his benefactor and declared that, ". . . henceforth I shall consider myself and my friends as belonging to your interest and we hold ourselves ready to vote at the next election in accordance with your noble wishes, and if, in time to come, it should appear that any service of mine might be useful to you, your commands will only honour, and elevate in the opinion of the World, your humble and devoted servant, Wendell Markworthy."

Thus far Mr Norrell had never found it necessary to elevate Mr Markworthy in the opinion of the world by honouring him with any commands, but it now appeared (it was Childermass that had found it out) that Mr Markworthy had used the money to secure for himself and his brother clerkships in the East India Company. They had gone to India and ten years later had returned very rich men. Having never received any instructions from Mr Norrell, his first patron, as to which way to vote, Mr Markworthy had followed the lead of Mr Bonnell, his superior at the East India Company, and had encouraged all his friends to do the same. He had made himself very useful to Mr Bonnell, who was in turn a great friend of the politician, Sir Walter Pole. In the busy worlds of trade and government this gentleman owes that one a favour, while he in his turn is owed a favour by someone else, and so on until a chain is formed of promises and obligations. In this case the chain extended all the way from Mr Norrell to Sir Walter Pole and Sir Walter Pole was now a Minister.

# 6

# "Magic is not respectable, sir."

## October 1807

IT WAS A difficult time to be a Minister.

The war went from bad to worse and the Government was universally detested. As each fresh catastrophe came to the public's notice some small share of blame might attach itself to this or that person, but in general everyone united in blaming the Ministers, and they, poor things, had no one to blame but each other – which they did more and more frequently.

It was not that the Ministers were dull-witted – upon the contrary there were some brilliant men among them. Nor were they, upon the whole, bad men; several led quite blameless domestic lives and were remarkably fond of children, music, dogs, landscape painting. Yet so unpopular was the Government that, had it not been for the careful speeches of the Foreign Secretary, it would have been almost impossible to get any piece of business through the House of Commons.

The Foreign Secretary was a quite peerless orator. No matter how low the Government stood in the estimation of everyone, when the Foreign Secretary stood up and spoke – ah! how different everything seemed then! How quickly was every bad thing discovered to be the fault of the previous administration (an evil set of men who wedded general stupidity to wickedness of purpose). As for the present Ministry, the Foreign Secretary said that not since the days of Antiquity had the world seen gentlemen so virtuous, so misunderstood and so horribly misrepresented by their enemies. They were all as wise as Solomon, as noble as Caesar and as courageous as Mark Antony; and no one in the world so much resembled Socrates in point of honesty as the Chancellor of the Exchequer. But in spite of all these virtues and abilities none of the Ministers' plans to defeat the French ever seemed to come to anything and even their cleverness was complained of. Country gentlemen who read in their newspapers the speeches of this or that Minister would mutter to themselves that he was certainly a clever fellow. But the country gentlemen were not made comfortable by this thought. The country gentlemen had a strong suspicion that cleverness was somehow unBritish. That sort of restless, unpredictable brilliance belonged most of all to Britain's arch-enemy, the Emperor Napoleon Buonaparte; the country gentlemen could not approve it.

Sir Walter Pole was forty-two and, I am sorry to say, quite as clever as any one else in the Cabinet. He had quarrelled with most of the great politicians of the age at one time or another and once, when they were both very drunk, had been struck over the head with a bottle of madeira by Richard Brinsley Sheridan. Afterwards Sheridan remarked to the Duke of York, "Pole accepted my apologies in a handsome, gentleman-like fashion. Happily he is such a plain man that one scar more or less can make no significant difference."

To my mind he was not so very plain. True, his features were all extremely bad; he had a great face half as long again as other faces, with a great nose (quite sharp at the end) stuck into it, two dark eyes like clever bits of coal and two little stubby eyebrows like very small fish swimming bravely in a great sea of face. Yet, taken together, all these ugly parts made a rather pleasing whole. If you had seen that face in repose (proud and not a little melancholy), you would have imagined that it must always look so, that no face in existence could be so ill-adapted to express feeling. But you could not have been more wrong.

Nothing was more characteristic of Sir Walter Pole than *Surprize*. His eyes grew large, his eyebrows rose half an inch upon his face and he leant suddenly backwards and altogether he resembled nothing so much as a figure in the engravings of Mr Rowlandson or Mr Gillray. In public life *Surprize* served Sir Walter very well. "But, surely," he cried, "You cannot mean to say —!" And, always supposing that the gentleman who was so foolish as to suggest — in Sir Walter's hearing was no friend or yours, or if you have that sort of mischief in you that likes to see blunt wits confounded by sharp ones, you would be entertained. On days when he was full of cheerful malice Sir Walter was better than a play in Drury-lane. Dull gentlemen in both Houses grew perplexed, and avoided him when they could. (Old Lord So-and-so waves his stick at Sir Walter as he trots down the little stone passage that connects the House of Commons to the Horse-Guards, and cries over his shoulder, "I will not speak to you, sir! You twist my words! You give me meanings I never intended!")

Once, while making a speech to a mob in the City, Sir Walter had memorably likened England and her politicians to an orphaned young lady left in the care of a pack of lecherous, avaricious old men. These scoundrels, far from offering the young lady protection from the wicked world, stole her inheritance and plundered her house. And if Sir Walter's audience stumbled on some of his vocabulary (the product of an excellent classical education) it did not much matter. All of them were capable of imagining the poor young lady standing on her bed in her petticoats while the leading Whig politicians of the day ransacked her closets and sold off all her bits of things to the rag man. And all the young gentlemen found themselves pleasantly shocked by the picture.

Sir Walter had a generous spirit and was often kind-hearted. He told someone once that he hoped his enemies all had reason to fear him and his friends reason to love him – and I think that upon the whole they did. His cheerful manner, his kindness and cleverness, the great station he now held in the world – these were even more to his credit as he maintained them in the face of problems that would almost certainly have brought down a lesser man. Sir Walter was distressed for money. I do not mean that he merely lacked for cash. Poverty is one thing, Sir Walter's debts quite another. Miserable situation! – and all the more bitter since it was no fault of his: *he* had never been extravagant and he had certainly never been foolish, but he was the son of one imprudent man and the grandson of another. Sir Walter had been born in debt. Had he been a different sort of man, then all might have been well. Had he been at all inclined to the Navy then he might have made his fortune in prize money; had he loved farming he might have improved his lands and made his money with corn. Had he even been a Minister fifty years before he might have lent out Treasury-money at twenty per cent interest and pocketed the profit. But what can a modern politician do? – he is more likely to spend money than make it.

Some years ago his friends in Government had got him the position of Secretary-in-Ordinary to the Office of Supplication, for which he received a special hat, a small piece of ivory and seven hundred pounds a year. There were no duties attached to the place because no one could remember what the Office of Supplication was supposed to do or what the small piece of ivory was for. But then Sir Walter's friends went out and new Ministers came in, declaring that they were going to abolish sinecures, and among the many offices and places which they pruned from the tree of Government was the Office of Supplication.

By the spring of 1807 it seemed as if Sir Walter's political career must be pretty much at an end (the last election had cost him almost two thousand pounds). His friends were almost frantic. One of those friends, Lady Winsell, went to Bath where, at a concert of Italian music, she made the acquaintance of some people called Wintertowne, a widow and her daughter. A week later Lady Winsell wrote to Sir Walter: "It is exactly what I have always wished for you. Her mother is all for a great marriage and will make no difficulties – or at least if she does then I rely upon *you* to charm them away. As for the money! I tell you, my dear friend, when they named the sum that is to be hers, tears sprang into my eyes! What would you say to one thousand a year? I will say nothing of the young person herself – when you have seen her you shall praise her to me much more ably than ever I could to you."

At about three o'clock upon the same day that Mr Drawlight attended the recital by the Italian lady, Lucas, Mr Norrell's footman, knocked upon the door of a house in Brunswick-square where Mr Norrell had been summoned to meet Sir Walter. Mr Norrell was admitted to the house and was shown to a very fine room upon the first floor.

The walls were hung with a series of gigantic paintings in gilded frames of great complexity, all depicting the city of Venice, but the day was overcast, a cold stormy rain had set in, and Venice – that city built of equal parts of sunlit marble and sunlit sea – was drowned in a London gloom. Its aquamarine-blues and cloud-whites and glints of gold were dulled to the greys and greens of drowned things. From time to time the wind flung a little sharp rain against the window (a melancholy sound) and in the grey light the well-polished surfaces of tulipwood *chiffoniers* and walnut writing-tables had all become black mirrors, darkly reflecting one another. For all its splendour, the room was peculiarly comfortless; there were no candles to light the gloom and no fire to take off the chill. It was as if the housekeeping was under the direction of someone with excellent eyesight who never felt the cold.

Sir Walter Pole rose to receive Mr Norrell and begged the honour of presenting Mrs Wintertowne and her daughter, Miss Wintertowne. Though Sir Walter spoke of *two* ladies, Mr Norrell could perceive only *one*, a lady of mature years, great dignity and magisterial aspect. This puzzled Mr Norrell. He thought Sir Walter must be mistaken, and yet it would be rude to contradict

Sir Walter so early in the interview. In a state of some confusion, Mr Norrell bowed to the magisterial lady.

"I am very glad to meet you, sir," said Sir Walter. "I have heard a great deal about you. It seems to me that London talks of very little else but the extraordinary Mr Norrell," and, turning to the magisterial lady, Sir Walter said, "Mr Norrell is a magician, ma'am, a person of great reputation in his native county of Yorkshire."

The magisterial lady stared at Mr Norrell.

"You are not at all what I expected, Mr Norrell," remarked Sir Walter. "I had been told you were a *practical* magician – I hope you are not offended, sir – it is merely what I was told, and I must say that it is a relief to me to see that you are nothing of the sort. London is plagued with a great number of mock-sorcerers who trick the people out of their money by promising them all sorts of unlikely things. I wonder, have you seen Vinculus, who has a little booth outside St Christopher Le Stocks? He is the worst of them. You are a *theoretical* magician, I imagine?" Sir Walter smiled encouragingly. "But they tell me that you have something to ask me, sir."

Mr Norrell begged Sir Walter's pardon but said that he was indeed a practical magician; Sir Walter looked surprized. Mr Norrell hoped very earnestly that he would not by this admission lose Sir Walter's good opinion.

"No, no. By no means," murmured Sir Walter politely.

"The misapprehension under which you labour," said Mr Norrell, "by which I mean, of course, the belief that all practical magicians must be charlatans – arises from the shocking idleness of English magicians in the last two hundred years. I have performed one small feat of magic – which the people in York were kind enough to say they found astounding – and yet I tell you, Sir Walter, any magician of modest talent might have done as much. This general lethargy has deprived our great nation of its best support and left us defenceless. It is this deficiency which I hope to supply. Other magicians may be able to neglect their duty, but I cannot; I am come, Sir Walter, to offer you my help in our present difficulties."

"Our present difficulties?" said Sir Walter. "You mean the war?" He opened his small black eyes very wide. "My dear Mr Norrell! What has the war to do with magic? Or magic to do with the war? I believe I have heard what you did in York, and I hope the housewives were grateful, but I scarcely see how we can apply such magic to the war! True, the soldiers get very dirty, but then, you know," and he began to laugh, "they have other things of think of."

Poor Mr Norrell! He had not heard Drawlight's story of how the fairies had washed the people's clothes and it came as a great shock to him. He assured Sir Walter that he had never in his life washed linen – not by magic nor by any other means – and he told Sir Walter what he had really done. But, curiously, though Mr Norrell was able to work feats of the most breath-taking wonder, he was only able to describe them in his usual dry manner, so that Sir Walter was left with the impression that the spectacle of half a thousand stone figures in York Cathedral all speaking together had been rather a dull affair and that he had been fortunate in being elsewhere at the time. "Indeed?" he said. "Well, that is most interesting. But I still do not quite understand how . . ."

Just at that moment someone coughed, and the moment that Sir Walter heard the cough he stopped speaking as if to listen.

Mr Norrell looked round. In the furthest, most shadowy corner of the room a young woman in a white gown lay upon a sopha, with a white shawl wrapped tightly around her. She lay quite still. One hand pressed a handkerchief to her mouth. Her posture, her stillness, everything about her conveyed the strongest impression of pain and ill-health.

So certain had Mr Norrell been that the corner was unoccupied, that he was almost as startled by her sudden appearance as if she had come there by someone else's magic. As he watched she was seized by a fit of coughing that continued for some moments, and during that time Sir Walter appeared most uncomfortable. He did not look at the young woman (though he looked everywhere else in the room). He picked up a gilt ornament from a little table by his side, turned it over, looked at its underneath, put it down again. Finally he coughed – a brief clearing of the throat as though to suggest that everyone coughed – coughing was the most natural thing in the world – coughing could never, under any circumstances, be cause for alarm. The young woman upon the sopha came at last to the end of her own coughing fit, and lay quite still and quiet, though her breathing did not seem to come easily.

Mr Norrell's gaze travelled from the young lady to the great, gloomy painting that hung above her and he tried to recollect what he had been speaking of.

"It is a marriage," said the majestic lady.

"I beg your pardon, madam?" said Mr Norrell.

But the lady only nodded in the direction of the painting and bestowed a stately smile upon Mr Norrell.

The painting which hung above the young lady shewed, like every other picture in the room, Venice. English cities are, for the most part, built upon hills; their streets rise and fall, and it occurred to Mr Norrell that Venice, being built upon the sea, must be the flattest, as well as the queerest, city in the world. It was the flatness which made the painting look so much like an exercise in perspective; statues, columns, domes, palaces, and cathedrals stretched away to where they met a vast and melancholy sky, while the sea that lapped at the walls of those buildings was crowded with ornately carved and gilded barges, and those strange black Venetian vessels that so much resemble the slippers of ladies in mourning.

"It depicts the symbolic marriage of Venice to the Adriatic," said the lady (whom we must now presume to be Mrs Wintertowne), "a curious Italian ceremony. The paintings which you see in this room were all bought by the late Mr Wintertowne during his travels on the Continent; and when he and I were married they were his wedding-gift to me. The artist – an Italian – was then quite unknown in England. Later, emboldened by the patronage he received from Mr Wintertowne, he came to London."

Her manner of speech was as stately as her person. After each sentence she paused to give Mr Norrell time to be impressed by the information it contained.

"And when my dear Emma is married," she continued, "these paintings shall be my wedding-present to her and Sir Walter."

Mr Norrell inquired if Miss Wintertowne and Sir Walter were to be married soon.

"In ten days' time!" answered Mrs Wintertowne triumphantly.

Mr Norrell offered his congratulations.

"You are a magician, sir?" said Mrs Wintertowne. "I am sorry to hear it. It is a profession I have a particular dislike to." She looked keenly at him as she said so, as though her disapproval might in itself be enough to make him renounce magic instantly and take up some other occupation.

When he did not she turned to her prospective son-in-law. "My own stepmother, Sir Walter, placed great faith in a magician. After my father's death he was always in the house. One could enter a room one was quite sure was empty and find him in a corner half hidden by a curtain. Or asleep upon the sopha with his dirty boots on. He was the son of a leather tanner and his low origins were frankly displayed in all he did. He had long, dirty hair and a face like a dog, but he sat at our table like a gentleman. My stepmother deferred to him in all she did and for seven years he governed our lives completely."

"And your own opinion was disregarded, ma'am?" said Sir Walter. "I am surprized at that!"

Mrs Wintertowne laughed. "I was only a child of eight or nine when it began, Sir Walter. His name was Dreamditch and he told us constantly how happy he was to be our friend, though my

brother and I were equally constant in assuring him that we considered him no friend of ours. But he only smiled at us like a dog that has learned how to smile and does not know how to leave off. Do not misunderstand me, Sir Walter. My stepmother was in many ways an excellent woman. My father's esteem for her was such that he left her six hundred a year and the care of his three children. Her only weakness was foolishly to doubt her own capabilities. My father believed that, in understanding and in knowledge of right and wrong and in many other things, women are men's equals and I am entirely of his opinion. My stepmother should not have shrunk from the charge. When Mr Wintertowne died *I* did not."

"No, indeed, ma'am," murmured Sir Walter.

"Instead," continued Mrs Wintertowne, "she placed all her faith in the magician, Dreamditch. He had not an ounce of magic in him and was consequently obliged to invent some. He made rules for my brother, my sister and me, which, he assured my stepmother, would keep us safe. We wore purple ribbons tied tightly round our chests. In our room six places were laid at the table, one for each of us and one for each of the spirits which Dreamditch said looked after us. He told us their names. What do you suppose they were, Sir Walter?"

"I have not the least idea in the world, ma'am."

Mrs Wintertowne laughed. "Meadowlace, Robin Summerfly and Buttercup. My brother, Sir Walter, who resembled myself in independence of spirit, would often say in my stepmother's hearing, 'Damn Meadowlace! Damn Robin Summerfly! Damn Buttercup!' and she, poor silly woman, would plead very piteously with him to stop. They did us no good those fairy spirits. My sister became ill. Often I went to her room and found Dreamditch there, stroking her pale cheeks and unresisting hand with his long yellow unclean fingernails. He was almost weeping, the fool. He would have saved her if he could. He made spells, but she died. A beautiful child, Sir Walter. For years I hated my stepmother's magician. For years I thought him a wicked man, but in the end, Sir Walter, I knew him to be nothing but a sad and pitiful fool."

Sir Walter turned in his chair. "Miss Wintertowne!" he said. "You spoke – but I did not hear what it was you said."

"Emma! What is it?" cried Mrs Wintertowne.

There was a soft sigh from the sopha. Then a quiet, clear voice said, "I said that you were quite wrong, Mama."

"Am I, my love?" Mrs Wintertowne, whose character was so forceful and whose opinions were handed down to people in the manner of Moses distributing the commandments, did not appear in the least offended when her daughter contradicted her. Indeed she seemed almost pleased about it.

"Of course," said Miss Wintertowne, "we must have magicians. Who else can interpret England's history to us and in particular her northern history, her black northern King? Our common historians cannot." There was silence for a moment. "I am fond of history," she said.

"I did not know that," said Sir Walter.

"Ah, Sir Walter!" cried Mrs Wintertowne. "Dear Emma does not waste her energies upon novels like other young women. Her reading has been extensive; she knows more of biography and poetry than any young woman I know."

"Yet I hope," said Sir Walter eagerly, leaning over the back of his chair to speak to his betrothed, "that you like novels as well, and then, you know, we could read to each other. What is your opinion of Mrs Radcliffe? Of Madame d'Arblay?"

But what Miss Wintertowne thought of these distinguished ladies Sir Walter did not discover for she was seized by a second fit of coughing which obliged her to struggle – with an appearance of great effort – into a sitting position. He waited some moments for an answer, but when her coughing had subsided she lay back on the sopha as before, with looks of pain and exhaustion, and closed her eyes.

Mr Norrell wondered that no one thought to go to her assistance. There seemed to be a sort of conspiracy in the room to deny that the poor young woman was ill. No one asked if they could bring her anything. No one suggested that she go to bed, which Mr Norrell – who was often ill himself – imagined would be by far the best thing for her.

"Mr Norrell," said Sir Walter, "I cannot claim to understand what this help is that you offer us . . ."

"Oh! As to particulars," Mr Norrell said, "I know as little of warfare as the generals and the admirals do of magic, and yet . . ."

". . . but whatever it is," continued Sir Walter, "I am sorry to say that it will not do. Magic is not respectable, sir. It is not," Sir Walter searched for a word, "serious. The Government cannot meddle with such things. Even this innocent little chat that you and I have had today, is likely to cause us a little embarrassment when people get to hear of it. Frankly, Mr Norrell, had I understood better what you were intending to propose today, I would not have agreed to meet you."

Sir Walter's manner as he said all this was far from unkind, but, oh, poor Mr Norrell! To be told that magic was not serious was a very heavy blow. To find himself classed with the Dreamditches and the Vinculuses of this world was a crushing one. In vain he protested that he had thought long and hard about how to make magic respected once more; in vain he offered to shew Sir Walter a long list of recommendations concerning the regulation of magic in England. Sir Walter did not wish to see them. He shook his head and smiled, but all he said was: "I am afraid, Mr Norrell, that I can do nothing for you."

When Mr Drawlight arrived at Hanover-square that evening he was obliged to listen to Mr Norrell lamenting the failure of all his hopes of succeeding with Sir Walter Pole.

"Well, sir, what did I tell you?" cried Drawlight. "But, oh! Poor Mr Norrell! How unkind they were to you! I am very sorry for it. But I am not in the least surprized! I have always heard that those Wintertownes were stuffed full of pride!"

But there was, I regret to say, a little duplicity in Mr Drawlight's nature and it must be said that he was not quite as sorry as he professed to be. This display of independence had provoked him and he was determined to punish Mr Norrell for it. For the next week Mr Norrell and Mr Drawlight attended only the quietest dinners and, without quite arranging matters so that Mr Norrell would find himself the guest of Mr Drawlight's shoemaker or the old lady who dusts the monuments in Westminster Abbey, Mr Drawlight took care that their hosts were people of as little consequence, influence, or fashion, as possible. In this way Drawlight hoped to create in Mr Norrell the impression that not only the Poles and Wintertownes slighted him, but the whole world, so that Mr Norrell might be brought to understand who was his true friend, and might become a little more accommodating when it came to performing those small tricks of magic that Drawlight had been promising for many months now.

Such were the hopes and schemes that animated the heart of Mr Norrell's dearest friend but, unfortunately for Mr Drawlight, so cast down was Mr Norrell by Sir Walter's rejection that he scarcely noticed the change in the style of entertainments and Drawlight succeeded in punishing no one but himself.

Now that Sir Walter was quite beyond Mr Norrell's reach, Mr Norrell became more and more convinced that Sir Walter was exactly the patron he wished for. A cheerful, energetic man, with pleasant, easy manners, Sir Walter Pole was everything that Mr Norrell was not. Therefore, reasoned Mr Norrell, Sir Walter Pole would have achieved everything that he *could* not. The influential men of the Age would have listened to Sir Walter.

"If only he had listened to me," sighed Mr Norrell one evening as he and Drawlight dined alone. "But I could not find the words to convince him. Of course I wish now that I had asked you or Mr Lascelles to come with me. Men of the world prefer to be talked to by other men of the world. I know that now. Perhaps I should have done some magic to shew him – turned the teacups into rabbits or the teaspoons into goldfish. At least then he would have believed me. But I do not think the old lady would have been pleased if I had done that. I do not know. What is your opinion?"

But Drawlight, who had begun to believe that if anyone had ever died of boredom then he was almost certain to expire within the next quarter of an hour, found that he had lost the will to speak and the best he could manage was a withering smile.

# 7

# An opportunity unlikely to occur again

## October 1807

"WELL, SIR! YOU have your revenge!" cried Mr Drawlight appearing quite suddenly in the library in Hanover-square.

"My revenge!" said Mr Norrell. "What do you mean?"

"Oh!" said Mr Drawlight. "Sir Walter's bride, Miss Wintertowne, is dead. She died this very afternoon. They were to be married in two days' time, but, poor thing, she is quite dead. A thousand pounds a year! – Imagine his despair! Had she only contrived to remain alive until the end of the week, what a difference it would have made! His need of the money is quite desperate – he is all to pieces. I should not be at all surprized if we were to hear tomorrow that he has cut his throat."

Mr Drawlight leant for a moment upon the back of a good, comfortable chair by the fire and, looking down, discovered a friend. "Ah, Lascelles, I declare. There you are behind the newspaper I see. How do you do?"

Meanwhile Mr Norrell stared at Mr Drawlight. "The young woman is dead, you say?" he said in amazement. "The young woman that I saw in that room? I can scarcely believe it. This is very unexpected."

"Oh! Upon the contrary," said Drawlight, "nothing was more probable."

"But the wedding!" said Mr Norrell. "All the necessary arrangements! They could not have known how ill she was."

"But I assure you," said Drawlight, "they did know. Everyone knew. Why! there was a fellow called Drummond, who saw her at Christmas at a private ball in Leamington Spa, and wagered Lord Carlisle fifty pounds that she would be dead within a month."

Mr Lascelles tutted in annoyance and put down his newspaper. "No, no," he said, "that was not Miss Wintertowne. You are thinking of Miss Hookham-Nix, whose brother has threatened to shoot her, should she bring disgrace upon the family – which everyone supposes she must do sooner or later. But it happened at Worthing – and it was not Lord Carlisle who took the bet but the Duke of Exmoor."

Drawlight considered this a moment. "I believe you are right," he said at last. "But it does not matter, for everyone *did* know that Miss Wintertowne was ill. Except of course the old lady. *She* thought her daughter perfection – and what can Perfection have to say to ill-health? Perfection is only to be admired; Perfection has only to make a great marriage. But the old lady has never allowed that Perfection might be ill – she could never bear to hear the subject mentioned. For all Miss Wintertowne's coughs and swoonings upon the ground and lyings-down upon the sopha, I never heard that any physician ever came near her."

"Sir Walter would have taken better care of her," said Lascelles, shaking out his newspaper before he began once more to read it. "One may say what one likes about his politics, but he is a sensible man. It is a pity she could not have lasted till Thursday."

"But, Mr Norrell," said Drawlight turning to their friend, "you look quite pale and sick! You are shocked, I dare say, at the spectacle of a young and innocent life cut off. Your good feelings, as ever, do you credit, sir – and I am entirely of your opinion – the thought of the poor young lady crushed out of existence like a lovely flower beneath someone's boot – well, sir, it cuts my heart like a knife – I can hardly bear to think of it. But then, you know, she was very ill and must have died at some time or other – and by your own account she was not very kind to *you*. I know it is not the fashion to say so, but I am the sternest advocate in the world for young people giving respectful attention to scholarly old persons such as yourself. Impudence, and sauciness, and everything of that sort I hate."

But Mr Norrell did not appear to hear the comfort his friend was so kind as to give him and when at last he spoke his words seemed chiefly addressed to himself, for he sighed deeply and murmured, "I never thought to find magic so little regarded here." He paused and then said in a quick, low voice, "It is a very dangerous thing to bring someone back from the dead. It has not been done in three hundred years. I could not attempt it!"

This was rather extraordinary and Mr Drawlight and Mr Lascelles looked round at their friend in some surprize.

"Indeed, sir," said Mr Drawlight, "and no one proposes that you should."

"Of course I know thc form of it," continued Mr Norrell as if Drawlight had not spoken, "but it is precisely the sort of magic that I have set my face against! – It relies so much upon . . . It relies so much . . . That is to say the outcome must be entirely unpredictable. – Quite out of the magician's power to determine. No! I shall not attempt it. I shall not even think of it."

There was a short silence. But despite the magician's resolve to think no more about the dangerous magic, he still fidgeted in his chair and bit his finger-ends and breathed very quick and exhibited other such signs of nervous agitation.

"My dear Mr Norrell," said Drawlight slowly, "I believe I begin to perceive your meaning. And I must confess that I think the idea an excellent one! You have in mind a great act of magic, a testimony to your extraordinary powers! Why, sir! Should you succeed all the Wintertownes and Poles in England will be on your doorstep soliciting the acquaintance of the wonderful Mr Norrell!"

"And if he should fail," observed Mr Lascelles, drily, "every one else in England will be shutting his door against the notorious Mr Norrell."

"My dear Lascelles," cried Drawlight, "what nonsense you talk! Upon my word, there is nothing in the world so easy to explain as failure – it is, after all, what every body does all the time."

Mr Lascelles said that that did not follow at all, and they were just beginning to argue about it when an anguished cry burst from the lips of their friend, Mr Norrell.

"Oh, God! What shall I do? What shall I do? I have laboured all these months to make my profession acceptable in the eyes of men and still they despise me! Mr Lascelles, you know the world, tell me . . ."

"Alas, sir," interrupted Mr Lascelles quickly, "I make a great point of never giving advice to any one." And he went back to his newspaper.

"My dear Mr Norrell!" said Drawlight (who did not wait to be asked for *his* opinion). "Such an opportunity is hardly likely to occur again . . ." (A potent argument this, and one which caused Mr Norrell to sigh very deeply.) ". . . and I must say I do not think that I could forgive myself if I allowed you to pass it by. With one stroke you return to us that sweet young woman – whose death no one can hear of without shedding a tear; you restore a fortune to a worthy gentleman; *and* you re-establish magic as a power in the realm for generations to come! Once you have proved the virtue of your skills – their utility and so forth – who will be able to deny magicians their dues of veneration and praise? They will be quite as much respected as admirals, a great deal more than generals, and probably as much as archbishops and lord chancellors! I should not be at all surprized if His Majesty did not immediately set up a convenient arrangement of degrees with magicians-in-ordinary and magicians-canonical, non-stipendiary magicians and all that sort of thing. And you, Mr Norrell, at the top as Arch-Magician! And all this with one stroke, sir! With one stroke!"

Drawlight was pleased with this speech; Lascelles, rustling the paper in his irritation, clearly had a great many things to say in contradiction of Drawlight, but had put it out of his power to say any of them by his declaration that he never gave advice.

"There is scarcely any form of magic more dangerous!" said Mr Norrell in a sort of horrified whisper. "It is dangerous to the magician and dangerous to the subject."

"Well, sir," said Drawlight reasonably, "I suppose you are the best judge of the danger as it applies to yourself, but the subject, as you term her, is dead. What worse can befall her?"

Drawlight waited a moment for a reply to this interesting question, but Mr Norrell made none.

"I shall now ring for the carriage," Drawlight declared and did so. "I shall go immediately to Brunswick-square. Have no fear, Mr Norrell, I have every expectation that all our proposals will meet with most ready acquiesence on all sides. I shall return within the hour!"

After Drawlight had hurried away, Mr Norrell sat for a quarter of an hour or so simply staring in front of him and though Lascelles did not believe in the magic that Mr Norrell said would be done (nor, therefore, in the danger that Mr Norrell said would be braved) he was glad that he could not see what Mr Norrell seemed to see.

Then Mr Norrell roused himself and took down five or six books in a great hurry and opened them up – presumably searching out those passages which were full of advice for magicians who wished to awaken dead young ladies. This occupied him until another three-quarters of an hour had passed, when a little bustle could be heard outside the library, and Mr Drawlight's voice preceded him into the room.

". . . the greatest favour in the world! So very much obliged to you . . ." Mr Drawlight danced through the library-door, his face one immense smile. "All is well, sir! Sir Walter did hold back a little at first, but all is well! He asked me to convey to you his gratitude for your kind attention, but he did not think that it could do any good. *I* said that if he were thinking of the thing getting out afterwards and being talked about, then he need not fear at all, for we had no wish to see him embarrassed – and that Mr Norrell's one desire was to be of service to him and that Lascelles and I were discretion itself – but he said he did not mind about that, for people would always laugh at a Minister, only he had rather Miss Wintertowne were left sleeping now – which he thought more respectful of her present situation. My dear Sir Walter! cried I, how can you say so? You cannot mean that a rich and beautiful young lady would gladly quit this life on the very eve of her marriage – when you yourself were to be the happy man! Oh! Sir Walter! – I said – *you* may not believe in Mr Norrell's magic, but what can it hurt to try? Which the old lady saw the sense of immediately and added her arguments to mine – and she told me of a magician she had known in her childhood, a most talented person and a devoted friend to all her family, who had prolonged her sister's life several years beyond what any one had expected. I tell you, Mr Norrell, nothing can express the gratitude Mrs Wintertowne feels at your goodness and she begs me to say to you that you are to come immediately – and Sir Walter himself says that he can see no sense in putting it off – so I told Davey to wait at the door and on no account to go anywhere else. Oh! Mr Norrell, it is to be a night of reconciliations! All misunderstandings, all unfortunate constructions which may have been placed on one or two ill-chosen words – all, all are to be swept away! It is to be quite like a play by Shakespeare!"

Mr Norrell's greatcoat was fetched and he got into the carriage; and from the expression of surprize upon his face when the carriage-doors opened and Mr Drawlight jumped in one side and Mr Lascelles jumped in the other I am tempted to suppose that he had not originally intended that those two gentlemen should accompany him to Brunswick-square.

Lascelles threw himself into the carriage, snorting with laughter and saying that he had never in his life heard of anything so ridiculous and comparing their snug drive through the London streets in Mr Norrell's carriage to ancient French and Italian fables in which fools set sail in milk-pails to fetch the moon's reflection from the bottom of a duckpond – all of which might well have offended Mr Norrell had Mr Norrell been in spirits to attend to him.

When they arrived at Brunswick-square they found, gathered upon the steps, a little crowd of people. Two men ran out to catch the horses' heads and the light from the oil-lamp above the steps shewed the crowd to be a dozen or so of Mrs Wintertowne's servants all on the look-out for the magician who was to bring back their young lady. Human nature being what it is, I dare say there may have been a few among them who were merely curious to see what such a man might look like. But many shewed in their pale faces signs that they had been grieving and these were, I think, prompted by some nobler sentiment to keep their silent vigil in the cold midnight street.

One of them took a candle and went before Mr Norrell and his friends to shew them the way, for the house was very dark and cold. They were upon the staircase when they heard Mrs Wintertowne's voice calling out from above, "Robert! Robert! Is it Mr Norrell? Oh! Thank God, sir!" She appeared before them very suddenly in a doorway. "I thought you would never come!" And then, much to Mr Norrell's consternation, she took both his hands in her own and, pressing them hard, entreated him to use his most potent spells to bring Miss Wintertowne back to life. Money was not to be thought of. He might name his price! Only say that he would return her darling child to her. He must promise her that he would!

Mr Norrell cleared his throat and was perhaps about to embark upon one of his long, uninteresting expositions of the philosophy of modern magic, when Mr Drawlight glided forward, took Mrs Wintertowne's hands and rescued them both.

"Now I beg of you, my dear madam," cried Drawlight, "to be

more tranquil! Mr Norrell is come, as you see, and we must try what his power may do. He begs that you will not mention payment again. Whatever he does tonight will be done for friendship's sake . . ." And here Mr Drawlight stood upon tiptoes and lifted his chin to look over Mrs Wintertowne's shoulder to where Sir Walter Pole was standing within the room. Sir Walter had just risen from his chair and stood a little way off, regarding the newcomers. In the candlelight he was pale and hollow-eyed and there was about him a kind of gauntness which had not been there before. Mere common courtesy said that he ought to have come forward to speak to them, but he did not do so.

It was curious to observe how Mr Norrell hesitated in the doorway and exhibited great unwillingness to be conducted further into the house until he had spoken to Sir Walter. "But I must just speak to Sir Walter! Just a few words with Sir Walter! – I shall do my utmost for you, Sir Walter!" he called out from the door. "Since the young lady is, ahem!, not long gone from us, I may say that the situation is promising. Yes, I think I may go so far as to say that the situation is a promising one. I shall go now, Sir Walter, and do my work. I hope, in due course, I shall have the honour of bringing you good news!"

All the assurances that Mrs Wintertowne begged for – and did not get – from Mr Norrell, Mr Norrell was now anxious to bestow upon Sir Walter who clearly did not want them. From his sanctuary in the drawing-room Sir Walter nodded and then, when Mr Norrell still lingered, he called out hoarsely, "Thank you, sir. Thank you!" And his mouth stretched out in a curious way. It was, perhaps, meant for a smile.

"I wish with all my heart, Sir Walter," called out Mr Norrell, "that I might invite you to come up with me and to see what it is I do, but the curious nature of this particular magic demands solitude. I will, I hope, have the honour of shewing you some magic upon another occasion."

Sir Walter bowed slightly and turned away.

Mrs Wintertowne was at that moment speaking to her servant, Robert, and Drawlight took advantage of this slight distraction to pull Mr Norrell to one side and whisper frantically in his ear: "No, no, sir! Do not send them away! My advice is to gather as many of them around the bed as can be persuaded to come. It is, I assure you, the best guarantee of our night's exploits being generally broadcast in the morning. And do not be afraid of making a little bustle to impress the servants – your best incantations if you please! Oh! What a noodle-head I am! Had only I thought to bring some Chinese powders to throw in the fire! I don't suppose that you have any about you?"

Mr Norrell made no reply to this but asked to be brought without delay to where Miss Wintertowne was.

But though the magician particularly asked to be taken there alone, his dear friends, Mr Drawlight and Mr Lascelles, were not so unkind as to leave him to face this great crisis of his career alone and consequently the three of them together were conducted by Robert to a chamber upon the second floor.

# 8

# A gentleman with thistle-down hair

## October 1807

THERE WAS NO one there.

Which is to say there was someone there. Miss Wintertowne lay upon the bed, but it would have puzzled philosophy to say now whether she were someone or no one at all.

They had dressed her in a white gown and hung a silver chain about her neck; they had combed and dressed her beautiful hair and put pearl-and-garnet earrings in her ears. But it was extremely doubtful whether Miss Wintertowne cared about such things any more. They had lit candles and laid a good fire in the hearth, they had put roses about the room, which filled it with a sweet perfume, but Miss Wintertowne could have lain now with equal composure in the foulest-smelling garret in the city.

"And she was quite tolerable to look at, you say?" said Mr Lascelles.

"You never saw her?" said Drawlight. "Oh! she was a heavenly creature. Quite divine. An angel."

"Indeed? And such a pinched-looking ruin of a thing now! I shall advise all the good-looking women of my acquaintance not to die," said Mr Lascelles. He leaned closer. "They have closed her eyes," he said.

"Her eyes were perfection," said Drawlight, "a clear dark grey, with long, dark eye-lashes and dark eye-brows. It is a pity you never saw her – she was exactly the sort of creature you would have admired." Drawlight turned to Mr Norrell. "Well, sir, are you ready to begin?"

Mr Norrell was seated in a chair next to the fire. The resolute, businesslike manner, which he had adopted on his arrival at the house, had disappeared; instead he sat with neck bowed, sighing heavily, his gaze fixed upon the carpet. Mr Lascelles and Mr Drawlight looked at him with that degree of interest appropriate to the character of each – which is to say that Mr Drawlight was all fidgets and bright-eyed anticipation, and Mr Lascelles all cool, smiling scepticism. Mr Drawlight took a few respectful steps back from the bed so that Mr Norrell might more conveniently approach it and Mr Lascelles leant against a wall and crossed his arms (an attitude he often adopted in the theatre).

Mr Norrell sighed again. "Mr Drawlight, I have already said that this particular magic demands complete solitude. I must ask you to wait downstairs."

"Oh, but, sir!" protested Drawlight. "Surely such intimate friends as Lascelles and I can be no inconvenience to you? We are the quietest creatures in the world! In two minutes' time you will have quite forgotten that we are here. And I must say that I consider our presence as absolutely essential! For who will broadcast the news of your achievement tomorrow morning if not Lascelles and myself? Who will describe the ineffable grandeur of the moment when your magicianship triumphs and the young woman rises from the dead? Or the unbearable pathos of the moment when you are forced to admit defeat? You will not do it half so well yourself, sir. You know that you will not."

"Perhaps," said Mr Norrell. "But what you suggest is entirely impossible. I will not, *cannot* begin until you leave the room."

Poor Drawlight! He could not force the magician to begin the magic against his will, but to have waited so long to see some magic and then to be excluded! It was almost more than he could bear. Even Mr Lascelles was a little disappointed for he had hoped to witness something very ridiculous that he could laugh at.

When they had gone Mr Norrell rose wearily from his seat and took up a book that he had brought with him. He opened it at a place he had marked with a folded letter and placed it upon a little table so that it would be to hand if he needed to consult it. Then he began to recite a spell.

It took effect almost immediately because suddenly there was something green where nothing green had been before and a fresh, sweet smell as of woods and fields wafted through the room. Mr Norrell stopped speaking.

Someone was standing in the middle of the room: a tall, handsome person with pale, perfect skin and an immense amount of hair, as pale and shining as thistle-down. His cold, blue eyes glittered and he had long dark eye-brows, which terminated in an upward flourish. He was dressed exactly like any other gentleman, except that his coat was of the brightest green imaginable – the colour of leaves in early summer.

"*O Lar!*" began Mr Norrell in a quavering voice. "*O Lar! Magnum opus est mihi tuo auxilio. Haec virgo mortua est et familia eius eam ad vitam redire vult.*"[1] Mr Norrell pointed to the figure on the bed.

At the sight of Miss Wintertowne the gentleman with the thistle-down hair suddenly became very excited. He spread wide his hands in a gesture of surprized delight and began to speak Latin very rapidly. Mr Norrell, who was more accustomed to seeing Latin written down or printed in books, found that he could not follow the language when it was spoken so fast, though he did recognize a few words here and there, words such as "*formosa*" and "*venusta*" which are descriptive of feminine beauty.

Mr Norrell waited until the gentleman's rapture had subsided and then he directed the gentleman's attention to the mirror above

---

[1] "O Fairy. I have great need of your help. This virgin is dead and her family wish her to be returned to life."

the mantelpiece. A vision appeared of Miss Wintertowne walking along a narrow rocky path, through a mountainous and gloomy landscape. "*Ecce mortua inter terram et caelum!*" declared Mr Norrell. "*Scito igitur, O Lar, me ad hanc magnam operam te elegisse quia . . .*"[2]

"Yes, yes!" cried the gentleman suddenly breaking into English. "You elected to summon *me* because my genius for magic exceeds that of all the rest of my race. Because I have been the servant and confidential friend of Thomas Godbless, Ralph Stokesey, Martin Pale *and* of the Raven King. Because I am valorous, chivalrous, generous and as handsome as the day is long! That is all quite understood! It would have been madness to summon anyone else! We both know who *I* am. The question is: who in the world are *you?*"

"I?" said Mr Norrell, startled. "I am the greatest magician of the Age!"

The gentleman raised one perfect eye-brow as if to say he was surprized to hear it. He walked around Mr Norrell slowly, considering him from every angle. Then, most disconcerting of all, he plucked Mr Norrell's wig from his head and looked underneath, as if Mr Norrell were a cooking pot on the fire and he wished to know what was for dinner.

"I . . . I am the man who is destined to restore magic to England!" stammered Mr Norrell, grabbing back his wig and replacing it, slightly askew, upon his head.

"Well, obviously you are *that*!" said the gentleman. "Or I should not be here! You do not imagine that I would waste my time upon a three-penny hedge-sorcerer, do you? But *who* are you? That is what I wish to know. What magic have you done? Who was your master? What magical lands have you visited? What enemies have you defeated? Who are your allies?"

Mr Norrell was extremely surprized to be asked so many questions and he was not at all prepared to answer them. He

[2] "Here is the dead woman between earth and heaven! Know then, O Fairy, that I have chosen you for this great task because . . ."

wavered and hesitated before finally fixing upon the only one to which he had a sensible answer. "I had no master. I taught myself."

"How?"

"From books."

"Books!" (This in a tone of the utmost contempt.)

"Yes, indeed. There is a great deal of magic in books nowadays. Of course, most of it is nonsense. No one knows as well as I how much nonsense is printed in books. But there is a great deal of useful information too and it is surprizing how, after one has learnt a little, one begins to see . . ."

Mr Norrell was beginning to warm to his subject, but the gentleman with the thistle-down hair had no patience to listen to other people talk and so he interrupted him.

"Am I the first of my race that you have seen?"

"Oh, yes!"

This answer seemed to please the gentleman with the thistle-down hair and he smiled. "So! Should I agree to restore this young woman to life, what would be my reward?"

Mr Norrell cleared his throat. "What sort of thing . . .?" he said, a little hoarsely.

"Oh! That is easily agreed!" cried the gentleman with the thistle-down hair. "My wishes are the most moderate things in the world. Fortunately I am utterly free from greed and sordid ambition. Indeed, you will find that my proposal is much more to your advantage than mine – such is my unselfish nature! I simply wish to be allowed to aid you in all your endeavours, to advise you upon all matters and to guide you in your studies. Oh! and you must take care to let all the world know that your greatest achievements are due in larger part to me!"

Mr Norrell looked a little ill. He coughed and muttered something about the gentleman's generosity. "Were I the sort of magician who is eager to entrust all his business to another person, then your offer would be most welcome. But unfortunately . . . I fear . . . In short I have no notion of employing you – or indeed any other member of your race – ever again."

A long silence.

"Well, this is ungrateful indeed!" declared the gentleman, coldly. "I have put myself to the trouble of paying you this visit. I have listened with the greatest good nature to your dreary conversation. I have borne patiently with your ignorance of the proper forms and etiquette of magic. And now you scorn my offer of assistance. Other magicians, I may say, have endured all sorts of torments to gain my help. Perhaps I would do better to speak to the other one. Perhaps he understands better than you how to address persons of high rank and estate?" The gentleman glanced about the room. "I do not see him. Where is he?"

"Where is who?"

"The other one."

"The other what?"

"Magician!"

"Magici . . ." Mr Norrell began to form the word but it died upon his lips. "No, no! There is no other magician! I am the only one. I assure you I am the only one. Why should you think that . . . ?"

"*Of course* there is another magician!" declared the gentleman, as if it were perfectly ridiculous to deny anything quite so obvious. "He is your dearest friend in all the world!"

"I have no friends," said Mr Norrell.

He was utterly perplexed. Whom might the fairy mean? Childermass? Lascelles? *Drawlight?*

"He has red hair and a long nose. And he is very conceited – as are all Englishmen!" declared the gentleman with the thistle-down hair.

This was no help. Childermass, Lascelles and Drawlight were all very conceited in their ways, Childermass and Lascelles both had long noses, but none of them had red hair. Mr Norrell could make nothing of it and so he returned, with a heavy sigh, to the matter in hand. "You will not help me?" he said. "You will not bring the young woman back from the dead?"

"I did not say so!" said the gentleman with the thistle-down hair, in a tone which suggested that he wondered why Mr Norrell should think *that*. "I must confess," he continued, "that in recent centuries I have grown somewhat bored of the society of my family and servants. My sisters and cousins have many virtues to recommend them, but they are not without faults. They are, I am sorry to say, somewhat boastful, conceited and proud. This young woman," he indicated Miss Wintertowne, "she had, I dare say, all the usual accomplishments and virtues? She was graceful? Witty? Vivacious? Capricious? Danced like sunlight? Rode like the wind? Sang like an angel? Embroidered like Penelope? Spoke French, Italian, German, Breton, Welsh and many other languages?"

Mr Norrell said he supposed so. He believed that those were the sorts of things young ladies did nowadays.

"Then she will be a charming companion for me!" declared the gentleman with the thistle-down hair, clapping his hands together.

Mr Norrell licked his lips nervously. "What exactly are you proposing?"

"Grant me half the lady's life and the deal is done."

"Half her life?" echoed Mr Norrell.

"Half," said the gentleman with the thistle-down hair.

"But what would her friends say if they learnt I had bargained away half her life?" asked Mr Norrell.

"Oh! They will never know any thing of it. You may rely upon me for that," said the gentleman. "Besides, she has no life now. Half a life is better than none."

Half a life did indeed seem a great deal better than none. With half a life Miss Wintertowne might marry Sir Walter and save him from bankruptcy. Then Sir Walter might continue in office and lend his support to all Mr Norrell's plans for reviving English magic. But Mr Norrell had read a great many books in which were described the dealings of other English magicians with persons of this race and he knew very well how deceitful they could be. He thought he saw how the gentleman intended to trick him.

"How long is a life?" he asked.

The gentleman with the thistle-down hair spread his hands in a gesture of the utmost candour. "How long would you like?"

Mr Norrell considered. "Let us suppose she had lived until she was ninety-four. Ninety-four would have been a good age. She is nineteen now. That would be another seventy-five years. If you were to bestow upon her another seventy-five years, then I see no reason why you should not have half of it."

"Seventy-five years then," agreed the gentleman with the thistle-down hair, "exactly half of which belongs to me."

Mr Norrell regarded him nervously. "Is there any thing more we must do?" he asked. "Shall we sign something?"

"No, but I should take something of the lady's to signify my claim upon her."

"Take one of these rings," suggested Mr Norrell, "or this necklace about her neck. I am sure I can explain away a missing ring or necklace."

"No," said the gentleman with the thistle-down hair. "It ought to be something . . . Ah! I know!"

Drawlight and Lascelles were seated in the drawing-room where Mr Norrell and Sir Walter Pole had first met. It was a gloomy enough spot. The fire burnt low in the grate and the candles were almost out. The curtains were undrawn and no one had put up the shutters. The rattle of the rain upon the windows was very melancholy.

"It is certainly a night for raising the dead," remarked Mr Lascelles. "Rain and trees lash the window-panes and the wind moans in the chimney – all the appropriate stage effects, in fact. I am frequently struck with the play-writing fit and I do not know that tonight's proceedings might not inspire me to try again – a tragi-comedy, telling of an impoverished minister's desperate attempts to gain money by any means, beginning with a mercenary marriage and ending with sorcery. I should think it might be received very well. I believe I shall call it, *'Tis Pity She's a Corpse*."

Lascelles paused for Drawlight to laugh at this witticism, but Drawlight had been put out of humour by the magician's refusal to allow him to stay and witness the magic, and all he said was: "Where do you suppose they have all gone?"

"I do not know."

"Well, considering all that you and I have done for them, I think we have deserved better than this! It is scarcely half an hour since they were so full of their gratitude to us. To have forgotten us so soon is very bad! And we have not been offered so much as a bit of cake since we arrived. I dare say it is rather too late for dinner – though I for one am famished to death!" He was silent a moment. "The fire is going out too," he remarked.

"Then put some more coals on," suggested Lascelles.

"What! And make myself all dirty?"

One by one all the candles went out and the light from the fire grew less and less until the Venetian paintings upon the walls became nothing but great squares of deepest black hung upon walls of a black that was slightly less profound. For a long time they sat in silence.

"That was the clock striking half-past one o'clock!" said Drawlight suddenly. "How lonely it sounds! Ugh! All the horrid things one reads of in novels always happen just as the church bell tolls or the clock strikes some hour or other in a dark house!"

"I cannot recall an instance of any thing very dreadful happening at half-past one," said Lascelles.

At that moment they heard footsteps on the stairs – which quickly became footsteps in the passageway. The drawing-room door was pushed open and someone stood there, candle in hand.

Drawlight grasped for the poker.

But it was Mr Norrell.

"Do not be alarmed, Mr Drawlight. There is nothing to be afraid of."

Yet Mr Norrell's face, as he raised up his candlestick, seemed to tell a different story; he was very pale and his eyes were wide and not yet emptied, it seemed, of the dregs of fear. "Where is Sir Walter?" he asked. "Where are the others? Miss Wintertowne is asking for her mama."

Mr Norrell was obliged to repeat the last sentence twice before the other two gentlemen could be made to understand him.

Lascelles blinked two or three times and opened his mouth as if in surprize, but then, recovering himself, he shut his mouth again and assumed a supercilious expression; this he wore for the remainder of the night, as if he regularly attended houses where young ladies were raised from the dead and considered this particular example to have been, upon the whole, a rather dull affair. Drawlight, in the meantime, had a thousand things to say and I dare say he said all of them, but unfortunately no one had attention to spare just then to discover what they were.

Drawlight and Lascelles were sent to find Sir Walter. Then Sir Walter fetched Mrs Wintertowne, and Mr Norrell led that lady, tearful and trembling, to her daughter's room. Meanwhile the news of Miss Wintertowne's return to life began to penetrate other parts of the house; the servants learnt of it and were overjoyed and full of gratitude to Mr Norrell, Mr Drawlight and Mr Lascelles. A butler and two manservants approached Mr Drawlight and Mr Lascelles and begged to be allowed to say that if ever Mr Drawlight or Mr Lascelles could benefit from any small service that the butler or the manservants might be able to render them, they had only to speak.

Mr Lascelles whispered to Mr Drawlight that he had not realized before that doing kind actions would lead to his being addressed in such familiar terms by so many low people – it was most unpleasant – he would take care to do no more. Fortunately the low people were in such glad spirits that they never knew they had offended him.

It was soon learnt that Miss Wintertowne had left her bed and, leaning upon Mr Norrell's arm, had gone to her own sitting-room where she was now established in a chair by her fire and that she had asked for a cup of tea.

Drawlight and Lascelles were summoned upstairs to a pretty little sitting-room where they found Miss Wintertowne, her mother, Sir Walter, Mr Norrell and some of the servants.

One would have thought from their looks that it had been Mrs Wintertowne and Sir Walter who had journeyed across several supernatural worlds during the night, they were so grey-faced and drawn; Mrs Wintertowne was weeping and Sir Walter passed his hand across his pale brow from time to time like someone who had seen horrors.

Miss Wintertowne, on the other hand, appeared quite calm and collected, like a young lady who had spent a quiet, uneventful evening at home. She was sitting in a chair in the same elegant gown that she had been wearing when Drawlight and Lascelles had seen her last. She rose and smiled at Drawlight. "I think, sir, that you and I scarcely ever met before, yet I have been told how much I owe to you. But I fear it is a debt quite beyond any repaying. That I am here at all is in a large part due to your energy and insistence. Thank you, sir. Many, many thanks."

And she held out both her hands to him and he took them.

"Oh! Madam!" he cried, all bows and smiles. "It was, I do assure you, the greatest hon . . ."

And then he stopped and was silent a moment. "Madam?" he said. He gave a short, embarrassed laugh (which was odd enough in itself – Drawlight was not easily embarrassed). He did not let go of her hands, but looked around the room as if in search of someone to help him out of a difficulty. Then he lifted one of her own hands and shewed it to her. She did not appear in any way alarmed by what she saw, but she did look surprized; she raised the hand so that her mother could see it.

The little finger of her left hand was gone.

## 9

# Lady Pole

## October 1807

It has been remarked (by a lady infinitely cleverer than the present author) how kindly disposed the world in general feels to young people who either die or marry. Imagine then the interest that surrounded Miss Wintertowne! No young lady ever had such advantages before: for she died upon the Tuesday, was raised to life in the early hours of Wednesday morning, and was married upon the Thursday; which some people thought too much excitement for one week.

The desire to see her was quite universal. The full stretch of most people's information was that she had lost a finger in her passage from one world to the next and back again. This was most tantalizing; was she changed in any other way? No one knew.

On Wednesday morning (which was the morning that followed her happy revival) the principals in this marvellous adventure seemed all in a conspiracy to deprive the Town of news; morning-callers at Brunswick-square learnt only that Miss Wintertowne and her mother were resting; in Hanover-square it was exactly the same – Mr Norrell was very much fatigued – it was entirely impossible that he see any body; and as for Sir Walter Pole, no body was quite certain where to find him (though it was strongly suspected that he was at Mrs Wintertowne's house in Brunswick-square). Had it not been for Mr Drawlight and Mr Lascelles (benevolent souls!) the Town would have been starved of information of any sort, but they drove diligently about London making their appearance in a quite impossible number of drawing-rooms, morning-rooms, dining-rooms and card-rooms. It is impossible to say how many dinners Drawlight was invited to sit down to that day – and it is fortunate that he was never at any time much of an eater or he might have done some lasting damage to his digestion. Fifty times or more he must have described how, after Miss Wintertowne's restoration, Mrs Wintertowne and he had wept together; how Sir Walter Pole and he had clasped each other's hand; how Sir Walter had thanked him most gratefully and how he had begged Sir Walter not to think of it; and how Mrs Wintertowne had insisted that Mr Lascelles and he both be driven home in her very own carriage.

Sir Walter Pole had left Mrs Wintertowne's house at about seven o'clock and had gone back to his lodgings to sleep for a few hours, but at about midday he returned to Brunswick-square just as the Town had supposed. (How our neighbours find us out!) By this time it had become apparent to Mrs Wintertowne that her daughter now enjoyed a certain celebrity; that she had, as it were, risen to public eminence overnight. As well as the people who left their cards at the door, great numbers of letters and messages of congratulation were arriving every hour for Miss Wintertowne, many of them from people of whom Mrs Wintertowne had never heard. "Permit me, madam," wrote one, "to entreat you to shake off the oppression of that shadowy vale which has been revealed to you."

That unknown persons should think themselves entitled to comment upon so private a matter as a death and a resurrection, that they should vent their curiosity in letters to her daughter was a circumstance to excite Mrs Wintertowne's utmost displeasure; she had a great deal to say in censure of such vulgar, ill-bred beings, and upon his arrival at Brunswick-square Sir Walter was obliged to listen to all of it.

"My advice, ma'am," he said, "is to think no more about it. As we politicians well know a policy of dignity and silence is our best defence against this sort of impertinence."

"Ah! Sir Walter!" cried his mother-in-law to be. "It is very gratifying to me to discover how frequently our opinions agree! Dignity and silence. Quite. I do not think we can ever be too discreet upon the subject of poor, dear Emma's sufferings. After tomorrow I for one am determined never to speak of it again."

"Perhaps," said Sir Walter, "I did not mean to go so far. Because, you know, we must not forget Mr Norrell. We shall always have a standing reminder of what has happened in Mr Norrell. I fear he must often be with us – after the service he has done us we can scarcely ever shew him consideration enough." He paused and then added with a wry twist of his ugly face, "Happily Mr Norrell himself has been so good as to indicate how he thinks *my* share of the obligation might best be discharged." This was a reference to a conversation which Sir Walter and Mr Norrell had had at four o'clock that morning, when Mr Norrell had waylaid Sir Walter upon the stairs and talked to him at great length about his plans to baffle the French by magic.

Mrs Wintertowne said that she would, of course, be glad to distinguish Mr Norrell with marks of special respect and consideration; any one might know how highly she regarded him. Quite apart from his great magicianship – which, said Mrs Wintertowne, there was no need to mention when he came to the house – he seemed a very good sort of old gentleman.

"Indeed," said Sir Walter. "But for now our most pressing concern must be that Miss Wintertowne should not undertake more than she is equal to – and it was of this that I particularly wished to speak to you. I do not know what may be your opinion but it seems to me that it would be as well to put off the wedding for a week or two."

Mrs Wintertowne could not approve of such a plan; all the arrangements were made and so much of the wedding-dinner cooked. Soup, jellies, boiled meats, pickled sturgeon and so forth were all ready; what was the good of letting it all spoil now, only to have it all to do over again in a week or so? Sir Walter had nothing to say to arguments of domestic economy, and so he suggested that they ask Miss Wintertowne to say whether or not she felt strong enough.

And so they rose from their seats in the icy drawing-room (where this conversation had taken place) and went up to Miss Wintertowne's sitting-room on the second-floor where they put the question to her.

"Oh!" said she. "I never felt better in my life. I feel very strong and well. Thank you. I have been out already this morning. I do not often walk. I rarely feel equal to exercise, but this morning I felt as if the house were a prison. I longed to be outside."

Sir Walter looked very concerned. "Was that wise?" He turned to Mrs Wintertowne. "Was that well done?"

Mrs Wintertowne opened her mouth to protest but her daughter only laughed and exclaimed, "Oh! Mama knew nothing of it, I assure you. I went out while she was asleep in her room. Barnard went with me. And I walked round Brunswick-square twenty times. Twenty! – is not that the most ridiculous thing you ever heard? But I was possessed of such a desire to walk! Indeed I would have run, I think, if it were at all possible, but in London, you know . . ." She laughed again. "I wanted to go further but Barnard would not let me. Barnard was in a great flutter and worry lest I should faint away in the road. She would not let me go out of sight of the house."

They stared at her. It was – apart from anything else – probably the longest speech Sir Walter had ever heard her utter. She was sitting very straight with a bright eye and blooming complexion – the very picture of health and beauty. She spoke so rapidly and with such expression; she looked so cheerful and was so exceedingly animated. It was as if Mr Norrell had not only restored her to life, but to twice or thrice the amount of life she had had before.

It was very odd.

"Of course," said Sir Walter, "if you feel well enough to take exercise, then I am sure that no one would wish to prevent you – nothing is so likely to make you strong, and to ensure your continuing health, as regular exercise. But perhaps, for the present, it would be as well not to go out without telling any one. You should have someone more than Barnard to guard you. From tomorrow, you know, I may claim that honour for myself."

"But you will be busy, Sir Walter," she reminded him. "You will have all your Government business to attend to."

"Indeed, but . . ."

"Oh! I know that you will be pretty constantly engaged with business affairs. I know I must not expect anything else."

She seemed so cheerfully resigned to his neglecting her that he could not help opening his mouth to protest – but the justice of what she said prevented him from saying a word. Ever since he had first seen her at Lady Winsell's house in Bath he had been greatly struck by her beauty and elegance – and had quickly concluded that it would be a very good thing, not only to marry her as soon as it could conveniently be contrived, but also to get better acquainted with her – for he had begun to suspect that, setting aside the money, she might suit him very well as a wife. He thought that an hour or so of conversation might accomplish a great deal towards setting them upon that footing of perfect unreserve and confidence which was so much to be desired between husband and wife. He had high hopes that such a tête-à-tête would soon provide ample proofs of their mutual sympathies and tastes. Several things she had said had encouraged him to hope that it might be so. And being a man – and a clever one – and forty-two years old, he naturally had a great deal of information and a great many opinions upon almost every subject you care to mention, which he was eager to communicate to a lovely woman of nineteen – all of which, he thought, she could not fail but to find quite enthralling. But, what with *his* great preoccupation with business and *her* poor health they had yet to have this interesting conversation; and now she told him that she expected things to continue much the same after they were married. She did not appear to resent it. Instead, with her new, lively spirits, she seemed quite entertained that he should ever have deceived himself that matters could be otherwise.

Unfortunately he was already late for an appointment with the Foreign Secretary so he took Miss Wintertowne's hand (her whole, right hand) and kissed it very gallantly; told her how much he looked forward to the morrow that would make him the happiest of men; attended politely – hat in hand – to a short speech by Mrs Wintertowne upon the subject; and left the house resolving to consider the problem further – just as soon, in fact, as he could find the time.

Upon the following morning the wedding did indeed take place at St George's Hanover-square. It was attended by almost all of His Majesty's Ministers, two or three of the Royal Dukes, half a dozen admirals, a bishop and several generals. But I am sorry to say that, vital as such great men must always be to a Nation's peace and prosperity, on the day that Miss Wintertowne married Sir Walter Pole, no body cared tuppence for any of them. The man who drew most eyes, the man whom every body whispered to his neighbour to point out to him, was the magician, Mr Norrell.

# 10

# The difficulty of finding employment for a magician

## October 1807

Sir Walter intended to introduce the subject of magic among the other Ministers by degrees, allowing them to grow gradually accustomed to the idea before proposing that they make trial of Mr Norrell in the war. He was afraid that they would oppose him; he was sure that Mr Canning would be sarcastic, that Lord Castlereagh would be uncooperative, and the Earl of Chatham merely bemused.

But all of these fears were entirely unfounded. The Ministers, he soon discovered, were quite as alive to the novelty of the situation as any one else in London. The next time the cabinet met at Burlington House[1]

[1] Burlington House in Piccadilly was the London residence of the Duke of Portland, the First Minister of the Treasury (whom many people nowadays like to call the *Prime Minister* in the French style). It had been erected in an Age when English noblemen were not afraid to rival their Monarch in displays of power and wealth and it had no equal for beauty anywhere in the capital. As for the Duke himself, he was a most respectable old person, but, poor man, he did not accord with any body's idea of what a Prime Minister ought to be. He was very old and sick. Just at present he lay in a curtained room somewhere in a remote part of the house, stupefied by laudanum and dying by degrees. He was of no utility whatsoever to his country and not much to his fellow Ministers. The only advantage of his leadership as far as they could see was that it allowed them to use his magnificent house as their meeting-place and to employ his magnificent servants to fetch them any little thing they might fancy out of his cellar. (They generally found that governing Great Britain was a thirsty business.)

they declared themselves eager to employ England's only magician. But it was by no means clear what ought to be done with him. It had been two hundred years since the English Government had last commissioned a magician and they were a little out of the habit of it.

"*My* chief problem," explained Lord Castlereagh, "is in finding men for the Army – a quite impossible task, I assure you; the British are a peculiarly unmilitary race. But I have my eye on Lincolnshire; I am told that the pigs in Lincolnshire are particularly fine and by eating them the population grows very stout and strong. Now what would suit me best would be a general spell cast over Lincolnshire so that three or four thousand young men would all at once be filled with a lively desire to become soldiers and fight the French." He looked at Sir Walter rather wistfully. "Would your friend know of such a spell, Sir Walter, do you think?"

Sir Walter did not know but he said he would ask Mr Norrell.

Later that same day Sir Walter called upon Mr Norrell and put the question to him. Mr Norrell was delighted. He did not believe that anyone had ever proposed such a piece of magic before and begged Sir Walter to convey his compliments to Lord Castlereagh as the possessor of a most original brain. As to whether or not it were possible; "The difficulty lies in confining the application of the spell to Lincolnshire – and to young men. There is a danger that if we were successful – which I flatter myself we would be – then Lincolnshire – and several of the neighbouring counties – might be entirely emptied of people."

Sir Walter went back to Lord Castlereagh and told him no.

The next magic which the Ministers proposed pleased Mr Norrell a great deal less. The resurrection of Lady Pole engrossed the thoughts of everyone in London and the Ministers were by no means exempt from the general fascination. Lord Castlereagh began it when he asked the other Ministers who was it that Napoleon Buonaparte had feared most in all the world? Who had always seemed to know what the wicked French emperor would do next? Who had inflicted so resounding a defeat upon the French that they dare not stick their French noses out of their ports? Who had united in one person all the virtues that make up an Englishman? Who else, said Lord Castlereagh, but Lord Nelson? Clearly the first thing to be done was to bring back Lord Nelson from the dead. Lord Castlereagh begged Sir Walter's pardon – perhaps he had not understood something – but why they were wasting time talking about it?

Whereupon Mr Canning, an energetic and quarrelsome person, replied quickly that of course Lord Nelson was sadly missed, Nelson had been the Nation's hero, Nelson had done everything Lord Castlereagh said he did. But when all was said and done – and Mr Canning meant no disrespect to the Navy, that most glorious of British institutions – Nelson had only been a sailor, whereas the late Mr Pitt had been everything.[2] If anyone dead was going to be brought back to life then really there was no choice – it must be Pitt.

Lord Chatham (who was also the late Mr Pitt's brother) naturally seconded this proposal but he wondered why they had to make a choice – why not resurrect both Pitt and Nelson? It would only be a question of paying the magician twice and there could not be any objection to that, he supposed?

Then other Ministers proposed other dead gentlemen as candidates for restoration until it seemed that half the vaults in England might be emptied. Very soon they had quite a long list and were, as usual, starting to argue about it.

"This will not do," said Sir Walter. "We must begin somewhere and it seems to me that every one of us was helped to his present position by the friendship of Mr Pitt. We would do very wrong to give some other gentleman the preference."

---

[2] William Pitt the Younger (1759–1806). It is very doubtful that we will ever see his like again, for he became Prime Minister at the age of twenty-four and led the country from that day forth, with just one brief interval of three years, until his death.

A messenger was sent to fetch Mr Norrell from Hanover-square to Burlington House. Mr Norrell was led into the magnificent painted saloon where the Ministers were sitting. Sir Walter told him that they were contemplating another resurrection.

Mr Norrell turned very pale and muttered something of how his special regard for Sir Walter had compelled him to undertake a sort of magic which otherwise he would not have attempted – he really had no wish to make a second attempt – the Ministers did not know what they were asking.

But when Mr Norrell understood better *who* it was that they proposed as a candidate, he looked a great deal relieved and was heard to say something about the condition of the *body*.

Then the Ministers thought how Mr Pitt had been dead for almost two years, and that, devoted as they had been to Pitt in his life, they really had very little desire to see him in his present condition. Lord Chatham (Mr Pitt's brother) remarked sadly that poor William would certainly have come a good deal unravelled by now.

The subject was not mentioned again.

A week or so later Lord Castlereagh proposed sending Mr Norrell to the Netherlands or possibly Portugal – places where the Ministers entertained faint hopes of gaining some foothold against Buonaparte – where Mr Norrell might do magic under the direction of the generals and the admirals. So Admiral Paycocke, an ancient red-faced seaman, and Captain Harcourt-Bruce of the 20th Light Dragoons were dispatched as a joint military and naval expedition to Hanover-square to take an observation of Mr Norrell.

Captain Harcourt-Bruce was not only dashing, handsome and brave, he was also rather romantic. The reappearance of magic in England thrilled him immensely. He was a great reader of the more exciting sort of history – and his head was full of ancient battles in which the English were outnumbered by the French and doomed to die, when all at once would be heard the sound of strange, unearthly music, and upon a hilltop would appear the Raven King in his tall, black helmet with its mantling of raven-feathers streaming in the wind; and he would gallop down the hillside on his tall, black horse with a hundred human knights and a hundred fairy knights at his back, and he would defeat the French by magic.

*That* was Captain Harcourt-Bruce's idea of a magician. *That* was the sort of thing which he now expected to see reproduced on every battlefield on the Continent. So when he saw Mr Norrell in his drawing-room in Hanover-square, and after he had sat and watched Mr Norrell peevishly complain to his footman, first that the cream in his tea was too creamy, and next that it was too watery – well, I shall not surprize you when I say he was somewhat disappointed. In fact he was so downcast by the whole undertaking that Admiral Paycocke, a bluff old gentleman, felt rather sorry for him and only had the heart to laugh at him and tease him very moderately about it.

Admiral Paycocke and Captain Harcourt-Bruce went back to the Ministers and said it was absolutely out of the question to send Mr Norrell anywhere; the admirals and the generals would never forgive the Government if they did it. For some weeks that autumn it seemed the Ministers would never be able to find employment for their only magician.

# 11

# Brest

## November 1807

IN THE FIRST week of November a squadron of French ships was preparing to leave the port of Brest which lies on the west coast of Brittany in France. The intention of the French was to cruise about the Bay of Biscay looking for British ships to capture or, if they were unable to do that, to prevent the British from doing any thing which they appeared to want to do.

The wind blew steadily off the land. The French sailors made their preparations quickly and efficiently and the ships were almost ready when heavy black clouds appeared suddenly and a rain began to fall.

Now it was only natural that such an important port as Brest should contain a great number of people who studied the winds and the weather. Just as the ships were about to set sail several of these persons hurried down to the docks in great excitement to warn the sailors that there was something very queer about the rain: the clouds, they said, had come from the north, whereas the wind was blowing from the east. The thing was impossible, but it had happened. The captains of the ships just had time to be astonished, incredulous or unnerved – as their characters dictated – when another piece of news reached them.

Brest harbour consists of an inner bay and an outer, the inner bay being separated from the open sea by a long thin peninsula. As the rain grew heavier the French officers in charge of the ships learnt that a great fleet of British ships had appeared in the outer bay.

How many ships were there? The officers' informants did not know. More than could be easily counted – perhaps as many as a hundred. Like the rain, the ships had seemingly arrived in a single instant out of an empty sea. What sort of ships were they? Ah! That was the strangest thing of all! The ships were all ships of the line, heavily armed two- and three-decked warships.

This was astonishing news. The ships' great number and their great size was, in truth, more puzzling than their sudden appearance. The British Navy blockaded Brest continually, but never with more than twenty-five ships at a time, of which only ten or twelve were ships of the line, the remainder being agile little frigates, sloops and brigs.

So peculiar was this tale of a hundred ships that the French captains did not believe it until they had ridden or rowed to Lochrist or Camaret Saint-Julien or other places where they could stand upon the clifftops and see the ships for themselves.

Days went by. The sky was the colour of lead and the rain continued to fall. The British ships remained stubbornly where they were. The people of Brest were in great dread lest some of the ships might attempt to come up to the town and bombard it. But the British ships did nothing.

Stranger still was the news that came from other ports in the French Empire, from Rochefort, Toulon, Marseilles, Genoa, Venice, Flushing, Lorient, Antwerp and a hundred other towns of lesser importance. They too were blockaded by British fleets of a hundred or so warships. It was impossible to comprehend. Added together these fleets contained more warships than the British possessed. Indeed they contained more warships than there were upon the face of the earth.

The most senior officer at Brest at that time was Admiral Desmoulins. He had a servant, a very small man no bigger than an eight-year-old child, and as dark as a European can be. He looked as if he had been put into the oven and baked for too long and was now rather overdone. His skin was the colour of a coffee-bean and the texture of a dried-up rice-pudding. His hair was black, twisted and greasy like the spines and quills you may observe on the less succulent parts of roasted chickens. His name was Perroquet (which means parrot). Admiral Desmoulins was very proud of Perroquet; proud of his size, proud of his cleverness, proud of his agility and most of all, proud of his colour. Admiral Desmoulins often boasted that he had seen blacks who would appear fair next to Perroquet.

It was Perroquet who sat in the rain for four days studying the ships through his eye-glass. Rain spurted from his child-size bicorn hat as if from two little rainspouts; it sank into the capes of his child-size coat, making the coat fearfully heavy and turning the wool into felt; and it ran in little streams down his baked, greasy skin; but he paid it not the slightest attention.

After four days Perroquet sighed, jumped to his feet, stretched himself, took off his hat, gave his head a good scratch, yawned and said, "Well, my Admiral, they are the queerest ships I have ever seen and I do not understand them."

"In what way, Perroquet?" asked the Admiral.

Gathered on the cliffs near Camaret Saint-Julien with Perroquet were Admiral Desmoulins and Captain Jumeau, and rain spurted from *their* bicorn hats and turned the wool of *their* coats into felt and filled their boots with half an inch of water.

"Well," said Perroquet, "the ships sit upon the sea as if they were becalmed and yet they are not becalmed. There is a strong westerly wind which ought by rights to blow them on to these rocks, but does it? No. Do the ships beat off? No. Do they reduce sail? No. I cannot count the number of times the wind has changed since I have sat here, but what have the men on those ships done? Nothing."

Captain Jumeau, who disliked Perroquet and was jealous of his influence with the Admiral, laughed. "He is mad, my Admiral. If the British were really as idle or ignorant as he says, their ships would all be heaps of broken spars by now."

"They are more like pictures of ships," mused Perroquet, paying the Captain no attention, "than the ships themselves. But a queerer thing still, my Admiral, is that ship, the three-decker at the northernmost tip of the line. On Monday it was just like the others but now its sails are all in tatters, its mizzen mast is gone and there is a ragged hole in its side."

"Huzza!" cried Captain Jumeau. "Some brave French crew has inflicted this damage while we stand here talking."

Perroquet grinned. "And do you think, Captain, that the British would permit one French ship to go up to their hundred ships and blow one of them to bits and then sail calmly away again? Ha! I should like to see you do it, Captain, in your little boat. No, my Admiral, it is my opinion that the British ship is melting."

"Melting!" declared the Admiral in surprize.

"The hull bulges like an old woman's knitting bag," said Perroquet. "And the bowsprit and the spritsail yard are drooping into the water."

"What idiotic nonsense!" declared Captain Jumeau. "How can a ship melt?"

"I do not know," said Perroquet, thoughtfully. "It depends upon what it is made of."

"Jumeau, Perroquet," said Admiral Desmoulins, "I believe that our best course will be to sail out and examine those ships. If the British fleet seems likely to attack, we will turn back, but in the meantime perhaps we may learn something."

So Perroquet and the Admiral and Captain Jumeau set sail in the rain with a few brave men; for sailors, though they face hardship with equanimity, are superstitious, and Perroquet was not the only person in Brest who had noticed the queerness of the British ships.

After they had gone some way, our adventurers could see that the strange ships were entirely grey and that they glittered; even under that dark sky, even in all that drenching rain they shone. Once, for a moment, the clouds parted and a ray of sunlight struck the sea. The ships disappeared. Then the clouds closed and the ships were there again.

"Dear God!" cried the Admiral. "What does all this mean?"

"Perhaps," said Perroquet uneasily, "the British ships have all been sunk and these are their ghosts."

Still the strange ships glittered and shone, and this led to some discussion as to what they might be made of. The Admiral thought perhaps iron or steel. (Metal ships indeed! The French are, as I have often supposed, a very whimsical nation.)

Captain Jumeau wondered if they might not be of silver paper.

"Silver paper!" exclaimed the Admiral.

"Oh, yes!" said Captain Jumeau. "Ladies, you know, take silver paper and roll it into quills and make little baskets of it, which they then decorate with flowers and fill with sugar plums."

The Admiral and Perroquet were surprized to hear this, but Captain Jumeau was a handsome man, and clearly knew more of the ways of ladies than they did.

But if it took one lady an evening to make a basket, how many ladies would it take to make a fleet? The Admiral said it made his head hurt to think of it.

The sun came out again. This time, since they were closer to ships, they could see how the sunlight shone *through* them and made them colourless until they were just a faint sparkle upon the water.

"Glass," said the Admiral, and he was near to the mark, but it was clever Perroquet who finally hit upon the truth.

"No, my Admiral, it is the rain. They are made of rain."

As the rain fell from the heavens the drops were made to flow together to form solid masses – pillars and beams and sheets, which someone had shaped into the likeness of a hundred ships.

Perroquet and the Admiral and Captain Jumeau were consumed with curiosity to know who could have made such a thing and they agreed he must be a master-rainsmith.

"But not only a master-rainsmith!" exclaimed the Admiral, "A master-puppeteer! See how they bob up and down upon the water! How the sails billow and fall!"

"They are certainly the prettiest things that ever I saw, my Admiral," agreed Perroquet, "but I repeat what I said before; he knows nothing of sailing or seamanship, whoever he is."

For two hours the Admiral's wooden ship sailed in and out of the rain-ships. Being ships of rain they made no sound at all – no creaking of timber, no slap of sail in the wind, no call of sailor to his mate. Several times groups of smooth-faced men of rain came to the ship's rail to gaze out at the wooden ship with its crew of flesh-and-blood men, but what the rain-sailors were thinking, no one could tell. Yet the Admiral, the Captain and Perroquet felt themselves to be perfectly safe, for, as Perroquet remarked, "Even if the rain-sailors wish to fire upon us, they only have rain-cannonballs to do it with and we will only get wet."

Perroquet and the Admiral and Captain Jumeau were lost in admiration. They forgot that they had been tricked, forgot that they had wasted a week and that for a week the British had been slipping into ports on the Baltic coast and ports on the Portuguese coast and all sorts of other ports where the Emperor Napoleon Buonaparte did not want them to go. But the spell which held the ships in place appeared to be weakening (which presumably explained the melting ship at the northernmost point of the fleet). After two hours it stopped raining and in the same moment the spell broke, which Perroquet and the Admiral and Captain Jumeau knew by a curious twist of their senses, as if they had tasted a string quartet, or been, for a moment, deafened by the sight of the colour blue. For the merest instant the rain-ships became mist-ships and then the breeze gently blew them apart.

The Frenchmen were alone upon the empty Atlantic.

# 12

# The Spirit of English Magic urges Mr Norrell to the Aid of Britannia

## December 1807

On a day in December two great draycarts happened to collide in Cheapside. One, which was loaded with barrels of sherry-wine, overturned. While the draymen argued about which of them was to blame, some passers-by observed that sherry-wine was leaking from one of the barrels. Soon a crowd of drinkers gathered with glasses and pint-pots to catch the sherry, and hooks and bars to make holes in those casks which were still undamaged. The draycarts and crowd had soon so effectively stopt up Cheapside that queues of carriages formed in all the neighbouring streets, Poultry, Threadneedle-street, Bartholomew-lane and, in the other direction, Aldersgate, Newgate and Paternoster-row. It became impossible to imagine how the knot of carriages, horses and people would ever get undone again.

Of the two draymen one was handsome and the other was fat and, having made up their quarrel, they became a sort of Bacchus and Silenus to the revel. They decided to entertain both themselves and their followers by opening all the carriage-doors to see what the rich people were doing inside. Coachmen and footmen tried to prevent this impertinence but the crowd were too many to be held off and too drunk to mind the blows of the whip which the crosser sort of coachmen gave them. In one of these carriages the fat drayman discovered Mr Norrell and cried, "What! Old Norrell!" The draymen both climbed into the carriage to shake Mr Norrell's hand and breathe sherry fumes all over him and assure him that they would lose no time in moving everything out of the way so that he – the hero of the French Blockade – might pass. Which promise they kept and respectable people found their horses unhitched and their carriages pushed and shoved into tanners' yards and other nasty places, or backed into dirty brick-lanes where they got stuck fast and all the varnish was scraped off; and when the draymen and their friends had made this triumphal path for Mr Norrell they escorted him and his carriage along it, as far as Hanover-square, cheering all the way, flinging their hats in the air and making up songs about him.

Everyone, it seemed, was delighted with what Mr Norrell had done. A large part of the French Navy had been tricked into remaining in its ports for eleven days and during that time the British had been at liberty to sail about the Bay of Biscay, the English Channel and the German Sea, just as it pleased and a great many things had been accomplished. Spies had been deposited in various parts of the French Empire and other spies brought back to England with news about what Buonaparte was doing. British merchant ships had unloaded their cargoes of coffee and cotton and spices in Dutch and Baltic ports without any interference.

Napoleon Buonaparte, it was said, was scouring France to find a magician of his own – but with no success. In London the Ministers were quite astonished to find that, for once, they had done something the Nation approved.

Mr Norrell was invited to the Admiralty, where he drank madeira-wine in the Board Room. He sat in a chair close to the fire and had a long comfortable chat with the First Lord of the Admiralty, Lord Mulgrave, and the First Secretary to the Admiralty, Mr Horrocks. Above the fireplace there were carvings of nautical instruments and garlands of flowers which Mr Norrell greatly admired. He described the beautiful carvings in the library at Hurtfew Abbey; "And yet," said Mr Norrell, "I envy you, my lord. Indeed I do. Such a fine representation of the instruments of your profession! I wish that I might have done the same. Nothing looks so striking. Nothing, I believe, inspires a man with such eagerness to begin his day's work as the sight of his instruments neatly laid out – or their images in good English oak as we have here. But really a magician has need of so few tools. I will tell you a little trick, my lord, the more apparatus a magician carries about with him – coloured powders, stuffed cats, magical hats and so forth – the greater the fraud you will eventually discover him to be!"

And what, inquired Mr Horrocks politely, were the few tools that a magician did require?

"Why! Nothing really," said Mr Norrell. "Nothing but a silver basin for seeing visions in."

"Oh!" cried Mr Horrocks. "I believe I would give almost any thing to see *that* magic done – would not you, my lord? Oh, Mr Norrell, might we prevail upon you to shew us a vision in a silver basin?"

Usually Mr Norrell was the last man in the world to satisfy such idle curiosity, but he had been so pleased with his reception at the Admiralty (for the two gentlemen paid him a world of compliments) that he agreed almost immediately and a servant was dispatched to find a silver basin; "A silver basin about a foot in diameter," said Mr Norrell, "which you must fill with clean water."

The Admiralty had lately sent out orders for three ships to rendezvous south of Gibraltar and Lord Mulgrave had a great curiosity to know whether or not this had occurred; would Mr Norrell be able to find it out? Mr Norrell did not know, but promised to try. When the basin was brought and Mr Norrell bent over it, Lord Mulgrave and Mr Horrocks felt as if nothing else could have so conjured up the ancient glories of English magic;

they felt as if they were living in the Age of Stokesey, Godbless and the Raven King.

A picture appeared upon the surface of the water in the silver basin, a picture of three ships riding the waves of a blue sea. The strong, clear light of the Mediterranean shone out into the gloomy December room and lit up the faces of the three gentlemen who peered into the bowl.

"It moves!" cried Lord Mulgrave in astonishment.

It did indeed. The sweetest white clouds imaginable were gliding across the blue sky, the ships rode the waves and tiny people could be seen moving about them. Lord Mulgrave and Mr Horrocks had no difficulty in recognizing HMS *Catherine of Winchester*, HMS *Laurel* and HMS *Centaur*.

"Oh, Mr Norrell!" cried Mr Horrocks. "The *Centaur* is my cousin's ship. Can you shew me Captain Barry?"

Mr Norrell fidgeted about and drew in his breath with a sharp hiss and stared fiercely at the silver basin, and by and by appeared a vision of a pink-faced, gold-haired, overgrown cherub of a man walking about a quarterdeck. This, Mr Horrocks assured them, was his cousin, Captain Barry.

"He looks very well, does he not?" cried Mr Horrocks. "I am glad to know he is in such good health."

"Where are they? Can you tell?" Lord Mulgrave asked Mr Norrell.

"Alas," said Mr Norrell, "this art of making pictures is the most imprecise in the world.[1] I am delighted to have had the honour of shewing your lordship some of His Majesty's ships. I am yet more pleased that they are the ones you want – which is frankly more than I expected – but I fear I can tell you nothing further."

So delighted was the Admiralty with all that Mr Norrell had accomplished that Lord Mulgrave and Mr Horrocks soon looked about them to see what other tasks they could find for the

[1] Four years later during the Peninsular War Mr Norrell's pupil, Jonathan Strange, had similar criticisms to make about this form of magic.

magician. His Majesty's Navy had recently captured a French ship of the line with a very fine figurehead in the shape of a mermaid with bright blue eyes, coral-pink lips, a great mass of sumptuous golden curls artistically strewn with wooden representations of starfish and crabs, and a tail that was covered all over with silver-gilt as if it might be made of gingerbread inside. It was known that before it had been captured, the ship had been at Toulon, Cherbourg, Antwerp, Rotterdam and Genoa, and so the mermaid had seen a great deal of enemy defences and of the Emperor Napoleon Buonaparte's great scheme of ship-building which was going forward at that time. Mr Horrocks asked Mr Norrell to put a spell on her so that she might tell all she knew. This Mr Norrell did. But though the mermaid could be made to speak she could not at first be brought to answer any questions. She considered herself the implacable enemy of the British and was highly delighted to be given powers of speech so that she could express her hatred of them. Having passed all her existence among sailors she knew a great many insults and bestowed them very readily on anyone who came near her in a voice that sounded like the creaking of masts and timbers in a high wind. Nor did she confine herself to abusing Englishmen with words. There were three seamen that had work to do about the ship, but the moment that they got within reach of the mermaid's wooden arms she picked them up in her great wooden hands and threw them in the water.

Mr Horrocks who had gone down to Portsmouth to talk to her, grew tired of her and told her that he would have her chopped up and made a bonfire of. But, though French, she was also very brave and said she would like to see the man that would try to burn her. And she lashed her tail and waved her arms menacingly; and all the wooden starfish and crabs in her hair bristled.

The situation was resolved when the handsome young Captain who had captured her ship was sent to reason with her. He was able to explain to her in clear, comprehensible French the rightness of the British cause and the terrible wrongness of the French one, and whether it were the persuasiveness of his words or the handsomeness of his face that convinced her I do not know, but she told Mr Horrocks all he wished to know.

Mr Norrell rose every day to new heights of public greatness and an enterprising printmaker called Holland who had a print-shop in St Paul's Churchyard was inspired to commission an engraving of him to be sold in the shop. The engraving shewed Mr Norrell in the company of a young lady, scantily dressed in a loose smock. A great quantity of stiff, dark material swirled and coiled about the young lady's body without ever actually touching it and, for the further embellishment of her person, she wore a crescent moon tucked in among the tumbling locks of her hair. She had taken Mr Norrell (who appeared entirely astonished by the proceedings) by the arm and was energetically pulling him up a flight of stairs and pointing in most emphatic manner towards a lady of mature years who sat at the top. The lady of mature years was attired like the young lady in smock and draperies, with the handsome addition of a Roman helmet on her head; she appeared to be weeping in the most uninhibited fashion, while an elderly lion, her only companion, lay at her feet with a gloomy expression upon his countenance. This engraving, entitled *The Spirit of English Magic urges Mr Norrell to the Aid of Britannia*, was an immense success and Mr Holland sold almost seven hundred copies in a month.

Mr Norrell did not go out so much as formerly; instead he stayed at home and received respectful visits from all sorts of great people. It was not uncommon for five or six coronet-coaches to stop at his house in Hanover-square in the space of one morning. He was the still same silent, nervous little man he had always been and, had it not been for Mr Drawlight and Mr Lascelles, the occupants of those carriages must have found their visits dull indeed. Upon such occasions Mr Drawlight and Mr Lascelles supplied all the conversation. Indeed Mr Norrell's dependence upon these two gentlemen increased daily. Childermass had once said that it would be an odd sort of magician that would employ Drawlight, yet Mr Norrell now employed him constantly; Drawlight was forever being driven about in Mr Norrell's carriage upon Mr Norrell's business. Every day he came early to Hanover-square to tell Mr Norrell what was being said about the Town, who was rising, who falling, who was in debt, who in love, until Mr Norrell, sitting alone in his library, began to know as much of the Town's business as any City matron.

More surprizing, perhaps, was Mr Lascelles's devotion to the cause of English magic. The explanation, however, was quite simple. Mr Lascelles was one of that uncomfortable breed of men who despise steady employment of any sort. Though perfectly conscious of his own superior understanding, he had never troubled to acquire any particular skills or knowledge, and had arrived at the age of thirty-nine entirely unfitted for any office or occupation. He had looked about him and seen men, who had worked diligently all the years of their youth, risen to positions of power and influence; and there is no doubt that he envied them. Consequently it was highly agreeable to Mr Lascelles to become counsellor-in-chief to the greatest magician of the Age, and have respectful questions put to him by the King's Ministers. Naturally, he made a great shew of being the same careless, indifferent gentleman as before, but in truth he was extremely jealous of his new-found importance. He and Drawlight had come to an understanding one night in the Bedford over a bottle of port. Two friends, they had agreed, were quite sufficient for a quiet gentleman such as Mr Norrell, and they had formed an alliance to guard each other's interest and to prevent any other person from gaining any influence over the magician.

It was Mr Lascelles who first encouraged Mr Norrell to think of publication. Poor Mr Norrell was constantly affronted by people's misconceptions concerning magic and was forever lamenting the general ignorance upon the subject. "They ask me to shew them fairy-spirits," he complained, "and unicorns and manticores and things of that sort. The *utility* of the magic I have done is entirely lost on them. It is only the most frivolous sorts of magic that excite their interest."

Mr Lascelles said, "Feats of magic will make your *name* known everywhere, sir, but they will never make your *opinions* understood. For that you must publish."

"Yes, indeed," cried Mr Norrell, eagerly, "and I have every intention of writing a book – just as you advise – only I fear it will be many years before I have leisure enough to undertake it."

"Oh! I quite agree – a book would mean a world of work," said Mr Lascelles, languidly, "but I had no notion of a book. Two or three articles was what I had in mind. I dare say there is not an editor in London or Edinburgh who would not be delighted to publish any little thing you cared to send him – you may make your choice of the periodicals, but if you take my advice, sir, you will chuse *The Edinburgh Review*. There is scarcely a household in the kingdom with any pretensions to gentility that does not take it. There is no quicker way of making your views more widely understood."

Mr Lascelles was so persuasive upon the subject and conjured up such visions of Mr Norrell's articles upon every library-table and Mr Norrell's opinions discussed in every drawing-room that, had it not been for the great dislike that Mr Norrell had to *The Edinburgh Review*, he would have sat down there and then to begin writing. Unfortunately, *The Edinburgh Review* was a publication renowned chiefly for radical opinions, criticism of the Government and opposition to the war with France – none of which Mr Norrell could approve.

"Besides," said Mr Norrell, "I really have no desire to write reviews of other people's books. Modern publications upon magic are the most pernicious things in the world, full of misinformation and wrong opinions."

"Then sir, you may say so. The ruder you are, the more the editors will be delighted."

"But it is my own opinions which I wish to make better known, not other people's."

"Ah, but, sir," said Lascelles, "it is precisely by passing judgements upon other people's work and pointing out their errors that readers can be made to understand your own opinions better. It is the easiest thing in the world to turn a review to one's own ends. One only need mention the book once or twice and for the rest of the article one may develop one's theme just as one chuses. It is, I assure you, what every body else does."

"Hmm," said Mr Norrell thoughtfully, "you may be right. But, no. It would seem as if I were lending support to what ought never to have been published in the first place."

And upon this point Mr Norrell proved unpersuadable.

Lascelles was disappointed; *The Edinburgh Review* far surpassed its rivals in brilliance and wit. Its articles were devoured by everyone in the kingdom from the meanest curate to the Prime Minister. Other publications were very dull in comparison.

He was inclined to abandon the notion altogether and had almost forgotten all about it when he happened to receive a letter from a young bookseller named Murray. Mr Murray respectfully requested that Mr Lascelles and Mr Drawlight would do him the honour of permitting him to wait upon them at any hour and upon any day to suit them. He had, he said, a proposal to put before them, a proposal which concerned Mr Norrell.

Lascelles and Drawlight met the bookseller at Mr Lascelles's house in Bruton-street a few days later. His manner was energetic and businesslike and he laid his proposal before them immediately.

"Like every other inhabitant of these isles, gentlemen, I have been amazed and delighted at the recent extraordinary revival of English magic. And I have been equally struck by the enthusiasm with which the British Public has greeted this reappearance of an art long thought dead. I am convinced that a periodical devoted to magic would achieve a wide circulation. Literature, politics, religion and travel are all very well – they will always be popular subjects for a periodical, but magic – real, practical magic like Mr Norrell's – has the advantage of complete novelty. I wonder, gentlemen, if you could tell me whether Mr Norrell would look favourably upon my proposal? I have heard that Mr Norrell has a great deal to say upon the subject. I have heard that Mr Norrell's opinions are quite surprizing! Of course we all learnt a little of the history and theory of magic in our schoolrooms, but it is so long since any magic was practised in these islands that I dare say what we have been taught is full of errors and misconceptions."

"Ah!" cried Mr Drawlight. "How perceptive of you, Mr Murray! How happy it would make Mr Norrell to hear you say so! Errors and misconceptions – exactly so! Whenever, my dear sir, you are privileged to enjoy Mr Norrell's conversation – as I have been upon many occasions – you will learn that such is the exact state of affairs!"

"It has long been the dearest wish of Mr Norrell's heart," said Lascelles, "to bring a more precise understanding of modern magic before a wider audience, but alas, sir, private wishes are often frustrated by public duties, and the Admiralty and the War Office keep him so busy."

Mr Murray replied politely that of course all other considerations must give way before the great consideration of the war and Mr Norrell was a National Treasure. "But I hope that some way might be found to arrange matters so that the chief burden did not fall upon Mr Norrell's shoulders. We would employ an editor to plan each issue, solicit articles and reviews, make changes – all under Mr Norrell's guidance, naturally."

"Ah, yes!" said Lascelles. "Quite. All under Mr Norrell's guidance. We would insist upon that."

The interview ended very cordially upon both sides with Lascelles and Drawlight promising to speak to Mr Norrell immediately.

Drawlight watched Mr Murray leave the room. "A Scotchman," he said as soon as the door was closed.

"Oh, quite!" agreed Lascelles. "But I do not mind that. The Scotch are often very able, very canny in business. I believe this might do very well."

"He seemed quite a respectable person – almost a gentleman in fact. Except that he has a queer trick of fixing his right eye upon one while his other eye travels the room. I found that a little disconcerting."

"He is blind in his right eye."

"Indeed?"

"Yes. Canning told me. One of his schoolmasters stuck a pen-knife in it when he was boy."

"Dear me! But, just imagine, my dear Lascelles! A whole periodical devoted to one person's opinions! I would never have believed it possible! The magician will be astonished when we tell him."

Mr Lascelles laughed. "He will consider it the most natural thing in the world. His vanity is beyond any thing."

As Lascelles had predicted, Mr Norrell found nothing extraordinary in the proposal, but straightaway he began to make difficulties. "It is an excellent plan," he said, "but unfortunately completely impracticable. I have no time to edit a periodical and I could scarcely entrust so important a task to any one else."

"I was quite of the same mind, sir," said Mr Lascelles, "until I thought of Portishead."

"Portishead? Who is Portishead?" asked Mr Norrell.

"Well," said Lascelles, "He *was* a theoretical magician, but . . ."

"A theoretical magician?" interrupted Mr Norrell in alarm. "You know what I think of that!"

"Ah, but you have not heard what follows," said Lascelles. "So great is his admiration of *you*, sir, that on being told you did not approve of theoretical magicians he immediately gave up his studies."

"Did he indeed?" said Mr Norrell, somewhat placated by this information.

"He has published one or two books. I forget what exactly – a history of sixteenth-century magic for children or something of that sort.[2] I really feel that you might safely entrust the periodical to Lord Portishead, sir. There is no danger of him publishing any thing of which you disapprove; he is known as one of most honourable men in the kingdom. His first wish will be to please you, I am quite certain."[3]

Somewhat reluctantly Mr Norrell agreed to meet Lord Portishead and Mr Drawlight wrote a letter summoning him to Hanover-square.

Lord Portishead was about thirty-eight years of age. He was very tall and thin with long, thin hands and feet. He habitually wore a whitish coat and light-coloured breeches. He was a gentle soul whom everything made uncomfortable: his excessive height made him uncomfortable; his status as a former theoretical magician made him uncomfortable (being an intelligent man he knew that Mr Norrell disapproved of him); meeting such polished men of the world as Drawlight and Lascelles made him uncomfortable and meeting Mr Norrell – who was his great hero – made him most uncomfortable of all. At one point he became so agitated that he began to sway backwards and forwards – which, taken in conjunction with his height and whitish clothes, gave him the appearance of a silver-birch tree in a high wind.

---

[2] In this speech Mr Lascelles has managed to combine all Lord Portishead's books into one. By the time Lord Portishead gave up the study of magic in early 1808 he had published three books: *The Life of Jacques Belasis*, pub. Longman, London, 1801, *The Life of Nicholas Goubert*, pub. Longman, London, 1805, and *A Child's History of the Raven King*, pub. Longman, London, 1807, engravings by Thomas Bewick. The first two were scholarly discussions of two sixteenth-century magicians. Mr Norrell had no great opinion of them, but he had a particular dislike of *A Child's History*. Jonathan Strange, on the other hand, thought this an excellent little book.

[3] "It was odd that so wealthy a man – for Lord Portishead counted large portions of England among his possessions – should have been so very self-effacing, but such was the case. He was besides a devoted husband and the father of ten children. Mr Strange told me that to see Lord Portishead play with his children was the most delightful thing in the world. And indeed he was a little like a child himself. For all his great learning he could no more recognize evil than he could spontaneously understand Chinese. He was the gentlest lord in all of the British aristocracy."

*The Life of Jonathan Strange* by John Segundus, pub. John Murray, London, 1820.

Despite his nervousness he managed to convey his great sense of the honour done to him in being summoned to meet Mr Norrell. Indeed so gratified was Mr Norrell by Lord Portishead's extreme deference towards him that he graciously gave his permission for Lord Portishead to study magic again.

Naturally Lord Portishead was delighted, but when he heard that Mr Norrell desired him to sit for long periods of time in a corner of Mr Norrell's own drawing-room, soaking up Mr Norrell's opinions upon modern magic, and then to edit, under Mr Norrell's direction, Mr Murray's new periodical, it seemed that he could conceive of no greater happiness.

The new periodical was named *The Friends of English Magic*, the title being taken from Mr Segundus's letter to *The Times* in the previous spring. Curiously none of the articles which appeared in *The Friends of English Magic* were written by Mr Norrell, who was found to be entirely incapable of finishing a piece of writing; he was never satisfied with what he had written. He could never be sure that he had not said too much or too little.[4]

---

[4] *The Friends of English Magic* was first published in February 1808 and was an immediate success. By 1812 Norrell and Lascelles were boasting of a circulation in excess of 13,000, though how reliable this figure may be is uncertain.

From 1808 until 1810 the editor was nominally Lord Portishead but there is little doubt that both Mr Norrell and Lascelles interfered a great deal. There was a certain amount of disagreement between Norrell and Lascelles as to the general aims of the periodical. Mr Norrell wished *The Friends of English Magic* first to impress upon the British Public the great importance of English modern magic, secondly to correct erroneous views of magical history and thirdly to vilify those magicians and classes of magicians whom he hated. He did not desire to explain the procedures of English magic within its pages – in other words he had no intention of making it in the least informative. Lord Portishead, whose admiration of Mr Norrell knew no bounds, considered it his first duty as editor to follow Norrell's numerous instructions. As a result the early issues of *The Friends of English Magic* are rather dull and often puzzling – full of odd omissions, contradictions and evasions. Lascelles, on the other hand, understood very well how the periodical might be used to gain support for the revival of English magic and he was anxious to make it lighter in tone. He grew more and more irritated at Portishead's cautious approach. He manoeuvred and from 1810 he and Lord Portishead were joint editors.

John Murray was the publisher of *The Friends of English Magic* until early

There is not much to interest the serious student of magic in the early issues and the only entertainment to be got from them is contained in several articles in which Portishead attacks on Mr Norrell's behalf: gentleman-magicians; lady-magicians; street-magicians; vagabond-magicians; child-prodigy-magicians; the Learned Society of York Magicians; the Learned Society of Manchester Magicians; learned societies of magicians in general; any other magicians whatsoever.

---

[4] *cont'd* 1815 when he and Norrell quarrelled. Deprived of Norrell's support, Murray was obliged to sell the periodical to Thomas Norton Longman, another publisher. In 1816 Murray and Strange planned to set up a rival periodical to *The Friends of English Magic*, entitled *The Famulus*, but only one issue was ever published.

13

# The magician of Threadneedle-street

## December 1807

THE MOST FAMOUS street-magician in London was undoubtedly Vinculus. His magician's booth stood before the church of St Christopher Le Stocks in Threadneedle-street opposite the Bank of England, and it would have been difficult to say whether the bank or the booth were the more famous.

Yet the reason for Vinculus's celebrity – or notoriety – was a little mysterious. He was no better a magician than any of the other charlatans with lank hair and a dirty yellow curtain. His spells did not work, his prophecies did not come true and his trances had been proven false beyond a doubt.

For many years he was much addicted to holding deep and weighty conference with the Spirit of the River Thames. He would fall into a trance and ask the Spirit questions and the voice of the Spirit would issue forth from his mouth in accents deep, watery and windy. On a winter's day in 1805 a woman paid him a shilling to ask the Spirit to tell her where she might find her runaway husband. The Spirit provided a great deal of quite surprizing information and a crowd began to gather around the booth to listen to it. Some of the bystanders believed in Vinculus's ability and were duly impressed by the Spirit's oration, but others began to taunt the magician and his client. One such jeerer (a most ingenious fellow) actually managed to set Vinculus's shoes on fire while Vinculus was speaking. Vinculus came out of his trance immediately: he leapt about, howling and attempting to pull off his shoes and stamp out the fire at one and the same time. He was throwing himself about and the crowd were all enjoying the sight immensely, when something popt out of his mouth. Two men picked it up and examined it: it was a little metal contraption not more than an inch and a half long. It was something like a mouth-organ and when one of the men placed it in his own mouth he too was able to produce the voice of the Spirit of the River Thames.

Despite such public humiliations Vinculus retained a certain authority, a certain native dignity which meant that he, among all the street-magicians of London, was treated with a measure of respect. Mr Norrell's friends and admirers were continually urging him to pay a visit to Vinculus and were surprized that he shewed no inclination to do it.

On a day in late December when storm clouds made Alpine landscapes in the sky above London, when the wind played such havoc in the heavens that the city was one moment plunged in gloom and the next illuminated by sunlight, when rain rattled upon the windowpane, Mr Norrell was seated comfortably in his library before a cheerful fire. The tea table spread with a quantity of good things stood before him and in his hand was Thomas Lanchester's *The Language of Birds*. He was turning the pages in search of a favourite passage when he was nearly frightened out of his wits by a voice suddenly saying very loudly and contemptuously, "Magician! You think that you have amazed everyone by your deeds!"

Mr Norrell looked up and was astonished to find that there was someone else in the room, a person he had never seen before, a thin, shabby, ragged hawk of a man. His face was the colour of three-day-old milk; his hair was the colour of a coal-smoke-and-ashes London sky; and his clothes were the colour of the Thames at dirty Wapping. Nothing about him – face, hair, clothes – was particularly clean, but in all other points he corresponded to the common notion of what a magician should look like (which Mr Norrell most certainly did not). He stood very erect and the expression of his fierce grey eyes was naturally imperious.

"Oh, yes!" continued this person, glaring furiously at Mr Norrell. "You think yourself a very fine fellow! Well, know this, Magician! Your coming was foretold long ago. I have been expecting you these past twenty years! Where have you been hiding yourself?"

Mr Norrell sat in amazed silence, staring at his accuser with open mouth. It was as if this man had reached into his breast, plucked out his secret thought and held it up to the light. Ever since his arrival in the capital Mr Norrell had realized that he had indeed been ready long ago; he could have been doing magic for England's benefit years before; the French might have been defeated and English magic raised to that lofty position in the Nation's regard which Mr Norrell believed it ought to occupy. He was tormented with the idea that he had betrayed English magic by his dilatoriness. Now it was as if his own conscience had taken concrete form and started to reproach him. This put him somewhat at a disadvantage in dealing with the mysterious stranger. He stammered out an inquiry as to who the person might be.

"I am Vinculus, magician of Threadneedle-street!"

"Oh!" cried Mr Norrell, relieved to find that at least he was no supernatural apparition. "And you have come here to beg I suppose? Well, you may take yourself off again! I do not recognize you as a brother-magician and I shall not give you any thing! Not money. Not promises of help. Not recommendations to other people. Indeed I may tell you that I intend . . ."

"Wrong again, Magician! I want nothing for myself. I have come to explain your destiny to you, as I was born to do."

"Destiny? Oh, it's prophecies, is it?" cried Mr Norrell contemptuously. He rose from his chair and tugged violently at the bell pull, but no servant appeared. "Well, now I really have nothing to say to people who pretend to do prophecies. *Lucas!* Prophecies are without a doubt one of the most villainous tricks which rascals like you play upon honest men. Magic cannot see into the future and magicians who claimed otherwise were liars. *Lucas!*"

Vinculus looked round. "I hear you have all the books that were ever written upon magic," he said, "and it is commonly reported that you have even got back the ones that were lost when the library of Alexandria burnt – and know them all by heart, I dare say!"

"Books and papers are the basis of good scholarship and sound knowledge," declared Mr Norrell primly. "Magic is to be put on the same footing as the other disciplines."

Vinculus leaned suddenly forward and bent over Mr Norrell with a look of the most intense, burning concentration. Without quite meaning to, Mr Norrell fell silent and he leaned towards Vinculus to hear whatever Vinculus was about to confide to him.

"*I reached out my hand,*" whispered Vinculus, "*England's rivers turned and flowed the other way . . .*"

"I beg your pardon?"

"*I reached out my hand,*" said Vinculus, a little louder, "*my enemies's blood stopt in their veins . . .*" He straightened himself, opened wide his arms and closed his eyes as if in a religious ecstasy of some sort. In a strong, clear voice full of passion he continued:

"*I reached out my hand; thought and memory flew out of my enemies' heads like a flock of starlings;*
*My enemies crumpled like empty sacks.*
*I came to them out of mists and rain;*
*I came to them in dreams at midnight;*
*I came to them in a flock of ravens that filled a northern sky at dawn;*
*When they thought themselves safe I came to them in a cry that broke the silence of a winter wood . . .*"

"Yes, yes!" interrupted Mr Norrell. "Do you really suppose that this sort of nonsense is new to me? Every madman on every street-corner screams out the same threadbare gibberish and every vagabond with a yellow curtain tries to make himself mysterious by reciting something of the sort. It is in every third-rate book on magic published in the last two hundred years! 'I came to them in a flock of ravens!' What does that *mean*, I should like to know? Who came to whom in a flock of ravens? *Lucas!*"

Vinculus ignored him. His strong voice overpowered Mr Norrell's weak, shrill one.

"*The rain made a door for me and I went through it;*
*The stones made a throne for me and I sat upon it;*
*Three kingdoms were given to me to be mine forever;*
*England was given to me to be mine forever.*
*The nameless slave wore a silver crown;*
*The nameless slave was a king in a strange country . . .*"

"Three kingdoms!" exclaimed Mr Norrell. "Ha! Now I understand what this nonsense pretends to be! A prophecy of the Raven King! Well, I am sorry to tell you that if you hope to impress me by recounting tales of that gentleman you will be disappointed. Oh, yes, you are entirely mistaken! There is no magician whom I detest more!"[1]

"*The weapons that my enemies raised against me are venerated in Hell as holy relics;*
*Plans that my enemies made against me are preserved as holy texts;*
*Blood that I shed upon ancient battlefields is scraped from the stained earth by Hell's sacristans and placed in a vessel of silver and ivory.*
*I gave magic to England, a valuable inheritance*

[1] The Raven King was traditionally held to have possessed three kingdoms: one in England, one in Faerie and one, a strange country on the far side of Hell.

*But Englishmen have despised my gift*
*Magic shall be written upon the sky by the rain but they shall not be able to read it;*
*Magic shall be written on the faces of the stony hills but their minds shall not be able to contain it;*
*In winter the barren trees shall be a black writing but they shall not understand it . . .*"

"It is every Englishman's birthright to be served by competent and well-educated magicians," interrupted Mr Norrell. "What do you offer them instead? Mystical ramblings about stones and rain and trees! This is like Godbless who told us that we should learn magic from wild beasts in the forest. Why not pigs in the sty? Or stray dogs, I wonder? This is not the sort of magic which civilized men wish to see practised in England nowadays!" He glared furiously at Vinculus and, as he did so, something caught his eye.

Vinculus had dressed himself with no particular care. His dirty neckcloth had been negligently wound about his neck and a little gap of unclean skin shewed between neckcloth and shirt. In that space was a curious curving mark of a vivid blue, not unlike the upward stroke of a pen. It might have been a scar – the relic of a street brawl perhaps – but what it most resembled was that barbaric painting of the skin which is practised by the natives of the South Sea islands. Curiously Vinculus, who was able to stand entirely at his ease in another man's house railing at him, seemed embarrassed by this mark and when he saw that Mr Norrell had observed it he put his hand to his throat and plucked at the cloth to hide it.

"*Two magicians shall appear in England . . .*"

A sort of exclamation broke from Mr Norrell, an exclamation that began as a cry and ended as a soft, unhappy sigh.

"*The first shall fear me; the second shall long to behold me;*
*The first shall be governed by thieves and murderers; the second shall conspire at his own destruction;*

*The first shall bury his heart in a dark wood beneath the snow, yet still feel its ache;*
*The second shall see his dearest possession in his enemy's hand . . .*"

"Oh! Now I know that you have come here with no other aim but to wound me! False Magician, you are jealous of my success! You cannot destroy my magic and so you are determined to blacken my name and destroy my peace . . ."

"*The first shall pass his life alone; he shall be his own gaoler;*
*The second shall tread lonely roads, the storm above his head, seeking a dark tower upon a high hillside . . .*"

Just then the door opened and two men ran in.

"Lucas! Davey!" screeched Mr Norrell, hysterically. "Where have you been?"

Lucas began to explain something about the bell-cord.

"What? Seize hold of him! Quickly!"

Davey, Mr Norrell's coachman, was built on the same generous scale as others of his profession and had the strength that comes from daily opposing his will to that of four high-bred coach-horses in the prime of life. He took hold of Vinculus around his body and his throat. Vinculus struggled energetically. He did not neglect in the meantime to continue berating Mr Norrell:

"*I sit upon a black throne in the shadows but they shall not see me.*
*The rain shall make a door for me and I shall pass through it;*
*The stones shall make a throne for me and I shall sit upon it . . .*"

Davey and Vinculus careered against a little table upsetting a pile of books that stood upon it.

"Aaaah! Be careful!" exclaimed Mr Norrell, "For God's sake be careful! He will knock over that ink pot! He will damage my books!"

Lucas joined Davey in endeavouring to pinion Vinculus's wild, windmilling arms, while Mr Norrell scampered round the library a great deal faster than any one had seen him move for many years, gathering up books and putting them out of harm's way.

"*The nameless slave shall wear a silver crown,*" gasped Vinculus – Davey's arm tightening about his throat rendered his oration decidedly less impressive than before. Vinculus made one last effort and pulled the upper part of his body free of Davey's grasp and shouted, "*The nameless slave shall be a king in a strange country . . .*" Then Lucas and Davey half-pulled, half-carried him out of the room.

Mr Norrell went and sat down in the chair by the fire. He picked up his book again but he found that he was a great deal too agitated to return to his reading. He fidgeted about, bit his fingernails, walked about the room, returned constantly to those volumes which had been displaced in the struggle and examined them for signs of damage (there were none), but most of all he went to the windows and peered out anxiously to see if any one was watching the house. At three o'clock the room began to grow dusky. Lucas returned to light the candles and mend the fire and just behind him was Childermass.

"Ah!" cried Mr Norrell. "At last! Have you heard what happened? I am betrayed on all sides! Other magicians keep watch upon me and plot my downfall! My idle servants forget their duties. It is a matter of complete indifference to them whether my throat is cut or not! And as for you, you villain, you are the very worst of all! I tell you this man appeared so suddenly in the room – *as if by magic!* And when I rang the bell and cried out *no one came!* You must put aside all your other work. Your only task now is to discover what spells this man employed to gain entry to the house! Where did he learn his magic? What does he know?"

Childermass gave his master an ironical look. "Well, if that is my only task, it is done already. There was no magic. One of the kitchenmaids left the pantry window open and the sorcerer climbed in and crept about the house until he found you. That is all. No one came because he had cut the bell-cord and Lucas and the others did not hear you shout. They heard nothing until he started to rant and then they came immediately. Is that not so, Lucas?"

Lucas, kneeling at the hearth with the poker in his hand, agreed that that was exactly how it had been. "And so I tried to tell you, sir. Only you would not listen."

But Mr Norrell had worked himself up into such a frenzy of anxiety over Vinculus's supposed magical powers that this explanation had at first little power to soothe him. "Oh!" he said. "But still I am certain he means me harm. Indeed he has done me great harm already."

"Yes," agreed Childermass, "very great harm! For while he was in the pantry he ate three meat-pies."

"And two cream cheeses," added Lucas.

Mr Norrell was forced to admit to himself that this did not seem much like the actions of a great magician, but still he could not be entirely easy until he had vented his anger upon someone. Childermass and Lucas being most conveniently to hand, he began with them and treated them to a long speech, full of invective against Vinculus as the greatest villain who ever lived and ending with several strong hints about the bad ends that impudent and neglectful servants came to.

Childermass and Lucas, who had been obliged to listen to something of this sort practically every week since they had entered Mr Norrell's service, felt no particular alarm, but merely waited until their master had talked out his displeasure, whereupon Childermass said: "Leaving aside the pies and cheeses, he has put himself to a great deal of trouble and risked a hanging to pay you this visit. What did he want?"

"Oh! To deliver a prophecy of the Raven King's. Hardly an original idea. It was quite as impenetrable as such ramblings generally are. There was something about a battlefield and something about a throne and something about a silver crown, but the chief burden of what he had to say was to boast of another magician – by which I suppose he meant himself."

Now that Mr Norrell was reassured that Vinculus was not a terrible rival he began to regret that he had ever been led on to argue with him. It would have been far better, he thought, to maintain a lofty and magisterial silence. He comforted himself with the reflection that Vinculus had looked a great deal less imposing when Lucas and Davey were dragging him from the room. Gradually this thought and the consciousness of his own infinitely superior education and abilities began to make him feel comfortable again. But alas! such comfort was short-lived. For, on taking up *The Language of Birds* again, he came upon the following passage:

> *. . . There is nothing else in magic but the wild thought of the bird as it casts itself into the void. There is no creature upon the earth with such potential for magic. Even the least of them may fly straight out of this world and come by chance to the Other Lands. Where does the wind come from that blows upon your face, that fans the pages of your book? Where the harum-scarum magic of small wild creatures meets the magic of Man, where the language of the wind and the rain and the trees can be understood, there we will find the Raven King . . .*[2]

The next time that Mr Norrell saw Lord Portishead (which happened two days later) he immediately went up to his lordship and addressed him with the following words: "I hope, my lord, that you will have some very sharp things to say about Thomas Lanchester in the periodical. For years I have admired *The Language of Birds* as a valiant attempt to place before the reader a clear and comprehensive description of the magic of the *Aureate* magicians, but upon closer examination I find his writing is tainted with their worst characteristics . . . He is mystical, my lord! He is mystical!"

[2] Thomas Lanchester, *Treatise concerning the Language of Birds*, Chapter 6.

# 14

# Heart-break Farm

## January 1808

Some thirty years before Mr Norrell arrived in London with a plan to astonish the world by restoring English magic, a gentleman named Laurence Strange came into his inheritance. This comprised a house in an almost ruinous state, some barren lands and a mountain of debts and mortgages. These were grave ills indeed, but, thought Laurence Strange, they were nothing that the acquisition of a large sum of money might not cure; and so like many other gentlemen before and after him, he made it his business to be particularly agreeable to heiresses whenever he met with any, and, being a handsome man with elegant manners and a clever way of talking, in no time at all he had captivated a Miss Erquistoune, a young Scottish lady with £900 a year.

With the money Miss Erquistoune brought him, Laurence Strange repaired his house, improved his lands and repaid his debts. Soon he began to make money instead of owing it. He extended his estate and lent out money at fifteen per cent. In these and other similar pursuits he found occupation for every waking hour. He could no longer be at the trouble of shewing his bride much attention. Indeed he made it quite plain that her society and conversation were irksome to him; and she, poor thing, had a very hard time of it. Laurence Strange's estate was in Shropshire, in a retired part of the country near the Welsh border. Mrs Strange knew no one there. She was accustomed to city life, to Edinburgh balls and Edinburgh shops and the clever conversation of her Edinburgh friends; the sight of the high, gloomy hills forever shrouded in Welsh rain was very dispiriting. She bore with this lonely existence for five years, before dying of a chill she had caught while taking a solitary walk on those same hills in a storm.

Mr and Mrs Strange had one child who was, at the time of his mother's death, about four years of age. Mrs Strange had not been buried more than a few days when this child became the subject of a violent quarrel between Laurence Strange and his late wife's family. The Erquistounes maintained that in accordance with the terms of the marriage settlement a large part of Mrs Strange's fortune must now be put aside for her son for him to inherit at his majority. Laurence Strange – to no one's very great surprize – claimed that every penny of his wife's money was his to do with as he liked. Both parties consulted lawyers and two separate lawsuits were started, one in the Doctors Commons in London and one in the Scottish courts. The two lawsuits, Strange *versus* Erquistoune and Erquistoune *versus* Strange, went on for years and years and during this time the very sight of his son became displeasing to Laurence Strange. It seemed to him that the boy was like a boggy field or a copse full of diseased trees – worth money on paper but failing to yield a good annual return. If English law had entitled Laurence Strange to sell his son and buy a better one, he probably would have done it.[1]

Meanwhile the Erquistounes realized that Laurence Strange had it in his power to make his son every bit as unhappy as his wife had been, so Mrs Strange's brother wrote urgently to Laurence Strange suggesting that the boy spend some part of every year at his own house in Edinburgh. To Mr Erquistoune's great surprize, Mr Strange made no objection.[2]

---

[1] Eventually, both lawsuits were decided in favour of Laurence Strange's son.
[2] Upon the contrary Laurence Strange congratulated himself on avoiding paying for the boy's food and clothes for months at a time. So may a love of money make an intelligent man small-minded and ridiculous.

So it was that Jonathan Strange spent half of every year of his childhood at Mr Erquistoune's house in Charlotte-square in Edinburgh, where, it is to be presumed, he learnt to hold no very high opinion of his father. There he received his early education in the company of his three cousins, Margaret, Maria and Georgiana Erquistoune.[3] Edinburgh is certainly one of the most civilized cities in the world and the inhabitants are full as clever and as fond of pleasure as those of London. Whenever he was with them Mr and Mrs Erquistoune did everything they could to make him happy, hoping in this way to make up for the neglect and coldness he met with at his father's house. And so it is not to be wondered at if he grew up a little spoilt, a little fond of his own way and a little inclined to think well of himself.

Laurence Strange grew older and richer, but no better.

A few days before Mr Norrell's interview with Vinculus, a new manservant came to work at Laurence Strange's house. The other servants were very ready with help and advice: they told the new manservant that Laurence Strange was proud and full of malice, that everybody hated him, that he loved money beyond any thing, and that he and his son had barely spoken to each other for years and years. They also said that he had a temper like the devil and that upon no account whatsoever must the new manservant do any thing to offend him, or things would go the worse for him.

The new manservant thanked them for the information and promised to remember what they had said. But what the other servants did not know was that the new manservant had a temper to rival Mr Strange's own; that he was sometimes sarcastic, often rude, and that he had a very high opinion of his own abilities and a correspondingly low one of other people's. The new manservant did not mention his failings to the other servants for the simple

[3] Strange's biographer, John Segundus, observed on several occasions how Strange preferred the society of clever women to that of men. *Life of Jonathan Strange*, pub. John Murray, London, 1820.

reason that he knew nothing of them. Though he often found himself quarrelling with his friends and neighbours, he was always puzzled to discover the reason and always supposed that it must be their fault. But in case you should imagine that this chapter will treat of none but disagreeable persons, it ought to be stated at once that, whereas malice was the beginning and end of Laurence Strange's character, the new manservant was a more natural blend of light and shade. He possessed a great deal of good sense and was as energetic in defending others from real injury as he was in revenging imaginary insults to himself.

Laurence Strange was old and rarely slept much. Indeed it would often happen that he found himself more lively at night than during the day and he would sit up at his desk, writing letters and conducting his business. Naturally one of the servants always sat up as well, and a few days after he had first entered the household, this duty fell to the new manservant.

All went well until a little after two o'clock in the morning when Mr Strange summoned the new manservant and asked him to fetch a small glass of sherry-wine. Unremarkable as this request was, the new manservant did not find it at all easy to accomplish. Having searched for the sherry-wine in the usual places, he was obliged to wake first the maid, and ask her where the butler's bedroom might be, and next the butler and ask him where the sherry-wine was kept. Even then the new manservant had to wait some moments more while the butler talked out his surprize that Mr Strange should ask for sherry-wine, a thing he hardly ever took. Mr Strange's son, Mr Jonathan Strange – added the butler for the new manservant's better understanding of the household – was very fond of sherry-wine and generally kept a bottle or two in his dressing-room.

In accordance with the butler's instructions the new manservant fetched the sherry-wine from the cellars – a task which involved much lighting of candles, much walking down long stretches of dark, cold passage-ways, much brushing dirty old cobwebs from his clothes, much knocking of his head against rusty old implements hanging from musty old ceilings, and much wiping of blood and dirt from his face afterwards. He brought the glass to Mr Strange who drank it straight down and asked for another.

The new manservant felt that he had seen enough of the cellars for one night and so, remembering what the butler had said, he went upstairs to the dressing-room of Mr Jonathan Strange. Entering cautiously he found the room apparently unoccupied, but with candles still burning. This did not particularly surprize the new manservant who knew that conspicuous among the many vices peculiar to rich, unmarried gentlemen is wastefulness of candles. He began to open drawers and cupboards, pick up chamber-pots and look into them, look under tables and chairs, and peer into flower-vases. (And if you are at all surprized by all the places into which the new manservant looked, then all I can say is that he had more experience of rich, unmarried gentlemen than you do, and knew that their management of household affairs is often characterized by a certain eccentricity.) He found the bottle of sherry-wine, much as he had expected, performing the office of a boot-jack inside one of its owner's boots.

As the new manservant poured the wine into the glass, he happened to glance into a mirror that was hanging on the wall and discovered that the room was was not, after all, empty. Jonathan Strange was seated in a high-backed, high-shouldered chair watching every thing that the new manservant did with a look of great astonishment upon his face. The new manservant said not a word in explanation – for what explanation could he have given that a gentleman would have listened to? A servant would have understood him in an instant. The new manservant left the room.

Since his arrival in the house the new manservant had entertained certain hopes of rising to a position of authority over the other servants. It seemed to him that his superior intellects and greater experience of the world made him a natural lieutenant for the two Mr Stranges in any difficult business they might have; in his fancy they already said to him such things as: "As you know, Jeremy, these are serious matters, and I dare not trust any one but you with their execution." It would be going too far to say that he immediately abandoned these hopes, but he could not disguise from himself that Jonathan Strange had not seemed greatly pleased to discover someone in his private apartment pouring wine from his private supply.

Thus the new manservant entered Laurence Strange's writing-room with fledgling ambition frustrated and spirits dangerously irritated. Mr Strange drank the second glass of sherry straight down and remarked that he thought he would have another. At this the new manservant gave a sort of strangled shout, pulled his own hair and cried out, "Then why in God's name, you old fool, did you not say so in the first place? I could have brought you the bottle!"

Mr Strange looked at him in surprize and said mildly that of course there was no need to bring another glass if it was such a world of trouble to him.

The new manservant went back to the kitchen (wondering as he did so, if in fact he had been a little curt). A few minutes later the bell sounded again. Mr Strange was sitting at his desk with a letter in his hand, looking out through the window at the pitch-black, rainy night. "There is a man that lives up on the hill opposite," he said, "and this letter, Jeremy, must be delivered to him before break of day."

Ah! thought the new manservant, how quickly it begins! An urgent piece of business that must be conducted under the cover of night! What can it mean? – except that already he has begun to prefer *my* assistance to that of the others. Greatly flattered he declared eagerly that he would go straightaway and took the letter which bore only the enigmatic legend, "Wyvern". He inquired if the house had a name, so that he might ask someone if he missed his way.

Mr Strange began to say that the house had no name, but then he stopt himself and laughed. "You must ask for Wyvern of Heart-break Farm," he said. He told the new manservant that he must leave the high-road by a broken wicket that stood opposite Blackstock's ale-house; behind the wicket he would find a path that would take him straight to Heart-break Farm.

So the new manservant fetched a horse and a stout lantern and rode out on to the high-road. It was a dismal night. The air was a great confusion of noisy wind and bitter, driving rain which got into all the gaps in his clothing so that he was very soon chilled to death.

The path that began opposite Blackstock's ale-house and wound up the hill was fearfully overgrown. Indeed it scarcely deserved the name of "path", for young saplings grew in the middle of it, which the strong wind took and turned into rods to lash the new manservant as he struggled past. By the time he had travelled half a mile he felt as if he had fought several strong men one after the other (and being a hot-headed sort of person who was always getting into quarrels in public places it was a sensation perfectly familiar to him). He cursed Wyvern for a negligent, idle fellow who could not even keep his hedges in order. It was only after an hour or so that he reached a place which might have been a field once, but which was now a wilderness of briars and brambles and he began to regret that he had not brought an axe with him. He left the horse tied to a tree and tried to push his way through. The thorns were large, sharp and plentiful; several times he found himself pinned into the briar-bushes in so many places and in such an elaborate fashion (an arm up here, a leg twisted behind him) that he began to despair of ever getting out again. It seemed odd that any one could live behind such a high hedge of thorns, and he began to think that it would be no great surprize to discover that Mr Wyvern had been asleep for a hundred years or so. Well, I shall not mind *that* so much, he thought, so long as I am not expected to kiss him.

As a sad, grey dawn broke over the hillside he came upon a

ruined cottage which did not so much seem to have broken its heart, as its neck. The chimney wall sagged outwards in a great bow and the chimney tottered above it. A landslide of stone tiles from the roof had left holes where the timbers shewed like ribs. Elder-trees and thorn-bushes filled the interior and, in the vigour of their growth, had broken all the windows and pushed the doors out of the door-frames.

The new manservant stood in the rain for some time contemplating this dismal sight. On looking up he saw someone striding down the hillside towards him; a fairy-tale figure with a large and curious hat upon his head and a staff in his hand. As the figure drew closer it proved to be a yeoman-farmer, a sensible-looking man whose fantastic appearance was entirely due to his having folded a piece of canvas about his head to keep the rain off.

He greeted the new manservant thus: "Man! What have you done to yourself? You are all over blood and your good clothes are in tatters!"

The new manservant looked down at himself and discovered this was true. He explained that the path was overgrown and full of thorns.

The farmer looked at him in amazement. "But there is a good road," he cried, "not a quarter of a mile to the west that you could have walked in half the time! Who in the world directed you to come by that old path?"

The new manservant did not answer but instead asked if the farmer knew where Mr Wyvern of Heart-break Farm might be found?

"That is Wyvern's cottage, but he has been dead five years. Heart-break Farm, you say? Who told you it was called that? Someone has been playing tricks upon you. Old paths, Heart-break Farm indeed! But then I dare say it is as good a name as any; Wyvern did indeed break his heart here. He had the misfortune, poor fellow, to own some land which a gentleman in the valley took a fancy to and when Wyvern would not sell it, the gentleman sent ruffians in the middle of the night to dig up all the beans and carrots and cabbages that Wyvern had planted and when that did not work he put lawsuits upon him – poor Wyvern knew nothing of the law and could not make head or tail of it."

The new manservant thought about this for a moment. "And I fancy," he said at last, "that I could tell you the name of that gentleman."

"Oh!" said the farmer. "Anyone could do that." He looked a little closer at the new manservant. "Man," he said, "you are white as a milk pudding and shivering fit to break yourself in pieces!"

"I am cold," said the new manservant.

Then the farmer (who said his name was Bullbridge) was very pressing with the new manservant to return with him to his own fireside where he could warm himself and take something to eat and drink, and perhaps lie down a spell. The new manservant thanked him but said he was cold, that was all.

So Bullbridge led the new manservant back to his horse (by a way which avoided the thorns) and shewed him the proper way to the road and then the new manservant went back to Mr Strange's house.

A bleak, white sun rose in a bleak, white sky like an allegorical picture of despair and, as he rode, it seemed to the new manservant that the sun was poor Wyvern and that the sky was Hell, and that Wyvern had been put there by Mr Strange to be tormented for ever.

Upon his return the other servants gathered about him. "Ah, lad!" cried the butler in his concern. "What a sight you are! Was it the sherry-wine, Jeremy? Did you make him angry over the sherry-wine?"

The new manservant toppled off the horse on to the ground. He grasped the butler's coat and begged the butler to bring him a fishing-rod, explaining that he needed it to fish poor Wyvern out of Hell.

From this and other such coherent speeches the other servants quickly deduced that he had taken a cold and was feverish. They put him to bed and sent a man for the physician. But Laurence Strange got to hear about it and he sent a second messenger after the first to tell the physician he was not wanted. Next Laurence Strange said that he thought he would take some gruel and told the butler that he wanted the new manservant to bring it to him. This prompted the butler to go in search of Mr Jonathan Strange, to beg him to do something, but Jonathan Strange had, it seemed, got up early to ride to Shrewsbury and was not expected back until the following day. So the servants were obliged to get the new manservant out of bed, dress him, put the tray of gruel into his unresisting hand, and push him through the door. All day long Mr Strange maintained a steady succession of minor requests, each of which – and Mr Strange was most particular about this – was for the new manservant to carry out.

By nightfall the new manservant was as hot to the touch as a iron kettle and talked wildly of oyster-barrels. But Mr Strange declared his intention of sitting up another night and said that the new manservant should wait upon him in the writing-room.

The butler pleaded bravely with his master to let him sit up instead.

"Ah! but you cannot conceive what a fancy I have taken to this fellow," said Mr Strange, his eyes all bright with dislike, "and how I wish to have him always near me. You think he does not look well? In *my* opinion he only wants fresh air." And so saying he unfastened the window above his writing-table. Instantly the room became bitter-cold and a handful of snow flakes blew in from outside.

The butler sighed, and propped the new manservant (who had begun to fall down again) more securely against the wall, and secretly put hand-warmers in his pockets.

At midnight the maid went in to take Mr Strange some gruel. When she returned to the kitchen she reported that Mr Strange had found the hand-warmers and taken them out and put them on the table. The servants went sorrowfully to bed, convinced that the new manservant would be dead by morning.

Morning came. The door to Mr Strange's writing-room was closed. Seven o'clock came and no one rang the bell for the servant; no one appeared. Eight o'clock came. Nine o'clock. Ten. The servants wrung their hands in despair.

But what they had forgot – what, indeed, Laurence Strange had forgot – was that the new manservant was a young, strong man, whereas Laurence Strange was an old one – and some of what the new manservant had been made to suffer that night, Laurence Strange had been forced to share. At seven minutes past ten the butler and the coachman ventured in together and found the new manservant upon the floor fast asleep, his fever gone. On the other side of the room, seated at his writing-table was Laurence Strange, frozen to death.

When the events of those two nights became more generally known there was a great curiosity to see the new manservant, such as there might be to see a dragonslayer or a man who had toppled a giant. Of course the new manservant was glad to be thought remarkable, and as he told and re-told the story he discovered that what he had *actually* said to Mr Strange when he asked for the third glass of sherry-wine was: "Oh! it may suit you very well now, you wicked old sinner, to abuse honest men and drive them into their graves, but a day is coming – and not far off either – when you shall have to answer for every sigh you have forced from an honest man's breast, every tear you have wrung from a widow's eye!" Likewise it was soon well known in the neighbourhood that when Mr Strange had opened the window with the kind intention of starving the new manservant to death with cold the new manservant had cried out, "Cold at first, Laurence Strange, but hot at last! Cold at first, hot at last!" – a prophetic reference to Mr Strange's present situation.

# 15

## "How is Lady Pole?"

### January 1808

"How is Lady Pole?"

In every part of the Town and among all stations and degrees of citizen the question was to be heard. In Covent-garden at break of dawn, costermongers asked flower-girls, "How is Lady Pole?". In Ackermann's in the Strand, Mr Ackermann himself inquired of his customers (members of the nobility and persons of distinction) whether they had any news of Lady Pole. In the House of Commons during dull speeches, Members of Parliament whispered the question to their neighbours (each regarding Sir Walter out of the corner of his eye as he did so). In Mayfair dressing-rooms in the early hours of the morning, maids begged their mistresses' pardons, ". . . but was Lady Pole at the party tonight? And how is her ladyship?"

And so the question went round and round; "How is Lady Pole?"

And, "Oh!" (came back the reply), "her ladyship is very well, exceedingly well."

Which demonstrates the sad poverty of the English language, for her ladyship was a great deal more than well. Next to her ladyship every other person in the world looked pale, tired, half-dead. The extraordinary energy she had exhibited the morning after her resurrection had never left her; when she took her walk people stared to see a lady get on so fast. And as for the footman who was meant to attend her, he, poor fellow, was generally many yards in the rear, red-faced and breathless. The Secretary of War, coming out of Drummond's in Charing Cross one morning, was brought into sudden and unexpected conjunction with her ladyship walking rapidly along the street and was quite overturned. She helped him to his feet, said she hoped she had not hurt him and was gone before he could think of a reply.

Like every other young lady of nineteen Lady Pole was wild for dancing. She would dance every dance at a ball without ever once losing her breath and was dismayed that everyone went away so soon. "It is ridiculous to call such a half-hearted affair a ball!" she told Sir Walter. "We have had scarcely three hours dancing!" And she marvelled too at the frailty of the other dancers. "Poor things! I pity them."

Her health was drunk by the Army, the Navy and the Church. Sir Walter Pole was regularly named as the most fortunate man in the Kingdom and Sir Walter himself was quite of the same opinion. Miss Wintertowne – poor, pale, sick Miss Wintertowne – had excited his compassion, but Lady Pole, in a constant glow of extraordinary good health and happy spirits, was the object of his admiration. When she accidentally knocked the Secretary of War to the ground he thought it the best joke in the world and spoke of it to everyone he met. He privately confided to Lady Winsell, his particular friend, that her ladyship was exactly the wife to suit him – so clever, so lively, so everything he could have wished for. He was particularly struck by her independent opinions.

"She advised me last week that the Government ought not to send money and troops to the King of Sweden – which is what we have decided – but instead to lend our support to the Governments of Portugal and Spain and make these countries the bases of our operations against Buonaparte. At nineteen, to have thought so deeply upon all manner of things and to have come to so many conclusions about them! At nineteen, to contradict all the Government so boldly! Of course I told her that she ought to be in Parliament!"

Lady Pole united in one person all the different fascinations of Beauty, Politics, Wealth and *Magic*. The fashionable world had no doubt but that she was destined to become one of its most brilliant leaders. She had been married almost three months now; it was time to embark upon the course that Destiny and the fashionable world had marked out for her. Cards were sent out for a magnificent dinner-party to be held in the second week of January.

The first dinner-party of a bride's career is a momentous occasion, entailing a world of small anxieties. The accomplishments which have won her acclaim in the three years since she left the schoolroom are no longer enough. It is no longer enough to dress exquisitely, to chuse jewels exactly appropriate to the occasion, to converse in French, to play the pianoforte and sing. Now she must turn her attention to French cooking and French wines. Though other people may advise her upon these important matters, her own taste and inclinations must guide her. She is sure to despise her mother's style of entertaining and wish to do things differently. In London fashionable people dine out four, five times a week. However will a new bride – nineteen years old and scarcely ever in a kitchen before – think of a meal to astonish and delight such jaded palates?

Then there are the servants. In the new bride's new house the footmen are all new to their business. If something is needed quickly – candles, a different sort of fork, a heavy cloth in which to carry a hot soup tureen – will they be able to find it? In the case of Lady Pole's establishment at no. 9 Harley-street the problems were multiplied threefold. Half of the servants were from Northamptonshire – from her ladyship's estate at Great Hitherden – and half were newly hired in London; and as everybody knows there is a world of difference between country servants and London servants. It is not a matter of duties exactly. Servants must cook and clean and fetch and carry in Northamptonshire just as in

London. No, the distinction lies more in the manner in which those duties are carried out. Say a country squire in Northamptonshire visits his neighbour. The visit over, the footman fetches the squire's greatcoat and helps the squire on with it. While he is doing so it is only natural for the footman to inquire respectfully after the squire's wife. The squire is not in the least offended and responds with some inquiries of his own. Perhaps the squire has heard that the footman's grandmother fell over and hurt herself while cutting cabbages in her garden and he wishes to know if she is recovered. The squire and the footman inhabit a very small world and have known each other from childhood. But in London this will never do. A London footman must not address his master's guests. He must look as if he did not know there were such things as grandmothers and cabbages in the world.

At no. 9 Harley-street Lady Pole's country servants were continually ill at ease, afraid of going wrong and never sure of what was right. Even their speech was found fault with and mocked. Their Northamptonshire accent was not always intelligible to the London servants (who, it must be said, made no very great efforts to understand them) and they used words like goosegogs, sparrow-grass, betty-cat and battle-twigs, when they should have said gooseberries, asparagus, she-cat and earwigs.

The London servants delighted in playing tricks on the country servants. They gave Alfred, a young footman, plates of nasty, dirty water and told him it was French soup and bade him serve it up to the other servants at dinner. Often they gave the country servants messages to pass on to the butcher's boy, the baker and the lamplighter. The messages were full of London slang and the country servants could make neither head nor tail of them, but to the butcher's boy, the baker and the lamplighter, who understood them very well, they were both vulgar and insulting. The butcher's boy punched Alfred in the eye on account of what was said to him, while the London servants hid in the larder, to listen and laugh.

Naturally, the country servants complained vigorously to Lady Pole (whom they had known all their lives) about the manner in which they were persecuted and Lady Pole was shocked to find that all her old friends were unhappy in their new home. But she was inexperienced and uncertain how to proceed. She did not doubt the truth of what the country servants said for a moment, but she feared making matters worse.

"What ought I to do, Sir Walter?" she asked.

"Do?" said Sir Walter in surprize. "Do nothing. Leave it all to Stephen Black. By the time Stephen has finished with them they will all be as meek as lambs and as harmonious as blackbirds."

Before his marriage Sir Walter had had only one servant, Stephen Black, and Sir Walter's confidence in this person knew scarcely any bounds. At no. 9 Harley-street he was called "butler", but his duties and responsibilities extended far beyond the range of any ordinary butler: he dealt with bankers and lawyers on Sir Walter's behalf; he studied the accounts of Lady Pole's estates and reported to Sir Walter upon what he found there; he hired servants and workmen without reference to any one else; he directed their work and paid bills and wages.

Of course in many households there is a servant who by virtue of his exceptional intelligence and abilities is given authority beyond what is customary. But in Stephen's case it was all the more extraordinary since Stephen was a negro. I say "extraordinary", for is it not generally the case that a negro servant is the least-regarded person in a household? No matter how hardworking he or she may be? No matter how clever? Yet somehow Stephen Black had found a way to thwart this universal principle. He had, it is true, certain natural advantages: a handsome face and a tall, well-made figure. It certainly did him no harm that his master was a politician who was pleased to advertise his liberal principles to the world by entrusting the management of his house and business to a black servant.

The other servants were a little surprized to find they were put under a black man – a sort of person that many of them had never even seen before. Some were inclined to be indignant at first and told each other that if he dared to give them an order they would return him a very rude answer. But whatever their intentions, they discovered that when they were actually in Stephen's presence they did nothing of the sort. His grave looks, air of authority and reasonable instructions made it very natural to do whatever he told them.

The butcher's boy, the baker, the lamplighter and other similar new acquaintances of the Harley-street servants shewed great interest in Stephen from the first. They asked the Harley-street servants questions about Stephen's mode of life. What did he eat and drink? Who were his friends? Where did he like to go whenever he should happen to be at liberty to go anywhere? When the Harley-street servants replied that Stephen had had three boiled eggs for breakfast, the Secretary at War's Welsh valet was a great friend of his and that he had attended a servants' ball in Wapping the night before, the butcher's boy, the baker and the lamplighter were most grateful for the information. The Harley-street servants asked them why they wished to know. The butcher's boy, the baker and the lamplighter were entirely astonished. Did the Harley-street servants really not know? The Harley-street servants really did not. The butcher's boy, the baker and the lamplighter explained that a rumour had been circulating London for years to the effect that Stephen Black was not really a butler at all. Secretly he was an African prince, the heir to a vast kingdom, and it was well known that as soon as he grew tired of being a butler he would return there and marry a princess as black as himself.

After this revelation the Harley-street servants watched Stephen out of the corners of their eyes and agreed among themselves that nothing was more likely. In fact, was not their own obedience to Stephen the best proof of it? For it was hardly likely that such independent, proud-spirited Englishmen and women would have submitted to the authority of a *black man*, had they not instinctively felt that respect and reverence which a commoner feels for a king!

Meanwhile Stephen Black knew nothing of these curious speculations. He performed his duties diligently as he had always done. He continued to polish silver, train the footmen in the duties of *service à la française*, admonish the cooks, order flowers, linen, knives and forks and do all the thousand and one things necessary to prepare house and servants for the important evening of the magnificent dinner-party. When it finally came, everything was as splendid as his ingenuity could make it. Vases of hot-house roses filled the drawing-room and dining-room and lined the staircase. The dining-table was laid with a heavy white damask cloth and shone with all the separate glitters that silver, glass and candlelight can provide. Two great Venetian mirrors hung upon the wall and on Stephen's instructions these had been made to face each other, so that the reflections doubled and tripled and twice-tripled the silver and the glasses and the candles, and when the guests finally sat down to dinner they appeared to be gently dissolving in a dazzling, golden light like a company of the blessed in glory.

Chief among the guests was Mr Norrell. What a contrast now with that period when he had first arrived in London! Then he had been disregarded – a Nobody. Now he sat among the highest in the land and was courted by them! The other guests continually directed remarks and questions to him and seemed quite delighted by his short, ungracious replies: "I do not know whom you mean," or "I have not the pleasure of that gentleman's acquaintance," or "I have never been to the place you mention."

Some of Mr Norrell's conversation – the more entertaining part – was supplied by Mr Drawlight and Mr Lascelles. They sat upon either side of him, busily conveying his opinions upon modern magic about the table. Magic was a favourite subject that evening. Finding themselves at one and the same time in the presence of England's only magician and of the most famous subject of his magic, the guests could neither think nor talk of any thing else.

Very soon they fell to discussing the numerous claims of successful spells which had sprung up all over the country following Lady Pole's resurrection.

"Every provincial newspaper seems to have two or three reports," agreed Lord Castlereagh. "In the *Bath Chronicle* the other day I read about a man called Gibbons in Milsom-street who awoke in the night because he heard thieves breaking into his house. It seems that this man has a large library of magical books. He tried a spell he knew and turned the housebreakers into mice."

"Really?" said Mr Canning. "And what happened to the mice?"

"They all ran away into holes in the wainscotting."

"Ha!" said Mr Lascelles. "Believe me, my lord, there was no magic. Gibbons heard a noise, feared a housebreaker, said a spell, opened a door and found – not housebreakers, but mice. The truth is, it was mice all along. All of these stories prove false in the end. There is an unmarried clergyman and his sister in Lincoln called Malpas who have made it their business to look into supposed instances of magical occurrences and they have found no truth in any of them."

"They are such admirers of Mr Norrell, this clergyman and his sister!" added Mr Drawlight, enthusiastically. "They are so delighted that such a man has arisen to restore the noble art of English magic! They cannot bear that other people should tell falsehoods and claim to imitate his great deeds! They hate it that other people should make themselves seem important at Mr Norrell's expense! They feel it as a personal affront! Mr Norrell has been so kind as to supply them with certain infallible means of establishing beyond a doubt the falsity of all such claims and Mr Malpas and Miss Malpas drive about the country in their phaeton confounding these imposters!"

"I believe you are too generous to Gibbons, Mr Lascelles," said Mr Norrell in his pedantic fashion. "It is not at all certain that he did not have some malicious purpose in making his false claim. At the very least he lied about his library. I sent Childermass to see it and Childermass says there is not a book earlier than 1760. Worthless! Quite worthless!"

"Yet we must hope," said Lady Pole to Mr Norrell, "that the clergyman and his sister will soon uncover a magician of genuine ability – someone to help you, sir."

"Oh! But there is no one!" exclaimed Drawlight. "No one at all! You see, in order to accomplish his extraordinary deeds Mr Norrell shut himself away for years and years reading books. Alas, such devotion to the interests of one's country is very rare! I assure you there is no one else!"

"But the clergyman and his sister must not give up their search," urged her ladyship. "I know from my own example how much labour is involved in one solitary act of magic. Think how desirable it would be if Mr Norrell were provided with an assistant."

"Desirable yet hardly likely," said Mr Lascelles. "The Malpases have found nothing to suggest that any such person is in existence."

"But by your own account, Mr Lascelles, they have not been looking!" said Lady Pole. "Their object has been to expose false magic, not find new magicians. It would be very easy for them, as they drive about in their phaeton, to make some inquiries as to who does magic and who has a library. I am certain they will not mind the extra trouble. They will be glad to do what they can to help you, sir." (This to Mr Norrell.) "And we shall all hope that they soon succeed, because I think you must feel a little lonely."

In due course a suitable proportion of the fifty or so dishes was deemed to have been eaten and the footmen took away what was left. The ladies withdrew and the gentlemen were left to their wine. But the gentlemen found they had less pleasure in each other's society than usual. They had got to the end of all they had to say about magic. They had no relish for gossiping about their acquaintance and even politics seemed a little dull. In short they felt that they should like to have the pleasure of looking at Lady Pole again, and so they told Sir Walter – rather than asked him – that he missed his wife. He replied that he did not. But this was not allowed to be possible; it was well known that newly married gentlemen were never happy apart from their wives; the briefest of absences could depress a new husband's spirits and interfere with his digestion. Sir Walter's guests asked each other if they thought he looked bilious and they agreed that he did. He denied it. Ah, he was putting a brave face on it, was he? Very good. But clearly it was a desperate case. They would have mercy on him and go and join the ladies.

In the corner by the sideboard Stephen Black watched the gentlemen leave. Three footmen – Alfred, Geoffrey and Robert – remained in the room.

"Are we to go and serve the tea, Mr Black?" inquired Alfred, innocently.

Stephen Black raised one thin finger as a sign they were to stay where they were and he frowned slightly to shew they were to be silent. He waited until he was sure the gentlemen were out of hearing and then he exlaimed, "What in the world was the matter with everyone tonight? Alfred! I know that you have not often been in such company as we have tonight, but that is no reason to forget all your training! I was astonished at your stupidity!"

Alfred mumbled his apologies.

"Lord Castlereagh asked you to bring him *partridges with truffles*. I heard him most distinctly! Yet you brought him a *strawberry jelly*! What were you thinking of?"

Alfred said something rather indistinct in which only the word "fright" was distinguishable.

"You had a fright? What fright?"

"I thought I saw a queer figure standing behind her ladyship's chair."

"Alfred, what are you talking about?"

"A tall person with a head of shining silver hair and a green coat. He was leaning down to look at her ladyship. But the next moment there was no one at all."

"Alfred, look to that end of the room."

"Yes, Mr Black."

"What do you see?"

"A curtain, Mr Black."

"And what else?"

"A chandelier."

"A green velvet curtain and a chandelier ablaze with candles. That is your green-coated, silver-headed person, Alfred. Now go and help Cissie put away the china and do not be so foolish in future." Stephen Black turned to the next footman. "Geoffrey! Your behaviour was every bit as bad as Alfred's. I swear your thoughts were somewhere else entirely. What have you to say for yourself?"

Poor Geoffrey did not answer immediately. He was blinking his eyes and pressing his lips together and generally doing all those things that a man will do when he is trying not to cry. "I am sorry, Mr Black, but it was the music that distracted me."

"What music?" asked Stephen. "There was no music. There! Listen! That is the string quartet just starting up in the drawing-room. They have not played until now."

"Oh, no, Mr Black! I mean the pipe and fiddle that were playing in the next room all the time the ladies and gentlemen were at dinner. Oh, Mr Black! It was the saddest music that I ever heard. I thought it would break my heart!"

Stephen stared at him in perplexity. "I do not understand you," he said. "There was no pipe and fiddle." He turned to the last footman, a solid-looking, dark-haired man of forty or so. "And Robert! I scarcely know what to say to you! Did we not talk yesterday?"

"We did, Mr Black."

"Did I not tell you how much I relied upon you to set an example to the others?"

"Yes, Mr Black."

"Yet half a dozen times this evening you went to the window! What were you thinking of? Lady Winsell was looking round for someone to bring her a clean glass. Your business was at the table, attending to her ladyship's guests, not at the window."

"I am sorry, Mr Black, but I heard a knocking at the window."

"A knocking? What knocking?"

"Branches beating against the glass, Mr Black."

Stephen Black made a little gesture of impatience. "But, Robert, there is no tree near the house! You know very well there is not."

"I thought a wood had grown up around the house," said Robert.

"What?" cried Stephen.

## 16

# Lost-hope

## January 1808

THE SERVANTS IN Harley-street continued to believe that they were haunted by eerie sights and mournful sounds. The cook, John Longridge, and the kitchenmaids were troubled by a sad bell. The effect of the bell, explained John Longridge to Stephen Black, was to bring vividly to mind everyone they had ever known who had died, all the good things they had ever lost and every bad thing which had ever happened to them. Consequently, they had become dejected and low and their lives were not worth living.

Geoffrey and Alfred, the two youngest footmen, were tormented by the sound of the fife and violin which Geoffrey had first heard on the night of the dinner-party. The music always appeared to come from the next room. Stephen had taken them all over the house and proved that nowhere was any one playing any such instruments, but it did no good; they continued afraid and unhappy.

Most bewildering of all, in Stephen's opinion, was the behaviour of Robert, the eldest footman. Robert had struck Stephen from the first as a sensible man, conscientious, reliable – in short the last person in the world to fall prey to imaginary fears. Yet Robert still insisted that he could hear an invisible wood growing up around the house. Whenever he paused in his work, he heard ghostly branches scraping at the walls and tapping upon the windows, and tree-roots slyly extending themselves beneath the foundations and prising apart the bricks. The wood was old, said Robert, and full of malice. A traveller in the wood would have as much to fear from the trees as from another person hiding there.

But, argued Stephen, the nearest wood of any size was four miles away upon Hampstead Heath and even there the trees were quite domesticated. They did not crowd around people's houses and try to destroy them. Stephen could say what he liked; Robert only shook his head and shivered.

Stephen's only consolation was that this peculiar mania had erased all the servants' other differences. The London servants no longer cared that the country servants were slow of speech and had old-fashioned manners. The country servants no longer complained to Stephen that the London servants played tricks upon them and sent them on imaginary errands. All the servants were united by the belief that the house was haunted. They sat in the kitchen after their work was done and told stories of all the other houses that they had ever heard of where there were ghosts and horrors, and of the horrible fates that had befallen the people who lived there.

One evening, about a fortnight after Lady Pole's dinner-party, they were gathered about the kitchen fire, engaged in this favourite occupation. Stephen soon grew tired of listening to them and retired to his own little room to read a newspaper. He had not been there more than a few minutes when he heard a bell ringing. So he put down his newspaper, put on his black coat and went to see where he was wanted.

In the little passage-way that connected the kitchen to the butler's room was a little row of bells and beneath the bells the names of various rooms were neatly inscribed in brown paint: *The Venetian Drawing-room*; *The Yellow Drawing-room*; *The Dining-room*; *Lady Pole's Sitting-room*; *Lady Pole's Bed-chamber*; *Lady Pole's Dressing-room*; *Sir Walter's Study*; *Sir Walter's Bed-chamber*; *Sir Walter's Dressing-room*; *Lost-hope*.

"Lost-hope?" thought Stephen. "What in the world is that?"

He had paid the carpenter that very morning for the work in putting up the bells and he had entered the amount in his account-book: *To Amos Judd, for putting up 9 bells in the kitchen passageway and painting the names of the rooms beneath, 4 shillings*. But now there were ten bells. And the bell for Lost-hope was ringing violently.

"Perhaps," thought Stephen, "Judd means it as a joke. Well, he shall be fetched back tomorrow and made to put it right."

Not knowing quite what else to do, Stephen went up to the ground floor and looked in every room; all were empty. And so he climbed the staircase to the first floor.

At the top of the staircase was a door which he had never seen before.

"Who's there?" whispered a voice from behind the door. It was not a voice Stephen knew and, though it was only a whisper, it was curiously penetrating. It seemed to get into Stephen's head by some other means than his ears.

"There is someone upon stairs!" insisted the whispering voice. "Is it the servant? Come here, if you please! I need you!"

Stephen knocked and went in.

The room was every bit as mysterious as the door. If anyone had asked Stephen to describe it, he would have said it was decorated in the Gothic style – this being the only explanation he could think of to account for its extraordinary appearance. But it had none of the usual Gothic embellishments such as one might see depicted in the pages of Mr Ackermann's *Repository of the Arts*. There were no pointed mediaeval arches, no intricately carved wood, no ecclesiastical motifs. The walls and floor of the room were of plain grey stone, very worn and uneven in places. The ceiling was of vaulted stone. One small window looked out upon a starlit sky. The window had not so much as a scrap of glass in it and the winter wind blew into the room.

A pale gentleman with an extraordinary quantity of silvery, thistle-down hair was looking at his reflection in an old cracked mirror with an air of deep dissatisfaction. "Oh, there you are!" he said, glancing sourly at Stephen. "A person may call and call in this house, but no one comes!"

"I am very sorry, sir," said Stephen, "but no one told me you were here." He supposed the gentleman must be a guest of Sir Walter's or Lady Pole's – which explained the gentleman, but not the room. Gentlemen are often invited to stay in other people's houses. Rooms hardly ever are.

"In what way may I serve you, sir?" asked Stephen.

"How stupid you are!" cried the gentleman with the thistle-down hair. "Don't you know that Lady Pole is to attend a ball tonight at my house? My own servant has run off and hidden himself somewhere. How can I appear by the side of the beautiful Lady Pole in this condition?"

The gentleman had cause for complaint: his face was unshaven, his curious hair was a mass of tangles and he was not dressed, but only wrapped in an old-fashioned powdering gown.

"I shall be with you in an instant, sir," Stephen assured him. "But first I must find the means to shave you. You do not happen to know what your servant has done with the razor, I suppose?"

The gentleman shrugged.

There was no dressing-table in the room. Indeed there was very little furniture of any description. There was the mirror, an old three-legged milking stool and a queer carved chair that appeared to be made of bones. Stephen did not quite believe that they were human bones, although they did look remarkably like it.

Atop the milking stool, next to a pretty little box, Stephen found a delicate silver razor. A battered pewter basin full of water stood upon the floor.

Curiously there was no fireplace in the room, but only a rusting iron brazier full of hot coals, that spilt its dirty ashes on the floor. So Stephen heated the basin of water on the brazier and then he shaved the gentleman. When he had finished, the gentleman inspected his face and pronounced himself excessively pleased.

He removed his gown and stood patiently in his dressing-trousers while Stephen massaged his skin with a bristle-brush. Stephen could not help but observe that, whereas other gentlemen grow red as lobsters under such treatment, this gentleman remained as pale as ever and the only difference was that his skin took on a whitish glow as of moonlight or mother-of-pearl.

His clothes were the finest Stephen had ever seen; his shirt was exquisitely laundered and his boots shone like black mirrors. But best of all were a dozen or so white muslin neckcloths, each as thin as a cobweb and as stiff as music paper.

It took two hours to complete the gentleman's toilet, for he was, Stephen found, extremely vain. During this time the gentleman became more and more delighted with Stephen. "I tell you that my own ignorant fellow has not got half your skill at dressing hair," he declared, "and when it comes to the delicate art of tying a muslin neckcloth, why! he cannot be made to understand it at all!"

"Well, sir, it is exactly the sort of task I like," said Stephen. "I wish I could persuade Sir Walter to take more care of his clothes, but political gentlemen have no leisure for thinking of such things."

Stephen helped the gentleman on with his leaf-green coat (which was of the very best quality and most fashionable cut), then the gentleman went over to the milking stool and picked up the little box that lay there. It was made of porcelain and silver, and was about the size of a snuff box but a little longer than snuff boxes generally are. Stephen made some admiring remark about the colour which was not exactly pale blue and not exactly grey, not precisely lavender and not precisely lilac.

"Yes, indeed! It is beautiful," agreed the gentleman enthusiastically. "And very hard to make. The pigment must be mixed with the tears of spinsters of good family, who must live long lives of impeccable virtue and die without ever having had a day of true happiness!"

"Poor ladies!" said Stephen. "I am glad it is so rare."

"Oh! It is not the tears that make it rare – I have bottles full of those – it is the skill to mix the colour."

The gentleman had by now become so affable, so willing to talk that Stephen had no hesitation in asking him, "And what do you keep in such a pretty little box, sir? Snuff?"

"Oh, no! It is a great treasure of mine that I wish Lady Pole to wear at my ball tonight!" He opened the box and shewed Stephen a small, white finger.

At first this struck Stephen as a little unusual, but his surprize faded in a moment and if any one had questioned him about it just then, he would have replied that gentlemen often carried fingers about with them in little boxes and that this was just one of many examples he had seen.

"Has it been in your family long, sir?" he asked, politely.

"No, not long."

The gentleman snapped shut the box and put it in his pocket.

Together, he and Stephen admired his reflection in the mirror. Stephen could not help but notice how they perfectly complemented each other: gleaming black skin next to opalescent white skin, each a perfect example of a particular type of masculine beauty. Exactly the same thought seemed to strike the gentleman.

"How handsome we are!" he said in a wondering tone. "But I see now that I have made a horrible blunder! I took you for a servant in this house! But that is quite impossible! Your dignity and handsomeness proclaim you to be of noble, perhaps kingly birth! You are a visitor here, I suppose, as I am. I must beg your pardon for imposing upon you and thank you for the great service you have done me in making me ready to meet the beautiful Lady Pole."

Stephen smiled. "No, sir. I am a servant. I am Sir Walter's servant."

The gentleman with the thistle-down hair raised his eye-brow in astonishment. "A man as talented and handsome as yourself ought not be a servant!" he said in a shocked tone. "He ought to be the ruler of a vast estate! What is beauty for, I should like to know, if not to stand as a visible sign of one's superiority to everyone else? But I see how it is! Your enemies have conspired together to deprive you of all your possessions and to cast you down among the ignorant and lowly!"

"No, sir. You are mistaken. I have always been a servant."

"Well, I do not understand it," declared the gentleman with the thistle-down hair, with a puzzled shake of his head. "There is some mystery here and I shall certainly look into it just as soon as I am at liberty. But, in the meantime, as a reward for dressing my hair so well and all the other services you have done me, you shall attend my ball tonight."

This was such a very extraordinary proposal that for a moment Stephen did not know quite what to say. "Either he is mad," he thought, "or else he is some sort of radical politician who wishes to destroy all distinctions of rank."

Aloud he said, "I am very sensible of the honour you do me, sir, but only consider. Your other guests will come to your house expecting to meet ladies and gentlemen of their own rank. When they discover that they are consorting with a servant I am sure they will feel the insult very keenly. I thank you for your kindness, but I should not wish to embarrass you or offend your friends."

This seemed to astonish the gentleman with the thistle-down hair even more. "What nobility of feeling!" he cried. "To sacrifice your own pleasure to preserve the comfort of others! Well, it is a thing, I confess, that would never occur to me. And it only increases my determination to make you my friend and do everything in my power to aid you. But you do not quite understand. These guests of mine on whose account you are so scrupulous, they are all my vassals and subjects. There is not one of them who would dare to criticize *me* or any one I chose to call my friend. And if they did, why! we could always kill them! But really," he added as if he were suddenly growing bored of this conversation, "there is very little use debating the point since you are already here!"

With that the gentleman walked away and Stephen found that he was standing in a great hall where a crowd of people were dancing to sad music.

Once again he was a little surprized but, as before, he grew accustomed to the idea in a moment and began to look about him. Despite all that the gentleman with the thistle-down hair had said upon the point, he was a little apprehensive at first that he would be recognized. A few glances about the room were enough to reassure him that there were no friends of Sir Walter present – indeed there was no one Stephen had ever seen before and in his neat black clothes and clean white linen he believed he might very easily pass for a gentleman. He was glad that Sir Walter had never required him to wear livery or a powdered wig, which would have marked him out as a servant in an instant.

Everyone was dressed in the very height of fashion. The ladies wore gowns of the most exquisite colours (though, to own the truth, very few of them were colours that Stephen could remember having seen before). The gentlemen wore knee breeches and white stockings and coats of brown, green, blue and black, their linen was a sparkling, shining white and their kid gloves had not so much as a stain or mark upon them.

But in spite of all the fine clothes and gaiety of the guests, there were signs that the house was not so prosperous as once it had been. The room was dimly lit by an insufficient number of tallow candles, and there was just one viol and one fife to provide the music.

"That must be the music that Geoffrey and Alfred spoke of," thought Stephen. "How odd that I could not hear it before! It is every bit as melancholy as they said."

He made his way to a narrow unglazed window and looked out upon a dark, tangled wood under starlight. "And this must be the wood which Robert talks about. How malevolent it looks! And is there a bell, I wonder?"

"Oh, yes!" said a lady who was standing close by. She wore a gown the colour of storms, shadows and rain and a necklace of broken promises and regrets. He was surprized to find himself addressed by her since he was quite certain that he had not spoken his thoughts out loud.

"There is indeed a bell!" she told him, "It is high up in one of the towers."

She was smiling and regarding him with such frank admiration that Stephen thought it only polite to say something.

"This is certainly a most elegant assembly, madam. I do not know when I last saw so many handsome faces and graceful figures gathered together in one place. And every one of them in the utmost bloom of youth. I confess that I am surprized to see no older people in the room. Have these ladies and gentlemen no mothers and fathers? No aunts or uncles?"

"What an odd remark!" she replied, laughing. "Why should the Master of Lost-hope House invite aged and unsightly persons to his ball? Who would want to look at them? Besides we are not so young as you suppose. England was nothing but dreary wood and barren moor when last we saw our sires and dams. But wait! See! There is Lady Pole!"

Between the dancers Stephen caught a glimpse of her ladyship. She was wearing a blue velvet gown and the gentleman with the thistle-down hair was leading her to the top of the dance.

Then the lady in the gown the colour of storms, shadows and rain inquired if he would like to dance with her.

"Gladly," he said.

When the other ladies saw how well Stephen danced, he found he could have any partner he wished for. After the lady in the gown the colour of storms, shadows and rain he danced with a young woman who had no hair, but who wore a wig of shining beetles that swarmed and seethed upon her head. His third partner complained bitterly whenever Stephen's hand happened to brush against her gown; she said it put her gown off its singing; and, when Stephen looked down, he saw that her gown was indeed covered with tiny mouths which opened and sang a little tune in a series of high, eerie notes.

Although in general the dancers followed the usual custom and changed partners at the end of two dances, Stephen observed that the gentleman with the thistle-down hair danced with Lady Pole the whole night long and that he scarcely spoke to any other person in the room. But he had not forgotten Stephen. Whenever Stephen chanced to catch his eye, the gentleman with the thistle-down hair smiled and bowed his head and gave every sign of wishing to convey that, of all the delightful circumstances of the ball, what pleased him most was to see Stephen Black there.

# 17

# The unaccountable appearance of twenty-five guineas

## January 1808

THE BEST GROCER's in Town is Brandy's in St James's-street. I am not alone in that opinion; Sir Walter Pole's grandfather, Sir William Pole, declined to purchase coffee, chocolate or tea from any other establishment, declaring that in comparison with Mr Brandy's Superfine High Roasted Turkey Coffee, all other coffees had a mealy flavour. It must be said, however, that Sir William Pole's patronage was a somewhat mixed blessing. Though liberal in his praise and always courteous and condescending to the shop-people, he was scarcely ever known to pay a bill and when he died, the amount of money owing to Brandy's was considerable. Mr Brandy, a short-tempered, pinched-faced, cross little old man, was beside himself with rage about it. He died shortly afterwards, and was presumed by many people to have done so on purpose and to have gone in pursuit of his noble debtor.

At Mr Brandy's death, the business came into the possession of his widow. Mr Brandy had married rather late in life and my readers will not be much surprized, I dare say, to learn that Mrs Brandy had not been entirely happy in her marriage. She had quickly discovered that Mr Brandy loved to look at guineas and shillings more than he had ever loved to look at her – though *I* say it must have been a strange sort of man that did not love to look at her, for she was everything that was delightful and amiable, all soft brown curls, light blue eyes and a sweet expression. It would seem to me that an old man, such as Mr Brandy, with nothing to recommend him but his money, ought to have treasured a young, pretty wife, and studied hard to please her in everything he could; but he did not. He had even denied her a house of her own to live in – which was something he could have afforded very easily. So loath had he been to part with a sixpence that he declared they should live in the little room above the shop in St. James's Street, and for the twelve years of her marriage this apartment served Mrs Brandy as parlour, bedroom, dining-parlour and kitchen. But Mr Brandy had not been dead three weeks when she bought a house in Islington, near the Angel, and acquired three maids, whose names were Sukey, Dafney and Delphina.

She also employed two men to attend the customers in the shop. John Upchurch was a steady soul, hard-working and capable. Toby Smith was a red-haired, nervous man whose behaviour often puzzled Mrs Brandy. Sometimes he would be silent and unhappy and at other times he would be suddenly cheerful and full of unexpected confidences. From certain discrepancies in the accounts (such as may occur in any business) and from the circumstances of Toby looking miserable and ill at ease whenever she questioned him about it, Mrs Brandy had begun to fear that he might be pocketing the difference. One January evening her dilemma took a strange turn. She was sitting in her little parlour above the shop when there was a knock upon the door and Toby Smith came shuffling in, quite unable to meet her eye.

"What's the matter, Toby?"

"If you please, ma'am," said Toby looking this way and that, "the money won't come right. John and me have counted it out again and again, ma'am, and cast up the sums a dozen times or more, but we cannot make head or tail of it."

Mrs Brandy tutted and sighed and asked by how much they were out.

"Twenty-five guineas, ma'am."

"Twenty-five guineas!" cried Mrs Brandy in horror. "Twenty-five guineas! How could we possibly have lost so much? Oh! I hope you are mistaken, Toby. Twenty-five guineas! I would not have supposed there to be so much money in the shop! Oh, Toby!" she cried, as another thought struck her. "We must have been robbed!"

"No, ma'am," said Toby. "Beg your pardon, ma'am, but you mistake. I did not mean to say we are twenty-five guineas short. We are over, ma'am. By that amount."

Mrs Brandy stared at him.

"Which you may see for yourself, ma'am," said Toby, "if you will just come down to the shop," and he held the door open for her with an anxious, pleading expression upon his face. So Mrs Brandy ran downstairs into the shop and Toby followed after her.

It was about nine o'clock on a moonless night. The shutters were all put up and John and Toby had extinguished the lamps. The shop ought to have been as dark as the inside of a tea-caddy, but instead it was filled with a soft, golden light which appeared to emanate from something golden which lay upon the counter-top.

A heap of shining guineas was lying there. Mrs Brandy picked up one of the coins and examined it. It was as if she held a ball of soft yellow light with a coin at the bottom of it. The light was odd. It made Mrs Brandy, John and Toby look quite unlike themselves: Mrs Brandy appeared proud and haughty, John looked sly and deceitful and Toby wore an expression of great ferocity. Needless to say, all of these were qualities quite foreign to their characters. But stranger still was the transformation that the light worked upon the dozens of small mahogany drawers that formed one wall of the shop. Upon other evenings the gilt lettering upon the drawers proclaimed the contents to be such things as: *Mace (Blades)*, *Mustard (Unhusked)*, *Nutmegs*, *Ground Fennel*, *Bay Leaves*,

*Pepper of Jamaica*, *Essence of Ginger*, *Caraway*, *Peppercorns* and *Vinegar* and all the other stock of a fashionable and prosperous grocery business. But now the words appeared to read: *Mercy (Deserved)*, *Mercy (Undeserved)*, *Nightmares*, *Good Fortune*, *Bad Fortune*, *Persecution by Families*, *Ingratitude of Children*, *Confusion*, *Perspicacity* and *Veracity*. It was as well that none of them noticed this odd change. Mrs Brandy would have been most distressed by it had she known. She would not have had the least notion what to charge for these new commodities.

"Well," said Mrs Brandy, "they must have come from somewhere. Has any one sent today to pay their bill?"

John shook his head. So did Toby. "And, besides," added Toby, "no one owes so much, excepting, of course, the Duchess of Worksop and frankly, ma'am, in that case . . ."

"Yes, yes, Toby, that will do," interrupted Mrs Brandy. She thought for a moment. "Perhaps," she said, "some gentleman, wishing to wipe the rain from his face, pulled out his handkerchief, and so caused the money to tumble out of his pocket on to the floor."

"But we did not find it upon the floor," said John, "it was here in the cash-box with all the rest."

"Well," said Mrs Brandy, "I do not know what to say. Did anyone pay with a guinea today?"

No, said Toby and John, no one had paid today with a guinea, let alone twenty-five such guineas or twenty-five such persons.

"And such yellow guineas, ma'am," remarked John, "each one the very twin of all the others, without a spot of tarnish upon any of them."

"Should I run and fetch Mr Black, ma'am?" asked Toby.

"Oh, yes!" said Mrs Brandy, eagerly. "But then again, perhaps no. We ought not to trouble Mr Black unless there is any thing very wrong. And nothing is wrong, is it, Toby? Or perhaps it is. I cannot tell."

The sudden and unaccountable arrival of large sums of money is such a very rare thing in our Modern Age that neither Toby nor John was able to help their mistress decide whether it were a wrong thing or a right.

"But, then," continued Mrs Brandy, "Mr Black is so clever. I dare say he will understand this puzzle in an instant. Go to Harley-street, Toby. Present my compliments to Mr Black and say that if he is at liberty I should be glad of a few moments' conversation with him. No, wait! Do not say that, it sounds so presumptuous. You must apologize for disturbing him and say that whenever he should happen to be at liberty I should be grateful – no, honoured – no, grateful – I should be grateful for a few moments' conversation with him."

Mrs Brandy's acquaintance with Stephen Black had begun when Sir Walter had inherited his grandfather's debts and Mrs Brandy had inherited her husband's business. Every week or so Stephen had come with a guinea or two to help pay off the debt. Yet, curiously, Mrs Brandy was often reluctant to accept the money. "Oh! Mr Black!" she would say, "Pray put the money away again! I am certain that Sir Walter has greater need of it than I. We did such excellent business last week! We have got some carracca chocolate in the shop just at present, which people have been kind enough to say is the best to be had any where in London – infinitely superior to other chocolate in both flavour and texture! – and they have been sending for it from all over Town. Will not you take a cup, Mr Black?"

Then Mrs Brandy would bring the chocolate in a pretty blue-and-white china chocolate-pot, and pour Stephen a cup, and anxiously inquire how he liked it; for it seemed that, even though people had been sending for it from all over Town, Mrs Brandy could not feel quite convinced of its virtues until she knew Stephen's opinion. Nor did her care of him end with making him chocolate. She was solicitous for his health. If it happened to be a cold day, she would be concerned that he was not warm enough; if it were raining she would worry that he might catch a cold; if it were a hot, dry day she would insist that he sit by a window overlooking a little green garden to refresh himself.

When it was time for him to go, she would revive the question of the guinea. "But as to next week, Mr Black, I cannot say. Next week I may need a guinea very badly – people do not always pay their bills – and so I will be so bold as to ask you to bring it again on Wednesday. Wednesday at about three o'clock. I shall be quite disengaged at three o'clock and I shall be sure to have a pot of chocolate ready, as you are so kind as to say you like it very much."

The gentlemen among my readers will smile to themselves and say that women never did understand business, but the ladies may agree with me that Mrs Brandy understood her business very well, for the chief business of Mrs Brandy's life was to make Stephen Black as much in love with her as she was with him.

In due course Toby returned, not with a message from Stephen Black, but with Stephen himself and Mrs Brandy's anxiety about the coins was swept away by a new and altogether more pleasant agitation. "Oh, Mr Black! We did not expect to see you so soon! I did not imagine you would be at liberty!"

Stephen stood in the darkness outside the radiance cast by the strange coins. "It does not matter where I am tonight," he said in a dull tone quite unlike his usual voice. "The house is all at sixes and sevens. Her ladyship is not well."

Mrs Brandy, John and Toby were shocked to hear this. Like every other citizen of London they took a close interest in everything that concerned her ladyship. They prided themselves upon their connexion with all sorts of aristocratic persons, but it was the patronage of Lady Pole which gave them the greatest satisfaction. Nothing pleased them so much as being able to assure people that when Lady Pole sat down to breakfast, her ladyship's roll was spread with Mrs Brandy's preserves and her coffee cup was filled with coffee made with Mrs Brandy's beans.

Mrs Brandy was suddenly struck with a most unpleasant idea.

"I hope her ladyship did not eat something which disagreed with her?" she asked.

"No," said Stephen with a sigh, "it is nothing of that sort. She complains of aches in all her limbs, odd dreams and feeling cold. But mostly she is silent and out of spirits. Her skin is icy to the touch."

Stephen stepped into the queer light.

The strange alterations which it had made to the appearance of Toby, John and Mrs Brandy were nothing to the changes it worked upon Stephen: his native handsomeness increased five-, seven-, tenfold; he acquired an expression of almost supernatural nobility; and, most extraordinary of all, the light somehow seemed to concentrate in a band around his brow so that he appeared to have been crowned with a diadem. Yet, just as before, none of those present noticed anything out of the common.

He turned the coins over in his thin black fingers. "Where were they, John?"

"Here in the cash-box with all the rest of the money. Where in the world can they have come from, Mr Black?"

"I am as puzzled as you are. I have no explanation to offer." Stephen turned to Mrs Brandy. "My chief concern, ma'am, is that you should protect yourself from any suspicion that you have come by the money dishonestly. I think you must give the money to a lawyer. Instruct him to advertise in *The Times* and *The Morning Chronicle* to discover if any one lost twenty-five guineas in Mrs Brandy's shop."

"A lawyer, Mr Black!" cried Mrs Brandy, horrified. "Oh, but that will cost a world of money!"

"Lawyers always do, ma'am."

At that moment a gentleman in St. James's-street passed Mrs Brandy's shop and, discerning a golden radiance shining out of the chinks in the shutters, realized that someone was within. He happened to be in need of tea and sugar and so he knocked upon the door.

"Customer, Toby!" cried Mrs Brandy.

Toby hurried to open the door and John put the money away. The instant that he closed the lid of the cash-box, the room became dark and for the first time they realized that they had been seeing each other by the light of the eerie coins. So John ran around, re-lighting the lamps and making the place look cheerful and Toby weighed out the things which the customer wanted.

Stephen Black sank into a chair and passed his hand across his forehead. He looked grey-faced and tired to death.

Mrs Brandy sat down in the chair next to his and touched his hand very gently. "You are not well, my dear Mr Black."

"It is just that I ache all over – as a man does who has been dancing all night." He sighed again and rested his head upon his hand.

Mrs Brandy withdrew her hand. "I did not know there was a ball last night," she said. There was a tinge of jealousy to her words. "I hope you had a most delightful time. Who were your partners?"

"No, no. There was no ball. I seem to have all the pains of dancing, without having had any of the pleasure." He raised his head suddenly. "Do you hear that?" he asked.

"What, Mr Black?"

"That bell. Tolling for the dead."

She listened a moment. "No, I do not hear any thing. I hope you will stay to supper, my dear Mr Black? It would do us so much honour. I fear it will not be a very elegant meal. There is very little. Hardly anything at all. Just some steamed oysters and a pigeon-pie and a harrico of mutton. But an old friend like you will make allowances, I am sure. Toby can fetch some . . ."

"Are you certain you do not hear it?"

"No."

"I cannot stay." He looked as if he meant to say something more – indeed he opened his mouth to say it, but the bell seemed to intrude itself upon his attention again and he was silent. "Good evening to you!" He rose and, with a rapid half-bow, he walked out.

In St James's-street the bell continued to toll. He walked like a man in a fog. He had just reached Piccadilly when an aproned porter carrying a basket full of fish came very suddenly out of a little alleyway. In trying to get out of the porter's way, Stephen collided with a stout gentleman in a blue coat and a Bedford hat who was standing on the corner of Albemarle-street.

The stout gentleman turned and saw Stephen. Instantly he was all alarm; he saw a black face close to his own face and black hands near his pockets and valuables. He paid no attention to Stephen's expensive clothes and respectable air but, immediately concluding that he was about to be robbed or knocked down, he raised his umbrella to strike a blow in his own defence.

It was the moment that Stephen had dreaded all his life. He supposed that constables would be called and he would be dragged before the magistrates and it was probable that even the patronage and friendship of Sir Walter Pole would not save him. Would an English jury be able to conceive of a black man who did not steal and lie? A black man who was a respectable person? It did not seem very likely. Yet now that his fate had come upon him, Stephen found he did not care very much about it and he watched events unfold as though he were watching a play through thick glass or a scene at the bottom of a pond.

The stout gentleman opened his eyes wide in fright, anger and indignation. He opened his mouth wide to begin accusing Stephen but in that moment he began to change. His body became the trunk of a tree; he suddenly sprouted arms in all directions and all the arms became branches; his face became a bole and he shot up twenty feet; where his hat and umbrella had been there was a thick crown of ivy.

"An oak tree in Piccadilly," thought Stephen, not much interested. "That is unusual."

Piccadilly was changing too. A carriage happened to be passing.

It clearly belonged to someone of importance for as well as the coachman upon his box, two footmen rode behind; there was a coat of arms upon the door and it was drawn by four matched greys. As Stephen watched the horses grew taller and thinner until they seemed about to disappear entirely and at that point they were suddenly transformed into a grove of delicate silver birches. The carriage became a holly bush and the coachman and the footmen became an owl and two nightingales which promptly flew away. A lady and gentleman walking along together suddenly sprouted twigs in every direction and became an elder-bush, a dog became a shaggy clump of dry bracken. The gas lamps that hung above the street were sucked up into the sky and became stars in a fretwork of winter trees and Piccadilly itself dwindled to a barely discernible path through a dark winter wood.

But just as in a dream where the most extraordinary events arrive complete with their own explanation and become reasonable in an instant, Stephen found nothing to be surprized at. Rather, it seemed to him that he had always known that Piccadilly stood in close proximity to a magical wood.

He began to walk along the path.

The wood was very dark and quiet. Above his head the stars were the brightest he had ever seen and the trees were nothing more than black shapes, mere absences of stars.

The thick grey misery and stupidity which had enveloped his mind and spirit all day disappeared and he began to muse upon the curious dream he had the night before about meeting a strange green-coated person with thistle-down hair who had taken him to a house where he had danced all night with the queerest people.

The sad bell sounded much clearer in the wood than it had in London and Stephen followed the sound along the path. In a very short while he came to an immense stone house with a thousand windows. A feeble light shone out of some of these openings. A high wall surrounded the house. Stephen passed through (though he did not quite understand how, for he saw no sign of a gate) and found himself in a wide and dreary courtyard where skulls, broken bones, and rusting weapons were scattered about, as if they had lain there for centuries. Despite the size and grandeur of the house its only entrance was a mean little door and Stephen had to bend low to pass through. Immediately he beheld a vast crowd of people all dressed in the finest clothes.

Two gentlemen stood just inside the door. They wore fine dark coats, spotless white stockings and gloves and dancing pumps. They were talking together, but the moment Stephen appeared, one turned and smiled.

"Ah, Stephen Black!" he said. "We have been waiting for you!"

At that moment the viol and pipe started up again.

# 18

# Sir Walter consults gentlemen in several professions

## February 1808

LADY POLE SAT by the window, pale and unsmiling. She said very little and whenever she did say any thing her remarks were odd and not at all to the point. When her husband and friends anxiously inquired what the matter was, she replied that she was sick of dancing and wished to dance no more. As for music, it was the most detestable thing in the world – she wondered that she had never realized it before.

Sir Walter regarded this lapse into silence and indifference as highly alarming. It was altogether too like that illness which had caused her ladyship so much suffering before her marriage and ended so tragically in her early death. Had she not been pale before? Well, she was pale now. Had she not been cold before? She was so again.

During her ladyship's previous illness no doctor had ever attended her and naturally doctors everywhere resented this as an insult to their profession. "Oh!" they cried whenever Lady Pole's name was mentioned, "the magic which brought her back to life was no doubt very wonderful, but if only the proper medicines had been administered in time then there would have been no need for the magic in the first place."

Mr Lascelles had been right when he declared the fault to be entirely Mrs Wintertowne's. She detested doctors and had never allowed one to come near her daughter. Sir Walter, however, was hindered by no such prejudice; he sent immediately for Mr Baillie.

Mr Baillie was a Scottish gentleman who had long been considered the foremost practitioner of his profession in London. He had written a great many books with important-sounding titles and he was Physician Extraordinary to the King. He had a sensible face and carried a gold-topped stick as a symbol of his pre-eminence. He answered Sir Walter's summons swiftly, eager to prove the superiority of medicine to magic. The examination done, he came out again. Her ladyship was in excellent health, he said. She had not got so much as a cold.

Sir Walter explained again how different she was today from what she had been only a few days ago.

Mr Baillic regarded Sir Walter thoughtfully. He said he believed he understood the problem. Sir Walter and her ladyship had not been married long, had they? Well, Sir Walter must forgive him, but doctors were often obliged to say things which other people would not. Sir Walter was not accustomed to married life. He would soon discover that married people often quarrelled. It was nothing to be ashamed of – even the most devoted couples disagreed sometimes, and when they did it was not uncommon for one partner to pretend an indisposition. Nor was it always the lady that did so. Was there perhaps something that Lady Pole had set her heart upon? Well, if it were a small thing, like a new gown or a bonnet, why not let her have it since she wanted it so much? If it were a large thing like a house or a visit to Scotland, then perhaps it would be best to talk to her about it. Mr Baillie was sure that her ladyship was not an unreasonable person.

There was a pause during which Sir Walter stared at Mr Baillie down his long nose. "Her ladyship and I have not quarrelled," he said at last.

Ah, said Mr Baillie in a kindly fashion. It might well appear to Sir Walter that there had been no quarrel. It was often the case that gentlemen did not observe the signs. Mr Baillie advised Sir Walter to think carefully. Might he not have said something to vex her ladyship? Mr Baillie did not speak of blame. It was all part of the little accommodations that married people must make in beginning their life together.

"But it is not Lady Pole's character to behave like a spoilt child!"

No doubt, no doubt, said Mr Baillie. But her ladyship was very young and young persons ought always be permitted some licence for folly. Old heads did not sit upon young shoulders. Sir Walter ought not to expect it. Mr Baillie was rather warming to his subject. He had examples to hand (drawn from history and literature) of sober-minded, clever men and women who had all done foolish things in their youth, however a glance at Sir Walter's face persuaded him that he should press the point no further.

Sir Walter was in a similar situation. He too had several things to say and a great mind to say some of them, but he felt himself on uncertain ground. A man who marries for the first time at the age of forty-two knows only too well that almost all his acquaintance are better qualified to manage his domestic affairs than him. So Sir Walter contented himself with frowning at Mr Baillie and then, since it was almost eleven o'clock, he called for his carriage and his secretary and drove to Burlington House where he had an appointment to meet the other Ministers.

At Burlington House he walked through pillared courtyards and gilded ante-rooms. He mounted great marble staircases that were overhung by painted ceilings in which impossible numbers of painted gods, goddesses, heroes and nymphs tumbled out of blue skies or reclined on fluffy white clouds. He was bowed at by a whole host of powdered, liveried footmen until he came to the room where the Ministers were looking at papers and arguing with one another.

"But why do you not send for Mr Norrell, Sir Walter?" asked

Mr Canning, the moment he heard what the matter was. "I am astonished that you have not already done so. I am sure that her ladyship's indisposition will prove to be nothing more than some slight irregularity in the magic which brought her back to life. Mr Norrell can make some small adjustment to a spell and her ladyship will be well again."

"Oh, quite!" agreed Lord Castlereagh. "It seems to me that Lady Pole has gone beyond physicians. You and I, Sir Walter, are set upon this earth by the Grace of God, but her ladyship is here by the grace of Mr Norrell. Her hold upon life is different from the rest of us – theologically and, I dare say, medically as well."

"Whenever Mrs Perceval is unwell," interjected Mr Perceval, a small, precise lawyer of unremarkable aspect and manners who held the exalted position of Chancellor of the Exchequer, "the first person I apply to is her maid. After all, who knows a lady's state of health better than her maid? What does Lady Pole's maid say?"

Sir Walter shook his head. "Pampisford is as mystified as I am. She agreed with me that her ladyship was in excellent health two days ago and now she is cold, pale, listless and unhappy. That is the beginning and end of Pampisford's information. That and a great deal of nonsense about the house being haunted. I do not know what is the matter with the servants just now. They are all in an odd, nervous condition. One of the footmen came to me this morning with a tale of meeting someone upon the stairs at midnight. A person with a green coat and a great quantity of pale, silvery hair."

"What? A ghost? An apparition?" asked Lord Hawkesbury.

"I believe that is what he meant, yes."

"How very extraordinary! Did it speak?" asked Mr Canning.

"No. Geoffrey said it gave him a cold, disdainful look and passed on."

"Oh! Your footman was dreaming, Sir Walter. He was certainly dreaming," said Mr Perceval.

"Or drunk," offered Mr Canning.

"Yes, that occurred to me too. So naturally I asked Stephen Black," said Sir Walter, "but Stephen is as foolish as the rest of them. I can scarcely get him to speak to me."

"Well," said Mr Canning, "you will not, I think, attempt to deny that there is something here that suggests magic? And is it not Mr Norrell's business to explain what other people cannot? Send for Mr Norrell, Sir Walter!"

This was so reasonable that Sir Walter began to wonder why he had not thought of it himself. He had the highest opinion of his own abilities and did not think he would generally miss so obvious a connection. The truth was, he realized, that he did not really *like* magic. He had never liked it – not at the beginning when he had supposed it to be false and not now that it had proved to be real. But he could hardly explain this to the other Ministers – he who had persuaded them to employ a magician for the first time in two hundred years!

At half-past three he returned to Harley-street. It was the eeriest part of a winter day. Twilight was turning all the buildings and people to blurred, black nothingnesses while, above, the sky remained a dizzying silver-blue and was full of cold light. A winter sunset was painting a swathe of rose-colour and blood-colour at the end of all the streets – pleasing to the eyes but somehow chilling to the heart. As Sir Walter gazed from his carriage-window, he thought it fortunate that he was not in any way a fanciful person. Someone else might have been quite unsettled by the combination of the disagreeable task of consulting a magician and this queer, black-and-bloody dissolution of the London streets.

Geoffrey opened the door of no. 9 Harley-street and Sir Walter rapidly mounted the stairs. On the first floor he passed the Venetian drawing-room where her ladyship had been sitting that morning. A sort of presentiment made him look inside. At first it did not seem as though any body could be there. The fire was low in the grate, creating a sort of second twilight within the room. No body had lit a lamp or candle yet. And then he saw her.

She was sitting very upright in a chair by the window. Her back was towards him. Everything about her – chair, posture, even the folds of her gown and shawl – was precisely the same as when he had left her that morning.

The moment he reached his study, he sat down and wrote an urgent message to Mr Norrell.

Mr Norrell did not come immediately. An hour or two passed. At last he arrived with an expression of fixed calm upon his face. Sir Walter met him in the hall and described what had happened. He then proposed that they go upstairs to the Venetian drawing-room.

"Oh!" said Mr Norrell, quickly. "From what you tell me, Sir Walter, I am quite certain there is no need to trouble Lady Pole because, you see, I fear I can do nothing for her. Much as it pains me to say this to you, my dear Sir Walter – for as you know I should always wish to serve you when I can – but whatever it is that has distressed her ladyship I do not believe that it is in the power of magic to remedy."

Sir Walter sighed. He ran his hand through his hair and looked unhappy. "Mr Baillie found nothing wrong and so I thought . . ."

"Oh! But it is precisely that circumstance which makes me so certain that I cannot help you. Magic and medicine are not always so distinct from one another as you seem to imagine. Their spheres often overlap. An illness may have both a medical cure and a magical one. If her ladyship were truly ill or if, God forbid!, she were to die again, then certainly there is magic to cure or restore her. But forgive me, Sir Walter, what you have described seems more a spiritual ailment than a physical one and as such belongs neither to magic nor medicine. I am no expert in these matters but perhaps a clergyman might be found to answer better?"

"But Lord Castlereagh thought – I do not know if it is true – Lord Castlereagh thought that since Lady Pole owes her life to magic – I confess that I did not understand him very well, but I believe he meant to say that since her ladyship's life is founded upon magic, she would only be susceptible to cure by magic."

"Indeed? Lord Castlereagh said that? Oh! He is quite mistaken, but I am most intrigued that he should have thought of it. That is what used to be called the Meraudian Heresy.[1] A twelfth-century abbot of Rievaulx dedicated himself to its destruction and was later made a saint. Of course the theology of magic has never been a favourite subject of mine, but I believe I am correct in saying that in the sixty-ninth chapter of William Pantler's *Three Perfectible States of Being* . . ."[2]

Mr Norrell seemed about to embark upon one of his long, dull speeches upon the history of English magic, full of references to books no one had ever heard of. Sir Walter interrupted him with, "Yes, yes! But do you have any notion who the person with the green coat and the silver hair might be?"

"Oh!" said Mr Norrell. "You think there was somebody then? But that seems to me most unlikely. Might it not be something more in the nature of a dressing gown left hanging on a hook by a negligent servant? Just where one does not expect to see it? I myself have often been badly startled by this wig which you see now upon my head. Lucas ought to put it away each night – he knows he ought – but several times now he has left it on its wig stand on the mantelpiece where it is reflected in the mirror above the fireplace

---

[1] This theory was first expounded by a Cornish magician called Meraud in the twelfth century and there were many variants. In its most extreme form it involves the belief that any one who has been cured, saved or raised to life by magic is no longer subject to God and His Church, though they may owe all sorts of allegiance to the magician or fairy who has helped them.

Meraud was arrested and brought before Stephen, King of Southern England, and his bishops at a Council in Winchester. Meraud was branded, beaten and stripped half-naked. Then he was cast out. The bishops ordered that no one should help him. Meraud tried to walk from Winchester to Newcastle, where the Raven King's castle was. He died on the way.

The Northern English belief that certain sorts of murderers belong not to God or to the Devil but to the Raven King is another form of the Meraudian Heresy.

[2] *Three Perfectible States of Being* by William Pantler, pub. Henry Lintot, London, 1735. The three perfectible beings are angels, men and fairies.

and resembles nothing so much in the world as two gentlemen with their heads together, whispering about me."

Mr Norrell blinked his small eyes rapidly at Sir Walter. Then, having declared that he could do nothing, he wished Sir Walter good evening and left the house.

Mr Norrell went straight home. As soon as he arrived at his house in Hanover-square he immediately went up to a little study upon the second floor. This was a quiet room at the back of the house, overlooking the garden. The servants never entered when he was working in this room and even Childermass needed some unusually pressing reason to disturb him there. Though Mr Norrell rarely gave warning of when he intended to use this little study, it was one of the rules of the household that it was always kept in readiness for him. Just now a fire was burning brightly in the grate and all the lamps were lit, but someone had neglected to draw the curtains and consequently the window had become a black mirror, in which the room was reflected.

Mr Norrell sat down at the desk which faced the window. He opened a large volume, one of many upon the desk, and began to murmur a spell to himself.

A coal falling from the grate, a shadow moving in the room, caused him to look up. He saw his own alarmed reflection in the dark window and he saw someone standing behind him – a pale, silvery face with a mass of shining hair around it.

Mr Norrell did not turn but instead addressed the reflection in the window in a bitter, angry tone. "When you said that you would take half the young lady's life, I thought you would permit her to remain with her friends and family for half seventy-five years. I thought it would appear as if she had simply died!"

"I never said so."

"You cheated me! You have not helped me at all! You risk undoing everything by your tricks!" cried Mr Norrell.

The person in the window made a sound of disapproval. "I had hoped that I would find you more reasonable at our second meeting. Instead you are full of arrogance and unreasonable anger against me! *I* have kept to the terms of our agreement! I have done what you asked and taken nothing that was not mine to take! If you were truly concerned for the happiness of Lady Pole, you would rejoice that she is now placed among friends who truly admire and esteem her!"

"Oh! As to that," said Mr Norrell, scornfully, "I do not care one way or the other. What is the fate of one young woman compared to the success of English magic? No, it is her husband that concerns me – the man for whom I did all this! He is brought quite low by your treachery. Supposing he should not recover! Supposing he were to resign from Government! I might never find another ally so willing to help me.[3] I shall certainly never again have a Minister so much in my debt!"

"Her husband, is it? Well, then I shall raise him up to some lofty position! I shall make him much greater than any thing he could achieve by his own efforts. He shall be Prime Minister. Or Emperor of Great Britain perhaps? Will that suit you?"

"No, no!" cried Mr Norrell. "You do not understand! I merely want him to be pleased with me and to talk to the other Ministers and to persuade them of the great good that my magic can do the country!"

"It is entirely mysterious to me," declared the person in the window, haughtily, "why you should prefer the help of this person to mine! What does he know of magic? Nothing! *I* can teach you to raise up mountains and crush your enemies beneath them! I can make the clouds sing at your approach. I can make it spring when you arrive and winter when you leave. I can . . ."

"Oh, yes! And all you want in return is to shackle English magic to your whims! You will steal Englishmen and women away from

[3] It is clear from this remark that Mr Norrell did not yet comprehend how highly the Ministers in general regarded him nor how eager they were to make use of him in the war.

their homes and make England a place fit only for your degenerate race! The price of your help is too high for me!"

The person in the window did not reply directly to these accusations. Instead a candlestick suddenly leapt from its place on a little table and flew across the room, shattering a mirror on the opposite wall and a little china bust of Thomas Lanchester.

Then all was quiet.

Mr Norrell sat in a state of fright and trembling. He looked down at the books spread out upon his desk, but if he read, then it was in a fashion known only to magicians, for his eye did not travel over the page. After an interval of several minutes he looked up again. The person reflected in the window was gone.

Everyone's plans concerning Lady Pole came to nothing. The marriage – which for a few short weeks had seemed to promise so much to both partners – lapsed into indifference and silence upon her part and into anxiety and misery upon his. Far from becoming a leader of the fashionable world, she declined to go any where. No one visited her and the fashionable world very soon forgot her.

The servants at Harley-street grew reluctant to enter the room where she sat, though none of them could have said why. The truth was that there hung about her the faintest echo of a bell. A chill wind seemed to blow upon her from far away and caused any one who came near her to shiver. So she sat, hour after hour, wrapped in her shawl, neither moving nor speaking, and bad dreams and shadows gathered about her.

# 19

# The Peep-O'Day-Boys

## February 1808

CURIOUSLY, NO ONE noticed that the strange malady that afflicted her ladyship was to a precision the same as that which afflicted Stephen Black. He too complained of feeling tired and cold, and on the rare occasions that either of them said any thing, they both spoke in a low, exhausted manner.

But perhaps it was not so curious. The different styles of life of a lady and a butler tend to obscure any similarities in their situations. A butler has his work and must do it. Unlike Lady Pole, Stephen was not suffered to sit idly by the window, hour after hour, without speaking. Symptoms that were raised to the dignity of an illness in Lady Pole were dismissed as mere low spirits in Stephen.

John Longridge, the cook at Harley-street, had suffered from low spirits for more than thirty years, and he was quick to welcome Stephen as a newcomer to the freemasonry of melancholy. He seemed glad, poor fellow, of a companion in woe. In the evenings when Stephen would sit at the kitchen table with his head buried in his hands, John Longridge would come and sit down on the other side of the table, and begin commiserating with him.

"I condole with you, sir, indeed I do. Low spirits, Mr Black, are the very worst torment that a man can be afflicted with. Sometimes it seems to me that all of London resembles nothing so much as cold pease porridge, both in colour and consistency. I see people with cold-pease-porridge faces and cold-pease-porridge hands walking down cold-pease-porridge streets. Ah, me! How bad I feel then! The very sun up in the sky is cold and grey and porridge-y, and has no power to warm me. Do you often feel chilled, sir?" John Longridge would lay his hand upon Stephen's hand. "Ah, Mr Black, sir," he would say, "you are cold as the tomb."

Stephen felt he was like a person sleepwalking. He did not live any more; he only dreamed. He dreamed of the house in Harley-street and of the other servants. He dreamed of his work and his friends and of Mrs Brandy. Sometimes he dreamed of things that were very strange – things that he knew, in some small, chilly, far-off part of himself, ought not to be. He might be walking along a hallway or up the stairs in the house in Harley-street and he would turn and see other hallways and staircases leading off into the distance – hallways and staircases which did not belong there. It would be as if the house in Harley-street had accidentally got lodged inside a much larger and more ancient edifice. The passageways would be stone-vaulted and full of dust and shadows. The stairs and floors would be so worn and uneven that they would more resemble stones found in nature than architecture. But the strangest thing of all about these ghostly halls was that they would be quite familiar to Stephen. He did not understand why or how, but he would catch himself thinking, "Yes, just beyond that corner is the Eastern Armoury." Or, "Those stairs lead to the Disemboweller's Tower."

Whenever he saw these passageways or, as he sometimes did, sensed their presence without actually perceiving them, then he would feel a little more lively, a little more like his old self. Whatever part of him it was that had frozen up (his soul? his heart?) unfroze itself the merest hair's breadth and thought, curiosity and feeling began to pulse again within him. But for the rest nothing amused him; nothing satisfied him. All was shadows, emptiness, echoes and dust.

Sometimes his restless spirit would cause him to go on long, solitary wanders through the dark winter streets around Mayfair and Piccadilly. On one such evening in late February he found himself outside Mr Wharton's coffee-house in Oxford-street. It was a place he knew well. The upper-room was home to the Peep-O'Day-Boys, a club for the grander sort of male servants in London's grand houses. Lord Castlereagh's valet was a notable member; the Duke of Portland's coachman was another and so was Stephen. The Peep-O'Day-Boys met upon the third Tuesday of every month and enjoyed the same pleasures as the members of any other London club – they drank and ate, gambled, talked politics and gossiped about their mistresses. On other evenings of the month it was the habit of Peep-O'Day-Boys who happened to find themselves disengaged to repair to the upper-room of Mr Wharton's coffee-house, there to refresh their spirits with the society of their fellows. Stephen went inside and mounted the stairs to the upper-room.

This apartment was much like the corresponding part of any similar establishment in the city. It was as full of tobacco smoke as such resorts of the masculine half of society usually are. It was panelled in dark wood. Partitions of the same wood divided off the room into boxes so that customers were able to enjoy being in a little wooden world all their own. The bare floor was kept pleasant with fresh sawdust everyday. White cloths covered the tables and oil-lamps were kept clean and their wicks trimmed. Stephen sat down in one of the boxes and ordered a glass of port which he then proceeded to stare at gloomily.

Whenever one of the Peep-O'Day-Boys passed Stephen's box, they would stop for a word with Stephen and he would raise a hand to them in half-hearted salutation, but tonight he did not trouble himself to answer them. This had happened, Oh!, two or three times, when suddenly Stephen heard someone say in a vivid whisper, "You are quite right to pay them no attention! For, when all is said and done, what are they but servants and drudges? And when, with my assistance, you are elevated to your rightful place at the very pinnacle of nobility and greatness, it will be a great comfort to you to remember that you spurned their friendship!" It was only a whisper, yet Stephen heard it most distinctly above the voices and laughter of the Peep-O'Days and other gentlemen. He had the odd idea that, though only a whisper, it could have passed through stone or iron or brass. It could have spoken to you from a thousand feet beneath the earth and you would have still heard it. It could have shattered precious stones and brought on madness.

This was so very extraordinary that for a moment he was roused from his lethargy. A lively curiosity to discover who had spoken took hold of him and he looked around the room but saw no one he did not know. So he stuck his head round the partition and looked into the next box. It contained one person of very striking appearance. He appeared very much at his ease. His arms were resting on the tops of the partition and his booted feet were resting on the table. He had several remarkable features, but the chief among them was a mass of silvery hair, as bright and soft and shining as thistle-down. He winked at Stephen. Then he rose from his own box and came and sat in Stephen's.

"I may as well tell you," he said, speaking in a highly confidential manner, "that this city has not the hundredth part of its former splendour! I have been gravely disappointed since my return. Once upon a time, to look upon London was to look upon a forest of towers and pinnacles and spires. The many-coloured flags and banners that flew from each and every one dazzled the eye! Upon every side one saw stone carvings as delicate as fingerbones and as intricate as flowing water! There were houses ornamented with stone dragons, griffins and lions, symbolizing the wisdom, courage and ferocity of the occupants, while in the gardens of those same houses might be found flesh-and-blood dragons, griffins and lions, locked in strong cages. Their roars, which could be clearly heard in the street, terrified the faint-of-heart. In every church a blessed saint lay, performing miracles hourly at the behest of the populace. Each saint was confined within an ivory casket, which was secreted in a jewel-studded coffin, which in turn was displayed in a magnificent shrine of gold and silver that shone night and day with the light of a thousand wax candles! Every day there was a splendid procession to celebrate one or other of these blessed saints, and London's fame passed from world to world! Of course in those days the citizens of London were wont to come to *me* for advice about the construction of their churches, the arrangement of their gardens, the decoration of their houses. If they were properly respectful in their petitions I would generally give them good counsel. Oh, yes! When London owed its appearance to *me* it was beautiful, noble, peerless. But now . . ."

He made an eloquent gesture, as if he had crumpled London into a ball in his hand and thrown it away. "But how stupid you look when you stare at me so! I have put myself to any amount of trouble to pay you this visit – and you sit there silent and sullen, with your mouth hanging open! You are surprized to see me, I dare say, but that is no reason to forget all your good manners. Of course," he remarked in the manner of someone making a great concession, "Englishmen are often all amazement in my presence – *that* is the most natural thing in the world – but you and I are such friends that I think I have deserved a better welcome than this!"

"Have we met before, sir?" asked Stephen in astonishment. "I have certainly dreamt of you. I dreamt that you and I were together in an immense mansion with endless, dusty corridors!"

" 'Have we met before, sir?' " mocked the gentleman with the thistle-down hair. "Why! What nonsense you talk! As if we had not attended the same feasts and balls and parties every night for weeks and weeks!"

"Certainly in my dreams . . ."

"I had not thought you could be so dull-witted!" cried the gentleman. "Lost-hope is not a *dream*! It is the oldest and most beautiful of my mansions – which are numerous – and it is quite as real as Carlton House.[1] In fact it is a great deal more so! Much of

[1] The London home of the Prince of Wales in Pall Mall.

the future is known to me and I tell you that Carlton House will be levelled to the ground in twenty years' time and the city of London itself will endure, oh!, scarcely another two thousand years, whereas Lost-hope will stand until the next age of the World!" He looked ridiculously pleased with this thought, and indeed it must be said that his natural manner seemed to be one of extreme self-congratulation. "No, it is no dream. You are merely under an enchantment which brings you each night to Lost-hope to join our fairy revels!"

Stephen stared at the gentleman uncomprehendingly. Then, remembering that he must speak or lay himself open to accusations of sullenness and bad manners, he gathered his wits and stammered out, "And . . . And is the enchantment yours, sir?"

"But of course!"

It was clear from the pleased air with which he spoke that the gentleman with the thistle-down hair considered that he had bestowed the greatest of favours upon Stephen by enchanting him. Stephen thanked him politely for it. ". . . although," he added, "I cannot imagine what I have done to deserve such kindness from you. Indeed, I am sure I have done nothing at all."

"Ah!" cried the gentleman, delighted. "Yours are excellent manners, Stephen Black! You could teach the proud English a thing or two about the proper respect that is due to persons of quality. *Your* manners will bring you good luck in the end!"

"And those golden guineas in Mrs Brandy's cash box," said Stephen, "were they yours too?"

"Oh! Have you only just guessed it? But only observe how clever I have been! Remembering all that you told me about how you are surrounded night and day by enemies who wish you harm, I conveyed the money to a friend of yours. Then when you and she marry, the money will be yours."

"How did . . . ." began Stephen and stopt. Clearly there was no part of his life that the gentleman did not know about and nothing with which the gentleman did not feel entitled to interfere. "But you are mistaken about my enemies, sir," he said, "I do not have any."

"My dear Stephen!" cried the gentleman, greatly amused, "*Of course* you have enemies! And the chief among them is that wicked man who is your master and Lady Pole's husband! He forces you to be his servant and do his bidding night and day. He sets tasks before you that are entirely unsuited to a person of your beauty and nobility. And why does he do these things?"

"I suppose because . . ." began Stephen.

"Precisely!" declared the gentleman triumphantly. "Because in the fulsomeness of his wickedness he has captured you and girded you with chains and now he triumphs over you, dancing about and howling with wicked laughter to see you in such straits!"

Stephen opened his mouth to protest that Sir Walter Pole had never done any of those things; that he had always treated Stephen with great kindness and affection; that when Sir Walter was younger he had paid money he could ill afford so that Stephen could go to school; and that later, when Sir Walter was poorer still, they had often eaten the same food and shared the same fire. As for triumphing over his enemies, Stephen had often seen Sir Walter wear a very self-satisfied smirk when he believed he had scored a point against his political opponents, but he had never seen him dance about or howl with wicked laughter. Stephen was about to say these things, when the mention of the word "chains" seemed to send a sort of silent thunderbolt through him. Suddenly in his fancy he saw a dark place – a terrible place – a place full of horror – a hot, rank, closed-in place. There were shadows in the darkness and the slither and clank of heavy iron chains. What this image meant or where it had come from he had not the least idea. He did not think it could be a memory. Surely he had never been in such a place?

". . . If he ever were to discover that every night you and she escape from him to be happy in my house, why! he would be thrown instantly into fits of jealousy and would, I dare say, try to kill you both. But fear not, my dear, dear Stephen! I will take good care he never finds out. Oh! How I detest such selfish people! *I* know what it is to be scorned and slighted by the proud English and put to perform tasks that are beneath one's dignity. I cannot bear to see the same fate befall you!" The gentleman paused to caress Stephen's cheek and brow with his icy white fingers, which produced a queer tingling sensation in Stephen's skin. "You cannot conceive what a warm interest I feel in you and how anxious I am to do you some lasting service! – which is why I have conceived a plan to make you the king of some fairy kingdom!"

"I . . . I beg your pardon, sir. I was thinking of something else. A king, you say? No, sir. I could not be a king. It is only your great kindness to me that makes you think it possible. Besides I am very much afraid that fairyland does not quite agree with me. Ever since I first visited your house I have been stupid and heavy. I am tired morning, noon and night and my life is a burden to me. I dare say the fault is all mine, but perhaps mortals are not formed for fairy bliss?"

"Oh! That is simply the sadness you feel at the dreariness of England compared to the delightful life you lead at my house where there is always dancing and feasting and everyone is dressed in their finest clothes!"

"I dare say you are right, sir, yet if you were to find it in your heart to release me from this enchantment, I should be very grateful to you."

"Oh! But that is impossible!" declared the gentleman. "Do you not know that my beautiful sisters and cousins – for each of whom, I may say, kings have killed each other and great empires fallen into decay – all quarrel over who will be your next dancing-partner? And what would they say if I told them you would come to Lost-hope no more? For amongst my many other virtues I am a most attentive brother and cousin and always try to please the females in my household when I can. And as for declining to become a king, there is nothing, I assure you, more agreeable than having everyone bow before one and call one by all sorts of noble titles."

He resumed his extravagant praises of Stephen's beauty, dignified countenance and elegant dancing – all of which he seemed to consider the chief qualifications for the ruler of a vast kingdom in Faerie – and he began to speculate upon which kingdom would suit Stephen best. "Untold-Blessings is a fine place, with dark, impenetrable forests, lonely mountains and uncrossable seas. It has the advantage of being without a ruler at present – but then it has the disadvantage that there are twenty-six other claimants already and you would be plunged straightaway into the middle of a bloody civil war – which perhaps you would not care for? Then there is the Dukedom of Pity-Me. The present Duke has no friends to speak of. Oh, but I could not bear to see any friend of mine ruler of such a miserable little place as Pity-Me!"

# 20

# The unlikely milliner

## February 1808

THOSE PEOPLE WHO had expected the war to be over now that the magician had appeared upon the scene were soon disappointed. "Magic!" said Mr Canning, the Foreign Secretary. "Do not speak to me of magic! It is just like everything else, full of setbacks and disappointments."

There was some justice in this, and Mr Norrell was always happy to give long, difficult explanations of why something was not possible. Once, in making one of these explanations, he said something which he later regretted. It was at Burlington House and Mr Norrell was explaining to Lord Hawkesbury, the Home Secretary,[1] that something or other could not be attempted since it would take, oh!, at least a dozen magicians working day and night. He made a long, tedious speech about the pitiful state of English magic, ending, "I would it were otherwise but, as your lordship is aware, our talented young men look to the Army, the Navy and the Church for their careers. My own poor profession is sadly neglected." And he gave a great sigh.

Mr Norrell meant nothing much by this, except perhaps to draw attention to his own extraordinary talent, but unfortunately Lord Hawkesbury took up quite another idea.

---

[1] Robert Banks Jenkinson, Lord Hawkesbury (1770–1828). On the death of his father in December 1808 he became the Earl of Liverpool. For the next nine years he would prove to be one of Mr Norrell's most steady supporters.

"Oh!" he cried. "You mean we need more magicians? Oh, yes! I quite see that. Quite. A school perhaps? Or a Royal Society under His Majesty's patronage? Well, Mr Norrell, I really think we will leave the details to you. If you will be so good as to draw up a memorandum upon the subject I shall be glad to read it and submit its proposals to the other Ministers. We all know your skill at drawing up such things, so clear and so detailed and your handwriting so good. I dare say, sir, we shall find you a little money from somewhere. When you have time, sir. There is no hurry. I know how busy you are."

Poor Mr Norrell! Nothing could be less to his taste than the creation of other magicians. He comforted himself with the thought that Lord Hawkesbury was an exemplary Minister, devoted to business, with a thousand and one things to think about. Doubtless he would soon forget all about it.

But the very next time that Mr Norrell was at Burlington House Lord Hawkesbury came hurrying up to him, crying out, "Ah! Mr Norrell! I have spoken to the King about your plan for making new magicians. His Majesty was very pleased, thought the idea an excellent one and asked me to tell you that he will be glad to extend his patronage to the scheme."

It was fortunate that before Mr Norrell could reply, the sudden arrival of the Swedish Ambassador in the room obliged his lordship to hurry away again.

But a week or so later Mr Norrell met Lord Hawkesbury again, this time at a special dinner given by the Prince of Wales in honour of Mr Norrell at Carlton House. "Ah! Mr Norrell, there you are! I don't suppose that you have the recommendations for the Magicians School about you? Only I have just been speaking to the Duke of Devonshire and he is most interested – thinks he has a house in Leamington Spa which would be just the thing and has asked me questions about the curriculum and whether there would be prayers and where the magicians would sleep – all sorts of things I have not the least idea about. I wonder – would you be so kind as to speak to him? He is just over there by the mantelpiece – he has seen us – he is coming this way. Your Grace, here is Mr Norrell ready to tell you all about it!"

It was with some difficulty that Mr Norrell was able to convince Lord Hawkesbury and the Duke of Devonshire that a school would take up far too much time and moreover he had yet to see any young men with sufficient talent to make the attempt worthwhile. Reluctantly his Grace and his lordship were obliged to agree and Mr Norrell was able to turn his attention to a far more agreeable project: that of destroying the magicians already in existence.

The street-sorcerers of the City of London had long constituted a standing irritation of his spirits. While he was still unknown and unregarded, he had begun to petition members of the Government and other eminent gentlemen for the removal of these vagabond magicians. Naturally, the moment that he attained public eminence he doubled and tripled his efforts. His first idea was that magic ought to be regulated by the Government and magicians ought to be licensed (though naturally he had no idea of any one being licensed but himself). He proposed that a proper regulatory Board of Magic be established, but in this he was too ambitious.

As Lord Hawkesbury said to Sir Walter; "We have no wish to offend a man who has done the country such service, but in the middle of a long and difficult war to demand that a Board be set up with Privy Councillors and Secretaries and Lord knows what else! And for what? To listen to Mr Norrell talk and to pay Mr Norrell compliments! It is quite out of the question. My dear Sir Walter, persuade him to some other course, I beg you."

So the next time that Sir Walter and Mr Norrell met (which was at Mr Norrell's house in Hanover-square) Sir Walter addressed his friend with the following words.

"It is an admirable purpose, sir, and no one quarrels with it, but a Board is precisely the wrong way of going about it. Within the City of London – which is where the problem chiefly lies – the

Board would have no authority. I tell you what we shall do; tomorrow you and I shall go to the Mansion House to wait upon the Lord Mayor and one or two of the aldermen. I think we shall soon find some friends for our cause."

"But, my dear Sir Walter!" cried Mr Norrell. "It will not do. The problem is not confined to London. I have looked into it since I left Yorkshire . . ." (Here he delved about in a pile of papers upon a little table at his elbow to fetch out a list.) "There are twelve street-sorcerers in Norwich, two in Yarmouth, two in Gloucester, six in Winchester, *forty-two* in Penzance! Why! Only the other day, one – a dirty female – came to my house and would not be satisfied without seeing me, whereupon she demanded that I give her a paper – a certificate of competence, no less! – testifying to my belief that she could do magic. I was never more astonished in my life! I said to her, 'Woman . . .' "

"As to the other places that you mention," said Sir Walter, interrupting hastily. "I think you will find that once London rids itself of this nuisance then the others will be quick to follow. They none of them like to feel themselves left behind."

Mr Norrell soon found that it was just as Sir Walter had predicted. The Lord Mayor and the aldermen were eager to be part of the glorious revival of English magic. They persuaded the Court of Common Council to set up a Committee for Magical Acts and the Committee decreed that only Mr Norrell was permitted to do magic within the City boundaries and that other persons who "set up booths or shops, or otherwise molested the citizens of London with claims to do magic" were to be expelled forthwith.

The street-sorcerers packed up their little stalls, loaded their shabby possessions into handcarts and trudged out of the City. Some took the trouble to curse London as they left, but by and large they bore the change in their fortunes with admirable philosophy. Most had simply settled it in their own minds that henceforth they would give up magic and become instead beggars and thieves and, since they had indulged in beggary and thievery in an amateur way for years, the wrench was not so great as you might imagine.

But one did not go. Vinculus, the magician of Threadneedle-street, stayed in his booth and continued to foretell unhappy futures and to sell petty revenges to slighted lovers and resentful apprentices. Naturally, Mr Norrell complained very vigorously to the Committee for Magical Acts about this state of affairs since Vinculus was the sorcerer whom he hated most. The Committee for Magical Acts dispatched beadles and constables to threaten Vinculus with the stocks but Vinculus paid them no attention, and he was so popular among London's citizens that the Committee feared a riot if he was removed by force.

On a bleak February day Vinculus was in his magician's booth beside the church of St Christopher Le Stocks. In case there are any readers who do not remember the magicians' booths of our childhood, it ought to be stated that in shape the booth rather resembled a Punch and Judy theatre or a shopkeeper's stall at a fair and that it was built of wood and canvas. A yellow curtain, ornamented to half its height with a thick crust of dirt, served both as a door and as a sign to advertise the services that were offered within.

On this particular day Vinculus had no customers and very little hope of getting any. The City streets were practically deserted. A bitter grey fog that tasted of smoke and tar hung over London. The City shopkeepers had heaped coals upon their fires and lit every lamp they possessed in a vain attempt to dispel the dark and the cold, but today their bow windows cast no cheerful glow into the streets: the light could not penetrate the fog. Consequently no one was enticed into the shops to spend money and the shopmen in their long white aprons and powdered wigs stood about at their ease, chatting to each other or warming themselves at the fire. It was a day when any one with something to do indoors stayed indoors to do it, and any one who was obliged to go outside did so quickly and got back inside again as soon as he could.

Vinculus sat gloomily behind his curtain half frozen to death, turning over in his mind the names of the two or three ale-house-keepers who might be persuaded to sell him a glass or two of hot spiced wine on credit. He had almost made up his mind which of them to try first when the sounds of someone stamping their feet and blowing upon their fingers seemed to suggest that a customer stood without. Vinculus raised the curtain and stepped outside.

"Are you the magician?"

Vinculus agreed a little suspiciously that he was (the man had the air of a bailiff).

"Excellent. I have a commission for you."

"It is two shillings for the first consultation."

The man put his hand in his pocket, pulled out his purse and put two shillings into Vinculus's hand.

Then he began to describe the problem that he wished Vinculus to magic away. His explanation was very clear and he knew exactly what it was that he wished Vinculus to do. The only problem was that the more the man talked, the less Vinculus believed him. The man said that he had come from Windsor. That was perfectly possible. True, he spoke with a northern accent, but there was nothing odd in that; people often came down from the northern counties to make their fortunes. The man also said he was the owner of a successful millinery business – now that seemed a good deal less likely, for any one less like a milliner it was difficult to imagine. Vinculus knew little enough about milliners but he did know that they generally dress in the very height of fashion. This fellow wore an ancient black coat that had been patched and mended a dozen times. His linen, though clean and of a good quality, would have been old-fashioned twenty years ago. Vinculus did not know the names of the hundred and one little fancy articles that milliners make, but he knew that milliners know them. This man did not; he called them "fol-de-lols".

In the freezing weather the ground had become an unhappy compound of ice and frozen mud and as Vinculus was writing down the particulars in a greasy little book, he somehow missed his footing and fell against the unlikely milliner. He tried to stand but so treacherous was the icy ground that he was obliged to use the other man as a sort of ladder to climb up. The unlikely milliner looked rather appalled to have strong fumes of ale and cabbage breathed in his face and bony fingers grabbing him all over, but he said nothing.

"Beg pardon," muttered Vinculus, when at last he was in an upright position again.

"Granted," said the unlikely milliner politely, brushing from his coat the stale crumbs, gobbets of matted grease and dirt and other little signs of Vinculus having been there.

Vinculus too was adjusting his clothes which had got somewhat disarranged in his tumble.

The unlikely milliner continued with his tale.

"So, as I say, my business thrives and my bonnets are the most sought-after in all of Windsor and scarcely a week goes by but one of the Princesses up at the Castle comes to order a new bonnet or fol-de-lol. I have put a great golden plaster image of the Royal Arms above my door to advertise the royal patronage I enjoy. Yet still I cannot help but think that millinery is a great deal of work. Sitting up late at night sewing bonnets, counting my money and so forth. It seems to me that my life might be a great deal easier if one of the Princesses were to fall in love with me and marry me. Do you have such a spell, Magician?"

"A love spell? Certainly. But it will be expensive. I generally charge four shillings for a spell to catch a milkmaid, ten shillings for a seamstress and six guineas for a widow with her own business. A Princess . . . Hmm." Vinculus scratched his unshaven cheek with his dirty fingernails. "Forty guineas," he hazarded.

"Very well."

"And which is it?" asked Vinculus.

"Which what is what?" asked the unlikely milliner.

"Which Princess?"

"They are all pretty much the same, aren't they? Does the price vary with the Princess?"

"No, not really. I will give you the spell written upon a piece of paper. Tear the paper in two and sew half inside the breast of your coat. You need to place the other half in a secret place inside the garments of whichever Princess you decide upon."

The unlikely milliner looked astonished. "And how in the world can I do that?"

Vinculus looked at the man. "I thought you just said that you sewed their bonnets?"

The unlikely milliner laughed. "Oh yes! Of course."

Vinculus stared at the man suspiciously. "You are no more a milliner than I am a . . . a . . ."

"A magician?" suggested the unlikely milliner. "You must certainly admit that it is not your only profession. After all you just picked my pockets."

"Only because I wished to know what sort of villain you are," retorted Vinculus, and he shook his arm until the articles he had taken from the pockets of the unlikely milliner fell out of his sleeve. There were a handful of silver coins, two golden guineas and three or four folded sheets of paper. He picked up the papers.

The sheets were small and thick and of excellent quality. They were all covered in close lines of small, neat handwriting. At the top of the first sheet was written, *Two Spells to Make an Obstinate Man leave London and One Spell to Discover what My Enemy is doing Presently*.

"The magician of Hanover-square!" declared Vinculus.

Childermass (for it was he) nodded.

Vinculus read through the spells. The first was intended to make the subject believe that every London churchyard was haunted by the people who were buried there and that every bridge was haunted by the suicides who had thrown themselves from it. The subject would see the ghosts as they had appeared at their deaths with all the marks of violence, disease and extreme old age upon them. In this way he would become more and more terrified until he dared not pass either a bridge or a church – which in London is a serious inconvenience as the bridges are not more than a hundred yards apart and the churches considerably less. The second spell was intended to persuade the subject that he would find his one true love and all sorts of happiness in the country and the third spell – the one to discover what your enemy was doing – involved a mirror and had presumably been intended by Norrell to enable Childermass to spy upon Vinculus.

Vinculus sneered. "You may tell the Mayfair magician that his spells have no effect upon me!"

"Indeed?" said Childermass, sarcastically. "Well, that is probably because I have not cast them."

Vinculus flung the papers down upon the ground. "Cast them now!" He folded his arms in an attitude of defiance and made his eyes flash as he did whenever he conjured the Spirit of the River Thames.

"Thank you, but no."

"And why not?"

"Because, like you, I do not care to be told how to conduct my business. My master has ordered me to make sure that you leave London. But I intend to do it in my way, not his. Come, I think it will be best if you and I have a talk, Vinculus."

Vinculus thought about this. "And could this talk take place somewhere warmer? An ale-house perhaps?"

"Certainly if you wish."

The papers with Norrell's spells upon them were blowing about their feet. Vinculus stooped down, gathered them together and, paying no regard to the bits of straw and mud sticking to them, put them in the breast of his coat.

# 21

# The cards of Marseilles

## February 1808

THE ALE-HOUSE WAS called the Pineapple and had once been the refuge and hiding-place of a notorious thief and murderer. This thief had had an enemy, a man as bad as himself. The thief and his enemy had been partners in some dreadful crime, but the thief had kept both shares of the spoils and sent a message to the magistrates telling them where his enemy might be found. As soon as the enemy had escaped from Newgate, he had come to the Pineapple in the dead of night with thirty men. He had set them to tear the slates off the roof and unpick the very bricks of walls until he could reach inside and pluck out the thief. No one had seen what happened next but many had heard the dreadful screams issuing from the pitch-black street. The landlord had discovered that the Pineapple's dark reputation was good for business and consequently he had never troubled to mend his house, other than by applying timber and pitch to the holes, which gave it the appearance of wearing bandages as if it had been fighting with its neighbours.

Three greasy steps led down from the street-door into a gloomy parlour. The Pineapple had its own particular perfume, compounded of ale, tobacco, the natural fragrance of the customers and the unholy stink of the Fleet River, which had been used as a sewer for countless years. The Fleet ran beneath the Pineapple's foundations and the Pineapple was generally supposed to be sinking into it. The walls of the parlour were ornamented with cheap engravings – portraits of famous criminals of the last century who had all been hanged and portraits of the King's dissolute sons who had not been hanged yet.

Childermass and Vinculus sat down at a table in a corner. A shadowy girl brought a cheap tallow candle and two pewter tankards of hot spiced ale. Childermass paid.

They drank in silence a while and then Vinculus looked up at Childermass. "What was all that nonsense about bonnets and princesses?"

Childermass laughed. "Oh, that was just a notion I had. Ever since the day you appeared in his library my master has been petitioning all his great friends to help him destroy you. He asked Lord Hawkesbury and Sir Walter Pole to complain to the King on his behalf. I believe he had an idea that His Majesty might send the Army to make war upon you, but Lord Hawkesbury and Sir Walter said that the King was unlikely to put himself to a great deal of trouble over one yellow-curtained, ragged-arsed sorcerer. But it occurred to me that if His Majesty were to learn that you had somehow threatened the virgin state of his daughters, he might take a different view of the matter."[1] Childermass took another draught of his spiced ale. "But tell me, Vinculus, don't you tire of fake spells and pretend oracles? Half your customers come to laugh at you. They no more believe in your magic than you do. Your day is over. There is a real magician in England now."

Vinculus gave a little snort of disgust. "The magician of Hanover-square! All the great men in London sit telling one another that they never saw a man so honest. But I know magicians and I

---

[1] The King was a most loving and devoted father to his six daughters, but his affection was such that it led him to act almost as if he were their jailer. He could not bear the thought that any of them might marry and leave him. They were required to lead lives of quite intolerable dullness with the ill-tempered Queen at Windsor Castle. Out of the six only one contrived to get married before she was forty.

know magic and I say this: all magicians lie and this one more than most."

Childermass shrugged as if he would not trouble to deny it.

Vinculus leaned forward across the table. "*Magic shall be written on the faces of the stony hills, but their minds shall not be able to contain it. In winter the barren trees shall be a black writing but they shall not understand it.*"

"Trees and hills, Vinculus? When did you last see a tree or a hill? Why don't you say that magic is written on the faces of the dirty houses or that the smoke writes magic in the sky?"

"It is not my prophecy!"

"Ah, yes. Of course. You claim it as a prophecy of the Raven King. Well there is nothing unusual in that. Every charlatan I ever met was the bearer of a message from the Raven King."

"*I sit upon a black throne in the shadows*," muttered Vinculus, "*but they shall not see me. The rain shall make a door for me and I shall pass through it.*"

"Quite. So, since you did not write this prophecy yourself, where did you find it?"

For a moment Vinculus looked as if he would not answer, but then he said, "It is written in a book."

"A book? What book? My master's library is extensive. He knows of no such prophecy."

Vinculus said nothing.

"Is it your book?" asked Childermass.

"It is in my keeping."

"And where did *you* get a book? Where did you steal it?"

"I did not steal it. It is my inheritance. It is the greatest glory and the greatest burden that has been given to any man in this Age."

"If it is really valuable then you can sell it to Norrell. He has paid great prices for books before now."

"The magician of Hanover-square will never own this book. He will never even see it."

"And where do you keep such a great treasure?"

Vinculus laughed coldly as if to say it was not very likely that he would tell that to the servant of his enemy.

Childermass called to the girl to bring them some more ale. She brought it and they drank for a while longer in silence. Then Childermass took a pack of cards from the breast of his coat and shewed them to Vinculus. "The cards of Marseilles. Did you ever see their like before?"

"Often," said Vinculus, "but yours are different."

"They are copies of a set belonging to a sailor I met in Whitby. He bought them in Genoa with the intention of using them to discover the hiding places of pirates' gold, but when he came to look at them, he found that he could not understand them. He offered to sell them to me, but I was poor and could not pay the price he asked. So we struck a bargain: I would tell him his fortune and in return he would lend me the cards long enough to make copies. Unfortunately his ship set sail before I was able to complete the drawings and so half are done from memory."

"And what fortune did you tell him?"

"His true one. That he would be drowned dead before the year was out."

Vinculus laughed approvingly.

It seemed that when Childermass had made the bargain with the dead sailor he had been too poor even to afford paper and so the cards were drawn upon the backs of ale-house bills, laundry lists, letters, old accounts and playbills. At a later date he had pasted the papers on to coloured cardboard, but in several instances the printing or writing on the other side shewed through, giving them an odd look.

Childermass laid out nine cards in a line. He turned over the first card.

Beneath the picture was a number and a name: *VIIII. L'Ermite*. It shewed an old man in a monkish robe with a monkish hood. He carried a lantern and walked with a stick as if he had come near to losing the use of his limbs through too much sitting and studying. His face was pinched and suspicious. A dry atmosphere seemed to rise up and envelop the observer as if the card itself were peppery with dust.

"Hmm!" said Childermass . "For the present your actions are governed by a hermit. Well, we knew that already."

The next card was *Le Mat*, which is the only picture card to remain numberless, as if the character it depicts is in some sense outside the story. Childermass's card shewed a man walking along a road beneath a summer tree. He had a stick to lean upon and another stick over his shoulder with a handkerchief bundle hanging from it. A little dog skipped after him. The figure was intended to represent the fool or jester of ancient times. He had a bell in his hat and ribbons at his knees which Childermass had coloured red and green. It appeared that Childermass did not know quite how to interpret this card. He considered a while and then turned over the next two cards: *VIII. La Justice*, a crowned woman holding a sword and a pair of scales; and *The Two of Wands*. The wands were crossed and might among other things be thought to represent a crossroads.

Childermass let out a brief burst of laughter. "Well, well!" he said, crossing his arms and regarding Vinculus with some amusement. "This card here," he tapped *La Justice*, "tells me you have weighed your choices and come to a decision. And this one," he indicated *The Two of Wands*. "tells me what your decision is: you are going wandering. It seems I have wasted my time. You have already made up your mind to leave London. So many protestations, Vinculus, and yet you always intended to go!"

Vinculus shrugged, as if to say, what did Childermass expect?

The fifth card was the *Valet de Coupe*, the Page of Cups. One naturally thinks of a page as being a youthful person, but the picture shewed a mature man with bowed head. His hair was shaggy and his beard was thick. In his left hand he carried a heavy cup, yet it could not be that which gave such an odd, strained expression to his countenance – not unless it were the heaviest cup in the world. No, it must be some other burden, not immediately apparent. Owing to the materials which Childermass had been compelled to use to construct his cards this picture had a most peculiar look. It had been drawn upon the back of a letter and the writing shewed through the paper. The man's clothes were a mass of scribble and even his face and hands bore parts of letters.

Vinculus laughed when he saw it as though he recognized it. He gave the card three taps in friendly greeting. Perhaps it was this that made Childermass less certain than he had been before. "You have a message to deliver to someone," he said in an uncertain tone.

Vinculus nodded. "And will the next card shew me this person?" he asked.

"Yes."

"Ah!" exclaimed Vinculus and turned over the sixth card himself.

The sixth card was the *Cavalier de Baton*. The Knight of Wands. A man in a broad-brimmed hat sat upon a horse of a pale colour. The countryside through which he rode was indicated by a few rocks and tufts of grass at his horse's hooves. His clothes were well-made and expensive-looking, but for some inexplicable reason he was carrying a heavy club. Even to call it a club was to make it sounder grander than it was. It was scarcely more than a thick branch torn from a tree or hedge; there were still twigs and leaves protruding from it.

Vinculus picked up the card and studied it carefully.

The seventh card was *The Two of Swords*. Childermass said nothing but immediately turned over the eighth card – *Le Pendv*, The Hanged Man. The ninth card was *Le Monde*, The World. It shewed a naked female figure dancing; in the four corners of the card were an angel, an eagle, a winged bull and a winged lion – the symbols of the evangelists.

"You may expect a meeting," said Childermass, "leading to an ordeal of some sort, perhaps even death. The cards do not say whether you survive or not, but whatever happens, this," he touched the last card, "says that you will achieve your purpose."

"And do you know what I am now?" asked Vinculus.

"Not exactly, but I know more of you than I did."

"You see that I am not like the others," said Vinculus.

"There is nothing here that says you are anything more than a charlatan," said Childermass and he began to collect his cards.

"Wait," said Vinculus, "I will tell your fortune."

Vinculus took the cards and laid out nine. Then he turned them over one by one: *XVIII La Lune*, *XVI La Maison Dieu* reversed, *The Nine of Swords*, *Valet de Baton*, *The Ten of Batons* reversed, *II La Papesse*, *X La Rove de Fortvne*, *The Two of Coins*, *The King of Cups*. Vinculus looked at them. He picked up *La Maison Dieu* and examined it, but he said nothing at all.

Childermass laughed. "You are right, Vinculus. You are not like the others. That is my life – there on the table. But you cannot read it. You are a strange creature – the very reverse of all the magicians of the last centuries. They were full of learning but had no talent. You have talent and no knowledge. You cannot profit by what you see."

Vinculus scratched his long, sallow cheek with his unclean fingernails.

Childermass began again to gather up his cards, but once again Vinculus prevented him and indicated that they should lay out the cards again.

"What?" asked Childermass in surprize. "I have told you your fortune. You have failed to tell me mine. What more is there?"

"I am going to tell his fortune."

"Whose? Norrell's? But you will not understand it."

"Shuffle the cards," said Vinculus, stubbornly.

So Childermass shuffled the cards and Vinculus took nine and laid them out. Then he turned over the first card. *IIII. L'Emperevr*. It shewed a king seated upon a throne in the open air with all the customary kingly accoutrements of crown and sceptre. Childermass leaned forward and examined it.

"What is it?" asked Vinculus.

"I do not seem to have copied this card very well. I never noticed before. The inking is badly done. The lines are thick and smudged so that the Emperor's hair and robe appear almost black. And someone has left a dirty thumbprint over the eagle. The Emperor should be an older man than this. I have drawn a young man. Are you going to hazard an interpretation?"

"No," said Vinculus and indicated by a contemptuous thrust of his chin that Childermass should turn the next card.

*IIII. L'Emperevr.*

There was a short silence.

"That is not possible," said Childermass. "There are not two Emperors in this pack. I know there are not."

If anything the king was younger and fiercer than before. His hair and robes were black and the crown upon his head had become a thin band of pale metal. There was no trace of the thumbprint upon the card, but the great bird in the corner was now decidedly black and it had cast off its eagle-like aspects and settled itself into a shape altogether more English: it had become a raven.

Childermass turned over the third card. *IIII. L'Emperevr.* And the fourth. *IIII. L'Emperevr.* By the fifth the number and name of the card had disappeared, but the picture remained the same: a young, dark-haired king at whose feet strutted a great, black bird. Childermass turned over each and every card. He even examined the remainder of the pack, but in his anxiety to see he fumbled and the cards somehow fell everywhere. Black Kings crowded about Childermass, spinning in the cold, grey air. Upon each card was the same figure with the same pale, unforgiving gaze.

"There!" said Vinculus softly. "That is what you may tell the magician of Hanover-square! That is his past and his present and his future!"

Needless to say when Childermass returned to Hanover-square and told Mr Norrell what had occurred, Mr Norrell was very angry. That Vinculus should continue to defy Mr Norrell was bad

enough; that he should claim to have a book and Mr Norrell not be able read it was considerably worse; but that he should pretend to tell Mr Norrell's fortune and threaten him with pictures of Black Kings was absolutely unbearable.

"He tricked you!" declared Mr Norrell, angrily. "He hid your own cards and supplanted them with a deck of his own. I am amazed you were so taken in!"

"Quite," agreed Mr Lascelles, regarding Childermass coldly.

"Oh, to be sure, Vinculus is nothing but conjuring tricks," agreed Drawlight. "But still I should have liked to have seen it. I am as fond as any thing of Vinculus. I wish you had told me, Mr Childermass, that you were going to see him. I would have come with you."

Childermass ignored Lascelles and Drawlight and addressed Mr Norrell. "Even supposing that he is an able enough conjuror to perform such a trick – which I am very far from allowing – how was he to know I possessed such a thing as a pack of Marseilles cards? How was he to know when you did not?"

"Aye, and it was as well for you that I did not know! Telling fortunes with picture cards – it is everything I despise! Oh, it has been a very ill-managed business from start to finish!"

"And what of this book that the sorcerer claims to have?" asked Lascelles.

"Yes, indeed," said Mr Norrell. "That odd prophecy. I dare say it is nothing, yet there were one or two expressions which suggested great antiquity. I believe it would be best if I examined that book."

"Well, Mr Childermass?" asked Lascelles.

"I do not know where he keeps it."

"Then we suggest you find out."

So Childermass set spies to follow Vinculus and the first and most surprizing discovery they made was that Vinculus was married. Indeed he was a great deal more married than most people. His wives were five in number and they were scattered throughout the various parishes of London and the surrounding towns and villages. The eldest was forty-five and the youngest fifteen and each was entirely ignorant of the existence of the other four. Childermass contrived to meet with each of them in turn. To two of them he appeared in the character of the unlikely milliner; to another he presented himself as a customs officer; for the benefit of the fourth he became a drunken, gambling rogue; and he told the fifth that, though he appeared to the world to be a servant of the great Mr Norrell of Hanover-square, he was in secret a magician himself. Two tried to rob him; one said she would tell him any thing he wanted to know as long as he paid for her gin; one tried to make him go with her to a Methodist prayer meeting; and the fifth, much to everyone's surprize, fell in love with him. But in the end all his playacting was for nothing because none of them were even aware that Vinculus possessed such a thing as a book, let alone where he kept it.

Mr Norrell refused to believe this and in his private study on the second floor he cast spells and peered into a silver dish of water, examining the lodgings of Vinculus's five wives, but nowhere was there any thing resembling a book.

Meanwhile on the floor above, in a little room set aside for his own particular use, Childermass laid out his cards. The cards had all returned to their original form, except for *The Emperevr* who had not shaken off his Raven-Kingish look. Certain cards appeared over and over again, among them *The Ace of Cups* – an ecclesiastical-looking chalice of such elaborate design that it more resembled a walled city on a stalk – and *II. La Papesse*. According to Childermass's way of thinking both these cards stood for something hidden. The suit of Wands also appeared with quite unwonted frequency, but they were always in the higher numbers, the Seven, the Eight, the Nine and Ten. The more Childermass gazed at these rows of wands the more they appeared to him to be lines of writing. Yet at the same time they were a barrier, an obstacle to understanding, and so Childermass came to believe that Vinculus's book, whatever it was, was in an unknown language.

# 22

# The Knight of Wands

## February 1808

JONATHAN STRANGE WAS a very different sort of person from his father. He was not avaricious; he was not proud; he was not ill-tempered and disagreeable. But though he had no striking vices, his virtues were perhaps almost as hard to define. At the pleasure parties of Weymouth and in the drawing-rooms of Bath he was regularly declared to be "the most charming man in the world" by the fashionable people he met there, but all that they meant by this was that he talked well, danced well, and hunted and gambled as much as a gentleman should.

In person he was rather tall and his figure was considered good. Some people thought him handsome, but this was not by any means the universal opinion. His face had two faults: a long nose and an ironic expression. It is also true that his hair had a reddish tinge and, as everybody knows, no one with red hair can ever truly be said to be handsome.

At the time of his father's death he was much taken up with a scheme to persuade a certain young lady to marry him. When he arrived home from Shrewsbury on the day of his father's death and the servants told him the news, his first thoughts were to wonder how his suit would be affected. Was she more likely to say yes now? Or less?

This marriage ought to have been the easiest matter in the world to arrange. Their friends all approved the match and the lady's brother – her only relation – was scarcely less ardent in wishing for it than Jonathan Strange himself. True, Laurence Strange had objected strongly to the lady's poverty, but he had put it out of his power to make any serious difficulty when he froze himself to death.

But, though Jonathan Strange had been the acknowledged suitor of this young lady for some months, the engagement – hourly expected by all their acquaintance – did not follow. It was not that she did not love him; he was quite certain that she did, but sometimes it seemed as if she had fallen in love with him for the sole purpose of quarrelling with him. He was quite at a loss to account for it. He believed that he had done everything she wanted in the way of reforming his behaviour. His card-playing and other sorts of gambling had dwindled away almost to nothing and he drank very little now – scarcely more than a bottle a day. He had told her that he had no objection to going to church more if that would please her – as often, say, as once a week – twice, if she would like it better – but she said that she would leave such matters to his own conscience, that they were not the sort of thing that could be dictated by another person. He knew that she disliked his frequent visits to Bath, Brighton, Weymouth and Cheltenham and he assured her that she had nothing to fear from the women in those places – doubtless they were very charming, but they were nothing to him. She said that was not what concerned her. *That* had not even occurred to her. It was just that she wished he could find a better way to occupy his time. She did not mean to moralize and no one loved a holiday better than her, but perpetual holidays! Was that really what he wanted? Did that make him happy?

He told her that he quite agreed with her and in the past year he had continually been forming plans to take up this or that profession or regular train of study. The plans themselves were very good. He thought he might seek out a destitute poetic genius and become his patron; he thought he would study law; look for fossils on the beach at Lyme Regis; buy an ironworks; study iron-founding; ask a fellow he knew about new methods of agriculture; study theology; and finish reading a fascinating work on engineering which he was almost certain he had put down on a little table at the furthest corner of his father's library two or three years ago. But to each of these projected courses some formidable obstacle was found to exist. Destitute poetic geniuses were harder to come by than he had imagined;[1] lawbooks were dull; he could not remember the name of the fellow who knew about agriculture; and the day that he intended to start for Lyme Regis it was raining heavily.

And so on and so on. He told the young lady that he heartily wished that he had gone into the Navy years ago. Nothing in the world would have suited him so well! But his father would never have agreed to it and he was twenty-eight now. It was far too late to take up a naval career.

The name of this curiously dissatisfied young woman was Arabella Woodhope and she was the daughter of the late curate

---

[1] It appears that Strange did not abandon the notion of a poetical career easily. In *The Life of Jonathan Strange*, pub. John Murray, London, 1820, John Segundus describes how, having been disappointed in his search for a poet, Strange decided to write the poems himself. "Things went very well upon the first day; from breakfast to dinner he sat in his dressing gown at the little writing table in his dressing room and scribbled very fast upon several dozen sheets of quarto. He was very delighted with everything he wrote and so was his valet, who was a literary man himself and who gave advice upon the knotty questions of metaphor and rhetoric, and who ran about gathering up the papers as they flew about the room and putting them in order and then running downstairs to read the most exhilarating parts to his friend, the under-gardener. It really was astonishing how quickly Strange wrote; indeed the valet declared that when he put his hand close to Strange's head he could feel a heat coming off it because of the immense creative energies within. On the second day Strange sat down to write another fifty or so pages and immediately got into difficulties because he could not think of a rhyme for " 'let love suffice'. 'Sunk in vice' was not promising; 'a pair of mice' was nonsense, and 'what's the price?' merely vulgar. He struggled for an hour, could think of nothing, went for a ride to loosen his brains and never looked at his poem again."

of St Swithin's in Clunbury.[2] At the time of Laurence Strange's death she was paying an extended visit to some friends in the Gloucestershire village where her brother was a curate. Her letter of condolence reached Strange on the morning of the funeral. It expressed everything that was proper – sympathy for his loss tempered by an understanding of the elder Mr Strange's many failings as a parent. But there was something more besides. She was concerned about him. She regretted her absence from Shropshire. She did not like him being alone and friendless at such a time.

His mind was made up upon the instant. He could not imagine that he was ever likely to find himself in a more advantageous situation. She would never be more full of anxious tenderness than she was at this moment and he would never be richer. (He could not quite believe that she was as indifferent to his wealth as she claimed.) He supposed he ought to allow a proper interval between his father's funeral and his proposal of marriage. Three days seemed about right, so on the morning of the fourth day he ordered his valet to pack his clothes and his groom to make his horse ready and he set off for Gloucestershire.

He took with him the new manservant. He had spoken at length to this man and had found him to be energetic, resourceful and able. The new manservant was delighted to be chosen (though his vain spirit told him that this was the most natural thing in the world). But now that the new manservant has passed the giant-toppling stage of his career – now that he has, as it were, stepped out of myth and into the workaday world, it will perhaps be found more convenient to give him his name like an ordinary mortal. His name was Jeremy Johns.

Upon the first day they endured nothing but the commonplace adventures which befall any traveller: they quarrelled with a man who set his dog to bark at them for no reason and there was an

[2] A village five or six miles from Strange's home.

alarm about Strange's horse which began to shew signs of being sickly and which then, upon further investigation, was discovered to be in perfect health. On the morning of the second day they were riding through a pretty landscape of gently sloping hills, winter woods and prosperous-looking, tidy farms. Jeremy Johns was occupied in practising the correct degree of haughtiness for the servant of a gentleman newly come into an extensive property and Jonathan Strange was thinking about Miss Woodhope.

Now that the day had arrived when he was to see her again he began to have some doubts of his reception. He was glad to think she was with her brother – dear, good Henry who saw nothing but good in the match and who, Strange was quite certain, never failed to encourage his sister to think favourably of it. But he had some doubts about the friends with whom she was staying. They were a clergyman and his wife. He knew nothing of them, but he had the natural distrust that a young, rich, self-indulgent man feels for members of the clergy. Who could say what notions of extraordinary virtue and unnecessary self-sacrifice they might be daily imparting to her?

The low sun cast immense shadows. Ice and frost sparkled upon the branches of the trees and in hollows of the fields. Catching sight of a man ploughing a field, he was reminded of the families who lived upon his land and whose welfare had always been cause for concern to Miss Woodhope. An ideal conversation began to develop in his head. *And what are your intentions regarding your tenants?* she would ask – *Intentions?* he would say – *Yes*, she would say. *How will you ease their burdens? Your father took every penny he could from them. He made their lives miserable – I know he did*, Strange would say, *I have never defended my father's actions – Have you lowered the rents yet?* she would say. *Have you talked to the parish council? Have you thought about almshouses for the old people and a school for the children?*

"It is really quite unreasonable for her to be talking of rents, almhouses and a school," thought Strange gloomily. "After all, my father only died last Tuesday."

"Well, that is odd!" remarked Jeremy Johns.

"Hmmm?" said Strange. He discovered that they had halted at a white gate. At the side of the road was a neat little white-painted cottage. It was newly built and had six sides and Gothic windows.

"Where is the toll-keeper?" asked Jeremy Johns.

"Hmmm?" said Strange.

"It is a tollhouse, sir. See, there is the board with the list of money to pay. But there is no one about. Shall I leave them sixpence?"

"Yes, yes. As you wish."

So Jeremy Johns left the toll upon the doorstep of the cottage and opened the gate so that Strange and he could pass through. A hundred yards further on they entered a village. There was an ancient stone church with winter's golden light upon it, an avenue of ancient, twisted hornbeams that led somewhere or other, and twenty or so neat stone cottages with smoke rising up from their chimneys. A stream ran by the side of the road. It was bordered by dry, yellow grasses with pendants of ice hanging from them.

"Where are all the people?" said Jeremy.

"What?" said Strange. He looked around and saw two little girls looking out of a cottage window. "There," he said.

"No, sir. Those are children. I meant grown-ups. I do not see any."

This was true; there were none to be seen. There were some chickens strutting about, a cat sitting on some straw in an ancient cart and some horses in a field, but no people. Yet as soon as Strange and Jeremy Johns left the village, the reason for this queer state of affairs became apparent. A hundred yards or so from the last house in the village a crowd was gathered round a winter hedge. They carried an assortment of weapons – billhooks, sickles, sticks and guns. It was a very odd picture, both sinister and a little ridiculous. Any one would have thought that the village had decided to make war upon hawthorn bushes and elder-trees. The low winter sun shone full upon the villagers, gilding their clothes and weapons and their strange, intent expressions. Long, blue shadows streamed behind them. They were completely silent and whenever one of them moved, he did so with great care as though afraid of making a noise.

As they rode by, Strange and Jeremy stood up in the stirrups and craned their necks to catch a glimpse of whatever it was that the villagers were looking at.

"Well, that is odd!" exclaimed Jeremy when they were past. "There was nothing there!"

"No," said Strange, "there was a man. I am not surprized you could not see him. At first I took him for a hedge-root, but it was definitely a man – a grey, gaunt, weather-worn man – a man remarkably like a hedge-root, but a man nevertheless."

The road led them into a dark winter wood. Jeremy John's curiosity had been excited and he wondered who the man could be and what the villagers were intending to do to him. Strange answered once or twice at random, but soon fell to thinking of Miss Woodhope.

"It will be best to avoid discussing the changes brought on by my father's death," he thought. "It is altogether too dangerous. I will begin with light, indifferent subjects – the adventures of this journey for example. Now, what has happened that will amuse her?" He looked up. Dark, dripping trees surrounded him. "There must have been something." He remembered a windmill he had seen near Hereford with a child's red cloak caught up on one of the sails. As the sails turned the cloak was one moment being dragged through the slush and the mud and the next flying through the air like a vivid scarlet flag. "Like an allegory of something or other. Then I can tell her about the empty village and the children at the window peeping out between the curtains, one with a doll in her hand and the other with a wooden horse. Next come the silent crowd with their weapons and the man beneath the hedge."

*Oh!* she was certain to say, *Poor man! What happened to him? – I do not know*, Strange would say. *But surely you stayed to help him*, she would say. *No*, Strange would say. *Oh!*, she would say . . .

"Wait!" cried Strange, reining in his horse. "This will not do at all! We must go back. I do not feel easy in my mind about the man under the hedge."

"Oh!" cried Jeremy Johns, in relief. "I am very glad to hear you say so, sir. Neither am I."

"I don't suppose you thought to bring a set of pistols, did you?" said Strange.

"No, sir."

"D—!" said Strange and then flinched a little, because Miss Woodhope did not approve of oaths. "What about a knife? Something of that sort?"

"No, nothing, sir. But do not fret." Jeremy jumped off his horse and went delving about in the undergrowth. "I can make us some clubs out of these branches which will do almost as well as pistols."

There were some stout branches which someone had cut from a coppice of trees and left lying on the ground. Jeremy picked one up and offered it to Strange. It was scarcely a club, more a branch with twigs growing out of it.

"Well," said Strange, doubtfully, "I suppose that it is better than nothing."

Jeremy equipped himself with another branch just the same, and, thus armed, they rode back to the village and the silent crowd of people.

"You there!" cried Strange, singling out a man dressed in a shepherd's smock with a number of knitted shawls tied over it and a wide-brimmed hat upon his head. He made a few flourishing gestures with his club in what he hoped was a threatening manner. "What . . . ?"

Upon the instant several of the crowd turned together and put their fingers to their lips.

Another man came up to Strange. He was dressed rather more respectably than the first in a coat of brown cord. He touched his fingers to his hat and said very softly, "Beg pardon, sir, but could not you take the horses further off? They stamp their feet and breathe very loud."

"But . . ." began Strange.

"Hush, sir!" whispered the man, "Your voice. It is too loud. You will wake him up!"

"Wake him up? Who?"

"The man under the hedge, sir. He is a magician. Did you never hear that if you wake a magician before his time, you risk bringing his dreams out of his head into the world?"

"And who knows what horrors he is dreaming of!" agreed another man, in a whisper.

"But how . . ." began Strange. Once again several people among the crowd turned and frowned indignantly at him and made signs that he was to speak more softly.

"But how do you know he is a magician?" he whispered.

"Oh! He has been in Monk Gretton for the past two days, sir. He tells everyone he is a magician. On the first day he tricked some of our children into stealing pies and beer from their mothers' larders, saying that they were for the Queen of the Fairies. Yesterday he was found wandering in the grounds of Farwater Hall, which is our great house here, sir. Mrs Morrow – whose property it is – hired him to tell her fortune, but all he said was that her son, Captain Morrow, has been shot dead by the French – and now, poor lady, she has lain down upon her bed and says she will lie there until she dies. And so, sir, we have had enough of this man. We mean to make him go. And if he will not, we shall send him to the workhouse."

"Well, that seems most reasonable," whispered Strange. "But what I do not understand is . . ."

Just at that moment the man under the hedge opened his eyes. The crowd gave a sort of soft, communal gasp and several people took a step or two backwards.

The man extracted himself from the hedge. This was no easy task because various parts of it – hawthorn twigs, elder branches, strands of ivy, mistletoe and witches' broom – had insinuated themselves among his clothes, limbs and hair during the night or glued themselves to him with ice. He sat up. He did not seem in the least surprized to find he had an audience; indeed one would almost have supposed from his behaviour that he had been expecting it. He looked at them all and gave several disparaging sniffs and snorts.

He ran his fingers through his hair, removing dead leaves, bits of twig and half a dozen earwigs. "I reached out my hand," he muttered to no one in particular. "England's rivers turned and flowed the other way." He loosened his neckcloth and fished out some spiders which had taken up residence inside his shirt. In doing so, he revealed that his neck and throat were ornamented with an odd pattern of blue lines, dots, crosses and circles. Then he wrapped his neckcloth back about his neck and, having thus completed his toilet to his satisfaction, he rose to his feet.

"My name is Vinculus," he declared. Considering that he had just spent a night under a hedge his voice was remarkably loud and clear. "For ten days I have been walking westwards in search of a man who is destined to be a great magician. Ten days ago I was shewn a picture of this man and now by certain mystic signs I see that it is you!"

Everyone looked around to see who he meant.

The man in the shepherd's smock and the knitted shawls came up to Strange and plucked at his coat. "It is you, sir," he said.

"Me?" said Strange.

Vinculus approached Strange.

"*Two magicians shall appear in England*," he said.
"*The first shall fear me; the second shall long to behold me;*
*The first shall be governed by thieves and murderers; the second shall conspire at his own destruction;*
*The first shall bury his heart in a dark wood beneath the snow, yet still feel its ache;*
*The second shall see his dearest possession in his enemy's hand . . .*"

"I see," interrupted Strange. "And which am I, the first or the second? No, do not tell me. It does not matter. Both sound entirely dreadful. For someone who is anxious that I should become a magician, I must say you do not make the life sound very appealing. I hope to be married soon and a life spent in dark woods surrounded by thieves and murderers would be inconvenient to say the least. I suggest you chuse someone else."

"I did not chuse you, Magician! You were chosen long ago."

"Well, whoever it was, they will be disappointed."

Vinculus ignored this remark and took a firm grasp of the bridle of Strange's horse as a precaution against his riding off. He then proceeded to recite in its entirety the prophecy which he had already performed for the benefit of Mr Norrell in the library at Hanover-square.

Strange received it with a similar degree of enthusiasm and when it was done, he leant down from his horse and said very slowly and distinctly, "I do not know any magic!"

Vinculus paused. He looked as if he was prepared to concede that this might be a legitimate obstacle to Strange's becoming a great magician. Happily the solution occurred to him immediately; he stuck his hand into the breast of his coat and pulled out some sheets of paper with bits of straw sticking to them. "Now," he said, looking even more mysterious and impressive than before, "I have here some spells which . . . No, no! I cannot *give* them to you!" (Strange had reached out to take them.) "They are precious objects. I endured years of torment and suffered great ordeals in order to possess them."

"How much?" said Strange.

"Seven shillings and sixpence," said Vinculus.

"Very well."

"Surely you do not intend to give him any money, sir?" asked Jeremy Johns.

"If it will stop him talking to me, then, yes, certainly."

Meanwhile the crowd was regarding Strange and Jeremy Johns

in no very friendly manner. Their appearance had coincided more or less with Vinculus's waking and the villagers were starting to wonder if they might not be two apparitions from Vinculus's dreams. The villagers began to accuse one another of having woken Vinculus up. They were just starting to quarrel about it when an official-looking person in an important-looking hat arrived and informed Vinculus that he must go to the workhouse as a pauper. Vinculus retorted that he would do no such thing as he was not a pauper any longer – he had seven shillings and sixpence! And he dangled the money in the man's face in a very impertinent fashion. Just as a fight seemed certain to ensue from one cause or another, peace was suddenly restored to the village of Monk Gretton by the simple expedient of Vinculus turning and walking off one way and Strange and Jeremy Johns riding off another.

Towards five o'clock they arrived at an inn in the village of S— near Gloucester. So little hope had Strange that his meeting with Miss Woodhope would be productive of any thing but misery to them both that he thought he would put it off until the following morning. He ordered a good dinner and went and sat down by the fire in a comfortable chair with a newspaper. But he soon discovered that comfort and tranquillity were poor substitutes for Miss Woodhope's company and so he cancelled the dinner and went immediately to the house of Mr and Mrs Redmond in order to begin being unhappy as soon as possible. He found only the ladies at home, Mrs Redmond and Miss Woodhope.

Lovers are rarely the most rational beings in creation and so it will come as no surprize to my readers to discover that Strange's musings concerning Miss Woodhope had produced a most inexact portrait of her. Though his imaginary conversations might be said to describe her *opinions*, they were no guide at all to her *disposition* and *manners*. It was *not* her habit to harass recently bereaved persons with demands that they build schools and almshouses. Nor did she find fault with everything they said. She was not so unnatural.

She greeted him in a very different manner from the cross, scolding young lady of his imaginings. Far from demanding that he immediately undo every wrong his father had ever done, she behaved with particular kindness towards him and seemed altogether delighted to see him.

She was about twenty-two years of age. In repose her looks were only moderately pretty. There was very little about her face and figure that was in any way remarkable, but it was the sort of face which, when animated by conversation or laughter, is completely transformed. She had a lively disposition, a quick mind and a fondness for the comical. She was always very ready to smile and, since a smile is the most becoming ornament that any lady can wear, she had been known upon occasion to outshine women who were acknowledged beauties in three counties.

Her friend, Mrs Redmond, was a kindly, placid creature of forty-five. She was not rich, widely travelled or particularly clever. Under other circumstances she would have been puzzled to know what to say to a man of the world like Jonathan Strange, but happily his father had just died and that provided a subject.

"I dare say you are a great deal occupied just now, Mr Strange," she said. "I remember when my own father died, there was a world of things to do. He left so many bequests. There were some china jugs that used to stand upon the kitchen mantelpiece at home. My father wished a jug to be given to each of our old servants. But the descriptions of the jugs in his will were most confusing and no one could tell which jug was meant for which person. And then the servants quarrelled and they all desired to be given the yellow jug with pink roses. Oh! I thought I would never be done with those bequests. Did your father leave many bequests, Mr Strange?"

"No, madam. None. He hated everybody."

"Ah! That is fortunate, is it not? And what shall you do now?"

"Do?" echoed Strange.

"Miss Woodhope says your poor, dear father bought and sold things. Shall you do the same?"

"No, madam. If I have my way – and I believe I shall – my father's business will all be wound up as soon as possible."

"Oh! But then I dare say you will be a good deal taken up with farming? Miss Woodhope says your estate is a large one."

"It is, madam. But I have tried farming and I find it does not suit me."

"Ah!" said Mrs Redmond, wisely.

There was a silence. Mrs Redmond's clock ticked and the coals shifted in the grate. Mrs Redmond began to pull about some embroidery silks that lay in her lap and had got into a fearful knot. Then her black cat mistook this activity for a game and stalked along the sopha and tried to catch at the silks. Arabella laughed and caught up the cat and started to play with it. This was exactly the sort of tranquil domestic scene that Strange had set his heart upon (though he did not want Mrs Redmond and was undecided about the cat) and it was all the more desirable in his eyes since he had never met with anything other than coldness and disagreeableness in his childhood home. The question was: how to persuade Arabella that it was what she wanted too? A sort of inspiration came over him and he suddenly addressed Mrs Redmond again. "In short, madam, I do not think that I shall have the time. I am going to study magic."

"Magic!" exclaimed Arabella, looking at him in surprize.

She seemed about to question him further, but at this highly interesting moment Mr Redmond was heard in the hall. He was accompanied by his curate, Henry Woodhope – the same Henry Woodhope who was both brother to Arabella and childhood friend to Jonathan Strange. Naturally there were introductions and explanations to get through (Henry Woodhope had not known Strange was coming) and for the moment Strange's unexpected announcement was forgotten.

The gentlemen were just come from a parish meeting and as soon as everyone was seated again in the drawing-room, Mr Redmond and Henry imparted various items of parish news to

Mrs Redmond and Arabella. Then they inquired about Strange's journey, the state of the roads and how the farmers got on in Shropshire, Herefordshire and Gloucestershire (these being the counties Strange had travelled through). At seven o'clock the tea things were brought in. In the silence that followed, while they were all eating and drinking, Mrs Redmond remarked to her husband, "Mr Strange is going to be a magician, my love." She spoke as if it were the most natural thing in the world, because to her it was.

"A magician?" said Henry, quite astonished. "Why should you want to do that?"

Strange paused. He did not wish to tell his real reason – which was to impress Arabella with his determination to do something sober and scholarly – and so he fell back upon the only other explanation he could think of. "I met a man under a hedge at Monk Gretton who told me that I was a magician."

Mr Redmond laughed, approving the joke. "Excellent!" he said.

"Did you, indeed?" said Mrs Redmond.

"I do not understand," said Henry Woodhope.

"You do not believe me, I suppose?" said Strange to Arabella.

"Oh, on the contrary, Mr Strange!" said Arabella with an amused smile. "It is all of a piece with your usual way of doing things. It is quite as strong a foundation for a career as I should expect from you."

Henry said, "But if you are going to take up a profession – and I cannot see why you should want one at all, now that you have come into your property – surely you can chuse something better than magic! It has no practical application."

"Oh, but I think you are wrong!" said Mr Redmond. "There is that gentleman in London who confounds the French by sending them illusions! I forget his name. What is it that he calls his theory? Modern magic?"

"But how is that different from the old-fashioned sort?" wondered Mrs Redmond. "And which will you do, Mr Strange?"

"Yes, do tell us, Mr Strange," said Arabella, with an arch look. "Which will you do?"

"A little of both, Miss Woodhope. A little of both!" Turning to Mrs Redmond, he said, "I purchased three spells from the man under the hedge. Should you like to see one, madam?"

"Oh, yes, indeed!"

"Miss Woodhope?" asked Strange.

"What are they for?"

"I do not know. I have not read them yet." Jonathan Strange took the three spells Vinculus had given him out of his breast pocket and gave them to her to look at.

"They are very dirty," said Arabella.

"Oh! We magicians do not regard a little dirt. Besides I dare say they are very old. Ancient, mysterious spells such as these are often . . ."

"The date is written at the top of them. 2nd February 1808. That is two weeks ago."

"Indeed? I had not observed."

"*Two Spells to Make an Obstinate Man leave London,*" read Arabella. "I wonder why the magician would want to make people leave London?"

"I do not know. There are certainly too many people in London, but it seems a great deal of work to make them leave one at a time."

"But these are horrible! Full of ghosts and horrors! Making them think that they are about to meet their one true love, when in truth the spell does nothing of the sort!"

"Let me see!" Strange snatched back the offending spells. He examined them rapidly and said, "I promise you I knew nothing of their content when I purchased them – nothing whatsoever. The truth is that the man I bought them from was a vagabond and quite destitute. With the money I gave him he was able to escape the workhouse."

"Well, I am glad of that. But his spells are still horrible and I hope you will not use them."

"But what of the last spell? *One Spell to Discover what My Enemy is doing Presently*. I think you can have no objection to that? Let me do the last spell."

"But will it work? You do not have any enemies, do you?"

"None that I know of. And so there can be no harm in attempting it, can there?"

The instructions called for a mirror and some dead flowers,[3] so Strange and Henry lifted a mirror off the wall and laid it upon the table. The flowers were more difficult; it was February and the only flowers Mrs Redmond possessed were some dried lavender, roses and thyme.

"Will these do?" she asked Strange.

He shrugged. "Who knows? Now . . ." He studied the instructions again. "The flowers must be placed around, like so. And then I draw a circle upon the mirror with my finger like this. And quarter the circle. Strike the mirror thrice and say these words . . ."

"Strange," said Henry Woodhope, "where did you get this nonsense?"

"From the man under the hedge. Henry, you do not listen."

"And he seemed honest, did he?"

"Honest? No, not particularly. He seemed, I would say, cold. Yes, 'cold' is a good word to describe him and 'hungry' another."

"And how much did you pay for these spells?"

"Henry!" said his sister. "Did you not just hear Mr Strange say that he bought them as an act of charity?"

Strange was absent-mindedly drawing circles upon the surface of the mirror and quartering them. Arabella, who was sitting next to him, gave a sudden start of surprize. Strange looked down.

"Good God!" he cried.

---

[3] Mr Norrell appears to have adapted it from a description of a Lancashire spell in Peter Watershippe's *Death's Library* (1448).

In the mirror was the image of a room, but it was not Mrs Redmond's drawing-room. It was a small room, furnished not extravagantly but very well. The ceiling – which was high – gave the idea of its being a small apartment within a large and perhaps rather grand house. There were bookcases full of books and other books lay about on tables. There was a good fire in the fireplace and candles on the desk. A man worked at a desk. He was perhaps fifty and was dressed very plainly in a grey coat. He was a quiet, unremarkable sort of man in an old-fashioned wig. Several books lay open on his desk and he read a little in some and wrote a little in others.

"Mrs Redmond! Henry!" cried Arabella. "Come quickly! See what Mr Strange has done!"

"But who in the world is he?" asked Strange, mystified. He lifted the mirror and looked under it, apparently with the idea that he might discover there a tiny gentleman in a grey coat, ready to be questioned. When the mirror was replaced upon the table the vision of the other room and the other man was still there. They could hear no sounds from the other room but the flames of the fire danced in the grate and the man, with his glinting spectacles on his nose, turned his head from one book to another.

"Why is he your enemy?" asked Arabella.

"I have not the least idea."

"Do you owe him money, perhaps?" asked Mr Redmond.

"I do not *think* so."

"He could be a banker. It looks a little like a counting house," suggested Arabella.

Strange began to laugh. "Well, Henry, you can cease frowning at me. If I am a magician, I am a very indifferent one. Other adepts summon up fairy-spirits and long-dead kings. I appear to have conjured the spirit of a banker."

# Volume II

# JONATHAN STRANGE

"Can a magician kill a man by magic?" Lord Wellington asked Strange. Strange frowned. He seemed to dislike the question. "I suppose a magician might," he admitted, "but a gentleman never could."

# 23

# The Shadow House

## July 1809

On a summer's day in 1809 two riders were travelling along a dusty country lane in Wiltshire. The sky was of a deep, brilliant blue, and beneath it England lay sketched in deep shadows and in hazy reflections of the sky's fierce light. A great horse-chestnut leant over the road and made a pool of black shadow, and when the two riders reached the shadow it swallowed them up so that nothing remained of them except their voices.

". . . and how long will it be before you consider publication?" said one. "For you must, you know. I have been considering the matter and I believe it is the first duty of every modern magician to publish. I am surprized Norrell does not publish."

"I dare say he will in time," said the other. "As to my publishing, who would wish to read what I have written? These days, when Norrell performs a new miracle every week, I cannot suppose that the work of a purely *theoretical* magician would be of much interest to any body."

"Oh! You are too modest," said the first voice. "You must not leave every thing to Norrell. Norrell cannot do every thing."

"But he can. He does," sighed the second voice.

How pleasant to meet old friends! For it is Mr Honeyfoot and Mr Segundus. Yet why do we find them on horseback? – a kind of exercise which agrees with neither of them and which neither takes regularly, Mr Honeyfoot being too old and Mr Segundus too poor. And on such a day as this! So hot that it will make Mr Honeyfoot first sweat, and then itch, and then break out in red pimples; a day of such dazzling brightness that it is certain to bring on one of Mr Segundus's headachs. And what are they doing in Wiltshire?

It had so happened that, in the course of his labours on behalf of the little stone figure and the girl with the ivy-leaves in her hair, Mr Honeyfoot had discovered something. He believed that he had identified the murderer as an Avebury man. So he had come to Wiltshire to look at some old documents in Avebury parish church. "For," as he had explained to Mr Segundus, "if I discover *who* he was, then perhaps it may lead me to discover who was the girl and what dark impulse drove him to destroy her." Mr Segundus had gone with his friend and had looked at all the documents and helped him unpick the old Latin. But, though Mr Segundus loved old documents (no one loved them more) and though he put great faith in what they could achieve, he secretly doubted that seven Latin words five centuries old could explain a man's life. But Mr Honeyfoot was all optimism. Then it occurred to Mr Segundus that, as they were already in Wiltshire, they should take the opportunity to visit the Shadow House which stood in that county and which neither of them had ever seen.

Most of us remember hearing of the Shadow House in our schoolrooms. The name conjures up vague notions of magic and ruins yet few of us have any very clear recollection of why it is so important. The truth is that historians of magic still argue over its significance – and some will be quick to tell you that it is of no significance whatsoever. No great events in English magical history took place there; furthermore, of the two magicians who lived in the house, one was a charlatan and the other was a woman – neither attribute likely to recommend its possessor to the gentleman-magicians and gentleman-historians of recent years – and yet for two centuries the Shadow House has been known as one of the most magical places in England.

It was built in the sixteenth century by Gregory Absalom, court magician to King Henry VIII and to Queens Mary and Elizabeth. If we measure a magician's success by how much magic he does, then Absalom was no magician at all, for his spells hardly ever took effect. However, if instead we examine the amount of money a magician makes and allow that to be our yardstick, then Absalom was certainly one of the greatest English magicians who ever lived, for he was born in poverty and died a very rich man.

One of his boldest achievements was to persuade the King of Denmark to pay a great handful of diamonds for a spell which, Absalom claimed, would turn the flesh of the King of Sweden into water. Naturally the spell did nothing of the sort, but with the money he got for half these jewels Absalom built the Shadow House. He furnished it with Turkey carpets and Venetian mirrors and glass and a hundred other beautiful things; and, when the house was completed, a curious thing happened – or may have happened – or did not happen at all. Some scholars believe – and others do not – that the magic which Absalom had pretended to do for his clients began to appear of its own accord in the house.

On a moonlit night in 1610 two maids looked out of a window on an upper floor and saw twenty or thirty beautiful ladies and handsome gentlemen dancing in a circle on the lawn. In February 1666 Valentine Greatrakes, an Irishman, held a conversation in Hebrew with the prophets Moses and Aaron in a little passageway near the great linen press. In 1667 Mrs Penelope Chelmorton, a visitor to the house, looked in a mirror and saw a little girl of three or four years old looking out. As she watched, she saw the child grow up and grow older and she recognized herself. Mrs Chelmorton's reflection continued to age until there was nought but a dry, dead corpse in the mirror. The reputation of the Shadow House is based upon these and a hundred other such tales.

Absalom had one child, a daughter named Maria. She was born in the Shadow House and lived there all her life, scarcely ever leaving it for more than a day or two. In her youth the house was visited by kings and ambassadors, by scholars, soldiers and poets.

Even after the death of her father, people came to look upon the end of English magic, its last strange flowering on the eve of its long winter. Then, as the visitors became fewer, the house weakened and began to decay and the garden went to the wild. But Maria Absalom refused to repair her father's house. Even dishes that broke were left in cracked pieces on the floor.[1]

In her fiftieth year the ivy was grown so vigorous and had so far extended itself that it grew inside all the closets and made much of the floor slippery and unsafe to walk upon. Birds sang as much within the house as without. In her hundredth year the house and woman were ruinous together – though neither was at all extinguished. She continued another forty-nine years, before dying one summer morning in her bed with the leaf shadows of a great ash-tree and the broken sunlight falling all around her.

As Mr Honeyfoot and Mr Segundus hurried towards the Shadow House on this hot afternoon, they were a little nervous in case Mr Norrell should get to hear of their going (for, what with admirals and Ministers sending him respectful letters and paying him visits, Mr Norrell was growing greater by the hour). They feared lest he should consider that Mr Honeyfoot had broken the

[1] Some scholars (Jonathan Strange among them) have argued that Maria Absalom knew exactly what she was about when she permitted her house to go to rack and ruin. It is their contention that Miss Absalom did what she did in accordance with the commonly-held belief that all ruined buildings belong to the Raven King. This presumably would account for the fact that the magic at the Shadow House appeared to grow stronger *after* the house fell into ruin.

"All of Man's works, all his cities, all his empires, all his monuments will one day crumble to dust. Even the houses of my own dear readers must – though it be for just one day, one hour – be ruined and become houses where the stones are mortared with moonlight, windowed with starlight and furnished with the dusty wind. It is said that in that day, in that hour, our houses become the possessions of the Raven King. Though we bewail the end of English magic and say it is long gone from us and inquire of each other how it was possible that we came to lose something so precious, let us not forget that it also waits for us at England's end and one day we will no more be able to escape the Raven King than, in this present Age, we can bring him back." *The History and Practice of English Magic* by Jonathan Strange, pub. John Murray, London, 1816.

terms of his contract. So, in order that as few people as possible should know what they were about, they had told no one where they were going and had set off very early in the morning and had walked to a farm where they could hire horses and had come to the Shadow House by a very roundabout way.

At the end of the dusty, white lane they came to a pair of high gates. Mr Segundus got down from his horse to open them. The gates had been made of fine Castillian wrought iron, but were now rusted to a dark, vivid red and their original form was very much decayed and shrivelled. Mr Segundus's hand came away with dusty traces upon it as if a million dried and powdered roses had been compacted and formed into the dreamlike semblance of a gate. The curling iron had been further ornamented with little bas-reliefs of wicked, laughing faces, now ember-red and disintegrating, as if the part of Hell where these heathens were now resident was in the charge of an inattentive demon who had allowed his furnace to get too hot.

Beyond the gate were a thousand pale pink roses and high, nodding cliffs of sunlit elm and ash and chestnut and the blue, blue sky. There were four tall gables and a multitude of high grey chimneys and stone-latticed windows. But the Shadow House had been a ruined house for well over a century and was built as much of elder-trees and dog roses as of silvery limestone and had in its composition as much of summer-scented breezes as of iron and timber.

"It is like the Other Lands," said Mr Segundus, pressing his face into the gate in his enthusiasm, and receiving from it an impression of its shape apparently in powdered roses.[2] He pulled open the

[2] When people talk of "the Other Lands", they generally have in mind Faerie, or some such other vague notion. For the purposes of general conversation such definitions do very well, but a magician must learn to be more precise. It is well known that the Raven King ruled three kingdoms: the first was the Kingdom of Northern England that encompassed Cumberland, Northumberland, Durham, Yorkshire, Lancashire, Derbyshire and part of Nottinghamshire. The other two were called "the King's Other Lands". One was part of Faerie and the other was commonly supposed to be a country on the far side of Hell, sometimes called "the Bitter Lands". The King's enemies said that he leased it from Lucifer.

gate and led in his horse. Mr Honeyfoot followed. They tied up their horses by a stone basin and began to explore the gardens.

The grounds of the Shadow House did not perhaps deserve the name, "gardens". No one had tended them for over a hundred years. But nor were they a wood. Or a wilderness. There is no word in the English language for a magician's garden two hundred years after the magician is dead. It was richer and more disordered than any garden Mr Segundus and Mr Honeyfoot had ever seen before.

Mr Honeyfoot was highly delighted with everything he saw. He exclaimed over a great avenue of elms where the trees stood almost to their waists, as it were, in a sea of vivid pink foxgloves. He wondered aloud over a carving of a fox which carried a baby in its mouth. He spoke cheerfully of the remarkable magical atmosphere of the place, and declared that even Mr Norrell might learn something by coming here.

But Mr Honeyfoot was not really very susceptible to atmospheres; Mr Segundus, on the other hand, began to feel uneasy. It seemed to him that Absalom's garden was exerting a strange kind of influence on him. Several times, as Mr Honeyfoot and he walked about, he found himself on the point of speaking to someone he thought he knew. Or of recognizing a place he had known before. But each time, just as he was about to remember what he wanted to say, he realized that what he had taken for a friend was in fact only a shadow on the surface of a rose bush. The man's head was only a spray of pale roses and his hand another. The place that Mr Segundus thought he knew as well as the common scenes of childhood was only a chance conjunction of a yellow bush, some swaying elder branches and the sharp, sunlit corner of the house. Besides he could not think who was the friend or what was the place. This began to disturb him so much that, after half an hour, he proposed to Mr Honeyfoot that they sit for a while.

"My dear friend!" said Mr Honeyfoot, "What is the matter?

Are you ill? You are very pale – your hand is trembling. Why did you not speak sooner?"

Mr Segundus passed his hand across his head and said somewhat indistinctly that he believed that some magic was about to take place. He had a most definite impression that that was the case.

"Magic?" exclaimed Mr Honeyfoot. "But what magic could there be?" He looked about him nervously in case Mr Norrell should appear suddenly from behind a tree. "I dare say it is nothing more than the heat of the day which afflicts you. I myself am very hot. But we are blockheads to remain in this condition. For here is comfort! Here is refreshment! To sit in the shade of tall trees – such as these – by a sweet, chattering brook – such as this – is generally allowed to be the best restorative in the world. Come, Mr Segundus, let us sit down!"

They sat down upon the grassy bank of a brown stream. The warm, soft air and the scent of roses calmed and soothed Mr Segundus. His eyes closed once. Opened. Closed again. Opened slowly and heavily . . .

He began to dream almost immediately.

*He saw a tall doorway in a dark place. It was carved from a silver-grey stone that shone a little, as if there was moonlight. The doorposts were made in the likeness of two men (or it might only be one man, for both were the same). The man seemed to stride out of the wall and John Segundus knew him at once for a magician. The face could not clearly be seen, only enough to know that it would be a young face and a handsome one. Upon his head he wore a cap with a sharp peak and raven wings upon each side.*

*John Segundus passed through the door and for a moment saw only the black sky and the stars and the wind. But then he saw that there was indeed a room, but that it was ruinous. Yet despite this, such walls as there were, were furnished with pictures, tapestries and mirrors. But the figures in the tapestries moved about and spoke to each other, and not all the mirrors gave faithful reproductions of the room; some seemed to reflect other places entirely.*

*At the far end of the room in an uncertain compound of moonlight and candlelight someone was sitting at a table. She wore a gown of a very ancient style and of a greater quantity of material than John Segundus could have supposed necessary, or even possible, in one garment. It was of a strange, old, rich blue; and about the gown, like other stars, the last of the King of Denmark's diamonds were shining still. She looked up at him as he approached – two curiously slanting eyes set farther apart than is generally considered correct for beauty and a long mouth curved into a smile, the meaning of which he could not guess at. Flickers of candlelight suggested hair as red as her dress was blue.*

*Suddenly another person arrived in John Segundus's dream – a gentleman, dressed in modern clothes. This gentleman did not appear at all surprized at the finely dressed (but somewhat outmoded) lady, but he did appear very astonished to find John Segundus there and he reached out his hand and took John Segundus by the shoulder and began to shake him . . .*

Mr Segundus found that Mr Honeyfoot had grasped his shoulder and was gently shaking him.

"I beg your pardon!" said Mr Honeyfoot. "But you cried out in your sleep and I thought perhaps you would wish to be woken."

Mr Segundus looked at him in some perplexity. "I had a dream," he said. "A most curious dream!"

Mr Segundus told his dream to Mr Honeyfoot.

"What a remarkably magical spot!" said Mr Honeyfoot, approvingly. "Your dream – so full of odd symbols and portents – is yet another proof of it!"

"But what does it *mean*?" asked Mr Segundus.

"Oh!" said Mr Honeyfoot, and stopt to think a while. "Well, the lady wore blue, you say? Blue signifies – let me see – immortality, chastity and fidelity; it stands for Jupiter and can be represented by tin. Hmmph! Now where does that get us?"

"Nowhere, I think," sighed Mr Segundus. "Let us walk on."

Mr Honeyfoot, who was anxious to see more, quickly agreed to this proposal and suggested that they explore the interior of the Shadow House.

In the fierce sunlight the house was no more than a towering, green-blue haze against the sky. As they passed through the doorway to the Great Hall, "Oh!" cried Mr Segundus.

"Why! What is it now?" asked Mr Honeyfoot, startled.

Upon either side of the doorway stood a stone image of the Raven King. "I saw these in my dream," said Mr Segundus.

In the Great Hall Mr Segundus looked about him. The mirrors and the paintings that he had seen in his dream were long since gone. Lilac and elder trees filled up the broken walls. Horse-chestnuts and ash made a roof of green and silver that flowed and dappled against the blue sky. Fine gold grasses and ragged robin made a latticework for the empty stone windows.

At one end of the room there were two indistinct figures in a blaze of sunlight. A few odd items were scattered about the floor, a kind of magical debris: some pieces of paper with scraps of spells scribbled upon them, a silver basin full of water and a half-burnt candle in an ancient brass candlestick.

Mr Honeyfoot wished these two shadowy figures a good morning and one replied to him in grave and civil tones, but the other cried out upon the instant, "Henry, it is he! That is the fellow! That is the very man I described! Do you not see? A small man with hair and eyes so dark as to be almost Italian – though the hair has grey in it. But the expression so quiet and timid as to be English without a doubt! A shabby coat all dusty and patched, with frayed cuffs that he has tried to hide by snipping them close. Oh! Henry, this is certainly the man! You sir!" he cried, suddenly addressing Mr Segundus. "Explain yourself!"

Poor Mr Segundus was very much astonished to hear himself and his coat so minutely described by a complete stranger – and the description itself of such a peculiarly distressing sort! Not at all polite. As he stood, trying to collect his thoughts, his interlocutor moved into the shade of an ash-tree that formed part of the north wall of the hall and for the first time in the waking world Mr Segundus beheld Jonathan Strange.

Somewhat hesitantly (for he was aware as he said it how strangely it sounded) Mr Segundus said, "I have seen you, sir, in my dream, I think."

This only enraged Strange more. "The dream, sir, was mine! I lay down on purpose to dream it. I can bring proofs, witnesses that the dream was mine. Mr Woodhope," he indicated his companion, "saw me do it. Mr Woodhope is a clergyman – the rector of a parish in Gloucestershire – I cannot imagine that his word could be doubted! I am rather of the opinion that in England a gentleman's dreams are his own private concern. I fancy there is a law to that effect and, if there is not, why, Parliament should certainly be made to pass one immediately! It ill becomes another man to invite himself into them." Strange paused to take breath.

"Sir!" cried Mr Honeyfoot hotly. "I must beg you to speak to this gentleman with more respect. You have not the good fortune to know this gentleman as I do, but should you have that honour you will learn that nothing is further from his character than a wish to offend others."

Strange made a sort of exclamation of exasperation.

"It is certainly very odd that people should get into each other's dreams," said Henry Woodhope. "Surely it cannot really have been the same dream?"

"Oh! But I fear it is," said Mr Segundus with a sigh. "Ever since I entered this garden I have felt as if it were full of invisible doors and I have gone through them one after the other, until I fell asleep and dreamt the dream where I saw this gentleman. I was in a greatly confused state of mind. I knew it was not me that had set these doors ajar and made them to open, but I did not care. I only wanted to see what was at the end of them."

Henry Woodhope gazed at Mr Segundus as if he did not entirely understand this. "But I still think it cannot be the *same* dream, you know," he explained to Mr Segundus, as if to a rather stupid child. "What did you dream of?"

"Of a lady in a blue gown," said Mr Segundus. "I supposed that it was Miss Absalom."

"Well, *of course*, it was Miss Absalom!" cried Strange in great exasperation as if he could scarcely bear to hear any thing so obvious mentioned. "But unfortunately the lady's appointment was to meet one gentleman. She was naturally disturbed to find two and so she promptly disappeared." Strange shook his head. "There cannot be more than five men in England with any pretensions to magic, but one of them must come here and interrupt my meeting with Absalom's daughter. I can scarcely believe it. I am the unluckiest man in England. God knows I have laboured long enough to dream that dream. It has taken me three weeks – working night and day! – to prepare the spells of summoning, and as for the . . ."

"But this is marvellous!" interrupted Mr Honeyfoot. "This is wonderful! Why! Not even Mr Norrell himself could attempt such a thing!"

"Oh!" said Strange, turning to Mr Honeyfoot. "It is not so difficult as you imagine. First you must send out your invitation to the lady – any spell of summoning will do. I used Ormskirk.[3] Of course the troublesome part was to adapt Ormskirk so that both Miss Absalom and I arrived in my dream at the same time –

---

[3] Paris Ormskirk (1496–1587), a schoolmaster from the village of Clerkenwell near London. He wrote several treatises on magic. Though no very original thinker, he was a diligent worker who set himself the task of assembling and sifting through all the spells of summoning he could find, to try to uncover one reliable version. This took him twelve years, during which time his little house on Clerkenwell-green filled up with thousands of small pieces of paper with spells written on them. Mrs Ormskirk was not best pleased, and she, poor woman, became the original of the magician's wife in stock comedies and second-rate novels – a strident, scolding, unhappy person.

The spell that Ormskirk eventually produced became very popular and was widely used in his own century and the two following ones; but, until Jonathan Strange made his own alterations to the spell and brought forth Maria Absalom into his own dream and Mr Segundus's, I never heard of any one who had the least success with it – perhaps for the reasons that Jonathan Strange gives.

Ormskirk is so loose that the person one summons might go pretty well anywhere at any time and feel that they had fulfilled their obligations – *that*, I admit, was not an easy task. And yet, you know, I am not displeased with the results. Second I had to cast a spell upon myself to bring on a magic sleep. Of course I have heard of such spells but confess that I have never actually seen one, and so, you know, I was obliged to invent my own – I dare say it is feeble enough, but what can one do?"

"Good God!" cried Mr Honeyfoot. "Do you mean to say that practically all this magic was your own invention?"

"Oh! well," said Strange, "as to that . . . I had Ormskirk – I based everything on Ormskirk."

"Oh! But might not Hether-Gray be a better foundation than Ormskirk?" asked Mr Segundus.[4] "Forgive me. I am no practical magician but Hether-Gray has always seemed to me so much more reliable than Ormskirk."

"Indeed?" said Strange. "Of course I have heard of Hether-Gray. I have recently begun to correspond with a gentleman in Lincolnshire who says he has a copy of Hether-Gray's *The Anatomy of a Minotaur*. So Hether-Gray is really worth looking into, is he?"

Mr Honeyfoot declared that Hether-Gray was no such thing, that his book was the most thick-headed nonsense in the world; Mr Segundus disagreed and Strange grew more interested, and less mindful of the fact that he was supposed to be angry with Mr Segundus.

For who can remain angry with Mr Segundus? I dare say there are people in the world who are able to resent goodness and amiability, whose spirits are irritated by gentleness – but I am glad to say that Jonathan Strange was not of their number. Mr Segundus offered his apologies for spoiling the magic and Strange,

[4] Mr Segundus's good sense seems to have deserted him at this point. Charles Hether-Gray (1712–89) was another historio-magician who published a famous spell of summoning. His spell and Ormskirk's are equally bad; there is not a pin to chuse between them.

with a smile and a bow, said that Mr Segundus should think of it no more.

"I shall not ask, sir," said Strange to Mr Segundus, "if you are a magician. The ease with which you penetrate other people's dreams proclaims your power." Strange turned to Mr Honeyfoot, "But are you a magician also, sir?"

Poor Mr Honeyfoot! So blunt a question to be applied to so tender a spot! He was still a magician at heart and did not like to be reminded of his loss. He replied that he *had* been a magician not so many years before. But he had been obliged to give it up. Nothing could have been further from his own wishes. The study of magic – of good English magic – was, in his opinion, the most noble occupation in the world.

Strange regarded him with some surprize. "But I do not very well comprehend you. How could any one make you give up your studies if you did not wish it?"

Then Mr Segundus and Mr Honeyfoot described how they had been members of the Learned Society of York Magicians, and how the society had been destroyed by Mr Norrell.

Mr Honeyfoot asked Strange for his opinion of Mr Norrell.

"Oh!" said Strange with a smile. "Mr Norrell is the patron saint of English booksellers."

"Sir?" said Mr Honeyfoot.

"Oh!" said Strange. "One hears of Mr Norrell in every place where the book trade is perpetrated from Newcastle to Penzance. The bookseller smiles and bows and says, 'Ah sir, you are come too late! I *had* a great many books upon subjects magical and historical. But I sold them all to a very learned gentleman of Yorkshire.' It is always Norrell. One may buy, if one chuses, the books that Norrell has left behind. I generally find that the books that Mr Norrell leaves behind are really excellent things for lighting fires with."

Mr Segundus and Mr Honeyfoot were naturally all eagerness to be better acquainted with Jonathan Strange, and he seemed just as anxious to talk to them. Consequently, after each side had made and answered the usual inquiries ("Where are you staying?" "Oh! the George in Avebury." "Well, that is remarkable. So are we."), it was quickly decided that all four gentlemen should ride back to Avebury and dine together.

As they left the Shadow House Strange paused by the Raven King doorway and asked if either Mr Segundus or Mr Honeyfoot had visited the King's ancient capital of Newcastle in the north. Neither had. "This door is a copy of one you will find upon every corner there," said Strange. "The first in this fashion were made when the King was still in England. In that city it seems that everywhere you turn the King steps out of some dark, dusty archway and comes towards you." Strange smiled wryly. "But his face is always half hidden and he will never speak to you."

At five o'clock they sat down to dinner in the parlour of the George inn. Mr Honeyfoot and Mr Segundus found Strange to be a most agreeable companion, lively and talkative. Henry Woodhope on the other hand ate diligently and when he was done eating, he looked out of the window. Mr Segundus feared that he might feel himself neglected, and so he turned to him and complimented him upon the magic that Strange had done at the Shadow House.

Henry Woodhope was surprized. "I had not supposed it was a matter for congratulation," he said. "Strange did not say it was anything remarkable."

"But, my dear sir!" exclaimed Mr Segundus. "Who knows when such a feat was last attempted in England?"

"Oh! I know nothing of magic. I believe it is quite the fashionable thing – I have seen reports of magic in the London papers. But a clergyman has little leisure for reading. Besides I have known Strange since we were boys and he is of a most capricious character. I am surprized this magical fit has lasted so long. I dare say he will soon tire of it as he has of everything else." With that he rose from the table and said that he thought he would walk about the village for a while. He bade Mr Honeyfoot and Mr Segundus a good evening and left them.

"Poor Henry," said Strange, when Mr Woodhope had gone. "I suppose we must bore him horribly."

"It is most good-natured of your friend to accompany you on your journey, when he himself can have no interest in its object," said Mr Honeyfoot.

"Oh, certainly!" said Strange. "But then, you know, he was forced to come with me when he found it so quiet at home. Henry is paying us a visit of some weeks, but ours is a very retired neighbourhood and I believe I am a great deal taken up with my studies."

Mr Segundus asked Mr Strange when he began to study magic.

"In the spring of last year."

"But you have achieved so much!" cried Mr Honeyfoot. "And in less than two years! My dear Mr Strange, it is quite remarkable!"

"Oh! Do you think so? It seems to me that I have hardly done any thing. But then, I have not known where to turn for advice. You are the first of my brother-magicians that I ever met with, and I give you fair warning that I intend to make you sit up half the night answering questions."

"We shall be delighted to help you in any way we can," said Mr Segundus, "But I very much doubt that we can be of much service to you. We have only ever been *theoretical* magicians."

"You are much too modest," declared Strange. "Consider, for example, how much more extensive your reading has been than mine."

So Mr Segundus began to suggest authors whom Strange might not yet have heard of and Strange began to scribble down their names and works in a somewhat haphazard fashion, sometimes writing in a little memorandum book and other times writing upon the back of the dinner bill and once upon the back of his hand. Then he began to question Mr Segundus about the books.

Poor Mr Honeyfoot! How he longed to take part in this interesting conversation! How, in fact, he *did* take part in it, deceiving no one but himself by his little stratagems. "Tell him he must read Thomas Lanchester's *The Language of Birds*," he said, addressing Mr Segundus, rather than Strange. "Oh!" he said. "I know you have no opinion of it, but I think one may learn many things from Lanchester."

Whereupon Mr Strange told them how, to his certain knowledge, there had been four copies of *The Language of Birds* in England not more than five years ago: one in a Gloucester bookseller's; one in the private library of a gentleman-magician in Kendal; one the property of a blacksmith near Penzance who had taken it in part payment for mending an iron-gate; and one stopping a gap in a window of the boys' school in the close of Durham Cathedral.

"But where are they now?" cried Mr Honeyfoot. "Why did you not purchase a copy?"

"By the time that I came to each place Norrell had got there before me and bought them all," said Mr Strange. "I never laid eyes upon the man, and yet he thwarts me at every turn. That is why I hit upon this plan of summoning up some dead magician and asking him – or her – questions. I fancied a *lady* might be more sympathetic to my plight, and so I chose Miss Absalom."[5]

Mr Segundus shook his head. "As a means of getting knowledge, it strikes me as more dramatic than convenient. Can you not think of an easier way? After all, in the Golden Age of English magic, books were much rarer than they are now, yet men still became magicians."

"I have studied histories and biographies of the *Aureates* to discover how they began," said Strange, "but it seems that in those days, as soon as any one found out he had some aptitude for

---

[5] In mediaeval times conjuring the dead was a well-known sort of magic and there seems to have been a consensus that a dead magician was both the easiest spirit to raise and the most worth talking to.

magic, he immediately set off for the house of some other, older, more experienced magician and offered himself as a pupil."[6]

"Then you should apply to Mr Norrell for assistance!" cried Mr Honeyfoot, "Indeed you should. Oh! yes, I know," seeing that Mr Segundus was about to make some objection, "Norrell is a little reserved, but what is that? Mr Strange will know how to overcome his timidity I am sure. For all his faults of temper, Norrell is no fool and must see the very great advantages of having such an assistant!"

Mr Segundus had many objections to this scheme, in particular Mr Norrell's great aversion to other magicians; but Mr Honeyfoot, with all the enthusiasm of his eager disposition, had no sooner conceived the idea than it became a favourite wish and he could not suppose there would be any drawbacks. "Oh! I agree," he said, "that Norrell has never looked very favourably upon us *theoretical* magicians. But I dare say he will behave quite differently towards an *equal*."

Strange himself did not seem at all averse to the idea; he had a natural curiosity to see Mr Norrell. Indeed Mr Segundus could not help suspecting that he had already made up his mind upon the point and so Mr Segundus gradually allowed his doubts and objections to be argued down.

"This is a great day for Great Britain, sir!" cried Mr Honeyfoot.

---

[6] There have been very few magicians who did not learn magic from another practitioner. The Raven King was not the first British magician. There had been others before him – notably the seventh-century half-man, half-demon, Merlin – but at the time the Raven King came into England there were none. Little enough is known about the Raven King's early years, but it is reasonable to suppose that he learnt both magic and kingship at the court of a King of Faerie. Early magicians in mediaeval England learnt their art at the court of the Raven King and these magicians trained others.

One exception may be the Nottinghamshire magician, Thomas Godbless (1105?–82). Most of his life is entirely obscure to us. He certainly spent some time with the Raven King, but this seems to have been late in his life when he had already been a magician for years. He is perhaps one example that a magician may be self-created – as of course were both Gilbert Norrell and Jonathan Strange.

"Look at all that one magician has been able to accomplish! Only consider what two might do! Strange and Norrell! Oh, it sounds very well!" Then Mr Honeyfoot repeated "Strange and Norrell" several times over, in a highly delighted manner that made Strange laugh very much.

But like many gentle characters, Mr Segundus was much given to changes of mind. As long as Mr Strange stood before him, tall, smiling and assured, Mr Segundus had every confidence that Strange's genius must receive the recognition it deserved – whether it be with Mr Norrell's help, or in spite of Mr Norrell's hindrance; but the next morning, after Strange and Henry Woodhope had ridden off, his thoughts returned to all the magicians whom Mr Norrell had laboured to destroy, and he began to wonder if Mr Honeyfoot and he might not have misled Strange.

"I cannot help thinking," he said, "that we should have done a great deal better to warn Mr Strange to avoid Mr Norrell. Rather than encouraging him to seek out Norrell we should have advised him to hide himself!"

But Mr Honeyfoot did not understand this at all. "No gentleman likes to be told to hide," he said, "and if Mr Norrell should mean any harm to Mr Strange – which I am very far from allowing to be the case – then I am sure that Mr Strange will be the first to find it out."

## 24

# Another magician

## September 1809

Mr Drawlight turned slightly in his chair, smiled, and said, "It seems, sir, that you have a rival."

Before Mr Norrell could think of a suitable reply, Lascelles asked what was the man's name.

"Strange," said Drawlight.

"I do not know him," said Lascelles.

"Oh!" cried Drawlight. "I think you must. Jonathan Strange of Shropshire. Two thousand pounds a year."

"I have not the least idea whom you mean. Oh, but wait! Is not this the man who, when an undergraduate at Cambridge, frightened a cat belonging to the Master of Corpus Christi?"

Drawlight agreed that this was the very man. Lascelles knew him instantly and they both laughed.

Meanwhile Mr Norrell sat silent as a stone. Drawlight's opening remark had been a terrible blow. He felt as if Drawlight had turned and struck him – as if a figure in a painting, or a table or a chair had turned and struck him. The shock of it had almost taken his breath away; he was quite certain he would be ill. What Drawlight might say next Mr Norrell dared not think – something of greater powers, perhaps – of wonders performed beside which Mr Norrell's own would appear pitiful indeed. And he had taken such pains to ensure there could be no rivals! He felt like the man who goes about his house at night, locking doors and barring windows, only to hear the certain sounds of someone walking about in an upstairs room.

But as the conversation progressed these unpleasant sensations lessened and Mr Norrell began to feel more comfortable. As Drawlight and Lascelles talked of Mr Strange's Brighton pleasure-trips and visits to Bath and Mr Strange's estate in Shropshire, Mr Norrell thought he understood the sort of man this Strange must be: a fashionable, shallow sort of man, a man not unlike Lascelles himself. That being so (said Mr Norrell to himself) was it not more probable that "You have a rival," was addressed, not to himself, but to Lascelles? This Strange (thought Mr Norrell) must be Lascelles's rival in some love affair or other. Norrell looked down at his hands clasped in his lap and smiled at his own folly.

"And so," said Lascelles, "Strange is now a magician?"

"Oh!" said Drawlight, turning to Mr Norrell. "I am sure that not even his greatest friends would compare his talents to those of the estimable Mr Norrell. But I believe he is well enough thought of in Bristol and Bath. He is in London at present. His friends hope that you will be kind enough to grant him an interview – and may I express a wish to be present when two such practitioners of the art meet?"

Mr Norrell lifted his eyes very slowly. "I shall be happy to meet Mr Strange," he said.

Mr Drawlight was not made to wait long before he witnessed the momentous interview between the two magicians (which was just as well for Mr Drawlight hated to wait). An invitation was issued and both Lascelles and Drawlight made it their business to be present when Mr Strange waited upon Mr Norrell.

He proved neither as young nor as handsome as Mr Norrell had feared. He was nearer thirty than twenty and, as far as another gentleman may be permitted to judge these things, not handsome at all. But what was very unexpected was that he brought with him a pretty young woman: Mrs Strange.

Mr Norrell began by asking Strange if he had brought his writing? He would, he said, very much like to read what Mr Strange had written.

"My writing?" said Strange and paused a moment. "I am afraid, sir, that I am at a loss to know what you mean. I have written nothing."

"Oh!" said Mr Norrell. "Mr Drawlight told me that you had been asked to write something for *The Gentleman's Magazine* but perhaps . . ."

"Oh, that!" said Strange. "I have scarcely thought about it. Nichols assured me he did not need it until the Friday after next."

"A week on Friday and not yet begun!" said Mr Norrell, very much astonished.

"Oh!" said Strange. "I think that the quicker one gets these things out of one's brain and on to the paper and off to the printers, the better. I dare say, sir," and he smiled at Mr Norrell in a friendly manner, "that you find the same."

Mr Norrell, who had never yet got any thing successfully out of his brain and off to the printers, whose every attempt was still at some stage or other of revision, said nothing.

"As to what I shall write," continued Strange, "I do not quite know yet, but it will most likely be a refutation of Portishead's article in *The Modern Magician*.[1] Did you see it, sir? It put me in a rage for a week. He sought to prove that modern magicians have no business dealing with fairies. It is one thing to admit that we have lost the power to raise such spirits – it is quite another to renounce all intention of ever employing them! I have no patience with any such squeamishness. But what is most extraordinary is that I have yet to see any criticism of Portishead's article anywhere. Now that we have something approaching a magical

[1] *The Modern Magician* was one of several magical periodicals set up following the first appearance of *The Friends of English Magic* in 1808. Though not appointed by Mr Norrell, the editors of these periodicals never dreamt of deviating from orthodox magical opinion as laid down by Mr Norrell.

community I think we would be very wrong to let such thick-headed nonsense pass unreproved."

Strange, apparently thinking that he had talked enough, waited for one of the other gentlemen to reply.

After a moment or two of silence Mr Lascelles remarked that Lord Portishead had written the article at Mr Norrell's express wish and with Mr Norrell's aid and approval.

"Indeed?" Strange looked very much astonished.

There was a silence of some moments and then Lascelles languidly inquired how one learnt magic these days?

"From books," said Strange.

"Ah, sir!" cried Mr Norrell. "How glad I am to hear you say so! Waste no time, I implore you, in pursuing any other course, but apply yourself constantly to reading! No sacrifice of time or pleasure can ever be too great!"

Strange regarded Mr Norrell somewhat ironically and then remarked, "Unfortunately lack of books has always been a great obstacle. I dare say you have no conception, sir, how few books of magic there are left in circulation in England. All the booksellers agree that a few years ago there were a great many, but now . . ."

"Indeed?" interrupted Mr Norrell, hurriedly. "Well, that is very odd to be sure."

The silence which followed was peculiarly awkward. Here sat the only two English magicians of the Modern Age. One confessed he had no books; the other, as was well known, had two great libraries stuffed with them. Mere common politeness seemed to dictate that Mr Norrell make some offer of help, however slight; but Mr Norrell said nothing.

"It must have been a very curious circumstance," said Mr Lascelles after a while, "that made you chuse to be a magician."

"It was," said Strange. "Most curious."

"Will you not tell us what that circumstance was?"

Strange smiled maliciously. "I am sure that it will give Mr Norrell great pleasure to know that he was the cause of my becoming a magician. One might say in fact that Mr Norrell made me a magician."

"I?" cried Mr Norrell, quite horrified.

"The truth is, sir," said Arabella Strange quickly, "that he had tried everything else – farming, poetry, iron-founding. In the course of a year he ran through a whole variety of occupations without settling to any of them. He was bound to come to magic sooner or later."

There was another silence, then Strange said, "I had not understood before that Lord Portishead wrote at your behest, sir. Perhaps you will be so good as to explain something to me. I have read all of his lordship's essays in *The Friends of English Magic* and *The Modern Magician* but have yet to see any mention of the Raven King. The omission is so striking that I am beginning to think it must be deliberate."

Mr Norrell nodded. "It is one of my ambitions to make that man as completely forgotten as he deserves," he said.

"But surely, sir, without the Raven King there would be no magic and no magicians?"

"That is the common opinion, certainly. But even it were true – which I am very far from allowing – he has long since forfeited any entitlement to our esteem. For what were his first actions upon coming into England? To make war upon England's lawful King and rob him of half his kingdom! And shall you and I, Mr Strange, let it be known that we have chosen such a man as our model? That we account *him* the first among us? Will that make our profession respected? Will that persuade the King's ministers to put their trust in us? I do not think so! No, Mr Strange, if we cannot make his name forgotten, then it is our duty – yours and mine – to broadcast our hatred of him! To let it be known everywhere our great abhorrence of his corrupt nature and evil deeds!"

It was clear that a great disparity of views and temper existed between the two magicians and Arabella Strange seemed to think that there was no occasion for them to continue any longer in the same room to irritate each other more. She and Strange left very shortly afterwards.

Naturally, Mr Drawlight was the first to pronounce upon the new magician. "Well!" he said rather *before* the door had closed upon Strange's back. "I do not know what may be your opinion, but I never was more astonished in my life! I was informed by several people that he was a handsome man. What could they have meant, do you suppose? With such a nose as he has got and that hair. Reddish-brown is such a fickle colour – there is no wear in it – I am quite certain I saw some grey in it. And yet he cannot be more than – what? – thirty? thirty-two perhaps? She, on the other hand, is quite delightful! So much animation! Those brown curls, so sweetly arranged! But I thought it a great pity that she had not taken more trouble to inform herself of the London fashions. The sprigged muslin she had on was certainly very pretty, but I should like to see her wear something altogether more stylish – say forest-green silk trimmed with black ribbons and black bugle-beads. That is only a first thought, you understand – I may be struck with quite a different idea when I see her again."

"Do you think that people will be curious about him?" asked Mr Norrell.

"Oh! certainly," said Mr Lascelles.

"Ah!" said Mr Norrell. "Then I am very much afraid – Mr Lascelles, I would be very glad if you could advise me – I am very much afraid that Lord Mulgrave may send for Mr Strange. His lordship's zeal for using magic in the war – excellent in itself, of course – has had the unfortunate effect of encouraging him to read all sorts of books on magical history and forming opinions about what he finds there. He has devised a plan to summon up witches to aid me in defeating the French – I believe he is thinking of those half-fairy, half-human women to whom malicious people were used to apply when they wished to harm their neighbours – the sort of witches, in short, that Shakespeare describes in *Macbeth*. He asked me to invoke three or four, and was not best pleased that I refused to do it. Modern magic can do many things, but summoning up witches could bring a world of trouble upon everyone's head. But now I fear he might send for Mr Strange instead. Mr Lascelles, do not you think that he might? And then Mr Strange might try it, not understanding any thing of the danger. Perhaps it would be as well to write to Sir Walter asking if he would be so good as to have a word in his lordship's ear to warn him against Mr Strange."

"Oh!" said Lascelles. "I see no occasion for that. If *you* think that Mr Strange's magic is not safe then it will soon get about."

Later in the day a dinner was given in Mr Norrell's honour at a house in Great Titchfield-street, at which Mr Drawlight and Mr Lascelles were also present. It was not long before Mr Norrell was asked to give his opinion of the Shropshire magician.

"Mr Strange," said Mr Norrell, "seems a very pleasant gentleman and a very talented magician who may yet be a most creditable addition to our profession, which has certainly been somewhat depleted of late."

"Mr Strange appears to entertain some very odd notions of magic," said Lascelles. "He has not troubled to inform himself of the modern ideas on the subject – by which I mean, of course, Mr Norrell's ideas, which have so astonished the world with their clarity and succinctness."

Mr Drawlight repeated his opinion that Mr Strange's red hair had no wear in it and that Mrs Strange's gown, though not exactly fashionable, had been of a very pretty muslin.

At about the same time that this conversation was taking place another set of people (among them Mr and Mrs Strange) was sitting down to dinner in a more modest dining-parlour in a house in Charterhouse-square. Mr and Mrs Strange's friends were naturally anxious to know their opinion of the great Mr Norrell.

"He says he hopes that the Raven King will soon be forgot," said Strange in amazement. "What do you make of that? A magician who hopes the Raven King will soon be forgot! If the Archbishop of Canterbury were discovered to be working secretly to suppress all knowledge of the Trinity, it would make as much sense to me."

"He is like a musician who wishes to conceal the music of Mr Handel," agreed a lady in a turban eating artichokes with almonds.

"Or a fishmonger who hopes to persuade people that the sea does not exist," said a gentleman helping himself to a large piece of mullet in a good wine sauce.

Then other people proposed similar examples of folly and everyone laughed except Strange who sat frowning at his dinner.

"I thought you meant to ask Mr Norrell to help you," said Arabella.

"How could I when we seemed to be quarrelling from the first moment we met?" cried Strange. "He does not like me. Nor I him."

"Not like you! No, perhaps he did not *like* you. But he did not so much as look at any other person the whole time we were there. It was as if he would eat you up with his eyes. I dare say he is lonely. He has studied all these years and never had any body he could explain his mind to. Certainly not to those disagreeable men – I forget their names. But now that he has seen you – and he knows that he could talk to you – well! it would be very odd if he did not invite you again."

In Great Titchfield-street Mr Norrell put down his fork and dabbed at his lips with his napkin. "Of course," he said, "he must apply himself. I urged him to apply himself."

Strange in Charterhouse-square said, "He told me to apply myself. – To what? I asked. – To reading he said. I was never more astonished in my life. I was very near asking him what I was supposed to read when he has all books."

The next day Strange told Arabella that they could go back to Shropshire any time she pleased – he did not think that there was any thing to keep them in London. He also said that he had resolved to think no more about Mr Norrell. In this he was not entirely successful for several times in the next few days Arabella found herself listening to a long recital of all Mr Norrell's faults, both professional and personal.

Meanwhile in Hanover-square Mr Norrell constantly inquired of Mr Drawlight what Mr Strange was doing, whom he visited, and what people thought of him.

Mr Lascelles and Mr Drawlight were a little alarmed at this development. For more than a year now they had enjoyed no small degree of influence over the magician and, as his friends, they were courted by admirals, generals, politicians, any one in fact who wished to know Mr Norrell's opinion upon this, or wished Mr Norrell to do that. The thought of another magician who might attach himself to Mr Norrell by closer ties than Drawlight or Lascelles could ever hope to forge, who might take upon himself the task of advising Mr Norrell was very disagreeable. Mr Drawlight told Mr Lascelles that Norrell should be discouraged from thinking of the Shropshire magician and, though Mr Lascelles's whimsical nature never permitted him to agree outright with any one, there is little doubt that he thought the same.

But three or four days after Mr Strange's visit, Mr Norrell said, "I have been considering the matter very carefully and I believe that something ought to be done for Mr Strange. He complained of his lack of materials. Well, of course, I can see that that might . . . In short I have decided to make him a present of a book."

"But, sir!" cried Drawlight. "Your precious books! You must not give them away to other people – especially to other magicians who may not use them as wisely as yourself!"

"Oh!" said Mr Norrell. "I do not mean one of my own books. I fear I could not spare a single one. No, I have purchased a volume from Edwards and Skittering to give Mr Strange. The choice was, I confess, a difficult one. There are many books which, to be perfectly frank, I would not be quite comfortable in recommending to Mr Strange yet; he is not ready for them. He would imbibe all sorts of wrong ideas from them. This book," Mr Norrell looked at it in an anxious sort of way, "has many faults – I fear it has a great many. Mr Strange will learn no actual magic from it. But it has a great deal to say on the subjects of diligent research and the perils of committing oneself to paper too soon – lessons which I hope Mr Strange may take to heart."

So Mr Norrell invited Strange to Hanover-square again and as on the previous occasion Drawlight and Lascelles were present, but Strange came alone.

The second meeting took place in the library at Hanover-square. Strange looked about him at the great quantities of books, but said not a word. Perhaps he had got to the end of his anger. There seemed to be a determination on both sides to speak and behave more cordially.

"You do me great honour, sir," said Strange when Mr Norrell gave him his present. "*English Magic* by Jeremy Tott." He turned the pages. "Not an author I have ever heard of."

"It is a biography of his brother, a theoretical magio-historian of the last century called Horace Tott," said Mr Norrell.[2] He explained about the lessons of diligent research and not committing oneself to paper that Strange was to learn. Strange smiled politely, bowed, and said he was sure it would be most interesting.

Mr Drawlight admired Strange's present.

Mr Norrell gazed at Strange with an odd expression upon his face as though he would have been glad of a little conversation with him, but had not the least idea how to begin.

Mr Lascelles reminded Mr Norrell that Lord Mulgrave of the Admiralty was expected within the hour.

---

[2] Horace Tott spent an uneventful life in Cheshire always intending to write a large book on English magic, but never quite beginning. And so he died at seventy-four, still imagining he might begin next week, or perhaps the week after that.

"You have business to conduct, sir," said Strange. "I must not intrude. Indeed I have business for Mrs Strange in Bond-street that must not be neglected."

"And perhaps one day," said Drawlight, "we shall have the honour of seeing a piece of magic worked by Mr Strange. I am excessively fond of seeing magic done."

"Perhaps," said Strange.

Mr Lascelles rang the bell for the servant. Suddenly Mr Norrell said, "I should be glad to see some of Mr Strange's magic now – if he would honour us with a demonstration."

"Oh!" said Strange. "But I do not . . ."

"It would do me great honour," insisted Mr Norrell.

"Very well," said Strange, "I shall be very glad to shew you something. It will be a little awkward, perhaps, compared to what you are accustomed to. I very much doubt, Mr Norrell, that I can match you in elegance of execution."

Mr Norrell bowed.

Strange glanced two or three times around the room in search of some magic to do. His glance fell upon a mirror that hung in the depths of a corner of the room where the light never penetrated. He placed *English Magic* by Jeremy Tott upon the library-table so that its reflection was clearly visible in the mirror. For some moments he stared at it and nothing happened. And then he made a curious gesture; he ran both hands through his hair, clasped the back of his neck and stretched his shoulders, as a man will do who eases himself of the cramps. Then he smiled and altogether looked exceedingly pleased with himself.

Which was odd because the book looked exactly as it had done before.

Lascelles and Drawlight, who were both accustomed to seeing – or hearing about – Mr Norrell's wonderful magic, were scarcely impressed by this; indeed it was a great deal less than a common conjuror might manage at a fairground. Lascelles opened his mouth – doubtless to say some scathing thing – but was forestalled by Mr Norrell suddenly crying out in a tone of wonder, "But that is remarkable! That is truly . . . My dear Mr Strange! I never even heard of such magic before! It is not listed in Sutton-Grove. I assure you, my dear sir, it is not in Sutton-Grove!"

Lascelles and Drawlight looked from one magician to the other in some confusion.

Lascelles approached the table and stared hard at the book. "It is a little longer than it was perhaps," he said.

"I do not think so," said Drawlight.

"It is tan leather now," said Lascelles. "Was it blue before?"

"No," said Drawlight, "it was always tan."

Mr Norrell laughed out loud; Mr Norrell, who rarely even smiled, laughed at them. "No, no, gentlemen! You have not guessed it! Indeed you have not! Oh! Mr Strange, I cannot tell how much . . . but they do not understand what it is you have done! Pick it up!" he cried. "Pick it up, Mr Lascelles!"

More puzzled than ever Lascelles put out his hand to grasp the book, but all he grasped was the empty air. The book lay there in appearance only.

"He has made the book and its reflection change places," said Mr Norrell. "The real book is over there, in the mirror." And he went to peer into the mirror with an appearance of great professional interest. "But how did you do it?"

"How indeed?" murmured Strange; he walked about the room, examining the reflection of the book upon the table from different angles like a billiards-player, closing one eye and then the other.

"Can you get it back?" asked Drawlight.

"Sadly, no," said Strange. "To own the truth," he said at last, "I have only the haziest notion of what I did. I dare say it is just the same with you, sir, one has a sensation like music playing at the back of one's head – one simply knows what the next note will be."

"Quite remarkable," said Mr Norrell.

What was perhaps rather more remarkable was that Mr Norrell, who had lived all his life in fear of one day discovering a rival, had finally seen another man's magic, and far from being crushed by the sight, found himself elated by it.

Mr Norrell and Mr Strange parted that afternoon on very cordial terms, and upon the following morning met again without Mr Lascelles or Mr Drawlight knowing any thing about it. This meeting ended in Mr Norrell's offering to take Mr Strange as a pupil. Mr Strange accepted.

"I only wish that he had not married," said Mr Norrell fretfully. "Magicians have no business marrying."

## 25

# The education of a magician

### September–December 1809

On the first morning of Strange's education, he was invited to an early breakfast at Hanover-square. As the two magicians sat down at the breakfast-table, Mr Norrell said, "I have taken the liberty of drawing up a plan of study for you for the next three or four years."

Strange looked a little startled at the mention of three or four years, but he said nothing.

"Three or four years is such a very short time," continued Mr Norrell with a sigh, "that, try as I can, I cannot see that we will achieve very much."

He passed a dozen or so sheets of paper to Strange. Each sheet was covered in three columns of Mr Norrell's small, precise handwriting; each column contained a long list of different sorts of magic.[1]

Strange looked them over and said that there was more to learn than he had supposed.

"Ah! I envy you, sir," said Mr Norrell. "Indeed I do. The *practice* of magic is full of frustrations and disappointments, but the *study* is a continual delight! All of England's great magicians are one's companions and guides. Steady labour is rewarded by

[1] Naturally, Mr Norrell based his syllabus upon the classifications contained in *De Generibus Artium Magicarum Anglorum* by Francis Sutton-Grove.

increase of knowledge and, best of all, one need not so much as look upon another of one's fellow creatures from one month's end to the next if one does not wish it!"

For a few moments Mr Norrell seemed lost in contemplation of this happy state, then, rousing himself, he proposed that they deny themselves the pleasure of Strange's education no longer but go immediately into the library to begin.

Mr Norrell's library was on the first floor. It was a charming room in keeping with the tastes of its owner who would always chuse to come here for both solace and recreation. Mr Drawlight had persuaded Mr Norrell to adopt the fashion of setting small pieces of mirror into odd corners and angles. This meant that one was constantly meeting with a bright gleam of silver light or the sudden reflection of someone in the street where one least expected it. The walls were covered with a light green paper, with a pattern of green oak leaves and knobbly oak twigs, and there was a little dome set into the ceiling which was painted to represent the leafy canopy of a glade in spring. The books all had matching bindings of pale calf leather with their titles stamped in neat silver capitals on the spine. Among all this elegance and harmony it was somewhat surprizing to observe so many gaps among the books, and so many shelves entirely empty.

Strange and Mr Norrell seated themselves one on each side of the fire.

"If you will permit me, sir," said Strange, "I should like to begin by putting some questions to you. I confess that what I heard the other day concerning fairy-spirits entirely astonished me, and I wondered if I might prevail upon you to talk to me a little upon this subject? To what dangers does the magician expose himself in employing fairy-spirits? And what is your opinion of their utility?"

"Their utility has been greatly exaggerated, the danger much underestimated," said Mr Norrell.

"Oh! Is it your opinion that fairies are, as some people think, demons?" asked Strange.

"Upon the contrary. I am quite certain that the common view of them is the correct one. Do you know the writings of Chaston upon the subject? It would not surprize me if Chaston turned out to have come very near the truth of it.[2] No, no, my objection to fairies is quite another thing. Mr Strange, tell me, in your opinion why does so much English magic depend – or appear to depend – upon the aid of fairy-spirits?"

Strange thought a moment. "I suppose because all English magic comes from the Raven King who was educated at a fairy court and learnt his magic there."

"I agree that the Raven King has every thing to do with it," said Mr Norrell, "but not, I think, in the way you suppose. Consider, if you will, Mr Strange, that all the time the Raven King ruled Northern England, he also ruled a fairy kingdom. Consider, if you will, that no king ever had two such diverse races under his sway. Consider, if you will, that he was as great a king as he was a magician – a fact which almost all historians are prone to overlook. I think there can be little doubt that he was much preoccupied with the task of binding his two peoples together – a task which he accomplished, Mr Strange, *by deliberately exaggerating the role of fairies in magic*. In this way he increased his human subjects' esteem for fairies, he provided his fairy subjects with useful occupation, and made both peoples desire each other's company."

"Yes," said Strange, thoughtfully, "I see that."

"It seems to me," continued Mr Norrell, "that even the greatest of *Aureate* magicians miscalculated the extent to which fairies are necessary to human magic. Look at Pale! He considered his fairy-servants so essential to the pursuit of his art that he wrote that his greatest treasures were the three or four fairy-spirits living in his

---

[2] Richard Chaston (1620–95). Chaston wrote that men and fairies both contain within them a faculty of reason and a faculty of magic. In men reason is strong and magic is weak. With fairies it is the other way round: magic comes very naturally to them, but by human standards they are barely sane.

house! Yet my own example makes it plain that almost all *respectable* sorts of magic are perfectly achievable without assistance from any one! What have I ever done that has needed the help of a fairy?"

"I understand you," said Strange, who imagined that Mr Norrell's last question must be rhetorical. "And I must confess, sir, that this idea is quite new to me. I have never seen it in any book."

"Neither have I," said Mr Norrell. "Of course there are some sorts of magic which are entirely impossible without fairies. There may be times – and I sincerely hope that such occasions will be rare – when you and I shall have to treat with those pernicious creatures. Naturally we shall have to exercise the greatest caution. Any fairy we summon will almost certainly have dealt with English magicians before. He will be eager to recount for us all the names of the great magicians he has served and the services he has rendered to each. He will understand the forms and precedents of such dealings a great deal better than we do. It puts us – will put us – at a disadvantage. I assure you, Mr Strange, nowhere is the decline of English magic better understood than in the Other Lands."

"Yet fairy-spirits hold a great fascination for ordinary people," mused Strange, "and perhaps if you were occasionally to employ one in your work it might help make our art more popular. There is still a great deal of prejudice against using magic in the war."

"Oh! Indeed!" cried Mr Norrell, irritably. "People believe that magic begins and ends with fairies! They scarcely consider the skill and learning of the magician at all! No, Mr Strange, that is no argument with me for employing fairies! Rather the reverse! A hundred years ago the magio-historian, Valentine Munday, denied that the Other Lands existed. He thought that the men who claimed to have been there were all liars. In this he was quite wrong, but his position remains one with which I have a great deal of sympathy and I wish we could make it more generally believed. Of course," said Mr Norrell thoughtfully, "Munday went on to deny that America existed, and then France and so on. I believe that by the time he died he had long since given up Scotland and was beginning to entertain doubts of Carlisle . . . I have his book here."[3] Mr Norrell stood up and fetched it from the shelves. But he did not give it to Strange straightaway.

After a short silence Strange said, "You advise me to read this book?"

"Yes, indeed. I think you should read it," said Mr Norrell.

Strange waited, but Norrell continued to gaze at the book in his hand as though he were entirely at a loss as to how to proceed. "Then you must give it to me, sir," said Strange gently.

"Yes, indeed," said Mr Norrell. He approached Strange cautiously and held the book out for several moments, before suddenly tipping it up and off into Strange's hand with an odd gesture, as though it was not a book at all, but a small bird which clung to him and would on no account go to any one else, so that he was obliged to trick it into leaving his hand. He was so intent upon this manoeuvre that fortunately he did not look up at Strange who was trying not to laugh.

Mr Norrell remained a moment, looking wistfully at his book in another magician's hand.

But once he had parted with one book the painful part of his ordeal seemed to be over. Half an hour later he recommended another book to Strange and went and got it with scarcely any fuss. By midday he was pointing out books on the shelves to Strange and allowing him to fetch them down for himself. By the end of the day Mr Norrell had given Strange a quite extraordinary number of books to read, and said that he expected him to have read them by the end of the week.

---

[3] *The Blue Book: being an attempt to expose the most prevalent lies and common deceptions practised by English magicians upon the King's subjects and upon each other*, by Valentine Munday, pub. 1698.

A whole day of conversation and study was a luxury they could not often afford; generally they were obliged to spend some part of every day in attending to Mr Norrell's visitors – whether these were the fashionable people whom Mr Norrell still believed it essential to cultivate or gentlemen from the various Government departments.

By the end of a fortnight Mr Norrell's enthusiasm for his new pupil knew no bounds. "One has but to explain something to him once," Norrell told Sir Walter, "and he understands it immediately! I well remember how many weeks I laboured to comprehend Pale's Conjectures Concerning the Foreshadowing of Things To Come, yet Mr Strange was master of this exceptionally difficult theory in little more than four hours!"

Sir Walter smiled. "No doubt. But I think you rate your own achievements too low. Mr Strange has the advantage of a teacher to explain the difficult parts to him, whereas you had none – *you* have prepared the way for him and made everything smooth and easy."

"Ah!" cried Mr Norrell. "But when Mr Strange and I sat down to talk of the Conjectures some more, I realized that they had a much wider application than I had supposed. It was his questions, you see, which led me to a new understanding of Dr Pale's ideas!"

Sir Walter said, "Well, sir, I am glad that you have found a friend whose mind accords so well with your own – there is no greater comfort."

"I agree with you, Sir Walter!" cried Mr Norrell. "Indeed I do!"

Strange's admiration for Mr Norrell was of a more restrained nature. Norrell's dull conversation and oddities of behaviour continued to grate upon his nerves; and at about the same time as Mr Norrell was praising Strange to Sir Walter, Strange was complaining of Norrell to Arabella.

"Even now I scarcely know what to make of him. He is, at one and the same time, the most remarkable man of the Age and the most tedious. Twice this morning our conversation was interrupted because he *thought* he heard a mouse in the room – mice are a particular aversion of his. Two footmen, two maids and I moved all the furniture about looking for the mouse, while he stood by the fireplace, rigid with fear."

"Has he a cat?" suggested Arabella. "He should get a cat."

"Oh, but that is quite impossible! He hates cats even more than mice. He told me that if he is ever so unlucky as to find himself in the same room as a cat, then he is sure to be all over red pimples within an hour."

It was Mr Norrell's sincere wish to educate his pupil thoroughly, but the habits of secrecy and dissimulation which he had cultivated all his life were not easily thrown off. On a day in December, when snow was falling in large, soft flakes from heavy, greenish-grey clouds, the two magicians were seated in Mr Norrell's library. The slow drifting motion of the snow outside the windows, the heat of the fire and the effects of a large glass of sherry-wine which he had been so ill-advised as to accept when Mr Norrell offered it, all combined to make Strange very heavy and sleepy. His head was supported upon his hand and his eyes were almost closing.

Mr Norrell was speaking. "Many magicians," he said, steepling his hands, "have attempted to confine magical powers in some physical object. It is not a difficult operation and the object can be any thing the magician wishes. Trees, jewels, books, bullets, hats have all been employed for this purpose at one time or another." Mr Norrell frowned hard at his fingertips. "By placing some of his power in whatever object he chuses, the magician hopes to make himself secure from those wanings of power, which are the inevitable result of illness and old age. I myself have often been severely tempted to do it; my own skills can be quite overturned by a heavy cold or a bad sore throat. Yet after careful consideration I have concluded that such divisions of power are most ill-advised. Let us examine the case of rings. Rings have long been considered peculiarly suitable for this sort of magic by virtue of their small size. A man may keep a ring continually upon his finger for years, without exciting the smallest comment – which would not be the case if he shewed the same attachment to a book or a pebble – and yet there is scarcely a magician in history who, having once committed some of his skill and power to a magic ring, did not somehow lose that ring and was put to a world of trouble to get it back again. Take for example, the twelfth-century Master of Nottingham, whose daughter mistook his ring of power for a common bauble, put it on her finger, and went to St Matthew's Fair. This negligent young woman . . ."

"What?" cried Strange, suddenly.

"What?" echoed Mr Norrell, startled.

Strange gave the other gentleman a sharp, questioning look. Mr Norrell gazed back at him, a little frightened.

"I beg your pardon, sir," said Strange, "but do I understand you aright? Are we speaking of magical powers that are got by some means into rings, stones, amulets – things of that sort?"

Mr Norrell nodded cautiously.

"But I thought you said," said Strange. "That is," he made some effort to speak more gently, "I *thought* that you told me some weeks ago that magic rings and stones were a fable."

Mr Norrell stared at his pupil in alarm.

"But perhaps I was mistaken?" said Strange.

Mr Norrell said nothing at all.

"I was mistaken," said Strange again. "I beg your pardon, sir, for interrupting you. Pray, continue."

But Mr Norrell, though he appeared greatly relieved that Strange had resolved the matter, was no longer equal to continuing and instead proposed that they have some tea; to which Mr Strange agreed very readily.[4]

That evening Strange told Arabella all that Mr Norrell had

[4] The story of the Master of Nottingham's daughter (to which Mr Norrell never returned) is worth recounting and so I set it down here.

The fair to which the young woman repaired was held on St Matthew's Feast in Nottingham. She spent a pleasant day, going about among the booths, making purchases of linens, laces and spices. Sometime during the

said and all that he, Strange, had said in reply.

"It was the queerest thing in the world! He was so frightened at having been found out, that he could think of nothing to say. It fell to me to think of fresh lies for him to tell me. I was

[4] *cont'd* afternoon she happened to turn suddenly to see some Italian tumblers who were behind her and the edge of her cloak flew out and struck a passing goose. This bad-tempered fowl ran at her, flapping its wings and screaming. In her surprize she dropt her father's ring, which fell into the goose's open gullet and the goose, in *its* surprize, swallowed it. But before the Master of Nottingham's daughter could say or do any thing the gooseherd drove the goose on and both disappeared into the crowd.

The goose was bought by a man called John Ford who took it back to his house in the village of Fiskerton and the next day his wife, Margaret Ford, killed the goose, plucked it and drew out its innards. In its stomach she found a heavy silver ring set with a crooked piece of yellow amber. She put it down on a table near three hens' eggs that had been gathered that morning.

Immediately the eggs began to shake and then to crack open and from each egg something marvellous appeared. From the first egg came a stringed instrument like a viol, except that it had little arms and legs, and played sweet music upon itself with a tiny bow. From the next egg emerged a ship of purest ivory with sails of fine white linen and a set of silver oars. And from the last egg hatched a chick with strange red-and-gold plumage. This last was the only wonder to survive beyond the day. After an hour or two the viol cracked like an eggshell and fell into pieces and by sunset the ivory ship had set sail and rowed away through the air; but the bird grew up and later started a fire which destroyed most of Grantham. During the conflagration it was observed bathing itself in the flames. From this circumstance it was presumed to be a phoenix.

When Margaret Ford realized that a magic ring had somehow fallen into her possession, she was determined to do magic with it. Unfortunately she was a thoroughly malicious woman, who tyrannized over her gentle husband, and spent long hours pondering how to revenge herself upon her enemies. John Ford held the manor of Fiskerton, and in the months that followed he was loaded with lands and riches by greater lords who feared his wife's wicked magic.

Word of the wonders performed by Margaret Ford soon reached Nottingham, where the Master of Nottingham lay in bed waiting to die. So much of his power had gone into the ring that the loss of it had made him first melancholy, then despairing and finally sick. When news of his ring finally came he was too ill to do any thing about it.

His daughter, on the other hand, was thoroughly sorry for bringing this misfortune on her family and thought it her duty to try and get the ring back; so without telling any one what she intended she set off along the riverbank to the village of Fiskerton.

She had only got as far as Gunthorpe when she came upon a very dreadful

obliged to conspire with him against myself."

"But I do not understand," said Arabella. "Why should he contradict himself in this odd way?"

"Oh! He is determined to keep some things to himself. That

---

[4] *cont'd* sight. A little wood was burning steadily with fierce flames lapping every part of it. The black bitter smoke made her eyes sting and her throat ache, yet the wood was not consumed by the fire. A low moan issued from the trees as if they cried out at such unnatural torment. The Master's daughter looked round for someone to explain this wonder to her. A young woodsman, who was passing, told her, "Two weeks ago, Margaret Ford stopt in the wood on the road from Thurgarton. She rested under the shade of its branches, drank from its stream and ate its nuts and berries, but just as she was leaving a root caught her foot and made her fall, and when she rose from the ground a briar was so impertinent as to scratch her arm. So she cast a spell upon the wood and swore it would burn for ever."

The Master's daughter thanked him for the information and walked on for a while. She became thirsty and crouched down to scoop up some water from the river. All at once a woman – or something very like a woman – half-rose out of the water. There were fish-scales all over her body, her skin was as grey and spotted as a trout's and her hair had become an odd arrangement of spiny grey trout fins. She seemed to glare at the Master's daughter, but her round cold fish-eyes and stiff fishskin were not well adapted to reproduce human expressions and so it was hard to tell.

"Oh! I beg your pardon!" said the Master's daughter, startled.

The woman opened her mouth, shewing a fish throat and mouth full of ugly fish teeth, but she seemed unable to make a sound. Then she rolled over and plunged back into the water.

A woman who was washing clothes on the riverbank explained to the Master's daughter, "That is Joscelin Trent who is so unfortunate as to be the wife of a man that Margaret Ford likes. Out of jealousy Margaret Ford has cast a spell on her and she is forced, poor lady, to spend all her days and nights immersed in the shallows of the river to keep her enchanted skin and flesh from drying out, and as she cannot swim she lives in constant terror of drowning."

The Master's daughter thanked the woman for telling her this.

Next the Master's daughter came to the village of Hoveringham. A man and his wife who were both squeezed together atop a little pony advised her not to enter the village, but led her around it by narrow lanes and paths. From a little green knoll the Master's daughter looked down and saw that everyone in the village wore a thick blindfold round his eyes. They were not at all used to their self-created blindness and constantly banged their faces against walls, tripped over stools and carts, cut themselves on knives and tools and burnt themselves in the fire. As a consequence they were covered in gashes and wounds, yet not one of them removed his blindfold.

"Oh!" said the wife. "The priest of Hoveringham has been bold enough to

much is obvious – and I suppose he cannot always remember what is to be a secret and what is not. You remember that I told you there are gaps among the books in his library? Well, it seems that the very day he accepted me as his pupil, he ordered five shelves to

---

[4] *cont'd* denounce the wickedness of Margaret Ford from his pulpit. Bishops, abbots and canons have all been silent, but this frail old man defied her and so she has cursed the whole village. It is their fate to have vivid images of all their worst fears constantly before their eyes. These poor souls see their children starve, their parents go mad, their loved ones scorn and betray them. Wives and husbands see each other horribly murdered. And so, though these sights be nought but illusions, the villagers must blindfold themselves or else be driven mad by what they see."

Shaking her head over the appalling wickedness of Margaret Ford, the Master's daughter continued on her way to John Ford's manor, where she found Margaret and her maidservants, each with a wooden stick in her hand, driving the cows to their evening's milking.

The Master's daughter went boldly up to Margaret Ford. Upon the instant Margaret Ford turned and struck her with her stick. "Wicked girl!" she cried. "I know who you are! My ring has told me. I know that you plan to lie to me, who have never done you any harm at all, and ask to become my servant. I know that you plan to steal my ring. Well, know this! I have set strong spells upon my ring. If any thief were foolish enough to touch it, then within a very short space of time bees and wasps and all kinds of insects would fly up from the earth and sting him; eagles and hawks and all kinds of birds would fly down from the sky and peck at him; then bears and boars and all kinds of wild creatures would appear and tear and trample him to pieces!"

Then Margaret Ford beat the Master's daughter soundly, and told the maids to put her to work in the kitchen.

Margaret Ford's servants, a miserable, ill-treated lot, gave the Master's daughter the hardest work to do and whenever Margaret Ford beat them or raged at them – which happened very often – they relieved their feelings by doing the same to her. Yet the Master's daughter did not allow herself to become low-spirited. She stayed working in the kitchen for several months and thought very hard how she might trick Margaret Ford into dropping the ring or losing it.

Margaret Ford was a cruel woman, quick to take offence and her anger, once roused, could never be appeased. But for all that she adored little children; she took every opportunity to nurse babies and once she had a child in her arms she was gentleness itself. She had no child of her own and no one who knew her doubted that this was a source of great sorrow to her. It was widely supposed that she had expended a great deal of magic upon trying to conceive a child, but without success.

One day Margaret Ford was playing with a neighbour's little girl, and saying how if she ever were to have a child then she would rather it were a girl

be emptied and the books sent back to Yorkshire, because they were too dangerous for me to read."

"Good Lord! However did you find that out?" asked Arabella, much surprized.

---

[4] *cont'd* and how she would wish it to have a creamy white skin and green eyes and copper curls (this being Margaret Ford's own colouring).

"Oh!" said the Master's daughter innocently "The wife of the Reeve in Epperstone has a baby of exactly that description, the prettiest little creature that ever you saw."

Then Margaret Ford made the Master's daughter take her to Epperstone and shew her the Reeve's wife's baby, and when Margaret Ford saw that the baby was indeed the sweetest, prettiest child that ever there was (just as the Master's daughter had said) she announced to the horrified mother her intention of taking the child away with her.

As soon as she had possession of the Reeve's wife's baby Margaret Ford became almost a different person. She spent her days in looking after the baby, playing with her and singing to her. Margaret Ford became contented with her lot. She used her magic ring a great deal less than she had before and scarcely ever lost her temper.

So things went on until the Master of Nottingham's daughter had lived in Margaret Ford's house for almost a year. Then one summer's day Margaret Ford, the Master's daughter, the baby and the other maids took their midday meal upon the banks of the river. After eating, Margaret Ford rested in the shade of a rose-bush. It was a hot day and they were all very sleepy.

As soon as she was certain that Margaret Ford was asleep the Master's daughter took out a sugar-plum and shewed it to the baby. The baby, knowing only too well what should be done to sugar-plums, opened its mouth wide and the Master's daughter popped it in. Then, as quick as she could and making sure that none of the other maids saw what she did, she slipped the magic ring from Margaret Ford's finger.

Then, "Oh! Oh!" she cried. "Wake up, madam! The baby has taken your ring and put it in her mouth! Oh, for the dear child's sake, undo the spell. Undo the spell!"

Margaret Ford awoke and saw the baby with its cheek bulging out, but for the moment she was too sleepy and surprized to understand what was happening.

A bee flew past and the Master's daughter pointed at it and screamed. All the other maids screamed too. "Quickly, madam, I beg you!" cried the Master's daughter. " Oh!" She looked up. "Here are the eagles and hawks approaching! Oh!" She looked into the distance. "Here are the bears and boars running to tear the poor little thing to pieces!"

Margaret Ford cried out to the ring to stop the magic which it did immediately, and almost at the same moment the baby swallowed the sugar-plum. While Margaret Ford and the maids begged and coaxed the baby and shook it to make it cough up the magic ring, the Master of

"Drawlight and Lascelles told me. They took great pleasure in it."

"Ill-natured wretches!"

Mr Norrell was most disappointed to learn that Strange's education must be interrupted for a day or two while he and Arabella sought for a house to live in. "It is his wife that is the problem," Mr Norrell explained to Drawlight, with a sigh. "Had he been a single man, I dare say he would not have objected to coming and living here with me."

Drawlight was most alarmed to hear that Mr Norrell had entertained such a notion and, in case it were ever revived, he took the precaution of saying, "Oh, but sir! Think of your work for the Admiralty and the War Office, so important and so confid-

---

[4] *cont'd* Nottingham's daughter began to run along the riverbank towards Nottingham.

The rest of the story has all the usual devices. As soon as Margaret Ford discovered how she had been tricked she fetched horses and dogs to chase the Master's daughter. Upon several occasions the Master's daughter seemed lost for sure – the riders were almost upon her and the dogs just behind her. But the story tells how she was helped by all the victims of Margaret Ford's magic: how the villagers of Hoveringham tore off their blindfolds and, in spite of all the horrifying sights they saw, rushed to build barricades to prevent Margaret Ford from passing; how poor Joscelin Trent reached up out of the river and tried to pull Margaret Ford down into the muddy water; how the burning wood threw down flaming branches upon her.

The ring was returned to the Master of Nottingham who undid all the wrongs Margaret Ford had perpetrated and restored his own fortune and reputation.

There is another version of this story which contains no magic ring, no eternally-burning wood, no phoenix – no miracles at all, in fact. According to this version Margaret Ford and the Master of Nottingham's daughter (whose name was Donata Torel) were not enemies at all, but the leaders of a fellowship of female magicians that flourished in Nottinghamshire in the twelfth century. Hugh Torel, the Master of Nottingham, opposed the fellowship and took great pains to destroy it (though his own daughter was a member). He very nearly succeeded, until the women left their homes and fathers and husbands and went to live in the woods under the protection of Thomas Godbless, a much greater magician than Hugh Torel. This less colourful version of the story has never been as popular as the other but it is this version which Jonathan Strange said was the true one and which he included in *The History and Practice of English Magic*.

ential! The presence of another person in the house would impede it greatly."

"Oh, but Mr Strange is going help me with that!" said Mr Norrell. "It would be very wrong of me to deprive the country of Mr Strange's talents. Mr Strange and I went down to the Admiralty last Thursday to wait upon Lord Mulgrave. I believe that Lord Mulgrave was none too pleased at first to see that I had brought Mr Strange . . ."

"That is because his lordship is accustomed to your superior magic! I dare say he thinks that a mere *amateur* – however talented – has no business meddling with Admiralty matters."

". . . but when his lordship heard Mr Strange's ideas for defeating the French by magic he turned to me with a great smile upon his face and said, 'You and I, Mr Norrell, had grown stale. We wanted new blood to stir us up, did we not?' "

"Lord Mulgrave said *that*? To *you*?" said Drawlight. "That was abominably rude of him. I hope, sir, that you gave him one of your looks!"

"What?" Mr Norrell was engrossed in his own tale and had no attention to spare for whatever Mr Drawlight might be saying. " 'Oh!' I said to him – I said, 'I am quite of your mind, my lord. But only wait until you have heard the rest of what Mr Strange has to say. You have not heard the half of it!' "

It was not only the Admiralty – the War Office and all the other departments of Government had reason to rejoice at the advent of Jonathan Strange. Suddenly a good many things which had been difficult before were made easy. The King's Ministers had long treasured a plan to send the enemies of Britain bad dreams. The Foreign Secretary had first proposed it in January 1808 and for over a year Mr Norrell had industriously sent the Emperor Napoleon Buonaparte a bad dream each night, as a result of which nothing had happened. Buonaparte's empire had not foundered and Buonaparte himself had ridden into battle as coolly as ever. And so eventually Mr Norrell was instructed to leave off. Privately Sir Walter and Mr Canning thought that the plan had failed because Mr Norrell had no talent for creating horrors. Mr Canning complained that the nightmares Mr Norrell had sent the Emperor (which chiefly concerned a captain of Dragoons hiding in Buonaparte's wardrobe) would scarcely frighten his children's governess let alone the conqueror of half of Europe. For a while he had tried to persuade the other Ministers that they should commission Mr Beckford, Mr Lewis and Mrs Radcliffe to create dreams of vivid horror that Mr Norrell could then pop into Buonaparte's head. But the other Ministers considered that to employ a magician was one thing, novelists were quite another and they would not stoop to it.

With Strange the plan was revived. Strange and Mr Canning suspected that the wicked French Emperor was proof against such insubstantial evils as dreams, and so they decided to begin this time with his ally, Alexander, the Emperor of Russia. They had the advantage of a great many friends at Alexander's court: Russian nobles who had made a great deal of money selling timber to Britain and were anxious to do so again, and a brave and ingenious Scottish lady who was the wife of Alexander's valet.

On learning that Alexander was a curiously impressionable person much given to mystical religion, Strange decided to send him a dream of eerie portents and symbols. For seven nights in succession Alexander dreamt a dream in which he sat down to a comfortable supper with Napoleon Buonaparte at which they were served some excellent venison soup. But no sooner had the Emperor tasted the soup, than he jumped up and cried, "J'ai une faim qui ne saurait se satisfaire de potage."[5] whereupon he turned into a she-wolf which ate first Alexander's cat, then his dog, then his horse, then his pretty Turkish mistress. And as the she-wolf set to work to eat up more of Alexander's friends and relations, her

[5] "I have a hunger which soup can never satisfy!"

womb opened and disgorged the cat, dog, horse, Turkish mistress, friends, relations, etc. again, but in horrible misshapen forms. And as she ate she grew; and when she was as big as the Kremlin, she turned, heavy teats swaying and maw all bloody, intent on devouring all of Moscow.

"There can be nothing dishonourable in sending him a dream which tells him that he is wrong to trust Buonaparte and that Buonaparte will betray him in the end," explained Strange to Arabella. "I might, after all, send him a letter to say as much. He *is* wrong and nothing is more certain than that Buonaparte *will* betray him in the end."

Word soon came from the Scottish lady that the Russian Emperor had been exceedingly troubled by the dreams and that, like King Nebuchadnezzar in the Bible, he had sent for astrologers and soothsayers to interpret it for him – which they very soon did.

Strange then sent more dreams to the Russian Emperor. "And," he told Mr Canning, "I have taken your advice and made them more obscure and difficult of interpretation that the Emperor's sorcerers may have something to do."

The indefatigable Mrs Janet Archibaldovna Barsukova was soon able to convey the satisfying news that Alexander neglected the business of government and war, and sat all day musing upon his dreams and discussing them with astrologers and sorcerers; and that whenever a letter came for him from the Emperor Napoleon Buonaparte he was seen to turn pale and shudder.

# 26

## Orb, crown and sceptre

### September 1809

EVERY NIGHT WITHOUT fail Lady Pole and Stephen Black were summoned by the sad bell to dance in Lost-hope's shadowy halls. For fashion and beauty these were, without a doubt, the most splendid balls Stephen had ever seen, but the fine clothes and smart appearance of the dancers made an odd contrast with the mansion itself which exhibited numerous signs of poverty and decay. The music never varied. The same handful of tunes were scraped out by a single violin, and tooted out by a single pipe. The greasy tallow-candles – Stephen could not help but observe with his butler's eye how there were far too few of them for such a vast hall – cast up strange shadows that spun across the walls as the dancers went through their figures.

On other occasions Lady Pole and Stephen took part in long processions in which banners were carried through dusty, ill-lit halls (the gentleman with the thistle-down hair having a great fondness for such ceremonies). Some of the banners were ancient and decaying pieces of dense embroidery; others represented the gentleman's victories over his enemies and were in fact made from the preserved skins of those enemies, their lips, eyes, hair and clothes having been embroidered on to their yellow skins by his female relations. The gentleman with the thistle-down hair never grew tired of these pleasures and he never appeared to entertain the slightest doubt that Stephen and Lady Pole were equally delighted with them.

Though changeable in all else, he remained constant in two things: his admiration of her ladyship and his affection for Stephen Black. The latter he continued to demonstrate by making Stephen extravagant gifts and by sending him strange pieces of good fortune. Some of the gifts were made, as before, to Mrs Brandy on Stephen's behalf and some were sent directly to Stephen for, as the gentleman told Stephen cheerfully, "Your wicked enemy will know nothing about it!" (He meant Sir Walter.) "I have very cleverly blinded him with my magic and it will never occur to him to wonder about it. Why! You could be made Archbishop of Canterbury tomorrow and he would think nothing of it! No one would." A thought appeared to strike him. "Would you like to be Archbishop of Canterbury tomorrow, Stephen?"

"No, thank you, sir."

"Are you quite certain? It is scarcely any trouble and if the Church has any attraction for you . . . ?"

"I promise you, sir, it has none."

"Your good taste as ever does you credit. A mitre is a wretchedly uncomfortable sort of thing to wear and not at all becoming."

Poor Stephen was assailed by miracles. Every few days something would occur to profit him in some way. Sometimes the actual value of what he gained was unremarkable – perhaps no more than a few shillings – but the means by which it came to him were always extraordinary. Once, for example, he received a visit from the overseer of a farm who insisted that, some years before, he had met Stephen at a cockfight near Richmond in the North Riding of Yorkshire and that Stephen had wagered him that the Prince of Wales would one day do something to bring disgrace upon the country. As this had now happened (the overseer cited the Prince's desertion of his wife as the shameful deed) the overseer had come to London by the stagecoach to bring Stephen twenty-seven shillings and sixpence – which, he said, was the amount of the wager. It was useless for Stephen to insist that he had never been to a cockfight or to Richmond in Yorkshire; the overseer would not be content until Stephen had taken the money.

A few days after the overseer's visit a large grey dog was discovered standing in the road opposite the house in Harley-street. The poor creature was drenched by the rain and splattered with mud and bore every sign of having travelled a great distance. More curious still, it had a document grasped between its jaws. The footmen, Robert and Geoffrey, and John Longridge, the cook, did their best to get rid of it by shouting and hurling bottles and stones at it, but the dog bore this treatment philosophically and declined to move until Stephen Black had come out in the rain and taken the document from its mouth. Then it went away with a quietly contented air, as if congratulating itself upon a difficult task well done. The document proved to be a map of a village in Derbyshire and shewed, among other surprizing things, a secret door let into the side of a hill.

Another time Stephen received a letter from the mayor and aldermen of Bath describing how, two months before, the Marquess of Wellesley had been in Bath and had done nothing during his stay but talk of Stephen Black and his remarkable honesty, intelligence and faithfulness to his master. So impressed had the mayor and the aldermen been by his lordship's report, that they had immediately ordered a medal, celebrating Stephen's life and virtues, to be struck. When five hundred medals had been made, the mayor and the aldermen had ordered them to be distributed to the chief householders of Bath amid general rejoicing. They enclosed a medal for Stephen, and begged that whenever he next found himself in Bath he would make himself known to them so that they might hold a magnificent dinner in his honour.

None of these miracles did any thing to raise poor Stephen's spirits. They only served to emphasize the eerie character of his present life. He knew that the overseer, dog and the mayor and the aldermen were all acting against their natures: overseers loved money – they did not give it away for no good reason; dogs did not patiently pursue strange quests for weeks on end; and mayors and aldermen did not suddenly develop a lively interest in negro servants they had never seen. Yet none of his friends seemed to think there was any thing remarkable about the course his life was taking. He was sick of the sight of gold and silver, and his little room at the top of the house in Harley-street was full of treasures he did not want.

He had been almost two years under the gentleman's enchantment. He had often pleaded with the gentleman to release him – or, if not him, then Lady Pole – but the gentleman would not hear of it. So Stephen had roused himself to try and tell someone about what he and Lady Pole suffered. He was anxious to discover if there were precedents for their case. He had faint hopes of finding someone who would help free them. The first person he had spoken to was Robert, the footman. He had warned Robert that he was about to hear a private revelation of a secret woe, and Robert had looked suitably solemn and interested. But, when Stephen began to speak, he found to his own astonishment that it was upon quite a different matter; he found himself delivering a very earnest and learned discourse upon the cultivation and uses of peas and beans – a subject he knew nothing about. Worse still, some of his information was of a most unusual nature and would have frankly astonished any farmer or gardener who had heard it. He explained the different properties of beans either planted or gathered by moonlight, by moondark, at Beltane or on Midsummer's Night, and how these properties were changed if you sowed or gathered the beans with a silver trowel or knife.

The next person to whom he attempted to describe his trouble was John Longridge. This time he found himself delivering an exact account of Julius Caesar's dealings and experiences in Britain. It was clearer and more detailed than any scholar could have managed, tho' he had studied the subject for twenty years or more. Once again it contained information that was not set down in any book.[1]

He made two more attempts to communicate his horrible situation. To Mrs Brandy he delivered an odd defence of Judas Iscariot in which he declared that in all Iscariot's last actions he was following the instructions of two men called John Copperhead and John Brassfoot whom Iscariot had believed to be angels; and to Toby Smith, Mrs Brandy's shopman, he gave a list of all the people in Ireland, Scotland, Wales and England who had been stolen away by fairies in the last two hundred years. None of them were people he had ever heard of.

Stephen was obliged to conclude that, try as he might, he *could not* speak of his enchantment.

The person who suffered most from his strange silences and dismal spirits was, without a doubt, Mrs Brandy. She did not

---

[1] Stephen described how, not long after Julius Caesar had arrived upon these shores, he had left his army and wandered into a little green wood. He had not gone far when he came upon two young men, sighing deeply and striking the ground in their frustration. Both were remarkably handsome and both were dressed in the finest linens dyed with the rarest dyes. Julius Caesar was so struck with the noble appearance of these young men that he asked them all sorts of questions and they answered him candidly and without the least diffidence. They explained how they were both plaintiffs at a court nearby. The court was held every Quarter Day to settle arguments and punish wrongdoers among their people, but unfortunately the race to which they belonged was a peculiarly wicked and quarrelsome one, and just at present no suits could be heard because they could not find an impartial judge; every venerable person among them either stood accused of a crime, or else had been found to have some other close connexion with one of the suits. On hearing this Caesar was struck with pity for them and immediately offered to be their judge himself – to which they eagerly agreed.

They led him a short way through the wood to a grassy hollow between smooth green hills. Here he found a thousand or so of the handsomest men and women that he had ever seen. He sat down upon the hillside and heard all their complaints and accusations; and when he had heard them he gave judgements so wise that everyone was delighted and no one went away feeling himself ill-used.

So pleased were they with Julius Caesar's judgements that they offered him any thing he liked as payment. Julius Caesar thought for a moment and said that he would like to rule the world. This they promised him.

understand that he had changed to the whole world, she only saw that he had changed towards *her*. One day at the beginning of September Stephen paid her a visit. They had not met for some weeks, which had made Mrs Brandy so unhappy that she had written to Robert Austin, and Robert had gone to Stephen and scolded him for his neglect. However once Stephen had arrived in the little parlour above the shop in St James's-street, no one could have blamed Mrs Brandy if she had wished him immediately away again. He sat with his head in his hand, sighing heavily, and had nothing to say to her. She offered him Constantia-wine, marmalade, an old-fashioned wigg bun – all sorts of delicacies – but he refused them all. He wanted nothing; and so she sat down on the opposite side of the fire and resumed her needlework – a nightcap which she was despondently embroidering for him.

"Perhaps," she said, "you are tired of London and of me, and you wish to return to Africa?"

"No," said Stephen.

"I dare say Africa is a remarkably charming place," said Mrs Brandy, who seemed determined to punish herself by sending Stephen immediately to Africa. "I have always heard that it is. With oranges and pineapples everywhere one looks, and sugar canes and chocolate trees." She had laboured fourteen years in the grocery trade and had mapped out her world in its stock. She laughed bitterly. "It seems that I would fare very ill in Africa. What need have people of shops when they have only to stretch out their hand and pluck the fruit of the nearest tree? Oh, yes! I should be ruined in no time in Africa." She snapped a thread between her teeth. "Not that I should not be glad to go tomorrow," She poked the thread viciously into the needle's innocent eye, "if any one were to ask me."

"Would you go to Africa for my sake?" asked Stephen in surprize.

She looked up. "I would go any where for your sake," she said. "I thought you knew that."

They regarded one another unhappily.

Stephen said that he must return and attend to his duties in Harley-street.

Outside in the street, the sky darkened and rain began to fall. People put up umbrellas. As Stephen walked up St James's-street, he saw a strange sight – a black ship sailing towards him through the grey rainy air above the heads of the crowd. It was a frigate, some two feet high, with dirty, ragged sails and peeling paint. It rose and fell, mimicking the motion of ships at sea. Stephen shivered a little to see it. A beggar emerged from the crowd, a negro with skin as dark and shining as Stephen's own. Fastened to his hat was this ship. As he walked he ducked and raised his head so that his ship could sail. As he went he performed his curious bobbing and swaying movements very slowly and carefully for fear of upsetting his enormous hat. The effect was of a man dancing amazingly slowly. The beggar's name was Johnson. He was a poor, crippled sailor who had been denied a pension. Having no other means of relief, he had taken to singing and begging to make a livelihood, in which he had been most successful and he was known throughout the Town for the curious hat he wore. Johnson held out his hand to Stephen, but Stephen looked away. He always took great care not to speak to, or in any way acknowledge, negroes of low station. He feared that if he were seen speaking to such people it might be supposed that he had some connexion with them.

He heard his name cried out, and he jumped as if he had been scalded, but it was only Toby Smith, Mrs Brandy's shopman.

"Oh! Mr Black!" cried Toby, hurrying up. "There you are! You generally walk so fast, sir! I was sure you would be in Harley-street by now. Mrs Brandy sends her compliments, sir, and says you left this by your chair."

Toby held out a silver diadem, a delicate band of metal of a size to fit Stephen's head exactly. It had no ornament other than a few odd signs and queer letters cut into its surface.

"But this is not mine!" said Stephen.

"Oh!" said Toby, blankly, but then he appeared to decide that Stephen was joking. "Oh, Mr Black, as if I have not seen it upon your head a hundred times!" Then he laughed and bowed and ran back to the shop, leaving Stephen with the diadem in his hand.

He crossed over Piccadilly into Bond-street. He had not gone far when he heard shouting, and a tiny figure came running down the street. In stature the figure appeared no more than four or five years old, but its dead-white, sharp-featured face belonged to a much older child. It was followed at a distance by two or three men, shouting "Thief!" and "Stop him!"

Stephen sprang into the thief's path. But though the young thief could not entirely escape Stephen (who was nimble), Stephen was not quite able to fasten on to the thief (who was slippery). The thief held a long bundle wrapped in a red cloth, which he somehow contrived to tip into Stephen's hands, before darting in among a crowd of people outside Hemmings's, the goldsmith. These people were but newly emerged from Hemmings's and knew nothing of the pursuit, so they did not spring apart when the thief arrived among them. It was impossible to say which way he went.

Stephen stood, holding the bundle. The cloth, which was a soft, old velvet, slipped away, revealing a long rod of silver.

The first of the pursuers to arrive was a dark, handsome gentleman sombrely, but elegantly dressed in black. "You had him for a moment," he said to Stephen.

"I am only sorry, sir," said Stephen, "that I could not hold him for you. But, as you see, I have your property." Stephen offered the man the rod of silver and the red velvet cloth but the man did not take them.

"It was my mother's fault!" said the gentleman, angrily. "Oh! How could she be so negligent? I have told her a thousand times that if she left the drawing-room window open, sooner or later a thief would come in by it. Have I not said so a hundred times,

Edward? Have I not said so, John?" The latter part of this speech was addressed to the gentleman's servants, who had come running up after their master. They lacked breath to reply, but were able to assure Stephen by emphatic nods that the gentleman had indeed said so.

"All the world knows that I keep many treasures at my house," continued the gentleman, "and yet she continues to open the window in spite of my entreaties! And now, of course, she sits weeping for the loss of this treasure which has been in my family for hundreds of years. For my mother takes great pride in our family and all its possessions. This sceptre, for example, is proof that we are descended from the ancient kings of Wessex, for it belonged to Edgar or Alfred or someone of that sort."

"Then you must take it back, sir," urged Stephen. "Your mother, I dare say, will be much relieved to see it safe and sound."

The gentleman reached out to take the sceptre, but suddenly drew back his hand. "No!" he cried. "I will not! I vow I will not. If I were to return this treasure to my mother's keeping, then she would never learn the evil consequences of her negligence! She would never learn to keep the window shut! And who knows what I might lose next? Why, I might come home tomorrow to an empty house! No, sir, you must keep the sceptre! It is a reward for the service you did me in trying to catch hold of the thief."

The gentleman's servants all nodded as if they saw the sense of this, and then a coach drew up and gentleman and servants all got into it and drove away.

Stephen stood in the rain with a diadem in one hand and a sceptre in the other. Ahead of him were the shops of Bond-street, the most fashionable shops in all the kingdom. In their windows were displayed silks and velvets, headdresses of pearl and peacock feathers, diamonds, rubies, jewels and every sort of gold and silver trinkets.

"Well," thought Stephen, "doubtless he will be able to make all sorts of eerie treasures for me out of the contents of those shops. But I shall be cleverer than him. I shall go home by another way."

He turned into a narrow alleyway between two buildings, crossed a little yard, passed through a gate, down another alleyway and emerged in a little street of modest houses. It was quite deserted here and strangely quiet. The only sound was the rain striking the cobblestones. Rain had darkened all the fronts of the houses until they appeared to be almost black. The occupants of the houses seemed a very frugal lot, for not one of them had lit a lamp or a candle despite the gloominess of the day. Yet the heavy cloud did not cover the sky completely and a watery white light shewed at the horizon, so that between the dark sky and the dark earth the rain fell in bright silver shafts.

A shining something rolled suddenly out of a dark alleyway and skittered unevenly over the wet cobblestones, coming to a stop directly in front of Stephen.

He looked at it and heaved a great sigh when he saw that it was, as he expected, a little silver ball. It was very battered and old-looking. At the top where there ought to have been a cross to signify that all the world belonged to God, there was a tiny open hand. One of the fingers was broken off. This symbol – the open hand – was one that Stephen knew well. It was one of those employed by the gentleman with the thistle-down hair. Only last night Stephen had taken part in a procession and carried a banner bearing this very emblem through dark, windswept courtyards and along avenues of immense oak-trees in whose unseen branches the wind soughed.

There was the sound of a window sash being raised. A woman poked her head out of a window at the top of the house. Her hair was all in curl papers. "Well, pick it up!" she cried, glaring furiously at Stephen.

"But it is not mine!" he called up to her.

"It is not his, he says!" This made her angrier still. "And I suppose I did not just see it fall out of your pocket and roll away! And I suppose my name is not Mariah Tompkins! And I suppose I do not labour night and day to keep Pepper-street clean and tidy, but you must come here a-purpose to throw away your rubbish!"

With a heavy sigh, Stephen picked up the orb. He found that, whatever Mariah Tompkins said or believed, if he put it in his pocket there was a very real danger of it tearing the cloth, it was so heavy. So he was obliged to walk through the rain, sceptre in one hand, orb in the other. The diadem he put on his head, as the most convenient place for it, and attired in this fashion he walked home.

On arriving at the house in Harley-street, he went down to the area and opened the kitchen door. He found himself, not in the kitchen as he had expected, but in a room he had never seen before. He sneezed three times.

A moment was enough to reassure him that he was not at Lost-hope. It was a quite commonplace sort of room – the sort of room, in fact, that one might find in any well-to-do house in London. It was, however, remarkably untidy. The inhabitants, who were presumably new to the house, appeared to be in the middle of unpacking. All the articles usually belonging to a sitting-room and study were present: card-tables, work-tables, reading-tables, fire-irons, chairs of varying degrees of comfortableness and usefulness, mirrors, tea-cups, sealing-wax, candle-sticks, pictures, books (a great number of these), sanders, ink-stands, pens, papers, clocks, balls of string, footstools, fire-screens and writing-desks. But they were all jumbled together and standing upon one another in new and surprizing combinations. Packing-cases and boxes and bundles were scattered about, some unpacked, some half-unpacked and some scarcely begun. The straw from the packing-cases had been pulled out and now lay scattered about the room and over the furniture, which had the effect of making everything dusty and causing Stephen to sneeze twice more. Some of the straw had even got into the fireplace so that there was a very real danger of the whole room going up in a conflagration at any moment.

The room contained two people: a man whom Stephen had never seen before and the gentleman with the thistle-down hair.

The man he had never seen before was seated at a little table in front of the window. Presumably he ought to have been unpacking his things and setting his room in order, but he had abandoned this task and was presently engaged in reading a book. He broke off every now and then to look things up in two or three other volumes that lay on the table; to mutter excitedly to himself; and to dash down a note or two in an ink-splashed little book.

Meanwhile the gentleman with the thistle-down hair sat in an arm-chair on the opposite side of the fireplace, directing at the other man a look of such extreme malevolence and irritation as made Stephen fear for the man's life. Yet the moment the gentleman with the thistle-down hair beheld Stephen, he became all delight, all affability. "Ah, there you are!" he cried. "How noble you look in your kingly accoutrements!"

There happened to be a large mirror standing opposite the door. For the first time Stephen saw himself with the crown, sceptre and orb. He looked every inch a king. He turned to look at the man at the table to discover how he bore with the sudden appearance of a black man in a crown.

"Oh! Do not concern yourself about *him*!" said the gentleman with the thistle-down hair. "He can neither see nor hear us. He has no more talent than the other one. Look!" He screwed up a piece of paper and threw it energetically at the man's head. The man did not flinch or look up or appear to know any thing about it.

"The other one, sir?" said Stephen. "What do you mean?"

"That is the younger magician. The one lately arrived in London."

"Is it indeed? I have heard of him, of course. Sir Walter thinks highly of him. But I confess I have forgotten his name."

"Oh! Who cares what his name is! What matters is that he is just as stupid as the other one and very near as ugly."

"What?" said the magician, suddenly. He turned away from his book and looked around the room with a slightly suspicious air. "Jeremy!" he called out very loudly.

A servant put his head around the door, but did not trouble himself so far as to come into the room. "Sir?" he said.

Stephen's eyes opened very wide at this lazy behaviour – it was a thing he would never have allowed in Harley-street. He made a point of staring very coldly at the man to shew him what he thought of him before he remembered that the man could not see him.

"These London houses are shockingly built," said the magician. "I can hear the people in the next house."

This was interesting enough to tempt the servant called Jeremy all the way into the room. He stood and listened.

"Are all the walls so thin?" continued the magician. "Do you suppose there can be something wrong with them?"

Jeremy knocked on the wall which divided the house from its neighbour. It responded with as dull and quiet a sound as any stout, well-built wall in the kingdom. Making nothing of this, he said, "I do not hear any thing, sir. What were they saying?"

"I believe I heard one of them call the other stupid and ugly."

"Are you sure, sir? It is two old ladies that live upon that side."

"Ha! That proves nothing. Age is no guarantee of any thing these days."

With this remark the magician appeared suddenly to grow tired of this conversation. He turned back to his book and started reading.

Jeremy waited a moment and then, since his master appeared to have forgotten all about him, he went away again.

"I have not thanked you yet, sir," said Stephen to the gentleman, "for these wonderful gifts."

"Ah, Stephen! I am glad I have pleased you. The diadem, I confess, is your own hat transformed by magic. I would have greatly preferred to give you a real crown, but I was entirely unable to lay my hand upon one at such short notice. You are disappointed, I dare say. Although now I come to think of it, the King of England has several crowns, and rarely makes use of any of them."

He raised his hands in the air and pointed upwards with two immensely long white fingers.

"Oh!" cried Stephen, suddenly realizing what the gentleman was about. "If you think of casting spells to bring the King of England here with one of his crowns – which I imagine you do, since you are all kindness – then I beg that you will spare yourself the trouble! I have no need of one at the moment, as you know, and the King of England is such an old gentleman – would it not perhaps be kinder to let him stay at home?"

"Oh, very well!" said the gentleman, lowering his hands.

For lack of any other occupation, he reassumed his abuse of the new magician. Nothing about the man pleased him. He ridiculed the book he was reading, found fault with the make of his boots, and was entirely unable to approve of his height (despite the fact that he was exactly the same height as the gentleman with the thistle-down hair – as was proved when they both happened to stand up at the same time.)

Stephen was anxious to return to his duties in Harley-street, but he feared that if he left them alone together then the gentleman might start throwing something more substantial than paper at the magician. "Shall you and I walk to Harley-street together, sir?" he asked. "Then you may tell me how your noble actions have moulded London and made it glorious. That is always so very entertaining. I never grow tired of hearing about it."

"Gladly, Stephen! Gladly!"

"Is it far, sir?"

"Is what far, Stephen?"

"Harley-street, sir. I do not know where we are."

"We are in Soho-square and no, it is not far at all!"

When they reached the house in Harley-street the gentleman took a most affectionate farewell of Stephen, urging him not to feel sad at this parting and reminding him that they would meet again that very night at Lost-hope. ". . . when a most charming ceremony will be held in the belfry of the Easternmost Tower. It commemorates an occasion which happened – oh! five hundred years ago or so – when I cleverly contrived to capture the little children of my enemy and we pushed them out of the belfry to their deaths. Tonight we will re-enact this great triumph! We will dress straw dolls in the children's blood-stained clothes and fling them down on to the paving stones and then we will sing and dance and rejoice over their destruction!"

"And do you perform this ceremony every year, sir? I feel sure I would have remembered it if I had seen it before. It is so very . . . striking."

"I am glad you think so. I perform it whenever I think of it. Of course it was a great deal more striking when we used real children."

# 27

# The magician's wife

## December 1809–January 1810

THERE WERE NOW two magicians in London to be admired and made much of and I doubt if it will come as much surprize to any one to learn that, of the two, London preferred Mr Strange. Strange was everyone's idea of what a magician ought to be. He was tall; he was charming; he had a most ironical smile; and, unlike Mr Norrell, he talked a great deal about magic and had no objection to answering any body's questions on the subject. Mr and Mrs Strange attended a great many evening- and dinner-parties, and at some point in the proceedings Strange would generally oblige the company with a shew of one of the minor sorts of magic. The most popular magic he did was to cause visions to appear upon the surface of water.[1]

---

[1] On May 14th, 1810 Strange wrote to John Segundus:

". . . There is a great passion here for seeing visions, which I am always glad to satisfy whenever I can. Whatever Norrell may say, it is very little trouble and nothing delights the layman so much. My only complaint is that people always end by asking me to shew them their relations. I was in Tavistock-square on Tuesday at the house of a family called Fulcher. I spilt some wine upon the table, did the magic and shewed them a sea-battle which was at that moment raging in the Bahamas, a view of a ruined Neapolitan monastery by moonlight and finally the Emperor Napoleon Buonaparte drinking a cup of chocolate with his feet in a steaming bowl of water.

"The Fulchers were well-bred enough to seem interested in what I was doing, but at the end of the evening they asked me if I might be able to shew them their aunt who lives in Carlisle. For the next half an hour Arabella and I

Unlike Norrell, he did not use a silver basin which was the traditional vessel for seeing visions in. Strange said that really one could see so little in a basin that it was scarcely worth the trouble of casting the spells. He preferred instead to wait until the servants had cleared the dishes off the table and removed the cloth, then he would tip a glass of water or wine over the table and conjure visions into the pool. Fortunately his hosts were generally so delighted with the magic that they hardly ever complained of their stained, spoilt tables and carpets.

For their part Mr and Mrs Strange were settled in London much to their satisfaction. They had taken a house in Soho-square and Arabella was deep in all the pleasant cares connected with a new home: commissioning elegant new furniture from the cabinet-makers, entreating her friends to help her to some steady servants and going every day to the shops.

One morning in mid-December she received a message from one of the shopmen at Haig and Chippendale's Upholstery (a most attentive person) to say that a bronze silk with alternate satin and watered stripes had just arrived in the shop and he believed it might be the very thing for Mrs Strange's drawing-room curtains. This necessitated a little re-organization of Arabella's day.

"It appears from Mr Sumner's description to be very elegant," she told Strange at breakfast, "and I expect to like it very much. But if I chuse bronze-coloured silk for the curtains, then I believe I must give up any notion of having a wine-coloured velvet for the chaise-longue. I do not think bronze-colour and wine-colour will look well together. So I shall to go to Flint and Clark's to look at the wine-coloured velvet again, and see if I can bear to give it up. Then I will go to Haig and Chippendale's. But that means I will have no time to visit your aunt – which I really ought to do as she is

---

[1] *cont'd* were obliged to converse with each other while the family stared, enraptured, at the spectacle of an old lady seated by the fire, in a white cap, knitting." *Letters and Miscellaneous Papers of Jonathan Strange*, ed. John Segundus, pub. John Murray, London, 1824.

leaving for Edinburgh this morning. I want to thank her for finding Mary for us."

"Mmm?" said Strange, who was eating hot rolls and preserves, and reading *Curiose Observations upon the Anatomie of Faeries* by Holgarth and Pickle.[2]

"Mary. The new maid. You saw her last night."

"Ah," said Strange, turning a page.

"She seems a nice, pleasant girl with quiet ways. I am sure we will be very happy with her. So, as I was saying, I would be very grateful, Jonathan, if you would call upon your aunt this morning. You can walk down to Henrietta-street after breakfast and thank her for Mary. Then you can come to Haig and Chippendale's and wait for me there. Oh! And could you look in at Wedgwood and Byerley's and ask the people when the new dinner-service will be ready? It will be scarcely any trouble. It is very nearly on your way." She looked at him doubtfully. "Jonathan, are you listening to me?"

"Mmm?" said Strange, looking up. "Oh, entirely!"

So Arabella, attended by one of the footmen, walked to Wigmore-street where Flint and Clark had their establishment. But on this second viewing of the wine-coloured velvet she concluded that, though very handsome, it was altogether too sombre. So then she walked on, all anticipation, to St Martin's-lane to behold the bronze-coloured silk. When she arrived at Haig and Chippendale's she found the shopman waiting for her, but not her husband. The shopman was most apologetic but Mr Strange had not been there all morning.

She went out into the street again.

"George, do you see your master anywhere?" she asked the footman.

"No, madam."

[2] One of Mr Norrell's books. Mr Norrell mentioned it, somewhat obliquely, when Mr Segundus and Mr Honeyfoot waited upon him in early January 1807.

A grey rain was beginning to fall. A sort of premonition inspired her to look in at the window of a bookseller's. There she discovered Strange, talking energetically to Sir Walter Pole. So she went into the shop, bid Sir Walter good morning and sweetly inquired of her husband if he had visited his aunt or looked in at Wedgwood and Byerley's.

Strange seemed somewhat perplexed by the question. He looked down and discovered that he had a large book in his hand. He frowned at it as if he could not imagine how it had got there. "I *would* have done so, my love, of course," he said, "only Sir Walter has been talking to me all this while which has quite prevented me from beginning."

"It has been entirely my fault," Sir Walter hastily assured Arabella. "We have a problem with our blockade. It is the usual sort of thing and I have been telling Mr Strange about it in the hope he and Mr Norrell will be able to help us."

"And can you help?" asked Arabella.

"Oh, I should think so," said Strange.

Sir Walter explained that the British Government had received intelligence that some French ships – possibly as many as ten – had slipped through the British blockade. No one knew where they had gone or what they intended to do when they got there. Nor did the Government know where to find Admiral Armingcroft who was supposed to prevent this sort of thing happening. The Admiral and his fleet of ten frigates and two ships of the line had quite disappeared – presumably he had gone in pursuit of the French. There was a promising young captain, presently stationed at Madeira, and if the Admiralty had only been able to discover what was happening and *where* it was happening, they would have gladly put Captain Lightwood in charge of four or five more ships and sent him there. Lord Mulgrave had asked Admiral Greenwax what he thought they ought to do and Admiral Greenwax had asked the Ministers and the Ministers said that the Admiralty ought to consult Mr Strange and Mr Norrell immediately.

"I would not have you think that the Admiralty is entirely helpless without Mr Strange," smiled Sir Walter. "They have done what they can. They sent one of the clerks, a Mr Petrofax, to Greenwich to seek out a childhood friend of Admiral Armingcroft's to ask him, with his superior knowledge of the Admiral's character, what he thought the Admiral would do under such circumstances. But when Mr Petrofax got to Greenwich the Admiral's childhood friend was drunk in bed, and Mr Petrofax was not sure that he understood the question."

"I dare say Norrell and I will be able to suggest something," said Strange, thoughtfully, "but I think I should like to see the problem on a map."

"I have all the necessary maps and papers at my house. One of our servants will bring them to Hanover-square later today and then perhaps you will be so kind as to talk to Norrell . . ."

"Oh! But we can do that now!" said Strange. "Arabella does not mind waiting a few moments! You do not mind, do you?" he said to his wife. "I am meeting Mr Norrell at two o'clock and I believe that if I can explain the problem to him straightaway then we may be able to return an answer to the Admiralty before dinner."

Arabella, like a sweet, compliant woman and good wife, put all thoughts of her new curtains aside for the moment and assured both gentlemen that in such a cause it was no trouble to her to wait. It was settled that Mr and Mrs Strange would accompany Sir Walter to his house in Harley-street.

Strange took out his watch and looked at it. "Twenty minutes to Harley-street. Three-quarters of an hour to examine the problem. Then another fifteen minutes to Soho-square. Yes, there is plenty of time."

Arabella laughed. "He is not always so scrupulous, I assure you," she said to Sir Walter, "but he was late on Tuesday for an appointment with Lord Liverpool and Mr Norrell was not best pleased."

"That was not my fault," said Strange. "I was ready to leave the house in good time but I could not find my gloves." Arabella's teasing accusation of lateness continued to vex him and on the way to Harley-street he examined his watch as though in hopes of discovering something about the operation of Time which had hitherto gone unnoticed and which would vindicate him. When they reached Harley-street he thought he had it. "Ha!" he cried suddenly. "I know what it is. My watch is wrong!"

"I do not think so," said Sir Walter, taking out his own watch and shewing it to Strange. "It is precisely noon. Mine says the same."

"Then why do I hear no bells?" said Strange. "Do you hear bells?" he said to Arabella.

"No, I hear nothing."

Sir Walter reddened and muttered something about the bells in this parish and the neighbouring ones being no longer rung.

"Really?" asked Strange. "Why in the world not?"

Sir Walter looked as if he would have thanked Strange to keep his curiosity to himself, but all he said was, "Lady Pole's illness has left her nerves in a sad condition. The tolling of a bell is peculiarly distressing to her and I have asked the vestries of St Mary-le-bone and St Peter if they would, out of consideration for Lady Pole's nerves, forbear from ringing the church bells, and they have been so obliging as to agree."

This was rather extraordinary, but then it was generally agreed that Lady Pole's illness was a rather extraordinary thing with symptoms quite unlike any other. Neither Mr nor Mrs Strange had ever seen Lady Pole. No one had seen her for two years.

When they arrived at no. 9 Harley-street Strange was anxious to begin looking at Sir Walter's documents straightaway but he was obliged to curb his impatience while Sir Walter satisfied himself that Arabella would not lack for amusement in their absence. Sir Walter was a well-bred man and greatly disliked leaving any guest alone in his house. To abandon a lady was particularly bad. Strange on the other hand was anxious to be on time for his appointment with Mr Norrell, so as fast as Sir Walter could suggest diversions, Strange was endeavouring to prove that Arabella needed none of them.

Sir Walter shewed Arabella the novels in the bookcase, and recommended Mrs Edgeworth's *Belinda* in particular as being likely to amuse her. "Oh," said Strange, interrupting, "I read *Belinda* to Arabella two or three years ago. Besides, you know, I do not think we will be so long that she will have time to finish a *three-volume* novel."

"Then perhaps some tea and seed-cake . . . ?" Sir Walter said to Arabella.

"But Arabella does not care for seed-cake," interrupted Strange, absent-mindedly picking up *Belinda* himself and beginning to read the first volume, "It is a thing she particularly dislikes."

"A glass of madeira, then," said Sir Walter. "You will take some madeira, I am sure. Stephen! . . . Stephen, fetch Mrs Strange a glass of madeira."

In the eerie, silent fashion peculiar to high-trained London servants, a tall black servant appeared at Sir Walter's elbow. Mr Strange seemed quite startled by his sudden arrival and stared hard at him for several moments, before he said to his wife, "You do not want madeira, do you? You do not want any thing."

"No, Jonathan. I do not want any thing," agreed his wife, laughing at their odd argument. "Thank you, Sir Walter, but I am perfectly content to sit here quietly and read."

The black servant bowed and departed as silently as he had come, and Strange and Sir Walter went off to talk of the French fleet and the missing English ships.

But when she was left alone, Arabella found that she was not after all in a mood for reading. On looking round the room in search of amusement her eye was caught by a large painting. It was a landscape comprising woods and a ruined castle perched on top of a cliff. The trees were dark and the ruins and cliff were touched with gold by the light of a setting sun; the sky by contrast was full of light and glowed with pearly colour. A large portion of the foreground was occupied by a silvery pool in which a young woman appeared to be drowning; a second figure bent over her – whether man, woman, satyr or faun, it was impossible to determine and, though Arabella studied their postures carefully, she could not decide whether it was the intention of the second figure to save the young woman or murder her. When she had tired of looking at this painting Arabella wandered out into the passage to look at the pictures there but, as these were for the most part watercolour views of Brighton and Chelmsford, she found them very dull.

Sir Walter and Strange could be heard talking in another room.

". . . extraordinary thing! Yet he is an excellent fellow in his way," said Sir Walter's voice.

"Oh! I know who you mean! He has a brother who is the organist at Bath Cathedral," said Strange. "He has a black-and-white cat that walks about the Bath streets just ahead of him. Once, when I was in Milsom-street . . ."

A door stood open, through which Arabella could see a very elegant drawing-room with a great number of paintings that appeared to be more splendid and richly coloured than any she had yet seen. She went in.

The room seemed to be full of light, although the day was every bit as grey and forbidding as it had been before. "So where does all this light come from?" wondered Arabella. "It is almost as if it shines out of the paintings, but that is impossible." The paintings were all of Venice[3] and certainly the great quantities of sky and sea which they contained made the room seem somehow insubstantial.

---

[3] These were Venetian paintings which Mr Norrell had seen at Mrs Wintertowne's house two years before. Mrs Wintertowne had informed Mr Norrell at the time that she intended to give them to Sir Walter and Miss Wintertowne as a wedding-present.

When she had done examining the paintings upon one wall, she turned to cross to the opposite wall and immediately discovered – much to her mortification – that she was not alone. A young woman was sitting before the fire on a blue sopha, regarding her with some curiosity. The sopha had a rather high back, which was the reason Arabella had not observed her before.

"Oh! I do beg your pardon!"

The young woman said nothing.

She was a remarkably elegant woman with a pale, perfect skin and dark hair most gracefully arranged. She wore a gown of white muslin and an Indian shawl of ivory, silver and black. She seemed altogether too well dressed to be a governess and too much at home to be a lady's companion. Yet if she were a guest in the house, why had Sir Walter not introduced her?

Arabella curtsied to the young woman and, blushing slightly, said, "I thought there was no one here! I beg your pardon for intruding upon you." She turned to leave.

"Oh!" said the young woman. "I hope you do not think of going! I so rarely see any one – scarcely any one at all! And besides you wished to see the paintings! You cannot deny it, you know, for I saw you in that mirror as you entered the room and your intention was plain." A large Venetian mirror hung above the fireplace. It had a most elaborate frame which was also made of mirror-glass and it was decorated with the ugliest glass flowers and scrolls imaginable. "I hope," said the young woman, "that you will not allow me to prevent you."

"But I fear I disturb you," said Arabella.

"Oh, but you do not!" The young woman gestured towards the paintings, "Pray. Continue."

So, feeling it would be a still worse breach of manners to refuse, Arabella thanked the young woman and went and examined the other paintings, but she did it less minutely than before because she was conscious that the young woman watched her in the mirror the entire time.

When she had finished, the young woman asked Arabella to sit. "And how do they please you?" she asked.

"Well," said Arabella, "they are certainly very beautiful. I particularly like the pictures of processions and feasts – we have nothing like them in England. So many fluttering banners! So many gilded boats and exquisite costumes! But it seems to me that the artist loves buildings and blue skies more than people. He has made them so small, so insignificant! Among so many marble palaces and bridges they seem almost lost. Do not you think so?"

This seemed to amuse the young woman. She smiled a wry smile. "Lost?" she said. "Oh, I should think they are indeed lost, poor souls! For, when all is said and done, Venice is only a labyrinth – a vast and beautiful labyrinth to be sure, but a labyrinth nonetheless and none but its oldest inhabitants can be sure of finding their way about – or, at least, that is my understanding."

"Indeed?" said Arabella. "That must certainly be very inconvenient. But then the sensation of being lost in a labyrinth must be so delightful! Oh! I believe I should give almost any thing to go there!"

The young woman regarded her with an odd, melancholy smile. "If you had spent months, as I have done, wearily parading through endless dark passageways, you would think very differently. The pleasures of losing oneself in a maze pall very quickly. And as for curious ceremonies, processions and feasts, well . . ." She shrugged. "I quite detest them!"

Arabella did not very well comprehend her, but thought that it might help if she discovered who the young woman was, and so she inquired as to her name.

"I am Lady Pole."

"Oh! Of course!" said Arabella and wondered why she had not thought of this before. She told Lady Pole her own name and that her husband had business with Sir Walter, which was the reason of her being there.

A sudden burst of loud laughter was heard from the direction of the library.

"They are supposed to be talking of the war," Arabella observed to her ladyship, "but either the war has got a great deal more entertaining recently, or else – as I suspect – they have left business far behind and have got to gossiping about their acquaintance. Half an hour ago Mr Strange could think of nothing but his next appointment, but now I suppose Sir Walter has drawn him off to talk of other things and I dare say he has forgot all about it." She smiled to herself as wives do when they pretend to criticize their husbands, but are really boasting of them. "I really do believe he is the most easily distracted creature in the world. Mr Norrell's patience must be sorely tried sometimes."

"Mr Norrell?" said Lady Pole.

"Mr Strange has the honour to be Mr Norrell's pupil," said Arabella.

She expected her ladyship to reply with some praise for Mr Norrell's extraordinary magical ability or some words of gratitude for his kindness. But Lady Pole said nothing and so Arabella continued in an encouraging tone, "Of course we have heard a great deal of the wonderful magic which Mr Norrell performed on your ladyship's behalf."

"Mr Norrell has been no friend to me," said Lady Pole in a dry, matter-of-fact tone. "I had far better be dead than be as I am."

It was such a shocking thing to hear that for several moments Arabella could think of nothing to say. She had no reason to love Mr Norrell. He had never done her any kindness – indeed he had several times gone out of his way to shew how little he regarded her, but for all that he was the only other representative of her husband's profession. So, just as the wife of an admiral will always take the part of the Navy or the wife of a bishop will speak up in favour of the Church, Arabella felt obliged to say something in defence of the other magician. "Pain and suffering are the very worst of companions and no doubt your ladyship grows heartily sick of them. No one in the world could blame you for wishing to be rid of them . . ." (Yet even as Arabella spoke these words, she was thinking, "It is very odd but she does not look ill. Not in the least.") "But if what I hear be true, then your ladyship is not without solace in your suffering. I must confess that I have never heard your ladyship's name spoken without its being accompanied by some praise for your devoted husband. Surely you would not gladly leave him? Surely, your ladyship, you must feel a little grateful to Mr Norrell – if only for Sir Walter's sake."

Lady Pole did not reply to this; instead she began to question Arabella about her husband. How long had he practised magic? How long had he been Mr Norrell's pupil? Was his magic generally successful? Did he perform magic by himself or only under Norrell's direction?

Arabella did her best to answer all the questions adding, "If there is any thing your ladyship would like me to ask Mr Strange on your behalf, if there is any service he can do, then your ladyship has only to name it."

"Thank you. But what I have to tell you is as much for your husband's sake as mine. I think Mr Strange ought to hear how I was left to a horrible fate by Mr Norrell. Mr Strange should know what sort of man he has to deal with. Will you tell him?"

"Of course. I . . ."

"Promise me that you will."

"I will tell Mr Strange any thing your ladyship wishes."

"I should warn you that I have made many attempts to tell people of my misery and I have never yet succeeded."

As Lady Pole said this something happened which Arabella did not quite understand. It was as if something in one of the paintings had moved, or someone had passed behind one of the mirrors, and the conviction came over her once again that this room was no room at all, that the walls had no real solidity but instead the room were only a sort of crossroads where strange winds blew upon Lady Pole from faraway places.

"In 1607," began Lady Pole, "a gentleman named Redeshawe in Halifax, West Yorkshire inherited £10 from his aunt. He used the money to buy a Turkish carpet, which he then brought home and spread over the stone flags of his parlour. Then he drank some beer and fell asleep in a chair by the fire. He awoke at two in the morning to find the carpet covered with three or four hundred people, each about two or three inches high. Mr Redeshawe observed that the most important individuals among them, both men and women, were gorgeously attired in gold and silver armour and that they rode white rabbits – which were to them as elephants are to us. When he asked what they were doing, one brave soul among them climbed up to his shoulder and bellowed in his ear that they intended to fight a battle according to the rules of Honoré Bonet and Mr Redeshawe's carpet was exactly suited to their purpose because the regularity of the patterns helped the heralds determine that each army was positioned correctly and took no unfair advantage over the other. However Mr Redeshawe did not chuse that a battle should be fought upon his new carpet and so he took a broom and . . . No, wait!" Lady Pole stopt and suddenly covered her face with her hands. "That is not what I wished to say!"

She began again. This time she told a story of a man who had gone hunting in a wood. He had become separated from his friends. His horse had caught its hoof in a rabbit-hole and he had tumbled off. As he fell he had had the strangest impression that he was somehow falling into the rabbit-hole. When he picked himself up he found he was in a strange country lit by its own sun and nurtured by its own rain. In a wood very like the one he had just left, he found a mansion where a party of gentlemen – some of them rather odd – were all playing cards together.

Lady Pole had just got to the part where the gentlemen invited the lost huntsman to join them, when a slight sound – scarcely more than an indrawn breath – made Arabella turn. She discovered that Sir Walter had entered the room and was gazing down at his wife in dismay.

"You are tired," he said to her.

Lady Pole looked up at her husband. Her expression at that moment was curious. There was sadness in it and pity too and, oddly enough, a little amusement. It was as if she were saying to herself, "Look at us! What a sad pair we make!" Aloud she said, "I am only as tired as I usually am. I must have walked for miles and miles last night. And danced for hours too!"

"Then you must rest," he insisted. "Let me take you upstairs to Pampisford and she will take care of you."

At first her ladyship seemed inclined to resist him. She seized Arabella's hand and held it, as if to shew him that she would not consent to be parted from her. But then just as suddenly she gave it up and allowed him to lead her away.

At the door she turned. "Goodbye, Mrs Strange. I hope they will let you come again. I hope you will do me that honour. I see no one. Or rather, I see whole roomfuls of people, but not a Christian among them."

Arabella stepped forward, intending to shake Lady Pole's hand and to assure her that she would gladly come again, but Sir Walter had already removed her ladyship from the room. For the second time that day Arabella was left alone in the house in Harley-street.

A bell began to toll.

Naturally she was a little surprized after all that Sir Walter had said about the bells of Mary-le-bone standing silent out of deference to Lady Pole's illness. This bell sounded very sad and far-away and it brought before her imagination all sorts of melancholy scenes . . .

*. . . bleak, wind-swept fens and moors; empty fields with broken walls and gates hanging off their hinges; a black, ruined church; an open grave; a suicide buried at a lonely crossroads; a fire of bones blazing in the twilit snow; a gallows with a man swinging from its arm; another man crucified upon a wheel; an ancient spear plunged into the mud with a strange talisman, like a little leather finger, hanging from it; a scarecrow whose black rags blew about so violently in the wind that he seemed about to leap into the grey air and fly towards you on vast black wings . . .*

"I must beg your pardon if you have seen any thing here to disturb you," said Sir Walter, coming suddenly back into the room.

Arabella caught hold of a chair to steady herself.

"Mrs Strange? You are not well." He took hold of her arm and helped her sit down. "May I fetch someone? Your husband? Her ladyship's maid?"

"No, no," said Arabella, a little out of breath. "I want no one, nothing. I thought . . . I did not know you were here. That is all."

Sir Walter stared at her in great concern. She tried to smile at him, but she was not quite sure that the smile turned out well.

He put his hands in his pockets, took them out, ran his fingers through his hair, and sighed deeply. "I dare say her ladyship has been telling you all sorts of odd tales," he said, unhappily.

Arabella nodded.

"And hearing them has distressed you. I am very sorry for it."

"No, no. Not at all. Her ladyship did talk a little of . . . of what seemed rather odd, but I did not mind it. Not in the least! I felt a little faint. But do not connect the two, I beg you! It was nothing to do with her ladyship! I had a sort of foolish idea that there was a sort of mirror before me with all sorts of strange landscapes in it and I thought I was falling into it. I suppose I must have been about to faint and your coming in just then prevented it. But it is very odd. I never did such a thing before."

"Let me fetch Mr Strange."

Arabella laughed. "You may if you wish, but I assure you he will be a great deal less concerned about me than you are. Mr Strange has never been much interested in other people's indispositions. His own are quite another matter! But, there is no need to fetch any body. See! I am myself again. I am perfectly well."

There was a little pause.

"Lady Pole . . ." began Arabella and paused, not knowing quite how to continue.

"Her ladyship is generally calm enough," said Sir Walter, "not exactly at peace, you understand, but calm enough. But on the rare occasions when any one new comes to the house, it always excites her to these outlandish speeches. I am sure you are too good to repeat any thing of what she has said."

"Oh! Of course! I would not repeat it for the world!"

"You are very kind."

"And may . . . may I come again? Her ladyship seems to wish it very much and I would be very happy in the acquaintance."

Sir Walter took a long moment to consider this proposal. Finally he nodded. Then he somehow turned his nod into a bow. "I shall consider that you do us both great honour," he said. "Thank you."

Strange and Arabella left the house in Harley-street and Strange was in high spirits. "I see the way to do it," he told her. "Nothing could be simpler. It is a pity that I must wait for Norrell's opinion before beginning or I believe I might solve the entire problem in the next half hour. As I see it, there are two crucial points. The first . . . Whatever is the matter?"

With a little "Oh!" Arabella had stopt.

It had suddenly occurred to her that she had given two entirely contradictory promises: one to Lady Pole to tell Strange about the gentleman in Yorkshire who had purchased a carpet; and the second to Sir Walter not to repeat any thing that Lady Pole had said. "It is nothing," she said.

"And which of the many occupations that Sir Walter was preparing for you did you fix upon?"

"None of them. I . . . I saw Lady Pole and we had some conversation together. That is all."

"Did you indeed? A pity I was not with you. I should have liked to see the woman who owes her life to Norrell's magic. But I have not told you what happened to me! You remember how the negro servant came in very suddenly? Well, just for a moment I had the distinct impression that there was a tall black king standing there, crowned with a silver diadem and holding a shining silver sceptre and an orb – but when I looked again there was no one there but Sir Walter's negro servant. Is not that absurd?" Strange laughed.

Strange had gossiped so long with Sir Walter that he was almost an hour late for his appointment with Mr Norrell and Mr Norrell was very angry. Later the same day Strange sent a message to the Admiralty to say that Mr Norrell and he had looked into the problem of the missing French ships and that they believed they were in the Atlantic, on their way to the West Indies where they intended to cause some mischief. Furthermore the two magicians thought that Admiral Armingcroft had guessed correctly what the French were doing and had gone after them. The Admiralty, on the advice of Mr Strange and Mr Norrell, sent orders to Captain Lightwood to follow the Admiral westwards. In due course some of the French ships were captured and those that were not fled back to their French ports and stayed there.

Arabella's conscience was sorely racked over the two promises she had made. She put the problem to several matrons, friends of hers in whose good sense and careful judgement she reposed a great deal of confidence. Naturally she presented it in an ideal form without naming any one or mentioning any of the particular circumstances. Unfortunately this had the effect of making her dilemma entirely incomprehensible and the wise matrons were unable to help her. It distressed her that she could not confide in Strange, but clearly even to mention it would be to break her word to Sir Walter. After much deliberation she decided that a promise to a person *in* their senses ought to be more binding than a promise to someone *out of* their senses. For, after all, what was to be gained by repeating the nonsensical ramblings of a poor madwoman? So she never told Strange what Lady Pole had said.

A few days later, Mr and Mrs Strange were at a house in Bedford-square attending a concert of Italian music. Arabella found much to enjoy, but the room where they sat was not quite warm and so in a little pause that ensued when a new singer was joining the musicians, she slipped away without any fuss to fetch her shawl from where it lay in another room. She was just wrapping it around herself when there was a whisper of sound behind her and she looked up to see Drawlight, approaching her with the rapidity of a dream and crying out, "Mrs Strange! How glad I am to see you! And how is dear Lady Pole? I hear that you have seen her?"

Arabella agreed reluctantly that she had.

Drawlight drew her arm through his as a precaution against her running away, and said, "The trouble I have been at to procure an invitation to that house you would scarcely believe! None of my efforts have met with the least success! Sir Walter puts me off with one paltry excuse after another. It is always exactly the same – her ladyship is ill or she is a little better, but she is never well enough to see any body."

"Well, I suppose . . ." offered Arabella.

"Oh! Quite!" interrupted Drawlight. "*If* she is ill, then of course the rabble must be kept away. But that is no reason for excluding *me*. I saw her when she was a *corpse*! Oh, yes! You did not know that, I dare say? On the night he brought her back from the dead Mr Norrell came to me and pleaded with me to accompany him to the house. His words were, 'Come with me, my dear Drawlight, for I do not think that my spirits can support the sight of a lady, young, fair and innocent, cut off in the sweetest period of existence!' She stays in the house and sees no one. Some people think that her resurrection has made her proud and unwilling to mix with ordinary mortals. But I think the truth is quite different. I believe that her death and resurrection have bred in her a taste for odd experiences. Do not you think they might? It seems to me entirely possible that she takes something in order to see horrors! I suppose you saw no evidence of any thing of that sort? She took no sips from a glass of odd-coloured liquid? There was no folded paper pushed hurriedly into a pocket as you entered the room? – A paper such as might contain a teaspoon or two of powder? No? Laudanum generally comes in a little blue glass vial two or three inches high. In cases of addiction the family always believe that they can conceal the truth, but it is quite in vain. It is always found out in the end." He gave an affected laugh, "*I* always find it out."

Arabella gently removed her arm from his and begged his pardon. She was quite unable to supply him with the information he required. She knew nothing of any little bottles or powders.

She returned to the concert with much less agreeable feelings than she had taken away.

"Odious, odious little man!"

# 28

# The Duke of Roxburghe's library

## November 1810–January 1811

AT THE END of 1810 the Government's situation was about as bad as it could possibly be. Bad news met the Ministers at every turn. The French were everywhere triumphant; the other great European powers who had once combined with Britain to fight the Emperor Napoleon Buonaparte (and who had subsequently been defeated by him) now discovered their mistake and became instead his allies. At home, trade was destroyed by the war and men in every part of the kingdom were bankrupted; the harvest failed two years together. The King's youngest daughter fell ill and died, and the King went mad from grief.

The war destroyed every present comfort and cast a deep gloom over the future. Soldiers, merchants, politicians and farmers all cursed the hour that they were born, but magicians (a contrary breed of men if ever there was one) were entirely delighted by the course events were taking. Not for many hundreds of years had their art been held in such high regard. Many attempts to win the war had ended in disaster and magic now seemed the greatest hope Britain had. There were gentlemen from the War Office and all the various boards and offices of the navy who were most anxious to employ Mr Norrell and Mr Strange. The press of business at Mr Norrell's house in Hanover-square was often so great that visitors were obliged to wait until three or four in the morning before Mr Strange and Mr Norrell were able to attend to them. This was no very great trial as long as there was a crowd of gentlemen in Mr Norrell's drawing-room, but woe to the one who was last, for it is never a pleasant thing to have to wait in the middle of night outside a closed door and know that behind the door are two magicians doing magic.[1]

A story which was circulating at the time (one heard it everywhere one went) was the tale of the Emperor Napoleon Buonaparte's bungled attempts to find a magician of his own. Lord Liverpool's spies[2] reported that the Emperor was so jealous of the success of English magicians that he had sent out officers to search through all his Empire for some person or persons with magical abilities. Thus far, however, all that they had discovered was a Dutchman called Witloof who had a magic wardrobe. The wardrobe had been taken to Paris in a barouche-landau. At Versailles, Witloof had promised the Emperor that he could find the answer to any question inside the wardrobe.

According to the spies, Buonaparte had asked the wardrobe the following three questions: "Would the baby the Empress was expecting be male?"; "Would the Czar of Russia change sides again?"; "When would the English be defeated?"

Witloof had gone inside the wardrobe and come out with the

---

[1] Among the forms of magic which Strange and Norrell performed in 1810 were: causing an area of sea in the Bay of Biscay to silt up and a vast wood of monstrous trees to appear there (thus destroying twenty French ships); causing unusual tides and winds to baffle French ships and destroy French crops and livestock; the fashioning of rain into fleets of ships, walled cities, gigantic figures, flights of angels, etc., etc., in order to frighten, confuse or charm French soldiers and sailors; bringing on night when the French were expecting day and vice versa.

All the above are listed in *De Generibus Artium Magicarum Anglorum* by Francis Sutton-Grove.

[2] The previous Secretary of War, Lord Castlereagh, had quarrelled violently with Mr Canning in late 1809. The two gentlemen had fought a duel, after which both had been obliged to resign from the Government. The present Secretary of War, Lord Liverpool, was in fact the same person as Lord Hawkesbury, who has been mentioned before in these pages. He had left off one title and assumed another when his father died in December 1808.

following answers: "Yes," "No," and "In four weeks time". Every time Witloof entered the wardrobe there was the most hideous noise as if half the demons in Hell were screaming inside it, clouds of little silver stars issued from the cracks and hinges and the wardrobe rocked slightly upon its ball-and-claw feet. After the three questions had been answered, Buonaparte regarded the wardrobe silently for some moments, and then he strode over and pulled open the doors. Inside he found a goose (to make the noises) and some saltpetre (to produce the silver stars) and a dwarf (to ignite the saltpetre and prod the goose). No one knew for certain what had happened to Witloof and the dwarf, but the Emperor had eaten the goose for dinner the following day.

In the middle of November the Admiralty invited Mr Norrell and Mr Strange to Portsmouth to review the Channel Fleet, an honour usually reserved for admirals, heroes and kings. The two magicians and Arabella went down to Portsmouth in Mr Norrell's carriage. Their entrance into the town was marked by a salute of guns from all the ships in the harbour and all the arsenals and forts that surrounded it. They were rowed about among the ships at Spithead, accompanied by a whole array of admirals, flag officers and captains in their several barges. Other less official boats went too, full of the good citizens of Portsmouth come to look at the two magicians and wave and cheer. On returning to Portsmouth Mr Norrell and Mr and Mrs Strange looked over the dock-yard and in the evening a grand ball was given in their honour at the Assembly Rooms and all the town was illuminated.

The ball was generally reckoned a very delightful affair. There was one slight annoyance early on when some of the guests were foolish enough to make some remarks to Mr Norrell upon the pleasantness of the occasion and the beauty of the ballroom. Mr Norrell's rude reply immediately convinced them that he was a cross, disagreeable man, unwilling to talk to any one below the rank of admiral. However they found ample compensation for this disappointment in the lively, unreserved manners of Mr and Mrs

Strange. *They* were happy to be introduced to Portsmouth's principal inhabitants and they spoke admiringly of Portsmouth, of the ships they had seen and of things naval and nautical in general. Mr Strange danced every dance without exception, Mrs Strange only sat out for two and they did not return to their rooms at the Crown until after two o'clock in the morning.

Having got to bed a little before three, Strange was not best pleased to be woken again at seven by a knock on the door. He got up and found one of the inn-servants standing in the hallway.

"Beg pardon, sir," said the man, "but the port-admiral has sent to say the *False Prelate* is run upon Horse Sand. He has sent Captain Gilbey to fetch one of the magicians but the other magician has the headach and will not go."

This was not perhaps as perfectly comprehensible as the man intended, and Strange suspected that, even if he had been rather more awake, he would not have understood it. Nevertheless it was clear that *something* had occurred and that he was required to go *somewhere*. "Tell Captain Whatever-it-is to wait," he said with a sigh. "I am coming."

He dressed and went downstairs. In the coffee-room he found a handsome young man in a captain's uniform who was pacing up and down. This was Captain Gilbey. Strange remembered him from the ballroom – an intelligent-seeming man with pleasant manners. He looked greatly relieved to see Strange and explained that a ship, the *False Prelate*, had run upon one of the shoals at Spithead. It was an awkward situation. The *False Prelate* might be got off without serious damage or she might not. In the meantime the port-admiral sent his compliments to Mr Norrell and Mr Strange and begged that one or both of them go with Captain Gilbey to see if there was any thing that they could do.

A gig stood outside the Crown with one of the inn-servants at the horse's head. Strange and Captain Gilbey got into it and Captain Gilbey drove them briskly through the town. The town was beginning to stir with a certain air of hurry and alarm.

Windows were opening; heads in nightcaps were poking out of them and shouting down questions; people in the street were shouting back answers. A great many people seemed to be hurrying in the same direction as Captain Gilbey's carriage.

When they reached the ramparts, Captain Gilbey halted. The air was cold and damp and there was a fresh breeze blowing off the sea. A little way out a huge ship was lying on her side. Sailors very small and black and far away could be seen clinging to the rail and clambering down the side of the ship. A dozen or so rowing boats and small sailing vessels were crowded around her. Some of the occupants of these boats appeared to be holding energetic conversations with the sailors on the ship.

To Strange's unnautical eye, it looked very much as if the ship had simply lain down and gone to sleep. He felt that if he had been the Captain he would have spoken to her sternly and made her get up again.

"But surely," he said, "dozens of ships go in and out of Portsmouth all the time. How could such a thing happen?"

Captain Gilbey shrugged. "I am afraid it is not so remarkable as you suppose. The master might not be familiar with the channels of Spithead, or he might be drunk."

A large crowd was assembling. In Portsmouth every inhabitant has some connexion with the sea and ships, and some interest of his own to preserve. The daily talk about the place is of the ships going in and out of the harbour and the ships that lie at anchor at Spithead. An event such as this was of almost universal concern. It drew not only the regular loungers of the place (who were numerous enough), but also the steadier citizens and tradesmen, and of course every naval gentleman who had leisure to go and see. A vigorous argument was already taking place over what the master of the ship had done wrong, and what the port admiral must do to put it right. As soon as the crowd understood who Strange was and what he had come to do, it was glad to transfer the benefit of its many opinions to him. Unfortunately a great deal of nautical language was employed and Strange had at best an indistinct impression of his informants' meaning. After one explanation he made the mistake of inquiring what "beating off" and "heaving to" meant, which led to such a very perplexing explanation of the principles of sailing that he understood a great deal less at the end of it than he had at the beginning.

"Well!" he said. "The chief problem is surely that she is on her side. Shall I simply turn her upright? That would be quite easy to accomplish."

"Good Lord! No!" cried Captain Gilbey. "That will not do at all! Unless it is done in the most careful manner imaginable her keel would almost certainly snap in two. Everybody would drown."

"Oh!" said Strange.

His next attempt to help fared even worse. Something somebody said about a fresher breeze blowing the ship off the sandbank at high water caused him to think that a strong wind might help. He raised his hands to begin conjuring one up.

"What are you doing?" asked Captain Gilbey.

Strange told him.

"No! No! No!" cried the Captain, appalled.

Several people seized Strange bodily. One man started shaking him vigorously, as though he thought that he might in this way dispel any magic before it took effect.

"The wind is the from south-west," explained Captain Gilbey. "If it grows stronger, it will batter the ship against the sands and almost certainly break her up. Everybody will drown!"

Someone else was heard to remark that he could not for the life of him understand why the Admiralty thought so highly of this fellow whose ignorance was so astonishing.

A second man replied sarcastically that he might not be much of a magician but at least he danced very well.

A third person laughed.

"What is the sand called?" asked Strange.

Captain Gilbey shook his head in an exasperated fashion to convey that he had not the least idea what Strange was talking about.

"The . . . the place . . . the thing on which the ship is caught," urged Strange. "Something about horses?"

"The shoal is called Horse Sand," said Captain Gilbey coldly and turned away to speak to someone else.

For the next minute or two no one paid any attention to the magician. They watched the progress of the sloops and brigs and barges around the *False Prelate* and they looked to the skies and talked of how the weather was changing and where the wind would be at high water.

Suddenly several people called attention to the water. Something odd had appeared there. It was a large, silvery something with a long, oddly-shaped head and hair like long pale weeds waving behind it. It seemed to be swimming towards the *False Prelate*. No sooner had the crowd begun to exclaim and wonder about this mysterious object than several more appeared. The next moment there were a whole host of silvery shapes – more than a man could count – all swimming towards the ship with great ease and speed.

"What in the world are they?" asked a man in the crowd.

They were much too large to be men and not at all like fish or dolphins.

"They are horses," said Strange.

"Where did they come from?" asked another man.

"I made them," said Strange, "out of the sand. Out of Horse Sand, to be precise."

"But will they not dissolve?" asked one of the crowd.

"And what are they for?" asked Captain Gilbey.

Strange said, "They are made of sand and sea-water and magic, and they will last as long as there is work for them to do. Captain Gilbey, get one of the boats to take a message to the Captain of the *False Prelate* to say that his men should lash the horses to the ship, as many of them as they can. The horses will pull the ship off the shoal."

"Oh!" said Captain Gilbey. "Very well. Yes, of course."

Within half an hour of the message reaching the *False Prelate*, the ship was clear of the shoal and the sailors were busy putting the sails to rights and doing the thousand and one things which sailors do (things which are quite as mysterious in their way as the actions of magicians). However, it ought to be said that the magic did not work quite as Strange intended. He had not imagined there would be much difficulty in capturing the horses. He supposed that the ship would have plenty of ropes to make the halters and he had tried to regulate the magic so that the horses would be as biddable as possible. But sailors in general do not know much of horses. They know the sea and that is all. Some of the sailors did their best to catch hold of the horses and harness them, but many had not the least idea how to begin or they were too afraid of the silvery, ghostly creatures to go anywhere near them. Of the hundred horses that Strange created only about twenty were eventually harnessed to the ship. These twenty were certainly instrumental in pulling the *False Prelate* off the sand, but equally useful was the great trough in the sandbank which appeared as more and more horses were created out of it.

In Portsmouth opinion was divided over whether Strange had done something glorious in saving the *False Prelate* or whether he had merely used the disaster to improve his own career. Many of the captains and officers about the place said that the magic he had done had been of a very showy sort and was obviously intended more to draw attention to his own talent and impress the Admiralty than to save the ship. Nor were they best pleased about the sand-horses. These did not just disappear when their work was done, as Strange had said they would; instead they swam about Spithead for a day and a half, after which they lay down and became sandbanks in new and entirely unexpected places. The masters and pilots of Portsmouth complained to the port-admiral that Strange had permanently altered the channels and shoals in Spithead so that the Navy would now have all the expense and trouble of taking soundings and surveying the anchorage again.

However, in London, where the Ministers knew as little of ships and seamanship as Strange, only one thing was clear: Strange had saved a ship, the loss of which would have cost the Admiralty a vast amount of money.

"One thing that the rescue of the *False Prelate* demonstrates," remarked Sir Walter Pole to Lord Liverpool, "is the very great advantage of having a magician upon the spot, able to deal with a crisis as it occurs. I know that we considered sending Norrell somewhere and were forced to give it up, but what of Strange?"

Lord Liverpool considered this. "I think," he said, "we could only justify sending Mr Strange to serve with one of the generals if we were reasonably confident of that general shortly achieving some sort of success against the French. Anything else would be an unforgivable waste of Mr Strange's talents which, God knows, we need badly enough in London. Frankly the choice is not great. Really there is no one but Lord Wellington."

"Oh, quite!"

Lord Wellington was in Portugal with his army and so his opinion could not be easily ascertained, but by an odd coincidence his wife lived at no. 11 Harley-street, just opposite Sir Walter's own house. When Sir Walter went home that evening he knocked at Lady Wellington's door and asked her ladyship what she thought Lord Wellington would say to the idea of a magician. But Lady Wellington, a small, unhappy person whose opinion was not much valued by her husband, did not know.

Strange, on the other hand, was delighted with the proposal. Arabella, though somewhat less delighted, gave her assent very readily. The greatest obstacle to Strange's going proved to be, to no one's great surprize, Norrell. In the past year Mr Norrell had grown to rely a great deal upon his pupil. He consulted Strange upon all those matters which in bygone days had been referred to

Drawlight and Lascelles. Mr Norrell talked of nothing but Mr Strange when Strange was away, and talked to no one *but* Strange when Strange was present. His feelings of attachment seemed all the stronger for being entirely new; he had never felt truly comfortable in any one's society before. If, in a crowded drawing-room or ballroom, Strange contrived to escape for a quarter of an hour, Mr Norrell would send Drawlight after him to discover where he had gone and whom he was talking to. Consequently, when Mr Norrell learnt there was a plan to send his only pupil and friend to the war he was shocked. "I am astonished, Sir Walter," he said, "that you should even suggest such a thing!"

"But every man must be prepared to make sacrifices for the sake of his country during a war," said Sir Walter with some irritation, "and thousands have already done so, you know."

"But they were *soldiers*!" cried Mr Norrell. "Oh! I dare say a soldier is very valuable in his way but that is nothing to the loss the Nation would sustain if any thing were to happen to Mr Strange! There is, I understand, a school at High Wycombe where 300 officers are trained every year. I would to God that I were so fortunate as to have 300 magicians to educate! If I had, then English magic might be in a much more promising situation than it is at present!"

After Sir Walter had tried and failed, Lord Liverpool and the Duke of York undertook to speak to Mr Norrell on the subject, but Mr Norrell could not be persuaded by any of them to view Strange's proposed departure with any thing other than horror.

"Have you considered, sir," said Strange, "the great respect that it will win for English magic?"

"Oh, I dare say it might," said Mr Norrell peevishly, "but nothing is so likely to evoke the Raven King and all that wild, mischievous sort of magic as the sight of an English magician upon a battlefield! People will begin to think that we raise fairy-spirits and consult with owls and bears. Whereas it is my hope for English magic that it should be regarded as a quiet, respectable sort of profession – the sort of profession in fact . . ."

"But, sir," said Strange, hastily interrupting a speech he had heard a hundred times before, "I shall have no company of fairy knights at my back. And there are other considerations which we would do very wrong to ignore. You and I have often lamented that we are continually asked to do the same sorts of magic over and over again. I dare say the exigencies of the war will require me to do magic that I have not done before – and, as we have often observed to each other, sir, the practice of magic makes the theory so much easier to understand."

But the two magicians were too different in temperament ever to come to an agreement upon such a point. Strange spoke of braving the danger in order to win glory for English magic. His language and metaphors were all drawn from games of chance and from war and were scarcely likely to find favour with Mr Norrell. Mr Norrell assured Mr Strange that he would find war very disagreeable. "One is often wet and cold upon a battlefield. You will like it a great deal less than you suppose."

For several weeks in January and February 1811 it seemed as if Mr Norrell's opposition would prevent Strange's going to war. The mistake that Sir Walter, Lord Liverpool, the Duke of York and Strange had all made was to appeal to Mr Norrell's nobility, patriotism and sense of duty. There is no doubt that Mr Norrell possessed these virtues, but there were other principles which were stronger in him and which would always counter any higher faculty.

Fortunately there were two gentlemen at hand who knew how to manage matters rather better. Lascelles and Drawlight were as anxious as every body else that Strange should go to Portugal and in their opinion the best method to achieve it was to play upon Mr Norrell's anxiety over the fate of the Duke of Roxburghe's library.

This library had long been a thorn in Mr Norrell's side. It was one of the most important private libraries in the kingdom – second only to Mr Norrell's own. It had a curious, poignant history. Some fifty years before, the Duke of Roxburghe, a most intelligent, civilized and respectable gentleman, had chanced to fall in love with the Queen's sister and had applied to the King for permission to marry her. For various reasons to do with court etiquette, form and precedence the King had refused. Heartbroken, the Duke and the Queen's sister made a solemn promise to love each other for ever and never upon any inducement to marry any one else. Whether the Queen's sister kept her side of the bargain I do not know, but the Duke retired to his castle in the Scottish borders and, to fill his lonely days, he began to collect rare books: exquisite illuminated mediaeval manuscripts and editions of the very first printed books produced in the workshops of men of such genius as William Caxton of London and Valdarfer of Venice. By the early years of the century the Duke's library was one of the wonders of the world. His Grace was fond of poetry, chivalry, history and theology. He had no particular interest in magic, but all old books delighted him and it would have been very odd if one or two magical texts had not found their way into his library.

Mr Norrell had written to the Duke a number of times begging to be allowed to examine and perhaps purchase any books of magic which the Duke possessed. The Duke, however, felt no inclination to satisfy Mr Norrell's curiosity and, being immensely wealthy, he did not want Mr Norrell's money. Having been true to his promise to the Queen's sister through many a long year, the Duke had no children and no obvious heir. When he died a large number of his male relatives were seized by a strong conviction that they were the next Duke of Roxburghe. These gentlemen took their claims before the Committee of Privileges of the House of Lords. The Committee considered and came to the conclusion that the new Duke was either Major-General Ker or Sir James Innes, but as to which of them it might be the Committee was not quite certain and it settled itself to consider the matter further. By early 1811 it had still not come to a decision.

On a cold, wet Tuesday morning Mr Norrell was seated with

Mr Lascelles and Mr Drawlight in the library at Hanover-square. Childermass was also in the room, writing letters to various Government departments upon Mr Norrell's behalf. Strange had gone to Twickenham with Mrs Strange to visit a friend.

Lascelles and Drawlight were speaking of the lawsuit between Ker and Innes. One or two seemingly random allusions upon Lascelles's part to the famous library caught Mr Norrell's attention.

"What do we know of these men?" he asked Lascelles. "Have they any interest in the practice of magic?"

Lascelles smiled. "You may be easy on that score, sir. I assure you the only thing that Innes or Ker cares for is to be Duke. I do not think I have ever seen either of them so much as open a book."

"Indeed? They do not care for books? Well, that is most reassuring." Mr Norrell thought for a moment. "But supposing one of them were to come into possession of the Duke's library and chanced to find some rare magical text upon a shelf and become curious about it. People are curious about magic, you know. That has been one of the more regrettable consequences of my own success. This man might read a little and find himself inspired to try a spell or two. It is, after all, exactly how I began myself when as a boy of twelve I opened a book from my uncle's library and found inside a single page torn from a much older volume. The instant I read it, the conviction took hold of me that I must be a magician!"

"Indeed? That is most interesting," said Lascelles, in tones of complete boredom. "But it is hardly, I think, likely to happen to Innes or Ker. Innes must be in his seventies and Ker about the same. Neither man is in search of a new career."

"Oh! But have they no young relatives? Relatives who are perhaps avid readers of *The Friends of English Magic* and *The Modern Magician*? Relatives who would seize upon any books of magic the instant they laid eyes upon them! No, forgive me, Mr Lascelles, but I cannot regard the advanced age of the two gentlemen as any security at all!"

"Very well. But I doubt, sir, if these young thaumatomanes[3] whom you describe so vividly will have any opportunity to view the library. In order to pursue their claim to the dukedom, both Ker and Innes have incurred vast legal expenses. The first concern of the new Duke, whoever he may be, will be to pay off his lawyers. His first act upon entering Floors Castle will be to look around for something to sell.[4] I shall be very much surprized if the library is not put up for sale within a week of the Committee giving its decision."

"A book sale!" exclaimed Mr Norrell in alarm.

"What are you afraid of now?" asked Childermass, looking up from his writing. "A book sale is generally the thing most calculated to please you."

"Oh! but that was before," said Mr Norrell, "when no one in the kingdom had the least interest in books of magic except me, but now I fear a great many people might try to buy them. I dare say there might be accounts in *The Times*."

"Oh!" cried Drawlight. "If the books are bought by someone else you may complain to the Ministers! You may complain to the Prince of Wales! It is not in the interests of the Nation that books of magic should be in any one's possession but your own, Mr Norrell."

"Except Strange," said Lascelles. "I do not think the Prince of Wales or the Ministers would have any objections to Strange's owning the books."

"That is true," agreed Drawlight. "I had forgot Strange."

Mr Norrell looked more alarmed than ever. "But Mr Strange will understand that it is proper for the books to be mine," he said. "They should be collected together in one library. They ought not to be separated." He looked about hopefully for someone to agree with him. "Naturally," he continued, "I shall have no objection to

[3] Thaumatomane: a person possessed of a passion for magic and wonders, *Dictionary of the English Language* by Samuel Johnson.
[4] Floors Castle is the home of the Dukes of Roxburghe.

Mr Strange reading them. Everyone knows how many of my books – my own precious books – I have lent to Mr Strange. That is . . . I mean, it would depend upon the subject."

Drawlight, Lascelles and Childermass said nothing. They did indeed know how many books Mr Norrell had lent Mr Strange. They also knew how many he had withheld.

"Strange is a gentleman," said Lascelles. "He will behave as a gentleman and expect you to do the same. If the books are offered privately to you and you alone, then I think you may buy them, but if they are auctioned, he will feel entitled to bid against you."

Mr Norrell paused, looked at Lascelles and licked his lips nervously. "And how do you suppose the books will be sold? By auction or by private transaction?"

"Auction," said Lascelles, Drawlight and Childermass together.

Mr Norrell covered his face with his hands.

"Of course," said Lascelles, slowly as if the idea were just occurring to him at that moment, "if Strange were abroad, he would not be able to bid." He took a sip of his coffee. "Would he?"

Mr Norrell looked up with new hope in his face.

Suddenly it became highly desirable that Mr Strange should go to Portugal for a year or so.[5]

---

[5] The Committee of Privileges eventually decided in favour of Sir James Innes and, just as Mr Lascelles had predicted, the new Duke immediately put the library up for sale.

The auction in the summer of 1812 (while Strange was in the Peninsula) was possibly the most notable bibliographic event since the burning of the library at Alexandria. It lasted for forty-one days and was the cause of at least two duels.

Among the Duke's books there were found seven magical texts, all of them extraordinary.

*Rosa et Fons* was a mystical meditation upon magic by an unknown fourteenth-century magician.

*Thomas de Dundelle*, a hitherto undiscovered poem by Chrétien de Troyes, was a colourful version of the life of Thomas Dundale, the Raven King's first human servant.

---

[5] *cont'd* *The Book of Loveday Ingham* was an account of the day-to-day occupations of a fifteenth-century magician in Cambridge.

*Exercitatio Magica Nobilissima* was a seventeenth-century attempt to describe all of English magic.

*The History of Seven* was a very muddled work, partly in English, partly in Latin and partly in an unknown fairy language. Its age could not be guessed at, the author could not be identified and the purpose of the said author in writing the book was entirely obscure. It appeared to be, upon the whole, the history of a city in Faerie, called "Seven", but the information was presented in a very confusing style and the author would frequently break off from his narrative to accuse some unspecified person of having injured him in some mysterious way. These parts of the text more resembled an indignant letter than any thing else.

*The Parliament of Women* was an allegorical sixteenth-century description of the wisdom and magic that belongs particularly to women.

But by far the most wonderful was *The Mirrour of the Lyf of Ralph Stokesie*, which along with a first edition of Boccaccio's *Decameron* was put up for auction on the last day. Even Mr Norrell had been entirely ignorant of the existence of this book until that day. It appeared to have been written by two authors, one a fifteenth-century magician called William Thorpe, the other Ralph Stokesey's fairy servant, Col Tom Blue. For this treasure Mr Norrell paid the quite unheard-of sum of 2,100 guineas.

Such was the general respect for Mr Norrell that not a single gentleman in the room bid against him. But a lady bid against him for every book. In the weeks before the auction Arabella Strange had been very busy. She had written numerous letters to Strange's relations and paid visits to all her friends

[5] *cont'd* in London in attempt to borrow enough money to buy some of the books for her husband, but Norrell outbid her for every one.

Sir Walter Scott, the author, was present and he described the end of the auction. "Such was Mrs Strange's disappointment at losing *The Life of Ralph Stokesey* that she sat in tears. At that moment Mr Norrell walked by with the book in his hand. Not a word, not a glance did this man have for his pupil's wife. I do not know when I last saw behaviour so little to my liking. Several people observed this treatment and I have heard some harsh things said of Norrell. Even Lord Portishead, whose admiration of the magician knows no bounds, admits that he thinks Norrell has behaved remarkably ill towards Mrs Strange."

But it was not only Mr Norrell's treatment of Mrs Strange that drew unfavourable comment. In the weeks that followed the auction scholars and historians waited to hear what new knowledge was to be found in the seven wonderful books. In particular they were in high hopes that *The Mirrour of the Lyf of Ralph Stokesey* would provide answers to some of the most puzzling mysteries in English magic. It was commonly supposed that Mr Norrell would reveal his new discoveries in the pages of *The Friends of English Magic* or that he would cause copies of the books to be printed. He did neither of these things. One or two people wrote him letters asking him specific questions. He did not reply. When letters appeared in the newspapers complaining of this behaviour he was most indignant. After all he was simply acting as he had always done – acquiring valuable books and then hiding them away where no man else could see them. The difference was that in the days when he was an unknown gentleman no one had thought any thing of it, but now the eyes of the world were upon him. His silence was wondered at and people began to remember other occasions when Mr Norrell had acted in a rude or arrogant manner.

# 29

## At the house of José Estoril

### January–March 1811

"I HAVE BEEN THINKING, sir, that my leaving for the Peninsula will be the cause of many changes in your dealings with the War Office," said Strange. "I am afraid that when I am gone you will not find it so convenient to have people knocking at the door at all hours of the day and night, asking for this or that piece of magic to be performed forthwith. There will be no one but you to attend to them. When will you sleep? I think we must persuade them to some other way of doing things. If I can be of any assistance in arranging matters, I should be glad to do so. Perhaps we should invite Lord Liverpool to dine one evening this week?"

"Oh, yes indeed!" said Mr Norrell in high good humour with this proof of Strange's considerateness. "You must be there. You explain everything so well! You have only to say a thing and Lord Liverpool understands immediately!"

"Then shall I write to his lordship?"

"Yes, do! Do!"

It was the first week of January. The date of Strange's departure was not yet fixed, but was likely to be soon. Strange sat down and wrote the invitation. Lord Liverpool replied very promptly and the next day but one saw him at Hanover-square.

It was the habit of Mr Norrell and Jonathan Strange to spend the hour before dinner in Mr Norrell's library and it was in this room that they received his lordship. Childermass was also present, ready to act as clerk, counsellor, messenger or servant just as circumstances should require.

Lord Liverpool had never seen Mr Norrell's library and before he sat down he took a little turn about the room. "I had been told, sir," he said, "that your library was one of the Wonders of the Modern World, but I never imagined any thing half so extensive."

Mr Norrell was very well pleased. Lord Liverpool was exactly the sort of guest he liked – one who admired the books but shewed no inclination to take them down from the shelves and read them.

Then Strange said, addressing Mr Norrell, "We have not spoken yet, sir, about the books I should take to the Peninsula. I have made a list of forty titles, but if you think it can be improved upon I should be glad of your advice." He pulled a folded sheet from a jumble of papers on a table and handed it to Mr Norrell.

It was not a list to delight Mr Norrell's soul. It was full of first thoughts crossed-out, second thoughts crossed-out and third thoughts put in at angles and made to wriggle around other words that were in the way. There were ink blots, titles misspellt, authors misnamed and, most confusing of all, three lines of a riddle-poem that Strange had begun composing as a farewell-present for Arabella. Nevertheless it was not this that made Mr Norrell grow pale. It had never occurred to him before that Strange would need books in Portugal. The idea of forty precious volumes being taken into a country in a state of war where they might get burnt, blown up, drowned or dusty was almost too horrible to contemplate. Mr Norrell did not know a great deal about war, but he suspected that soldiers are not generally your great respecters of books. They might put their dirty fingers on them. They might tear them! They might – horror of horrors! – read them and try the spells! Could soldiers read? Mr Norrell did not know. But with the fate of the entire Continent at stake and Lord Liverpool in the room, he realized how very difficult it would be – impossible in fact – to refuse to lend them.

He turned with a look of desperate appeal to Childermass.

Childermass shrugged.

Lord Liverpool continued to gaze about him in a calm manner. He appeared to be thinking that the temporary absence of forty books or so would scarcely be noticed among so many thousands.

"I should not wish to take more than forty," continued Strange in a matter-of-fact tone.

"Very wise, sir," said Lord Liverpool. "Very wise. Do not take more than you can conveniently carry about."

"Carry about!" exclaimed Mr Norrell, more shocked than ever. "But surely you do not intend to take them from place to place? You must put them in a library the moment you arrive. A library in a castle will be best. A stout, well-defended castle . . ."

"But I fear they will do me little good in a library," said Strange with infuriating calmness. "I shall be in camps and on battlefields. And so must they."

"Then you must place them in a box!" said Mr Norrell. "A very sturdy wooden box or perhaps an iron chest! Yes, iron will be best. We can have one made specially. And then . . ."

"Ah, forgive me, Mr Norrell," interrupted Lord Liverpool, "but I strongly advise Mr Strange against the iron chest. He must not trust to any provision being made for him in the carts. The soldiers need the carts for their equipment, maps, food, ammunition and so on. Mr Strange will occasion the Army the least inconvenience if he carries all his possessions on a mule or donkey as the officers do." He turned to Strange. "You will need a good, strong mule for your baggage and your servant. Purchase some saddlebags at Hewley and Ratt's and place the books in them. Military saddlebags are most capacious. Besides, on a cart the books would almost certainly be stolen. Soldiers, I am sorry to say, steal everything." He thought for a moment and then added, "Or at least ours do."

How the dinner went after that Mr Norrell knew very little. He was dimly aware that Strange and his lordship talked a great deal and laughed a great deal. Several times he heard Strange say, "Well, that is decided then!" And he heard his lordship reply, "Oh, certainly!" But what they were talking about, Mr Norrell neither knew nor cared. He wished he had never come to London. He wished he had never undertaken to revive English magic. He wished he had stayed at Hurtfew Abbey, reading and doing magic for his own pleasure. None of it, he thought, was worth the loss of forty books.

After Lord Liverpool and Strange had gone he went to the library to look at the forty books and hold them and treasure them while he could.

Childermass was still there. He had taken his dinner at one of the tables and was now doing the household accounts. As Mr Norrell entered, he looked up and grinned. "I believe Mr Strange will do very well in the war, sir. He has already out-manoeuvred you."

On a bright, moonlit night in early February a British ship called *St Serlo's Blessing*[1] sailed up the Tagus and landed at Black-horse square in the middle of the city of Lisbon. Among the first to disembark were Strange and his servant, Jeremy Johns. Strange had never been in a foreign country before and he found that the consciousness of being so now and the important military and naval bustle that was going on all around him was quite exhilarating. He was eager to begin doing magic.

"I wonder where Lord Wellington is," he said to Jeremy Johns. "Do you suppose any of these fellows will know?" He looked with some curiosity at a vast, half-built arch at one end of the square. It had a very military appearance and he would not have been at all surprized to learn that Wellington was somewhere at the rear of it.

---

[1] *St Serlo's Blessing* had been captured from the French. Its French name was *Le Temple Foudroyé*. Saint Serlo's Blessing was, of course, the name of one of the four magical woods which surrounded and protected the Raven King's capital city, Newcastle.

"But it is two o'clock in the morning, sir," said Jeremy. "His lordship will be asleep."

"Oh, do you think so? With the fate of all Europe in his hands? I suppose you may be right."

Reluctantly, Strange agreed that it would be better to go to the hotel now and look for Lord Wellington in the morning.

They had been recommended to a hotel in Shoemaker-street which belonged to a Mr Prideaux, a Cornishman. Mr Prideaux's guests were almost all British officers who had just returned to Portugal from England or who were waiting for ships to take them on leave of absence. It was Mr Prideaux's intention that during their stay at his hotel the officers should feel as much at home as possible. In this he was only partly successful. Do whatsoever he might, Mr Prideaux found that Portugal continually intruded itself upon the notice of his guests. The wallpaper and furnishings of the hotel might all have been brought originally from London, but a Portuguese sun had shone on them for five years and faded them in a peculiarly Portuguese manner. Mr Prideaux might instruct the cook to prepare an English bill of fare but the cook was Portuguese and there was always more pepper and oil in the dishes than the guests expected. Even the guests' boots had a faintly Portuguese air after the Portuguese bootboy had blacked them.

The next morning Strange rose rather late. He ate a large breakfast and then strolled about for an hour or so. Lisbon proved to be a city well provided with arcaded squares, elegant modern buildings, statues, theatres and shops. He began to think that war could not be so very dreadful after all.

As he returned to the hotel he saw four or five British officers, gathered in the doorway, conversing eagerly together. This was just the opportunity he had hoped for. He went up to them, begged their pardon for interrupting, explained who he was and asked where in Lisbon Lord Wellington might be found.

The officers turned and gave him a rather surprized look as if they thought the question a wrong one, though he could not tell why it should be. "Lord Wellington is not in Lisbon," said one, a man in the blue jacket and white breeches of the Hussars.

"Oh! When is he coming back?" asked Strange.

"Back?" said the officer. "Not for weeks – months, I expect. Perhaps never."

"Then where will I find him?"

"Good God!" said the officer. "He might be anywhere."

"Don't you know where he is?" asked Strange.

The officer looked at him rather severely. "Lord Wellington does not stay in one place," he said. "Lord Wellington goes wherever he is needed. And Lord Wellington," he added for Strange's better understanding, "is needed *everywhere*."

Another officer who wore a bright scarlet jacket liberally adorned with silver lace, said in a rather more kindly tone, "Lord Wellington is in the Lines."

"In the Lines?" said Strange.

"Yes."

Unfortunately this was not quite the clear and helpful explanation that the officer intended it to be. But Strange felt that he had demonstrated his ignorance long enough. His desire to ask questions had quite evaporated.

"Lord Wellington is in the Lines." It was a very curious phrase and if Strange had been obliged to hazard a guess at its meaning he believed he would have said it was some sort of slang for being drunk.

He went back into the hotel and told the porter to find Jeremy Johns. If any one was going to appear ignorant and foolish in front of the British Army he had much rather it was Jeremy.

"There you are!" he said when Jeremy appeared. "Go and find a soldier or officer and ask him where I shall find Lord Wellington."

"Certainly, sir. But don't you want to ask him yourself?"

"Quite impossible. I have magic to do."

So Jeremy went out and after a very brief interval he returned.

"Have you found it out?" asked Strange.

"Oh yes, sir!" said Jeremy, cheerfully. "There is no great secret about it. Lord Wellington is in the Lines."

"Yes, but what does that mean?"

"Oh, I beg your pardon, sir! The gentleman said it so naturally. As if it were the most commonplace thing in the world. I thought you would know."

"Well, I do not. Perhaps I had better ask Prideaux."

Mr Prideaux was delighted to be of assistance. There was nothing simpler in the world. Mr Strange must go to the Army's Headquarters. He was certain to find his lordship there. It was a half day's ride from the city. Perhaps a little more. "As far as from Tyburn to Godalming, sir, if you can picture it."

"Well, if you would be so good as to shew me on a map . . ."

"Lord bless you, sir!" said Mr Prideaux, much amused. "You would never find it on your own. I must find a man to take you."

The person whom Mr Prideaux found was an Assistant Commissary with business in Torres Vedras, a town four or five miles further on than Headquarters. The Assistant Commissary declared himself very happy to ride with Strange and shew him the way.

"Now, at last," thought Strange, "I am making progress."

The first part of the journey was through a pleasant landscape of fields and vineyards scattered here and there with pretty little white-painted farms and stone-built windmills with brown canvas sails. Large numbers of Portuguese soldiers in brown uniforms were continually going to and fro along the road and there were also a few British officers whose brighter uniforms of scarlet or blue appeared – to Strange's patriotic eye at any rate – more manly and warlike. After they had been riding for three hours they saw a line of mountains rising up from the plain like a wall.

As they entered a narrow valley between two of the highest mountains the Assistant Commissary said, "This is the beginning of the Lines. You see that fort there high up on one side of the pass?" He pointed to the right. The "fort" appeared to have started out life as a windmill, but had recently received all sorts of additions in the way of bastions, battlements and gun embrasures. "And the other fort on the other side of the pass?" added the Assistant Commissary. He pointed to the left. "And then on the next rocky outcrop another little fort? And then – though you can't see it, since today is dull and cloudy – there is another beyond that. And so on and so on. A whole line of forts from the Tagus to the sea! But that is not all! There are two more lines to the north of us. Three lines in all!"

"It is certainly impressive. And did the Portuguese do this?"

"No, sir. Lord Wellington did it. The French mayn't pass here. Why, sir! a beetle mayn't pass unless that beetle has a paper with Lord Wellington's writing on it! And that, sir, is why the French Army sits at Santarem and can get no further, while you and I sleep safe in our beds at Lisbon!"

Very soon they left the road and took a steep and winding lane that led up the hillside to the tiny village of Pero Negro. Strange was struck by the difference between war, as he had imagined it, and war, as it actually was. He had pictured Lord Wellington sitting in some grand building in Lisbon, issuing orders. Instead he found him in a place so small that it barely would have qualified as a village in England.

The Army's Headquarters proved to be an entirely unremarkable house in a plain cobbled yard. Strange was informed that Lord Wellington had gone out to inspect the Lines. No one knew when he would return – probably not until dinner. No one had any objection to Strange's waiting – providing he did not get in their way.

But from the first moment of his entering the house Strange found himself subject to that peculiarly uncomfortable Natural Law which states that whenever a person arrives at a place where he is not known, then wherever he stands he is sure to be in the way. He could not sit because the room he had been placed in contained no chairs – presumably in case the French should somehow penetrate the house and hide behind them – so he took up a position in front of a window. But then two officers came in and one of them wished to demonstrate some important military characteristic of the Portuguese landscape, for which purpose it was necessary to look out of the window. They glared at Strange who moved to stand in front of a half-curtained arch.

Meanwhile a voice was calling every moment from the passageway for someone named Winespill to bring the gunpowder barrels and to do it quickly. A soldier of very small stature and with a slight hunchback entered the room. He had a vivid purple birthmark on his face and appeared to be wearing part of the uniform of every regiment in the British Army. This, presumably, was Winespill. Winespill was unhappy. He could not find the gunpowder. He hunted in cupboards, under staircases and on balconies. He called back every now and then "One moment!" – until the moment came when he thought to look behind Strange, behind the curtain and under the arch. Immediately he shouted out that he had found the casks of gunpowder now and he would have seen them earlier only Someone – here he gave Strange a very black look – was standing in front of them.

The hours passed slowly. Strange was back at his station by the window and almost falling asleep, when he realized from certain sounds of bustle and disruption that Someone of Importance had just entered the house. The next moment three men swept into the room and Strange found himself at last in the presence of Lord Wellington.

How to describe Lord Wellington? How can such a thing be necessary or even possible? His face is everywhere one looks – a cheap print upon the wall of the coaching inn – a much more elaborate one, embellished with flags and drums, at the top of the Assembly-room staircase. Nowadays no young lady of average romantic feeling will reach the age of seventeen without purchasing at least one picture of him. She will think a long, aquiline nose infinitely preferable to a short, stubby one and consider it the worst misfortune of her life that he is married already. To make up for it she fully intends to name her first-born son, Arthur. Nor is she alone in her devotion. Her younger brothers and sisters are every bit as fanatical. The handsomest toy soldier in an English nursery is always called Wellington and has more adventures than the rest of the toy box put together. Every schoolboy impersonates Wellington at least once a week, and so do his younger sisters. Wellington embodies every English virtue. He is Englishness carried to perfection. If the French carry Napoleon in their bellies (which apparently they do), then we carry Wellington in our hearts.[2]

Just at present Lord Wellington was none too pleased about something.

"My orders were perfectly clear, I think!" he said to the other two officers. "The Portuguese were to destroy all the corn that they could not carry away, so that it should not fall into the hands of the French. But I have just spent half the day watching the French soldiers going into the caves at Cartaxo and bringing out sacks again."

"It was very hard for the Portuguese farmers to destroy their corn. They feared to be hungry," explained one of the officers.

The other officer made the hopeful suggestion that perhaps it was not corn that the French had found in the sacks, but something else altogether less useful. Gold or silver, perhaps?

Lord Wellington eyed him coolly. "The French soldiers took the sacks to the windmills. The sails were going round in plain view! Perhaps you think they were milling gold? Dalziel, complain to the Portuguese authorities, if you please!" His gaze, darting angrily about the room, came to rest upon Strange. "Who is that?" he asked.

The officer called Dalziel murmured something in his lordship's ear.

[2] Of course it may be objected that Wellington himself was *Irish*, but a patriotic English pen does not stoop to answer such quibbling.

"Oh!" said Lord Wellington and then, addressing Strange, he said, "You are the magician." The faintest note of inquiry pervaded his remark.

"Yes," said Strange.

"Mr Norrell?"

"Ah, no. Mr Norrell is in England. I am Mr Strange."

Lord Wellington looked blank.

"The other magician," explained Strange.

"I see," said Lord Wellington.

The officer called Dalziel stared at Strange with an expression of surprize, as if he thought that once Lord Wellington had told Strange who he was, it was rather ill-bred of him to insist on being someone else.

"Well, Mr Strange," said Lord Wellington, "I fear you have had a wasted journey. I must tell you frankly that if I had been able to prevent your coming I would have done so. But now that you are here I shall take the opportunity to explain to you the great nuisance which you and the other gentleman have been to the Army."

"Nuisance?" said Strange.

"Nuisance," repeated Lord Wellington. "The visions you have shewn the Ministers have encouraged them to believe that they understand how matters stand in Portugal. They have sent me a great many more orders and interfered to a far greater extent than they would have done otherwise. Only I know what needs to be done in Portugal, Mr Strange, since only I am acquainted with all the circumstances. I do not say that you and the other gentleman may not have done some good elsewhere – the Navy seem pleased – I know nothing of that – but what I *do* say is that I need no magician here in Portugal."

"But surely, my lord, here in Portugal magic is liable to no such misuse, since I shall be wholly at your service and under your direction."

Lord Wellington gave Strange a sharp look. "What I chiefly need is men. Can you make more?"

"Men? Well, that depends on what your lordship means. It is an interesting question . . ." To Strange's great discomfort, he found he sounded exactly like Mr Norrell.

"Can you make more?" interrupted his lordship.

"No."

"Can you make the bullets fly any quicker to strike the French? They fly very quickly as it is. Can you perhaps upturn the earth and move the stones to build my Redoubts, Lunettes and Other Defensive Works?"

"No, my lord. But, my lord . . ."

"The name of the chaplain to the Headquarters is Mr Briscall. The name of the chief medical officer is Dr McGrigor. Should you decide to stay in Portugal then I suggest you make yourself known to these gentlemen. Perhaps you may be of some use to them. You are none to me." Lord Wellington turned away and immediately shouted for someone named Thornton to get dinner ready. In this way Strange was given to understand that the interview was at an end.

Strange was used to deferential treatment from Government Ministers. He was accustomed to being addressed as an equal by some of the highest in the land. To find himself suddenly classed with the chaplains and doctors of the Army – mere supernumeraries – was very bad indeed.

He spent the night – very uncomfortably – at Pero Negro's only inn and as soon as it was light he rode back to Lisbon. When he arrived back at the hotel in Shoemaker-street, he sat down and wrote a long letter to Arabella describing in great detail the shocking way he was treated. Then, feeling a little better, he decided that it was unmanly to complain and so he tore the letter up.

He next made a list of all the sorts of magic which Norrell and he had done for the Admiralty and tried to decide which would suit Lord Wellington best. After careful consideration he concluded that there were few better ways of adding to the misery of the

French Army than by sending it storms of thunder and drenching rain. He immediately determined upon writing his lordship a letter offering to do this magic. A definite course of action is always a cheering thing and Strange's spirits rose immediately – until, that is, he happened to glance out of the window. The skies were black, the rain was coming down in torrents and a fierce wind was blowing. It looked as if it might very well thunder in a short while. He went in search of Mr Prideaux. Prideaux confirmed that it had been raining like this for weeks – that the Portuguese thought it would continue for a good long while – and, yes, the French were indeed very unhappy.

Strange pondered this for a while. He was tempted to send Lord Wellington a note offering to make it *stop* raining, on the principle that it must be very uncomfortable for the British soldiers as well – but in the end he decided that the whole question of weather-magic was too vexed until he understood the war and Lord Wellington better. In the meantime he settled upon a plague of frogs as the best thing to drop on the heads of the French soldiers. It was highly Biblical and what, thought Strange, could be more respectable than that?

The next morning he was sitting gloomily in his hotel room, pretending to read one of Norrell's books but actually watching the rain, when there was a knock at the door. It was a Scottish officer in the uniform of the Hussars who looked inquiringly at Strange and said, "Mr Norrell?"

"I am not . . . Oh, never mind! What can I do for you?"

"Message for you from Headquarters, Mr Norrell." The young officer presented Strange with a piece of paper.

It was his own letter to Wellington. Someone had scrawled over it in thick, blue pencil the single word, "Denied".

"Whose writing is that?" asked Strange.

"Lord Wellington's, Mr Norrell."

"Ah."

The next day Strange wrote Wellington another note, offering to make the waters of the River Tagus rise up and overwhelm the French. This at least provoked Wellington into writing a rather longer reply explaining that at present the entire British Army and most of the Portuguese Army were *between* the Tagus and the French and consequently Mr Strange's suggestion was not found to be at all convenient.

Strange refused to be deterred. He continued to send Wellington one proposal every day. All were rejected.

On a particularly gloomy day at the end of February he was passing through the hallway of Mr Prideaux's hotel on his way to a solitary dinner when he almost collided with a fresh-faced young man in English clothes. The young man begged his pardon and asked if he knew where Mr Strange was to be found.

"I am Strange. Who are you?"

"My name is Briscall. I am Chaplain to the Headquarters."

"Mr Briscall. Yes. Of course."

"Lord Wellington has asked me to pay you a visit," explained Mr Briscall. "He said something about your aiding me by magic?" Mr Briscall smiled. "But I believe his real reason is that he hopes I may be able to dissuade you from writing to him every day."

"Oh!" said Strange. "I shall not stop until he gives me something to do."

Mr Briscall laughed. "Very well, I shall tell him."

"Thank you. And is there any thing I can do for you? I have never done magic for the Church before. I will be frank with you, Mr Briscall. My knowledge of ecclesiastical magic is very slight, but I should be glad to be of use to someone."

"Hmm. I will be equally frank with you, Mr Strange. My duties are really very simple. I visit the sick and wounded. I read the soldiers the services and try and get them a decent burial when they are killed, poor fellows. I do not see what you could do to help."

"Neither does any one else," said Strange with a sigh. "But come, have dinner with me? At least I shall not have to eat alone."

This was quickly agreed to and the two men sat down in the hotel dining-parlour. Strange found Mr Briscall to be a pleasant dinner companion who was happy to tell all he knew of Lord Wellington and the Army.

"Soldiers are not in general religious men," he said, "but then I never expected that they would be and I have been greatly helped by the circumstance that all the chaplains before me went on leave almost as soon as they arrived. I am the first to stay – and the men are grateful to me for that. They look very kindly on any one who is prepared to share their hard life."

Strange said he was sure of it.

"And what of you, Mr Strange? How do you get on?"

"I? I do not get on at all. No one wants me here. I am addressed – on the rare occasions when any one speaks to me at all – quite indiscriminately as Mr Strange or Mr Norrell. No one seems to have any notion that these might be *distinct* persons."

Briscall laughed.

"And Lord Wellington rejects all my offers of help as soon as I make them."

"Why? What have you offered him?"

Strange told him about his first proposal to send a plague of frogs to fall on the French from the sky.

"Well, I am really not at all surprized he refused *that*!" said Briscall, contemptuously. "The French cook frogs and eat them, do they not? It is a vital part of Lord Wellington's plan that the French should starve. You might as well have offered to drop roast chickens on their heads or pork pies!"

"It is not my fault," said Strange, a little stung. "I would be only too glad to take Lord Wellington's plans into consideration – only I do not know what they are. In London the Admiralty told us their intentions and we shaped our magic accordingly."

"I see," said Briscall. "Forgive me, Mr Strange – perhaps I have not understood very well – but it seems to me that you have a great advantage here. In London you were obliged to rely upon the

Admiralty's opinion as to what might be happening hundreds of miles away – and I dare say the Admiralty was quite often mistaken. Here you can go and see for yourself. Your experience is no different from my own. When I first arrived no one took the least notice of me either. I drifted from one regiment to another. No one wanted me."

"And yet now you are a part of Wellington's Staff. How did you do it?"

"It took time, but in the end I was able to prove my usefulness to his lordship – and I am sure you will do the same."

Strange sighed. "I try. But all I seem to do is demonstrate my superfluousness. Over and over again!"

"Nonsense! As far as I can see you have only made one real mistake – and that is in remaining here in Lisbon. If you take my advice, you will leave as soon as you can. Go and sleep on the mountains with the men and the officers! You will not understand them until you do. Talk to them. Spend your days with them in the deserted villages beyond the Lines. They will soon love you for it. They are the best fellows in the world."

"Really? It was reported in London that Wellington had called them the scum of the earth."

Briscall laughed as if being the scum of the earth were a very minor sort of indiscretion and indeed a large part of the Army's charm. This was, thought Strange, an odd position for a clergyman to take.

"Which are they?" he asked.

"They are both, Mr Strange. They are both. Well, what do you say? Will you go?"

Strange frowned. "I do not know. It is not that I fear hardship and discomfort, you understand. I believe I can endure as much of that sort of thing as most men. But I know no one there. I seem to have been in every body's way since I arrived and without friends to go to . . ."

"Oh! That is easily remedied! This is not London or Bath where one needs letters of introduction. Take a barrel of brandy – and a case or two of Champagne if your servant can carry them. You will soon have a very wide acquaintance among the officers if you have brandy and Champagne to spare."

"Really? It is as simple as that, is it?"

"Oh, to be sure! But do not trouble to take any red wine. They have plenty of that already."

A few days later Strange and Jeremy Johns left Lisbon for the country beyond the Lines. The British officers and men were a little surprized to find a magician in their midst. They wrote letters home to their friends describing him in a variety of uncomplimentary ways and wondering what in the world he was doing there. But Strange did as Mr Briscall had advised. Every officer he met was invited to come and drink Champagne with him that evening after dinner. They soon excused him the eccentricity of his profession. What mattered was that one could always meet with some very jolly fellows at Strange's bivouack and something decent to drink.

Strange also took up smoking. It had never really appealed to him as a pastime before, but he discovered that a ready supply of tobacco was quite invaluable for striking up conversations with the enlisted men.

It was an odd sort of life and an eerie sort of landscape. The villages beyond the Lines had all been emptied of inhabitants on Lord Wellington's instructions and the crops burnt. The soldiers of both armies went down to the deserted villages and helped themselves to whatever looked useful. On the British side it was not unusual to come upon sophas, wardrobes, beds, chairs and tables standing on a hillside or in a woodland glade. Occasionally one would find whole bed-chambers or drawing-rooms, complete with shaving equipment, books and lamps, but minus the impediment of walls and ceiling.

But if the British Army suffered inconvenience from the wind and the rain, then the plight of the French Army was far, far worse.

Their clothes were in rags and they had nothing to eat. They had been staring at Lord Wellington's Lines since the previous October. They could not attack the British Army – it had three lines of impregnable forts behind which to retreat at any moment it chose. Nor did Lord Wellington trouble to attack the French. Why should he, when Hunger and Disease were killing his enemies faster than he could? On the 5th of March the French struck camp and turned north. Within a very few hours Lord Wellington and the British Army were in pursuit. Jonathan Strange went with them.

One very rainy morning about the middle of the month Strange was riding at the side of a road along which the 95th Rifles were marching. He happened to spy some particular friends of his a little way ahead. Urging his horse to a canter, he soon caught up with them.

"Good morning, Ned," he said, addressing a man he had reason to regard as a thoughtful, sensible sort of person.

"Good morning, sir," said Ned, cheerfully.

"Ned?"

"Yes, sir?"

"What is it that you chiefly desire? I know it is an odd question, Ned, and you will excuse my asking it. But I really need to know."

Ned did not answer immediately. He sucked in his breath and furrowed his brow and exhibited other signs of deep thinking. Meanwhile his comrades helpfully told Strange what they chiefly desired – things such as magic pots of gold that would never be empty and houses carved out of a single diamond. One, a Welshman, sang out dolefully, "Toasted cheese! Toasted cheese!" several times – which caused the others to laugh a good deal, Welshmen being naturally humorous.

Meanwhile Ned had got to the end of his ruminations. "New boots," he said.

"Really?" said Strange in surprize.

"Yes, sir," answered Ned. "New boots. It is these d—d Portuguese roads." He gestured ahead at the collection of stones and pot-holes that the Portuguese were pleased to call a road. "They tear a man's boots to ribbons and at night his bones ache from walking over them. But if I had new boots, oh! wouldn't I be fresh after a day's march? Couldn't I just fight the French then? Couldn't I just make Johnny sweat for it?"

"Your appetite for the fray does you great credit, Ned," said Strange. "Thank you. You have given me an excellent answer." He rode off, followed by a great many shouts of "When will Ned be getting his boots, then?" and "Where's Ned's boots?"

That evening Lord Wellington's headquarters were set up in a once-splendid mansion in the village of Lousão. The house had once belonged to a wealthy and patriotic Portuguese nobleman, José Estoril, but he and his sons had all been tortured and killed by the French. His wife had died of a fever, and various stories were in circulation concerning the sad fate of his daughters. For many months it had been a very melancholy place, but now Wellington's Staff had arrived to fill it with the sound of their noisy jokes and arguments, and the gloomy rooms were made almost cheerful by the officers in their coats of red and blue passing in and out.

The hour before dinner was one of the busiest of the day and the room was crowded with officers bringing reports or collecting orders, or simply gathering gossip. At one end of the room was a very venerable, ornate and crumbling stone staircase which led to a pair of ancient doors. Behind the doors, it was said, Lord Wellington was hard at work devising new plans to defeat the French, and it was a curious fact that everyone who came into the room was sure to cast a respectful glance up to the top of that staircase. Two of Wellington's senior staff, the Quartermaster-General, Colonel George Murray, and the Adjutant-General, General Charles Stewart, were seated one upon either side of a large table, both busily engaged in making arrangements for the disposal of the Army upon the following day. And I pause here merely to observe that if, upon reading the words "Colonel" and "General", you fancy these are two *old* men sitting at the table, you could not be more wrong. It is true that when the French war had begun eighteen years before, the British Army had been commanded by some very venerable old persons many of whom had passed their whole careers without glimpsing a battlefield. But the years had gone by and these old generals were all retired or dead and it had been found more convenient to replace them with younger, more energetic men. Wellington himself was only a little more than forty and most of his senior officers were younger still. The room in José Estoril's house was a room of young men, all fond of a fight, all fond of dancing, all quite devoted to Lord Wellington.

The March evening, though rainy, was mild – as mild as May in England. Since his death, José Estoril's garden had grown wild and in particular a great number of lilac trees had appeared, crowding against the walls of the house. These trees were now all in flower and the windows and shutters of the house stood open to let in the damp, lilac-scented air. Suddenly Colonel Murray and General Stewart found that both they and their important papers were being comprehensively showered with drops of water. On looking up in some indignation they saw Strange, outside on the verandah unconcernedly shaking the water off his umbrella.

He entered the room and bid good evening to various officers with whom he had some acquaintance. He approached the table and inquired if he might possibly speak to Lord Wellington. General Stewart, a proud, handsome man, made no reply other than to shake his head vigorously. Colonel Murray, who was a gentler and more courteous soul, said he feared it would not be possible.

Strange glanced up the venerable staircase to the great carved doors behind which his lordship sat. (Curious how everyone who entered knew instinctively where he was to be found. Such is the fascination that great men exert!) Strange shewed no inclination to go. Colonel Murray supposed that he must be feeling lonely.

A tall man with vivid black eyebrows and long black mustaches to match approached the table. He wore the dark blue jacket and gold braid of the Light Dragoons. "Where have you put the French prisoners?" he demanded of Colonel Murray.

"In the belfry," said Colonel Murray.

"That will do," said the man. "I only ask because last night Colonel Pursey put three Frenchmen in a little shed, thinking they could do no harm there. But it seems some lads of the 52nd had previously put some chickens in the shed and during the night the Frenchmen ate the chickens. Colonel Pursey said that this morning several of his lads were eyeing the Frenchmen in a very particular manner as if they were wondering how much of the flavour of the chickens had got into the Frenchmen and whether it might not be worth cooking one of them to find out."

"Oh!" said Colonel Murray. "There is no danger of any thing like that happening tonight. The only other creatures in the belfry are the rats and I should think that if any one is going to eat any one else, the rats will eat the Frenchmen."

Colonel Murray, General Stewart and the man with black mustaches began to laugh, when suddenly they were interrupted by the magician saying, "The road between Espinhal and Lousão is abominably bad." (This was the road along which a substantial part of the British Army had come that day.)

Colonel Murray agreed that the road was very bad indeed.

Strange continued, "I cannot tell how many times today my horse stumbled into pot-holes and slipped in the mud. I was certain she would fall lame. Yet it was no worse than any of the other roads that I have seen since I arrived here, and tomorrow I understand some of us must go where there are no roads whatsoever."

"Yes," said Colonel Murray, wishing very heartily that the magician would go away.

"Through flooded rivers and stony plains, and through woods and thickets, I suppose," said Strange. "That will be very bad for all of us. I dare say we shall make very poor progress. I dare say we shall not get on at all."

"It is one of the disadvantages of waging war in such a backward, out-of-the-way place as Portugal," said Colonel Murray.

General Stewart said nothing but the angry look he gave the magician expressed quite clearly his opinion that perhaps Mr Strange would make better progress if he and his horse took themselves back to London.

"To take forty-five thousand men and all their horses and carts and equipment, across such an abominable country! No one in England would believe it possible." Strange laughed. "It is a pity that his lordship cannot spare a moment to talk to me, but perhaps you will be so good as to give him a message. Say this: Mr Strange presents his compliments to Lord Wellington and says that if it is of any interest to his lordship to have a nice, well-made road for the Army to march along tomorrow, then Mr Strange will be glad to conjure one up for him. Oh! And if he wishes he may have bridges too, to replace the ones the French have blown up. Good evening to you." With that Strange bowed to both gentlemen, picked up his umbrella and left.

Strange and Jeremy Johns had been unable to find anywhere to stay in Lousão. None of the gentlemen who found quarters for the generals and told the rest of the soldiers which damp field they were to sleep in, had made any provision for the magician and his servant. Strange had eventually agreed terms for a tiny upstairs room with a man who kept a little wine shop a few miles down the road to Miranda de Corvo.

Strange and Jeremy ate the supper the wine-shop owner had provided for them. It was a stew and their evening's entertainment chiefly consisted in trying to guess what had gone into it.

"What the devil is that?" asked Strange, holding up his fork. On the end of it was something whitish and glistening that curled over and under itself.

"A fish perhaps?" ventured Jeremy.

"It looks more like a snail," said Strange.

"Or part of someone's ear," added Jeremy.

Strange stared at it a moment longer. "Would you like it?" he asked.

"No, thank you, sir," said Jeremy with a resigned glance into his own cracked plate, "I have several of my own."

When they had finished supper and when the last candle had burnt out there seemed nothing else to do but go to bed – and so they did. Jeremy curled up upon one side of the room and Strange lay down upon the other. Each had devised his own bed from whatever materials had taken his fancy. Jeremy had a mattress fashioned out of his spare clothes and Strange had a pillow formed chiefly of books from Mr Norrell's library.

All at once there came the sound of someone's horse galloping up the road to the little wine-shop. This was quickly followed by the sound of someone's boots pounding up the rickety stairs, which in turn was followed by the sound of someone's fist pounding on the ramshackle door. The door opened and a smart young man in the uniform of the Hussars half-tumbled into the room. The smart young man was somewhat out of breath but managed to convey, between gulps of air, that Lord Wellington presented his compliments to Mr Strange and that if it was at all convenient to Mr Strange Lord Wellington would like to speak to him immediately.

At José Estoril's house Wellington was at dinner with a number of his staff officers and other gentlemen. Strange could have sworn that the gentlemen at the table had all been engaged in the liveliest conversation up to the moment when he entered the room, but now all fell silent. This rather suggested that they had been talking about him.

"Ah, Strange!" cried Lord Wellington, raising a glass in greeting. "There you are! I have had three *aides-de-camp* looking for you all evening. I wished to invite you to dinner, but my boys could not find you. Sit down anyway and have some Champagne and dessert."

Strange looked rather wistfully at the remains of the dinner which the servants were clearing away. Among other good things Strange believed he recognized were the remains of some roast geese, the shells from buttered prawns, half a ragoo of celery, and the ends of some spicy Portuguese sausages. He thanked his lordship and sat down. A servant brought him a glass of Champagne and he helped himself to almond-tart and dried cherries.

"And how do you like the war, Mr Strange?" asked a fox-haired, fox-faced gentleman at the other end of the table.

"Oh, it is a little confusing at first, like most things," said Strange, "but having now experienced many of the adventures a war affords, I grow used to it. I have been robbed – once. I have been shot at – once. Once I found a Frenchman in the kitchen and had to chase him out, and once the house I was sleeping in was set on fire."

"By the French?" inquired General Stewart.

"No, no. By the English. There was a company of the 43rd who were apparently very cold that night and so they set fire to the house to warm themselves."

"Oh, that always happens!" said General Stewart.

There was a little pause and then another gentleman in a cavalry uniform said, "We have been talking – arguing rather – about magic and how it is done. Strathclyde says that you and the other magician have given every word in the Bible a number, and you look for the words to make up the spell and then you add the numbers together and then you do something else and then . . ."

"*That* was not what I said!" complained another person, presumably Strathclyde. "You have not understood at all!"

"I am afraid I have never done any thing remotely resembling what you describe," said Strange. "It seems rather complicated and I do not think it would work. As to how I do magic, there are many, many procedures. As many, I dare say, as for making war."

"I should like to do magic," said the fox-haired, fox-faced

gentleman at the other end of the table. "I should have a ball every night with fairy music and fairy fireworks and I would summon all the most beautiful women out of history to attend. Helen of Troy, Cleopatra, Lucrezia Borgia, Maid Marian and Madame Pompadour. I should bring them all here to dance with you fellows. And when the French appeared on the horizon, I would just," he waved his arm vaguely, "do something, you know, and they would all fall down dead."

"Can a magician kill a man by magic?" Lord Wellington asked Strange.

Strange frowned. He seemed to dislike the question. "I suppose a magician might," he admitted, "but a gentleman never could."

Lord Wellington nodded as if this was just as he would have expected. And then he said, "This road, Mr Strange, which you have been so good as to offer us, what sort of road would it be?"

"Oh! The details are the easiest thing in the world to arrange, my lord. What sort of road would you like?"

The officers and gentlemen around Lord Wellington's dinner-table looked at each other; they had not given the matter any thought.

"A chalk road, perhaps?" said Strange, helpfully. "A chalk road is pretty."

"Too dusty in the dry and a river of mud in the rain," said Lord Wellington. "No, no. A chalk road will never do. A chalk road is scarcely better than no road at all."

"What about a cobbled road?" suggested Colonel Murray.

"Cobbles will make the men's boots wear out," said Wellington.

"And besides the artillery will not like it," said the fox-haired, fox-faced gentleman, "They will have a devil of a time dragging the guns along a cobbled road."

Someone else suggested a gravel road. But that, thought Wellington, was liable to the same objection as a chalk road: it would become a river of mud in the rain – and the Portuguese *did* seem to think that it would rain again tomorrow.

"No," said his lordship, "I believe, Mr Strange, that what would suit us best would be a road along the Roman pattern, with a nice ditch upon either side to drain off the water and good flat stones well fitted together on top."

"Very well," said Strange.

"We set off at daybreak," said Wellington.

"Then, my lord, if someone would be good enough to shew me where the road ought to go, I shall see to it immediately."

By morning the road was in place and Lord Wellington rode along it on Copenhagen – his favourite horse – and Strange rode beside him on Egyptian – who was *his* favourite horse. In his customary decisive manner Wellington pointed out those things which he particularly liked about the road and those things which he did not like; ". . . But really I have hardly any criticisms to make. It is an excellent road! Only make it a little wider tomorrow, if you please."

Lord Wellington and Strange agreed that as a general rule the road should be in place a couple of hours before the first regiment stepped on to it and disappear an hour after the last soldier had passed along it. This was to prevent the French Army from gaining any benefit from the roads. The success of this plan depended on Wellington's Staff providing Strange with accurate information as to when the Army was likely to begin and end marching. Obviously these calculations were not always correct. A week or so after the first appearance of the road Colonel Mackenzie of the 11th Foot came to see Lord Wellington in a great temper and complained that the magician had allowed the road to disappear before his regiment could reach it.

"By the time we got to Celorico, my lord, it was disappearing under our feet! An hour after that it had vanished entirely. Could not the magician summon up visions to find out what the different regiments are doing? I understand that this is something he can do very easily! Then he could make sure that the roads do not disappear until everyone has finished with them."

Lord Wellington said sharply, "The magician has a great deal to do. Beresford needs roads.[3] I need roads. I really cannot ask Mr Strange to be forever peering into mirrors and bowls of water to discover where every stray regiment has got to. You and your lads must keep up, Colonel Mackenzie. That is all."

Shortly after this the British Headquarters received intelligence of something that had befallen a large part of the French Army as it was marching from Guarda to Sabugal. A patrol had been sent out to look at the road between the two towns, but some Portuguese had come along and told the patrol that this was one of the English magician's roads and was certain to disappear in an hour or two taking everyone upon it to Hell – or possibly England. As soon as this rumour reached the ears of the soldiers they declined absolutely to walk along the road – which was in fact perfectly real and had existed for almost a thousand years. Instead the French followed some serpentine route over mountains and through rocky valleys that wore out their boots and tore their clothes and delayed them for several days.

Lord Wellington could not have been more delighted.

[3] There were three great fortresses which guarded the border into Spain: Almeida, Badajoz and Ciudad Rodriguez. In the early months of 1811 all three were held by the French. While Wellington advanced upon the Almeida he despatched General Beresford with the Portuguese Army to besiege the fortress of Badajoz further south.

30

# The book of Robert Findhelm

## January–February 1812

A MAGICIAN'S HOUSE IS expected to have certain peculiarities, but the most peculiar feature of Mr Norrell's house was, without a doubt, Childermass. In no other household in London was there any servant like him. One day he might be observed removing a dirty cup and wiping crumbs from a table like a common footman. The next day he would interrupt a room full of admirals, generals and noblemen to tell them in what particulars he considered them mistaken. Mr Norrell had once publicly reprimanded the Duke of Devonshire for speaking at the same time as Childermass.

On a misty day at the end of January 1812 Childermass entered the library at Hanover-square where Mr Norrell was working and briefly informed him that he was obliged to go away upon business and did not know when he would return. Then, having given the other servants various instructions about the work they were to do in his absence, he mounted his horse and rode away.

In the three weeks that followed Mr Norrell received four letters from him: one from Newark in Nottinghamshire, one from York in the East Riding of Yorkshire, one from Richmond in the North Riding of Yorkshire and one from Sheffield in the West Riding of Yorkshire. But the letters were only about business matters and threw no light upon his mysterious journey.

He returned one night in the second half of February. Lascelles and Drawlight had dined at Hanover-square and were in the drawing-room with Mr Norrell when Childermass entered. He came directly from the stables; his boots and breeches were splashed with mud and his coat was still damp with rain.

"Where in the world have you been?" demanded Mr Norrell.

"In Yorkshire," said Childermass, "making inquiries about Vinculus."

"Did you see Vinculus?" asked Drawlight, eagerly.

"No, I did not."

"Do you know where he is?" asked Mr Norrell.

"No, I do not."

"Have you found Vinculus's book?" asked Lascelles.

"No, I have not."

"Tut," said Lascelles. He eyed Childermass disapprovingly. "If you take my advice, Mr Norrell, you will not permit Mr Childermass to waste any more time upon Vinculus. No one has heard or seen any thing of him for years. He is probably dead."

Childermass sat down upon the sopha like a man who had a perfect right to do so and said, "The cards say he is not dead. The cards say he is still alive and still has the book."

"The cards! The cards!" cried Mr Norrell. "I have told you a thousand times how I detest any mention of those objects! You will oblige me by removing them from my house and never speaking of them again!"

Childermass threw his master a cool look. "Do you wish to hear what I have learnt or not?" he asked.

Mr Norrell nodded sullenly.

"Good," said Childermass. "In your interest, Mr Norrell, I have taken care to improve my acquaintance with all Vinculus's wives. It has always seemed to me nigh on impossible that one of them did not know something that would help us. It seemed to me that all I had to do was to go with them to enough gin-houses, buy them enough gin, and let them talk, and eventually one of them would reveal it to me. Well, I was right. Three weeks ago Nan Purvis told me a story which finally put me on the track of Vinculus's book."

"Which one is Nan Purvis?" inquired Lascelles.

"The first. She told me something that happened twenty or thirty years ago when Vinculus and she were first married. They had been drinking at a gin-house. They had spent their money and exhausted their credit and it was time to return to their lodgings. They staggered along the street and in the gutter they saw a creature even worse for drink than themselves. An old man was lying there, dead drunk. The filthy water flowed around him and over his face, and it was only by chance that he did not drown. Something about this wretch caught Vinculus's eye. It seemed that he recognized him. He went and peered at him. Then he laughed and gave the old man a vicious kick. Nan asked Vinculus who the old man was. Vinculus said his name was Clegg. She asked how he knew him. Vinculus replied angrily that he did not know Clegg. He said he had never known Clegg! What was more, he told her, he was determined never to know him! In short there was no one in the world whom he despised more than Clegg! When Nan complained that this was not a very full explanation, Vinculus grudgingly said that the man was his father. After this he refused to say any more."

"But what has this to do with any thing?" interrupted Mr Norrell. "Why do you not ask these wives of Vinculus's about the *book*?"

Childermass looked annoyed. "I did so, sir. Four years ago. You may remember I told you. None of them knew any thing about it."

With an exasperated wave of his hand Mr Norrell indicated that Childermass was to continue.

"Some months later Nan was in a tavern, listening to an account of a hanging at York that someone was reading from a newspaper. Nan loved to hear of a good hanging and this report particularly impressed her because the name of the man who had been executed was Clegg. It stuck in her mind and that evening she told Vinculus. To her surprize, she found that he already knew all about it and that it was indeed his father. Vinculus was delighted Clegg had been hanged. He said Clegg richly deserved it. He said Clegg had been guilty of a terrible crime – the worst crime committed in England in the last hundred years."

"What crime?" asked Lascelles.

"At first Nan could not bring it to mind," said Childermass. "But with a little persistent questioning and the promise of more gin she remembered. He had stolen a book."

"A book!" exclaimed Mr Norrell.

"Oh, Mr Norrell!" cried Drawlight. "It must be the same book. It must be Vinculus's book!"

"Is it?" asked Mr Norrell.

"I believe so," said Childermass.

"But did this woman know what the book was?" said Mr Norrell.

"No, that was the end of Nan's information. So I rode north to York, where Clegg had been tried and executed, and I examined the records of the Quarter Sessions. The first thing I discovered was that Clegg was originally from Richmond in Yorkshire. Oh yes!" Here Childermass glanced meaningfully at Mr Norrell. "Vinculus is, by descent at least, a Yorkshireman.[1] Clegg began life as a tightrope walker at the northern fairs, but as tightrope-walking is not a trade that combines well with drinking – and Clegg was a famous drinker – he was obliged to give it up. He returned to Richmond and hired himself out as a servant on a prosperous farm. He did well there and impressed the farmer with his cleverness, so that he began to be entrusted with more and more business. From time to time he would go drinking with bad companions and on these occasions he never stopped at one bottle

[1] Yorkshire was part of the Raven King's kingdom of Northern England. Childermass and Norrell's respect for Vinculus would have increased a little, knowing that he was, like them, a Northerner.

or two. He drank until the spigots gave out and the cellars were emptied. He was mad-drunk for days and in that time he got up to all sorts of mischief – thieving, gambling, fighting, destruction of property – but he always made sure that these wild adventures took place far away from the farm and he always had some plausible excuse to explain his absence so that his master, the farmer, never suspected any thing was amiss, though the other servants knew all about it. The farmer's name was Robert Findhelm. He was a quiet, kindly, respectable sort of man – the sort of man easily deceived by a rogue like Clegg. The farm had been in his family for generations, but once, long ago, it had been one of the granges of the Abbey of Easby . . ."

Mr Norrell drew in his breath sharply and fidgeted in his chair.

Lascelles looked inquiringly at him.

"Easby Abbey was one of the foundations of the Raven King," explained Mr Norrell.

"As was Hurtfew," added Childermass.

"Indeed!" said Lascelles in surprize.[2] "I confess that after all you have said about him, I am surprized that you live in a house so closely connected to him."

"You do not understand," said Mr Norrell, irritably. "We are speaking of Yorkshire, of John Uskglass's Kingdom of Northern England where he lived and ruled for three hundred years. There is scarcely a village, scarcely a field even, that does not have some close connexion with him."

Childermass continued. "Findhelm's family possessed something else that had once belonged to the Abbey – a treasure that had been given into their keeping by the last Abbot and which was handed down from father to son with the land."

"A book of magic?" asked Norrell, eagerly.

---

[2] Many people besides Lascelles remarked upon the odd circumstance that Mr Norrell who hated any mention of the Raven King should have lived in a house built of stones quarried upon the King's instruction, and upon land which the King had once owned and knew well.

"If what they told me in Yorkshire is true, it was more than a book of magic. It was The Book of Magic. A book written by the Raven King and set down in his own hand."

There was a silence.

"Is this possible?" Lascelles asked Mr Norrell.

Mr Norrell did not answer. He was sitting deep in thought, wholly taken up with this new, and not altogether pleasant, idea.

At last he spoke, but it was more as if he were speaking his thoughts out loud, rather than answering Lascelles's question. "A book belonging to Raven King or written by him is one of the great follies of English magic. Several people have imagined that they have found it or that they know where it is hidden. Some of them were clever men who might have written important works of scholarship but instead wasted their lives in pursuit of the King's book. But that is not to say that such a book might not exist somewhere . . ."

"And if it did exist," urged Lascelles, "and if it were found – what then?"

Mr Norrell shook his head and would not reply.

Childermass answered for him. "Then all of English magic would have to be reinterpreted in the light of what was found there."

Lascelles raised an eyebrow. "Is this true?" he asked.

Mr Norrell hesitated and looked very much as if he would like to say that it was not.

"Do *you* believe that this was the King's book?" Lascelles asked Childermass.

Childermass shrugged. "Findhelm certainly believed it. In Richmond I discovered two old people who had been servants in Findhelm's house in their youth. They said that the King's book was the pride of his existence. He was Guardian of The Book first, and all else – husband, parent, farmer – second." Childermass paused. "The greatest glory and the greatest burden given to any man in this Age," he mused. "Findhelm seems to have been a theoretical magician himself in a small way. He bought books about magic and paid a magician in Northallerton to teach him. But one thing struck me as very curious – both these old servants insisted that Findhelm never read the King's book and had only the vaguest notion of what it contained."

"Ah!" exclaimed Mr Norrell, softly.

Lascelles and Childermass looked at him.

"So he could not read it," said Mr Norrell. "Well, that is very . . ." He fell silent, and began to chew on his fingernails.

"Perhaps it was in Latin," suggested Lascelles.

"And why do you assume that Findhelm did not know Latin?" replied Childermass with some irritation. "Just because he was a farmer . . ."

"Oh! I meant no disrespect to farmers in general, I assure you," laughed Lascelles. "The occupation has its utility. But farmers are not in general known for their classical scholarship. Would this person even have recognized Latin when he saw it?"

Childermass retorted that of course Findhelm would have recognized Latin. He was not a fool.

To which Lascelles coldly replied that he had never said he was.

The quarrel was becoming heated when they were both suddenly silenced by Mr Norrell saying slowly and thoughtfully, "When the Raven King first came into England, he could not read and write. Few people could in those days – even kings. And the Raven King had been brought up in a fairy house where there was no writing. He had never even seen writing before. His new human servants shewed it to him and explained its purpose. But he was a young man then, a very young man, perhaps no more than fourteen or fifteen years of age. He had already conquered kingdoms in two different worlds and he had all the magic a magician could desire. He was full of arrogance and pride. He had no wish to read other men's thoughts. What were other men's thoughts compared to his own? So he refused to learn to read and write Latin – which was what his servants wanted – and instead he invented a writing of his own to preserve his thoughts for later times. Presumably this writing mirrored the workings of his own mind more closely than Latin could have done. That was at the very beginning. But the longer he remained in England, the more he changed, becoming less silent, less solitary – less like a fairy and more like a man. Eventually he consented to learn to read and write as other men did. But he did not forget his own writing – the King's Letters, as it is called – and he taught it to certain favoured magicians so that they might understand his magic more perfectly. Martin Pale mentions the King's Letters and so does Belasis, but neither of them had ever seen so much as a single penstroke of it. If a piece of it has survived and in the King's own hand, then certainly . . ." Mr Norrell fell silent again.

"Well, Mr Norrell," said Lascelles, "you are full of surprizes tonight! So much admiration for a man you have always claimed to hate and despise!"

"My admiration does not lessen my hatred one whit!" said Mr Norrell, sharply. "I said he was a great magician. I did not say he was a good man or that I welcomed his influence upon English magic. Besides what you have just heard was my private opinion and not for public circulation. Childermass knows. Childermass understands."

Mr Norrell glanced nervously at Drawlight, but Drawlight had stopped listening some time ago – just as soon as he discovered that Childermass's story concerned no one in the fashionable world, but only Yorkshire farmers and drunk servants. At present he was busy polishing his snuff box with his handkerchief.

"So Clegg stole this book?" said Lascelles to Childermass. "Is that what you are going to tell us?"

"In a manner of speaking. In the autumn of 1754 Findhelm gave the book to Clegg and told him to deliver it to a man in the village of Bretton in the Derbyshire Peak. Why, I do not know. Clegg set off and on the second or third day of his journey he reached Sheffield. He stopped at a tavern, and there he fell in with a man, a blacksmith by trade, whose reputation as a drinker was almost as extraordinary as his own. They began a drinking contest that lasted two days and two nights. At first they simply drank to see which of them could drink the most, but on the second day they began to set each other mad, drunken challenges. There was a barrel of salted herrings in the corner. Clegg challenged the blacksmith to walk across a floor of herrings. An audience had gathered by this time and all the lookers-on and the loungers-about emptied out the herrings and paved the floor with fish. Then the blacksmith walked from one end of the room to the other till the floor was a stinking mess of pulped fish and the blacksmith was bloody from head to foot with all the falls he had taken. Then the blacksmith challenged Clegg to walk along the edge of the tavern roof. Clegg had been drunk for a whole day by this time. Time after time the onlookers thought he was about to fall and break his worthless neck, but he never did. Then Clegg challenged the blacksmith to roast and eat his shoes – which the blacksmith did – and finally, the blacksmith challenged Clegg to eat Robert Findhelm's book. Clegg tore it into strips and ate it piece by piece."

Mr Norrell gave a cry of horror. Even Lascelles blinked in surprize.

"Days later," said Childermass, "when Clegg awoke he realized what he had done. He made his way down to London and four years after that he tumbled a serving girl in a Wapping tavern, who was Vinculus's mother."

"But surely the explanation is clear!" cried Mr Norrell. "The book is not lost at all! The story of the drinking contest was a mere invention of Clegg's to blind Findhelm to the truth! In reality he kept the book and gave it to his son! Now if we can only discover . . ."

"But why?" said Childermass. "Why should he go to all this trouble in order to procure the book for a son he had never seen and did not care about? Besides Vinculus was not even born when Clegg set off on the road to Derbyshire."

Lascelles cleared his throat. "For once, Mr Norrell, I agree with Mr Childermass. If Clegg still had the book or knew where it was to be found, then surely he would have produced it at his trial or tried to use it to bargain for his life."

"And if Vinculus had profited so much from his father's crime," added Childermass, "why did he hate his father? Why did he rejoice when his father was hanged? Robert Findhelm was quite sure that the book was destroyed – that is plain. Nan told me Clegg had been hanged for stealing a book, but the charge Robert Findhelm brought against him was not theft. The charge Findhelm brought against him was book-murder. Clegg was the last man in England to be hanged for book-murder."[3]

"So why does Vinculus claim to have this book if his father ate it?' said Lascelles in a wondering tone. "The thing is not possible."

"Somehow Robert Findhelm's inheritance has passed to Vinculus, but how it happened I do not pretend to understand," said Childermass.

"What of the man in Derbyshire?" asked Mr Norrell, suddenly. "You said that Findhelm was sending the book to a man in Derbyshire."

Childermass sighed. "I passed through Derbyshire on my way back to London. I went to the village of Bretton. Three houses and an inn high on a bleak hill. Whoever the man was that Clegg was sent to seek out, he is long dead. I could discover nothing there."

Stephen Black and the gentleman with the thistle-down hair were seated in the upper room of Mr Wharton's coffee-house in Oxford-street where the Peep-O'Day-Boys met.

The gentleman was speaking, as he often did, of his great affection for Stephen. "Which reminds me," he said; "I have been meaning for many months to offer you an apology and an explanation."

---

[3] Book-murder was a late addition to English magical law. The wilful destruction of a book of magic merited the same punishment as the murder of a Christian.

"An apology to me, sir?"

"Yes, Stephen. You and I wish for nothing in the world so much as Lady Pole's happiness, yet I am bound by the terms of the magician's wicked agreement to return her to her husband's house each morning where she must while away the long day until evening. But, clever as you are, you must surely have observed that there are no such constraints upon you and I dare say you are wondering why I do not take you away to Lost-hope House to be happy for ever and for ever."

"I have wondered about that, sir," agreed Stephen. He paused because his whole future seemed to depend upon the next question. "Is there something which prevents you?"

"Yes, Stephen. In a way there is."

"I see," said Stephen. "Well, that is most unfortunate."

"Would not you like to know what it is?" asked the gentleman.

"Oh yes, sir! Indeed, sir!"

"Know then," said the gentleman, putting on grave and important looks quite unlike his usual expression, "that we fairy-spirits know something of the future. Often Fate chuses us as her vessels for prophecy. In the past we have lent our aid to Christians to allow them to achieve great and noble destinies – Julius Caesar, Alexander the Great, Charlemagne, William Shakespeare, John Wesley and so forth.[4] But often our knowledge of things to come is misty and . . ." The gentleman gestured furiously as if he were brushing away thick cobwebs from in front of his face. ". . . imperfect. Out of my dear love for you, Stephen, I have traced the smoke of burning cities and battlefields and prised dripping, bloody guts out of dying men to discover your future. You are indeed destined to be a king! I must say that I am not in the least surprized! I felt strongly from the first that you should be a king and it was most unlikely that I should be wrong. But more than

[4] Not all the Worthies referred to by the gentleman are Christian. Just as we refer to a great many diverse tribes and races as "fairies", so they commonly name us "Christians" regardless of our religion, race or era.

this, I believe I know which kingdom is to be yours. The smoke and guts and all the other signs state quite clearly that it is to be a kingdom where you have already been! A kingdom with which you are already closely connected."

Stephen waited.

"But do you not see?" cried the gentleman, impatiently. "It must be England! I cannot tell you how delighted I was when I learnt this important news!"

"England!" exclaimed Stephen.

"Yes, indeed! Nothing could be more beneficial for England herself than that you should be her King. The present King is old and blind and as for his sons, they are all fat and drunk! So now you see why I cannot take you away to Lost-hope. It would be wholly wrong of me to remove you from your rightful kingdom!"

Stephen sat for a moment, trying to comprehend. "But might not the kingdom be somewhere in Africa?" he said at last. "Perhaps I am destined to find my way back there and perhaps by some strange portent the people will recognize me as the descendant of one of their kings?"

"Perhaps," said the gentleman, doubtfully. "But, no! That cannot be. For you see it is a kingdom where *you have already been*. And you never were in Africa. Oh, Stephen! How I long for your wonderful destiny to be accomplished. On that day I shall ally my many kingdoms to Great Britain – and you and I shall live in perfect amity and brotherhood. Think how our enemies will be confounded! Think how eaten up with rage the magicians will be! How they will curse themselves that they did not treat us with more respect!"

"But I think that you must be mistaken, sir. I cannot rule England. Not with this . . ." He spread out his hands in front of him. *Black skin*, he thought. Aloud he continued, "Only you, sir, with your partiality for me, could think such a thing possible. Slaves do not become kings, sir."

"Slave, Stephen? Whatever do you mean?"

"I was born into slavery, sir. As are many of my race. My mother was a slave on an estate in Jamaica that Sir Walter's grandfather owned. When his debts grew too great Sir William went to Jamaica to sell the estate – and one of the possessions which he brought back with him was my mother. Or rather he intended to bring her back to be a servant in his house, but during the voyage she gave birth to me and died."

"Ha!" exclaimed the gentleman in triumph. "Then it is exactly as I have said! You and your estimable mother were enslaved by the wicked English and brought low by their machinations!"

"Well, yes, sir. That is true in a sense. But I am not a slave now. No one who stands on British soil can be a slave. The air of England is the air of liberty. It is a great boast of Englishmen that this is so." *And yet*, he thought, *they own slaves in other countries*. Out loud he said, "From the moment that Sir William's valet carried me as a tiny infant from the ship I was free."

"Nevertheless we should punish them!" cried the gentleman. "We can easily kill Lady Pole's husband, and then I will descend into Hell and find his grandfather, and then . . ."

"But it was not Sir William and Sir Walter who did the enslaving," protested Stephen. "Sir Walter has always been very much opposed to the slave trade. And Sir William was kind to me. He had me christened and educated."

"Christened? What? Even your name is an imposition of your enemies? Signifying slavery? Then I strongly advise you to cast it off and chuse another when you ascend the throne of England! What was the name your mother called you?"

"I do not know, sir. I am not sure that she called me any thing."

The gentleman narrowed his eyes as a sign that he was thinking hard. "It would be a strange sort of mother," he mused, "that did not name her child. Yes, there will be a name that belongs to you. Truly belongs to you. That much is clear to me. The name your mother called you in her heart during those precious moments when she held you in her arms. Are you not curious to know what it was?"

"Certainly, sir. But my mother is long dead. She may never have told that name to another soul. Her own name is lost. Once when I was a boy I asked Sir William, but he could not remember it."

"Doubtless he knew it well, but in his malice would not tell it to you. It would need someone very remarkable to recover your name, Stephen – someone of rare perspicacity, with extraordinary talents and incomparable nobility of character. Me, in fact. Yes, that is what I will do. As a token of the love I bear you, I will find your true name!"

# 31

## Seventeen dead Neapolitans

### April 1812–June 1814

THERE WERE IN the British Army at that time a number of "exploring officers" whose business it was to talk to the local people, to steal the French Army's letters and always to know the whereabouts of the French troops. Let your notions of war be as romantic as they may, Wellington's exploring officers would always exceed them. They forded rivers by moonlight and crossed mountain ranges under the searing sun. They lived more behind French lines than English ones and knew everyone favourable to the British cause.

The greatest of these exploring officers was, without a doubt, Major Colquhoun Grant of the 11th Foot. Often the French would look up from whatever they were doing and see Major Grant on horseback, observing them from atop a far-off hill. He would peer at them through his telescope and then make notes about them in his little notebook. It made them most uncomfortable.

One morning in April 1812, quite by chance, Major Grant found himself caught between two French cavalry patrols. When it became clear that he could not outride them he abandoned his horse and hid in a little wood. Major Grant always considered himself to be a soldier rather than a spy, and, as a soldier, he made it a point of honour to wear his uniform at all times. Unfortunately the uniform of the 11th Foot (as of almost all infantry regiments) was bright scarlet and as he hid amongst the budding spring leaves the French had no difficulty whatsoever in perceiving him.

For the British the capture of Grant was a calamity akin to losing a whole brigade of ordinary men. Lord Wellington immediately sent out urgent messages – some to the French generals proposing an exchange of prisoners and some to the *guerrilla* commanders,[1] promising them silver dollars and weapons aplenty if they could effect Grant's rescue. When neither of these proposals produced any results Lord Wellington was obliged to try a different plan. He hired one of the most notorious and ferocious of all the *guerrilla* chieftains, Jeronimo Saornil, to convey Jonathan Strange to Major Grant.

"You will find that Saornil is rather a formidable person," Lord Wellington informed Strange before he set off, "but I have no fears upon that account, because frankly, Mr Strange, so are you."

Saornil and his men were indeed as murderous a set of villains as you could wish to see. They were dirty, evil-smelling and unshaven. They had sabres and knives stuck into their belts and rifles slung over their shoulders. Their clothes and saddle-blankets were covered with cruel and deadly images: skulls and crossbones; hearts impaled upon knives; gallows; crucifixions upon cartwheels; ravens pecking at hearts and eyes; and other such pleasant devices. These images were formed out of what appeared at first to be pearl buttons but which, on closer examination, proved to be the teeth of all the Frenchmen they had killed. Saornil, in particular, had so many teeth attached to his person that he rattled whenever he moved, rather as if all the dead Frenchmen were still chattering with fear.

---

[1] *Guerrilla* – a Spanish word meaning "little war". *Guerrilla* bands were groups of Spaniards numbering between dozens and thousands who fought and harassed the French armies. Some were led by ex-soldiers and maintained an impressive degree of military discipline. Others were little more than bandits and devoted as much of their energies to terrifying their own unfortunate countrymen as they did to fighting the French.

Surrounded as they were by the symbols and accoutrements of death, Saornil and his men were confident of striking terror into everyone they met. They were therefore a little disconcerted to find that the English magician had outdone them in this respect – he had brought a coffin with him. Like many violent men they were also rather superstitious. One of them asked Strange what was inside the coffin. He replied carelessly that it contained a man.

After several days of hard riding the *guerrilla* band brought Strange to a hill which overlooked the principal road leading out of Spain and into France. Along this road, they assured Strange, Major Grant and his captors were sure to pass.

Saornil's men set up camp nearby and settled themselves to wait. On the third day they saw a large party of French soldiers coming along the road and, riding in the middle of them, in his scarlet uniform, was Major Grant. Immediately Strange gave instructions for his coffin to be opened. Three of the *guerrilleros* took crowbars and prised off the lid. Inside they found a pottery person – a sort of mannikin made from the same rough red clay which the Spanish use to make their colourful plates and jugs. It was life-size, but very crudely made. It had two holes for eyes and no nose to speak of. It was, however, carefully dressed in the uniform of an officer of the 11th Foot.

"Now," said Strange to Jeronimo Saornil, "when the French outriders reach that rock there, take your men and attack them."

Saornil took a moment to digest this, not least because Strange's Spanish had several eccentricities of grammar and pronunciation.

When he had understood he asked, "Shall we try to free *El Bueno Granto*?" (*El Bueno Granto* was the Spaniards' name for Major Grant.)

"Certainly not!" replied Strange. "Leave *El Bueno Granto* to me!"

Saornil and his men went halfway down the hill to a place where thin trees made a screen that hid them from the road. From here they opened fire. The French were taken entirely by surprize. Some were killed; many others wounded. There were no rocks and very few bushes – scarcely any where to hide – but the road was still before them, offering a good chance of outrunning their attackers. After a few minutes of panic and confusion the French gathered up their wits and their wounded and sped away.

As the *guerrilleros* climbed back up the hill, they were very doubtful that any thing had been accomplished; after all, the figure in the scarlet uniform had still been among the Frenchmen as they rode off. They reached the place where they had left the magician and were amazed to find he was no longer alone. Major Grant was with him. The two men were sitting sociably on a rock, eating cold chicken and drinking claret.

". . . Brighton is all very well," Major Grant was saying, "but I prefer Weymouth."

"You amaze me," replied Strange. "I detest Weymouth. I spent one of the most miserable weeks of my life there. I was horribly in love with a girl called Marianne and she snubbed me for a fellow with an estate in Jamaica and a glass eye."

"That is not Weymouth's fault," said Major Grant. "Ah! Capitán Saornil!" He waved a chicken leg at the chieftain by way of greeting. "Buenos Días!"

Meanwhile the officers and soldiers of the French escort continued on their way to France and when they reached Bayonne they delivered their prisoner into the keeping of the Head of Bayonne's Secret Police. The Head of the Secret Police came forward to greet what he confidently believed to be Major Grant. He was somewhat disconcerted when, on reaching out to shake the Major's hand, the entire arm came away in his hand. So surprized was he that he dropped it on the ground where it shattered into a thousand pieces. He turned to make his apologies to Major Grant and was even more appalled to discover large black cracks appearing all over the Major's face. Next, part of the Major's head fell off – by which means he was discovered to be completely hollow inside – and a moment later he fell to bits like the Humpty-Dumpty person in *Mother Goose's Melody*.

On July 22nd Wellington fought the French outside the ancient university city of Salamanca. It was the most decisive victory for any British Army in recent years.

That night the French Army fled through the woods that lay to the south of Salamanca. As they ran, the soldiers looked up and were amazed to see flights of angels descending through the dark trees. The angels shone with a blinding light. Their wings were as white as swans' wings and their robes were the shifting colours of mother-of-pearl, fish scales or skies before thunder. In their hands they held flaming lances and their eyes blazed with a divine fury. They flew through the trees with astonishing rapidity and brandished their lances in the faces of the French.

Many of the soldiers were stricken with such terror that they turned and ran back towards the city – towards the pursuing British Army. Most were too amazed to do any thing but stand and stare. One man, braver and more resolute than the rest, tried to understand what was happening. It seemed to him highly unlikely that Heaven should suddenly have allied itself with France's enemies; after all such a thing had not been heard of since Old Testament times. He noticed that though the angels threatened the soldiers with their lances, they did not attack them. He waited until one of the angels swooped down towards him and then he plunged his sabre into it. The sabre encountered no resistance – nothing but empty air. Nor did the angel exhibit any signs of hurt or shock. Immediately the Frenchman called out to his compatriots that there was no reason to be afraid; these were nothing but illusions produced by Wellington's magician; they could not harm them.

The French soldiers continued along the road, pursued by the phantom angels. As they came out of the trees they found themselves on the bank of the River Tormes. An ancient bridge crossed the river, leading into the town of Alba de Tormes. By an error on the part of one of Lord Wellington's allies this bridge had been left entirely unguarded. The French crossed over and escaped through the town.

Some hours later, shortly after dawn, Lord Wellington rode wearily across the bridge at Alba de Tormes. With him were three other gentlemen: Lieutenant-Colonel De Lancey who was the Army's Deputy Quartermaster; a handsome young man called Fitzroy Somerset who was Lord Wellington's Military Secretary; and Jonathan Strange. All of them were dusty and battle-stained and none of them had been to bed for some days. Nor was there much likelihood of their doing so soon since Wellington was determined to continue his pursuit of the fleeing French.

The town with its churches, convents and mediaeval buildings stood out with perfect clarity against an opalescent sky. Despite the hour (it was not much after half past five) the town was already up. Bells were already being rung to celebrate the defeat of the French. Regiments of weary British and Portuguese soldiers were filing through the streets and the townspeople were coming out of their houses to press gifts of bread, fruit and flowers on them. Carts bearing wounded men were lined up against a wall while the officer in charge sent men to seek out the hospital and other places to receive them. Meanwhile five or six plain-faced, capable-looking nuns had arrived from one of the convents and were going about among the wounded men giving them draughts of fresh milk from a tin cup. Small boys whom nobody could persuade to stay in bed were excitedly cheering every soldier they saw and forming impromptu victory parades behind any that did not seem to mind it.

Lord Wellington looked about him. "Watkins!" he cried, hailing a soldier in an artillery uniform.

"Yes, my lord?" said the man.

"I am in search of my breakfast, Watkins. I don't suppose you have seen my cook?"

"Sergeant Jefford said he saw your people going up to the castle, my lord."

"Thank you, Watkins," said his lordship and rode on with his party.

The Castle of Alba de Tormes was not much of a castle. Many years ago at the start of the war the French had laid siege to it and with the exception of one tower it was all in ruins. Birds and wild creatures now made nests and holes where once the Dukes of Alba had lived in unimaginable luxury. The fine Italian murals for which the castle had once been famous were a great deal less impressive now that the ceilings were all gone and they had been subjected to the rough caresses of rain, hail, sleet and snow. The dining-parlour lacked some of the convenience that other dining-parlours have; it was open to the sky and there was a young birch tree growing in the middle of it. But this troubled Lord Wellington's servants not one whit; they were accustomed to serve his lordship his meals in far stranger places. They had set a table beneath the birch tree and spread it with a white cloth. As Wellington and his companions rode up to the castle they had just begun to lay it with plates of bread rolls, slices of Spanish ham, bowls of apricots and dishes of fresh butter. Wellington's cook went off to fry fish, devil kidneys and make coffee.

The four gentlemen sat down. Colonel De Lancey remarked that he did not believe he could remember when his last meal had been. Somebody else agreed and then they all silently applied themselves to the serious business of eating and drinking.

They were just beginning to feel a little more like their usual selves and grow a little more conversational when Major Grant arrived.

"Ah! Grant," said Lord Wellington. "Good Morning. Sit down. Have some breakfast."

"I will in a moment, my lord. But first I have some news for you. Of rather a surprizing sort. It seems the French have lost six cannon."

"Cannon?" said his lordship, not much interested. He helped himself to a bread roll and some devilled kidneys. "Of course they have lost cannon. Somerset!" he said, addressing his Military Secretary. "How many pieces of French cannon did I capture yesterday?"

"Eleven, my lord."

"No, no, my lord," said Major Grant. "I beg your pardon, but you misunderstand. I am not speaking of the cannon that were captured during the battle. These cannon were never in the battle. They were on their way from General Caffarelli in the north to the French Army. But they did not arrive in time for the battle. In fact they never arrived at all. Knowing that you were in the vicinity, my lord, and pressing the French hard, General Caffarelli was anxious to deliver them with all dispatch. He made up his escort out of the first thirty soldiers that came to hand. Well, my lord, he acted in haste and has repented at leisure for it seems that ten out of thirty were Neapolitan."

"Neapolitan! Were they indeed?" said his lordship.

De Lancey and Somerset exchanged pleased looks with one another and even Jonathan Strange smiled.

The truth was that, although Naples was part of the French Empire, the Neapolitans hated the French. The young men of Naples were forced to fight in the French Army but they took every opportunity they could to desert, often running away to the enemy.

"But what of the other soldiers?" asked Somerset. "Surely we must assume that they will prevent the Neapolitans doing much mischief?"

"It is too late for the other soldiers to do any thing," said Major Grant. "They are all dead. Twenty pairs of French boots and twenty French uniforms are, at this very moment, hanging in the shop of an old clothes dealer in Salamanca. The coats all have long slits in the back, such as might be made by an Italian stiletto, and they are all over blood stains."

"So, the cannon are in the hands of a pack of Italian deserters, are they?" said Strange. "What will they do? Start a war of their own?"

"No, no!" said Grant. "They will sell them to the highest bidder. Either to you, my lord or to General Castanos." (This was the name of the General in charge of the Spanish Army.)

"Somerset!" said his lordship. "What ought I to give for six French cannon? Four hundred dollars?"

"Oh! It is certainly worth four hundred dollars to make the French feel the consequences of their foolishness, my lord. But what I do not understand is why we have not heard something from the Neapolitans already. What can they be waiting for?"

"I believe I know the answer to that," said Major Grant. "Four nights ago two men met secretly in a little graveyard upon a hillside not far from Castrejon. They wore ragged French uniforms and spoke a sort of Italian. They conferred a while and when they parted one went south towards the French Army at Cantalapiedra, the other went north towards the Duero. My lord, it is my belief that the Neapolitan deserters are sending messages to their countrymen to come and join them. I dare say they believe that with the money that you or General Castanos will give them for the guns, they will all be able to sail back to Naples in a golden ship. There is probably not a man among them who does not have a brother or cousin in some other French regiment. They do not wish to return home and face their mothers and grandmothers without bringing their relations with them."

"I have always heard that Italian women are rather fierce," agreed Colonel De Lancey.

"All we need to do, my lord," continued Major Grant, "is find some Neapolitans and question them. I am certain we will find that they know where the thieves are and where the guns are."

"Are there any Neapolitans among yesterday's prisoners?" asked Wellington.

Colonel De Lancey sent a man to find out.

"Of course," continued Wellington, thoughtfully, "it would suit me much better to pay nothing at all. Merlin!" (This was his name for Jonathan Strange.) "If you will be so good as to conjure up a vision of the Neapolitans, perhaps we will gain some clue as to where they and the guns are to be found and then we can simply go and get them!"

"Perhaps," said Strange.

"I dare say there will be an oddly shaped mountain in the background," said his lordship cheerfully, "or a village with a distinctive church tower. One of the Spanish guides will soon recognize the place."

"I dare say," said Strange.

"You do not seem very sure of it."

"Forgive me, my lord, but – as I think I have said before – visions are precisely the wrong sort of magic for this sort of thing."[2]

"Well, have you any thing better to suggest?" asked his lordship.

---

[2] *Jonathan Strange to John Segundus*, Madrid, Aug. 20th, 1812.

"Whenever someone or something needs to be found, Lord Wellington is sure to ask me to conjure up a vision. It never works. The Raven King and the other *Aureates* had a sort of magic for finding things and persons. As I understand it they began with a silver basin of water. They divided the surface of the water into quarters with glittering lines of light. (By the by, John, I really cannot believe that you are having as much difficulty as you say in creating these lines. I *cannot* describe the magic any more clearly. They are the simplest things in the world!) The quarters represent Heaven, Hell, Earth and Faerie. It seems that you employ a spell of election to establish in which of these realms the person or thing you seek is to be found – but how it goes on from there I have not the least idea, and neither does Norrell. If I only had this magic! Wellington or his staff is forever giving me tasks which I cannot do or which I must leave half-completed because I do not have it. I feel the lack of it almost daily. Yet I have no time for experiment. And so, John, I would be infinitely obliged to you if you could spend a little time attempting this spell and let me know *immediately* if you have the least success."

There is nothing in any of John Segundus's surviving papers to suggest that he had any success in his attempts to retrieve this magic. However in the autumn of 1814 Strange realised that a passage in Paris Ormskirk's *Revelations of Thirty-Six Other Worlds* – long thought to be a description of a shepherd's counting rhyme – was in fact a somewhat garbled version of precisely this spell. By late 1814 both Strange and Mr Norrell were performing this magic with confidence.

"No, my lord. Not at present."

"Then it is decided!" said Lord Wellington. "Mr Strange, Colonel De Lancey and Major Grant can turn their attention to the discovery of these guns. Somerset and I will go and annoy the French." The brisk manner in which his lordship spoke suggested that he expected all of these things to start happening very soon. Strange and the gentlemen of the Staff swallowed the rest of their breakfast and went to their various tasks.

At about midday Lord Wellington and Fitzroy Somerset were seated upon their horses on a slight ridge near the village of Garcia Hernandez. On the stony plain below several brigades of British Dragoons were preparing to charge some squadrons of cavalry which formed the rearguard of the French Army.

Just then Colonel De Lancey rode up.

"Ah, Colonel!" said Lord Wellington. "Have you found me any Neapolitans?"

"There are no Neapolitans among the prisoners, my lord," said De Lancey. "But Mr Strange suggested we look among the dead upon yesterday's battlefield. By magical means he has identified seventeen corpses as Neapolitan."

"Corpses!" said Lord Wellington, putting down his telescope in surprize. "What in the world does he want corpses for?"

"We asked him that, my lord, but he grew evasive and would not answer. However he has asked that the dead men be put somewhere safe where they will be neither lost nor molested."

"Well, I suppose one ought not to employ a magician and then complain that he does not behave like other people," said Wellington.

At that moment an officer standing close by cried out that the Dragoons had increased their pace to a gallop and would soon be upon the French. Instantly the eccentricities of the magician were forgotten; Lord Wellington put his telescope to his eye and every man present turned his attention to the battle.

Strange meanwhile had returned from the battlefield to the castle at Alba de Tormes. In the Armoury Tower (the only part of the castle still standing) he had found a room that no one was using and had appropriated it. Scattered about the room were Norrell's forty books. They were all still more or less in one piece, though some were decidedly battered-looking. The floor was covered with Strange's notebooks and pieces of paper with scraps of spells and magical calculations scribbled on them. On a table in the centre of the room stood a wide and shallow silver bowl, filled with water. The shutters had been pulled tight and the only light in the room came from the silver bowl. All in all it was a veritable magician's cave and the pretty Spanish maid who brought coffee and almond biscuits at regular intervals was quite terrified and ran out again as soon as she had put down her trays.

An officer of the 18th Hussars called Whyte had arrived to assist Strange. Captain Whyte had lived for a time at the house of the British Envoy in Naples. He was adept at languages and understood the Neapolitan dialect perfectly.

Strange had no difficulty in conjuring up the visions but, just as he had predicted, the visions gave very little clue as to where the men were. The guns, he discovered, were half hidden behind some pale yellow rocks – the sort of rocks which were scattered liberally throughout the Peninsula – and the men were camped in a sparse woodland of olive and pine trees – the sort of woodland in fact that one might discover by casting one's glance in any direction.

Captain Whyte stood at Strange's side and translated everything the Neapolitans said into clear, concise English. But, though they stared into the silver bowl all day they learnt very little. When a man has been hungry for eighteen months, when he has not seen his wife or sweetheart for two years, when he has spent the last four months sleeping upon mud and stones his powers of conversation tend to be somewhat dulled. The Neapolitans had very little to say to each other and what they did say chiefly concerned the food they wished they were eating, the charms of the absent wives and sweethearts they wished they were enjoying, and the soft feather mattresses they wished they were sleeping upon.

For half the night and most of the following day Strange and Captain Whyte remained in the Armoury Tower, engaged in the dull work of watching the Neapolitans. Towards the evening of the second day an *aide-de-camp* brought a message from Wellington. His lordship had set up his Headquarters at a place called Flores de Avila and Strange and Captain Whyte were summoned to attend him there. So they packed up Strange's books and the silver bowl and gathered their other possessions and set off along the hot, dusty roads.

Flores de Avila proved to be rather an obscure place; none of the Spanish men and women whom Captain Whyte accosted had heard of it. But when two of Europe's greatest armies have recently travelled along a road, they cannot help but leave some signs of their passing; Strange and Captain Whyte found that their best plan was to follow the trail of discarded baggage, broken carts, corpses and feasting black birds. Against a background of empty, stone-strewn plains these sights resembled nothing so much as images from a mediaeval painting of Hell and they provoked Strange to make a great many gloomy remarks upon the Horror and Futility of War. Ordinarily Captain Whyte, a professional soldier, would have felt inclined to argue, but he too was affected by the sombre character of their surroundings and only answered, "Very true, sir. Very true."

But a soldier ought not to dwell too long on such matters. His life is full of hardship and he must take his pleasure where he can. Though he may take time to reflect upon the cruelties that he sees, place him among his comrades and it is almost impossible for his spirits not to rise. Strange and Captain Whyte reached Flores de Avila at about nine o'clock and within five minutes they were greeting their friends cheerfully, listening to the latest gossip about Lord Wellington and making a great many inquiries about the previous day's battle – another defeat for the French. One would scarcely suppose they had seen any thing to distress them within the last twelvemonth.

The Headquarters had been set up in a ruined church on a hillside above the village and there Lord Wellington, Fitzroy Somerset, Colonel De Lancey and Major Grant were waiting to meet them.

For all that he had won two battles in as many days Lord Wellington was not in the best of tempers. The French Army, famed throughout Europe for the rapidity of its marches, had got away from him and was now well on the way to Valladolid and safety. "It is a perfect mystery to me how they get on so fast," he complained, "and I would give a great deal to catch up with them and destroy them. But this is the only army I have and if I wear it out I cannot get another."

"We have heard from the Neapolitans with the guns," Major Grant informed Strange and Captain Whyte. "They are asking a hundred dollars a piece for them. Six hundred dollars in all."

"Which is too much," said his lordship briefly. "Mr Strange, Captain Whyte, I hope you have good news for me?"

"Hardly, my lord," said Strange. "The Neapolitans are in a wood. But as to where that wood might be I have not the least idea. I am not sure how to progress. I have exhausted everything I know."

"Then you must quickly learn something else!"

For a moment Strange looked as if he was going to return his lordship an angry reply, but thinking better of it he sighed and inquired whether the seventeen dead Neapolitans were being kept safe.

"They have been put in the bell tower," said Colonel De Lancey. "Sergeant Nash has charge of them. Whatever you want them for, I advise you to use them soon. I doubt they will last much longer in this heat."

"They will last another night," said Strange. "The nights are cold." Then he turned and went out of the church.

Wellington's Staff watched him go with some curiosity. "You know," said Fitzroy Somerset, "I really cannot help wondering what he is going to do with seventeen corpses."

"Whatever it is," said Wellington, dipping his quill in the ink and beginning a letter to the Ministers in London, "he does not relish the thought of it. He is doing everything he can to avoid it."

That night Strange did a sort of magic he had never done before. He attempted to penetrate the dreams of the Neapolitan company. In this he was perfectly successful.

One man dreamt that he was chased up a tree by a vicious Roast Leg of Lamb. He sat in the tree weeping with hunger while the Leg of Lamb ran round and round and thrust its knob of bone at him in a menacing way. Shortly afterwards the Leg of Lamb was joined by five or six spiteful Boiled Eggs who whispered the most dreadful lies about him.

Another man dreamt that, as he was walking through a little wood, he met his dead mother. She told him that she had just looked down a rabbit hole and seen Napoleon Buonaparte, the King of England, the Pope and the Czar of Russia at the bottom. The man went down the rabbit hole to see, but when he arrived at the bottom he discovered that Napoleon Buonaparte, the King of England, the Pope and the Czar of Russia were in fact all the same person, a huge blubbering great man as big as a church with rusty iron teeth and burning cartwheels for eyes. "Ha!" sneered this ogre. "You did not think we were really different people, did you?" And it reached into a bubbling cauldron that stood nearby and pulled out the dreamer's little son and ate him. In short the Neapolitans' dreams, though interesting, were not very illuminating.

Next morning at about ten o'clock Lord Wellington was sitting at a makeshift desk in the chancel of the ruined church. He looked up and saw Strange entering the church. "Well?" he asked.

Strange sighed and said, "Where is Sergeant Nash? I need him to bring out the dead bodies. With your permission, my lord, I will try some magic that I heard of once."[3]

News quickly got about Headquarters that the magician was going to do something to the dead Neapolitans. Flores de Avila was a tiny place, scarcely more than a hundred dwellings. The previous evening had proved very dull for an army of young men who had just won a great victory and who felt inclined to celebrate and it was considered highly probable that Strange's magic would prove the best entertainment of the day. A small crowd of officers and men soon gathered to see it.

---

[3] Strange knew of it as a piece of magic done by the Raven King. Most of the King's magic was mysterious, beautiful, subtle, and so it comes as some surprize to us to learn that he should have employed any spell so brutal.

In the mid-thirteenth century several of the King's enemies were attempting to form an alliance against him. Most of its members were known to him: the King of France was one, the King of Scotland another, and there were several disaffected fairies who gave themselves grandiose titles and who may, or may not, have governed the vast territories they claimed. There were also other personages more mysterious, but even greater. The King had for most of his reign been on good terms with most angels and demons, but now it was rumoured that he had quarrelled with two: Zadkiel who governs mercy and Alrinach who governs shipwreck.

The King does not seem to have been greatly worried by the activities of the alliance. But he became more interested when certain magical portents seemed to shew that one of his own noblemen had joined with them and was plotting against him. The man he suspected was Robert Barbatus, Earl of Wharfdale, a man so known for his cunning and manipulative ways that he was nicknamed the Fox. In the King's eyes there was no greater crime than betrayal.

When the Fox's eldest son, Henry Barbatus, died of a fever, the Raven King had his body taken out of its grave and he brought him back to life to tell what he knew. Thomas of Dundale and William Lanchester both had a deep disgust for this particular sort of magic and pleaded with the King to employ some other means. But the King was bitterly angry and they could not dissuade him. There were a hundred other forms of magic he could have used, but none were so quick or so direct and, like most great magicians, the Raven King was nothing if not practical.

It was said that in his fury the Raven King beat Henry Barbatus. In life Henry had been a splendid young man, much admired for his handsome face and graceful manners, much feared for his knightly prowess. That such a noble knight should have been reduced to a cowering, whimpering doll by the King's magic made William Lanchester very angry and was the cause of a bitter quarrel between the two of them which lasted several years.

The church had a stone terrace which overlooked a narrow valley and a prospect of pale, towering mountains. Vineyards and olive groves clothed the slopes. Sergeant Nash and his men fetched the seventeen corpses from the bell tower and propped them up in a sitting position against a low wall that marked the edge of the terrace.

Strange walked along, looking at each in turn. "I thought I told you," he said to Sergeant Nash, "that I particularly did not want any one interfering with the corpses."

Sergeant Nash looked indignant. "I am sure, sir," he said, "that none of our lads has touched them. But my lord," he said, appealing to Lord Wellington, "there was scarcely a corpse on the battlefield that those Spanish irregulars had not done something to . . ." He expatiated on the various national failings of the Spanish and concluded that if a man so much as went to sleep where the Spanish could find him he would be sorry for it when he woke up.

Lord Wellington waved impatiently at the man to make him be quiet. "I do not see that they are very much mutilated," he said to Strange. "Does it matter if they are?"

Strange muttered blackly that he supposed it did not except that he had to look at them.

Indeed, most of the wounds that the Neapolitans bore appeared to have been the ones that killed them, but all of them had been stripped naked and several had had their fingers cut off – the better to remove their rings. One had been a handsome young man, but his beauty was very much marred now that someone had plucked out his teeth (to make false teeth) and cut off most of his black hair (to make wigs).

Strange told a man to fetch a sharp knife and a clean bandage. When the knife was brought he took off his coat and rolled up the sleeve of his shirt. Then he began muttering to himself in Latin. He next made a long, deep cut in his arm, and when he had got a good strong spurt of blood, he let it splash over the heads of the corpses, taking care to anoint the eyes, tongue and nostrils of each. After a moment the first corpse roused itself. There was a horrible rasping

sound as its dried-out lungs filled with air and its limbs shook in a way that was very dreadful to behold. Then one by one the corpses revived and began to speak in a guttural language which contained a much higher proportion of screams than any language known to the onlookers.

Even Wellington looked a little pale. Only Strange continued apparently without emotion.

"Dear God!" cried Fitzroy Somerset, "What language is that?"

"I believe it is one of the dialects of Hell," said Strange.

"Is it indeed?" said Somerset. "Well, that is remarkable."

"They have learnt it very quickly," said Lord Wellington, "They have only been dead three days." He approved of people doing things promptly and in a businesslike fashion. "But do you speak this language?" he asked Strange.

"No, my lord."

"Then how are we to talk to them?"

For answer Strange grasped the head of the first corpse, pulled open its jabbering jaws and spat inside its mouth. Instantly it began to speak in its native, *earthly* language – a thick Neapolitan dialect of Italian, which to most people was quite as impenetrable and almost as horrible as the language it had been speaking before. It had the advantage, however, of being perfectly comprehensible to Captain Whyte.

With Captain Whyte's help Major Grant and Colonel De Lancey interrogated the dead Neapolitans and were highly pleased by the answers they returned. Being dead, the Neapolitans were infinitely more anxious to please their questioners than any living informer could have been. It seemed that shortly before their deaths at the battle of Salamanca, these wretches had each received a secret message from their countrymen hidden in the woods, informing them of the capture of the cannon and telling them to make their way to a village a few leagues north of the city of Salamanca, from where they would easily be able to find the wood by following secret signs chalked on trees and boulders.

Major Grant took a small detachment of cavalry and within a few days he returned with both guns and deserters. Wellington was delighted.

Unfortunately, Strange was entirely unable to discover the spell for sending the dead Neapolitans back to their bitter sleep.[4] He made several attempts, but these had very little effect except that once he made all seventeen corpses suddenly shoot up until they were twenty feet tall and strangely transparent, like huge water-colour paintings of themselves done on thin muslin banners. When Strange had returned them to their normal size, the problem of what should be done with them remained.

At first they were placed with the other French prisoners. But the other prisoners protested loudly about being confined with such shambling, shuffling horrors. ("And really," observed Lord Wellington as he eyed the corpses with distaste, "one cannot blame them.")

So when the prisoners were sent back to England the dead Neapolitans remained with the Army. All that summer they travelled in a bullock cart and on Lord Wellington's orders they were shackled. The shackles were intended to restrict their movements and keep them in one place, but the dead Neapolitans were not afraid of pain – indeed they did not seem to feel it – so it was very little trouble to them to extricate themselves from their shackles, sometimes leaving pieces of themselves behind. As soon as they were free they would go in search of Strange and begin pleading with him in the most pitiful manner imaginable to restore them to the fullness of life. They had seen Hell and were not anxious to return there.

In Madrid the Spanish artist, Francisco Goya, made a sketch in red chalk of Jonathan Strange surrounded by the dead Neapolitans. In the picture Strange is seated on the ground. His gaze is cast down and his arms hang limp at his sides and his whole

[4] To end the "lives" of the corpses you cut out their eyes, tongues and hearts.

attitude speaks of helplessness and despair. The Neapolitans crowd around him; some are regarding him hungrily; others have expressions of supplication on their faces; one is putting out a tentative finger to stroke the back of his hair. It is, needless to say, quite different from any other portrait of Strange.

On the 25th of August Lord Wellington gave an order for the dead Neapolitans to be destroyed.[5]

Strange was in some anxiety lest Mr Norrell get to hear of the magic he had done at the ruined church at Flores de Avila. He made no mention of it in his own letters and he begged Lord Wellington to leave it out of his Dispatches.

"Oh, very well!" said his lordship. Lord Wellington was not in any case particularly fond of writing about magic. He disliked having to deal with any thing he did not understand extremely well. "But it will do very little good," he pointed out. "Every man that has written a letter home in the last five days will have given his friends a very full account of it."

"I know," said Strange, uncomfortably, "but the men always exaggerate what I do and perhaps by the time people in England have made allowances for the usual embellishments it will not appear so very remarkable. They will merely imagine that I healed some Neapolitans that were wounded or something of that sort."

The raising of the seventeen dead Neapolitans was a good example of the sort of problem faced by Strange in the latter half of the war. Like the Ministers before him, Lord Wellington was becoming more accustomed to using magic to achieve his ends and

---

[5] "Concerning the dead Italian soldiers I can only say that we greatly regretted such cruelty to men who had already suffered a great deal. But we were obliged to act as we did. They could not be persuaded to leave the magician alone. If they had not killed him, then they would have certainly driven him mad. We were obliged to set two men to watch him while he slept to keep the dead men from touching him and waking him up. They had been so battered about since their deaths. They were not, poor fellows, a sight any one wished to see upon waking. In the end we made a bonfire and threw them on it."

*Lord Fitzroy Somerset to his brother*, 2nd Sept., 1812.

he demanded increasingly elaborate spells from his magician. However, unlike the Ministers, Wellington had very little time or inclination for listening to long explanations of why a thing was not possible. After all, he regularly demanded the impossible of his engineers, his generals and his officers and he saw no reason to make an exception of his magician. "Find another way!" was all he would say, as Strange tried to explain that such-and-such a piece of magic had not been attempted since 1302 – or that the spell had been lost – or that it had never existed in the first place. As in the early days of his magicianship, before he had met Norrell, Strange was obliged to invent most of the magic he did, working from general principles and half-remembered stories from old books.

In the early summer of 1813 Strange again performed a sort of magic the like of which had not been done since the days of the Raven King: he moved a river. It happened like this. The war that summer was going well and everything Lord Wellington did was crowned with success. However it so happened that one particular morning in June the French found themselves in a more advantageous position than had been the case for some time. His lordship and the other generals immediately gathered together to discuss what could be done to correct this highly undesirable situation. Strange was summoned to join them in Lord Wellington's tent. He found them gathered round a table upon which was spread a large map.

His lordship was in really excellent spirits that summer and he greeted Strange almost affectionately. "Ah, Merlin! There you are! Here is our problem! We are on this side of the river and the French are on the other side, and it would suit me much better if the positions were reversed."

One of the generals began to explain that if they marched the Army west *here*, and then built a bridge across the river *here*, and then engaged the French *here* . . .

"It will take too long!" declared Lord Wellington. "Far too long! Merlin, could not you arrange for the Army to grow wings and fly over the French? Could you do that, do you think?" His lordship was perhaps half-joking, but only half. "It is only a matter of supplying each man with a little pair of wings. Take Captain Macpherson for example," he said, eyeing an enormous Scotsman. "I have a great fancy to see Macpherson sprout wings and flutter about."

Strange regarded Captain Macpherson thoughtfully. "No," he said at last, "but I would be grateful, my lord, if you would permit me to borrow him – and the map – for an hour or two."

Strange and Captain Macpherson peered at the map for some time, and then Strange went back to Lord Wellington and said it would take too long for every man in the army to sprout wings, but it would take no time at all to move the river and would that do? "At the moment," said Strange, "the river flows south here and then twists northwards here. If upon the other hand it flowed north instead of south and twisted southwards here, then, you see, we would be on the north bank and the French on the south."

"Oh!" said his lordship. "Very well."

The new position of the river so baffled the French that several French companies, when ordered to march north, went in entirely the wrong direction, so convinced were they that the direction *away* from the river must be north. These particular companies were never seen again and so it was widely supposed that they had been killed by the Spanish *guerrilleros*.

Lord Wellington later remarked cheerfully to General Picton that there was nothing so wearying for troops and horses as constant marching about and that in future he thought it would be better to keep them all standing still, while Mr Strange moved Spain about like a carpet beneath their feet.

Meanwhile the Spanish Regency Council in Cadiz became rather alarmed at this development and began to wonder whether, when they finally regained their country from the French, they would recognize it. They complained to the Foreign Secretary (which many people thought ungrateful). The Foreign Secretary persuaded Strange to write the Regency Council a letter promising that after the war he would replace the river in its original position and also ". . . any thing else which Lord Wellington requires to be moved during the prosecution of the war." Among the many things which Strange moved were: a wood of olive trees and pines in Navarra;[6] the city of Pamplona;[7] and two churches in the town of St Jean de Luz in France.[8]

On the 6th April 1814 the Emperor Napoleon Buonaparte abdicated. It is said that when Lord Wellington was told he performed a little dance. When Strange heard the news he laughed aloud, and then suddenly stopped and murmured, "Dear God! What will

[6] Colonel Vickery had reconnoitred the wood and discovered it to be full of French soldiers waiting to shoot at the British Army. His officers were just discussing what to do about it when Lord Wellington rode up. "We could go round it, I suppose," said Wellington, "but that will take time and I am in a hurry. Where is the magician?"

Someone went and fetched Strange.

"Mr Strange!" said Lord Wellington. "I can scarcely believe that it will be much trouble to you to move these trees! A great deal less, I am sure, than to make four thousand men walk seven miles out of their way. Move the wood, if you please!"

So Strange did as he was asked and moved the wood to the opposite side of the valley. The French soldiers were left cowering on a barren hillside and very quickly surrendered to the British.

[7] Owing to a mistake in Wellington's maps of Spain the city of Pamplona was not exactly where the British had supposed it to be. Wellington was deeply disappointed when, after the Army had marched twenty miles in one day, they did *not* reach Pamplona which was discovered to be ten miles further north. After swift discussion of the problem it was found to be more convenient to have Mr Strange move the city, rather than change all the maps.

[8] The churches in St Jean de Luz were something of an embarrassment. There was no reason whatsoever to move them. The fact of the matter was that one Sunday morning Strange was drinking brandy for breakfast at a hotel in St Jean de Luz with three Captains and two lieutenants of the 16th Light Dragoons. He was explaining to these gentlemen the theory behind the magical transportation of various objects. It was an entirely futile undertaking: they would not have understood him very well had they been sober and neither they nor Strange had been entirely sober for two days. By way of an illustration Strange swapped the positions of the two churches with the congregations still inside them. He fully intended to change them round again before the people came out, but shortly afterwards he was called away to a game of billiards and never thought of it again. Indeed despite Strange's many assurances he never found the time or inclination to replace river, wood, city, or indeed any thing at all in its original position.

they do with us now?" It was presumed at the time that this somewhat enigmatic remark referred to the Army, but afterwards several people wondered if he might perhaps have been talking about himself and the other magician.

The map of Europe was created anew: Buonaparte's new kingdoms were dismantled and the old ones put back in their place; some kings were deposed; other were restored to their thrones. The peoples of Europe congratulated themselves on finally vanquishing the Great Interloper. But to the inhabitants of Great Britain it suddenly appeared that the war had had an entirely different purpose: it had made Great Britain the Greatest Nation in the World. In London Mr Norrell had the satisfaction of hearing from everyone that magic – his magic and Mr Strange's – had been of vital importance in achieving this.

One evening towards the end of May Arabella returned home from a Victory Dinner at Carlton House. She had heard her husband spoken of in terms of the warmest praise, toasts had been made in his honour and the Prince Regent had said a great many complimentary things to her. Now it was just after midnight and she was sitting in the drawing-room reflecting that all she needed to complete her happiness was her husband home again, when one of the maids burst in and cried out, "Oh, madam! The master is here!"

Someone came into the room.

He was a thinner, browner person than she remembered. His hair had more grey in it and there was a whitish scar above his left eyebrow. The scar was not recent, but she had never seen it before. His features were what they had always been, but somehow his air was different. This scarcely seemed to be the person she had been thinking of only a moment ago. But before she could be disappointed, or awkward, or any of the things she had feared she would be when he at last came home, he looked around the room with a quick, half-ironic glance that she knew in an instant. Then he looked at her with the most familiar smile in the world and said, "I'm home."

* * *

The next morning they still had not said a hundredth part of all they had to tell each other.

"Sit there," said Strange to Arabella.

"In this chair?"

"Yes."

"Why?"

"So that I may look at you. I have not looked at you for three years and I have long felt the lack of it. I must supply the deficiency."

She sat down, but after a moment or two she began to smile. "Jonathan, I cannot keep my countenance if you stare at me like that. At this rate you will have supplied the deficiency in half an hour. I am sorry to disappoint you, but you never did look at me so very often. You always had your nose in some dusty old book."

"Untrue. I had entirely forgotten how quarrelsome you are. Hand me that piece of paper. I shall make a note of it."

"I shall do no such thing," said Arabella, laughing.

"Do you know what my first thought upon waking this morning was? I thought I ought to get up and shave and breakfast before some other fellow's servant took all the hot water and all the bread rolls. Then I remembered that all the servants in the house were mine and all the hot water in the house was mine and all the bread rolls were mine too. I do not think I was ever so happy in my life."

"Were you never comfortable in Spain?"

"In a war one is either living like a prince or a vagabond. I have seen Lord Wellington – his Grace, I should say[9] – sleeping under a tree with only a rock for a pillow. At other times I have seen thieves

[9] The British Government made Lord Wellington a Duke. At the same time there was a great deal of talk of ennobling Strange. "A baronetcy is the least he will expect," said Lord Liverpool to Sir Walter, "and we would be perfectly justified in doing something more – what would you say to a viscountcy?" The reason that none of this ever happened was because, as Sir Walter pointed out, it was entirely impossible to bestow a title on Strange without doing something for Norrell and somehow no one in the Government liked Norrell well enough to wish to do it. The thought of having to address Mr Norrell as "Sir Gilbert" or "my lord" was somehow rather depressing.

and beggars snoring upon feather-beds in palace bed-chambers. War is a very topsy-turvy business."

"Well, I hope you will not find it dull in London. The gentleman with the thistle-down hair said that once you had tasted war, you were sure to be bored at home."

"Ha! No, indeed! What, with everything clean, and just so? And all one's books and possessions so close to hand and one's wife just before one whenever one looks up? What does . . . ? Who did you say it was? The gentleman with what sort of hair?"

"Thistle-down. I am sure you must know the person I mean. He lives with Sir Walter and Lady Pole. At least, I am not sure he lives there, but I see him whenever I go to the house."

Strange frowned. "I do not know him. What is his name?"

But Arabella did not know. "I have always supposed him to be a relation of Sir Walter or Lady Pole. How queer it is that I never thought to ask him his name. I have had, oh! hours of conversation with him!"

"Have you indeed? I am not sure that I approve of that. Is he handsome?"

"Oh, yes! Very! How odd that I do not know his name! He is very entertaining. Quite unlike most people one meets."

"And what do you talk of?"

"Oh, everything! But it always ends in him wishing to give me presents. On Monday last he wanted to fetch me a tiger from Bengal. On Wednesday he wished to bring me the Queen of Naples – because, he said, she and I are so much alike that we were sure to be the best of friends and on Friday he wished to send a servant to bring me a music-tree . . ."

"A music-tree?"

Arabella laughed. "A music-tree! He says that somewhere on a mountain with a storybook name there grows a tree which bears sheet music instead of fruit and the music is far superior to any other. I can never quite tell whether he believes his own tales or not. Indeed, there have been occasions when I have wondered if he is mad. I always make some excuse or other for not accepting his presents."

"I am glad. I should not at all have cared to come home and find the house full of tigers and queens and music-trees. Have you heard from Mr Norrell recently?"

"Not recently, no."

"Why are you smiling?" asked Strange.

"Was I? I did not know. Well then, I will tell you. He once sent me a message and that is all."

"Once? In three years?"

"Yes. About a year ago there was a rumour that you had been killed at Vitoria and Mr Norrell sent Childermass to ask if it was true. I knew no more than he did. But that evening Captain Moulthrop arrived. He had landed at Portsmouth not two days before and had come straight here to tell me that there was not a word of truth in it. I shall never forget his kindness! Poor young man! His arm had been amputated only a month or so before and he was still suffering very much. But there is a letter for you from Mr Norrell on the table. Childermass brought it yesterday."

Strange got up and went to the table. He picked up the letter and turned it over in his hands. "Well, I suppose I shall have to go," he said doubtfully.

The truth was that he was not looking forward to meeting his old tutor with any very great enthusiasm. He had become accustomed to independence of thought and action. In Spain he had had his instructions from the Duke of Wellington but what magic he did to fulfil those instructions had been entirely his own decision. The prospect of doing magic under Mr Norrell's direction again was not an appealing one; and after months spent in the company of Wellington's bold, dashing young officers, the thought of long hours with only Mr Norrell to talk to was a little grim.

Yet in spite of his misgivings it was a very cordial meeting. Mr Norrell was so delighted to see him, so full of questions about the precise nature of the spells he had employed in Spain, so full of praise for all that had been achieved, that Strange almost began to feel he had misjudged his tutor.

Naturally enough Mr Norrell would not hear of Strange's giving up his role as Mr Norrell's pupil. "No, no, no! You must return here! We have a great deal to do. Now the war is over, all the real work is ahead of us. We must establish magic for the Modern Age! I have had the most gratifying assurances from several Ministers who were anxious to assure me of the utter impossibility of their continuing to govern the country without the aid of our magic! And despite everything that you and I have done there are misconceptions! Why! Only the other day I overheard Lord Castlereagh tell someone that you had, at the Duke of Wellington's insistence, employed Black Magic in Spain! I was swift to assure his lordship that you had employed nothing but the most modern methods."

Strange paused and then inclined his head slightly in a manner which Mr Norrell certainly took for acquiescence. "But we were speaking of whether or not I should continue as your pupil. I have mastered all the sorts of magic on the list you made four years ago. You told me, sir, before I went to the Peninsula, that you were entirely delighted with my progress – as I dare say you remember."

"Oh! But that was barely a beginning. I have made another list while you were in Spain. I shall ring for Lucas to fetch it from the library. Besides, there are *other books*, you know, which I wish you to read." He blinked his little blue eyes nervously at Strange.

Strange hesitated. This was a reference to the library at Hurtfew Abbey which Strange had still not seen.

"Oh, Mr Strange!" exclaimed Mr Norrell. "I am very glad that you have come home, sir. I am very glad to see you! I hope we may have many hours of conversation. Mr Lascelles and Mr Drawlight have been here a great deal . . ."

Strange said he was sure of it.

". . . but there is no talking to them about magic. Come back tomorrow. Come early. Come to breakfast!"

32

# The King

## November 1814

EARLY IN NOVEMBER 1814 Mr Norrell was honoured by a visit from some very noble gentlemen – an earl, a duke and two baronets – who came, they said, to speak to him upon a matter of the utmost delicacy and were so discreet themselves that half an hour after they had begun talking Mr Norrell was still entirely ignorant of what they wished him to do.

It emerged that, elevated as these gentlemen were, they were the representatives of one still greater – the Duke of York – and they had come to speak to Mr Norrell about the madness of the King. The King's sons had recently paid a visit to their father and had been very shocked by his sad condition; and, though all of them were selfish and some of them were dissolute and none of them were much given to making sacrifices of any sort, they had all told each other how they would give any amount of money and cut off any number of limbs to make the King a little more comfortable.

But, just as the King's children quarrelled amongst themselves as to which doctor their father should have, so they now quarrelled as to whether or not a magician should attend the King. Chief in opposition to the idea was the Prince Regent. Many years before, during the life of the great Mr Pitt, the King had suffered a severe bout of madness and the Prince had ruled in his place, but then the King had recovered and the Prince had found his powers and privileges stripped away from him. Of all the tiresome situations in the world, thought the Prince Regent, the most tiresome was to rise from one's bed in a state of uncertainty as to whether or not one was the ruler of Great Britain. So perhaps the Prince might be forgiven for wishing that the King remain mad or, at least, only gain such relief as Death would supply.

Mr Norrell, who had no wish to offend the Prince Regent, declined to offer his assistance, adding that he doubted very much whether the King's illness were susceptible of treatment by magic. So the King's second son, the Duke of York, who was a military gentleman, asked the Duke of Wellington if he thought that Mr Strange might be persuaded to visit the King.

"Oh! I am certain of it!" replied the Duke of Wellington. "Mr Strange is always glad of an opportunity to do magic. Nothing pleases him more. The tasks I set him in Spain posed all sorts of difficulties and, though he made a great shew of complaining, the truth was he could not have been more delighted. I have a great opinion of Mr Strange's abilities. Spain is, as your Royal Highness knows, one of the most uncivilized places in the world, with scarcely any thoroughfare superior to a goat track from one end of the country to the other. But thanks to Mr Strange my men had good English roads to take them wherever they were needed and if there was a mountain or a forest or a city in our way, why! Mr Strange simply moved it somewhere else."

The Duke of York remarked that King Ferdinand of Spain had sent a letter to the Prince Regent complaining that many parts of his kingdom had been rendered entirely unrecognizable by the English magician and demanding that Mr Strange return and restore the country to its original form.

"Oh," said the Duke of Wellington, not much interested, "they are still complaining about that, are they?"

As a consequence of this conversation Arabella Strange came downstairs one Thursday morning to find her drawing-room full of the King's male offspring. There were five of them; their Royal

Highnesses the Dukes of York, Clarence, Sussex, Kent and Cambridge. They were all between forty and fifty years of age. All had been handsome once, but all were rather fond of eating and drinking, and consequently all were growing rather stout.

Mr Strange was standing with his elbow on the mantelpiece, one of Mr Norrell's books in his hand and a polite look of interest upon his face, while their Royal Highnesses all talked at the same time and interrupted one another in their eagerness to describe the terrible pathos of the King's situation.

"Were you to see how His Majesty dribbles his bread and milk when he eats," said the Duke of Clarence to Arabella with tears in his eyes, "how full of imaginary fears he is and how he holds long conversations with Mr Pitt who has been dead this age . . . well, my dear, you could not help but be brought very low by the sight." The Duke took Arabella's hand and began to stroke it, apparently under the impression that she was the parlour-maid.

"All of His Majesty's subjects are very sorry that he is ill," said Arabella. "None of us can think of his suffering with indifference."

"Oh, my dear!" cried the Duke delighted, "How it touches my heart to hear you say so!" and he planted a large wet royal kiss upon her hand and looked at her very tenderly.

"If Mr Norrell does not consider it a subject capable of treatment by magic then frankly I do not think the chances are good," said Strange. "But I will gladly wait upon His Majesty."

"In that case," said the Duke of York, "there is only the problem of the Willises."

"The Willises?" said Strange.

"Oh, indeed!" cried the Duke of Cambridge. "The Willises are more impertinent than any one can imagine."

"We must be careful not to vex the Willises too much," warned the Duke of Clarence, "or they are sure to revenge themselves upon His Majesty."

"The Willises will have a great many objections to Mr Strange visiting the King," sighed the Duke of Kent.

The Willises were two brothers who owned a madhouse in Lincolnshire. For many years now they had attended the King whenever His Majesty had happened to become mad. And whenever he had happened to be in his right mind the King had repeatedly told everyone how much he hated the Willises and how deeply he resented their cruel treatment of him. He had extracted promises from the Queen and the Dukes and the Princesses that, should he ever become mad again, they would not surrender him to the Willises. But it had done no good. At the first sign of delirium the Willises had been sent for, and they had come immediately and locked the King in a room and clapped him in a strait waistcoat and given him strong, purging medicines.

I believe it will puzzle my readers (for it puzzled everyone else) that a king should be so little able to command his own fate. But consider with what alarm the rumour of madness is greeted in private families. Consider then how much greater the alarm when the sufferer is the King of Great Britain! If you or I go mad, it is a misfortune for ourselves, our friends and family. When a king goes mad, it is a disaster for the whole Nation. Frequently in the past King George's illness had left it entirely uncertain who should govern the country. There were no precedents. No one had known what to do. It was not that the Willises were liked or respected – they were not. It was not that their treatments granted the King any relief from his torments – they did not. The secret of the Willises' success was that they were cool when everyone else was in a panic. They embraced a responsibility which everyone else was most anxious to avoid. In return they demanded absolute control of the King's person. No one was permitted to speak to the King without a Willis being present. Not the Queen, not the Prime Minister. Not even the King's thirteen sons and daughters.

"Well, said Strange when all this had been explained to him, "I admit that I would much rather speak to His Majesty without the encumbrance of other people – particularly people unfavourable to my purpose. However, I have upon occasion baffled the entire French Army. I dare say I can manage two doctors. Leave the Willises to me."

Strange refused to discuss the matter of a fee until he had seen the King. He would make no charge for visiting His Majesty, which the Dukes – who all had gambling debts to pay and houses full of illegitimate children to feed and educate – thought very handsome of him.

Early the next day Strange rode out to Windsor Castle to see the King. It was a sharp, cold morning and a thick, white mist lay everywhere. On the way he cast three small spells. The first ensured that the Willises would sleep long past their customary hour; the second spell caused the wives and servants of the Willises to forget to wake them; and the third made sure that when the Willises finally woke, none of their clothes or boots would be in the places where they had left them. Two years earlier Strange would have scrupled to play even so slight a trick as this upon two strangers, but now he did not give it a second thought. Like many other gentlemen who had been in Spain with the Duke of Wellington, he had begun unconsciously to imitate his Grace, part of whose character it was always to act in the most direct way possible.[1]

Towards ten o'clock he crossed the River Thames by the little wooden bridge at the village of Datchet. He passed along the lane between the river and the Castle wall and entered the town of Windsor. At the Castle-gate he told the sentry who he was and his business with the King. A servant in a blue uniform appeared to escort him to the King's apartments. The servant was a civil, intelligent sort of man and, as often happens with servants in grand places, he was excessively proud of the Castle and every thing to do with it. His chief pleasure in life laying in shewing people around the Castle and in fancying them astonished, awed

[1] In *The Life of Jonathan Strange*, John Segundus discusses other ways in which he believes Strange's later actions were influenced by the Duke of Wellington.

and amazed. "Surely this cannot be your first visit to the Castle, sir?" was his first question to Strange.

"Upon the contrary. I was never here in my life."

The man looked shocked. "Then, sir, you have missed one of the noblest sights that England has to offer!"

"Indeed? Well, I am here now."

"But you are here on business, sir," answered the servant in a reproving tone, "and will not, I dare say, have leisure to examine everything properly. You must come again, sir. In summer. And in case you should be a married gentleman, I take the liberty of observing that ladies are always particularly delighted with the Castle."

He led Strange through a courtyard of impressive size. Long ago, in times of war it must have provided a refuge for a large number of people and their livestock and there were still a few ancient buildings in a very simple style that bore witness to the military character which the Castle had originally possessed. But as time had gone on the desire for kingly pomp and splendour had begun to outweigh more utilitarian considerations and a magnificent church had been built which filled up most of the space. This church (called the Chapel, but in truth more like a Cathedral) displayed all the complexity and elaborateness of which the Gothic style is capable. It was hedged about with prickly stone buttresses, crowned with stone pinnacles and it bulged with chapels, oratories and vestries.

The servant took Strange past a steep mound with smooth sides, surmounted by the round tower which is the most easily recognizable part of the Castle when viewed from a distance. Passing through a mediaeval gateway, they entered another courtyard. This was almost as magnificently proportioned as the first courtyard, but whereas the other had been peopled with servants, soldiers and household officials, this was silent and empty.

"It is a great pity that you did not come here a few years ago, sir," said the servant. "At that time it was possible to visit the King and Queen's Apartments upon application to the housekeeper, but His Majesty's illness has made that impossible."

He led Strange to an imposing Gothic entrance in the middle of a long range of stone buildings. As they mounted a flight of stone stairs he continued to bemoan the many obstacles which stood in the way of Strange's seeing the Castle. He could not help but suppose Strange's disappointment to be very great. "I have it!" he declared suddenly. "I will shew you St George's Hall! Oh, it is not a hundredth part of what you ought to see, sir, but still it will give you a notion of the sublimity of which Windsor Castle is capable!"

At the top of the stairs he turned to the right and went swiftly through a hall with arrangements of swords and pistols upon the walls. Strange followed. They entered a long and lofty hall, some two or three hundred feet long.

"There!" said the servant with as much satisfaction as if he had built and decorated it himself.

Tall, arched windows along the south wall let in the cold, misty light. The lower part of the walls was panelled with pearwood and the panels all had carved and gilded borders. The upper part of the walls and the ceiling were covered with paintings of gods and goddesses, kings and queens. The ceiling shewed Charles II in the process of being carried up to eternal glory upon a white and blue cloud, surrounded by fat, pink cherubs. Generals and diplomats laid trophies at his feet, while Julius Caesar, Mars, Hercules and various important personages stood about in some embarrassment, having been suddenly struck with a mortifying consciousness of their inferiority to the British King.

All of this was most magnificent, but the painting which caught Strange's eye was a huge mural that stretched the entire length of the north wall. In the middle were two kings seated upon two thrones. On each side stood or knelt knights, ladies, courtiers, pages, gods and goddesses. The left-hand part of the painting was steeped in sunlight. The king upon this side was a strong, handsome man who displayed all the vigour of youth. He was dressed in a pale robe and his hair was golden and curling. There was a laurel wreath upon his brow and a sceptre in his hand. The people and gods who attended him were all equipped with helmets, breastplates, spears and swords, as if the artist wished to suggest that this king only attracted the most warlike of men and gods to be his friends. In the right-hand part of the painting the light grew dim and dusky, as if the artist meant to depict a summer's twilight. Stars shone above and around the figures. The king on this side was pale-skinned and dark-haired. He wore a black robe and his expression was unfathomable. He had a crown of dark ivy leaves and in his left hand he held a slim ivory wand. His entourage was composed largely of magical creatures: a phoenix, a unicorn, a manticore, fauns and satyrs. But there were also some mysterious persons: a male figure in a monklike robe with his hood pulled down over his face, a female figure in a dark, starry mantle with her arm thrown over her eyes. Between the two thrones stood a young woman in a loose white robe with a golden helmet upon her head. The warlike king had placed his left hand protectively upon her shoulder; the dark king held out his right hand towards her and she had extended her hand to his so that their fingertips lightly touched.

"The work of Antonio Verrio, an Italian gentleman," said the servant. He pointed to the king upon the left. "That is Edward the Third of Southern England." He pointed to the king upon the right, "And that is the Magician-King of Northern England, John Uskglass."

"Is it though?" said Strange, greatly interested. "I have seen statues of him of course. And engravings in books. But I do not think I ever saw a painting before. And the lady between the two kings, who is she?"

"That is Mrs Gwynn, one of the mistresses of Charles II. She is meant to represent Britannia."

"I see. It is something, I suppose, that he still has a place of honour in the King's house. But then they put him in Roman dress and make him hold hands with an actress. I wonder what he would say to that?"

The servant led Strange back through the weapon-lined room to a black door of imposing size overtopped with a great jutting marble pediment.

"I can take you no further than this, sir. My business ends here and the Dr Willises' begins. You will find the King behind that door." He bowed and went back down the stairs.

Strange knocked on the door. From somewhere inside came the sound of a harpsichord and someone singing.

The door opened to reveal a tall, broad fellow of thirty or forty. His face was round, white, pockmarked and bedabbled with sweat like a Cheshire cheese. All in all he bore a striking resemblance to the man in the moon who is reputed to be made of cheese. He had shaved himself with no very high degree of skill and here and there on his white face two or three coarse black hairs appeared – rather as if a family of flies had drowned in the milk before the cheese was made and their legs were poking out of it. His coat was of rough brown drugget and his shirt and neckcloth were of the coarsest linen. None of his clothes were particularly clean.

"Yes?" he said, keeping his hand upon the door as if he intended to shut it again at the least provocation. He had very little of the character of a palace servant and a great deal of the character of a madhouse attendant, which was what he was.

Strange raised his eyebrow at this rude behaviour. He gave his name rather coldly and said he had come to see the King.

The man sighed. "Well, sir, I cannot deny that we were expecting you. But, you see, you cannot come in. Dr John and Dr Robert . . ." (These were the names of the two Willis brothers) ". . . are not here. We have been expecting them every minute for the past hour and a half. We do not understand where they can have got to."

"That is most unfortunate," said Strange. "But it is none of my concern. I have no desire to see the gentlemen you mention. My business is with the King. I have a letter signed by the Archbishops of Canterbury and York granting me permission to visit His Majesty today." Strange waved the letter in the man's face.

"But you must wait, sir, until Dr John and Dr Robert come. They will not allow any one to interfere with their system of managing the King. Silence and seclusion are what suits the King best. Conversation is the very worst thing for him. You can scarcely imagine, sir, what terrible harm you might do to the King merely by speaking to him. Say you were to mention that it is raining. I dare say you would consider that the most innocent remark in the world. But it might set the King a-thinking, you see, and in his madness his mind runs on from one thing to another, enraging him to a most dangerous degree. He might think of times in the past when it rained and his servants brought him news of battles that were lost, and daughters that were dead, and sons that had disgraced him. Why! It might be enough to kill the King outright! Do you want to kill the King, sir?"

"No," said Strange.

"Well, then," said the man coaxingly, "do you not see, sir, that it would be far better to wait for Dr John and Dr Robert?"

"Thank you, but I think I will take my chances. Conduct me to the King if you please."

"Dr John and Dr Robert will be very angry," warned the man.

"I do not care if they are," replied Strange coolly.

The man looked entirely astonished at this.

"Now," said Strange, with a most determined look and another flourish of his letter, "will you let me see the King or will you defy the authority of two Archbishops? That is a very grave matter, punishable by . . . well, I do not exactly know what, but something rather severe, I should imagine."

The man sighed. He called to another man (as rough and dirty as himself) and told him to go immediately to the houses of Dr John and Dr Robert to fetch them. Then with great reluctance he stood aside for Strange to enter.

The proportions of the room were lofty. The walls were panelled in oak and there was a great deal of fine carving. More royal and symbolic personages lounged about upon clouds on the ceiling. But it was a dreary place. There was no covering upon the floor and it was very cold. A chair and a battered-looking harpsichord were the only furniture. An old man was seated at the harpsichord with his back to them. He was dressed in a dressing-gown of ancient purple brocade. There was a crumpled nightcap of scarlet velvet on his head and dirty broken slippers on his feet. He was playing with great vigour and singing loudly in German. When he heard the sound of approaching footsteps he stopped.

"Who's there?" he demanded. "Who is it?"

"The magician, Your Majesty," said the madhouse attendant.

The old man seemed to consider this a moment and then he said in a loud voice, "It is a profession to which I have a particular dislike!" He struck the keys of his harpsichord again and resumed his loud singing.

This was rather a discouraging beginning. The madhouse attendant gave an impertinent snigger and walked off, leaving Strange and the King alone. Strange took a few paces further into the room and placed himself where he might observe the King's face.

It was a face in which all the misery of madness was compounded by the misery of blindness. The eyes had irises of clouded blue and whites as discoloured as rotten milk. Long locks of whitish hair streaked with grey hung down on either side of cheeks patched with broken veins. As the King sang, spittle flew from his slack red lips. His beard was almost as long and white as his hair. He was nothing at all like the pictures Strange had seen of him, for they had been made when he was in his right mind. With his long hair, long beard and long, purple robe, what he chiefly resembled was someone very tragic and ancient out of Shakespeare – or, rather, two very tragic and ancient persons out of Shakespeare. In his madness and his blindness he was Lear and Gloucester combined.

Strange had been cautioned by the Royal Dukes that it was contrary to Court etiquette to speak to the King unless the King addressed him first. However there seemed little hope of this since the King disliked magicians so much. So when the King ceased his playing and singing again, he said, "I am Your Majesty's humble servant, Jonathan Strange of Ashfair in Shropshire. I was Magician-in-Ordinary to the Army during the late war in Spain where, I am happy to say, I was able to do Your Majesty some service. It is the hope of Your Majesty's sons and daughters that my magic might afford Your Majesty some relief from your illness."

"Tell the magician I do not see him!" said the King airily.

Strange did not trouble to make any reply to this nonsensical remark. Of course the King could not see him, the King was blind.

"But I see his companion *very well*!" continued His Majesty in an approving tone. He turned his head as though to gaze at a point two or three feet to the left of Strange. "With such silver hair as he has got, I think I ought to be able to see him! He looks a very wild fellow."

So convincing was this speech that Strange actually turned to look. Of course there was no one.

In the past few days he had searched Norrell's books for something pertinent to the King's condition. There were remarkably few spells for curing madness. Indeed he had found only one, and even then he was not sure that was what it was meant for. It was a prescription in Ormskirk's *Revelations of Thirty-Six Other Worlds*. Ormskirk said that it would dispel illusions and correct wrong ideas. Strange took out the book and read through the spell again. It was a peculiarly obscure piece of magic, consisting only of the following words:

*Place the moon at his eyes and her whiteness shall devour the false sights the deceiver has placed there.*
*Place a swarm of bees at his ears. Bees love truth and will destroy the deceiver's lies.*

*Place salt in his mouth lest the deceiver attempt to delight him with the taste of honey or disgust him with the taste of ashes.*
*Nail his hand with an iron nail so that he shall not raise it to do the deceiver's bidding.*
*Place his heart in a secret place so that all his desires shall be his own and the deceiver shall find no hold there.*

*Memorandum. The colour red may be found beneficial.*

However, as Strange read it through, he was forced to admit that he had not the least idea what it meant.[2] How was the magician supposed to fetch the moon to the afflicted person? And if the second part were correct, then the Dukes would have done better to employ a beekeeper instead of a magician. Nor could Strange believe that their Royal Highnesses would be best pleased if he began piercing the King's hands with iron nails. The note about the colour red was odd too. He thought he remembered hearing or reading something about red but he could not at present recall what it was.

The King, meanwhile, had fallen into conversation with the imaginary silver-haired person. "I beg your pardon for mistaking you for a common person," he said. "You may be a king just as you say, but I merely take the liberty of observing that I have never heard of any of your kingdoms. Where is Lost-hope? Where are the Blue Castles? Where is the City of Iron Angels? I, on the other hand, am King of *Great Britain*, a place everyone knows and which is clearly marked on all the maps!" His Majesty paused, presumably to attend to the silver-haired person's reply for he suddenly cried out, "Oh, do not be angry! Pray, do not be angry! You are a king and I am a king! We shall all be kings together!

[2] The likelihood was that neither did Ormskirk. He had simply written down a spell that someone else had told him or that he had found in another book. This is a perennial problem with the writings of the *Argentine* magicians. In their anxiety to preserve any scrap of magical knowledge, they were often obliged to set down what they themselves did not understand.

And there is really no need for either of us to be angry! I shall play and sing for you!" He drew a flute from the pocket of his dressing-gown and began to play a melancholy air.

As an experiment Strange reached forward and plucked off His Majesty's scarlet nightcap. He watched closely to see if the King grew any more mad without it, but after several minutes of observation he was forced to admit that he could see no difference. He put the nightcap back on.

For the next hour and a half he tried all the magic he could think of. He cast spells of remembering, spells of finding, spells of awakening, spells to concentrate the mind, spells to dispel nightmares and evil thoughts, spells to find patterns in chaos, spells to find a path when one was lost, spells of demystification, spells of discernment, spells to increase intelligence, spells to cure sickness and spells to repair a limb that is shattered. Some of the spells were long and complicated. Some were a single word. Some had to be said out loud. Some had only to be thought. Some had no words at all but consisted of a single gesture. Some were spells that Strange and Norrell had employed in some form or other every day for the last five years. Some had probably not been used for centuries. Some used a mirror; two used a tiny bead of blood from the magician's finger; and one used a candle and a piece of ribbon. But they all had this in common: they had no effect upon the King whatsoever.

At the end of this time: "Oh, I give up!" thought Strange.

His Majesty, who had been happily unconscious of the magic directed at him, was chatting confidentially to the person with the silver hair that only he could see. "Have you been sent here for ever or can you go away again? Oh, do not stay to be caught! This is a bad place for kings! They put us in strait waistcoats! The last time I was permitted to go out of these rooms was on a Monday in 1811. They tell me that was three years ago, but they lie! By my calculation, it will be two hundred and forty-six years on Saturday fortnight!"

"Poor, unhappy gentleman!" thought Strange. "Shut away in

this cold, melancholy place without friends or amusements! Small wonder time passes so slowly for him. Small wonder he is mad!"

Out loud he said, "I shall be very happy to take you outside, Your Majesty, if you wish it."

The King paused in his chatter and turned his head slightly. "Who said that?" he demanded.

"I did, Your Majesty. Jonathan Strange, the magician." Strange made the King a respectful bow, before recollecting that His Majesty could not see it.

"Great Britain! My dear Kingdom!" cried the King. "How I should love to see her again – especially now that it is summertime. The trees and meadows are all decked in their brightest finery and the air is sweet as cherry-tart!"

Strange glanced out of the window at the white, icy mist and the skeletal winter trees. "Quite so. And I would account it a great honour if Your Majesty would accompany me outside."

The King seemed to consider this proposal. He took off one of his slippers and attempted to balance it upon his head. When this did not work, he put the slipper back on, took a tassel that hung from the end of his dressing-gown cord and sucked upon it thoughtfully. "But how do I know that you are not a wicked demon come to tempt me?" he asked at last in a tone of the most complete reasonableness.

Strange was somewhat lost for an answer to this question. While he was considering what to say, the King continued, "Of course if you are a wicked demon, then you should know that I am Eternal and cannot die. If I discover that you are my Enemy, I shall stamp my foot and send you straight back to Hell!"

"Really? Your Majesty must teach me the trick of that. I should like to know something so useful. But permit me to observe that, with such powerful magic at your command, Your Majesty has nothing to fear from accompanying me outside. We should leave as quickly and discreetly as we can. The Willises are sure to be here soon. Your Majesty must be very quiet!"

The King said nothing, but he tapped his nose and looked very sly.

Strange's next task was to discover a way out without alerting the madhouse attendants. The King was no help at all in this regard. When asked where the various doors led to, he gave it as his opinion that one door led to America, another to Everlasting Perdition and a third might possibly be the way to next Friday. So Strange picked one – the one the King thought led to America – and quickly escorted His Majesty through several rooms. All had painted ceilings in which English monarchs were depicted as dashing about the sky in fiery chariots, vanquishing persons who symbolized Envy, Sin and Sedition, and establishing Temples of Virtue, Palaces of Eternal Justice and other useful institutions of that sort. But though the ceilings were full of the most intense activity, the rooms beneath them were forlorn, threadbare and full of dust and spiders. The furniture was all covered up with sheets so that it appeared as if these chairs and tables must have died some time ago and these were their gravestones.

They came to a sort of back-staircase. The King, who had taken Strange's warning to be quiet very much to heart, insisted upon tip-toeing down the stairs in the highly exaggerated manner of a small child. This took some time.

"Well, Your Majesty," said Strange, cheerfully, when at last they reached the bottom, "I think we managed that rather well. I do not hear any sounds of pursuit. The Duke of Wellington would be glad to employ either of us as Intelligence Officers. I do not believe that Captain Somers-Cocks or Colquhoun Grant himself could have crossed enemy territory with more . . ."

He was interrupted by the King playing a very loud, very triumphant blare upon his flute.

"D—!" said Strange and listened for sounds of the madhouse attendants coming or, worse still, the Willises.

But nothing happened. Somewhere close at hand there was an odd, irregular thumping and clattering, accompanied by screams and wailing – rather as if someone were being beaten by a whole cupboardful of brooms at once. Apart from that, all was quiet.

A door opened on to a broad stone terrace. From here the land descended steeply and at the foot of the slope lay a Park. On the right a long, double line of winter trees could be just seen.

Arm in arm the King and Strange walked along the terrace to the corner of the Castle. Here Strange found a path leading down the slope and into the Park. They descended this path and had not walked far into the Park when they came upon an ornamental pool, bounded by a low stone rim.[3] At its centre stood a little stone pavilion decorated with carved creatures. Some resembled dogs – except that their bodies were long and low like lizards and each had a row of spines along its back. Others were meant to represent curved stone dolphins which had somehow contrived to fasten themselves to the walls. On the roof half a dozen classical ladies and gentlemen were sitting in classical attitudes, holding vases. It had clearly been the architect's intention that fountains of water should gush out of the mouths of all these strange animals and out of the vases on the roof and tumble decoratively into the pool, but just now all was frozen and silent.

Strange was about to make some remark on the melancholy sight which this frozen pool presented, when he heard several shouts. He looked back and saw that a group of people was descending the slope of the Castle very rapidly. As they drew nearer he saw that they were four in number: two gentlemen he had never seen before and the two madhouse attendants – the one with the face like a Cheshire cheese and the one who had been sent to fetch the Willises. They all looked angry.

The gentlemen hurried up, frowning in an important, offended sort of manner. They shewed every symptom of having dressed in a

---

[3] This pool and the line of trees were all that remained of a vast ornamental garden planned by King William III which had been begun, but never completed. It had been abandoned when the cost proved far too great. The land had been allowed to return to its former state of Park and meadow.

great hurry. One was attempting to fasten the buttons of his coat, but without much success. As soon as he did up the buttons, they flew open again. He was about Mr Norrell's age and wore an old-fashioned wig (rather like Mr Norrell's) which from time to time made a little jump and spun round on his head. But he differed from Mr Norrell in that he was rather tall, rather handsome and had an imposing, decisive manner. The other gentleman (who was several years younger) was plagued by his boots, which seemed to have developed opinions of their own. While he was struggling to walk forwards, they were attempting to carry him off in an entirely different direction. Strange could only suppose that his earlier magic had been rather more successful than he had expected and had made the clothes themselves difficult to manage.

The tallest gentleman (the one who wore the playful wig) gave Strange a furious stare. "Upon whose authority is the King outside?" he demanded.

Strange shrugged. "Mine, I suppose."

"You! Who are you?"

Not liking the manner in which he was addressed, Strange retorted, "Who are you?"

"I am Dr John Willis. This is my brother, Dr Robert Darling Willis. We are the King's physicians. We have charge of the King's person by order of the Queen's Council. No one is allowed to see His Majesty without our permission. I ask you again: who are you?"

"I am Jonathan Strange. I have come at the request of their Royal Highnesses the Dukes of York, Clarence, Sussex, Kent and Cambridge to see whether or not His Majesty might be cured by magic."

"Ha!" cried Dr John contemptuously. "Magic! That is chiefly used for killing Frenchmen, is it not?"

Dr Robert laughed in a sarcastic manner. But the effect of cold, scientific disdain was rather spoilt when his boots suddenly carried him off with such force that he banged his nose against a tree.

"Well, Magician!" said Dr John. "You mistake your man if you think you may mistreat me and my servants with impunity. You will admit, I dare say, that you glued the doors of the Castle shut by magic, so that my men could not prevent you leaving?"

"Certainly not!" declared Strange. "I did nothing of the sort! I *might* have done it," he conceded, "if there had been any need. But your men are as idle as they are impertinent! When His Majesty and I left the Castle they were nowhere to be seen!"

The first madhouse attendant (the one with a face like a Cheshire cheese) almost exploded upon hearing this. "That is not true!" he cried. "Dr John, Dr Robert, I beg that you will not listen to these lies! Martin here," he indicated the other madhouse attendant, "has had his voice entirely taken from him. He could not make a sound to raise the alarm!" The other madhouse attendant mouthed and gestured furiously in confirmation. "As for me, sir, I was in the passageway at the bottom of the stairs, when the door opened at the top. I was just readying myself to speak to this magician – and some strong words I was going to give him too, sir, on your behalf – when I was pulled by magic into a broom cupboard and the door shut fast upon me . . ."

"What nonsense!" cried Strange.

"Nonsense, is it?" cried the man. "And I suppose you did not make the brooms in the cupboard beat me! I am all over bruises."

This, at least, was perfectly true. His face and hands were covered in red marks.

"There, Magician!" cried Dr John, triumphantly. "What do you say now? Now that all your tricks are exposed?"

"Oh, really!" said Strange. "He has done that to himself to make his story more convincing!"

The King blew a vulgar noise on his flute.

"Be assured," said Dr John, "that the Queen's Council will soon hear of your impudence!" Then, turning away from Strange, he cried out, "Your Majesty! Come here!"

The King skipped nimbly behind Strange.

"You will oblige me by returning the King to my care," said Dr John.

"I will do no such thing," declared Strange.

"And you know how lunatics should be treated, do you?" said Dr Robert with a sneer. "You have studied the matter?"

"I know that to keep a man without companionship, to deny him exercise and a change of air cannot possibly cure any thing," said Strange. "It is barbaric! I would not keep a dog so."

"In speaking as you do," added Dr Robert, "you merely betray your ignorance. The solitude and tranquility of which you complain so vigorously are the cornerstones of our whole system of treating the King."

"Oh!" said Strange. "You call it a system, do you? And what does it consist of, this system?"

"There are three main principles," declared Dr Robert. "Intimidation . . ."

The King played a few sad notes upon his flute . . .

". . . isolation . . ."

. . . which became a lonely little tune . . .

". . . and restraint."

. . . ending in a long note like a sigh.

"In this way," continued Dr Robert, "all possible sources of excitement are suppressed and the patient is denied material with which to construct his fantasies and improper notions."

"But in the end," added Dr John, "it is by the imposition of his will upon his patient that the doctor effects his cure. It is the forcefulness of the doctor's own character which determines his success or failure. It was observed by many people that our father could subdue lunatics merely by fixing them with his eye."

"Really?" said Strange, becoming interested in spite of himself. "I had never thought of it before, but something of the sort is certainly true of magic. There are all sorts of occasions when the success of a piece of magic depends upon the forcefulness of the magician's character."

"Indeed?" said Dr John, glancing briefly to his left.

"Yes. Take Martin Pale for example. Now he . . ." Strange's eyes involuntarily followed where Dr John had looked. One of the madhouse attendants – the one who could not speak – was creeping around the ornamental pool towards the King with a pale-coloured something in his hands. Strange could not think at first what it could be. And then he recognized it. It was a strait waistcoat.

Several things happened at once. Strange shouted something – he did not know what – the other madhouse attendant lunged towards the King – both Willises attempted to grab Strange – the King blew piercing shrieks of alarm on his flute – and there was an odd noise as if a hundred or so people had all cleared their throats at once.

Everyone stopped and looked about them. The sound appeared to have come from the little stone pavilion at the centre of the frozen pool. Suddenly out of the mouths of each stone creature a dense white cloud appeared, as if they had all exhaled at once. The breath-clouds glittered and sparkled in the thin, misty light, and then fell upon the ice with a faint tinkling sound.

There was a silence, followed immediately by a horrible sound like blocks of marble being ripped apart. Then the stone creatures tore themselves from the walls of the pavilion and began to crawl and waddle down and across the ice towards the Willises. Their blank stone eyes rolled in their sockets. They opened their stone mouths and from every stone throat came a plume of water. Stone tails snaked from side to side and stone legs went stiffly up and down. The lead pipes which conducted water to their mouths extended magically behind them.

The Willises and the madhouse attendants stared, quite unable to comprehend what was happening. The grotesque creatures crawled, dragging their pipes behind them and dousing the Willises with water. The Willises shrieked and leapt about, more from fright than because of any real hurt they had sustained.

The madhouse attendants ran away and as to the Willises remaining any longer with the King, there could be no question of it. In the cold air their drenched clothes were turning icy.

"Magician!" cried Dr John, as he turned to run back to the Castle. "Why! It is just another name for liar! Lord Liverpool shall know of it, Magician! He shall know how you use the King's physicians! Ow! Ow!" He would have said more but the stone figures on the roof of the pavilion had stood up and begun pelting him with stones.

Strange merely bestowed a contemptuous smile on both Willises. But he was acting more confident than he felt. The truth was he was beginning to feel decidedly uncomfortable. Whatever magic had just been done, had not been done by him.

# 33

## *Place the moon at my eyes*

### November 1814

IT WAS MOST mysterious. Could someone in the Castle be a magician? One of the servants perhaps? Or one of the Princesses? It did not seem likely. Could it be Mr Norrell's doing? Strange pictured his tutor sitting in his little room upon the second floor at Hanover-square peering into his silver dish, watching all that had happened and finally driving away the Willises with magic. It was possible, he supposed. Bringing statues to life was, after all, something of a speciality of Mr Norrell's. It had been the first magic to bring him to the public notice. And yet, and yet . . . Why would Mr Norrell suddenly decide to help him? Out of the kindness of his heart? Hardly. Besides there had been a dark humour in the magic which was not like Norrell at all. The magician had not merely wanted to frighten the Willises; he had wanted to make them ridiculous. No, it could not be Norrell. But who then?

The King did not seem in the least fatigued. In fact he was more inclined to dance and skip about and generally rejoice over the defeat of the Willises. So, thinking that further exercise would certainly do His Majesty no harm, Strange walked on.

The white mist had erased all detail and colour from the landscape and left it ghostly. Earth and sky were blended together in the same insubstantial grey element.

The King took Strange's arm in a most affectionate manner and seemed to have quite forgot that he disliked magicians. He began to talk about the things that preoccupied him in his madness. He was convinced that a great many disasters had befallen Great Britain since he had become mad. He seemed to imagine that the wreck of his own reason must be matched by a corresponding wreck of the kingdom. Chief among these delusions was the belief that London had been drowned in a great flood. ". . . and when they came to me and said that the cold, grey waters had closed over the dome of St Paul's Cathedral and that London was become a domain of fishes and sea-monsters, my feelings are not to be described! I believe I wept for three weeks together! Now the buildings are all covered in barnacles and the markets sell nothing but oysters and sea-urchins! Mr Fox told me that three Sundays ago he went to St Vedast in Foster-lane where he heard an excellent sermon preached by a turbot.[1] But I have a plan for my kingdom's restoration! I have dispatched ambassadors to the King of the Fishes with proposals that I should marry a mermaid and so end the strife between our two great Nations! . . ."

The other subject which preoccupied His Majesty was that of the silver-haired person whom only he could see. "He says he is a king," he whispered eagerly, "but I believe he is an angel! With all that silver hair I think it very likely. And those two Evil Spirits – the ones you were talking to – he has been abusing them most horribly. It is my belief he has come to smite them and cast them into a fiery pit! Then, no doubt, he will carry you and me away to glory in Hanover!"

"Heaven," said Strange. "Your Majesty means Heaven."

They walked on. Snow began to fall, a slow tumble of white over a pale grey world. It was very quiet.

---

[1] Charles James Fox, a radical politician who had died some eight years before. This remark proves how far the King's wits were deranged: Mr Fox was a celebrated atheist who would never upon any inducement have entered a church.

Suddenly the sound of a flute was heard. The music was unutterably lonely and mournful, but at the same time full of nobility.

Thinking that it must be the King who was playing, Strange turned to watch. But the King was standing with his hands at his side and his flute in his pocket. Strange looked around. The mist was not dense enough to hide anyone who might have been standing near them. There was no one. The Park was empty.

"Ah, listen!" cried the King. "He is describing the tragedy of the King of Great Britain. That run of notes there! That is for past powers all gone! That melancholy phrase! That is for his Reason destroyed by deceitful politicians and the wicked behaviour of his sons. That little tune fit to break your heart – that is for the beautiful young creature whom he adored when he was a boy and was forced by his friends to give up. Ah, God! How he wept then!"

Tears rolled down the King's face. He began to perform a slow, grave dance, waving his body and his arms from side to side and spinning slowly over the ground. The music moved away, deeper into the Park and the King danced after it.

Strange was mystified. The music seemed to be leading the King in the direction of a grove of trees. At least Strange had supposed it was a grove. He was almost certain that a moment ago he had seen a dozen trees – probably fewer. But now the grove had become a thicket – no, a wood – a deep, dark wood where the trees were ancient and wild. Their great branches resembled twisted limbs and their roots tumbling nests of snakes. They were twined about thickly with ivy and mistletoe. There was a little path between the trees; it was pitted with deep, ice-rimmed hollows and fringed with frost-stiffened weeds. Pale pinpricks of light deep within the wood suggested a house where no house ought to be.

"Your Majesty!" cried Strange. He ran after the King and caught him by the hands. "Your Majesty must forgive me, but I do not quite like the look of those trees. I think perhaps that we would be as well to return to the Castle."

The King was quite enraptured by the music and did not wish to leave. He grumbled and pulled his arm away from Strange's grasp. Strange caught him again and half-led, half-dragged him back towards the gate.

But the invisible flute-player did not seem inclined to give them up so easily. The music suddenly grew louder; it was all around them. Another tune crept in almost imperceptibly and blended sweetly with the first.

"Ah! Listen! Oh, listen!" cried the King, spinning round. "He is playing for you now! That harsh melody is for your wicked tutor who will not teach you what you have every right to learn. Those discordant notes describe your anger at being prevented from making new discoveries. That slow, sad march is for the great library he is too selfish to shew you."

"How in the world . . ." began Strange and then stopped. He heard it too – the music that described his whole life. He realized for the first time how full of sadness his existence was. He was surrounded by mean-spirited men and women who hated him and were secretly jealous of his talent. He knew now that every angry thought he had ever had was justified and that every generous thought was misplaced. His enemies were despicable and his friends were treacherous. Norrell (naturally) was worst of all, but even Arabella was weak and unworthy of his love.

"Ah!" sighed His Majesty, "So you have been betrayed too."

"Yes," said Strange, sadly.

They were facing the wood again. The lights among the trees – tiny as they were – conveyed to Strange a strong idea of the house and its comforts. He could almost see the soft candlelight falling upon the comfortable chairs, the ancient hearths where cheerful fires blazed, the glasses of hot spiced wine which would be provided to warm them after their walk through the dark wood. The lights suggested other ideas too. "I think there is a library," he said.

"Oh, certainly!" declared the King, clapping his hands together in his enthusiasm. "You shall read the books and when your eyes grow tired, I shall read them to you! But we must hurry! Listen to the music! He grows impatient for us to follow him!"

His Majesty reached out to take Strange's left arm. In order to accommodate him, Strange found that he must move something he was holding in his left hand. It was Ormskirk's *Revelations of Thirty-Six Other Worlds*.

"Oh, *that*!" he thought. "Well, I do not need that any longer. There are sure to be better books at the house in the wood!" He opened his hand and let *Revelations* fall upon the snowy ground.

The snow fell thicker. The flute-player played. They hurried towards the wood. As they ran, the King's scarlet nightcap fell over his eyes. Strange reached up and straightened it. As he did so, he suddenly remembered what it was that he knew about the colour red: it was powerful protection against enchantment.

"Hurry! Hurry!" cried the King.

The flute-player played a series of rapid notes which rose and fell to mimic the sound of the wind. A real wind appeared out of nowhere and half-lifted, half-pushed them over the ground towards the wood. When it set them down again they were a great deal nearer to the wood.

"Excellent!" cried the King.

The nightcap caught Strange's eye again.

. . . *Protection against enchantment* . . .

The flute-player conjured up another wind. This one blew the King's nightcap off.

"No matter! No matter!" cried the King cheerfully. "He has promised me nightcaps a-plenty when we get to his house."

But Strange let go of the King's arm and staggered back through the snow and the wind to fetch it. It lay in the snow, bright scarlet among all the misty shades of white and grey.

. . . *Protection against enchantment* . . .

He remembered saying to one of the Willises that in order to practise magic successfully a magician must employ the forcefulness of his own character; why should he think of that now?

*Place the moon at my eyes* (he thought) *and her whiteness shall devour the false sights the deceiver has placed there.*

The moon's scarred white disc appeared suddenly – not in the sky, but somewhere else. If he had been obliged to say exactly where, he would have said that it was inside his own head. The sensation was not a pleasant one. All he could think of, all he could see was the moon's face, like a sliver of ancient bone. He forgot about the King. He forgot he was a magician. He forgot Mr Norrell. He forgot his own name.

He forgot everything except the moon . . .

The moon vanished. Strange looked up and found himself in a snowy place a little distance from a dark wood. Between him and the wood stood the blind King in his dressing-gown. The King must have walked on when he stopped. But without his guide to lean on, the King felt lost and afraid. He was crying out, "Magician! Magician! Where are you?"

The wood no longer struck Strange as a welcoming place. It appeared to him now as it had at first – sinister, unknowable, *unEnglish.* As for the lights, he could barely see them; they were the merest pricks of white in the darkness and suggested nothing except that the inhabitants of the house could not afford many candles.

"Magician!" cried the King.

"I am here, Your Majesty."

*Place a swarm of bees at my ears* (he thought). *Bees love truth and will destroy the deceiver's lies.*

A low murmuring noise filled his ears, blocking out the music of the flute-player. It was very like language and Strange thought that in a little while he would understand it. It grew, filling his head and his chest to the very tips of his fingers and toes. Even his hair seemed electrified and his skin buzzed and shook with the noise. For one horrible moment he thought that his mouth was full of bees and that there were bees buzzing and flying under his skin, in his guts and his ears.

The buzzing stopped. Strange heard the flute-player's music again but it did not sound as sweet as before and it no longer seemed to be describing his life.

*Place salt in my mouth* (he thought) *lest the deceiver attempt to delight me with the taste of honey or disgust me with the taste of ashes.*

This part of the spell had no effect whatsoever.[2]

*Nail my hand with an iron nail so that I shall not raise it to do the deceiver's bidding.*

"Aaaghh! Dear God!" screamed Strange. There was an excruciating pain in the palm of his left hand. When it ceased (as suddenly as it had begun) he no longer felt compelled to hurry towards the wood.

*Place my heart in a secret place so that all my desires shall be my own and the deceiver shall find no hold there.*

He pictured Arabella, as he had seen her a thousand times, prettily dressed and seated in a drawing-room among a crowd of people who were all laughing and talking. He gave her his heart. She took it and placed it quietly in the pocket of her gown. No one observed what she did.

Strange next applied the spell to the King and at the last step he gave the King's heart to Arabella to keep in her pocket. It was interesting to observe the magic from the outside. There had been so many unusual occurrences in the King's poor head that the moon's sudden appearance there seemed to occasion him no surprize. But he did not care for the bees; he was brushing them away for some time afterwards.

When the spell was finished, the flute-player abruptly ceased playing.

"And now, Your Majesty," said Strange, "I think it is time we returned to the Castle. You and I, Your Majesty, are a British King and a British magician. Though Great Britain may desert us,

[2] When Strange reviewed the morning's events afterwards he could only suppose that the flute-player had made no attempt to deceive him by his sense of taste.

we have no right to desert Great Britain. She may have need of us yet."

"True, true! I swore an oath at my coronation always to serve her! Oh, my poor country!" The King turned and waved in the direction he supposed the mysterious flute-player to be. "Goodbye! Goodbye, dear sir! God bless you for your kindness to George III!"

*Revelations of Thirty-Six Other Worlds* lay half-covered up by the snow. Strange picked it up and brushed off the snow. He looked back. The dark wood had gone. In its place was a most innocent clump of five leafless beech trees.

On the ride back to London Strange was deep in thought. He was aware that he ought to have been disturbed by his experience at Windsor, perhaps even frightened. But his curiosity and excitement far exceeded his uneasiness. Besides, whatever, or whoever, had done the magic, he had defeated them and imposed his will upon theirs. They had been strong, but he had been stronger. The whole adventure had confirmed something he had long suspected: that there was more magic in England than Mr Norrell admitted.

Consider the matter from whichever point of view he would, he continually came back to the silver-haired person whom only the King could see. He tried to recall what exactly the King had said about this person, but he could recall nothing beyond the simple fact of his silver hair.

He reached London at about half past four. The city was growing dark. Lights were glowing in all the shops, and the lamplighters were out in the streets. When he got to the corner of Oxford-street and New Bond-street he turned aside and rode to Hanover-square. He found Mr Norrell in his library, drinking tea.

Mr Norrell was, as ever, delighted to see the other magician and he was eager to hear all about Strange's visit to the King.

Strange told him how the King was kept a solitary prisoner in his own palace, and he listed the spells he had done. But of the drenching of the Willises, the enchanted wood and the invisible flute-player he said not a word.

"I am not at all surprized that you could not help His Majesty," said Mr Norrell. "I do not believe that even the *Aureate* magicians could cure madness. In fact I am not sure that they tried. They seem to have considered madness in quite a different light. They held madmen in a sort of reverence and thought they knew things sane men did not – things which might be useful to a magician. There are stories of both Ralph Stokesey and Catherine of Winchester consulting with madmen."

"But it was not only magicians, surely?" said Strange. "Fairies too had a strong interest in madmen. I am sure I remember reading that somewhere."

"Yes, indeed! Some of our most important writers have remarked upon the strong resemblance between madmen and fairies. Both are well known for talking without sense or connexion – I dare say you noticed something of the sort with the King. But there are other similarities. Chaston, as I remember, has several things to say upon the subject. He gives the example of a lunatic in Bristol who each morning told his family of his intention to take his walk in company with one of the dining chairs. The man was quite devoted to this article of furniture, considered it one of his closest friends, and held imaginary conversations with it in which they discussed the walk they would take and the likelihood of meeting other tables and chairs. Apparently, the man became quite distressed whenever any one proposed sitting upon the chair. Clearly the man was mad, but Chaston says that fairies would not consider his behaviour as ridiculous as we do. Fairies do not make a strong distinction between the animate and the inanimate. They believe that stones, doors, trees, fire, clouds and so forth all have souls and desires, and are either masculine or feminine. Perhaps this explains the extraordinary sympathy for madness which fairies exhibit. For example, it used to be well known that when fairies hid themselves from general sight, lunatics were often able to perceive them. The most celebrated instance which I can recall was of a mad boy called Duffy in Chesterfield in Derbyshire in the fourteenth century, who was the favourite of a mischievous fairy-spirit which had tormented the town for years. The fairy took a great fancy to this boy and made him extravagant presents – most of which would have scarcely been of any use to him in his right mind and were certainly no use to him in his madness – a sailing boat encrusted with diamonds, a pair of silver boots, a singing pig . . ."

"But why did the fairy pay Duffy all these attentions?"

"Oh! He told Duffy they were brothers in adversity. I do not know why. Chaston wrote that a great many fairies harboured a vague sense of having been treated badly by the English. Though it was a mystery to Chaston – as it is to me – why they should have thought so. In the houses of the great English magicians fairies were the first among the servants and sat in the best places after the magician and his lady. Chaston has a great many interesting things to say upon the subject. His best work is the *Liber Novus*." Mr Norrell frowned at his pupil. "I am sure I have recommended it to you half a dozen times," he said. "Have you not read it yet?"

Unfortunately, Mr Norrell did not always recall with absolute precision which books he wished Strange to read and which books he had sent to Yorkshire for the express purpose of keeping them out of Strange's reach. The *Liber Novus* was safe on a shelf in the library at Hurtfew Abbey. Strange sighed and remarked that the moment Mr Norrell put the book into his hand he would be very glad to read it. "But in the meantime, sir, perhaps you would be so good as to finish the tale of the fairy of Chesterfield."

"Oh, yes! Now where was I? Well, for a number of years nothing went wrong for Duffy and nothing went right for the town. A wood grew up in the market square and the townspeople could not conduct their business. Their goats and swine grew wings and flew away. The fairy turned the stones of the half-built parish church into sugar loaves. The sugar grew hot and sticky under the sun and part of the church melted. The town smelt like a giant pastry-cook's. Worse still dogs and cats came and licked at the church, and birds, rats and mice came and nibbled at it. So the townspeople were left with a half-eaten, misshapen church – which was not at all the effect that they had in mind. They were obliged to apply to Duffy and beg him to plead with the fairy on their behalf. But he was sullen and would not help them because he remembered how they had mocked him in the past. So they were obliged to pay the poor, mad wretch all sorts of compliments on his cleverness and handsomeness. So then Duffy pleaded with the fairy and, ah!, what a difference then! The fairy stopped tormenting them and he turned the sugar church back into stone. The townspeople cut down the wood in the market place and bought new animals. But they could never get the church quite right again. Even today there is something odd about the church in Chesterfield. It is not quite like other churches."

Strange was silent a moment. Then he said, "Is it your opinion, Mr Norrell, that fairies have left England completely?"

"I do not know. There are many stories of Englishmen and women meeting with fairies in out-of-the-way places in the last three or four hundred years, but as none of these people were scholars or magicians their evidence cannot be said to be worth a great deal. When you and I summon fairies – I mean," he added hastily, "if we were so ill-advised as to do such a thing – then, providing we cast our spells correctly, the fairies will appear promptly. But where they come from or by what paths they travel is uncertain. In John Uskglass's day very plain roads were built that led out of England into Faerie – wide green roads between high green hedges or stone walls. Those roads still exist, but I do not think fairies use them nowadays any more than Christians. The roads are all overgrown and ruined. They have a lonely look and I am told that people avoid them."

"People believe that fairy roads are unlucky," said Strange.

"They are foolish," said Norrell. "Fairy roads cannot hurt them. Fairy roads lead nowhere at all."[3]

"And what of the half-human descendants of fairies? Do they inherit their forefathers' knowledge and powers?" asked Strange.

"Oh! That is quite another question. Many people nowadays have surnames that reveal their ancestors' fairy origins. Otherlander and Fairchild are two. Elfick is another. And Fairey, obviously. I remember there was a Tom Otherlander who worked upon one of our farms when I was a child. But it is quite rare for any of these descendants of fairies to exhibit the least magical talent. Indeed more often than not they have a reputation for malice, pride and laziness – all vices for which their fairy-ancestors were well known."

---

[3] Whether Mr Norrell was right to say that fairy roads can do no harm is debatable. They are eerie places and there are dozens of tales of the strange adventures which befell people who attempted to travel along them. The following is one of the better known. It is hard to say what precisely was the fate suffered by the people in the road – certainly it is not a fate you or I would wish to share.

In Yorkshire in the late sixteenth century there was a man who had a farm. Early one morning in summer he went out with two or three of his men to begin the hay-making. A white mist lay upon the land and the air was cool. Along one side of the field there was an ancient fairy road bounded by high hawthorn hedges. Tall grass and young saplings grew in the road and even on the brightest day it was dim and shadowy. The farmer had never seen any one on the fairy road, but that morning he and his men looked up and saw a group of people coming along it. Their faces were strange and they were outlandishly dressed. One among them – a man – strode ahead of the others. He left the road and came into the field. He was dressed in black and was young and handsome; and though they had never seen him before, the farmer and his men knew him immediately – it was the Magician King, John Uskglass. They knelt before him and he raised them up. He told them that he was on a journey and they brought him a horse, and some food and drink. They went and fetched their wives and children, and John Uskglass blessed them and gave them good fortune.

The farmer looked doubtfully at the strange people who remained in the fairy road; but John Uskglass told the farmer not to be afraid. He promised him that the people could do him no harm. Then he rode away.

The strange people in the ancient road lingered a little while, but when the first rays of the strong summer sun touched them they disappeared with the mist.

The next day Strange met with the Royal Dukes and told them how much he regretted that he had been unable to alleviate the King's madness. Their Royal Highnesses were sorry to hear it, but they were not at all surprized. It was the outcome they had expected and they assured Strange that they did not blame him in the least. In fact they were pleased with all he had done and they particularly liked that he had not charged them a fee. As a reward they granted him their Royal Warrants. This meant that he could, if he wished, put gilt and plaster images of all their five coats of arms above his door in Soho-square, and he was at liberty to tell any one he liked that he was Magician to the Royal Dukes by appointment.

Strange did not tell the Dukes that he deserved their gratitude more than they knew. He was quite certain he had saved the King from some horrible fate or other. He simply did not know what it was.

## 34

# On the edge of the desert

### November 1814

STEPHEN AND THE gentleman with the thistle-down hair were walking through the streets of a strange town.

"Are you not growing weary, sir?" asked Stephen. "I know that I am. We have been walking here for hours."

The gentleman let out a burst of high-pitched laughter. "My dear Stephen! You have only just this instant arrived! A moment ago you were at Lady Pole's house, being forced to perform some menial task at the bidding of her wicked husband!"

"Oh!" said Stephen. He realized that the last thing he remembered was cleaning the silver in his little room near the kitchen, but that seemed like, oh!, years ago.

He looked around him. There was nothing here he recognized. Even the smell of the place, a mixture of spices, coffee, rotting vegetables and roasting meats, was new to him.

He sighed. "It is this magic, sir. It is so very confusing."

The gentleman squeezed his arm affectionately.

The town appeared to be built upon a steep hillside. There did not seem to be any proper streets, but only narrow alleyways composed mainly of steps that wound up and down between the houses. The houses themselves were of the utmost simplicity; one might say severity. The walls were made of earth or clay, painted white, the doorways had plain wooden doors and the windows had plain wooden shutters. The steps of the alleys were also painted white. In all the town there did not seem to be so much as a spot of colour anywhere to relieve the eye: no flower in a flowerpot upon a windowsill, no painted toy left where a child had abandoned it in a doorway. Walking through these narrow streets was, thought Stephen, rather like losing oneself in the folds of an enormous linen napkin.

It was eerily silent. As they went up and down the narrow steps they heard the murmur of grave conversation coming from the houses, but there was no laughter, no song, no child's voice raised in excitement. From time to time they met an inhabitant of the town; a solemn, dark-faced man dressed in a white robe and pantaloons with a white turban upon his head. All carried walking-sticks – even the young men – though in truth none of them seemed to be very young; the inhabitants of this town had been born old.

They saw only one woman (at least the gentleman with the thistle-down hair said it was a woman). She stood at her husband's side robed from the crown of her head to the tip of her toe in a single garment the colour of shadows. When Stephen first saw her she had her back to him and it seemed in keeping with the dream-like atmosphere of the place that as she turned slowly towards him, he saw that her face was not a face at all, but a panel of densely embroidered cloth of the same dusky hue as the rest of her garment.

"These people are very strange," whispered Stephen. "But they do not appear to be surprized to find us here."

"Oh!" said the gentleman. "It is part of the magic I have done that you and I should appear to them as two of their number. They are quite convinced that they have known us since childhood. Moreover you will find that you understand them perfectly and they will understand you – in spite of the obscurity of their language which is scarcely comprehensible to their own countrymen twenty-five miles away!"

Presumably, Stephen thought, it was also part of the magic that the town's inhabitants should not notice how loud the gentleman spoke and how his words echoed from every white-washed corner.

The street they were descending turned a corner and ended abruptly at a low wall that had been put there to prevent unwary pedestrians from tumbling off the hill. From this spot the surrounding country could be viewed. A desolate valley of white rock lay before them under a cloudless sky. A hot wind blew across it. It was a world from which all flesh had been stripped, leaving only the bones.

Stephen would have supposed that this place was a dream or part of his enchantment, had not the gentleman with the thistle-down hair informed him excitedly that this was, ". . . Africa! Your ancestral soil, my dear Stephen!"

"But," thought Stephen, "my ancestors did not live here, I am sure. These people are darker than Englishmen, but they are far fairer than me. They are Arabs, I suppose." Out loud he said, "Are we going anywhere in particular, sir?"

"To see the market, Stephen!"

Stephen was glad to hear it. The silence and emptiness were oppressive. The market presumably would have some noise, some bustle.

But the market of this town proved to be of a very curious character. It was situated close to the high town walls just by a great wooden gate. There were no stalls, no crowds of eager people going about to view the wares. Instead everyone who felt at all inclined to buy any thing sat silently upon the ground with his hands folded while a market official – a sort of auctioneer – carried the goods about and shewed them to the prospective buyers. The auctioneer named the last price he had been offered and the buyer either shook his head or offered a higher one. There was not a great deal of variety in the goods – there were some bales of fine cloth and some embroidered articles, but mostly it was carpets. When Stephen remarked upon this to his companion, the gentleman replied, "Their religion is of the strictest sort, Stephen. Almost everything is forbidden to them except carpets."

Stephen watched them as they went mournfully about the market, these men whose mouths were perpetually closed lest they spoke some forbidden word, whose eyes were perpetually averted from forbidden sights, whose hands refrained at every moment from some forbidden act. It seemed to him that they did little more than half-exist. They might as well have been dreams or ghosts. In the silent town and the silent countryside only the hot wind seemed to have any real substance. Stephen felt he would not be surprized if one day the wind blew the town and its inhabitants entirely away.

Stephen and the gentleman seated themselves in a corner of the market beneath a tattered brown awning.

"Why are we here, sir?" asked Stephen.

"So that we may have some quiet conversation, Stephen. A most serious matter has arisen. I am sorry to have to tell you that all our wonderful plans have been rudely overturned and once again it is the magicians who thwart us! Never was there such a rascally pair of men! Their only pleasure, I think, is in demonstrating their contempt of us! But one day, I believe . . ."

The gentleman was a great deal more interested in abusing the magicians than he was in making his meaning clear and so it was some time before Stephen was able to understand what had happened. It seemed that Jonathan Strange had paid a visit to the King of England – for what reason the gentleman did not explain – and the gentleman had gone too with the idea first of seeing what the magician did and secondly of looking at the King of England.

". . . and I do not know how it is, but for some reason I never paid my respects to His Majesty before. I discovered him to be a most delightful old person! Very respectful to me! We had a great deal of conversation! He has suffered much from the cruel treatment of his subjects. The English take great pleasure in humbling the great and the noble. A great many Worthies throughout history have suffered from their vicious persecutions – people such as Charles I, Julius Caesar and, above all, you and me!"

"I beg your pardon, sir. But you mentioned plans. What plans are these?"

"Why, our plans to make you King of England, of course! You had not forgotten?"

"No, indeed! But . . ."

"Well! I do not know what may be your opinion, dearest Stephen," declared the gentleman, not waiting to find out, "but I confess I grow weary of waiting for your wonderful destiny to happen of its own accord. I am very much inclined to anticipate the tardy Fates and make you King myself. Who knows? Perhaps I am meant to be the noble instrument that raises you to the lofty position that is yours by right! Nothing seems so likely! Well! While the King and I were talking, it occurred to me that the first step to making you King was to get rid of him! Observe! I meant the old man no harm. Upon the contrary! I wrapped his soul in sweetness and made him happier than he has been in many a long year. But this would not do for the magician! I had barely begun to weave an enchantment when the magician began to work against me. He employed ancient fairy magic of immense power. I was never more surprized in my life! Who could have supposed that he would have known how to do such a thing?"

The gentleman paused in his tirade long enough for Stephen to say, "Grateful as I am for your care of me, sir, I feel obliged to observe that the present King has thirteen sons and daughters, the eldest of whom is already governing the country. Even if the King were dead, the Crown would certainly pass to one of them."

"Yes, yes! But the King's children are all fat and stupid. Who wishes to be governed by such frights? When the people of England understand that they might instead be governed by you, Stephen – who are all elegance and charm and whose noble countenance would look so well upon a coin – why! they must be very dull indeed if they are not immediately delighted and rush to support your cause!"

The gentleman, thought Stephen, understood the character of Englishmen a great deal less than he supposed.

At that moment their conversation was interrupted by a most barbaric sound – a great horn was being blown. A number of men rushed forward and heaved the great town gates shut. Thinking that perhaps some danger threatened the town, Stephen looked round in alarm. "Sir, what is happening?"

"Oh, it is these people's custom to shut the gate every night against the wicked heathen," said the gentleman, languidly, "by which they mean everyone except themselves. But tell me your opinion, Stephen? What should we do?"

"Do, sir? About what?"

"The magicians, Stephen! The magicians! It is clear to me now that as soon as your wonderful destiny begins to unfold, they are certain to interfere. Though why it should matter to them who is King of England, I cannot tell. I suppose being ugly and stupid themselves, they prefer to have a king the same. No, they are our enemies and consequently it behoves us to seek a way to destroy them utterly. Poison? Knives? Pistols? . . ."

The auctioneer approached, holding out yet another carpet. "Twenty silver pennies," he said in a slow, deliberate tone as if he were pronouncing a righteous doom upon all the world.

The gentleman with the thistle-down hair regarded the carpet thoughtfully. "It is possible, of course," he said, "to imprison someone within the pattern of a carpet for a thousand years or so. That is a particularly horrible fate which I always reserve for people who have offended me deeply – as have these magicians! The endless repetition of colour and pattern – not to mention the irritation of the dust and the humiliation of stains – never fails to render the prisoner completely mad! The prisoner always emerges from the carpet determined to wreak revenge upon all the world and then the magicians and heroes of that Age must join together to kill him or, more usually, imprison him a second time for yet more thousands of years in some even more ghastly prison. And so he goes on growing in madness and evil as the millennia pass. Yes, carpets! Perhaps . . ."

"Thank you," said Stephen to the auctioneer, quickly, "but we have no wish to buy this carpet. Pray, sir, pass on."

"You are right, Stephen," said the gentleman. "Whatever their faults these magicians have proved themselves most adept at avoiding enchantments. We must find some other way to crush their spirits so that they no longer have the will to oppose us! We must make them wish they had never taken up the practice of magic!"

# 35

## The Nottinghamshire gentleman

### November 1814

During Strange's three-year absence Mr Drawlight and Mr Lascelles had enjoyed a little revival of their influence over Mr Norrell. Any one wishing to talk to Mr Norrell or ask for Mr Norrell's assistance had been obliged to apply first to them. They had advised Mr Norrell upon the best way of managing the Ministers and the Ministers upon the best way of managing Mr Norrell. As friends and counsellors of England's most eminent magician their acquaintance had been solicited by all the wealthiest and most fashionable people in the kingdom.

After Strange's return they continued to wait upon Mr Norrell as assiduously as ever, but now it was Strange's opinion which Mr Norrell most wished to hear and Strange's advice which he sought before any other. Naturally, this was not a state of affairs to please them and Drawlight, in particular, did all that was in his power to increase those little annoyances and resentments which each magician occasionally felt at the behaviour of the other.

"I cannot believe that I do not know something that would harm him," he said to Lascelles. "There are some very odd stories about what he did in Spain. Several people have told me that he raised a whole army of dead soldiers to fight the French. Corpses with shattered limbs and eyes hanging by a thread and every sort of horror that you can imagine! What do you suppose Norrell would say if he heard that?"

Lascelles sighed. "I wish I could convince you of the futility of trying to manufacture a quarrel between them. They will do that themselves sooner or later."

A few days after Strange's visit to the King a crowd of Mr Norrell's friends and admirers gathered in the library at Hanover-square with the object of admiring a new portrait of the two magicians by Mr Lawrence.[1] Mr Lascelles and Mr Drawlight

[1] This portrait, now lost, hung in Mr Norrell's library from November 1814 until the summer of the following year when it was removed. It has not been seen since.

The following extract from a volume of memoirs describes the difficulties experienced by Mr Lawrence (later Sir Thomas Lawrence) in painting the portrait. It is also of interest for the light it sheds upon the relationship of Norrell and Strange in late 1814. It seems that, in spite of many provocations, Strange was still struggling to bear patiently with the older magician and to encourage others to do the same.

"The two magicians sat for the picture in Mr Norrell's library. Mr Lawrence found Mr Strange to be a most agreeable man and Strange's part of the portrait progressed very well. Mr Norrell, on the other hand, was very restless from the start. He would shift about in his chair and crane his neck as if he were trying to catch sight of Mr Lawrence's hands – a futile endeavour as the easel stood between them. Mr Lawrence supposed he must be anxious about the picture and assured him it went well. Mr Lawrence added that Mr Norrell might look if he wished, but this did nothing to cure Mr Norrell's fidgets.

All at once Mr Norrell addressed Mr Strange, who was in the room and busy writing a letter to one of the Ministers. 'Mr Strange, I feel a draught! I do believe that the window behind Mr Lawrence is open! Pray, Mr Strange, go and see if the window is open!' Without looking up, Strange replied, 'No, the window is not open. You are mistaken.' A few minutes later Mr Norrell thought he heard a pie-seller in the square and begged Mr Strange to go to the window and look out, but once again Mr Strange refused. Next it was a duchess's coach that Mr Norrell heard. He tried everything that he could think of to make Mr Strange go to the window, but Mr Strange would not go. This was very odd, and Mr Lawrence began to suspect that all Mr Norrell's agitation had nothing to with imaginary draughts or pie-sellers or duchesses but that it had something to do with the painting.

So when Mr Norrell went out of the room Mr Lawrence asked Mr Strange what the matter was. At first Mr Strange insisted that nothing was wrong, but Mr Lawrence was determined to find out and pressed Mr Strange to tell him the truth. Mr Strange sighed. 'Oh, very well! He has got it into his head that you are copying spells out of his books behind your easel.'

were there, as were Mr and Mrs Strange and several of the King's Ministers.

The portrait shewed Mr Norrell in his plain grey coat and his old-fashioned wig. Both coat and wig seemed a little too large for him. He appeared to have withdrawn inside them and his small, blue eyes looked out at the world with a curious mixture of fearfulness and arrogance that put Sir Walter Pole in mind of his valet's cat. Most people, it seemed, were having to put themselves to a little effort to find any thing flattering to say of Mr Norrell's half of the picture, but everyone was happy to admire Strange's half. Strange was painted behind Mr Norrell, half-sitting, half-leaning against a little table, entirely at his ease, with his mocking half-smile and his eyes full of smiles and secrets and spells – just as magicians' eyes should be.

"Oh! it is an excellent thing," enthused a lady. "See how the darkness of the mirror behind the figures sets off Mr Strange's head."

"People always imagine that magicians and mirrors go together," complained Mr Norrell. "There is no mirror in that part of my library."

"Artists are tricky fellows, sir, forever reshaping the world according to some design of their own," said Strange. "Indeed they are not unlike magicians in that. And yet he has made a curious piece of work of it. It is more like a door than a mirror – it is

---

[1] *cont'd* Mr Lawrence was shocked. He had painted the greatest in the land and never before been suspected of stealing. This was not the sort of treatment he expected.

'Come,' said Mr Strange, gently, 'do not be angry. If any man in England deserves our patience, it is Mr Norrell. All the future of English magic is on his shoulders and I assure you he feels it very keenly. It makes him a little eccentric. What would be your sensations, I wonder, Mr Lawrence, if you woke one morning and found yourself the only artist in Europe? Would not you feel a little lonely? Would you not feel the watchful gaze of Michelangelo and Raphael and Rembrandt and all the rest of them upon you, as if they both defied and implored you to equal their achievements? Would you not sometimes be out of spirits and out of temper?' "

From *Recollections of Sir Thomas Lawrence during an intimacy of nearly thirty years by Miss Croft*

so dark. I can almost feel a draught coming from it. I do not like to see myself sitting so close to it – I am afraid that I may catch cold."

One of the Ministers, who had never been in Mr Norrell's library before, made some admiring remark about its harmonious proportions and style of fitting up, which led other people to say how beautiful they thought it.

"It is certainly a very fine room," agreed Drawlight, "but it is really nothing in comparison with the library at Hurtfew Abbey! That is truly a charming room. I never in my life saw any thing so delightful, so complete. There are little pointed arches and a dome with pillars in the Gothic style and the carvings of leaves – dried and twisted leaves, as if withered by some horrid winter blast, all done in good English oak and ash and elm – are the most perfect things I ever saw. 'Mr Norrell,' I said, when I saw them, 'there are depths in you that we have not suspected. You are quite a Romantic, sir.' "

Mr Norrell looked as if he did not much like to hear the library at Hurtfew talked about so much, but Mr Drawlight continued regardless: "It is like being in a wood, a pretty little wood, late in the year, and the bindings of the books, being all tan and brown and dry with age, compound that impression. Indeed there are as many books, it seems, as the leaves in a wood." Mr Drawlight paused. "And were you ever at Hurtfew, Mr Strange?"

Strange replied that he had not yet had that pleasure.

"Oh, you should go," Drawlight smiled spitefully. "Indeed you should. It is truly wonderful."

Norrell looked anxiously at Strange but Strange did not reply. He had turned his back on them all and was gazing intently at his own portrait.

As the others moved away and began to speak of something else, Sir Walter murmured, "You must not mind his malice."

"Mmmm?" said Strange. "Oh, it is not that. It is the mirror. Does it not look as if one could just walk into it? It would not be so difficult I think. One could use a spell of revelation. No, of unravelling. Or perhaps both. The way would be clear before one. One step forward and away." He looked around him and said, "And there are days when I would be away."

"Where?" Sir Walter was surprized; there was no place he found so much to his liking as London with its gaslights and its shops, its coffee-houses and clubs, its thousand pretty women and its thousand varieties of gossip and he imagined it must be the same for every one.

"Oh, wherever men of my sort used to go, long ago. Wandering on paths that other men have not seen. Behind the sky. On the other side of the rain."

Strange sighed again and his right foot tapped impatiently on Mr Norrell's carpet, suggesting that, if he did not make up his mind soon to go to the forgotten paths, then his feet would carry him there of their own accord.

By two o'clock the visitors had gone and Mr Norrell, who was rather anxious to avoid any conversation with Strange, went upstairs and hid himself away in his little room at the back of the house on the second floor. He sat down at his table and began to work. Very soon he had forgot all about Strange and the library at Hurtfew and all the disagreeable sensations which Drawlight's speech had produced. He was therefore somewhat dismayed when a few minutes later there was a knock at the door and Strange walked in.

"I beg your pardon for disturbing you, sir," he said, "but there is something I wish to ask you."

"Oh!" said Mr Norrell nervously. "Well, of course I am always very happy to answer any questions you may have, but just now there is a piece of business which I fear I cannot neglect. I have spoken to Lord Liverpool about our plan to secure the coast of Great Britain from storms by magic and he is quite delighted with it. Lord Liverpool says that every year property to the value of many hundreds of thousands of pounds is destroyed by the sea. Lord Liverpool says that he considers the preservation of property to be the first task of magic in peacetime. As always his lordship wishes it done immediately and it is a great deal of work. The county of Cornwall alone will take a week. I fear we must postpone our conversation until some other time."

Strange smiled. "If the magic is as urgent as that, sir, then I had better assist you and we can talk while we work. Where do you begin?"

"At Yarmouth."

"And what are you using? Belasis?"

"No, not Belasis. There is a reconstruction of Stokesey's magic for calming stormy waters in Lanchester's *Language of Birds*. I am not so foolish as to suppose that Lanchester greatly resembles Stokesey but he is the best we have. I have made some revisions to Lanchester and I am adding Pevensey's spells of Ward and Watch."[2] Mr Norrell pushed some papers towards Strange. Strange studied the papers and then he too began to work.

After a while Strange said, "I recently found a reference in Ormskirk's *Revelations of Thirty-Six Other Worlds* to the kingdom

---

[2] Francis Pevensey, sixteenth-century magician. Wrote *Eighteen Wonders to be found in the House of Albion*. We know that Pevensey was trained by Martin Pale. The *Eighteen Wonders* has all the characteristics of Pale's magic, including his fondness for complicated diagrams and intricate magical apparatus.

For many years Francis Pevensey occupied a minor but respectable place in English magical history as a follower of Martin Pale and it was a great surprize to everyone when he suddenly became the subject of one of the bitterest controversies in eighteenth-century magical theory.

It began in 1754 with the discovery of a number of letters in the library of a gentleman in Stamford in Lincolnshire. They were all in an antique hand and signed by Martin Pale. The magical scholars of the period were besides themselves with joy.

But upon closer examination the letters proved to be *love letters* with no word of magic in them from beginning to end. They were of the most passionate description imaginable: Pale compared his beloved to a sweet shower of rain falling upon him, to a fire at which he warmed himself, to a torment that he preferred to any comfort. There were various references to milk-white breasts and perfumed legs and long soft, brown hair in which stars became entangled, and other things not at all interesting to the magical scholars who had hoped for magic spells.

Pale was much addicted to writing his beloved's name – which was Francis – and in one letter he made a sort of punning poem or riddle upon her surname: Pevensey. At first the eighteenth-century magical scholars were inclined to argue that Pale's mistress must have been the sister or wife of the that lies behind mirrors, a kingdom which is apparently full of the most convenient roads by which a traveller may get from one place to another."

This would not ordinarily have been a subject to please Mr Norrell, but he was so relieved to discover that Strange did not intend to quarrel with him about the library at Hurtfew that he grew quite communicative. "Oh yes, indeed! There is indeed a path which joins all the mirrors of the world. It was well-known to the Great Mediaevals. No doubt they trod it often. I fear I cannot give you any more precise information. The writers I have seen all describe it in different ways. Ormskirk says it is a road across a wide, dark moor, whereas Hickman calls it a vast house with many dark passages and great staircases.[3] Hickman says that within this house there are stone bridges spanning deep chasms and canals of black water flowing between stone walls – to what destination or for what purpose no one knows." Suddenly Mr Norrell was in an

---

[2] *cont'd* other Francis Pevensey. In the sixteenth century Francis had been a common name for both men and women. Then Charles Hether-Gray published seven different extracts from the letters which mentioned *Eighteen Wonders in the House of Albion* and shewed plainly that Pale's mistress and the author of the book were one and the same person.

William Pantler argued that the letters were forgeries. The letters had been found in the library of a Mr Whittlesea. Mr Whittlesea had a wife who had written several plays, two of which had been performed at the Drury Lane Theatre. Clearly, said Pantler, a woman who would stoop to writing plays would stoop to any thing and he suggested that Mrs Whittlesea had forged the letters ". . . in order to elevate her Sex above the natural place that God had ordained for it . . ." Mr Whittlesea challenged William Pantler to a duel and Pantler, who was a scholar through and through and knew nothing of weapons, apologized and published a formal retraction of his accusations against Mrs Whittlesea.

Mr Norrell was quite happy to employ Pevensey's magic, since he had settled it in his own mind long ago that Pevensey was a man. As to the letters – since they contained no word of magic he did not concern himself with them. Jonathan Strange took a different view. According to him only one question needed to be asked and answered in order to settle the matter: would Martin Pale have taught a woman magic? The answer was, again according to Strange, yes. After all Martin Pale claimed to have been taught by a woman – Catherine of Winchester.

[3] Thaddeus Hickman (1700–38), author of a life of Martin Pale.

excellent humour. To sit quietly doing magic with Mr Strange was to him the very height of enjoyment. "And how does the article for the next *Gentleman's Magazine* come along?" he asked.

Strange thought for a moment. "I have not quite completed it," he said.

"What is it about? No, do not tell me! I greatly look forward to reading it! Perhaps you will bring it with you tomorrow?"

"Oh! Tomorrow certainly."

That evening Arabella entered the drawing-room of her house in Soho-square and was somewhat surprized to discover that the carpet was now covered with small pieces of paper upon which were written spells and notes and fragments of Norrell's conversation. Strange was standing in the middle of the room, staring down at the papers and pulling his hair.

"What in the world can I put in the next article for the *Gentleman's Magazine*?" he demanded.

"I do not know, my love. Has Mr Norrell made no suggestion?"

Strange frowned. "For some reason he thinks it is already done."

"Well, what about trees and magic?" suggested Arabella. "You were only saying the other day how interesting the subject is and very much neglected."

Strange took a clean sheet of paper and began rapidly scribbling notes upon it. "Oak trees can be befriended and will aid you against your enemies if they think your cause is just. Birch woods are well known for providing doors into Faerie. Ash-trees will never cease to mourn until the Raven King comes home again.[4]

[4] The ivy promised to bind England's enemies
Briars and thorns promised to whip them
The hawthorn said he would answer any question
The birch said he would make doors to other countries
The yew brought us weapons
The raven punished our enemies
The oak watched the distant hills
The rain washed away all sorrow
This traditional English saying supposedly lists the various contracts which John Uskglass, the Raven King, made on England's behalf with the forests.

No, no! That will never do. I cannot say that. Norrell would have a fit." He crumpled up the paper and threw it in the fire.

"Oh! Then perhaps you will listen for a moment to what I have to say," said Arabella. "I paid a visit to Lady Westby's house today, where I met a very odd young lady who seems to be under the impression that you are teaching her magic."

Strange looked up briefly. "I am not teaching any one magic," he said.

"No, my love," said Arabella patiently, "I know that you are not. That is what makes it so extraordinary."

"And what is the name of this confused young person?"

"Miss Gray."

"I do not know her."

"A smart, stylish girl, but not handsome. She is apparently very rich and absolutely wild for magic. Everybody says so. She has a fan decorated with your pictures – yours and Mr Norrell's – and she has read every word that you and Lord Portishead have ever published."

Strange stared thoughtfully at her for several seconds, so that Arabella mistakenly supposed he must be considering what she had just said. But when he spoke it was only to say in a tone of gentle reproof, "My love, you are standing on my papers." He took her arm and moved her gently aside.

"She told me that she has paid you four hundred guineas for the privilege of being your pupil. She says that in return you have sent her letters with descriptions of spells and recommendations of books to read."

"Four hundred guineas! Well, that is odd. I might forget a young lady, but I do not think I could forget four hundred guineas." A piece of paper caught Strange's eye and he picked it up and began to read it.

"I thought at first that she might have invented this story in order to make me jealous and cause a quarrel between us, but her mania does not seem to be of that sort. It is not your person she admires, it is your profession. I cannot make head nor tail of it. What can these letters be? Who can have written them?"

Strange picked up a little memorandum book (it happened to be Arabella's housekeeping book and nothing to do with him at all) and began to scribble notes in it.

"Jonathan!"

"Mmm?"

"What should I say to Miss Gray when I see her next?"

"Ask her about the four hundred guineas. Tell her I have not received it yet."

"Jonathan! This is a serious matter."

"Oh! I quite agree. There are few things as serious as four hundred guineas."

Arabella said again that it was the oddest thing in the world. She told Strange that she was quite concerned upon Miss Gray's account and she said she wished he would speak to Miss Gray so that the mystery might be resolved. But she said all this for her own satisfaction, since she knew perfectly well that he was no longer attending to her.

A few days later Strange and Sir Walter Pole were playing at billiards at the Bedford in Covent-garden. The game had come to an *impasse* as Sir Walter had begun, as usual, to accuse Strange of transporting billiard balls about the table by magic.

Strange declared that he had done no such thing.

"I saw you touch your nose," complained Sir Walter.

"Good God!" cried Strange. "A man may sneeze, mayn't he? I have a cold."

Two other friends of Strange and Sir Walter, Lieutenant-Colonel Colquhoun Grant and Colonel Manningham, who were watching the game, said that if Strange and Sir Walter merely wished to quarrel then was it entirely necessary for them to occupy the billiards table to do it? Colquhoun Grant and Colonel Manningham hinted that there were other people – more interested in the game itself – who were waiting to play. This, developing into a more general argument, unfortunately led two country gentlemen to put their heads round the door and inquire when the table might be free for a game, unaware that on Thursday evenings the billiards room at the Bedford was generally considered to be the personal property of Sir Walter Pole and Jonathan Strange and their particular friends.

"Upon my word," said Colquhoun Grant, "I do not know. But probably not for a very long while."

The first of the two country gentlemen was a thick-set, solid-looking person with a coat of heavy brown cloth and boots which would have appeared more to advantage at some provincial market than in the fashionable surroundings of the Bedford. The second country gentleman was a limp little man with an expression of perpetual astonishment.

"But, sir," said the first man, addressing Strange in tones of the utmost reasonableness, "you are talking, not playing. Mr Tantony and I are from Nottinghamshire. We have ordered our dinner but are told we must wait another hour before it is ready. Let us play while you have your chat and then we will be only too glad to give up the table to you again."

His manner as he said this was perfectly polite, yet it rather rankled with Strange's party. Everything about him plainly spoke him to be a farmer or a tradesman and they were not best pleased that he took it upon himself to order them about.

"If you examine the table," said Strange, "you will see that we have just begun. To ask a gentleman to break off before his game is ended – well, sir, it is a thing that is never done at the Bedford."

"Ah! Is it not?" said the Nottinghamshire gentleman pleasantly. "Then I beg your pardon. But perhaps you will not object to telling me whether you think it will be a short game or a long one?"

"We have already told you," said Grant. "We do not know." He gave Strange a look which plainly said, "This fellow is very stupid."

It was at this point that the Nottinghamshire gentleman began to suspect that Strange's party were not merely unhelpful, but that they intended to be rude to him. He frowned and indicated the limp little man with the astonished expression who stood at his side. "It is Mr Tantony's first visit to London and he does not desire to come again. I particularly wished to shew him the Bedford Coffee-house, but I did not think to find the people so very disobliging."

"Well, if you do not like it here," said Strange, angrily, "then I can only suggest that you go back home to wherever it is . . . Nothing-shire, I think you said?"

Colquhoun Grant gave the Nottinghamshire gentleman a very cool look and remarked to nobody in particular, "It is no wonder to me that farming is in such a parlous condition. Farmers nowadays are always upon the gad. One meets with them at all the idlest haunts in the kingdom. They consult nothing but their own pleasure. Is there no wheat to be sown in Nottinghamshire, I wonder? No pigs to be fed?"

"Mr Tantony and I are not farmers, sir!" exclaimed the Nottinghamshire gentleman indignantly. "We are brewers. Gatcombe and Tantony's Entire Stout is our most celebrated beer and it is famed throughout three counties!"

"Thank you, but we have beer and brewers enough in London already," remarked Colonel Manningham. "Pray, do not stay upon our account."

"But we are not here to sell beer! We have come for a far nobler purpose than that! Mr Tantony and I are enthusiasts for magic! We consider that it is every patriotic Englishman's duty to interest himself in the subject. London is no longer merely the capital of Great Britain – it is the centre of our magical scholarship. For many years it was Mr Tantony's dearest wish that he might learn magic, but the art was in such a wretched condition that it made him despair. His friends bade him be more cheerful. We told him that it is when things are at their worst that they start to mend.

And we were right, for almost immediately there appeared two of the greatest magicians that England has ever known. I refer of course to Mr Norrell and Mr Strange! The wonders which they have performed have given Englishmen cause to bless the country of their birth again and encouraged Mr Tantony to hope that he might one day be of their number."

"Indeed? Well, it is my belief that he will be disappointed," observed Strange.

"Then, sir, you could not be more wrong!" cried the Nottinghamshire gentleman triumphantly. "Mr Tantony is being instructed in the magical arts by Mr Strange himself!"

Unfortunately, Strange happened at that moment to be leaning across the table, balanced upon one foot to take aim at a billiard ball. So surprized was he at what he heard that he missed the shot entirely, struck his cue against the side of the table and promptly fell over.

"I think there must be some mistake," said Colquhoun Grant.

"No, sir. No mistake," said the Nottinghamshire gentleman with an air of infuriating calmness.

Strange, getting up from the floor, asked, "What does he look like, this Mr Strange?"

"Alas," said the Nottinghamshire gentleman, "I cannot give you any precise information upon that point. Mr Tantony has never met Mr Strange. Mr Tantony's education is conducted entirely by letters. But we have great hopes of seeing Mr Strange in the street. We go to Soho-square tomorrow expressly for the purpose of looking at his house."

"Letters!" exclaimed Strange.

"I would think an education by correspondence must of a very inferior sort," said Sir Walter.

"Not at all!" cried the Nottinghamshire gentleman. "Mr Strange's letters are full of sage advice and remarkable insights into the condition of English magic. Why, only the other day Mr Tantony wrote and asked Mr Strange for a spell to make it stop raining – we get a great deal of rain in our part of Nottinghamshire. The very next day Mr Strange wrote back and said that, though there were indeed spells that could move rain and sunshine about, like pieces on a chessboard, he would never employ them except in the direst need, and he advised Mr Tantony to follow his example. English magic, said Mr Strange, had grown up upon English soil and had in a sense been nurtured by English rain. Mr Strange said that in meddling with English weather, we meddled with England, and in meddling with England we risked destroying the very foundations of English magic. We thought that a very striking instance of Mr Strange's genius, did we not, Mr Tantony?" The Nottinghamshire man gave his friend a little shake which made him blink several times.

"Did you ever say that?" murmured Sir Walter.

"Why! I think I did," answered Strange. "I believe I said something of the sort . . . when would it have been? Last Friday, I suppose."

"And to whom did you say it?"

"To Norrell, of course."

"And was there any other person in the room?"

Strange paused. "Drawlight," he said slowly.

"Ah!"

"Sir," said Strange to the Nottinghamshire gentleman. "I beg your pardon if I offended you before. But you must admit that there was something about the way in which you spoke to me which was not quite . . . In short I have a temper and you piqued me. I am Jonathan Strange and I am sorry to tell you that I never heard of you or Mr Tantony until today. I suspect that Mr Tantony and I are both the dupes of an unscrupulous man. I presume that Mr Tantony pays me for his education? Might I ask where he sends the money? If it is to Little Ryder-street then I shall have the proof I need."

Unfortunately the Nottinghamshire gentleman and Mr Tantony had formed an idea of Strange as a tall, deep-chested man with a long white beard, a ponderous way of speaking and an antiquated mode of dress. As the Mr Strange who stood before them was slender, clean-shaven, quick of speech and dressed exactly like every other rich, fashionable gentleman in London, they could not at first be persuaded that this was the right person.

"Well, that is easily resolved," said Colquhoun Grant.

"Of course," said Sir Walter, "I will summon a waiter. Perhaps the word of a servant will do what the word of a gentleman cannot. John! Come here! We want you!"

"No, no, no!" cried Grant, "That was not what I meant at all. John, you may go away again. We do not want you. There are any number of things which Mr Strange could do which would prove his incomparable magicianship far better than any mere assurances. He is after all the Greatest Magician of the Age."

"Surely," said the Nottinghamshire man with a frown, "that title belongs to Mr Norrell?"

Colquhoun Grant smiled. "Colonel Manningham and I had the honour, sir, to fight with his Grace the Duke of Wellington in Spain. I assure you we knew nothing of Mr Norrell there. It was Mr Strange – this gentleman here – whom we trusted. Now, if he were to perform some startling act of magic then I do not think you could doubt any longer and then I am sure your great respect for English magic and English magicians would not allow you to remain silent a moment longer. I am sure you would wish to tell him all you know about these forged letters." Grant looked at the Nottinghamshire gentleman inquiringly.

"Well," said the Nottinghamshire gentleman, "you are a very queer set of gentlemen, I must say, and what you can mean by spinning me such a tale as this, I do not know. For I tell you plainly I will be very much surprized if the letters prove to be forgeries when every line, every word breathes good English magic!"

"But," said Grant, "if, as we suppose, this scoundrel made use of Mr Strange's own words to concoct his lies, then that would explain it, would it not? Now, in order to prove that he is who we say he is, Mr Strange shall now shew you something that no man living has ever seen!"

"Why?" said the Nottinghamshire man. "What will he do?"

Grant smiled broadly and turned to Strange, as if he too were suddenly struck with curiosity. "Yes, Strange, tell us. What will you do?"

But it was Sir Walter who answered. He nodded in the direction of a large Venetian mirror which took up most of one wall and was at that moment reflecting only darkness, and he declared, "He will walk into that mirror and he will not come out again."

36

# All the mirrors of the world

## November 1814

THE VILLAGE OF Hampstead is situated five miles north of London. In our grandfathers' day it was an entirely unremarkable collection of farmhouses and cottages, but the existence of so rustic a spot close to London attracted large numbers of people to go there to enjoy the sweet air and verdure. A racecourse and bowling-green were built for their amusement. Bun shops and tea-gardens provided refreshment. Rich people bought summer cottages there and Hampstead soon became what it is today: one of the favourite resorts of fashionable London society. In a very short space of time it has grown from a country village to a place of quite respectable size – almost a little town.

Two hours after Sir Walter, Colonel Grant, Colonel Manningham and Jonathan Strange had quarrelled with the Nottinghamshire gentleman a carriage entered Hampstead on the London road and turned into a dark lane which was overhung with elder bushes, lilacs and hawthorns. The carriage drove to a house at the end of the lane where it stopped and Mr Drawlight got out.

The house had once been a farmhouse, but it had been much improved in recent years. Its small country windows – more useful for keeping out the cold than letting in the light – had all been made large and regular; a pillared portico had replaced the mean country doorway; the farm-yard had been entirely swept away and a flower garden and shrubbery established in its place.

Mr Drawlight knocked upon the door. A maidservant answered his knock and immediately conducted him to a drawing-room. The room must once have been the farmhouse-parlour, but all signs of its original character had disappeared beneath costly French wallpapers, Persian carpets and English furniture of the newest make and style.

Drawlight had not waited there more than a few minutes when a lady entered the room. She was tall, well-formed and beautiful. Her gown was of scarlet velvet and her white neck was set off by an intricate necklace of jet beads.

Through an open door across the passageway could be glimpsed a dining-parlour, as expensively got up as the drawing-room. The remains of a meal upon the table shewed that the lady had dined alone. It seemed that she had put on the red gown and black necklace for her own amusement.

"Ah, madam!" cried Drawlight leaping up. "I hope you are well?"

She made a little gesture of dismissal. "I suppose I am well. As well as I can be with scarcely any society and no variety of occupation."

"What!" cried Drawlight in a shocked voice. "Are you all alone here?"

"I have one companion – an old aunt. She urges religion upon me."

"Oh, madam!" cried Drawlight. "Do not waste your energies upon prayers and sermons. You will get no comfort there. Instead, fix your thoughts upon *revenge*."

"I shall. I do," she said simply. She sat down upon the sopha opposite the window. "And how are Mr Strange and Mr Norrell?"

"Oh, busy, madam! Busy, busy, busy! I could wish for their sakes, as well as yours, that they were less occupied. Only yesterday Mr Strange inquired most particularly after you. He wished to know if you were in good spirits. 'Oh! Tolerable,' I told him, 'merely tolerable.' Mr Strange is shocked, madam, frankly shocked at the heartless behaviour of your relations."

"Indeed? I wish that his indignation might shew itself in more practical ways," she said coolly. "I have paid him more than a hundred guineas and he has done nothing. I am tired of trying to arrange matters through an intermediary, Mr Drawlight. Convey to Mr Strange my compliments. Tell him I am ready to meet him wherever he chuses at any hour of the day or night. All times are alike to me. I have no engagements."

"Ah, madam! How I wish I could do as you ask. How Mr Strange wishes it! But I fear it is quite impossible."

"So you say, but I have heard no reason – at least none that satisfies me. I suppose Mr Strange is nervous of what people will say if we are seen together. But our meeting may be quite private. No one need know."

"Oh, madam! You have quite misunderstood Mr Strange's character! Nothing in the world would please him so much as an opportunity to shew the world how he despises your persecutors. It is entirely upon your account that he is so circumspect. He fears . . ."

But what Mr Strange feared the lady never learnt, for at that moment Drawlight stopt suddenly and looked about him with an expression of the utmost perplexity upon his face. "What in the world was that?" he asked.

It was as if a door had opened somewhere. Or possibly a series of doors. There was a sensation as of a breeze blowing into the house and bringing with it the half-remembered scents of childhood. There was a shift in the light which seemed to cause all the shadows in the room to fall differently. There was nothing more definite than that, and yet, as often happens when some magic is occurring, both Drawlight and the lady had the strongest impression that nothing in the visible world could be relied upon any more. It was as if one might put out one's hand to touch any thing in the room and discover it was no longer there.

A tall mirror hung upon the wall above the sopha where the lady sat. It shewed a second great white moon in a second tall dark window and a second dim mirror-room. But Drawlight and the lady did not appear in the mirror-room at all. Instead there was a kind of an indistinctness, which became a sort of shadow, which became the dark shape of someone coming towards them. From the path which this person took, it could clearly be seen that the mirror-room was not like the original at all and that it was only by odd tricks of lighting and perspective – such as one might meet with in the theatre – that they appeared to be the same. It seemed that the mirror-room was actually a long corridor. The hair and coat of the mysterious figure were stirred by a wind which could not be felt in their own room and, though he walked briskly towards the glass which separated the two rooms, it was taking him some time to reach it. But finally he reached the glass and then there was a moment when his dark shape loomed very large behind it and his face was still in shadow.

Then Strange hopped down from the mirror very neatly, smiled his most charming smile and bid both Drawlight and the lady, "Good evening."

He waited a moment, as if allowing someone else time to speak and then, when no one did, he said, "I hope you will be so kind, madam, as to forgive the lateness of my visit. To say the truth the way was a little more meandering than I had anticipated. I took a wrong turning and very nearly arrived in . . . well, I do not quite know where."

He paused again, as if waiting for someone to invite him to sit down. When no one did, he sat down anyway.

Drawlight and the lady in the red gown stared at him. He smiled back at them.

"I have been getting acquainted with Mr Tantony," he told Drawlight. "A most pleasant gentleman, though not very talkative. His friend, Mr Gatcombe, however, told me all I wished to know."

"You are Mr Strange?" asked the lady in the red gown.

"I am, madam."

"This is most fortunate. Mr Drawlight was just explaining to me why you and I could never meet."

"It is true, madam, that until tonight circumstances did not favour our meeting. Mr Drawlight, pray make the introductions."

Drawlight muttered that the lady in the red gown was Mrs Bullworth.

Strange rose, bowed to Mrs Bullworth and sat down again.

"Mr Drawlight has, I believe, told you of my horrible situation?" said Mrs Bullworth.

Strange made a small gesture with his head which might have meant one thing or might have meant another thing or might have meant nothing at all. He said, "A narration by an unconnected person can never match the tale told by someone intimately concerned with the events. There may be vital points which Mr Drawlight has, for one reason or another, omitted. Indulge me, madam. Let me it hear from you."

"All?"

"All."

"Very well. I am, as you know, the daughter of a gentleman in Northamptonshire. My father's property is extensive. His house and income are large. We are among the first people in that county. But my family have always encouraged me to believe that with my beauty and accomplishments I might occupy an even higher position in the world. Two years ago I made a very advantageous marriage. Mr Bullworth is rich and we moved in the most fashionable circles. But still I was not happy. In the summer of last year I had the misfortune to meet a man who is everything Mr Bullworth is not: handsome, clever, amusing. A few short weeks were enough to convince me that I preferred this man to any one I had ever seen." She gave a little shrug of her shoulders. "Two days before Christmas I left my husband's house in his company. I hoped – indeed expected – to divorce Mr

Bullworth and marry him. But that was not his intention. By the end of January we had quarrelled and my friend had deserted me. He returned to his house and all his usual pursuits, but there was to be no such revival of a former life for me. My husband cast me off. My friends refused to receive me. I was forced back upon the mercy of my father. He told me that he would provide for me for the rest of my life, but in return I must live in perfect retirement. No more balls for me, no more parties, no more friends. No more any thing." She gazed into the distance for a moment, as if in contemplation of all that she had lost, but just as quickly she shook off her melancholy and declared, "And now to business!" She went to a little writing-table, opened a drawer and drew out a paper which she offered to Strange. "I have, as you suggested, made a list of all the people who have betrayed me," she said.

"Ah, I told you to make a list, did I?" said Strange, taking the paper. "How businesslike I am! It is quite a long list."

"Oh!" said Mrs Bullworth. "Every name will be considered a separate commission and you shall have your fee for each. I have taken the liberty of writing by each name the punishment which I believe ought to be theirs. But your superior knowledge of magic may suggest other, more appropriate fates for my enemies. I should be glad of your recommendations."

" 'Sir James Southwell. Gout,' " read Strange.

"My father," explained Mrs Bullworth. "He wearied me to death with speeches upon my wicked character and exiled me for ever from my home. In many ways it is he who is the author of all my miseries. I wish I could harden my heart enough to decree some more serious illness for him. But I cannot. I suppose that is what is meant by the weakness of women."

"Gout is exceedingly painful," observed Strange. "Or so I am told."

Mrs Bullworth made a gesture of impatience.

" 'Miss Elizabeth Church,' " continued Strange. " 'To have her engagement broken off.' Who is Miss Elizabeth Church?"

"A cousin of mine – a tedious, embroidering sort of girl. No one ever paid her the least attention until I married Mr Bullworth. Yet now I hear she is to be married to a clergyman and my father has given her a banker's draft to pay for wedding clothes and new furniture. My father has promised Lizzie and the clergyman that he will use his interest to get them all sorts of preferments. Their way is to be made easy. They are to live in York where they will attend dinners and parties and balls, and enjoy all those pleasures which ought to have been mine. Mr Strange," she cried, growing more energetic, "surely there must be spells to make the clergyman hate the very sight of Lizzie? To make him shudder at the sound of her voice?"

"I do not know," said Strange. "I never considered the matter before. I suppose there must be." He returned to the list. " 'Mr Bullworth' . . ."

"My husband," she said.

". . . 'To be bitten by dogs.' "

"He has seven great black brutes and thinks more of them than of any human creature."

" 'Mrs Bullworth senior' – your husband's mother, I suppose – 'To be drowned in a laundry tub. To be choked to death on her own apricot preserves. To be baked accidentally in a bread oven.' That is three deaths for one woman. Forgive me, Mrs Bullworth, but the greatest magician that ever lived could not kill the same person three different ways."

"Do as much as you can manage," said Mrs Bullworth stubbornly. "The old woman is so insufferably proud of her housekeeping. She bored me to death upon the subject."

"I see. Well, this is all very Shakespearian. And so we come to the last name. 'Henry Lascelles.' I know this gentleman." Strange looked inquiringly at Drawlight.

Mrs Bullworth said, "That is the person under whose protection I left my husband's house."

"Ah! And what shall his fate be?"

"Bankruptcy," she said in a fierce, low voice. "Lunacy. Fire. A disfiguring disease. A horse to trample upon him! A villain to lie in wait for him and cut his face with a knife! A vision of horror to haunt him and drive away sleep night after night!" She rose and began to pace about the room. "Let every mean and dishonourable action he ever did be published in the newspaper! Let everyone in London shun him! Let him seduce some country girl who will go mad for love of him. Let her follow him wherever he goes for years and years. Let him become an object of ridicule because of her. Let her never leave him in peace. Let some mistake upon the part of an honest man lead to his being accused of a crime. Let him suffer all the indignities of trial and imprisonment. Let him be branded! Let him be beaten! Let him be whipped! And let him be executed!"

"Mrs Bullworth," said Strange, "pray, calm yourself."

Mrs Bullworth stopped pacing. She ceased calling down horrible fates upon Mr Lascelles's head, but still she could hardly have been said to be calm. Her breath came rapidly, she trembled all over and her face still worked furiously.

Strange watched until he judged her enough in command of herself to understand what he wanted to say and then he began, "I am sorry, Mrs Bullworth, but you have been the victim of a cruel deception. This," he glanced at Drawlight, "person has lied to you. Mr Norrell and I have never undertaken commissions for private individuals. We have never employed this person as an agent to find business for us. I never even heard your name until tonight."

Mrs Bullworth stared at him a moment and then turning upon Drawlight. "Is this true?"

Drawlight fixed his miserable gaze upon the carpet and mumbled some sort of speech in which only the words "madam" and "peculiar situation" were discernible.

Mrs Bullworth reached up and rang the bellpull.

The maid who had let Drawlight into the house reappeared.

"Haverhill," said Mrs Bullworth, "remove Mr Drawlight."

Unlike the majority of maids in fashionable households who are chosen mainly for their pretty faces, Haverhill was a competent-looking person of the middle age with strong arms and an unforgiving expression. But on this occasion she was required to do very little since Mr Drawlight was only too grateful for the opportunity to remove himself. He picked up his stick and scuttled out of the room the moment Haverhill opened the door.

Mrs Bullworth turned to Strange. "Will you help me? Will you do what I ask? If the money is not sufficient . . ."

"Oh, the money!" Strange made a dismissive gesture. "I am sorry, but as I have just told you, I do not undertake private commissions."

She stared at him, and then said in a wondering tone, "Can it be that you are entirely unmoved by the misery of my situation?"

"Upon the contrary, Mrs Bullworth, a system of morality which punishes the woman and leaves no share of blame to the man seems to me quite detestable. But beyond that I will not go. I will not hurt innocent people."

"Innocent!" she cried. "Innocent! Who is innocent? No one!"

"Mrs Bullworth, there is nothing to be said. I can do nothing for you. I am sorry."

She regarded him sourly. "Hmm, well. At least you have the grace to refrain from recommending repentance or good works or needlework or whatever it is the other fools hold up as a cure for a blank life and a broken heart. Nevertheless I think it will be best for both of us if this interview is brought to a conclusion. Good night, Mr Strange."

Strange bowed. As he left the room he gave a wistful glance at the mirror above the sopha, as if he would have preferred to depart by that means, but Haverhill held the door open and common politeness obliged him to go through it.

Having neither horse nor carriage, he walked the five miles from Hampstead to Soho-square. On arriving at his own front door he discovered that although it was almost two o'clock in the morning there was a light in every window of the house. Before he could even fish in his pocket for his doorkey, the door was flung open by Colquhoun Grant.

"Good heavens! What are you doing here?" cried Strange.

Grant did not trouble to answer him, but instead turned back into the house and called, "He is here, ma'am! He is quite safe."

Arabella came running, almost tumbling, out of the drawing-room, followed a moment later by Sir Walter. Then Jeremy Johns and several of the servants appeared in the passageway leading to the kitchen.

"Has something happened? Is something wrong?" asked Strange, gazing at them all in surprize.

"Blockhead!" laughed Grant, striking him affectionately on the head. "We were concerned about you! Where in the world have you been?"

"Hampstead."

"Hampstead!" exclaimed Sir Walter. "Well, we are very glad to see you!" He glanced at Arabella and added nervously, "I fear we have made Mrs Strange anxious for no good reason."

"Oh!" said Strange to his wife. "You were not afraid, were you? I was perfectly well. I always am."

"There, ma'am!" declared Colonel Grant cheerfully. "It is just as I told you. In Spain Mr Strange was often in great peril, but we were never in the least concerned about him. He is too clever to come to any harm."

"Must we stand in the hallway?" asked Strange. On the way from Hampstead he had been thinking about magic and he had intended to continue doing so at home. Instead, he found a house full of people all talking together. It put him out of humour.

He led the way into the drawing-room and asked Jeremy to bring him some wine and something to eat. When they were all seated he said, "It was just as we supposed. Drawlight has been arranging for Norrell and I to perform every sort of Black Magic you can think of. I found him with a most excitable young woman who wanted me to inflict torments upon her relations."

"How horrible!" said Colonel Grant.

"And what did Drawlight say?" asked Sir Walter. "How did he explain himself?"

"Ha!" Strange let out a short burst of uncheerful laughter. "He did not say any thing. He simply ran away – which was a pity, as I had a great mind to challenge him to a duel."

"Oh!" said Arabella suddenly. "It is duels now, is it?"

Sir Walter and Grant both looked at her in alarm, but Strange was too absorbed in what he was saying to notice her angry expression. "Not that I suppose he would have accepted, but I should have liked to frighten him a little. God knows he deserves it."

"But you have not said any thing about this kingdom, path – whatever it is – behind the mirror," said Colonel Grant. "Did it answer your expectations?"

Strange shook his head. "I do not have the words to describe it. All that Norrell and I have done is as nothing in comparison! And yet we have the audacity to call ourselves magicians! I wish I could give you an idea of its grandeur! Of its size and complexity! Of the great stone halls that lead off in every direction! I tried at first to judge their length and number, but soon gave up. There seemed no end to them. There were canals of still water in stone embankments. The water appeared black in the gloomy light. I saw staircases that rose up so high I could not see the top of them, and others that descended into utter blackness. Then suddenly I passed under an arch and found myself upon a stone bridge that crossed a dark, empty landscape. The bridge was so vast that I could not see the end of it. Imagine a bridge that joined Islington to Twickenham! Or York to Newcastle! And everywhere in the halls and on the bridge I saw his likeness."

"Whose likeness?" asked Sir Walter.

"The man that Norrell and I have slandered in almost everything we have written. The man whose name Norrell can hardly bear to hear mentioned. The man who built the halls, canals, bridge, everything! John Uskglass, the Raven King! Of course, the structure has fallen into disrepair over the centuries. Whatever John Uskglass once used these roads for, it seems he no longer needs them. Statues and masonry have collapsed. Shafts of light break in from God-knows-where. Some halls are blocked, while others are flooded. And I will tell you something else very curious. There were a great number of discarded shoes everywhere I went. Presumably they belonged to other travellers. They were of a very ancient style and much decayed. From which I conclude that these passages have been little frequented in recent years. In all the time I was walking I only saw one other person."

"You saw someone else?" said Sir Walter.

"Oh, yes! At least I think it was a person. I saw a shadow moving along a white road that crossed the dark moor. You must understand that I was upon the bridge at the time and it was much higher than any bridge I have ever seen in this world. The ground appeared to be several thousand feet beneath me. I looked down and saw someone. If I had not been so set upon finding Drawlight, I would certainly have found a way down and followed him or her, for it seems to me that there could be no better way for a magician to spend his time than in conversation with such a person."

"But would such a person be safe?" asked Arabella.

"Safe?" said Strange, contemptuously. "Oh, no. I do not think so. But then I flatter myself that neither am I particularly *safe*. I hope I have not missed my chance. I hope that when I return tomorrow I will find some clue as to where the mysterious figure went."

"Return!" exclaimed Sir Walter. "But are you sure . . . ?"

"Oh!" cried Arabella, interrupting. "I see how it is to be! You will be walking these paths every moment Mr Norrell can spare you, while I remain here in a condition of the most miserable suspense, wondering if I am ever to see you again!"

Strange looked at her in surprize. "Arabella? Whatever is the matter?"

"The matter! You are set upon putting yourself in the most horrible danger and you expect me to say nothing about it!"

Strange made a sort of gesture of combined appeal and helplessness, as if he were calling upon Sir Walter and Grant to bear witness how exceedingly unreasonable this was. He said, "But when I told you I was going to Spain, you were perfectly composed, even though a vicious war was raging there at the time. This, on the other hand, is quite . . ."

"Perfectly composed? I assure you I was nothing of the kind! I was horribly afraid for you – as were all the wives and mothers and sisters of the men in Spain. But you and I agreed that you had a duty to go. And besides, in Spain you had the entire British Army with you, whereas there you will be perfectly alone. I say 'there', but none of us knows where 'there' is!"

"I beg your pardon, but I know exactly where it is! It is the King's Roads. Really, Arabella, I think it is a little late in the day to decide you do not like my profession!"

"Oh, that is not fair! I have never said a word against your profession. I think it one of the noblest in the world. I am proud beyond measure of what you and Mr Norrell have done and I have never objected in the least to your learning whatever new magic you saw fit – but until today you have always been content to make your discoveries in books."

"Well, no longer. To confine a magician's researches to the books in his library, well, you might just as well tell an explorer that you approve his plan to search for the source of, of – whatever it is those African rivers are called – on the condition that he never steps outside Tunbridge Wells!"

Arabella gave an exclamation of exasperation. "I thought you meant to be a magician not an explorer!"

"It is the same thing. An explorer cannot stay at home reading maps other men have made. A magician cannot increase the stock of magic by reading other men's books. It is quite obvious to me that sooner or later Norrell and I must look beyond our books!"

"Indeed? That is obvious to you, is it? Well, Jonathan, I very much doubt that it is obvious to Mr Norrell."

Throughout this exchange Sir Walter and Lieutenant-Colonel Grant looked as uncomfortable as any two people can who inadvertently find themselves witnesses to a little outburst of marital disharmony. Nor was their situation improved by the consciousness that just at present neither Arabella nor Strange was feeling particularly well disposed towards them. They had already had to endure some sharp words from Arabella when they had confessed their part in encouraging Strange to perform the dangerous magic. Now Strange was directing angry glances at them, as if he wondered by what right they had come to his house in the middle of the night and put his usually sweet-tempered wife out of temper. As soon as there was any thing like a pause in the conversation, Colonel Grant muttered something incoherent about the lateness of the hour and about their kind hospitality being more than he deserved and about wishing them all good night. But then, as no one paid the slightest attention to his speech, he was obliged to continue where he was.

Sir Walter, however, was of a more resolute character. He concluded that he had been wrong in sending Strange upon the mirror-path and he was determined to do what he could to put matters right. Being a politician, he was never dissuaded from giving any body his opinion by the mere fact that they were not inclined to hear it. "Have you read every book upon magic?" he demanded of Strange.

"What? No, of course not! You know very well I have not!" said Strange. (He was thinking of the books in the library at Hurtfew.)

"These halls that you saw tonight, do you know where they all lead?" asked Sir Walter.

"No," said Strange.

"Do you know what the dark land is that the bridge crosses?"

"No, but . . ."

"Then, surely it would be better to do as Mrs Strange suggests and read all you can about these roads, before returning to them," said Sir Walter.

"But the information in books is inaccurate and contradictory! Even Norrell says so and he has read everything there is to read about them. You may be certain of that!"

Arabella, Strange and Sir Walter continued to argue for another half hour until everyone was cross and wretched and longing to go to bed. Only Strange seemed at all comfortable with these descriptions of eerie, silent halls, unending pathways and vast, dark landscapes. Arabella was genuinely frightened by what she had heard and even Sir Walter and Colonel Grant felt decidedly unsettled. Magic, which had seemed so familiar just hours before, so *English*, had suddenly become inhuman, unearthly, *otherlandish*.

As for Strange, it was his decided opinion that they were the most incomprehensible and infuriating set of people in the country. They did not appear to comprehend that he had done something entirely *remarkable*. It would not be going too far (he thought) to say that this had been the most extraordinary achievement of his career so far. No English magician since Martin Pale had been on the King's Roads. But instead of congratulating him and praising his skill – which any one else would have done – all they did was complain in a Norrellish sort of way.

The following morning he awoke determined to return to the King's Roads. He greeted Arabella cheerfully, talked to her upon indifferent subjects and generally tried to pretend that the quarrel had been due to her tiredness and overwrought state the previous evening. But long before he could take advantage of this convenient fiction (and slip away to the Roads by the nearest large mirror) Arabella told him very plainly that she felt just the same as she had last night.

In the end is it not futile to try and follow the course of a quarrel between husband and wife? Such a conversation is sure to meander more than any other. It draws in tributary arguments and grievances from years before – all quite incomprehensible to any but the two people they concern most nearly. Neither party is ever proved right or wrong in such a case, or, if they are, what does it signify?

The desire to live in harmony and friendship with one's spouse is very strong, and Strange and Arabella were no different from other people in this respect. Finally, after two days arguing the point back and forth, they made each other a promise. He promised her not to go upon the King's Roads again until she said that he might. In return she promised him to grant him that permission just as soon as he convinced her that it was safe to do so.

# 37

# The Cinque Dragownes

## November 1814

SEVEN YEARS AGO Mr Lascelles's house in Bruton-street was generally reckoned to be one of the best in London. It had the sort of perfection that can only be achieved by a very rich, very idle man who devotes the greater part of his time to collecting pictures and sculpture and the greater part of his mental energies to chusing furniture and wallpapers. His taste was remarkably good and he had a talent for combining colours in new and quite striking ways. He was particularly fond of blues, greys and a sort of darkish, metallic bronze. Yet he never became sentimentally attached to his possessions. He sold paintings as frequently as he bought them and his house never deteriorated into that picture-gallery confusion which besets the homes of some collectors. Each of Lascelles's rooms contained only a handful of pictures and *objets d'art*, but that handful included some of the most beautiful and remarkable objects in all of London.

In the last seven years however the perfection of Mr Lascelles's house had become somewhat diminished. The colours were as exquisite as ever, but they had not been changed for seven years. The furnishings were expensive, but they represented what had been most fashionable seven years ago. In the last seven years no new paintings had been added to Lascelles's collection. In the last seven years remarkable antique sculptures had arrived in London from Italy, Egypt and Greece but other gentlemen had bought them.

What is more, there were signs that the owner of the house had been engaged in useful occupation, that he had, in short, been *working*. Reports, manuscripts, letters and Government papers lay upon every table and chair, and copies of *The Friends of English Magic* and books on magic were to be found in every room.

The truth was that, though Lascelles still affected to despise work, in the seven years since Mr Norrell had first arrived in London he had been busier than ever before. Though it had been his suggestion to appoint Lord Portishead editor of *The Friends of English Magic*, the manner in which his lordship had carried on his editorial duties had exasperated Lascelles to a degree scarcely to be borne. Lord Portishead had deferred to Mr Norrell in all things – had instantly executed all of Mr Norrell's unnecessary amendments – and, as a result, *The Friends of English Magic* had grown duller and more circumlocutious with every issue. In the autumn of 1810 Lascelles had contrived to have himself appointed joint editor. *The Friends of English Magic* had one of the largest subscriptions of any periodical in the kingdom; the work was not inconsiderable. In addition Lascelles wrote upon modern magic for other periodicals and newspapers; he advised the Government upon magical policy; he visited Mr Norrell almost every day and in his spare time he studied the history and theory of magic.

On the third day after Strange had paid his visit to Mrs Bullworth, Lascelles happened to be working hard in his library upon the next issue of *The Friends of English Magic*. Though it was a little after noon he had not yet found the time to shave and dress and was sitting in his dressing-gown amid a litter of books, papers, breakfast plates and coffee cups. A letter he wanted was missing and so he went to look for it. On entering the drawing-room he was surprized to find someone there.

"Oh!" he said. "It's you."

The wretched-looking creature who drooped in a chair by the fire raised his head. He said, "Your servant has gone to find you and tell you I am here."

"Ah!" said Lascelles and paused, apparently at a loss for something to say next. He sat down in the opposite chair, rested his head upon his hand and regarded Drawlight thoughtfully.

Drawlight's face was pale and his eyes were sunk in his head. His coat was dusty, his boots were but indifferently polished and even his linen had a wilted look.

"I think it most unkind of you," said Lascelles at last, "to accept money for arranging to have me ruined, crippled and driven mad. And from Maria Bullworth of all people! Why she should be so angry is quite beyond me! It was quite as much her doing as mine. I did not force her to marry Bullworth. I merely offered her an escape when she could no longer bear the sight of him. Is it true that she wanted Strange to inflict leprosy upon me?"

"Oh, probably," sighed Drawlight. "I really do not know. There was never the least danger in the world that any thing would happen to you. You sit there, every bit as rich, healthy and comfortable as ever you were, whereas I am the wretchedest being in London. I have not slept in three days. This morning my hands were shaking so much I could scarcely tie my cravat. No one knows what mortification it is to me to appear in this scarecrow condition. Not that any one will see me, so what does it matter? I have been turned away from every door in London. Yours is the only house where I am admitted." He paused. "I ought not to have told you that."

Lascelles shrugged. "What I do not understand," he said, "is how you expected to succeed with such a perfectly absurd scheme."

"It was not in the least absurd! Upon the contrary I was

scrupulous in my choice of . . . of *clients*. Maria Bullworth lives in perfect retirement from society. Gatcombe and Tantony are brewers! From Nottinghamshire! Who could have predicted that they and Strange would ever meet?"

"And what of Miss Gray? Arabella Strange met her at Lady Westby's house in Bedford-square."

Drawlight sighed. "Miss Gray was eighteen years old and lived with her guardians in Whitby. According to the terms of her father's will she was obliged to consult their wishes in everything she did until she was thirty-six. They detested London and were determined never to leave Whitby. Unfortunately they both caught colds and died very suddenly two months ago and the wretched girl immediately set off for the capital." Drawlight paused and licked his lips nervously. "Is Norrell very angry?"

"Beyond any thing I ever saw," said Lascelles softly.

Drawlight retreated a little further into his chair. "What will they do?"

"I do not know. Since your little adventure became known I have thought it best to absent myself from Hanover-square for a while. I heard from Admiral Summerhayes that Strange wished to call you out . . ." (Drawlight gave a sort of yelp of fright.) ". . . but Arabella disapproves of duelling and so nothing came of it."

"Norrell has no right to be angry with me!" declared Drawlight suddenly. "He owes everything to me! Magicianship is all very well, but had it not been for me taking him about and shewing him to people, no one would ever have heard of him. He could not do without me then, and he cannot do without me now."

"You think so?"

Drawlight's dark eyes grew larger than ever and he put a finger in his mouth as though to gnaw a fingernail for comfort, but finding that he was still wearing his gloves, he took it out again quickly. "I shall call again this evening," he said. "Shall you be at home?"

"Oh, probably! I have half-promised Lady Blessington to go to her salon, but I doubt that I shall go. We are horribly behind with the *Friends*. Norrell keeps plaguing us with contradictory instructions."

"So much work! My poor Lascelles! That will not suit you at all! What a slavedriver the old man is!"

After Drawlight had gone Lascelles rang for his servant. "I shall go out in an hour, Emerson. Tell Wallis to get my clothes ready . . . Oh, and Emerson! Mr Drawlight has expressed an intention of returning here later this evening. When he comes, do not upon any consideration admit him."

At the same time that the above conversation was taking place Mr Norrell, Mr Strange and John Childermass were gathered in the library at Hanover-square to discuss Drawlight's treachery. Mr Norrell sat in silence, staring into the fire while Childermass described to Strange how he had discovered another of Drawlight's dupes, an elderly gentleman in Twickenham called Palgrave who had given Drawlight two hundred guineas to have his life prolonged by another eighty years and his youth returned to him.

"I am not sure," continued Childermass, "that we will ever know for certain how many people have paid Drawlight in the belief that they were commissioning you to perform Black Magic. Both Mr Tantony and Miss Gray have received promises of some future position in a hierarchy of magicians, which Drawlight told them will soon exist and which I do not pretend to understand very well."

Strange sighed. "How we shall ever convince people that we had no part in it, I do not know. We should do something, but I confess that I have not the least idea what."

Suddenly Mr Norrell said, "I have been considering the matter very carefully during the last two days – indeed I may say that I have thought of little else – and I have come to the conclusion that we must revive the Cinque Dragownes!"[1]

There was a short silence and then Strange said, "I beg your pardon, sir. Did you say the Cinque Dragownes?"

Mr Norrell nodded. "It is quite clear to me that this villain should be tried by the Cinque Dragownes. He is guilty of False Magic and Evil Tendings. Happily the old mediaeval law has never been revoked."

"Old mediaeval law," said Childermass, with a short laugh, "required twelve magicians to sit in judgement in the Court of

[1] Les Cinque Dragownes (The Five Dragons). This court took its name not, as is generally supposed, from the ferocity of its judges, but from a chamber in the house of John Uskglass, the Raven King, in Newcastle where the judgements were originally given. This chamber was said to be twelve-sided and to be decorated by wonderful carvings, some of them the work of men and some of them the work of fairies. The most marvellous of all were the carvings of five dragons.

Crimes tried by the Cinque Dragownes included: "Evil Tendings" – magic with an inherently malevolent purpose; "False Magic" – pretending to do magic or promising to do magic which one either could not or did not intend to do; selling magic rings, hats, shoes, coats, belts, shovels, beans, musical instruments etc., etc. to people who could not be expected to control those powerful articles; pretending to be a magician or pretending to act on behalf of a magician; teaching magic to unsuitable persons, e.g. drunkards, madmen, children, persons of vicious habits and inclinations; and many other magical crimes committed by trained magicians and other Christians. Crimes against the person of John Uskglass were also tried by the Cinque Dragownes. The only category of magical crimes with which the Cinque Dragownes had nothing to do was crimes by fairies. These were dealt with by the separate court of Folflures.

In England in the twelfth, thirteenth and fourteenth centuries a thriving community of magicians and fairies was continually performing magic. Magic is notoriously difficult to regulate and, naturally enough, not all the magic that was done was well intentioned. John Uskglass seems to have devoted a great deal of time and energy to the creation of a body of law to govern magic and magicians. When the practice of magic spread throughout England, the southern English kings were only too grateful to borrow the wisdom of their northern neighbour. It is a peculiarity of that time that though England was divided into two countries with separate judiciary systems, the body of law which governed magic was the same for both. The southern English equivalent of the Cinque Dragownes was called the Petty Dragownes of London and was situated near Blackfriars.

Cinque Dragownes. There are not twelve magicians in England. You know very well there are not. There are two."

"We could find others," said Mr Norrell.

Strange and Childermass looked at him in astonishment.

Mr Norrell had the grace to appear a little embarrassed at contradicting all that he had maintained for seven years, but nevertheless he continued, "There is Lord Portishead and that dark little man in York who would not sign the agreement. That is two and I dare say," here he looked at Childermass, "you will find some more if you put your mind to it."

Childermass opened his mouth, presumably to say something of all the magicians he had already found for Mr Norrell – magicians who were magicians no longer now that Mr Norrell had their books, or had turned them out of their businesses or made them sign pernicious agreements or, in some other way, destroyed them.

"Forgive me, Mr Norrell," interrupted Strange, "but when I spoke of something being done, I meant an advertisement in the newspaper or something of that sort. I very much doubt that Lord Liverpool and the Ministers would allow us, for the sake of punishing one man, to revive a branch of English law that has been defunct for more than two hundred years. And even if they were so obliging as to permit it, I think we must assume that twelve magicians means twelve *practising* magicians. Lord Portishead and John Segundus are both theoretical magicians. Besides it is very likely that Drawlight will soon be prosecuted for fraud, forgery, theft and I do not know what else. I fail to see what advantage the Cinque Dragownes has over the common-law courts."

"The justice of the common-law courts is entirely unpredictable! The judge will know nothing of magic. The magnitude of this man's crimes will be entirely lost upon him. I am speaking of his crimes against English magic, his crimes against *me*. The Cinque Dragownes was renowned for its severity. I consider it our best security that he will be hanged."

"Hanged!"

"Oh, yes. I am quite determined to see him hanged! I thought that was what we were talking about." Mr Norrell blinked his small eyes rapidly.

"Mr Norrell," said Strange, "I am quite as angry with this man as you are. He is unprincipled. He is deceitful. He is everything I despise. But I will not be the cause of any one's death. I was in the Peninsula, sir. I have seen enough men die."

"But two days ago you wished to challenge him to a duel!"

Strange gave him an angry look. "That is quite another thing!"

"In any case," continued Mr Norrell, "I scarcely think Drawlight more to blame than you!"

"Me?" cried Strange, startled. "Why? What have I done?"

"Oh, you know very well what I mean! What in the world possessed you to go upon the King's Roads? Alone and entirely without preparation! You could hardly suppose that I would approve such a wild adventure! Your actions that night will do as much to bring magic into disrepute as anything that man has done. Indeed they will probably do more! No one ever did think well of Christopher Drawlight. It is no surprize to any one that he turns out a villain. But you are known everywhere as my pupil! You are the Second Magician in the land! People will think that I approved what you did. People will think that this is part of my plan for the restoration of English magic!"

Strange stared at his master. "God forbid, Mr Norrell, that you should feel compromised by any action of mine. Nothing, I assure you, could be further from my wishes. But it is easily remedied. If you and I part company, sir, then each of us may act independently. The world will judge each of us without reference to the other."

Mr Norrell looked very shocked. He glanced at Strange, glanced away again and muttered in a low voice that he had not meant *that*. He hoped Mr Strange knew he had not meant *that*. He cleared his throat. "I hope Mr Strange will make some allowance for the irritation of my spirits. I hope Mr Strange cares enough for English magic to bear with my fretfulness. He knows how important it is that he and I speak and act together for the good of English magic. It is altogether too soon for English magic to be exposed to the buffeting of contrary winds. If Mr Strange and I begin to contradict each other upon important matters of magical policy, then I do not believe that English magic will survive."

A silence.

Strange rose from his chair and made Mr Norrell a stiff, formal bow.

The next few moments were awkward. Mr Norrell looked as if he would have been glad to say something but was at a loss for a subject.

It so happened that Lord Portishead's new book, the *Essay on the Extraordinary Revival of English Magic, &c.*, had just arrived from the printer and was lying to hand upon a little table. Mr Norrell seized upon it. "What an excellent little work this is! And how devoted to our cause is Lord Portishead! After such a crisis one does not feel much inclined to trust any body – and yet I think we may always rely upon Lord Portishead!"

He handed Strange the book.

Strange turned the pages, thoughtfully. "He has certainly done everything we asked. Two long chapters attacking the Raven King and scarcely a mention of fairies at all. As I remember, his original manuscript had a long description of the Raven King's magic."

"Yes, indeed," said Mr Norrell. "Until you made those corrections, it was worthless. Worse than worthless – dangerous! But the long hours you spent with him, guiding his opinions, have all borne fruit! I am excessively pleased with it."

By the time Lucas brought in the tray with the tea-things the two magicians seemed like their natural selves again (though Strange was perhaps a little quieter than usual). The quarrel seemed mended.

Just before Strange left he asked if he might borrow Lord Portishead's book.

"Certainly!" cried Mr Norrell. "Keep it as your own! I have several other copies."

Despite all that Strange and Childermass had said against it Mr Norrell was unable to give up his plan to revive the Cinque Dragownes. The more he thought of it, the more it seemed to him that he would never enjoy peace again until there was a proper court of magical law in England. He felt that no punishment that might be meted out to Drawlight from any other quarter could ever satisfy him. So later that same day he sent Childermass to Lord Liverpool's house to beg the favour of a few minutes' conversation with his lordship. Lord Liverpool sent back a message that he would see Mr Norrell upon the following day.

At the appointed hour Mr Norrell waited upon the Prime Minister and explained his plan. When he had finished Lord Liverpool frowned.

"But magical law has fallen into disuse in England," said his lordship. "There are no lawyers trained to practise in such a court. Who would take the cases? Who would judge them?"

"Ah!" exclaimed Mr Norrell, producing a thick sheaf of papers. "I am glad your lordship asks such pertinent questions. I have drawn up a document describing the workings of the Cinque Dragownes. Sadly there are many lacunae in our knowledge, but I have suggested ways in which we might restore what has been lost. I have taken as my model the ecclesiastical courts of the Doctors Commons. As your lordship will see, we have a great deal of work before us."

Lord Liverpool glanced at the papers. "Too much work by far, Mr Norrell," he declared flatly.

"Oh, but it is very necessary I assure you! Very necessary indeed! How else will we regulate magic? How else will we guard against wicked magicians and their servants?"

"What wicked magicians? There is only Mr Strange and you."

"Well, that is true, but . . ."

"Do you feel particularly wicked at present, Mr Norrell? Is there some pressing reason that the British Government should establish a separate body of law to control your vicious tendencies?"

"No, I . . ."

"Or perhaps Mr Strange is exhibiting a strong inclination to murder, maim and steal?"

"No, but . . ."

"Then all we are left with is this Mr Drawlight – who, as far as I can tell, is not a magician at all."

"But his crimes are specifically magical crimes. Under English law he ought to be tried by the court of Cinque Dragownes – it is the proper place for him. These are the names of his crimes." Mr Norrell placed yet another list before the Prime Minister. "There! False Magic, Evil Tendings and Malevolent Pedagogy. No ordinary court is competent to deal with them."

"No doubt. But, as I have already observed, there is no one who can try the case."

"If your lordship will only cast your eye over page forty-two of my notes, I propose employing judges, advocates and proctors from the Doctors Commons. I could explain the principles of thaumaturgic law to them – it will take no more than a week or so. And I could lend them my servant, John Childermass, for as long as the trial lasts. He is a very knowledgeable man and could easily tell them when they were going wrong."

"What! The judge and lawyers to be coached in their duties by the plaintiff and his servant! Certainly not! Justice recoils from the idea!"

Mr Norrell blinked. "But what other security do I have that other magicians might not arise to challenge my authority and contradict me?"

"Mr Norrell, it is not the duty of the court – any court – to exalt one person's opinions above others! Not in magic nor in any other sphere of life. If other magicians think differently from you, then you must battle it out with them. You must prove the superiority of your opinions, as I do in politics. You must argue and publish and practise your magic and you must learn to live as I do – in the face of constant criticism, opposition and censure. That, sir, is the English way."

"But . . ."

"I am sorry, Mr Norrell. I will hear no more. That is an end of it. The Government of Great Britain is grateful to you. You have done your country immeasurable service. Any one may know how highly we prize you, but what you ask is quite impossible."

Drawlight's deception soon became common knowledge and, as Strange had predicted, a certain amount of blame attached to the two magicians. Drawlight was, after all, the bosom companion of one of them. It made an excellent subject for the caricaturists and several quite startling examples were published. One by George Cruikshank shewed Mr Norrell making a long speech to a group of his admirers about the nobility of English magic, while in a backroom Strange dictated a sort of bill of fare to a servant who chalked it upon a blackboard; "For killing a slight acquaintance by magic – twenty guineas. For killing a close friend – forty guineas. For killing a relation – one hundred guineas. For killing a spouse – four hundred guineas." In another caricature by Rowlandson a fashionable lady was walking in the street leading a fluffy little dog upon a leash. She was met by some of her acquaintance who began exclaiming over her dog: "La! Mrs Foulkes, what a sweet little pug!" "Yes," replied Mrs Foulkes, "it is Mr Foulkes. I paid Mr Strange and Mr Norrell fifty guineas to make my husband obedient to my every desire and this is the result."

There is no doubt that the caricatures and malicious paragraphs in the newspapers did the cause of English magic considerable damage. It was now possible for magic to be considered in quite a different light – not as the Nation's Greatest Defence, but as the tool of Malice and Envy.

And what of the people whom Drawlight had harmed? How did they view matters? There is no doubt that Mr Palgrave – the ancient, sick and disagreeable person who had hoped to live for ever – intended to prosecute Drawlight for fraud, but he was prevented from doing so by the circumstance of his dying suddenly the next day. His children and heirs (who all hated him) were rather pleased than otherwise to discover that his last days had been characterized by frustration, misery and disappointment. Nor did Drawlight have any thing to fear from Miss Gray or Mrs Bullworth. Miss Gray's friends and relations would not allow her to become embroiled in a vulgar court case and Mrs Bullworth's instructions to Drawlight had been so malicious as to make her culpable herself; she was powerless to strike at him. That left Gatcombe and Tantony, the Nottinghamshire brewers. As a practical man of business Mr Gatcombe was chiefly concerned to recover the money and sent bailiffs to London to fetch it. Unfortunately, Drawlight was unable to oblige Mr Gatcombe in this small particular, as he had spent it all long ago.

And so we come to Drawlight's real downfall, for no sooner had he escaped the gallows than his true Nemesis appeared in the already-cloudy sky of his existence, whirling through the air upon black wings to crush him. He had never been rich, indeed quite the reverse. He lived chiefly upon credit and by borrowing from his friends. Sometimes he won money at gambling clubs, but more often he encouraged foolish young Toms and Jerrys to gamble, and when they lost (which they invariably did) he would take them by the arm and, talking all the while, would lead them to this or that money-lender of his acquaintance. "I could not honestly recommend you to any other money-lender," he would tell them solicitously, "they require such monstrous amounts of interest – but Mr Buzzard is quite another sort. He is such a kindly old gentleman. He cannot bear to see any body denied a pleasure when he has the means of obtaining it for them. I truly think that he considers the lending of small sums of money more in the light of a work of charity than a business venture!"

For this small but important role in luring young men into debt, vice and ruination, Drawlight received payment from the money-lenders – generally four per cent of the first year's interest for the son of a commoner, six per cent for the son of a viscount or baronet and ten per cent for the son of an earl or duke.

News of his disgrace began to circulate. Tailors, hatters and glovemakers to whom he owed money became anxious and began to clamour for payment. Debts which he had confidently supposed might be put off for another four or five years were suddenly revived and made matters of urgency. Rough-faced men with sticks in their hands came pounding upon his door. He was advised by several people to go abroad immediately, but he could not quite believe that he was so entirely forsaken by his friends. He thought Mr Norrell would relent; he thought Lascelles, his dear, dear Lascelles, would help him. He sent them both respectful letters requesting the immediate loan of four hundred guineas. But Mr Norrell never replied and Lascelles only wrote to say that he made it a rule never to lend money to any one. Drawlight was arrested for debt upon the Tuesday morning and by the following Friday he was a prisoner in the King's Bench Prison.

On an evening towards the end of November, a week or so after these events, Strange and Arabella were sitting in the drawing-room at Soho-square. Arabella was writing a letter and Strange was plucking absent-mindedly at his hair and staring straight ahead of him. Suddenly he got up and went out of the room.

He reappeared an hour later with a dozen sheets of paper covered in writing.

Arabella looked up. "I thought the article for *The Friends of English Magic* was done," she said.

"This is not the article for *The Friends of English Magic*. It is a review of Portishead's book."

Arabella frowned. "But you cannot review a book which you yourself helped write."

"I believe I might. Under certain circumstances."

"Indeed! And what circumstances are those?"

"If I say it is an abominable book, a wicked fraud perpetrated upon the British public."

Arabella stared at him. "Jonathan!" she said at last.

"Well, it *is* an abominable book."

He handed her the sheaf of papers and she began to read them. The mantelpiece clock struck nine and Jeremy brought in the tea-things. When she had finished, she sighed. "What are you going to do?"

"I do not know. Publish it, I suppose."

"But what of poor Lord Portishead? If he has written things in his book that are wrong, then of course someone ought to say so. But you know very well that he only wrote them because you told him to. He will feel himself very ill used."

"Oh, quite! It is a wretched business from start to finish," said Strange unconcernedly. He sipped his tea and ate a piece of toast. "But that is not the point. Ought I to allow my regard for Portishead to prevent me from saying what I think is true? I do not think so. Do you?"

"But must it be you?" said Arabella with a miserable look. "Poor man, he will feel it so much more coming from you."

Strange frowned. "Of course it must be me. Who else is there? But, come. I promise you I will make him a very handsome apology just as soon as the occasion arises."

And with that Arabella was obliged to be content.

In the meantime Strange considered where he should send his review. His choice fell upon Mr Jeffrey, the editor of *The Edinburgh Review* in Scotland. *The Edinburgh Review,* it may be remembered, was a radical publication in favour of political reform, emancipation of Catholics and Jews, and all sorts of other things Mr Norrell did not approve. As a consequence, in recent years Mr Jeffrey had seen reviews and articles upon the Revival of English Magic appear in rival publications, while he, poor fellow, had none.

Naturally he was delighted to receive Strange's review. He was not in the least concerned about its astonishing and revolutionary content, since that was the sort of thing that he liked best. He wrote Strange a letter immediately, assuring him that he would publish it as soon as possible, and a couple of days later he sent Strange a haggis (a sort of Scotch pudding) as a present.

# 38

## From *The Edinburgh Review*

### January 1815

ART. XIII. *Essay on the Extraordinary Revival of English Magic, &c.* By JOHN WATERBURY, Lord PORTISHEAD, with an Account of the Magic done in the late Peninsular War: By JONATIIAN STRANGE, Magician-in-Ordinary to His Grace the Duke of WELLINGTON. London, 1814. John Murray.

As the valued aide and confidant of Mr NORRELL and the friend of Mr STRANGE, Lord PORTISHEAD is admirably fitted to write the history of recent magical events, for he has been at the centre of many of them. Each of Mr NORRELL and Mr STRANGE's achievements has been widely discussed in the newspapers and reviews, but Lord PORTISHEAD's readers will have their understanding much improved by having the tale set out for them in its entirety.

Mr NORRELL's more enthusiastic admirers would have us believe that he arrived in London in the Spring of 1807 fully formed as England's Greatest Magician and the First Phenomenon of the Age, but it is clear from PORTISHEAD's account that both he and STRANGE have grown in confidence and skill from very tentative beginnings. PORTISHEAD does not neglect to mention their failures as well as their successes. Chapter Five contains a tragi-comic account of their long-running argument with the HORSE GUARDS which began in 1810 when one of the generals had the original notion of replacing the Cavalry's horses with unicorns. In this way it was hoped to grant the soldiers the power of goring Frenchmen through their hearts. Unfortunately, this excellent plan was never implemented since, far from finding unicorns in sufficient number for the Cavalry's use, Mr NORRELL and Mr STRANGE have yet to discover a single one.

Of more dubious value is the second half of his lordship's book, wherein he leaves description behind and begins to lay down rules to determine what is, and is not, respectable English magic – in other words what shall be called White Magic and what Black. There is nothing new here. Were the reader to cast his eye over the offerings of the recent commentators upon Magic, he would begin to perceive a curious uniformity of opinion. All recite the same history and all use the same arguments to establish their conclusions.

Perhaps the time has come to ask why this should be so. In every other branch of Knowledge our understanding is enlarged by rational opposition and debate. Law, Theology, History and Science have their various factions. Why then, in Magic, do we hear nothing but the same tired arguments? One begins to wonder why any one troubles to argue at all, since everyone appears to be convinced of the same truths. This dreary monotone is particularly evident in recent accounts of ENGLISH MAGICAL HISTORY which are growing more eccentric with each retelling.

Eight years ago this very author published *A Child's History of the Raven King*, one of the most perfect things of its kind. It conveys to the reader a vivid sense of the eeriness and wonder of JOHN USKGLASS's magic. So why does he now pretend to believe that true English Magic began in the sixteenth century with MARTIN PALE? In Chapter 6 of the *Essay on the Extraordinary Revival of English Magic, &c.*, he declares that PALE consciously set out to purge English Magic of its darker elements. He does not attempt to present any evidence for this extraordinary claim – which is just as well, since no evidence exists.

According to PORTISHEAD's present view, the tradition which began with PALE was more perfectly elaborated by HICKMAN, LANCHESTER, GOUBERT, BELASIS *et al* (those we term the ARGENTINE magicians), and has now reached its glorious apogee with Mr NORRELL and Mr STRANGE. It is certainly a view that Mr STRANGE and Mr NORRELL have worked hard to perpetrate. But it simply will not do. MARTIN PALE and the ARGENTINE magicians never intended to lay the foundations of English Magic. In every spell they recorded, in every word they wrote, they were trying to re-create the glorious Magic of their predecessors (those we term the Golden Age or AUREATE magicians): THOMAS GODBLESS, RALPH DE STOKESEY, CATHERINE OF WINCHESTER and, above all, JOHN USKGLASS. MARTIN PALE was the devoted follower of these magicians. He never ceased to regret that he had been born two hundred years out of his proper time.

One of the most extraordinary characteristics of the revival of English Magic has been its treatment of JOHN USKGLASS. Nowadays it seems that his name is only spoken in order to revile him. It is as if Mr DAVY and Mr FARADAY and our other Great Men of Science felt obliged to begin their lectures by expressing their contempt and loathing of ISAAC NEWTON. Or as if our eminent Physicians prefaced every announcement of a new discovery in Medicine with a description of the wickedness of WILLIAM HARVEY.

Lord PORTISHEAD devotes a long chapter of his book to trying to prove that JOHN USKGLASS is not, as is commonly supposed, the founder of English Magic since there were magicians in these islands before his time. I do not deny it. But what I do most vehemently deny is that there was any *tradition of Magic* in England before JOHN USKGLASS.

Let us examine these earlier magicians that PORTISHEAD

makes so much of. Who were they? JOSEPH OF ARIMATHEA was one, a magician who came from the Holy Lands and planted a magic tree to protect England from harm – but I never heard that he stayed long enough to teach any of the inhabitants his skills. MERLIN was another but, as he was upon his mother's side *Welsh* and upon his father's *Infernal*, he will scarcely do for that pattern of respectable English Magic upon which PORTISHEAD, NORRELL and STRANGE have set their hearts. And who were MERLIN's pupils and followers? We cannot name a single one. No, for once the common view is the correct one: Magic had been long extinct in these islands until JOHN USKGLASS came out of Faerie and established his Kingdom of Northern England.

PORTISHEAD seems to have had some doubts upon this point himself and in case his arguments have failed to convince his readers he sets about proving that JOHN USKGLASS's magic was inherently wicked. But it is far from clear that the examples he chuses support this conclusion. Let us examine one of them. Everyone has heard of the four magical woods that surrounded JOHN USKGLASS's capital city of Newcastle. Their names were Great Tom, Asmody's Citadel, Petty Egypt and Serlo's Blessing. They moved from place to place and were known, upon occasion, to swallow up people who approached the city intending harm to the inhabitants. Certainly the notion of man-eating woods strikes us as eerie and horrible, but there is no evidence that JOHN USKGLASS's contemporaries found it so. It was a violent Age; JOHN USKGLASS was a mediaeval king and he acted as a mediaeval king should, to protect his city and his citizens.

Often it is difficult to decide upon the morality of USKGLASS's actions because his motives are so obscure. Of all the AUREATE magicians he is the most mysterious. No one knows why in 1138 he caused the moon to disappear from the sky and made it travel through all the lakes and rivers of England. We do not know why in 1202 he quarrelled with Winter and banished it from his kingdom, so that for four years Northern England enjoyed continual Summer. Nor do we know why for thirty consecutive nights in May and June of 1345 every man, woman and child in the kingdom dreamt that they had been gathered together upon a dark red plain beneath a pale golden sky to build a tall black tower. Each night they laboured, waking in the morning in their own beds completely exhausted. The dream only ceased to trouble them when, on the thirtieth night, the tower and its fortifications were completed. In all these stories – but particularly in the last – we have a sense of great events going on, but what they might be we cannot tell. Several scholars have speculated that the tall black tower was situated in that part of Hell which USKGLASS was reputed to lease from LUCIFER and that USKGLASS was building a fortress in order to prosecute a war against his enemies in Hell. However, MARTIN PALE thought otherwise. He believed that there was a connexion between the construction of the tower and the appearance in England three years later of the Black Death. JOHN USKGLASS's kingdom of Northern England suffered a good deal less from the disease than its southern neighbour and PALE believed that this was because USKGLASS had constructed some sort of defence against it.

But according to the *Essay on the Extraordinary Revival of English Magic* we have no business even to wonder about such things. According to Mr NORRELL and Lord PORTISHEAD the Modern Magician ought not to meddle with things only half-understood. But *I* say that it is precisely because these things are only half-understood that we must study them.

English Magic is the strange house we magicians inhabit. It is built upon foundations that JOHN USKGLASS made and we ignore those foundations at our peril. They should be studied and their nature understood so that we can learn what they will support and what they will not. Otherwise cracks will appear, letting in winds from God-knows-where. The corridors will lead us to places we never intended to go.

In conclusion PORTISHEAD's book – though containing many excellent things – is a fine example of the mad contradiction at the heart of Modern English Magic: our foremost magicians continually declare their intention of erasing every hint and trace of JOHN USKGLASS from English Magic, but how is this even possible? It is JOHN USKGLASS's magic that we do.

# 39

# The two magicians

## February 1815

OF ALL THE CONTROVERSIAL pieces ever published in *The Edinburgh Review*, this was the most controversial by far. By the end of January there scarcely seemed to be an educated man or woman from one end of the country to the other who had not read it and formed an opinion upon it. Though it was unsigned, everyone knew who the author was – Strange. Oh, certainly at the beginning some people hesitated and pointed to the fact that Strange was as much criticized as Norrell – perhaps more. But these people were judged very stupid by their friends. Was not Jonathan Strange known to be precisely the sort of whimsical, contradictory person who *would* publish against himself? And did not the author declare himself to be a magician? Who else could it possibly be? Who else could speak with so much authority?

When Mr Norrell had first come to London, his opinions had seemed very new and not a little eccentric. But since then people had grown accustomed to them and he had seemed no more than the Mirror of the Times when he said that magic, like the oceans themselves, should agree to be governed by Englishmen. Its boundaries were to be drawn up and all that was not easily comprehensible to modern ladies and gentlemen – John Uskglass's three-hundred-year reign, the strange, uneasy history of our dealings with fairies – might be conveniently done away with. Now Strange had turned the Norrellite view of magic on its head. Suddenly it seemed that all that had been learnt in every English childhood of the wildness of English magic might still be true, and even now on some long-forgotten paths, behind the sky, on the other side of the rain, John Uskglass might be riding still, with his company of men and fairies.

Most people thought the partnership between the two magicians must be broken up. In London there was a rumour that Strange had been to Hanover-square and the servants had turned him away. And there was another, contradictory rumour to the effect that Strange had *not* been to Hanover-square, but that Mr Norrell was sitting night and day in his library, waiting for his pupil, pestering the servants every five minutes to go and look out of the window to see if he were coming.

On a Sunday evening in early February Strange did at last call upon Mr Norrell. This much was certain because two gentlemen on their way to St George's, Hanover-square saw him standing on the steps of the house; saw the door opened; saw Strange speak to the servant; and saw him instantly admitted as one who had been long expected. The two gentlemen continued on their way to church where they immediately told their friends in the neighbouring pews what they had seen. Five minutes later a thin, saintly-looking young man arrived at the church. Under the pretext of saying his prayers, he whispered that he had just spoken to someone who was leaning out of the first-floor window of the house next door to Mr Norrell's and this person believed he could hear Mr Strange ranting and haranguing his master. Two minutes later it was being reported throughout the church that both magicians had threatened each other with a kind of magical excommunication. The service began and several of the congregation were seen to gaze longingly at the windows, as if wondering why those apertures were always placed so high in ecclesiastical buildings. An anthem was sung to the accompaniment of the organ and some people said later that above the sound of the music they had heard great rolls of thunder – a sure sign of magical disturbances. But other people said that they had imagined it.

All of which would have greatly astonished the two magicians who were at that moment standing silently in Mr Norrell's library, regarding each other warily. Strange, who had not seen his tutor for some days, was shocked at his appearance. His face was haggard and his body shrunken – he looked ten years older.

"Shall we sit down, sir?" said Strange. He moved towards a chair and Mr Norrell flinched at the suddenness of the movement. It was almost as if he were expecting Strange to hit him. The next moment, however, he had recovered himself enough to sit down.

Strange was not much more comfortable. In the last few days he had asked himself over and over again if he had been right to publish the review, and repeatedly he had come to the conclusion that he had been. He had decided that the correct attitude to take was one of dignified moral superiority softened by a very moderate amount of apology. But now that he was actually sitting in Mr Norrell's library again, he did not find it easy to meet his tutor's eye. His gaze fixed itself upon an odd succession of objects – a small porcelain figure of Dr Martin Pale; the doorknob; his own thumbnail; Mr Norrell's left shoe.

Mr Norrell, on the other hand, never once took his eyes from Strange's face.

After several moments' silence both men spoke at once.

"After all your kindness to me . . ." began Strange.

"You think that I am angry," began Mr Norrell.

Both paused and then Strange indicated that Mr Norrell should continue.

"You think that I am angry," said Mr Norrell, "but I am not. You think I do not know why you have done what you have done, but I do. You think you have put all your heart into that writing and that every one in England now understands you. What do they understand? Nothing. I understood you before you wrote a word." He paused and his face worked as if he were struggling to say something that lay very deep inside him. "What you wrote, you wrote for me. For me alone."

Strange opened his mouth to protest at this surprizing conclusion. But upon consideration he realized it was probably true. He was silent.

Mr Norrell continued. "Do you really believe that I have never felt the same . . . the same *longing* you feel? *It is John Uskglass's magic that we do*. Of course it is. What else should it be? I tell you, there were times when I was young when I would have done any thing, endured any thing, to find him and throw myself at his feet. I tried to conjure him up – Ha! That was the act of a very young, very foolish man – to treat a king like a footman and summon him to come and talk to me. I consider it one of the most fortunate circumstances of my life that I was unsuccessful! Then I tried to find him using the old spells of election. I could not even make the spells work. All the magic of my youth was wasted in trying to find him. For ten years I thought of nothing else."

"You never said any of this before, sir."

Mr Norrell sighed. "I wished to prevent you from falling into my error." He raised his hands in a gesture of helplessness.

"But by your own account, Mr Norrell, this was long ago when you were young and inexperienced. You are a very different magician now, and I flatter myself that I am no ordinary assistant. Perhaps if we were to try again?"

"One cannot find so powerful a magician unless he wishes to be found," declared Mr Norrell, flatly. "It is useless to make the attempt. Do you think he cares what happens to England? I tell you he does not. He abandoned us long ago."

"Abandoned?" said Strange, frowning. "That is rather a harsh word. I suppose years of disappointment would naturally incline one towards a conclusion of that sort. But there are many accounts of people who saw John Uskglass long after he had supposedly left England. The glovemaker's child in Newcastle,[1]

[1] In the late seventeenth century there was a glovemaker in the King's city of Newcastle who had a daughter – a bold little thing. One day this child, whom everyone supposed to be playing in some corner of her father's house, was missed. Her mother and father and brothers searched for her. The neighbours searched, but she was nowhere to be found. Then in the late afternoon they looked up and saw her coming down the muddy, cobbled hill. Some of them thought for a moment that they saw someone beside her in the dark winter street, but she came on alone. She was quite unharmed and her story, when they had pieced it together, was this:

She had left her father's house to go wandering in the city and had quickly come upon a street she had never seen before. This street was wide and well-paved and led her straight up, higher than she had ever been before, to the gate and courtyard of a great stone house. She had gone into the house and looked into many rooms, but all were silent, empty, full of dust and spiders. On one side of the house there was a suite of rooms where the shadows of leaves fell ceaselessly over walls and floor as if there were summer trees outside the windows, but there were no trees (and it was, in any case, winter). One room contained nothing but a high mirror. Room and mirror seemed to have quarrelled at some time for the mirror shewed the room to be filled with birds but the room was empty. Yet the glovemaker's child could hear birdsong all around her. There was a long dark corridor with a sound of rushing water as if some dark sea or river lay at the end of it. From the windows of some rooms she saw the city of Newcastle, but from others she saw a different city entirely and others shewed only high, wild moors and a cold blue sky.

She saw many staircases winding up inside the house, great staircases at first, which grew rapidly narrower and more twisting as she mounted higher in the house, until at the top they were only such chinks and gaps in the masonry that a child might notice and a child could slip through. The last of these led to a little door of plain wood.

Having no reason to fear she pushed it open but what she found on the other side made her cry out. It seemed to her that a thousand, thousand birds thronged the air, so that there was neither daylight nor darkness but only a great confusion of black wings. A wind seemed to come to her from far away and she had the impression of immense space as if she had climbed up to the sky and found it full of ravens. The glovemaker's child began to be very much afraid, but then she heard someone say her name. Instantly the birds disappeared and she found herself in a small room with bare stone walls and a bare stone floor. There was no furniture of any kind but, seated upon the floor, was a man who beckoned to her and called her by her name again and told her not to be afraid. He had long, ragged black hair and strange, ragged black clothes. There was nothing about him that suggested a king and

the Yorkshire farmer,[2] the Basque sailor . . ."[3]

Mr Norrell made a small sound of irritation. "Hearsay and superstition! Even if those stories are true – which I am very far from allowing – I have never understood how any of them knew

---

[1] *cont'd* the only symbol of his magicianship was the great silver dish of water at his side. The glovemaker's daughter stayed by the man's side for some hours until dusk, when he led her down through the house into the city to her home.

[2] See Chapter 33, footnote 3.

[3] Perhaps the eeriest tale told of John Uskglass's return was that told by a Basque sailor, a survivor of the Spanish king's great Armada. After his ship was destroyed by storms on the far northern coasts of England, the sailor and two companions had fled inland. They dared not go near villages, but it was winter and the frost was thick upon the ground; they feared they would die of the cold. As night came on they found an empty stone building on a high hillside of bare frozen earth. It was almost dark inside, but there were openings high in the wall that let in starlight. They lay down upon the earth floor and slept.

The Basque sailor dreamt that there was a king who watched him.

He woke. Above him dim shafts of grey light pierced the winter dark. In the shadows at the farthest end of the building he thought he saw a raised stone dais. As the light grew he saw something upon the dais: a chair or throne. A man sat upon the throne; a pale man with long black hair, wrapped in a black robe. Terrified, the man woke his fellows and shewed them the uncanny sight of the man who sat upon the throne. He seemed to watch them but he never moved, not so much as a finger; yet it did not occur to them to doubt that he was a living man. They stumbled to the door and ran away across the frozen fields.

The Basque sailor soon lost his companions: one man died of cold and heartbreak within the week; the other, determined to try and make his way back to the Bay of Biscay, began to walk south, and what became of him no one knows. But the Basque sailor stayed in Cumbria and was taken in by some farm people. He became a servant at that same farm and married a young girl from a neighbouring farm. All his life he told the story of the stone barn upon the high hills, and he was taught by his new friends and neighbours to believe that the man upon the black throne was the Raven King. The Basque sailor never found the stone barn again, and neither did his friends nor any of his children.

And all his life whenever he went into dark places he said, "I greet thee, Lord, and bid thee welcome to my heart" – in case the pale king with the long black hair should be seated in the darkness waiting for him. Across the expanses of northern England a thousand, thousand darknesses, a thousand, thousand places for the King to be. "I greet thee, Lord, and bid thee welcome to my heart."

that the person they had seen was John Uskglass. No portraits of him exist. Two of your examples – the glovemaker's child and the Basque sailor – did not in fact identify him as Uskglass. They saw a man in black clothes and other people *told* them later that it was John Uskglass. But it is really of very little consequence whether or not he returned at this or that time or was seen by this or that person. The fact remains that when he abandoned his throne and rode out of England he took the best part of English magic with him. From that day forth it began to decline. Surely that is enough in itself to mark him as our enemy? You are familiar, I dare say, with Watershippe's *A Faire Wood Withering*?"[4]

"No, I do not know it," said Strange. He gave Mr Norrell a sharp look that seemed to say he had not read it for the usual reason. "But I cannot help wishing, sir, that you had said some of this before."

"Perhaps I have been wrong to keep so much of my mind from you," said Mr Norrell, knotting his fingers together. "I am almost certain now that I have been wrong. But I decided long ago that Great Britain's best interests were served by absolute silence on these subjects and old habits are hard to break. But surely you see the task before us, Mr Strange? Yours and mine? Magic cannot wait upon the pleasure of a King who no longer cares what happens to England. We must break English magicians of their dependence on him. We must make them forget John Uskglass as completely as he has forgotten us."

[4] *A Faire Wood Withering* (1444) by Peter Watershippe. This is a remarkably detailed description by a contemporary magician of how English magic declined after John Uskglass left England. In 1434 (the year of Uskglass's departure) Watershippe was twenty-five, a young man just beginning to practise magic in Norwich. *A Faire Wood Withering* contains precise accounts of spells which were perfectly practicable as long as Uskglass and his fairy subjects remained in England but which no longer had any effect after their departure. Indeed it is remarkable how much of our knowledge of *Aureate* English magic comes from Watershippe. *A Faire Wood Withering* seems an angry book until one compares it with two of Watershippe's later books: *A Defence of my Deeds Written while Wrongly Imprisoned by my Enemies in Newark Castle* (1459/60) and *Crimes of the False King* (written 1461?, published 1697, Penzance).

Strange shook his head, frowning. "No. In spite of all you say, it still seems to me that John Uskglass stands at the very heart of English magic and that we ignore him at our peril. Perhaps I will be proved wrong in the end. Nothing is more likely. But on a matter of such vital importance to English magic I need to understand for myself. Do not think that I am ungrateful, sir, but I believe the period of our collaboration is over. It seems to me that we are too different . . ."

"Oh!" cried Mr Norrell. "I know that in character . . ." He made a gesture of dismissal. "But what does that matter? We are magicians. That is the beginning and end of me and the beginning and the end of you. It is all that either of us cares about. If you leave this house today and pursue your own course, who will you talk to? – as we are talking now? –there is no one. You will be quite alone." In a tone almost of pleading, he whispered, "Do not do this!"

Strange stared in perplexity at his master. This was by no means what he had expected. Far from being driven into a passion of fury by Strange's review, Mr Norrell seemed only to have been provoked into an outburst of honesty and humility. At that moment it seemed to Strange both reasonable and desirable to return to Mr Norrell's tutelage. It was only pride and the consciousness that he was certain to feel differently in an hour or two which prompted him to say, "I am sorry, Mr Norrell, but ever since I returned from the Peninsula it has not felt right to me to call myself your pupil. I have felt as if I was acting a part. To submit my writings for your approval so that you can make changes in any way that you see fit – it is what I can no longer do. It is making me say what I no longer believe."

"All, all is to be done in public," sighed Mr Norrell. He leaned forward and said with more energy, "Be guided by me. Promise me that you will publish nothing, speak nothing, do nothing until you are quite decided upon these matters. Believe me when I tell you that ten, twenty, even fifty years of silence is worth the satisfaction of knowing at the end that you have said what you ought – no more, no less. Silence and inaction will not suit you – I know that. But I promise to make what amends I can. You will not lose by it. If you have ever had cause to consider me ungrateful, you shall not find me so in future. I shall tell everyone how highly I prize you. We shall no longer be tutor and pupil. Let it be a partnership of equals! Have I not in any case learnt almost as much from you as you have from me? The most lucrative business shall all be yours! The books . . ." He swallowed slightly. "The books which I ought to have lent you and which I have kept from you, you shall read them! We will go to Yorkshire, you and I together – tonight if you wish it! – and I will give you the key to the library and you shall read whatever you desire. I . . ." Mr Norrell passed his hand across his brow, as if in surprize at his own words. "I shall not even ask for a retraction of the review. Let it stand. Let it stand. And in time, you and I, together, will answer all the questions you raise in it."

There was a long silence. Mr Norrell watched the other magician's face eagerly. His offer to shew Strange the library at Hurtfew was not without effect. For some moments Strange was clearly wavering in his determination to part with his master, but at last he said, "I am honoured, sir. You are not usually a man for a compromise, I know. But I think I must follow my own course now. I think we must part."

Mr Norrell closed his eyes.

At that moment the door opened. Lucas and one of the other footmen entered with the tea-tray.

"Come, sir," said Strange.

He touched his master's arm to rouse him a little and England's only two magicians took tea together for the last time.

Strange left Hanover-square at half past eight. Several people, lingering by their downstairs windows, saw him go. Other people, who scorned to watch themselves, had sent their maids and footmen to stand about the square. Whether Lascelles had made some arrangement of this sort is not known, but ten minutes after Strange had turned the corner into Oxford-street Lascelles knocked upon Mr Norrell's door.

Mr Norrell was still in the library, still in the chair he had been sitting in when Strange had left. He was staring fixedly at the carpet.

"Is he gone?" asked Lascelles.

Mr Norrell did not answer.

Lascelles sat down. "Our conditions? How did he receive them?"

Still no reply.

"Mr Norrell? You told him what we agreed? You told him that unless he publishes a retraction we shall be forced to reveal what we know of the Black Magic done in Spain? You told him that under no circumstances would you accept him any longer as a pupil?"

"No," said Mr Norrell. "I said none of those things."

"But . . ."

Mr Norrell sighed deeply. "It does not matter what I said to him. He is gone."

Lascelles was silent a moment and looked with some displeasure at the magician. Mr Norrell, still lost in his own thoughts, did not observe this.

Finally, Lascelles shrugged. "You were right in the beginning, sir," he said. "There can be only one magician in England."

"What do you mean?"

"I mean that *two* of any thing is a most uncomfortable number. *One* may do as he pleases. *Six* may get along well enough. But *two* must always struggle for mastery. *Two* must always watch each other. The eyes of all the world will be on *two*, uncertain which of them to follow. You sigh, Mr Norrell. You know that I am right. Henceforth we must consider Strange in all our plans – what he will say, what he will do, how to counter him. You have often told me that he is a remarkable magician. His brilliance was a great advantage when it was employed in your service. But that is all over now. Sooner or later he is sure to turn his talents against you. We cannot begin to guard against him too soon. I am speaking quite literally. His genius for magic is so great and his materials so poor and the end of it will be that he comes to believe that all things are permitted to a magician – be they house-breaking, theft or deception." Lascelles leant forward. "I do not mean that he is so depraved as to steal from you at this moment, but if a day ever comes when he is in great need, then it will appear to his undisciplined mind that any breach of trust, any violation of private property is justified." He paused. "You have made provision against thieves at Hurtfew? Spells of concealment?"

"Spells of concealment would be no protection against Strange!" declared Mr Norrell, angrily. "They would only serve to attract his eye! It would bring him straight to my most precious volumes! No, no, you are right." He sighed. "Something more is needed here. I must think."

Two hours after Strange's departure Mr Norrell and Lascelles left Hanover-square in Mr Norrell's carriage. Three servants accompanied them and they had every appearance on embarking on a long journey.

The following day, Strange, as whimsical and contradictory as ever, was inclined to regret his break with Mr Norrell. Mr Norrell's prediction that he would never again have any one to talk to about magic continually presented itself to his mind. He had been rehearsing their conversation. He was almost certain that all Norrell's conclusions concerning John Uskglass were wrong. As a consequence of what Mr Norrell had said he had developed a great many new ideas about John Uskglass, and now he was suffering all the misery of having no one to tell them to.

In the absence of a more suitable listener he went and complained to Sir Walter Pole in Harley-street.

"Since last night I have thought of fifty things I ought to have said to him. Now I suppose I shall have to put them in an article or a review – which will not be published until April at the earliest – and then he will have to instruct Lascelles or Portishead to write a repudiation – which will not appear until June or July. Five or six months to know what he would say to me! It is a very cumbersome way of conducting an argument, particularly when you consider that until yesterday I could simply have walked to Hanover-square and asked him what he thought. And I am certain now to get no sight nor smell of the books which matter! How is a magician to exist without books? Let someone explain *that* to me. It is like asking a politician to achieve high office without the benefit of bribes or patronage."

Sir Walter took no offence at this peculiarly uncivil remark, but charitably made allowances for the irritation of Strange's spirits. As a schoolboy at Harrow he had been forced to study magical history (which he had loathed) and he now cast his mind back to discover if he remembered any thing which might be useful. He found that he did not remember much – as much, he thought wryly, as might half-fill a very small wine-glass.

He thought for a moment or two and at last offered the following. "It is my understanding that the Raven King learnt all there is to know of English magic without the aid of any books – since there were none at that time in England – and so perhaps you could do the same?"

Strange gave him a very cool look. "And it is *my* understanding that the Raven King was the favourite foster-child of King Auberon, which, among other trifles, secured him an excellent magical education and a large kingdom of his own. I suppose that I could take to loitering in out-of-the-way copses and mossy glades in the hopes of being adopted by some fairy royalty but I rather think that they might find me a little tall for the purpose."

Sir Walter laughed. "And what shall you do now, without Mr Norrell to fill your days for you? Shall I tell Robson at the Foreign

Office to send you some magic to do? Only last week he was complaining that he is obliged to wait until all the work for the Admiralty and the Treasury is done before Mr Norrell has any time to spare for him."

"By all means. But tell him it cannot be for two or three months. We are going home to Shropshire. Both Arabella and I have a great desire to be in our own country and now that we need not consult the convenience of Mr Norrell, nothing remains to prevent our going."

"Oh!" said Sir Walter. "But you are not going immediately?"

"In two days' time."

"So soon?"

"Do not look so stricken! Really, Pole, I had no idea you were so fond of my company!"

"I am not. I was thinking of Lady Pole. It will be a sad change for her. She will miss her friend."

"Oh! Oh, yes!" said Strange, a little discomfited. "Of course!"

Later that morning Arabella made her parting visit to Lady Pole. Five years had made very little difference to her ladyship's beauty and none at all to her sad condition. She was as silent as ever and as indifferent to every pain or pleasure. Kindness or coldness left her equally unmoved. She passed her days sitting by the window in the Venetian drawing-room in the house in Harley-street. She never exhibited the least inclination for any occupation and Arabella was her only visitor.

"I wish you were not going," said her ladyship, when Arabella told her the news. "What sort of a place is Shropshire?"

"Oh! I fear I am a very partial judge. I believe that most people would agree that it is a pretty place with green hills and woods and sweet country lanes. Of course we shall have to wait for spring to enjoy it completely. But even in winter the views can be very striking. It is a peculiarly romantic county with a noble history. There are ruined castles and stones planted on the hilltops by who-knows-what people – and being so close to Wales it has often been fought over – there are ancient battlefields in almost every valley."

"Battlefields!" said Lady Pole. "I know only too well what that is like. To glance out of a window and see nothing but broken bones and rusting armour everywhere one looks! It is a very melancholy sight. I hope you will not find it too distressing."

"Broken bones and armour?" echoed Arabella. "No, indeed. Your ladyship misunderstands me. The battles were all long ago. There is nothing to see – certainly nothing to distress one."

"And yet, you know," continued Lady Pole, scarcely attending to her, "battles have been fought at some time or other almost everywhere. I remember learning in my schoolroom how London was once the scene of a particularly fierce battle. The people were put to death in horrible ways and the city was burnt to the ground. We are surrounded by the shadows of violence and misery all the days of our life and it seems to me that it matters very little whether any material sign remains or not."

Something changed in the room. It was as if cold, grey, beating wings had passed over their heads or as if someone had walked through the mirrors and cast a shadow into the room. It was an odd trick of the light which Arabella had often observed when she sat with Lady Pole. Not knowing what else to attribute it to, she supposed it must be because there were so many mirrors in the room.

Lady Pole shivered and pulled her shawl tighter round her. Arabella leaned forward and took her hand. "Come! Fix your thoughts upon more cheerful objects."

Lady Pole looked at her blankly. She had no more idea how to be cheerful than to fly.

So Arabella began to talk, hoping to distract her for a time from thinking of horrors. She spoke of new shops and new fashions. She described a very pretty ivory-coloured sarsenet she had seen in a window in Friday-street and a trimming of turquoise-coloured bugle beads she had seen somewhere else which would match the ivory sarsenet beautifully. She went on to relate what her dressmaker had said about bugle beads, and then to describe an extraordinary plant that the dressmaker possessed which stood in a pot on a little iron balcony outside the window and which had grown so tall in the space of a year that it had entirely blocked up a window on the floor above belonging to a candlestick-maker. Next came other surprizingly tall plants – Jack and his beanstalk – the giant at the top of the beanstalk – giants and giant-killers in general – Napoleon Buonaparte and the Duke of Wellington – the Duke's merits in every sphere of life except in one – the great unhappiness of the Duchess.

"Happily, it is what you and I have never known any thing of," she finished up, a little breathless, "to have one's peace continually cut up by the sight of one's husband paying attentions to other women."

"I suppose so," answered Lady Pole, somewhat doubtfully.

This annoyed Arabella. She tried to make allowances for all Lady Pole's oddities, but she found it rather hard to forgive her her habitual coolness towards her husband. Arabella could not visit at Harley-street as often as she did without being aware of how very devoted Sir Walter was to Lady Pole. If he ever thought that any thing might bring her pleasure or ease her sufferings in the slightest, then that thing was done in an instant, and Arabella could never observe without a pang the very meagre return he got for his pains. It was not that Lady Pole shewed any dislike towards him; but sometimes she scarcely seemed to know that he was there.

"Oh! But you do not consider what a blessing it is," said Arabella. "One of the best blessings of existence."

"What is?"

"Your husband's love."

Lady Pole looked surprized. "Yes, he does love me," she said at last. "Or at least he tells me that he does. But what good is that to me? It has never warmed me when I was cold – and I always am cold, you know. It has never shortened a long, dreary ball by so much as a minute or stopped a procession through long, dark, ghostly corridors. It has never saved me from any misery at all. Has the love of your husband ever saved you from any thing?"

"Mr Strange?" smiled Arabella. "No, never. I am more in the habit of saving him! I mean," she added quickly, since it was clear that Lady Pole did not understand her, "that he often meets with people who wish him to do magic on their behalf. – Or they have a great-nephew who wishes to learn magic from him. – Or they believe they have discovered a magic shoe or fork or some such nonsense. They mean no harm. Indeed they are generally most respectful. But Mr Strange is not the most patient of men and so I am obliged to go in and rescue him before he says something that he had much better not."

It was time for Arabella to be thinking of leaving and she began upon her goodbyes. Now that they might not meet again for many months she was particularly anxious to say something cheerful. "And I hope, my dear Lady Pole," she said, "that when you and I next meet you will be a great deal better and perhaps able to go out into society again. It is my dearest wish that one day we shall see each other at a theatre or in a ballroom . . ."

"A ballroom!" exclaimed Lady Pole in horror. "What in the world should make you say that? God forbid that you and I should ever meet in a ballroom!"

"Hush! Hush! I never meant to distress you. I forgot how you hate dancing. Come, do not weep! Do not think of it, if it makes you unhappy!"

She did her best to soothe her friend. She embraced her, kissed her cheek and her hair, stroked her hand, offered her lavender-water. Nothing did any good. For several minutes Lady Pole was entirely given over to a fit of weeping. Arabella could not quite understand what the matter was. But then again, what understanding could there be? It was part of her ladyship's complaint to be put in a fright by trifles, to be made unhappy by nothing at all. Arabella rang the bell to summon the maid.

Only when the maid appeared, did her ladyship at last make an effort to compose herself. "You do not understand what you have said!" she cried. "And God forbid that you should ever find out as I have. I shall try to warn you – I know it is hopeless, but I shall try! Listen to me, my dear, dear Mrs Strange. Listen as if your hopes of eternal salvation depended upon it!"

So Arabella looked as attentive as she possibly could.

But it was all to no end. This occasion proved no different from any other when her ladyship had claimed to have something of great importance to communicate to Arabella. She looked pale, took several deep breaths – and then proceeded to relate a very odd story about the owner of a Derbyshire leadmine who fell in love with a milkmaid. The milkmaid was everything the mine-owner had ever hoped for, except that her reflection always came several minutes too late into a mirror, her eyes changed colour at sunset and her shadow was often seen dancing wild dances when she herself was still.

After Lady Pole had gone upstairs, Arabella sat alone. "How stupid of me!" she thought. "When I know very well that any mention of dancing distresses her beyond measure! How can I have been so unguarded? I wonder what it was that she wished to tell me? I wonder if she knows herself? Poor thing! Without the blessing of health and reason, riches and beauty are worthless indeed!"

She was moralizing to herself in this strain, when a slight noise behind her caused her to look round. Immediately she rose from her seat and walked rapidly towards the door with hands outstretched.

"It is you! How glad I am to see you! Come! Shake hands with me. This will be our last meeting for a long time."

That evening she said to Strange, "One person at least is delighted that you have turned your attention to the study of John Uskglass and his fairy-subjects."

"Oh? And who is that?"
"The gentleman with the thistle-down hair."
"Who?"
"The gentleman who lives with Sir Walter and Lady Pole. I told you before."
"Oh, yes! I remember." There was a silence of some moments while Strange considered this. "Arabella!" he suddenly exclaimed. "Do you mean to tell me that you have still not learnt his name?" He began to laugh.
Arabella looked annoyed. "It is not my fault," she said. "He has never said his name and I have never remembered to ask him. But I am glad you take it so lightly. I thought at one time that you were inclined to be jealous."
"I do not remember that I was."
"How odd! I remember it quite distinctly."
"I beg your pardon, Arabella, but it is difficult to be jealous of a man whose acquaintance you made a number of years ago and whose name you have yet to discover. So he approves of my work, does he?"
"Yes, he has often told me that you will never get anywhere until you begin to study fairies. He says that that is what true magic is – the study of fairies and fairy magic."
"Indeed? He seems to have very decided views upon the subject! And what, pray, does he know about it? Is he a magician?"
"I do not think so. He once declared that he had never read a book upon the subject in his life."
"Oh! He is one of those, is he?" said Strange, contemptuously. "He has not studied the subject at all, but has managed to devise a great many theories about it. I meet with that sort very often. Well, if he is not a magician, what is he? Can you at least tell me that?"
"I think I can," said Arabella in the pleased manner of someone who has made a very clever discovery.
Strange sat expectantly.

"No," said Arabella, "I will not tell you. You will only laugh at me again."

"Probably."

"Well, then," said Arabella after a moment, "I believe he is a prince. Or a king. He is certainly of royal blood."

"What in the world should make you think that?"

"Because he has told me a great deal of his kingdoms and his castles and his mansions – though I confess they all have very odd names and I never heard of a single one before. I think he must be one of the princes that Buonaparte deposed in Germany or Swisserland."

"Indeed?" said Strange, with some irritation. "Well, now that Buonaparte has been defeated, perhaps he would like to go home again."

None of these half-explanations and guesses concerning the gentleman with the thistle-down hair quite satisfied him and he continued to wonder about Arabella's friend. The following day (which was to be the Stranges' last in London) he walked to Sir Walter's office in Whitehall with the express intention of discovering who the fellow was.

But when Strange arrived, he found only Sir Walter's private secretary hard at work.

"Oh! Moorcock! Good morning! Has Sir Walter gone?"

"He has just gone to Fife House,[5] Mr Strange. Is there any thing I can do for you?"

"No, I do not . . . Well, perhaps. There is something I always mean to ask Sir Walter and I never remember. I don't suppose that you are at all acquainted with the gentleman who lives at his house?"

"Whose house, sir?"

"Sir Walter's."

Mr Moorcock frowned. "A gentleman at Sir Walter's house? I cannot think whom you mean. What is his name?"

---

[5] Lord Liverpool's London home, a quaint, old, rambling mansion which stood by the Thames.

"That is what I wish to know. I have never seen the fellow, but Mrs Strange always seems to meet him the moment she steps out of the house. She has known him for years yet she has never been able to discover his name. He must be a very eccentric sort of person to make such a secret of it. Mrs Strange always calls him the gentleman with the silvery nose or the gentleman with the snow-white complexion. Or some odd name of that sort."

But Mr Moorcock only looked even more bewildered at this information. "I am very sorry, sir. I do not think I can ever have seen him."

# 40

## "Depend upon it; there is no such place."

### June 1815

The emperor Napoleon Buonaparte had been banished to the island of Elba. However His Imperial Majesty had some doubts whether a quiet island life would suit him – he was, after all, accustomed to governing a large proportion of the known world. And so before he left France he told several people that when violets bloomed again in spring he would return. This promise he kept.

The moment he arrived upon French soil he gathered an army and marched north to Paris in further pursuit of his destiny, which was to make war upon all the peoples of the world. Naturally he was eager to re-establish himself as *Emperor*, but it was not yet known where he would chuse to be Emperor *of*. He had always yearned to emulate Alexander the Great and so it was thought that he might go east. He had invaded Egypt once before and had some success there. Or he might go west: there were rumours of a fleet of ships at Cherbourg ready and waiting to take him to America to begin the conquest of a fresh, new world.

But wherever he chose, everyone agreed that he was sure to begin by invading Belgium and so the Duke of Wellington went to Brussels to await the arrival of Europe's Great Enemy.

The English newspapers were full of rumours: Buonaparte had assembled his army; he was advancing with appalling swiftness upon Belgium; he was there; he was victorious! Then the next day it would appear that he was still in his palace in Paris, never having stirred from there in the first place.

At the end of May, Jonathan Strange followed Wellington and the Army to Brussels. He had spent the past three months quietly in Shropshire thinking about magic and so it was hardly surprizing that he should feel a little bewildered at first. However after he had walked about for an hour or two he came to the conclusion that the fault was not in him, but in Brussels itself. He knew what a city at war looked like, and this was not it. There ought to have been companies of soldiers passing up and down, carts with supplies, anxious-looking faces. Instead he saw fashionable-looking shops and ladies lounging in smart carriages. True, there were groups of officers everywhere, but none of them appeared to have any idea of pursuing military business (one was expending a great deal of concentration and effort in mending a toy parasol for a little girl). There was a great deal more laughter and gaiety than seemed quite consistent with an imminent invasion by Napoleon Buonaparte.

A voice called out his name. He turned and found Colonel Manningham, an acquaintance of his, who immediately invited Strange to go with him to Lady Charlotte Greville's house. (This was an English lady who was living in Brussels.) Strange protested that he had no invitation and anyway he ought to go and look for the Duke. But Manningham declared that the lack of an invitation could not possibly matter – he was sure to be welcome – and the Duke was just as likely to be in Lady Charlotte Greville's drawing-room as anywhere else.

Ten minutes later Strange found himself in a luxurious apartment filled with people, many of whom he already knew. There were officers; beautiful ladies; fashionable gentlemen; British politicians; and representatives, so it seemed, of every rank and degree of British peer. All of them were loudly discussing the war and making jokes about it. It was quite a new idea to Strange:

war as a fashionable amusement. In Spain and Portugal it had been customary for the soldiers to regard themselves as martyred, maligned and forgotten. Reports in the British newspapers had always endeavoured to make the situation sound as gloomy as possible. But here in Brussels it was the noblest thing in the world to be one of his Grace's officers – and the second noblest to be his Grace's magician.

"Does Wellington really want all these people here?" whispered Strange to Manningham in amazement. "What will happen if the French attack? I wish I had not come. Someone is sure to begin asking me about my disagreement with Norrell, and I really do not want to talk about it."

"Nonsense!" Manningham whispered back. "No one cares about that here! And anyway here is the Duke!"

There was a little bustle and the Duke appeared. "Ah, Merlin!" he cried as his eye lighted upon Strange. "I am very glad to see you! Shake hands with me! You are acquainted with the Duke of Richmond, of course. No? Then allow me to make the introduction!"

If the assembly had been lively before, how much more spirited it became now his Grace was here! All eyes turned in his direction to discover whom he was talking to and (more interesting still) whom he was flirting with. One would not have supposed to look at him that he had come to Brussels for any other reason than to enjoy himself. But every time Strange tried to move away, the Duke fixed him with a look, as if to say, "No, *you* must stay. I have need of you!" Eventually, still smiling, he inclined his head and murmured in Strange's ear, "There, I believe that will do. Come! There is a conservatory at the other end of the room. We will be out of the crowd there."

They took their seats amid the palms and other exotic plants.

"A word of warning," said the Duke. "This is not Spain. In Spain the French were the detested enemy of every man, woman and child in the country. But here matters stand quite differently.

Buonaparte has friends in every street and in a great many parts of the Army. The city is full of spies. And so it is our job – yours and mine – to look as if nothing in the world were more certain than his defeat! Smile, Merlin! Take some tea. It will steady your nerves."

Strange tried a careless smile, but it immediately turned itself into an anxious frown and so, to draw his Grace's attention away from the deficiencies of his face, he inquired how his Grace liked the Army.

"Oh! It is a bad army at best. The most miscellaneous Army I ever commanded. British, Belgians, Dutch and Germans all mixed up together. It is like trying to build a wall out of half a dozen materials. Each material may be excellent in its way, but one cannot help wondering if the thing will hold together. But the Prussian Army has promised to fight with us. And Blücher is an excellent old fellow. Loves a fight." (This was the Prussian General.) "Unfortunately, he is also mad. He believes he is pregnant."

"Ah!"

"With a baby elephant."

"Ah!"

"But we must put you to work straightaway! Have you your books? Your silver dish? A place to work? I have a strong presentiment that Buonaparte will appear first in the west, from the direction of Lille. It is certainly the way I would chuse and I have letters from our friends in that city assuring me that he is hourly expected there. That is your task. Watch the western border for signs of his approach and tell me the instant you catch a glimpse of French troops."

For the next fortnight Strange summoned up visions of places where the Duke thought the French might appear. The Duke provided him with two things to help him: a large map and a young officer called William Hadley-Bright.

Hadley-Bright was one of those happy men for whom Fortune reserves her choicest gifts. Everything came easily to him. He was the adored only child of a rich widow. He had wanted a military career; his friends had got him a commission in a fashionable regiment. He had wanted excitement and adventure; the Duke of Wellington had chosen him to be one of his *aides-de-camp*. Then, just as he had decided that the one thing he loved more than soldiering was English magic, the Duke had appointed him to assist the sublime and mysterious Jonathan Strange. But only persons of a particularly sour disposition could resent Hadley-Bright's success; everyone else was disarmed by his cheerfulness and good nature.

Day after day Strange and Hadley-Bright examined ancient fortified cities in the west of Belgium; they peered at dull village streets; they watched vast, empty vistas of fields beneath even vaster prospects of watercolour clouds. But the French did not appear.

On a hot, sticky day in the middle of June they were seated at this interminable task. It was about three o'clock. The waiter had neglected to remove some dirty coffee-cups and a fly buzzed around them. From the open window came the mingled odours of horse-sweat, peaches and sour milk. Hadley-Bright, perched on a dining-chair, was demonstrating to perfection one of the most important skills of a soldier – that of falling asleep under any circumstances and at any time.

Strange glanced at his map and chose a spot at random. In the water of his silver dish a quiet crossroads appeared; nearby was a farm and two or three houses. He watched for a moment. Nothing happened. His eyes closed and he was on the point of dozing off when some soldiers dragged a gun into position beneath some elm-trees. They had a rather businesslike air. He kicked Hadley-Bright to wake him up. "Who are those fellows?" he asked.

Hadley-Bright blinked at the silver dish.

The soldiers at the crossroads wore green coats with red facings. There suddenly seemed to be a great many of them.

"Nassauers," said Hadley-Bright, naming some of Wellington's

German troops. "The Prince of Orange's boys. Nothing to worry about. What are you looking at?"

"A crossroads twenty miles south of the city. A place called Quatre Bras."

"Oh! There is no need to spend time on that!" declared Hadley-Bright with a yawn. "That is on the road to Charleroi. The Prussian Army is at the other end of it – or so I am told. I wonder if those fellows are supposed to be there?" He began to leaf through some papers describing the disposition of the various Allied armies. "No, I really don't think . . ."

"And what is *that*?" interrupted Strange, pointing at a soldier in a blue coat who had appeared suddenly over the opposite rise with his musket at the ready.

There was the merest pause. "A Frenchman," said Hadley-Bright.

"Is *he* supposed to be there?" asked Strange.

The one Frenchman had been joined by another. Then fifty more appeared. The fifty became two hundred – three hundred – a thousand! The hillside seemed to be breeding Frenchmen as a cheese breeds maggots. The next moment they all began to discharge their muskets upon the Nassauers at the crossroads. The engagement did not last long. The Nassauers fired their cannons. The Frenchmen, who appeared to have no cannons of their own, retreated over the hill.

"Ha!" cried Strange, delighted. "They are beaten! They have run away!"

"Yes, but where did they come from in the first place," muttered Hadley-Bright. "Can you look over that hill?"

Strange tapped the water and made a sort of twisting gesture above the surface. The crossroads vanished and in its place appeared an excellent view of the French Army – or, if not the whole Army, a very substantial part of it.

Hadley-Bright sat down like a marionette whose strings have been cut. Strange swore in Spanish (a language he naturally associated with warfare). The Allied armies were in entirely the wrong place. Wellington's divisions were in the west, ready to defend to the death all sorts of places that Buonaparte had no intention of attacking. General Blücher and the Prussian army were too far east. And here was the French Army suddenly popping up in the south. As matters stood at present, these Nassauers (who amounted to perhaps three or four thousand men) were all that lay between Brussels and the French.

"Mr Strange! Do something, I implore you!" cried Hadley-Bright.

Strange took a deep breath and opened wide his arms, as though he were gathering up all the magic he had ever learnt.

"Hurry, Mr Strange! Hurry!"

"I could move the city!" said Strange. "I could move Brussels! I could put it somewhere where the French will not find it."

"Put it where?" cried Hadley-Bright, grabbing Strange's hands and forcing them down again. "We are surrounded by armies. Our own armies! If you move Brussels you are liable to crush some of our regiments under the buildings and the paving stones. The Duke will not be pleased. He needs every man."

Strange thought some more. "I have it!" he cried.

A sort of breeze rushed by. It was not unpleasant – indeed it had the refreshing fragrance of the ocean. Hadley-Bright looked out of the windows. Beyond the houses, churches, palaces and parks were mountain-ridges that had not been there a moment ago. They were black, as if covered with pine trees. The air was much fresher – like air that had never been breathed before.

"Where are we?" asked Hadley-Bright.

"America," said Strange. And then by way of an explanation he added, "It always looks so empty on the maps."

"Dear God! But this is no better than before! Have you forgotten that we have only just signed a peace treaty with America? Nothing will excite the Americans' displeasure so much as the appearance of a European city on their soil!"

"Oh, probably! But there is no need for concern, I assure you. We are a long way from Washington or New Orleans or any of those places where the battles were. Hundreds of miles I expect. At least . . . That is to say I am not sure where exactly. Do you think it matters?"[1]

[1] The citizens of Brussels and the various armies occupying the city were intrigued to learn that they were now situated in a far-away country. Unfortunately they were much occupied in preparing for the coming battle (or in the case of the richer and more frivolous part of the population in preparing for the Duchess of Richmond's ball that evening) and hardly any one had leisure just then to go and discover what the country was like or who its inhabitants were. Consequently for a long time it was unclear where precisely Strange had put Brussels on that June afternoon.

In 1830 a trader and trapper named Pearson Denby was travelling through the Plains country. He was approached by a Lakota chief of his acquaintance, Man-afraid-of-the-Water. Man-afraid-of-the-Water asked if Denby could acquire for him some black lightning balls. Man-afraid-of-the-Water explained that he was intending to make war upon his enemies and had urgent need of the balls. He said that at one time he had had about fifty of the balls and he had always used them sparingly, but now they were all gone. Denby did not understand. He asked if Man-afraid-of-the-Water meant ammunition. No, said Man-afraid-of-the-Water. Like ammunition, but much bigger. He took Denby back to his camp and showed him a brass 5½–inch howitzer made by the Carron Company of Falkirk in Scotland. Denby was astonished and asked how Man-afraid-of-the-Water had acquired the gun in the first place. Man-afraid-of-the-Water explained that in some nearby hills lived a tribe called the Half-Finished People. They had been created very suddenly one summer, but their Creator had only given them one of the skills men need to live: that of fighting. All other skills they lacked; they did not know how to hunt buffalo or antelope, how to tame horses or how to make houses for themselves. They could not even understand each other since their crazy Creator had given them four or five different languages. But they had had this gun, which they had traded to Man-afraid-of-the-Water in exchange for food.

Intrigued, Denby sought out the tribe of Half-Finished People. At first they seemed like any other tribe, but then Denby noticed that the older men had an oddly European look and some of them spoke English. Some of their customs were the same as the Lakota tribes' but others seemed to be founded upon European military practice. Their language was like Lakota but contained a great many English, Dutch and German words.

A man called Robert Heath (otherwise Little-man-talks-too-much) told Denby that they had all deserted from several different armies and regiments on the afternoon of 15th June 1815 because a great battle was going to be fought the next day and they had all had a strong presentiment that they would die if they remained. Did Denby know if the Duke of Wellington or Napoleon Buonaparte was now King of France? Denby could not say. "Well, sir," said Heath philosophically, "Whichever of 'em it is, I dare say life goes on just the same for the likes of you and me."

Hadley-Bright dashed outside to find the Duke and tell him that, contrary to what he might have supposed, the French were now in Belgium, but he, the Duke, was not.

His Grace (who happened to be taking tea with some British politicians and Belgian countesses) received the news in his customary imperturbable fashion. But half an hour later he appeared in Strange's hotel with the Quartermaster General, Colonel De Lancey. He stared down at the vision in the silver dish with a grim expression. "Napoleon has humbugged me, by God!" he exclaimed. "De Lancey, you must write the orders as quickly as you can. We must gather the Army at Quatre Bras."

Poor Colonel De Lancey looked most alarmed. "But how do we deliver the orders to the officers with all the Atlantic between us?" he asked.

"Oh," said his Grace, "Mr Strange will take care of that." His eye was caught by something outside the window. Four horsemen were passing by. They had the bearing of kings and the expressions of emperors. Their skin was the colour of mahogany; their long hair was the shiny jet-black of a raven's wing. They were dressed in skins decorated with porcupine quills. Each was equipped with a rifle in a leather case, a fearsome-looking spear (as feathered as their heads) and a bow. "Oh, and De Lancey! Find someone to ask those fellows if they would like to fight tomorrow, would you? They look as if they could do the business."

An hour or so later, in the town of Ath twenty miles from Brussels (or, rather, twenty miles from where Brussels usually stood) a *pâtissier* took a batch of little cakes from the oven. After the cakes had cooled he drew a letter upon each one in pink icing – a thing he had never in his life done before. His wife (who knew not a word of English) laid the cakes in a wooden tray and gave the tray to the *sous-pâtissier*. The *sous-pâtissier* carried it to the Headquarters of the Allied Army in the town, where Sir Henry Clinton was issuing orders to his officers. The *sous-pâtissier* presented the cakes to Sir Henry. Sir Henry took one and was about to carry it to his mouth when Major Norcott of the 95th Rifles gave a cry of surprize. There in front of them, written in pink icing on little cakes, was a dispatch from Wellington instructing Sir Henry to move the 2nd Division of Infantry towards Quatre Bras with as little delay as possible. Sir Henry looked up in amazement. The *sous-pâtissier* beamed at him.

At about the same time the general in charge of the 3rd Division – a Hanoverian gentleman called Sir Charles Alten – was hard at work in a château twenty-five miles south-west of Brussels. He happened to look out of the window and observed a very small and oddly behaved rainstorm in the courtyard. It shed its rain in the centre of the courtyard and touched the walls not at all. Sir Charles was curious enough to go outside and look more closely. There, written in the dust with raindrops, was the following missive:

*Bruxelles, 15th June, 1815*

*The 3rd Division to move upon Quatre Bras immediately.*

*Wellington*

Meanwhile some Dutch and Belgian generals in Wellington's Army had discovered for themselves that the French were at Quatre Bras and were on their way there with the 2nd Netherlands Division. Consequently these generals (whose names were Rebecq and Perponcher) were more annoyed than enlightened when a great mass of songbirds alighted in the trees all around and began to sing:

*The Duke's ideas let us expound*
*At Quatre Bras the French are found*
*All his troops must gather round*
*To the crossroads all are bound*

"Yes, yes! We know!" cried General Perponcher, gesturing at the birds to shoo them away. "Be off, d— you!" But the birds only flew closer and some actually settled upon his shoulders and horse. They continued singing in the most officious manner possible:

*There reputations will be made*
*The Duke commands: be not afraid!*
*All the army's plans are laid*
*Go quickly now with your brigade!*

The birds accompanied the soldiers for all the remainder of the day, never ceasing for a moment to twitter and cheep the same aggravating song. General Rebecq – whose English was excellent – managed to catch hold of one of them and tried to teach it a new song, in the hopes that it might return to Jonathan Strange and sing it to him:

*The Duke's magician must be kicked*
*From Bruxelles to Maastricht*
*For playing tricks on honest men*
*To Maastricht and back again*[2]

At six o'clock Strange returned Brussels to European soil. Immediately those regiments which had been quartered inside the city marched out of the Namur Gate and down the road that led to Quatre Bras. That done, Strange was able to make his own preparations for war. He collected together his silver dish; half a dozen books of magic; a pair of pistols; a light summer coat with a number of unusually deep pockets; a dozen hard-boiled eggs; three flasks of brandy; some pieces of pork pie wrapped in paper; and a very large silk umbrella.

The next morning, with these necessaries stowed in various

[2] General Rebecq also made up a Dutch version of his jingle which was sung by his soldiers on the way to Quatre Bras. They taught it to their English comrades and it later became a child's skipping rhyme, both in England and the Netherlands.

places about his person and his horse, he rode with the Duke and his staff up to the crossroads at Quatre Bras. Several thousand Allied troops were assembled there now, but the French had yet to shew themselves. From time to time there was the sound of a musket, but it was scarcely more than you would hear in any English wood where gentlemen are shooting.

Strange was looking about him when a songthrush alighted upon his shoulder and began to chirrup:

*The Duke's ideas let us expound*
*At Quatre Bras the French are found . . .*

"What?" muttered Strange. "What are you doing here? You were supposed to have disappeared hours ago!" He made Ormskirk's sign to disperse a magic spell and the bird flew off. In fact, rather to his consternation, a whole flock of birds took flight at the same moment. He glanced round nervously to see if any one had noticed that he had bungled the magic; but everyone seemed busy with military concerns and he concluded they had not.

He found a position to his liking – in a ditch directly in front of Quatre Bras farmhouse. The crossroads was on his immediate right and the 92nd Foot, the Highland Regiment were on his left. He took the hard-boiled eggs out of his pockets and gave them to such of the Highlanders as thought they might like to eat them. (In peacetime some sort of introduction is generally required to make a person's acquaintance; in war a small eatable will perform the same office.) The Highlanders gave him some sweet, milky tea in return and soon they were chatting very companionably together.

The day was intensely hot. The road went down between the fields of rye, which seemed, under that bright sun, to glow with an almost supernatural brilliance. Three miles away the Prussian Army had already engaged with the French and there were faint sounds of guns booming and men shouting, like the ghosts of things to come. Just before noon drums and fierce singing were heard in the distance. The ground began to shake with the stamping of tens of thousands of feet, and through the rye towards them came the thick, dark columns of French infantry.

The Duke had given Strange no particular orders and so, when the fighting began, he set about performing all the magic he used to do on Spanish battlefields. He sent fiery angels to menace the French and dragons to breathe flames over them. These illusions were larger and brighter than any thing he had managed in Spain. Several times he climbed out of the ditch to admire the effect – in spite of the warnings of the Highlanders that he was liable to be shot at any moment.

He had been diligently casting such spells for three or four hours when something happened. Out on the battlefield, a sudden assault by the French Chasseurs threatened to envelop the Duke and his staff. These gentlemen were obliged to wheel round and ride pell-mell back to the Allied lines. The nearest troops happened to be the 92nd Foot.

"92nd!" cried the Duke. "Lie down!"

The Highlanders immediately lay down. Strange looked up from the ditch to see the Duke upon Copenhagen[3] skimming over their heads. His Grace was quite unharmed and indeed appeared more invigorated than alarmed by his adventure. He looked around to see what everyone was doing. His eye alighted upon Strange.

"Mr Strange! What are you doing? When I want a display of Vauxhall-Gardens magic I shall ask for it![4] The French saw plenty of this sort of thing in Spain – they are not in the least disturbed by it. But it is entirely new to the Belgians, Dutch and Germans in *my*

---

[3] Copenhagen, the Duke's famous chestnut horse, 1808–36.

[4] In 1810 Messrs George and Jonathan Barratt, the proprietors of Vauxhall Gardens, had offered Strange and Norrell a vast sum of money to stage displays of magic every night in the gardens. The magic which the Barratts were proposing was of exactly this sort – illusions of magical creatures, famous persons from the Bible and history etc., etc. Naturally enough, Mr Norrell had refused.

Army. I have just seen one of your dragons menace a company of Brunswickers in that wood. Four of them fell over. It will not do, Mr Strange! It simply will not do!" He galloped off.

Strange stared after him. He had half a mind to make some pointed remarks about the Duke's ingratitude to his friends, the Highlanders; but they seemed a little busy at the moment, being shot at by cannons and hacked at by sabres. So he picked up his map, climbed out of the ditch and made his way to the crossroads where the Duke's military secretary, Lord Fitzroy Somerset, was looking about him with an anxious air.

"My lord?" said Strange. "I need to ask you something. How is the battle going?"

Somerset sighed. "All will be well in the end. Of course it will. But half the Army is not here yet. We have scarcely any cavalry to speak of. I know you sent the divisions their orders very promptly but some of them were simply too far away. If the French get reinforcements before we get ours, then . . ." He shrugged.

"And if French reinforcements do come, which direction will they come from? The south, I suppose?"

"The south and south-east."

Strange did not return to the battle. Instead, he walked to Quatre Bras farm, just behind the British lines. The farm was quite deserted. Doors stood open; curtains billowed out of windows; a scythe and hoe had been thrown down in the dust in the haste to get away. In the milk-smelling gloom of the dairy he found a cat with some newborn kittens. Whenever the guns sounded (which was often) the cat trembled. He fetched her some water and spoke to her gently. Then he sat down upon the cool flagstones and placed his map before him.

He began to move the roads, lanes and villages to the south and east of the battlefield. First he changed the positions of two villages. Then he made all the roads that went east to west, run north to south. He waited ten minutes and then he put it all back the way it was. He made all the woods in the vicinity turn round and face the other way. Next he made the brooks flow in the wrong direction. Hour after hour he continued to change the landscape. It was intricate, tedious work – quite as dull as any thing he had done with Norrell. At half-past six he heard the Allied bugles sound the advance. At eight o'clock he stood up and stretched his cramped limbs. "Well," he remarked to the cat, "I have not the least idea whether that achieved any thing or not."[5]

Black smoke hung over the fields. Those dismal attendants of any battle, the crows and ravens, had arrived in their hundreds. Strange found his friends, the Highlanders, in a most forlorn condition. They had captured a house next to the road, but in doing so they had lost half their men and twenty-five of their thirty-six officers, including their colonel – a man whom many of them had regarded as a father. More than one grizzled-looking veteran was sitting with his head in his hands, weeping.

The French had apparently returned to Frasnes – the town they had come from that morning. Strange asked several people if this meant the Allies had won, but no one seemed to have any precise information upon this point.

He slept that night in Genappe, a village three miles up the road to Brussels. He was at breakfast when Captain Hadley-Bright appeared, bearing news: the Duke's Allies, the Prussian Army had received a terrible beating in the fighting of previous day.

---

[5] The accepted magical technique for creating confusion within roads, landscapes, rooms and other physical spaces is to make a labyrinth within them. But Strange did not learn this magic until February 1817.

Nevertheless this was arguably the decisive action of the campaign. Unknown to Strange, the French general, D'Erlon, was trying to reach the battlefield with 20,000 men. Instead he spent those crucial hours marching through a landscape which changed inexplicably every few minutes. Had he and his men succeeded in reaching Quatre Bras it is probable the French would have won and Waterloo would never have happened. Strange was piqued by the Duke's abruptness earlier in the day and did not mention to any one what he had done. Later he told John Segundus and Thomas Levy. Consequently historians of Quatre Bras were perplexed to account for D'Erlon's failure until John Segundus's *The Life of Jonathan Strange* was published in 1820.

"Are they defeated?" asked Strange.

"No, but they have retreated and so the Duke says we must do the same. His Grace has chosen somewhere to fight and the Prussians will meet us there. A place called Waterloo."

"Waterloo? What a ridiculously odd name!" said Strange.

"It is odd, is it not? I could not find it on the map."

"Oh!" said Strange. "This was continually happening in Spain! No doubt the fellow who told you got the name wrong. Depend upon it, there is no such place as Waterloo!"

A little after noon they mounted their horses and were about to follow the Army out of the village, when a message arrived from Wellington: a squadron of French lancers was approaching and could Mr Strange do something to annoy them? Strange, anxious to avoid another accusation of Vauxhall-Gardens magic, asked Hadley-Bright's advice. "What do cavalry hate the most?"

Hadley-Bright thought for a moment. "Mud," he said.

"Mud? Really? Yes, I suppose you are right. Well, there are few things more plain and workman-like than weather magic!"

The skies darkened. An inky thundercloud appeared; it was as large as all Belgium and so full and heavy that its ragged skirts seemed to brush the tops of the trees. There was a flash and the world turned bone-white for an instant. There was a deafening crack and the next moment the rain came down in such torrents that the earth boiled and hissed.

Within minutes the surrounding fields had turned to a quagmire. The French lancers were quite unable to indulge in their favourite sport of fast and dextrous riding; Wellington's rearguard got safely away.

An hour later Strange and Hadley-Bright were surprized to discover that there was indeed a place called Waterloo and that they had arrived at it. The Duke was sitting on his horse in the rain, gazing in high good humour at the filthy men, horses and carts. "Excellent mud, Merlin!" he called out cheerfully. "Very sticky and slippery. The French will not like it at all. More rain, if you please! Now, you see that tree where the road dips down?"

"The elm, your Grace?"

"The very one. If you will stand there during the battle tomorrow, I will be much obliged to you. I will be there some of the time, but probably not very often. My boys will bring you your instructions."

That evening the various divisions of the Allied Army took up positions along a shallow ridge south of Waterloo. Above them the thunder roared and the rain came down in torrents. From time to time deputations of bedraggled men approached the elm-tree and begged Strange to make it stop, but he only shook his head and said, "When the Duke tells me to stop, I shall."

But the veterans of the Peninsular War remarked approvingly that rain was always an Englishman's friend in times of war. They told their comrades: "There is nothing so comforting or familiar to us, you see – whereas other nations it baffles. It rained on the nights before Fuentes, Salamanca and Vitoria." (These were the names of some of Wellington's great victories in the Peninsula.)

In the shelter of his umbrella Strange mused on the battle to come. Ever since the end of the Peninsular War he had been studying the magic that the *Aureates* used in times of war. Very little was known about it; there were rumours – nothing more – of a spell which John Uskglass had used before his own battles. It foretold the outcome of present events. Just before nightfall Strange had a sudden inspiration. "There is no way of finding out what Uskglass did, but there is always Pale's Conjectures Concerning the Foreshadowing of Things To Come. That is very likely a watered-down version of the same thing. I could use that."

For a moment or two before the spell took effect, he was aware of all the sounds around him: rain splashing on metal and leather, and running down canvas; horses shuffling and snorting; Englishmen singing and Scotsmen playing bagpipes; two Welsh soldiers arguing over the proper interpretation of a Bible passage; the Scottish captain, John Kincaid, entertaining the American savages and teaching them to drink tea (presumably with the idea that once a man had learnt to drink tea, the other habits and qualities that make up a Briton would naturally follow).

Then silence. Men and horses began to disappear, few by few at first, and then more quickly – hundreds, thousands of them vanishing from sight. Great gaps appeared among the close-packed soldiers. A little further to the east an entire regiment was gone, leaving a hole the size of Hanover-square. Where, moments before, all had been life, conversation and activity, there was now nothing but the rain and the twilight and the waving stalks of rye. Strange wiped his mouth because he felt sick. "Ha!" he thought. "That will teach me to meddle with magic meant for kings! Norrell is right. Some magic is not meant for ordinary magicians. Presumably John Uskglass knew what to do with this horrible knowledge. I do not. Should I tell someone? The Duke? He will not thank me for it."

Someone was looking down at him; someone was speaking to him – a captain in the Horse Artillery. Strange saw the man's mouth move but he heard not a sound. He snapped his fingers to dismiss the spell. The captain was inviting him to come and share some brandy and cigars. Strange shivered and declined.

For the rest of the night he sat by himself under the elm-tree. Until this moment it had never seemed to him that his magicianship set him apart from other men. But now he had glimpsed the wrong side of something. He had the eeriest feeling – as if the world were growing older around him, and the best part of existence – laughter, love and innocence – were slipping irrevocably into the past.

At about half past eleven the next morning the French guns began to fire. The Allied artillery replied. The clear summer air between the two armies was filled with drifting veils of bitter, black smoke.

The French attack was chiefly directed at the Château of Hougoumont, an Allied outpost in the valley, whose woods and buildings were defended by the 3rd Foot Guards, Coldstream Guards, Nassauers and Hanoverians. Strange summoned vision after vision into his silver dish so that he could watch the bloody engagements in the woods around the château. He was in half a mind to move the trees to give the Allied soldiers a better shot at their attackers, but this sort of close hand-to-hand fighting was the very worst subject for magic. He reminded himself that in war a soldier may do more harm by acting too soon or too impetuously than by never acting at all. He waited.

The cannonade grew fiercer. British veterans told their friends that they had never known shot fall so fast and thick. Men saw comrades cut in half, smashed to pieces or beheaded by cannonballs. The very air shook with the guns' reverberations. "Hard pounding this," remarked the Duke coolly, and ordered the front ranks to withdraw behind the crest of the ridge and lie down. When it was over, the Allies lifted their heads to see the French infantry advancing through the smoke-filled valley: sixteen thousand men shoulder to shoulder in immense columns, all shouting and stamping together.

More than one soldier wondered if, at last, the French had found a magician of their own; the French infantrymen appeared much taller than ordinary men and the light in their eyes as they drew closer burnt with an almost supernatural fury. But this was only the magic of Napoleon Buonaparte, who knew better than any one how to dress his soldiers so they would terrify the enemy, and how to deploy them so that any onlooker would think them indestructible.

Now Strange knew exactly what to do. The thick, clogging mud was already proving a decided hindrance to the advancing soldiers. To hamper them further he set about enchanting the stalks of rye. He made them wind themselves around the Frenchmen's feet. The stalks were as tough as wires; the soldiers staggered and fell over. With luck, the mud would hold them down and they would be trampled by their comrades – or by the French cavalry who soon appeared behind them. But it was painstaking work and, in spite of all his efforts, this first magic of Strange's probably did no more harm against the French than the firing of a skilful British musketeer or rifleman.

An *aide-de-camp* flew up with impossible velocity and thrust a strip of goatskin into Strange's hand with a shout of, "Message from his Grace!" In an instant he was off again.

*French shells have set the Château of Hougoumont on fire. Put out the flames.*

*Wellington*

Strange summoned another vision of Hougoumont. The men there had suffered greatly since he had last seen the château. The wounded of both sides lay in every room. The haystack, outbuildings and château were all on fire. Black, choking smoke was everywhere. Horses screamed and wounded men tried to crawl away – but there was hardly anywhere to go. Meanwhile the battle raged on around them. In the chapel Strange found half a dozen images of saints painted on the walls. They were seven or eight feet tall and oddly proportioned – the work, it seemed, of an enthusiastic *amateur*. They had long, brown beards and large, melancholy eyes.

"They'll do!" he muttered. At his command the saints stepped down from the walls. They moved in a series of jerks, like marionettes, but they had a certain lightness and grace. They stalked through the ranks of wounded men to a well in one of the courtyards. Here they drew buckets of water which they carried to the flames. All seemed to be going well until two of them (possibly Saint Peter and Saint Jerome) caught fire and burnt up – being composed of nothing but paint and magic they burnt rather easily. Strange was trying to think how to remedy this situation when part of an exploded French shell hit the side of his silver dish, sending it spinning fifty yards to the right. By the time he had retrieved it, knocked out a large dent in its side and set it to rights, all the painted saints had succumbed to the flames. Wounded men and horses were burning. There were no more paintings upon the walls. Almost brought to tears by his frustration, Strange cursed the unknown artist for his idleness.

What else was there? What else did he know? He thought hard. Long ago John Uskglass would sometimes make a champion for himself out of ravens – birds would flock together to become a black, bristling, shifting giant who could perform any task with ease. On other occasions Uskglass would make servants out of earth.

Strange conjured a vision of Hougoumont's well. He drew the water out of the well in a sort of fountain; and then, before the fountain could spill on the ground, he forced it to take on the clumsy semblance of a man. Next he commanded the water-man to hurry to the flames and cast himself down upon them. In this way a stall in the stables was successfully doused and three men were saved. Strange made more as quickly as he could, but water is not an element that holds a coherent form easily; after an hour or so of this labour his head was spinning and his hands were shaking uncontroulably.

Between four and five o'clock something entirely unexpected happened. Strange looked up to see a brilliant mass of French cavalry approaching. Five hundred abreast they rode and twelve deep – yet the thunder of the guns was such that they made no sound that any one could hear; they seemed to come silently. "Surely," thought Strange, "they must realize that Wellington's infantry is unbroken. They will be cut to pieces." Behind him the infantry regiments were forming squares; some of the men called to Strange to come and shelter inside their square. This seemed like good advice and so he went.

From the relative safety of the square Strange watched the

cavalry's approach; the cuirassiers wore shining breast-plates and tall crested helmets; the lancers' weapons were embellished with fluttering pennants of red and white. They seemed scarcely to belong to this dull age. Theirs was the glory of ancient days – but Strange was determined to match it with an ancient glory of his own. The images of John Uskglass's servants burnt in his mind – servants made of ravens, servants made of earth. Beneath the French horsemen the mud began to swell and bubble. It shaped itself into gigantic hands; the hands reached up and pulled down men and horses. The ones who fell were trampled by their comrades. The rest endured a storm of musket-fire from the Allied infantry. Strange watched impassively.

When the French had been beaten back, he returned to his silver dish.

"Are you the magician?" said someone.

He spun round and was astonished to find a little, round, soft-looking person in civilian clothes who smiled at him. "Who in God's name are you?" he demanded.

"My name is Pink," explained the man. "I am a commercial traveller for Welbeck's Superior Buttons of Birmingham. I have a message from the Duke for you."

Strange, who was covered in mud and more tired than he had ever been in his life, took a moment to comprehend this. "Where are all the Duke's *aides-de-camp*?"

"He says that they are dead."

"What? Hadley-Bright is dead? What about Colonel Canning?"

"Alas," smiled Mr Pink, "I can offer no precise information. I came out from Antwerp yesterday to see the battle and when I espied the Duke I took the opportunity to introduce myself and to mention in passing the excellent qualities of Welbeck's Superior Buttons. He asked me as a particular favour to come and tell you that the Prussian army is on their way here and have reached Paris Wood, but, says his Grace, they are having the devil of a time . . ." (Mr Pink smiled and blinked to hear himself say such a soldierly

word.) ". . . the devil of a time in the little lanes and the mud, and would you be so good as to make a road for them between the wood and the battlefield?"

"Certainly," said Strange, rubbing some of the mud from his face.

"I will tell his Grace." He paused and asked wistfully, "Do you think his Grace would like to order some buttons?"

"I do not see why not. He is as fond of buttons as most men."

"Then, you know, we could put 'Supplier of Buttons to his Grace the Duke of Wellington' in all our advertisements." Mr Pink beamed happily. "Off I go then!"

"Yes, yes. Off you go." Strange created the road for the Prussians, but in later times he was always inclined to suppose he must have dreamt Mr Pink of Welbeck's Superior Buttons.[6]

Events seemed to repeat themselves. Again and again the French cavalry charged and Strange took refuge within the infantry square. Again the deadly horsemen swirled against the sides of the square like waves. Again Strange drew monstrous hands from the earth to pull them down. Whenever the cavalry withdrew the cannonade began again; he returned to his silver dish and made men out of water to put out the flames and succour the dying in ruined, desperate Hougoumont. Everything happened over and over, again and again; it was inconceivable that the fighting would ever end. He began to think it had always been like this.

"There must come a time when the musket-balls and cannon-shot run out," he thought. "And what will we do then? Hack at each other with sabres and bayonets? And if we all die, every one of us, who will they say has won?"

The smoke rolled back revealing frozen moments like tableaux in a ghostly theatre: at the farmhouse called La Haye Sainte the

---

[6] In actual fact Mr Pink was only one of the civilians whom the Duke pressed into service as unofficial *aides-de-camp* that day. Others included a young Swiss gentleman and another commercial traveller, this time from London.

French were climbing a mountain of their own dead to get over the wall and kill the German defenders.

Once Strange was caught outside the square when the French arrived. Suddenly, directly in front of him, was an enormous French cuirassier upon an equally enormous horse. His first thought was to wonder if the fellow knew who he was. (He had been told the entire French Army hated the English magician with a vivid, Latin passion.) His second thought was that he had left his pistols inside the infantry square.

The cuirassier raised his sabre. Without thinking, Strange muttered Stokesey's *Animam Evocare*. Something like a bee flew out of the breast of the cuirassier and settled in the palm of Strange's hand. But it was not a bee; it was a bead of pearly blue light. A second light flew out of the cuirassier's horse. The horse screamed and reared up. The cuirassier stared, puzzled.

Strange raised his other hand to smash horse and horseman out of existence. Then he froze.

*"And can a magician kill a man by magic?" the Duke had asked.*

*And he had answered, "A magician might, but a gentleman never could."*

While he was hesitating a British cavalry officer – a Scots Grey – swung round out of nowhere. He slashed the cuirassier's head open, from his chin, upwards through his teeth. The man toppled like a tree. The Scots Grey rode on.

Strange could never quite remember what happened after this. He believed that he wandered about in a dazed condition. He did not know for how long.

The sound of cheering brought him to himself. He looked up and saw Wellington upon Copenhagen. He was waving his hat – the signal that the Allies were to advance upon the French. But the smoke wreathed itself so thickly about the Duke that only the soldiers nearest to him could share in this moment of victory.

So Strange whispered a word and a little gap appeared in the billows. A single ray of evening sunlight shone down upon Wellington. All along the ridge the faces of the soldiers turned towards him. The cheering grew louder.

"There," thought Strange, "that is the proper use of English magic."

He followed the soldiers and the retreating French down through the battlefield. Scattered about among the dead and the dying were the great earthen hands he had created. They seemed frozen in gestures of outrage and horror as if the land itself despaired. When he came level with the French guns that had done the Allied soldiers such profound injury, he did one last act of magic. He drew more hands out of the earth. The hands grasped the cannons and pulled them under.

At the Inn of Belle Alliance on the far side of the battlefield, he found the Duke with the Prussian General, Prince Blücher. The Duke nodded to him and said, "Come to dinner with me."

Prince Blücher shook his hand warmly and said a great many things in German (none of which Strange understood). Then the old gentleman pointed to his stomach wherein lay the illusory elephant and made a wry face as if to say, "What can one do?"

Strange stepped outside and immediately he almost walked into Captain Hadley-Bright. "I was told you were dead!" he cried.

"I was sure you would be," replied Hadley-Bright.

There was a pause. Both men felt faintly embarrassed. The ranks of dead and wounded stretched away upon all sides as far as the eye could see. Simply being alive at that moment seemed, in some indefinable way, ungentlemanly.

"Who else survived? Do you know?" asked Hadley-Bright.

Strange shook his head. "No."

They parted.

At Wellington's Headquarters in Waterloo that night the table was laid for forty or fifty people. But when the dinner-hour came, only three men were there: the Duke, General Alava (his Spanish attaché) and Strange. Whenever the door opened the Duke turned his head to see if it was one of his friends, alive and well; but no one came.

Many places at that table had been laid for gentlemen who were either dead or dying: Colonel Canning, Lieutenant-Colonel Gordon, Major-General Picton, Colonel De Lancey. The list would grow longer as the night progressed.

The Duke, General Alava and Mr Strange sat down in silence.

# 41

# Starecross

## Late September–December 1815

Fortune, it seemed, could not be persuaded to smile upon Mr Segundus. He had come to live in York with the aim of enjoying the society and conversation of the city's many magicians. But no sooner had he got there than all the other magicians were deprived of their profession by Mr Norrell, and he was left alone. His little stock of money had dwindled considerably and in the autumn of 1815 he was forced to seek employment.

"And it is not to be supposed," he remarked to Mr Honeyfoot with a sigh, "that I shall be able to earn very much. What am I qualified to do?"

Mr Honeyfoot could not allow this. "Write to Mr Strange!" he advised. "He may be in need of a secretary."

Nothing would have pleased Mr Segundus better than to work for Jonathan Strange, but his natural modesty would not allow him to propose it. It would be a shocking thing to put himself forward in such a way. Mr Strange might be embarrassed to know how to answer him. It might even look as if he, John Segundus, considered himself Mr Strange's equal!

Mr and Mrs Honeyfoot assured him that if Mr Strange did not like the idea he would very soon say so – and so there could be no possible harm in asking him. But upon this point Mr Segundus proved unpersuadable.

Their next proposal, however, pleased him better. "Why not see if there are any little boys in the town who wish to learn magic?" asked Mrs Honeyfoot. Her grandsons – stout little fellows of five and seven – were just now of an age to begin their education and so the subject rather occupied her mind.

So Mr Segundus became a tutor in magic. As well as little boys, he also discovered some young ladies whose studies would have more usually been confined to French, German and music, but who were now anxious to be instructed in theoretical magic. Soon he was asked to give lessons to the young ladies' older brothers, many of whom began to picture themselves as magicians. To young men of a studious turn of mind, who did not desire to go into the Church or the Law, magic was very appealing, particularly since Strange had triumphed on the battlefields of Europe. It is, after all, many centuries since clergymen distinguished themselves on the field of war, and lawyers never have.

In the early autumn of 1815 Mr Segundus was engaged by the father of one of his pupils upon an errand. This gentleman, whose name was Palmer, had heard of a house in the north of the county that was being sold. Mr Palmer did not wish to buy the house, but a friend had told him that there was a library there worth examining. Mr Palmer was not at leisure just then to go and see for himself. Though he trusted his servants in many other matters, their talents did not quite run to scholarship, so he asked Mr Segundus to go in his place, to find out how many books there were and what their condition might be and whether they were worth purchasing.

Starecross Hall was the principal building in a village which otherwise comprised a handful of stone cottages and farmhouses. Starecross itself stood in a most isolated spot, surrounded on all sides by brown, empty moors. Tall trees sheltered it from storms and winds – yet at the same time they made it dark and solemn. The village was amply provided with tumbledown stone walls and tumbledown stone barns. It was very quiet; it felt like the end of the world.

There was a very ancient and worn-looking packhorse bridge that crossed a deep beck of fast-running water. Bright yellow leaves flowed swiftly upon the dark, almost-black water, making patterns as they went. To Mr Segundus the patterns looked a little like magical writing. "But then," he thought, "so many things do."

The house itself was a long, low, rambling building, constructed of the same dark stone as the rest of the village. Its neglected gardens, garths and courts were filled with deep drifts of autumn leaves. It was hard to know who would wish to buy such a house. It was much too large for a farmhouse, yet altogether too gloomy and remote for a gentleman's residence. It might have done for a parsonage except that there was no church. It might have done for an inn, except that the old pack-road that had once passed through the village had fallen into disuse and the bridge was all that remained of it.

No one came in answer to Mr Segundus's knock. He observed that the front door was ajar. It seemed rather impertinent simply to go inside, but after four or five minutes of fruitless knocking he did so.

Houses, like people, are apt to become rather eccentric if left too much on their own; this house was the architectural equivalent of an old gentleman in a worn dressing-gown and torn slippers, who got up and went to bed at odd times of day, and who kept up a continual conversation with friends no one else could see. As Mr Segundus wandered about in search of whoever was in charge, he found a room which contained nothing but china cheese-moulds, all stacked one upon another. Another room had heaps of queer red clothes, the like of which he had never seen before – something between labourers' smocks and clergymen's robes. The kitchen had very few of those articles that usually belong to kitchens, but it did have the skull of an alligator in a glass case; the skull had a great grin and seemed very pleased with itself, though Mr Segundus did not know why it should be. There was one room that could only be reached by a queer arrangement of steps and staircases, where the pictures all seemed to have been chosen by someone with an inordinate love of fighting; there were pictures of men fighting, boys fighting, cocks fighting, bulls fighting, dogs fighting, centaurs fighting and even a startling depiction of two beetles locked in combat. Another room was almost empty except for a doll's house standing on a table in the middle of the floor; the doll's house was an exact copy of the real house – except that inside the doll's house a number of smartly dressed dolls were enjoying a peaceful and rational existence together: making doll-sized cakes and loaves of bread, entertaining their friends with a diminutive harpsichord, playing casino with tiny cards, educating miniature children, and dining upon roast turkeys the size of Mr Segundus's thumbnail. It formed a strange contrast with the bleak, echoing reality.

He seemed to have looked in every room, but he still had not found the library and he still had not found any people. He came to a small door half-hidden by a staircase. Behind it was a tiny room – scarcely more than a closet. A man in a dirty white coat with his boots propped up on the table was drinking brandy and staring at the ceiling. After a little persuasion this person agreed to shew him where the library was.

The first ten books Mr Segundus looked at were worthless – books of sermons and moralizing from the last century, or descriptions of persons whom no one living cared about. The next fifty were very much the same. He began to think his task would soon be done. But then he stumbled upon some very interesting and unusual works of geology, philosophy and medicine. He began to feel more sanguine.

He worked steadily for two or three hours. Once he thought he heard a carriage arrive at the house, but he paid it no attention. At the end of that time he was suddenly aware that he was extremely hungry. He had no idea whether any arrangements had been made for his dinner or not, and the house was a long way from the nearest inn. He went off in search of the negligent man in the tiny room to ask him what could be done. In the labyrinth of rooms and corridors he was lost immediately. He wandered about opening every door, feeling more and more hungry, and more and more out of temper with the negligent man.

He found himself in an old-fashioned parlour with dark oak panelling and a mantelpiece the size of a young triumphal arch. Directly before him a lovely young woman was sitting in a deep window-seat, gazing out at the trees and the high, bare hills beyond. He had just time enough to notice that her left hand lacked a little finger, when suddenly she was not there at all – or perhaps it was more accurate to say she changed. In her place was a much older, stouter woman, a woman about Mr Segundus's own age, dressed in a violet silk gown, with an Indian shawl about her shoulders and a little dog in her lap. This lady sat in exactly the same attitude as the other, gazing out of the window with the same wistful expression.

All these details took but a moment to apprehend, yet the impression made upon Mr Segundus by the two ladies was unusually vivid – almost supernaturally so – like images in a delirium. A queer shock thrilled through his whole being, his senses were overwhelmed and he fainted away.

When he came to himself he was lying on the floor and two ladies were leaning over him, with exclamations of dismay and concern. Despite his confusion he quickly comprehended that neither lady was the beautiful young woman with the missing finger whom he had seen first. One was the lady with the little dog whom he had seen *second*, and the other was a thin, fair-haired, equally mature lady of unremarkable face and figure. It appeared that she had been in the room all along, but she had been seated *behind* the door and so he had not observed her.

The two ladies would not permit him to stand up or attempt any movement of his limbs. They would scarcely allow him to speak; they warned him sternly it would bring on another fainting fit.

They fetched cushions for his head, and blankets to keep him warm (he protested he was perfectly warm to begin with, but they would not listen to him). They dispensed lavender water and *sal volatile*. They stopt a draught they thought might be coming from under one of the doors. Mr Segundus began to suspect that they had had an uneventful morning, and that when a strange gentleman had walked into the room and dropt down in a swoon, they were rather pleased than otherwise.

After quarter of an hour of this treatment he was permitted to sit in a chair and sip weak tea unaided.

"The fault is entirely mine," said the lady with the little dog. "Fellowes told me that the gentleman had come from York to see the books. I ought to have made myself known to you before. It was too great a shock coming upon us like that!"

The name of this lady was Mrs Lennox. The other was Mrs Blake, her companion. They generally resided in Bath and they had come to Starecross so that Mrs Lennox might see the house one more time before it was sold.

"Foolish, is it not?" said Mrs Lennox to Mr Segundus. "The house has stood vacant for years and years. I ought to have sold it long ago, but when I was a child I spent several summers here which were particularly happy."

"You are still very pale, sir," offered Mrs Blake. "Have you eaten any thing today?"

Mr Segundus confessed that he was very hungry.

"Did not Fellowes offer to fetch your dinner?" asked Mrs Lennox in surprize.

Fellowes was presumably the negligent servant in the tiny room. Mr Segundus did not like to say that he had barely been able to rouse Fellowes to speak to him.

Fortunately, Mrs Lennox and Mrs Blake had brought an ample dinner with them and Fellowes was, at that moment, preparing it. Half an hour later the two ladies and Mr Segundus sat down to dine in an oak-panelled room with a melancholy view of autumn trees. The only slight inconvenience was that the two ladies wished Mr Segundus, in his invalid character, to eat light, easily digestible foods, whereas in truth he was very hungry and wanted fried beefsteaks and hot pudding.

The two ladies were glad of a companion and asked him a great many questions about himself. They were most interested to learn that he was a magician; they had never met one before.

"And have you found any magical texts in my library?" asked Mrs Lennox.

"None, madam," said Mr Segundus. "But magical books, valuable ones, are very rare indeed. I would have been most surprized to find any."

"Now that I think of it," mused Mrs Lennox, "I believe there were a few. But I sold them all years ago to a gentleman who lived near York. Just between ourselves I thought him a little foolish to pay me such a great sum for books no one wanted. But perhaps he was wise after all."

Mr Segundus knew that "the gentleman who lived near York" had probably not paid Mrs Lennox one quarter the proper value of the books, but it does no good to say such things out loud and so he smiled politely, and kept his reflections to himself.

He told them about his pupils, both male and female, and how clever they were and how eager to learn.

"And since you encourage them with such praise," said Mrs Blake, kindly, "they are sure to fare better under your tutelage than they would with any other master."

"Oh! I do not know about that," said Mr Segundus.

"I had not quite understood before," said Mrs Lennox, with a thoughtful air, "how universally popular the study of magic has become. I had thought that it was confined to those two men in London. What are their names? Presumably, Mr Segundus, the next step is a school for magicians? Doubtless that is where you will direct your energies?"

"A school!" said Mr Segundus. "Oh! But that would require –

well, I do not know what exactly – but a great deal of money and a house."

"Perhaps there would be difficulty in acquiring pupils?" said Mrs Lennox.

"No, indeed! I can think of four young men immediately."

"And if you were to advertise . . ."

"Oh! But I would never do that!" said Mr Segundus, rather shocked. "Magic is the noblest profession in the world – well, the second noblest perhaps, after the Church. One ought not to soil it with commercial practices. No, I would only take young men upon private recommendation."

"Then all that remains is for someone to find you a little money and a house. Nothing could be easier. But I dare say your friend, Mr Honeyfoot, of whom you speak with such regard, would wish to lend you the money. I dare say he would want to claim that honour for his own."

"Oh, no! Mr Honeyfoot has three daughters – the dearest girls in the world. One of them is married and another is engaged and the third cannot make up her mind. No, Mr Honeyfoot must think of his family. His money is quite tied up."

"Then I can tell you my hope with a clear conscience! Why should I not lend you the money?"

Mr Segundus was all amazement and for several moments quite at a loss for an answer. "You are very kind, madam!" he stammered at last.

Mrs Lennox smiled. "No, sir. I am not. If magic is as popular as you say – and I shall, of course, ascertain the opinion of other people upon this point – then I believe the profits will be handsome."

"But my experience of business is woefully small," said Mr Segundus. "I should fear to make a mistake and lose you your money. No, you are very kind and I thank you with all my heart, but I must decline."

"Well, if you dislike the notion of becoming a borrower of

money – and I know it does not suit everyone – then that is easily solved. The school shall be mine – mine alone. I will bear the expence and the risk. You will be master of the school and our names will appear upon the prospectus together. After all, what better purpose for this house could there be than as a school for magicians? As a residence it has many drawbacks, but its advantages as a school are considerable. It is a very isolated situation. There is no shooting to speak of. There would be little opportunity for the young men to gamble or hunt. Their pleasures will be quite restricted and so they will apply themselves to their studies."

"I would not chuse young men who gamble!" said Mr Segundus, rather shocked.

She smiled again. "I do not believe you have ever given your friends a moment's anxiety – except for worrying that this wicked world would quickly take advantage of someone so honest."

After dinner Mr Segundus dutifully returned to the library and in the early evening he took his leave of the two ladies. They parted in a most friendly manner and with a promise on Mrs Lennox's side that she would soon invite him to Bath.

On the way back he gave himself stern warnings not to place any reliance on these wonderful plans for Future Usefulness and Happiness, but he could not help indulging in ideal pictures of teaching the young men and of their extraordinary progress; of Jonathan Strange coming to visit the school; of his pupils being delighted to discover that their master was a friend and intimate of the most famous magician of the Modern Age; of Strange saying to him, "It is all excellent, Segundus. I could not be better pleased. Well done!"

It was after midnight when he got home, and it took all his resolve not to run to Mr Honeyfoot's house immediately to tell them the news. But the following morning when he arrived at the house at a very early hour, their raptures were scarcely to be described. They were full of the happiness he had hardly dare allow himself to feel. Mrs Honeyfoot still had a great deal of the schoolgirl in her and she caught up her husband's hands and danced around the breakfast-table with him as the only possible means of expressing what she felt. Then she took Mr Segundus's hands and danced around the table with *him*, and when both magicians protested against any more dancing, she continued by herself. Mr Segundus's only regret (and it was a very slight one) was that Mr and Mrs Honeyfoot did not feel the *surprize* of the thing quite as he intended they should; their opinion of him was so high that they found nothing particularly remarkable in great ladies wishing to establish schools solely for his benefit.

"Shc may consider herself very lucky to have found you!" declared Mr Honeyfoot. "For who is better fitted to direct a school for magicians? No one!"

"And after all," reasoned Mrs Honeyfoot, "what else has she to do with her money? Poor, childless lady!"

Mr Honeyfoot was convinced that Mr Segundus's fortune was now made. His sanguine temper would not permit him to expect less. Yet he had not lived so long in the world without acquiring some sober habits of business and he told Mr Segundus that they would make some inquiries about Mrs Lennox, who she was and whether she was as rich as she seemed.

They wrote to a friend of Mr Honeyfoot's who lived in Bath. Fortunately Mrs Lennox was well known as a great lady, even in Bath, a city beloved by the rich and the elevated. She had been born rich and married an even richer husband. This husband had died young and not much regretted, leaving her at liberty to indulge her active temperament and clever mind. She had increased her fortune with good investments and careful management of her lands and estates. She was famed for her bold, decisive temper, her many charitable activities and the warmth of her friendship. She had houses in every part of the kingdom, but resided chiefly at Bath with Mrs Blake.

Meanwhile Mrs Lennox had been asking the same sort of questions about Mr Segundus, and she must have been pleased with the answers because she soon invited him up to Bath where every detail of the projected school was quickly decided.

The next months were spent in repairing and fitting up Starecross Hall. The roof leaked, two chimneys were blocked and part of the kitchen had actually fallen down. Mr Segundus was shocked to discover how much everything would cost. He calculated that if he did not clear the second chimney, made do with old country settles and wooden chairs instead of buying new furniture, and confined the number of servants to three, he could save £60. His letter to this effect produced an immediate reply from Mrs Lennox; she informed him he was not spending enough. His pupils would all be from good families; they would expect good fires and comfort. She advised him to engage nine servants, in addition to a butler and a French cook. He must completely refurnish the house and purchase a cellar of good French wines. The cutlery, she said, must all be silver and the dining-service Wedgwood.

In early December Mr Segundus received a letter of congratulation from Jonathan Strange, who promised to visit the school the following spring. But in spite of everyone's good wishes and everyone's endeavours, Mr Segundus could not get rid of the feeling that the school would never actually come into being; something would occur to prevent it. This idea was constantly at the back of his thoughts, do what he would to suppress it.

One morning around the middle of December he arrived at the Hall and found a man seated, quite at his ease, upon the steps. Though he did not believe he had ever seen the man before, he knew him instantly: he was Bad Fortune personified; he was the Ruin of Mr Segundus's Hopes and Dreams. The man was dressed in a black coat of an old-fashioned cut, as worn and shabby as Mr Segundus's own, and he had mud on his boots. With his long, ragged dark hair he looked like the portent of doom in a bad play.

"Mr Segundus, you cannot do this!" he said in a Yorkshire accent.

"I beg your pardon?" said Mr Segundus.

"The school, sir. You must give up this notion of a school!"

"What?" cried Mr Segundus, bravely pretending that he did not know the man spoke an inevitable truth.

"Now, sir," continued the dark man, "you know me and you know that when I say a thing is so, that thing will be so – however much you and I might privately regret it."

"But you are quite mistaken," said Mr Segundus. "I do not know you. At least I do not believe I ever saw you before."

"I am John Childermass, Mr Norrell's servant. We last talked nine years ago, outside the Cathedral in York. When you confined yourself to a few pupils, Mr Segundus, I was able to turn a blind eye. I said nothing and Mr Norrell remained in ignorance of what you were doing. But a regular school for grown-up magicians, that is a different matter. You have been too ambitious, sir. He knows, Mr Segundus. He knows and it is his desire that you wind up the business immediately."

"But what has Mr Norrell or Mr Norrell's desires to do with me? *I* did not sign the agreement. You should know that I am not alone in this undertaking. I have friends now."

"That is true," said Childermass, mildly amused. "And Mrs Lennox is a very rich woman, and an excellent woman for business. But does she have the friendship of every Minister in the Cabinet like Mr Norrell? Does she have his influence? Remember the Society of Learned Magicians, Mr Segundus! Remember how he crushed them!"

Childermass waited a moment and then, since the conversation appeared to be at an end, he strode off in the direction of the stables.

Five minutes later he reappeared on a big, brown horse. Mr Segundus was standing, just as before, with his arms crossed, glaring at the paving-stones.

Childermass looked down at him. "I am sorry it ends like this, sir. Yet, surely all is not lost? This house is just as suited to another kind of school as it is for a magical one. You would not think it to look at me, but I am a very fine fellow with a wide acquaintance among great people. Chuse some other sort of school and the next time I hear that a lord or lady has need of such an establishment for their little lordlings, I will send them your way."

"I do not want another kind of school!" said Mr Segundus, peevishly.

Childermass smiled his sideways smile and rode away.

Mr Segundus travelled to Bath and informed his patroness of their dismal situation. She was full of indignation that some gentleman she had never even met should presume to instruct her in what she could and could not do. She wrote Mr Norrell an angry letter. She got no reply, but her bankers, lawyers and partners in other business ventures suddenly found themselves in receipt of odd letters from great people of their acquaintance, all complaining in an oblique fashion of Mr Segundus's school. One of the bankers – an argumentative and obdurate old person – was unwise enough to wonder publicly (in the lobby of the House of Commons) what a school for magicians in Yorkshire could possibly have to do with him. The result was that several ladies and gentlemen – friends of Mr Norrell – withdrew their patronage from his bank.

In Mrs Honeyfoot's drawing-room in York a few evenings later Mr Segundus sat with his head in his hands, lamenting. "It is as if some evil fortune is determined to torment me, holding out great prizes in front of me, only to snatch them away again."

Mrs Honeyfoot clucked sympathetically, patted his shoulder and offered the same damning censure of Mr Norrell with which she had consoled both Mr Segundus and Mr Honeyfoot for the past nine years: to wit, that Mr Norrell seemed a very odd gentleman, full of queer fancies, and that she would never understand him.

"Why not write to Mr Strange?" said Mr Honeyfoot, suddenly. "He will know what to do!"

Mr Segundus looked up. "Oh! I know that Mr Strange and Mr

Norrell have parted, but still I should not like to be a cause of argument between them."

"Nonsense!" cried Mr Honeyfoot. "Have you not read the recent issues of *The Modern Magician*? This is the very thing Strange wants! – some principle of Norrellite magic that he can attack openly and so bring the whole edifice tumbling down. Believe me, he will consider himself obliged to you for the opportunity. You know, Segundus, the more I think of it, the more I like this plan!"

Mr Segundus thought so too. "Let me only consult Mrs Lennox and if she is in agreement, then I shall certainly do as you suggest!"

Mrs Lennox's ignorance concerning recent magical events was extensive. She knew very little of Jonathan Strange other than his name and that he had some vague connexion to the Duke of Wellington. But she was quick to assure Mr Segundus that if Mr Strange disliked Mr Norrell, then she was very much in his favour. So on the 20th December Mr Segundus sent Strange a letter informing him of Gilbert Norrell's actions in regard to the school at Starecross Hall.

Unfortunately, far from leaping to Mr Segundus's defence, Strange never even replied.

# 42

# Strange decides to write a book

## June–December 1815

It may very easily be imagined with what pleasure Mr Norrell received the news that on his return to England Mr Strange had gone straight to Shropshire.

"And the best part of it is," Mr Norrell told Lascelles, "that in the country he is unlikely to publish any more of those mischievous articles upon the magic of the Raven King."

"No indeed, sir," said Lascelles, "for I very much doubt that he will have time to write them."

Mr Norrell took a moment to consider what this might mean.

"Oh! Have you not heard, sir?" continued Lascelles. "Strange is writing a book. He writes to his friends of nothing else. He began very suddenly about two weeks ago and is, by his own account, making very rapid progress. But then we all know with what ease Strange writes. He has sworn to put the entirety of English magic into his book. He told Sir Walter that he would be greatly astonished if he could cram it all into two volumes. He rather thinks that it will need three. It is to be called *The History and Practice of English Magic* and Murray has promised to publish it when it is done."

There could scarcely have been worse news. Mr Norrell had always intended to write a book himself. He intended to call it *Precepts for the Education of a Magician* and he had begun it when he had first become tutor to Mr Strange. His notes already filled two shelves of the little book-lined room on the second floor. Yet he had always spoken of his book as something for the distant future. He had a quite unreasonable terror of committing himself to paper which eight years of London adulation had not cured. All his volumes of private notes and histories and journals had yet to be seen by anyone (except, in a few instances, by Strange and Childermass). Mr Norrell could never believe himself ready to publish: he could never be sure that he had got at the truth; he did not believe he had thought long enough upon the matter; he did not know if it were a fit subject to place before the public.

As soon as Mr Lascelles had gone, Mr Norrell called for a silver dish of clear water to be brought to him in his room on the second floor.

In Shropshire, Strange was working upon his book. He did not look up, but suddenly he smiled a little wryly and wagged his finger at the empty air as if to tell some unseen person *No*. All the mirrors in the room had been turned to face the wall and, though Mr Norrell spent several hours bent over his silver dish, by the end of the evening he was no wiser.

On an evening at the beginning of December Stephen Black was polishing silver in his room at the end of the kitchen-passage. He looked down and discovered that the strings of his polishing-apron were untying themselves. It was not that the bow had come loose (Stephen had never tied a lazy bow in his life), but rather that the strings were snaking about in a bold, decisive way like apron-strings that knew what they were about. Next his polishing-sleeves and polishing-gloves slipped off his arms and hands and folded themselves up neatly upon the table. Then his coat leapt from the chairback where he had hung it. It took firm hold of him and helped him on with itself. Finally the butler's room itself disappeared.

Suddenly he was standing in a small apartment panelled in dark wood. A table took up most of the space. The table was laid with a cloth of scarlet linen with a deep and ornate border of gold and silver. It was crowded with gold and silver dishes and the dishes were heaped with food. Jewelled ewers were filled with wine. Wax candles in gold candlesticks made a blaze of light and incense burnt in two golden censers. Besides the table the only other furniture were two carved wooden chairs draped with cloth of gold and made luxurious with embroidered cushions. In one of these chairs the gentleman with the thistle-down hair was sitting.

"Good evening, Stephen!"

"Good evening, sir."

"You look a little pale tonight, Stephen. I hope you are not unwell."

"I am merely a little out of breath, sir. I find these sudden removals to other countries and continents a little perplexing."

"Oh! But we are still in London, Stephen. This is the Jerusalem Coffee-house in Cowper's-court. Do you not know it?"

"Oh, yes indeed, sir. Sir Walter would often sup here with his rich friends when he was a bachelor. It is just that it was never so magnificent before. As for this banquet, there are hardly any dishes here I recognize."

"Oh! That is because I have ordered an exact copy of a meal I ate in this very house four or five hundred years ago! Here is a haunch of roasted wyvern and a pie of honeyed hummingbirds. Here is roasted salamander with a relish of pomegranates; here a delicate fricassee of the combs of cockatrices spiced with saffron and powdered rainbows and ornamented with gold stars! Now sit you down and eat! That will be the best cure for your dizziness. What will you take?"

"It is all very wonderful, sir, but I believe I see some plain pork steaks which look very good indeed."

"Ah, Stephen! As ever your noble instincts have led you to pick the choicest dish of all! Though the pork steaks are indeed quite plain, they have been fried in fat that was rendered down from the exorcised ghosts of black Welsh pigs that wander through the hills of Wales at night terrifying the inhabitants of that deplorable country! The ghostliness and ferocity of the pigs lends the steaks a wonderful flavour which is quite unlike any other! And the sauce which accompanies them is made from cherries that were grown in a centaur's orchard!"

Taking up a jewelled and gilded ewer, the gentleman poured Stephen a glass of ruby-red wine. "This wine is one of the vintages of Hell – but do not allow yourself to be dissuaded from tasting it upon that account! I dare say you have heard of Tantalus? The wicked king who baked his little son in a pie and ate him? He has been condemned to stand up to his chin in a pool of water he cannot drink, beneath a vine laden with grapes he cannot eat. This wine is made from those grapes. And, since the vine was planted there for the sole purpose of tormenting Tantalus, you may be sure the grapes have an excellent flavour and aroma – and so does the wine. The pomegranates too are from Persephone's own orchard."

Stephen tasted the wine and the pork steaks. "It is altogether excellent, sir. What was the occasion when you dined here before?"

"Oh! I and my friends were celebrating our departure for the Crusades. William of Lanchester[1] was here and Tom Dundell[2] and many other noble lords and knights, both Christian and fairy. Of course it was not a coffee-house then. It was an inn. From where we sat we looked out over a wide courtyard surrounded by carved and gilded pillars. Our servants, pages and squires went to and fro, making everything ready for us to wreak a terrible vengeance upon our wicked enemies! On the other side of the courtyard were the stables where were housed not only the most beautiful horses in England, but three unicorns that another fairy – a cousin of mine –

[1] William of Lanchester was John Uskglass's seneschal and favourite servant, and consequently one of the most important men in England.
[2] Thomas of Dundale, John Uskglass's first human servant. See footnote 2, Chapter 45.

was taking to the Holy Lands to pierce our enemies through and through. Several talented magicians were seated at the table with us. They in no way resembled the horrors that pass for magicians nowadays. They were as handsome in their persons as they were accomplished in their art! The birds of the air stooped to hear their commands. The rains and the rivers were their servants. The north wind, the south wind, etc., etc., only existed to do their bidding. They spread their hands and cities crumbled – or sprang up whole again! What a contrast to that horrible old man who sits in a dusty room, muttering to himself and turning the pages of some ancient volume!" The gentlemen ate some cockatrice fricassee thoughtfully. "The other one is writing a book," he said.

"So I have heard, sir. Have you been to look at him recently?"

The gentleman frowned. "I? Did you just not hear me say that I consider these magicians the stupidest, most abominable men in England? No, I have not seen him above twice or three times a week since he left London. When he writes, he cuts his nibs rather square with a old pen-knife. *I* should be ashamed to use so battered and ugly an old knife, but these magicians endure all sorts of nastiness that you and I would shudder at! Sometimes he gets so lost in what he is writing that he forgets to mend his nib and then the ink splatters on to his paper and into his coffee and he pays it no attention at all."

Stephen reflected how odd it was that the gentleman, who lived in a partly ruinous house surrounded by the grisly bones of bygone battles, should be so sensitive to disorder in other people's houses. "And what of the subject of the book, sir?" he asked. "What is your opinion of that?"

"It is most peculiar! He describes all the most important appearances of my race in this country. There are accounts of how we have intervened in Britain's affairs for Britain's good and the greater glory of the inhabitants. He continually gives it as his opinion that nothing is so desirable as that the magicians of this Age should immediately summon us up and beg for our assistance.

Can you make any thing of this, Stephen? I cannot. When I wished to bring the King of England to my house and shew him all sorts of polite attentions, this same magician thwarted me. His behaviour upon that occasion seemed calculated to insult me!"

"But I think, sir," said Stephen, gently, "that perhaps he did not quite understand who or what you were."

"Oh! who can tell what these Englishmen understand? Their minds are so peculiar! It is impossible to know what they are thinking! I fear you will find it so, Stephen, when you are their King!"

"I really have no wish to be King of anywhere, sir."

"You will feel very differently when you are King. It is just that you are cast down at the thought of being excluded from Lost-hope and all your friends. Be easy upon that score! I too would be miserable if I thought that your elevation would be the means of parting us. But I see no necessity for you to reside permanently in England merely because you are its monarch. A week is the utmost any person of taste could be expected to linger in such a dull country. A week is more than enough!"

"But what of my duties, sir? It is my understanding that kings have a great deal of business, and as little as I want to be King, I should not wish . . ."

"My dear Stephen!" cried the gentleman in affectionate but amused delight. "That is what seneschals are for! They can perform all the dull business of government, while you remain with me at Lost-hope to enjoy our usual pleasures. You will return here every so often to collect your taxes and the tribute of conquered nations and put them into a bank. Oh, I suppose that once in a while it will be prudent to stay in England long enough to have your portrait painted so that the populace may adore you all the more. Sometimes you may graciously permit all the most beautiful ladies in the land to wait in line to kiss your hands and fall in love with you. Then, all your duties performed to perfection, you can return to Lady Pole and me with a good conscience!" The gentleman paused and grew unusually thoughtful. "Though I must confess," he said at last, "that my delight in the beautiful Lady Pole is not so overpowering as once it was. There is another lady whom I like much more. She is only moderately pretty, but the deficiency in beauty is more than compensated for by her lively spirits and sweet conversation. And this other lady has one great advantage over Lady Pole. As you and I both know, Stephen, however often Lady Pole visits my house, she must always go away again in accordance with the magician's agreement. But in the case of this lady, there will be no need for any such foolish agreement. Once I have obtained her, I shall be able to keep her always at my side!"

Stephen sighed. The thought of some other poor lady held prisoner at Lost-hope for ever and a day was melancholy indeed! Yet it would be foolish to suppose that he could do any thing to prevent it and it might be that he could turn it to Lady Pole's advantage. "Perhaps, sir," he said, respectfully, "in that case you would consider releasing her ladyship from her enchantment? I know her husband and friends would be glad to have her restored to them."

"Oh! But I shall always regard Lady Pole as a most desirable addition to all our entertainments. A beautiful woman is always good company and I doubt if her ladyship has her equal for beauty in England. There are not many to equal her in Faerie. No, what you suggest is entirely impossible. But to return to the subject in hand. We must decide upon a scheme to pluck this other lady from her home and carry her off to Lost-hope. I know, Stephen, that you will be all the more eager to help me when I tell you that I consider the removal of this lady from England as quite essential to our noble aim of making you King. It will be a terrible blow to our enemies! It will cast them down into utter despair! It will produce strife and dissension amongst them. Oh, yes! It will be all good things to us and all bad to them! We would fail in our lofty duties if we did any thing less!"

Stephen could make very little of this. Was the gentleman speaking of one of the Princesses at Windsor Castle? It was well known that the King had gone mad when his youngest and favourite daughter died. Perhaps the gentleman with the thistle-down hair supposed that the loss of another Princess might actually kill him, or loosen the wits of some other members of the Royal Family.

"Now, my dear Stephen," said the gentleman. "The question before us is: how may we fetch the lady away without any one noticing – particularly the magicians!" He considered a moment. "I have it! Fetch me a piece of moss-oak!"

"Sir?"

"It must be about your own girth and as tall as my collar bone."

"I would gladly fetch it for you immediately, sir. But I do not know what moss-oak is."

"Ancient wood that has been sunk in peat bogs for countless centuries!"

"Then, sir, I fear we are not very likely to find any in London. There are no peat bogs here."

"True, true." The gentleman flung himself back in his chair and stared at the ceiling while he considered this tricky problem.

"Would any other sort of wood suit your purposes, sir?" asked Stephen, "There is a timber merchant in Gracechurch-street, who I dare say . . ."

"No, no," said the gentleman, "This must be done . . ."

At that instant Stephen experienced the queerest sensation: he was plucked out of his chair and stood upon his feet. At the same moment the coffee-house disappeared and was replaced by a pitch-black, ice-cold nothingness. Though he could see nothing at all, Stephen had the sense that he was in a wide, open place. A bitter wind howled about his ears and a thick rain seemed to be falling upon him from all directions at once.

". . . properly," continued the gentleman in exactly the same tone as before. "There is a very fine piece of moss-oak hereabouts.

At least I think I remember . . ." His voice, which had been somewhere near Stephen's right ear, moved away. "Stephen!" he cried, "Have you brought a flaughter, a rutter and a tusker?"

"What, sir? Which, sir? No, sir. I have not brought any of those things. To own the truth, I did not quite understand that we were going any where." Stephen found that his feet and ancles were deep in cold water. He tried to step aside. Immediately the ground lurched most alarmingly and he sank suddenly into it up to the middle of his calves. He screamed.

"Mmm?" inquired the gentleman.

"I . . . I would never presume to interrupt you, sir. But the ground appears to be swallowing me up."

"It is a bog," said the gentleman, helpfully.

"It is certainly a most terrifying substance." Stephen attempted to mimic the gentleman's calm, uninterested tone. He knew only too well that the gentleman set a great value upon dignity in every situation and he feared that if he let the gentleman hear how terrified he was, there was every possibility that the gentleman would grow disgusted with him and wander off, leaving him to be sucked into the bog. He tried to move, but found nothing solid beneath his feet. He flailed about, almost fell and the only result was that his feet and legs slipped a little further into the watery mud. He screamed again. The bog made a series of most unpleasant sucking noises.

"Ah, God! I take the liberty of observing, sir, that I am sinking by degrees. Ah!" He began to slip sideways. "You have often been so kind as to express an affection for me, sir, and to say how much you prefer my society to that of any other person. If it would not inconvenience you in any way, perhaps I might prevail upon you to rescue me from this horrible bog?"

The gentleman did not trouble to reply. Instead Stephen found himself plucked by magic out of the bog and stood upon his feet. He was quite weak with fright and would have liked to lie down, but dared not move. The ground here seemed solid enough, but it was unpleasantly wet and he had no idea where the bog was.

"I would gladly help you, sir," he called into the darkness, "but I dare not move for fear of falling into the bog again!"

"Oh, it does not matter!" said the gentleman. "In truth, there is nothing to do but wait. Moss-oak is most easily discovered at dawn."

"But dawn is not for another nine hours!" exclaimed Stephen in horror.

"No, indeed! Let us sit down and wait."

"Here, sir? But this is a dreadful place. Black and cold and awful!"

"Oh, quite! It is most disagreeable!" agreed the gentleman with aggravating calmness. He fell silent then and Stephen could only suppose that he was pursuing this mad plan of waiting for the dawn.

The icy wind blew upon Stephen; the damp seeped up into every part of his being; the blackness pressed down upon him; and the long hours passed with excruciating slowness. He had no expectation of being able to sleep, but at some time during the night he experienced a little relief from the misery of his situation. It was not that he fell asleep exactly, but he did fall to dreaming.

In his dream he had gone to the pantry to fetch someone a slice of a magnificent pork pie. But when he cut the pie open he found that there was very little pork inside it. Most of the interior was taken up by the city of Birmingham. Within the pie-crust forges and smithies smoked and engines pounded. One of the citizens, a civil-looking person, happened to stroll out from the cut that Stephen had made and when his glance fell upon Stephen, he said . . .

Just then a high, mournful sound broke in upon Stephen's dream – a slow, sad song in an unknown language and Stephen understood without ever actually waking that the gentleman with the thistle-down hair was singing.

It may be laid down as a general rule that if a man begins to sing, no one will take any notice of his song except his fellow human beings. This is true even if his song is surpassingly beautiful. Other men may be in raptures at his skill, but the rest of creation is, by and large, unmoved. Perhaps a cat or a dog may look at him; his horse, if it is an exceptionally intelligent beast, may pause in cropping the grass, but that is the extent of it. But when the fairy sang, the whole world listened to him. Stephen felt clouds pause in their passing; he felt sleeping hills shift and murmur; he felt cold mists dance. He understood for the first time that the world is not dumb at all, but merely waiting for someone to speak to it in a language it understands. In the fairy's song the earth recognized the names by which it called itself.

Stephen began to dream again. This time he dreamt that hills walked and the sky wept. Trees came and spoke to him and told him their secrets and also whether or not he might regard them as friends or enemies. Important destinies were hidden inside pebbles and crumpled leaves. He dreamt that everything in the world – stones and rivers, leaves and fire – had a purpose which it was determined to carry out with the utmost rigour, but he also understood that it was possible sometimes to persuade things to a different purpose.

When he awoke it was dawn. Or something like dawn. The light was watery, dim and incomparably sad. Vast, grey, gloomy hills rose up all around them and in between the hills there was a wide expanse of black bog. Stephen had never seen a landscape so calculated to reduce the onlooker to utter despair in an instant.

"This is one of your kingdoms, I suppose, sir?" he said.

"My kingdoms?" exclaimed the gentleman in surprize. "Oh, no! This is Scotland!"

The gentleman disappeared suddenly – and reappeared a moment later with an armful of tools. There was an axe and a spit and three things Stephen had never seen before. One was a little like a hoe, one was a little like a spade and the last was a very strange object, something between a spade and a scythe. He handed all of them to Stephen, who examined them with a puzzled air. "Are they new, sir? They shine so brightly."

"Well, obviously one cannot employ tools of ordinary metal for such a magical undertaking as I am proposing. These are made of a compound of quicksilver and starshine. Now, Stephen, we must look for a patch of ground where the dew has not settled and if we dig there we are sure to find moss-oak!"

All through the glen all the grasses and tiny coloured bog-plants were covered with dew. Stephen's clothes, hands, hair and skin had a velvety, grey bloom, and the gentleman's hair – which was always extraordinary – had added the sparkle of a million tiny spheres of water to its customary brilliance. He appeared to be wearing a jewelled halo.

The gentleman walked slowly across the glen, his eyes fixed upon the ground. Stephen followed.

"Ah!" cried the gentleman. "Here we are!"

How the gentleman knew this, Stephen could not tell.

They were standing in the middle of a boggy expanse, exactly like every other part of the glen. There was no distinguishing tree or rock nearby to mark the spot. But the gentleman strode on with a confident air until he came to a shallow depression. In the middle of the depression was a long, broad stripe where there was no dew at all.

"Dig here, Stephen!"

The gentleman proved surprizingly knowledgeable about the art of peat cutting. And though he did none of the actual work himself he carefully instructed Stephen how to cut away the uppermost layer of grasses and moss with one tool, how to cut the peat with another tool and how to lift out the pieces with a third.

Stephen was unaccustomed to hard labour and he was soon out of breath and every part of him ached. Fortunately, he had not cut down very far when he struck something much harder than the peat.

"Ah!" cried the gentleman, very well pleased. "That is the moss oak. Excellent! Now, Stephen, cut around it!"

This was easier said than done. Even when Stephen had cut away enough of the peat to expose the moss-oak to the air it was still very difficult to see what was oak and what was peat – both were black, wet and oozing. He dug some more and he began to suspect that, though the gentleman called it a log, this was in fact an entire tree.

"Could you not lift it out by magic, sir?" he asked.

"Oh, no! No, indeed! I shall ask a great deal of this wood and therefore it is incumbent upon us to make its passage from the bog into the wider world as easy as we can! Now, do you take this axe, Stephen, and cut me a piece as tall as my collar-bone. Then with the spit and the tusker we will prise it out!"

It took them three more hours to accomplish the task. Stephen chopped the wood to the size the gentleman had asked for, but the task of manoeuvring it out of the bog was more than one man could manage and the gentleman was obliged to descend into the muddy, stinking hole with him and they strained and pulled and heaved together.

When at last they had finished, Stephen threw himself upon the ground in a condition of the utmost exhaustion, while the gentleman stood, regarding his log with delight.

"Well," he said, "that was a great deal easier than I had imagined."

Stephen suddenly found himself once more in the upper room of the Jerusalem Coffee-house. He looked at himself and at the gentleman. Their good clothes were in tatters and they were covered from head to foot with bog-mud.

For the first time he was able to see the log of moss-oak properly. It was as black as sin, extremely fine-grained, and it oozed black water.

"We must dry it out before it will be fit for any thing," he said.

"Oh, no!" said the gentleman with a brilliant smile. "For my purposes it will do very well as it is!"

# 43

# The curious adventure of Mr Hyde

## December 1815

ONE MORNING IN the first week of December Jeremy knocked upon the door of Strange's library at Ashfair House and said that Mr Hyde begged the favour of a few minutes' conversation with him.

Strange was not best pleased to be interrupted. Since he had been in the country he had grown almost as fond of quiet and solitude as Norrell. "Oh, very well!" he muttered.

Delaying only to write another paragraph, look up three or four things in a biography of Valentine Greatrakes, blot his paper, correct some spellings and blot his paper again, he went immediately to the drawing-room.

A gentleman was sitting alone by the fire, staring pensively into the flames. He was a vigorous-looking, active sort of man of fifty or so years, dressed in the stout clothes and boots of a gentleman-farmer. On a table at his side there was a little glass of wine and a small plate of biscuits. Clearly Jeremy had decided that the visitor had sat alone long enough to require some refreshment.

Mr Hyde and Jonathan Strange had been neighbours all their lives, but the marked differences in their fortunes and tastes had meant that they had never been more than common acquaintances. This was in fact the first time they had met since Strange had become a magician.

They shook hands.

"I dare say, sir," began Mr Hyde, "you are wondering what can bring me to your door in such weather."

"Weather?"

"Yes, sir. It is very bad."

Strange looked out of the window. The high hills surrounding Ashfair were sheathed in snow. Every branch, every twig bore its burden of snow. The very air seemed white with frost and mist.

"So it is. I had not observed. I have not been out of the house since Sunday."

"Your servant tells me that you are very much occupied with your studies. I beg your pardon for interrupting you, but I have something to tell you which can wait no longer."

"Oh! There is no explanation necessary. And how is your . . ." Strange paused and tried to remember whether Mr Hyde had a wife, any children, brothers, sisters or friends. He found he was entirely without information upon the subject. "Farm," he finished. "I recollect it is at Aston."

"It is nearer to Clunbury."

"Clunbury. Yes."

"All is well with me, Mr Strange, except for something rather . . . unsettling which happened to me three days ago. I have been debating with myself ever since whether I ought to come and speak to you about it. I have asked the advice of my friends and my wife and all are agreed that I ought to tell you what I have seen. Three days ago I had business on the Welsh side of the border, with David Evans – I dare say you know him, sir?"

"I know him by sight. I have never spoken to him. Ford knows him, I believe." (Ford was the agent who managed all the business of Strange's estate.)

"Well, sir, David Evans and I had finished our business by two o'clock and I was very anxious to get home. There was a thick snow lying everywhere and the roads between here and Llanfair Waterdine were very bad. I dare say you do not know it, sir, but

David Evans's house is high up on a hill with a long view westwards and the moment he and I stepped outside we saw great grey clouds full of snow coming towards us. Mrs Evans, Davey's mother, pressed me to stay with them and come home the next day, but Evans and I talked it over and we both agreed that all would be well providing I left instantly and came home by the most direct way possible – in other words I should ride up to the Dyke and cross over into England before the storm was upon me."[1]

"The Dyke?" said Strange, frowning, "That is a steep ride – even in summer – and a very lonely place if any thing were to happen to you. I do not think I would have attempted it. But I dare say you know these hills and their temper better than I."

"Perhaps you are wiser than I was, sir. As I rode up to the Dyke a hard, high wind began to blow and it caught up the snow that had already fallen and carried it up into the air. The snow stuck to my horse's coat and to my own greatcoat so that when I looked down we were as white as the hillside, as white as the air. As white as everything. The wind made eerie shapes with the snow so that I seemed to be surrounded by spinning ghosts and the kind of evil spirits and bad angels that are in the Arabian lady's stories. My poor horse – who is not generally a nervous beast – seemed to be seeing all manner of things to frighten him. As you may imagine, I was beginning to wish very heartily that I had accepted Mrs Evans's hospitality when I heard the sound of a bell tolling."

"A bell?" said Strange.

"Yes, sir."

"But what bell could there have been?"

"Well, none at all, sir, in that lonely place. Indeed it is a wonder to me that I could have heard any thing at all what with the horse snorting and the wind howling."

[1] The Dyke is a great wall of earth and stones, now much decayed, which divides Wales from England – the work of Offa, an eighth-century Mercian king, who had learnt by experience to distrust his Welsh neighbours.

Strange, who imagined that Mr Hyde must have come in order to have this queer bell explained to him, began to talk of the magical significance of bells: how bells were used as a protection against fairies and other evil spirits and how a bad fairy might sometimes be frightened away by the sound of a church bell. And yet, at the same time, it was well known that fairies loved bells; fairy magic was often accompanied by the tolling of a bell; and bells often sounded when fairies appeared. "I cannot explain this odd contradiction," he said. "Theoretical magicians have puzzled over it for centuries."

Mr Hyde listened to this speech with every appearance of politeness and attentiveness. When Strange had finished, Mr Hyde said, "But the bell was just the beginning, sir."

"Oh!" said Strange, a little annoyed. "Very well. Continue."

"I got so far up the hill that I could see the Dyke where it runs along the top. There were a few bent trees, some broken-down walls of loose stones. I looked to the south and I saw a lady walking very fast along the Dyke towards me . . ."

"A lady!"

"I saw her very clearly. Her hair was loose and the wind was setting it on end and making it writhe about her head." Mr Hyde gestured with his hands to shew how the lady's hair had danced in the snowy air. "I think I called out to her. I know that she turned her head and looked at me, but she did not stop or slow her pace. She turned away again and walked on along the Dyke with all the snowy wraiths around her. She wore only a black gown. No shawl. No pelisse. And that made me very afraid for her. I thought that some dreadful accident must have befallen her. So I urged my horse up the hill, as fast as the poor creature could go. I tried to keep her in sight the whole time, but the wind kept carrying the snow into my eyes. I reached the Dyke and she was nowhere to be seen. So I rode back and forth along the Dyke. I searched and cried myself hoarse – I was sure she must have fallen down behind a heap of stones or snow, or tripped in some rabbit-hole. Or

perhaps been carried away by the person who had done her the evil in the first place."

"The evil?"

"Well, sir, I supposed that she must have been carried to the Dyke by someone who meant her harm. One hears such terrible things nowadays."

"You knew the lady?"

"Yes, sir."

"Who was it?"

"Mrs Strange."

There was a moment's silence.

"But it could not have been," said Strange, perplexed. "Mr Hyde, if any thing of a distressing nature had happened to Mrs Strange, I think someone would have told me. I am not so shut up with my books as that. I am sorry, Mr Hyde, but you are mistaken. Whoever this poor woman was, it was not Mrs Strange."

Mr Hyde shook his head. "If I saw you, sir, in Shrewsbury or Ludlow, I might not know you immediately. But Mrs Strange's father was curate of my parish for forty-seven years. I have known Mrs Strange – Miss Woodhope as she was then – since she was an infant taking her first steps in Clunbury churchyard. Even if she had not looked at me I would have known her. I would have known her by her figure, by her way of walking, by her everything."

"What did you do after you had lost sight of the woman?"

"I rode straight here – but your servant would not let me in."

"Jeremy? The man you spoke to just now?"

"Yes. He told me that Mrs Strange was safe within. I confess that I did not believe him and so I walked around your house and looked in at all the windows, until I saw her seated upon a sopha in this very room." Mr Hyde pointed to the sopha in question. "She was wearing a pale blue gown – not black at all."

"Well, there is nothing remarkable in that. Mrs Strange never wears black. It is not a colour I like to see a young woman wear."

Mr Hyde shook his head and frowned. "I wish I could convince you, sir, of what I saw. But I see that I cannot."

"And I wish I could explain it to you. But I cannot."

They shook hands at parting. Mr Hyde looked solemnly at Strange and said, "I never wished her harm, Mr Strange. Nobody could be more thankful that she is safe."

Strange bowed slightly. "And we intend to keep her so."

The door closed upon Mr Hyde's back.

Strange waited a moment and then went to find Jeremy. "Why did not you tell me that he had been here before?"

Jeremy made a sort of snorting noise of derision. "I believe I know better, sir, than to trouble you with such nonsense! Ladies in black dresses walking about in snow-storms!"

"I hope you did not speak too harshly to him."

"Me, sir? No, indeed!"

"Perhaps he was drunk. Yes, I expect that was it. I dare say he and David Evans were celebrating the successful conclusion of their business."

Jeremy frowned. "I do not think so, sir. David Evans is a Methodist preacher."

"Oh! Well, yes. I suppose you are right. And indeed it is not much like a hallucination brought on by drunkenness. It is more the sort of thing one might imagine if one took opium after reading one of Mrs Radcliffe's novels."

Strange found himself unsettled by Mr Hyde's visit. The thought of Arabella – even an ideal, imaginary Arabella – lost in the snow, wandering upon the hilltops, was disturbing. He could not help but be reminded of his own mother, who had taken to walking those same hills alone to escape the miseries of an unhappy marriage and who had caught a chill in a rainstorm and died.

That evening at dinner he said to Arabella, "I saw John Hyde today. He thought he saw you walking upon the Dyke last Tuesday in the middle of a snow-storm."

"No!"

"Yes."

"Poor man! He must have been a good deal startled."

"I believe he was."

"I shall certainly visit Mr and Mrs Hyde when Henry is here."

"You seem intent upon visiting every body in Shropshire when Henry is here," said Strange. "I hope you will not be disappointed."

"Disappointed! What do you mean?"

"Only that the weather is bad."

"Then we will tell Harris to drive slowly and carefully. But he would do that anyway. And Starling is a very steady horse. It takes a great deal of snow and ice to frighten Starling. He is not easily daunted. Besides, you know, there are people whom Henry *must* visit – people who would be most unhappy if he did not. Jenny and Alwen – my father's two old servants. They talk of nothing but Henry's coming. It is five years since they saw him last and they are scarcely likely to last another five years, poor things."

"Very well! Very well! I only said that the weather would be bad. That is all."

But that was not quite all. Strange was aware that Arabella had high hopes of this visit. She had seen her brother only rarely since her marriage. He had not come to Soho-square as often as she would have liked and, once there, he had never stayed as long as she wished. But this Christmas visit would restore all their old intimacy. They would be together among all the scenes of their childhood and Henry had promised to stay almost a month.

Henry arrived and at first it seemed that Arabella's dearest wishes would all be answered. The conversation at dinner that evening was very animated. Henry had a great deal of news to relate about Great Hitherden, the Northamptonshire village where he was Rector.[2]

Great Hitherden was a large and prosperous village. There were several gentlemen's families in the neighbourhood. Henry was highly pleased with the respectable place he occupied in its society. After a long description of his friends and their dinner-parties and balls, he ended by saying, "But I would not have you think that we neglect charitable works. We are a very active neighbourhood. There is much to do and many distressed persons. The day before yesterday I paid a visit to a poor, sick family and I found Miss Watkins already at the cottage, dispensing money and good advice. Miss Watkins is a very compassionate young lady." Here he paused as if expecting someone to say something.

Strange looked blank; then, suddenly, a thought seemed to strike him. "Why, Henry, I do beg your pardon. You will think us very remiss. You have now mentioned Miss Watkins five times in ten minutes and neither Bell nor I have made the least inquiry about her. We are both a little slow tonight – it is this cold Welsh air – it chills the brain – but now that I have awoken to your meaning I shall be happy to quiz you about her quite as much as you could wish for. Is she fair or dark? A brown complexion or a pale one? Does she favour the piano or the harp? What are her favourite books?"

Henry, who suspected he was being teased, frowned and seemed inclined to say no more about the lady.

Arabella, with a cool look at her husband, took up the inquiries in a gentler style and soon got out of Henry the following

[2] At the time of Strange and Arabella's marriage Henry had been Rector of Grace Adieu in Gloucestershire. While there he had conceived a wish to marry a young lady of the village, a Miss Parbringer. But Strange had not approved the young lady or her friends. The living of Great Hitherden had happened to fall vacant at this time and so Strange persuaded Sir Walter Pole, in whose gift it lay, to appoint Henry. Henry had been delighted. Great Hitherden was a much larger place than Grace Adieu and he soon forgot the unsuitable young lady.

information – that Miss Watkins had only lately removed to the neighbourhood of Great Hitherden – that her Christian name was Sophronia – that she lived with her guardians, Mr and Mrs Swoonfirst (persons to whom she was distantly related) – that she was fond of reading (though Henry could not say precisely what) – that her favourite colour was yellow – and that she had a particular dislike of pineapples.

"And her looks? Is she pretty?" asked Strange.

The question seemed to embarrass Henry.

"Miss Watkins is not generally considered one of the first in beauty, no. But then upon further acquaintance, you know – that is worth a great deal. People of both sexes, whose looks are very indifferent at the beginning, may appear almost handsome on further acquaintance. A well-informed mind, nice manners and a gentle nature – all of these are much more likely to contribute to a husband's happiness than mere transient beauty."

Strange and Arabella were a little surprized at this speech. There was a pause and then Strange asked, "Money?"

Henry looked quietly triumphant. "Ten thousand pounds," he said.

"My dear Henry!" cried Strange.

Later, when they were alone, Strange said to Arabella, "As I understand it, Henry is to be congratulated upon his cleverness. It seems that he has found the lady before any one else could. I take it that she has not been overpowered by offers – there is something in her face or figure that protects her from a too universal admiration."

"But I do not think that it can be only the money," said Arabella, who was inclined to defend her brother. "I think there must be some liking too. Or Henry would not have thought of it."

"Oh, I dare say," said Strange. "Henry is a very good fellow. And, besides, I never interfere, as you know."

"You are smiling," said Arabella, "which you have no right to do. *I* was just as clever as Henry in my time. I do not believe that any one had thought of marrying you, with your long nose and unamiable disposition, until it occurred to me to do so."

"That is true," said Strange thoughtfully. "I had forgotten that. It is a family failing."

The next day Strange stayed in the library while Arabella and Henry drove out to visit Jenny and Alwen. But the enjoyment of the first few days did not last long. Arabella soon discovered that she no longer had a great deal in common with her brother. Henry had passed the last seven years in a small country village. She, on the other hand, had been in London where she had observed at close hand some of the most important events of recent years. She had the friendship of more than one Cabinet Minister. She was acquainted with the Prime Minister and had danced several times with the Duke of Wellington. She had met the Royal Dukes, curtsied to the Princesses and could always rely upon a smile and a word from the Prince Regent whenever she happened to be at Carlton House. As for her large acquaintance with every one connected with the glorious revival of English magic, *that* went without saying.

But, while she was greatly interested in all her brother's news, he had next to no interest in hers. Her descriptions of London life drew no more than a polite, "Ah, indeed?" from him. Once when she was speaking of something the Duke of Wellington had said to her and relating what she had said in reply, Henry turned and looked at her with a raised eye-brow and a bland smile – a look and smile which said very plainly, "I do not believe you." Such behaviour wounded her. She did not believe she was boasting – such encounters had been part of the daily tenor of her London life. She realized with a little pang that whereas his letters had always delighted her, he must have found her replies tedious and affected.

Meanwhile, poor Henry had dissatisfactions of his own. When he had been a boy he had greatly admired Ashfair House. Its size, its situation and the great importance of its owner in the neighbourhood of Clun, had all seemed equally wonderful to him. He had always looked forward to the day when Jonathan Strange would inherit and he could visit Ashfair in the important character of Friend of The Master. Now that all of this had come to pass he discovered that he did not really enjoy being there. Ashfair was inferior to many houses that he had seen in the intervening years. It had almost as many gables as windows. Its rooms were all low-ceilinged and oddly shaped. The many generations of inhabitants had placed the windows in the walls just as it had pleased them – without any thought to the general appearance of the house – and the windows themselves were darkened, every one, by the roses and ivy growing up the walls. It was an old-fashioned house – the sort of house in fact, as Strange expressed it, which a lady in a novel might like to be persecuted in.

Several houses in the neighbourhood of Great Hitherden had recently been improved and elegant new cottages built for ladies and gentlemen with rustic inclinations and so – partly because it was impossible for Henry to keep any thing connected to his parish to himself – and partly because he was intending to be married soon and so his mind rather ran upon domestic improvements – he was quite unable to refrain from giving Strange advice upon the matter. He was particularly distressed by the position of the stable yard which, as he told Strange, "One is obliged to walk through to get to the southerly part of the pleasure-grounds and the orchard. You could very easily pull it down and build it again somewhere else."

Strange did not exactly reply to this, but instead suddenly addressed his wife. "My love, I hope you like this house? I am very much afraid that I never thought to ask you before. Say if you do not and we shall instantly remove elsewhere!"

Arabella laughed and said that she was quite satisfied with the house. "And I am sorry, Henry, but I am just as satisfied with the stable-yard as with everything else."

Henry tried again. "Well, surely, you will agree that a great improvement could be made simply by cutting down those trees that crowd about the house so much and darken every room? They grow just as they please – just where the acorn or seed fell, I suppose."

"What?" asked Strange, whose eyes had wandered back to his book during the latter part of the conversation.

"The trees," said Henry.

"Which trees?"

"Those," said Henry, pointing out of the window to a whole host of ancient and magnificent oaks, ashes and beech trees.

"As far as neighbours go, those trees are quite exemplary. They mind their own affairs and have never troubled me. I rather think that I will return the compliment."

"But they are blocking the light."

"So are you, Henry, but I have not yet taken an axe to you."

The truth was that, though Henry saw much to criticize in the grounds and position of Ashfair, this was not his real complaint. What really disturbed him about the house was the all-pervading air of magic. When Strange had first taken up the profession of magic, Henry had not thought any thing of it. At that time news of Mr Norrell's wonderful achievements was only just beginning to spread throughout the kingdom. Magic had seemed little more than an esoteric branch of history, an amusement for rich, idle gentlemen; and Henry still somehow contrived to regard it in that light. He prided himself upon Strange's wealth, his estate, his important pedigree, but not upon his magic. He was always a little surprized whenever any one congratulated him on his close connexion with the Second Greatest Magician of the Age.

Strange was a long way from Henry's ideal of a rich English gentleman. He had pretty well abandoned those pursuits with which gentlemen in the English countryside customarily occupy their time. He took no interest in farming or hunting. His neighbours went shooting – Henry heard their shots echoing in the snowy woods and fields and the barking of their dogs – but

Strange never picked up a gun. It took all Arabella's persuasion to make him go outside and walk about for half an hour. In the library the books that had belonged to Strange's father and grandfather – those works in English, Greek and Latin which every gentleman has upon his shelves – had all been removed and piled up upon the floor to make room for Strange's own books and notebooks.[3] Periodicals concerned with the practice of magic, such as *The Friends of English Magic* and *The Modern Magician*, were everywhere scattered about the house. Upon one of the tables in the library there stood a great silver dish, which was sometimes full of water. Strange would often sit for half an hour peering into the water, tapping the surface and making odd gestures and writing down notes of what he saw there. On another table amid a jumble of books there lay a map of England upon which Strange was marking the old fairy roads which once led out of England to who-knows-where.

There were other things too which Henry only half-understood but which he disliked even more. He knew for instance that Ashfair's rooms often had an odd look, but he did not see that this was because the mirrors in Strange's house were as likely as not to be reflecting the light of half an hour ago, or a hundred years ago. And in the morning, when he awoke, and at night, just before he fell asleep, he heard the sound of a distant bell – a sad sound, like the bell of a drowned city heard across a waste of ocean. He never really thought of the bell, or indeed remembered any thing about it, but its melancholy influence stayed with him through the day.

He found relief for all his various disappointments and dis-satisfactions in drawing numerous comparisons between the way things were done in Great Hitherden and the way they were done in Shropshire (much to the detriment of Shropshire), and in

[3] The books Strange possessed were, of course, books *about* magic, not books *of* magic. The latter were all in the possession of Mr Norrell. *C.f.* Chapter 1, footnote 5.

wondering aloud that Strange should study so hard – "quite as if he had no estate of his own and all his fortune was still to make." These remarks were generally addressed to Arabella, but Strange was often in earshot and pretty soon Arabella found herself in the unenviable position of trying to keep the peace between the two of them.

"When I want Henry's advice," said Strange, "I shall ask for it. What business is it of his, I should like to know, where I chuse to build my stables? Or how I spend my time?"

"It is very aggravating, my love," agreed Arabella, "and no one should wonder if it put you out of temper, but only consider . . ."

"My temper! It is he who keeps quarrelling with me!"

"Hush! Hush! He will hear you. You have been very sorely tried and any one would say that you have borne it like an angel. But, you know, I think he means to be kind. It is just that he docs not express himself very well, and for all his faults we shall miss him greatly when he is gone."

Upon this last point Strange did not perhaps look as convinced as she could have wished. So she added, "Be kind to Henry? For my sake?"

"Of course! Of course! I am patience itself. You know that! There used to be a proverb – quite defunct now – something about priests sowing wheat and magicians sowing rye, all in the same field. The meaning is that priests and magicians will never agree.[4]

[4] The meaning was perhaps a little more than this. As early as the twelfth century it was recognized that priests and magicians are in some sense rivals. Both believe that the universe is inhabited by a wide variety of supernatural beings and subject to supernatural forces. Both believe that these beings can be petitioned through spells or prayers and so be persuaded to help or hinder mankind. In many ways the two cosmologies are remarkably similar, but priests and magicians draw very different conclusions from this understanding.

Magicians are chiefly interested in the usefulness of these supernatural beings; they wish to know under what circumstances and by what means angels, demons and fairies can be brought to lend their aid in magical practices. For their purposes it is almost irrelevant that the first class of beings is divinely good, the second infernally wicked and the third morally suspect.

I never found it so until now. I believe I was on friendly terms with the London clergy. The Dean of Westminster Abbey and the Prince Regent's chaplain are excellent fellows. But Henry irks me."

On Christmas-day the snow fell thick and fast. Whether from the vexations of recent days or from some other cause, Arabella awoke in the morning quite sick and wretched with a headach, and unable to rise from her bed. Strange and Henry were obliged to keep each other company the whole day. Henry talked a great deal about Great Hitherden and in the evening they played ecarte. This was a game they were both rather fond of. It might perhaps have produced a more natural state of enjoyment, but halfway through the second game Strange turned over the nine of spades and was immediately struck by several new ideas concerning the magical significance of this card. He abandoned the game, abandoned Henry and took the card with him to the library to study it. Henry was left to his own devices.

Sometime in the early hours of the following morning he woke – or half-woke. There was a faint silvery radiance in the room which might easily have been a reflection of the moonlight on the snow

---

[4] *cont'd* Priests on the other hand are scarcely interested in any thing else.

In mediaeval England attempts to reconcile the two cosmologies were doomed to failure. The Church was quick to identify a whole host of different heresies of which an unsuspecting magician might be guilty. The Meraudian Heresy has already been mentioned.

Alexander of Whitby (1230s?-1302) taught that the universe is like a tapestry only parts of which are visible to us at a time. After we are dead we will see the whole and then it will be clear to us how the different parts relate to each other. Alexander was forced to issue a retraction of his thesis and priests were henceforth on the lookout for the Whitbyian Heresy. Even the humblest of village magicians was obliged to become a cunning politician if he or she wished to avoid accusations of heresy.

This is not to say that all magicians avoided confusing religion and magic. Many "spells" which have come down to us exhort such-and-such a saint or holy person to help the magician. Surprizingly the source of the confusion was often the magicians' fairy-servants. Most fairies were forcibly baptized as soon as they entered England and they soon began to incorporate references to Saints and Apostles into their magic.

outside. He thought he saw Arabella, dressed and seated on the foot of the bed with her back towards him. She was brushing her hair. He said something to her – or at least thought he said something.

Then he went back to sleep.

At about seven o'clock he woke properly, anxious to get to the library and work for an hour or two before Henry appeared. He rose quickly, went to his dressing-room and rang for Jeremy Johns to come and shave him.

At eight o'clock Arabella's maid, Janet Hughes, knocked on the bed-chamber door. There was no reply and Janet, thinking her mistress might still have the headach, went away again.

At ten o'clock Strange and Henry breakfasted together. Henry had decided to spend the day shooting and was at some pains to persuade Strange to go with him.

"No, no. I have work to do, but that need not prevent your going. After all you know these fields and woods as well as I. I can lend you a gun and dogs can be found from somewhere, I am sure."

Jeremy Johns appeared and said that Mr Hyde had returned. He was in the hall and had asked to speak to Strange on a matter of urgency.

"Oh, what does the fellow want this time?" muttered Strange.

Mr Hyde entered hurriedly, his face grey with anxiety.

Suddenly Henry exclaimed, "What in the world does that fellow think he is doing? He is neither in the room nor out of it!" One of Henry's several sources of vexation at Ashfair was the servants who rarely behaved with that degree of ceremony that Henry considered proper for members of such an important household. On this occasion Jeremy Johns had begun to leave the room but had only got as far as the doorway, where, half-hidden by the door, he and another servant were conducting a conversation in urgent whispers.

Strange glanced at the doorway, sighed and said, "Henry, it really does not matter. Mr Hyde, I . . ."

Meanwhile Mr Hyde, whose agitation appeared to have been increased by this delay, burst out, "An hour ago I saw Mrs Strange again upon the Welsh hills!"

Henry gave a start and looked at Strange.

Strange gave Mr Hyde a very cool look and said, "It is nothing, Henry. Really it is nothing."

Mr Hyde flinched a little at this, but there was a sort of stubbornness in him that helped him bear it. "It was upon Castle Idris and just as before, Mrs Strange was walking away from me and I did not see her face. I tried to follow her and catch up with her, but, just as before, I lost sight of her. I know that the last time it was accounted no more than a delusion – a phantom made by my own brain out of the snow and wind – but today is clear and calm and I know that I saw Mrs Strange – as clearly, sir, as I now see you."

"The last time?" said Henry in confusion.

Strange, somewhat impatiently, began to thank Mr Hyde for his great good nature in bringing them this . . . (He was not quite able to find the word he wanted.) "But as I know Mrs Strange to be safe within my own house, I dare say you will not be surprized, if I . . ."

Jeremy came back into the room rather suddenly. He went immediately to Strange and bent and whispered in his ear.

"Well, speak, man! Tell us what is the matter!" said Henry.

Jeremy looked rather doubtfully at Strange, but Strange said nothing. He covered his mouth with his hand and his eyes went this way and that, as if he were suddenly taken up with some new, and not very pleasant, idea.

Jeremy said, "Mrs Strange is no longer in the house, sir. We do not know where she is."

Henry was questioning Mr Hyde about what he had seen on the hills and barely giving him time to answer one question before asking another. Jeremy Johns was frowning at them both. Strange, meanwhile, sat silently, staring in front of him. Suddenly he stood up and went rapidly out of the room.

"Mr Strange!" called Mr Hyde. "Where are you going?"

"Strange!" cried Henry.

As nothing could be done or decided without him, they had no choice but to follow him. Strange mounted the stairs to his library on the first floor and went immediately to the great silver dish that stood upon one of the tables.

"Bring water," he said to Jeremy Johns.

Jeremy Johns fetched a jug of water and filled the dish.

Strange spoke a single word and the room seemed to grow twilit and shadowy. In the same moment the water in the dish darkened and became slightly opaque.

The lessening of the light terrified Henry.

"Strange!" he cried. "What are we doing here? The light is failing! My sister is outside. We ought not to remain in the house a moment longer!" He turned to Jeremy Johns as the only person present likely to have any influence with Strange. "Tell him to stop! We must start to search!"

"Be quiet, Henry," said Strange.

He drew his finger over the surface of the water twice. Two glittering lines of light appeared, quartering the water. He made a gesture above one of the quarters. Stars appeared in it and more lines, veinings and webs of light. He stared at this for some moments. Then he made a gesture above the next quarter. A different pattern of light appeared. He repeated the process for the third and fourth quarters. The patterns did not remain the same. They shifted and sparkled, sometimes appearing like writing, at other times like the lines of a map and at other times like constellations of stars.

"What is all this meant to do?" asked Mr Hyde, in a wondering tone.

"Find her," said Strange. "At least, that is what it is supposed to do."

He tapped one of the quarters. Instantly the other three patterns disappeared. The remaining pattern grew until it filled the surface of the water. Strange divided it into quarters, studied it for a while and then tapped one of the quarters. He repeated this process several times. The patterns grew denser and began more and more to resemble a map. But the further Strange got, the more doubting his expression grew and the less sure he seemed of what the dish was shewing him.

After several minutes Henry could bear it no longer. "For God's sake, this is no time for magic! Arabella is lost! Strange, I beg you! Leave this nonsense and let us look for her!"

Strange said nothing in reply but he looked angry and struck the water. Instantly the lines and stars disappeared. He took a deep breath and began again. This time he proceeded in a more confident manner and quickly reached a pattern he seemed to consider relevant. But far from drawing any useful information from it, he sat instead regarding it with a mixture of dismay and perplexity.

"What is it?" asked Mr Hyde in alarm. "Mr Strange, do you see your wife?"

"I can make no sense of what the spell is telling me! It says she is not in England. Not in Wales. Not in Scotland. Not in France. I cannot get the magic right. You are right, Henry. I am wasting time here. Jeremy, fetch my boots and coat!"

A vision blossomed suddenly on the face of the water. In an ancient, shadowy hall a crowd of handsome men and lovely women were dancing. But as this could have no conceivable connexion with Arabella, Strange struck the surface of the water again. The vision vanished.

Outside, the snow lay thick upon everything. All was frozen, still and silent. The grounds of Ashfair were the first places to be searched. When these proved to contain hardly so much as a wren or a robin, Strange, Henry, Mr Hyde and the servants began to search the roads.

Three of the maidservants went back to the house where they went into attics that had scarcely been disturbed since Strange had been a boy. They took an axe and a hammer and broke open chests that had been locked fifty years before. They looked into closets and drawers, some of which could hardly have contained the body of an infant, let alone that of a grown woman.

Some of the servants ran to houses in Clun. Others took horses and rode to Clunton, Purslow, Clunbury and Whitcott. Soon there was not a house in the neighbourhood that did not know Mrs Strange was missing and not a house that did not send someone to join the search. Meanwhile the women of these houses kept up their fires and made all manner of preparations so that should Mrs Strange be brought to *that* house, she should instantly have as much warmth, nourishment, and comfort as one human being can benefit from at a time.

The first hour brought them Captain John Ayrton of the 12th Light Dragoons, who had been with Wellington and Strange in the Peninsula and at Waterloo. His lands adjoined those of Strange. They were the same age and had been neighbours all their lives, but Captain Ayrton was so shy and reserved a gentleman that they had rarely exchanged more than twenty words in the course of a year. In this crisis he arrived with maps and a quiet, solemn promise to Strange and Henry to give them all the assistance that was in his power.

It was soon discovered that Mr Hyde was not the only person to have seen Arabella. Two farm labourers, Martin Oakley and Owen Bullbridge, had also seen her. Jeremy Johns learnt this from some friends of the two men, whereupon he instantly took the first horse he could lay his hands upon and rode to the snowy fields on the banks of the Clun river where Oakley and Bullbridge had joined the general search. Jeremy half-escorted them, half-herded them back to Clun to appear before Captain Ayrton, Mr Hyde, Henry Woodhope and Strange.

They discovered that Oakley and Bullbridge's account contradicted Mr Hyde's in odd ways. Mr Hyde had seen Arabella on the bare snowy hillsides of Castle Idris. She had been walking northwards. He had seen her at precisely nine o'clock and, just as before, he had heard bells ringing.

Oakley and Bullbridge, on the other hand, had seen her hurrying through the dark winter trees some five miles east of Castle Idris, yet they too claimed to have seen her at precisely nine o'clock.

Captain Ayrton frowned and asked Oakley and Bullbridge to explain how they had known it was nine o'clock, since, unlike Mr Hyde, neither of them possessed a pocket-watch. Oakley replied that they had thought it must be nine o'clock because they had heard bells ringing. The bells, Oakley thought, belonged to St George's in Clun. But Bullbridge said that they were *not* the bells of St George's – that the bells he had heard were many, and that St George's had but one. He had said that the bells he had heard were sad bells – funeral bells, he thought – but, when asked to explain what he meant by this, he could not.

The two accounts agreed in all other details. In neither was there any nonsense about black gowns. All three men said she had been wearing a white gown and all agreed that she had been walking rather fast. None of them had seen her face.

Captain Ayrton set the men to search the dark winter woods in groups of four and five. He set women to find lanterns and warm clothing and he set riders to cover the high, open hills around Castle Idris. He put Mr Hyde – who would be satisfied with nothing else – in charge of them. Ten minutes after Oakley and Bullbridge had finished speaking, all were gone. As long as daylight lasted they searched, but daylight could not last long. They were only five days from the Winter Solstice: by three o'clock the light was fading; by four it was gone altogether.

The searchers returned to Strange's house, where Captain Ayrton intended to review what had been done so far and hoped to determine what ought to be done next. Several of the ladies of the neighbourhood were also present. They had tried waiting in their own houses for news of Mrs Strange's fate and found it a lonely, anxious business. They had come to Ashfair partly in case they were needed, but chiefly so that they might take comfort in each other's society.

The last to arrive were Strange and Jeremy Johns. They came, booted and muddy, direct from the stables. Strange was ashen-faced and hollow-eyed. He looked and moved like a man in dream. He would probably not even have sat down, had Jeremy Johns not pushed him into a chair.

Captain Ayrton laid out his maps upon the table and began to question each of the search parties about where they had been and what they had found – which was nothing at all.

Every man and woman present thought how the neatly drawn lines and words upon the maps were in truth ice-covered pools and rivers, silent woods, frozen ditches and high, bare hills and every one of them thought how many sheep and cattle and wild creatures died in this season.

"I think I woke last night . . ." said a hoarse voice, suddenly. They looked round.

Strange was still seated in the chair where Jeremy had placed him. His arms hung at his sides and he was staring at the floor. "I think I woke last night. I do not know when exactly. Arabella was sitting at the foot of the bed. She was dressed."

"You did not say this before," said Mr Hyde.

"I did not remember before. I thought I had dreamt it."

"I do not understand," said Captain Ayrton. "Do you mean to say that Mrs Strange may have left your house during the night?"

Strange seemed to cast about for an answer to this highly reasonable question, but without success.

"But surely," said Mr Hyde, "you must know if she was there or not in the morning?"

"She was there. Of course she was there. It is ridiculous to suggest . . . At least . . ." Strange paused. "That is to say I was thinking about my book when I rose and the room was dark."

Several people present began to think that as a husband

Jonathan Strange, if not absolutely neglectful, was at least curiously unobservant of his wife, and some of them were led to eye him doubtingly and run through in their minds the many reasons why an apparently devoted wife might suddenly run away into the snow. Cruel words? A violent temper? The dreadful sights attendant on a magician's work – ghosts, demons, horrors? The sudden discovery that he had a mistress somewhere and half a dozen natural children?

Suddenly there was a shout from outside in the hall. Afterwards no one could say whose voice it had been. Several of Strange's neighbours who were standing nearest the door went to see what the matter was. Then the exclamations of those people drew out the rest.

The hall was dark at first, but in a moment candles were brought and they could see that someone was standing at the foot of the stairs.

It was Arabella.

Henry rushed forward and embraced her; Mr Hyde and Mrs Ayrton told her how glad they were to see her safe and sound; other people began to express their amazement and to inform any one who would listen that they had not had the least idea of her being there. Several of the ladies and maids gathered around her, asking her questions. Was she hurt? Where had she been? Had she got lost? Had something happened to distress her?

Then, as sometimes will happen, several people became aware at the same time of something rather odd: Strange had said nothing, made no movement towards her – nor, for that matter, had she spoken to him or made any movement towards him.

The magician stood, staring silently at his wife. Suddenly he exclaimed, "Good God, Arabella! What have you got on?"

Even by the candles' uncertain, flickering light it was quite plain that she was wearing a black gown.

## 44

# Arabella

## December 1815

"YOU MUST BE chilled to the bone!" declared Mrs Ayrton, taking one of Arabella's hands. "Oh, my dear! You are as cold as thc grave!"

Another lady ran and fetched one of Arabella's shawls from the drawing-room. She returned carrying a blue Indian cashmere with a delicate border of gold and pink threads, but when Mrs Ayrton wrapped it around her, the black gown seemed to extinguish all its prettiness.

Arabella, with her hands folded in front of her, looked at them all with a calm, indifferent expression upon her face. She did not trouble to answer any of their kind inquiries. She seemed neither surprized nor embarrassed to find them there.

"Where in the world have you been?" demanded Strange.

"Walking," she said. Her voice was just as it had always been.

"Walking! Arabella, are you quite mad? In three feet of snow? Where?"

"In the dark woods," she said, "among my soft-sleeping brothers and sisters. Across the high moors among the sweet-scented ghosts of my brothers and sisters long dead. Under the grey sky through the dreams and murmurs of my brothers and sisters yet to come."

Strange stared at her. "What?"

With such gentle questioning as this to encourage her, it surprized no one that she said no more and at least one of the ladies began to think that it was her husband's harshness that made her so quiet and made her answer in such odd strain.

Mrs Ayrton put her arm around Arabella and gently turned her towards the stairs. "Mrs Strange is tired," she said firmly. "Come, my dear, let you and I go up to . . ."

"Oh, no!" declared Strange. "Not yet! I wish to know where that gown came from. I beg your pardon, Mrs Ayrton, but I am quite determined to . . ."

He advanced towards them, but then stopt suddenly and stared down at the floor in puzzlement. Then he carefully stepped out of the way of something. "Jeremy! Where did this water come from? Just where Mrs Strange was standing."

Jeremy Johns brought a candelabra to the foot of the stairs. There was a large pool. Then he and Strange peered at the ceiling and the walls. The other manservants became interested in the problem and so did the gentlemen.

While the men were thus distracted, Mrs Ayrton and the ladies led Arabella quietly away.

The hall at Ashfair was as old-fashioned as the rest of the house. It was panelled in cream-painted elmwood. The floor was well-swept stone flags. One of the manservants thought that the water must have seeped up from under the stones and so he went and fetched an iron rod to poke about at them to prove that one of them was loose. But he could not make them move. Nowhere was there any sign of where the water could have crept in. Someone else thought that perhaps Captain Ayrton's two dogs might have shed the water. The dogs were carefully examined. They were not in the least wet.

Finally they examined the water itself.

"It is black and there are tiny scraps of something in it," pointed out Strange.

"It looks like moss," said Jeremy Johns.

They continued to wonder and exclaim for some time until a complete lack of any success obliged them to abandon the matter. Shortly afterwards the gentlemen left, taking their wives with them.

At five o'clock Janet Hughes went up to her mistress's bedchamber and found her lying upon the bed. She had not even troubled to take off the black dress. When Janet asked her if she felt unwell, Arabella replied that she had a pain in her hands. So Janet helped her mistress undress and then went and told Strange.

On the second day Arabella complained of a pain which went from the top of her head all down her right side to her feet (or at least that was what they supposed she meant when she said, "from my crown to the tips of my roots"). This was sufficiently alarming for Strange to send for Mr Newton, the physician at Church Stretton. Mr Newton rode over to Clun in the afternoon, but apart from the pain he could find nothing wrong and he went away cheerfully, telling Strange that he would return in a day or two.

On the third day she died.

# Volume III

# JOHN USKGLASS

It is the contention of Mr Norrell of Hanover-square that everything belonging to John Uskglass must be shaken out of modern magic, as one would shake moths and dust out of an old coat. What does he imagine he will have left? If you get rid of John Uskglass you will be left holding the empty air.

Jonathan Strange, Prologue to *The History and Practice of English Magic*, pub. John Murray, London, 1816

# 45

# Prologue to *The History and Practice of English Magic*

## by Jonathan Strange

IN THE LAST months of 1110 a strange army appeared in Northern England. It was first heard of near a place called Penlaw some twenty or thirty miles north-west of Newcastle. No one could say where it had come from – it was generally supposed to be an invasion of Scots or Danes or perhaps even of French.

By early December the army had taken Newcastle and Durham and was riding west. It came to Allendale, a small stone settlement that stands high among the hills of Northumbria, and camped one night on the edge of a moor outside the town. The people of Allendale were sheep-farmers, not soldiers. The town had no walls to protect it and the nearest soldiers were thirty-five miles away, preparing to defend the castle of Carlisle. Consequently, the townspeople thought it best to lose no time in making friends with the strange army. With this aim in mind several pretty young women set off, a company of brave Judiths determined to save themselves and their neighbours if they could. But when they arrived at the place where the army had their camp the women became fearful and hung back.

The camp was a dreary, silent place. A thick snow was falling and the strange soldiers lay, wrapped in their black cloaks, upon the snowy ground. At first the young women thought the soldiers must be dead – an impression which was strengthened by the great multitude of ravens and other black birds which had settled over the camp, and indeed upon the prostrate forms of the soldiers themselves – yet the soldiers were not dead; from time to time one would stir himself and go attend to his horse, or brush a bird away if it tried to peck at his face.

At the approach of the young women a soldier got to his feet. One of the women shook off her fears and went up to him and kissed him on the mouth.

His skin was very pale (it shone like moonlight) and entirely without blemish. His hair was long and straight like a fall of dark brown water. The bones of his face were unnaturally fine and strong. The expression of the face was solemn. His blue eyes were long and slanting and his brows were as fine and dark as pen-strokes with a curious flourish at the end. None of this worried the girl in the least. For all she knew every Dane, Scot and Frenchman ever born is eerily beautiful.

He took well enough to the kiss and allowed her to kiss him again. Then he paid her back in kind. Another soldier rose from the ground and opened his mouth. Out of it came a sad, wailing sort of music. The first soldier – the one the girl had kissed – began to coax her to dance with him, pushing her this way and that with his long white fingers until she was dancing in a fashion to suit him.

This went on for some time until she became heated with the dance and paused for a moment to take off her cloak. Then her companions saw that drops of blood, like beads of sweat, were forming on her arms, face and legs, and falling on to the snow. This sight terrified them and so they ran away.

The strange army never entered Allendale. It rode on in the night towards Carlisle. The next day the townspeople went cautiously up to the fields where the army had camped. There they found the girl, her body entirely white and drained of blood while the snow around her was stained bright red.

By these signs they recognized the *Daoine Sidhe* – the Fairy Host.

Battles were fought and the English lost every one. By Christmas the Fairy Host was at York. They held Newcastle, Durham, Carlisle and Lancaster. Aside from the exsanguination of the maid of Allendale the fairies displayed very little of the cruelty for which their race is famed. Of all the towns and fortifications which they took, only Lancaster was burnt to the ground. At Thirsk, north of York, a pig offended a member of the Host by running out under the feet of his horse and causing it to rear up and fall and break its back. The fairy and his companions hunted the pig and when they had caught it they put its eyes out. Generally, however, the arrival of the Host at any new place was a cause of great rejoicing among animals both wild and domesticated as if they recognized in the fairies an ally against their common foe, Man.

At Christmas, King Henry summoned his earls, bishops, abbots and the great men of his realm to his house in Westminster to discuss the matter. Fairies were not unknown in England in those days. There were long-established fairy settlements in many places, some hidden by magic, some merely avoided by their Christian neighbours. King Henry's counsellors agreed that fairies were naturally wicked. They were lascivious, mendacious and thieving; they seduced young men and women, confused travellers, and stole children, cattle and corn. They were astonishingly indolent: they had mastered the arts of masonry, carpentry and carving thousands of years ago but, rather than take the trouble to build themselves houses, most still preferred to live in places which they were pleased to call castles but which were in fact *brugh* – earth barrows of great antiquity. They spent their days drinking and dancing while their barley and beans rotted in the fields, and their beasts shivered and died on the cold hillside. Indeed, all King Henry's advisers agreed that, had it not been for their extraordinary magic and near immortality, the entire fairy race would have long since perished from hunger and thirst. Yet this feckless, improvident people had invaded a well-defended Christian kingdom, won every battle they had fought and had ridden from place to place securing each stronghold as they came to it. All this spoke of a measure of purposefulness which no fairy had ever been known to possess.

No one knew what to make of it.

In January the Fairy Host left York and rode south. At the Trent they halted. So it was at Newark on the banks of the Trent that King Henry and his army met the *Daoine Sidhe* in battle.

Before the battle a magic wind blew through the ranks of King Henry's army and a sweet sound of pipe music was heard, which caused a great number of the horses to break free and flee to the fairy side, many taking their unlucky riders with them. Next, every man heard the voices of his loved ones – mothers, fathers, children, lovers – call out to him to come home. A host of ravens descended from the sky, pecking at the faces of the English and blinding them with a chaos of black wings. The English soldiers not only had the skill and ferocity of the *Sidhe* to contend with, but also their own fear in the face of such eerie magic. It is scarcely to be wondered at that the battle was short and that King Henry lost. At the moment when all fell silent and it became clear beyond any doubt that King Henry had been defeated the birds for miles around began singing as if for joy.

The King and his counsellors waited for some chieftain or king to step forward. The ranks of the *Daoine Sidhe* parted and someone appeared.

He was rather less than fifteen years old. Like the *Daoine Sidhe* he was dressed in ragged clothes of coarse black wool. Like them his dark hair was long and straight. Like them, he spoke neither English nor French – the two languages current in England at that time – but only a dialect of Faerie.[1] He was pale and handsome

[1] No one in England nowadays knows this language and all we have left of it is a handful of borrowed words describing various obscure magical techniques. Martin Pale wrote in *De Tractatu Magicarum Linguarum* that it was related to the ancient Celtic languages.

and solemn-faced, yet it was clear to everyone present that he was human, not fairy.

By the standards of the Norman and English earls and knights, who saw him that day for the first time, he was scarcely civilized. He had never seen a spoon before, nor a chair, nor an iron kettle, nor a silver penny, nor a wax candle. No fairy clan or kingdom of the period possessed any such fine things. When King Henry and the boy met to divide England between them, Henry sat upon a wooden bench and drank wine from a silver goblet, the boy sat upon the floor and drank ewe's milk from a stone cup. The chronicler, Orderic Vitalis, writing some thirty years later, describes the shock felt by King Henry's court when they saw, in the midst of all these important proceedings, a *Daoine Sidhe* warrior lean across and begin solicitously plucking lice out of the boy's filthy hair.

There was among the Fairy Host a young Norman knight called Thomas of Dundale.[2] Though he had been a captive in Faerie for many years he remembered enough of his own language (French) to make the boy and King Henry understand each other.

King Henry asked the boy his name.

The boy replied that he had none.[3]

King Henry asked him why he made war on England.

The boy said that he was the only surviving member of an aristocratic Norman family who had been granted lands in the north of England by King Henry's father, William the Conqueror.

[2] Variously Thomas de Dundelle or Thomas de Donvil. It seems that several of Henry's noblemen recognized Thomas as the younger son of a powerful Norman magnate who had disappeared one Christmas fourteen years before. Given the circumstances of his return it is doubtful whether they felt particularly pleased to have him back.

[3] When he was a child in Faerie the *Sidhe* had called him a word in their own language which, we are told, meant "Starling", but he had already abandoned that name by the time he entered England. Later he took to calling himself by his father's name – John d'Uskglass – but in the early part of his reign he was known simply by one of the many titles his friends or enemies gave him: the King; the Raven King; the Black King; the King in the North.

The men of the family had been deprived of their lands and their lives by a wicked enemy named Hubert de Cotentin. The boy said that some years before his father had appealed to William II (King Henry's brother and predecessor) for justice, but had received none. Shortly afterwards his father had been murdered. The boy said that he himself had been taken by Hubert's men while still a baby and abandoned in the forest. But the *Daoine Sidhe* had found him and taken him to live with them in Faerie. Now he had returned.

He had a very young man's belief in the absolute rightness of his own cause and the absolute wrongness of everyone else's. He had settled it in his own mind that the stretch of England which lay between the Tweed and the Trent was a just recompense for the failure of the Norman kings to avenge the murders of his family. For this reason and no other King Henry was suffered to retain the southern half of his kingdom.

The boy said that he was already a king in Faerie. He named the fairy king who was his overlord. No one understood.[4]

That day he began his unbroken reign of more than three hundred years.

At the age of fourteen he had already created the system of magic that we employ today. Or rather that we would employ if we could; most of what he knew we have forgotten. His was a perfect blending of fairy magic and human organization – their powers were wedded to his own terrifying purposefulness. There is no reason that we know of to explain why one stolen Christian child should suddenly emerge the greatest magician of any age. Other children, both before and since, have been held captive in the borderlands of Faerie, but none other ever profited from the experience in the way he did. By comparison with his achievements all our efforts seem trivial, insignificant.

It is the contention of Mr Norrell of Hanover-square that

[4] The name of this *Daoine Sidhe* King was particularly long and difficult. Traditionally he has always been known as Oberon.

everything belonging to John Uskglass must be shaken out of modern magic, as one would shake moths and dust out of an old coat. What does he imagine he will have left? If you get rid of John Uskglass you will be left holding the empty air.

From *The History and Practice of English Magic*, volume I, by Jonathan Strange, published by John Murray, 1816

# 46

## "The sky spoke to me . . ."

### January 1816

IT WAS A dark day. A chill wind blew snowflakes against the windows of Mr Norrell's library where Childermass sat writing business letters. Though it was only ten o'clock in the morning the candles were already lit. The only sounds were the coals being consumed in the grate and the scratch of Childermass's pen against the paper.

> Hanover-square
> *To Lord Sidmouth, the Home Secretary* Jan. 8th, 1816.
>
> My lord,
> Mr Norrell desires me to inform you that the spells to prevent flooding of the rivers in the County of Suffolk are now complete. The bill will be sent to Mr Wynne at the Treasury today . . .

*Somewhere a bell was tolling, a mournful sound. It was very far away. Childermass barely noticed it and yet, under the influence of the bell, the room around him grew darker and lonelier.*

> . . . The magic will keep the waters within the confines of the rivers' customary courses. However Mr Leeves, the young engineer employed by the Lord Lieutenant of Suffolk to assess

> the strength of the present bridges and other structures adjacent to the rivers, has expressed some doubts . . .

*The image of a dreary landscape was before him. He saw it very vividly as if it were somewhere he knew well or a painting that he had seen every day for years and years. A wide landscape of brown, empty fields and ruined buildings beneath a bleak, grey sky . . .*

> . . . whether the bridges over the Stour and the Orwell are capable of withstanding the more violent flow of water which will certainly ensue at times of heavy rains. Mr Leeves recommends an immediate and thorough examination of the bridges, mills and fords in Suffolk, beginning with the Stour and Orwell. I am told that he has already written to your lordship about this matter . . .

*He was no longer merely thinking of the landscape. It seemed to him that he was actually there. He was standing in an old road, rutted and ancient, that wound up a black hill towards the sky where a great flock of black birds was gathering . . .*

> . . . Mr Norrell has declined to put a period to the magic. It is his private opinion that it will last as long as the rivers themselves, however he begs leave to recommend to your lordship that the spells be re-examined in twenty years. On Tuesday next Mr Norrell will begin to put in place the same magic for the County of Norfolk . . .

*The birds were like black letters against the grey of the sky. He thought that in a moment he would understand what the writing meant. The stones in the ancient road were symbols foretelling the traveller's journey.*

Childermass came to himself with a start. The pen jerked from his hand and the ink splattered over the letter.

He looked around in confusion. He did not appear to be dreaming. All the old, familiar objects were there: the shelves of books, the mirror, the ink pot, the fire-irons, the porcelain figure of Martin Pale. But his confidence in his own senses was shaken. He no longer trusted that the books, the mirrors, the porcelain figure were really there. It was as if everything he could see was simply a skin that he could tear with one fingernail and find the cold, desolate landscape behind it.

*The brown fields were partly flooded; they were strung with chains of chill, grey pools. The pattern of the pools had meaning. The pools had been written on to the fields by the rain. The pools were a magic worked by the rain, just as the tumbling of the black birds against the grey was a spell that the sky was working and the motion of grey-brown grasses was a spell that the wind made. Everything had meaning.*

Childermass leapt up away from the desk and shook himself. He took a hurried turn around the room and rang the bell for the servant. But even as he waited the magic began to reassert itself. By the time Lucas appeared he was no longer certain if he were in Mr Norrell's library or standing upon an ancient road . . .

He shook his head violently and blinked several times. "Where is my master?" he said, "Something is wrong."

Lucas gazed at him in some concern. "Mr Childermass? Are you ill, sir?"

"Never mind that. Where is Mr Norrell?"

"He is at the Admiralty, sir. I thought you knew. The carriage came for him over an hour ago. I dare say he will be back shortly."

"No," said Childermass, "that cannot be. He cannot have gone. Are you sure that he is not upstairs doing magic?"

"Quite sure, sir. I saw the carriage leave with the master inside it. Let me send Matthew for a physician, Mr Childermass. You look very ill."

Childermass opened his mouth to protest that he was not ill at all, but just at that moment . . .

*. . . the sky looked at him. He felt the earth shrug because it felt him upon its back.*

*The sky spoke to him.*

*It was a language he had never heard before. He was not even certain there were words. Perhaps it only spoke to him in the black writing the birds made. He was small and unprotected and there was no escape. He was caught between earth and sky as if cupped between two hands. They could crush him if they chose.*

*The sky spoke to him again.*

*"I do not understand," he said.*

He blinked and found that Lucas was bending over him. His breath was coming in gasps. He put out his hand and his hand brushed something at his side. He turned to look at it and was puzzled to discover that it was a chair-leg. He was lying on the floor. "What . . . ?" he asked.

"You are in the library, sir," said Lucas. "I think you fainted."

"Help me up. I need to talk to Norrell."

"But I told you already, sir . . ."

"No," said Childermass. "You are wrong. He must be here. He must be. Take me upstairs."

Lucas helped him up and out of the room, but when they reached the stairs he very nearly collapsed again. So Lucas called for Matthew, the other footman, and together they half-supported, half-carried Childermass to the little study upon the second floor where Mr Norrell performed his most private magic.

Lucas opened the door. Inside, a fire was burning in the grate. Pens, pen-knives, pen-holders and pencils were placed neatly in a little tray. The inkwell was filled and the silver cap placed on it. Books and notebooks stood stacked neatly or tidied away. Everything was dusted and polished and in perfect order. Clearly Mr Norrell had not been there that morning.

Childermass pushed the footmen away from him. He stood and gazed at the room in some perplexity.

"You see, sir?" said Lucas. "It is just as I told you. The master is at the Admiralty."

"Yes," said Childermass.

But it made no sense to him. If the eerie magic was not Norrell's, then whose could it be? "Has Strange been here?" he asked.

"No, indeed!" Lucas was indignant. "I hope I know my duties better than to let Mr Strange in the house. You still look queer, sir. Let me send for a physician."

"No, no. I am better. I am a great deal better. Here, help me to a chair." Childermass collapsed into a chair with a sigh. "What in God's name are you both staring at?" He waved them both away. "Matthew, have you no work to do? Lucas, fetch me a glass of water!"

He was still dazed and dizzy, but the sick feeling in his stomach had lessened. He could picture the landscape in every detail. The image of it was fixed in his head. He could taste its desolation, its otherworldliness, but he no longer felt in danger of losing himself in it. He could think.

Lucas returned with a tray with a wine-glass and a decanter full of water. He poured a glass of water and Childermass drank it off.

There was a spell Childermass knew. It was a spell to detect magic. It could not tell you what the magic was or who was performing it; it simply told you whether there was any magic occurring or not. At least that was what it was supposed to do. Childermass had only ever tried it once and there had been nothing. He had no way of knowing whether or not it worked.

"Fill the glass again," he told Lucas.

Lucas did so.

This time Childermass did not drink from the glass. Instead he muttered some words at it. Then he held it up to the light and peered through it, turning slowly until he had surveyed every part of the room through the glass.

There was nothing.

"I am not even sure what I am looking for," he murmured. To Lucas he said, "Come. I need your help."

They returned to the library. Childermass held up the glass again and said the words and looked through it.

Nothing.

He approached the window. For a moment he thought he saw something at the bottom of the glass like a pearl of white light.

"It is in the square," he said.

"What is in the square?" asked Lucas.

Childermass did not answer. Instead, he looked out of the window. Snow covered the muddy cobbles of Hanover-square. The black railings that surrounded the enclosure in the centre shewed sharply against the whiteness. Snow was still falling and there was a sharp wind. Despite this there were several people in the square. It was well known that Mr Norrell lived in Hanover-square and people came here, hoping to catch a glimpse of him. Just now a gentleman and two young ladies (all, doubtless, fanatics for magic) were standing in front of the house, gazing at it in some excitement. A little further off a dark young man was lounging against the railings. Near him was an ink-seller with a ragged coat and a little barrel of ink upon his back. On the right there was another lady. She had turned away from the house and was walking slowly in the direction of Hanover-street, but Childermass had the notion that she had been among the onlookers only a moment before. She was fashionably and expensively dressed in a dark green pelisse trimmed with ermine, and she carried a large ermine muff.

Childermass knew the ink-seller well – he had often bought ink from him. The others were, he thought, all strangers. "Do you recognize anyone?" he asked.

"That dark-haired fellow." Lucas pointed to the young man

leaning against the railings. "That is Frederick Marston. He has been here several times to ask Mr Norrell to take him as a pupil, but Mr Norrell has always refused to see him."

"Yes. I think you told me about him." Childermass studied the people in the square a moment longer and then he said, "Unlikely as it seems, one of them must be performing some sort of magic. I need to go down and see. Come. I cannot do this without you."

In the square the magic was stronger than ever. The sad bell tolled inside Childermass's head. Behind the curtain of snow the two worlds flickered back and forth, like images in a magic lantern – one moment Hanover-square, one moment dreary fields and a black writing upon the sky.

Childermass held up the wine-glass in preparation to saying the words of the spell, but there was no need. It blazed with a soft white light. It was the brightest thing in the whole of that dark winter's day, its light clearer and purer than any lamp could be and it threw curious shadows upon the faces of Childermass and Lucas.

*The sky spoke to him again. This time he thought it was a question. Great consequences hung upon his answer. If he could just understand what was being asked and find the correct words in which to frame his reply, then something would be revealed – something that would change English magic for ever, something that Strange and Norrell had not even guessed at yet.*

*For a long moment he struggled to understand. The language or spell seemed tantalizingly familiar now. In a moment, he thought, he would grasp it. After all, the world had been speaking these words to him every day of his life – it was just that he had not noticed it before . . .*

Lucas was saying something. Childermass must have begun to fall again because he now found that Lucas was grasping him under the arms and dragging him upright. The wine-glass lay shattered upon the cobbles and the white light was split across the snow.

". . . the queerest thing," said Lucas. "That's it, Mr Childermass. Up you come. I have never known you taken like this. Are you sure, sir, that you don't want to go inside? But, here is Mr Norrell. He will know what to do."

Childermass looked to the right. Mr Norrell's carriage was turning into the square from George-street.

The ink-seller saw it too. Immediately he approached the gentleman and two young ladies. He made them a respectful bow and spoke to the gentleman. All three turned their heads and looked at the carriage. The gentleman reached into a pocket and gave the ink-seller a coin. The ink-seller bowed again and withdrew.

Mr Marston, the dark young man, did not need any one to tell him that this was Mr Norrell's carriage. As soon as he observed its approach, he stood away from the railings and moved forward.

Even the fashionably dressed lady had turned and was walking back towards the house, apparently with the intention of looking at England's Foremost Magician.

The carriage stopped in front of the house. The footman descended from the box and opened the door. Mr Norrell stepped out. He was so wrapped up in mufflers that his shrunken little form appeared almost stout. Immediately Mr Marston hailed him and began to say something to him. Mr Norrell shook his head impatiently and waved Mr Marston away.

The fashionably dressed lady passed Childermass and Lucas. She was very pale and solemn-looking. It occurred to Childermass that she would probably have been considered handsome by the people who cared about such things. Now that he looked at her properly he began to think that he knew her. "Lucas," he murmured, "who is that woman?"

"I am sorry, sir. I don't think I ever saw her before."

At the foot of the carriage steps Mr Marston was growing more insistent and Mr Norrell was growing angrier. Mr Norrell looked around; he saw Lucas and Childermass close at hand and beckoned to them.

Just then the fashionably dressed lady took a step towards him. For a moment it seemed that she too was going to address him, but that was not her intention. She took a pistol from her muff and, with all the calm in the world, aimed it at his heart.

Mr Norrell and Mr Marston both stared at her.

Several things happened at once. Lucas loosed his hold of Childermass – who dropt like a stone to the ground – and ran to help his master. Mr Marston seized hold of the lady around her waist. Davey, Mr Norrell's coachman, jumped down from his box and grabbed the arm which held the pistol.

Childermass lay amid the snow and shards of glass. He saw the woman shrug herself free of Mr Marston's grasp with what seemed like remarkable ease. She pushed him to the ground with such force that he did not get up again. She put one small, gloved hand to Davey's chest and Davey was flung several yards backwards. Mr Norrell's footman – the one who had opened the carriage door – tried to knock her down, but his blow had not the least effect upon her. She put her hand upon his face – it looked like the lightest touch in the world – he crumpled to the ground. Lucas she simply struck with the pistol.

Childermass could make very little sense of what was happening. He dragged himself upright and stumbled forward for half a dozen yards, scarcely knowing whether he was walking upon the cobblestones of Hanover-square or an ancient road in Faerie.

Mr Norrell stared at the lady in the utmost horror, too frightened to cry out or run away. Childermass put up his hands to her in a gesture of conciliation. "Madam . . ." he began.

She did not even look at him.

The dizzying fall of white flakes confused him. Try as he might, he could not keep his hold upon Hanover-square. The eerie landscape was claiming him; Mr Norrell would be killed and there was nothing he could do to prevent it.

Then something strange happened.

*Something strange happened. Hanover-square disappeared. Mr Norrell, Lucas and all the rest of them disappeared.*

*But the lady remained.*

*She stood facing him, upon the ancient road, beneath the sky with its tumble and seethe of black birds. She raised her pistol and aimed it out of Faerie and into England at Mr Norrell's heart.*

*"Madam," said Childermass again.*

*She looked at him with a cold, burning fury. There was nothing in the world he could say to deter her. Nothing in this world nor any other. And so he did the only thing he could think of. He seized hold of the barrel of the pistol.*

*There was a shot, an intolerably loud sound.*

It was the force of the noise, Childermass supposed, which pushed him back into England.

Suddenly he was half-sitting, half-lying in Hanover-square with his back to the carriage-steps. He wondered where Norrell was and whether he was dead. He supposed he ought to go and find out, but he found he did not much care about it and so he stayed where he was.

It was not until a surgeon arrived that he understood that the lady had indeed shot someone and that the someone was himself.

The rest of that day and most of the following one passed in a confusion of pain and laudanum-dreams. Sometimes Childermass thought he was standing on the ancient road under the speaking sky, but now Lucas was with him talking of maids-of-honour and coal-scuttles. A tight-rope was strung across the sky and a great many people were walking on it. Strange was there and so was Norrell. They both had piles of books in their hands. There was John Murray, the publisher, and Vinculus and many others. Sometimes the pain in Childermass's shoulder escaped from him and ran about the room and hid. When this happened he thought it became a small animal. No one else knew it was there. He supposed he ought to tell them so that they could chase it out.

Once he caught sight of it; it had flame-coloured fur, brighter than a fox . . .

On the evening of the second day he was lying in bed with a much clearer notion of who he was, and where he was, and what had happened. At about seven o'clock Lucas entered the room, carrying one of the dining-chairs. He placed it by the bed. A moment later Mr Norrell entered the room and sat upon it.

For some moments Mr Norrell did nothing but stare at the counterpane with an anxious expression. Then he muttered a question.

Childermass did not hear what was said, but he naturally supposed that Mr Norrell must be inquiring about his health, so he began to say that he hoped he would be better in a day or two.

Mr Norrell interrupted him and said again more sharply, "Why were you performing Belasis's Scopus?"

"What?" asked Childermass.

"Lucas said that you were doing magic," said Mr Norrell. "I made him describe it to me. Naturally I recognized Belasis's Scopus."[1] His face grew sharp and suspicious. "Why were you performing it? And – which is even more to the point – where in the world did you learn such a thing? How can I do my work when I am constantly betrayed in this manner? It is astonishing to me that I have achieved any thing at all, when I am surrounded by servants who learn spells behind my back and pupils who set themselves to undo my every accomplishment!"

Childermass gave him a look of mild exasperation. "You taught it to me yourself."

"I?" cried Mr Norrell, his voice several pitches higher than usual.

"It was before you came to London, in the days when you kept

[1] The spell to detect magic appears in *The Instructions* by Jacques Belasis.

to your library at Hurtfew, when I used to go about the country for you buying up valuable books. You taught me the spell in case I should ever meet with any one who claimed to be a practical magician. You were afraid that there might be another magician who could . . ."

"Yes, yes," said Mr Norrell, impatiently. "I remember now. But that does not explain why you were performing it in the square yesterday morning."

"Because there was magic everywhere."

"Lucas did not notice any thing."

"It is not part of Lucas's duties to know when there is magic going on. That falls to me. It was the strangest thing I ever knew. I kept thinking that I was somewhere else entirely. I believe that for a while I was in real danger. I do not understand very well where the place was. It had some curious features – which I will describe to you in a moment – but it was certainly not England. I think it was Faerie. What sort of magic produces such an effect? And where was it coming from? Can it be that that woman was a magician?"

"Which woman?"

"The woman who shot me."

Mr Norrell made a small sound of irritation. "That bullet affected you more than I supposed," he said contemptuously. "If she had been a great magician, do you really suppose that you could have thwarted her so easily? There was no magician in the square. Certainly not that woman."

"Why? Who was she?"

Mr Norrell was silent a moment. Then he said, "Sir Walter Pole's wife. The woman I brought back from the dead."

Childermass was silent a moment. "Well, you astonish me!" he said at last. "I can think of several people who have good cause to aim a pistol at your heart, but for the life of me I cannot understand why this woman should be one of them."

"They tell me she is mad," said Mr Norrell. "She escaped the people who were set to watch her and came here to kill me – which, as I think you will agree, is proof enough of her madness." Mr Norrell's small grey eyes looked away. "After all I am known everywhere as her benefactor."

Childermass was barely listening to him. "But where did she get the pistol? Sir Walter is a sensible man. It is hard to imagine that he leaves firearms in her way."

"It was a duelling pistol – one of a pair that belongs to Sir Walter. It is kept in a locked box in a locked writing-desk in his private study. Sir Walter says that until yesterday he would have taken an oath that she knew nothing about it. As to how she contrived to get the key – both keys – that is a mystery to every one."

"It does not seem much of a mystery to me. Wives, even mad wives, have ways of getting what they want from husbands."

"But Sir Walter did not have the keys. That is the strange part of it. These pistols were the only firearms in the house and Sir Walter had some natural concerns for the security of his wife and possessions since he is so frequently away from home. The keys were in the keeping of the butler – that tall black man – I dare say you know who I mean. Sir Walter cannot understand how he came to make such a mistake. Sir Walter says he is generally the most reliable and trustworthy fellow in the world. Of course one never really knows what servants are thinking," continued Mr Norrell blithely, forgetting that he was speaking to one at that moment, "yet it can hardly be supposed that this man bears any grudge against me. I never spoke three words to him in my life. Of course," he continued, "I could prosecute Lady Pole for trying to kill me. Yesterday I was quite determined upon it. But it has been represented to me by several people that I must consider Sir Walter. Lord Liverpool and Mr Lascelles both say so, and I believe that they are right. Sir Walter has been a good friend to English magic. I should not wish to give Sir Walter any reason to regret that he has been my friend. Sir Walter has given me his solemn oath that she will be put away somewhere in the country where she will see no one and no one will see her."

Mr Norrell did not trouble to ascertain Childermass's wishes upon this point. Despite the fact that it was Childermass who was lying upon the bed sick with pain and loss of blood, and that Mr Norrell's injuries had consisted chiefly of a slight headach and a small cut upon one finger, it was clear to Mr Norrell that he was the more sinned against of the two.

"So what was the magic?" asked Childermass.

"Mine, of course!" declared Mr Norrell, angrily. "Who else's should it be? It was the magic I did to bring her back from the dead. That was what you felt and that is what Belasis's Scopus revealed. It was early in my career and I dare say there were some irregularities that may have caused it to take an odd turn and . . ."

"An odd turn?" cried Childermass, hoarsely. He was seized with a fit of coughing. When he had regained his breath, he said, "At every moment I was in danger of being transported to some realm where everything breathed magic. The sky spoke to me! Everything spoke to me! How could that have been?"

Mr Norrell raised an eyebrow. "I do not know. Perhaps you were drunk."

"And have you ever known me to be drunk in the performance of my duties?" asked Childermass, icily.

Mr Norrell shrugged defensively. "I have not the least idea what you do. It seems to me that you have been a law unto yourself from the first moment you entered my house."

"But surely the idea is not so strange when considered in the light of ancient English magic," insisted Childermass. "Have you not told me that *Aureates* regarded trees, hills, rivers and so on as living creatures with thoughts, memories and desires of their own? The *Aureates* thought that the whole world habitually worked magic of a sort."

"Some of the *Aureates* thought so, yes. It is a belief that they imbibed from their fairy-servants, who attributed some of their own extraordinary magic to their ability to talk to trees and rivers and so forth, and to form friendships and alliances with them. But there is no reason to suppose that they were right. My own magic does not rely upon any such nonsensical ideas."

"The sky spoke to me," said Childermass. "If what I saw was true, then . . ." He paused.

"Then what?" asked Mr Norrell.

In his weakened state Childermass had been thinking aloud. He had meant to say that if what he had seen was true, then everything that Strange and Norrell had ever done was child's-play and magic was a much stranger and more terrifying thing than any of them had thought of. Strange and Norrell had been merely throwing paper darts about a parlour, while real magic soared and swooped and twisted on great wings in a limitless sky far, far above them.

But then he realized that Mr Norrell was unlikely to take a very sanguine view of such ideas and so he said nothing.

Curiously, Mr Norrell seemed to guess his thoughts anyway.

"Oh!" he cried in a sudden passion. "Very well! You are there, are you? Then I advise you to go and join Strange and Murray and all the other traitors immediately! I believe you will find that their ideas suit your present frame of mind much better! I am sure that they will be very glad to have you. And you will be able to tell them all my secrets! I dare say they will pay you handsomely for it. I shall be ruined and . . ."

"Mr Norrell, calm yourself. I have no intention of taking up any new employment. You are the last master I shall ever have."

There was another short silence which perhaps allowed Mr Norrell time to reflect upon the inappropriateness of quarrelling with the man who had saved his life only yesterday. In a more reasonable tone he said, "I dare say no one has told you yet. Strange's wife is dead."

"What?"

"Dead. I had the news from Sir Walter. Apparently she went for a walk in the snow. Most ill-advised. Two days later she was dead."

Childermass felt cold. The dreary landscape was suddenly very close, just beneath the skin of England. He could almost fancy himself upon the ancient road again . . .

*. . . and Arabella Strange was on the road ahead of him. Her back was turned towards him and she walked on alone into the chill, grey lands, under the magic-speaking sky . . .*

"I am told," continued Mr Norrell, quite oblivious to Childermass's sudden pallor and laboured breathing, "that Lady Pole has been made very unhappy by the death of Mrs Strange. Her distress has been out of all reason. It seems they were friends. I did not know that until now. Had I had known it, I might perhaps have . . ." He paused and his face worked with some secret emotion. "But it cannot matter now – one of them is mad and the other one is dead. From all that Sir Walter can tell Lady Pole seems to consider me in some way culpable for Mrs Strange's death." He paused. Then, in case there should be any doubt about the matter, he added, "Which is nonsense, of course."

Just then the two eminent physicians whom Mr Norrell had employed to attend Childermass entered the room. They were surprized to see Mr Norrell in the room – surprized and delighted. Their smiling countenances and bowing, bobbing forms said what a very pleasing instance of the great man's condescension they thought it that he should pay this visit to his servant. They told him that they had rarely seen a household where the master was so careful of the health of his inferiors or where the servants were so attached to their master by ties, less of duty, than of respect and fond regard.

Mr Norrell was at least as susceptible to flattery as most men and he began to think that perhaps he was indeed doing something unusually virtuous. He extended his hand with the intention of patting Childermass's hand in a friendly and condescending manner. However, upon meeting Childermass's cold stare, he thought better of it, coughed and left the room.

Childermass watched him go.

*All magicians lie and this one more than most*, Vinculus had said.

# 47

## "A black lad and a blue fella – that ought to mean summat."

### Late January 1816

SIR WALTER POLE's carriage was travelling along a lonely road in Yorkshire. Stephen Black rode on a white horse at its side.

On either hand empty moors the colour of a bruise stretched up to a dark sky that threatened snow. Grey, misshapen rocks were strewn about, making the landscape appear still more bleak and uncouth. Occasionally a low ray of sunlight would pierce the clouds, illuminating for a moment a white, foaming stream, or striking a pot-hole full of water that would suddenly become as dazzling as a fallen silver penny.

They came to a crossroads. The coachman halted the horses and stared gloomily at the place where, in his opinion, the fingerpost ought to have been.

"There are no milestones," said Stephen, "nothing to say where any of these roads might lead to."

"Always supposing they go anywhere at all," said the coachman, "which I am beginning to doubt." He took a snuff-box from his pocket and inhaled a large pinch of it.

The footman who sat on the box beside the coachman (and who was by far the coldest and most miserable of the three) comprehensively cursed Yorkshire, all Yorkshiremen and all Yorkshire roads.

"We ought to be travelling north or north-east, I think," said Stephen. "But I have got a little turned around on this moor. Do you have any idea which way is north?"

The coachman, to whom this question was addressed, said that all the directions looked pretty northern to him.

The footman gave a short, uncheerful laugh.

Finding that his companions were of no help, Stephen did what he always did under such circumstances; he took the whole charge of the journey upon himself. He instructed the coachman to take one road, while he took another. "If I have success, I will come and find you, or send a messenger. If you have success, deliver your charge and do not worry about me."

Stephen rode along, looking doubtfully at all the lanes and tracks he came to. Once he met with another lone rider and asked for directions, but the man proved to be a stranger to the moor like himself and had never heard of the place Stephen mentioned.

He came at last to a narrow lane that wound between two walls, built – as is the custom in that part of England – of dry stones without any mortar. He turned down the lane. On either hand a row of bare winter trees followed the line of the walls. As the first flakes of snow floated down he crossed a narrow packhorse bridge and entered a village of dour stone cottages and tumbledown walls. It was very quiet. There was scarcely more than a handful of buildings and he quickly found the one he sought. It was a long, low hall with a paved courtyard in front of it. He surveyed the low roofs, the old-fashioned casements and the moss-covered stones with an air of the deepest dissatisfaction. "Halloo!" he called. "Is there any one there?"

The snow began to fall thicker and faster. From somewhere at the side of the house two manservants came running. They were neatly and cleanly dressed, but their nervous expressions and clumsy air made Stephen wince, and wish that he had had the training of them.

For their part they stared to see a black man upon a milk-white mare in their yard. The braver of the two bobbed a sort of half-bow.

"Is this Starecross Hall?" asked Stephen.

"Yes, sir," said the courageous servant.

"I am here on business for Sir Walter Pole. Go and fetch your master."

The man ran off. A moment later the front door opened and a thin, dark person appeared.

"You are the madhouse-keeper?" inquired Stephen. "You are John Segundus?"

"Yes, indeed!" cried Mr Segundus. "Welcome! Welcome!"

Stephen dismounted and threw the reins to the servant. "This place is the very devil to find! We have been driving about this infernal moor for an hour. Can you send a man to bring her ladyship's carriage here? They took the road to the left of this one at the crossroads two miles back."

"Of course. At once," Mr Segundus assured him. "I am sorry you have had difficulties. The house is, as you see, extremely secluded, but that is one of the reasons that it suits Sir Walter. His lady is well, I hope?"

"Her ladyship is very much fatigued by the journey."

"Everything is ready for her reception. At least . . ." Mr Segundus led the way inside. "I am aware that it must be very different from what she is accustomed to . . ."

At the end of a short stone passage they came to a room which was a pleasant contrast with the bleak and sombre surroundings. It spoke nothing but comfort and welcome. It had been fitted up with paintings and pretty furniture, with soft carpets and cheerfully glowing lamps. There were footstools for her ladyship's feet if she felt weary, screens to protect her from a draught if she felt cold, and books to amuse her, should she wish to read.

"Is it not suitable?" asked Mr Segundus, anxiously. "I see by your face that it is not."

Stephen opened his mouth to tell Mr Segundus that what he

saw was quite different. He saw what her ladyship would see when she entered the room. Chairs, paintings and lamps were all quite ghostly. Behind them lay the far more substantial and solid forms of Lost-hope's bleak, grey halls and staircases.

But it was no use trying to explain any of this. The words would have changed as he spoke them; they would have turned into some nonsense about beer brewed from anger and longings for revenge; or girls whose tears turned to opals and pearls when the moon waxed and whose footprints filled with blood when the moon waned. So he contented himself with saying, "No, no. It is perfectly satisfactory. Her ladyship requires nothing more."

To many people this might have seemed a little cool – especially if they had worked as hard as Mr Segundus – but Mr Segundus made no objection. "So this is the lady whom Mr Norrell brought back from the dead?" he said.

"Yes," said Stephen.

"The single act upon which the whole restoration of English magic is founded!"

"Yes," said Stephen.

"And yet she tried to kill him! It is a very strange business altogether! Very strange!"

Stephen said nothing. These were not, in his opinion, fit subjects for the madhouse-keeper to ponder on; and it was most unlikely that he would hit upon the truth of the matter if he did.

To draw Mr Segundus's thoughts away from Lady Pole and her supposed crime, Stephen said, "Sir Walter chose this establishment himself. I do not know whose advice he took. Have you been a madhouse-keeper long?"

Mr Segundus laughed. "No, not long at all. About two weeks in fact. Lady Pole will be my first charge."

"Indeed!"

"I believe Sir Walter considers my lack of experience to be an advantage rather than otherwise! Other gentlemen in this profession are accustomed to exercise all sorts of authority over their charges and impose restraints upon them – something Sir Walter is very much opposed to in the case of his wife. But, you see, I have no such habits to break. Her ladyship will meet with nothing but kindness and respect in this house. And, apart from such little precautions as may suggest themselves to our good sense – such as keeping guns and knives out of her way – she will be treated as a guest in this house and we will strive to make her happy."

Stephen inclined his head in acceptance of these proposals. "How did you come to it?" he asked.

"The house?" asked Mr Segundus.

"No, madhouse-keeping."

"Oh! Quite by accident. Last September I had the great good fortune to meet a lady called Mrs Lennox, who has since become my benefactress. This house belongs to her. For some years she had tried to find a good tenant for it, but without success. She took a liking to me and wished to do me a kindness; so she determined upon establishing a business here and placing me in charge of it. Our first thought was a school for magicians, but . . ."

"Magicians!" exclaimed Stephen in surprize. "But what have you to do with magicians?"

"I am one myself. I have been one all my life."

"Indeed!"

Stephen looked so very much affronted by this news that Mr Segundus's natural impulse was to apologize to him – though what sort of apology one could offer for being a magician he did not know. He went on. "But Mr Norrell did not approve our plan for a school and he sent Childermass here to warn me against it. Do you know John Childermass, sir?"

"I know him by sight," said Stephen. "I have never spoken to him."

"At first Mrs Lennox and I had every intention of opposing him – Mr Norrell, I mean, not Childermass. I wrote to Mr Strange, but my letter arrived on the morning that his wife disappeared and, as I dare say you know, the poor lady died a few days later."

For a moment Stephen looked as if he were about to say something, but then he shook his head and Mr Segundus continued. "Without Mr Strange to help us, it was clear to me that we must abandon the school. I travelled up to Bath to inform Mrs Lennox. She was full of kindness and told me we would soon fix on another plan. But I confess I left her house in a very despondent frame of mind. I had not gone many steps when I saw a strange sight. In the middle of the road was a figure in tattered black rags. His sore, reddened eyes were empty of all reason and hope. He dashed his arms against the phantoms that assaulted him and cried out, entreating them to have pity on him. Poor soul! The sick in body may sometimes find respite in sleep, but I knew instinctively that this man's demons would follow him even into his dreams. I put a few coins into his hand and continued on my way. I am not aware that I thought of him particularly on the journey back, but as I stepped across the threshold of this house something very curious happened. I had what I think I must call a vision. I saw the madman in all his ravings standing in the hall – just as I had seen him in Bath – and I realized something. I realized that this house with its silence and its seclusion might be kind to persons distressed in mind. I wrote to Mrs Lennox and she approved my new plan. You said you did not know who had recommended me to Sir Walter. It was Childermass. Childermass had said he would help me if he could."

Stephen said, "It might be best, sir, if you were to avoid any mention of your profession or of the school, at least at the beginning. There is nothing in the world – in this world or any other – that would give her ladyship greater pain than to find herself in thrall to another magician."

"Thrall!" exclaimed Mr Segundus, in astonishment. "What an odd word that is! I sincerely hope that no one will ever consider themselves in thrall to me! Certainly not this lady!"

Stephen studied him for a moment. "I am sure you are a very different sort of magician from Mr Norrell," he said.

"I hope I am," said Mr Segundus, seriously.

An hour later a little commotion was heard in the yard. Stephen and Mr Segundus went out to receive her ladyship. The horses and carriage had been entirely unable to cross the packhorse bridge and Lady Pole had been obliged to walk the last fifty yards or so of her journey. She entered the courtyard of the Hall with some trepidation, glancing round at the bleak, snowy scene; and it seemed to Stephen that only the cruellest of hearts could look upon her, with all her youth, beauty and sad affliction, and not wish to offer her all the protection in their power. Inwardly he cursed Mr Norrell.

Something in her appearance seemed to startle Mr Segundus. He looked down at her left hand, but the hand was gloved. He recovered himself immediately and welcomed her to Starecross Hall.

In the drawing-room Stephen brought tea for them.

"I am told your ladyship has been greatly distressed by the death of Mrs Strange," said Mr Segundus. "May I offer my condolences?"

She turned away her head to hide her tears. "It would be more to the point to offer them to her, not me," she said. "My husband offered to write to Mr Strange and beg the favour of borrowing a picture of Mrs Strange, so that a copy might be made to console me. But what good would that do? After all, I am scarcely likely to forget her face when she and I attend the same balls and processions every night – and shall do for the rest of our lives, I presume. Stephen knows. Stephen understands."

"Ah, yes," said Mr Segundus. "Your ladyship has a horror of dancing and music, I know. Be assured that they will not be allowed here. Here we shall have nothing that is not cheerful, nothing that does not promote your happiness." He spoke to her of the books he planned they should read together and the walks they could take in spring, if her ladyship liked.

To Stephen, occupied among the tea-things, it seemed the most innocuous of conversations – except that once or twice he observed Mr Segundus glance from her ladyship to himself and back again, in a sharp, penetrating manner that both puzzled him and made him uncomfortable.

The carriage, coachman, maid and footman were all to remain at Starecross Hall with Lady Pole; Stephen, however, was to return to Harley-street. Early the next morning, while her ladyship was at breakfast, he went in to take his leave of her.

As he bowed to her, she gave a laugh half-melancholy, half-amused. "It is very ridiculous to part so, when you and I both know that we will be together again in a few hours. Do not be concerned about me, Stephen. I shall be more comfortable here. I feel I shall."

Stephen went out to the stable-yard where his horse stood waiting. He was just putting on his gloves when a voice came behind him. "I beg your pardon!"

Mr Segundus was there, as hesitant and unassuming as ever. "May I ask you something? What is the magic that surrounds you and her ladyship?" He put up his hand as if he intended to brush Stephen's face with his fingertips. "There is a red-and-white rose at your mouth. And another at hers. What does that mean?"

Stephen put his hand up to his mouth. There was nothing there. But for a moment he had some wild notion of telling Mr Segundus everything – all about his enchantment and the enchantment of the two women. He pictured Mr Segundus somehow understanding him; Mr Segundus proving to be an extraordinary magician – much greater than Strange or Norrell – who would find a way to thwart the gentleman with the thistle-down hair. But these were very fleeting fancies. A moment later Stephen's native distrust of Englishmen – and of English magicians in particular – reasserted itself.

"I do not understand you," he said quickly. He mounted his horse and rode away without another word.

The winter roads that day were some of the worst he had ever seen. The mud had been frozen into ruts and ridges as hard as iron. Fields and roads were thickly covered with white frost and an icy mist added to the general gloom.

His horse was one of the gentleman's innumerable gifts. She was a milk-white mare without so much as a single black hair anywhere. She was, besides, swift and strong, and as affectionately disposed towards Stephen as a horse can be to a man. He had named her Firenze and he doubted that the Prince Regent himself or the Duke of Wellington had a better horse. It was one of the peculiarities of his strange, enchanted life that it did not matter where he went, no one remarked upon the incongruity of a negro servant possessing the finest horse in the kingdom.

About twenty miles south of Starecross Hall he came to a small village. There was a sharp corner as the road passed between a large, elegant house and garden upon the right and a row of tumbledown stables upon the left. Just as Stephen was passing the entrance to the house, a carriage came suddenly out of the sweep and very nearly collided with him. The coachman looked round to see what had caused his horses to shy and forced him to rein them in. Seeing nothing but a black man, he lashed out at him with his whip. The blow missed Stephen but struck Firenze just above the right eye. Pained and startled, she reared up and lost her footing on the icy road.

There was a moment when everything seemed to tumble over. When Stephen was next able to comprehend what was happening, he found that he was on the ground. Firenze had fallen. He had been thrown clear, but his left foot was still caught in the stirrup and the leg was twisted in a most alarming way – he was sure it must be broken. He freed his foot and sat for a moment feeling sick and stunned. There was a sensation of something wet trickling down his face and his hands had been scraped raw by the fall. He tried to stand and found with relief that he could; the leg seemed bruised, but not broken.

Firenze lay snorting, her eyes rolling wildly. He wondered why she did not try to right herself or at least kick out. A sort of involuntary shuddering possessed her frame but apart from that she was still. Her legs were stiff and seemed to stick out at awkward angles to each other. Then it came to him: she could not move; her back was broken.

He looked at the gentleman's house, hoping that someone would come and help him. A woman appeared for a moment at a window. Stephen had a brief impression of elegant clothes and a cold, haughty expression. As soon as she had satisfied herself that the accident had produced no harm to any one or any thing belonging to her she moved away and Stephen saw no more of her.

He knelt down by Firenze and stroked her head and shoulder. From out of a saddlebag he drew a pistol, a powder flask, a ramrod and a cartridge. He loaded and primed the pistol. Then he stood and drew the hammer back to full cock.

But he found he could go no further. She had been too good a friend to him; he could not kill her. He was on the point of giving up in despair when there was a rattle in the lane behind him. Around the corner came a cart drawn by a great, shambling, placid-looking horse. It was a carrier's cart and in the cart sat the carrier himself, a big barrel-shaped man with a round, fat face. He was dressed in an ancient coat. When he saw Stephen, he reined in his horse. "Eh, lad! What's to do?"

Stephen gestured at Firenze with the pistol.

The carrier climbed down from his cart and came over to Stephen. "She was a pretty beast," he said in a kindly tone. He clapped Stephen on the shoulder and breathed sympathetic cabbage smells over him. "But, lad! Tha cannot help her now."

He looked from Stephen's face to the pistol. He reached out and gently raised the barrel until it pointed at Firenze's shuddering head. When Stephen still did not fire, he said, "Shall I do it for thee, lad?"

Stephen nodded.

The carrier took the pistol. Stephen looked away. There was a shot – a horrible sound – followed immediately by a wild cawing and the rush of wings as all the birds in the neighbourhood took flight at once. Stephen looked back. Firenze convulsed once and then was still.

"Thank you," he said to the carrier.

He heard the carrier walk away and he thought the man was gone, but in a moment he returned, nudged Stephen again and handed him a black bottle.

Stephen swallowed. It was gin of the roughest sort. He coughed.

Despite the fact that the cost of Stephen's clothes and boots could have bought the carrier's cart and horse twice over, the carrier assumed the cheerful superiority that white generally feels for black. He considered the matter and told Stephen that the first thing they must do was to arrange for the carcass to be removed. "She's a valuable beast – dead or alive. Your master won't be best pleased when he finds soom other fella has got t'horse and t'money."

"She was not my master's horse," said Stephen, "She was mine."

"Eh!" said the carrier. "Look at that!"

A raven had alighted upon Firenze's milk-white flank.

"No!" cried Stephen and moved to shoo the bird away.

But the carrier stopped him. "Nay, lad! Nay! That's lucky. I do not know when I saw a better omen!"

"Lucky!" said Stephen, "What are you talking about?"

"'Tis the sign of the old King, ain't it? A raven upon summat white. Old John's banner!"[1]

The carrier informed Stephen that he knew of a place close by where, he said, the people would for a price help Stephen make arrangements for disposing of Firenze. Stephen climbed upon the box and the carrier drove him to a farm.

The farmer had never seen a black man before and was quite

[1] John Uskglass's arms were the Raven-in-Flight (properly called the Raven Volant), a black raven on a white field.

astonished to find such an otherlandish creature in his yard. Despite all evidence to the contrary, he could not bring himself to believe that Stephen was speaking English. The carrier, who sympathized with the farmer in his confusion, stood beside Stephen, kindly repeating everything he said for the farmer's better understanding. But it made no difference. The farmer took no notice of either of them, but merely gaped at Stephen and made remarks about him to one of his men who stood equally entranced. The farmer wondered whether the black came off when Stephen touched things and he made other speculations of an even more impertinent and disagreeable nature. All Stephen's careful instructions concerning the disposal of Firenze's carcass went for nothing, until the farmer's wife returned from a nearby market. She was a very different sort of person. As far as she was concerned a man in good clothes with a costly horse (albeit a dead one) counted for a gentleman – let him be whatsoever colour he chose. She told Stephen of a cats-meat man who took the dead horses from the farm and who would dispose of the flesh and sell the bones and hooves for glue. She told him what the cats-meat man would pay and promised to arrange everything if she could keep one third of the money. To this Stephen agreed.

Stephen and the carrier came out of the farmyard into the lane.

"Thank you," said Stephen. "This would have been much more difficult without your help. I will pay you for your trouble, of course. But I fear I must trouble you further. I have no means of getting home. I would be very much obliged if you could take me as far as the next post-inn."

"Nay!" said the carrier. "Put th' little purse away, lad, I'll tek thee to Doncaster and it'll cost thee nowt."

In truth Stephen would have much preferred to go to the next post-inn, but the carrier seemed so pleased to have found a companion that it seemed kinder and more grateful to go with him.

The cart progressed towards Doncaster by degrees, travelling along country lanes and coming at inns and villages from odd directions, taking them by surprize. They delivered a bed-stead in this place, and a fruitcake in that place, and took up no end of oddly shaped parcels. Once they stopped at a very small cottage that stood by itself behind a high bare hedge in the middle of a wood. There they received from the hands of an ancient maid a bony, old, black-painted bird-cage containing a very small canary. The carrier informed Stephen that it had belonged to an old lady who had died and it was to be delivered to her great-niece south of Selby.

Not long after the canary had been secreted in the back of the carriage, Stephen was startled by a series of thunderous snores issuing unexpectedly from the same place. It seemed impossible that such a very loud noise should have come out of such a very small bird and Stephen concluded that there was another person in the cart, someone he had not yet been privileged to see.

The carrier produced from a basket a large pork pie and a hunk of cheese. He cut a piece off the pie with a large knife and seemed about to offer it to Stephen when he was struck by a doubt. "Do black lads eat the same as us?" he asked as if he thought they might possibly eat grass, or moonbeams.

"Yes," said Stephen.

The carrier gave Stephen the piece of pie and some cheese.

"Thank you. Does not your other passenger want something?"

"He might. When he wakes. I took him up at Ripon. He'd no money. I thowt as how he'd be someone to talk to. He were chatty enough at first but he went to sleep at Boroughbridge and he's done nowt else since."

"Very tiresome of him."

"I don't mind it. I have you to talk to now."

"He must be very tired," mused Stephen. "He has slept through the shot that finished my horse, the visit to the foolish farmer, the bed-stead and the canary – all the events of the day in fact. Where is he going?"

"Him? Nowhere. He wanders about from place to place. He is persecuted by soom famous man in London and cannot stay long anywhere – or t'oother chap's servant might catch up wi' him."

"Indeed?"

"He is blue," remarked the carrier.

"Blue?" said Stephen, mystified.

The carrier nodded.

"What? Blue with cold? Or has he been beaten?"

"Nay, lad. He is as blue as thou art black. Eh! I have a black lad and a blue fella in my cart! I niver heard o' anyone that did that before. Now if to see a black lad is good luck – which it must be, like cats – then to see a black lad and a blue fella together in one place ought to mean summat. But what?"

"Perhaps it does mean something," offered Stephen, "but not for you. Perhaps it means something for him. Or me."

"Nay, that can't be right," objected the carrier. "It's me it's happening to."

Stephen considered the unknown man's odd colour. "Does he have a disease?" he asked.

"Could be," said the carrier, unwilling to commit himself.

After they had eaten, the carrier began to nod and pretty soon he was fast asleep with the reins in his hands. The cart continued serenely along the road under the captainship of the horse – a beast of excellent sense and judgement.

It was a weary journey for Stephen. The sad exile of Lady Pole and the loss of Firenze depressed his spirits. He was glad to be relieved of the carrier's conversation for a while.

Once he heard a sort of muttering, suggesting that the blue man was waking up. At first he could not tell what the blue man was saying and then he heard very clearly, "*The nameless slave shall be king in a strange country.*"

That made him shiver; it reminded him so forcibly of the gentleman's promise to make him King of England.

It grew dark. Stephen halted the horse, got down from the box and lit the three ancient lanterns that hung about the cart. He was about to get back upon the box when a ragged, unkempt-looking person climbed suddenly out of the back and jumped down upon the icy ground to stand in front of him.

The unkempt person regarded Stephen by the lanterns' light. "Are we there yet?" he asked in a hoarse tone.

"Are we where?" asked Stephen.

The man considered this for a moment and then decided to rephrase his original question. "Where are we?" he asked.

"Nowhere. Between somewhere called Ulleskelf and another place called Thorpe Willoughby, I believe."

Though the man had asked for this information he did not seem much interested in it when it was given to him. His dirty shirt was open to the waist and Stephen could see that the carrier's description of him had been of a most misleading nature. He was not blue in the same way that Stephen was black. He was a thin, disreputable hawk of a man, whose skin in its natural state ought to have been the same colour as every other Englishman's, but it was covered in a strange patterning of blue lines, flourishes, dots and circles.

"Do you know John Childermass, the magician's servant?" he asked.

Stephen was startled – as any body would be who was asked the same question twice in two days by complete strangers. "I know him by sight. I have never spoken to him."

The man grinned and winked. "He has been looking for me for eight years. Never found me yet. I have been to look at his master's house in Yorkshire. It stands in a great park. I should have liked to steal something. When I was at his house in London I ate some pies."

It was a little disconcerting to find oneself in the company of a self-confessed thief, yet Stephen could not help but feel some sort of fellowship with someone who wished to rob the magician. After all, if it had not been for Mr Norrell Lady Pole and he would never have fallen under an enchantment. He reached into his pocket and pulled out two crown coins. "Here!" he said.

"And what is that for?" asked the man suspiciously (but he took the coins anyway).

"I am sorry for you."

"Why?"

"Because, if what I am told is true, you have no home."

The man grinned again and scratched his dirty cheek. "And if what *I* am told is true, you have no name!"

"What?"

"I have a name. It is Vinculus." He grabbed Stephen's hand. "Why do you try to pull away from me?"

"I do not," said Stephen.

"Yes, you did. Just then."

Stephen hesitated. "Your skin is marked and discoloured. I thought perhaps the marks meant you had a disease of some sort."

"That is not what my skin means," said Vinculus.

"Means?" said Stephen. "That is an odd word to use. Yet it is true – skin can mean a great deal. Mine means that any man may strike me in a public place and never fear the consequences. It means that my friends do not always like to be seen with me in the street. It means that no matter how many books I read, or languages I master, I will never be any thing but a curiosity – like a talking pig or a mathematical horse."

Vinculus grinned. "And mine means the opposite of yours. It means you will be raised up on high, Nameless King. It means your kingdom is waiting for you and your enemy shall be destroyed. It means the hour is almost come. *The nameless slave shall wear a silver crown; the nameless slave shall be a king in a strange country* . . ."

Then, keeping tight hold of Stephen's hand, Vinculus recited the whole of his prophecy. "There," he said when he was done, "now I have told it to the two magicians and I have told it to you. The first part of my task is done."

"But I am not a magician," said Stephen.

"I never said you were," answered Vinculus. Without warning he released Stephen's arm, pulled his ragged coat tight around him, plunged into the darkness beyond the glow of the lanterns and was gone.

A few days later the gentleman with the thistle-down hair expressed a sudden desire to see a wolf hunt, something he had apparently not done for several centuries.

There happened to be one going on in southern Sweden just then and so he instantly transported himself and Stephen to the place. Stephen found himself standing upon a great branch that belonged to an ancient oak in the midst of a snowy forest. From here he had an excellent view of a little clearing where a tall wooden pole had been planted in the ground. On top of the pole was an old wooden cartwheel, and on top of the cartwheel a young goat was securely tied. It bleated miserably.

A family of wolves crept out of the trees, with frost and snow clogging their fur, their gaze fixed hungrily upon the goat. No sooner had they appeared, than dogs could be heard in every part of the forest and riders could be glimpsed approaching at great speed. A pack of hounds came pouring into the clearing; the two foremost dogs leapt upon a wolf and together the three creatures became a single snapping, snarling, biting, thrashing knot of bodies, legs and teeth. The hunters galloped up and shot the wolf. The other wolves went streaming into the dark trees, and the dogs and hunters followed.

As soon as the sport waned in one place, the gentleman carried himself and Stephen through the air by magic, to wherever it was likely to be better. In this fashion they progressed from treetop to treetop, from hill to rocky outcrop. Once they travelled to the top of a church tower in a village of wooden houses, where the windows and doors were made in quaint, fairy-tale shapes and the roofs were dusted with powdery snow that glittered in the sunlight.

They were waiting in a quiet part of the wood for the hunters to appear, when a single wolf passed by their tree. He was the handsomest of his kind, with fine, dark eyes and a pelt the colour of wet slate. He looked up into the tree and addressed the gentleman in a language that sounded like the chatter of water over stones and the sighing of wind amongst bare branches and the crackle of fire consuming dead leaves.

The gentleman answered him in the same speech, then gave a careless laugh and waved him away with his hand.

The wolf bestowed one last reproachful glance upon the gentleman and ran on.

"He begs me to save him," the gentleman explained.

"Oh, could you not do it, sir? I hate to see these noble creatures die!"

"Tender-hearted Stephen!" said the gentleman, fondly. But he did not save the wolf.

Stephen was not enjoying the wolf hunt at all. True, the hunters were brave and their hounds were faithful and eager; but it was too soon after the loss of Firenze for him to take pleasure in the deaths of any creature, especially one as strong and handsome as the wolf. Thinking of Firenze reminded him that he had not yet told the gentleman about his meeting with the blue-skinned man in the cart and the prophecy. He did so now.

"Really? Well, that is most unexpected!" declared the gentleman.

"Have you heard this prophecy before, sir?"

"Yes, indeed! I know it well. All my race do. It is a prophecy of . . ." Here the gentleman said a word which Stephen did not understand.[2] "Whom you know better by his English name, John Uskglass, the Raven King. But what I do not understand is how it has survived in England. I did not think Englishmen interested themselves in such matters any more."

[2] Presumably the Raven King's original *Sidhe* name, which Jonathan Strange thought meant "Starling".

"The nameless slave! Well, that is me, sir, is it not? And this prophecy seems to tell how I will be a king!"

"Well, of course you are going to be a king! I have said so, and I am never wrong in these matters. But dearly as I love you, Stephen, this prophecy does not refer to you at all. Most of it is about the restoration of English magic, and the part you have just recited is not really a prophecy at all. The King is remembering how he came into his three kingdoms, one in England, one in Faerie, one in Hell. By the nameless slave he means himself. He was the nameless slave in Faerie, the little Christian child hidden in the *brugh*, brought there by a very wicked fairy who had stolen him away out of England."

Stephen felt oddly disappointed, though he did not know why he should be. After all he did not wish to be king of anywhere. He was not English; he was not African. He did not belong anywhere. Vinculus's words had briefly given him the sense of belonging to something, of being part of a pattern and of having a purpose. But it had all been illusory.

# 48

## The Engravings

### Late February–March 1816

"YOU ARE CHANGED. I am quite shocked to see you."

"Am I? You surprize me. I am perhaps a little thinner, but I am not aware of any other change."

"No, it is in your face, your air, your . . . something."

Strange smiled. Or rather he twisted something in his face and Sir Walter supposed that he was smiling. Sir Walter could not really recall what his smile had looked like before.

"It is these black clothes," said Strange. "I am like a leftover piece of the funeral, condemned to walk about the Town, frightening people into thinking of their own mortality."

They were in the Bedford coffee-house in Covent-garden, chosen by Sir Walter as a place where they had often been very merry in the past and which might therefore do something to cheer Strange's spirits. But on such an evening as this even the Bedford was somewhat deficient in cheerfulness. Outside, a cold black wind was pulling people this way and that, and driving a thick black rain into their eyes. Inside, rooms full of damp, unhappy gentlemen were producing a kind of gloomy, domesticated fog, which the waiters were attempting to dispel by putting extra shovelsful of coals on the fire and getting extra glassesful of hot spiced wine into the gentlemen.

When Sir Walter had come into the room he had discovered

Strange writing furiously in a little book. He nodded towards the book and remarked, "You have not given up magic then?"

Strange laughed.

Sir Walter took this to mean he had not – which Sir Walter was glad of, for Sir Walter thought a great deal of a man's having a profession and believed that useful, steady occupation might cure many things which other remedies could not. Only he did not quite like the laugh – a hard, bitter exclamation which he had never heard from Strange before. "It is just that you said . . ." he began.

"Oh, I said a great many things! All sorts of odd ideas crept into my brain. Excess of grief may bring on quite as fine a bout of madness as an excess of any thing else. Truth to tell, I was not quite myself for a time. Truth to tell, I was a little wild. But, as you see, that is all past now."

But – truth to tell – Sir Walter did not see at all.

It was not quite enough to say that Strange had changed. In some senses he was just what he had always been. He smiled as often as before (though it was not quite the same smile). He spoke in the same ironic, superficial tone as he had always done (while giving the impression of scarcely attending to his own words). His words and his face were what all his friends remembered – with this difference: that the man behind them seemed only to be acting a part while his thoughts and his heart were somewhere else entirely. He looked out at them all from behind the sarcastic smile and none of them knew what he was thinking. He was more like a magician than ever before. It was very curious and no one knew what to make of it, but in some ways he was more like Norrell.

He wore a mourning ring on the fourth finger of his left hand with a thin strand of brown hair inside it and Sir Walter noticed that he continually touched it and turned it upon his finger.

They ordered a good dinner consisting of a turtle, three or four beefsteaks, some gravy made with the fat of a green goose, some lampreys, escalloped oysters and a small salad of beet root.

"I am glad to be back," said Strange. "Now that I am here I intend to make as much mischief as I can. Norrell has had everything his own way for far too long."

"He is already in agonies whenever your book is mentioned. He is forever inquiring of people if they know what is in it."

"Oh, but the book is only the beginning! And besides it will not be ready for months. We are to have a new periodical. Murray wishes to bring it forward as quickly as possible. Naturally it will be a very superior production. It is to be called *The Famulus*[1] and is intended to promote *my* views on magic."

"And these are very different from Norrell's, are they?"

"But, of course! My chief idea is to examine the subject rationally without any of the restrictions and limitations that Norrell imposes upon it. I am confident that such a re-examination will rapidly open up new avenues worthy of exploration. For, when you consider the matter, what does our so-called restoration of English magic amount to? What have Norrell and I actually done? Some weaving of illusions with clouds, rain, smoke etc. – the easiest things in the world to accomplish! Bestowing life and speech upon inanimate objects – well, I grant you, that is quite sophisticated. Sending storms and bad weather to our enemies – I really cannot emphasize how simple weather-magic is. What else? Summoning up visions – well, that might be impressive if either of us could manage it with any degree of skill, but neither of us can. Now! Compare that sorry reckoning with the magic of the *Aureates*. They persuaded sycamore and oak woods to join with them against their enemies; they made wives and servants for themselves out of flowers; they transformed themselves into mice, foxes, trees, rivers, etc.; they made ships out of cobwebs, houses out of rosebushes . . ."

"Yes, yes!" interrupted Sir Walter. "I understand that you are

[1] *Famulus*: a Latin word meaning a servant, especially the servant of a magician.

impatient to try all these different sorts of magic. But though I do not much like saying it, it seems to me that Norrell may be right. Not all these sorts of magic will suit us nowadays. Shape-changing and so on were all very well in the past. It makes a vivid incident in a story, I grant you. But surely, Strange, you would not want to practise it? A gentleman cannot change his shape. A gentleman scorns to seem any thing other than what he is. You yourself would never wish to appear in the character of a pastry-cook or a lamplighter . . ."

Strange laughed.

"Well then," said Sir Walter, "consider how much worse it would be to appear as a dog or a pig."[2]

"You are deliberately chusing low examples."

"Am I? A lion, then! Would you like to be a lion?"

"Possibly. Perhaps. Probably not. But that is not the point! I agree that shape-changing is a sort of magic which requires delicate handling, but that is not to say that some useful application might not exist. Ask the Duke of Wellington whether he would have liked to be able to turn his exploring officers into foxes or mice and have them slip about the French camps. I assure you his Grace will not be so full of qualms."

---

[2] Sir Walter is voicing a commonly-held concern. Shape-changing magic has always been regarded with suspicion. The *Aureates* generally employed it during their travels in Faerie or other lands beyond England. They were aware that shape-changing magic was particularly liable to abuses of every sort. For example in London in 1232 a nobleman's wife called Cecily de Walbrook found a handsome pewter-coloured cat scratching at her bed-chamber door. She took it in and named it Sir Loveday. It ate from her hand and slept upon her bed. What was even more remarkable, it followed her everywhere, even to church where it sat curled up in the hem of her skirts, purring. Then one day she was seen in the street with Sir Loveday by a magician called Walter de Chepe. His suspicions were immediately aroused. He approached Cecily and said, "Lady, the cat that follows you – I fear it is no cat at all." Two other magicians were fetched and Walter and the others said spells over Sir Loveday. He turned back into his true shape – that of a minor magician called Joscelin de Snitton. Shortly afterwards Joscelin was tried by the Petty Dragownes of London and sentenced to have his right hand cut off.

"I do not think you could have persuaded Colquhoun Grant to become a fox."[3]

"Oh! Grant would not have minded being a fox as long as he could have been a fox in a uniform. No, no, we need to turn our attention to the *Aureates*. A great deal more energy ought to be applied to the study of the life and magic of John Uskglass and when we . . ."

"That is the one thing you must not do. Do not even think of it."

"What are you talking about?"

"I am serious, Strange. I say nothing against the *Aureates* in general. Indeed, upon the whole, I think you are right. Englishmen take great pride in their ancient magical history – in Godbless, Stokesey, Pale and the rest. They do not like to read in their newspapers that Norrell makes light of their achievements. But you are liable to fall into the opposite mistake. Too much talk of other kings is bound to make the Government nervous. Particularly when we are liable to be overrun by Johannites at any moment."

"Johannites? Who are the Johannites?"

"What? Good Lord, Strange! Do you never look into a newspaper?"

Strange looked a little put out. "My studies take up a great deal of my time. All of it in fact. And besides, you know, in the past month I can plead distractions of a very particular nature."

"But we are not speaking of the past month. There have been Johannites in the northern counties for four years."

"Yes, but who are they?"

"They are craftsmen who creep into mills at dead of night and destroy property. They burn down factory-owners' houses. They hold pernicious meetings inciting the common people to riotous acts and they loot marketplaces."[4]

---

[3] It has already been described how Lt-Col. Colquhoun Grant's devotion to his scarlet uniform had led to his capture by the French in 1812.

[4] The common people in Northern England considered that they had suffered a great deal in recent years – and with good reason. Poverty and lack of employment had added to the general misery which the war with the French had produced. Then just when the war was over a new threat to their

"Oh, *machine-breakers*. Yes, yes, I understand you now. It is just that you misled me by that odd name. But what have machine-breakers to do with the Raven King?"

"Many of them are, or rather claim to be, his followers. They daub the Raven-in-Flight upon every wall where property is destroyed. Their captains carry letters of commission purporting to come from John Uskglass and they say that he will shortly appear to re-establish his reign in Newcastle."

"And the Government believes them?" asked Strange in astonishment.

"Of course not! We are not so ridiculous. What we fear is a great deal more mundane – in a word, revolution. John Uskglass's banner is flying everywhere in the north from Nottingham to Newcastle. Of course we have our spies and informers to tell us what these fellows are doing and thinking. Oh, I do not say that they all believe that John Uskglass is coming back. Most are as rational as you or I. But they know the power of his name among the common people. Rowley Fisher-Drake, the Member for Hampshire, has brought forward a Bill in which he proposes to make it illegal to raise the Raven-in-Flight. But we cannot forbid people to fly their own flag, the flag of their legitimate King."[5] Sir Walter sighed and poked a beefsteak upon his plate with a fork. "Other countries," he said, "have stories of kings who will return at times of great need. Only in England is it part of the constitution."

Strange waved a fork impatiently at the Minister. "But all that is politics. It is nothing to do with me. I am not going to call for the

---

[4] *cont'd* happiness had arisen – remarkable new machines which produced all sorts of goods cheaply and put them out of work. It is scarcely to be wondered at that certain individuals among them had taken to destroying the machines in an attempt to preserve their livelihoods.

[5] There could be no neater illustration than this of the curious relation in which the Government in London stood to the northern half of the Kingdom. The Government represented the King of England but the King of England was only the King of the southern half. Legally he was the steward of the northern half maintaining the rule of law until such time as John Uskglass chose to return.

re-establishment of John Uskglass's kingdom. My only wish is to examine, in a calm and rational manner, his accomplishments as a magician. How can we restore English magic until we understand what it is we are supposed to be restoring?"

"Then study the *Aureates*, but leave John Uskglass in the obscurity in which Norrell has placed him."

Strange shook his head. "Norrell has poisoned your minds against John Uskglass. Norrell has bewitched you all."

They ate in silence for a while and then Strange said, "Did I ever tell you that there is a portrait of him at Windsor Castle?"

"Who?"

"Uskglass. A fanciful scene painted upon a wall of one of the state rooms by some Italian painter. It shews Edward III and John Uskglass – warrior-king and magician-king seated side by side. It has been almost four hundred years since John Uskglass went out of England and still the English cannot quite make up their minds whether to adore him or hate him."

"Ha!" exclaimed Sir Walter. "In the north they know exactly what to think of him. They would exchange the rule of Westminster for his rule tomorrow if they could."[6]

[6] Naturally, at various times pretenders have arisen claiming to be John Uskglass and have attempted to take back the kingdom of Northern England. The most famous of these was a young man called Jack Pharaoh who was crowned in Durham Cathedral in 1487. He had the support of a large number of northern noblemen and also of a few fairies who remained at the King's city of Newcastle. Pharaoh was a very handsome man with a kingly bearing. He could do simple magic and his fairy supporters were quick to do more whenever he was present and to attribute it to him. He was the son of a pair of vagabond-magicians. While still a child he was seen at a fair by the Earl of Hexham who noted his striking resemblance to descriptions of John Uskglass. Hexham paid the boy's parents seven shillings for him. Pharaoh never saw them again. Hexham kept him at a secret place in Northern England where he was trained in kingly arts. In 1486 the Earl produced Pharaoh and he began his brief reign as King of Northern England. Pharaoh's main problem was that too many people knew about the deception. Pharaoh and Hexham soon quarrelled. In 1490 Hexham was murdered on Pharaoh's orders. Hexham's four sons joined with Henry VII of Southern England to attack Pharaoh and at the Battle of Worksop in 1493 Pharaoh was defeated. Pharaoh was kept in the Tower of London and executed in 1499.

A week or so later the first issue of *The Famulus* was published and, owing to the sensational nature of one of the articles, the entire run sold out within two days. Mr Murray, who was soon to publish the first volume of Strange's *The History and Practice of English Magic*, was filled with a happy anticipation of making a very large profit. The article which so thrilled the public was a description of how magicians might summon up dead people for the purposes of learning useful information from them. This shocking (but deeply interesting) subject caused such a sensation that several young ladies were reported to have fainted merely upon learning that *The Famulus* was in the house.[7] No one could imagine Mr Norrell ever approving such a publication and so every body who did not like Mr Norrell took a particular pleasure in buying a copy.

In Hanover-square Mr Lascelles read it out loud for the benefit

---

[6] *cont'd* Other pretenders, more or less successful, were Piers Blackmore and Davey Sans-chaussures. The last pretender was known simply as the Summer King since his true identity was never discovered. He first appeared near Sunderland in May 1536 shortly after Henry VIII dissolved the monasteries. It is thought that he may have been a monk from one of the great northern abbeys – Fountains, Rievaulx or Hurtfew. The Summer King differed from Pharaoh and Blackmore in that he had no support from the northern aristocracy, nor did he attempt to gain any. His appeal was to the common people. In some ways his career was more mystical than magical. He healed the sick and taught his followers to revere nature and wild creatures – a creed which seems closer to the teachings of the twelfth-century magician, Thomas Godbless, than any thing John Uskglass ever proposed. His ragged band made no attempt to capture Newcastle or indeed to capture any thing at all. All through the summer of 1536 they wandered about Northern England, gaining supporters wherever they appeared. In September Henry VIII sent an army against them. They were not equipped to fight. Most ran away back to their homes but a few remained and fought for their King and were massacred at Pontefract. The Summer King may have been among the dead or he may have simply vanished.

[7] Consulting dead magicians may strike us as highly sensational, but it is a magical procedure with a perfectly respectable history. Martin Pale claimed to have learnt magic from Catherine of Winchester (who was a pupil of John Uskglass). Catherine of Winchester died two hundred years before Martin Pale was born. John Uskglass himself was reputed to have had conversations with Merlin, the Witch of Endor, Moses and Aaron, Joseph of Arimathea and other venerable and ancient magicians.

of Mr Norrell. "'. . . Where the magician is deficient in skill and knowledge – and this must include all modern magicians, our National Genius in such matters being sadly fallen off from what it was in former times – then he or she might be best advised to conjure up the spirit of someone who was in life a magician or had at least some talent for the art. For, if we are uncertain of the path ourselves, it is best to call on someone in possession of a little knowledge and who is able, as it were, to meet us halfway.'"

"He will undo every thing!" cried Norrell with a wild passion. "He is determined to destroy me!"

"It is certainly very aggravating," remarked Lascelles with all the calm in the world, "and after he swore to Sir Walter that he had given up magic when his wife died."

"Oh! We might all die – half of London might be swept away, but Strange will always do magic – he cannot help himself. He is too much a magician ever to stop now. And the magic that he will do is evil – and I do not know how I shall prevent him!"

"Pray, calm yourself, Mr Norrell," said Lascelles, "I am sure you will soon think of something."

"When is his book to be published?"

"Murray's advertisements say that the first volume will appear in August."

"The first volume!"

"Oh, yes! Did you not know? It will be a three-volume work. The first volume lays before the public the complete history of English magic. The second volume furnishes them with a precise understanding of its nature and the third provides the foundation for its future practice."

Mr Norrell groaned aloud, bowed his head and hid his face in his hands.

"Of course," said Lascelles thoughtfully, "as mischievous as the text undoubtedly will be, what I find even more alarming are the engravings . . ."

"Engravings?" cried Mr Norrell, aghast. "What engravings are these?"

"Oh," said Lascelles, "Strange has discovered some emigrant or other who has studied under all the best masters of Italy, France and Spain and he is paying this man a most extravagant amount of money to make the engravings."

"But what are they of? What is the subject?"

"What indeed?" said Lascelles with a yawn. "I have not the least idea." He took up *The Famulus* again and began to read silently to himself.

Mr Norrell sat for some time deep in thought, chewing at his fingernails. By and by he rang the bell and sent for Childermass.

East of the City of London lies the suburb of Spitalfields, famed far and wide as a place where wonderful silks are made. There is not now, nor ever will be, silk produced any where else in England of so fine a quality as Spitalfields silk. In the past good houses were built to accommodate the silk merchants, master-weavers and dyers who prospered from the trade. But, though the silk that comes out of the weavers' attics nowadays is every bit as remarkable as ever it was, Spitalfields itself is much fallen off. Its houses have grown dirty and shabby. The wealthy merchants have moved to Islington, Clerkenwell and (if they are very wealthy indeed) to the parish of Mary-le-bone in the west. Today Spitalfields is inhabited by the low and the poor and is much plagued with small boys, thieves and other persons inimicable to the peace of the citizens.

On a particularly gloomy day when a cold, grey rain fell in the dirty streets and pooled in the mud, a carriage came down Elder-street in Spitalfields and stopped at a tall, thin house. The coachman and footman belonging to this carriage wore deep mourning. The footman jumped down from the box, put up a black umbrella and held it up as he opened the door for Jonathan Strange to get out.

Strange paused a moment on the pavement to adjust his black

gloves and to cast his glance up and down Elder-street. Apart from two mongrel dogs industriously excavating a heap of refuse, the street was deserted. Yet he continued to look about him until his eye was caught by a doorway on the opposite side of the street.

It was the most unremarkable of doorways – the entrance to a merchant's warehouse or some such. Three worn stone steps led up to a massive black door of venerable construction, surmounted by a great jutting pediment. The door was much papered over with tattered playbills and notices informing the reader that upon such-and-such a day at such-and-such a tavern all the property of Mr So-and-so Esq. (Bankrupt) would be put up for sale.

"George," said Strange to the footman who held the umbrella, "do you draw?"

"I beg your pardon, sir?"

"Were you ever taught drawing? Do you understand its principles? Fore-grounds, side-screens, perspective, that sort of thing?"

"Me, sir? No, sir."

"A pity. It was part of my education. I could draw you a landscape or portrait perfectly proficient and perfectly uninteresting. Exactly like the productions of any other well-educated *amateur*. Your late mistress had none of the advantages of expensive drawing-masters that I had, yet I believe she had more talent. Her watercolours of people and children would horrify a fashionable drawing-master. He would find the figures too stiff and the colours too bright. But Mrs Strange had a genius for capturing expressions both of face and figure, for finding charm and wit in the most commonplace situations. There is something in her pictures, altogether lively and pretty which . . ." Strange broke off and was silent a moment. "What was I saying? Oh, yes. Drawing teaches habits of close observation that will always be useful. Take that doorway for instance . . ."

The footman looked at the doorway.

". . . Today is cold, dark, rainy. There is very little light and therefore no shadows. One would expect the interior of that doorway to be gloomy and dim; one would not expect that shadow to be there – I mean the strong shadow going from left to right, keeping the left-hand of the doorway in utter blackness. And I believe I am right in saying that even if today were sunny and bright, a shadow would fall in the opposite direction. No, that shadow is altogether an oddity. It is not a thing that appears in Nature."

The footman looked at the coachman for some assistance, but the coachman was determined not to be drawn in and stared off into the distance. "I see, sir," said the footman.

Strange continued to regard the doorway with the same expression of thoughtful interest. Then he called out, "Childermass! Is that you?"

For a moment nothing happened and then the dark shadow which Strange objected to so strongly moved. It came away from the doorway like a wet sheet being peeled from a bed and as it did so, it changed and shrank and altered and became a man: John Childermass.

Childermass smiled his wry smile. "Well, sir, I could not expect to stay hidden from you for long."

Strange sniffed. "I have been expecting you this past week or more. Where have you been?"

"My master did not send me until yesterday."

"And how is your master?"

"Oh, poorly, sir, very poorly. He is beset with colds and headachs and tremblings in his limbs. All his usual symptoms when someone has vexed him. And no one vexes him as you do."

"I am pleased to hear it."

"By the by, sir, I have been meaning to tell you. I have some money at Hanover-square for you. Your fees from the Treasury and the Admiralty for the last quarter of 1814."

Strange opened his eyes in surprize. "And does Norrell really intend to let me have my share? I had supposed that money was gone for good."

Childermass smiled. "Mr Norrell knows nothing about it. Shall I bring the money tonight?"

"Certainly. I shall not be at home, but give it to Jeremy. Tell me, Childermass, I am curious. Does Norrell know that you go about making yourself invisible and turning yourself into shadows?"

"Oh, I have picked up a little skill here and there. I have been twenty-six years in Mr Norrell's service. I would have to be a very dull fellow to have learnt nothing at all."

"Yes, of course. But that was not what I asked. Does Norrell *know*?"

"No, sir. He suspects, but he chuses not to *know*. A magician who passes his life in a room full of books must have someone to go about the world for him. There are limits to what you can find out in a silver dish of water. You know that."

"Hmm. Well, come on, man! See what you were sent to see!"

The house had a much neglected, almost deserted air. Its windows and paint were very dirty and the shutters were all put up. Strange and Childermass waited upon the pavement while the footman knocked at the door. Strange had his umbrella and Childermass was entirely indifferent to the rain falling upon him.

Nothing happened for some time and then something made the footman look down into the area and he began a conversation with someone no one else could see. Whoever this person was, Strange's footman did not think much of them; his frown, his way of standing with both hands on his hips, the manner in which he admonished them, all betrayed the severest impatience.

After a while the door was opened by a very small, very dirty, very frightened servant-girl. Jonathan Strange, Childermass and the footman entered and, as they did so, each glanced down at her and she, poor thing, was frightened out of her wits to be looked at by so many tall, important-looking people.

Strange did not trouble to send up his name – it seemed so unlikely that they could have persuaded the little servant-girl to do it. Instead, instructing Childermass to follow him, Strange ran up the stairs and passed directly into one of the rooms. There in an obscure light made by many candles burning in a sort of fog – for the house seemed to produce its own weather – they found the engraver, M'sieur Minervois, and his assistant, M'sieur Forcalquier.

M'sieur Minervois was not a tall man; he was slight of figure. He had long hair, as fine, dark, shining and soft as a skein of brown silk. It brushed his shoulders and fell into his face whenever he stooped over his work – which was almost all the time. His eyes too were remarkable – large, soft and brown, suggesting his southern origins. M'sieur Forcalquier's looks formed a striking contrast to the extreme handsomeness of his master. He had a bony face with deep sunken eyes, a shaven head covered in pale bristles. But for all his cadaverous, almost skeletal, aspect he was of a most courteous disposition.

They were refugees from France, but the distinction between a refugee and an enemy was altogether too fine a one for the people of Spitalfields. M'sieur Minervois and M'sieur Forcalquier were known everywhere as French spies. They endured much on account of this unjust reputation: gangs of Spitalfields boys and girls thought it the best part of any holiday to lie in wait for the two Frenchmen and beat them and roll them in the dirt – an article in which Spitalfields was peculiarly rich. On other days the Frenchmen's neighbours relieved their feelings by surliness and catcalls and refusing to sell them any thing they might want or need. Strange had been of some assistance in mediating between M'sieur Minervois and his landlord and in arguing this latter gentleman into a more just understanding of M'sieur Minervois's character and situation – and by sending Jeremy Johns into all the taverns in the vicinity to drink gin and get into conversations with the natives of the place and to make it generally known that the two Frenchmen were the protégés of one of England's two magicians – "and," said Strange, raising a finger to Jeremy in instruction, "if they reply that Norrell is the greater of the two, you may let it pass – but say to them that I have a shorter temper and am altogether more sensitive to slights to my friends." M'sieur Minervois and M'sieur Forcalquier were grateful to Strange for his efforts, but, under such dismal circumstances, they had found that their best friend was brandy, taken with a strict regularity throughout the day.

They stayed shut up inside the house in Elder-street. The shutters were closed day and night against the inhospitableness of Spitalfields. They lived and worked by candlelight and had long since broken off all relations with clocks. They were rather amazed to see Strange and Childermass, being under the impression that it was the middle of the night. They had one servant – the tiny, wide-eyed orphan girl – who could not understand them and who was very much afraid of them and whose name they did not know. But in a careless, lofty way, the two men were kind to her and had given her a little room of her own with a feather-bed in it and linen sheets – so that she thought the gloomy house a very paradise. Her chief duties were to go and fetch them food and brandy and opium – which they then divided with her, keeping the brandy and opium for themselves, but giving her most of the food. She also fetched and heated water for their baths and their shaving – for both were rather vain. But they were entirely indifferent to dirt or disorder in the house, which was just as well for the little orphan knew as much of housekeeping as she did of Ancient Hebrew.

There were sheets of thick paper on every surface and inky rags. There were pewter dishes containing ancient cheese rinds and pots containing pens and pieces of charcoal. There was an elderly bunch of celery that had lived too long and too promiscuously in close companionship with the charcoal for its own good. There were engravings and drawings pinned directly on to every part of the panelling and the dark, dirty wallpaper – there was one of Strange that was particularly good.

At the back of the house in a smutty little yard there was an apple tree which had once been a country tree – until grey London had come and eaten up all its pleasant green neighbours. Once in a fit of industriousness some unknown person in the house had picked all the apples off the tree and placed them on all of the windowsills, where they had lain for several years now – becoming first old apples, then swollen corpses of apples and finally mere ghosts of apples. There was a very decided smell about the place – a compound of ink, paper, seacoals, brandy, opium, rotting apples, candles, coffee – all mingled with the unique perfume exuded by two men who work day and night in a rather confined space and who never under any circumstances can be induced to open a window.

The truth was that Minervois and Forcalquier often forgot that there were such places as Spitalfields or France upon the face of the earth. They lived for days at a time in the little universe of the engravings for Strange's book – and these were very odd things indeed.

They shewed great corridors built more of shadows than any thing else. Dark openings in the walls suggested other corridors so that the engravings appeared to be of the inside of a labyrinth or something of that sort. Some shewed broad steps leading down to dark underground canals. There were drawings of a vast dark moor, across which wound a forlorn road. The spectator appeared to be looking down on this scene from a great height. Far, far ahead on that road there was a shadow – no more than a scratch upon the road's pale surface – it was too far off to say if it were man or woman or child, or even a human person, but somehow its appearance in all that unpeopled space was most disquieting.

One picture showed the likeness of a lonely bridge that spanned some immense and misty void – perhaps the sky itself – and, though the bridge was constructed of the same massive masonry as the corridors and the canals, upon either side tiny staircases wound down, clinging to the great supports of the bridge. These staircases were frail-looking things, built with far less skill than the bridge, but there were many of them winding down through the clouds to God-knew-where.

Strange bent over these things, with a concentration to rival Minervois's own, questioning, criticizing and proposing. Strange and the two engravers spoke French to each other. To Strange's surprize Childermass understood perfectly and even addressed one or two questions to Minervois in his own language. Unfortunately, Childermass's French was so strongly accented by his native Yorkshire that Minervois did not understand and asked Strange if Childermass was Dutch.

"Of course," remarked Strange to Childermass, "they make these scenes altogether too Roman – too like the works of Palladio and Piranesi, but they cannot help that – it is their training. One can never help one's training, you know. As a magician I shall never quite be Strange – or, at least, not Strange alone – there is too much of Norrell in me."

"So this is what you saw upon the King's Roads?" said Childermass.

"Yes."

"And what is the country that the bridge crosses?"

Strange looked at Childermass ironically. "I do not know, Magician. What is your opinion?"

Childermass shrugged. "I suppose it is Faerie."

"Perhaps. But I am beginning to think that what we call Faerie is likely to be made up of many countries. One might as well say 'Elsewhere' and say as much."

"How far distant are these places?"

"Not far. I went there from Covent-garden and saw them all in the space of an hour and a half."

"Was the magic difficult?"

"No, not really."

"And will you tell me what it was?"

"With the greatest good will in the world. You need a spell of revelation – I used Doncaster. And another of dissolution to melt the mirror's surface. There are no end of dissolution spells in the books I have seen, but as far as I can tell, they are all perfectly useless so I was obliged to make my own – I can write it down for you if you wish. Finally one must set both of these spells within an overarching spell of path-finding. That is important, otherwise I do not see how you would ever get out again." Strange paused and looked at Childermass. "You follow me?"

"Perfectly, sir."

"Good." There was a little pause and then Strange said, "Is it not time, Childermass, that you left Mr Norrell's service and came to me? There need be none of this servant nonsense. You would simply be my pupil and assistant."

Childermass laughed. "Ha, ha! Thank you, sir. Thank you! But Mr Norrell and I are not done with each other. Not yet. And, besides, I think I would be a very bad pupil – worse even than you."

Strange, smiling, considered a moment. "That is a good answer," he said at last, "but not quite good enough, I am afraid. I do not believe that you can truly support Norrell's side. One magician in England! One opinion upon magic! Surely you do not agree with that? There is at least as much contrariness in your character as in mine. Why not come and be contrary with me?"

"But then I would be obliged to agree with you, sir, would I not? I do not know how it will end with you and Norrell. I have asked my cards to tell me, but the answer seems to blow this way and that. What lies ahead is too complex for the cards to explain clearly and I cannot find the right question to ask them. I tell you what I will do. I will make you a promise. If you fail and Mr Norrell wins, then I will indeed leave his service. I will take up your cause, oppose him with all my might and find arguments to vex him – and then there shall still be two magicians in England and two opinions upon magic. But, if he should fail and you win, I will do the same for you. Is that good enough?"

Strange smiled. "Yes, that is good enough. Go back to Mr Norrell and present my compliments. Tell him I hope he will be pleased with the answers I have given you. If there is any thing else he wishes to know, you will find me at home tomorrow at about four."

"Thank you, sir. You have been very frank and open."

"And why should I not? It is Norrell who likes to keep secrets, not I. I have told you nothing that is not already in my book. In a month or so, every man, woman and child in the kingdom will be able to read it and form their own opinions upon it. I really cannot see that there is any thing Norrell can do to prevent it."

# 49

# Wildness and madness

## March 1816

A FEW DAYS AFTER the visit to the engravers Strange invited Sir Walter and Lord Portishead to dinner. Both gentlemen had dined with Strange upon many occasions, but this was the first time they had entered the house in Soho-square since the death of Mrs Strange. They found it sadly changed. Strange seemed to have reverted to all his old bachelor habits. Tables and chairs were fast disappearing under piles of papers. Half-finished chapters of his book were to be found in every part of the house and in the drawing-room he had even taken to making notes upon the wallpaper.

Sir Walter started to remove a pile of books from a chair.

"No, no!" cried Strange, "Do not move those! They are in a very particular order."

"But where shall I sit?" asked Sir Walter in some perplexity.

Strange made a small sound of exasperation as if this were a most unreasonable request. Nevertheless he moved the books and only once became distracted in the process and fell to reading one of them. As soon as he had read through the passage twice and made a note of it upon the wallpaper he was able to attend to his guests again.

"I am very pleased to see you here again, my lord," he said to Portishead. "I have been asking everyone about Norrell – as much, I believe, as he has been asking about me. I hope you have a great deal to tell me."

"I thought I had already told you all about that," said Sir Walter, plaintively.

"Yes, yes. You told me where Norrell has been and whom he has been speaking to and how he is regarded by all the Ministers, but I am asking his lordship about *magic* and what you understand about magic would barely . . ."

". . . fill a square inch of wallpaper?" offered Sir Walter.

"Quite. Come, my lord. Tell me. What has Mr Norrell been doing lately?"

"Well," said Lord Portishead, "at the request of Lord Liverpool he has been working on some magic to help guard against Napoleon Buonaparte ever escaping again – and he has been studying the *Discourses upon the Kingdom of Light and the Kingdom of Darkness*. He believes he has made some discoveries."

"What is this?" cried Strange in alarm. "Something new in the *Discourses*?"[1]

"It is something he has found on page 72 of Cromford's edition. A new application of the Spell to Conjure Death. I do not understand it very well.[2] Mr Norrell seems to think that the principle might be adapted to cure diseases in men and animals – by conjuring the disease to come forth out of the body as if it were a demon."

"Oh, *that*!" exclaimed Strange in relief. "Yes, yes! I know what you mean now. I made the connexion last June. So Norrell has only just arrived there, has he? Oh, excellent!"

[1] Scholars of magic are always particularly excited about any new discovery concerning the great Dr Pale. He occupies an unique position in English magical history. Until the advent of Strange and Norrell he was the only noteworthy practical magician who wrote down his magic for other people to read. Naturally his books are esteemed above all others.

[2] For centuries this passage was considered an interesting curiosity, but of no practical value since no one nowadays believes that Death is a person capable of being interrogated in the manner Pale suggests.

"Many people were surprized that he did not take another pupil after you," continued Lord Portishead, "and I know that he has received a number of applications. But he has taken none of them. Indeed I do not believe he even spoke to the young men in question or answered their letters. His standards are so very exacting and no one comes up to you, sir."

Strange smiled. "Well, all that is just as I would have expected. He can scarcely bear the existence of a second magician. A third will probably be the death of him. I shall soon have the advantage of him. In the struggle to decide the character of English magic the sides will be very unevenly matched. There will only be one Norrellite magician and dozens of Strangite magicians. Or at least, as many as I can educate. I am thinking of setting up Jeremy Johns as a sort of anti-Childermass. He can go about the country seeking out all the people whom Norrell and Childermass have persuaded out of the study of magic and then he and I can persuade them back into it. I have had conversations with several young men already. Two or three are very promising. Lord Chaldecott's second son, Henry Purfois, has read a great many fourth-rate books about magic and fifth-rate biographies of magicians. It makes his conversation a little tedious, but he is scarcely to blame for that, poor fellow. Then there is William Hadley-Bright who was one of Wellington's *aides-de-camp* at Waterloo, and an odd little man called Tom Levy who is presently employed as a dancing-master in Norwich."

"A dancing-master?" frowned Sir Walter. "But is that really the sort of person whom we should be encouraging to take up magic? Surely it is a profession that ought to be reserved for gentlemen?"

"I do not see why. And besides I like Levy best. He is the first person I have met in years who regards magic as something to be enjoyed – and he is also the only one of the three who has managed to learn any practical magic. He made the window frame over there sprout branches and leaves. I dare say you were wondering why it is in that odd condition."

"To own the truth," said Sir Walter, "the room is so full of oddities that I had not even noticed."

"Of course Levy did not intend that it should remain like that," said Strange, "but after he did the magic he could not make it go back – and neither could I. I suppose I must tell Jeremy to find a carpenter to repair it."

"I am delighted you have found so many young men to suit you," said Sir Walter. "That bodes well for English magic."

"I have also had several applications from young ladies," said Strange.

"Ladies!" exclaimed Lord Portishead.

"Of course! There is no reason why women should not study magic. That is another of Norrell's fallacies."

"Hmm. They come thick and fast now," remarked Sir Walter.

"What do?"

"Norrell's fallacies."

"What do you mean by that?"

"Nothing! Nothing! Do not take offence. But I notice you do not mention taking any ladies as pupils yourself."

Strange sighed. "It is purely a matter of practicalities. That is all. A magician and his pupil must spend a great deal of time together, reading and discussing. Had Arabella not died, then I believe I might have taken female pupils. But now I would be obliged to rely upon chaperones and all sorts of tediousness that I do not have patience for at the moment. My own researches must come first."

"And what new magic are you intending to shew us, Mr Strange?" asked Lord Portishead, eagerly.

"Ah! I am glad you ask me that! I have been giving the matter a great deal of consideration. If the revival of English magic is to continue – or rather if it is not to remain under the sole direction of Gilbert Norrell – then I must learn something new. But new magic is not easily come by. I could go upon the King's Roads and try and reach those countries where magic is the general rule, rather than the exception."

"Good God!" exclaimed Sir Walter. "Not this again! Are you quite mad? I thought we had agreed that the King's Roads were far too dangerous to justify . . ."

"Yes, yes! I am well acquainted with your opinions. You lectured me long enough upon the subject. But you do not let me finish! I merely name possibilities. I shall not go upon the King's Roads. I gave my word to my . . . to Arabella that I would not."[3]

There was a pause. Strange sighed and his expression darkened. He was clearly now thinking of something – or someone – else.

Sir Walter observed quietly, "I always had the highest regard for Mrs Strange's judgement. You cannot do better than follow her advice. Strange, I sympathize – of course you wish to do new magic – any scholar would – but surely the only safe way to learn magic is from books?"

"But I do not have any books!" exclaimed Strange. "Good God! I promise to be as meek and stay-at-home as any maiden aunt if the Government will just pass a law saying Norrell must shew me his library! But as the Government will not do me this kindness, I have no choice but to increase my knowledge in any way I can."

"So what will you do?" asked Lord Portishead.

"Summon a fairy," said Strange, briskly. "I have made several attempts already."

"Did not Mr Norrell lay it down as a general rule that summoning fairies is full of hazards?" asked Sir Walter.

"There is not much that Mr Norrell does not regard as full of hazards," said Strange in tones of some irritation.

"True." Sir Walter was satisfied. After all, summoning fairies was a long-established part of English magic. All the *Aureates* had done it and all the *Argentines* had wished to.

---

[3] Most of us are naturally inclined to struggle against the restrictions our friends and family impose upon us, but if we are so unfortunate as to lose a loved one, what a difference then! Then the restriction becomes a sacred trust.

"But are you sure that it is even possible, sir?" asked Lord Portishead. "Most authorities agree that fairies hardly ever visit England any more."

"That is indeed the general opinion, yes," agreed Strange, "but I am almost certain that I was in company with one in November 1814, a month or two before Norrell and I parted."

"Were you indeed!" exclaimed Lord Portishead.

"You never mentioned this before," said Sir Walter.

"I was quite unable to mention it before," said Strange. "My position as Norrell's pupil depended upon my never breathing a word of it. Norrell would have fallen over in a blue fit at the least suggestion of such a thing."

"What did he look like, Mr Strange?" asked Lord Portishead.

"The fairy? I do not know. I did not see him. I heard him. He played music. There was someone else present who, I believe, both heard and saw him. Now, consider the advantages of dealing with such a person! No magician, living or dead, could teach me as much. Fairies are the source of everything we magicians desire. Magic is their native condition! As for the disadvantages, well, there is only the usual one – that I have almost no idea how to accomplish it. I have cast spells by the dozen, done everything I ever heard or read of, to try and get this fairy back again, but it has all been to no avail. I cannot for the life of me tell why Norrell expends so much energy in proscribing what no one can achieve. My lord, I don't suppose you know any spells for raising fairies?"

"Many," said Lord Portishead, "but I am sure you will have tried them all already, Mr Strange. We look to you, sir, to reconstruct for us all that has been lost."

"Oh!" sighed Strange. "Sometimes I think that nothing has been lost. The truth is that it is all at the library at Hurtfew."

"You said there was another person present who both saw and heard the fairy?" said Sir Walter.

"Yes."

"And I take it that this other person was not Norrell?"

"No."

"Very well then. What did this other person say?"

"He was . . . confused. He believed he was seeing an angel, but owing to his general style of living and habits of mind he did not find this quite as extraordinary as you might think. I beg your pardon but discretion forbids me to say any thing more of the circumstances."

"Yes, yes! Very well! But your companion saw the fairy. Why?"

"Oh, I know why. There was something very particular about him which enabled him to see fairies."

"Well, can you not use that somehow?"

Strange considered this. "I do not see how. It is a mere chance like one man having blue eyes and another brown." He was silent a moment, musing. "But then again perhaps not. Perhaps you are right. It is not such a very outlandish notion when you come to consider it. Think of the *Aureates*! Some of them were the fairies' near-neighbours in wildness and madness! Think of Ralph Stokesey and his fairy-servant, Col Tom Blue! When Stokesey was a young man there was scarcely any thing to chuse between them. Perhaps I am too tame, too *domestic* a magician. But how *does* one work up a little madness? I meet with mad people every day in the street, but I never thought before to wonder how they got mad. Perhaps I should go wandering on lonely moors and barren shores. That is always a popular place for lunatics – in novels and plays at any rate. Perhaps wild England will make me mad."

Strange got up and went to the drawing-room window, as if he expected to be able to survey wild England from there – although all it shewed was the very ordinary sight of Soho-square in a thick and mizzling rain. "I think you may have hit upon something, Pole."

"I?" cried Sir Walter, somewhat alarmed at where his remarks appeared to be leading, "I meant to suggest no such thing!"

"But, Mr Strange," reasoned the gentle Lord Portishead, "you cannot possibly mean this. For a man of such erudition as you possess to propose that he become a . . . a vagabond. Well, sir, it is a very shocking thought."

Strange crossed his arms and took another look at Soho-square and said, "Well, I shall not go today." And then he smiled his self-mocking smile and looked almost like his old self. "I shall wait," he said, "until it stops raining."[4]

---

[4] Even John Uskglass who had three kingdoms to rule over and all of English magic to direct was not entirely free from this tendency to go on long mysterious journeys. In 1241 he left his house in Newcastle in some mysterious fashion known only to magicians. He told a servant that he would be found asleep upon a bench in front of the fire in one day's time.

The following day the servant and members of the King's household looked for the King upon the bench in front of the fire, but he was not there. They looked for him every morning and every evening but he did not appear.

William, Earl of Lanchester, governed in his stead and many decisions were postponed "until the King shall return". But as time went on many people were inclined to doubt that this would ever happen. Then, a year and a day after his departure, the King was discovered, sleeping on the bench before the fire.

He did not seem aware that any thing untoward had happened and he told no one where he had been. No one dared ask him if he had always intended to be away so long or if something terrible had happened. William of Lanchester summoned the servant and asked him to repeat yet again the exact words that the King had said. Could it be that he had actually said he would be away for a year and a day?

Perhaps said the man. The King was generally quietly spoken. It was quite possible that he had not heard correctly.

# 50

## *The History and Practice of English Magic*

### April to late September 1816

STRANGE'S FRIENDS WERE glad to be assured that he did not intend to give up his comfortable houses, his good income and his servants to go and be a gypsy in the wind and the rain, but still very few of them were entirely comfortable with his new practices. They had good reason to fear that he had lost all restraint and was prepared to indulge in any and all kinds of magic. His promise to Arabella kept him from the King's Roads for the present, but all Sir Walter's warnings could not prevent him from continually talking and wondering about John Uskglass and his fairy subjects.

By the end of April, Strange's three new pupils, thc Honourable Henry Purfois, William Hadley-Bright and Tom Levy, the dancing-master, had all taken lodgings near Soho-square. Every day they attended Strange's house to study magic. In the intervals between directing their magical education Strange worked at his book and performed magic on behalf of the Army and the East India Company. He had also received applications for assistance from the Corporation of Liverpool and the Society of Merchant Venturers in Bristol.

That Strange should still receive commissions from official bodies – or indeed from any one at all – so incensed Mr Norrell that he complained to Lord Liverpool, the Prime Minister, about it.

Lord Liverpool was not sympathetic. "The generals may do as they wish, Mr Norrell. The Government does not interfere in military matters, as well you know.[1] The generals have employed Mr Strange as their magician for a number of years and they see no reason to stop simply because you and he have quarrelled. As for the East India Company I am told that its officials applied to you in the first place and that you declined to help them."

Mr Norrell blinked his little eyes rapidly. "My work for the Government – my work for you, my lord – takes up so much of my time. I cannot, in conscience, neglect it for the sake of a private company."

"And believe me, Mr Norrell, we are grateful. Yet I need scarcely tell you how vital the success of the East India Company is to the prosperity of the Nation and the Company's need for a magician is immense. It has fleets of ships at the mercy of storms and bad weather; it has vast territories to administer and its armies are continually harassed by Indian princelings and bandits. Mr Strange has undertaken to controul the weather around the Cape and in the Indian Ocean and he has offered advice on the best use of magic in hostile territories. The Directors of the East India Company believe that Mr Strange's experience in the Spanish Peninsula will prove invaluable. It is yet another demonstration of Britain's sore need for more magicians. Mr Norrell, as diligent as you are, you cannot be everywhere and do everything – and no one expects that you should. I hear that Mr Strange has taken pupils. It would please me immensely to hear that you intended to do the same."

Despite Lord Liverpool's approval, the education of the three new magicians, Henry Purfois, William Hadley-Bright and Tom Levy, progressed no more smoothly than Strange's own six years before. The only difference was that whereas Strange had had

[1] This was not in the least true. It had been the Duke of Wellington's bitterest complaint during the Peninsular War that the Government interfered constantly.

Norrell's evasiveness to contend with, the young men were continually thwarted by Strange's low spirits and restlessness.

By early June the first volume of *The History and Practice of English Magic* was finished. Strange delivered it to Mr Murray and it surprized no one when, on the following day, he told Henry Purfois, William Hadley-Bright and Tom Levy that they must defer their magical education for a while as he had decided to go abroad.

"I think it an excellent plan!" said Sir Walter as soon as Strange told him of it. "A change of scene. A change of society. It is exactly what I would prescribe for you. Go! Go!"

"You do not think that it is too soon?" asked Strange anxiously. "I shall be leaving Norrell in possession of London so to speak."

"You think we have such short memories as that? Well, we shall make every endeavour not to forget you in the space of a few months. Besides, your book will be published soon and that will serve as a standing reminder to us all of how ill we get on without you."

"That is true. There is the book. It will take Norrell months to refute forty-six chapters and I shall be back long before he is finished."

"Where shall you go?"

"Italy, I think. The countries of southern Europe have always had a strong attraction for me. I was often struck by the appearance of the countryside when I was in Spain – or at least I believe I would have found it very striking had it not been covered in soldiers and gunsmoke."

"I hope you will write occasionally? Some token of your impressions?"

"Oh! I shall not spare you. It is the right of a traveller to vent their frustration at every minor inconvenience by writing of it to their friends. Expect long descriptions of everything."

As often happened these days, Strange's mood darkened suddenly. His light, ironic air evaporated upon the instant and he sat frowning at the coal-scuttle. "I wondered if you . . ." he said at last. "That is, I wish to ask you . . ." He made a sound of exasperation at his own hesitancy. "Would you convey a message to Lady Pole from me? I would be most grateful. Arabella was greatly attached to her ladyship and I know she would not have liked me to leave England without sending some message to Lady Pole."

"Certainly. What shall I tell her?"

"Oh! Simply give her my heartfelt wishes for her better health. Whatever you think best. It does not matter what you say. But you must say that the message is from Arabella's husband. I wish her ladyship to understand that her friend's husband has not forgotten her."

"With the greatest goodwill," said Sir Walter. "Thank you."

Strange had half-expected that Sir Walter would invite him to speak to Lady Pole himself, but Sir Walter did not. No one even knew whether her ladyship was still at the house in Harley-street. There was a rumour circulating the Town that Sir Walter had sent her to the country.

Strange was not alone in wishing to go abroad. It had suddenly become very fashionable. For far too long the British had been confined to their own island by the war with Buonaparte. For far too long they had been forced to satisfy their desire to look upon new scenes and curious people by visits to the Scottish Highlands or the English Lakes or the Derbyshire Peak. But now the war was over they could go to the Continent and see mountains and shores of quite a different character. They could view for themselves those celebrated works of art which hitherto they had only seen in books of engravings. Some went abroad hoping to find that it was cheaper to live on the Continent than at home. Some went to avoid debts or scandal and some, like Strange, went to find a tranquillity that eluded them in England.

Bruxelles

*Jonathan Strange to John Segundus* Jun. 12th, 1816.

> I am, as far as I can tell, about a month behind Lord Byron.[2] In every town we stop at we discover innkeepers, postillions, officials, burghers, potboys and all kinds and sorts of ladies whose brains still seem somewhat deranged from their brief exposure to his lordship. And though my companions are careful to tell people that I am that dreadful being, an English magician, I am clearly nothing in comparison to an English poet and everywhere I go I enjoy the reputation – quite new to me, I assure you – of the quiet, good Englishman, who makes no noise and is no trouble to any one . . .

It was a queer summer that year. Or rather it was no summer at all. Winter had extended its lease into August. The sun was scarcely seen. Thick grey clouds covered the sky; bitter winds blew through towns and withered crops; storms of rain and hail, enlivened by occasional displays of thunder and lightning, fell upon every part of Europe. In many ways it was worse than winter: the long hours of daylight denied people the consolation of darkness which would have hidden all these miseries for a while.

London was half empty. Parliament was dissolved and the Members of Parliament had all gone to their country houses, the better to stare at the rain. In London Mr John Murray, the publisher, sat in his house in Albermarle-street. At other times Mr Murray's rooms were the liveliest in London – full of poets, essayists, reviewers and all the great literary men of the kingdom. But the great literary men of the kingdom had gone to the country. The rain pattered upon the window and the wind moaned in the chimney. Mr Murray heaped more coals upon the fire and then sat down at his desk to begin reading that day's letters. He picked

[2] Lord Byron left England in April 1816 in the face of mounting debts, accusations of cruelty to his wife and rumours that he had seduced his sister.

each letter up and held it close to his left eye (the right being quite blind and useless).

It so happened that on this particular day there were two from Geneva in Swisserland. The first was from Lord Byron complaining of Jonathan Strange and the second was from Strange complaining of Byron. The two men had met at Mr Murray's house a handful of times, but until now they had never got acquainted. Strange had visited Byron at Geneva a couple of weeks before. The meeting had not been a success.

Strange (who was just now in a mood to place the highest value upon matrimony and all that he had lost in Arabella) was unsettled by Byron's domestic arrangements. "I found his lordship at his pretty villa upon the shores of the lake. He was not alone. There was another poet called Shelley, Mrs Shelley and another young woman – a girl really – who called herself Mrs Clairmont and whose relationship to the two men I did not understand. If you know, do not tell me. Also present was an odd young man who talked nonsense the entire time – a Mr Polidori."

Lord Byron, on the other hand, took exception to Strange's mode of dress. "He wore half-mourning. His wife died at Christmas, did she not? But perhaps he thinks black makes him look more mysterious and wizardly."

Having taken an immediate dislike to each other, they had progressed smoothly to quarrelling about politics. Strange wrote: "I do not quite know how it happened, but we immediately fell to talking of the battle of Waterloo – an unhappy subject since I am the Duke of Wellington's magician and they all hate Wellington and idolize Buonaparte. Mrs Clairmont, with all the impertinence of eighteen, asked me if I was not ashamed to be an instrument in the fall of so sublime a man. No, said I."

Byron wrote: "He is a great partisan for the Duke of W. I hope for your sake, my dear Murray, that his book is more interesting than he is."

Strange finished: "People have such odd notions about magicians. They wanted me to tell them about *vampyres*."

Mr Murray was sorry to find that his two authors could not agree better, but he reflected that it probably could not be helped since both men were famous for quarrelling: Strange with Norrell, and Byron with practically everybody.[3]

When he had finished reading his letters, Mr Murray thought he would go downstairs to the bookshop. He had printed a very large number of copies of Jonathan Strange's book and he was anxious to know how it was selling. The shop was kept by a man called Shackleton who looked exactly as you would wish a bookseller to look. He would never have done for any other sort of shopman – certainly not for a haberdasher or milliner who must be smarter than his customers – but for a bookseller he was perfect. He appeared to be of no particular age. He was thin and dusty and spotted finely all over with ink. He had an air of learning tinged with abstraction. His nose was adorned with spectacles; there was a quill pen stuck behind his ear and a half-unravelled wig upon his head.

"Shackleton, how many of Mr Strange's book have we sold today?" demanded Mr Murray.

"Sixty or seventy copies, I should think."

"Excellent!" said Mr Murray.

Shackleton frowned and pushed his spectacles further up his nose. "Yes, you would think so, would you not?"

"What do you mean?"

---

[3] Despite the seeming lack of sympathy between the two men, something about Strange must have impressed Byron. His next poem, *Manfred*, begun in September or October of the same year, was about a magician. Certainly Manfred does not greatly resemble Jonathan Strange (or at least not the respectable Strange whom Byron so disliked). He much more resembles Byron with his self-obsession, his self-loathing, his lofty disdain for his fellow men, his hints of impossible tragedies and his mysterious longings. Nevertheless Manfred is a magician who passes his time in summoning up spirits of the air, earth, water and fire to talk to him. It was as if Byron, having met a magician who disappointed him, created one more to his liking.

Shackleton took the pen from behind his ear "A great many people have come twice and bought a copy both times."

"Even better! At this rate we shall overtake Lord Byron's *Corsair*! At this rate we shall need a second printing by the end of next week!" Then, observing that Shackleton's frown did not grow any less, Mr Murray added, "Well, what is wrong with that? I dare say they want them as presents for their friends."

Shackleton shook his head so that all the loose hairs of his wig jiggled about. "It is queer. I have never known it happen before."

The shop door opened and a young man entered. He was small in stature and slight in build. His features were regular and, truth to tell, he would have been quite handsome had it not been for his rather unfortunate manner. He was one of those people whose ideas are too lively to be confined in their brains and spill out into the world to the consternation of passers-by. He talked to himself and the expression of his face changed constantly. Within the space of a single moment he looked surprized, insulted, resolute and angry – emotions which were presumably the consequences of the energetic conversations he was holding with the ideal people inside his head.

Shops, particularly London shops, are often troubled with lunatics and Mr Murray and Shackleton were immediately upon their guard. Nor were their suspicions at all allayed when the young man fixed Shackleton with a piercing look of his bright blue eyes and cried, "This is treating your customers well! This is gentility!" He turned to Mr Murray and addressed him thus, "Be advised by me, sir! Do not buy your books here. They are liars and thieves!"

"Liars and thieves?" said Mr Murray. "No, you are mistaken, sir. I am sure we can convince you that you are."

"Ha!" cried the young man and gave Mr Murray a shrewd look to shew he had now understood that Mr Murray was not, as he had first supposed, a fellow customer.

"I am the proprietor," explained Mr Murray hurriedly. "We

do not rob people here. Tell me what the matter is and I will be glad to serve you in any way I can. I am quite sure it is all a misunderstanding."

But the young man was not in the least mollifed by Mr Murray's polite words. He cried, "Do you deny, sir, that this establishment employs a rascally cheat of magician – a magician called Strange?"

Mr Murray began to say something of Strange being one of his authors, but the young man could not wait to hear him. "Do you deny, sir, that Mr Strange has put a spell upon his books to make them disappear so that a man must buy another? And then another!" He wagged a finger at Shackleton and looked sly. "You are going to say you don't remember me!"

"No, sir, I am not. I remember you very well. You were one of the first gentlemen to buy a copy of *The History and Practice of English Magic* and then you came back about a week later for another."

The young man opened his eyes very wide. "I was obliged to buy another!" he cried indignantly. "The first one disappeared!"

"Disappeared?" asked Mr Murray, puzzled. "If you have lost your book, Mr . . . er, then I am sorry for it, but I do not quite understand how any blame can attach to the bookseller."

"My name, sir, is Green. And I did not lose my book. It disappeared. Twice." Mr Green sighed deeply, as a man will who finds he has to deal with fools and feeble-minded idiots. "I took the first book home," he explained, "and I placed it upon the table, on top of a box in which I keep my razors and shaving things." Mr Green mimed putting the book on top of the box. "I put the newspaper on top of the book and my brass candlestick and an egg on top of that."

"An egg?" said Mr Murray.

"A hard-boiled egg! But when I turned around – not ten minutes later! – the newspaper was directly on top of the box and the book was gone! Yet the egg and the candlestick were just where they had always been. So a week later I came back and bought another copy – just as your shopman says. I took it home. I put it on the mantelpiece with *Cooper's Dictionary of Practical Surgery* and stood the teapot on top. But it so happened that when I made the tea I dislodged both books and they fell into the basket where the dirty washing is put. On Monday, Jack Boot – my servant – put the dirty linen into the basket. On Tuesday the washerwoman came to take the dirty linen away, but when the bedsheets were lifted away, *Cooper's Dictionary of Practical Surgery* was there at the bottom of the basket but *The History and Practice of English Magic* was gone!"

These speeches, suggesting some slight eccentricities in the regulation of Mr Green's household, seemed to offer hope of an explanation.

"Could you not have mistook the place where you put it?" offered Mr Shackleton.

"Perhaps the laundress took it away with your sheets?" suggested Mr Murray.

"No, no!" declared Mr Green.

"Could someone have borrowed it? Or moved it?" suggested Shackleton.

Mr Green looked amazed at this suggestion. "Who?" he demanded.

"I . . . I have no idea. Mrs Green? Your servant?"

"There is no Mrs Green! I live alone! Except for Jack Boot and Jack Boot cannot read!"

"A friend, then?"

Mr Green seemed about to deny that he had ever had any friends.

Mr Murray sighed. "Shackleton, give Mr Green another copy and his money for the second book." To Mr Green he said, "I am glad you like it so well to buy another copy."

"Like it!" cried Mr Green, more astonished than ever. "I have not the least idea whether I like it or not! I never had a chance to open it."

After he had gone, Mr Murray lingered in the shop a while

making jokes about linen-baskets and hard-boiled eggs, but Mr Shackleton (who was generally as fond of a joke as any one) refused to be entertained. He looked thoughtful and anxious and insisted several times that there was something queer going on.

Half an hour later Mr Murray was in his room upstairs gazing at his bookcase. He looked up and saw Shackleton.

"He is back," said Shackleton.

"What?"

"Green. He has lost his book again. He had it in his right-hand pocket, but by the time he reached Great Pulteney-street it was gone. Of course I told him that London is full of thieves, but you must admit . . ."

"Yes, yes! Never mind that now!" interrupted Mr Murray. "My own copy is gone! Look! I put it here, between d'Israeli's *Flim-Flams* and Miss Austen's *Emma*. You can see the space where it stood. What is happening, Shackleton?"

"Magic," said Shackleton, firmly. "I have been thinking about it and I believe Green is right. There is some sort of spell operating upon the books, and upon us."

"A spell!" Mr Murray opened his eyes wide. "Yes, I suppose it must be. I have never experienced magic at first hand before. I do not think that I shall be in any great hurry to do so again. It is most eerie and unpleasant. How in the world is a man to know what to do when nothing behaves as it should?"

"Well," said Shackleton, "if I were you I would begin by consulting with the other booksellers and discover if their books are disappearing too, then at least we will know if the problem is a general one or confined to us."

This seemed like good advice. So leaving the shop in charge of the office-boy, Mr Murray and Shackleton put on their hats and went out into the wind and rain. The nearest bookseller was Edwards and Skittering in Piccadilly. When they got there they were obliged to step aside to make way for a footman in blue livery. He was carrying a large pile of books out of the shop.

Mr Murray had scarcely time to think that both footman and livery looked familiar before the man was gone.

Inside they found Mr Edwards deep in conversation with John Childermass. As Murray and Shackleton came in, Mr Edwards looked round with a guilty expression, but Childermass was just as usual. "Ah, Mr Murray!" he said. "I am glad to see you, sir. This spares me a walk in the rain."

"What is happening?" demanded Mr Murray. "What are you doing?"

"Doing? Mr Norrell is purchasing some books. That is all."

"Ha! If your master means to suppress Mr Strange's book by buying up all the copies, then he will be disappointed. Mr Norrell is a rich man but he must come to the end of his fortune at last and I can print books as fast as he can buy them."

"No,' said Childermass. "You can't."

Mr Murray turned to Mr Edwards. "Robert, Robert! Why do you let them tyrannize over you in this fashion?"

Poor Mr Edwards looked most unhappy. "I am sorry, Mr Murray, but the books were all disappearing. I have had to give more than thirty people their money back. I stood to lose a great deal. But now Mr Norrell has offered to buy up my entire stock of Strange's book and pay me a fair price for them, and so I . . ."

"Fair?" cried Shackleton, quite unable to bear this. "Fair? What is fair about it, I should like to know? Who do you suppose is making the books disappear in the first place?"

"Quite!" agreed Mr Murray. Turning to Childermass, he said, "You will not attempt to deny that all this is Norrell's doing?"

"No, no. Upon the contrary Mr Norrell is eager to declare himself responsible. He has a whole list of reasons and will be glad to tell them to any one who will listen."

"And what are these reasons?" asked Mr Murray, coldly.

"Oh, the usual sort of thing, I expect," said Childermass, looking, for the first time, slightly evasive. "A letter is being prepared which tells you all about it."

"And you think that will satisfy me, do you? A letter of apology?"

"Apology? I doubt you will get much in the way of an apology."

"I intend to speak to my attorney," said Mr Murray, "this very afternoon."

"Of course you do. We should not expect any thing less. But be that as it may, it is not Mr Norrell's intention that you should lose money by this. As soon as you are able to give me an account of all that you have spent in the publication of Mr Strange's book, I am authorized to give you a banker's draft for the full amount."

This was unexpected. Mr Murray was torn between his desire to return Childermass a very rude answer and his consciousness that Norrell was depriving him of a great deal of money and ought in fairness to pay him.

Shackleton poked Mr Murray discreetly in the arm to warn him not to do any thing rash.

"What of my profit?" asked Mr Murray, trying to gain a little time.

"Oh, you wish that to be taken into consideration, do you? That is only fair, I suppose. Let me speak to Mr Norrell." With that Childermass bowed and walked out of the shop.

There was no reason for Mr Murray and Shackleton to remain any longer. As soon as they were out in the street again, Mr Murray turned to Shackleton and said, "Go down to Thames-street . . ." (This was the warehouse where Mr Murray kept his stock.) ". . . and find out if any of Mr Strange's books are left. Do not allow Jackson to put you off with a short answer. Make him shew them to you. Tell him I need him to count them and that he must send me the reckoning within the hour."

When Mr Murray arrived back at Albermarle-street he found three young men loitering in his shop. They shut up their books the moment they saw him, surrounded him in an instant and began talking at once. Mr Murray naturally supposed that they must have come upon the same errand as Mr Green. As two of them were very tall and all of them were loud and indignant, he became rather nervous and signalled to the office-boy to run and fetch help. The office-boy stayed exactly where he was and watched the proceedings with an expression of unwonted interest upon his face.

Some rather violent exclamations from the young men such as, "Desperate villain!" and "Abominable scoundrel!" did little to reassure Mr Murray, but after a few moments he began to understand that it was not he whom they were abusing, but Norrell.

"I beg your pardon, gentlemen," he said, "but if it is not too much trouble, I wonder if you would do me the kindness of informing me who you are?"

The young men were surprized. They had supposed they were better known than that. They introduced themselves. They were Strange's three pupils-in-waiting, Henry Purfois, William Hadley-Bright and Tom Levy.

William Hadley-Bright and Henry Purfois were both tall and handsome, while Tom Levy was a small, slight figure with dark hair and eyes. As has already been noted, Hadley-Bright and Purfois were well-born English gentlemen, while Tom was an ex-dancing-master whose forefathers had all been Hebrew. Happily Hadley-Bright and Purfois took very little notice of such distinctions of rank and ancestry. Knowing Tom to be the most talented amongst them, they generally deferred to him in all matters of magical scholarship, and, apart from calling him by his given name (while he addressed them as Mr Purfois and Mr Hadley-Bright) and expecting him to pick up books they left behind them, they were very much inclined to treat him as an equal.

"We cannot sit about doing nothing while this villain, this monster destroys Mr Strange's great work!" declared Henry Purfois. "Give us something to do, Mr Murray! That is all we ask!"

"And if that something could involve running Mr Norrell through with a very sharp sabre, then so much the better," added William Hadley-Bright.

"Can one of you go after Strange and bring him back?" asked Mr Murray.

"Oh, certainly! Hadley-Bright is your man for that!" declared Henry Purfois. "He was one of the Duke's *aides-de-camp* at Waterloo, you know. There is nothing he likes better than dashing about on a horse at impossible speeds."

"Do you know where Mr Strange has gone?" asked Tom Levy.

"Two weeks ago he was in Geneva," said Mr Murray. "I had a letter from him this morning. He may be still there. Or he may have gone on to Italy."

The door opened and Shackleton walked in, his wig hung with drops of rain as if he had decorated it with innumerable glass beads. "All is well," he said eagerly to Mr Murray. "The books are still in their bales."

"You saw them with your own eyes?"

"Yes, indeed. I dare say it takes a good deal of magic to make ten thousand books disappear."

"I wish I could be so sanguine," said Tom Levy. "Forgive me, Mr Murray, but from all I ever heard of Mr Norrell once he has set himself a task he works tirelessly at it until it is accomplished. I do not believe we have time to wait for Mr Strange to come back."

Shackleton looked surprized to hear any one pronounce with such confidence upon magical matters.

Mr Murray hastily introduced Strange's three pupils. "How much time do you think we have?" he asked Tom.

"A day? Two at the most? Certainly not enough time to find Mr Strange and bring him back. I think, Mr Murray, that you must put this into our hands and we must try a spell or two to counteract Norrell's magic."

"Are there such spells?" asked Mr Murray, eyeing the novice-magicians doubtfully.

"Oh, hundreds!" said Henry Purfois.

"Do you know any of them?" asked Mr Murray.

"We know *of* them," said William Hadley-Bright. "We could probably put a fairly decent one together. What an excellent thing it would be if Mr Strange came back from the Continent and we had saved his book! That would rather make him open his eyes, I think!"

"What about Pale's Invisible What-D'ye-Call-It and Thingumajig?" asked Henry Purfois.

"I know what you mean," said William Hadley-Bright.

"A really remarkable procedure of Dr Pale's," Henry Purfois informed Mr Murray. "It turns a spell around and inflicts it upon its maker. Mr Norrell's own books would go blank or disappear! Which is, after all, no more than he deserves."

"I am not sure Mr Strange would be so delighted if he came back and found we had destroyed England's foremost magical library," said Tom. "Besides in order to perform Pale's Invisible Reflection and Protection we would have to construct a Quiliphon."

"A what?" said Mr Murray.

"A Quiliphon," said William Hadley-Bright. "Dr Pale's works are full of such machines for doing magic. I believe that in appearance it is something between a trumpet and a toasting fork . . ."

". . . and there are four metal globes on top that go round and round," added Henry Purfois.

"I see," said Mr Murray.

"Building a Quiliphon would take too long," said Tom, firmly. "I suggest we turn our attention to De Chepe's Prophylaxis.[4] That

---

[4] Walter De Chepe was an early thirteenth-century London magician. His procedure, Prophylaxis, protects a person, city or object from magic spells. Supposedly it closely follows a piece of fairy magic. It is reputed to be very strong. Indeed the only problem with this spell is its remarkable efficacy. Sometimes objects become impervious to human or fairy agency of any sort whether magical or not. Thus if Strange's students had succeeded in casting the spell over one of Strange's books, it is quite possible that no one would have been able to pick up the book or turn its pages.

In 1280 the citizens of Bristol ordered the town's magicians to cast de Chepe's Prophylaxis over the whole town to protect it from the magic spells of its enemies. Unfortunately so successful was the magic that everyone in the town, all the animals and all the ships in the harbour became living statues. No one could move; water stopped flowing within the boundaries; even the flames in the hearth were frozen. Bristol remained like this for a whole month until John Uskglass came from his house in Newcastle to put matters right.

is very quick to implement and, correctly done, should hold off Norrell's magic for a while – long enough to get a message to Mr Strange."

Just then the door opened and an untidy-looking fellow in a leather apron entered the shop. He was somewhat discomfited to find the eyes of all the room upon him. He made a little bobbing bow, handed a piece of paper to Shackleton and quickly made his escape.

"What is it, Shackleton?" asked Mr Murray.

"A message from Thames-street. They have looked inside the books. They are all blank – not a word left upon any of the pages. I am sorry, Mr Murray, but *The History and Practice of English Magic* is gone."

William Hadley-Bright stuck his hands in his pockets and gave a low whistle.

As the hours progressed it became clear that not a single copy of Strange's book remained in circulation. William Hadley-Bright and Henry Purfois were all for calling Mr Norrell out, until it was represented to them that Mr Norrell was an elderly gentleman who rarely took exercise and had never been seen with a sword or a pistol in his hand. There were no circumstances under which it would be fair or honourable for two men in the prime of life (one of them a soldier) to challenge him to a duel. Hadley-Bright and Purfois accepted this with a good grace, but Purfois could not help looking hopefully about the room for a person of equal decrepitude to Mr Norrell. He gazed speculatively at Shackleton.

Other friends of Strange appeared to condole with Mr Murray and give vent to some of the fury they felt at what Mr Norrell had done. Lord Portishead arrived and gave an account of the letter he had sent to Mr Norrell breaking off their friendship and the letter he had sent to Lascelles resigning as editor of *The Friends of English Magic* and cancelling his subscription.

"Henceforth, gentlemen," he told Strange's pupils, "I consider myself as belonging solely to your party."

Strange's pupils assured his lordship he had done the right thing and would never regret it.

At seven o'clock Childermass arrived. He walked into the crowded room with as much composure as if he were walking into church. "Well, how much have you lost, Mr Murray?" he asked. He took out his memorandum book and picked up a quill from Mr Murray's desk and dipped it in the ink.

"Put your book away again, Mr Childermass," said Mr Murray. "I do not want your money."

"Indeed? Be careful, sir, how you let these gentlemen influence you. Some of them are young and have no responsibilities . . ." Childermass gave a cool glance to Strange's three pupils and to the several officers in uniform who stood about the room. "And others are rich and a hundred pounds more or less is nothing to them." Childermass looked at Lord Portishead. "But you, Mr Murray, are a man of business and business ought to be your first consideration."

"Ha!" Mr Murray crossed his arms and looked triumphantly at Childermass with his one good eye. "You think I am in desperate need of the money – but, you see, I am not. Offers of loans from Mr Strange's friends have been arriving all evening. I believe I might set up a whole new business if I chose! But I desire you will take a message to Mr Norrell. It is this. He will pay in the end – but upon our terms, not his. We intend to make him pay for the new edition. He shall pay for the advertisements for his rival's book. That will give him greater pain than any thing else could, I believe."

"Oh, indeed! If it ever happens," said Childermass, drily. He turned towards the door. Then he paused and, staring for a moment at the carpet, seemed to debate something within himself. "I will tell you this," he said. "The book is not destroyed however it may seem at present. I have dealt my cards and asked them if there are any copies left. It seems that two remain. Strange has one and Norrell the other."

*   *   *

For the next month London talked of little else but the astonishing thing that Mr Norrell had done, but as to whether it were the wickedness of Strange's book or the spitefulness of Mr Norrell which was most to blame, London was divided. People who had bought copies were furious at the loss of their books and Mr Norrell did not help matters by sending his servants to their houses with a guinea (the cost of the book) and the letter in which he explained his reasons for making their books disappear. A great many people found themselves more insulted than ever and some of them immediately summoned their attorneys to begin proceedings against Mr Norrell.[5]

In September the Ministers returned from the country to London and naturally Mr Norrell's extraordinary actions formed one of the main topics of conversation at their first meeting.

"When we first employed Mr Norrell to do magic on our behalf," said one, "we had no idea of permitting him to intrude his spells into people's houses and alter their possessions. In some ways it is a pity that we do not have that magical court he is always proposing. What is it called?"

[5] The letter contained two implications which were considered particularly offensive: first, that the purchasers were not clever enough to understand Strange's book; and second, that they did not possess the moral judgement to decide for themselves if the magic Strange was describing was good or wicked.

The Norrellites had fully expected that the destruction of Strange's book would be controversial and they were prepared to receive a great deal of criticism, however the harm done to their own cause by the letter was entirely unintentional. Mr Norrell had been supposed to shew the letter to Mr Lascelles before it was sent out. If Lascelles had seen it, then the language and expressions would have undergone considerable modification and presumably have been less offensive to the recipients.

Unfortunately, there was a misunderstanding. Mr Norrell asked Childermass if Lascelles had made his amendments. Childermass thought they were speaking of an article for *The Friends of English Magic* and said that he had. And so the letter went out uncorrected. Lascelles was furious and accused Childermass of having purposely encouraged Mr Norrell to damage his own cause. Childermass vehemently denied doing any such thing.

From this time on relations between Lascelles and Childermass (never good) worsened rapidly and soon Lascelles was hinting to Mr Norrell that Childermass had Strangite sympathies and was secretly working to betray his master.

"The Cinque Dragownes," said Sir Walter Pole.

"I presume he must be guilty of some magical crime or other?"

"Oh, certainly! But I have not the least idea what. John Childermass probably knows, but I very much doubt that he would tell us."

"It does not matter. There are several suits against him in the common courts for theft."

"Theft!" said another Minister in surprize. "I find it very shocking that a man who has done the country such service should be prosecuted for such a low crime!"

"Why?" asked the first. "He has brought it upon himself."

"The problem is," said Sir Walter, "that the moment he is asked to defend himself he will respond by saying something about the nature of English magic. And no one is competent to argue that subject except Strange. I think we must be patient. I think we must wait until Strange comes back."

"Which raises another question," said another Minister. "There are only two magicians in England. How can we decide between them? Who can say which of them is right and which is wrong?"

The Ministers looked at each other in perplexity.

Only Lord Liverpool, the Prime Minister, was unperturbed. "We will know them as we know other men," he declared, "by the fruits that they bear."[6]

There was a pause for the Ministers to reflect that the fruits Mr Norrell was currently bearing were not very promising: arrogance, theft and malice.

It was agreed that the Home Secretary should speak to Mr Lascelles privately and ask that he would convey to Mr Norrell the extreme displeasure of the Prime Minister and all the Ministers at what Mr Norrell had done.

There seemed no more to be said, but the Ministers were unable to leave the subject without indulging in a little gossip. They had

[6] "Wherefore by their fruits ye shall know them." St Matthew, 7,16.

all heard how Lord Portishead had severed himself from Mr Norrell. But Sir Walter was able to tell them how Childermass – who up to this moment had seemed like his master's shadow – had distanced himself from Mr Norrell's interests and spoken to Strange's assembled friends as an independent person, assuring them that the book was not destroyed. Sir Walter sighed deeply. "I cannot help thinking that in many ways this is a worse sign than all the rest. Norrell never was a good judge of men, and now the best of his friends are deserting him – Strange is gone, John Murray and now Portishead. If Childermass and Norrell quarrel there will only be Henry Lascelles left."

Strange's friends all sat down that evening and wrote him letters full of indignation. The letters would take two weeks to reach Italy, but Strange moved about so much that it might be another two weeks before they found him. At first Strange's friends felt confident that the instant he read them he would immediately set out for England in a blaze of anger, ready to contend with Norrell in the courts and the newspapers. But in September they received news which made them think that perhaps they would have to wait a while after all.

As long as Strange had been travelling towards Italy he had seemed generally to be in good spirits. His letters had been full of cheerful nonsense. But as soon as he arrived there his mood changed. For the first time since Arabella's death he had no work to do and nothing to distract him from his widowed state. Nothing he saw pleased him and for some weeks it seemed that he could only find any relief for his misery in continual change of scene.[7] In

[7] ". . . I cannot tell you any thing of Piacenza," Strange wrote to Henry Woodhope, "as I did not stay long enough to see it. I arrived in the evening. After dinner I thought I would walk about for a half hour, but on entering the main piazza, I was immediately struck by a tall urn standing upon a pedestal with its long, black shadow trailing upon the stones. Two or three strands of ivy or some other creeping plant emerged from the neck of the urn but they were quite dead. I cannot say why, but this seemed to me so deeply melancholy that I could not bear it. It was like an allegory of loss, death and misery. I returned to the inn, went immediately to bed and in the morning left for Turin."

early September he reached Genoa. Liking this place a little better than other Italian towns he had seen, he stayed almost a week. During this time an English family arrived at the hotel where he was staying. Though he had previously declared to Sir Walter his intention of avoiding the society of Englishmen while he was abroad, Strange struck up an acquaintance with this family. In no time at all he was writing letters back to England full of praise for the manners, cleverness and kindness of the Greysteels. At the end of the week he travelled to Bologna, but finding no pleasure there he very soon returned to Genoa to remain with the Greysteels until the end of the month when they all planned to travel together to Venice.

Naturally, Strange's friends were very glad that he had found some agreeable company, but what intrigued them most were several references in Strange's letters to the daughter of the family, who was young and unmarried and in whose society Strange seemed to take a particular pleasure. The same interesting idea occurred to several of his friends at once: what if he were to marry again? A pretty young wife would cure his gloomy spirits better than any thing else could, and best of all she would distract him from that dark, unsettling magic he seemed so set upon.

There were more thorns in Mr Norrell's side than Strange. A gentleman called Knight had begun a school for magicians in Henrietta-street in Covent-garden. Mr Knight was not a practical magician, nor did he pretend to be. His advertisement offered young gentlemen: "a thorough Education in Theoretical Magic and English Magical History upon the same principles which guided our Foremost Magician, Mr Norrell, in teaching his Illustrious Pupil, Jonathan Strange." Mr Lascelles had written Mr Knight an angry letter in which he declared that Mr Knight's school could not possibly be based upon the principles mentioned since these were known only to Mr Norrell and Mr Strange. Lascelles threatened Mr Knight with exposure as a fraud if he did not immediately dismantle his school.

Mr Knight had written a polite letter back in which he begged to differ. He said that, upon the contrary, Mr Norrell's system of education was well known. He directed Mr Lascelles's attention to page 47 of *The Friends of English Magic* from the Autumn of 1810 in which Lord Portishead had declared that the only basis for training up more magicians approved by Mr Norrell was that devised by Francis Sutton-Grove. Mr Knight (who declared himself a sincere admirer of Mr Norrell's) had bought a copy of Sutton-Grove's *De Generibus Artium Magicarum Anglorum* and studied it. He took the opportunity to wonder whether Mr Norrell would do him the honour of becoming the school's Visiting Tutor and giving lectures and so forth. He had intended to tutor four young men, but he had been so overpowered by applications that he had been obliged to rent another house to accommodate them and hire more teachers to teach them. Other schools were being proposed in Bath, Chester and Newcastle.

Almost worse than the schools were the shops. Several establishments in London had begun to sell magical philtres, magic mirrors and silver basins which, the manufacturers claimed, had been specially constructed for seeing visions in. Mr Norrell had done what he could to halt the trade, with diatribes against them in *The Friends of English Magic*. He had persuaded the editors of all the other magical publications over which he had any influence to publish articles explaining that there never ever had been any such thing as magical mirrors, and that the magic performed by magicians using mirrors (which were in any case only a few sorts and hardly any that Mr Norrell approved) were performed using ordinary mirrors. Nevertheless the magical articles continued to sell out as fast as the shopkeepers could put them on the shelves and some shopkeepers were considering whether they ought not to give up their other business and devote their whole shop to magical accoutrements.

# 51

# A family by the name of Greysteel

## October to November 1816

Campo Santa Maria Zobenigo, Venice
*Jonathan Strange to Sir Walter Pole* Oct. 16th, 1816.

We left *terra firma* at Mestre. There were two gondolas. Miss Greysteel and her aunt were to go in one, and the doctor and I were to go in the other. But whether there was some obscurity in my Italian when I explained it to the *gondolieri* or whether the distribution of Miss Greysteel's boxes and trunks dictated another arrangement I do not know, but matters did not fall out as we had planned. The first gondola glided out across the lagoon with all the Greysteels inside it, while I still stood upon the shore. Dr Greysteel stuck his head out and roared his apologies, like the good fellow that he is, before his sister – who I think is a little nervous of the water – pulled him back in again. It was the most trivial incident yet somehow it unnerved me and for some moments afterwards I was prey to the most morbid fears and imaginings. I looked at my gondola. Much has been said, I know, about the funereal appearance of these contraptions – which are something between a coffin and a boat. But I was struck by quite another idea. I thought how much they resembled the black-painted, black-curtained conjuring boxes of my childhood – the sort of boxes into which quack-sorcerers would put country people's handkerchiefs and coins and lockets. Sometimes these articles could never be got back – for which the sorcerer was always very sorry – "but fairy-spirits, Sir, is very giddy, wexatious creatures." And all the nursemaids and kitchenmaids I ever knew when I was a child, always had an aunt, who knew a woman, whose first cousin's boy had been put into just such a box, and had never been seen again. Standing on the quayside at Mestre I had a horrible notion that when the Greysteels got to Venice they would open up the gondola that should have conveyed me there and find nothing inside. This idea took hold of me so strongly that for some minutes I forgot to think of any thing else and there were actual tears standing in my eyes – which I think may serve to shew how nervous I have become. It is quite ridiculous for a man to begin to be afraid that he is about to disappear. It was towards evening and our two gondolas were as black as night and quite as melancholy. Yet the sky was the coldest, palest blue imaginable. There was no wind or hardly any, and the sea was nothing but the sky's mirror. There were immeasurable spaces of still cold light above us and immeasurable spaces of still cold light beneath. But the city ahead of us received no illumination either from sky or lagoon, and appeared like a vast collection of shadow-towers and shadow-pinnacles, all pierced with tiny lights and set upon the shining water. As we entered Venice the water became crowded with scraps and rubbish – splinters of wood and hay, orange peels and cabbage stalks. I looked down and saw a ghostly hand for a moment – it was only a moment – but I quite believed that there was a woman beneath the dirty water, trying to find her way back to the light. Of course it was only a white glove, but the fright, while it lasted, was very great. But you are not to worry about me. I am very well occupied, working on the second volume of *The History and Practice* and when I am not working I am generally with the Greysteels, who are just such a set of people as you yourself would like – cheerful, independent, and well-informed. I confess to being a little fretful that I have heard nothing as yet of how the first volume was received. I am tolerably certain of its being a great triumph – I *know* that when he read it, N. fell down on the floor in a jealous fit and foamed at the mouth – but I cannot help wishing that someone would write and tell me so.

Campo Santa Maria Zobenigo, Venice
*Jonathan Strange to John Murray* Oct. 27th, 1816.

. . . from eight separate persons of what Norrell has done. Oh, I *could* be angry. I *could*, I dare say, wear out both my pen and myself in a long tirade – but to what end? I do not *chuse* to be governed any longer by this impudent little man. I shall return to London in the early spring, as I planned, and we shall have a new edition. We shall have lawyers. I have my friends, just as he has his. Let him say in court (if he dares) why he thinks that Englishmen have become children and may not know the things that their forefathers knew. And if he dares to use magic against me again, then we shall have some counter-magic and then we shall finally see who is the Greatest Magician of the Age. And I think, Mr Murray, that you will be best advised to print a great many more copies than before – this has been one of Norrell's most notorious acts of magic and I am sure that people will like to see the book that forced him to it. By the by when you print the new edition we shall have corrections – there are some horrible blunders. Chapters six and forty-two are particularly bad . . .

Harley-street, London
*Sir Walter Pole to Jonathan Strange* Oct. 1st, 1816.

. . . a bookseller in St Paul's Churchyard, Titus Watkins, has printed up a very nonsensical book and is selling it as Strange's lost *History and Practice of English Magic*. Lord Portishead says some of it is copied out of Absalom[1] and some of it is nonsense. Portishead wonders which you will find the most insulting – the Absalom part or the nonsense. Like a good fellow, Portishead contradicts this imposition wherever he goes, but a great many people have already been taken in and Watkins has certainly made money. I am glad you like Miss Greysteel so much . . .

Campo Santa Maria Zobenigo, Venice

*Jonathan Strange to John Murray* Nov. 16th., 1816.

My dear Murray,
You will be pleased, I think, to hear that some good at least has come from the destruction of *The History and Practice of English Magic* – I have made up my quarrel with Lord Byron. His lordship knows nothing of the great controversies which are rending English magic in two and frankly cares less. But he has the greatest respect for books. He informs me that he is constantly on guard lest your over-cautious pen, Mr Murray, should alter some of his own poems and render some of the more *surprizing* words a little more respectable. When he heard that a whole book had been magicked out of existence by the author's enemy, his indignation was scarcely to be described. He sent me a long letter, vilifying Norrell in the liveliest terms. Of all the letters I received upon that sad occasion, this is my favourite. No Englishman alive can equal his lordship for an insult. He arrived in Venice about a week ago and we met at Florian's.[2] I confess to being a little anxious lest he should bring that insolent young person, Mrs Clairmont, but happily she was nowhere to beseen. Apparently he dismissed her some time ago. Our new friendly relations have been sealed by the discovery that we share a fondness for billiards; I play when I am thinking about magic and he plays when he is hatching his poems . . .

[1] *The Tree of Learning* by Gregory Absalom (1507–99)
[2] A famous café on the San Marco Piazza.

The sunlight was as cold and clear as the note struck by a knife on a fine wine-glass. In such a light the walls of the Church of Santa Maria Formosa were as white as shells or bones – and the shadows on the paving stones were as blue as the sea.

The door to the church opened and a little party came out into the campo. These ladies and gentlemen were visitors to the city of Venice who had been looking at the interior of the church, its altars and objects of interest, and now that they had got out of it, they were inclined to be talkative and filled up the water-lapped silence of the place with loud, cheerful conversation. They were excessively pleased with the Campo Santa Maria Formosa. They thought the façades of the houses very magnificent – they could not praise them highly enough. But the sad decay, which buildings, bridges and church all displayed, seemed to charm them even more. They were Englishmen and, to them, the decline of other nations was the most natural thing in the world. They belonged to a race blessed with so sensitive an appreciation of its own talents (and so doubtful an opinion of any body else's) that they would not have been at all surprized to learn that the Venetians themselves had been entirely ignorant of the merits of their own city – until Englishmen had come to tell them it was delightful.

One lady, having got to the end of her raptures, began to speak of the weather to the other lady.

"You know, it is a very odd thing, my dear, but when we were in the church, while you and Mr Strange were looking at the pictures, I just popped my head out of the door and I thought then that it was raining and I was very much afraid that you would get wet."

"No, aunt. See, the stones are perfectly dry. There is not a spot of rain upon them."

"Well then, my dear, I hope that you are not inconvenienced by this wind. It is a little sharp about the ears. We can always ask Mr Strange and papa to walk a little faster if you do not like it."

"Thank you, aunt, but I am perfectly comfortable. I like this breeze – I like the smell of the sea – it clears the brain, the senses – every thing. But perhaps, aunt, *you* do not like it."

"Oh no, my dear. I never mind any such thing. I am quite hardy. I only think of you."

"I know you do, aunt," said the young lady. The young lady was perhaps aware that the sunlight and breeze which shewed Venice to so much advantage, made its canals so blue and its marble so mystically bright, did as much – or almost as much – for her. Nothing could so well draw attention to the translucency of Miss Greysteel's complexion, as the rapid progression across it of sunlight and shadow. Nothing could be so becoming to her white muslin gown as the breeze which blew it about.

"Ah," said the aunt, "now papa is showing Mr Strange some new thing or other. Flora, my dear, would not you like to see?"

"I have seen enough. You go, aunt."

So the aunt hurried away to the other end of the campo and Miss Greysteel walked slowly on to the little white bridge that stood just by the church, fretfully poking the point of her white parasol between the white paving stones and murmuring to herself, "I have seen enough. Oh, I have seen *quite* enough!" The repetition of this mysterious exclamation did not appear to afford her spirits much relief – indeed it only served to make her more melancholy, and to make her sigh more frequently.

"You are very quiet today," said Strange suddenly. She was startled. She had not known he was so close by.

"Am I? I was not aware of it." But she then gave her attention to the view and was silent for several moments. Strange leant back against the bridge, folded his arms and looked very intently at her.

"Quiet," he repeated, "and a little sad, I think. And so, you know, I must talk to you."

This made her smile in spite of herself. "Must you?" she said. But then the very act of smiling and of speaking to him seemed to give her pain and so she sighed and looked away again.

"Indeed. Because, whenever *I* am melancholy you talk to me of cheerful things and cure my low spirits and so I must now do the same for *you*. That is what friendship is."

"Openness and honesty, Mr Strange. Those are the best foundations for friendship, I think."

"Oh! You think me secretive. I see by your face that you do. You may be right, but I . . . That is . . . No, I dare say you are right. It is not, I suppose, a profession that encourages . . ."

Miss Greysteel interrupted him. "I did not mean a fling at your profession. Not at all. All professions have their different sorts of discretion. *That*, I think, is quite understood."

"Then I do not understand you."

"It is no matter. We should rejoin my aunt and papa."

"No, wait, Miss Greysteel, it will not do. Who else will put me right, when I am going wrong, if not you? Tell me – whom do you think I deceive?"

Miss Greysteel was silent a moment and then, with some reluctance, said, "Your friend of last night, perhaps?"

"My friend of last night! What do you mean?"

Miss Greysteel looked very unhappy. "The young woman in the gondola who was so anxious to speak to you and so unwilling – for a full half hour – that any one else should."

"Ah!" Strange smiled and shook his head. "No, you have run away with a wrong idea. She is not my friend. She is Lord Byron's."

"Oh! . . ." Miss Greysteel reddened a little. "She seemed rather an agitated young person."

"She is not best pleased with his lordship's behaviour." Strange shrugged. "Who is? She wished to discover if I were able to influence his lordship and I was at some pains to persuade her that there is not now, nor ever was, I think, magic enough in England to do that."

"You are offended."

"Not in the least. Now I believe we are closer to that good understanding which you require for friendship. Will you shake hands with me?"

"With the greatest goodwill," she said.

"Flora? Mr Strange?" cried Dr Greysteel, striding up to them. "What is this?"

Miss Greysteel was a little confused. It was of the greatest importance to her that her aunt and father should have a good opinion of Mr Strange. She did not want them to know that she herself had suspected him of wrongdoing. She feigned not to have heard her father's question and began to speak energetically of some paintings in the Scuola di Giorgio degli Schiavoni that she had a great desire to see. "It is really no distance. We could go now. You will come with us, I hope?" she said to Strange.

Strange smiled ruefully at her. "I have work to do."

"Your book?" asked Dr Greysteel.

"Not today. I am working to uncover the magic which will bring forth a fairy-spirit to be my assistant. I have lost count of how many times I have tried – and how many ways. And never, of course, with the least success. But such is the predicament of the modern magician! Spells which were once taken for granted by every minor sorcerer in England are now so elusive that we despair of ever getting them back. Martin Pale had twenty-eight fairy servants. I would count myself fortunate to have one."

"Fairies!" exclaimed Aunt Greysteel. "But by all accounts they are very mischievous creatures! Are you quite certain, Mr Strange, that you really wish to burden yourself with such a troublesome companion?"

"My dear aunt!" said Miss Greysteel. "Mr Strange knows what he is doing."

But Aunt Greysteel was concerned and to illustrate her point she began to speak of a river that flowed through the village in Derbyshire where she and Dr Greysteel had grown up. It had been enchanted by fairies long ago and as a consequence had shrunk from a noble torrent to a gentle brook and, though this had happened centuries and centuries ago, the local population still remembered and resented it. They still talked of the workshops they might have set up and the industries they might have founded if only the river had been strong enough to supply the power.[3]

Strange listened politely and when she had finished he said, "Oh, to be sure! Fairies are naturally full of wickedness and exceedingly difficult to control. Were I successful, I should certainly have to take care whom my fairy – or fairies – associated with." He cast a glance at Miss Greysteel. "Nevertheless their power and knowledge are such that a magician cannot lightly dispense with their help – not unless he is Gilbert Norrell. Every fairy that ever drew breath has more magic in his head, hands and heart than could be contained in the greatest library of magical books that ever existed."[4]

"Has he indeed?" said Aunt Greysteel. "Well, that is remarkable."

Dr Greysteel and Aunt Greysteel wished Strange success with his magic and Miss Greysteel reminded him that he had promised to go with her one day soon to look at a pianoforte which they had heard was for hire from an antiquarian who lived near the Campo San Angelo. Then the Greysteels went on to the rest of the day's pleasures while Strange returned to his lodgings near Santa Maria Zobenigo.

Most English gentlemen who come to Italy nowadays write poems or descriptions of their tour, or they make sketches. Italians

[3] Aunt Greysteel is probably speaking of the Derwent. Long ago, when John Uskglass was still a captive child in Faerie, a king in Faerie foretold that if he came to adulthood, then all the old fairy kingdoms would fall. The king sent his servants into England to bring back an iron knife to kill him. The knife was forged by a blacksmith on the banks of the Derwent and the waters of the Derwent were used to cool the hot metal. However, the attempt to kill John Uskglass failed and the king and his clan were destroyed by the boy-magician. When John Uskglass entered England and established his kingdom, his fairy-followers went in search of the blacksmith. They killed him and his family, destroyed his house and laid magic spells upon the Derwent to punish it for its part in making the wicked knife.

[4] The views Strange is expressing at this point are wildly optimistic and romantic. English magical literature is full of examples of fairies whose powers were weak or who were stupid or ignorant.

who wish to rent apartments to these gentlemen are well advised to provide them with rooms where they can pursue these occupations. Strange's landlord, for example, had set aside a shadowy little chamber at the top of his house for his tenant's use. It contained an ancient table with four carved gryphons to serve for its legs; there was a sea-captain's chair, a painted wooden cupboard such as one might find in a church and a wooden figure two or three feet tall, which stood upon a pillar. It represented a smiling man holding something round and red in his hand, which might have been an apple, might have been a pomegranate or might have been a red ball. It was difficult to imagine quite where this gentleman could have come from: he was a little too cheerful for a saint in a church and not quite comical enough for a coffee-house sign.

Strange had found the cupboard to be damp and full of mildew and so he had abandoned it and placed his books and papers in heaps about the floor. But he had made a sort of friend of the wooden figure and, as he worked, he constantly addressed remarks to it, such as, "What is your opinion?" and "Doncaster or Belasis? What do you suggest?"[5] and "Well? Do you see him? I do not,"

---

[5] Jacques Belasis was reputed to have created an excellent spell for summoning fairy-spirits. Unfortunately the only copy of Belasis's masterpiece, *The Instructions*, was at the library at Hurtfew and Strange had never seen it. All he knew of it were vague descriptions in later histories and so it must be assumed that Strange was re-creating this magic and had only the flimsiest notion of what he was aiming at.

By contrast, the spell commonly attributed to the Master of Doncaster is very well known and appears in a number of widely available works. The identity of the Master of Doncaster is not known. His existence is deduced from a handful of references in *Argentine* histories to thirteenth-century magicians acquiring spells and magic "from Doncaster". Moreover, it is far from clear that all the magic attributed to the Master of Doncaster is the work of one man. This has led magio-historians to postulate a second magician, even more shadowy than the first, the Pseudo-Master of Doncaster. If, as has been convincingly argued, the Master of Doncaster was really John Uskglass, then it is logical to assume that the spell of summoning was created by the Pseudo-Master. It seems highly unlikely that John Uskglass would have had any need of a spell to summon fairies. His court was, after all, full of them.

and once in tones of extreme exasperation, "Oh! Be quiet, will you?"

He took out a paper on which he had scribbled a spell. He moved his lips as magicians do when they are reciting magic words. When he had finished, he glanced about the room as though he half-expected to find another person there. But whomever it was that he hoped to see, he did not see them. He sighed, crumpled the spell into a ball and threw it at the little wooden figure. Then he took another sheet of paper – made some notes – consulted a book – retrieved the first piece of paper from the floor – smoothed it out – studied it for half an hour, pulling at his hair all the while – crumpled it up again and threw it out the window.

A bell had begun to toll somewhere. It was a sad and lonely sound which made the hearer think of wild forlorn places, dark skies and emptiness. Some of these ideas must have occurred to Strange because he became distracted and stopped what he was doing and glanced out of the window as though to reassure himself that Venice had not suddenly become an empty, silent ruin. But the scene outside was the usual one of bustle and animation. Sunlight shone on blue water. The campo was crowded with people: there were Venetian ladies coming to Santa Maria Zobenigo, Austrian soldiers strolling about arm-in-arm and looking at everything, shopkeepers trying to sell them things, urchins fighting and begging, cats going about their secret business.

Strange returned to his work. He took off his coat and rolled up the sleeve of his shirt. Next he left the room and returned with a knife and a small white basin. He used the knife to let some blood from his arm. He put the basin on the table and peered into it to see if he had got enough, but the loss of blood must have affected him more than he supposed because in a moment of faintness he knocked the table and the bowl fell upon the floor. He cursed in Italian (a good cursing language) and looked around for something to wipe up the blood.

It so happened that there was some white cloth lying bundled up on top of the table. It was a nightshirt which Arabella had sewn in the early years of their marriage. Without realizing what it was, Strange reached out for it. He had almost grasped it, when Stephen Black stept out of the shadows and handed him a rag. Stephen accompanied the action with that faint half-bow that is second nature to a well-trained servant. Strange took the rag and mopped up the blood (somewhat ineffectually), but of Stephen's presence in the room he appeared to know nothing at all. Stephen picked up the nightshirt, shook out the creases, carefully folded it up and placed it neatly on a stool in the corner.

Strange threw himself back into his chair, caught the damaged part of his arm upon the edge of the table, swore again and covered his face with his hands.

"What in the world is he trying to do?" asked Stephen Black in a hushed tone.

"Oh, he is attempting to summon me!" declared the gentleman with the thistle-down hair. "He wishes to ask me all sorts of questions about magic! But there is no need to whisper, my dear Stephen. He can neither see nor hear you. They are so ridiculous, these English magicians! They do everything in such a roundabout way. I tell you, Stephen, watching this fellow try to do magic is like watching a man sit down to eat his dinner with his coat on backwards, a blindfold round his eyes and a bucket over his head! When did you ever see *me* perform such nonsensical tricks? Draw forth my own blood or scribble words on paper? Whenever I wish to do something, I simply speak to the air – or to the stones – or to the sunlight – or the sea – or to whatever it is and politely request them to help me. And then, since my alliances with these powerful spirits were set in place thousands of years ago, they are only too glad to do whatever I ask."

"I see," said Stephen. "But, though the magician is ignorant, he has still succeeded. After all, you are here, sir, are you not?"

"Yes, I dare say," said the gentleman in an irritated tone. "But that does not detract from the fact that the magic that brought me here is clumsy and inelegant! Besides what does it profit him? Nothing! I do not chuse to shew myself to him and he knows no magic to counteract that. Stephen! Quick! Turn the pages of that book! There is no breeze in the room and it will perplex him beyond any thing. Ha! See how he stares! He half-suspects that we are here, but he cannot see us. Ha, ha! How angry he is becoming! Give his neck a sharp pinch! He will think it is a mosquito!"

# 52

# The old lady of Cannaregio

## End of November 1816

SOME TIME BEFORE he had left England Dr Greysteel had received a letter from a friend in Scotland, begging that, if he were to get as far as Venice, he would pay a visit to a certain old lady who lived there. It would be, said the Scottish friend, an act of charity, since this old lady, once rich, was now poor. Dr Greysteel thought he remembered hearing once that she was of some odd, mixed parentage – as it might be half-Scottish, half-Spanish or perhaps half-Irish, half-Hebrew.

Dr Greysteel had always intended to visit her, but what with inns and carriages, sudden removals and changes of plan, he had discovered, on arriving at Venice, that he could no longer lay his hand on the letter and no longer retained a very clear impression of its contents. Nor had he any note of her name – nothing but a little scrap of paper with the direction where she might be found.

Aunt Greysteel said that under such very difficult circumstances as these, they would do best to send the old lady a letter informing her of their intention to call upon her. Though, to be sure, she added, it would look very odd that they did not know her name – doubtless she would think them a sad, negligent sort of people. Dr Greysteel looked uncomfortable, and sniffed and fidgeted a good deal, but he could think of no better plan and so they wrote the note forthwith and gave it to their landlady, so that she might deliver it to the old lady straightaway.

Then came the first odd part of the business, for the landlady studied the direction, frowned and then – for reasons which Dr Greysteel did not entirely comprehend – sent it to her brother-in-law on the island of Giudecca.

Some days later this same brother-in-law – an elegant little Venetian lawyer – waited upon Dr Greysteel. He informed Dr Greysteel that he had sent the note, just as Dr Greysteel had requested, but Dr Greysteel should know that the lady lived in that part of the city which was called Cannaregio, in the Ghetto – where the Jews lived. The letter had been delivered into the hands of a venerable Hebrew gentleman. There had been no reply. How did Dr Greysteel wish to proceed? The little Venetian lawyer was happy to serve Dr Greysteel in any way he could.

In the late afternoon Miss Greysteel, Aunt Greysteel, Dr Greysteel and the lawyer (whose name was Signor Tosetti), glided through the city in a gondola – through that part of the city which is called St Mark's where they saw men and women preparing for the night's pleasures – past the landing of Santa Maria Zobenigo, where Miss Greysteel turned back to gaze at a little candlelit window, which might have belonged to Jonathan Strange – past the Rialto where Aunt Greysteel began to tut and sigh and wish very much that she saw more shoes upon the children's feet.

They left the gondola at the Ghetto Nuovo. Though all the houses of Venice are strange and old, those of the Ghetto seemed particularly so – as if queerness and ancientness were two of the commodities this mercantile people dealt in and they had constructed their houses out of them. Though all the streets of Venice are melancholy, these streets had a melancholy that was quite distinct – as if Jewish sadness and Gentile sadness were made up according to different recipes. Yet the houses were very plain and the door upon which Signor Tosetti knocked was black enough and humble enough to have done for any Quaker meeting-house in England.

The door was opened by a manservant who let them into the house and into a dark chamber panelled with dried-out, ancient-looking wood that smelt of nothing so much as the sea.

There was a door in this chamber that was open a little. From where he stood Dr Greysteel could see ancient, battered-looking books in thin leather bindings, silver candlesticks that had sprouted more branches than English candlesticks generally do, mysterious-looking boxes of polished wood – all of which Dr Greysteel took to be connected with the Hebrew gentleman's religion. Hung upon the wall was a doll or puppet as tall and broad as a man, with huge hands and feet, but dressed like a woman, with its head sunk upon its breast so that its face could not be seen.

The manservant went through this door to speak to his master. Dr Greysteel whispered to his sister that the servant was decent-looking enough. Yes, said Aunt Greysteel, except that he wore no coat. Aunt Greysteel said that she had often noticed that male servants were always liable to present themselves in their shirt-sleeves and that it was often the case that if their masters were single gentlemen then nothing would be done to correct this bad habit. Aunt Greysteel did not know why this should be. Aunt Greysteel supposed that the Hebrew gentleman was a widower.

"Oh!" said Dr Greysteel, peeping through the half-open doorway. "We have interrupted him at his dinner."

The venerable Hebrew gentleman wore a long, dusty black coat and had a great beard of curly grey and white hairs and a black skullcap on top of his head. He was seated at a long table upon which was laid a spotless white linen cloth and he had tucked a generous portion of this into the neck of his black robe to serve him as a napkin.

Aunt Greysteel was very shocked that Dr Greysteel should be spying through chinks in doorways and attempted to make him stop by poking at him with her umbrella. But Dr Greysteel had come to Italy to see everything he could and saw no reason to make an exception of Hebrew gentlemen in their private apartments.

This particular Hebrew gentleman did not seem inclined to interrupt his dinner to wait upon an unknown English family; he appeared to be instructing the manservant in what to say to them.

The servant came back and spoke to Signor Tosetti and when he had finished Signor Tosetti bowed low to Aunt Greysteel and explained that the name of the lady they sought was Delgado and that she lived at the very top of the house. Signor Tosetti was a little annoyed that none of the Hebrew gentleman's servants seemed willing to shew them the way and announce their arrival, but, as he said, their party was one of bold adventurers and doubtless they could find their way to the top of a staircase.

Dr Greysteel and Signor Tosetti took a candle each. The staircase wound up into the shadows. They passed many doors which, although rather grand, had a queer, stunted look about them – for in order to accommodate all the people, the houses in the Ghetto had been built as tall and with as many storeys as the householders had dared – and to compensate for this all the ceilings were rather low. At first they heard people talking behind these doors and at one they heard a man singing a sad song in an unknown language. Then they came to doors that stood open shewing only darkness; a cold, stale draught came from each. The last door, however, was closed. They knocked, but no one answered. They called out they were come to wait upon Mrs Delgado. Still no reply. And then, because Aunt Greysteel said that it was foolish to come so far and just go away again, they pushed open the door and went inside.

The room – which was scarcely more than an attic – had all the wretchedness that old age and extreme poverty could give it. It contained nothing that was not broken, chipped or ragged. Every colour in the room had faded, or darkened, or done what it must until it was grey. There was one little window that was open to the evening air and shewed the moon, although it was a little surprizing that the moon with her clean white face and fingers should condescend to make an appearance in that dirty little room.

Yet this was not what made Dr Greysteel look so alarmed, made him pull at his neckcloth, redden and go pale alternately, and draw great breaths of air. If there was one thing which Dr Greysteel disliked more than another, it was cats – and the room was full of cats.

In the midst of the cats sat a very thin person on a dusty, wooden chair. It was lucky, as Signor Tosetti had said, that the Greysteels were all bold adventurers, for the sight of Mrs Delgado might well have been a little shocking to nervous persons. For though she sat very upright – one would almost have said that she was poised, waiting for something – she bore so many of the signs and disfigurings of extreme old age that she was losing her resemblance to other human beings and began instead to resemble other orders of living creatures. Her arms lay in her lap, so extravagantly spotted with brown that they were like two fish. Her skin was the white, almost transparent skin of the extremely old, as fine and wrinkled as a spider's web, with veins of knotted blue.

She did not rise at their entrance, nor make any sign that she had noticed them at all. But perhaps she did not hear them. For, though the room was silent, the silence of half a hundred cats is a peculiar thing, like fifty individual silences all piled one on top of another.

So the Greysteels and Signor Tosetti, practical people, sat down in the terrible little room and Aunt Greysteel, with her kind smile and solicitous wishes that every one should be made comfortable and easy, began their addresses to the old lady.

"I hope, my dear Mrs Delgado, that you will forgive this intrusion, but my niece and I wished to do ourselves the honour of waiting upon you." Aunt Greysteel paused in case the old lady wished to make a reply, but the old lady said nothing. "What an airy situation you have here, ma'am! A dear friend of mine – a Miss Whilesmith – lodges in a little room at the top of a house in

Queen's square in Bath – a room much like your own, Mrs Delgado – and she declares that in summer she would not exchange it for the best house in the city – for she catches the breezes that nobody else gets and is perfectly cool when great people stifle in their rich apartments. And she has everything so neat and tidy and just to hand, whenever she wants it. And her only complaint is that the girl from the second back pair is always putting hot kettles on the staircase – which, as you know Mrs Delgado – can be so very displeasing if you chance to strike your foot against one of them. Do you suffer much inconvenience from the staircase, ma'am?"

There was a silence. Or rather some moments passed filled with nothing but the breathing of fifty cats.

Dr Greysteel dabbed at his sweating brow with his handkerchief and shifted about inside his clothes. "We are here, ma'am," he began, "at the particular request of Mr John McKean of Aberdeenshire. He wishes to be remembered to you. He hopes that you are well and sends every good wish for your future health."

Dr Greysteel spoke rather louder than usual, for he had begun to suspect that the old lady was deaf. This had no other effect, however, than to disturb the cats, many of which began to stalk around the room, brushing against each other and sending up sparks into the twilight air. A black cat dropped from somewhere or other on to the back of Dr Greysteel's chair and walked it as if it were a tightrope.

Dr Greysteel took a moment to recover himself and then said, "May we take back some report of your health and situation to Mr McKean, ma'am?"

But the old lady said nothing.

Miss Greysteel was next. "I am glad, ma'am," she said, "to see you so well provided with good friends. They must be a great comfort to you. That little honey-coloured puss at your feet – what an elegant form she has! And such a dainty way of washing her face! What do you call her?"

But the old lady did not answer.

So, prompted by a glance from Dr Greysteel, the little Venetian lawyer began to relate much of what had already been said, but this time in Italian. The only difference was that now the old lady no longer troubled to look at them, but fixed her gaze upon a great grey cat, which was, in its turn, looking at a white cat, which was, in *its* turn staring at the moon.

"Tell her that I have brought her money," said Dr Greysteel to the lawyer. "Tell her it is a gift made to her on behalf of John McKean. Tell her she must not thank me . . ." Dr Greysteel waved his hand vigorously as if a reputation for generous deeds and benevolent actions were a little like a mosquito and he hoped in this way to prevent one from landing on him.

"Mr Tosetti," said Aunt Greysteel, "you are not well. You are pale, sir. Will you have a glass of water? I am sure that Mrs Delgado could furnish you with a glass of water."

"No, Madamina Greysteel, I am not ill. I am . . ." Signor Tosetti looked round the room to find the word he wanted. "Fearful," he whispered.

"Fearful?" whispered Dr Greysteel. "Why? What of?"

"Ah, Signor Dottore, this is a terrible place!" returned the other in a whisper, and his eyes wandered in a kind of horror first to where one of the cats was licking its paw, in preparation to washing its face, and then back to the old lady, as if in expectation of seeing her perform the same action.

Miss Greysteel whispered that in their concern to shew Mrs Delgado attention they had come in too great a number and arrived too suddenly at her door. Clearly they were the first visitors she had had in years. Was it any wonder her wits seemed temporarily to be wandering? It was too severe a trial!

"Oh, Flora!" whispered Aunt Greysteel. "Only think! To pass years and years without society of any kind!"

To be all whispering together in such a small room – for the old lady was not three feet distant from any of them – appeared to Dr

Greysteel to be very ridiculous and, from not knowing what else to do, he became rather irritable with his companions, so that his sister and daughter judged it best to go.

Aunt Greysteel insisted on taking a long and fond farewell of the old lady, telling her that they would all return when she was feeling better – which Aunt Greysteel hoped would be soon.

Just as they passed through the door, they looked back. At that moment a new cat appeared upon the sill of the window with a stiff, spiky something in its mouth – a thing remarkably like a dead bird. The old lady made a little joyous sound and sprang with surprizing energy out of her chair. It was the oddest sound in all the world and bore not the slightest resemblance to human speech. It made Signor Tosetti, in his turn, cry out in alarm and pull the door shut, and hide whatever it was that the old lady was about to do next.[1]

---

[1] Signor Tosetti later confessed to the Greysteels that he believed he knew who the old lady of Cannaregio was. He had heard her story often as he went about the city, but until he had seen her with his own eyes he had dismissed it as a mere fable, a tale to frighten the young and foolish.

It seems her father had been a Jew, and her mother was descended from half the races of Europe. As a child she had learnt several languages and spoke them all perfectly. There was nothing she could not make herself mistress of if she chose. She learnt for the pleasure of it. At sixteen she spoke – not only French, Italian and German – which are part of any lady's commonplace accomplishments – but all the languages of the civilized (and uncivilized) world. She spoke the language of the Scottish Highlands (which is like singing). She spoke Basque, which is a language which rarely makes any impression upon the brains of any other race, so that a man may hear it as often and as long as he likes, but never afterwards be able to recall a single syllable of it. She even learnt the language of a strange country which, Signor Tosetti had been told, some people believed still existed, although no one in the world could say where it was. (The name of this country was Wales.)

She travelled through the world and appeared before kings and queens; archdukes and archduchesses; princes and bishops; Grafs and Grafins, and to each and every one of these important people she spoke in the language he or she had learnt as a child and every one of them proclaimed her a wonder.

And at last she came to Venice.

But this lady had never learnt to moderate her behaviour in any thing. Her appetite for learning was matched by her appetite in other things and she had married a man who was the same. This lady and her husband came at

[1] *cont'd* *Carnevale* and never went away again. All their wealth they gambled away in the *Ridottos*. All their health they lost in other pleasures. And one morning, when all of Venice's canals were silver and rose-coloured with the dawn, the husband lay down upon the wet stones of the Fondamenta dei Mori and died and there was nothing anyone could do to save him. And the wife would perhaps have done as well to do the same – for she had no money and nowhere to go. But the Jews remembered that she had some claim to their charity, being in a manner of speaking a Jewess herself (though she had never before acknowledged it) or perhaps they felt for her as a suffering creature (for the Jews have endured much in Venice). However it was, they gave her shelter in the Ghetto. There are different stories of what happened next, but what they all agree upon is that she lived among the Jews, but she was not one of them. She lived quite alone and whether the fault was hers or whether the fault was theirs I do not know. And a great deal of time went by and she did not speak to a living soul and a great wind of madness howled through her and overturned all her languages. And she forgot Italian, forgot English, forgot Latin, forgot Basque, forgot Welsh, forgot every thing in the world except Cat – and that, it is said, she spoke marvellously well.

# 53

## A little dead grey mouse

### End of November 1816

THE FOLLOWING EVENING in a room where Venetian gloom and Venetian magnificence mingled in a highly romantic and satisfactory manner, the Greysteels and Strange sat down to dinner together. The floor was of cracked, worn marble, all the colours of a Venetian winter. Aunt Greysteel's head, in its neat white cap, was set off by the vast, dark door that loomed in the distance behind her. The door was surmounted by dim carvings and resembled nothing so much as some funerary monument wreathed in dreary shadows. On the plaster walls, were the ghosts of frescoes painted in the ghosts of colours, all glorifying some ancient Venetian family whose last heir had drowned long ago. The present owners were as poor as church mice and had not been able to repair their house for many years. It was raining outside and, what was more surprizing, inside too; from somewhere in the room came the disagreeable sound of large quantities of water dripping liberally upon floor and furniture. But the Greysteels were not to be made gloomy, nor put off a very good dinner, by such trifles as these. They had banished the funereal shadows with a good blaze of candlelight and were masking the sound of dripping water with laughter and conversation. They were generally bestowing a cheerful Englishness on that part of the room where they sat.

"But I do not understand," said Strange, "Who takes care of the old woman?"

Dr Greysteel said, "The Jewish gentleman – who seems a very charitable old person – provides her with a place to live, and his servants put dishes of food for her at the foot of the stairs."

"But as to how the food is conveyed to her," exclaimed Miss Greysteel, "no one knows for certain. Signor Tosetti believes that her cats carry it up to her."

"Such nonsense!" declared Dr Greysteel. "Whoever heard of cats doing anything useful!"

"Except for staring at one in a supercilious manner," said Strange. "That has a sort of moral usefulness, I suppose, in making one feel uncomfortable and encouraging sober reflection upon one's imperfections."

The Greysteels' odd adventure had supplied a subject of conversation since they had sat down to dinner. "Flora, my dear," said Aunt Greysteel, "Mr Strange will begin to think we cannot talk of any thing else."

"Oh! Do not trouble upon my account," said Strange. "It is curious and we magicians collect curiosities, you know."

"Could you cure her by magic, Mr Strange?" asked Miss Greysteel.

"Cure madness? No. Though it is not for want of trying. I was once asked to visit a mad old gentleman to see what I could do for him and I believe I cast stronger spells upon that occasion than upon any other, but at the end of my visit he was just as mad as ever."

"But there might be recipes for curing madness, might there not?" asked Miss Greysteel eagerly. "I dare say the *Aureate* magicians might have had one." Miss Greysteel had begun to interest herself in magical history and her conversation these days was full of words like *Aureate* and *Argentine*.

"Possibly," said Strange, "but if so, then the prescription has been lost for hundreds of years."

"And if it were a thousand years, then I am sure that it need be no impediment to *you*. You have related to us dozens of examples of spells which were thought to be lost and which you have been able to recover."

"True, but generally I had some idea of how to begin. I never heard of a single instance of an *Aureate* magician curing madness. Their attitude towards madness seems to have been quite different from ours. They regarded madmen as seers and prophets and listened to their ramblings with the closest attention."

"How strange! Why?"

"Mr Norrell believed it was something to do with the sympathy which fairies feel for madmen – that and the fact that madmen can perceive fairy-spirits when no one else can." Strange paused. "You say this old woman is very mad?" he said.

"Oh, yes! I believe so."

In the drawing-room after dinner Dr Greysteel fell soundly asleep in his chair. Aunt Greysteel nodded in hers, waking every now and then to apologize for her sleepiness and then promptly falling asleep again. So Miss Greysteel was able to enjoy a tête-a-tête with Strange for the rest of the evening. She had a great deal to say to him. On his recommendation she had recently been reading Lord Portishead's *A Child's History of the Raven King* and she wished to ask him about it. However, he seemed distracted and several times she had the disagreeable impression that he was not attending to her.

The following day the Greysteels visited the Arsenal and were full of admiration for its gloom and vastness, they idled away an hour or two in curiosity shops (where the shopkeepers seemed nearly as quaint and old-fashioned as the curiosities themselves), and they ate ices at a pastry-cook's near the Church of San Stefano. To all the pleasures of the day Strange had been invited, but early in the morning Aunt Greysteel had received a short note presenting his compliments and thanks, but he had come quite by accident upon a new line of inquiry and dare not leave it, ". . . and scholars, madam, as you know by the example of your own brother, are the most selfish beings in creation and think that devotion to their researches excuses any thing . . ." Nor did he appear the next day when they visited the Scuola di Santa Maria della Carità. Nor the following one when they went by gondola to Torcello, a lonely, reed-choked island shrouded in grey mists where the first Venetian city had been raised, been magnificent, been deserted and finally crumbled away, all long, long ago.

But, though Strange was shut away in his rooms near Santa Maria Zobenigo, doing magic, Dr Greysteel was spared the anguish of missing him greatly by the frequency with which his name was mentioned among them. If the Greysteels walked by the Rialto – and if the sight of that bridge drew Dr Greysteel on to talk of Shylock, Shakespeare and the condition of the modern theatre, then Dr Greysteel was sure to have the benefit of Strange's opinions upon all these subjects – for Miss Greysteel knew them all and could argue for them quite as well as for her own. If, in a little curiosity shop, the Greysteels were struck by a painting of a quaint dancing bear, then it only served as an opportunity for Miss Greysteel to tell her father of an acquaintance of Mr Strange who had a stuffed brown bear in a glass case. If the Greysteels ate mutton, then Miss Greysteel was sure to be reminded of an occasion, of which Mr Strange had told her, when he had eaten mutton at Lyme Regis.

On the evening of the third day Dr Greysteel sent Strange a message proposing that the two of them should take a coffee and a glass of Italian spirit together. They met at Florian's a little after six o'clock.

"I am glad to see you," said Dr Greysteel, "but you look pale. Are you remembering to eat? To sleep? To take exercise?"

"I believe I ate something today," said Strange, "although I really cannot recall what it was."

They talked for a while of indifferent matters, but Strange was distracted. Several times he answered Dr Greysteel almost at random. Then, swallowing the last of his *grappa*, he took out his pocket-watch and said, "I hope you will forgive my hurrying away. I have an engagement. And so, good night."

Dr Greysteel was a little surprized at this and he could not help but wonder what sort of an engagement it might be. A man might behave badly any where in the world, but it seemed to Dr Greysteel that in Venice he might behave worse and do so more frequently. No other city in the world was so bent upon providing opportunities for every sort of mischief and Dr Greysteel happened to be particularly concerned at this period that Strange should have a character beyond reproach. So he inquired with as careless an air as he could manage whether the appointment was with Lord Byron?

"No, indeed. To own the truth," Strange narrowed his eyes and grew confidential, "I believe I may have found someone to aid me."

"Your fairy?"

"No. Another human being. I have high hopes of this collaboration. Yet at the same time I am not quite sure how the other person will greet my proposals. You will understand that under such circumstances I have no desire to keep them waiting."

"No, indeed!" exclaimed Dr Greysteel. "Go! Go!"

Strange walked away and became one of the many black figures on the piazza, all with black faces and no expressions, hurrying across the face of moon-coloured Venice. The moon itself was set among great architectural clouds so that there appeared to be another moon-lit city in the sky, whose grandeur rivalled Venice and whose great palaces and streets were crumbling and falling into ruins, as if some spirit in a whimsical mood had set it there to mock the other's slow decline.

Meanwhile, Aunt Greysteel and Miss Greysteel had taken advantage of the doctor's absence to return to the terrible little room at the top of the house in the Ghetto. They had come in secret, having an idea that Dr Greysteel, and perhaps even Mr

Strange, might try to prevent them going, or else insist upon accompanying them – and they had no wish for male companionship upon this occasion.

"They will want to be talking about it," said Aunt Greysteel, "they will be trying to guess how she came to this sad condition. But what good will that do? How does that help her?"

Miss Greysteel had brought some candles and a candlestick. She lit the candle so that they could see what they were doing. Then, out of their baskets they took a nice savoury dish of veal fricassee that filled the stale, desperate room with a good smell, some fresh white rolls, some apples and a warm shawl. Aunt Greysteel placed the plate of veal fricassee before Mrs Delgado, but she found that Mrs Delgado's fingers and fingernails were as curved and stiff as claws, and she could not coax them round the handles of the knife and fork.

"Well, my dear," said Aunt Greysteel at last, "she shews great interest in it, and I am sure it will do her good. But I think we will leave her to eat it in whatever way she thinks best."

They went down into the street. As soon as they were outside Aunt Greysteel exclaimed, "Oh, Flora! Did you see? She had her supper already prepared. There was a little china saucer – quite a pretty saucer – rather like my tea-service with rosebuds and forget-me-nots – and she had laid a mouse in it – a little dead grey mouse!"

Miss Greysteel looked thoughtful. "I dare say a head of chicory – boiled and dressed with a sauce, as they prepare it here – looks a little like a mouse."

"Oh my dear!" said Aunt Greysteel. "You know it was nothing of the sort . . ."

They were walking through the Ghetto Vecchio towards Cannaregio canal when Miss Greysteel turned suddenly away into the shadows and disappeared from sight.

"Flora! What is the matter?" cried Aunt Greysteel. "What do you see? Do not linger, my love. It is so very dark here among the houses. Dearest! Flora!"

Miss Greysteel moved back into the light as quickly as she had gone away. "It is nothing, aunt," she said. "Do not be startled. It is only that I thought I heard someone say my name and I went to see. I thought it was someone I knew. But there is no one there."

At the *Fondamenta* their gondola was waiting for them. The oarsman handed them in and then, with slow strokes, moved away. Aunt Greysteel made herself snug under the covering in the centre of the boat. Rain began to patter upon the canvas. "Perhaps when we get home we shall find Mr Strange with papa," she said.

"Perhaps," said Miss Greysteel.

"Or maybe he has gone to play billiards with Lord Byron again," said Aunt Greysteel. "It is odd that they should be friends. They seem such very different gentlemen."

"Oh, indeed! Though Mr Strange told me that he found Lord Byron a great deal less agreeable when he met him in Swisserland. His lordship was with some other poetical people who claimed all his attention and whose company he clearly preferred to that of any one else. Mr Strange says that he was barely civil."

"Well, that is very bad. But not at all surprizing. Should not you be afraid to look at him, my love? Lord Byron, I mean. I think that perhaps I might – a little."

"No, I should not be afraid."

"Well, my love, that is because you are more clear-headed and steady than other people. Indeed I do not know what there is in the world that you would be afraid of."

"Oh! I do not think it is because of any extraordinary courage on my part. As to extraordinary virtue – I cannot tell. I was never yet much tempted to do any thing very bad. It is only that Lord Byron could never have any power over me or sway the least of my thoughts or actions. I am quite safe from him. But that is not to say that there might not be someone in the world – I do not say that I have seen him yet – whom I would be a little afraid to look at sometimes – for fear that he might be looking sad – or lost – or thoughtful, or – what, you know, might seem worst of all – brooding on some private anger or hurt and so not knowing or caring if I looked at him at all."

In the little attic at the top of the house in the Ghetto, Miss Greysteel's candles guttered and went out. The moon shone down into the nightmare apartment and the old lady of Cannaregio began to devour the veal fricassee which the Greysteel ladies had brought her.

She was about to swallow the last bite when an English voice suddenly said, "Unfortunately, my friends did not stay to perform the introductions and it is always an awkward business, is it not, madam, when two people are left together in a room to get acquainted? My name is Strange. Yours, madam, though you do not know it, is Delgado, and I am delighted to meet you."

Strange was leaning against the windowsill with his arms crossed, looking intently at her.

She, on the other hand, took as little notice of him as she had of Aunt Greysteel or Miss Greysteel or any of her visitors of the last few days. She took as little notice of him as a cat takes of any body who does not interest it.

"Let me first assure you," said Strange, "that I am not one of those tiresome visitors who have no real purpose for their visit and nothing to say for themselves. I have a proposal to make to you, Mrs Delgado. It is our excellent fortune, madam, that you and I should meet at this time. I am able to give you your heart's desire and in return you shall give me mine."

Mrs Delgado made no sign that she had heard any of this. She had turned her attention to the saucer with the dead mouse and her ancient mouth gaped to devour it.

"Really, madam!" cried Strange. "I must insist that you put off your dinner for a moment and attend to what I am saying." He leant forward and removed the saucer. For the first time Mrs Delgado seemed to know he was there. She made a little mew of displeasure and looked resentfully at him.

"I want you to teach me how to be mad. The idea is so simple, I wonder I did not think of it before."

Mrs Delgado growled very low.

"Oh! You question the wisdom of my proceedings? You are probably right. To wish madness upon oneself is very rash. My tutor, my wife and my friends would all be angry if they knew any thing of it." He paused. The sardonic expression disappeared from his face and the light tone disappeared from his voice. "But I have cast off my tutor, my wife is dead and I am separated from my friends by twenty miles of chill water and the best part of a continent. For the first time since I took up this odd profession, I am not obliged to consult any one else. Now, how to begin? You must give me something – something to serve as a symbol and vessel of your madness." He glanced around the room. "Unfortunately, you do not appear to possess any thing, except your gown . . ." He looked down at the saucer which he held in his hand. ". . . and this mouse. I believe I prefer the mouse."

Strange began to say a spell. There was a burst of silver lights in the room. It was something between white flames and the glittering effect which fireworks produce. For a moment it hung in the air between Mrs Delgado and Strange. Then Strange made a gesture as if he intended to throw it at her; the light flew towards her and, just for a moment, she was bathed in a silver radiance. Suddenly Mrs Delgado was nowhere to be seen and in her place was a solemn, sulky girl in an old-fashioned gown. Then the girl too disappeared to be replaced by a beautiful young woman with a wilful expression. She was followed swiftly by an older woman of imperious bearing but with a glint of impending madness in her eyes. All the women Mrs Delgado had ever been flickered for an instant in the chair. Then all of them disappeared.

On the chair was only a heap of crumpled silk. Out of it stepped a little grey cat. The cat jumped daintily down, sprang up on the windowsill and vanished into the darkness.

"Well, that worked," said Strange. He picked up the half-rotten dead mouse by its tail. Instantly he became interesting to several of the cats who mewed and purred and rubbed themselves against his legs to attract his attention.

He grimaced. "And what was John Uskglass forced to endure, I wonder, in order to forge English magic?"

He wondered if he would notice any difference. Would he find, after he had done the spell, that he was trying to guess if he were mad now? Would he stand about, trying to think mad thoughts to discover if any of them seemed more natural? He took a last look around at the world, opened his mouth and gingerly lowered the mouse into it . . .

*It was like plunging beneath a waterfall or having two thousand trumpets sound in one's ear. Everything he thought before, everything he knew, everything he had been was swept away in a great flood of confused emotion and sensation. The world was made again in flame-like colours that were impossible to bear. It was shot through with new fears, new desires, new hatreds. He was surrounded by great presences. Some had wicked mouths full of teeth and huge, burning eyes. There was a thing like a horribly crippled spider that reared up beside him. It was full of malice. He had something in his mouth and the taste of it was unspeakable. Unable to think, unable to know, he found from God-knows-where the presence of mind to spit it out. Someone screamed . . .*

He found that he was lying on his back staring up into a confusion of darkness, roof beams and moonlight. A shadowy face appeared and peered into his own face in an unnerving manner. Its breath was warm, damp and malodorous. He had no recollection of lying down, but then he did not have much recollection of any thing. He wondered vaguely if he were in London or Shropshire. There was the queerest sensation all over his body as if several cats were walking on him at once. After a moment he raised his head and found that this was indeed the case.

He sat up and the cats leapt away. The full moon shone down

through a broken window. Then, mounting from recollection to recollection, he began to piece the evening together. He remembered the spell by which he had transformed the old woman, his plan to bring madness upon himself in order to see the fairy. At first it seemed to him so distant that he thought he must be remembering events that had happened, oh!, perhaps a month or so ago. Yet here he was in the room and he found by his pocket-watch that scarcely any time had passed at all.

He managed to rescue the mouse. By luck his arm had fallen upon it and kept it safe from the cats. He tucked it into his pocket and left the room hurriedly. He did not want to remain there a moment longer; the room had been nightmarish to begin with – now it seemed to him a place of untold horror.

He met several people on the stairs, but they took not a scrap of notice of him. He had previously cast a spell over the inhabitants of the house and they were quite convinced that they saw him every day, that he frequented these rooms regularly, and that nothing was more natural than that he should be there. But if any one had asked them who he was, they would have been quite unable to say.

He walked back to his lodgings at Santa Maria Zobenigo. The old woman's madness still seemed to infect him. People he passed in the street were strangely changed; their expressions seemed ferocious and unintelligible, and even their gait was lumbering and ugly. "Well one thing is clear," he thought, "the old woman was very mad indeed. I could not possibly summon the fairy in that condition."

The next day he rose early and immediately after breakfast began the process of reducing the flesh and guts of the mouse to a powder, according to various well-known principles of magic. The bones he preserved intact. Then he turned the powder into a tincture. This had two advantages. First (and by no means least), it was considerably less repulsive to swallow a few drops of tincture than to put a dead mouse in his mouth. Secondly, he believed that in this way he might be able to regulate the degree of madness he imposed upon himself.

By five o'clock he had a darkish brown liquid, which smelt chiefly of the brandy he had used to make the tincture. He decanted it into a bottle. Then he carefully counted fourteen drops into a glass of brandy and drank it.

After a few minutes he looked out of the window and into the Campo Santa Maria Zobenigo. People were walking up and down. The backs of their heads were hollowed out; their faces were nothing but thin masks at the front. Within each hollow a candle was burning. This was so plain to him now, that he wondered he had never noticed it before. He imagined what would happen if he went down into the street and blew some of the candles out. It made him laugh to think of it. He laughed so much that he could no longer stand. His laughter echoed round and round the house. Some small remaining shred of reason warned him that he ought not to let the landlord and his family know what he was doing so he went to bed and muffled the sound of his laughter in the pillows, kicking his legs from time to time with the sheer hilarity of the idea.

Next morning he awoke in bed, fully dressed and with his boots still on. Apart from the dull, greasy feeling that generally results from sleeping in one's clothes, he believed he was much as usual. He washed, shaved and put on fresh clothes. Then he went out to take something to eat and drink. There was a little coffee-house he liked on the corner of the Calle de la Cortesia and the Campo San Angelo. All seemed well until the waiter approached his table and put the cup of coffee down upon it. Strange looked up and saw a glint in the man's eye like a tiny candle-flame. He found he could no longer recall whether people had candles in their heads or not. He knew that there was a world of difference between these two notions: one was sane and the other was not, but he could not for the life of him remember which was which.

This was a little unsettling.

"The only problem with the tincture," he thought, "is that it is really quite difficult to judge when the effects have worn off. I had not thought of that before. I suppose I ought to wait a day or two before trying it again."

But at midday his impatience got the better of him. He felt better. He was inclining to the view that people did *not* have candles in their heads. "And anyway," he thought, "it does not much matter which it is. The question has no relevance to my present undertaking." He put nine drops of the tincture into a glass of Vin Santo and drank it down.

Immediately he became convinced that all the cupboards in the house were full of pineapples. He was certain that there were other pineapples under his bed and under the table. He was so alarmed by this thought that he felt hot and cold all over and was obliged to sit down on the floor. All the houses and *palazzi* in the city were full of pineapples and outside in the streets people were carrying pineapples, hidden under their clothes. He could smell the pineapples everywhere – a smell both sweet and sharp.

Some time later there was a knock at his door. He was surprized to find it was now evening and the room was quite dark. The knock sounded again. The landlord was at the door. The landlord began to talk, but Strange could not understand him. This was because the man had a pineapple in his mouth. How he had managed to cram the whole thing in there, Strange could not imagine. Green, spiky leaves emerged slowly out of his mouth and then were sucked back in again as he spoke. Strange wondered if perhaps he ought to go and fetch a knife or a hook and try and fish the pineapple out, in case the landlord should choke. But at the same time he did not care much about it. "After all," he thought with some irritation, "it is his own fault. He put it there."

The next day in the coffee-house on the corner of the Calle de la Cortesia one of the waiters was cutting up a pineapple. Strange, huddled over his coffee, shuddered to see it.

He had discovered that it was easier – far easier than any one could have supposed – to make oneself mad, but like all magic it was full of obstacles and frustrations. Even if he succeeded in summoning the fairy (which did not seem very likely), he would be in no condition to talk to him. Every book he had ever read on the subject urged magicians to be on their guard when dealing with fairies. Just when he needed all his wits, he would have scarcely any wits at all.

"How am I supposed to impress him with the superiority of my magicianship if all I can do is babble about pineapples and candles?" he thought.

He spent the day pacing up and down his room, breaking off every now and then to scribble notes upon bits of paper. When evening came he wrote down a spell for summoning fairies and put it on the table. Then he put four drops of tincture into a glass of water and swallowed it.

This time the tincture affected him quite differently. He was not assailed by any peculiar beliefs or fears. Indeed in many ways he felt better than he had in a long time: cooler, calmer, less troubled. He found that he no longer cared very much about magic. Doors slammed in his mind and he went wandering off into rooms and hallways inside himself that he had not visited in years. For the first ten minutes or so he became the man he had been at twenty or twenty-two; after that he was someone else entirely – someone he had always had the power to be, but for various reasons had never actually become.

His first desire after taking the tincture was to go to a *Ridotto*. It seemed ridiculous that he should have been in Venice since the beginning of October and never visited one. But on examining his pocket-watch he discovered that it was only eight o'clock. "That is much too early," he remarked to no one in particular. He was feeling talkative and looked round for someone to confide in. For lack of any one better, he settled upon the little wooden figure in the corner. "There will be no one worth seeing for three or four hours yet," he told it.

To fill the time he thought he might go and find Miss Greysteel. "But I suppose her aunt and father will be there." He made a small sound of irritation. "Dull! Dull! Dull! Why do pretty women always have such herds of relatives?" He looked at himself in a mirror. "Dear God! This neckcloth looks as if it was tied by a ploughman."

He spent the next half hour tying and re-tying the neckcloth until he was satisfied with it. Then he discovered that his finger-nails were longer than he liked and not particularly clean. He went to look for a pair of scissars to cut them with.

The scissars were on the table. And something else besides. "What have we here?" he asked. "Papers! Papers with magic spells on them!" This struck him as highly amusing. "You know, it is the queerest thing," he told the little wooden figure, "but I know the fellow who wrote this! His name is Jonathan Strange – and now that I think about it, I think these books belong to him." He read a little further. "Ha! You will never guess what idiocy he is engaged in now! Casting spells to summon fairies! Ha! Ha! He tells himself he is doing it to get himself a fairy-servant and further the cause of English magic. But really he is only doing it to terrify Gilbert Norrell! He has come hundreds of miles to the most luxurious city in the world and all he cares about is what some old man in London thinks! How ridiculous!"

He put the piece of paper down again in disgust and picked up the scissars. He turned and just avoided striking his head against something. "What in the world . . . ?" he began.

A black ribbon hung from the ceiling. At the end of it were a few tiny bones, a phial of some dark liquid – blood perhaps – and a piece of paper with writing on it, all tied up together. The length of the ribbon was such that a person moving about the room was almost certain to knock against it sooner or later. Strange shook his head in disbelief at other people's stupidity. Leaning against the table, he began to cut his nails.

Several minutes passed. "He had a wife, you know," he remarked to the little wooden figure. He brought his hand near to the candlelight to examine his nails. "Arabella Woodhope. The most charming girl in all the world. But dead. Dead, dead, dead." He picked up a nail-buffer from the table and began to polish his nails with it. "In fact, now that I come to think of it, was I not in love with her myself? I think I must have been. She had the sweetest way of saying my name and smiling at the same time, and every time she did so, my heart turned over." He laughed. "You know, it is really very ridiculous, but I cannot actually remember what my name is. Laurence? Arthur? Frank? I wish Arabella were here. She would know. And she would tell me too! She is not one of those women who tease one and insist upon making a game of everything long after it has ceased to be amusing. By God, I wish she were here! There is an ache here." He tapped his heart. "And something hot and hard inside here." He tapped his forehead. "But half an hour's conversation with Arabella would put both right, I am sure. Perhaps I ought to summon this fellow's fairy and ask him to bring her here. Fairies can summon the dead, can they not?" He picked up the spell from the table and read it again. "There is nothing to this. It is the simplest thing in the world."

He rattled off the words of the spell and then, because it seemed important to do so, he went back to shining his nails.

In the shadows by the painted cupboard there was a person in a leaf-green coat – a person with hair the colour of thistle-down – a person with an amused, superior sort of smile upon his face.

Strange was still intent upon his nails.

The gentleman with the thistle-down hair walked very rapidly over to where Strange stood and put out his hand to pull Strange's hair. But before he could do so, Strange looked directly at him and said, "I don't suppose that you happen to have such a thing as a pinch of snuff, do you?"

The gentleman with the thistle-down hair froze.

"I have looked in every pocket of this damned coat," continued Strange, perfectly unaware of the gentleman's astonishment, "but there is not a snuff box anywhere. I cannot imagine what I was thinking of to come out without one. Kendal Brown is what I generally take, if you have it."

As he spoke he fished in his pockets again. But he had forgotten about the little bone-and-blood posy that hung from the ceiling and as he moved, he knocked his head against it. The posy swung back, swung forward again and struck him fairly in the middle of his forehead.

# 54

# A little box, the colour of heartache

## 1st and 2nd December 1816

THERE WAS A kind of snap in the air, followed immediately by a faint breeze and a new freshness, as if some stale odour had suddenly been swept from the room.

Strange blinked two or three times.

His first thought upon coming to himself was that his whole elaborate scheme had worked; here was someone – without a doubt a fairy – standing before him. His second thought was to wonder what in the world he had been doing. He pulled out his pocket-watch and examined it; almost an hour had passed since he had drunk the tincture.

"I beg your pardon," he said, "I know it is an odd question, but have I asked any thing of you yet?"

"Snuff," said the gentleman with the thistle-down hair.

"Snuff?"

"You asked me for a pinch of snuff."

"When?"

"What?"

"When did I ask you for snuff?"

"A moment ago."

"Ah! Ah. Good. Well, you need not trouble yourself. I do not need it now."

The gentleman with the thistle-down hair bowed.

Strange was conscious that his confusion shewed in his face. He remembered all the stern warnings he had read against letting members of this tricksy race suspect that they know more than oneself. So he covered up his perplexity with sarcastic looks. Then, remembering that it is generally considered even more perilous to appear superior and so make the fairy-spirit angry, he covered up his sarcasm with a smile. Finally he went back to looking puzzled.

He did not notice that the gentleman was at least as uncomfortable as himself.

"I have summoned you here," he said, "because I have long desired one of your race to aid me and instruct me in magic." He had rehearsed this little pronouncement several times and was pleased to find that it sounded both confident and dignified. Unfortunately he immediately spoilt the effect by adding anxiously, "Did I mention that before?"

The gentleman said nothing.

"My name is Jonathan Strange. Perhaps you have heard of me? I am at a most interesting point in my career. I believe it is no exaggeration to say that the entire future of English magic depends upon my actions in the coming months. Agree to help me and your name will be as famous as those of Col Tom Blue and Master Witcherley!"[1]

"Tut!" declared the gentleman in disgust. "Low persons!"

"Really?" said Strange. "I had no idea." He pressed on. "It was your . . ." He paused to find the right phrase. ". . . *kind attentions* to the King of England that first brought you to my notice. Such power! Such inventiveness! English magic today lacks spirit! It lacks fire and energy! I cannot tell you how bored I am of the same dull spells to solve the same dull problems. The glimpse I had of your magic proved to me that it is quite different. You could surprize me. And I long to be surprized!"

[1] Col Tom Blue was of course the most famous servant of Ralph Stokesey; Master Witcherley assisted Martin Pale.

The gentleman raised one perfect fairy eye-brow, as if he would not object in the least to surprizing Jonathan Strange.

Strange continued excitedly. "Oh! and I may as well tell you immediately that there is an old person in London called Norrell – a magician of sorts – who will be driven into fits of rage the moment he learns that you have allied yourself to me. He will do his best to thwart us but I dare say you and I will be more than a match for him."

The gentleman appeared to have stopped listening. He was glancing about the room, fixing his gaze first upon one object, then upon another.

"Is there something in the room which displeases you?" asked Strange. "I beg you will tell me if that is the case. I dare say your magical sensibilities are much finer than my own. But even in my case there are certain things which can disrupt my ability to do magic – I believe it is so with all magicians. A salt-cellar, a rowan-tree, a fragment of the consecrated host – these all make me feel decidedly unsettled. I do not say I *cannot* do magic in their presence, but I always need to take them into account in my spells. If there is something here you dislike, you have only to say so and I shall be happy to remove it."

The gentleman stared at him a moment as if he had not the least idea what Strange was talking about. Then suddenly he exclaimed, "My magical sensibilities, yes! How clever of you! My magical sensibilities are, as you suppose, quite tremendous! And just now they inform me that you have recently acquired an object of great power! A ring of disenchantment? An urn of visibility? Something of that nature? My congratulations! Shew me the object and I shall immediately instruct you as to its history and proper use!"

"Actually no," said Strange, surprized. "I have nothing of that sort."

The gentleman frowned. He looked hard, first at a chamber-pot half-hidden under the table, then at a mourning-ring that contained a miniature of an angel painted on ivory, and finally at a painted pottery jar that had once contained candied peaches and plums. "Perhaps you have come upon it by accident?" he asked. "Such objects can be very powerful even if the magician has no idea that they are present."

"I really do not think so," said Strange. "That jar, for instance, was purchased in Genoa from a confectioner's. And there were dozens in the shop, just the same. I cannot see why one would be magical and the others not."

"No, indeed," agreed the gentleman. "And really there does not seem to be any thing here apart from the usual objects. I mean," he added quickly, "the objects that I would expect to find in the apartments of a magician of your genius."

There was a short pause.

"You make no reply to my offer," said Strange. "You are undecided until you know more of me. That is just as it should be. In a day or two I will do myself the honour of soliciting your company again and we shall talk some more."

"It has been a most interesting conversation!" said the gentleman.

"The first of many, I hope," said Strange, politely, and bowed.

The gentleman bowed in return.

Then Strange released the gentleman from the spell of summoning and he promptly disappeared.

Strange's excitement was immense. He supposed he ought to sit down and make sober, scholarly notes of what he had seen, but it was difficult to keep from dancing, laughing and clapping his hands. He actually performed several figures of a country-dance, and if the carved wooden figure had not been attached by its feet to a wooden pillar he would certainly have made it his partner and whirled about the room with it.

When the dancing fit left him he was sorely tempted to write to Norrell. In fact he did sit down and begin a letter full of triumph and steeped in sarcasm. ("You will no doubt be *delighted* to learn . . .") But then he thought better of it. "It will only provoke him to make my house disappear, or something. Ha! How furious he will be when I arrive back in England. I must publish the news immediately I return. I shall not wait for the next issue of *The Famulus*. That would take much too long. Murray will complain but I cannot help that. *The Times* would be best. I wonder what he meant by all that nonsense about rings of power and chamber-pots? I suppose he was trying to account for my success in summoning him."

Upon the whole he could not have been more pleased with himself if he had conjured up John Uskglass himself and had half an hour of civil conversation with him. The only unsettling part of the business was the memory – returning to him in scraps and fragments – of the form his madness had taken this time. "I think I turned into Lascelles or Drawlight! How perfectly horrible!"

The next morning Stephen Black had business to conduct for Sir Walter. He paid a visit to a banker in Lombard-street; he spoke to a portrait-painter in Little-Britain; he delivered instructions to a woman in Fetter-lane about a gown for Lady Pole. His next appointment was at the office of an attorney. A soft, heavy snow was falling. All around him were the customary sounds of the City: the snorting and stamping of the horses, the rattle of the carriages, the cries of the street-vendors, the slamming of doors and the padding of feet through the snow.

He was standing at the corner of Fleet-street and Mitre-court. He had just taken out his pocket-watch (a present from the gentleman with the thistle-down hair), when every sound ceased as if it had been cut off with a knife. For a moment it seemed he must have been struck deaf. But almost before he could feel any alarm he looked round and realized that this was not the only peculiarity. The street was suddenly empty. There were no people, no cats, no dogs, no horses, no birds. Everyone was gone.

And the snow! That was the oddest thing of all. It hung, suspended in the air, in huge, soft white flakes, as big as sovereigns.

"Magic!" he thought in disgust.

He walked a little way down Mitre-court, looking in the windows of the shops. Lamps were still lit; goods were lying heaped or scattered over the counters – silks, tobacco, sheet-music; fires were still burning in the hearths but their flames were frozen. He looked back and discovered that he had made a sort of tunnel through the three-dimensional lace-work of snow. It was, of all the strange things he had seen in his life, the strangest.

From out of nowhere a furious voice cried, "I thought myself quite safe from him! What tricks can he be using?" The gentleman with the thistle-down hair suddenly appeared immediately before Stephen, with blazing face and glittering eyes.

The shock was so great that for a moment Stephen feared he would drop down in a swoon. But he was well aware how highly the gentleman prized coolness and composure, so he hid his fright as best he could and gasped, "Safe from whom, sir?"

"Why, the magician, Stephen! The magician! I thought that he must have acquired some potent object that would reveal my presence to him. But I could not see any thing in his rooms and he swore that he had nothing of the sort. Just to be sure I have circled the globe in the past hour and examined every ring of power, every magical chalice and quern. But none of them are missing. They are all exactly where I thought they were."

From this rather incomplete explanation Stephen deduced that the magician must have succeeded in summoning and speaking to the gentle-man with the thistle-down hair. "But surely, sir," he said, "there was a time when you wished to aid the magicians and do magic with them and gain their gratitude. That is how you came to rescue Lady Pole, is it not? Perhaps you will find you like it better than you think."

"Oh, perhaps! But I really do not think so. I tell you, Stephen, apart from the inconvenience of having him summon me whenever he chuses, it was the dreariest half hour I have spent in many a long age. I have never heard any one talk so much! He is quite the most conceited person I have ever met. People like that who must be continually talking themselves and have no time to listen to any one else are quite disgusting to me."

"Oh, indeed, sir! It is most vexatious. And I dare say that, since you will be busy with the magician, we will have to put off making me King of England?"

The gentleman said something very fierce in his own language – presumably a curse. "I believe you are right – and that makes me angrier than all the rest put together!" He thought for a moment. "But then again, it may not be so bad as we fear. These English magicians are generally very stupid. They usually want the same things. The poor ones desire an unending supply of turnips or porridge; the rich ones want yet more riches, or power over the whole world; and the young ones want the love of some princess or queen. As soon as he asks for one of those things, I will grant it to him. It is sure to bring a world of trouble on his head. It always does. He will become distracted and then you and I can pursue our plan to make you King of England! Oh, Stephen! How glad I am that I came to you! I always hear better sense from you than from anyone else!" Upon the instant the gentleman's anger evaporated and he was full of delight. The sun actually appeared from behind a cloud and all the strange, suspended fall of snow glittered and blazed around them (though whether this was the gentleman's doing or no, Stephen could not tell).

He was about to point out that he had not actually suggested any thing, but in that instant the gentleman disappeared. All the people, horses, carriages, cats and dogs immediately reappeared, and Stephen walked straight into a fat woman in a purple pelisse.

Strange rose from his bed in excellent spirits. He had slept for eight hours without interruption. For the first time in weeks he had not got up in the middle of the night to do magic. As a reward to himself for his success in summoning the fairy, he decided that today should be a holiday. Shortly after ten o'clock, he presented himself at the *palazzo* where the Greysteels were staying and found the family at their breakfast. He accepted their invitation to sit down, ate some hot rolls, drank some coffee and told Miss Greysteel and Aunt Greysteel that he was entirely at their service.

Aunt Greysteel was happy to give up her share of the favour to her niece. Miss Greysteel and Strange passed the forenoon in reading books about magic together. These were books that he had lent to her or that she had bought upon his recommendation. They were Portishead's *A Child's History of the Raven King*, Hickman's *Life of Martin Pale* and Hether-Gray's *The Anatomy of a Minotaur*. Strange had read them when he first began to study magic and he was amused to discover how simple, almost innocent, they seemed to him now. It was the most agreeable thing in the world to read them to Miss Greysteel, and answer her questions, and listen to her opinions upon them – eager, intelligent and, it seemed to him, slightly over-serious.

At one o'clock, after a light repast of cold meat, Aunt Greysteel declared that they had all sat still long enough and she proposed a walk. "I dare say, Mr Strange, that you will be glad of the fresh air. Scholars often neglect exercise."

"We are very sad fellows, madam," agreed Strange, cheerfully.

It was a fine day. They wandered through the narrow streets and alleys and chanced upon a happy succession of intriguing objects: a carving of a dog with a bone in its mouth; a shrine to a saint that none of them recognized; a set of windows whose curtains seemed at first to be made of heavy swags of the most exquisite lace, but which were found upon closer examination to be only spiders' webs – vast, intermingling spiders' webs which permeated every part of the room inside. They had no guide to tell them about these things; there was no one standing near whom they could ask; and so they entertained themselves by making up their own explanations.

Just before twilight they entered a chilly, stony, little square with a well at its centre. It was a curiously blank and empty place.

The ground was paved with ancient stones. The walls were pierced with surprizingly few windows. It was as if the houses had all been offended by something the square had done and had resolutely turned their backs and looked the other way. There was one tiny shop that appeared to sell nothing but Turkish Delight of an infinite number of varieties and colours. It was closed, but Miss Greysteel and Aunt Greysteel peered into the window and wondered aloud when it might open and whether they would be able to find their way back to it.

Strange walked about. He was thinking of nothing in particular. The air was very cold – pleasantly so – and overhead the first star of evening appeared. He became aware of a peculiar scraping sound behind him and he turned to see what was making it.

In the darkest corner of the little square something was standing – a thing the like of which he had never seen before. It was black – so black that it might have been composed of the surrounding darkness. Its head or top took the form of an old-fashioned sedan chair, such as one might occasionally see conveying a dowager about Bath. It had windows with black curtains pulled across. But beneath the windows it dwindled into the body and legs of a great black bird. It wore a tall black hat and carried a thin, black walking-stick. It had no eyes, yet Strange could tell it was looking at him. It was scraping the tip of the walking-stick across the paving stones with a horrible jerking motion.

He supposed he ought to feel afraid. He supposed that he ought perhaps to do some magic to try and fend it off. Spells of dispersal, spells of dismissal, spells of protection flowed through his brain but he somehow failed to catch hold of any of them. Although the thing reeked of evil and malevolence, he had a strong sense that it was no danger to himself or any one else just at present. It seemed more like a sign of evil-yet-to-come.

He was just beginning to wonder how the Greysteels bore with this sudden appearance of horror in their midst when something shifted in his brain; the thing was no longer there. In its place stood the stout form of Dr Greysteel – Dr Greysteel in black clothes, Dr Greysteel with a walking-stick in his hand.

"Well?" called out Dr Greysteel.

"I . . . I beg your pardon!" Strange called back. "Did you speak? I was thinking of . . . of something else."

"I asked you if you intended to dine with us tonight!"

Strange stared at him.

"What is the matter? Are you sick?" asked Dr Greysteel. He looked rather probingly at Strange as if he saw something in the magician's face or manner he did not like.

"I am perfectly well, I assure you," said Strange. "And I will dine with you gladly. I should like nothing better. Only I have promised Lord Byron that I will play billiards with him at four."

"We should find a gondola to take us back," said Dr Greysteel. "I believe Louisa is more tired than she admits to." (He meant Aunt Greysteel.) "Where do you meet his lordship? Where shall we tell the fellow to take you?"

"Thank you," said Strange, "but I shall walk. Your sister was right. I am in need of fresh air and exercise."

Miss Greysteel was a little disappointed to find that Strange was not to return with them. The two ladies and the magician took a somewhat prolonged leave of each other and reminded each other several times that they were all to meet again in a few hours, until Dr Greysteel began to lose patience with them all.

The Greysteels walked off in the direction of the *Rio*. Strange followed at a distance. Despite his cheerful assurances to Dr Greysteel, he was feeling badly shaken. He tried to persuade himself that the apparition had been nothing more than a trick of the light, but it would not do. He was obliged to admit to himself that what it most resembled was a return of the old lady's madness.

"It is really most aggravating! The effects of the tincture seemed to have worn off entirely! Well, pray God, I do not need to drink any more of it. If this fairy refuses to serve me, I shall simply have to find another way of summoning someone else."

He emerged from the alley into the clearer light of the *Rio* and saw that the Greysteels had found a gondola and that someone – a gentleman – was helping Miss Greysteel into it. He thought at first that it was a stranger, but then he saw that this person had a head of shining thistle-down hair. He hurried to meet him.

"What a beautiful young woman!" said the gentleman, as the gondola pulled away from the quayside. His eyes sparkled with brilliance. "And she dances most delightfully, I expect?"

"Dances?" said Strange. "I do not know. We were supposed to attend a ball together in Genoa, but she had the toothach and we did not go. I am surprized to see you. I had not expected that you would come until I summoned you again."

"Ah, but I have been thinking about your proposal that we do magic together! And I now perceive it to be an excellent plan!"

"I am pleased to hear it," said Strange, suppressing a smile. "But tell me something. I have been trying to summon you for weeks. Why did you not come before?"

"Oh! That is easily explained!" declared the gentleman, and he began a long story about a cousin of his who was very wicked and very jealous of all his talents and virtues; who hated all English magicians; and who had somehow contrived to distort Strange's magic so that the gentleman had not known of the summons until last night. It was an exceedingly complicated tale and Strange did not believe a word of it. But he thought it prudent to look as if he did and so he bowed his acceptance.

"And to shew you how sensible I am of the honour you do me," finished up the gentleman, "I will bring you any thing you desire."

"Any thing?" repeated Strange, with a sharp look. "And this offer is – if I understand correctly – in the nature of a binding agreement. You cannot deny me something once I have named it?"

"Nor would I wish to!"

"And I can ask for riches, dominion over all the world? That sort of thing?"

"Exactly!" said the gentleman with a delighted air. He raised his hands to begin.

"Well, I do not want any of those things. What I chiefly want is information. Who was the last English magician you dealt with?"

A moment's pause.

"Oh, you do not want to hear about that!" declared the gentleman. "I assure you it is very dull. Now, come! There must be something you desire above all else? A kingdom of your own? A beautiful companion? Princess Pauline Borghese is a most delightful woman and I can have her here in the twinkling of an eye!"

Strange opened his mouth to speak and then stopt a moment. "Pauline Borghese, you say? I saw a picture of her in Paris."[2] Then, recollecting himself, he continued, "But I am not interested in that just at present. Tell me about magic. How would I go about turning myself into a bear? Or a fox? What are the names of the three magical rivers that flow through the Kingdom of Agrace?[3] Ralph Stokesey thought that these rivers influenced events in England; is that true? There is mention in *The Language of Birds* of a group of spells that are cast by manipulating colours; what can you tell me about that? What do the stones in the Doncaster Squares represent?"

The gentleman threw up his hands in mock surprize. "So many questions!" He laughed; it was clearly meant to be a merry, carefree laugh, but it sounded a little forced.

"Well then, tell me the answer to one of them. Any one you like."

The gentleman only smiled pleasantly.

Strange stared at him in undisguised vexation. Apparently the offer did not extend to knowledge, only objects. "And if I wanted to give myself a present, I would go and buy something!" thought

[2] This lady was the most beautiful and tempestuous of Napoleon Buonaparte's sisters, much given to taking lovers and posing, unclothed, for statues of herself.

[3] Agrace is the name sometimes given to John Uskglass's third Kingdom. This Kingdom was thought to lie on the far side of Hell.

Strange. "If I wanted to see Pauline Borghese, I would simply go to her and introduce myself. I do not need magic for that! How in the world do I . . ." A thought struck him. Out loud he said, "Bring me something that you gained from your last dealings with an English magician!"

"What?" said the gentleman, startled. "No, you do not want that! It is worthless, utterly worthless! Think again!"

Clearly he was much perturbed by Strange's request – though Strange could not tell why he should be. "Perhaps," he thought, "the magician gave him something valuable and he is loath to give it up. No matter. Once I have seen what it is, and learnt what I can from it I shall give it back to him. That ought to persuade him of my good intentions."

He smiled politely: "A binding agreement, I think you said? I shall expect it – whatever it is – later this evening!"

At eight o'clock he dined with the Greysteels in their gloomy dining-hall.

Miss Greysteel asked him about Lord Byron.

"Oh!" said Strange. "He does not intend to return to England. He can write poems anywhere. Whereas in my own case, English magic was shaped by England – just as England herself was shaped by magic. The two go together. You cannot separate them."

"You mean," said Miss Greysteel, frowning a little, "that English minds and history and so forth were shaped by magic. You are speaking metaphorically."

"No, I was speaking quite literally. This city, for example, was built in the common way . . ."

"Oh!" interrupted Dr Greysteel, laughing. "How like a magician that sounds! The slight edge of contempt when he speaks of things being done in the common way!"

"I do not think that I intended any disrespect. I assure you I have the greatest regard for things done in the common way. No, my point was merely that the boundaries of England – its very shape was determined by magic."

Dr Greysteel sniffed. "I am not sure of this. Give me an example."

"Very well. There once was a very fine town stood on the coast of Yorkshire whose citizens began to wonder why it was that their King, John Uskglass, should require taxes from them. Surely, they argued, so great a magician could conjure up all the gold he wanted from the air. Now there is no harm in wondering, but these foolish people did not stop there. They refused to pay and began to plot with the King's enemies. A man is best advised to consider carefully before he quarrels with a magician and still more with a king. But when these two characters are combined in one person, Why! then the peril is multiplied a hundred times. First a wind came out of the north and blew through the town. As the wind touched the beasts of the town they grew old and died – cows, pigs, fowls and sheep – even the cats and dogs. As the wind touched the town itself houses became ruins before the very eyes of the unhappy householders. Tools broke, pots shattered, wood warped and split, brick and stone crumbled into dust. Stone images in the church wore away as if with extreme age, until, it was said, every face of every statue appeared to be screaming. The wind whipped up the sea into strange, menacing shapes. The townspeople, very wisely, began to run from the town and when they reached the higher ground they looked back and were just in time to see the remains of the town slip slowly under the cold, grey waves."

Dr Greysteel smiled. "Let the government be who they may – Whigs, Tories, emperors or magicians – they take it very ill when people do not pay their taxes. And shall you include these tales in your next book?"

"Oh, certainly. I am not one of those miserly authors who measure out their words to the last quarter ounce. I have very liberal ideas of authorship. Anyone who cares to pay Mr Murray their guinea will find that I have thrown the doors of my warehouse wide open and that all my learning is up for sale. My readers may stroll about and chuse at their leisure."

Miss Greysteel gave this tale a moment or two of serious consideration. "He was certainly provoked," she said at last, "but it was still the act of a tyrant."

Somewhere in the shadows footsteps were approaching.

"What is it, Frank?" asked Dr Greysteel.

Frank, Dr Greysteel's servant, emerged from the gloom.

"We have found a letter and a little box, sir. Both for Mr Strange." Frank looked troubled.

"Well, do not stand and gape so. Here is Mr Strange, sat just at your elbow. Give him his letter and his little box."

Frank's expression and attitude all declared him to be tussling with some great perplexity. His scowl suggested that he believed himself to be quite out of his depth. He made one last attempt to communicate his vexation to his master. "We found the letter and the little box on the floor just inside the door, sir, but the door was locked and bolted!"

"Then someone must have unlocked and unbolted it, Frank. Do not be making mysteries," said Dr Greysteel.

So Frank gave the letter and box to Strange and wandered away into the darkness again, muttering to himself and inquiring of the chairs and tables he met on the way what sort of blockhead they took him for.

Aunt Greysteel leaned over and politely entreated Mr Strange to use no ceremony – he was with friends and should read his letter directly. This was very kind of her, but a little superfluous, since Strange had already opened the paper and was reading his letter.

"Oh, aunt!" cried Miss Greysteel, picking up the little box which Frank had placed on the table. "See, how beautiful!"

The box was small and oblong and apparently made of silver and porcelain. It was a beautiful shade of blue, but then again not exactly blue, it was more like lilac. But then again, not exactly lilac either, since it had a tinge of grey in it. To be more precise, it was the colour of heartache. But fortunately neither Miss Greysteel nor Aunt Greysteel had ever been much troubled by heartache and so they did not recognize it.

"It is certainly very pretty," said her aunt. "Is it Italian, Mr Strange?"

"Mmm?" said Strange. He glanced up. "I do not know."

"Is there anything inside?" asked Aunt Greysteel.

"Yes, I believe so," said Miss Greysteel, beginning to open it.

"Flora!" cried Dr Greysteel and shook his head sharply at his daughter. He had an idea that the box might be a present which Strange intended to give to Flora. He did not like this idea, but Dr Greysteel did not think himself competent to judge the sorts of behaviour in which a man like Strange – a fashionable man of the world – might consider himself licensed to indulge.

Strange, with his nose still deep in the letter, saw and heard none of this. He took up the little box and opened it.

"Is there any thing inside, Mr Strange?" asked Aunt Greysteel.

Strange shut the box quickly again. "No, madam, nothing at all." He put the box in his pocket and immediately summoned Frank and asked for a glass of water.

He left the Greysteels very soon after dinner and went straight to the coffee-house on the corner of the Calle de la Cortesia. The first glimpse of the contents of the box had been very shocking and he had a strong desire to be among people when he opened it again.

The waiter brought his brandy. He took a sip and opened the box.

At first he supposed that the fairy had sent him a replica of a small, white, amputated finger, made of wax or some such material and very lifelike. It was so pale, so drained of blood, that it seemed almost to be tinged with green, with a suggestion of pink in the grooves around the fingernail. He wondered that any one should labour so long to produce any thing quite so horrible.

But the moment he touched it he realized it was not wax at all. It was icy cold, and yet the skin moved in the same way as the skin moved upon his own finger and the muscles could be detected beneath the skin, both by touch and sight. It was, without a doubt, a human finger. From the size of it he thought it was probably a child's finger or perhaps the smallest finger of a woman with rather delicate hands.

"But why would the magician give him a finger?" he wondered. "Perhaps it was the magician's finger? But I do not see how that can be, unless the magician were either a child or a woman." It occurred to him that he had heard something about a finger once, but for the moment he could not remember what it was. Oddly enough although he did not remember *what* he had been told, he thought he remembered *who* had told him. It had been Drawlight. ". . . which explains why I did not pay a great deal of attention. But why would Drawlight have been talking of magic? He knew little and cared less."

He drank some more brandy. "I thought that if I had a fairy to explain everything to me, then all the mysteries would become clear. But all that has happened is that I have acquired another mystery!"

He fell to musing upon the various stories he had heard concerning the great English magicians and their fairy-servants. Martin Pale with Master Witcherley, Master Fallowthought and all the rest. Thomas Godbless with Dick-come-Tuesday; Meraud with Coleman Gray; and most famous of all, Ralph Stokesey and Col Tom Blue.

When Stokesey first saw Col Tom Blue, he was a wild, unruly person – the last fairy in the world to ally himself to an English magician. So Stokesey had followed him into Faerie, to Col Tom Blue's own castle[4] and had gone about invisibly and discovered many interesting things.[5] Strange was not so naive as to suppose

[4] *Brugh*, the ancient *Sidhe* word for the homes of the fairies, is usually translated as castle or mansion, but in fact means the interior of a barrow or hollow hill.

[5] Stokesey summoned Col Tom Blue to his house in Exeter. When the fairy refused for the third time to serve him, Stokesey made himself invisible and

that the story as it had come down to children and magio-historians was an accurate description of what had happened. "Yet there is probably some truth in it somewhere," he thought. "Perhaps Stokesey managed to penetrate Col Tom Blue's castle and that proved to Col Tom Blue that he was a magician to be reckoned with. There is no reason that I could not do something similar. After all this fairy knows nothing of my skills or achievements. If I were to pay him an unexpected visit, it would prove to him the extent of my power."

---

[5] *cont'd* followed Col Tom Blue out of the town. Col Tom Blue walked along a fairy road and soon arrived in a place that was not England. There was a low brown hill by a pool of still water. In answer to Col Tom Blue's command a door opened in the hillside and he went inside. Stokesey went after him.

In the centre of the hill Stokesey found an enchanted hall where everyone was dancing. He waited until one of the dancers came close. Then he rolled a magic apple towards her and she picked it up. Naturally it was the best and most beautiful apple in all the worlds that ever were. As soon as the fairy woman had eaten it, she desired nothing so much as another one just the same. She looked around, but saw no one. "Who sent me that apple?" she asked. "The East Wind," whispered Stokesey. On the next night Stokesey again followed Col Tom Blue inside the hill. He watched the dancers and again he rolled an apple towards the woman. When she asked who had sent it to her, he replied that it was the East Wind. On the third night he kept the apple in his hand. The fairy woman left the other dancers and looked round. "East Wind! East Wind!" she whispered. "Where is my apple?" "Tell me where Col Tom Blue sleeps," whispered Stokesey, "and I will give you the apple." So she told him: deep in the ground, on the northernmost edge of the *brugh*.

On the following nights Stokesey impersonated the West Wind, the North Wind and the South Wind and he used his apples to persuade other inhabitants of the mound to give him information about Col Tom Blue. From a shepherd he learnt what animals guarded Col Tom Blue while he slept – a wild she-pig and an even wilder he-goat. From Col Tom Blue's nurse he learnt what Col Tom Blue held in his hand while he slept – a very particular and important pebble. And from a kitchen-boy he learnt what three words Col Tom Blue said every morning upon waking.

In this way Stokesey learnt enough to gain power over Col Tom Blue. But before he could use his new knowledge, Col Tom Blue came to him and said he had reconsidered: he believed he would like to serve Stokesey after all.

What had happened was this: Col Tom Blue had discovered that the East Wind, the West Wind, the North Wind and the South Wind had all been asking questions about him. He had no idea what he could have done to offend these important personages, but he was seriously alarmed. An alliance with a powerful and learned English magician suddenly seemed a great deal more attractive.

He thought back to the misty, snowy day at Windsor when he and the King had almost stumbled into Faerie, lured by the gentleman's magic. He thought of the wood and the tiny lights within it that had suggested an ancient house. The King's Roads could certainly take him there, but – leaving aside his promise to Arabella – he had no desire to find the gentleman by magic he had already done. He wanted this to be something new and startling. When he next saw the gentleman he wanted to be full of the confidence and exhilaration that a successful new spell always bestowed on him.

"Faerie is never very far away," he thought, "and there are a thousand ways of getting there. Surely I ought to be able to find one of them?"

There was a spell he knew of that could make a path between any two beings the magician named. It was an old spell – just a step away from fairy magic. The paths it would make could certainly cross the boundaries between worlds. Strange had never used it before and he had no idea of what the path would like look or how he would follow it. Still he believed he could do it. He muttered the words to himself, made a few gestures, and named himself and the gentleman as the two beings between whom the path should be drawn.

There was a shift as sometimes happened at the start of magic. It was as if an invisible door had opened and closed, leaving him upon the other side of it. Or as if all the buildings in the city had turned round and everything was now facing in another direction. The magic appeared to have worked perfectly – something had certainly happened – but he could see no result. He considered what to do next.

"It is probably only a matter of perception – and I know how to cure that." He paused. "It is vexatious. I had much rather not use it again, but still, once more is not likely to hurt."

He reached into the breast of his coat and brought out the tincture of madness. The waiter brought him a glass of water and he carefully tipped in one tiny drop. He drank it down.

He looked around and perceived for the first time the line of glittering light which began at his foot, crossed the tiled floor of the coffee-house and led out of the door. It was very like those lines which he had often made to appear upon the silver dish of water. He found that if he looked directly at it, it disappeared. But if he kept it in the corner of his eye he could see it very well.

He paid the waiter and stepped out into the street. "Well," he said, "that is truly remarkable."

# 55

## *The second shall see his dearest possession in his enemy's hand*

Night of 2nd/3rd December 1816

IT WAS AS if that fate which had always seemed to threaten the city of Venice had overtaken her in an instant; but instead of being drowned in water, she was drowned in trees. Dark, ghostly trees crowded the alleys and squares, and filled the canals. Walls were no obstacle to them. Their branches pierced stone and glass. Their roots plunged deep beneath paving stones. Statues and pillars were sheathed in ivy. It was suddenly – to Strange's senses at any rate – a great deal quieter and darker. Trailing beards of mistletoe hid lamps and candles and the dense canopy of branches blocked out the moon.

Yet none of Venice's inhabitants appeared to notice the least change. Strange had often read how men and women could be cheerfully oblivious to magic going on around them, but never before had he seen an example of it. A baker's apprentice was carrying a tray of bread on his head. As Strange watched, the man neatly circumvented all the trees he did not know were there and ducking this way and that to avoid branches which would have poked his eye out. A man and a woman dressed for the ballroom or the *Ridotto*, with cloaks and masks, came down the Salizzada San Moisè together, arm in arm, heads together, whispering. A great tree stood in their way. They parted quite naturally, passed one on each side of the tree and joined arms again on the other side.

Strange followed the line of glittering light down an alley to the quayside. The trees went on where the city stopped, and the line of light led through the trees.

He did not much care for the idea of stepping into the sea. At Venice there is no gently sloping beach to lead one inch by inch into the water; the stone world of the city ends at the quayside and the Adriatic begins immediately. Strange had no notion how deep the water might be just here, but he was tolerably certain that it was deep enough to drown in. All he could do was hope that the glittering path which led him through the wood would also prevent him from drowning.

Yet at the same time it pleased his vanity to think how much better suited he was to this adventure than Norrell. "He could never be persuaded to step into the sea. He hates getting wet. Who was it that said a magician needs the subtlety of a Jesuit, the daring of a soldier and the wits of a thief? I believe it was meant for a insult, but it has some truth in it."

He stepped off the quayside.

Instantly the sea became more ethereal and dreamlike, and the wood became more solid. Soon the sea was scarcely more than a faint silver shimmer among the dark trees and a salty tang mingling with the usual scents of a night-time wood.

"I am," thought Strange, "the first English magician to enter Faerie in almost three hundred years."[1] He felt excessively pleased at the thought and rather wished there were someone there to see him do it and be astonished. He realized how tired he was of books and silence, how he longed for the times when to be a magician meant journeys into places no Englishman had ever seen. For the first time since Waterloo he was actually doing something. Then it

[1] The last English magician to enter Faerie willingly before Strange was Dr Martin Pale. He made many journeys there. The last was probably some time in the 1550s.

occurred to him that, rather than congratulating himself, he ought to be looking about him and seeing if there were any thing he could learn. He applied himself to studying his surroundings.

The wood was not quite an English wood, though it was very like it. The trees were a little too ancient, a little too vast and a little too fantastic in shape. Strange had the strong impression that they possessed fully formed characters, with loves, hates and desires of their own. They looked as if they were accustomed to being treated equally with men and women, and expected to be consulted in matters that concerned them.

"This," he thought, "is just as I would have expected, but it ought to stand as a warning to me of how different this world is from my own. The people I meet here are sure to ask me questions. They will want to trick me." He began to imagine the sorts of questions they might ask him and to prepare a variety of clever answers. He felt no fear; a dragon might appear for all he cared. He had come so far in the last two days; he felt as if there was nothing he could not do if he tried.

After twenty minutes or so of walking the glittering line led him to the house. He recognized it immediately; its image had been so sharp and clear before him that day in Windsor. Yet at the same time it was different. In Windsor it had appeared bright and welcoming. Now he was struck by its overwhelming air of poverty and desolation. The windows were many, but very small and most of them were dark. It was much bigger than he expected – far larger than any earthly dwelling. "The Czar of Russia may have a house as large as this," he thought, "or perhaps the Pope in Rome. I do not know. I have never been to those places."

It was surrounded by a high wall. The glittering line seemed to stop at the wall. He could not see any opening. He muttered Ormskirk's Spell of Revelation, followed immediately by Taillemache's Shield, a charm to ensure safe passage through enchanted places. His luck held and immediately a mean little gate appeared. He passed through it and found himself in a wide grey courtyard.

It was full of bones that glimmered whitely in the starlight. Some skeletons were clad in rusting armour; the weapons that had destroyed them were still tangled with their ribs or poking out of an eye-socket.

Strange had seen the battlefields of Badajoz and Waterloo; he was scarcely perturbed by a few ancient skeletons. Still it was interesting. He felt as if he really were in Faerie now.

Despite the dilapidation of the house he had the strongest suspicion that there was something magical about its appearance. He tried Ormskirk's Revelation again. Immediately the house shifted and changed and he could see that it was only partly built of stone. Some of what had appeared to be walls, buttresses and towers was now revealed as a great mound of earth – a hillside in fact.

"*It is a brugh*!" he thought in great excitement.[2]

He passed under a low doorway and found himself immediately in a vast room filled with people dancing. The dancers were dressed in the finest clothes imaginable, but the room itself seemed in the very worst state of repair. Indeed at one end, part of a wall had collapsed and lay in a heap of rubble. The furnishings were few and shabby, the candles were of the poorest sort and there was only one fiddler and one piper to provide the music.

No one appeared to be paying Strange the least attention and so he stood among the people near the wall and watched the dance. In many ways the entertainment here was less foreign to him than, say, a *conversazione*[3] in Venice. The manners of the guests seemed more English and the dance itself was very like the country dances that are enjoyed by ladies and gentlemen from Newcastle to Penzance every week of the year.

It occurred to him that once upon a time he had been fond of dancing, and so had Arabella. But after the war in Spain he had hardly danced with her – or indeed with any one else. Wherever he

[2] See Chapter 54, footnote 4.
[3] Italian party.

had gone in London – whether to a ballroom or Government office – there had always been too many people to talk to about magic. He wondered if Arabella had danced with other people. He wondered if he had asked her. "Though if I did think to ask her," he thought with a sigh, "I clearly did not listen to her answers – I cannot remember any thing about it."

"Good God, sir! What are you doing here?"

Strange turned to see who spoke. The one thing he was not prepared for was that the first person he should meet should be Sir Walter Pole's butler. He could not remember the fellow's name, though he had heard Sir Walter speak it a hundred times. Simon? Samuel?

The man grasped Strange by the arm and shook him. He seemed highly agitated. "For God's sake, sir, what are you doing here? Don't you know that he hates you?"

Strange opened his mouth to deliver one of the clever ripostes but then hesitated. Who hated him? Norrell?

In the complexity of the dance the man was whisked away. Strange looked for him again and caught sight of him on the other side of the room. The man glared furiously at Strange as if he were angry at him for not leaving.

"How odd," thought Strange. "And yet of course they would do that. They would do the thing you least expected. Probably it is not Pole's butler at all. Probably it is only a fairy in his likeness. Or a magical illusion." He began to look around for his own fairy.

"Stephen! Stephen!"

"I am here, sir!" Stephen turned and found the gentleman with the thistle-down hair at his elbow.

"The magician is here! He is here! What can he want?"

"I do not know, sir."

"Oh! He has come here to destroy me! I know he has!"

Stephen was astonished. For a long time he had imagined that the gentleman was proof against any injury. Yet here he was in a condition of the utmost anxiety and fright.

"But why would he want to do that, sir?" asked Stephen in a soothing tone. "I think it far more likely that he has come here to rescue . . . to take home his wife. Perhaps we should release Mrs Strange from her enchantment and permit her to return home with her husband? And Lady Pole too. Let Mrs Strange and Lady Pole return to England with the magician, sir. I am sure that will be enough to mollify his anger against you. I am sure I can persuade him."

"What? What are you talking about? Mrs Strange? No, no, Stephen! You are quite mistaken! Indeed you are! He has not so much as mentioned our dear Mrs Strange. You and I, Stephen, know how to appreciate the society of such a woman. He does not. He has forgotten all about her. He has a new sweetheart now – a bewitching young woman whose lovely presence I hope one day will add lustre to our own balls! There is naught so fickle as an Englishman! Oh, believe me! He has come to destroy me! From the moment he asked me for Lady Pole's finger I knew that he was far, far cleverer than I had ever guessed before. Advise me, Stephen. You have lived among these Englishmen for years. What ought I to do? How can I protect myself? How can I punish such wickedness?"

Through all the dullness and heaviness of his enchantment Stephen struggled to think clearly. A great crisis was upon him, he was sure of it. Never before had the gentleman asked for his help so openly. Surely he ought to be able to turn the situation to his advantage? But how? And he knew from long experience that none of the gentleman's moods lasted long; he was the most mercurial being in the world. The smallest word could turn his fear into a blazing rage and hatred – if Stephen misspoke now, then far from freeing himself and the others, he might goad the gentleman into destroying them all. He gazed about the room in search of inspiration.

"What shall I do, Stephen?" moaned the gentleman. "What shall I do?"

Something caught Stephen's eye. Beneath a black arch stood a familiar figure: a fairy woman who habitually wore a black veil that went from the crown of her head to the tips of her fingers. She never joined in the dancing; she half-walked, half-floated among the dancers and the standers-by. Stephen had never seen her speak to any one, but when she passed by there was a faint smell of graveyards, earth and charnel houses. He could never look upon her without feeling a shiver of apprehension, but whether she was malignant, cursed, or both, he did not know.

"There are people in this world," he began, "whose lives are nothing but a burden to them. A black veil stands between them and the world. They are utterly alone. They are like shadows in the night, shut off from joy and love and all gentle human emotions, unable even to give comfort to each other. Their days are full of nothing but darkness, misery and solitude. You know whom I mean, sir. I . . . I do not speak of blame . . ." The gentleman was gazing at him with fierce intensity. "But I am sure we can turn the magician's wrath away from you, if you will only release . . ."

"Ah!" exclaimed the gentleman and his eyes widened with understanding. He held up his hand as a sign for Stephen to be silent.

Stephen was certain that he had gone too far. "Forgive me," he whispered.

"Forgive?" said the gentleman in a tone of surprize. "Why, there is nothing to forgive! It is long centuries since any one spoke to me with such forthrightness and I honour you for it! Darkness, yes! Darkness, misery and solitude!" He turned upon his heel and walked away into the crowd.

Strange was enjoying himself immensely. The eerie contradictions of the ball did not disturb him in the least; they were just what he would have expected. Despite the poverty of the great hall, it was still in part an illusion. His magician's eye perceived that at least part of the room was beneath the earth.

A little way off a fairy woman was regarding him steadily. She was dressed in a gown the colour of a winter sunset and carried a delicate, glittering fan strung with something which might have been crystal beads – but which more resembled frost upon leaves and the fragile pendants of ice that hang from twigs.

A dance was at that moment starting up. No one appeared to claim the fairy woman's hand, so upon an impulse Strange smiled and bowed and said, "There is scarcely any one here who knows me. So we cannot be introduced. Nevertheless, madam, I should be greatly honoured if you would dance with me."

She did not answer him or smile in return, but she took his proffered hand and allowed him to lead her to the dance. They took their places in the set and stood for a moment without saying a word.

"You are wrong to say no one knows you," she said suddenly. "I know you. You are one of the two magicians who is destined to return magic to England." Then she said, as if reciting a prophecy or something that was commonly known, "*And the name of one shall be Fearfulness. And the name of the other shall be Arrogance* . . . Well, clearly you are not Fearfulness, so I suppose you must be Arrogance."

This was not very polite.

"That is indeed my destiny," Strange agreed. "And an excellent one it is!"

"Oh, you think so, do you?" she said, giving him a sideways look. "Then why haven't you done it yet?"

Strange smiled. "And what makes you think, madam, that I have not?"

"Because you are standing here."

"I do not understand."

"Did not you listen to the prophecy when it was told to you?"

"The prophecy, madam?"

"Yes, the prophecy of . . ." She finished by saying a name, but it was in her own language and Strange could not make it out.[4]

"I beg your pardon?"

"The prophecy of the King."

Strange thought back to Vinculus climbing out from under the winter hedge with bits of dry, brown grass and empty seed pods stuck to his clothes; he remembered Vinculus reciting something in the winter lane. But what Vinculus had said he had no idea. He had had no notion of becoming a magician just then and had not paid any attention. "I believe there was a prophecy of some sort, madam," he said, "but to own the truth it was long ago and I do not remember. What does the prophecy say we must do? – the other magician and I?"

"Fail."

Strange blinked in surprize. "I . . . I do not think . . . Fail? No, madam, no. It is too late for that. Already we are the most successful magicians since Martin Pale."

She said nothing.

Was it too late to fail? wondered Strange. He thought of Mr Norrell in the house in Hanover-square, of Mr Norrell at Hurtfew Abbey, of Mr Norrell complimented by all the Ministers and politely attended to by the Prince Regent. It was perhaps a little ironic that he of all people should take comfort from Norrell's success, but at that moment nothing in the world seemed so solid, so unassailable. The fairy woman was mistaken.

For the next few minutes they were occupied in going down the dance. When they had resumed their places in the set, she said, "You are certainly very bold to come here, Magician."

"Why? What ought I to fear, madam?"

She laughed. "How many English magicians do you suppose have left their bones lying in this *brugh*? Beneath these stars?"

---

[4] Presumably John Uskglass's *Sidhe* name.

"I have not the least idea."

"Forty-seven."

Strange began to feel a little less comfortable.

"Not counting Peter Porkiss, but he was no magician. He was only a *cowan*."[5]

"Indeed."

"Do not pretend that you know what I mean," she said sharply. "When it is as plain as Pandemonium that you do not."

Strange was once again perplexed what to reply. She seemed so bent upon being displeased. But then again, he thought, what was so unusual about it? In Bath and London and all the cities of Europe ladies pretended to scold the men they meant to attract. For all he knew she was just the same. He decided to treat her severe manner as a kind of flirtation and see if that soothed her. So he laughed lightly and said, "It seems you know a great deal of what has passed in this *brugh*, madam." It gave him a little thrill of excitement to say the word, a word so ancient and romantic.

She shrugged. "I have been a visitor here for four thousand years."[6]

"I should be very glad to talk you about it whenever you are at liberty."

"Say rather when *you* are next at liberty! Then I shall have no objection to answering any of your questions."

"You are very kind."

"Not at all. A hundred years from tonight then?"

"I . . . I beg your pardon?"

---

[5] A particular problem in mediaeval England was the great abundance of *cowans*. It is a term (now obsolete) properly applied to any unqualified or failed craftsmen, but here has special application to magicians.

[6] Several authorities have noted that long-lived fairies have a tendency to call any substantial period of time "four thousand years". The fairy lady simply means she has known the *brugh* time out of mind, before any one troubled to reckon up time into years, centuries and millennia. Many fairies, when asked, will say they are four thousand years old; they mean they do not know their age; they are older than human civilization – or possibly than humankind.

But she seemed to feel she had talked enough and he could get nothing more from her but the most commonplace remarks upon the ball and their fellow-dancers.

The dance ended; they parted. It had been the oddest and most unsettling conversation of Strange's life. Why in the world should she think that magic had not yet been restored to England? And what was all that nonsense about a hundred years? He consoled himself with the thought that a woman who passed much of her life in an echoing mansion in a deep, dark wood was unlikely to be very well informed upon events in the wider worlds.

He rejoined the watchers by the wall. The course of the next dance brought a particularly lovely woman close to him. He was struck by the contrast between the beauty of her face and the deep, settled unhappiness of her expression. As she raised her hand to join hands with her partner, he saw that her little finger was missing.

"Curious!" he thought and touched the pocket of his coat where the box of silver and porcelain lay. "Perhaps . . ." But he could not conceive any sequence of events which would result in a magician giving the fairy a finger belonging to someone in the fairy's own household. It made no sense. "Perhaps the two things are not connected at all," he thought.

But the woman's hand was so small and white. He was sure that the finger in his pocket would fit it perfectly. He was full of curiosity and determined to go and speak to her and ask her how she had lost her finger.

The dance had ended. She was speaking to another lady, who had her back to him.

"I beg your pardon . . ." he began.

Instantly the other lady turned. It was Arabella.

She was dressed in a white gown with an overdress of pale blue net and diamonds. It glittered like frost and snow, and was far prettier than any gown she had possessed when she lived in England. In her hair were sprays of some tiny, star-like blossoms and there was a black velvet ribbon tied around her throat.

She gazed at him with an odd expression – an expression in which surprize was mixed with wariness, delight with disbelief. "Jonathan! Look, my love!" she said to her companion. "It is Jonathan!"

"Arabella . . ." he began. He did not know what he meant to say. He held out his hands to her; but she did not take them. Without appearing to know what she did, she withdrew slightly and joined her hands with those of the unknown woman, as if this was now the person to whom she went for comfort and support.

The unknown woman looked at Strange in obedience to Arabella's request. "He looks as most men do," she remarked, coldly. And then, as if she felt the meeting were now concluded, "Come," she said. She tried to lead Arabella away.

"Oh, but wait!" said Arabella softly. "I think that he must have come to help us! Do not you think he might have?"

"Perhaps," said the unknown woman in a doubtful tone. She stared at Strange again. "No. I do not think so. I believe he came for another reason entirely."

"I know that you have warned me against false hopes," said Arabella, "and I have tried to do as you advise. But he is here! I was sure he would not forget me so soon."

"Forget you!" exclaimed Strange. "No, indeed! Arabella, I . . ."

"*Did* you come here to help us?" asked the unknown woman, suddenly addressing Strange directly.

"What?" said Strange. "No, I . . . You must understood that until now I did not know . . . Which is to say, I do not quite understand . . ."

The unknown woman made a small sound of exasperation. "Did you or did you not come here to help us? It is a simple enough question I should think."

"No," said Strange. "Arabella, speak to me, I beg you. Tell me what has . . ."

"There? You see?" said the unknown woman to Arabella. "Now let you and me find a corner where we can be peaceful together. I believe I saw an unoccupied bench near the door."

But Arabella would not be persuaded to walk away just yet. She continued to gaze at Strange in the same odd way; it was as if she were looking at a picture of him, rather than the flesh-and-blood man. She said, "I know you do not put a great deal of faith in what men can do, but . . ."

"I put no faith in them at all," interrupted the unknown woman. "I know what it is to waste years and years upon vain hopes of help from this person or that. No hope at all is better than ceaseless disappointment!"

Strange's patience was gone. "You will forgive my interrupting you, madam," he said to the unknown woman, "though I observe you have done nothing but interrupt since I joined you! I fear I must insist on a minute's private conversation with my wife! Perhaps if you will have the goodness to retire a pace or two . . ."

But neither she nor Arabella was attending to him. They were directing their gaze a little to his right. The gentleman with thistle-down hair was just at his shoulder.

Stephen pushed through the crowd of dancers. His conversation with the gentleman had been most unnerving. Something had been decided upon, but the more Stephen thought about it, the more he realized he had not the least idea what it was. "It is still not too late," he muttered as forced his way through. "It is not still too late." Part of him – the cold, uncaring, enchanted half – wondered what he meant by that. Not too late to save himself? To save Lady Pole and Mrs Strange? The magician?

Never had the lines of dancers seemed so long, so like a fence barring his way. On the other side of the room he thought he saw a head of gleaming, thistle-down hair. "Sir!" he cried. "Wait! I must speak with you again!"

The light changed. The sounds of music, dancing and conversation were swept away. Stephen looked around, expecting to find himself in a new city or upon another continent. But he was still in the great hall of Lost-hope. It was empty; the dancers and musicians were gone. Three people remained: Stephen himself and, some way off, the magician and the gentleman with the thistle-down hair.

The magician called out his wife's name. He hastened towards a dark door as if he intended to dash off into the house in search of her.

"Wait!" cried the gentleman with the thistle-down hair. The magician turned and Stephen saw that his face was black with anger, that his mouth was working as if a spell were about to explode out of him.

The gentleman with the thistle-down hair raised his hands. *The great hall was filled with a flock of birds. In the blink of an eye they were there; in the blink of an eye they were gone.*

The birds had struck Stephen with their wings. They had knocked the breath out of him. When he recovered enough to lift his head, he saw that the gentleman with the thistle-down hair had raised his hands a second time.

*The great hall was full of spinning leaves. Winter-dry and brown they were, turning in a wind that had come out of nowhere. In the blink of an eye they were there; in the blink of an eye they were gone.*

The magician was staring wildly. He did not seem to know what to do in the face of such overwhelming magic. "He is lost," thought Stephen.

The gentleman with the thistle-down hair raised his hands a third time. *The great hall was full of rain – not a rain of water, a rain of blood. In the blink of an eye it was there; in the blink of an eye it was gone.*

The magic ended. In that instant the magician disappeared and the gentleman with the thistle-down hair dropped to the floor, like a man in a swoon.

"Where is the magician, sir?" cried Stephen, rushing to kneel beside him. "What has happened?"

"I have sent him back to Altinum's sea colony,"[7] he said in a hoarse whisper. He tried to smile, but seemed quite unable. "I have done it, Stephen! I have done what you advised! It has taken all my strength. My old alliances have been stretched to their utmost limit. But I have changed the world! Oh! I have dealt him such a blow! Darkness, misery and solitude! He will not hurt us any more!" He attempted a triumphant laugh, but it turned into a fit of coughing and retching. When it was done he took Stephen's hand. "Do not be concerned about me, Stephen. I am a little tired, that is all. You are a person of remarkable vision and penctration. Henceforth you and I are no longer friends: we are brothers! You have helped me defeat my enemy and in return I shall find your name. I shall make you King!" His voice faded to nothing.

"Tell me what you have done!" whispered Stephen.

But the gentleman closed his eyes.

Stephen remained kneeling in the ballroom, grasping the gentleman's hand. The tallow candles went out; the shadows closed about them.

[7] Meaning Venice: Altinum was the city on Italy's eastern coast whence came the first inhabitants of Venice.

# 56

# The Black Tower

## 3rd/4th December 1816

Dr Greysteel was asleep and dreaming. In his dream someone was calling for him and something was required of him. He was anxious to oblige whoever it was and so he went to this place and that, searching for them; but he did not find them and still they called his name. Finally he opened his eyes.

"Who's there?" he asked.

"It's me, sir. Frank, sir."

"What's the matter?"

"Mr Strange is here. He wants to speak to you, sir."

"Is something wrong?"

"He don't say, sir. But, I think there must be."

"Where is he, Frank?"

"He won't come in, sir. He won't be persuaded. He's outside, sir."

Dr Greysteel lowered his legs out of the bed and drew in his breath sharply. "It's cold, Frank!" he said.

"Yes, sir." Frank helped Dr Greysteel on with his dressing-gown and slippers. They padded through numerous dark rooms, across acres of dark marble floors. In the vestibule a lamp was burning. Frank pulled back the great iron double doors and then he picked up the lamp and went outside. Dr Greysteel followed him.

A flight of stone steps descended into darkness. Only the smell of the sea, the lap of water against stone and a certain occasional glitter and shifting-about of the darkness gave the observer to understand that at the bottom of the steps there was a canal. A few houses round about had lamps burning in windows or upon balconies. Beyond this all was silence and darkness.

"There is no one here!" cried Dr Greysteel. "Where is Mr Strange?"

For answer Frank pointed off to the right. A lamp bloomed suddenly under a bridge and by its light Dr Greysteel saw a gondola, waiting. The *gondoliero* poled his boat towards them. As it approached, Dr Greysteel could see there was a passenger. Despite all that Frank had said, it took a moment or two for Dr Greysteel to recognize him. "Strange!" he cried. "Good God! What has happened? I did not know you! My . . . my . . . my dear friend." Dr Greysteel's tongue stumbled, trying to find a suitable word. He had grown accustomed in the last few weeks to the idea that he and Strange would soon stand in a much closer relationship. "Come inside! Frank, quick! Fetch a glass of wine for Mr Strange!"

"No!" cried Strange in a hoarse, unfamiliar voice. He spoke urgently in Italian to the *gondoliero*. His Italian was considerably more fluent than Dr Greysteel's and Dr Greysteel did not understand him, but the meaning soon became clear when the *gondoliero* began to move his boat away.

"I cannot come inside!" cried Strange. "Do not ask me!

"Very well, but tell me what has happened."

"I am cursed!"

"Cursed? No! Do not say so."

"But I do say so. I have been wrong from start to finish! I told this fellow to take me a little way off. It is not safe for me to be too close to your house. Dr Greysteel! You must send your daughter away!"

"Flora! Why?"

"There is someone nearby who means her harm!"

"Good God!"

Strange's eyes grew wider. "There is someone who means to bind her to a life of ceaseless misery! Slavery and subjugation to a wild spirit! An ancient prison built as much of cold enchantments as of stone and earth. Wicked, wicked! And then again, perhaps not so wicked after all – for what does he do but follow his nature? How can he help himself?"

Neither Dr Greysteel nor Frank could make any thing of this.

"You are ill, sir," said Dr Greysteel. "You have a fever. Come inside. Frank can make you a soothing drink to take away these evil thoughts. Come inside, Mr Strange." He drew away slightly from the steps so that Strange might approach, but Strange took no notice.

"I thought . . ." began Strange, and then stopt immediately. He paused so long it seemed he had forgotten what he was going to say, but then he began again. "I thought," he began again, "that Norrell had only lied to me. But I was wrong. Quite wrong. He has lied to everybody. He has lied to us all." Then he spoke to the *gondoliero* and the gondola moved away into the darkness.

"Wait! Wait!" cried Dr Greysteel, but it was gone. He stared into the darkness, hoping that Strange would reappear, but he did not.

"Should I go after him, sir?" asked Frank.

"We do not know where he has gone."

"I dare say he has gone home, sir. I can follow him on foot."

"And say what to him, Frank? He would not listen to us just now. No, let us go inside. There is Flora to consider."

But once inside Dr Greysteel stood helpless, quite at a loss to know what to do next. He suddenly looked as old as his years. Frank took him gently by the arm and led him down a dark stone staircase into the kitchen.

It was a very small kitchen to service so many large marble rooms upstairs. In daylight it was a dank, gloomy place. There was only one window. It was high up on the wall, just above the level of the water outside, and it was covered by a heavy iron grille. This meant that most of the room was below the level of the canal. Yet after their encounter with Strange, it seemed a warm and friendly place. Frank lit more candles and stirred the fire into life. Then he filled a kettle to make them both some tea.

Dr Greysteel, seated in a homely kitchen chair, stared into the fire, lost in thought. "When he spoke of someone meaning harm to Flora . . ." he said at last.

Frank nodded as if he knew what came next.

". . . I could not help thinking he meant himself, Frank," said Dr Greysteel. "He fears he will do something to hurt her and so he comes to warn me."

"That's it, sir!" agreed Frank. "He comes here to warn us. Which shews that he is a good man at heart."

"He is a good man," said Dr Greysteel, earnestly. "But something has happened. It is this magic, Frank. It must be. It is a very queer profession and I cannot help wishing he were something else – a soldier or a clergyman or a lawyer! What will we tell Flora, Frank? She will not want to go – you may be sure of that! She will not want to leave him. Especially when . . . when he is sick. What can I tell her? I ought to go with her. But then who will remain in Venice to take care of Mr Strange?"

"You and I will stay here and help the magician, sir. But send Miss Flora away with her aunt."

"Yes, Frank! That's it! That's what we shall do!"

"Tho' I must say, sir," added Frank, "that Miss Flora scarcely needs people to take care of her. She is not like other young ladies." Frank had lived long enough with the Greysteels to catch the family habit of regarding Miss Greysteel as someone of exceptional abilities and intelligence.

Feeling that they had done all that they could for the present, Dr Greysteel and Frank went back to bed.

But it is one thing to form plans in the middle of the night, it is quite another to carry them out in the broad light of day. As Dr Greysteel had predicted, Flora objected in the strongest terms to being sent away from Venice and from Jonathan Strange. She did not understand. Why must she go?

Because, said Dr Greysteel, he was ill.

All the more reason to stay then, she said. He would need someone to nurse him.

Dr Greysteel tried to imply that Strange's illness was contagious, but he was, by principle and inclination, an honest man. He had had little practice at lying and he did it badly. Flora did not believe him.

Aunt Greysteel scarcely understood the change of plan any better than her niece. Dr Greysteel could not stand against their united opposition and so he was obliged to take his sister into his confidence and tell her what had happened during the night. Unfortunately he had no talent for conveying atmospheres. The peculiar chill of Strange's words was entirely absent from his explanation. Aunt Greysteel understood only that Strange had been incoherent. She naturally concluded that he had been drunk. This, though very bad, was not unusual among gentlemen and seemed no reason for them all to remove to another city.

"After all, Lancelot," she said, "I have known *you* very much the worse for wine. There was the time we dined with Mr Sixsmith and you insisted upon saying good night to all the chickens. You went out into the yard and pulled them one by one out of the henhouse and they all escaped and ran about and half of them were eaten by the fox. I never saw Antoinette so angry with you." (Antoinette was the Doctor's late wife.)

This was an old story and very demeaning. Dr Greysteel listened with mounting exasperation. "For God's sake, Louisa! I am a physician! I know drunkenness when I see it!"

So Frank was brought in. He remembered much more precisely what Strange had said. The visions he conjured up of Flora shut away in prison for all eternity were quite enough to terrify her aunt. In a very short space of time Aunt Greysteel was as eager as any one else to send Flora away from Venice. However she insisted upon one thing – something which had never occurred to Dr Greysteel and Frank: she insisted that they tell Flora the truth.

It cost Flora Greysteel a great deal of pain to hear that Strange had lost his reason. She thought at first they must be mistaken, and even when they had persuaded her that it might be true, she was still certain there was no necessity for her to leave Venice; she was sure he would never hurt her. But she could now see that her father and aunt believed otherwise and that they would never be comfortable until she went. Most reluctantly she agreed to leave.

Shortly after the departure of the two ladies, Dr Greysteel was sitting in one of the *palazzo*'s chill marble rooms. He was comforting himself with a glass of brandy and trying to find the courage to go and look for Strange, when Frank entered the room and said something about a black tower.

"What?" said Dr Greysteel. He was in no mood to be puzzling out Frank's eccentricities.

"Come to the window and I will shew you, sir."

Dr Greysteel got up and went to the window.

Something was standing in the centre of Venice. It could best be described as a black tower of impossible vastness. The base of it seemed to cover several acres. It rose up out of the city into the sky and the top of it could not be seen. From a distance its colour was uniformly black and its texture smooth. But there were moments when it seemed almost translucent, as if it were made of black smoke. One caught glimpses of buildings behind – or possibly even *within* – it.

It was the most mysterious thing Dr Greysteel had ever seen. "Where can it have come from, Frank? And what has happened to the houses that were there before?"

Before these or any other questions could be answered, there was a loud, official-sounding knock upon the door. Frank went to answer it. He returned a moment later with a small crowd of people, none of whom Dr Greysteel had ever seen before. Two of them were priests, and there were three or four young men of military bearing who all wore brightly coloured uniforms decorated with an extravagant amount of gold lace and braid. The most handsome of the young men stepped forward. His uniform was the most splendid of all and he had long yellow moustaches. He explained that he was Colonel Wenzel von Ottenfeld, secretary to the Austrian Governor of the city. He introduced his companions; the officers were Austrian like himself, but the priests were Venetian. This in itself was enough to cause Dr Greysteel some surprize; the Venetians hated the Austrians and the two races were hardly ever seen in each other's company.

"You are the Sir Doctor?" said Colonel von Ottenfeld. "The friend of the *Hexenmeister*[1] of the Great Vellinton?"

Dr Greysteel agreed that he was.

"Ah! Sir Doctor! We are beggars under your feet today!" Von Ottenfeld put on a melancholy expression which was much enhanced by his long, drooping moustaches.

Dr Greysteel said he was astonished to hear it.

"We come today. We ask your . . ." Von Ottenfeld frowned and snapped his fingers. "*Vermittlung. Wir bitten um Ihre Vermittlung. Wie kann man das sagen?*" There was some discussion how this word ought to be translated. One of the Italian priests suggested "intercession".

"Yes, yes," agreed von Ottenfeld, eagerly. "We ask your intercession from us to the *Hexenmeister* of the Great Vellinton. Sir Doctor, we esteem very much the *Hexenmeister* of the Great Vellinton. But now the *Hexenmeister* of the Great Vellinton has done something. What calamity! The people of Venice are afraid. Many must leave their houses and go away!"

"Ah!" said Dr Greysteel, knowingly. He thought for a moment and comprehension dawned. "Oh! You think Mr Strange has something to do with this Black Tower."

"No!" declared von Ottenfeld. "It is not a Tower. It is the Night! What calamity!"

[1] German for magician.

"I beg your pardon?" said Dr Greysteel and looked to Frank for help. Frank shrugged.

One of the priests, whose English was a little more robust, explained that when the sun had risen that morning, it had risen in every part of the city except one – the parish of Santa Maria Zobenigo, which was where Strange lived. There, Night continued to reign.

"Why does the *Hexenmeister* of the Great Vellinton this?" asked von Ottenfeld, "We do not know. We beg you go, Sir Doctor. Ask him, please, for the sun to come back to Santa Maria Zobenigo? Ask him, respectfully, to do no more magic in Venice?"

"Of course I will go," said Dr Greysteel. "It is a most distressing situation. And, though I am quite sure that Mr Strange has not done this deliberately – that it will prove to be all a mistake – I will gladly help in any way I can."

"Ah!" said the priest with the good English, anxiously, and put up his hand, as if he feared that Dr Greysteel would rush out to Santa Maria Zobenigo upon the instant. "But you will take your servant, please? You will not go alone?"

Snow was falling thickly. All of Venice's sad colours had become shades of grey and black. St Mark's Piazza was a faint grey etching of itself done on white paper. It was quite deserted. Dr Greysteel and Frank stumped through the snow together. Dr Greysteel carried a lantern and Frank held a black umbrella over the Doctor's head.

Beyond the Piazza rose up the Black Pillar of Night; they passed beneath the arch of the Atrio and between the silent houses. The Darkness began halfway across a little bridge. It was the eeriest thing in the world to see how the flakes of snow, falling aslant, were sucked suddenly into it, as if it were a living thing that ate them up with greedy lips.

They took one last look at the silent white city and stepped into the Darkness.

The alleys were deserted. The inhabitants of the parish had fled to relatives and friends in other parts of the city. But the cats of Venice – who are as contrary a set of creatures as the cats of any other city – had flocked to Santa Maria Zobenigo to dance and hunt and play in the Endless Night which seemed to them to be a sort of high holiday. In the Darkness cats brushed past Dr Greysteel and Frank; and several times Dr Greysteel caught sight of glowing eyes watching him from a doorway.

When they reached the house where Strange lodged it was quiet. They knocked and called out, but no one came. Finding the door was unlocked, they pushed it open. The house was dark. They found the staircase and went up to Strange's room at the top of the house where he did magic.

After all that had happened they were rather expecting something remarkable, to find Strange in conversation with a demon or haunted by horrible apparitions. It was somewhat disconcerting that the scene which presented itself was so ordinary. The room looked as it had upon numerous occasions. It was lit by a generous number of candles and an iron stove gave out a welcome heat. Strange was at the table, bending over his silver dish with a pure white light radiating up into his face. He did not look up. A clock ticked quietly in the corner. Books, papers and writing things were thickly scattered over every surface as usual. Strange passed the tip of his finger over the surface of the water and struck it twice very gently. Then he turned and wrote something in a book.

"Strange," said Dr Greysteel.

Strange glanced up. He did not look so frantic as he had the night before, but his eyes had the same haunted look. He regarded the doctor for a long moment without any sign of recognition. "Greysteel," he murmured at last. "What are you doing here?"

"I have come to see how you are. I am concerned about you."

Strange made no reply to this. He turned back to his silver dish and made a few gestures over it. But immediately he seemed dissatisfied with what he had done. He took a glass and poured some water into it. Then he took a tiny bottle and carefully tipped two drops of liquid into the glass.

Dr Greysteel watched him. There was no label upon the bottle; the liquid was amber-coloured; it could have been any thing.

Strange observed Dr Greysteel's eyes upon him. "I suppose you are going to say I ought not to take this. Well, you may spare yourself the trouble!" He drank it down in one draught. "You will not say so when you know the reason!"

"No, no," said Dr Greysteel in his most placating tone – the one he employed for his most difficult patients. "I assure you I was going to say nothing of the kind. I only wish to know if you are in pain? Or ill? I thought last night that you were. Perhaps I can advise . . ." He stopped. He smelt something. It was quite overpowering – a dry, musty scent mixed with something rank and animal; and the curious thing was that he recognized it. Suddenly he could smell the room where the old woman lived: the mad old woman with all the cats.

"My wife is alive," said Strange. His voice was hoarse and thick. "Ha! There! You did not know that!"

Dr Greysteel turned cold. If there was any thing Strange could have said to alarm him even more, this was probably it.

"They told me she was dead!" continued Strange. "They told me that they had buried her! I cannot believe I was so taken in! She was enchanted! She was stolen from me! And that is why I need this!" He waved the little bottle of amber-coloured liquid in the doctor's face.

Dr Greysteel and Frank took a step or two backwards. Frank muttered in the doctor's ear. "All is well, sir. All is well. I shall not let him harm you. I have the measure of him. Do not fear."

"I cannot go back to the house," said Strange. "He has expelled me and he will not let me go back. The trees will not let me pass. I have tried spells of disenchantment, but they do not work. They do not work . . ."

"Have you been doing magic since last night?" asked Dr Greysteel.

"What? Yes!"

"I am very sorry to hear it. You should rest. I dare say you do not remember very much of last night . . ."

"Ha!" exclaimed Strange with bitterest irony. "I shall never forget the smallest detail!"

"Is that so? Is that so?" said Dr Greysteel in the same soothing tone. "Well, I cannot conceal from you that your appearance alarmed me. You were not yourself. It was the consequence, I am sure, of overwork. Perhaps if I . . ."

"Forgive me, Dr Greysteel, but, as I have just explained, my wife is *enchanted*; she is a prisoner beneath the earth. Much as I would like to continue this conversation, I have far more pressing matters to attend to!"

"Very well. Calm yourself. Our presence here distresses you. We will go away again and come back tomorrow. But before we go, I must say this: the Governor sent a delegation to me this morning. He respectfully requests that you refrain from performing magic for the present . . ."

"Not do magic!" Strange laughed – a cold, hard, humourless sound. "You ask me to stop now? Quite impossible! What did God make me a magician for, if not for this?" He returned to his silver dish and began to draw signs in the air, just above the surface of the water.

"Then at least free the parish from this Unnatural Night. Do that at least, for me? For friendship's sake? For Flora's sake?"

Strange paused in the middle of a gesture. "What are you talking about? What Unnatural Night? What is unnatural about it?"

"For God's sake, Strange! It is almost noon!"

For a moment Strange said nothing. He looked at the black window, at the darkness in the room and finally at Dr Greysteel. "I had not the least idea," he whispered, aghast. "Believe me! This is not my doing!"

"Whose is it then?"

Strange did not reply; he stared vacantly about the room.

Dr Greysteel feared it would only vex him to be questioned more about the Darkness, and so he simply asked, "Can you bring the daylight back?"

"I . . . I do not know."

Dr Greysteel told Strange that they would come again the next day and he took the opportunity once more to recommend sleep as an excellent remedy.

Strange was not listening, but, just as Dr Greysteel and Frank were leaving, he took hold of the doctor's arm and whispered, "May I ask you something?"

Dr Greysteel nodded.

"Are you not afraid that it will go out?"

"What will go out?" asked Dr Greysteel.

"The candle." Strange gestured to Dr Greysteel's forehead. "The candle inside your head."

Outside, the Darkness seemed eerier than ever. Dr Greysteel and Frank made their way silently through the night streets. When they reached the daylight at the western extremity of St Mark's Piazza, both breathed a great sigh of relief.

Dr Greysteel said, "I am determined to say nothing to the Governor about the overturn of his reason. God knows what the Austrians might do. They might send soldiers to arrest him – or worse! I shall simply say that he is unable to banish the Night just now, but that he means no harm to the city – for I am quite certain he does not – and that I am sure of persuading him to set matters right very soon."

The next day when the sun rose Darkness still covered the parish of Santa Maria Zobenigo. At half past eight Frank went out to buy milk and fish. The pretty, dark-eyed peasant-girl who sold milk from the milk-barge in the San Lorenzo-canal liked Frank and always had a word and a smile for him. This morning she handed him up his jug of milk and asked, "*Hai sentito che lo stregone inglese è pazzo*?" (Have you heard that the English magician is mad?)

In the fish-market by the Grand Canal a fisherman sold Frank three mullet, but then almost neglected to take the money because his attention was given to the argument he was conducting with his neighbour as to whether the English magician had gone mad because he was a magician, or because he was English. On the way home two pale-faced nuns scrubbing the marble steps of a church wished Frank a good morning and told him that they intended to say prayers for the poor, mad English magician. Then just as he was almost at the house-door, a white cat stepped out from under a gondola seat, sprang on to the quayside and gave him a look. He waited for it to say something about Jonathan Strange, but it did not.

"How in God's name did this happen?" asked Dr Greysteel, sitting up in bed. "Do you think Mr Strange went out and spoke to someone?"

Frank did not know. Out he went again and made some inquiries. It seemed that Strange had not yet stirred from the room at the top of the house in Santa Maria Zobenigo; but Lord Byron (who was the one person in all the city who treated the appearance of Eternal Night as a sort of entertainment) had visited him at about five o'clock the previous evening and had found him still doing magic and raving about candles, pineapples, dances that went on for centuries and dark woods that filled the streets of Venice. Byron had gone home and told his mistress, his landlord and his valet; and, as these were all sociable people much given to spending their evenings among large groups of talkative friends, the number of people who knew by morning was quite remarkable.

"Lord Byron! Of course!" cried Dr Greysteel. "I forgot all about him! I must go and warn him to be discreet."

"I think it's a little late for that, sir," said Frank.

Dr Greysteel was obliged to admit the truth of this. Nevertheless he felt he should like to consult someone. And who better than Strange's other friend? So that evening he dressed carefully and went in his gondola to the house of the Countess Albrizzi. The Countess was a clever Greek lady of mature years, who had published some books upon sculpture; but her chief delight was to give *conversazioni* where all sorts of fashionable and learned people could meet each other. Strange had attended one or two, but until tonight Dr Greysteel had never troubled about them.

He was shewn to a large room on the *piano nobile*. It was richly decorated with marble floors, wonderful statues, and painted walls and ceilings. At one end of the room the ladies sat in a semi-circle around the Countess. The men stood at the other end. From the moment he entered the room Dr Greysteel felt the eyes of the other guests upon him. More than one person was pointing him out to his neighbour. There was little doubt but that they were talking of Strange and the Darkness.

A small, handsome man was standing by the window. He had dark, curly hair and a full, soft, red mouth. It was a mouth which would have been striking upon a woman, but on a man it was simply extraordinary. With his small stature, carefully chosen clothes and dark hair and eyes, he had a little of the look of Christopher Drawlight – but only if Drawlight had been fearfully clever. Dr Greysteel went up to him directly, and said, "Lord Byron?"

The man turned to see who spoke. He did not look best pleased to be addressed by a dull, stout, middle-aged Englishman. Yet he could not deny who he was. "Yes?"

"My name is Greysteel. I am a friend of Mr Strange."

"Ah!" said his lordship. "The physician with the beautiful daughter!"

Dr Greysteel, in his turn, was not best pleased to hear his daughter spoken of in such terms by one of the most notorious rakes in Europe, yet he could not deny that Flora was beautiful. Putting it aside for the moment, he said, "I have been to see Strange. All my worst fears are confirmed. His reason is quite overturned."

"Oh, quite!" agreed Byron. "I was with him again a few hours ago and could not get him to talk of any thing but his dead wife and how she is not really dead, but merely enchanted. And now he shrouds himself in Darkness and works Black Magic! There is something rather admirable in all this, do you not agree?"

"Admirable?" said the doctor sharply. "Say pitiable rather! But do you think he made the Darkness? He told me quite plainly that he had not."

"But of course he made it!" declared Byron. "A Black World to match his Black Spirits! Who would not blot out the sun sometimes? The difference is that when one is a magician, one can actually do it."

Dr Greysteel considered this. "You may be right," he conceded. "Perhaps he created the Darkness and then forgot about it. I do not think he always remembers what he has said or done. I have found that he retains very little impression of my earlier conversations with him."

"Ah. Well. Quite," said his lordship, as if there was nothing very surprizing in this and that he too would be glad to forget the doctor's conversation just as soon as he could. "Were you aware that he has written to his brother-in-law?"

"No, I did not know that."

"He has instructed the fellow to come to Venice to see his dead sister."

"Do you think he will come?" asked Dr Greysteel.

"I have not the least idea!" Lord Byron's tone implied that it was somewhat presumptuous of Dr Greysteel to expect the Greatest Poet of the Age to interest himself in such matters. There was a moment or two of silence and then he added in a more natural tone, "To own the truth, I believe he will not come. Strange shewed me the letter. It was full of disjointed ramblings and reasonings that none but a madman – or a magician! – could understand."

"It is a very bitter thing," said Dr Greysteel. "Very bitter indeed! Only the day before yesterday we were walking with him. He was in such cheerful spirits! To have gone from complete sanity to complete madness in the space of one night, I cannot understand it. I wonder if there might not be some physical cause. Some infection perhaps?"

"Nonsense!" declared Byron. "The causes of his madness are purely metaphysical. They lie in the vast chasm between that which one is, and that which one desires to become, between the soul and the flesh. Forgive me, Dr Greysteel, but this is a matter of which I have experience. Of this I can speak with authority."

"But . . ." Dr Greysteel frowned and paused to collect his thoughts. "But the period of intense frustration appeared to be over. His work was going well."

"All I can tell you is this. Before this peculiar obsession with his dead wife, he was full of quite another matter: John Uskglass. You must have observed that? Now I know very little of English magicians. They have always seemed to me a parcel of dull, dusty old men – except for John Uskglass. He is quite another matter! The magician who tamed the Otherlanders![2] The only magician to defeat Death! The magician whom Lucifer himself was forced to treat as an equal! Now, whenever Strange compares himself to this sublime being – as he must from time to time – he sees himself for what he truly is: a plodding, earth-bound mediocrity! All his achievements – so praised up in the desolate little isle[3] – crumble to dust before him! That will bring on as fine a bout of despair as you could wish to see. *This is to be mortal, And seek the things beyond mortality.*" Lord Byron paused for a moment, as if committing the last remark to memory in case he should want to put it in a poem. "I myself was touched with something of the same melancholia when I was in the Swiss mountains in September. I wandered about, hearing avalanches every five minutes – as if God was bent upon my destruction! I was full of regrets and immortal longings.

[2] A somewhat poetical name for fairies.
[3] Lord Byron is speaking of Great Britain.

Several times I was sorely tempted to blow my brains out – and I would have done it too, but for the recollection of the pleasure it would give my mother-in-law."

Lord Byron might shoot himself any day of the week for all that Dr Greysteel cared. But Strange was another matter. "You think him capable of self-destruction?" he asked, anxiously.

"Oh, certainly!"

"But what is to be done?"

"Done?" echoed his lordship, slightly perplexed. "Why would you want to do any thing?" Then, feeling that they had talked long enough about someone else, his lordship turned the conversation to himself. "Upon the whole I am glad that you and I have met, Dr Greysteel. I brought a physician with me from England, but I was obliged to dismiss him at Genova. Now I fear my teeth are coming loose. Look!"[4] Byron opened his mouth wide and displayed his teeth to Dr Greysteel.

Dr Greysteel gently tugged on a large, white tooth. "They seem very sound and firm to me," he said.

"Oh! Do you think so? But not for long, I fear. I grow old. I wither. I can feel it." Byron sighed. Then, struck by a more cheerful thought, he added, "You know, this crisis with Strange could not have come at a better time. I am by chance writing a poem about a magician who wrestles with the Ineffable Spirits who rule his destiny. Of course, as a model for my magician Strange is far from perfect – he lacks the true heroic nature; for that I shall be obliged to put in something of myself."

A lovely young Italian girl passed by. Byron tilted his head to a very odd angle, half-closed his eyes and composed his features to suggest that he was about to expire from chronic indigestion. Dr Greysteel could only suppose that he was treating the young woman to the Byronic profile and the Byronic expression.

[4] See Byron's letter to Augusta Leigh, October 28th, 1816.

# 57

# The Black Letters[1]

## December 1816

Santa Maria Zobenigo, Venice

*Jonathan Strange to the Reverend Henry Woodhope* Dec. 3rd, 1816.

My dear Henry,

You must prepare yourself for wonderful news. *I have seen Arabella.* I have seen her and spoken to her. Is that not glorious? Is that not the best of all possible news? You will not believe me. You will not understand it. Be assured it was not a dream. It was not drunkenness, or madness, or opium. Consider: you have only to accept that last Christmas at Clun we were half-enchanted, and all becomes believable, all becomes possible. It is ironic, is it not, that I of all people did not recognize magic when it wrapped itself about me? In my own defence I may say that it was of a quite unexpected nature and came from a

[1] Strange's later Venetian letters (in particular his letters to Henry Woodhope) have been known by this name since their publication in London in January 1817. Lawyers and magical scholars will doubtless continue to argue over whether or not the publication was legal. Certainly Strange never gave his permission and Henry Woodhope has always maintained that neither did he. Henry Woodhope also said that the published letters had been altered and added to, presumably by Henry Lascelles and Gilbert Norrell. In his *The Life of Jonathan Strange* John Segundus published what he and Woodhope claimed were the originals. It is these versions which are reprinted here.

quarter I could never have foreseen. Yet to my shame other people were quicker-witted than me. John Hyde knew that something was wrong and tried to warn me, but I did not listen to him. Even you, Henry, told me quite plainly that I was too taken up with my books, that I neglected my responsibilities and my wife. I resented your advice and on several occasions gave you a rude answer. I am sorry for it now and humbly beg your pardon. Blame me as much as you want. You cannot think me half so much at fault as I think myself. But to come to the point of all this. I need you to come here to Venice. Arabella is in a place not very far distant from here, but she cannot leave it and I cannot go there – at least [several lines expunged]. My friends here in Venice are well-meaning souls, but they plague me with questions. I have no servant and there is something here which makes it hard for me to go about the city unobserved. Of this I shall say no more. My dear, good Henry, please do not make difficulties. Come straightaway to Venice. Your reward will be Arabella safe and well and restored to us. For what other reason has God made me the Greatest Magician of the Age if not for this?
Your brother,
S

Santa Maria Zobenigo, Venice
*Jonathan Strange to the Reverend Henry Woodhope* Dec. 6th, 1816.

My dear Henry,
I have been somewhat troubled in my conscience since I wrote to you last. You know that I have never lied to you, but I confess that I have not told you enough for you to form an accurate opinion of how matters stand with Arabella at present. She is not dead but . . . [12 lines crossed out and indecipherable] . . . under the earth, within the hill which they call the *brugh*. Alive, yet not alive – not dead either – *enchanted*. It has been their habit

since time immemorial to steal away Christian men and women and make servants of them, or force them – as in this case – to take part in their dreary pastimes: their dances, their feasts, their long, empty celebrations of dust and nothingness. Among all the reproaches which I heap on my own head the bitterest by far is that I have betrayed her – she whom my first duty was to protect.

Santa Maria Zobenigo, Venice

*Jonathan Strange to the Reverend Henry Woodhope* Dec. 15th, 1816.

My dear Henry,

It grieves me to tell you that I now have better grounds for the uneasiness I told you of in my last letter.[2] I have done everything I can think of to break the bars of her black prison, but without success. There is no spell that I know of that can make the smallest dent in such ancient magic. For aught I know there is no such spell in the whole English canon. Stories of magicians freeing captives from Faerie are few and far between. I cannot now recall a single one. Somewhere in one of his books Martin Pale describes how fairies can grow tired of their human guests and expel them without warning from the *brugh*; the poor captives find themselves back home, but hundreds of years after they left it. Perhaps that is what will happen. Arabella will return to England long after you and I are dead. That thought freezes my blood. I cannot disguise from you that there is a black mood upon me. Time and I have quarrelled. All hours are midnight now. I had a clock and a watch, but I destroyed them both. I could not bear the way they mocked me. I do not

---

[2] This letter has never been found. It is probable that Strange never sent it. According to Lord Byron (letter to John Murray, Dec. 31st, 1816.) Strange would often write long letters to his friends and then destroy them. Strange confessed to Byron that he quickly became confused as to which he had and had not sent.

> sleep. I *cannot* eat. I take wine – and something else. Now at times I become a little wild. I shake and laugh and weep for a time – I cannot say *what* time; perhaps an hour, perhaps a day. But enough of that. Madness is the key. I believe I am the first English magician to understand that. Norrell was right – he said we do not need fairies to help us. He said that madmen and fairies have much in common, but I did not understand the implications then, and neither did he. Henry, you cannot conceive of how desperately I need you here. Why do you not come? Are you ill? I have received no replies to my letters, but this may mean that you are already on the road to Venice and this letter may perhaps never reach you.

"Darkness, misery and solitude!" cried the gentleman in high glee. "That is what I have inflicted upon him and that is what he must suffer for the next hundred years! Oh! How cast down he is! I have won! I have won!" He clapped his hands and his eyes glittered.

In Strange's room in the parish of Santa Maria Zobenigo three candles were burning: one upon the desk, one upon the top of the little painted cupboard and one in a wall-sconce by the door. An observer of the scene might have supposed them to be the only lights in all the world. From Strange's window nothing could be seen but night and silence. Strange, unshaven, with red-rimmed eyes and wild hair, was doing magic.

Stephen stared at him with mingled pity and horror.

"And yet he is not so solitary as I would like," remarked the gentleman, in a displeased tone. "There is someone with him."

There was indeed. A small, dark man in expensive clothes was leaning against the little painted cupboard, watching Strange with an appearance of great interest and enjoyment. From time to time he would take out a little notebook and scribble in it.

"That is Lord Byron," said Stephen.

"And who is he?"

"A very wicked gentleman, sir. A poet. He quarrelled with his wife and seduced his sister."

"Really? Perhaps I will kill him."

"Oh, do not do that, sir! True, his sins are very great, and he has been more or less driven out of England, but even so . . ."

"Oh! I do not care about his crimes against other people! I care about his crimes against *me*! He ought not to be here. Ah, Stephen, Stephen! Do not look so stricken. Why should you care what becomes of one wicked Englishman? I tell you what I will do: because of the great love I bear you, I will not kill him now. He may have another, oh!, another five years of life! But at the end of that he must die!"[3]

"Thank you, sir," said Stephen, gratefully. "You are all generosity."

Suddenly Strange raised his head and cried out, "I know you are there! You can hide from me if you wish, but it is too late! I know you are there!"

"Who are you talking to?" Byron asked him.

Strange frowned. "I am being watched. Spied upon!"

"Are you indeed? And do you know by whom?

"By a fairy and a butler!"

"A butler, eh?" said his lordship, laughing. "Well, one may say what one likes about imps and goblins, but butlers are the worst of them!"

"What?" said Strange.

The gentleman with the thistle-down hair was looking anxiously about the room. "Stephen! Can you see my little box anywhere?"

"Little box, sir?"

"Yes, yes! You know what I mean! The little box containing dear Lady Pole's finger!"

"I do not see it, sir. But surely the little box does not matter any more? Now that you have defeated the magician?"

[3] Byron died of a chill five years later in Greece.

"Oh, there it is!" cried the gentleman. "See? You had put your hand down upon the table and accidentally hidden it from my view."

Stephen moved his hand away. After a moment he said, "You do not pick it up, sir."

To this remark the gentleman made no reply. Instead, he immediately returned to abusing the magician and glorying in his own victory.

"It is not his any more!" thought Stephen, with a thrill of excitement. "He may not take it! It belongs to the magician now! Perhaps the magician can use it somehow to free Lady Pole!" Stephen watched and waited to see what the magician would do. But at the end of half an hour he was forced to admit that the signs were scarcely hopeful. Strange strode about the room, muttering magic spells to himself and looking entirely deranged; Lord Byron questioned him about what he was doing and the answers that Strange gave were wild and incomprehensible (though quite to the taste of Lord Byron). And, as for the little box, Strange never once looked at it. For all that Stephen could tell, he had forgotten all about it.

# 58

# Henry Woodhope pays a visit

## December 1816

"You have done quite right in coming to me, Mr Woodhope. I have made a careful study of Mr Strange's Venetian correspondence and, aside from the general horror of which you rightly speak, there is much in these letters which is hidden from the layman. I think I may say without vanity that, at this moment, I am the only man in England who is capable of understanding them."

It was twilight, three days before Christmas. In the library at Hanover-square the candles and lamps had not yet been lit. It was that curious time of day when the sky is bright and full of colour, but all the streets are dim and shadowy. Upon the table there was a vase of flowers, but in the fading light it appeared to be a black vase of black flowers.

Mr Norrell sat by the window with Strange's letters in his hands. Lascelles sat by the fire, regarding Henry Woodhope coolly.

"I confess to having been in a condition of some distress ever since I first received these letters," said Henry Woodhope to Mr Norrell. "I have not known whom to turn to for help. To be truthful I have no interest in magic. I have not followed the fashionable quarrels about the subject. But everyone says that you are England's greatest magician – and you were once Mr Strange's tutor. I shall be very grateful to you, sir, for any advice you are able to give me."

Mr Norrell nodded. "You must not blame Mr Strange," he said. "The magical profession is a dangerous one. There is no other which so lays a man open to the perils of vanity. Politics and Law are harmless in comparison. You should understand, Mr Woodhope, that I tried very hard to keep him with me, to guide him. But his genius – which makes us all admire him – is the very thing which leads his reason astray. These letters shew that he has strayed much further than I could ever have supposed."

"Strayed? Then you do not believe this queer tale of my sister being alive?"

"Not a word of it, sir, not a word of it. It is all his own unhappy imaginings."

"Ah!" Henry Woodhope sat silent for a moment as if he were deciding upon the relative degrees of disappointment and relief that he felt. He said, "And what of Mr Strange's curious complaint that Time has stopt? Can you make any thing of this, sir?"

Lascelles said, "We understand from our correspondents in Italy that for some weeks Mr Strange has been surrounded by Perpetual Darkness. Whether he has done this deliberately or whether it is a spell gone wrong we do not know. There is also the possibility that he has offended some Great Power and that this is the result. What is certain is that some action upon Mr Strange's part has caused a disturbance in the Natural Order of Things."

"I see," said Henry Woodhope.

Lascelles looked at him rather severely. "It is something which Mr Norrell has striven hard all his life to avoid."

"Ah," said Henry. He turned to Mr Norrell. "But what should I do, sir? Ought I to go to him as he begs me to?"

Mr Norrell sniffed. "The most important question is, I believe, how soon we may contrive to bring him back to England, where his friends may care for him and bring to a rapid end the delusions that beset him."

"Perhaps if you were to write to him, sir?"

"Ah, no. I fear my little stock of influence with Mr Strange all ran out some years ago. It was the war in Spain that did the mischief. Before he went to the Peninsula he was very content to stay with me and learn all I could teach him, but afterwards . . ." Mr Norrell sighed. "No, we must rely upon you, Mr Woodhope. You must make him come home and, since I suspect that your going to Venice could only prolong his stay in that city and persuade him that one person at least gives credit to his imaginings, then I most strongly urge you not to go."

"Well, sir, I must confess that it makes me very glad to hear you say so. I shall certainly do as you advise. If you could pass me my letters I shall trouble you no longer."

"Mr Woodhope," said Lascelles. "Do not be in such a hurry, I beg you! Our conversation is by no means concluded. Mr Norrell has answered all your questions candidly and without reservation. Now you must return the favour."

Henry Woodhope frowned and looked puzzled. "Mr Norrell has relieved me of a great deal of anxiety. If there is any way in which I can serve Mr Norrell, then, of course, I shall be very happy. But I do not quite understand . . ."

"Perhaps I do not make myself clear," said Lascelles, "I mean of course that Mr Norrell requires your help so that he may help Mr Strange. Is there any thing else you can tell us of Mr Strange's Italian tour? What was he like before he fell into this sad condition? Was he in good spirits?"

"No!" said Henry indignantly, as though he thought some insult was implied in the question. "My sister's death weighed very heavily on him! At least at first it did. At first he seemed very unhappy. But when he reached Genoa everything changed." He paused. "He writes no word of it now, but before his letters were full of praise for a young lady – one of the party he is travelling with. And I could not help suspecting that he was thinking of marrying again."

"A second marriage!" exclaimed Lascelles, "And so soon after the death of your sister? Dear me! How very shocking! How very distressing for you."

Henry nodded unhappily.

There was a little pause and then Lascelles said, "I hope he gave no sign of this fondness for the society of other ladies before? I mean when Mrs Strange was alive. It would have caused her great unhappiness."

"No! No, of course not!" cried Henry.

"I beg your pardon if I have offended you. I certainly meant no disrespect to your sister – a most charming woman. But such things are not uncommon, you know. Particularly among men of a certain stamp of mind." Lascelles reached over to the table where Strange's letters to Henry Woodhope lay. He poked at them with one finger until he found the one he wanted. "In this letter," he said, running his eye over it, "Mr Strange has written, 'Jeremy has told me that you did not do what I asked. But it is no matter. Jeremy has done it and the outcome is exactly as I imagined.'" Lascelles put down the letter and smiled pleasantly at Mr Woodhope. "What did Mr Strange ask you to do that you did not do? Who is Jeremy and what was the outcome?"

"Mr Strange . . . Mr Strange asked me to exhume my sister's coffin." Henry looked down. "Well, of course, I would not. So Strange wrote to his servant, a man called Jeremy Johns. A very arrogant fellow!"

"And Johns exhumed the body?"

"Yes. He has a friend in Clun who is a gravedigger. They did it together. I can scarcely describe my feelings when I discovered what this person had done."

"Yes, quite. But what did they discover?"

"What ought they to discover but my poor sister's corpse? However they chose to say they did not. They chose to put about a ridiculous tale."

"What did they say?"

"I do not repeat servants' tittle-tattle."

"Of course you do not. But Mr Norrell desires that you put aside this excellent principle for a moment and speak openly and candidly – as he has spoken to you."

Henry bit his lip. "They said the coffin contained a log of black wood."

"No body?" said Lascelles.

"No body," said Henry.

Lascelles looked at Mr Norrell. Mr Norrell looked down at his hands in his lap.

"But what has my sister's death to do with any thing?" asked Henry with a frown. He turned to Mr Norrell. "I understood from what you said before that there was nothing extraordinary about my sister's death. I thought you said no magic had taken place?"

"Oh! Upon the contrary!" declared Lascelles. "Certainly there was some magic taking place. There can be no doubt about that! The question is whose was it?"

"I beg your pardon?" asked Henry.

"Of course it is too deep for me!" said Lascelles. "It is a matter which only Mr Norrell can deal with."

Henry looked in confusion from one to the other.

"Who is with Strange now?" asked Lascelles. "He has servants, I suppose?"

"No. No servants of his own. He is attended, I believe, by his landlord's servants. His friends in Venice are an English family. They seem a very odd set of people, very much addicted to travelling, the females as much as the gentleman."

"Name?"

"Greystone or Greyfield. I do not remember exactly."

"And where are they from, these people called Greystone or Greyfield?"

"I do not know. I do not believe Strange ever told me. The gentleman was a ship's doctor, I believe, and his wife – who is dead – was French."

Lascelles nodded. The room was now so dim that Henry Woodhope could not see the faces of the other two men.

"You look pale and tired, Mr Woodhope," remarked Mr Lascelles. "Perhaps the London air does not agree with you?"

"I do not sleep very well. Since these letters began to arrive I have dreamt of nothing but horrors."

Lascelles nodded. "Sometimes a man may know things in his heart that he will not whisper in the open air, even to himself. You are very fond of Mr Strange, are you not?"

Henry Woodhope might perhaps be excused for looking a little puzzled at this since he had not the least idea what Lascelles was talking about, but all he said was, "Thank you for your advice, Mr Norrell. I will certainly do as you suggest and now, I wonder if I might take back my letters?"

"Ah! Well, as to that," said Lascelles, "Mr Norrell wonders if he might borrow them for a time? He believes there is still much to learn from them." Henry Woodhope looked as if he was about to protest, so Lascelles added in a somewhat reproachful tone, "He is only thinking of Mr Strange! It is all for the good of Mr Strange."

So Henry Woodhope left the letters in the possession of Mr Norrell and Lascelles.

When he was gone Lascelles said, "Our next step must be to send someone to Venice."

"Yes, indeed!" agreed Mr Norrell. "I should dearly love to know the truth of the matter."

"Ah, yes, well." Lascelles gave a short, contemptuous laugh. "*Truth . . .*"

Mr Norrell blinked his little eyes rapidly at Lascelles, but Lascelles did not explain what he meant. "I do not know who we can send," continued Mr Norrell. "Italy is a very great distance. The journey takes almost two weeks, I understand. I could not spare Childermass for half so long."

"Hmm," said Lascelles, "I was not necessarily thinking of Childermass. Indeed there are several arguments against sending

Childermass. You yourself have often suspected him of Strangite sympathies. It appears to me highly undesirable that the two of them should be alone together in a foreign country where they can plot against us. No, I know whom we can send."

The next day Lascelles's servants went out into various parts of London. Some of the places they visited were highly disreputable like the slums and rookeries of St Giles, Seven Dials and Saffron-hill; others were grand and patrician like Golden-square, St James's and Mayfair. They gathered up a strange miscellany of persons: tailors, glove-makers, hat-makers, cobblers, money-lenders (a great many of these), bailiffs and sponging-house-keepers; and they brought them all back to Lascelles's house in Bruton-street. When they were assembled in the kitchen (the master of the house having no intention of receiving such people in the drawing-room) Lascelles came down and paid each of them a sum of money on behalf of someone else. It was, he told them with a cold smile, an act of charity. After all if a man cannot be charitable at Christmas, when can he be?

Three days later, on St Stephen's Day, the Duke of Wellington appeared suddenly in London. For the past year or so his Grace had been living in Paris, where he was in charge of the Allied Army of Occupation. Indeed it would scarcely be an exaggeration to say that at present the Duke of Wellington ruled France. Now the question had arisen whether the Allied Army ought to remain in France or go to its various homes (which was what the French wanted). All that day the Duke was closeted with the Foreign Secretary, Lord Castlereagh, to discuss this important matter and in the evening he dined with the Ministers at a house in Grosvenor-square.

They had scarcely begun to eat when the conversation lapsed (a rare thing among so many politicians). The Ministers seemed to be waiting for someone to say something. The Prime Minister, Lord Liverpool, cleared his throat a little nervously and said, "We do not think you will have heard, but it is reported from Italy that Strange has gone mad."

The Duke paused for a moment with his spoon halfway to his mouth. He glanced round at them all and then continued eating his soup.

"You do not appear very much disturbed at the news," said Lord Liverpool.

His Grace dabbed at his lips with his napkin. "No," he said. "I am not."

"Will you give us your reasons?" asked Sir Walter Pole.

"Mr Strange is eccentric," said the Duke. "He might seem mad to the people around him. I dare say they are not used to magicians."

The Ministers did not appear to find this quite as convincing an argument as Wellington intended they should. They offered him examples of Strange's madness: his insistence that his wife was not dead, his curious belief that people had candles in their heads and the even odder circumstance that it was no longer possible to transport pineapples into Venice.

"The watermen who carry fruit from the mainland to the city say that the pineapples fly out of their boats as if they had been fired out of a cannon," said Lord Sidmouth, a small, dried-up-looking person. "Of course they carry other sorts of fruit as well – apples and pears and so on. None of these occasion the least disturbance, but several people have been injured by the flying pineapples. Why the magician should have taken such a dislike to this particular fruit, no one knows."

The Duke was not impressed. "None of this proves any thing. I assure you, he did much more eccentric things in the Peninsula. But if he is indeed mad, then he has some reason for being so. If you will take my advice, gentlemen, you will not worry about it."

There was a short silence while the Ministers puzzled this out.

"You mean to say he might have become mad *deliberately*?" said one in an incredulous tone.

"Nothing is more likely," said the Duke.

"But why?" asked another.

"I have not the least idea. In the Peninsula we learnt not to question him. Sooner or later it would become clear that all his incomprehensible and startling actions were part of his magic. Keep him to his task, but shew no surprize at any thing he does. That, my lords, is the way to manage a magician."

"Ah, but you have not heard all yet," said the First Lord of the Admiralty eagerly. "There is worse. It is reported that he is surrounded by Constant Darkness. The Natural Order of Things is overturned and a whole parish in the city of Venice has been plunged into Ceaseless Night!"

Lord Sidmouth declared, "Even you, your Grace, with all your partiality for this man must admit that a Shroud of Eternal Darkness does not bode well. Whatever the good this man has done for the country, we cannot pretend that a Shroud of Eternal Darkness bodes well."

Lord Liverpool sighed. "I am very sorry this has happened. One could always speak to Strange as if he were an ordinary person. I had hoped that he would interpret Norrell's actions for us. But now it seems we must first find someone to interpret Strange."

"We could ask Mr Norrell," suggested Lord Sidmouth.

"I do not think we can expect an impartial judgement from that quarter," said Sir Walter Pole.

"So what ought we to do?" asked the First Lord of the Admiralty.

"We shall send a letter to the Austrians," said the Duke of Wellington with his customary decisiveness. "A letter reminding them of the warm interest that the Prince Regent and the British Government will always feel in Mr Strange's welfare; reminding them of the great debt owed by all Europe to Mr Strange's gallantry and magicianship during the late wars. Reminding them of our great displeasure were we to learn that any harm had come to him."

"Ah!" said Lord Liverpool. "But that is where you and I differ, your Grace. It seems to me that if harm does come to Strange, it will not come from the Austrians. It is far more likely to come from Strange himself."

In the middle of January a bookseller named Titus Watkins published a book called *The Black Letters* which purported to be letters from Strange to Henry Woodhope. It was rumoured that Mr Norrell had paid all the expences of the edition. Henry Woodhope swore that he had never given his permission for the letters to be published. He also said that some of them had been changed. References to Norrell's dealings with Lady Pole had been removed and other things had been put in, many of which seemed to suggest that Strange had murdered his wife by magic.

At about the same time one of Lord Byron's friends – a man called Scrope Davies – caused a sensation when he let it be known that he intended to prosecute Mr Norrell upon Lord Byron's account for attempting to acquire Lord Byron's private correspondence by means of magic. Scrope Davies went to a lawyer in Lincoln's Inn and swore an affidavit in which he stated the following. He had recently received several letters from Byron in which his lordship referred to the Pillar of Constant Darkness which covered the Parish of Mary Sobendigo [sic] in Venice, and to the madness of Jonathan Strange. Scrope Davies had placed the letters on his dressing-table in his rooms in Jermyn-street, St James's. One evening – he thought the 7th of January – he was dressing to go to his club. He had just picked up a hairbrush when he happened to notice that the letters were skipping about like dry leaves caught in a breeze. But there was no breeze to account for the movement and at first he was puzzled. He picked up the letters and saw that the handwriting on the pages was behaving strangely too. The pen-strokes were coming unhitched from their moorings and lashing about like clothes-lines in a high wind. It suddenly came to him that the letters must be under the influence of magic spells. He was a gambler by profession and, like all successful gamblers, he was quick-witted and cool-headed. He quickly placed the letters inside a Bible, in the pages of St Mark's Gospel. He told some friends afterwards that, though he was entirely ignorant of magical theory, it had seemed to him that nothing was so likely to foil an unfriendly spell as Holy Writ. He was right; the letters remained in his possession and unaltered. It was a favourite joke afterwards in all the gentlemen's clubs that the most extraordinary aspect of the whole business was not that Mr Norrell should have tried to acquire the letters, but that Scrope Davies – a notorious rake and drunk – should possess a *Bible.*

## 59

# Leucrocuta, the Wolf of the Evening

## January 1817

On a morning in the middle of January Dr Greysteel stepped out of his street-door and stood a moment to straighten his gloves. Looking up, he happened to observe a small man who was sheltering from the wind in the doorway opposite.

All doorways in Venice are picturesque – and sometimes the people who linger in them are too. This fellow was rather small and, despite his evident poverty, he seemed to possess a strong degree of foppishness. His clothes were exceedingly worn and shabby-looking, but he had tried to improve them by shining whatever could be shone and brushing what could not. He had whitened his old, yellowing gloves with so much chalk that he had left little chalky fingerprints upon the door beside him. At first glance he appeared to be wearing the proper equipment of a fop – namely a long watch-chain, a bunch of watch-seals and a lorgnette; but a moment's further observation shewed that he had no watch-chain, only a gaudy gold ribbon which he had carefully arranged to hang from a buttonhole. Likewise his watch seals proved to be nothing of the sort; they were a bunch of tin hearts, crosses and talismans of the Virgin – the sort that Italian pedlars sell for a frank or two. But it was his lorgnette which was best of all – all fops and dandies love lorgnettes. They employ them to stare quizzically at those less fashionable than themselves. Presumably this odd little man felt naked without one and so he had hung a large kitchen spoon in its place.

Dr Greysteel took careful note of these eccentricities so that he might amuse a friend with them. Then he remembered that his only friend in the city was Strange, and Strange no longer cared about such things.

Suddenly the little man left the doorway and came up to Dr Greysteel. He put his head on one side and said in English, "You are Dr Greyfield?"

Dr Greysteel was surprized to be addressed by him and did not immediately reply.

"You are Dr Greyfield? The friend of the magician?"

"Yes," said Dr Greysteel, in a wondering tone. "But my name is Greysteel, sir, not Greyfield."

"A thousand apologies, my dear Doctor! Some stupid person has misinformed me of your name! I am quite mortified. You are, I assure you, the last person in the world to whom I should wish to give offence! My respect for the medical profession is boundless! And now you stand there in all the dignity of poultices and pulse-taking and you say to yourself, 'Who is this odd creature that dares to address me in the street, as if I were a common person?' Permit me to introduce myself! I come from London – from Mr Strange's friends who, when they heard how far his wits had become deranged, were thrown into such fits of anxiety that they took the liberty of dispatching me to come and find out how he is!"

"Hmm!" said Dr Greysteel. "Frankly I could have wished them more anxious. I first wrote to them at the beginning of December – six weeks ago, sir! Six weeks ago!"

"Oh, quite! Very shocking, is it not? They are the idlest creatures in the world! They think of nothing but their own convenience! While you remain here in Venice – the magician's one true friend!" He paused. "That is correct, is it not?" he asked in quite a different voice. "He has no friends but you?"

"Well, there is Lord Byron . . ." began Dr Greysteel.

"Byron!" exclaimed the little man. "Really? Dear me! Mad, *and* a friend of Lord Byron!" He sounded as if he did not know which was worse. "Oh! My dear Dr Greysteel. I have a thousand questions to ask you! Is there somewhere you and I can talk privately?"

Dr Greysteel's street-door was just behind them, but his distaste for the little man was growing every moment. Anxious as he was to help Strange and Strange's friends, he had no wish to invite the fellow into his house. So he muttered something about his servant being in town on an errand just now. There was a little coffee-house a few streets away; why did they not go there?

The little man was all smiling acquiescence.

They set off for the coffee-house. Their way lay by the side of a canal. The little man was upon Dr Greysteel's right hand, closest to the water. He was talking and Dr Greysteel was looking around. The doctor's eyes happened to be directed towards the canal and he saw how, without warning, a wave appeared – a single wave. This was odd enough in itself, but what followed was even more surprizing. The wave rushed towards them and slopped over the stone rim of the canal and, as it did so, it changed shape; watery fingers reached out towards the little man's foot as if they were trying to pull him in. The moment the water touched him, he leapt back with an oath, but he did not appear to notice that any thing unusual had occurred and Dr Greysteel said nothing of what he had seen.

The interior of the coffee-house was a welcome refuge from the chill, damp, January air. It was warm and smoky – a little gloomy perhaps, but the gloom was a comfortable one. The brown-painted walls and ceiling were darkened with age and tobacco smoke, but they were also made cheerful by the glitter of wine bottles, the gleam of pewter tankards, and the sparkle of highly varnished pottery and gold-framed mirrors. A damp, indolent spaniel lay on the tiles in front of stove. It shook its head and sneezed when the tip of Dr Greysteel's cane accidentally brushed its ear.

"I ought to warn you," said Dr Greysteel after the waiter had brought coffee and brandy, "that there are all sorts of rumours circulating in the town concerning Mr Strange. People say he has summoned witches and made a servant for himself out of fire. You will know not to be taken in by such nonsense, but it is as well to be prepared. You will find him sadly changed. It would be foolish to pretend otherwise. But he is still the same at heart. All his excellent qualities, all his merits are just what they always were. Of that I have no doubt."

"Indeed? But tell me, is it true he has eaten his shoes? Is it true that he has turned several people into glass and then thrown stones at them?"

"Eaten his shoes?" exclaimed Dr Greysteel. "Who told you that?"

"Oh! Several people – Mrs Kendal-Blair, Lord Pope, Sir Galahad Denehey, the Miss Underhills . . ." The little man rattled off a long list of names of English, Irish and Scottish ladies and gentlemen who were currently residing in Venice and the surrounding towns.

Dr Greysteel was astounded. Why would Strange's friends wish to consult with these people in preference to himself? "But did you not hear what I just said? This is exactly the sort of foolish nonsense I am talking about!"

The little man laughed pleasantly. "Patience! Patience, my dear Doctor! My brain is not so quick as yours. While you have been sharpening yours up with anatomy and chemistry, mine has languished in idleness." He rattled on a while about how he had never applied himself to any regular course of study and how his teachers had despaired of him and how his talents did not lie in that direction at all.

But Dr Greysteel no longer troubled to listen to him. He was thinking. It occurred to him that a while ago the little man had begged to introduce himself, yet somehow he had neglected actually to do it. Dr Greysteel was about to ask him his name when the little man asked a question that swept everything else from his mind.

"You have a daughter, do you not?"

"I beg your pardon?"

The little man, apparently thinking Dr Greysteel was deaf, repeated the question a little louder.

"Yes, I have, but . . ." said Dr Greysteel.

"And they say that you have sent her out of the city?"

"They! Who are they? What has my daughter to do with any thing?"

"Oh! Only that they say she went immediately after the magician went mad. It seems to shew that you were fearful of some harm coming to her!"

"I suppose you got this from Mrs Kendal-Blair and so forth," said Dr Greysteel. "They are nothing but a pack of fools."

"Oh, I dare say! But *did* you send your daughter away?"

Dr Greysteel said nothing.

The little man put his head first on one side and then on the other. He smiled the smile of someone who knows a secret and is preparing to astound the world with it. "You know, of course," he said, "that Strange murdered his wife?"

"What?" Dr Greysteel was silent a moment. A kind of laugh burst out of him. "I do not believe it!"

"Oh! But you must believe it," said the little man, leaning forward. His eyes glittered with excitement. "It is what everybody knows! The lady's own brother – a most respectable man – a clergyman – a Mr Woodhope – was there when the lady died and saw with his own eyes."

"What did he see?"

"All sorts of suspicious circumstances. The lady was bewitched. She was entirely enchanted and scarcely knew what she did from morning to night. And no one could explain it. It was all her husband's doing. Of course he will try to use his magic to evade punishment, but Mr Norrell, who is *devoured*, quite *devoured* with pity for the poor lady, will thwart him. Mr Norrell is determined that Strange shall be brought to justice for his crimes."

Dr Greysteel shook his head. "Nothing you say shall make me believe this slander. Strange is an honourable man!"

"Oh, quite! And yet the practice of magic has destroyed stronger minds than his. Magic in the wrong hands can lead to the annihilation of every good quality, the magnification of every bad one. He defied his master – the most patient, wise, noble, good . . ."

The little man, trailing adjectives, seemed no longer to remember what he meant to say; he was distracted by Dr Greysteel's penetrating observation of him.

Dr Greysteel sniffed. "It is a curious thing," he said slowly. "You say that you are sent by Mr Strange's friends, yet you have neglected to tell me who these friends are. It is certainly a very particular sort of friend that voices it everywhere that a man is a murderer."

The little man said nothing.

"Was it Sir Walter Pole, perhaps?"

"No," said the little man in a considering tone, "not Sir Walter."

"Mr Strange's pupils, then? I have forgot their names."

"Everybody always does. They are the most unmemorable men in the world."

"Was it them?"

"No."

"Mr Norrell?"

The little man was silent.

"What is your name?" asked Dr Greysteel.

The little man tipped his head one way and then another. But finding no way of avoiding such a direct question, he replied, "Drawlight."

"Oh, ho, ho! Here's a pretty accuser! Yes, indeed, your word will carry a great deal of weight against an honest man, against the Duke of Wellington's own magician! Christopher Drawlight! Famed throughout England as a liar, a thief and a scoundrel!"

Drawlight blushed and blinked at the doctor resentfully. "It suits you to say so!" he hissed. "Strange is a rich man and you intended to marry your daughter to him! Where is the honour in that, my dear Doctor? Where is the honour in that?"

Dr Greysteel made a sound of mixed exasperation and anger. He rose from his seat. "I shall visit every English family in the Veneto. I shall warn them not to speak to you! I am going now. I wish you no good morning! I take no leave of you!" And so saying, he flung some coins upon the table and left.

The last part of this exchange had been loud and angry. The waiters and coffee-house people looked curiously at Drawlight as he sat alone. He waited until there seemed little chance of meeting the doctor in the street and then he too left the coffee-house. As he passed along the streets, the water in the canals stirred in the oddest way. Waves appeared and followed him, occasionally making little darts and forays at his feet, slopping over the brim of the canal. But he observed none of this.

Dr Greysteel was as good as his word. He paid visits to all the British families in the city and warned them not speak to Drawlight. Drawlight did not care. He turned his attention to the servants, waiters and *gondolieri*. He knew from experience that this class of person often knew a great deal more than the masters they served; and if they did not, why!, he was able to rectify that situation by telling them something himself. Soon a great many people knew that Strange had murdered his wife; that he had tried to marry Miss Greysteel by force in the Cathedral of Saint Mark and had only been prevented by the arrival of a troop of Austrian soldiers; and that he had agreed with Lord Byron that they should hold their future wives and mistresses in common. Drawlight told any lie about Strange that occurred to him, but his powers of invention were not great and he was glad to seize upon any little half-rumour, any half-formed thought in the minds of his informers.

A *gondoliero* introduced him to a draper's wife, Marianna Segati – Byron's mistress. Through an interpreter, Drawlight paid her a world of compliments and told her scandalous secrets about great ladies in London, who, he assured her, were nowhere near as pretty as herself. She told him that, according to Lord Byron, Strange kept to his room, drinking wine and brandy, and doing magic spells. None of this was very interesting, but she did tell Drawlight the little she knew about the magician in Lord Byron's poem; how he consorted with wicked spirits and defied the gods and all humankind. Drawlight conscientiously added these fictions to his edifice of lies.

But of all the inhabitants of Venice the one Drawlight desired most as a confidant was Frank. Dr Greysteel's insults had rankled with him and he had soon determined that the best revenge would be to make a traitor of his manservant. So he sent Frank a letter inviting him to a little wine-shop in San Polo. Somewhat to his surprize, Frank agreed to come.

At the appointed hour Frank arrived. Drawlight ordered a jug of rough red wine and poured them both a tumblerful.

"Frank?" he began in a soft, wistful sort of voice. "I spoke to your master the other day – as I dare say you know. He seems a very stern sort of old fellow – not at all kind. I hope you are happy in your situation, Frank? I only mention it because a dear friend of mine, whose name is Lascelles, was saying only the other day how hard it is to find good servants in London and if only someone would help him to a good manservant he believed he would pay almost any money."

"Oh!" said Frank.

"Do you think you might like to live in London, Frank?"

Frank drew circles on the table with some spilt wine in a considering sort of way. "I might," he said.

"Because," continued Drawlight, eagerly. "if you were able to do me one or two little services, then I would be able to tell my friend of your helpfulness and I am sure he would say immediately that you were the man for him!"

"What sort of services?" asked Frank.

"Oh! Well, the first is the easiest thing in the world! Indeed the moment I tell you what it is, you will be eager to do it – even if there were no reward at all. You see, Frank, I fear something quite horrible will soon happen to your master and his daughter. The magician means them a world of harm. I tried to warn your master, but he is so stubborn he would not listen to me. I can scarcely sleep for thinking of it. I curse my stupidity that I could not explain myself better. But they trust you, Frank. You could drop a few hints – not to your master, but to his sister and daughter – about Strange's wickedness, and put them on their guard." Then Drawlight explained about the murder of Arabella Strange and the pact with Byron to hold their women in common.

Frank nodded warily.

"We need to be on our guard against the magician," said Drawlight. "The others are all taken in by his lies and deceit – your master in particular. So it is vital that you and I gather up all the intelligence we can so that we can reveal his wicked plans to the world. Now, tell me Frank, is there any thing you have observed, any word the magician let fall accidentally, any thing at all that has excited your suspicions?"

"Well, now that you mention it," said Frank, scratching his head, "There is one thing."

"Really?"

"I have not told any one else about this. Not even my master."

"Excellent!" smiled Drawlight.

"Only I cannot explain it very well. 'Tis easier to shew you."

"Oh, certainly! Where do we go?"

"Just come outside. You can see it from here."

So Frank and Drawlight went outside, and Drawlight looked

about him. It was the most commonplace Venetian scene imaginable. There was a canal just before them and on the other side a tawny-coloured church. A servant was plucking some pigeons in front of an open door; their dirty feathers were scattered in a greyish, whitish circle in front of her. Everywhere was a jumble of buildings, statues, lines of washing and flowerpots. And in the distance towered the sheer, smooth face of the Darkness.

"Well, perhaps not exactly here," admitted Frank. "The buildings get in the way. Take a few steps forward and you will see it perfectly."

Drawlight took a few steps forward. "Here?" he asked, still looking about him.

"Yes, just there," said Frank. And he kicked him into the canal.

A resounding splash.

Frank lingered a little longer to shout out some reflections upon Drawlight's moral character, calling him a lying, underhand scoundrel; a low dog; a venomous, cowardly blackguard; a snake; and a swine. These remarks certainly relieved Frank's feelings, but they were rather lost upon Drawlight who was by this time under the water and could not hear them.

The water had hit him like a blow, stinging his whole body and knocking the breath out of him. He fell through murky depths. He could not swim and was certain he would drown. But he had not been in the water more than a few seconds when he felt himself plucked up by a strong current and borne away at great speed. By some accident the action of water brought him to the surface every now and then and he was able to snatch a breath. Moment after moment he continued in a state of the most abject terror, quite unable to save himself. Once the racing water bore him up high and for an instant he saw the sunlit quayside (a place he did not recognize); he saw white, foaming water dashing at the stones, soaking people and houses; he saw people's shocked faces. He understood that he had not been driven out to sea, as he had supposed, but even then it did not occur to him that the current was in any way *unnatural*. Sometimes it carried him on vigorously in one direction; sometimes all was confusion and he was certain that his end was upon him. Then suddenly the water seemed to grow tired of him; the motion ceased upon the instant and he was thrown up on to some stone steps. He was vaguely aware of cold air and buildings around him.

He drew in great, shuddering, body-racking breaths of air and, just as it became easier to breathe, he vomited up quantities of cold salt water. Then for a long time he simply lay there with his eyes closed, as a man might lie upon a lover's breast. He had no thought of any thing at all. If any desires remained in him, then they were simply to lie there for ever. Much later he became aware, firstly, that the stones were probably very dirty and, secondly, that he was fearfully cold. He began to wonder why it was so quiet and why no one came to help him.

He sat up and opened his eyes.

Darkness was all around him. Was he in a tunnel? A cellar? Under the earth! Any of these would have been quite horrible since he had not the least idea how he had got there or how he was going to get out again. But then he felt a thin, chill wind upon his cheek; he looked up and saw the white, winter stars. Night!

"No, no, no!" he pleaded. He shrank back against the stones of the quay, whimpering.

The buildings were dark and utterly silent. The only live, bright things were the stars. Their constellations looked to Drawlight like gigantic, glittering letters – letters in an unknown alphabet. For all he knew the magician had formed the stars into these letters and used them to write a spell against him. All that could be seen in any direction was black Night, stars and silence. There was no light in any of the houses and, if what Drawlight had been told was true, there were no people in any of the houses. Unless, of course, the magician was there.

With great reluctance he stood up and looked around. Nearby was a little bridge. On the other side of the bridge an alley disappeared between the high walls of dark houses. He could go that way or he could chuse the pavement by the side of the canal. It was frosted with starlight and looked particularly eerie and exposed. He chose the alley and darkness.

He crossed the bridge and passed between the houses. Almost immediately the alley opened out into a square. Several other alleys led away from the square. Which way should he go? He thought of all the black shadows he would have to pass, all the silent doorways. Suppose he never got out! He felt sick and faint with fear.

There was a church in the square. Even by starlight its façade was a monstrous thing. It bulged with pillars and bristled with statues. Angels with outspread wings held trumpets to their lips; a shadowy figure held out its arms beneath a stone canopy; blind faces gazed down at Drawlight from dark arches.

"How do I know the magician is not there?" he thought. He began to examine each black figure in turn to see if it was Jonathan Strange. Once he had begun, it was difficult to stop; he fancied that if he looked away for a moment one of the figures would move. He had almost persuaded himself that it was safe to walk away from the church when something caught his eye – the merest possible irregularity in the deep blackness of the doorway. He looked closer. There was something – or someone – lying on the steps. A man. He lay stretched out upon the stones as if in a swoon, face down, with his arm thrown over his head.

For several moments – oh! but it seemed like an eternity! – Drawlight waited to see what would happen.

Nothing happened.

Then it came to him in an instant: the magician was dead! Perhaps in his madness he had killed himself! The sense of joy and relief was overwhelming. In his excitement he laughed out loud – an extraordinary sound in all the silence. The dark figure in the

dark doorway did not stir. He drew closer until he was leaning over the figure. There was no sound of breathing. He wished that he had a stick to poke it.

Without warning, the figure turned over.

Drawlight gave a little yelp of fright.

Silence. Then, "I know you!" whispered Strange.

Drawlight tried to laugh. He had always employed laughter as a means to placate his victims. Laughter was a soothing thing, was it not? All friends together? But all that came out of his mouth was a queer braying sound.

Strange stood up and took a few steps towards Drawlight. Drawlight backed away. In the starlight Drawlight could see the magician more clearly. He could begin to trace the features of the man he had known. Strange's feet were bare. His coat and shirt hung open and he had clearly not shaved in days.

"I know you," whispered Strange again. "You are . . . You are . . ." He moved his hands through the empty air as if tracing magical symbols. "You are a Leucrocuta!"

"A Loo . . . ?" echoed Drawlight.

"You are the Wolf of the Evening! You prey upon men and women! Your father was a hyena and your mother a lioness! You have the body of a lion; your hooves are cloven. You cannot look behind you. You have one long tooth and no gums. Yet you can take human shape and lure men to you with a human voice!"

"No, no!" pleaded Drawlight. He wanted to say more; he wanted to say that he was none of those things, that Strange was quite mistaken, but his mouth was too dry and weak from terror; it was no longer able to form the words.

"And now," said Strange calmly, "I shall return you to your proper form!" He raised his hands. "Abracadabra!" he cried.

Drawlight fell to the ground, screaming over and over again; and Strange burst into such peals of laughter – eerie, mad laughter – that he bent double and staggered about the square.

Eventually the fear of one man and the hilarity of the other subsided; Drawlight realized that he had *not* been transformed into the horrible, nightmare creature; and Strange grew calmer, almost severe.

"Leucrocuta," he whispered, "stand up."

Still whimpering, Drawlight got to his feet.

"Leucrocuta, why did you come here? No, wait! I know this." Strange snapped his fingers. "I brought you here. Leucrocuta, tell me: why do you spy on me? What have I ever done that is secret? Why did you not come here and ask me? I would have told you everything!"

"They made me do it. Lascelles and Norrell. Lascelles paid my debts so I could leave the King's Bench.[1] I have always been your friend." Drawlight faltered slightly; it seemed unlikely that even a madman would believe this.

Strange raised his head, as if he gave Drawlight a defiant look, but in the Darkness Drawlight could not see his expression. "I have been mad, Leucrocuta!" he hissed. "Did they tell you that? Well, it is true. I have been mad and I will be so again. But since you came to this city I have refrained from . . . I have refrained from certain spells, so that when I saw you I would be in my right mind. My old mind. So that I would know you, and I would know what I meant to say to you. I have learnt many things in the Darkness, Leucrocuta, and one of them is this: I cannot do this alone. I have brought you here to help me."

"Have you? I am glad! I will do any thing! Thank you! Thank you!" But as he spoke Drawlight wondered how long Strange meant to keep him there; the thought turned his heart to water.

"What is . . . What is . . ." Strange appeared to be having difficulty catching hold of his thoughts. He trawled his hands through the air. "What is the name of Pole's wife?"

"Lady Pole?"

"Yes, but I mean . . . her other names?"

---

[1] The prison where Drawlight was imprisoned for debt in November 1814.

"Emma Wintertowne?"

"Yes, that is it. Emma Wintertowne. Where is she? Now?"

"They have taken her to a madhouse in Yorkshire. It is supposed to be a great secret, but I found it out. I knew a man in the King's Bench whose son's sweetheart is a mantua-maker and she knew all about it because she was employed to make Lady Pole's Yorkshire clothes – it is very cold in Yorkshire. They have taken her to a place called Star-something – Lady Pole I mean, not the mantua-maker. Stare-something. Wait! I will tell you! I know this, I swear! Starecross Hall in Yorkshire."

"Starecross? I know that name."

"Yes, yes, you do! Because the tenant is a friend of yours. He was once a magician in Newcastle or York or one of those northern places – only I do not know his name. It seems that Mr Norrell did him an unkindness once – or maybe twice. So when Lady Pole became mad, Childermass thought to mend matters a little by recommending him as a madhouse-keeper to Sir Walter."

There was a silence. Drawlight wondered how much Strange had understood. Then Strange said, "Emma Wintertowne is not mad. She appears mad. But that is Norrell's fault. He summoned a fairy to raise her from the dead and in exchange he gave the fairy all sorts of rights over her. This same fairy threatened the liberty of the King of England and has enchanted at least two more of His Majesty's subjects, one of them my wife!" He paused. "Your first task, Leucrocuta, is to tell John Childermass what I have just told you and to deliver this to him."

Strange took something out of a pocket of his coat and handed it to Drawlight. It appeared to be a small box like a snuff box, except it was a little longer and narrower than snuff boxes usually are. Drawlight took it and put it in his own pocket.

Strange gave a long sigh. The effort of speaking coherently seemed to exhaust him. "Your second task is . . . Your second task is to take a message to all the magicians in England. Do you understand me?"

"Oh, yes! But . . ."

"But what?"

"But there is only one."

"What?"

"There is only one magician, sir. Now that you are here, only one magician remains in England."

Strange seemed to consider this for a moment. "My pupils," he said. "My pupils are magicians. All the men and women who ever wanted to be Norrell's pupils are magicians. Childermass is another. Segundus another. Honeyfoot. The subscribers to the magical journals. The members of the old societies. England is full of magicians. Hundreds! Thousands perhaps! Norrell refused them. Norrell denied them. Norrell silenced them. But they are magicians nonetheless. Tell them this." He passed his hand across his forehead and breathed hard for a moment. "Tree speaks to stone; stone speaks to water. It is not so hard as we have supposed. Tell them to read what is written in the sky. Tell them to ask the rain! All of John Uskglass's old alliances are still in place. I am sending messengers to remind the stones and the sky and the rain of their ancient promises. Tell them . . ." But again Strange could not find the words he wanted. He drew something in the air with a gesture. "I cannot explain it," he said. "Leucrocuta, do you understand?"

"Yes. Oh, yes!" said Drawlight, though he had not the least idea what Strange was talking about.

"Good. Now repeat to me the messages I have given you. Tell them back to me."

Drawlight did so. Long years of collecting and repeating malicious gossip about his acquaintance had made him adept at remembering names and facts. He had the first message perfectly, but the second had descended to a few garbled sentences about magicians standing in the rain, looking at stones.

"I will shew you," said Strange, "and then you will understand. Leucrocuta, if you perform these three tasks, I shall take no revenge on you. I shall not harm you. Deliver these three messages and you may return to your night-hunts, to your devouring of men and women."

"Thank you! Thank you!" breathed Drawlight, gratefully, until a horrible realization gripped him. "Three! But, sir, you only gave me two!"

"Three messages, Leucrocuta," said Strange, wearily. "You must deliver three messages."

"Yes, but you have not told me what the third is!"

Strange made no reply. He turned away, muttering to himself.

In spite of all his terror, Drawlight had a great desire to get hold of the magician and shake him. He might have done it too, if he thought it would do any good. Tears of self-pity began to trickle down his face. Now Strange would kill him for not performing the third task and it was not his fault.

"Leucrocuta," said Strange, suddenly returning. "Bring me a drink of water!"

Drawlight looked around. In the middle of the square there was a well. He went over to it and found a horrible old iron cup attached to the stones by a length of rusting chain. He pushed aside the well-cover, drew up a pail of water and dipped the cup into the water. He hated touching it. Curiously, after everything that had happened to him that day it was the iron cup he hated the most. All of his life he had loved beautiful things, but now everything that surrounded him was horrible. It was the magicians' fault. How he hated them!

"Sir? Lord Magician?" he called out. "You will have to come here to drink." He shewed the iron chain by way of an explanation.

Strange came forward, but he did not take the proffered cup. Instead he took a tiny phial out of his pocket and handed it to Drawlight. "Put six drops in the water," he said.

Drawlight took out the stopper. His hand was trembling so

much that he feared he would pour the whole thing on the ground. Strange did not appear to notice; Drawlight shook in some drops.

Strange took the cup and drank the water down. The cup fell from his hand. Drawlight was aware – he did not know how exactly – that Strange was changed. Against the starry sky the black shape of his figure sagged and his head drooped. Drawlight wondered if he were drunk. But how could a few drops of any thing make a man drunk? Besides he did not smell of strong liquor; he smelt like a man who had not washed himself or his linen for some weeks; and there was another smell too – one that had not been there a minute ago – a smell like old age and half a hundred cats.

Drawlight had the strangest feeling. It was something he had felt before when magic was about to happen. Invisible doors seemed to be opening all around him; winds blew on him from far away, bringing scents of woods, moors and bogs. Images flew unbidden into his mind. The houses around him were no longer empty. He could see inside them as if the walls had been removed. Each dark room contained – not a person exactly – a Being, an Ancient Spirit. One contained a Fire; another a Stone; yet another a Shower of Rain; yet another a Flock of Birds; yet another a Hillside; yet another a Small Creature with Dark and Fiery Thoughts; and on and on.

"What are they?" he whispered, in amazement. He realized that all the hairs on his head were standing on end as if he had been electrified. Then a new, different sensation took him: it was a sensation not unlike falling, and yet he remained standing. It was as if his mind had fallen down.

*He thought he stood upon an English hillside. Rain was falling; it twisted in the air like grey ghosts. Rain fell upon him and he grew thin as rain. Rain washed away thought, washed away memory, all the good and the bad. He no longer knew his name. Everything was washed away like mud from a stone. Rain filled him up with thoughts and memories of its own. Silver lines of water covered the hillside, like intricate lace, like the veins of an arm.*

*Forgetting that he was, or ever had been, a man, he became the lines of water. He fell into the earth with the rain.*

*He thought he lay beneath the earth, beneath England. Long ages passed; cold and rain seeped through him; stones shifted within him. In the Silence and the Dark he grew vast. He became the earth; he became England. A star looked down on him and spoke to him. A stone asked him a question and he answered it in its own language. A river curled at his side; hills budded beneath his fingers. He opened his mouth and breathed out spring . . .*

*He thought he was pressed into a thicket in a dark wood in winter. The trees went on for ever, dark pillars separated by thin, white slices of winter light. He looked down. Young saplings pierced him through and through; they grew up through his body, through his feet and hands. His eye-lids would no longer close because twigs had grown up through them. Insects scuttled in and out of his ears; spiders built nests and webs in his mouth. He realized he had been entwined in the wood for years and years. He knew the wood and the wood knew him. There was no saying any longer what was wood and what was man.*

*All was silent. Snow fell. He screamed . . .*

Blackness.

Like rising up from beneath dark waters, Drawlight came to himself. Who it was that released him – whether Strange, or the wood, or England itself – he did not know, but he felt its contempt as it cast him back into his own mind. The Ancient Spirits withdrew from him. His thoughts and sensations shrank to those of a Man. He was dizzy and reeling from the memory of what he had endured. He examined his hands and rubbed the places on his body where the trees had pierced him. They seemed whole enough; oh, but they hurt! He whimpered and looked around for Strange.

The magician was a little way off, crouching by a wall, muttering magic to himself. He struck the wall once; the stones bulged, changed shape, became a raven; the raven opened its wings and, with a loud caw, flew up towards the night sky. He struck the wall again: another raven emerged from the wall and flew away. Then another and another, and on and on, thick and fast they came until all the stars above were blotted out by black wings.

Strange raised his hand to strike again . . .

"Lord Magician," gasped Drawlight. "You have not told me what the third message is."

Strange looked round. Without warning he seized Drawlight's coat and pulled him close. Drawlight could feel Strange's stinking breath on his face and for the first time he could see his face. Starlight shone on fierce, wild eyes, from which all humanity and reason had fled.

"Tell Norrell I am coming!" hissed Strange. "Now, go!"

Drawlight did not need to be told twice. He sped away through the darkness. Ravens seemed to pursue him. He could not see them, but he heard the beating of their wings and felt the currents in the air that those wings created. Halfway across a bridge he tumbled without warning into dazzling light. Instantly he was surrounded by the sound of birdsong and of people talking. Men and women were walking and talking and going about their everyday pursuits. Here was no terrible magic – only the everyday world – the wonderful, beautiful everyday world.

Drawlight's clothes were still drenched in sea-water and the weather was cruelly cold. He was in a part of the city he did not recognize. No one offered to help him and for a long time he walked about, lost and exhausted. Eventually he happened upon a square he knew and was able to make his way back to the little tavern where he rented a room. By the time he reached it, he was weak and shivering. He undressed and rinsed the salt from his body as best he could. Then he lay down on his little bed.

For the next two days he lay in a fever. His dreams were unspeakable things, filled with Darkness, Magic and the Long, Cold Ages of the Earth. And all the time he slept he was filled with dread lest he wake to find himself under the earth or crucified by a winter wood.

By the middle of the third day he was recovered enough to get up and go to the harbour. There he found an English ship bound for Portsmouth. He shewed the captain the letters and papers Lascelles had given him, promising a large fee to the ship that bore him back to England and signed by two of the most famous bankers in Europe.

By the fifth day he was on a ship bound for England.

A thin, cold mist lay upon London, mimicking – or so it seemed – the thin, cold character of Stephen's existence. Lately his enchantment weighed upon him more heavily than ever. Joy, affection and peace were all strangers to him now. The only emotions that pierced the clouds of magic around his heart were of the bitterest sort – anger, resentment and frustration. The division and estrangement between him and his English friends grew ever deeper. The gentleman might be a fiend, but when he spoke of the pride and self-importance of Englishmen, Stephen found it hard to deny the justice of what he said. Even Lost-hope, dreary as it was, was sometimes a welcome refuge from English arrogance and English malice; there at least Stephen had never needed to apologize for being what he was; there he had only ever been treated as an honoured guest.

On this particular winter's day Stephen was in Sir Walter Pole's stables in the Harley-street mews. Sir Walter had recently purchased a pair of very fine greyhounds, much to the delight of his male servants, who idled away a large part of every day in visiting the dogs and admiring them and talking with varying degrees of knowledge and understanding of their likely prowess in the field. Stephen knew he ought to check this bad habit, but he found he did not really care enough to do it. Today when Robert, the footman, had invited him to come and see the dogs, Stephen, far from scolding him, had put on his hat and coat and gone with him.

Now he watched Robert and the grooms fussing over the dogs. He felt as if he was on the other side of a thick and dirty pane of glass.

Suddenly each man straightened himself and filed out of the stables. Stephen shivered. Experience had taught him that such unnatural behaviour invariably announced the arrival of the gentleman with the thistle-down hair.

Now here he was, lighting up the cramped, dark stables with the brilliance of his silver hair, and the glitter of his blue eyes, and the brightness of his green coat; full of loud talk and laughter; never doubting for a moment that Stephen was as delighted to see him as he was to see Stephen. He was as pleased with the dogs as the servants had been, and called on Stephen to admire them with him. He spoke to them in his own language and the dogs leapt up and barked joyously, seeming more enamoured of him than any one they had ever seen before.

The gentleman said, "I am reminded of an occasion in 1413 when I came south to visit the new King of Southern England. The King, a gracious and valiant person, introduced me to his court, telling them of my many marvellous accomplishments, extensive kingdoms, chivalrous character etc., etc. However one of his noblemen chose not to attend to this instructive and elevating speech. Instead he and his followers stood gossiping and laughing together. I was – as you may imagine – much offended by this treatment and determined to teach them better manners! The next day these wicked men were hunting hares near Hatfield Forest. Coming upon them all unawares, I had the happy notion of turning the men into hares and the hares into men. First the hounds tore their masters to pieces, and then the hares – now in the shape of men – found themselves able to inflict a terrible revenge upon the hounds who had chased and harried them." The gentleman paused to receive Stephen's praises for this feat, but before Stephen could utter a word, the gentleman exclaimed, "Oh! Did you feel that?"

"Feel what, sir?" asked Stephen.

"All the doors shook!"

Stephen glanced at the stable doors.

"No, not those doors!" said the gentleman. "I mean the doors between England and everywhere else! Someone is trying to open them. Someone spoke to the Sky and it was not me! Someone is giving instructions to the Stones and Rivers and it is not me! Who is doing that? Who is it? Come!"

The gentleman seized Stephen's arm and they seemed to rise up in the air, as if they were suddenly stood upon a mountain or a very high tower. Harley-street mews disappeared and a new scene presented itself to Stephen's eyes – and then another, and then another. Here was a port with a crowd of masts as thick as a forest – it seemed to fly away beneath their feet and was immediately replaced by a grey, winter sea and ships in full sail bending to the wind – next came a city with spires and splendid bridges. Curiously there was scarcely any sensation of movement. It felt more as if the world was flying towards Stephen and the gentleman, while they remained still. Now came snow-covered mountains with tiny people toiling up them – next a glassy lake with dark peaks all around it – then a level country with tiny towns and rivers spread across it like a child's toy.

There was something ahead of them. At first it looked like a black line that cut the sky in half. But as they drew nearer, it became a Black Pillar that reached up from the earth and had no end.

Stephen and the gentleman came to rest high above Venice (as to what they might be resting *upon*, Stephen was determined not to consider). The sun was setting and the streets and buildings beneath them were dark, but the sea and sky were full of light in which shades of rose, milky-blue, topaz and pearl were all blended harmoniously together. The city seemed to float in a radiant void.

For the most part the Black Pillar was as smooth as obsidian, but, just above the level of the house-roofs, twists and spirals of darkness were billowing out from it and drifting away through the air. What they could be, Stephen could not imagine.

"Is it smoke, sir? Is the tower on fire?" asked Stephen.

The gentleman did not reply, but as they drew closer Stephen saw that it was not smoke. A dark multitude was flying out of the Tower. They were ravens. Thousands upon thousands of ravens. They were leaving Venice and flying back in the direction Stephen and the gentleman had come.

One flock wheeled towards them. The air was suddenly tumultuous with the beating of a thousand wings, and loud with a thrumming, drumming noise. Clouds of dust and grit flew into Stephen's eyes, nose and throat. He bent low and cupped his hand over his nose to shut out the stench.

When they were gone, he asked in amazement, "What are they, sir?"

"Creatures the magician has made," said the gentleman. "He is sending them back to England with instructions for the Sky and the Earth and the Rivers and the Hills. He is calling up all the King's old allies. Soon they will attend to English magicians, rather than to me!" He gave a great howl of mingled anger and despair. "I have punished him in ways that I never punished my enemies before! Yet still he works against me! Why does he not resign himself to his fate? Why does he not despair?"

"I never heard that he lacked courage, sir," said Stephen. "By all accounts he did many brave things in the Peninsula."

"Courage? What are you talking about? This is not courage! This is malice, pure and simple! We have been negligent, Stephen! We have let the English magicians get the advantage of us. We must find a way to defeat them! We must redouble our efforts to make you King!"

# 60

# Tempest and lies

## February 1817

Aunt Greysteel had rented a house in Padua within sight of the fruit market. It was very convenient for everywhere and only eighty sechinis a quarter (which comes to about 38 guineas). Aunt Greysteel was very well pleased with her bargain. But it sometimes happens that when one acts quickly and with great resolve, all the indecisiveness and doubt comes afterwards, when it is too late. So it was in this case: Aunt Greysteel and Flora had not been living in the house a week, when Aunt Greysteel began to find fault with it and began to wonder if, in fact, she ought to have taken it at all. Although ancient and pretty, its gothic windows were rather small and several of them were fenced about with stone balconies; in other words it was inclined to be dark. This would never have been a problem before, but just at present Flora's spirits required support, and (thought Aunt Greysteel) gloom and shadows – be they ever so picturesque – might not in fact be the best thing for her. There were moreover some stone ladies who stood about the courtyard and who had, in the course of the years, acquired veils and cloaks of ivy. It was no exaggeration to say that these ladies were in imminent danger of disappearing altogether and every time Aunt Greysteel's eye fell upon them, she was put in mind of Jonathan Strange's poor wife, who had died so young and so mysteriously, and whose unhappy fate seemed to have driven her husband mad. Aunt Greysteel hoped that no such melancholy notions occurred to Flora.

But the bargain had been made and the house had been taken, so Aunt Greysteel set about making it as cheerful and bright as she could. She had never squandered candles or lamp oil in her life, but in her endeavour to raise Flora's spirits she put all questions of expence aside. There was a particularly gloomy spot on the stairs, where a step turned in an odd way that no one could possibly have predicted, and lest any one should tumble down and break their neck, Aunt Greysteel insisted upon a lamp being placed upon a shelf just above the step. The lamp burnt day and night and was a continual affront to Bonifazia, the elderly Italian maid who came with the house and who was an even more economical person than Aunt Greysteel herself.

Bonifazia was an excellent servant, but much inclined to criticism and long explanations of why the instructions she had just been given were wrong or impossible to carry out. She was aided in her work by a slow, put-upon sort of young man called Minichello, who greeted any order with a low, grumbling murmur of dialect words, quite impossible to comprehend. Bonifazia treated Minichello with such familiar contempt that Aunt Greysteel supposed they must be related, though she had yet to obtain any precise information upon this point.

So what with the arrangements for the house, the daily battles with Bonifazia and all the discoveries, pleasant or otherwise, attendant upon a sojourn in a new town, Aunt Greysteel's days were full of interesting occupation; but her chief and most sacred duty at this time was to try and find amusement for Flora. Flora had fallen into habits of quiet and solitude. If her aunt spoke to her she answered cheerfully enough, but few indeed were the conversations that she began. In Venice Flora had been the chief instigator of all their pleasures; now she simply fell in with whatever projects of exploration Aunt Greysteel proposed. She preferred those occupations that require no companion. She walked alone, read alone, sat alone in the sitting-room or in the ray of faint sunshine which sometimes penetrated the little courtyard at about one o'clock. She was less open-hearted and confiding than before; it was as if someone – not necessarily Jonathan Strange – had disappointed her and she was determined to be more independent in future.

In the first week in February there was a great storm in Padua. It happened at about the middle of the day. The storm came very suddenly out of the east (from the direction of Venice and the sea). The old men who frequented the town's coffee-houses said that there had been no sign of it moments before. But other people were not much inclined to take any notice of this; after all it was winter and storms must be expected.

First a great wind blew through the town. It was no respecter of doors or windows, this wind. It seemed to find out chinks that no one knew existed and it blew almost as fiercely within the houses as without. Aunt Greysteel and Flora were together in a little sitting-room on the first floor. The window-panes began to rattle and some crystals that hung from a chandelier began to jingle. Then the pages of a letter that Aunt Greysteel was writing escaped from beneath her hand and went flying about the room. Outside the window, the skies darkened and it became as black as night; sheets of blinding rain began to descend.

Bonifazia and Minichello entered the sitting-room. They came under the pretext of finding out Aunt Greysteel's wishes concerning the storm, but in truth Bonifazia wanted to join with Aunt Greysteel in exclamations of astonishment at the violence of the wind and rain (and a fine duet they made of it too, albeit in different languages). Minichello came presumably because Bonifazia did; he regarded the storm gloomily, as if he suspected it of having been arranged on purpose to make work for him.

Aunt Greysteel, Bonifazia and Minichello were all at the window and saw how the first stroke of lightning turned the whole familiar scene into something quite Gothic and disturbing, full of pallid, unearthly glare and unexpected shadows. This was followed by a crack of thunder that shook the whole room. Bonifazia murmured appeals to the Virgin and several saints. Aunt Greysteel, who was equally alarmed, might well have been glad of the same refuge, but as a member of the communion of the Church of England, she could only exclaim, "Dear me!" and, "Upon my word!" and "Lord bless me!" – none of which gave her much comfort.

"Flora, my love," she called out in a voice that quavered slightly, "I hope you are not frightened. It is a very horrid storm."

Flora came to the window and took her aunt's hand and told her that it was sure to be over very soon. Another stroke of lightning illuminated the town. Flora dropped her aunt's hand, undid the window-fastening and stepped eagerly out on to the balcony.

"Flora!" exclaimed Aunt Greysteel.

She was leaning into the howling darkness with both hands upon the balustrade, quite oblivious of the rain that soaked her gown or of the wind that pulled at her hair.

"My love! Flora! Flora! Come out of the rain!"

Flora turned and said something to her aunt, but what it was they could not hear.

Minichello followed her on to the balcony and, with a surprizing delicacy (though without relinquishing for a moment his native gloominess), he managed to herd her inside again, using his large, flat hands to guide her, in the same way shepherds use hurdles to direct sheep.

"Can you not see?" exclaimed Flora. "There is someone there! There, at the corner! Can you tell who it is? I thought . . ." She fell silent abruptly and whatever it was that she thought, she did not say.

"Well, my love, I hope you are mistaken. I pity any one who is in the street at this moment. I hope they will find some shelter as soon as they can. Oh, Flora! How wet you are!"

Bonifazia fetched towels and then she and Aunt Greysteel immediately set about drying Flora's gown, turning her round and round between them, and sometimes trying to give her a turn in contrary directions. At the same time both were giving Minichello urgent instructions, Aunt Greysteel in stumbling, yet insistent Italian, and Bonifazia in rapid Veneto dialect. The instructions, like the turns, may well have been at odds with each other, because Minichello did nothing, except regard them with a baleful expression.

Flora gazed over the bowed heads of the two women into the street. Another stroke of lightning. She stiffened, as if she had been electrified, and the next moment she wriggled out of the clutches of aunt and maid, and ran out of the room.

They had no time to wonder where she was going. The next half hour was one of titanic domestic struggle: of Minichello trying to close shutters in the teeth of the storm; of Bonifazia stumbling about in the dark, looking for candles; of Aunt Greysteel discovering that the Italian word she had been using to mean "shutter" actually meant "parchment". Each of them in turn lost his or her temper. Nor did Aunt Greysteel feel that the situation was much improved when all the bells in the town began to ring at once, in accordance with the belief that bells (being blessed objects) can dispel storms and thunder (which are clearly works of the Devil).

At last the house was secured – or very nearly. Aunt Greysteel left Bonifazia and Minichello to complete the work and, forgetting that she had seen Flora leave the sitting-room, she returned thither with a candle for her niece. Flora was not there, but Aunt Greysteel observed that Minichello still had not closed the shutters in that room.

She mounted the stairs to Flora's bed-chamber: Flora was not there either. Nor was she in the little dining-parlour, nor in Aunt Greysteel's own bed-chamber, nor in the other, smaller sitting-room which they sometimes used after dinner. The kitchen, the vestibule and the gardener's room were tried next; she was not in any of those places.

Aunt Greysteel began to be seriously frightened. A cruel little voice whispered in her ear that whatever mysterious fate had befallen Jonathan Strange's wife, it had begun when she had disappeared very unexpectedly in bad weather.

"But that was snow, not rain," she told herself. As she went about the house, looking for Flora, she kept repeating to herself, "Snow, not rain. Snow, not rain." Then she thought, "Perhaps she was in the sitting-room all along. It was so dark and she is so quiet, I may well not have perceived her."

She returned to the room. Another stroke of lightning gave it an unnatural aspect. The walls became white and ghastly; the furniture and other objects became grey, as if they had all been turned to stone. With a horrible jolt, Aunt Greysteel realized that there was indeed a second person in the room – a woman, *but not Flora* – a woman in a dark, old-fashioned gown, standing with a candle in a candlestick, looking at her – a woman whose face was entirely in shadow, whose features could not be seen.

Aunt Greysteel grew cold all over.

There was a crack of thunder: then pitch-black darkness, except for the two candle flames. But somehow the unknown woman's candle seemed to illuminate nothing at all. Queerer still the room seemed to have grown larger in some mysterious way; the woman and her candle were strangely distant from Aunt Greysteel.

Aunt Greysteel cried out, "Who is there?"

No one answered.

"Of course," she thought, "she is Italian. I must ask her again in Italian. Perhaps she has wandered into the wrong house in the confusion of the storm." But try as she might, she could not at that moment think of a single Italian word.

Another flash of lightning. There was the woman, standing just as she had been before, facing Aunt Greysteel. "It is the ghost of Jonathan Strange's wife!" she thought. She took a step forward, and so did the unknown woman. Suddenly realization and relief came upon her in equal measures; "It is a mirror! Oh! How foolish! How foolish! To be afraid of my own reflection!" She was so relieved she almost laughed out loud, but then she paused; it had not been foolish to be frightened, not foolish at all; *there had been no mirror in that corner until now.*

The next flash of lightning shewed the mirror to her. It was ugly and much too large for the room; she knew she had never seen it before in her life.

She hurried out of the room. She felt she would be able to think more clearly away from the sight of the baleful mirror. She was halfway up the stairs when some sounds that seemed to originate in Flora's bed-chamber made her open the door and look inside.

There was Flora. She had lit the candles they had placed for her and was in the middle of pulling her gown over her head. The gown was sopping wet. Her petticoat and stockings were no better. Her shoes were tumbled on the floor at the side of the bed; they were quite soaked and spoilt with rain.

Flora looked at her aunt with an expression in which guilt, embarrassment, defiance and several other things more difficult of interpretation were mixed together. "Nothing! Nothing!" she cried.

This, presumably, was the answer to some question she expected her aunt to put to her, but all that Aunt Greysteel said was: "Oh, my dear! Where have you been? Whatever made you go out in such weather?"

"I . . . I went out to buy some embroidery silk."

Aunt Greysteel must have looked a good deal astonished at this, because Flora added doubtfully, "I did not think the rain would last so long."

"Well, my love, I must say I think you acted rather foolishly, but you must have been a good deal frightened! Was it that that made you cry?"

"Cry! No, no! You are mistaken, aunt. I have not been crying. It is rain, that is all."

"But you are . . ." Aunt Greysteel stopped. She had been going to say, *you are crying now*, but Flora shook her head and turned away. For some reason she had wrapped her shawl into a bundle and Aunt Greysteel could not help thinking that if she had not done that the shawl would have given her some protection from the rain and she would not now be so wet. From out of the bundle she took a little bottle half full of an amber-coloured liquid. She opened a drawer, and put it inside.

"Flora! Something very peculiar has happened. I do not know quite how to tell you, but there is a mirror . . ."

"Yes, I know," said Flora, quickly. "It belongs to me."

"Belongs to you!" Aunt Greysteel was more perplexed than ever. A pause of some moments' duration. "Where did you buy it?" she asked. It was all she could think of to say.

"I do not remember exactly. It must have been delivered just now."

"But surely no one would deliver any thing in the middle of a storm! And even if any body had been so foolish as to do such a thing, they would have knocked upon the door – and not done it in this strange, secret way."

To these very reasonable arguments Flora made no reply.

Aunt Greysteel was not sorry to let the subject drop. She was quite sick of storms and frights and unexpected mirrors. The question of *why* the mirror had appeared was now resolved and so, for the present, she put aside the question of *how* it had appeared. She was glad to fall back upon the more soothing subjects of Flora's gown and Flora's shoes and the likelihood of Flora's catching cold and the necessity for Flora drying herself immediately and putting on her dressing-gown and coming and sitting by the fire in the sitting-room and eating something hot.

When they were both in the sitting-room again, Aunt Greysteel said, "See! The storm is almost passed. It seems to be going back towards the coast. How odd! I thought that was the direction it came from. I suppose your embroidery silks were ruined by the rain along with everything else."

"Embroidery silks?" said Flora. Then, remembering, "Oh! I did not get so far as the shop. It was, as you say, a foolish undertaking."

"Well, we can go out later and get whatever you need. How sorry I am for the poor market people! Everything on the stalls will have been spoilt. Bonifazia is making your gruel, my love. I wonder if I told her to use the new milk?"

"I do not remember, aunt."

"I had better go and just mention it."

"I can go, aunt," said Flora, proposing to stand up.

But her aunt would not hear of it. Flora must remain exactly where she was, at the fire-side, with her feet upon a footstool.

It was becoming lighter by the moment. Before proceeding to the kitchen, Aunt Greysteel surveyed the mirror. It was very large and ornate; the sort of mirror, in fact, that is made on the island of Murano in the Venetian Lagoon. "I confess I am surprized at you liking this mirror, Flora. It has so many scrolls and curlicues and glass flowers. Generally you prefer simple things."

Flora sighed and said she supposed she had acquired a taste for what was sumptuous and elaborate since she had been in Italy.

"Was it expensive?" asked Aunt Greysteel. "It looks expensive."

"No. Not expensive at all."

"Well, that is something, is it not?"

Aunt Greysteel went down the stairs to the kitchen. She was feeling a good deal recovered, and felt confident that the train of shocks and alarms of which the morning seemed to have been composed was now at an end. But in this she was quite wrong.

Standing in the kitchen with Bonifazia and Minichello were two men she had never seen before. Bonifazia did not appear to have begun making Flora's gruel. She had not even fetched the oatmeal and milk out of the pantry.

The moment Bonifazia laid eyes upon Aunt Greysteel, she took her by the arm and unleashed a flood of eager dialect words upon her. She was speaking of the storm – that much was clear – and saying it was evil, but beyond that Aunt Greysteel understood very little. To her absolute astonishment it was Minichello who helped her comprehend it. In a very reasonable counterfeit of the English language he said, "The magician Engliss makes it. The magician Engliss makes the *tempesta*."

"I beg your pardon?"

With frequent interruptions from Bonifazia and the two men, Minichello informed her that in the midst of the storm several people had looked up and seen a cleft in the black clouds. But what they had seen through the cleft had astonished and terrified them; it had not been the clear azure they were expecting, but a black, midnight sky full of stars. The storm had not been natural at all; it had been contrived in order to hide the approach of Strange's Pillar of Darkness.

This news was soon known all over the town and the citizens were greatly disturbed by it. Until now the Pillar of Darkness had been a horror confined to Venice, which seemed – to the Paduans at least – a natural setting for horrors. Now it was clear that Strange had stayed in Venice by choice rather than enchantment. Any city in Italy – any city in the world might suddenly find itself visited by Eternal Darkness. This was bad enough, but for Aunt Greysteel it was much worse; to all her fear of Strange was added the unwelcome conviction that Flora had lied. She debated with herself whether it was more likely that her niece had lied because she was under the influence of a spell, or because her attachment to Strange had weakened her principles. She did not know which would be worse.

She wrote to her brother in Venice, begging him to come. In the meantime she determined to say nothing. For the rest of the day she observed Flora closely. Flora was much as usual, except that there sometimes seemed to be a tinge of penitence in her behaviour to her aunt, where no tinge ought to have been.

At one o'clock on the next day – some hours before Aunt Greysteel's letter could have reached him – Dr Greysteel arrived with Frank from Venice. They told her that it had been no secret in Venice when Strange left the parish of Santa Maria Zobenigo and went to *terrafirma*. The Pillar of Darkness had been seen from many parts of the city, moving across the face of the sea. Its surface had flickered and twists and spirals of Darkness had darted in and out, so that it appeared to be made of black flames. How Strange had contrived to cross over the water – whether he had travelled in a boat, or whether his passage had been purely magical – was not known. The storm by which he had tried to hide his approach had not been conjured up until he got to Strà, eight miles from Padua.

"I tell you, Louisa," said Dr Greysteel, "I would not exchange with him now upon any consideration. Everyone fled at his approach. From Mestre to Strà he could not have seen another living creature – nothing but silent streets and abandoned fields. Henceforth the world is an empty place to him."

A few moments before, Aunt Greysteel had been thinking of Strange with no very tender feelings, but the picture that her brother conjured up was so shocking that tears started into her eyes. "And where is he now?" she asked in a softened tone.

"He has gone back to his rooms in Santa Maria Zobenigo," said Dr Greysteel. "All is just as it was. As soon as we heard he had been in Padua, I guessed what his object was. We came as soon as we could. How is Flora?"

Flora was in the drawing-room. She had been expecting her father – indeed she seemed relieved that the interview had come at last. Dr Greysteel had scarcely got out his first question when she burst forth with her confession. It was the release of an overcharged heart. Her tears fell abundantly and she admitted that she had seen Strange. She had seen him in the street below and known that he was waiting for her and so she had run out of the house to meet him.

"I will tell you everything, I promise," she said. "But not yet. I have done nothing wrong. I mean . . ." She blushed. ". . . apart from the falsehoods I told my aunt – for which I am very sorry. But these secrets are not mine to tell."

"But why must there be secrets at all, Flora?" asked her father. "Does that not tell you that there is something wrong? People whose intentions are honourable do not have secrets. They act openly."

"Yes, I suppose . . . Oh, but that does not apply to magicians! Mr Strange has enemies – that terrible old man in London and others besides! But you must not scold me for doing wrong. I have tried so hard to do good and I believe I have! You see, there is a sort of magic which he has been practising and which is destroying him – and yesterday I persuaded him to give it up! He made me a promise to abandon it completely."

"But, Flora!" said her father, sadly. "This distresses me more than all the rest. That you should regard yourself as entitled to exact promises from him is something which requires explanation. Surely you must see that? My dear, are you engaged to him?"

"No, papa!" Another burst of tears. It took a great many caresses from her aunt to restore her to tolerable calm. When she could speak again, she said, "There is no engagement. It is true that I was attached to him once. But that is all over and done with. You must not suspect me of it! It was for friendship's sake that I asked him to promise me. And for his wife's sake. He thinks he is doing it for her, but I know that she would not want him to do magic so destructive of his health and reason – whatever the object, however desperate the circumstances! She is no longer able to guide his actions – and so it fell to me to speak on her behalf."

Dr Greysteel was silent. "Flora," he said after a minute or two, "you forget, my dear, that I have seen him often in Venice. He is in no condition to keep promises. He will not even remember what promise he has made."

"Oh! But he will! I have arranged matters so that he must!"

A fresh return of tears seemed to shew that she was not quite as free of love as she claimed. But she had said enough to make her father and aunt a little easier in their minds. They were convinced that her attachment to Jonathan Strange must come to a natural close sooner or later. As Aunt Greysteel said later that evening, Flora was not the sort of girl to spend years in longing for an impossible love; she was too rational a creature.

Now that they were all together again Dr Greysteel and Aunt Greysteel were eager to continue their travels. Aunt Greysteel wished to go to Rome to see the ancient buildings and artefacts which they had heard were so remarkable. But Flora no longer had any interest in remains or works of art. She was happiest, she said, where she was. Most of the time she would not even leave the house unless absolutely forced to it. When they proposed a walk or a visit to a church with a Renaissance altarpiece, she declined to accompany them. She would complain that it was raining or that the streets were wet – all of which was true; there was a great deal of rain in Padua that winter, but the rain had never troubled her before.

Her aunt and father were patient, though Dr Greysteel in particular thought it a little hard. He had not come to Italy to sit quietly in an apartment half the size of the rooms in his own comfortable house in Wiltshire. In private he grumbled that it was perfectly possible to read novels or embroider in Wiltshire (these were now Flora's favourite pursuits) and a good deal cheaper too, but Aunt Greysteel scolded him and made him hush. If this was the way in which Flora intended to grieve for Jonathan Strange, then they must let her.

Flora did propose one expedition, but that was of a most peculiar sort. After Dr Greysteel had been in Padua about a week she announced that she had a great desire to be upon the sea.

Did she mean a sea-voyage, they asked. There was no reason why they should not go to Rome or Naples by sea.

But she did not mean a sea-voyage. She did not wish to leave Padua. No, what she would like would be to go out in a yacht or other sort of boat. Only for an hour or two, perhaps less. But she would like to go immediately. The next day they repaired to a small fishing village.

The village had no particular advantages of situation, prospect, architecture or history – in fact it had very little to recommend it at all, other than its proximity to Padua. Dr Greysteel inquired in the little wine-shop and at the priest's house until he heard of two steady fellows who would be willing to take them out upon the water. The men had no objection to taking Dr Greysteel's money, but they were obliged to point out that there was nothing to see; there would have been nothing to see even in good weather. But it was not good weather; it was raining – hard enough to make an excursion on the water most uncomfortable, not quite hard enough to dispel the heavy, grey mist.

"Are you sure, my love, that this is what you want?" asked Aunt Greysteel. "It is a dismal spot and the boat smells very strongly of fish."

"I am quite sure, Aunt," said Flora and climbed into the boat and settled herself at one end. Her aunt and father followed her. The mystified fishermen sailed out until all that could be seen in any direction was a shifting mass of grey water confined by walls of dull, grey mist. The fishermen looked expectantly at Dr Greysteel. He, in turn, looked questioningly at Flora.

Flora took no notice of any of them. She was seated, leaning against the side of the boat in a pensive attitude. Her right arm was stretched out over the water.

"There it is again!" cried Dr Greysteel.

"There is what again?" asked Aunt Greysteel, irritably.

"That smell of cats and mustiness! A smell like the old woman's room. The old woman we visited in Cannaregio. Is there a cat on board?"

The question was absurd. Every part of the fishing-boat was visible from every other part; there was no cat.

"Is any thing the matter, my love?" asked Aunt Greysteel. There was something in Flora's posture she did not quite like. "Are you ill?"

"No, Aunt," said Flora, straightening herself and adjusting her umbrella. "I am well. We can go back now if you wish."

For a moment Aunt Greysteel saw a little bottle floating upon the waves, a little bottle with no stopper. Then it sank beneath the water and was gone for ever.

This peculiar expedition was the last time for many weeks that Flora would shew any inclination to go out. Sometimes Aunt Greysteel would try to persuade her to sit in a chair by the window so that she could see what was going on in the street. In an Italian street there is often something amusing going on. But Flora was greatly attached to a chair in a shadowy corner, beneath the eerie mirror; and she acquired a peculiar habit of comparing the picture of the room as it was contained in the mirror and the room as it really was. She might, for example, suddenly become interested in a shawl that was thrown across a chair and look at its reflection and say, "That shawl looks different in the mirror."

"Does it?" Aunt Greysteel would say, puzzled.

"Yes. It looks brown in the mirror, whereas in truth it is blue. Do not you think so?"

"Well, my dear, I am sure you are right, but it looks just the same to me."

"No," Flora would say, with a sigh, "you are right."

## 61

# Tree speaks to Stone; Stone speaks to Water

### January–February 1817

When Mr Norrell had destroyed Strange's book, public opinion in England had been very much against him and very much in favour of Strange. Comparisons were made, both publicly and privately, between the two magicians. Strange was open, courageous and energetic, whereas secrecy seemed to be the beginning and end of Mr Norrell's character. Nor was it forgotten how, when Strange was in the Peninsula in the service of his country, Norrell had bought up all the books of magic in the Duke of Roxburghe's library so that no one else could read them. But by the middle of January the newspapers were full of reports of Strange's madness, descriptions of the Black Tower and speculations concerning the magic which held him there. An Englishman called Lister had been at Mestre on the Italian coast on the day Strange had left Venice and gone to Padua. Mr Lister had witnessed the passage of the Pillar of Darkness over the sea and sent back an account to England; three weeks later accounts appeared in several London newspapers of how it had glided silently over the face of the waters. In the space of a few short months Strange had become a symbol of horror to his countrymen: a damned creature – scarcely human.

But Strange's sudden fall from grace did little to benefit Mr

Norrell. He received no new commissions from the Government and, worse yet, commissions from other sources were cancelled. In early January the Dean of St Paul's Cathedral had inquired whether Mr Norrell might be able to discover the burial place of a certain dead young woman. The young woman's brother wished to erect a new monument to all the members of his family. This entailed moving the young woman's coffin, but the Dean and Chapter were most embarrassed to discover that her burial place had been written down wrongly and they did not know where she was. Mr Norrell had assured him that it would be the easiest thing in the world to find her. As soon as the Dean informed him of the young lady's name and one or two other details he would do the magic. But the Dean did not send Mr Norrell her name. Instead an awkwardly phrased letter had arrived in which the Dean made many elaborate apologies and said how he had recently been struck by the inappropriateness of clergymen employing magicians.

Lascelles and Norrell agreed that the situation was a worrying one.

"It will be difficult to sustain the restoration of English magic if no new magic is done," said Lascelles. "At this crisis it is imperative that we bring your name and achievements continually before the public."

Lascelles wrote articles for the newspapers and he denounced Strange in all the magical journals. He also took the opportunity to review the magic that Mr Norrell had done in the past ten years and suggest improvements. He decided that he and Mr Norrell should go down to Brighton to look at the wall of spells that Mr Norrell and Jonathan Strange had cast around Britain's coast. It had occupied the greater part of Mr Norrell's time for the past two years and had cost the Government a vast sum of money.

So on a particularly icy, windy day in February they stood together at Brighton and contemplated a wide stretch of featureless grey sea.

"It is invisible," said Lascelles.

"Invisible, yes!" agreed Mr Norrell, eagerly, "But no less efficacious for that! It will protect the cliffs from erosion, people's houses from storm, livestock from being swept away and it will capsize any enemies of Britain who attempt to land."

"But could you not have placed beacons at regular intervals to remind people that the magic wall is there? Burning flames hovering mysteriously over the face of the waters? Pillars shaped out of sea-water? Something of that sort?"

"Oh!" said Mr Norrell. "To be sure! I could create the magical illusions you mention. They are not at all difficult to do, but you must understand that they would be purely ornamental. They would not strengthen the magic in any way whatsoever. They would have no practical effect."

"Their effect," said Lascelles, severely, "would be to stand as a constant reminder to every onlooker of the works of the great Mr Norrell. They would let the British people know that you are still the Defender of the Nation, eternally vigilant, watching over them while they go about their business. It would be worth ten, twenty articles in the Reviews."

"Indeed?" said Mr Norrell. He promised that in future he would always bear in mind the necessity of doing magic to excite the public imagination.

They stayed that night in the Old Ship Tavern and the following morning they returned to London. As a rule Mr Norrell detested long journeys. Though his carriage was a most superior example of the carriage-makers' art with everything in the way of iron springs and thick-padded seats, still he felt every bump and dent in the road. After half an hour or so, he would begin to suffer from pains in his back and aches in his head and queasinesses in his stomach. But upon this particular morning he scarcely gave any thought to his back or his stomach at all. From the first moment of setting off from the Old Ship he was in a curiously nervous condition, beset by unexpected ideas and half-formed fears.

Through the carriage glass he saw great numbers of large black birds – whether ravens or crows he did not know, and in his magician's heart he was sure that they meant something. Against the pale winter sky they wheeled and turned, and spread their wings like black hands; and as they did so each one became a living embodiment of the Raven-in-Flight: John Uskglass's banner. Mr Norrell asked Lascelles if he thought the birds were more numerous than usual, but Lascelles said he did not know. After the birds the next thing to haunt Mr Norrell's imagination were the wide, cold puddles that were thickly strewn across every field. As the carriage passed along the road each puddle became a silver mirror for the blank, winter sky. To a magician there is very little difference between a mirror and a door. England seemed to be wearing thin before his eyes. He felt as if he might pass through any of those mirror-doors and find himself in one of the other worlds which once bordered upon England. Worse still, he was beginning to think that other people might do it. The Sussex landscape began to look uncomfortably like the England described in the old ballad:

*This land is all too shallow*
*It is painted on the sky*
*And trembles like the wind-shook rain*
*When the Raven King passed by*[1]

For the first time in his life Mr Norrell began to feel that perhaps there was too much magic in England.

When they reached Hanover-square Mr Norrell and Lascelles went immediately to the library. Childermass was there, seated at a desk. A pile of letters lay in front of him and he was reading one of them. He looked up when Mr Norrell entered the room. "Good! You are back! Read this."

[1] See Chapter 3, footnote 1.

"Why? What is it?"

"It is from a man called Traquair. A young man in Nottinghamshire has saved a child's life by magic and Traquair was a witness to it."

"Really, Mr Childermass!" said Lascelles, with a sigh. "I thought you knew better than to trouble your master with such nonsense." He glanced at the pile of opened letters; one had a large seal displaying someone's arms. He stared at it for several moments before he realized that he knew it well and snatched it up. "Mr Norrell!" he cried. "We have a summons from Lord Liverpool!"

"At last!" exclaimed Mr Norrell. "What does he say?"

Lascelles took a moment to read the letter. "Only that he begs the favour of our attendance at Fife House upon a matter of the utmost urgency!" He thought rapidly. "It is probably the Johannites. Liverpool ought to have requested your assistance years ago to deal with the Johannites. I am glad he realizes it at last. And as for you," he said, turning upon Childermass, "are you quite mad? Or do you have some game of your own to play? You chatter on about false claims of magic, while a letter from the Prime Minister of England lies unattended on the desk!"

"Lord Liverpool can wait," said Childermass to Mr Norrell. "Believe me when I tell you that you need to know the contents of this letter!"

Lascelles gave a snort of exasperation.

Mr Norrell looked from one to the other. He was entirely at a loss. For years he had been accustomed to rely upon both of them, and their quarrels (which were becoming increasingly frequent) unnerved him completely. He might have stood there, unable to chuse between them, for some time, had not Childermass decided matters by seizing his arm and pulling him bodily into a small, panelled ante-chamber which led off the library. Childermass shut the door with a bang and leant on it.

"Listen to me. This magic happened at a grand house in Nottinghamshire. The grown-ups were talking in the drawing-room; the servants were busy and a little girl wandered off into the garden. She climbed a high wall that borders a kitchen-garden and walked along the top of it. But the wall was covered in ice and she tumbled down and fell through the roof of a hot-house. The glass broke and pierced her in many places. A servant heard her screaming. There was no surgeon nearer than ten miles away. One of the party, a young man called Joseph Abney, saved her by magic. He drew the shards of glass out of her and mended the broken bones with Martin Pale's Restoration and Rectification,[2] and he stopped the flow of blood using a spell which he claimed was Teilo's Hand."[3]

"Ridiculous!" declared Mr Norrell. "Teilo's Hand has been lost for hundreds of years and Pale's Restoration and Rectification is a very difficult procedure. This young man would have had to study for years and years . . ."

"Yes, I know – and he admits that he has hardly studied at all. He barely knew the names of the spells, let alone their execution. Yet Traquair said that he performed the spells fluidly, without hesitation. Traquair and the other people who were present spoke to him and asked him what he was doing – the girl's father was much alarmed to see Abney perform magic upon her – but, so far as they could tell, Abney did not hear them. Afterwards he was like a man coming out of a dream. All he could say was: 'Tree speaks to stone; stone speaks to water.' He seemed to think that the trees and the sky had told him what to do."

"Mystical nonsense!"

"Perhaps. And yet I do not think so. Since we came to London I have read hundreds of letters from people who think they can do magic and are mistaken. But this is different. This is true. I would

---

[2] Restoration and Rectification was a spell which reversed the effects of a recent calamity.

[3] Teilo's Hand was an ancient fairy spell which halted all sorts of things: rain, fire, wind, coursing water or blood. It presumably was named after the fairy who had first taught it to an English magician.

stake money upon it. Besides there are other letters here from people who have tried spells – and the spells have worked. But what I do not understand is . . ."

But at that moment the door against which Childermass was leaning was subject to a great rattling and shaking. A blow hit it and Childermass was thrown away from the door and against Mr Norrell. The door opened to reveal Lucas and, behind him, Davey the coachman.

"Oh!" said Lucas, somewhat surprized. "I beg your pardon, sir. I did not know you were here. Mr Lascelles said the door had jammed shut, and Davey and I were trying to free it. The carriage is ready, sir, to take you to Lord Liverpool."

"Come, Mr Norrell!" cried Lascelles from within the library. "Lord Liverpool is waiting!"

Mr Norrell cast a worried glance at Childermass and went.

The journey to Fife House was not a very pleasant one for Mr Norrell: Lascelles was full of spite towards Childermass and lost no time in venting it.

"Forgive me for saying so, Mr Norrell," he said, "but you have no one but yourself to blame. Sometimes it seems like wisdom to allow an intelligent servant a certain degree of independence – but one always regrets it in the end. That villain has grown in insolence until he thinks nothing of contradicting you and insulting your friends. My father whipped men for less – a great deal less, I assure you. And I should like, oh! I should like . . ." Lascelles twitched and fidgeted, and threw himself back upon the cushions. In a moment he said in a calmer tone, "I advise you to consider, sir, if your need of him is really as great as you think? How many of his sympathies are with Strange, I wonder? Yes, that is the real question, is it not?" He looked out of the glass at the bleak, grey buildings. "We are here. Mr Norrell, I beg that you will remember what I told you. Whatever the difficulties of the magic which his lordship requires, do not dwell upon them. A long explanation will not make them grow any less."

Mr Norrell and Lascelles found Lord Liverpool in his study, standing by the table where he conducted a great deal of his business. With him was Lord Sidmouth, the Home Secretary. They fixed Mr Norrell with solemn looks.

Lord Liverpool said, "I have here letters from the Lord Lieutenants of Lincolnshire, Yorkshire, Somerset, Cornwall, Warwickshire and Cumbria . . ." (Lascelles could scarcely refrain from giving a sigh of pleasure at the magic and the money that seemed to be in prospect.) ". . . all complaining of the magic that has recently occurred in those counties!"

Mr Norrell blinked his little eyes rapidly. "I beg your pardon?"

Lascelles said quickly, "Mr Norrell knows nothing of any magic done in those places."

Lord Liverpool gave him a cool look as if he did not believe him. There was a pile of papers on the table. Lord Liverpool picked one up at random. "Four days ago in the town of Stamford," he said, "a Quaker girl and her friend were telling each other secrets. They heard a noise and discovered their younger brothers listening at the door. Full of indignation, they chased the boys into the garden. There they joined hands and recited a charm. The boys' ears leapt off their heads and flew away. It was not until the boys had made a solemn oath never to do such a thing ever again, that the ears could be coaxed back out of the bare rose-bushes – which was where they had alighted – and persuaded to return to the boys' heads."

Mr Norrell was more perplexed than ever. "I am, of course, sorry that these badly behaved young women have been studying magic. That members of the Female Sex should study magic at all is, I may say, a thing I am very much opposed to. But I do not quite see . . ."

"Mr Norrell," said Lord Liverpool, "these girls were *thirteen*. Their parents are adamant that they have never so much as seen a magical text. There are no magicians in Stamford, no magic books of any kind."

Mr Norrell opened his mouth to say something, realized he was quite at a loss and fell silent.

Lascelles said, "This is very odd. What explanation did the girls give?"

"The girls told their parents that they looked down and saw the spell written upon the path in grey pebbles. They said the stones told them what to do. Other people have since examined the path; there are indeed some grey pebbles, but they form no symbols, no mystical writing. They are ordinary grey pebbles."

"And you say that there have been other instances of magic, in other places besides Stamford?" said Mr Norrell.

"Many other instances and many other places – mostly, but by no means solely, in the north, and almost all within the past two weeks. Seventeen fairy roads have opened up in Yorkshire. Of course the roads have existed since the reign of the Raven King, but it is centuries since they actually led anywhere and the local inhabitants allowed them to become overgrown. Now without warning they are clear again. The weeds are gone and the inhabitants report that they can see strange destinations at the end of them – places no one has ever seen before."

"Has any one . . . ?" Mr Norrell paused and licked his lips. "Has any one come down the roads?"

"Not yet," said Lord Liverpool. "But presumably it is only a matter of time."

Lord Sidmouth had been impatient to speak for some moments. "This is worst of all!" he declared in a passion, "It is one thing to change Spain by magic, Mr Norrell, but this is England! Suddenly we border upon places no one knows any thing about – places no one has ever even heard of! I can scarcely describe my feelings at this juncture. It is not treason exactly – I do not think there is even a name for what you have done!"

"But I did not do it!" said Mr Norrell in a tone of desperation.

"Why would I? I detest fairy roads! I have said so upon many occasions." He turned to Lord Liverpool. "I appeal to your lordship's memory. Have I ever given you reason to suppose that I approve of fairies or their magic? Have I not censured and condemned them at every turn?"

This was the first thing that Mr Norrell had said that seemed in any way to mollify the Prime Minister. He inclined his head slightly. "But if it is not your doing, whose is it?"

This question seemed to strike at some particularly vulnerable spot in Mr Norrell's soul. He stood, eyes staring, mouth opening and closing, entirely unable to answer.

Lascelles, however, was in complete command of himself. He had not the least idea in the world whose magic it was, nor did he care. But he did know precisely what answer would serve his and Mr Norrell's interest best. "Frankly I am surprized that your lordship need put the question," he said, coolly. "Surely the wickedness of the magic proclaims its author; it is Strange."

"Strange!" Lord Liverpool blinked. "But Strange is in Venice!"

"Mr Norrell believes that Strange is no longer the master of his own desires," said Lascelles. "He has done all sorts of wicked magic; he has trafficked with creatures that are enemies of Great Britain, of Christianity, of Mankind itself! This catastrophe may be some sort of experiment of his, which has gone awry. Or it may be that he has done it deliberately. I feel it only right to remind your lordship that Mr Norrell has warned the Government on several occasions of the great danger to the Nation from Strange's present researches. We have sent your lordship urgent messages, but we have received no replies. Fortunately for us all Mr Norrell is what he always was: firm and resolute and watchful." As he spoke, Lascelles's glance fell upon Mr Norrell, who was at the moment the very picture of everything which was dismayed, defeated and impotent.

Lord Liverpool turned to Mr Norrell. "Is this your opinion also, sir?"

Mr Norrell was lost in thought, murmuring over and over, "This is my doing. This is my doing." Although he spoke to himself, it was just loud enough for everyone else in the room to hear.

Lascelles's eyes widened; but he was master of himself in an instant. "It is only natural that you feel that now, sir," he said quickly, "but in a while you will realize that nothing could be further from the truth. When you taught Mr Strange magic, you could not have known that it would end like this. No one could have known."

Lord Liverpool looked more than a little irritated at this attempt to make Mr Norrell appear in the character of a victim. For years and years Mr Norrell had set himself up as the chief magician in England and if magic had been done in England then Lord Liverpool considered him partly responsible at least. "I ask you again, Mr Norrell. Answer me plainly, if you please. Is it your opinion that this was done by Strange?"

Mr Norrell looked at each gentleman in turn. "Yes," he said in a frightened voice.

Lord Liverpool gave him a long, hard look. Then he said, "The matter shall not rest here, Mr Norrell. But whether it is Strange or not, one thing is clear. Great Britain already has a mad King; a mad magician would be the outside of enough. You have repeatedly asked for commissions; well, here is one. Prevent your pupil from returning to England!"

"But . . ." began Mr Norrell. Then he caught sight of Lascelles's warning glance and fell silent.

Mr Norrell and Lascelles returned to Hanover-square. Mr Norrell went immediately to the library. Childermass was working at the table as before.

"Quick!" cried Mr Norrell, "I need a spell which no longer works!"

Childermass shrugged. "There are thousands. Chauntlucet;[4] Daedalus's Rose;[5] the Unrobed Ladies;[6] Stokesey's Vitrification[7] . . ."

"Stokesey's Vitrification! Yes! I have a description of that!"

Mr Norrell rushed to a shelf and pulled out a book. He searched for a page, found it and looked hurriedly around the room. On a table near the fireside stood a vase of mistletoe, ivy, red-berried holly and some sprays of a winter-flowering shrub. He fixed his eye upon the vase and began to mutter to himself.

All the shadows in the room did something odd, something not easy to describe or explain. It was as if they all turned and faced another way. Even when they were motionless again Childermass and Lascelles would have been hard pressed to say whether they were the same as they had been or not.

Something fell out of the vase and shattered upon the table with a tinkling sound.

Lascelles went over to the table and examined it. One of the branches of holly had been turned into glass. The glass branch had been too heavy for the vase and so it had toppled out; two or three unbroken holly leaves lay on the table.

"That spell has not worked for almost four hundred years," said Mr Norrell. "Watershippe specifically mentions it in *A Faire Wood*

[4] Chauntlucet: a mysterious and ancient spell which encourages the moon to sing. The song the moon knows is apparently very beautiful and can cure leprosy or madness in any who hear it.

[5] Daedalus's Rose: a fairly complicated procedure devised by Martin Pale for preserving emotions, vices and virtues in amber or honey or beeswax. When the preserving medium is warmed, the imprisoned qualities are released. The Rose has – or rather had – a huge number of applications. It could be used to dispense courage to oneself or inflict cowardice on one's enemy; it could provoke love, lust, nobility of purpose, anger, jealousy, ambition, self-sacrifice, etc., etc.

[6] Like many spells with unusual names, the Unrobed Ladies was a great deal less exciting than it sounded. The ladies of the title were only a kind of woodland flower which was used in a spell to bind a fairy's powers. The flower was required to be stripped of leaves and petals – hence the "unrobing".

[7] Stokesey's Vitrification turns objects – and people – to glass.

*Withering* as one of the spells which worked in his youth and was entirely ineffective by the time he was twenty!"

"Your superior skill . . ." began Lascelles.

"My superior skill has nothing to do with it!" snapped Mr Norrell. "I cannot do magic that is not there. Magic is returning to England. Strange has found a way to bring it back."

"Then I was right, was I not?" said Lascelles. "And our first task is to prevent him returning to England. Succeed in that and Lord Liverpool will forgive a great many other things."

Mr Norrell thought for a moment. "I can prevent him arriving by sea," he said.

"Excellent!" said Lascelles. Then something in the way Mr Norrell had phrased this last statement gave him pause. "Well, he is scarcely likely to come any other way. He cannot fly!" He gave a light laugh at the idea. Then another thought struck him. "Can he?"

Childermass shrugged.

"I do not know what Strange might be capable of by now," said Mr Norrell. "But I was not thinking of that. I was thinking of the King's Roads."

"I thought the King's Roads led to Faerie," said Lascelles.

"Yes, they do. But not only Faerie. The King's Roads lead everywhere. Heaven. Hell. The Houses of Parliament . . . They were built by magic. Every mirror, every puddle, every shadow in England is a gate to those roads. I cannot set a lock upon all of them. No body could. It would be a monstrous task! If Strange comes by the King's Roads then I know nothing to prevent him."

"But . . ." began Lascelles.

"I cannot prevent him!" cried Mr Norrell, wringing his hands. "Do not ask me! But . . ." He made a great effort to calm himself. ". . . I *can* be ready to receive him. The Greatest Magician of the Age. Well, soon we shall see, shall we not?"

"If he comes to England," said Lascelles, "where will he go first?"

"Hurtfew Abbey," said Childermass. "Where else?"

Mr Norrell and Lascelles were both about to answer him, but at that moment Lucas entered the room with a silver tray upon which lay a letter. He offered it to Lascelles. Lascelles broke the seal and read it rapidly.

"Drawlight is back," he said. "Wait for me here. I will return within a day."

## 62

## *I came to them in a cry that broke the silence of a winter wood*

### Early February 1817

FIRST LIGHT IN early February: a crossroads in the middle of a wood. The space between the trees was misty and indistinct; the darkness of the trees seeped into it. Neither of the two roads was of any importance. They were rutted and ill-maintained; one was scarcely more than a cart-track. It was an out-of-the-way place, marked on no map. It did not even have a name.

Drawlight was waiting at the crossroads. There was no horse standing nearby, no groom with a trap or cart, nothing to explain how he had come there. Yet clearly he had been standing at the crossroads for some time; his coat-sleeves were white with frost. A faint click behind him made him spin round. But there was nothing: only the same stretch of silent trees.

"No, no," he muttered to himself. "It was nothing. A dry leaf fell – that is all." There was a sharp snap, as ice cracked wood or stone. He stared again, with eyes addled by fear. "It was only a dry leaf," he murmured.

There was a new sound. For a moment he was all in a panic, uncertain where it was coming from; until he recognized it for what it was: horses' hooves. He peered up the road. A dim, grey smudge in the mist shewed where a horse and rider were approaching.

"He is here at last. He is here," muttered Drawlight and hastened forward. "Where have you been?" he cried. "I have been waiting here for hours."

"So?" said Lascelles's voice. "You have nothing else to do."

"Oh! But you are wrong! You could not be more wrong. You must take me to London as quickly as possible!"

"All in good time." Lascelles emerged from the mist and reined in his horse. His fine clothes and hat were beaded with a silvery dusting of dew.

Drawlight regarded him for a moment and then, with something of his old character, said sulkily, "How nicely you are dressed! But really, you know, it is not very clever of you to parade your wealth like that. Are not you afraid of robbers? This is a very horrid spot. I dare say there are all sorts of desperate characters close at hand."

"You are probably right. But you see I have my pistols with me, and am quite as desperate as any of them."

Drawlight was struck by a sudden thought. "Where is the other horse?" he asked.

"What?"

"The other horse! The one that is to take me to London! Oh, Lascelles, you noodlehead! How am I to get to London without a horse?"

Lascelles laughed. "I would have thought you would be glad to avoid it. Your debts may have been paid off – *I* have paid them – but London is still full of people who hate you and will do you an ill turn if they can."

Drawlight stared as if he had understood none of this. In a shrill, excited voice, he cried, "But I have instructions from the magician! He has given me messages to deliver to all sorts of people! I must begin immediately! I must not delay a single hour!"

Lascelles frowned. "Are you drunk? Are you dreaming? Norrell has not asked you to do any thing. If he had tasks for you, he would convey them through me, and besides . . ."

"Not Norrell. Strange!"

Lascelles sat stock still upon his horse. The horse shifted and fidgeted, but Lascelles moved not at all. Then, in a softer, more dangerous voice, he said, "What in the world are you talking about? Strange? How dare you talk to me of Strange? I advise you to think very carefully before you speak again. I am already seriously displeased. Your instructions were quite plain, I think. You were to remain at Venice until Strange left. But here you are. And there he is."

"I could not help it! I had to leave! You do not understand. I saw him and he told me . . ."

Lascelles held up his hand. "I have no wish to conduct this conversation in the open. We will go a little way into the trees."

"Into the trees!" The little colour that was left in Drawlight's face drained away. "Oh, no! Not for the world! I will not go there! Do not ask me!"

"What do you mean?" Lascelles looked round, a little less comfortable than before. "Has Strange set the trees to spy on us?"

"No, no. That is not it. I cannot explain it. They are waiting for me. They know me! I cannot go in there!" Drawlight had no words for what had happened to him. He held out his arms for a moment as if he thought he could shew Lascelles the rivers that had curled about his feet, the trees that had pierced him, the stones that had been his heart and lungs and guts.

Lascelles raised his riding-whip. "I have no idea what you are talking about." He urged his horse at Drawlight and flourished the whip. Poor Drawlight had never possessed the least physical courage and he was driven, whimpering, into the trees. A briar caught the edge of his sleeve and he screamed.

"Oh, do be quiet!" said Lascelles. "Any one would think there is murder going on."

They walked on until they came to a small clearing. Lascelles got down from his horse and tethered him to a tree. He removed the two pistols from the saddle-holsters and stuck them in the pockets of his great coat. Then he turned to Drawlight. "So you actually saw Strange? Good. Excellent, in fact. I was sure you were too cowardly to face him."

"I thought he would change me into something horrible."

Lascelles surveyed Drawlight's stained clothing and haunted face with some distaste. "Are you sure he did not do it?"

"What?" said Drawlight.

"Why did you not simply kill him? There, in the Darkness? You were alone, I presume? No one would have known."

"Oh, yes. That is very likely, is it not? He is tall and clever and quick and cruel. I am none of those things."

"I would have done it," said Lascelles.

"Would you? Well then, you are very welcome to go to Venice and try."

"Where is he now?"

"In the Darkness – in Venice – but he is coming to England."

"He said so?"

"Yes, I told you – I have messages: one for Childermass, one for Norrell and one for all the magicians in England."

"And what are they?"

"I am to tell Childermass that Lady Pole was not raised from the dead in the way Norrell said – he had a fairy to help him and the fairy has done things – wrong things – and I am to give Childermass a little box. That is the first message. And I am to tell Norrell that Strange is coming back. That is the third message."

Lascelles considered. "This little box, what does it contain?"

"I do not know."

"Why? Is it sealed shut in some way? By magic?"

Drawlight shut his eyes and shook his head. "I do not know that either."

Lascelles laughed out loud. "You do not mean to tell me that you have had a box in your possession for weeks and not tried to open it? You of all people? Why, when you used to come to my house, I never dared leave you alone for a moment. My letters would have been read; my business would have been common knowledge by the next morning."

Drawlight's glance sank to the ground. He seemed to shrink inside his clothes. He grew, if it were possible, several degrees more miserable. One might have supposed that he was ashamed to hear his past sins described, but it was not that. "I am afraid," he whispered.

Lascelles made a sound of exasperation. "Where is the box?" he cried. "Give it to me!"

Drawlight reached into a pocket of his coat and brought out something wrapped in a dirty handkerchief. The handkerchief was tied into many wonderfully complicated knots to guard against the box coming open of its own accord. Drawlight gave it to Lascelles.

With a series of grimaces, expressive of extreme distaste, Lascelles set himself to undo the knots. When he had done so, he opened the box.

A moment's silence.

"You are a fool," said Lascelles and shut the box with a snap and put it in his own pocket.

"Oh! But I have to . . ." began Drawlight, reaching out ineffectually.

"You said that there were three messages. What is the other one?"

"I do not think you will understand it."

"What? You understand it, yet I will not? You must have grown a great deal cleverer in Italy."

"That is not what I meant."

"Then what do you mean? Tell me quickly. I am growing bored of this conversation."

"Strange said that tree speaks to stone. Stone speaks to water. He said magicians can learn magic from woods and stones and such. He said John Uskglass's old alliances still held."

"John Uskglass, John Uskglass! How sick I am of that name!

Yet they all rattle on about him nowadays. Even Norrell. I cannot understand why; his day was done four hundred years ago."

Drawlight held out his hand again. "Give me back my box. I must . . ."

"What the devil is the matter with you? Do not you understand? Your messages will never be delivered – except for the one to Norrell and that I shall deliver myself."

A howl of anguish burst from Drawlight. "Please, please! Do not make me fail him! You do not understand. He will kill me! Or worse!"

Lascelles spread his arms and glanced around, as if asking the wood to bear witness how ridiculous this was. "Do you honestly believe that I would allow you to destroy Norrell? Which is to say destroy *me*?"

"It is not my fault! It is not my fault! I dare not disobey him!"

"Worm, what will you do between two such men as Strange and me? You will be crushed."

Drawlight made a little sound, like a whimper of fear. He gazed at Lascelles with strange, addled eyes. He seemed about to say something. Then, with surprizing speed, he turned and fled through the trees.

Lascelles did not trouble to follow him. He simply raised one of the pistols, aimed it and fired.

The bullet struck Drawlight in the thigh, producing, for one instant, a red, wet flowering of blood and flesh in the white and grey woods. Drawlight screamed and fell with a crash into a patch of briars. He tried to crawl away but his leg was quite useless and, besides, the briars were catching at his clothes; he could not pull free of them. He turned his head to see Lascelles advance upon him; fear and pain rendered his features entirely unrecognizable.

Lascelles fired the second pistol.

The left side of Drawlight's head burst open, like an egg or an orange. He convulsed several times and was still.

Although there was no one there to see, and although his blood was pounding in his ears, in his chest, in his everything, Lascelles would not permit himself to appear in the least disturbed: that, he felt, would not have been the behaviour of a gentleman.

He had a valet who was much addicted to accounts of murders and hangings in *The Newgate Calendar* and *The Malefactor's Register*. Sometimes Lascelles would amuse himself by picking up one of these volumes. A prominent characteristic of these histories was that the murderer, however bold he was during the act of murder, would soon afterwards be overcome with emotion, leading him to act in strange, irrational ways that were always his undoing. Lascelles doubted there was much truth in these accounts, but for safety's sake he examined himself for signs of remorse or horror. He found none. Indeed his chief thought was that there was one less ugly thing in the world. "Really," he said to himself, "if he had known three or four years ago that it would come to this, he would have begged me to do it."

There was a rustling sound. To Lascelles's surprize he saw that a small shoot was poking out of Drawlight's right eye (the left one had been destroyed by the pistol blast). Strands of ivy were winding themselves about his neck and chest. A holly shoot had pierced his hand; a young birch had shot up through his foot; a hawthorn had sprung up through his belly. He looked as if he been crucified upon the wood itself. But the trees did not stop there; they kept growing. A tangle of bronze and scarlet stems blotted out his ruined face, and his limbs and body decayed as plants and other living things took strength from them. Within a short space of time nothing of Christopher Drawlight remained. The trees, the stones and the earth had taken him inside themselves, but in their shape it was possible still to discern something of the man he had once been.

"That briar was his arm, I think," mused Lascelles. "That stone . . . his heart perhaps? It is small enough and hard enough." He laughed. "That is the ridiculous thing about Strange's magic," he said to no one at all. "Sooner or later it all works against him." He mounted on his horse and rode back towards the road.

# 63

## *The first shall bury his heart in a dark wood beneath the snow, yet still feel its ache*

### Mid February 1817

MORE THAN TWENTY-EIGHT hours had passed since Lascelles had left Hanover-square and Mr Norrell was half frantic. He had promised Lascelles they would wait for him, but now he feared they would arrive at Hurtfew Abbey to find Strange in possession of the library.

No one in the house at Hanover-square was permitted to go to bed that night and by morning everyone was tired and wretched.

"But why do we wait at all?" asked Childermass. "What good do you suppose *he* will be when Strange comes?"

"I place great reliance on Mr Lascelles. You know I do. He is my only adviser now."

"You still have me," said Childermass.

Mr Norrell blinked his small eyes rapidly. They seemed to be half a sentence away from, *but you are only a servant*. Mr Norrell said nothing.

Childermass seemed to understand him anyway. He made a small sound of disgust and walked off.

At six o'clock in the evening the library door was thrown open and Lascelles walked in. He looked as he had never looked before: his hair was dishevelled, his neckcloth was stained with dust and sweat, and there were mud-splashes on his greatcoat and boots.

"We were right, Mr Norrell!" he cried. "Strange is coming!"

"When?" said Mr Norrell, turning pale.

"I do not know. He has not been so kind as to furnish us with those details, but we should leave for Hurtfew Abbey as soon as possible!"

"We can go immediately. All is in readiness. So you actually saw Drawlight? Is he here?" Mr Norrell leant sideways to see if he could catch a glimpse of Drawlight behind Lascelles.

"No, I did not see him. I waited for him, but he never came. But do not fear, sir!" (Mr Norrell was on the point of interrupting.) "He has sent a letter. We have all the intelligence we need."

"A letter! May I see it?"

"Of course! But there will be time enough for that on the journey. We must be off. You need not delay on my account. My wants are few and what I do not have, I can very easily do without." (This was perhaps a little surprizing. Lascelles's wants had never been few before. They had been numerous and complicated.) "Come, come, Mr Norrell. Rouse yourself. Strange is coming!" He strode out of the room again. Mr Norrell heard later from Lucas that he had not even asked for water to wash or for any thing to drink. He had simply gone to the carriage, thrown himself into a corner and waited.

By eight o'clock they were on their way to Yorkshire. Mr Norrell and Lascelles were inside the carriage; Lucas and Davey were upon the box; Childermass was on horseback. At the Islington tollgate Lucas paid the keeper. There was a smell of snow in the air.

Mr Norrell gazed idly at a shop window ablaze with lamplight. It was a superior sort of shop with an uncluttered interior and elegant modern chairs for the customers to sit upon; in fact it was so very refined an establishment that it was by no means clear what it sold. A heap of brightly coloured somethings lay tossed upon a chair, but whether they were shawls or materials for gowns or something else entirely, Mr Norrell could not tell. There were three women in the shop. One was a customer – a smart, stylish person in a spencer like a Hussar's uniform, complete with fur trim and frogging. On her head was a little Russian fur cap; she kept touching the back of it as if she feared it would fall off. The shopkeeper was more discreetly dressed in a plain dark gown, and there was besides a little assistant who looked on respectfully and bobbed a nervous little curtsey whenever any one chanced to look at her. The customer and the shopkeeper were not engaged in business; they were talking together with a great deal of animation and laughter. It was a scene as far removed from Mr Norrell's usual interests as it was possible to be, yet it went to his heart in a way he could not understand. He thought fleetingly of Mrs Strange and Lady Pole. Then something flew between him and the cheerful scene – something like a piece of the darkness made solid. He thought that it was a raven.

The toll was paid. Davey shook the reins and the carriage moved on towards the Archway.

Snow began to fall. A sleety wind buffeted the sides of the carriage and made it rock from side to side; it penetrated every chink and crack, and chilled shoulders, noses and feet. Mr Norrell was not made any more comfortable by the fact that Lascelles appeared to be in a very odd mood. He was excited, almost elated, though Mr Norrell could not tell why he should be. When the wind howled, he laughed, as if he suspected it of trying to frighten him and wished to shew it that it was mistaken.

When he saw that Mr Norrell was observing him, he said, "I have been thinking. This is the merest nothing! You and I, sir, will soon get the better of Strange and his tricks. What a pack of old women the Ministers are! They disgust me! All this alarm over one lunatic! It makes me laugh to think of it. Of course Liverpool and Sidmouth are the very worst of them! For years they have hardly dared put their noses out of their front doors for fear of Buonaparte and now Strange has sent them into fits merely by going insane."

"Oh, but you are wrong!" declared Mr Norrell. "Indeed, you

are! The threat from Strange is immense – Buonaparte was nothing to it – but you have not told me what Drawlight said. I should very much like to see his letter. I will tell Davey to stop at the Angel in Hadley and then . . ."

"But I do not have it. I left it at Bruton-street."

"Oh! But . . ."

Lascelles laughed. "Mr Norrell! Do not concern yourself! Do I not tell you that it does not matter? I recall it exactly."

"What does it say?"

"That Strange is mad and imprisoned in Eternal Darkness – all of which we knew before – and . . ."

"What form does his madness take?" asked Mr Norrell.

The merest pause.

"Talking nonsense mostly. But then he did that before, did he not?" Lascelles laughed. Catching sight of Mr Norrell's expression, he continued more soberly, "He babbles about trees, and stones, and John Uskglass, and," (glancing round for inspiration), "invisible coaches. And oh, yes! This will amuse you! He has stolen fingers off the hands of several Venetian maidens. Stolen them clean away! Keeps the stolen fingers in little boxes!"

"Fingers!" said Mr Norrell in alarm. This seemed to suggest some unpleasant associations to him. He thought for a moment but could make nothing of it. "Did Drawlight describe the Darkness? Did he say any thing that might help us understand it?"

"No. He saw Strange, and Strange gave him a message for you. He says that he is coming. That is the substance of the letter."

They fell into silence. Mr Norrell began to doze without intending to; but several times in his dreams he heard Lascelles whispering to himself in the darkness.

At midnight they changed horses at the Haycock Inn at Wansford. Lascelles and Mr Norrell waited in the public parlour, a large, plain apartment with wood-panelled walls, a sanded floor and two great fireplaces.

The door opened and Childermass walked in. He went straight

to Lascelles and addressed him in the following words: "Lucas says there is a letter from Drawlight telling what he has seen in Venice."

Lascelles half-turned his head, but he did not look at Childermass.

"May I see it?" asked Childermass.

"I left it at Bruton-street," said Lascelles.

Childermass looked a little surprized. "Very well then," he said. "Lucas can fetch it. We will hire a horse for him here. He will catch up with us again before we reach Hurtfew."

Lascelles smiled. "I said Bruton-street, did I not? But do you know? – I do not think it is there. I believe I left it at the inn, the one in Chatham where I waited for Drawlight. They will have thrown it away." He turned back to the fire.

Childermass scowled at him for a moment or two. Then he strode out of the room.

A manservant came to say that hot water, towels and other necessaries had been set out in two bed-chambers so that Mr Norrell and Lascelles might refresh themselves. "And it's a blind-man's holiday in the passage-way, gentlemen," he said cheerfully, "so I've lit you a candle each."

Mr Norrell took his candle and made his way along the passage-way (which was indeed very dark). Suddenly Childermass appeared and seized his arm. "What in the world were you thinking of?" he hissed. "To leave London without that letter?"

"But he says he remembers what it contains," pleaded Mr Norrell.

"Oh! And you believe him, do you?"

Mr Norrell made no reply. He went into the room that had been made ready. He washed his hands and face and, as he did so, he caught a glimpse in the mirror of the bed behind him. It was heavy, old fashioned and – as often happens at inns – much too large for the room. Four carved mahogany columns, a high dark canopy and bunches of black ostrich feathers at each corner all

contrived to give it a funereal look. It was as if someone had brought him into the room and shewn him his own tomb. He began to have the strangest feeling – the same feeling he had had at the tollgate, watching the three women – the feeling that something was coming to an end and that all his choices had now been made. He had taken a road in his youth, but the road did not lead where he had supposed; he was going home, but home had become something monstrous. In the half-dark, standing by the black bed, he remembered why he had always feared the darkness as a child: the darkness belonged to John Uskglass.

*For always and for always*
*I pray remember me*
*Upon the moors, beneath the stars*
*With the King's wild company*

He hurried from the room, back to the warmth and lights of the public parlour.

A little after six o'clock a grey dawn came up that was scarcely any dawn at all. White snow fell through a grey sky on to a grey and white world. Davey was so liberally coated in snow that one might have supposed that someone had ordered a wax-works model of him and the plaster mould was being prepared.

All that day a succession of post-horses laboured to bring the carriage through snow and wind. A succession of inns provided hot drinks and a brief respite from the weather. Davey and Childermass – who, as coachman and rider, were undoubtedly the most exhausted of the party – derived the least benefit from these halts; they were generally in the stables arguing with the innkeeper about the horses. At Grantham the innkeeper infuriated Childermass by proposing to rent them a stone-blind horse. Childermass swore he would not take it; the innkeeper on the other hand swore it was the best horse he had. There was very little choice and they ended by hiring it. Davey said afterwards that it was an excellent beast, hard-working and all the more obedient to his instructions since it had no other means of knowing where to go or what to do. Davey himself lasted as far as the Newcastle Arms at Tuxford and there they were obliged to leave him. He had driven more than a hundred and thirty miles and was, said Childermass, so tired he could barely speak. Childermass hired a postillion and they travelled on.

An hour or so before sunset the snow ceased and the skies cleared. Long blue-black shadows overlaid the bare fields. Five miles out of Doncaster they passed the inn that is called the Red House (by reason of its painted walls). In the low winter sun it blazed like a house of fire. The carriage went on a little way and then halted.

"Why are we stopping?" cried Mr Norrell from within.

Lucas leant down from the box and said something in reply, but the wind carried his voice away and Mr Norrell did not hear what it was.

Childermass had left the highway and was riding across a field. The field was filled with ravens. As he passed, they flew up with a great croaking and cawing. On the far side of the field was an ancient hedge with an opening and two tall holly-trees, one on each side. The opening led into another road or lane, bounded by hedges. Childermass halted there and looked first one way and then the other. He hesitated. Then he shook his reins and the horse trotted between the trees, into the lane and out of sight.

"He has gone into the fairy road!" cried Mr Norrell in alarm.

"Oh!" said Lascelles. "Is that what it is?"

"Yes, indeed!" said Mr Norrell. "That is one of the more famous ones. It is reputed to have joined Doncaster to Newcastle by way of two fairy citadels."

They waited.

After about twenty minutes Lucas climbed down from the box. "How long ought we to stay here, sir?" he asked.

Mr Norrell shook his head. "No Englishman has stept over the boundaries into Faerie since Martin Pale three hundred years ago. It is perfectly possible that he will never come out again. Perhaps . . ."

Just then Childermass reappeared and galloped back across the field.

"Well, it is true," he told Mr Norrell. "The paths to Faerie are open again."

"What did you see?" asked Mr Norrell.

"The road goes on a little way and then leads into a wood of thorn trees. At the entrance to the wood there is a statue of a woman with her hands outstretched. In one hand she holds a stone eye and in the other a stone heart. As for the wood itself . . ." Childermass made a gesture, perhaps expressive of his inability to describe what he had seen, or perhaps of his powerlessness in the face of it. "Corpses hang from every tree. Some might have died as recently as yesterday. Others are no more than age-old skeletons dressed in rusting armour. I came to a high tower built of rough-hewn stones. The walls were pierced with a few tiny windows. There was a light at one of them and the shadow of someone looking out. Beneath the tower was a clearing with a brook running through it. A young man was standing there. He looked pale and sickly, with dead eyes, and he wore a British uniform. He told me he was the Champion of the Castle of the Plucked Eye and Heart. He had sworn to protect the Lady of the Castle by challenging any one who approached with the intent of harming or insulting her. I asked him if he had killed all the men I had seen. He said he had killed some of them and hung them upon the thorns – as his predecessor had done before him. I asked him how the Lady intended to reward him for his service. He said he did not know. He had never seen her or spoken to her. She remained in the Castle of the Plucked Eye and Heart; he stayed between the brook and the thorn trees. He asked me if I intended to fight him. I reminded him that I had neither insulted nor harmed his lady. I told him I was a servant and bound to return to my master who was at that moment waiting for me. Then I turned my horse and rode back."

"What?" cried Lascelles. "A man offers to fight you and you run away. Have you no honour at all? No shame? A sickly face, dead eyes, an unknown person at the window!" He gave a snort of derision. "These are nothing but excuses for your cowardice!"

Childermass flinched as if he had been struck and seemed about to return a sharp answer, but he was interrupted by Mr Norrell. "Upon the contrary! Childermass did well to leave as soon as he could. There is always more magic in such a place than appears at first sight. Some fairies delight in combat and death. I do not know why. They are prepared to go to great lengths to secure such pleasures for themselves."

"Please, Mr Lascelles," said Childermass, "if the place has a strong appeal for you, then go! Do not stay upon our account."

Lascelles looked thoughtfully at the field and the gap in the hedge. But he did not move.

"You do not like the ravens perhaps?" said Childermass in a quietly mocking tone.

"No one likes them!" declared Mr Norrell. "Why are they here? What do they mean?"

Childermass shrugged. "Some people think that they are part of the Darkness that envelops Strange, and which, for some reason, he has made incarnate and sent back to England. Other people think that they portend the return of John Uskglass."

"John Uskglass. Of course," said Lascelles. "The first and last resort of vulgar minds. Whenever any thing happens, it must be because of John Uskglass! I think, Mr Norrell, it is time for another article in *The Friends* reviling that gentleman. What shall we say? That he was unChristian? UnEnglish? Demonic? Somewhere I believe I have a list of the Saints and Archbishops who denounced him. I could easily work that up."

Mr Norrell looked uncomfortable. He glanced nervously at the Tuxford postillion.

"If I were you, Mr Lascelles," said Childermass, softly, "I would speak more guardedly. You are in the north now. In John Uskglass's own country. Our towns and cities and abbeys were built by him. Our laws were made by him. He is in our minds and hearts and speech. Were it summer you would see a carpet of tiny flowers beneath every hedgerow, of a bluish-white colour. We call them John's Farthings. When the weather is contrary and we have warm weather in winter or it rains in summer the country people say that John Uskglass is in love again and neglects his business.[1] And when we are sure of something we say it is as safe as a pebble in John Uskglass's pocket."

Lascelles laughed. "Far be it from me, Mr Childermass, to disparage your quaint country sayings. But surely it is one thing to pay lip-service to one's history and quite another to talk of bringing back a King who numbered Lucifer himself among his allies and overlords? No one wants that, do they? I mean apart from a few Johannites and madmen?"

"I am a North Englishman, Mr Lascelles," said Childermass. "Nothing would please me better than that my King should come home. It is what I have wished for all my life."

It was nearly midnight when they arrived at Hurtfew Abbey. There was no sign of Strange. Lascelles went to bed, but Mr Norrell walked about the house, examining the condition of certain spells that had long been in place.

Next morning at breakfast Lascelles said, "I have been wondering if there were ever magical duels in the past? Struggles between two magicians? – that sort of thing."

---

[1] It has often been observed that the Northern English, though never wavering in their loyalty to John Uskglass, do not always treat him with the respect he commands in the south. In fact Uskglass's subjects take a particular delight in stories and ballads that shew him at a decided disadvantage, *c.f.* the tale of John Uskglass and the Charcoal Burner of Ullswater or the tale of the Hag and the Sorceress. There are many versions of the latter (some of them quite vulgar); it tells how Uskglass almost lost his heart, his kingdoms and his power to a common Cornish witch.

Mr Norrell sighed. "It is difficult to know. Ralph Stokesey seems to have fought two or three magicians by magic – one a very powerful Scottish magician, the Magician of Athodel.[2] Catherine of Winchester was once driven to send a young magician to Granada by magic. He kept disturbing her with inconvenient proposals of marriage when she wanted to study and Granada was the furthest place she could think of at the time. Then there is the curious tale of the Cumbrian charcoal-burner . . ."[3]

"And did such duels ever end in the death of one of the magicians?"

"What?" Mr Norrell stared at him, horror-struck. "No! That is to say, I do not know. I do not think so."

Lascelles smiled. "Yet the magic must exist surely? If you gave your mind to it, I dare say you could think of a half a dozen spells that would do the trick. It would be like a common duel with pistols or swords. There would be no question of a prosecution afterwards. Besides, the victor's friends and servants would be perfectly justified in helping him shroud the matter in all possible secrecy."

Mr Norrell was silent. Then he said, "It will not come to that."

Lascelles laughed. "My dear Mr Norrell! What else can it possibly come to?"

Curiously, Lascelles had never been to Hurtfew Abbey before. Whenever, in days gone by, Drawlight had gone to stay there,

[2] Like John Uskglass, the Magician of Athodel ruled his own island or kingdom. Athodel seems to have been one of the Western Isles of Scotland. But either it has sunk or else it is, as some people think, invisible. Some Scottish historians like to see Athodel as evidence of the superiority of Scottish magic over English; John Uskglass's kingdom, they argue, has fallen and is in the hands of the Southern English, whereas Athodel remains independent. Since Athodel is both invisible and inaccessible this is a difficult proposition to prove or disprove.

[3] In the tale of John Uskglass and the Charcoal Burner of Ullswater, Uskglass engages in a contest of magic with a poor charcoal-burner and loses. It bears similarities to other old stories in which a great ruler is outwitted by one of his humblest subjects and, because of this, many scholars have argued that it has no historical basis.

Lascelles had always contrived to have a previous engagement. A sojourn at a country house in Yorkshire was Lascelles's idea of purgatory. At best he fancied Hurtfew must be like its owner – dusty, old-fashioned and given to long, dull silences; at worst he pictured a rain-lashed farmhouse upon a dark, dreary moor. He was surprized to find that it was none of these things. There was nothing of the Gothic about it. The house was modern, elegant and comfortable and the servants were far from the uncouth farmhands of his imagination. In fact they were the same servants who waited upon Mr Norrell in Hanover-square. They were London-trained and well acquainted with all Lascelles's preferences.

But any magician's house has its oddities, and Hurtfew Abbey – at first sight so commodious and elegant – seemed to have been constructed upon a plan so extremely muddle-headed, that it was quite impossible to go from one side of the house to the other without getting lost. Later that morning Lascelles was informed by Lucas that he must on no account attempt to go to the library alone, but only in the company of Mr Norrell or Childermass. It was, said Lucas, the first rule of the house.

Naturally, Lascelles had no intention of obeying such a prohibition, delivered to him by a servant. He examined the eastern part of the house and found the usual arrangement of morning-room, dining-room, drawing-room – but no library. He concluded that the library must lie in the unexplored, western part. He set off and immediately found himself back in the room he had just left. Thinking he must have taken a wrong turn, he tried again. This time he arrived at one of the sculleries where a small, unclean, sniffling maid first wiped her nose on the back of her hand and then used that same hand to wash the cooking pots. No matter which path he chose, it returned him immediately to either morning-room or the scullery. He grew very sick of the sight of the little maid, and she did not seem exactly overjoyed to see him. But though he wasted an entire morning on this fruitless endeavour it never occurred to him to attribute his failure to any thing other than a peculiarity of Yorkshire architecture.

For the next three days Mr Norrell kept to the library as much as he could. Whenever he saw Lascelles he was sure to hear some fresh complaint about Childermass; while Childermass kept harassing him with demands that he search for Drawlight's letter by magic. In the end he found it easier to avoid them both.

Nor did he divulge to either of them something he had discovered which worried him a great deal. Ever since he and Strange had parted he had been in the habit of summoning up visions to try and discover what Strange was doing. But he had never succeeded. One night, about four weeks ago, he had not been able to sleep. He had got up and performed the magic. The vision had not been very distinct, but he had seen a magician in the darkness, doing magic. He had congratulated himself on penetrating Strange's counterspells at last; until it occurred to him that he was looking at a vision of himself in his own library. He had tried again. He had varied the spells. He named Strange in different ways. It did not matter. He was forced to conclude that English magic could no longer tell the difference between himself and Strange.

Letters arrived from Lord Liverpool and the Ministers with angry descriptions of more magic which no one could explain. Mr Norrell wrote back, promising his earliest attention to these matters just as soon as Strange had been defeated.

On the third evening after their arrival Mr Norrell, Lascelles and Childermass were gathered together in the drawing-room. Lascelles was eating an orange. He had a little pearl-handled fruit knife with a jagged blade, which he used to cut the peel. Childermass was laying out his cards upon a little table. He had been reading the cards for the past two hours. It was a measure of how far Mr Norrell was distracted by the present situation that he made not the slightest objection. Lascelles, on the other hand, was driven half-mad by those cards. He was certain that one of the subjects of all those layings-out and turnings-over was himself. In this he was perfectly correct.

"How I detest this inactivity!" he said, abruptly. "What can Strange be waiting for, do you suppose? We do not even know for certain that he will come."

"He will come," said Childermass.

"And how do you know that?" asked Lascelles. "Because you have told him to?"

Childermass did not respond. Something he had seen in the cards had claimed his attention. His glance flickered over them. Suddenly he rose from the table. "Mr Lascelles! You have a message for me!"

"I?" said Lascelles, in surprize.

"Yes, sir."

"What do you mean?"

"I mean that someone has recently given you a message for me. The cards say so. I would be grateful if you would deliver it to me."

Lascelles gave a snort of contempt. "I am not any body's messenger – yours least of all!"

Childermass ignored this. "Who is the message from?" he asked.

Lascelles said nothing. He went back to his knife and his orange.

"Very well," said Childermass and he sat down and laid out the cards again.

Mr Norrell, in a state of great apprehension, watched them. His hand fluttered up towards the bell-cord, but after a moment's consideration he changed his mind and went in search of a servant himself. Lucas was in the dining-room, laying the table. Mr Norrell told him what was going on. "Can not something be done to separate them?" he asked. "They might be cooler in a while. Has no message come for Mr Lascelles? Is there nothing that needs Childermass's attention? Can you not invent something? What about dinner? Can it be ready?"

Lucas shook his head. "There is no message. Mr Childermass will do as he pleases – he always does. And you ordered dinner for half-past nine, sir. You know you did."

"I wish Mr Strange were here," said Mr Norrell, miserably. "He would know what to say to them. He would know what to do."

Lucas touched his master's arm as if trying to rouse him. "Mr Norrell? We are trying to prevent Mr Strange from coming here – if you remember, sir?"

Mr Norrell looked at him in some irritation. "Yes, yes! I know that! But still."

Mr Norrell and Lucas returned to the drawing-room together. Childermass was turning over his last card. Lascelles was staring with great determination at a newspaper.

"What do the cards say?" said Mr Norrell to Childermass.

Mr Norrell asked the question, but Childermass spoke his answer to Lascelles. "They say that you are a liar and a thief. They say that there is more than a message. You have been given something – an object – something of great value. It is meant for me and yet you retain it."

A short silence.

Lascelles said coldly, "Mr Norrell, how long do you intend that I shall be insulted in this manner?"

"I ask you for the last time, Mr Lascelles," said Childermass, "will you give me what is mine?"

"How dare you address a gentleman in such a fashion?" asked Lascelles.

"And is it the act of a gentleman to steal from me?" replied Childermass.

Lascelles turned a dead white. "Apologize!" he hissed. "Apologize to me or I swear, you whoreson, you dregs of every Yorkshire gutter, I will teach you better manners."

Childermass shrugged. "Better a whoreson than a thief!"

With a cry of rage, Lascelles seized him and thrust him against the wall so hard that Childermass's feet actually left the ground. He shook Childermass and the paintings on the wall rattled in their frames.

Curiously, Childermass seemed defenceless against Lascelles. His arms had somehow got pinned against Lascelles's body and though he struggled hard, he seemed unable to free them. It was over in a moment. Childermass nodded briefly at Lascelles as if to say Lascelles had won.

But Lascelles did not release him. Instead, he leant hard against him, keeping him trapped against the wall. Then he reached down and picked up the pearl-handled knife with the jagged edge. He drew the blade slowly across Childermass's face, cutting him from eye to mouth.

Lucas let out a cry, but Childermass said nothing at all. He somehow freed his left hand and raised it. It was closed in a tight fist. They remained like that for a moment – a tableau – then Childermass dropped his hand.

Lascelles smiled broadly. He let Childermass go and turned to Mr Norrell. In a calm, quiet voice he addressed him thus: "I will not suffer any excuses to be made for this person. I have been insulted. If this person were of a rank to be noticed by me, I should certainly call him out. He knows it. His inferior condition protects him. If I am to remain another moment in this house, if I am to continue as your friend and adviser, then this person must leave your service this minute! After tonight I can never hear his name spoken by you or any of your servants again on pain of dismissal. I hope, sir, that this is sufficiently plain?"

Lucas took the opportunity to hand Childermass a surreptitious napkin.

"Well, sir," said Childermass to Mr Norrell, wiping the blood from his face, "which of us is it to be?"

A long moment of silence. Then in a hoarse voice quite unlike his usual tone, Mr Norrell said, "You must go."

"Goodbye, Mr Norrell," said Childermass, bowing. "You have

made the wrong choice, sir – as usual!" He gathered up his cards and left.

He went up to his bare little attic bedroom and lit the candle which stood upon a table. There was a cracked, cheap looking-glass hanging on the wall. He examined his face. The cut was ugly. His neckcloth and the right shoulder of his shirt were soaked in blood. He washed the wound as best he could. Then he washed and dried his hands.

Carefully he took something out of his coat-pocket. It was a box, the colour of heartache, about the size of a snuff box but a little longer. He whispered to himself, "A man cannot help his training."[4]

He opened it. For a moment or two he looked thoughtful; he scratched his head and then cursed because he had very nearly dropt blood into it. He snapped it shut and put it in his pocket.

It did not take long to collect his possessions. There was a mahogany case containing a pair of pistols, a small purse of money, a razor, a comb, a toothbrush, a bit of soap, some clothes (all as ancient as the ones he was wearing) and a small parcel of books, including a Bible, *A Child's History of the Raven King* by Lord Portishead and a copy of Paris Ormskirk's *Revelations of Thirty-Six Other Worlds*. Mr Norrell had paid Childermass well for years, but what he did with his money no one knew. As Davey and Lucas had often remarked to each other, he certainly did not spend it.

Childermass packed everything into a battered valise. There was a dish of apples upon the table. He wrapped them in a cloth and added them to the valise. Then, holding the napkin to his face, he went downstairs. He was in the stable-yard before he remembered that his pen, ink and memorandum book were still in the drawing-room. He had put them on a side-table while he read his

---

[4] At the engravers' house in Spitalfields in the early spring of 1816, Strange had told Childermass, "One can never help one's training, you know . . ."

Childermass had had several careers before he became Mr Norrell's servant and adviser. His first was as a highly talented child pick-pocket. His mother, Black Joan, had once managed a small pack of dirty, ragged child-thieves that had worked the towns of the East Riding in the late 1770s.

cards. "Well, it is too late to go back," he thought. "I shall have to buy others."

There was a party waiting for him in the stables: Davey, Lucas, the grooms and several of the manservants who had managed to slip away from the house. "What are you all doing here?" he asked, in surprize. "Holding a prayer meeting?"

The men glanced at each other.

"We saddled Brewer for you, Mr Childermass," said Davey. Brewer was Childermass's horse, a big, unhandsome stallion.

"Thank you, Davey."

"Why did you let him do it, sir?" asked Lucas. "Why did you let him cut you?"

"Don't fret about it, lad. It's of no consequence."

"I brought bandages. Let me bind up your face."

"Lucas, I need my wits tonight and I cannot think if I am all over bandages."

"But it will leave a terrible scar if the lips of the wound are not closed."

"Let it. No one will complain if I am less beautiful than I was. Just give me another clout[5] to staunch the flow. This one is soaked through. Now, lads, when Strange comes . . ." He sighed. "I do not know what to tell you. I have no advice. But if you get a chance to help them, then do it."

"What?" asked one manservant. "Help Mr Norrell and Mr Lascelles?"

"No, you blockhead! Help Mr Norrell and Mr Strange. Lucas, tell Lucy, Hannah and Dido that I said goodbye and wished them well – and good, obedient husbands when they want them." (These were three housemaids who were particular favourites of Childermass.)

Davey grinned. "And you yourself willing to do the job, sir?" he said.

---

[5] A Yorkshire word meaning "cloth".

Childermass laughed – then flinched at the pain in his face. "Well, for Hannah perhaps," he said. "Goodbye, lads."

He shook hands with all of them and was a little taken aback when Davey, who for all his strength and size was as sentimental as a schoolgirl, insisted on embracing him and actually shed tears. Lucas gave him a bottle of Mr Norrell's best claret as a parting gift.

Childermass led Brewer out of the stables. The moon had risen. He had no difficulty in following the sweep out of the pleasure-grounds into the park. He was just crossing over the bridge when the sudden realization came upon him that there was magic going on. It was as if a thousand trumpets had sounded in his ear or a dazzling light had shone out of the darkness. The world was entirely different from what it had been a moment before, but what that difference was he could not at first make out. He looked round.

Directly above the park and house there was a patch of night-sky shoved in where it did not belong. The constellations were broken. New stars hung there – stars that Childermass had never seen before. They were, presumably, the stars of Strange's Eternal Darkness.

He took one last look at Hurtfew Abbey and galloped away.

All the clocks began to strike at the same moment. This in itself was extraordinary enough. For fifteen years Lucas had been trying to persuade the clocks of Hurtfew to tell the hour together and they had never done so until this moment. But what o'clock it might be was hard to say. The clocks struck on and on, long past twelve, telling the time of a strange, new era.

"What in the world is that hideous sound?" asked Lascelles.

Mr Norrell stood up. He rubbed his hands together – with him always a sign of great nervousness and strain. "Strange is here," said, quickly. He spoke a word. The clocks were silent.

The door burst open. Mr Norrell and Mr Lascelles turned with faces all alarm, in full expectation of seeing Strange standing there. But it was only Lucas and two of the other servants.

"Mr Norrell!" began Lucas. "I think . . ."

"Yes, yes! I know! Go to the store-room at the foot of the kitchen-stairs. In the chest under the window you will find lead chains, lead padlocks and lead keys. Bring them here! Quickly!"

"And I will go and fetch a pair of pistols," declared Lascelles.

"They will do no good," said Mr Norrell.

"Oh! You would be surprized how many problems a pair of pistols can solve!"

They returned within five minutes. There was Lucas, looking reluctant and unhappy, holding the chains and locks; Lascelles with his pistols; and four or five more manservants.

"Where do you suppose he is?" asked Lascelles.

"In the library. Where else?" said Mr Norrell. "Come."

They left the drawing-room and entered the dining-room. From here they passed into a short corridor which contained an inlaid ebony sideboard, the marble statue of a centaur and its foal, and a painting of Salome carrying St John's head on a silver platter. There were two doors ahead of them. The one on the right had an unfamiliar look to Lascelles, as if he had never seen it before. Mr Norrell led them through it and they immediately found themselves – back in the drawing-room.

"Wait," said Mr Norrell in confusion. He looked behind him. "I must have . . . No. Wait. I have it now! Come!"

Once again they passed through the dining-room into the corridor. This time they went through the door upon the left. It too led straight back to the drawing-room.

Mr Norrell gave a loud, despairing cry. "He has broken my labyrinth and woven another against me!"

"In some ways, sir," remarked Lascelles, "I could have wished that you had not taught him so well."

"Oh! I never taught him to do this – and you may be sure that he never learnt it from any one else! Either the Devil taught him or he learnt it this very night in my house. This is the genius of my enemy! Lock a door against him and all that happens is that he learns first how to pick a lock and second how to build a better one against you!"

Lucas and the other servants lit more candles as if light could somehow help them see through Strange's spells and help them distinguish reality from magic. Soon each of the three apartments was ablaze with light. Candlesticks and candelabras were crowded upon every surface, but it only served to confuse them more. They went from dining-room to drawing-room, from drawing-room to corridor – "Like foxes in a stopt earth," said Lascelles. But, try as they might, they could not leave the three apartments.

Time passed. It was impossible to say how much. The clocks had all turned to midnight. Every window shewed the black of Eternal Night and the unknown stars.

Mr Norrell stopt walking. He closed his eyes. His face was as dark and tight as a fist. He stood quite still and only his lips moved slightly. Then he opened his eyes briefly and said, "Follow me." Closing his eyes again, he walked. It was as if he were following the plan of an entirely different house that had somehow got wedged inside his own. The turns he took, the rights and lefts, made a new path – one he had never taken before.

After three or four minutes he opened his eyes. There before him was the corridor he had been searching for – the one with the floor of stone flags – and at the end of it the tall shadowy shape of the library door.

"Now, we shall see what he is doing!" he cried. "Lucas, keep the lead chains and locks ready. There is no better prophylactic against magic than lead. We will bind his hands and that will hinder him a little. Mr Lascelles, how quickly do you suppose we might get a letter to one of the Ministers?" He was a little surprized that none of them made any reply and so he turned.

He was quite alone.

A little way off he heard Lascelles say something; his cold, languid voice was unmistakable. He heard one of the other servants reply and then Lucas. But gradually all the noise grew less. The sounds of the servants rushing from room to room were gone. There was silence.

# 64

## Two versions of Lady Pole

### Mid February 1817

"WELL!" SAID LASCELLES. "That was unexpected!" He and the servants were gathered at the north wall of the dining-room – a wall through which Mr Norrell had just walked, with all the composure in the world.

Lascelles put out his hand and touched it; it was perfectly solid. He pressed it hard; it did not move.

"Did he mean to do that, do you think?" wondered one of the servants.

"I do not think it much matters what he meant," said Lucas. "He has gone to be with Mr Strange now."

"Which is as much as to say he has gone to the Devil!" added Lascelles.

"What will happen now?" asked another servant.

No one answered him. Images of magical battles flitted through the minds of everyone present: Mr Norrell hurling mystical cannonballs at Strange; Strange calling up devils to come and carry Mr Norrell away. They listened for sounds of a struggle. There were none.

A shout came from the next room. One of the servants had opened the drawing-room door and found the breakfast-room on the other side of it. Beyond the breakfast-room was Mr Norrell's sitting-room, and beyond that, his dressing-room. The old sequence of rooms was suddenly re-established; the labyrinth was broken.

The relief of this discovery was very great. The servants immediately abandoned Lascelles and went down to the kitchen, the natural refuge and solace of their class. Lascelles – just as naturally – sat down in solitary state in Mr Norrell's sitting-room. He had some idea of staying there until Mr Norrell returned. Or if Mr Norrell never came back, of waiting for Strange and then shooting him. "After all," he thought, "what can a magician do against a lead ball? Between the pistol firing and his heart exploding, there is no time for magic."

But such thoughts as these provided only a temporary comfort. The house was too silent, the darkness too magical. He was too aware of the servants gathered together sociably in one place, and the two magicians doing God-knew-what in another place, and himself, alone, in a third place. There was an old longcase clock that stood in one corner of the room, a last remnant of Mr Norrell's childhood home in York. This clock had, like all the others in the house, turned to midnight when Strange arrived. But it had not done so willingly; it protested very volubly against such an unexpected turn of events. Its ticking was all askew; it seemed to be drunk – or possibly in a fever – and from time to time it made a sound that was remarkably like an indrawn breath; and every time it did so Lascelles thought that Strange had entered the room and was about to say something.

He got up and followed the servants to the kitchen.

The kitchen at Hurtfew Abbey was very much like the undercroft of a great church, full of classical angles and classical gloom. In the centre of the room was a huge number of tallow candles and gathered there was every servant that Lascelles had ever seen at Hurtfew, and a great many that he had not. He leant against a pillar at the top of a flight of steps.

Lucas glanced up at him. He said, "We have been discussing what to do, sir. We shall leave within the half hour. We can do Mr

Norrell no good by staying here and may do ourselves some harm. That is our intention, sir, but if you have another opinion I shall be glad to hear it."

"My opinion!" exclaimed Lascelles. He looked all amazement, and only part of it was feigned. "This is the first time I was ever asked my *opinion* by a footman. Thank you, but I believe I shall decline my share of this . . ." He thought for a moment, before settling upon the most offensive word in his vocabulary. ". . . *democracy*."

"As you wish, sir," said Lucas, mildly.

"It must be daylight in England by now," said one of the maids, looking longingly at the windows set high in the walls.

"This is England, silly girl!" declared Lascelles.

"No, sir. Begging your pardon," said Lucas, "but it is not. England is a natural place. Davey, how long to turn the horses out?"

"Oh!" cried Lascelles. "You are all very bold, I must say, to discuss your thievery in front of me! What? You think I shall not speak out against you? On the contrary I shall see you all hanged!"

Some of the servants nervously eyed the pistols in Lascelles's hands. Lucas, however, ignored him.

The servants soon agreed that those among them who had relations or friends in the neighbourhood would go to them. The rest would be dispatched with the horses to the various farms which stood upon Mr Norrell's estate.

"So, you see, sir," said Lucas to Lascelles, "nobody is stealing. Nobody is a thief. All of Mr Norrell's property is to remain on Mr Norrell's land – and we will take as good care of his horses as if they were still in his stables, but it would be a wicked cruelty to leave any creature in this Perpetual Darkness."

Sometime later the servants left Hurtfew (there was no saying exactly how much later it was – their pocket-watches, like the clocks, had all turned to midnight). With baskets and valises slung over their arms and knapsacks on their backs, they led the horses by the halter. There were also two donkeys and a goat who had always lived in the stables because the horses found him agreeable company. Lascelles followed at a distance; he had no desire to appear part of this rag-tag and bobtail procession, but neither did he want to be left alone in the house.

Ten yards short of the river they walked out of the Darkness into the Dawn. There was a sudden rush of scents upon the air – scents of frost, winter earth and the nearby river. The colours and shapes of the park seemed simplified, as if England had been made afresh during the night. To the poor servants, who had been in some doubt whether they would ever see any thing but Dark and stars again, the sight was an exceedingly welcome one.

Their watches had started up again and they found by a general consultation that it was a quarter to eight.

But the alarms of that night were not quite over yet. Two bridges now led across the river where only one had been before.

Lascelles came hurrying up. "What is that?" he demanded, pointing at the new bridge.

An old servant – a man with a beard like a miniature white cloud stuck to the end of his chin – said that it was a fairy bridge. He had seen it in his youth. It had been built long ago, when John Uskglass still ruled Yorkshire. It had fallen into disrepair and been dismantled in the time of Mr Norrell's uncle.

"And yet here it is, back again," said Lucas with a shudder.

"And what lies on the other side?" asked Lascelles.

The old servant said that it had led to Northallerton once upon a time, by way of various queer places.

"Does it meet up with the road we saw near the Red House?" asked Lascelles.

The old servant shook his head. He did not know.

Lucas was losing patience. He wished to be away.

"Fairy roads are not like Christian roads," he said. "Often they do not go where they are supposed to at all. But what does it matter? Nobody here is going to put so much as a foot upon the wicked thing."

"Thank you," said Lascelles, "but I believe I shall make up my own mind upon that point." He hesitated a moment and then strode forward on to the fairy bridge.

Several of the servants called out to him to come back.

"Oh, let him go!" cried Lucas, tightening his hold upon a basket which contained his cat. "Let him be damned if he wishes! I am sure no one could deserve it more." He threw Lascelles one last, hearty look of dislike and followed the others into the Park.

Behind them the Black Pillar rose up into the grey Yorkshire sky and the end of it could not be seen.

Twenty miles away Childermass was crossing over the packhorse bridge that led into Starecross village. He rode through the village to the Hall and dismounted.

"Hey! Hey!" He banged on the door with his whip. He shouted some more and gave the door a few vigorous kicks.

Two servants appeared. They had been alarmed enough by all the shouting and banging, but when they held up their candle and found that its author was a wild-eyed, cutthroat-looking person with a slit in his face and his shirt all bloody, they were not in the least reassured.

"Do not stand there gawping!" he told them. "Go fetch master! He knows me!"

Ten minutes more brought Mr Segundus in a dressing-gown. Childermass, waiting impatiently just within the door, saw that as he came along the passage his eyes were closed and the servant led him by the hand. It looked for all the world as if he had gone blind. The servant placed him just before Childermass. He opened his eyes.

"Good Lord, Mr Childermass!" he cried. "What happened to your face?"

"Someone mistook it for an orange. And you, sir? What has happened to you? Have you been ill?"

"No, not ill." Mr Segundus looked embarrassed. "It is living in constant proximity to strong magic. I had not realized before how weakening that can be. To a person who is susceptible to it, I mean. The servants feel no effects whatsoever, I am glad to say."

There was a queer insubstantiality about him. He looked as if he were painted on the air. The merest draught from a gap in the casement took his hair and made little corkscrews and curlicues of it, as if it weighed nothing at all.

"I suppose that is what you have come about," he continued. "But you should tell Mr Norrell that I have done nothing but study the occurrences that presented themselves. I confess I have made a few notes, but really he has nothing to complain about."

"What magic?" asked Childermass. "What are you talking about? And you need not concern yourself any longer about Mr Norrell. He has problems of his own and knows nothing of my being here. What have you been doing, Mr Segundus?"

"Only watching and recording – as a magician should." Mr Segundus leant forward eagerly. "And I have come to some surprizing conclusions concerning Lady Pole's illness!"

"Oh?"

"In my opinion it is not madness at all. It is magic!" Mr Segundus waited for Childermass to be amazed. He looked a little disappointed when Childermass simply nodded.

"I have something that belongs to her ladyship," said Childermass. "Something she has long missed. So I beg that you will do me the kindness of taking me to her."

"Oh, but . . ."

"I mean her no harm, Mr Segundus. And I believe I may be able to do her some good. I swear it by Bird and Book. By Bird and Book."[1]

---

[1] This is an old Northern English oath. John Uskglass's arms shewed a Raven-in-Flight upon a white field (Argent, Raven Volant); those of his Chancellor, William Lanchester, shewed the same with the addition of an open book (Argent, Raven Volant above an open book).

For much of the thirteenth century John Uskglass devoted himself to scholarship and magic, abandoning the business of government to Lanchester. Lanchester's arms were displayed in all the great courts of law and upon many important legal documents. Consequently, the people fell into the habit of swearing by Bird and Book, the elements of those arms.

"I cannot take you to her," said Mr Segundus. He put up his hand to forestall Childermass's objection. "I do not mean that I am unwilling. I mean I *cannot*. Charles will take us." He indicated the servant at his side.

This seemed rather eccentric, but Childermass was in no mood to argue about it. Mr Segundus grasped Charles's arm and closed his eyes.

Behind the stone-and-oak passages of Starecross Hall, a vision of another house leapt up. Childermass saw high corridors that stretched away into unthinkable distances. It was as if two transparencies had been put into a magic lantern at the same time, so that one picture overlaid the other. The impression of walking through both houses at once rapidly brought on a sensation akin to sea-sickness. Confusion mounted in his mind and, had he been alone, he would soon have been at a loss to know which way to go. He could not tell whether he was walking or falling, whether he climbed one step, or mounted a staircase of impossible length. Sometimes he seemed to be skimming across an acre of stone flags, while at the same time he was scarcely moving at all. His head spun and he felt sick.

"Stop! Stop!" he cried and sank to the ground with his eyes closed.

"It affects you badly," said Mr Segundus. "Worse even than me. Close your eyes and take hold of my arm. Charles will lead us both."

They walked on, eyes closed. Charles guided them round a right-hand turning and up a staircase. At the top of the staircase there was a murmured conversation between Mr Segundus and someone. Charles drew Childermass forward. Childermass had the impression of entering a room. It smelt of clean linen and dried roses.

"This is the person you wish me to see?" said a woman's voice. There was something odd about it, as if it were coming from two places at once, as if there were an echo. "But I know this person! He is the magician's servant! He is . . ."

"I am the person your ladyship shot," said Childermass and he opened his eyes.

He saw not one woman, but two – or perhaps it would be more accurate to say he saw the same woman doubled. Both sat in the same posture, looking up at him. They occupied the same space, so that he had the same giddy feeling in looking at her as he had had walking through the corridors.

One version of Lady Pole sat in the house in Yorkshire; she wore an ivory-coloured morning dress and regarded him with calm indifference. The other version was fainter – more ghostly. She sat in the gloomy, labyrinthine house, dressed in a blood-red evening gown. There were jewels or stars in her dark hair and she regarded him with fury and hatred.

Mr Segundus pulled Childermass to the right. "Stand just here!" he said, excitedly. "Now close one eye! Can you see it? Observe! A red-and-white rose where her mouth ought to be."

"The magic affects us differently," said Childermass. "I see something very strange, but I do not see that."

"You are very bold to come here," said both versions of Lady Pole, addressing Childermass, "considering who you are and whom you represent."

"I am not here on Mr Norrell's business. To own the truth I am not entirely sure who it is I represent. I think it is Jonathan Strange. It is my belief that he sent me a message – and I think it was about your ladyship. But the messenger was prevented from reaching me and the message was lost. Do you know, your ladyship, what Mr Strange might have wished to tell me about you?"

"Yes," said both versions of Lady Pole.

"Will you tell me what it is?"

"If I speak," they said, "I shall speak nothing but madness."

Childermass shrugged his shoulders. "I have passed twenty years in the society of magicians. I am accustomed to it. Speak."

So she (or they) began. Immediately Mr Segundus took a memorandum book out of a pocket of his night-gown and began to scribble notes. But, in Childermass's eyes, the two versions of Lady Pole were no longer speaking as one. The Lady Pole who sat in Starecross Hall told a tale about a child who lived near Carlisle,[2] but the woman in the blood-red gown seemed to be telling quite a different story. She wore a fierce expression and emphasized her words with passionate gestures – but what she said Childermass could not tell; the whimsical tale of the Cumbrian child drowned it out.

"There! You see!" exclaimed Mr Segundus, as he finished scribbling his notes. "This is what makes them think her mad – these odd stories and tales. But I have made a list of all that she has told me and I have begun to find correspondences between them and ancient fairy lore. I am sure that if you and I were to make inquiries we would discover some reference to a set of fairies who had some close connexion with songbirds. They may not have been songbird-herds. That, you will agree, sounds a little too much like settled occupation for such a feckless race – but they may have pursued a particular sort of magic related to songbirds. And it may have suited one of their number to tell an impressionable child that she was a songbird-herd."

"Perhaps," said Childermass, not much interested. "But that was not what she meant to tell us. And I have remembered the magical significance of roses. They stand for silence. That

[2] One autumn morning the Cumbrian child went out into her grandmother's garden. In a forgotten corner she discovered a house about the height and largeness of a bee-skep, built of spiders' webs stiffened and whitened with hoar-frost. Inside the lacy house was a tiny person who at times appeared immeasurably old and at other times no older than the child herself. The little person told the Cumbrian child that she was a songbird-herd and that for ages past it had been her task to watch over the fieldfares, redwings and mistle-thrushes in that part of Cumbria. All winter the Cumbrian child and the songbird-herd played together and the progress of their friendship was not in the least impeded by the difference in their sizes. In fact the songbird-herd generally did away with this obstacle by making herself as large as the Cumbrian child – or sometimes by making them both as small as birds, or beetles, or snowflakes. The songbird-herd introduced the Cumbrian child to many odd and interesting persons, some of whom lived in houses even more eccentric and delightful than the songbird-herd's own.

is why you see a red-and-white rose – it is a muffling spell."

"A muffling spell!" said Mr Segundus, in amazement. "Yes, yes! I see that! I have read about such things. But how do we break it?"

From his coat-pocket Childermass took a little box, the colour of heartache. "Your ladyship," he said, "give me your left hand."

She laid her white hand in Childermass's lined, brown one. Childermass opened the box, took out the finger and laid it against the empty place.

Nothing happened.

"We must find Mr Strange," said Mr Segundus. "Or Mr Norrell. They may be able to mend it!"

"No," said Childermass. "There is no need. Not now. You and I are two magicians, Mr Segundus. And England is full of magic. How many years' study do we have between us? We must know something to the point. What about Pale's Restoration and Rectification?"

"I know the form of it," said Mr Segundus. "But I have never been a *practical* magician."

"And you never will be, if you do not try. Do the magic, Mr Segundus."

So Mr Segundus did the magic.[3]

The finger flowed into the hand, making a seamless whole. In the same instant the impression of endless, dreary corridors surrounding them disappeared; the two women before Childermass's eyes resolved themselves into one.

Lady Pole rose slowly from her chair. Her eyes went rapidly this way and that, like someone who was seeing the world anew.

[3] Like most of Martin Pale's magic, Restoration and Rectification involves the use of a tool or key made specifically for the purpose. In this case the key is a small cross-like object made of two thin pieces of metal. The four arms of the cross represent past state and future state, wholeness (or wellness) and incompleteness (or sickness). As he later reported in *The Modern Magician*, Mr Segundus used a spoon and a bodkin from Lady Pole's dressing-case which Lady Pole's maid tied together with a ribbon.

Everyone in the room could see she was changed. There was animation and fire in every feature. Her eyes glowed with a furious light. She raised both arms; her hands were clenched in tight fists, as if she intended to bring them down upon someone's head.

"I have been *enchanted*!" she burst out. "Bargained away for the sake of a wicked man's career!"

"Good God!" cried Mr Segundus. "My dear Lady Pole . . ."

"Compose yourself, Mr Segundus!" said Childermass. "We have no time for trivialities. Let her speak!"

"I have been dead within and almost-dead without!" Tears started from her eyes and she struck her own breast with her clenched hand. "And not only me! Others suffer even now! – Mrs Strange and my husband's servant, Stephen Black!"

She recounted the cold, ghostly balls she had endured, the dreary processions she had been forced to take part in and the strange handicap that would not allow her and Stephen Black to speak of their predicament.

Mr Segundus and the servants heard each new revelation with mounting horror; Childermass sat and listened with impassive expression.

"We must write to the editors of the newspapers!" cried Lady Pole. "I am determined upon public exposure!"

"Exposure of whom?" asked Mr Segundus.

"The magicians, of course! Strange and Norrell!"

"Mr Strange?" faltered Mr Segundus. "No, no, you are mistaken! My dear Lady Pole, take a moment to consider what you are saying. I have not a word to say for Mr Norrell – his crimes against you are monstrous! But Mr Strange has done no harm – not knowingly at any rate. Surely he is more sinned against than sinning?"

"Oh!" cried Lady Pole. "Upon the contrary! I consider him by far the worse of the two. By his negligence and cold, masculine magic he has betrayed the best of women, the most excellent of wives!"

Childermass stood up.

"Where are you going?" asked Mr Segundus.

"To find Strange and Norrell," said Childermass.

"Why?" cried Lady Pole, rounding on him. "To warn them? So that they can prepare themselves against a woman's vengeance? Oh, how these men protect one another!"

"No, I am going to offer them my assistance to free Mrs Strange and Stephen Black."

Lascelles walked on. The path entered a wood. At the entrance to the wood was the statue of the woman holding the plucked eye and heart – just as Childermass had described. Corpses hung from the thorn-trees in various states of decay. Snow lay on the ground and it was very quiet.

After a while he came to the tower. He had imagined it to be a fanciful, otherlandish sort of place; "But really," he thought, "it is very plain, like the castles of the Scottish border country."

High in the tower was a single window glowing with candlelight and the shadow of someone watching. Lascelles noticed something else too, something that Childermass had either not seen, or else had not troubled to report: the trees were full of serpent-like creatures. They had heavy, sagging forms. One was in the process of swallowing whole a fresh, meaty-looking corpse.

Between the trees and the brook was the pale young man. His eyes were empty and there was a slight dew upon his brow. His uniform was, thought Lascelles, that of the 11th Light Dragoons.

Lascelles addressed him thus: "One of our countrymen approached you a few days ago. He spoke to you. You challenged him. Then he ran away. He was a dark, ill-favoured fellow. A person of despicable habits and base origins."

If the pale young man recognized Childermass from this description, he shewed no sign of it. In a dead voice he said, "I am the Champion of the Castle of the Plucked Eye and Heart. I offer challenges to . . ."

"Yes, yes!" cried Lascelles, impatiently. "I do not care about that. I have come here to fight. To erase the stain upon England's honour that was made by that fellow's cowardice."

The figure at the window leaned forward eagerly.

The pale young man said nothing.

Lascelles made a sound of exasperation. "Very well! Believe that I mean this woman all sorts of harm if it pleases you. It matters not one whit to me! Pistols?"

The pale young man shrugged.

There being no seconds to act for them, Lascelles told the young man that they would stand at twenty paces and he measured the ground himself.

They had taken their positions and were about to fire, when something occurred to Lascelles. "Wait!" he cried. "What is your name?"

The young man stared dully at him. "I do not remember," he said.

They both fired their pistols at the same time. Lascelles had the impression that, at the last moment, the young man turned his pistol and deliberately fired wide. Lascelles did not care: if the young man was a coward then so much the worse for him. His own ball flew with pleasing exactitude to pierce the young man's breast. He watched him die with the same intense interest and sense of satisfaction that he had felt when he had killed Drawlight.

He hung the body upon the nearest thorn-tree. Then he amused himself by taking shots at the decaying bodies and the serpents. He had not been engaged in this pleasant occupation for more than an hour when he heard the sounds of hooves upon the woodland path. From the opposite direction, from Faerie rather than England, a dark figure upon a dark horse was approaching.

Lascelles spun round. "I am the Champion of the Castle of the Plucked Eye and Heart," he began . . .

## 65

# The ashes, the pearls, the counterpane and the kiss

### Mid February 1817

As LUCAS AND the others were leaving Hurtfew Abbey, Stephen was dressing in his bed-chamber at the top of the house in Harley-street.

London is a city with more than its fair share of eccentricities, but of all the surprizing places it contained at this time the most extraordinary was undoubtedly Stephen's bed-chamber. It was full of things that were precious, rare or wonderful. If the Cabinet, or the gentlemen who direct the Bank of England, had been somehow able to acquire the contents of Stephen's bed-chamber their cares would have all been over. They could have paid off Britain's debts and built London anew with the change. Thanks to the gentleman with the thistle-down hair Stephen possessed crown jewels from who-knew-what kingdoms, and embroidered robes that had once belonged to Coptic popes. The flowerpots upon his windowsill contained no flowers, but only ruby-and-pearl crosses, carved jewels and the insignia of long-dead military orders. Inside his small cupboard was a piece of the ceiling of the Sistine Chapel and the thigh-bone of a Basque saint. St Christopher's hat hung upon a peg behind the door and a marble statue of Lorenzo de Medici by Michael Angel (which had stood, until recently, upon the great man's tomb in Florence) occupied most of the floor.

Stephen was shaving himself in a little mirror balanced upon Lorenzo de Medici's knee when the gentleman appeared at his shoulder.

"The magician has returned to England!" he cried. "I saw him last night in the King's Roads, with the Darkness wrapped about him like a mystical cloak! What does he want? What can he be planning? Oh! This will be the end of me, Stephen! I feel it! He means me great harm!"

Stephen felt a chill. The gentleman was always at his most dangerous in this mood of agitation and alarm.

"We should kill him!" said the gentleman.

"Kill him? Oh no, sir!"

"Why not? We could be rid of him for ever! I could bind his arms, eyes and tongue with magic, and you could stab him through the heart!"

Stephen thought rapidly. "But his return may have nothing to do with you at all, sir," he offered. "Consider how many enemies he has in England – human enemies, I mean. Perhaps he has come back to continue his quarrel with one of them."

The gentleman looked doubtful. Any reasoning that did not contain a reference to himself was always difficult for him to follow. "I do not think *that* very likely," he said.

"Oh, but yes!" said Stephen, beginning to feel upon surer ground. "There have been terrible things written about him in the newspapers and the magical journals. There is a rumour that he killed his wife. Many people believe it. Were it not for his present situation, he would very likely have been arrested by now. And it is common knowledge that the other magician is the author of all these lies and half-truths. Probably, Strange has come to take revenge upon his master."

The gentleman stared at Stephen for a moment or two. Then he laughed, his spirits as elevated as moments before they had been the reverse. "We have nothing to fear Stephen!" he cried, in delight. "The magicians have quarrelled and hate each other! Yet they are nothing without one another. How glad that makes me! How happy I am to have you to advise me! And it so happens that I intend to give you a wonderful present today – something you have long desired!"

"Indeed, sir?" said Stephen with a sigh. "That will be most delightful."

"Yet we ought to kill someone," said the gentleman, immediately reverting to his former subject. "I have been quite put out of temper this morning and someone ought to die for it. What do you say to the old magician? – Oh, but wait! That would oblige the younger one, which I do not want to do! What about Lady Pole's husband? He is tall and arrogant and treats you like a servant!"

"But I *am* a servant, sir."

"Or the King of England! Yes, that is an excellent plan! Let you and I go immediately to the King of England. Then you can put him to death and be King in his place! Do you have the orb, crown and sceptre that I gave you?"

"But the laws of Great Britain do not allow . . ." began Stephen.

"The laws of Great Britain! Pish tush! What nonsense! I thought you would have understood by now that the laws of Great Britain are nothing but a flimsy testament to the idle wishes and dreams of mankind. According to the ancient laws by which my race conducts itself, a king is most commonly succeeded by the person who killed him."

"But, sir! Remember how much you liked the old gentleman when you met him?"

"Hmm, that is true. But in a matter of such importance I am willing to put aside my personal feelings. The difficulty is that we have too many enemies, Stephen! There are too many wicked persons in England! I know! I shall ask some of my allies to tell us who is our greatest enemy of all. We must be careful. We must be cunning. We must frame our question with exactitude.[1] I shall ask

[1] It is all very well in fairy-tales to ask, "Who is the fairest of them all?" But in reality no magic, fairy or human, could ever be persuaded to answer such an imprecise question.

the North Wind and the Dawn to bring us immediately into the presence of the one person in England whose existence is the greatest threat to me! And then we can kill him, whoever he is. You observe, Stephen, that I make reference to my own life, but I consider your fate and mine as bound so closely together that there is scarcely any difference between us. Whosoever is a danger to me, is a danger to you also! Now take up your crown and orb and sceptre and say a last farewell to the scenes of your slavery! It may be that you shall never see them again!"

"But . . ." began Stephen.

It was too late. The gentleman raised his long, white hands and gave a sort of flourish.

Stephen expected to be brought before one or other of the magicians – possibly both. Instead the gentleman and he found themselves upon a wide, empty moor covered in snow. More snow was falling. On one side the ground rose up to meet the heavy, slate-coloured sky; on the other was a misty view of far-away, white hills. In all that desolate landscape there was only one tree – a twisted hawthorn not far from where they stood. It was, thought Stephen, very like the country around Starecross Hall.

"Well, that is very odd!" said the gentleman. "I do not see any body at all, do you?"

"No, sir. No one," said Stephen, in relief. "Let us return to London."

"I cannot understand . . . Oh, but wait! Here is someone!"

Half a mile or so away there seemed to be a road or track of some sort. A horse and cart were coming slowly along it. When the cart drew level with the hawthorn tree, it stopped and someone got out. This person began to stump across the moor towards them.

"Excellent!" cried the gentleman. "Now we shall see our wickedest and most powerful enemy! Put on your crown, Stephen! Let him tremble before our power and majesty! Excellent! Raise your sceptre! Yes, yes! Hold forth your orb! How handsome you look! How regal! Now, Stephen, since we have a little time before he arrives . . ." The gentleman gazed at the little figure in the distance labouring across the snowy moor. ". . . I have something else to tell you. What is the date today?"

"The fifteenth of February, sir. St Anthony's Day."

"Ha! A dreary saint indeed! Well, in future the people of England will have something better to celebrate on the fifteenth of February than the life of a monk who keeps the rain off people and finds their lost thimbles!"[2]

"Will they indeed, sir? And what is that?"

"The Naming of Stephen Black!"

"I beg your pardon, sir?"

"I told you, Stephen, that I would find your true name!"

"What! Did my mother really name me, sir?"

"Yes, indeed! It is all just as I supposed! – which is scarcely surprizing since I am rarely wrong in such matters. She named you with a name in her own tongue. With a name she had heard often among her own people when she was a young girl. She named you, but she did not tell the name to a single soul. She did not even whisper it into your infant ear. She had no time because Death stole upon her and took her unawares."

A picture rose up in Stephen's mind – the dark, fusty hold of the ship – his mother, worn out by the pains of childbirth, surrounded by strangers – himself a tiny infant. Did she even speak the language of the other people on board? He had no way of knowing. How alone she must have felt! He would have given a great deal at that moment to be able to reach out and comfort her, but all the years of his life lay between them. He felt his heart harden another degree against the English. Only a few minutes ago he had struggled to persuade the gentleman not to kill Strange, but why should he care what became of one Englishman? Why should he care what became of any of that cold, callous race?

---

[2] St Anthony of Padua. Several of his miracles involve preserving from rain congregations to whom he was preaching, or maid-servants with whom he was friendly. He also helps people find things they have lost.

With a sigh, he put these thoughts aside and discovered that the gentleman was still talking.

". . . It is a most edifying tale and demonstrates to perfection all those qualities for which I am especially famed; namely self-sacrifice, devoted friendship, nobility of purpose, perceptiveness, ingenuity and courageousness."

"I beg your pardon, sir?"

"The story of my finding your name, Stephen, which I am now going to relate! Know then that your mother died in the hold of a ship, the *Penlaw*,[3] that was sailing from Jamaica to Liverpool. And then," he added in a matter-of-fact tone, "the English sailors stripped her body and flung it into the sea."

"Ah!" breathed Stephen.

"Now, as you may imagine, this made the task of recovering your name extremely difficult. After thirty or forty years, all that was left of your mother was four things: her screams in childbirth, which had sunk into the planks of the ship; her bones, which was all that was left of her, once the flesh and softer parts had been devoured by fishes . . ."

"Ah!" exclaimed Stephen again.

". . . her gown of rose-coloured cotton which had passed into the possession of a sailor; and a kiss which the captain of the ship had stolen from her, two days earlier. Now," said the gentleman (who was clearly enjoying himself immensely), "you will observe with what cleverness and finesse I traced the passage of each part of her through the world, until I was able to recover them and so divine your glorious name! The *Penlaw* sailed on to Liverpool where the wicked grandfather of Lady Pole's wicked husband disembarked with his servant – who carried your own infant person in his arms. On the *Penlaw*'s next voyage, which was to Leith in Scotland, it met with a storm and was wrecked. Various spars and bits of broken hull were cast up upon the rocky shore,

[3] Penlaw is the name of the place in Northumbria where John Uskglass and his fairy army first appeared in England.

including the planks that contained your mother's screams. These were taken by a very poor man to make a roof and walls for his house. I found the house very easily. It stood upon a windy promontory, overlooking a stormy sea. Inside, several generations of the poor man's family were living in the utmost poverty and degradation. Now, you should know, Stephen, that wood has a stubborn, proud nature; it does not readily tell what it knows – even to its friends. It is always easier to deal with the ashes of the wood, rather than wood itself. So I burnt the poor man's house to the ground, placed the ashes in a bottle and continued on my way."

"Burnt, sir! I hope no one was hurt!"

"Well, some people were. The strong, young men were able to run out of the conflagration in time, but the older, enfeebled members of the family, the women and infants were all burnt to death."

"Oh!"

"Next I traced the history of her bones. I believe I mentioned before that she was cast into the ocean where, due to the movement of the waters and the importunate interference of the fishes, the body became bones, the bones became dust, and the dust was very soon transformed by a bed of oysters into several handfuls of the most beautiful pearls. In time the pearls were harvested and sold to a jeweller in Paris, who created a necklace of five perfect strands. This he sold to a beautiful French Comtesse. Seven years later the Comtesse was guillotined and her jewels, gowns and personal possessions became the property of a Revolutionary official. This wicked man was, until quite recently, the mayor of a small town in the Loire valley. Late at night he would wait until all his servants had gone to bed and then, in the privacy of his bed-chamber, he would put on the Comtesse's jewels and gowns and other finery and parade up and down in front of a large mirror. Here I found him one night, looking, I may say, very ridiculous. I strangled him upon the spot – using the pearl necklace."

"Oh!" said Stephen.

"I took the pearls, let the miserable corpse fall to the ground and passed on. Next I turned my attention to your mother's pretty rose-coloured gown. The sailor who had acquired it, kept it among his things for a year or two until he happened to find himself in a cold, miserable little hamlet on the eastern coast of America called Piper's Grave. There he met a tall, thin woman and, wishing to impress her, he gave her the gown as a present. The gown did not fit this woman (your mother, Stephen, had a sweetly rounded, feminine figure), but she liked the colour and so she cut it up and sewed the pieces into a counterpane with some other cheap materials. The rest of this woman's history is not very interesting – she married several husbands and buried them all, and by the time I found her she was old and withered. I plucked the counterpane off her bed as she slept."

"You did not kill her, did you, sir?" asked Stephen, anxiously.

"No, Stephen. Why would I? Of course it was a bitter night with four feet of snow and a raging north wind outside. She may have died of the cold. I do not know. So we come at last to the kiss and the captain who stole it from her."

"Did you kill him, sir?"

"No, Stephen – though I would certainly have done so to punish him for his insult to your esteemed mother, but he was hanged in the town of Valletta twenty-nine years ago. Fortunately he had kissed a great many other young women before he died and the virtue and strength of your mother's kiss had been conveyed to them. So all I had to do was to find them and extract what was left of your mother's kiss."

"And how did you do that, sir?" asked Stephen, though he feared that he knew the answer all too well.

"Oh! It is easy enough once the women are dead."

"So many people dead, just to find my name," sighed Stephen.

"And I would gladly have killed twice that number – nay, a hundred times – nay, a hundred thousand times or more! – so great is the love I bear you, Stephen. With the ashes that were her screams and the pearls that were her bones and the counterpane that was her gown and the magical essence of her kiss, I was able to divine your name – which I, your truest friend and most noble benefactor, will now . . . Oh, but here is our enemy! As soon as we have killed him, I will bestow your name upon you. Beware, Stephen! There will probably be a magical combat of some sort. I dare say I shall have to take on different forms – cockatrices, raw head and bloody bones, rains of fire, etc., etc. You may wish to stand back a little!"

The unknown person drew closer. He was as thin as a Banbury cheese, with a hawk-like, disreputable-looking face. His coat and shirt were in rags and his boots were broken and full of holes.

"Well!" said the gentleman after a moment. "I could not be more astonished! Have you ever seen this person before, Stephen?"

"Yes, sir. I must confess that I have. This is the man I told you about. The one with the strange disfiguration who told me the prophecy. His name is Vinculus."

"Good day to you, King!" said Vinculus to Stephen. "Did I not tell you the hour was almost come? And now it has! The rain shall make a door for you and you shall go through it! The stones shall make a throne for you and you shall sit upon it!" He surveyed Stephen with a mysterious satisfaction, as if the crown, orb and sceptre were somehow all his doing.

Stephen said to the gentleman, "Perhaps the Venerable Beings to whom you applied are mistaken, sir. Perhaps they have brought us to the wrong person."

"Nothing seems more likely," agreed the gentleman. "This vagabond is scarcely any threat to any one. To me least of all. But as the North Wind and the Dawn have taken the trouble to point him out to us, it would be most disrespectful to them not to kill him."

Vinculus seemed curiously unmoved by this proposal. He gave a laugh. "Try if you can do it, Fairy! You will discover that I am very hard to kill!"

"Are you indeed?" said the gentleman. "For I must confess that it looks to me as if nothing would be easier! But then you see I am very adept at killing all sorts of things! I have slain dragons, drowned armies and persuaded the earthquakes and tempests to devour cities! You are a man. You are all alone – as all men are. I am surrounded by ancient friends and allies. Rogue, what do you have to counter that?"

Vinculus thrust out his dirty chin at the gentleman in a gesture of the utmost contempt. "A book!" he said.

It was an odd thing to say. Stephen could not help thinking that if Vinculus had indeed possessed a book he would have been well advised to sell it and buy a better coat.

The gentleman turned his head to gaze with sudden intensity at a distant line of white hills. "Oh!" he exclaimed with as much violence as if he had been struck. "Oh! They have stolen her from me! Thieves! Thieves! English thieves!"

"Who, sir?"

"Lady Pole! Someone has broken the enchantment!"

"The magic of Englishmen, Fairy!" cried Vinculus. "The magic of Englishmen is coming back!"

"Now you see their arrogance, Stephen!" cried the gentleman, spinning round to bestow a look of vivid fury upon Vinculus. "Now you see the malice of our enemies! Stephen, procure me some rope!"

"Rope, sir? There is none for miles around, I am sure. Let you and I . . ."

"No rope, Fairy!" jeered Vinculus.

But something was happening in the air above them. The lines of sleet and snow were somehow twisting together. They snaked across the sky towards Stephen. Without warning a length of strong rope fell into his hand.

"There!" cried the gentleman, triumphantly. "Stephen, look!

Here is a tree! One tree in all this desolate waste, exactly where we need it! But England has always been my friend. She has always served me well. Throw the rope over a branch and let us hang this rogue!"

Stephen hesitated, uncertain for the moment how to prevent this new disaster. The rope in his hand seemed to grow impatient with him; it jumped away and divided itself neatly into two lengths. One snaked across the ground to Vinculus and trussed him tight and the other quickly formed itself into a well-made noose and hung itself neatly over a branch.

The gentleman was in high glee, his spirits quite restored at the prospect of a hanging. "Do you dance, rogue?" he asked Vinculus. "I shall teach you some new steps!"

Everything took on the character of a nightmare. Events happened quickly and seamlessly, and Stephen never found the right moment to intervene or the right words to say. As for Vinculus himself, he behaved very oddly throughout his entire execution. He never appeared to understand what was happening to him. He said not another word, but he did make several exclamations of exasperation as if he was being put to some serious inconvenience and it was putting him out of temper.

Without any appearance of exertion the gentleman took hold of Vinculus and placed him beneath the noose. The noose draped itself about his neck and hoisted him abruptly into the air; at the same time the other rope unwound itself from his body and folded itself neatly on the ground.

Vinculus kicked his feet uselessly in the empty air; his body jerked and spun. For all his boast of being hard to kill, his neck broke very easily – the snapping sound could be clearly heard on the empty moor. A jerk or two more and he was finished.

Stephen – forgetting that he had determined to hate all Englishmen – covered his face with his hands and wept.

The gentleman danced round and sang to himself, as a child will when something has pleased it particularly; and when he was done he said in a conversational tone, "Well, that was disappointing! He did not struggle at all. I wonder who he was?"

"I told you, sir," said Stephen, wiping his eyes. "He is the man who told me that prophecy. He has a strange disfiguration upon his body. Like writing."

The gentleman pulled off Vinculus's coat, shirt and neckcloth. "Yes, there it is!" he said in mild surprize. He scratched with one nail at a little circle on Vinculus's right shoulder to see if it would come off. Finding it did not, he lost interest.

"Now!" he said. "Let us go and cast a spell upon Lady Pole."

"A spell, sir!" said Stephen. "But why would we wish to do that?"

"Oh! So that she will die within a month or two. It is – apart from any thing else – very traditional. It is very rare that any one released from an enchantment is permitted to live long – certainly not if I have enchanted them! Lady Pole is not far away and the magicians must be taught that they may not oppose us with impunity! Come, Stephen!"

# 66

# Jonathan Strange and Mr Norrell

## Mid February 1817

Mr Norrell turned and looked back along the corridor which had once led from the library to the rest of the house. If he had had any confidence that it could take him back to Lascelles and the servants, he would have gone down it. But he was quite certain that Strange's magic would simply return him to this spot.

There was a sound from within the library and he gave a start of terror. He waited, but no one appeared. After a moment he realized that he knew what the sound was. He had heard it a thousand times before – it was the sound of Strange exclaiming in exasperation over some passage in a book. It was such a very familiar sound – and so closely connected in Mr Norrell's mind with the happiest period of his existence – that it gave him the courage to open the door and go inside.

The first thing that struck him was the immense quantity of candles. The room was full of light. Strange had not troubled to find candlesticks; he had simply stuck the candles to tables or to bookshelves. He had even stuck them to piles of books. The library was in imminent danger of catching fire. There were books everywhere – scattered over tables, tumbled on the floor. Many had been laid face-down on the floor, so that Strange should not lose his place.

Strange was standing at the far end of the room. He was a much thinner person than Mr Norrell remembered. He had shaved himself with no extraordinary degree of perfection and his hair was ragged. He did not look up at Mr Norrell's approach.

"Seven people from Norwich in 1124," he said, reading from the book in his hand. "Four from Aysgarth in Yorkshire at Christmas in 1151, twenty-three at Exeter in 1201, one from Hathersage in Derbyshire in 1243 – all enchanted and stolen away into Faerie. It was a problem he never solved."

He spoke with such calm that Mr Norrell – who was rather expecting to be blasted with a bolt of magic at any moment – looked round to see if someone else was in the room. "I beg your pardon?" he asked.

"John Uskglass," said Strange, still not troubling to turn around. "He could not prevent fairies stealing away Christian men and women. Why should I suppose that I might be capable of something he was not?" He read a little further. "I like your labyrinth," he said conversationally. "Did you use Hickman?"

"What? No. De Chepe."

"De Chepe! Really?" For the first time Strange looked directly at his master. "I had always supposed him to be a very minor scholar without an original thought in his head."

"He was never much to the taste of people who like the showier sorts of magic," said Mr Norrell, nervously, uncertain of how long this civil mood of Strange's might last. "He was interested in labyrinths, magical pathways, spells which may be effected by following certain steps and turns – things of that sort. There is a long description of his magic in Belasis's *Instructions* . . ." He paused. ". . . which you have never seen. The only copy is here. It is on the third shelf by the window." He pointed and discovered that the shelf had been emptied. "Or it might be on the floor," he offered. "In that pile."

"I shall look in a moment," Strange assured him.

"Your own labyrinth was quite remarkable," said Mr Norrell. "I have been half the night trying to escape it."

"Oh, I did what I usually do in such circumstances," said Strange, carelessly. "I copied you and added some refinements. How long has it been?"

"I beg your pardon?"

"How long have I been in the Darkness?"

"Since the beginning of December."

"And what month is it now?"

"February."

"Three months!" exclaimed Strange. "Three months! I thought it had been years!"

Mr Norrell had imagined this conversation many times. Each time he had pictured Strange angry and vengeful, and himself putting forth powerful arguments of self-justification. Now that they had finally met, Strange's unconcern was utterly bewildering. The distant pains Mr Norrell had long felt in his small, shrivelled soul awakened. They grew claws and rent at him. His hands began to shake.

"I have been your enemy!" he burst out. "I destroyed your book – all except my own copy! I have slandered your name and plotted against you! Lascelles and Drawlight have told everyone that you murdered your wife! I have let them believe it!"

"Yes," said Strange.

"But these are terrible crimes! Why are you not angry?"

Strange seemed to concede that this was a reasonable question. He thought for a moment. "I suppose it is because I have been many things since last we met. I have been trees and rivers and hills and stones. I have spoken to stars and earth and wind. One cannot be the conduit through which all English magic flows and still be oneself. I would have been angry, you say?"

Mr Norrell nodded.

Strange smiled his old, ironic smile. "Then be comforted! I dare say I shall be so again. In time."

"And you have done all this just to thwart me?" asked Mr Norrell.

"To thwart you?" said Strange, in astonishment. "No! I have done this to save my wife!"

There was a short silence during which time Mr Norrell found it impossible to meet Strange's eye. "What do you want from me?" he asked in a low voice.

"Only what I have always wanted – your help."

"To break the enchantments?"

"Yes."

Mr Norrell considered this for a moment. "The hundredth anniversary of an enchantment is often most auspicious," he said. "There are several rites and procedures . . ."

"Thank you," said Strange, with more than a tinge of his old sarcastic manner, "but I believe I was hoping for something a little more immediate in its effect."

"The death of the enchanter puts an end to all such contracts and enchantments, but . . ."

"Ah, yes! Quite!" interrupted Strange, eagerly. "The death of the enchanter! I thought of it often in Venice. With all of English magic at my disposal there were so many ways I could have killed him. Sent him hurtling down from great heights. Burned him with bolts of lightning. Raised up mountains and crushed him beneath them. Had it been my freedom at stake, I would have certainly attempted it. But it was not my freedom – it was Arabella's – and if I had tried and failed – if I had been killed – then her fate would have been sealed forever. So I set to thinking some more. And I thought how there was one man in all the world – in all the worlds that ever were – who would know how to defeat my enemy. One man who could advise me what I ought to do. I realized the time had come to speak to him."

Mr Norrell looked more alarmed than ever. "Oh! But I must tell you that I no longer regard myself as your superior. My reading has been a great deal more extensive than yours, it is true, and I will give you what help I can, but I can offer you no security that I will be any more successful than you."

Strange frowned. "What? What are you talking about? I do not mean you! I mean John Uskglass. I want your help in summoning John Uskglass."

Mr Norrell breathed hard. The very air seemed to quiver as if a deep note had been sounded. He was aware, to an almost painful degree, of the darkness surrounding them, of the new stars above them and of the silence of the stopt clocks. It was one Great Black Moment going on for ever, pressing down upon him, suffocating him. And in that Moment it cost no effort to believe that John Uskglass was near – a mere spell away; the deep shadows in the far corners of the room were the folds of his robe; the smoke from the guttering candles was the raven mantling of his helm.

Strange, however, seemed oppressed by no such immortal fears. He leant forward a little, with an eager half-smile. "Come, Mr Norrell," he whispered. "It is very dull working for Lord Liverpool. You must feel it so? Let other magicians cast protection spells over cliffs and beaches. There will be plenty of them to do it soon! Let you and me do something extraordinary!"

Another silence.

"You are afraid," said Strange, drawing back displeased.

"Afraid!" burst out Norrell. "Of course I am afraid! It would be madness – absolute madness – to be any thing else! But that is not my objection. It will not work. Whatever you hope to gain by it, it will not work. Even if we succeeded in bringing him forth – which we might very well do, you and I together – he will not help you in the way you imagine. Kings do not satisfy idle curiosity – this King least of all."

"You call it idle curiosity . . . ?" began Strange.

"No, no!" said Norrell, interrupting hastily. "*I* do not. I merely represent to you how it will appear to *him*. What will he care about two lost women? You are thinking of John Uskglass as if he were an ordinary man. I mean a man like you or me. He was brought up and educated in Faerie. The ways of the *brugh* were natural to him – and most *brughs* contained captive Christians – he was one himself. It will not seem so extraordinary to him. He will not understand."

"Then I will explain it to him. Mr Norrell, I have changed England to save my wife. I have changed the world. I shall not flinch from summoning up one man; let him be as tremendous as he may. Come, sir! There is very little sense in arguing about it. The first thing is to bring him here. How do we begin?"

Mr Norrell sighed. "It is not like summoning any one else. There are difficulties peculiar to any magic involving John Uskglass."

"Such as?"

"Well, for one thing we do not know what to call him. Spells of summoning require the magician to be most particular about names. None of the names by which we call John Uskglass were really his own. He was, as the histories tell, stolen away into Faerie, before he could be christened – and so he became the nameless child in the *brugh*. 'The nameless slave' was one of the ways in which he referred to himself. Of course the fairies gave him a name after their own fashion, but he cast that off when he returned to England. As for all his titles – the Raven King, the Black King, the King of the North – these are what other people called him, not what he called himself."

"Yes, yes!" declared Strange, impatiently. "I know all that! But surely John Uskglass was his true name?"

"Oh! By no means. That was the name of a young Norman aristocrat who died, I believe, in the summer of 1097. The King – our John Uskglass – claimed that man as his father, but many people have disputed whether they were really related at all. I do not suppose that this muddle of names and titles is accidental. The King knew that he would always draw the eyes of other magicians to him and so he protected himself from the nuisance of their magic by deliberately confusing their spells."

"So what ought I to do?" Strange snapped his fingers. "Advise me!"

Mr Norrell blinked his small eyes. He was unaccustomed to think so rapidly. "If we use an ordinary English spell of summoning – and I strongly advise that we do, as they cannot be bettered – then we can make the elements of the spell do the work of identification for us. We will need an envoy, a path and a handsel.[1] If we chuse tools that already know the King, and know him well, then it will not matter that we cannot name him properly, they will find him, bring him and bind him, without our help! Do you see?"

In spite of all his terror, he was growing more animated at the prospect of magic – new magic! – to be performed with Mr Strange.

"No," said Strange. "I do not see at all."

"This house is built upon the King's land, with stones from the King's abbey. A river runs by it – not more than two hundred yards from this room; that river has often borne the King in his royal barge upon its waters. In my kitchen-garden are a pear-tree and an apple-tree – the direct descendants of some pips spat out by the King when he sat one summer's evening in the Abbot's garden. Let the old abbey stones be our envoy; let the river be our path; let next year's apples and pears from those trees be our handsel. Then we may name him simply 'The King'. These stones, this river, those trees know none other!"

"Good," said Strange. "And what spell do you recommend? Are there any in Belasis?"

"Yes, three."

"Are they worth trying?"

"No, not really." Mr Norrell opened a drawer and drew out a piece of paper. "This is the best I know. I am not in the habit of

[1] These are the customary three elements of a traditional English summoning spell. The envoy finds the person summoned, the path brings him to the summoner and the handsel (or gift) binds him to come.

using summoning spells – but if I were, this is the one I would use." He passed it to Strange.

It was covered with Mr Norrell's small, meticulous handwriting. At the top was written, "Mr Strange's spell of summoning."

"It is the one you used to summon Maria Absalom,"[2] explained Norrell. "I have made some amendments. I have omitted the *florilegium* which you copied word for word from Ormskirk. I have, as you know, no opinion of *florilegia* in general and this one seems particularly nonsensical. I have added an epitome of preservation and deliverance, and a skimmer of supplication – though I doubt that either will help us much in this case."[3]

"It is as much your work as mine now," observed Strange. There was no trace of rivalry or resentment in his voice.

"No, no," said Norrell. "All the fabric of it is yours. I have merely neatened the edges."

"Good! Then we are ready, are we not?"

"There is one more thing."

"What is it?"

"There are certain precautions that are necessary to secure Mrs Strange's safety," explained Mr Norrell.

---

[2] At the Shadow House in July 1809, Mr Segundus, Mr Honeyfoot and Henry Woodhope being present.

[3] "*Florilegium*", "epitome" and "skimmer" are all terms for parts of spells. In the thirteenth and fourteenth centuries fairies in England were fond of adding to their magic, exhortations to random collections of Christian saints. Fairies were baffled by Christian doctrine, but they were greatly attracted to saints, whom they saw as powerful magical beings whose patronage it was useful to have. These exhortations were called *florilegia* (lit. cullings or gatherings of flowers) and fairies taught them to their Christian masters. When the Protestant religion took hold in England and saints fell out of favour, *florilegia* degenerated into meaningless collections of magical words and bits of other spells, thrown in by the magician in the hope that some of them might take effect.

An epitome is a highly condensed form of a spell inserted within another spell to strengthen or enlarge it. In this case an epitome of preservation and deliverance is intended to protect the magician from the person summoned. A skimmer is a sprinkling of words or charms (from a dialect word of Northern English, meaning to brighten or sparkle). A skimmer of supplication encourages the person summoned to aid the magician.

Strange cast a glance at him as if he thought it a little late in the day for Mr Norrell to be thinking of Arabella's safety, but Mr Norrell had hurried to a bookshelf and was busy delving in a large volume and did not notice.

"The spell is written in Chaston's *Liber Novus*. Ah, yes! Here it is! We must build a magical road and make a door so that Mrs Strange may come safely out of Faerie. Otherwise she might be trapped there for ever. It might take us centuries to find her."

"Oh, that!" said Strange. "I have done it already. And appointed a doorkeeper to meet her when she comes out. All is in readiness."

He took the merest stub of a candle, placed it in a candlestick and lit it.[4] Then he began to recite the spell. He named the abbey-stones as the envoy sent to seek the King. He named the river as the path the King was to come. He named next year's apples and pears from Mr Norrell's trees as the handsel the King was to receive. He named the moment of the flame's dying as the time when the King was to appear.

The candle guttered and went out . . .

. . . and in that moment . . .

. . . in that moment the room was full of ravens. Black wings filled the air like great hands gesturing, filled Strange's vision like a tumult of black flames. He was struck at from every side by wings and claws. The cawing and the croaking were deafening. Ravens battered walls, battered windows, battered Strange himself. He covered his head with his hands and fell to the floor. The din and strife of wings continued a little while longer.

Then, in the blink of an eye, they were gone and the room was silent.

---

[4] The last element of a successful summoning spell is temporal. The magician must somehow convey to the summoned person *when* he is meant to appear, otherwise (as Strange once observed) the summoned person might appear at any time and feel he had fulfilled his obligations. A candle stub is a very convenient device: the magician instructs the person summoned to appear when the flame goes out.

The candles had all been extinguished. Strange rolled on to his back, but for some moments he could do nothing but stare into the Darkness. "Mr Norrell?" he said at last.

No one answered.

In the pitch-black darkness he got to his feet. He succeeded in finding one of the library desks and felt about until his hand met with an upturned candle. He took his tinderbox from his pocket and lit it.

Raising it above his head, he saw that the room was in the last extremes of chaos and disorder. Not a book remained upon a shelf. Tables and library steps had been overturned. Several fine chairs had been reduced to firewood. A thick drift of raven feathers covered everything, as if a black snow had fallen.

Norrell was half-lying, half-sitting on the floor, his back against a desk. His eyes were open, but blank-looking. Strange passed the candle before his face. "Mr Norrell?" he said again.

In a dazed whisper, Norrell said, "I believe we may assume that we have his attention."

"I believe you are right, sir. Do you know what happened?"

Still in a whisper Norrell said, "The books all turned into ravens. I had my eye upon Hugh Pontifex's *The Fountain of the Heart* and I saw it change. He used it often, you know – that chaos of black birds. I have been reading about it since I was a boy. That I should live to see it, Mr Strange! That I should live to see it! It has a name in the *Sidhe* language, the language of his childhood, but the name is lost."[5] He suddenly seized Strange's hand. "Are the books safe?"

Strange picked up one from the floor. He shook the raven feathers off it and glanced at the title: *Seven Doors and Forty-two Keys* by Piers Russinol. He opened it and began to read at random. "*. . . and there you will find a strange country like a chessboard, where alternates barren rock with fruitful orchards, wastes of thorns with fields of*

[5] The chaos of ravens and wind is also described in the tale of the Newcastle glovemaker's child (Chapter 39, footnote 1).

*bearded corn, water meadows with deserts. And in this country, the god of magicians, Thrice-Great Hermes, has set a guard upon every gate and every bridge: in one place a ram, in another place serpent . . .* Does that sound right?" he asked doubtfully.

Mr Norrell nodded. He took out his pocket handkerchief and dabbed the blood from his face with it.

The two magicians sat upon the floor amid the books and feathers, and for a little while they said nothing at all. The world had shrunk to the breadth of a candle's light.

Finally, Strange said, "How near to us must he be in order to do magic like that?"

"John Uskglass? For aught I know he can do magic like that from a hundred worlds away – from the heart of Hell."

"Still it is worth trying to find out, is it not?"

"Is it?" asked Norrell.

"Well, for example, if we found he was close by, we could . . ." Strange considered a moment. "We could go to him."

"Very well," sighed Norrell. He did not sound or look very hopeful.

The first – and indeed only – requirement for spells of location is a silver dish of water. At Hurtfew Abbey Mr Norrell's dish had stood upon a little table in the corner of the room, but the table had been destroyed by the violence of the ravens and the dish was nowhere to be seen. They searched for a while and eventually found it in the fireplace, upside-down beneath a mess of raven feathers and damp, torn pages from books.

"We need water," said Norrell. "I always made Lucas get it from the river. Water that has travelled rapidly is best for location magic – and Hurtfew's river is quick-flowing even in summer. I will fetch it."

But Mr Norrell was not much in the habit of doing any thing for himself and it was a little while before he was out of the house. He stood on the lawn and stared up at stars he had never seen before. He did not feel as if he were inside a Pillar of Darkness in the middle of Yorkshire; he felt more as if the rest of the world had fallen away and he and Strange were left alone upon a solitary island or promontory. The idea distressed him a great deal less than one might have supposed. He had never much cared for the world and he bore its loss philosophically.

At the river's edge he knelt down among the frozen grasses to fill the dish with water. The unknown stars shone up at him from the depths. He stood up again (a little dizzy from the unaccustomed exertion) – and immediately he had an overwhelming sense of magic going on – much stronger than he had ever felt it before. If any one had asked him to describe what was happening, he would have said that all of Yorkshire was turning itself inside out. For a moment he could not think which direction the house lay in. He turned, stumbled and walked straight into Mr Strange, who for some reason was standing directly behind him. "I thought you were going to remain in the library!" he said in surprize.

Strange glared at him. "I did remain in the library! One moment I was reading Goubert's *Gatekeeper of Apollo*. The next moment I was here!"

"You did not follow me?" asked Norrell.

"No, of course not! What is happening? And what in God's name is taking you so long?"

"I could not find my greatcoat," said Norrell, humbly. "I did not know where Lucas had put it."

Strange raised one eye-brow, sighed and said, "I presume you experienced the same as me? Just before I was plucked up and brought here, there was a sensation like winds and waters and flames, all mixed together?"

"Yes," said Norrell.

"And a faint odour, as of wild herbs and mountainsides?"

"Yes," said Norrell.

"Fairy magic?"

"Oh!" said Norrell. "Undoubtedly! This is part of the same spell that keeps you here in Eternal Darkness." He looked around. "How extensive is it?"

"What?"

"The Darkness."

"Well, it is hard for me to know exactly since it moves around with me. But other people have told me that it is the size of the parish in Venice where I lived. Say half an acre?"

"Half an acre! Stay here!" Mr Norrell put the silver dish of water down upon the frozen ground. He walked off in the direction of the bridge. Soon all that was visible of him was his grey wig. In the starlight it resembled nothing so much as a little stone tortoise waddling away.

The world gave another twist and suddenly the two magicians were standing together on the bridge over the river at Hurtfew.

"What in the world . . . ?" began Strange.

"You see?" said Norrell, grimly. "The spell will not allow us to move too far from one another. It has gripped me too. I dare say there was some regrettable impreciseness in the fairy's magic. He has been careless. I dare say he named you as the English magician – or some such vague term. Consequently, his spell – meant only for you – now entraps any English magician who stumbles into it!"

"Ah!" said Strange. He said nothing more. There did not seem any thing to say.

Mr Norrell turned towards the house. "If nothing else, Mr Strange," he said, "this is an excellent illustration of the need for great preciseness about names in spells!"

Behind him Strange raised his eyes heavenward.

In the library they placed the silver dish of water on a table between them.

It was very odd but the discovery that he was now imprisoned in Eternal Darkness with Strange seemed to have raised Mr Norrell's spirits rather than otherwise. Cheerfully he reminded Strange that they still had not found a way to name John Uskglass and that this

was certain to be a great obstacle in finding him – by magic or any other means.

Strange, with his head propped up on his hands, stared at him gloomily. "Just try John Uskglass," he said.

So Norrell did the magic, naming John Uskglass as the person they sought. He divided the surface of the water into quarters with lines of glittering light. He gave each quarter a name: Heaven, Hell, Earth and Faerie. Instantly a speck of bluish light shone in the quarter that represented Earth.

"There!" said Strange, leaping up triumphantly. "You see, sir! Things are not always as difficult as you suppose."

Norrell tapped the surface of the quarter; the divisions disappeared. He redrew them, naming them afresh: "England, Scotland, Ireland, Elsewhere." The speck of light appeared in England. He tapped the quarter, redrew the divisions and examined the result. And on and on, he went, refining the magic. The speck glowed steadily.

He made a soft sound of exclamation.

"What is it?" asked Strange.

In a tone of wonder, Norrell said, "I think we may have succeeded after all! It says he is here. In Yorkshire!"

67

# The hawthorn tree

## February 1817

CHILDERMASS WAS CROSSING a lonely moorland. In the middle of the moor a misshapen hawthorn tree stood all alone and from the tree a man was hanging. He had been stripped of his coat and shirt, revealing in death what he had doubtless kept hidden during his life: that his skin bore a strange deformation. His chest, back and arms were covered with intricate blue marks, marks so dense that he was more blue than white.

As he rode up to the tree, Childermass wondered if the murderer had written upon the body as a joke. When he had been a sailor he had heard tales of countries where criminals's confessions were written on to their bodies by various horrible means before they were killed. From a distance the marks looked very like writing, but as he got closer he saw that they were beneath the skin.

He got down from his horse and swung the body round until it was facing him. The face was purple and swollen; the eyes were bulging and filled with blood. He studied it until he could discern in the distorted features a face he knew. "Vinculus," he said.

Taking out his pocket-knife, he cut the body down. Then he pulled off Vinculus's breeches and boots, and surveyed the body: the corpse of a forked animal on a barren, winter moor.

The strange marks covered every inch of skin – the only exceptions were his face, hands, private parts and the soles of his feet. He looked like a blue man wearing white gloves and a white mask. The more Childermass looked at him, the more he felt that the marks meant something. "This is the King's Letters," he said at last. "This is Robert Findhelm's book."

Just then it started to snow with a flurry of sharp, icy flakes. The wind blew harder.

Childermass thought of Strange and Norrell twenty miles away and he laughed out loud. What did it matter who read the books at Hurtfew? The most precious book of all lay naked and dead in the snow and the wind.

"So," he said, "it has fallen to me, has it? 'The greatest glory and the greatest burden given to any man in this Age.' "

At present the burden was more obvious than the glory. The book was in a most inconvenient form. He had no idea how long Vinculus had been dead or how soon he might begin to rot. What to do? He could take his chances and throw the body over his horse. But a freshly hanged corpse would be difficult to explain to any one he met on the road. He could hide the body and go and fetch a horse and cart. How long would it take? And supposing that in the meantime someone found the body and took it. There were doctors in York who would pay money for corpses and no questions asked.

"I could cast a spell of concealment," he thought.

A spell of concealment would certainly hide it from human eyes, but there were dogs, foxes and crows to consider. They could not be deceived by any magic Childermass knew. The book had been eaten once already. He had no wish to risk it happening a second time.

The obvious thing was to make a copy, but his memorandum book, pen and ink were lying upon the table in the drawing-room in the Darkness of Hurtfew Abbey. So what then? He could scratch a copy on to the frozen earth with a stick – but that was no better than what he had already. If only there had been some trees, he might have been able to strip the bark and burn some wood and write upon the bark with the ashes. But there was only this one twisted hawthorn.

He looked at his pocket-knife. Perhaps he ought to copy the book on to his own body? There were several things in favour of this plan. First, who was to say that the positioning upon Vinculus's body did not carry some meaning with it? The closer to the head, the more important the text? Any thing was possible. Second, it would make the book both secret and secure. He would not have to worry about any one stealing it. Whether he intended to shew it to Strange or Norrell, he had not yet decided.

But the writing upon Vinculus's body was both dense and intricate. Even if he were able to force his knife to mimic all those delicate dots, circles and flourishes exactly – which he doubted – he would have to cut quite deep to make the marks permanent.

He took off his greatcoat and his ordinary coat. He undid the wrist of his shirt and rolled up his sleeve. As an experiment, he cut one of the symbols on the inside of Vinculus's arm into the same place upon his own arm. The result was not promising. There was so much blood that it was difficult to see what he was doing and the pain made him feel faint.

"I can afford to lose some blood in this cause, but there is so much writing – it would surely kill me. Besides, how in the world could I copy what is written on his back? I will put him over my horse and if any one challenges me – well, I will fire at them if needs be. That is a plan. It is not a very good plan, but it is a plan." He put on his coat and his greatcoat again.

Brewer had wandered off a little way and was cropping at some dry grasses, which the wind had exposed. Childermass walked over to him. Out of his valise he took a length of strong rope and the box containing his pistols. He rammed a ball into each pistol and primed them with powder.

He turned back to make sure that all was right with the body. Someone – a man – was bending over it. He shoved the pistols into the pockets of his greatcoat and began to run, calling out.

The man wore black boots and a black travelling coat. He was half-stooping, half-kneeling on the snowy ground beside Vinculus. For a brief moment Childermass thought it was Strange – but this man was not quite so tall and was somewhat slighter in figure. His dark clothes were clearly expensive and looked fashionable. Yet his straight, dark hair was longer than any fashionable gentleman would have worn it; it gave him something of the look of a Methodist preacher or a Romantic poet. "I know him," thought Childermass. "He is a magician. I know him well. Why can I not think what his name is?"

Out loud he said, "The body is mine, sir! Leave it be!"

The man looked up. "Yours, John Childermass?" he said with a mildly ironic air, "I thought it was mine."

It was a curious thing but despite his clothes and his air of cool authority, his speech sounded uncouth – even to Childermass's ears. His accent was northern – of that there was no doubt – but Childermass did not recognize it. It might have been Northumbrian, but it was tinged with something else – the speech of the cold countries that lie over the North Sea and – which seemed more extraordinary still – there was more than a hint of French in his pronunciation.

"Well, you are mistaken." Childermass raised his pistols. "I will fire upon you, if I have to, sir. But I would much rather not. Leave the body to me and go on your way."

The man said nothing. He regarded Childermass a moment longer and then, as if he had become bored with him, turned back to his examination of the body.

Childermass looked round for a horse or a carriage – some indication of how the man had got here. There was nothing. In all the wide moor there were only the two men, the horse, the corpse and the hawthorn tree.

"Yet there must be a carriage somewhere," he thought. "There is not so much as a spot of mud on his coat and none on his boots. He looks as if he has just come fresh from his valet. Where are his servants?"

This was a discomfiting thought. Childermass doubted he would have much difficulty in overpowering this pale, thin, poetical-looking person, but a coachman and two or three stout footmen would be another matter entirely.

"Does the land hereabouts belong to you, sir?" he asked.

"Yes."

"And where is your horse? Where is your carriage? Where are your servants?"

"I have no horse, John Childermass. I have no carriage. And only one of my servants is here."

"Where?"

Without troubling to look up, the man raised his arm and pointed a thin, pale finger.

Childermass looked behind him in confusion. There was no one there. Just the wind blowing across the snowy tussocks. What did he mean? Was it the wind or the snow? He had heard of mediaeval magicians who claimed these and other natural forces as servants. Then comprehension dawned on him. "What? No, sir, you are mistaken! I am not your servant!"

"You boasted of it, not three days ago," said the man.

There was only one person who had any claim to be Childermass's master. Was this, in some mysterious fashion, Norrell? An aspect of Norrell? In the past, magicians had sometimes appeared in different forms according to the qualities which made up their character. Childermass tried to think what part of Gilbert Norrell's character might suddenly manifest as a pale, handsome man with a peculiar accent and an air of great authority. He reflected that strange things had happened recently, but nothing as queer as that. "Sir!" he cried. "I have warned you! Let the body be!"

The man bent closer to Vinculus's corpse. He plucked something out of his own mouth – a tiny pearl of light faintly tinged with rose and silver. He placed it in Vinculus's mouth. The corpse shivered. It was not like the shudder of a sick man, nor yet like the shiver of a healthy one; it was like the shiver of a bare birch wood as spring breathes upon it.

"Move away from the body, sir!" cried Childermass. "I will not ask you again!"

The man did not even trouble to look up. He passed the tip of his finger over the body as if he were writing upon it.

Childermass aimed the right-hand pistol somewhat wide of the man's left shoulder, intending to frighten him away. The pistol fired perfectly; a cloud of smoke and a smell of gunpowder rose from the pan; sparks and more smoke disgorged from the barrel.

But the lead refused to fly. It hung in the air as if in a dream. It twisted, swelled and changed shape. Suddenly it put forth wings, turned into a lapwing and flew away. In the same instant Childermass's mind grew as quiet and fixed as a stone.

The man moved his finger over Vinculus and all the patterns and symbols flowed and swirled as if they had been written upon water. He did this for a while and when he was satisfied, he stopped and stood up.

"You are wrong," he said to Childermass. "He is not dead." He came and stood directly before Childermass. With as little ceremony as a parent who cleans something from a child's face, the man licked his finger and daubed a sort of symbol on each of Childermass's eye-lids, on his lips and over his heart. Then he gave Childermass's left hand a knock, so that the pistol fell to the ground. He drew another symbol on Childermass's palm. He turned and seemed about to depart, but glancing back and apparently as an afterthought, he made a final gesture over the cut in Childermass's face.

The wind shook the falling snow and made it spin and twist about. Brewer made a sound as if something had disturbed him. Briefly, the snow and the shadows seemed to form a picture of a thin, dark man in a greatcoat and boots. The next moment the illusion was gone.

* * *

Childermass blinked. "Where am I wandering to?" he asked himself irritably. "And what am I doing talking to myself? This is no time to be wool-gathering!" There was a smell of gunpowder. One of his pistols lay in the snow. When he picked it up it was still warm as if he had recently discharged it. That was odd, but he had no time to be properly surprized because a sound made him look up.

Vinculus was getting up off the ground. He did it clumsily, in jerks, like something new-born that has not yet discovered what its limbs are for. He stood for a moment, his body swaying and his head twitching from side to side. Then he opened his mouth and screamed at Childermass. But the sound that came out of his mouth was no sound at all; it was the emptied skin of sound without flesh or bones.

It was, without a doubt, the strangest thing Childermass had ever seen: a naked blue man with blood-engorged eyes, silently screaming in the middle of a snow-covered moor. It was such a very extraordinary situation that for some moments he was at a loss to know what to do. He wondered if he ought to try the spell called Gilles de Marston's Restoration of Flown Tranquillity, but on further consideration, he thought of something better. He took out the claret that Lucas had given him and shewed it to Vinculus. Vinculus grew calmer and fixed his gaze upon it.

A quarter of an hour later they were seated together on a tussock beneath the hawthorn, breakfasting on the claret and a handful of apples. Vinculus had put on his shirt and breeches and was wrapped in a blanket that belonged to Brewer. He had recovered from his hanging with surprizing rapidity. His eyes were still blood-shot, but they were less alarming to look at than before. His speech was hoarse and liable to be interrupted at any moment by fits of violent coughing, but it was comprehensible.

"Someone tried to hang you," Childermass told him. "I do not know who or why. Luckily I found you in time and cut you down." As he said this, he felt a faint question disturb his thoughts.

In his mind's eye he saw Vinculus, dead on the ground, and a thin, white hand, pointing. Who had that been? The memory slipped away from him. "So tell me," he continued, "how does a man become a book? I know that your father was given the book by Robert Findhelm and that he was supposed to take the book to a man in the Derbyshire hills."

"The last man in England who could read the King's letters," croaked Vinculus.

"But your father did not deliver the book. Instead he ate it in the drinking contest in Sheffield."

Vinculus took another drink from the bottle and wiped his mouth with the back of his hand. "Four years later I was born and the King's Letters were written on my infant body. When I was seventeen, I went to look for the man in the Derbyshire hills – he lived just long enough for me to find him out. That was a night indeed! A starlit, summer night, when the King's Book and the last Reader of the King's Letters met and drank wine together! We sat upon the brow of the hill at Bretton, looking out over England, and he read England's destiny from me."

"And that was the prophecy which you told to Strange and Norrell?"

Vinculus, who had been seized with a fit of coughing, nodded. When he was able to speak again, he added, "And also to the nameless slave."

"Who?" said Childermass with a frown. "Who is that?"

"A man," replied Vinculus. "It has been part of my task to bear his story. He began as a slave. Will soon be a king. His true name was denied him at his birth."

Childermass pondered this description for a moment or two. "You mean John Uskglass?" he said.

Vinculus made a noise of exasperation. "If I meant John Uskglass, I would say so! No, no. He is not a magician at all. He is a man like any other." He thought for a moment. "But black," he added.

"I have never heard of him," said Childermass.

Vinculus looked at him with amusement. "Of course not. You have lived your life in the Mayfair magician's pocket. You only know what he knows."

"So?" said Childermass, stung. "That is not so very trifling, is it? Norrell is a clever man – and Strange another. They have their faults, as other men do, but their achievements are still remarkable. Make no mistake; I am John Uskglass's man. Or would be, if he were here. But you must admit that the restoration of English magic is their work, not his."

"Their work!" scoffed Vinculus. "Theirs? Do you still not understand? They *are* the spell John Uskglass is doing. That is all they have ever been. And he is doing it now!"

# 68

## "Yes."

### February 1817

IN THE SILVER dish of water the speck of light flickered and disappeared.

"What!" cried Strange. "What has happened? Quickly, Mr Norrell!"

Norrell tapped the water's surface, redrew the lines of light and whispered a few words, but the water in the dish remained dark and still. "He is gone," he said.

Strange closed his eyes.

"It is very odd," continued Norrell, in a tone of wonder. "What do you suppose he was doing in Yorkshire?"

"Oh!" cried Strange. "I dare say he came here on purpose to make me mad!" With a cry of mingled rage and self-pity he demanded, "Why will he not attend to me? After everything I have done, why does he not care enough to look at me? To speak to me?"

"He is an old magician and an old king," answered Norrell briefly. "Two things that are not easily impressed."

"All magicians long to astonish their masters. I have certainly astonished *you*. I wanted to do the same to him."

"But your real purpose is to free Mrs Strange from the enchantment," Norrell reminded him.

"Yes, yes. That is right," said Strange, irritably. "Of course it is. Only . . ." He did not finish his thought.

There was a silence and then Norrell, who had been looking thoughtful, said, "You mentioned magicians always wishing to impress their masters. I am reminded of something which happened in 1156 . . ."

Strange sighed.

". . . In that year John Uskglass suffered some strange malady – as he did from time to time. When he recovered, a celebration was held at his house in Newcastle. Kings and queens brought presents of immense value and splendour – gold, rubies, ivory, rare spices. Magicians brought magical things – clouds of revelation, singing trees, keys to mystical doors and so on – each one trying to outdo the other. The King thanked them all in the same grave manner. Last of all came the magician, Thomas Godbless. His hands were empty. He had no gift. He lifted his head and said, 'Lord, I bring you the trees and hills. I bring you the wind and the rain.' The kings and queens, the great lords and ladies and the other magicians were amazed at his impudence. It appeared to them as if he had done nothing at all. But for the first time since he had been ill, the King smiled."

Strange considered this. "Well," he said. "I am afraid I am with the kings and queens. I can make nothing of it. Where did you get this tale?"

"It is in Belasis's *Instructions*. In my youth I studied the *Instructions* with a passionate devotion and I found this passage particularly intriguing. I concluded that Godbless had somehow persuaded the trees and the hills and so on to greet John Uskglass in some mystical fashion, to bow down before him as it were. I was pleased to have understood something that Belasis had not, but I thought no more about it – I had no use for such magic. Years later I discovered a spell in Lanchester's *The Language of Birds*. Lanchester got it from an older book, now lost. He admitted that he did not know what it was for, but I believe it is the spell Godbless used – or one very like it. If you are serious in your intention of talking to John Uskglass, suppose we cast it now? Suppose we ask England to greet him?"

"What will that achieve?" asked Strange.

"Achieve? Nothing! At least, nothing directly. But it will remind John Uskglass of the bonds between him and England. And it will shew a sort of respectfulness on our part, which is surely more in keeping with the behaviour a king expects from his subjects."

Strange shrugged. "Well," he said. "I have nothing better to suggest. Where is your copy of *The Language of Birds*?"

He looked about the room. Every book lay where it had fallen the moment it had ceased to be a raven. "How many books are there?" he asked.

"Four or five thousand," said Norrell.

The magicians took a candle each and began to search.

The gentleman with the thistle-down hair strode rapidly along the walled lane which led to the village of Starecross. Stephen stumbled after him, on his way from one death to another.

England seemed to him to be nothing but horrors and misery now. The very shapes of the trees were like frozen screams. A bunch of dry leaves hung from a branch and rattled in the wind – that was Vinculus upon the hawthorn tree. The corpse of a rabbit ripped apart by a fox lay upon the path – that was Lady Pole, soon to be killed by the gentleman.

Death upon death, horror upon horror; and there was nothing Stephen could do to prevent any of it.

At Starecross Hall Lady Pole was seated at a desk in her sitting-room, writing furiously. The desk was scattered with sheets of paper, all covered with handwriting.

There was a knock and Mr Segundus entered the room. "I beg your pardon!" he said. "Might I inquire? Do you write to Sir Walter?"

She shook her head. "These letters are to Lord Liverpool and the editor of *The Times*!"

"Indeed?" said Mr Segundus. "Well, I have, in fact, just

finished a letter of my own – to Sir Walter – but nothing, I am sure, will delight him so much as a line or two in your ladyship's own hand, assuring him that you are well and disenchanted."

"But your own letter will do that. I am sorry, Mr Segundus, but while my dear Mrs Strange and poor Stephen remain in the power of that wicked spirit, I can spare no thought for any thing else! You must send these letters off straight away! And when they are done I shall write to the Archbishop of Canterbury and the Prince Regent!"

"You do not think perhaps that Sir Walter is the proper person to apply to such exalted gentlemen? Surely . . . ?"

"No, indeed!" she cried, all indignation. "I have no notion of asking people to perform services for me which I can do perfectly well for myself. I do not intend to go, in the space of one hour, from the helplessness of enchantment to another sort of helplessness! Besides, Sir Walter will not be able to explain half so well as me the true hideousness of Mr Norrell's crimes!"

Just then another person entered the room – Mr Segundus's manservant, Charles, who came to say that something very odd was happening in the village. The tall black man – the person who had originally brought her ladyship to Starecross – had appeared with a silver diadem upon his head, and with him was a gentleman with thistle-down hair, wearing a bright green coat.

"Stephen! Stephen and the enchanter!" cried Lady Pole. "Quickly, Mr Segundus! Summon up all your powers! We depend upon you to defeat him! You must free Stephen as you freed me!"

"Defeat a fairy!" exclaimed Mr Segundus in horror. "Oh, but no! I could not. It would take a far greater magician . . ."

"Nonsense!" she cried, with shining eyes. "Remember what Childermass told you. Your years of study have prepared you! You have simply to try!"

"But I do not know . . ." he began, helplessly.

But it did not much matter what he knew. The moment she

finished speaking she ran from the room – and, since he considered himself bound to protect her, he was obliged to run after her.

At Hurtfew the two magicians had found *The Language of Birds* – it lay open on the table at the page where the fairy spell was printed. But the problem of finding a name for John Uskglass remained. Norrell sat crouched over the silver dish of water doing location spells. They had already run through all the titles and names they could think of, and the location spell did not recognize a single one. The water in the silver dish remained dark and featureless.

"What of his fairy name?" said Strange.

"That is lost," replied Norrell.

"Did we try the King of the North yet?"

"Yes."

"Oh." Strange thought for a moment and then said, "What was that curious appellation you mentioned before? Something you said he called himself? The nameless something?"

"The nameless slave?"

"Yes. Try that."

Norrell looked very doubtful. But he cast the spell for the nameless slave. Instantly a speck of bluish light appeared. He proceeded and the nameless slave proved to be in Yorkshire – in very much the same place where John Uskglass had appeared before.

"There!" exclaimed Strange, triumphantly. "All our anxiety was quite needless. He is still here."

"But I do not think that is the same person," interrupted Norrell. "It looks different somehow."

"Mr Norrell, do not be fanciful, I beg you! Who else could it be? How many nameless slaves can there possibly be in Yorkshire?"

This was so very reasonable a question that Mr Norrell offered no further objections.

"And now for the magic itself," said Strange. He picked up the book and began to recite the spell. He addressed the trees of

England; the hills of England; the sunlight, water, birds, earth and stones. He addressed them all, one after the other, and exhorted them to place themselves in the hands of the nameless slave.

Stephen and the gentleman came to the packhorse bridge that led into Starecross.

The village was quiet; there was hardly any one to be seen. In a doorway a girl in a print-gown and woollen shawl was tipping milk from wooden pails into cheese-vats. A man in gaiters and a broad-brimmed hat came down a lane at the side of the house; a dog trotted at his side. When the man and the dog rounded the corner, the girl and the man greeted each other smilingly and the dog barked his pleasure. It was the sort of simple, domestic scene that would ordinarily have delighted Stephen, but in his present mood he could only feel a chill; if the man had reached out and struck the girl – or strangled her – he would have felt no surprize.

The gentleman was already on the packhorse bridge. Stephen followed him and . . .

. . . and everything changed. The sun came out from behind a cloud; it shone through the winter trees; hundreds of small, bright patches of sunlight appeared. The world became a kind of puzzle or labyrinth. It was like the superstition which says that one must not walk upon lines between flag stones – or the strange magic called the Doncaster Squares which is performed upon a board like a chessboard. Suddenly everything had meaning. Stephen hardly dared take another step. If he did so – if, for example, he stepped into *that* shadow or *that* spot of light, then the world might be forever altered.

"Wait!" he thought, wildly. "I am not ready for this! I have not considered. I do not know what to do!"

But it was too late. He looked up.

*The bare branches against the sky were a writing and, though he did not want to, he could read it. He saw that it was a question put to him by the trees.*

"Yes," he answered them.

Their age and their knowledge belonged to him.

*Beyond the trees was a high, snow-covered ridge, like a line drawn across the sky. Its shadow was blue upon the snow before it. It embodied all kinds of cold and hardness. It hailed Stephen as a King it had long missed. At a word from Stephen it would tumble down and crush his enemies. It asked Stephen a question.*

"Yes," he told it.

Its scorn and strength were his for the taking.

*The black beck beneath the packhorse bridge sang its question to him.*

"Yes," he said.

*The earth said . . .*

"Yes," he said.

*The rooks and magpies and redwings and chaffinches said . . .*

"Yes," he said.

*The stones said . . .*

"Yes," said Stephen. "Yes. Yes. Yes."

Now all of England lay cupped in his black palm. All Englishmen were at his mercy. Now every insult could be revenged. Now every injury to his poor mother could be paid back a thousandfold. All of England could be laid waste in a moment. He could bring houses crashing down upon the occupants' heads. He could command hills to fall and valleys to close their lips. He could summon up centaurs, snuff out stars, steal the moon from the sky. Now. Now. Now.

Now came Lady Pole and Mr Segundus, running down from the Hall in the pale winter sunlight. Lady Pole looked at the gentleman with eyes ablaze with hatred. Poor Mr Segundus was all confusion and dismay.

The gentleman turned to Stephen and said something. Stephen could not hear him: the hills and the trees spoke too loud. But, "Yes," he said.

The gentleman laughed gaily and raised his hands to cast spells on Lady Pole.

Stephen closed his eyes. He spoke a word to the stones of the packhorse bridge.

*Yes, said the stones.* The bridge reared up like a raging horse and cast the gentleman into the beck.

Stephen spoke a word to the beck.

*Yes, said the beck.* It grasped the gentleman in a grip of iron and bore him swiftly away.

Stephen was aware that Lady Pole spoke to him, that she tried to catch hold of his arm; he saw Mr Segundus's pale, astonished face, saw him say something; but he had no time to answer them. Who knew how long the world would consent to obey him? He leapt down from the bridge and ran along the bank.

The trees seemed to greet him as he ran past; they spoke of old alliances and reminded him of times gone by. The sunlight called him King and spoke its pleasure at finding him here. He had no time to tell them he was not the person they imagined.

He came to a place where the land rose steeply upon either side of the beck – a deep dale in the moor, a place where millstones were quarried. Scattered around the sides of the dale were great, round, hewn stones, each of them half the height of a man.

The surface of the beck seethed and boiled where the gentleman was imprisoned. Stephen knelt upon a flat stone and leant over the water. "I am sorry," he said. "You intended nothing but kindness, I know."

The gentleman's hair streamed out like silver snakes in the dark water. His face was a terrible sight. In his fury and hatred he began to lose his resemblance to humankind: his eyes grew further apart, there was fur upon his face and his lips rolled back from his teeth in a snarl.

A voice inside Stephen's mind said: "If you kill me, you will never know your name!"

"I am the nameless slave," said Stephen. "That is all I have ever been – and today I am content to be nothing more."

He spoke a word to the millstones. They flew up in the air and flung themselves down upon the gentleman. He spoke to the boulders and rocks; they did the same. The gentleman was old beyond telling, and very strong. Long after his bones and flesh must have been crushed to pieces, Stephen could feel whatever was left of him struggling to bind itself back together by magic. So Stephen spoke to the stony shoulders of the dale and asked them to help him. Earth and rock crumbled; it heaped itself on top of the millstones and the rocks until there was a hill standing there as high as the sides of the dale.

For years Stephen had felt as if a pane of dirty, grey glass hung between him and the world; the moment that the last spark of the gentleman's life was extinguished, the pane shattered. Stephen stood a moment, gasping for breath.

But his allies and servants were growing doubtful. There was a question in the minds of the hills and the trees. They began to know that he was not the person they had taken him for – that all this was borrowed glory.

One by one he felt them withdraw. As the last one left him, he fell, empty and insensible, to the ground.

In Padua the Greysteels had already breakfasted and were gathered together in the little sitting-room on the first floor. They were not in the best of spirits this morning. There had been a disagreement. Dr Greysteel had taken to smoking a pipe indoors – a thing to which Flora and Aunt Greysteel were very much opposed. Aunt Greysteel had tried to argue him out of it, but Dr Greysteel had proved stubborn. Pipe-smoking was a pastime he was particularly fond of and he felt that he ought to be permitted an indulgence or two, to make up for their never going anywhere any more. Aunt Greysteel said that he ought to smoke his pipe outside. Dr Greysteel replied that he could not because it was raining. It was difficult to smoke a pipe in the rain – the rain made the tobacco wet.

So he was smoking the pipe and Aunt Greysteel was coughing; and Flora, who was disposed to blame herself, glanced at each from time to time with an unhappy expression. Things had gone on like this for about an hour when Dr Greysteel happened to look up and exclaimed in amazement, "My head is black! Completely black!"

"Well, what do you expect if you smoke a pipe?" replied his sister.

"Papa," asked Flora, putting down her work in alarm, "what do you mean?"

Dr Greysteel was staring at the mirror – the very same mirror which had so mysteriously appeared when day had turned to night and Strange had come to Padua. Flora went and stood behind his chair, so that she could see what he saw. Her exclamation of surprize brought Aunt Greysteel to join her.

Where Dr Greysteel's head ought to have been in the mirror was a dark spot that moved and changed shape. The spot grew in size until gradually it began to resemble a figure fleeing down an immense corridor towards them. The figure drew closer, and they could see it was a woman. Several times she looked back as she ran, as if in fear of something behind her.

"What has frightened her to make her run like that?" wondered Aunt Greysteel. "Lancelot, can you see any thing? Does any one chase after her? Oh, poor lady! Lancelot, is there any thing you can do?"

Dr Greysteel went to the mirror, placed his hand upon it and pushed, but the surface was as hard and smooth as mirrors usually are. He hesitated for a moment, as though debating with himself whether to try a more violent approach.

"Be careful, papa!" cried Flora in alarm. "You must not break it!"

The woman within the mirror drew nearer. For a moment she appeared directly behind it and they could see the elaborate embroidery and beading of her gown; then she mounted up upon the frame as on a step. The surface of the mirror became softer, like a dense cloud or mist. Flora hastened to push a chair against the wall so that the lady might more easily descend. Three pairs of hands were raised to catch her, to pull her away from whatever it was that frightened her.

She was perhaps thirty or thirty-two years of age. She was dressed in a gown the colour of autumn, but she was breathless and a little disordered from running. With a frantic look she surveyed the unknown room, the unknown faces, the unfamiliar look of everything. "Is this Faerie?" she asked.

"No, madam," answered Flora.

"Is it England?"

"No, madam." Tears began to course down Flora's face. She put her hand on her breast to steady herself. "This is Padua. In Italy. My name is Flora Greysteel. It is a name quite unknown to you, but I have waited for you here at your husband's desire. I promised him I would meet you here."

"Is Jonathan here?"

"No, madam."

"You are Arabella Strange," said Dr Greysteel in amazement.

"Yes," she said.

"Oh, my dear!" exclaimed Aunt Greysteel, one hand flying to cover her mouth and the other to her heart. "Oh, my dear!" Then both hands fluttered around Arabella's face and shoulders. "Oh, my dear!" she exclaimed for the third time. She burst into tears and embraced Arabella.

Stephen awoke. He was lying on the frozen ground in a narrow dale. The sunlight was gone. It was grey and cold. The dale was choked with a great wall of millstones and boulders and earth – an eerie tomb. The wall had dammed the beck, but a little water still seeped through and was now spreading across the ground. Stephen's crown, sceptre and orb lay a little distance away in pools of dirty water. Wearily he stood up.

In the distance he could hear someone calling, "Stephen! Stephen!" He thought it was Lady Pole.

"I cast off the name of my captivity," he said. "It is gone." He picked up the crown, the sceptre and orb, and began to walk.

He had no notion of where he was going. He had killed the gentleman and he had allowed the gentleman to kill Vinculus. He could never go home – if home it had been in the first place. What would an English judge and jury say to a black man who was a murderer twice over? Stephen had done with England and England had done with him. He walked on.

After a while it seemed to him that the landscape was no longer as English as it had been. The trees that now surrounded him were immense, ancient things, their boughs twice the thickness of a man's body and curved into strange, fantastical shapes. Though it was winter and the briars were bare, a few roses still bloomed here, blood-red and snow-white.

England lay behind him. He did not regret it. He did not look back. He walked on.

He came to a long, low hill, and in the middle of the hill was an opening. It was more like a mouth than a door, yet it did not have an evil look. Someone was standing there, just within the opening, waiting for him. "I know this place," he thought. "It is Lost-hope! But how can that be?"

It was not simply that the house had become a hill, everything seemed to have undergone a revolution. The wood was suddenly possessed of a spirit of freshness, of innocence. The trees no longer threatened the traveller. Between their branches were glints of a serene winter sky of coldest blue. Here and there shone the pure light of a star – though whether they were stars of morning or stars of evening he could no longer remember. He looked around for the ancient bones and rusting armour – those ghastly emblems of the gentleman's bloodthirsty nature. To his surprize he found that they were everywhere – beneath his feet, stuffed into hollows of the tree roots, tangled up with briars and brambles. But they were in a far more advanced state of decay than he remembered; they were moss-covered, rust-eaten and crumbling into dust. In a little while nothing would be left of them.

The figure within the opening was a familiar one; he had often attended the balls and processions at Lost-hope. But he too was changed; his features had become more fairy-like; his eyes more glittering; his eye-brows more extravagant. His hair curled tightly like the fleece of a young lamb or like young ferns in spring, and there was a light dusting of fur upon his face. He looked older, yet at the same time more innocent. "Welcome!" he cried.

"Is this truly Lost-hope?" asked the person who had once been Stephen Black.

"Yes, grandfather."

"But I do not understand. Lost-hope was a great mansion. This is . . ." The person who had once been Stephen Black paused. "I do not have a word for what this is."

"This is a *brugh*, grandfather! This is the world beneath the hill. Lost-hope is changing! The old King is dead. The new King approaches! And at his approach the world sheds its sorrow. The sins of the old King dissolve like morning mist! The world assumes the character of the new. His virtues fill up the wood and the wold!"

"The new King?" The person who had once been Stephen Black looked down at his own hands. In one was the sceptre and in the other the orb.

The fairy smiled at him, as if wondering why he should be surprized. "The changes you wrought here far surpass any thing you did in England."

They passed through the opening into a great hall. The new King sat down upon an ancient throne. A crowd of people came and gathered around him. Some faces he knew, others were unfamiliar to him, but he suspected that this was because he had never seen them as they truly were before. For a long time he was silent.

"This house," he told them at last, "is disordered and dirty. Its inhabitants have idled away their days in pointless pleasures and in celebrations of past cruelties – things that ought not to be remembered, let alone celebrated. I have often observed it and often regretted it. All these faults, I shall in time set right."[1]

The moment the spell took effect a great wind blew through Hurtfew. Doors banged in the Darkness; black curtains billowed out in black rooms; black papers were swept from black tables and made to dance. A bell – taken from the original Abbey long ago and since forgotten – rang frantically in a little turret above the stables.

In the library, visions appeared in mirrors and clock-faces. The wind blew the curtains apart and visions appeared in the windows too. They followed thick and fast upon one another, almost too rapid to comprehend. Mr Norrell saw some that seemed familiar: the shattered branch of holly in his own library at Hanover-square; a raven flying in front of St Paul's Cathedral so that for a moment it was the living embodiment of the Raven-in-Flight; the great black bed in the inn at Wansford. But others were entirely strange to him: a hawthorn tree; a man crucified upon a thicket; a crude wall of stones in a narrow valley; an unstoppered bottle floating on a wave.

Then all the visions disappeared, except for one. It filled one of the tall library windows, but what it was a vision *of*, Mr Norrell was at a loss to know. It resembled a large, perfectly round, black stone of almost impossible brilliance and glossiness, set into a thin ring of rough stone and mounted upon what appeared to be a

---

[1] A surprizing number of kings and princes of Faerie have been human. John Uskglass, Stephen Black and Alessandro Simonelli are just three. Fairies are, by and large, irredeemably indolent. Though they are fond of high rank, honours and riches, they detest the hard work of government.

black hillside. Mr Norrell thought of it as a hillside because it bore some resemblance to a moor where the heather is all burnt and charred – except that this hillside was not the black of burnt things, it was the black of wet silk or well-shone leather. Suddenly the stone did something – it moved or spun. The movement was almost too quick to grasp but Mr Norrell was left with the sickening impression that it had blinked.

The wind died away. The bell above the stable ceased to ring.

Mr Norrell breathed a long sigh of relief that it was over. Strange was standing with his arms crossed, deep in thought, staring at the floor.

"What did you make of that?" asked Mr Norrell. "The last was by far the worst. I thought for a moment it was an eye."

"It was an eye," said Strange.

"But what could it belong to? Some horror or monster, I suppose! Most unsettling!"

"It was monstrous," agreed Strange. "Though not quite in the way you imagine. It was a raven's eye."

"A raven's eye! But it filled the whole window!"

"Yes. Either the raven was immensely large or . . ."

"Or?" quavered Mr Norrell.

Strange gave a short, uncheerful laugh. "Or we were ridiculously small! Pleasant, is it not, to see oneself as others see one? I said I wanted John Uskglass to look at me and I think, for a moment he did. Or at least one of his lieutenants did. And in that moment you and I were smaller than a raven's eye and presumably as insignificant. Speaking of John Uskglass, I do not suppose that we know where he is?"

Mr Norrell sat down at the silver dish and began to work. After five minutes or so of patient labour, he said, "Mr Strange! There is no sign of John Uskglass – nothing at all. But I have looked for Lady Pole and Mrs Strange. Lady Pole is in Yorkshire and Mrs Strange is in Italy. There is no shadow of their presence in Faerie. Both are completely disenchanted!"

There was a silence. Strange turned away abruptly.

"It is more than a little odd," continued Mr Norrell in a tone of wonder. "We have done everything we set out to do, but *how* we did it, I do not pretend to understand. I can only suppose that John Uskglass simply saw what was amiss and stretched out his hand to put it right! Unfortunately, his obligingness did not extend to freeing us from the Darkness. That remains."

Mr Norrell paused. This then was his destiny! – a destiny full of fear, horror and desolation! He sat patiently for a few moments in expectation of falling prey to some or all of these terrible emotions, but was forced to conclude that he felt none of them. Indeed, what seemed remarkable to him now were the long years he had spent in London, away from his library, at the beck and call of the Ministers and the Admirals. He wondered how he had borne it.

"I am glad I did not recognize the raven's eye for what it was," he said cheerfully, "or I believe I would have been a good deal frightened!"

"Indeed, sir," said Strange hoarsely. "You were fortunate there! And I believe I am cured of wanting to be looked at! Henceforth John Uskglass is welcome to ignore me for as long as he pleases."

"Oh, indeed!" agreed Mr Norrell. "You know, Mr Strange, you really should try to rid yourself of the habit of wishing for things. It is a dangerous thing in a magician!" He began a long and not particularly interesting story about a fourteenth-century magician in Lancashire who had often made idle wishes and had caused no end of inconvenience in the village where he lived, accidentally turning the cows into clouds and the cooking pots into ships, and causing the villagers to speak in colours rather than words – and other such signs of magical chaos.

At first Strange barely answered him and such replies as he made were random and illogical. But gradually he appeared to listen with more attention, and he spoke in his usual manner.

Mr Norrell had many talents, but penetration into the hearts of men and women was not one of them. Strange did not speak of the restoration of his wife, so Mr Norrell imagined that it could not have affected him very deeply.

# 69

## Strangites and Norrellites

### February–spring 1817

CHILDERMASS RODE AND Vinculus walked at his side. All around them was spread the wide expanse of snow-covered moor, appearing, with all its various hummocks and hills, like a vast feather mattress. Something of the sort may have occurred to Vinculus because he was describing in great detail the soft, pillowy bed he intended to sleep in that night and the very large dinner he intended to eat before he retired there. There was no doubt that he expected Childermass to pay for these luxuries, and it would not have been particularly surprizing if Childermass had had a word or two to say about them, but Childermass said nothing. His mind was wholly taken up with the problem of whether or not he ought to shew Vinculus to Strange and Norrell. Certainly there was no one in England better qualified to examine Vinculus; but, on the other hand, Childermass could not quite predict how the magicians would act when faced with a man who was also a book. Childermass scratched his cheek. There was a faint, well-healed scar upon it – the merest silvery line upon his brown face.

Vinculus had stopped talking and was standing in the road. His blanket had fallen from him and he was eagerly pushing back the sleeves of his coat.

"What is it?" asked Childermass. "What is the matter?"

"I have changed!" said Vinculus. "Look!" He took off his coat and opened his shirt. "The words are different! On my arms! On my chest! Everywhere! This is not what I said before!" Despite the cold, he began to undress. Then, when he was quite naked again, he celebrated his transformation by dancing about gleefully like a blue-skinned devil.

Childermass dismounted from his horse with feelings of panic and desperation. He had succeeded in preserving John Uskglass's book from death and destruction; and then, just when it seemed secure, the book itself had defeated him by changing.

"We must get to an inn as soon as we can!" he declared. "We must get paper and ink! We must make a record of exactly what was written upon you before. You must search every corner of your memory!"

Vinculus stared at him as if he thought he must have taken leave of his senses. "Why?" he asked.

"Because it is John Uskglass's magic! John Uskglass's thoughts! The only record any one ever had of them. We must preserve every scrap we can!"

Vinculus remained unenlightened. "Why?" he asked again. "John Uskglass did not think it worth preserving."

"But why should you change all of a sudden? There is no rhyme or reason in it!"

"There is every sort of reason," said Vinculus. "I was a Prophecy before; but the things that I foretold have come to pass. So it is just as well I have changed – or I would have become a History! A dry-as-dust History!"

"So what are you now?"

Vinculus shrugged his shoulders. "Perhaps I am a Receipt-Book! Perhaps I am a Novel! Perhaps I am a Collection of Sermons!" He was excessively diverted by these thoughts and cackled to himself and capered about some more.

"I hope you are what you have always been – a Book of Magic. But what are you saying? Vinculus, do you mean to tell me that you never learnt these letters?"

"I am a Book," said Vinculus, stopping in mid-caper. "I am *the* Book. It is the task of the Book to bear the words. Which I do. It is the task of the Reader to know what they say."

"But the last Reader is dead!"

Vinculus shrugged as if that were none of his concern.

"You must know something!" cried Childermass, growing almost wild with exasperation. He seized Vinculus's arm. "What about this? This symbol like a horned circle with a line through it. It occurs over and over again. What does it mean?"

Vinculus pulled his arm away again. "It means last Tuesday," he said. "It means three pigs, one of 'em wearing a straw hat! It means Sally went a-dancing in the moon's shadow and lost a little rosy purse!" He grinned and wagged a finger at Childermass. "I know what you are doing! You hope to be the next Reader!"

"Perhaps," said Childermass. "Though I cannot, for the life of me, tell how I shall begin. Yet I cannot see that any one else has a better claim to be the next Reader. But whatever else happens, I shall not let you out of my sight again. Henceforth, Vinculus, you and I shall be each other's shadow."

Vinculus's mood soured upon the instant. Gloomily he dressed himself again.

Spring returned to England. Birds followed ploughs. Stones were warmed by the sun. Rains and winds grew softer, and were fragranced with the scents of earth and growing things. Woods were tinged with a colour so soft, so subtle that it could scarcely be said to be a colour at all. It was more the *idea* of a colour – as if the trees were dreaming green dreams or thinking green thoughts.

Spring returned to England, but Strange and Norrell did not. The Pillar of Darkness covered Hurtfew Abbey and Norrell did not come out of it. People speculated upon the probability of Strange having killed Norrell, or Norrell having killed Strange, the different degrees to which each deserved it, and whether or not someone ought to go and find out.

But before any one could reach a conclusion concerning these interesting questions the Darkness disappeared – taking Hurtfew Abbey with it. House, park, bridge and part of the river were all gone. Roads that used to lead to Hurtfew now led back upon themselves or to dull corners of fields and copses that no one wished to visit. The house in Hanover-square and both Strange's houses – the one in Soho-square and his home in Clun[1] – suffered the same queer fate. In London the only creature in the world who could still find the house in Soho-square was Jeremy Johns' cat, Bullfinch. Indeed, Bullfinch did not appear to be aware that the house was in any way changed and he continued to go there whenever he wished, slipping between number 30 and number 32, and everyone who saw him do it agreed that it was the oddest sight in the world.[2]

Lord Liverpool and the other Ministers said a great deal publicly about their regret at Strange and Norrell's disappearance, but privately they were glad to be relieved of such a peculiar problem. Neither Strange nor Norrell had proved as respectable as they once had seemed. Both had indulged in, if not Black Magic, then certainly magic of a darker hue than seemed desirable or legitimate. Instead, the Ministers turned their attention to the great number of new magicians who had suddenly sprung up.

---

[1] For years afterwards the people of Clun said that if you stood, slightly upon tiptoes, close by a particular tree in winter at full moon and craned your neck to look between the branches of another tree, then it was possible still to see Ashfair in the distance. In the moonlight and snow the house looked very eerie, lost and lonely. In time, however, the trees grew differently and Ashfair was seen no more.

[2] This is by no means unusual as the following passage from *The Modern Magician* (Autumn, 1812) shews. "Where is Pale's house? Where Stokesey's? Why has no one ever seen them? Pale's house was in Warwick. The very street was known. Stokesey's house faced the cathedral in Exeter. Where is the Raven King's castle in Newcastle? Every one who saw it proclaimed it to be the first house for beauty and splendour in all the world – but has any one ever seen it in the Modern Age? No. Is there any record of it being destroyed? No. It simply disappeared. All these houses exist somewhere, but when the magician goes away or dies, they disappear. *He* may enter and leave as he pleases, but no one else may find them."

These magicians had performed scarcely any magic and were largely uneducated; nevertheless they promised to be every bit as quarrelsome as Strange and Norrell themselves, and some means of regulating them would quickly have to be found. Suddenly Mr Norrell's plans for reviving the Court of Cinque Dragownes (which had seemed so irrelevant before) were found to be of the utmost pertinence.[3]

In the second week of March a paragraph appeared in the *York Chronicle*, addressed to former members of the Learned Society of York Magicians, and also to any one who might wish to become a member of that society. It invited them to come to the Old Starre Inn on the following Wednesday (this being the day upon which the society had traditionally met).

This curious announcement offended at least as many of the former members of the York society as it pleased. Placed as it was in a newspaper, it could be read by everyone who possessed a penny. Furthermore the author (who was not named) appeared to have taken it upon himself to invite people to join the York society – something which he clearly had no right to do, whoever he was.

When the interesting evening came the former members arrived at the Old Starre to find fifty or so magicians (or would-be magicians) assembled in the Long Room. The most comfortable seats were all taken and the former members (who included Mr Segundus, Mr Honeyfoot and Dr Foxcastle) were obliged to take their places upon a little dais some distance from the fireplaces. The situation had this advantage however: they had an excellent view of the new magicians.

It was not a sight calculated to bring joy to the bosoms of the former members. The assembly was made up of the most mis-

[3] Many of the new magicians applied to Lord Liverpool and the Ministers for permission to go and find Strange and Norrell. Some gentlemen were so thoughtful as to append lists of equipment, both magical and mundane, which they thought they might need and which they hoped that the Government would be kind enough to supply. One, a man called Beech in Plymouth, asked for the loan of the Inniskilling Dragoons.

cellaneous people. ("With scarcely," observed Dr Foxcastle, "a gentleman among them.") There were two farmers and several shopkeepers. There was a pale-faced young man with light-coloured hair and an excitable manner, who was telling his neighbours that he was quite certain the announcement had been placed in the newspaper by Jonathan Strange himself and Strange would doubtless arrive at any moment to teach them all magic! There was also a clergyman – which was rather more promising. He was a clean-shaven, sober-looking person of fifty or sixty in black clothes. He was accompanied by a dog, as grey-haired and respectable as himself, and a young, striking-looking, female person in a red velvet gown. This seemed rather less respectable. She had dark hair and a fierce expression.

"Mr Taylor," said Dr Foxcastle to an acolyte of his, "perhaps you would be so good as to go and give that gentleman a hint that we do not bring members of our family to these meetings."

Mr Taylor scurried away.

From where they sat the former members of the York Society observed that the clean-shaven clergyman was more flinty than his quiet face suggested and that he returned Mr Taylor quite a sharp answer.

Mr Taylor came back with the following message. "Mr Redruth begs the society's pardon but he is not a magician at all. He has a great deal of interest in magic, but no skill. It is his daughter who is the magician. He has one son and three daughters and he says they are all magicians. The others did not wish to attend the meeting. He says that they have no wish to consort with other magicians, preferring to pursue their studies privately at home without distractions."

There was a pause while the former members tried, and failed, to make any sense of this.

"Perhaps his dog is a magician too," said Dr Foxcastle and the former members of the society laughed.

It soon became clear that the newcomers fell into two distinct parties. Miss Redruth, the young lady in the red velvet gown, was one of the first to speak. Her voice was low and rather hurried. She was not used to speaking in public and not all of the magicians caught her words, but her delivery was very passionate. The burden of what she had to say seemed to be that Jonathan Strange was everything! Gilbert Norrell nothing! Strange would soon be vindicated and Norrell universally reviled! Magic would be freed from the shackles that Gilbert Norrell had placed upon it! These observations, together with various references to Strange's lost masterpiece, *The History and Practice of English Magic*, drew angry responses from several other magicians to the effect that Strange's book was full of wicked magic and Strange himself was a murderer. He had certainly murdered his wife[4] and had probably murdered Norrell too.

The discussion was growing yet more heated when it was interrupted by the arrival of two men. Neither looked in the least respectable. Both had long, ragged hair and wore ancient coats. However, while one seemed to be nothing more or less than a vagabond, the other was considerably neater in his appearance and had about him an air of business – almost, one might say, of authority.

The vagabonding fellow did not even trouble to look at the York society; he simply sat down upon the floor and demanded gin and hot water. The other strode to the centre of the room and regarded them all with a wry smile. He bowed in the direction of Miss Redruth and addressed the magicians with the following words.

"Gentlemen! Madam! Some of you may remember me. I was with you ten years ago when Mr Norrell did the magic in York Cathedral. My name is John Childermass. I was, until last month, the servant of Gilbert Norrell. And this," he indicated the man sitting on the floor, "is Vinculus, a some-time street sorcerer of London."

Childermass got no further. Everyone began speaking at once. The former members of the York Society were dismayed to find

[4] This slander was not entirely discredited until Arabella Strange herself returned to England in early June 1817.

that they had left their comfortable firesides to come here and be lectured by a servant. But while these gentlemen were unburdening themselves of their indignation, most of the newcomers were affected quite differently. They were all either Strangites or Norrellites; but not one of them had ever laid eyes on his hero and to be seated in such proximity to a person who had actually known and spoken to him wound them up to an unprecedented pitch of excitement.

Childermass was not in the least discomfited by the uproar. He simply waited until it was quiet enough for him to speak and then he said, "I have come to tell you that the agreement with Gilbert Norrell is void. Null and void, gentlemen. You are magicians once more, if you wish to be."

One of the new magicians shouted out to know if Strange were coming. Another wished to know if Norrell were coming.

"No, gentlemen," said Childermass. "They are not. You must make do with me. I do not think Strange and Norrell will be seen again in England. At least not in this generation."

"Why?" asked Mr Segundus. "Where have they gone?"

Childermass smiled. "Wherever magicians used to go. Behind the sky. On the other side of the rain."

One of the Norrellites remarked that Jonathan Strange was wise to remove himself from England. Otherwise he would have certainly been hanged.

The excitable young man with the light-coloured hair retorted spitefully that the whole pack of Norrellites would soon find themselves at a grave disadvantage. Surely the first principle of Norrellite magic was that everything must be based upon books? And how were they going to do that when the books had all disappeared with Hurtfew Abbey?[5]

---

[5] There are very few modern magicians who do not declare themselves to be either Strangite or Norrellite, the only notable exception being John Childermass himself. Whenever he is asked he claims to be in some degree both. As this is like claiming to be both Whig and Tory at the same time, no one understands what he means.

"You do not need the library at Hurtfew, gentlemen," said Childermass. "Nor yet the library in Hanover-square. I have brought you something much better. A book Norrell long desired, but never saw. A book Strange did not even know existed. I have brought you John Uskglass's book."

More shouting. More uproar. In the midst of all of which Miss Redruth appeared to be making a speech in defence of John Uskglass, whom she insisted upon calling his Grace, the King, as if he were at any moment about to enter Newcastle and resume the government of Northern England.

"Wait!" cried Dr Foxcastle, his loud, important voice gradually overpowering first those nearest him, and then the rest of the assembly. "I see no book in this rogue's hands! Where is it? This is a trick, gentlemen! He wants our money, I'll be bound. Well, sir?" (This to Childermass.) "What do you say? Bring out your book – if indeed it exists!"

"On the contrary, sir," said Childermass, with his long, dark, one-sided grin. "I want nothing of yours. Vinculus! Stand up!"

In the house in Padua the first concern of the Greysteels and their servants was to make Mrs Strange as comfortable as they could; and each had his or her own way of doing it. Dr Greysteel's comfort chiefly took a philosophical form. He searched his memory for examples from history of people – particularly ladies – who had triumphed over adverse circumstances, often with the help of their friends. Minichello and Frank, the two manservants, ran to open doors for her – often whether she wanted to go through them or not. Bonifazia, the maid, preferred to treat a year's sojourn in Faerie as if it had been rather a severe sort of cold and brought her strengthening cordials throughout the day. Aunt Greysteel sent all over the town for the best wines and the rarest delicacies; and she purchased the softest, down-filled cushions and pillows, as if she hoped that by laying her head on them Arabella might be induced to forget all that had happened to her. But of all the various sorts of consolation that were offered her, that which seemed to suit Arabella best was Flora's company and Flora's conversation.

One morning they were sitting together at their needlework. Arabella put down her work with a gesture of impatience and went to the window. "There is a spirit of restlessness upon me," she said.

"It is to be expected," said Flora, gently. "Be patient. In time your spirits will be what they were before."

"Will they?" said Arabella, with a sigh. "Truth to own, I really do not remember what I was like before."

"Then I will tell you. You were always cheerful – tho' often left to your own devices. You were hardly ever out of temper – tho' often severely provoked. Your every speech was remarkable for its wit and genius – tho' you got no credit for it and almost always received a flat contradiction."

Arabella laughed. "Good Heavens! What a prodigy I was! But," she said with a wry look, "I am not inclined to put much trust in this portrait, since you never saw me."

"Mr Strange told me. Those are his words."

"Oh!" said Arabella. She turned her face away.

Flora cast her eyes down and said softly, "When he returns, he will do more to restore you to yourself than any one else could. You will be happy again." She glanced up.

Arabella was silent for a moment. She said, "I am not sure that we will see each other again."

Flora took up her needlework again. After a moment she said, "It is very odd that he should have gone back to his old master at last."

"Is it? There seems nothing very extraordinary in it to me. I never thought the quarrel would last as long as it did. I thought they would have been friends again by the end of the first month."

"You quite astonish me!" said Flora. "When Mr Strange was with us he did not have a good word to say for Mr Norrell – and Mr Norrell has published the most dreadful things about Mr Strange in the magical journals."

"Oh, I dare say!" said Arabella, entirely unimpressed. "But that was just their nonsense! They are both as stubborn as Old Scratch. I have no cause to love Mr Norrell – far from it. But I know this about him: he is a magician first and everything else second – and Jonathan is the same. Books and magic are all either of them really cares about. No one else understands the subject as they do – and so, you see, it is only natural that they should like to be together."

As the weeks went by Arabella smiled and laughed more often. She became interested in everything that concerned her new friends. Her days were taken up with sociable meals, errands and the pleasant obligations of friendship – small domestic matters with which her sore mind and wounded spirit were glad to refresh themselves. Of her absent husband she thought very little, except to be grateful for his consideration in placing her with the Greysteels.

There happened to be a young Irish captain in Padua just then and several people were of the opinion that he admired Flora – though Flora said that he did not. He had led a company of cavalry into the teeth of the severest gunfire at Waterloo; yet his courage all seemed to desert him where Flora was concerned. He could not look at her without blushing and was most alarmed whenever she entered a room. Generally he found it easier to apply to Mrs Strange for intelligence of when Flora might be walking in the Prato della Valle (a beautiful garden at the heart of the city) or when she might next visit the Baxters (some mutual friends); and Arabella was always glad to help him.

But there were some consequences of her captivity which she could not easily shake off. She was accustomed to dancing all night, and sleep did not come easily to her. Sometimes at night she could still hear a mournful fiddle and a pipe playing fairy tunes, compelling her to dance – though it was the last thing in the world that she wanted to do.

"Talk to me," she would say to Flora and Aunt Greysteel. "Talk to me and I think I can master it."

Then one or both of them would sit up with her and talk to her of everything they could think of. But sometimes Arabella found that the impulse to movement – any sort of movement – was too strong to be denied, and then she would take to pacing the bedchamber she shared with Flora; and on several occasions Dr Greysteel and Frank kindly sacrificed their own sleep to walk with her in the night-streets of Padua.

On one such night in April they were strolling about near to the Cathedral; Arabella and Dr Greysteel were speaking of their departure for England which had been arranged for the following month. Arabella found the prospect of being amongst all her English friends again a little daunting and Dr Greysteel was reassuring her. Suddenly Frank gave an exclamation of surprize and pointed upwards.

The stars were shifting and changing; in the patch of sky above them were new constellations. A little further on was an ancient-looking stone arch. There was nothing exactly unusual in this; Padua is a city full of intriguing doorways, arches and arcades. But this arch was not like the others. Padua is built of mediaeval bricks and consequently many of its streets are a pleasing pink-gold colour. This arch was built of dour, dark northern stones and upon each side was a statue of John Uskglass, his face half-hidden by a cap with raven wings. Just within the arch a tall figure was standing.

Arabella hesitated. "You will not go far?" she said to Dr Greysteel.

"Frank and I shall be here," Dr Greysteel told her. "We shall not move from this spot. You have only to call us."

She went on alone. The person within the doorway was reading. He looked up as she approached, with the old, dear expression of not quite remembering where he was or what he had do with the world outside his book.

"You have not brought a thunderstorm with you this time," she said.

"Oh, you heard about that, did you?" Strange gave a slightly self-conscious laugh. "That was a little overdone perhaps. Not altogether in the best of taste. I believe I spent too much time in Lord Byron's society when I was in Venice. I caught something of his style."

They walked on a little and at every moment new patterns of stars appeared above their heads.

"You look well, Arabella," he said. "I feared . . . What did I fear? Oh! a thousand different things. I feared you would not speak to me. But here you are. I am very glad to see you."

"And now your thousand fears can be laid to rest," she said. "At least as far as they concern me. Have you found any thing yet to dispel the Darkness?"

"No, not yet. Though, to own the truth, we have been so busy recently – some new conjectures concerning naiads – that we have scarcely had time to apply ourselves seriously to the problem. But there are one or two things in Goubert's *Gatekeeper of Apollo* which look promising. We are optimistic."

"I am glad. I am miserable when I think of you suffering."

"Do not be miserable, I beg you. Apart from any thing else, I do not suffer. A little perhaps at first, but not now. And Norrell and I are hardly the first English magicians to labour under an enchantment. Robert Dymoke fell foul of a fairy in the twelfth century and thereafter could not speak but only sing – which, I am sure, is not so pleasant as it sounds. And there was a fourteenth-century magician who had a silver foot – which must have been very disagreeable. Besides who is to say that the Darkness may not be of advantage to us? We intend to go out of England and are likely to meet with all sorts of tricksy persons. An English magician is an impressive thing. Two English magicians are, I suppose, twice as impressive – but when those two English magicians are shrouded in an Impenetrable Darkness – ah, well! That, I should think, is enough to strike terror into the heart of any one short of a demi-god!"

"Where will you go?"

"Oh, there are plenty of places. This world is only one among so many, and it does not do for a magician to become too – what shall I say? – too *parochial*."

"But will Mr Norrell like it?" she asked, doubtfully. "He was never fond of travelling – not even as far as Portsmouth."

"Ah! But that is one of the advantages of our particular mode of travel. He need never leave the house if he does not wish it. The world – all worlds – will come to us." He paused and looked about him. "I had better not go further. Norrell is a little way off. For various reasons to do with the enchantment, it is best that we do not stray very far from each other. Arabella," he said, with a degree of seriousness unusual to him, "it hurt me more than I could bear to think of you under the earth. I would have done any thing – any thing at all – to fetch you safely out."

She took his hands and her eyes were shining. "And you did it," she whispered. They looked at each other for a long moment, and in that moment all was as it used to be – it was as if they had never parted; but she did not offer to go into the Darkness with him and he did not ask her.

"One day," he said, "I shall find the right spell and banish the Darkness. And on that day I will come to you."

"Yes. On that day. I will wait until then."

He nodded and seemed about to depart, but then he hesitated. "Bell," he said, "do not wear black. Do not be a widow. Be happy. That is how I wish to think of you."

"I promise. And how shall I think of you?"

He considered a moment and then laughed. "Think of me with my nose in a book!"

They kissed once. Then he turned upon his heel and disappeared into the Darkness.

## ACKNOWLEDGEMENTS

Thanks are first due to the immensely wonderful, much-missed Giles Gordon. I was proud to say he was my agent. I still am.

And special thanks to Jonny Geller for everything since Giles has been gone.

For encouragement when this book began: Geoff Ryman, Alison Paice (also much missed), and Tinch Minter and her writing group, especially Julian Hall.

For encouragement along the way: my parents Janet and Stuart, Patrick and Teresa Nielsen Hayden, Ellen Datlow, Terri Windling and Neil Gaiman whose generosity to other writers never ceases to amaze me.

For everyone who helped with languages: Stuart Clarke, Samantha Evans, Patrick Marcel and Giorgia Grilli. For help with knotty problems of Napoleonic military and naval history: Nicholas Blake (needless to say, the remaining errors are entirely my responsibility). For immensely perceptive comments and suggestions: Antonia Till. For writing books that were continually helpful: Elizabeth Longford (*Wellington*) and Christopher Hibbert and Ben Weinreb (*The London Encyclopedia*).

To Jonathan Whiteland, who cheerfully gives his time and expertise so that Macs can run and books be written.

And, above all, to Colin who did everything else so I could write, who never complained, and without whom it is most unlikely this book would ever have seen the light of day.

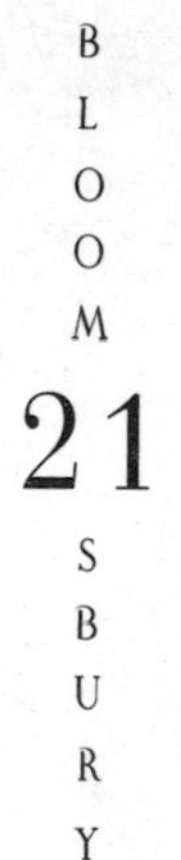


# SUSANNA CLARKE

# Jonathan Strange & Mr Norrell

A READING GUIDE

# ABOUT THE BOOK

## *In brief*

Centuries ago, when magic still existed in England, the greatest magician of them all was the Raven King. A human child brought up by fairies, the Raven King blended fairy wisdom and human reason to create English magic. Now, at the beginning of the nineteenth century, he is barely more than a legend, and England, with its mad King and its dashing poets, no longer believes in practical magic.

Then the reclusive Mr Norrell of Hurtfew Abbey appears and causes the statues of York Cathedral to speak and move. News spreads of the return of magic to England and, persuaded that he must help the government in the war against Napoleon, Mr Norrell goes to London. There he meets a brilliant young magician and takes him as a pupil. Jonathan Strange is charming, rich and arrogant. Together, they dazzle the country with their feats.

But the partnership soon turns to rivalry. Mr Norrell has never conquered his lifelong habits of secrecy, while Strange will always be attracted to the wildest, most perilous magic. He becomes fascinated by the shadowy figure of the Raven King, and his heedless pursuit of long-forgotten magic threatens not only his partnership with Norrell but everything that he holds dear.

## *In detail*

*Jonathan Strange & Mr Norrell* began with a kind of waking dream. As Susanna Clarke puts it: 'I could picture a tall, charming, rather Byronic Englishman in nineteenth-century clothes standing in a campo in Venice, talking to a well-to-do English family. But I knew nothing whatsoever about him – apart from the fact that he was more dangerous and wild than he appeared, and that he was something to do with magic.' This enigmatic, charismatic Englishman was to become Jonathan Strange, and when Clarke encountered – on a jigsaw – a dusty-looking gentleman wearing an eighteenth-century wig and sitting in a library, the rivalry between Strange and the bookish, secretive Mr Norrell of Hurtfew Abbey was born. During an illness that required her to rest a great deal, Clarke re-read Tolkien's *Lord of the Rings*, and when she finished she decided to try writing a novel of magic and fantasy. She had long admired the fantasy writing of Ursula K. Le Guin and Alan Garner, but also loved the historical fiction of Rosemary Sutcliff and the novels of Jane Austen. These various influences were to come together in a novel which is part magical fantasy, part scrupulously researched historical novel, with teasing faux-academic footnotes referencing a bibliography of magical books entirely of her own invention.

Susanna Clarke's story is set in an alternative version of nineteenth-century England during the Napoleonic wars. She spent hours reading military history to get the details of the battles just right, since she felt that the more accurate these details were, the more real the magic would seem. In this alternative world magic is a dying art, practised by only two people – our eponymous heroes – and is otherwise an academic rather than a practical discipline. Although most of the tradition of English magic to which the novel refers is invention, one of the magicians, Valentine Greatrakes (or Greatorex) actually existed: he was a celebrated Irish healer who toured England in 1666 curing people by the laying on of hands. Clarke included details of fairy behaviour taken from Scottish, Irish, Welsh and English folklore – for example, their habitation of hollow hills, and their habit of stealing Christians (and dancing with them all night). As the story develops, and especially under the influence of the mysterious Raven King, the very landscape becomes suffused with magic. As Clarke says, 'England can still seem a pretty magical place to me. Sometimes a feature of a landscape – a line of trees in a field; a perfectly ordinary house on a hill – can have the eeriest effect upon you that you can't quite explain.'

Susanna Clarke is writing a second book set in the same world as *Jonathan Strange & Mr Norrell* – something of a challenge, even for her. As she once said to an interviewer, 'I have a bit of a problem now that the fairy roads are all open ... what do I do with them?'

# ABOUT THE AUTHOR

Susanna Clarke was born in Nottingham in 1959, the eldest daughter of a Methodist Minister. A nomadic childhood was spent in towns in Northern England and Scotland. She was educated at St Hilda's College, Oxford, and has worked in various areas of non-fiction publishing. In 1990 she left London and went to Turin to teach English to stressed-out executives of the Fiat motor company. The following year she taught English in Bilbao.

She returned to England in 1992 and spent the rest of that year in County Durham, in a house that looked out over the North Sea. *Jonathan Strange & Mr Norrell*, her first novel, was published in 2004 in more than thirty countries, and shortlisted for the Whitbread First Novel Award and the Guardian First Book Award. It won the British Book Awards Newcomer of the Year, the Hugo Award and the World Fantasy Award in 2005. *The Ladies of Grace Adieu*, a collection of her short stories, some set in the world of *Jonathan Strange & Mr Norrell*, was published by Bloomsbury in 2006.

Susanna Clarke lives in Cambridge with her partner, the novelist and reviewer Colin Greenland.

## FOR DISCUSSION

- Sir Walter Pole likens England in the novel to 'an orphaned young lady left in the care of a pack of lecherous, avaricious old men' who 'stole her inheritance and plundered her house' (page 82). What is the narrator's view of the government ministers, aristocrats and military figures who hold the reins of power in Regency England? Do you think satire plays an important part in the novel?

- *Jonathan Strange & Mr Norrell* interweaves fictional characters with real figures from nineteenth-century England, including, among others, King George III, the publisher John Murray, the Duke of Wellington and the poet Byron. What is the effect of mixing fact and fiction in this way? Does the author use any other techniques to convince us of the 'truth' of her narrative? Is this kind of writing 'fantasy' or 'historical fiction'?

- 'Magicians have no business marrying,' says Mr Norrell, of Strange's relationship with Arabella. Why does Norrell take such a dim view of Strange's marriage to Arabella? What does the novel have to say about marriage in general and the nature of relationships between men and women in the society it depicts?

- How does Susanna Clarke's use of the language and idiom of the nineteenth century add to the atmosphere of the book?

Do the tone of her narrator or her choice of words remind you of any other writers?

- An interview with Susanna Clarke in *Time* magazine suggested that, if it had not already been taken, 'Sense and Sensibility' would have been a good alternative title for *Jonathan Strange & Mr Norrell*. How do Strange and Norrell differ in their motivations for reviving English magic, and in their temperaments? Arabella Strange observes that 'a great disparity of views and temper existed between the two magicians'. Do they have any similarities? Why do you think the author created two contrasting central characters?

- What part does madness play in the novel?

- Clarke's narrative is heavily footnoted with references to books, stories, and historical documents both real and imagined. These extensive notes – many of them transfixing short stories in their own right – hint at a much broader historical canvas against which the events in the novel take place. Is this construction successful? Does it add credibility to the fictional universe Clarke has created? Does it detract from the main narrative in any way?

- 'Can a magician kill a man by magic?'Lord Wellington asked Strange. Strange frowned. He seemed to dislike the question. 'I suppose a magician might,' he admitted, 'but a gentleman never could' (page 389).

- According to the narrator of the story, Strange, Norrell, the York magicians, Lascelles and Lord Byron are all 'gentlemen', but Stephen Black and Childermass are not. Is the quality of being a 'gentleman' in the novel related to integrity? And if not, what is it dependent on? How does your opinion of characters such as Stephen Black, Childermass and Vinculus change over the course of the novel?

- How important is humour in the book? Do you think it is important to the author to make her readers laugh?

- How much truth is there in Vinculus' early prophecy to Jonathan Strange (page 252)? What different kinds of knowledge and wisdom are explored in the book?

## ALSO BY SUSANNA CLARKE

*The Ladies of Grace Adieu and other stories*

## SUGGESTED FURTHER READING

*Pride and Prejudice* by Jane Austen
*The Crimson Petal and the White* by Michel Faber
*The Earthsea Trilogy* by Ursula K. Le Guin
*The Magician's Nephew* by C. S. Lewis
*Perdido Street Station* by China Miéville
*Quicksilver* by Neal Stephenson
*Great Expectations* by Charles Dickens
*The Lord of the Rings* by J. R. R. Tolkien
*Stardust* by Neil Gaiman and Charles Vess
*The Quincunx* by Charles Palliser
*Thursbitch* by Alan Garner
*The Kingdoms of Elfin* by Sylvia Townsend Warner

For further resource material, including an interview with the author, reviews and extra material by Susanna Clarke, visit www.jonathanstrange.com.

# SUSANNA CLARKE'S FAVOURITE BOOKS

## *Children's book/s*

As a child I was a Narnian. I read *The Lion, the Witch and the Wardrobe* by C. S. Lewis and looked hopefully into the backs of wardrobes. It seemed to me then that imaginary places are quite as real as real ones. It still does.

It's a commonplace criticism of Tolkien that he couldn't write about women because he lived the circumscribed, masculine life of an Oxford Don. In many ways Lewis lived an even narrower life, with no offspring of his own and for a long time no wife, and yet he writes such admirably real children. The children's speech may be dated, but they are very recognisable with all their quarrelling and courage, predictable selfishnesses and unexpected generosities.

Lewis and Tolkien both created worlds that don't centre on human beings. Narnia is largely a kingdom of talking animals; Middle Earth contains Men but they're not necessarily the most interesting or important race. It's one of the things fantasy does particularly well – reminds us that there are other things in the universe besides us.

My favourite children's books of This Moment Now are Diana Wynne Jones' Chrestomanci books, particularly *The Lives of Christopher Chant*. Each night Christopher gets out of bed, walks round a corner by the fireplace and visits different worlds. Because he is a very small boy, nothing about this strikes him as particularly strange, but as soon as adults learn about it

Christopher is set a series of sinister tasks. Vivid and astonishingly imaginative.

### *Classic*

When I first read *Emma* Emma herself was, I suppose, ten or eleven years older than me. Now I am more than twice her age. But I am still as fascinated by her, still as comfortable in her company. She is clever, but misinterprets everyone and everything; she is snobbish, but generous; she is critical of other people, but most of all of herself.

Even among Austen's books *Emma* is curiously unmelodramatic. There is melodrama in Austen's other books, though mostly it happens off-stage. Girls are seduced and made pregnant, wives abscond with heartless men and once a young lady falls from a stone quay on to her head. But in *Emma* the most dramatic things that happen are that someone mysteriously delivers a piano to a young lady's house, an ignorant clergyman refuses to dance with a penniless girl and a picnic no one really wanted to go on turns out badly. *Emma* centres on homely things – taking care of an aged parent, the pleasures of talking to a good friend, the irritation caused by a shrill and silly new neighbour – but as the perfect plot unwinds the heartaches, surprises and suspense rival the most gothic of novels.

## *Contemporary book*

The contemporary author who fascinates me above all others is the comics writer, Alan Moore, especially the five volumes of *Promethea*. It begins with Sophie Bangs, a New York student, who discovers she can become Promethea, a beautiful 'science-heroine' with Graeco-Egyptian armour, magical powers and the ability to fly. So far, so familiar. But the book continues in the most weird and wonderful ways, becoming, among other things, an exploration of Hermetic magic and the Tarot, an account of a journey through Heaven and a user's guide to the end of the world. Above all it is a hymn to the splendours of the human imagination. Promethea herself is, in some mystical fashion, the personification of the human imagination. As she says to the reader at the end, 'I'm real and I'm the best friend you ever had. Who do you think got you all this cool stuff?'

Many of the pleasures are in the lesser characters: Sophie's maddening, ditsy best friend, Stacia; Sonny Baskerville, 'New York's first multiple personality mayor'; and Weeping Gorilla who is a comic-book character within the comic, an enormous gorilla who appears on billboards everywhere, weeping and spouting self-pitying clichés ('The garage says it's the clutch.'). My favourite quotation is from celebrity mass murderer, the Painted Doll: 'Oh they said God was dead, all those beatniks and snooty-ass Frenchmen. Not me. I knew better. I said to them, "Wait boys! Don't break cover yet awhile. He might be faking."'

## *Top 10*

To give my Top 10 Books of All Time is clearly quite impossible. These, in no particular order, are my Top 10 Books of All Time This Week.

*The Man who was Thursday* by G. K. Chesterton.
All of Sherlock Holmes
*Emma* by Jane Austen
*Promethea* by Alan Moore
The Chrestomanci books by Diana Wynne Jones
*Bleak House* by Charles Dickens
The works of P. G. Wodehouse
*The Private Memoirs and Confessions of a Justified Sinner* by James Hogg
*The Adventures of Huckleberry Finn* by Mark Twain
The Narnia books by C. S. Lewis

B L O O M 21 S B U R Y

| | |
|---|---|
| *Cat's Eye* | Margaret Atwood |
| *A Prayer for Owen Meany* | John Irving |
| *The English Patient* | Michael Ondaatje |
| *Snow Falling on Cedars* | David Guterson |
| *Fugitive Pieces* | Anne Michaels |
| *Harry Potter and the Philosopher's Stone* | J. K. Rowling |
| *Easy Riders, Raging Bulls* | Peter Biskind |
| *The Map of Love* | Ahdaf Soueif |
| *Holes* | Louis Sachar |
| *Marrying the Mistress* | Joanna Trollope |
| *Kitchen Confidential* | Anthony Bourdain |
| *Witch Child* | Celia Rees |
| *If Nobody Speaks of Remarkable Things* | Jon McGregor |
| *Middlesex* | Jeffrey Eugenides |
| *The Little Friend* | Donna Tartt |
| *Frankie & Stankie* | Barbara Trapido |
| *A Gathering Light* | Jennifer Donnelly |
| *The Kite Runner* | Khaled Hosseini |
| *The Promise of Happiness* | Justin Cartwright |
| *Jonathan Strange & Mr Norrell* | Susanna Clarke |
| *The Two of Us* | Sheila Hancock |

## Praise for *Jonathan Strange & Mr Norrell*

'Absolutely compelling ... irresistible ... I could not stop reading until I'd finished it ... It's an astonishing achievement. I can't think of anything that is remotely like it' Charles Palliser

'*Jonathan Strange & Mr Norrell* is unquestionably the finest English novel of the fantastic written in the last seventy years. It's funny, moving, scary, otherworldly, practical and magical, a journey through light and shadow – a delight to read' Neil Gaiman

'Dazzling, witty and gleefully entertaining ... A triumph of traditional imaginative storytelling, this is an energetic, engaging and inventive tale that simply kidnaps the lucky reader to participate in a rare experience' *Irish Times*

'A nourishing, nineteenth-century-style novel that will warm readers through any number of dark and stormy nights ... a big, bubbling cauldron of a book' *Daily Telegraph*

'To be honest, my topic for a gathering, my page-turner, my mind-improver, my talking point and my train reading are all one and the same book: *Jonathan Strange & Mr Norrell* ... I am literally unable to put it down' Julian Fellows, *Tatler*

'Full of spells, bad weather, statues that talk, haunted ballrooms and sinister gentlemen with thistledown hair ... be enchanted! *****' *Elle*

'Brimming with cod-academic references and myths, pert drawing-room comedy and genuinely chilling fantasy, this will appeal to devotees of Sarah Waters as much as to Harry Potter fans' *Marie Claire*

'Compelling: Clarke's tale of magicians and fairies is a prodigious achievement' *Sunday Times*

# Software Engineering

Edited by Merlin Dorfman and Richard H. Thayer
Foreword by Barry W. Boehm

Original contributions by:

A. Frank Ackerman
Doug Bell
Keith Bennett
Barry Boehm
Pearl Brereton
David Budgen
Mary Beth Chrissis
Bill Curtis
Merlin Dorfman
Richard E. Fairley
Stuart R. Faulk
Roger U. Fujii
Hassan Gomaa
Patrick A.V. Hall
Patricia W. Hurst
Lingzi Jin
John J. Marciniak
Ian Morrey
Linda Northrop
James D. Palmer
Mark Paulk
Roger S. Pressman
John Pugh
Robert J. Remington
Paul Rook
Richard H. Thayer
Dolores Wallace
Charles Weber

IEEE Computer Society Press
Los Alamitos, California

Washington • Brussels • Tokyo

**Library of Congress Cataloging-in-Publication Data**

Software engineering / Merlin Dorfman and Richard H. Thayer; foreword by Barry W. Boehm;
original contributions by A. Frank Ackerman... [et al.].
p. cm.
Includes bibliographical references.
ISBN 0-8186-7609-4
1. Software engineering. I. Dorfman, M. (Merlin) II. Thayer, Richard H.
QA76.758.S6454 1997
005.1—dc20 96-15910
CIP

IEEE Computer Society Press
10662 Los Vaqueros Circle
P.O. Box 3014
Los Alamitos, CA 90720-1314



IEEE Computer Society Press Order Number BP07609
Library of Congress Number 96-15910
ISBN 0-8186-7609-4

Additional copies can be ordered from

IEEE Computer Society Press
Customer Service Center
10662 Los Vaqueros Circle
P.O. Box 3014
Los Alamitos, CA 90720-1314
Tel: (714) 821-8380
Fax: (714) 821-4641
Email: cs.books@computer.org

IEEE Service Center
445 Hoes Lane
P.O. Box 1331
Piscataway, NJ 08855-1331
Tel: (908) 981-1393
Fax: (908) 981-9667
mis.custserv@computer.org

IEEE Computer Society
13, avenue de l'Aquilon
B-1200 Brussels
BELGIUM
Tel: +32-2-770-2198
Fax: +32-2-770-8505
euro.ofc@computer.org

IEEE Computer Society
Ooshima Building
2-19-1 Minami-Aoyama
Minato-ku, Tokyo 107
JAPAN
Tel: +81-3-3408-3118
Fax: +81-3-3408-3553
tokyo.ofc@computer.org



Assistant Publisher: Matt Loeb
Technical Editor: Jon Butler
Acquisistions Editor: Bill Sanders
Acquisitions Assistant: Cheryl Smith
Advertising/Promotions: Tom Fink
Production Editor: Lisa O'Conner
Cover Design: Alex Torres

Printed in the United States of America by Edwards Brothers, Incorporated

The Institute of Electrical and Electronics Engineers, Inc.

## Contributors of Original Papers

**Dr. A. Frank Ackerman**, Institute for Zero Defects Software, 5130 Birkdale Way, San Jose, CA 95138-2111, USA

**Dr. Doug Bell,** School of Computing and Management Science, Sheffield Hallam University, Hallamshire Business Park, 100 Napier Street, Sheffield S11 8HB, England, UK

**Prof. Keith H. Bennett**, Center for Software Maintenance, University of Durham, Durham DH1 3LE England, U.K.

**Dr. Barry W. Boehm**, Center for Software Engineering, University of Southern California, Los Angeles, CA, 90089-0781, USA

**Dr. Pearl Brereton**, Department of Computer Science, University of Keele, Keele, Staffordshire ST5 5BG England, U.K.

**Prof. David Budgen**, Department of Computer Science, University of Keele, Keele, Staffordshire ST5 5BG England, U.K.

**Ms. Mary Beth Chrissis**, Software Engineering Institute (SEI), Carnegie Mellon University, Pittsburgh, PA 15213-3890, USA

**Dr. Bill Curtis**, TeraQuest Metrics, P.O. Box 200490, Austin, TX 78720-0490, USA

**Mr. Jon K. Digerness (Illustrator)**, North Coast Graphics, 7418 Kanai Avenue, Citrus Heights, CA 95621, USA

**Dr. Merlin Dorfman,** Lockheed Martin Missiles & Space Company, Inc., P.O. Box 3504, Sunnyvale, CA 94088-3504, USA

**Dr. Richard E. Fairley**, Colorado Technical University, 4435 N. Chestnut Street, Colorado Springs, CO 80907-3896, USA

**Dr. Stuart R. Faulk**, Department of Computer and Information Science, Deschutes Hall, University of Oregon, Eugene, OR, 97403, USA

**Mr. Roger U. Fujii**, Logicon, Inc., 255 West Fifth Street, San Pedro, CA 90733-0471, USA

**Dr. Hassan Gomaa**, Department of Information and Software Systems Engineering, George Mason University, Fairfax, VA 22030-4444, USA

**Prof. Patrick (Pat) A.V. Hall**, Faculty of Math and Computing, The Open University, Walton Hall, Milton Keynes MK7 6AA England, U.K.

**Ms. Patricia W. Hurst**, Fastrak Training, Inc., 9175 Guilford Rd., Suite 300, Columbia, MD 21046, USA

**Dr. Lingzi Jin**, Department of Computer Science, Nanjing University, People's Republic of China 210093

**Mr. John J. Marciniak**, Kaman Sciences Corporation, 2560 Huntington Avenue, Suite 100, Alexandria, VA 22303-1416, USA

**Mr. Ian Morrey,** School of Computing and Management Science, Sheffield Hallam University, Hallamshire Business Park, 100 Napier Street, Sheffield S11 8HD, England, UK

**Ms. Linda M. Northrop**, Software Engineering Institute (SEI), Carnegie Mellon University, Pittsburgh, PA 15213-3890, USA

**Dr. James D. Palmer**, 860 Cashew Way, Fremont, CA 94536-2646, USA

**Mr. Mark C. Paulk**, Software Engineering Institute (SEI), Carnegie Mellon University, Pittsburgh, PA 15213-3890, USA

**Dr. Roger S. Pressman**, R.S. Pressman & Associates, Inc., 620 East Slope Drive, Orange, CT 06477, USA

**Prof. John Pugh,** School of Computer Science, Carleton University, Ottawa, Canada

**Dr. Robert J. Remington**, Lockheed Martin Missiles & Space Company, Inc., P.O. Box 3504, Sunnyvale, CA 94088-3504, USA

**Mr. Paul Rook**, The Centre for Software Reliability, City University, Northampton Square, London, EC1V 0HB England, U.K. (deceased)

**Dr. Richard H. Thayer**, Department of Computer Science, 6000 J Street, California State University at Sacramento, Sacramento, CA 95819, USA.

**Ms. Dolores R. Wallace**, Computer Systems Laboratory, National Institute of Standards and Technology, Gaithersburg, MD 20899-0001, USA

**Mr. Charles V. Weber**, Lockheed Martin Federal Systems Company, 6304 Spine Road, Boulder, CO 80301-3320, USA

# Foreword

Barry Boehm
*Center for Software Engineering*
*University of Southern California, Los Angeles, California*

This tutorial volume is very timely because its subject, software engineering, is currently going through an identity crisis, leaving many people wondering where, how, and if its previous precepts still apply. When commercial-off-the-shelf (COTS) products drive the nature of a software system, what is the role of a "requirements specification?" When user interface software is developed via pointing and clicking on a screen, how relevant are metrics such as lines of code or errors per line of code? When organizations are developing software product line families, how relevant are techniques oriented toward development of a single isolated software product?

Given the magnitude of these changes, there is a temptation to toss all of the old practices out the window and either embrace one of the latest "silver bullet" solutions or reinvent processes from scratch. Unfortunately, as the Brooks article indicates, silver-bullet solutions do not address all aspects of the software problem. And, as seen in the Gibbs article, colossal software disasters such as the Denver International Airport and the FAA Advanced Automation System await projects that neglect previous wisdom in such areas as early error elimination and stabilizing software requirements.

All this is happening while software is coming onto center stage as the key empowering technology of the Information Age. Without software, one cannot enter or exit the information superhighway. Without software, a Cray supercomputer is a rather expensive loveseat and a Powerbook laptop is a rather expensive paperweight. If their software is bungled, our cars, radiation therapy machines, bank accounts—and we ourselves—can get into big trouble.

Fortunately, there is a great deal of wisdom available about how to do software projects properly. A major difficulty is that the wisdom appears in many places, without a framework of guidelines on how to apply it in changing situations.

Resolving that difficulty is what makes this software engineering tutorial volume very helpful as well as very timely. Chapter 1 provides overall perspectives on software engineering issues. Chapter 2 emphasizes a critical guideline: that software engineering needs to concentrate not just on the software, but on the system and mission that the software supports. Chapters 4 and 5 elaborate on techniques for addressing both software and systems aspects in software requirements engineering and design. These chapters particularly illuminate such key areas as concurrent systems, real-time systems, and user-intensive systems. They also address new techniques such as object-oriented system development and formal methods. Chapter 7 on verification, validation, and testing places Chapter 9 on software quality and quality assurance in proper perspective by emphasizing that quality is not tested into the software, but planned, prepared for, and sustained throughout the development cycle.

Chapter 10, software project management, covers the advantages and limitations of quantitative approaches to managing software projects. Quantitative models and methods enable software project managers and their stakeholders (users, customers, developers, maintainers, interfacers, and so forth) to reason about tradeoffs among cost, schedule, functionality, performance, and quality before committing to a course of action.

These models also provide the foundation for plans that enable managers to monitor the progress of projects and to keep them under control. However, since, software development is a people-intensive activity, strict "manage by the numbers" approaches must be tempered by people-oriented approaches. These emphasize such considerations as empowerment, delegation, and development of shared values in getting people to create systems with conceptual integrity, and in establishing organizations that enable people to fulfill their needs for belonging, achievement, recognition, and self-actualization.

The final paper in Chapter 10 and the first two papers in Chapter 11 provide perspectives on the use of risk management as the key for tailoring software projects to their particular objectives, available capabilities, and environment. Risk management offers guidelines for determining when and how much to invest in such activities as domain engineering, COTS package evaluation, prototyping, configuration management, and quality assurance; and for determining what and how much to include in successive increments of a software product. The final paper in Chapter 11 provides an overview of the Software Engineering Institute's highly influential Capability Maturity Model for assessing the maturity of one's software engineering management processes.

Chapter 12 presents some balanced views of software technology capabilities such as computer-aided software engineering (CASE) tools, reusable components, and prototyping tools, reinforcing the point in Chapter 1 that none of these serves as a silver bullet for eliminating software problems. Finally, the paper in Chapter 13 on education reinforces the point in Chapter 2 that software engineers need to learn how to deal with systems, not just the software portions of the systems.

Of course, this book is not a silver bullet either. Readers will need to exercise considerable judgment in applying its insights to their particular project situations. But it performs a valuable service in assembling and organizing the insights, and pointers to more detailed techniques, into a framework within which the appropriate insights can be recalled and applied.

# Software Engineering

Merlin Dorfman
Richard H. Thayer

## Preface

This tutorial describes the current state of the practice of software engineering. The purpose for writing this tutorial is twofold:

1. There is a need for a set of papers that can be used for a senior or graduate class in software engineering for those faculty members who prefer to use a set of definitive papers rather than a textbook, while relieving the instructor of the need to obtain copyright clearance from dozens of publishers.
2. There are software professionals who would like to have a preselected volume of the best papers in the field of software engineering, for self-study or for a training course in industry.

For the purposes of this tutorial, software engineering is defined as an engineering discipline that applies sound scientific, mathematical, management, and engineering principles to the successful building of large computer programs (software).

> **software engineering**. (1) The application of a systematic, disciplined, quantifiable approach to the development, operation, and maintenance of software, that is, the application of engineering to software. (2) The study of approaches as in (1).

Software systems are built within an organizational structure called a software project. A *successful* software project delivers its planned products within schedule and budget and meets its defined functional and quality requirements.

Software engineering includes software requirements analysis; software design; modern programming methods; testing procedures; verification and validation; software configuration management; software quality assurance; tools for analysis and design; corporate software policies, strategies and goals; project management planning, organizing, staffing, directing, and controlling; as well as the foundations of computer science.

In our opinion, good tutorial papers have the following characteristics:

- They define the basic terms
- They cover the state of the practice for the given topic thoroughly and evenly
- They avoid new, unproved concepts (other than to list them as future possibilities)
- They do not try to sell one tool or concept over all others
- They are easy to read
- They are organized in a hierarchical manner (top-level concepts discussed first, second level concepts discussed next, and so forth)
- They provide additional references
- They come from a refereed journal (unless written specifically for the tutorial)
- They were written by an expert in the area (to assure all of the above)

Our criteria are of course idealized. Even these "rules" can be violated if there is a good reason.

In addition, to keep the whole tutorial under 500 pages, each article should be no longer than 10–12 journal pages.

Our intent was to use the best and most current leading papers in the field. To assure that our intent was fulfilled, we sent survey forms to over 200 of the leading researchers and practitioners of software engineering in the US, Canada, Europe, and Asia, asking what papers they would like to see in a software engineering tutorial. Seventy survey forms were returned. In a surprisingly large number of the basic specialty areas of software engineering, there were no recent, high-quality overview papers identified. It appears that, as a discipline matures, people no longer write overview papers. There have been very few acceptable papers on the fundamentals of software engineering published in the last ten or so years. Therefore the editors contacted some of the leading authors and practitioners in the major subfields of software engineering and asked them to write papers for us. A list of the contributors can be found on Page v; we are grateful that they took time from their busy schedules to write for this tutorial.

Our tutorial is divided into four parts and 13 chapters.

Part One includes Chapters 1, 2, and 3 and provides an overview of software engineering in the context of current issues and the engineering of large complex systems. Chapter 1 describes the problems that occur in developing software, sometimes called the "software crisis." Chapters 2 and 3 present the concepts of system engineering of software-intensive systems, and of engineering of software products, as the solution to the "software crisis."

Part Two, Chapters 4 through 8, describes software engineering from the viewpoint of the phases of the software life cycle: requirements, design, implementation (coding), testing, and maintenance. Chapter 4, *Software Requirements Engineering and Software Design*, discusses the state of the practice in requirements and design. Originally requirements engineering and design were separate chapters, but most papers on the subject combine the two topics so we did as well. Chapter 5, *Software Development Methodologies*, also combines approaches supporting analysis and design. Because of their growing importance, special attention was paid to object-oriented and formal methods. Chapter 6, *Coding*, describes programming activities as they affect software engineering and vice versa. Chapter 7, *Software Validation, Verification, and Testing*, and Chapter 8, *Software Maintenance*, describe the state of the practice in those areas of specialization.

Part Three consists of Chapters 9, 10, and 11 and takes a phase-independent view of the software development process and its management. Chapter 9 looks at software quality assurance in the larger context of ensuring conformance to the development process, as well as in the traditional smaller-scale context. The chapter also looks at configuration management, standards, and reliability engineering as keys to building quality into software products. Chapter 10 discusses software project management and some related topics such as software cost estimation and risk management. Chapter 11 looks at the software development process and how it fits into the larger scope of the software life cycle.

Part Four discusses software technology and education. Chapter 12, *Software Technology*, discusses how technology is transitioned from theory to practice as well as software re-engineering and reuse, computer-aided software engineering (CASE), and software metrics. Chapter 13 contains a single paper on the topic of education for software professionals.

This tutorial is a companion document to the below-listed software engineering tutorials. Duplication of papers has been kept to a minimum. In a few cases, particularly important papers are duplicated in order that each tutorial can stand alone.

- R.H. Thayer, editor, *Tutorial: Software Engineering Project Management,* IEEE Computer Society Press, Los Alamitos, Calif., 1988 (revision in process).
- R.H. Thayer and M. Dorfman (eds.), *System and Software Requirements Engineering,* IEEE Computer Society Press, Los Alamitos, Calif., 1990 (revision in process).
- R.H. Thayer and A. D. McGettrick (eds.), *Software Engineering—A European Perspective,* IEEE Computer Society Press, Los Alamitos, Calif., 1993.

We would like to acknowledge the support provided by the following people.

- Ms Catherine Harris and Dr. William Sanders, managing editors of IEEE Computer Society Press
- IEEE volunteer editors under the direction of Prof. Jon Butler of the Naval Postgraduate School
- Fernando Proaño, a graduate student at Sacramento State University, who assisted us with the survey mentioned above

Merlin Dorfman, Ph.D.
Lockheed Martin Missiles and Space Company
Sunnyvale, California, USA

Richard H. Thayer, Ph.D.
California State University, Sacramento
Sacramento, California, USA

# Contents

# Chapter 1

# Issues—The Software Crisis

## 1. Introduction to Chapter

The term "software crisis" has been used since the late 1960s to describe those recurring system development problems in which software development problems cause the entire system to be late, over budget, not responsive to the user and/or customer requirements, and difficult to use, maintain, and enhance. The late Dr. Winston Royce, in his paper *Current Problems* [1], emphasized this situation when he said in 1991:

> The construction of new software that is both pleasing to the user/buyer and without latent errors is an unexpectedly hard problem. It is perhaps the most difficult problem in engineering today, and has been recognized as such for more than 15 years. It is often referred to as the "software crisis". It has become the longest continuing "crisis" in the engineering world, and it continues unabated.

This chapter describes some of the current issues and problems in system development that are caused by software—software that is late, is over budget, and/or does not meet the customers' requirements or needs.

*Software* is the set of instructions that govern the actions of a programmable machine. Software includes application programs, system software, utility software, and firmware. Software does not include data, procedures, people, and documentation. In this tutorial, "software" is synonymous with "computer programs."

Because software is invisible, it is difficult to be certain of development progress or of product completeness and quality. Software is not governed by the physical laws of nature: there is no equivalent of Ohm's Law, which governs the flow of electricity in a circuit; the laws of aerodynamics, which act to keep an aircraft flying stably in the air; or Maxwell's Equations, which describe the radiation of energy from an antenna.

In addition, software is not manufactured like hardware; it does not have a production phase nor manufactured spare parts like hardware; it is typically custom-built, not assembled from existing components like hardware. Even in today's society, software is viewed with suspicion by many individuals, such as senior managers and customers, as somewhat akin to "black magic."

The result is that software is one of the most difficult artifacts of the modern world to develop and build.

## 2. Introduction to Papers

The opening paper fortuitously appeared in a recent issue of *Scientific American* as the editors were casting about for a way to incorporate a recent rash of high-publicity software problems into the motivation for this tutorial. The paper defines and presents essentially all the major issues currently plaguing software development and maintenance. The article is "popular" rather than technical in the sense that it is journalistic in style and focuses on popular perceptions of software as "black magic," but it raises many issues that software professionals need to be familiar with. It is also worth noting that many of the problems described are partly or largely due to non-software issues such as politics, funding, and external constraints, but again the software professional needs to know that problems unrelated to software engineering must overcome if software projects are to be successful.

The term "software crisis" not unexpectedly originated with the military, for that is where large, complex "real-time" software was first developed. More recently, as civilian and commercial software systems have approached and exceeded military systems in size, complexity, and performance requirements, the "software crisis" has occurred in these environments as well. It is noteworthy that the *Scientific American* article mentions military systems only peripherally.

The article begins with a discussion of the highly-publicized and software-related failure of the baggage system at the new Denver International Airport. As of the date of the article, opening of the airport had been delayed four times, for almost a year, at a cost to the airport authority of over $1 million a day.

Almost as visible in recent months, and also mentioned in the article, are failures of software development for the Department of Motor Vehicles (DMV) of the State of California, and for the advanced air traffic control system of the US Federal Aviation Administration (FAA). The DMV project involved attempts to merge existing, separately developed systems that managed driver's licenses and vehicle registrations. As has been pointed out in the press [2], the State of California has had problems with computer projects of over $1 billion in value, and the problems resulted from the acquisition policies of the State of California (how contractors and consultants are selected and managed by the State), and from hardware-software integration difficulties, as well as from causes strictly related to software development.

The article identifies the first use of the term "software engineering" in a 1968 conference of the NATO Science Committee in Garmisch, Germany. (See also the Bauer article in this Tutorial.) Many approaches that have been proposed to improve software development are discussed; the author feels that most of these ideas have not lived up to the expectations of their originators. Also discussed is the idea that there are no "silver bullets." (See the article by Brooks in this chapter.)

The *Scientific American* article looks favorably on the use of formal specification methods to solve the problem of software quality, and on "software reuse" (the ability to use a software product developed for one application again later for another application) to solve the productivity or cost problem.

The Software Engineering Institute's Capability Maturity Model was also favorably mentioned (see the article by Paulk, Curtis, Chrissis, and Weber in this Tutorial) as a motivation to software developers to improve their practices. The paper reports an SEI finding that approximately 75 percent of all software developers do not have any formal process or any productivity or quality metrics.

Because software development depends on an educated workforce and good communications rather than on a fixed plant of any kind, software is inherently a suitable export product for developing countries. Although the US is still strong in software design and project management, the article notes that third world countries—notably India and Far Eastern countries—are capable of producing many more "lines of code" per dollar.

A sidebar by Dr. Mary Shaw provides a view of software engineering's history, and of how that history may serve as a roadmap for software engineering's future. Finally, the paper urges education of computer science students in software engineering as an essential step toward resolving the software crisis.

The second and last article in this chapter, "No Silver Bullets: Essence and Accidents of Software Engineering," is by Fred Brooks, one of the legendary figures in software engineering. He has been called the father of software engineering project management in the United States. He worked at IBM in the 1960s and was the software project manager for the OS/360 operating system.

This paper, which he wrote in 1987, states that "no single technique exists to solve the software crisis, that there is no silver bullet." The easy problems ("accidents") have been solved and the remaining difficulties are "essential." He views the solution to the software crisis as a collection of many software engineering tools and techniques that, used in combination, will reduce or eliminate software problems. Although Brooks sees no single solution to the software crisis, no single technology or management technique, he does see encouragement for the future through disciplined, consistent efforts to develop, propagate, and exploit many of the software tools and techniques that are being developed today. (In a report, also written in 1987 [3], Brooks states his belief that most software development problems of the US Department of Defense are managerial rather than technical.)

Brooks believes the hard part of building software is the specification and design of a system, not the coding and testing of the final product. As a result, he believes that building software will always be hard. There is no apparent simple solution. Brooks describes the three major advances in software development as:

- The use of high level languages
- The implementation of time-sharing to improve the productivity of programmers and the quality of their products
- Unified programming environment

Brooks also cites the Ada language, object-oriented programming, artificial intelligence, expert systems, and "automatic" programming (automated generation of code from system specification and design) as technologies with the potential for improving software. From the perspective of another eight years, the AI-related technologies for the most part have yet to fulfill the potential that Brooks saw for them in 1987.


1. Royce, Winston, "Current Problems," in *Aerospace Software Engineering: A Collection of Concepts*, edited by Christine Anderson and Merlin Dorfman, American Institute of Aeronautics, Inc., Washington DC, 1991.
2. "State Fears a Computer Nightmare: Costly 'Screw-Ups' Found in Many Government Projects," *Sacramento Bee*, Sacramento, Calif., June 16, 1994.
3. "Report of the Defense Science Board Task Force on Military Software," Office of the Under Secretary of Defense for Acquisition, Department of Defense, Washington, DC, Sept. 1987.

# Software's Chronic Crisis

by W. Wayt Gibbs, *staff writer*

Denver's new international airport was to be the pride of the Rockies, a wonder of modern engineering. Twice the size of Manhattan, 10 times the breadth of Heathrow, the airport is big enough to land three jets simultaneously—in bad weather. Even more impressive than its girth is the airport's subterranean baggage-handling system. Tearing like intelligent coal-mine cars along 21 miles of steel track, 4,000 independent "telecars" route and deliver luggage between the counters, gates and claim areas of 20 different airlines. A central nervous system of some 100 computers networked to one another and to 5,000 electric eyes, 400 radio receivers and 56 bar-code scanners orchestrates the safe and timely arrival of every valise and ski bag.

At least that is the plan. For nine months, this Gulliver has been held captive by Lilliputians—errors in the software that controls its automated baggage system. Scheduled for takeoff by last Halloween, the airport's grand opening was postponed until December to allow BAE Automated Systems time to flush the gremlins out of its $193-million system. December yielded to March. March slipped to May. In June the airport's planners, their bond rating demoted to junk and their budget hemorrhaging red ink at the rate of $1.1 million a day in interest and operating costs, conceded that they could not predict when the baggage system would stabilize enough for the airport to open.

To veteran software developers, the Denver debacle is notable only for its visibility. Studies have shown that for every six new large-scale software systems that are put into operation, two others are canceled. The average software development project overshoots its schedule by half; larger projects generally do worse. And some three quarters of all large systems are "operating failures" that either do not function as intended or are not used at all.

The art of programming has taken 50 years of continual refinement to reach this stage. By the time it reached 25, the difficulties of building big software loomed so large that in the autumn of 1968 the NATO Science Committee convened some 50 top programmers, computer scientists and captains of industry to plot a course out of what had come to be known as the software crisis. Although the experts could not contrive a road map to guide the industry toward firmer ground, they did coin a name for that distant goal: software engineering, now defined formally as "the application of a systematic, disciplined, quantifiable approach to the development, operation and maintenance of software."

A quarter of a century later software engineering remains a term of aspiration. The vast majority of computer code is still handcrafted from raw programming languages by artisans using techniques they neither measure nor are able to repeat consistently. "It's like musket making was before Eli Whitney," says Brad J. Cox, a professor at George Mason University. "Before the industrial revolution, there was a nonspecialized approach to manufacturing goods that involved very little interchangeability and a maximum of craftsmanship. If we are ever going to lick this software crisis, we're going to have to stop this hand-to-mouth, every-programmer-builds-everything-from-the-ground-up, preindustrial approach."

The picture is not entirely bleak. Intuition is slowly yielding to analysis as programmers begin using quantitative measurements of the quality of the software they produce to improve

"Software's Chronic Crisis" by W.W. Gibbs from *Scientific American*, Sept. 1994, pp. 86–95.

the way they produce it. The mathematical foundations of programming are solidifying as researchers work on ways of expressing program designs in algebraic forms that make it easier to avoid serious mistakes. Academic computer scientists are starting to address their failure to produce a solid corps of software professionals. Perhaps most important, many in the industry are turning their attention toward inventing the technology and market structures needed to support interchangeable, reusable software parts.

"Unfortunately, the industry does not uniformly apply that which is well-known best practice," laments Larry E. Druffel, director of Carnegie Mellon University's Software Engineering Institute. In fact, a research innovation typically requires 18 years to wend its way into the repertoire of standard programming techniques. By combining their efforts, academia, industry and government may be able to hoist software development to the level of an industrial-age engineering discipline within the decade. If they come up short, society's headlong rush into the information age will be halting and unpredictable at best.

### Shifting Sands

"We will see massive changes [in computer use] over the next few years, causing the initial personal computer revolution to pale into comparative insignificance," concluded 22 leaders in software development from academia, industry and research laboratories this past April. The experts gathered at Hedsor Park, a corporate retreat near London, to commemorate the NATO conference and to analyze the future directions of software. "In 1968 we knew what we wanted to build but couldn't," reflected Cliff Jones, a professor at the University of Manchester. "Today we are standing on shifting sands."

The foundations of traditional programming practices are eroding swiftly, as hardware engineers churn out ever faster, cheaper and smaller machines. Many fundamental assumptions that programmers make—for instance, their acceptance that everything they produce will have defects—must change in response. "When computers are embedded in light switches, you've got to get the software right the first time because you're not going to have a chance to update it," says Mary M. Shaw, a professor at Carnegie Mellon.

"The amount of code in most consumer products is doubling every two years," notes Remi H. Bourgonjon, director of software technology at Philips Research Laboratory in Eindhoven. Already, he reports, televisions may contain up to 500 kilobytes of software; an electric shaver, two kilobytes. The power trains in new General Motors cars run 30,000 lines of computer code.

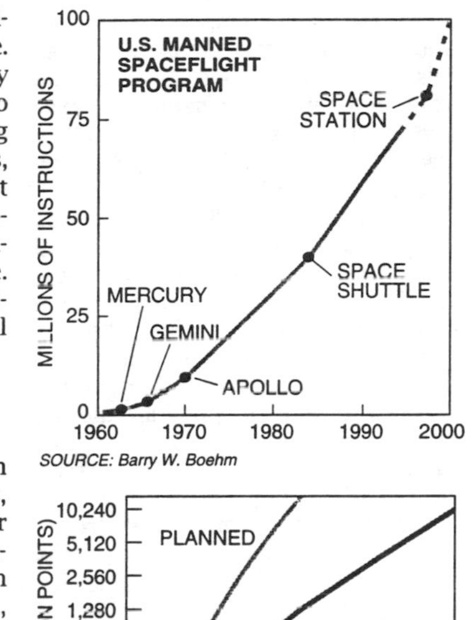

SOURCE: Barry W. Boehm

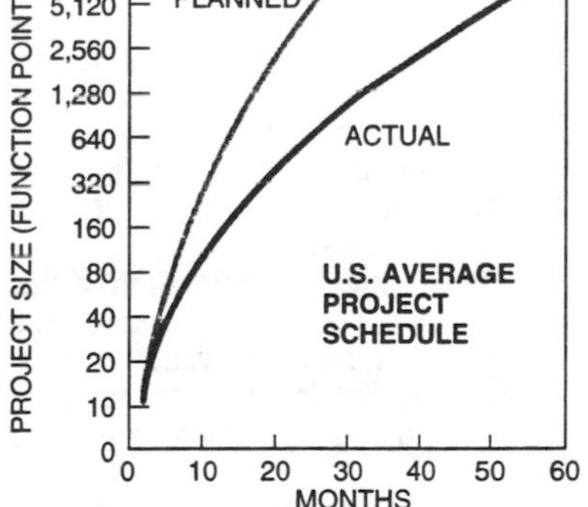

SOURCE: Software Productivity Research

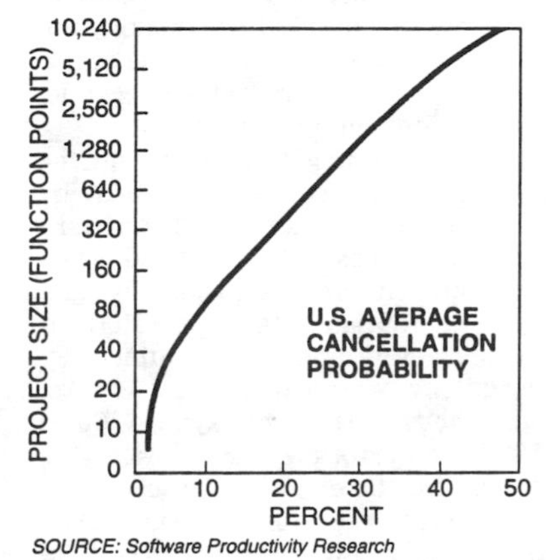

SOURCE: Software Productivity Research

**SOFTWARE IS EXPLODING in size as society comes to rely on more powerful computer systems (*top*). That faith is often rewarded by disappointment as most large software projects overrun their schedules (*middle*) and many fail outright (*bottom*)—usually after most of the development money has been spent.**

Getting software right the first time is hard even for those who care to try. The Department of Defense applies rigorous—and expensive—testing standards to ensure that software on which a mission depends is reliable. Those standards were used to certify *Clementine,* a satellite that the DOD and the National Aeronautics and Space Administration directed into lunar orbit this past spring. A major part of the Clementine mission was to test targeting software that could one day be used in a space-based missile defense system. But when the satellite was spun around and instructed to fix the moon in its sights, a bug in its program caused the spacecraft instead to fire its maneuvering thrusters continuously for 11 minutes. Out of fuel and spinning wildly, the satellite could not make its rendezvous with the asteroid Geographos.

Errors in real-time systems such as *Clementine* are devilishly difficult to spot because, like that suspicious sound in your car engine, they often occur only when conditions are just so [see "The Risks of Software," by Bev Littlewood and Lorenzo Strigini; SCIENTIFIC AMERICAN, November 1992]. "It is not clear that the methods that are currently used for producing safety-critical software, such as that in nuclear reactors or in cars, will evolve and scale up adequately to match our future expectations," warned Gilles Kahn, the scientific director of France's INRIA research laboratory, at the Hedsor Park meeting. "On the contrary, for real-time systems I think we are at a fracture point."

Software is buckling as well under tectonic stresses imposed by the inexorably growing demand for "distributed systems": programs that run cooperatively on many networked computers. Businesses are pouring capital into distributed information systems that they hope to wield as strategic weapons. The inconstancy of software development can turn such projects into Russian roulette.

Many companies are lured by goals that seem simple enough. Some try to reincarnate obsolete mainframe-based software in distributed form. Others want to plug their existing systems into one another or into new systems with which they can share data and a friendlier user interface. In the technical lingo, connecting programs in this way is often called systems integration. But Brian Randell, a computer scientist at the University of Newcastle upon Tyne, suggests that "there is a better word than integration, from old R.A.F. slang: namely, 'to graunch,' which means 'to make to fit by the use of excessive force.'"

It is a risky business, for although

software seems like malleable stuff, most programs are actually intricate plexuses of brittle logic through which data of only the right kind may pass. Like handmade muskets, several programs may perform similar functions and yet still be unique in design. That makes software difficult to modify and repair. It also means that attempts to graunch systems together often end badly.

In 1987, for example, California's Department of Motor Vehicles decided to make its customers' lives easier by merging the state's driver and vehicle registration systems—a seemingly straightforward task. It had hoped to unveil convenient one-stop renewal kiosks last year. Instead the DMV saw the projected cost explode to 6.5 times the expected price and the delivery date recede to 1998. In December the agency pulled the plug and walked away from the seven-year, $44.3-million investment.

Sometimes nothing fails like success. In the 1970s American Airlines constructed SABRE, a virtuosic, $2-billion flight reservation system that became part of the travel industry's infrastructure. "SABRE was the shining example of a strategic information system because it drove American to being the world's largest airline," recalls Bill Curtis, a consultant to the Software Engineering Institute.

Intent on brandishing software as effectively in this decade, American tried to graunch its flight-booking technology with the hotel and car reservation systems of Marriott, Hilton and Budget. In 1992 the project collapsed into a heap of litigation. "It was a smashing failure," Curtis says. "American wrote off $165 million against that system."

The airline is hardly suffering alone. In June IBM's Consulting Group released the results of a survey of 24 leading companies that had developed large distributed systems. The numbers were unsettling: 55 percent of the projects cost more than expected, 68 percent overran their schedules and 88 percent had to be substantially redesigned.

The survey did not report one critical statistic: how reliably the completed programs ran. Often systems crash because they fail to expect the unexpected. Networks amplify this problem. "Distributed systems can consist of a great set of interconnected single points of failure, many of which you have not identified beforehand," Randell explains. "The complexity and fragility of these systems pose a major challenge."

The challenge of complexity is not only large but also growing. The bang that computers deliver per buck is doubling every 18 months or so. One result is "an order of magnitude growth in system size every decade—for some industries, every half decade," Curtis says. To keep up with such demand, programmers will have to change the way that they work. "You can't build skyscrapers using carpenters," Curtis quips.

### Mayday, Mayday

When a system becomes so complex that no one manager can comprehend the entirety, traditional development processes break down. The Federal Aviation Administration (FAA) has faced this problem throughout its decade-old attempt to replace the nation's increasingly obsolete air-traffic control system [see "Aging Airways," by Gary Stix; SCIENTIFIC AMERICAN, May].

The replacement, called the Advanced Automation System (AAS), combines all the challenges of computing in the 1990s. A program that is more than a million lines in size is distributed across hundreds of computers and embedded into new and sophisticated hardware, all of which must respond around the clock to unpredictable real-time events. Even a small glitch potentially threatens public safety.

To realize its technological dream, the FAA chose IBM's Federal Systems Company, a well-respected leader in software development that has since been purchased by Loral. FAA managers expected (but did not demand) that IBM would use state-of-the-art techniques to estimate the cost and length of the project. They assumed that IBM would screen the requirements and design drawn up for the system in order to catch mistakes early, when they can be fixed in hours rather than days. And the FAA conservatively expected to pay about $500 per line of computer code, five times the industry average for well-managed development processes.

According to a report on the AAS project released in May by the Center for Naval Analysis, IBM's "cost estimation and development process tracking used inappropriate data, were performed inconsistently and were routinely ignored" by project managers. As a result, the FAA has been paying $700 to $900 per line for the AAS software. One reason for the exorbitant price is that "on average every line of code developed needs to be rewritten once," bemoaned an internal FAA report.

Alarmed by skyrocketing costs and tests that showed the half-completed system to be unreliable, FAA administrator David R. Hinson decided in June to cancel two of the four major parts of the AAS and to scale back a third. The $144 million spent on these failed programs is but a drop next to the $1.4 billion invested in the fourth and central piece: new workstation software for air-traffic controllers.

That project is also spiraling down the drain. Now running about five years late and more than $1 billion over budget, the bug-infested program is being scoured by software experts at Carnegie Mellon and the Massachusetts Institute of Technology to determine whether it can be salvaged or must be canceled outright. The reviewers are scheduled to make their report in September.

Disaster will become an increasingly common and disruptive part of software development unless programming takes on more of the characteristics of an engineering discipline rooted firmly in science and mathematics [*see box on page 92*]. Fortunately, that trend has already begun. Over the past decade industry leaders have made significant progress toward understanding how to measure, consistently and quantitatively, the chaos of their development processes, the density of errors in their products and the stagnation of their programmers' productivity. Researchers are already taking the next step: finding practical, repeatable solutions to these problems.

### Proceeds of Process

In 1991, for example, the Software Engineering Institute, a software think tank funded by the military, unveiled its Capability Maturity Model (CMM). "It provides a vision of software engineering and management excellence," beams David Zubrow, who leads a project on empirical methods at the institute. The CMM has at last persuaded many programmers to concentrate on measuring the process by which they produce software, a prerequisite for any industrial engineering discipline.

Using interviews, questionnaires and the CMM as a benchmark, evaluators can grade the ability of a programming team to create predictably software that meets its customers' needs. The CMM uses a five-level scale, ranging from chaos at level 1 to the paragon of good management at level 5. To date, 261 organizations have been rated.

"The vast majority—about 75 percent—are still stuck in level 1," Curtis reports. "They have no formal process, no measurements of what they do and no way of knowing when they are on the wrong track or off the track altogether." (The Center for Naval Analysis concluded that the AAS project at IBM Federal Systems "appears to be at a low 1 rating.") The remaining 24 percent of projects are at levels 2 or 3.

Only two elite groups have earned the highest CMM rating, a level 5. Motorola's Indian programming team in Bangalore holds one title. Loral's (formerly IBM's) on-board space shuttle software project claims the other. The Loral team has learned to control bugs so well that it can reliably predict how many will be found in each new version of the software. That is a remarkable feat, considering that 90 percent of American programmers do not even keep count of the mistakes they find, according to Capers Jones, chairman of Software Productivity Research. Of those who do, he says, few catch more than a third of the defects that are there.

Tom Peterson, head of Loral's shuttle software project, attributes its success to "a culture that tries to fix not just the bug but also the flaw in the testing process that allowed it to slip through." Yet some bugs inevitably escape detection. The first launch of the space shuttle in 1981 was aborted and delayed for two days because a glitch prevented the five on-board computers from synchronizing properly. Another flaw, this one in the shuttle's rendezvous program, jeopardized the *Intelsat-6* satellite rescue mission in 1992.

Although the CMM is no panacea, its promotion by the Software Engineering Institute has persuaded a number of leading software companies that quantitative quality control can pay off in the long run. Raytheon's equipment division, for example, formed a "software engineering initiative" in 1988 after flunking the CMM test. The division began pouring $1 million per year into refining rigorous inspection and testing guidelines and training its 400 programmers to follow them.

Within three years the division had jumped two levels. By this past June, most projects—including complex radar and air-traffic control systems—were finishing ahead of schedule and under budget. Productivity has more than doubled. An analysis of avoided rework costs revealed a savings of $7.80 for every dollar invested in the initiative. Impressed by such successes, the U.S. Air Force has mandated that all its software developers must reach level 3 of the CMM by 1998. NASA is reportedly considering a similar policy.

### Mathematical Re-creations

Even the best-laid designs can go awry, and errors will creep in so long as humans create programs. Bugs squashed early rarely threaten a project's deadline and budget, however. Devastating mistakes are nearly always those in the initial design that slip undetected into the final product.

Mass-market software producers, because they have no single customer to please, can take a belated and brute-force approach to bug removal: they release the faulty product as a "beta" version and let hordes of users dig up the glitches. According to Charles Simonyi, a chief architect at Microsoft, the new version of the Windows operating system will be beta-tested by 20,000 volunteers. That is remarkably effective, but also expensive, inefficient and—since mass-produced PC products make up less than 10 percent of the $92.8-billion software market in the U.S.—usually impractical.

Researchers are thus formulating several strategies to attack bugs early or to avoid introducing them at all. One idea is to recognize that the problem a system is supposed to solve always changes as the system is being built. Denver's airport planners saddled BAE with $20 million worth of changes to the design of its baggage system long after construction had begun. IBM has been similarly bedeviled by the indecision of FAA managers. Both companies naively assumed that once their design was approved, they would be left in peace to build it.

Some developers are at last shedding that illusion and rethinking software as something to be grown rather than built. As a first step, programmers are increasingly stitching together quick prototypes out of standard graphic interface components. Like an architect's scale model, a system prototype can help clear up misunderstandings between customer and developer before a logical foundation is poured.

Because they mimic only the outward behavior of systems, prototypes are of little help in spotting logical inconsistencies in a system's design. "The vast majority of errors in large-scale software are errors of omission," notes Laszlo A. Belady, director of Mitsubishi Electric Research Laboratory. And models do not make it any easier to detect bugs once a design is committed to code.

When it absolutely, positively has to be right, says Martyn Thomas, chairman of Praxis, a British software company, engineers rely on mathematical analysis to predict how their designs will behave in the real world. Unfortunately, the mathematics that describes physical systems does not apply within the synthetic binary universe of a computer program; discrete mathematics, a far less mature field, governs here. But using the still limited tools of set theory and predicate calculus, computer scientists have contrived ways to translate specifications and programs into the language of mathematics, where they can be analyzed with theoretical tools called formal methods.

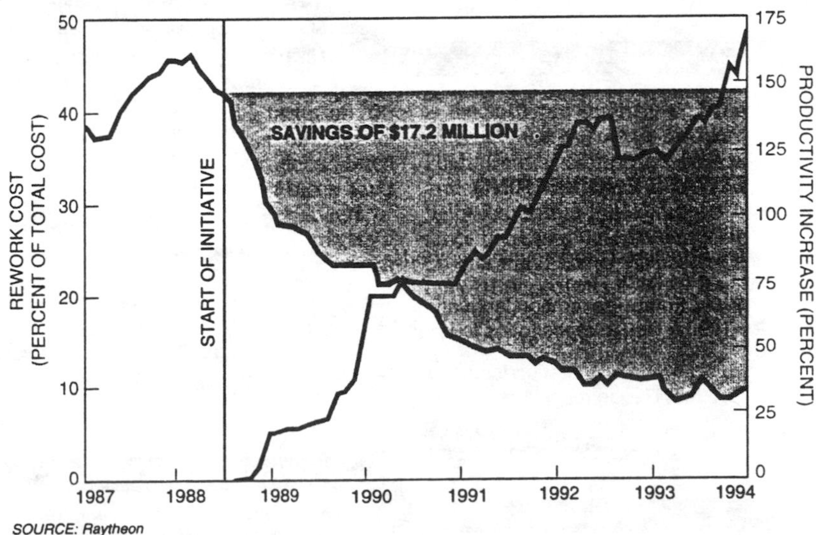


**RAYTHEON HAS SAVED $17.2 million in software costs since 1988, when its equipment division began using rigorous development processes that doubled its programmers' productivity and helped them to avoid making expensive mistakes.**

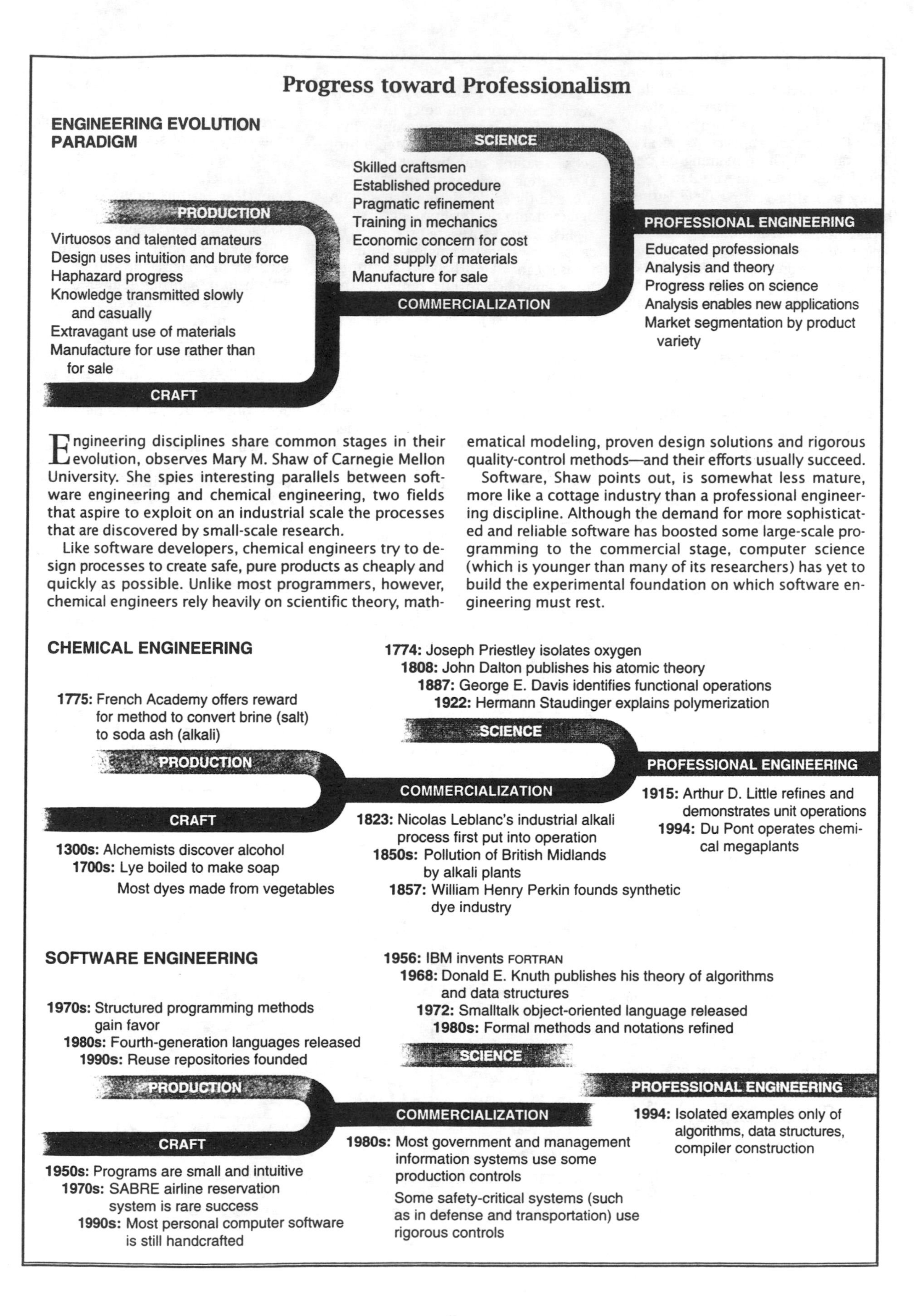
Progress toward Professionalism
ENGINEERING EVOLUTION PARADIGM
CRAFT
Virtuosos and talented amateurs
Design uses intuition and brute force
Haphazard progress
Knowledge transmitted slowly and casually
Extravagant use of materials
Manufacture for use rather than for sale
PRODUCTION
COMMERCIALIZATION
Skilled craftsmen
Established procedure
Pragmatic refinement
Training in mechanics
Economic concern for cost and supply of materials
Manufacture for sale
SCIENCE
PROFESSIONAL ENGINEERING
Educated professionals
Analysis and theory
Progress relies on science
Analysis enables new applications
Market segmentation by product variety

Engineering disciplines share common stages in their evolution, observes Mary M. Shaw of Carnegie Mellon University. She spies interesting parallels between software engineering and chemical engineering, two fields that aspire to exploit on an industrial scale the processes that are discovered by small-scale research.

Like software developers, chemical engineers try to design processes to create safe, pure products as cheaply and quickly as possible. Unlike most programmers, however, chemical engineers rely heavily on scientific theory, mathematical modeling, proven design solutions and rigorous quality-control methods—and their efforts usually succeed.

Software, Shaw points out, is somewhat less mature, more like a cottage industry than a professional engineering discipline. Although the demand for more sophisticated and reliable software has boosted some large-scale programming to the commercial stage, computer science (which is younger than many of its researchers) has yet to build the experimental foundation on which software engineering must rest.

CHEMICAL ENGINEERING
CRAFT
1300s: Alchemists discover alcohol
1700s: Lye boiled to make soap
Most dyes made from vegetables
PRODUCTION
1775: French Academy offers reward for method to convert brine (salt) to soda ash (alkali)
COMMERCIALIZATION
1823: Nicolas Leblanc's industrial alkali process first put into operation
1850s: Pollution of British Midlands by alkali plants
1857: William Henry Perkin founds synthetic dye industry
SCIENCE
1774: Joseph Priestley isolates oxygen
1808: John Dalton publishes his atomic theory
1887: George E. Davis identifies functional operations
1922: Hermann Staudinger explains polymerization
PROFESSIONAL ENGINEERING
1915: Arthur D. Little refines and demonstrates unit operations
1994: Du Pont operates chemical megaplants
SOFTWARE ENGINEERING
CRAFT
1950s: Programs are small and intuitive
1970s: SABRE airline reservation system is rare success
1990s: Most personal computer software is still handcrafted
PRODUCTION
1970s: Structured programming methods gain favor
1980s: Fourth-generation languages released
1990s: Reuse repositories founded
COMMERCIALIZATION
1980s: Most government and management information systems use some production controls
Some safety-critical systems (such as in defense and transportation) use rigorous controls
SCIENCE
1956: IBM invents FORTRAN
1968: Donald E. Knuth publishes his theory of algorithms and data structures
1972: Smalltalk object-oriented language released
1980s: Formal methods and notations refined
PROFESSIONAL ENGINEERING
1994: Isolated examples only of algorithms, data structures, compiler construction

Praxis recently used formal methods on an air-traffic control project for Britain's Civil Aviation Authority. Although Praxis's program was much smaller than the FAA's, the two shared a similar design problem: the need to keep redundant systems synchronized so that if one fails, another can instantly take over. "The difficult part was guaranteeing that messages are delivered in the proper order over twin networks," recalls Anthony Hall, a principal consultant to Praxis. "So here we tried to carry out proofs of our design, and they failed, because the design was wrong. The benefit of finding errors at that early stage is enormous," he adds. The system was finished on time and put into operation last October.

Praxis used formal notations on only the most critical parts of its software, but other software firms have employed mathematical rigor throughout the entire development of a system. GEC Alsthom in Paris is using a formal method called "B" as it spends $350 million to upgrade the switching- and speed-control software that guides the 6,000 electric trains in France's national railway system. By increasing the speed of the trains and reducing the distance between them, the system can save the railway company billions of dollars that might otherwise need to be spent on new lines.

Safety was an obvious concern. So GEC developers wrote the entire design and final program in formal notation and then used mathematics to prove them consistent. "Functional tests are still necessary, however, for two reasons," says Fernando Mejia, manager of the formal development section at GEC. First, programmers do occasionally make mistakes in proofs. Secondly, formal methods can guarantee only that software meets its specification, not that it can handle the surprises of the real world.

Formal methods have other problems as well. Ted Ralston, director of strategic planning for Odyssey Research Associates in Ithaca, N.Y., points out that reading pages of algebraic formulas is even more stultifying than reviewing computer code. Odyssey is just one of several companies that are trying to automate formal methods to make them less onerous to programmers. GEC is collaborating with Digilog in France to commercialize programming tools for the B method. The beta version is being tested by seven companies and institutions, including Aerospatiale, as well as France's atomic energy authority and its defense department.

On the other side of the Atlantic, formal methods by themselves have yet to catch on. "I am skeptical that Americans are sufficiently disciplined to apply formal methods in any broad fashion," says David A. Fisher of the National Institute of Standards and Technology (NIST). There are exceptions, however, most notably among the growing circle of companies experimenting with the "clean-room approach" to programming.

The clean-room process attempts to meld formal notations, correctness proofs and statistical quality control with an evolutionary approach to software development. Like the microchip manufacturing technique from which it takes its name, clean-room development tries to use rigorous engineering techniques to consistently fabricate products that run perfectly the first time. Programmers grow systems one function at a time and certify the quality of each unit before integrating it into the architecture.

Growing software requires a whole new approach to testing. Traditionally, developers test a program by running it the way they intend it to be used, which often bears scant resemblance to real-world conditions. In a clean-room process, programmers try to assign a probability to every execution path—correct and incorrect—that users can take. They then derive test cases from those statistical data, so that the most common paths are tested more thoroughly. Next the program runs through each test case and times how long it takes to fail. Those times are then fed back, in true engineering fashion, to a model that calculates how reliable the program is.

Early adopters report encouraging results. Ericsson Telecom, the European telecommunications giant, used clean-room processes on a 70-programmer project to fabricate an operating system for its telephone-switching computers. Errors were reportedly reduced to just one per 1,000 lines of program code; the industry average is about 25 times higher. Perhaps more important, the company found that development productivity increased by 70 percent, and testing productivity doubled.

### No Silver Bullet

Then again, the industry has heard tell many times before of "silver bullets" supposedly able to slay werewolf projects. Since the 1960s developers have peddled dozens of technological innovations intended to boost productivity—many have even presented demonstration projects to "prove" the verity of their boasts. Advocates of object-oriented analysis and programming, a buzzword du jour, claim their approach represents a paradigm shift that will deliver "a 14-to-1 improvement in productivity," along with higher quality and easier maintenance, all at reduced cost.

There are reasons to be skeptical. "In the 1970s structured programming was also touted as a paradigm shift," Curtis recalls. "So was CASE [computer-assisted software engineering]. So were third-, fourth- and fifth-generation languages. We've heard great promises for technology, many of which weren't delivered."

Meanwhile productivity in software development has lagged behind that of more mature disciplines, most notably computer hardware engineering. "I think of software as a cargo cult," Cox says. "Our main accomplishments were imported from this foreign culture of hardware engineering—faster machines and more memory." Fisher tends to agree: adjusted for inflation, "the value added per worker in the industry has been at $40,000 for two decades," he asserts. "We're not seeing any increases."

"I don't believe that," replies Richard A. DeMillo, a professor at Purdue University and head of the Software Engineering Research Consortium. "There has been improvement, but everyone uses different definitions of productivity." A recent study published by Capers Jones—but based on necessarily dubious historical data—states that U.S. programmers churn out twice as much code today as they did in 1970.

The fact of the matter is that no one really knows how productive software developers are, for three reasons. First, less than 10 percent of American companies consistently measure the productivity of their programmers.

Second, the industry has yet to settle on a useful standard unit of measurement. Most reports, including those published in peer-reviewed computer science journals, express productivity in terms of lines of code per worker per month. But programs are written in a wide variety of languages and vary enormously in the complexity of their operation. Comparing the number of lines written by a Japanese programmer using C with the number produced by an American using Ada is thus like comparing their salaries without converting from yen to dollars.

Third, Fisher says, "you can walk into a typical company and find two guys sharing an office, getting the same salary and having essentially the same credentials and yet find a factor of 100 difference in the number of instructions per day that they produce." Such enormous individual differences tend to swamp the much smaller effects of technology or process improvements.

After 25 years of disappointment with apparent innovations that turned out to be irreproducible or unscalable, many researchers concede that computer science needs an experimental branch to separate the general results from the accidental. "There has always been this assumption that if I give you a method, it is right just because I told you so," complains Victor R. Basili, a professor at the University of Maryland. "People are developing all kinds of things, and it's really quite frightening how bad some of them are," he says.

Mary Shaw of Carnegie Mellon points out that mature engineering fields codify proved solutions in handbooks so that even novices can consistently handle routine designs, freeing more talented practitioners for advanced projects. No such handbook yet exists for software, so mistakes are repeated on project after project, year after year.

DeMillo suggests that the government should take a more active role. "The National Science Foundation should be interested in funding research aimed at verifying experimental results that have been claimed by other people," he says. "Currently, if it's not groundbreaking, first-time-ever-done research, program officers at the NSF tend to discount the work." DeMillo knows whereof he speaks. From 1989 to 1991 he directed the NSF's computer and computation research division.

Yet "if software engineering is to be an experimental science, that means it needs laboratory science. Where the heck are the laboratories?" Basili asks. Because attempts to scale promising technologies to industrial proportions so often fail, small laboratories are of limited utility. "We need to have places where we can gather data and try things out," DeMillo says. "The only way to do that is to have a real software development organization as a partner."

There have been only a few such partnerships. Perhaps the most successful is the Software Engineering Laboratory, a consortium of NASA's Goddard Space Flight Center, Computer Sciences Corp. and the University of Maryland. Basili helped to found the laboratory in 1976. Since then, graduate students and NASA programmers have collaborated on "well over 100 projects," Basili says, most having to do with building ground-support software for satellites.

### Just Add Water

Musket makers did not get more productive until Eli Whitney figured out how to manufacture interchangeable parts that could be assembled by any skilled workman. In like manner, software parts can, if properly standardized, be reused at many different scales. Programmers have for decades used libraries of subroutines to avoid rewriting the same code over and over. But these components break down when they are moved to a different programming language, computer platform or operating environment. "The tragedy is that as hardware becomes obsolete, an excellent expression of a sorting algorithm written in the 1960s has to be rewritten," observes Simonyi of Microsoft.

Fisher sees tragedy of a different kind. "The real price we pay is that as a specialist in any software technology you cannot capture your special capability in a product. If you can't do that, you basically can't be a specialist." Not that some haven't tried. Before moving to NIST last year, Fisher founded and served as CEO of Incremental Systems. "We were truly world-class in three of the component technologies that go into compilers but were not as good in the other seven or so," he states. "But we found that there was no practical way of selling compiler components; we had to sell entire compilers."

So now he is doing something about that. In April, NIST announced that it was creating an Advanced Technology Program to help engender a market for component-based software. As head of the program, Fisher will be distributing $150 million in research grants to software companies willing to attack the technical obstacles that currently make software parts impractical.

The biggest challenge is to find ways of cutting the ties that inherently bind programs to specific computers and to other programs. Researchers are investigating several promising approaches, including a common language that could be used to describe software parts, programs that reshape components to match any environment, and components that have lots of optional features a user can turn on or off.

Fisher favors the idea that components should be synthesized on the fly. Programmers would "basically capture how to do it rather than actually doing it," producing a recipe that any computer could understand. "Then when you want to assemble two components, you would take this recipe and derive compatible versions by adding additional elements to their interfaces. The whole thing would be automated," he explains.

Even with a $150-million incentive and market pressures forcing companies to find cheaper ways of producing software, an industrial revolution in software is not imminent. "We expect to see only isolated examples of these technologies in five to seven years—and we may not succeed technically either," Fisher hedges. Even when the technology is ready, components will find few takers unless they can be made cost-effective. And the cost of software parts will depend less on the technology involved than on the kind of market that arises to produce and consume them.

Brad Cox, like Fisher, once ran a software component company and found it hard going. He believes he has figured out the problem—and its solution. Cox's firm tried to sell low-level program parts analogous to computer chips. "What's different between software ICs [integrated circuits] and silicon ICs is that silicon ICs are made of atoms, so they abide by conservation of mass, and people therefore know how to buy and sell them robustly," he says. "But this interchange process that is at the core of all commerce just does not work for things that can be copied in nanoseconds." When Cox tried selling the parts his programmers had created, he found that the price the market would bear was far too low for him to recover the costs of development.

The reasons were twofold. First, recasting the component by hand for each customer was time-consuming; NIST hopes to clear this barrier with its Advanced Technology Program. The other factor was not so much technical as cultural: buyers want to pay for a component once and make copies for free.

"The music industry has had about a century of experience with this very problem," Cox observes. "They used to sell tangible goods like piano rolls and sheet music, and then radio and television came along and knocked all that into a cocked hat." Music companies adapted to broadcasting by setting up agencies to collect royalties every time a song is aired and to funnel the money back to the artists and producers.

Cox suggests similarly charging users each time they use a software compo-

## A Developing World

Since the invention of computers, Americans have dominated the software market. Microsoft alone produces more computer code each year than do any of 100 nations, according to Capers Jones of Software Productivity Research in Burlington, Mass. U.S. suppliers hold about 70 percent of the worldwide software market.

But as international networks sprout and large corporations deflate, India, Hungary, Russia, the Philippines and other poorer nations are discovering in software a lucrative industry that requires the one resource in which they are rich: an underemployed, well-educated labor force. American and European giants are now competing with upstart Asian development companies for contracts, and in response many are forming subsidiaries overseas. Indeed, some managers in the trade predict that software development will gradually split between Western software engineers who design systems and Eastern programmers who build them.

"In fact, it is going on already," says Laszlo A. Belady, director of Mitsubishi Electric Research Laboratory. AT&T, Hewlett-Packard, IBM, British Telecom and Texas Instruments have all set up programming teams in India. The Pact Group in Lyons, France, reportedly maintains a "software factory" in Manila. "Cadence, the U.S. supplier of VLSI design tools, has had its software development sited on the Pacific rim for several years," reports Martyn Thomas, chairman of Praxis. "ACT, a U.K.-based systems house, is using Russian programmers from the former Soviet space program," he adds.

So far India's star has risen fastest. "Offshore development [work commissioned in India by foreign companies] has begun to take off in the past 18 to 24 months," says Rajendra S. Pawar, head of New Delhi-based NIIT, which has graduated 200,000 Indians from its programming courses. Indeed, India's software exports have seen a compound annual growth of 38 percent over the past five years; last year they jumped 60 percent—four times the average growth rate worldwide.

About 58 percent of the $360-million worth of software that flowed out of India last year ended up in the U.S. That tiny drop hardly makes a splash in a $92.8-billion market. But several trends may propel exports beyond the $1-billion mark as early as 1997.

The single most important factor, Pawar asserts, is the support of the Indian government, which has eased tariffs and restrictions, subsidized numerous software technology parks and export zones, and doled out five-year tax exemptions to software exporters. "The opening of the Indian economy is acting as a very big catalyst," Pawar says.

It certainly seems to have attracted the attention of large multinational firms eager to reduce both the cost of the software they need and the amount they build in-house. The primary cost of software is labor. Indian programmers come so cheap—$125 per unit of software versus $925 for an American developer, according to Jones—that some companies fly an entire team to the U.S. to work on a project. More than half of India's software exports come from such "body shopping," although tightened U.S. visa restrictions are stanching this flow.

Another factor, Pawar observes, is a growing trust in the quality of overseas project management. "In the past two years, American companies have become far more comfortable with the offshore concept," he says. This is a result in part of success stories from leaders like Citicorp, which develops banking systems in Bombay, and Motorola, which has a top-rated team of more than 150 programmers in Bangalore building software for its Iridium satellite network.

Offshore development certainly costs less than body shopping, and not merely because of saved airfare. "Thanks to the time differences between India and the U.S., Indian software developers can act the elves and the shoemaker," working overnight on changes requested by managers the previous day, notes Richard Heeks, who studies Asian computer industries at the University of Manchester in England.

Price is not everything. Most Eastern nations are still weak in design and management skills. "The U.S. still has the best system architects in the world," boasts Bill Curtis of the Software Engineering Institute. "At large systems, nobody touches us." But when it comes to just writing program code, the American hegemony may be drawing to a close.

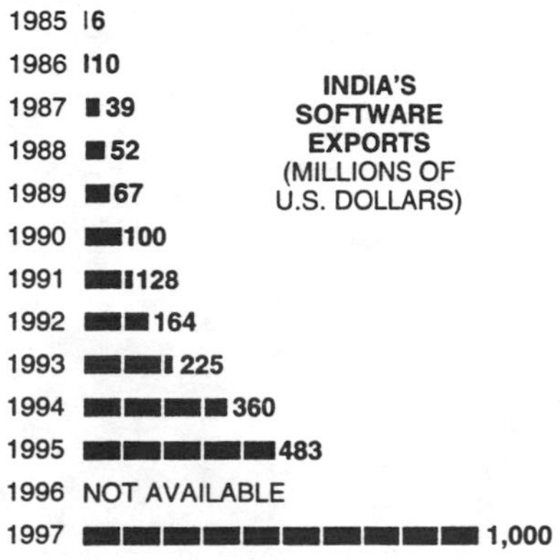

**INDIA'S SOFTWARE EXPORTS** (MILLIONS OF U.S. DOLLARS)

| Year | Exports |
|---|---|
| 1985 | 6 |
| 1986 | 10 |
| 1987 | 39 |
| 1988 | 52 |
| 1989 | 67 |
| 1990 | 100 |
| 1991 | 128 |
| 1992 | 164 |
| 1993 | 225 |
| 1994 | 360 |
| 1995 | 483 |
| 1996 | NOT AVAILABLE |
| 1997 | 1,000 |

*SOURCES: NIIT, NASSCOM*

nent. "In fact," he says, "that model could work for software even more easily than for music, thanks to the infrastructure advantages that computers and communications give us. Record players don't have high-speed network links in them to report usage, but our computers do."

Or will, at least. Looking ahead to the time when nearly all computers are connected, Cox envisions distributing software of all kinds via networks that link component producers, end users and financial institutions. "It's analogous to a credit-card operation but with tentacles that reach into PCs," he says. Although that may sound ominous to some, Cox argues that "the Internet now is more like a garbage dump than a farmer's market. We need a national infrastructure that can support the distribution of everything from Grandma's cookie recipe to Apple's window managers to Addison-Wesley's electronic books." Recognizing the enormity of the cultural shift he is proposing, Cox expects to press his cause for years to come through the Coalition for Electronic Markets, of which he is president.

The combination of industrial process control, advanced technological tools and interchangeable parts promises to transform not only how programming is done but also who does it. Many of the experts who convened at Hedsor Park agreed with Belady that "in the future, professional people in most fields will use programming as a tool, but they won't call themselves programmers or think of themselves as spending their time programming. They will think they are doing architecture, or traffic planning or film making."

That possibility begs the question of who is qualified to build important systems. Today anyone can bill herself as a software engineer. "But when you have 100 million user-programmers, frequently they will be doing things that are life critical—building applications that fill prescriptions, for example," notes Barry W. Boehm, director of the Center for Software Engineering at the University of Southern California. Boehm is one of an increasing number who suggest certifying software engineers, as is done in other engineering fields.

Of course, certification helps only if programmers are properly trained to begin with. Currently only 28 universities offer graduate programs in software engineering; five years ago there were just 10. None offer undergraduate degrees. Even academics such as Shaw, DeMillo and Basili agree that computer science curricula generally provide poor preparation for industrial software development. "Basic things like designing code inspections, producing user documentation and maintaining aging software are not covered in academia," Capers Jones laments.

Engineers, the infantry of every industrial revolution, do not spontaneously generate. They are trained out of the bad habits developed by the craftsmen that preceded them. Until the lessons of computer science inculcate a desire not merely to build better things but also to build things better, the best we can expect is that software development will undergo a slow, and probably painful, industrial evolution.

FURTHER READING

ENCYCLOPEDIA OF SOFTWARE ENGINEERING. Edited by John J. Marciniak. John Wiley & Sons, 1994.

SOFTWARE 2000: A VIEW OF THE FUTURE Edited by Brian Randell, Gill Ringland and Bill Wulf. ICL and the Commission of European Communities, 1994.

FORMAL METHODS: A VIRTUAL LIBRARY. Jonathan Bowen. Available in hypertext on the World Wide Web as http://www.comlab.ox.ac.uk/archive/formal-methods.html

# No Silver Bullet

## Essence and Accidents of Software Engineering

Frederick P. Brooks, Jr.
University of North Carolina at Chapel Hill

**Fashioning complex conceptual constructs is the *essence; accidental* tasks arise in representing the constructs in language. Past progress has so reduced the accidental tasks that future progress now depends upon addressing the essence.**

Of all the monsters that fill the nightmares of our folklore, none terrify more than werewolves, because they transform unexpectedly from the familiar into horrors. For these, one seeks bullets of silver that can magically lay them to rest.

The familiar software project, at least as seen by the nontechnical manager, has something of this character; it is usually innocent and straightforward, but is capable of becoming a monster of missed schedules, blown budgets, and flawed products. So we hear desperate cries for a silver bullet—something to make software costs drop as rapidly as computer hardware costs do.

But, as we look to the horizon of a decade hence, we see no silver bullet. There is no single development, in either technology or in management technique, that by itself promises even one order-of-magnitude improvement in productivity, in reliability, in simplicity. In this article, I shall try to show why, by examining both the nature of the software problem and the properties of the bullets proposed.

Skepticism is not pessimism, however. Although we see no startling breakthroughs—and indeed, I believe such to be inconsistent with the nature of software—many encouraging innovations are under way. A disciplined, consistent effort to develop, propagate, and exploit these innovations should indeed yield an order-of-magnitude improvement. There is no royal road, but there is a road.

The first step toward the management of disease was replacement of demon theories and humours theories by the germ theory. That very step, the beginning of hope, in itself dashed all hopes of magical solutions. It told workers that progress would be made stepwise, at great effort, and that a persistent, unremitting care would have to be paid to a discipline of cleanliness. So it is with software engineering today.

### Does it have to be hard?—Essential difficulties

Not only are there no silver bullets now in view, the very nature of software makes it unlikely that there will be any—no inventions that will do for software productivity, reliability, and simplicity what electronics, transistors, and large-scale integration did for computer hardware.

This article was first published in *Information Processing '86*, ISBN No. 0-444-70077-3, H.-J. Kugler, ed., Elsevier Science Publishers B.V. (North-Holland) © IFIP 1986.

Reprinted from *Computer*, Vol. 20, No. 4, Apr. 1987, pp. 10–19.

We cannot expect ever to see twofold gains every two years.

First, one must observe that the anomaly is not that software progress is so slow, but that computer hardware progress is so fast. No other technology since civilization began has seen six orders of magnitude in performance-price gain in 30 years. In no other technology can one choose to take the gain in *either* improved performance *or* in reduced costs. These gains flow from the transformation of computer manufacture from an assembly industry into a process industry.

Second, to see what rate of progress one can expect in software technology, let us examine the difficulties of that technology. Following Aristotle, I divide them into *essence*, the difficulties inherent in the nature of software, and *accidents,* those difficulties that today attend its production but are not inherent.

The essence of a software entity is a construct of interlocking concepts: data sets, relationships among data items, algorithms, and invocations of functions. This essence is abstract in that such a conceptual construct is the same under many different representations. It is nonetheless highly precise and richly detailed.

*I believe the hard part of building software to be the specification, design, and testing of this conceptual construct, not the labor of representing it and testing the fidelity of the representation.* We still make syntax errors, to be sure; but they are fuzz compared with the conceptual errors in most systems.

If this is true, building software will always be hard. There is inherently no silver bullet.

Let us consider the inherent properties of this irreducible essence of modern software systems: complexity, conformity, changeability, and invisibility.

**Complexity.** Software entities are more complex for their size than perhaps any other human construct because no two parts are alike (at least above the statement level). If they are, we make the two similar parts into a subroutine—open or closed. In this respect, software systems differ profoundly from computers, buildings, or automobiles, where repeated elements abound.

Digital computers are themselves more complex than most things people build: They have very large numbers of states. This makes conceiving, describing, and testing them hard. Software systems have orders-of-magnitude more states than computers do.

Likewise, a scaling-up of a software entity is not merely a repetition of the same elements in larger sizes, it is necessarily an increase in the number of different elements. In most cases, the elements interact with each other in some nonlinear fashion, and the complexity of the whole increases much more than linearly.

The complexity of software is an essential property, not an accidental one. Hence, descriptions of a software entity that abstract away its complexity often abstract away its essence. For three centuries, mathematics and the physical sciences made great strides by constructing simplified models of complex phenomena, deriving properties from the models, and verifying those properties by experiment. This paradigm worked because the complexities ignored in the models were not the essential properties of the phenomena. It does not work when the complexities are the essence.

Many of the classic problems of developing software products derive from this essential complexity and its nonlinear increases with size. From the complexity comes the difficulty of communication among team members, which leads to product flaws, cost overruns, schedule delays. From the complexity comes the difficulty of enumerating, much less understanding, all the possible states of the program, and from that comes the unreliability. From complexity of function comes the difficulty of invoking function, which makes programs hard to use. From complexity of structure comes the difficulty of extending programs to new functions without creating side effects. From complexity of structure come the unvisualized states that constitute security trapdoors.

Not only technical problems, but management problems as well come from the complexity. It makes overview hard, thus impeding conceptual integrity. It makes it hard to find and control all the loose ends. It creates the tremendous learning and understanding burden that makes personnel turnover a disaster.

**Conformity.** Software people are not alone in facing complexity. Physics deals

The Photo Source International Inc.

with terribly complex objects even at the "fundamental" particle level. The physicist labors on, however, in a firm faith that there are unifying principles to be found, whether in quarks or in unified-field theories. Einstein argued that there must be simplified explanations of nature, because God is not capricious or arbitrary.

No such faith comforts the software engineer. Much of the complexity that he must master is arbitrary complexity, forced without rhyme or reason by the many human institutions and systems to which his interfaces must conform. These differ from interface to interface, and from time to time, not because of necessity but only because they were designed by different people, rather than by God.

In many cases, the software must conform because it is the most recent arrival on the scene. In others, it must conform because it is perceived as the most conformable. But in all cases, much complexity comes from conformation to other interfaces; this complexity cannot be simplified out by any redesign of the software alone.

**Changeability.** The software entity is constantly subject to pressures for change. Of course, so are buildings, cars, computers. But manufactured things are infrequently changed after manufacture; they are superseded by later models, or essential changes are incorporated into later-serial-number copies of the same basic design. Call-backs of automobiles are really quite infrequent; field changes of computers somewhat less so. Both are much less frequent than modifications to fielded software.

In part, this is so because the software of a system embodies its function, and the function is the part that most feels the pressures of change. In part it is because software can be changed more easily—it is pure thought-stuff, infinitely malleable. Buildings do in fact get changed, but the high costs of change, understood by all, serve to dampen the whims of the changers.

All successful software gets changed. Two processes are at work. First, as a software product is found to be useful, people try it in new cases at the edge of or beyond the original domain. The pressures for extended function come chiefly from users who like the basic function and invent new uses for it.

Second, successful software survives beyond the normal life of the machine vehicle for which it is first written. If not new computers, then at least new disks, new displays, new printers come along; and the software must be conformed to its new vehicles of opportunity.

In short, the software product is embedded in a cultural matrix of applications, users, laws, and machine vehicles. These all change continually, and their changes inexorably force change upon the software product.

**Invisibility.** Software is invisible and unvisualizable. Geometric abstractions are powerful tools. The floor plan of a building helps both architect and client evaluate spaces, traffic flows, views. Contradictions and omissions become obvious.

---

**Despite progress in restricting and simplifying software structures, they remain inherently unvisualizable, and thus do not permit the mind to use some of its most powerful conceptual tools.**

---

Scale drawings of mechanical parts and stick-figure models of molecules, although abstractions, serve the same purpose. A geometric reality is captured in a geometric abstraction.

The reality of software is not inherently embedded in space. Hence, it has no ready geometric representation in the way that land has maps, silicon chips have diagrams, computers have connectivity schematics. As soon as we attempt to diagram software structure, we find it to constitute not one, but several, general directed graphs superimposed one upon another. The several graphs may represent the flow of control, the flow of data, patterns of dependency, time sequence, name-space relationships. These graphs are usually not even planar, much less hierarchical. Indeed, one of the ways of establishing conceptual control over such structure is to enforce link cutting until one or more of the graphs becomes hierarchical.[1]

In spite of progress in restricting and simplifying the structures of software, they remain inherently unvisualizable, and thus do not permit the mind to use some of its most powerful conceptual tools. This lack not only impedes the process of design within one mind, it severely hinders communication among minds.

## Past breakthroughs solved accidental difficulties

If we examine the three steps in software-technology development that have been most fruitful in the past, we discover that each attacked a different major difficulty in building software, but that those difficulties have been accidental, not essential, difficulties. We can also see the natural limits to the extrapolation of each such attack.

**High-level languages.** Surely the most powerful stroke for software productivity, reliability, and simplicity has been the progressive use of high-level languages for programming. Most observers credit that development with at least a factor of five in productivity, and with concomitant gains in reliability, simplicity, and comprehensibility.

What does a high-level language accomplish? It frees a program from much of its accidental complexity. An abstract program consists of conceptual constructs: operations, data types, sequences, and communication. The concrete machine program is concerned with bits, registers, conditions, branches, channels, disks, and such. To the extent that the high-level language embodies the constructs one wants in the abstract program and avoids all lower ones, it eliminates a whole level of complexity that was never inherent in the program at all.

The most a high-level language can do is to furnish all the constructs that the programmer imagines in the abstract program. To be sure, the level of our thinking about data structures, data types, and operations is steadily rising, but at an ever-decreasing rate. And language development approaches closer and closer to the sophistication of users.

Moreover, at some point the elaboration of a high-level language creates a tool-mastery burden that increases, not reduces, the intellectual task of the user who rarely uses the esoteric constructs.

**Time-sharing.** Time-sharing brought a major improvement in the productivity of programmers and in the quality of their product, although not so large as that brought by high-level languages.

Time-sharing attacks a quite different difficulty. Time-sharing preserves immediacy, and hence enables one to maintain an overview of complexity. The slow turnaround of batch programming means that one inevitably forgets the minutiae, if not the very thrust, of what one was thinking when he stopped programming and called for compilation and execution. This interruption is costly in time, for one must refresh one's memory. The most serious effect may well be the decay of the grasp of all that is going on in a complex system.

Slow turnaround, like machine-language complexities, is an accidental rather than an essential difficulty of the software process. The limits of the potential contribution of time-sharing derive directly. The principal effect of time-sharing is to shorten system response time. As this response time goes to zero, at some point it passes the human threshold of noticeability, about 100 milliseconds. Beyond that threshold, no benefits are to be expected.

**Unified programming environments.** Unix and Interlisp, the first integrated programming environments to come into widespread use, seem to have improved productivity by integral factors. Why?

They attack the accidental difficulties that result from using individual programs *together*, by providing integrated libraries, unified file formats, and pipes and filters. As a result, conceptual structures that in principle could always call, feed, and use one another can indeed easily do so in practice.

This breakthrough in turn stimulated the development of whole toolbenches, since each new tool could be applied to any programs that used the standard formats.

Because of these successes, environments are the subject of much of today's software-engineering research. We look at their promise and limitations in the next section.

## Hopes for the silver

Now let us consider the technical developments that are most often advanced as potential silver bullets. What problems do they address—the problems of essence, or the remaining accidental difficulties? Do they offer revolutionary advances, or incremental ones?

**Ada and other high-level language advances.** One of the most touted recent de-

## To slay the werewolf

Why a silver bullet? Magic, of course. Silver is identified with the moon and thus has magic properties. A silver bullet offers the fastest, most powerful, and safest way to slay the fast, powerful, and incredibly dangerous werewolf. And what could be more natural than using the moon-metal to destroy a creature transformed under the light of the full moon?

The legend of the werewolf is probably one of the oldest monster legends around. Herodotus in the fifth century BC gave us the first written report of werewolves when he mentioned a tribe north of the Black Sea, called the Neuri, who supposedly turned into wolves a few days each year. Herodotus wrote that he didn't believe it.

Sceptics aside, many people have believed in people turning into wolves or other animals. In medieval Europe, some people were killed because they were thought to be werewolves. In those times, it didn't take being bitten by a werewolf to become one. A bargain with the devil, using a special potion, wearing a special belt, or being cursed by a witch could all turn a person into a werewolf. However, medieval werewolves could be hurt and killed by normal weapons. The problem was to overcome their strength and cunning.

Enter the fictional, not legendary, werewolf. The first major werewolf movie, *The Werewolf of London*, in 1935 created the two-legged man-wolf who changed into a monster when the moon was full. He became a werewolf after being bitten by one, and could be killed only with a silver bullet. Sound familiar?

Actually, we owe many of today's ideas about werewolves to Lon Chaney Jr.'s unforgettable 1941 portrayal in *The Wolf Man*. Subsequent films seldom strayed far from the mythology of the werewolf shown in that movie. But that movie strayed far from the original mythology of the werewolf.

Would you believe that before fiction took over the legend, werewolves weren't troubled by silver bullets? Vampires were the ones who couldn't stand them. Of course, if you rely on the legends, your only salvation if unarmed and attacked by a werewolf is to climb an ash tree or run into a field of rye. Not so easy to find in an urban setting, and hardly recognizable to the average movie audience.

What should you watch out for? People whose eyebrows grow together, whose index finger is longer than the middle finger, and who have hair growing on their palms. Red or black teeth are a definite signal of possible trouble.

Take warning, though. The same symptoms mark people suffering from hypertrichosis (people born with hair covering their bodies) or porphyria. In porphyria, a person's body produces toxins called porphyrins. Consequently, light becomes painful, the skin grows hair, and the teeth may turn red. Worse for the victim's reputation, his or her increasingly bizarre behavior makes people even more suspicious of the other symptoms. It seems very likely that the sufferers of this disease unwittingly contributed to the current legend, although in earlier times they were evidently not accused of murderous tendencies.

It is worth noting that the film tradition often makes the werewolf a rather sympathetic character, an innocent transformed against his (or rarely, her) will into a monster. As the gypsy said in *The Wolf Man*,

Even a man who is pure at heart,
And says his prayers at night,
Can become a wolf when the wolfbane blooms,
And the moon is full and bright.

—*Nancy Hays*
*Assistant Editor*

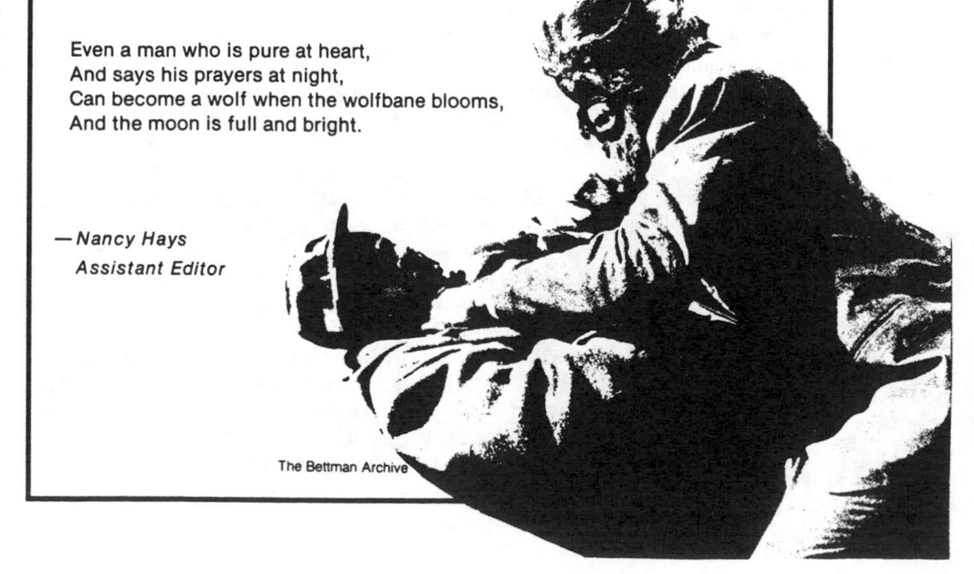

The Bettman Archive

velopments is Ada, a general-purpose high-level language of the 1980's. Ada not only reflects evolutionary improvements in language concepts, but indeed embodies features to encourage modern design and modularization. Perhaps the Ada philosophy is more of an advance than the Ada language, for it is the philosophy of modularization, of abstract data types, of hierarchical structuring. Ada is over-rich, a natural result of the process by which requirements were laid on its design. That is not fatal, for subsetted working vocabularies can solve the learning problem, and hardware advances will give us the cheap MIPS to pay for the compiling costs. Advancing the structuring of software systems is indeed a very good use for the increased MIPS our dollars will buy. Operating systems, loudly decried in the 1960's for their memory and cycle costs, have proved to be an excellent form in which to use some of the MIPS and cheap memory bytes of the past hardware surge.

Nevertheless, Ada will not prove to be the silver bullet that slays the software productivity monster. It is, after all, just another high-level language, and the biggest payoff from such languages came from the first transition—the transition up from the accidental complexities of the machine into the more abstract statement of step-by-step solutions. Once those accidents have been removed, the remaining ones will be smaller, and the payoff from their removal will surely be less.

I predict that a decade from now, when the effectiveness of Ada is assessed, it will be seen to have made a substantial difference, but not because of any particular language feature, nor indeed because of all of them combined. Neither will the new Ada environments prove to be the cause of the improvements. Ada's greatest contribution will be that switching to it occasioned training programmers in modern software-design techniques.

**Object-oriented programming.** Many students of the art hold out more hope for object-oriented programming than for any of the other technical fads of the day.[2] I am among them. Mark Sherman of Dartmouth notes on CSnet News that one must be careful to distinguish two separate ideas that go under that name: *abstract data types* and *hierarchical types.* The concept of the abstract data type is that an object's type should be defined by a name, a set of proper values, and a set of proper operations rather than by its storage structure, which should be hidden. Examples are Ada packages (with private types) and Modula's modules.

Hierarchical types, such as Simula-67's classes, allow one to define general interfaces that can be further refined by providing subordinate types. The two concepts are orthogonal—one may have hierarchies without hiding and hiding without hierarchies. Both concepts represent real advances in the art of building software.

Each removes yet another accidental difficulty from the process, allowing the designer to express the essence of the design without having to express large amounts of syntactic material that add no information content. For both abstract types and hierarchical types, the result is to remove a higher-order kind of accidental difficulty and allow a higher-order expression of design.

**Many students of the art hold out more hope for object-oriented programming than for other technical fads of the day.**

Nevertheless, such advances can do no more than to remove all the accidental difficulties from the expression of the design. The complexity of the design itself is essential, and such attacks make no change whatever in that. An order-of-magnitude gain can be made by object-oriented programming only if the unnecessary type-specification underbrush still in our programming language is itself nine-tenths of the work involved in designing a program product. I doubt it.

**Artificial intelligence.** Many people expect advances in artificial intelligence to provide the revolutionary breakthrough that will give order-of-magnitude gains in software productivity and quality.[3] I do not. To see why, we must dissect what is meant by "artificial intelligence."

D.L. Parnas has clarified the terminological chaos[4]:

> Two quite different definitions of AI are in common use today. AI-1: The use of computers to solve problems that previously could only be solved by applying human intelligence. AI-2: The use of a specific set of programming techniques known as heuristic or rule-based programming. In this approach human experts are studied to determine what heuristics or rules of thumb they use in solving problems. . . . The program is designed to solve a problem the way that humans seem to solve it.
>
> The first definition has a sliding meaning. . . . Something can fit the definition of AI-1 today but, once we see how the program works and understand the problem, we will not think of it as AI any more. . . . Unfortunately I cannot identify a body of technology that is unique to this field. . . . Most of the work is problem-specific, and some abstraction or creativity is required to see how to transfer it.

I agree completely with this critique. The techniques used for speech recognition seem to have little in common with those used for image recognition, and both are different from those used in expert systems. I have a hard time seeing how image recognition, for example, will make any appreciable difference in programming practice. The same problem is true of speech recognition. The hard thing about building software is deciding what one wants to say, not saying it. No facilitation of expression can give more than marginal gains.

Expert-systems technology, AI-2, deserves a section of its own.

**Expert systems.** The most advanced part of the artificial intelligence art, and the most widely applied, is the technology for building expert systems. Many software scientists are hard at work applying this technology to the software-building environment.[3,5] What is the concept, and what are the prospects?

An *expert system* is a program that contains a generalized inference engine and a rule base, takes input data and assumptions, explores the inferences derivable from the rule base, yields conclusions and advice, and offers to explain its results by retracing its reasoning for the user. The inference engines typically can deal with fuzzy or probabilistic data and rules, in addition to purely deterministic logic.

Such systems offer some clear advantages over programmed algorithms designed for arriving at the same solutions to the same problems:

- Inference-engine technology is developed in an application-independent way, and then applied to many uses. One can justify much effort on the inference engines. Indeed, that technology is well advanced.
- The changeable parts of the application-peculiar materials are en-

coded in the rule base in a uniform fashion, and tools are provided for developing, changing, testing, and documenting the rule base. This regularizes much of the complexity of the application itself.

The power of such systems does not come from ever-fancier inference mechanisms, but rather from ever-richer knowledge bases that reflect the real world more accurately. I believe that the most important advance offered by the technology is the separation of the application complexity from the program itself.

How can this technology be applied to the software-engineering task? In many ways: Such systems can suggest interface rules, advise on testing strategies, remember bug-type frequencies, and offer optimization hints.

Consider an imaginary testing advisor, for example. In its most rudimentary form, the diagnostic expert system is very like a pilot's checklist, just enumerating suggestions as to possible causes of difficulty. As more and more system structure is embodied in the rule base, and as the rule base takes more sophisticated account of the trouble symptoms reported, the testing advisor becomes more and more particular in the hypotheses it generates and the tests it recommends. Such an expert system may depart most radically from the conventional ones in that its rule base should probably be hierarchically modularized in the same way the corresponding software product is, so that as the product is modularly modified, the diagnostic rule base can be modularly modified as well.

The work required to generate the diagnostic rules is work that would have to be done anyway in generating the set of test cases for the modules and for the system. If it is done in a suitably general manner, with both a uniform structure for rules and a good inference engine available, it may actually reduce the total labor of generating bring-up test cases, and help as well with lifelong maintenance and modification testing. In the same way, one can postulate other advisors, probably many and probably simple, for the other parts of the software-construction task.

Many difficulties stand in the way of the early realization of useful expert-system advisors to the program developer. A crucial part of our imaginary scenario is the development of easy ways to get from program-structure specification to the automatic or semiautomatic generation of diagnostic rules. Even more difficult and important is the twofold task of knowledge acquisition: finding articulate, self-analytical experts who know *why* they do things, and developing efficient techniques for extracting what they know and distilling it into rule bases. The essential prerequisite for building an expert system is to have an expert.

The most powerful contribution by expert systems will surely be to put at the service of the inexperienced programmer the experience and accumulated wisdom of the best programmers. This is no small contribution. The gap between the best software engineering practice and the average practice is very wide—perhaps wider than in any other engineering discipline. A tool that disseminates good practice would be important.

**"Automatic" programming.** For almost 40 years, people have been anticipating and writing about "automatic programming," or the generation of a program for solving a problem from a statement of the problem specifications. Some today write as if they expect this technology to provide the next breakthrough.[5]

Parnas[4] implies that the term is used for glamor, not for semantic content, asserting,

> In short, automatic programming always has been a euphemism for programming with a higher-level language than was presently available to the programmer.

He argues, in essence, that in most cases it is the solution method, not the problem, whose specification has to be given.

One can find exceptions. The technique of building generators is very powerful, and it is routinely used to good advantage in programs for sorting. Some systems for integrating differential equations have also permitted direct specification of the problem, and the systems have assessed the parameters, chosen from a library of methods of solution, and generated the programs.

These applications have very favorable properties:

• The problems are readily characterized by relatively few parameters.

• There are many known methods of solution to provide a library of alternatives.

• Extensive analysis has led to explicit rules for selecting solution techniques, given problem parameters.

It is hard to see how such techniques generalize to the wider world of the ordinary software system, where cases with such neat properties are the exception. It is hard even to imagine how this breakthrough in generalization could occur.

**Graphical programming.** A favorite subject for PhD dissertations in software engineering is graphical, or visual, programming—the application of computer graphics to software design.[6,7] Sometimes the promise held out by such an approach is postulated by analogy with VLSI chip design, in which computer graphics plays so fruitful a role. Sometimes the theorist justifies the approach by considering flowcharts as the ideal program-design medium and by providing powerful facilities for constructing them.

Nothing even convincing, much less exciting, has yet emerged from such efforts. I am persuaded that nothing will.

In the first place, as I have argued elsewhere,[8] the flowchart is a very poor abstraction of software structure. Indeed, it is best viewed as Burks, von Neumann, and Goldstine's attempt to provide a desperately needed high-level control language for their proposed computer. In the pitiful, multipage, connection-boxed form to which the flowchart has today been elaborated, it has proved to be useless as a design tool—programmers draw

The Bettman Archive

flowcharts after, not before, writing the programs they describe.

Second, the screens of today are too small, in pixels, to show both the scope and the resolution of any seriously detailed software diagram. The so-called "desktop metaphor" of today's workstation is instead an "airplane-seat" metaphor. Anyone who has shuffled a lap full of papers while seated between two portly passengers will recognize the difference—one can see only a very few things at once. The true desktop provides overview of, and random access to, a score of pages. Moreover, when fits of creativity run strong, more than one programmer or writer has been known to abandon the desktop for the more spacious floor. The hardware technology will have to advance quite substantially before the scope of our scopes is sufficient for the software-design task.

More fundamentally, as I have argued above, software is very difficult to visualize. Whether one diagrams control flow, variable-scope nesting, variable cross-references, dataflow, hierarchical data structures, or whatever, one feels only one dimension of the intricately interlocked software elephant. If one superimposes all the diagrams generated by the many relevant views, it is difficult to extract any global overview. The VLSI analogy is fundamentally misleading—a chip design is a layered two-dimensional description whose geometry reflects its realization in 3-space. A software system is not.

**Program verification.** Much of the effort in modern programming goes into testing and the repair of bugs. Is there perhaps a silver bullet to be found by eliminating the errors at the source, in the system-design phase? Can both productivity and product reliability be radically enhanced by following the profoundly different strategy of proving designs correct before the immense effort is poured into implementing and testing them?

I do not believe we will find productivity magic here. Program verification is a very powerful concept, and it will be very important for such things as secure operating-system kernels. The technology does not promise, however, to save labor. Verifications are so much work that only a few substantial programs have ever been verified.

Program verification does not mean error-proof programs. There is no magic here, either. Mathematical proofs also can be faulty. So whereas verification might reduce the program-testing load, it cannot eliminate it.

More seriously, even perfect program verification can only establish that a program meets its specification. The hardest part of the software task is arriving at a complete and consistent specification, and much of the essence of building a program is in fact the debugging of the specification.

**Environments and tools.** How much more gain can be expected from the exploding researches into better programming environments? One's instinctive reaction is that the big-payoff problems—hierarchical file systems, uniform file formats to make possible uniform program interfaces, and generalized tools—were the first attacked, and have been solved. Language-specific smart editors are developments not yet widely used in practice, but the most they promise is freedom from syntactic errors and simple semantic errors.

**Language-specific smart editors promise at most freedom from syntactic errors and simple semantic errors.**

Perhaps the biggest gain yet to be realized from programming environments is the use of integrated database systems to keep track of the myriad details that must be recalled accurately by the individual programmer and kept current for a group of collaborators on a single system.

Surely this work is worthwhile, and surely it will bear some fruit in both productivity and reliability. But by its very nature, the return from now on must be marginal.

**Workstations.** What gains are to be expected for the software art from the certain and rapid increase in the power and memory capacity of the individual workstation? Well, how many MIPS can one use fruitfully? The composition and editing of programs and documents is fully supported by today's speeds. Compiling could stand a boost, but a factor of 10 in machine speed would surely leave think-time the dominant activity in the programmer's day. Indeed, it appears to be so now.

More powerful workstations we surely welcome. Magical enhancements from them we cannot expect.

## Promising attacks on the conceptual essence

Even though no technological breakthrough promises to give the sort of magical results with which we are so familiar in the hardware area, there is both an abundance of good work going on now, and the promise of steady, if unspectacular progress.

All of the technological attacks on the accidents of the software process are fundamentally limited by the productivity equation:

$$\textit{time of task} = \sum_i (\textit{frequency})_i \times (\textit{time})_i$$

If, as I believe, the conceptual components of the task are now taking most of the time, then no amount of activity on the task components that are merely the expression of the concepts can give large productivity gains.

Hence we must consider those attacks that address the essence of the software problem, the formulation of these complex conceptual structures. Fortunately, some of these attacks are very promising.

**Buy versus build.** The most radical possible solution for constructing software is not to construct it at all.

Every day this becomes easier, as more and more vendors offer more and better software products for a dizzying variety of applications. While we software engineers have labored on production methodology, the personal-computer revolution has created not one, but many, mass markets for software. Every newsstand carries monthly magazines, which sorted by machine type, advertise and review dozens of products at prices from a few dollars to a few hundred dollars. More specialized sources offer very powerful products for the workstation and other Unix markets. Even software tools and environments can be bought off-the-shelf. I have elsewhere proposed a marketplace for individual modules.[9]

Any such product is cheaper to buy than to build afresh. Even at a cost of one hundred thousand dollars, a purchased piece of software is costing only about as much as one programmer-year. And delivery is immediate! Immediate at least for products that really exist, products whose developer can refer products to a happy user. Moreover, such products tend to be much better documented and somewhat better maintained than home-grown software.

The development of the mass market is, I believe, the most profound long-run trend in software engineering. The cost of software has always been development cost, not replication cost. Sharing that cost among even a few users radically cuts the per-user cost. Another way of looking at it is that the use of *n* copies of a software system effectively multiplies the productivity of its developers by *n*. That is an enhancement of the productivity of the discipline and of the nation.

The key issue, of course, is applicability. Can I use an available off-the-shelf package to perform my task? A surprising thing has happened here. During the 1950's and 1960's, study after study showed that users would not use off-the-shelf packages for payroll, inventory control, accounts receivable, and so on. The requirements were too specialized, the case-to-case variation too high. During the 1980's, we find such packages in high demand and widespread use. What has changed?

Not the packages, really. They may be somewhat more generalized and somewhat more customizable than formerly, but not much. Not the applications, either. If anything, the business and scientific needs of today are more diverse and complicated than those of 20 years ago.

The big change has been in the hardware/software cost ratio. In 1960, the buyer of a two-million dollar machine felt that he could afford $250,000 more for a customized payroll program, one that slipped easily and nondisruptively into the computer-hostile social environment. Today, the buyer of a $50,000 office machine cannot conceivably afford a customized payroll program, so he adapts the payroll procedure to the packages available. Computers are now so commonplace, if not yet so beloved, that the adaptations are accepted as a matter of course.

There are dramatic exceptions to my argument that the generalization of software packages has changed little over the years: electronic spreadsheets and simple database systems. These powerful tools, so obvious in retrospect and yet so late in appearing, lend themselves to myriad uses, some quite unorthodox. Articles and even books now abound on how to tackle unexpected tasks with the spreadsheet. Large numbers of applications that would formerly have been written as custom programs in Cobol or Report Program Generator are now routinely done with these tools.

Many users now operate their own computers day in and day out on various applications without ever writing a program. Indeed, many of these users cannot write new programs for their machines, but they are nevertheless adept at solving new problems with them.

I believe the single most powerful software-productivity strategy for many organizations today is to equip the computer-naive intellectual workers who are on the firing line with personal computers and good generalized writing, drawing, file, and spreadsheet programs and then to turn them loose. The same strategy, carried out with generalized mathematical and statistical packages and some simple programming capabilities, will also work for hundreds of laboratory scientists.

**Requirements refinement and rapid prototyping.** The hardest single part of building a software system is deciding precisely what to build. No other part of the conceptual work is as difficult as establishing the detailed technical requirements, including all the interfaces to people, to machines, and to other software systems. No other part of the work so cripples the resulting system if done wrong. No other part is more difficult to rectify later.

Therefore, the most important function that the software builder performs for the client is the iterative extraction and refinement of the product requirements. For the truth is, the client does not know what he wants. The client usually does not know what questions must be answered, and he has almost never thought of the problem in the detail necessary for specification. Even the simple answer—"Make the new software system work like our old manual information-processing system" —is in fact too simple. One never wants exactly that. Complex software systems are, moreover, things that act, that move, that work. The dynamics of that action are hard to imagine. So in planning any software-design activity, it is necessary to allow for an extensive iteration between the client and the designer as part of the system definition.

I would go a step further and assert that it is really impossible for a client, even working with a software engineer, to specify completely, precisely, and correctly the exact requirements of a modern software product before trying some versions of the product.

Therefore, one of the most promising of the current technological efforts, and one that attacks the essence, not the accidents, of the software problem, is the development of approaches and tools for rapid prototyping of systems as prototyping is part of the iterative specification of requirements.

A *prototype software system* is one that simulates the important interfaces and performs the main functions of the intended system, while not necessarily being bound by the same hardware speed, size, or cost constraints. Prototypes typically perform the mainline tasks of the application, but make no attempt to handle the exceptional tasks, respond correctly to invalid inputs, or abort cleanly. The purpose of the prototype is to make real the conceptual structure specified, so that the client can test it for consistency and usability.

Much of present-day software-acquisition procedure rests upon the assumption that one can specify a satisfactory system in advance, get bids for its construction, have it built, and install it. I think this assumption is fundamentally wrong, and that many software-acquisition problems

The Bettman Archive

spring from that fallacy. Hence, they cannot be fixed without fundamental revision—revision that provides for iterative development and specification of prototypes and products.

**Incremental development—grow, don't build, software.** I still remember the jolt I felt in 1958 when I first heard a friend talk about *building* a program, as opposed to *writing* one. In a flash he broadened my whole view of the software process. The metaphor shift was powerful, and accurate. Today we understand how like other building processes the construction of software is, and we freely use other elements of the metaphor, such as *specifications, assembly of components,* and *scaffolding*.

The building metaphor has outlived its usefulness. It is time to change again. If, as I believe, the conceptual structures we construct today are too complicated to be specified accurately in advance, and too complex to be built faultlessly, then we must take a radically different approach.

Let us turn to nature and study complexity in living things, instead of just the dead works of man. Here we find constructs whose complexities thrill us with awe. The brain alone is intricate beyond mapping, powerful beyond imitation, rich in diversity, self-protecting, and self-renewing. The secret is that it is grown, not built.

So it must be with our software systems. Some years ago Harlan Mills proposed that any software system should be grown by incremental development.[10] That is, the system should first be made to run, even if it does nothing useful except call the proper set of dummy subprograms. Then, bit by bit, it should be fleshed out, with the subprograms in turn being developed—into actions or calls to empty stubs in the level below.

I have seen most dramatic results since I began urging this technique on the project builders in my Software Engineering Laboratory class. Nothing in the past decade has so radically changed my own practice, or its effectiveness. The approach necessitates top-down design, for it is a top-down growing of the software. It allows easy backtracking. It lends itself to early prototypes. Each added function and new provision for more complex data or circumstances grows organically out of what is already there.

The morale effects are startling. Enthusiasm jumps when there is a running system, even a simple one. Efforts redouble when the first picture from a new graphics software system appears on the screen, even if it is only a rectangle. One always has, at every stage in the process, a working system. I find that teams can *grow* much more complex entities in four months than they can *build*.

The same benefits can be realized on large projects as on my small ones.[11]

**Table 1. Exciting vs. useful but unexciting software products.**

| Exciting Products | |
|---|---|
| Yes | No |
| Unix | Cobol |
| APL | PL/1 |
| Pascal | Algol |
| Modula | MVS/370 |
| Smalltalk | MS-DOS |
| Fortran | |

**Great designers.** The central question in how to improve the software art centers, as it always has, on people.

We can get good designs by following good practices instead of poor ones. Good design practices can be taught. Programmers are among the most intelligent part of the population, so they can learn good practice. Hence, a major thrust in the United States is to promulgate good modern practice. New curricula, new literature, new organizations such as the Software Engineering Institute, all have come into being in order to raise the level of our practice from poor to good. This is entirely proper.

Nevertheless, I do not believe we can make the next step upward in the same way. Whereas the difference between poor conceptual designs and good ones may lie in the soundness of design method, the difference between good designs and great ones surely does not. Great designs come from great designers. Software construction is a *creative* process. Sound methodology can empower and liberate the creative mind; it cannot inflame or inspire the drudge.

The differences are not minor—they are rather like the differences between Salieri and Mozart. Study after study shows that the very best designers produce structures that are faster, smaller, simpler, cleaner, and produced with less effort.[12] The differences between the great and the average approach an order of magnitude.

A little retrospection shows that although many fine, useful software systems have been designed by committees and built as part of multipart projects, those software systems that have excited passionate fans are those that are the products of one or a few designing minds, great designers. Consider Unix, APL, Pascal, Modula, the Smalltalk interface, even Fortran; and contrast them with Cobol, PL/I, Algol, MVS/370, and MS-DOS. (See Table 1.)

Hence, although I strongly support the technology-transfer and curriculum-development efforts now under way, I think the most important single effort we can mount is to develop ways to grow great designers.

No software organization can ignore this challenge. Good managers, scarce though they be, are no scarcer than good designers. Great designers and great managers are both very rare. Most organizations spend considerable effort in finding and cultivating the management prospects; I know of none that spends equal effort in finding and developing the great designers upon whom the technical excellence of the products will ultimately depend.

My first proposal is that each software organization must determine and proclaim that great designers are as important to its success as great managers are, and that they can be expected to be similarly nurtured and rewarded. Not only salary, but the perquisites of recognition—office size, furnishings, personal technical equipment, travel funds, staff support—must be fully equivalent.

How to grow great designers? Space does not permit a lengthy discussion, but some steps are obvious:

- Systematically identify top designers as early as possible. The best are often not the most experienced.
- Assign a career mentor to be responsible for the development of the prospect, and carefully keep a career file.
- Devise and maintain a career-development plan for each prospect, including carefully selected apprenticeships with top designers, episodes of advanced formal education, and short courses, all interspersed with solo-design and technical-leadership assignments.
- Provide opportunities for growing designers to interact with and stimulate each other.□

## Acknowledgments

I thank Gordon Bell, Bruce Buchanan, Rick Hayes-Roth, Robert Patrick, and, most especially, David Parnas for their insights and stimulating ideas, and Rebekah Bierly for the technical production of this article.


## References


1. D.L. Parnas, "Designing Software for Ease of Extension and Contraction," *IEEE Trans. Software Engineering,* Vol. 5, No. 2, Mar. 1979, pp. 128-138.
2. G. Booch, "Object-Oriented Design," *Software Engineering with Ada,* 1983, Benjamin/Cummings, Menlo Park, Calif.
3. *IEEE Trans. Software Engineering* (special issue on artificial intelligence and software engineering), J. Mostow, guest ed., Vol. 11, No. 11, Nov. 1985.
4. D.L. Parnas, "Software Aspects of Strategic Defense Systems," *American Scientist,* Nov. 1985.
5. R. Balzer, "A 15-Year Perspective on Automatic Programming," *IEEE Trans. Software Engineering* (special issue on artificial intelligence and software engineering), J. Mostow, guest ed., Vol. 11, No. 11, Nov. 1985, pp. 1257-1267.
6. *Computer* (special issue on visual programming), R.B. Graphton and T. Ichikawa, guest eds., Vol. 18, No. 8, Aug. 1985.
7. G. Raeder, "A Survey of Current Graphical Programming Techniques," *Computer* (special issue on visual programming), R.B. Graphton and T. Ichikawa, guest eds., Vol. 18, No. 8, Aug. 1985, pp. 11-25.
8. F.P. Brooks, *The Mythical Man-Month,* 1975, Addison-Wesley, Reading, Mass., New York, Chapter 14.
9. Defense Science Board, *Report of the Task Force on Military Software,* in press.
10. H.D. Mills, "Top-Down Programming in Large Systems," in *Debugging Techniques in Large Systems,* R. Ruskin, ed., Prentice-Hall, Englewood Cliffs, N.J., 1971.
11. B.W. Boehm, "A Spiral Model of Software Development and Enhancement," 1985, TRW tech. report 21-371-85, TRW, Inc., 1 Space Park, Redondo Beach, CA 90278.
12. H. Sackman, W.J. Erikson, and E.E. Grant, "Exploratory Experimental Studies Comparing Online and Offline Programming Performance," *CACM,* Vol. 11, No. 1, Jan. 1968, pp. 3-11.

# Chapter 2

# System and Software System Engineering

## 1. Introduction to Chapter

Figure 2.1 reflects the interfaces of three related disciplines; system engineering, software system engineering, and software engineering.

*System engineering* is the overall technical management of a system development project. It is a logical sequence of activities and decisions that transform an operational need to a description of system configuration. The product of system engineering is documents, not physical systems. System engineering includes:

- Problem definition
- Solution analysis
- Process planning
- Process control
- Product evaluation

*Software system engineering* is concerned with the development of software using the same mechanism and approach as system engineering, that is, the logical sequence of activities and decisions that transform an operational need to a description of a software system and its documentation. Software system engineering is a relatively new concept, probably less than ten years old, and as a result is not as well defined as system engineering. Software system engineering (similarly to system engineering) includes:

- Requirements analysis and specifications
- Software design
- Process planning
- Process control
- Software verification, validation, and testing

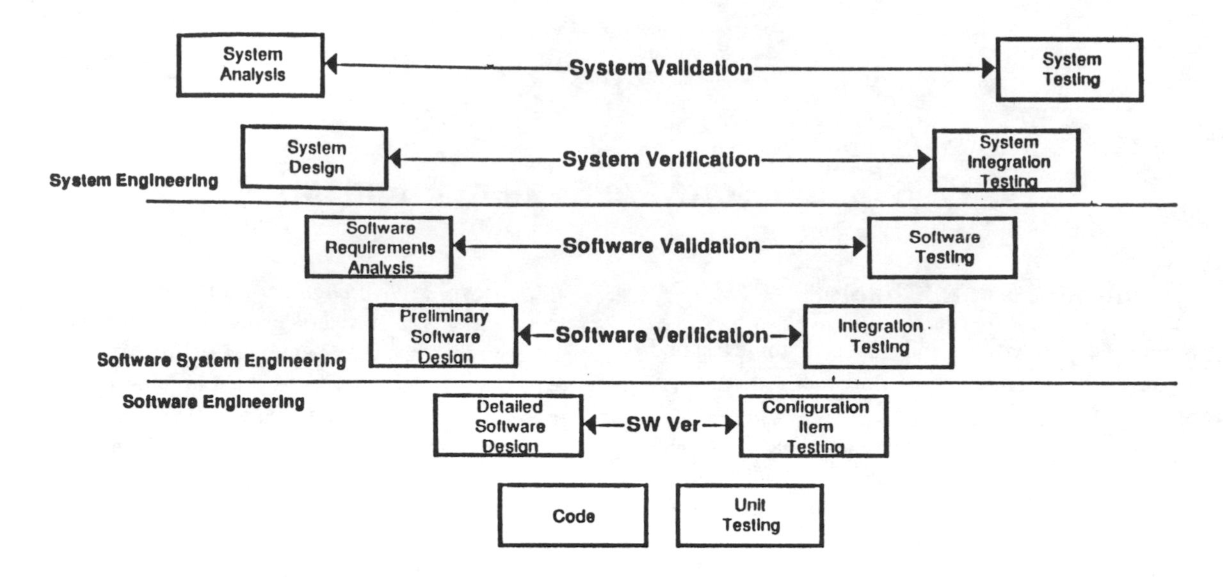


*Figure 2.1. System and software system engineering process model*

*Software engineering* has been defined as the practical application of computer science and other disciplines to the analysis, design, construction, and maintenance of the software and the associated documentation. It can also be considered to be the systematic application of methods, tools, and techniques to achieve its stated requirements objective for a software system.

Software engineering is built on the concepts of system engineering. Several authors (such as Andriole and Freeman [see paper in this chapter] and Sage and Palmer [1]) have recently argued for the use of the term *software system engineering* as a replacement for the term *software engineering*. This tutorial will take the more conservative viewpoint and refer to software development, either at the system level or at the detail level, as the more conventional *software engineering*. Much thought was given, however, to titling this IEEE tutorial *Software System Engineering*, and the importance of software system engineering in the software development process cannot be overemphasized [2]:

> System engineering and software system engineering are often overlooked in a software development project. Systems that are all software and/or run on commercial, off-the-shelf computers are often considered just software projects, not system projects, and no effort is expended to develop a system engineering approach. Ignoring the systems aspects of the project often results in software that will not run on or with the hardware selected, will not integrate with hardware and other software systems, and frequently contributes to the so-called "software crisis."

## 2. Introduction to Papers

The first short paper, "Engineering a Small System," by Kurt Skytte, introduces the concept of system engineering. He argues that system engineering, once done only on government projects or by large aerospace companies, can and should be applied to small systems in the commercial arena.

Skytte's intent was to describe how system engineering can be applied to "small" systems. The author, and the editors of this Tutorial, believe that it provides a very good outline for applying system engineering to a system of any size.

The paper by Stephen Andriole and Peter Freeman on "Software System Engineering: The Case for New Discipline" is one of the few papers that shows a relationship between system engineering and software engineering. The authors propose that software engineering and system engineering be integrated into a concept called "software system engineering." As the Tutorial editors have already stated, it is clear that software engineering developed from system engineering in the early 1960s and 1970s. The editors therefore concur with the concept of developing software through the software system engineering methodology.

The third paper, "The Concept of Operations: The Bridge From Operational Requirements To Technical Specifications," was written by Richard Fairley and Richard Thayer. (Thayer is one of the Tutorial editors.) This paper presents the relatively new concept of developing a "needs" document that bridges the gap between the customer and the more formal software requirements specifications. This paper describes the role of the *concept of operations* (ConOps) document in the specification and development of a software-intensive system. It also describes the process of developing a ConOps, its uses and benefits, who should develop it, and when it should be developed. The paper compares the ConOps to other forms of operational concept documents. A detailed outline of the ConOps document is provided as an appendix to the paper.


1. Sage, Andrew P. and James D. Palmer, *Software System Engineering*, John Wiley & Sons, Inc., New York, 1990.

2. Thayer, Richard H., and Winston W. Royce, "Software System Engineering," in "*Tutorial: System and Software Requirements Engineering*," IEEE Computer Society Press, Los Alamitos, Calif., 1990.

# Engineering a small system

*Once the preserve of large government projects, systems engineering can benefit commercial products, as well*

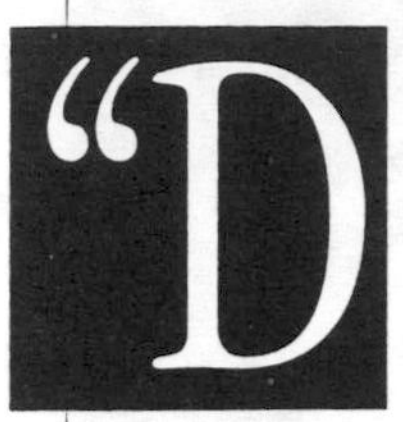

"Do it right the first time" is the slogan of systems engineering. The approach can benefit all types of development projects, small as well as large, because the objective is the same: to design a high-quality product as fast and efficiently as possible.

Perhaps the most cogent definition of systems engineering is given in the *1988 Chambers Science and Technology Dictionary*: "A logical process of activities which transforms a set of requirements arising from a specific mission objective into a full description of a system which fulfills the objective in an optimum way. It ensures that all aspects of a project have been considered and integrated into a consistent whole."

In other words, systems engineering translates a customer's stated need into a set of requirements and specifications for a system's performance and configuration. The process defines all the resources and special tools needed plus the stages in the product's development. It also sets up checkpoints at each stage in the design cycle to ensure that objectives are met and that defects are identified and corrected as early as possible, thus minimizing their impact on the development schedule and on the product's cost and quality. The final system is then validated against the original requirements and specifications.

For decades now systems-engineering techniques have been standard in the U.S. Department of Defense and applied to large commercial products like airliners. But they have not been widely applied to the engineering of medium-sized or relatively small commercial products like medical diagnostic equipment or industrial test and measurement instruments. That situation, however, may be changing. Organizations such as the U.S. Food and Drug Administration (FDA) and the International Organization for Standardization (ISO) are establishing guidelines—for example, the ISO standard 9001—on how quality should be addressed during the development of products. A development process based on the analytical techniques of systems engineering also can help meet this goal.

Kurt Skytte AnalySys Consulting Inc.

**START WITH NEEDS.** Perhaps the prime assumption underpinning systems engineering is that a product should be designed to fulfill customers' actual needs; only by solving a real problem better than any competition does a product become truly successful. As identified through marketing surveys and other mechanisms, the customers' needs inspire the formal written requirements the product must fulfill. On those requirements are based the system's technical specifications, which form part of the documents that are the key references for the design.

Self-evident as this approach may seem, it is surprisingly common for companies to develop products with little or no customer input. Even when a large market exists, a product can fail when the customer's real needs are poorly understood. For example, both General Electric Ultrasound in Milwaukee, Wis., and Philips Ultrasound in Santa Ana, Calif., have introduced ultrasound medical imaging instruments that would have sold in greater numbers had the interfaces been better tailored to the needs of the intended users. The GE product put a touch screen over the image monitor—but imaging gel and other contaminants on the ultrasound technician's fingers quickly accumulated, smudging the screen and blurring the diagnostic image.

The problem with the Philips instrument was different. Ultrasound imaging instruments typically have many separate controls, and Philips sought to reduce that number by incorporating a mouse. But ultrasound technicians want to concentrate on the diagnostic image, not be distracted by computer icons, and to progress through an examination as quickly as possible. Clicking the buttons on the mouse was neither fast nor interactive enough to suit their needs.

**REDUCE REDESIGN.** Another assumption behind systems engineering is that the system as a whole must be carefully planned out to minimize its redesign. For a long time the largest source of project delays, redesign typically becomes necessary because the product requirements were poorly defined or changed, the engineering specifications were inferior, or the basic design's ability to meet the original requirements was not thoroughly reviewed.

The full effect of inadequate planning is rarely detected until late in the development cycle, sometimes even into the system's design validation phase. The later any design defects are detected, the more time and money any redesign will need. Moreover, late changes often compromise the product's reliability and maintenance costs, perhaps even affecting its profitability and success. Spending extra time up front completing and clarifying the basic requirements always pays high dividends in the end.

Even so, the best-written requirements can be undermined if unnecessary changes to them are allowed after design is started. During this phase, the product is often embellished in ways not specified originally. Commonly called "creeping elegance," these additions are sometimes made without an awareness that such changes may delay the schedule and add to the life-cycle costs.

In Japan, such companies as Matsushita Communication Industrial Co.'s Instrument Division in Yokohama and Toshiba American Medical Systems Inc. in Tustin, Calif., manage both to prevent and profit from creeping elegance. As new ideas or requirements surface, they are collected not for ongoing projects, but for later upgrades or new products.

To be sure, companies must at times react to market shifts or exploit some new discovery by changing product requirements, but the resulting stretchout of schedule and increase in cost should be clearly grasped and properly integrated into the product's development plan.

**SPECS DRIVE DESIGN.** A third essential assumption of systems engineering is that specifications for the system as a whole, as well as for the details of individual components, should direct the design process. A system-level design specification defines the system's architecture in terms of functional segments and their interfaces. Taking the time to architect the system properly can minimize the system's complexity, lower its cost, and improve its reliability, manufacturability, and serviceability. It is also important for the final top-level design and architecture to show how these objectives can be balanced in terms of life-cycle costs, not near-term objectives.

Performance specifications must also be captured so that they can be compared with measured system performance during design verification.

**SCALING DOWN.** Systems engineering on large government projects is rigorous and detailed. For smaller commercial applica-

Reprinted from *IEEE Spectrum*, Vol. 31, No. 3, Mar. 1994, pp. 63–65.

tions, it can be streamlined to reduce the overhead while retaining the benefits.

Whatever its size, though, a company using systems engineering development must proceed through six phases: requirements development, system design, detail design, system integration, system optimization, and design validation. During each phase, formal documents are written, capturing all elements of the design. These documents then become the references that drive the design process.

**Phase 1: Requirements development.** The first step in designing any system is identifying the objectives it must fulfill. Since life-cycle costs hinge on this early planning, enough time and resources absolutely must be allocated to researching the system's requirements.

In a commercial environment, the product's objectives should be determined by surveying the needs of potential customers. Next, a team should be formed to develop the specification describing the product's functional requirements. This team should include representatives from marketing, engineering, manufacturing, field service, and any other group that will influence the system's functions and life-cycle costs.

The specification should cover each of the system's required functions in detail, including a description of the user interfaces with objectives for response time, types of input and output devices (visual or auditory), and any application-specific information that relates ergonomic requirements to the typical user's environment. Each function must be associated with a specific type of control, and each requirement for user feedback must be associated with an output device. The functional-requirement specification, however, defines only *what* has to be designed into the product, not *how* it is to be designed.

One of the trickier aspects of this first phase is determining which features and functions are of the most value to the product. The first draft of a functional specification for a new product often resembles an indiscriminate list of features found in existing products. One way to identify the most valuable features is to use quality function deployment (QFD), a technique that—through developing a series of matrices—can help rank product attributes in order of their importance to the customer. Understanding which of these attributes matter most will aid the team in making sound decisions when tradeoffs must be made.

The functional-requirement specification is complete when the project team is willing to commit itself to a set of functions, recognizing that the completeness of the document describing them is vital to the quality of the final system, and that any changes made to the document after it is released to the design engineers will directly affect product quality, production schedule, and life-cycle costs.

**Phase 2: System design.** The next step is to translate the completed functional requirements into an architecture and a set of system-level design specifications that together meet the original customer needs. It is essential now to translate all the functional requirements into design specifications, making sure that none is overlooked.

The architecture document must identify each subsystem and component, specify all the intended relationships among them, and delineate clearly how each will fulfill one of the documented functional requirements. Performance requirements should be specified quantitatively, in terms that can be measured in the final system.

For any small project, such as an instrument containing only a couple of circuit boards, writing a single system-level specification may suffice. For a larger project, such as a medical ultrasound imaging system, it is preferable to have one top-level document specify the system's architecture and performance requirements, and separate specifications define the functional and performance requirements for each subsystem. The subsystem specifications would also identify and specify the requirements for each circuit board within the subsystem.

One of the more perplexing aspects of the system-design phase is the proper allocation of functions to hardware and software. If that allocation is suboptimal, the product may end up with overly expensive hardware or overly complex software. For an intricate system such as an ultrasound imaging system, computer-aided engineering (CAE) tools are useful for comparing choices of implementation, developing critical performance specifications, and verifying signal-processing algorithms before starting the designs of subsystems and components.

Ideally, a single simulation tool would address all the necessary levels of simulation from behavior modeling through algorithm development and down to the level of hardware details. But currently, different CAE tools must address those needs [see table at right]. Any modeling or simulations begun during this phase should be revisited later to optimize the system's performance.

Part of the system-design phase is to develop a plan for the integration of the system. This plan should define the order in which the components will be assembled into larger units, whose function will be verified before proceeding to the next step in the assembly. The plan should identify the acceptance criteria for hardware (such as printed-circuit boards and other components) and software for those units, identify any needs for special test fixtures or tools, and assess the number of support personnel required to complete the assembly.

For more complex systems, a coordinated

## Systems-engineering checklist

Here is a checklist of the steps essential to applying systems-engineering principles to the design of smaller commercial products:

**Requirements phase**

- Consult potential customers to ascertain their actual needs.
- Have a multidisciplinary project team take that statement of needs and use it to develop a detailed specification describing the product's functional requirements.

**System-design phase**

- Develop a system architecture that supports specified product requirements.
- Develop system-design specifications that document the system's architecture, system-level performance specifications, and the functional requirements of each subsystem and component.
- If necessary, use simulations and other analytical techniques to verify that top-level design concepts support all specified product requirements.
- Define the system's life-cycle cost model.

**Detail design phase**

- Design the hardware and software as described in the system-design specifications.
- Schedule several detail-design reviews to make quite sure that the hardware and software meet the specifications.
- Build and test each component to verify that the design objectives have been met.
- Develop plans for integrating the components and subsystems into the entire system, and for testing the system.
- Compare the actual costs of designing the hardware and software with the cost estimates to verify that cost objectives are being met.

**System integration phase**

- Integrate the components and subsystems into a prototype system and verify its functionality.

**Design verification and optimization phase**

- Verify that all performance specifications are met over all specified operating conditions.
- Optimize the system's design by minimizing any differences found between expected and measured performance.

**System validation phase**

- Evaluate the final product's configuration to ensure that it complies with the original functional-requirements specification.

test plan helps ensure that any special resources or equipment will be on hand to test and optimize the system. For efficiency, this plan should identify key performance benchmarks.

**Phase 3: Detail design.** Now, and only now, do engineers begin to design the hardware and software that will implement the top system-level specifications. Every aspect of these designs should be documented by drawings and written descriptions, which will ultimately support the development and manufacturing processes. From the detail-design phase emerge tested and verified components ready for integration into the system.

The design teams should use the system-level design specifications as the primary technical reference for all designs. Moreover, several times during the detail-design phase, the designs should be reviewed against the systems-level specification to see that its objectives are being met.

**Phase 4: System integration.** At last, it is time to put all the components and subsystems together. They should be assembled in the order defined by the integration plan, which was mapped out during the system-design phase, and verified to work.

**Phase 5: Design verification and optimization.** After it has been established that the system works properly, it is necessary to test that it performs just like or better than the requirements of the system-design specification. If the system was properly designed, the scope and range of the optimization parameters should be embedded within the control software or hardware so that adjustments are easy. The system is optimized when differences between the expected and measured performance of all its functions have been minimized.

**Phase 6: System validation.** Finally, it is time to ensure that the final system design complies with the functional-requirements specification. This is the last overall check of the system before its design is released to manufacturing.

Every state of the machine and every function described in the original functional requirements must be tested to validate the system. Since today most systems have some kind of embedded computer, functionality is usually dictated by the control software and much of the validation is bound up with the testing of the software design. Every time the software is modified or changed, the system must be re-validated. In fact, the ability to validate a system design quickly can enhance its upgradeability and maintainability. Automated test tools that can simulate user inputs and then monitor for correct responses can speed this process.

**BEYOND CONCURRENT ENGINEERING.** A well-conceived systems-engineering process shares some of the same development objectives as concurrent engineering. Premised on multidisciplinary project teams, concurrent engineering helps to ensure that all elements of the product life cycle are factored into the design, and overlaps development phases whenever possible to save time.

In some ways systems engineering may be viewed as a refinement of concurrent engineering. It takes the basic concept of multidisciplinary design teams and adds to it guidelines for formal development phases.

By adopting a structured approach to development that is scaled to the needs of the project, it is possible to eliminate some of the remaining sources of design defects and development risks. Development time is further shortened, and product quality and profitability are enhanced.

**TO PROBE FURTHER.** Because the use of system engineering principles in developing modest-sized commercial products is a fairly new concept, information on it must be taken from more general systems-engineering sources. The National Council on Systems Engineering (NCOSE) has established a working group to specifically address commercial systems-engineering practices; contact NCOSE at 333 Cobalt Way, Suite 107, Sunnyvale, CA 94086.

Benjamin S. Blanchard and Walter J. Fabrycky's textbook *Systems Engineering and Analysis* (Prentice Hall, Englewood Cliffs, N.J., 1990) is an excellent overview of systems-engineering concepts, design methods, and commonly used analytical tools.

All aspiring system architects should also read Eberhardt Rechtin's classic *Systems Architecting: Creating and Building Complex Systems* (Prentice Hall, Englewood Cliffs, N. J., 1991), which defines the role and responsibilities of the system architect and lists what knowledge, skill, and other pertinent traits are required. Rechtin's article "The Art of Systems Architecting" *(IEEE Spectrum*, October 1992, pp. 66–69) introduces a number of design heuristics that can be used, along with analytical techniques, to develop the architectures for systems.

The author wishes to thank Michael Brendel and Christopher Chapman of Siemens Medical Systems Inc. (Ultrasound Group), Issaquah, Wash., for their helpful insights. ◆

*ABOUT THE AUTHOR. Kurt Skytte is the president of AnalySys Consulting, in Alamo, Calif., which specializes in consulting for the development of medical and analytical instruments. Before founding AnalySys Consulting, he was systems engineering manager at Siemens Ultrasound Inc. from 1986 to 1992. Before going to Siemens, he was a hardware design engineer and project leader for the Instrument Division of Varian Associates in Walnut Creek, Calif., for six years.*

## Tools for computer-aided systems-engineering design

| Company | Product name | Development of requirements | Simulation and modeling | High-level software modeling and development | DSP simulations | Algorithm development |
|---|---|---|---|---|---|---|
| International TechneGroup Inc. Milford, Ohio | QFD/Capture | ● | | | | |
| Ascent Logic Corp. San Jose, Calif. | RDD | | ● | | | |
| I-Logix Inc. Santa Clara, Calif. | Statemate | | ● | | | |
| General Electric Co. King of Prussia, Pa. | OMTool | | | ● | | |
| Interactive Development Environments Inc. San Francisco | Software Through Pictures | | ● | ● | | |
| Popkin Software & Systems Inc. New York City | System Architect | | ● | ● | | |
| ProtoSoft Inc. Houston, Texas | Paradigm Plus | | | ● | | |
| Comdisco Systems Inc. Foster City, Calif. | SPW | | ● | | ● | ● |
| Mathworks Inc. Natick, Mass. | Matlab | | | | ● | ● |
| Mentor Graphics Corp. San Jose, Calif. | DSP Station | | ● | | ● | ● |
| Signal Technology Inc. Santa Barbara, Calif. | NIPower | | ● | | ● | ● |

DSP = digital signal processing. Source: Kurt Skytte

# Software systems engineering: the case for a new discipline

by Stephen J. Andriole and Peter A. Freeman

**One of the hallmarks of the modern world is the creation of complex systems. The discipline of systems engineering is often utilised in this activity and, as many of these systems are also software-intensive, the discipline of software engineering becomes one of the critical technologies that must be utilised. In these cases, both disciplines address the same subject, the creation of complex software-intensive systems, albeit from different perspectives. In this paper, we examine the current state of each discipline, analyse and compare each along several dimensions, and conclude by presenting the case for a new discipline, *software systems engineering*, which combines the essential elements of both disciplines.**

## 1 Introduction

Our working premise is simple; software-intensive systems (regardless of their application domains) are among the most important, yet hardest to create and maintain, artifacts of modern society. Thirty years ago, there were few large-scale software-intensive systems. Today they pervade the public and private sectors. We now live with a systems infrastructure that is sometimes nearly impossible to maintain. We often spend too much for too little increase in functionality and quality, and seem to learn relatively little from our mistakes. Despite every effort to enhance the process, we have, in fact, created a 'software crisis'.

Our interest here is in improving the development of software-intensive systems. As researchers, educators and practitioners, we have found that a systematic approach to the overall task, such as that provided by the discipline of *systems* engineering, is necessary. We have also observed that, when the creation or modification of software is a part of the task, additional systematic procedures, such as those provided by *software* engineering, are necessary. In short, we have found that the creation of software-intensive systems demands more than what is traditionally in either of the fields. Although there is no shortage of references that describe software engineering [1] or systems engineering [2], there are only a few [3] that have looked at the intersection. Our purpose here is to continue the analysis of the intersection; in the process, we hope to outline the terms of a productive marriage.

## 2 Definitions

Modern homes represent complex systems that could not have been designed or constructed by one professional. Software-intensive systems are similarly complex, although they are often designed, developed and maintained by professionals with narrow disciplinary perspectives. An information system for naïve users, who have to input, locate and route documents, should not be designed and developed by programmers, computer scientists, cognitive psychologists, or electrical engineers, but by all of these, and perhaps other professionals.

We noted above that it sometimes seems that, as a discipline, we are not learning from our experience. We believe this flat learning curve is traceable to our unwillingness to pluralise the systems design process. It is dangerous to see systems only from the bottom-up or from the top-down, only as a programmer or only as a psychologist. It is essential that we redefine the systems analysis, modelling, design, and development processes from a multidisciplinary perspective.

*Systems engineering* is a problem-solving process with roots in behavioural, computer, engineering, management and mathematical sciences. According to at least one source [4], the systems engineering process is a

'*... logical sequence of activities and decisions transforming an operational need into a description of system performance parameters and a preferred system configuration ...*'

The US federal government has developed a systems engineering 'standard' [4] definition:

'*Systems engineering is the application of scientific and engineering efforts to (a) transform operational need into a description of system performance parameters and a system configuration through the use of an iterating process of definition, synthesis, analysis, design, test, and evaluation; (b) integrate related technical*

"Software System Engineering: The Case for a New Discipline" by S.J. Andriole and P.A. Freeman
from *Software Eng. J.*, Vol. 8, No. 3, May 1993, pp. 165–179. 

*parameters and ensure compatibility of all physical, functional, and program interfaces in a manner that optimizes the total system definition and design; (c) integrate reliability, maintainability, safety, survivability, human, and other such factors into the total engineering effort to meet cost, schedule, and technical performance objectives.'*

Eisner [5] defines systems engineering as 'an iterative process of top-down synthesis, development, and operation of a real-world system that satisfies, in a near optimal manner, the full range of requirements for the system'. In fact, most definitions of systems engineering [2, 5–9] focus on the process by which operational needs and specific requirements are converted into working systems against a backdrop of cost, time and talent constraints.

*Software engineering* cannot claim a widely held definition. The definition first stated by Naur and Randall [10] still captures the overall pattern of the field (and is used, for example, by Pressman [1]):

*'The establishment and use of sound engineering principles in order to obtain economically software that is reliable and works efficiently on real machines.'*

Boehm [11] echoes this definition:

*'Software engineering is the application of science and mathematics by which the capabilities of computer equipment are made useful to man via computer programs, procedures, and associated documentation.'*

Boehm's mention of mathematics foreshadows today's increasing emphasis on formal methods and, in fact, provides a tie to the non-engineering view of the creation of software as a mathematical activity. The mathematical definition of software creation is, in our view, a valid viewpoint within the realm of programming and program design, but its scope does not encompass the full range of issues with which software engineering must deal. Mills [12] notes that software engineering is between systems engineering and systems integration, is focused on software-intensive systems, and involves a mathematically disciplined design process. This view, and the work that he pioneered at IBM, is perhaps the best documented instance of a software engineering methodology.

The operational definition that we have used [13] for some years, and the one that we endorse here, is concisely stated as follows:

*'Software engineering is the systematic application of methods, tools, and knowledge to achieve stated technical, economic, and human objectives for a software-intensive system.'*

## 3 Scope of the disciplines

The creation of a complex artifact involves both time duration and a wide range of activities. These two dimensions (time and activity) provide a framework for describing the scope of a discipline.

*Time duration* is bounded by the time before which a system does not exist and the time after which it no longer exists (or is out of service and of no interest). Within these extremes, there are four major time divisions:

- pre-development;
- initial development;
- operation-and-modification;
- decommissioning.

*Activities* present a harder subject to explicate. To provide some structure, we have chosen the following framework of activities associated with the creation of software-intensive systems:

- ☐ purely technical activities:
  - creating technical work products (such as designs or test plans);
  - modifying existing technical work products;
  - studying work products to derive some information (e.g. producing a scenario from a requirements specification or testing a program);
- ☐ purely managerial activities:
  - planning;
  - acquiring resources;
  - allocating resources;
  - controlling;
  - evaluating;
- ☐ ancillary/mixed activities:
  - producing, modifying, studying non-technical work product (such as user documentation or needs statements);
  - requirements engineering;
  - acceptance testing;
  - training;
  - support (such as tool building, travel, physical space planning).

### *3.1 Time and activities scope of systems engineering*

In many respects, *systems engineering* is a composite field that borrows from a wide range of areas and formal disciplines. Without these contributions, the field itself could not exist; yet without the organising systems engineering life-cycle, they remain unco-ordinated islands of expertise.

Systems engineering is also domain-independent. The design and development principles are generic. They have been applied to any number of substantive problems. Systems engineering is thus, to some people, a meta-design strategy, more than a tactical course of action. In truth, the process directly addresses both objectives.

The state-of-the-art is difficult to assess in either a methodological or applications vacuum. Some aspects of systems engineering have evolved more impressively than others. The process by which system requirements are identified, modelled and validated, for example, has evolved dramatically over the past two decades. Today it is commonplace to hear about the 'requirements engineering' process, where a set of qualitative and quantitative tools are used to elicit and represent systems requirements at all levels. Trade-off analyses are now conducted with the aid of several powerful techniques, such as computer-assisted cost-benefit and more qualitative multi-attribute utility assessment techniques. Suffice to say that the systems engineering process has evolved along with its core areas and disciplines, while maintaining a design whole greater than the sum of its methodological parts.

Eisner [5] regards the systems engineering process as consisting of the following 'elements'. These elements directly address *time duration* and *activities*:

- 1. requirements analysis;
- 2. requirements allocations;
- 3. functional analysis;
- 4. functional allocation;
- 5. specification analysis;
- 6. specification allocation;
- 7. specification development;
- 8. preliminary design:
  A. system level;
  B. sub-system level;
- 9. interface definition;
- 10. schedule development;
- 11. preliminary cost-analysis;
- 12. technical performance measurement;
- 13. trade-off/alternative analysis;
- 14. pre-planned product improvement;
- 15. final design:
  A. system level;
  B. sub-system level;
- 16. schedule update;
- 17. cost update;
- 18. fabrication;
- 19. coding;
- 20. preliminary testing;
- 21. debugging and reconfiguration;
- 22. testing and integration;
- 23. updates:
  A. schedule;
  B. cost;
  C. technical performance measurement;
- 24. documentation;
- 25. training;
- 26. production.

The US government's 'Systems engineering management guide' [14] describes the process in detail. Eisner presents a graphic look at the process in Fig. 1.

In terms of the four major *time dimensions* identified above, systems engineering is concerned with all phases of the systems design and development process. Systems engineers are concerned with the pre-development phase, especially as it pertains to the identification and verification of system requirements. Systems engineers design and develop prototypes during the initial (and subsequent) development phases, especially as they pertain to the operation and modification of systems. Systems engineers are even concerned with the decommissioning of systems as decommissioned systems are the springboard to new generation systems.

The *activities* taxonomy maps directly onto the systems engineering process. Systems engineers are at once scientists, technologists and managers. In practice, of course, it is difficult to find such talent in one or two professionals.

The intersection of technical and managerial activities presumes the conversion of requirements into working systems. The systems engineering process represents the integration and synthesis of tools, techniques, methods and findings for the explicit purpose of fielding operational systems.

One of the key differences between software engineering and systems engineering is the extent to which managerial activities are pursued and integrated with technical ones. Whereas software engineers worry a great deal about software project management, they tend to restrict their concern to those technical activities connected with the design and development of software. The systems engineer, even for a software-intensive system, worries about all the system components and how to manage their technical development.

### *3.2 Time and activities scope of software engineering*

When we look at the *time scope* of software engineering, it is no surprise to find that its focus is on the initial phase, with emerging interest in the pre-development time frame. *Pre-development* (including needs analysis, requirements analysis, project planning etc. that go on before technical development can begin) is a phase in the systems life-cycle in which software engineers are becoming increasingly involved (a phase, as suggested above, that has preoccupied systems engineering since its inception). The methods of software engineering are intended to assist in those aspects of the requirements engineering process that deal with software, especially when it comes to validating those requirements and turning them into technical specifications that trigger technical development.

*Initial development* is the phase in the life-cycle of a system in which it first comes into 'tangible' being. In the case of software-intensive systems, this typically involves turning requirements into software specifications, creating architectural and detailed designs for the software systems, programming, testing, and integration of the software, not only internally, but also with the hardware.

The *operation and modification* phase in a system's life-cycle is not addressed by software engineering, except with respect to the modification of existing systems about which it has a good deal to say.

*Decommissioning* of software-intensive systems for the most part is a relatively trivial phase (as far as the software aspect is concerned) and one of which there is very little experience. Software engineering does not address this phase of a system's life-cycle.

When we turn to the range of *activities* encompassed by software engineering, the situation is not as clear, at least in part because non-technical activities tend to be ill defined.

In the area of purely managerial activities, software engineering provides the mechanisms for dealing with project resources in some cases (estimation techniques, configuration management, performance measurement), but does not (for the most part) address how those mechanisms should be used in the overall organisation of a project. The one exception to this is in the area of technical project management, where specific techniques and models of the software development process are often

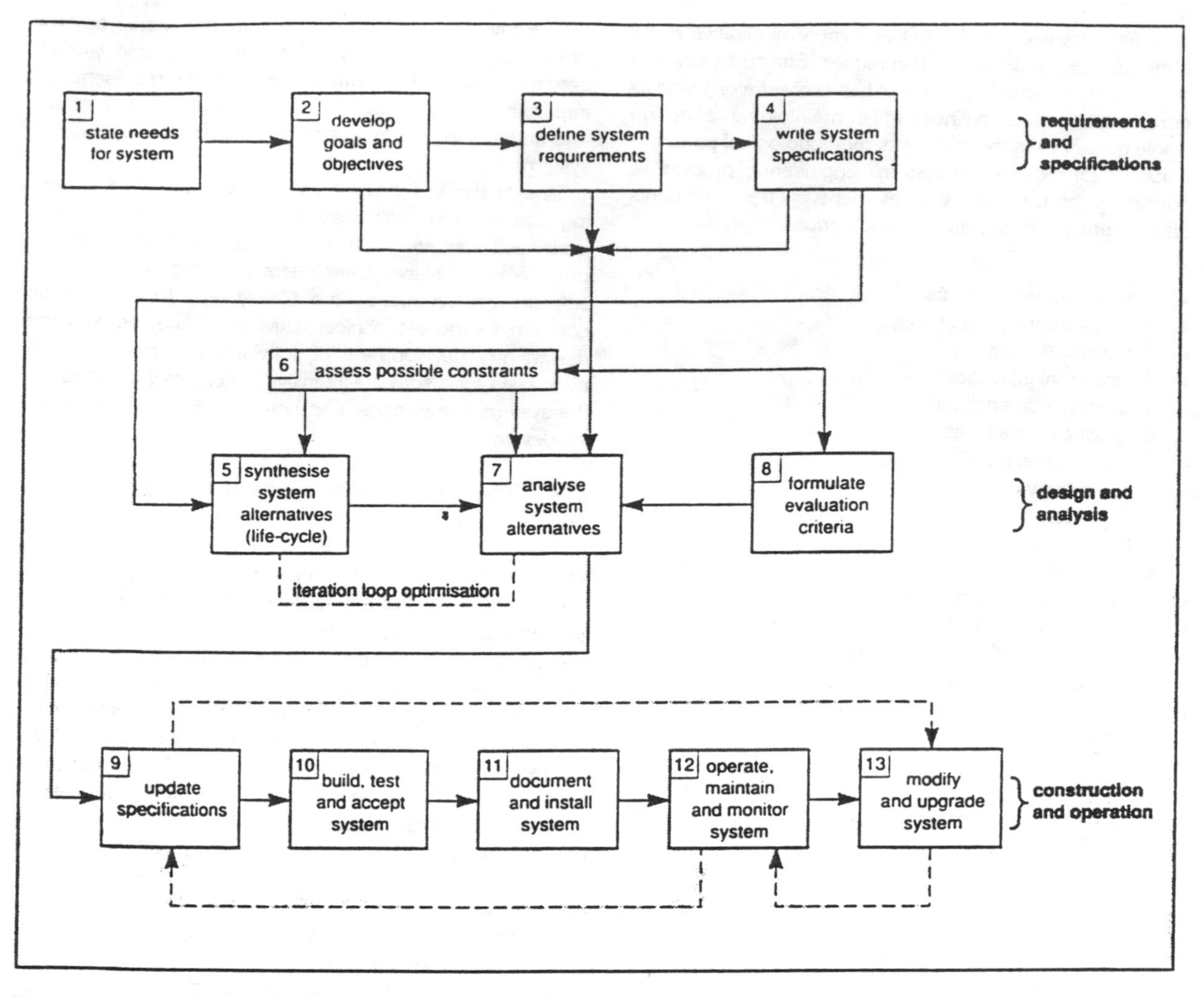


**Fig. 1 Generic systems engineering process [5]**

incorporated into elements of the software engineering discipline.

When we look at the ancillary/mixed activities, we find that software engineering does not, for example, address general issues of training, but clearly incorporates work on training software engineers. In the case of requirements engineering, acceptance testing and work on non-technical work products, software engineering as a discipline tries to deal with such activities from the technical aspect, without claiming total purview. In the area of support, software engineering involvement ranges from almost total in the case of tools to nothing in the case of travel or physical space planning.

A major theme of software engineering (in its short history) has been the search for the 'right' development life-cycle model to guide the process of creating software. The most widely known is the so-called 'waterfall' model shown in Fig. 2. First introduced by Royce [15] and popularised by Boehm [11], it describes the generic process that many software engineers follow, at least to some extent. Much criticism of the waterfall model has ensued, however, which has resulted in more refined models. One of the more popular of these, also from Boehm [16], is shown in Fig. 3. Boehm's 'spiral model' stresses prototyping and risk assessment, two relatively new concepts to software engineering (although quite familiar for decades to systems engineers).

### 3.3 *Comparative scopes*

Fig. 4 compares the level of involvement of software engineering and systems engineering over the time frame of a system's life. Of particular interest here is the relative emphasis that systems engineering places on the front-end requirements analysis, modelling and validation processes (often via prototyping). Systems engineers tend to spend much more time and effort on requirements than software engineers, although it is certainly true that software engineers have begun to appreciate the importance of needs analysis, user requirements modelling, and organisational requirements profiling.

## 4 Structure of the disciplines

One means of analysing and understanding a discipline is to look at its structural parts, its *processes* and *objects*. It is also useful to consider *constraints*, *paradigms* and *principles*.

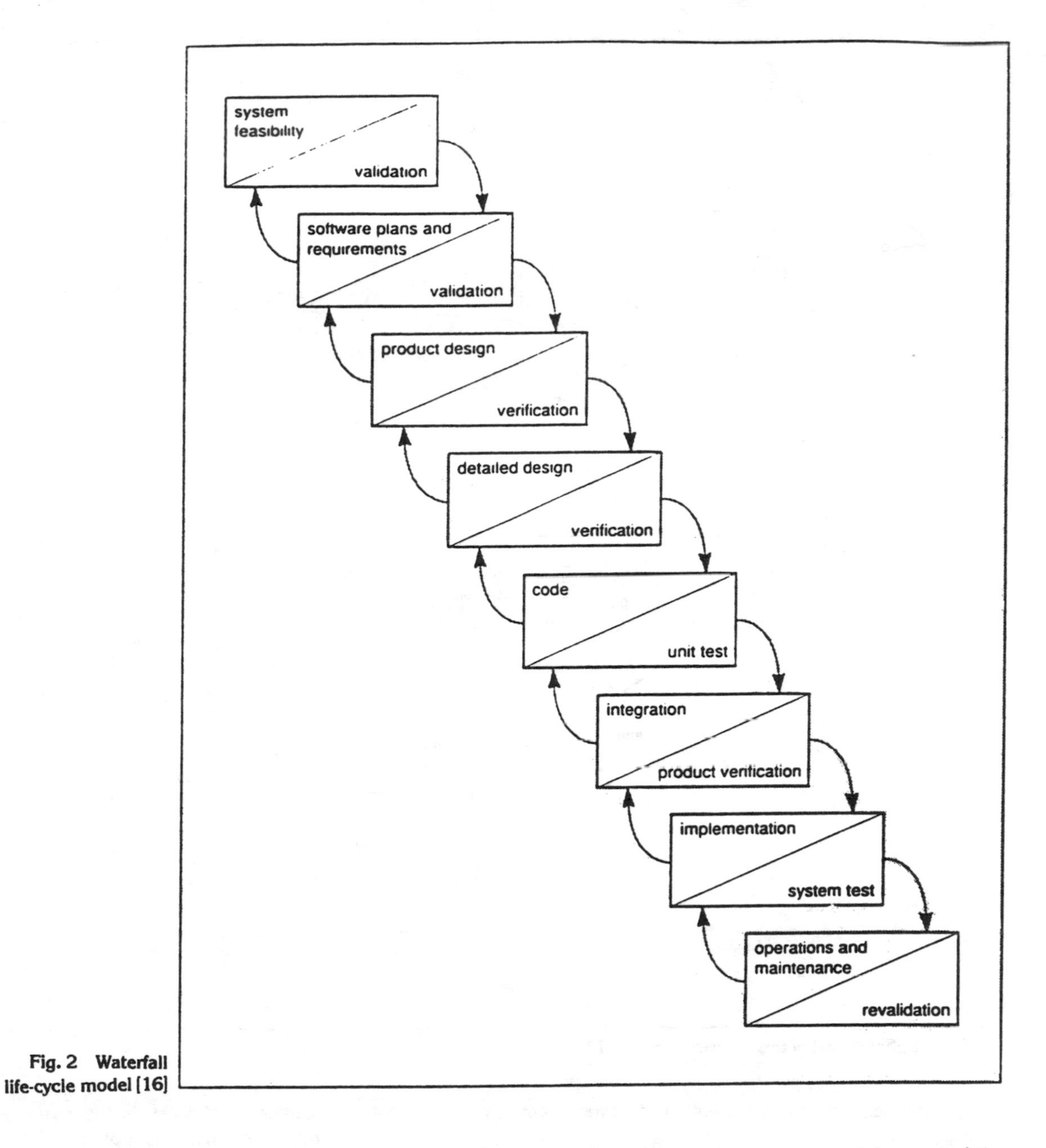


**Fig. 2 Waterfall life-cycle model [16]**

### *4.1 Systems engineering structure*

Fig. 1 from Eisner [5] presents the generic *systems engineering* process, which is reduced to three major activities: requirements and specifications, design and analysis, and construction and operation. Eisner suggests that the system engineering process is inextricably tied to technical project management, as proposed in Fig. 5. Note that Eisner locates the generic systems engineering process between technical program planning and control and a set of engineering speciality areas.

As suggested above, systems engineering is domain-independent and -driven. The systems engineering process, with its attendant 'principles' (see below), can be applied to transportation, space, weapons, command and control, urban, and, of course, information and software systems engineering problems.

The intersection between management and technology also often poses problems. What plays well in the technical 'trenches' often violates some managerial *constraints*. Systems engineers have difficulty with projecting precisely how much time and money it will take to implement design A over design B. It is also sometimes difficult to 'size up' from a prototype to a working system.

What are the systems engineering 'watchwords', the key influential *principles*? The first principle is system and user requirements specification. Multidisciplinary systems engineering (MSE) calls for the identification, definition and validation of requirements on multiple levels that suggest how requirements interrelate and how they might be satisfied through design. Note again that this is a pre-design principle.

Another key principle is iteration or the recognition that it is impossible to capture requirements the first time through a system concept. MSE assumes the need for iteration, in all phases of the design and development process. Rapid prototyping assumes the need to iterate on user requirements, alternative system concepts, software

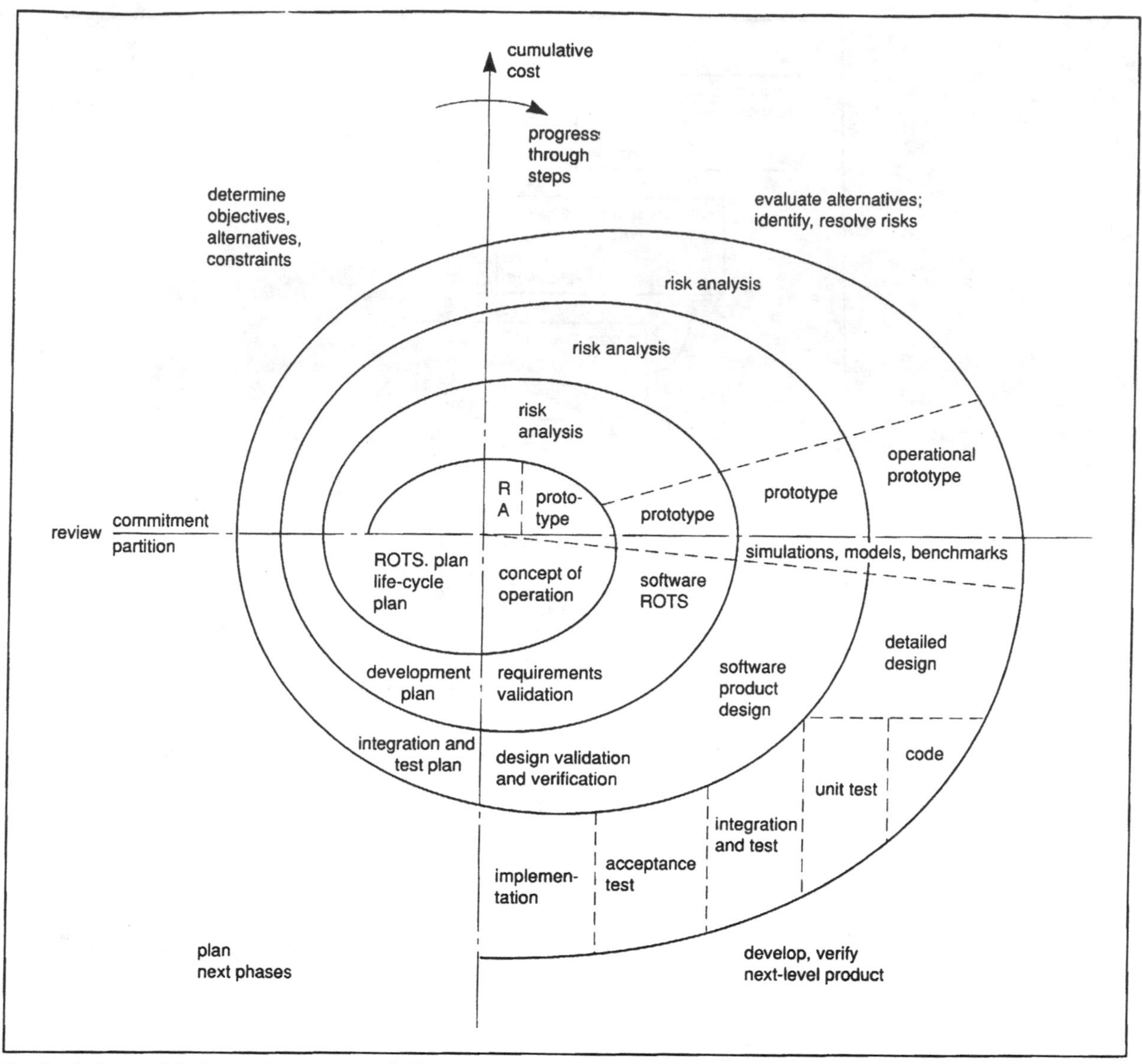


**Fig. 3 Spiral model of the software process [11]**

requirements, testing and evaluation and even documentation.

Yet another key concept is synthesis or the ability to integrate disparate components into a coherent cost-effective whole greater than the sum of the components. The process of creative synthesis has been described elsewhere [17] but not formally represented. Although there are steps that suggest what and where to synthesise elements of the design, there are far fewer guidelines for instructing the information systems engineer about how to proceed. Nevertheless, synthesis remains an important part of the MSE process and one that is well suited to a multidisciplinary perspective.

Trade-off analysis is always part of the MSE process. The mix among requirements, constraints and alternative designs yields a continuous need to evaluate, prioritise, and test. Which interface should we use and why? Why not use the other one? What about the software language; why C and not Ada? Which requirement is more important and why? How do we rank requirements? How do we weigh the importance of the evaluative criteria?

Last, but certainly not least, is the essential need to remain as multidisciplinary as possible. This calls for expertise that cuts across the social, behavioural, computer, mathematical, engineering, management, and even physical sciences. Note, however, that information systems engineers cannot be expected to know all there is to know about these fields and disciplines; an attitude that accepts contributions, regardless of their disciplinary race, creed or religion, is what keeps the door open to creative problem-solving. Systems engineers whose staff are clones of themselves will fail far more often than when their staff are from backgrounds of diverse experience and opinion. Maintaining inventories of analytical methods organised around the MSE cycle is another good idea. The key is to make certain that you have looked beyond the obvious or what you have done (over and over again) before; analytical inertia is not necessarily your friend.

The working *paradigm* is not Kuhnian [18] in a strict sense, nor is it easily definable from any perspective. Systems engineers practise a process that is iterative, multidisciplinary and flexible. They borrow from many

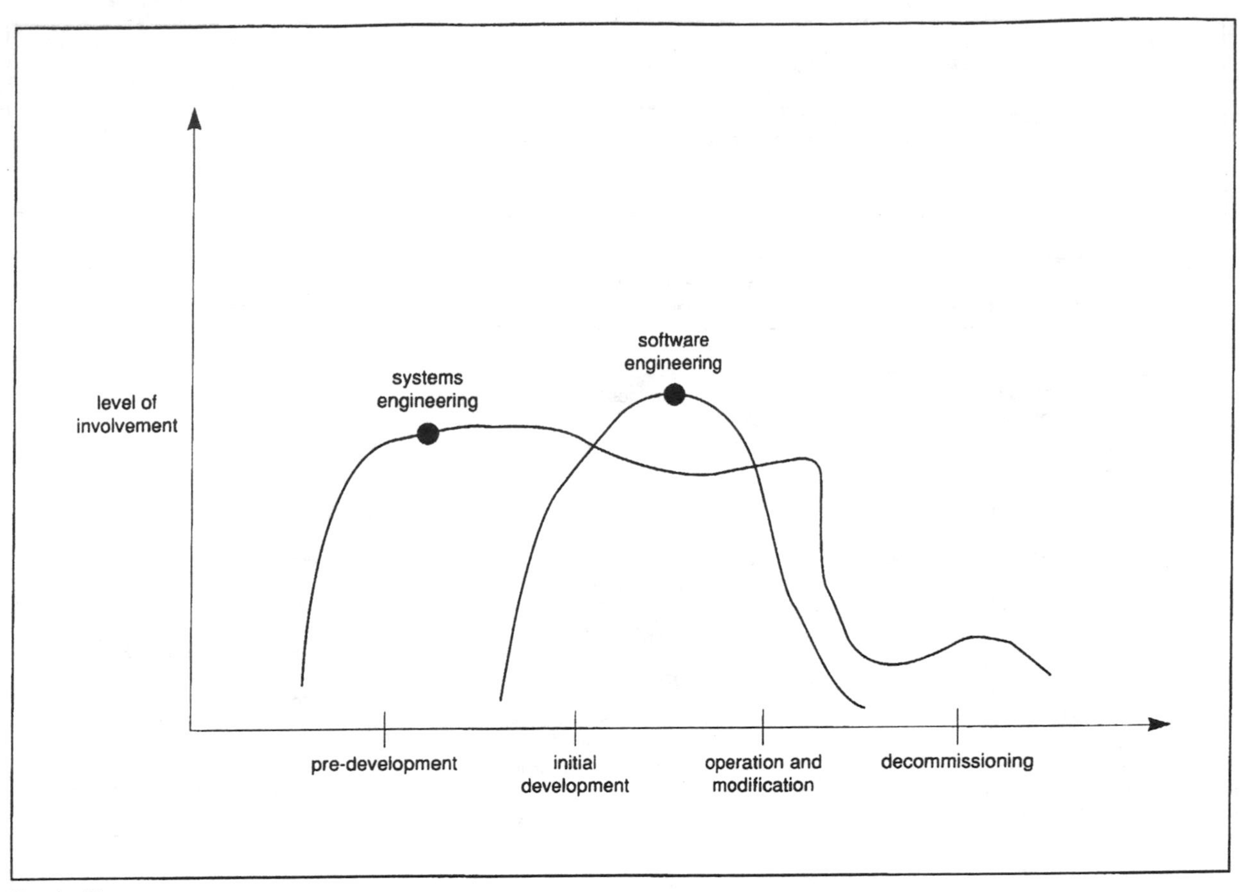


**Fig. 4 Time scope**

fields and disciplines. Their creed is essentially practical, although they respect the need for basic research to keep their applied tools honed.

### *4.2 Software engineering structure*

A widely used software engineering textbook [1] implicitly specifies the *processes* of software engineering:

- needs analysis
- requirements analysis
- specification
- architectural design
- detailed design
- programming
- unit testing
- integration testing
- management
- documentation
- performance analysis
- program analysis.

The Ada Methodman study, which represented the thinking of many people in the US Department of Defense world at that time, identified eight basic processes of software development:

- ☐ analysis
- ☐ functional specification
- ☐ design
- ☐ implementation
- ☐ validation
- ☐ evolution
- ☐ management
- ☐ communication.

A more conceptual treatment [13] views all of software engineering as the following basic processes that manipulate representations:

- choose locale and operation.
- gather external information.
- change representation.
- extract information from representation.
- evaluate representation.

Lehman *et al.* [19] take a similar, but more formal, approach to model the processes of software engineering as a set of transformations. Likewise, Kerola [20] and those who have extended his work [21] focus on the intellectual activities that a system developer employs in the course of creating a system.

We try not to consolidate or reconcile these different views here. We can move forward with our structural analysis, however, by positing a set of 'basic' processes that capture the mainstream view of what is going on (at the technical level) in software engineering. They include

☐ *analysis*: understanding something by separating it into component parts.

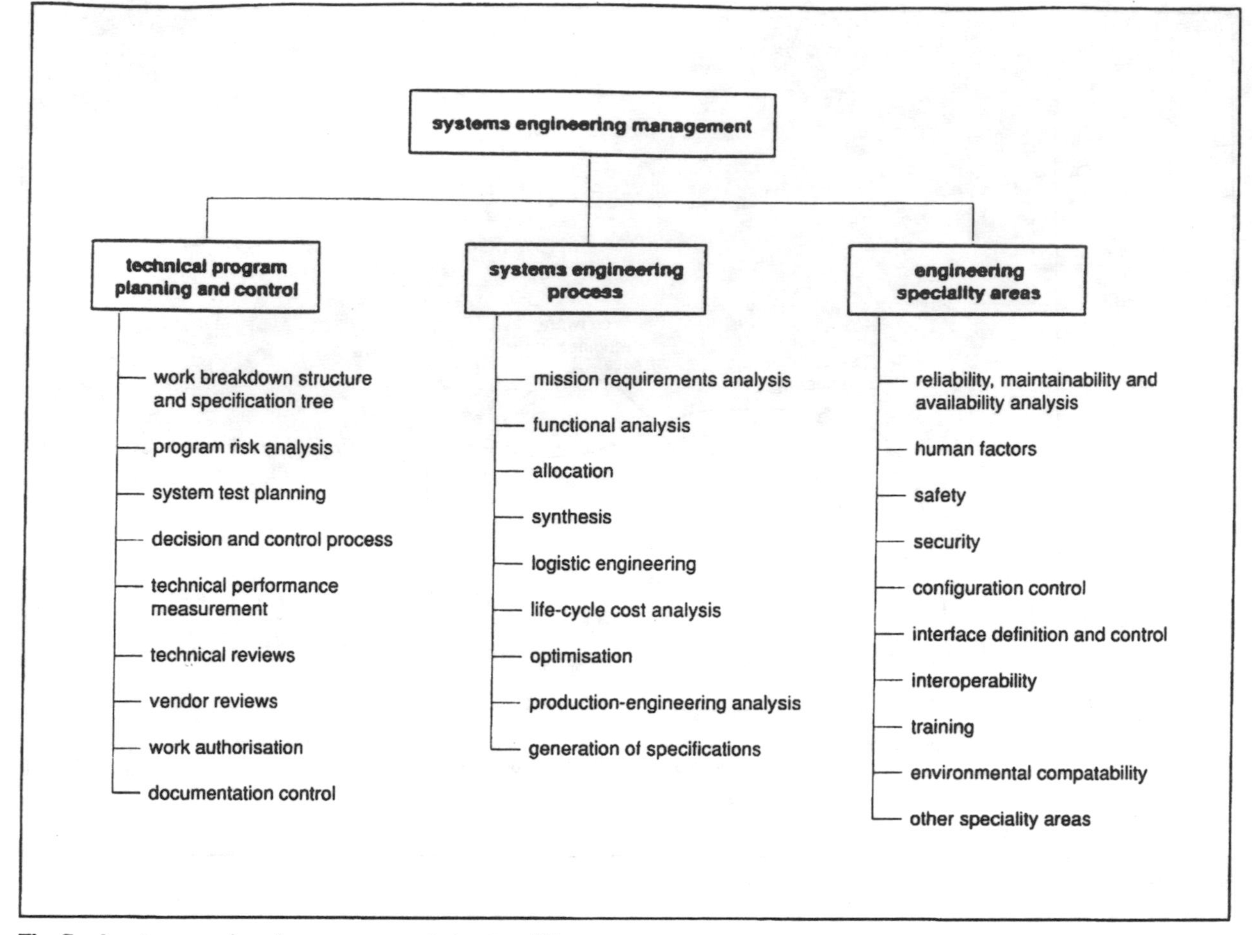


**Fig. 5 A systems engineering management structure [5]**

☐ *specification*: describing something by its external characteristics.
☐ *design*: devising an artifact that meets a set of objectives.
☐ *programming*: building a coherent set of instructions for a processor that will cause it to exhibit a desired behaviour.
☐ *testing*: determining empirically if an artifact meets a stated set of specifications.
☐ *verification*: determining if a step in the development process has been correctly carried out.
☐ *validation*: determining if a description of a system, or the system itself, properly meets the expectations of the customer.
☐ *modification (commonly called 'maintenance')*: making changes to an existing artifact.

A generally held view is that software engineering must address all of the *objects* of importance in the technical development of software, including (but not limited to) specifications, designs, programs, test results and project schedules. There is again active research underway concerned with devising effective repositories for all the 'project information' in development; this work is usually associated with work on development environments. As with processes, however, we can provide a schema for describing the objects that must be dealt with by software engineering:

- *development prologues*: needs statements, requirements specifications etc.
- *technical system descriptions*: specifications, designs, data descriptions etc.
- *system aggregations*: systems, integrated hardware and software etc.
- *installed systems*: base-line systems, versions etc.
- *derived information*: operating measurements, error reports etc.

A fundamental concern in any system of action is what are the constraints against the arbitrary application of processes to objects. In the case of software engineering, there are several generic constraints:

☐ incompleteness of most software representations.
☐ inaccuracy of many software representations.
☐ absence of robust models of standard systems.
☐ paucity of observed data concerning the results of software engineering processes.
☐ inability to observe many things of interest.
☐ incomplete and changing map between reality and models of reality.

As with the objects and processes of software engineering, the newness of the field and the relative sparsity of theoretical/conceptual work means that there is no widespread agreement on 'fundamental' *principles*. The following, however, would probably appear on most lists:

- modularity
- information-hiding
- abstraction
- step-wise refinement
- decomposition
- systematic processes.

Similarly, the *paradigms*, or overall patterns of action, of software engineering are limited at this juncture:

☐ reticulated, structured development (phases, defined work products, set relationships between activities).
☐ formal development (use of 'formal' methods wherever possible; not necessarily mutually exclusive of other paradigms).
☐ evolving development (use of prototypes; continual development).
☐ kernel development (starting with a small, central core of functionality and mechanisms, grow the desired system by accretion of additional mechanisms).

## 5 Depth of the disciplines

*Systems engineering* comprises a core process, the systems engineering technical and management life-cycle, surrounded by all of the fields and disciplines recognised by modern analytical scientists. Its depth is very much a function of the depth of the systems engineers assigned to a problem.

As a formal field, it is important to note that 'real' engineers (mechanical, electrical, chemical) sometimes wonder where systems engineering fits in the overall engineering continuum. 'Peterson's Guide to Engineering' does not place systems engineering in the engineering section; rather, systems engineering finds itself in the same section as operations research and industrial engineering.

Whereas we can date systems engineering back to the 1950s, its actual practice has come and gone over the years; there have been countless large-scale systems development projects that did not embrace the generic systems engineering (nor, for that matter, any) life-cycle. At the same time, perhaps because of some monumental failures, there is a growing appreciation for structured design and development. One measure is the number of undergraduate and graduate programs now in existence and the popularity of these programs; at the University of Virginia, for example, the systems engineering problem is the largest undergraduate program in the engineering school.

One of the problems with this field is the fear that it educates and trains professionals who are 'a mile wide and an inch deep', i.e. in its attempt to introduce as many disciplines as possible into the systems engineering process, the field has become too diffuse and too broad. Our view is that the broad, multidisciplinary perspective is precisely the strength of the field, and that practitioners who are truly free from the biases inherent in single-discipline-based solutions will always make the best problem-solvers.

As we have observed, *software engineering* is still a developing field. Specifically, there is very little 'theory' in the sense of compact, rigorous, potentially verifiable descriptions of the essence of software engineering; very little objective data on the results of 'doing' software engineering; essentially no data describing the artifacts that are produced nor multiple paradigms for software engineers to follow; and disagreement over the value of many elements of the field. Software engineering is thus very early in its evolutionary development. Only a few ideas have been adopted and later discarded, although a few (such as structured programming) have been relegated to a position of less importance as their role became better understood. In the area of life-cycle or process modelling, there has also been a maturing in the understanding of what is needed, but in most of the technical methods of producing software, we are still dealing with first-generation ideas. (There is also disagreement over what the research agenda should contain.)

Sophistication of a field can also be evaluated in terms of the use of existing knowledge from outside the field (such as mathematics or computer science), the degree of dependence on results from other parts of the field, and the degree to which the constructs of the field address the subject matter. In this area, software engineering must also be ranked as unsophisticated (especially as compared to systems engineering, which openly trades on a multidisciplinary perspective).

Although a software engineer may use computer science extensively, the techniques of software engineering (such as structuring a system to enhance maintainability or organising testing on the basis of expected systemic payoff) do not rely heavily on any outside field. Advancement in different parts of software engineering, likewise, tend not to be too interdependent. Although we might think that producing new computer-aided software engineering (CASE) tools would be closely tied to our understanding of the nature and value of different design methods, this is not normally what happens. The last point, of how well software engineering addresses its subject, is one that must at this time (due to the lack of objective data) be largely subjective. The strongly held belief of some (including ourselves) is that the methods and principles of software engineering, when properly applied, make a significant difference and thus *do* address the problems the field is supposed to be addressing. Despite the numerous anecdotes and some quantitative data, we are nowhere near being able to assert the value of software engineering in the same way that medical science can assert the value of certain treatment protocols or drugs.

We have already noted that software engineering is not nearly as widely used as it might seem or as even the meagre objective data would indicate is sensible. A recent anonymous letter to the editor of *Software*, commenting on a previous article, provides an insight to a situation which is probably more widespread than most would care to admit:

'*This project is represented to the public as state-of-the-art defense, but the simulation (and much other design) work is done in Fortran, a language originally conceived before I could drive (I'm 50 now). It runs on an operating system that was conceived before my son was (and he's a junior in dental school). It is administered by a DP group that let the default file-compare program exist for years with a known error that caused it to report no differences for files that were in fact different. It is used by engineers who are rewarded for finding and using workarounds to get the job done rather than for fixing the real problems.'*

In short, along the dimension of *usage*, software engineering is not yet very deep.

## 6 Requirements for a discipline to be used in the creation of software-intensive systems

The requirements for a basic and applied discipline to optimally support the design, development, testing and maintenance of software-intensive systems are many and varied. Those that we regard as essential include the following:

- the ability to indicate common alternatives for the elements of a design process over which one may have control; for example, by indicating types of design methods that can be used for detailed design or specifying what information should formally be provided to developers.
- the ability to force alternative problem-solving methods, tools and techniques onto the design process, to remain multidisciplinary in the face of single-minded solutions.
- the ability to identify, model and validate (especially user) requirements to an extent that permits communication to users and conversion to alternative forms, such as diagrams and prototypes.
- the ability to provide the means (including norms from practice) for choosing among alternatives; for example, by providing criteria that permit us to match design methods to specific types of applications, or by providing indications of current practice in building information repositories for development.
- the ability to specify in great detail, and from multiple notations, software requirements in adaptive, flexible specifications; the ability to utilise to their fullest potential available methods, techniques and computer-based tools.
- the ability to influence optimal software production methods, techniques and tools, including variants of structured programming, CASE and other environments.
- the ability to provide guidance for utilising elements, for example, by indicating how to put together multiple design methods for a complex task and what to do when they are insufficient.
- the ability to clearly delineate what subjects belong in curricula, both basic and applied, for educating/training members of the discipline; for example, by indicating that the study of design methods is included in the discipline, whereas study of the basic mathematics that may underlie them belongs to another discipline.
- the ability to characterise the artifacts that are produced by applying the discipline, both in theoretical and empirical terms; for example, designs that can be characterised in terms of prescribed properties and in terms of what is found to exist in practice.
- the ability to indicate the range and characteristics of problems (objectives) with which the approach is prepared to deal; for example, by delimiting design problems to those involving the design of software and procedures, but excluding those concerned with the design of business organisations.
- the ability to provide measures and standards by which the artifacts produced and the processes utilised can be measured; for example, by providing measurable quality criteria for a design, along with expected norms for those criteria.
- the ability to review its own theory and practice to feed the processes of metrics development, research agenda setting, and educational and training program development.

The assumption made here is that it is possible to define a field in terms of activity/process/object-based requirements; the above list attempts to develop such a set of 'living' requirements.

## 7 Comparative advantages and suggested syntheses

Table 1 shows how well (or badly) systems engineering and software engineering currently satisfy the above requirements. We have used a simple (H/high, M/medium, L/low) scaling of the state of each discipline's capabilities. Much more importantly, however, the Table was developed to assist in the synthesis of strengths from the two disciplines. (The two *major* differences are highlighted in ***bold italic***; '*minor*' differences are in **bold** only.)

It is interesting that the most diagnostic requirements for software systems engineering appear to be those that address the front-end of the systems design and development process. This is consistent with the findings of a number of field studies of why systems fail and with perceptions of major problems with the requirements analysis, modelling, prototyping and verification processes; problems that systems engineers have recognised, and addressed, for years. Where structured criteria-based qualitative and quantitative trade-off analysis has been an essential part of the systems engineering process, it is only considered critical to a handful of today's software engineers.

This 'finding' is extremely important as (perhaps harshly) it can be said that software engineers have not (lip service to the contrary) spent a great deal of time on front-end system and user requirements identification, definition, or validation. Instead, there has been a desire to 'get coding' as soon as possible. Consequently, there are a large number of 'failures' that can be traced directly to inadequate requirements analyses. Software engineers have also historically avoided the systematic development and evaluation of alternative definitions and designs throughout the software engineering process. Criteria-based alternative design evaluation, for example, is seldom conducted by software engineers; nor is there much emphasis on prioritising requirements with reference to constraints in formal (or even informal) trade-off analyses. All such activity is automatic to systems engineering; without such activity, software engineers risk proceeding prematurely to design and coding (as has often been the case).

Table 1 also suggests the ranges of methods, tools and techniques from systems and software engineering that can complement one another, which can together create a

**Table 1 Systems software engineering comparative advantages**

| | System engineering | Software engineering |
|---|---|---|
| Alternative design methods | H | M |
| Multidisciplinary orientation | *H* | *L* |
| User requirements analysis and prototyping | *H* | *L* |
| Criteria-based trade-off analysis | *H* | *L* |
| Detailed software specifications | M | H |
| Optimal software production | M | H |
| Methods integration (re-)planning | M | L |
| Education and training curricula | M | M |
| Artifact profiling | M | M |
| Applications range assessment | M | M |
| Measurements and standards | M | M |
| Processes/metrics introspection | M | M |

more powerful discipline for converting requirements into cost-effective software-intensive systems. This is important because there are many methods, processes, models and computer-based tools that software engineers tend to overlook, and *vice versa*. The Table suggests that we look at each discipline's strengths and identify the methods, tools, processes, and techniques that explain its comparative advantage; where appropriate, these methods, models, processes, tools and techniques can be invited onto the software systems engineering team.

## 8 Software systems engineering

Our working premise remains that solutions are more easily found in broad disciplinary perspectives, rather than through narrow analytical lenses. The above analysis suggests that there will be benefits in adopting and synthesising the tools and techniques of systems engineering and software engineering, to yield a more powerful and adaptive approach to systems analysis, design, development, evaluation, and maintenance of software-intensive systems. For example, note that reference to systems analysis and design itself represents an expansion of the traditional role of software engineers, just as the maintenance of software-intensive systems is an activity outside the expertise of the typical systems engineer.

In the following, we outline the new discipline at this particular point in time, a snapshot of what it is, what it can do, its concerns, and how it should help prepare those who will perpetuate its application and evolution. The following sections thus address the conceptual, operational, educational and research bases for software systems engineering.

### *8.1 The conceptual basis*

One of the major differences between what we propose here and more conventional definitions of disciplines or fields of inquiry is its explicit commitment to practice, research *and* education. Many disciplines evolved from some key ideas, models or theorems, usually after some exotic applications, and over time developed educational correlates. Some fields and disciplines have remained largely in academia, with relatively short, applied track records. We propose here to think about software systems engineering simultaneously as a practical, educational and research enterprise in order to enhance its relevance in all three theatres.

Fig. 6 shows the proposed conceptual basis. It organises the disciplines according to its infrastructure, enabling technologies, application modules, issues in the practice, domains, and, by implication, the educational and research activities necessary to support the evolution and application of the discipline.

### *8.2 The operational basis*

Fig. 7 shows a proposed new life-cycle that integrates all of the above into a prescriptive agenda. It represents the disciplines, analytical foci, and procedural realities (such as iteration and prototyping) that must be part of the software-intensive systems design and development process.

This life-cycle bears a resemblance to Boehm's spiral model [16] as a graphical device to represent the fact that the software systems engineer must make multiple passes through similar activities (concept development, prototyping, specification, design, implementation in the next level of technology). It also can trace some heritage back to Kerola [20] and others who first observed that system development involves a set of basic activities, such as planning, design, implementation, and testing, all of which are in operation (to some extent) throughout the life-cycle, being repeated with different emphases and contexts.

Looking down the time axis, the four quadrants represent four major collections of system development activities: goal setting, planning, design and construction. Each of these is an abstraction for a myriad of development activities, some of which span two quadrants. Depending on the position on the time axis, these activities take on different specific meanings. For example, needs analysis (labelled here as a 'goal setting' activity) at early stages of development is concerned with understanding the needs of the entire context in which a proposed system will be

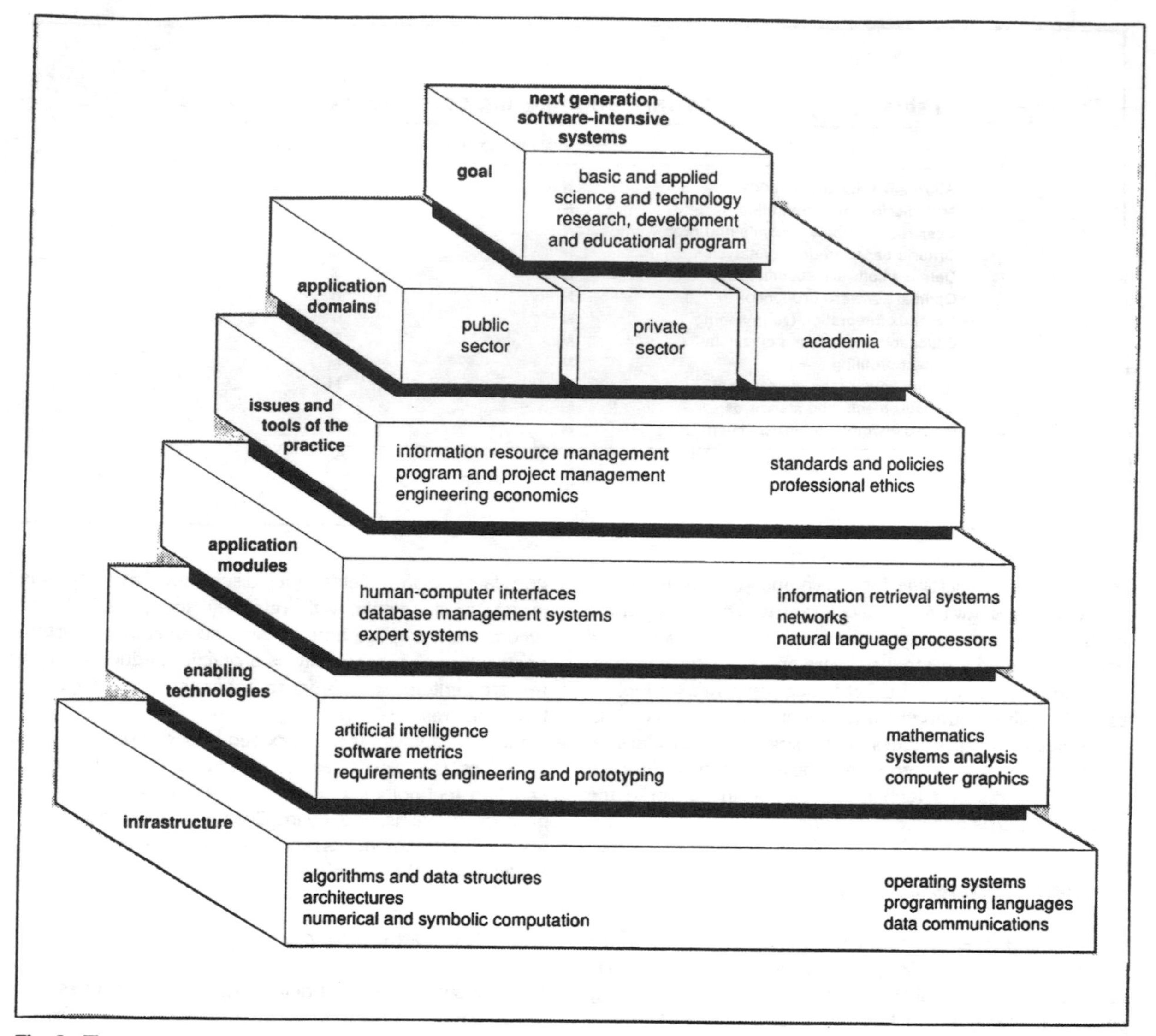


**Fig. 6 The conceptual basis of software systems engineering,**

embedded (thus involving potential owners, clients, users and operators of the system). At later stages of development, however, the needs analysis activities might be concerned with determining the needs of a VDT operator (thus involving psychologists, terminal operators and medical experts).

The following definitions are intended to provide a non-exclusive outline of the activities that might be found in each quadrant.

☐ *Goal setting* includes enterprise analysis, mission 'planning', needs analysis and most of the activities often associated with requirements engineering. Goal setting is front-end intensive and oriented to most aspects of the initial requirements analysis process.

☐ *Planning* includes those activities that focus on or directly affect a large amount of development work, until the next planning phase appears in the life-cycle. This includes prototyping, which provides fundamental information to help us decide how to proceed, project planning, which lays out detailed work schedules, and specification activities, which provide the detailed 'work orders' for future work.

☐ *Design* includes those activities that devise the structures (orgnisational, hardware of all sorts, software, procedural) which, when implemented, will provide the suitably constrained functionality needed to meet the goals. We differentiate between high-level (architectural) and detailed design. Crossing into the construction realm are those activities concerned with individual components. In the case of software, this is the detailed programming activity.

☐ *Construction* activities include the various levels of testing which range from unit or component testing to acceptance or field testing. The various activities involved in measuring a system's performance and effects are included in this quadrant.

In the three-dimensional solid described by this life-cycle, different fields of expertise and different people can be seen to touch different quadrants at different levels (times). The volumes thus described are, of course, highly irregu-

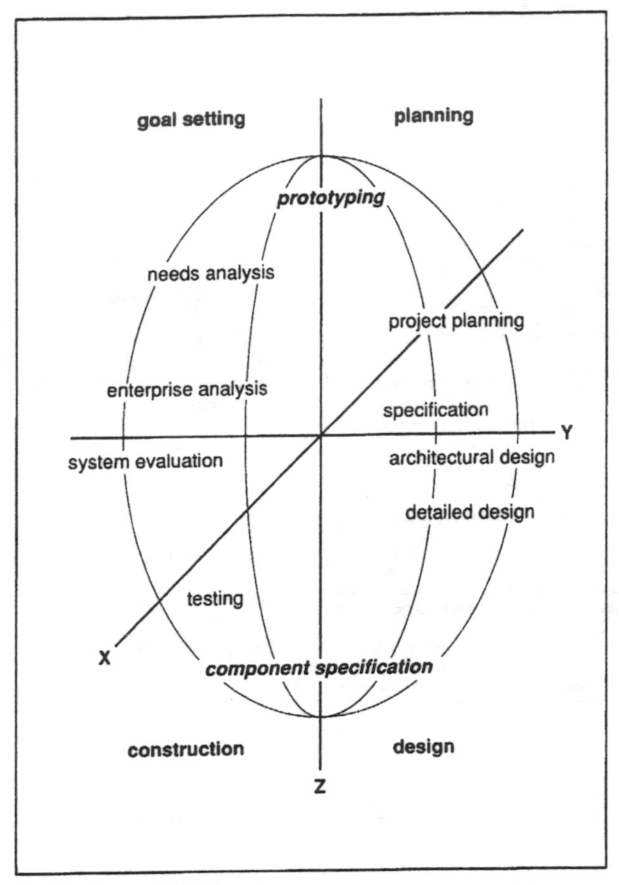


**Fig. 7 Integrated life-cycle**

lar. For example, psychology (in a broad sense) might come into play in the early stages of goal setting by providing an insight into the workings of a large organisation and the potential effects of a new software-intensive way of doing business; at a later stage by providing detailed parameters for VDT formats; and during operation of a system, by providing us with the methodology for evaluating the effect of a system on its clients.

Progress over time in creating, operating and modifying a software-intensive system is represented by a spiral path downward through the solid. Although such a path can represent the 'centroid' of project activity over time, it is important to remember that a complex system will involve many (perhaps thousands) of people whose activities may be spread over a large volume of the model.

Operationally, software systems engineering will encompass an egg-shaped solid centred on the Z-axis of this model. On a linear scale, this volume of activities will be centred rather high up on the Z-axis as, once a system is fully operational, the involvement decreases rapidly (except when major modifications are needed). Likewise, the extent of the activities in the X-Y plane is not regular, reaching out during certain activities to include other expertise and contracting in other places. Overall, however, the extent of activities carried out by the software systems engineer is limited at the start, expands to a maximum during design and construction of the actual system, and tapers off once the system is fully operational and modifications have either ceased or decreased to a very low level.

### 8.3 The educational basis

The kind of educational programs necessary to sustain the discipline are today not in place. Although there are certainly institutions with broad perspectives, there are far too many institutions working well within conventional disciplinary boundaries. One of our key assumptions is that the nature of emerging software-intensive problems demands new educational programs. We believe that it will be impossible for narrowly defined disciplines to address problems that are moving more towards analytical content and away from data-oriented transactional content. Unfortunately, the nature of education and educational institutions makes change very slow.

We propose that software systems engineers should be educated using a new core program and a set of electives that crosscuts the requisite disciplines. Such a curriculum should follow the conceptual and operational bases for the field as outlined above, incorporating elements of traditional systems engineering, software engineering, behavioural, management and computer science, as well as the mathematical and engineering fundamentals necessary to those disciplines.

An essential characteristic of the curriculum is that it must prepare the student for life-long learning in and communication with other disciplines, such as management, psychology and the various traditional engineering fields. Another important aspect of the proposed curriculum is that it must be heavily experiential, focusing on the application of formal knowledge in the context of realistic development exercises.

### 8.4 The research basis

The research agenda should take two forms; one is a 'maintenance' agenda comprising the continuation of the fundamental research issues and questions in the discipline, and the other pushes the state-of-the-practice and the state-of-the-expectation. Fig. 8 identifies these items. The two-tier research agenda addresses the immediate and longer term futures. Like the life-cycle and the educational program, it must be flexible and adaptive to changing applications needs and emerging technology opportunities.

Fig. 8 identifies a set of research aims organised around the conceptual basis of the field presented in Fig. 7. Short-term research aims are 'maintenance' areas, and the longer term ones are part 'wish list' and part necessity. Note also that there is at least one area that appears on both lists; human–computer interaction research. There may well be others that need our immediate and continual attention.

The sort-term list includes areas such as systems and user requirements modelling, the codification of existing basic and applied knowledge, the development of quality metrics, the improvement of our evaluation and testing methods and tools, research into real-time software-intensive systems design and development, the development of computer-aided software systems engineering (CASSE) tools, and research into the promise of conceptual and algorithmic reuse etc. The longer term research goals include the development of interoperability protocols, procedures for optimal multiprocessing program-

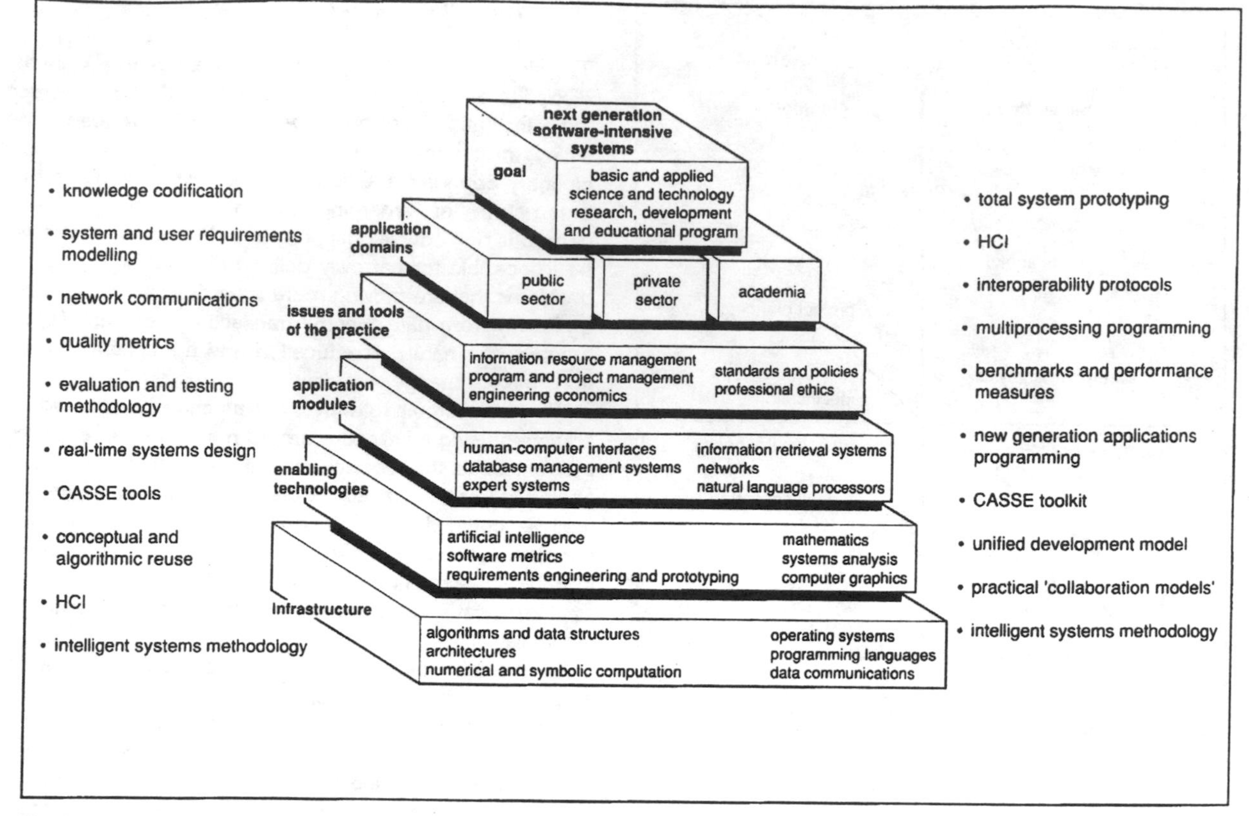


**Fig. 8 A research agenda**

ming, the development of a full-blow CASSE tool kit, a 'unified development model' etc.

These lists will, of course, change over time as new ideas are developed and others fall by the wayside. New hardware technology will also alter the list, as will breakthroughs in software productivity, prototyping and end-user computing.

## 9 Concluding remarks

We have provided an analysis of the fields of systems engineering and software engineering along several dimensions. Based on these analyses and our experience in all aspects of the fields, we have synthesised a case for a new field of software systems engineering. Although only in outline form here, we have provided the basis for conceptual, operational, educational and research activity in this new field. The simple message of this paper is that the systems problems of the coming decades will be software-intensive and they will demand results of these suggested activities.

## 10 Acknowledgments

Support for Dr. Andriole's research was provided by the Pennsylvania Ben Franklin Technology Center and Drexel University's College of Information Studies. Dr. Freeman's research was supported by the Virginia Center for Innovative Technology (CIT), the George Mason University Center for Software Systems Engineering and the Georgia Institute of Technology's College of Computing.

## 11 References

[1] PRESSMAN, R.S.: 'Software engineering: a practitioner's approach' (McGraw-Hill Book Co., New York, 1987) 2nd edn.

[2] CHESTNUT, H.: 'Systems engineering methods' (Wiley, New York, 1967)

[3] SAGE, A.P., and PALMER, J.D.: 'Software systems engineering' (John Wiley, New York, 1989)

[4] Department of Defense (DOD): 'Engineering management'. MIL-STD-499A (USAF), 1 May 1974, pp. 11–18

[5] EISNER, H.: 'Computer-aided systems engineering' (Prentice-Hall, Englewood Cliffs, New Jersey, 1988)

[6] BLANCHARD, K., and FABRYCKY, S.: 'System engineering' (Prentice-Hall, Englewood Cliffs, New Jersey, 1981)

[7] SAGE, A.P.: 'Methodology for large scale systems' (McGraw-Hill, New York, 1977)

[8] HALL, A.D.: 'Methodology for systems engineering' (Van Nostrand, Princeton, New Jersey, 1962)

[9] GOODE, H., and MACHOL, R.E.: 'Systems engineering: an introduction to the design of large scale systems' (McGraw-Hill, New York, 1957)

[10] NAUR, P., and RANDALL, B. (Eds.): 'Software engineering (report on a meeting held October 1968) NATO Science Committee, Brussels, Belgium, 1969

[11] BOEHM, B.W.: 'Software engineering', *IEEE Trans.*, 1976, **C-25**, (12), pp. 1226–1241

[12] MILLS, H.D.: 'Principles of software engineering', *IBM Syst. J.*, 1980, **19**, (4), pp. 414–420

[13] FREEMAN, P., and VON STAA, A.: 'Towards a theory of software engineering'. Working paper, Washington DC, November 1984 (available from PAF)

[14] Defense Systems Management College (DSMC): 'Systems engineering management guide' (Washington, DC, Fort Belvoir, 1986)

[15] ROYCE, W.: 'Managing the development of large software systems'. Proc. WESCON, August 1970

[16] BOEHM, B.W.: 'A spiral model of software development', *Computer*, 1988, (5), pp. 61–72

[17] SMITH, C.: 'Analytical methods for systems engineering' a taxonomy of analytical methods'. George Mason University, School of Information Technology and Engineering, 1988

[18] KUHN, T.S.: 'The structure of scientific revolutions' (Unviersity of Chicago Press, Chicago, 1970) 2nd edn.

[19] LEHMAN, M.M., STENNING, V., and TURSKI, W.M.: 'Another look at software design methodology', *SIGSOFT Softw. Eng. Notes*, 1984, **9**, (2), pp. 38–53

[20] KEROLA, P., and FREEMAN, P.A.: 'Comparison of lifecycle models'. Proc. 5th Int. Conf. on Software Engineering, IEEE Computer Society, Los Alamitos, California, 1981, pp. 90–99

[21] IIVARI, J., and KOSKELA, E.: 'The PIOCO model for IS design', *MIS Quarterly*, 1987, **11**, (3)

---



The paper was first received on 14 April 1992 and in revised form 11 January 1993.

Stephen J. Andriole is Director, Center for Multidisciplinary Information Systems Engineering, College of Information Studies, Drexel University, Philadelphia, PA 19104, USA; Peter A. Freeman is Dean, College of Computing, Georgia Institute of Technology, Atlanta, GA 30332-0280, USA.

# The Concept of Operations: The Bridge from Operational Requirements to Technical Specifications*

Richard E. Fairley
*Colorado Technical University*

Richard H. Thayer
*California State University, Sacramento*

## Abstract

This paper describes the role of a Concept of Operations (ConOps) document in specification and development of a software-intensive system. It also describes the process of developing a ConOps, its uses and benefits, who should develop it, and when it should be developed. The ConOps described in this paper is compared to other forms of operational concept documents. A detailed outline for ConOps documents is provided in an appendix to the paper.

## Introduction

The goal of software engineering is to develop and modify software-intensive systems that satisfy user needs, on schedule and within budget. Accurate communication of operational requirements from those who need a software-intensive system to those who will build the system is thus the most important step in the system development process. Traditionally, this information has been communicated as follows: The developer analyzes users' needs and buyer's requirements and prepares a requirements specification that defines the developers' understanding of those needs and requirements.[1] The users and buyer review the requirements specification and attempt to verify that the developer has correctly understood their needs and requirements. A draft users' manual is sometimes written by the developer to assist users and buyer in determining whether the proposed system will operate in a manner consistent with their needs and expectations. A prototype of the user interface may be constructed to demonstrate the developers' understanding of the desired user interface.

This traditional way of specifying software requirements introduces several problems: First, the buyer may not adequately convey the needs of the user community to the developer, perhaps because the buyer does not understand those needs. Second, the developer may not be expert in the application domain, which inhibits communication. Third, the users and buyer often find it difficult to understand the requirements produced by the developer. Fourth, the developer's requirements specification typically specifies system attributes such as functions, performance factors, design constraints, system interfaces, and quality attributes, but typically contains little or no information concerning operational characteristics of the specified system [ANSI/IEEE Std 830-1984]. This leaves the users and buyer uncertain as to whether the requirements specification describes a system that will provide the needed operational capabilities.

A draft version of the users' manual can provide some assurance that the developer understands user/buyer needs and expectations, but a draft version of the manual may not be written. If it is written, considerable time and effort have usually been spent by the time it is available for review. Major changes can require significant rework. Furthermore, it is difficult to demonstrate that the correspondences among technical specifications, users' manual, and (undocumented) operational requirements are complete and consistent.

A prototype of the user interface can be helpful, but there is a danger that demonstration of an acceptable user interface will be taken as assurance that the developer understands all of the users' operational needs. In summary, the traditional approach does not facilitate communication among users, buyer, and developer; nor does it emphasize the importance of specifying the operational requirements for the envisioned system.

---

* An ealier version of this paper appeared in *Annals of Software Engineering*, 1996.

1 Users are those who will interact with the new or modified system in the performance of their daily work activities; users include operators and maintainers. The buyer is a representative of the user community (or communities) who provides the interface between users and developer: the developer is the organization that will build (or modify) and deliver the system.

Concept analysis helps users clarify their operational needs, thereby easing the problems of communication among users, buyer, and developer. Development of a Concept of Operation document (ConOps) to record the results of concept analysis provides a bridge from user needs into the system development process. Ideally, concept analysis and development of the ConOps document are the first steps in the development process; however, (as discussed below) developing a ConOps at later stages of the system lifecycle is also cost-effective.

Subsequent sections of this paper describe the evolution of the ConOps technique, the concept analysis process, the Concept of Operations document, roles to be played by a ConOps, some guidelines on when and how to develop a ConOps, development scenarios and a process for developing the ConOps, the recommended format for a ConOps, and some issues concerning maintenance of a ConOps throughout the development process and the operational life of a software system.

## History of the ConOps Approach

One of the earliest reports on formalizing the description of operational concepts for a software system is contained in a 1980 TRW report by R.J. Lano: "A Structured Approach for Operational Concept Formulation" [TRW SS-80-02]. The importance of a well-defined operational concept (for example, definition of system goals, missions, functions, components) to the success of system development is emphasized in the report. The report presented tools, techniques, and procedures for more effectively accomplishing the system engineering tasks of concept formulation, requirements analysis and definition, architecture definition, and system design.

In 1985, the Joint Logistics Commanders' Joint Regulation "Management of Computer Resources in Defense Systems" was issued. This Joint Regulation included DoD-STD-2167, which contained a Data Item Description (DID) entitled "Operational Concept Document" (OCD) [DI-ECRS-8x25, DoD-Std-2167, 1985]. The purpose of this DID was to describe the mission of the system, its operational and support environments, and the functions and characteristics of the computer system within an overall system. The OCD DID was folded into the System/Segment Design Document [DI-CMAN-80534, DoD-Std-2167A, 1988] in the revised version of DoD-STD-2167 [DoD-Std-2167A].

Operational concepts were moved into Section 3 of the System/Segment Design Document (SSDD), which tended to place emphasis on overall system concepts rather than software concepts. Because the OCD was no longer a stand-alone document in 2167A, many users of 2167A did sufficiently emphasize operational concepts. For software-only projects, use of the SSDD was often waived. In these cases, there was no other place within the 2167A DIDs to record operational concepts for a software-intensive system. As a result, several other government agencies, including NASA and the Federal Aviation Administration, produced their own versions of the original 2167 DID for documenting operational concepts within the 2167A framework.

Another DoD standard, DoD-Std-7935A for development of information systems, required that the functional description of the proposed information system be contained in Section 2 of that document. The Functional Description in 7935A provided little guidance on how to develop a ConOps document; furthermore, it was very specific to the information systems domain, emphasized functionality only, and allowed little flexibility for new methods and techniques of software system development.

In recognition of the importance of well-defined operational concepts to successful development of a software system, Mil-Std 498 for Software Development and Documentation, which has replaced 2167A and 7935A, includes a Data Item Description for an Operational Concept Document (OCD). The authors of this paper played a leading role in developing the draft version of the Operational Concept Document (OCD) for the Harmonization Working Group that prepared Mil-Std-498. The OCD in Mil-Std 498 is similar to the ConOps outline contained in Appendix A of this paper. IEEE Standard 1498, the commercial counterpart of Mil-Std-498 (which currently exists in draft form) incorporates an OCD similar to the one in Appendix A.

The American Institute of Aeronautics and Astronautics (AIAA) published a document titled "Operational Concept Document (OCD) Preparation Guidelines" [AIAA OCD 1992]. The AIAA OCD compares favorably with the ConOps presented in this paper; however, in the opinion of this paper's authors, the tone and language used in the AIAA OCD is biased to the developer's view of user needs rather than the users' operational view. The AIAA OCD is also biased toward embedded, real-time systems.

A major goal for the ConOps presented here is to provide a means for users of information processing systems, who are knowledgeable in their application domain but not expert in software engineering, to describe their needs and wants from their point of view; in other words, the recommended Guide is more user-oriented than existing standards and guidelines, which tend to be systems-oriented and developer-oriented.

Another difference between existing standards and the ConOps recommended in this paper is that this paper emphasizes the importance of describing both the current system's and the proposed system's characteristics, even though that may result in some redundancy in the document. The advantages of redundancy are considered to outweigh the problems.

## The Concept Analysis Process

Concept analysis is the process of analyzing a problem domain and an operational environment for the purpose of specifying the characteristics of a proposed system from the users' perspective. The traditional system development process emphasizes functionality with little concern for how that functionality will be used. Concept analysis emphasizes an integrated view of a system and its operational characteristics, rather than focusing on individual functions or pieces of a system. A major goal of concept analysis is to avoid development of a system in which each individual function meets its specifications, but the system as a whole fails to meet the users' needs.

Concept analysis should be the first step taken in the overall system development process. It identifies the various classes of users and modes of operation,[2] and provides users with a mechanism for defining their needs and desires. Concept analysis is also useful to surface different users' (and user groups') needs and viewpoints, and to allow the buyer (or multiple buyers) to state their requirements for the proposed system. This process is essential to the success of the subsequent system development effort. Users have an opportunity to express their needs and desires, but they are also required to state which of those needs are essential, which are desirable, and which are optional. In addition, they must prioritize the desired and optional needs. Prioritized user needs provide the basis for establishing an incremental development process and for making trade-offs among operational needs, schedule, and budget.

Concept analysis helps to clarify and resolve vague and conflicting needs, wants, and opinions by reconciling divergent views. In the case where several user groups (or buyer groups) have conflicting needs, viewpoints, or expectations, concept analysis can aid in building consensus. In some cases, it may be determined that no single system can satisfy all of the divergent needs and desires of multiple user groups and buyer agencies. It is better to make that determination earlier rather than later.

Concept analysis is an iterative process that should involve various people. The analysis group should include representatives from the user, buyer, and developer organizations, plus any other appropriate parties such as training and operational support. In cases where a development organization has not been selected at the time of concept analysis, the developer role may be filled by in-house development experts or consultants.

The results of concept analysis are recorded in the ConOps document, which serves as a framework to guide the analysis process and provides the foundation document for all subsequent system development activities (analysis, design, implementation, and validation). The ConOps document should say everything about the system that the users and buyer need to communicate to those who will develop the system.

The ConOps document should be repeatedly reviewed and revised until all involved parties agree on the resulting document. This iterative process helps bring to the surface many viewpoints, needs, wants, and scenarios that might otherwise be overlooked.

## The Concept of Operations (ConOps) Document

The ConOps document describes the results of the conceptual analysis process. The document should contain all of the information needed to describe the users' needs, goals, expectations, operational environment, processes, and characteristics for the system under consideration. Essential elements of a ConOps include:

- A description of the current system or situation
- A description of the needs that motivate development of a new system or modification of an existing system
- Modes of operation for the proposed system
- User classes and user characteristics
- Operational features of the proposed system
- Priorities among proposed operational features
- Operational scenarios for each operational mode and class of user
- Limitations of the proposed approach
- Impact analysis for the proposed system

A detailed outline for a ConOps document containing these elements is provided in Appendix A to this paper.

---

2 Diagnostic mode, maintenance mode, degraded mode, emergency mode, and backup mode must be included, as appropriate, in the set of operational modes for a system environment, processes, and characteristics for the system under consideration.

A ConOps document should, in contrast to a requirements specifications, be written in narrative prose, using the language and terminology of the users' application domain. It should be organized to tell a story, and should make use of visual forms (diagrams, illustrations, graphs, and so forth) whenever possible. Although desirable, it is not necessary that the needs and wants expressed in a ConOps be quantified; that is, users can state their desire for "fast response" or "reliable operation." These desires are quantified during the process of mapping the ConOps to the requirements specification and during the flow-down of requirements to the system architecture. During system development, the impact of trade-offs among quantified system attributes (such as response time and reliability) must be explored within the limits of available time, money, and the state of technology.

A ConOps document should be tailored for the application domain, operational environment, and intended audience. This means that the terminology, level of abstraction, detail, technical content, and presentation format should adhere to the objectives for that particular ConOps document. The following points are worth making in this regard:

1. A ConOps document must be written in the users' language. This does not necessarily imply that it cannot use technical language, but rather that it should be written in the users' technical language if the users are experts in a technical domain. If the ConOps document is written by the buyer or developer the authors must avoid use of terminology associated with their own discipline.
2. The level of detail contained in a ConOps should be appropriate to the situation. For example, there may be instances wherein a high-level description of the current system or situation is sufficient. In other instances, a detailed description of the current system or situation may be necessary. For example, there may be no current system: A detailed statement of the situation that motivates new system development with extensively specified operational scenarios for the envisioned system may be required. Or, the new system may be a replacement for an existing system to upgrade technology while adding new capabilities. In this case, a brief description of the existing system would be appropriate, with more detail on the new capabilities to be provided. The level of detail also depends on whether the ConOps document is for a system as a whole, or whether there will be separate ConOps documents for each system segment (for example, checkout, launch, on-orbit, and ground support elements for a spacecraft system) with an umbrella ConOps that describes operational aspects of the entire system.
3. The presentation format used in a ConOps document will vary, depending on the application of the document. In some user communities, textual documents are the tradition, while in others, storyboards are used. Examples of this difference can be seen by comparing the styles of communication in the information processing and command-and-control domains, for instance. The presentation format should be adjusted to accommodate the intended audience of the ConOps, although the use of visual forms is recommended for all audiences.
4. The comprehensive outline of a ConOps document, as presented in Appendix A, may not apply to every system or situation. If a particular paragraph of the outline does not apply to the situation under consideration, it should be marked "Not Applicable (N/A);" however, for each paragraph marked N/A, a brief justification stating why that paragraph is not applicable should be provided in place of the paragraph. "Not Applicable" should be used only when the authors of a ConOps are confident that the paragraph does not apply to the situation, and not simply because the authors don't have the required information. For example, if the authors do not know whether alternatives and trade-offs were considered (paragraph 8.3 of the ConOps outline), they should determine that fact. In the interim period, the paragraph can be marked "TBD." If they determine no alternatives or trade-offs were considered, the paragraph can be marked "not applicable." In this case, a brief justification stating why alternatives and trade-offs were not considered should be included.

To summarize, the ConOps format presented in Appendix A should be tailored to produce an efficient and cost-effective mechanism for documenting user needs and for maintaining traceability to those needs throughout the development process.

## Roles for ConOps Documents

The ConOps document can fill one of several roles, or some combination thereof:

1. To communicate users' and buyer's needs/requirements to the system developers. The ConOps author might be a buyer, presenting users' views to a developer; or a user presenting the users' view to a buyer and/or a developer. In this case, the ConOps is used by the developer as the basis for subsequent development activities.
2. To communicate a developer's understanding to users and/or buyer. The developer might produce a ConOps document as an aid in communicating the technical requirements to users and buyer, or to explain a possible solution strategy to the users and/or buyer. In this case, the ConOps is reviewed by the users and buyer to determine whether the proposed approach meets their needs and expectations.
3. To communicate a buyer's understanding of user needs to a developer. In this case, the buyer would develop the ConOps, obtain user concurrence, and use the ConOps to present user needs and operational requirements to the developer.
4. To document divergent needs and differing viewpoints of various user groups and/or buyers. In this case, each user group and/or buyer might develop (or commission development of) a ConOps to document their particular needs and viewpoints. This would be done as a prelude to obtaining a consensus view (see Role 5), or to determine that no single system can satisfy all of the various users' needs and buyers' requirements.
5. To document consensus on the system's characteristics among multiple users, user groups, or multiple buyers. In this case, the ConOps provides a mechanism for documenting the consensus view obtained from divergent needs, visions, and viewpoints among different users, user groups, and buyers before further development work proceeds.
6. To provide a means of communication between system engineers and software developers. In this case, the ConOps would describe user needs and operational requirements for the overall system (hardware, software, and people) and provide a context for the role of software within the total system.
7. To provide common understanding among multiple system/software developers. In cases where multiple system development and/or software development organizations are involved, the ConOps can provide a common understanding of how the software fits into the overall system, and how each software developer's part fits into the software portion of the system. In this case, there may be multiple ConOps documents, related in a hierarchical manner that mirrors the system partitioning.

Variations on, and combinations of, these roles might be found under differing circumstances. For example, the ConOps process might play Roles 4 and 5 to obtain and document consensus among user groups and buyers prior to developer selection; the consensus ConOps document would then fill Role 1 by providing the basis for subsequent development activities by the developer.

Additional roles for the ConOps include:

8. Providing a mechanism to document a system's characteristics and the users' operational needs in a manner that can be verified by the users without requiring them to have any technical knowledge beyond what is required to perform their job functions.
9. Providing a place for users to state their desires, visions, and expectations without requiring them to provide quantified, testable specifications. For example, the users could express their need for a "highly reliable" system, and their reasons for that need, without having to produce a testable reliability requirement.
10. Providing a mechanism for users and buyer(s) to express their thoughts and concerns on possible solution strategies. In some cases, there may be design constraints that dictate particular approaches. In other cases, there may be a variety of acceptable solution strategies. The ConOps allows users and buyer(s) to record design constraints, the rationale for those constraints, and to indicate the range of acceptable solution strategies.

## When Should the ConOps be Developed?

Development of a ConOps document should be the first step in the overall development process, so that it can serve as a basis for subsequent development activities.

The ConOps might be developed

1. Before the decision is made to develop a system. In this case, the ConOps document would be used to support the decision process.
2. Before the request for proposals (RFP) or in-house project authorization is issued. The ConOps would be included in the RFP package or project authorization.
3. As the first task after award of contract, so that the developer can better understand the users' needs and expectations before subsequent system development activities are started.

In cases (1) and (2), development of the ConOps document will be initiated by the users or the buyer (although the document author might be a developer; possibly the developer who will later develop the system). In case (3), development of the ConOps can be initiated by, and/or developed by, the user, buyer, or developer.

Concept analysis and preparation of a ConOps document can also be quite useful even if initiated at a later stage of the system life cycle. If, during system development, so many diverging opinions, needs, visions, and viewpoints surface that the development process cannot continue successfully, a ConOps document can provide a common vision of the system. The ConOps document for the Hubble Space Telescope System is a good example of this situation [Hubble 1983]. It was written after several attempts to develop a requirements specification; however, potential users of the space telescope could not agree on the operational requirements. The ConOps document provided the vehicle for obtaining a consensus, which in turn provided a basis for generating detailed operational requirements.

The developer who is building a system might want to develop a ConOps document, even as the requirements specifications are being generated. The developer might want the ConOps as a high-level overview and introduction to the system to serve as a guideline for the development team. Developers concerned about understanding user needs might develop a ConOps document as an aid to successfully developing a system that meets the users' needs and expectations.

A ConOps document might be developed during the operational phase of the system life cycle to support users, operators, and maintainers of the system. It might happen that potential system users do not want to use it because they do not understand the system's operational capabilities, or because they do not understand how the system would fit into their working environment. To solve these problems, the buyer or the developer might develop a ConOps document to "sell" the system to potential users.

A ConOps is also helpful to new users, operators, and maintainers who need to understand the operational characteristics of a system. The ConOps can also be used to explain the system's operational characteristics to prospective buyers who were not involved in initial system development.

If the involved parties deem it to be useful, a ConOps document can be developed at any time during the system life cycle; however, some major benefits of the document and the process of developing it are lost if it is developed after the requirements specification is baselined.

## Scenarios for Developing the ConOps

Ideally, concept analysis and development of the ConOps document should be done by the users. However, depending on the purpose and timing of development, the ConOps might be developed by the users, the buyer, or the developer. Regardless of who develops the ConOps, it must reflect the views of, and be approved by, the user community.

A high degree of user involvement in concept analysis and review of the ConOps document is crucial to a successful outcome, even if concept analysis and development of the ConOps document are done by the buyer or the developer. In these cases, the buyer or developer must engage the users in the process to ensure a correct and comprehensive understanding of the current system or situation and the users' needs, visions, and expectations for the new system. One way to ensure the necessary interactions is to establish an interdisciplinary team consisting of representatives from all user groups, from the buyer(s), and from the developer(s). However, the focus must never be allowed to shift from the users' operational perspective to the buyer's or developer's perspective.

One benefit of having the users write the ConOps document is that it ensures the focus will stay on user-related issues. However, the users may not know how to develop a ConOps document or be able to realistically envision what a new system can accomplish, that is they may not know the capabilities of existing technology. To reduce the impact of these problems, qualified personnel can be brought in to assist the users in developing the ConOps document.

One benefit of having the developers write the ConOps document is that they will, in most cases, have comprehensive knowledge of available technologies, and thus may be able to propose alternative (and better) ways of solving the users' problems. Another benefit of a developer-produced ConOps is that the ConOps analysis process will provide the developer with a good understanding of the users' problems, needs, and expectations, which facilitates subsequent development activities.

An advantage of a buyer-developed ConOps is that the buyer may have a good understanding of the user community, the developer organization, the political realities of the situation, and the budgetary constraints that may exist. This knowledge can be invaluable in producing a ConOps for a system that will satisfy user needs and that can be delivered within political and budgetary constraints.

Regardless of who takes primary responsibility for producing the ConOps document, it is important that all parties (users, buyers, developers) be involved in the analysis process and that everyone contribute their particular viewpoint to development of the ConOps.

## A Development Process for the ConOps

The approach described below is intended as a guideline. If the approach conflicts with what seems to be most appropriate in a specific situation, the guideline should be modified to fit that situation. For instance, there may be no current system; or the new system may be a modification of a current system; or the new system may be a total replacement for an outdated (manual or automated) system. Topics emphasized in the ConOps may be different in each situation.

1. Determine the objectives, roles, and team members for the ConOps process. This will normally be determined by the situation that motivates development of the ConOps document.
2. Tailor the recommended ConOps document format and obtain agreement on an outline for the ConOps document. This is important so that everyone understands the agreed-upon format and content areas of the document.
3. Describe the overall objectives and shortcomings of the current system. Also, determine and document the overall objectives for the new or modified system. If there is no current system, describe the situation that motivates development of a new system.
4. If there is an existing system, describe the that system's scope and boundaries, and identify any external systems and the interfaces to them. Also, establish and describe in general terms the scope and boundaries for the new or modified system, and identify the major external systems and interfaces to it.
5. Describe operational policies and constraints that apply to the current system or situation and any changes to those policies and constraints for the new system.
6. Describe the features of the current system or situation. This includes the system's operational characteristics, operational environment and processes, modes of operation, user classes, and the operational support and maintenance environments.
7. State the operational policies and constraints that will apply to the new or modified system.
8. Determine the operational characteristics of the proposed system, that is, describe the characteristics the proposed system must possess to meet the users' needs and expectations.
9. Document operational scenarios for the new or modified system. Scenarios are specified by recording, in a step-by-step manner, the sequences of actions and interactions between a user and the system. The following approach can be used to develop and document operational scenarios:

   - Develop a set of scenarios that, to the extent possible, covers all modes of operation, all classes of users, and all specific operations and processes of the proposed system.
   - Walk through each scenario with the appropriate users and record information concerning normal operating states and unusual conditions that are relevant to the operation of the proposed system.
   - During the walk-throughs, establish new scenarios to cover abnormal operations such as exception handling, stress load handling, and handling of incomplete and incorrect data.
   - Establish new scenarios whenever a branch in the thread of operation is encountered. Typically, walking through the "normal" scenarios will uncover additional scenarios. Different users may also have different views of some sce-

narios. If these variations are significant, include them as separate scenarios.

- Repeatedly develop scenarios until all operations, and all significant variations of those operations, are covered.
- For each operational scenario, develop an associated test scenario to be used in validating the operational aspects of the delivered system in the user environment. Establish traceability between operational scenarios and test scenarios.

10. After the scenarios have been developed, validate the description of the proposed system and the operational scenarios by walking through all of the scenarios with representatives from all user groups and all classes of users for all operational modes.
11. Obtain consensus on priorities among the operational scenarios and features of the proposed system. Group the scenarios and operational features into essential, desirable, and optional categories; prioritize scenarios and features within the desirable and optional categories. Also, describe scenarios and features considered but not included in the proposed system.
12. Analyze and describe the operational and organizational impacts the proposed system will have on users, buyer(s), developers, and the support/maintenance agencies. Also, include significant impacts on these groups during system development.
13. Describe the benefits, limitations, advantages, and disadvantages of the proposed system, compared to the present system or situation.

## Recommended Format of a ConOps Document

The recommended format of a ConOps document accommodates the objective of describing a proposed system from the users' point of view, in user terminology. The following format is recommended. Appendix A contains a detailed version of this outline.

1. Introduction to the ConOps document and to the system described in the document.
2. List of all documents referenced in the ConOps document.
3. Description of the current system or situation, including scope and objectives of the current system, operational policies and constraints, modes of operation, classes of users, and the support environment for the current system. If there is no existing system, describe the reasons that motivate development of a new system.
4. Nature of proposed changes and/or new features, including the justification for those changes and/or features.
5. Operational concepts for the proposed system, including scope and objectives for the proposed system, operational policies and constraints, modes of operation, classes of users, and the support environment for the proposed system.
6. Operational scenarios describing how the proposed system is to perform in its environment, relating system capabilities and functions to modes of operation, classes of users, and interactions with external systems.
7. Operational and organizational impacts on the users, buyers, developers, and the support and maintenance agencies, during system development and after system installation.
8. Alternative and trade-offs considered but not included in the new or modified system; analysis of benefits, limitations, advantages, and disadvantages of the new or modified system.
9. Notes, acronyms and abbreviations, appendices, and glossary of terms

This organization of a ConOps document provides a logical flow of information beginning with a description of the current system, transitioning through considerations of needed changes and the rationale for such changes, and leading to a description of the new or modified system. This will guide the reader through the description of the systems (both the current system or situation and the proposed system) in a simple and intuitive way.

## Maintaining the ConOps

A ConOps should be a living document that is updated and maintained throughout the entire life cycle (development process and operational life) of the software product. During system development, the ConOps document must be updated to keep users informed of the operational impacts of changes in requirements, the system design, operational policies, the operational environment, and other users' needs. During the operational life of the software product, the

ConOps must be updated to reflect the evolutionary changes to the system.

It is important to maintain the ConOps document under configuration control, and to ensure that user and buyer representatives are members of the change control board for the ConOps. Placing the ConOps under configuration control will protect the document from uncontrolled changes, and through the formal process of updating and notification, help to keep all parties informed of changes. A major benefit of this approach is that users and buyers are involved in reviewing and approving the changes. This minimizes the surprise factor that can occur when a delivered system is not the same as the system users thought they agreed to at the requirements review.

The ConOps document should also be updated and maintained under configuration control throughout the operational life of the associated system. During the operational life of the system, a ConOps can aid the support, maintenance, and enhancement activities for the system in much the same way that it helped during development. Specifically, it can be used to communicate new operational needs and impacts that result in modifications, upgrades, and enhancements. Furthermore, the ConOps provides a communication tool to familiarize new personnel with the system and the application domain.

Traceability should be established and maintained among the ConOps document, the system/software requirements specifications, and the acceptance/regression test scenarios. It is important for the developer (or maintainer) to be able to demonstrate to the users, buyer, and themselves that every essential user need stated in the ConOps document, and the desirable and optional features implemented, can be traced to and from the system specifications and to and from the delivered capabilities in the final product.

## Summary and Conclusions

This paper has described the evolution of the ConOps approach, the conceptual analysis process, the Concept of Operations document, roles to be played by a ConOps, some guidelines on when to develop a ConOps, development scenarios and a development process for developing the ConOps, the recommended format for a ConOps, and some issues concerning the maintenance of a ConOps throughout the development process and operational life of a software system.

As software engineers, we become so involved in the technology of software development and modification that we sometimes forget our fundamental charter: to develop and modify software-intensive systems that satisfy user needs, on time and within budget. Performing conceptual analysis and developing and maintaining a Concept of Operations document provides the bridge from users' operational requirements to technical specifications. All subsequent work products (requirements specs, design documents, source code, test plans, users' manual, training aids, and maintenance guide, for example) should flow from the ConOps. Maintaining the ConOps and the traceability of work products to the ConOps will not guarantee success; however, it can increase the probability that we will develop systems that satisfy users' needs for efficient and effective tools that help them accomplish their work activities.

## Acknowledgments

The authors would like to acknowledge the support of the following individuals in preparing the ConOps Guide: Per Bjorke, Dr. Merlin Dorfman, Dr. Lisa Friendly, and Jane Radatz.

## References

**[AIAA OCD, 1992]** AIAA Recommended Technical Practice, Operational Concept Document (OCD), Preparation Guidelines, Software Systems Technical Committee, American Institute of Aeronautics and Astronautics (AIAA), Mar. 1, 1992.

**[ANSI/IEEE Std 830-1984]** ANSI/IEEE Standard 830-1984: IEEE Guide for Software Requirements Specifications, The Institute of Electrical and Electronic Engineers, Inc., approved by the American National Standards Institute July 20, 1984.

**[DI-CMAN-80534, DoD-Std-2167A, 1988]** System/Segment Design Document (SSDD), DI-CMAN-80534, U.S. Department of Defense, Feb. 29, 1988.

**[DI-ECRS-8x25, DoD-Std-2167, 1985]** Operational Concept Document (OCD), DI-[ECRS-8x25] U.S. Department of Defense, June 4, 1985.

**[DoD-Std-2167A, 1988]** Military Standard: Defense System Software, Development, DoD-Std-2167A, U.S. Department of Defense, Feb. 29, 1988.

**[DoD-Std-7935A, 1988]** Functional Description (FD), DoD Automated Information Systems (AIS) Documentation Standards, DoD-Std-7935A, U.S. Department of Defense, Oct. 31, 1988, pp. 19–37.

**[Hubble, 1983]** Science Operations Concept, Part 1 (Final), Space Telescope Science Institute, Prepared for NASA Goddard Space Flight Center, Greenbelt, MD, May 1983.

**[Lano, 1988]** Lano, R.J., "A Structured Approach For Operational Concept Formulation (OCF)," TRW-SS-80-02, TRW Systems Engineering and Integration Division, Redondo Beach, Calif., Jan. 1980. Also in *Tutorial: Software Engineering Project Management*, edited by R. Thayer, Computer Society Press, Los Alamitos, Calif., 1988.

## Appendix A

## Outline for a Concept of Operations Document

# Chapter 3

# Software Engineering

## 1. Introduction to Chapter

*Software* can be considered a product of engineering just like an airplane, automobile, television, or any other object that requires a high degree of skill to turn a raw material into a usable product. Software:

- Is an entity (not a document)
- Is generally a component of a larger system (hardware/software)
- Replaces previously engineered hardware components
- Must interface with other hardware or software systems
- Must be tested before being put to use
- Is too large and complex to build without a plan (specification)
- Is expensive to build

The term *software engineering* was coined in 1967 by Professor Friedrich Bauer at a pre-conference meeting in Germany. (See the paper by Bauer in this chapter.) It was first applied as a technology in the mid-1970s and was accepted as a job title in the late 1970s. Today, most software positions (programming or engineering) are advertised as software engineering.

The purpose of software engineering was to introduce an engineering discipline to software development. It is applied to try to solve or reduce the problems of late deliveries, cost overruns, and failure to meet requirements that plagued software projects starting in the 1960s.

## 2. Introduction to Papers

The centerpiece of this chapter is an original paper by the well-known author and consultant, Roger Pressman. As indicated in the *Preface*, one of the problems of software engineering is the shortage of basic papers. Once something is described, practitioners and academics apparently move on to research or to the finer points of argument, abandoning the need to occasionally update the fundamentals. Dr. Pressman undertook the task of updating the basic papers on software engineering to the current state of practice. Pressman discusses technical and management aspects of software engineering. He surveys existing high-level models of the software development process (linear sequential, prototyping, incremental, evolutionary, and formal) and discusses management of people, the software project, and the software process. He discusses quality assurance and configuration management as being equally as important as technical and management issues. He reviews some of the principles and methods that form the foundation of the current practice of software engineering, and concludes with a prediction that three issues, reuse, re-engineering, and a new generation of tools, will dominate software engineering for the next ten years or so.

Pressman's most recent book is "*A Manager's Guide to Software Engineering*" (McGraw-Hill, 1993).

Paper number two credits Professor Friedrich L. Bauer with coining the phrase "software engineering." In 1967, the NATO Science Committee set about organizing a conference on the problems of building large-scale software systems. The conference was to be held in Garmisch, Germany, in 1968. At a pre-conference meeting, Professor Bauer, of Munich Technical University, proposed that the conference be called "Software Engineering" as a means of attracting attention. This one-page paper, which is the foreword from an earlier IEEE Tutorial, *Software Engineering—A European Perspective*,[1] explains the history behind the term and, as such, is included in this tutorial to give full credit to Professor Bauer.

The last paper in this chapter is a another historical perspective, the paper by Buxton entitled "Software Engineering—20 Years on and 20 Years Back." This paper provides another historical note on the origin and use of the term "software engineering." Professor Buxton is in a unique position to define the past history of software engineering as he was one of the main reporters and documentors of the second NATO software engineering conference in Rome in 1969.

1. Thayer, R. H., and A. D. McGettrick, eds., *Software Engineering—A European Perspective*, IEEE Computer Society Press, Los Alamitos, Calif., 1993.

# Software Engineering

Roger S. Pressman, Ph.D.

*As software engineering approaches its fourth decade, it suffers from many of the strengths and some of the frailties that are experienced by humans of the same age. The innocence and enthusiasm of its early years have been replaced by more reasonable expectations (and even a healthy cynicism) fostered by years of experience. Software engineering approaches its mid-life with many accomplishments already achieved, but with significant work yet to do.*

*The intent of this paper is to provide a survey of the current state of software engineering and to suggest the likely course of the aging process. Key software engineering activities are identified, issues are presented, and future directions are considered. There will be no attempt to present an in-depth discussion of specific software engineering topics. That is the job of other papers presented in this book.*

## 1.0 Software Engineering—Layered Technology[1]

Although hundreds of authors have developed personal definitions of software engineering, a definition proposed by Fritz Bauer [1] at the seminal conference on the subject still serves as a basis for discussion:

> [Software engineering is] the establishment and use of sound engineering principles in order to obtain economically software that is reliable and works efficiently on real machines.

Almost every reader will be tempted to add to this definition. It says little about the technical aspects of software quality; it does not directly address the need for customer satisfaction or timely product delivery; it omits mention of the importance of measurement and metrics; it does not state the importance of a mature process. And yet, Bauer's definition provides us with a baseline. What are the "sound engineering principles" that can be applied to computer software development? How to "economically" build software so that it is "reliable"? What is required to create computer programs that work "efficiently" on not one but many different "real machines"? These are the questions that continue to challenge software engineers.

Software engineering is a layered technology. Referring to Figure 1, any engineering approach (including software engineering) must rest on an organizational commitment to quality. Total quality management and similar philosophies foster a continuous process improvement culture, and it is this culture that ultimately leads to the development of increasingly more mature approaches to software engineering. The bedrock that supports software engineering is a quality focus.

The foundation for software engineering is the process layer. Software engineering process is the glue that holds the technology layers together and enables rational and timely development of computer software. Process defines a framework for a set of *key process areas* [2] that must be established for effective delivery of software engineering technology. The key process areas form the basis for management control of software projects, and establish the context in which technical methods are applied, deliverables (models, documents, data reports, forms, and so on) are produced, milestones are established, quality is ensured, and change is properly managed.

Software engineering methods provide the technical "how to's" for building software. Methods encompass a broad array of tasks that include: requirements analysis, design, program construction, testing, and maintenance. Software engineering methods rely on a set of basic principles that govern each area of the technology and include modeling activities, and other descriptive techniques.

Software engineering tools provide automated or semiautomated support for the process and the methods. When tools are integrated so that information created by one tool can be used by another, a system for the support of software development, called computer-aided software engineering (CASE), is established. CASE combines software, hardware, and a software engineering database (a repository containing important information about analysis, design, program construction, and testing) to create a software engineering environment that is analogous to CAD/CAE (computer-aided design/engineering) for hardware.

1 Portions of this paper have been adapted from *A Manager's Guide to Software Engineering* [19] and *Software Engineering: A Practitioner's Approach* (McGraw-Hill, fourth edition, 1997) and are used with permission.

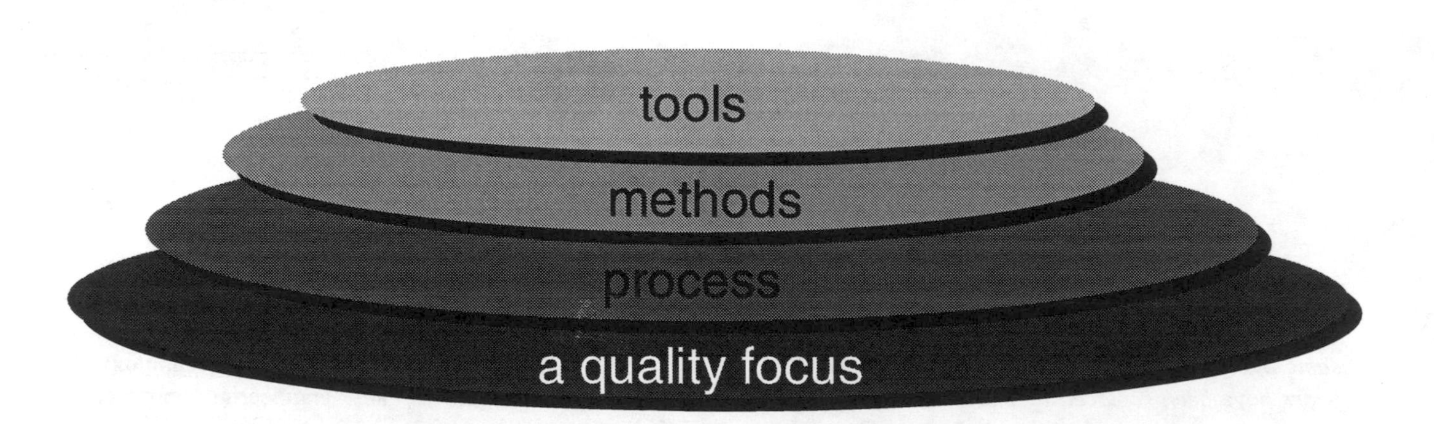


*Figure 1. Software engineering layers*

## 2.0 Software Engineering Process Models

Software engineering incorporates a development strategy that encompasses the process, methods, and tools layers described above. This strategy is often referred to as a *process model* or a *software engineering paradigm.* A process model for software engineering is chosen based on the nature of the project and application, the methods and tools to be used, and the controls and deliverables that are required. Four classes of process models have been widely discussed (and debated). A brief overview of each is presented in the sections that follow.

### 2.1 Linear, Sequential Models

Figure 2 illustrates the *linear sequential* model for software engineering. Sometimes called the "classic life cycle" or the "waterfall model," the linear sequential model demands a systematic, sequential approach to software development that begins at the system level and progresses through analysis, design, coding, testing, and maintenance. The linear sequential model is the oldest and the most widely used paradigm for software engineering. However, criticism of the paradigm has caused even active supporters to question its efficacy. Among the problems that are sometimes encountered when the linear sequential model is applied are:

1. Real projects rarely follow the sequential flow that the model proposes. Although the linear model can accommodate iteration, it does so indirectly. As a result, changes can cause confusion as the project team proceeds.
2. It is often difficult for the customer to state all requirements explicitly. The linear sequential model requires this and has difficulty accommodating the natural uncertainty that exists at the beginning of many projects.
3. The customer must have patience. A working version of the program(s) will not be available until late in the project time span. A major blunder, if undetected until the working program is reviewed, can be disastrous.

*Figure 2. The linear, sequential paradigm*

## 2.2 Prototyping

Often, a customer defines a set of general objectives for software, but does not identify detailed input, processing, or output requirements. In other cases, the developer may be unsure of the efficiency of an algorithm, the adaptability of an operating system, or the form that human-machine interaction should take. In these, and many other situations, a prototyping paradigm may offer the best approach.

The prototyping paradigm (Figure 3) begins with requirements gathering. Developer and customer meet and define the overall objectives for the software, identify whatever requirements are known, and outline areas where further definition is mandatory. A "quick design" then occurs. The quick design focuses on a representation of those aspects of the software that will be visible to the customer/user (for example, input approaches and output formats). The quick design leads to the construction of a prototype. The prototype is evaluated by the customer/user and is used to refine requirements for the software to be developed. Iteration occurs as the prototype is tuned to satisfy the needs of the customer, while at the same time enabling the developer to better understand what needs to be done.

Ideally, the prototype serves as a mechanism for identifying software requirements. If a working prototype is built, the developer attempts to make use of existing program fragments or applies tools (report generators, and window managers, for instance) that enable working programs to be generated quickly.

Both customers and developers like the prototyping paradigm. Users get a feel for the actual system and developers get to build something immediately. Yet, prototyping can also be problematic for the following reasons:

1. The customer sees what appears to be a working version of the software, unaware that the prototype is held together "with chewing gum and baling wire" or that in the rush to get it working we haven't considered overall software quality or long-term maintainability. When informed that the product must be rebuilt, the customer cries foul and demands that "a few fixes" be applied to make the prototype a working product. Too often, software development management relents.

2. The developer often makes implementation compromises in order to get a prototype working quickly. An inappropriate operating system or programming language may be used simply because it is available and known; an inefficient algorithm may be implemented simply to demonstrate capability. After a time, the developer may become familiar with these choices and forget all the reasons why they were inappropriate. The less-than-ideal choice has now become an integral part of the system.

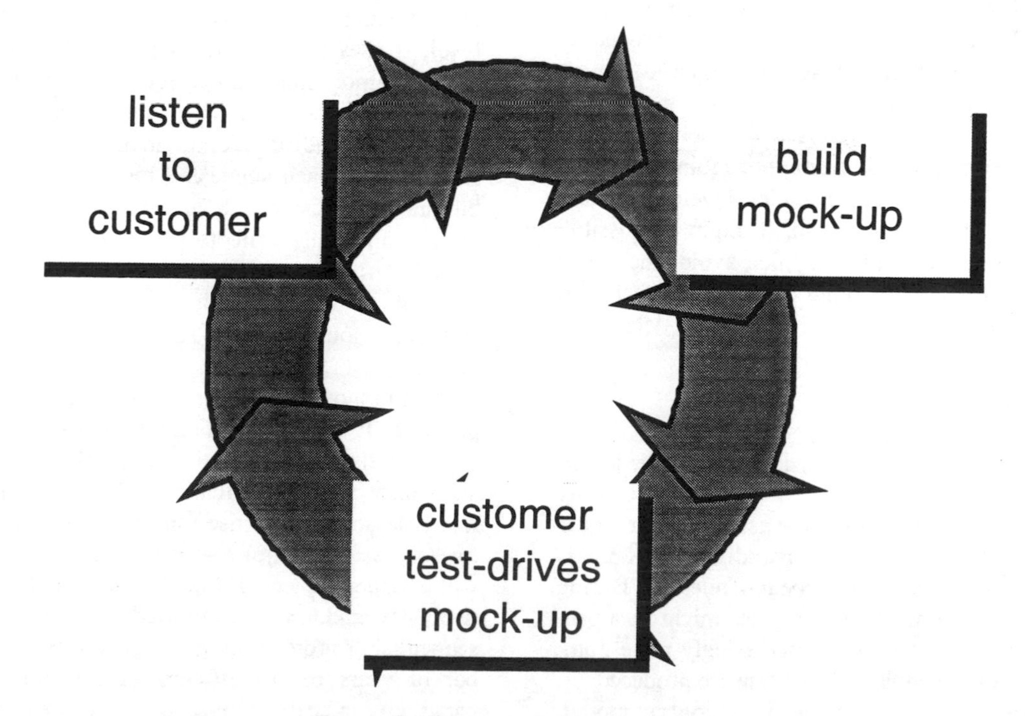


*Figure 3. The prototyping paradigm*

Although problems can occur, prototyping is an effective paradigm for software engineering. The key is to define the rules of the game at the beginning; that is, the customer and developer must both agree that the prototype is built to serve as a mechanism for defining requirements. It is then discarded (at least in part) and the actual software is engineered with an eye toward quality and maintainability.

When an incremental model is used, the first increment is often a *core product*. That is, basic requirements are addressed, but many supplementary features (some known, others unknown) remain undelivered. The core product is used by the customer (or undergoes detailed review). As a result of use and/or evaluation, a plan is developed for the next increment. The plan addresses the modification of the core product to better meet the needs of the customer and the delivery of additional features and functionality. This process is repeated following the delivery of each increment, until the complete product is produced.

The incremental process model, like prototyping (Section 2.2) and evolutionary approaches (Section 2.4), is iterative in nature. However, the incremental model focuses on the delivery of an operational product with each increment. Early increments are "stripped down" versions of the final product, but they do provide capability that serves the user and also provide a platform for evaluation by the user.

Incremental development is particularly useful when staffing is unavailable for a complete implementation by the business deadline that has been established for the project. Early increments can be implemented with fewer people. If the core product is well received, then additional staff (if required) can be added to implement the next increment. In addition, increments can be planned to manage technical risks. For example, a major system might require the availability of new hardware that is under development and whose delivery date is uncertain. It might be possible to plan early increments in a way that avoids the use of this hardware, thereby enabling partial functionality to be delivered to end users without inordinate delay.

### 2.4 Evolutionary Models

The *evolutionary* paradigm, also called the *spiral model* [3] couples the iterative nature of prototyping with the controlled and systematic aspects of the linear model. Using the evolutionary paradigm, software is developed in a series of incremental releases. During early iterations, the incremental release might be a prototype. During later iterations, increasingly more complete versions of the engineered system are produced.

Figure 4 depicts a typical evolutionary model. Each pass around the spiral moves through six task regions:

- **customer communication**—tasks required to establish effective communication between developer and customer
- **planning**—tasks required to define resources, time lines and other project-related information
- **risk assessment**—tasks required to assess both technical and management risks
- **engineering**—tasks required to build one or more representations of the application
- **construction and release**—tasks required to construct, test, install, and provide user support (for example, documentation and training)
- **customer evaluation**—tasks required to obtain customer feedback based on evaluation of the software representations created during the engineering stage and implemented during the installation stage.

Each region is populated by a series of tasks adapted to the characteristics of the project to be undertaken.

The spiral model is a realistic approach to the development of large scale systems and software. It uses an "evolutionary" approach [4] to software engineering, enabling the developer and customer to understand and react to risks at each evolutionary level. It uses prototyping as a risk reduction mechanism, but more importantly, it enables the developer to apply the prototyping approach at any stage in the evolution of the product. It maintains the systematic stepwise approach suggested by the classic life cycle but incorporates it into an iterative framework that more realistically reflects the real world. The spiral model demands a direct consideration of technical risks at all stages of the project, and if properly applied, should reduce risks before they become problematic.

But like other paradigms, the spiral model is not a panacea. It may be difficult to convince customers (particularly in contract situations) that the evolutionary approach is controllable. It demands considerable risk assessment expertise, and relies on this expertise for success. If a major risk is not discovered, problems will undoubtedly occur. Finally, the model itself is relatively new and has not been used as widely as the linear sequential or prototyping paradigms. It will take a number of years before efficacy of this important new paradigm can be determined with absolute certainty.

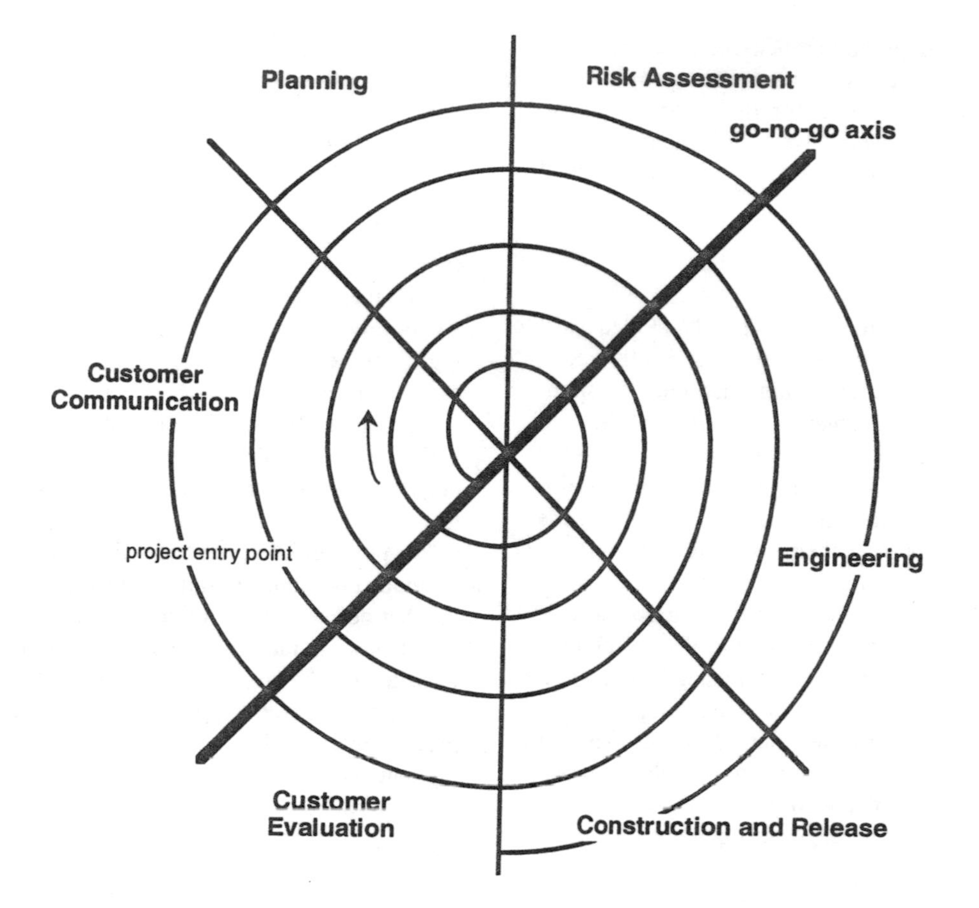


*Figure 4. The evolutionary model*

### 2.5 The Formal Methods Model

The formal methods paradigm encompasses a set of activities that leads to formal mathematical specification of computer software. Formal methods enable a software engineer to specify, develop, and verify a computer-based system by applying a rigorous, mathematical notation. A variation on this approach, called cleanroom software engineering [5, 6], is currently applied by a limited number of companies.

When formal methods are used during development, they provide a mechanism for eliminating many of the problems that are difficult to overcome using other software engineering paradigms. Ambiguity, incompleteness, and inconsistency can be discovered and corrected more easily—not through ad hoc review, but through the application of mathematical analysis. When formal methods are used during design, they serve as a basis for program verification and therefore enable the software engineer to discover and correct errors that might otherwise go undetected.

Although not yet a mainstream approach, the formal methods model offers the promise of defect-free software. Yet, concern about its applicability in a business environment has been voiced:

1. The development of formal models is currently quite time-consuming and expensive.
2. Because few software developers have the necessary background to apply formal methods, extensive training is required.
3. It is difficult to use the models as a communication mechanism for technically unsophisticated customers.

These concerns notwithstanding, it is likely that the formal methods approach will gain adherents among software developers who must build safety-critical software (such as aircraft avionics and medical devices) and among developers that would suffer severe economic hardship should software errors occur.

## 3.0 The Management Spectrum

Effective software project management focuses on the three P's: *people, problem, and process*. The order is not arbitrary. The manager who forgets that software engineering work is an intensely human endeavor will never have success in project management. A manager who fails to encourage comprehensive customer communication early in the evolution of a project risks building an elegant solution for the wrong problem. Finally, the manager who pays little attention to the process runs the risk of inserting competent technical methods and tools into a vacuum.

### 3.1 People

The cultivation of motivated, highly skilled software people has been discussed since the 1960s [see 7, 8, 9]. The Software Engineering Institute has sponsored a *people-management maturity model* "to enhance the readiness of software organizations to undertake increasingly complex applications by helping to attract, grow, motivate, deploy, and retain the talent needed to improve their software development capability." [10]

The people-management maturity model defines the following key practice areas for software people: recruiting, selection, performance management, training, compensation, career development, organization, and team and culture development. Organizations that achieve high levels of maturity in the people-management area have a higher likelihood of implementing effective software engineering practices.

### 3.2 The Problem

Before a project can be planned, objectives and scope should be established, alternative solutions should be considered, and technical and management constraints should be identified. Without this information, it is impossible to develop reasonable cost estimates, a realistic breakdown of project tasks, or a manageable project schedule that is a meaningful indicator of progress.

The software developer and customer must meet to define project objectives and scope. In many cases, this activity occurs as part of structured customer communication process such as *joint application design* [11, 12]. Joint application design (JAD) is an activity that occurs in five phases: project definition, research, preparation, the JAD meeting, and document preparation. The intent of each phase is to develop information that helps better define the problem to be solved or the product to be built.

### 3.3 The Process

A software process (see discussion of process models in Section 2.0) can be characterized as shown in Figure 5. A few framework activities apply to all software projects, regardless of their size or complexity. A number of *task sets*—tasks, milestones, deliverables, and quality assurance points—enable the framework activities to be adapted to the characteristics of the software project and the requirements of the project team. Finally, umbrella activities—such as software quality assurance, software configuration management, and measurement—overlay the process model. Umbrella activities are independent of any one framework activity and occur throughout the process.

In recent years, there has been a significant emphasis on process "maturity." [2] The Software Engineering Institute (SEI) has developed a comprehensive assessment model predicated on a set of software engineering capabilities that should be present as organizations reach different levels of process maturity. To determine an organization's current state of process maturity, the SEI uses an assessment questionnaire and a five-point grading scheme. The grading scheme determines compliance with a capability maturity model [2] that defines key activities required at different levels of process maturity. The SEI approach provides a measure of the global effectiveness of a company's software engineering practices and establishes five process maturity levels that are defined in the following manner:

**Level 1: Initial**—The software process is characterized as ad hoc, and occasionally even chaotic. Few processes are defined, and success depends on individual effort.

**Level 2: Repeatable**—Basic project management processes are established to track cost, schedule, and functionality. The necessary process discipline is in place to repeat earlier successes on projects with similar applications.

**Level 3: Defined**—The software process for both management and engineering activities is documented, standardized, and integrated into an organization-wide software process. All projects use a documented and approved version of the organization's process for developing and maintaining software. This level includes all characteristics defined for level 2.

**Level 4: Managed**—Detailed measures of the software process and product quality are collected. Both the software process and products are quantitatively understood and controlled using detailed measures. This level includes all characteristics defined for level 3.

**Level 5: Optimizing**—Continuous process improvement is enabled by quantitative feedback from the process and from testing innovative ideas and technologies. This level includes all characteristics defined for level 4.

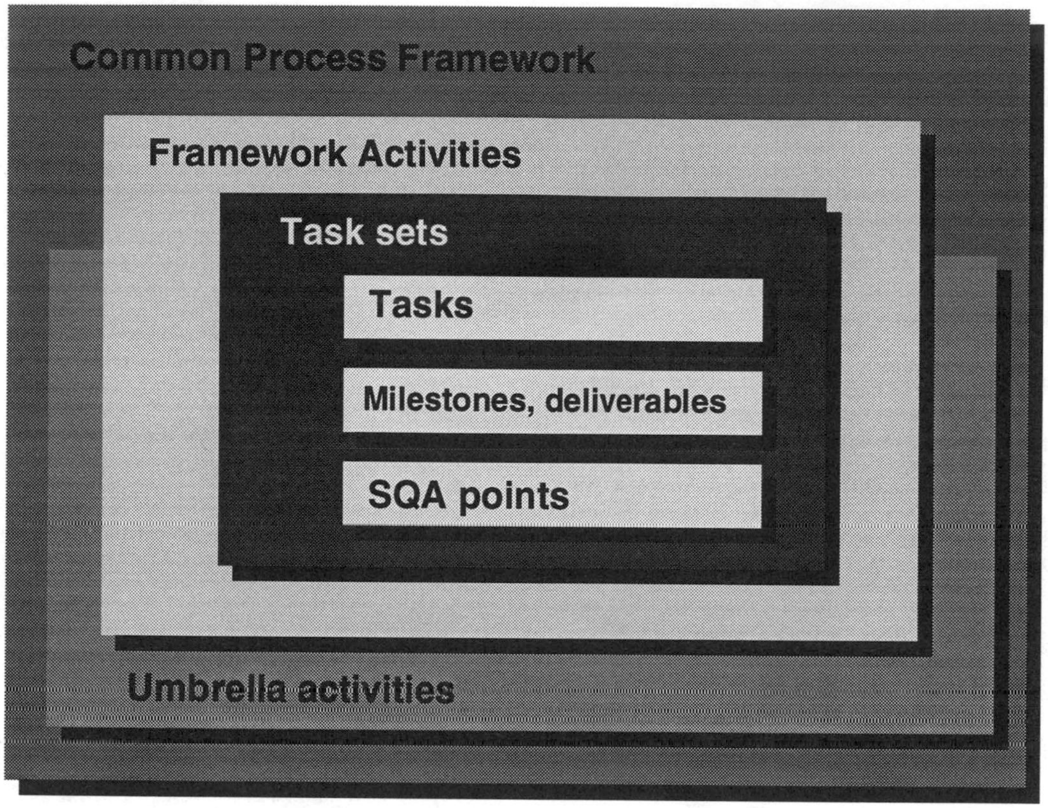

*Figure 5. A common process framework*

The five levels defined by the SEI are derived as a consequence of evaluating responses to the SEI assessment questionnaire that is based on the CMM. The results of the questionnaire are distilled to a single numerical grade that helps indicate an organization's process maturity.

The SEI has associated key process areas (KPAs) with each maturity level. The KPAs describe those software engineering functions (for example, software project planning and requirements management) that must be present to satisfy good practice at a particular level. Each KPA is described by identifying the following characteristics:

- *goals*—the overall objectives that the KPA must achieve
- *commitments*—requirements (imposed on the organization) that must be met to achieve the goals, provide proof of intent to comply with the goals
- *abilities*—those things that must be in place (organizationally and technically) that will enable the organization to meet the commitments
- *activities*—the specific tasks that are required to achieve the KPA function
- *methods for monitoring implementation*—the manner in which the activities are monitored as they are put into place
- *methods for verifying implementation*—the manner in which proper practice for the KPA can be verified.

Eighteen KPAs (each defined using the structure noted above) are defined across the maturity model and are mapped into different levels of process maturity.

Each KPA is defined by a set of *key practices* that contribute to satisfying its goals. The key practices are policies, procedures, and activities that must occur before a key process area has been fully instituted. The SEI defines *key indicators* as "those key practices or components of key practices that offer the greatest insight into whether the goals of a key process area have been achieved." Assessment questions are designed to probe for the existence (or lack thereof) of a key indicator.

## 4.0 Software Project Management

Software project management encompasses the following activities: measurement, project estimating, risk analysis, scheduling, tracking, and control. A comprehensive discussion of these topics is beyond the scope of this paper, but a brief overview of each topic will enable the reader to understand the breadth of management activities required for a mature software engineering organizations.

### 4.1 Measurement and Metrics

To be most effective, software metrics should be collected for both the process and the product. Process-oriented metrics [14, 15] can be collected during the process and after it has been completed. Process metrics collected during the project focus on the efficacy of quality assurance activities, change management, and project management. Process metrics collected after a project has been completed examine quality and productivity. Process measures are normalized using either lines of code or function points [13], so that data collected from many different projects can be compared and analyzed in a consistent manner. Product metrics measure technical characteristics of the software that provide an indication of software quality [15, 16, 17, 18]. Measures can be applied to models created during analysis and design activities, the source code, and testing data. The mechanics of measurement and the specific measures to be collected are beyond the scope of this paper.

### 4.2 Project Estimating

Scheduling and budgets are often dictated by business issues. The role of estimating within the software process often serves as a "sanity check" on the predefined deadlines and budgets that have been established by management. (Ideally, the software engineering organization should be intimately involved in establishing deadlines and budgets, but this is not a perfect or fair world.)

All software project estimation techniques require that the project have a bounded scope, and all rely on a high level functional decomposition of the project and an assessment of project difficulty and complexity. There are three broad classes of estimation techniques [19] for software projects:

- **Effort estimation techniques**. The project manager creates a matrix in which the left-hand column contains a list of major system functions derived using functional decomposition applied to project scope. The top row contains a list of major software engineering tasks derived from the common process framework. The manager (with the assistance of technical staff) estimates the effort required to accomplish each task for each function.
- **Size-Oriented Estimation**. A list of major system functions is derived using functional decomposition applied to project scope. The "size" of each function is estimated using either lines of code (LOC) or function points (FP). Average productivity data (for instance, function points per person month) for similar functions or projects are used to generate an estimate of effort required for each function.
- **Empirical Models**. Using the results of a large population of past projects, an empirical model that relates product size (in LOC or FP) to effort is developed using a statistical technique such as regression analysis. The product size for the work to be done is estimated and the empirical model is used to generate projected effort (for example, [20]).

In addition to the above techniques, a software project manager can develop estimates by analogy. This is done by examining similar past projects then projecting effort and duration recorded for these projects to the current situation.

### 4.3 Risk Analysis

Almost five centuries have passed since Machiavelli said: "I think it may be true that fortune is the ruler of half our actions, but that she allows the other half to be governed by us... [fortune] is like an impetuous river... but men can make provision against it by dykes and banks." Fortune (we call it risk) is in the back of every software project manager's mind, and that is often where it stays. And as a result, risk is never adequately addressed. When bad things happen, the manager and the project team are unprepared.

In order to "make provision against it," a software project team must conduct risk analysis explicitly. Risk analysis [21, 22, 23] is actually a series of steps that enable the software team to perform risk identification, risk assessment, risk prioritization, and risk management. The goals of these activities are: (1) to identify those risks that have a high likelihood of occurrence, (2) to assess the consequence (impact) of each risk should it occur, and (3) to develop a plan for mitigating the risks when possible, monitoring factors that may indicate their arrival, and developing a set of contingency plans should they occur.

### 4.4 Scheduling

The process definition and project management activities that have been discussed above feed the scheduling activity. The common process framework provides a work breakdown structure for scheduling. Available human resources, coupled with effort estimates and risk analysis, provide the task interdependencies, parallelism, and time lines that are used in constructing a project schedule.

### 4.5 Tracking and Control

Project tracking and control is most effective when it becomes an integral part of software engineering work. A well-defined process framework should provide a set of milestones that can be used for project tracking. Control focuses on two major issues: quality and change.

To control quality, a software project team must establish effective techniques for software quality assurance, and to control change, the team should establish a software configuration management framework.

## 5.0 Software Quality Assurance

In his landmark book on quality, Philip Crosby [24] states:

> The problem of quality management is not what people don't know about it. The problem is what they think they do know...
>
> In this regard, quality has much in common with sex. Everybody is for it. (Under certain conditions, of course.) Everyone feels they understand it. (Even though they wouldn't want to explain it.) Everyone thinks execution is only a matter of following natural inclinations. (After all, we do get along somehow.) And, of course, most people feel that problems in these areas are caused by other people. (If only they would take the time to do things right.)

There have been many definitions of software quality proposed in the literature. For our purposes, software quality is defined as: *Conformance to explicitly stated functional and performance requirements, explicitly documented development standards, and implicit characteristics that are expected of all professionally developed software.*

There is little question that the above definition could be modified or extended. In fact, the precise definition of software quality could be debated endlessly. But the definition stated above does serve to emphasize three important points:

1. Software requirements are the foundation from which quality is assessed. Lack of conformance to requirements is lack of quality.
2. A mature software process model defines a set of development criteria that guide the manner in which software is engineered. If the criteria are not followed, lack of quality will almost surely result.
3. There is a set of implicit requirements that often go unmentioned (for example, the desire for good maintainability). If software conforms to its explicit requirements but fails to meet implicit requirements, software quality is suspect.

Almost two decades ago, McCall and Cavano [25, 26] defined a set of quality factors that were a first step toward the development of metrics for software quality. These factors assessed software from three distinct points of view: (1) product operation (using it); (2) product revision (changing it), and (3) product transition (modifying it to work in a different environment, that is., "porting" it). These factors include:

- *Correctness*. The extent to which a program satisfies its specification and fulfills the customer's mission objectives.
- *Reliability*. The extent to which a program can be expected to perform its intended function with required precision.
- *Efficiency*. The amount of computing resources and code required by a program to perform its function.
- *Integrity*. Extent to which access to software or data by unauthorized persons can be controlled.
- *Usability*. Effort require to learn, operate, prepare input, and interpret output of a program.
- *Maintainability*. Effort require to locate and fix an error in a program. [Might be better termed "correctability"].
- *Flexibility*. Effort required to modify an operational program.
- *Testability*. Effort required to test a program to insure that it performs its intended function.
- *Portability*. Effort required to transfer the program from one hardware and/or software system environment to another.
- *Reusability*. Extent to which a program [or parts of a program] can be reused in other

applications—related to the packaging and scope of the functions that the program performs.

- *Interoperability.* Effort required to couple one system to another.

The intriguing thing about these factors is how little they have changed in almost 20 years. Computing technology and program architectures have undergone a sea change, but the characteristics that define high-quality software appear to be invariant. The implication: An organization that adopts factors such as those described above will build software today that will exhibit high quality well into the first few decades of the twenty-first century. More importantly, this will occur regardless of the massive changes in computing technologies that are sure to come over that period of time.

Software quality is designed into a product or system. It is not imposed after the fact. For this reason, *software quality assurance* (SQA) actually begins with the set of technical methods and tools that help the analyst to achieve a high-quality specification and the designer to develop a high-quality design.

Once a specification (or prototype) and design have been created, each must be assessed for quality. The central activity that accomplishes quality assessment is the formal technical review. The *formal technical review* (FTR)—conducted as a *walk-through* or an *inspection* [27]—is a stylized meeting conducted by technical staff with the sole purpose of uncovering quality problems. In many situations, formal technical reviews have been found to be as effective as testing in uncovering defects in software [28].

*Software testing* combines a multistep strategy with a series of test case design methods that help ensure effective error detection. Many software developers use software testing as a quality assurance "safety net." That is, developers assume that thorough testing will uncover most errors, thereby mitigating the need for other SQA activities. Unfortunately, testing, even when performed well, is not as effective as we might like for all classes of errors. A much better strategy is to find and correct errors (using FTRs) before getting to testing.

The degree to which formal *standards and procedures* are applied to the software engineering process varies from company to company. In many cases, standards are dictated by customers or regulatory mandate. In other situations standards are self-imposed. An assessment of compliance to standards may be conducted by software developers as part of a formal technical review, or in situations where independent verification of compliance is required, the SQA group may conduct its own audit.

A major threat to software quality comes from a seemingly benign source: changes. Every change to software has the potential for introducing error or creating side effects that propagate errors. The change control process contributes directly to software quality by formalizing requests for change, evaluating the nature of change, and controlling the impact of change. Change control is applied during software development and later, during the software maintenance phase.

*Measurement* is an activity that is integral to any engineering discipline. An important objective of SQA is to track software quality and assess the impact of methodological and procedural changes on improved software quality. To accomplish this, *software metrics* must be collected.

*Record keeping and recording* for software quality assurance provide procedures for the collection and dissemination of SQA information. The results of reviews, audits, change control, testing, and other SQA activities must become part of the historical record for a project and should be disseminated to development staff on a need-to-know basis. For example, the results of each formal technical review for a procedural design are recorded and can be placed in a "folder" that contains all technical and SQA information about a module.

## 6.0 Software Configuration Management

Change is inevitable when computer software is built. And change increases the level of confusion among software engineers who are working on a project. Confusion arises when changes are not analyzed before they are made, recorded before they are implemented, reported to those who should be aware that they have occurred, or controlled in a manner that will improve quality and reduce error. Babich [29] discusses this when he states:

> The art of coordinating software development to minimize... confusion is called *configuration management.* Configuration management is the art of identifying, organizing, and controlling modifications to the software being built by a programming team. The goal is to maximize productivity by minimizing mistakes.

*Software configuration management* (SCM) is an umbrella activity that is applied throughout the software engineering process. Because change can occur at any time, SCM activities are developed to (1) identify change, (2) control change, (3) ensure that change is being properly implemented and (4) report change to others who may have an interest.

A primary goal of software engineering is to improve the ease with which changes can be accommodated and reduce the amount of effort expended when changes must be made.

## 7.0 The Technical Spectrum

There was a time—some people still call it "the good old days"—when a skilled programmer created a program like an artist creates a painting: she just sat down and started. Pressman and Herron [30] draw other parallels when they write:

> At one time or another, almost everyone laments the passing of the good old days. We miss the simplicity, the personal touch, the emphasis on quality that were the trademarks of a craft. Carpenters reminisce about the days when houses were built with mahogany and oak, and beams were set without nails. Engineers still talk about an earlier era when one person did all the design (and did it right) and then went down to the shop floor and built the thing. In those days, people did good work and stood behind it.
>
> How far back do we have to travel to reach the good old days? Both carpentry and engineering have a history that is well over 2,000 years old. The disciplined way in which work is conducted, the standards that guide each task, the step by step approach that is applied, have all evolved through centuries of experience. *Software engineering* has a much shorter history.

During its short history, the creation of computer programs has evolved from an art form, to a craft, to an engineering discipline. As the evolution took place, the free-form style of the artist was replaced by the disciplined methods of an engineer. To be honest, we lose something when a transition like this is made. There's a certain freedom in art that can't be replicated in engineering. But we gain much, much more than we lose.

As the journey from art to engineering occurred, basic principles that guided our approach to software problem analysis, design and testing slowly evolved. And at the same time, methods were developed that embodied these principles and made software engineering tasks more systematic. Some of these "hot, new" methods flashed to the surface for a few years, only to disappear into oblivion, but others have stood the test of time to become part of the technology of software development.

In this section we discuss the basic principles that support the software engineering methods and provide an overview of some of the methods that have already "stood the test of time" and others that are likely to do so.

### 7.1 Software Engineering Methods—The Landscape

All engineering disciplines encompass four major activities: (1) the definition of the problem to be solved, (2) the design of a solution that will meet the customer's needs; (2) the construction of the solution, and (4) the testing of the implemented solution to uncover latent errors and provide an indication that customer requirements have been achieved. Software engineering offers a variety of different methods to achieve these activities. In fact, the methods landscape can be partitioned into three different regions:

- conventional software engineering methods
- object-oriented approaches
- formal methods

Each of these regions is populated by a variety of methods that have spawned their own culture, not to mention a sometimes confusing array of notation and heuristics. Luckily, all of the regions are unified by a set of overriding principles that lead to a single objective: to create high quality computer software.

Conventional software engineering methods view software as an information transform and approach each problem using an input-process-output viewpoint. Object-oriented approaches consider each problem as a set of classes and work to create a solution by implementing a set of communicating objects that are instantiated from these classes. Formal methods describe the problem in mathematical terms, enabling rigorous evaluation of completeness, consistency, and correctness.

Like competing geographical regions on the world map, the regions of the software engineering methods map do not always exist peacefully. Some inhabitants of a particular region cannot resist religious warfare. Like most religious warriors, they become consumed by dogma and often do more harm that good. The regions of the software engineering methods landscape can and should coexist peacefully, and tedious debates over which method is best seem to miss the point. Any method, if properly applied within the context of a solid set of software engineering principles, will lead to higher quality software than an undisciplined approach.

### 7.2 Problem Definition

A problem cannot be fully defined and bounded until it is communicated. For this reason, the first step in any software engineering project is customer communication. Techniques for customer communication [11, 12] were discussed earlier in this paper. In essence, the developer and the customer must develop an effective mechanism for defining and negotiating the basic requirements for the software project. Once this has been accomplished, requirements analysis begins. Two options are available at this stage: (1) the creation of a prototype that will assist the developer and the customer in better understanding the system to be build, and/or (2) the creation of a detailed set of analysis models that describe the data, function, and behavior for the system.

#### 7.2.1 Analysis Principles

Today, analysis modeling can be accomplished by applying one of several different methods that populate the three regions of the software engineering methods landscape. All methods, however, conform to a set of analysis principles [31]:

1. **The data domain of the problem must be modeled.** To accomplish this, the analyst must define the data objects (entities) that are visible to the user of the software and the relationships that exist between the data objects. The content of each data object (the object's attributes) must also be defined.
2. **The functional domain of the problem must be modeled.** Software functions transform the data objects of the system and can be modeled as a hierarchy (conventional methods), as services to classes within a system (the object-oriented view), or as a succinct set of mathematical expressions (the formal view).
3. **The behavior of the system must be represented.** All computer-based systems respond to external events and change their state of operation as a consequence. Behavioral modeling indicates the externally observable states of operation of a system and how transition occurs between these states.
4. **Models of data, function, and behavior must be partitioned.** All engineering problem-solving is a process of elaboration. The problem (and the models described above) are first represented at a high level of abstraction. As problem definition progresses, detail is refined and the level of abstraction is reduced. This activity is called partitioning.
5. **The overriding trend in analysis is from essence toward implementation.** As the process of elaboration progresses, the statement of the problem moves from a representation of the essence of the solution toward implementation-specific detail. This progression leads us from analysis toward design.

#### 7.2.2 Analysis Methods

A discussion of the notation and heuristics of even the most popular analysis methods is beyond the scope of this paper. The problem is further compounded by the three different regions of the methods landscape and the local issues specific to each. Therefore, all that we can hope to accomplish in this section is to note similarities among the different methods and regions:

- All analysis methods provide a notation for describing data objects and the relationships that exist between them.
- All analysis methods couple function and data and provide a way for understanding how function operates on data.
- All analysis methods enable an analyst to represent behavior at a system level, and in some cases, at a more localized level.
- All analysis methods support a partitioning approach that leads to increasingly more detailed (and implementation-specific models).
- All analysis methods establish a foundation from which design begins, and some provide representations that can be directly mapped into design.

For further information on analysis methods in each of the three regions noted above, the reader should review work by Yourdon [32], Booch [33], and Spivey [34].

### 7.3 Design

M.A. Jackson [35] once said: "The beginning of wisdom for a computer programmer [software engineer] is to recognize the difference between getting a program to work, and getting it *right*." Software design is a set of basic principles and a pyramid of modeling methods that provide the necessary framework for "getting it right."

#### 7.3.1 Design Principles

Like analysis modeling, software design has

spawned a collection of methods that populate the conventional, object-oriented, and formal regions that were discussed earlier. Each method espouses its own notation and heuristics for accomplishing design, but all rely on a set of fundamental principles [31] that are outlined in the paragraphs that follow:

1. **Data and the algorithms that manipulate data should be created as a set of interrelated abstractions**. By creating data and procedural abstractions, the designer models software components that have characteristics leading to high quality. An abstraction is self-contained; it generally implements one well-constrained data structure or algorithm; it can be accessed using a simple interface; the details of its internal operation need not be known for it to be used effectively; it is inherently reusable.
2. **The internal design detail of data structures and algorithms should be hidden from other software components that make use of the data structures and algorithms**. Information hiding [36] suggests that modules be "characterized by design decisions that (each) hides from all others." Hiding implies that effective modularity can be achieved by defining a set of independent modules that communicate with one another only that information that is necessary to achieve software function. The use of information hiding as a design criterion for modular systems provides greatest benefits when modifications are required during testing and later, during software maintenance. Because most data and procedures are hidden from other parts of the software, inadvertent errors (and resultant side effects) introduced during modification are less likely to propagate to other locations within the software.
3. **Modules should exhibit independence**. That is, they should be loosely coupled to each other and to the external environment and should exhibit functional cohesion. Software with *effective modularity*, that is, independent modules, is easier to develop because function may be compartmentalized and interfaces are simplified (consider ramifications when development is conducted by a team). Independent modules are easier to maintain (and test) because secondary effects caused by design/code modification are limited; error propagation is reduced; and reusable modules are possible.
4. **Algorithms should be designed using a constrained set of logical constructs**. This design approach, widely know as *structured programming* [37], was proposed to limit the procedural design of software to a small number of predictable operations. The use of the structured programming constructs (sequence, conditional, and loops) reduces program complexity and thereby enhances readability, testability, and maintainability. The use of a limited number of logical constructs also contributes to a human understanding process that psychologists call *chunking*. To understand this process, consider the way in which you are reading this page. You do not read individual letters; but rather, recognize patterns or chunks of letters that form words or phrases. The structured constructs are logical chunks that allow a reader to recognize procedural elements of a module, rather than reading the design or code line by line. Understanding is enhanced when readily recognizable logical forms are encountered.

### 7.3.2 The Design Pyramid

Like analysis, a discussion of even the most popular design methods is beyond the scope of this paper. Our discussion here will focus on a set of design activities that should occur regardless of the method that is used.

Software design should be accomplished by following a set of design activities as illustrated in Figure 6. *Data design* translates the data model created during analysis into data structures that meet the needs of the problem. *Architectural design* differs in intent depending upon the designer's viewpoint. Conventional design creates hierarchical software architectures, while object-oriented design views architecture as the message network that enables objects to communicate. *Interface design* creates implementation models for the human-computer interface, the external system interfaces that enable different applications to interoperate, and the internal interfaces that enable program data to be communicated among software components. Finally, *procedural design* is conducted as algorithms are created to implement the processing requirements of program components.

Like the pyramid depicted in Figure 6, design should be a stable object. Yet, many software developers do design by taking the pyramid and standing it on its point. That is, design begins with the creation of procedural detail, and as a result, interface, architectural, and data design just happen. This approach, common among people who insist upon coding the program with no explicit design activity, invariably leads to low-quality software that is difficult to test, challenging to extend, and frustrating to maintain. For a stable, high-quality product, the design approach must also be stable. The design pyramid provides the degree of stability necessary for good design.

### 7.4 Program Construction

The glory years of third-generation programming languages are rapidly coming to a close. Fourth-generation techniques, graphical programming methods, component-based software construction, and a variety of other approaches have already captured a significant percentage of all software construction activities, and there is little debate that their penetration will grow.

And yet, some members of the software engineering community continue to debate "the best programming language." Although entertaining, such debates are a waste of time. The problems that we continue to encounter in the creation of high-quality computer-based systems have relatively little to do with the means of construction. Rather, the challenges that face us can only be solved through better or innovative approaches to analysis and design, more comprehensive SQA techniques, and more effective and efficient testing. It is for this reason that construction is not emphasized in this paper.

### 7.5 Software Testing

Glen Myers [38] states three rules that can serve well as testing objectives:

1. Testing is a process of executing a program with the intent of finding an error.
2. A good test case is one that has a high probability of finding an as-yet-undiscovered error.
3. A successful test is one that uncovers an as-yet-undiscovered error.

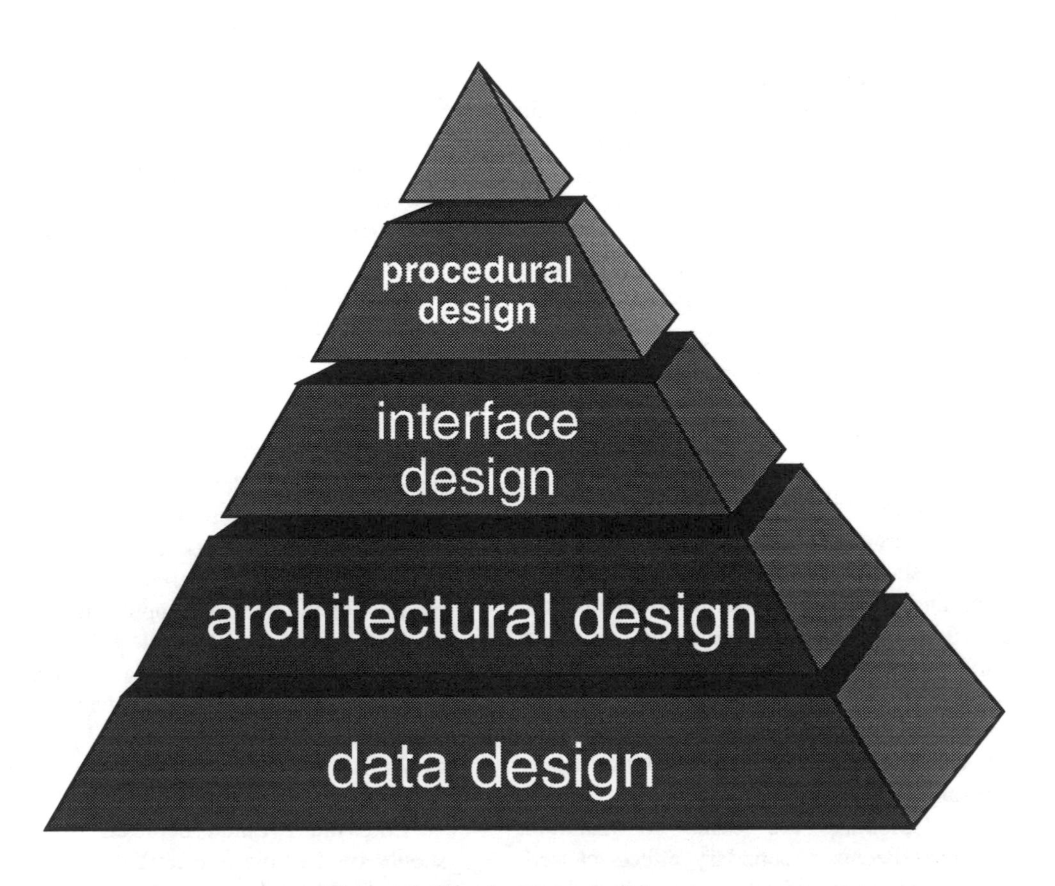


*Figure 6. The design pyramid*

These objectives imply a dramatic change in viewpoint. They move counter to the commonly held view that a successful test is one in which no errors are found. Our objective is to design tests that systematically uncover different classes of errors and to do so with a minimum of time and effort.

If testing is conducted successfully (according to the objective stated above), it will uncover errors in the software. As a secondary benefit, testing demonstrates that software functions appear to be working according to specification, that performance requirements appear to have been met. In addition, data collected as testing is conducted provides a good indication of software reliability and some indication of software quality as a whole. But there is one thing that testing cannot do: testing cannot show the absence of defects, it can only show that software defects are present. It is important to keep this (rather gloomy) statement in mind as testing is being conducted.

### 7.5.1 Strategy

A strategy for software testing integrates software test-case design techniques into a well-planned series of steps that result in the successful construction of software. It defines a template for software testing—a set of steps into which we can place specific test-case design techniques and testing methods.

A number of software testing strategies have been proposed in the literature. All provide the software developer with a template for testing, and all have the following generic characteristics:

- Testing begins at the module level and works incrementally "outward" toward the integration of the entire computer-based system.
- Different testing techniques are appropriate at different points in time.
- Testing is conducted by the developer of the software and (for large projects) an independent test group.
- Testing and debugging are different activities, but debugging must be accommodated in any testing strategy.

A strategy for software testing must accommodate low-level tests that are necessary to verify that a small source code segment has been correctly implemented, intermediate-level tests designed to uncover errors in the interfaces between modules, and high-level tests that validate major system functions against customer requirements. A strategy must provide guidance for the practitioner and a set of milestones for the manager. Because the steps of the test strategy occur at a time when deadline pressure begins to rise, progress must be measurable and problems must surface as early as possible.

### 7.5.2 Tactics

The design of tests for software and other engineered products can be as challenging as the initial design of the product itself. Recalling the objectives of testing, we must design tests that have the highest likelihood of finding the most errors with a minimum of time and effort.

Over the past two decades a rich variety of test-case design methods have evolved for software. These methods provide the developer with a systematic approach to testing. More importantly, methods provide a mechanism that can help to ensure the completeness of tests and provide the highest likelihood for uncovering errors in software.

Any engineered product (and most other things) can be tested in one of two ways: (1) knowing the specified function that a product has been designed to perform, tests can be conducted that demonstrate each function is fully operational; (2) knowing the internal workings of the product, tests can be conducted to ensure that "all gears mesh"; that is, internal operation performs according to specification and all internal components have been adequately exercised. The first test approach is called *black-box testing* and the second, *white-box testing* [38].

When computer software is considered, black-box testing alludes to tests that are conducted at the software interface. Although they are designed to uncover errors, black-box tests are also used to demonstrate that software functions are operational; that input is properly accepted, and output is correctly produced; that the integrity of external information (such as data files) is maintained. A black-box test examines some aspect of a system with little regard for the internal logical structure of the software.

White-box testing of software is predicated on close examination of procedural detail. Logical paths through the software are tested by providing test cases that exercise specific sets of conditions and/or loops. The status of the program may be examined at various points to determine if the expected or asserted status corresponds to the actual status.

## 8.0 The Road Ahead & The Three R's

Software is a child of the latter half of the twentieth century—a baby boomer. And like its human counterpart, software has accomplished much while at the same time leaving much to be accomplished. It appears that the economic and business environment of the next ten years will be dramatically different than anything that baby boomers have yet experienced.

Staff downsizing, the threat of outsourcing, and the demands of customers who won't take "slow" for an answer require significant changes in our approach to software engineering and a major reevaluation of our strategies for handling hundreds of thousands of existing systems [39].

Although many existing technologies will mature over the next decade, and new technologies will emerge, it's likely that three existing software engineering issues—I call them the three R's—will dominate the software engineering scene.

### 8.1 Reuse

We must build computer software faster. This simple statement is a manifestation of a business environment in which competition is vicious, product life cycles are shrinking, and time to market often defines the success of a business. The challenge of faster development is compounded by shrinking human resources and an increasing demand for improved software quality.

To meet this challenge, software must be constructed from reusable components. The concept of software reuse is not new, nor is a delineation of its major technical and management challenges [40]. Yet without reuse, there is little hope of building software in time frames that shrink from years to months.

It is likely that two regions of the methods landscape may merge as greater emphasis is placed on reuse. Object-oriented development can lead to the design and implementation of inherently reusable program components, but to meet the challenge, these components must be demonstrably defect free. It may be that formal methods will play a role in the development of components that are proven correct prior to their entry in a component library. Like integrated circuits in hardware design, these "formally" developed components can be used with a fair degree of assurance by other software designers.

If technology problems associated with reuse are overcome (and this is likely), management and cultural challenges remain. Who will have responsibility for creating reusable components? Who will manage them once they are created? Who will bear the additional costs of developing reusable components? What incentives will be provided for software engineers to use them? How will revenues be generated from reuse? What are the risks associated with creating a reuse culture? How will developers of reusable components be compensated? How will legal issues such as liability and copyright protection be addressed? These and many other questions remain to be answered. And yet, component reuse is our best hope for meeting the software challenges of the early part of the twenty-first century.

### 8.2 Reengineering

Almost every business relies on the day-to-day operation of an aging software plant. Major companies spend as much as 70 percent or more of their software budget on the care and feeding of legacy systems. Many of these systems were poorly designed more than decade ago and have been patched and pushed to their limits. The result is a software plant with aging, even decrepit systems that absorb increasingly large amounts of resource with little hope of abatement. The software plant must be rebuilt, and that demands a reengineering strategy.

Reengineering takes time; it costs significant amounts of money, and it absorbs resources that might be otherwise occupied on immediate concerns. For all of these reasons, reengineering is not accomplished in a few months or even a few years. Reengineering of information systems is an activity that will absorb software resources for many years.

A paradigm for reengineering includes the following steps:

- *inventory analysis*—creating a prioritized list of programs that are candidates for reengineering
- *document restructuring*—upgrading documentation to reflect the current workings of a program
- *code restructuring*—recoding selected portions of a program to reduce complexity, ready the code for future change, and improve understandability
- *data restructuring*—redesigning data structures to better accommodate current needs; redesign the algorithms that manipulate these data structures
- *reverse engineering*—examine software internals to determine how the system has been constructed
- *forward engineering*—using information obtained from reverse engineering, rebuild the application using modern software engineering practices and principles.

### 8.3 Retooling

To achieve the first two R's, we need a third R—a new generation of software tools. In retooling the software engineering process, we must remember the mistakes of the 1980s and early 1990s. At that time, CASE tools were inserted into a process vacuum, and failed to meet expectations. Tools for the next ten years will address all aspects of the methods landscape. But they should emphasize reuse and reengineering.

## 9.0 Summary

As each of us in the software business looks to the future, a small set of questions is asked and re-asked. Will we continue to struggle to produce software that meets the needs of a new breed of customers? Will generation X software professionals repeat the mistakes of the generation that preceded them? Will software remain a bottleneck in the development of new generations of computer-based products and systems? The degree to which the industry embraces software engineering and works to instantiate it into the culture of software development will have a strong bearing on the final answers to these questions. And the answers to these questions will have a strong bearing on whether we should look to the future with anticipation or trepidation.

## References


[1] Naur, P. and B. Randall (eds.), *Software Engineering: A Report on a Conference Sponsored by the NATO Science Committee*, NATO, 1969.

[2] Paulk, M. et al., *Capability Maturity Model for Software*, Software Engineering Institute, Carnegie Mellon University, Pittsburgh, PA, 1993.

[3] Boehm, B., "A Spiral Model for Software Development and Enhancement," *Computer*, Vol. 21, No. 5, May 1988, pp. 61–72.

[4] Gilb, T., *Principles of Software Engineering Management*, Addison-Wesley, Reading, Mass., 1988.

[5] Mills, H.D., M. Dyer, and R. Linger, "Cleanroom Software Engineering," *IEEE Software*, Sept. 1987, pp. 19–25.

[6] Dyer, M., *The Cleanroom Approach to Quality Software Development*, Wiley, New York, N.Y., 1992.

[7] Cougar, J. and R. Zawacki, *Managing and Motivating Computer Personnel*, Wiley, New York, N.Y., 1980.

[8] DeMarco, T. and T. Lister, *Peopleware*, Dorset House, 1987.

[9] Weinberg, G., *Understanding the Professional Programmer*, Dorset House, 1988.

[10] Curtis, B., "People Management Maturity Model," *Proc. Int'l Conf. Software Eng.*, IEEE CS Press, Los Alamitos, Calif., 1989, pp. 398–399.

[11] August, J.H., *Joint Application Design*, Prentice-Hall, Englewood Cliffs, N.J., 1991.

[12] Wood, J. and D. Silver, *Joint Application Design*, Wiley, New York, N.Y., 1989.

[13] Dreger, J.B., *Function Point Analysis*, Prentice-Hall, Englewood Cliffs, N.J., 1989.

[14] Hetzel, B., *Making Software Measurement Work*, QED Publishing, 1993.

[15] Jones, C., *Applied Software Measurement*, McGraw-Hill, New York, N.Y., 1991.

[16] Fenton, N.E., *Software Metrics*, Chapman & Hall, 1991.

[17] Zuse, H., *Software Complexity*, W. deGruyer & Co., Berlin, 1990.

[18] Lorenz, M. and J. Kidd, *Object-Oriented Software Metrics*, Prentice-Hall, Englewood Cliffs, N.J., 1994.

[19] Pressman, R.S., *A Manager's Guide to Software Engineering*, McGraw-Hill, New York, N.Y., 1993.

[20] Boehm, B., *Software Engineering Economics*, Prentice-Hall, Englewood Cliffs, N.J., 1981.

[21] Charette, R., *Application Strategies for Risk Analysis*, McGraw-Hill, New York, N.Y., 1990.

[22] Jones, C., *Assessment and Control of Software Risks*, Yourdon Press, 1993.

[24] Crosby, P., *Quality is Free*, McGraw-Hill, New York, N.Y., 1979.

[25] McCall, J., P. Richards, and G. Walters, "Factors in Software Quality," three volumes, NTIS AD-A049-014, 015, 055, Nov. 1977.

[26] Cavano, J.P. and J.A. McCall, "A Framework for the Measurement of Software Quality," *Proc. ACM Software Quality Assurance Workshop*, ACM Press, New York, N.Y., 1978, pp. 133–139.

[27] Freedman, D and G. Weinberg, *The Handbook of Walkthroughs, Inspections and Technical Reviews*, Dorset House, 1990.

[28] Gilb, T. and D. Graham, *Software Inspection*, Addison-Wesley, Reading, Mass., 1993.

[29] Babich, W., *Software Configuration Management*, Addison-Wesley, Reading, Mass., 1986.

[30] Pressman, R. and S. Herron, Software Shock, Dorset House, 1991.

[31] Pressman, R., *Software Engineering: A Practitioner's Approach*, 3rd ed., McGraw-Hill, New York, N.Y., 1992.

[32] Yourdon, E., *Modern Structured Analysis*, Yourdon Press, 1989.

[33] Booch, G., *Object-Oriented Analysis & Design*, Benjamin-Cummings, 1994.

[34] Spivey, M., *The Z Notation*, Prentice-Hall, Englewood Cliffs, N.J., 1992.

[35] Jackson, M., *Principles of Program Design*, Academic Press, New York, N.Y., 1975.

[36] Parnas, D.L., "On Criteria to be used in Decomposing Systems into Modules," *Comm. ACM*, Vol. 14, No. 1, Apr. 1972, pp. 221–227.

[37] Linger, R., H. Mills, and B. Witt, *Structured Programming*, Addison-Wesley, Reading, Mass., 1979.

[38] Myers, G., *The Art of Software Testing*, Wiley, New York, N.Y., 1979.

[38] Beizer, B., *Software Testing Techniques*, 2nd ed., VanNostrand Reinhold, 1990.

[39] Pressman, R., "Software According to Nicollo Machiavelli," *IEEE Software*, Jan. 1995, pp. 101–102.

[40] Tracz, W., *Software Reuse: Emerging Technology*, IEEE CS Press, Los Alamitos, Calif., 1988.

# Foreword

In the mid-1960s, there was increasing concern in scientific quarters of the Western world that the tempestuous development of computer hardware was not matched by appropriate progress in software. The software situation looked more to be turbulent. Operating systems had just been the latest rage, but they showed unexpected weaknesses. The uneasiness had been lined out in the NATO Science Committee by its US representative, Dr. I.I. Rabi, the Nobel laureate and famous, as well as influential, physicist. In 1967, the Science Committee set up the Study Group on Computer Science, with members from several countries, to analyze the situation. The German authorities nominated me for this team. The study group was given the task of "assessing the entire field of computer science," with particular elaboration on the Science Committee's consideration of "organizing a conference and, perhaps, at a later date,...setting up...an International Institute of Computer Science."

The study group, concentrating its deliberations on actions that would merit an international rather than a national effort, discussed all sorts of promising scientific projects. However, it was rather inconclusive on the relation of these themes to the critical observations mentioned above, which had guided the Science Committee. Perhaps not all members of the study group had been properly informed about the rationale of its existence. In a sudden mood of anger, I made the remark, "The whole trouble comes from the fact that there is so much tinkering with software. It is not made in a clean fabrication process," and when I found out that this remark was shocking to some of my scientific colleagues, I elaborated the idea with the provocative saying, "What we need is *software engineering*."

This remark had the effect that the expression "software engineering," which seemed to some to be a contradiction in terms, stuck in the minds of the members of the group. In the end, the study group recommended in late 1967 the holding of a Working Conference on Software Engineering, and I was made chairman. I had not only the task of organizing the meeting (which was held from October 7 to October 10, 1968, in Garmisch, Germany), but I had to set up a scientific program for a subject that was suddenly defined by my provocative remark. I enjoyed the help of my cochairmen, L. Bolliet from France, and H.J. Helms from Denmark, and in particular the invaluable support of the program committee members, A.J. Perlis and B. Randall in the section on design, P. Naur and J.N. Buxton in the section on production, and K. Samuelson, B. Galler, and D. Gries in the section on service. Among the 50 or so participants, E.W. Dijkstra was dominant. He actually made not only cynical remarks like "the dissemination of error-loaded software is frightening" and "it is not clear that the people who manufacture software are to be blamed. I think manufacturers deserve better, more understanding users." He also said already at this early date, "Whether the correctness of a piece of software can be guaranteed or not depends greatly on the structure of the thing made," and he had very fittingly named his paper "Complexity Controlled by Hierarchical Ordering of Function and Variability," introducing a theme that followed his life the next 20 years. Some of his words have become proverbs in computing, like "testing is a very inefficient way of convincing oneself of the correctness of a program."

With the wide distribution of the reports on the Garmisch conference and on a follow-up conference in Rome, from October 27 to 31, 1969, it emerged that not only the phrase *software engineering*, but also the idea behind this, became fashionable. Chairs were created, institutes were established (although the one which the NATO Science Committee had proposed did not come about because of reluctance on the part of Great Britain to have it organized on the European continent), and a great number of conferences were held. The present volume shows clearly how much progress has been made in the intervening years.

The editors deserve particular thanks for paying so much attention to a tutorial. In choosing the material, they have tried to highlight a number of software engineering initiatives whose origin is European. In particular, the more formal approach to software engineering is evident, and they have included some material that is not readily available elsewhere. The tutorial nature of the papers is intended to offer readers an easy introduction to the topics and indeed to the attempts that have been made in recent years to provide them with the tools, both in a handcraft and intellectual sense, that allow them now to call themselves honestly *software engineers*.

Friedrich L. Bauer

Reprinted from *Software Engineering—A European Perspective,* R.H. Thayer and A.D. McGettrick, eds., p. vi.

# Software Engineering—20 Years On and 20 Years Back*

J. N. Buxton
*Department of Computing, Kings College, London*

This paper gives a personal view of the development of software engineering, starting from the NATO conferences some 20 years ago, looking at the current situation and at possible lines of future development. Software engineering is not presented as separate from computer science but as the engineering face of the same subject. It is proposed in the paper that significant future developments will come from new localized computing paradigms in specific application domains.

## 20 YEARS BACK

The start of the development of software engineering as a subject in its own right, or perhaps more correctly as a new point of view on computing, is particularly associated with the NATO conferences in 1968 and 1969. The motivations behind the first of these meetings was the dawning realization that major software systems were being fuilt by groups consisting essentially of gifted amateurs. The endemic problems of the "software crisis"—software was late, over budget, and unreliable—already affected small and medium systems for well-coordinated applications and would clearly have even more serious consequences for the really big systems which were being planned.

People in the profession typically had scientific backgrounds in mathematics, the sciences, or electronics. In 1968 we had already achieved the first big breakthrough in the subject—the development of high-level programming languages—and the second was awaited. The time was ripe for the proposition which was floated by the NATO Science Committee, and by Professor Fritz Bauer of Munich, among others, that we should consider the subject as a branch of engineering; other professions built big systems of great complexity and by and large they called themselves "engineers," and perhaps we should consider whether we should do the same. Our big systems problems seemed primarily to be on the software side and the proposition was that it might well help to look at software development from the standpoint of the general principles and methods of engineering. And so, the first NATO Conference on Software Engineering was convened in Garmisch Parten-Kirchen in Bavaria.

It was an inspiring occasion. Some 50 people were invited from among the leaders in the field and from the first evening of the meeting it was clear that we shared deep concerns about the quality of software being built at the time. It was not just late and over budget; even more seriously we could see, and on that occasion we were able to share our anxieties about, the safety aspects of future systems.

The first meeting went some way to describing the problems—the next meeting was scheduled to follow after a year which was to be devoted to study of the techniques needed for its solution. We expected, of course, that a year spent in studying the application of engineering principles to software development would show us how to solve the problem. It turned out that after a year we had not solved it and the second meeting in Rome was rather an anticlimax. However, the software engineering idea was now launched: it has steadily gathered momentum over some 20 years. Some would no doubt say that it has become one of the great bandwagons of our time; however, much has been achieved and many central ideas have been developed: the need for management as well as technology, the software lifecycle, the use of toolsets, the application of quality assurance techniques, and so on.

So during some 20 years, while the business has expanded by many orders of magnitude, we have been able to keep our heads above water. We have put computers to use in most fields of human endeavor, we

*Address correspondence to Professor J. N. Buxton, Department of Computing, Kings College London, Strand, London WC2R2LS, England.*

*The paper is a written version of the keynote address at the International Conference on Software Engineering, Pittsburgh, May, 1989.

Reprinted from *J. Systems and Software,* Vol. 13, J.N. Buxton, "Software Engineering—20 Years On and 20 Years Back," pp. 153–155, 1990, with kind permission from Elsevier Science–NL, Sara Burgerhartstraat 25; 1055 KV Amsterdam, The Netherlands.

have demonstrated that systems of millions of lines of code taking hundreds of man-years can be built to acceptable standards, and our safety record, while not perfect, has so far apparently not been catastrophic. The early concepts of 20 years ago have been much developed: the lifecycle idea has undergone much refinement, the toolset approach has been transformed by combining unified toolsets with large project data bases, and quality control and assurance is now applied as in other engineering disciplines. We now appreciate more clearly that what we do in software development can well be seen as engineering, which must be underpinned by scientific and mathematical developments which produce laws of behavior for the materials from which we build: in other words, for computer programs.

## THE PRESENT

So, where is software engineering today? In my view there is indeed a new subject of "computing" which we have to consider. It is separate from other disciplines and has features that are unique to the subject. The artifacts we build have the unique property of invisibility and furthermore, to quote David Parnas, the state space of their behavior is both large and irregular. In other words, we cannot "see" an executing program actually running; we can only observe its consequences. These frequently surprise us and in this branch of engineering we lack the existence of simple physical limits on the extent of erroneous behavior. If you build a bridge or an airplane you can see it and you can recognize the physical limitations on its behavior—this is not the case if you write a computer program.

The subject of computing has strong links and relationships to other disciplines. It is underpinned by discrete mathematics and formal logic in a way strongly analogous to the underpinning of more traditional branches of engineering by physics and continuous mathematics. We expect increasing help from relevant mathematics in determining laws of behavior for our systems and of course we rely on electronics for the provision of our hardware components. A computer is an electronic artifact and is treated as such when it is being built or when it fails; at other times we treat it as a black box and assume it runs our program perfectly.

At the heart of the subject, however, we have the study of software. We build complex multilayered programs which eventually implement applications for people—who in turn treat the software as a black box and assume it will service their application perfectly.

So, where and what is software engineering? I do not regard it as a spearate subject. Building software is perhaps the central technology in computing and much of what we call software engineering is, in my view, the face of computing which is turned toward applications. The subject of computing has three main aspects: computer science is the face turned to mathematics, from which we seek laws of behavior for programs; computer architecture is the face turned to the electronics, from which we build our computers; and software engineering is the face turned toward the users, whose applications we implement. I think the time has come to return to a unified view of our subject—software engineering is not something different from computer science or hardware design—it is a different aspect or specialty within the same general subject of computing.

## 20 YEARS ON

To attempt to answer the question, Where should we go next and what of the next 20 years? opens interesting areas of speculation. As software engineers, our concerns are particularly with the needs of the users and our aims are to satisfy these needs. Our techniques involve the preparation of computer programs and I propose to embark on some speculation based on a study of the levels of language inwhich these programs are written.

The traditional picture of the process of implementing an application is, in general, as follows. The user presents a problem, expressed in his own technical terminology or language, which could be that of commerce, nuclear physics, medicine or whatever, to somebody else who speaks a different language in the professional sense. This is the language of algorithms and this person devises an algorithmic solution to the specific user problem, i.e., a solution expressed in computational steps, sequences, iterations, choices. This person we call the "systems analyst" and indeed, in the historical model much used in the data processing field, this person passes the algorithms on to a "real programmer" who thinks and speaks in the codeof the basic computer hardware.

The first major advance in computing was the general introduction of higher level languages such as FORTRAN and COBOL—as in effect this eliminated from all but some specialized areas the need for the lower level of language, i.e., achine or assembly code programming. The separate roles of systems analyst and programmer have become blurred into the concept of the software engineer who indeed thinks in algorithms but expresses these directly himself in one of the fashionable languages of the day. This indeed is a breakthrough and has given us an order of magnitude advance, whether we measure it in terms of productivity, size of application we can tackle, or quality of result.

Of course we have made other detailed advances—we have refined our software engineering techniques, we have devised alternatives to algorithmic programming in functional and rule-based systems, and we have done much else. But in general terms we have not succeeded in making another general advance across the board in the subject.

In some few areas, however, there have been real successes which have brought computing to orders of magnitude more people with applications. These have been in very specific application areas, two of which spring to mind—spreadsheets and word processors. In my view, study of these successes gives us most valuable clues as to the say ahead for computing applications.

The spreadsheet provides a good example for study. The generic problem of accountancy is the presentation of a set of figures which are perhaps very complexly related but which must be coherent and consistent. The purpose is to reveal a picture of the formal state of affairs of an enterprise (so far, of course, as the accountatn thinks it wise or necessary to reveal it). The traditional working language of the accountatn is expressed in rows and columns of figures on paper together with their relationships. Now, the computer-based spreadsheet system automates the piece of paper and gives it magical extra properties which maintain consistency of the figure under the relationships between them as specified by the accountant, while he adjusts the figures. In effect, the computer program automates the generic problem rather than any specific set of accounts and so enables the accountant to express his problem of the moment and to seek solutions in his own professional language. He need know nothing, for example, of algorithms, high-level languages, or von Neuman machines, and the intermediary stages of the systems analyst and programmer have both disappeared from his view.

The same general remarks can be applied to word processing. Here what the typist sees is in effect a combination of magic correcting typewriter and filing cabinet—and again the typist need know nothing of algorithms. In both these examples there has been conspicuous success in introduction. And there are others emerging, e.g., hypertext. And historically there is much in the thesis that relates to the so-called 4GLs and, even earlier, to simulation languages in the 1960s.

Let me return to the consideration of levels of language, and summarize the argument so far. I postulated a traditional model for complete applications in which a specific user problem, expressed in the language of the domain of application, underwent a two-stage translation: first into algorithms (or some language of similar level such as functional applications or Horn logic clauses) and second down into machine code. Our first breakthrough was to automate the lower of these stages by the introduction of high-level languages, primarily algorithmic. I now postulate that the second breakthrough will come in areas where we can automate the upper stage. Examples can already be found: very clearly in specific closed domains such as spreadsheets and word processors but also in more diffuse areas addressed by very high-level languages such as 4GLs and simulation generators.

Perhaps I should add a word here about object-orientedness, as this is the best known buzz word of today. I regard an object-oriented approach as a halfway house to the concept I am proposing. Objects indeed model those features of the real world readily modelable as classes of entities—that is why we invented the concept in the simulation languages of the early 1960s. However, the rules of behavior of the object are still expressed algorithmically and so an object-oriented system still embodies a general purpose language.

It is central to the argument to realize that spreadsheets and such can be used by people who do not readily think in terms of algorithms. The teaching of programming has demonstrated over many years that thinking in algorithms is a specific skill and most people have little ability in transposing problems from their own domains into algorithmic solutions. Attempts to bring the use of computers to all by teaching them programming do not work; providing a service to workers in specific domains directly in the language of that domain, however, does work and spectacularly so.

## CONCLUSIONS

I come to the conclusion, therefore, that the most promising activity for the next 20 years is the search for more domains of applications in which the language used to express problems in the domain is closed, consistent, and logically based. Then we can put forward generic computer-based systems which enable users in the domain to express their problems in the language of the application and to be given solutions in their own terms. To use another buzz word of the day, I look for non-specific but localized paradigms for computing applications.

Of course this is not all that we might expect to do in the next 20 years. We can do much more in developing the underpinning technology in the intermediate levels between the user and the machine. Most of our work will still be devoted to the implementing of systems to deliver solutions to specific problems. But while we proceed with the day-to-day activities of software engineering or of the other faces of computing with which we may be concerned, wemight be wise to look out for opportunities to exploit new application domains where we can see ways to raise the "level of programming language" until it becomes the same as the professional language of that domain. Then, we will achieve another breakthrough.

# Chapter 4

# Software Requirements Engineering and Software Design

## 1. Introduction to Chapter.

This Tutorial initially contained one chapter on requirements engineering and one chapter on design. As the papers began to accumulate, it became apparent that the topics ought to be treated together: it is not always clear when requirements engineering stops and design starts, and many of the tools and techniques are common to both disciplines. The Tutorial was therefore reorganized to cover the basics of requirements and design in one chapter and to focus on methodologies in the next.

### 1.1 Introduction to Software Requirements

A *software requirement* can be defined as:

- A software capability needed by the user to solve a problem or achieve an objective.
- A software capability that must be met or possessed by a system or system component to satisfy a contract, specification, standard, or other formally imposed document.

*Software requirements engineering* consists of the following five activities:

- *Software requirements elicitation*—The process through which the customers (buyers and/or users) and the developer (contractor) of a software system discover, review, articulate, and understand the users' needs and the constraints on the software and the development activity.
- *Software requirements analysis*—Reasoning about and analyzing the customers' and users' needs to arrive at a definition of software requirements
- *Software requirements specification*—Development of a document that clearly and precisely records each of the requirements of the software system
- *Software requirements verification*—Ensuring that the software requirements specification is in compliance with the system requirements, conforms to document standards of the requirements phase, and is an adequate basis for the architectural (preliminary) design phase
- *Software requirements management*—Planning and controlling the requirements elicitation, specification, analysis, and verification activities

This chapter concerns itself primarily with the activities of analysis and specification. Discussions of the other elements of requirements engineering can be found in other chapters in this Tutorial.

Software requirements may be categorized as follows:

- Functional requirements
- Performance requirements
- External interface requirements
- Design constraints
- Quality requirements

The last four categories are sometimes referred to as non-functional requirements or constraints.

### 1.2. Introduction to Software Design

*Software design* can be defined as the use of scientific principles, technical information, and imagination in the definition of a software system to perform specified functions with maximum economy and efficiency. Software design is also defined as the activity of transforming a statement of what is required to be accomplished into a plan for implementing the requirements on a computer.

Others, in their attempts to separate the disciplines of requirements analysis and design, have defined analysis as being what the customer or user is interested in and design as being what the customer or user is not interested in, that is, the customer or user doesn't care about the details of how the system is implemented. A fourth view is that requirements may be implemented in more than one way, while design is the selected approach to implementation. The terms "what" and "how" are also used: requirements are "what" a system must do, and design is "how" the requirements are met.

Software design has two stages, *architectural design* and *detailed design. Architectural design* (sometimes called preliminary design) is the process of defining a collection of software components, their functions, and their interfaces to establish a framework for the development of a software system. *Detailed design* (sometimes called critical design) is the process of refining and expanding the software architectural design to describe the internals of the components (the algorithms, processing logic, data structures, and data definitions). Detailed design is complete when the description is sufficient for implementation, that is, coding.

## 2. Introduction to Papers

The first paper in this chapter, by Stuart Faulk of the US Naval Research Laboratory, is an overview of software requirements engineering. Faulk shows that "requirements problems are persistent, pervasive, and costly," and describes the difficulties that arise in the development and documentation of software requirements. He shows how a disciplined approach can help solve requirements problems. He summarizes current and emerging methods for software requirements engineering, and concludes with the observation that, while it may be impossible to do a perfect job of software requirements, a careful, systematic approach, carried out by properly trained and supported people, can contribute to a successful software development.

The second paper in this section is "Software Design: An Introduction," by David Budgen of the University of Keele, UK. Professor Budgen is the author of the recent and well-received textbook entitled "Software Design."[1]

This overview paper describes the software engineering activity of software design, terminating in a software design description (sometimes called a design specification). Budgen defines three aspects of software design:

1. *Representative* part (usually textual in form)
2. *Process* part (the procedure to be followed in developing the design model)
3. A set of *heuristics* (conveying non-procedural knowledge, such as quality attributes)

A design viewpoint as described by Budgen is an abstract description of a particular set of attributes or properties that can be used to describe design elements. They are defined as:

- *Function* viewpoint (describes what a design element does)
- *Behavioral* viewpoint (describes the transformation that occurs in response to events)
- *Structural* viewpoint (describes how elements of the solution are related)
- *Data modeling* (describes the relationships that are inherent in the design elements)

Finally Budgen delineates the changes in software design since the 1960s.

The third paper in this chapter is an original contribution by Hassan Gomaa of George Mason University, author of the recent textbook *Software Design Methods for Concurrent and Real-Time Systems*.[2] Gomaa's paper, entitled "Design Methods for Concurrent and Real Time Systems," demonstrates some of the features of software engineering as applied to designing concurrent and real-time computer-based systems. This paper discusses and compares the concepts and criteria used by software design methods for developing large-scale concurrent and real-time systems. Concurrence is addressed by task structuring while modifiability is addressed by module structuring. In addition, the behavioral aspects of a real-time system are addressed by means of finite state machines. Several real-time analysis and design tools and methods are discussed, such as DARTS, Jackson System Development, and object-oriented design.

The last paper in this section is another application-oriented paper by Robert Remington of Lockheed Martin Missiles & Space Co. Remington's paper, "Computer Human Interface Software Development Survey," familiarizes the reader with available information sources as well as recent trends in human-computer interface design, development, and evaluation. The paper describes several earlier surveys that provide the computer professional with an introduction to human-computer interface concepts, methods, and tools. It emphasizes that without good human-computer interface many systems are difficult to use and may not be used.

This paper emphasizes the need to use basic human interface design principles such as rapid prototyping techniques to obtain user feedback early and continuously throughout the design process, and systematic usability testing to validate designs.


1. Budgen, David, *Software Design*, Addison-Wesley, Publishing Company, Wokingham, England; Reading, Massachusetts, 1993
2. Gomaa, Hassan, "Software Design Methods for Concurrent and Real-Time Systems," SEI Series in Software Engineering, Addison-Wesley Publishing Company, Reading, Mass., 1993.

# Software Requirements: A Tutorial

Stuart R. Faulk

"The hardest single part of building a software system is deciding precisely what to build. No other part of the conceptual work is as difficult as establishing the detailed technical requirements . . . No other part of the work so cripples the resulting system if done wrong. No other part is as difficult to rectify later."

[Brooks 87]

## 1. Introduction

Deciding precisely what to build and documenting the results is the goal of the requirements phase of software development. For many developers of large, complex software systems, requirements are their biggest software engineering problem. While there is considerable disagreement on how to solve the problem, few would disagree with Brooks' assessment that no other part of a development is as difficult to do well or as disastrous in result when done poorly. The purpose of this tutorial is to help the reader understand why the apparently simple notion of "deciding what to build" is so difficult in practice, where the state of the art does and does not address these difficulties, and what hope we have for doing better in the future.

This paper does not survey the literature but seeks to provide the reader with an understanding of the underlying issues. There are currently many more approaches to requirements than one can cover in a short paper. This diversity is the product of two things: different views about which of the many problems in requirements is pivotal, and different assumptions about the desirable characteristics of a solution. This paper attempts to impart a basic understanding of the requirements problem and its many facets, as well as the trade-offs involved in attempting a solution. Thus forearmed, readers can assess the claims of different requirements methods and their likely effectiveness in addressing the readers' particular needs.

We begin with basic terminology and some historical data on the requirements problem. We examine the goals of the requirements phase and the problems that can arise in attempting those goals. As in Brooks's article [Brooks 87], much of the discussion is motivated by the distinction between the difficulties inherent in what one is trying to accomplish (the "essential" difficulties) and those one creates through inadequate practice ("accidental" difficulties). We discuss how a disciplined software engineering process helps address many of the accidental difficulties and why the focus of such a disciplined process is on producing a written specification of the detailed technical requirements. We examine current technical approaches to requirements in terms of the specific problems each approach seeks to address. Finally, we examine technical trends and discuss where significant advances are likely to occur in the future.

## 2. Requirements and the Software Life Cycle

A variety of software life-cycle models have been proposed with an equal variety of terminology. Davis [Davis 88] provides a good summary. While differing in the detailed decomposition of the steps (for example, prototyping models) or in the surrounding management and control structure (for example, to manage risk), there is general agreement on the core elements of the model. Figure 1 [Davis 93] is a version of the common model that illustrates the relationship between the software development stages and the related testing and acceptance phases.

When software is created in the context of a larger hardware and software system, system requirements are defined first, followed by system design. System design includes decisions about which parts of the system requirements will be allocated to hardware and which to software. For software-only systems, the life-cycle model begins with software requirements analysis. From this point on, the role of software requirements in the development model is the same whether or not the software is part of a larger system, as shown in Figure 2 [Davis 93]. For this reason, the remainder of our discussion does not distinguish whether or not software is developed as part of a larger system. For an overview of system versus software issues, the reader is referred to Dorfman and Thayer's survey [Thayer 90].

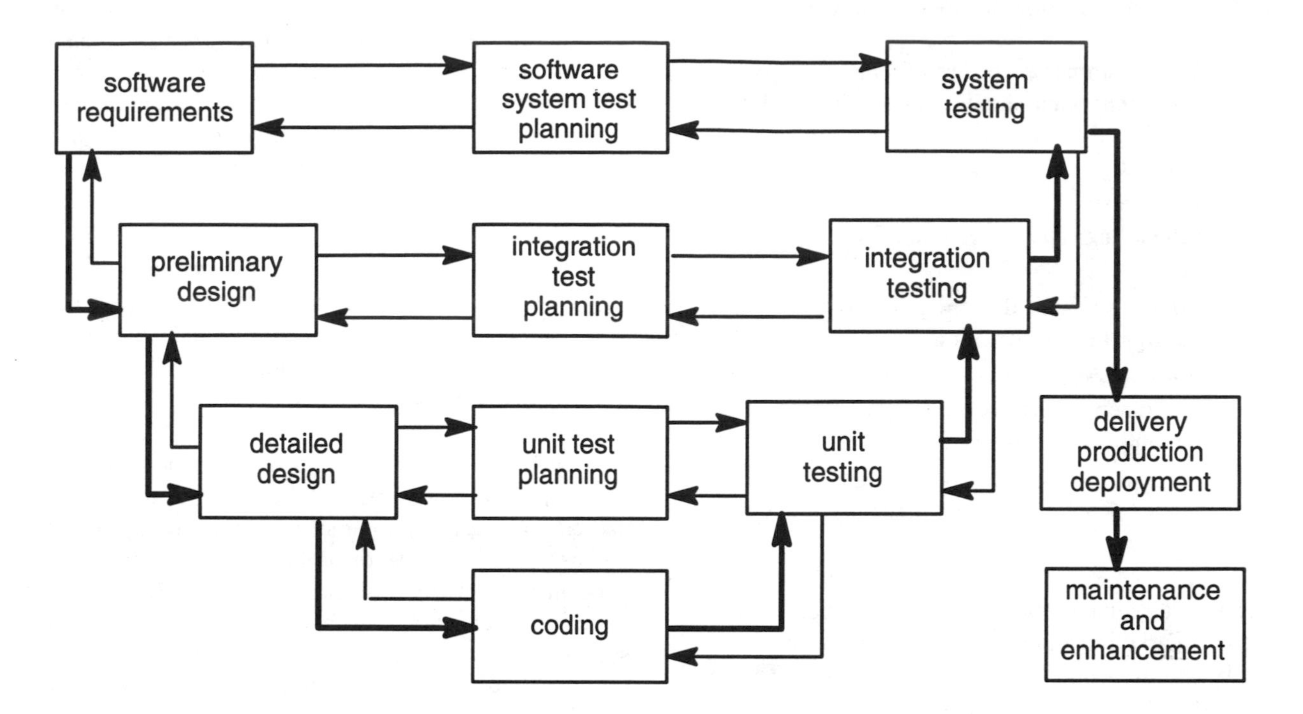


*Figure 1. Software life cycle*

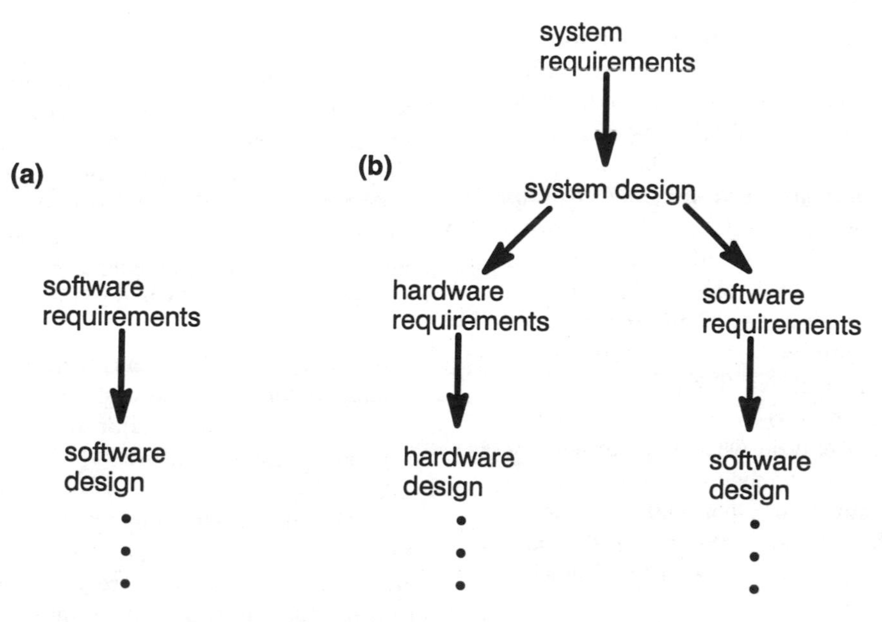


*Figure 2. Development paths: (a) software, (b) systems*

In a large system development, the software requirements specification may play a variety of roles:

- For customers, the requirements typically document what should be delivered and may provide the contractual basis for the development.
- For managers, it may provide the basis for scheduling and a yardstick for measuring progress.
- For the software designers, it may provide the "design-to" specification.
- For coders, it defines the range of acceptable implementations and is the final authority on the outputs that must be produced.
- For quality assurance personnel, it is the basis for validation, test planning, and verification.

The requirements may also used by such diverse groups as marketing and governmental regulators.

It is common practice (for example, see [Thayer 90]) to classify software requirements as "functional" or "nonfunctional." While definitions vary somewhat in detail, "functional" typically refers to requirements defining the acceptable mappings between system input values and corresponding output values. "Nonfunctional" then refers to all other constraints including, but not limited to, performance, dependability, maintainability, reusability, and safety.

While widely used, the classification of requirements as "functional" and "nonfunctional" is confusing in its terminology and of little help in understanding common properties of different kinds of requirements. The word "function" is one of the most overloaded in computer science, and its only rigorous meaning, that of a mathematical function, is not what is meant here. The classification of requirements as functional and non-functional offers little help in understanding common attributes of different types of requirements since it partitions classes of requirements with markedly similar qualities (for example, output values and output deadlines) while grouping others that have commonality only in what they are not (for example, output deadlines and maintainability goals).

A more useful distinction is between what can be described as "behavioral requirements" and "developmental quality attributes" with the following definitions [Clements 95]:

- *Behavioral requirements*—Behavioral requirements include any and all information necessary to determine if the runtime behavior of a given implementation is acceptable. The behavioral requirements define all constraints on the system outputs (for example, value, accuracy, timing) and resulting system state for all possible inputs and current system state. By this definition, security, safety, performance, timing, and fault tolerance are all behavioral requirements.
- *Developmental quality attributes*—Developmental quality attributes include any constraints on the attributes of the system's static construction. These include properties like testability, changeability, maintainability, and reusability.

Behavioral requirements have in common that they are properties of the runtime behavior of the system and can (at least in principle) be validated objectively by observing the behavior of the running system, independent of its method of implementation. In contrast, developmental quality attributes are properties of the system's static structures (for example, modularization) or representation. Developmental quality attributes have in common that they are functions of the development process and methods of construction. Assessment of developmental quality attributes are necessarily relativistic—for example, we do not say that a design is or is not maintainable but that one design is more maintainable than another.

## 3. A Big Problem

Requirements problems are persistent, pervasive, and costly. Evidence is most readily available for the large software systems developed for the US government, since the results are a matter of public record. As soon as software became a significant part of such systems, developers identified requirements as a major source of problems. For example, developers of the early Ballistic Missile Defense System noted that:

> In nearly every software project that fails to meet performance and cost goals, requirements inadequacies play a major and expensive role in project failure [Alford 79].

Nor has the problem mitigated over the intervening years. A recent study of problems in mission-critical defense systems identified requirements as a major problem source in two thirds of the systems examined [GAO 92]. This is consistent with results of a survey of large aerospace firms that identified requirements as the most critical software development problem [Faulk 92]. Likewise, studies by Lutz

[Lutz 92] identified functional and interface requirements as the major source of safety-related software errors in NASA's Voyager and Galileo spacecraft.

Results of industry studies in the 1970s described by Boehm [Boehm 81], and since replicated a number of times, showed that requirements errors are the most costly. These studies all produced the same basic result: The earlier in the development process an error occurs and the later the error is detected, the more expensive it is to correct. Moreover, the relative cost rises quickly. As shown in Figure 3, an error that costs a dollar to fix in the requirements phase may cost $100 to $200 to fix if it is not corrected until the system is fielded or in the maintenance phase.

The costs of such failures can be enormous. For example, the 1992 GAO report notes that one system, the Cheyenne Mountain Upgrade, will be delivered eight years late, exceed budget by $600 million, and have less capability than originally planned, largely due to requirements-related problems. Prior GAO reports [GAO 79] suggest that such problems are the norm rather than the exception. While data from private industry is less readily available, there is little reason to believe that the situation is significantly different.

In spite of presumed advances in software engineering methodology and tool support, the requirements problem has not diminished. This does not mean that the apparent progress in software engineering is illusory. While the features of the problem have not changed, the applications have grown significantly in capability, scale, and complexity. A reasonable conclusion is that the growing ambitiousness of our software systems has outpaced the gains in requirements technology, at least as such technology is applied in practice.

## 4. Why Are Requirements Hard?

It is generally agreed that the goal of the requirements phase is to establish and specify precisely what the software must do without describing how to do it. So simple seems this basic intent that it is not at all evident why it is so difficult to accomplish in practice. If what we want to accomplish is so clear, why is it so hard? To understand this, we must examine more closely the goals of the requirements phase, where errors originate, and why the nature of the task leads to some inherent difficulties.

Most authors agree in principle that requirements should specify "what" rather than "how." In other words, the goal of requirements is to understand and specify the *problem* to be solved rather than the *solution*. For example, the requirements for an automated teller system should talk about customer accounts, deposits, and withdrawals rather than the software algorithms and data structures. The most basic reason for this is that a specification in terms of the problem captures the actual requirements without overconstraining the subsequent design or implementation. Further, solutions in software terms are typically more complex, more difficult to change, and harder to understand (particularly for the customer) than a specification of the problem.

Unfortunately, distinguishing "what" from "how" itself represents a dilemma. As Davis [Davis 88], among others, points out, the distinction between what and how is necessarily a function of perspective. A specification at any chosen level of system decomposition can be viewed as describing the "what" for the next level. Thus customer needs may define the "what" and the decomposition into hardware and software the corresponding "how." Subsequently, the behavioral requirements allocated to a software component define its "what," the software design, the "how," and so on. The upshot is that requirements cannot be effectively discussed at all without prior agreement on which system one is talking about and at what level of decomposition. One must agree on what constitutes the problem space and what constitutes the solution space—the analysis and specification of requirements then properly belongs in the problem space.

| Stage | Relative Repair Cost |
|---|---|
| Requirements | 1–2 |
| Design | 5 |
| Coding | 10 |
| Unit test | 20 |
| System test | 50 |
| Maintenance | 200 |

*Figure 3: Relative cost to repair a software error in different stages*

In discussing requirements problems, one must also distinguish the development of large, complex systems from smaller efforts (for example, developments by a single or small team of programmers). Large system developments are multiperson efforts. They are developed by teams of tens to thousands of programmers. The programmers work in the context of an organization typically including management, systems engineering, marketing, accounting, and quality assurance. The organization itself must operate in the context of outside concerns also interested in the software product, including the customer, regulatory agencies, and suppliers.

Even where only one system is intended, large systems are inevitably multiversion as well. As the software is being developed, tested, and even fielded, it evolves. Customers understand better what they want, developers understand better what they can and cannot do within the constraints of cost and schedule, and circumstances surrounding development change. The results are changes in the software requirements and, ultimately, the software itself. In effect, several versions of a given program are produced, if only incrementally. Such unplanned changes occur in addition to the expected variations of planned improvements.

The multiperson, multiversion nature of large system development introduces problems that are both quantitatively and qualitatively different from those found in smaller developments. For example, scale introduces the need for administration and control functions with the attendant management issues that do not exist on small projects. The quantitative effects of increased complexity in communication when the number of workers rises are well documented by Brooks [Brooks 75]. In the following discussion, it is this large system development context we will assume, since that is the one in which the worst problems occur and where the most help is needed.

Given the context of multiperson, multiversion development, our basic goal of specifying what the software must do can be decomposed into the following subgoals:

1. Understand precisely what is required of the software.
2. Communicate the understanding of what is required to all of the parties involved in the development.
3. Provide a means for controlling the production to ensure that the final system satisfies the requirements (including managing the effects of changes).

It follows that the source of most requirements errors is in the failure to adequately accomplish one of these goals, that is:

1. The developers failed to understand what was required of the software by the customer, end user, or other parties with a stake in the final product.
2. The developers did not completely and precisely capture the requirements or subsequently communicate the requirements effectively to other parties involved in the development.
3. The developers did not effectively manage the effects of changing requirements or ensure the conformance of down-stream development steps including design, code, integration, test, or maintenance to the system requirements.

The end result of such failures is a software system that does not perform as desired or expected, a development that exceeds budget and schedule or, all too frequently, failure to deliver any working software at all.

### 4.1 Essential Difficulties

Even our more detailed goals appear straightforward; why then do so many development efforts fail to achieve them? The short answer is that the mutual satisfaction of these goals, in practice, is inherently difficult. To understand why, it is useful to reflect on some points raised by Brooks [Brooks 87] on why software engineering is hard and on the distinction he makes between essential difficulties—those inherent in the problem, and the accidental difficulties—those introduced through imperfect practice. For though requirements are inherently difficult, there is no doubt that these difficulties are many times multiplied by the inadequacies of current practice.

The following essential difficulties attend each (in some cases all) of the requirements goals:

- *Comprehension.* People do not know what they want. This does not mean that people do not have a general idea of what the software is for. Rather, they do not begin with a precise and detailed understanding of what functions belong in the software, what the output must be for every possible input, how long each operation should take, how one decision will affect another, and so on.

Indeed, unless the new system is simply a reconstruction of an old one, such a detailed understanding at the outset is unachievable. Many decisions about the system behavior will depend on other decisions yet unmade, and expectations will change as the problem (and attendant costs of alternative solutions) is better understood. Nonetheless, it is a precise and richly detailed understanding of expected behavior that is needed to create effective designs and develop correct code.

- *Communication.* Software requirements are difficult to communicate effectively. As Brooks points out, the conceptual structures of software systems are complex, arbitrary, and difficult to visualize. The large software systems we are now building are among the most complex structures ever attempted. That complexity is arbitrary in the sense that it is an artifact of people's decisions and prior construction rather than a reflection of fundamental properties (as, for example, in the case of physical laws). To make matters worse, many of the conceptual structures in software have no readily comprehensible physical analogue so they are difficult to visualize.

  In practice, comprehension suffers under all of these constraints. We work best with regular, predictable structures, can comprehend only a very limited amount of information at one time, and understand large amounts of information best when we can visualize it. Thus the task of capturing and conveying software requirements is inherently difficult.

  The inherent difficulty of communication is compounded by the diversity of purposes and audiences for a requirements specification. Ideally, a technical specification is written for a particular audience. The brevity and comprehensibility of the document depend on assumptions about common technical background and use of language. Such commonality typically does not hold for the many diverse groups (for example, customers, systems engineers, managers) that must use a software requirements specification.

- *Control.* Inherent difficulties attend control of software development as well. The arbitrary and invisible nature of software makes it difficult to anticipate which requirements will be met easily and which will decimate the project's budget and schedule if, indeed, they can be fulfilled at all. The low fidelity of software planning has become a cliche, yet the requirements are often the best available basis for planning or for tracking to a plan.

  This situation is made incalculably worse by software's inherent malleability. Of all the problems bedeviling software managers, few evoke such passion as the difficulties of dealing with frequent and arbitrary changes to requirements. For most systems, such changes remain a fact of life even after delivery. The continuous changes make it difficult to develop stable specifications, plan effectively, or control cost and schedule. For many industrial developers, change management is the most critical problem in requirements.

- *Inseparable concerns.* In seeking solutions to the foregoing problems, we are faced with the additional difficulty that the issues cannot easily be separated and dealt with, piecemeal. For example, developers have attempted to address the problem of changing requirements by baselining and freezing requirements before design begins. This proves impractical because of the comprehension problem—the customer may not fully know what he wants until he sees it. Similarly, the diversity of purposes and audiences is often addressed by writing a different specification for each. Thus there may be a system specification, a set of requirements delivered to customer, a distinct set of technical requirements written for the internal consumption of the software developers, and so on. However, this solution vastly increases the complexity, provides an open avenue for inconsistencies, and multiplies the difficulties of managing changes.

These issues represent only a sample of the inherent dependencies between different facets of the requirements problem. The many distinct parties with an interest in a system's requirements, the many different roles the requirements play, and the interlocking nature of software's conceptual structures, all introduce dependencies between concerns and impose conflicting constraints on any potential solution.

The implications are twofold. First we are constrained in the application of our most effective strategy for dealing with complex problems—divide and conquer. If a problem is considered in isolation, the solution is likely to aggravate other difficulties. Effective solutions to most requirements difficulties must simultaneously address more than one problem. Second, developing practical solutions requires making difficult trade-offs. Where different problems have conflicting constraints, compromises must be made. Because the trade-offs result in different gains or losses to the different parties involved, effective compromises require negotiation. These issues are considered in more detail when we discuss the properties of a good requirements specification.

### 4.2 Accidental Difficulties

While there is no doubt that software requirements are inherently difficult to do well, there is equally no doubt that common practice unnecessarily exacerbates the difficulty. We use the term "accidental" in contrast to "essential," not to imply that the difficulties arise by chance but that they are the product of common failings in management, elicitation, specification, or use of requirements. It is these failings that are most easily addressed by improved practice.

- *Written as an afterthought.* It remains common practice that requirements documentation is developed only after the software has been written. For many projects, the temptation to rush into implementation before the requirements are adequately understood proves irresistible. This is understandable. Developers often feel like they are not really doing anything when they are not writing code; managers are concerned about schedule when there is no visible progress on the implementation. Then too, the intangible nature of the product mitigates toward early implementation. Developing the system is an obvious way to understand better what is needed and make visible the actual behavior of the product. The result is that requirements specifications are written as an afterthought (if at all). They are not created to guide the developers and testers but treated as a necessary evil to satisfy contractual demands.

  Such after-the-fact documentation inevitably violates the principle of defining what the system must do rather than the how since it is a specification of the code as written. It is produced after the fact so it is not planned or managed as an essential part of the development but is thrown together. In fact, it is not even available in time to guide implementation or manage development.

- *Confused in purpose.* Because there are so many potential audiences for a requirements specification, with different points of view, the exact purpose of the document becomes confused. An early version is used to sell the product to the customer, so it includes marketing hype extolling the product's virtues. It is the only documentation of what the system does, so it provides introductory, explanatory, and overview material. It is a contractual document, so it is intentionally imprecise to allow the developer latitude in the delivered product or the customer latitude in making no-cost changes. It is the vehicle for communicating decisions about software details to designers and coders, so it incorporates design and implementation. The result is a document in which it is unclear which statements represent real requirements and which are more properly allocated to marketing, design, or other documentation. It is a document that attempts to be everything to everyone and ultimately serves no one well.

- *Not designed to be useful.* Often, in the rush to implementation, little effort is expended on requirements. The requirements specification is not expected to be useful and, indeed, this turns out to be a self-fulfilling prophecy. Because the document is not expected to be useful, little effort is expended on designing it, writing it, checking it, or managing its creation and evolution. The most obvious result is poor organization. The specification is written in English prose and follows the author's stream of consciousness or the order of execution [Heninger 80].

  The resulting document is ineffective as a technical reference. It is unclear which statements represent actual requirements. It is unclear where to put or find particular requirements. There is no effective procedure for ensuring that the specification is consistent or complete. There is no systematic way to manage requirements changes. The specification is difficult to use and difficult to maintain. It quickly becomes out of date and loses whatever usefulness it might originally have had.

- *Lacks essential properties.* Lack of forethought, confusion of purpose, or lack of careful design and execution all lead to requirements that lack properties critical to good technical specifications. The requirements, if documented at all, are redundant, inconsistent, incomplete, imprecise, and inaccurate.

Where the essential difficulties are inherent in the problem, the accidental difficulties result from a failure to gain or maintain intellectual control over what is to be built. While the presence of the essential difficulties means that there can be no "silver bullet" that will suddenly render requirements easy, we can remove at least the accidental difficulties through a well thought out, systematic, and disciplined development process. Such a disciplined process then provides a stable foundation for attacking the essential difficulties.

## 5. Role of a Disciplined Approach

The application of discipline in analyzing and specifying software requirements can address the accidental difficulties. While there is now general agreement on the desirable qualities of a software development approach, the field is insufficiently mature to have standardized the development process. Nonetheless, it is useful to examine the characteristics of an idealized process and its products to understand where current approaches are weak and which current trends are promising. In general, a complete requirements approach will define:

- *Process*: The (partially ordered) sequence of activities, entrance and exit criteria for each activity, which work product is produced in each activity, and what kind of people should do the work.
- *Products*: The work products to be produced and, for each product, the resources needed to produce it, the information it contains, the expected audience, and the acceptance criteria the product must satisfy.

Currently, there is little uniformity in different author's decomposition of the requirements phase or in the terminology for the activities. Davis [Davis 88] provides a good summary of the variations. Following Davis's integrated model and terminology [Davis 93], the requirements phase consists of two conceptually distinct but overlapping activities corresponding to the first two goals for requirements enumerated previously:

1. *Problem analysis*: The goal of problem analysis is to understand precisely what problem is to be solved. It includes identifying the exact purpose of the system, who will use it, the constraints on acceptable solutions, and the possible trade-offs between conflicting constraints.
2. *Requirements specification*: The goal of requirements specification is to create a document, the Software Requirements Specification (SRS), describing exactly what is to be built. The SRS captures the results of problem analysis and characterizes the set of acceptable solutions to the problem.

In practice, the distinction between these activities is conceptual rather than temporal. Where both are needed, the developer typically switches back and forth between analysis of the problem and documentation of the results. When problems are well understood, the analysis phase may be virtually nonexistent. When the system model and documentation are standardized or based on existing specifications, the documentation paradigm may guide the analysis [Hester 81].

### 5.1 Problem Analysis

Problem analysis is necessarily informal in the sense that there is no effective, closed-end procedure that will guarantee success. It is an information-acquiring, -collating, and -structuring process through which one attempts to understand all the various parts of a problem and their relationships. The difficulty in developing an effective understanding of large, complex software problems has motivated considerable effort to structure and codify problem analysis.

The basic issues in problem analysis are:

- How to effectively elicit a complete set of requirements from the customer or other sources?
- How to decompose the problem into intellectually manageable pieces?
- How to organize the information so it can be understood?
- How to communicate about the problem with all the parties involved?

- How to resolve conflicting needs?
- How to know when to stop?

### 5.2 Requirements Specification

For substantial developments, the effectiveness of the requirements effort depends on how well the SRS captures the results of analysis and how useable the specification is. There is little benefit to developing a thorough understanding of the problem if that understanding is not effectively communicated to customers, designers, implementors, testers, and maintainers. The larger and more complex the system, the more important a good specification becomes. This is a direct result of the many roles the SRS plays in a multiperson, multiversion development [Parnas 86]:

1. The SRS is the primary vehicle for agreement between the developer and customer on exactly what is to be built. It is the document reviewed by the customer or his representative and often is the basis for judging fulfillment of contractual obligations.
2. The SRS records the results of problem analysis. It is the basis for determining where the requirements are complete and where additional analysis is necessary. Documenting the results of analysis allows questions about the problem to be answered only once during development.
3. The SRS defines what properties the system must have and the constraints on its design and implementation. It defines where there is, and is not, design freedom. It helps ensure that requirements decisions are made explicitly during the requirements phase, not implicitly during programming.
4. The SRS is the basis for estimating cost and schedule. It is management's primary tool for tracking development progress and ascertaining what remains to be done.
5. The SRS is the basis for test plan development. It is the tester's chief tool for determining the acceptable behavior of the software.
6. The SRS provides the standard definition of expected behavior for the system's maintainers and is used to record engineering changes.

For a disciplined software development, the SRS is the primary technical specification of the software and the primary control document. This is an inevitable result of the complexity of large systems and the need to coordinate multiperson development teams. To ensure that the right system is built, one must first understand the problem. To ensure agreement on what is to be built and the criteria for success, the results of that understanding must be recorded. The goal of a systematic requirements process is thus the development of a set of specifications that effectively communicate the results of analysis.

Requirement's accidental difficulties are addressed through the careful analysis and specification of a disciplined process. Rather than developing the specification as an afterthought, requirements are understood and specified before development begins. One knows what one is building before attempting to build it. The SRS is the primary vehicle for communicating requirements between the developers, managers, and customers, so the document is designed to be useful foro that purpose. A useful document is maintained.

## 6. Requirements for the Software Requirements Specification

The goals of the requirements process, the attendant difficulties, and the role of the requirements specification in a disciplined process determine the properties of a "good" requirements specification. These properties do not mandate any particular specification method but do describe the characteristics of an effective method.

In discussing the properties of a good SRS, it is useful to distinguish semantic properties from packaging properties [Faulk 92]. Semantic properties are a consequence of what the specification says (that is, its meaning or semantics). Packaging properties are a consequence of how the requirements are written—the format, organization, and presentation of the information. The semantic properties determine how effectively an SRS captures the software requirements. The packaging properties determine how useable the resulting specification is. Figure 4 illustrates the classification of properties of a good SRS.

An SRS that satisfies the semantic properties of a good specification is:

- *Complete*. The SRS defines the set of acceptable implementations. It should contain all the information needed to write software that is acceptable to the customer and no more. Any implementation that satisfies every statement in the requirements is an acceptable product. Where information is not available before development begins, areas of incompleteness must be explicitly indicated [Parnas 86].

| SRS Semantic Properties | SRS Packaging Properties |
|---|---|
| Complete | Modifiable |
| Implementation independent | Readable |
| Unambiguous and consistent | Organized for reference and review |
| Precise | |
| Verifiable | |

*Figure 4. Classification of SRS properties*

- *Implementation independent.* The SRS should be free of design and implementation decisions unless those decisions reflect actual requirements.
- *Unambiguous and consistent.* If the SRS is subject to conflicting interpretation, the different parties will not agree on what is to be built or whether the right software has been built. Every requirement should have only one possible interpretation. Similarly, no two statements of required behavior should conflict.
- *Precise.* The SRS should define exactly the required behavior. For each output, it should define the range of acceptable values for every input. The SRS should define any applicable timing constraints such as minimum and maximum acceptable delay.
- *Verifiable.* A requirement is verifiable if it is possible to determine unambiguously whether a given implementation satisfies the requirement or not. For example, a behavioral requirement is verifiable if it is possible to determine, for any given test case (that is, an input and an output), whether the output represents an acceptable behavior of the software given the input and the system state.

An SRS[1] that satisfies the packaging properties of a good specification is:

- *Modifiable.* The SRS must be organized for ease of change. Since no organization can be equally easy to change for all possible changes, the requirements analysis process must identify expected changes and the relative likelihood of their occurrence. The specification is then organized to limit the effect of likely changes.
- *Readable.* The SRS must be understandable by the parties that use it. It should clearly relate the elements of the problem space as understood by the customer to the observable behavior of the software.
- *Organized for reference and review.* The SRS is the primary technical specification of the software requirements. It is the repository for all the decisions made during analysis about what should be built. It is the document reviewed by the customer or his representatives. It is the primary arbitrator of disputes. As such, the document must be organized for quick and easy reference. It must be clear where each decision about the requirements belongs. It must be possible to answer specific questions about the requirements quickly and easily.

To address the difficulties associated with writing and using an SRS, a requirements approach must provide techniques addressing both semantic and packaging properties. It is also desirable that the conceptual structures of the approach treat the semantic and packaging properties as distinct concerns (that is, as independently as possible). This allows one to change the presentation of the SRS without changing its meaning.

In aggregate, these properties of a good SRS represent an ideal. Some of the properties may be unachievable, particularly over the short term. For example, a common complaint is that one cannot develop complete requirements before design begins because the customer does not yet fully understand what he wants or is still making changes. Further, different SRS "requirements" mitigate toward conflicting solutions. A commonly cited example is the use of English prose to express requirements. English is readily understood but notoriously ambiguous and imprecise. Conversely, formal languages are precise and unambiguous, but can be difficult to read.

Although the ideal SRS may be unachievable, possessing a common understanding of what constitutes

1. Reusability is also a packaging property and becomes an attribute of a good specification where reusability of requirements specifications is a goal.

an ideal SRS is important [Parnas 86] because it:

- provides a basis for standardizing an organization's processes and products,
- provides a standard against which progress can be measured, and,
- provides guidance—it helps developers understand what needs to be done next and when they are finished.

Because it is so often true that (1) requirements cannot be fully understood before at least starting to build the system, and (2) a perfect SRS cannot be produced even when the requirements are understood, some approaches advocated in the literature do not even attempt to produce a definitive SRS. For example, some authors advocate going directly from a problem model to design or from a prototype implementation to the code. While such approaches may be effective on some developments, they are inconsistent with the notion of software development as an engineering discipline. The development of technical specifications is an essential part of a controlled engineering process. This does not mean that the SRS must be entire or perfect before anything else is done but that its development is a fundamental goal of the process as a whole. That we may currently lack the ability to write good specifications in some cases does not change the fact that it is useful and necessary to try.

## 7. State of the Practice

Over the years, many analysis and specification techniques have evolved. The general trend has been for software engineering techniques to be applied first to coding problems (for example, complexity, ease of change), then to similar problems occurring earlier and earlier in the life cycle. Thus the concepts of structured programming led eventually to structured design and analysis. More recently, the concepts of object-oriented programming have led to object-oriented design and analysis. The following discussion characterizes the major schools of thought and provides pointers to instances of methods in each school. The general strengths and weaknesses of the various techniques are discussed relative to the requirements difficulties and the desirable qualities of analysis and specification methods.

It is characteristic of the immature state of requirements as a discipline that the more specific one gets, the less agreement there is. There is not only disagreement in terminology, approach, and the details of different methods, there is not even a commonly accepted classification scheme. The following general groupings are based on the evolution of the underlying concepts and the key distinctions that reflect paradigmatic shifts in requirements philosophy.

### 7.1 Functional Decomposition

Functional decomposition was originally applied to software requirements to abstract from coding details. Functional decomposition focuses on understanding and specifying what processing the software is required to do. The general strategy is to define the required behavior as a mapping from inputs to outputs. Ideally, the analysis proceeds top down, first identifying the function associated with the system as a whole. Each subsequent step decomposes the set of functions into steps or sub-functions. The result is a hierarchy of functions and the definitions of the functional interfaces. Each level of the hierarchy adds detail about the processing steps necessary to accomplish the more abstract function above. The function above controls the processing of its subfunctions. In a complete decomposition, the functional hierarchy specifies the "calls" structure of the implementation. One example of a methodology based on functional decomposition is Hamilton and Zeldin's Higher Order Software [Hamilton 76].

The advantage of functional decomposition is that the specification is written using the language and concepts of the implementors. It communicates well to the designers and coders. It is written in terms of the solution space so the transition to design and code is straightforward.

Common complaints are that functional specifications are difficult to communicate, introduce design decisions prematurely, and difficult to use or change. Because functional specifications are written in the language of implementation, people who are not software or systems experts find them difficult to understand. Since there are inevitably many possible ways of decomposing functions into subfunctions, the analyst must make decisions that are not requirements. Finally, since the processing needed in one step depends strongly on what has been done the previous step, functional decomposition results in components that are closely coupled. Understanding or changing one function requires understanding or changing all the related functions.

As software has increased in complexity and become more visible to nontechnical people, the need for methods addressing the weaknesses of functional decomposition has likewise increased.

### 7.2 Structured Analysis

Structured analysis was developed primarily as a

means to address the accidental difficulties attending problem analysis and, to a lesser extent, requirements specification, using functional decomposition. Following the introduction of structured programming as a means to gain intellectual control over increasingly complex programs, structured analysis evolved from functional decomposition as a means to gain intellectual control over system problems.

The basic assumption behind structured analysis is that the accidental difficulties can be addressed by a systematic approach to problem analysis using [Svoboda 90]:

- a common conceptual model for describing all problems,
- a set of procedures suggesting the general direction of analysis and an ordering on the steps,
- a set of guidelines or heuristics supporting decisions about the problem and its specification, and
- a set of criteria for evaluating the quality of the product.

While structured analysis still contains the decomposition of functions into subfunctions, the focus of the analysis shifts from the processing steps to the data being processed. The analyst views the problem as constructing a system to transform data. He analyzes the sources and destinations of the data, determines what data must be held in storage, what transformations are done on the data, and the form of the output.

Common to the structured analysis approaches is the use of data flow diagrams and data dictionaries. Data flow diagrams provide a graphic representation of the movement of data through the system (typically represented as arcs) and the transformations on the data (typically represented as nodes). The data dictionary supports the data flow diagram by providing a repository for the definitions and descriptions of each data item on the diagrams. Required processing is captured in the definitions of the transformations. Associated with each transformation node is a specification of the processing the node does to transform the incoming data items to the outgoing data items. At the most detailed level, a transformation is defined using a textual specification called a "MiniSpec." A MiniSpec may be expressed in several different ways including English prose, decision tables, or a procedure definition language (PDL).

Structured analysis approaches originally evolved for management information systems (MIS). Examples of widely used strategies include those described by DeMarco [DeMarco 78] and Gane and Sarson [Gane 79]. "Modern" structured analysis was introduced to provide more guidance in modeling systems as data flows as exemplified by Yourdon [Yourdon 89]. Structured analysis has also been adapted to support specification of embedded control systems by adding notations to capture control behavior. These variations are collectively known as structured analysis/real-time (SA/RT). Major variations of SA/RT have been described by Ward and Mellor [Ward 86] and Hatley and Pirbhai [Hatley 87]. A good summary of structured analysis concepts with extensive references is given by Svoboda [Svoboda 90].

Structured analysis extends functional decomposition with the notion that there should be a systematic (and hopefully predictable) approach to analyzing a problem, decomposing it into parts, and describing the relationships between the parts. By providing a well-defined process, structured analysis seeks to address, at least in part, the accidental difficulties that result from ad hoc approaches and the definition of requirements as an afterthought. It seeks to address problems in comprehension and communication by using a common set of conceptual structures—a graphic representation of the specification in terms of those structures—based on the assumption that a decomposition in terms of the data the system handles will be clearer and less inclined to change than one based on the functions performed.

While structured analysis techniques have continued to evolve and have been widely used, there remain a number of common criticisms. When used in problem analysis, a common complaint is that structured analysis provides insufficient guidance. Analysts have difficulty deciding which parts of the problem to model as data, which parts to model as transformations, and which parts should be aggregated. While the gross steps of the process are reasonably well defined, there is only very general guidance (in the form of heuristics) on what specific questions the analyst needs to answer next. Similarly, practitioners find it difficult to know when to stop decomposition and addition of detail. In fact, the basic structured analysis paradigm of modeling requirements as data flows and data transformations requires the analyst to make decisions about intermediate values (for example, form and content of stored data and the details of internal transformations) that are not requirements. Particularly in the hands of less experienced practitioners, data flow models tend to incorporate a variety of detail that properly belongs to design or implementation.

Many of these difficulties result from the weak constraints imposed by the conceptual model. A goal of the developers of structured analysis was to create a very general approach to modeling systems; in fact, one that could be applied equally to model human enterprises, hardware applications, software applications of different kinds, and so on. Unfortunately, such generality can be achieved only by abstracting away any semantics that are not common to all of the types of systems potentially being modeled. The conceptual model itself can provide little guidance relevant to a particular system. Since the conceptual model applies equally to requirements analysis and design analysis, its semantics provide no basis for distinguishing the two. Similarly, such models can support only very weak syntactic criteria for assessing the quality of structured analysis specifications. For example, the test for completeness and consistency in data flow diagrams is limited to determining that the transformations at each level are consistent in name and number with the data flows of the level above.

This does not mean one cannot develop data flow specifications that are easy to understand, communicate effectively with the user, or capture required behavior correctly. The large number of systems developed using structured analysis show that it is possible to do so. However, the weakness of the conceptual model means that a specification's quality depends largely on the experience, insight, and expertise of the analyst. The developer must provide the necessary discipline because the model itself is relatively unconstrained.

Finally, structured analysis provides little support for producing an SRS that meets our quality criteria. Data flow diagrams are unsuitable for capturing mathematical relations or detailed specifications of value, timing, or accuracy so the detailed behavioral specifications are typically given in English or as pseudocode segments in the MiniSpecs. These constructs provide little or no support for writing an SRS that is complete, implementation independent, unambiguous, consistent, precise, and verifiable. Further, the data flow diagrams and attendant dictionaries do not, themselves, provide support for organizing an SRS to satisfy the packaging goals of readability, ease of reference and review, or reusability. In fact, for many of the published methods, there is no explicit process step, structure, or guidance for producing an SRS, as a distinct development product, at all.

### 7.3 Operational Specification

The operational[2] approach focuses on addressing two of the essential requirements dilemmas. The first is that we often do not know exactly what should be built until we build it. The second is the problem inherent in moving from a particular specification of requirements (what to build) to a design that satisfies those requirements (how to build it). The closer the requirements specification is to the design, the easier the transition, but the more likely it is that design decisions are made prematurely.

The operational approach seeks to address these problems, among others, by supporting development of executable requirements specifications. Key elements of an operational approach are: a formal specification language and an engine for executing well-formed specifications written in the language. Operational approaches may also include automated support for analyzing properties of the formal specification and for transforming the specification into an equivalent implementation. A good description of the operational approach, its rationale, and goals is given by Zave [Zave 82].

The underlying reasoning about the benefits of the operational approach is as follows:

- Making the requirements specification itself executable obviates the dilemma that one must build the system to know what to build. The developer writes the requirements specification in a formal language. The specification may then be executed to validate that the customer's needs have been captured and the right system specified (for example, one can apply scenarios and test cases). The approach is presumed to require less labor and be more cost-effective than conventional prototyping because a separate requirements specification need not be produced; the specification and the "prototype" are the same thing.
- Operational specifications allow the developer to abstract from design decisions while simplifying the transition from requirements to design and implementation. Transition to design and implementation is both simple and automatable because the behavioral requirements are already expressed in terms of computational mechanisms. During design, one makes decisions concerning efficiency, resource management, and target language realization that are abstracted from the operational specification.

For general applications, operational approaches have achieved only limited success. This is at least in part due to the failure to achieve the necessary semantic distinction between an operational computational model and conventional programming. The benefits of the approach are predicated on the assumption that the

2. We use the term "operational" here specifically to denote approaches based on executable specifications in the sense of Zave [Zave 82]. The term is sometimes used to contrast with axiomatic specification–that is not the meaning here.

operational model can be written in terms of the problem domain, without the need to introduce conceptual structures belonging to the solution domain. In practice, this goal has proven elusive. To achieve generality, operational languages have typically had to introduce implementation constructs. The result is not a requirements specification language but a higher-level programming language. As noted by Parnas [Parnas 85b] and Brooks [Brooks 87], the specification ends up giving the solution method rather than the problem statement. Thus, in practice, operational specifications do not meet the SRS goal of implementation independence.

The focus of operational specification is on the benefits of early simulation rather than on the properties of the specification as a reference document. Since executability requires formality, operational specifications necessarily satisfy the SRS semantic properties of being unambiguous, consistent, precise, and verifiable. The ability to validate the specification through simulation also supports completeness. However, as discussed, these properties have not been achieved in concert with implementation independence. Further, the methods discussed in the literature put little emphasis on the communication or packaging qualities of the specification, except as these qualities overlap with desirable design properties. Thus, there may be some support for modifiability but little for readability or organizing an SRS for reference and review.

### 7.4 Object Oriented Analysis (OOA)

There is currently considerable discussion in the literature, and little agreement, on exactly what should and should not be considered "object oriented." OOA has evolved from at least two significant sources: information modeling and object oriented design. Each has contributed to current views of OOA, and the proponents of each emphasize somewhat different sets of concepts. For the purposes of this tutorial, we are not interested in which method is by some measure "more object oriented" but in the distinct contributions of the object-oriented paradigm to analysis and specification. For an overview of OOA concepts and methods, see Balin's article [Balin 94]; Davis's book [Davis 93] includes both discussion and examples. Examples of recent approaches self-described as object oriented include work by Rumbaugh [Rumbaugh 91], Coad and Yourdon [Coad 91], Shlaer and Mellor [Shlaer 88], and Selic, Gullekson, and Ward [Selic 94].

OOA techniques differ from structured analysis in their approach to decomposing a problem into parts and in the methods for describing the relationships between the parts. In OOA, the analyst decomposes the problem into a set of interacting objects based on the entities and relationships extant in the problem domain. An object encapsulates a related set of data, processing, and state (thus, a significant distinction between object-oriented analysis and structured analysis is that OOA encapsulates both data and related processing together). Objects provide externally accessible functions, typically called services or methods. Objects may hide information about their internal structure, data, or state from other objects. Conversely, they may provide processing, data, or state information through the services defined on the object interface. Dynamic relationships between objects are captured in terms of message passing (that is, one object sends a message to invoke a service or respond to an invocation). The analyst captures static relationships in the problem domain using the concepts of aggregation and classification. Aggregation is used to capture whole/part relationships. Classification is used to capture class/instance relationships (also called "is-a" or inheritance relationships).

The structural components of OOA (for example, objects, classes, services, aggregation) support a set of analytic principles. Of these, two directly address requirements problems:

1. From information modeling comes the assumption that a problem is easiest to understand and communicate if the conceptual structures created during analysis map directly to entities and relationships in the problem domain. This principle is realized in OOA through the heuristic of representing problem domain objects and relationships of interest as OOA objects and relationships. Thus an OOA specification of a vehicle registration system might model vehicles, vehicle owners, vehicle title, and so on [Coad 90] as objects. The object paradigm is used to model both the problem and the relevant problem context.
2. From early work on modularization by Parnas [Parnas 72] and abstract data types, by way of object-oriented programming and design, come the principles of information hiding and abstraction. The principle of information hiding guides one to limit access to information on which other parts of the system should not depend. In an OO specification of requirements, this principle is applied to hide details of design and implementation. In OOA, behavior requirements are specified in terms of the data and services provided on the object interfaces; how those services are implemented is encapsulated by the object.

The principle of abstraction says that only the relevant or essential information should be presented. Abstraction is implemented in OOA by defining object interfaces that provide access only to essential data or state information encapsulated by an object (conversely hiding the incidentals).

The principles and mechanisms of OOA provide a basis for attacking the essential difficulties of comprehension, communication, and control. The principle of problem-domain modeling helps guide the analyst in distinguishing requirements (what) from design (how). Where the objects and their relationships faithfully model entities and relationships in the problem, they are understandable by the customer and other domain experts; this supports early comprehension of the requirements.

The principles of information hiding and abstraction, with the attendant object mechanisms, provide mechanisms useful for addressing the essential problems of control and communication. Objects provide the means to divide the requirements into distinct parts, abstract from details, and limit unnecessary dependencies between the parts. Object interfaces can be used to hide irrelevant detail and define abstractions providing only the essential information. This provides a basis for managing complexity and improving readability. Likewise objects provide a basis for constructing reusable requirements units of related functions and data.

The potential benefits of OOA are often diluted by the way the key principles are manifest in particular methods. While the objects and relations of OOA are intended to model essential aspects of the application domain, this goal is typically not supported by a corresponding conceptual model of the domain behavior. As for structured analysis, object-modeling mechanisms and techniques are intentionally generic rather than application specific. One result is insufficient guidance in developing appropriate object decompositions. Just as structured analysis practitioners have difficulty choosing appropriate data flows and transformations, OOA practitioners have difficulty choosing appropriate objects and relationships.

In practice, the notion that one can develop the structure of a system, or a requirements specification, based on physical structure is often found to be oversold. It is true that the elements of the physical world are usually stable (especially relative to software details) and that real-world-based models have intuitive appeal. It is not, however, the case that everything that must be captured in requirements has a physical analog. An obvious example is shared state information. Further, many real-world structures are themselves arbitrary and likely to change (for example, where two hardware functions are put on one physical platform to reduce cost). While the notion of basing requirements structure on physical structure is a useful heuristic, more is needed to develop a complete and consistent requirements specification.

A further difficulty is that the notations and semantics of OOA methods are typically based on the conceptual structures of software rather than those of the problem domain the analyst seeks to model. Symptomatic of this problem is that analysts find themselves debating about object language features and their properties rather than about the properties of the problem. An example is the use of message passing, complete with message passing protocols, where one object uses information defined in another. In the problem domain it is often irrelevant whether information is actively solicited or passively received. In fact there may be no notion of messages or transmission at all. Nonetheless one finds analysts debating about which object should initiate a request and the resulting anomaly of passive entities modeled as active. For example, to get information from a book one might request that the book "read itself" and "send" the requested information in a message. To control an aircraft the pilot might "use his hands and feet to 'send messages' to the aircraft controls which in turn send messages to the aircraft control surfaces to modify themselves" [Davis 93]. Such decisions are about OOA mechanisms or design, not about the problem domain or requirements.

A more serious complaint is that most current OOA methods inadequately address our goal of developing a good SRS. Most OOA approaches in the literature provide only informal specification mechanisms, relying on refinement of the OO model in design and implementation to add detail and precision. There is no formal basis for determining if a specification is complete, consistent, or verifiable. Further, none of the OOA techniques discussed directly address the issues of developing the SRS as a reference document. The focus of all of the cited OOA techniques is on problem analysis rather than specification. If the SRS is addressed at all, the assumption is that the principles applied to problem understanding and modeling are sufficient, when results are documented, to produce a good specification. Experience suggests otherwise. As we have discussed, there are inherent trade-offs that must be made to develop a specification that meets the needs of any particular project. Making effective trade-offs requires a disciplined and thoughtful approach to the SRS itself, not just the problem. Thus, while OOA provide the means to address packaging issues, there is typically little methodological emphasis on issues like modifiability or organization of a specification for reference and review.

### 7.5 Software Cost Reduction (SCR) Method

Where most of the techniques thus far discussed focus on problem analysis, the requirements work at the US Naval Research Laboratory (NRL) focused equally on issues of developing a good SRS. NRL initiated the Software Cost Reduction (SCR) project in 1978 to demonstrate the feasibility and effectiveness of advanced software engineering techniques by applying them to a real system, the Operational Flight Program (OFP) for the A-7E aircraft. To demonstrate that (then-academic) techniques such as information hiding, formal specification, abstract interfaces, and cooperating sequential processes could help make software easier to understand, maintain, and change, the SCR project set out to reengineer the A-7E OFP.

Since no existing documentation adequately captured the A-7E's software requirements, the first step was to develop an effective SRS. In this process, the SCR project identified a number of properties a good SRS should have and a set of principles for developing effective requirements documentation [Heninger 80]. The SCR approach uses formal, mathematically based specifications of acceptable system outputs to support development of a specification that is unambiguous, precise, and verifiable. It also provided techniques for checking a specification for a variety of completeness and consistency properties. The SCR approach introduced principles and techniques to support our SRS packaging goals, including the principle of separation of concerns to aid readability and support ease of change. It also includes the use of a standard structure for an SRS specification and the use of tabular specifications that improve readability, modifiability, and facilitate use of the specification for reference and review.

While other requirements approaches have stated similar objectives, the SCR project is unique in having applied software engineering principles to develop a standard SRS organization, a specification method, review method [Parnas 85a], and notations consistent with those principles. The SCR project is also unique in making publicly available a complete, model SRS of a significant system [Alspaugh 92].

A number of issues were left unresolved by the original SCR work. While the product of the requirements analysis was well documented, the underlying process and method were never fully described. Since the original effort was to reengineer an existing system, it was not clear how effective the techniques would be on a new development. Since the developers of the A-7E requirements document were researchers, it was also unclear whether industrial developers would find the rather formal method and notation useable, readable, or effective. Finally, while the A-7E SRS organization is reasonably general, many of the specification techniques are targeted to real-time, embedded applications. As discussed in the following section, more recent work by Parnas [Parnas 91], NRL [Heitmeyer 95a,b], and others [Faulk 92] has addressed many of the open questions about the SCR approach.

## 8. Trends and Emerging Technology

While improved discipline will address requirement's accidental difficulties, addressing the essential difficulties requires technical advances. Significant trends, in some cases backed by industrial experience, have emerged over the past few years that offer some hope for improvement:

- *Domain specificity*: Requirements methods will provide improved analytic and specification support by being tailored to particular classes of problems. Historically, requirements approaches have been advanced as being equally useful to widely varied types of applications. For example, structured analysis methods were deemed to be based on conceptual models that were "universally applicable" (for example, [Ross 77]); similar claims have been made for object-oriented approaches.

Such generality comes at the expense of ease of use and amount of work the analyst must do for any particular application. Where the underlying models have been tailored to a particular class of applications, the properties common to the class are embedded in the model. The amount of work necessary to adapt the model to a specific instance of the class is relatively small. The more general the model, the more decisions that must be made, the more information that must be provided, and the more tailoring that must be done. This provides increased room for error and, since each analyst will approach the problem differently, makes solutions difficult to standardize. In particular, such generality precludes standardization of sufficiently rigorous models to support algorithmic analysis of properties like completeness and consistency.

Similar points have been expressed in a recent paper by Jackson [Jackson 94]. He points out that some of the characteristics separating real engineering disciplines from what is euphemistically described as "software engineering" are well-understood procedures, mathematical models, and standard designs specific to narrow classes of applications. Jackson points out the need for software methods based on the conceptual structures and mathematical models of behavior inherent in a given problem domain (for example, publication, command and control, accounting, and so on). Such common underlying constructs can provide the engineer guidance in developing the specification for a particular system.

- *Practical formalisms*: Like so many of the promising technologies in requirements, the application of formal methods is characterized by an essential dilemma. On one hand, formal specification techniques hold out the only real hope for producing specifications that are precise, unambiguous, and demonstrably complete or consistent. On the other, industrial practitioners widely view formal methods as impractical. Difficulty of use, inability to scale, readability, and cost are among the reasons cited. Thus, in spite of significant technical progress and a growing body of literature, the pace of adoption by industry has been extremely slow.

In spite of the technical and technical transfer difficulties, increased formality is necessary. Only by placing behavioral specification on a mathematical basis will we be able to acquire sufficient intellectual control to develop complex systems with any assurance that they satisfy their intended purpose and provide necessary properties like safety. The solution is better formal methods—methods that are practical given the time, cost, and personnel constraints of industrial development.

Engineering models and the training to use them are de rigueur in every other discipline that builds large, complex, or safety-critical systems. Builders of a bridge or skyscraper who did not employ proven methods or mathematical models to predict reliability and safety would be held criminally negligent in the event of failure. It is only the relative youth of the software discipline that permits us to get away with less. But, we cannot expect great progress overnight. As Jackson [Jackson 94] notes, the field is sufficiently immature that "the prerequisites for a more mathematical approach are not in place." Further, many of those practicing our craft lack the background required of licensed engineers in other disciplines [Parnas 89]. Nonetheless, sufficient work has been done to show that more formal approaches are practical and effective in industry. For an overview of formal methods and their role in practical developments, refer to Rushby's summary work [Rushby 93].

- *Improved tool support*: It remains common to walk into the office of a software development manager and find the shelves lined with the manuals for CASE tools that are not in use. In spite of years of development and the contrary claims of vendors, many industrial developers have found the available requirements CASE tools of marginal benefit.

Typically, the fault lies not so much with the tool vendor but with the underlying method or methods the tool seeks to support. The same generality, lack of strong underlying conceptual model, and lack of formality that makes the methods weak limits the benefits of automation. Since the methods do not adequately constrain the problem space and offer little specific guidance, the corresponding tool cannot actively support the developer in making difficult decisions. Since the model and SRS are not standardized, its production eludes effective automated support. Since the underlying model is not formal, only trivial syntactic properties of the specification can be evaluated. Most such tools provide little more than a graphic interface and requirements database.

Far more is now possible. Where the model, conceptual structures, notations, and process are standardized, significant automated support becomes possible. The tool can use information about the state of the specification and the process to guide the developer in making the next step. It can use standardized templates to automate rote portions of the SRS. It can use the underlying mathematical model to determine to what extent the specification is complete and consistent. While only the potential of such tools has yet been demonstrated, there are sufficient results to project the benefits (for example, [Heitmeyer 95b], [Leveson 94]).

- *Integrated paradigms*: One of the Holy Grails of software engineering has been the integrated software development environment. Much of the frustration in applying currently available methods and tools is the lack of integration, not just in the tool interfaces, but in the underlying models and conceptual structures. Even where an approach works well for one phase of development, the same techniques are either difficult to use in the next phase or there is no clear transition path. Similarly tools are either focused on a small subset of the many tasks (for example, analysis but not documentation) or attempt to address the entire life cycle but support none of it well. The typical development employs a hodgepodge of software engineering methodologies and ad hoc techniques. Developers often build their own software to bridge the gap between CASE platforms.

In spite of a number of attempts, the production of a useful, integrated set of methods and supporting environment has proven elusive. However, it now appears that there is sufficient technology available to provide, if not a complete solution, at least the skeleton for one.

The most significant methodological trend can be described as convergent evolution. In biology, convergent evolution denotes a situation where common evolutionary pressures lead to similar characteristics (morphology) in distinct species. An analogous convergence is ongoing in requirements. As different schools of thought have come to understand and attempt to address the weaknesses and omissions in their own approaches, the solutions have become more similar. In particular, the field is moving toward a common understanding of the difficulties and common assumptions about the desired qualities of solutions. This should not be confused with the bandwagon effect that often attends real or imaginary paradigm shifts (for example, the current rush to object-oriented everything). Rather, it is the slow process of evolving common understanding and changing conventional practices.

Such trends and some preliminary results are currently observable in requirements approaches for embedded software. In the 1970s, the exigencies of national defense and aerospace applications resulted in demand for complex, mission-critical software. It became apparent early on that available requirements techniques addressed neither the complexity of the systems being built nor the stringent control, timing, and accuracy constraints of the applications. Developers responded by creating a variety of domain-specific approaches. Early work by TRW for the US Army on the Ballistic Missile Defense system produced the Software Requirements Engineering Method (SREM) [Alford 77] and supporting tools. Such software problems in the Navy led to the SCR project. Ward, Mellor, Hatley, and Pirbhai ([Ward 86], [Hatley 87]) developed extensions to structured analysis techniques targeted to real-time applications. Work on the Israeli defense applications led Harel to develop statecharts [Harel 87] and the supporting tool Statemate.

The need for high-assurance software in mission- and safety-critical systems also led to the introduction of practical formalisms and integrated tools support. TRW developed REVS [Davis 77] and other tools as part of a complete environment supporting SREM and other phases of the life cycle. The SCR project developed specification techniques based on mathematical functions and tabular representations [Heninger 80]. These allowed a variety of consistency and completeness checks to be performed by inspection. Harel introduced a compact graphic representation of finite state machines with a well-defined formal semantics. These features were subsequently integrated in the Statemate tool that supported symbolic execution of statecharts for early customer validation and limited code generation. All of these techniques began to converge on an underlying model based on finite state automata.

More recent work has seen continuing convergence toward a common set of assumptions and similar solutions. Recently, Ward and colleagues have developed the Real-Time Object-Oriented Modeling (ROOM) method [Selic 94]. ROOM integrates concepts from operational specification, object-oriented analysis, and statecharts. It employs an object-oriented modeling approach with tool support. The tool is based on a simplified statechart semantics and supports symbolic execution and some code generation. The focus of ROOM currently remains on problem modeling and the transition to design, and execution rather than formal analysis.

Nancy Leveson and her colleagues have adapted statecharts to provide a formally based method for embedded system specification [Jaffe 91]. The approach has been specifically developed to be useable and readable by practicing engineers. It employs both the graphical syntax of statecharts and a tabular representation of functions similar to those used in the SCR approach. Its underlying formal model is intended to support formal analysis of system properties, with an emphasis on safety. The formal model also supports symbolic execution. These techniques have been applied to develop a requirements specification for parts of the Federal Aviation Administration's safety-critical Traffic Alert and Collision Avoidance System (TCAS) [Leveson 94].

Extensions to the SCR work have taken a similar direction. Parnas and Madey have extended the SCR approach to create a standard mathematical model for embedded system requirements [Parnas 91]. Heitmeyer and colleagues at NRL have extended the Parnas/Madey work by defining a corresponding formal model for the SCR approach [Heitmeyer 95b]. This formal model has been used to develop a suite of prototype tools supporting analysis of requirements properties like completeness and consistency [Heitmeyer

95a]. The NRL tools also support specification-based simulation and are being integrated with other tools to support automated analysis of application-specific properties like safety assertions. Concurrent work at the Software Productivity Consortium by Faulk and colleagues [Faulk 92] has integrated the SCR approach with object-oriented and graphic techniques and defined a complete requirements analysis process including a detailed process for developing a good SRS. These techniques have been applied effectively in development of requirements for Lockheed's avionics upgrade on the C-130J aircraft [Faulk 94]. The C-130J avionics software is a safety-critical system of approximately 100K lines of Ada code.

Other recent work attempts to increase the level of formality and the predictability of the problem analysis process and its products. For example, Potts and his colleagues are developing process models and tools to support systematic requirements elicitation that include a formal structure for describing discussions about requirements [Potts 94]. Hsia and his colleagues, among others, are investigating formal approaches to the use of scenarios in eliciting and validating requirements [Hsia 94]. Recent work by Boehm and his colleagues [Boehm 94] seeks to address the accidental difficulties engendered by adversarial software procurement processes.

While none of the works mentioned can be considered a complete solution, it is clear that (1) the work is converging toward common assumptions and solutions, (2) the approaches all provide significantly improved capability to address both accidental and essential requirements difficulties, and (3) the solutions can be effectively applied in industry.

## 9. Conclusions

Requirements are intrinsically hard to do well. Beyond the need for discipline, there are a host of essential difficulties that attend both the understanding of requirements and their specification. Further, many of the difficulties in requirements will not yield to technical solution alone. Addressing all of the essential difficulties requires the application of technical solutions in the context of human factors such as the ability to manage complexity or communicate to diverse audiences. A requirements approach that does not account for both technical and human concerns can have only limited success. For developers seeking new methods, the lesson is caveat emptor. If someone tells you his method makes requirements easy, keep a hand on your wallet.

Nevertheless, difficulty is not impossibility and the inability to achieve perfection is not an excuse for surrender. While all of the approaches discussed have significant weaknesses, they all contribute to the attempt to make requirements analysis and specification a controlled, systematic, and effective process. Though there is no easy path, experience confirms that the use of *any* careful and systematic approach is preferable to an ad hoc and chaotic one. Further good news is that, if the requirements are done well, chances are much improved that the rest of the development will also go well. Unfortunately, ad hoc approaches remain the norm in much of the software industry.

A final observation is that the benefits of good requirements come at a cost. Such a difficult and exacting task cannot be done properly by personnel with inadequate experience, training, or resources. Providing the time and the means to do the job right is the task of responsible management. The time to commit the best and brightest is before, not after, disaster occurs. The monumental failures of a host of ambitious developments bear witness to the folly of doing otherwise.

## 10. Further Reading

Those seeking more depth on requirements methodologies than this tutorial can provide should read Alan Davis' book *Software Requirements: Objects, Functions, and States* [Davis 93]. In addition to a general discussion of issues in software requirements, Davis illustrates a number of problem analysis and specification techniques with a set of common examples and provides a comprehensive annotated bibliography.

For a better understanding of software requirements in the context of systems development, the reader is referred to the book of collected papers edited by Thayer and Dorfman, *System and Software Requirements Engineering* [Thayer 90]. This tutorial work contains in one volume both original papers and reprints from many of the authors discussed above. The companion volume, *Standards, Guidelines, and Examples on System and Software Requirements Engineering* [Dorfman 90] is a compendium of international and US government standards relating to system and software requirements and provides some illustrating examples.

For enjoyable reading as well as insightful commentary on requirements problems, methods, and a host of requirements-related issues, the reader is referred to Michael Jackson's recent book, *Software Requirements and Specifications: A Lexicon of Practice, Principles, and Prejudice.* [Jackson 95]

## Acknowledgments

C. Colket at SPAWAR, E. Wald at ONR and A. Pyster at the Software Productivity Consortium supported the development of this report. The quality of this paper has been much improved thanks to thoughtful reviews by Paul Clements, Connie Heitmeyer, Jim Kirby, Bruce Labaw, Richard Morrison, and David Weiss.

## References

[Alford 77] Alford, M., "A Requirements Engineering Methodology for Real-Time Processing Requirements," *IEEE Trans. Software Eng.*, Vol. 3, No. 1, Jan. 1977, pp. 60–69.

[Alford 79] Alford, M. and J. Lawson, "Software Requirements Engineering Methodology (Development)," *RADC-TR-79-168*, U.S. Air Force Rome Air Development Center, June 1979.

[Alspaugh 92] Alspaugh, T. et al., *Software Requirements for the A-7E Aircraft*, NRL/FR/5530-92-9194, Naval Research Laboratory, Washington, D.C., 1992.

[Balin 94] Balin, S., "Object-Oriented Requirements Analysis," in *Encyclopedia of Software Engineering*, J. Marciniak ed., John Wiley & Sons, New York, N.Y., 1994, pp. 740–756.

[Basili 81] Basili, V. and D. Weiss, "Evaluation of a Software Requirements Document by Analysis of Change Data," *Proc. 5th Int'l Conf. Software Eng.*, IEEE CS Press, Los Alamitos, Calif., 1981, pp. 314–323.

[Boehm 81] Boehm, B., *Software Engineering Economics*, Prentice-Hall, Englewood Cliffs, N.J., 1981.

[Boehm 94] Boehm, B. et al., "Software Requirements as Negotiated Win Conditions," *Proc. 1st Int'l Conf. Requirements Eng.*, IEEE CS Press, Los Alamitos, Calif., 1994, pp. 74–83.

[Brooks 75] Brooks, F., *The Mythical Man-Month*, Addison-Wesley, Reading, Mass., 1975.

[Brooks 87] Brooks, F., "No Silver Bullet: Essence and Accidents of Software Engineering," *Computer*, Apr. 1987, pp. 10–19.

[CECOM 89] *Software Methodology Catalog: Second Edition*, Technical report C01-091JB-0001-01, US Army Communications-Electronics Command, Fort Monmouth, N.J., Mar. 1989.

[Clements 95] Clements, P., private communication, May 1995.

[Coad 90] Coad, P. and E. Yourdon, *Object Oriented Analysis*, Prentice-Hall, Englewood Cliffs, N.J., 1990.

[Davis 77] Davis, C. and C. Vick, "The Software Development System," *IEEE Trans. Software Eng.*, Vol. 3, No. 1, Jan. 1977, pp. 69–84.

[Davis 88] Davis, A., "A Taxonomy for the Early Stages of the Software Development Life Cycle," *J. Systems and Software*, Sept. 1988, pp. 297–311.

[Davis 93] Davis, A., *Software Requirements (Revised): Objects, Functions, and States*, Prentice-Hall, Englewood Cliffs, N.J., 1993.

[DeMarco 78] DeMarco, T., *Structured Analysis and System Specification*, Prentice-Hall Englewood Cliffs, N.J., 1978.

[Dorfman 90] Dorfman, M. and R. Thayer, eds., *Standards, Guidelines, and Examples on System and Software Requirements Engineering*, IEEE CS Press, Los Alamitos, Calif., 1990.

[Faulk 92] Faulk, S. et al., "The Core Method for Real-Time Requirements," *IEEE Software*, Vol. 9, No. 5, Sept. 1992.

[Faulk 93] Faulk, S. et al., *Consortium Requirements Engineering Guidebook*, Version 1.0, SPC-92060-CMC, Software Productivity Consortium, Herndon, Virginia, 1993.

[Faulk 94] Faulk, S. et al., "Experience Applying the CoRE Method to the Lockheed C-130J," *Proc. 9th Ann. Conf. Computer Assurance*, IEEE Press, Piscataway, N.J., 1994, pp. 3–8.

[GAO 79] US General Accounting Office, *Contracting for Computer Software Development—Serious Problems Require Management Attention to Avoid Wasting Additional Millions*, Report FGMSD-80-4, November 1979.

[GAO 92] US General Accounting Office, *Mission Critical Systems: Defense Attempting to Address Major Software Challenges*, GAO/IMTEC-93-13, December 1992.

[Gane 79] Gane, C. and T. Sarson, *Structured Systems Analysis*, Prentice-Hall, New Jersey, 1979.

[Hamilton 76] Hamilton, M. and S. Zeldin, "Higher Order Software-A Methodology for Defining Software," *IEEE Trans. Software Eng.*, Vol. 2, No. 1, Jan. 1976, pp. 9–32.

[Harel 87] Harel, D., "Statecharts: a Visual Formalism for Complex Systems," *Science of Computer Programming 8*, 1987, pp. 231–274.

[Hatley 87] Hatley, D. and I. Pirbhai, *Strategies for Real-Time Specification*, Dorset House, New York, N.Y., 1987.

[Heitmeyer 95a] Heitmeyer, C., B. Labaw, and D. Kiskis, "Consistency Checking of SCR-Style Requirements Specifications," *Proc. 2nd IEEE Int'l Symp. Requirements Eng.*, IEEE CS Press, Los Alamitos, Calif., 1995, pp. 56–63.

[Heitmeyer 95b] Heitmeyer, C., R. Jeffords, and B. Labaw, *Tools for Analyzing SCR-Style Requirements Specifications: A Formal Foundation*, NRL Technical Report NRL-7499, U.S. Naval Research Laboratory, Washington, DC, 1995.

[Heninger 80] Heninger, K., "Specifying Software Requirements for Complex Systems: New Techniques and Their Application," *IEEE Trans. Software Eng.*, Vol. 6, No. 1, Jan. 1980.

[Hester 81] Hester, S., D. Parnas, and D. Utter, "Using Documentation as a Software Design Medium," *Bell System Technical J.*, Vol. 60, No. 8, Oct. 1981, pp. 1941–1977.

[Hsia 94] Hsia, P. et al., "Formal Approach to Scenario Analysis," *IEEE Software*, Mar. 1994, pp. 33–41.

[Jackson 83] Jackson, M., *System Development*, Prentice-Hall, Englewood Cliffs, N.J., 1983.

[Jackson 94] Jackson, M., "Problems, Methods, and Specialization," *IEEE Software*, Nov. 1994, pp. 57–62.

[Jackson 95] Jackson, M., *Software Requirements and Specifications: A Lexicon of Practice, Principles, and Prejudice*, ACM Press/Addison Wesley, Reading, Mass., 1995.

[Jaffe 91] Jaffe, M. et al., "Software Requirements Analysis for Real-Time Process-Control Systems," *IEEE Trans. Software Eng.*, Vol. 17, No. 3, Mar. 1991, pp. 241–257.

[Leveson 94] Leveson, N. et al., "Requirements Specification for Process-Control Systems," *IEEE Trans. Software Eng.*, Vol. 20, No. 9, Sept. 1994.

[Lutz 93] Lutz, R., "Analyzing Software Requirements Errors in Safety-Critical Embedded Systems," *Proc. IEEE Int'l Symp. Requirements Eng.*, IEEE CS Press, Los Alamitos, Calif., 1993, pp. 126–133.

[Parnas 72] Parnas, D., "On the Criteria to be Used in Decomposing Systems into Modules," *Comm. ACM*, Vol. 15, No. 12, Dec. 1972, pp. 1053–1058.

[Parnas 85a] Parnas, D. and D. Weiss, "Active Design Reviews: Principles and Practices," *Proc. 8th Int'l Conf. Software Eng.*, IEEE CS Press, Los Alamitos, Calif., 1985.

[Parnas 85b] Parnas, D. "Software Aspects of Strategic Defense Systems," *American Scientist*, Sept. 1985, pp. 432–440.

[Parnas 86] Parnas, D. and P. Clements, "A Rational Design Process: How and Why to Fake It," *IEEE Trans. Software Eng.*, Vol. 12, No. 2, Feb. 1986, pp. 251–257.

[Parnas 89] Parnas, D., *Education for Computing Professionals*, Technical Report 89-247, Department of Computing and Information Science, Queens University, Kingston, Ontario, 1989.

[Parnas 91] Parnas, D. and J. Madey, *Functional Documentation for Computer Systems Engineering* (Version 2), CRL Report No. 237, McMaster University, Hamilton, Ontario, Canada, Sept. 1991.

[Potts 94] Potts, C., K. Takahashi, and A. Anton, "Inquiry-Based Requirements Analysis," *IEEE Software*, Mar. 1994, pp. 21–32.

[Shlaer 88] Shlaer, S. and S. Mellor, *Object-Oriented Systems Analysis: Modeling the World in Data*, Prentice-Hall, Englewood Cliffs, N.J., 1988.

[Ross 77] Ross, D. and K. Schoman Jr., "Structured Analysis for Requirements Definitions," *IEEE Trans. Software Eng.*, Vol. 3, No. 1, Jan. 1977, pp. 6–15.

[Rumbaugh 91] Rumbaugh, M. Blaha et al, *Object-Oriented Modeling and Design*, Prentice-Hall, Englewood Cliffs, N.J., 1991.

[Rushby 93] Rushby, J., *Formal Methods and the Certification of Critical Systems*, CSL Technical Report SRI-CSL-93-07, SRI International, Menlo Park, Calif., Nov., 1993.

[Selic 94] Selic, B., G. Gullekson, and P. Ward, *Real-Time Object-Oriented Modeling*, John Wiley & Sons, New York, N.Y., 1994.

[Svoboda 90] Svoboda, C., "Structured Analysis," in *Tutorial: System and Software Requirements Engineering*, R. Thayer and M. Dorfman, eds., IEEE CS Press, Los Alamitos, Calif., 1990, pp. 218–237.

[Thayer 90] Thayer, R. and M. Dorfman, eds., *Tutorial: System and Software Requirements Engineering*, IEEE CS Press, Los Alamitos, Calif., 1990.

[Ward 86] Ward, P. and S. Mellor, *Structured Development for Real-Time Systems*, Vols. 1, 2, and 3, Prentice-Hall, Englewood Cliffs, N.J., 1986.

[Yourdon 89] Yourdon, E., *Modern Structured Analysis*, Yourdon Press/Prentice-Hall, Englewood Cliffs, N.J., 1989.

[Zave 82] Zave, P., "An Operational Approach to Requirements Specification for Embedded Systems," *IEEE Trans. Software Eng.*, Vol. 8, No. 3, May 1982, pp. 250–269.

# Software Design: An Introduction

David Budgen

## 1. The Role of Software Design

A question that should be asked (and preferably answered!) at the beginning of an overview paper such as this, is

*What exactly is the purpose of design?*

and the answer that we will be assuming is along the lines of

*"To produce a workable (implementable) solution to a given problem."*

where in our context, the eventual "solution" involves producing an artifact that will be in the form of software.

This end goal is one that we need to keep in mind in seeking to provide a concise review of some of the many factors and issues that are involved in designing software-based systems. We also need to remember the corollary to this: that the key measure of the appropriateness of any solution is that of *fitness for purpose.*

The significant characteristic of design as a problem-solving approach is that there is rarely (indeed, almost never) only one solution to a problem. So we cannot hope to identify some systematic way of finding the answer, as occurs in the physical and mathematical sciences. Instead, the designer needs to work in a creative manner to identify the properties required in the solution and then seek to devise a structure that possesses them.

This characteristic can be illustrated by a very simple example of a design task that will be familiar to many, and which is based upon that major trauma of life: moving house! When we move to a new house or apartment, we are faced with a typical design problem in deciding where our furniture is to be placed. We may also be required to assist the removal company by supplying them with an abstract description of our intentions.

There are of course many ways in which furniture can be arranged within a house or apartment. We need to decide in which room each item needs to be placed, perhaps determined chiefly by functionality, and then to decide exactly where it might go in the room. We might choose to focus our attention on getting a good balance of style in one room at the expense of another. We also need to consider the constraints imposed by the configuration of the house, so that furniture does not block doors or windows, and power outlets remain accessible.

So this simple example exhibits all of the main characteristics that are to be found in almost all design problems [1]: no single "right" solution; many factors and constraints to be balanced in choosing a solution; no one measure of "quality;" and no particular process that can ensure that we can even identify an acceptable solution!

### 1.1 The software design process

An important task for a designer is to formulate and develop some form of abstract design model that represents his or her ideas about a solution. Accepting that these activities that underpin the design process are creative ones, the next question that should be asked is why is it that the task of designing software seems to be even more intractable and less well understood than other forms of design? In [2], Fred Brooks has suggested that some software properties that contribute to this include:

- *The complexity of software*, with no two parts ever being quite alike, and with a process or system having many possible states during execution.
- *The problem of conformity* that arises because of the very pliable nature of software, with software designers being expected to tailor software around the needs of hardware, of existing systems, or to meet other sources of "standards."
- *The (apparent) ease of changeability*, leading to constant requirements for change from users, who fail to appreciate the true costs implied by changes.
- *The invisibility of software* so that our descriptions of design ideas lack any visual link to the form of the end product, and hence are unable to help with comprehension in the same way as usually occurs with descriptions of more physical structures.

Empirical studies of the activities involved in designing software [3, 4, 5] suggest that designers use a number of techniques to reduce the effects of at least some of these properties. These techniques include the use of abstract "mental models" of their solutions, which can then be mentally executed to simulate the final system behaviour; reusing parts of previous solutions; and making notes about future (detailed) intentions as reminders for later stages in development.

Even where designers use a particular strategy to help with developing a design model, they may still deviate from this in an opportunistic manner either:

- to *postpone* making a decision where information is not yet available; or
- to define components for which the information is ready to hand, in *anticipation* of further developments in the design.

The use of an opportunistic strategy should not be taken to imply that design decisions are being made in an *unstructured* manner. Rather, this corresponds to a situation where the designer is making use of his or her own experience and knowledge of the problem domain to help adapt their problem-solving strategy, by identifying those aspects of the solution that need to be given most attention in the early stages [6].

Where a designer lacks experience, or is unfamiliar with the type of problem being solved, then one means of acquiring the experience of others is through the use of a *software design method.* Clearly, to transfer all of the different forms of knowledge that allow the designer to use opportunistic development strategies would be difficult, and design methods are therefore limited to encouraging those forms of design practice that can be prescribed in a *procedural* manner. To do so, they provide:

1. A *representation part* consisting of a set of notations that can be used to describe a design model of the form that the method seeks to develop.
2. A *process part* that describes how the model is to be developed, expressed as a set of steps, with each step representing a transformation of the model.
3. A *set of heuristics* that provide guidance on how the process part should be modified or adapted in order to cope with particular forms of problem. These may consist of alternative procedures, or may identify useful "rules of thumb."

One important point that should be made here: Designing software is rarely a completely *unconstrained* process. The designer not only has to produce a solution to a given problem but must also meet other customer-imposed requirements. These *constraints* may include the need to design a solution that can be implemented in a particular programming language; or one that will work within a particular environment or operating system. Constraints therefore act to limit the "solution space" that is available to the designer.

### 1.2 Design in the software development cycle

Constraints can affect the design process as well as the form of the product. Designing software is not an isolated and independent activity. The eventual system as implemented will be expected to meet a whole set of user needs (reminding us of the criterion of "fitness for purpose"), where these needs are likely to have been determined by some process of *requirements elicitation.* The activities of *analysis* may be used to identify the form of solution that will meet the user's needs, and the designer is then required to provide a solution that conforms to that form. But of course, the activities of all those tasks will interact, largely because each activity is likely to lead to the identification of inconsistencies between requirements and solution, as ideas about the latter develop.

In a like manner, a designer must provide a set of specifications for those who are to construct a system. These need to be as clear, complete, and unambiguous as possible, but of course it is likely that further needs for change will be identified during implementation. The designer also needs to "think ahead" in planning a solution, since few software systems are used for long without being altered and extended. So designing for "maintenance" (a term that is usually a circumlocution for "extensive further development") is another factor that may influence the form of the solution that is adopted.

### 1.3 Design qualities

The features of a system that may be considered as representative of our ideas of quality are apt to be dependent upon the specific relationship that we have to the system. We began by suggesting that *fitness for purpose* was a paramount need of any system, but of course, this is not an absolute measure of quality, nor one that can be measured in any direct manner. Simply doing the job correctly and within the resource constraints identified may not be enough to achieve fitness for purpose. For example, if it is anticipated that a system will be used for at least ten years, involving modification at frequent intervals, then our notions of fitness for purpose are very likely to incorporate ideas about how easily the structure of the design will accommodate the likely changes. On the other hand, if the need is for a solution that is extremely short-term, but urgent, we may place much more priority on getting a system that works than on ensuring that it can also be modified and extended.

We do not have space here for a discussion of quality factors, but a useful group to note are those that are usually referred to as the "*ilities*". The exact membership of this group may depend upon context, but the key ones are generally accepted as being *reliability, efficiency, maintainability*, and *usability*. The ilities can be considered to describe rather abstract and "top-level" properties of the eventual system, and these are not easily assessed from design information alone.

Indeed, it has generally proved to be difficult to apply any systematic form of measurement to design information. While at the level of implementation, basic code measurements (metrics) can at least be gathered by counting lexical tokens [7], the variability and the weak syntax and semantics of design notations make such an approach much less suitable for designs. More practical approaches to assessment at this level of abstraction usually involve such activities as design walk-throughs and reviews [8].

## 2 Describing Designs

### 2.1 Recording the design model: design viewpoints

In this section we examine some of the ways in which a designer's ideas about the design model can be visualised by using various forms of description.

A major need for the designer is to be able to select and use a set of abstractions that describe those properties of the design model that are relevant to the design decisions that need to be made. This is normally achieved by using a number of representation forms, where such forms can be used for:

- documenting and exploring the details of the design model;
- explaining the designer's ideas to others (including the customer, the implementors, managers, reviewers, and so forth);
- checking for consistency and completeness of the design model.

Because software design methods must rely upon constructing a design model through a fixed set of procedures, they each use an associated set of representations to describe the properties identified through following the procedures. This forms both a strength and a weakness of design methods: The representations support the procedures by helping the designer visualise those aspects of the design that are affected by the procedures; but they may also limit the designer's vision. (Indeed, the act of deviating from the procedures of a method in order to draw some other form of diagram to help highlight some issue is a good example of what was earlier termed *opportunistic* behaviour on the part of a designer.)

The representations used in software design can be grouped according to their *purpose*, since this identifies the forms of property they seek to describe. One such grouping, explored in some detail in [9] is based upon the concept of the *design viewpoint*. A design viewpoint can be regarded as being a "projection" from the design model that displays certain of the properties of the design model, as is shown schematically in Figure 1. The four viewpoints shown there are:

1. The *behavioural* viewpoint, describing the causal links between external events and system activities during program execution.
2. The *functional* viewpoint, describing what the system does.
3. The *structural* viewpoint, describing the interdependencies of the constructional components of the system, such as subprograms, modules, and packages.
4. The *data modelling* viewpoint, describing the relationships that exist between the data objects used in the system.

### 2.2 Design representation forms

The three principal forms of description normally used to realise the design viewpoints are text, diagrams, and mathematical expressions.

**Textual descriptions**

Text is of course widely used, both on its own, and in conjunction with the other two forms. We can structure it by using such forms as headings, lists (numbered, bullets), and indentation, so as to reflect the structure of the properties being described. However, text on its own does have some limitations, in particular:

- The presence of any form of structure that is implicitly contained in the information can easily be obscured if its form does not map easily onto lists and tables.
- Natural language is prone to ambiguity that can only be resolved by using long and complex sequences of text (as is amply demonstrated by any legal document!)

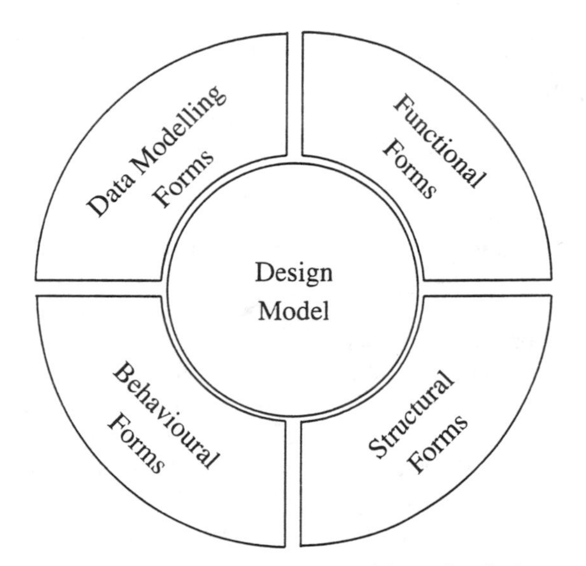


*Figure 1. Design viewpoints projected from the design model.*

**Diagrammatical descriptions**

There is a long tradition of drawing diagrams to provide abstractions in science and engineering, and even though the "invisibility" factor makes the form of these less intuitive when used to describe software, they are still very useful. Since they will form the main examples later in this section, we will not elaborate on their forms here, other than to identify the following properties as those that seem to characterise the more widely used and "successful" forms:

- *A small number of symbols.* The symbols in a diagram describe the "elements" that are modelled by that form of diagram, and the number of symbols is often in inverse pro portion to the degree of abstraction provided. Most of the widely used forms use only four or five different symbols, including circles, lines (arcs), and boxes.
- *A hierarchical structure.* The complex interactions that occur between software components together with the abstract nature of the components means that diagrams with many different symbols are often very difficult to understand. To help overcome this, many diagrammatical forms allow the use of a hierarchy of diagrams, with symbols at one level being expanded at another level with the same set of symbols, as is shown schematically in Figure 2.

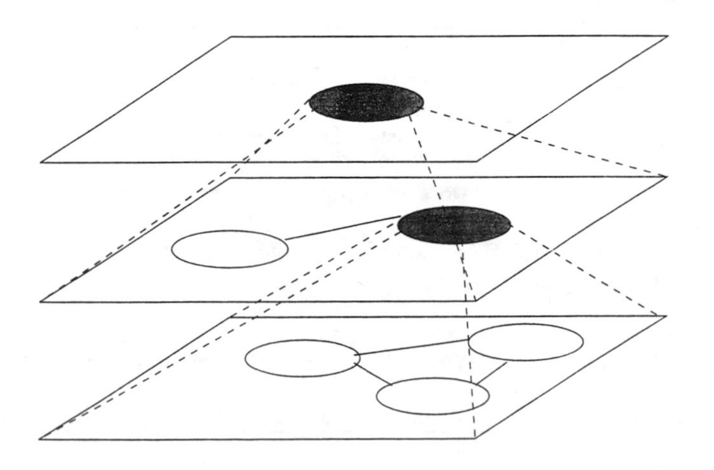

*Figure 2. Use of hierarchy in representations.*

- *Simplicity of symbol forms.* Ideally, *any* notation should be capable of being drawn using a pencil and paper only (or a white-board). Complicated symbols that require the support of specialised diagram drawing software can limit the ease with which designers communicate their ideas to others.

**Mathematical descriptions**

Mathematical notations are of course ideally suited to providing concise abstractions of ideas, and so it is hardly surprising that these have been employed in what we generally term the Formal Description Techniques, or FDTs. However, the very terse nature of mathematical descriptions, and the precision that they provide, are not necessarily compatible with the designer's need for abstraction, since they may demand early resolution of issues that the designer may wish to defer.

So far, FDTs have found their main use in specification roles, especially in providing unambiguous descriptions of requirements and descriptions of detailed design features. In both of these roles, their form makes them well suited to exploring the completeness and consistency of the specification, although less so to its development [10].

### 2.3 Some examples of design representations

To conclude this section we provide some simple examples of diagrammatical notations used for the four design viewpoints. This is a very small selection from the very large range of forms that have been proposed and used (for a fuller survey, see reference [9]). Table 1 provides a summary of some widely used representations, the viewpoints that they provide, and the related design properties that they describe. (It should be noted that the conventions used in these notations do vary between different groups of users.)

**The Statechart**

Statecharts provide a means of modelling the behaviour of a system when viewed as a finite-state machine, [11] while providing better scope for hierarchical decomposition and composition than is generally found in behavioural representation forms.

A state is denoted by a box with rounded corners and directed arcs denote transitions. The latter are labelled with a description of the event causing the transition and, optionally, with a parenthesised condition. The hierarchy of states is shown by encapsulating state symbols.

A description of the actions of an aircraft "entity" within an air traffic control system is shown in Figure 3. Note that the short curved arc denotes the "default initial state" that is entered when an instance of the entity is added to the system. (For clarity, not all transitions have been labelled in this example.)

**The Jackson Structure Diagram**

This notation is very widely used under a variety of names. Its main characteristic is that it can describe the ordered structure of an "object" in terms of the three classical structuring forms of sequence, selection and iteration. For this particular example, we will show its use for modelling functional properties, although it is also used for modelling data structure and for describing time-ordered behaviour.

*Table 1. Design representations and viewpoints.*

| Representation Form | Viewpoints | Design properties |
|---|---|---|
| Data-Flow Diagram (DFD) | Functional | Information flow; dependency of operations on other operations. |
| Entity-Relationship Diagram (ERD) | Data modelling | Static relationships between subprograms; decomposition into subprograms |
| Structure Chart | Structural and functional | Invocation hierarchy between subprograms; decomposition into subprograms |
| Structure Diagram (Jackson) | Functional, data modelling, behavioural | Algorithm forms; sequencing of data components; sequencing of actions. |
| Pseudocode | Functional | Algorithm forms |
| State Transition Diagram (STD) | Behavioural | State model describing how events cause transitions in entities. |
| Statechart | Behavioural | System-wide state model, including parallelism, hierarchy, and abstraction. |

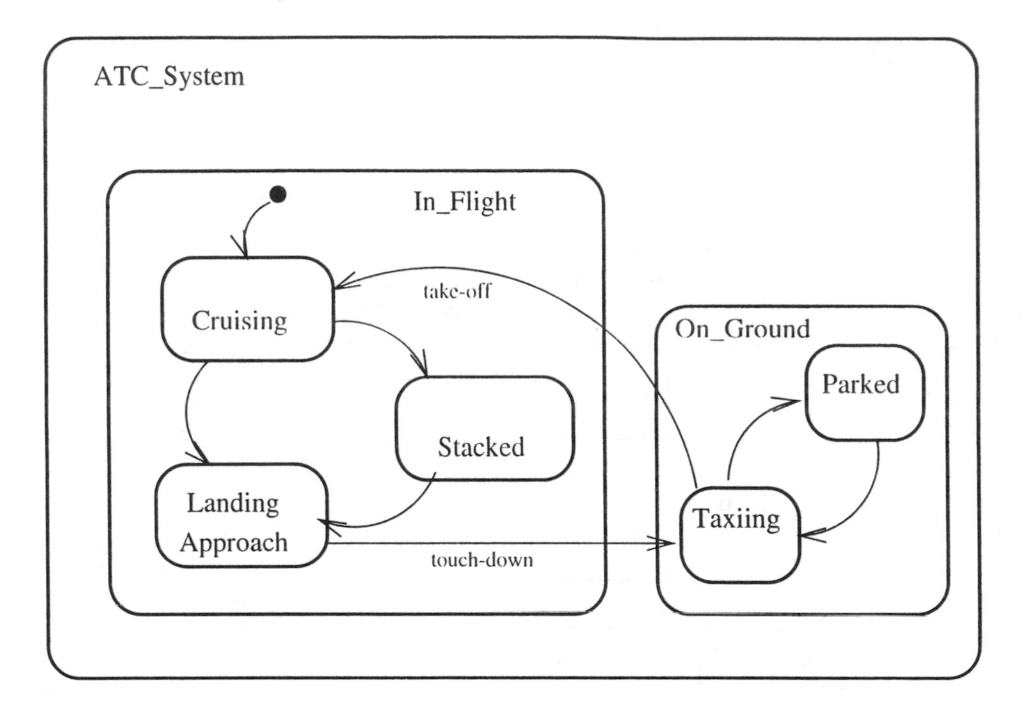


*Figure 3. An example Statechart.*

Figure 4 provides a simple functional description of the (British) approach to making tea. Points to note are:

- Each level is an expanded (and hence, less abstract) description of a box in the level above.
- Sequence is denoted by an ordered line of boxes, selection by a set of boxes with circles in the upper corner, and iteration by a box with an asterisk in the upper corner.
- The structuring forms should not be mixed in a group on a level. (Hence the action "put tea in the pot" forms an abstraction within a sequence, and this is then expanded separately as an iterated set of actions.)

**The Structure Chart**

This notation captures one aspect of constructional information, namely the invocation hierarchy that exists between subprogram units. While the tree-like form is similar to that of the Jackson Structure Diagram, the interpretation is very different, in that the elements (boxes) in a Structure Chart represent physical entities (subprograms) and the hierarchy shown is one of invocation (transfer of control) rather than of abstraction. Figure 5 shows a very simple example of this notation. (There are different forms used to show information about parameter passing; this is just one of them.)

The structural viewpoint is concerned with the physical properties of a design, and hence it is one that may need to describe many attributes of design elements. For this reason, no one single notation can effectively project all of the relevant relationships (such as encapsulation, scope of shared information, invocation), and so an effective description of the structural viewpoint is apt to involve the use of more than a single representation.

**The Entity-Relationship Diagram**

The Entity-Relationship Diagram (ERD) is commonly used for modelling the details of the inter-relationships that occur between data elements in a system, although it may also perform other modelling roles [12]. Figure 6 shows a very simple example of one form of ERD containing two entities (boxes), a relationship (diamond) and the relevant attributes of the entities. Additional conventions are used to show whether the nature of a relationship is one-to-one, one-to-many or many-to-many. (In the example, the relationship is many-to-one between the entities "aircraft" and "landing stack," since one stack may contain many aircraft.)

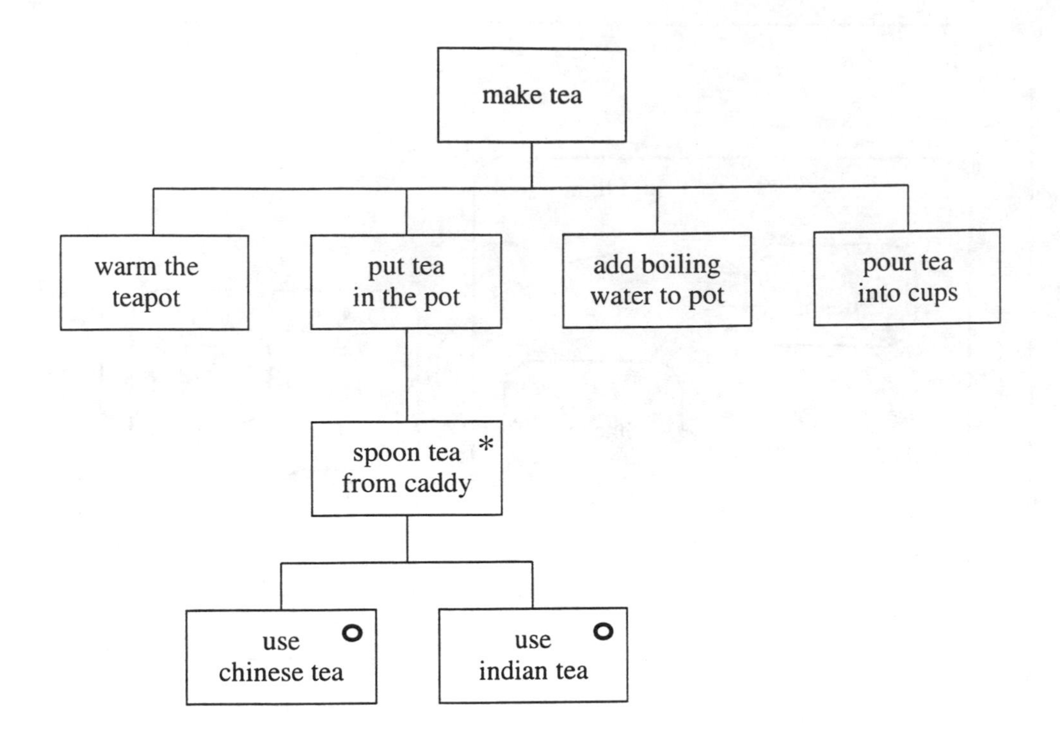


*Figure 4. An example of a Jackson Structure Diagram.*

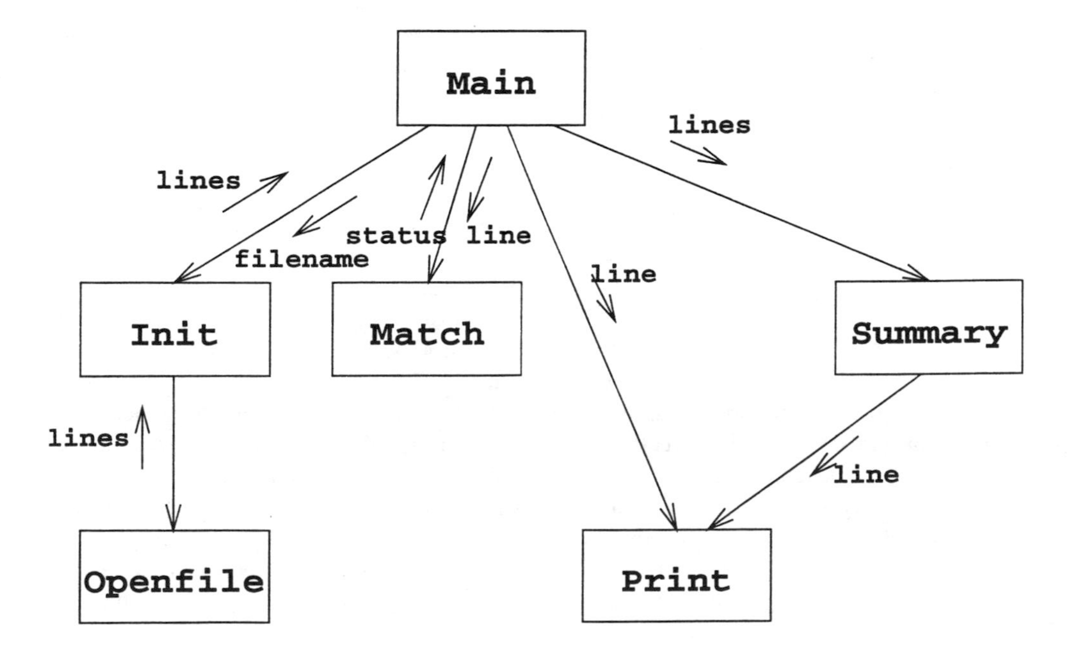


*Figure 5. A simple Structure Chart.*

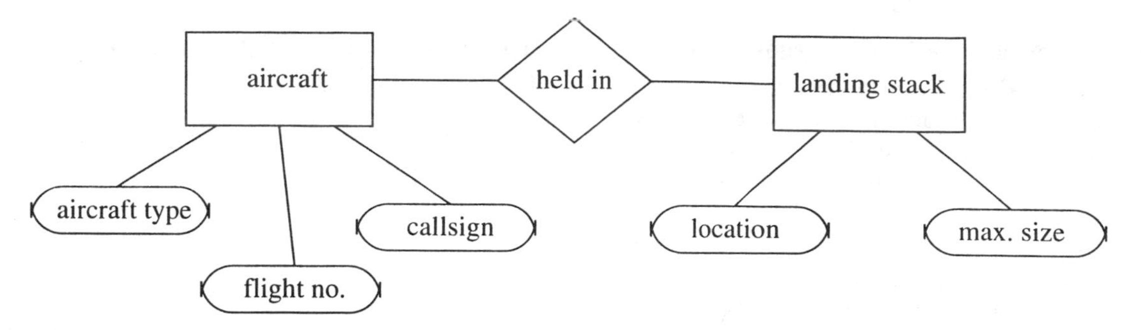


*Figure 6. A simple Entity-Relationship Diagram.*

## 3 Software Design Practices and Design Methods

Section 1.1 introduced the concept of a *software design method* as a means of transferring "knowledge" to less experienced designers. This section explores this concept a little further.

### 3.1 Rationale for software design methods

The use of "methods" for software design has no parallel in any other stage of software development. We do not have "testing methods" or even "programming methods." When teaching programming, we commonly provide the student with a set of "programming metaphors," together with a set of application paradigms such as trees and stacks that make use of these.

The partial analogy with programming points to one of the problems that hinders teaching about design, namely that of scale. Novice programmers can use the abstractions provided in a programming language to construct actual programs, and in the process receive feedback that can assist with revising their ideas and understanding during both compilation and execution of the programs. In contrast, novice designers have no equivalent sources of feedback to indicate where their ideas might be inconsistent, and have little or no chance of comparing an eventual implementation against the abstract design ideas. So "method knowledge" may be our only practical means for transferring experience, however inadequate this might be. (As an example, it is rather as though programmers were taught to solve all needs for iteration by using only the FOR construct.)

Other roles for software design methods include:

- Establishing common goals and styles for a *team* of developers.
- Generating "consistent" documentation that may assist with future maintenance by helping the maintainers to recapture the original design model.
- Helping to make some of the features of a problem more explicit, along with their influence upon the design.

Constraints that limit their usefulness are:

- The *process part* of a method provides relatively little detailed guidance as to how a problem should be solved. It may indicate how the design model is to be developed, but not what should go into this for a given problem.
- The need to use a procedural form (do this, then do that, then...) leads to practices that conflict with the behaviour observed in experienced designers. Decisions have to be made on a method-based schedule, rather than according to the needs of the problem.

So, while at the present time software design methods probably provide the most practical means of transferring design knowledge, we cannot claim that they are particularly successful.

### 3.2 Design strategies

Design methods embody strategies (indeed, this is where they particularly diverge from the practices of experienced designers, since the latter are observed to adapt a strategy opportunistically in order to meet the needs of a problem). Four widely-used strategies are:

**Top-down:** As the name implies, this is based upon the idea of separating a large problem into smaller ones, in the hope that the latter will be easier to solve. While relatively easy to use, it has the disadvantage that important structural decisions may need to be made at an early stage, so that any subsequent need for modification may require extensive reworking of the whole design.

**Compositional:** As implied, this involves identifying a set of "entities" that can be modelled and which can then be assembled to create a model for the complete solution. While the earlier stages may be simple, the resultant model can become very complex.

**Organisational:** A strategy of this form is used where the needs of the development organisation and its management structures impose constraints upon the design process. This may require that project (and design) team members may be transferred at arbitrary times, so that the method should help with the transfer between old and new team members. A good example of this form is SSADM [13].

**Template:** Templates can be used in those rare cases where some general paradigm describes a reasonably large domain of problems. The classical example of this form is that of compiler design, and indeed, this is probably the only really good example.

Whatever the strategy adopted, the process part of a method is usually described as a sequence of *steps*. Each step alters the design method, either by *elaborating* the details of the model, or by *transforming* them, adding new attributes to create new viewpoint descriptions. Steps may involve many activities, and provide a set of milestones that can be used to monitor the progress of a design.

The choice of design strategy and associated method has significant implications for the resulting solution structure, or architecture. Shaw's comparative review of design forms for a car cruise-control system [14] demonstrates the wide range of solution architectures that have been produced from the use of 11 different design methods. But of course, this still leaves open the question of how to know in advance which of these is likely to be the most appropriate solution, and hence the most appropriate method! Any choice of a design method may also be further influenced by prior experience, as well as by social, political, historical, business and other nontechnical factors, none of which can be easily quantified (or accommodated in this review).

## 4. Features of Some Software Design Methods

A review paper such as this cannot examine the workings of software design methods in any detail. So in this section, we briefly review the significant features of a number of well-established design methods, chosen to provide a reasonable range of examples of strategy and form. For fuller descriptions and references, see [9].

Our review starts with two first-generation design methods that provide examples of both compositional and decompositional strategies. After that, we look at two examples of second-generation methods, which typically exhibit much more complex design models.

### 4.1 Jackson Structured Programming (JSP)

JSP was one of the earliest design methods and provides a useful paradigm for the method-based approach to transferring and developing design knowledge. It is deliberately aimed at a very tightly constrained domain of application, and hence can be more prescriptive in its process part than is normal. In addition, it is an algorithm design method, whereas the other methods are aimed at larger systems and produce structural plans. On occasion, JSP may therefore be useful for localised design tasks within a larger system design task. JSP uses a compositional strategy.

The *representation part* of JSP is provided by the ubiquitous Jackson Structure Diagram. This is used both for modelling data structures and also for functional modelling.

The *process part* of JSP is summarised in Table 2. For each step we describe its purpose and also whether it elaborates or transforms the design model.

The heuristics of JSP are highly developed. *Read-ahead, back-tracking,* and *program inversion* have been widely documented and discussed. Between them, they provide a set of "adaptations" to the basic process, and they can be used to resolve some of the more commonly-encountered difficulties in applying JSP to practical problems.

*Table 2. Summary of the JSP process part.*

| | | |
|---|---|---|
| Step 1 | Draw Structure Diagrams for inputs and outputs | *elaboration* |
| Step 2 | Merge these to create the program Structure Diagram | *transformation* |
| Step 3 | List the operations and allocate to program elements | *elaboration* |
| Step 4 | Convert program to text | *elaboration* |
| Step 5 | Add conditions | *elaboration* |

## 4.2 Structured Systems Analysis and Structured Design

Like JSP, this is a relatively old method, and can be considered as an extension of the functional top-down approach to design. It consists of an "analysis" component and a "design" component. (For the purposes of this paper, the activities of analysis are considered to be integral with those of design.)

During the analysis phase (Steps 1 and 2), the designer constructs a functional model of the system (using "physical" Data-Flow Diagrams) and then uses this to develop a functional model of the solution (using "logical" DFDs). This is usually supplemented by some degree of data modelling, and some real-time variants also encourage the development of behavioural descriptions using State Transition Diagrams (STDs).

In the design phase (Steps 3 to 5), this model is gradually transformed into a structural model, based on a hierarchy of subprograms, and described by using Structure Charts. There is relatively little support for using ideas such as information hiding, or for employing any packaging concepts other than the subprogram.

The *representation part* therefore uses both DFDs and Structure Charts for the primary notations, and sometimes involves the use of ERDs and STDs.

The *process part* is summarised in Table 3, using the same format as previously.

The heuristics are far less well-defined than those of JSP. One of them is intended to help with determining which "bubble" in the DFD acts as the "central transform," while others are used to help restructure and reorganise the solution after the major Transform Analysis Step (Step 4) has generated the structural viewpoint for the design model.

As a method, this one has strong intuitive attractions, but suffers from the disadvantage of having a large and relatively disjoint transformation step.

## 4.3 Jackson System Development (JSD)

JSD encourages the designer to create a design model around the notion of modelling the behaviour of active "entities." In the initial stages, these entities are related to the problem, but gradually the emphasis changes to use entities that are elements of the solution.

A characteristic of second-generation design methods is that they involve constructing much more complex design models from the start, usually involving the use of more than one design viewpoint. As a result, they generally use a sequence of elaboration steps to modify the design model, rather than providing any major transformation steps.

The *representation part* of JSD makes use of *Entity-Structure Diagrams* (ESDs) to model the time-ordered behaviour of long-lived problem entities. (These diagrams use a different interpretation of the basic Jackson Structure Diagram.) The function and structure of the resulting network of interacting "processes" is then modelled using *System Specification Diagrams* (SSDs).

The *process part* can be described in terms of three stages [9,15], which can be further subdivided to form six major design activities. Table 4 provides a very basic summary of these activities, using the same format as before.

*Table 3. Summary of the process part of SSA and SD.*

| | | |
|---|---|---|
| Step 1 | Develop a top-level description | *elaboration* |
| Step 2 | Develop a model of the problem (SSA) | *elaboration* |
| Step 3 | Subdivide into DFDs describing transactions | *elaboration* |
| Step 4 | Transform into Structure Charts | *transformation* |
| Step 5 | Refine and recombine into system description | *elaboration* |

*Table 4. Summary of the JSD process part.*

| | | |
|---|---|---|
| 1. Entity Analysis | Identify and model problem entities | *elaboration* |
| 2. Initial Model Phase | Complete the problem model network | *elaboration* |
| 3. Interactive Function Step | Add new solution entities | *elaboration* |
| 4. Information Function Step | Add new solution entities | *elaboration* |
| 5. System Timing Step | Resolve synchronisation issues | *elaboration* |
| 6. Implementation | Physical design mappings | *elaboration* |

The *heuristics* of JSD owe quite a lot to JSP, with both back-tracking and program inversion being recognisable adaptions of these ideas to a larger scale. An additional technique is that of state vector separation which can be used to increase implementational efficiency via a form of "reentrancy."

### 4.4 Object-Oriented Design

The topics of "what is an object?" and "how do we design with objects?" are both well beyond the scope of this paper. Some ideas about the nature of objects can be found in [16] and in [17].

It can be argued that object-oriented analysis and design techniques are still evolving (perhaps not as rapidly as was once hoped). The Fusion method [12] provides a useful example of one of the more developed uses of these ideas, and one that has brought together a number of techniques (hence its name).

The *representation part* of such methods is often a weakness, being used to document decisions at a later stage, rather than to help model the solution. Fusion seeks to make extensive use of diagrammatical forms, and especially of variations upon the Entity-Relationship Diagram.

The *process part* is described in Table 5 and includes both analysis and design activities. There are no identifiable heuristics available for such a recent method. (A fuller methodological analysis of Fusion as well as of the other methods described in this section is provided in reference [18].) A problem with object-oriented methods is that they do encourage the designer to make decisions about "structure" at a much earlier stage than "process"-oriented methods (including JSD), and hence bind the design to implementation-oriented physical issues before the details of the abstract design model have been fully worked through.

## 5. Conclusion

This paper has sought to review both our current understanding of how software systems are designed (and why that process is a complex one) and also how current software design methods attempt to provide frameworks to assist with this. As can be seen, even the second-generation design methods still provide only limited help with many aspects of designing a system.

We have not discussed the use of support tools. Many design support tools still provide little more than diagram editing facilities and support for version control. In particular, they tend to bind the user to a particular set of notations, and hence to a specific design process. Inevitably, this is an area of research that lags behind research into design practices.

Overall, while our understanding of how software is designed is slowly improving [19], it seems likely that this will provide an active area of research for many years to come.

## References


[1] H.J. Rittel and M.M. Webber, "Planning Problems are Wicked Problems," N. Cross, ed., *Developments in Design Methodology*, Wiley, 1984, pp. 135–144.

[2] F.P. Brooks Jr., "No Silver Bullet: Essence and Accidents of Software Engineering," *Computer*, Apr. 1987, pp. 10–19.

[3] B. Adelson and E. Soloway, "The Role of Domain Experience in Software Design," *IEEE Trans. Software Eng.*, Vol. SE-11, No. 11, Nov. 1985, pp. 1351–1360.

[4] R. Guindon and B. Curtis, "Control of Cognitive Processes during Software Design: What Tools are needed?" in *Proc. CHI'88*, ACM Press, New York, N.Y., 1988, pp. 263–268.

[5] W. Visser and J.-M. Hoc, "Expert Software Design Strategies," in *Psychology of Programming*, Academic Press, New York, N.Y., 1990.

[6] B. Hayes-Roth and F. Hayes-Roth, "A Cognitive Model of Planning," *Cognitive Science*, Vol. 3, 1979, pp. 275–310.

[7] N.E. Fenton, *Software Metrics: A Rigorous Approach*, Chapman & Hall, 1991.


*Table 5. The Fusion design process.*

| Phase | Step | Action |
|---|---|---|
| Analysis | 1. | Develop the Object Model |
| Analysis | 2. | Determine the System Interface |
| Analysis | 3. | Development of the Interface Model |
| Analysis | 4. | Check the Analysis Models |
| Design | 5. | Develop Object Interaction Graphs |
| Design | 6. | Develop Visibility Graphs |
| Design | 7. | Develop Class Descriptions |
| Design | 8. | Develop Inheritance Graphs |

[8] D.L. Parnas and D.M. Weiss, "Active Design Reviews: Principles and Practices," *J. Systems & Software*, Vol. 7, 1987, pp. 259–265.

[9] D. Budgen, *Software Design,* Addison-Wesley, Wokingham, Berkshire, 1993.

[10] G. Friel and D. Budgen, "Design Transformation and Abstract Design Prototyping," *Information and Software Technology*, Vol. 33, No. 9, Nov. 1991, pp. 707–719.

[11] D. Harel, "On Visual Formalisms," *Comm. ACM*, Vol. 31, No. 5, May 1988, pp. 514–530.

[12] D. Coleman, et al., *Object-Oriented Development: The Fusion Method,* Prentice-Hall, Englewood Cliffs, N.J., 1994.

[13] E. Downs, P. Clare, and I. Coe, *SSADM: Structured Systems Analysis and Design Method: Application and Context,* Prentice-Hall, Englewood Cliffs, N.J., 2nd ed., 1992.

[14] M. Shaw, "Comparing Architectural Design Styles," *IEEE Software*, Vol. 12, No. 6, Nov. 1995, pp. 27–41.

[15] J. Cameron, *JSP & JSD: The Jackson Approach to Software Development,* 2nd ed., IEEE Computer Society Press, Los Alamitos, Calif., 1989.

[16] G. Booch, *Object-Oriented Analysis and Design,* Benjamin/Cummings, Redwood City, Calif., 1994.

[17] A. Snyder, "The Essence of Objects: Concepts and Terms," *IEEE Software*, Jan. 1993, pp. 31–42.

[18] D. Budgen, "'Design Models' from Software Design methods," *Design Studies*, Vol. 16, No. 3, July 1995, pp. 293–325.

[19] B.I. Blum, "A Taxonomy of Software Development Methods," *Comm. ACM*, Vol. 37, No. 11, Nov. 1994, pp. 82–94.

# Design Methods for Concurrent and Real-Time Systems

Hassan Gomaa
*Department of Information and Software Systems Engineering*
*George Mason University*
*Fairfax, Virginia 22030-4444*

## Abstract

*This paper discusses and compares the concepts and criteria used by software design methods for developing large-scale concurrent and real-time systems. Concurrency is addressed by task structuring while modifiability is addressed by module structuring. In addition, the behavioral aspects of a real-time system are addressed by means of finite state machines. The Real-Time Structured Analysis and Design, DARTS, Jackson System Development, Naval Research Lab, and Object-Oriented Design methods are presented and compared from the perspective of how they address these concepts. Two related design methods for real-time systems, which build on the previous methods, ADARTS$^{SM}$ (Ada-based Design Approach for Real-Time Systems) and CODARTS (Concurrent Design Approach for Real-Time Systems), are also briefly described.*

## 1. Introduction

With the massive reduction in the cost of microprocessor and semiconductor chips—and the large increase in microprocessor performance over the past few years—real-time and distributed real-time microcomputer-based systems are a very cost-effective solution to many problems. Nowadays, more and more commercial, industrial, military, medical, and consumer products are microcomputer based and either software controlled or have a crucial software component to them.

This paper presents an overview of the design of concurrent systems, as well as an important category of concurrent systems: real-time systems. The paper starts by describing three key design concepts for large-scale concurrent and real-time systems: concurrency, modularity, and finite state machines. After introducing these concepts, this paper describes and compares five software design methods for concurrent and real-time systems that use these concepts. It then describes two related design methods for concurrent and real-time systems, ADARTS (Ada-based Design Approach for Real-Time Systems) and CODARTS (Concurrent Design Approach for Real-Time Systems), which build on these earlier methods.[1]



## 2. Design Concepts For Concurrent and Real-Time Systems

### 2.1 Concurrent Tasks

In the early days of computing, most computer systems were batch programs. Each program was sequential and ran off line. Today, with the proliferation of interactive systems and the tendency toward distributed microcomputer systems, many systems are concurrent in nature. A characteristic of a concurrent system is that it typically has many activities occurring in parallel. It is often the case that the order of incoming events is not predictable, and the events may overlap.

The concept of concurrent tasks, also frequently referred to as concurrent processes, is fundamental in the design of these systems. A concurrent system consists of many tasks that execute in parallel. The design concepts for concurrent systems are generally applicable to real-time systems and distributed applications.

A task represents the execution of a sequential program or sequential component of a concurrent program. Each task deals with one sequential thread of execution; hence no concurrency is allowed within a task. However, overall system concurrency is obtained by having multiple tasks that execute in parallel. From time to time, the tasks must communicate and synchronize their operations with each other. The concurrent tasking concept has been applied extensively in the design of operating systems, real-time systems,

---

[1] The material presented in this paper is excerpted from *Software Design Methods for Concurrent and Real-Time Systems*, by Hassan Gomaa, copyright 1993 by Addison-Wesley Publishing Company, Inc. Reprinted with permission of the publisher.

interactive systems, distributed systems, parallel systems, and in simulation applications.

Criteria for task structuring have been developed to guide a software designer in decomposing a real-time system into concurrent tasks. The main consideration in identifying tasks is the asynchronous nature of the functions within the system. The task structuring criteria were first described in the DARTS (Design Approach for Real-Time Systems) method (3,4) and later refined for the ADARTS and CODARTS methods (6).

### 2.2 Modularity

Modularity provides a means of decomposing a system into smaller, more manageable units with well-defined interfaces between them. However, there are many definitions of the term "module." The two definitions used in this paper are those used by the Structured Design (9,10,19) and the Naval Research Laboratory Software Cost Reduction (NRL) (11,12,13) methods. In Structured Design, a module usually means a function or procedure. In the NRL method, a module is an information hiding module (IHM) that contains the hidden information as well as the access procedures to it.

The module cohesion and coupling criteria, which originated from the work of Constantine and Myers in Structured Design (9,19), are criteria for decomposing a system into modules, where a module usually means a procedure or function. Cohesion is a criterion for identifying the strength or unity within a module. Coupling is a measure of the connectivity between modules. The goal of Structured Design is to develop a design in which the modules have strong cohesion and low coupling.

Functional cohesion, where the module performs one specific function, was considered the strongest form of cohesion (19). However, the informational cohesion criterion was added later by Myers (9) to identify information hiding modules. Data coupling is considered the lowest form of coupling (9,19), in which parameters are passed between modules. Undesirable forms of coupling include common coupling, where global data is used.

The Information Hiding principle was first proposed by Parnas (11) as a criterion for decomposing a software system into modules. The principle states that each module should hide a design decision that is considered likely to change. Each changeable decision is called the secret of the module. The reasons for applying information hiding are to provide modules that are modifiable and understandable and hence maintainable. Because information hiding modules are usually self-contained, they have a greater potential for reuse than most procedural modules.

### 2.3 Finite State Machines

Finite state machines address the behavioral aspects of real-time systems. They are particularly important in real-time design as real-time systems are frequently state dependent, that is, their actions depend not only on their inputs but also on what previously happened in the system.

A finite state machine may be used for modeling the behavioral aspects of a real-time system. It is a conceptual machine with a given number of states; it can be in only one of the states at any specific time. State transitions are changes in state that are caused by input events. In response to an input event, the system may transition to the same or to a different state. Furthermore, an output event may be optionally generated. Notations used to define finite state machines are the state transition diagram and the state transition table or matrix.

Finite state machine are used by several real-time design methods including Real-Time Structured Analysis, DARTS, the Naval Research Laboratory Software Cost Reduction Method, and Object-Oriented Design.

## 3. Survey of Software Design Methods for Concurrent and Real-Time Systems

Due to the importance of the design concepts described in the previous section, three important objectives for a design method for concurrent and real-time systems should be:

- the capability of structuring a system into concurrent tasks,
- the development of modifiable and potentially reusable software through the use of information hiding,
- definition of the behavioral aspects of a real-time system using finite state machines.

A fourth important objective for real-time systems is the ability to analyze the performance of a design to determine that it will meet its performance requirements.

### 3.1 Real-Time Structured Analysis and Design (RTSAD)

Real-Time Structured Analysis (RTSA) (7,18) is an extension of Structured Analysis to address the needs of real-time systems. Two variations of RTSA have been developed, the Ward/Mellor (18) and Hatley Pirbhai (7) approaches.

The first step in RTSA is to develop the system context diagram. The system context diagram defines the boundary between the system to be developed and the external environment. The context diagram shows all the inputs to the system and outputs from the system.

Next, a data flow/control flow decomposition is performed. The system is structured into functions (called transformations or processes) and the interfaces between them are defined in the form of data flows or event flows. Transformations may be data or control transformations. The system is structured as a hierarchical set of data flow/control flow diagrams that may be checked for completeness and consistency. Each leaf-node data transformation on a data flow diagram is defined by writing a minispecification (also referred to as a process specification), usually in Structured English. A data dictionary is developed that defines all data flows, event flows, and data stores.

The real-time extensions to Structured Analysis are motivated by a desire to represent more precisely the behavioral characteristics of the system being developed. With the Ward/Mellor approach (18), this is achieved primarily through the use of state transition diagrams, event flows, and integrating the state transition diagrams with data flow diagrams through the use of control transformations. Each state transition diagram shows the different states of the system (or subsystem). It also shows the input events that cause state transitions, and output events resulting from state transitions. A state transition diagram is executed by a control transformation.

After developing the specification using RTSA, the next step is to allocate transformations to processors, although little guidance is provided for this purpose. Transformations on a given processor are then structured into modules using Structured Design. Structured Design (SD) (9,10,19) uses the criteria of module coupling and cohesion in conjunction with two design strategies, Transform and Transaction Analysis, to develop a design starting from an RTSA specification. However, because SD is a program design method, the issue of structuring a system into concurrent tasks is not addressed.

An example of RTSA is given in Figures 1 and 2. Figure 1 shows a state transition diagram for the Automobile Cruise Control System (6). Figure 2 shows a data flow/control flow diagram, in which the Cruise Control control transformation executes the Cruise Control state transition diagram shown in Figure 1.

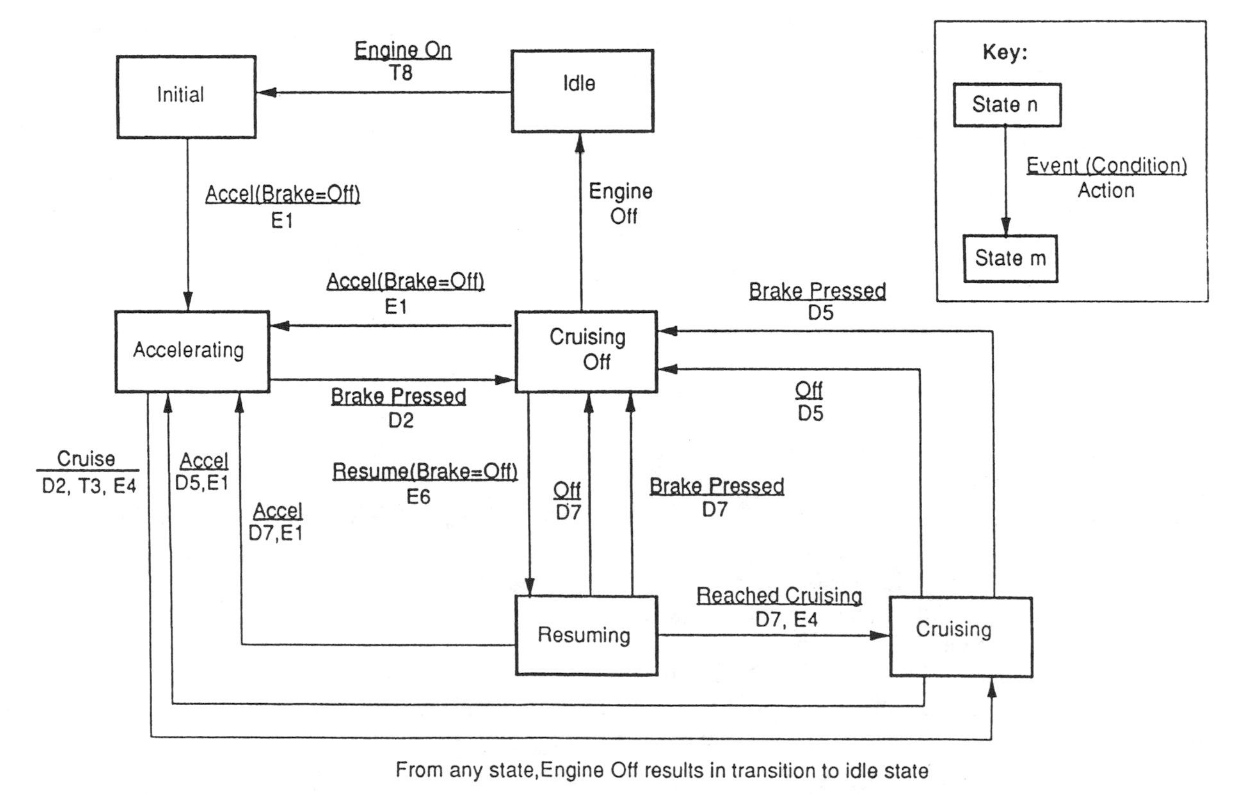


*Figure 1. Cruise control system state transition diagram*

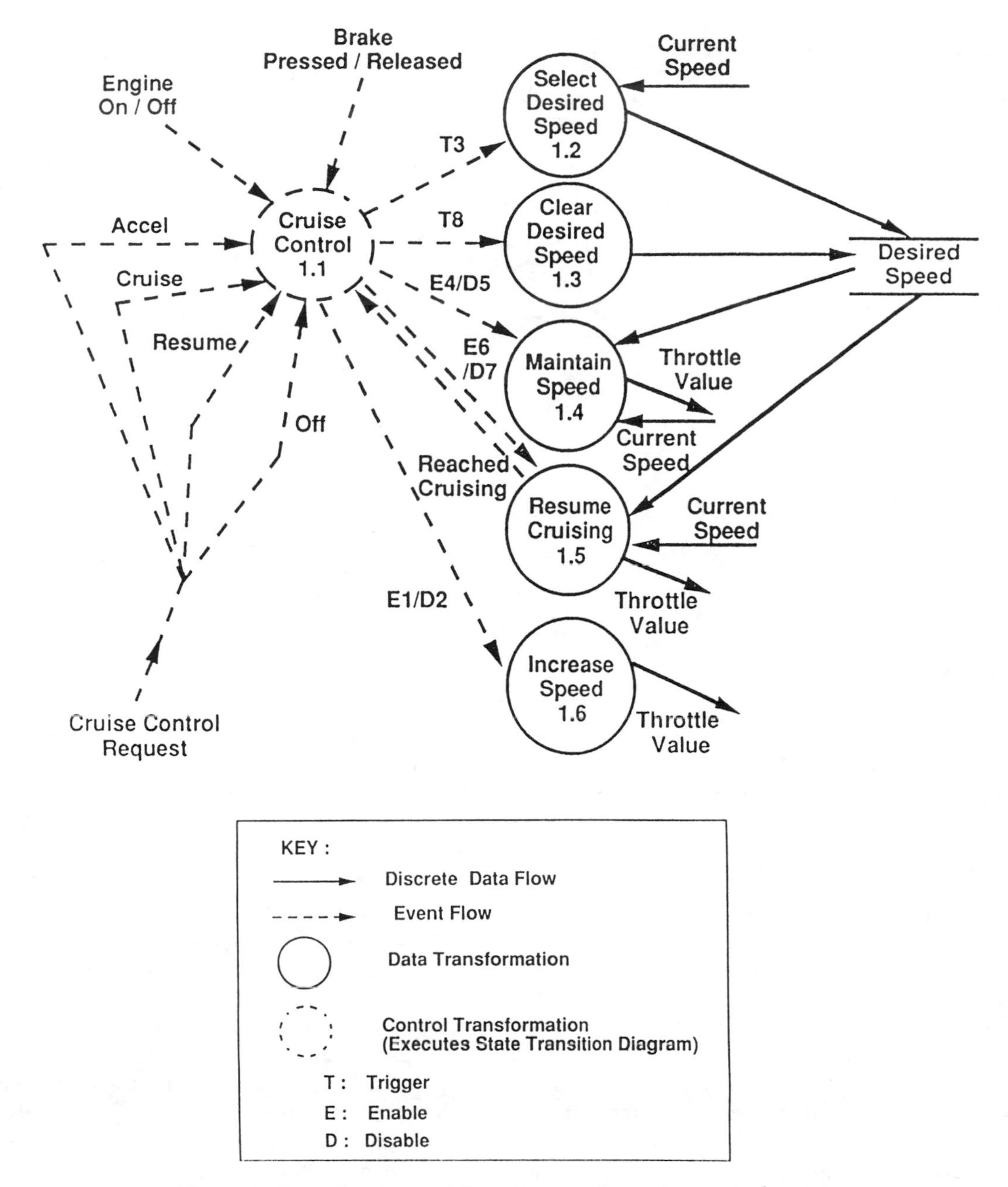


*Figure 2. Data flow/control flow diagram for cruise control system*

For example, if the Cruise Control control transformation receives the Accel event flow while the system is in Initial state, (and providing the brake is not pressed), the car enters Accelerating state. An action is associated with this transition, namely the data transformation Increase Speed is enabled (action E1 on Figures 1 and 2). It remains active while the vehicle is in Accelerating state, outputing to the throttle on a regular basis so that the car accelerates automatically.

An example of a structure chart for the Cruise Control System is shown in Figure 3. The main module, Perform Automobile Cruise Control, has a cyclic loop in which it determines when to call its subordinate modules. These are Get Cruise Control Input, which reads the car's input sensors, Determine Speed, to compute the current speed of the car, Control Speed, which controls the throttle when the car is under automatic control, and Display Speed.

### 3.2 DARTS

The DARTS (Design Approach for Real-Time Systems) design method (3,4,5) emphasizes the decomposition of a real-time system into concurrent tasks and defining the interfaces between these tasks.

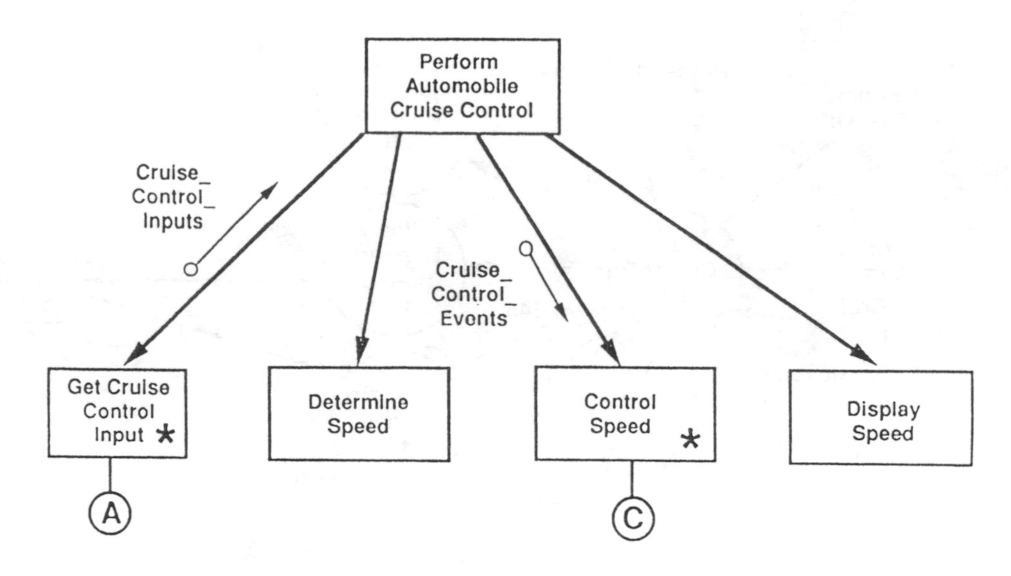


*Figure 3. Structure chart for cruise control system*

DARTS may be considered an extension of Real-Time Structured Analysis and Structured Design. It addresses a key limitation of Real-Time Structured Analysis and Design, that of not adequately addressing task structuring. DARTS uses a set of task structuring criteria for identifying the concurrent tasks in the system as well as a set of guidelines for defining the communication and synchronization interfaces between tasks. Each task, which represents a sequential program, is then designed using Structured Design.

After developing a system specification using Real-Time Structured Analysis, the next step in DARTS is to structure the system into concurrent tasks. The task structuring criteria assist the designer in this activity. The main consideration in identifying the tasks is the concurrent nature of the transformations within the system. In DARTS, the task structuring criteria are applied to the leaf-level data and control transformations on the hierarchical set of data flow/control flow diagrams developed using Real-Time Structured Analysis. Thus, a transformation is grouped with other transformations into a task, based on the temporal sequence in which they are executed.

A preliminary Task Architecture Diagram is drawn showing the tasks identified using the task structuring criteria. An example of a Task Architecture Diagram for the cruise control system is given in Figure 4. Several of the tasks are I/O tasks, including Monitor Cruise Control Input, which is an asynchronous device input task, and Monitor Auto Sensors, which is a periodic, temporally cohesive task that samples the brake and engine sensors. Cruise Control is a control task that executes the cruise control state transition diagram.

In the next step, task interfaces are defined by analyzing the data flow and control flow interfaces between the tasks identified in the previous stage. Task interfaces take the form of message communication, event synchronization, or information hiding modules (IHMs). Message communication may be either loosely or tightly coupled. Event synchronization is provided in cases where no data is passed between tasks. Information hiding modules are used for hiding the contents and representation of data stores and state transition tables. Where an IHM is accessed by more than one task, the access procedures must synchronize the access to the data.

Figure 4 also shows the interfaces between tasks. Thus, the Cruise Control task receives loosely coupled cruise control messages in its message queue while it sends tightly coupled Speed Command messages to Auto Speed Control. Current Speed and Desired Speed are information hiding modules that synchronize access to the data they encapsulate.

Once the tasks and their interfaces have been defined, each task, which represents the execution of a sequential program, is designed. Using the Structured Design method, each task is structured into modules. An example of a structure chart for the Cruise Control task is given in Figure 5. The task is dormant until it receives a cruise control message. The Cruise Control state transition module encapsulates the cruise control state transition diagram, implemented as a table. The Get operation of the Current Speed IHM and the Update operation of the Desired Speed IHM are invoked from within this task.

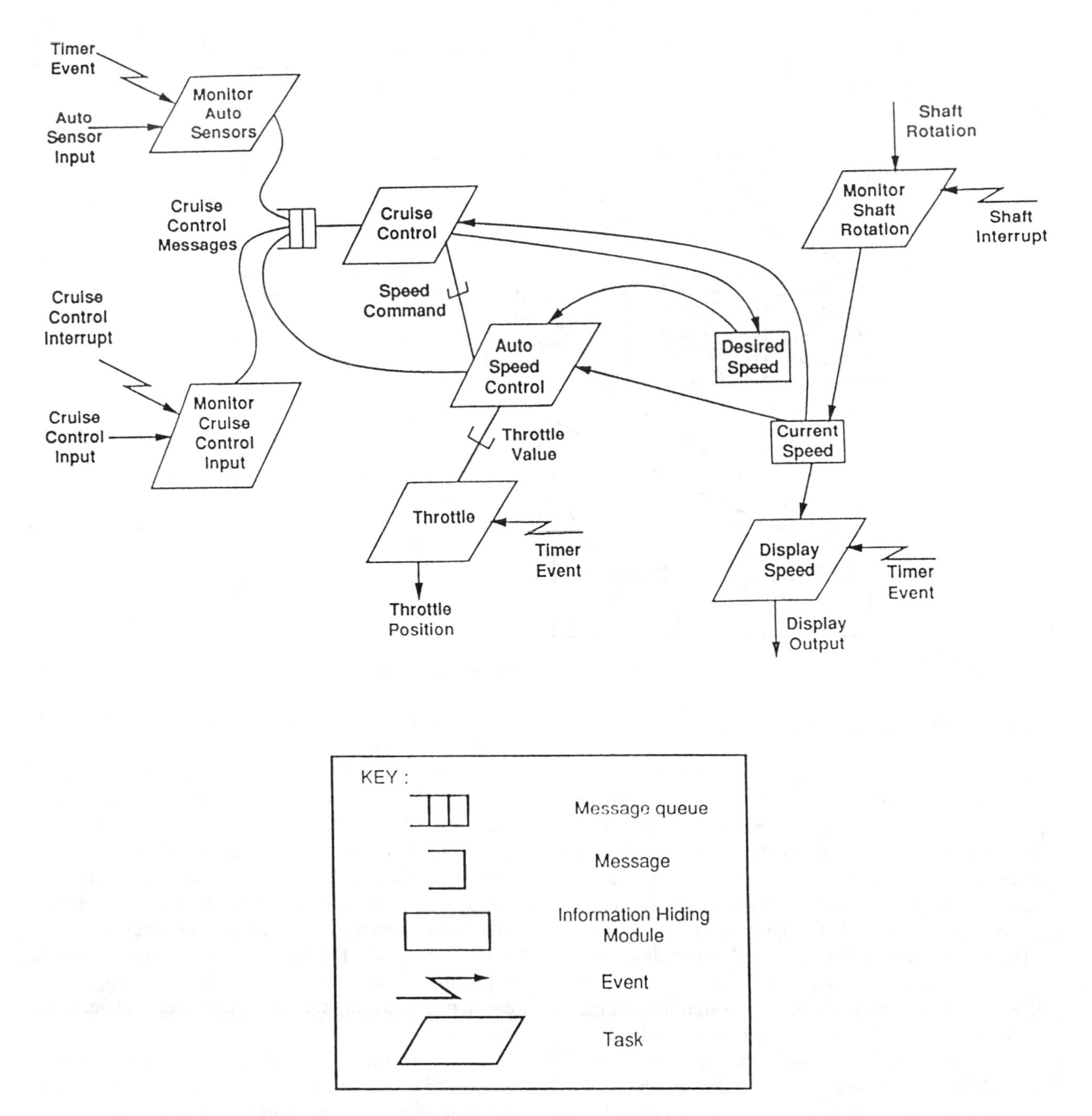


*Figure 4. Task architecture diagram for cruise control system*

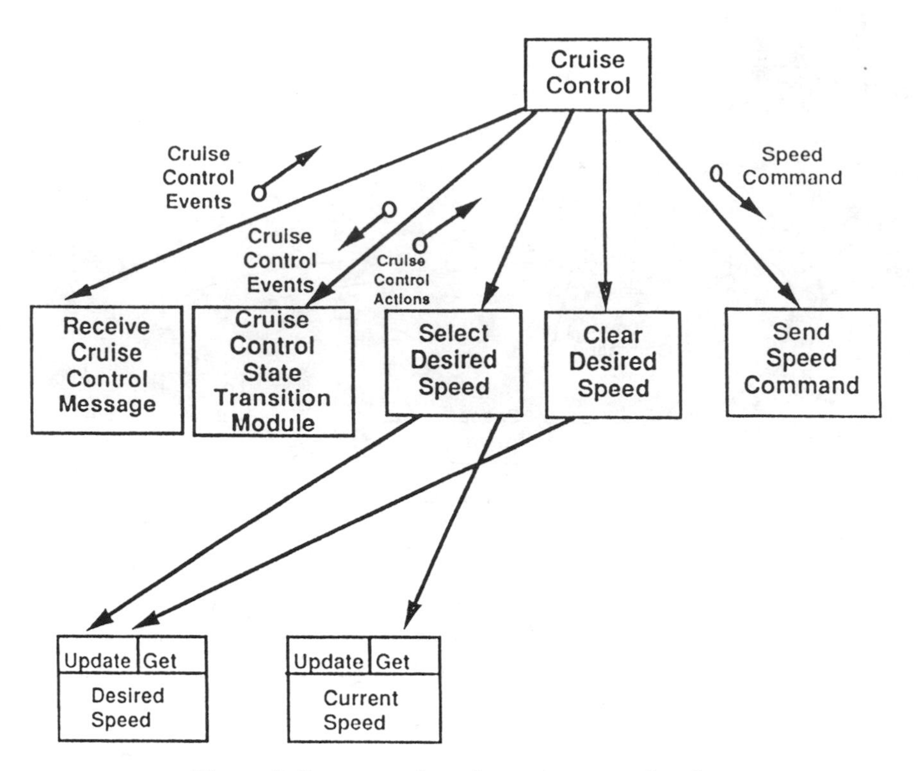


*Figure 5. Structure chart for cruise control task*

### 3.3 Jackson System Development

Concurrency is also an important theme in Jackson System Development (JSD) (8), which is a modeling approach to software design. A fundamental concept of JSD is that the design should model reality first before considering the functions of the system. The system is considered a simulation of the real world. The functions of the system are then added to this simulation.

There are three phases in JSD, the modeling, network, and implementation phases. The first phase of JSD is the Modeling Phase. A JSD design models the behavior of real-world entities over time. Each entity is mapped onto a software task (referred to as a process in JSD). During the Modeling Phase, the real-world entities are identified. The entity is defined in terms of the events (referred to as actions in JSD) it experiences. An entity structure diagram is developed in which the sequence of events experienced by the entity is explicitly shown.

Each real-world entity is modeled by means of a concurrent task called a model task. This task faithfully models the entity in the real world and has the same basic structure as the entity. Since real-world entities usually have long lives, each model task typically also has a long life.

An example of an entity structure diagram for a model task is given in Figure 6. The diagram is represented in terms of sequence, selection, and iterations of events. Figure 6 shows the structure of the Shaft model task. Shaft consists of an iteration of Shaft revolution events, one for each revolution of the shaft.

During the Network Phase, the communication between tasks is defined, function is added to model tasks, and function tasks are added. Communication between tasks is in the form of data streams of messages or by means of state vector inspections. In the first case, a producer task sends a message to a consumer, whereas in the latter case a task may read data belonging to another task. A network diagram is developed showing the communication between the model tasks.

The functions of the system are considered next. Some simple functions are added to the model tasks. Other independent functions are represented by function tasks. The network diagram is updated to show the function tasks and their communication with other function or model tasks.

An example of a network diagram is given in Figure 7. Data streams correspond to message queues between tasks and are shown as circles. In Figure 7, the Cruise Control task sends Speed Command messages to the Throttle task. A state vector corresponds to internal data maintained by a task and is shown as a diamond. Only the task that maintains its state vector can write to it, but other tasks may read from it. In Figure 7, the Shaft task maintains a state vector, Current Speed, which is read by the Cruise Control task.

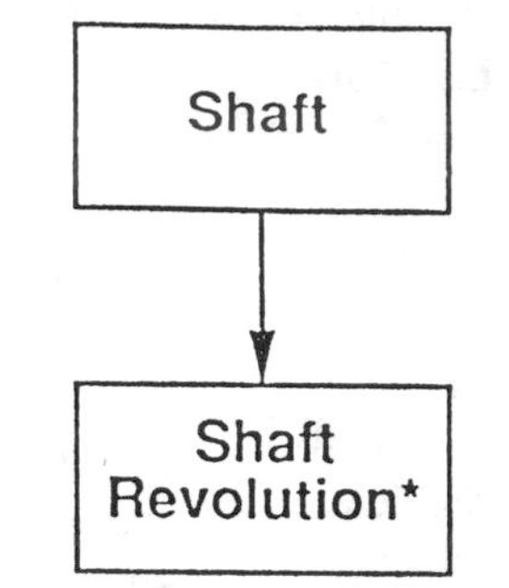


*Figure 6. JSD entity structure diagram*

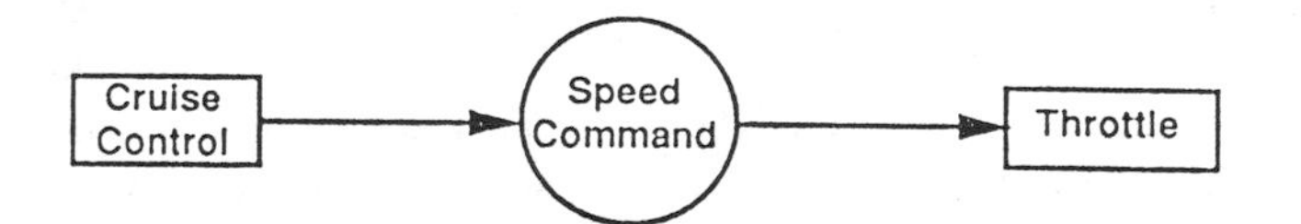


Data Stream (message) connection

State Vector Connection

*Figure 7. JSD network diagrams*

During the Implementation Phase, the JSD specification, consisting of potentially very large numbers of logical tasks, is mapped onto an implementation version, which is directly executable. Originally, with the emphasis on data processing, the specification was mapped onto one program using the concept of program inversion. During the implementation phase, JSD specifications can be mapped to concurrent designs, for example, Ada implementations (15).

### 3.4 NRL Method

The Naval Research Laboratory Software Cost Reduction Method (NRL) originated to address the perceived growing gap between software engineering principles advocated in academia and the practice of software engineering in industry and government (13). These principles formed the basis of a design method that was first applied to the development of a complex real-time system, namely the Onboard Flight Program for the US Navy's A-7E aircraft. Several principles were refined as a result of experience in applying them in this project.

The NRL method starts with a black box requirements specification. This is followed by a module-structuring phase in which modules are structured according to the information hiding critcrion. Thc usc of information hiding emphasizes that each aspect of a system that is considered likely to change, such as a system requirement, a hardware interface, or a software design decision, should be hidden in a separate information hiding module. Each module has an abstract interface that provides the external view of the module to its users.

To manage the complexity of handling large numbers of modules, the NRL method organizes information hiding modules into a tree-structured, information hiding module hierarchy and documents them in a module guide. The module hierarchy is a decomposition hierarchy. Thus only the leaf modules of the hierarchy are executable. The main categories of information hiding modules, as determined on the A7 project, are:

- *Hardware hiding modules.* These modules are categorized further into extended computer modules and device interface modules. Extended computer modules hide the characteristics of the hardware/software interface that are likely to change. Device interface modules hide the characteristics of I/O devices that are likely to change.

- *Behavior hiding modules.* These modules hide the behavior of the system as specified by the functions defined in the requirements specification. Thus changes to the requirements affect these modules.
- *Software decision modules.* These modules hide decisions made by the software designers that are likely to change.

After designing and documenting the module structure, the abstract interface specification for each leaf module in the module hierarchy is developed. This specification defines the external view of the information hiding module, including the operations provided by the module and the parameters for these operations.

The NRL method also advocates design for extension and contraction. This is achieved by means of the uses hierarchy, which is a hierarchy of operations (access procedures or functions) provided by the information hiding modules, and allows the identification of system subsets. Task structuring is considered orthogonal to module structuring (14). It is carried out later in the NRL method, and few guidelines are provided for identifying tasks.

An example of an information hiding module hierarchy for the cruise control system is given next. The module hierarchy consists of device interface modules and behavior hiding modules. There is a device interface module for each I/O device, a state transition module to hide the structure and contents of the state transition table, and data abstraction modules to encapsulate the data that needs to be stored.

Device Interface Modules
  Cruise Control Lever
  Engine Sensor
  Brake Sensor
  Drive Shaft Sensor
  Throttle Mechanism
  Display

Behavior Hiding Modules
  State Transition Module
    Cruise Control
  Data Abstraction Modules
    Desired Speed
    Current Speed
Function Driver Modules
  Speed Control

### 3.5 Object-Oriented Design

Object-Oriented Design (OOD), as described by Booch (1), is also based on the concept of information hiding. An object is an information hiding module that has state and is characterized by the operations it provides for other objects and the operations it uses (provided by other objects). Booch later extended his version of OOD to include classes and inheritance (2).

An informal strategy is used for identifying objects. Initially, Booch advocated identifying objects by underlining all nouns (which are candidates for objects) and verbs (candidates for operations) in the specification. However, this is not practical for large-scale systems. Booch later advocated the use of Structured Analysis as a starting point for the design, and then identifying objects from the data flow diagrams by applying a set of object structuring criteria [1], which are based on information hiding. Most recently, Booch [2] has advocated determining classes and objects directly by analyzing the problem domain and applying object structuring criteria such as those described in [17], which model objects in the problem domain using information modeling techniques.

Next, the semantics of the classes and objects are identified. This involves determining each object's interface. The operations provided by each object are determined, as well as the operations it uses from other objects. Preliminary class and object diagrams are developed.

The third step, identifying the relationships among classes and objects, is an extension of the previous step. Objects are instances of classes, and for similar objects it is necessary to determine if they belong to the same class or different classes. Static and dynamic dependencies between objects are determined; the class and object diagrams are refined. In the final step, the classes and objects are implemented. The internals of each object are developed, which involves designing the data structures and internal logic of each object.

An example of an object diagram for the cruise control system is given in Figure 8. Some objects are tangible objects that model concrete entities in the problem domain such as the engine, brake, and shaft objects. Other objects are abstract: Cruise Control is a control object that executes the Cruise Control state transition diagram, while Current Speed and Desired Speed encapsulate data that must be stored.

An example of a class diagram is shown in Figure 9, which shows how the inheritance and uses relationships are employed on the same diagram. Current

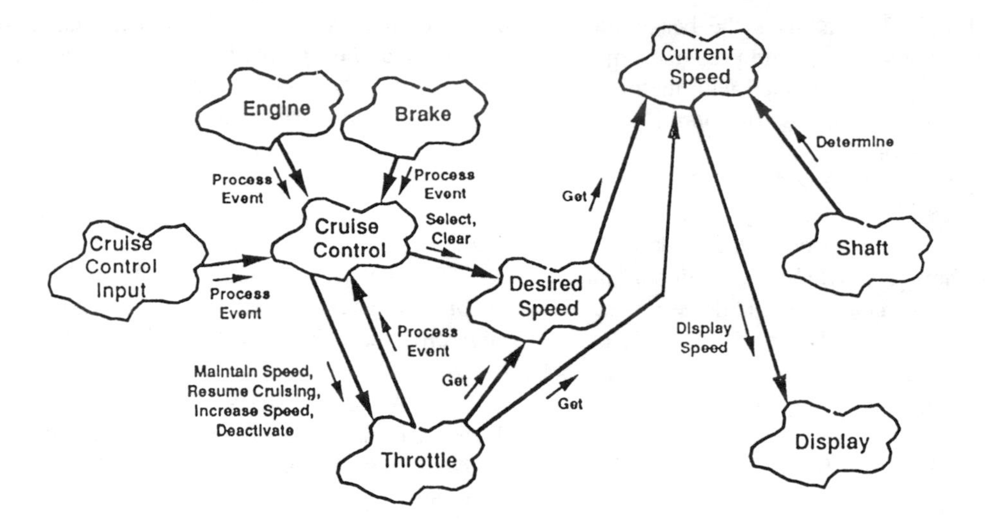


*Figure 8. Example of object diagram for cruise control system*

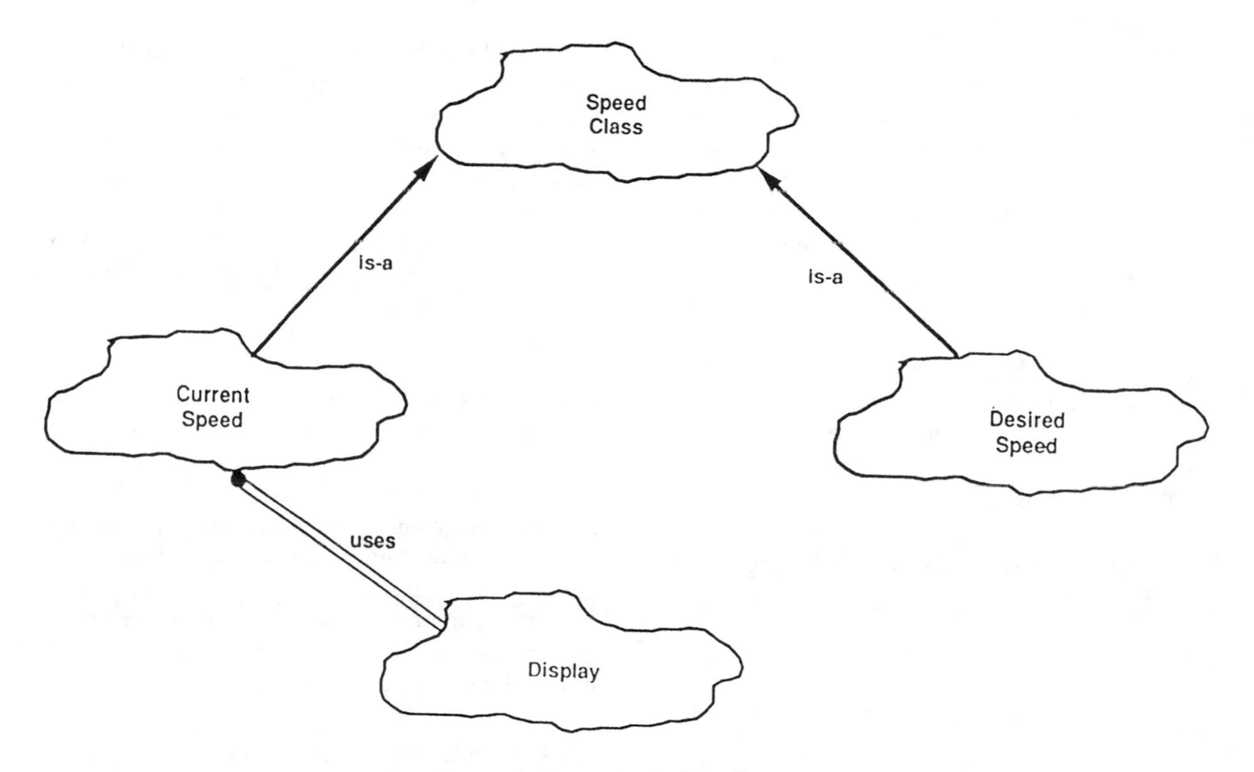


*Figure 9. Example of class diagram*

Speed and Desired Speed are subclasses of the Speed Class; they have the same overall structure as Speed, but they also introduce some changes through inheritance. In addition, Current Speed uses Display.

### 3.6 Comparison of Concurrent and Real-Time Design Methods

This section compares the design methods with respect to the objectives described in the first section.

Real-Time Structured Analysis and Design is weak in task structuring and information hiding. Structured Design does not address the issues of structuring a system into tasks. Furthermore, in its application of information hiding, Structured Design lags behind the Naval Research Lab method and Object-Oriented Design. Although Structured Design can be used for designing individual tasks, it is considered inadequate for designing real-time systems because of its weaknesses in the areas of task structuring and information hiding. However, RTSA does address the behavioral aspects of a system using state transition diagrams and tables, which have been well integrated with the functional decomposition through the use of control transformations and specifications.

DARTS addresses the weaknesses of RTSAD in the task structuring area by introducing the capability of applying the task structuring criteria and defining task interfaces. Although DARTS uses information hiding for encapsulating data stores, it does not use information hiding as extensively as NRL and OOD. Thus, it uses the Structured Design method, and not information hiding, for structuring tasks into procedural modules. DARTS addresses finite state machines as it uses RTSA as a front-end to the design method. During design, each finite state machine is mapped to a concurrent task. JSD also addresses task structuring. However, it does not support information hiding or finite state machines.

Both the NRL and OOD methods emphasize the structuring of a system into information hiding modules (objects) but place less emphasis on task structuring. Both NRL and OOD encapsulate finite state machines in information hiding modules. OOD uses the same criteria for identifying tasks (active objects) as information hiding modules (passive objects). This is contrary to the DARTS and NRL method, which both consider task structuring orthogonal to module structuring.

In conclusion, each of the methods addresses one or two of the objectives. However, none of them supports all of the objectives. Furthermore, none of the methods addresses to any great extent the performance analysis of real-time designs.

## 4. The ADARTS and CODARTS Design Methods

### 4.1 Introduction

This section describes two related methods, ADARTS (Ada-based Design Approach for Real-Time Systems and CODARTS (Concurrent Design Approach for Real-Time Systems), which build on the methods described in the previous section. Whereas ADARTS is Ada oriented, CODARTS is language independent. However, the two methods have a common approach to task and module structuring.

ADARTS and CODARTS attempt to build on the strengths of the NRL, OOD, JSD, and DARTS methods by emphasizing both information hiding module structuring and task structuring. Key features of both ADARTS and CODARTS are the principles for decomposing a real-time system into concurrent tasks and information hiding modules. To achieve the goal of developing maintainable and reusable software components, the two methods incorporate a combination of the NRL module structuring criteria and the OOD object structuring criteria. To achieve the goal of structuring a system into concurrent tasks, they use a set of task structuring criteria that are a refinement of those originally developed for the DARTS design method.

Using the NRL method, it is often a large step from the black box requirements specification to the module hierarchy, and because of this it is sometimes difficult to identify all the modules in the system. Instead, ADARTS starts with a behavioral model developed using Real-Time Structured Analysis. CODARTS provides an alternative approach to Real-Time Structured Analysis for analyzing and modeling the system, namely Concurrent Object-Based Real-Time Analysis (COBRA), as described in the next section.

Both the task structuring criteria and the module structuring criteria are applied to the objects and/or functions of the behavioral model, which are represented by data and control transformations on the data flow/control flow diagrams. When performing task and module structuring, the behavioral model is viewed from two perspectives, dynamic and static structuring. The dynamic view is provided by the concurrent tasks, which are determined using the task structuring criteria. The static view is provided by the information hiding modules, which are determined using the module-structuring criteria. Guidelines are then provided for integrating the task and module views.

The task structuring criteria are applied first, followed by the module structuring criteria, although it is intended that applying the two sets of criteria should be an iterative exercise. The reason for applying the task-structuring criteria first is to allow an early performance analysis of the concurrent tasking design to be made, an important consideration in real-time systems.

### 4.2 Steps in Using ADARTS and CODARTS

1. *Develop Environmental and Behavioral Model of System.* ADARTS uses RTSA for analyzing and modeling the problem domain (18), while CODARTS uses the COBRA method (6). COBRA provides an alternative decomposition strategy to RTSA for concurrent and real-time systems. It uses the RTSA notation but addresses limitations of RTSA by providing comprehensive guidelines for performing a system decomposition. COBRA provides guidelines for developing the envi-

ronmental model based on the system context diagram. It provides structuring criteria for decomposing a system into subsystems, which may potentially be distributed. It also provides criteria for determining the objects and functions within a subsystem. Finally, it provides a behavioral approach for determining how the objects and functions within a subsystem interact with each other using event sequencing scenarios.

2. *Structure the system into distributed subsystems.* This is an optional step taken for distributed concurrent and distributed real-time applications. Thus CODARTS for Distributed Applications (CODARTS/DA) provides criteria for structuring a system into subsystems that can execute on geographically distributed nodes and communicate over a network by means of messages. CODARTS/DA builds on and substantially refines and extends the ideas from DARTS for Distributed Applications (DARTS/DA) (5).
3. *Structure the system (or subsystem) into concurrent tasks.* The concurrent tasks in the system (or subsystem of a distributed application) are determined by applying the task structuring criteria. The inter-task communication and synchronization interfaces are defined. Task structuring is applied to the whole system in the case of a nondistributed design. In the case of a distributed design, where the subsystems have already been defined, task structuring is applied to each subsystem. The performance of the concurrent tasking design is analyzed. As this step is also carried out in DARTS, an example of a task architecture diagram is given in Figure 4.
4. *Structure the system into information hiding modules.* The information hiding modules in the system are determined by applying the module structuring criteria, which are based on the NRL and OOD methods. An information hiding module hierarchy is created in which the information hiding modules are categorized. As this step is similar to the NRL method, an example of a module hierarchy is given in Section 3.4.
5. *Integrate the task and module views.* Tasks, determined using the task structuring criteria of Step 3, and information hiding modules, determined using the module structuring criteria of Step 4, are now integrated to produce a software architecture. An example of a software architecture diagram for the Cruise Control problem is given in Figure 10. This shows the same tasks as on the task architecture diagram (Figure 4) with the information hiding modules (Section 3.4) added.
6. *Develop an Ada-based architectural design.* This step is used in ADARTS to address the Ada-specific aspects of the design. In this step, Ada support tasks are added and Ada task interfaces are defined. Additional tasks are usually required in an Ada application to address loosely coupled inter-task communication and synchronization of access to shared data (6). An example of an Ada architecture diagram is given in Figure 11, in which a Cruise Control Event buffering task replaces the Cruise Control message queue, and task entries are explicitly defined.
7. *Define component interface specifications for tasks and modules.* These represent the externally visible view of each component.
8. *Develop the software incrementally.*

## 5. Conclusions

This paper has described the concepts and criteria used by software design methods for developing large-scale concurrent and real-time systems. After surveying and comparing five different methods, two related software design methods for concurrent and real-time systems, ADARTS and CODARTS, which build on these methods, have been described. ADARTS and CODARTS use the task structuring criteria for identifying concurrent tasks and the information hiding module-structuring criteria for identi-fying information hiding modules. The survey, as well as the description of ADARTS and CODARTS, are covered in considerably more detail in (6). In addition, a design can be analyzed from a performance perspective by applying real-time scheduling theory (16), as described in (6).

With the proliferation of low-cost workstations and personal computers operating in a networked environment, the interest in designing concurrent and real-time systems, particularly distributed applications (6), is likely to grow rapidly in the next few years.

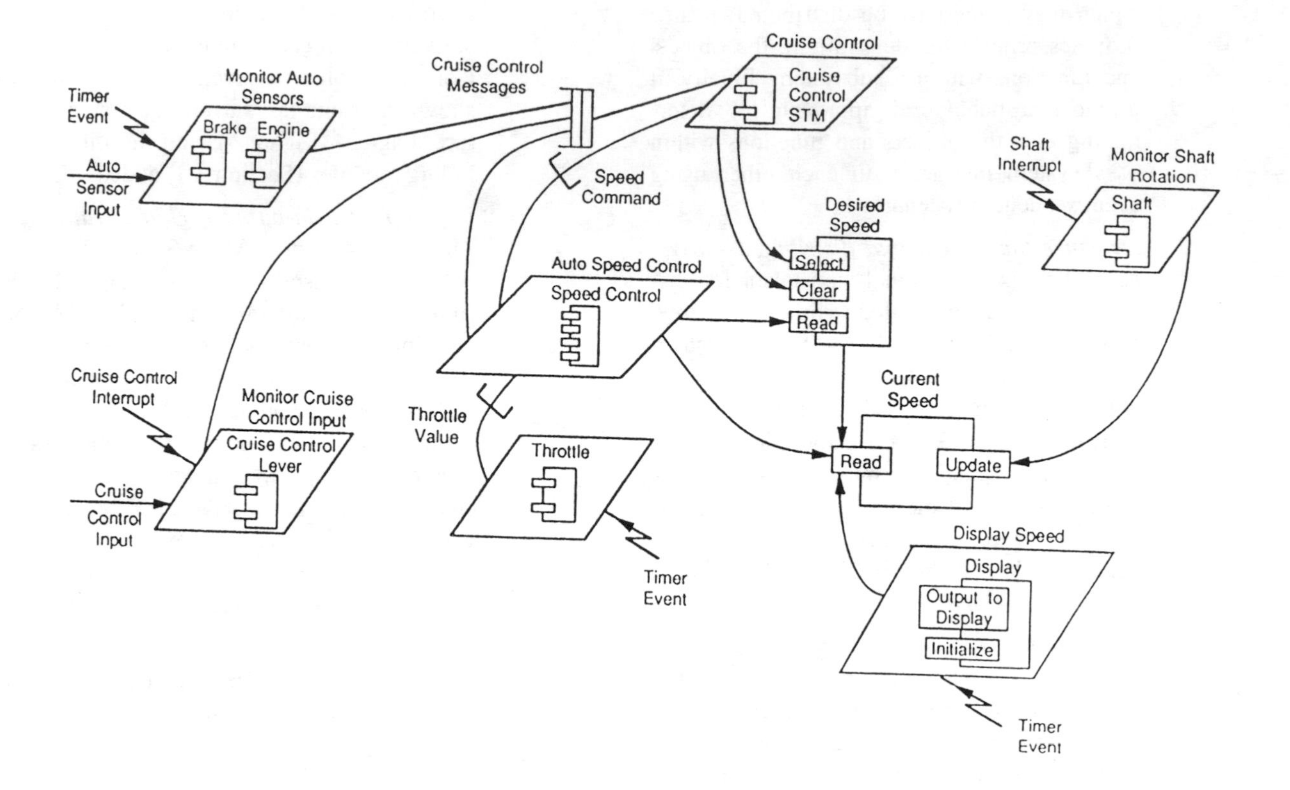


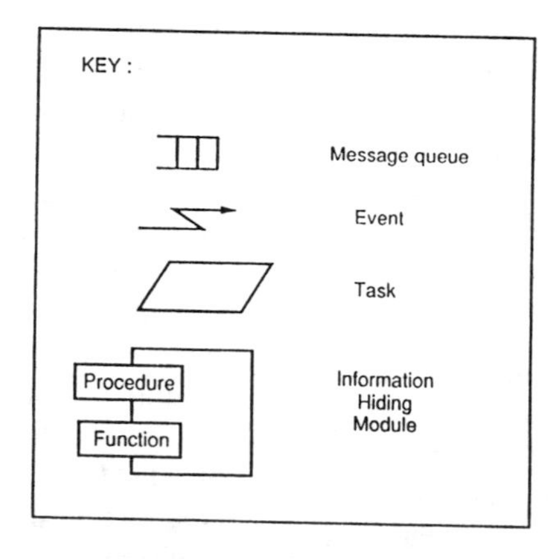


*Figure 10. Cruise control system software architecture diagram*

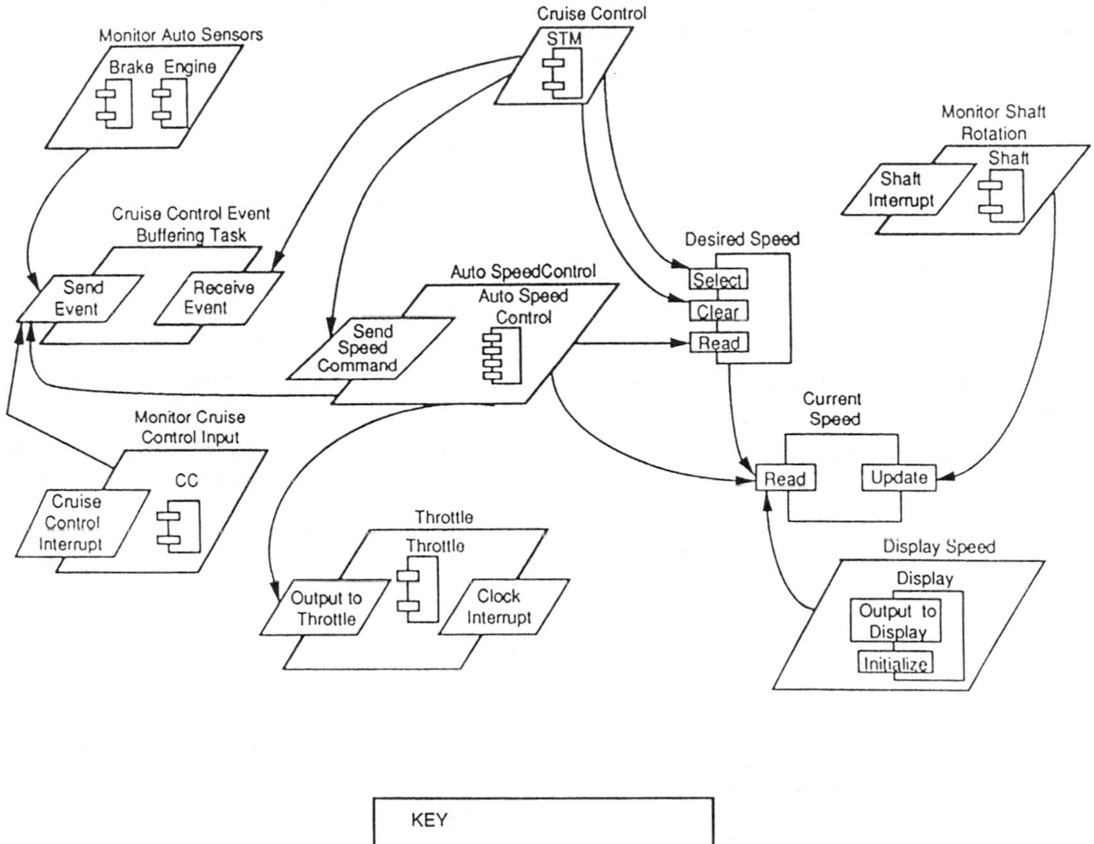


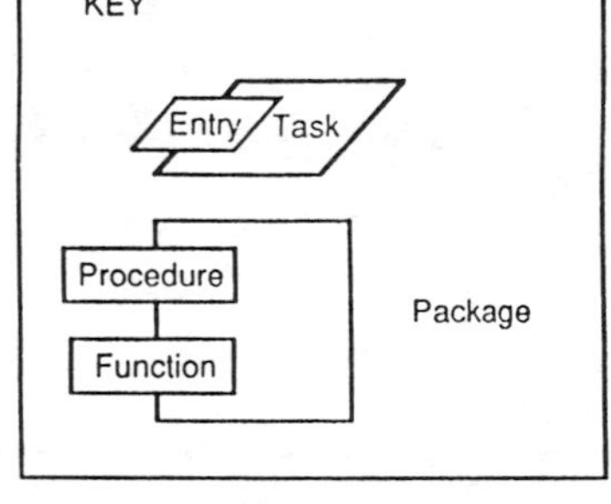


*Figure 11. Cruise control system Ada architecture diagram*

## Acknowledgments

The author gratefully acknowledges the Software Productivity Consortium's sponsorship of the development of the ADARTS$^{SM}$ method. The author also gratefully acknowledges the contributions of Mike Cochran, Rick Kirk, and Elisa Simmons, particularly during the ADARTS validation exercise [20]. Acknowledgments are also due to David Weiss for his thoughtful comments during the formative stages of ADARTS.

## References

(1) G. Booch, "Object Oriented Development," *IEEE Trans. Software Eng.*, Feb. 1986.

(2) G. Booch, *Object-Oriented Design with Applications*, Benjamin Cummings, 1991.

(3) H. Gomaa, "A Software Design Method for Real-Time Systems," *Comm. ACM*, Vol. 27, No. 9, Sept. 1984, pp. 938–949.

(4) H. Gomaa, "Software Development of Real-Time Systems," *Comm. ACM*, Vol. 29, No. 7, July 1986, pp. 657–668.

(5) H. Gomaa, "A Software Design Method for Distributed Real-Time Applications," *J. Systems and Software*, Feb. 1989.

(6) H. Gomaa, *Software Design Methods for Concurrent and Real-Time Systems*, Addison-Wesley, Reading, Mass., 1993.

(7) D. Hatley and I. Pirbhai, *Strategies for Real-Time System Specification*, Dorset House, 1988.

(8) M.A. Jackson, *System Development*, Prentice-Hall, Englewood Cliffs, N.J., 1983.

(9) G. Myers, *Composite/Structured Design*, Van Nostrand Reinhold, 1978.

(10) M. Page-Jones, *The Practical Guide to Structured Systems Design*, 2nd ed., Yourdon Press, 1988.

(11) D.L. Parnas, "On the Criteria to be Used In Decomposing Systems into Modules," *Comm. ACM*, Dec. 1972.

(12) D.L. Parnas, "Designing Software for Ease of Extension and Contraction," *IEEE Trans. Software Eng.*, Mar. 1979.

(13) D.L. Parnas, P. Clements, and D. Weiss, "The Modular Structure of Complex Systems," *Proc. 7th Int'l Conf. Software Eng.*, 1984.

(14) D.L. Parnas and S.R Faulk, "On Synchronization in Hard Real-Time Systems," *Comm. ACM*, Vol. 31, No. 3, Mar. 1988, pp. 274–287.

(15) Sanden B., *Software Systems Construction*, Prentice-Hall, Englewood Cliffs, N.J., 1994.

(16) L. Sha and J.B. Goodenough, "Real-Time Scheduling Theory and Ada," *Computer*, Vol. 23, No. 4, Apr. 1990, pp. 53–62. Also CMU/SEI-89-TR-14, Software Engineering Institute, Pittsburgh, Pa., 1989.

(17) Shlaer S. and S. Mellor, *Object Oriented Systems Analysis*, Prentice-Hall, Englewood Cliffs, N.J., 1988.

(18) P. Ward and S. Mellor, *Structured Development for Real-Time Systems*, Vols. 1 and 2, Prentice-Hall, Englewood Cliffs, N.J., 1985.

(19) E. Yourdon and L. Constantine, *Structured Design*, Prentice-Hall, Englewood Cliffs, N.J., 1979.

(20) M. Cochran and H. Gomaa, "Validating the ADARTS Software Design Method for Real-Time Systems," *Proc ACM Tri-Ada Conf.*, 1991.

# Computer-Human Interface Software Development Survey

Robert J. Remington
*Lockheed Martin Missiles and Space*
*Sunnyvale, California*
*CHI Rapid Prototyping and Usability Laboratory*

## Introduction

A young software engineer was recently assigned the responsibility to develop a graphical user interface for a modern command and control system. After pondering the assignment for a few hours he went to the project leader and asked: "Do you know if anyone has ever written a paper or report that might help me design a good user interface?"

The question, as well as the answer to the question, provides a rather persuasive case for including a chapter on computer human interface (CHI) in a software engineering tutorial.

The young software engineer's question reflects the fact that many of today's software engineering professionals have received no formal training in, and relatively little exposure to, the world of CHI software development. The answer to the young software engineer's question, if taken literally, is *no*! There is no single paper or report that, if followed religiously, will automatically lead to a good CHI design. There is no magic pill! However, there is a tremendous wealth of knowledge that can be drawn upon to help user interface developers deal with the full range of decision-making situations likely to be encountered in a typical CHI software development project.

A brief discussion of terminology might prevent some confusion as readers begin to explore the documents referenced in this survey. The term CHI will be used to refer to both the general field of *computer-human interaction*, and the *computer-human interface* (that is, the user interface that allows the person using the computer access to the facilities offered by the computer). There is no real difference between the term CHI and the term *HCI* as used in many of the technical references. People who prefer to use the name human-computer interaction, or HCI for short, tend to be making a statement that the human comes before the computer. Indeed, the human should take precedence over the computer in substantive matters such as user interface design. However, in the case of just deciding between two names, it can be argued that CHI rolls off the tongue more gracefully than HCI.

### Scope and Objectives

The main objective of this chapter is to familiarize the reader with available informational sources as well as *recent* trends in CHI design, development, and evaluation. There are several earlier surveys that can provide computer science professionals with a more comprehensive introduction to CHI concepts, methods, and tools than will be offered by this brief snapshot of the current state of the CHI technology. For example, Hartson and Hix (1989) provide an extensive 92-page survey focusing on "the management of the computer science, or constructional, aspects of human-computer interface development." Similarly, Perlman (1989) provides a complete CHI course module that covers "the issues, information sources, and methods used in the design, implementation, and evaluation of user interfaces." Bass and Coutaz (1989) provide a 112-page document that introduces concepts and techniques relevant to the design and implementation of user interfaces. The present chapter should be viewed as a supplement to this excellent body of CHI knowledge, a supplement that concentrates on a few significant developments that have taken place since these earlier surveys were published.

### Increased Importance of CHI

The first recent trend worth noting concerns the tremendous increase in interest being directed toward the topic of CHI by both the computer industry and user communities. There are several good reasons for the increased attention paid to CHI design and development. There is growing competitive pressure for improved user interfaces for computer software products in the marketplace. Improvement in user interface design was singled out at the 1993 Fall Comdex in Las Vegas by the software industry's leaders, including Microsoft's Bill Gates, as the biggest challenge now facing the computer industry. It is becoming more apparent to both industry and government user communities that CHI design can have a major impact on overall system performance, total life cycle costs, and user acceptance. User interface design largely determines operator performance, and how much training is required for users to reach an acceptable level of productivity. Ease-of-use and ease-of-learning have become key factors in the marketing campaigns for most consumer software products.

With the emergence of interactive graphical user interfaces (GUIs) we have seen a dramatic increase in the complexity and quantity of the CHI software component for new systems. While well-designed GUIs tend to make life more pleasant for end-users, programming them can be a very difficult, time-consuming, and error-prone process. Failure of traditional software methods and tools to deal effectively with this complex task can easily result in projects that are late and over budget, and excessive life-cycle costs of reworking poor-quality software that fails to meet user requirements. Most of the major software companies have recently experienced long delays in getting important products to the marketplace. These highly publicized failures to meet schedules and to gain user acceptance have taken a significant toll on these companies in terms of lost revenue, lost credibility, and depressed stock value.

In recent years, the development of complex software has dominated the cost of computer-based business and military application solutions, far outstripping the hardware costs. The software portion of the cost of most major computer-based systems has been estimated to run about 80 percent of the total system cost. Estimates for the CHI software component for a modern system range from 30-80 percent of the total lines of programming code. Myers and Rosson (1992) report the results of a formal survey of user interface programming. Based upon the results from 74 recent software projects it was found that an average of 48 percent of the code was devoted to the user interface portion. The average time spent on the user interface portion was 45 percent during the design phase, 50 percent during the implementation phase, and 37 percent during the maintenance phase. The most common problems reported by user interface developers included defining user requirements, writing help text, achieving consistency, learning how to use the tools, and getting acceptable graphics performance.

The increased interest in the issues and problems related to CHI software development has been accompanied by an explosion in the number of publications. Well over a thousand papers covering CHI-related topics were published in professional journals and conference proceedings in 1993 and 1994. This trend has been accompanied by an unprecedented number of books on the subject. Just a few of the new publications are referenced here. Shneiderman (1992) is a much-improved second edition of a classic CHI reference work. The book by Dix et al. (1993) provides a broad coverage of the important CHI topics with an emphasis on design methods. Barfield (1993) has written a book aimed at those who are just becoming involved in CHI design, either through academic study or as practitioners. Bass and Dewan (1993) provide a collection of papers on several topics related to advanced user interface software development environments. The book by Hix and Hartson (1994) emphasizes the user interface development *process* independently of current implementation considerations. Blattner and Dannenberg (1992) focus on the issues and problems related to the recent introduction of multimedia and multimodality into user interface design. Tognazzini (1992) has written an entertaining book with many lessons for the design of graphical user interfaces, in particular the Macintosh user interface. Finally, Baecker, et al. (1994) offer a complete course in human-computer interaction with their 900-page volume that pulls together relevant materials from the research community; professional practice, and real-world applications.

## CHI Design

### Iterative Design Process

The simplified design-implementation-evaluation CHI development life-cycle model presented in Figure 1, from Perlman (1990), shows many of the main influences on design. They include experience with other systems, guidelines, and standards based upon human factors research, the results of evaluating previous versions, and requirements derived from task analysis. Ideally, modern CHI development tools and techniques are used to implement a prototype or the actual system based on a requirements-driven design specification. The resulting design is evaluated against system design specifications, and by means of formal usability testing of a functional prototype or working system. The actual CHI development cycle should involve several iterations of the feedback and design refinement process shown in Figure 1.

This is particularly true of complex interactive computer systems, for which the requirements cannot be fully specified at the beginning of the design cycle. For a better understanding of the iterative CHI development process and key techniques such as task analysis, rapid prototyping, and usability testing, see Bass and Coutaz (1991), Helander (1988), Nielsen (1992), and Salvendy (1987). Curtis and Hefley (1992) provide an interesting article describing the need to integrate the user interface engineering process into the overall product engineering process throughout its life cycle.

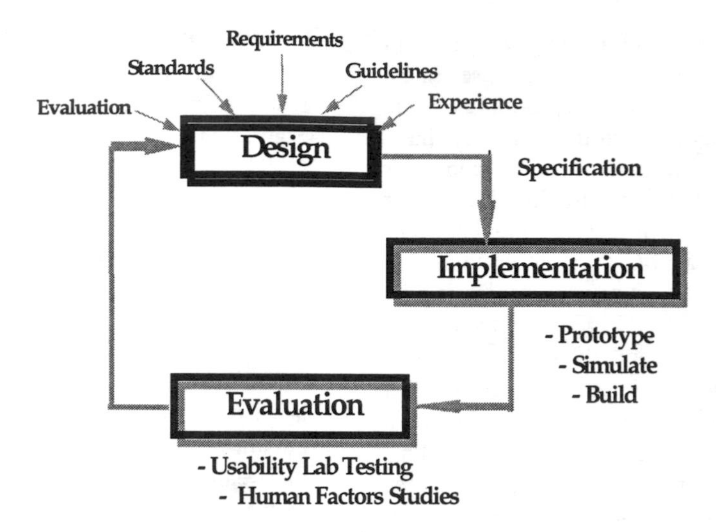


*Figure 1. The design/implementation/evaluation CHI development process from Perlman (1990)*

**Theories, Models, and Research Foundations**

With the focus of this survey on recent developments, a reader with little exposure to the field of CHI might have formed the impression that it has a short heritage of only a few years. This is definitely not the case. Human factors professionals have systematically researched the relationships between computer user interface design characteristics and user performance and acceptance since the early sixties. This research originally went under the name of *man-machine interface* research. To human factors professionals, with strong backgrounds in experimental psychology, terms such as "ease-of-use" and "ease-of-learning" have a definite meaning. For example, systematic analysis of error rates associated with alternative CHI designs has been useful in isolating inherent design characteristics highly correlated with user errors across a wide range of tasks.

The human factors approach to system design provides a conceptual model that is useful to those who are committed to designing user-oriented products. The user is viewed as an integral component of a working system. As the most important part of the system, all other components, including computer software and hardware, are adapted to match state-of-the-art knowledge regarding human capabilities, limitations, expectations, and preferences.

The Gillan and Breedin (1990) study suggests that the training and experience of the human factors specialist leads to a different way of thinking about the user interface than the way that non-human factors systems developers think. An important part of human factors training consists of developing a working knowledge of basic human capabilities (for example, memory, attention, perception, and psycho-motor skills). It is likely that this knowledge is useful in producing user interfaces designs that do not place excessive demands on users' cognitive abilities and motor skills. It has been demonstrated that such designs lead to increased user productivity and lower error rates.

For example, Bailey (1993) found that CHI designs produced by human factors specialists allowed users to complete tasks in 60 percent of the time required for designs produced by programmers. Mismatches between CHI designs and users' capabilities and expectations have resulted in many documented cases of human errors, some of which resulted in fatal accidents. For example, Casey (1993) reports a case where a poorly designed, and inadequately tested, computer-based user interface that controlled a radiotherapy accelerator was responsible for a fatal accident involving the delivery of a lethal proton beam powered by 25 million electron volts!

Bailey (1993) presents some evidence that the iterative design methodology alone can improve designs only within a limited range. Studies by Jeffries et al. (1991) and Karat et al. (1992) indicate that successful design is the result of a combination of techniques and knowing when and how to apply them. Mayhew (1992) attempts to provide a "tool kit of design methods or principles needed by software development professionals." Borenstein (1992) offers entertaining views on most important CHI topics, including the value of CHI research. He proclaims that "the biggest danger in remaining ignorant about basic HCI research is not that you'll miss something, but that you'll hear something inaccurate and reach incorrect conclusions based on a misunderstanding of the latest research." Shneiderman's (1992) three pillars of successful user interface development presented in Figure 2 illustrates the model for building user interfaces that enhance user acceptance and product success.

In the past decade, human factors researchers have been joined by other disciplines, including computer science, cognitive psychology, and graphic design. For example, the ACM Special Interest Group on Computer Human Interaction (SIG-CHI), composed mostly of human factors and computer science professionals, was formed in 1983. The CHI '94 Conference held in Boston was attended by more than 2,500 people including academic researchers and educators from various disciplines; CHI designers and developers involved in all phases of product design and development; and managers and users from major corporations. In the past few years we have seen a significant increase in research related to improving CHI design, development tools, and enabling technologies.

Marcus (1992) provides a concise survey of the strategic pursuits of leading human interface research and development centers. Over 350 representative articles and lab reviews from 63 CHI research and development centers were examined to identify research goals and their supporting technology developments. The resulting CHI research findings and technology developments have given us better theoretical models, new user interface design principles, and innovative CHI enabling technologies that will lead to more natural forms of human computer interaction.

While the topic of next-generation user interfaces is beyond the scope of this survey, several CHI researchers including Nielsen (1993), Myers (1992), Staples (1993), Baecker et al. (1994), and Blattner (1994) attempt to give us a look into the future of CHI.

### CHI Guidelines, Standards and Style Guides

The use of technical reference sources in product design is a critical aspect of the engineering process. Development of CHI design guidance based upon a large body of accumulated knowledge was a lively pursuit in the mid-1980s. These early attempts to turn the wealth of information derived from empirical human factors research, associated theories and models of human information processing, and real-world experience into practical design information resulted in various CHI design *guideline* documents. The Smith and Mosier (1986) document, containing almost 1,000 guidelines for designing user interface software, is one of the more comprehensive CHI design guides. Identification and application of the particular principles and guidelines that apply to a given CHI software design project can be very difficult, but often a rewarding part of the CHI design process. These guidelines require careful and intelligent interpretation and application, which often depends on thorough analysis of the system environment, including functions and critical user tasks.

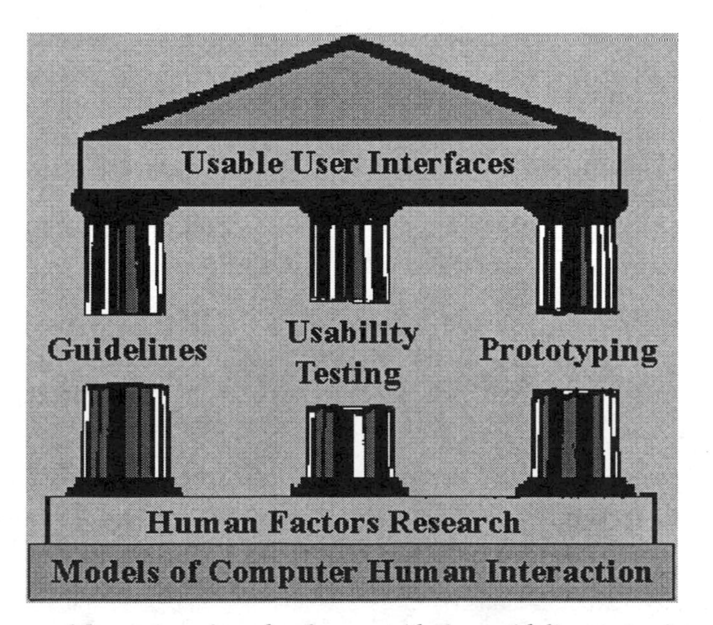


*Figure 2. Three pillars of successful user interface development (design guidelines, user interface rapid prototyping, and usability laboratories for iterative testing) rest on a foundation of theories and experimental research. Shneiderman (1992)*

One of the key principles of good user interface design found in all the early guidelines concerned the value of maintaining *consistency* in both the look and feel of the user interface. Consistency helps the user to develop an accurate model of the system's user environment. An accurate model fosters user acceptance and allows users to apply old skills to new applications and programs. The most direct way to achieve consistency across applications and software environments is to create CHI *standards.* The demand for standardization of fundamental aspects of the "look" and "feel" of CHI software by the user communities within business and government organizations, and software developers, has been growing in recent years.

Unfortunately, much of the recent user interface standards activities have been undertaken in the cause of the "GUI wars," and have little to do with design principles and guidelines derived from CHI research and practice. In the late 1980's a tremendous amount of effort was devoted to the creation of multiple GUIs, all aimed at preventing non-technical users from dropping into that four-letter word, Unix! The resulting proliferation of GUIs, and associated toolkits (such as Motif, OpenLook, CXI, and XUI) based upon X Window System technology, prompted a flurry of standardization activities. An early attempt at practicing safe Unix and the formation of several IEEE standards groups to deal with problems caused by too many Unix GUIs are reported by Remington (1989, 1990). By the end of 1993 OSF/Motif emerged as the victorious GUI in the Unix world.

Each of the remaining participants in the battle for the GUI market—including OSF/Motif, Macintosh, Microsoft Windows, and IBM's OS/2 Presentation Manager—have published style guides that are intended to provide precise look-and-feel user interface specifications. A comparison of the three major interface styles is presented in Figure 3. These three major GUI software platforms have several things in common, including a point-and-click direct manipulation interaction style, an object-action metaphor, and similar GUI building blocks or widgets sets (for example, pull-down menus, radio buttons, check boxes, list boxes, spin boxes, and icons). Most of the enhancements made to the Motif 2.0 release were aimed at making the Motif widget set more compatible with Microsoft Windows and IBM's OS/2 Presentation Manager. The most obvious difference between the major platforms as seen in Figure 3 is differing graphic styles. For example, notice the heavy reliance on 3D visual cues in the Motif graphic style. Other less obvious differences include a different number of mouse buttons and associated functions, different keyboard functional mappings, differences in terminology, and window management differences.

Even strict adherence to one of these user interface specifications does not necessarily result in a highly usable product. They do not provide adequate guidance in many critical aspects of CHI design. For example, the OSF Motif 2.0 Style Guide (1994) provides only a single recommendation regarding the use of color. Being told to "use color as a redundant aspect of the interface" is not much help in this problematic area of user interface design! Tognazzini (1992) notes that even with the publication of the Apple Human Interface Guidelines to help developers write Macintosh-standard user interfaces, there was an alarming growth of programs that "followed all the specifics of Apple guidelines, but were clearly not Macintosh."

There has been an increase in activity related to the production of open systems CHI standards and style guides. For example, the POSIX-sponsored IEEE P1201.2 Recommended Practice for Graphical User Interface Drivability [IEEE, 1993] specifies those elements and characteristics of all graphical user interfaces that should be consistent to permit users to transfer easily from one look and feel or application to another with minimal interference, errors, confusion, relearning, and retraining. In theory, it should be possible to define a core set of GUI elements and characteristics that support "drivability" across multiple look and feel GUIs, in the same sense that the standardization of critical automobile controls allows us to drive most makes and models without special training. Topics covered include terminology, keyboard usage, mouse or pointing device usage, menus, controls, windows, user guidance and help, and common user actions. This recommended practice does not dictate a particular software implementation or graphical style, only that the user interface meets the recommendations. The following are typical recommended practices aimed at enhancing drivability:

> *"When menu items are chosen from the keyboard, the menu item chosen should not depend upon the case (that is, shifted or unshifted, upper case, lower case, or mixed case) of character(s) entered from the keyboard."*

> *"If the system supports more than one level of undo, then the system should provide a distinct indication (for example, dim the undo control item) when no more undos are possible."*

> *"If the pointer is moved out of the active area of an armed button while SELECT [mouse button] is held down, the button should be disarmed."*

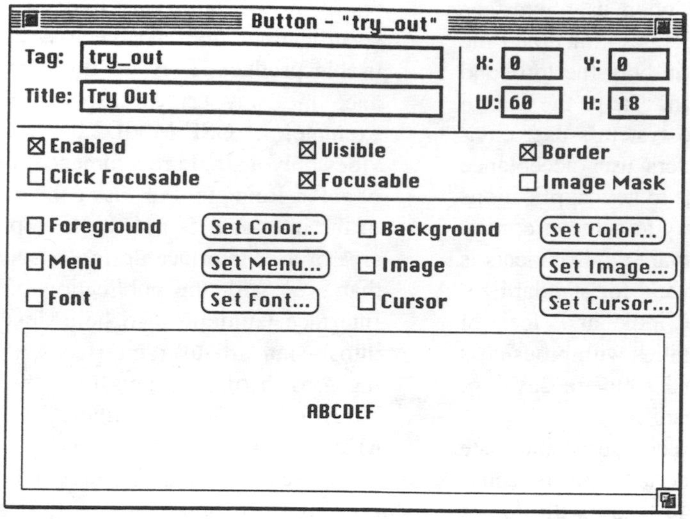

Button - "try_out"

Tag: try_out  X: 0  Y: 0
Title: Try Out  W: 60  H: 18

☒ Enabled ☒ Visible ☒ Border
☐ Click Focusable ☒ Focusable ☐ Image Mask

☐ Foreground [Set Color...] ☐ Background [Set Color...]
☐ Menu [Set Menu...] ☐ Image [Set Image...]
☐ Font [Set Font...] ☐ Cursor [Set Cursor...]

ABCDEF

*Macintosh Look-and-Feel*

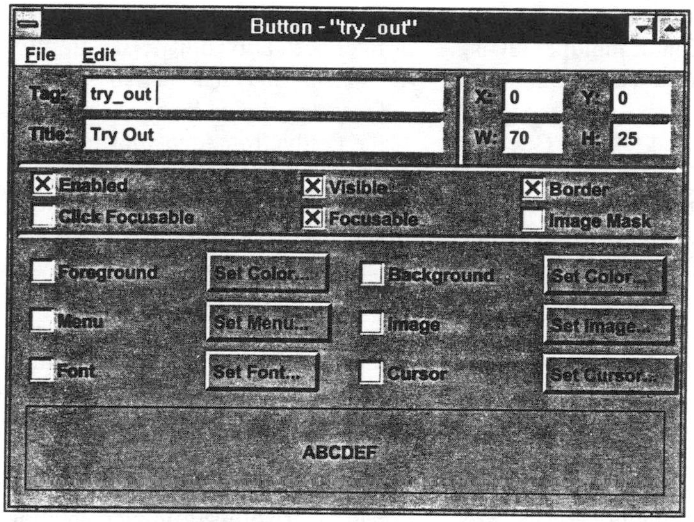

Button - "try_out"

File Edit

Tag: try_out  X: 0  Y: 0
Title: Try Out  W: 70  H: 25

☒ Enabled ☒ Visible ☒ Border
☐ Click Focusable ☒ Focusable ☐ Image Mask

☐ Foreground [Set Color...] ☐ Background [Set Color...]
☐ Menu [Set Menu...] ☐ Image [Set Image...]
☐ Font [Set Font...] ☐ Cursor [Set Cursor...]

ABCDEF

*Windows Look-and-Feel*

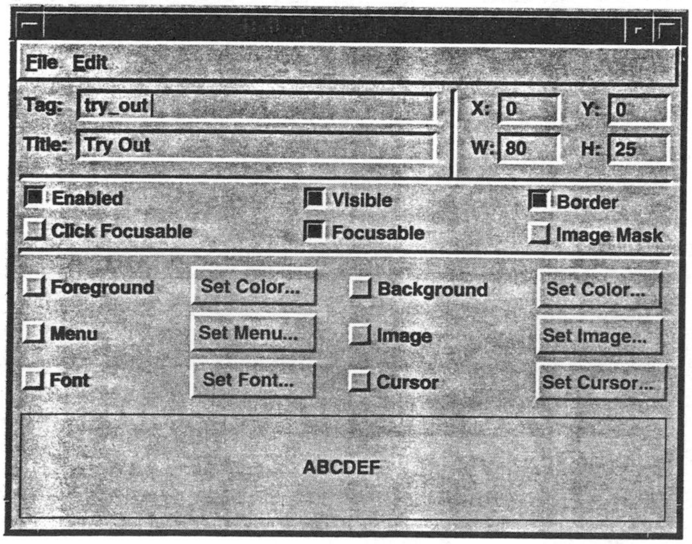

File Edit

Tag: try_out  X: 0  Y: 0
Title: Try Out  W: 80  H: 25

Enabled Visible Border
Click Focusable Focusable Image Mask

Foreground [Set Color...] Background [Set Color...]
Menu [Set Menu...] Image [Set Image...]
Font [Set Font...] Cursor [Set Cursor...]

ABCDEF

*Motif Look-and-Feel*

*Figure 3. A comparison of the three major GUI styles*

Adherence to the one-hundred-plus recommendations offered in the IEEE 1201.2 document would undoubtedly eliminate the major sources of confusion users currently experience when they transfer from one major platform to another.

**Rapid Prototyping**

The technique of rapid prototyping, or creating a limited, but functional, user interface to be given a "test-drive" early in the design process to gain user feedback, has proven to be a major new development in the CHI development process. Feedback resulting from the use of prototypes can be used to refine the user interface specification, leading to a user interface that is more in tune with users' expectations and capabilities. Software products with this type of user interface have a better chance of gaining wider user acceptance, and being used in a more productive fashion by the intended user population. By permitting early identification of CHI design problems, prototypes allow developers to explore solutions while they are still technically and economically feasible. It costs significantly more to rid software of errors during operation than during design. A majority of errors are not actually coding bugs, but design problems due to misunderstanding and miscommunication of user requirements. The book by Wiklund (1994) contains several detailed case studies that show "before and after" examples of improvements in GUI designs resulting from user feedback based on experience with prototypes. In some cases, cost benefits related to CHI design improvements are analyzed and reported. These include reduced customer support and service costs, reduced customer training costs, increased user productivity, and avoidance of costly delays in the product development schedule in order to fix major usability problems before going to market.

Rapid prototyping can serve an important role as an "enabling technology" by allowing designers to quickly implement and test the viability of new forms of computer human interaction. CHI designers have found that one of the main benefits of rapid prototyping is that it often provides the "breathing room" needed to experiment with optional design concepts, including innovative user interface concepts being developed at various CHI research laboratories. In the absence of a rapid prototyping approach, there is a tendency to grab onto a familiar user interface style and begin the coding process without entertaining new alternatives.

We have seen a major breakthrough in the area of CHI prototyping technology in the past few years. The products of the first-generation rapid prototyping tools consisted of user interface "look and feel" simulations driven with proprietary throw-away code. Modern CHI development tools, such as those described in the following section, have successfully evolved into tools that support both CHI rapid prototyping and software development. Now, the user interface prototype produced for early user testing becomes the actual GUI code for the delivered product. These second-generation CHI rapid development tools are available for each of the major GUI software environments including Microsoft Windows, OSF Motif, Sun's OpenLook, and Apple Macintosh.

## CHI Implementation

**Development Tools: Introduction**

The dramatic increase in the complexity and quantity of software associated with the user interface component of modern computer systems has prompted tremendous interest in the development and application of new tools that will expedite the production of usable CHI software. The resulting outpouring of commercially available CHI software development tools is another significant trend that has occurred in the past few years. It is interesting to note that only a handful of user interface toolkits are described in the three 1989 surveys of CHI developments referenced at the beginning of this chapter. Most of these earlier proprietary toolkits have dropped by the wayside, making way for a variety of more powerful, fully supported commercial tools with established track records in dealing with large-scale and small-scale user interface development projects.

A survey of the major CHI development tools shows that they vary greatly in their capabilities with respect to their ability to allow rapid modifications, to create functional prototypes, to deal with interactive graphics, and to generate directly usable code. They also vary regarding the degree of programming skill required to use them.

Myers and Rosson (1992) provide a simplified but useful taxonomy for user interface tools ranging from the more primitive *window system and widget toolkits,* to the *Interactive Design Tools (IDTs)* and the *User Interface Management Systems (UIMS).* Both IDTs and UIMS are generally designed to speed the development of GUIs by allowing developers to "draw," rather than hand code, significant portions of their user interfaces. They provide graphical tools that help developers to create and arrange the basic building blocks, or widgets, for a particular GUI environment such as buttons, sliders, pull-down menus, dialog boxes, scrolling lists, and other controls for applications. For example, they normally provide a palette showing the GUI building block widgets available in a given GUI toolkit, and allow the designer to interactively select, position, and size the desired widgets. Widget properties can be easily viewed and set via a special editor. Figure 4 shows the widget palette for one of the more popular Motif GUI development toolkits.

In addition to laying out the "look" of the CHI, most modern GUI development tools provide a test mode that allows developers to view and modify screens before generating and compiling various types of programming code (such as C, C++, Ada, and UIL). For IDTs, testing of interface behavior is usually confined to demonstrating the selection of various interface objects (for example, button or menu option) without actually executing associated callback behavior (that is, what happens in the application when the user presses buttons, selects menu options, or operates a scroll bar). This is because most IDTs have no way of dynamically executing the code without first compiling it. IDT-generated sources usually require extensive editing to include the code for the callbacks.

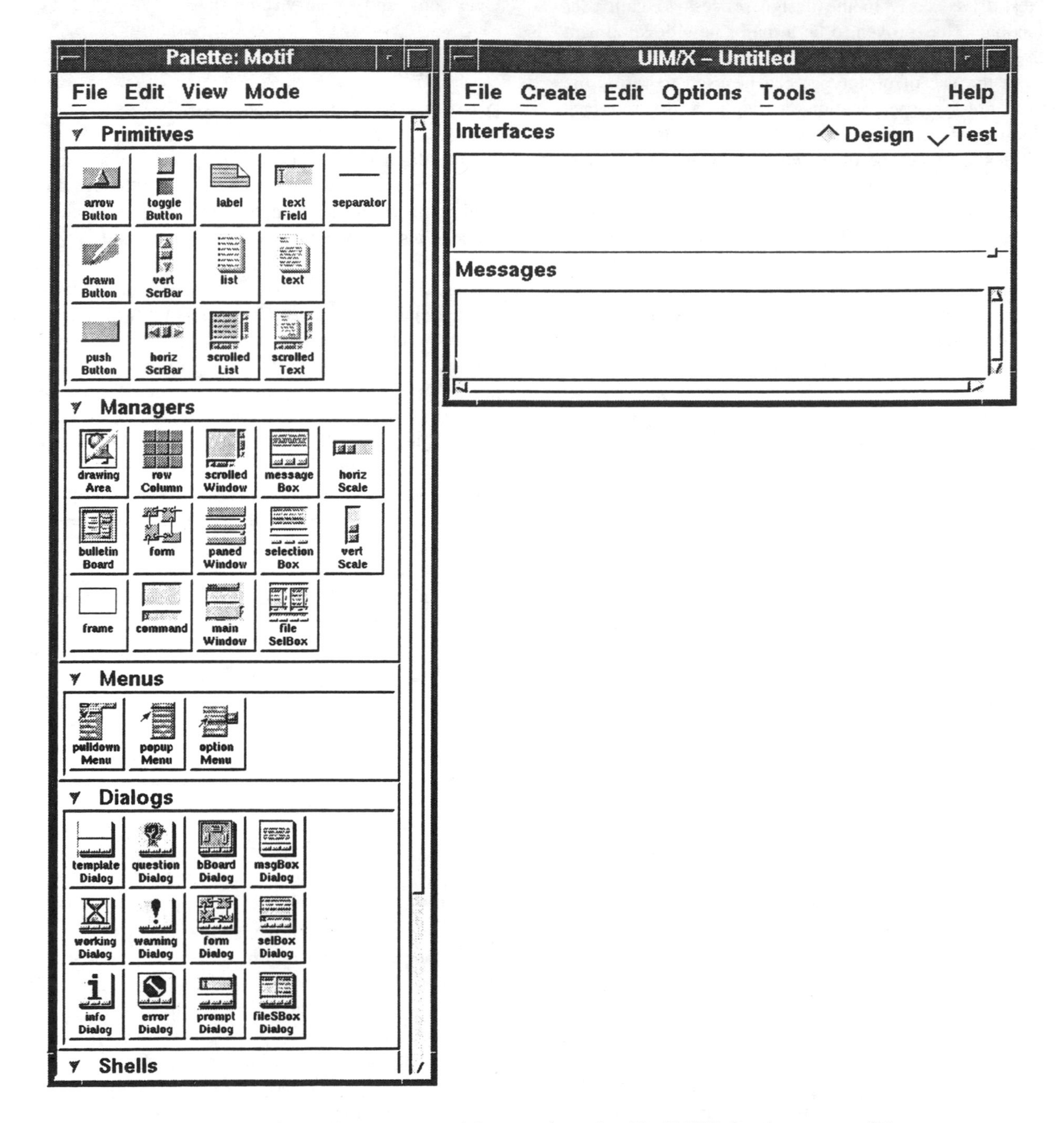


*Figure 4. Widget palette for one of the more popular Motif GUI development toolkits*

On the other hand, UIMS are generally more expensive and comprehensive tools designed to eliminate much of the hand-coding ordinarily required to (1) activate widgets, (2) feed data to be displayed by widgets, and (3) define callback functions to control the application functions. In addition to common GUI layout capabilities, they provide facilities to develop and test user interface behavior, usually with some sort of built-in interpreter. Some UIMSs separate the user interface from the application code, so the user interface is not embedded into the application code. With this separation, the CHI developer can easily create and modify the user interface without affecting the data source, permitting concurrent application development and rapid prototyping associated with early usability testing and user requirements definition.

Many of the more mature interface builders and UIMSs are now second-generation products that offer a form of visual programming. This lets developers use point-and-click and direct manipulation techniques to create a substantial portion of the CHI without writing programming code. The Myers and Rosson (1992) survey results showed that 34 percent of the systems were implemented using a toolkit, 27 percent made use of a UIMS, 14 percent used an IDT, and 26 percent used no tools. The projects using UIMSs or interface builders spent 41 percent of their time on the user interface. The study provides some good evidence that the currently available CHI software tools can be used to speed development and cut the cost of developing modern GUI-based CHIs.

**Development Tools: Selection**

"*Horses for courses*" is a simple phrase used in England to indicate that a particular approach may be best suited for a particular situation. In the CHI development tool arena, you must be knowledgeable about both the nature of the CHI development project to be undertaken (that is, the type of race course), and the relative strengths and weaknesses of the various tools that are available to do the job (the race horses). Selection of the appropriate tool(s) is often a difficult and time-consuming task. It is a task that is becoming more and more complex in the face of an increasing number of commercially available tools and the associated competing and confusing marketing claims.

First, the developer must identify the target GUI environment(s). Second, with the nature, scope, and schedule of the development project in mind, the developer must decide whether or not to use a UIMS, an IDT, or resort to programming with low-level tools such as Xlib, MacApp, or Microsoft Windows API.

There are several competing development tools for each of the major GUI environments including Motif, Open Look, Macintosh, Microsoft Windows and Windows NT, and OS/2 Presentation Manager. The requirement to develop a portable GUI to run across various Unix platforms, as well as the major non-Unix operating systems such as Microsoft Windows, OS2, and Macintosh, further complicates matters. There are, however, several tools for developing a GUI that is portable across these major platforms (for example, XVT, Neuron Data Open Interface, and Visix Galaxy).

There are often more than a dozen candidate development tools for a given CHI development project. The creation of a prioritized list of requirements, or selection criteria, is usually required to aid in the short listing process. It typically takes an experienced person three to four weeks to perform an unbiased and honest evaluation of a single CHI development tool. If schedule or budget constraints preclude a proper hands-on evaluation of how each tool handles a representative sample case, then it is often helpful to talk to other developers who have used the tool and to review evaluations reported in various professional trade journals. For example, the *IEEE Software* Tools Fair report by Forte (1992), the comparison of six GUI tools by Armstrong (1992), and a review of user interface development tools by Topper (1993) are representative of the unbiased coverage of the major GUI development tools available from professional journals. Unfortunately, the shelf life of a software tools trade study tends to be very short. New product releases about every six months tend to negate the value of earlier product comparisons related to important functional and performance capabilities.

**Development Tools: Future Trends**

There is still much room for improvement in CHI software tools. Current commercially available tools deal mainly with the graphical appearance and behavior of only limited parts of an application's user interface. They do not adequately support the construction of many application classes such as data visualization, command and control, and domain-specific editors. In addition, none of the commercially available GUI development tools *actively* assist developers in the design of critical and problematic areas of user interface design. For example, they do not actively assist designers in the proper use of color, font selection, screen layout, functional grouping, and selection of appropriate interaction techniques. As a result, many of the CHIs produced with today's best GUI toolkits are characterized by (1) operator fatigue due to the use of illegible fonts and color combinations, (2) operator confusion due to graphical clutter and poor screen layout, and (3) excessive operator error due to poor design and inconsistent implementation of critical interaction techniques.

Several CHI tool development projects, such as UIDE (Foley, et al. 1993), Marquise (Myers, et al., 1993), Humanoid (Szekely, et al. 1993), and CHIRP (Remington, 1994) show great promise for the future. We can expect to see many of the innovative concepts embodied in these projects (for example, intelligent design assistants and demonstrational interfaces) become commercially available the near future. The result will be development tools that exploit the strengths of both human designers and computers in the CHI design process. We can also expect to see advances in CHI development tools that closely parallel new advances in CHI enabling technologies, which will support the development of more natural forms of human-computer interaction. Figure 5 presents an example of the advances in CHI software development environments that we can expect to see as research prototypes emerge from the laboratory into commercial products.

The CHIRP Toolkit (Remington, 1994) is an integrated set of tools supporting the rapid development of CHI design and concept of operations demonstrations, and training simulations for the command and control applications domain. In addition to providing typical access to the basic building block widgets, it allows the developer to use higher-level prefabricated reusable interface modules (such as a panel of buttons and screen layout templates) application graphics libraries and interactive routines (for example, maps, globes, image and signal processing, and orbital mechanics displays). CHIRP provides an embedded Design Assistant that makes use of a CHI standards and guidelines knowledge-base to actively assist the interface designer in dealing with selected problematic aspects of CHI design.

## CHI Evaluation

### Usability Evaluation: Trends

In the past few years, many companies have gradually realized that it is not good business for major product usability flaws to be found by their customers after the product is released for operational use. Many of the most successful computer hardware and software companies (for instance, Apple Computers, Microsoft, Hewlett-Packard, Silicon Graphics Inc., and Intuit) attribute much of the success of their best-selling products (Macintosh personal computers, Word for Windows, LaserJet printers, SGI workstations, and Quicken Personal Financial software, respectively) to early usability testing. It is noteworthy that these were among the first companies to establish usability laboratories. The Usability Professionals Association, formed by 30 specialists at the CHI '92 Conference, now has over 1700 members and held their own conference in July 1994 with more than 350 attendees.

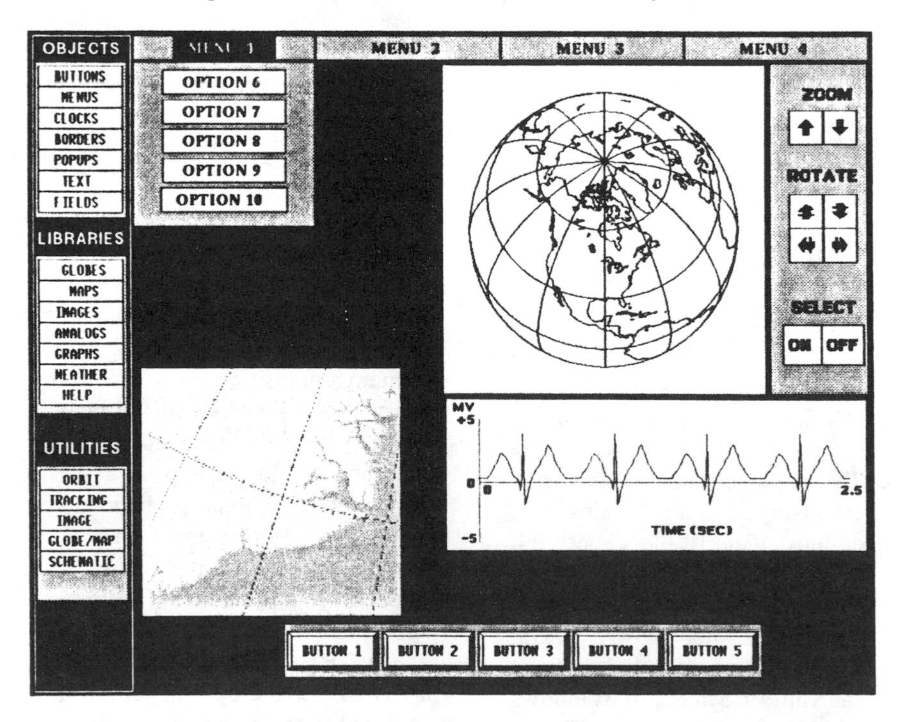


*Figure 5. A developer's view of the CHIRP Toolkit (Remington, 1994)*

*Figure 6. A typical usability laboratory in use*

Usability testing typically involves systematic observation of a sample of the potential user population performing representative tasks with an early version or prototype of the target software product in a controlled laboratory environment. Details of each user's behavior are usually captured by videotape, audio recordings, computer- logging programs, and expert observers. One-way viewing windows allow unobtrustive observation of users. Figure 6 shows a typical usability laboratory in action.

Users are encouraged to "think aloud" as they are performing a task. Quantitative behavioral measures such as the number of errors, time to complete tasks, the frequency of on-line and hard copy documentation accesses, and the number of frustration responses (for instance, pounding the table, cursing, or crying) are recorded and analyzed. Qualitative measures such as users' subjective opinions are also collected by means of post-test questionnaires and structured interviews. The results of well-designed and properly executed usability tests normally provide a clear identification of potentially serious usability problems, as well as useful insights regarding possible solutions. Highlight videos showing users working with a system can provide developers with very persuasive evidence of design flaws that detract from product usability.

For those interested in learning more about planning and conducting a usability test, analyzing data, and using the results to improve both products and processes, Dumas and Redish (1993) have written a practical guide to usability testing. Nielsen (1993) presents a more philosophical view of usability engineering in general, in an attempt to "provide concrete advice and methods that can be systematically employed to ensure a high degree of usability in the final user interface." Wiklund (1994) has edited a book in which usability specialists from 17 leading companies provide informative case studies of successful usability testing programs.

Jeffries et al. (1991) provide experimental evidence regarding the strengths and weaknesses of usability testing with respect to other techniques for isolating usability problems including cognitive walkthroughs, guidelines, and heuristic evaluation. It was found that many of the most severe design flaws could only be identified with usability testing. For example, for an early version of the popular HP-VUE desktop environment, deleting your home directory made it impossible to log in at a later time. An inadvertent action of one of the usability test subjects led to the identification of this problem. None of the other methods were successful in locating this design flaw.

It is possible to develop usability metrics. Bevan and Macleod (1994) present an overview of the ESPRIT Metrics for Usability Standards in Computing (MUSiC) Project. The MUSiC project was a three-year effort to develop comprehensive and efficient techniques for usability assessment at various stages of the development life cycle. The project has resulted in development of several usability measurement methods that have been empirically tested and validated. It has also produced tools that assist in the collection of usability data. For example, the Diagnostic Recorder for Usability Measurement (DRUM) is a software tool that provides support in video control and analysis of logged data and calculation of usability metrics. The Software Usability Measurement Inventory (SUMI), developed as part of the MUSiC project measures user satisfaction and thus assesses user-perceived software quality.

Finally, based on an analysis of 11 usability studies, Nielsen and Landauer (1993) report that the detection of problems as a function of number of users tested or heuristic evaluators employed is well modeled as a Poisson process. The mathematical model resulting from this effort should prove useful in planning the amount of evaluation required to achieve desired levels of thoroughness or benefits, similar to the model developed by Dalal and Mallows (1990) to decide when to stop testing software for programming bugs.

In summary, there is no proven single technique for developing highly usable CHI software. However, an approach involving basic human factors design principles, rapid prototyping tools and techniques to obtain user feedback early and continuously throughout the entire design process, and systematic usability testing to validate designs normally results in products that are both useful and usable. Such an approach also tends to reduce the risk of serious design flaws that result in user acceptance problems and costly rework. Usability will be increasingly viewed as one of the key characteristics of software product quality. A product's software quality plan should include the critical usability characteristics that, if not met, would make the product undesirable or not needed by customers or end users. The field of CHI is currently experiencing a period of increased visibility, accelerated growth, and exciting innovation. It is important for us to continuously exploit the latest CHI design, implementation, evaluation methods, and enabling technologies to provide more usable products and systems. This is especially true today, with computer users becoming more demanding in terms of their expectations for software products that are easier to learn, less intimidating, and simply more fun to use!

## References


Armstrong, J., "Six GUI Builders Face Off," *SunWorld*, Dec. 1992, pp. 67–74.

Bailey, G., "Iterative Methodology and Designer Training in Human-Computer Interface Design," *Conf. Proc. Human Factors in Computing Systems INTERCHI '93*, 1993, pp. 198–205.

Barfield, L., *The User Interface: Concepts and Design,* Addison-Wesley, Wokingham, England, 1993.

Bass, L. and Coutaz, J., "Human-Machine Interaction Considerations for Interactive Software," Software Engineering Institute Technical Report CMU/SEI-89-TR-4, Feb. 1989.

Bass, L. and Coutaz, J., *Developing Software for the User Interface,* Addison-Wesley, Reading, Mass., 1991.

Bass, L. and Dewan, P., *User Interface Software,* Wiley, New York, N.Y., 1993.

Bevan, N. and Macleod, M., "Behaviour and Information Technology" in *Usability Measurement in Context,* 1994, Vol. 13, Nos. 1 and 2, pp. 132–145.

Blattner, M., "In Our Image: Interface Design in the 1990s," *IEEE Multimedia*, Vol. 1, No. 1, 1994, pp. 25–36.

Blattner, M. and Dannenberg, L., *Multimedia Interface Design,* ACM Press, New York, N.Y., 1992.

Borenstein, N., *Programming as if People Mattered: Friendly Programs, Software Engineering, and other Noble Delusions*, Princeton University Press, Princeton, N.J., 1992.

Baecker, R., et al., *Readings in Human-Computer Interaction: Toward the Year 2000*, Morgan Kaufmann, San Mateo, Calif., 1994.

Casey, S., *Set Phaser on Stun: And Other True Tales of Design, Technology and Human Error*, Aegean Publishing Company, Santa Barbara, Calif., 1993.

Constantine, L., "More than Just a Pretty Face: Designing for Usability," *Proc. Software Development '94 Conf.*, 1994, pp. 361–369.

Corbett, M., Macleod, M. and Kelly, M., "Quantitative Usability Evaluation," *Proc. 5th Int'l Conf. Human-Computer Interaction*, 1993, pp. 313–318.

Curtis, B. and Hefley, B., "Defining a Place for Interface Engineering," *IEEE Software*, Mar. 1992, pp. 84–86.

Dalal, S. and Mallows, C., "Some Graphical Aids for Deciding When to Stop Testing Software," *IEEE J. Selected Areas Comm.,* Vol. 8, No. 2, Feb. 1990, pp. 169–175.

Dix, A., et al., *Human-Computer Interaction*, Prentice Hall, New York, N.Y., 1993.

Forte, G., "Tool Fair: Out of the Lab, Onto the Shelf." *IEEE Software*, May 1992, pp. 70–77.

Hartson, H. and Hix, D., "Human-Computer Interface Development: Concepts and Systems for Its Management." *ACM Computing Surveys*, Vol. 21. No 1, Mar. 1989.

Hix, D. and Hartson, H., *Developing User Interfaces: Ensuring Usability Through Product and Process*, John Wiley, New York, N.Y., 1994.

Helander, M. (Editor). *Handbook of Human-Computer Interaction,* North-Holland, Amsterdam, 1988.

IEEE, "Recommended Practice for Graphical User Interface Drivability," *P1201.2 Balloting Draft 2*, Sponsored by the Portable Applications Standards Committee of the IEEE Computer Society, Aug. 1993.

Jeffries, R., et al., "User Interface Evaluation in the Real World: A Comparison of Four Techniques," *CHI'91 Human Factors in Computing Systems Conf. Proc.*, ACM Press, New York, N.Y., 1991, pp. 119–124.

Karat, J. (ed.), *Taking Software Design Seriously: Practical Techniques for Human-Computer Interaction Design,* Academic Press, San Diego, Calif., 1991.

Karat, C., Campbell, R., and Fiegel, T., "Comparison of Empirical Testing and Walkthrough Methods in User Interface Evaluation," *SIGCHI'92 Human Factors in Computing Systems Proc.*, ACM Press, New York, N.Y., 1992, pp. 397–404.

Marcus, A., "A Comparison of User Interface Research and Development Centers," *Proc. Hawaii Int'l Conf. System Sciences*, Vol. 2, IEEE CS Press, Los Alamitos, Calif., 1992, pp. 741–752.

Mayhew, D., *Principles and Guidelines in Software User Interface Design*, Prentice Hall, Englewood Cliffs, N.J., 1992.

Myers, B., "Demonstrational Interfaces: A Step Beyond Direct Manipulation," *Computer,* Aug. 1992, pp. 61–73.

Myers, B. and Rosson, M., "Survey of User Interface Programming," *SIGCHI' 92: Human Factors in Computing Systems Conf. Proc.,* ACM Press, New York, N.Y., 1992.

Nielsen, J., "The Usability Engineering Life Cycle," *Computer*, Mar. 1992, pp. 12–22.

Nielsen, J., *Usability Engineering*, Academic Press, San Diego, Calif., 1993.

Nielsen, J., "Noncommand User Interfaces," *Comm. ACM*, Vol. 36, No. 4, 1993, pp. 83–99.

Nielsen, J. and Landauer, T., "A Mathematical Model of the Finding of Usability Problems," *Proc. Human Factors in Computing Systems INTERCHI '93 Conf.,* 1993, ACM Press, New York, N.Y., pp. 206–213.

*Open Software Foundation, OSF/Motif Style Guide Revision 2.0*, Prentice Hall, Englewood Cliffs, N.J., 1994.

Perlman. G., "User Interface Development," *Software Engineering Institute Curriculum Module,* SEI-CM-17-1.1, Nov. 1989.

Perlman, G., "Teaching User Interface Development," *IEEE Software*, Nov. 1990, pp. 85–86.

Remington, R., "X Windows: Coming to a Screen in Your Area," *Seybold's Outlook on Professional Computing*, Vol. 8, No. 5, Dec. 1989.

Remington, R., "Practicing Safe Unix on Your Dell Station with the IXI Desktop Shell," *Seybold's Outlook on Professional Computing*, Vol. 8, No. 10, May 1990.

Remington, R., "CHIRP: The Computer Human Interface Rapid Prototyping and Design Assistant Toolkit," *Proc. CHI '94: Human Factors in Computing Systems Conference Companion,* ACM Press, New York, N.Y., 1994, pp. 113–114.

Salvendy, G. (Editor), *Handbook of Human Factors*, John Wiley and Sons, New York, N.Y., 1987.

Shneiderman, B., *Designing the User Interface: Strategies for Effective Human-Computer Interaction,* Second Ed., Addison-Wesley, New York, N.Y., 1992.

Smith, S. and Mosier, J., "Guidelines for Designing User Interface Software," *Mitre Corporation Report #10090*, Bedford, Mass., 1986.

Staples, L., "Representation in Virtual Space: Visual Convention in the Graphical User Interface," *Proc. Human Factors in Computing Systems INTERCHI '93,* ACM Press, New York, N.Y., 1993, pp. 348–354.

Tognazzini, B., *Tog on Interface,* Addison-Wesley Publishing Company, Inc., 1992.

Topper, A., "Review of User Interface Development Tools." *American Programmer*, Oct. 1993.

Wiklund, M., (Editor), *Usability in Practice: How Companies Develop User-Friendly Products*, Academic Press, Cambridge, Mass, 1994.

# Chapter 5

# Software Development Methodologies

## 1. Introduction to Chapter

A *methodology*, as generally defined in software engineering and used in this Tutorial, is a set of software engineering methods, policies, procedures, rules, standards, techniques, tools, languages, and other methodologies for analyzing and specifying requirements and design. These methodologies can be used to:

- aid in determination of the software requirements and design
- represent the software requirements and design specifications prior to the beginning of either design or coding.

In order to be an acceptable methodology, a software requirements and/or design methodology must have the following attributes:

- *The methodology is documented*—the procedure for using this methodology exists in a document or users' manual
- *The methodology is repeatable*—each application of the methodology is the same
- *The methodology is teachable*—sufficient detailed procedures and examples exist that qualified people can be instructed in the methodology

SOFTWARE DEVELOPMENT METHODOLOGIES

- *The methodology is based on proven techniques*—the methodology implements proven fundamental procedures or other simpler methodologies
- *The methodology has been validated*—the methodology has been shown to work correctly on a large number of applications
- The methodology is appropriate to the problem to be solved

## 2. Introduction to Papers

The first paper, by Linda Northrop of the Software Engineering Institute, is an overview of object-oriented technology. This is an original paper based on her article in the 1994 *Encyclopedia of Software Engineering*. [1]

She begins with an interesting history of the object-oriented methodologies, giving credit to the original developers. In the object-oriented development model, systems are viewed as cooperative objects that encapsulate structure and behavior. She then provides a description of object-oriented programming, object-oriented design, and lastly object-oriented analysis. Although this is the reverse order from that in which these activities usually take place, the methods and tools were developed in this sequence.

She briefly describes how to transition a software development organization to object-oriented development and takes a look at possible future trends.

The second paper, by A.G. Sutcliffe, entitled "Object-Oriented Systems Development: Survey of Structured Methods," includes a description of some of the modern object-oriented analysis and design techniques, as well as a survey of the structured analysis and design methods.

Sutcliffe's paper discusses object-oriented programming and programming languages, as well as new methods of object-oriented analysis and design. The paper also defines many of the object-oriented concepts such as abstraction, encapsulation, and inheritance. Further, the paper describes some of the current object-oriented methods such as hierarchical object-oriented design (HOOD), object-oriented system design (OOSD), object-oriented system analysis (OOSA) by Schlaer and Mellor, and object-oriented analysis (OOA) by Coad and Yourdon.

The paper is particularly valuable, and is included in this chapter, because it compares object-oriented development with other methodologies such as structured analysis (developed by Yourdon and Softech in the 1970s), and the Structured System Analysis and Design Method (SSADM) used in the United Kingdom and elsewhere in Europe. The author's purpose in describing these structured methods is to determine whether or not these methods support any of the object-oriented concepts.

The third paper in this chapter, "Structured System Analysis and Design Method," by Caroline Ashworth of Scion Ltd., discusses SSADM, a popular analysis technique used in Europe and particularly in the United Kingdom. SSADM was originally developed for the government of the UK by Learmonth and Burchett Management Systems (LBMS) and has a commercial counterpart called LSDM (LBMS System Development Methodology).

SSADM is one of the better-known structured methods used in Europe. It is controlled by a UK government agency, the Central Computer and Telecommunications Agency (CCTA), which is part of HM Treasury. SSADM was introduced in 1981, and by 1987 more than 600 UK government projects were using the methodology. SSADM has the following characteristics:

- Data structure is developed at an early stage
- SSADM separates logical design from physical design
- SSADM provides three different views of the system--data structure view, data flow view, and entity life history view
- SSADM contains elements of both top-down and bottom-up approaches
- User involvement is encouraged through the use of easily understood, non-technical diagrammatic techniques supported by short, simple narrative descriptions
- Quality assurance reviews and walkthroughs are encouraged throughout the process
- SSADM forms the project documentation and is used in subsequent steps (that is, it is "self-documenting")

SSADM is similar to the structured analysis and structured design approach popular in the US, with the exception of the process known as the entities life history.

The Ashworth paper was written in 1988 and describes SSADM Version 3.x. Version 4 was released in 1990 but differed only in detail around some of the techniques, particularly in the interface area. Since then Version 4+ has been in development, with a somewhat broader scope and an emphasis on customization of the method to each individual site. No firm documentation has been developed on Version 4 or 4+, so the Ashworth paper is still the best description of SSADM available [2].

The fourth and last paper in this section is "A Review of Formal Methods" by Robert Vienneau of the Kaman Sciences Corporation. This paper is an extract from a longer report with the same title [3]. The author defines a formal method in software development as a method that provides a formal language describing a software artifact (for example, specification, design, source code) such that formal proofs are possible in principle about properties of the artifacts so expressed. Formal methods support precise and rigorous specification of those aspects of a computer system capable of being expressed in the language. Formal methods are considered to be an alternative to requirements analysis methods such as structured analysis and object-oriented analysis. The paper says that formal methods can provide more precise specifications, better communications, and higher quality and productivity.

There is a range of opinion on the proper scope of validity for formal methods with the current state of technology. The Vienneau article agrees with the Tutorial editors' views that claims of reduced errors and improved reliability through the use of formal methods are as yet unproven. This point of view is also expressed in [4]. However, there is a body of opinion that takes the more expansive view that, in critical systems such as microcode, secure systems, and perhaps safety applications, the use of formal methods to specify requirements is an important aid in detecting flaws in the requirements. This opinion is represented in [5] and [6], but even this view recognizes that the use of formal methods is expensive and there are very few applications willing to pay the cost.


1. Northrop, Linda M., "Object-Oriented Development," in *Encyclopedia of Software Engineering*, John J. Marciniak (ed.), John Wiley & Sons, Inc., New York, 1994, pp. 729–736.
2. Hall, Patrick A. V., private communication.
3. Vienneau, Robert, *A Review of Formal Methods,* Kaman Science Corporation, Utica, NY, May 26, 1993, pp. 3–15 and 27–33.
4. Fenton, Norman, Shari Lawrence Pfleeger, and Robert L. Glass, "Science and Substance: A Challenge to Software Engineers," *IEEE Software*, Vol. 11, No. 4, July 1994, pp. 86–95.
5. Gerhart, Susan, Dan Craigen, and Ted Ralston, "Experience with Formal Methods in Critical Systems," *IEEE Software*, Vol 11, No. 1, Jan. 1994, pp. 21–29.
6. Bowen, Jonathan P., and Michael G. Hinchley, "Ten Commandments of Formal Methods," *Computer*, Vol. 28, No. 4, Apr. 1995, pp. 56–63.

# Object-Oriented Development

Linda M. Northrop
*Software Engineering Institute*

## Historical Perspective

The object-oriented model for software development has become exceedingly attractive as the best answer to the increasingly complex needs of the software development community. What was first viewed by many as a research curiosity and an impractical approach to industrial strength software is now being enthusiastically embraced. Object-oriented versions of most languages have or are being developed. Numerous object-oriented methodologies have been proposed. Conferences, seminars, and courses on object-oriented topics are extremely popular. New journals and countless special issues of both academic and professional journals have been devoted to the subject. Contracts for software development that specify object-oriented techniques and languages currently have a competitive edge. Object-oriented development is to the 1990s what structured development was to the 1970s, and the object-oriented movement is still accelerating.

Concepts like "objects" and "attributes of objects" actually date back to the early 1950s when they appeared in early works in *Artificial Intelligence* (Berard, 1993). However, the real legacy of the object-oriented movement began in 1966 when Kristen Nygaard and Ole-Johan Dahl moved to higher levels of abstraction and introduced the language Simula. Simula provided encapsulation at a more abstract level than subprograms; data abstraction and classes were introduced in order to simulate a problem. During approximately this same time frame, Alan Kay was working at the University of Utah on a personal computer that he hoped would be able to support graphics and simulation. Due to both hardware and software limitations, Flex, Kay's computer venture, was unsuccessful. However, his ideas were not lost, and surfaced again when he joined Xerox at Palo Alto Research Center (PARC) in the early 1970s.

At PARC he was a member of a project that espoused the belief that computer technologies are the key to improving communication channels between people and between people and machines. The group developed Smalltalk, based upon this conviction and influenced by the class concept in Simula; the turtle ideas LOGO provided in the Pen classes; the abstract data typing in CLU; and the incremental program execution of LISP. In 1972, PARC released the first version of Smalltalk. About this time the term "object-oriented" was coined. Some people credit Alan King who is said to have used the term to characterize Smalltalk. Smalltalk is considered to be the first true object-oriented language (Goldberg, 1983), and today Smalltalk remains the quintessential object-oriented language. The goal of Smalltalk was to enable the design of software in units that are as autonomous as possible. Everything in the language is an object; that is, an instance of a class. Objects in this nascent Smalltalk world were associated with nouns. The Smalltalk effort supported a highly interactive development environment and prototyping. This original work was not publicized and was viewed with academic interest as highly experimental.

Smalltalk-80 was the culmination of a number of versions of the PARC Smalltalk and was released to the non-Xerox world in 1981. The August 1981 issue of *Byte* featured the Smalltalk efforts. On the cover of the issue was a picture of a hot air balloon leaving an isolated island that symbolized the launch of the PARC object-oriented ideas. It was time to start publicizing to the software development community. The impact was gradual at first but mounted to the current level of flurry about object-oriented techniques and products. The balloon was in fact launched and there was an effect. The early Smalltalk research in environments led to window, icon, mouse, and pull-down window environments. The Smalltalk language influenced the development in the early to mid-1980s of other object-oriented languages, most notably: Objective-C (1986), C++ (1986), Self (1987), Eiffel (1987), and Flavors (1986). The application of object orientation was broadened. Objects no longer were associated just with nouns, but also with events and processes. In 1980, Grady Booch pioneered with the concept of object-oriented design (Booch, 1982). Since then others have followed suit, and object-oriented analysis techniques have also begun to be publicized. In 1985, the first commercial object-oriented database system was introduced. The 1990s brought an ongoing investigation of object-oriented domain analysis, testing, metrics, and management. The current new frontiers in object technology are design patterns, distributed object systems, and Web-based object applications.

## Motivation

Why has the object-oriented movement gained such momentum? In reality, some of its popularity probably stems from the hope that it, like so many other earlier software development innovations, will address the crying needs for greater productivity, reliability, maintainability, and manageability. However, aside from the hope that object-orientation is in fact the "silver bullet," there are many other documented arguments to motivate its adoption.

Object-oriented development adds emphasis on direct mapping of concepts in the problem domain to software units and their interfaces. Furthermore, it is felt by some that based upon recent studies in psychology, viewing the world as objects is more natural since it is closer to the way humans think. Objects are more stable than functions; what most often precipitates software change is change in required functionality, not change in the players, or objects. In addition, object-oriented development supports and encourages the software engineering practices of information hiding, data abstraction, and encapsulation. In an object, revisions are localized. Object-orientation results in software that is easily modified, extended, and maintained (Berard, 1993).

Object-orientation extends across the life cycle in that a consistent object approach is used from analysis through coding. Moreover, this pervading object approach quite naturally spawns prototypes that support rapid application development. The use of object-oriented development encourages the reuse of not only software but also design and analysis models. Furthermore, object technology facilitates interoperability; that is, the degree to which an application running on one node of a network can make use of a resource at a different node of the network. Object-oriented development also supports the concurrency, hierarchy, and complexity present in many of today's software systems. It is currently necessary to build systems—not just black-box applications. These complex systems are often hierarchically composed of different kinds of subsystems. Object-oriented development supports open systems; there is much greater flexibility to integrate software across applications. Finally, use of the object-oriented approach tends to reduce the risk of developing complex systems, primarily because system integration is diffused throughout the life cycle (Booch, 1994).

## Object-Oriented Model

The object-oriented model is more than a collection of new languages. It is a new way of thinking about what it means to compute and about how information can be structured. In the object-oriented model, systems are viewed as cooperating objects that encapsulate structure and behavior and which belong to classes that are hierarchically constructed. All functionality is achieved by messages that are passed to and from objects. The object-oriented model can be viewed as a conceptual framework with the following elements: abstraction, encapsulation, modularity, hierarchy, typing, concurrence, persistence, reusability, and extensibility.

The emergence of the object-oriented model does not mark any sort of computing revolution. Instead, object-orientation is the next step in a methodical evolution from both procedural approaches and strictly data-driven approaches. Object-orientation is the integration of procedural and data-driven approaches. New approaches to software development have been precipitated by both programming language developments and increased sophistication and breadth in the problem domains for which software systems are being designed. While in practice the analysis and design processes ideally precede implementation, it has been the language innovations that have necessitated new approaches to design and, later, analysis. Language evolution in turn has been a natural response to enhanced architecture capabilities and the ever increasingly sophisticated needs of programming systems. The impetus for object-oriented software development has followed this general trend. Figure 1 depicts the many contributing influences.

Perhaps the most significant factors are the advances in programming methodology. Over the past several decades, the support for abstraction in languages has progressed to higher levels. This abstraction progression has gone from address (machine languages), to name (assembly languages), to expression (first-generation languages, such as FORTRAN), to control (second-generation languages, such as COBOL) to procedure and function (second- and early third-generation languages, such as Pascal), to modules and data (late third-generation languages, such as Modula 2), and finally to objects (object-based and object-oriented languages). The development of Smalltalk and other object-oriented languages as discussed above necessitated the invention of new analysis and design techniques.

These new object-oriented techniques are really the culmination of the structured and database approaches. In the object-oriented approach, the smaller scale concerns of data flow-orientation, like coupling and cohesion, are very relevant. Similarly, the behavior within objects will ultimately require a function-oriented design approach. The ideas of the entity relationship (ER) approach to data modeling from the database technology are also embodied in the object-oriented model.

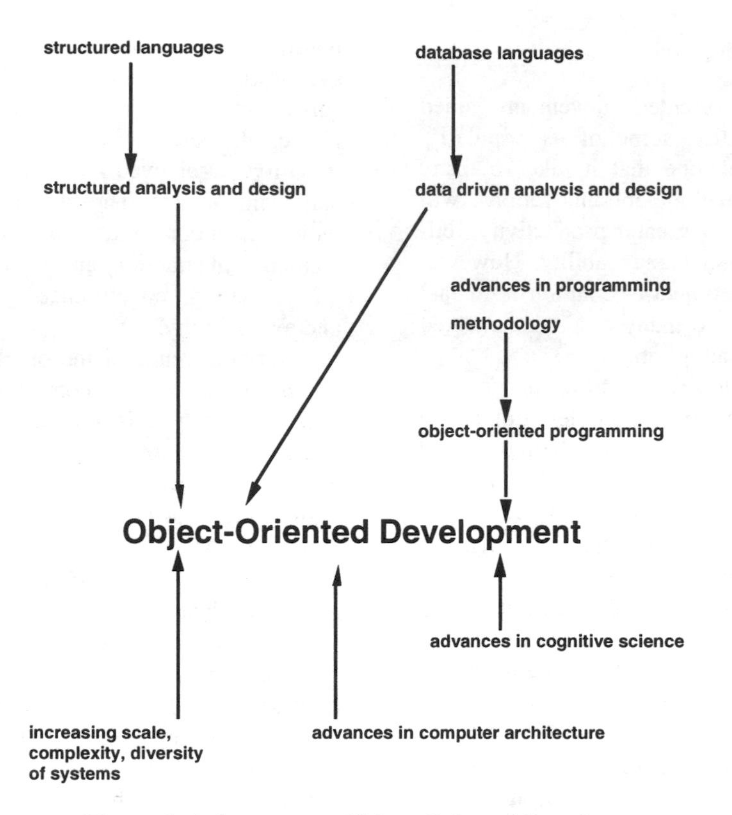


*Figure 1. Influences on Object-Oriented Development*

Advances in computer architecture, both in the increased capability combined with decrease in cost, and in the introduction of objects into hardware (capability systems and hardware support for operating systems concepts) have likewise affected the object-oriented movement. Object-oriented programming languages are frequently memory and MIPS intensive. They required and are now utilizing added hardware power. Philosophy and cognitive science have also influenced the advancement of the object-oriented model in their hierarchy and classification theories (Booch, 1991). And finally, the ever-increasing scale, complexity, and diversity of computer systems have helped both propel and shape object technology.

Because there are many and varied influences on object-oriented development, and because this approach has not reached maturity, there is still some diversity in thinking and terminology. All object-oriented languages are not created equal nor do they refer to the same concepts with consistent verbiage across the board. And though there is a movement toward some unification, there is no complete consensus on how to do object-oriented analysis and object-oriented design nor on the symbology to use to depict these activities. Nevertheless, object-oriented development has proven successful in many applications including: air traffic control, animation, banking, business data processing, command and control systems, computer-aided design (CAD), computer-integrated manufacturing, databases, document preparation, expert systems, hypermedia, image recognition, mathematical analysis, music composition, operating systems, process control, robotics, space station software, telecommunications, telemetry systems, user interface design, and VLSI design. It is unquestionable that object-oriented technology has moved into the mainstream of industrial-strength software development.

## Object-Oriented Programming

### Concepts

Since the object-oriented programming efforts predate the other object-oriented development techniques, it is reasonable to focus first on object-oriented programming. In object-oriented programming, programs are organized as cooperating collections of objects, each of which is an instance of some class and whose classes are all members of a hierarchy of classes united via inheritance relations. Object-oriented languages are characterized by the following: object creation facility, message-passing capability, class capability, and inheritance. While these concepts can and have been used individually in other languages, they complement each other in a unique synergistic way in object-oriented languages.

Figure 2 illustrates the procedural programming model.

To achieve desired functionality, arguments are passed to a procedure and results are passed back. Object-oriented languages involve a change of perspective. As depicted in Figure 3, functionality is achieved through communication with the interface of an object. An object can be defined as an entity that encapsulates state and behavior; that is, data structures (or attributes) and operations. The state is really the information needed to be stored in order to carry out the behavior. The interface, also called the protocol, of the object is the set of messages to which it will respond.

Messaging is the way objects communicate and therefore the way that functionality is achieved. Objects respond to the receipt of messages by either performing an internal operation, also sometimes called a method or routine, or by delegating the operation to be performed by another object. All objects are instances of classes, which are sets of objects with similar characteristics, or from another viewpoint; a template from which new objects may be created. The method invoked by an object in response to a message is determined by the class of this receiver object. All objects of a given class use the same method in response to similar messages. Figure 4 shows a DOG class and objects instantiated from the dog class. All the DOG objects respond in the same way to the messages sit, bark, and roll. All DOG objects will also have the same state (data structures), though the values contained in what are typically called state variables can vary from DOG object to DOG object.

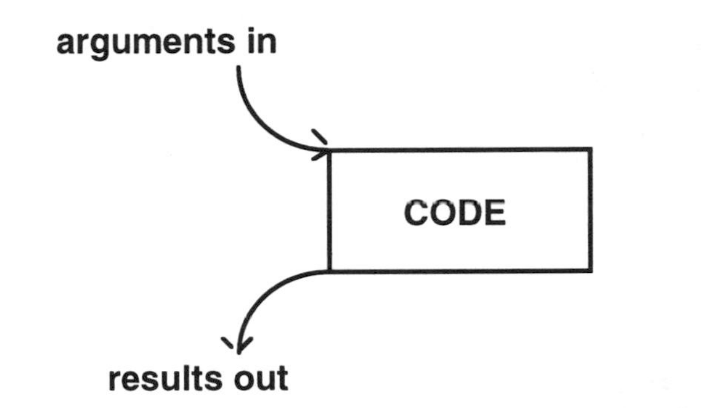


*Figure 2. Procedural Model*

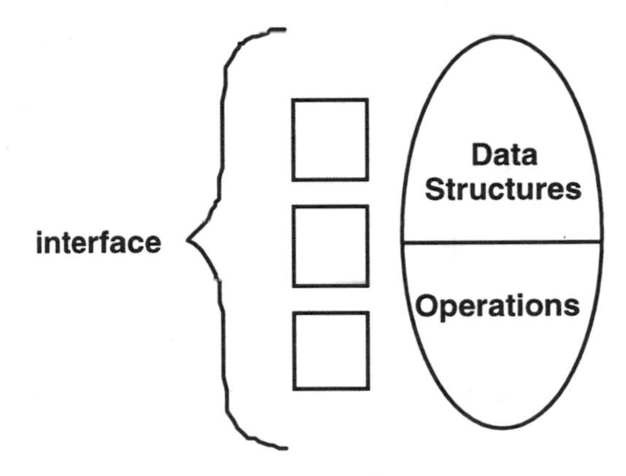


*Figure 3. Object-Oriented Model*

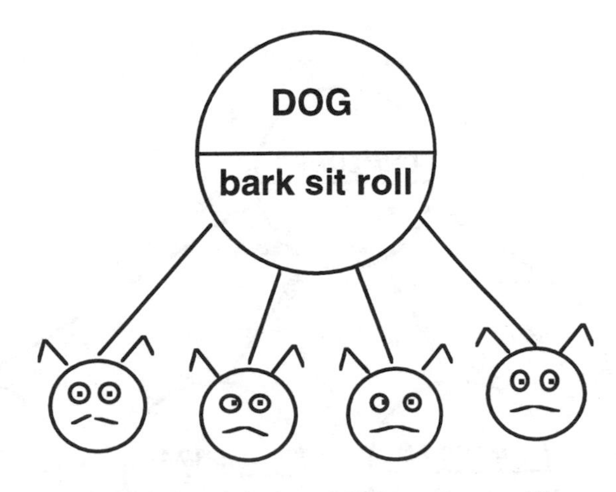


*Figure 4. Instantiation of Objects From a Class*

Classes can be arranged in a hierarchy. A subclass will inherit state and behavior from its superclass higher in the inheritance hierarchy structure. Inheritance can be defined as the transfer of a class' capabilities and characteristics to its subclasses. Figure 5 shows a subclass DOBERMAN of the original DOG class. An object of the DOBERMAN class will have the bark, sit, and roll behavior of the DOG class, but in addition, it will have the kill behavior particular to the DOBERMAN class. When a message is sent to an object, the search for the corresponding method begins in the class of the object and will progress up the superclass chain until such a method is found or until the chain has been exhausted (when an error would occur). In some languages, it is possible for a given class to inherit from more than one superclass. This capability is called *multiple inheritance*. When dynamic binding is present, inheritance results in polymorphism. Polymorphism essentially describes the phenomenon that a given message sent to an object will be interpreted differently at execution based upon subclass determination. Figure 6 illustrates a superclass UNMEMBER with its subclasses. If the message "speak" is sent to an object, at execution time it will be determined where the appropriate speak method will be found based upon the current subclass association of the object. Thus the polymorphism means that the speak capability will vary and in fact will be determined at execution.

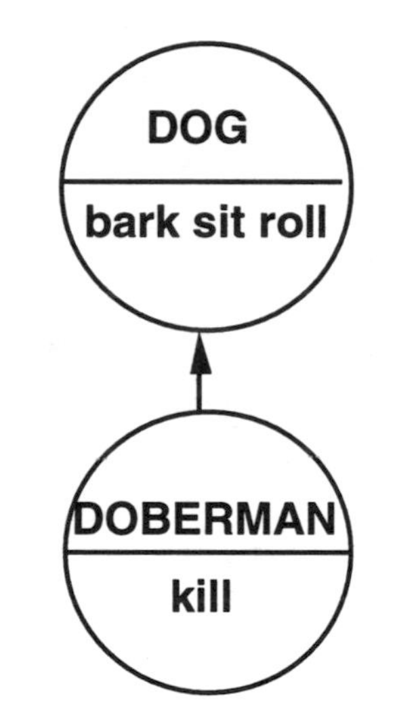


*Figure 5. Inheritance*

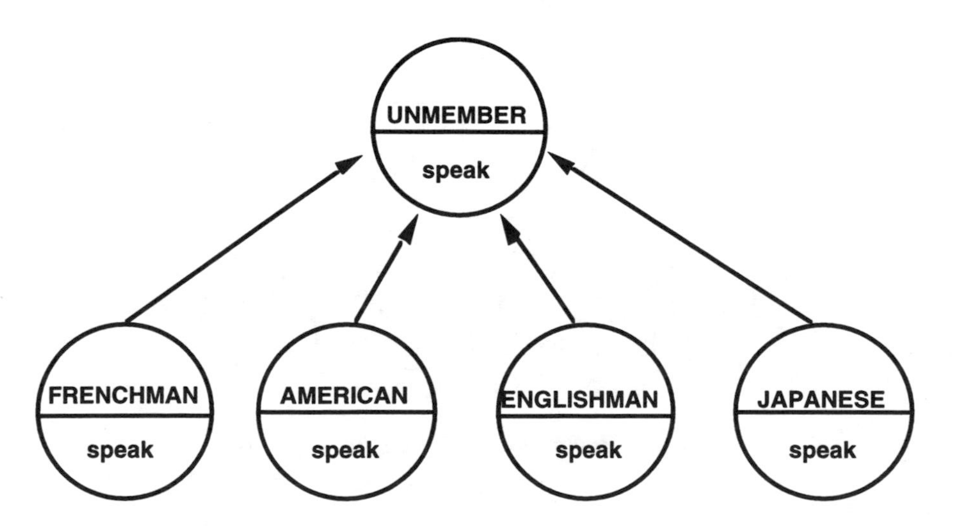


*Figure 6. Polymorphism*

*Table 1. Object-Oriented Languages*

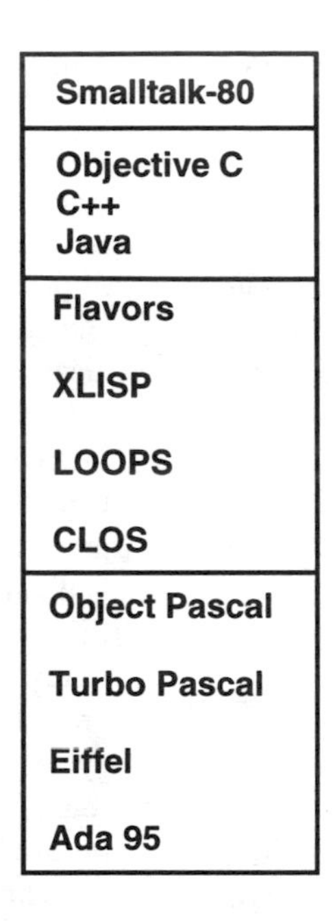

| Smalltalk-80 |
|---|
| Objective C<br>C++<br>Java |
| Flavors<br>XLISP<br>LOOPS<br>CLOS |
| Object Pascal<br>Turbo Pascal<br>Eiffel<br>Ada 95 |

It is possible for a method to not be actually defined in the superclass but still be included in the interface and hence be inherited by subclasses. One calls such a superclass an *abstract class*. Abstract classes do not have instances and are used only to create subclasses. For example, UNMEMBER would be an abstract class if the method for the message speak was not defined in UNMEMBER. Including speak in the interface of UNMEMBER, however, would dictate that speak would be a message common to all subclasses of UNMEMBER, but the exact speak behavior would vary with each subclass. Abstract classes are used to capture commonality without determining idiosyncratic behavior.

**Languages**

There are essentially four branches of object-oriented languages: Smalltalk-based, C-based, LISP-based, and Pascal-based. Simula is actually the common ancestor of all of these languages. The terminology and capability of the object-oriented languages varies considerably. A sampling of popular object-oriented languages in each branch is given in Table 1. The Smalltalk-based languages include the five versions, including Smalltalk-80, developed at PARC as well as Digitalk Smalltalk and other such versions. Smalltalk- 80 is considered the truest object-oriented language, although it and the others in this group do not have multiple inheritance capability.

In the C-based category are languages that are derived from C. Objective-C was developed by Brad Cox, has an extensive library, and has been used successfully to build large systems. C++ was written by Bjarne Stroustrup of AT&T Bell Labs. C's STRUCT concept is extended in C++ to provide class capability with data hiding. Polymorphism is implemented by virtual functions, which deviate from the normal C typing that is still resolved at compilation.

C++ Version 2.0 includes multiple inheritance. C++ is a popular choice in many software areas, especially those where UNIX is preferred. Similar to C and C++ but much simpler is Java, the latest object-oriented language that hit the software development scene with great fanfare in 1995. Java, developed at Sun Microsystems, in addition to being object-oriented has the capability to compile programs into binary format (applets) that can be executed on many platforms without compilation, providing embedded executable content for Web-based applications. Java is strongly typed and has multithreading and synchronization mechanisms like Ada, yet is high-performance and portable like C.

The many dialects including LOOPS, Flavors, Common LOOPS, and New Flavors, in the LISP-based branch were precipitated by knowledge representation research. Common LISP Object System (CLOS) was an effort to standardize object-oriented LISP. The Pascal-based languages include among others Object Pascal and Turbo Pascal as well as Eiffel. Object Pascal was developed by Apple and Niklaus Wirth for the Macintosh. The class library for Object Pascal is MacApp. Turbo Pascal, developed by Borland, followed the Object Pascal lead. Eiffel was released by

Bertrand Meyer of Interactive Software Engineering, Inc. in 1987. Eiffel is a full object-oriented language that has an Ada-like syntax and operates in a UNIX environment. Ada as it was originally conceived in 1983 was not object-oriented in that it did not support inheritance and polymorphism. In 1995, an object-oriented version of Ada was released. Though object-oriented, Ada 95 continues to differ from other object-oriented languages in its definition of a class in terms of types.

There are also languages that are referred to as *object-based.* A sample of object-based languages appears in Table 2. Object-based languages differ from object-oriented languages ostensibly in their lack of inheritance capability. It should be noted that while Ada 95 is object-oriented, its predecessor, Ada, is object-based.

## Object-Oriented Software Engineering

### Life Cycle

While the object-oriented languages are exciting developments, coding is not the primary source of problems in software development. Requirements and design problems are much more prevalent and much more costly to correct. The focus on object-oriented development techniques, therefore, should not be strictly on the programming aspects, but more appropriately on the other aspects of software engineering. The promise object-oriented methodologies hold for attacking complexity during analysis and design and accomplishing analysis and design reuse is truly significant. If it is accepted that object-oriented development is more than object-oriented coding, then a whole new approach, including life cycle, must be adopted (Booch, 1994).

The most widely accepted life cycle to date is the waterfall/structured life cycle (Lorenz, 1993). The waterfall organization came into existence to stem the ad hoc approaches that had led to the software crisis as it was first noted in the late 60s. A version of the waterfall life cycle is pictured in Figure 7.

As shown, the process is sequential; activities flow in primarily one direction. There is little provision for change and the assumption is that the system is quite clearly understood during the initial stages. Unfortunately, any software engineering effort will inherently involve a great deal of iteration, whether it is scheduled or not. Good designers have been described as practitioners who work at several levels of abstraction and detail simultaneously (Curtis, 1989). The waterfall life cycle simply does not accommodate real iteration. Likewise, prototyping, incremental builds, and program families are misfits. The waterfall/structured life cycle is also criticized for placing no emphasis on reuse and having no unifying model to integrate the phases (Korson, 1990).

The object-oriented approach begins with a model of the problem and proceeds with continuous object identification and elaboration. It is inherently iterative and inherently incremental. Figure 8 illustrates a version of the water fountain life cycle that has been used to describe the object-oriented development process (Henderson-Sellers, 1990). The fountain idea conveys that the development is inherently iterative and seamless. The same portion of the system is usually worked on a number of times with functionality being added to the evolving system with each iteration. Prototyping and feedback loops are standard. The seamlessness is accounted for in the lack of distinct boundaries during the traditional activities of analysis, design, and coding.

*Table 2. Object-Based Languages*

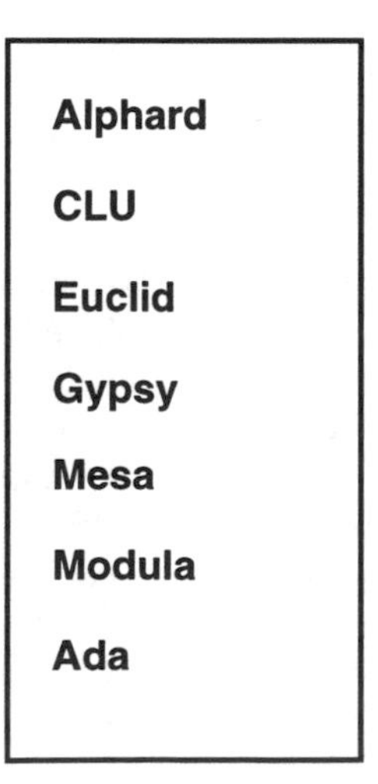

| |
|---|
| Alphard |
| CLU |
| Euclid |
| Gypsy |
| Mesa |
| Modula |
| Ada |

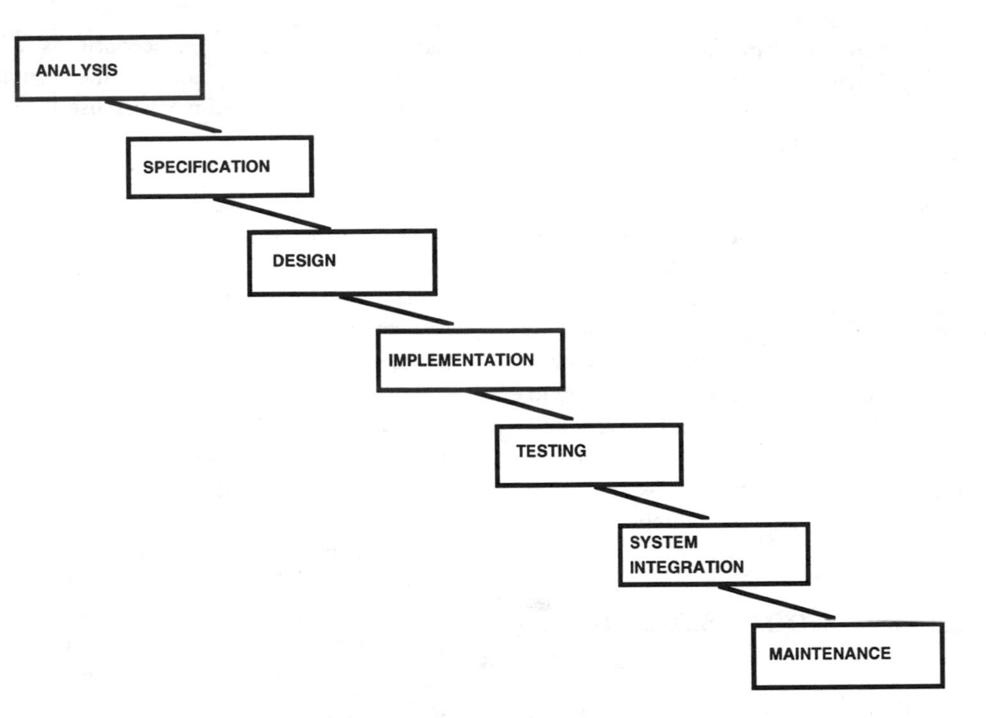


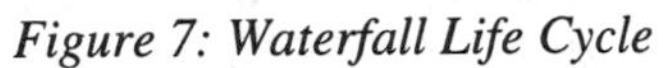

*Figure 7: Waterfall Life Cycle*

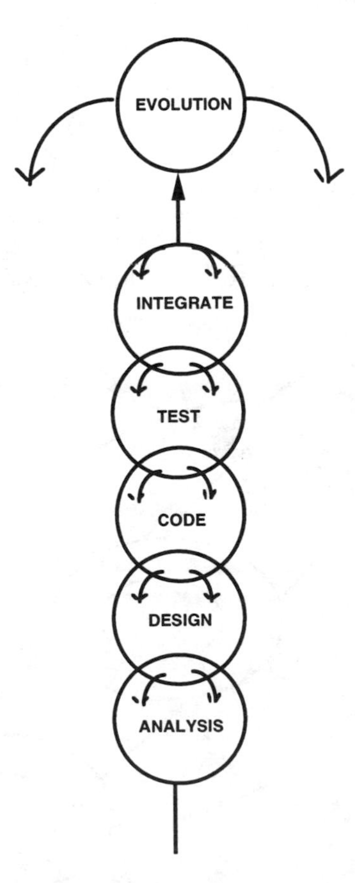


*Figure 8. Water Fountain Life Cycle for Object-Oriented Software Development*

The reason for removing the boundaries is that the concept of object permeates; objects and their relationships are the medium of expression for analysis, design, and implementation. There is also a switch of effort from coding to analysis and an emphasis on data structure before function. Furthermore, the iterative and seamless nature of object-oriented development makes the inclusion of reuse activities natural.

More recently a life cycle that has both a macro- and a microview has been proposed to increase the manageability of object-oriented development (Booch, 1994). The macro phases in Figure 9 are: *analysis*, to discover and identify the objects; *design*, to invent and design objects; and *implementation*, to create objects. Built into each macrophase is a microphase depicting the iteration. This life cycle suggests Boehm's Spiral Model (Boehm, 1988).

**Object-Oriented Analysis (OOA) and Object-Oriented Design (OOD)**

Since object-oriented technology is still relatively new, there are, as noted above, a number of approaches to Object-Oriented Analysis and Design. Most of them use graphical representations, an idea that was likely inherited from structured methodologies. Object-oriented analysis builds on previous information modeling techniques, and can be defined as a method of analysis that examines requirements from the perspective of the classes and objects found in the vocabulary of the problem domain. Analysis activities yield black-box objects that are derived from the problem domain. Scenarios are often used in object-oriented approaches to help determine necessary object behavior. A scenario is a sequence of actions that takes place in the problem domain. Frameworks have become very useful in capturing an object-oriented analysis for a given problem domain and making it reusable for related applications. Basically, a framework is a skeleton of an application or application subsystem implemented by concrete and abstract classes. In other words, a framework is a specialization hierarchy with abstract superclasses that depicts a given problem domain. One of the drawbacks of all current object-oriented analysis techniques is their universal lack of formality.

During object-oriented design, the object focus shifts to the solution domain. Object-oriented design is a method of design encompassing the process depicting both logical and physical as well as static and dynamic models of the system under design (Booch, 1994).

In both analysis and design there is a strong undercurrent of reuse. Researchers in object technology are now attempting to codify design patterns, which are a kind of reusable asset that can be applied to different domains. Basically, a design pattern is a recurring design structure or solution that when cataloged in a systematic way can be reused and can form the basis of design communication (Gamma, 1994).

OOD techniques were actually defined before OOA techniques were conceived. There is difficulty in identifying and characterizing current OOA and OOD techniques because as described above, the boundaries between analysis and design activities in the object-oriented model are fuzzy. Given that problem, the following descriptions provide an overview to some of the OOA and OOD techniques being used.

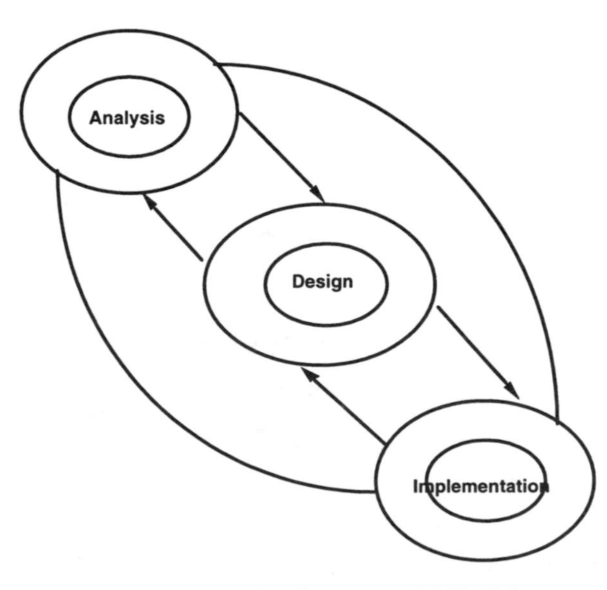


*Figure 9. Iterative/Incremental Life Cyle*

Meyer uses language as a vehicle for expressing design. His approach is really not classifiable as an OOD technique (Meyer, 1988). Booch's OOD techniques extend his previous Ada work. He advocates a "round-trip gestalt" process during which: objects are identified, semantics of the objects are identified, relationships are identified, implementation is accomplished, and iteration occurs. Originally he used class diagrams, class category diagrams, class templates, and object diagrams to record design (Booch, 1991). More recently he has taken ideas from other methods and woven them into his work. Behavior is described with Harel Statecharts in conjunction with interaction or annotated object diagrams (Booch 94).

Wirfs-Brock's OOD technique is driven by delegation of responsibilities. Class responsibility cards (CRC) are used to record classes responsible for specific functionality and collaborators with the responsible classes. The initial exploration of classes and responsibilities is followed by detailed relationship analysis and implementation of subsystems (Wirfs-Brock, 1990).

Rumbaugh et al. use three kinds of models to describe a system: the object model, which is a static structure of the objects in a system; the dynamic model, which describes the aspects of a system that change over time; and the functional model, which describes the data value transformations within a system. Object diagrams, state diagrams, and data flow diagrams are used to represent the three models, respectively (Rumbaugh, 1991).

In their OOA technique, Coad and Yourdon advocate the following steps: find classes and objects, identify structures and relationships, determine subjects, define attributes, and define services to determine a multilayer object-oriented model. The layers corresponds to the steps, namely: class and object layer, subject layer, structure layer, attribute layer, and service layer, respectively. Their OOD technique is both multilayer and multicomponent. The layers are the same as in analysis. The components include: problem domain, human interaction, task management, and data management.

Ivar Jacobson offers Objectory, an object-oriented software engineering method developed by Objective Systems in Sweden. Jacobson's method has a strong focus on a particular kind of scenario referred to as a "use-case." The use-cases become the basis for the analysis model, which gives way to the design model when the use-cases are formalized by interaction diagrams. The use-cases also drive the testing in a testing phase that Objectory makes explicit. Objectory is the most complete industrial method to date (Jacobson, 1992).

There are also other published OOA and OOD techniques as well as variations of the above that are not listed here. In recent years, as the methods have been evolving, there has been considerable convergence. In late 1995 Booch, Rumbaugh, and Jacobson joined forces and proposed the first draft of a Unified Method, which promises to add some welcome consensus and stability (Booch, 1995).

**Management Issues**

As organizations begin to shift to object-oriented development techniques, the management activities that support software development also necessarily have to change. A commitment to objects requires a commitment to change processes, resources, and organizational structure (Goldberg, 1995). The seamless, iterative, prototyping nature of object-oriented development eliminates traditional milestones. New milestones have to be established. Also, some of the ways in which measurements were made are less appropriate in an object-oriented context. LOC (lines of code) is definitely not helpful. Number of classes reused, inheritance depth, number of class-to-class relationships, coupling between objects, number of classes, and class size are more meaningful measurements. Most work in object-oriented metrics is relatively new, but references are beginning to surface (Lorenz, 1993).

Resource allocation needs to be reconsidered as does team organization. Smaller development teams are suggested (Booch, 1994), as is cultivation of reuse experts. Incentives should be based on reuse, not LOC. An entirely new mind set is required if reuse is to really be operative. Libraries and application frameworks have to be supported and built along with contracted application software. Long-term investment strategies are imperative as well as the processes and commitment to evolve and maintain these reuse assets.

Regarding quality assurance, typical review and testing activities are still essential, but their timing and definition must be changed. For example, a walkthrough could involve enacting a scenario of interacting objects proposed to effect some specific functionality. Testing of object-oriented systems is another area that needs to be more completely addressed. Release in terms of a steady stream of prototypes requires a flavor of configuration management that differs from that which is being used to control products generated using structured techniques.

Another management concern ought to be appropriate tool support. An object-oriented development environment is essential. Also needed are: a browser for class library, an incremental compiler, debuggers that know about class and object semantics, graphics support for design and analysis notation and reference checking, configuration management and version control tools, and a database application that functions as a class librarian. Tools are now available but need to be evaluated based upon the purpose, the organization, and the method chosen.

Estimates can also be problematic until there is object-oriented development history to substantiate proposed development estimates of resource and cost. Cost of current and future reuse must be factored into the equation. Finally, management must be aware of the risks involved in moving to an object-oriented approach. There are potential performance risks such as: cost of message passing, explosion of message passing, class encumbrance, paging behavior, dynamic allocation and destruction overhead. There are also start-up risks including: acquisition of appropriate tools, strategic and appropriate training, and development of class libraries.

## Object-Oriented Transition

There are documented success stories, but there are also implicit recommendations. The transition needs to progress through levels of absorption before assimilation into a software development organization actually occurs. This transition period can take considerable time. Training is essential. Pilot projects are recommended. Combination of structured and object-oriented approaches are not recommended. There is growing evidence that success requires a total object-oriented approach for at least the following reasons: traceability improvement, reduction in significant integration problems, improvement in conceptual integrity of process and product, minimization of need for objectification and deobjectification, and maximization of the benefits of object-orientation (Berard, 1993).

## Future

In summary, object-oriented development is a natural outgrowth of previous approaches and has great promise for software development in many application domains. Paraphrasing Maurice Wilkes in his landmark 29-year reprise of his 1967 ACM Turing Lecture, "Objects are the most exciting innovation in software since the 70s" (Wilkes, 1996). Object-oriented development is not, however, a panacea and has not yet reached maturity. The full potential of objects has not been realized. Yet while the future of object-oriented development cannot be defined, the predictions of the early 1990s (Winblad, 1990) are already materializing. Class libraries and application frameworks are becoming readily available in the marketplace. Transparent information access across applications and environments is conceivable. Environments in which users can communicate among applications and integrated object-oriented multimedia tool kits are emerging. It is likely that the movement will continue to gain in popularity and techniques will mature significantly as experience increases. It is also likely that object-orientation will eventually be replaced or absorbed into an approach that deals at an even higher level of abstraction. Of course these are just predictions. In the not too distant future, talk about objects will no doubt be passé, but for now there is much to generate genuine enthusiasm.

## References


E.V. Berard, *Essays on Object-Oriented Software Engineering*, Vol. 1, Prentice-Hall, Inc., Englewood Cliffs, N.J., 1993.

B. Boehm, "A Spiral Model of Software Development and Enhancement," in Thayer, Richard, ed., *Software Engineering Project Management*, IEEE Computer Society Press, Los Alamitos, Calif., 1988.

G. Booch and J. Rumbaugh, "Introduction to the United Method," *OOPSLA '95 Tutorial Notes*, 1995.

G. Booch, *Object-Oriented Analysis and Design With Applications*, Addison-Wesley, Reading, Mass., 1994.

G. Booch, "Object-Oriented Design," *Ada Letters*, Vol. I, No. 3, Mar.-Apr. 1982, pp. 64–76.

G. Booch, *Object-Oriented Design with Applications*, The Benjamin/ Cummings Publishing Company, Inc., Redwood City, Calif., 1991.

T. Budd, *An Introduction to Object-Oriented Programming*, Addison-Wesley Publishing Company, Inc., New York, N.Y., 1991.

P. Coad and J. Nicola, *Object-Oriented Programming*, Prentice-Hall, Inc., Englewood Cliffs, N.J., 1993.

P. Coad and E. Yourdon, *Object-Oriented Analysis*, 2nd Ed., Prentice-Hall, Inc., Englewood Cliffs, N.J., 1991.

P. Coad and E. Yourdon, *Object-Oriented Design*, Prentice-Hall, Inc., Englewood Cliffs, N.J., 1991.

B.J. Cox, *Object-Oriented Programming: An Evolutionary Approach*, Addison-Wesley, Reading, Mass., 1986.

B. Curtis, "...But You Have to Understand. This Isn't the Way We Develop Software At Our Company," MCC Technical Report No. STP-203-89, Microelectronics and Computer Technology Corporation, Austin, Texas, 1989.

M. Fowler, "A Comparison of Object-Oriented Analysis and Design Methods," *OOPSLA '95 Tutorial Notes*, 1995.

I.E. Gamma et al., *Design Patterns*, Addison-Wesley, Reading, Mass., 1995.

A. Goldberg and P. Robson, *Smalltalk-80: The Language and Its Implementation*, Addison-Wesley, Reading, Mass., 1983.

A. Goldberg and K. Rubin, *Succeeding With Objects*, Addison-Wesley, Reading, Massachusetts, 1995.

B. Henderson-Sellers and J.M. Edwards, "The Object-Oriented Systems Life Cycle," *Comm. ACM*, Sept. 1990, pp. 143–159.

I. Jacobson et al., *Object Oriented Software Engineering*, Addison-Wesley, Reading, Mass., 1992.

T. Korson and J. McGregor, "Understanding Object-Oriented: A Unifying Paradigm," *Comm. ACM*, Sept. 1990, pp. 41–60.

M. Lorenz, *Object-Oriented Software Development*, Prentice-Hall, Inc., Englewood Cliffs, N.J., 1993.

B. Meyer, *Object-Oriented Software Construction*, Prentice-Hall, Inc., Englewood Cliffs, N.J., 1988.

D. Monarchi and G. Puhr, "A Research Typology for Object-Oriented Analysis and Design, *Comm. ACM*, Sept. 1992, pp. 35–47.

R. Pressman, *Software Engineering A Practitioner's Approach*, 3rd Ed., McGraw-Hill, Inc., New York, N.Y., 1992.

J. Rumbaugh, et al., *Object-Oriented Modeling and Design*, Prentice-Hall, Inc., Englewood Cliffs, N.J., 1991.

S. Shlaer and S.J. Mellor, *Object-Oriented Systems Analysis: Modeling the World in Data*, Yourdon Press: Prentice-Hall, Englewood Cliffs, N.J., 1988.

A.L. Winblad, S.D. Edwards, and D.R. King, *Object-Oriented Software*, Addison-Wesley Publishing Company, Inc., Reading, Mass., 1990.

R. Wirfs-Brock, B. Wilkerson, and L. Wiener, *Designing Object-Oriented Software*, Prentice-Hall, Inc., Englewood Cliffs, N.J., 1990.

M. Wilkes, "Computers Then and Now—Part 2," Invited Talk, ACM Computer Science Conference, Philadelphia, Penn., 1996.

# Object-oriented systems development: survey of structured methods

A G Sutcliffe

*Concepts of object-oriented system programming and system design are reviewed in the light of previous research on systems development methodologies. Key principles are identified and a selection of system development methods is then judged against these principles to determine their concordance with object-oriented design. The advantages of object-oriented system development are reviewed in the light of the study of structured system development methods.*

*object-oriented, object-oriented systems, structured methods, systems analysis and design*

Object-oriented programming (OOP) has been the subject of several studies[1-3] that describe the principles of the object-oriented (OO) approach and their incorporation in the new generation of programming languages such as C++, Eiffel, and Smalltalk. In contrast, the object-oriented approach has received little attention in studies on system development methods. This paper aims to redress that balance and explore how OO concepts are being integrated into structured systems development methods.

Apart from the extensive interest in OOP languages, OO approaches have received some attention in office automation[4,5]. More recently, several methods have appeared claiming to be 'object-oriented' (OOSA (Object-Oriented Systems Analysis)[6], OOA (Object-Oriented Analysis)[7], and HOOD (Hierarchically Object-Oriented Design)[8]. As yet object-oriented system (OOS) development methods are not in widespread commercial practice, although interest in OO concepts continues to grow. One unanswered question is what are the essential differences between OO methods and those from the more classical 'structured camp', e.g. Structured Systems Analysis and Design Method (SSADM), Jackson System Development (JSD), and Structured Analysis/Structured Design (SA/SD). If OO methods are to become accepted, the advantages over and differences from previous methods have to be established and then the implications of migration paths from current techniques to OO methods should be made clear. This paper aims to throw some light on these questions by examining how current system development methods fit criteria for OO development.

First, OO concepts are described within the context of system development, then a selection of system development methods is reviewed.

## OBJECT-ORIENTED CONCEPTS

OO development is claimed to improve software design for reliability and maintenance. Further claims are that the development process is made more efficient by reuse. The justification for these claims rests on three principles: abstraction, encapsulation, and inheritance.

### Abstraction

OO approaches have been based on modelling structures in the real world. Programming languages that facilitate this modelling and support its implementation are said to create more maintainable and reliable systems with reusable program components[3].

Objects are an abstraction of parts of real-world systems and model composite units of structure and activity. Cook[3] points out that there are two roles that objects fulfil: an implementation role related to improving the maintainability of programs, and a modelling role, which addresses the problems of correct specification of system requirements. OOS development should emphasize the latter role, while supplying the necessary specifications to enhance maintainability in implementation.

### Encapsulation

Encapsulation is the concept that objects should hide their internal contents from other system components to improve maintainability. By making part of the design local, objects limit the volatility of change in the system. The encapsulated parts of objects are hidden to insulate them from the effects of system modifications.

### Inheritance

Objects should have generic properties, i.e., support reusability by property inheritance from superclass to subclass[3]. By organizing objects in class hierarchies, lower-level objects can receive properties from higher-level objects. This facilitates reuse of more general, higher-level objects by specialization.

Two forms of inheritance may be supported: hierarchi-

Department for Business Computing, School of Informatics, The City University, Northampton Square, London EC1V 0HB, UK

Reprinted from *Information and Software Technology,* Vol. 33, No. 6, July/Aug. 1991, A.G. Sutcliffe, "Object-Oriented Systems Development: Survey of Structured Methods," pp. 433–442, 1991, with kind permission from Elsevier Science–NL, Sara Burgerhartstraat 25; 1055 KV Amsterdam, The Netherlands.

cal, in which a child object can inherit only from its parent object, or multiple, when an object can inherit properties from several parent objects. Multiple inheritance may result in 'polymorphism', with one component having different properties in several new locations, as it is specialized in child objects.

These principles contribute to the OO model of systems, which is composed of a network of objects communicating by messages. Each object specifies both data and activity and may share properties according to a classification hierarchy. To enable comparison of methods, the basic principles of the OO approach need to be situated in a comparative framework that addresses not only OO concepts, but also more traditional models of structured methods. The ISO meta-schema (ISO TC97)[9] is taken as a starting point.

### Evaluation of modelling components

The first question to resolve is what is an object, and what is the difference between objects and more traditional concepts such as entities and functions. The starting point may be taken from the entity definition given in the ISO TC97 report[9]:

> Any concrete or abstract thing of interest including association among things.

The ISO report makes distinctions about entities on three levels:

- Entity instances — the actual occurrence of one example of an entity type.
- Entity type — a type defined by a set of common properties to which all instances belong.
- Entity class — all possible entity types for which a proposition holds, i.e., the set of instances for a particular entity type.

These definitions accord with the OO approach. Besides entities, the other system components recognised by the ISO report are propositions (i.e., rules), constraints, which specify the behaviour of entities, and events, which are defined as 'The fact that something has happened in either the universe of discourse, or the environment or in the information system'. Events are modelled as messages in the OO approach, i.e., messages communicate events to which objects respond. Objects record states, i.e., an unchanging reality altered by transitions from one state to another, and react to events by changing state[10]. Events are modelled as messages passed within a network of objects, and thereby controlling their behaviour[3,10]. Rules, however, are more problematic.

The ISO separation of entities representing data structures from rules specifying control does not match the OO concept because objects specify a composite of data and activity. In the ISO meta-model, entities are not considered to possess attributes, instead attributes are regarded as entities in their own right. This is contrary to OO approaches in which attributes are components of objects. Furthermore, the ISO view of relationships does not fit the OO conceptualization of relationships between objects being either caused by events or specified in terms of a classification hierarchy.

Object orientation, therefore, shares many of the ISO concepts, but by no means all. The main point of divergence is the separation of activity and data specification, a point that re-emerges when individual methods are considered. Within the perspective of systems development, the convergence of objects and traditional concepts may be summarized as:

- Objects are close to the entity concept, i.e., something of interest defined by a collection of attributes, although objects add activity to the entity.
- Objects are a type with one or more instances of the type, essentially the same as the entity-type concept.
- Objects instances may be changed by events in the outside world or within the system and record a state resulting from change.

Objects may have more or less activity associated with them. At one extreme are data-oriented objects, which undergo no operations other than simple updates to their attributes. In contrast, a task-oriented object may possess few data items and much complex algorithmic processing. An example of the latter is a mathematical calculation in an engineering system.

Given that objects may show variable structures and properties, a useful classification is given by Booch[10], who divides objects into actors, agents, and servers. Actors are objects that perform actions which influence other objects in the system, and have similarities with tasks and procedures; servers are the recipients of an actor's activity and are related to the database entity concept; and, finally, agents are an amalgam of both characteristics. In practice, the mix of object types within a system will reflect the application, e.g., real-time systems will have more actors, whereas data retrieval systems will have more servers.

So far the components of an OO model have been contrasted with more traditional concepts. However, conceptual models are only one facet of methods. The next section develops the comparison from modelling features into an evaluation framework.

## EVALUATION PROCEDURE

A meta-model of OO development is illustrated in Figure 1, summarizing the components of OO conceptual models, the principles of the approach, and the OO conceptualization of the development life-cycle. Methods should advise practitioners how to proceed as well as giving them the tools with which to analyse and design systems. Four dimensions are used in the evaluation framework:

- Conceptual modelling: the method should contain a means of modelling applications, and in the perspective of this study, the model should meet OO criteria.

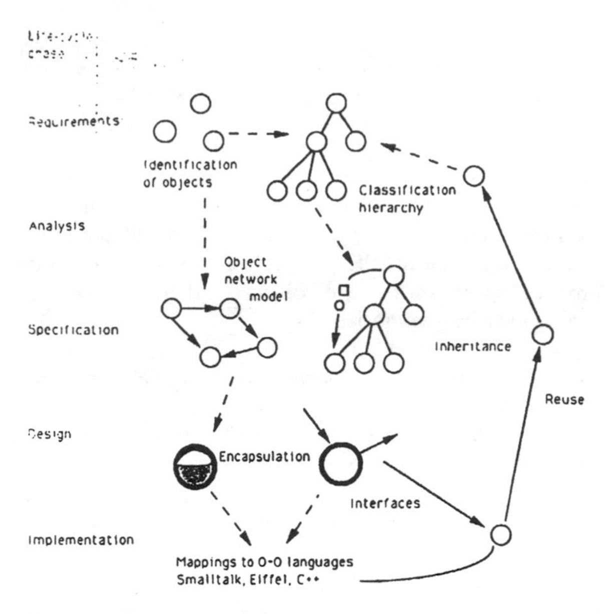


*Figure 1. Summary of object-oriented meta-model*

- Procedural guidance: a method should have clear steps telling the analyst how to conduct analysis, specification, and design.
- Transformations: methods should give heuristics, rules, and algorithms for changing specifications into designs. Ideally, these steps should be automatable.
- Design products: the results of specification and design should be clearly described, ideally delivering executable designs as code.

This schema was derived from previous studies[11] and shares many criteria with other evaluation frameworks[12]. Systems development methods may be classified into different groups that share some common approach or philosophical background[11]. Representative methods from different groups were selected for comparison against the following framework.

**Conceptual modelling**

- The data and processing control parts of a system are modelled in one unit rather than separately.
- The method produces a network system model of objects communicating by messages.
- The method explicitly models object types and instances.
- Classification of objects is supported with property inheritance.

**Procedure and guidance**

- The method should guide the analyst towards identifying and describing objects.
- Guidance should be available for analysis, specification, and design phases.

**Transformations and products**

- Design transformations should support change of OO specifications into designs implementable in OOP languages.

**Table 1. Feature analysis of object-oriented methods**

| Method | Abstraction | Classification | Inheritance | Encapsulation | Coverage (R-A-S-D-I) |
|---|---|---|---|---|---|
| HOOD | Y | Y | Partial | Y | ------ |
| OOSD | Y | Y | Y | Y | ------ |
| OOSA | Y | Partial | - | - | ----- |
| OOA | Y | Y | Y | - | ------ |
| ObjectOry | Y | Y | Y | Partial | ------- |

Key: Y = Yes.

R-A-S-D-I in coverage refers to Requirements Analysis, Analysis, Specification, Design, and Implementation. The measure of coverage is judged from the methods procedures and notations.

In the following sections, a selection of system development methods, chosen to cover diverse backgrounds from real-time to information-processing applications, is analysed to review how well they accord with OO concepts.

First, OO methods are reviewed for their support of OO principles, then traditional structured methods are surveyed in terms of their modelling perspective (data, process, or event)[12] and their potential fit to the OO approach. Selected methods are illustrated with specifications using the case study described in the Appendix. Space precludes illustration of all of the methods. Comparison of methods' specification is not the intention of this paper; instead, selected specifications are given to illuminate the differences between OO and non-OO methods.

## OBJECT-ORIENTED METHODS

The claims of OO methods can now be evaluated using the OO meta-model. Each method is evaluated in terms of its fit with OO method criteria and its coverage in terms of analysis and design.

### Hierarchical Object-Oriented Design (HOOD)[8]

As may be expected, this method scores well on OO properties (see Table 1). HOOD encourages modelling of objects explicitly, although there is little guidance for early analysis stages and structured analysis and design techniques are even recommended for the purpose. Objects are modelled in a hierarchical manner, with inheritance of properties between parent and child objects. There is strong emphasis on the object interface specification and encapsulation. A system network of objects communicating by messages is created with control by event messages. HOOD uses Booch's conception of actor and server objects.

HOOD supports object classes, but inheritance specification is not detailed and reuse support is not explicit. The method is better developed in the design phase and gives explicit transformations into Ada. Overall, HOOD incorporates many OO properties, but it is a real-time design method, consequently data specification and associated inheritance mechanisms receive less attention.

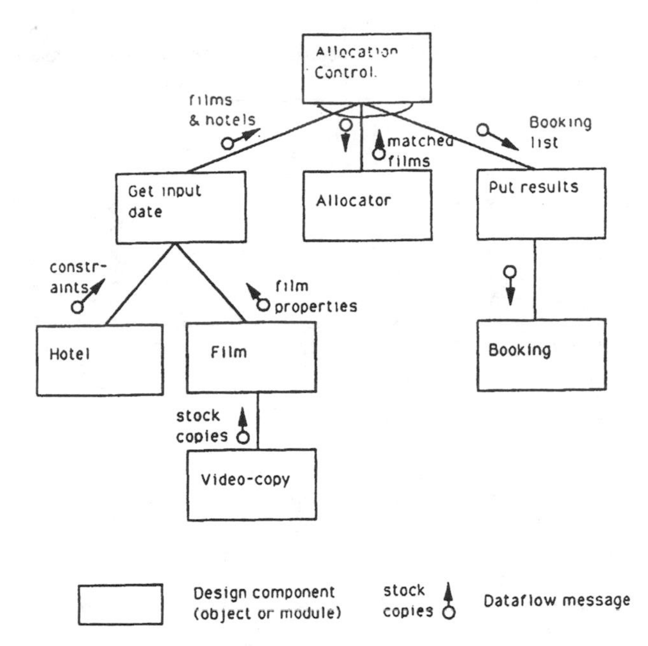


*Figure 2. Object model of VI application produced by OOSD method*

*OOSD design showing structure chart notation. Some design components are shared with other methods, e.g., objects Film, Hotel, Video-copy, and Booking. Other components have been added by OOSD method, e.g., Allocation control, Put results*

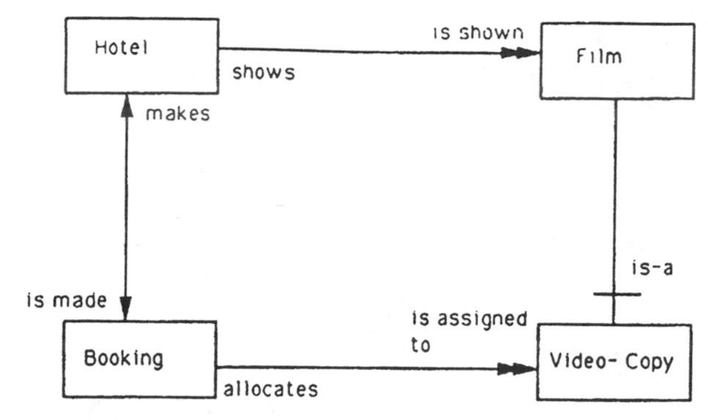


*Figure 3. Object model of VI application produced by OOSA*

*Because OOSA takes data-modelling approach, more active objects, e.g., Clerk, Allocator, are not specified in object network. This functionality would be described in dataflow diagrams*

## Object-Oriented System Design (OOSD)[13]

This method assumes that an analysis phase has identified and partially specified objects. OOSD provides a detailed notation for object classes and management of inheritance. Inter-object communication is also specified in terms of event/message types. The method supplies detailed notation for interface description and encapsulation, with local data and services. Part of an OOSD specification of the case study application is given in Figure 2. The system is modelled either as a sequentially executed hierarchy using the Yourdon structure chart notation or as an asynchronous network of processes with monitors.

No analysis advice is given, so coverage of OOSD is necessarily restricted to the design phase. The notation can become overcrowded and difficult to read.

## Object-Oriented Systems Analysis (OOSA)[6]

Shaler and Mellor's method is described with a case study prototyping approach. It gives many heuristics for object identification and analysis, which help initial abstraction and object modelling. OOSA owes its ancestry to the data-modelling approach and many of its recommendations are indistinguishable from entity-relationship modelling.

The method models an object relationship network with subclasses. State-transition specifications are constructed for each object and functions are modelled with dataflow diagrams. The object relationship model is illustrated in Figure 3. The method does produce a composite activity-data model, but this is achieved by attachment of activity to the data model, essentially merging dataflow diagrams and state-transition models with entities. The procedure for achieving this synthesis is not explicit. The main criticism of OOSA is its lack of support for inheritance. Classes are supported, but only inheritance of object properties is modelled. Inheritance of services is not considered and reuse is not explicitly supported. In addition, the method is underspecified in the design phase.

## Object-Oriented Analysis (OOA)[7]

OOA covers all OO concepts, although it is an analysis method, hence coverage of design issues is weak (see Table 1). Classification and inheritance are modelled and abstraction is helped by the structure layer, which gives an overview of object groupings for large systems. Objects are a composite data activity specification. Three links between objects are supported: relationship connections, which are modelled in the familiar data model crow's feet notation, classification hierarchies, and message passing. The resulting specification can appear overcrowded, although Coad and Yourdon separate the complexity into different layers (Subject, Structure, Attribute, Service) and build the specification incrementally. An OOA specification showing the object model in the service layer is depicted in Figure 4.

The method uses hierarchical inheritance and masking rather than multiple inheritance, and specification of encapsulation and object interfaces is not as detailed as in OOSD or HOOD. Overall, however, it does meet many OO criteria.

## ObjectOry[14]

This method supports OO concepts of classification, encapsulation, and inheritance. Abstraction is promoted by levels in design from higher-level system views to lower block and component levels. ObjectOry adds concepts of user-centred design 'uses cases' to the OO approach for specification of the user interfaces and tasks provided by object services. Use cases are specified

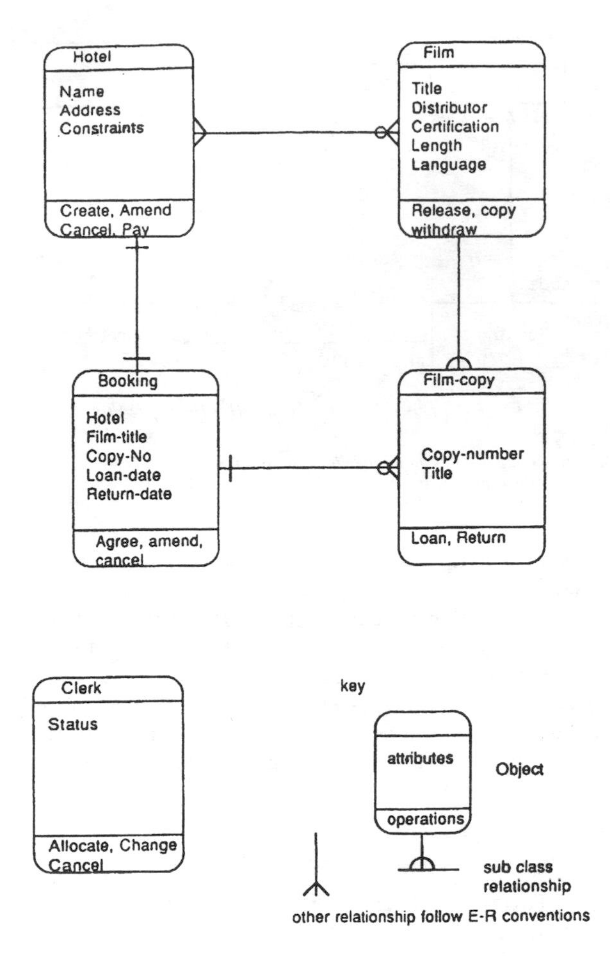


*Figure 4. Object model for VI system produced by OOA method*

with dataflow diagrams, and this functional specification is then mapped on to object services.

The composite data and activity definition of objects is not strongly enforced and services (described as processes) are also regarded as objects. Reuse is supported by component libraries, and design transformations to real-time languages are given (CHILL and Ada). Guidance for analysis is less comprehensive and the target applications of ObjectOry, like HOOD, appear to be real-time and engineering systems.

## Summary of OO methods

The coverage of OO methods is variable and not all methods meet the necessary range of criteria. HOOD and OOSD give comprehensive design notations, but are weak on prescriptive guidance. Indeed, guidance in the analysis phase is totally absent. HOOD does fulfil most OO criteria, but does not completely support property inheritance, probably because its real-time orientation does not necessitate specification of complex data structures within objects. OOSA produces an object model with fewer components as a consequence of its data-modelling heritage, whereas OOA is more likely to identify actor as well as server objects. OOA meets many OO criteria and gives procedural advice, although its coverage of the design phase is not extensive. Consequently, no complete OO method exists, although all the issues are addressed separately in different methods.

**Table 2. Summary of method specification models and approaches**

| Method | Functional process | Data relationship | Event sequence | Coverage (R-A-S-D-I) | Application |
|---|---|---|---|---|---|
| IE | Y | Y | Y | ---------- | IS |
| ISAC | Y | Y | N | ----- | IS |
| SASD | Y | N | Y | -------- | IS |
| SSADM | Y | Y | Y | ---------- | IS |
| SADT | Y | Y | N | ----- | IS, RT |
| JSD | N | Y | Y | ------------ | IS, RT |
| NIAM | Y | Y | N | -------- | IS (data intensive) |
| Mascot | Y | N | N | -------- | RT |

Key: Y = Yes, N = No.
Coverage of the life-cycle: Requirements (R), Analysis (A) Specification (S), Design (D), Implementation (I).
Application: IS = information systems, RT = real-time.

**Table 3. Summary of structured methods' object-oriented features**

| | Object model | Data + activity | Encapsulation | Types + instances | Classification |
|---|---|---|---|---|---|
| IE | Poss | N | N | Y | N |
| ISAC | Y | N | N | N | N |
| SASD | Y | N | N | N | N |
| SSADM | Y | N | N | Y | N |
| SADT | Y | N | N | N | N |
| JSD | Y | Y | Y | Y | N |
| NIAM | Poss | Poss | N | Y | Y |
| Mascot | Y | Y | Y | Y | N |

Notes:
(1) For the object model, Poss means an object model could possibly be constructed from the data model in these methods.
(2) To score Y for the object model, methods have to specify a concurrent network of message-passing processes, however these processes may be functional or data-oriented. This can be cross-checked on column two, which records whether data and processing are modelled together in an object.

## REVIEW OF OBJECT ORIENTEDNESS OF SYSTEMS DEVELOPMENT METHODS

A summary feature analysis of the methods investigated is given in Table 2. The types of model employed by methods are categorized as functional/process (typically represented by dataflow diagrams), data relationship (entity-relationship diagrams), or event (entity life histories). The feature analysis also includes the approximate life-cycle coverage of each method. For further details of method comparisons, see Loucopoulos *et al.*[11] and Olle *et al.*[12]. A summary of the OO features is illustrated in Table 3 and described in more detail in the following sections.

## Information Engineering (IE)[15]

Data modelling is an important component of IE, which encourages object modelling of the data components of a system. Functional specification uses process dependency and action diagrams, separated from data modelling, thereby discouraging common data and control specification. Cross-referencing of functions to entities is provided for and state-transition diagrams explicitly associate event-creating operations with entities, giving a partial OO specification.

Concepts of type-instance are supported; also IE encourages conceptual modelling of business processes leading towards object orientation. A data model composed of entities and relationships gives a network specification for the static part of systems, but separation during analysis of processing from data and the emphasis on functional decomposition means that IE cannot be regarded as truly object-oriented.

## Information systems activity and change analysis (ISAC)[16]

This method advocates top-down functional decomposition of processing and data in separate specifications as activity and data diagrams. Emphasis is placed on analysis of change, and processes are viewed as transforming data, which encourages a partial OO approach. Type-instance and classification concepts are not supported. Even though a network model of processes and data structures is produced, the separation of data from system control makes ISAC more functionally oriented than object-oriented.

## Structured Analysis/Structured Design (SASD)[17–19]

SASD uses top-down functional decomposition to analyse systems in terms of a network of processes connected by dataflow messages (see Figure 5). The method is based on principles of functional cohesion, which groups actions pertaining to a single goal in processing units, and coupling, which aims for low interdependence between system components. Dataflow diagrams specify the system as a network of communicating functions, which is transformed into a hierarchical design. The method does not support any OO concepts, separates data and process specification, and encourages specification of functionally based system components. More recent versions have added state-transition diagrams and bottom-up analysis driven by event identification[19]. This creates more potential for expressing OO specifications.

## Structured Systems Analysis and Design Method (SSADM)[20]

SSADM is a composite method derived from structured analysis, structured design and data analysis. Process analysis is by dataflow diagramming and separated from data analysis, which employs an entity-relationship

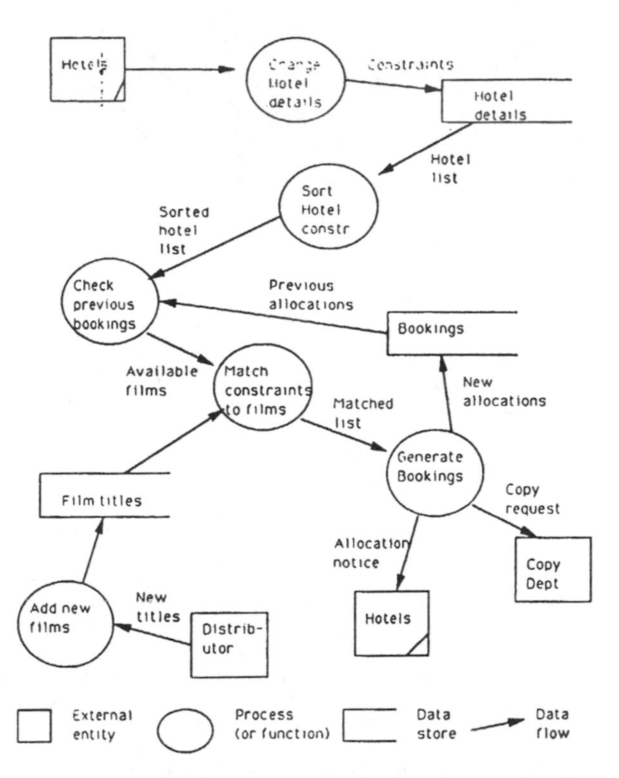


*Figure 5. Dataflow diagram specification of VI application using SSA*

approach. As with IE, data analysis encourages object orientation, but the separation of processing from data specification and use of top-down functional decomposition results in specification of functionally related processing structures. As a result most of the views expressed about IE also apply to SSADM. Entity life histories do associate processing events with data objects, but this is just one modelling view within the method. In version 4 of SSADM it forms a major theme within the overall specification and hence encourages OO specifications. Although SSADM does encourage data abstraction by conceptual modelling, functional modelling is also supported and hence it cannot be said to be truly object-oriented.

## Structured Analysis and Design Technique (SADT)[21]

SADT uses top-down decomposition to analyse systems in successively increasing levels of detail. Specification uses network diagrams of processes connected by data flows, control messages, and mechanisms. The method does encourage modelling of real-world problems, but constructs separate activity and data models using the same box and arrow notation. More emphasis is placed on activity modelling. SADT does not support type-instance concepts, although some classification is possible in the hierarchical decomposition of data. The separation of process specification from data makes this method unsuitable for an OO approach.

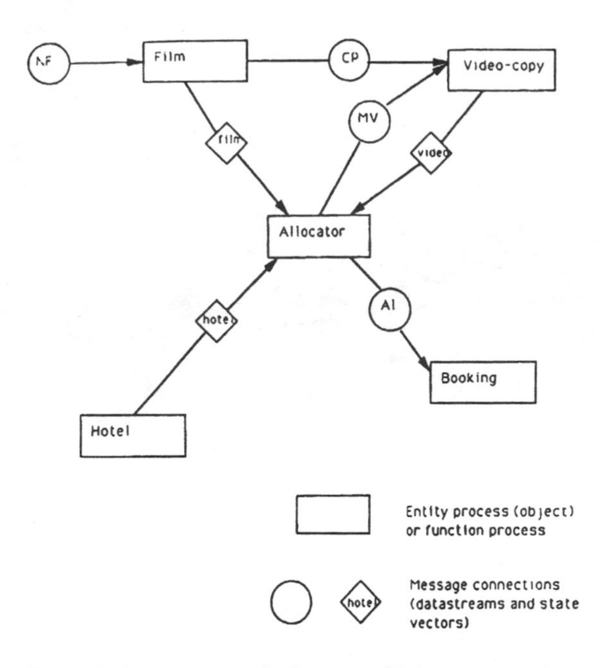


*Figure 6. System network diagram of VI system produced by JSD*

## Jackson System Development (JSD)[22,23]

JSD produces system models based on networks of concurrent communicating processes, with a type-instance concept, although classification and property inheritance is not supported. System control is modelled in terms of time-ordering of actions associated with entities, and more recent versions have placed more emphasis on data analysis, resulting in an object model that combines data and operations. A JSD system specification diagram (see Figure 6) shows a network of communicating processes similar to an object model. Because of its emphasis on an entity-life-history approach, JSD has much in common with OO methods, although it does not explicitly support all OO concepts. Even though object classification is not supported, JSD does advocate alternative views on an object, called entity roles.

## Nijssen's Information Analysis Method (NIAM)[24]

NIAM is a conceptual-modelling method that concentrates on data specification during the early parts of the analysis life-cycle. Based on the ANSI/SPARC schema, it supports data abstraction with conceptual modelling, thereby encouraging object orientation. Process analysis is by addition of semantic constraints to the data model and by specification of transactions for data input and output using a rule-based approach. Type-instance concepts are supported, as is classification by entity subtypes, so NIAM can be said to possess some OO properties, although it does not support inheritance. However, emphasis on constraint-based processing tightly coupled to relationship roles in the data model does detract from the OO approach.

## Mascot-3[25]

Mascot advocates functional decomposition of systems, however, recent versions have introduced modular concepts of encapsulation and clearly defined interfaces for system components. Mascot system specifications consist of a network of communicating processes, and hierarchical abstraction is supported. Mascot has a type-instance concept for implementing many instances of software modules from one template 'type'. However, it does not explicitly support classification of objects, although some inheritance of communication procedures between modules is provided for by the access interface. Encapsulation is encouraged by the strongly typed interface specification of modules.

Mascot gives little guidance during early analysis, and other functional methods such as structured analysis and CORE[26] are recommended. Overall, Mascot encourages the analyst to produce a functionally oriented specification because of its imprecise early stages and emphasis on functional decomposition, although its implementation does incorporate OO features.

## Summary of method evaluation

Methods using functional decomposition (e.g., SASD) encourage identification of goal-related components in systems (see Figure 5), in contrast to the OO approach (see Figures 3 and 4), which promotes system components more compatible with data models. SASD encourages specification of a hierarchy of task/procedural units that are unrelated to the objects on which the tasks act.

Although it may be argued that functions are essentially objects containing only activity, a method's viewpoint will influence modelling. An analyst trained in the functional approach will naturally identify goal-related modules using the principles of cohesion and functional decomposition[17,18]. In contrast an analyst using an OO viewpoint will identify modules that relate to a model of the real world without prejudice to processing goals. However, OO methods such as OOSD and HOOD do not encourage a specific view on object identity, so it is possible to argue that structured analysis and design modules are equivalent to actor objects in Booch's sense. Resolution of this dichotomy may depend on the fit of method and application, with real-time methods (e.g., HOOD, ObjectOry) tending towards functional, actor-type objects. For information systems, data-oriented objects may be more suitable.

Consequently for information systems, structured methods with a data-modelling heritage (e.g., IE, SSADM) are closer to the OO approach. Data modelling encourages specification of the static aspects of object structures. Unfortunately, data modelling ignores dynamic system components, and as a result these methods generally borrow functional specification for the dynamic parts of the system from methods such as structured analysis. Process specification that relies on functional decomposition will bias implementation towards functionally based structures. Another method in this group is NIAM, which emphasizes semantic data modelling, combining entities and rules in one model. In spite of this, NIAM does not explicitly attach all the system activity specified as rules to objects.

JSD views entities as being active and creates a system model explicitly based on real-world objects, combining data and control within one structure. JSD, however, does not support object classification. Instead, it advocates multiple views of an object in terms of roles that could be used to specify property sharing. Mascot cannot be regarded as truly object-oriented because it uses functional decomposition to identify modules. However, Mascot, in common with other real-time methods, does include OO concepts such as encapsulation.

In summary, current structured methods using an entity-modelling and/or entity-life-history approach have potential to evolve towards object orientation. Classification and encapsulation are supported, but separately in different methods. Inheritance is not supported, although data-oriented methods could incorporate these features, as illustrated by the evolution of OOSA and OOA.

## DISCUSSION

The first part of the discussion reviews OO concepts proposed by previous studies, followed by discussion of the object orientedness of system development methods.

### Object-oriented concepts

Objects are close relatives of abstract data types[27], which first brought specification of data structures and operations together. Objects, however, go beyond abstract data types, which emphasize control from a viewpoint of constraints on data structures, to encompass a wide range of system components. Booch[10] defines objects as entities characterized by their actions, essentially composite specifications of the active, processing and the static, data-related components of systems. Reviewers of OOP have also defined objects as being composite specifications of data and control/actions[1,3], combined with properties to enhance program maintenance and reusability of modules.

The importance of modelling systems that can respond to change is discussed by Maclennan[27], who points out that there is a dichotomy between valued-oriented and OO programming. The former being based on mathematics is concerned with unchanging definitions and alias values; object orientation, however, is about change and the tasks of recording and responding to it. Maclennan[27] develops this point to demonstrate that many current programming languages are value- rather than object-oriented.

While current programming languages rarely support OO principles, a new generation of languages has been developed to support object programming, some of which (e.g., C++, Smalltalk) have gained widespread acceptance. To reap the rewards of improved maintainability and reusability which these languages offer, system development methods need an OO approach, otherwise procedural specifications will continue to be implemented, failing to reap the advantages of OO design.

### General conclusions

Principles of OO development have been devised to tackle problems of poor specification, the lack of maintainability, and the need for software reusability. It may be argued that use of a particular system development method will not bias implementation of OO systems and that OO designs may be derived from any specification. This view is unrealistic, as demonstrated in this study by the different specifications produced by application of OO and non-OO methods. However, data model and OO specifications show considerable convergence, suggesting a feasible migration path from structured methods such as JSD, IE, and SSADM towards further object orientation.

Functionally based development methods (e.g., Structured Analysis) are less well suited to development of OO systems. If functionally based methods are used, the designer would have to map functional components on to objects, a difficult task that may require re-specification of large parts of the system. Some attempts have tried to graft functionality on to objects in an *ad hoc* manner[28], resulting in muddled specification of objects without a clear modelling basis. More recent developments have taken the entity model as the starting point for object definitions and then used dataflow design to model services, alias functionality[6,7].

The functional bias problem arises with OO real-time methods (e.g., HOOD), which either leave the analytic phase underspecified or recommend use of methods based on functional decomposition and procedural dependency (e.g., SADT[21] and CORE[26]) as front-ends for requirements analysis and early specification stages. The OOSD method[14] builds on structured design concepts and develops a notation and design procedure for object-like modules. The method, however, does not cover requirements analysis and specification. OO analysis methods offer coverage of the early life-cycle phases[6,7], by integrating object specification with dataflow diagram specification and entity-relationship analysis, although only the Coad and Yourdon method meets all the OO modelling requirements. OO analysis does not offer good coverage in early life-cycle phases, but no design transformations are included. All of these methods have yet to be proven in practice and have little computer-aided software engineering (CASE) tool support, but they do lend support to the importance of the data model in OO concepts.

Within the current generation of structured system development methods only JSD has a truly OO approach to modelling, even though it does not support classification. However, data-modelling approaches using rules applied to data structures, as found in NIAM's semantic data model, may also provide a promising way forward. The derivation of OO specification as created by the Coad and Yourdon method demonstrates that method evolution is possible and practical. Further evidence of evolution moves may be the importance attached to entity life histories, essentially Jackson techniques, in version 4 of SSADM.

Migration to object orientation, however, will largely depend on system developers being convinced of the benefits of the approach. Thorough evaluations of OO claims for improved maintainability and reuse have not been published, if they exist at all. Object models alone are unlikely to be sufficient to promote extensive reuse as none of the OO methods contains procedures or explicit modelling techniques for reusable system development. Initial studies of this problem suggest considerable problems exist in specifying generic objects[29]. Furthermore, because much information about domains is contained in the relationships between objects and in propositional statements object models alone may be insufficient for specification of applications. OO methods may need to move in the direction of semantic data modelling e.g., TAXIS[30] and CML[31], to augment the data/activity specification of objects with richer semantics. The inter-relationship between objects and system control could also present problems for OO methods, as recognised by Nierstrasz[4]. Modelling techniques to specify inter-object communication and message-passing control will have to progress beyond concepts of client-server objects as found in HOOD.

If, to paraphrase Rentsch's[1] prediction, 'object oriented systems development will be in the 1990's what structured design was in the 1970's', system development methods will have to pay more attention to OO concepts and approaches. On the other hand, proponents of the OO approach will have to demonstrate the validity of their claims by evaluation in industrial-scale applications.

## ACKNOWLEDGEMENTS

The author is grateful to colleagues at City University, Alwyn Jones and John Crinnon, for their comments and suggestions.

This work was based on research within the AMADEUS project 1229(1252), partially funded by the Esprit programme of the Commission of the European Communities.

## REFERENCES

1 **Rentsch, T** 'Object oriented programming' *SIGPLAN Notices* Vol 17 No 9 (1982) pp 51–61
2 **Cohen, A T** 'Data abstraction, data encapsulation and object oriented programming' *SIGPLAN Notices* Vol 17 No 1 (1984) pp 31–35
3 **Cook, S** 'Languages and object oriented programming' *Soft. Eng. J.* Vol 1 No 2 (1986) pp 73–80
4 **Nierstrasz, O M** 'An object-oriented system' in **Tsichritzis, D (ed)** *Office automation* Springer-Verlag (1985)
5 **Tsichritzis, D** 'Objectworld' in **Tsichritzis, D (ed)** *Office automation* Springer-Verlag (1985)
6 **Shaler, S and Mellor, S J** *Object oriented systems analysis* Yourdon Press (1988)
7 **Coad, P and Yourdon, E** *Object oriented analysis* Yourdon Press (1990)
8 **Robinson, P J (ed)** *The HOOD manual, issue 2.1* European Space Agency, Noordwijk, The Netherlands (1987)
9 **van Griethyuysen (ed)** 'Concepts and terminology for the conceptual schema and the information base, computers and information processing' *ISO/TC97/SC5/WG3* International Organization for Standardization, Geneva, Switzerland (1982)
10 **Booch, G** 'Object oriented development' *IEEE Trans. Soft. Eng.* Vol 12 No 2 (1986) pp 211–221
11 **Loucopoulos, P, Black, W J, Sutcliffe, A G and Layzell, P J** 'Towards a unified view of system development methods' *Int. J. Inf. Manage.* Vol 7 No 4 (1987) pp 205–218
12 **Olle, T W *et al.*** *A framework for the comparative evaluation of information systems methodologies* Addison-Wesley (1989)
13 **Wasserman, A, Pircher, P A and Muller, R J** 'Concepts of object oriented design' *Technical report* Interactive Development Environments, San Francisco, CA, USA (1989)
14 **Jacobsen, I** 'Object oriented development in an industrial environment' in *Proc. OOPSLA-87* ACM Press (1987) pp 183–191
15 **Macdonald, I G** 'Information engineering — an improved, automatable methodology for the design of data sharing systems' in **Olle, T W, Sol, H G and Verrijn-Stuart, A A (eds)** *Information systems design methodologies: improving the practice* North-Holland (1986)
16 **Lundeberg, M, Goldkuhl, G and Nilsson, A** *Information systems development: a systematic approach* Prentice Hall (1981)
17 **DeMarco, T** *Structured analysis and system specification* Yourdon Press (1978)
18 **Yourdon, E and Constantine, L** *Structured design* Yourdon Press (1977)
19 **Yourdon, E** *Modern systems analysis* Prentice Hall (1990)
20 **Longworth, P G and Nicholls, D** *SSADM—Structured Systems Analysis and Design Method* NCC Publications (1986)
21 **Ross, D T and Schoman, K G** 'Structured analysis for requirements definition' *IEEE Trans. Soft. Eng.* Vol 3 No 1 (1977) pp 1–65
22 **Jackson, M A** *System development* Prentice Hall (1983)
23 **Sutcliffe, A G** *Jackson System Development* Prentice Hall (1988)
24 **Nijssen, G M** *A conceptual framework for organisational aspects of future data bases* Control Data Corporation, Brussels, Belgium (1978)
25 **Simpson, H** 'The Mascot method' *Soft. Eng. J.* Vol 1 No 3 (1986) pp 103–120
26 **Mullery, G** 'CORE — a method for controlled requirements specification' in *Proc. 4th Int. Conf. Software Engineering* IEEE (1979)
27 **Maclennan, B** 'Values and objects in programming languages' *SIGPLAN Notices* Vol 17 No 12 (1982) pp 75–81
28 **Balin, S C** 'An object oriented requirements specification method' *Commun. ACM* Vol 32 No 5 (1989) pp 608–620
29 **Sutcliffe, A G** 'Towards a theory of abstraction: some investigations into the object oriented paradigm' *Technical report* City University, London, UK (1991)
30 **Greenspan, S J and Mylopoulos, J** 'A knowledge representation approach to software engineering: the TAXIS project' in *Proc. Canadian Information Processing Society* Ontario, Canada (1983) pp 163–174
31 **Jarke, M** 'DAIDA: conceptual modelling and knowledge based support for information systems development process' in *Software engineering in Esprit (Techniques et Science Informatiques)* Vol 9 No 2 Dunod-AFCET (1990)

## APPENDIX: CASE STUDY

A complete description of this case study can be obtained from the author. A summary is presented here.

Video International hires video tapes of films to hotels, who then transmit videos to guests via internal cable TV networks. Films are hired from distributors, who charge a rental fee based on the popularity of the film and the duration hired. Video International has contracts with hotels to supply a set number of films as specified by the hotel. Films are hired in blocks of one or more weeks and it is usual for hotels to offer guests a choice of four to five films. Hotels impose constraints on the type of film they wish to accept. Some hotels have a policy on non-violent films, some films may offend religious values, while other hotels accept films with specific running lengths. In addition, all hotels do not wish to be allocated the same film twice. Hotels may also change their film preferences from time to time.

The problem is to satisfy the demand for films from the available titles within constraints imposed by individual hotels. The hiring history of each hotel has to be examined to determine which films they have not received. Films are allocated to hotels and the appropriate number of copies are made for the demand. Video copies are delivered to hotels. Sometimes video tapes break and the copy has to be replaced. Records of the hotel video booking log have to be updated, showing which film copies have been allocated to each hotel for each week. Revenue is calculated from these logs, however, billing is not within the remit of the investigation.

# Structured systems analysis and design method (SSADM)

CAROLINE M ASHWORTH

*Abstract: The structured systems analysis and design method (SSADM) is the standard structured method used for computer projects in UK government departments. It is also being adopted as a standard by various other bodies. Responsibility for SSADM belongs to the Central Computer and Telecommunications Agency (CCTA), HM Treasury although support and training may be acquired through commercial organizations.*

*SSADM has certain underlying principles and consists of six stages which are broken down into a number of steps and tasks. Within this framework, a number of structured techniques are used and documents produced.*

*SSADM may be compared with methods that use some of the same techniques. Two other methods (Yourdon and Arthur Young's Information Engineering) are briefly described and some comparisons drawn with SSADM.*

*Keywords: systems analysis, methodologies, information systems, JSP, quality assurance.*

In 1980 the UK Government initiated a lengthy procedure to select a structured method to be the standard throughout all computer projects in UK government departments. Most of the better-known structured methods were considered, but the method selected was put together specifically for the purpose by UK consultancy, Learmonth and Burchett Management Systems (LBMS). This method was seen to integrate several relatively mature structured techniques (and a newer technique) into a clear procedural framework leading from the analysis of the current system through to the physical design of the new system. After an initial hand-over period, the Central Computer and Telecommunications Agency (CCTA), HM Treasury is now the design authority. It has recently applied to register SSADM as a certification trademark.

Since its introduction in 1981, the use of SSADM has grown to the extent that in 1987 more than 600 government projects are estimated to have used or are using SSADM. SSADM has also been adopted as a standard by public utilities, local government, health authorities, foreign governments and several large private sector organizations. SSADM is now widely available outside the Government. The National Computing Centre (NCC) has a collaborative agreement with the CCTA for the development and administration of SSADM and publishes the official reference manual[1]. The method is also described in a recently published book by Downs, Clare and Coe[2].

The experience from the many government projects has been channelled back into the development of the method through several mechanisms including:

- SSADM user group
- SSADM consultants from the CCTA who support projects
- private sector organizations
- NCC

The current version in use is the third since the introduction of the method. As a result of the experience in use, together with the mechanisms for using this experience in developing and enhancing the method, SSADM can claim to be one of the most mature methods in use in the UK.

SSADM was initially designed to be used in conjunction with two other UK government standards, the Prompt project management and control methodology[3] and structured design method (SDM), a version of Jackson structured programming[4]. The method also works in the context of fourth generation technology and it is now used extensively with a variety of application generators.

## BASIC PRINCIPLES

The basic principles of SSADM are shared, to a varying degree, by many of the modern structured methods of systems analysis and design. These principles underpin the whole development life cycle and should be referred to when proposing to tailor the method for specific project circumstances.

### Data-driven

All application systems have an underlying, generic data structure which changes little over time, although processing requirements may change. Within SSADM, it is a central principle that this underlying data structure is developed from an early stage, checked

Scicon Ltd, Wavendon Tower, Wavendon, Milton Keynes, Bucks MK17 8LX, UK

Reprinted from *Information and Software Technology,* Vol. 30, No. 3, Apr. 1988, C. Ashworth, "Structured System Analysis and Design Method (SSADM)," pp. 153–163, 1988, with kind permission from Elsevier Science–NL, Sara Burgerhartstraat 25; 1055 KV Amsterdam, The Netherlands.

against the processing and reporting requirements and finally built into the system's architecture.

### Differentiation between logical and physical

SSADM separates logical design from physical design. A hardware/software independent logical design is produced which can be translated into an initial physical design. This helps the developers to address one problem at a time and prevents unnecessary constraints being added at too early a stage in development. This also helps communication with users who may not be computer literate but are able to validate a logical specification or design of their system.

### Different views of the system

Three different views of the system are developed in analysis. These views are closely related to one another and are cross-checked for consistency and completeness. The equal weight given to these three techniques and the prescriptive procedures for checking them against one another is a strength of the SSADM approach. The views are:

- underlying structure of the system's data (the logical data structure),
- how data flows into and out of the system and is transformed within the system (data flow diagrams),
- how the system data is changed by events over time (entity life histories).

### Top-down and bottom-up

SSADM contains elements of both top-down and bottom-up approaches. In the early stages of a project, top-down techniques such as data flow diagramming and logical data structuring are used. In the logical design stage bottom-up techniques such as relational data analysis are used to provide more of the detail and then reconciled with the top-down views to produce a validated logical design.

### User involvement

It is considered important that end users have involvement in, and commitment to, the development of the system from an early stage. By ensuring that the specification and design match the user's requirements at each stage, the risk of producing the 'wrong' system is reduced and the possible problems can be solved before they become unmanageable.

User involvement is encouraged by the use of easily understood, non-technical diagrammatic techniques supported by short, simple narrative descriptions. Users participate in formal quality assurance reviews and informal 'walkthroughs' and should 'sign off' each stage before the developers progress to the next.

As the techniques of SSADM do not require skill in computer systems, it has been found that an ideal situation is one in which a user representative works full-time within the development team. This provides a constant supply of knowledge about the system and provides a bridge between the developers and users.

### Quality assurance

The use of informal quality assurance reviews and walkthroughs is encouraged throughout the method. Formal quality assurance reviews are held at the end of each SSADM stage. The end products for the stage are scrutinized for quality, completeness, consistency and applicability by users, developers and experienced systems staff external to the project. Each stage can therefore be signed off to act as a baseline for the subsequent stage.

### Self documenting

The products of each SSADM step form the project documentation and are used in subsequent steps. It becomes important that the documentation is completed at the relevant time within the project instead of being left until the project is complete, as often happens when timescales are short. This ensures that the documentation is up-to-date at all times.

## OVERVIEW OF SSADM

The structured techniques fit into a framework of steps and stages, each with defined inputs and outputs. Also, there are a number of forms and documents that are specified which add information to that held within the diagrams. Thus, SSADM consists of three features of equal importance:

- structure of the method,
- structured techniques and their interrelationship,
- documents and forms produced.

### Structure of the method

Figure 1 shows the stages of an SSADM project. Each stage is broken down into a number of steps which define inputs, outputs and tasks to be performed. The products of each step and the interfaces between steps are clearly defined in the SSADM documentation[1].

The structure of the method illustrates several features of the SSADM approach. First, the current system, in its current implementation, is studied to gain an understanding of the environment of the new system. This view of the current system is used to build the specification of the required system. However, the required system is not constrained by the way in which the current system is implemented. The specification of requirements is detailed to the extent that detailed technical options can be formulated. The detailed design is completed at the logical level before implementation issues are addressed. Finally, the logical design is converted into physical design by the

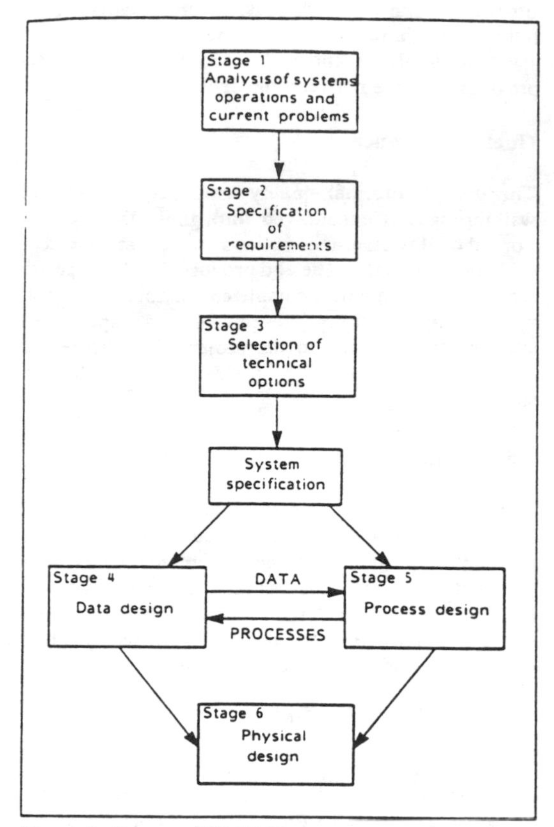


*Figure 1. Stages of SSADM*

application of simple (first cut) rules. The resulting design is tuned using the technique of physical design control before implementation. The breakdown of each stage into constituent steps is shown at annex A at the end of this paper.

### *Stage one: Analysis system operation and current problems*

The current system is investigated for several reasons, for example, the analysts learn the terminology and function of the users' environment. The data required by the system can be investigated. The current system provides the users with a good introduction to the techniques and the boundaries of the investigation can be clearly set.

The second reason illustrates one of the principles of SSADM that the underlying structure of the data of a system will not change much over time. Even though the introduction of a new computer system may change the functions (a computer system can increase what can be tackled by users), the underlying data required to perform the functions will not change much. If there is no current system, for example where there is a new law that requires support, this stage consists of initiating the project and beginning to document the new requirements.

### *Stage two: Specification of requirements*

In order that the new system will not be constrained by the current implementation, there are a number of steps within this stage to gradually lead the analysts away from the current system towards a fresh view of the requirements.

First, the current system view built up in stage one is redrawn to extract what the system does without any indication of how this is achieved. The resulting picture is the logical view of the current system. This allows the analyst to concentrate on what functions are performed in the current system and to make decisions about what must be included in the new system.

The current system is surpassed by the business system options (BSOs) which are completed next. The BSOs express the requirements in a number of different ways to reflect the different ways in which the system might be organized. These are not implementation decisions, although they may constrain the way the system is implemented. Instead, this is a way of taking a fresh view of what the system is required to do and how the business can be organized to make the best use of the system. Based upon the selected business system option, a detailed specification of the required system is built up and checked extensively.

### *Stage three: Selection of technical options*

At this stage, if the purchase of new computer equipment is required, the development team have enough information to compile the different implementation options for the system. Each option costed out and the benefits weighed against the costs to help the user choose the final solution. This might form the basis for competitive tendering for the final system hardware.

### *Stage four: Logical data design*

This stage builds up the logical data design so that all the required data will be included. It applies a relational analysis technique to groups of data items in the system to act as a cross-check on the data definition built up in stage two. The final data design is checked against the logical processes, developed in stage five, to ensure that all the data needed by the processes is present in the data design.

### *Stage five: Logical process design*

The definition developed in stage two is expanded to a low level of detail so that the implementor can be given the detail necessary to build the system. This processing definition is checked against the data definitions derived in stage four.

### *Stage six: Physical design*

The complete logical design, both data and processing, is converted into a design that will run on the target environment. The initial physical design is tuned on paper before being implemented so that it will meet the performance requirements of the system. In this stage, much of the documentation required during the system implementation is produced. The implementation of the system takes place, traditionally, after this stage when the detailed program specifications are used as the basis for program design and coding, possibly using a program design method such as Jackson structured programming[4].

## Structured techniques

The techniques of SSADM give standards for how each step and task is to be performed. The rules of the syntax and notation of each technique are supplemented with guidelines on how it should be applied in a particular step. The diagrammatic techniques of SSADM are data flow diagrams, logical data structuring, entity life histories and logical dialogue design. In addition, there are techniques and procedures that are not diagrammatic including:

- relational data analysis (TNF)
- first cut rules
- physical design control
- quality assurance reviewing
- project estimating

The SSADM reference material gives clear guidelines on each of the techniques and, more importantly, shows how they are interrelated and can be used to cross-check one another. The principal diagrammatic techniques and procedures are described in more detail below.

### *a. Logical data structure (LDS)*

This is a method for describing what information should be held by the system. The approach used in SSADM is similar to entity modelling in other methods. A diagram is produced showing the entities and their relationships, this is further documented by a set of entity description forms detailing their data contents.

A logical data structure (LDS) is produced for the current system. This is extended to meet the requirements of the new system, resulting in a required system LDS. This LDS becomes the composite logical data design (CLDD) by comparison with the results of relational data analysis. The CLDD is used as the basis for the physical data design.

The major conventions of LDSs are summarized in Figure 2. These conventions are the same for the CLDD.

An entity can be thought of as either a 'thing' of significance to the system about which information will be held or a group of related data items that can be uniquely identified by a key. Which view predominates is influenced by the way in which the logical data structures are built up within SSADM; the former view is adopted when starting the whole process in Stage one and gradually the latter view is adopted so that by the time the composite logical data design is completed, the structure is thought of as 'system data'.

A relationship is a logical association between two entities. Within SSADM, only one-to-many relationships are permitted (one-to-one relationships are resolved by merging the entities and many-to-many relationships are resolved by inserting a 'link' entity). The 'crow's foot' indicates the 'many' end of the relationship. The relationships are validated by checking the assertions that, for example, an instance of 'overdrawn status' is related to many instances of 'customer' and that an instance of 'customer' will always be related to one, and only one, instance of 'overdrawn status'. If it is possible that 'customer' could exist without 'overdrawn status', then this relationship becomes optional, indicated by a small circle on the relationship. In Figure 2 the exclusive notation for relationships is illustrated, showing that instances of the two relationships to 'personal customer' and 'company' will never exist concurrently for the same 'bank account' entity.

### *b. Data flow diagrams (DFDs)*

A data flow diagram[5, 10] is a diagrammatic representation of the information flows within a system, showing how information enters and leaves the system; what changes the information; and where information is stored. Data flow diagrams are an important technique of systems analysis as a means of *boundary definition*. The diagrams clearly show the boundaries and scope of the system being represented. They also *check the completeness of analysis*. The construction of the diagrams, and their cross-comparison with the other major SSADM techniques, help ensure that all information flows, stores of information and activities within the system have been considered. DFDs denote the major functional areas of the system, and therefore the programs or program suites required. They may be

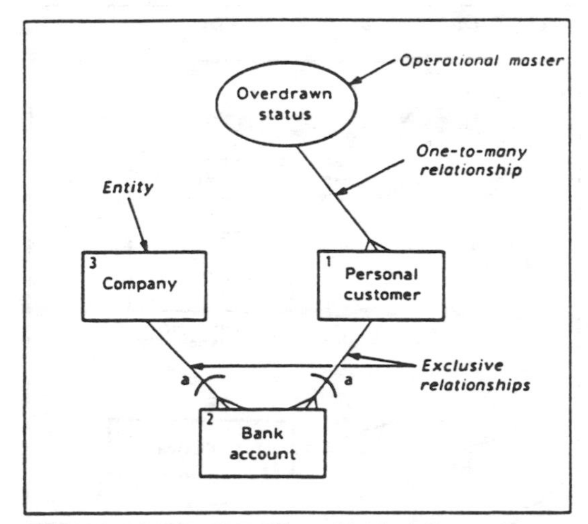


*Figure 2. Major conventions of logical data structures*

used to represent a physical system or a logical abstraction of a system.

In SSADM four sets of data flow diagrams are developed. First, the current physical. The current system is modelled in its present implementation. Second, the logical. The purely logical representation of the current system is extracted from the current physical DFDs. Third, the business system options. Several proposed designs are developed, each satisfying the requirements of the new system. Each of these is expressed as an overview, known as a business system option. Fourth, using the selected business system option and the logical data flow diagrams, a full set of data flow diagrams representing the new system is developed. The relationship between the different sets of data flow diagrams is represnted in Figure 3. The conventions of DFDs are illustrated in Figure 4.

External entities are sources or recipients of data, processes transform the data within the system and data stores are repositories of information. Data stores are closely related to entities on the logical data structure.

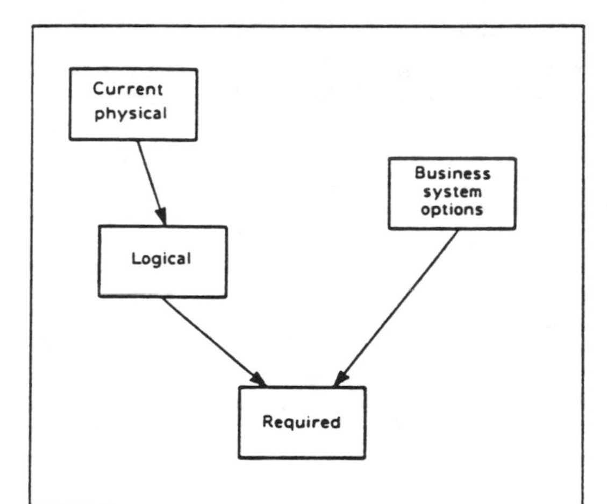


*Figure 3. Data flow diagrams in SSADM*

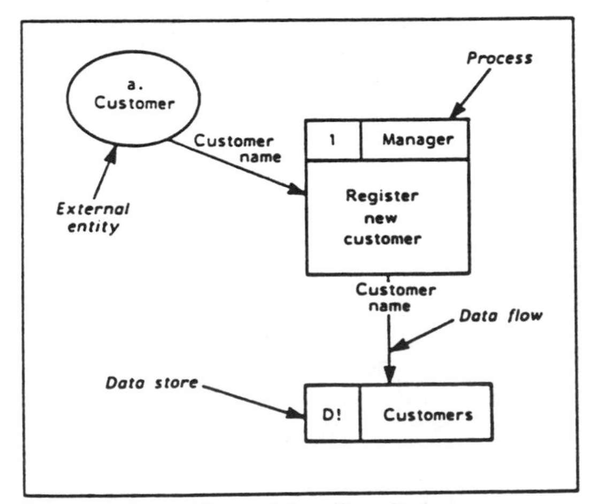


*Figure 4. Conventions of data flow diagrams*

Each process can be decomposed into a lower level data flow diagram, successively adding detail through each level.

### c. Entity life histories (ELHs)

These are models of how the system's data is changed over time by events acting on entities. For each entity the sequence, selection and iteration of events affecting it are shown using a notation derived from Jackson[4].

An event is whatever triggers a process to update system data. As it would be too complicated to model the entire set of events for a whole system at once, the effects of the events upon each entity from the logical data structure are modelled. These individual views of the event sequences are drawn together in an entity/event matrix (ELH matrix) and process outlines. The major conventions of the entity life history technique are shown in Figure 5. The state indicators are a re-expression of the structure of the entity life history and may be used in validation in the implemented system.

### d. Logical dialogue outlines

Logical dialogue outlines were introduced in version three of SSADM to allow developers to specify requirements for man-machine dialogues at an early stage in the development. The prototyping of dialogues using a screen painter, or similar rapid development software, to demonstrate the man-machine interface to users is obviously more effective in the specification of user requirements for dialogues, so dialogue outlines are designed to be used generally where prototyping

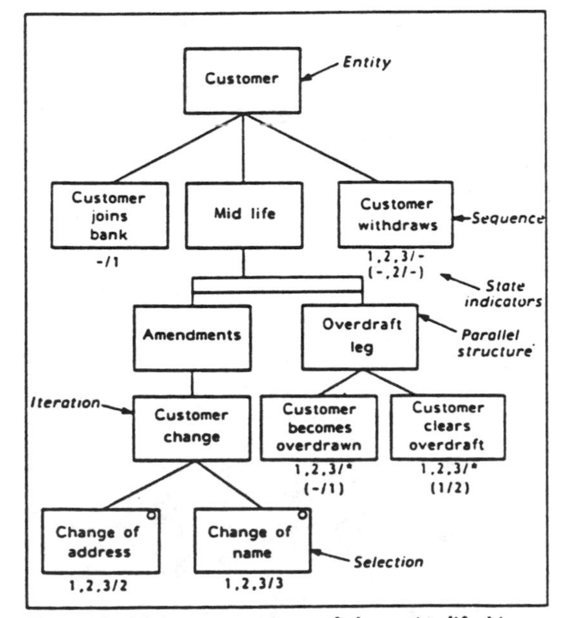


*Figure 5. Major conventions of the entity life history technique*

facilities are not available. A logical dialogue outline is produced for each non-trivial online event or enquiry identified during analysis. Thus, this technique is used towards the end of requirements definition in stage two. The data items flowing across the man-machine boundary are detailed, the sequence of logical 'screens' and an overview of the processing done to satisfy the dialogue are modelled using a flow-chart style notation. It is also possible to add the requirements for the time taken at each stage of the dialogue, points at which users will be required to make decisions, an indication of some messages that might be used and a cross-reference to operations on process outlines. An extract from a simple logical dialogue outline is shown in Figure 6. It is possible to create 'levels' by reflecting the context of one or more logical dialogue outlines on a higher-level outline called a logical dialogue control.

### e. Relational data analysis (TNF)

Relational data analysis, based upon Codd's aproach[6], is used in the logical design stage of SSADM (Stage four) where it complements the logical data structuring done during requirements analysis. The merging of the two techniques results in the composite logical data design (CLDD) which is the basis for the physical database or file design.

Any collection of data items that have been defined without direct reference to the logical data structure can be used as an input to relational data analysis or normalization. Commonly, the input/output descriptions or screen definitions are used as inputs to this technique.

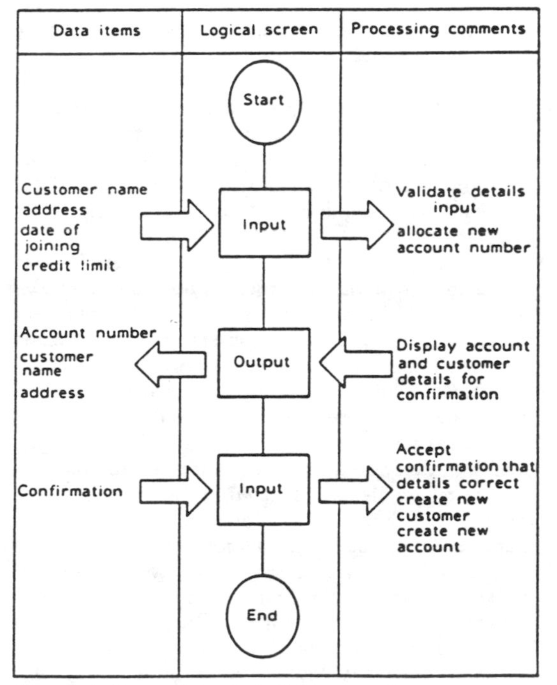


*Figure 6. Example logical dialogue outline*

Normalization consists of a progression from the original, unnormalized, data through several refinements (normal forms) until the data items are arranged to eliminate any repeating items or duplication. The results of performing this analysis on several different groups of data items are merged or optimized to give sets of data items that should correspond to the entities on the logical data structure. At this point, the logical data structure is merged with the results of the normalization.

The process of relational data analysis ensures that all data items required by the system are included in the system's data structure. Also, it is a good way to ensure that the data is fully understood. Although the rules of normalization appear to be mechanical, to apply them effectively the underlying relationships between data items must be well understood.

### f. First cut rules and physical design control

The conversion of the logical process and data design into a workable physical design takes place in two phases. First, simple rules are applied which roughly convert the logical design into a corresponding design for the target environment. This design might work, but would probably not be efficient or exploit the features of the particular hardware or software that will be used. Therefore, the 'first cut' design is tuned using a process called physical design control. This consists of successively calculating the time taken to execute certain critical transactions, modifying the design slightly and recalculating until the performance objectives (defined in stage three) are met.

### g. Quality assurance reviewing

SSADM places emphasis on holding formal quality assurance reviews at the end of each stage. It is important to ensure that the products from each stage are technically correct and that they meet the objectives of the users. The work for the second stage of SSADM has its foundations in the work done in the first stage. This principle applies throughout the project: each stage builds on the work done in the previous stage. There is a high risk that all subsequent work will be poor if the foundations are poor.

A formal sign-off by a group consisting principally of users emphasizes the joint responsibility for the project of both the users and the project team. This ensures the ongoing active interest of the users in the project and avoids the situation commonly encountered in systems analysis and design where communication between the project team and the users is minimal during the development phase leading to the implemented system not meeting the users' requirements.

Products from each stage should be reviewed by a team comprising responsible users who will have the authority to authorize the continuation of the project and at least one person with a good understanding of SSADM who will be referred to here as the 'technical reviewer'. This should be done on a formal basis to force the correction of errors identified by the reviewers before work is allowed to proceed to the subsequent stages.

The following procedures are an example of how quality assurance reviewing is undertaken within SSADM.

**Before the review**

All participants receive an invitation to the review meeting one week in advance of the meeting, together with a copy of all the documents they will be required to review. If any of the reviewers is unfamiliar with the conventions of the diagrams, then the analysts might arrange to explain the aspects of the diagrams that are relevant to a reviewer. This can be done on a one-to-one basis but can be achieved more efficiently when a number of people are involved. This is done by organizing a presentation to state the purpose and basic conventions of the diagrams with a more general discussion about quality assurance review procedures.

**The review meeting**

The actual review would not be more than one to two hours long. The chairman is either a user who has been closely involved with the project or the project team manager. The meeting should not attempt to solve the difficulties that might arise but should highlight errors for subsequent resolution away from the meeting. An analyst from the project team walks through the documentation being reviewed and invites comments from the reviewers. A list of errors is compiled by the chairman and agreed by the meeting. The reviewers may decide that the documentation contains no errors and meets its objectives in which case will sign the stage off at this meeting. More commonly, there will be a number of non-critical errors detected in which case the documentation may be signed off provided that certain follow-up action is taken and subsequently agreed by the reviewers out of the meeting. If there are numerous errors and the reviewers are not confident that the project team has met the objectives of the stage, then a date for another quality assurance review is set and the documentation failed.

**After the review**

Any necessary corrections are made to the documentation within a week of the review and circulated to the members of the review team. If the errors are only minor, the reviewers may sign it off individually. If the errors are more severe, the documentation is reviewed a second time at another review meeting.

The resources required to hold a quality assurance review are significant and should not be underestimated when the project plan is being prepared. At least three elaspsed weeks should be allowed for each formal review and one to two weeks for informal reviews. It is a temptation to cut this time when project timescales are tight. But compared to the weeks or months that might be wasted later in the project on trying to sort out compounded errors arising from poor quality assurance, it is time well spent.

*h. Project estimating*

Project estimating guidelines have been developed from experience and may be made available to project managers. They are based upon the techniques, steps and stages of SSADM. Certain factors will make timescales longer or shorter, for example the number of user areas and the complexity of the project. The estimating guidelines are applied after an initial data flow diagram and logical data structure have been drawn. The number of processes and entities on these initial diagrams give an indication of the number of diagrams that will be completed throughout the project. The results of the estimating guidelines are refined throughout the project. The estimates produced at the beginning of a project will not be accurate but will give some idea of the order of magnitude of a project.

## Documents and forms

Documentation standards define how the products of this development activity should be presented. The forms are either supporting detail of the techniques or additional non-diagrammatic information. In the former category are entity descriptions and elementary function descriptions; in the latter category are the problems/requirements list and function catalogues.

In addition to forms, there are several working documents, principally matrices, which are used to help the start-up to some of the techniques. An entity matrix is used to identify relationships between entities as an initial step in the logical data structuring techniques and an entity-event (ELH) matrix is used as a basis for entity life histories.

One of the most central documents in the analysis stages of SSADM is the problem/requirement list. It is used as a checklist of all the factors that must be accounted for in the new system and can be used to measure the success of a project by checking that all the problems and requirements have a corresponding solution.

It is tempting for the analyst to accept a user requirement written by the users without any additional analysis work. Experience has shown that a statement of requirements produced by users will often include detail such as 'I need a terminal linked to a central mainframe' rather than 'I need my data to be up-to-date at all times and I will need to be able to access the data during the hours of nine to five'. It is the analyst's responsibility to make sure that the requirements and problems are stated in logical terms. It is important to have this logical statement of requirements so that the final solution does not become constrained. It must be left to the systems analyst/designer to specify the best solution to fit the users requirements not allowing the user's preconceptions to be carried through to an ill-judged implementation.

The problem/requirement list is initiated in stage one, the survey of the current system. During the analysis of requirements, the problem/requirement list is expanded to include design constraints and requirements for the system auditing, controls and security.

## AUTOMATED SUPPORT FOR SSADM

One of the principle features required of the method chosen to become SSADM was that it was designed to be supported by automated support tools. A simple database tool was introduced by the CCTA soon after the introduction of the method to act as a prototype for future support tools. From experience of the use of this tool together with other tools, such as CAD and word-processing software, it was possible to define the desirable features of a software tool to support SSADM. Some of these features are summarized here, in no particular sequence:

- automatic production of documentation,
- assistance in creating and amending SSADM diagrams,
- enforcement of diagram syntax,
- enforcement and help with the rules of the method,
- consistency and completeness checking,
- traceability of specification through to logical and physical design,
- automatic generation of elements of the design,
- presentation of the information in different formats and combinations,
- integration of diagram information with data dictionary information.

There are several software tools to support SSADM and there is a growing number of other tools that can be used to support aspects of SSADM. These other tools are either designed to support other similar methods or are tailorable to a number of different methods including SSADM. They provide varying support to such techniques as data flow diagramming, entity modelling, functional decomposition, relational data analysis, action diagramming and database design. Some provide generation of database definitions and program code. These tools are generally single user, running on IBM PC/AT or compatible hardware, although some multiuser tools are becoming available.

## TRENDS IN DEVELOPMENT

Developments in the area of SSADM are driven principally by user experience (ease of use) and the need for automation. Advanced state-of-the-art ideas must also always be considered to ensure better techniques are not ignored. The whole method must remain consistent through any changes made and, being a government standard method, fit in with other standards that have been set.

### User experience

Some SSADM projects often develop their own interpretation of the ways in which techniques can be used successfully in their particular environment. Occasionally, these local practices can have wider applicability and developers of SSADM have been keen to introduce well-tried new ideas that have been shown to be beneficial in practice. As well as developing new practices, projects have introduced new forms or pointed out gaps in the method where inadequacies have become apparent.

It is important to take this type of experience into account because it is wasteful for different projects to start again from the beginning when an improvement is required. The benefits of standardization should not be diluted by too many local variants.

An example of a development introduced as a result of user experience is the logical dialogue design element of SSADM. Several different projects perceived a need to be able to model human-computer interactions in the analysis stage of the method and were inventing their own approaches. The experiences gained as a result of this were integrated into SSADM after several pilot uses of the techniques in projects.

### The need for automation

It is generally considered to be a fact that methods will become more automated as the technology of software tools increases. The trend towards automation will determine the competitiveness of methods in the future. Methods will be determined by the tools available to support them. Eventually, the method and tool will become synonymous and the manual structured methods will fall into disuse. This means that the development of SSADM must always take into account whether particular ideas will be readily automated or whether they will make automation more difficult. This consideration is often in direct opposition to the wish to enhance the usability of the manual method as it stands currently. If a technique has strict rules of syntax associated with it, the manual use of it will seem arduous; however, a software tool needs to have a large number of such rules defined in order to give the best possible support for the technique.

As a move towards automation, the CCTA commissioned a detailed entity model of SSADM. The production of this model meant that many definitions had to be made tighter and rules had to take the place of guidelines.

## COMPARISON WITH OTHER METHODS

SSADM is most readily compared with other methods that employ data flow diagrams as a major technique of analysis and design. These include the Yourdon method[7] and Arthur Young's information engineering method[8]. A brief overview of these methods and a comparison with SSADM follow.

## Yourdon method

The Yourdon method is based upon the approach of DeMarco[5]. Data flow diagrams are used to build a number of models of the system required. A logical (essential) view of the required system is developed supported by an entity-relationship diagram, a data dictionary and process descriptions. An implementation-dependent view (implementation model) is developed from the logical diagram by assigning processes to processors and showing how the system will be organized. The data flow diagrams are developed down to a low level of detail. The bottom-level processes that constitute a program or module are drawn together into a program structure which becomes the program design. In addition, certain extensions have been added to the basic notation to cope with realtime control aspects of systems. A controlling process which enables, disables and triggers the transformation processes may be represented by state transition diagrams which form the basis for design. The entity-relationship diagrams are used as the basis for database design.

The main different between the Yourdon method and SSADM is that there is no structure of steps, stages and deliverables and detailed task lists defined in the Yourdon method. A sequence is implied by the way in which each model is developed but it is left to the developer to build project management and review procedures around the techniques.

Another difference is in the approach to process design. In the Yourdon method, the design is derived through successive decomposition of the data flow diagrams. Each bottom-level process is described by a detailed process description or mini-spec. In SSADM, the data flow diagrams are used mostly in the requirements specification; the process definition is taken through to design using the events identified from entity life histories: each event is expanded by a process outline which is subsequently converted into a program specification.

SSADM emphasizes the fact that three different views of the system are developed and compared in analysis whereas the principal technique that is used throughout the Yourdon method is data flow diagramming. The entity-relationship diagram developed in the Yourdon method is not given as much emphasis as the data flow diagrams. The Yourdon data dictionary is defined in terms of the contents of data flows and data stores whereas in SSADM the data is defined with reference to the logical data structure.

## Arthur Young information engineering method (AY-IEM)

Arthur Young information engineering method (AY-IEM)[8] is based upon the concepts described by James Martin[9]. Within this basic framework, Arthur Young have developed a detailed method which requires the use of their software tool, information engineering workbench (IEW), to implement the concepts fully.

The method consists of a number of steps and stages leading from strategy to construction. Emphasis is placed upon the data model as the foundation for good system design. The data model developed is similar to the logical data structure of SSADM. Data flow diagrams are fully integrated with the data model. The data flow diagrams are also cross-referenced to a function decomposition diagram which effectively summarizes the hierarchy of processes within the data flow diagrams. The detail of processing is defined in terms of action diagrams.

Both AY information engineering and SSADM contain steps and stages. SSADM has detailed task lists with define inputs, outputs and activities whereas AY information engineering concentrates upon stressing the aims and objectives of each step and stage, leaving more freedom to choose the most appropriate way of achieving the objectives. Information engineering concentrates more upon providing a set of techniques and tools, together with a project framework and allowing the developer to decide upon the best way of combining them to meet the objectives. This means that there are no specified inputs and outputs of steps and no forms to fill in. The central database, or encyclopoedia, of the tools contains all the necessary information to support the developer.

Other differences between the two methods include the fact that SSADM uses a third view in analysis provided by the entity life history technique and information engineering has action diagrams and structure charts to define the structure of the processes.

## CONCLUSION

SSADM has been used in a large number of projects principally in the area of government data processing systems. Several of the larger projects are now live and their implementation was considered to be a success. Experience shows that the method has improved the quality of systems analysis and design. The role of a central group in introducing, promoting, controlling and supporting SSADM has been a major contributor in ensuring its success.

## References


1 **Longworth, G and Nichols, D** *The SSADM Manual* National Computer Centre, Manchester, UK (1987)

2 **Downs, Clare and Coe** *Structured Systems Analysis and Design Method – Application and Context* Prentice-Hall, (1988)

3 **Yeates, D** *Systems Project Management* Pitman Publishing Ltd, London, UK (1986)

4 **Jackson, M A** *Principles of Program Design* Academic Press, London, UK (1975)

5 **DeMarco, T** *Structured Analysis and System Specification* Prentice-Hall, Englewood Cliffs, NJ, USA (1979)

6 **Codd, E R** 'A relational model of data for large shared data banks' *Commun. ACM* Vol 13 No 6 (June 1970) pp 377–387

7 *Yourdon Method.* Yourdon Europe, 15–17 Ridgmount Street London WC1 7BH, UK

8 *Arthur Young Information Engineering Method,* Arthur Young, Rolls House, 7 Rolls Buildings, Fetter Lane, London EC4A 1NH, UK

9 **Martin, J** 'Information Engineering' Savant Research Studies, 2 New Street, Carnforth, Lancs LA5 9BX, UK (1986)

10 **Gane, C and Sarson, T** *Structured Systems Analysis: Tools and Techniques* Prentice-Hall Englewood Cliffs, NJ, USA (1979)

□

## Annex A

*Stage 1*

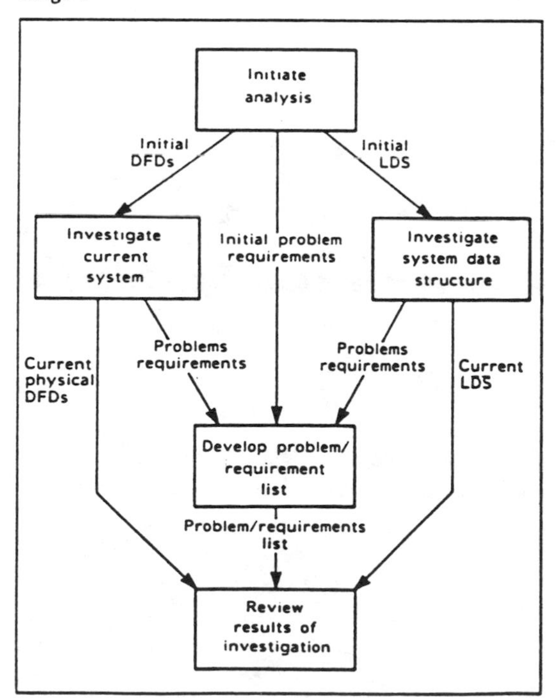


*Stage 2*

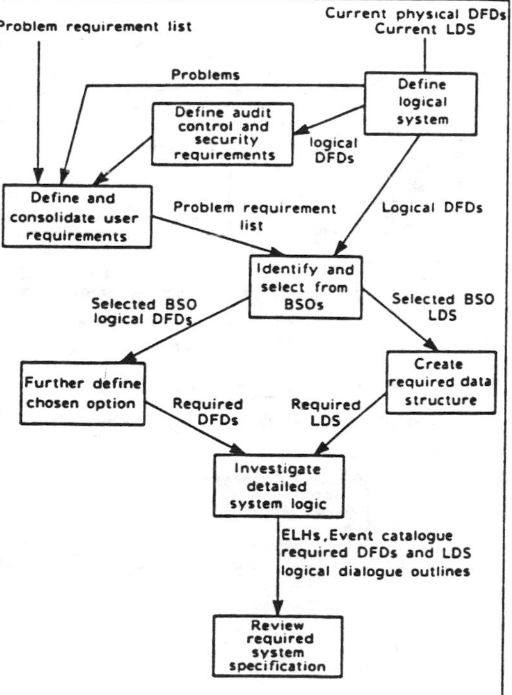

*Stage 3*

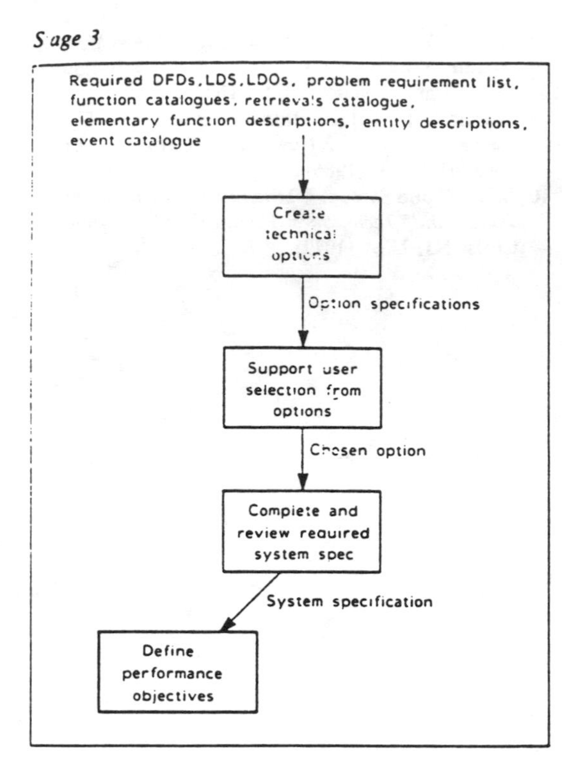

Required DFDs, LDS, LDOs, problem requirement list, function catalogues, retrievals catalogue, elementary function descriptions, entity descriptions, event catalogue
Create technical options
Option specifications
Support user selection from options
Chosen option
Complete and review required system spec
System specification
Define performance objectives

*Stage 6*

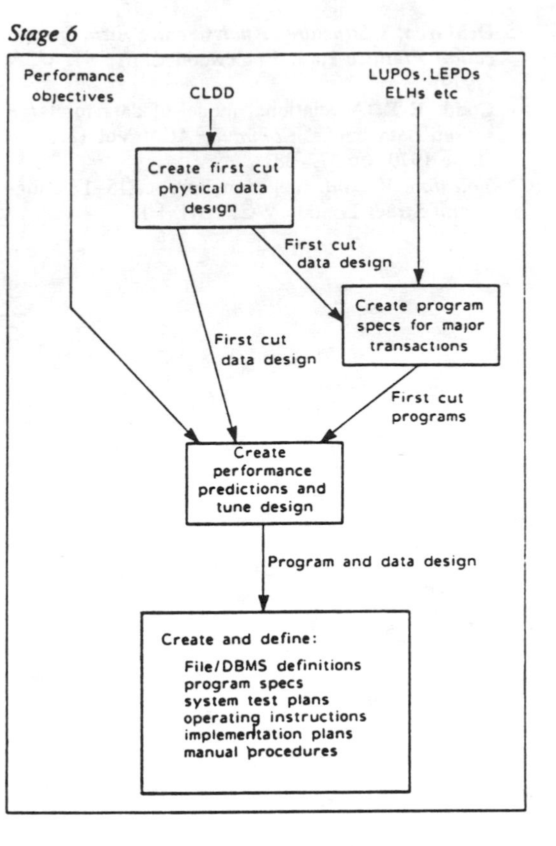

Performance objectives
CLDD
LUPOs, LEPDs ELHs etc
Create first cut physical data design
First cut data design
Create program specs for major transactions
First cut data design
First cut programs
Create performance predictions and tune design
Program and data design
Create and define:
File/DBMS definitions
program specs
system test plans
operating instructions
implementation plans
manual procedures

*Stage 4*

*Stage 5*

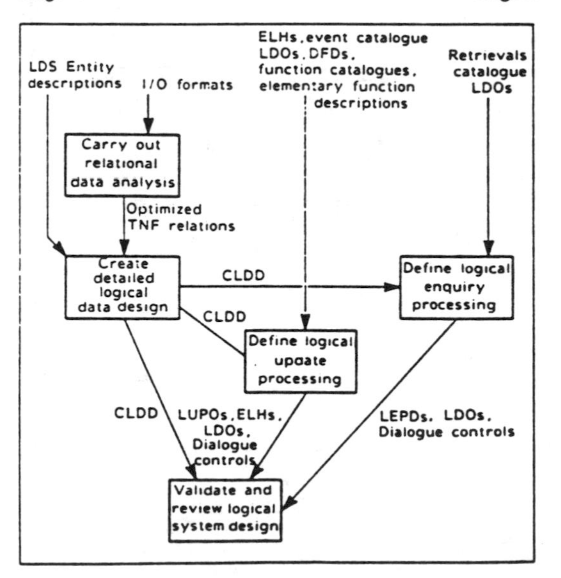

LDS Entity descriptions
I/O formats
ELHs, event catalogue LDOs, DFDs, function catalogues, elementary function descriptions
Retrievals catalogue LDOs
Carry out relational data analysis
Optimized TNF relations
Create detailed logical data design
CLDD
Define logical enquiry processing
CLDD
Define logical update processing
CLDD
LUPOs, ELHs, LDOs, Dialogue controls
LEPDs, LDOs, Dialogue controls
Validate and review logical system design

# A Review of Formal Methods

*Prepared for:*
*Rome Laboratory*
*RL/C3C*
*Griffiss AFB, NY 13441-5700*

*Prepared by:*
*Robert Vienneau*
*Kaman Sciences Corporation*
*258 Genesee Street*
*Utica, New York 13502-4627*

## Introduction

The seventies witnessed the structured programming revolution. After much debate, software engineers became convinced that better programs result from following certain precepts in program design. Recent imperative programming languages provide constructs supporting structured programming. Achieving this consensus did not end debate over programming methodology. Quite the contrary, a period of continuous change began, with views on the best methods of software development mutating frequently. Top-down development, modular decomposition, data abstraction, and, most recently, object oriented design are some of the jargon terms that have arisen to describe new concepts for developing large software systems. Both researchers and practitioners have found it difficult to keep up with this onslaught of new methodologies.

There is a set of core ideas that lies at the base of these changes. Formal methods have provided a unifying philosophy and central foundation upon which these methodologies have been built. Those who understand this underlying philosophy can more easily adopt these and other programming techniques. This report provides the needed understanding of formal methods to guide a software manager in evaluating claims related to new methodologies. It also provides an overview for the software engineer and a guide to the literature. Ample examples are provided to fully convey the flavor of using formal methods.

The underlying philosophy for formal methods has not changed in over two decades. Nevertheless, this approach is a revolutionary paradigm shift from conventional notions about computer programming. Many software engineers have adopted the new methodologies that grew out of this work without understanding or even being aware of the root concepts.

The traditional notion of programming looks at the software engineer's task as the development of code to instruct a physically existing machine to compute a desired result. Existing computers possess many idiosyncrasies reflecting hardware engineering concerns. Likewise user interfaces and the desired function can be expected to introduce additional complexities. In the traditional view of programming, these details can be expected to appear in a design, or even a specification, at all levels of abstraction. The engineer's job is seen as the introduction of more details and tricks to get the utmost in speed and performance out of computers. Since software development is therefore a "cut and fit" process, such complex systems can be expected to be full of bugs. A careful testing process is seen as the means of detecting and removing these bugs.

The mindset behind formal methods is directly opposite to the traditional view. It is the job of the hardware engineer, language designer, and compiler writer to provide a machine for executing code, not the reverse:

> Originally I viewed it as the function of the abstract machine to provide a truthful picture of the physical reality. Later, however, I learned to consider the abstract machine as the 'true' one, because that is the only one we can "think" it is the physical machine's purpose to supply "a working model," a (hopefully!) sufficiently accurate physical simulation of the true, abstract machine...It used to be the program's purpose to instruct our computers; it became the computer's purpose to execute our programs. [Dijkstra 76]

"A Review of Formal Methods" by R. Vienneau extracted from *A Review of Formal Methods*,
Kaman Science Corporation, 1993, pp. 3–15 and 27–33. Reprinted with permission.

The software engineer's task is to produce several models or descriptions of a system for an abstract machine, with accompanying proofs that models at lower levels of abstraction correctly implement higher-level models. Only this design process can ensure high levels of quality, not testing. Edsger Dijkstra has asserted that testing can demonstrate the presence of faults, not their absence. Since software engineers must be able to read and reason about designs, implementation details must be prevented from influencing the expression of designs as long as possible. A separation of concerns exists here, and if microefficiency concerns are allowed to dominate, produced code will reflect a design that cannot be convincingly demonstrated correct by anyone.

The contrast between these views is controversial (for example, see the discussion engendered in the ACM Forum by [DeMillo 79], [Fetzer 88], [Dijkstra 89], or [Gries 91]). Advocates of formal methods argue that many have adopted structured programming and top-down development without really understanding the underlying formalism [Mills 86]. A concern with formal methods can produce more rigorous specifications, even if they are expressed in English [Meyer 85]. Designs and code will be easier to reason about, even if fully formal proofs are never constructed. Critics focus on the difficulties in scaling up to large systems, the impracticalities of formalizing many inherently complex aspects of systems (for example, user interactions and error- checking code), and the radical retraining needed for the large population of already existing software engineers.

This report's purpose is not to advocate one or another position on formal methods. Rather, it overviews the technical basis for formal methods, while critically noting weaknesses. Polemics are avoided, but enough information is reviewed to allow the reader to form an informed judgment on formal methods. Formal methods are beginning to see more widespread industrial use, especially in Europe. Their use is characteristic of organizations with a Defined (Level 3) process or better, as specified in the process maturity framework developed by the Software Engineering Institute [Humphrey 88]. Formal methods have the potential of engendering further revolutionary changes in practice and have provided the underlying basis of past changes. These reasons make it imperative that software managers and engineers be aware of the increasingly widespread debate over formal methods.

## Definition and Overview of Formal Methods

Wide and narrow definitions of formal methods can be found in the literature. For example, Nancy Leveson states:

> A broad view of formal methods includes all applications of (primarily) discrete mathematics to software engineering problems. This application usually involves modeling and analysis where the models and analysis procedures are derived from or defined by an underlying mathematically- precise foundation. [Leveson 90]

A more narrow definition, however, better conveys the change in practice recommended by advocates of formal methods. The definition offered here is based on that in [Wing 90], and has two essential components. First, formal methods involve the essential use of a formal language. A formal language is a set of strings over some well-defined alphabet. Rules are given for distinguishing those strings, defined over the alphabet, that belong to the language from strings that do not.

Second, formal methods in software support formal reasoning about formulae in the language. These methods of reasoning are exemplified by formal proofs. A proof begins with a set of axioms, which are to be taken as statements postulated to be true. Inference rules state that if certain formulas, known as premises, are derivable from the axioms, then another formula, known as the consequent, is also derivable. A set of inference rules must be given in each formal method. A proof consists of a sequence of well-defined formulae in the language in which each formula is either an axiom or derivable by an inference rule from previous formulae in the sequence. The last axiom in the sequence is said to be proven. The following definition summarizes the above discussion:

> A formal method in software development is a method that provides a formal language for describing a software artifact (for instance, specifications, designs, or source code) such that formal proofs are possible, in principle, about properties of the artifact so expressed.

Often, the property proven is that an implementation is functionally correct, that is, it fulfills its specification. Thus, either the formal language associated with a method permits a system to be described by at least two levels of abstraction or two languages are provided for describing a specification and its implementation. The method provides tools with which an implementation can be proven to satisfy a specification. To be practically useful, the method should also provide heuristics and guidelines for developing elegant specifications and for developing implementations and proofs in parallel.

The concept of formalism in formal methods is borrowed from certain trends in 19th and 20th century mathematics. The development of consistent non-Euclidean geometries, in which supposedly parallel lines may intersect, led mathematicians to question their methods of proof and to search for more rigorous foundations. Eventually, these foundations came to be seen as describing numbers, sets, and logic. Leading mathematicians in this movement included Karl Weierstrass, Gottlob Frege, Giuseppe Peano, and David Hilbert. By the turn of the century, a foundation seemed to be in place, but certain strange examples and antinomies caused mathematicians to question the security of their foundations and even their own intuition on fundamental matters. A mechanical method of manipulating symbols was thus invented to investigate these questions. Due to fundamental discoveries of Kurt Godel, Thoralf Skolem, and Leopold Lowenheim, the results of using this method were ambiguous. Nevertheless, the axiomatic method became widely used in advanced mathematics, especially after impetus was added to this tendency by an extremely influential group of French mathematicians writing around World War II under the pseudonym of Nicholas Bourbaki [Kline 80].

Formal methods are merely an adoption of the axiomatic method, as developed by these trends in mathematics, for software engineering. In fact, Edsger Dijkstra has suggested, somewhat tongue-in-cheek, that computer science be renamed Very Large Scale Application of Logic (VLSAL) [Dijkstra 89]. Mastery of formal methods in software requires an understanding of this mathematics background. Mathematical topics of interest include formal logic, both the propositional calculus and predicate logic, set theory, formal languages, and automata such as finite state machines. The full flavor of the relevant mathematics cannot be conveyed here.

## Use of Formal Methods

How are the mathematics of formal languages applied in software development? What engineering issues have been addressed by their application? Formal methods are of global concern in software engineering. They are directly applicable during the requirements, design, and coding phases and have important consequences for testing and maintenance. They have influenced the development and standardization of many programming languages, the programmer's most basic tool. They are important in ongoing research that may change standard practice, particularly in the areas of specifications and design methodology. They are entwined with lifecycle models that may provide an alternative to the waterfall model, namely rapid prototyping, the Cleanroom variant on the spiral model, and "transformational" paradigms.

## What Can be Formally Specified

Formal methods support precise and rigorous specifications of those aspects of a computer system capable of being expressed in the language. Since defining what a system should do and understanding the implications of these decisions are the most troublesome problems in software engineering, this use of formal methods has major benefits. In fact, practitioners of formal methods frequently use formal methods solely for recording precise specifications, not for formal verifications ([Hall 90] and [Place 90]).

Some of the most well-known formal methods consist of or include specification languages for recording a system's functionality. These methods include:

- Z (pronounced "Zed")
- Communicating Sequential Processes (CSP)
- Vienna Development Method (VDM)
- Larch
- Formal Development Methodology (FDM).

Formal methods can be used to specify aspects of a system other than functionality. The emphasis of this report is on functionality since such techniques are currently the most well-known, developed, and of general interest. Software safety and security are other areas where formal methods are sometimes applied in practice. The benefits of proving that unsafe states will not arise, or that security will not be violated, can justify the cost of complete formal verifications of the relevant portions of a software system. Formal methods can deal with many other areas of concern to software engineers but, other than in research organizations, have not been much used for dealing with issues unrelated to functionality, safety, and security. Areas in which researchers are exploring formal methods include fault tolerance, response time, space efficiency, reliability, human factors, and software structure dependencies [Wing 90].

Formal methods can include graphical languages. Data Flow Diagrams (DFDs) are the most well-known graphical technique for specifying the function of a system. DFDs can be considered a semi-formal method, and researchers have explored techniques for treating DFDs in a completely formal manner. Petri nets provide another well-known graphical technique, often used in distributed systems [Peterson 77]. Petri nets are a fully formal technique. Finally, finite state machines are often presented in tabular form. This does not decrease the formalism in the use of finite state machines. So the definition of formal methods provided earlier is quite encompassing.

Software engineers produce models and define the properties of systems at several levels of abstraction. Formal methods can be employed at each level. A specification should describe what a system should do, but not how it is done. More details are provided in designs, with the source code providing the most detailed model. For example, Abstract Data Types (ADTs) frequently are employed at intermediate levels of abstraction. ADTs, being mathematical entities, are perfect candidates for formal treatment and are often so treated in the literature.

Formal methods are not confined to the software components of large systems. System engineers frequently use formal methods. Hardware engineers also use formal methods, such as VHSIC Hardware Description Language (VHDL) descriptions, to model integrated circuits before fabricating them.

**Reasoning about a Formal Description**

Once a formal description of a system has been produced, what can be done with it? Usable formal methods provide a variety of techniques for reasoning about specifications and drawing implications. The completeness and consistency of a specification can be explored. Does a description imply a system should be in several states simultaneously? Do all legal inputs yield one and only one output? What surprising results, perhaps unintended, can be produced by a system? Formal methods provide reasoning techniques to explore these questions.

Do lower level descriptions of a system properly implement higher level descriptions? Formal methods support formal verification, the construction of formal proofs that an implementation satisfies a specification. The possibility of constructing such formal proofs was historically the principle driver in the development of formal methods. Prominent technology for formal verification includes Edsger Dijkstra's "weakest precondition" calculus ([Dijkstra 76] and [Gries 81]) and Harlan Mills' "functional correctness" approach [Linger 79].

**Tools and Methodology**

Developments in supporting tools and methodologies have accompanied the development of technology for formalizing software products. The basic idea is that the ultimate end-product of development is not solely a working system. Of equal importance are specifications and proofs that the program meets its specification. A proof is very hard to develop after the fact. Consequently, proofs and programs should be developed in parallel, with close interconnections in the development history. Since programs must be proven correct, only those constructions that can be clearly understood should be used. This is the primary motivation that many early partisans had for advocating structured programming.

A challenge is to apply these ideas on large scale projects. Formal specifications seem to scale up much easier than formal verifications. Nevertheless, ideas relating to formal verifications are applicable to projects of any size, particularly if the level of formality is allowed to vary. David Gries recommends a design methodology incorporating certain heuristics that support more reliable and provable designs [Gries 81]. Harlan Mills has spent considerable effort developing the Cleanroom approach, a lifecycle in which formal methods, inspections, and reliability modeling and certification are integrated in a social process for producing software ([Mills 87] and [Dyer 92]).

Formal methods have also inspired the development of many tools. These tools may bring formal methods into more widespread practice, although interestingly enough, many advocates of formal methods are not strong believers in tools. An obvious example of such tools are program provers. Some tools animate specifications, thereby converting a formal specification into an executable prototype of a system. Other tools derive programs from specifications through various automated transformations. Under some approaches a program is found as a solution to an equation in a formal language. Transformational implementation suggests a future in which many software systems are developed without programmers, or at least with more automation, higher productivity, and less labor ([Agresti 86] and [KBSE 92]).

In some sense, no programmer can avoid formal methods, for every programming language is, by definition, a formal language. Ever since Algol 60 was introduced, standards defining programming languages have used a formal notation for defining language syntax, namely Backus-Naur Form (BNF). Usually, standards do not formally define the semantics of programming languages, although, in principle, they could. The convention of using natural language descriptions for defining language semantics is due to not having yet developed settled techniques for defining all constructs included in large languages. Nevertheless, formal methods have resulted in one widely agreed criterion for evaluating language features: how simply can one formally reason about a program with a proposed new feature? The formal specification of language semantics is a lively area of research. In particular, formal methods have always been an interest of the Ada community, even before standardization ([London 77], [McGettrick 82] and [Preston 88]).

### Limitations of Formal Methods

Given the applicability of formal methods throughout the lifecycle, and their pervasive possibilities for almost all areas of software engineering, why are they not more widely visible? Part of the problem is educational. Revolutions are not made by conversion, but by the old guard passing away. More recent university graduates tend to be more willing to experiment with formal methods.

On the other hand, the only barrier to the widespread transition of this technology is not lack of knowledge on the part of practitioners. Formal methods do suffer from certain limitations. Some of these limitations are inherent and will never be overcome. Other restrictions, with research and practice, will be removed as formal methods are transitioned into wider use.

### The Requirements Problem

The inherent limitations in formal methods are neatly summarized in the oft-repeated aphorism, "You cannot go from the informal to the formal by formal means." In particular, formal methods can prove that an implementation satisfies a formal specification, but they cannot prove that a formal specification captures a user's intuitive informal understanding of a system. In other words, formal methods can be used to verify a system, but not to validate a system. The distinction is that validation shows that a product will satisfy its operational mission, while verification shows that each step in the development satisfies the requirements imposed by previous steps [Boehm 81].

The extent of this limitation should not be underemphasized. One influential field study, [Curtis 88], found that the three most important problems in software development are:

- The thin spread of application domain knowledge
- Changes in and conflicts between requirements
- Communication and coordination problems.

Successful projects were often successful because of the role of one or two key exceptional designers. These designers had a deep understanding of the applications domain and could map the applications requirements to computer science concerns. These findings suggest the reduction of informal application knowledge to a rigorous specification is a key problem area in the development of large systems.

Empirical evidence does suggest, however, that formal methods can make a contribution to the problem of adequately capturing requirements. The discipline of producing a formal specification can result in fewer specification errors. Furthermore, implementors without an exceptional designer's knowledge of the application area commit less errors when implementing a formal specification than when relying on hazy knowledge of the application [Goel 91]. These benefits may exist even when the final specification is expressed in English, not a formal language [Meyer 85]. A specification acts as a "contract" between a user and a developer. The specification describes the system to be delivered. Using specifications written in a formal language to complement natural language descriptions can make this contract more precise. Finally, developers of automated programming environments, which use formal methods, have developed tools to interactively capture a user's informal understanding and thereby develop a formal specification [Zeroual 91].

Still, formal methods can never replace deep application knowledge on the part of the requirements engineer, whether at the system or the software level. The application knowledge of the exceptional designer is not limited to one discipline. For example, an avionics application might require knowledge of flight control, navigation, signal processing, and electronic countermeasures. Whether those drawing on interdisciplinary knowledge in developing specifications come to regard formal methods as just another discipline making their life more complicated, or an approach that allows them to simply, concisely, and accurately record their findings, will only be known with experience and experimentation.

### Physical Implementations

The second major gap between the abstractions of formal methods and concrete reality lies in the nature of any actual physically existing computer. Formal methods can verify that an implementation satisfies a specification when run on an idealized abstract machine, but not when run on any physical machine.

Some of the differences between typical idealized machines and physical machines are necessary for humanly-readable correctness proofs. For instance, an abstract machine might be assumed to have an infinite memory, while every actual machine has some upper limit. Similarly, physical machines cannot implement real numbers, as axiomatically described by mathematicians, while proofs are most simply constructed assuming the existence of mathematically precise reals. No reason in principle exists why formal methods cannot incorporate these limitations. The proofs will be much messier and less elegant, and they will be limited to a particular machine.

A limitation in principle, however, does exist here. Formal proofs can show with certainty, subject to mistakes in calculation, that given certain assumptions, a program is a correct implementation of a specification. What cannot be formally shown is that those assumptions are correct descriptions of an actual physical system. A compiler may not correctly implement a language as specified. So a proof of a program in that language will fail to guarantee the execution behavior of the program under that compiler. The compiler may be formally verified, but this only moves the problem to a lower level of abstraction. Memory chips and gates may have bugs. No matter how thoroughly an application is formally verified, at some point one must accept that an actual physical system satisfies the axioms used in a proof. Explanations must come to an end sometime.

Both critics [Fetzer 88] and developers ([Dijkstra 76] and [Linger 79]) of formal methods are quite aware of this limitation, although the critics do not always seem to be aware of the developers' explicit statements on this point. This limitation does not mean formal methods are pointless. Formal proofs explicitly isolate those locations where an error may occur. Errors may arise in providing a machine that implements the abstract machine, with sufficient accuracy and efficiency, upon which proofs are based. Given this implementation, a proof vastly increases confidence in a program [Merrill 83].

Although no prominent advocate of formal methods recommends testing be avoided entirely, it is unclear what role testing can play in increasing confidence in the areas not addressed by formal methods. The areas addressed by testing and formal methods may overlap, depending on the specific methodologies employed. From an abstract point of view, the question of what knowledge or rational belief can be provided by testing is the riddle of the rational basis for induction. How can an observation that some objects of a given type have a certain property ever convince anyone that all objects of that type have the property? Why should a demonstration that a program produces the correct outputs for some inputs ever lead to a belief that the program is likely to produce the correct output for all inputs? If a compiler correctly processes certain programs, as defined by a syntactical and semantic standard, why should one conclude that any semantic axiom in the standard can be relied upon for a formal proof of the correctness of a program not used in testing the compiler? Over two centuries ago, the British philosopher David Hume put related questions at the center of his epistemology.

Two centuries of debate have not reached a consensus on induction. Still, human beings are inclined to draw these conclusions. Software developers exhibit the same inclination in testing computer programs. Formal methods will never entirely supplant testing, nor do advocates intend them to do so. In principle, a gap always exists between physical reality and what can be formally verified. With more widespread use of formal methods, however, the role of testing will change.

**Implementation Issues**

The gaps between users' intentions and formal specifications and between physical implementations and abstract proofs create inherent limitations to formal methods, no matter how much they may be developed in the future. There are also a host of pragmatic concerns that reflect the current state of the technology.

The introduction of a new technology into a large-scale software organization is not a simple thing, particularly a technology as potentially revolutionary as formal methods. Decisions must be made about whether the technology should be completely or partially adopted. Appropriate accompanying tools need to be acquired. Current personnel need to be retrained, and new personnel may need to be hired. Existing practices need to be modified, perhaps drastically. All of these issues arise with formal methods. Optimal decisions depend on the organization and the techniques for implementing formal methods. Several schemes exist, with various levels of feasibility and impact.

The question arises, however, whether formal methods are yet suitable for full-scale implementation. They are most well-developed for addressing issues of functionality, safety, and security, but even for these mature methods, serious questions exist about their ability to scale up to large applications. In much academic work, a proof of a hundred lines of code was seen as an accomplishment. The applicability of such methods to a commercial or military system, which can be over a million lines of code, is seriously in doubt. This issue of scaling can be a deciding factor in the choice of a method. Harlan Mills claims his program function approach applies easier on large systems than Dijkstra's competing predicate calculus method [Mills 86]. Likewise, the languages considered in academic work tend to be extremely simplified compared to real-world programming languages.

One frequently adopted scheme for using formal methods on real-world projects is to select a small subset of components for formal treatment, thus finessing the scalability problem. These components might be selected under criteria of safety, security, or criticality. Components particularly amenable to formal proof might be specifically selected. In this way, the high cost of formal methods is avoided for the entire project, but only incurred where project requirements justify it. Under this scheme, the issue of scaling is avoided, for formal methods are never applied on a large scale.

Decisions about tool acquisition and integration need to be carefully considered. Advocates of formal methods argue that they should be integrated into the design process. One does not develop a specification and an implementation and then attempt to prove the implementation satisfies the specification. Rather, one designs the implementation and proof in parallel, with continual interaction. Sometimes discussion about automated verifiers suggests that the former approach, not the latter, provides an implementation model ([DeMillo 79] and [Merrill 83]). Selective implementation of formal methods on small portions of large projects may make this integration difficult to obtain.

Another approach can have much more global impacts. Perhaps the entire waterfall lifecycle should be scrapped. An alternate approach is to develop formal specifications at the beginning of the lifecycle and then automatically derive the source code for the system. Maintenance, enhancements, and modifications will be performed on the specifications, with this derivation process being repeated. Programmers are replaced by an intelligent set of integrated tools, or at least given very strong guidance by these tools. Knowledge about formal methods then becomes embodied in the tools, with Artificial Intelligence techniques being used to direct the use of formal methods. This revolutionary programmerless methodology is not here yet, but it is providing the inspiration for many tool developers. For example, this vision is close to that of Rome Laboratory's Knowledge-Based Software Engineering project [KBSE 92].

A third alternative is to partially introduce formal methods by introducing them throughout an organization or project, but allowing a variable level of formality. In this sense, informal verification is an argument meant to suggest that details can be filled in to provide a completely formal proof. The most well-known example of this alternative is the Cleanroom methodology, developed by Harlan Mills [Mills 87]. Given varying levels of formality, tools are much less useful under this approach. The Cleanroom methodology involves much more than formal methods, but they are completely integrated into the methodology. Other technologies involved include the spiral lifecycle, software reliability modeling, a specific testing approach, reliability certification, inspections, and statistical process control. Thus, although this approach allows partial experimentation with formal methods, it still requires drastic changes in most organizations.

No matter to what extent an organization decides to adopt formal methods, if at all, training and education issues arise. Most programmers have either not been exposed to the needed mathematical background, or do not use it in their day-to-day practice. Even those who thoroughly understand the mathematics may have never realized its applicability to software development. Set theory is generally taught in courses in pure mathematics, not computer programming. Even discrete mathematics, a standard course whose place in the university curriculum owes much to the impetus of computer science professional societies, is often not tied to software applications. Education in formal methods should not be confined to degreed university programs for undergraduates newly entering the field. Means need to be found, such as seminars and extension courses, for retraining an existing workforce. Perhaps this educational problem is the biggest hurdle to the widespread transition of formal methods.

## Specification Methods

Formal methods were originally developed to support verifications, but higher interest currently exists in specification methods. Several methods and languages can be used for specifying the functionality of computer systems. No single language, of those now available, is equally appropriate for all methods, application domains, and aspects of a system. Thus, users of formal specification techniques need to understand the strength and weaknesses of different methods and languages before deciding on which to adopt. This section briefly describes characteristics of different methods now available.

The distinction between a specification method and a language is fundamental. A method states what a specification must say. A language determines in detail how the concepts in a specification can be expressed [Lamport 89]. Some languages support more than one method, while most methods can be used in several specification languages. Some methods are more easily used with certain languages.

### Semantic Domains

A formal specification language contains an alphabet of symbols and grammatical rules that define well-formed formulae. These rules characterize a language's "syntactic domain." The syntax of a language shows how the symbols in the language are put together to form meaningless formulae. Neither the nature of the objects symbolized nor the meanings of the relationships between them are characterized by the syntax of a language.

Meanings, or interpretations of formulae, are specified by the semantics of a language. A set of objects, known as the language's "semantic domain," can provide a model of a language. The semantics are given by exact rules which state what objects satisfy a specification. For example, Cartesian Geometry shows how theorems in Euclidean Geometry can be modeled by algebraic expressions. A language can have several models, but some will seem more natural than others.

A specification is a set of formulae in a formal language. The objects in the language's semantic domain that satisfy a given specification can be nonunique. Several objects may be equivalent as far as a particular specification is concerned. Because of this nonuniqueness, the specification is at a higher level of abstraction than the objects in the semantic domain. The specification language permits abstraction from details that distinguish different implementations, while preserving essential properties. Different specification methods defined over the same semantic domain allow for specifying different aspects of specified objects. These concepts can be defined more precisely using mathematics. The advantage of this mathematics is that it provides tools for formal reasoning about specifications. Specifications can then be examined for completeness and consistency.

Specification languages can be classified by their semantic domains. Three major classes of semantic domains exist [Wing 90]:

- Abstract Data Type specification languages
- Process specification languages
- Programming languages.

ADT specification languages can be used to specify algebras. An ADT 'defines the formal properties of a data type without defining implementation features' [Vienneau 91]. Z, the Vienna Development Method, and Larch are examples of ADT specification languages. Process specification languages specify state sequences, event sequences, streams, partial orders, and state machines. C.A.R. Hoare's Communicating Sequential Processes (CSP) is the most well-known process specification language.

Programming languages provide an obvious example of languages with multiple models. Predicate transformers provide one model, functions provide another model, and the executable machine instructions that are generated by compiling a program provide a third model. Formal methods are useful in programming because programs can be viewed both as a set of commands for physical machines and as abstract mathematical objects as provided by these alternative models.

**Operational and Definitional Methods**

The distinction between operational and definitional methods provides another important dimension for classifying formal methods [Avizienis 90]. Operational methods have also been described as constructive or model-oriented [Wing 90]. In an operational method, a specification describes a system directly by providing a model of the system. The behavior of this model defines the desired behavior of the system. Typically, a model will use abstract mathematical structures, such as relations, functions, sets, and sequences. An early example of a model-based method is the specification approach associated with Harlan Mills' functional correctness approach. In this approach, a computer program is defined by a function from a space of inputs to a space of outputs. In effect, a model-oriented specification is a program written in a very high-level language. It may actually be executed by a suitable prototyping tool.

Definitional methods are also described as property-oriented [Wing 90] or declarative [Place 90]. A specification provides a minimum set of conditions that a system must satisfy. Any system that satisfies these conditions is functionally correct, but the specification does not provide a mechanical model showing how to determine the output of the system from the inputs. Two classes of definitional methods exist, algebraic and axiomatic. In algebraic methods, the properties defining a program are restricted to equations in certain algebras. Abstract Data Types are often specified by algebraic methods. Other types of axioms can be used in axiomatic methods. Often these axioms will be expressed in the predicate calculus. Edsger Dijkstra's method of specifying a program's function by preconditions and postconditions is an early example of an axiomatic method.

**Use of Specification Methods**

Different specification methods are more advantageous for some purposes than others. In general, formal methods provide for more precise specifications. Misunderstandings and bugs can be discovered earlier in the lifecycle. Since the earlier a fault is detected, the cheaper it can be removed; formal specification methods can dramatically improve both productivity and quality. Cost savings can only be achieved if formal methods are used appropriately. How to best use them in a specific environment can only be determined through experimentation.

Formal specifications should not be presented without a restatement of the specification in a natural language. In particular, customers should be presented with the English version, not a formal specification. Very few sponsors of a software development project will be inclined to read a specification whose presentation is entirely in a formal language.

Whether an ADT or process specification language should be adopted depends on the details of the project and the skills of the analysts. Choosing between operational and definitional methods also depends on project-specific details and experience. Generally, programmers are initially more comfortable with operational methods since they are closer to programming. Operational specifications may lead to over-specification. They tend to be larger than definitional specifications. Their complexity thus tends to be greater, and relationships among operations tend to be harder to discern.

Definitional specifications are generally harder to construct. The appropriate axioms to specify are usually not trivial. Consistency and completeness may be difficult to establish. Usually completeness is more problematic than consistency. Intuition will tend to prevent the specification of inconsistent axioms. Whether some axioms are redundant, or more are needed, is less readily apparent. Automated tools are useful for guidance in answering these questions [Guttag 77].

## Conclusions

This report has briefly surveyed various formal methods and the conceptual basis of these techniques. Formal methods can provide:

- More precise specifications
- Better internal communication
- An ability to verify designs before executing them during test
- Higher quality and productivity.

These benefits will come with costs associated with training and use. Hard and fast rules do not exist on how to properly vary the level of formalism on a project or on how to transition the use of formal methods into an organization. Their enthusiastic use certainly depends on the organization's members perceiving a need that formal methods can fill. No change is likely to be achievable in an organization that is satisfied with its current practice.

Even if formal methods are not integrated into an organization's process, they can still have positive benefits. Consider a group whose members have been educated in the use of formal methods, but are not encouraged to use formal methods on the job. These programmers will know that programs can be developed to be fault-free from the first execution. They will have a different attitude to both design and testing, as contrasted to programmers who have not been so exposed to formal methods. They will be able to draw on a powerful set of intellectual tools when needed. They will be able to use formal methods on a personal basis and, to a limited extent, to communicate among one another. If management provides the appropriate milieu, this group can be expected to foster high quality attitudes with consequent increases in both productivity and quality.

To get their full advantages, formal methods should be incorporated into a software organization's standard procedures. Software development is a social process, and the techniques employed need to support that process. How to fully fit formal methods into the lifecycle is not fully understood. Perhaps there is no universal answer, but only solutions that vary from organization to organization.

### The Cleanroom as a Lifecycle with Integrated Use of Formal Methods

Harlan Mills has developed the Cleanroom methodology [Mills 87], which is one approach for integrating formal methods into the lifecycle. The Cleanroom approach combines formal methods and structured programming with Statistical Process Control (SPC), the spiral lifecycle and incremental releases, inspections, and software reliability modeling. It fosters attitudes, such as emphasizing defect prevention over defect removal, that are asociated with high quality products in non-software fields.

Cleanroom development begins with the requirements phase. Ideally, specifications should be developed in a formal language, although the Cleanroom approach allows the level of formality to vary. The Cleanroom lifecycle uses incremental releases to support SPC. Cleanroom-developed specifications include:

- Explicit identification of functionality to be included in successive releases
- Failure definitions, including levels of severity
- The target reliability as a probability of failure-free operation
- The operational profile for each increment, that is, the probability distribution of user inputs to the system
- The reliability model that will be applied in system test to demonstrate reliability.

The design and coding phases of Cleanroom development are distinctive. Analysts must develop proofs of correctness along with designs and codes. These proofs use functional correctness techniques and are meant to be human-readable. They serve a social role and are not intended to be automatically checked by automated verification tools. Inspections are emphasized for reviewing designs, proofs, and code. The design process is intended to prevent the introduction of defects. In keeping with this philosophy, the Cleanroom methodology includes no unit or integration test phase. In fact, coders are actually forbidden to compile their programs. Cleanroom development takes its name from just this aspect of the methodology. Testing is completely separated from the design process, and analysts are not permitted to adopt the attitude that quality can be tested in. Instead, they must produce readable programs which can be convincingly shown correct by proof.

Testing does play a very important role in Cleanroom development. It serves to verify that reliability goals are being attained. Given this orientation, testing is organized differently than in traditional methods. Unit and integration testing do not exist. Functional methods, not structural testing methods, are employed. Furthermore, the testing process is deliberately designed to meet the assumptions of the chosen software reliability model. Test cases are statistically chosen from the specified operational profile. Although faults are removed when detected, the testing group's responsibility is not to improve the product to meet acceptable failure-rate goals. Rather, the testing group exists to perform reliability measurement and certification.

When testing fails to demonstrate the desired reliability goal is met, the design process is altered. The level of formality may be increased, or more inspections may be planned. Testing and incremental builds are combined to provide feedback into the development process under a Statistical Process Control philosophy as tailored for software. Formal methods are embodied in an institutional structure designed to foster a "right the first time" approach. The Cleanroom methodology draws upon evolving concepts of the best practice in software, including formal methods. The Cleanroom approach is beginning to generate interest and experimentation in organizations unassociated with Harlan Mills and International Business Machines [Selby 87].

### Technologies Supported by Formal Methods

Researchers are drawing on formal methods in developing tools and techniques that may not be state-of-the-practice for several years. Lifecycle paradigms that rely on automatically transforming specifications to executable code are necessarily formal. Many software development tools, whether standalone or integrated into a common environment, draw on formal methods. Consequently, as software development becomes more tool intensive, formal methods will be more heavily used. Inasmuch as these formal methods are embodied in the tools, tool users may not be fully aware of the embedded formalism. Tool users who are trained in formal methods will be able to wield some of these tools more effectively. Formal methods, through their use in tools, have the promise of being able to transform the software development lifecycle from a labor-intensive error-prone process to a capital-intensive high quality process.

Emerging technologies that are increasingly widespread today also draw on formal methods. A knowledge of formal methods is needed to completely understand these popular technologies and to use them most effectively. These technologies include:

- Rapid prototyping
- Object Oriented Design (OOD)
- Structured programming
- Formal inspections.

Rapid prototyping depends on the ability to quickly construct prototypes of a system to explore their ability to satisfy user needs. Using executable specifications to describe a system at a high level is a typical approach. The tool that compiles the specification fills in the details. Specifications constructed under a rapid prototyping methodology, if executable, are by definition in a formal language. Often the languages used in prototyping tools involve the same set theoretical and logical concepts used in formal specification methods not intended for prototyping.

OOD is another increasingly well-known technology that is based on formal methods. Abstract Data Types provide a powerful basis for many classes in Object Oriented systems. Furthermore, at least one pure object oriented language, Eiffel, has assertions, preconditions, postconditions, and loop invariants built into the language to a certain extent. Simple boolean expressions are checked during execution of an Eiffel program, but not all assertions, such as those with existential and universal quantifiers, can be expressed in the language [Meyer 88]. Thus, formal methods can be usefully combined with object oriented techniques.

The connection between formal methods and structured programming is very close. Structured programming is a set of heuristics for producing high quality code. Only a limited set of constructs should be used. Programs should be developed in a top-down fashion. The historical source for these heuristics lies in formal methods. Programs developed with these precepts will be capable of being rigorously proven correct. Consequently, they will also be capable of being understood intuitively and nonrigorously. Structured programming cannot be completely understood without understanding the rigorous mathematical techniques associated with formal methods. Adopting formal methods is a natural progression for software development teams who employ structured programming techniques.

Inspections throughout the lifecycle have been shown to increase both productivity and quality. A rigorous methodology has been defined for inspections [Fagan 76]. Those participating in inspections play specified roles: moderator, author, coder, tester, and so on. Inspections should be organized to include representatives from specified departments (for example, Quality Assurance) within a software organization. Fault data is collected during inspections and analyzed to ensure the development process is under control. Inspections rely on the ability of individuals to reason about software products and to convince others of the correctness of their reasoning. Training in formal methods provides inspection team members with a powerful language to communicate their trains of reasoning. Formal and semi-formal verifications can lead to more effective inspections. The Cleanroom methodology demonstrates the potential synergy between formal methods and inspections.

## Summary

Formal methods promise to yield benefits in quality and productivity. They provide an exciting paradigm for understanding software and its development, as well as a set of techniques for use by software engineers. Over the last 20 years, researchers have drawn on formal methods to develop certain software technologies that are currently becoming increasingly popular and are dramatically altering software development and maintenance. Further revolutionary advances based on formal methods are highly likely considering research currently in the pipeline.

Many organizations have experience with the use of formal methods on a small scale. Formal methods are typically used in organizations attaining a Level 3 rating and above on the Software Engineering Institute's process maturity framework. Increasingly, recently trained software engineers have had some exposure to formal methods. Nevertheless, their full scale use and transition is not fully understood. An organization that can figure out how to effectively integrate formal methods into their current process will be able to gain a competitive advantage.

## References


[Agresti 86] W.W. Agresti, *New Paradigms for Software Development*, IEEE Computer Society Press, Los Alamitos, Calif., 1986.

[Aho 86] A.V. Aho, R. Sethi, and J.D. Ullman, *Compilers: Principles, Techniques, and Tools*, Addison-Wesley, Reading, Mass., 1986.

[Avizienis 90] A. Avizienis and C.-S. Wu, "A Comparative Assessment of Formal Specification Techniques," *Proc. 5th Ann. Knowledge-Based Software Assistant Conf.*, 1990.

[Baber 91] R.L. Baber, *Error-Free Software: Know-how and Know-why of Program Correctness*, John Wiley & Sons, New York, N.Y., 1991.

[Backus 78] J. Backus, "Can Programming Be Liberated from the von Neumann Style? A Functional Style and Its Algebra of Programs," *Comm. ACM*, Vol. 21, No. 8, Aug. 1978.

[Boehm 81] B.W. Boehm, *Software Engineering Economics*, Prentice- Hall, Inc., Englewood Cliffs, N.J., 1981.

[Curtis 88] B. Curtis, H. Krasner, and N. Iscoe, "A Field Study of the Software Design Process for Large Systems," *Comm. ACM*, Vol. 31, No. 11, Nov.1988.

[DeMillo 79] R. DeMillo, R. Lipton, and A. Perlis, "Social Processes and Proofs of Theorems and Programs," *Comm. ACM*, Vol. 22, No. 5, May 1979.

[DeRemer 76] F. DeRemer and H.H. Kron, "Programming-in-the-Large Versus Programming-in-the-Small," *IEEE Trans. Software Eng.*, Vol. SE-2, No. 2, June 1976, pp. 312–327.

[Dijkstra 76] E.W. Dijkstra, *A Discipline of Programming*, Prentice Hall, Englewood Cliffs, N.J., 1976.

[Dijkstra 89] E.W. Dijkstra, "On the Cruelty of Really Teaching Computer Science," *Comm. ACM*, Vol. 32, No. 12, Dec. 1989.

[Dyer 92] M. Dyer, *The Cleanroom Approach to Quality Software Development*, John Wiley & Sons, New York, N.Y., 1992.

[Fagan 76] M.E. Fagan, "Design and Code Inspections to Reduce Errors in Program Development," *IBM Systems J.*, Vol. 15, No. 3, 1976.

[Fetzer 88] J.H. Fetzer, "Program Verification: The Very Idea," *Comm. ACM*, Vol. 31, No. 9, Sept. 1988.

[Goel 91] A.L. Goel and S.N. Sahoo, "Formal Specifications and Reliability: An Experimental Study," *Proc. Int'l Symp. Software Reliability Eng.* IEEE Computer Society Press, Los Alamitos, Calif., 1991, pp. 139–142.

[Gries 81] D. Gries, *The Science of Programming*, Spring-Verlag, New York, N.Y., 1981.

[Gries 91] D. Gries, "On Teaching and Calculation," *Comm. ACM*, Vol. 34, No. 3, Mar. 1991.

[Guttag 77] J. Guttag, "Abstract Data Types and the Development of Data Structures," *Comm. ACM*, Vol. 20, No. 6, June 1977.

[Hall 90] A. Hall, "Seven Myths of Formal Methods," *IEEE Software*, Vol. 7, No. 5, Sept. 1990, pp. 11–19.

[Hoare 85] C.A.R. Hoare, *Communicating Sequential Processes*, Prentice-Hall International, 1985.

[Hoare 87] C.A.R. Hoare, "Laws of Programming," *Comm. ACM*, Vol. 30, No. 8, Aug. 1987.

[Humphrey 88] W.S. Humphrey, "Characterizing the Software Process: A Maturity Framework," *IEEE Software*, Vol. 5, No. 2, Mar. 1988, pp. 73–79.

[KBSE 92] *Proc. 7th Knowledge-Based Software Eng. Conf.*, 1992.

[Kline 80] M. Kline, *Mathematics: The Loss of Certainty*, Oxford University Press, 1980.

[Lamport 89] L. Lamport, "A Simple Approach to Specifying Concurrent Systems," *Comm. ACM,* Vol. 32, No. 1, Jan. 1989.

[Leveson 90] N.G. Leveson, "Guest Editor's Introduction: Formal Methods in Software Engineering," *IEEE Trans. Software Eng.*, Vol. 16, No. 9, Sept. 1990, pp. 929–931.

[Linger 79] R.C. Linger, H.D. Mills, and B.I. Witt, *Structured Programming: Theory and Practice*, Addison-Wesley Publishing Company, Reading, Mass., 1979.

[London 77] R.L. London, "Remarks on the Impact of Program Verification on Language Design," in *Design and Implementation of Programming Languages*, Springer-Verlag, New York, N.Y., 1977.

[Lyons 77] J. Lyons, *Noam Chomsky*, Penguin Books, Revised Edition 1977.

[McGettrick 82] Andrew D. McGettrick, *Program Verification using Ada,* Cambridge University Press, 1982.

[Merrill 83] G. Merrill, "Proofs, Program Correctness, and Software Engineering," *SIGPLAN Notices*, Vol. 18, No. 12, Dec. 1983.

[Meyer 85] B. Meyer, "On Formalism in Specifications," *IEEE Software*, Vol. 2, No. 1, Jan. 1985, pp. 6–26.

[Meyer 88] B. Meyer, *Object-Oriented Software Construction*, Prentice-Hall, Englewood Cliffs, N.J., 1988.

[Mills 86] H.D. Mills, "Structured Programming: Retrospect and Prospect," *IEEE Software,* Vol. 3, No. 6, Nov. 1986, pp. 58–66.

[Mills 87] H.D. Mills, Michael Dyer, and Richard C. Linger, "Cleanroom Software Engineering," *IEEE Software*, Vol. 4, No. 5, Sept. 1987, pp. 19–25.

[Peterson 77] J.L. Peterson, "Petri Nets," *Computing Surveys*, Vol. 9, No. 3, Sept. 1977.

[Place 90] P.R.H. Place, W. Wood, and M. Tudball, *Survey of Formal Specification Techniques for Reactive Systems*, Software Engineering Institute, CMU/SEI-90-TR-5, May 1990.

[Preston 88] D. Preston, K. Nyberg, and R. Mathis, "An Investigation into the Compatibility of Ada and Formal Verification Technology," *Proc. 6th Nat'l Conf. Ada Technology*, 1988.

[Selby 87] R.W. Selby, V.R. Basili, and F.T. Baker, "Cleanroom Software Development: An Empirical Evaluation," *IEEE Trans. Software Eng.*, Vol. SE-13, No. 9, Sept. 1987, pp. 1027–1037.

[Spivey 88] J.M. Spivey, *Understanding Z: A Specification Language and its Formal Semantics*, Cambridge University Press, 1988.

[Stolyar 70] A.A. Stolyar, *Introduction to Elementary Mathematical Logic*, Dover Publications, 1970.

[Suppes 72] P. Suppes, *Axiomatic Set Theory*, Dover Publications, 1972.

[Terwilliger 92] R.B. Terwilliger, "Simulating the Gries/Dijkstra Design Process," *Proc. 7th Knowledge-Based Software Eng. Conf.,* IEEE Computer Society Press, Los Alamitos, Calif., 1992, pp. 144–153.

[Vienneau 91] R. Vienneau, *An Overview of Object Oriented Design,* Data & Analysis Center for Software, Apr. 30, 1991.

[Wing 90] J.M. Wing, "A Specifier's Introduction to Formal Methods," *Computer*, Vol. 23, No. 9, Sept. 1990, pp. 8–24.

[Zeroual 91] K. Zeroual, "KBRAS: A Knowledge-Based Requirements Acquisition System," *Proc. 6th Ann. Knowledge-Based Software Eng. Conf.,* IEEE Computer Society Press, Los Alamitos, Calif., 1991, pp. 38–47.

# Chapter 6

# Coding

## 1. Introduction to Chapter

This chapter is deemed essential by the Tutorial editors in order to complete the classic life cycle model of a software development, that is, requirements, design, implementation and testing. Coding, along with unit testing, is in the implementation phase of a software development. The coding aspect of software engineering is considered very important in the final product but is a relatively mature discipline and as such receives less discussion than the other phases. However, the editors have selected two papers that are appropriate for this Tutorial. The first describes the history and possible future of structured programming; the second covers the application of programming languages to software engineering.

The editors selected the term "coding" over the term "programming" as more appropriate to a discussion of the activities in relationship to software engineering. The term "programming" is not well defined and could include such activities as analysis, design, coding and testing—many of the activities we include in software engineering. Coding, on the other hand, is more precisely defined as translating a low-level (or detailed-level) software design into a language capable of operating a computing machine.

CODING

## 2. Introduction to Papers

The first paper, by Harlan Mills, entitled "Structured Programming: Retrospect and Prospect," is from one of the tutorials that periodically appear in the IEEE publication *IEEE Software*. This paper discusses the origin of the term "structured programming," which first appeared in Edsger Dijkstra's 1969 article "Structured Programming" [1]. The paper also looks at the impact of structured programming on software development, as well as some of the earlier experiences such as the classic New York Times project for which Mills was the project manager. Structured programming is a corollary to Dijkstra's proposal to prohibit the unconditional "goto." [2] Mills brings up the concept of cleanroom software development and discusses how it relates to the structured programming approach.

Harlan Mills was one of the true pioneers of software engineering in both academic and industrial settings. He was a major contributor to the state of the art and the state of the practice for more than 30 years. His recent death saddened his many friends and deprives the profession of one of its most prolific contributors.

The second and last paper in this chapter is based upon a chapter in a book, *Software Engineering: A Programming Approach* [3]. The book's authors, Doug Bell, Ian Morrey, and John Pugh, revised and updated the chapter for this Tutorial. The paper discusses the features that a good programming language should have from the viewpoint of software engineering, that is, the features that assist the software development process.

The authors divide the discussion into "programming in the small" and "programming in the large." Programming in the small concerns itself with those language features that support the programming of modules or small programs. These features include simplicity, clarity, and the language's syntax and facilities for control and data abstraction. Programming in the large is concerned with those features that support programs that are made up of many components. These features include facilities for separately compiling individually developed modules, features for controlling the interaction between components, and support tools associated with the language.

There is tendency to interpret programming in the small as "coding" and programming in the large as "software engineering." The authors of this paper avoid that interpretation and describe how programming in the small also applies to software engineering.


1. Dijkstra, Edsger W., "Structured Programming," in *Software Engineering Techniques*, J.N. Buxton and B. Randell, eds., NATO Science Committee, Rome, 1969, pp. 88–93.

2. Dijkstra, E., "GOTO Statement Considered Harmful," *Comm. ACM*, Vol. 11, No. 3, Mar. 1968.

3. Bell, Doug, Ian Morrey, and John Pugh, *Software Engineering: A Programming Approach,* Prentice Hall International, Englewood Cliffs, N.J., 1987.

# Structured Programming: Retrospect and Prospect

Harlan D. Mills, IBM Corp.

***Structured programming has changed how programs are written since its introduction two decades ago. However, it still has a lot of potential for more change.***

Edsger W. Dijkstra's 1969 "Structured Programming" article[1] precipitated a decade of intense focus on programming techniques that has fundamentally altered human expectations and achievements in software development.

Before this decade of intense focus, programming was regarded as a private, puzzle-solving activity of writing computer instructions to work as a program. After this decade, programming could be regarded as a public, mathematics-based activity of restructuring specifications into programs.

Before, the challenge was in getting programs to run at all, and then in getting them further debugged to do the right things. After, programs could be expected to both run and do the right things with little or no debugging. Before, it was common wisdom that no sizable program could be error-free. After, many sizable programs have run a year or more with no errors detected.

**Impact of structured programming.** These expectations and achievements are not universal because of the inertia of industrial practices. But they are well-enough established to herald fundamental change in software development.

Even though Dijkstra's original argument for structured programming centered on shortening correctness proofs by simplifying control logic, many people still regard program verification as academic until automatic verification systems can be made fast and flexible enough for practical use.

By contrast, there is empirical evidence[2] to support Dijkstra's argument that infor-

## Introducing the fundamental concepts series

A group of leading software engineers met in Columbia, Maryland, in September 1982 to provide recommendations for advancing the software engineering field. The participants were concerned about the rapid changes in the software development environment and about the field's ability to effectively deal with the changes.

The result was a report issued six months later and printed in the January 1985 issue of *IEEE Software* ("Software Engineering: The Future of a Profession" by John Musa) and in the April 1983 *ACM Software Engineering Notes* ("Stimulating Software Engineering Progress — A Report of the Software Engineering Planning Group").

The group's members were members of the IEEE Technical Committee on Software Engineering's executive board, the ACM Special Interest Group on Software Engineering's executive committee, and the IEEE Technical Committee on VLSI.

In the area of software engineering technology creation, the highest priority recommendation was to "commission a 'best idea' monograph series. In each monograph, an idea from two to four years ago, adjudged a 'best idea' by a panel of experts, would be explored from the standpoint of how it was conceived, how it has matured over the years, and how it has been applied. A key objective here is to both stimulate further development and application of the idea and encourage creation of new ideas from the divergent views of the subject."

Another way to state the objectives of the series is to (1) explain the genesis and development of the research idea so it will help other researchers in the field and (2) transfer the idea to the practicing software engineer.

After the report was published in this magazine, an editorial board was created to implement the series. John Musa, then chairman of the IEEE Technical Committee on Software Engineering, and Bill Riddle, then chairman of ACM SIGSE, appointed the following board members:

- Bruce Barnes, of the National Science Foundation,
- Meir Lehman, of Imperial College, as adviser,

Reprinted from *IEEE Software*, Vol. 3, No. 4, Nov. 1986, pp. 58–66.

KEVIN REAGAN

mal, human verification can be reliable enough to replace traditional program debugging before system testing. In fact, structured programming that includes human verification can be used as the basis for software development under statistical quality control.[3]

It seems that the limitations of human fallibility in software development have been greatly exaggerated. Structured programming has reduced much of the unnecessary complexity of programming

- Peter Neumann, of SRI International (and no longer with the board),
- Norman Schneidewind, of the Naval Postgraduate School, as editor-in-chief, and
- Marv Zelkowitz, of the University of Maryland.

Rather than produce a monograph series, the board decided that *IEEE Software* would be a better medium for the series, since it reaches a large readership. Furthermore, the magazine's editor-in-chief, Bruce Shriver of IBM, strongly supported the series' objectives.

I am delighted that Harlan Mills, an IBM fellow, agreed to write the first article, "Structured Programming: Retrospect and Prospect," in this series. I am also grateful for Bruce Shriver's enthusiastic support and for agreeing to publish the series in *IEEE Software*. Future articles in this series will appear in this magazine. I also thank the *IEEE Software* reviewers for the excellent job they did of refereeing Mills's article.

In presenting this series, the editorial board is not advocating the idea of this or any article published. Rather, our purpose is to be an agent for the transfer of technology to the software engineering community. We believe it is the readers who should evaluate the significance to software engineering of the ideas we present.

The board is very interested in your opinions on this article and on the general concept of the series. Do you think it is a good idea? Has the article helped you to better understand the origins, concepts, and application of structured programming? What topics would you like covered? Please send your thoughts and opinions to Norman Schneidewind, Naval Postgraduate School, Dept. AS, Code 54Ss, Monterey, CA 93943.

Norman Schneidewind

Norman Schneidewind
Series Editor-in-Chief

and can increase human expectations and achievements accordingly.

**Early controversies.** Dijkstra's article proposed restricting program control logic to three forms — sequence, selection, and iteration — which in languages such as Algol and PL/I left no need for the goto instruction. Until then, the goto statement had seemingly been the foundation of stored-program computing. The ability to branch arbitrarily, based on the state of data, was at the heart of programming ingenuity and creativity. The selection and iteration statements had conditional branching built in implicitly, but they seemed a pale imitation of the possibilities inherent in the goto.

As a result, Dijkstra's proposal to prohibit the goto was greeted with controversy: "You must be kidding!" In response to complex problems, programs were being produced with complex control structures — figurative bowls of spaghetti, in which simple sequence, selection, and iteration statements seemed entirely inadequate to express the required logic. No wonder the general practitioners were skeptical: "Simple problems, maybe. Complex problems, not a chance!"

In fact, Dijkstra's proposal was far broader than the restriction of control structures. In "Notes on Structured Programming"[4] (published in 1972 but privately circulated in 1970 or before), he discussed a comprehensive programming process that anticipated stepwise refinement, top-down development, and program verification.

However, Dijkstra's proposal could, indeed, be shown to be theoretically sound by previous results from Corrado Boehm and Giuseppe Jacopini[5] who had showed that the control logic of any flowchartable program — any bowl of spaghetti — could be expressed without gotos, using sequence, selection, and iteration statements.

So the combination of these three basic statements turned out to be more powerful than expected, as powerful as any flowchartable program. That was a big surprise to rank and file programmers.

Even so, Dijkstra's proposal was still greeted with controversy: "It can't be practical." How could the complex bowls of spaghetti written at that time otherwise be explained? Formal debates were held at conferences about practicality, originality, creativity, and other emotional issues in programming, which produced more heat than light.

## Early industrial experience

**The *New York Times* project.** An early published result in the use of structured programming in a sizable project helped calibrate the practicality issue. F. Terry Baker reported on a two-year project carried out by IBM for the *New York Times*, delivered in mid-1971, that used structured programming to build a system of some 85,000 lines of code.[6] Structured programming worked!

The project used several new techniques simultaneously: chief-programmer team organization, top-down development by stepwise refinement, hierarchical modularity, and functional verification of programs. All were enabled by structured programming.

The *New York Times* system was an on-line storage and retrieval system for newspaper reference material accessed through more than a hundred terminals — an advanced project in its day. The *Times* system met impressive performance goals — in fact, it achieved throughputs expected in an IBM 360/Model 50 using an interim hardware configuration of a Model 40. The IBM team also achieved an impressive level of productivity — a comprehensive internal study concluded that productivity, compared to other projects of similar size and complexity, was a factor of five better.

***Unlike a spaghetti program, a structured program defines a natural hierarchy among its instructions.***

In this case, since the *New York Times* had little experience in operating and maintaining a complex, on-line system, IBM agreed to maintain the system for the newspaper over the first year of operation. As a result, the exact operational experience of the system was also known and published by Baker.[7]

The reliability of the system was also a pleasant surprise. In a time when on-line software systems typically crashed several times a day, the *Times* software system crashed only once that year.

The number of changes required, for any reason, was 25 during that year, most of them in a data editing subsystem that was conceived and added to the system after the start of the project. Of these, about a third were external specification changes, a third were definite errors, and a third interpretable either way.

The rate of definite errors was only 0.1 per thousand lines of code. The highest quality system of its complexity and size produced to that time by IBM, the *Times* project had a major effect on IBM software development practices.

**The structure theorem and its top-down corollary.** Even though structured programming has been shown to be possible and practical, there is still a long way to go to achieve widespread use and benefits in a large organization. In such cases, education and increased expectations are more effective than exhortations, beginning with the management itself.

The results of Boehm and Jacopini were especially valuable to management when recast into a so-called structure theorem,[8] which established the existence of a structured program for any problem that permitted a flowchartable solution.

As an illustration, hardware engineering management implicitly uses and benefits from the discipline of Boolean algebra and logic, for example, in the result that any combinational circuit can be designed with Not, And, and Or building blocks. If an engineer were to insist that these building blocks were not enough, his credibility as an engineer would be questioned.

The structure theorem permits management by exception in program design standards. A programmer cannot claim the problem is too difficult to be solved with a structured program. To claim that a structured program would be too inefficient, a program must be produced as proof. Usually, by the time a structured program is produced, the problem is understood much better than before, and a good solution has been found. In certain cases, the final solution may not be structured — but it should be well-documented and verified as an exceptional case.

The lines of text in a structured program can be written in any order. The history of which lines were written first and how they were assembled into the final structured program are immaterial to its execution. However, because of human abilities and fallibilities, the order in which lines of a structured program are written can greatly affect the correctness and completeness of the program.

For example, lines to open a file should be written before lines to read and write the file. This lets the condition of the file be checked when coding a file read or write statement.

The key management benefit from top-down programming was described in the top-down corollary[8] to the structure theorem. The lines of a structured program can be written chronologically so that every line can be verified by reference only to lines already written, and not to lines yet to be written.

Unlike a spaghetti program, a structured program defines a natural hierarchy among its instructions, which are repeatedly nested into larger and larger parts of the program by sequence, selection, and iteration structures. Each part defines a subhierarchy executed independently of its surroundings in the hierarchy. Any such part can be called a program stub and given a name — but, even more importantly, it can be described in a specification that has no control properties, only the effect of the program stub on the program's data.

The concept of top-down programming, described in 1971,[9] uses this hierarchy of a structured program and uses program stubs and their specifications to decompose program design into a hierarchy of smaller, independent design problems. Niklaus Wirth discussed a similar concept of stepwise refinement at the same time.[10]

**Using the top-down corollary.** The top-down corollary was counterintuitive in the early 1970's because programming was widely regarded as a synthesis process of assembling instructions into a program rather than as an analytic process of restructuring specifications into a program. Furthermore, the time sequence in which lines of text were to be written was counter to common programming practice.

For example, the corollary required that the JCL (job-control language) be written first, the LEL (linkage-editor language) next, and ordinary programs in programming languages last. The custom then was to write them in just the reverse order. Further, the hard inner loops, usually worked out first, had to be written last under the top-down corollary. In fact, the top-down corollary forced the realization that the linkage editor is better regarded as a language processor than a utility program.

It is easy to misunderstand the top-down corollary. It does not claim that the thinking should be done top-down. Its benefit is in the later phases of program design, after the bottom-up thinking and perhaps some trial coding has been accomplished. Then, knowing where the top-down development is going, the lines of the structured program can be checked one by one as they are produced, with no need to write later lines to make them correct. In large designs, the top-down process should look ahead several levels in the hierarchy, but not necessarily to the bottom.

The *New York Times* team used both the structure theorem and its top-down corollary. While the proof of the structure theorem (based on that of Boehm and Jacopini) seemed more difficult to understand, the team felt the application of the top-down corollary was more challenging in program design, but correspondingly more rewarding in results.

For example, with no special effort or prestated objectives, about half of the *Times* modules turned out to be correct after their first clean compile. Other techniques contributed to this result, including chief-programmer team organization, highly visible program development library procedures, and intensive program reading. However, these techniques were permitted to a great extent by top-down structured programming, particularly in the ability to defer and delegate design tasks through specifications of program stubs.

***Dijkstra's proposal to prohibit the goto was greeted with controversy: "You must be kidding!"***

**NASA's Skylab project.** In 1971-74, a much larger but less publicized project demonstrated similar benefits of top-down structured programming in software development by IBM for the NASA Skylab space laboratory's system. In comparison, the NASA Apollo system (which carried men to the Moon several times) had been developed in 1968-71, starting before structured programming was proposed publicly.

While the *New York Times* project involved a small team (originally four but enlarged to 11) over two years, Apollo and Skylab each involved some 400 programmers over consecutive three years of development. In each system, the software was divided into two major parts, of similar complexity: (1) a simulation system for flight controller and astronaut training and (2) a mission system for spacecraft control during flight.

In fact, these subsystems are mirror images in many ways. For example, the simulation system estimates spacecraft behavior from a rocket engine burn called for by an astronaut in training, while the mission system will observe spacecraft behavior from a rocket engine burn called for by an astronaut in flight.

Although less spectacular than Apollo, the Skylab project of manned space study of near-Earth space was in many ways more challenging. The software for the Skylab simulation system was about double the size of Apollo's, and the complexity was even greater.

The Skylab software project was initiated shortly after the original proposals for structured programming, and a major opportunity for methodology comparison arose. The Skylab mission system was developed by the same successful methods used for both subsystems in Apollo. But the Skylab simulation system was developed with the then-new method of top-down structured programming under the initiative of Sam E. James.

The Skylab results were decisive. In Apollo, the productivity of the programmers in both simulation and mission systems was very similar, as to be expected. The Skylab mission system was developed with about the same productivity and integration difficulty as experienced on both Apollo subsystems.

But the Skylab simulation system, using top-down structured programming, showed a productivity increase by a factor of three and a dramatic reduction in integration difficulty.

Perhaps most revealing was the use of computer time during integration. In most projects of the day, computer time would increase significantly during integration to deal with unexpected systems problems. In the Skylab simulation system, computer time stayed level throughout integration.

**Language problems.** By this time (the mid-1970's), there was not much debate about the practicality of structured programming. Doubtless, some diehards were not convinced, but the public arguments disappeared.

Even so, only the Algol-related languages permitted direct structured programming with sequence, selection and iteration statements in the languages. Assembly languages, Fortran, and Cobol were conspicuous problems for structured programming.

One approach with these languages is to design in structured forms, then hand-translate to the source language in a final coding step. Another approach is to create a language preprocessor to permit final coding in an extended language to be mechanically translated to the source language. Both approaches have drawbacks.

The first approach requires more discipline and dedication than many programming groups can muster. It is tempting to use language features that are counter to structured programming.

The second approach imposes a discipline, but the programs actually compiled in the target language will be the result of mechanical translation themselves, with artificial labels and variables that make reading difficult. The preprocessing step can also be cumbersome and expensive, so the temptation in debugging is to alter the mechanically generated target code directly, much like patching assembly programs, with subsequent loss of intellectual control.

As a result of these two poor choices of approach, much programming in assembly languages, Fortran, and Cobol has been slow to benefit from structured programming.

Paradoxically, assembly language programming is probably the easiest to adapt to structured programming through the use of macroassemblers. For example, the Skylab simulation and mission systems were both programmed in assembly language, with the simulation system using structured programming through a macroassembler.

Both Fortran and Cobol have had their language definitions modified to permit direct structured programming, but the bulk of programming in both languages — even today — probably does not benefit fully from structured programming.

## Current theory and practice

**Mathematical correctness of structured programs.** With the debate over and the doubters underground, what was left to learn about structured programming? It turned out that there was a great deal to learn, much of it anticipated by Dijkstra in his first article.[1]

The principal early discussions about structured programming in industry focused on the absence of gotos, the theoretical power of programs with restricted control logic, and the syntactic and typographic aspects of structured programs (indentation conventions and pretty printing, stepwise refinement a page at a time).

These syntactic and typographic aspects permitted programmers to read each other's programs daily, permitted them to conduct structured walk-throughs and program inspections, and permitted managers to understand the progress of software development as a process of stepwise refinement that allowed progressively more accurate estimates of project completion.

When a project was claimed to be 90-percent done with solid top-down structured programming, it would take only 10 percent more effort to complete it (instead of possibly another 90 percent!).

However, Dijkstra's first article on structured programming did not mention syntax, typography, readability, stepwise refinement, or top-down development. Instead, his main argument for structured programming was to shorten the mathematical proofs of correctness of programs! That may seem a strange argument when almost no one then (and few now) bothered to prove their programs correct anyway. But it was an inspired piece of prophecy that is still unfolding.

***The ideas of structured programming, mathematical correctness, and high-level languages are mutually independent.***

The popularizations of structured programming have emphasized its syntactic and superficial aspects because they are easiest to explain. But that is only half the story — and less than half the benefit — because there is a remarkable synergy between structured programming and the mathematical correctness of programs. And there have been many disappointments for people and organizations who have taken the structured-programming-made-easy approach without mathematical rigor.

Two reasons that Dijkstra's argument about the size of proofs of correctness for structured programs seems to be inspired prophecy are

- The proof of program's correctness is a singularly appropriate definition for its necessary and sufficient documentation. No gratuitous or unnecessary ideas are needed and the proof is sufficient evidence that the program satisfies its specification.
- The size of a correctness proof seems at least a partial measure of the complexity of a program. For example, a long program with few branches may be simpler to prove than a shorter one with many loops — and it may be less complex, as well. Or, tricky use of variables and operations may reduce the number of branches but will make the proof longer.

However, unless programmers understand what proofs of correctness are, these insights will not be realized. That was the motivation of the article "How to Write Correct Programs and Know It."[9] Then, whether structured programs are proved correct or not, this understanding will implicitly reduce complexity and permit better documentation.

In fact, Dijkstra's argument shows that the mathematical correctness of programs was an independent and prior idea to structured programming (even anticipated by writings of von Neumann and Turing). Yet it was strange and unknown to most programmers at the time. It is curious, although the earliest computers were motivated and justified by the solution of numerical problems of mathematics (such as computing ballistic tables), that the programming of such computers was not widely viewed as a mathematical activity.

Indeed, when it was discovered that computers could be used in business data processing, dealing with mostly character data and elementary arithmetic, the relation between programming and mathematics seemed even more tenuous.

As the Skylab project showed, structured programming is also independent of high-level languages. As treated syntactically and superficially, structured programming may have seemed dependent on high-level languages. But this is not true. Of course, high-level languages have improved programmer productivity as well, but that is a separate matter.

The ideas of structured programming, mathematical correctness, and high-level languages are mutually independent.

**Program functions and correctness.** A terminating program can be regarded as a rule for a mathematical function that converts an initial state of data into a final state, whether the problem being solved is considered mathematical or not.

For example, a payroll program defines a mathematical function just as a matrix inversion program does. Even nonterminating programs, such as operating systems and communication systems, can be expressed as a single nonterminating loop that executes terminating subprograms endlessly.

The function defined by any such terminating program is simply a set of ordered pairs: the initial and final states of data that can arise in its execution. That matrix inversion seems more mathematical than payroll processing is a human cultural illusion, an illusion not known to or shared by computers.

Since programs define mathematical functions, which thereby abstract out all details of execution — including even which language or which computer is used — it is possible to discuss the correctness of a program with respect to its specification as a purely mathematical question. Such a specification is a relation. If the specification admits no ambiguity of the correct final state for a given initial state, the specification will be a function.

For example, a square root specification that requires an answer correct to eight decimal places (so any more places can be arbitrary) is a relation. But a sort specification permits only one final ordering of any initial set of values, and is thus a function.

A program will be correct with respect to a specification if and only if, for every initial value permissible by the specification, the program will produce a final value that corresponds to that initial value in the specification.

A little notation will be helpful. Let function $f$ be defined by program $P$, and relation $r$ be a specification ($r$ is possibly a function). Then program $P$ is correct with respect to relation $r$ if and only if a certain correctness equation between $f$ and $r$ holds, as follows: $\text{domain}(f \cap r) = \text{domain}(r)$.

To see this, note that $f \cap r$ consists of just those pairs of $r$ correctly computed by $P$, so $\text{domain}(f \cap r)$ consists of all initial values for which $P$ computes correct final values. But $\text{domain}(r)$ is just the set of initial values for which $r$ specifies acceptable final values, so it should equal $\text{domain}(f \cap r)$.

Such an equation applies equally to a payroll program or a matrix inversion program. Both can be mathematically correct, regardless of human interpretations of whether the computation is mathematical or not.

To picture this correctness equation, we can diagram $f$ and $r$ in a Venn diagram with projections of these sets of ordered pairs into their domain sets (see Figure 1). The correctness equation requires that the two domain sets $D(f \cap r)$ and $D(r)$ must coincide.

*Mathematical correctness proofs.* In principle, a direct way to prove the mathematical correctness of a program is clear. Start with a program $P$ and the specification $r$. Determine from $P$ its function $f$ and whether the correctness equation between $f$ and $r$ holds.

In practice, given a spaghetti program, such a proof may be impractical — even impossible — because of the program's complexity. But a structured program with the same function $f$ will be simpler to prove correct because of the discipline on its control structure. In retrospect, the reason lies in an algebra of functions that can be associated with structured programming.

It is easy to see in principle why a program is a rule for a function. For any initial state from which the program terminates normally (does not abort or loop endlessly), a unique final state is determined. But unlike classical mathematical function rules (such as given by polynomial expressions, trigonometric expressions, and the like), the function rules determined by programs can be quite arbitrary and complex. The final state, even though unique, may not be easily described because of complex dependencies among individual instructions.

For a spaghetti program, the only reasonable way to think of the program as a rule for a function is to imagine it being executed with actual data — by mental simulation. For small programs, a limited generic simulation may be possible (for example, "for negative values the program is executed in this section").

But for a structured program, there is a much more powerful way to think of it: as a function rule that uses simpler functions. For example, any sequence, selection, or iteration defines a rule for a function that uses the functions of its constituent parts.

*Algebra of part functions.* The remarkable thing about building these functions from the nested parts of a structured program is that the rules for constructing them are very simple and regular. They are simply described as operations in a certain algebra of functions.

The rules for individual instructions depend on the programming language. For example, the rule for an assignment statement $x := y + z$ is that the final state is exactly the same as the initial state except that the value attached to identifier $x$ is changed to the value attached to identifier $y$ plus the value attached to identifier $z$.

The rule for sequence is function composition. For example, if statements $s1$, $s2$ have functions $f1$, $f2$, the function for the sequence $s1; s2$ will be the composition $f1 \circ f2 = \{<x,y>\} : y = f2(f1(x))\}$.

It is important to note that the rules at each level use the functions at the next lower level, and not the rules at the next lower level. That is, a specific program part determines the rule of a function, but the rule itself is not used at higher levels. This means that any program part can be safely changed at will to another with the same function, even though it represents a different rule.

For example, the program parts $x := y$ and If $x \neq y$ Then $x := y$ define different rules for the same function and can be exchanged at will.

*Axiomatic and functional verification.* There is a curious paradox today between university and industry. While program correctness proofs are widely taught in universities for toy programs, most academics not deeply involved in the subject

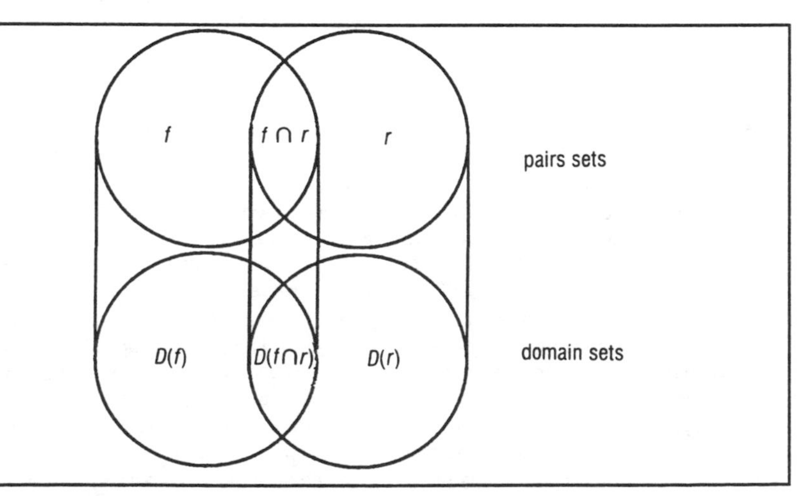


**Figure 1. Correctness equation diagram with projections of the ordered pair sets into their domain sets.**

regard program correctness as academic. Their motivation is cultural: "You'd never want to do this in practice, but it is good for you to know how to do it."

On the other hand, the IBM Software Engineering Institute curriculum is centered on the idea of program correctness exactly because it is not academic. Rather, it provides a practical method of reasoning about large programs that leads to much improved quality and productivity in software development.

There is also a simple answer to this paradox. Academics primarily teach a form of program correctness, called axiomatic verification, applied directly to toy programs, while the IBM Software Engineering Institute teaches a different form called functional verification in a way intended to scale up to large programs.

Axiomatic verification proves correctness by reasoning about the effect of programs on data. This reasoning takes the form of predicates on data at various places in the program that are invariant during execution. The relations between these predicates are given by axioms of the programming language (hence the name), and the entry/exit predicates together define the program function in an alternative form. Tony Hoare has given a beautiful explanation for this reasoning as a form of natural deduction, now called Hoare logic.[11]

Functional verification is based on function theory from the outset. For example, a simple assignment statement $x := y + z$ defines a function that can be denoted by $[x := y + z]$ and then used as a function in the algebra of structured-program part functions. In practice, functional verification is harder to teach but easier to scale up to large programs because of the presence of algebraic structure in an explicit form.

The most critical difference in practice between axiomatic and functional verification arises in the treatment of loops. In axiomatic verification, a loop invariant must be invented for every loop. In functional verification, during stepwise refinement, no such loop invariants are required because they are already embodied in the loop specification function or relation.[8]

Axiomatic verification can be explained directly in terms of program variables and the effects of statements on them, concretely in any given programming language. But when programs get large, the number of program variables get large, too — while the number of functions remains just one. The variable-free theory scales up to a more complex function rather than to many more variables.

Such a function may be defined in two lines of mathematical notation or a hundred pages of English. But its mathematical form is the same: a set of ordered pairs. There are many more opportunities for ambiguity and fallibility in a hundred pages of English, but increased individual fallibility can be countered by checks and balances of well-managed teams, rather than abandoning the methodology.

As a result, the functional verification of a top-level design of a 100,000 lines has the same form as for a low-level design of 10 lines: There is one function rule to be verified by using a small number of functions at the next level. The function defines a mapping from initial states to final states. These states will eventually be represented as collections of values of variables, but can be reasoned about as abstract objects directly in high-level design.

**_Eliminate the use of arrays in structured programs, and use instead data abstractions without arbitrary access._**

While most of this reasoning is in the natural language of the application, its rules are defined by the algebra of functions, which is mathematically well-defined and can be commonly understood among designers and inspectors. There is considerable evidence that this informal kind of reasoning in mathematical forms can be effective and reliable in large software systems (exceeding a million lines) that are designed and developed top-down with very little design backtracking.[12]

There is yet another way to describe the reasoning required to prove the correctness of structured programs. The predicates in program variables of axiomatic verification admit an algebra of predicates whose operations are called predicate transformers in a classic book by Edsger Dijkstra,[13] and followed in a beautiful elaboration by David Gries.[14]

## Looking to the future

**Data-structured programming.** The objective of reducing the size of formal correctness proofs can be reapplied to structured programs with a surprising and constructive result. In carrying out proofs of structured programs, the algebraic operations on the functions involved are the same at every level, but the functions become more complex in the upper parts of the hierarchy.

Two features in the data of the program have a large effect on the size of formal proofs: (1) The sheer number of program variables that define the data and (2) assignments to arrays.

Arrays represent arbitrary access to data just as gotos represent arbitrary access to instructions. The cost of this access shows up directly in the length and complexity of proofs that involve array assignments. For example, an array assignment, say $x[i] := y[j+k]$ refers to three previous assignments to $i$, $j$, and $k$. The values of $i$ or $j+k$ may be out of range, and certainly must be accounted for if in range. Furthermore, array $x$ will be altered at location $i$, and this fact must be accounted for the next time $x$ is accessed again for the same value of $i$ (which may be the value of another variable $m$).

Dijkstra's treatment of arrays[13] is very illuminating evidence of their complexity. Gries has also given the predicate transformers for array assignments,[14] which are much more complex than for simple assignments.

Happily, there is a way to address both of these proof expanders in one stroke: eliminate the use of arrays in structured programs, and use instead data abstractions without arbitrary access. Three simple such abstractions come to mind immediately: sets, stacks, and queues — the latter two data structures with LIFO and FIFO access disciplines. No pointers are required to assign data to or from stacks or queues, so fewer variables are involved in such assignments.

Furthermore, the proofs involving assignments to sets, stacks, and queues are much shorter than proofs involving arrays. It takes a good deal more thinking to design programs without arrays, just as it takes more thinking to do without gotos. But the resulting designs are better thought out, easier to prove, and have more function per instruction than array programs.

For example, the array-to-array assignment $x[i] := y[j+k]$ is but one of four instructions needed to move an item of data from $y$ to $x$ (assignments required for $x$, $i$, $j$, and $k$).

On the other hand, a stack to queue assignment, such as back($x$) := top($y$) moves the top of stack $y$ to the back of queue $x$ with no previous assignments. Of course it takes more planning to have the right item at the top of stack $y$ when it is needed for the back of queue $x$.

This discipline for data access, using stacks and queues instead of arrays, has been used in developing a complex language processing system of some 35,000 lines.[2] Independent estimates of its size indicates a factor of up to five more function per instruction than would be expected with array designs.

The design was fully verified, going to system test without the benefit of program debugging of any kind. System testing revealed errors of mathematical fallibility in the program at a rate of 2.5 per thousand instructions, all easily found and fixed. The kernel of the system (some 20,000 instructions) has been operating for two years since its system test with no errors detected.

**Functional verification instead of unit debugging.** The functional verification of structured programs permits the production of high-quality software without unit debugging. Just as gotos and arrays have seemed necessary, so unit debugging has also seemed necessary. However, practical experience with functional verification has demonstrated that software can be developed without debugging by the developers with some very beneficial results.

This latent ability in programmers using functional verification has a surprising synergy with statistical testing at the system level — that is, testing software against user-representative, statistically-generated input.[3] Statistical testing has not been used much as a development technique — and indeed for good reason in dealing with software that requires considerable defect removal just to make it work at all, let alone work reliably. However, statistical testing of functionally verified structured programs is indeed effective.

**Cleanroom software development.** The combined discipline of no unit debugging and statistical testing is called cleanroom software development. The term "cleanroom" refers to the emphasis on defect prevention instead of defect removal, as used in hardware fabrication, but applied now to the design process rather than the manufacturing process.

In fact, cleanroom software development permits the development of software under statistical quality control by iterating incremental development and testing. Early increments can be tested statistically for scientific estimates of their quality and for management feedback into the development process for later increments to achieve prescribed levels of quality.

At first glance, no unit debugging in software development seems strange, because unit debugging appears to be such an easy way to remove most of the defects that might be in the software. However, unit debugging is a good way to inadvertently trade simple blunders for deep system errors through the tunnel vision of debugging. And the very prospect of unit testing invites a dependence on debugging that undermines concentration and discipline otherwise possible.

More positively, eliminating unit testing and debugging leads to several benefits:

- more serious attention to design and verification as an integrated personal activity by each programmer,

***The latent ability of people in new technologies is a source of continual amazement to experts.***

- more serious attention to design and verification inspection by programming teams,
- preserving the design hypothesis for statistical testing and control (debugging compromises the design),
- selecting qualified personnel by their ability to produce satisfactory programs without unit debugging, and
- high morale of qualified personnel.

On the other hand, user-representative, statistical testing of software never before debugged provides several benefits:

- valid scientific estimates of the software's reliability and the rate of its growth in reliability when errors are discovered and fixed during system testing,
- forced recognition by programmers of the entire specification input space and program design by specification decomposition (instead of getting a main line running then adding exception logic later), and
- the most effective way to increase the reliability of software through testing and fixing.

The evidence is that industrial programming teams can produce software with unprecedented quality. Instead of coding in 50 errors per thousand lines of code and removing 90 percent by debugging to leave five errors per thousand lines, programmers using functional verification can produce code that has never been executed with less than five errors per thousand lines and remove nearly all of them in statistical system testing.

Furthermore, the errors found after functional verification are qualitatively different than errors left from debugging. The functional verification errors are due to mathematical fallibility and appear as simple blunders in code — blunders that statistical tests can effectively uncover.

**Limits of human performance.** The latent ability of people in new technologies is a source of continual amazement to experts. For example, 70 years ago, experts could confidently predict that production automobiles would one day go 70 miles an hour. But how many experts would have predicted that 70-year-old grandmothers would be driving them?!

Thirty years ago, experts were predicting that computers would be world chess champions, but not predicting much for programmers except more trial and error in writing the programs that would make chess champions out of the computers. As usual, it was easy to overestimate the future abilities of machines and underestimate the future abilities of people. Computers are not chess champions yet, but programmers are exceeding all expectations in logical precision.

From the beginning of computer programming, it has been axiomatic that errors are necessary in programs because people are fallible. That is indisputable, but is not very useful without quantification. Although it is the fashion to measure errors per thousand lines of code, a better measure is errors released per person-year of software development effort.

Such a measure compensates for the differences in complexity of programs — high complexity programs have more errors per thousand lines of code but also require more effort per thousand lines of code. It normalizes out complexity differences and has the further advantage of relating errors to effort rather than product, which is more fundamental.

For example, the *New York Times* released error rate was about one error per person-year of effort. That was considered an impossible goal before that time, but it is consistently bettered by advanced programming teams today.

An even better result was achieved by Paul Friday in the 1980 census software system for the distributed control of the national census data collection and communications network. The real-time software contained some 25,000 lines, developed with structured programming and functional verification, and ran throughout the production of the census (almost a year) with no errors detected.

Friday was awarded a gold medal, the highest award of the Commerce Department (which manages the Census Bureau), for this achievement. Industrial software experts, looking at the function provided, regard the 25,000 lines as very economical, indeed. (It seems to be characteristic of high-quality, functionally verified software to have more function per line than is usual.)

At 2500 lines of code per person-year for software of moderate complexity, and one error per 10 person-years of effort, the result is one expected error for a 25,000-line software system. Conversely, a 25,000-line software system should prove to be error-free with appreciable probability.

These achievements already exist. With data structured programming, functional verification and cleanroom software development (and good management), we can expect another factor of 10 improvement in this dimension of performance in the next decade.

Structured programming has reduced much of the unnecessary complexity of programming and can increase human expectations and achievements accordingly. Even so, there is much yet to be done. It is not enough to teach university students how to verify the correctness of toy programs without teaching them how to scale up their reasoning to large and realistic programs. A new undergraduate textbook[15] seeks to address this issue.

Better software development tools are needed to reduce human fallibility. An interactive debugger is an outstanding example of what is not needed — it encourages trial-and-error hacking rather than systematic design, and also hides marginal people barely qualified for precision programming. A proof organizer and checker is a more promising direction.

It is not enough for industrial management to count lines of code to measure productivity any more than they count words spoken per day by salesmen. Better management understandings are needed for evaluating programming performance, as are increased investment in both education and tools for true productivity and quality.

But the principal challenge for management is to organize and focus well-educated software engineers in effective teams. The limitations of human fallibility, while indisputable, have been greatly exaggerated, especially with the checks and balances of well-organized teams. □


## Acknowledgments

I appreciate the early help of the Fundamental Concepts in Software Engineering Series' editorial board, especially its editor-in-chief, Norman Schneidewind, in materially shaping this article. Key technical suggestions and improvements, due to David Gries and *IEEE Software*'s referees, are appreciated very much.


## References


1. Edsger W. Dijkstra, "Structured Programming," in *Software Engineering Techniques*, J.N. Buxton and B. Randell, eds., NATO Science Committee, Rome, 1969, pp. 88-93.
2. Harlan D. Mills and Richard C. Linger, "Data Structured Programming: Program Design without Arrays and Pointers," *IEEE Trans. Software Eng.*, Vol. SE-12, No. 2, Feb. 1986, pp. 192-197.
3. Paul A. Currit, Michael Dyer, and Harlan D. Mills, "Certifying the Reliability of Software," *IEEE Trans. Software Eng.*, Vol. SE-12, No. 1, Jan. 1986, pp. 3-11.
4. O.J. Dahl, Edsger W. Dijkstra, and C.A.R. Hoare, *Structured Programming*, Academic Press, New York, 1972.
5. Corrado Boehm and Giuseppe Jacopini, "Flow Diagrams, Turing Machines, and Languages with Only Two Formation Rules," *Comm. ACM*, Vol. 9, No. 5, May 1966, pp. 366-371.
6. F. Terry Baker, "Chief-Programmer Team Management of Production Programming," *IBM Systems J.*, Vol. 1, No. 1, 1972, pp. 56-73.
7. F. Terry Baker, "System Quality Through Structured Programming," *AFIPS Conf. Proc. FJCC, Part 1*, 1972, pp. 339-343.
8. Richard C. Linger, Harlan D. Mills, and Bernard I. Witt, *Structured Programming: Theory and Practice*, Addison-Wesley, Reading, Mass., 1979.
9. Harlan D. Mills, *Software Productivity*, Little, Brown, and Co., Boston, 1983.
10. Niklaus Wirth, "Program Development by Stepwise Refinement," *Comm. ACM*, Vol. 14, No. 4, April 1971, pp. 221-227.
11. C.A.R. Hoare, "An Axiomatic Basis for Computer Programming," *Comm. ACM*, Vol. 12, No. 10, Oct. 1969, pp. 576-583.
12. Anthony J. Jordano, "DSM Software Architecture and Development," *IBM Technical Directions*, Vol. 10, No. 3, 1984, pp. 17-28.
13. Edsger W. Dijkstra, *A Discipline of Programming*, Prentice-Hall, Englewood Cliffs, N.J., 1976.
14. David Gries, *The Science of Programming*, Springer-Verlag, New York, 1981.
15. Harlan D. Mills et al., *Principles of Computer Programming: A Mathematical Approach*, Allyn and Bacon, Rockleigh, N.J., 1987.

# The Programming Language

Doug Bell
*School of Computing and Management Science*
*Sheffield Hallam University*
*Hallamshire Business Park*
*Sheffield S11 8HB, UK,*

Ian Morrey
*School of Computing and Management Science*
*Sheffield Hallam University*
*Hallamshire Business Park*
*Sheffield S11 8HB, UK*

John Pugh
*School of Computer Science*
*Carleton University*
*Ottawa, Canada*

## 1. Introduction

Everyone involved in programming has their favourite programming language, or language feature they would like to have available. This paper does not present a survey of programming languages, nor is it an attempt to recommend one language over another. Rather, we wish to discuss the features that a good programming language should have from the viewpoint of the software engineer. We limit our discussion to 'traditional' procedural languages such as Fortran, Cobol, Pascal, C, and Ada. The main thrust will be a discussion of the features a language should provide to assist the software development process. That is, what features encourage the development of software that is reliable, maintainable, and efficient?

It is important to realise that programming languages are very difficult animals to evaluate and compare. For example, although it is often claimed that language X is a general-purpose language, in practice languages tend to be used within particular communities. Thus, Cobol is often the preferred language of the data processing community; Fortran, the language of the scientist and engineer; C, the language of the systems programmer; and Ada, the language for developing real-time or embedded computer systems. Cobol is not equipped for applications requiring complex numerical computation, just as the data description facilities in Fortran are poor and ill-suited to data processing applications.

Programming languages are classified in many ways, for example, "high-level" or "low-level." A high-level language such as Cobol, Fortran, or Ada, is said to be problem-oriented and to reduce software production and maintenance costs. A low-level language such as assembler is said to be machine-oriented and to allow programmers complete control over the efficiency of their programs. Between high- and low-level languages, another class, the systems implementation language or high-level assembler, has emerged. Languages such as C attempt to bind into a single language the expressive power of a high-level language and the ultimate control that only a language that provides access at the register and primitive machine instruction level can provide. Languages may also be classified using other concepts such as whether they are block-structured or not, whether they are weakly or strongly typed, and whether they are compiled or interpreted.

The selection of a programming language for a particular project will be influenced by many factors not directly related to the programming language itself. For example, many organisations have a substantial investment in a particular programming language. Over a period of time, hundreds of thousands of lines of code may have been developed, and the programming staff will have built up considerable expertise with the language. In such a situation, there is often considerable resistance to change even if a "superior" language is available. There are other factors that can influence programming language selection. The software developer may be bound by a contract that actually specifies the implementation language. Decisions by the U.S. government to support Cobol and, more recently, Ada, considerably influenced the acceptance of those languages. Support from suppliers of major software components, such as language compilers and database management systems, will influence language selection for many developers. If an apparent bug appears in a compiler, for example, they need to know that they can pick up the telephone and get the supplier to help them. Similarly, the availability of software tools such as language-sensitive editors, debugging systems and project management tools may favour one programming language over another. The development of language-based programming environments that combine the programming language with an extensive set of development tools, such as UNIX (for C) and the Ada Programming Support Environment (APSE) will be an increasing influence on language selection.

Although the factors discussed above may influence the choice of programming language for a particular project, it is still most important to define what characteristics we expect from a programming language for software engineering. It is useful to divide the discussion into those features required to support *programming in the small* and those required to support *programming in the large*. By programming in the small, we mean those features of the language required to support the coding of individual program modules or small programs. In this category, we include the simplicity, clarity, and orthogonality of the language, the language syntax, and facilities for control and data abstraction. By programming in the large, we mean those features of the language that support the development of large programs. Here, we define a "large" program as one whose size or complexity dictates that it be developed by a number of programmers and which consists of a collection of individually developed program modules. In this category we include facilities for the separate compilation of program modules, features for controlling the interaction between program modules, high-level functional and data abstraction tools, and programming environments or support tools associated with the language.

## 2. Programming in the Small

### 2.1 Simplicity, Clarity, and Orthogonality

An important current school of thought argues that the only way to ensure that programmers will consistently produce reliable programs is to make the programming language simple. For programmers to become truly proficient in a language, the language must be small and simple enough that it can be understood in its entirety. The programmer can then use the language with confidence, probably without recourse to a language manual.

Cobol and PL/1 are examples of languages that are large and unwieldy. The ANSI standard for Cobol is 3 cm thick. By contrast, somewhat unfairly, the Pascal standard is 3 mm thick. What are the problems of large languages? Because they contain so many features, some are seldom used and, consequently, rarely fully understood. Also, since language features must not only be understood independently but also in terms of their interaction with each other, the larger the number of features, the more complex it will be to understand their interactions.

Although smaller, simpler languages are clearly desirable, the software engineer of the near future will have to wrestle with existing large, complex languages. For example, to meet the requirements laid down by its sponsors, the U.S. Department of Defense, the programming language Ada is a large and complex language requiring a three hundred page reference manual to describe it.

The clarity of a language is also an important factor. In recent years, there has been a marked and welcome trend to design languages for the programmers who program in them rather than for the machines the programs are to run on. Many older languages incorporate features that reflect the instruction sets of the computers they were originally designed to be executed on. The language designers of the sixties were motivated to prove that high-level languages could generate efficient code. Although we will be forever grateful to them for succeeding in proving this point, they introduced features into languages, such as Cobol and Fortran, that are clumsy and error-prone from the programmers' viewpoint. Moreover, even though the languages have subsequently been enhanced with features reflecting modern programming ideas, the original features still remain.

A programming language is the tool that programmers use to communicate their intentions. It should therefore be a language that accords with what people find natural, unambiguous, and meaningful—in other words, clear. Perhaps language designers are not the best judges of the clarity of a new language feature. A better approach to testing a language feature may be to set up controlled experiments in which subjects are asked to answer questions about fragments of program code. This experimental psychology approach is gaining some acceptance and some results are discussed later in the section on control abstractions. A programmer can only write reliable programs if he or she understands precisely what every language construct does. The quality of the language definition and supporting documentation are critical. Ambiguity or vagueness in the language definition erodes a programmer's confidence in the language. It should not be necessary to have to write a program fragment to confirm the semantics of some language feature.

Programming languages should also display a high degree of orthogonality. This means that it should be possible to combine language features freely; special cases and restrictions should not be prevalent. Although more orthogonal than many other languages, Pascal displays a lack of orthogonality in a number of areas. For example, it is entirely reasonable for a programmer to infer that values of all scalar types can be both read and written. In Pascal this is generally true, with the exception that booleans may be written but not read, and that enumerated types may not be read or written. Similarly, one would expect that functions would be able to return values of any type, rather than be restricted to returning values of only scalar types. A lack of orthogonality in a language has an unsettling effect on programmers; they no longer have the confidence to make generalizations and inferences about the language.

It is no easy matter to design a language that is simple, clear, and orthogonal. Indeed, in some cases these goals would seem to be incompatible with one another. A language designer could, for the sake of orthogonality, allow combinations of features that are not very useful. Simplicity would be sacrificed for increased orthogonality! While we await the simple, clear, orthogonal programming language of the future, these concepts remain good measures with which the software engineer can evaluate the programming languages of today.

**2.2 Language Syntax**

The syntax of a programming language should be consistent, natural, and promote the readability of programs. Syntactic flaws in a language can have a serious effect on program development. For example, studies have shown that syntax errors due to the misuse of semi-colons are ten times more likely to occur in a language using the semi-colon as a separator than in a language using it as a terminator. Another syntactic flaw found in languages is the use of BEGIN .. END pairs or bracketing conventions for grouping statements together. Omitting an END or closing bracket is a very common programming error. The use of explicit keywords, such as END IF and END WHILE, leads to fewer errors and more readily understandable programs. Programs are also easier to maintain.

The static, physical layout of a program should reflect as far as is possible the dynamic algorithm that the program describes. There are a number of syntactic concepts to help achieve this goal. The ability to freely format a program allows the programmer the freedom to use techniques such as indentation and blank lines to highlight the structure and improve the readability of a program. Older languages such as Fortran and Cobol imposed a fixed formatting style on the programmer. Components of statements were constrained to lie within certain columns on each input source line. These constraints are not intuitive to the programmer; rather, they date back to the time when programs were normally presented to the computer in the form of decks of 80-column punched cards. A program statement was normally expected to be contained on a single card.

The readability of a program can also be improved by the use of *meaningful identifiers* to name program objects. Limitations on the length of names, as found in early versions of BASIC (2 characters) and Fortran (6 characters), force the programmer to use unnatural, cryptic, and error-prone abbreviations. These restrictions were dictated by the need for efficient programming language compilers. Arguably, programming languages should be designed to be convenient for the programmer rather than the compiler and the ability to use meaningful names, irrespective of their length, enhances the self-documenting properties of a program.

Another factor that affects the readability of a program is the consistency of language syntax. For example, operators should not have different meanings in different contexts. The operator '=' should not double as both the assignment operator and the equality operator. Similarly, it should not be possible for the meaning of language keywords to change under programmer control. The keyword IF, for example, should be used solely for expressing conditional statements. If the programmer is able to define an array with the identifier IF, the time required to read and understand the program will be increased as we must now examine the context in which the identifier IF is used to determine its meaning.

**2.3 Control Abstractions**

A programming language for software engineering must provide a small but powerful set of control structures to describe the flow of execution within a program unit. In the late sixties and seventies there was considerable debate as to what control structures were required. The advocates of structured programming have largely won the day and there is now a reasonable consensus of opinion as to what kind of primitive control structures are essential. A language must provide primitives for the three basic structured programming constructs: sequence, selection, and repetition. There are, however, considerable variations both in the syntax and the semantics of the control structures found in modern programming languages. Early programming languages, such as Fortran, did not provide a rich set of control structures. The programmer used a set of low-level control structures, such as the unconditional branch or GOTO statement and the logical IF to express the control flow within a program. These low-level control structures provide the programmer with too much freedom to construct poorly structured programs. In particular, uncontrolled use of the GOTO statement for controlling program flow leads to programs that are hard to read and unreliable.

There is now general agreement that higher level control abstractions must be provided and should consist of:

- *Sequence*—to group together a related set of program statements
- *Selection*—to select whether a group of statements should be executed or not based on the value of some condition.
- *Repetition*—to repeatedly execute a group of statements.

This basic set of primitives fits in well with the top-down philosophy of program design; each primitive has a single entry point and a single exit point. These primitives are realized in similar ways in most programming languages. For brevity, we will look in detail only at representative examples from common programming languages.

### 2.3.1 Selection

Ada provides two basic selection constructs; the first, the IF statement, provides one or two-way selection and the second, the CASE statement, provides a convenient multi-way selection structure. When evaluating the conditional statements in a programming language, the following factors must be considered.

- Does the language use explicit closing symbols, such as END IF, thus avoiding the 'dangling else' problem?
- Nested conditional statements can quite easily become unreadable. Does the language provide any help? For example, the readability of "chained" IF statements can be improved by the introduction of an ELSIF clause. In particular, this eliminates the need for multiple ENDIF's to close a series of nested IF's.
- The expressiveness of the case statement is impaired if the type of the case selector is restricted. It should not have to be an integer.
- Similarly, it should be easy to specify multiple alternative case choices (for example, 1 | 5 | 7 meaning 1 or 5 or 7) and a range of values as a case choice (for example, Monday .. Friday or 1 .. 99).
- The reliability of the case statement is enhanced if the case choices must specify actions for **ALL** the possible values of the case selector. If not, the semantics should, at least, clearly state what will happen if the case expression evaluates to an unspecified choice. The ability to specify an action for all unspecified choices through a WHEN OTHERS or similar clause is optimal.

It would be natural to think that there would no longer be any controversy over language structures for selection. The IF-THEN-ELSE is apparently well-established. However, the lack of symmetry in the **IF** statement has been criticised. While it is clear that the THEN part is carried out if the condition is true, the ELSE part is instead tagged on at the end to cater for all other situations. Experimental evidence suggests that significantly fewer bugs will result if the programmer is required to restate the condition (in its negative form) prior to the ELSE as shown below:

```
IF condition THEN
   statement_1
NOT condition ELSE
   statement_2
ENDIF
```

### 2.3.2 Repetition

Control structures for repetition traditionally fall into two classes: loop structures where the number of iterations is fixed, and those where the number of iterations is controlled by the evaluation of some condition. The usefulness and reliability of the FOR statement for fixed length iterations can be affected by a number of issues:

- The type of the loop control variable should not be limited to integers. Any ordinal type should be allowed. However, reals should not be allowed. For example, how many iterations are specified by the following:

```
FOR X := 0.0 TO 1.0 STEP 0.33 DO
```

It is not at all obvious, and things are made worse by the fact, that computers represent real values only approximately. (Note how disallowing the use of reals as loop control variables conflicts with the aim of orthogonality).

- The semantics of the FOR is greatly affected by the answers to the following questions. When and how many times are the initial expression, final expression, and step expressions evaluated? Can any of these expressions be modified within the loop? What is of concern here is whether or not it is clear how many iterations of the loop will be performed. If the expressions can be modified and the expressions are recomputed on each iteration, then there is a distinct possibility of producing an infinite loop.
- Similar problems arise if the loop control variable can be modified within the loop. A conservative but safe approach similar to that taken by Pascal (which precludes assignment into the loop control variable) is preferred.
- The scope of the loop control variable is best limited to the FOR statement. If it is not, then what should its value be on exit from the loop, or should it be undefined?

Condition controlled loops are far simpler in form. Almost all modern languages provide a leading decision repetition structure (WHILE .. DO) and some, for convenience, also provide a trailing decision form (REPEAT .. UNTIL). The WHILE form continues to iterate while a condition evaluates to true. Since the test appears at the head of the form, the WHILE performs zero or many iterations of the loop body. The REPEAT, on the other hand, iterates until a condition is true. The test appears following the body of the loop ensuring that the REPEAT performs at least one iteration.

The WHILE and REPEAT structures are satisfactory for the vast majority of iterations we wish to specify. For the most part, loops that terminate at either their beginning or end are sufficient. However, there are situations, notably when encountering some exceptional condition, where it is appropriate to be able to branch out of a repetition structure at an arbitrary point within the loop. Often it is necessary to break out of a series of nested loops rather than a single loop. In many languages, the programmer is limited to two options. The terminating conditions of each loop can be modified to accommodate the "exceptional" exit and IF statements can be used within the loop to transfer control to the end of the loop should the exceptional condition occur. This solution is clumsy at best and considerably decreases the readability of the code. A second, and arguably better, solution is to use the much-maligned GOTO statement to branch directly out of the loops. Ideally however, since there is a recognised need for *N and a half* times loops, the language should provide a controlled way of exiting from one or more loops. Ada provides such a facility where an orderly EXIT may be made but only to the statement following the loop(s).

### 2.4 Data Types and Strong Typing

A significant part of the software engineer's task is concerned with how to model, within a program, objects from some problem domain. Programming, after all, is largely the manipulation of data. In the words of Niklaus Wirth, the designer of Pascal, Algorithms + Data Structures = Programs. The data description and manipulation facilities of a programming language should therefore allow the programmer to represent 'real-world' objects easily and faithfully. In recent years, increasing attention has been given to the problem of providing improved data abstraction facilities for programmers. Discussion has largely centered around the concept of a data type, the advantages of strongly typed languages, and language features to support abstract data types. The latter is an issue best considered in the context of 'programming in the large' and will therefore be discussed later.

A data type is a set of data objects and a set of operations applicable to all objects of that type. Almost all languages can be thought of as supporting this concept to some extent. Many languages require the programmer to explicitly define the type (for example, integer or character) of all objects to be used in a program and, to some extent or another, depending on the individual language, this information prescribes the operations that can be applied to the objects. Thus, we could state, for example, that Fortran, Cobol, C, Pascal, and Ada are all typed languages. However, only Pascal (mostly) and Ada would be considered strongly typed languages.

A language is said to be *strongly typed* if it can be determined at compile-time whether or not each operation performed on an object is consistent with the type of that object. Operations inconsistent with the type of an object are considered illegal. A strongly typed language therefore forces the programmer to consider more closely how objects are to be defined and used within a program. The additional information provided to the compiler by the programmer allows the compiler to perform automatic type-checking operations and discover type inconsistencies. Studies have shown that programs written in strongly typed languages are clearer, more reliable, and more portable. Strong typing necessarily places some restrictions on what a programmer may do with data objects. However, this apparent decrease in flexibility is more than compensated for by the increased security and reliability of the ensuing programs. Languages such as Lisp, APL, and POP-2 allow a variable to change its type at run-time. This is known as *dynamic typing* as opposed to the *static typing* found in languages where the type of an object is permanently fixed.

Where dynamic typing is employed, type checking must occur at run-time rather than compile-time. Dynamic typing provides additional freedom and flexibility but at a cost. More discipline is required on the part of the programmer so that the freedom provided by dynamic typing is not abused. That freedom is often very useful, even necessary, in some applications—for example, problem-solving programs that use sophisticated artificial intelligence techniques for searching complex data structures would be very difficult to write in languages without dynamic typing.

What issues need to be considered when evaluating the data type facilities provided by a programming language? We suggest the following list:

- Does the language provide an adequate set of primitive data types?
- Can these primitives be combined in useful ways to form aggregate or structured data types?
- Does the language allow the programmer to define new data types? How well do such new data types integrate with the rest of the language?
- To what extent does the language support the notion of strong typing?
- When are data types considered equivalent?
- Are type conversions handled in a safe and secure manner?
- Is it possible for the programmer to circumvent automatic type checking operations?

### 2.4.1 Primitive Data Types

Programmers are accustomed to having a rudimentary set of primitive data types available. We have come to expect that the primitive types, *Boolean*, *Character*, *Integer*, and *Real*, together with a supporting cast of operations (relational, arithmetic etc.) will be provided. For each type, it should be possible to clearly define the form of the literals or constants that make up the type. For example , the constants *true* and *false* make up the set of constants for the type *Boolean*.

Similarly, we should be able to define the operations for each type. For the type *Boolean*, these might include the operations =, <>, NOT, AND, and OR. For certain application domains, advanced computation facilities such as extended precision real numbers or long integers might be essential. The ability to specify the range of integers and reals and the precision to which reals are represented reduces the dependence on the physical characteristics, such as the word size, of a particular machine and thus increases the portability of programs. Types should only be associated with objects through explicit declarations. Implicit declarations, such as those allowed in Fortran, where, by default, undeclared variables beginning with the letters "I" through "N" are considered to be of type integer, should be avoided. The use of such conventions encourages the use of cryptic names.

The *Pointer* data type is provided by modern languages such as Pascal and Ada but not by older languages such as Fortran and Cobol. Pointers provide the programmer with the ability to refer to a data object indirectly. We can manipulate the object 'pointed' to or referenced by the pointer. Pointers are particularly useful in situations where the size of a data aggregate cannot be predicted in advance or where the structure of the aggregates are dynamically varying. Recursive data structures, such as lists and trees, are more easily described using pointers. Similarly, operations such as deleting an element from a linked list or inserting a new element into a balanced binary tree are more easily accomplished using pointers. Although such data types can be implemented using arrays, the mapping is less clear and certainly less flexible.

The use of pointers is not without pitfalls. The pointer is often mentioned in the same sentence as the infamous GOTO as a potential source for obtuse and error-prone code. A number of issues should be considered when evaluating a language's implementation of pointers.

- Since the same data object may be referenced through more than one pointer variable, care must be taken not to create 'dangling references'. That is, a pointer that references a location that is no longer in use. Does the language provide any assistance in reducing the opportunities for such errors?
- The security of pointers is enhanced in languages, such as Ada and Pascal, that require the programmer to bind a pointer variable to reference only objects of a particular type. Programs written in languages, such as C, that allow pointers to dynamically reference

different types of object are often awkward to debug.

- What provisions, for example, scoping mechanisms, explicit programmer action, or garbage collection procedures, does the language provide for the reclamation of space that is no longer referenced by any pointer variable?

The readability, reliability, and data abstraction capabilities of a language are enhanced considerably if the programmer can extend the primitive data types provided as standard by the language. The ability to define user-defined types separates the languages Pascal and Ada from their predecessors. In addition to defining completely new types, it is also useful to be able to define types that are subranges of existing types. In a strongly typed language the compiler can automatically generate code to perform run-time checks to ensure that this will always be so. In a weakly typed language, the responsibility for adding such code falls on the programmer.

**2.4.2 Structured Data Types**

Composite data types allow the programmer to model structured data objects. The most common aggregate data abstraction provided by programming languages is the *array*; a collection of homogeneous elements that may be referenced through their positions within the collection. Arrays are characterised by the type of their elements and by the index or subscript range or ranges that specify the size, number of dimensions, and how individual elements of the array may be referenced. Individual elements of an array can be referenced by specifying the array name and an expression for each subscript. The implementation of arrays in programming languages raises the following considerations for the programmer.

- What restrictions are placed on the element type? For complete freedom of expression, there should be no restrictions. Similarly, the index type should be any valid subrange of any ordinal type.
- At what time must the size of an array be known? The utility of arrays in a programming language is governed by the time (compile-time or run-time) at which the size of the array must be known.
- What aggregate operations may be applied to arrays? For example, it is very convenient to be able to carry out array assignment between compatible arrays.
- Are convenient methods available for the initialisation of arrays?

The time at which a size must be bound to an array has important implications on how the array may be used. In Pascal, the size of an array must be defined statically. The size and subscript ranges are required to be known at compile-time. This has the advantage of allowing the compiler to generate code to automatically check for out of range subscripts. However, the disadvantage of this simple scheme is that, to allow the program to accommodate data sets of differing sizes, we often wish to delay determining the size of the array until run-time. A further problem exists in Pascal in that formal array parameters to procedures must also specify their size statically. This makes it impossible to write a general routine to manipulate an arbitrary-sized matrix. Rather, a specific routine must be defined for each particular size of matrix. This is very inconvenient and inefficient; many implementations of Pascal now include a feature (conformant arrays) to deal with this very problem. However, less restrictive approaches are to be found. Ada, for example, allows the specification of array types in which the subscript ranges are not fixed at compile-time.

Data objects in problem domains are not always simply collections of homogeneous objects. Rather, they are often collections of heterogeneous objects. Although such collections can be represented using arrays, most programming languages, but notably not Fortran, provide a *record* data aggregate. *Records* (or structures) are generalisations of arrays where the elements (or fields) may be of different types and where individual components are referenced by (field) name rather than by position. Each component of a record may be of any type including aggregate types such as arrays and records. Similarly, the element type of an array might be a record type.

Programming languages that provide data abstractions such as arrays and records and allow them to be combined orthogonally in this fashion allow a wide range of real data objects to be modelled in a natural fashion. This is not true of all languages; for example, Fortran. Components of records are selected by naming the required field rather than by providing a numeric subscript.

Sometimes, records whose structure is not completely fixed can be useful. Such records normally contain a special field, known as the tag field, the value of which determines the structure of the record. Records with varying structures are known as *variant records* or, since the record type can be thought of as a union of several subtypes based on some discriminating tag field, as *discriminated unions*. In Pascal, the implementation of variant records is very insecure. Pascal allows programmers to assign into the tag field of a variant record variable at any time. This logically indicates a dynamic change in the structure of the record. As a consequence no run-time checks are performed and the onus is on the programmer to write defensive code to ensure no illegal references to variant fields are made. Furthermore, Pascal allows the tag field to be omitted.

Variant records are one reason why Pascal is not considered as strongly typed as Ada. Ada adopts a safer approach, restricting the programmer to specify the tag field when a record variable is created and disallowing subsequent changes to the value of the tag field.

### 2.4.3 Strong versus Weak Typing

The debate as to whether strongly typed languages are preferable to weakly typed languages closely mirrors the earlier debate among programming language afficionados about the virtues of the GOTO statement. The pro-GOTO group argued that the construct was required and its absence would restrict programmers. The anti-GOTO group contended that indiscriminate use of the construct encouraged the production of "spaghetti-like" code. The result has been a compromise; the use of the GOTO is restricted to cases where it is clearly the most convenient control structure to use.

The anti-strongly typed languages group similarly argue that some classes of programs are very difficult, if not impossible, to write in strongly typed languages. The pro-strongly typed languages group argue that the increased reliability and security outweigh these disadvantages. We believe that a similar compromise will be struck; strong typing will be generally seen as most desirable but languages will provide well-defined escape mechanisms to circumvent type checking for those instances where it is truly required.

What programmer flexibility is lost in a strongly typed language? Weakly typed languages such as Fortran and C provide little compile-time type-checking support. However, they do provide the ability to view the representation of an object as different types. For example, using the EQUIVALENCE statement in Fortran, a programmer is able to subvert typing. This language feature is dangerous; programs using it will be unclear and not be portable. Variant records in Pascal can be used in a similar, underhand fashion to circumvent type-checking operations.

To a small number of systems programming applications, the ability to circumvent typing to gain access to the underlying physical representation of data is essential. How should this be provided in a language that is strongly typed? The best solution seems to be to force the programmer to state *explicitly* in the code that he or she wishes to violate the type checking operations of the language. This approach is taken by Ada where an object may be reinterpreted as being of a different type only by using the UNCHECKED_CONVERSION facility.

The question of conversion between types is inextricably linked with the strength of typing in a language. Fortran, being weakly typed, performs many conversions (or coercions) implicitly during the evaluation of arithmetic expressions. These implicit conversions may result in a loss of information and can be dangerous to the programmer. Fortran allows mixed mode arithmetic and freely converts reals to integers on assignment. Pascal and strongly typed languages perform implicit conversions **only** when there will be no accompanying loss of information. Thus, an assignment of an integer to a real variable will result in implicit conversion of the integer to a real. However, an attempt to assign a real value to an integer variable will result in a type incompatibility error. Such an assignment must be carried out using an explicit conversion function. That is, the programmer is forced by the language to explicitly consider the loss of information implied by the use of the conversion function.

## 2.5 Procedural Abstraction

Procedural or algorithmic abstraction is one of the most powerful tools in the programmer's arsenal. When designing a program, we abstract *what* should be done before we specify *how* it should be done. Program designs evolve as layers of abstractions; each layer specifying more detail than the layer above. Procedural abstractions in programming languages, such as procedures and functions, allow the layered design of a program to be accurately reflected in the modular structure of the program text. Even in relatively small programs, the ability to factor a program into small, functional modules is essential; factoring increases the readability and maintainability of programs. What does the software engineer require from a language in terms of support for procedural abstraction? We suggest the following list of requirements.

- An adequate set of primitives for defining procedural abstractions, including support for recursion.
- Safe and efficient mechanisms for controlling communication between program units.
- Simple, clearly defined mechanisms for controlling access to data objects defined within program units.

The basic procedural abstraction primitives provided in programming languages are *procedures* and *functions*. Procedures can be thought of as extending the statements of the language while functions can be thought of as extending the operators of the language. When a procedure is called, it achieves its effect by modifying the environment of the program unit that called it. Optimally, this effect is communicated to the calling program unit in a controlled fashion by the modification of the parameters passed to the procedure. Functions, like their mathematical counterparts, may return only a single value and must therefore be embedded within expressions.

The power of procedural abstraction is that it allows the programmer to consider the procedure or function as an independent entity performing a well-described task largely independent of the rest of the program. It is critical that the interface between program units be small and well defined if we are to achieve independence between units. Procedures should only accept and return information through their parameters. Functions should accept but not return information through their parameters. A single result should be returned as the result of invoking a function.

Unfortunately, programming languages do not enforce even these simple, logical rules. It is largely the responsibility of the programmer to ensure that procedures and functions do not have side effects. The programming language itself does not prevent programmers from directly accessing and modifying data objects defined outside of the local environment of the procedure or function. Many abstractions, particularly those that manipulate recursive data structures such as lists, graphs, and trees, are more concisely described recursively. Amongst widely used languages, Cobol and Fortran do not support recursion directly.

**2.5.1 Parameter Passing Mechanisms**

Programmers require three basic modes of interaction through parameters:

- *Input Parameters* to allow a procedure or function *read-only* access to an actual parameter. The actual parameter is purely an input parameter; the procedure or function should not be able to modify the value of the actual parameter.
- *Output Parameters* to allow a procedure *write-only* access to an actual parameter. The actual parameter is purely an output parameter; the procedure should not be able to read the value of the actual parameter.
- *Input-Output Parameters* to allow a procedure *read-write* access to an actual parameter. The value of the actual parameter may be modified by the procedure.

Note that, by definition, Output and Input-Output parameters should not be supplied to functions. Most programming languages, including Fortran and Pascal, do not automatically enforce this restriction. Again, the onus is on the programmer not to write functions with side-effects. These same languages also, unfortunately, restrict the type of result that may be returned from functions to scalar types only. Ada only allows Input variables to functions but side effects may still occur through modification of non-local variables.

A number of parameter-passing schemes are employed in programming languages but no language provides a completely safe and secure parameter-passing mechanism. Fortran employs only a single parameter passing mode; *call by reference*. This mode equates to Input-Output parameters. Thus, undesirably, all actual parameters in Fortran may potentially be changed by any subroutine or function. The programmer is responsible for ensuring the safe implementation of Input and Output parameters. Using call by reference, the location of the actual parameter is bound to the formal parameter. The formal and actual parameter names are thus *aliases*; modification of the formal parameter automatically modifies the actual parameter. This method is particularly appropriate for passing large, aggregate data structures as parameters as no copying of the values of the parameters will be carried out.

Pascal uses both call by reference (*VAR* parameters) and *call by value*. Call by reference is used for both Input-Output and Output parameters while call by value provides a more secure implementation of Input parameters. When parameters are passed by value, a copy of the value of the actual parameter is passed to the formal parameter, which acts as a variable local to the procedure; modification of the formal parameter therefore does not modify the value of the actual parameter. This method is inefficient for passing large, aggregate data structures, as copies must be made. In such situations, it is commonplace to pass the data structure by reference even if the parameter should not be modified by the procedure.

*Call by value-result* is often used as an alternative to call by reference for Input-Output parameters. It avoids the use of aliases at the expense of copying. Parameters passed by value-result are initially treated as in call by value; a copy of the value of the actual parameter is passed to the formal parameter that again acts as a local variable. Manipulation of the formal parameter does not immediately affect the actual parameter. On exit from the procedure, the final value of the formal is assigned into the actual parameter.

*Call by result* may be used as an alternative to call by reference for Output parameters. Parameters passed by value are treated exactly as those passed by value-result except that no initial value is assigned to the local formal parameter.

The parameter-passing mechanisms used in Ada (*in*, *out*, and *in out*) are described in a similar fashion to the input, output, and input-output parameters described above and would therefore seem to be ideal. However, Ada does not specify whether they are to be implemented using sharing or copying. Though beneficial to the language implementor, since the space requirements of the parameter can be used to determine whether sharing or copying should be used, this decision can be troublesome to the programmer. In the presence of aliases, call by value-result and call by reference may return different results.

### 2.5.2 Scoping Mechanisms and Information Hiding

It should not be necessary for the programmer to know the implementation details of a procedure or a function in order to use it. In particular, the programmer should not need to consider the names used within the procedure or function. Large programs use thousands of names; the names used within a procedure should not influence the choice of names outside it. Similarly, objects used within the procedure, other than output or input-output parameters, should have no effect outside the procedure. When programs are developed by more than one programmer these issues become critical. Programmers must be able to develop routines independently of each other. The software engineer requires that a language support the concept of *information hiding*; concealing information that is not required. Advanced language features for the support of information hiding will be discussed in the next section. We limit discussion here to the control of access to data objects through scoping.

Programming languages use the concept of *scope* to control the visibility of names. The scope of a name in a program is the part of the program in which the name may be referenced. Support for scoping varies from language to language. BASIC provides no scoping and all names may therefore be referenced anywhere in a program. That is, all variables are *global*. This severely limits the usefulness of the language for the development of large programs.

The unit of scope in Fortran is the subroutine or function. Since subroutines and functions may not be nested, the scope of a name is the subroutine or function in which it is implicitly or explicitly declared. That is, all names are *local* to the program unit in which they are declared. There are no global names although the same effect may be achieved through the use of shared COMMON blocks.

Algol, Pascal, and Ada are known as *block-structured* languages. They use the more sophisticated concept of nested program blocks to control the scope of names. The scope of a name is the block (program, procedure, or function) in which it is declared. The multi-level scoping control offered by block-structured languages is of great assistance to the software engineer. Names may be re-used within the same program safely. More importantly, some information hiding is now possible.

## 3. Programming In The Large

The programming of very large, complex software projects, or programming in the large, introduces many new problems for the software engineer. First, what are the characteristics of such software systems? The size of the code is an obvious factor. Large systems consist of tens of thousands of lines of source code; systems with hundreds of thousands of lines are not uncommon. Projects of this size must be developed by teams of programmers; for very large projects the programming team may consist of hundreds of programmers. Such systems are implemented over a long period of time and when completed are expected to undergo continual maintenance and enhancement over an extended lifetime. Many of the problems associated with such large projects are logistical, caused by the sheer size of the task and the number of personnel involved. Methodologies for managing such projects have been developed and clearly many software tools, other than the programming language being used, are required to assist and control the development of such large systems. A recent trend has been to integrate these software tools with a particular programming language to form an integrated software development environment. An example of this is the Ada Programming Support Environment (APSE). In this section, we concentrate on support for programming in the large at the programming language level.

What support can we expect from a programming language? The programmer's chief tool in managing complexity is abstraction. Abstraction allows the programmer to keep a problem intellectually manageable. The programming language must therefore provide mechanisms that can be used to encapsulate the most common abstractions used by programmers: functional (or procedural) abstraction and data abstraction. The simplest mechanism, provided by nearly all programming languages, is the procedure: a program unit that allows the encapsulation of a functional abstraction. Programming in the large requires that higher level abstraction primitives than the procedure be provided.

The use of abstractions promotes modularity, which itself encourages the production of reusable code, and promotes the notion of information hiding. Modularity and module independence are essential in an environment where individual modules will most often be developed by different programmers. The programming language can support development in multi-programmer environments by providing mechanisms for hiding from a user irrelevant details concerning the implementation of a module.

Additionally, the interface between modules must be carefully controlled. It is essential to eliminate the possibility that the implementation of one module may affect another module in some unanticipated manner. This is also important when a system is being maintained or enhanced in some way. It must be possible to localise the effect of some system enhancement or error fix to specific modules of the system; side effects of changes should not propagate throughout the complete system.

Clearly, many of these issues are as much system design issues as they are programming language issues. No programming language will solve the problems of a poor system design. On the other hand, the implementation of a good system design can be hampered if the implementation language is of limited expressive power. If modules are to be developed independently, the programming language must also provide facilities for the independent compilation of program modules. In addition, the language should provide strong type-checking across module boundaries to ensure the consistency of calls to externally defined modules.

### 3.1 Functional and Data Abstraction

Functional abstraction is the traditional abstraction tool of the programmer. Programming methodologies such as top-down, stepwise refinement rely totally on functional abstraction. In programming language terms, such abstractions can be thought of as extending the operations provided by the language and appear within programs in the form of procedures and functions. In recent years, increasing attention has been paid to the notion of data abstraction. Many program design decisions involve:

- selecting an internal representation for some set of data objects from the problem domain.
- defining the operations to be performed on those objects.

In programming language terms, this can be thought of as extending the built-in primitive data types provided by a language with new *abstract data types*. The two abstraction mechanisms are complementary and are often used in concert with one another. Functional abstraction is often used to describe the implementation of the operations on abstract data types.

What do we require in terms of programming language support for data abstraction? An abstract data type consists of a set of objects and a set of operations that can be applied to those objects. The power of an abstraction mechanism is that it permits understanding of the essential ideas whilst suppressing irrelevant details. Thus, programming languages should support the concept of information hiding; that is, users should be provided with sufficient information to use the data type but nothing more. The most common way of achieving this is to separate out the specification of the data type from its implementation and to implement protection (scoping) mechanisms to ensure the privacy of information that should not be accessible to users. Users of a data type should be provided with a specification of the effect of each of the operations provided and a description of how to use each operation. They should not be required to know the representation of the data type nor be able to access it other than indirectly through an operation provided by the type. In summary, programming language support for abstraction should include:

- high-level encapsulation mechanisms for both functional and data abstraction.
- a clear separation between the specification (the users' view) of an abstraction and its implementation (the implementor's view).
- protection mechanisms to prevent user access to private information.
- support for the reusable program modules, that is, provision of library facilities and simple mechanisms for importing library modules into user programs.

#### 3.1.1 Abstraction in Pascal

Pascal provides support for functional abstraction at the level of the procedure or function. There are no standard mechanisms to encapsulate collections of procedures although many non-standard extensions exist. Programming language support for abstract data types is variable; many programming languages, including Pascal, only provide support for what might be termed *transparent* data types: data types whose representation may be directly accessed by the programmer. That is, the representation is visible, not hidden. Pascal provides little support for data abstraction. There is no way of encapsulating a data type into a single program module. The data type and the application program are inextricably mixed. There is no clear mapping between the logical data type specified by the designer and the physical modules of the program. The lack of an encapsulation mechanism and the strict ordering (CONST, TYPE, VAR ..) of declarations enforced by Pascal poses almost insurmountable organisation problems in programs that require the use of multiple data types.

### 3.1.2 Abstraction in Ada

Ada provides far greater support for programming in the large than Pascal. Ada provides encapsulation mechanisms at the subprogram and package level. A package can encapsulate simply a collection of related procedures or can be used to encapsulate an abstract data type. A package consists of two parts; a specification and a body (or implementation). Each of these parts may be separately compiled. The specification can be used by the programmer to describe to users how to use the package and to determine what components of the package are to be visible to the user. The package body contains the implementation of all procedures belonging to the package and is not normally seen by users of the package. Thus, Ada satisfies our requirements for a high-level encapsulation mechanism and for a clear separation between the specification of an abstraction and its implementation.

Logically, details of the representation of the type should be in the package body rather than the specification. Unfortunately, Ada requires that details of the representation be provided in the specification. This enables the specification and body of the package to be compiled separately. However, the representation of the type is declared as private and described in the private part of the specification and is thus automatically protected from access by users of the type.

Unlike in Pascal, it is not possible for the Ada programmer to directly reference the representation of the type. Indeed, the representation of the type could be altered by the implementor without impacting on users of the type. Ada promotes reusable software by viewing packages as resources that should normally reside in a library from where they may be imported into any program, and it is the responsibility of the Ada programmer to explicitly state the dependency relationships between modules.

### 3.1.3 Generics—An advanced abstraction mechanism

The strong typing philosophy of programming languages such as Pascal and Ada can have a detrimental effect on programming efficiency. For example, suppose we defined a stack of integers as an abstract data type with the normal stack operations of Push and Pop, and so forth. If we subsequently needed another stack type, but one in which the elements were booleans rather than integers, then clearly the specification and implementation would be identical apart from the different stack element types. In Pascal, our only recourse would be to duplicate the stack data type; Push and Pop operations and a different representation would have to be provided for each of the two stack types. A more powerful stack abstraction is required that allows the stack element type to be parameterised.

The generic facility found in Ada and other languages provides a partial answer to this problem. Generics allow programmers to define templates (or patterns) for packages and procedures. These templates may then be used to instantiate actual packages and procedures with different parameters. Notwithstanding generics, statically typed programming languages restrict programmer flexibility in dealing with abstract data types. For example, in a statically typed language such as Ada all packages must be instantiated at compile-time. It is not possible, for example, to create stacks whose element types are determined dynamically or where the elements in the stack may not all be of the same type.

## 3.2 Separate Compilation

A programming language is ill-suited for the development of large, complex programs if it does not provide facilities for the separate compilation of program modules. Large programs must necessarily be developed by teams of programmers; individual programmers must be able to work independently and at the same time access programs written by other members of the team. Programming language support is required for the integration of routines that have been developed separately. Additional support in this area is often provided by environmental tools such as linkers, cross-reference generators, file librarians, and source code control systems. What support should the programming language itself provide? We suggest the following:

- independent compilation of program modules.
- easy access to libraries of precompiled software.
- the ability to integrate routines written in different languages.
- strong type checking across module boundaries.
- the ability to avoid the unnecessary recompilation of pre-compiled modules.

One of the foremost reasons for the continued popularity of Fortran is the tremendous resource of reusable software available to scientists and engineers through the readily accessible libraries of scientific and engineering subroutines. Fortran provides independent compilation of modules at the subroutine level and easy access to library routines but performs no run-time checking of calls to external routines. It is the responsibility of the programmer to check that the correct number and type of parameters are used in the calling program.

Standard Pascal provides no support for separate compilation. All modules must be integrated into a single, large program that is then compiled. In order to support the development of large programs, many implementations support language extensions that provide at least independent compilation, access to libraries, and the ability to integrate assembly language routines into Pascal programs. The major disadvantage of this approach is that programs using these non-standard extensions are no longer immediately portable.

Ada provides far greater support for separate compilation than Pascal or Fortran. Both subprograms and packages may be compiled as separate modules with strong type checking across module boundaries to ensure that they are used in accordance with their specifications. The specification and implementation of a package may be compiled in two separate parts. This has a number of advantages for the software engineer. The strong type checking ensures that all specifications stay in line with their implementations. Also, it means that once the specification for a package has been compiled, modules that use that package may also be compiled (even before the implementation of the package has been completed).

## 4. Summary

In this paper we have surveyed the characteristics that a programming language should have from the viewpoint of the software engineer. In summary, the following issues have been considered fundamentally important.

A programming language should:

- be well matched to the application area of the proposed project
- be clear and simple, and display a high degree of orthogonality
- have a syntax that is consistent and natural, and that promotes the readability of programs
- provide a small but powerful set of control abstractions
- provide an adequate set of primitive data abstractions
- support strong typing
- provide support for scoping and information hiding
- provide high-level support for functional and data abstraction
- provide a clear separation of the specification and the implementation of program modules
- support separate compilation

While software engineers, language designers and programmers might argue about the inclusion of particular items on the above list (or may suggest other issues that have been excluded), it is apparent that the features of an implementation language can have a profound effect on the success or failure of a project. Moreover, the programming task should not be isolated from its wider software engineering context.

## 5. Bibliography


Watt, D.A. *Programming Language Concepts and Paradigms*, Prentice Hall, Englewood Cliffs, N.J., 1990.

Meyer, B. *Introduction to the Theory of Programming Languages*, Prentice Hall, Englewood Cliffs, N.J., 1990.

Bell, D., Morrey, I. and Pugh, J. *Software Engineering—A Programming Approach*, Prentice Hall, Englewood Cliffs, N.J., 1992.

Booch, G. and Bryan, D. *Software Engineering with Ada*, Addison-Wesley, Reading, Mass., 1994.

# Chapter 7

# Software Validation, Verification, and Testing

## 1. Introduction to Chapter

In the past, testing was considered to be a separate phase of the software life cycle that followed coding. Two developments have caused this idea to be reconsidered. First, the linear sequential view of the life cycle is now only one of many possible approaches, so the activities that precede or follow another activity cannot always be stated completely and in advance. Second, the activity of ensuring that software is correct is no longer considered to take place only after the code has been written—it takes place throughout the software development process.

This second viewpoint has led to the concept of validation and verification (V&V) as a unified approach to identifying and resolving software problems and high-risk issues early in the software cycle [1]. V&V can also be defined as a software system engineering process employing a rigorous methodology for evaluating the correctness and quality of the software product through the software lifecycle [2]. However, in some contexts, validation and verification retain separate, independent definitions:

SOFTWARE VALIDATION,
VERIFICATION, AND
TESTIN

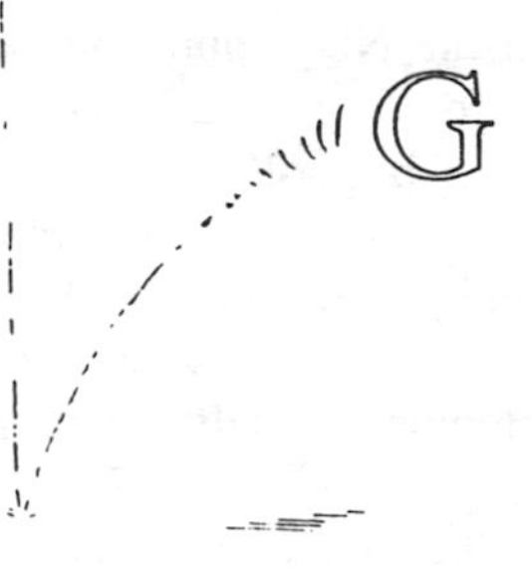

- *Verification and Validation* (V&V)—the process of determining whether the requirements for a system or component are complete and correct, the products of each development phase fulfill the requirements or conditions imposed by the previous phase, and the final system or component complies with specified requirements [3].
- *Verification*—the process of determining whether or not the products of a given phase of the software development cycle fulfill the requirements established for them at the end of the previous phase. Verification answers the question, "Are we building the system right?"
- *Validation*—the determination of the correctness of the final program or software produced from a development project with respect to the user's needs and requirements. Validation answers the question, "Are we building the right system?" [1]

Readers interested in a more extensive treatment of software verification and validation than can be provided in this Tutorial are referred to a recent publication by Robert O. Lewis [4].

This Tutorial takes the viewpoint that testing is integral to a program of ensuring the correctness of the software product, so the topics of V&V and testing are treated together in this chapter.

## 2. Introduction to Papers

The first paper on software verification and validation is a revision and updating of the US National Institute of Standards and Technology (NIST) Special Publication 500-165. Both the NIST publication and the new paper were written by Roger Fujii and Dolores Wallace. This paper describes software V&V and its objectives and recommended tasks, and provides guidance for selecting techniques to perform the task. It explains the differences between V&V and quality assurance, and how development, quality assurance, V&V, and other software engineering practitioners can use V&V techniques to produce quality software.

The second article, an original paper by Frank Ackerman, describes software inspections, undoubtedly one of the best tools available to the software engineering practitioner to assure a quality software system. Software inspections were developed and described by Michael Fagan [5], who worked for IBM in the 1970s. Essentially, software inspections are a form of peer review (like walkthroughs), which use the ability of individuals, not under pressure, willing to discuss freely the work being done to find errors in a software artifact.

Ackerman's paper provides a description of an inspection, the steps that the team must go through to ensure a quality inspection, a description of the people involved in a software inspection, and the benefits and results of a good software inspection. Ackerman also shows that properly applied software inspections are cost-effective through early detection of software errors.

The third paper in this chapter is an original paper by John Marciniak on the subject of reviews and audits. This paper is an update to Marciniak's article of the same title in the *Encyclopedia of Software Engineering* [6]. In addition to writing that article, Marciniak edited the entire encyclopedia. In this paper, Marciniak describes a review as a process during which a work product or a set of work products is presented to project personnel, managers, users, customers, and/or interested parties for consent or approval. Types of reviews include audits, peer reviews, design reviews, formal qualification reviews, requirements reviews and test reviews. A definition is provided for each of these review types.

Marciniak also defines two categories of reviews: formal reviews, which are required by contract commitment, and informal reviews, which, although not contractually required, are held because of their perceived benefits. He also integrates reviews, audits, walkthroughs, and inspections into the software development life cycle and shows when a given review might be held as well as the impact this review has on the life cycle and its products. He does not describe the activities of an inspection, only those of a walkthrough.

The fourth paper, on traceability, was written for this Tutorial by James Palmer of George Mason University. Palmer defines traceability and a number of other related terms. He notes that traceability should be established among requirements, design, code, test, and implementation. He then describes the state of the practice, and the benefits of establishing and maintaining traceability during system development. He notes that, even with tool support, establishment of traceability is a labor-intensive process, because it is necessary to read and understand the system documents (requirements, design, test plans, and so forth) in order to define those elements that trace to each other.

Palmer describes an ideal process for establishing traceability and explains why the actual process used in practice is different. He states that it is difficult or impossible to establish the "return on investment" of traceability, because, while the cost is easy to determine, the benefit is in errors or rework avoided and in reducing the risk of building an unsatisfactory product. He describes the current state of tool support for traceability. Most tools require the user to establish traceability; the tools then manage the resulting database and provide information conveniently. Some tools, however, provide semi-automated approaches that assist the user in establishing traceability. Palmer concludes with a summary of current research and a projection of future tools and technology for traceability.

The final paper in this chapter is "A Review of Software Testing," by David Coward of Bristol Polytechnic in the UK. The paper was taken from an earlier IEEE Tutorial, *Software Engineering: A European Perspective*. The author acknowledges that, until software can be built perfectly, there will be some need for software testing. The principal objective of testing, according to Coward, is to gain confidence in the software.

Coward divides testing into two categories, functional and non-functional. Functional testing addresses whether the program produces the correct output. Non-functional testing addresses such elements as quality, design constraints, and interface specifications.

The author describes and recommends several testing strategies, for example:

- *Functional versus structural testing—Functional testing* requires you to derive test data from the functions (requirements) of a system. *Structural testing* requires you to derive test data from the structure (design) of the system, and includes program proving, symbolic execution, and anomaly analysis. The terms "black box" and "white box," respectively, are also used to describe these two forms of testing.
- *Static versus dynamic analysis—Static analysis* involves measuring the system under test when it is not running. *Dynamic analysis* requires that the software be executed and relies on instrumenting the program to measure internal data and logic states as well as outputs.

Coward emphasizes the need to separate software developers from software testers in order to ensure that the software is given a rigorous test. The author provides a very good bibliography of testing references at the end of his paper.


1. Boehm, B.W., "Verifying and Validating Software Requirements and Design Specifications," *IEEE Software*, Vol. 1, No. 1, Jan. 1984, pp. 75–88.
2. *IEEE Standards for Verification and Validation Plans Seminar*, The Institute of Electrical and Electronics Engineers, Inc., Piscataway, NJ, 1987.
3. IEEE Standard 610.12, *IEEE Standard Glossary of Software Engineering Terminology*, The Institute of Electrical and Electronics Engineers, Inc., Piscataway, NJ, 1993.
4. Lewis, Robert O., Independent Verification & Validation: A Life Cycle Engineering Process for Quality Software, Wiley and Sons, New York, 1992.
5. Fagan, M.E., "Design and Code Inspections to Reduce Errors in Program Development," *IBM Systems J.*, Vol. 15, No. 3, 1976, pp. 182–211.
6. Marciniak, John J., Editor-in-Chief, *Encyclopedia of Software Engineering*, 2 vols., John Wiley, New York, 1994.

# Software Verification and Validation (V&V)

Roger U. Fujii
*Logicon, Incorporated*
*222 West Sixth Street*
*San Pedro, CA 90733-0471*

Dolores R. Wallace
*National Computer Systems Laboratory*
*National Institute of Standards and Technology*
*Gaithersburg, MD 20899*

## Abstract

*Software engineering standards tie together to provide a strong framework for ensuring quality computer systems. Standards for software verification and validation (V&V), a systems engineering approach to ensure quality software, support the requirements of standards for project management and quality assurance. When used together, they contribute to safe, secure, reliable, and maintainable computer systems.*

*This report describes software V&V, its objectives, recommended tasks, and guidance for selecting techniques to perform the tasks. It explains differences between V&V and quality assurance, and how development, quality assurance, V&V, and other software engineering practitioners can use V&V techniques to produce quality software. While two studies of V&V's cost-effectiveness have different conclusions, an analysis of the parameters of those studies suggests that the benefits of V&V outweigh the costs associated with it.*

*This report describes six existing software engineering standards for software verification and validation. A description is provided on which standards contain guidance for scoping the V&V effort, planning the V&V effort, and managing the V&V effort.*

## 1. Introduction

The purpose of this paper is to provide a brief introduction to Software Verification and Validation (V&V). Traditionally, software V&V is defined as a systems engineering methodology to ensure that quality (that is, emphasizing correctness, reliability, and usability) is built into the software during development. The analysis and test activities performed by V&V evaluate and assess the software products and development processes during each software life cycle phase in parallel with, not after the completion of, the development effort. This evaluation and assessment provides early identification of errors, assessment of software performance, compliance with requirements, identification of program risks, and assessment of the quality of development processes and products. Because software is becoming an integral part of linking the system together, V&V ensures that the examined software performs correctly within the system context (that is, system performance, system stimuli and operating environment, user features across the system, among others).

Software V&V is complementary to and supportive of quality assurance, project management, systems engineering, and development. V&V utilizes unique V&V techniques in addition to well-proven techniques used by these other complementary development functional groups. V&V uses these techniques to (1) unravel the details of the software product or process; (2) examine each individual detail piece to determine its correctness; and (3) determine completeness, correctness, and other quality attributes when the pieces are viewed as a whole from an unbiased persepective. Figure 1 illustrates how V&V activities supports the other functional groups (that is, development, systems engineering, and quality assurance) of the development effort.

By examining the software in detail and assessing the detailed pieces against the total system requirements, software V&V attacks two of the major contributors to software failures: (1) incorrect or missing requirements (lack of understanding the problem to be solved by software); and (2) poor organization in software architecture and failure to plan effectively (managing information complexity). Our modern software paradigms and techniques can assist in deal-

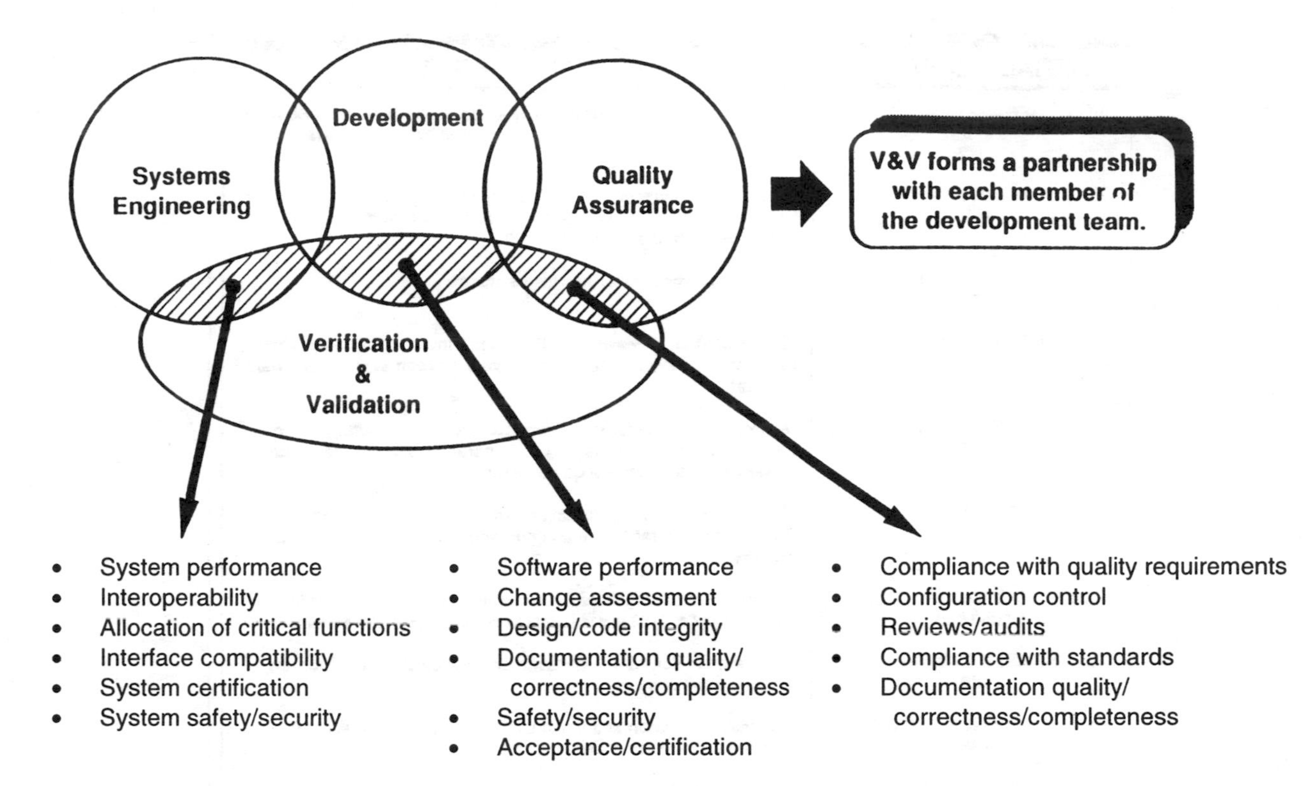


*Figure 1. Relationship of V&V to the development team*

ing with these causes of primary software failures, and software V&V in particular is a powerful technique to address these types of failures.

In the remainder of the paper, the primary V&V techniques used in life cycle phase will be described. A section of the paper will describe a selction of standards on software V&V that are representative of the currect standards used by United States Federal agencies, industries, and academia.

## 2. Overview Of Software Verification and Validation

In 1961, a software error caused the destruction of a Mariner payload on board a radio-controlled Atlas booster. The Atlas guidance software had used incorrect radar data to compute navigation and steering commands. The cause was a simple programming error of misusing a hyphen on previous data rather than on the corrected, extrapolated data.

This simple but expensive error led the Air Force to require independent review of the guidance equations and software implementation of all future mission-critical space launches. This need to ensure software quality and to have high confidence in the correct performance of the system gave birth to the methodology of software verification and validation. At a time when missile guidance theories and computer technologies were still in their infancy and many unknowns were yet to be solved, software V&V proved highly successful in providing the independent assessment of the proposed technical solution's correctness. Through early identification and correction of errors, V&V also succeeded in developing higher confidence in the system. Program managers made better decisions because they now had the technical insight and advanced notice of risk-prone areas to make informed decisions. Since then, software V&V has become a powerful risk management tool.

As these and other benefits of V&V became apparent in improved software quality, including safety and security, complex information systems outside the Department of Defense began using the V&V methodology. Today, the methodology has proliferated throughout the Department of Defense (DOD) services, the Federal Aviation Administration, and the National Aeronautics and Space Administration, as well as medical and nuclear power industries. The history of the growth of V&V is shown in Figure 2; some agencies, like the Food and Drug Administration, are presently deciding how to incorporate V&V requirements into their policies and procedures regarding medical devices.

In many cases, V&V is governed by standards establishing software development, project management, and software quality assurance requirements. Government and industry began to develop V&V standards because managers needed a specification of

| INITIAL RELEASE | STANDARD/REGULATION |
|---|---|
| AFR 122-9/-10<br>1970 | "Design Certification Program for Nuclear Weapon System Software and Firmware" for Air Force nuclear weapon systems software (mandatory) |
| AFR 800-14<br>1975 | "Acquisition Management: Acquisition and Support Procedures for Computer Resources in Systems" for acquisition of major Air Force embedded computer systems |
| MIL-STD-1679<br>1978 | "Software Development " for Navy systems |
| JCMPO INST 8020.1<br>1981 | "Safety Studies, Reviews, and Evaluation Involving Nuclear Weapon Systems" for Navy nuclear cruise missile weapon systems software (mandatory) |
| ANSI/IEEE - ANS 7.4.3.2<br>1982 | "Application Criteria for Programmable Digital Computer Systems in Safety Systems of Nuclear Power Generating Stations" for Nuclear power generation embedded software |
| FIPSPUB101<br>1983 | "Guideline for Lifecycle Validation, Verification, and Testing of Computer Software" for general guidance to computer software industry |
| DoD-STD-2167A and 2168<br>1985-1988 | "Defense System Software Development: Quality Program" for development of DoD mission critical computer system software |
| ANSI/IEEE-STD 1012<br>1986 | "Standard for Software Verification and Validation Plans" for any software development |
| NASA SMAP GUIDEBOOKS<br>1986 | "Software Verificaton and Validation for Project Managers" for software intensive systems for NASA |
| FIPSPUB132<br>1987 | "Guideline for Software Verification and Validation Plans" for uniform and minimum requirements of V&V; adopts ANSI/IEEE 1012 |
| ANSI/ANS 10.4<br>1987 | "Guidelines for V&V of Scientific and Engineering Computer Programs for the Nuclear Industry" for scientific and engineering programs (R&D) for nuclear power industry |
| ARMY REG 50-4<br>1986 | "Software Studies and Reviews of Nuclear Weapon Systems" for Army nuclear weapon system software |
| AFSCP 800-5<br>1988 | "Software Independent Verification and Validation" for Air Force systems with potential to cause death, system loss, more than $550K damage to equipment, or severe illness/injury |
| FAA STD 0-26 (DRAFT)<br>---- | "National Aerospace System Software Development" for national airspace system-advanced automation system |
| FDA XXX<br>---- | "Reviewer Guidance for Computer Controlled Medical Devices" for computer controlled medical devices. |

4/89-0035-SMV-6480

*Figure 2. History of V&V standards*

this methodology for contract procurements and for monitoring the technical performance of V&V efforts.

### 2.1. Objectives of V&V

Software V&V comprehensively analyzes and tests software during all stages of its development and maintenance in parallel with the development process to

- determine that it performs its intended functions correctly,
- ensure that it performs no unintended functions, and
- measure and assess the quality and reliability of software.

As a systems engineering discipline, software V&V also assesses, analyzes, and tests the software on how it interfaces with, influences the performance of, or reacts to stimuli from the system elements. These systems elements include the following:

- hardware including all hardware directly or indirectly influenced by the software,
- users that interface with the software or other system components,
- external software linked to the system,
- and system environment (such as stimuli, inputs, operating conditions).

A software error needs the system elements to be present for the error to cause an effect. Software performing correctly in one set of conditions or system environment could fail under different system stimuli. Therefore, in order to determine software correctness, software V&V must always consider the system when performing V&V analysis and testing. When performed in parallel with software development, V&V yields several benefits:

- uncovers high risk errors early, giving the design team time to evolve a comprehensive solution rather than forcing them into a makeshift fix to accommodate software deadlines.
- evaluates the correctness of products against system and software requirements.
- provides management with in-depth technical visibility into the quality and progress of the development effort that is continuous and comprehensive, not just at major review milestones (which may occur infrequently).
- provides the user an incremental preview of system performance, with the chance to make early adjustments.
- provides decision criteria for whether or not to proceed to the next development phase.

### 2.2 Responsibilities of V&V Versus Other Groups

While the techniques of V&V may be applied by anyone involved in software development and maintenance, a comprehensive V&V effort is often administered by a specific group. Similarly, a project may have developers who are from the end-user organization or who may be contractors or subcontractors. Other groups may be quality assurance, configuration management, and data management. The organizational structure of a project depends on many characteristics (for example, size, complexity, purpose of the software, corporate culture, project standards, contractual requirements). Often these groups are separate, but in many instances, especially for small projects, the structure is not as diverse. On these projects, the functions described in this section must still be performed but may be distributed differently.

A functional view demonstrates how V&V and other groups complement their software quality responsibilities. The software development group builds the software product to satisfy the established quality and performance requirements. The group relies on its quality assurance group, systems engineering, requirements analysts, designers, programmers, testers, data and configuration management specialists, documentation specialists, and others.

The quality assurance group verifies that the development process and products conform to established standards and procedures. Via reviews, audits, inspections, and walk-throughs, it acts as a formal check and balance to monitor and evaluate software as it is being built. The software systems engineering group ensures that the software product satisfies system requirements and objectives. It uses techniques such as simulations to gain reasonable assurance that system requirements are satisfied.

The configuration and data management groups monitor and control the software program versions and data during its development, using such techniques as formal audits, change control records, traceability of requirements, and sign-off records. The user group must provide assurance that the software product satisfies user requirements and operational needs. Typically, it uses techniques such as formal design reviews and acceptance testing.

Like software systems engineering, the V&V group is responsible for verifying that the software product at each life cycle phase satisfies software quality attributes and that the software product at each phase satisfies the requirements of the previous phase. In addition, V&V is responsible for validating that the software satisfies overall system requirements and objectives. The activities are directed at the software, but V&V must consider how the software interacts with the rest of the system, including hardware, users, other software, and with other external systems. V&V maintains its own configuration and data management functions on programs, data, and documentation received from the development organization to assure V&V discrepancy reports are against controlled documents and to repeat V&V tests against controlled software releases. V&V responsibilities may vary for different projects; some examples are provided in Section 2.3.

V&V documentation, evaluation, and testing are different from those conducted by other groups. The quality assurance group reviews documents for compliance to standards. V&V performs a check on the technical correctness of the document contents. V&V may perform in-depth evaluation by such activities as rederiving the algorithms from basic principles, computing timing data to verify response time requirements, and developing control flow diagrams to identify missing and erroneous requirements. V&V may suggest, if appropriate, alternative approaches. V&V testing is usually separate from the development group's testing. In some cases, V&V may use development test plans and results and supplement them with additional tests.

### 2.3 Organizing a V&V Effort

A major influence on the responsibilities of V&V, and its relationship to other groups, is to whom V&V reports. Four methods of organizing a V&V effort are described: independent; embedded in the development system engineering group; embedded in the development quality assurance group; and embedded in the user group.

The traditional approach is that the V&V group is independent of the development group and is called *independent V&V* or IV&V. As IV&V, the V&V group reports directly to the system program manager, often the acquisition organization, who manages the separate development and IV&V teams. In this relationship, the V&V organization establishes formal procedures for receiving software releases and documentation from the development team. V&V sends all evaluation reports and discrepancy reports to both the program manager and development group. To maintain an unbiased technical viewpoint, V&V may selectively use results or procedures from the quality assurance or systems engineering groups.

The V&V tasks are oriented toward engineering analysis (for example, algorithm analysis, control/data flow analysis) and comprehensive testing (such as simulation). The objective is to develop an independent assessment of the software quality and to determine whether the software satisfies critical system requirements. Advantages of this approach are detailed analysis and test of software requirements; an independent determination of how well the software performs; and early detection of high-risk software and system errors. Disadvantages are higher cost to the project and additional development interfaces.

When the V&V group is embedded in development's systems engineering group, the V&V tasks are to review the group's engineering analyses (for instance, algorithm development, sizing/timing) and testing (like test evaluation or review of the adequacy of the development test planning document). In some instances, the V&V organization may be the independent test team for the systems engineering group, sharing some test data generated by the systems engineering group. V&V's results are reviewed and monitored by the systems engineering and quality assurance groups. An independent V&V group reporting to the systems engineering group is another alternative. Advantages to using systems engineering personnel in the V&V tasks are minimum cost impact to the project; no system learning for the staff; and no additional development interfaces. A disadvantage is the loss of engineering analysis objectivity.

When the V&V group is embedded in the development's quality assurance group, its tasks take on a monitoring, auditing, and reviewing content (for example, audit performance, audit support, test witnessing, walk-through support, documentation review). In these tasks, the V&V group is part of quality assurance and maintains its relationship to systems engineering and other development groups in the same manner as quality assurance. The main advantages of embedding V&V as part of quality assurance are low cost to the project and bringing V&V analysis capabilities into reviews, audits, and inspections. A disadvantage is the loss of an independent software systems analysis and test capability.

When the V&V group is embedded in the user group, its tasks are an extension of the users' responsibilities. The tasks consist of configuration management support of development products, support of formal reviews, user documentation evaluation, test witnessing, test evaluation of the development test planning documents, and user testing support (for example, user acceptance testing and installation and checkout testing).

As an extension of the user group, the V&V group would receive formal software product deliverables and provide comments and data to the development project management that distributes the information to its own development team. An advantage of this approach is the strong systems engineering and user perspective that can be brought to bear on the software product during development. Main disadvantages are loss of detailed analysis and test of incremental software products (since these typically are not formal deliverables) and error detection and feedback to the development team constrained by the frequency of formal product deliverables. If the user group has an IV&V group reporting to it, then the disadvantages can be overcome. However, in this instance, the project incurs the disadvantage of having an additional development interface.

### 2.4 Applying V&V to a Software Life Cycle

The minimum recommended V&V tasks that are required by the ANSI/IEEE Standard for Software Verification and Validation Plans (SVVP) [1] for the development phases are shown in Figure 3. They are considered effective and applicable to all types of software applications. Tailoring V&V for a specific project is accomplished by adding tasks to the minimum set or, when appropriate, deleting V&V tasks. Figures 4a and 4b list additional V&V tasks in the life cycle phase where they most likely can be applied, and considerations that one might use to assign the tasks to V&V. The SVVP standard requires V&V management tasks spanning the entire software life cycle and V&V tasks for operations and maintenance.

| PHASE | TASKS | KEY ISSUES |
|---|---|---|
| Concept | Concept-documentation evaluation | Satisfy user needs; constraints of interfacing systems |
| Requirements Definition | Traceability analysis | Trace of requirements to concept |
| | Requirements validation | Correctness, consistency, completeness, accuracy, readability, and testability; satisfaction of system requirements |
| | Interface analysis | Hardware, software, and operator interfaces |
| | Begin planning for V&V system testing | Compliance with functional requirements; performance at interfaces; adequacy of user documentation; performance at boundaries |
| | Begin planning for V&V acceptance testing | Compliance with acceptance requirements |
| Design | Traceability analysis | Trace of design to requirements |
| | Design evaluation | Correctness; design quality |
| | Interface analysis | Correctness; data items across interface |
| | Begin planning for V&V component testing | Compliance to design; timing and accuracy; performance at boundaries |
| | Begin planning for V&V integration testing | Compliance with functional requirements; timing and accuracy; performance at stress limits |
| Implementation | Traceability analysis | Trace of source code to design |
| | Code evaluation | Correctness; code quality |
| | Interface analysis | Correctness; data/control access across interfaces |
| | Component test execution | Component integrity |
| Test | V&V integration-test execution | Correctness of subsystem elements; subsystem interface requirements |
| | V&V system-test execution | Entire system at limits and user stress conditions |
| | V&V acceptance-test execution | Performance with operational scenarios |
| Installation and Checkout | Installation-configuration audit | Operations with site dependencies; adequacy of installation procedure |
| | V&V final report generation | Disposition of all errors; summary of V&V results |

4/89-0036-SMV-6480

*Figure 3. Minimum set of recommended V&V tasks*

| V&V Issues | Algorithm Analysis | Analytic Modeling | Assertion Generation | Assertion Processing | Cause Effect Graphing | Code Auditor | Comparator | Control Flow Analyzer | Criticality Analysis | Cross Reference Generator | Data Base Analyzer | Data Flow Analyzer | Design Compliance Analyzer | Execution Time Estimator | Formal Review | Formal Verification | Functional Testing | Inspections | Interactive Test Aids | Interface Checker | Metrics | Mutation Analysis | PDL Processor | Peer Review | Physical Units Testing | Regression Testing | Requirements Parsing | Roundoff Analysis | Simulations | Sizing | Software Monitors | Specification Base | Structural Testing | Symbolic Execution | Test Coverage Analyzer | Test Data Generator | Test Drivers | Test Support Facilities | Timing | Tracing | Walkthroughs |
|---|---|---|---|---|---|---|---|---|---|---|---|---|---|---|---|---|---|---|---|---|---|---|---|---|---|---|---|---|---|---|---|---|---|---|---|---|---|---|---|---|---|
| Acceptance Tests | | | | | | | | | ■ | | | | | | | | | | | | | | | | | ■ | ■ | | | | | ■ | | | | ■ | | ■ | | ■ | |
| Accuracy | ■ | ■ | | | | | | | | | | | | | | | | ■ | | | ■ | | | | | | | ■ | | | | | | | | | | | | | |
| Algorithm Efficiency | ■ | ■ | | | | | | | | | | | | | | | | | | | ■ | | | | | | | | | ■ | | | | | | | | | ■ | | |
| Assertion Violations | | | ■ | ■ | | | | ■ | | | | ■ | | | | ■ | | | | ■ | | | | | | | | | | | | | | ■ | | | | | | | |
| Bottlenecks | | ■ | | | ■ | | | ■ | | | | ■ | | ■ | | | | | | | | | | | | | | | | | ■ | ■ | ■ | | | | | | ■ | | |
| Boundary Test Cases | | | | | ■ | | | ■ | | | | ■ | | | | | ■ | | ■ | | | ■ | | | | | | | ■ | ■ | ■ | ■ | | | ■ | ■ | ■ | ■ | ■ | | |
| Branch & Path Identification | | | | | ■ | | | ■ | | | | ■ | | | | | ■ | | ■ | | | ■ | | | | | | | ■ | ■ | ■ | ■ | | | ■ | ■ | ■ | ■ | ■ | ■ | |
| Branch Testing | | | | | ■ | | | ■ | | | | ■ | | | | | ■ | | ■ | | | ■ | | | | | | | ■ | ■ | ■ | ■ | | | ■ | ■ | ■ | ■ | ■ | ■ | |
| Call Structure Of Modules | | | | | ■ | | | ■ | | ■ | | ■ | | | | | | | | ■ | ■ | | ■ | | | | ■ | | | | | | | | | | | | | | |
| Checklist (Reqmts, Design, Code) | | | | | | ■ | ■ | | | | | | ■ | | | | | ■ | | | | | | | | | ■ | | | | | | | | | | | | | | ■ |
| Code Reading | | | | | | ■ | ■ | | | | | | | | ■ | | | ■ | | | | | | ■ | | | | | | | | | | | | | | | | | |
| Component Tests | | | | | ■ | | | ■ | | ■ | ■ | | | | | | ■ | | ■ | ■ | | | | | ■ | ■ | ■ | | ■ | | ■ | ■ | | | ■ | ■ | ■ | ■ | ■ | ■ | |
| Consistency In Computation | ■ | | | | | | | | | | | | ■ | | | | | | | ■ | | | | | ■ | | ■ | ■ | | | | | | | | | | | | | |
| Data Characteristics | | | ■ | | | | | | | ■ | ■ | ■ | | | | | | | | | | | | | ■ | | | | | | | | | | | | | | | | |
| Design Evaluation | | | | | ■ | | | ■ | ■ | | | ■ | ■ | | | | | | | | | | ■ | | | | | | | | | | | | | | ■ | | | | |
| Design To Code Correlation | | | | | | | ■ | | ■ | | | | ■ | | | | | | | | | | | | | | | | | | | | | | | | | | | | |
| Dynamic Testing Of Assertions | | | ■ | ■ | ■ | | | ■ | | | | ■ | | | | | | | ■ | | | | | | | | ■ | | ■ | | ■ | ■ | | | ■ | ■ | ■ | ■ | | | |
| Error Propagation | ■ | ■ | ■ | ■ | ■ | | | ■ | ■ | | | ■ | ■ | | ■ | | | | | ■ | | | | | | | | | | | | | ■ | | | ■ | | | | | ■ |
| Environment Interaction | | | | | | | | | ■ | | | ■ | | | | | | | ■ | ■ | | | | | | | ■ | | ■ | | ■ | ■ | | | | ■ | ■ | ■ | | | |
| Evaluation Of Program Paths | | | | | ■ | | | | ■ | | | ■ | | | | ■ | | | ■ | | | | | | | | | | | | | | ■ | ■ | | ■ | | | | | |
| Execution Monitoring | | | | | | | | | | | | | | | | | | | ■ | | | | | | | | | | ■ | | ■ | | | | | | | ■ | | | |
| Execution Sampling | | | | | | | | | | | | | | ■ | | | | | | | | | | | | | | | ■ | | ■ | | | | | | | ■ | | | |
| Execution Support | | | | | | | | | | | | | ■ | | | | | | ■ | | | | | | | | | | ■ | | ■ | | | | | ■ | | ■ | | | |
| Expected Vs Actual Results | | | | | ■ | | ■ | ■ | | | | ■ | | | | ■ | | | | | | | | | | | | | | | | | | | | | | | | | |
| Feasibility | | ■ | | | | | | | ■ | | | | | | | | | | | | | | | | | | ■ | | ■ | | | | | | | ■ | | | | | |
| File Sequence Error | | | | | | | | ■ | | | ■ | ■ | | | | | ■ | | | | | | | | | | | | ■ | | ■ | ■ | | | | ■ | | ■ | | | |
| Formal Specification Evaluation | | | | ■ | ■ | | | ■ | | | ■ | | | | ■ | ■ | | ■ | | | ■ | | | ■ | | | ■ | | | | | | | | | | | | | | ■ |
| Global Information Flow | | | | | ■ | | | ■ | | | ■ | ■ | | | | | | | | ■ | | | | | | | | | | | | | | | | | | | | | |
| Go-No-Go Decisions | | | | | | | | | ■ | | | | | | ■ | | | ■ | | | | | | ■ | | | | | | | | | | | | | | | | | ■ |
| Hierarchical Interrelationship Of Modules | | | | | ■ | | | ■ | ■ | ■ | | ■ | | | | | | | | ■ | ■ | | ■ | | | | ■ | | | | | | | | | | | | | | |
| Information Flow Consistency | | | | | | ■ | | ■ | ■ | ■ | | ■ | ■ | | | | | ■ | | | | | | | | | ■ | | | | | | | | | | | | | | |
| Inspections | | | | | | | | | | | | | ■ | | | | | ■ | | | | | | | | | | | | | | | | | | | | | | | ■ |
| Integration Tests | | | | | | | | ■ | ■ | ■ | | ■ | ■ | | | | | | ■ | ■ | | | | | | ■ | ■ | | ■ | | ■ | ■ | ■ | | ■ | ■ | ■ | ■ | | ■ | |

2/89-0118-MSW-6360

Figure 4a. Cross-reference of V&V issues to V&V techniques/tools (part 1)

TECHNIQUE/TOOLS

V&V ISSUES

| Technique/Tools | Inter-module Structure | Loop Invariants | Manual Simulation | Module Invocation | Numerical Roundoff | Numerical Stability | Parameter Checking | Path Testing | Physical Units | Portability | Processing Efficiency |
|---|---|---|---|---|---|---|---|---|---|---|---|
| Algorithm Analysis | | | | | ■ | ■ | | | | | ■ |
| Analytic Modeling | | | | | ■ | ■ | | | | | ■ |
| Assertion Generation | | ■ | | | | | | | ■ | | |
| Assertion Processing | | | | | | | | | | | |
| Cause Effect Graphing | ■ | ■ | | ■ | | | | ■ | | | |
| Code Auditor | | ■ | | ■ | | | ■ | ■ | | ■ | |
| Comparator | | | | | | | | | | | |
| Control Flow Analyzer | ■ | ■ | | ■ | | | | ■ | | | ■ |
| Criticality Analysis | ■ | | | | | | | ■ | | ■ | |
| Cross Reference Generator | ■ | ■ | | ■ | | | ■ | ■ | ■ | | |
| Data Base Analyzer | | | | | | | | | | | ■ |
| Data Flow Analyzer | ■ | ■ | | ■ | | | | ■ | | | ■ |
| Design Compliance Analyzer | ■ | ■ | | ■ | | | | | | | |
| Execution Time Estimator | | | | | | | | | | | ■ |
| Formal Review | | | | | | | | | | | |
| Formal Verification | | | | | | | | | | | |
| Functional Testing | | | | | | | | ■ | | | |
| Inspections | | ■ | ■ | ■ | | | | | | | |
| Interactive Test Aids | | | | | | | | ■ | | | ■ |
| Interface Checker | | | | ■ | | | ■ | | ■ | | |
| Metrics | | | | | | | | ■ | | | ■ |
| Mutation Analysis | | | | | | | | | | | |
| PDL Processor | | ■ | | ■ | | | | | | | |
| Peer Review | | | ■ | | | | | | | | |
| Physical Units Testing | | | | ■ | | | ■ | | | | |
| Regression Testing | | | | | | | | | | | |
| Requirements Parsing | | | | ■ | | | | ■ | | | |
| Roundoff Analysis | | | | | ■ | ■ | | | | | |
| Simulations | ■ | | | | | | | ■ | | | |
| Sizing | | | | | | | | | | | |
| Software Monitors | | | | | | | | ■ | | | ■ |
| Specification Base | | | | | | | | ■ | | | |
| Structural Testing | ■ | | | | | | ■ | | | | |
| Symbolic Execution | | | | | | | | | | | |
| Test Coverage Analyzer | ■ | | | | | | | ■ | | | |
| Test Data Generator | ■ | | | | | | | ■ | | | |
| Test Drivers | ■ | | | | | | | ■ | | | |
| Test Support Facilities | | | | | | | | ■ | | | |
| Timing | | | | | | | | | | | |
| Tracing | | | | | | | | ■ | | | |
| Walkthroughs | | | ■ | | | | ■ | | | | |

| Technique/Tools | Program Execution Characteristics | Proof Of Correctness | Requirements Evaluation | Requirements Indexing | Requirements To Design Correlation | Retest/Reevaluation After Change | Space Utilization Evaluation | Standards Check | Statement Coverage/Testing | Status Reviews | System Performance Prediction |
|---|---|---|---|---|---|---|---|---|---|---|---|
| Algorithm Analysis | | | | | | | ■ | | | | ■ |
| Analytic Modeling | | | | | | | | | | | ■ |
| Assertion Generation | | | | | | | | | | | |
| Assertion Processing | | | | | | | | | | | |
| Cause Effect Graphing | | | | | | ■ | | | | | |
| Code Auditor | | ■ | | | | ■ | | ■ | | | ■ |
| Comparator | | | | | | ■ | | ■ | | | |
| Control Flow Analyzer | | | | | | ■ | | | | | ■ |
| Criticality Analysis | | | ■ | ■ | ■ | ■ | | | | | |
| Cross Reference Generator | | | | | | ■ | | | | | |
| Data Base Analyzer | | | | | | | ■ | | | | |
| Data Flow Analyzer | | | | | | ■ | | | | | ■ |
| Design Compliance Analyzer | | ■ | | | | ■ | | ■ | | | |
| Execution Time Estimator | ■ | | | | | | ■ | | | | ■ |
| Formal Review | | | | | | | | | | ■ | |
| Formal Verification | | ■ | | | | | | | | | |
| Functional Testing | ■ | | | | | ■ | | | ■ | | ■ |
| Inspections | | | | | | ■ | ■ | | | ■ | |
| Interactive Test Aids | ■ | | | | | | ■ | | ■ | | |
| Interface Checker | | | ■ | | | ■ | | | | | |
| Metrics | ■ | | ■ | ■ | | | | ■ | ■ | | |
| Mutation Analysis | | | | | | ■ | | | | | |
| PDL Processor | | | | | | ■ | | ■ | | | |
| Peer Review | | | | | | ■ | | | | ■ | |
| Physical Units Testing | | | | | | | | | | | |
| Regression Testing | | | | | | ■ | | | | | |
| Requirements Parsing | | ■ | ■ | ■ | ■ | ■ | | ■ | ■ | | |
| Roundoff Analysis | | | | | | | | | | | |
| Simulations | ■ | | | | | ■ | | | ■ | | ■ |
| Sizing | | | | | | ■ | ■ | | | | |
| Software Monitors | ■ | | | | | ■ | ■ | | ■ | | ■ |
| Specification Base | ■ | | | | | ■ | | | ■ | | ■ |
| Structural Testing | ■ | | | | | | | | | | |
| Symbolic Execution | ■ | ■ | | | | ■ | | | | | |
| Test Coverage Analyzer | ■ | | | | | ■ | | | ■ | | |
| Test Data Generator | | | | | | ■ | | | ■ | | ■ |
| Test Drivers | ■ | | | | | | | | | | |
| Test Support Facilities | ■ | | | | | ■ | | | ■ | | ■ |
| Timing | ■ | | | | | ■ | | | | | |
| Tracing | | ■ | | ■ | ■ | ■ | | | ■ | | |
| Walkthroughs | | | | | | ■ | | | | ■ | |

| Technique/Tools | System Tests | Technical Reviews | Test Case Preparation | Test Thoroughness | Type Checking | Uninitialized Variables | Unused Variables | Variable References | Variable Snapshots/Tracing | Walkthroughs |
|---|---|---|---|---|---|---|---|---|---|---|
| Algorithm Analysis | | | | | | | | | | |
| Analytic Modeling | | | | | | | | | | |
| Assertion Generation | | | | | | | | | | |
| Assertion Processing | | | | | | | | | | |
| Cause Effect Graphing | ■ | | | | | | | | | |
| Code Auditor | ■ | | | | ■ | ■ | ■ | ■ | | |
| Comparator | ■ | | | | | | | | | |
| Control Flow Analyzer | | | ■ | | | | | | | |
| Criticality Analysis | | | ■ | ■ | | | | | | |
| Cross Reference Generator | | | | | ■ | ■ | ■ | ■ | | |
| Data Base Analyzer | | | | | | ■ | | | | |
| Data Flow Analyzer | | | ■ | | | ■ | ■ | ■ | | |
| Design Compliance Analyzer | ■ | | | | | ■ | ■ | ■ | | |
| Execution Time Estimator | ■ | | | | | | | | | |
| Formal Review | | | | | | | | | | |
| Formal Verification | | ■ | | | | | | | | |
| Functional Testing | ■ | | ■ | ■ | | ■ | ■ | ■ | ■ | |
| Inspections | | ■ | | | | | | | | |
| Interactive Test Aids | | | | | | ■ | ■ | ■ | ■ | |
| Interface Checker | | | ■ | | ■ | | | | | |
| Metrics | | | | | | | | | | |
| Mutation Analysis | | | ■ | | | | | | | |
| PDL Processor | | | | | | ■ | | | | |
| Peer Review | | ■ | | ■ | | | | | | ■ |
| Physical Units Testing | | | | | ■ | | | | | |
| Regression Testing | ■ | | | | | | | | | |
| Requirements Parsing | ■ | | | | | | | | | |
| Roundoff Analysis | | | | | | | | | | |
| Simulations | ■ | | | | | ■ | ■ | ■ | ■ | |
| Sizing | | | | | | | | | | |
| Software Monitors | ■ | | | | | ■ | ■ | ■ | ■ | |
| Specification Base | ■ | | ■ | ■ | | | | | | |
| Structural Testing | | | | | | | | | | |
| Symbolic Execution | | | | | | | | | | |
| Test Coverage Analyzer | | | | ■ | | ■ | ■ | ■ | ■ | |
| Test Data Generator | ■ | | ■ | ■ | | ■ | ■ | | | |
| Test Drivers | ■ | | | | | | | | | |
| Test Support Facilities | ■ | | | ■ | | ■ | ■ | ■ | ■ | |
| Timing | | | | | | | | | | |
| Tracing | | | ■ | ■ | | ■ | ■ | ■ | | |
| Walkthroughs | ■ | ■ | | | | | | | | ■ |

*Figure 4b. Cross-reference of V&V issues to V&V techniques/tools (part 2).*

These V&V tasks can be applied to different life cycle models simply by mapping traditional phases to the new model. Examples include variations of the traditional waterfall, Boehm's spiral development [2], rapid prototyping, or evolutionary development models [3]. The V&V tasks are fully consistent with the ANSI/IEEE standard for software life cycle processes [4]. The SVVP standard specifies minimum input and output requirements for each V&V task; a V&V task may not begin without specific inputs, and is not completed until specific outputs are completed.

### 2.4.1 Management of V&V

Management tasks for V&V span the entire life cycle. These tasks are to plan the V&V process; coordinate and interpret performance and quality of the V&V effort; report discrepancies promptly to the user or development group; identify early problem trends and focus V&V activities on them; provide a technical evaluation of the software performance and quality at each major software program review (so a determination can be made of whether the software product has satisfied its requirements well enough to proceed to the next phase); and assess the full impact of proposed software changes. The output of the V&V activities consists of the Software Verification and Validation Plan (SVVP), task reports, phase summary reports, final report, and discrepancy report.

Major steps in developing the V&V plan are as follows:

- Define the quality and performance objectives (for example, verify conformance to specifications, verify compliance with safety and security objectives, assess efficiency and quality of software, and assess performance across the full operating environment).
- Characterize the types of problems anticipated in the system and define how they would show up in the software.
- Select the V&V analysis and testing techniques to effectively detect the system and software problems.

The plan may include a tool acquisition and development plan and a personnel training plan. The SVVP is a living document, constantly being revised as knowledge accumulates about the characteristics of the system, the software, and the problem areas in the software.

An important V&V management activity is to monitor the V&V technical progress and quality of results. At each V&V phase, planned V&V activities are reviewed and new tasks are added to focus on the critical performance/quality functions of the software and its system. The monitoring activity conducts formal reviews of V&V discrepancy reports and technical evaluation results to provide a check of their correctness and accuracy. V&V studies (reference) have shown that responding to discrepancy reports and V&V evaluation reports consumes the largest portion of a development group's interface time with the V&V group.

Boehm and Papaccio [5] report that the Pareto analysis, that is, 20 percent of the problems cause 80 percent of the rework costs, applies to software; they recommend that V&V "focus on identifying and eliminating the specific high-risk problems to be encountered by a software project." Part of the V&V management activities is to define and use methods to address these problems of rework and risk management. One method of providing early delivery of information is to have the development team deliver incremental documents (for example, draft portions) and "software builds" to V&V. A software build represents a basic program skeleton containing portions of the full software capabilities. Each successive build integrates additional functions into the skeleton, permitting early software deliveries to V&V in an orderly development process. Based on discrepancy or progress reports, software program management can make the technical and management decisions to refocus the V&V and development team onto the program's specific problem areas of the software.

Criticality analysis, a method to locate and reduce high-risk problems, is performed at the beginning of a project. It identifies the functions and modules that are required to implement critical program functions or quality requirements (such as safety and security). The steps of the analysis are:

- Develop a block diagram or control-flow diagram of the system and its software. Each block or control flow box represents a system or software function (module).
- Trace each critical function or quality requirement through the block or control flow diagram.
- Classify all traced software functions (modules) as critical to either the proper execution of critical software functions or the quality requirements.
- Focus additional analysis on these traced software functions (modules).
- Repeat criticality analysis for each life cycle phase to observe whether the implementation details shift the emphasis of the criticality.

The criticality analysis may be used along with the cross-reference matrix of Figure 4 to identify V&V techniques to address high-risk concerns.

### 2.4.2 Concept Definition Evaluation

In this phase, the principal V&V task is to evaluate the concept documentation to determine whether the defined concept satisfies user needs and project objectives (for example, statement of need, project initiation memo) in terms of system performance requirements, feasibility (for example, overestimation of hardware capabilities), completeness, and accuracy. The evaluation also identifies major constraints of interfacing systems and constraints/limitations of the proposed approach and assesses the allocation of system functions to hardware and software, where appropriate. The evaluation assesses the criticality of each software item defined in the concept.

Most of the techniques in the cross-reference matrix of Figure 4 are described in a publication from the National Institute of Standards and Technology (formerly the National Bureau of Standards), the National Bureau of Standards Special Publication 500-93, "Software Validation, Verification, and Testing Technique and Tool Reference Guide" [6]. In Figure 4, the techniques are mapped against specific V&V issues [7] which they address.

While the use of the cross-reference matrix for selecting V&V techniques and tools is applicable to all phases, its use is illustrated in this report only for examining how concept feasibility is determined. Of several techniques for determining feasibility of a software concept and architecture, those most commonly used are requirements parsing, analytic modeling, and simulation. These give the V&V analyst a way to parse the desired performance requirements from other concept data; analytically model the desired performance; and, by creating a simulation of the proposed operating environment, execute test data to determine whether the resulting performance matches the desired performance. Criticality analysis is especially useful during concept definition to identify the critical functions and their distribution within the system architecture. Test data generation defines the performance limits of the proposed system concept; the predicted performance can be verified by using the simulation to execute the test scenario.

### 2.4.3 Requirements Analysis

Poorly specified software requirements (for example, incorrect, incomplete, ambiguous, or not testable) contribute to software cost overruns and problems with reliability due to incorrect or misinterpreted requirements or functional specifications. Software often encounters problems in the maintenance phase because general requirements (such as maintainability, quality, and reusability) were not accounted for during the original development. The problem of outdated requirements is intensified by the very complexity of the problems being solved (which causes uncertainty in the intended system performance requirements) and by continual changes in requirements to incorporate new technologies. V&V tasks verify the completeness of all the requirements.

The most commonly used V&V tasks for requirements analysis are control flow analysis, data flow analysis, algorithm analysis, and simulation. Control and data flow analysis are most applicable for real-time and data-driven systems. These flow analyses transform logic and data requirements text into graphic flows that are easier to analyze than the text. PERT, state transition, and transaction diagrams are examples of control flow diagrams. Algorithm analysis involves rederivation of equations or evaluation of the suitability of specific numerical techniques. Simulation is used to evaluate the interactions of large, complex systems with many hardware, user, and other interfacing software components.

Another activity in which V&V plays an important role is test management. V&V looks at all testing for the software system and ensures that comprehensive testing is planned. V&V test planning begins in the requirements phase and spans almost the full range of life cycle phases. Test planning activities encompass four separate types of testing—component, integration, system, and acceptance testing. The planning activities result in documentation for each test type consisting of a test plan, test design, test case, and test procedure documents.

Component testing verifies the design and implementation of software units or modules. Integration testing verifies functional requirements as the software components are integrated, directing attention to internal software interfaces and external hardware and operator interfaces. System testing validates the entire software program against system requirements and software performance objectives. V&V system tests validate that the software executes correctly in a simulated system environment. They do not duplicate or replace the user and development team's responsibilities of testing the entire system requirements (for example, those pertaining to hardware, software, and users).

Acceptance testing validates the software against V&V acceptance criteria, defining how the software should perform with other completed software and hardware. One of the distinctions between V&V system and acceptance testing is that the former uses a laboratory environment in which some system features are simulated or performed by nonoperational hardware or software, and the latter uses an operational environment with final configurations of other system hardware and software. V&V acceptance testing usually consists of tests to demonstrate that the software will execute as predicted by V&V system testing in the operational environment. Full acceptance testing is the responsibility of the user and the development systems engineering group.

#### 2.4.4 Design Evaluation

The minimum set of design phase V&V tasks—traceability, interface analysis, and design evaluation—assures that (1) requirements are not misrepresented or incompletely implemented, (2) unintended requirements are not designed into the solution by oversight or indirect inferences, and (3) requirements are not left out of the design. Design errors can be introduced by implementation constraints relating to timing, data structures, memory space, and accuracy, even though the basic design satisfies the functional requirements.

The most commonly used V&V tasks are algorithm analysis, database analysis, timing/sizing analysis, and simulation. In this phase, algorithm analysis examines the correctness of the equations or numerical techniques as in the requirements analysis phase, but also examines truncation and round-off effects, numerical precision of word storage and variables (for example, single- versus extended-precision arithmetic), and data-typing influences. Database analysis is particularly useful for programs that store program logic in data parameters. A logic analysis of these data values is required to determine the effect these parameters have on program control. Timing/sizing analysis is useful for real-time programs having response time requirements and constrained memory execution space requirements.

#### 2.4.5 Implementation (Code) Evaluation

Clerical and syntactical errors have been greatly reduced through use of structured programming and reuse of code, adoption of programming standards and style guides, availability of more capable computer languages, better compiler diagnostics and automated support, and, finally, more knowledgeable programmers. Nevertheless, problems still occur in translating design into code and can be detected with some V&V analyses.

Commonly used V&V tasks are control flow analysis, database analysis, regression analysis, and sizing/timing analysis. For large code developments, control flow diagrams showing the hierarchy of main routines and their subfunctions are useful in understanding the flow of program control. Database analysis is performed on programs with significant data storage to ensure that common data and variable regions are used consistently between all call routines; data integrity is enforced and no data or variable can be accidentally overwritten by overflowing data tables; and data typing and use are consistent throughout all program elements.

Regression analysis is used to reevaluate requirements and design issues whenever any significant code change is made. This technique ensures project awareness of the original system requirements. Sizing/timing analysis is done during incremental code development and compared against predicted values. Significant deviations between actual and predicted values is a possible indication of problems or the need for additional examination.

Another area of concern to V&V is the ability of compilers to generate object code that is functionally equivalent to the source code, that is, reliance on the correctness of the language compiler to make data-dependent decisions about abstract, programmer-coded information. For critical applications, this problem is solved by validating the compiler or by validating that the object code produced by the compiler is functionally equivalent to the source.

Other tasks indicated in Figure 4 for code evaluation are walk-throughs, code inspections, and audits. These tasks occur in interactive meetings attended by a team that usually includes at least one member from the development group. Other members may belong to the development group or to other groups involved in software development. The duration of these meetings is usually no more than a few hours in which code is examined on a line-by-line basis.

In these dynamic sessions, it may be difficult to examine the code thoroughly for control logic, data flow, database errors, sizing, timing and other features that may require considerable manual or automated effort. Advance preparation for these activities may be necessary and includes additional V&V tasks shown in Figure 4. The results of these tasks provide appropriate engineering information for discussion at meetings where code is evaluated. Regardless of who conducts or participates in walk-throughs and inspections, V&V analyses may be used to support these meetings.

#### 2.4.6 Testing

As already described, V&V test planning is a major portion of V&V test activities and spans several phases. A comprehensive test management approach to testing recognizes the differences in objectives and strategies of different types of testing. Effective testing requires a comprehensive understanding of the system. Such understanding develops from systematically analyzing the software's concept, requirements, design, and code. By knowing internal software details, V&V testing is effective at probing for errors and weaknesses that reveal hidden faults. This is considered structural, or white-box, testing. It often finds errors for which some functional, or black-box, test cases can produce the correct output despite internal errors.

Functional test cases execute part or all of the system to validate that the user requirement is satisfied; these test cases cannot always detect internal errors that will occur under special circumstances. Another V&V test technique is to develop test cases that violate software requirements. This approach is effective at uncovering basic design assumption errors and unusual operational use errors. In general, the process of V&V test planning is as effective in detecting errors as test executions.

The most commonly used optional tasks are regression analysis and test, simulation, and user document evaluation. User document evaluation is performed for systems having an important operator interface. For these systems, V&V reviews the user documentation to verify that the operating instructions are consistent with the operating characteristics of the software. The system diagnostic messages and operator recovery procedures are examined to ensure their accuracy and correctness with the software operations.

#### 2.4.7 Installation and Checkout Activities

During installation and checkout, V&V validates that the software operates correctly with the operational hardware system and with other software, as specified in the interface specifications. V&V may verify the correctness and adequacy of the installation procedures and certify that the verified and validated software is the same as the executable code delivered for installation. There may be several installation sites with site-dependent parameters. V&V verifies that the program has been accurately tailored for these parameters and that the configuration of the delivered product is the correct one for each installation.

Optional V&V tasks most commonly used in this phase are regression analysis and test, simulation, and test certification. Any changes occurring from installation and test are reviewed using regression analysis and test to verify that our basic requirement and design assumptions affecting other areas of the program have not been violated. Simulation is used to test operator procedures and to help isolate any installation problems. Test certification, especially in critical software systems, is used to demonstrate that the delivered software product is identical to the software product subjected to V&V.

#### 2.4.8 Operations and Maintenance Evaluation and Test

For each software change made in the operations and maintenance phase, all life cycle phase V&V activities of Figure 3 are considered and possibly repeated to ensure that nothing is overlooked. V&V activities are added or deleted to address the type of software change made. In many cases, an examination of the proposed software change shows that V&V needs to repeat its activities on only a small portion of the software. Also, some V&V activities such as concept documentation evaluation require little or no effort to verify a small change. Small changes can have subtle but significant side effects in a software program.

If V&V is not done in the normal software development phase, then the V&V in the maintenance phase must consider performing a selected set of V&V activities for earlier life cycle phases. Some of the activities may include generating requirements or design information from source code, a process known as reverse engineering. While costly and time-consuming, it is necessary when the need exists for a rigorous V&V effort.

### 2.5 Effectiveness of V&V

The effectiveness of V&V varies with project size and complexity, and V&V staff experience. Two study results are provided as follows:

Radatz's 1981 study [8] for Rome Air Development Center reported V&V effectiveness results for four large IV&V projects ranging from 90K to 176K lines of code. The projects were real-time command and control, missile tracking, and avionics programs and a time-critical batch trajectory computation program. The projects varied from 2.5 to 4 years to develop. Two projects started V&V at the requirements phase, one at the code phase, and one at testing. The V&V organization used a staff of 5 to 12 persons per project.

In 1982, McGarry [9] reported on three small projects at the Software Engineering Laboratory (SEL) at NASA Goddard Space Flight Center. Three flight dynamics projects ranging in size from 10K to 50K lines of code were selected. V&V was involved in requirements and design verification, separate system testing, and validation of consistency from start to finish. The V&V effort lasted 18 months and used a staff averaging 1.1, peaking at 3, persons.

Based on these studies, some positive effects of V&V on a software project include:

| Radatz Study | McGarry Study |
|---|---|
| • Errors were detected early in the development—50 percent to 89 percent detected before development testing began.<br>• Large number of discrepancies were reported (total 1,259) on average of over 300 per program. | • Rates of uncovering errors early in the development cycle were better. |
| • V&V found an average 5.5 errors per thousand lines of code. | • V&V found 2.3 errors per thousand lines of code. |
| • Over 85 percent of the errors affected reliability and maintainability. | • Reliability of the software was no different from other SEL projects. |
| • Effect on programmer productivity was very positive—total savings per error of 1.3 to 6.1 hours. | • Productivity of the development teams was the lowest of any SEL project (due to the V&V interface). |
| • The largest savings amounted to 92–180 percent of V&V costs. | • Cost rate to fix all discovered errors was no less than in any other SEL project. |

- Better quality (for example, complete, consistent, readable, testable) and more stable requirements.
- More rigorous development planning, at least to interface with the V&V organization.
- Better adherence by the development organization to programming language and development standards and configuration management practices.
- Early error detection and reduced false starts.
- Better schedule compliance and progress monitoring.
- Greater project management visibility into interim technical quality and progress.
- Better criteria and results for decision-making at formal reviews and audits.

Some negative effects of V&V on a software development project include:

- Additional project cost of V&V (10–30 percent).
- Additional interface involving the development team, user, and V&V organization (for example, attendance at V&V status meeting, anomaly resolution meeting).
- Lower development staff productivity if programmers and engineers spend time explaining the system to V&V analysts and resolving invalid anomaly reports.

Some steps can be taken to minimize the negative effects and to maximize the positive effects of V&V. To recover much of the V&V costs, V&V is started early in the software requirements phase. The interface activities for documentation, data, and software deliveries between developer and V&V groups should be considered as an inherently necessary step required to evaluate intermediate development products. This is a necessary by-product of doing what's right in the beginning.

To offset unnecessary costs, V&V must organize its activities to focus on critical areas of the software so that it uncovers critical errors for the development group and thereby results in significant cost savings to the development process. To do this, V&V must use its criticality analysis to identify critical areas and it must scrutinize each discrepancy before release to ensure that no false or inaccurate information is released to prevent the development group from wasting time on inaccurate or trivial reports.

To eliminate the need to have development personnel train the V&V staff, it is imperative that V&V select personnel who are experienced and knowledgeable about the software and its engineering application. When V&V engineers and computer scientists reconstruct the specific details and idiosyncracies of the software as a method of reconfirming the correctness of engineering and programming assumptions, they often find subtle errors. They gain detailed insight into the development process and an ability to spot critical errors early. The cost of the development interface is minimal, and at times nonexistent, when the V&V assessment is independent.

## 3. Standards and Guidelines For Planning and Managing V&V

The documents in Figure 5 establish guidelines for planning and managing a V&V effort. Their activities produce information that satisfies the life cycle requirements of standards governing projects. They have the following features:

| PROCEDURE | AFSC 800-5 | ANS 10.4 | FIPSPUB 132 | FIPSPUB 101 | ANSI/IEEE STD 1012 | JPL |
|---|---|---|---|---|---|---|
| **SCOPE THE V&V EFFORT** | | | | | | |
| Criticalty Assessment | ■ | | | | | |
| Organization | ■ | ■ | | | | |
| Costing | ■ | | | | | |
| **PLAN THE V&V EFFORT** | | | | | | |
| Planning Preparation | | ■ | ■ | ■ | ■ | |
| Objectives | | ■ | ■ | ■ | ■ | ■ |
| General Task Selection | ■ | ■ | ■ | ■ | ■ | ■ |
| Minimum, Required | | | ■ | | ■ | |
| Optional | | | ■ | | ■ | |
| Recommendations for Criticality Levels | ■ | | | ■ | | |
| Test Management | | | ■ | | ■ | |
| Test Types | | | ■ | ■ | ■ | ■ |
| Objectives | | | ■ | | ■ | |
| Documentation | | | ■ | | ■ | |
| Coverage | | ■ | ■ | ■ | ■ | ■ |
| Planning | ■ | ■ | ■ | ■ | ■ | ■ |
| Planning V&V for Maintenance | | ■ | ■ | ■ | ■ | |
| **MANAGE THE V&V EFFORT** | | | | | | |
| V&V Management Tasks | | | ■ | | ■ | |
| Reporting | | ■ | ■ | | ■ | |

GUIDANCE

4/89-0040-SMV-6480

*Figure 5. Planning V&V with guidance from V&V documents*

- Require V&V to determine how well evolving and final software products comply with their requirements.
- Permit users to select specific techniques to satisfy their application needs.
- Identify a broad spectrum of V&V analysis and test activities.

Brief descriptions of each document follow:

The NIST issued the Federal Information Processing Standards Publication "Guideline for Lifecycle Validation, Verification and Testing," in 1983 [10]. This document was followed in 1987 with the "Guideline for Software Verification and Validation Plans," [11] which adopted the ANSI/IEEE standard for V&V planning [1]. Reference to the guideline, FIPSPUB132, includes reference to the ANSI/IEEE specifications.

FIPSPUB101 permits performance of V&V activities by developers, the same organization, or some independent group [10]. FIPSPUB132/IEEE1012 does not require independence; it does require the SVVP to "define the relationship of V&V to other efforts such as development, quality assurance, configuration or data management, or end user" [1,11]. Internal and external lines of communication to V&V must be defined; V&V could occur independently or within one of the other efforts.

The Air Force pamphlet, "AFSC /AFLCP 800-5 Software Independent Verification and Validation," [12] is concerned only with software IV&V. It describes V&V activities typically performed by an independent V&V group separate from the developer's quality assurance group required by DOD-STD-2167A Standard, "Defense System Software Development" [13]. The AF pamphlet provides the criteria for selecting an independent V&V group.

The V&V activities of "Guidelines for the Verification and Validation of Scientific and Engineering Computer Programs for the Nuclear Industry," ANS 10.4, [14] may be performed by the program developer, as a task separate from development, or by an IV&V agent. The guideline contains an example of a division of V&V responsibilities.

The "Independent Verification and Validation of Computer Software: Methodology" from the Jet Propulsion Laboratory (JPL) [15] states that V&V activities should be performed independently of the development organization to ensure effectiveness and integrity of the V&V effort. The document allows flexibility in selecting the extent of the detailed V&V effort it describes.

## 4. Summary

Software V&V is a proven systems engineering discipline for generating correct and quality software. In addition to early error detection and correction benefits, software V&V has become a powerful risk management tool by providing the detailed technical insight into the "true" performance of the software. All software V&V is performed with a system perspective to ensure that the software is solving the "right problem."

## Acknowledgments

The following people have provided substantive guidance to the authors through their reviews of this report: Dr. William Bryan, Grumman Data Systems; Fletcher Buckley, General Electric Company; Taz Daughtrey, Babcock and Wilcox; Dr. Herbert Hecht, SoHar, Incorporated; Tom Kurihara, Department of Defense; Dr. Jerome Mersky, Logicon, Incorporated; George Tice, Mentor Graphics Corporation; Dr. Richard Thayer, California State University–Sacramento, and Dr. N. Pat Wilburn, Columbia Software.

## References

[1] ANSI/IEEE Std.1012-1986, "Standard for Software Verification and Validation Plans," IEEE, Inc., New York, NY, Nov. 1986.

[2] Boehm, B.W., "A Spiral Model of Software Development and Enhancement," *Computer*, May 1988, pp. 61–72.

[3] Davis, A.M., E.H. Bersoff, and E.R. Comer, "A Strategy for Comparing Alternative Software Development Life Cycle Models," *IEEE Trans. Software Eng.*, Vol. 14, No. 10, Oct. 1988, pp. 1453-1461.

[4] ANSI/IEEE 1074-1991, "Standard for Software Life Cycle Processes," IEEE, Inc., New York, NY.

[5] Boehm, B.W., and P.N. Papaccio, "Understanding and Controlling Software Costs," *IEEE Trans. Software Eng.*, Oct. 1988.

[6] Powell, P.B., "Software Validation, Verification and Testing Technique and Tool Reference Guide," *National Bureau of Standards Special Publication 500-93*, National Institute of Standards and Technology, Gaithersburg, MD 20899, 1982.

[7] Adrion, W.R., M.A. Branstad, and J.C. Cherniavsky, "Validation, Verification, and Testing of Computer Software," *ACM Computing Surveys*, Vol. 14, No. 2, June 1982.

[8] Radatz, J.W., "Analysis of IV&V Data," RADC-TR-81-145, Logicon, Inc., Rome Air Development Center, Griffiss AFB, NY, June 1981.

[9] McGarry, F., and G. Page, "Performance Evaluation of an Independent Software Verification and Integration Process," NASA Goddard, Greenbelt, MD, SEL 81-110, September 1982.

[10] "Guideline for Lifecycle Validation, Verification and Testing of Computer Software," FIPSPUB101, National Institute of Standards and Technology, Gaithersburg, MD 20899, 1983.

[11] "Guideline for Software Verification and Validation Plans," FIPSPUB132, National Institute of Standards and Technology, Gaithersburg, MD 20899, 1987.

[12] AFSC/AFLCP 800-5 Air Force Systems Command and Air Force Logistics Command Software Independent Verification and Validation, Washington, DC, 22 May 1988.

[13] DoD-Std-2167A Military Standard Defense System Software Development, AMSC No. 4327, Department of Defense, Washington, DC, Feb. 29, 1988.

[14] ANSI/ANS-10.4-1987, "Guidelines for the Verification and Validation of Scientific and Engineering Computer Programs for the Nuclear Industry," American Nuclear Society, La Grange Park, IL 1987.

[15] Blosiu, J.O., "Independent Verification and Validation of Computer Software: Methodology," National Aeronautics and Space Administration, Jet Propulsion Laboratory, Pasadena, Calif., JPL D-576, Feb. 9, 1983.

# Software Inspections and the Cost Effective Production of Reliable Software

A. Frank Ackerman*
*Institute for Zero Defect Software*
*San Jose, California*

*Software inspections were first defined for IBM by M. E. Fagan in 1976 [FGN76]. Since that time they have been used within IBM [DBN81] and other organizations [PEL82]. An IEEE software engineering standard covering inspections was approved in 1988 [IEEE88]. This paper describes software inspections as they were used in a large telecommunications R&D organization, and the technology transfer program that was used for their effective implementation. It also describes the placement of software inspections within the overall development process, and discusses their use in conjunction with other verification and validation techniques.*

## 1. Introduction

The routine production of software products of high reliability produced within budget and on schedule continues to be an elusive goal. The root cause of the difficulty is that although software development can be conceptualized as an industrial process [FGN76], most of the individual steps of this process must be performed by individual "intellectual artisans." The scope of an artisan's work is inherently difficult to bound, the techniques employed can not be specified precisely, and the quality of the resulting products is variable. By contrast, in a well-organized industrial process, each individual operation is clearly delineated, the techniques employed are clearly defined, and the whole process can be managed in such a way that it predictably produces products of specified quality. Software inspections, as defined in this paper, were first employed by M.E. Fagan in 1974 at the IBM Corporation as a method for reducing variability in the quality of individual operations in a software development process. Inspections also facilitated tighter, more rational process control [FGN76].

This paper is based on the results of a software engineering technology transfer program to implement software inspections at a large telecommunications R&D organization. Used for more than two years on a wide variety of applications, the program trained more than 2,400 software developers and managers in 40 different projects. The current evaluation of such programs is that software inspections can indeed produce the quality and productivity benefits claimed by M.E. Fagan, but that the implementation of software inspections within a development organization is a challenging task. This task requires not only a sound understanding of software development technology, but also a keen appreciation of the behavior and motivation of individual developers and the organizational culture in which these individuals work.

Sections 2, 3, and 4 of this paper describes software inspections and how they can be used to improve the industrial production of software products. Section 5 discusses the relationship of software inspections to other verification tasks. Section 6 describes a method for implementing software inspections within development organizations.

## 2. Software Inspections Overview

Software inspections are designed to address the three major tasks of process management: planning, measurement, and control. For software development, the corresponding tasks are (1) the definition of a software development process as a clearly defined series of individual operations, (2) the collection of quantitative quality data at different points in the process, and (3) the use of this data for improving the process.

The individual operations within a complete development process can be delineated by specifying explicit exit criteria to be met by the work products produced by each operation. The process can then be "thought of as a continuous process during which sequential sets of exit criteria are satisfied, the last set in the entire series requiring a well-defined end product" [FGN76]. For example, the exit criteria for the completion of module coding might be: compilation with no faults, no warnings from a portability checker, and no violations from a standards checker.

* This paper is adapted from an earlier paper, "Software Inspections and the Industrial Production of Software," by the author, Priscilla J. Fowler, and Robert G. Ebenau, which appeared in *Software Validation*, H.I. Hausen, ed., Elsevier, Amsterdam, 1984, pp. 13–40.

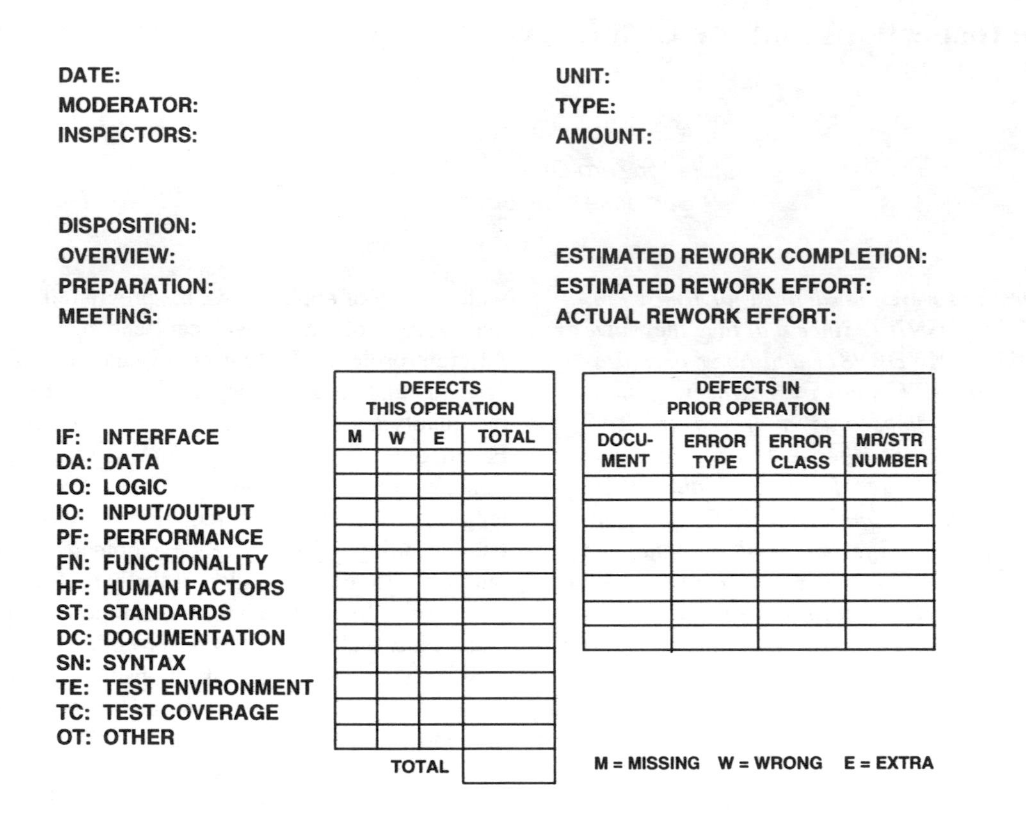

DATE:
MODERATOR:
INSPECTORS:

UNIT:
TYPE:
AMOUNT:

DISPOSITION:
OVERVIEW:
PREPARATION:
MEETING:

ESTIMATED REWORK COMPLETION:
ESTIMATED REWORK EFFORT:
ACTUAL REWORK EFFORT:

| | DEFECTS THIS OPERATION | | | |
|---|---|---|---|---|
| | M | W | E | TOTAL |
| IF: INTERFACE | | | | |
| DA: DATA | | | | |
| LO: LOGIC | | | | |
| IO: INPUT/OUTPUT | | | | |
| PF: PERFORMANCE | | | | |
| FN: FUNCTIONALITY | | | | |
| HF: HUMAN FACTORS | | | | |
| ST: STANDARDS | | | | |
| DC: DOCUMENTATION | | | | |
| SN: SYNTAX | | | | |
| TE: TEST ENVIRONMENT | | | | |
| TC: TEST COVERAGE | | | | |
| OT: OTHER | | | | |
| | | | TOTAL | |

| DEFECTS IN PRIOR OPERATION | | | |
|---|---|---|---|
| DOCU-MENT | ERROR TYPE | ERROR CLASS | MR/STR NUMBER |
| | | | |
| | | | |
| | | | |
| | | | |
| | | | |
| | | | |
| | | | |

M = MISSING W = WRONG E = EXTRA

*Figure 1. Software inspection data*

The operations which make up a particular development process, and the exit criteria which define their completion, are dependent on the particular application, the development techniques being used, and the culture of the organization. The only essential requirements are that the criteria be explicit, unambiguous, and verifiable.

One of the mechanisms used to collect quantitative quality data at defined points in the development process is a software inspection. A software inspection is a group review process that is used to detect and correct defects in a software work product. It is a formal, technical activity that is performed by the work product author and a small peer group on a limited amount of material. It produces a formal, quantitative report on the resources expended and the results achieved.

Software inspections are often compared to walk-throughs [YRD78] and indeed there are many similarities. But there are major differences in focus and intent. Walk-throughs are generally considered to be a developer technique that can be used by individuals to improve the quality of their work. Inspections, on the other hand, are intended to be a process management tool that will not only improve the quality of individual work products, but will also produce data that can be used for rational, quantitative decision-making. Thus, within each development process, software inspections must be formally and rigorously defined and they must be executed according to specification. More details on software inspections are provided in the next section.

An example of the data collected for an individual software inspection is shown in Figure 1.[1] The use of these data for process control is illustrated in Figure 2. In Figure 2, inspection data is shown as being used in three different ways: feed-back, feed-forward, and feed-into. For example, a series of design inspections might reveal an unexpectedly high percentage of data definition defects that could indicate a need for better

[1] Figure 1 uses the term "defects" rather than "errors," which is the term used by Fagan [FGN76]. The reason for this change of terminology is to be consistent with IEEE Std 729-1983, *IEEE Standard Glossary of Software Engineering Terminology*. All the terms used in this paper are consistent with this standard unless otherwise noted.

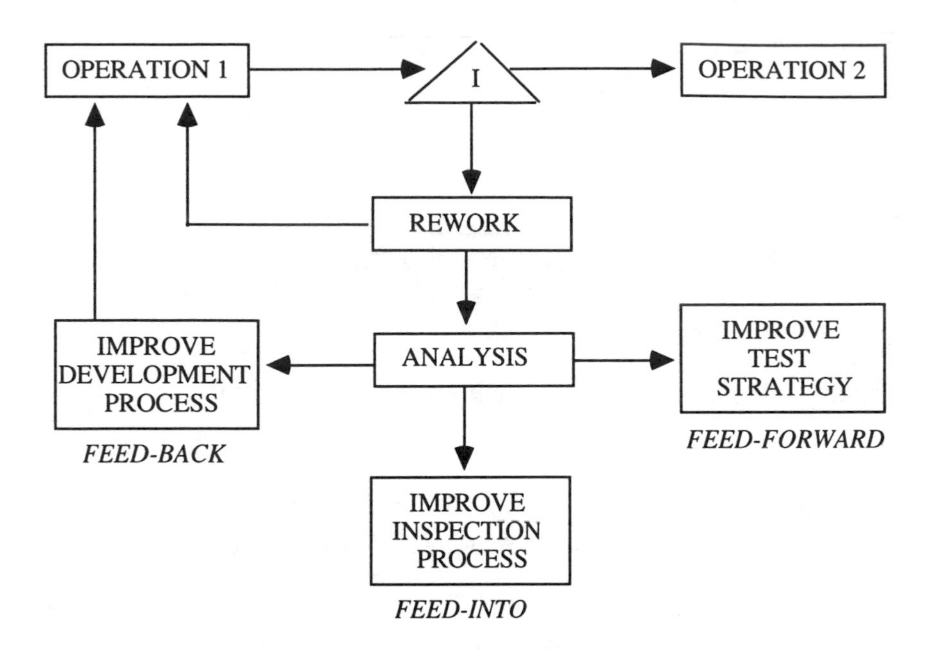


*Figure 2. The use of inspection data*

control of documentation for data layouts, that is, a need for a process adjustment to assure higher quality in subsequent work products. Information feed-forward can provide intelligence on treatment adjustments for individual work products. For example, a work product that was found to have an unusually high percentage of logic defects could be subjected to more rigorous testing.

The third use of inspection data (feed-into) can provide effectiveness and quality data about the inspection operations themselves. (For example, Are work products being examined carefully? are inspectors sufficiently prepared? and so on.) The collection and analysis of inspection data in conjunction with other process measures, such as reports on quality and productivity from testing operations, allows individual inspection operations to be adjusted for overall effectiveness. Thus, used properly, software inspections are self-regulating. They have repeatedly proven to be an effective method for improving both quality and productivity.

In his paper, Fagan reports on the effectiveness of software inspections applied to the development of a moderately complex component of a large operating system [FGN76]. Software inspections were held on detail designs, on cleanly compiled code, and at the completion of unit test. The result was a 23 percent productivity improvement and a 38 percent quality improvement, when compared with the development of a similar component that used walk-throughs.

In a trial of software inspections on a time-sharing system component upgrade at a large telecommunications R&D organization, software inspections were held on 1,482 noncommentary lines of source code after clean compile and some unit testing. The results were that 32 failures were detected by inspections with a total documented expenditure of 116 staff hours. The product (which altogether contained 8,940 lines of old, new, and changed code) was then subjected to system test, which detected 21 failures with an estimated expenditure of 162 staff hours.

## 3. Software Inspection Specifics

**The Software Inspection Process**. Each software inspection is itself a five or six-step process that is carried out by a designated moderator, by the author of the work product being inspected, and by at least one other peer inspector. The six steps are:

- Planning
- Overview
- Preparation
- Meeting
- Rework
- Follow-up

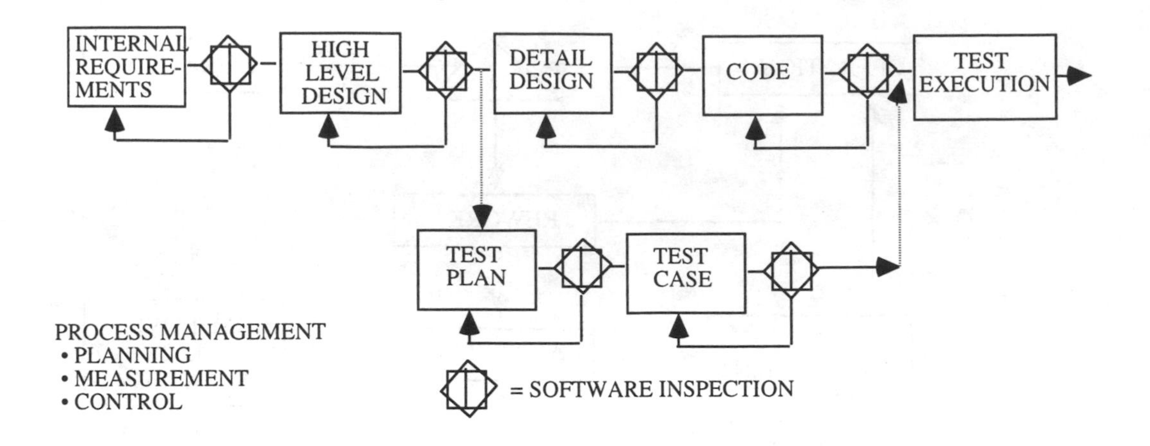


*Figure 3. Software development process*

Planning for an inspection begins when an author's work product meets the entry criteria established for this type of inspection. The first step is to select a moderator—a peer developer responsible for carrying out the inspection. A moderator may be selected by the author or a first-line manager from among a pool of qualified developers, or may be selected from an independent group with overall responsibility for the conduct of inspections for that organization. Since the moderator has overall responsibility for the inspection, including the final decision on the work product's disposition at the end of the inspection, it is important that he or she be as objective as possible. One way to ensure this is to specify that the moderator not be a member of a group that has direct production responsibility for the work product being inspected.

The moderator's first task is to meet with the author and to verify that the work product to be inspected meets the entry criteria for this type of inspection. When the work product meets these criteria, the next step is to decide whether or not to hold an overview, to select the other inspectors, and to schedule the overview and the meeting.

A software inspection overview is a presentation that is made to provide inspectors with any background information they may need in order to properly inspect the author's work product. Typically, an overview is given by an author, and it often covers material pertinent to a number of inspections. For example, for the time-sharing system component cited above, a single overview of the whole system was held for all prospective inspectors before beginning any of the individual inspections.

Another use of an overview is to provide a tutorial session on a specialized design or implementation technique that is used in the work product to be inspected, for example, a specialized enqueue and dequeue technique for synchronizing independent processes. The purpose of the overview is educational; the only inspection data collected during this step are the author's preparation time and the time the author and the inspectors spend at the overview presentation.

Preparation for a software inspection is an individual activity. The author prepares by collecting all the material required for this inspection and by completing an Inspection Profile Form (see Form 1 at the end of this paper). The other inspectors prepare by studying the work product to be inspected and by completing an Inspection Preparation Log (see Form 2). The purpose of individual preparation is to develop an understanding of the work product and to note places where this understanding is incomplete, or where the work product appears to have defects. Obvious defects are noted during this step, but detailed analysis and classification of defects is deferred to the inspection meeting.

The inspection meeting is conducted by the moderator. There is an established agenda that consists of:

- Introduction
- Establishing preparedness
- Examining the material and recording defects
- Reviewing defect list
- Determining disposition
- Debriefing.

During the introduction, the moderator introduces the inspectors and the material to be examined and states the purpose of the meeting. Preparedness is established by having each inspector report his or her preparation time as entered on the Inspection Preparation Log. The moderator sums these times for entry on the Inspection Management Report (see Form 3). If the moderator feels that preparation has been insufficient for an effective meeting, he or she may postpone the meeting.

Examining the material and recording defects are the major activities of an inspection meeting. At the meeting, one of the inspectors takes the role of reader and paces the group through the material by paraphrasing each "line" or section of the material aloud for the group. As the reader proceeds through the material in what he or she has selected as the most effective sequence for defect detection, the inspectors (including the reader) interrupt with questions and concerns. Each of these is either handled immediately or tabled. Whenever the group agrees, or the moderator rules, that a defect has been detected, the recorder for that inspection notes the location, description, class, and type on the Inspection Defect List (Form 4). (The role of recorder can be assumed by the moderator or any other inspector other than the author.)

After the reading and recording of defects, the moderator has the recorder review the Defect List to make sure that all defects have been recorded and correctly classified. After this is done, the inspectors determine the disposition of the material: "meets," "rework," or "re-inspect." The disposition of "meets" is given when the work product as inspected meets the exit criteria (or needs only trivial corrections) required for that type of inspection. The disposition of "re-inspect" is given when rework will change the work product in a substantial way.

Since an inspection meeting is to determine and record defects in a peer's work product, there is always the potential that interpersonal tension will develop during the meeting. An experienced moderator will note this and after the meeting initiate a suitable "debriefing exercise" to give these tensions opportunity for safe release. The debriefing exercise that we teach in our inspections training classes simply gives each participant an opportunity to briefly share his or her experience of the meeting in a supportive atmosphere.

Our experience with the interpersonal aspect of inspections is that problems in this area can be significant when inspections are initially introduced in a project, but they tend to disappear as inspections become a routine procedure. The two-day workshop we give to all inspectors considers the interpersonal problems associated with the use of inspections throughout the course and the final lecture deals with this area exclusively. Given this training, our experience is that most groups are able to handle any initial start-up problems without undue difficulty.

From the above description, it may appear that an inspection meeting is a formidable affair. It is not. The formality of the agenda, the assigned rules, the specified defect classification, and the limited purpose of the meeting all serve to create an effective meeting in which all the participants know what is to be done, and how to do it. With a modicum of training (described in a subsequent section), a synergistic team effort develops during the meeting that produces a result superior to the sum of what could be accomplished by isolated individual efforts. The meeting often develops the spirit of a detective drama because each participant's remarks provide clues in a vigorous effort to detect defects.

Inspection rework is performed by the author. It consists simply of correcting the defects noted in the Inspection Defect List.

The follow-up step is the responsibility of the moderator. It consists of verifying the corrections made during rework and completing the Inspection Management Report and the Inspection Defect Summary Report (Form 5).

Figure 4 gives a schematic of the overall process. Rework, and/or Follow-up may be skipped if the disposition is "meets."

**Software Inspection Roles**. Routine, effective, and hassle-free execution of an inspection process is facilitated by recognizing the specific inspection roles mentioned above. The following table provides a brief summary of the roles in an inspection.

| | |
|---|---|
| Author | the producer (or current owner) of the subject work product |
| Moderator | an inspector responsible for organizing, executing, and reporting a software inspection |
| Reader | an inspector who guides the examination of the work product at the meeting |
| Recorder | an inspector who enters all the defects found during the meeting on the Inspection Defect List (Form 4) |
| Inspector | a member of an inspection team other than the author. Often chosen to represent a specific development role: designer, tester, technical writer, for example |

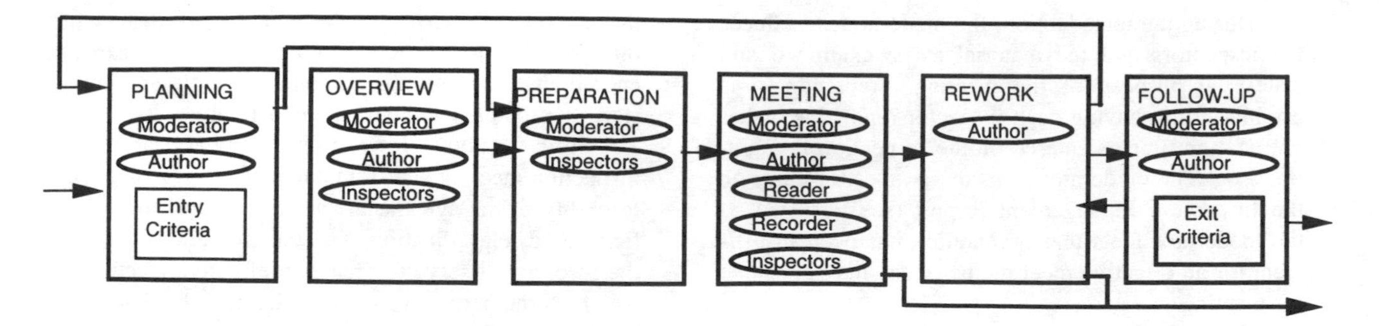


*Figure 4. Software inspection process*

In Figure 4 each role is associated with the step in which it participates.

**Software Inspections As A Process Control Tool**. As described in the previous section, the use of software inspections as a process control tool requires that they be employed at specified points throughout the development process. Figure 3 provides an example of a development process with software inspections being applied to internal requirements, high-level design, detail design, coding, test plans, and test cases. Within a development process each of these inspections is defined by specifying:

- Entry criteria
- Exit criteria
- Recommended participants
- Defect classifications
- Defect detection strategies.

Entry criteria are the pro-form conditions that a work product must meet before it is considered ready for inspection. These generally include the development operation exit criteria that would apply if an inspection were not specified for that operation, but they also include requirements for an effective inspection. For example, the entry criteria for a code inspection would require a clean compile, but it would also specify that the material to be inspected have visible line numbers and that the pertinent requirements, design, and change information be included as part of the inspection package.

Exit criteria are the completion conditions for an inspection. Typically, these are the correction of all detected defects and the documentation of any uncorrected defects in the project problem-tracking system.

Since a software inspection is a cooperative process that relies on group synergy, the selection of participants is an important issue. At inspections held early in the development process, for example, at requirements or high-level design, both the user and system test viewpoints should be represented, as well as that of the developers responsible for implementation. The representation of all of these points of view will sometimes require inspection teams as large as seven or eight. At inspections held later in the development process, for example, code inspections, teams of three or four developers concerned only with detail design, coding, and unit test are effective [BCK81].

Strategies for detecting defects depend on the type of inspection, the kind of material, and the defect categories. In Fagan's implementations [FGN76], the inspectors are provided with checklists keyed to the defect types. In our implementations we have stressed "understanding" during preparation rather than defect detection. So a checklist organized by defect type is not appropriate. What we are now tending to provide are "preparation guidelines" that are keyed to the organization of the material being inspected. For example, for high-level designs it is important to verify that the functionality being specified in the design is in one-to-one correspondence with the requirements. Hence a high-level design preparation guideline might provide useful questions to be asked of each part of each subprogram and module design to check for this correspondence.

As described in the previous section, defect counts are used as process control data. Thus, the precise classification of defects is an essential part of the specification of each type of inspection. For software inspections, a defect is defined to be noncompliance with a product specification or document standard. Thus, as shown in Figure 1, defects are categorized by type and class. The classes, as defined by Fagan, are M="missing", E="extra," and W="wrong" [FGN76]. "Missing" is used for material that is called for in the specification or the standard, but is absent. "Extra" is used for material that exceeds the specification or the standard. "Wrong" is used for material that should be present, and is present, but contains a flaw.

Defect-type classifications depend on the nature of the material being inspected and on the specific development process. It should be possible to classify any defect easily and unambiguously during an inspection meeting. Furthermore, the resulting defect counts, when taken over time, should yield useful process control information. The thirteen defect types listed in Figure 1 form a generic set that has been used as a starting point with many different development projects. The appropriate types for each kind of inspection are selected from these thirteen and given definitions that apply to a particular inspection for a given project. An example of this kind of tailoring is given in Figure 5. An example of the kind of material inspected for these particular defects is given in Figure 6.

**Other Aspects of the Use of Software Inspections**. My experience with the implementation of software inspections in many development organizations is that the introduction of this technique often provides additional benefits beyond the measurable improvements in productivity and quality. One of the motivations in establishing software inspections as a standard part of a development process is that the use of inspections makes a frequently opaque operation more visible. Unlike a number of other software engineering techniques, software inspections are adaptable enough to be effective with primitive methodologies.

Every software project must produce code, and it is always possible to define an initial set of useful error types and detection strategies for a code inspection. Hence, about the only project for which inspections cannot be applied to at least the code is a project where the individual code modules are very large (greater than 500 lines) and are so badly structured that they cannot be partitioned. In my experience I have found that the use of the basic notions of structured programming is widespread so the occurrence of large, unstructured modules is rare.

When it is clear to the developers that their management supports their use of inspections as a technique for making improvements in quality and productivity, the experience of performing code inspections leads rapidly into consideration of other software engineering techniques. In many projects the precision of the inspection process points out the usefulness of a separate requirements document, and this in turn can lead to a better understanding of the usefulness of design documentation. Furthermore, when some of these other techniques are implemented, the data collected by inspections can be used to quantify the quality improvements achieved by these techniques.

---

**Performance (PF)**
- There is a plausible argument that the component will not meet the performance objectives stated in the requirements.

**Data (DA)**
- Missing or extra item in an Input, Output, or Update section.
- Incorrect or missing data type in an Input, Output, or Update section.

**Interface (IF)**
- Missing or extra routine call in a Processing section.
- An incorrect Invocation section.

**Functionality (FN)**
- In a Processing section a step is missing, extra, or erroneous.
- In a Processing section logical conditions are missing, extra, or erroneous.

**Documentation (DC)**
- The content of a Description section is. incomplete or misleading.
- The description of a data item is ambiguous.
- A processing step is not clearly described.

**Standard (ST)**
- An applicable standard in the Project Standards Manual is violated.

**Syntax (SN)**
- A defect in grammar, punctuation, or spelling.

**Other (OT)**
- A defect that does not fall under any of the types given above.

*Figure 5. Example of High-Level Design Inspection Defect Types*

**SUBPROGRAM: prcl**

**TITLE:** Print in columns

**DESCRIPTION:** This subprogram formats an input file into a columnized output file.

**INPUTS:**

| | |
|---|---|
| -l | optional length command |
| -k | optional number of columns |
| -w | optional page width command |
| *filename* | input file |

**UPDATES: N/A**

**OUTPUTS:**

| | |
|---|---|
| Formatted output | listed to standard output file |
| Error message | to standard error file |
| Status | process status code |

**PROCESSING:**

1. Formats input file into **k** columns per page on standard output.
2. If error detected sends error message to standard error file.
3. Return status code of 0 for normal exit or 1 for error exit.

**INVOCATION:** Called form the shell using the following format:
**prcl** [**-l**integer] [**-k**integer] [**-w**integer] filename

*Figure 6. Example of High-Level Design Specification*

The process of inspecting all the work products produced by a given development operation exposes thc development group as a whole to both good and bad examples. The inspection both develops and enforces group norms for quality workmanship. Participating in inspections thus eliminates much of the ambiguity about what is expected of each developer. Participating in inspections also spreads detail technical information around. This is especially important in projects where much of the essential information isn't formally written down. Finally, although project management is strongly warned against formally using detailed inspection data for personnel evaluation, the process does provide individuals with an objective means for dynamically assessing the quality of their work. For example, if I know the overall project defect rate for detail designs, I can use that information to motivate improvements in my own work, while also realizing that the inspection process will correct my mistakes before they become public.[2]

[2] At the completion of one trial of inspections at IBM [IBM77], a study was made of individual defect rates. During the course of the project defect rates decreased for all the developers. The software inspection process has the potential for enhancing professional growth and increasing job satisfaction.

## 4. Software Inspections Data and Process Control

The collection and analysis of data is the essential feature that sets software inspections apart from other peer review techniques, for example, walk-throughs as described by Yourdon [YRD78].

The first use of inspection data is made by the first-line manager. The inspection disposition of "meets," "rework," or "reinspect," and the estimated effort and dates for rework provide essential process scheduling information. If the amount of rework is extensive, and scheduling constraints are tight, the manager may need to negotiate a reduction in the amount of functionality to be delivered. Some of the defects can then be documented with trouble reports so that they can be addressed during the next development cycle, and the rework limited to the corrections that can be made without impacting the scheduled delivery to the next operation.

The next use of inspection data is made by the developers or verifiers who receive the work product at later stages in the process. The Inspection Defect Summary Report[3] is essentially an "intelligence" report on the state of the work product at the time it was inspected. Although these defects are normally corrected during the rework step, the data nonetheless points to potential weak spots in the product.

The data on the amount of material inspected, the amount of inspector preparation, and the speed with which the material was examined during the meeting can be used by a quality assurance function to assess the effectiveness of an inspection. In a study performed by F.O. Buck at IBM [BCK81], it was found that inspection preparation and examination rates during the meeting were significant predictors of an effective inspection. For example, during the course of one development project inspection teams that inspected design and code at, or less than, the recommended rate found more than 100 percent more defects per thousand lines of code than did teams that exceeded this recommended rate. Furthermore, for a series of 106 inspections held as part of an inspection training effort, it was found that unless a team prepared for the recommended amount of time, it would, on the average, inspect faster, (less effectively) than the recommended rate.

The determination of recommended inspection and preparation rates is a quality assurance responsibility. The optimal rate depends on the type of material and the application. For code the initial recommendation is to plan for a rate of 100 lines of code per hour. This recommendation is derived from the study by Buck [BCK81] and has been substantiated in experience. For straightforward application code, some of our projects are reporting higher rates. On the other hand, for inspections of performance sensitive microcode, one project reported a rate of 40 lines of code per hour. Within each project, the reported rates should be scrutinized by quality assurance by studying the number and kinds of defects uncovered at different rates for similar workproducts.

The above are all examples of the immediate use of data from individual inspections. When inspection data are accumulated over time, summarized, and used in conjunction with other process data, rational, real-time control of a software development process becomes a possibility. For example, one of the standard inspection reports is the normalized distribution of the types of defects detected at each inspection point during designated time periods (Figure 7).

When a report such as this shows that a particular process is experiencing higher than normal defect percentages during initial development increments, it may be possible to remedy the problem and improve the quality of subsequent workproducts. For example, the sample report in Figure 7 shows that about one in every four defects is a documentation problem, an unexpectedly high percentage for this type of inspection. Perhaps the documentation standards for this work product are confusing; perhaps some of the developers need additional training in the application of these standards. At any rate, the inspection report has indicated the need for further investigation and remedy.

By comparing the defect detection and correction efficiencies between different inspection points and testing points, project management can make informed decisions for optimizing a development process overall. For example, in [DBN81], J.A. Dobbins and R.D. Buck report that an analysis of inspection data in their organization led to a shift in emphasis from code inspections to design inspections. They also report that an analysis of test reports led to the realization that an additional interface inspection needed to be added to their development process.

## 5. Software Inspections and Other Verification Techniques

As discussed above, software inspections are a process control tool, and are thus designed to work in cooperation with any other technique employed during a development process. In particular, the above discussion assumes that a development process employing software inspections will also employ testing,[4] reviews, and audits. Proof-of-correctness techniques are currently not widely used for the industrial production of software, but as argued by R.A. De Millo, et al., [DML79] a proof is a social process, not a formal one, and hence the use of proof techniques is also compatible with the use of software inspections.

[3] The Inspection Defect List (Form 4) is private to the inspection team. It is only used during the meeting to collect raw data and during follow-up. The data contained on the Defect List is sumarized by the moderator on the Inspection Defect Summary Report (Form 5).

[4] "Testing" refers to the process of exercising or evaluating a system or system component by automated (not manual) means to verify that it satisfies specified requirements or to identify differences between expected and actual results.

INSPECTION: DETAIL DESIGN FROM: 03/20/82 TO 09/01/82
NUMBER: 23 AMOUNT: 2751PC

| Defect Type | Defect Category Missing | Wrong | Extra | Total Defect | Defect % |
|---|---|---|---|---|---|
| IF (Interface) | 5 | 17 | 1 | 23 | 6.6 |
| DA (Data) | 3 | 21 | 1 | 25 | 7.2 |
| LO (Logic) | 32 | 40 | 14 | 77 | 24.8 |
| IO (Input/Output) | 7 | 9 | 3 | 19 | 5.5 |
| PF (Performance) | 0 | | | | |
| FN (Functionality) | 5 | 7 | 2 | 14 | 4.0 |
| HF (Human Factors) | 3 | 2 | 5 | 10 | 2.9 |
| ST (Standards) | 25 | 24 | 3 | 52 | 14.9 |
| DC (Documentation) | 37 | 51 | 10 | 92 | 28.1 |
| SN (Syntax) | 4 | 9 | 1 | 14 | 4.0 |
| TE (Test Environment) | 0 | | | | |
| TC (Test Coverage) | 0 | | | | |
| OT (Other) | 2 | 5 | | 7 | 2.0 |
| | 123 | 185 | 40 | 348 | 100.0 |

*Figure 7. Software Inspection Summary Report. (Simulated Data)*

Testing and software inspections both have the same purpose, that is, to discover defects [MRS79]. Within a given software development process, they play complementary and supporting roles. The first thing to note in discussing the relationship of software inspections and testing is that software inspections may be employed early in the development process while testing, since it requires executable units of code, cannot complete until these units have been specified, designed, and compiled. Since the cost of detecting and correcting defects in a software product rises exponentially as one proceeds through the development process [BHM76], the use of inspections as an adjunct to testing can often result in cost savings. To fully understand the relationship between inspections and testing, it is necessary to distinguish the different kinds of testing that are performed in the course of developing a software product. Below we discuss the relationship between unit testing, system testing, and software inspections.

In unit testing, an individual unit of program production (a function, or a collection of functions) is subjected to detailed testing to discover if there are any input combinations that will cause the unit to behave in an unexpected manner, or to produce incorrect results. Since it is practically impossible to test all input combinations, the art of unit testing is that of specifying a limited set of inputs that will most likely reveal defects. One of the concepts used for the specification of such input sets is that of code coverage, for example, that all statements be executed or all branches be executed. In practice, it is extremely difficult to specify input sets that give 100 percent branch coverage; but detailed design and code inspections are a line-by-line examination of designs and code, and hence provide 100 percent coverage because all branches are considered. For processes where data is being collected on the relative effort and effectiveness of unit testing and software inspections, rational judgments can be made on which to use, or how they should be combined.

For system testing, the situation is different because this operation exercises many units (including the entire system) and thus provides an opportunity for defect detection beyond the scope of the inspection of individual units. However, there is still a use for inspections in this area. For example, in one case cited above [DBN81], the detection of a large number of interface defects during a test operation led to the creation of a special interface inspection to detect and correct these defects prior to this testing operation. The overall result was an improvement in productivity. The reason for this is that one inspection may find a number of errors that are then corrected all at once, while testing tends to find and correct defects one by one.

A further use of software inspections in relation to testing is in the use of test plan and test case inspections [LRS75]. The purpose of these inspections is to improve the effectiveness of the test operation by improving the defect detection potential of the tests. An application of test plan and test case inspections at IBM reported that the number of test cases was increased by 30 percent, but that the overall result was an 85 percent improvement in test productivity [EBN81].

By definition, software inspections are a small peer group process whose purpose is the detection and correction of defects. When development work products must be examined by larger groups, or by management, software inspections do not apply. Nor do they apply when the purpose of the examination is other than defect detection, for example, the consideration of architectural or design alternatives. Each of these cases calls for procedures specifically designed to achieve the desired objectives.

The proper design and execution of various kinds of review procedures is beyond the scope of this paper, but we can make some suggestions on the use of reviews in relationship to inspections. Where it is the case that the purpose of a manual examination of a work product is strictly to detect and correct defects, then inspections have been shown to be superior to other review procedures [FGN76], and in addition, they provide data for process management. Of course, in order to detect defects in a work product there must be a clear understanding of the product specifications and document standards.

Often the use of a special review procedure will be dictated by considerations other than verification, and the question then arises as to whether the review subsumes the defect detection and correction function of an inspection, or whether an inspection should be held in addition to the review. In general, the answer to this question is that if it appears that an inspection might be of benefit, then the inspection can be implemented and the resulting inspection data can then decide the question.

Audits by definition[5] involve an agent external to the process being examined. Except for special cases, for example, the auditing of financial software by outside auditors, auditing of software development work products is not an efficient verification technique because it involves the duplication of technical expertise within an auditing function.

Procedural audits are another matter. In the case of software inspections, it is assumed that a quality assurance function has responsibility for auditing inspection procedures to ensure (1) that the procedures are being performed as specified, and (2) that the procedures, when faithfully executed, are producing the intended results in quality and productivity. In this application of audits, inspection reports become input to the audit operation.

Where formal verification techniques, such as Dijkstra's discipline of programming [DJK76], are being utilized as part of the design and implementation operations, software inspections are a natural choice for a peer examination technique. Where automatic verifiers are used in a development process, the situation is similar to that in which a compiler is employed. The compiler is assumed to operate correctly, and the problem is that of saying the right things in the higher level language. Software inspections can be applied to the verification of correctness conditions just as they are to compiler input.

Walk-throughs, as described in [IEEE88], are often compared to inspections. The essential differences between inspections and walk-throughs are: (1) walk-throughs are not a formally documented and implemented development process, (2) walk-throughs do not create quality records that can be used for process improvement, (3) walk-throughs do not create quality records that provide evidence that detected defects have been corrected and the corrections verified.

Terminology is not the issue here. A software development work product verification process that does not have the three characteristics just listed does not satisfy the requirements of ISO 9001; more is required. Furthermore, a process that can be managed and relied on throughout the life of an organization is needed. Walk-throughs, as the term is used here, do not meet these requirements.

## 6. A Software Inspection Implementation Program

**The Development and Training Environment.** Installing software inspections as an effective technique in a development organization can be a difficult job since it involves changing the behavior of a whole organization. The required behavior changes are not large, but they must be coordinated between the developers, first-level management, project management, and software quality assurance. In addition, for long-running projects, the changes must be planned and executed within existing scheduling constraints.

This section describes a comprehensive inspections implementation program that was carried out in the early eighties at a large telecommunications R&D organization. Similar programs have since been used in many other organizations for the successful installation of effective inspection processes.

In the subject organization each project was an independent organizational entity. The management of each project had the responsibility for choosing the appropriate means of achieving project objectives, and a wide variety of approaches were employed. The approach that was selected depended largely on the past experience of the managers and senior developers. Tools, techniques, and procedures were borrowed freely between projects, but generally they were tailored, or reimplemented to fit the project's perception of its needs.

[5] IEEE-Std-729, op cit, gives two definitions. The first is "an independent review for the purpose of assessing compliance."

Within the subject organization, the systems training department had the responsibility for providing software engineering training in subject matter that was applicable to a number of different projects. For example, it provided training in the use of the Unix operating system, the C language, microprocessor application design, data communications, and so on.

Within the systems training department, the system development technology group had responsibility for developing and delivering training in software engineering methodologies that could be utilized by a variety of application areas regardless of the specific implementation techniques being utilized. Figure 8 shows the subject matter covered by this group's curriculum.

During the course of developing the software inspections program within this curriculum, it became apparent that if this training program wanted to use actual, effective implementations of software inspections on individual projects as its measure of success, it would have to take a novel approach. The approach that was developed was called *consultative training* and became the group's primary method of software engineering technology transfer. Consultative training utilized a project-oriented view of the subject matter of software engineering, as shown in Figure 9 [EMR83].

**Software Inspection Program Design Concepts**. For software inspections, the application of the consultative training concept resulted in the following program design concepts:

- The software inspections program was focused on entire software projects, as opposed to traditional training focused on individual developers. Within Bell Laboratories, individual software projects normally correspond with a single organizational element, for example, a group or a department, and hence this approach allowed us to work in concert with project management as well as the developers. It also allowed us to schedule the various implementation steps at the project's convenience.

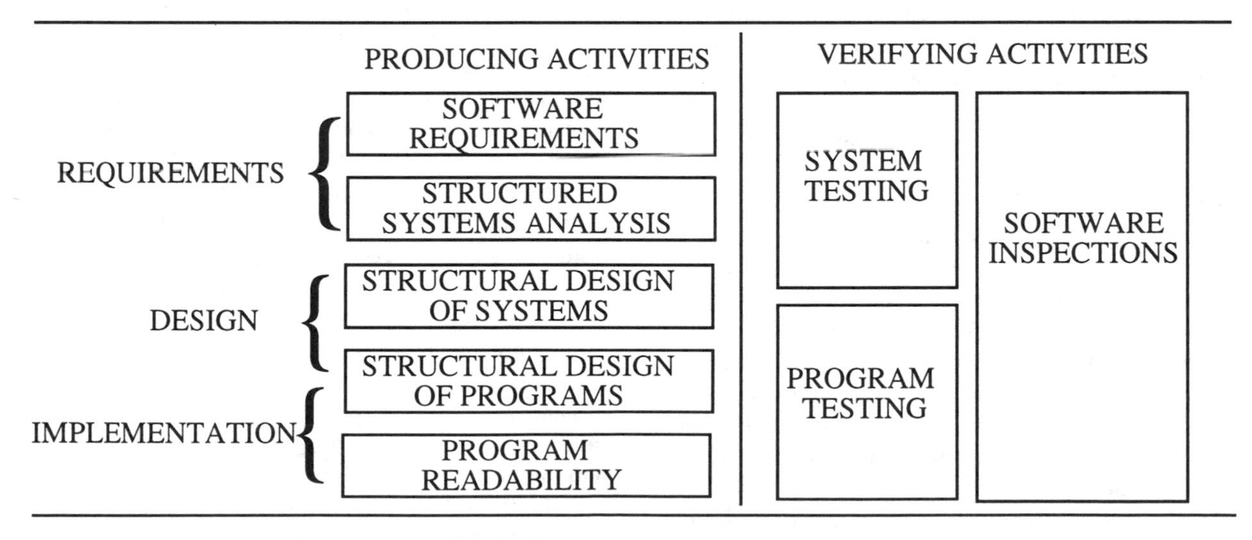


*Figure 8. Our original software engineering curriculum*

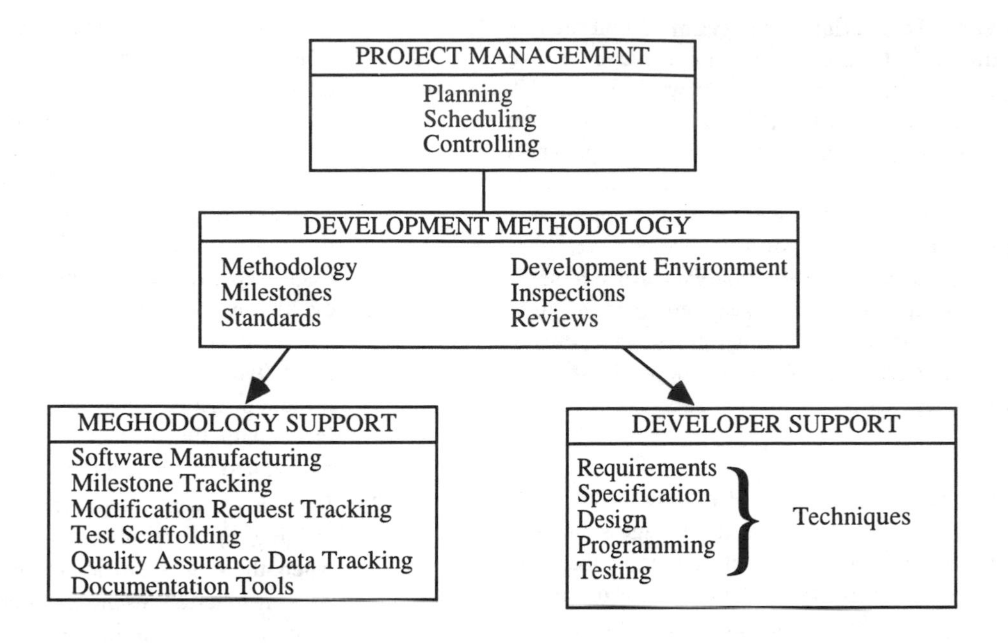


*Figure 9. Project-Oriented View of Software Engineering*

- Within each project, our major concern was with motivating and training developers and first-line managers. We obtained the support of upper management and coordinated the program with them, but we avoided a top-down approach. Our assumption was that effective behavioral change cannot be dictated from above.[6]

- We employed formal classroom training as a major part of our program, but we also provided direct consulting. We assisted projects in selecting the appropriate inspection points within their existing methodology, and we helped specify the entry and exit criteria, defect types and detection strategies, and the recommended participants. As part of this effort we supplied each project with first drafts of a Project Inspection Manual that contained our initial suggestions for the specification of each type of inspection the project would use. This manual also contained inspection data collection forms tailored to the project's needs.

- We entered into an ongoing relationship with each client project and provided whatever assistance was appropriate when problems arose. In particular, we performed evaluation and review activities to determine whether the project was in fact following its procedures, whether these procedures were in fact producing the desired results, and whether the overall perception of the developers and first-line managers was that inspections were making a positive contribution to their project.

- In order to make our formal classroom training directly applicable to an individual project, we separated the teaching and exercise material into two classes: (1) that which taught principles and techniques generic to any application of software inspections, and (2) that which considered aspects that could be specialized for a particular project. This meant, for example, that we could apply the project's own definitions of defect types and detection strategies against class exercise material developed from actual project work products.

- Wherever possible, software inspections were introduced into a project on a trial basis. A trial allowed a shakedown of the software inspection procedures in the project environment, and also allowed the project to directly experience the benefits of inspections before making a full-scale commitment.

---

[6] This is no longer an assumption. In the few instances where we violated this principle, we were emphatically taught its general validity.

**Software Inspections Program Implementation**. To implement the concepts just discussed above we designed the six-step program shown in Figure 10. This formal approach to the delivery of this program allowed us to keep track of each project's progress through its implementation plan. It also helped us manage and allocate our own resources among the constantly changing needs of our clients, and it at times provided a structure for charging for our services. This six-step program also served to make clear to each project what its responsibilities were during each step of the program. Each of these six steps is described below.

1. *Software Inspections Overview.* The overview was a presentation to managers and key developers on a project. It introduced the software inspections technique, discussed how it would be carried out, what the expected benefits would be, what the costs would be, and what project resources would be required for implementation. At the conclusion of this presentation, the project decided whether or not it wished to proceed with a software inspections implementation program at that time and, if it did, who on the project would have responsibility for initiating the effort.
2. *Needs-Assessment.* The needs-assessment activity consisted of meeting with the project members who were assigned to initiate the program, and one or two members of the software inspection program staff. Project members first presented an overview of the project, including the nature of the application, project resources and schedules, and the development environment. Project members and the software inspections program staff then determined training requirements and schedules, project development phase demarcations with appropriate software inspection types, and a schedule and participants for the trial use of software inspections. The trial period was designed to correspond to some part of the project's development cycle so that any defect data from the project's normal quality assurance procedures could be used later in evaluating the use of software inspections on that project. A software inspections coordinator, who would have responsibility for the project's inspection program, and who interfaced with the inspection program staff was designated by project management.
3. *Implementation Support.* The classroom training on inspections was most effective when there was sufficient time in the project's inspection implementation schedule to prepare (1) an initial draft of the project's software inspections manual and (2) practice inspection material based on an actual project work product. These materials were produced through a joint effort between the software inspections staff and the project's software inspections coordinator. This effort supplemented the inspections staff's understanding of inspections in general with essential information about the project's specific environment. The inspections staff involvement in turn overcame the project's lack of expertise and, more subtly, provided an outside impetus toward completing work that was not directly related to the immediate development schedule. The inspections staff involvement also provided the coordinator with psychological support—the coordinator, after all, must deal directly with his or her colleagues' resistance to changes in project procedures.

| COURSE/ACTIVITY | AUDIENCE | PURPOSE | LENGTH |
|---|---|---|---|
| 1. Software Inspections Overview | Project Management<br>Key Developers | To provide decision base | ½ Day class |
| 2. Software Inspections Needs Assessment | Project Management<br>Key Developers | To plan project use of process | ½–1 Day consulting |
| 3. Implementation | Inspections Coordinator | Design and document project process | 1–2 Days support |
| 4. Software Inspections Workshop | Project Development Groups | To provide developer training | 2 Day class |
| 5. Software Inspections Management Seminar | Project Management | To provide management training | ½ Day class |
| 6. Software Inspections Review and Evaluation | Project Management<br>Key Developers | To "tune" the process | Interview as needed |

*Figure 10. The Bell Labs Software Inspections Program*

4. *Developer Workshop.* The developer workshop taught the steps needed to prepare for, participate in, and lead an inspection. A major section of the workshop was a full-scale practice inspection that inspected the project material especially prepared for this purpose, and that utilized draft copies of the project's inspections manual. This exercise thus not only provided the developers with experience in the inspection technique generally, but it also gave them a chance to trial the specific procedures that would be used on their project, and a chance to offer their own suggestions for improving these procedures. The workshop concluded with a discussion of project implementation considerations by the software inspections coordinator who worked with the training staff to tailor the program to the project.
5. *Management Seminar.* In the initial implementation period of inspections on a project, the inspections staff sought to maximize the involvement of the developers on whom the success of the technique ultimately depended and to minimize involvement by management. Once inspections began to take hold, however, there was a need to provide management with additional information. In fact, project management ultimately has a key role to play in a successful project implementation of inspections. This role was discussed with the developers in the workshop, and skepticism about whether or not management will play its role properly was blunted by the inspections staff's commitment to bring the developers' concerns directly to the management. For small projects, this could be handled informally; for large projects, a half-day seminar was used for this purpose.
6. *Evaluation and Review.* At the conclusion of a trial, and at appropriate intervals thereafter, a project should review its software inspection procedures to determine what changes, if any, should be made in its procedures. In this step, the software inspections program staff evaluated the project's inspection process using project inspection data, direct observation of inspection meetings, and formal interviews with participating developers and their first-level managers. The collected data was then evaluated and presented, along with recommendations for improvements, to the project's software inspections coordinator and to interested developers and managers.

The results of this program were positive. Of the 42 projects that participated in the program by the middle of 1984, 25 were using inspections as an established part of their development process, 4 were trailing inspections, and 5 had training scheduled. The remaining 8 projects did not immediately continue the program for a variety of reasons: one project did not follow the training with the necessary implementation resources, in another the supervisor sabotaged the process by attending inspection meetings, and so on. The review and evaluation step described above was completed for 6 projects.

Data for one completed evaluation was obtained from a series of 40 interviews with developers and project management, from inspection records, and by direct observation. The results were that:

- inspections were being consistently used;
- the developers and managers were enthusiastic and supportive of the inspection process; and
- more than 90 percent of those interviewed felt that inspections increased product quality and enhanced developer growth, with a majority perceiving no delay in production schedules as a result of using inspections.

These results have been corroborated by other studies and by less formal project evaluations. The bottom line is that this approach to the implementation of software inspections is effective. However, there were still some problems:

**Timing and Initial Implementation**. The least effective software inspection is the code inspection since it can find errors only after the completion of requirements, design, and coding. Yet one large project chose to restrict the initial application of inspections to code because they had just implemented a new methodology that contained detailed procedures for design reviews. Had we been able to start our work with this project a few months sooner, most likely we would have been able to convince them to use design inspections rather than reviews. Our philosophy has been to work with whatever opportunities have presented themselves to us and to let the effectiveness of the inspection technique speak for itself over the long haul

**Data Collection and Analysis**. Most projects agree in theory with the need to collect and analyze data on the effectiveness of the inspection process. They understand the potential benefits from having the data: immediate and well-documented results from software inspection meetings; indication of troublesome areas in system implementation in time for preventive measures, such as redesign or more thorough testing; and measures of the costs of the inspection process versus other defect detection and correction methods. However, few projects as yet are willing to invest in other than the most minimal of data collection and analysis efforts. Fear of misuse of the information is one problem. Another is limited staff for doing the work involved. One answer is more mechanized support for data collection and analysis, and then more specific procedures for how to use the results.

**Management Support**. Management support is key to the success of any new technique. If a sustained commitment to spending the resources required is not maintained, failure is certain, and much effort will be wasted. A well-defined trial use of software inspections helps give management a good measure of the benefits and costs of using software inspections in their particular projects.

Continued success is possible, however, only when management uses inspections in a way that is consistent with other project objectives and with developer expectations. One failure we experienced was the direct result of the management's lack of proper support and encouragement for developers in implementing this process.

## 7. Conclusions

Software inspections have been shown [FGN76] [IBM77] [PEL82] [MCK81] [EBN81a] to be an efficient and effective method for improving project productivity and product quality in a wide variety of industrial software development environments. Software inspections can be effectively employed together with testing, product reviews, procedural audits, and formal verification techniques. The successful installation of software inspections within ongoing projects is complex, but well-conceived and supported programs have been successful in numerous development organizations.

## References


[ACK82] Ackerman, A.F., Ackerman, A.S., and Ebenau, R.G., "A Software Inspections Training Program," *Proc. COMPSAC 82* IEEE Computer Society Press, Los Alamitos, Calif., 1982, pp. 443–444.

[BCK81] Buck, F.O., "Indicators of Quality Inspection," IBM Technical Report TR21.802, Systems Communications Division, Kingston, N.Y., 1981.

[BHM76] Boehm, B.W., "Software Engineering," *IEEE Trans. Computers*, Dec. 1976, pp. 1,226–1,241.

[DML79] DeMillo, R.A., Lipton, R.J., and Perles, A.J., "Social Processes and Proofs of Theories and Programs," *Comm. ACM,* Vol. 22, No. 5, 1979, pp. 271–280.

[DBN81] Dobbins, J.A. and Buck, R.D., "Software Quality in the 80's," *Proc. Trends and Applications Symp.,* IEEE Computer Society Press, Los Alamitos, Calif., 1981, pp. 31–37.

[DJK76] Dijkstra, E.W., *A Discipline of Programming*, Prentice-Hall, Englewood Cliffs, N.J., 1976.

[EBN81] Ebenau, R.G., Private communication

[EBN81a] Ebenau, R.G., "Inspecting For Software Quality," *Proc. 2nd Nat'l Symp. EDP Quality Assurance*, 1981, DPMA Education Foundation, produced by U. S. Professional Development Institute, Inc., 12611 Davon Drive, Silver Spring, Md. 20904

[EMR83] Emerson, T.J., et al., "Training For Software Engineering Technology Transfer," *Workshop on Software Engineering Technology,* IEEE Computer Society Press, Los Alamitos, Calif., 1983, pp. 34–41.

[FGN76] Fagan, M.E., "Design and Code Inspections to Reduce Errors in Program Development," *IBM System J.*, Vol. 15, No. 3, 1976.

[IBM77] "Inspections in Application Development—Introduction and Implementation Guidelines," IBM publication GC20-2000, July 1977, IBM Technical Publications, Department 824, 1133 Westchester Avenue, White Plains, N.Y. 10604

[IEEE88] IEEE, ANSI/IEEE Std 1028-1988, Standard for Software Reviews and Audits.

[LRS75] Larson, R.R., "Test Plan and Test Case Inspection Specifications," Technical Report TR21.586, April 4, 1975, IBM Corporation, Kingston, N.Y.

[MCK81] McCormick, K.K., "The Results of Using a Structured Methodology, Software Inspections, and a New Hardware/Software Configuration on Application Systems," *Proc. 2nd National Symp. EDP Quality Assurance*, 1981, DPMA Education Foundation, produced by US Professional Development Institute, Inc., 12611 Davan Drive, Silver Spring, MD 20904.

[MRS79] Myers, G.J., *The Art of Software Testing*, John Wiley & Sons, New York, N.Y., 1979.

[PEL81] Peele, R., "Design Code Inspection Pilot Project Evaluation," *Proc. 2nd Nat'l Symp. EDP Quality Assurance*, DPMA Education Foundation, produced by US Professional Development Institute, Inc. 12611 Davan Drive, Silver Spring, MD 20904.

[PEL82] Peele, R., "Code Inspections at First Union Corporation," *Proc. COMPSAC 82*, IEEE Computer Society Press, Los Alamitos, Calif., 1982, pp. 445–446.

[YRD78] Yourdon, E., *Structured Walkthroughs*, Yourdon, Inc., 1978.

# INSPECTION PROFILE

System: ______________ Release: ______ Increment: ______ Date: ________

Unit: ________________________________

Inspection type:

- ☐ Internal Requirements ☐ Detail Design ☐ Test Plan
- ☐ High Level Design ☐ Code ☐ Test Cases

Size of material: _______________ (unit) _________________________

Is this a re-inspection: ☐ No ☐ Yes

Summary of open items: ____________________________________________

_________________________________________________________________

_________________________________________________________________

_________________________________________________________________

Other comments: __________________________________________________

_________________________________________________________________

_________________________________________________________________

_________________________________________________________________

Prepared by: _____________________________________________________

Form 1: Sample software inspection profile form

# INSPECTION PREPARATION LOG

System: ______________ Release: ______ Increment: ______ Date: ________

Unit: ________________________________

Inspector: __________________ Room: _________ Phone: _________________

Role: ☐ Author ☐ Moderator ☐ Peer Inspector

Overview attendance: ☐ No ☐ Yes

Date received Inspection Package: ________________________

| | date: | time: |
|---|---|---|
| Preparation Log: | ____________ | ____________ |
| | ____________ | ____________ |
| | ____________ | ____________ |
| | ____________ | ____________ |
| Total Preparation: | | ____________ hours |

CONCERNS

| Location | Description |
|---|---|
| ____________ | ______________________________ |
| | ______________________________ |
| | ______________________________ |
| ____________ | ______________________________ |
| | ______________________________ |
| | ______________________________ |
| ____________ | ______________________________ |
| | ______________________________ |
| | ______________________________ |
| ____________ | ______________________________ |
| | ______________________________ |

Form 2: Sample inspection preparation log

# INSPECTION MANAGEMENT REPORT

System:____________ Release: _____ Increment:___ Inspection date: _____

Unit:________________________________

Moderator:________________ Room:________ Phone:________________

Inspection type:

☐ Internal Requirements ☐ Detail Design ☐ Test Plan

☐ High Level Design ☐ Code ☐ Test Cases

Overview held: ☐ No ☐ Yes Overview duration: ____________

Number attending: ____________

Number of inspection meetings:________ Total meeting duration:________

Total number of inspectors:____________ Total preparation time:________

Module disposition: ☐ meets ☐ follow-up ☐ re-inspect

Estimated rework effort:__________ (days)

Rework to be completed by:____________

Actual rework effort:___________________

Re-inspection scheduled for:____________

Other inspectors:

____________________________ ____________________________

____________________________ ____________________________

____________________________ ____________________________

____________________________ ____________________________

Moderator certification:______________________ Date: __________________

Additional comments:________________________________________________

____________________________________________________________________

____________________________________________________________________

____________________________________________________________________

____________________________________________________________________

Form 3: Sample software inspection management report

# INSPECTION DEFECT LIST

System:__________ Release:____ Increment:_____ Date: __________

Unit:________________________________

Moderator: __________________ Room:________ Phone:________________

Inspection type:

- ☐ Internal Requirements
- ☐ High Level Design
- ☐ Detail Design
- ☐ Code
- ☐ Test Plan
- ☐ Test Cases

| Document: | Location: | Defect Description: | Defect Type: | Defect Class: |
|---|---|---|---|---|
| | | | | |
| | | | | |
| | | | | |
| | | | | |
| | | | | |
| | | | | |
| | | | | |
| | | | | |
| | | | | |
| | | | | |
| | | | | |
| | | | | |
| | | | | |
| | | | | |
| | | | | |
| | | | | |
| | | | | |
| | | | | |
| | | | | |

Error type: IF=Interface DA=Data LO=Logic IO=Input/Output PF=Performanc HF=Human factors ST=Standards DC=Documentation SN=Syntax OT=Other

Error class: M=Missing W=Wrong E=Extra

Error stage: RQ=Requirements HL=High Level Design DD=Detail Design CD=Code TP=Test Plan TC=Test Case

Page____ of____

Form 4: Sample software inspection defect list

# INSPECTION SUMMARY

System: ____________ Release: ____ Increment: ____ Inspection Date: ____
Unit: ______________________________
Moderator: ________________ Room: ________ Phone: ________________

Inspection type:

☐ Internal Requirements ☐ Detail Design ☐ Test Plan
☐ High Level Design ☐ Code ☐ Test Cases

| Error | | DEFECTS THIS OPERATION | | | |
|---|---|---|---|---|---|
| | | M | W | E | Total |
| IF: | Interface | | | | |
| DA: | Data | | | | |
| LO: | Logic | | | | |
| IO: | Input/Output | | | | |
| PF: | Performanc | | | | |
| HF: | Human factors | | | | |
| ST: | Standards | | | | |
| DC: | Documentation | | | | |
| SN: | Syntax | | | | |
| TE: | Test Environment | | | | |
| TC: | Test Coverage | | | | |
| OT: | Other | | | | |
| | | | Total | | |

| DEFECT IN PRIOR OPERATIONS | | | |
|---|---|---|---|
| Defect Stage | Defect Type | Defect Class | MR Number |
| | | | |
| | | | |
| | | | |
| | | | |
| | | | |
| | | | |
| | | | |

Major Errors This Stage:
Requirement=IF+PF+HF
High Level Design=IF+DA+LO+IO+PF+HF
Detail Design=IF+DA+LO+IO+PF
Code=IF+DA+LO+IO+PF
Test Plan=TE+TC
Test Case=TE+TC

| MAJOR DEFECT THIS OPERATION | |
|---|---|
| Defect Type | Total |
| | |
| | |
| | |
| | |
| | |
| | |
| Total | |

Form 5: Sample software inspections summary form

# Reviews and Audits

John J. Marciniak
*Kaman Sciences Corporation*

Reviews and audits are valuable tools used in software development projects, as well as in systems development. The distinction between software management and systems management, as well as software engineering and systems engineering, is becoming blurred as "systems" development involves an increasing integration of these disciplines. One example is in reengineering projects where the trade-off between new software development is intrinsically related to the development or use of new hardware. The economics of reengineering projects dictate the acquisition approach and the degree of hardware and software development. The types of reviews discussed apply equally to the total system environment; however, their genesis is in software development. Some of these review types will vary in area of application while others such as the Formal Inspection, are more pertinent to the practice of software development.

Reviews come in different forms and names. Some of these are: formal reviews, inspections, audits, and walk-throughs. In each of these categories, the terms have different connotation and meaning. For example, general management reviews include project reviews and management oversight. Irrespective of the use or purpose, the form of the review is most important. Thus, one has to distinguish between the review as a practice and its use in practice.

The most common characteristics that distinguish review forms are: purpose, scope, and method. It is the purpose of this article to introduce these forms, explain the basic differences between them, and provide insight in how they are applied in software development practice. In general the purpose and scope of the review will determine the method used and the degree of formality applied. In Table 1 we depict these general characteristics.

The scope of a review may range from the entire project to a review of the design, or a single document such as the users' guide. In general, the scope of a review does not appreciably affect the review procedure, only the impact that it has on the level and area of application. The purpose of a review may range from an audit or inspection of a specific product, to an assessment or completion of a development milestone. For example, to determine the adequacy of a design specification, an inspection may be used. To determine the status of the progress of development at various milestones such as the completion of software design, management reviews or walk-throughs may be used. The method may vary from free form, or informal, to a specific methodology such as formal inspections. A free-form, or less formal procedure, may be used in technical interchange meeting (TIMs), while a formal inspection may be applied to assess the status of a specific product at the various points in its development.

## Definitions

According to the *IEEE Standard Glossary of Software Engineering Terminology* (IEEE, 1990a), a review is

> A process or meeting during which a work product, or a set of work products, is presented to project personnel, managers, users, customers, or other interested parties for comment or approval. Types include code review, design review, formal qualification review, requirements review, and test readiness review.

This is the most general form and, as we shall see, is focused and customized depending on the specific purpose of the review.

Reviews are further classified according to formality. A formal review is typically one that is required by a contract commitment that is usually invoked through the application of a standard such as military standard 498 (MIL-STD-498), which are often more prevalent in government acquisition projects. The implication is that it is a contractual milestone witnessed by the customer or acquirer of the system, and normally denotes the completion of certain activities such as detailed design or system testing and results in a development or formal baseline for continued development of the software system.

*Table 1. Review Characteristics*

| Type | Scope | Purpose | Method |
|---|---|---|---|
| Reviews | Usually broad | Project progress assessment of milestone completion | Ad hoc |
| Walk-throughs | Fairly narrow | Assess specific development products | Static analysis of products |
| Inspections | Narrow | Assess specific development products | Noninteractive, fairly procedural |
| Audits | Narrow to broad | Check processes and products of development | Formal, mechanical and procedure |

In another perspective, Freedman and Weinberg use the following criteria to classify a formal review: (Freedman, 1990a)

1. A written report on the status of the product reviewed—a report that is available to everyone involved in the project, including management;
2. Active and open participation of everyone in the review group, following some traditions, customs, and written rules as to how such a review is to be conducted;
3. Full responsibility of all participants for the quality of the review—that is, for the quality of the information in the written report.

One can see that, from this description, the criteria shifts to certain responsibilities for the review participants as opposed to the contract vehicle.

As we see, there are different views as to the formality of the review. In contradistinction, informal reviews are those that are held which are not contractually required, or less formal from the perspective of Freedman and Weinberg, such as technical interchange meetings. The procedures applied for both formality types are similar, the principal difference being the rigor applied in the conduct of the review, for example, formal management of minutes.

There are other types of review classifications. For example, there are internal management reviews. (Marciniak, 1990) These may be periodic reviews of the project by senior management within the developing organization to assess progress or special reviews based on specific issues such as the impact of the development on other market areas. In the latter, management uses the review to provide general awareness of the direction of the project in order to take advantage of the resulting product in other market areas or to avoid conflict with other company projects.

Another major classification of reviews is the peer review. Peer reviews are usually walk-throughs, inspections, and round-robin reviews (Freedman, 1990b). The common characteristic of a peer review is that it is conducted by peers. A walk-through is normally a peer review; however, in many cases it is conducted with participants who are nonpeers. These reviews are normally confined to a single product such as a segment of the design, or a code unit, or component. The definitions of these reviews follows.

A Walk-through is

> A static analysis technique in which a designer or programmer leads members of the development team and other interested parties through a segment of documentation or code, and the participants ask questions and make comments about possible errors, violation of development standards, and other problems. (IEEE, 1990b)

Walk-throughs are sometimes referred to as structured walk-throughs (not to be confused with formal inspections, see below); however, according to Freedman and Weinberg they are one and the same (Freedman, 1990c). A walk-through is probably the most common review technique in a software project, and the method will vary based on individual implementation.

A special form of a walk-through is the Formal Inspection. The Formal Inspection was developed at IBM (Fagan, 1976) and is often referred to simply as Fagan Inspections. A principal distinguishing factor between a walk-through and a formal inspection is that the formal inspection is led by a moderator independent of the person responsible for the product, while the walk-through is led by a reader or presenter who may be the developer of the product.

In a formal inspection the collection of anomalies is carefully structured to capture statistical evidence of the effort. A formal inspection should not be confused with an inspection. The choice of the term is perhaps unfortunate as the formal inspection is a type of walk-through rather than an inspection. Hollocker discusses the procedures used for Formal Inspections; however, chooses to use the words "Software Inspection." (Hollocker, 1990)

## Inspection

An inspection is

> A static analysis technique that relies on visual examination of development products to detect errors, violations of developing standards, and other problems. Types include code inspection; design inspections. (IEEE, 1990c)

Freedman and Weinberg define inspection as "a method of rapidly evaluating material by confining attention to a few selected aspects, one at a time" (Freedman, 1990d). The inspection is carried out in an noninteractive manner, usually by a party that is detached from the developer.

The difference between inspections and audits is not obvious, and perhaps the difference is not pertinent. The differences are stated in Evans (Evans, 1987a).

An inspection normally has a narrow focus evaluating only a segment of the project environment. The inspection structure is very rigid and the evaluation criteria are predetermined based on a model of acceptability.

An audit may also have a narrow focus, but, in most cases, is use to evaluate the broader aspects of the project environment. Besides checking individual segments of the project infrastructure against plans, audits may evaluate the interrelationships between segments of the infrastructure. When assessing the implementation attributes, audits tend to be more "freewheeling" allowing the auditor to pursue paths not necessarily included in the initial audit.

Another view put forth in Evans, focuses on interaction (Evans 1987b). An audit is normally more interactive in that the auditor communicates with the project staff. In an inspection, the inspector uses a rigid set of guidelines or a checklist to assess the degree of compliance with the checklist or guidelines. In either event, the important thing is to focus on the purpose of the procedure, then apply the mechanism that is more appropriate for the project.

### Audits

An audit is much like an inspection; however, as indicated above, it tends to be of a broader nature and involve interactions with the project staff.

In the general form an audit is

> An independent examination of a work product or set of work products to assess compliance with specifications, standards, contractual agreements, or other criteria. (IEEE, 1990d)

The IEEE defines two specific forms of audits, the Functional Configuration Audit (FCA) and the Physical Configuration Audit (PCA).

A functional configuration audit (FCA) is

> An audit conducted to verify that the development of a configuration item has been completed satisfactorily, that the item has achieved the performance and functional characteristics specified in the functional or allocated configuration identification, and that its operational and support documents are complete and satisfactory. (IEEE, 1990e)

A physical configuration audit (PCA) is

> An audit conducted to verify that a configuration item, as built, conforms to the technical documentation that defined it. (IEEE, 1990f)

These two audits are formal audits because they are required by the contractual instruments that govern the development project. If there were no contractual instrument, the eventual user would still conduct a form of the above to verify the product. A simple example is buying an automobile. When the automobile is ordered, a spec sheet or contract is normally filled out calling for items such as fog lights and radios. A functional audit would verify that the radio performs, for example, that it plays the bands specified, while a physical audit would verify that the type of radio ordered is the one that is actually delivered with the automobile.

There are other types of audits that are conducted during the development process. For example, there are quality assurance audits that audit a particular process of development such as the conduct of reviews and walk-throughs. There are configuration management audits that audit the processes of configuration management. The distinguishing factor in these types of audits is that they are carried out by the function with that specific responsibility. For example, a software quality assurance (SQF) audit is carried out by the software quality assurance function, and it is based on SQA plans and procedures.

## Application in the life cycle

Reviews, audits, walk-throughs, and inspections are used to provide assessment of the progress, processes used, and products of the project. The program management plan, or software development plan, will normally specify the types of reviews used and the methods that are applied in their use. Certain reviews, as mentioned above, will be dictated by contract requirements, usually through the use of development standards such as IEEE Std 1498 (IEEE, 19XX). In Figure 1 we show a typical waterfall life cycle with examples of system development reviews and audits.

There are three parts to a review: the planning phase, the review conduct, and the post review phase. All are important to any successful review. The elimination or neglect of any of the phases will jeopardize a successful review.

In the planning phase, the actions generally include stating the purpose of the review, arranging for participants, ensuring that review materials are provided for their inspection well prior to the conduct of the review, making physical arrangements for the location and support required, and preparing an agenda. During the conduct of the review, it is important to follow the agenda in a disciplined manner. Generally speaking, the purpose of the review conduct is not to fix problems that are identified, but, to identify them and assign action for their resolution. Reviews can very easily get contentious so it is important to ensure that a moderator or review leader maintains control of the proceedings. A recorder or scribe has to be assigned to transcribe the proceedings into recorded form for the purpose of preparing a record of the review and a postreview action list. The postreview period can be flexible depending on the actions required. These are normally followed to completion by management and reported on at the next review. It is possible that another review may be required if the review results are unsatisfactory. Naturally, this could result in some project impact, usually of schedule and cost.

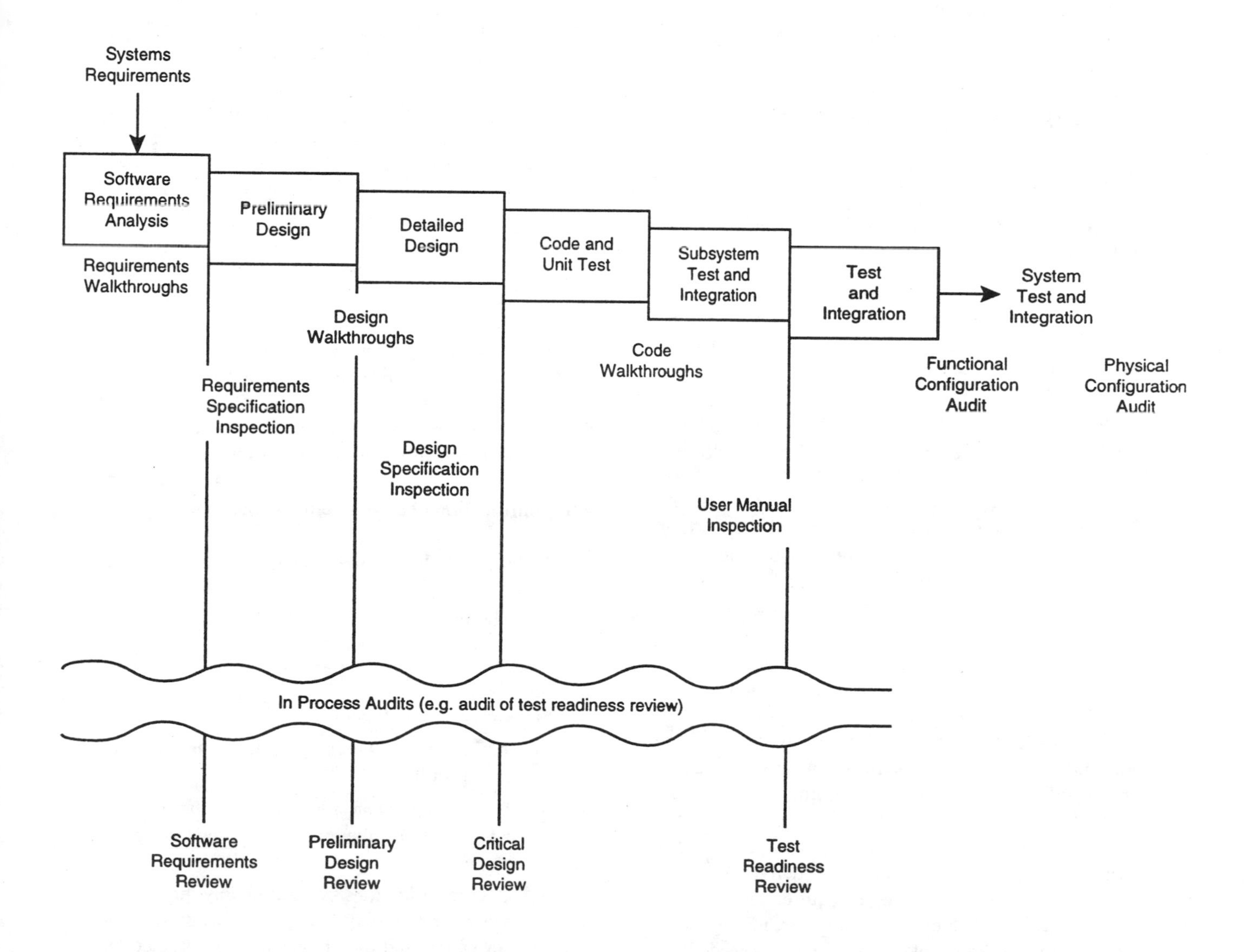


*Figure 1. Reviews in the software life cycle*

### Management Reviews

**Objective.** A management review is a formal management-team evaluation of a project-level plan or a project's status relative to such a plan. The review team communicates progress, coordinates the decision making within their span of control, and provides recommendations for:

- Making activities progress according to plan, based on an evaluation of product development status
- Changing project direction or identifying the need for alternative planning
- Maintaining global control of the project through adequate allocation of resources

Moreover, to further tailor this review process for an individual project milestone, specific objectives are to be identified in a "Statement of Objectives" made available before the review meeting. The management review concept can be applied to new development or to maintenance activities. It can also be useful in managing process improvement projects.

**People and Their Agendas.** Roles for the management review include:

- Leader
- Reporter
- Team member

The review leader is responsible for the administrative tasks pertaining to the review, for assuring that the review is conducted in an order manner, and for issuing any minutes or reports. The reporter is responsible for having the project status and all supporting documentation available for distribution before the meeting. This individual is also responsible for documenting the findings, decisions, and recommendations of the review team.

**When to Hold a Management Review.** Typically, the project planning documents (for example, Software Quality Assurance Plan, Software Development Plan, or Software Verification and Validation Plan) establish the need for conducting specific management reviews. As stated in these plans, a management review can be initiated by the completion of a project phase or specific software deliverable (for example, a planning document, a requirements specification, or a design document). Moreover, management reviews not required by plan may occur, as needed, to deal with any unscheduled events or contingencies.

A selected review leader establishes or confirms a statement of objectives for the meeting and verifies that any appropriate software deliverables and any other documents or reports available are sufficiently complete to support the review objectives. In addition to any applicable reference material supplied by project management, or requested by the review leader, these would include:

- A Statement of Objectives for the management review and its agenda
- Current project schedule, resource, and cost data
- Pertinent reports (for example, managerial review reports, technical review reports, or audit reports) from other reviews and/or audits already completed
- Software deliverable status or current disposition

**Procedures.** The review leader, having identified the team, schedules facilities for the meeting and distributes any materials needed by the review team for advanced preparation (for example, statement of objectives, agenda, or presentation requirements). In addition, the review leader might consider requesting that a project representative conduct an overview session for the review team. This overview can occur as part of the examination meeting or as a separate meeting. The management review process is considered complete when all issues identified in the review "Statement of Objectives" have been addressed and the management review report has been issued. Project management typically tracks any action items through to resolution. If a re-review is required, it would provide confirmation of action item completion.

**Output.** The Management Review Report identifies:

- The project being reviewed and the team that participated in that review
- Inputs to the review
- Review objectives
- Action item ownership, status, and tracking responsibility
- Project status and a list of issues that must be addressed for the project to meet its milestone
- Recommendations regarding any further reviews and audits, and a list of additional information and data that must be obtained before they can be executed

### The Walk-through

**Objective**. The walk-through process has much in common with both the general technical review process and the inspection process. It, too, is used to evaluate a specific software element and provide evidence that the software element satisfies its specifications and conforms to applicable standards. Its statement of objectives includes software element specific objectives. They also exist in the form of a checklist that varies with the product being presented. Objectives typically do not pertain to any additional constraints on the walk-through process.

Distinctions from other review processes, however, are established by unique objectives. The following always appear in the Statement of Objectives for the application of the walk-through process:

- Detect, identify, and describe software element defects
- Examine alternatives and stylistic issues
- Provide a mechanism that enables the authors to collect valuable feedback on their work, yet allows them to retain the decision-making authority for any changes

**People and Their Agendas**. Roles for the walk-through are similar to those for other review processes, with one important distinction. The leader responsible for conducting a specific walk-through, handling the administrative tasks pertaining to the walk-through, and ensuring that the walk-through is conducted in an orderly manner is usually the author.

The scribe is responsible for writing down all comments made during the walk-through that pertain to errors found, questions of style, omissions, contradictions, suggestions for improvement, or alternative approaches.

Each team member is responsible for reviewing any input material prior to the walk-through and participating during the walk-through to ensure that it meets its objective. Roles may be shared among the walk-through members.

**When to Hold the Walk-through Meeting**. The need for conducting walk-throughs, as with all product reviews, can be established either by local practice or in planning documents. Completion of a specific software element can trigger the walkthrough for the element. Additional walk-throughs can be conducted during development of the software element at the request of the author or management from various functional areas. A walk-through is conducted when the author indicates readiness.

**Procedures**. *Planning*. During the planning process phase the author:

- Identifies the walk-through team
- Schedules the meeting and selects the meeting place
- Distributes all necessary input materials to the participants, allowing for adequate preparation time

**Overview**. An overview presentation is made by the author as part of the walk-through meeting. Before that meeting, however, individual preparation is still required.

**Preparation**. During the preparation phase participants review the input material that was distributed to them and prepare a list of questions and issues to be brought up during the walk-through.

**Examination**. During the walk-through meeting:

- The author makes an overview presentation of the software element
- The author "walks through" the specific software element so that members of the walk-through team may ask questions or raise issues about the software element, and/or make notes documenting their concerns
- The scribe writes down comments and decisions for inclusion in the walk-through report

At the completion of the walk-through, the team may recommend a follow-up walk-through that follows the same process and would, at a minimum, cover areas changed by the author. The walk-through process is complete when the entire software element has been walked through in detail and all deficiencies, omissions, efficiency issues, and suggestions for improvement have been noted. The walk-through report is issued, as required by local standards.

**Output**. The walk-through report contains:

- Identification of the walk-through team
- Identification of the software element(s) being examined
- The statement of objectives that were to be handled during this walk-through meeting
- A list of the noted deficiencies, omissions, contradictions, and suggestions for improvement

- Any recommendations made by the walk-through team on how to dispose of deficiencies and unresolved issues. If follow-up walk-throughs are suggested, that should be mentioned in the report as well

**Formal Inspections**

**Objective.** A formal inspection, as stated earlier, is a variant of the procedure used for a structured walk-through. The differences are described in the following procedure and contrasted with the above procedures for a walk-through.

The objective of the formal inspection is to detect defects in the product being inspected by comparison with a checklist that typifies the types of defects that are common to the type of product being inspected. These are recorded and a statistical report is prepared so that evidential data is compiled. These data are used: to compare the product at this stage of development with later stages; compile a basis for statistical measure of the product; and to build an experience base to be used for other products in the same or similar projects.

**People and Their Agendas.** The roles in a formal inspection include a moderator, participants or inspectors, the preparer or developer of the product, and a recorder. The moderator is normally a peer who is selected for his/her technical expertise with the type of material. This person should be someone who is from outside the project. The participants are peers of the preparer and normally from the project staff to ensure that they are familiar with the project from a technical point of view.

**Procedures.** Prior to the inspection, the moderator makes arrangements for the inspection based on similar procedures used for a walk-through. The materials to be inspected, the checklists to be used, and the facilities where the inspection is to be located are all planning functions that need to be accomplished. The moderator controls the inspection process by walking through the code or design in a step-by-step manner. The peers comment on the product and these are recorded by the recorder.

It is important to identify the checklist that will be used and ensure that the recorder understands his/her duties with respect to recording the results. The checklist, which is the basis for the inspection, is composed of the common types of defects that are found in the product. For example, in a code inspection the following types of defects may be listed in the checklist (Vliet, 1993):

1. wrongful use of data: uninitialized variables, array index out of bounds, dangling pointers, and so forth;
2. faults in declarations, such as the use of undeclared variables, or the declaration of the same name in nested blocks;
3. faults in computations; division by zero, overflow, wrong use of variables of different types in one and the same expression, faults caused by an erroneous conception of operator priorities, etc.;
4. faults in relational expressions, such as using an incorrect operator, or an erroneous conception of priorities of Boolean operators;
5. faults in control flow, such as infinite loops, or a loop that gets executed n+1 or n-1 times rather than n;
6. faults in interfaces, such as an incorrect number of parameters, parameters of the wrong type, or an inconsistent use of global variables.

**When to Hold the Formal Inspection Meeting.** Inspections are regularly scheduled in accordance with project plans based on the status of a product. For example, periodic inspections of the product could be conducted at the preliminary design, detailed design, and implementation or code completion.

**Output.** The result of the inspection is a list of the defects that are found. Defects may be categorized according to severity. The defects are corrected after the inspection and the results are checked by the moderator. A reinspection may be called for if the product is deemed unsatisfactory to proceed.

**Audits**

**Objective.** Audits, performed in accordance with documented plans and procedures, provide an independent confirmation that product development and process execution adhere to standards, guidelines, specifications, and procedures. Audit personnel use objective audit criteria (for example, contracts and plans; standards, practices and conventions: or requirements and specifications) to evaluate:

- Software elements
- The processes for producing them
- Projects
- Entire quality programs

**People and Their Agendas**. It is the responsibility of the audit team leader to organize and direct the audit and to coordinate the preparation and issuance of the audit report. The audit team leader is ultimately responsible for the proper conduct of the audit and its reports, and makes sure that the audit team is prepared.

The entity initiating the audit is responsible for authorizing the audit. Management of the auditing organization assumes responsibility for the audit and the allocation of the necessary resources to perform the audit.

Those whose products and processes are being audited provide all relevant materials and resources and correct or resolve deficiencies cited by the audit team.

**When to Audit**. The need for an audit is established by one of the following events:

- A special project milestone, calendar date, or other criterion has been met and, as part of its charter, the auditing organization is to respond by initiating an audit.
- A special project milestone has been reached. The audit is initiated per earlier plans (for example, the Software Quality Assurance Plan, or Software Development Plan). This includes planned milestones for controlling supplier development.
- External parties (for example, regulatory agencies or end users) require an audit at a specific calendar date or project milestone. This may be in fulfillment of a contract requirement or as a prerequisite to contractual agreement.
- A local organizational element(s)(for example, project management, functional management, systems engineering, or internal quality assurance/control) has requested the audit, establishing a clear and specific need.

Perhaps the most important inputs required to assure the success of the audit are the purpose and scope of the audit. Observations and evaluations performed as part of the audit require objective audit criteria, such as contracts requirements, plans, specifications, procedures, guidelines, and standards. The software elements and processes to be audited need to be made accessible, as do any pertinent histories. Background information about the organization responsible for the products and processes being audited (for example, organization charts) are critical for both planning and execution of the audit.

**Procedures**. The auditing organization develops and documents an audit plan for each audit. This plan should, in addition to restating the audit scope, identify the:

- Project processes to be examined (provided as input) and the time frame for audit team observations
- Software to be examined (provided as input) and their availability where sampling is used, a statistically valid sampling methodology is used to establish selection criteria and sample use
- Reporting requirements (that is, results report, and, optionally, the recommendations report with their general format and distribution defined), whether recommendations are required or excluded should be explicitly stated
- Required follow-up activities
- Activities, elements, and procedures necessary to meet the scope of the audit
- Objective Audit Criteria that provide the basis for determining compliance (provided as input)
- Audit Procedures and Checklists
- Audit Personnel requirements (for example, number, skills, experience, and responsibilities)
- Organizations involved in the audit (for example, the organization whose products and processes are being audited)
- Date, time, place, agenda, and intended audience of "overview" session (optional)

The audit team leader prepares an audit team having the necessary background and (when allowed) notifies the involved organizations, giving them a reasonable amount of advance warning before the audit is performed. The notification should be written to include audit scope, the identification processes and products to be audited, and the auditors' identity.

An optional overview meeting with the audited organization is recommended to "kick off" the examination phase of the audit. The overview meeting, led by the audit team leader, provides:

- Overview of existing agents (for example, audit scope, plan and related contracts)
- Overview of production and processes being audited

- Overview of the audit process, its objectives, and outputs
- Expected contributions of the audited organization to the audit process (that is, the number of people to be interviewed, meeting facilities, et cetera)
- Specific audit schedule

The following preparations are required by the audit team:

- Understand the organization: It is essential to identify functions and activities performed by the audited organization and to identify functional responsibility
- Understand the products and processes: It is a prerequisite for the team to learn about the products and processes being audited through readings and briefings
- Understand the Objective Audit Criteria: It is important that the audit team become familiar with the objective and criteria to be used in the audit
- Prepare for the audit report: It is important to choose the administrative reporting mechanism that will be used throughout the audit to develop the report that follows the layout identified in the audit plan
- Detail the audit plan: Choose appropriate methods for each step in the audit program

In addition, the audit team leader makes the necessary arrangements for:

- Team orientation and training
- Facilities for audit interviews
- Materials, documents, and tools required by the audit procedures
- The software elements to be audited (for example, documents, computer files, personnel to be interviewed)
- Scheduling interviews

Elements that have been selected for audit are evaluated against the Objective Audit Criteria. Evidence is examined to the depth necessary to determine if these elements comply with specified criteria.

An audit is considered complete when:

- Each element(s) within the scope of the audit has been examined
- Findings have been presented to the audited organization
- Response to draft findings have been received and evaluated
- Final findings have been formally presented to the audited organization and initiating entity
- The audit report has been prepared and submitted to recipients designated in the audit plan
- The recommendation report, if required by plan, has been prepared and submitted to recipients designated in the audit plan
- All of the auditing organization's follow-up actions included in the scope (or contract) of the audit have been performed.

**Output**. Following a standard framework for audit reports, the draft and final audit reports contain:

- Audit Identification: Report title, audited organization, auditing organization, and date of the audit
- Scope: Scope of the audit, including an enumeration of the standards, specifications, practices, and procedures constituting the Objective Audit Criteria against which the audit of the software elements and processes were conducted
- Conclusions: A summary and interpretation of the audit findings, including the key items of nonconformance
- Synopsis: A listing of all the audited software elements and processes, and associated findings
- Follow-up: The type and timing of audit follow-up activities

Additionally, when stipulated by the audit plan, recommendations are provided to the audited organization, or the entity that initiated the audit. Recommendations are reported separately from results.

Comments and issues raised by the audited organization must be resolved. The final audit report should then be prepared, approved, and issued by the audit team leader to the organizations specified in the audit plan.

### Inspections

Inspections are limited forms of an audit. The procedures for conducting an inspection are similar to an audit except that they are limited due to the focus of the inspection.

## Future directions

As previously mentioned, the use of reviews and audits in the software development business is becoming more blurred because of the concentration on a systems perspective. Thus, we will see more emphasis on systems engineering. This will not change the mechanisms or practices that are used. They will be applied, however, in more of a systems management and engineering context. Thus, the use of specific review procedures will be more broadly applied in the development or acquisition of the system.

One trend that we currently see is the use of more interactive techniques. A walk-through is an interactive procedure. The moderator or inspector, participants, recorder—all communicate as the product is being "walked through". As systems development becomes more dynamic, as we already see in Web development, electronic techniques will enhance this procedure. It is possible to have an on-line review conducted across geographic distances. It is even possible to make dynamic changes to products as the capability to do so advances (for example, in the development of a home page as an element of Web site development). If a product such as a document is being reviewed, changes to it can be accomplished in real time. This will place more emphasis on the rigor or formality required of the process to properly control and account for changes. Configuration management will take on a real-time (and more dramatic) meaning in this environment.

Another trend that is quite possible is the more prevalent use of formal inspections. It has already been demonstrated that this technique has great benefit to the development of software. As software engineering progresses in maturity, there will be more emphasis on the attainment of specific attributes of the product. We should be able to relate the attainment software quality factors such as reliability, usability, and complexity described by the work of McCall and Bowen directly to the product (Vincent, 1988). Thus, the coupling or relationship of these factors to the product will be a more measured one. This will afford the quantifiable prediction of quality, and control of the product in order to meet these predictions. The implication is that checklists, based on experiential data associated with the attainment of specific quality attributes, will be more widely used.

## Summary

The different types of reviews used in a software development process range from informal technical reviews to formal reviews such as the FCA. The types and number of reviews are largely determined by the complexity and size of the project. In a project that is internal to an organization, reviews tend to be more informal compared to a project that is under contract. Normally, the number and types of reviews will be detailed in management plans with specific methods left to a procedures and standards handbook.

Although there are different reasons for conducting reviews, the principal purpose is to assess the progress or integrity of a process or product. Reviews are also important for gathering data. The systematic collection of data is essential for assessing the process in order to support process improvement programs as well as developing experiential data for applying to new projects. These data can support the prediction of various activities such as the quality of products through comparisons of previous data collected on prior projects.

Thus, reviews of all sorts provide a basic performance and assessment technique that bridges the individual project, and even the organization. They are the essential performance technique in software development practice.

Portions of this article have been excised from Software Reviews and Audits, Charles Hollocker, John Wiley & Sons, New York, N.Y., 1990.

## References

M. Evans and J. Marciniak, *Software Quality Assurance and Management*, John Wiley & Sons, New York, N.Y., 1987a, p. 115; 1987b, p. 229.

Michael Fagan, "Design and Code Inspection to Reduce Errors in Program Development," *IBM Systems J.*, Vol. 15, No. 3, 1976.

Daniel P. Freedman and Gerald M. Weinberg, *Walkthroughs, Inspections, and Technical Reviews*, Dorset House, New York, N.Y., Third Ed., 1990a, pp. 10–11; 1990b, p. 232; 1990c, p. 232; 1990d, p. 239.

Charles Hollocker, *Software Reviews and Audits*, John Wiley & Sons, New York, N.Y., 1990, pp. 44–48.

IEEE Std 610.12-1990, *Standard Glossary of Software Engineering Terminology*, IEEE, New York, N.Y., 1990a, p. 64;. 1990b, p. 81; 1990c, p. 40; 1990d, p. 11; 1990e, p. 35; 1990f, p. 55.

IEEE Std 1498, IEEE, New York, N.Y.

John J. Marciniak and Donald J. Reifer, *Software Acquisition Management*, John Wiley & Sons, New York, N.Y., 1990, p. 26.

Mil-Std-498, "Software Development and Documentation," Department of Defense, 1994.

J. Vincent, A. Waters, and J. Sinclair, *Software Quality Assurance*, Prentice-Hall, Englewood Cliffs, N.J., Vol. 1, 1988, pp. 11–28.

# Traceability

James D. Palmer
*Professor Emeritus, George Mason University*
*and Software Consultant*
*860 Cashew Way*
*Fremont, CA 94536*

## Abstract

*Traceability gives essential assistance in understanding the relationships that exist within and across software requirements, design, and implementation and is critical to the development process by providing a means of ascertaining how and why system development products satisfy stakeholder requirements, especially for large complex systems. Traceability provides a path to the validation and verification of stakeholder requirements to assure these needs are met by the delivered system, as well as information on testing procedures, performance measures, non-functional characteristics, and behavioral aspects for the delivered system. Both syntactic and semantic information are needed to successfully implement tracing. It is not enough to know the form; it is also necessary to know the substance of the entities to be traced.*

*However, traceability is often misunderstood, frequently misapplied, and seldom performed correctly. There are many challenges to achieving traceability, particularly the absence of automated techniques to assist in the identification of linkages from requirements to design, or test, or operation needed to trace entities within and across the system development process. One of the particular challenges to providing traceability to and from system level requirements is that it becomes necessary to utilize both the constructs of language semantics as well as syntax.*

*Traceability is introduced, and its place in a development process, coupled with the values and pitfalls are covered. The essentials of traceability are examined together with how to implement tracing within a development life cycle for large complex systems. Working definitions and related terms are provided to assure common understanding of the terminology and application of tracing in system and software development. A review of contemporary approaches to implement tracing with an overview of several of the Computer Supported Software (or System) Engineering (CASE) tools that purport to support tracing are given and future trends are examined.*

## Introduction

Successful system development depends on the ability to satisfy stakeholder needs and requirements and to reflect these in the delivered system. Requirements, design, and implementation that are complete, correct, consistent, and error free, play a major role in ensuring that the delivered system meets stakeholder needs. Critical keys to this are understanding and tracing the relationships that exist amongst system requirements, design, code, test, and implementation. Large-scale complex systems are initiated by stakeholder determination that a need exists that is not met by existing systems. From this beginning, system level requirements are developed to broadly outline the desired capabilities, which, in turn, are investigated to ascertain feasibility and practicality and examine trade-offs. Once the feasibility and practicality of the desired system have been determined to be necessary and sufficient to launch a new system (or significant modification of an existing or legacy system), design is completed and systems are constructed, tested, and fielded. It is essential to maintain traceability from the system requirements to operation and maintenance to assure that the delivered system meets the stated organizational needs of the stakeholder.

## System Life Cycle for Traceability Management

Generally, a system or process development life cycle is followed to produce the desired system. There are many life cycle models [1], and one of the simplest is the system development or waterfall life cycle model depicted in Figure 1. It also serves as the basis for most life cycle models in use today, such as the spiral model, the evolutionary model, and the prototyping model. Within any system development life cycle, requirements must be traced both forward and backward to assure that the correct system is being designed and produced, and that the correct design and production approaches are used.

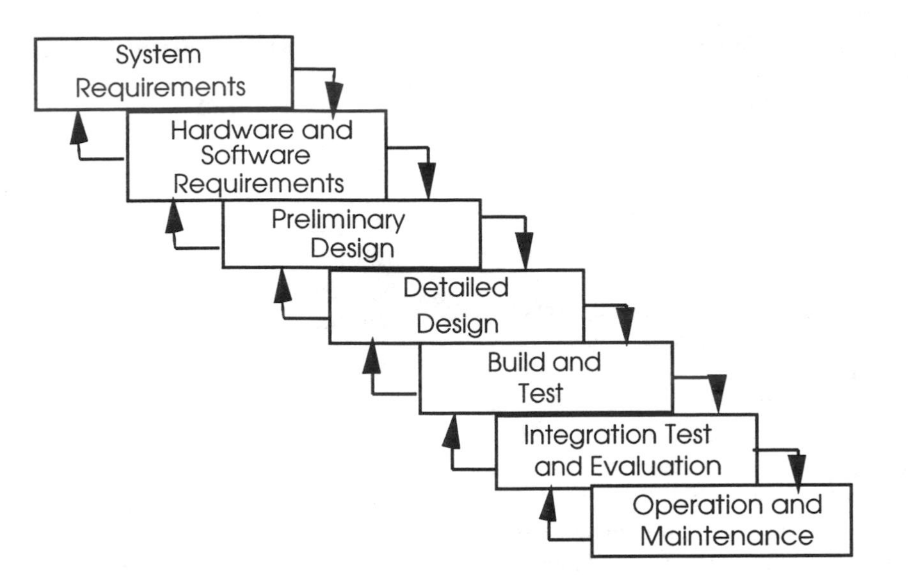


*Figure 1. Typical system and software development life cycle*

In the life cycle model of Figure 1, system requirements, usually prepared in natural language, are provided by the stakeholder to the developer. These system requirements, if they exist at all, may be poorly written and only vaguely define stakeholder desires for the new system. This may impact the ability to construct a system that will satisfy the stakeholder. From these system requirements, hardware and software requirements and specifications are prepared. Requirement and specification development are followed by preliminary design; detailed design; construction of the system including hardware and software; system integration, testing and evaluation; and finally installation including operation and maintenance.

These life cycle activities require documentation of needs and outcomes. Each must trace forward to the subsequent activity and backward to the preceding one. Clearly, traceability, both forward and backward, is essential to verify that the requirements of one phase translate to outcomes of that phase which become the requirements for the next phase, and so on through the development activity. Traceability is equally essential to validate that system requirements are satisfied during operation.

## Need for Traceability

Traceability is essential to verification and validation and is needed to better understand the processes used to develop the system and the products that result. It is needed for quick access to information, information abstraction, and to provide visualization into the techniques used for system development. Traceability is needed for change control, development process control, and risk control. Tracing provides insights to non-behavioral components such as quality, consistency, completeness, impact analysis, system evolution, and process improvement. It is equally important to have the capability to trace a requirement or design or code module to its origin, as well as test. Stakeholders recognize the value of properly tracing within and across the entities of a system through risk management insights, appropriate integration tests, and the delivery of a project that meets the needs statements of the requirements. [2]

Traceability supports assessment of under- or over designs; investigation of high-level behavior impact on detailed specifications, as well as non-functional requirements such as performance and quality factors. Moreover, traceability supports conflict detection by making it feasible to examine linkages within and across selected entities and by providing visibility into the entire system. Through tracing, there is the assurance that decisions made later in the system development life cycle are consistent with earlier decisions. Test cases check that coverage for code and integration testing and for requirements validation is provided. Traceability provides the basis for the development of an audit trail for the entire project by establishing the links within and across system entities, functions, behavior, and performance, for example.

While there is widespread acceptance of the necessity to trace, there is considerable controversy as to the ultimate need, purpose, and cost of tracing from requirements to delivered product. The controversy arises primarily because of the lack of automated approaches to implement the process and the concomitant time and effort that must be applied with any of the presently available support tools. Developers simply do not see the benefits that may accrue to the final product when traceability is fully implemented compared to the time and effort required.

## Problems and Issues Concerning Traceability

Difficulties related to tracing generally revolve around the necessity to manually add trace elements to requirements documents and subsequent work products from software development. Since these products have little or no direct consequence to the development team, assignment of trace elements generally has a low priority. The benefits of traceability are not seen until much later in the development life cycle, usually during validation testing and system installation and operation, and then primarily by integration testers and stakeholders rather than developers. Additionally, traceability is often misunderstood, frequently misapplied, and seldom performed correctly.

Issues and concerns emanate from the complexity of a project itself that must be confronted when implementing traceability. Each discipline, such as avionics, communications, navigation, security, or safety, may have languages, methods, and tools peculiar to the discipline. This results in a lack of ability to trace across disciplines, which, in turn, may lead to errors in traceability matrices used to provide linkages within and across disciplines. Some of the issues that need to be addressed by the stakeholder and developer at the time of system development include how to apportion projects by discipline, the type and nature of information that should be traced across different disciplines, and the types of tools that can be used to provide consistent and correct traceability across disciplines. Establishing threads across disciplines is also difficult due to language, method, and tool peculiarities.

Currently, there is no single modeling method or language sufficiently rich to represent all aspects of a large complex system and still be understandable to those involved. In tracing information across different disciplines and toolsets, and to provide threads across these, essential system properties and the classification schemes used are needed. Such properties and schemas do not usually exist. Thus, for verification and validation, traceability must always focus on a common denominator; the approved system requirements. Finally, internal consistency of the baseline documentation may not be adequate to support tracing. This latter is usually a significant problem in the modification of legacy systems.

## Definition of Terms

There are many terms that describe, delineate, or relate to traceability. Some of these correlate to the "how and why" for traceability, while others connect to the outcomes or "what" of traceability. In general, the basic meaning of the terms is first that provided by Webster's New Collegiate Dictionary [3], while the last meaning is given in the context of systems and software engineering, as an example of usage.

**Allocation:** The act of distributing; allotment or apportionment; as to assign or apportion functions to specific modules.

**Audit:** A formal checking of records, to determine that what was stated was accomplished; to examine and verify; as to confirm a stated capability is met in the software product.

**Behavior:** The way in which a system acts, especially in response to a stimulus; stimulus-response mechanisms; as activity or change in reliability across sub-systems.

**Bottom-up:** A design philosophy or policy that dictates the form and partitioning of the system from the basic functions that the system is to perform and moving up to the top level requirements; as a design policy that provides basic modules followed by top-level constructs.

**Classification:** A group of entities ranked together as possessing common characteristics or quality; the act of grouping or segregating into classes which have systematic relationships; a systematic grouping of entities based upon some definite scheme; as to classify requirements according to organizational or performance characteristics.

**Flowdown:** To move or circulate from upper to lower levels; as to trace a requirement from a top level to designs to code to test.

**Function:** The characteristic action or the normal or special action of a system; one aspect of a system is so related to another that there is a correspondence from one to the other when an action is taken; as an algorithm to provide the equations of motion.

**Hierarchy:** A series of objects or items divided or classified in ranks or orders; as in a type of structure in which each element or block has a level number (1= highest), and each element is associated with one or more elements at the next higher level and lower levels; as a single high level requirement decomposes to lower level requirements and to design and code.

**Impact Analysis:** Separation into constituent parts to examine or distinguish contact of one on another, a communicating force; as to focus on software changes and the traceable consequences; relating software requirements to design components.

**Policy:** Management or procedure based primarily on material interest; as a settled course or level to be followed for system security.

**Requirement:** A requisite condition; a required quality; to demand; to claim as by right or authority; to exact; as to demand system performance by the stakeholder.

**Thread:** To connect; as to pass a thread through; string together; as to link behaviors of a system together.

**Top-down:** A design philosophy or policy that dictates the form and partitioning of the system from the top-level requirements perspective to the lower level design components; as in a design policy for all activities from high-level requirements to design and code.

**Top-level requirement:** A requisite condition leveled by the stakeholder; as a system level requirement for security.

**Traceability:** The course or path followed; to follow or track down; to follow or study out in detail or step by step, especially by going backward over evidence (as to trace requirements from design); to discover or uncover by investigation; as to trace to the source; as to follow requirements from the top level to design and code and back; or as to identify and document the allocation/flowdown path (downward) and derivation path (upward) of requirements into the hierarchy. The Department of Defense (DoD) defines traceability in the Standard for Defense System Software Development DoD-Std-2167A to be a demonstration of completeness, necessity, and consistency. Specifically, DoD- Std -21267A defines traceability as: "(1) the document in question contains or implements all applicable stipulations of the predecessor document, (2) a given term, acronym, or abbreviation means the same thing in all documents, (3) a given item or concept is referred to by the same name or description in the documents, (4) all material in the successor document has its basis in the predecessor document, that is, no untraceable material has been introduced, and (5) the two documents do not contradict one another."

**Traceability Management:** To control and direct; guide; administer; give direction to accomplish an end; as to control and direct tracing from top level through to design and code.

**Tree:** A diagrammatic representation that indicates branching from an original stem; as software components derived from a higher level entity to more discrete lower level entities.

## State of the Practice of Traceability

Traceability management applies to the entire development life cycle from project initiation through operation and maintenance as shown in Figure 2. It is presently feasible to manage tracing using a combination of manual and automated assistance, thus providing some assurance that the development of a system meets the needs as provided by the stakeholder. An essential element of successful traceability management, provided by currently available CASE tools, is the ability to provide links from requirements forward to designs, code, test, and implementation, and backward from any of these activities to requirements once these links have been manually entered into the CASE tool.

Techniques currently in use to establish and maintain traceability from requirements through designs, code, test, and operation begin with manual identification of linkages. These linkages may be subsequently supported by document managers, a database, or CASE tools specifically designed for requirements traceability management.

## Contemporary Traceability Practices

Traceability has traditionally been accomplished by manually assigning and linking unique identifiers; that is, a sentence or paragraph (or other partition) requirement is assigned a particular alpha-numeric reference. This information is subsequently managed in a word processor or database, often through use of a CASE tool. Even with the use of a CASE tool, the initial identification of trace entities and linkages must be accomplished manually. By establishing a unique identification system and following this scheme throughout the life of the project, it is possible to trace these specific entities both forward and backward from

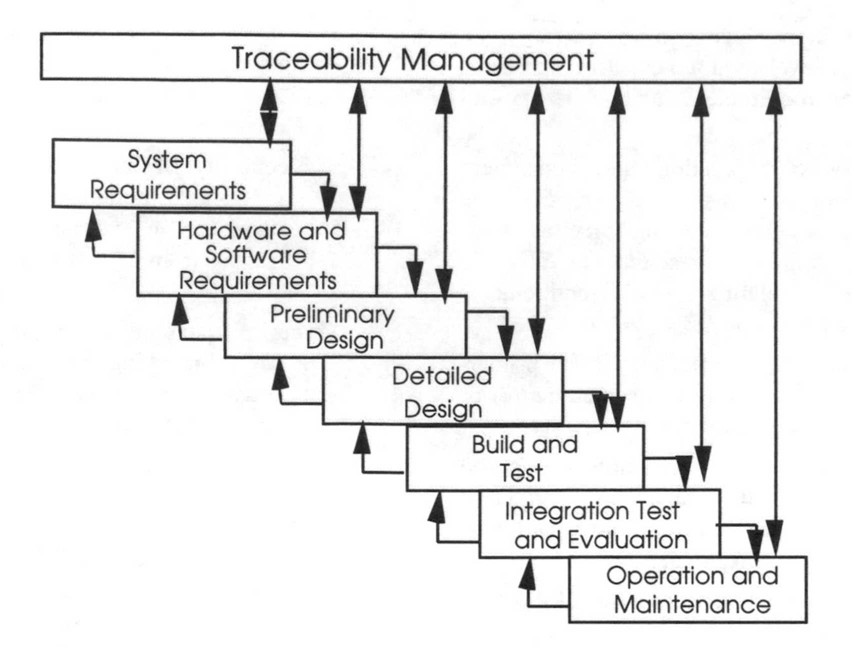


*Figure 2. Traceability management across the system development life cycle*

requirements to product. This unique identity may be linked within and across documents using manually derived traceability tables to assure full traceability over all aspects of the project.

A typical output of tracing is a traceability matrix that links high-level requirements to each and every other requirement or specification of the system. A typical traceability table for a large complex system is shown in Table 1. In this table, individual requirements in the Systems Requirements Document (SRD) have been manually linked to more detailed system requirements in the Systems Specification which in turn have been manually linked to particular specifications in the System Segments.

Other matrices or tables may provide more details such as cryptic messages, partial text, critical values, or the entire text. The system represented in the traceability table is configured as in Figure 3. The SRD represents stakeholder input, the SS represents the initial interpretation of these high level requirements by developers, and the segment specifications provide more detailed information to design. The Interface Control Document (ICD) provides linkages for all messages that occur within and across segments.

In most system development programs, there is the added expectation of continuous change in the system as requirements are added, modified, and deleted. Thus, the management of an ever-changing requirements base becomes a very important traceability function, as tracing provides a review of how the system requirements flowdown to lower levels and how lower level requirements are derived from higher levels. These traces may or may not contain information as to why the system is to be partitioned in a particular manner. As new requirements are added or existing ones are updated, deleted, or modified, the management process continues to provide traceability and impact analysis to assure that each of the changes is properly included in the system development process. This provides the major verification and validation procedure to assure stakeholder needs are met.

*Table 1. Traceability matrix for multi-segment system*

| SRD | SS | Segment 1 | Segment 2 | Segment 3 | ICD |
|---|---|---|---|---|---|
| 3.1.2.1 | 3.3.4.5<br>3.3.4.6 | 3.2.2.5.6<br>3.2.2.5.7<br>3.4.5.6.2 | 3.5.3.2 | | 3.1.4.6.7<br>3.1.4.6.8<br>3.1.4.6.9 |
| 3.4.3.1 | 3.6.7.2<br>3.8.4.3 | 3.5.2.5.1 | 3.7.4.3.1<br>3.7.4.3.2 | 3.6.4.5.2 | 3.3.2.4.5<br>3.3.2.4.7 |

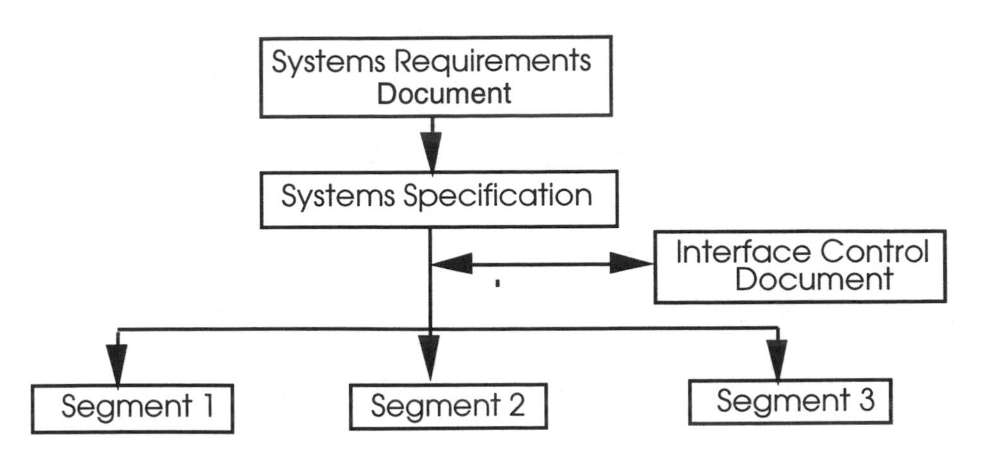


*Figure 3. Typical requirements classification schema for a large complex system*

Traceability is especially critical for the operation and maintenance phase. This is when significant stakeholder changes may be made and change impacts and impact analyses must be performed. Such changes are difficult to trace; however, without tracing it is nearly impossible to ascertain the extent of the full impact of additions, deletions, or modifications to the system.

## An Ideal Process for Traceability

To understand what must be traced, we need a defined process for developing system architectural views, classification schemes, as well as processes for specifying and verifying the products to be constructed. This is generally provided by the stakeholder in consort with the developer. The development of these views is necessary to partition the project for design and construction.

An ideal traceability process consists of the steps of identification, architecture selection, classification, allocation, and flowdown as depicted in Figure 4. The process begins with the identification of requirements at the system level, specification of system architecture, and selection of classification schema. Following this, allocations are made in accordance with the selected schema. Following allocation, the requirements flow down to design, code, and test. This top-down approach has proven most effective in the management of traceability for large scale complex projects.

However, this approach is basically a manual activity that requires significant investment of time and effort on the part of skilled personnel. The outcomes represent a system hierarchy along the lines of the classification structure used for the architectural allocations. It is also necessary to provide threads through the various behavioral and non-behavioral aspects of the project to complete the traceability process. These thread paths are manually assigned using approaches such as entity-relation-attribute diagrams. For example, tests are threaded back to requirements through code and design.

Once the system hierarchy, the architecture, and classification schema have been defined, identified system requirements are assigned to the top-level block of the hierarchy. At this time, they are added to the traceability database for storage, retrieval, and reuse. After appropriate analyses, these requirements are decomposed and flow down into more detailed requirements for each of the lower level blocks to which the requirement was allocated, as was shown in the example of Figure 3. The higher level requirements are sometimes referred to as parents and the lower level ones as children. Change notification should be rigorously traced to determine the impact of such activities on changes in cost, schedule, and feasibility of system design and implementation, on tests that must be conducted, and on support software and hardware.

## Actual Practice for Implementing Traceability

In actual practice, tracing is a labor intensive and aggravating task. Domain experts follow a process to decompose the system that is similar to that depicted in Figure 3. Once appropriate systems architectures are identified, a classification schema or schemas for purposes of allocation of requirements to system specific architectures is prepared and requirements are assigned to specific units. As examples of the types of classification schemes used, one may be centered on functional aspects of the project; such as navigation, communications, or threat assessment; another may concentrate on performance and security; while yet another may be focused on stakeholder organization. It is not feasible to enumerate, a priori- , all the ways in which the project may need to be partitioned and

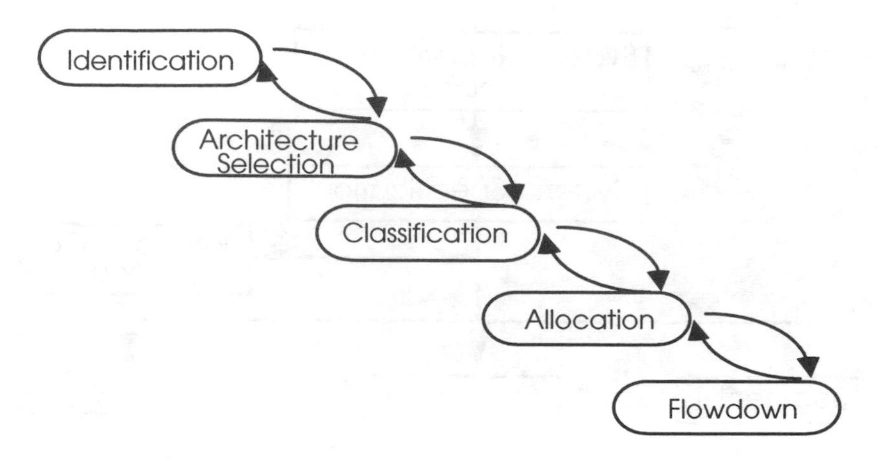


*Figure 4. The ideal traceability process*

viewed; thus, traceability becomes a continuous process as perspectives change and as requirements change. To validate these various views, there is only one common basis from which to form trace linkages, the system requirements.

The next step, after receipt of the requirements documents and delineation of the system architecture, is to determine the nature of the tracing to be accomplished. Several options are feasible; these include working with statements that contain "shall," "will," "should," "would," or similar verbs; or with entire paragraphs; or the total set of statements provided by the stakeholder. The strongest selection is "shall" statements, which may be the only contractually acceptable designation for a requirement. This is followed by the development of classification schemes according to function, data object, behavior, organization, or other approaches. Once the option(s) has been selected, the requirements are parsed according to the option and assigned a unique identity. For example, if "shall" has been selected as the option, sentences with "shall" as a verb are collected and are identified sequentially, while also retaining the original identification system provided by the stakeholder. This new identification system is maintained throughout the life of the project.

Syntactic and semantic information are both necessary to perform tracing. Language semantics are needed to assure the trace is related to the meaning or context of the requirement or set of requirements, while syntax is necessary to trace to a specific word or phrase, without regard to meaning or context. Integration of both constructs is required to provide for full traceability from natural language statements to the other steps as shown in Figure 2. Manual verification of outcomes is required to assure compliance with the intent and purpose of the tracing activity.

Next comes allocation according to the classification scheme. This likewise is a manual task, even with automated assistance from one of the available CASE tools, as most of these tools require the operator to physically establish the links from one entity to another for traceability. All linkages must be designated and maintained and traceability matrices are generated from these outcomes. If a CASE tool has been used that supports generation of traceability matrices, these are created automatically; otherwise, these matrices must be manually prepared. These steps are depicted graphically in Figure 5. These results are usually stored in a traceability database. The traceability linkages are subsequently designated and maintained across the entire development project from design to code to test to operation and maintenance.

## Return on Investment for Traceability

It is not feasible to measure the return on investment (ROI) for traceability. Although most of the costs associated with implementation can be documented, the benefits are quite difficult to ascertain unless comparative case studies are conducted. Costs of implementation include the investment of time and effort of domain experts to provide system architectural perspectives and classification schema, the initial cost of acquiring CASE tools to manage requirements traceability, and the expended costs of training and maintenance in the use of such tools. Due to the manual approaches required to establish architectural perspectives, classification schema, allocation, linkage, and system maintenance, fixing costs, while manageable, is a difficult task. These costs may be either estimated or accounted for with some degree of accuracy. This may be done for an ongoing project or by estimating the time, effort, capitalization costs, and expended costs involved.

The benefits are largely intangible and are related to the avoided costs associated with rework and possible failure of the product to satisfy stakeholders. To

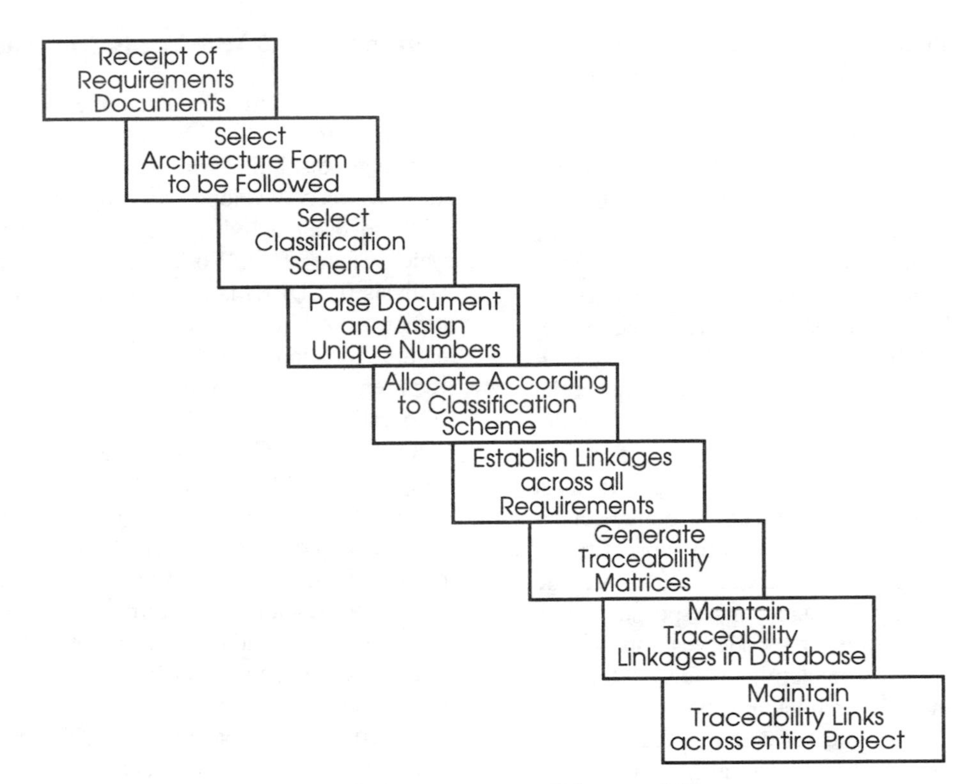


*Figure 5. Steps to accomplish traceability*

estimate the benefits, it would be necessary to prepare various scenarios, simulate the outcomes due to failure of various aspects of the development process, and estimate the value of avoiding these failures. Risk factors must also be taken into consideration in calculation of the potential benefits, including the potential that the project will not meet stakeholder needs. Assessing benefits without comparative analyses is generally not possible. Generating this information is considered to be unfeasible due to the costs of running such experiments and the need to develop realistic scenarios that may or may not ever be replicated in actual practice.

## Current Traceability Tools

Typical of the currently available automated (or semi-automated) assistance approaches to traceability are those that provide for traceability through a variety of syntactic language components: hypertext linking, unique identifiers, syntactical similarity coefficients, or combinations of these. In hypertext linking, the "hotword" or word/phrase to be linked to other requirements is manually identified and entered into the hypertext tool. Links are automatically made and maintained by the tool to provide forward and reverse traceability for the word selection. In the unique identifier approach, an identifier is assigned that remains with the individual requirement throughout the life of the project. To assure traceability, this unique identifier provides a "fan-out" capability within a hierarchical structure such that one system level ("A" level) requirement may be the parent to many "B" level requirements which, in turn, may be the parents for great numbers of "C" level requirements, as depicted in Table 1. Use of syntactic similarity coefficients ascertains whether or not a pre-defined set of words of a given requirement are found in another requirement. When the degree of similarity is above a pre-defined threshold, the two requirements in question are said to trace.

There are problems with each of these approaches. They do not consider the semantics or context in which the tracing is to occur. Hypertext linking finds the search text without regard to the placement in the text and without regard to the way in which the words are used. Use of a unique identifier provides access only to those requirements so identified with no perspective as to meaning or context. Syntactic similarity coefficient traceability is like hypertext linking in that it is indiscriminate as to the meaning and context of the requirement to be traced.

Commercially available requirements tools utilize straightforward traceability links that must be manually developed to relate requirements to other requirements and to design, code, and implementation. Current methods for implementing traceability with these commercial tools generally involve the manual provision of links within and across documents and then automated management of these documents. Traceability links are used to establish the one-to-one, one-to many, many-to-one, or many-to-many relationships that may exist, as may be seen from Table 1. As noted previously, linkages are not automatically established by tools during the development process, but must be manually generated. From this point, automated assistance is provided by the tool to manage traceability.

At present, there are no standards available to support tools for traceability, which has led to the development and use of a large number of commercial tools, each with differing methods, as well as proprietary tools developed by certain industries because it is considered to be a competitive advantage for most large complex projects. A number of commercially available tools have been developed to support traceability and a number of general CASE tools provide support to traceability management, especially from requirements forward to design, code, test, and operation. One of the common activities for all tools is manual development of architectural perspectives and classification schemas. Another common feature is the need to manually establish the initial linkages within and across all traceable entities. Once the initial linkages have been established, these tools effectively and efficiently manage a traceability database or word processor document.

## Common Tool Characteristics

There are some common tool characteristics that are deemed to be minimal to provide support for traceability. The tool must be well understood by and be responsive to users and match the characteristics of the development environment used by the developers. Tools must also accept and utilize the data that is provided in the form provided. In addition, the tool must be flexible, capable of operation in an automated assistance mode to support various activities and services; such as active and passive data checking; batch as well as on-line processing; addition, deletion, and modification of a requirement; customization to specific domain applications; dynamic database structure for change management; and a tailorable user interface. Traceability tools will never be fully automated, as human decision making is essential to the establishment of classification schema and system architecture designation. Human interaction and decision making is both desirable and necessary to maximize the interaction of the stakeholder/developer in the development of the project.

## Commercial CASE Tools for Traceability

Some commercially available tools have been developed for traceability link information expressed by a single discipline within a single phase, while others have been developed specifically to link requirements to other activities within the development life cycle. Cadre TeamWork for Real-Time Structured Analysis (CADRE) is a tool that operates on a single discipline within a single phase. Tools that link information from multiple disciplines and phases include: Requirements Traceability Manager (RTM) (Marconi Corporation) [4], SLATE (TD Technologies) [5], and DOORS (Zycad Corporation) [6]. These tools use an entity-relation-attribute-like schema to capture information on a system database, either relational or object-oriented, enable formation of queries about traceable entities, and for report generation. RTM uses a relational database structure to capture information and provide management, while DOORS provides an object-oriented database for management of information. SLATE follows a multi-user, client-server, object-oriented approach that provides dynamic representation of the system as it evolves.

Another method used by commercial tool vendors is the hypertext approach. In this approach, keywords or phrases are identified as being indicative of traces. These are linked through hypertext throughout the document or set of documents that comprise the requirements. An example of a tool that uses this approach is Document Director [7].

Some general-purpose analysis tools are also used for tracing. Some of the more robust tool sets include: Requirements Driven Design (RDD-100 by Ascent Logic) [8], which is used to document system conceptual models and Foresight [9], which is utilized to maintain a data dictionary and document system simulation.

Other tools and techniques that support requirements traceability include Software Requirements Methodology (SREM); Problem Statement Language/Problem Statement Analyzer (PSL/PSA); N2 charts; Requirement Networks (R-Nets); and ARTS (a database management system for requirements). Not all of the CASE tools support requirements traceability; however; most do support some form of requirements management.

## Future Trends and Conclusions

The future in traceability support lies in the development of the capability to deal directly with requirements in natural language, the ability to provide automated assistance to allocation of requirements to various architectural and classification systems, and the ability to manage these. From this automated assistance, it becomes feasible to provide for and manage a traceable baseline for the entire system.

The following issues are being addressed in ongoing research programs:

- automated allocation of entities to architectures and classifications
- traceability that is independent of methods used to develop architectures and classifications
- tracing product attributes from requirements to the lowest levels

Several research programs are working on the problems associated with natural language; the two addressing traceability are from George Mason University and Trident Systems. The Center for Software Systems Engineering at George Mason University has developed and applied an automated assistance approach to the problems of allocation of entities to architectures and classification called the Automated Integrated Requirements Engineering System (AIRES) [10]. Trident Systems intends to develop a CASE tool called RECAP (Requirements Capture) which is intended to manage natural language requirements [11].

AIRES provides an assessment framework and techniques for integrated application of both semantic and syntactic rules for effective, efficient, and comprehensive identification of traceable and non-traceable requirements in large complex multiple-segment systems. The framework provides for the categorization of requirements in classification structures through the application of a diverse combination of rules and procedures, each of which applies unique combinations of both semantic and syntactic classification rules and tables for the categorization of requirements. These serve as the basic building blocks of the assessment framework and may be applied either singly or in combinations. AIRES supports automated development of linkages that may be transferred electronically to commercially available traceability tools such as RTM for management of a requirements database and report generation. AIRES is presently available in prototype form and has been utilized in support of several large complex system development for traceability support [12].

RECAP, presently a conceptual design, is intended to provide a set of interfaces that permit the operator to manipulate natural language requirements. RECAP proposes to combine the information management and extraction capabilities of information retrieval system approaches with knowledge-base rules. It also intends to provide sequential and string search access to any portion of the document set. Quick access to information is proposed through keywords, sentence identifiers, or rule-based queries. The user will be required to provide information for resolution of ambiguity, mistakes in statements, and addition of missing items. RECAP is intended to aid the user in making these decisions. [11].

Information linked by these tracing tools is not dependent upon a model or discipline. It is possible to link entities as needed; for example, it may be desirable to link the estimated footprint, weight, and power usage of a piece of computer equipment (stored in a hardware modeling tool) to the estimated throughput and memory requirements for a piece of software (stored in a software modeling tool). To efficiently use these tracing tools, it is necessary to automatically transfer the information captured to CASE tools used downstream in the development life cycle. This is accomplished by tracing system definitions, system development processes, and interrelationships across system units.

While tracing from origination to final product is a difficult and arduous, manually intensive task at the present time, advances in technology should soon be commercially available to assist in automated allocation and classification procedures. These advances will make the traceability task much more reasonable, feasible, and supportable for large complex system developments due to the automated assistance provided for allocation and classification, the most labor intensive aspects of tracing. In each of the approaches, the CASE tool provides automated assistance to tracing, but requires human operator inputs only for decision-making activities. These tools represent a significant advance over the present state of the practice for traceability.

## References

[1] Sage, Andrew P. and Palmer, James D., *Software Systems Engineering*, John Wiley and Sons, New York, N.Y., 1990.

[2] White, Stephanie, "Tracing Product and Process Information when developing Complex Systems," *CSESAW '94,* 1994, pp. 45–50, NSWCDD/MP-94/122.

[3] *Webster's New Collegiate Dictionary*, Sixth Ed., G.&C. Merriam Co., Springfield, Mass., 1951.

[4] "RTM-Requirements & Traceability Management, Practical Workbook," GEC-Marconi Limited, Oct., 1993.

[5] Nallon, John, "Implementation of NSWC Requirements Traceability Models," *CSESAW*, 1994, pp. 15–22, NSWCDD/MP-94/122.

[6] Rundley, Nancy and Miller, William D., "DOORS to the Digitized Battlefield: Managing Requirements Discovery and Traceability," *CSESAW*, 1994, pp. 23–28.

[7] "Document Director-The Requirements Tool," B.G. Jackson Associates, 17629 E. Camino Real, Suite 720, Houston, Tex., 77058, 1989.

[8] "RDD-100-Release Notes Release 3.0.2.1, Oct., 1992," Requirements Driven Design, Ascent Logic Corporation, 180 Rose Orchard Way, #200, San Jose, Calif., 95134, 1992.

[9] Vertal, Michael D., "Extending IDEF: Improving Complex Systems with Executable Modeling," *Proc. 1994 Ann. Conf. for Business Re-engineering*, IDEF Users Group, Richmond, VA, May, 1994.

[10] Palmer, James D. and Evans Richard P., "An Integrated Semantic and Syntactic Framework for Requirements Traceability: Experience with System Level Requirements for a Large Complex Multi-Segment Project," *CSESAW*, 1994, pp. 9–14, NSWCDD/MP-94/122.

[11] Hugue, Michelle, Casey, Michael, Wood, Glenn, and Edwards, Edward, "RECAP: A REquirements CAPture Tool for Large Complex Systems," *CSESAW*, 1994, pp. 39–44, NSWCDD/MP-94/122.

[12] Palmer, James D. and Evans Richard P., "Software Risk Management: Requirements-Based Risk Metrics," *Proc. IEEE 1994 Int'l Conf. SMC*, IEEE Press, Piscataway, N.J., 1994.

# A review of software testing

P DAVID COWARD

*Abstract: Despite advances in formal methods of specification and improved software creation tools, there is no guarantee that the software produced meets its functional requirements. There is a need for some form of software testing. The paper introduces the aims of software testing. This is followed by a description of static and dynamic analysis, and, functional and structural testing strategies. These ideas are used to provide a taxonomy of testing techniques. Each technique is briefly described.*

*Keywords: software development, software testing, formal methods*

Before software is handed over for use, both the commissioner and the developer want the software to be correct. Unfortunately, what is meant by 'correct' is not clear. It is often taken to mean that the program matches the specification. However, the specification itself may not be correct. Correctness is then concerned with whether the software meets user requirements. Whatever the definition of correctness there is always the need to test a system.

Testing is one of the many activities that comprise the larger complex task of software development. The need for testing arises out of an inability to guarantee that earlier tasks in the software project have been performed adequately, and attempts to assess how well these tasks have been performed.

There is no agreed definition of testing. The term is often used to describe techniques of checking software by executing it with data. A wider meaning will be adopted in this paper: testing includes *any* technique of checking software, such as symbolic execution and program proving as well as the execution of test cases with data. Checking, implies that a comparison is undertaken. The comparison is made between the output from the test and an expected output derived by the tester. The expected output is based on the specification and is derived by hand.

Two terms often associated with testing are *verification* and *validation*. Verification refers to ensuring correctness from phase to phase of the software development cycle. Validation involves checking the software against the requirements. These strategies have been termed *horizontal* and *vertical* checks. Sometimes, verification is associated with formal proofs of correctness, while validation is concerned with executing the software with test data. This paper avoids these terms and instead refers only to *testing* and *checking*, both terms being used synonymously.

Testing may be subdivided into two categories: *functional* and *nonfunctional*.

Functional testing addresses itself to whether the program produces the correct output. It may be employed when testing a new program or when testing a program that has been modified. *Regression testing* is the name given to the functional testing that follows modification. Primarily, regression testing is undertaken to determine whether the correction has altered the functions of the software that were intended to remain unchanged. There is a need for the automatic handling of regression testing. Fischer[1] describes software for determining which tests need to be rerun following a modification.

Implementing the functions required by the customer will not necessarily satisfy *all* the requirements placed upon a software system. Additional requirements, which are the subject of nonfunctional testing, involve checking that the software:

- satisfies legal obligations,
- performs within specified response times,
- is written to a particular house style,
- meets documentation standards.

The scope of this paper is limited to addressing the testing of the commissioner's functional requirements. The literature is not united about the aims of software testing. The variety of aims seem to fall into one of two camps:

- testing is concerned with finding faults in the software,
- testing is concerned with demonstrating that there are no faults in the software.

These may be viewed as an individual's attitude towards testing which may have an impact on how testing is conducted. Aiming to find faults is a destructive process, whereas aiming to demonstrate that there are no faults is constructive. Adopting the latter strategy may cause the tester to be gentle with the software, thus, giving rise to the risk of missing inherent faults. The destructive stance is perhaps more likely to uncover faults because it is more probing. Weinberg[2] suggests that programmers regard the software they produce as an extension of their ego. To be destructive in testing is therefore difficult. NASA long ago established teams of software validators separate from the software creators[3] a practice which is

Department of Computer Studies, Bristol Polytechnic, Coldharbour Lane, Frenchay, Bristol BS16 1QY, UK

Reprinted from *Information and Software Technology,* Vol. 30, No. 3, Apr. 1988, P. David Coward, "A Review of Software Testing," pp. 189–198, 1988, with kind permission from Elsevier Science–NL, Sara Burgerhartstraat 25; 1055 KV Amsterdam, The Netherlands.

now widespread in large software development organizations.

There are a large number of questions about testing. How much testing should be undertaken? When should we have confidence in the software? When a fault is discovered, should we be pleased that it has been found, or dismayed that it existed? Does the discovery of a fault lead us to suspect that there are likely to be more faults? At what stage can we feel confident that all, or realistically most, of the faults have been discovered? In short, what is it that we are doing when we test software? To what extent is testing concerned with quality assurance?

Perhaps testing is about both finding faults *and* demonstrating their absence. The aim is to demonstrate the absence of faults. This is achieved by setting out to find them. These views are reconciled by establishing the notion of the 'thoroughness of testing'. Where testing has been thorough, faults found and corrected, retested with equal thoroughness, then one has established confidence in the software. If, on the other hand, there is no feel for the thoroughness of the test one has no means of establishing confidence in the results of the testing. Much work has been done to establish test metrics to assess the thoroughness of a set of tests and to develop techniques that facilitate thorough testing.

## Testing strategies

There are many widely differing testing techniques. But, for all the apparent diversity they cluster or separate according to their underlying principles. There are two prominent strategy dimensions: function/structural and static/dynamic. A solely functional strategy uses only the requirements defined in the specification as the basis for testing; whereas a structural strategy is based on the detailed design. A dynamic approach executes the software and assesses the performance, while a static approach analyses the software without recourse to its execution.

### *Functional* versus *structural testing*

A testing strategy may be based upon one of two starting points: either the specification or the software is used as the basis for testing. Starting from the specification the required functions are identified. The software is then tested to assess whether they are provided. This is known as *functional testing*. If the strategy is based on deriving test data from the structure of a system this is known as *structural testing*. Functions which are included in the software, but not required; for example, functions which relate to the access of data in a database but which are not specifically asked for by a user, are more likely to be identified by adopting a structural testing strategy in preference to a functional testing strategy.

### *Functional testing*

Functional testing involves two main steps. First, identify the functions which the software is expected to perform. Second, create test data which will check whether these functions are performed by the software. No consideration is given to *how* the program performs these functions.

There have been significant moves towards more systematic elicitation and expression of functional requirements[4–7]. These may be expected to lead to a more systematic approach to functional testing. Rules can be constructed for the direct identification of function and data from systematic design documentation. These rules do not take account of likely fault classes. Weyuker and Ostrand[8] have suggested that the next step in the development of functional testing, is a method of formal documentation which includes a description of faults associated with each part of the design as well as the design features themselves.

Howden[9] suggests this method be taken further. He claims that it is not sufficient to identify classes of faults for parts of the design. Isolation of particular properties of each function should take place. Each property will have certain fault classes associated with it. There are many classifications of faults. One detailed classification is given by Chan[10] and is a refinement of Van Tassel's[11] classification. Chan's classification consists of 13 groups which are subdivided to produce a total of 47 categories.

Functional testing has been termed a black box approach as it treats the program as a box with its contents hidden from view. Testers submit test cases to the program based on their understanding of the intended function of the program. An important component of functional testing is an *oracle*.

An oracle is someone who can state precisely what the outcome of a program execution will be for a particular test case. Such an oracle does not always exist and, at best, only imprecise expectations are available[12]. Simulation software provides a powerful illustration of the problem of determining an oracle. No precise expectation can be determined, the most precise expectation of output that can be provided is a range of plausible values.

### *Structural testing*

The opposite to the black box approach is the white box aproach. Here testing is based upon the detailed design rather than on the functions required of the program, hence the name structural testing.

While functional testing requires the execution of the program with test data, there are two possible scenarios for structural testing. The first scenario, and the one most commonly encountered, is to execute the program with test cases. Second, and less common, is where the functions of the program are compared with the required functions for congruence. The second of these approaches is characterized by symbolic execution and program proving.

Structural testing involving the execution of a program may require the execution of a single path through the program, or it may involve a particular level of coverage such as 100% of all statements have been executed. The notion of a minimally-thorough test has occupied researchers over the years, i.e. they have been trying to discover what is the minimum amount of testing that is required to ensure a degree of reliability. Some of these are shown below:

- All statements in the programs should be executed at least once[13].
- All branches in the program should be executed at least once[13].
- All linear code sequence and jumps (LCSAJs) in the program should be executed at least once[14]. An LCSAJ is a sequence of code ending with a transfer of control out of the linear code sequence.

Probably the most thorough set of test metrics has been specified by Miller[15] who listed 13 structure-based metrics for judging test thoroughness. Obviously, the best test is an exhaustive one where all possible paths through the program are tested. However, there are two obstacles to this goal which account for the existence of the above measures.

The first obstacle is the large number of possible paths. The number of paths is determined by the numbers of conditions and loops in the program. All combinations of the conditions must be considered and this causes a rapidly increasing number of combinations as the number of conditions increases. This is known as the combinatorial explosion of testing. Loops add to the combinatorial explosion and give rise to an excessively large number of paths. This is most acute when the number of iterations is not fixed but determined by input variables.

The second obstacle is the number of infeasible paths. An infeasible path is one which cannot be executed due to the contradiction of some of the predicates at conditional statements. Most developers, when asked, would be surprised at the existence of infeasible code in a system. However, such code can be quite extensive, for example, in a recent study of a sample of programs, which involve examining 1000 shortest paths, only 18 were found to be feasible[16].

As an example of path infeasibility consider the following block of code.

```
1  Begin
2    Readln (a);
3    If a>15
4    then
5      b:=b+1
6    else
7      c:=c+1;
8    if a<10
9    then
10     d:=d+1
11 end;
```

There are four paths through this block as follows:

*Path 1* lines 1,2,3,4,5,8,11.

*Path 2* 1,2,3,6,7,8,9,10,11.

*Path 3* 1,2,3,6,7,8,11.

*Path 4* 1,2,3,4,5,8,9,10,11.

*Path 1* can be executed so long as the value of *a* is greater than 15 after the execution of line 2.

*Path 2* can be executed so long as the value of *a* is less than 10 after the execution of line 2.

*Path 3* can be executed so long as the value of *a* lies in the range 10 to 15 inclusive after the execution of line 2.

*Path 4* cannot be executed regardless of the value of *a* because *a* cannot be both greater than 15 and less than 10 simultaneously. Hence this path is infeasible.

Even trivial programs contain a large number of paths. Where a program contains a loop which may be executed a variable number of times the number of paths increases dramatically. A path exists for each of the following circumstances: where the loop is not executed, where the loop is executed once, where the loop is executed twice etc.

The number of paths is dependent on the value of the variable controlling the loop. This poses a problem for a structural testing strategy. How many of the variable-controlled-loop-derived paths should be covered? Miller and Paige[17] sought to tackle this problem by introducing the notion of a level-i path and have employed testing metrics which utilize this notion.

A further difficulty in achieving 100% for any metric of testing coverage is the presence of island code. This is a series of lines of code, following a transfer of control or program termination, and which is not the destination of a transfer of control from elsewhere in the program. An example of island code is a procedure that is not invoked. Island code should not exist. It is caused by an error in the invocation of a required procedure, or the failure to delete redundant code following maintenance.

### *Static* versus *dynamic analysis*

A testing technique that does not involve the execution of the software with data is known as *static analysis*. This includes program proving, symbolic execution and anomaly analysis. Program proving involves rigorously specifying constraints on the input and output data sets for a software component such as a procedure using mathematics. The code that implements the procedure is then proved mathematically to meet its specification. Symbolic execution is a technique which executes a software system, with symbolic values for variables being used rather than the normal numerical or string values. Anomaly analysis searches the program source for anomalous features such as island code.

Dynamic analysis requires that the software be executed. It relies on the use of probes inserted into a program [18,19]. These are program statements which make calls to analysis routines that record the frequency of execution of elements of the program. As a result the tester is able to ascertain information such as the frequency that certain branches or statements are executed and also any areas of code that have not been exercised by the test.

Dynamic analysis can act as a bridge between functional and structural testing. Initially functional testing may dictate the set of test cases. The execution of these test cases may then be monitored by dynamic analysis. The program can then be examined structurally to determine test cases which will exercise the code left idle by the previous test. This dual approach results in the program being tested for the function required and the whole of the program being exercised. The latter feature ensures that the program does not perform any function that is not required.

## Taxonomy of testing techniques

It is only over the last 15 years that testing techniques have achieved importance. Consequently, there is no generally accepted testing technique taxonomy. The degree to which the techniques employ a static *versus* dynamic analysis or a functional *versus* structural strategy provides one possible basis for a simple classification of testing techniques. The following grid outlines one classification. The techniques in the grid are described later in the paper. Domain testing, described later in this section, has been included under both structural and functional strategies.

**Table 1. Simple classification of testing techniques**

| | Structural | Functiona |
|---|---|---|
| Static | Symbolic execution<br>Program proving<br>Anomaly analysis | |
| Dynamic | Computation testing<br>Domain testing<br>Automatic path-based test data generation<br>Mutation analysis | Random testing<br>Domain testing<br>Cause-effect graphing<br>Adaptive perturbation testing |

### *Static-structural*

No execution of the software is undertaken. Assessment is made of the soundness of the software by criteria other than its run-time behaviour. The features assessed vary with the technique. For example, anomaly analysis checks for peculiar features such as the existence of island code. On the other hand, program proving, aims to demonstrate congruence between the specification and the software.

#### *Symbolic execution*

Symbolic execution, sometimes referred to as symbolic evaluation, does not execute a program in the traditional sense of the word. The traditional notion of execution requires that a selection of paths through the program is exercised by a set of test cases. In symbolic execution actual data values are replaced by symbolic values. A program executed using inputs consisting of actual data values results in the output of a series of actual values. Symbolic execution on the other hand produces a set of expressions, one expression per output variable. Symbolic evaluation occupies a middle ground of testing between testing data and program proving. There are a number of symbolic execution systems[20–23].

The most common approach to symbolic execution is to perform an analysis of the program, resulting in the creation of a flow-graph. This is a directed graph which contains decision points and the assignments associated with each branch. By traversing the flow-graph from an entry point along a particular path a list of assignment statements and branch predicates is produced.

The resulting path is represented by a series of input variables, condition predicates and assignment statements. The execution part of the approach takes place by following the path from top to bottom. During this path traverse each input variable is given a symbol in place of an actual value. Thereafter, each assignment statement is evaluated so that it is expressed in terms of symbolic values of input variables and constants.

Consider paths 1–11 through the program in Figure 1. The symbolic values of the variables and the path condition at each branch are given in the right hand columns for the evaluation of this path.

At the end of the symbolic execution of a path the output variable will be represented by expressions in terms of symbolic values of input variables and constants. The output expressions will be subject to constraints. A list of these constraints is provided by the set of symbolic representations of each condition predicate along the path. Analysis of these constraints may indicate that the path is not executable due to a contradiction. This infeasibility problem is encountered by all forms of path testing.

A major difficulty for symbolic execution is the handling of loops (or iterations). Should the loops be symbolically evaluated once, twice, a hundred times or not at all? Some symbolic executors take a pragmatic approach. For each loop three paths are constructed, each path containing one of the following: no execution of the loop, a single execution of the loop and two executions of the loop.

| | | Path Condition | a | b | c | d |
|---|---|---|---|---|---|---|
| 1 | Begin | – | – | – | – | |
| 2 | Read a, b, c, d | – | a | b | c | d |
| 3 | a := a+b | – | a+b | b | c | d |
| 4 | IF a>c | a+b<=c | a+b | b | c | d |
| 5 | THEN d := d+1 | | | | | |
| 6 | ENDIF | a+b<=c | a+b | b | c | d |
| 7 | IF b=d | a+b<=c AND b<>d | a+b | b | c | d |
| 8 | THEN WRITE ('Success', a, d) | | | | | |
| 9 | ELSE WRITE ('Fail', a, d) | a+b<=c AND b<>d | a+b | b | c | d |
| 10 | ENDIF | a+b<=c AND b<>d | a+b | b | c | d |
| 11 | END | a+b<=c AND b<>d | a+b | b | c | d |

*Figure 1. Program fragment and symbolic values for a path*

*Partition analysis*

Partition analysis uses symbolic execution to identify subdomains of the input data domain. Symbolic execution is performed on both the software and the specification. The path conditions are used to produce the subdomains, such that each subdomain is treated identically by both the program and the specification. Where a part of the input domain cannot be allocated to such a subdomain then either a structural or functional (program or specification) fault has been discovered. In the system described by Richardson[24] the specification is expressed in a manner close to program code. This is impractical. Specifications need to be written at a higher level of abstraction if this technique is to prove useful.

*Program proving*

The most widely reported approach to program proving is the 'inductive assertion verification' method developed by Floyd[25]. In this method assertions are placed at the beginning and end of selected procedures. Each assertion describes the function of the procedure mathematically. A procedure is said to be correct (with respect to its input and output assertions) if the truth of its input assertion upon procedure entry ensures the truth of its output assertion upon procedure exit[26].

There are many similarities between program proving and symbolic execution. Neither technique executes with actual data and both examine the source code. Program proving aims to be more rigorous in its approach. The main distinction between program proving and symbolic execution is in the area of loop handling. Program proving adopts a theoretical approach in contrast to symbolic execution. An attempt is made to produce a proof that accounts for all possible iterations of the loop. Some symbolic execution systems make the assumption that if the loop is correct when not executed, when executed just once and when executed twice, then it will be correct for any number of iterations.

Program proving is carried out as the following steps:

- Construct a program.
- Examine the program and insert mathematical assertions at the beginning and end of all procedures blocks.
- Determine whether the code between each pair of start and end assertions will achieve the end assertion given the start assertion.
- If the code achieves the end assertions then the block has been proved correct.

If the code fails to achieve the end assertion then mistakes have been made in either the program or the proof. The proof and the program should be checked to determine which of these possibilities has occurred and appropriate corrections made.

DeMillo *et al*[27] describe how theorems and proofs can never be conceived as 'correct' but rather, only 'acceptable' to a given community. This acceptability is achieved by their being examined by a wide audience who can find no fault in the proof. Confidence in the proof increases as the number of readers, finding no faults, increases. This approach has clear parallels with the confidence placed in software. The wider the audience that has used the software and found no fault the more confidence is invested in the software.

When a program has been proved correct, in the sense that it has been demonstrated that the end assertions will be achieved given the initial assertions, then the program has achieved partial correctness. To achieve total correctness it must also be shown that the block will terminate, in other words the loops will terminate[28].

*Anomaly analysis*

The first level of anomaly analysis is performed by the compiler to determine whether the program adheres to the language syntax. This first level of analysis is not usually considered testing. Testing is usually deemed to commence when a syntactically correct program is produced.

The second level of anomaly analysis searches for anomalies that are not outlawed by the programming language. Examples of such systems which carry out such an analysis are Dave[29], Faces[30] and Toolpack[31]. Anomalies which can be discovered by these systems include:

- The existence of (island code) unexecutable code,
- Problems concerning array bounds,
- Failure to initialize variables,
- Labels and variables which are unused,
- Jumps into and out of loops.

Some systems will even detect high complexity and departure from programming standards.

Discovery of these classes of problem is dependent on the analysis of the code. The first phase of anomaly analysis is to produce a flow-graph. This representation of the software can now be easily scanned to identify anomalies. Determining infeasible paths is not within the bounds of anomaly analysis.

Some features of anomaly analysis have been grouped under the title of *data flow analysis*. Here, emphasis is placed on a careful analysis of the flow of data. Software may be viewed as flow of data from input to output. Input values contribute to intermediate values which, in turn, determine the output values. 'It is the ordered use of data implicit in this process that is the central objective of study in data flow analysis'[32] The anomalies detected by data flow analysis are:

- Assigning values to a variable which is not used later in the program,
- Using a variable (in an expression or condition) which has not previously been assigned a value,
- (Re)assigning a variable without making use of a previously assigned value.

Data flow anomalies may arise from mistakes such as misspelling, confusion of variable names and incorrect parameter passing. The existence of a data flow anomaly is not evidence of a fault, it merely indicates the possibility of a fault. Software that contains data flow anomalies may be less likely to satisfy the functional requirements than software which does not contain them.

The role of data flow analysis is one of a program critic drawing attention to peculiar uses of variables. These peculiarities must be checked against the programmer's intentions and, if in disagreement, the program should be corrected.

## *Dynamic-functional*

This class of technique executes test cases. No consideration is given to the detailed design of the software. Cause-effect graphing creates test cases from the rules contained in the specification. Alternatively, test cases may be generated randomly. Domain testing creates test cases based on a decomposition of the required functions. Adaptive testing attempts to create further, more effective, test cases by modifying previous test cases. In all the approaches there is the need for an oracle to pronounce on the correctness of the output.

### *Domain testing*

This is the least well defined of the dynamic-functional approaches. Test cases are created based on an informal classification of the requirements into domains. Either data or function may provide the basis for the domain partitioning. The test cases are executed and compared against the expectation to determine whether faults have been detected.

### *Random testing*

Random testing produces data without reference to the code or the specification. The main software tool required is a random number generator. Duran and Ntafos[33,34] describe how estimates of the operational reliability of the software can be derived from the results of random testing.

Potentially, there are some problems for random testing. The most significant is that it may seem that there is no guarantee to complete coverage of the program. For example, when a constraint on a path is an equality e.g. A=B+5 the likelihood of satisfying this constraint by random generation seems low. Alternatively, if complete coverage is achieved then it is likely to have generated a large number of test cases. The checking of the output from the execution would require an impractical level of human effort.

Intuitively, random testing would appear to be of little practical value. Some recent studies have attempted to counter this view by randomly testing instrumented programs[33-35]. Ince and Hekmatpour record that an average branch coverage of 93% was achieved for a small set of randomly generated test cases. The key to this approach is to examine only a small subset of the test results. The subset is chosen to give a high branch coverage.

### *Adaptive perturbation testing*

This technique is based on assessing the effectiveness of a set of test cases. The effectiveness measure is used to generate further test cases with the aim of increasing the effectiveness. Both Cooper[36] and Andrews[37] describe systems which undertake this automatically.

The cornerstone of the technique is the use of executable assertions which the software developer inserts into the software. An assertion is a statement about the reasonableness of values of variables. The aim is to maximize the number of assertion violations. An initial set of test cases are provided by the tester. These are executed and the assertion violations recorded. Each test case is now considered in turn. The single input parameter of the test case that contributes least to the assertion violation count is identified. Optimization routines are then used to find the best value to replace the discarded value such that the number of assertion violations is maximized. The test case is said to have undergone *perturbation*. This is repeated for each test case. The perturbed set of test cases are executed and the cycle is repeated until the number of violated assertions can be increased no further.

### *Cause-effect graphing*

The strength of cause-effect graphing lies in its power to explore input combinations. The graph is a combinatorial logic network, rather like a circuit, making use of only the Boolean logical operators AND, OR and NOT. Myers[38] describes a series of steps for determining cases using cause-effect graphs as follows:

- Divide the specification into workable pieces. A workable piece might be the specification for an individual transaction. This step is necessary because a cause-effect graph for a whole system would be too unwieldy for practical use.
- Identify causes and effects. A cause is an input stimulus, e.g. a command typed in at a terminal, an effect is an output response.
- Construct a graph to link the causes and effects in a way that represents the semantics of the specification. This is the *cause-effect graph*.
- Annotate the graph to show impossible effects and impossible combinations of causes.
- Convert the graph into a limited-entry decision table. Conditions represent the causes, actions represent the effects and rules (columns) represent the test cases.

In a simple case, say with three conditions, one may be tempted to feel that the cause-effect graph is an unnecessary intermediate representation. However, Myers illustrates the creation of test cases for a specification containing 18 causes. To progress immediately to the decision table would have given 262 potential test cases. The purpose of the cause-effect graph is to identify a small number of useful test cases.

### *Dynamic-structural*

Here the software is executed with test cases. Creation of the test cases is generally based upon an analysis of the software.

#### *Domain and computation testing*

Domain and computation testing are strategies for selecting test cases. They use the structure of the program and select paths which are used to identify domains. The assignment statements on the paths are used to consider the computations on the path. These approaches also make use of the ideas of symbolic execution.

A *path computation* is the set of algebraic expressions, one for each output variable, in terms of input variables and constants for a particular path. A *path condition* is the conjunction of constraint on the path. A path domain is the set of input values that satisfy the path condition. An empty path domain means that the path is infeasible and cannot be executed.

The class of error that results when a case follows the wrong path due to a fault in a conditional statement is termed a *domain error*. The class of error that results when a case correctly follows a path which contains faults in an assignment statement is termed a computation error.

Domain testing is based on the observation that points close to, yet satisfying boundary conditions are most sensitive to domain errors[39]. The domain testing strategy selects test data on and near the boundaries of each path domain[8,40].

Computation testing strategies focus on the detection of computation errors. Test data for which the path is sensitive to computation errors are selected by analysing the symbolic representation of the path computation[39]. Clarke and Richardson[24] list a set of guidelines for selecting test data for arithmetic and data manipulation computations.

#### *Automatic test data generation*

Use is made of automatic generation of test data when the program is to be executed and the aim is to achieve a particular level of courage indicated by a coverage metric.

It has been suggested that test data can be generated from a syntactic description of the test data expressed in, say, BNF[41]. This may seem novel as it is not usual to prepare such a syntactic description of the data, but it is a technique familiar to compiler writers[42,43]. In the case of compilers a carefully prepared data description: that of the programming language, is available. The principle may be transferable to test data generation in general.

Many automatic test data generators have used the approach of path identification and symbolic execution to aid the data generation process, for example, CASEGEN[23] and the FORTRAN testbed[44]. The system of predicates produced for a path is part-way to generating test data. If the path predicates cannot be solved due to a contradiction, then the path is infeasible. Any solution of these predicates will provide a series of data values for the input variables so providing a test case.

Repeated use of the path generation and predicate solving parts of such a system may produce a set of test cases in which one has confidence of high coverage of the program. The initial path generation will provide the highest coverage. Subsequent attempts to find feasible paths which incorporate remaining uncovered statements, branches and LCSAJs will prove increasingly difficult, some impossibly difficult.

A path-based approach which does not use symbolic execution is incorporated in the SMOTL system[45]. The system has a novel approach to minimizing the number of paths required to achieve full branch coverage.

A program that has been tested with a high coverage may still not meet its specification. This may be due to the omission in the program of one of the functions defined in the specification. Data that is generated from the specification would prove useful in determining such omissions. To achieve this automatically requires a rigorous means of specification. The increasing use of formal specification methods may provide the necessary foundations on which to build automated functional test data generators.

#### *Mutation analysis*

Mutation analysis is not concerned with creating test data, nor of demonstrating that the program is correct. It is concerned with the quality of a set of test data[46,47]. Other forms of testing use the test data to test the program. Mutation analysis uses the program to test the test data.

High quality test data will harshly exercise a program thoroughly. To provide a measure of how well the program has been exercised mutation analysis creates many, almost identical, programs. One change is made per mutant program. Each mutant program and the original program are then executed with the same set of test data. The output from the original program is then compared with the output from each mutant program in turn. If the outputs are different then that particular mutant is of little interest as the test data has discovered that there is a difference between the programs. This mutant is now *dead* and disregarded. A mutant which produced output that matches with the original is interesting. The change has not been detected by the test data, and the mutant is said to be *live*.

Once the output from all the mutants has been examined, a ratio of dead to live mutants will be available. A high proportion of live mutants indicates a poor set of test data. A further set of test data must be devised and the process repeated until the number of live mutants is small, indicating that the program has been well tested.

A difficulty for mutation analysis occurs when a mutant program is an equivalent program to the original program. Although the mutant is textually different from the original it will always produce the same results as the original program. Mutation analysis will record this as a live mutant even though no test data can be devised to kill it. The difficulty lies in the fact that determining the state of equivalence is, in general, unsolvable and hence cannot be taken into account when assessing the ratio of live to killed mutants.

Mutation analysis relies on the notion that if the test data discovers the single change that has been made to produce the mutant program then the test data will discover more major faults in the program. Thus, if the test data has not discovered any major faults, and a high proportion of the mutants have been killed, then the program is likely to be sound.

## Summary

The principal objective of software testing is to gain confidence in the software. This necessitates the discovery of both errors of omission and commission. Confidence arises from thorough testing. There are many testing techniques which aim to help achieve thorough testing.

Testing techniques can be assessed according to where along the two main testing strategy dimensions they fall. The first dimension, the functional-structural dimension, assesses the extent to which the function description in the specification, as opposed to the detailed design of the software, is used as a basis for testing. The second dimension, the static-dynamic dimension, considers the degree to which the technique executes the software and assesses its run-time behaviour, as opposed to inferring its run-time behaviour from an examination of the software. These two dimensions can be used to produce four categories of testing technique:

- static-functional
- static-structural
- dynamic-functional
- dynamic-structural

As with all classifications this one is problematic at the boundaries. Some techniques appear to belong equally well in two categories.

The aims of testing techniques range from: demonstrating correctness for all input classes (e.g. program proving), to, showing that for a particular set of test cases no faults were discovered (e.g. random testing). Debate continues as to whether correctness can be proved for life-size software and about what can be inferred when a set of test cases finds no errors. A major question facing dynamic testing techniques is whether the execution of a single case demonstrates anything more than that the software works for that particular case. This has led to work on the identification of domains leading to the assertion that a text case represents a particular domain of possible test cases.

Many of the structural techniques rely on the generation of paths through the software. These techniques are hampered by the lack of a sensible path generation strategy. There is no clear notion of what constitutes a *revealing* path worthy of investigation, as opposed to a *concealing* path which tells the tester very little.

Testers often utilize their experience of classes of faults associated with particular functions and data types to create additional test cases. To date there is no formal way of taking account of these heuristics.

Symbolic execution looks to be a promising technique. Yet, few full symbolic execution systems currently exist[48]. Of the experimental systems that have been developed none address commercial data processing software written in languages such as COBOL.

Whenever a program is executed with data values, or symbolically evaluated, the success of the testing lies in the ability to recognize that errors have occurred. Who is responsible for deeming an output correct? The notion of an oracle is used to overcome this difficulty. Whoever commissions the software is deemed capable of assessing whether the results are correct. This may be satisfactory in many situations such as commercial data processing software. However, there are instances when this is not a solution. For example, software to undertake calculations in theoretical physics may be developed precisely because the calculations could not be undertaken by hand.

One of the few pieces of empirical data on testing techniques is provided in a study by Howden[49]. The study tested six programs of various types using several different testing techniques. The results are encouraging for the use of symbolically evaluated expressions for output variables. Out of a total of 28 errors five were discovered where it would be 'possible for the incorrect variable to take on the values of the correct variable during testing on actual data, thus hiding the presence of the error.' The paper concluded that the testing strategy most likely to produce reliable software was one that made use of a variety of techniques. Over the last few years effort has been directed at construction of integrated, multitechnique software development environments.

Formal proofs, dynamic testing techniques and symbolic execution used together look likely to provide a powerful testing environment. What is necessary now is an attempt to overcome the division that has arisen between the formalists and the structuralists. The level of mathematics required by many approaches to program proving is elementary in comparison with the abilities necessary to produce the software itself. On the other hand, the formalists must resist the temptation to proclaim that their approach is not just necessary but that it is also sufficient. For the production of correct software the wider the range of testing techniques used the better the software is likely to be.

## References


1 **Fischer, K F** 'A test case selection method for the validation of software maintenance modification' *Proc. COMPSAC 1977*, pp 421–426 (1977)
2 **Weinberg, G M** *The Psychology of Computer Programming* Van Nostrand Reinhold (1971)
3 **Spector, A and Gifford, D** 'Case study: the space shuttle primary computer system' *Commun. ACM* Vol 27 No 9 (1984) pp 874–900
4 **DeMarco, T** *Structured Analysis and System Specification,* Yourden Press (1981)
5 **Hayes, I** *Specification Case Studies* Prentice-Hall International (1987)
6 **Jackson, M** *Principles of Program Design*, Academic Press (1975)
7 **Jones, C B** *Systematic Software Development using VDM* Prentice-Hall International (1986)
8 **Weyuker, F J and Ostrand, T J** 'Theories of program testing and the application of revealing subdomains' (IEEE) *Trans. Software Eng.* Vol 6 No 3 (1980) pp 236–246
9 **Howden, W E** 'Errors, design properties and functional program tests' *Computer Program Testing* (**Eds Chandrasekaran, B and Radicchi, S**) North-Holland, (1981)
10 **Chan, J** *Program debugging methodology* M Phil Thesis, Leicester Polytechnic (1979)
11 **Van Tassel, D** *Program Style, Design, Efficiency, Debugging and Testing* Prentice-Hall (1978)
12 **Weyuker, E J** 'On testing non-testable programs' *The Comput. J.* Vol 25 No 4 (1982) pp 465–470
13 **Miller, J C and Maloney, C J** Systematic mistake analysis of digital computer programs, *Commun. ACM* pp 58–63 Vol 6 (1963)
14 **Woodward, M R, Hedley, D and Hennell, M A** 'Experience with path analysis and testing of programs' (IEEE) *Trans. Software Eng.* Vol 6 No 6 (1980) pp 278–285
15 **Miller, E F** 'Software quality assurance' *Presentation* London, UK (14–15 May 1984)
16 **Hedley, D and Hennell, M A** 'The cause and effects of infeasible paths in computer programs' *Proc. Eight Int. Conf. Software Eng.* (1985)
17 **Miller, E F and Paige, M R** Automatic generation of software tescases, *Proc. Eurocomp Conf.* pp 1–12 (1974)
18 **Knuth, D E and Stevenson, F R** 'Optimal measurement points for program frequency count' *BIT* Vol 13 (1973)
19 **Paige, M R and Benson, J P** 'The use of software probes in testing FORTRAN programs' *Computer* pp 40–47 (July 1974)
20 **Boyer, R S, Elpas, B and Levit, K N** 'SELECT – a formal system for testing and debugging programs by symbolic execution' *Proc. Int. Conf. Reliable Software* pp 234–244 (1975)
21 **Clarke, L A** 'A system to generate test data and symbolically execute programs' (IEEE) *Trans. Software Eng.* Vol 2 No 3 (1976) pp 215–222
22 **King, J C** Symbolic execution and program testing, *Commun. ACM* Vol 19 No 7 (1976) pp 385–394
23 **Ramamoothy, C V, Ho, S F and Chen, W J** 'On the automated generation of program test data' (IEEE) *Trans. Software Eng.* Vol 2 No 4 (1976) pp 293–300
24 **Richardson, D J and Clarke L A** 'A partition analysis method to increase program reliability' *Proc. Fifth Int. Conf. Software Eng.* pp 244–253 (1981)
25 **Floyd, R W** 'Assigning meaning to programs' *Proc. of the Symposia in Applied Mathematics* Vol 19 pp 19–32 (1967)
26 **Hantler, S L and King, J C** 'An introduction to proving the correctness of programs' *Computing Surveys* Vol 18 No 3 (1976) pp 331–353
27 **Demillo, R A, Lipton, R J and Perlis, A J** 'Social processes and proofs of theorems and programs' *Commun. ACM* Vol 22 No 5 (1979) pp 271–280
28 **Elpas, B, Levitt, K N, Waldinger, R J and Wakemann, A** 'An assessment of techniques for proving program correctness' *Computing Surveys* Vol 4 No 2 (1972) pp 97–147
29 **Osterweil, L J and Fosdick, L D** 'Some experience with DAVE- a FORTRAN program analyser' *Proc. AFIPS Conf.* pp 909–915 (1976)
30 **Ramamoorthy, C V and Ho, S F** 'FORTRAN automatic code evaluation system' *Rep. M-466* Electron. Resl Lab, University California, Berkeley, CA, USA (August 1974)
31 **Osterweil, L J** 'TOOLPACK – An experimental software development environment research project (IEEE) *Trans. Software Eng.* Vol 9 No 6 (1983) pp 673–685
32 **Fosdik, L D and Osterwell, L J** 'Data flow analysis in software reliability' *Computing Surveys* Vol 8 No 3 (1976) pp 305–330
33 **Duran, J W and Ntafos, S C** 'A report on random testing' *Proc. Fifth Int. Conf. Software Eng.* pp 179–183 (1981)
34 **Duran, J W and Ntafos, S C** 'An evaluation of random testing' (IEEE) *Trans. Software Eng.* Vol 10 No 4 (1984) pp 438–444
35 **Ince, D C and Hekmatpour, S** 'An evaluation of some black-box testing methods' *Technical report No 84/7* Computer Discipline, Faculty of Mathematics, Open University, Milton Keynes,UK (1984)
36 **Cooper, D W** 'Adaptive testing' *Proc. Second Int. Conf. Software Eng.* pp 223–226 (1976)
37 **Andrews, D and Benson, J P** 'An automated program testing methodology and its implementation' *Proc. Fifth Int. Conf. Software Eng.* pp 254–261 (1981)
38 **Myers, G J** *The Art of Software Testing* John Wiley (1979)
39 **Clarke, L A and Richardson, D J** 'The application of error-sensitive testing strategies to debugging' *ACM SIGplan Notices* Vol 18 No 8 (1983) pp 45–52
40 **White, L J and Cohen, E I** 'A domain strategy for computer program testing' (IEEE) *Trans. Software Eng.* Vol 6 No 3 (1980) pp 247–257

41 **Ince, D C** The automatic generation of test data, *The Comput. J.* Vol 30 No 1 (1987) pp 63–69

42 **Bazzichi, F and Spadafora, I** 'An automatic generator for compiler testing' (IEEE) *Trans. Software Eng.* Vol 8 No 4 (1982) pp 343–353

43 **Payne, A J** 'A formalized technique for expressing compiler exercisers', *SIGplan Notices* Vol 13 No 1 (1978) pp 59–69

44 **Hedley, D** *Automatic test data generation and related topics* PhD Thesis, Liverpool University (1981)

45 **Bicevskis, J, Borzovs, J, Straujums, U, Zarins, A and Miller, E F** 'SMOTL – a system to construct samples for data processing program debugging' (IEEE) *Trans. Software Eng.* Vol 5 No 1 (1979) pp 60–66

46 **Budd, T A and Lipton, R J** 'Mutation analysis of decision table programs' *Proc. Conf. Information Science and Systems* pp 346–349 (1978)

47 **Budd, T A, Demillo, R A, Lipton, R J and Sayward, F G** 'Theoretical and empirical studies on using program mutation to test the functional correctness of programs' *Proc. ACM Symp. Principles of Prog. Lang.* pp 220–222 (1980)

48 **Coward, P D** 'Symbolic execution systems – a review' *The Software Eng. J.* (To appear)

49 **Howden, W** 'An evaluation of the effectiveness of symbolic testing' *Software Pract. Exper.* Vol 8 (1978) pp 381–397 □

# Chapter 8

# Software Maintenance

## 1. Introduction to Chapter

### 1.1 Overview of Software Maintenance

Conventional wisdom says that software maintenance represents from 40 to 70 percent of the total cost of a software system. The major reason that so much money is spent on software maintenance is that maintenance is a term often used to describe many things that are not really "maintenance" but might be categorized as software development, for example, correcting a delivered software system that was not specified, designed, programmed, or tested correctly in the first place. It is not unheard of for developers to say during testing, "...let's fix this problem during the maintenance phase, after the system is delivered." Often, developers and customers agree that enhancements or changes that are identified during development will not be implemented until the maintenance phase, so as not to delay delivery of the originally specified capabilities.

### 1.2 Categories of Software Maintenance

The term *maintenance* may be used to refer to enhancements made to improve software performance, maintainability, or understandability, as well as to fix mistakes.

Software maintenance includes changes that result from new or changing requirements. Maintenance may involve activities designed to make the system easier to understand and to work with, such as restructuring or redocumenting the software system. Optimization of code to make it run faster or use storage more efficiently might be included. These types of maintenance are called *perfective maintenance* and account for some 60 to 70 percent of the overall maintenance effort.

Other modifications are made to a system to satisfy or accommodate changes in the processing environment. These are required changes and are not normally under the control of the software maintainer. These changes may include changes to rules, laws, and regu-

SOFTWARE MAINTEN

lations that affect the system, as well as changes to enable the software to run on new hardware. This type of maintenance is called *adaptive maintenance.*

And, lastly, error correction that is required to keep the system operational is called *corrective maintenance*. Corrective maintenance is usually a reactive process to failures in the software system.

## 2. Introduction to Paper

This chapter consists of only one paper. Prof. Keith Bennett, a leading authority on software maintenance in the UK, wrote the paper specifically for this Tutorial. Prof. Bennett defines and describes the maintenance process and points out that as software development has matured more funds are now spent on the maintenance of many software systems than was spent on their development.

Maintenance terminology is defined. To the conventionally defined types of maintenance (perfective, adaptive, and corrective), Bennett has added a new category, preventive maintenance.

Professor Bennett describes software maintenance from the points of view of:

- Management and the organization
- Process models
- Technical issues

The paper discusses why software maintenance is such a major problem. Management may or may not look favorably on software maintenance activities. In one regard, maintenance can be looked at as a drain on resources; on the opposite side, maintenance is required to keep a product competitive. Therefore, software maintenance activities need to be justified in terms of "return on investment."

The author looks at the IEEE Standard for Software Maintenance [1] as one of the best maintenance processes. He describes the activities of software maintenance and the quality control over each activity.

Prof. Bennett points out that the technology required for software maintenance is similar to that needed for new development. He discusses the need for configuration management, traceability, impact analysis, metrics, and CASE tools.

Next Bennett discusses legacy systems, typically large, old, much-modified software systems that are expensive and difficult to maintain but would also be very expensive to replace with new systems. He discusses options other than continued maintenance or replacement, including re-engineering and reverse engineering. Finally research topics in software maintenance are discussed, and the vehicles for maintenance technology (conferences, journals, organizations, and research programs) are presented.

1. IEEE Std 1912-1992, *Standard for Software Maintenance*, The Institute of Electrical and Electronics Engineers, Inc., Piscataway, NJ, 1993.

# Software Maintenance: A Tutorial

Keith H. Bennett
*Computer Science Department*
*University of Durham*
*Durham, UK*
*tel: +44 91 374 4596*
*fax: +44 91 374 2560*
Email: keith.bennett@durham.ac.uk

## 1. Objectives for the Reader

The objectives of this tutorial are:

- to explain what is meant by software maintenance.
- to show how software maintenance fits into other software engineering activities
- to explain the relationship between software maintenance and the organization
- to explain the best practice in software maintenance in terms of a process model
- to describe important maintenance technology such as impact analysis
- to explain what is meant by a legacy system and describe how reverse engineering and other techniques may be used to support legacy systems.

## 2. Overview of Tutorial

This tutorial starts with a short introduction to the field of software engineering, thereby providing the context for the constituent field of software maintenance. It focuses on solutions, not problems, but an appreciation of the problems in software maintenance is important. The solutions are categorized in a three layer model: organizational issues; process issues; and technical issues.

Our presentation of organizational solutions to maintenance concentrates on software as an asset whose value needs to be sustained.

We explain the process of software maintenance by describing the IEEE standard for the maintenance process. Although this is only a draft standard at present, it provides a very sensible approach which is applicable to many organizations.

Technical issues are explained by concentrating on techniques of particular importance to maintenance. For example, configuration management and version control are as important for initial development as for maintenance, so these are not addressed. In contrast, coping with the ripple (domino) effect is only found during maintenance, and it is one of the crucial technical problems to be solved. We describe solutions to this.

By this stage the tutorial will have presented the typical iterative maintenance process that is used, at various levels of sophistication, in many organizations. However, the software may become so difficult and expensive to maintain that special, often drastic action is needed. The software is then called a "legacy system," and the particular problems of and solutions to coping with legacy code are described.

The tutorial is completed by considering some fruitful research directions for the field.

## 3. The Software Engineering Field

Software maintenance is concerned with modifying software once it is delivered to a customer. By that definition it forms a sub-area of the wider field of Software Engineering [IEEE91], which is defined as:

> the application of the systematic, disciplined, quantifiable approach to the development, operation and maintenance of software; that is the application of engineering to software.

It is helpful to understand trends and objectives of the wider field in order to explain the detailed problems and solutions concerned with maintenance. McDermid's definition in the Software Engineer's Reference book embodies the spirit of the engineering approach. He states that [MCDER 91]:

> software engineering is; the science and art of specifying, designing, implementing and evolving—with economy, time limits and elegance—programs, documentation and operat-

ing procedures whereby computers can be made useful to man.

Software Engineering is still a very young discipline and the term itself was only invented in 1968. Modern computing is only some 45 years old; yet within that time we have gained the ability to solve very difficult and large problems. Often these huge projects consume thousands of person-years or more of design. The rapid increase in the size of the systems which we tackle, from 100 line programs 45 years ago to multi-million line systems now, presents many problems of dealing with *scale*, so it is not surprising that evolving such systems to meet continually changing user needs is difficult.

Much progress has been made over the past decade in improving our ability to construct high quality software which does meet users' needs. Is it feasible to extrapolate these trends? Baber (BABE 91) has identified three possible futures for software engineering:

(a) Failures of software systems are common, due to limited technical competence and developers. This is largely an extrapolation of the present situation.

(b) The use of computer systems is limited to those application in which there is a minimal risk to the public. There is wide spread scepticism about the safety of software based systems. There may be legislation covering the use of software in safety critical and safety related systems.

(c) The professional competence and qualifications of software designers are developed to such a high level that even very challenging demands can be met reliably and safely. In this vision of the future, software systems would be delivered on time, fully meet their requirements, and be applicable in safety critical systems.

In case (a), software development is seen primarily as a craft activity. Option (b) is unrealistic; software is too important to be restricted in this way. Hence there is considerable interest within the software engineering field in addressing the issues raised by (c). In this tutorial, we feel (c) defines the goal of software maintenance and addresses *evolving* systems.

A root problem for many software systems, which also causes some of the most difficult problems for software maintenance, is complexity. Sometimes this arises because a system is migrated from hardware to software in order to gain the additional functionality found in software. Complexity should be a result of implementing an inherently complex application (for example in a tax calculation package, which is deterministic but non-linear; or automation of the UK Immigration Act, which is complex and ambiguous). The main tools to control complexity are modular design and building systems as separated layers of abstraction that separate concerns. Nevertheless, the combination of scale and application complexity mean that it is infeasible for one person alone to understand the complete software system.

## 4. Software Maintenance

Once software has been initially produced, it then passes into the *maintenance* phase. The IEEE definition of software maintenance is as follows [IEEE91]:

> software maintenance is the process of modifying the software system or component after delivery to correct faults, improve performance or other attributes, or adapt to a change in environment.

Some organizations use the term software maintenance to refer only to the implementation of very small changes (for example, less than one day), and the term software development to refer to all other modifications and enhancements. However, to avoid confusion, we shall continue to use the IEEE standard definition.

Software maintenance, although part of software engineering, is by itself of major economic importance. A number of surveys over the last 15 years have shown that for most software, software maintenance occupies anything between 40 and 90 percent of total life cycle costs. (see [FOST93] for a review of such surveys) A number of surveys have also tried to compute the total software maintenance costs in the UK and in the US. While these figures need to be treated with a certain amount of caution, it seems clear that a huge amount of money is being spent on software maintenance.

The inability to undertake maintenance quickly, safely, and cheaply means that for many organizations, a substantial *applications backlog* occurs. The Management Information Services Department is unable to make changes at the rate required by marketing or business needs. End-users become frustrated and often adopt PC solutions in order to short circuit the problems. They may then find that a process of rapid prototyping and end-user computing provides them (at least in the short term) with quicker and easier solutions than those supplied by the Management Information Systems Department.

In the early decades of computing, software maintenance comprised a relatively small part of the software life cycle; the major activity was writing new programs for new applications. In the late 1960s and 1970s, management began to realize that old software does not simply die, and at that point the software maintenance started to be recognized as a significant activity. An anecdote about the early days of electronic data processing in banks illustrates this point. In the 1950s, a large US bank was about to take the major step of employing its very first full-time programmer. Management raised the issue of what would happen to this person once the programs had been written. The same bank now has several buildings full of data processing staff.

In the 1980s, it was becoming evident that old architectures were severely constraining new design. In another example from the US banking system, existing banks had difficulty modifying their software in order to introduce automatic teller machines. In contrast, new banks writing software from scratch found this relatively easy. It has also been reported in the UK that at least two mergers of financial organizations were unable to go ahead due to the problems of integrating software from two different organizations.

In the 1990s, a large part of the business needs of many organization has now been implemented so that business change is represented by evolutionary change to the software, not revolutionary change, and that most so-called development is actually enhancement and evolution.

## 5. Types of Software Maintenance

Leintz and Swanson [LEIN78][LEIN80] undertook a survey which categorized maintenance into four different categories.

(1) *Perfective maintenance*; changes required as a result of user requests (also known as *evolutive* maintenance)

(2) *Adaptive maintenance*; changes needed as a consequence of operated system, hardware, or DBMS changes

(3) *Corrective maintenance*; the identification and removal of faults in the software

(4) *Preventative maintenance*; changes made to software to make it more maintainable

The above categorization is very useful in helping management to understand some of the basic costs of maintenance. However, it will be seen from Section 9 that the processes for the four types are very similar, and there is little advantage in distinguishing them when designing best practice maintenance processes.

It seems clear from a number of surveys that the majority of software maintenance is concerned with evolution deriving from user requested changes.

The important requirement of software maintenance for the client is that changes are accomplished quickly and cost effectively. The reliability of the software should at worst not be degraded by the changes. Additionally, the maintainability of the system should not degrade, otherwise future changes will be progressively more expensive to carry out. This phenomenon was recognized by Lehman, and expressed in terms of his well known laws of evolution [LEHE80][LEHE84]. The first law of continuing change states that *a program that is used in a real world environment necessarily must change or become progressively less useful in that environment.*

This argues that software evolution is not an undesirable attribute and essentially it is only useful software that evolves. Lehman's second law of increasing complexity states that *as an evolving program changes, its structure tends to become more complex. Extra resources must be devoted to preserving the semantics and simplifying the structure.* This law argues that things will become much worse unless we do something about it. The problem for most software is that nothing has been done about it, so changes are increasingly more expensive and difficult. Ultimately, maintenance may become too expensive and almost infeasible: the software then becomes known as a *legacy system* (see section 11). Nevertheless, it may be of essential importance to the organization.

## 6. Problems of Software Maintenance

Many technical and managerial problems occur when changing software quickly, reliably, and cheaply. For example, user changes are often described in terms of the *behavior* of the software system and must be interpreted as changes to the source code. When a change is made to the code, there may be substantial consequential changes, not only in the code itself, but within documentation, design, and test suites, (this is termed the *domino*, or *ripple effect*). Many systems under maintenance are very large, and solutions which work for laboratory scale pilots will not scale up to industrial sized software. Indeed it may be said that any program which is small enough to fit into a textbook or to be understood by one person does not have maintenance problems.

There is much in common between best practice in software engineering in general, and software maintenance in particular. Software maintenance problems essentially fall into three categories:

(a) *Alignment with organizational objectives.* Initial software development is usually project based with a defined timescale, and budget. The main emphasis is to deliver on time and within budget to meet user needs. In contrast, software maintenance often has the objective of extending the life of a software system for as long as possible. In addition, it may be driven by the need to meet user demand for software updates and enhancements. In both cases, return on investment is much less clear, so that the view at senior management level is often of a major activity consuming large resources with no clear quantifiable benefit for the organization.

(b) *Process issues.* At the process level, there are many activities in common with software development. For example, configuration management is a crucial activity in both. However, software maintenance requires a number of additional activities not found in initial development. Initial requests for changes are usually made to a "help desk" (often part of a larger end-user support unit), which must assess the change (as many change requests derive from misunderstanding of documentation) and, if it is viable, then pass it to a technical group who can assess the cost of making the change. Impact analysis on both the software and the organization, and the associated need for system comprehension, are crucial issues. Further down the life cycle, it is important to be able to perform regression tests on the software so that the new changes do not introduce errors into the parts of the software that were not altered.

(c) *Technical issues.* There are a number of technical challenges to software maintenance. As noted above, the ability to construct software that it is easy to comprehend is a major issue [ROBS91]. A number of studies have shown that the majority of time spent in maintaining software is actually consumed in this activity. Similarly, testing in a cost effective way provides major challenges. Despite the emergence of methods based on discrete mathematics (for example, to prove that an implementation meets its specification), most current software is tested rather than verified, and the cost of repeating a full test suite on a major piece of software can be very large in terms of money and time. It will be better to select a sub-set of tests that only stressed those parts of the system that had been changed, together with the regression tests. The technology to do this is still not available, despite much useful progress. As an example, it is useful to consider a major billing package for an industrial organization. The change of the taxation rate in such a system should be a simple matter; after all, generations of students are taught to place such constants at the head of the program so only a one line edit is needed. However, for a major multi-national company dealing with taxation rates in several countries with complex and different rules for tax calculations (that is, complex business rules), the change of the taxation rate may involve a huge expense.

Other problems are related to the lower status of software maintenance compared with software development. In the manufacture of a consumer durable, the majority of the cost lies in production, and it is well understood that design faults can be hugely expensive. In contrast, the construction of software is automatic, and development represents almost all the initial cost. Hence in conditions of financial stringency, it is tempting to cut costs by cutting back design. This can have a very serious effect on the costs of subsequent maintenance.

One of the problems for management is assessing a software product to determine how easy it is to change. This leaves little incentive for initial development projects to construct software that is easy to evolve. Indeed, lucrative maintenance contracts may follow a software system where shortcuts have been taken during its development [WALT94].

We have so far stressed the *problems* of software maintenance in order to differentiate it from software engineering in general. However, much is known about best practice in software maintenance, and there are excellent case studies, such as the US Space Shuttle on-board flight control software system, which demonstrate that software can be evolved carefully and with improving reliability. The remainder of this paper is focused on solutions rather than problems. The great majority of software in use today is neither geriatric nor state of the art, and the tutorial addresses this type of software. It describes a top-down approach to successful maintenance, addressing:

(a) Software Maintenance and the organization
(b) Process models
(c) Technical Issues

In particular, we shall focus on the new proposed IEEE standard for software maintenance process, which illustrates the improving maturity of the field.

## 7. Organizational Aspects of Maintenance

In 1987, Colter (COLT87) stated that the major problem of software maintenance was not technical, but managerial. Software maintenance organizations were failing to relate their work to the needs of the business, and therefore it should not be a surprise that the field suffered from low investment and poor status, compared to initial development which was seen as a revenue and profit generator.

Initial software development is product-oriented; the aim is to deliver an artifact within budget and timescale. In contrast, software maintenance is much closer to a *service*. In many Japanese organizations, for example, (BENN94), software maintenance is seen at senior management level primarily as a means of ensuring continued satisfaction with the software; it is closely related to quality. The customer expects the software to continue to evolve to meet his or her changing needs, and the vendor must respond quickly and effectively or lose business. In Japan, it is also possible in certain circumstances to include software as an asset on the balance sheet. These combine to ensure that software maintenance has a high profile with senior management in Japan.

Like any other activity, software maintenance requires financial investment. We have already seen that within senior management, maintenance may be regarded simply as a drain on resources, or distant to core activities, and it becomes a prime candidate for funding reduction and even elimination. Software maintenance thus needs to be expressed in terms of return on investment. In many organizations undertaking maintenance for other internal divisions, the service is rarely charged out as a revenue-generating activity from a profit center. In the UK defense sector, there has been a major change in practice in charging for maintenance. Until recently, work would be charged to Government on the time taken to do the work plus a profit margin. Currently, competitive tendering (procurement) is used for specific work packages.

Recently there has been a trend for software maintenance to be *outsourced*; in other words, a company will contract out its software maintenance to another which specializes in this field. Companies in India and China are becoming increasingly competitive in this market. This is sometimes done for peripheral software, as the company is unwilling to release the software used in its core business. An outsourcing company will typically spend a number of months assessing the software before it will accept a contract. Increasingly, *service level agreements* between the maintenance organization (whether internal or external) and the customer are being used as a contractual mechanism for defining the maintenance service that will be provided. The UK Central Computer and Telecommunications Agency has produced a series of guidelines on good practice in this area, in the form of the Information Technology Infrastructure Library (ITIL93).

When new software is passed over to the customer, payment for subsequent maintenance must be determined. At this stage, primary concerns are typically:

- repair of errors on delivery
- changes to reflect an ambiguous specification

Increasingly, the former is being met by some form of warranty to bring software in line with other goods (although much commodity software is still ringed with disclaimers). Hence, the vendor pays. The latter is much more difficult to resolve and addresses much more than the functional specification. For example, if the software is not delivered in a highly maintainable form, there will be major cost implications for the purchaser.

Recently, Foster [FOST93] proposed an interesting investment cost model which regards software as a corporate asset which can justify financial support and sustain its value. Foster uses his model to determine the optimum release strategy for a major software system. This is hence a business model, allowing an organization the ability to calculate return on investment in software by methods comparable with investment in other kinds of assets. Foster remarks that many papers on software maintenance recognize that it is a little understood area, but it consumes vast amounts of money. With such large expenditure, even small technical advances must be worth many times that cost. The software maintenance manager, however, has to justify investment into an area which does not directly generate income. Foster's approach allows a manager to derive a model for assessing the financial implications of the proposed change of activity, thereby providing the means to calculate both cost and benefit. By expressing the result in terms of return on investment, the change can be ranked against competing demands for funding.

Some work has been undertaken in applying predictive cost modeling to software maintenance, based on the COCOMO techniques. The results of such work remain to be seen.

The AMES project [HATH94, BOLD94, BOLD95] is addressing the development of methods and tools to aid application management, where application management is defined as:

> the contracted responsibility for the management and execution of all activities related to the maintenance of existing applications.

Its focus is on the formalization of many of the issues raised in this section, and in particular, customer-supplier relations. It is developing a maturity model to support the assessment in a quantitative and systematic way of this relationship.

## 8. Process Models

Process management [IEEE91] is defined as:

> the direction, control and coordination of work performed to develop a product or perform a service.

This definition therefore encompasses software maintenance and includes quality, line management, technical, and executive processes. A mature engineering discipline is characterized by mature well-understood processes, so it is understandable that modeling software maintenance, and integrating it with software development, is an area of active concern [MCDER91]. A software process model may be defined [DOWS85] as:

> a purely descriptive representation of the software process, representing the attributes of a range of particular software processes and being sufficiently specific to allow reasoning about them.

The foundation of good practice is a mature process, and the Software Engineering Institute at Carnegie-Mellon University has pioneered the development of a scale by which process maturity may be measured. A questionnaire approach is used to assess the maturity of an organization and also provides a metric for process improvement. More recently, the BOOTSTRAP project has provided an alternative maturity model from a European perspective.

A recent IEEE draft standard for software maintenance [IEEE94] promotes the establishment of better understood processes and is described in the next section. It reflects the difference between maintenance and initial development processes, and, although it is only a draft, it represents many of the elements of good practice in software maintenance. The model is based on an iterative approach of accepting a stream of change requests (and error reports), implementing the changes, and, after testing, forming new software releases. This model is widely used in industry, in small to medium-sized projects, and for in-house support. It comprises four key stages:

- **Help desk**: the problem is received, a preliminary analysis undertaken, and if the problem is sensible, it is accepted.
- **Analysis**: a managerial and technical analysis of the problem is undertaken to investigate and cost alternative solutions.
- **Implementation**: the chosen solution is implemented and tested.
- **Release:** the change (along with others) is released to the customer.

Most best practice models (for instance, that of Hinley [HINL92]) incorporate this approach, though it is often refined into much more detailed stages (as in the IEEE model described in the next section). Wider aspects of the software maintenance process, in the form of applications management, are addressed in [HATH94].

## 9. IEEE Standard for Software Maintenance

### 9.1 Overview of the standard

This new proposed standard describes the process for managing and executing software maintenance activities. Almost all the standard is relevant for software maintenance. The focus of the standard is in a seven stage activity model of software maintenance, which incorporates the following *stages*:

Problem Identification
Analysis
Design
Implementation
System Test
Acceptance Test
Delivery

Each of the seven activities has five associated attributes; these are:

Input life cycle products
Output life cycle products
Activity definition
Control
Metrics

A number of these, particularly in the early stages of the maintenance process, are already addressed by existing IEEE standards.

As an example, we consider the second activity in the process model, the *analysis phase*. This phase accepts as its input a validated problem report, together with any initial resource estimates and other repository information, plus project and system documentation if available. The process is seen as having two substantial components. First of all, feasibility analysis is undertaken which assesses the impact of the modification, investigates alternative solutions, assesses short and long term costs, and computes the benefit value of making the change. Once a particular approach has been selected, then the second stage of detailed analysis is undertaken. This determines firm requirements of the modification, identifies the software involved, and requires a test strategy and an implementation plan to be produced.

In practice, this is one of the most difficult stages of software maintenance. The change may effect many aspects of the software, including not only documentation, test suites, and so on, but also the environment and even the hardware. The standard insists that all affected components shall be identified and brought in to the scope of the change.

The standard also requires that at this stage a test strategy is derived comprising at least three levels of test, including unit testing, integration testing, and user-orientated functional acceptance tests. It is also required to supply regression test requirements associated with each of these levels of test.

### 9.2 Structure of the standard

The standard also establishes quality control for each of the seven phases. For example, for the analysis phase, the following controls are required as a minimum:

1. Retrieve the current version of project and systems documentation from the configuration control function of the organization
2. Review the proposed changes and an engineering analysis to assess the technical and economic feasibility and to assess correctness
3. Consider the integration of the proposed change within the existing software
4. Verify that all appropriate analysis and project documentation is updated and properly controlled
5. Verify that the testing organization is providing a strategy for testing the changes and that the change schedule can support the proposed test strategy
6. Review the resource estimates and schedules and verification of their accuracy
7. Undertake a technical review to select the problem reports and proposed enhancements to be implemented and released. The list of changes shall be documented

Finally, at the end of the analysis phase, a risk analysis is required to be performed. Any initial resource estimate will be revised, and a decision that includes the customer is made on whether to proceed onto the next phase.

The phase deliverables are also specified, again as a minimum as follows:

1. Feasibility report for problem reports
2. Detailed analysis report
3. Updated requirements
4. Preliminary modification list
5. Development, integration and acceptance test strategy
6. Implementation plan

The contents of the analysis report is further specified in greater detail by the proposed standard.

The proposed standard suggests the following metrics are taken during the analysis phase:

Requirement changes
Documentation area rates
Effort per function area
Elapsed time
Error rates generated, by priority and type.

The proposed standard also includes appendices which provide guidelines on maintenance practice. These are not part of the standard itself, but are included as useful information. For example, in terms of our analysis stage, the appendix provides a short commentary on the provision of change on impact analysis. A further appendix addresses supporting maintenance technology, particularly re-engineering and reverse engineering. A brief description of these processes is also given.

### 9.3 Assessment of the Proposed Standard

The standard represents a welcome step forward in establishing a process standard for software maintenance. A strength of the approach is that it is based on existing IEEE standards from other areas in software engineering. It accommodates practical necessities, such as the need to undertake emergency repairs.

On the other hand, it is clearly oriented towards classic concepts of software development and maintenance. It does not cover issues such as rapid application development and end-user computing, nor does it address executive level issues in the process model nor establish boundaries for the scope of the model.

The process model corresponds approximately to level two in the SEI five level model. The SEI model is forming the basis of the SPICE process assessment standards initiative.

Organizations may well be interested in increasing the maturity of their software engineering processes. Neither the proposed IEEE standard nor the SEI model give direct help in process improvement. Further details of this may be found in [HINL92]. Additionally, there is still little evidence in practice that improving software process maturity actually benefits organizations, and the whole edifice is based on the assumption that the success of the product is determined by the process. That this is not necessarily true is demonstrated by the success of certain commodity software.

It is useful to note that the International Standards Organization [ISO90] have published a draft standard for a process model to assess the quality (including maintainability) of software. Many technical problems in measurement remain unsolved, however.

## 10. Technical Aspects of Software Maintenance

### 10.1 Technical issues

Much of the technology required for software maintenance is similar to that needed for initial development, but with minor changes. For example, configuration management and version control are indispensable for both. Information relating to development and maintenance will be kept in a repository. For maintenance, the repository will be used to hold frequently occurring queries handled by the help desk. Metrics data for product and process will be similar. CASE tools, supporting graphical representation of software, are widely used in development and maintenance. These topics are described in other Chapters, and here we concentrate on issues of specific importance to maintenance.

In our description of the IEEE standard process model we identified the need for impact analysis. This is a characteristic of software maintenance that is not needed in initial software development. We shall present further details of this technique as an example of the technology needed to support software maintenance.

In the above process model, it was necessary to determine the cost of making a change to meet a software change request. In this section we examine how impact analysis can help this activity. To amplify the analysis needed, the user-expressed problem must first of all be translated into software terms to allow the maintenance team to decide if the problem is viable for further work or if it should be rejected. It then must be localized; this step determines the origin of the anomaly by identifying the primary components to the system which must be altered to meet the new requirement.

Next, the above step may suggest several solutions, all of which are viable. Each of these must be investigated, primarily using impact analysis. The aim is to determine all changes which are consequence to the primary change. It must be applied to all software components, not just code. At the end of impact analysis, we are in the position to make a decision on the best implementation route or to make no change. Weiss [WEIS 89] has shown, for three NASA projects, the primary source of maintenance changes deriving from user problem reports:

| | |
|---|---|
| Requirements Phase | 19 percent |
| Design Phase | 52 percent |
| Coding Phase | 7 percent |

He noted that 34 percent of changes affected only one component and 26 percent affected two components.

### 10.2 The Problem

One of the major difficulties of software maintenance which encourages maintainers to be cautious is that a change made at one place in the system may have a ripple effect elsewhere, so consequence changes must be made. In order to carry out a consistent change, maintainers must investigate all such ripple effects, such as the impact of the change assessed and changes possibly made in all affected contexts. Yau [YAU87] defines this as:

> ripple effect propagation is a phenomenon by which changes made to a software component along the software life cycle (specification, design, code, or test phase) have a tendency to be felt in other components.

As a very simple example, a maintainer may wish to remove a redundant variable X. It is obviously necessary to also remove all applied occurrences of X, but for most high level languages the compiler can detect and report undeclared variables. This is hence a very simple example of an impact which can be determined by *static analysis*. In many cases, ripple effects cannot determine statically, and dynamic analysis must be used. For example, an assignment to an element of an array, followed by the use of a subscripted variable, may or may not represent a ripple effect depending on the particular elements accessed. In large programs containing pointers aliases, for instance, the problem is much harder. We shall define the problem of impact analysis [WILD93] as:

> the task for assessing the effects for making the set of changes to a software system.

The starting point for impact analysis is an explicit set of primary software objects which the maintainer intends to modify. He or she has determined the set by relating the change request to objects such as variables, assignments, goals, an so on. The purpose of impact analysis is ensuring that the change has been correctly and consistently bounded. The impact analysis stage identifies a set of further objects impacted by changes in the primary sector. This process is repeated until no further candidate objects can be identified.

### 10.3 Traceability

In general, we require traceability of information between various software artifacts in order to assess impact in software components. Traceability is defined [IEEE91] as:

> Traceability is a degree to which a relationship can be established between two or more products of the development process, especially products having a predecessor successor or master subordinate relationship to one another.

Informally, traceability provides us with semantic links which we can then use to perform impact analysis. The links may relate similar components such as design documents or they may link between different types such as a specification to code.

Some types of traceability links are very hard to determine. For example, even a minor alteration of the source code may have performance implications which causes a real time system to fail to meet a specification. It is not surprising that the majority of work in impact analysis has been undertaken at the code level, as this is the most tractable. Wilde [WILD89] provides a good review of code level impact analysis techniques.

Many modern programming languages are based on using static analysis to detect or stop ripple effect. The use of modules with opaque types, for example, can prevent at compile time several unpleasant types of ripple effect. Many existing software systems are unfortunately written in older languages, using programming styles (such as global aliased variables) which make the potential for ripple effects much greater, and their detection much harder.

More recently, Munro and Turver [TURV94] have described an approach which has placed impact analysis within the overall software maintenance process. The major advance is that documentation is included within the objects analyzed; documentation is modeled using a ripple propagation graph and it is this representation that is used for analysis. The approach has the advantage that it may be set in the early stages of analysis to assess costs without reference to the source code.

Work has also been undertaken recently to establish traceability links between HOOD design documents [FILL94] in order to support impact analysis of the design level.

In a major research project at Durham, formal semantic preserving transformations are being used to derive executable code from formal specifications and in reverse engineering to derive specifications from existing code. The ultimate objective is to undertake maintenance at the specification level rather than the code level, and generate executable code automatically or semi-automatically. The transformation technique supports the derivation of the formal traceability link between the two representations, and research is underway to explore this as a means of enhancing ripple effect across wider sections of the life cycle (see WARD93,WARD94,WARD94a, YOUN94, BENN95, BENN95b for more details).

## 11. Legacy Systems

### 11.1 Legacy problems

There is no standard definition of a legacy system; but many in industry will recognize the problem. A legacy system is typically very old, and has been heavily modified over the years to meet continually evolving needs. It is also very large, so that a team is needed to support it; although none of the original members of the software development team may still be around. It will be based on old technology, and be written in out-of-date languages such as Assembler. Documentation will not be available and testing new releases is a major difficulty. Often the system is supporting very large quantities of live data.

Such systems are surely a candidate for immediate replacement. The problem is that the software is often at the core of the business and replacing it would be a huge expense. While less than ideal, the software works and continues to do useful things.

An example of a legacy system is the billing software for a telecommunications company. The software was developed many years ago when the company was owned by the Government, and the basic service sold was restricted to a telephone connection to each premises. The system is the main mechanism for generating revenue and it supports a huge on-line database of paying customers.

Over the years the software has been maintained to reflect the changing telecommunications business: from government to private ownership; from simple call charging to wide ranging and complex (and competitive) services; from single country to international organizations with highly complex VAT (value added tax) systems. The system now comprises several million lines of source code.

While the process of maintenance to meet continually evolving customer needs is becoming better understood, and more closely linked with software engineering in general, dealing with legacy software is still very hard. It has been estimated that there are 70 billion lines of COBOL in existence that are still doing useful work. Much of the useful software being written today will end up as legacy software in 20 years time. Software which is 40 years old is being used in mission critical applications.

It is easy to argue that the industry should never have ended up in the position of relying on such software. It is unclear whether steps are being taken to avoid the problem for modern software. There seems to be a hope that technology such as object-oriented design will solve the problems for future generations, though there is as yet little positive evidence.

In this section, we shall analyze why it might be useful not just to discard the legacy system and start again. In the subsequent section, we shall present solutions to dealing with legacy systems.

### 11.2 Analysis of legacy systems

In some cases, discarding the software and starting again may be the courageous, although expensive, solution following analysis of the business need and direction and the state of the software. Often the starting point is taking an inventory of the software, as this may be unknown. As a result of analysis, the following solutions for the legacy system may be considered:

- carry on as now, possibly subcontracting the maintenance.
- replace software with a package.
- re-implement from scratch.
- discard software and discontinue.
- freeze maintenance and phase in new system.
- encapsulate the old system and call as a server to the new.
- reverse engineer the legacy system and develop a new software suite.

In the literature, case studies addressing these types of approaches are becoming available. The interest of this tutorial is focused on reverse engineering, as it appears to be the most fruitful approach. Increasing interest is being shown in encapsulation as a way of drawing a boundary round the legacy system. The new system is then evolved so that it progressively takes over functionality from the old, until the latter becomes redundant. Currently, few successful studies have been published, but it is consistent with the move to distributed open systems based on client-server architectures.

### 11.3 Reverse Engineering

Chikofsky and Cross [CHIK90] have defined several terms in this field which are now generally accepted. Reverse engineering is:

> the process of analyzing a subject system to identify the system's components and their inter-relationships, and to create representations of the system in another form or at higher levels of abstraction.

It can be seen that reverse engineering is *passive*; it does not change the system, or result in a new one, though it may add new representations to it. For example, a simple reverse engineering tool may produce call graphs and control flow graphs from source code. These are both higher level abstractions, though in neither case is the original source code changed. Two important types of reverse engineering are redocumentation, which is:

> the creation or revision of a semantically equivalent representation within the same relative abstraction layer;

and design recovery, which:

> involves identifying meaningful higher level abstractions beyond those obtained directly by examining the system itself.

The main motivation is to provide help in program comprehension; most maintainers have little choice but to work with source codes in the absence of any documentation. Concepts such as procedure structures and control flow are important mechanisms by which the maintainer understands the system, so tools have been constructed to provide representations to help the process.

If good documentation existed (including architectural, design, and test suite documentation) reverse engineering would be unnecessary. However, the types of documentation needed for maintenance are probably different than those produced during typical initial development. As an example, most large systems are too big for one person to maintain; yet the maintainer rarely needs to see a functional decomposition or object structure; he or she is trying to correlate external behavior within internal descriptions. In these circumstances, *slicing* offers help: slicing is a static analysis technique in which only those source code statements which can affect a nominated variable are displayed.

Pragmatically, many maintainers cover lineprinter listings with notes and stick-on pieces of paper. In an attempt to simulate this, Foster and Munro [FOST87] and Younger [YOUN93] have built tools to implement a hypertext form of documentation which is managed incrementally by the maintainer who is able to attach "notes" to the source code. An advantage of this approach is that it does not attempt to redocument the whole system; documentation is provided by the maintainer, in the form preferred, only for the "hot-spots." Those parts of the code which are stable, and are never studied by the maintainer (often large parts), do not have to be redocumented, thereby saving money.

For a description of a reverse engineering method, see [EDWA95].

### 11.4 Program comprehension

Program comprehension is a topic in its own right and has stimulated an annual IEEE workshop. Documentation is also an active area; see for example Knuth's WEB [KNUT84], and also Gilmore [GILM90] for details of issues concerned with psychology. In [YOUN93], there is a useful list of criteria for software maintenance documentation:

- integrated source code, via traceability links
- integrated call graphs, control graphs, etc.
- integration of existing documentation (if any)
- incremental documentation
- informal update by maintainer.
- quality assurance on the documentation.
- configuration management and version control of all representations.
- information hiding to allow abstraction
- team use.

It may be decided that active change of the legacy system is needed. Restructuring is:

> the transformation from one representation to another at the same relative level of abstraction, while preserving the system's external behavior.

Lehman's second law argues that such remedial action is essential in a system which is undergoing maintenance; otherwise, the maintainability will degrade and the cost of maintenance correspondingly increases. Examples include:

- control flow restructuring to remove "spaghetti" code.
- converting monolithic code to use parameterized procedures.
- identifying modules and abstract data types.
- removing dead code and redundant variables.
- simplifying aliased/common and global variables

Finally, Re-engineering is:

> the examination and alteration of the subject system to reconstitute it in a new form, and the subsequent implementation of the new form.

Re-engineering is the most radical (and expensive) form of alteration. It is not likely to be motivated simply by wanting more maintainable software. For example, owners of on-line systems produced in the 1960s and 1970s would like to replace the existing character based input/output with a modern graphical user interface. This is usually very difficult to achieve, so it may be necessary to undertake substantial redesign.

### 11.5 Reverse and re-engineering

In [BENN93], a list of 26 decision criteria for considering reverse engineering is presented. In abbreviated form, these are:

#### Management criteria

- enforcing product and process standards (such as the IEEE draft standard introduced above)

- permit better maintenance management
- legal contesting of reverse engineering legislation
- better audit trails

**Quality criteria**

- simplification of complex software
- facilitating detection of errors
- removing side effects
- improve code quality
- undertaking major design repair correction
- production of up-to-date documentation
- preparing full test suites
- improving performance
- bringing into line with practices elsewhere in the company
- financial auditing
- facilitate quality audits (such as ISO9000)

**Technical criteria**

- to allow major changes to be made
- to discover the underlying business model
- to discover the design, and requirements specification
- to port the system
- to establish a reuse library
- to introduce technical innovation such as fault tolerance or graphic interfaces
- to reflect evolving maintenance processes
- to record many different types of high level representations
- to update tool support
- disaster recovery

It is useful to amplify two of the above points. Firstly, many legacy systems represent years of accumulated experience, and this experience may now no longer be represented anywhere else. Systems analysis cannot start with humans and hope to introduce automation; the initial point is the software which contains the business rules.

Secondly, it is not obvious that a legacy system, which has been modified over many years, does actually have a high level, coherent representation. Is it simply the original system plus the aggregation of many accumulated changes? The evidence is not so pessimistic. The current system reflects a model of current reality, and it is that model we are trying to discover.

### 11.6 Techniques

Work on simplifying control flow and data flow graphs has been undertaken for many years. A very early result showed that any control graph (for instance, using unstructured goto's) can be restructured into a semantically equivalent form using sequences, if-then-else-if conditionals, and loops, although this may cause flag variables to be introduced. A good review of this type of approach can be found in the Redo Compendium [ZUYL93]. This work is generally mature, and commercial tools exist for extracting, displaying, and manipulating graphical representations of source code. In [WARD93], an approach using formal transformations is described which is intended to support the human maintainer, rather than act as a fully automated tool. This work shows that much better simplification is achievable, such as the conversion of monolithic code with aliased variables to well-structured code using parameterized procedures.

Much research in reverse engineering, especially in the USA, has been based on the program plan or cliché approach, pioneered by Rich and Waters [RICH90]. This is based on the recognition that many programs use a relatively small number of generic design ideas, which tend to be used over and over again. Reverse engineering should then attempt to find such plans in existing source code by matching from a set of patterns in a library. This would appear to have had some modest success, but there are many open issues. For example, how should patterns be represented? How generic are they? And how good is the matching process? This approach shares many of the problems of libraries of reusable components.

Most researchers aim to make their approach source language independent, so that different languages may be handled by adding front ends. Thus, design of intermediate languages is an important issue. In [ZUYL93], an approach called UNIFORM is described.

Ward [WARD93] uses a formally defined wide spectrum language WSL as the heart of his system. A wide spectrum language is used as the representational format because only one language is then needed for both low and high levels of abstractions and intermediary points. The approach has been shown to work for large (80K line) assembler programs and also for very challenging benchmark cases such as the Schorr-Waite graph-marking algorithm.

Further details are given in [BULL92] and [BULL94]. ([BULL94] also contains a useful review of other transformation systems).

Cimitile and his colleagues have done research on producing tools and methods for discovering abstract data types in existing code [CANF94]. Sneed [SNEE91, as well asNYAR95, SNEE93], has presented his experience in reverse engineering large commercial COBOL systems using partial tool support.

It is encouraging to observe that most new promising approaches to reverse engineering address two basic properties of legacy systems:

- they are very large, and "toy" solutions are not applicable
- they must be taken as they are, not how the engineer would like them to be. Often this means "on-off" solutions.

## 12. Research Questions

Although software maintenance tends to be regarded in academic circles as of minor importance, it is of major commercial and industrial significance. It is useful to end the tutorial with a brief review of promising trends.

There are many interesting research problems to be solved which can lead to important commercial benefits. There are also some grand challenges which lie at the heart of software engineering.

How do we change software quickly, reliably, and safely? In safety critical systems for example, enormous effort is expended in producing and validating software. If we wish to make a minor change to the software, do we have to repeat the entire validation or can we make the cost of the change proportionally in some way to its size? There are several well publicized cases where very minor changes to important software has caused major crashes and failures in service. A connected problem lies in the measurement of how easily new software can be changed. Without this, it is difficult to purchase software knowing that a reduced purchase price may mean enormous maintenance costs later on. Almost certainly, solution to this problem will involve addressing process issues as well as attributes of the product itself. This is a major problem for Computer Science. A new approach is described in [SMIT95].

In practice, much existing software has evolved in ad-hoc ways and has suffered the fate predicted by Lehman's laws. Despite its often central role of many organizations, such legacy systems provide a major headache. Management and technical solutions are needed to address the problems of legacy systems; otherwise, we shall be unable to move forward and introduce new technology because of our commitments and dependence on old technology.

It is often thought that the move to end-user computing, open systems, and client service systems will remove this problem. In practice, it may well make it considerably worse. A system which is comprised of many components, from many different sources by horizontal and vertical integration, and possibly across a widely distributed network, poses major problems when any of those components change. For further details of this issue, see [BENN94b].

## 13. Professional support

Over the last 10 years, professional activity in software maintenance has increased considerably. The annual International Conference on Software Maintenance, sponsored by the IEEE, represents the major venue which brings academics and practitioners together to discuss and present the latest results and experiences. Also relevant is the IEEE workshop on program comprehension. The proceedings of both conferences are published by the IEEE Computer Society Press.

In Europe, the main annual event is the annual European workshop on Software maintenance, organized in Durham. This is mainly aimed at practitioners, and again the proceedings are published.

The *Journal of Software Maintenance — Practice & Experience*, which appears bi-monthly, acts as a journal of record for significant research and practice advances in the field.

Finally, aspects of software maintenance are increasingly being taught in University courses, and PhD graduates are starting to appear who have undertaken research in the field.

## 14. Conclusions

We have described a three level approach to considering software maintenance in terms of the impact on the organization, on the process, and on technology supporting that process. This has provided a framework in which to consider maintenance. Much progress has been made in all three areas and we have described briefly recent work on the establishment of a standard maintenance process model. The adoption of such models, along with formal process assessment and improvement, will do much to improve the best practice and average practice in the software maintenance.

We have also described a major problem that distinguishes software maintenance: coping with legacy systems. We have presented several practical techniques for addressing such systems.

Thus we have presented software maintenance not as a problem but as a solution. However, there are still major research issues of strategic industrial importance to be solved. We have defined these as, firstly, to learn how to evolve software quickly and cheaply; and secondly, how to deal with large legacy systems. When a modern technology such as object-oriented systems claim to improve the situation, the claim is based largely on hope with little evidence of actual improvement. Such technology may introduce new maintenance problems (see for example [SMIT92, TURN93, TURN95] for new testing methods associated with object oriented programs). As usual, there are no magic bullets, and the Japanese principle of *Kaizen*—the progressive and incremental improvement of practices—is likely to be more successful.

## Acknowledgments

Much of the work at Durham in Software Maintenance has been supported by SERC (now EPSRC) and DTI funding, together with major grants from IBM and British Telecom. I am grateful to colleagues at Durham for discussions which lead to ideas presented in this paper, in particular to Martin Ward and Malcolm Munro. A number of key ideas have arisen from discussions with Pierrick Fillon. Thanks are due to Cornelia Boldyreff for reading drafts of this paper.

## References

BABE91 Baber R.L., "Epilogue: Future Developments," in *Software Engineer's Reference Book*, ed. McDermid, Butterworth-Heinemann, 1991.

BENN93 Bennett, K.H., "An Overview of Maintenance and Reverse Engineering," in *The REDO Compendium*, ed. van Zuylen, Wiley, 1993.

BENN94 Bennett, K.H., "Software Maintenance in Japan." Report published under the auspices of the U.K. Department of Trade and Industry, Sept. 1994. Available from the Computer Science Department, University of Durham, South Road, Durham, DH1 3LE, UK.

BENN94b Bennett, K.H., "Theory and Practice of Middle-out Programming to Support Program Understanding," *Proc IEEE Conf. Program Comprehension*, IEEE Computer Society Press, Los Alamitos, Calif., 1994, pp. 168–175.

BENN95 Bennett, K.-H. and Ward, M.P. "Formal Methods for Legacy Systems," *J. Software Maintenance: Research and Practice,* Vol. 7, No. 3, May-June 1995, pp. 203–219.

BENN95b Bennett, K.H. and Yang, H., "Acquisition of ERA Models from Data Intensive Code," *Proc IEEE Int'l Conf. Software Maintenance,* IEEE Computer Society Press, Los Alamitos, Calif., 1995, pp. 116–123.

BOLD94 Boldyreff C., Burd E., and Hather R., "An Evaluation of the State of the Art for Application Management," *Proc. Int'l Conf. Software Maintenance,* IEEE Computer Society Press, Los Alamitos, Calif., 1994, pp. 161–169.

BOLD95 Boldyreff, C., Burd E., Hather R.M., Mortimer R.E., Munro M., and Younger E.J., "The AMES Approach to Application Understanding: A Case Study," *Proc. Int'l Conf. Software Maintenance,* IEEE Computer Society Press, Los Alamitos, Calif, 1995, pp. 182-191.

BULL94 Bull, T., "Software Maintenance by Program Transformation in a Wide Spectrum Language, PhD. thesis, Department of Computer Science, University of Durham. 1994.

BULL92 Bull, T.M., Bennett, K.H., and Yang, H., "A Transformation System for Maintenance—Turning Theory into Practice," *Proc. IEEE Conf. Software Maintenance*, IEEE Computer Society Press, Los Alamitos, Calif., 1992, pp. 146–155.

CANF94 Canfora, G., Cimitile, A., and Munro, M., "RE2: Reverse Engineering and Reuse Re-engineering," *J. Software Maintenance: Research & Practice,* Vol. 6, No. 2, Mar.-Apr. 1994, pp. 53–72.

COLT87 Colter, M., "The Business of Software Maintenance," *Proc. 1st Workshop Software Maintenance,* University of Durham, Durham, 1987. Available from the Computer Science Department (see BENN94).

DOWS85 Dowson M. and Wilden J.C., "A Brief Report on the International Workshop on the Software Process and Software Environment," *ACM Software Engineering Notes*, Vol. 10, 1985, pp. 19–23.

EDWA95 Edwards, H.M., Munro M., and West, R., "The RECAST Method for Reverse Engineering," Information Systems Engineering Library, CCTA, HMSO, ISBN:1 85 554705 8, 1995.

FILL94 Fillon P., "An Approach to Impact Analysis in Software Maintenance," MSc. Thesis, University of Durham, 1994.

FOST87 Foster, J. and Munro, M., "A Documentation Method Based on Cross-Referencing," *Proc. IEEE Conf. Software Maintenance*, IEEE Computer Society Press, Los Alamitos, Calif., 1987.

FOST93 Foster, J., "Cost Factors in Software Maintenance," PhD thesis, Computer Science Department, University of Durham, 1993.

GILM90 Gilmore, D., "Expert Programming Knowledge: A Strategic Approach," in *Psychology of Programming*, Hoc, J.M., Green, T.R.G., Samurcay, R., and Gilmore, D.J., Ed., Academic Press, New York, N.Y., 1990.

HATH94 Hather, R, Burd, L., and Boldyreff, C., "A Method for Application Management Maturity Assessment," *Proc. Centre for Software Reliability Conference*, 1994 (to be published).

HINL92 Hinley, D.S. and Bennett K.H., "Developing a Model to Manage the Software Maintenance Process," *Proc. Conf. Software Maintenance,* IEEE Computer Society Press, Los Alamitos, Calif, 1992, pp. 174–182.

IEEE91 IEEE Std. 610.12-1990, *IEEE Standard Glossary of Software Engineering Terminology*, IEEE, 1991, New York.

IEEE94 *IEEE Standard for Software Maintenance* (unapproved draft). IEEE ref. P1219, IEEE, 1994, New York.

ISO90 "Information Technology—Software Product Evaluation—Quality Characteristics and Guidlelines for Their Use," International Standards Organization ISO/IEC JTC1 Draft International Standard 9126.

ITIL93 Central Computer & Telecommunications Agency, "The IT Infrastructure Library," CCTA, Gildengate House, Upper Green Lane, Norwich, NR3 1DW.

KNUT84 Knuth, D.E., "Literate Programming," *Comp. J.*, Vol. 27, No. 2, 1984, pp. 97–111.

LEHE80 Lehman, M.M., "Programs, Lifecycles and the Laws of Software Evolution," *Proc. IEEE*, Vol. 19, 1980, pp. 1060–1076.

LEHE84 Lehman, M.M., "Program Evolution," *Information Processing Management*, Vol. 20, 1984, pp. 19–36.

LEIN78 Lientz, B., Swanson, E.B., and Tompkins, G.E., "Characteristics of Applications Software Maintenance" *Comm. ACM*, Vol. 21, 1978, pp. 466–471.

LEIN80 Leintz, B. and Swanson, E.B., *Software Maintenance Management*, Addison-Wesley, Reading, Mass., 1980.

McDER91 SERB McDermid J., ed., *Software Enginering Reference Book,* Butterworth-Heinemann, 1991.

LEVE93 Leveson N.G. and Turner C.S., "An Investigation of the Therac-25 Accidents," *Computer*, Vol. 26, No. 7, July 1993, pp. 18–41.

NYAR95 Nyary E. and Sneed H., "Software Maintenance Offloading at the Union Bank of Switzerland," *Proc IEEE Int'l Conf. Software Maintenance,* IEEE Computer Society Press, Los Alamitos, Calif., 1995, pp. 98–108.

RICH90 Rich, C. and Waters, R.C., *The Programmer's Apprentice*, Addison-Wesley, Reading, Mass., 1990.

ROBS91 Robson, D.J. et al., "Approaches to Program Comprehension," *J. Systems Software*, Vol. 14, No. 1, 1991.

SMIT92 Smith M.D. and Robson D.J., "A Framework for Testing Object-Oriented Programs," *J. Object-Oriented Programming*, Vol. 5, No. 3, June 1992, pp. 45–53.

SMIT95 Smith S.R., Bennett K.H., and Boldyreff C., "Is Maintenance Ready for Evolution?" *Proc. IEEE Int'l Conference Software Maintenance*, IEEE Computer Society Press, Los Alamitos, Calif., 1995, pp. 367–372.

SNEE91 Sneed H., "Economics of Software Reengineering," *J. Software Maintenance: Research and Practice*, Vol. 3, No. 3, Sept. 1991, pp. 163–182.

SNEE93 Sneed H. and Nyary E., "Downsizing Large Application Programs," *Proc. IEEE Int'l Conf. Software Maintenance,* IEEE Computer Society Press, Los Alamitos, Calif., 1993, pp. 110–119.

TURN93 Turner C.D. and Robson D.J., "The State-based Testing of Object-Oriented Programs," Proc. *IEEE Conf. Software Maintenance*, IEEE Computer Society Press, Los Alamitos, Calif., 1993, pp. 302–310.

TURN95 Turner C.D. and Robson D.J., "A State-Based Approach to the Testing of Class-Based Programs," *Software—Concepts and Tools*, Vol 16, No. 3, 1995, pp. 106-112.

TURV94 Turver R.J. and Munro M., "An Early Impact Analysis technique for Software Maintenance, *J. Software Maintenance: Research and Practice*, Vol. 6, No. 1, Jan. 1994, pp. 35–52.

WALT94 Walton D.S., "Maintainability Metrics," *Proc. Centre for Software Reliability Conf.*, Dublin, 1994. Available from Centre for Software Reliability, City University, London, UK.

WARD93 Ward M.P., "Abstracting a Specification from Code," *J. Software Maintenance: Practice and Experience,* Vol. 5, No. 2, June 1993, pp. 101–122.

WARD94 Ward M.P., "Reverse Engineering through Formal Transformation," *Computer J.*, Vol. 37, No 9, 1994.

WARD94a Ward M.P., "Language Oriented Programming," *Software—Concepts and Tools*, Vol. 15, 1994, pp. 147–161.

WEIS89 Weiss D.M., "Evaluating Software Development by Analysis of Change," PhD dissertation, Univ. of Maryland, USA.

WILD93 Wilde N., "Software Impact Analysis: Processes and Issues," Durham University Technical Report 7/93, 1993.

YAU87 Yau S.S. and Liu S., "Some Approaches to Logical Ripple Effect Analysis," Technical Report, SERC, USA, 1987.

YOUN93 Younger, E., "Documentation," in *The REDO Compendium*, van Zuylen, ed., Wiley, 1993.

YOUN94 Younger E. and Ward M.P., "Inverse Engineering a Simple Real Time Program," *J. Software Maintenance: Research and Practice*, Vol. 6, 1994, pp. 197–234.

ZUYL90 van Zuylen, H., ed., *The REDO Compendium,* Wiley, 1993.

# Chapter 9

## Software Quality and Quality Assurance

### 1. Introduction to Chapter

*Software quality assurance* (SQA), unlike verification and validation, is primarily concerned with assuring the quality of the software development process rather than the quality of the product. Quality assurance includes development standards and the methods and procedures used in ensuring that the standards are complied with. IEEE Standard 610.12-1990 [1] provides two definitions for software quality assurance:

- A planned and systematic pattern of all actions necessary to provide adequate confidence that an item or product conforms to established technical requirements
- A set of activities designed to evaluate the process by which products are developed or manufactured

SQA cannot be properly implemented without the use of *standards*. Standards are accepted procedures for describing a process or product. Standards exist in order that there be a common understanding of how something should be developed or what attributes it should possess at delivery.

Software standards are primarily (but not entirely) documentation standards. Proper documentation of software products (such as requirements specifications, project plans, code, and test procedures) is a very critical part of software engineering. Software is invisible; documentation makes it visible. Product visibility makes it possible to track progress against the project's plans.

Often included with quality assurance in the category of process assurance is software configuration management. *Configuration management* (CM) is a discipline for applying technical and administrative direction and surveillance in order to [1]:

SOFTWARE QUALITY AND QUALITY ASSURANCE

- Identify and document the functional and physical characteristics of a configuration item
- Control characteristics of those items
- Record and report change processing and implementation status
- Verify compliance with specified requirements

Configuration management is also the mechanism for maintaining the various baselines. The elements of configuration management are (adapted from IEEE Standard 610.12-1990 [2]:

- *Configuration Item*—Any aggregation of a hardware/software system, or any of its portions, that satisfies an end-use function and is designated by the customer or developer for configuration management.
- *Configuration identification*—The process of designating the hardware/software configuration items in a system and recording their characteristics.
- *Configuration control*—The process of evaluating, approving or disapproving, and coordinating changes to hardware/software configuration items after formal establishment of their configuration identification.
- *Configuration status accounting*—The recording and reporting of the information that is needed to manage a hardware/software configuration effectively, including a listing of the approved configuration identification, the status of proposed changes to configuration, and the implementation status of approved changes.
- *Configuration auditing*—The process of verifying that all required hardware/software configuration items have been produced, that the current version agrees with specified requirements, that the technical documentation completely and accurately describes the configuration items, and that all change requests have been resolved.
- *Configuration control board* (CCB)—The authority responsible for evaluating and approving or disapproving proposed engineering changes to the hardware/software configuration that are under formal configuration control, and ensuring implementation of the approved changes.
- *Software development library*—A software library containing computer-readable and human-readable information relevant to a software development effort.

CM is sometimes grouped into formal CM and informal CM.

*Formal* configuration management (also called external CM or baseline CM) is used to manage the configuration between the customer/user and the developer. CM is also frequently used to maintain the configuration after delivery during the maintenance and operations phase of the life cycle. The configuration control board is the agency responsible for managing the configuration.

*Informal* configuration management (also called internal CM or developmental CM) is used for maintaining configuration control for products under development, such as plans, specifications, versions, test procedures and test results, and deliverable (but not yet delivered) documents. The project manager acts as the CCB and an individual called the product support librarian provides the accounting and auditing.

## 2. Overview of Papers

The first paper in this chapter is an original article by Patricia Hurst of Fastrak Training, Inc. Hurst reviews the history of software quality assurance (SQA) and its role in software development. She provides a number of reasons for developers to practice good SQA, ranging from a moral obligation to develop a high-quality product to the pressures of competition. She surveys current world-wide initiatives in software quality improvement and provides two definitions, one comparatively narrow and one broad, of SQA.

Next Hurst describes those SQA functions carried out across an entire development organization as well as on a particular project. Finally she reviews how a software developer would organize and carry out the SQA functions. She also notes that an effective program of software quality assurance has proven to be cost-effective in many environments.

The next paper dates from 1984 but is still the best overview of software configuration management (SCM). Ed Bersoff defines configuration management as the discipline of identifying the configuration of a system at discrete points in time for the purpose of systematically controlling changes to the configuration and maintaining the integrity and traceability of the configuration throughout the system life cycle. Configuration management keeps track of the various artifacts developed during the lifetime of a software project through identifying, controlling, auditing, and status accounting of the various software development products.

Bersoff reminds us that controlling code is *not*

enough; the documentation that enables us to use and operate the code must also be controlled. This paper also provides a lengthy description of the program support library (PSL). Bersoff discusses the major problems involved in deciding how to properly manage the software configuration: too much control is cumbersome; too little control invites disaster.

The third paper in this chapter is entitled "Evaluating Software Engineering Standards" and was written by Shari Lawrence Pfleeger, Norm Fenton, and Stella Page of the Center for Software Reliability at the University of London. While not specifically a tutorial paper as described in the Preface, this paper does provide a definition of standards and an overview of the types of standards, their presumed benefits, and a comparison of the characteristics of software standards with those in other fields of specialization. The paper then reports on a study of the effectiveness of standards in industrial practice. The study revealed that in many cases it was impossible to determine whether or not the standards were being followed (because compliance was not testable); that in cases where compliance was testable, management was not aware that compliance was less than complete; and that software standards, far more than those in other fields, apply to the process of development rather than to the final product. The authors also conclude that progress is needed in defining, collecting, and analyzing software metrics before the effectiveness of standards can be judged adequately—an excellent lead-in to the metrics articles in Chapter 12 of this Tutorial.

The authors note that the body of software standards is large and growing: as of the date of the article there were over 250 software engineering standards worldwide, and the IEEE computer society typically completes several new standards or revisions per year. At the time of this writing, the US Department of Defense is in the midst of a major initiative to reduce the use of standards and specifications that are peculiar to the military environment, and to use commercial standards, especially process standards, wherever possible. Thus, the highly dynamic nature of the body of software standards can be expected to continue.

To provide a benchmark on the status of standards as of the date of this Tutorial, one of the editors (Richard Thayer) has surveyed and listed the software standards currently available worldwide. This survey is included as an Appendix to the Tutorial.

The last paper in the chapter was written by John Musa and William Everett of AT&T Bell Laboratories. It introduces a discipline that the authors call *software reliability engineering*. The authors include a number of activities, taking place during all phases of the life cycle, as part of software-reliability engineering, for example:

- Defining the quality factors (reliability and others) that the software should attain
- Helping determine the architecture and process to meet the reliability goal
- Predicting reliability from the product and process
- Measuring the reliability during testing
- Managing reliability during operations and maintenance
- Using measured reliability to improve the development process

Musa and Everett distinguish between *failures* (behavior of the software that does not meet requirements) and *faults* (the defects in the code that cause the failures). They note that failures can be measured by execution time or by calendar time, and that all faults are not equally likely to cause failures—faults in software functions that are used more frequently by the end user will cause more failures than faults in less-used functions. It should also be noted that not all failures are equal: failures in critical functions may be of more consequence to the users.

By orienting the test program toward critical functions and portions of the program executed most frequently, it is possible to leverage testing to eliminate a higher percentage of the failures that will occur in operations and that will be of greatest consequence to the users.

Finally, the authors define areas where research may bring about further improvement in the discipline of software-reliability engineering. They rate reliability prediction as the most important research area. Estimation of the number of faults in the software at the start of testing (based on errors found in earlier phases) and estimating failure intensity during unit testing are also promising areas.


1. IEEE Standard 610.12-1990, *IEEE Standard Glossary of Software Engineering Terminology*, The Institute of Electrical and Electronics Engineers, Inc., Piscataway, NJ, 1990.

2. IEEE Standard 610.12-1990, *IEEE Standard Glossary of Software Engineering Terminology*, The Institute of Electrical and Electronics Engineers, Inc., Piscataway, NJ, 1990.

# Software Quality Assurance: A Survey of an Emerging View

Patricia W. Hurst
Fastrak Training, Inc.
Columbia, MD

**Abstract**

Since the mid 1980s, the term "quality assurance" has assumed increasing importance in the software development industry. The once accepted practice of relying on back-end testing to assure quality is fading with the recognition that quality must be addressed from conception, through development, and throughout the maintenance activities. Quality programs are being organized and implemented by many organizations using the Capability Maturity Model developed by the Software Engineering Institute for guidance. This survey article provides a historical perspective and rationale for quality assurance, discusses U. S. and international initiatives to improve quality, defines an emerging view of quality assurance as a subset of a broader Quality Management concern, defines the functions required for a Quality Management program, and presents an organizational structure to support these functions.

## INTRODUCTION

Since the mid 1980s, the term "quality assurance" has assumed increasing importance in the software development industry. It is being recognized that quality must be addressed throughout the software life cycle in order to supply software products which meet the needs of our society and its consumers. The once accepted practice of relying on back-end testing of the product to assure quality is fading with the recognition that quality must be addressed from conception, through development, and throughout the maintenance activities.

This recognition has not been sudden, but has emerged over the decades since software was first produced in the 1940s. This emergence has occurred as many software products and systems have repeatedly failed to meet expectations in terms of costs, schedules, functionality, and corrective maintenance. These failed expectations have continued in spite of numerous improvements in platforms, operating systems, languages, development methodologies, computer-aided software engineering (CASE) tools, and management practices. The industry has diligently searched for a "silver bullet" to eliminate the nightmares experienced by developers. However, the community is learning, as has virtually every other area of engineering, that advances in quality and productivity do not occur simply through new technologies. Rather, improvement requires attention to the processes used to develop and maintain software products.

This survey article provides a historical perspective and rationale for quality assurance, discusses U. S. and international initiatives to improve quality, defines an emerging view of quality assurance as a subset of a broader Quality Management concern, defines the functions required for a Quality Management program, and presents an organizational structure to support these functions.

## BACKGROUND

From a historical perspective, the early years through the 1960s can be viewed as the functional era of software engineering, the 1970s as the schedule era, and the 1980s as the cost era [5]. In the late 1960s, the focus began to shift from the singular issue of "what functions should the software perform," to the broader recognition that software was expensive, of insufficient quality, hard to schedule, and difficult to manage. Thus, the focus in the 1970s was placed on planning and controlling of software projects. Life-cycle models which defined development phases were introduced and project planning and tracking procedures emerged. In the 1980s, information technology spread through every facet of our institutions and became available to individuals as well. Driven by competition, issues of productivity became more significant and various models used for estimating costs were developed by organizations in industry and academia. In the mid 1980s, quality issues emerged and have subsequently increased in importance. The decade of the 1990s is already being characterized as the "quality era" [34]. As society's dependence on software increases and technology provides for expanding functionality, the demand for quality intensifies. For vendors of software to compete in the marketplace at home and abroad, quality is becoming more of a necessity. In this decade, quality has become a key issue in how software is conceived, developed and maintained for the broad and diverse customer base.

With this focus on quality, the software industry is recognizing that producing quality products requires a concern for not only quality of product but quality of process as well. In a 1987 article, "No Silver Bullet" [8], Brooks argued that the difficulties of software development are inevitable for they arise not from accident, but from software's inescapable essence — the complexity of interlocking constructs. Indeed, for 25 years, software engineers have sought methods which they hoped would provide a technological "fix" for the software crisis. Although small improvement can be made by the use of specific methods, there is little empirical evidence to support the hypothesis that such fixes can radically improve the way we develop software systems [21]. While attention to quality issues may not slay the dragon of software complexity and satisfy Brook's yardstick for a technological breakthrough of a tenfold improvement in quality or productivity, or both, there is growing evidence that it can provide a significant step in that direction. Several companies [11, 16, 17, 28, 54, 56] have reported increases in quality and productivity by focusing on improving the quality of their development processes.

## RATIONALE

There are many reasons for wanting to improve software processes and quality. These include a moral obligation, customer satisfaction, cost effectiveness, predictability, application demand, and international competition.

**Moral obligation.** The increasing reliance on software in life-critical systems morally obligates the producers to provide products that are reliable in performing their needed functions and can be counted on to do no harm. The realities of software fragility are evident in critical systems that we build. As examples [36], a Patriot missile timing error may have contributed to the deaths of 28 soldiers in Dhahran during the Gulf War and software has been suspect in the Therac-25 radiation-therapy machine which has been implicated in at least two deaths.

**Customer satisfaction.** From the customer's view, quality is conformance to expectations and requirements. Customers today often have multiple sources from which to select products or services; they are increasingly demanding more assurances that their expectations will be met.

**Cost effectiveness.** With the increase in size and complexity of software systems, the costs have correspondingly increased. With the decrease in hardware costs over the years, the cost of labor has become a major contributor to development costs. Improved development processes are needed to make more efficient use of personnel resources.

**Predictability.** The need for better predictability of costs, schedules and product quality is driven by customer demands and cost concerns. For example, a Federal Aviation Administration (FAA) project to develop new workstation software for air-traffic controllers was reported in 1994 to be bug-infested and running five years late accompanied by $1 billion over budget [23]. A 1994 survey by IBM's Consulting Group [23] of leading companies that developed large distributed systems showed that 55% of the projects cost more than expected, 68% overran their schedules and 88% had to be substantially redesigned.

**Application demand.** The demands for software continue to increase in terms of size, complexity, and new domains. Modern, windows-based commercial products average 100,000 lines of code (LOC) [33]. Operating and data-base management systems often exceed one million LOC and complex telephone switching systems are up to 10 million LOC [37]. Because hardware capabilities rapidly advance, an order of magnitude growth in system size every decade is expected for many industries. Such growth in system size is stressing our cultural tradition founded in the prowess of the individual programmer.

**International competition.** The 21st century will be very competitive for software vendors in the global marketplace. Software is a labor intensive activity. Third world countries, with low wage earners, looking to "leap frog" into the technological age have discovered that software can be key to a competitive strategy for their future. Past practices that enabled U. S. software producers to achieve supremacy will not suffice and bold steps are needed to ensure that our software industry will not fall to foreign competition. Other industries such as automotive, steel, and consumer

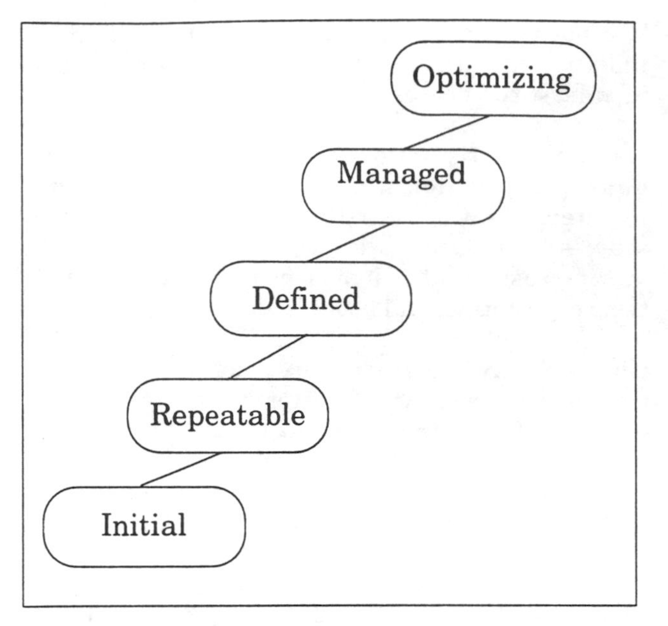


**Figure 1. SEI Capability Maturity Model**

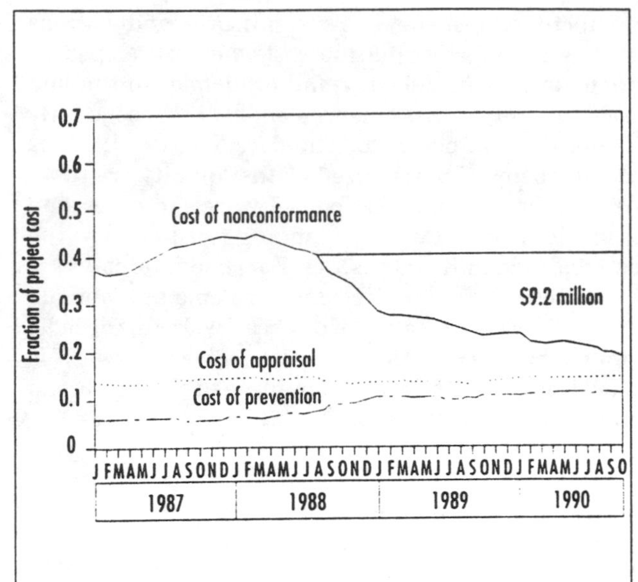


**Figure 2. Raytheon's Savings Due to Rework**

electronics faced the same challenge and in their hesitation to change, lost marketshare. The challenge for the software industry will be to provide customer satisfaction at a competitive price.

## QUALITY IMPROVEMENT INITIATIVES

A movement to improve software development emerged in the mid 1980s. Shortcomings in managing development and maintenance processes were recognized as prime inhibitors of growth in software productivity and quality. This movement focused on the underlying foundation of development efforts — a foundation composed of people, tasks, tools, methods, and a well-defined and documented process. Several initiatives to provide the needed foundation have been undertaken.

**Software Engineering Institute.** In November 1986, the Software Engineering Institute (SEI) began developing a process-maturity framework that would help developers improve their software process. This work has evolved into the Capability Maturity Model (CMM) Version 1.1 [44] which presents recommended practices in a number of key process areas that have been shown to enhance the software development and maintenance capability of an organization. The CMM provides a rating scale composed of five maturity levels as shown in Figure 1. It is based on the principles of incremental and continuous process improvement espoused by Walter Shewart, W. Edwards Deming, Joseph Juran, and Philip Crosby.

Many organizations in the U. S. are using the SEI model as a catalyst for change. For example, the Air Force has mandated that all of its software development organizations must reach Level 3 of the CMM by 1998 [23]. A similar directive has been issued by the Navy and NASA is considering such a policy [23]. Industry organizations using the CMM include large and small companies.

Improvement efforts have shown that the return on investment is high and published results demonstrate this cost effectiveness. Results from a two year effort to progress to Level 3 at the Software Engineering Division of Hughes Aircraft [28] indicate a $2 million per year savings. Intangible benefits cited include increased pride in work, quality of work life, and in general, fewer problems. Raytheon achieved similar results over a three-year improvement effort that took the Equipment Division from a Level 2 to a Level 3 [17]. Their analysis, as shown in Figure 2, indicates that $9.2 million was saved by reducing rework on a base of nearly $115 million in development costs. During the past several years, Computer Sciences Corporation has experienced about a 20% annual increase in productivity and quality [11]. This is a result of applying the SEI approach as well as other ongoing improvement activities. Procase Corporation, a smaller company which is a producer of CASE tools, progressed from a Level 1 to a Level 2 over an 18-month period [54]. The company is now shipping releases close to a 6-month cycle compared with a previous 30-month cycle.

The CMM represents a broad consensus of the software community on best practices and is providing guidance for many organizational software process-improvement efforts.

**ISO 9000-3**. Another method for assessing the ability of an organization to produce software with predictability and quality is *ISO 9000-3, Guidelines for the Application of ISO 9001 to the Development, Supply, and Maintenance of Software*, which is part of the ISO 9000 series of standards published by the International Standards Organization (ISO) [2]. These standards describe the requirements for various types of companies and organizations doing business in the European Community.

**BOOTSTRAP.** BOOTSTRAP [35], a project under the auspices of the European Strategic Programme for Research in Information Technology (ESPRIT), applied the SEI model to the European software industry. Although the CMM maturity levels are still recognizable, the assessment methodology yields more detailed capability profiles of organizations and projects. As of 1993, 90 projects in 37 organizations had been assessed with results showing that 73% of the organizations were at Level 1 with the remainder at Level 2.

**SPICE.** In 1993, the International Standards Group for Software Engineering sponsored the Software Process Improvement and Capability dEtermination (SPICE) project which has been endorsed by the international community [18]. Its objective is to develop an international standard for software process assessment by building on the best features of existing software assessment methods such as the SEI model.

**Other Models.** Other improvement models have been developed and used by large companies, such as Hewlett-Packard's Software Quality and Productivity Analysis (SQPA) [25]. Models have also been developed as an adjunct to consulting services, such as those offered by R. S. Pressman & Associates, Inc., Howard Rubin & Associates, and Capers Jones through Software Productivity Research, Inc.

## QUALITY ASSURANCE DEFINITION

Over a decade ago, Buckley [9] stated, "You can wander into any bar in town and get into a fight over quality assurance." This is still true. There are various definitions of quality assurance and related concepts. Definitions provided by the IEEE [32] and by the CMM [44] are as follows:

**IEEE Definition 1.** A planned and systematic pattern of all actions necessary to provide adequate confidence that an item or product conforms to established technical requirements.

**IEEE Definition 2.** A set of activities designed to evaluate the process by which products are developed or manufactured.

**CMM Definition of Purpose.** The purpose of quality assurance is to provide management with appropriate visibility into the process being used by the software project and of the products being built.

The first IEEE definition is very broad in scope and includes plans and subsequent actions taken by a project's development personnel as well as by others in organizational support roles. Such plans address areas such as project planning and tracking, development process models, deliverable and in-process documentation, reviews and audits, requirements management, configuration management, verification and validation procedures, and training. The *IEEE Standard for Software Quality Assurance Plans* [31] provides the contents of such a comprehensive plan.

The second IEEE definition of quality assurance and the CMM definition of its purpose are similar and narrower in scope. The key phrases are "to evaluate" and to provide "appropriate visibility into" the process being used to develop the software products. These definitions imply an oversight function concerned with assuring that defined processes are in place for the development and support activities required to produce a quality product and with assuring that these processes are being complied with.

To bridge this chasm between the broad and the narrow definitions, terms such as "Quality Management" and "Quality Program" are being used to encompass the broad spectrum of quality-oriented activities while the term "Quality Assurance" is applied to the oversight function. The terms are in a state of evolution and are being influenced by the increasing popularity of the CMM among developer organizations.

In the remainder of this paper, the terms Quality Management (QM) and Quality Assurance (QA) will be used in conformance with this emerging new view.

## QUALITY MANAGEMENT FUNCTIONS

Quality Management is concerned with quality-related activities across the spectrum of a software development organization. Since consistency is needed

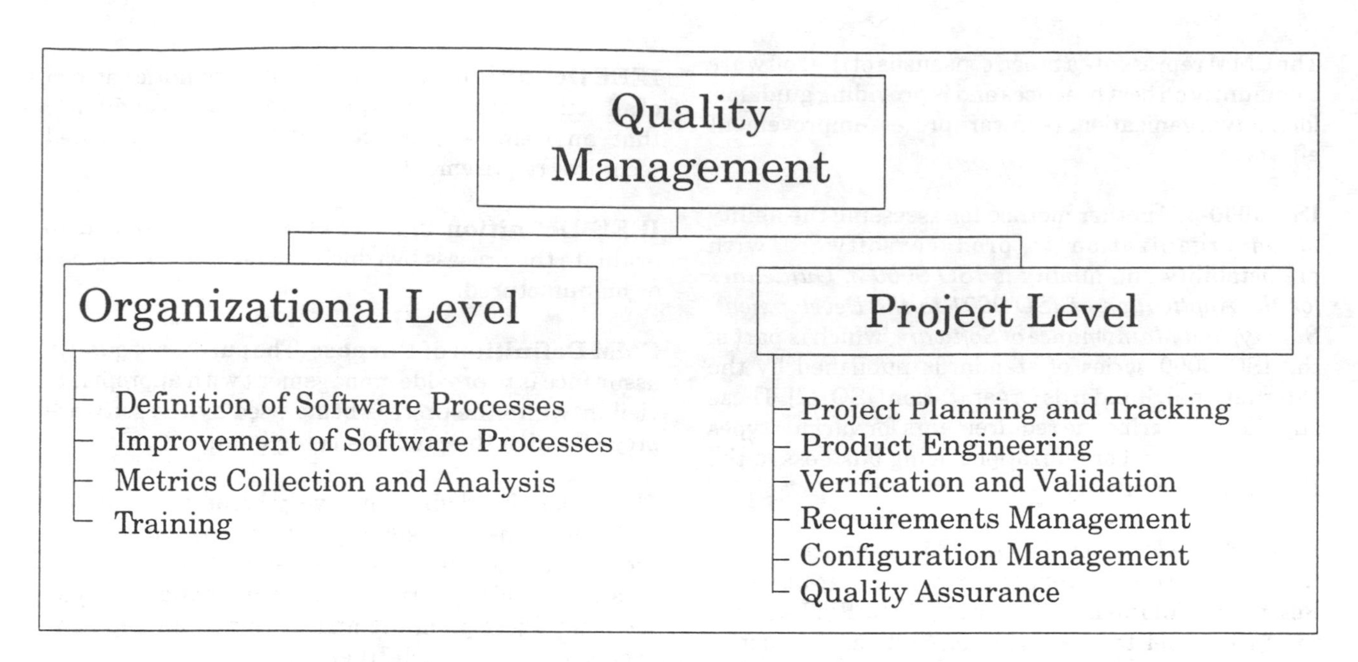


**Figure 3. Primary Quality Management Functions**

both for reliable prediction of schedules, costs, and product quality and for improvement over time, a primary goal is to provide for consistency across a multitude of individual software projects. This applies to the various processes and methodologies used by the various projects. Thus, QM must address quality functions at two levels, the organizational and the project levels. The organizational-level functions include those necessary to define and support the processes and methodologies which will be used by individual projects within the organization. The project-level functions include those necessary to carry out the defined processes, using the defined methodologies, for a specific project. The primary functions addressed by QM are shown in Figure 3.

**Organizational Level Functions**

Primary functions at the organizational level include definition and improvement of software development processes, metrics collection and analysis, and training.

**Definition of Software Development Processes**. This function is to define and document the processes which development projects will follow. These processes encompass the activities, procedures, documentation, and standards required to carry out the QM functions shown at the project level.

Software process models are at the heart of improving the way software is developed and thus the quality of the resultant products. While a life-cycle model, such as the waterfall, spiral, or evolutionary, defines the high-level activities for the development effort, a process model is a more detailed decomposition and is usually displayed as a network of activities.

A software process model defines the various development activities which must be performed. For each activity, the model defines information or documents which must be available for the activity to occur, work-products that are produced, standards that must be met, methodologies and tools that must be used, verification and validation procedures that will be applied, configuration management activities that will be applied, and quality assurance activities that will be applied. Thus, a process model integrates the various quality management activities appropriate for a project.

Automated support is available for modeling and enacting a defined process. These tools aid in ensuring that the personnel participating on a project follow the defined process. A description of several tools is given in [52]. Examples include Process Weaver from Cap Gemini, InConcert from Xsoft Inc., and Process Engineer from Learmonth & Burchett Management Systems.

Procedures and standards apply to various products during a project's life. Document templates are typically developed for deliverable and non-deliverable work-products such as the project plan, the requirement specifications, user and operator manuals, various design documents, and test plans. Documents which contains descriptions of the processes and procedures

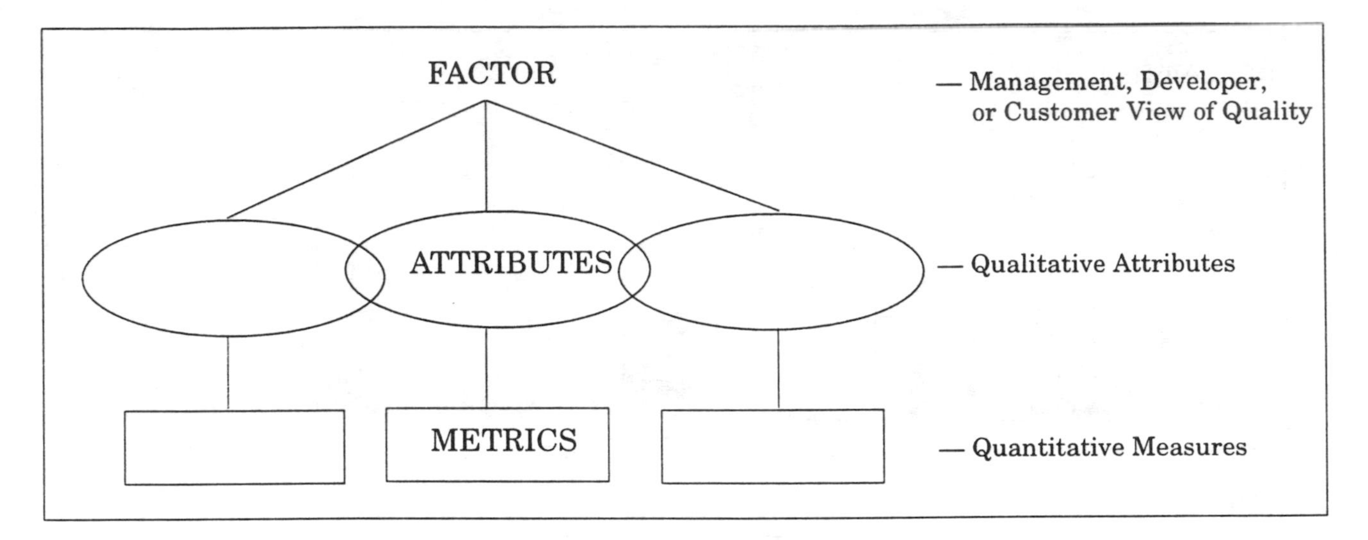


**Figure 4. Software Metrics Framework**

to be followed on individual projects, such as for configuration management, verification and validation, and quality assurance activities, are also required. Coding standards include expectations and restrictions on items such as descriptive comments, programming languages, control structures, data structures, naming conventions, source-code size, and operating system interfaces.

Defined processes are used, perhaps with tailoring, by individuals on specific projects to guide them in performing their work according to expectations.

**Improvement of Software Development Processes.** Improving development processes requires evaluating the current processes being used and products produced, identifying areas that are weak, and modifying the defined processes in these areas. It also includes follow-up evaluation to ensure that the modifications are indeed improving productivity and/ or product quality.

**Metrics Collection and Analysis.** Software metrics play an important role in evaluating and improving the development processes and the software products. Such improvement results in increased productivity and quality, and reduced cycle time, all of which improve a company's competitiveness. Although there are a number of successful metrics programs in industry [16, 24, 25, 38. 48, 59], only about 25% of application development organizations have a formal metrics program [59]. Implementation of metrics is a complex issue as indicated in a survey by Howard Rubin & Associates, as mentioned in [39], that reported two out of three measurement efforts either failed or were discontinued after two years.

An example of a successful metrics program is found within Motorola. Their six sigma program has a quality goal of no more than 3.4 defects per million lines of code. One Motorola Division achieved a 50X reduction in released-software defect density within 3.5 years [16].

An example of a small software group that has benefited from a measurement program is from Eastman Kodak Company [56]. Since 1990, the group has measured the time spent in different work phases on development and maintenance projects. Distribution trends have been used to set quantitative improvement goals, identify opportunities that can increase productivity, and develop heuristics to assist with estimating new projects. The focus has been on improving up-front activities such as requirements analysis, instituting design and code inspections, and formalizing software quality assurance practices. A notable result has been a reduction in the corrective maintenance effort from 13.5% to a steady state of less than 2%.

Metrics can be classified into two broad categories — process metrics and product metrics. Process metrics can be used to improve the development and maintenance processes. Examples include defects associated with testing and inspections, defect containment efficiency, and labor consumed. Product metrics can be used to improve the software and its associated products. Examples include complexity of the design, the size of the source code, and the usability of the documentation produced.

A popular approach to defining product metrics is through a hierarchical framework [51, 53]. A three-level framework is shown in Figure 4. The first level

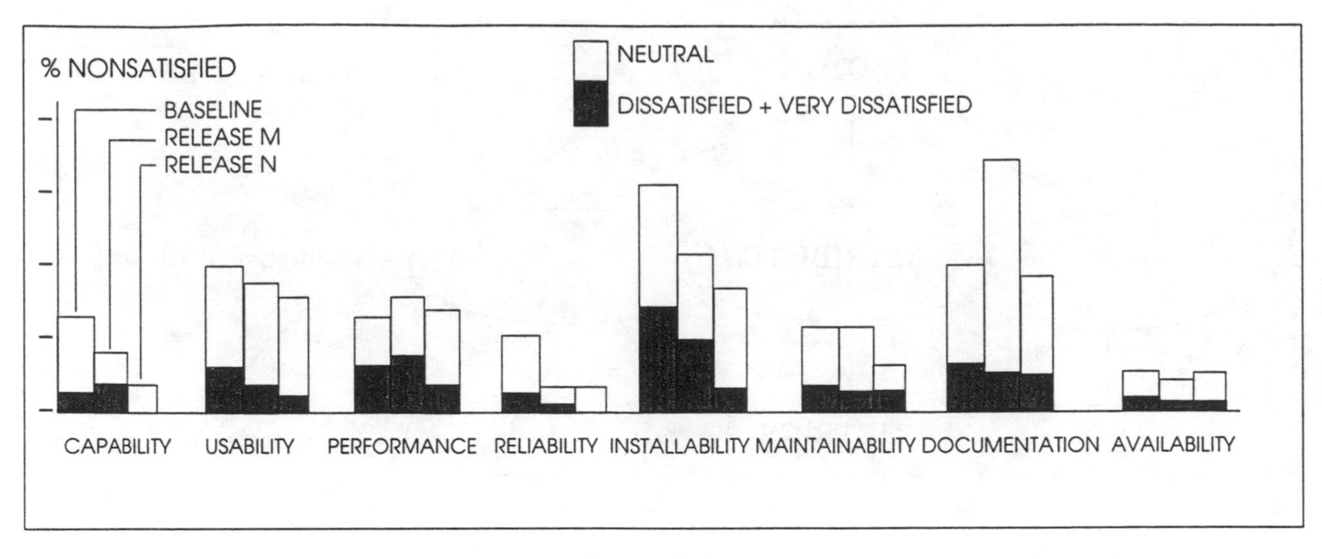


**Figure 5. Monitoring Software Quality in Terms of Customer Satisfaction**

establishes high-level quality factors; the second identifies the software attributes which define the factor; and the third identifies the metrics which can be used to measure the degree of presence of each attribute, and thus the quality factor. For example, the quality factor "maintainability" may be decomposed into three attributes: consistency, simplicity and modularity; the attribute simplicity may be decomposed into metrics describing the LOC and the maximum loop-nesting level for a module. The framework can be used for individual modules or for a system to enforce standards and to measure deviations from quality goals. Commonly accepted quality factors include correctness, reliability, efficiency, integrity, usability, maintainability, testability, flexibility, portability, reusability, and interoperability [46]. The concept of a metrics framework is supported by several commercial packages such as Logiscope marketed by Verilog, Inc.

Another example of quality factors, with focus on customer satisfaction/dissatisfaction, is found in the CUPRIMDA model used by IBM's AS/400 Division as part of a corporate strategy of market-driven quality (MDQ) [34]. CUPRIMDA is an acronym for eight quality factors as shown in Figure 5. Each factor is defined through a set of metrics and used to measure products across different releases and against benchmarked competitors. This information is used to improve the process and as a result, the product, in areas contributing to low customer satisfaction.

In a similar way of measuring customer satisfaction, the Hewlett-Packard Company focuses on FURPS (functionality, usability, reliability, performance, and supportability) [24, 25]. Similar dimensions of quality are used by other companies.

A useful approach for developing a set of metrics is provided by the "goal/question/metric" paradigm [3, 4]. It is well described by Grady[25]: "The basic principle behind the paradigm is that each organization or project has a set of goals. For each goal there is a set of questions that you might ask to help you understand whether you are achieving your goal. Many of these questions have answers that can be measured. To the extent that the questions are a complete set, and to the extent the metric data satisfactorily answers the questions, you can measure whether you are meeting goals." The relationships among goals, questions, and metrics are shown in Figure 6. This approach was used in brainstorming sessions by the Hewlett-Packard's Software Metrics Council as an initial step in defining a set of software maintenance metrics [25]. As such, the "metrics" were not precisely defined but provided a platform for further discussion, feedback and refinement. An example follows:

**Goal:** Minimize Engineering Effort and Schedule

**Question:** Where are the resources going and where are the worst rework loops in the process?

**Metrics:** Engineering months by product/ component/activity.

Increasingly, a metrics program is being viewed by industry and government organizations as a powerful tool for improving the quality of products and processes in software development. The IEEE has developed standards for productivity metrics [30] and software

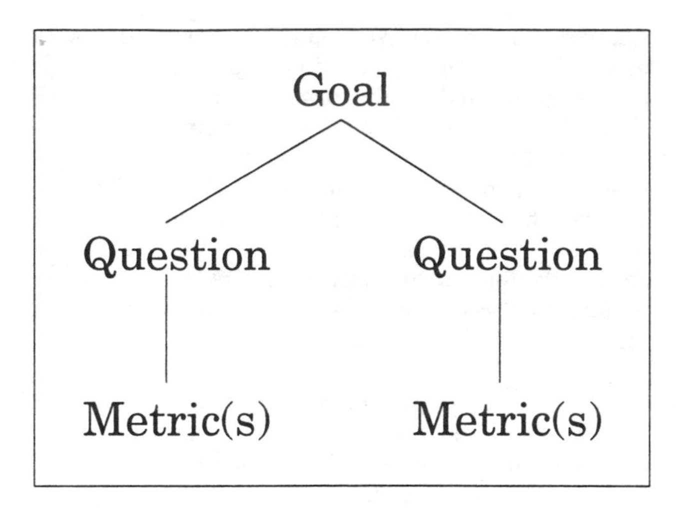


**Figure 6. Goal/Question/Metric Paradigm**

quality metrics [29]. The Department of Defense (DoD) is developing a software-metrics database which is to become a national repository for all DoD organizations, on both in-house and contracted projects, and for others who choose to contribute [40]. An Air Force policy requires software-intensive programs, whether embedded, command and control, or management information systems, to have a metrics program which collects the core attributes of size, effort, schedule, quality and rework [40].

Metrics programs are well supported by vendor tools. Software Productivity Research provides Checkpoint for estimating staffing and quality levels. Industry baselines for productivity and quality measures are provided through products such as SLIM from Quantitative Software Management and several from Howard Rubin & Associates. McCabe & Associates provides a toolset to support the analysis of software structure.

A comprehensive metrics training program is provided through METKIT, a product produced by an ESPRIT project [1]. The industrial package consists of 18 modules, a computer-aided instruction system, and a textbook [21].

**Training**. For a viable quality program, the organization needs to provide for training of personnel in their processes, standards, and metrics program. Management, technical and support staff who are to be involved in the project-level activities should be included.

**Project Level Functions**

The primary functions at the project level are implementations of the defined processes established by the organization as standards to be followed by all software projects within the organization. These functions include project planning and tracking, product engineering, verification and validation, requirements management, configuration management, and quality assurance.

**Project Planning and Tracking**. Project planning is performed at the beginning of a project and includes defining the work to be performed, estimating resources required, and producing a schedule. The planning process itself adheres to the process defined at the organization level and the resultant plan should incorporate processes defined for the other project-level functions described below. Tailoring of the defined processes may be necessary for a specific project and is performed during the planning phase. The project tracking functions involve assessing the status of the work and work-products as the project progresses, evaluating adherence to the plan, and taking action to correct any deviation.

**Product Engineering**. Product engineering involves following the defined software process model, with the appropriate methods and tools, to develop the software and associated products. Activities defined by product engineering include requirements analysis, design, implementation, and testing.

**Verification and Validation (V&V)**. V&V is "the process of determining whether the requirements for a system or component are complete and correct, the products of each development phase fulfill the requirements or conditions imposed by the previous phase, and the final system or component complies with specified requirements" [32]. This process should be integrated into the software process model and includes "gate-keeping" activities at each process step to ensure freedom from defects and compliance with standards and requirements. Example activities include producing traceability matrices, holding technical reviews and inspections, and performing unit, integration and system testing. Reviews and inspections are particularly important V&V activities.

The idea of software reviews has been around almost as long as software. Babbage and von Neumann regularly asked colleagues to examine their programs [22]. By the 1970s, various review methods had emerged and were called walkthroughs, structured walkthroughs, and code inspections. Petroski, in his text *To Engineer is Human* [47] states that "it is the essence of modern engineering not only to be able to check one's own work, but also to have one's work checked and to be able to check the work of others." The value of reviews is based on the fact that the cost of fixing a defect rises dramatically the later it is found in the development cycle. Reviews of requirements, design, and code allow early detection of defects and thus, lower costs.

Over the years, many companies have reported their experiences with inspections [19, 50, 58]. At Bell-Northern Research, code inspections uncovered approximately 80% of all defects on an ultralarge project of 2.5 million lines of code [50].

**Requirements Management (RM).** Software requirements are essential for proper planning of software development activities. Requirements management includes ensuring that requirements are well defined, agreed to by appropriate parties, used for project planning, and modified according to a defined procedure. The modification procedure must ensure that later changes are incorporated properly and that project plans are updated accordingly. If appropriate, the requirements may be placed under the full rigor of formal configuration management.

**Configuration Management (CM).** The purpose of CM [44] is to "establish and maintain the integrity of the products of the software project throughout the project's software life cycle." This involves identifying the software work products — called configuration items — to be placed under CM control and providing the technical and administrative procedures required to ensure that approved baselined versions exist at specific points during the project, that changes are incorporated in a defined manner, and that the status of configurations items are accounted for. Examples of work products that may be designated as configuration items include the project plan, the requirements, the architectural design, the source code, and the user manual.

CM has been addressed by many organizations [41]. About 80% of organizations examined in one survey have well-developed mechanisms for controlling changes to requirements, design, and code. There are a number of automated tools, which support elements of CM, especially for source code. Examples include Digital Equipment Corporation's VMS, Softool Corporation's CCC, and Expertware Inc.'s CMVision. However, many CM tools were developed on mainframe machines and few fully support the needs required in distributed client-server environments [10].

**Quality Assurance.** QA, as noted previously, is an oversight function providing assurance that all processes defined in the project plan are followed. Thus, QA ensures that all product engineering, V&V, RM and CM activities are carried out as planned and that work products conform to standards. QA also assures that the project plan itself was developed according to defined procedures and meets the standards for the organization. QA functions are performed through a series of reviews, audits, and consultations.

QA reviews ensure documented processes are followed and that planned activities such as project reviews and inspections are held. QA personnel may attend technical and management reviews and may attend work-product inspections. Their presence, however, is not as a technical contributor with responsibility for detecting technical-content errors. Their presence is to observe that the meeting processes are being implemented as planned and to note deviations. For example, they may note that the moderator of a code inspection did not distribute materials in advance and that the inspectors are not prepared. They may also evaluate effectiveness of the meeting procedures and make recommendations for change. QA personnel may perform reviews to ensure proper records, status-accounting reports, and other physical documents are present and are being used as planned. For example, QA may periodically review the project manager's records to ensure that monthly reports, inspection meeting reports, and testing reports are being produced, distributed and saved according to procedures. QA may also review CM records to ensure that monthly reports are being produced, distributed and saved according to procedures.

QA may audit a variety of work products for which standards have been established. This includes auditing of deliverable work-products such as code and manuals prior to delivery. Similar to attending reviews, their purpose is not to detect technical-content errors but to ensure that all items are present, that all standards are complied with, and that all activities, such as completion of test-traceability matrices, have been completed prior to delivery. QA may also review non-deliverable work-products, such as design documents and test plans, for standards compliance.

QA personnel provide consulting services throughout the project life from initial planning through final product delivery. This includes advising the project management on implementing and tailoring the organizational processes and standards as well as advising on corrective actions required to eliminate discrepancies detected during reviews and audits.

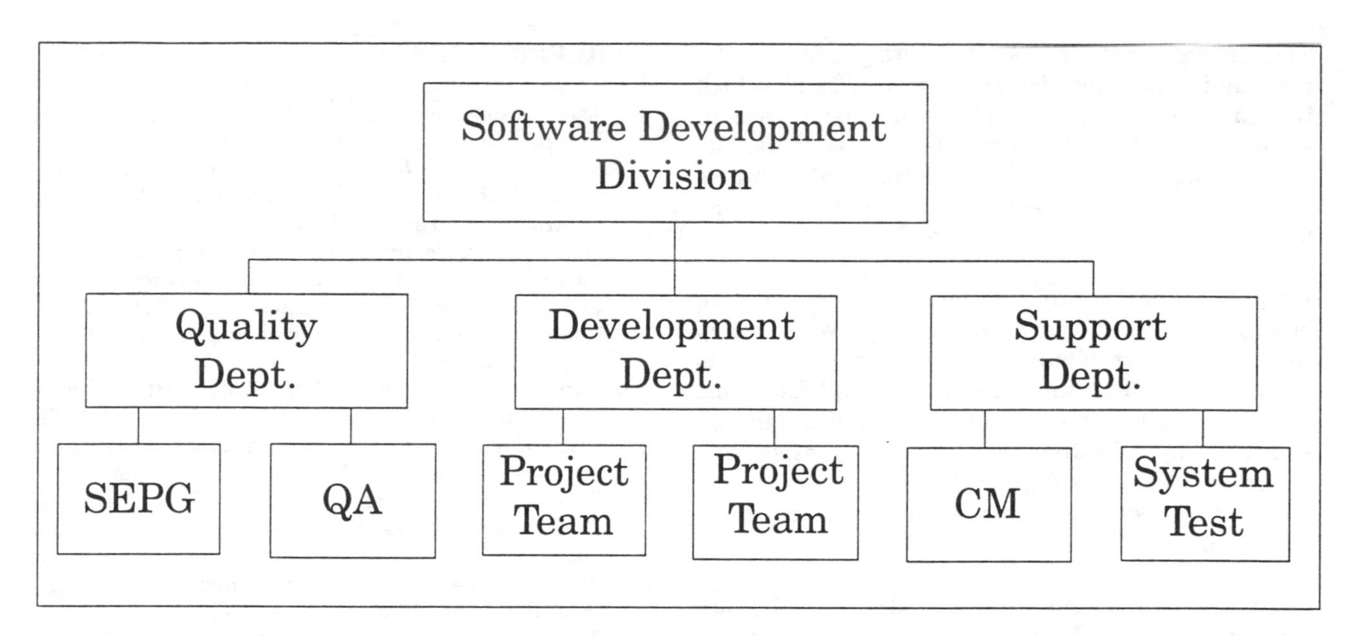


**Figure 7. Organizational Structure Supporting Quality Management Activities**

An important part of the QA function is reporting to project management and to senior management regarding the status of project adherence to defined processes as described in the project plan. Noncompliance issues that cannot be resolved within the software project are addressed by senior management.

The QM functions defined at the organizational and project levels provide a comprehensive set of well-integrated processes needed for prediction and control of project costs and schedule and of product quality.

## QUALITY MANAGEMENT ORGANIZATION

The organization of personnel and other resources required to carry out the development and QM functions is a critical element of success in implementing a quality program. The organizational structure used to define roles and responsibilities of personnel can vary depending on the resources, skills, and culture inherent in the organization itself. The structure presented in this section is a composite based on the author's experience as an instructor and consultant for organizations seeking to institute a QM program, and thus, is intended as a representative structure. The structure is shown in Figure 7. Some alternatives are described in the text.

**Software Engineering Process Group (SEPG).** The SEPG is responsible for capturing, documenting, maintaining and disseminating the organization's software process activities. The SEI's CMM requires an SEPG, or similar group, for Level 3 [44]. In the context of this paper, the SEPG performs the functions defined at the organizational level, which include definition and improvement of software development processes, metrics collection and analysis, and training.

Many software development organizations are in the early stage of implementing QM functions with primary focus on definining the various processes required. As such, the SEPG may not be considered a permanent organizational entity with traditional line management as shown, but instead may report to a "Steering Committee" composed of managers who will implement the defined procedures on software projects. The Steering Committee would include the division and department managers and the project team, QA, CM, and Test managers. In this early stage, "working groups" are created to define and document a specific process(es) which will become the organizational standard. For example, a requirements working group would be responsible for defining and documenting the process to be followed by individual projects for requirements management. The working groups report to the SEPG. The SEPG and the working groups are typically staffed with software development personnel on a part- or full-time basis.

**Quality Assurance (QA).** The QA group is responsible for assuring defined processes are followed by those organizational entities carrying out the project-level QM function. Thus, the QA group performs those QA functions defined at the project level which include reviews, audits, and consultations.

The QA organization is staffed with personnel who have in-depth knowledge of the processes for which they are providing oversight; thus, experience in software engineering is a desirable pre-requisite. The organization may have part- or full-time staff positions and may rotate software engineers into QA positions for a period of time.

**Project Team**. The project team includes the software project manager and software engineers who develop the software and related products. This group performs all project-level QM functions except for QA functions. The project manager is responsible for project planning and tracking and software engineers are responsible for product engineering, verification and validation (other than system testing),and requirements management.

**Configuration Management (CM).** The CM group performs the configuration management activities for all projects in the organization. It is not uncommon in small development organizations, however, for the project team to perform these functions for a specific project.

**System Test.** The system test group is responsible for the independent V&V activity of testing the complete system prior to delivery. It is not uncommon in small development organizations, however, for the project team to perform these functions for a project.

## SUMMARY

The future prospects for improvement in software quality appear promising. Quality Management programs are being organized and implemented by many development organizations using the Capability Maturity Model developed by the Software Engineering Institute for guidance. Quality Assurance as an entity of Quality Management is emerging as an important oversight function to ensure that documented processes are being followed and that they are effective. Organizations such as Hughes Aircraft, Motorola, Raytheon, and IBM have shown that improvements in quality and productivity go hand-in-hand in the field of software development, as has been shown in other industries such as manufacturing. The technologies needed for improvement are defined and available to organizations through methodologies and supporting tools. Quality initiatives by industry and by government agencies provide strong incentives for a change in culture from the ad-hoc development processes of the past decades to a more defined structure for the future. Only through a focus on quality issues can the U. S. software industry maintain its supremacy and meet the challenges of the competitive 21st century.

## REFERENCES


1. Ashley, Nicholas, “METKIT: Training in How to Use Measurement as a Software Management Tool,” *Software Quality Journal*, 3, 1994, pp. 129-136.
2. Bamford, Robert and Deibler, William, “Comparing, Contrasting ISO 9001 and the SEI Capability Maturity Model,” *IEEE Computer*, October 1993, pp. 68-70.
3. Basili, V. R. and Weiss, D. M., "A Methodology for Collecting Valid Software Engineering Data," *IEEE Transactions on Software Engineering*, Vol. SE-10, No. 6, November 1984.
4. Basili, V. R. and Rombach, H. D., "Tailoring the Software Process to Project Goals and Environments," *IEEE Proceedings of the Ninth InternationalConference on Software Engineering*, Monterey, CA, April 1987.
5. Basili, V.R. and Musa, J. D., “The Future Engineering of Software: A Management Perspective,” *IEEE Computer*, Vol. 24, No. 9, September 1991, pp. 90-96.
6. Basili, Victor *et al*, “Technology Transfer at Motorola,” *IEEE Software*, March 1994, pp. 70-76.
7. Brooks, F. P., *The Mythical Man-Month*, Addison-Wesley, 1975.
8. Brooks, Fred, “No Silver Bullet: Essence and Accidents of Software Engineering,” *IEEE Computer*, April 1987.
9. Buckley, Fletcher J., “Software Quality Assurance,” *IEEE Transactions on Software Engineering*, January 1984, pp. 36-41.
10. Buckley, Fletcher J., “Implementing a Software Configuration Management Environment,” *IEEE Computer*, February 1994, pp. 56-61.
11. Card, David, “The SEI Software Process Improvement Approach: A Case Study,” *Software Engineering Strategies*, November/December 1993, pp. 7-14.
12. Crosby, P. B., *Quality is Free: The Art of Making Quality Certain*, McGraw-Hill, 1979.
13. Crosby, Philip, *Quality Without Tears*, McGraw-Hill, 1984.
14. Curtis, B. and Paulk, M., “Creating a Software Process Improvement Program,” *Information and Software Technology*, June/July, 1993, pp. 381-386.
15. Cusumano, Michael, *Japan's Software Factories: A Challenge to U. S. Management*, M.I.T. Press, 1991.
16. Daskalantonakis, Michael, “A Practical View of Software Measurement and Implementation Experiences within Motorola, *IEEE Transactions on Software Engineering*, November 1992, pp. 998-1010.
17. Dion, Raymond, “Elements of a Process-Improvement Program,” *IEEE Software*, July 1992, pp. 83-85.
18. Dorling, A., “SPICE: Software Process Improvement and Capability dEtermination,” *Information and Software Technology*, June/July 1993, pp. 404-406.
19. Ebenau, Robert G., “Predictive Quality Control with Software Inspections,” *CrossTalk*, June 1994, pp. 9-16.
20. Fenton, Norman, *Software Metrics: A Rigorous Approach*, Chapman & Hall, 1991.
21. Fenton, Norman, “How Effective Are Software Engineering Methods?” *The Journal of Systems and Software*, 22, 1993, pp. 141-146.
22. Freedman, D. P. and Weinberg, G. M., “Reviews, Walkthroughs, and Inspections,” *IEEE Transactions on Software Engineering*, January 1984.

23. Gibbs, W. Wayt, "Software's Chronic Crisis," *Scientific American*, September 1994, pp. 86-95.
24. Grady, R. B. and Caswell, D. L., *Software Metrics: Establishing a Company-wide Program*, Prentice-Hall, 1986.
25. Grady, Robert B., *Practical Software Metrics for Project Management and Process Improvement*, Prentice-Hall, 1992.
26. Hausler, P. A., Linger, R. C., and Trammell, C. J., "Adopting Cleanroom Software Engineering With a Phased Approach," *IBM Systems Journal*, Vol. 33, No. 1, 1994, pp. 89-109.
27. Humphrey, Watts, *Managing the Software Process*, Addison-Wesley, 1989.
28. Humphrey, W., Snyder, T. and Willis, R., "Software Process Improvement at Hughes Aircraft," *IEEE Software*, July 1991.
29. *IEEE Standard for a Software Quality Metrics Methodology*, IEEE Std 1061-1992, IEEE, 1992.
30. *IEEE Standard for Software Productivity Metrics,* IEEE Std 1045-1992, IEEE, 1992.
31. *IEEE Standard for Software Quality Assurance Plans*, IEEE 730-1989, IEEE, 1989.
32. *IEEE Standard Glossary of Software Engineering Terminology*, Std 610.12-1990, IEEE, 1990.
33. Jones, Capers, "Determining Software Schedules," *IEEE Computer*, February 1995, pp. 73-75.
34. Kan, S. H., Basili, V. R., and Shapiro, L. N., "Software Quality: An Overview from the Perspective of Total Quality Management," *IBM Systems Journal*, Vol. 33, No. 1, 1994, pp. 4-19.
35. Kuvaja, Pasc and Biccgo, Adriana, "BOOTSTRAP — a European Assessment Methodology", *Software Quality Journal*, 3, 1994, 99 117-127.
36. Lutz, Michael, "Complex Software: Unsafe at any Level," *IEEE Software*, November 1994, pp. 110-111.
37. Marciniak, John J., Editor-in-Chief, "Quality Assurance", *Encyclopedia of Software Engineering*, Volume 2, John Wiley & Sons, 1994, pp. 941-958.
38. McGarry, F. E., "Results of 15 Years of Measurement in the SEL," *Proceedings: Fifteenth Annual Software Engineering Workshop*, NASA/Goddard Space Flight Center, November, 1990.
39. Miluk, G. "Cultural Barriers to Software Measurement," *Proceedings: First International Conference on Applications of Software Measurement*, November 1990.
40. Mosemann, Lloyd K., "Predictability", *Crosstalk*, August 1994, pp. 2-6.
41. Oliver, Paul, "Using a Process Assessment to Improve Software Quality," *Software Engineering Strategies*, March/April, 1993, pp. 14-20.
42. Over, James, "Motivation for Process-Driven Development," *Crosstalk*, January 1993, pp. 17-24.
43. Parnas, E. W. and Weiss, D. M., "Active Design Reviews: Principles and Practices," *Proceedings of ICSE '85* (London, England, Aug. 28-30), IEEE Computer Society, 1985, pp. 132-136.
44. Paulk, Mark C. *et al.*, *Capability Maturity Model for Software, Version 1.1*, CMU/SEI-93-TR-24, Software Engineering Institute, 1993.
45. Paulk, Mark *et al.*, "Capability Maturity Model, Version 1.1," *IEEE Software*, July 1993, pp. 18-26.
46. Perry, William, "Quality Concerns in Software Development," *Information Systems Management*, Spring 1992, pp. 48-52.
47. Petroski, Henry, *To Engineer is Human*, St. Martin's Press, 1985.
48. Pfleeger, S. L., Fitzgerald, J. C., and Porter, A., "The CONTEL Software Metrics Program," *Proceeding: First International Conference on Applications of Software Measurement*, November, 1990.
49. Pressman, Roger, "Assessing Software Engineering Practices for Successful Technology Transition," *Software Engineering Strategies*, 1992, pp. 6-14.
50. Russell, Glen W., "Experience with Inspections in Ultralarge-Scale Developments," *IEEE Software*, January 1991, pp. 25-30.
51. Schulmeyer, G. Gordon and McManus, James I., *Handbook of Software Quality Assurance*, Van Nostrand Reinhold, 1987.
52. Sharon, David and Bell, Rodney, "Tools that Bind: Creating Integrated Environments," *IEEE Software*, March 1995, pp. 76-85.
53. *Specification of the Software Quality Attributes, Vol. 1, 2, and 3*, RADC-TR-85-37, Rome Laboratories, 1985.
54. Sudlow, Bill, "Moving from Chaos to SEI Level 2", *Software Development*, December 1994, pp. 37-40.
55. *The Project Management Body of Knowledge*(Draft), Project Management Institute, August 1994.
56. Weigers, Karl, "Lessons from Software Work Effort Metrics," *Software Development*, October 1994, pp. 37-47.
57. Weinberg, Gerald and Freedman Daniel, *Handbook of Walkthorughs, Inspections, and Technical Reviews, Third Ed.*, Dorset House, 1990.
58. Weller, Edward F., "Lessons from Three Years of Inspection Data," *IEEE Software*, September 1993, pp. 38-45.
59. Yourdon, Ed, "Software Metrics," *Application Development Strategies*, Vol. VI, No. 11, November 1994, pp. 1-16.


---

ABOUT THE AUTHOR

**PATRICIA W. HURST** is a senior lecturer/instructor with Fastrak Training, Inc. in Columbia, MD. Her seminars and workshops include software engineering topics such as quality assurance, project management, process modeling and risk management. She is the author of *Software Quality Assurance: Control, Metrics and Testing*, a course published by Technology Exchange Company, Reading, MA. She is past Editor and Publisher of *Deadline Newsletter*, a bimothly publication of abstracts from leading journals and other publications of interest to the software-engineering community.

# Elements of Software Configuration Management

EDWARD H. BERSOFF, SENIOR MEMBER, IEEE

***Abstract*—Software configuration management (SCM) is one of the disciplines of the 1980's which grew in response to the many failures of the software industry throughout the 1970's. Over the last ten years, computers have been applied to the solution of so many complex problems that our ability to manage these applications has all too frequently failed. This has resulted in the development of a series of "new" disciplines intended to help control the software process.**

**This paper will focus on the discipline of SCM by first placing it in its proper context with respect to the rest of the software development process, as well as to the goals of that process. It will examine the constituent components of SCM, dwelling at some length on one of those components, configuration control. It will conclude with a look at what the 1980's might have in store.**

***Index Terms*—Configuration management, management, product assurance, software.**

## Introduction

SOFTWARE configuration management (SCM) is one of the disciplines of the 1980's which grew in response to the many failures of our industry throughout the 1970's. Over the last ten years, computers have been applied to the solution of so many complex problems that our ability to manage these applications in the "traditional" way has all too frequently failed. Of course, tradition in the software business began only 30 years ago or less, but even new habits are difficult to break. In the 1970's we learned the hard way that the tasks involved in managing a software project were not linearly dependent on the number of lines of code produced. The relationship was, in fact, highly exponential. As the decade closed, we looked back on our failures [1], [2] trying to understand what went wrong and how we could correct it. We began to dissect the software development process [3], [4] and to define techniques by which it could be effectively managed [5]-[8]. This self-examination by some of the most talented and experienced members of the software community led to the development of a series of "new" disciplines intended to help control the software process.

While this paper will focus on the particular discipline of SCM, we will first place it in its proper context with respect to the rest of the software development process, as well as to the goals of that process. We will examine the constituent components of SCM, dwelling at some length on one of those components, configuration control. Once we have woven our way through all the trees, we will once again stand back and take a brief look at the forest and see what the 1980's might have in store.

Manuscript received April 15, 1982; revised December 1, 1982 and October 18, 1983.

The author is with BTG, Inc., 1945 Gallows Rd., Vienna, VA 22180.

## SCM in Context

It has been said that if you do not know where you are going, any road will get you there. In order to properly understand the role that SCM plays in the software development process, we must first understand what the goal of that process is, i.e., where we are going. For now, and perhaps for some time to come, software developers are people, people who respond to the needs of another set of people creating computer programs designed to satisfy those needs. These computer programs are the tangible output of a thought process—the conversion of a thought process into a product. The goal of the software developer is, or should be, the construction of a product which closely matches the real needs of the set of people for whom the software is developed. We call this goal the achievement of "product integrity." More formally stated, product integrity (depicted in Fig. 1) is defined to be the intrinsic set of attributes that characterize a product [9]:

- that fulfills user functional needs;
- that can easily and completely be traced through its life cycle;
- that meets specified performance criteria;
- whose cost expectations are met;
- whose delivery expectations are met.

The above definition is pragmatically based. It demands that product integrity be a measure of the satisfaction of the real needs and expectations of the software user. It places the burden for achieving the software goal, product integrity, squarely on the shoulders of the developer, for it is he alone who is in control of the development process. While, as we shall see, the user can establish safeguards and checkpoints to gain visibility into the development process, the prime responsibility for software success is the developer's. So our goal is now clear; we want to build software which exhibits all the characteristics of product integrity. Let us make sure that we all understand, however, what this thing called software really is. We have learned in recent times that equating the terms "software" and "computer programs" improperly restricts our view of software. Software is much more. A definition which can be used to focus the discussion in this paper is that software is information that is:

- structured with logical and functional properties;
- created and maintained in various forms and representations during the life cycle;
- tailored for machine processing in its fully developed state.

So by our definition, software is not simply a set of computer programs, but includes the documentation required to define, develop, and maintain these programs. While this notion is not very new, it still frequently escapes the software

Reprinted from *IEEE Trans. Software Eng.*, Vol. SE-10, No. 1, Jan. 1984, pp. 79–87. 

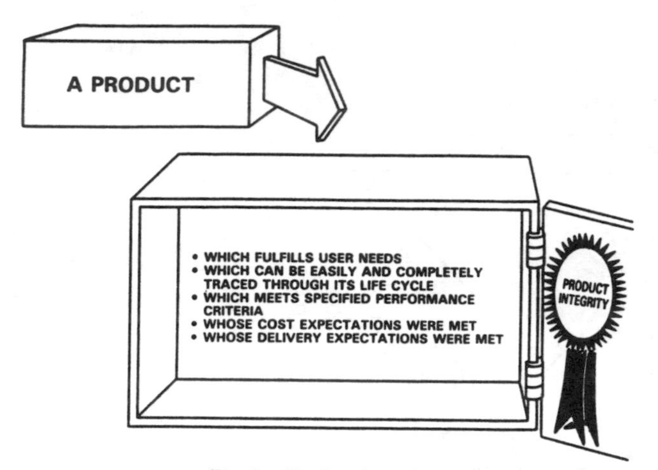


Fig. 1. Product integrity.

development manager who assumes that controlling a software product is the same as controlling computer code.

Now that we more fully appreciate what we are after, i.e., to build a software product with integrity, let us look at the one road which might get us there. We have, until now, used the term "developer" to characterize the organizational unit responsible for converting the software idea into a software product. But developers are, in reality, a complex set of interacting organizational entities. When undertaking a software project, most developers structure themselves into three basic discipline sets which include:

- project management,
- development, and
- product assurance.

Project management disciplines are both inwardly and outwardly directed. They support general management's need to see what is going on in a project and to ensure that the parent or host organization consistently develops products with integrity. At the same time, these disciplines look inside a project in support of the assignment, allocation, and control of all project resources. In that capacity, project management determines the relative allocation of resources to the set of development and product assurance disciplines. It is management's prerogative to specify the extent to which a given discipline will be applied to a given project. Historically, management has often been handicapped when it came to deciding how much of the product assurance disciplines were required. This was a result of both inexperience and organizational immaturity.

The development disciplines represent those traditionally applied to a software project. They include:

- analysis,
- design,
- engineering,
- production (coding),
- test (unit/subsystem),
- installation,
- documentation,
- training, and
- maintenance.

In the broadest sense, these are the disciplines required to take a system concept from its beginning through the development life cycle. It takes a well-structured, rigorous technical approach to system development, along with the right mix of development disciplines to attain product integrity, especially for software. The concept of an ordered, procedurally disciplined approach to system development is fundamental to product integrity. Such an approach provides successive development plateaus, each of which is an identifiable measure of progress which forms a part of the total foundation supporting the final product. Going sequentially from one baseline (plateau) to another with high probability of success, necessitates the use of the right development disciplines at precisely the right time.

The product assurance disciplines which are used by project management to gain visibility into the development process include:

- configuration management,
- quality assurance,
- validation and verification, and
- test and evaluation.

Proper employment of these product assurance disciplines by the project manager is basic to the success of a project since they provide the technical checks and balances over the product being developed. Fig. 2 represents the relationship among the management, development, and product assurance disciplines. Let us look at each of the product assurance disciplines briefly, in turn, before we explore the details of SCM.

Configuration management (CM) is the discipline of identifying the configuration of a system at discrete points in time for the purpose of systematically controlling changes to the configuration and maintaining the integrity and traceability of the configuration throughout the system life cycle. Software configuration management (SCM) is simply configuration management tailored to systems, or portions of systems, that are comprised predominantly of software. Thus, SCM does not differ substantially from the CM of hardware-oriented systems, which is generally well understood and effectively practiced. However, attempts to implement SCM have often failed because the particulars of SCM do not follow by direct analogy from the particulars of hardware CM and because SCM is a less mature discipline than that of hardware CM. We will return to this subject shortly.

Quality assurance (QA) as a discipline is commonly invoked throughout government and industry organizations with reasonable standardization when applied to systems comprised only of hardware. But there is enormous variation in thinking and practice when the QA discipline is invoked for a software development or for a system containing software components. QA has a long history, and much like CM, it has been largely developed and practiced on hardware projects. It is therefore mature, in that sense, as a discipline. Like CM, however, it is relatively immature when applied to software development. We define QA as consisting of the procedures, techniques, and tools applied by professionals to insure that a product meets or exceeds prespecified standards during a product's development cycle; and without specific prescribed standards, QA entails insuring that a product meets or

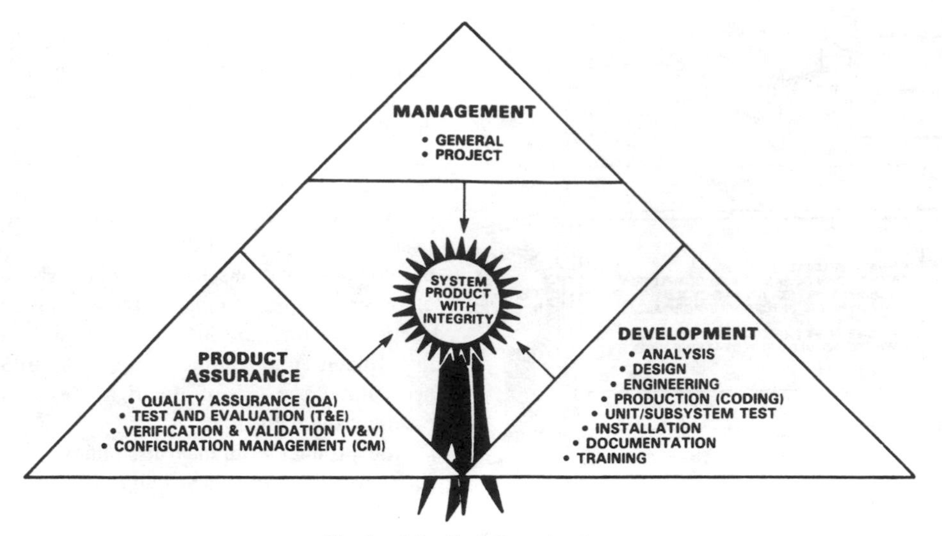


Fig. 2. The discipline triangle.

exceeds a minimum industrial and/or commercially acceptable level of excellence.

The QA discipline has not been uniformly treated, practiced or invoked relative to software development. First, very few organizations have software design and development standards that compare in any way with hardware standards for detail and completeness. Second, it takes a high level of software expertise to assess whether a software product meets prescribed standards. Third, few buyer organizations have provided for or have developed the capability to impose and then monitor software QA endeavors on seller organizations. Finally, few organizations have been concerned over precisely defining the difference between QA and other product assurance disciplines, CM often being subservient to QA or vice versa in a given development organization. Our definition of software given earlier suggests still another reason for the software QA discipline being in the same state as SCM so far as its universal application within the user, buyer, and seller communities. Software, as a form of information, cannot be standardized; only structures for defining/documenting software can be standardized. It follows that software development techniques can only be meaningfully standardized in relation to information structures, not information content.

The third of the four product assurance disciplines is validation and verification (V&V). Unlike CM and QA, V&V has come into being expressly for the purpose of coping with software and its development. Unlike QA, which prinicipally deals with the problem of a product's adherence to preestablished standards, V&V deals with the issue of how well software fulfills functional and performance requirements and the assurance that specified requirements are indeed stated and interpreted correctly. The verification part of V&V assures that a product meets its prescribed goals as defined through baseline documentation. That is, verification is a discipline imposed to ascertain that a product is what it was intended to be relative to its preceding baseline. The validation part of V&V, by contrast, is levied as a discipline to assure that a product not only meets the objectives specified through baseline documentation, but in addition, does the right job. Stated another way, the validation discipline is invoked to insure that the end-user gets the right product. A buyer or seller may have misinterpreted user requirements or, perhaps, requirements have changed, or the user gets to know more about what he needs, or early specifications of requirements were wrong or incomplete or in a state of flux. The validation process serves to assure that such problems do not persist among the user, buyer, and seller. To enhance objectivity, it is often desirable to have an independent organization, from outside the developing organization, perform the V&V function.

The fourth of the product assurance disciplines is test and evaluation (T&E), perhaps the discipline most understood, and yet paradoxically, least practiced with uniformity. T&E is defined as the discipline imposed outside the development project organization to independently assess whether a product fulfills objectives. T&E does this through the execution of a set of test plans and procedures. Specifically in support of the end user, T&E entails evaluating product performance in a live or near-live environment. Frequently, particularly within the miliatry arena, T&E is a major undertaking involving one or more systems which are to operate together, but which have been individually developed and accepted as stand-alone items. Some organizations formally turn over T&E responsibility to a group outside the development project organization after the product reaches a certain stage of development, their philosophy being that developers cannot be objective to the point of fully testing/evaluating what they have produced.

The definitions given for CM, QA, V&V, and T&E suggest some overlap in required skills and functions to be performed in order to invoke these disciplines collectively for product assurance purposes. Depending on many factors, the actual overlap may be significant or little. In fact, there are those who would argue that V&V and T&E are but subset functions of QA. But the contesting argument is that V&V and T&E have come into being as separate disciplines because conventional QA methods and techniques have failed to do an adequate job with respect to providing product assurance, particularly for computer-centered systems with software components. Management must be concerned with minimizing the application of excessive and redundant resources to address the overlap of these disciplines. What is important is that all the functions defined above are performed, not what they are called or who carries them out.

### The Elements of SCM

When the need for the discipline of configuration management finally achieved widespread recognition within the software engineering community, the question arose as to how closely the software CM discipline ought to parallel the extant hardware practice of configuration management. Early SCM authors and practitioners [10] wisely chose the path of commonality with the hardware world, at least at the highest level. Of course, hardware engineering is different from software engineering, but broad similarities do exist and terms applied to one segment of the engineering community can easily be applied to another, even if the specific meanings of those terms differ significantly in detail. For that reason, the elements of SCM were chosen to be the same as those for hardware CM. As for hardware, the four components of SCM are:

- identification,
- control,
- auditing, and
- status accounting.

Let us examine each one in turn.

*Software Configuration Identification:* Effective management of the development of a system requires careful definition of its baseline components; changes to these components also need to be defined since these changes, together with the baselines, specify the system evolution. A system baseline is like a snapshot of the aggregate of system components as they exist at a given point in time; updates to this baseline are like frames in a movie strip of the system life cycle. The role of software configuration identification in the SCM process is to provide labels for these snapshots and the movie strip.

A baseline can be characterized by two labels. One label identifies the baseline itself, while the second label identifies an update to a particular baseline. An update to a baseline represents a baseline plus a set of changes that have been incorporated into it. Each of the baselines established during a software system's life cycle controls subsequent system development. At the time it is first established a software baseline embodies the actual software in its most recent state. When changes are made to the most recently established baseline, then, from the viewpoint of the software configuration manager, this baseline and these changes embody the actual software in its most recent state (although, from the viewpoint of the software developer, the actual software may be in a more advanced state).

The most elementary entity in the software configuration identification labeling mechanism is the software configuration item (SCI). Viewed from an SCM perspective, a software baseline appears as a set of SCI's. The SCI's within a baseline are related to one another via a tree-like hierarchy. As the software system evolves through its life cycle, the number of branches in this hierarchy generally increases; the first baseline may consist of no more than one SCI. The lowest level SCI's in the tree hierarchy may still be under development and not yet under SCM control. These entities are termed design objects or computer program components (see Fig. 3). Each baseline and each member in the associated family of updates will exist in one or more forms, such as a design document, source code on a disk, or executing object code.

In performing the identification function, the software configuration manager is, in effect, taking snapshots of the SCI's. Each baseline and its associated updates collectively represents the evolution of the software during each of its life cycle stages. These stages are staggered with respect to one another. Thus, the collection of life cycle stages looks like a collection of staggered and overlapping sequences of snapshots of SCI trees. Let us now imagine that this collection of snapshot sequences is threaded, in chronological order, onto a strip of movie film as in Fig. 4. Let us further imagine that the strip of movie film is run through a projector. Then we would see a history of the evolution of the software. Consequently, the identification of baselines and updates provides an explicit documentation trail linking all stages of the software life cycle. With the aid of this documentation trail, the software developer can assess the integrity of his product, and the software buyer can assess the integrity of the product he is paying for.

*Software Configuration Control:* The evolution of a software system is, in the language of SCM, the development of baselines and the incorporation of a series of changes into the baselines. In addition to these changes that explicitly affect existing baselines, there are changes that occur during early stages of the system life cycle that may affect baselines that do not yet exist. For example, some time before software coding begins (i.e., some time prior to the establishment of a design baseline), a contract may be modified to include a software warranty provision such as: system downtime due to software failures shall not exceed 30 minutes per day. This warranty provision will generally affect subsequent baselines but in a manner that cannot be explicitly determined *a priori*. One role of software configuration control is to provide the administrative mechanism for precipitating, preparing, evaluating, and approving or disapproving all change proposals throughout the system life cycle.

We have said that software, for configuration management purposes, is a collection of SCI's that are related to one another in a well-defined way. In early baselines and their associated updates, SCI's are specification documents (one or more volumes of text for each baseline or associated update); in later baselines and their associated updates, each SCI may manifest itself in any or all of the various software representations. Software configuration control focuses on managing changes to SCI's (existing or to be developed) in all of their representations. This process involves three basic ingredients.

1) Documentation (such as administrative forms and supporting technical and administrative material) for formally precipitating and defining a proposed change to a software system.

2) An organizational body for formally evaluating and

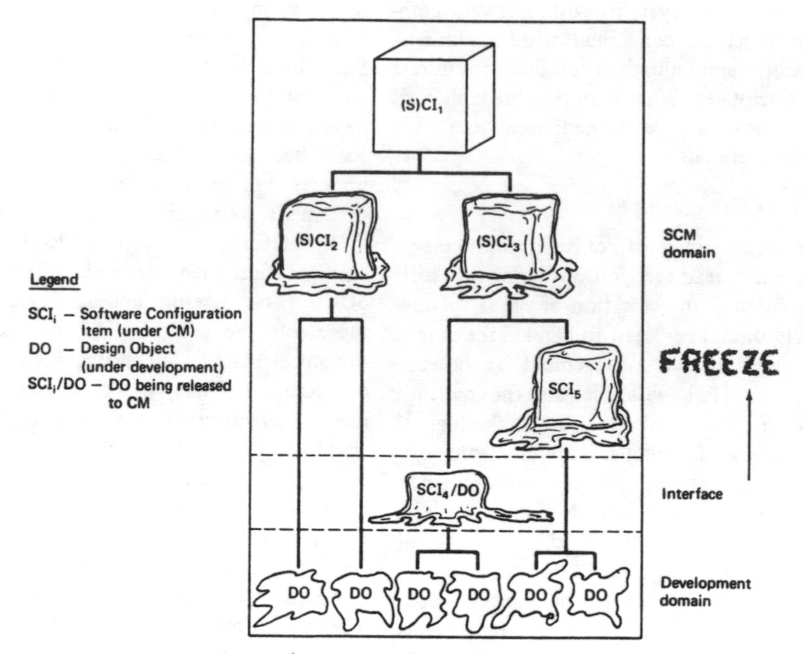


Fig. 3. The development/SCM interface.

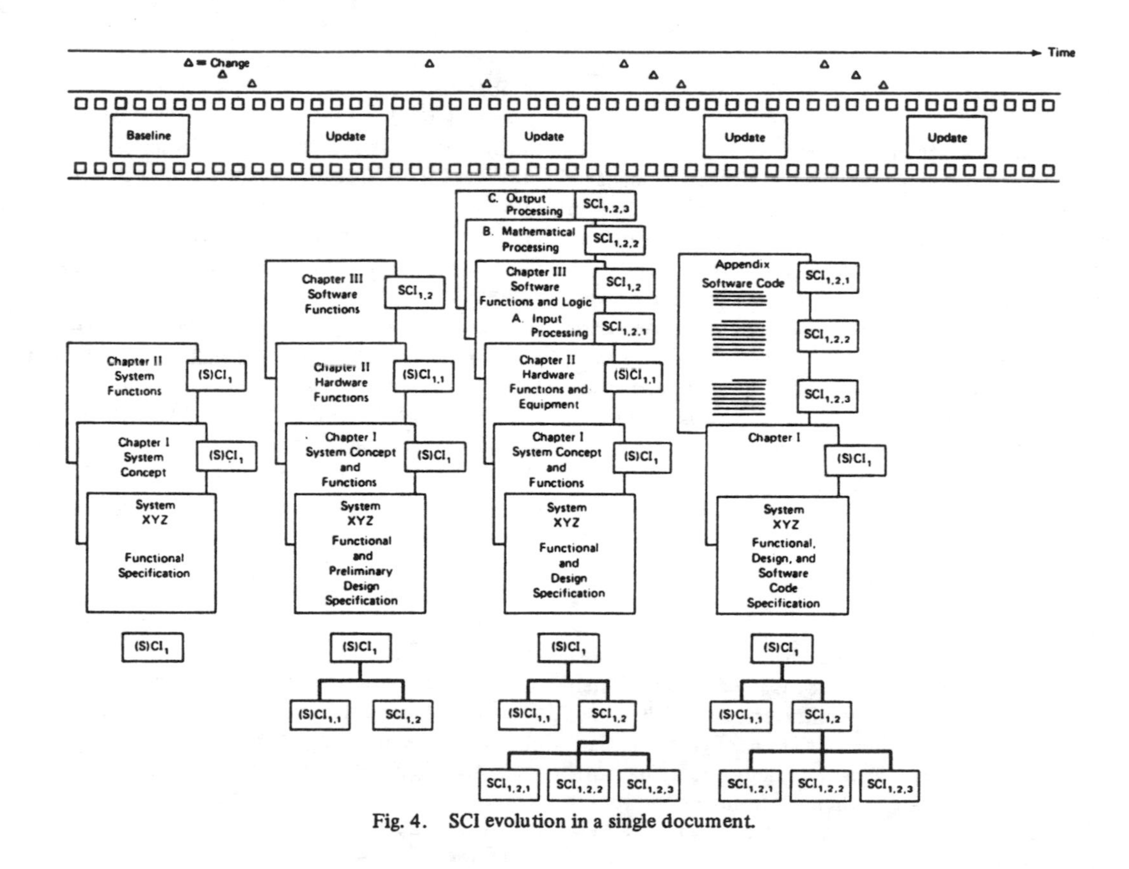


Fig. 4. SCI evolution in a single document.

approving or disapproving a proposed change to a software system (the Configuration Control Board).

3) Procedures for controlling changes to a software system.

The Engineering Change Proposal (ECP), a major control document, contains information such as a description of the proposed change, identification of the originating organization, rationale for the change, identification of affected baselines and SCI's (if appropriate), and specification of cost and schedule impacts. ECP's are reviewed and coordinated by the CCB, which is typically a body representing all organizational units which have a vested interest in proposed changes.

Fig. 5 depicts the software configuration control process.

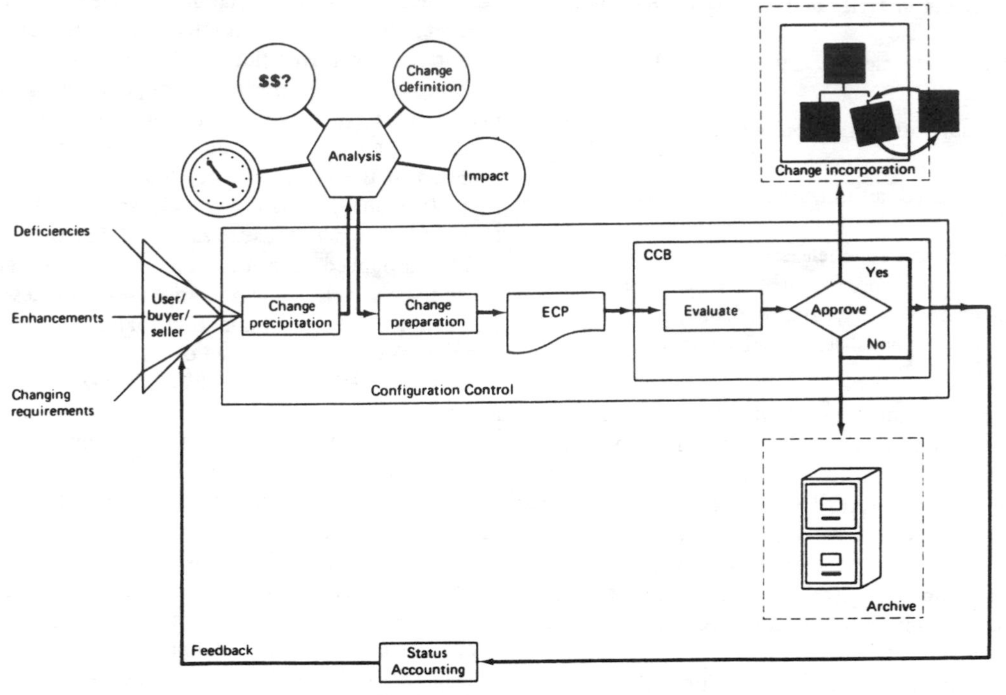


Fig. 5. The control process.

As the figure suggests, change incorporation is not an SCM function, but monitoring the change implementation process resulting in change incorporation is. Fig. 5 also emphasizes that the analysis that may be required to prepare an ECP is also outside the SCM purview. Note also from the figure how ECP's not approved by the CCB are not simply discarded but are archived for possible future reference.

Many automated tools support the control process. The major ones aid in controlling software change once the coding stage has been reached, and are generically referred to as program support libraries (PSL's). The level of support provided by PSL's, however, varies greatly. As a minimum, a PSL should provide a centralized and readily available repository for authoritative versions of each component of a software system. It should contain the data necessary for the orderly development and control of each SCI. Automation of other functions, such as library access control, software and document version maintenance, change recording, and document reconstruction, greatly enhance both the control and maintenance processes. These capabilities are currently available in systems such as SOFTOOL's change and configuration control environment (CCC).

A PSL supports a developmental approach in which project personnel work on a common visible product rather than on independent components. In those PSL's which include access controls, project personnel can be separately assigned read/write access to each software document/component, from programs to lines of code. Thus, all project personnel are assured ready access to the critical interface information necessary for effective software development. At the same time, modifications to various software components, whether sanctioned baselines or modules under development, can be closely controlled.

Under the PSL concept, the programmer operates under a well-defined set of parameters and exercises a narrower span of detailed control. This minimizes the need for explicit communication between analysts and programmers and makes the inclusion of new project personnel less traumatic since interface requirements are well documented. It also minimizes the preparation effort for technical audits.

Responsibility for maintenance of the PSL data varies depending on the level of automation provided. For those systems which provide only a repository for data, a secretary/librarian is usually responsible for maintaining the notebooks which will contain the data developed and used by project personnel and for maintenance of the PSL archives. More advanced PSL systems provide real time, on-line access to data and programs and automatically create the records necessary to fully trace the history of the development. In either case the PSL provides standardization of project recordkeeping, ensures that system documentation corresponds to the current system configuration, and guarantees the existence of adequate documentation of previous versions.

A PSL should support three main activities: code development, software management, and configuration control. Support to the development process includes support to design, coding, testing, documentation, and program maintenance along with associated database schema and subschema. A PSL provides this support through:

- storage and maintenance of software documentation and code,
- support to program compilation/testing,
- support for the generation of program/system documentation.

Support to the management of the software development process involves the storage and output of programming data such as:

- collection and automatic reporting of management data related to program development,

- control over the integrity and security of the data in the PSL,
- separation of the clerical activity related to the programming process.

PSL's provide support to the configuration control process through:

- access and change authorization control for all data in the library,
- control of software code releases,
- automatic program and document reconstruction,
- automatic change tracking and reporting,
- assurance of the consistency between documentation, code, and listings.

A PSL has four major components: internal libraries in machine-readable form, external libraries in hardcopy form, computer procedures, and office procedures. The components of a PSL system are interlocked to establish an exact correspondence between the internal units of code and external versions (such as listings) of the developing systems. This continuous correspondence is the characteristic of a PSL that guarantees ongoing visibility and identification of the developing system.

Different PSL implementations exist for various system environments with the specifics of the implementation dependent upon the hardware, software, user, and operating environment. The fundamental correspondence between the internal and external libraries in each environment, however, is established by the PSL librarian and computer procedures. The office procedures are specified in a project CM Plan so that the format of the external libraries is standard across software projects, and internal and external libraries are easily maintainable.

Newer PSL systems minimize the need for both office and computer procedures through the implementation of extensive management functionality. This functionality provides significant flexibility in controlling the access to data and allocating change authority, while providing a variety of status reporting capabilities. The availability of management information, such as a list of all the software structures changed to solve a particular Software Trouble Report or the details on the latest changes to a particular software document, provides a means for the control function to effectively operate without burdening the development team with cumbersome procedures and administrative paperwork. Current efforts in PSL refinement/development are aimed at linking support of the development environment with that of the configuration control environment. The goal of such systems is to provide an integrated environment where control and management information is generated automatically as a part of a fully supported design and development process.

*Software Configuration Auditing:* Software configuration auditing provides the mechanism for determining the degree to which the current state of the software system mirrors the software system pictured in baseline and requirements documentation. It also provides the mechanism for formally establishing a baseline. A baseline in its formative stages (for example, a draft specification document that appears prior to the existence of the functional baseline) is referred to as a "to-be-established" baseline; the final state of the auditing process conducted on a to-be-established baseline is a sanctioned baseline. The same may be said about baseline updates.

Software configuration auditing serves two purposes, configuration verification and configuration validation. Verification ensures that what is intended for each software configuration item as specified in one baseline or update is actually achieved in the succeeding baseline or update; validation ensures that the SCI configuration solves the right problem (i.e., that customer needs are satisfied). Software configuration auditing is applied to each baseline (and corresponding update) in its to-be-established state. An auditing process common to all baselines is the determination that an SCI structure exists and that its contents are based on all available information.

Software auditing is intended to increase software visibility and to establish traceability throughout the life cycle of the software product. Of course, this visibility and traceability are not achieved without cost. Software auditing costs time and money. But the judicious investment of time and money, particularly in the early stages of a project, pays dividends in the latter stages. These dividends include the avoidance of costly retrofits resulting from problems such as the sudden appearance of new requirements and the discovery of major design flaws. Conversely, failing to perform auditing, or constraining it to the later stages of the software life cycle, can jeopardize successful software development. Often in such cases, by the time discrepancies are discovered (if they are), the software cannot be easily or economically modified to rectify the discrepancies. The result is often a dissatisfied customer, large cost overruns, slipped schedules, or cancelled projects.

Software auditing makes visible to management the current status of the software in the life cycle product audited. It also reveals whether the project requirements are being satisfied and whether the intent of the preceding baseline has been fulfilled. With this visibility, project management can evaluate the integrity of the software product being developed, resolve issues that may have been raised by the audit, and correct defects in the development process. The visibility afforded by the software audit also provides a basis for the establishment of the audited life cycle product as a new baseline.

Software auditing provides traceability between a software life cycle product and the requirements for that product. Thus, as life cycle products are audited and baselines established, every requirement is traced successively from baseline to baseline. Disconnects are also made visible during the establishment of traceability. These disconnects include requirements not satisfied in the audited product and extraneous features observed in the product (i.e., features for which no stated requirement exists).

With the different point of view made possible by the visibility and traceability achieved in the software audit, management can make better decisions and exercise more incisive control over the software development process. The result of a software audit may be the establishment of a baseline, the redirection of project tasking, or an adjustment of applied project resources.

The responsibility for a successful software development project is shared by the buyer, seller, and user. Software auditing uniquely benefits each of these project participants. Appropriate auditing by each party provides checks and balances over the development effort. The scope and depth of the audits undertaken by the three parties may vary greatly. However, the purposes of these differing forms of software audit remain the same: to provide visibility and to establish traceability of the software life cycle products. An excellent overview of the software audit process, from which some of the above discussion has been extracted, appears in [11].

*Software Configuration Status Accounting:* A decision to make a change is generally followed by a time delay before the change is actually made, and changes to baselines generally occur over a protracted period of time before they are incorporated into baselines as updates. A mechanism is therefore needed for maintaining a record of how the system has evolved and where the system is at any time relative to what appears in published baseline documentation and written agreements. Software configuration status accounting provides this mechanism. Status accounting is the administrative tracking and reporting of all software items formally identified and controlled. It also involves the maintenance of records to support software configuration auditing. Thus, software configuration status accounting records the activity associated with the other three SCM functions and therefore provides the means by which the history of the software system life cycle can be traced.

Although administrative in nature, status accounting is a function that increases in complexity as the system life cycle progresses because of the multiple software representations that emerge with later baselines. This complexity generally results in large amounts of data to be recorded and reported. In particular, the scope of software configuration status accounting encompasses the recording and reporting of:

1) the time at which each representation of a baseline and update came into being;

2) the time at which each software configuration item came into being;

3) descriptive information about each SCI;

4) engineering change proposal status (approved, disapproved, awaiting action);

5) descriptive information about each ECP;

6) change status;

7) descriptive information about each change;

8) status of technical and administrative documentation associated with a baseline or update (such as a plan prescribing tests to be performed on a baseline for updating purposes);

9) deficiencies in a to-be-established baseline uncovered during a configuration audit.

Software configuration status accounting, because of its large data input and output requirements, is generally supported in part by automated processes such as the PSL described earlier. Data are collected and organized for input to a computer and reports giving the status of entities are compiled and generated by the computer.

## The Management Dilemma

As we mentioned at the beginning of this paper, SCM and many of the other product assurance disciplines grew up in the 1970's in response to software failure. The new disciplines were designed to achieve visibility into the software engineering process and thereby exercise some measure of control over that process. Students of mathematical control theory are taught early in their studies a simple example of the control process. Consider being confronted with a cup of hot coffee, filled to the top, which you are expected to carry from the kitchen counter to the kitchen table. It is easily verified that if you watch the cup as you carry it, you are likely to spill more coffee than if you were to keep your head turned away from the cup. The problem with looking at the cup is one of overcompensation. As you observe slight deviations from the straight-and-level, you adjust, but often you adjust too much. To compensate for that overadjustment, you tend to overadjust again, with the result being hot coffee on your floor.

This little diversion from our main topic of SCM has an obvious moral. There is a fundamental propensity on the part of the practitioners of the product assurance disciplines to overadjust, to overcompensate for the failures of the development disciplines. There is one sure way to eliminate failure completely from the software development process, and that is to stop it completely. The software project manager must learn how to apply his resources intelligently. He must achieve visibility and control, but he must not so encumber the developer so as to bring progress to a virtual halt. The product assurers have a virtuous perspective. They strive for perfection and point out when and where perfection has not been achieved. We seem to have a binary attitude about software; it is either correct or it is not. That is perhaps true, but we cannot expect anyone to deliver perfect software in any reasonable time period or for a reasonable sum of money. What we need to develop is software that is good enough. Some of the controls that we have placed on the developer have the deleterious effect of increasing costs and expanding schedules rather than shrinking them.

The dilemma to management is real. We must have the visibility and control that the product assurance disciplines have the capacity to provide. But we must be careful not to overcompensate and overcontrol. This is the fine line which will distinguish the successful software managers of the 1980's from the rest of the software engineering community.


## Acknowledgment

The author wishes to acknowledge the contribution of B. J. Gregor to the preparation and critique of the final manuscript.


## References


[1] "Contracting for computer software development—Serious problems require management attention to avoid wasting additional millions," General Accounting Office, Rep. FGMSD 80-4, Nov. 9, 1979.

[2] D. M. Weiss, "The MUDD report: A case study of Navy software development practices," Naval Res. Lab., Rep. 7909, May 21, 1975.

[3] B. W. Boehm, "Software engineering," *IEEE Trans. Comput.*, vol. C-25, pp. 1226–1241, Dec. 1976.

[4] *Proc. IEEE* (Special Issue on Software Engineering), vol. 68, Sept. 1980.

[5] E. Bersoff, V. Henderson, and S. Siegel, "Attaining software product integrity," *Tutorial: Software Configuration Management*, W. Bryan, C. Chadbourne, and S. Siegel, Eds., Los Alamitos, CA, IEEE Comput. Soc., Cat. EHO-169-3, 1981.

[6] B. W. Boehm *et al.*, *Characteristics of Software Quality, TRW Series of Software Technology*, vol. 1. New York: North-Holland, 1978.

[7] T. A. Thayer, *et al.*, *Software Reliability, TRW Series of Software Technology*, vol. 2. New York: North-Holland, 1978.

[8] D. J. Reifer, Ed., *Tutorial: Automated Tools for Software Eng.*, Los Alamitos, CA, IEEE Comput. Soc., Cat. EHO-169-3, 1979.

[9] E. Bersoff, V. Henderson, and S. Siegel, *Software Configuration Management*. Englewood Cliffs, NJ: Prentice-Hall, 1980.

[10] ——, "Software configuration management: A tutorial," *Computer*, vol. 12, pp. 6–14, Jan. 1979.

[11] W. Bryan, S. Siegel, and G. Whiteleather, "Auditing throughout the software life cycle: A primer," *Computer*, vol. 15, pp. 56–67, Mar. 1982.

[12] "Software configuration management," Naval Elec. Syst. Command, Software Management Guidebooks, vol. 2, undated.

# Evaluating Software Engineering Standards

**Shari Lawrence Pfleeger, Norman Fenton, and Stella Page**
**Centre for Software Reliability**

**Given the more than 250 software engineering standards, why do we sometimes still produce less than desirable products? Are the standards not working, or being ignored?**

Software engineering standards abound; since 1976, the Software Engineering Standards Committee of the IEEE Computer Society has developed 19 standards in areas such as terminology, documentation, testing, verification and validation, reviews, and audits.[1] In 1992 alone, standards were completed for productivity and quality metrics, software maintenance, and CASE (computer-aided software engineering) tool selection. If we include work of the major national standards bodies throughout the world, there are in fact more than 250 software engineering standards. The existence of these standards raises some important questions. How do we know which practices to standardize? Since many of our projects produce less-than-desirable products, are the standards not working, or being ignored? Perhaps the answer is that standards have codified approaches whose effectiveness has not been rigorously and scientifically demonstrated. Rather, we have too often relied on anecdote, "gut feeling," the opinions of experts, or even flawed research, rather than on careful, rigorous software engineering experimentation.

This article reports on the results of the Smartie project (Standards and Methods Assessment Using Rigorous Techniques in Industrial Environments), a collaborative effort to propose a widely applicable procedure for the objective assessment of standards used in software development. We hope that, for a given environment and application area, Smartie will enable the identification of standards whose use is most likely to lead to improvements in some aspect of software development processes and products. In this article, we describe how we verified the practicality of the Smartie framework by testing it with corporate partners.

Suppose your organization is considering the implementation of a standard. Smartie should help you to answer the following questions:

- What are the potential benefits of using the standard?
- Can we measure objectively the extent of any benefits that may result from its use?
- What are the related costs necessary to implement the standard?
- Do the costs exceed the benefits?

Reprinted from *IEEE Software*, Vol. 11, No. 5, Sept. 1994, pp. 71–79.

To that end, we present Smartie in three parts. First, we analyze what typical standards look like, both in software engineering and in other engineering disciplines. Next, we discuss how to evaluate a standard for its applicability and objectivity. Finally, we describe the results of a major industrial case study involving the reliability and maintainability of almost two million lines of code.

## Software engineering standards

Standards organizations have developed standards for standards, including a definition of what a standard is. For example, the British Standards Institute defines a standard as

> A technical specification or other document available to the public, drawn up with the cooperation and consensus or general approval of all interests affected by it, based on the consolidated results of science, technology and experience, aimed at the promotion of optimum community benefits.[2]

Do software engineering standards satisfy this definition? Not quite. Our standards are technical specifications available to the public, but they are not always drawn up with the consensus or general approval of all interests affected by them. For example, airline passengers were not consulted when standards were set for building the A320's fly-by-wire software, nor were electricity consumers polled when software standards for nuclear power stations were considered. Of course, the same could be said for other standards; for example, parents may not have been involved in the writing of safety standards for pushchairs (strollers). Nevertheless, the intention of a standard is to reflect the needs of the users or consumers as well as the practices of the builders. More importantly, our standards are not based on the consolidated results of science, technology, and experience.[3] Programming languages are declared to be corporate or even national standards without case studies and experiments to demonstrate the costs and benefits of using them. Techniques such as cleanroom, formal specification, or object-oriented design are mandated before we determine under what circumstances they are most beneficial. Even when scientific analysis and evaluation exist, our standards rarely reference them. So even though our standards are laudably aimed at promoting community benefits, we do not insist on having those benefits demonstrated clearly and scientifically before the standard is published. Moreover, there is rarely a set of objective criteria that we can use to evaluate the proposed technique or process.

Thus, as Smartie researchers, we sought solutions to some of the problems with software engineering standards. We began our investigation by posing three simple questions that we wanted Smartie to help us answer:

- On a given project, what standards are used?
- To what extent is a particular standard followed?
- If a standard is being used, is it effective? That is, is it making a difference in quality or productivity?

### What is a standard — and what does it mean for software engineering?

Often, a standard's size and complexity make it difficult to determine whether a particular organization is compliant. If partial compliance is allowed, measurement of the degree of compliance is difficult, if not impossible — consider, for example, the ISO 9000 series and the 14 major activities it promotes.[4] The Smartie project suggests that large standards be considered as a set of smaller "ministandards." A ministandard is a standard with a cohesive, content-related set of requirements. In the remaining discussion, the term *standard* refers to a ministandard.

## What is a good standard?

We reviewed dozens of software engineering standards, including international, national, corporate, and organizational standards, to see what we could learn. For each standard, we wanted to know

- How good is the standard?
- What is affected by the standard?
- How can we determine compliance with the standard?
- What is the basis for the standard?

"Goodness" of the standard was difficult to determine, as it involved at least three distinct aspects. First, we wanted to know whether and how we can tell if the standard is being complied with. That is, a standard is not a good standard if there is no way of telling whether a particular organization, process, or piece of code complies with the standard. There are many examples of such "bad" standards. For instance, some testing standards require that all statements be tested "thoroughly"; without a clear definition of "thoroughly," we cannot determine compliance. Second, a standard is good only in terms of the success criteria set for it. In other words, we wanted to know what attributes of the final product (such as reliability or maintainability) are supposed to be improved by using the standard. And finally, we wanted to know the cost of applying the standard. After all, if compliance with the standard is so costly as to make its use impractical, or practical only in certain situations, then cost contributes to "goodness."

We developed a scheme to evaluate the degree of objectivity inherent in assessing compliance. We can classify each requirement being evaluated into one of four categories: reference only, subjective, partially objective, and completely objective. A reference-only requirement declares that something will happen, but there is no way to determine compliance; for example, "Unit testing shall be carried out." A subjective requirement is one in which only a subjective measure of conformance is possible; for example, "Unit testing shall be carried out effectively." A subjective requirement is an improvement over a reference-only requirement, but it is subject to the differing opinions of experts. A partially objective requirement involves a measure of conformance that is somewhat objective but still requires a degree of subjectivity; for example, "Unit testing shall be carried out so that all statements and the most probable paths are tested." An objective requirement is the most desirable kind, as conformance to it can be determined completely objectively; for example, "Unit testing shall be carried out so that all statements are tested."

Clearly, our goal as a profession should be to produce standards with require-

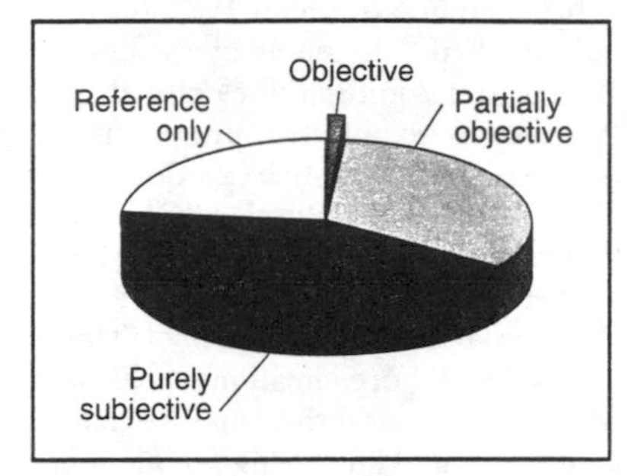


**Figure 1. Degree of objectivity in software engineering standards' requirements.**

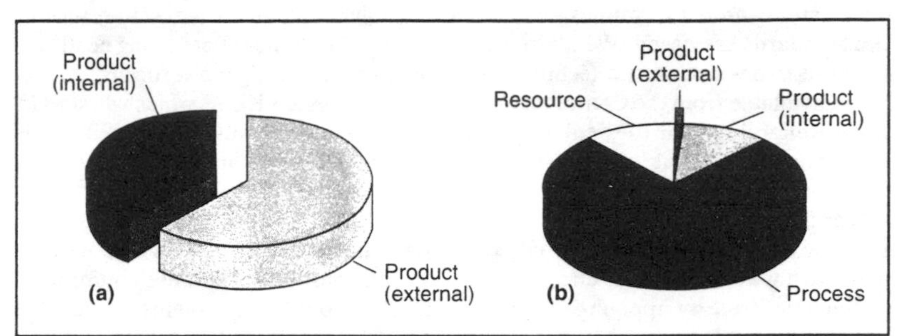


**Figure 2. A comparison of (a) BS4792 standard for safe pushchairs, with 29 requirements, and (b) DEF STD 00-55 for safe software, with 115 requirements, shows that software standards place more emphasis on process than on the final product.**

ments that are as objective as possible. However, as Figure 1 illustrates, the Smartie review of the requirements in software engineering standards indicates that we are a long way from reaching that goal.

# To what do our standards apply?

To continue our investigation, Smartie researchers reviewed software engineering standards to determine what aspect of software development is affected by each standard. We considered four distinct categories of requirements in the standards: process, internal product, external product, and resources. Internal product requirements refer to such items as the code itself, while external product requirements refer to what the user experiences, such as reliability. For examples of these categories, we turn to the British Defence Standard DEF STD 00-55 (interim),[5] issued by the Ministry of Defence (second revision in 1992) for the procurement of safety-critical software in defense equipment. Some are internal product requirements:

- Each module should have a single entry and exit.
- The code should be indented to show its structure.

Others are process requirements:

- The Design Team shall validate the Software Specification against Software Requirements by animation of the formal specification.

while some are resource requirements:

- All tools and support software . . . shall have sufficient safety integrity.
- The Design Authority shall demonstrate . . . that the seniority, authority, qualifications and experience of the staff to be employed on the project are satisfactory for the tasks assigned to them.

Typical of many software standards, DEF STD 00-55 has a mixture of all four types of requirements.

# Are software standards like other standards?

Standardization has made life easier in many disciplines. Because of standard voltage and plugs, an electrical appliance from Germany will work properly in Italy. A liter of petrol in one country is the same as a liter in another, thanks to standard measurement. These standards, products of other engineering disciplines, offer lessons that we can learn as software engineers. So the next step in the Smartie process was to examine other engineering standards to see how they differ from those in software engineering. In particular, we asked

- Is the mix of product, process, and resource roughly the same?
- Is the mix of objective and nonobjective compliance evaluation roughly the same?

The answer to both questions is a resounding no. To show just how different software engineering standards are, Figure 2 compares the British standard for pushchair safety with DEF STD 00-55, a software safety standard.

The figure shows what is true generally: Software engineering standards are heavy on process and light on product, while other engineering standards are the reverse. That is, software engineering standards reflect the implicit assumption that using certain techniques and processes, in concert with "good" tools and people, will necessarily result in a good product. Other engineering disciplines have far less faith in the process; they insist on evaluating the final product in their standards.

Another major difference between our standards and those of other engineering disciplines is in the method of compliance assessment. Most other disciplines include in their standards a description of the method to be used to assess compliance; we do not. In other words, other engineers insist that the proof of the pudding is in the eating: Their standards describe how the eating is to be done, and what the pudding should taste like, look like, and feel like. By contrast, software engineers prescribe the recipe, the utensils, and the cooking techniques, and then assume that the pudding will taste good. If our current standards are not effective, it may be because we need more objective standards and a more balanced mix of process, product, and resource requirements

# The proof of the pudding: Case studies

The Smartie framework includes far more than we can describe here — for example, guidelines for evaluating the experiments and case studies on which the standards are based. We address all of these issues in Smartie technical reports, available from the Centre for Software Reliability. For the remainder of this article, we focus on an aspect of Smartie that distinguishes it from other research on standards: its practicality. Because Smartie includes industrial partners, we have evaluated the effectiveness of Smartie itself by applying it to real-life situations. We present here two examples of the Smartie "reality check": (1) applying the framework to written standards for a major company and (2) evaluating the use of standards to meet specified goals.

Both examples involve Company X, a large, nationwide company whose services depend on software. The company is interested in using standards to enhance its software's reliability and maintainability. In the first example, we examine some of the company's programming standards to see if they can be improved. In the second example, we recommend changes to the way data is collected and analyzed, so that management can make better decisions about reliability and maintainability.

**Reality check 1: How good are the written standards?** We applied the Smartie techniques to a ministandard for using Cobol. The Cobol standard is part of a larger set of mandated standards, called programming guidelines, in the company's system development manual.

Using the guidelines reputedly "facilitate[s] the production of clear, efficient and maintainable Cobol programs." The guidelines were based on expert opinion, not on experiments and case studies demonstrating their effectiveness in comparison with not following the guidelines. This document is clearly designed as a standard rather than a set of guidelines, since "enforceability of the standards is MANDATORY," with "any divergence" being "permanently recorded."

We focused on the layout and naming conventions, items clearly intended to make the code easier to maintain. Layout requirements such as the following can be measured in a completely objective fashion:

- Each statement should be terminated by a full stop.
- Only one verb should appear on any one line.
- Each sentence should commence in column 12 and on a new line, second and subsequent lines being neatly indented and aligned vertically.... Exceptions are ELSE which will start in the same column as its associated IF and which will appear on a line of its own.

Each line either conforms or does not, and the proportion of lines conforming to all layout requirements represents overall compliance with the standard.

On the other hand, measuring conformance to some naming conventions can be difficult, because such measurements are subjective, as is the case with

- Names must be meaningful.

The Smartie approach recommends that the standard be rewritten to make it more objective. For example, improvements might include

**The Smartie framework has guidelines for evaluating the case studies on which the standards are based.**

- Names must be English or scientific words which themselves appear as identifiable concepts in the specification document(s).
- Abbreviations of names must be consistent.
- Hyphens must be used to separate component parts of names.

Conformance measures can then use the proportion of names that conform to the standard. Analysis of the commenting requirements also led to recommendations that would improve the degree of objectivity in measuring conformance.

**Reality check 2: Do the standards address the goals?** Company X collects reliability and maintainability data for many of its systems. The company made available to Smartie all of its data relating to a large system essential to its business.

Initiated in November 1987, the system had had 27 releases by the end of 1992. The 1.7 million lines of code for this system involve two programming languages: Cobol (both batch Cobol and CICS Cobol) and Natural (a 4GL). Less than a third of the code is Natural; recent growth (15.2 percent from 1991 to 1992) has been entirely in Cobol. Three corporate and organizational goals are addressed by measuring this system: (1) monitoring and improving product reliability, (2) monitoring and improving product maintainability, and (3) improving the overall development process. The first goal requires information about actual operational failures, while the second requires data on discovering and fixing faults. The third goal, process improvement, is at a higher level than the other two, so Smartie researchers focused primarily on reliability and maintainability as characteristics of process improvement.

The system runs continuously. Users report problems to a help desk whose staff determines whether the problem is a user error or a failure of the system to do something properly. Thus, all the data supplied to Smartie related to software failures rather than to documentation failures. The Smartie team received a complete set of failure information for 1991-92, so the discussion in this section refers to all 481 software failures recorded and fixed during that period. We reviewed the data to see how data collection and analysis standards addressed the overall goal of improving system reliability and maintainability. In many cases, we recommended a simple change that should yield additional, critical information in the future. The remainder of this section describes our findings.

A number is assigned to each "fault" report. We distinguish a fault (what the developer sees) from a failure (what the user sees).[6] Here we use "fault" in quotation marks, since failures are labeled as faults. A typical data point is identified by a "fault" number, the week it was reported, the system area and fault type, the week the underlying cause was fixed and tested, and the actual number of hours to repair the problem (that is, the time from when the maintenance group decides to clear the "fault" until the time when the fix is tested and integrated with the rest of the system). Smartie researchers analyzed this data and made several recommendations about how to improve data collection and analysis to

| Existing closure report | Revised closure report |
| --- | --- |
| Fault ID: F752<br>Reported: 18/6/92<br>Definition: Logically deleted work done records appear on enquiries<br>Description: Causes misleading information to users. Amend Additional Work Performed RDVIPG2A to ignore work done records with flag-amend = 1 or 2 | Fault ID: F752<br>Reported: 18/6/92<br>Definition: Logically deleted work done records appear on enquiries<br>Effect: Misleading information to users<br>Cause: Omission of appropriate flag variables for work done records<br>Change: Amend Additional Work Performed RDVIPG2A to ignore work done records with flag-amend = 1 or 2 |

**Figure 3. Examples of an existing closure report and a proposed revision.**

get a better picture of system maintainability. Nevertheless, the depth of data collection practiced at Company X is to be applauded. In particular, the distinction between hours-to-repair and time between problem-open ("week in") and problem-close ("week out") is a critical one that is not usually made in maintenance organizations.

The maintenance group designated 28 system areas to which underlying faults could be traced. Each system area name referred to a particular function of the system rather than to the system architecture. There was no documented mapping of programs or modules to system areas. A typical system area involved 80 programs, with each program consisting of 1,000 lines of code. The fault type indicated one of 11, many of which were overlapping. In other words, the classes of faults were not orthogonal, so it was possible to find more than one fault class appropriate for a given fault. In addition, there was no direct, recorded link between "fault" and program in most cases. Nor was there information about program size or complexity.

Given this situation, we made two types of recommendations. First, we examined the existing data and suggested simple changes to clarify and separate issues. Second, we extracted additional information by hand from many of the programs. We used the new data to demonstrate that enhanced data collection could provide valuable management information not obtainable with the current forms and data.

*Issue 1: Faults versus failures.* Because the cause of a problem (that is, a fault) is not always distinguished from the evidence to the user of that problem (that is, a failure), it is difficult to assess a system's reliability or the degree of user satisfaction. Furthermore, with no mapping from faults to failures, we cannot tell which particular parts or aspects of the system are responsible for most of the problems users are encountering.

- *Recommendation*: Define fault and failure, and make sure the maintenance staff understands the difference between the two. Then, consider failure reports separate from fault reports. For example, a design problem discovered during a design review would be described in a fault report; a problem in function discovered by a user would be described in a failure report.

*Issue 2: Mapping from program to system area.* Use of system areas to describe faults is helpful, but a mapping is needed from program name to system area. The current information does not reveal whether code in one system area leads to problems in another system area. The batch reporting and integration into the system of problem repairs compounds this difficulty because there is then no recorded link from program to fault. This information must have existed at some point in the maintenance process in order for the problem to be fixed; capturing it at the time of discovery is much more efficient than trying to elicit it well after the fact (and possibly incorrectly).

- *Recommendation:* Separate the system into well-defined system areas and provide a listing that maps each code module to a system area. Then, as problems are reported, indicate the system area affected. Finally, when the cause of the problem is identified, document the names of the program modules that caused the problem.

*Issue 3: Ambiguity and informality inherent in the incident closure reports.* The description of each problem reflects the creativity of the recorder rather than standard aspects of the problem. This lack of uniformity makes it impossible to amalgamate the reports and examine overall trends.

- *Recommendation:* The problem description should include the manifestation, effect, and cause of the problem, as shown in Figure 3. Such data would permit traceability and trend analysis.

*Issue 4: Fault classification scheme.* Because the scheme contains nonorthogonal categories, it is difficult for the maintainer to decide in which category a particular fault belongs. For this reason, some of the classifications may be arbitrary, resulting in a misleading picture when the faults are aggregated and tracked.

- *Recommendation:* Redefine fault categories so that there is no ambiguity or overlap between categories.

*Issue 5: Unrecoverable data.* By unrecoverable, we mean that the information we need does not exist in some documented form in the organization. For example, most of the problem report forms related a large collection of faults to a large collection of programs that were changed as a result. What appears to be unrecoverable is the exact mapping of program changes to a particular fault. On the other hand, some information was recoverable, but with great difficulty. For example, we re-created size information

**Table 1. Recoverable (documented) data versus nonrecoverable (undocumented) data.**

| Recoverable | Nonrecoverable |
|---|---|
| Size information for each module<br>Static/complexity information for each module<br>Mapping of faults to programs<br>Severity categories | Operational usage per system (needed for reliability assessment)<br>Success/failure of fixes (needed to assess effectiveness of maintenance process)<br>Number of repeated failures (needed for reliability assessment) |

manually from different parts of the data set supplied to us, and we could have related problem severity to problem cause if we had had enough time.

• *Recommendation:* The data in Table 1 would be useful if it were explicit and available to the analysts.

Figures 4 through 8 show what we can learn from the existing data; Figures 9 through 11 (page 78) show how much more we can learn using the additional data.

Since we have neither mean-time-between-failure data nor operational usage information, we cannot depict reliability directly. As an approximation, we examined the trend in the number of "faults" received per week. Figure 4 shows that there is great variability in the number of "faults" per week, suggesting that there is no general improvement in system reliability.

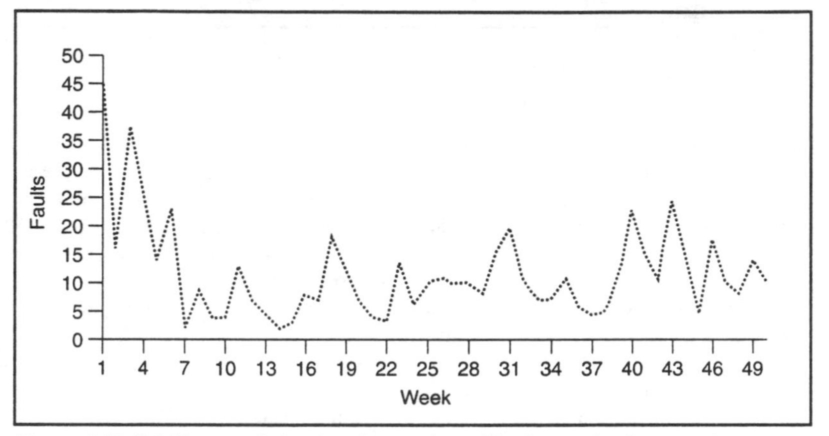


**Figure 4. Reliability trend charting the number of faults received per week.**

The chart in Figure 5 contrasts the "faults" received with the "faults" addressed and resolved ("actioned") in a given week. Notice that there is wide variation in the proportion of "faults" that are actioned each week. In spite of the lack-of-improvement trend, this chart provides managers with useful information; they can use it to begin an investigation into which "faults" are handled first and why.

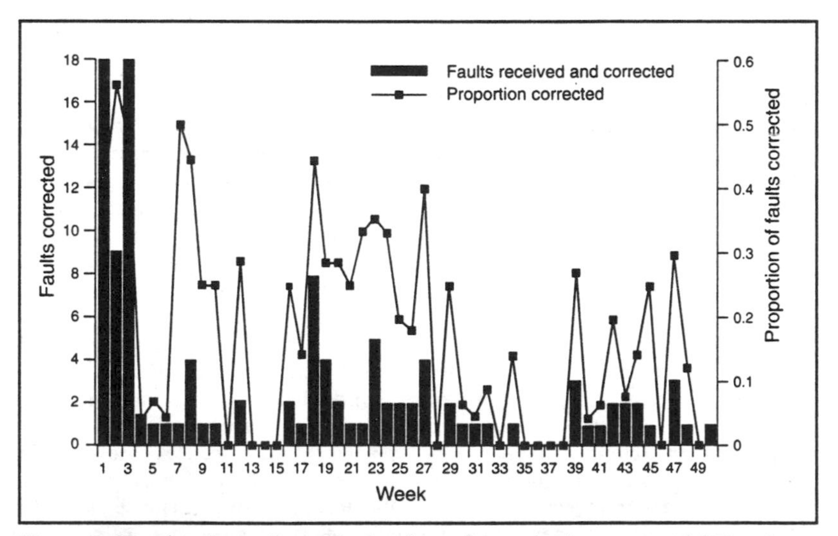


**Figure 5. Charting the faults received and acted upon in the same week helps show how Company X deals with software failures.**

Examining the number of "faults" per system area is also useful, and we display the breakdown in Figure 6. However, there is not enough information to know why particular system areas generate more "faults" than others. Without information such as size, complexity, and operational usage, we can draw no definitive conclusions. Similarly, an analysis of "faults" by fault type revealed that data and program faults dominated user, query, and other faults. However, the fault types are not orthogonal, so again there is little that we can conclude.

Figures 7 and 8 show, respectively, mean time to repair fault by system area and by fault type. This information highlights interesting variations, but our conclusions are still limited because of missing information about size.

The previous charts contain only the information supplied to us explicitly by Company X. The following charts reflect additional information that was recovered manually. As you can see, this re-

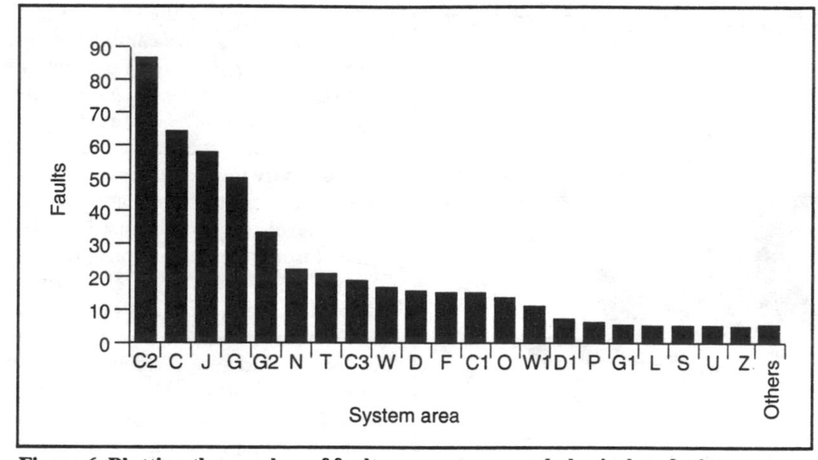


**Figure 6. Plotting the number of faults per system area helps isolate fault-prone system areas.**

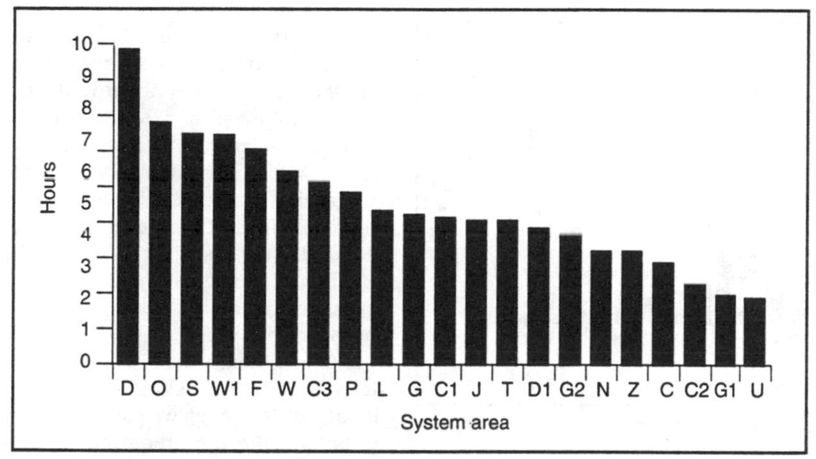


**Figure 7. Mean time to repair fault (by system area).**

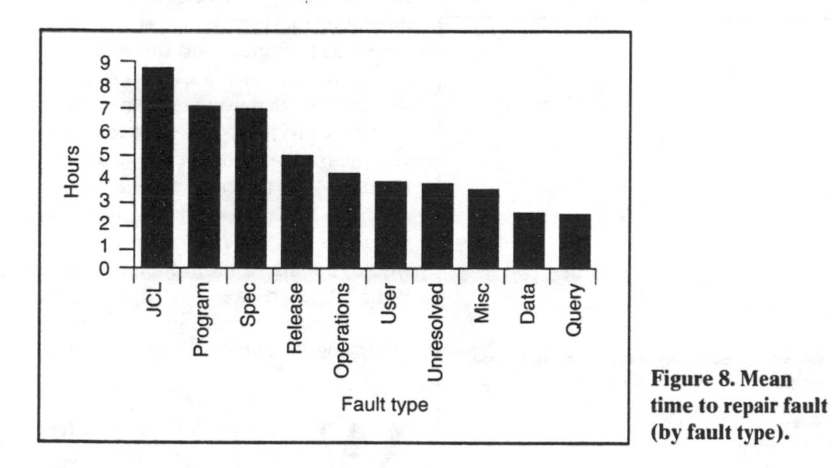


**Figure 8. Mean time to repair fault (by fault type).**

covered information enriches the management decisions that can be made on the basis of the charts.

By manually investigating the (poorly documented) link between individual programs and system areas, we examined the relationships among size, language, and system area. Figure 9 shows the variation between CICS Cobol and Natural in each of the main system areas examined. Recall that Figures 4, 5, and 6 revealed limited information about the distribution of "faults" in the overall system. However, by adding size data, the resulting graph in Figure 10 shows the startling result that C2 — one of the smallest system areas (with only 4,000 lines of code) — has the largest number of "faults." If the fault rates are graphed by system area, as in Figure 11, it is easy to see that C2 dominates the chart. In fact, Figure 11 shows that, compared with published industry figures, each system area except C2 is of very high quality; C2, however, is much worse than the industry average. Without size measurement, this important information would not be visible. Consequently, we recommended that the capture of size information be made standard practice at Company X.

These charts represent examples of our analysis. In each case, improvements to standards for measurement and collection are suggested in light of the organizational goals. Our recommendations reflect the need to make more explicit a small degree of additional information that can result in a very large degree of additional management insight. The current amount of information allows a manager to determine the status of the system; the additional data would yield explanatory information that would allow managers to be proactive rather than reactive during maintenance.

## Lessons learned in case studies

The Company X case study was one of several intended to validate the Smartie methodology, not only in terms of finding missing pieces in the methodology, but also by testing the practicality of Smartie for use in an industrial environment (the other case studies are not complete as of this writing). The first and most serious lesson learned in performing the case studies involved the lack of control. Because each investigation was retrospective, we could not

- require measurement of key productivity and quality variables,
- require uniformity or repetition of measurement,
- choose the project, team, or staff characteristics that might have eliminated confounding effects,

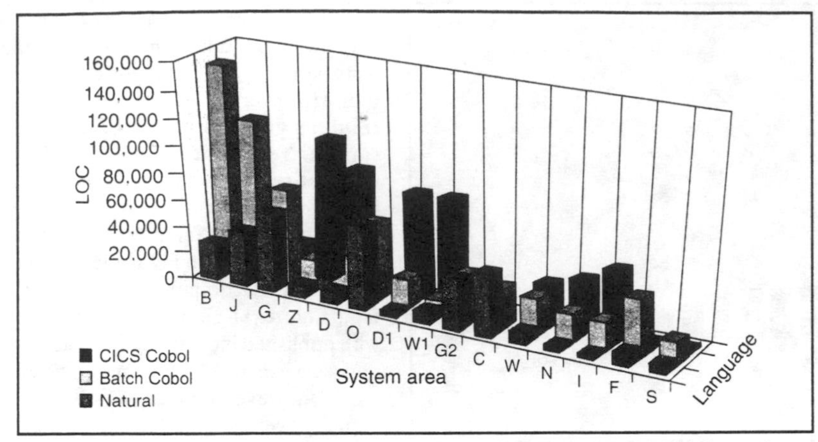


**Figure 9. System structure showing system areas with more than 25,000 lines of code and types of programming languages.**

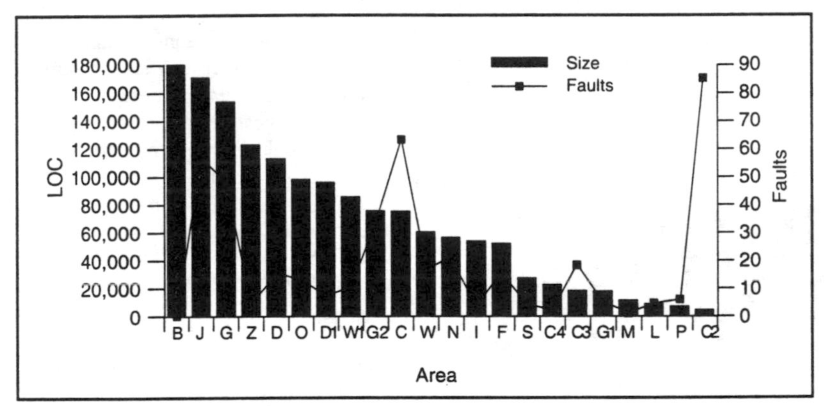


**Figure 10. System area size versus number of faults.**

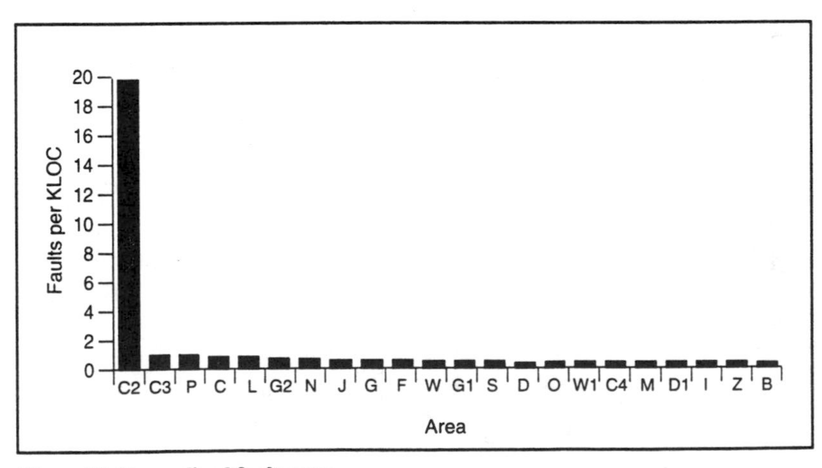


**Figure 11. Normalized fault rates.**

- choose or rewrite standards so that they were easy to apply and assess,
- choose the type of standard, or
- establish a baseline condition or environment against which to measure change.

The last point is the most crucial. Without a baseline, we cannot describe with confidence the effects of using (or not using) the standards. As a consequence, a great deal of expert (but nevertheless highly subjective) judgment was necessary in assessing the results of the case studies. It is also clear that a consistent level of control must be maintained throughout the period of the case study. There were many events, organizational and managerial as well as technical, that affected the outcome of the case study, and about which we had no input or control. In particular, lack of control led to incomplete or inconsistent data. For example, a single problem report usually included several problems related only by the time period in which the problems occurred. Or the description of a single type of problem varied from report to report, depending on the documentation style of the maintainer and the time available to write the description. With such inconsistency, it is impossible to aggregate the problem reports or fault information in a meaningful way; it is also impossible to evaluate the root causes of problems and relate them to the use of standards. Indeed, the very lack of standards in data collection and reporting inhibits us from doing a thorough analysis.

A final difficulty with our assessment derives from the lack of information about cost. Although we have Company X data on the time required to fix a problem, the company did not keep careful records on the cost of implementation or maintenance at a level that allows us to understand the cost implications of standards use. That is, even if we can show that using standards is beneficial for product quality, we cannot assess the trade-offs between the increase in quality and the cost of achieving that quality. Without such information, managers in a production environment would be loath to adopt standards, even if the standards were certifiably effective according to the Smartie (or any other) methodology.

We learned a great deal from reviewing standards and administering case studies. The first and most startling result of our work is that many standards are not really standards at all. Many "standards" are reference or subjective requirements, suggesting that they are really guidelines (since degree of compliance cannot be evaluated). Organizations with such standards should revisit their goals and revise the standards to address the goals in a more objective way.

We also found wide variety in conformance from one employee to another as well as from one module to another. In one of our case studies, management assured us that all modules were 100 percent compliant with the company's own structured programming standards, since it was mandatory company practice. Our review revealed that only 58 percent of the modules complied with the standards, even though the standards were clearly stated and could be objectively evaluated.

A related issue is that of identifying the portion of the project affected by the standard and then examining conformance only within that portion. That is, some standards apply only to certain types of modules, so notions of conformance must be adjusted to consider only that part of the system that is subject to the standard in the first place. For example, if a standard applies only to interface modules, then 50 percent compliance should mean that only 50 percent of the interface modules comply, not that 50 percent of the system is comprised of interface modules and that all of them comply.

More generally, we found that we have a lot to learn from standards in other engineering disciplines. Our standards lack objective assessment criteria, involve more process than product, and are not always based on rigorous experimental results.

Thus, we recommend that software engineering standards be reviewed and revised. The resulting standards should be cohesive collections of requirements to which conformance can be established objectively. Moreover, there should be a clearly stated benefit to each standard and a reference to the set of experiments or case studies demonstrating that benefit. Finally, software engineering standards should be better balanced, with more product requirements in relation to process and resource requirements. With standards expressed in this way, managers can use project objectives to guide standards' intention and implementation.

The Smartie recommendations and framework are practical and effective in identifying problems with standards and in making clear the kinds of changes that are needed. Our case studies have demonstrated that small, simple changes to standards writing, and especially to data collection standards, can improve significantly the quality of information about what is going on in a system and with a project. In particular, these simple changes can move the project from assessment to understanding. ■

## Acknowledgments

We gratefully acknowledge the assistance of other participants in the SERC/DTI-funded Smartie project: Colum Devine, Jennifer Thornton, Katie Perrin, Derek Jaques, Danny McComish, Eric Trodd, Bev Littlewood, and Peter Mellor.

## References

1. *IEEE Software Engineering Technical Committee Newsletter*, Vol. 11, No. 3, Jan. 1993, p. 4.

2. British Standards Institute, *British Standards Guide: A Standard for Standards*, London, 1981.

3. N. Fenton, S.L. Pfleeger, and R.L. Glass, "Science and Substance: A Challenge to Software Engineers," *IEEE Software*, Vol. 11, No. 4, July 1994, pp. 86-95.

4. International Standards Organization, *ISO 9000: Quality Management and Quality Assurance Standards — Guidelines for Selection and Use*, 1987 (with ISO 9001 - 9004).

5. Ministry of Defence Directorate of Standardization, *Interim Defence Standard 00-55: The Procurement of Safety-Critical Software in Defence Equipment, Parts 1-2*, Glasgow, Scotland, 1992.

6. P. Mellor, "Failures, Faults, and Changes in Dependability Measurement," *J. Information and Software Technology*, Vol. 34, No. 10, Oct. 1992, pp. 640-654.

# Software-Reliability Engineering: Technology for the 1990s

**John D. Musa** and **William W. Everett**, *AT&T Bell Laboratories*

***Software engineering is about to reach a new stage — the reliability stage — that stresses customers' operational needs. Software-reliability engineering will make this stage possible.***

Where will software engineering head in the 1990s? Not an easy question to answer, but a look at its history and recent evolution may offer some clues. Software engineering has evolved through several stages during its history, each adding a new expectation on the part of users:

- In the initial *functional* stage, functions that had been done manually were automated. The return on investment in automation was so large that *providing* the automated functions was all that mattered.
- The *schedule* stage followed. By this point, users' consciousness had been raised about the financial effects of having important operational capabilities delivered earlier rather than later. The need to introduce new systems and features on an orderly basis had become evident. Users were painfully aware of operational disruptions caused by late deliveries. Schedule-estimation and -management technology used for hardware systems was coupled with data and experience gained from software development and applied.
- The *cost* stage reflected the widespread use of personal computers, where price was a particularly important factor. Technology for estimating software productivity and cost and for engineering and managing it to some degree — however imperfect — was developed.
- We are now seeing the start of the fourth stage —*reliability*— which is based on engineering the level of reliability to be provided for a software-based system. It derives from the increasingly absolute operational dependence of most users on their information systems and the concomitant heavily increasing costs of failure. This stage must respond to the need to consider reliability as one of a set of factors (principally functionality, delivery date, cost, and reliability) that customers view as comprising quality. It must contend with the reality — not always fully recognized by users — that for any stage of tech-

Reprinted from *IEEE Software*, Vol. 7, No. 4, Nov. 1990, pp. 36–43.

nology, improving one of the quality factors may adversely affect one of the others.

In response to this challenge, a substantial technology — software-reliability engineering — has been developed[1] and is already seeing practical use.[2] Trends indicate that it will be extensively applied and perfected in the 1990s.

## What is it?

Software-reliability engineering is the applied science of predicting, measuring, and managing the reliability of software-based systems to maximize customer satisfaction. Reliability is the probability of failure-free operation for a specified period. Software-reliability engineering helps a product gain a competitive edge by satisfying customer needs more precisely and thus more efficiently.

Software-reliability engineering includes such activities as

- helping select the mix of principal quality factors (reliability, cost, and availability date of new features) that maximize customer satisfaction,
- establishing an operational (frequency of use) profile for the system's functions,
- guiding selection of product architecture and efficient design of the development process to meet the reliability objective,
- predicting reliability from the characteristics of both the product and the development process or estimating it from failure data in test, based on models and expected use,
- managing the development process to meet the reliability objective,
- measuring reliability in operation,
- managing the effects of software modification on customer operation with reliability measures,
- using reliability measures to guide development process improvement, and
- using reliability measures to guide software acquisition.

Software-reliability engineering works in concert with fault-tolerance, fault-avoidance, and fault-removal technologies, as well as with failure-modes and -effects analysis and fault-tree analysis. It should be applied in parallel with hardware-reliability engineering, since customers are interested in the reliability of the whole *system*.[3]

## Why is it important?

The intense international competition in almost all industries that developed in the late 1980s and that will probably increase in this decade has made software-reliability engineering an important technology for the 1990s. The sharply dropping costs of transportation and, particularly, communication, the rapidly increasing competitiveness of the Pacific Rim countries, the ascent of the European Economic Community, and the entry of the Communist bloc into the world economy all indicate the likely continued strength of this trend.

***There appears to be a strong correlation between interest in adopting reliability-engineering technology and the competitiveness of the organization or project concerned.***

The fact that the world economy has evolved from being labor-intensive to capital-intensive (with the Industrial Revolution) and now to information-intensive to meet this competition makes high-quality information processing critical to the viability of every institution. Thus, customers of software suppliers have become very demanding in their requirements. Fierce competition has sprung up between suppliers for their business.

It is no longer possible to tolerate one-dimensional conservatism when engineering quality factors. If you err on the safe side and build unneeded reliability into products, a competitor will offer your customers the reliability they do need at a lower price or with faster delivery or some combination of both. You must understand and deal with the real interactive multidimensionality of customer needs and make trade-offs. Above all, you must precisely specify, measure, and control the key quality factors.

We have observed an interesting phenomenon. There appears to be a strong correlation between interest in adopting reliability-engineering technology and the competitiveness of the organization or project concerned.

The arguments for achieving quality in software products are persuasive. A study[4] of factors influencing long-term return on investment showed that the top third of companies in customer-perceived quality averaged a return of 29 percent; the bottom third, 14 percent. Increased demand for quality also increases the importance of precisely measuring how well your competitors are doing in providing quality to the market.

It is also becoming increasingly important that the right level of reliability be achieved the first time around. In the past, without customer-oriented measures to guide us, we often approached reliability incrementally. We guessed what the customer wanted, provided an approximation to it, awaited the customer's dissatisfactions, and then tried to ameliorate them.

But the costs of operational disruption and recovery that the customer encounters due to failures have increased and are increasing relative to other costs. With

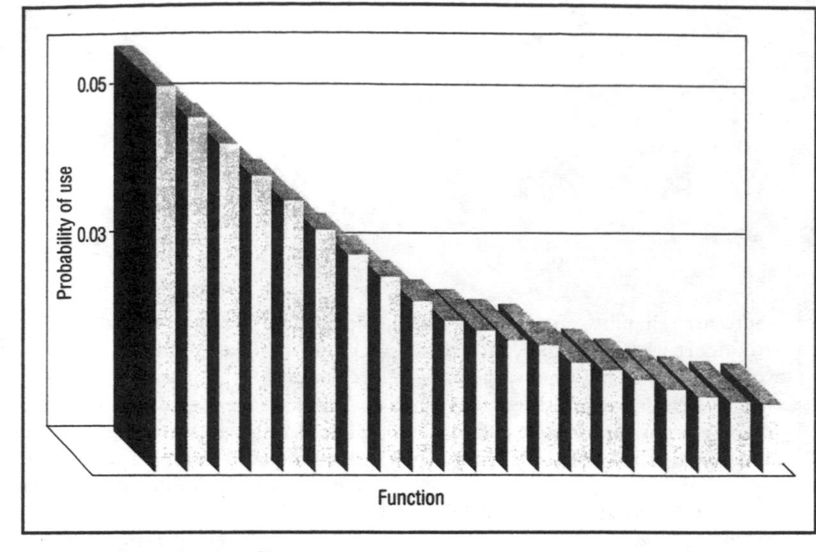


**Figure 1.** Operational profile.

such pressures, loss of confidence in a software supplier can be rapid. This trend argues for greatly increased and quantified communication between supplier and customer — from the start.

Thus, the application and perfection of sofware reliability engineering is rapidly growing in importance. It provides a measurement dimension of quality that has until recently been lacking, with very detrimental results.

## Basic concepts

To understand software-reliability engineering, you must start with some important definitions:

- A software *failure* is some behavior of the executing program that does not meet the customer's operational requirements.
- A software *fault* is a defect in the code that may cause a failure.

For example, if a command entered at a workstation does not result in the requisite display appearing, you have a failure. The cause of that failure may be a fault consisting of an incorrect argument in a calling statement to a subroutine.

Failures are customer-oriented; faults are developer-oriented.

New thinking in software-reliability engineering lets you combine functionality and reliability into one generic reliability figure, if desired. System requirements are interpreted both in terms of functions explicitly included in a product and in terms of those that the customer needs but that are not included in the product. If a function is lacking, the product is charged with a failure each time the customer needs the absent function. Thus a low level of functionality will result in a low level of reliability.

Of course, some objective basis for "needs" must be established, such as an analysis of the customer's operation or the union of all features of competitive products. Otherwise, the needs list could become an open-ended list of unrealistic wishes.

There are two alternative ways of expressing the software-reliability concept, which are related by a simple formula[1]:

- *Software reliability* proper is the probability of failure-free operation for a specified time duration.
- The other expression is *failure intensity*, the number of failures experienced per time period. Time is *execution time*: the actual time the processor is executing the program. As an example, a program with a reliability of 0.92 would operate without failure for 10 hours of execution with a probability of 0.92. Alternatively, you could say that the failure intensity is eight failures per thousand hours of execution.

Varying operational effects of failures can be handled by classifying failures by *severity*, usually measured by threat to human life or by economic impact. You can determine a reliability or failure intensity for each severity class, or you can combine the classes through appropriate weighting to yield a loss function like dollars per hour of operation.

Fault measures, often expressed as *fault density* or faults per thousand executable source lines, are generally not useful to customers. Although they can help developers probe the development process to try to understand the factors that influence it, you must relate them to measures like failure intensity and reliability if — as is proper — measures of customer satisfaction are to be the ultimate arbiters.

Another important concept is the *operational profile*. It is the set of the functions the software can perform with their probabilities of occurrence. Figure 1 shows a sample operational profile. The profile expresses how the customer uses or expects to use the software.[1,5]

**Setting improvement goals.** Companies' software-improvement goals have usually not been set from the customer's perspective. However, percentage-improvement goals stated in terms of the customer-oriented failure intensity (failures per thousand CPU hours) rather than the developer-oriented fault density (faults per thousand source lines) are both better in meeting the customer's needs and *much easier* to achieve.

Improving failure intensity is easier because you can take advantage of an operational profile that is usually nonuniform and concentrate your quality-improvement efforts on the functions used most frequently.

A simple example illustrates this point. For the same amount of testing, the failure intensity is proportional to the number of faults introduced into the code during development.[1] Let the proportionality factor be $k$. Assume that a system performs only two functions: function $A$ 90 percent of the time and function $B$ 10 percent. Suppose that the software contains 100 faults, with 50 associated with each function.

Improving the fault density by 10 times means that you must improve development over the entire program so that 90 fewer faults are introduced.

The current failure intensity is $0.9(50)k + 0.1(50)k$, or $50k$. If you concentrate your development efforts on the most frequently used function so it has no faults, the new failure intensity will be $0.1(50)k$, or $5k$.

You have reduced the failure intensity by a factor of 10 through improvements in development involving only a factor-of-two reduction in the number of faults (50 faults). A similar but more extended analysis could also take account of failure severity.

**Reliability models.** Models play an important role in relating reliability to the factors that affect it. To both represent the failure process accurately and have maximum usefulness, reliability models need two components:

- The *execution-time* component relates failures to execution time, properties of the software being developed, properties of the development environment, and properties of the operating environment. Failure intensity can decrease, remain fixed, or increase with execution time. The last behavior is not of practical interest. Decreasing failure intensity, shown in Figure 2, is common during system test because the removal of faults reduces the rate at which failures occur. Constant failure intensity usually occurs for systems released to the field, when systems are ordinarily stable and no fault removal occurs.
- The *calendar-time* component relates the passage of calendar time to execution time. During test, it is based on the fact that resources like testers, debuggers, and computer time are limited and that these resources, each at a different time, control the ratio between calendar time and execution time. During field operation, the relationship is simpler and depends only on how the computer is used.

## Life cycle

You apply software-reliability engineering in each phase of the life cycle: definition, design and implementation, validation, and operation and maintenance.[6] The definition phase focuses on developing a requirements specification for a product that can profitably meet some set of needs for some group of customers. System and software engineers develop product designs from the product requirements, and software engineers implement them in code in the design and implementation phase. Test teams, usually independent of the design and implementation teams, operate the product in the validation phase to see if it meets the requirements. In the operation and maintenance phase, the product is delivered to and used by the customer. The maintenance staff responds to customer requests for new features and to reported problems by developing and delivering software changes.

**Definition phase.** Good product definition is essential for success in the marketplace. The primary output of the definition phase is a product-requirements specification. The product's failure-intensity objective should be explicitly included.

The first step in setting the failure-intensity objective is to work with the customer to define what a failure is from the customer's perspective. Next, you categorize failures by *severity*, or the effect they have on the customer. Determine the customer's tolerance to failures of different severities and willingness to pay for reduced failure intensities in each failure-severity category.

Looking at the customer's experiences with past and existing products will help both of you determine the value of reliability. A larger market reduces the per-unit cost of reliability, making higher reliability more feasible.

Another consideration is assessing the reliability of competitors' products. You must also determine the effects of meeting the failure-intensity objective on delivery date.

You can then use the information developed in each of these steps to establish failure-intensity objectives, trading off product reliability, cost, and delivery date.

Customers generally view the foregoing communication very favorably. It greatly improves the match between product characteristics and customer needs, and it generally increases the customer's trust in the supplier.

Now, you need two other items:

- The operational profile, since the product's reliability may depend on how the product will be used.
- Estimates relating calendar time to execution time, so that failure-intensity objectives expressed in terms of calendar time (the form customers can relate to) can be translated into failure-intensity objectives expressed in terms of execution time (the form relevant to software).

So you can readily determine failure intensity in testing and in the field, you should consider building automatic failure identification and reporting into the system.

Two questions often asked about applying models during the definition phase are:

- How accurate are the reliability predictions made at this time?
- Is the effort to model reliability at this point worth it?

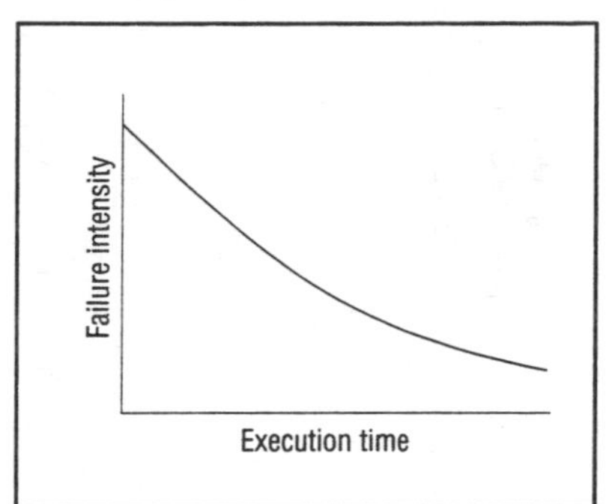


**Figure 2.** General appearance of the software-reliability model's execution-time component.

There is not enough information to give a definitive answer to the first question today, although there are some indications that the accuracy may be within a factor of three or four. Accuracy is likely to be determined and to improve as the field progresses and appropriate data is collected.

As to the second question, the effort would probably not be worth it if the modeling were carried no further than just predicting software reliability. However, the modeling should continue into the design and implementation, validation, and operation and maintenance phases. Particularly during the validation and the operation and maintenance phases, you can use modeling with collected data to track whether reliability objectives are being met. Also, you can use the results to refine the prediction process for the future.

The real utility of modeling becomes evident in this cycle of model, measure, and refine. Furthermore, applying models during the definition phase forces project teams to focus very early on reliability issues and baseline assumptions about the product's reliability *before* development begins.

**Design and implementation phase.** The first goal of the design and implementation phase is to turn the requirements specification into design specifications for the product and the development pro-

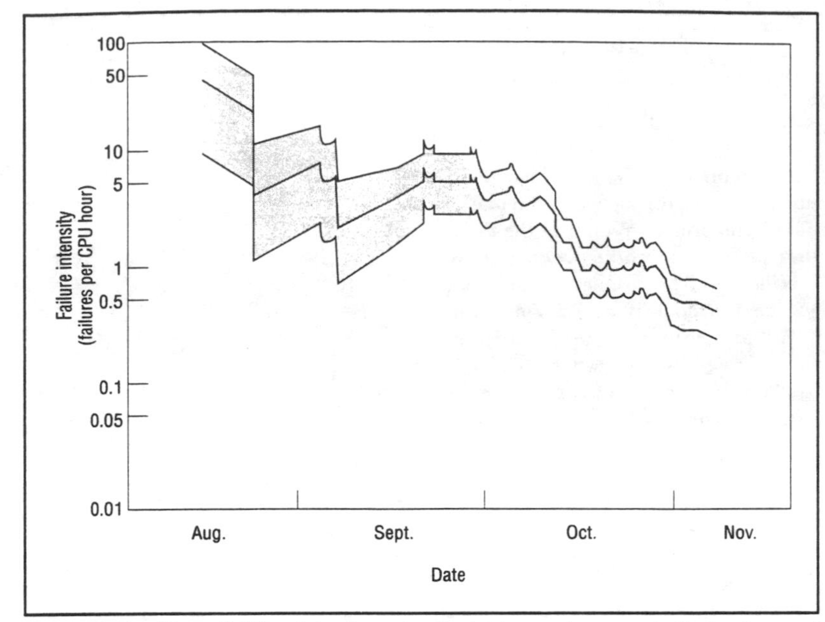


**Figure 3.** Tracking reliability status in system test. The center curve indicates the most likely value of failure intensity. The shaded area represents the interval within which the true failure intensity lies with 75-percent confidence. The *y* axis is logarithmic so the data can fit the graph.

cess. Then the process is implemented.

An early activity of this phase is allocating the system-reliability objective among the components. In some cases, you may want to consider different architectural options. You should analyze whether you can attain the reliability objective with the proposed design.

It will usually be necessary to identify critical functions for which failure may cause catastrophic effects. You should then identify the modules whose satisfactory operation is essential to the functions, using techniques like failure-modes and -effects analysis and fault-tree analysis. You can then single out the critical modules for special fault-avoidance or fault-removal activities. You may also use fault-tolerance techniques like periodic auditing of key variables during program execution and recovery blocks.

The design of the development process consists of determining the development activities to be performed with their associated time and resource requirements. Usually, more than one plan can meet the product requirements, but some plans are faster, less expensive, or more reliable than others.

The software-reliability-engineering part of the development-process design involves examining the controllable and uncontrollable factors that influence reliability. Controllable factors include such things as use or nonuse of design inspections, thoroughness of design inspections, and time and resources devoted to system test. Uncontrollable (or perhaps minimally controllable) factors are usually related to the product or the work environment; for example, program size, volatility of requirements, and average experience of staff.

You use the uncontrollable factors to predict the failure intensity that would occur without any attempt to influence it. You then choose suitable values of the controllable factors to achieve the failure-intensity objective desired within acceptable cost and schedule limits. Techniques now exist to predict the effects of some of the factors, and appropriate studies should be able to determine the effects of the others. The relationships between the factors and reliability must be expressed in simple terms that software engineers can intuitively understand. Otherwise, they are not likely to apply them.

You should construct a reliability time line to indicate goals for how reliability should improve as you progress through the life cycle from design through inspection to coding to unit test to system test to release. You use this time line to evaluate progress. If progress is not satisfactory, several actions are possible:

• Reallocate project resources (for example, from test team to debugging team or from low-usage to high-usage functions).

• Redesign the development process (for example, lengthening the system-test phase).

• Redesign subsystems that have low reliability.

• Respecify the requirements in negotiation with the customers (they might accept lower reliability for on-time delivery).

Reliability can't be directly measured in the design and coding stages. However, there is a good chance that indirect methods will be developed based on trends in finding design errors and later trends in discovering code faults by inspection or self-checking.

Syntactic faults are usually found by compilers or perhaps editors, so you should concentrate on *semantic* faults to predict reliability. In unit test, we anticipate that methods will be developed to estimate reliability from failure trends.

Another important activity is to certify the reliability of both acquired software and reused software (not only application software but also system software like operating-system and communication-interface software). You should establish the reliability of such components through testing with the operational profile expected for the new product.

The operational profile can help increase productivity and reduce cost during the design and implementation phase by helping guide where you should focus design resources.

Verification activities like inspections, unit test, and subsystem test are commonly conducted during the design and implementation phase. You can apply inspections to both design and code.

**Validation phase.** The primary thrust of validation is to certify that the product meets customer requirements and is suitable for customer use. Product validation for software generally includes system tests and field trials.

Software-reliability measurements are particularly useful in combination with reliability testing (also called longevity or stability testing). During reliability testing, you generally execute functions with relative frequencies that match what is specified in the operational profile. When fail-

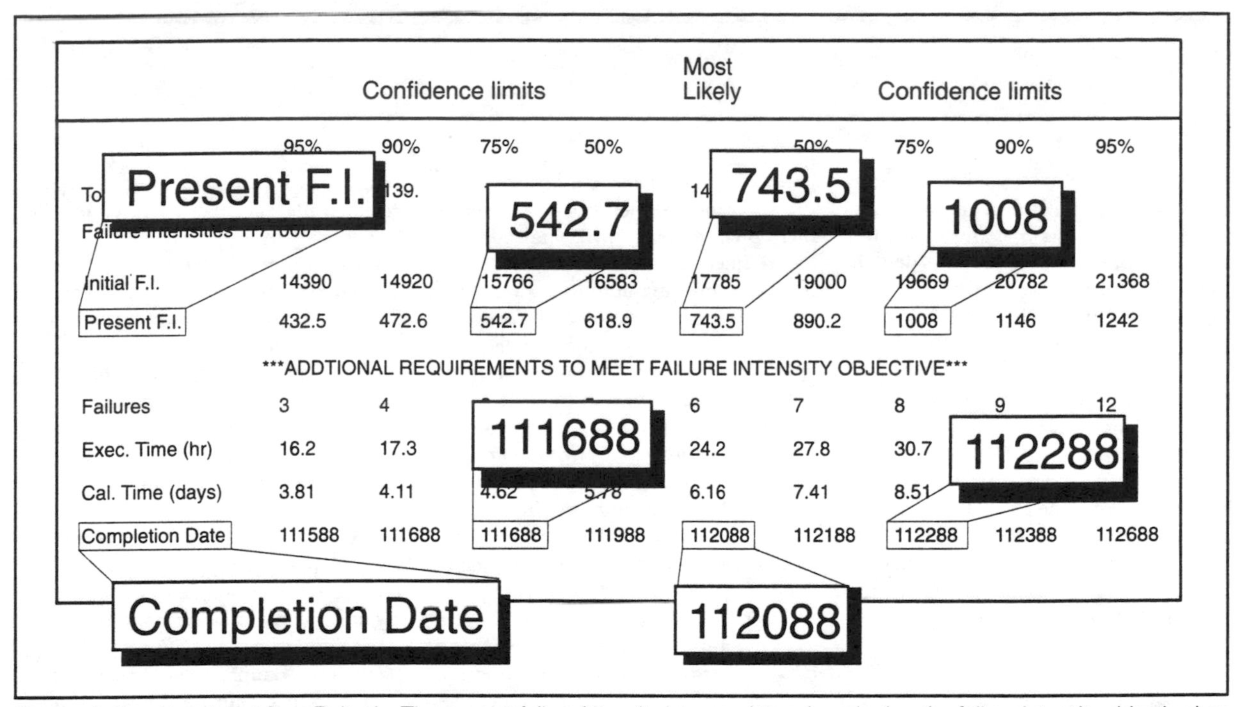


**Figure 4.** Sample printout from Reltools. The present failure intensity lets you determine whether the failure-intensity objective has been met. Key quantities are called out here for emphasis.

ures are experienced, developers start a correction process to identify and remove the faults causing them.

You may use multiple operational profiles, each relating to a different application with its associated market segment.

We expect it will be possible in the future to test using strategies with function-occurrence frequencies that depart from the operational profile. You would compensate for this departure from the profile by adjusting the measured failure intensities.

To obtain the desired reliability quantities, you first record failures and the corresponding execution times (from the start of test). Then you run a software-reliability-estimation program like Reltools (available from the authors), which uses statistical techniques to estimate the parameters of the software-reliability model's execution-time component, based on the recorded failure data. Applying the execution-time component with the estimated parameters, it determines such useful quantities as current failure intensity and the remaining execution time needed to meet the failure-intensity objective. It also uses the calendar-time component to estimate remaining calendar time needed for testing to achieve the failure-intensity objective.[7]

Managers and engineers can track reliability status during system test, as Figure 3 shows. The plot shows real project data. The downward trend is clear despite real-world perturbations due to statistical noise and departures of the project from underlying model assumptions. The actual improvement in failure intensity is about 70 to 1, a fact deemphasized by the need to use a logarithmic scale to fit the curves on the chart.

Problems are highlighted when the downward trend does not progress as expected, which alerts you before the problem gets too severe. Cray Research is one company that applies reliability tracking for this purpose as standard practice in its compiler development.

Figure 4 shows a sample printout produced by Reltools. The way it presents current failure intensity lets you determine whether the failure-intensity objective has been met. You can use this as a criterion for release, so you are confident that customer needs are met before shipping. There have been several demonstrations of the value of software reliability as a release criterion, including applications at AT&T[8] and Hewlett-Packard.[9] Cray Research[10] uses such a release criterion as standard practice.

**Operation and maintenance phase.** The primary thrust of the operation and maintenance phase is to move the product into the customers' day-to-day operations, support customers in their use of the product, develop new features needed by customers, and fix faults in the software that affect the customers' use of the product.

For those organizations that have operational responsibility for software products, reliability measurement can help monitor the operating software's reliability. You can use the results to determine if there is any degradation in reliability over time (for example, degradation caused by the introduction of additional faults when software fixes are installed). Software-reliability measurement can help you time the addition of new software features so reliability is not reduced below a tolerable level for the user.

Field-support engineers can use operational software-reliability measures to compare the customer's perceived level of reliability to the reliability measured by the supplier at release. Several factors could cause these measures to differ: different definitions of "failure," different operational profiles, or different versions of the software. Determining which factors contribute to the differences and feeding information back to the appropriate people is an important task.

You can also apply software-reliability engineering to maintenance. One prime example is using the frequency and severity of failures to rank the order for repairing underlying faults. In addition to other considerations, users usually consider failures in old functions more severe than those in new functions because their operations are likely to be more heavily affected by the old functions they depend on.

You can also use software-reliability-engineering methods to size the maintenance staff needed to repair faults reported from field sites. You can use the methods to estimate PROM production rates for firmware. Also, you can use them to estimate warranty costs. A potential use is to determine the optimum mix of fault-removal and new-feature activities in releases.

**Process improvement.** The most important activity that you can conduct near the end of the life cycle is a *root-cause analysis* of faults. Such an analysis determines when and how the faults are introduced and what changes should be made to the development process to reduce the number introduced in the future.

Also, if you have used a new technique, tool, or other "improvement" to the software-engineering process, you should try to evaluate its effect on reliability. This implies a comparison with another situation in which all product and process variables are held constant except the one whose effect is being checked. That can be difficult across projects, so it may be more feasible to test the "improvement" across subsystems of the same project.

## Research opportunities

The applications of software-reliability engineering described here have in most cases been based on existing capabilities, which in some instances have already been used on a pilot basis. However, some depend on extensions requiring studies, usually based on actual project data. The structure of this research appears reasonably clear, and in many cases it is well under way. There is of course some risk that all the extensions might not come to fruition.

**Predicting reliability.** The largest and most significant area of potential advance is the prediction of reliability before program execution from characteristics of the software product and the development process. Initial work[1] indicates that failure intensity is related to the number of faults remaining in the software at the start of system test, the size of the program in object instructions, the average processing speed of the computer running the software, and the fault-exposure ratio. The fault-exposure ratio represents the proportion of time that a hypothetical encounter of a fault, based on processing speed and program size, would result in failure.

Some evidence indicates that the fault-exposure ratio may be a constant. This needs to be verified over a range of projects. If not constant, it may vary with a few factors like some measures of program "branchiness" and "loopiness." These relationships would need to be developed.

The number of faults remaining at the start of system test is clearly related to program size. You can approximate it by the number of faults detected in system test and operation, provided the operating period totaled over all installations is large and the rate of detection of faults is approaching zero.

Studies indicate that it depends (to a lesser degree) on the number of specification changes, thoroughness of design documentation, average programmer skill level, percent of reviews accomplished, and percent of code read. It is possible that adding more factors would further improve such predictions; finding out requires a study of multiple projects.

The selection of appropriate factors might be aided by insight gained from root-cause analysis of why faults get introduced. Our experience indicates that the factors are most likely related to characteristics of the development process rather than the product itself.

Interestingly, complexity other than that due to size seems to average out for programs above the module level. Thus, it is not an operative factor. This fact appears to support the conjecture that the fault-exposure ratio may be constant.

**Estimating before test.** An area of challenge is to find a way to estimate the number of remaining faults based on patterns of data taken on design errors detected in design inspections and coding faults detected in desk-checking or code walkthroughs.

This estimate of remaining faults is needed to estimate software reliability before test for comparison with a reliability time line. One possibility would be to apply an analog of software-reliability-modeling and -estimation procedures to the values of inspection or walkthrough execution times at which you experience the design errors or code faults.

**Estimating during test.** Work is needed to develop ways of applying software-reliability theory to estimating failure intensity during unit test. There are two problems to deal with:

- the small sample sizes of failures and
- efficiently determining the operational profiles for units from the system's operational profile.

Estimating reliability from failure data in system test works fairly well, but improvements could be made in reducing estimation bias for both parameters and predicted quantities. Adaptive prediction, which feeds back the prediction results to improve the model, is showing considerable promise.

**Other opportunities.** Current work on developing algorithms to compensate for testing with run profiles that are different from the operational profile may open up a substantially expanded range of application for sofwtare-reliability engineering.

As software-reliability engineering is used on more and more projects, special problems may turn up, as is the case with any new technology. These offer excellent opportunities for those who can closely couple research and practice and communicate their results.

Software-reliability engineering, although not yet completely developed, is a discipline that is advancing at a rapid pace. Its benefits are clear. It is being practically applied in industry. And research is proceeding to answer many of the problems that have been raised. It is likely to advance further in the near future. This will put the practice of software engineering on a more quantitative basis. ❖

## Acknowledgments

The authors are grateful to Frank Ackerman, Jack Adams, Bob Brownlie, Mary Donnelly, Anthony Iannino, Tom Riedl, Sheldon Robinson, and the other authors in this special issue for their helpful reviews.

## References

1. J.D. Musa, A. Iannino, and K. Okumoto, *Software Reliability: Measurement, Prediction, Application*, McGraw-Hill, New York, 1987.
2. J.D. Musa, "Tools for Measuring Software Reliability," *IEEE Spectrum*, Feb. 1989, pp. 39-42.
3. L. Bernstein and C.M. Yuhas, "Taking the Right Measure of System Performance," *Computerworld*, July 30, 1984, pp. ID-1–ID-4.
4. R.D. Buzzell and B.T. Gale, *The PIMS Principles: Linking Strategy to Performance*, The Free Press, New York, 1987, p. 109.
5. W.K. Ehrlich, J.P. Stampfel, and J.R. Wu, "Application of Software-Reliability Modeling to Product Quality and Test Process," *Proc. 12th Int'l Conf. Software Eng.*, CS Press, Los Alamitos, Calif., pp. 108-116.
6. W.W. Everett, "Software-Reliability Measurement," *IEEE J. Selected Areas in Comm.*, Feb. 1990, pp. 247-252.
7. J.D. Musa and A.F. Ackerman, "Quantifying Software Validation: When to Stop Testing?" *IEEE Software*, May 1989, pp. 19-27.
8. P. Harrington, "Applying Customer-Oriented Quality Metrics," IEEE Software, Nov. 1989, pp. 71, 74.
9. H.D. Drake and D.E. Wolting, "Reliability Theory Applied to Software Testing," *Hewlett-Packard J.*, April 1987, pp. 35-39.
10. K.C. Zinnel, "Using Software-Reliability Growth Models to Guide Release Decisions," *Proc. IEEE Subcommittee Software-Reliability Eng.*, 1990, available from the authors.

# Chapter 10

## Software Project Management

### 1. Introduction to Chapter

*Management* can be defined as all the activities and tasks undertaken by one or more persons for the purpose of planning and controlling the activities of others in order to achieve an objective or complete an activity that could not be achieved by the others acting independently [1]. The classic management model as portrayed by well-known authors in the field of management [2], [3], [4], [5], [6] contains the following components:

Planning
Organizing
Staffing
Directing
Controlling

Project management is defined as a system of procedures, practices, technologies, and know-how that provides the planning, organizing, staffing, directing, and controlling necessary to successfully manage an engineering project. Know-how in this case means the skill, background, and wisdom necessary to apply knowledge effectively in practice [6].

A project is a temporary organizational structure that has an established beginning and end date, established goals and objectives, defined responsibilities, and a defined budget and schedule.

The importance of software project management is best illustrated by the following paragraphs extracted from two US Department of Defense (DoD) reports.

A report from the STARS (Software Technology for Adaptable, Reliable Systems) initiative states, "The manager plays a major role in software and systems development and support. The difference between

SOFTWARE PROJECT MANAGEMENT

success or failure—between a project being on schedule and on budget or late and over budget—is often a function of the manager's effectiveness [7]."

In a report to the Defense Science Board Task Force on Military Software, Fred Brooks states that "... today's major problems with software development are not technical problems, but management problems [8]."

## 2. Introduction to Papers

This chapter includes two papers on the overall management of software projects and three papers on the management of cost and risk as specific issues in software development.

The chapter begins with the classic of all classic software engineering papers, "The Mythical Man-Month," by Dr. Fred Brooks. No collection of papers on software engineering project management would be complete without this paper. Brooks could be considered the father of modern software engineering project management; his book, *The Mythical Man-Month: Essays on Software Engineering,* written in 1975, [9] was a best seller for 20 years and was republished in 1995. This paper, or, better yet, the book should be required reading for all software project managers.

The paper (and the book) is the source of such now-famous quotes as:

- "Adding manpower to a late software project only makes it later." ("Brooks's Law")
- "How does a project get to be a year late? ...One day at a time."
- "All programmers are optimists."
- "The man-month as a unit for measuring the size of a job is a dangerous and deceptive myth."

In the second paper in this chapter, Thayer expands on MacKenzie's and other papers and applies the concept of the universality of management to developing an overview of software engineering project management.

The paper takes a top-down approach to establishing a set of project management and software engineering project management responsibilities, activities, and tasks that should be undertaken by any manager who is assigned the responsibility of managing a software engineering project. It covers the management functions of planning, organizing, staffing, directing, and controlling, and it discusses in detail activities and tasks necessary to successfully manage a software development project.

The third paper in this chapter is a short essay by Tom De Marco entitled "Why Does Software Cost So Much?" In this article, De Marco quotes Dr. Jerry Weinberg: "Compared to what?" [10] This paper posits that software really does not cost too much. He reflects on the expectations of customers and users, which are perhaps unrealistic for an engineering discipline that is less than fifty years old.

De Marco points out that a major problem in the high cost of software is the unrealistic estimates that are made at the beginning of the software project. He says the assertion that software costs too much is typically a ploy by unknowledgeable managers and customers in an attempt to coerce the project manager into either estimating or developing the software for less cost.

The next paper, by F.J. Heemstra, presents a thorough overview of the state of the art in software cost estimation. Heemstra points out that it is very easy to ask the question, "Why are software overruns on budget and schedule so prevalent?" However, the answer is not so simple.

The author thoroughly discusses why software cost estimation is so difficult. The primary reason is that there is a lack of data on completed software projects. Without this data, it becomes very difficult to make project management estimates on future software costs.

The author goes into the many factors that influence software development effort and duration. He points out that the estimator must know, among other things, the size of the software project, required quality, requirements volatility (that is, the amount and rate of change of requirements), software complexity, the level of software reuse, the amount of documentation required, and the type of application.

The author also discusses the types of software cost-estimation techniques and tools. He points out that there are two main approaches that can be distinguished from each other—the top-down and the bottom-up approaches.

Heemstra also looks at some cost estimation models beginning with the principles of these models. He then presents an overview of COCOMO, function point analysis, the Putnam model, and others. He manages to pinpoint most of the major software cost-estimation techniques available today.

The fifth and last paper in this section is an original article, "Risk Management for Software Development," written by the late Paul Rook of the Center for Software Reliability in London and completed after Rook's death by Dr. Richard Fairley. The paper defines the many aspects of risk management such as risk, risk impact, risk exposure, and risk reduction or elimination. It restates the classic definition of risk as the "potential for realization of unwanted, negative consequences of an event." It concentrates on describing the importance of the relationship between risk management and project control and illustrates the sources of risk, how risk can be tackled, and how to carry out risk assessment, risk identification, and risk analysis. Risk management planning and risk resolution are also covered.

Mr. Rook's premature death in January 1995 was a blow to his friends and colleagues, and to the technology of software reliability. He will be sorely missed. The editors thank Dick Fairley for completing this paper.


1. Koontz, H., C. O'Donnell, and H. Weihrich, *Management*, 7th ed., McGraw-Hill Book Co., New York, N.Y., 1980.
2. Cleland, D.I., and W.R. King, *Management: A Systems Approach,* McGraw-Hill Book Company, New York, N.Y., 1972.
3. MacKenzie, R.A., "The Management Process in 3-D," *Harvard Business Rev.*, Nov.-Dec. 1969, pp. 80-87.
4. Blanchard, Benjamin S. and Walter J. Fabrycky, *System Engineering and Analysis*, Prentice Hall, Inc., Englewood Cliffs, N.J., Second Ed., 1990.
5. Kerzner, Harold, *Project Management: A Systems Approach to Planning, Scheduling, and Controlling*, 3rd ed., Van Nostrand Reinhold, New York, N.Y., 1989.
6. Thayer, R.H., "Software Engineering Project Management: A Top-Down View," R.H. Thayer (ed.), *Software Engineering Project Management*, IEEE Computer Society Press, Los Alamitos, Calif., 1988
7. *Strategy for a DOD Software Initiative*, Department of Defense Report, 1 Oct.1982.
8. *Report of the Defense Science Board Task Force on Military Software*, Office of the Under Secretary of Defense for Acquisition, Department of Defense, Washington D.C., September 1987.
9. F.P. Brooks, Jr., *The Mythical Man-Month: Essays on Software Engineering*, Addison-Wesley Publishing Co., Reading, Mass., 1975. Revised edition published 1995.
10. Weinberg, G., *Quality Software Management*, Volume 1: *Systems Thinking*, Dorset House, New York, N.Y., 1992.

# THE MYTHICAL MAN-MONTH

The above is an extract from the *Mythical Man-Month* by Frederick P. Brooks, Jr., copyright © 1975 by Addison-Wesley Publishing Company, Inc., Reading, Massachusetts, pages 14-26, 88-94, 153-160, and 177. Reprinted with permission. The extract was prepared by the editors of *Datamation* and published in *Datamation*, December 1974, pages 44-52.

## HOW DOES A PROJECT GET TO BE A YEAR LATE? . . . . . . ONE DAY AT A TIME.

By Frederick P. Brooks, Jr.

Dr. Brooks was part of the management team charged with developing the hardware for the IBM 360 system. In 1964 he became the manager of the Operating System/360 project; this trial by fire convinced him that managing a large software project is more like managing any other large undertaking than programmers believe and less like it than professional managers expect.

About his OS/360 project, he says: "Managing OS/360 development was a very educational experience, albeit a very frustrating one. The team, including F. M. Trapnell who succeeded me as manager, has much to be proud of. The system contains many excellences in design and execution, and it has been successful in achieving widespread use. Certain ideas, most noticeably device-independent input/output and external library management, were technical innovations now widely copied. It is now quite reliable, reasonably efficient, and very versatile.

The effort cannot be called wholly successful, however. Any OS/360 user is quickly aware of how much better it should be. The flaws in design and execution pervade especially the control program, as distinguished from language compilers. Most of the flaws date from the 1964-1965 design period and hence must be laid to my charge. Furthermore, the product was late, it took more memory than planned, the costs were several times the estimate, and it did not perform very well until several releases after the first."

Analyzing the OS/360 experiences for management and technical lessons, Dr. Brooks put his thoughts into book form. Addison-Wesley Publishing Company (Reading, Mass.) will offer "The Mythical Man-Month: Essays on Software Engineering", from which this article is taken, sometime next month.

**NO SCENE FROM PREHISTORY is quite so vivid as that of the mortal struggles of great beasts in the tar pits. In the mind's eye one sees dinosaurs, mammoths, and saber-toothed tigers struggling against the grip of the tar. The fiercer the struggle, the more entangling the tar, and no beast is so strong or so skillful but that he ultimately sinks.**

Large-system programming has over the past decade been such a tar pit, and many great and powerful beasts have thrashed violently in it. Most have emerged with running systems—few have met goals, schedules, and budgets. Large and small, massive or wiry, team after team has become entangled in the tar. No one thing seems to cause the difficulty—any particular paw can be pulled away. But the accumulation of simultaneous and interacting factors brings slower and slower motion. Everyone seems to have been surprised by the stickiness of the problem, and it is hard to discern the nature of it. But we must try to understand it if we are to solve it.

More software projects have gone awry for lack of calendar time than for all other causes combined. Why is this case of disaster so common?

First, our techniques of estimating are poorly developed. More seriously, they reflect an unvoiced assumption which is quite untrue, i.e., that all will go well.

Second, our estimating techniques fallaciously confuse effort with progress, hiding the assumption that men and months are interchangeable.

Third, because we are uncertain of our estimates, software managers often lack the courteous stubbornness required to make people wait for a good product.

Fourth, schedule progress is poorly monitored. Techniques proven and routine in other engineering disciplines are considered radical innovations in software engineering.

Fifth, when schedule slippage is recognized, the natural (and traditional) response is to add manpower. Like dousing a fire with gasoline, this makes matters worse, much worse. More fire requires more gasoline and thus begins a regenerative cycle which ends in disaster.

Schedule monitoring will be covered later. Let us now consider other aspects of the problem in more detail.

### Optimism

All programmers are optimists. Perhaps this modern sorcery especially attracts those who believe in happy endings and fairy godmothers. Perhaps the hundreds of nitty frustrations drive away all but those who habitually focus on the end goal. Perhaps it is merely that computers are young, programmers are younger, and the young are always optimists. But however the selection process works, the result is indisputable: "This time it will surely run," or "I just found the last bug."

So the first false assumption that underlies the scheduling of systems programming is that *all will go well*, i.e., that *each task will take only as long as it "ought" to take*.

The pervasiveness of optimism among programmers deserves more than a flip analysis. Dorothy Sayers, in her excellent book, *The Mind of the*

*Maker*, divides creative activity into three stages: the idea, the implementation, and the interaction. A book, then, or a computer, or a program comes into existence first as an ideal construct, built outside time and space but complete in the mind of the author. It is realized in time and space by pen, ink, and paper, or by wire, silicon, and ferrite. The creation is complete when someone reads the book, uses the computer or runs the program, thereby interacting with the mind of the maker.

This description, which Miss Sayers uses to illuminate not only human creative activity but also the Christian doctrine of the Trinity, will help us in our present task. For the human makers of things, the incompletenesses and inconsistencies of our ideas become clear only during implementation. Thus it is that writing, experimentation, "working out" are essential disciplines for the theoretician.

In many creative activities the medium of execution is intractable. Lumber splits; paints smear; electrical circuits ring. These physical limitations of the medium constrain the ideas that may be expressed, and they also create unexpected difficulties in the implementation.

Implementation, then, takes time and sweat both because of the physical media and because of the inadequacies of the underlying ideas. We tend to blame the physical media for most of our implementation difficulties; for the media are not "ours" in the way the ideas are, and our pride colors our judgment.

Computer programming, however, creates with an exceedingly tractable medium. The programmer builds from pure thought-stuff: concepts and very flexible representations thereof. Because the medium is tractable, we expect few difficulties in implementation; hence our pervasive optimism. Because our ideas are faulty, we have bugs; hence our optimism is unjustified.

In a single task, the assumption that all will go well has a probabilistic effect on the schedule. It might indeed go as planned, for there is a probability distribution for the delay that will be encountered, and "no delay" has a finite probability. A large programming effort, however, consists of many tasks, some chained end-to-end. The probability that each will go well becomes vanishingly small.

## The mythical man-month

The second fallacious thought mode is expressed in the very unit of effort used in estimating and scheduling: the man-month. Cost does indeed vary as the product of the number of men and the number of months. Progress does not. *Hence the man-month as a unit for measuring the size of a job is a dangerous and deceptive myth.* It implies that men and months are interchangeable.

Men and months are interchangeable commodities only when a task can be partitioned among many workers *with no communication among them* (Fig. 1). This is true of reaping wheat or picking cotton; it is not even approximately true of systems programming.

When a task cannot be partitioned

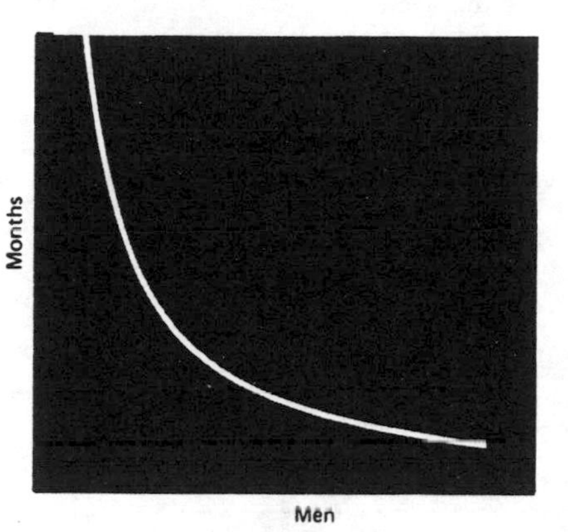


Fig. 1. The term "man-month" implies that if one man takes 10 months to do a job, 10 men can do it in one month. This may be true of picking cotton.

because of sequential constraints, the application of more effort has no effect on the schedule. The bearing of a child takes nine months, no matter how many women are assigned. Many software tasks have this characteristic because of the sequential nature of debugging.

In tasks that can be partitioned but which require communication among the subtasks, the effort of communication must be added to the amount of work to be done. Therefore the best that can be done is somewhat poorer than an even trade of men for months (Fig. 2).

The added burden of communication is made up of two parts, training and intercommunication. Each worker must be trained in the technology, the goals of the effort, the overall strategy, and the plan of work. This training cannot be partitioned, so this part of the added effort varies linearly with the number of workers.

V. S. Vyssotsky of Bell Telephone Laboratories estimates that a large project can sustain a manpower buildup of 30% per year. More than that strains and even inhibits the evolution of the essential informal structure and its communication pathways. F. J. Corbató of MIT points out that a long project must anticipate a turnover of 20% per year, and new people must be both technically trained and integrated into the formal structure.

Intercommunication is worse. If each part of the task must be separately coordinated with each other part, the effort increases as $n(n-1)/2$. Three workers require three times as much pairwise intercommunication as two; four require six times as much as two. If, moreover, there need to be conferences among three, four, etc., workers to resolve things jointly, matters get worse yet. The added effort of communicating may fully counteract the division of the original task and bring us back to the situation of Fig. 3.

Since software construction is inherently a systems effort—an exercise in complex interrelationships—communication effort is great, and it quickly

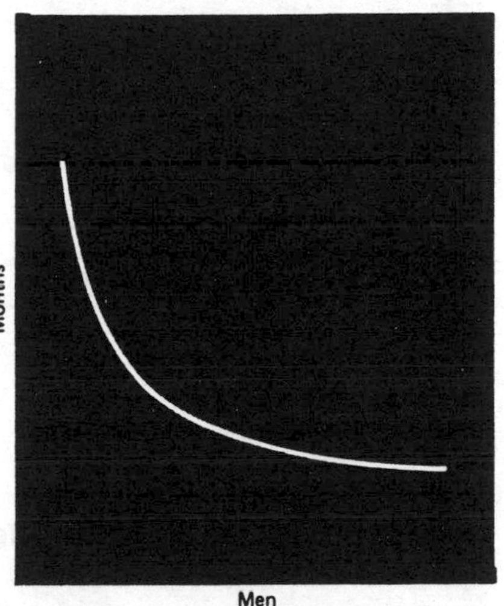


Fig. 2. Even on tasks that can be nicely partitioned among people, the additional communication required adds to the total work, increasing the schedule.

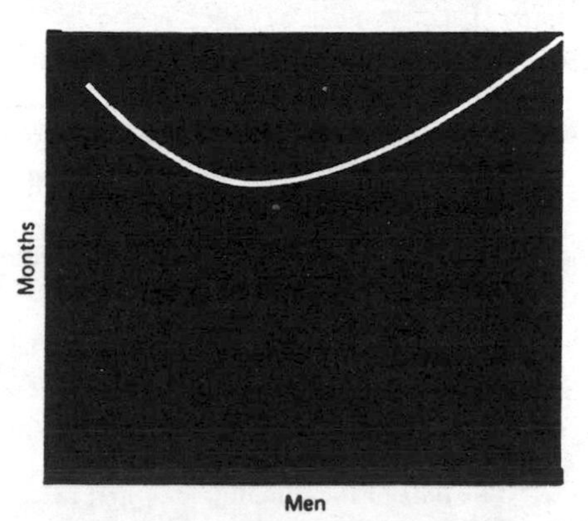


Fig. 3. Since software construction is complex, the communications overhead is great. Adding more men can lengthen, rather than shorten, the schedule.

dominates the decrease in individual task time brought about by partitioning. Adding more men then lengthens, not shortens, the schedule.

### Systems test

No parts of the schedule are so thoroughly affected by sequential constraints as component debugging and system test. Furthermore, the time required depends on the number and subtlety of the errors encountered. Theoretically this number should be zero. Because of optimism, we usually expect the number of bugs to be smaller than it turns out to be. Therefore testing is usually the most mis-scheduled part of programming.

For some years I have been successfully using the following rule of thumb for scheduling a software task:

⅓ planning

⅙ coding

¼ component test and early system test

¼ system test, all components in hand.

This differs from conventional scheduling in several important ways:

1. The fraction devoted to planning is larger than normal. Even so, it is barely enough to produce a detailed and solid specification, and not enough to include research or exploration of totally new techniques.
2. The *half* of the schedule devoted to debugging of completed code is much larger than normal.
3. The part that is easy to estimate, i.e., coding, is given only one-sixth of the schedule.

In examining conventionally scheduled projects, I have found that few allowed one-half of the projected schedule for testing, but that most did indeed spend half of the actual schedule for that purpose. Many of these were on schedule until and except in system testing.

Failure to allow enough time for system test, in particular, is peculiarly disastrous. Since the delay comes at the end of the schedule, no one is aware of schedule trouble until almost the delivery date. Bad news, late and without warning, is unsettling to customers and to managers.

Furthermore, delay at this point has unusually severe financial, as well as psychological, repercussions. The project is fully staffed, and cost-per-day is maximum. More seriously, the software is to support other business effort (shipping of computers, operation of new facilities, etc.) and the secondary costs of delaying these are very high, for it is almost time for software shipment. Indeed, these secondary costs may far outweigh all others. It is therefore very important to allow enough system test time in the original schedule.

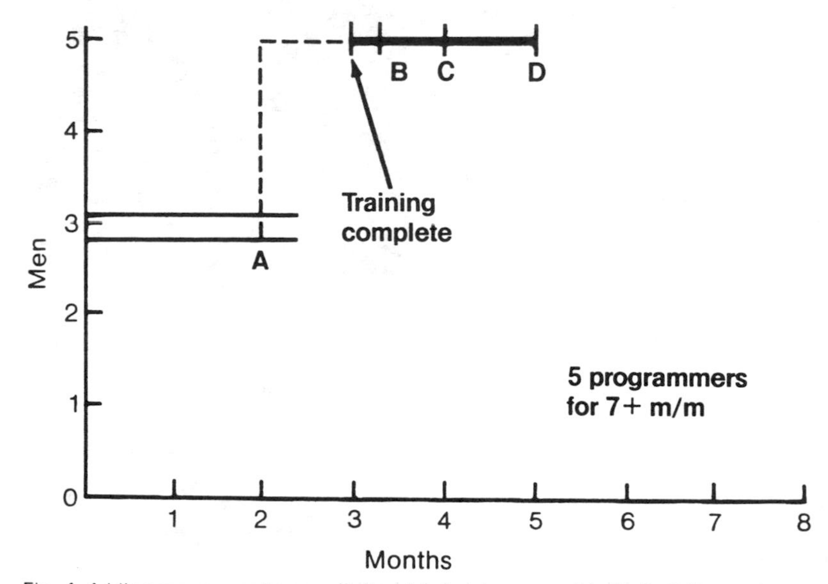


Fig. 4. Adding manpower to a project which is late may not help. In this case, suppose three men on a 12 man-month project were a month late. If it takes one of the three an extra month to train two new men, the project will be just as late as if no one was added.

### Gutless estimating

Observe that for the programmer, as for the chef, the urgency of the patron may govern the scheduled completion of the task, but it cannot govern the actual completion. An omelette, promised in ten minutes, may appear to be progressing nicely. But when it has not set in ten minutes, the customer has two choices—wait or eat it raw. Software customers have had the same choices.

The cook has another choice; he can turn up the heat. The result is often an omelette nothing can save—burned in one part, raw in another.

Now I do not think software managers have less inherent courage and firmness than chefs, nor than other engineering managers. But false scheduling to match the patron's desired date is much more common in our discipline than elsewhere in engineering. It is very difficult to make a vigorous, plausible, and job-risking defense of an estimate that is derived by no quantitative method, supported by little data, and certified chiefly by the hunches of the managers.

Clearly two solutions are needed. We need to develop and publicize productivity figures, bug-incidence figures, estimating rules, and so on. The whole profession can only profit from sharing such data.

Until estimating is on a sounder basis, individual managers will need to stiffen their backbones, and defend their estimates with the assurance that their poor hunches are better than wish-derived estimates.

### Regenerative disaster

What does one do when an essential software project is behind schedule? Add manpower, naturally. As Figs. 1 through 3 suggest, this may or may not help.

Let us consider an example. Suppose a task is estimated at 12 man-months and assigned to three men for four months, and that there are measurable mileposts A, B, C, D, which are scheduled to fall at the end of each month.

Now suppose the first milepost is not reached until two months have elapsed. What are the alternatives facing the manager?

1. Assume that the task must be done on time. Assume that only the first part of the task was misestimated. Then 9 man-months of effort remain, and two months, so 4½ men will be needed. Add 2 men to the 3 assigned.
2. Assume that the task must be done on time. Assume that the whole estimate was uniformly low. Then 18 man-months of effort remain, and two months, so 9 men will be needed. Add 6 men to the 3 assigned.
3. Reschedule. In this case, I like the advice given by an experienced hardware engineer, "Take no small slips." That is, allow enough time in the new schedule to ensure that the work can be carefully and

thoroughly done, and that rescheduling will not have to be done again.

4. Trim the task. In practice this tends to happen anyway, once the team observes schedule slippage. Where the secondary costs of delay are very high, this is the only feasible action. The manager's only alternatives are to trim it formally and carefully, to reschedule, or to watch the task get silently trimmed by hasty design and incomplete testing.

In the first two cases, insisting that the unaltered task be completed in four months is disastrous. Consider the regenerative effects, for example, for the first alternative (Fig. 4 preceding page). The two new men, however competent and however quickly recruited, will require training in the task by one of the experienced men. If this takes a month, *3 man-months will have been devoted to work not in the original estimate.* Furthermore, the task, originally partitioned three ways, must be repartitioned into five parts, hence some work already done will be lost and system testing must be lengthened. So at the end of the third month, substantially more than 7 man-months of effort remain, and 5 trained people and one month are available. As Fig. 4 suggests, the product is just as late as if no one had been added.

To hope to get done in four months, considering only training time and not repartitioning and extra systems test, would require adding 4 men, not 2, at the end of the second month. To cover repartitioning and system test effects, one would have to add still other men. Now, however, one has at least a 7-man team, not a 3-man one; thus such aspects as team organization and task division are different in kind, not merely in degree.

Notice that by the end of the third month things look very black. The March 1 milestone has not been reached in spite of all the managerial effort. The temptation is very strong to repeat the cycle, adding yet more manpower. Therein lies madness.

The foregoing assumed that only the first milestone was misestimated. If on March 1 one makes the conservative assumption that the whole schedule was optimistic one wants to add 6 men just to the original task. Calculation of the training, repartitioning, system testing effects is left as an exercise for the reader. Without a doubt, the regenerative disaster will yield a poorer product later, than would rescheduling with the original three men, unaugmented.

Oversimplifying outrageously, we state Brooks' Law:

**Adding manpower to a late software project makes it later.**

This then is the demythologizing of the man-month. The number of months of a project depends upon its sequential constraints. The maximum number of men depends upon the number of independent subtasks. From these two quantities one can derive schedules using fewer men and more months. (The only risk is product obsolescence.) One cannot, however, get workable schedules using more men and fewer months. More software projects have gone awry for lack of calendar time than for all other causes combined.

### Calling the shot

How long will a system programming job take? How much effort will be required? How does one estimate?

I have earlier suggested ratios that seem to apply to planning time, coding, component test, and system test. First, one must say that one does *not* estimate the entire task by estimating the coding portion only and then applying the ratios. The coding is only one-sixth or so of the problem, and errors in its estimate or in the ratios could lead to ridiculous results.

Second, one must say that data for building isolated small programs are not applicable to programming systems products. For a program averaging about 3,200 words, for example, Sackman, Erikson, and Grant report an average code-plus-debug time of about 178 hours for a single programmer, a figure which would extrapolate to give an annual productivity of 35,800 statements per year. A program half that size took less than one-fourth as long, and extrapolated productivity is almost 80,000 statements per year.[1]. Planning, documentation, testing, system integration, and training times must be added. The linear extrapolation of such spring figures is meaningless. Extrapolation of times for the hundred-yard dash shows that a man can run a mile in under three minutes.

Before dismissing them, however, let us note that these numbers, although not for strictly comparable problems, suggest that effort goes as a power of size *even* when no communication is involved except that of a man with his memories.

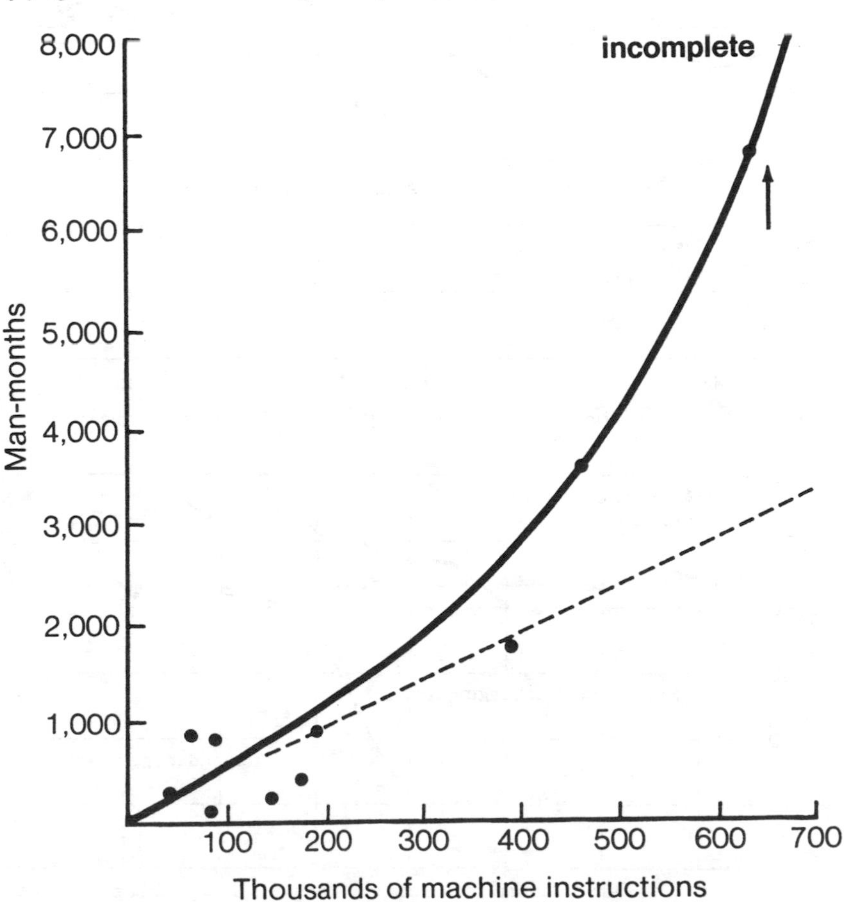


Fig. 5. As a project's complexity increases, the number of man-months required to complete it goes up exponentially.

Fig. 5 tells the sad story. It illustrates results reported from a study done by Nanus and Farr[2] at System Development Corp. This shows an exponent of 1.5; that is,

$$\text{effort} = (\text{constant}) \times (\text{number of instructions})^{1.5}$$

Another SDC study reported by Weinwurm[3] also shows an exponent near 1.5.

A few studies on programmer productivity have been made, and several estimating techniques have been proposed. Morin has prepared a survey of the published data.[4] Here I shall give only a few items that seem especially illuminating.

### Portman's data

Charles Portman, manager of ICL's Software Div., Computer Equipment Organization (Northwest) at Manchester, offers another useful personal insight.

He found his programming teams missing schedules by about one-half—each job was taking approximately twice as long as estimated. The estimates were very careful, done by experienced teams estimating man-hours for several hundred subtasks on a PERT chart. When the slippage pattern appeared, he asked them to keep careful daily logs of time usage. These showed that the estimating error could be entirely accounted for by the fact that his teams were only realizing 50% of the working week as actual programming and debugging time. Machine downtime, higher-priority short unrelated jobs, meetings, paperwork, company business, sickness, personal time, etc. accounted for the rest. In short, the estimates made an unrealistic assumption about the number of technical work hours per man-year. My own experience quite confirms his conclusion.

An unpublished 1964 study by E. F. Bardain shows programmers realizing only 27% productive time.[5]

| | Prog. units | Number of programmers | Years | Man-years | Program words | Words/ man-yr. |
|---|---|---|---|---|---|---|
| Operational | 50 | 83 | 4 | 101 | 52,000 | 515 |
| Maintenance | 36 | 60 | 4 | 81 | 51,000 | 630 |
| Compiler | 13 | 9 | 2¼ | 17 | 38,000 | 2230 |
| Translator (Data assembler) | 15 | 13 | 2½ | 11 | 25,000 | 2270 |

Table 1. Data from Bell Labs indicates productivity differences between complex problems (the first two are basically control programs with many modules) and less complex ones. No one is certain how much of the difference is due to complexity, how much to the number of people involved.

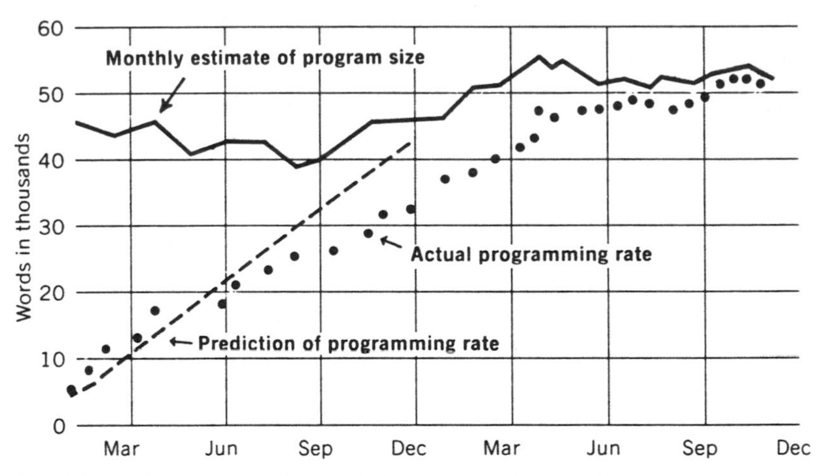


Fig. 6. Bell Labs' experience in predicting programming effort on one project.

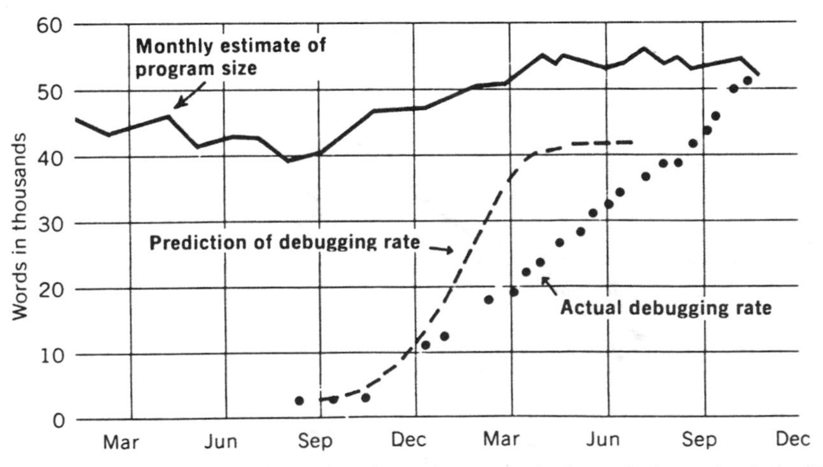


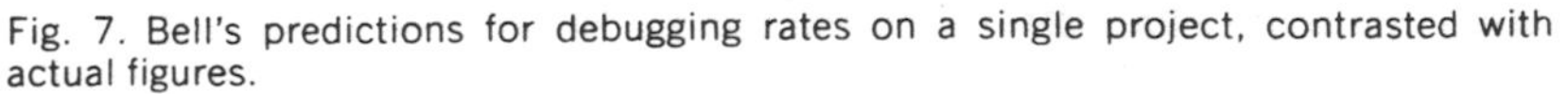

Fig. 7. Bell's predictions for debugging rates on a single project, contrasted with actual figures.

### Aron's data

Joel Aron, manager of Systems Technology at IBM in Gaithersburg, Maryland, has studied programmer productivity when working on nine large systems (briefly, *large* means more than 25 programmers and 30,000 deliverable instructions). He divides such systems according to interactions among programmers (and system parts) and finds productivities as follows:

| | |
|---|---|
| Very few interactions | 10,000 instructions per man-year |
| Some interactions | 5,000 |
| Many interactions | 1,500 |

The man-years do not include support and system test activities, only design and programming. When these figures are diluted by a factor of two to cover system test, they closely match Harr's data.

### Harr's data

John Harr, manager of programming for the Bell Telephone Laboratories' Electronic Switching System, reported his and others' experience in a paper at the 1969 Spring Joint Computer Conference.[6] These data are shown in Table 1 and Figs. 6 and 7.

Of these, Fig. 6 is the most detailed and the most useful. The first two jobs are basically control programs; the second two are basically language translators. Productivity is stated in terms of debugged words per man-year. This includes programming, component test, and system test. It is not clear how much of the planning effort, or effort in machine support, writing, and the like, is included.

The productivities likewise fall into two classifications: those for control programs are about 600 words per man-year; those for translators are about 2,200 words per man-year. Note that all four programs are of similar size—the variation is in size of the work groups, length of time, and number of modules. Which is cause and which is effect? Did the control programs require more people because they were more complicated? Or did they require more modules and more man-months because they were assigned more people? Did they take longer because of the greater complexity, or because more people were assigned? One can't be sure. The control programs were surely more complex. These uncertainties aside, the numbers describe the real productivities achieved on a large system, using present-day programming techniques. As such they are a real contribution.

Figs. 6 and 7 show some interesting data on programming and debugging rates as compared to predicted rates.

### OS/360 data

IBM OS/360 experience, while not available in the detail of Harr's data, confirms it. Productivities in range of 600-800 debugged instructions per man-year were experienced by control program groups. Productivities in the 2,000-3,000 debugged instructions per man-year were achieved by language translator groups. These include planning done by the group, coding component test, system test, and some support activities. They are comparable to Harr's data, so far as I can tell.

Aron's data, Harr's data, and the OS/360 data all confirm striking differences in productivity related to the complexity and difficulty of the task itself. My guideline in the morass of estimating complexity is that compilers are three times as bad as normal batch application programs, and operating systems are three times as bad as compilers.

### Corbató's data

Both Harr's data and OS/360 data are for assembly language programming. Little data seem to have been published on system programming productivity using higher-level languages. Corbató of MIT's Project MAC reports, however, a mean productivity of 1,200 lines of debugged PL/I statements per man-year on the MULTICS system (between 1 and 2 million words)[7]

This number is very exciting. Like the other projects, MULTICS includes control programs and language translators. Like the others, it is producing a system programming product, tested and documented. The data seem to be comparable in terms of kind of effort included. And the productivity number is a good average between the control program and translator productivities of other projects.

But Corbató's number is *lines* per man-year, not *words!* Each statement in his system corresponds to about three-to-five words of handwritten code! This suggests two important conclusions:

- Productivity seems constant in terms of elementary statements, a conclusion that is reasonable in terms of the thought a statement requires and the errors it may include.
- Programming productivity may be increased as much as five times when a suitable high-level language is used. To back up these conclusions, W. M. Taliaffero also reports a constant productivity of 2,400 statements/year in Assembler, FORTRAN, and COBOL.[8] E. A. Nelson has shown a 3-to-1 productivity improvement for high-level language, although his standard deviations are wide.[9]

### Hatching a catastrophe

When one hears of disastrous schedule slippage in a project, he imagines that a series of major calamities must have befallen it. Usually, however, the disaster is due to termites, not tornadoes; and the schedule has slipped imperceptibly but inexorably. Indeed, major calamities are easier to handle; one responds with major force, radical reorganization, the invention of new approaches. The whole team rises to the occasion.

But the day-by-day slippage is harder to recognize, harder to prevent, harder to make up. Yesterday a key man was sick, and a meeting couldn't be held. Today the machines are all down, because lightning struck the building's power transformer. Tomorrow the disc routines won't start testing, because the first disc is a week late from the factory. Snow, jury duty, family problems, emergency meetings with customers, executive audits—the list goes on and on. Each one only postpones some activity by a half-day or a day. And the schedule slips, one day at a time.

How does one control a big project on a tight schedule? The first step is to *have* a schedule. Each of a list of events, called milestones, has a date. Picking the dates is an estimating problem, discussed already and crucially dependent on experience.

For picking the milestones there is only one relevant rule. Milestones must be concrete, specific, measurable events, defined with knife-edge sharpness. Coding, for a counterexample, is "90% finished" for half of the total coding time. Debugging is "99% complete" most of the time. "Planning complete" is an event one can proclaim almost at will.[10]

Concrete milestones, on the other hand, are 100% events. "Specifications signed by architects and implementers," "source coding 100% complete, keypunched, entered into disc library," "debugged version passes all test cases." These concrete milestones demark the vague phases of planning, coding, debugging.

It is more important that milestones be sharp-edged and unambiguous than that they be easily verifiable by the boss. Rarely will a man lie about milestone progress, *if* the milestone is so sharp that he can't deceive himself. But if the milestone is fuzzy, the boss often understands a different report from that which the man gives. To supplement Sophocles, no one enjoys bearing bad news, either, so it gets softened without any real intent to deceive.

> None love
> the bearer of bad news.
> *Sophocles*

Two interesting studies of estimating behavior by government contractors on large-scale development projects show that:

1. Estimates of the length of an activity made and revised carefully every two weeks before the activity starts do not significantly change as the start time draws near, no matter how wrong they ultimately turn out to be.
2. *During* the activity, *over*estimates of duration come steadily down as the activity proceeds.
3. *Underestimates* do not change significantly during the activity until about three weeks before the scheduled completion.[11]

Sharp milestones are in fact a service to the team, and one they can properly expect from a manager. The fuzzy milestone is the harder burden to live with. It is in fact a millstone that grinds down morale, for it deceives one about lost time until it is irremediable. And chronic schedule slippage is a morale-killer.

### "The other piece is late"

A schedule slips a day; so what? Who gets excited about a one-day slip? We can make it up later. And the other piece ours fits into is late anyway.

A baseball manager recognizes a nonphysical talent, *hustle*, as an essential gift of great players and great teams. It is the characteristic of running faster than necessary, moving sooner than necessary, trying harder than necessary. It is essential for great programming teams, too. Hustle provides the cushion, the reserve capacity, that enables a team to cope with routine mishaps, to anticipate and forfend minor calamities. The calculated response, the measured effort, are the wet blankets that dampen hustle. As we have seen, one *must* get excited about a one-day slip. Such are the elements of catastrophe.

But not all one-day slips are equally disastrous. So some calculation of response is necessary, though hustle be dampened. How does one tell which slips matter? There is no substitute for a PERT chart or a critical-path schedule. Such a network shows who waits for what. It shows who is on the critical path, where any slip moves the end date. It also shows how much an activity can slip before it moves into the critical path.

The PERT technique, strictly speaking, is an elaboration of critical-path scheduling in which one estimates three times for every event, times corresponding to different probabilities of meeting the estimated dates. I do not find this refinement to be worth the extra effort, but for brevity I will call any critical path network a PERT chart.

The preparation of a PERT chart is the most valuable part of its use. Laying out the network, identifying the dependencies, and estimating the legs all force a great deal of very specific planning very early in a project. The first chart is always terrible, and one invents and invents in making the second one.

As the project proceeds, the PERT chart provides the answer to the demoralizing excuse, "The other piece is late anyhow." It shows how hustle is needed to keep one's own part off the critical path, and it suggests ways to make up the lost time in the other part.

## Under the rug

When a first-line manager sees his small team slipping behind, he is rarely inclined to run to the boss with this woe. The team might be able to make it up, or he should be able to invent or reorganize to solve the problem. Then why worry the boss with it? So far, so good. Solving such problems is exactly what the first-line manager is there for. And the boss does have enough real worries demanding his action that he doesn't seek others. So all the dirt gets swept under the rug.

But every boss needs two kinds of information, exceptions for action and a status picture for education.[12] For that purpose he needs to know the status of all his teams. Getting a true picture of that status is hard.

The first-line manager's interests and those of the boss have an inherent conflict here. The first-line manager fears that if he reports his problem, the boss will act on it. Then his action will preempt the manager's function, diminish his authority, foul up his other plans. So as long as the manager thinks he can solve it alone, he doesn't tell the boss.

Two rug-lifting techniques are open to the boss. Both must be used. The first is to reduce the role conflict and inspire sharing of status. The other is to yank the rug back.

## Reducing the role conflict

The boss must first distinguish between action information and status information. He must discipline himself *not* to act on problems his managers can solve, and *never* to act on problems when he is explicitly reviewing status. I once knew a boss who invariably picked up the phone to give orders before the end of the first para-

**SYSTEM/360 SUMMARY STATUS REPORT**
**05/369 LANGUAGE PROCESSORS + SERVICE PROGRAMS**
**AS OF FEBRUARY 01 • 1965**

A=APPROVAL
C=COMPLETED

•= REVISED PLANNED DATE
NE=NOT ESTABLISHED

| PROJECT | LOCATION | COMMITMNT ANNOUNCE RELEASE | OBJECTIVE AVAILABLE APPROVED | SPECS AVAILABLE APPROVED | SRL AVAILABLE APPROVED | ALPHA TEST ENTRY EXIT | COMP TEST START COMPLETE | SYS TEST START COMPLETE | BULLETIN AVAILABLE APPROVED | BETA TEST ENTRY EXIT |
|---|---|---|---|---|---|---|---|---|---|---|
| OPERATING SYSTEM | | | | | | | | | | |
| 12K DESIGN LEVEL (E) | | | | | | | | | | |
| ASSEMBLY | SAN JOSE | 04/--/4<br>12/31/5 | 10/28/4 C | 10/13/4 C<br>01/11/5 | 11/13/4 C<br>11/16/4 A | 01/15/5 C<br>02/22/5 | | | | 09/01/5<br>11/30/5 |
| FORTRAN | POK | 04/--/4 C<br>12/31/5 | 10/28/4 C | 10/21/4 C<br>01/22/5 | 12/17/4 C<br>12/19/4 A | 01/15/5 C<br>02/22/5 | | | | 09/01/5<br>11/30/5 |
| COBOL | ENDICOTT | 04/--/4 C<br>12/31/5 | 10/25/4 C | 10/15/4 C<br>01/20/5 A | 11/17/4 C<br>12/08/4 A | 01/15/5 C<br>02/22/5 | | | | 09/01/5<br>11/30/5 |
| RPG | SAN JOSE | 04/--/4 C<br>12/31/5 | 10/28/4 C | 09/30/4 C<br>01/05/5 A | 12/02/4 C<br>01/18/5 A | 01/15/5 C<br>02/22/5 | | | | 09/01/5<br>11/30/5 |
| UTILITIES | TIME/LIFE | 04/--/4 C<br>12/31/5 | 06/24/4 C | | 11/20/4 C<br>11/30/4 A | | | | | 09/01/5<br>11/30/5 |
| SORT 1 | POK | 04/--/4 C<br>12/31/5 | 10/28/4 C | 10/19/4 C<br>01/11/5 | 11/12/4 C<br>11/30/4 A | 01/15/5 C<br>03/22/5 | | | | 09/01/5<br>11/30/5 |
| SORT 2 | POK | 04/--/4 C<br>06/30/6 | 10/28/4 C | 10/19/4 C<br>01/11/5 | 11/12/4 C<br>11/30/4 A | 01/15/5 C<br>03/22/5 | | | | 03/01/6<br>05/30/6 |
| 44K DESIGN LEVEL (F) | | | | | | | | | | |
| ASSEMBLY | SAN JOSE | 04/--/4 C<br>12/31/5 | 10/28/4 C | 10/13/4 C<br>01/11/5 | 11.13.4 C<br>11/18/4 A | 02/15/5<br>03/22/5 | | | | 09/01/5<br>11/30/5 |
| COBOL | TIME/LIFE | 04/--/4 C<br>06/30/6 | 10/28/4 C | 10/15/4 C<br>01/20/5 A | 11/17/4 C<br>12/06/4 A | 02/15/5<br>03/22/5 | | | | 03/01/5<br>05/30/6 |
| NPL | HURSLEY | 04/--/4 C<br>03/31/6 | 10/28/4 C | | | | | | | |
| 2250 | KINGSTON | 03/30/4 C<br>03/31/6 | 11/05/4 C | 10/06/4 C<br>01/04/5 | 01/12/5 C<br>01/29/5 | 01/04/5 C<br>01/29/5 | | | | 01/03/6<br>NE |
| 2280 | KINGSTON | 06/30/4 C<br>09/30/6 | 11/05/4 C | | | 04/01/5<br>04/30/5 | | | | 01/28/6<br>NE |
| 200K DESIGN LEVEL (H) | | | | | | | | | | |
| ASSEMBLY | TIME/LIFE | | 10/28/4 C | | | | | | | |
| FORTRAN | POK | 04/--/4 C<br>06/30/6 | 10/28/4 C | 10/16/4 C<br>01/11/5 | 11/11/4 C<br>12/10/4 A | 02/15/5<br>03/22/5 | | | | 03/01/6<br>05/30/6 |
| NPL | HURSLEY | 04/--/4 C | 10/28/4 C | | | 07/--/5 | | | | 01/--/7 |
| NPL H | POK | 04/--/4 C | 03/30/4 C | | | 02/01/5<br>04/01/5 | | | | 10/15/5<br>12/15/5 |

Fig. 8. A report showing milestones and status in a key document in project control. This one shows some problems in OS development: specifications approval is late on some items (those without "A"); documentation (SRL) approval is overdue on another; and one (2250 support) is late coming out of alpha test.

graph in a status report. That response is guaranteed to squelch full disclosure.

Conversely, when the manager knows his boss will accept status reports without panic or preemption, he comes to give honest appraisals.

This whole process is helped if the boss labels meetings, reviews, conferences, as *status-review* meetings versus *problem-action* meetings, and controls himself accordingly. Obviously one may call a problem-action meeting as a consequence of a status meeting, if he believes a problem is out of hand. But at least everybody knows what the score is, and the boss thinks twice before grabbing the ball.

## Yanking the rug off

Nevertheless, it is necessary to have review techniques by which the true status is made known, whether cooperatively or not. The PERT chart with its frequent sharp milestones is the basis for such review. On a large project one may want to review some part of it each week, making the rounds once a month or so.

A report showing milestones and actual completions is the key document. Fig. 8 (preceding page), shows an excerpt from such a report. This report shows some troubles. Specifications approval is overdue on several components. Manual (SRL) approval is overdue on another, and one is late getting out of the first state (ALPHA) of the independently conducted product test. So such a report serves as an agenda for the meeting of 1 February. Everyone knows the questions, and the component manager should be prepared to explain why it's late, when it will be finished, what steps he's taking, and what help, if any, he needs from the boss or collateral groups.

V. Vyssotsky of Bell Telephone Laboratories adds the following observation:

*I have found it handy to carry both "scheduled" and "estimated" dates in the milestone report. The scheduled dates are the property of the project manager and represent a consistent work plan for the project as a whole, and one which is* a priori *a reasonable plan. The estimated dates are the property of the lowest level manager who has cognizance over the piece of work in question, and represents his best judgment as to when it will actually happen, given the resources he has available and when he received (or has commitments for delivery of) his prerequisite inputs. The project manager has to keep his fingers off the estimated dates, and put the emphasis on getting accurate, unbiased estimates rather than palatable optimistic estimates or self-protective conservative ones. Once this is clearly established in everyone's mind, the project manager can see quite a ways into the future where he is going to be in trouble if he doesn't do something.*

The preparation of the PERT chart is a function of the boss and the managers reporting to him. Its updating, revision, and reporting requires the attention of a small (one-to-three-man) staff group which serves as an extension of the boss. Such a "Plans and Controls" team is invaluable for a large project. It has no authority except to ask all the line managers when they will have set or changed milestones, and whether milestones have been met. Since the Plans and Controls group handles all the paperwork, the burden on the line managers is reduced to the essentials—making the decisions.

We had a skilled, enthusiastic, and diplomatic Plans and Controls group on the OS/360 project, run by A. M. Pietrasanta, who devoted considerable inventive talent to devising effective but unobtrusive control methods. As a result, I found his group to be widely respected and more than tolerated. For a group whose role is inherently that of an irritant, this is quite an accomplishment.

The investment of a modest amount of skilled effort in a Plans and Controls function is very rewarding. It makes far more difference in project accomplishment than if these people worked directly on building the product programs. For the Plans and Controls group is the watchdog who renders the imperceptible delays visible and who points up the critical elements. It is the early warning system against losing a year, one day at a time.

## Epilogue

The tar pit of software engineering will continue to be sticky for a long time to come. One can expect the human race to continue attempting systems just within or just beyond our reach; and software systems are perhaps the most intricate and complex of man's handiworks. The management of this complex craft will demand our best use of new languages and systems, our best adaptation of proven engineering management methods, liberal doses of common sense, and a God-given humility to recognize our fallibility and limitations.

## References


1. Sackman, H., W. J. Erikson, and E. E. Grant, "Exploratory Experimentation Studies Comparing Online and Offline Programming Performance," *Communications of the ACM*, 11 (1968), 3-11.
2. Nanus, B., and L. Farr, "Some Cost Contributors to Large-Scale Programs," *AFIPS Proceedings, SJCC*, 25 (1964), 239-248.
3. Weinwurm, G. F., *Research in the Management of Computer Programming*. Report SP-2059, 1965, System Development Corp., Santa Monica.
4. Morin, L. H., *Estimation of Resources for Computer Programming Projects*, M. S. thesis, Univ. of North Carolina, Chapel Hill, 1974.
5. Quoted by D. B. Mayer and A. W. Stalnaker, "Selection and Evaluation of Computer Personnel," *Proceedings 23 ACM Conference*, 1968, 661.
6. Paper given at a panel session and not included in the *AFIPS Proceedings*.
7. Corbató, F. J., *Sensitive Issues in the Design of Multi-Use Systems*. Lecture at the opening of the Honeywell EDP Technology Center, 1968.
8. Taliaffero, W. M., "Modularity the Key to System Growth Potential," *Software*, 1 (1971), 245-257.
9. Nelson, E. A., *Management Handbook for the Estimation of Computer Programming Costs*. Report TM-3225, System Development Corp., Santa Monica, pp. 66-67.
10. Reynolds, C. H., "What's Wrong with Computer Programming Management?" in *On the Management of Computer Programming*. Ed. G. F. Weinwurm. Philadelphia: Auerbach, 1971, pp. 35-42.
11. King, W. R., and T. A. Wilson, "Subjective Time Estimates in Critical Path Planning—a Preliminary Analysis," *Management Sciences*, 13 (1967), 307-320, and sequel, W. R. King, D. M. Witterrongel, and K. D. Hezel, "On the Analysis of Critical Path Time Estimating Behavior," *Management Sciences*, 14 (1967), 79-84.
12. Brooks, F. P., and K. E. Iverson, *Automatic Data Processing, System/360 Edition*. New York: Wiley, 1969, pp. 428-430. □

# Software Engineering Project Management

Richard H. Thayer
*California State University, Sacramento*
*Sacramento, CA 95819*

## Abstract

*This article describes the management functions of planning, organizing, staffing, directing, and controlling that are necessary to manage any enterprise or activity. The universality of these management concepts provides a framework for adapting these traditional management functions to ensure complete coverage of project management activities. From these general management functions and activities, this article derives the detailed activities and tasks that should be undertaken by any manager who is assigned the responsibility of managing a software engineering project.*

*This article describes those management procedures, practices, technologies, and skills necessary to successfully manage a software engineering project.*

## 1. Introduction

This article is about management, the universality of management concepts, and the activities and tasks of software engineering project management.

*Management* involves the activities and tasks undertaken by one or more persons for the purpose of planning and controlling the activities of others in order to achieve objectives that could not be achieved by the others acting alone. Management functions can be categorized as planning, organizing, staffing, directing, and controlling.

*Project management* is a system of management procedures, practices, technologies, skill, and experience that is necessary to successfully manage an engineering project. If the project product is software, then the act of managing the project is called *software engineering project management.* The *manager* of a software engineering project is called a *software engineering project manager*, a *software project manager*, or, in many cases, just project manager.

Software engineering projects are frequently part of larger, more comprehensive projects that include equipment (hardware), facilities, personnel, procedures, as well as software. Examples include aircraft systems, accounting systems, radar systems, inventory control systems, and railroad switching systems. These *systems engineering projects* are typically managed by one or more system project managers (sometimes called *program managers*) who manage projects composed of engineers, experts in the field of the application, scientific specialists, programmers, support personnel, and others. If the software to be delivered is a "stand-alone" software system (a system that does not involve development of other non-software components), the software engineering project manager may be called the system project manager.

*Universality of management* is a concept that comes from management science [Koontz and O'Donnell 1972], [Fayol 1949] and means:

- Management performs the same functions (planning, organizing, staffing, directing, and controlling) regardless of position in the organization or the enterprise managed.
- Management functions are characteristic duties of managers; management practices, methods, activities, and tasks are particular to the enterprise or job managed.

The universality of management concepts allows us to apply them to software engineering project management [Thayer and Pyster 1984].

This article describes a comprehensive set of software engineering project management functions, activities, and tasks that should be undertaken by any manager who is assigned the responsibility of managing a software engineering project. It covers the management functions of planning, organizing, staffing, directing, and controlling software projects and the detailed activities and specific tasks of project management necessary to successfully manage a software engineering project.

Section 2 lists some of the major issues of software engineering that pertain to project management. Section 3 partitions the functions of management into a detailed list of management activities. Sections 4 through 8 then partition these management activities into the detailed activities and tasks of a software engineering project manager. Section 9 provides a summary of the article.

## 2. Major Issues of Software Engineering

Over 70 percent of software development organizations develop their software through ad hoc and unpredictable methods [Zubrow et al. 1995]. These organizations (considered to be "immature" according to the Software Engineering Institute Capability Maturity Model) do not have an objective basis for determining software cost and schedule or judging software quality. Software development processes are generally improvised by practitioners and their management during the course of the project. The company does not have any standard practices or follow any existing practices. Each manager manages according to individual preference. Proved software engineering techniques such as in-depth requirements analysis, inspections, reviews, testing, and documentation are reduced or eliminated when the project falls behind in cost, schedule and/or the customer demands more functionality without increase in budget [Paulk et al. 1996].

The "software crisis" is identified by software that is late, over budget, and fails to meet the customer's and/or user's system requirements [Gibbs 1994]. Many if not most of these problems have been blamed on inadequate or inferior software project management.

The importance of software project management is best illustrated in the following paragraphs extracted from the indicated Department of Defense (DoD) reports.

- A report from the STARS initiative (STARS: Software Technology for Adaptable, Reliable Systems) states, "The manager plays a major role in software and systems development and support. The difference between success or failure—between a project being on schedule and on budget or late and over budget—is often a function of the manager's effectiveness." [DoD Software Initiative 1983].
- A Report to the Defense Science Board Task Force on Military Software, states that "... today's major problems with software development are not technical problems, but management problems." [Brooks 1987]
- A General Accounting Office (GAO) report that investigated the cost and schedule overrun of the C-17 said, "... software development has clearly been a major problem during the first 6 years of the program. In fact, the C-17 is a good example of how not to manage software development...." [GAO/IMTEC-92-48 C-17 Aircraft Software]

## 3. Functions and Activities of Management

This article presents a top-down overview of software engineering project management responsibilities, activities, and tasks that should be undertaken by any manager who is assigned the responsibility of managing a software engineering project. A top-down approach is used to partition and allocate top-level functions to lower-level activities and tasks.

Table 3.1 depicts the classic management model as portrayed by such well-known authors in the field of management as Kootz and O'Donnell [1972], and others [Rue and Byars 1983], [Cleland and King 1972], [MacKenzie 1969].

According to this model, management is partitioned into five separate functions or components: *planning, organizing, staffing, directing, and controlling* (see Table 3.1 for definitions or explanations of these functions). All the activities of management, such as budgeting, scheduling, establishing authority and responsibility relationships, training, communicating, allocating responsibility, and so forth fall under one of these five headings.

**Table 3.1: Major Functions of Management**

| Activity | Definition or Explanation |
|---|---|
| Planning | Predetermining a course of action for accomplishing organizational objectives |
| Organizing | Arranging the relationships among work units for accomplishing objectives and granting responsibility and authority to obtain those objectives |
| Staffing | Selecting and training people for positions in the organization |
| Directing | Creating an atmosphere that will assist and motivate people to achieve desired end results |
| Controlling | Establishing, measuring, and evaluating activity performance toward planned objectives |

The detailed activities and tasks that are particular to a software engineering project are defined and discussed in Sections 3 through 8. Each of these sections defines and discusses one of the five functions of management along with some of the major issues of the individual functions. The management activities from Table 3.1 are partitioned into one or more levels of detailed tasks, which are then discussed and/or illustrated in the appropriate section.

## 4. Planning a Software Engineering Project

### 4.1 Introduction and Definitions

Planning a software engineering project consists of the management activities that lead to selecting, among alternatives, future courses of action for the project and a program for completing those actions.

Planning thus involves specifying the *goals* and *objectives* for a project and the *strategies, policies, plans*, and *procedures* for achieving them. "Planning is deciding in advance what to do, how to do it, when to do it, and who is to do it" [Koontz and O'Donnell 1972].

Every software engineering project should start with a good plan. Uncertainties and unknowns, both within the software project environment and from external sources, make planning necessary. The act of planning focuses attention on project goals, objectives, uncertainties, and unknowns.

Table 4.1 provides an outline of the planning activities that must be accomplished by software project managers in planning their projects. The project manager is responsible for developing numerous types of plans.

The balance of this section discusses and provides greater detail on the activities outlined in Table 4.1.

### 4.2 Set Objectives and Goals for the Project

The first planning step for a software engineering project is determining what the project must accomplish, when it must be accomplished, and what resources are necessary. Typically, this involves analyzing and documenting the system and software requirements. The management requirements and constraints must be determined. Management constraints are often expressed as resource and schedule limitations.

Success criteria must also be specified. Success criteria would normally include delivering a software system that satisfies the requirements, is on time, and is within costs. However, there may be other criteria. For instance, success could include winning a follow-on contract. Other criteria might include increasing the size and scope of the present contract, or increasing the profit margin by winning an incentive award.

Success criteria might also be placed in a relative hierarchy of importance. For example, being on time might be more important than being within budget.

### 4.3 Develop Project Strategies

Another planning activity is developing and documenting a set of management strategies (sometime called strategic policies) for a project. Strategies are defined as long-range goals and the methods to obtain those goals. These long-range goals are usually developed at a corporate level; however, the project manager can have strategic plans within an individual projcct. This is particularly true if it is a

**Table 4.1: Planning Activities for Software Projects**

| Activity | Definition or Explanation |
|---|---|
| Set objectives and goals | Determine the desired outcome for the project. |
| Develop strategies | Decide major organizational goals and develop a general program of action for reaching those goals. |
| Develop policies | Make standing decisions on important recurring matters to provide a guide for decision making. |
| Forecast future situations | Anticipate future events or make assumptions about the future; predict future results or expectations from courses of action. |
| Conduct a risk assessment | Anticipate possible adverse events and problem areas; state assumptions; develop contingency plans; predict results of possible courses of action. |
| Determine possible courses of action | Develop, analyze, and/or evaluate different ways to conduct the project. |
| Make planning decisions | Evaluate and select a course of action from among alternatives. |
| Set procedures and rules | Establish methods, guides, and limits for accomplishing the project activity. |
| Develop project plans | Establish policies, procedures, rules, tasks, schedules, and resources necessary to complete the project. |
| Prepare budgets | Allocate estimated costs to project functions, activities, and tasks. |
| Document project plans | Record policy decisions, courses of action, budget, program plans, and contingency plans. |

large project. An example of a strategic plan might be to develop a new area of expertise or business for the organization by conducting a project in that area.

### 4.4 Develop Policies for the Project

*Policies* are predetermined management decisions. The project manager may establish policies for the project to provide guidance to supervisors and individual team members in making routine decisions. For example, it might be a policy of the project that status reports from team leaders are due in the project manager's office by close of business each Thursday. Policies can reduce the need for interaction on every decision and provide a sense of direction for the team members. In many cases, the project manager does not develop new policies for the project, but follows the policies established at the corporate level.

### 4.5 Forecast Future Situations

Determining future courses of action will be based on the current status and environment as well as the project manager's vision of the future. The project manager is responsible for forecasting situations that might impact the software project.

Forecasting is addressed in two steps. The first step involves predicting the future environment of the project and the second step involves predicting how the project will respond to the predicted future. Step one involves predicting future events, such as availability of personnel, the inflation rate, or availability of new computer hardware and the impact these future events will have on the software engineering project.

The second step involves predicting future activities of the project, such as specifying future expenditures of project resources and funds. The project manager is also responsible for estimating future risks and developing contingency plans for countering those risks.

### 4.6 Conduct a Risk Assessment for the Project

*Risk* is the likelihood of a specified hazardous or undesirable event occurring within a specified period or circumstance. The concept of risk has two elements: the frequency, or probability that a specified hazard might occur and the consequences of it. Risk factors must be identified and forecasts of situations that might adversely impact the software project must be prepared [Fairley and Rook 1996]. For example, there is serious doubt that the software can be developed for the amount specified in the contract. Should this occur, the results would be a loss of profit for the development company.

*Contingency plans* specify the actions to be taken should a risk (a potential problem) become a real problem. The risk becomes a problem when a predetermined risk-indicator metric crosses a predetermined threshold. For example, the budget has been over run by 12 percent at software specifications review (SSR). The preset threshold metric was 10 percent; therefore, the appropriate contingency plan must be put in effect. [Boehm 1987]

### 4.7 Determine Possible Courses of Action

In most projects there is more than one way to conduct the project, but not with equal cost, equal schedule, or equal risk. It is the project manager's responsibility to examine various approaches that could achieve the project objectives and satisfy the success criteria.

### 4.8 Make Planning Decisions for the Project

The project manager, in consultation with higher level management, the customer, and other appropriate parties, is responsible for choosing among the many possible courses of action those that are most appropriate for meeting project goals and objectives. The project manager is responsible for making tradeoff decisions involving cost, schedule, design strategies, and risks [Bunyard and Coward 1982].

### 4.9 Set Procedures and Rules for the Project

The project manager establishes procedures and rules for a project. In contrast to policies, *procedures* establish customary methods and provide detailed guidance for project activities. Procedures detail the exact manner for accomplishing an activity. For example, there may be a procedure for conducting design reviews.

In another contrast, a *rule* establishes specific and definite actions to be taken or not taken with respect to a given situation. A rule allows no discretion. For example, a rule might require two people to be on duty in the machine room at all times.

*Process standards* (in contrast to *product standards*) can be used to establish procedures. Process standards may be adopted from the corporate standards or written for a particular project. Process standards might cover topics such as reporting methods, reviews, and documentation preparation requirements.

### 4.10 Develop a Software Project Plan

A project plan specifies all of the actions necessary to successfully deliver a software product.

Typically, the plan specifies:

- The *tasks* to be performed by the software development staff in order to deliver the final software product. This usually requires partitioning the project activities into small, well-specified tasks. A useful tool for representing the partitioned project is the work breakdown structure (WBS).

- The *cost* and resources necessary to accomplish each project task [Boehm 1984].
- The project *schedule* that specifies dependencies among tasks, and establishes project milestones.

For further discussion of project planning see [Miller 1978].

### 4.11 Prepare Budgets for the Project

*Budgeting* involves placing cost figures on the project plan. The project manager is responsible for determining the cost of the project and allocating the budget to project tasks. Cost is the common denominator for all elements of the project plan. Requirements for personnel, computers, travel, office space, equipment, and so forth can only be compared and cost-tradeoffs made when these requirements are measured in terms of their monetary value.

### 4.12 Document Project Plans

The project manager is responsible for documenting the project plan [Fairley 1987] and for preparing other plans such as the software quality assurance plan, software configuration management plan, staffing plan, and the test plan. The project plan is the primary means of communicating with other entities that interface with the project.

## 5. Organizing a Software Engineering Project

### 5.1 Introduction and Definitions

*Organizing* a software engineering project involves developing an effective and efficient organizational structure for assigning and completing project tasks and establishing the authority and responsibility relationships among the tasks.

Organizing involves itemizing the project activities required to achieve the objectives of the project and then arranging these activities into logical clusters. It also involves assigning groups of activities to various organizational entities and then delegating responsibility and authority needed to carry out the activities.

The purpose of an organizational structure is to "focus the efforts of many on a selected goal" [Donnelly, Gibson, and Ivancevich 1975].

Table 5.1 provides an outline of the activities that must be accomplished by the project manager in organizing a project. The remainder of this section provides greater detail concerning the activities outlined in Table 5.1.

### 5.2 Identify and Group Project Tasks

The manager is responsible for reviewing the project requirements, defining the various tasks to be accomplished, sizing those tasks, and grouping those tasks. Titles and organizational entities are assigned to the assembly of tasks; for example, analysis tasks, design tasks, coding tasks, and testing tasks. This information enables the project manager to select an organizational structure to control these groups.

### 5.3 Select an Organizational Structure for the Project

After identifying and grouping project tasks, the project manager must select an organizational structure. A software development project can be organized using one of several different and overlapping organizational types. For example:

- *Conventional organization structure*—line or staff organization.
- *Project organization structure*—functional, project, or matrix.
- *Team structure*—Egoless, chief programmer, or hierarchical.

**Table 5.1: Organizing Activities for Software Project**

| Activity | Definition or Explanation |
|---|---|
| Identify and group project function, activities and tasks | Define, size, and categorize the project work. |
| Select organizational structures | Select appropriate structures to accomplish the project and to monitor, control, communicate, and coordinate. |
| Create organizational positions | Establish title, job descriptions, and job relationships for each project role. |
| Define responsibilities and authority | Define responsibilities for each organizational position and the authority to be granted for fulfilling those responsibilities. |
| Establish position qualifications | Define qualifications for persons to fill each position. |
| Document organizational decisions | Document titles, positions, job, descriptions, responsibilities, authorities, relationships, and position qualifications |

The project manager may not have the luxury of selecting the best project organizational type, since this may be determined by policy at the corporate level. Regardless of who does it, an organizational structure that matches the needs and goals of the project application and environment and facilitates communication between the organizational entities should be selected.

The following paragraphs describe these organizational considerations.

**5.3.1 Conventional Organizational Structures.** A *line* organization has the responsibility and authority to perform the work that represents the primary mission of the larger organizational unit. In contrast, a *staff* organization is a group of functional experts that has responsibility and authority to perform special activities that help the line organization do its work. All organizations in a company are either line or staff.

**5.3.2 Software Project Structures.** A project structure is a temporary organizational form that has been established for the purpose of developing and building a system that is too big to be done by one or, at most, a few people. In a software engineering project, a software system is to be built. A project structure can be superimposed on a line or staff organization.

**5.3.2.1 Functional Project Organization.** One type of project organization is a *functional* organization; a project structure is built around a software engineering function or group of similar functions. A project is accomplished either within a functional unit or, if multifunctional, by two or more functional units, and the work product is passed from function to function as the project passes through the life-cycle phases. Figure 5.1 illustrates the tasks and lines of authority of a functional organization used to develop a software product.

**5.3.2.2 Project Organization.** Another type of project organization is built around each specific project; a project manager is given the responsibility, authority, and resources for conducting the project [Middleton 1967]. (The project organization is sometimes called a *projected* organization to get away from the term "project organization."). The manager must meet project goals within the resources of the organization. The project manager usually has the responsibility to hire, discharge, train, and promote people within the project. Figure 5.2 illustrates the tasks and lines of authority of a project organization. Note that the software project manager has total control over the project and the assigned software personnel.

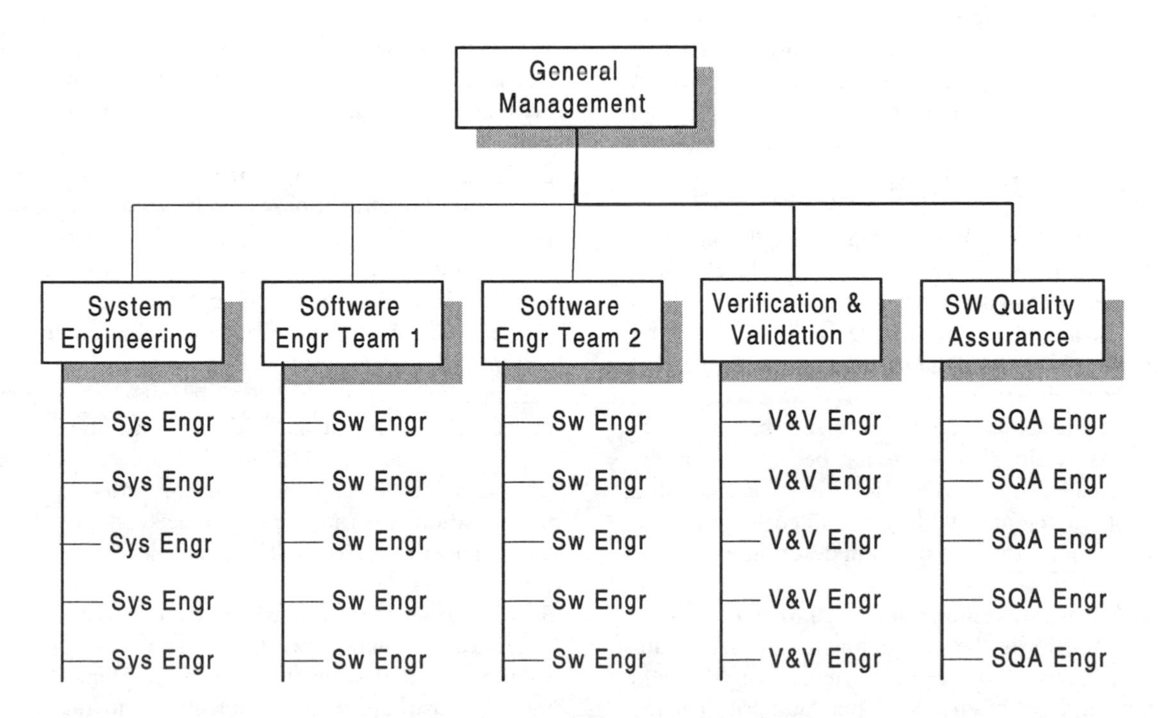


*Figure 5.1: Functional Project Organization*

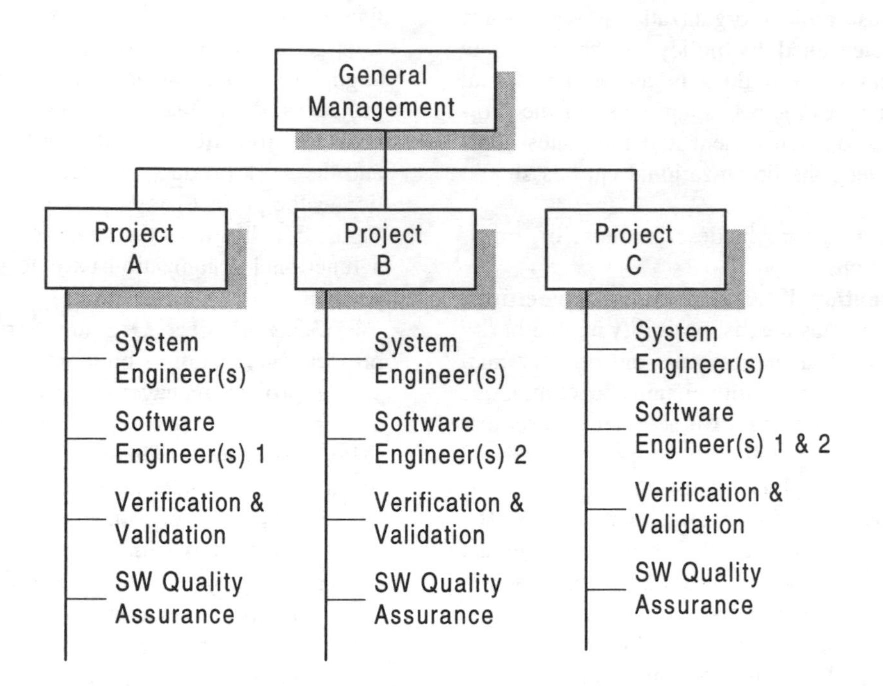


*Figure 5.2: Project Organization*

**5.3.2.3 Matrix Project Organization.** The third project organization is the *matrix* organization (sometimes called matrix project organization) and is a composite of the functional organization and the project organization [Stuckenbruck 1981]. The project manager is given responsibility and authority for completing the project. The functional managers provide the resources needed to conduct the project. In a matrix organization, the project manager usually does not have the authority to hire, discharge, train, or promote personnel within his project. Figure 5.3 illustrates the tasks and lines of authority in a matrix organization. Engineers labeled "A" are temporarily assigned to Project A, Engineers labeled "B" are temporarily assigned to Project B, Engineer labeled "C" are temporarily assigned to Project C.

Since each individual worker is "supervised" by two separates managers, the system is sometime called the "two boss" system.

Once the tasks are identified, sized, and grouped, and the organizational structure has been specified, the project manager must create job titles and position descriptions. Personnel will be recruited for the project using the job titles and position descriptions.

### 5.5 Define Responsibilities and Authority

*Responsibility* is the obligation to fulfill commitments. *Authority* is the right to make decisions and exert power. It is often stated that authority can be delegated, but responsibility cannot. [Koontz and O'Donnell 1976] support this view by defining responsibility as "the obligation owed by subordinates to their supervisors for exercising authority delegated to them in a way to accomplish results expected." Responsibility and authority for organizational activities or tasks should be assigned to the organizational position at the time the position is created or modified. The project manager is assigned and in turn assigns the responsibilities and the corresponding authorities to the various organizational positions within the project.

### 5.6 Establish Position Qualifications

Position qualifications must be identified for each position in the project. Position qualifications are established by considering issues such as the types of individuals needed for the project, the necessary experience in the area of the application, the required education (a B.S. in computer science or an M.S. in artificial intelligence), the required training, either before or after the project is initiated, and the required knowledge, such as FORTRAN, Lisp, or some other programming language. Establishing proper and accurate position qualifications will make it possible for the manager to correctly staff the project.

### 5.7 Document Organizational Structures

Lines of authority, tasks, and responsibilities should be documented in the project plan. Decisions must be justified, well documented, and made available to guide staffing of the project.

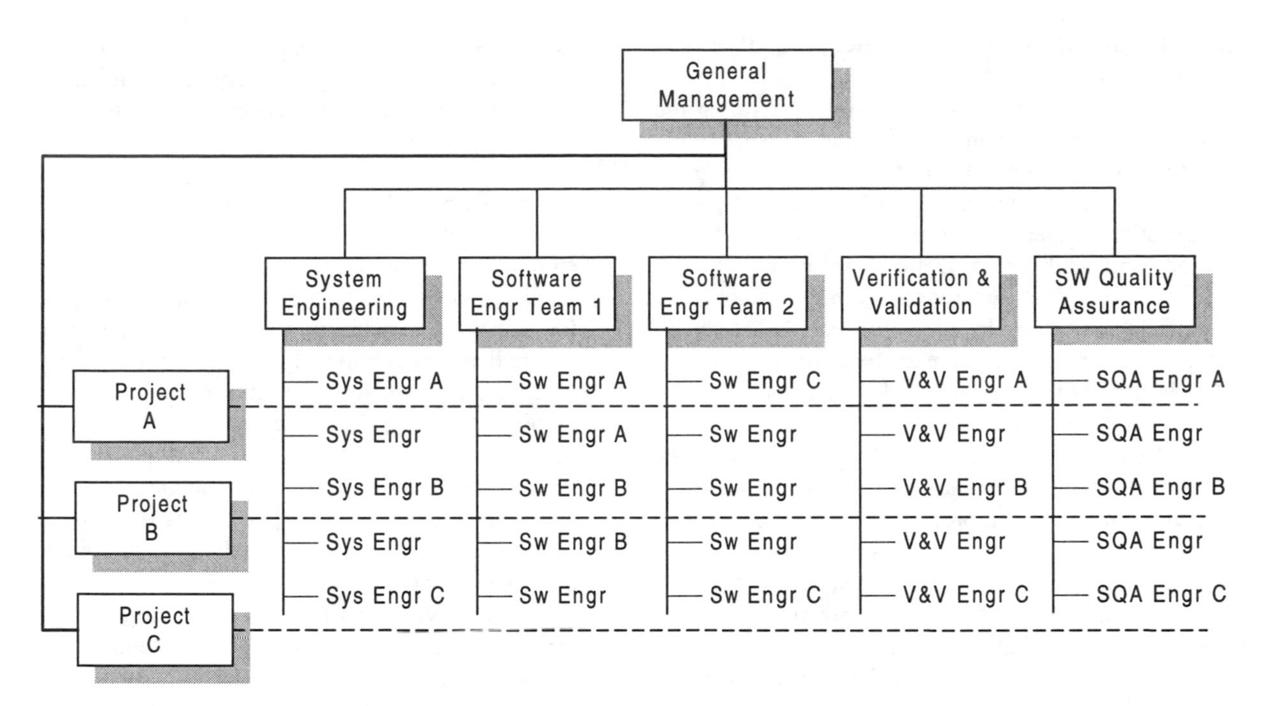


*Figure 5.3: Matrix Project Organization*

## 6. Staffing a Software Engineering Project

### 6.1 Introduction and Definitions

*Staffing* a software engineering project consists of all of the management activities that involve filling (and keeping filled) the positions that were established in the project organizational structure. This includes selecting candidates for the positions and training or otherwise developing candidates and incumbents to accomplish their tasks effectively. Staffing also involves terminating project personnel when necessary.

Staffing is not the same as organizing; staffing involves filling the roles created in the project organizational structure through selection, training, and development of personnel. The objective of staffing is to ensure that project roles are filled by personnel who are qualified (both technically and temperamentally) to occupy them.

Table 6.1 provides an outline of the activities and tasks that must be accomplished by project managers to staff their projects. The remainder of this section provides greater detail on the activities and tasks outlined in Table 6.1.

**Table 6.1: Staffing Activities for Software Projects**

| Activity | Definition or Explanation |
|---|---|
| Fill organizational positions | Select, recruit, or promote qualified people for each project position. |
| Assimilate assigned personnel newly | Orient and familiarize new people with the organization, facilities, and tasks to be done on the project. |
| Educate or train personnel | Make up deficiencies in position qualifications through training and education. |
| Provide for general development | Improve knowledge, attitudes, and skills of project personnel. |
| Evaluate and appraise personnel | Record and analyze the quantity and quality of project work as the basis for personnel evaluations. Set performance goals and appraise personnel periodically. |
| Compensate | Provide wages, bonuses, benefits, or other financial remuneration commensurate with project responsibilities and performance. |
| Terminate assignments | Transfer or separate project personnel as necessary. |
| Document staffing decisions | Record staffing plans, training plans and achievements, appraisal records, and compensations recommendations |

### 6.2 Fill Organizational Positions in a Software Project

The project manager is responsible for filling the positions that were established during organizational planning for the project. In staffing any software project, any number of factors should be considered, such as education, experience, training, motivation, commitment, and intelligence. Deficiencies in any of these factors can be offset by strengths in other factors. For example, deficiencies in education can be offset by better experience, a particular type of training, or enthusiasm for the job. Serious deficiencies should be cause for corrective action.

**6.2.1 Sources of Qualified Project Individuals.** One source of qualified individuals is personnel who transfer from within the project itself. It is the project manager's prerogative to move people from one task to another within a project. Another source is transfers from other projects within the organization. This can be done anytime, but often happens when another software engineering project is either phasing down or is canceled.

Other sources of qualified personnel are new hires from other companies through such methods as job fairs, referrals, headhunters, want ads, and unsolicited resumes. New college graduates can be recruited either through interviews on campus or through referrals from recent graduates who are now company employees.

**6.2.2 Selecting a Productive Software Staff.** Two metrics may indicate a productive software staff:

- *Amount of experience*—An experienced staff is more productive than an inexperienced staff [Boehm 1984]. Some of the best experience comes from having worked on software projects similar to the project being staffed.
- *Diversity of experience*—Diversity of experience is a reasonable predictor of productivity [Kruesi 1982]. It is better that the individuals under consideration have done well in several jobs over a period of time rather than one job for the same time period.

Other qualities indicative of a highly productive individual are communications skills (both oral and written), a college degree (usually in a technical field), being a self-starter, and experience in the application area of the project.

### 6.3 Assimilate Newly Assigned Software Personnel

The manager is responsible not only for hiring the people, but also for familiarizing them with any project procedures, facilities, and plans necessary to assure their effective integration into the project. In short, the project manager is responsible for introducing new employees to the company and the company to the employees.

### 6.4 Educate or Train Personnel as Necessary

It is not always possible to recruit or transfer employees with exactly those skills needed for a particular project. Therefore, the manager is responsible for educating and training the assigned personnel to ensure that they can meet the project requirements.

Education differs from training. *Education* involves teaching the basics, theory, and underlying concepts of a discipline with a view toward a long-term payoff. *Training* means teaching a skill or a knowledge of how to use, operate, or make something. The skill is typically needed in the near future and has a short term payoff.

Each individual within an organization must have a *training plan* that specifies career education and training goals and the steps each person will take in achieving those goals. To be successful, top management must actively support training programs.

### 6.5 Provide for General Development of the Project Staff

In addition to education and training, the project manager must ensure that project staff grows with the project and company. The manager must ensure that their professional knowledge will increase and that they maintain a positive attitude toward the project, the company, and the customers.

### 6.6 Evaluate and Appraise Project Personnel

The project manager is also responsible for periodically evaluating and appraising personnel. An appraisal provides feedback to staff members concerning the positive and negative aspects of their performance. This feedback allows the staff member to strengthen good qualities and improve those which are negative. Appraisals should be done at regular intervals and should concentrate on the individual's performance and not on personality, unless personality issues interfere with performance [Moneysmith 1984].

### 6.7 Compensate the Project Personnel

The manager—sometimes directly, sometimes indirectly—is responsible for determining the salary scale and benefits of project personnel. Benefits take on many forms. Most benefits are monetary or can be equated to money. These include stock options, a company car, first class tickets for all company trips, or a year-end bonus. Some benefits are nonmonetary but appeal to the self-esteem of the individual; examples are combat medals in the military, a reserve parking place at the company plant, or an impressive title on the door.

### 6.8 Terminate Project Assignments

The project manager is not only responsible for hiring people, but must also terminate assignments as necessary. "Terminate" includes reassigning personnel at the end of a successful project (a pleasant termination) and dismissing personnel due to project cancellation (an unpleasant termination). Termination can also occur by firing when an employee is determined to be unsatisfactory.

### 6.9 Document Project Staffing Decisions

Project managers should document their staffing plan and their evaluation and training policies for all to read. Each individual within an organization should have a personal training plan reflecting course work needed and progress made. Other staffing documents that might be produced include orientation plans and schedules, salary schedules, and promotion policies. The project manager and each individual employee should have a copy of his or her annual performance objectives signed by the employee and the project manager.

## 7. Directing a Software Engineering Project

### 7.1 Introduction and Definitions

Directing a software engineering project consists of management's motivational and interpersonal aspects that encourage project personnel to understand and contribute to project goals. Once subordinates are trained and oriented, the project manager has a continuing responsibility for clarifying their assignments, guiding them toward improved performance, and motivating them to work with enthusiasm and confidence toward achieving project goals.

Directing, like staffing, involves people. Directing is sometimes considered to be synonymous with leading (compare reference [Koontz and O'Donnell 1972] with reference [Koontz, O'Donnell, and Weihrich 1984]). Directing a project involves providing leadership to the project, day-to-day supervision of the project personnel, delegating authority to the lower organizational entities, coordinating activities of the project members, facilitating communications between project members and those outside the project, resolving conflicts, managing change, and documenting important decisions.

Table 7.1 provides an outline of leadership activities and tasks that must be accomplished by project managers and leadership teams for software projects. The remainder of this section discusses and provides greater detail on the activities outlined in Table 7.1.

### 7.2 Provide Leadership to the Project Team

The project manager provides leadership to the project management team by interpreting plans and requirements to them to ensure that everybody on the project team is working toward common goals. Leadership results from the power of the leader and his or her ability to guide and influence individuals. The project manager's power can be derived from his leadership position as project manager; this is called *positional power*. The project manager's power can also be derived from the manager's own "charm," sometimes called *charisma*; this is called *personal power*.

**Table 7.1: Directing Activities for Software Projects**

| Activity | Definition or Explanation |
|---|---|
| Provide leadership | Create an environment in which project members can accomplish their assignments with enthusiasm and confidence. |
| Supervise personnel | Provide day-to-day instructions, guidance, and discipline to help project members fulfill their assigned duties. |
| Delegate authority | Allow project personnel to make decisions and expend resources within the limitations and constraints of their roles. |
| Motivate personnel | Provide a work environment in which project personnel can satisfy their psychological needs. |
| Build teams | Provide a work environment in which project personnel can work together toward common project goals. Set performance goals for teams as well as for individuals. |
| Coordinate activities | Combine project activities into effective and efficient arrangements. |
| Facilitate communication | Ensure a free flow of correct information among project members. |
| Resolve conflicts | Encourage constructive differences of opinion and help resolve the resulting conflicts. |
| Manage changes | Stimulate creativity and innovation in achieving project goals. |
| Document directing decisions | Document decisions involving delegation of authority, communication and coordination, conflict resolution, and change management. |

### 7.3 Supervise Project Personnel

The project manager is responsible for overseeing the project members' work and providing day-to-day supervision of the personnel assigned to the project. It is the project manager's responsibility to provide guidance to and, when necessary, discipline project members to ensure that they fulfill their assigned duties.

### 7.4 Delegate Authority to the Appropriate Project Members

The software engineering project manager is also responsible for delegating authority to the project staff. Tasks are assigned to subgroups, teams, and individuals, and authority is delegated to these teams so that they can accomplish their tasks in an efficient and effective manner. Typically, a good project manager will always delegate authority down through the lowest possible level of the project [Raudsepp 1981].

### 7.5 Motivate Project Personnel

The project manager is responsible for motivating and inspiring personnel to do their best. Several motivational techniques from mainstream management are applicable to software engineering projects, such as management by objective, Maslow's hierarchy of needs [Maslow 1954], Herzberg's hygiene factors [Herzberg, Mausner, and Snyderman 1959], and sometimes just the charisma of the manager. The project manager should always acknowledge the special needs of the highly qualified, technically trained engineers and scientists who staff the project. It should also be noted that dollars will attract good software engineers to a company, but dollars will not keep them. For a further discussion of motivating software development personnel see [Fitz-enz 1978]. For another paper with a unique method of motivating computer people, see [Powell and Posner 1984].

### 7.6 Build Software Project Teams

As discussed in Section 5, software is built by project teams. *Team building* is the process of improving the interrelationship between team members in order to improve the efficiency and effectiveness of the team as a whole. Techniques such as team building exercises, "off-site" meetings, and group dynamics can be used to improve the capabilities of the team to be more productive as a group than the team members would be as individuals.

### 7.7 Coordinate Project Activities

*Coordination* is arranging project entities to work together toward common goals with minimum friction. Documents, policies, procedures, and so forth are viewed differently by various people. The task of the project manager is to reconcile differences in approach, effort, and schedule, and to resolve these differences for the benefit of the project.

### 7.8 Facilitate Communication

Along with coordination, the project manager is responsible for facilitating communication both within the project and between the project and other organizations. *Facilitate* means to expedite, ease, and assist in the progress of communication. *Communication*, in turn, is an information exchange among entities that are working toward common goals.

### 7.9 Resolve Conflicts

It is the project manager's responsibility to resolve conflicts among project staff members and between project staff and outside agencies in both technical and managerial matters. The project manager is not expected to be an expert in all aspects of the project; however, he or she should have the good judgment to recognize the best possible approach to solve a particular technical or managerial problem.

### 7.10 Manage Change that Impacts the Software Project

The project manager is responsible for encouraging independent thought and innovation in achieving project goals. A good manager must always accommodate change when change is cost-effective and beneficial to the project. [Kirchof and Adams 1986]

### 7.11 Document Directing Decisions

The project manager must document all tasks, assignments of authority and responsibility, and the outcome of conflict resolution. In addition, all decisions concerning lines of communication and coordination must be documented.

## 8. Controlling a Software Engineering Project

### 8.1 Introduction and Definitions

*Controlling* is collecting management activities used to ensure that the project goes according to plan. Performance and results are measured against plans, deviations are noted, and corrective actions are taken to ensure conformance of plans and actuals.

Control is a feedback system that provides information on how well the project is going. Control asks: Is the project on schedule? Is it within cost? Are there any potential problems that will cause slippages in meeting budget and schedule requirements? Controls also provide plans and approaches for eliminating the difference between the plans and/or standards and the actuals or results.

The control process also requires organizational structure, communication, and coordination. For example, who is responsible for assessing progress? Who will take action on reported problems?

Controlling methods and tools must be objective. Information must be quantified. The methods and tools must point out deviations from plans without regard to the particular people or positions involved. Control methods must be tailored to individual environments and managers. The methods must be flexible and adaptable to deal with the changing environment of the organization. Control also must be economical; the cost of control should not outweigh its benefits.

Control must lead to corrective action—either bringing the actual status back to plan, changing the plan, or terminating the project.

Table 8.1 provides an outline of the project management activities that must be accomplished by project managers to control their projects. The remainder of this section discusses the activities outlined in Table 8.1.

### 8.2 Develop Standards of Performance

The project manager is responsible for developing and specifying performance standards for the project. The project manager either develops standards and procedures for the project, adopts and uses standards developed by the parent organization, or uses standards developed by the customer or a professional society (for example see [IEEE Software Engineering Standards 1993]).

- *Standards*—A documented set of criteria used to specify, and determine the adequacy of, an action or object.
- *Software quality assurance*—A planned and systematic pattern of all actions necessary to provide adequate confidence that the item or product conforms to established technical requirements [IEEE-STD 729-1983]
- *Software configuration management*—A method for controlling and reporting on software status. SCM is the discipline of identifying the configuration of a system at discrete points in time for purposes of systematically controlling changes to this configuration and maintaining the integrity and traceability of this configuration throughout the system life cycle [Bersoff 1984].
- *Process and product metrics*—A measure of the degree to which a process or product possesses a given attribute.

### 8.3 Establish Monitoring and Reporting Systems

The project manager is responsible for establishing the methods of monitoring the software project and reporting project status. Monitoring and reporting systems must be specified in order to determine project status. The project manager needs feedback on the progress of the project and quality of the product to ensure that everything is going according to plan. The type, frequency, originator, and recipient of project reports must be specified. Status reporting tools to provide progress visibility, and not just resources used or time passed, must be implemented.

### 8.5 Measure and Analyze Results

The project manager is responsible for measuring the results of the project both during and at the end of the project. For instance, actual phase deliverables should be measured against planned phase deliverables. The measured results can be management (process) results and/or technical (product) results. An example of a process result would be the status of the project schedule. An example of a product result would be the degree to which the design specifications correctly interpreted the requirement specifications. Some of the tools and methods for measuring results are described in the following paragraphs.

**Table 8.1: Controlling Activities for Software Projects**

| Activity | Definition or Explanation |
|---|---|
| Develop standards of performance | Set goals that will be achieved when tasks are correctly accomplished. |
| Establish monitoring and reporting systems | Determine necessary data, who will receive it, when they will receive it, and what they will do with it to control the project. |
| Measure and Analyze results | Compare achievements with standards, goals, and plans, |
| Initiate corrective actions | Bring requirements, plans, and actual project status into conformance |
| Reward and discipline | Praise, remunerate, and discipline project personnel as appropriate |
| Document controlling methods | Document the standards of performance, monitoring and control systems and reward and discipline mechanisms. |

- *Binary tracking and work product specifications*—Specifies the objectives of the work, staffing requirements, the expected duration of the task, the resources to be used, the results to be produced, and any special considerations for the work. Binary track is the concept that a work pack is either done or not done (that is, assigned a numeric "1" or "0").
- *Unit development folders*—A specific form of development notebook that has proven to be useful and effective in collecting and organizing software products as they are produced [Ingrassia 1987].
- *Walkthroughs and inspections*—Reviews of a software product (design specifications, code, test procedures, and so on.) conducted by the peers of the group being reviewed [Ackerman 1996].
- *Independent auditing*—An independent review of a software project to determine compliance with software requirements, specifications, baselines, standards, policies, and software quality assurance plans.

### 8.6 Initiate Corrective Actions for the Project

If standards and requirements are not being met, the project manager must initiate corrective action. For instance, the project manager can change the plan or standard, use overtime or other procedures to get back on plan, or change the requirements, such as delivering less.

### 8.7 Reward and Discipline the Project Members

The project manager should reward people for meeting their standards and plans, and discipline those who without good reason do not. This should not be confused with the rewards and discipline given to workers for performing their assigned duties; that is a function of staffing. The system of rewards and discipline discussed here is a mechanism for controlling ability to meet a plan or standard.

### 8.8 Document Controlling Methods

The project manager must document all standards, software quality procedures, metrics and other means of measuring production and products. In addition, the manager must establish metrics for determining when corrective action must be initiated and determine in advance possible corrective action that can be taken.

## 9. Summary

Software engineering procedures and techniques do not alone guarantee a successful project. A good project manager can sometimes overcome or work around deficiencies in organization, staffing, budgets, standards, or other shortcomings. A poor manager stumbles over every problem, real or imaginary; no number of rules, policies, standards, or techniques will help. The methods and techniques discussed in this article, in the hands of a competent project manager, can significantly improve the probability of a successful project.

In this paper and in many other documents, the terms "project management" and "software engineering project management" are used interchangeably. This is because the management of a software engineering project and other types of projects require many of the same tools, techniques, approaches, and methods of mainstream management. The functions and general activities of management are the same at all levels; only the detailed activities and tasks are different.

## References


[Ackerman 1996] F.A. Ackerman, "Software Inspections and the Cost-Effective Production of Reliable Software," in *Software Engineering,* edited by M. Dorfman and R.H. Thayer, IEEE Computer Society Press, Los Alamitos, Calif., 1996.

[Bersoff 1984] E.H. Bersoff, "Elements of Software Configuration Management," *IEEE Trans. Software Eng.*, Vol. SE-10, No. 1, Jan. 1984, pp. 79–87. Reprinted in *Tutorial: Software Engineering Project Management,* edited by R.H. Thayer, IEEE Computer Society Press, Los Alamitos, Calif., 1988.

[Boehm 1984] B.W. Boehm, "Software Engineering Economics," *IEEE Trans. Software Eng.*, Vol. SE-10, No. 1, Jan. 1984, pp. 4-21.

[Boehm 1987] B.W. Boehm, *Tutorial: Software Risk Management*, IEEE Computer Society Press, Los Alamitos, Calif., 1989.

[Brooks 1987] "Report on the Defense Science Board Task Force on Military Software," Office of the Undersecretary of Defense for Acquisition, Department of Defense, Washington, DC, Sept. 1987.

[Cleland and King, 1972] D.I. Cleland and W.R. King, *Management: A Systems Approach,* See Table 5-1: Major Management Functions as Seen by Various Authors, McGraw-Hill Book Company, New York, NY, 1972.

[DoD Software Initiative 1983] *Strategy for a DoD Software Initiative*, Department of Defense Report, 1 Oct. 1982. (An edited public version was published in *Computer*, Nov. 1983.)

[Donnelly, Gibson, and Ivancevich 1975] J.H. Donnelly, Jr., J.L. Gibson, and J.M. Ivancevich, *Fundamentals of Management: Functions, Behavior, Models*, rev. ed., Business Publications, Inc., Dallas, TX, 1975.

[Fairley 1987] R.E. Fairley, "A Guide for Preparing Software Project Management Plans," in *Tutorial: Software Engineering Project Management*, edited by R.H. Thayer, IEEE Computer Society Press, Los Alamitos, Calif., 1988.

[Fairley and Rook 1996] R.E. Fairley and P. Rook, "Risk Management for Software Development," in *Software Engineering*, edited by M. Dorfman and R.H. Thayer, IEEE Computer Society Press, Los Alamitos, Calif., 1996.

[Fayol 1949] H. Fayol, *General and Industrial Administration*, Sir Isaac Pitman & Sons, Ltd., London, 1949.

[Fitz-enz 1978] J. Fitz-enz, "Who is the DP Professional?," *Datamation*, Sept. 1978, pp. 125–128. Reprinted in *Tutorial: Software Engineering Project Management*, edited by R.H. Thayer, IEEE Computer Society Press, Los Alamitos, Calif., 1988.

[GAO/IMTEC-92-48 C-17 Aircraft Software] "Embedded Computer Systems: Significant Software Problems on C-17 Must be Addresses," General Accounting Office GAO/IMTEC-92-48, Gaithersburg, MD 20877, May 1992

[Herzberg, Mausner, and Snyderman 1959] F. Herzberg, B. Mausner, and B.B. Snyderman, *The Motivation to work*, John Wiley & Son, New York, N.Y., 1959.

[IEEE-STD 729-1983] ANSI/IEEE Std. 729-1983, *IEEE Standard Glossary of Software Engineering Terminology*, IEEE, Inc., New York, NY, 1983.

[IEEE Software Engineering Standards 1993] Hardbound Edition of Software Engineering Standards, IEEE, New York, N.Y., 1993.

[Ingrassia 1987] F.S. Ingrassia, "The Unit Development Folder (UDF): A Ten-Year Perspective," in *Tutorial: Software Engineering Project Management,* edited by R.H. Thayer, IEEE Computer Society Press, Los Alamitos, Calif., 1988.

[Kirchof and Adams 1986] N.S. Kirchof and J.R. Adams, "Conflict Management for Project Managers: An Overview," extracted from *Conflict Management for Project Managers*, Project Management Institute, Feb. 1986, pages 1-13. Reprinted in *Tutorial: Software Engineering Project Management*, edited by R.H. Thayer, IEEE Computer Society Press, Los Alamitos, Calif., 1988.

[Koontz and O'Donnell, 1972] H. Koontz and C. O'Donnell, *Principles of Management: An Analysis of Managerial Functions,* 5th ed., McGraw-Hill Book Company, New York, N.Y., 1972.

[Koontz, O'Donnell, and Weihrich 1984] H. Koontz, C. O'Donnell and H. Weihrich, *Management*, 8th ed., McGraw-Hill Book Co., New York, NY, 1984.

[Kruesi 1982] B. Kruesi, seminar on "Software Psychology," California State University, Sacramento, Fall 1982.

[MacKenzie, 1969] R.A. MacKenzie, "The Management Process in 3-D," *Harvard Business Rev.*, Vol. 47, No. 6, Nov.-Dec. 1969, pp. 80–87. Reprinted in *Tutorial: Software Engineering Project Management*, edited by R.H. Thayer, IEEE Computer Society Press, Los Alamitos, Calif., 1988.

[Maslow 1954] A.H. Maslow, *Motivation and Personality*, Harper & Brothers, New York, N.Y., 1954.

[Middleton, 1967] C.J. Middleton, "How to Set Up a Project Organization," *Harvard Business Rev.,* Nov.-Dec. 1967, pp. 73–82.

[Miller 1978] W.B. Miller, "Fundamentals of Project Management," *J. Systems Management*, Vol. 29, No. 11, Issue 211, Nov. 1978, pp. 22–29.

[Moneysmith 1984] M. Moneysmith, "I'm OK—and You're Not," *Savvy*, Apr. 1984, pp. 37-38. Reprinted in *Tutorial: Software Engineering Project Management*, edited by R.H. Thayer, IEEE Computer Society Press, Los Alamitos, Calif., 1988.

[Paulk et al., 1996] M.C. Paulk, B. Curtis, M.B. Chrissis, and C.V. Weber, "The Capability Maturity Model for Software," in *Software Engineering*, edited by M. Dorfman and R.H. Thayer, IEEE Computer Society Press, Los Alamitos, Calif., 1996.

[Powell and Posner 1984] G.N. Powell and B.Z. Posner, "Excitement and Commitment: Keys to Project Success," *Project Management J.*, Dec. 1984, pp. 39–46. Reprinted in *Tutorial: Software Engineering Project Management*, edited by R.H. Thayer, IEEE Computer Society Press, Los Alamitos, Calif., 1988.

[Raudsepp 1981] E. Raudsepp, "Delegate Your Way to Success," *Computer Decisions,* Mar. 1981, pp. 157–164. Reprinted in *Tutorial: Software Engineering Project Management,* edited by R.H. Thayer, IEEE Computer Society Press, Los Alamitos, Calif., 1988.

[Rue and Byars, 1983] L.W. Rue and L.L. Byars, *Management: Theory and Application*, Richard D. Irwin, Inc., Homewood, Ill., 60430, 1983.

[Stuckenbruck 1981] L.C. Stuckenbruck, "The Matrix Organization," *A Decade of Project Management*, Project Management Institute 1981, pp. 157–169. Reprinted in *Tutorial: Software Engineering Project Management*, edited by R.H. Thayer, IEEE Computer Society Press, Los Alamitos, Calif., 1988.

[Thayer and Pyster 1984] R.H. Thayer and A.B. Pyster, "Guest Editorial: Software Engineering Project Management," *IEEE Trans. Software Eng.*, Vol. SE-10, No. 1, Jan. 1984.

[Zubrow, et al. 1995] D. Zubrow, J. Herbsleb, W. Hayes, and D. Goldenson presentation: "Process Maturity Profile of the Software Community 1995 Update," Nov. 1995, based on data up to September 1995 for most recent assessment of 440 organizations: ML1 - 70.2%; ML2 - 18.4%; ML3 - 10.2%; ML4 - 1%; ML5 - 0.2%. Source: email, Mark Paulk, Software Engineering Institution, 14 Feb 1996.

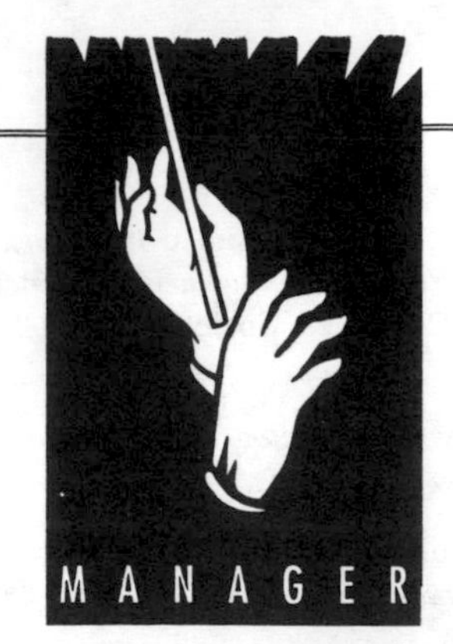


**How to get people and technology to work together.**

*Tom DeMarco, The Atlantic Systems Guild*

# WHY DOES SOFTWARE COST SO MUCH?

*When I took over as coeditor of this department, my intent was to keep it personal. In this spirit, I've turned down several contributions, but this column captures the very kind of controversial, entertaining, and educational insights I want to relay. Tom DeMarco is the author of four books on software and management, including (with Tom Lister) the recent Dorset-House book,* Peopleware: Productive Projects and Teams. *In 1986 he was awarded the J.D. Warnier Prize for lifetime contribution to the information sciences.*

*—Alan Davis*

IN THE ABSENCE OF MEANINGFUL standards, a new industry like ours comes to depend instead on folklore. As the industry matures, the first order of business is to recognize and question the folklore. For example, how you ask and how you answer the familiar question "Why does software cost so much?" tells much about what folklore you've grown up with.

Author and consultant Jerry Weinberg claims to have encountered this question more than any other in his long career (*Quality Software Management, Volume 1: Systems Thinking*, Dorset-House, 1992). The correct answer, he says, is "Compared to what?" There is a likable logic to that: Most of the things we do with software in the '90s are barely conceivable without software, so there is no valid basis of comparison.

**PEOPLE DON'T ASK THIS TO GET AN ANSWER. IT'S NOT A QUESTION, IT'S AN ASSERTION.**

Yet Jerry's answer, charming as it is, won't do you much good. At best it will just annoy the questioner. No answer is satisfactory because people don't ask that question to get an answer. "Why does software cost so much?" is not a question, it's an assertion. The assertion is that software costs too much.

The person who poses this nonquestion may seem to be motivated by intellectual curiosity: "Gee, I've always wondered, just why is it that software costs so much?" The real motivation, however, has nothing to do with curiosity and everything to do with getting the brutal assertion on the table.

It's a negotiating position: You are being put on notice that software costs are unconscionable and no budget or schedule you ask for will be considered reasonable. Your boss or user may agree to your budget, but only under *extreme* duress. Because the amount budgeted is already terribly, terribly excessive, it goes without saying that any slip or overrun is virtually a crime against nature.

In a recent interview (*Computer Design*, Aug. 1991, pp. 25-27), Cadre Technologies founder Lou Mazzucchelli observed that "software consumers are not satisfied with either the quantity or the quality of our output." Right on target. Software consumers in vast numbers are telling us that our efforts don't begin to measure up to their expectations. Software is much too expensive, takes too long to build, isn't solid enough, isn't easy enough to use — isn't good enough in any way.

I have a very grumpy question for those who complain that the software-development community hasn't measured up to their expectations: Where in hell did those expectations come from?

**A LITTLE DIATRIBE.** You and I and others like us built the software industry from scratch over the last 30 years. Out of thin air we made a $300 billion-a-year business. (See John E. Hopcroft and Dean B. Krafft, "Sizing the US Software Industry," *IEEE Spectrum*, Dec. 1987, pp. 58-62 to understand how I arrive at this figure.) In all of economic history, there has never been a more staggering accomplishment. $300 billion a year! Think of it. In the time it will take you to read this article, the software industry will generate something more than $12 million.

What has it taken to build this huge new industry so quickly? Hint: It wasn't just getting some programmers together and teaching them to sling code. It required the active participation of a marketplace. Somebody had to toady up huge quantities of money to buy all the software we built. And they did. Not only did they buy all we could produce at the cost we charged, they complained about not being able to buy even more, about the so-called backlog.

This growth was not the result of poor quality and poor productivity. The only conceivable explanation for the phenomenal success of the software industry is that it regularly delivered a quality and productivity far beyond the market's real expecta-

Editors: Alan Davis
University of Colorado
1867 Austin Bluffs Pkwy., Suite 200
Colorado Springs, CO 80933-7150
Internet adavis@zeppo.uccs.edu

Winston Royce
TRW
1 Federal Systems Park Dr.
STC 7165U
Fairfax, VA 22030
(703) 803-5025/6
fax: (703) 803-5108

Reprinted from *IEEE Software*, Vol. 10, No. 2, Mar. 1993, pp. 89–90.

tions. But all the time that our buyers (our managers and our users) were lining up to cash in on the bargain, they were complaining. This behavior is not a recent phenomenon: They didn't congratulate us for years and years and then become upset only during the downturn in the '90s. No, they complained all the way from zero to $300 billion.

I myself am a bit peeved by this. (Perhaps you could tell.) I feel like we have accomplished wonders and been yelled at the whole time. Through their actions and their words, our buyers have sent diametrically opposed messages.

Imagine how the Wright brothers would have felt had they had a similar reception. You are Orville. It's December 7, 1904, at Kitty Hawk, North Carolina, 7:30 a.m., and you're climbing up into Flyer One. "Let 'er rip," you say, or words to that effect. The engine coughs to life. You rev it up and there is movement. There is not just movement, there is speed. Speed and bumps and wind ... by God, you're up! You've done it. You've pulled off a miracle, and the world will never be the same. You are so elated you're barely even afraid. Cool as a cucumber, you bring the flyer down.

**CUSTOMERS COMPLAIN BECAUSE WE WORK HARDER WHEN THEY DO. BOY ARE WE DUMB.**

Just as you are coming to a stop, you notice a guy in a business suit, looking sourly at his watch. He says "Orville, I'm really disappointed in this project. I had great expectations and you've let me down. Here it is nearly eight a.m. and I have to be in LA for a dinner meeting tonight. And you guys are nowhere! You haven't invented the jet engine or the flight attendant or the airport or those cocktails in tiny bottles. You've let me down completely!" This is the guy Mazzucchelli was talking about.

**WHERE EXPECTATIONS COME FROM.** No one expected the software industry to achieve what it has achieved. Not a single futurist predicted the extraordinary productivity and quality we have accomplished. How is it possible that the industry is performing beyond our wildest expectations while every individual project is underperforming?

It's not. Those projects aren't underperforming at all. And their consumers know it. Pay attention to what they do, not what they say. The real message our consumers are telling us is that software is the best bargain they ever heard of. They complain to us because *they know we work harder when they do complain.* We have trained them to do this. When they complained in the past, we worked harder. We gave them more for their money (even more than the extraordinary bargain they would have gotten anyway) because they pretended to be discontent. Boy, are we dumb.

In a recent article, Albert L. Lederer and Jayesh Prasad set down some guidelines for better software cost estimating ("Nine Management Guidelines for Better Cost Estimating," *Comm ACM*, Feb. 1992, pp. 51-59). Their method involved a survey of some 400 professional software managers. What interested me was a tiny nugget tucked away in the commentary: The great majority of respondents reported that their software estimates were dismal — only about one in four projects come in at a cost "reasonably close" to the estimate. However, 43 percent said their current estimating method was "very" or "moderately" satisfactory (the two highest ratings).

What's going on here? Estimates bear little or no resemblance to reality but managers aren't dissatisfied? I think I'm beginning to understand. Maybe the purpose of the estimating process is not to come up with a realistic answer, but to come up with an *unrealistic* answer. Maybe the estimating process is not supposed to guide the manager as to what to expect. Rather, it's supposed to guide the manager as to what to *pretend* to expect.

This is the kind of process that tells your boss, for example, to set September 1994 as the expected delivery date. This "right" schedule is neither ridiculous nor feasible. That is, after all, the object of the exercise. The "right" schedule is one that is *utterly* impossible, but not *obviously* impossible.

**HOW DO MANAGERS KNOW?** It is a great tribute to quality software management that managers know how to set this "right" schedule. It isn't easy. In the abstract, at least, it is just as hard to predict a date that is just short of possible as to pick one that is safe and reasonable. Both require a prediction of product size as well as a correct assessment of team capability. How do our managers learn to do this? Again, we have trained them. They watch our faces when they set schedules. If we look relieved, they know they haven't turned the screws enough. If we just giggle, they know they've gone too far.

The assertion that software costs too much is part of a cost-containment ploy. The cynical notion that a "right" schedule is one that no one has a prayer of achieving is another part of that ploy. The constant refrain that software developers just are not productive enough is a goad. It appears to work because software developers are sincere and professional and a little dopey. The problem is that our industry is overgoaded. Our work is largely incompressible. When you're under pressure, your first response is to cut out extraneous activities: chats and bull sessions.

That may indeed be productive, but that's the end of it. As the pressure continues, there is nothing more you can do. You can't work faster; that just isn't possible. You might stay later, but that has a long-term cost: Overtime applied over months and months gives only an illusion of progress that is wiped out by compensatory "undertime," burnout, disillusionment, waste, and employee turnover.

**THE MORAL** As time pressure increases, the only real option is to pay for speed by reducing quality. I sometimes think, rather bitterly, that reduced quality is a conscious goal of those who pressure projects. They are saying "Loosen up, folks — learn to rush the product out the door without worrying so much about quality." This comes, of course, at the very moment that companies are paying lip service to quality as never before.

In the short run, paying for speed by reducing quality makes sense. In the long run, it will take us where it took the US automobile industry. We might win a few battles, but not the war.

If you ask the wrong question you'll never get the right answer. Instead of asking "Why does software cost so much?" we must begin to ask "What have we done to make it possible for present-day software to cost so little?" The answer to that question will help us continue the extraordinary level of achievement that has always distinguished the software industry. ◆

# Software cost estimation

F J Heemstra

*The paper gives an overview of the state of the art of software cost estimation (SCE). The main questions to be answered in the paper are: (1) What are the reasons for overruns of budgets and planned durations? (2) What are the prerequisites for estimating? (3) How can software development effort be estimated? (4) What can software project management expect from SCE models, how accurate are estimations which are made using these kind of models, and what are the pros and cons of cost estimation models?*

*software, cost estimation, project control, software cost estimation model*

## SIMPLE QUESTIONS, DIFFICULT ANSWERS

Judging by reports from everyday practice and findings in the literature, software projects regularly get out of hand and invariably the effort expended on development exceeds the estimated effort, resulting in the software being delivered after the planned date. There is no doubt that SCE is a serious problem for software project management. At first glance the questions to be answered are simple: How much time and effort will it cost to develop the software? What are the dominating cost factors? What are the important risk factors? Unfortunately, however, the answers are neither simple nor easy.

The article gives an overview of the field of software cost estimation (SCE). Special attention is paid to the use of SCE models. These models are one of the techniques project management can use to estimate and control the effort and duration of software development. The paper starts with a description of the importance of accurate cost estimates. From this it will be clear that SCE is not easy, and management is confronted with many problems. In the following section some reasons for the problems will be highlighted, the paper going on to explain which prerequisites are necessary for an estimate to be possible. It is important to have knowledge about the product that must be developed, the development process, the development means, the development personnel, and the user organization. Also it is necessary to have available a set of estimation methods and techniques. An overview of the existing techniques for cost estimation is given in the fifth section, and the sixth section describes the principles of cost estimation models with an overview of models available nowadays. The rest of the paper deals with one of these techniques, that is to say parametric models. The penultimate section offers a comparison of SCE models, focusing mainly on the question 'How accurate are estimates made as a result of using models?' Despite the fact that software cost estimation is in its infancy plus the shortcomings of the current SCE models, the use of models has several advantages. The last section deals with the pros and cons and gives a critical evaluation of the state of the art of the use of these models.

Faculty of Public Administration and Public Policy, Twente University, POB 217, Enschede, The Netherlands

## OVERSHOOTS OF SOFTWARE DEVELOPMENT COSTS

Estimation of effort and duration of software development has become a topic of growing importance. This is not surprising. It often happens that software is more expensive than estimated and completion is later than planned. Moreover it turns out that much software does not meet the demands of the customer. There are a number of examples of such automation projects. The development costs of the automation of the education funding in The Netherlands proved to be three times as much as expected. Delays and wrong payments are a daily occurrence (*Volkskrant*, 24 June 1987). The development of the software for the purpose of the house-rent subsidies, produced to government order, proved to be twice as much as planned (NRC *Handelsblad*, 28 February 1989). In September 1989 the Dutch media announced as front page news the results of a governmental audit concerning the automation for the police. It proved to be an expensive disaster. The development costs of a computerized identifying system were US$43 million instead of the estimated US$21 million. Furthermore the system did not answer the formulated goals. The findings of a well-known Dutch consultancy organization (Berenschot) were that the costs of the automation of the registration of the Dutch population at the municipal offices were more than twice as much as were estimated (*Volkskrant*, 5 January 1990). A few years ago the estimates of the costs were about US$25 million. New calculations show that there is a deficit of more than US$30 million.

A field study by the Eindhoven University of Technology[1] gives an overview of the present state of the art of

Reprinted from *Information and Software Technology,* Vol. 34, No. 10, Oct. 1992, F.J. Heemstra, "Software Cost Estimation," pp. 627–639, 1992, with kind permission from Elsevier Science–NL, Sara Burgerhartstraat 25; 1055 KV Amsterdam, The Netherlands.

the estimation and control of software development projects in 598 Dutch organizations. The most remarkable conclusions are:

- 35% of the participating organizations do not make an estimate
- 50% of the responding organizations record no data on an ongoing project
- 57% do not use cost-accounting
- 80% of the projects executed by the participating organizations have overruns of budgets and duration
- the mean overruns of budgets and duration are 50%

Van Lierop *et al.*[2] measured extensively whether development activities were executed according to plan. They investigated the reasons for the differences between plan and reality, and overall 80 development activities were measured. For all these activities 3203 hours were planned but 3838 hours were used, which means an overshoot of 20% on average of the planned number of hours. The duration of the activities (in days) proved to be 28% longer on average than planned. For all the activities 406 days of duration were planned, while the actual number of days proved to be 526.

In the literature the impression is given, mistakenly, that software development without overshoots of plans and budgets is not possible. This impression is inaccurate, and other measurements confirm this[3]. These show that 6% of all the activities had a shorter duration than planned and 58% were executed according to plan and were ready exactly on time. With regard to the development effort, it appeared that 25% of the activities needed less effort than estimated and 30% needed precisely the estimated effort. The reasons for the differences between plan and reality prove to be very specific for the development situation. In the organization where the measurements were taken the reasons were mainly related to things underestimation of the quantity of work, underestimation of the complexity of the application, and specifications which proved to be unrealistic from a technical point of view. In other organizations, where similar measurements were taken, other reasons were discovered. As a result, other control actions are, of course, necessary. This conclusion fits well with the results of research carried out by Beers[4]. Thirty experienced software developers, project managers, and others, were asked to give the reasons for unsuccessful software projects. The answers can be summarized briefly as 'many minds, many thoughts'. It was not possible to indicate just one reason. A long list of all kinds of reasons were given.

It is alarming that it is so difficult for organizations to control the development of software. This is sufficient reason to emphasize that software development cost estimation and control should take its place as a fully fledged branch within discipline of software development.

## WHAT MAKES SOFTWARE COST ESTIMATION SO DIFFICULT?

The main question, when confronting the abovementioned problems, is what it is that makes software cost estimation so difficult. There are many reasons and, without going into detail, some can be listed as follows:

(1) There is a lack of data on completed software projects. This kind of data can support project management in making estimates.
(2) Estimates are often done hurriedly, without an appreciation for the effort required to do a credible job. In addition, too often it is the case that an estimate is needed before clear specifications of the system requirements have been produced. Therefore, a typical situation is that estimators are being pressured to write an estimate too quickly for a system that they do not fully understand.
(3) Clear, complete and reliable specifications are difficult to formulate, especially at the start of a project. Changes, adaptations and additions are more the rule than the exception: as a consequence plans and budgets must be adapted too.
(4) Characteristics of software and software development make estimating difficult. For example, the level of abstraction, complexity, measurability of product and process, innovative aspects, etc.
(5) A great number of factors have an influence on the effort and time to develop software. These factors are called 'cost drivers'. Examples are size and complexity of the software, commitment and participation of the user organization, experience of the development team. In general these cost drivers are difficult to determine in operation.
(6) Rapid changes in information technology (IT) and the methodology of software development are a problem for a stabilization of the estimation process. For example, it is difficult to predict the influence of new workbenches, fourth and fifth generation languages, prototyping strategies, and so on.
(7) An estimator (mostly the project manager) cannot have much experience in developing estimates, especially for large projects. How many 'large' projects can someone manage in, for example, 10 years?
(8) An apparent bias of software developers towards underestimation. An estimator is likely to consider how long a certain portion of the software would take and then to extrapolate this estimate to the rest of the system, ignoring the non-linear aspects of software development, for example co-ordination and management.
(9) The estimator estimates the time it would take to perform the task personally, ignoring the fact that a lot of work will be done by less experienced people, and junior staff with a lower productivity rate.

(10) There exists a serious mis-assumption of a linear relation between the required capacity per unit of time and the available time. This would mean that software developed by 25 people in two years could be accomplished by 50 people in one year. The assumption is seriously wrong. According to Brooks[5] the crucial corollary is: 'Adding people to a late project only makes it later'.

(11) The estimator tends to reduce the estimates to some degree, in order to make the bid more acceptable.

## PREREQUISITES FOR SOFTWARE COST ESTIMATION

There are many ways to get to grips with the SCE problems. From an organizational perspective there are numerous ways to improve software project management: allocation of responsibilities; decision-making; organizing project work; monitoring and auditing of development tasks. Also software cost estimation can be looked at from a sociological and psychological point of view. This refers, for example, to commitment, organizing group cohesion, style of leadership, and so on. The technical side of the job is also an important issue to take into consideration. For example, the availability of good equipment such as design, programming, test and documentation tools, hardware facilities, etc.

There are many factors that have an influence on the effort and duration of software development. Several prerequisites must be fulfilled to address the problems listed above and to guarantee a sound basis for predicting effort, duration and the capacity to develop the software. These prerequisites are:

**Insight in the characteristics of:**

- the product (software) that has to be developed — WHAT
- the production means — WITH WHAT
- the production personnel — WHO
- the organization of the production — HOW
- the user/user organization — FOR WHOM

**Availability of:**

- Techniques and tools for software cost estimation.

In this section the attention will be focused on the WHAT, WITH WHAT, WHO, HOW and FOR WHOM factors, referred to as cost drivers in the literature. In the next section, SCE techniques and tools will be discussed.

There are many cost drivers. A study by Noth and Kretzschmar[6] found that more than 1200 different drivers were mentioned. Although there was considerable overlap in meaning, it is impossible to take them all into consideration during SCE. It is important for an organization to consider what are the most dominant cost factors. Within the context of this paper it is impossible to give an extended overview of the overwhelming number of drivers, so concentration will be on:

- a way of structuring the cost drivers
- listing the drivers which are commonly regarded as important
- some general considerations

Table 1 presents a structure of cost drivers in five categories. For each category the most important drivers are listed. From the literature and practice it is known that it is not easy to handle the cost drivers. When making an estimate one has to know which cost drivers are the most important in the specific situation, what the values are of the drivers, and what the influences are on effort and duration. In answering these questions it is important to pay attention to several issues:

*Definition* There is a lack of clear and accepted definitions for drivers, such as size, quality, complexity, experience, etc.

*Quantification* The majority of the cost drivers are hard to quantify. Often one has to use measures such as many, moderate, few, etc.

**Table 1. A structure of important cost drivers[7]**

| WHAT (product) | WITH WHAT (means) | WHO (personnel) | HOW (project) | FOR WHOM (user) |
|---|---|---|---|---|
| Size of the software | Computer constraints | Quality of | Requirements | Participation |
| | —execution time | personnel | project duration | |
| Required quality | —response time | | —stretch out | Number of users |
| | —memory capacity | Experience of | —compression | |
| Requirements volatility | | personnel | | Stability of user |
| | User of tools | | Basis for | organization, |
| Software complexity | | Quality | project control | procedures, way |
| | Use of modern | management | —matrix org. | of working |
| Level of reuse | programming techniques | | —project org. | |
| | —information hiding | Availability | —prototyping | Experience of user |
| Amount of documentation | —chief prog. team | for project | —incremental | with automation, |
| | —structured program | | —linear devel. | level of education |
| Type of application | —top-down design | | —software devel. | in automation |

*Objectivity* Subjectivity is a potential risk factor. What may be complex for developer A is not complex for developer B.

*Correlation* It is difficult to consider one driver by itself. A change in the value of driver A may have consequences in the values of several other cost drivers. This is a difficulty from the viewpoint of measurability.

*Relation between driver and effort* For estimation it is important to predict the relation between, for example, software size and the required effort, a specified quality level and required effort, etc. From the literature we know that there is little clarity about these relations.

*Calibration* It is impossible to talk about 'the most important' cost drivers in isolation. It differs from situation to situation.

*Effectivity and efficiency* There is conflict between effectivity and efficiency. From an effectivity perspective it is worthwhile to pay a lot of attention to, for example, user participation. For the efficiency of a project it is justifiable to avoid user involvement.

*Human factors* Almost all research agrees on the dominating influence of cost drivers, such as experience and quality of the personnel. This means that investment in 'good' developers is important.

*Reuse* In many studies reuse is regarded as (one of) the most important factors to increase productivity[8-10].

## SOFTWARE COST ESTIMATION: TECHNIQUES AND TOOLS

In the literature you can find a great number of techniques for estimating software development costs. Most of them are a combination of the following primary techniques[11]:

(1) Estimates made by an expert.
(2) Estimates based on reasoning by analogy.
(3) Estimates based on Price-to-Win.
(4) Estimates based on available capacity.
(5) Estimates based on the use of parametric models.

Furthermore two main approaches can be distinguished:

(1) Top-down
In the top-down approach the estimation of the overall project is derived from the global characteristics of the product. The total estimated cost is then split up among the various components.
(2) Bottom-up
In the bottom-up approach the cost of each individual component is estimated by the person who will be responsible for developing the component. The individual estimated costs are summed to get the overall cost estimate of the project.

The reliability of estimates based on expert judgement (1) depends a great deal to the degree in which a new project conforms with the experience and the ability of the expert to remember facts of historical projects. Mostly the estimates are qualitative and not objective. An important problem in using this method is that it is difficult for someone else to reproduce and use the knowledge and experience of an expert. This can lead to misleading situations where the rules of thumb of an expert are becoming general rules and used in inapplicable situations. Despite the disadvantages, this technique is usually used in situations where a first indication of effort and time is needed, especially in the first phases of software development in which the specifications of the product are vague and continually adapted.

The foundation of a cost estimation technique based on reasoning by analogy (2) is an analysed database of similar historical projects or similar project parts or modules. To find a similarity between a new project and one or more completed projects it is necessary to collect and record data and characteristics of old projects.

The Price-to-Win (3) technique can hardly be called an SCE technique. Primarily commercial motives play an important part in using this approach. It is remarkable that the estimates of organizations which use Price-to-Win are no less accurate than organizations which use other methods[7].

The basis of the estimation method which regards SCE as a capacity (4) problem is the availability of means, especially of personnel. An example is: 'Regarding our capacity planning, three men are available for the new project over the next four months. So the planned effort will be 12 man months'. If the specifications of the software are not clear, this method can be successful. An unfavourable side-effect is that in situations of overestimation the planned effort will be used completely. This effect is based on Parkinson's law that 'Work expands to fill the available volume'.

In parametric models (5) the development time and effort is estimated as a function of a number of variables. These variables represent the most important cost drivers. The nucleus of an estimation model is a number of algorithms and parameters. The values of the parameters and the kind of algorithms are, to a significant extent, based on the contents of a database of completed projects. In the next section a more comprehensive explanation of estimation models is given.

As mentioned earlier only 65% of the organizations which participated on the field study estimate a software project. Table 2 shows the frequency of use of the different techniques. The figures show that most organizations make use of data from past projects in some way. Obviously this works on an informal basis, because only 50% of the participating organizations record data from completed projects. Estimates based on expert judgement and the capacity method prove to be quite popular despite the disadvantages of these methods.

**Table 2. Use of cost estimation techniques (an organization can use more than one technique)**

| | Use (%) |
|---|---|
| Expert judgement | 25.5 |
| Analogy method | 60.8 |
| Price-to-Win | 8.9 |
| Capacity problem | 20.8 |
| Parametric models | 13.7 |

The next sections of this paper focus on the use of SCE models. There was a rapid growth of models in the 1970s. In the 1980s and the 1990s, however, few new models have been developed despite the increasing importance of controlling and estimating software development. Most of the 1970 models are of no interest to present industrial practitioners. There is a tendency towards automated versions (tools) of (combinations or refinements) existing models. An important question is whether this kind of model can solve all of the problems discussed above.

## SOFTWARE COST ESTIMATION MODELS

In this section, one estimation technique, namely SCE models, will be discussed and the principles of SCE models described, making a distinction between sizing and productivity models. The characteristics of some well-known models will also be given.

### The principles of SCE models

Most models found nowadays are two-stage models[7]. The first stage is a sizer and the second stage provides a productivity adjustment factor.

In the first stage an estimate regarding the size of the product to be developed is obtained. In practice several sizing techniques are used. The most well-known sizers nowadays are function points[12] and lines of code[11]. But other sizing techniques like 'software science'[13] and DeMarco's Bang method[14,15], have been defined. The result of a sizing model is the size/volume of the software to be developed, expressed as the number of lines of source code, number of statements, or the number of functions points.

In the second stage it is estimated how much time and effort it will cost to develop the software of the estimated size. First, the estimate of the size is converted into an estimate in nominal man-months of effort. As this nominal effort takes no advantage of knowledge concerning the specific characteristics of the software-product, the way the software-product will be developed and the production means, a number of cost influencing factors (cost drivers) are added to the model. The effect of these cost drivers must be estimated. This effect is often called a productivity adjustment factor. Application of this correction factor to the nominal estimation of effort provides a more realistic estimate.

Some models, like FPA[16], are focused more on the sizing stage. Others, like the well-known COCOMO model[11] on the productivity stage and some tools, such as Before You Leap[17] combine two models to cover both stages. Figure 1 shows the two stages in SCE models.

Figure 2 shows the sizing and the productivity stages in the context of general cost estimation. In Figure 2 five components of the general cost estimation structure are shown. Besides the sizing and productivity components, a phase distribution and sensitivity/risk analysis component are distinguished. In the phase distribution component the total effort and duration is split up over the phases and activities of a project. This division has to be based on empirical data of past projects. The sensitivity and risk analysis phase supports project management — especially at the start of a project when the uncertainty is great — in determining the risk factors of a project and the sensitivity of the estimates to the cost drivers settings. Again data on past projects provide an important input for this component. Before using a model for the first time validation is necessary, and it may also be necessary to calibrate the model. Mostly the environment in which the SCE model has been developed and the database of completed projects on which the model is based will differ from the project characteristics of the environment(s) in which the model is to be used. To make validation and calibration possible, data on historical projects have to be available in an organization. As already mentioned, this information is often lacking.

Most of the tools implementing SCE models do not support project management in all of these steps. The seven steps are:

(1) Creation of database of completed projects.
(2) Size estimation.
(3) Productivity estimation.
(4) Phase distribution.
(5) Sensitivity and risk analysis.
(6) Validation.
(7) Calibration.

Calibration and risk and sensitivity analysis are especially lacking.

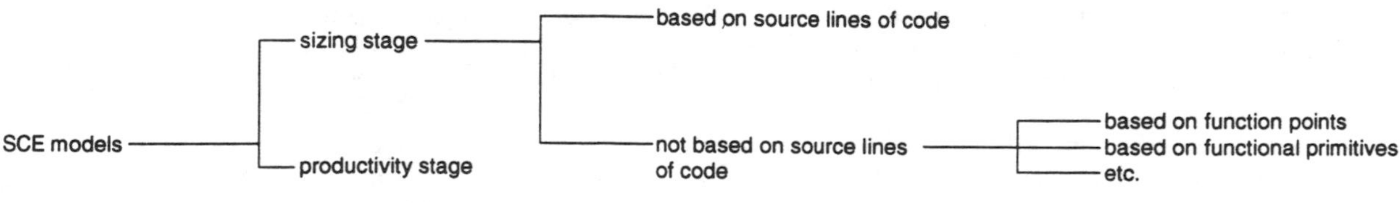

*Figure 1. Structuring of SCE models*

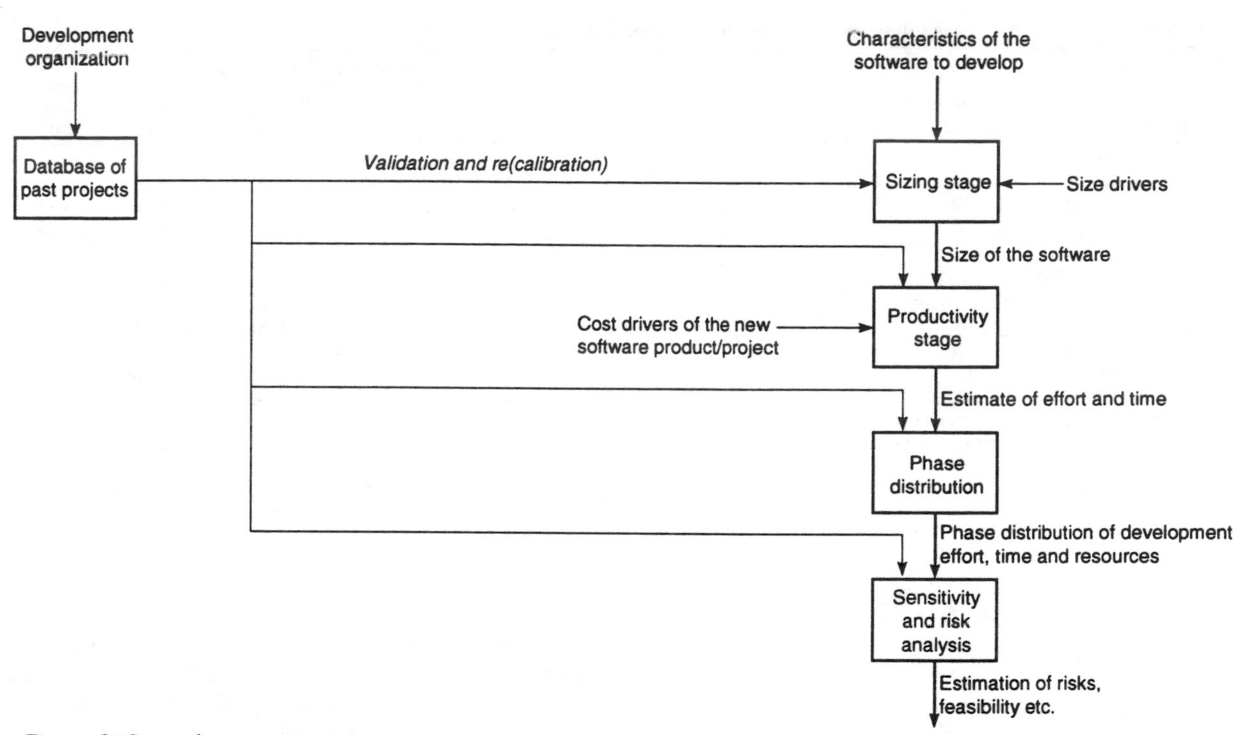


*Figure 2. General cost estimation structure*

## An overview of SCE models

In the past 10 years a number of SCE models have been developed. This section does not give an exhaustive treatment of all the models: the overview is limited to one example of a sizing model, one productivity model, some models which are relevant from an historical point of view, well documented and within the experience of the author, and some models which introduce new ideas.

**The COnstructive COst MOdel (COCOMO)**
COCOMO[11,18] is the best documented and most transparent model currently available. The main focus in COCOMO is upon estimating the influence of 15 cost drivers on the development effort. Before this can be done, an estimate of the software size must be available. COCOMO does not support the sizing estimation stage: it only gives several equations based on 63 completed projects at TRW. The equations represent the relations between size and effort and between effort and development time. The equations are shown in Table 3. A distinction is made between three development modes: the organic mode (stable development environment, less innovative, relatively small size); the embedded mode (developing within tight constraints, innovative, complex, high volatility of requirements); and the semi-detached mode (between organic and embedded mode).

The nominal effort is adjusted by the influence of 15 cost drivers. In Table 4 the 15 COCOMO cost drivers are listed with the adjustment for each driver value. For example: where the required reliability of the software is determined to be very high, the nominal effort has to be multiplied by 1.40. Furthermore COCOMO provides tables to apportion the adjusted estimated effort and development over the project phases and, in the detailed version of the model, to refine the adjustment for each phase. For example: the quality of the programmer has less influence in the feasibility phase than in the design phase. Thus phase dependent adjustment factors are used in the detailed model.

**Function point analysis (FPA)**
FPA has been developed by Albrecht[16] of IBM, and made widely available through the user groups *Guide and Share*. Albrecht was looking for a method to measure productivity in software development. For that purpose he developed FPA as an alternative measure to the number of lines of code. The method is programming language or fourth generation tool independent. The method has been refined several times by Rudolph[19,20], Albrecht and Gaffney[12], and Symons[21,22]. The principle of FPA is simple and is based on the number of 'functions' the software has to fulfil. These functions are

**Table 3. The relation between the nominal effort and size and between development time and effort. KDSI = number of delivered source instructions/1000**

| Development mode | Man-month (nominal) | Development time (nominal) |
|---|---|---|
| Organic | $3.2 * KDSI^{1.05}$ | $2.5 * MM (nom)^{0.38}$ |
| Semi-detached | $3.0 * KDSI^{1.12}$ | $2.5 * MM (nom)^{0.35}$ |
| Embedded | $2.8 * KDSI^{1.20}$ | $2.5 * MM (nom)^{0.32}$ |

**Table 4. The COCOMO cost drivers and their influence on the nominal effort**

| Cost drivers | Very low | Low | Average | High | Very high | Extra high |
|---|---|---|---|---|---|---|
| | Value of the cost drivers | | | | | |
| Required reliability | 0.75 | 0.88 | 1.00 | 1.15 | 1.40 | |
| Database size | | 0.94 | 1.00 | 1.08 | 1.16 | |
| Complexity software | 0.70 | 0.85 | 1.00 | 1.15 | 1.30 | 1.65 |
| Constraints execution time | | | 1.00 | 1.11 | 1.30 | 1.66 |
| Memory constraints | | | 1.00 | 1.06 | 1.21 | 1.56 |
| Hardware volatility | | 0.87 | 1.00 | 1.15 | 1.30 | |
| Response time constraints | | 0.87 | 1.00 | 1.07 | 1.15 | |
| Quality analysts | 1.46 | 1.19 | 1.00 | 0.86 | 0.71 | |
| Experience with application | 1.29 | 1.13 | 1.00 | 0.91 | 0.82 | |
| Quality programmers | 1.42 | 1.17 | 1.00 | 0.86 | 0.70 | |
| Hardware experience | 1.21 | 1.10 | 1.00 | 0.90 | | |
| Programming language experience | 1.14 | 1.07 | 1.00 | 0.95 | | |
| Use modern programming techniques | 1.24 | 1.10 | 1.00 | 0.91 | 0.82 | |
| Use software tools | 1.24 | 1.10 | 1.00 | 0.91 | 0.83 | |
| Project duration constraints | 1.23 | 1.08 | 1.00 | 1.04 | 1.10 | |

related to the types of data the software uses and generates. Within FPA the software is characterized by the five functions:

- the external input type
- the external output type
- the external inquiry type
- the logical internal file type
- the external interface file type

For each of these five types the number of simple, average and complex occurrences that are expected in the software is estimated. By weighting each number with an appropriate weight a number is obtained, the unadjusted number of function points. This indication for nominal size is then adjusted, using 14 technical characteristics. Figure 3 gives an overview of function point analysis.

**PRICE-S**

The PRICE-S model (Programming Review of Information Costing and Evaluation — Software) is developed and supported by RCA PRICE Systems. An important disadvantage with regard to COCOMO and FPA is that the underlying concepts and ideas are not publicly defined and the users are presented with the model as a black box. The user of PRICE sends the input to a time-sharing computer in the USA, UK, or France and gets back his estimates immediately. Despite this disadvantage and the high rental price, there are many users, especially in America. There is, however, an important motivation for American companies to use the model. The US Department of Defense demands a PRICE estimate for all quotations for a software project. PRICE has separate sizer and productivity function.

**The PUTNAM model**

This SCE model was developed by Putnam in 1974[23]. He based his model on the work of Norden[34]. For many projects at IBM, Norden plotted frequency distributions, in which he showed how many people were allocated to the development and maintenance of a software product during the life-cycle. The curves he made fitted very well with the Rayleigh curves. His findings were merely empirical. He found no explanations for the shape of the effort curve. On the assumptions of Norden, Putnam formulated his model. There is not enough space in this paper to explain the principles of the model and the reader is referred to Putnam[23,24], Putnam and Fitzsimmons[25] and Londeix[26].

**Before You Leap (BYL)**

BYL is a commercial package based on a link-up between FPA and COCOMO[17]. BYL starts with a calculation of the amount of net function points. This amount is then translated into source lines of code, taking in account the language used. For Cobol, for instance, one function point is equal to 105 SLOC, for LISP 64, etc. This estimate of the size in SLOC is precisely the necessary input for COCOMO and the COCOMO part of BYL, taking into account the influence on effort of the 15 COCOMO cost drivers, calculates the estimates of costs and time-scale.

**Estimacs**

Estimacs has been developed by H. Rubin[27-29] and Computer Associates[30], and is available as a software package. The model consists of nine modules: a function point module; a risk module; an effort module (to estimate development and maintenance effort), etc. The most important and extensive module is Effort. The user has to answer 25 input questions. These questions are partly related to the complexity of the user-organization and partly to the complexity and size of the software to be developed. The way Estimacs translates the input to an estimation of effort is not clear. Like many other models, Estimacs is a 'closed model'.

| Function count | | ⟵Max range: Factor * 2⟶ | | | | |
|---|---|---|---|---|---|---|
| | | Level of information processing function | | | | |
| Type ID | Description | Simple | Average | Complex | Total | |
| IT | External input | --*3 = -- | --*4 = --- | --*6 = --- | ----- | ↑ |
| OT | External output | --*4 = -- | --*5 = --- | --*7 = --- | ----- | Maximum |
| FT | Logical internal file | --*7 = -- | --*10 = -- | --*15 = -- | ----- | range |
| EI | External interface file | --*5 = -- | --*7 = --- | --*10 = -- | ----- | factor 2.5 |
| QT | External inquiry | --*3 = -- | --*4 = --- | --*6 = --- | ----- | ↓ |
| FC | | Total unadjusted function points | | | | |

| General information processing characteristics | | | | | |
|---|---|---|---|---|---|
| | Characteristics | DI | | Characteristics | DI |
| C1 | Data communications | --- | C8 | On-line update | --- |
| C2 | Distributed functions | --- | C9 | Complex processing | --- |
| C3 | Performance | --- | C10 | Re-usability | --- |
| C4 | Heavily used configuration | --- | C11 | Installation ease | --- |
| C5 | Transaction rate | --- | C12 | Operational ease | --- |
| C6 | On-line data entry | --- | C13 | Multiple sites | --- |
| C7 | End-user efficiency | --- | C14 | Facilitate change | --- |
| PC | | | | Total degree of influence | --- |

| DI Values | | | |
|---|---|---|---|
| Not present or no influence | = 0 | Average influence | = 3 |
| Insignificant influence | = 1 | Significant influence | = 4 |
| Moderate influence | = 2 | Strong influence, throughout | = 5 |

FC (Function count) ≡ Total unadjusted function points
PC (Process complexity) ≡ Total degree of influence
PCA (Process complexity adjustment) = 0.65 + 0.01 * PC
FP (Function point measure) = FC * PCA

*Figure 3. Overview of function point analysis*

**SPQR-20**

SPQR stands for Software Productivity, Quality and Reliability. The model has been developed by C. Jones[31]. SPQR claims to be applicable for all kinds of software projects as well as an estimate of duration, costs and effort to develop software; the model also gives an estimate of maintenance costs. SPQR uses FPA to size the volume of a program. The model is based on an extensive database of past projects. There are four versions of model, SPQR 10, 20, 50 and 100 (the numbers stand for the number of questions the model user has to answer and gives an indication of the degree of refinement of the versions). SPQR-20 is the only commercially available version at the moment, not marketed by C. Jones any more but overtaken by his Checkmark product.

**BIS-Estimator**

BIS-Estimator is completely different from the previously described models. According to the documentation[32] the model claims to be a 'knowledge-based tool'. This cannot be fully confirmed, because the principles of the model are secret for the most part. The model starts with a 'soft' estimate. This is a rough estimate of duration and effort based on (far too few) input questions. Next a 'hard' estimate is made for each phase. Based on the estimates by phase, by means of extrapolation, an estimate of the complete project is made. The 'hard' estimate has to be made at the start of and/or during each phase. The model has facilities to base the estimate upon a comparison with a number of projects, selected by the model user. A positive feature of the model is the evolutionary approach. This means that the estimation process changes during software development. As a result of the kind of questions, data and considerations, an estimate is based on the model changes for each phase.

Several models and computerized versions (tools) are available, but just a few of these have been described briefly above. Without going into detail, Table 5 gives a more extensive list of models and tools. The reader is referred to publications in the literature for a more comprehensive description of each. The models in the list are in chronological order (year of publication). The first 11 are ancient models and of no current interest to practitioners.

## COMPARISON OF SCE MODELS

During the past few years several empirical studies have been carried out to validate the various SCE models. Validation is important but difficult to do, because of the demand to capture large amounts of data about completed software projects. As mentioned before, data collection is not common in the software community. It is labour and time-intensive and requires an attitude not only focused on the constructive part but also on the analytical part of software engineering. Furthermore data collection, usable for validating SCE, is limited to a relative small number of software development organizations. Only a few organizations realize large software projects each year. Nevertheless, a number of validation research investigations have been carried out. In this section some of them will be discussed.

The models discussed earlier differ considerably. Experiments show that estimates made by the different models for the same project vary strongly. Furthermore the estimates differ very much from the real development cost and duration. To give an opinion upon the quality of SCE models, it must be known what kind of demands have to be made upon these models. In Table 6 an overview of these demands/requirements is presented. These requirements are a part of an evaluation method for SCE models. This method has been developed by Heemstra, Kusters and van Genuchten[1] and used to

**Table 5. SCE models and tools with references**

| Model | Source |
|---|---|
| SDC | Nelson, E A *Management handbook for the estimation of computer programming costs*, AD-A648750, Systems Development Corporation (1966) |
| TRW Wolverton | Wolverton, R W 'The cost of development large-scale software' *IEEE Trans. on computers*, Vol c-23, No 6 (June 1974) |
| TELECOTE | Frederic, B C *A professional model for estimating computer program development costs*. Telecote Research Inc. (1974) |
| BOEING | Black, R K D, Curnow, R P, Katz, R and Gray, M D 'BCS software production data' *Final technical report, RADC-TR-77-116*, Boeing Computer Services Inc. (March 1977) |
| IBM/FSD | Walston, C E and Felix, C P 'A method of programming measurement and estimating' *IBM System J.* Vol 16 (1977) |
| DOTY | Herd, J R, Postak, J N, Russell, W E and Stewart, K R 'Software cost estimation — study results. *Final technical report, RA-DC-TR-77-220*, Vol 1, DOTY Associates, Inc., Rockville, MD (1977) |
| ESD1 | Duquette, J A and Bourbon, G A 'ESD, A computerized model for estimating software life cycle costs' *FSD-TR-235* Vol 1 (April 1978) |
| SLIM | Putnam, L H 'A general empirical solution to the macro software sizing and estimating problem' *IEEE Trans. Soft. Eng.* SE-4, 4 (1978) |
| Surbock | Surbock, E K *Management software development* Projekten Berlin (1978) (In German) |
| GRC | Carriere, W M and Thibodeau, R 'Development of a logistic software cost estimating technique for foreign military sales' *GRC Report CR-3-839* (1979) |
| Grumman | Sandler, G and Bachowitz, B 'Software cost models — Grumman experience' *IEEE, quantitative software model conference* (1979) |
| PRICE-S | Freiman, F R and Park, R E 'The Price software cost model: RCA government systems division' *IEEE* (1979) |
| FPA | Albrecht, A J 'Measuring application development productivity' *Proc. of Joint SHARE/GUIDE/IBM application development symp.* (October 1979) |
| SLICE | Kustanowitz, A L 'System life cycle estimation (SLICE): a new approach to estimating resources for application program development' *IEEE first international computer software and application conference, Chicago* (1980) |
| FAST | Freiman, F R 'The FAST methodology' *J. of parametrics*, Vol 1 No 2 (1981) |
| Baily/Basili | Bailey, J W and Basili V R 'A meta-model for software development resource expenditures' *Proc. 5th Int. Conf. Soft. Engin., IEEE* (1981) |
| COCOMO | Boehm, B W *Software engineering economics* Prentice-Hall (1981) |
| SOFTCOST | Tausworthe, R C 'Deep space network software cost estimation model' Publication 81-7, *Jet Propulsion Laboratory*, Pasadena, CA (1981) |
| BANG | DeMarco, T *Controlling software projects: management, measurement and estimation* Yourdon Press, New York (1982) |
| JS 3/System-4/Seer | Jensen, R W 'An improved macrolevel software development resource estimation model' *Proc. 5th ISPA Conf.* St Louis MO (1983) |
| COPMO | Thebaut, S M and Shen, V Y 'An analytic resource model for large-scale software development' *Inf. Proc. Management*, Vol 20 No 1–2 (1984) |
| GECOMO | Gecomo 'Software tools for professionals' *GEC Software Documentation*, G & C Company, London (1985) |
| ESTIMACS | Computer Associates. CA-Estimacs *User Guide*, Release 5.0 (July 1986) |
| BYL | Before You Leap. *User's Guide*, Gordon Group (1986) |
| SPQR/Checkmark | Jones, C *Programming productivity* McGraw-Hill (1986) |
| Jeffery | Jeffery, D R 'A software development productivity model for MIS environments' *J. of Systems and Software* 7 (1987) |
| ESTIMATE/1 | Estimate/1. Documentative Method/1: Automated Project Estimating Aid. Arthur Anderson (1987) |
| BIS | BIS/Estimator. User Manual, version 4.4, BIS Applied System Ltd (1987) |
| SECOMO | Goethert, W B 'SECOMO' in Boehm, B W *Documentation of the seminar: software cost estimation using COCOMO and ADA COCOMO*, SAL, London. 1988' ITT Research Institute, Data & Analysis Center for Software. |

**Table 6. Requirements for SCE models**

| Model requirements | Application requirements | Implementation requirements |
|---|---|---|
| Linked to software control method | Possibilities for calibration | User-friendliness of the tool |
| Applicability at the start of a project | Accuracy of the estimations | Possibilities for sensitivity analyses |
| Fit with the data that is available during development | | Possibilities for risk analysis |
| Possible to adjust estimate due to changing objectives | | Open model, is it possible to see how the results were obtained |
| Definition of domain model is suitable for | | Clarity of input definition |
| | | Completeness and detail of output |

evaluate the eight models described above. The results of that evaluation are presented in Table 7 and described in more detail in Heemstra[7]. From the table it can be seen that there are only few plusses. The conclusion is that the quality of the models is poor and much improvement is necessary. The accuracy of the estimations were evaluated by several tests. The way the tests were executed and the results obtained will be described. The objectives of the tests were:

- to determine the accuracy of the estimate using SCE models in a semi-realistic situation
- to determine whether these models will be accepted by project management

After a severe selection procedure only two SCE models remained. These were the BYL and Estimacs models. During the tests 14 experienced project leaders were asked to make a number of estimates for a project that had actually been carried out. The project was described as if it was at the start of the project. The project leaders had to make three estimates. The first estimate of effort and duration (the 'manual' estimate) was made on the basis of the project leaders' knowledge and experience. Next, two estimates were made using the models selected. In conclusion, a final estimate was made on the basis of the project leaders' knowledge and experience together with the model estimates. Each estimate was evaluated directly using a questionnaire, and the tests ended with a discussion session. The results are presented in Table 8.

The real effort and duration were eight man-months and six months. The main conclusions of the experiment were that on the basis of the differences found between the estimates and reality, it has not been shown that the selected models can be used for a reliable estimation tool at an early stage of software development. All in all, the project leaders were not wildly enthusiastic about these tools, but they were, nevertheless, felt to be acceptable as a check-list and as a means of communication. It should be mentioned that the selected project is small. Most models are calibrated on data from medium/large projects.

Kemerer[33] shows that estimates of different models can differ considerably. For each model he investigated the difference between actual and estimated number of man-months. He used COCOMO, Estimacs, FPA and Putnam's model to estimate the required effort of 15 already realized projects. From Table 9 it can be seen that for both COCOMO and Putnam's model there were sharp overestimations. FPA and Estimacs gave distinctly better results with overshoots of 100% and 85%, respectively. A similar study was carried out by Rubin[29]. A project description was sent to Jensen (Jensen's model), Greene (Putnam's model SLIM) and Rook (GECOMO) and to himself (Rubin's model Estimacs).

**Table 7. Evaluation of models**

| | Models | | | | | | | |
|---|---|---|---|---|---|---|---|---|
| Requirements | COCOMO | PRICE | PUTNAM | FPA | BYL | ESTIMACS | SPQR | BIS |
| *Model requirements* | | | | | | | | |
| Linked to software control method | − − | − − | − − | − − | − − | + + | − − | − − |
| Applicable at an early stage | − − | − − | − − | + | + | + + | + | − |
| Using available data | + | − − | − − | − − | − − | − − | − − | + + |
| Adjustment to objectives | + | + | + | − − | − − | + | + + | − − |
| Definition of scope/domain | + | − | − | + + | − | − | − | + + |
| *Application requirements* | | | | | | | | |
| Calibration | − | − − | − − | − | + | + | − | − |
| Accuracy | nt | nt | nt | nt | t | t | nt | nt |
| *Implementation requirements* | | | | | | | | |
| User friendliness | + + | − | + | + | + + | + | + | + |
| Sensitivity analysis | − − | + | − − | − − | + + | + + | − | − |
| Risk analysis | − − | − − | − − | − − | − − | + + | + | − − |
| Open model/traceability | + + | − − | + + | + + | + + | − | − | + |
| Definition input | + + | − | + + | − | + | + | + | + |
| Completeness and detail output | + | + + | − | − | + + | + + | + + | + + |

+ + = satisfies the requirement; + = sufficient; − = insufficient; − − = the model does not satisfy the requirement; nt = the model was not tested on accuracy; t = the models were tested

Table 8. Some results of the tests. Duration is given in months, effort in man-months

| Variable | $\mu$ | $\sigma$ |
|---|---|---|
| Effort | | |
| Manual estimate | 28.4 | 18.3 |
| BYL estimate | 27.7 | 14.0 |
| Estimacs estimate | 48.5 | 13.9 |
| Final estimate | 27.7 | 12.8 |
| Duration | | |
| Manual estimate | 11.2 | 3.7 |
| BYL estimate | 8.5 | 2.4 |
| Final estimate | 12.1 | 3.4 |

The main purpose was to compare and contrast the different sort of information required by the four models. Also a comparison was made between the estimates obtained using the models, that is to say the number of man-months and the duration for the development of the selected project. From Table 10 it can be seen that the estimates vary significantly. Also Rubin's explanation is that the models are based on different databases of completed projects and have not been calibrated and the four participants made different assumptions in choosing the settings of the cost drivers.

## THE IMPORTANCE OF SCE MODELS

The field study, mentioned earlier in the paper, shows that SCE models are currently not generally accepted in organizations surveyed. Only 51 of the 364 organizations that estimate software development use models. An analysis showed that these 51 model-users make no better estimates than the non-model-users. These results are disappointing at first glance. It does not mean, however, that it makes no sense to spend further research effort on models. All the investigations mentioned before agree that the poor quality is primarily due to using the models wrongly. For example: use of models requires organizational bounded data of past projects. Most of the time models are used without calibration. If models cannot be adapted the result will be less accurate estimates. The majority of the models do not support calibration.

It is worth while to promote the development of better estimation tools, despite the shortcomings of the existing models. In this section some arguments are put forward that underline the necessity to invest more effort and time in the development of SCE models.

In making an estimate, especially at an early stage of development, a lot of uncertainty and fuzziness exists. It is not known which cost drivers play a part in the estimation and what the influence of the cost drivers will be. There are many participants involved in the project (project manager, customer, developer, user, etc.). Often they all have their own hidden agendas and goals conflicting with each other (minimalization of the costs, maximalization of the quality, minimalization of the duration, optimal use of

Table 9. Estimates of the actual and estimated number of man-months using four different models

| Models | Averages for all projects: Actual number of MM | Estimated number of MM | (Estimated divided by actual) * 100% |
|---|---|---|---|
| GECOMO | 219.25 | 1291.75 | 607.85 |
| Putnam | 219.25 | 2060.17 | 771.87 |
| FPA | 260.30 | 533.23 | 167.29 |
| Estimacs | 287.97 | 354.77 | 85.48 |

employees, etc.). For project management it is difficult to predict the progress of a project in such fuzzy situations. To make point estimations like 'duration will be 321 man-months of which 110 for analysis, 70 for design, etc.', will be of less importance. Such exact figures do not fit in with the nature of the problem. Project management will be more interested in a number of scenarios from which alternatives can be chosen and in the sensitiveness of an estimation to specific cost drivers. For example: what will be the result on the duration of the addition of two more analysts to the project: what will be the influence on effort if the available development time will be decreased sharply; what will be the result on effort and duration if the complexity of the software to be developed has been estimated too high or too low, etc. An approach of the estimation problem like this gives project management more insight and feeling for alternative solutions. Furthermore this approach offers a proper basis for project control. If an estimate proves to be sensible for changes of a specific cost driver, this provides a warning for project management to pay full attention to this cost driver during development.

Often project management will be confronted with little tolerance in defined duration, price and quality. In such cases project management wants support in choosing the values of the decision variables. What are the available possible choices to meet the given objectives. Which personnel in combination with which tools and by means of which kind of project organization are suitable as possible solutions. The conclusion is that there is no need for a rigid 'calculation tool'. This does not fit with the characteristics of the estimation problem, namely uncertainty, fuzziness, little structuring, and unclear and incomplete specifications.

An important prerequisite for successful estimation is the development, acceptance and use of a uniform set of

Table 10. Comparison of SCE models by Rubin[29]

| | | Effort | Duration |
|---|---|---|---|
| Mode | Jensen | 940 MM | 31 m |
| | Putnam | 200 MM | 17 m |
| | GECOMO | 363 MM | 23 m |
| | Estimacs | 17 100 hrs | 16 m |

MM = man-months; m = months

definitions and standards. This results in agreements such as:

- How many times an estimate is made for a project. For example: five times for each project that costs more than 12 man-months.
- In what phases during execution an estimate is made. For example: during the feasibility study, during the specification phase and after finishing the design.
- Which employees are involved in the estimation process. For example: project management, customers, developers.
- What will be estimated. For example: all development activities with regard to the phases feasibility, specification, design, etc. or all activities including training, documentation, etc.
- The output of an estimate. For example: costs in dollars, effort in man-months, duration in months.
- The factors which can be regarded as the most important cost drivers and have to be recorded. For example: size, reliability, type of application, quality of personnel, etc.
- A set of definitions. For example: volume will be expressed in function points, documentation contains of . . . , high complexity means . . . , etc.

The result will be a comprehensive list of standardized agreements. It is important that these are really applied in the subsequent project. An SCE model that meets requirements such as a set of clear definitions, measurable and relevant cost drivers, flexibility with regards to other control methods, etc. will result in a more structural approach to software cost estimation and control.

## CONCLUSIONS AND RECOMMENDATIONS

In this final section some concrete guidelines for controlling and estimating software development will be offered. Most of these guidelines have been discussed at different levels of detail in the previous sections.

### Determine the level of uncertainty

High uncertainty needs another approach of cost estimation and control than does low uncertainty. High uncertainty corresponds with risk analysis, estimating and margins, exploration oriented problem-solving, expert-oriented estimating techniques, etc. Low uncertainty corresponds with cost estimation models (calculation tools), experiences from past projects, realization oriented problem-solving, the estimate is regarded as a norm, etc.

### Cost estimation and data collection

Collection of data of completed projects is necessary for successful cost estimation. Cost models, estimation by analogy and experts require such data. It is no solution to use data collected from other organizations. The relevant data are different for each organization.

### Use more than one estimation technique

A lot of research shows that the quality of the current estimation techniques is poor. The lack of accurate and reliable estimation techniques combined with the financial, technical, organizational and social risks of software projects, require a frequent estimation during the development of an application and the use of more than one estimation technique. More and different techniques are required, especially at the milestones of the development phases. The level of knowledge of the software whose cost we are trying to estimate is growing during a project. A possibility is to use another model during a project, because more information and more *accurate* information is available; a cascade of techniques — for example Wide Band Delphi, Estimacs, DeMarco, COCOMO — is a possible solution.

### Cost estimation needs commitment

Software development has to be done by highly qualified professionals. For such people some characteristics are relevant, such as:

- individuality in work performance is important
- a good professional result of their work is important
- professionals want to be consulted in decisions, work planning, the desired result, etc.
- professionals do not want to be disturbed by management during the execution of their work

It is not wise to confront professional developers with a plan and estimate without any consultation. A hierarchical leadership is not suitable. In consulting the developers not only their expertise is used but also their involvement in the estimation process is increased. This results in a higher commitment than is necessary for the success of a project.

### Cost estimation: a management problem

Software cost estimation is often wrongly regarded as a technical problem that can be solved with calculation models, a set of metrics and procedures. However, the opposite is true. The 'human aspects' are much more important. The quality, experience and composition of the project team, the degree in which the project leader can motivate, kindle enthusiasm and commit his developers, has more influence on delivering the software in time and within budget than the use of rigid calculations.

## REFERENCES

1 **Heemstra, F J, Kusters, R and van Genuchten, M** 'Selections of software cost estimation models' *Report TUE/BDK* University of Technology Eindhoven (1989)

2 **Lierop van, F L G, Volkers, R S A, Genuchten, M van and Heemstra, F J** 'Has someone seen the software?' *Informatie* Vol 33 No 3 (1991) (In Dutch)

3 **Genuchten, van M I J M** 'Towards a software factory' *PhD Thesis*, University of Technology Eindhoven (1991)

4 **Beers** 'Problems, planning and knowledge, a study of the processes behind success and failure of an automation project' *PhD Series in general management. No 1* Faculty Industrial Engineering/Rotterdam School of Management, Erasmus University Rotterdam (1991) (In Dutch)

5 **Brooks, F B** *The mythical manmonth. Essays on software engineering* Addison-Wesley (1975)

6 **Noth, T and Kretzschmar, M** *Estimation of software development projects* Springer-Verlag (1984) (In German)

7 **Heemstra, F J** *How expensive is software? Estimation and control of software-development* Kluwer (1989) (In Dutch)

8 **Druffel, L E** 'Strategies for a DoD Software initiative' *CSS DUSD(RAT)* Washington, DC (1982)

9 **Conte, S D, Dunsmore, H F and Shen, V Y** *Software engineering metrics and models* Benjamin Cummins (1986)

10 **Reifer, D J** 'The economics of software reuse' *Proc. 14th Annual ISPA Conf.*, New Orleans (May 1991)

11 **Boehm, B W** *Software engineering economics* Prentice-Hall (1981)

12 **Albrecht, A J and Gaffney, J E** 'Software function, source lines of code, and development effort prediction: a software science validation' *IEEE Trans. Soft. Eng.* Vol SE-9 No 6 (1983)

13 **Halstead, M H** *Elements of software science* North-Holland (1977)

14 **DeMarco, T** *Controlling software projects: management, measurement and estimation* Yourdon Press, New York (1982)

15 **DeMarco, T** 'An algorithm for sizing software products' *Performance Evaluation Review* 12 pp 13–22 (1984)

16 **Albrecht, A J** 'Measuring application development productivity' *Proc. Joint SHARE/GUIDE/IBM application development symp.* (October 1979)

17 **Gordon** 'Before You Leap' *User's Guide* Gordon Group (1986)

18 **Boehm, B W** 'Software engineering economics' *IEEE Trans. Soft. Eng.* Vol 10 No 1 (January 1984)

19 **Rudolph, E E** 'Productivity in computer application development, Department of Management Studies' *Working paper No 9* University of Auckland (March 1983)

20 **Rudolph, E E** 'Function point analyses, cookbook' own edition from Rudolph (March 1983)

21 **Symons, C R** 'Function point analysis: difficulties and improvements' *IEEE Trans. Soft. Eng.* Vol 14 No 1 (January 1988)

22 **Symons, C R** *Software sizing and estimating—MARK II FPA* Wiley (1991)

23 **Putnam, L H** 'A general empirical solution to the macro software sizing and estimating problem' *IEEE Trans. Soft. Eng.* SE-4, 4 (1978)

24 **Putnam, L** 'Software costing estimating and life cycle control' *IEEE Computer Society Press* (1980)

25 **Putnam, L H and Fitzsimmons, A** 'Estimating software costs' *Datamation* (Sept. Oct. Nov. 1979)

26 **Londeix, B** *Cost estimation for software development* Addison-Wesley (1987)

27 **Rubin, H A** 'Interactive macro-estimation of software life cycle parameters via personal computer: a technique for improving customer/developer communication' *Proc. Symp. on application & assessment of automated tools for software development, IEEE*, San Francisco (1983)

28 **Rubin, H A** 'Macro and micro-estimation of maintenance effort: the estimacs maintenance models' *IEEE* (1984)

29 **Rubin, H A** 'A comparison of cost estimation tools' *Proc. 8th Int. Conf. Soft. Eng. IEEE* (1985)

30 **Computer Associates** CA-Estimacs *User Guide* Release 5.0 (July 1986)

31 **Jones, C** *Programming productivity* McGraw-Hill (1986)

32 **BIS/Estimator** *User manual version 4.4.* BIS Applied System Ltd. (1987)

33 **Kemerer, C F** 'An empirical validation of software cost estimation models' *Communications of the ACM* Vol 30 No 5 (May 1987)

34 **Norden, P V** *Useful tools for project management* (Operations research in research and development) Wiley (1963)

# Risk Management for Software Development

Richard Fairley
*Colorado Technical University*
*Colorado Springs, Colorado, USA*

Paul Rook
*The Centre for Software Reliability*
*City University, Northampton Square, London, UK*

## Keywords: Risk, Risk Management, Software Risk, Risk Exposure, Risk Factors

A risk is a potential problem; a problem is a risk that has materialized. By a problem, we mean an undesirable situation that will require time and resources to correct. In some cases the problem, should it occur, may be uncorrectable. A risk, being a potential problem, is characterized by:

- The probability that an undesired event might occur ($0<P<1$)
- A loss associated with occurrence of the undesired event

The loss associated with an undesired event is referred to as the *risk impact*. Sometimes, it is possible to quantify the loss in measurable terms, such as dollars or human lives. In other cases the loss is intangible; for example, loss of credibility or good will. In cases where loss can be quantified, the product of (probability * risk impact) is referred to as the *risk exposure*.

Probability and impact typically vary with time and circumstances. A small risk may become a large one, and conversely, a large risk may, with passing time, become a non-risk. For example, the probability of failing to achieve a desired result falls to zero upon attainment of the desired result. Furthermore, some risk factors may be interdependent so that reducing the probability and/or cost of one may increase the probability and/or cost of another. With hindsight, it will be determined that some potential problems occurred and others did not.

When we are dealing with risk in this general sense, it is not always easy to distinguish between single events, multiple events, continuous events, and interdependent events, or between cause and effect. In considering an undertaking, many risks may be identified. Systematic risk management requires that initial apprehensions be turned into specific root causes, and that the probabilities and potential losses be established. The specific outcome we wish to avoid must be explicitly stated in order to identify possible courses of action for risk reduction.

The first step in risk management for software development is to organize the development effort as a well-defined project having a schedule, a budget, a set of objectives to be achieved, and a set of skills needed to accomplish the work. Project objectives must be translated into a set of targets that cover, at least, cost (or effort), schedule, and product functionality, performance, and quality attributes.

In setting targets for a project, a subproject, or a development phase the following must be considered:

- *Constraints.* A constraint is an external condition imposed by forces over which project management has no control. There may be constraints on time, money, personnel, and other aspects of the work. There may also be design constraints imposed on the product. When a constraint is broken it may result in financial loss or cancellation of the project.
- *Estimates.* An estimate is a prediction of expected outcomes under certain circumstances. An estimate should be made for each of the project targets. Estimates should include ranges of values with associated probabilities, confidence levels, and most importantly, analyses of the assumptions underlying the estimates. Estimates must incorporate the process and product constraints placed on the project.
- *Types of targets.* Targets are set by the customer and by project management and speci-

fied in the project plan. Targets should include negotiated considerations of project constraints, and the estimate ranges and probabilities. These negotiations may involve the customer, management, and development staff.

- *Conditional minimax targets.* There may be a project attribute (cost, schedule, functionality, performance) that management and the customer desire to optimize. However, it may be that optimizing this target should only be achieved provided all other targets are achieved. Consequently, the optimization criteria must incorporate the full set of targets; otherwise, the desired attribute will be minimized or maximized at the expense of other attributes.

Risks are thus viewed as potential problems that, should they occur, will impact project targets. If there are no quantified targets, then there is no danger that the targets will not be achieved; risk management is meaningless unless targets are defined in measurable terms.

Identifying the risk factors for the various project targets allows risks to be traced through subsequent risk management plans, risk monitoring and reporting procedures, and corrective action.

## Risk Management and Project Management

The goal of traditional project management is to control pervasive risks that might hinder the development of a satisfactory product on time and within budget. Traditional project management uses systematic procedures to estimate and plan the work, lead and direct the staff, monitor progress, and control the project by replanning and reassigning resources as necessary. This remains the fundamental basis for project management and is not invalidated by any consideration of risk management. However, on its own, traditional project management is a recipe for "problem management" in that difficult decisions are addressed and actions taken only when problems arise. In this sense, project management is reactive, whereas risk management is proactive.

Risk Management consists of Risk Assessment followed by Risk Control (see Figure 1). Risk assessment provides informed decisions based on systematic assessment of things that might go wrong, the associated probabilities, and the severities of the impacts. Risk control is concerned with developing strategies and plans to abate the major risk factors, to resolve those risks that do become problems, and to continuously reassess risk. Real risk management occurs when significant decision making, planning, resources, money, and effort are expended to reduce the probabilities and/or impacts of identified risk factors. The extent to which time and effort are invested in these processes can be used as a test to determine whether risk management is being accomplished over and above traditional project management.

Risk management is not synonymous with project management, nor is it a replacement for project management, or something entirely separate. Rather, it is an explicit augmentation and extension of traditional project management, closely intertwined with the information gathering and decision making functions of project management. When a project is successful, it is not because there were no problems, but because the problems were overcome. Risk management does not guarantee success, but has the primary goal of identifying and responding to potential problems with sufficient lead time to avoid crisis situations, so that it becomes possible to conduct a project that meets its targets.

## Types of Risks

Risks can be categorized as Contractual/Environmental, Management/Process, Resources/Personnel, and Technical/Operational. The introduction of systematic risk management requires managers to abandon the idea that all risks on a technically difficult project are technical in nature. While some risks should indeed be identified as technical risks, there are also risks in the use of resources (especially personnel), risks in the way of working the project (management/process) and, just as importantly, risks to the project which are beyond the control of project management (contractual/environmental).

Figure 2 lists these four types of risk with some examples of each. All identified risks must be correctly typed. If risks that come from other sources are misidentified as technical risks, there is a danger they will be passed down from the management level to become the responsibility of the technical staff, who may not be able to control them. The result may be that these risk factors are not explicitly managed until they have become significant problems. Ensuring that all risks are fully addressed by management, the customer, and the developers requires explicit identification of the processes, team structures, responsibilities and authorities, and environmental/contractual factors. This is properly the domain of good traditional project management in any case, and a necessary prerequisite for successful risk control.

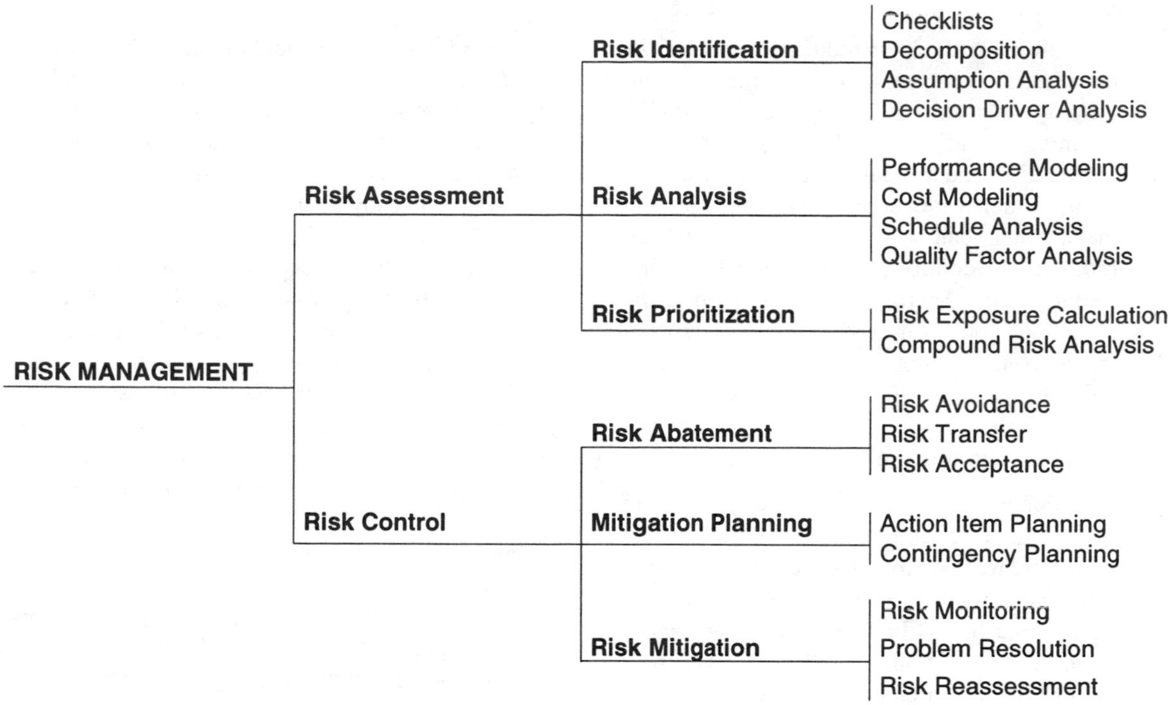

- RISK MANAGEMENT
  - Risk Assessment
    - Risk Identification
      - Checklists
      - Decomposition
      - Assumption Analysis
      - Decision Driver Analysis
    - Risk Analysis
      - Performance Modeling
      - Cost Modeling
      - Schedule Analysis
      - Quality Factor Analysis
    - Risk Prioritization
      - Risk Exposure Calculation
      - Compound Risk Analysis
  - Risk Control
    - Risk Abatement
      - Risk Avoidance
      - Risk Transfer
      - Risk Acceptance
    - Mitigation Planning
      - Action Item Planning
      - Contingency Planning
    - Risk Mitigation
      - Risk Monitoring
      - Problem Resolution
      - Risk Reassessment

*Figure 1. A Taxonomy for Risk Management (adapted from [Boehm89])*

| Contractual/Environmental | Management/Process | Personnel | Technical |
|---|---|---|---|
| "...to suffer the slings and arrows of outrageous fortune, or to take arms against a sea of troubles..."<br>Unreasonable customers<br>Nonperforming vendors and subcontractors<br>Dependencies on and demands from other projects<br>Inappropriate corporate policies<br>Change in management priorities | "It is best to do things systematically since we are only human and disorder is our worst enemy"<br>Unclear responsibilities and authorities<br>Ill-defined procedures<br>Inadequate control of development process<br>Inadequate support facilities and services<br>Lack of "visibility" | "though all men be made of one metal, yet they be not cast all in one mold"<br>Wrong people available<br>–lack of skills<br>–lack of training<br>–lack of expertise<br>Lack of staff continuity<br>Incorrect staffing<br>–too many people for the current task<br>–too few people for the current tasks | "The best laid plans..."<br>Requirements changes<br>–customer changes mind<br>–hidden implications emerge<br>Failure to meet requirements<br>–cannot produce a feasible design<br>–acceptance tests fail<br>Problems or errors detected<br>–inconsistent design<br>–missing components<br>–inadequate time for testing |

*Figure 2. Sources of Risk*

For purposes of risk control, risk factors fall into two categories:

- *Generic risks* are those risk factors common to all software projects. For example, costly late fixes (dealt with by early requirements and design verification), error-prone products (dealt with by verification, validation, and incremental testing throughout the life cycle), uncontrolled development processes (dealt with by planning and control based on well-defined processes), uncontrolled product (dealt with by configuration management and quality assurance), and poor communications (dealt with by documentation, reviews, and technical interchange meetings)

Over time, methods of reducing generic risks have become institutionalized in the tools and techniques used; for example, in project planning, configuration management, and verification and validation. In this sense, traditional software engineering and project management can be viewed as systematic approaches to controlling generic risk factors. Reduction of generic risk is evidenced in the choice of the overall development process (prototyping, incremental development, evolutionary development, design to cost, and so on) and the choice of methods, tools, and techniques used within that process.

Significant expenditures may be incurred in setting up a development process, acquiring tools, and training the managers and technical staff to cope with the generic risks inherent in a particular line of business. The outcomes of these risk reduction activities are the process(es), project plan(s), and work activities for each project. Generic risks for each phase of a software development project are controlled by explicitly designing the work processes of those phases.

- *Project-specific risks* are potential problems inherent to a particular project (for instance, insufficient personnel, key personnel not available when needed, unrealistic schedule and/or budget, inadequate requirements, shortfalls in externally supplied components or services, reliance on advances in the state of the art, and so on). Project-specific risks are dealt with in a Risk Management Plan which identifies the actions to be carried out should certain events occur. Risk management plans are especially useful when the customer, management, and developers agree that the project represents a risky undertaking.

A Risk Management Plan may contain both Action Plans and Contingency Plans. An action plan represents a decision to engage in a risk reduction activity that is to be conducted without further consideration; for example, acquiring training in a particular method or technique, acquiring work stations and software tools, or purchasing desks and work spaces. Like all plans, an action plan must specify a well-defined set of tasks, a schedule, a budget, and the responsibility and authority assigned to each involved person. A contingency plan is a risk reduction activity to be engaged in at some future time, should circumstances warrant; for example, rescoping the work or adding people should the schedule slip more than two weeks, or buying more memory or reducing functionality should the memory budget exceed its allocation by more than ten percent.

A contingency plan should contain the items illustrated by example in Figure 3. As illustrated in Figure 3, a contingency plan should describe the risk factor(s) dealt with by the plan, possible alternative courses of action to mitigate the risk factor(s) should it (they) become problem(s), the constraints on contingent actions, the risks created by the various possible alternatives, the risk indicator metric(s), the threshold value(s) of the indicator metric(s) that indicate the potential problem has become a real problem, the reset level for the indicator metric(s) that will signal resolution of the problem, the resources to be applied during the contingent action, the maximum duration of the contingency plan (after which the project goes into crisis mode), and the responsible party who will track the indicator metric(s) and implement the contingency plan. A project enters crisis mode when the maximum duration of a contingency plan is exceeded. A crisis is a "show-stopper;" all available resources are focused on solving the problem until the crisis is resolved or the project is rescoped or terminated.

Choosing the development process to be used is an essential risk reduction technique and is just as important as the risk reduction techniques identified in the risk management plan.

Various process models are summarized by Boehm [BOEHM89] as follows:

- *Buy COTS*: Buying a Commercial-Off-The-Shelf (COTS) product is a simple approach often overlooked in the enthusiasm to design and build something new, or because of the problems involved in administrative procedures required to buy rather than build. (Major risks for the COTS approach include failure to satisfy user needs, lack of compatibility with other system components, and the difficulties of integrating multiple COTS packages [Fairley94].)
- *Waterfall*: The sequential, single-pass requirements-design-code-test-maintain model.
- *Risk Reduction/Waterfall*: The waterfall model, preceded by one or more phases focused on reducing the risks of poorly understood requirements or architecture, technology uncertainties, potential performance shortfall, robustness issues, and so on.

1. Risk Factors: Software Size (256K limit)
   Processing Time (100 microsecond loop)
2. Alternatives: Prototyping
   Memory Overlays
   Buy Memory
   Faster Processor
   Incremental Development plus Technical Performance Measurement (ID + TPM)
3. Constraints: Schedule and Budget
4. Risk Created: Prototype: how to scale results?
   Overlays: execution time penalty
   Memory: hardware architectural constraints
   Processor: customer constraint
   ID + TPM: reduced functionality
   unmaintainable product
5. Selected Approach: Incremental Development plus TPM
   –partition design into a series of incremental builds
   –allocate 90% of memory and exection time to product functions
   –pursue incremental development based on partitioning
   –use TPM tracking on the memory and timing budgets
6. Risk Indicator Metrics: Cost Performance Indices (CPI) for memory and timing budgets
7. Thresholds for Contingent Action: either CPI > 1.10
8. Reset Levels: CPI < 1.05
9. Resources to be Applied: unlimited overtime for Sue Jones and Bill Williams
10. Maximum Duration: 2 weeks
11. Responsible Party: Sue Jones

*Figure 3. A Contingency Plan*

- *Capabilities-to-Requirements*: This model reverses the usual requirements-to-capabilities sequence inherent in the waterfall model. It begins with an assessment of the envelope of capabilities available from COTS or other reusable components, and then involves adjusting the requirements wherever possible to capitalize on the existing capabilities.
- *Transform*: This model relies on the availability of a generator that can automatically transform the specifications into code. If such a capability spans the system's growth envelope, the transform model may be most appropriate.
- *Evolutionary Development*: This approach involves developing an initial approximation to a desired software product, and evolving it into a final product based on feedback from users. This is a highly effective, low-risk approach if the system's growth envelope is covered by a 4GL, or if the system requirements are poorly understood but, the architecture of similar systems is well-understood, lowering the risk that the system will evolve into a configuration poorly supported by the architecture.
- *Evolutionary Prototyping*: This model is similar to evolutionary development, except that a prototype-quality system (low robustness) is acceptable.
- *Incremental Development*: This approach involves organizing a project into a series of builds that incrementally add increasing capabilities to the growing system. In contrast to the prototyping models, an incremental model requires that the requirements and architecture be (mostly) understood up-front and that the design be partitioned into a series of incremental builds. This is the preferred approach in many situations because, in contrast to the waterfall model, incremental integration and frequent demonstrations of progress are possible. Incremental development also lowers the risks of insufficient development personnel and failure to meet a fixed delivery date (with, perhaps, less than full capability).
- *Design-to-Cost and/or Design-to-Schedule*: This approach involves prioritizing the desired system capabilities, pruning the requirements to fit the time and money available, and organizing the architecture to

facilitate dropping lower-priority capabilities if it is determined that those capabilities cannot be realized within the available budget and/or schedule.

These last two process models (incremental development and design-to-cost/schedule) can often be combined with other process model alternatives.

Boehm lists the following factors as critical decision drivers for choosing a process model:

- *Growth envelope*: This refers to the foreseeable limits of growth to a system's size and diversity over the course of its life cycle. A high-growth envelope implies high risk of using limited-domain implementation strategy such as commercial-off-the-shelf products or 4GLs.
- *Available technologies*: Alternatively, technologies such as commercial off-the-shelf products, application generators, or 4GL capabilities that do cover a system's growth envelope may determine the most attractive process model. (A related process model is the "capabilities-to-requirements" model, in which the availability of powerful, easy-to-adapt capabilities or reusable components strongly influences the system requirements.)
- *Knowledge of requirements*: Ill-defined requirements imply process models that incorporate the user-feedback loops of prototyping and evolutionary development, as opposed to the waterfall model which has a high risk of developing software that does not satisfy user requirements.
- *Architecture understanding*: The lower the level of understanding of system architecture, the higher the risk of a pure top-down waterfall approach. On the other hand, a high level of architecture understanding lowers one of the risks of evolutionary development: that the system will evolve in directions that the architecture cannot support.
- *Robustness*: Systems that must be highly robust and error-free encounter high risks from informal process models such as evolutionary prototyping. More rigorous process models such as the incremental model reduce these risks, although the incremental model may need to be preceded by less formal prototyping phases to address requirements understanding or architecture-understanding risks.
- *Budget and schedule limitations*: May require a design-to-cost or design-to-schedule approach.
- *High-risk system nucleus*: May dictate an evolutionary or incremental development approach.

## Risk Management Procedures

The origins of risk management date from the 1800s when the concept of risk exposure (probability * cost) was used in the insurance industry to analyze data collected about fires and deaths. By the 1950s, decision theory and probabilistic modeling were being taught as academic subjects. Use of risk management in the petrochemical and construction industries dates from about 1980; recognition of risk management as an element of software engineering dates from about 1990. In the 1990s risk management is being applied to many diverse disciplines. In each discipline, the basic concepts of identifying, analyzing, planning, and controlling risks are used, although the terminology and procedures vary among disciplines. Figure 1 shows a suitable structure for risk management in a software development environment (adapted from [Boehm89]). As illustrated there, risk assessment is distinguished from risk control.

## Risk Assessment (Risk Identification, Risk Analysis, and Risk Prioritization)

Risk Assessment deals with determining the threats to a project, with particular emphasis placed on identifying, analyzing, and prioritizing major risk factors that might become problems.

The three explicit steps of Risk Assessment involve (i) identifying risk factors so that they are brought to the attention and understanding of senior engineers, managers, and customers; (ii) analyzing the risk factors so that numerical values can be assigned to the risk impacts, probabilities, and cost and benefits of alternative courses of action; and (iii) determining which risk factors have the highest priority for the expenditure of time and effort (money) to reduce their probabilities and/or impacts.

## Risk Identification

The techniques of risk identification rely on expertise and experience to identify specific risk factors for a project. Risk identification techniques include:

- risk-factor checklists
- cause-effect diagrams
- development process audits and capability assessments
- decomposition of plans to determine task dependencies
- decomposition of the design to find technical risk factors
- investigation of interface details
- examination of assumptions and decision drivers
- worst case scenarios
- group consensus techniques
- prototyping
- benchmarking
- simulation and modeling

Risk identification is improved by relying on past experience, often in the form of checklists (sometimes structured and quantified with weightings from historical data). The most useful checklists are those derived from local experience.

Customers and users, in addition to managers, lead engineers, and the development staff, need to be involved in the risk identification process. When a number of different organizations are involved in a development project, it is necessary to integrate the different perceptions—technical and organizational—of the different parties.

## Risk Analysis

The primary issue in risk analysis is developing solid, numerical values for the probabilities and impacts of various risk factors. These numbers can be developed by examining historical data, by using cost estimation tools, and by converting expert judgment into numbers (for instance, Low -> $0<P<0.3$; Medium -> $0.3<P<0.7$; High -> $0.7<P<1.0$).

Risk analysis techniques to be used depend on the types of risks being considered:

- *Risk of technical failure.* Techniques for analyzing technical risks include performance modeling, decision analysis, and cost-benefit analysis. Influence diagrams (fishbone or Ishikawa diagrams) can be used to identify areas of insufficient technical information. Various types of modeling, including simulation, benchmarking, and prototyping, can be used to analyze technical risk factors.
- *Risk of cost failure.* Techniques for analyzing cost risks include algorithmic cost models [Fairley93] and analysis of project assumptions. Monte Carlo simulation can be used to provide statistical ranges of cost based on probability distributions for the cost drivers [Fairley94].
- *Risk of schedule failure.* Techniques for analyzing schedule risks include algorithmic scheduling models, critical path methods, and PERT analysis. Probabilistic techniques, such as PERT and Monte Carlo simulation can provide ranges of probabilities for achieving various project milestones (including project completion) based on probabilistic values for the duration of the individual project tasks and the sequencing dependencies among those tasks.
- *Risk of operational failure.* Techniques for analyzing the risk of operational failure include performance modeling, reliability modeling, and quality factor analysis. By operational failure, we mean the risk that a project may produce a system that does not satisfy operational needs (that is, it does not possess the functional, performance, or other quality attributes the customer and users want and need). By operational risk, we do not mean the risk of hazard from a system in operation. Hazard is an intrinsic property or condition of a system that has the potential to cause an accident (hazard analysis constitutes a separate body of knowledge).

A risk factor may correspond to a single event, to a number of discrete events (any one of which may occur), or to a continuous distribution of possible events. Assessing the probabilities of discrete events and deriving probability distributions for continuous events is the most difficult part of risk analysis. Techniques available for determining these probabilities include expert judgment (especially expert group consensus techniques such as the Wideband Delphi technique), historical data, analogy, worst-case analysis, and what-if analysis. In many cases, these techniques provide a constructive framework for quantifying guesses (which is not all bad, provided the guesses are educated guesses). The best techniques are based on analysis of recorded data from past projects in the local environment.

## Risk Prioritization

The purpose of risk prioritization is to choose,

from the list of identified risk factors, a prioritized subset of manageable proportions. The obvious choices for the most important risk factors are, theoretically, those with the largest risk exposures. In practice, however, the decision is more complex.

The following are some factors to consider in selecting the risk items to be included the prioritized list:

- Size of the risk exposure of the risk factor relative to the size of the target
- Size of the risk exposure of the risk factor relative to the largest risk exposure of any risk factor.
- Confidence level of the risk assessor in the reliability of the risk assessment carried out for the risk factor.
- Risk exposure range (ER), where:

  $RER = (RE_{maximum} - RE_{minimum})/RE_{nominal}$

  and $Re_{maximum}$, $Re_{minimum}$, and $RE_{nominal}$ are the largest, smallest, and nominal values of risk exposures among the identified risk factors. Projects having a wide risk exposure range require careful prioritization of the list. It is not necessary to perform a detailed risk analysis for a project having a small estimate range, provided the risk assessors have adequate confidence in their estimates.
- Compound risks—a risk factor that is conditioned on another risk factor that is of high priority should also be ranked high on the list.
- Maximum number of risk factors that can be interpreted and acted upon.

In selecting the risk factors to place on the prioritized list, we must not forget the objective, which is to choose those risk factors that are primary candidates for 1) immediate risk-abating actions (rather than waiting until they later become problems) or 2) are of such concern that contingency plans should be developed to trigger explicit actions should they become problems (that is, when a risk indicator metric crosses a predetermined threshold, such as a schedule delay of more than two weeks or a performance shortfall of more than 100 milliseconds).

The prioritized list is a dynamic subset of the total list of risk factors. Risk assessment should be a continuous, on-going activity, and both the total list and the prioritized, managed list will change as the project progresses. Risk factors will disappear as their threat vanishes, new risks will be identified, and risk exposures will change with the passage of time or as the result of reducing or eliminating the risks.

## Risk Control (Risk Abatement Strategies, Risk Mitigation Planning, Risk Mitigation)

The conceptual basis of risk control, as in all control theory, is the feedback loop. Initial action plans are executed to reduce risk, and contingency plans are developed to trigger further risk-mitigating actions upon occurrence of certain events. As a project progresses, the operation is monitored to verify that risk factors are indeed being controlled and, if not, the project is redirected as appropriate, thus closing the control loop. The controller is the project manager who works with the project team to meet project targets by assessing risk and acting on the prioritized risk factors to protect against their possible consequences.

Risk control depends on the risk assessment procedures put in place at the beginning of a project. It is difficult to incorporate risk control into a project that has encountered problems as a result of the lack of risk assessment. The three explicit steps of risk control are (1) determining the best strategies for abating assessed risks, (2) producing risk mitigation plans, and (3) mitigating risks.

## Risk Abatement Strategies

In choosing where to expend effort, time, and money on risk-reducing activities, we need to first consider areas where we do not know enough about the risks involved—or even do not know what we don't know—and proceed to gain information by prototyping, simulation, surveys, benchmarks, reference checks, examining local history, consulting experts, and so on.

In dealing with known, assessed risks there are three strategies for risk abatement:

- *Risk avoidance*, for example, by reducing functionality or performance requirements, or buying more hardware—thus eliminating the source of the risk.
- *Risk transfer*, for example, by reallocating functionality or performance requirements into hardware, moving complexity into the human element, subcontracting to specialists, or realigning authority and responsibility.
- *Risk acceptance,* by which a risk factor is acknowledged, and responsibility accepted by all affected parties, with the understanding that the accepted risk will be explicitly managed and that, in spite of our best efforts, the project might encounter significant difficulties.

Risk transfer can be a risky strategy. If, for example, there is significant risk that a specialty subcontractor may fail to deliver a satisfactory component, that problem (should it materialize) will affect the outcome of the project. We must take care to distinguish risk transfer situations from those where we retain responsibility for the outcome and those where the transfer of risk results in a transfer of responsibility as well.

Risk abatement strategies are often based on expert judgment and local experience. For example, Figure 4 illustrates the top-ten risk factors identified by Boehm in his work environment at TRW, along with risk management techniques for abating those risks [Boehm89]. Depending on your work environment, the relative priorities among the risk factors in Figure 4 (and others not on the list) may be different. For example, item 6 in Figure 4 might be the most difficult risk factor in your environment; lack of well defined development processes (not on the list in Figure 4) might be a significant risk factor in your environment.

The costs as well as the benefits of alternative courses of action must be considered; it is not sensible to spend more on risk reduction than the cost to fix the resulting problem, should it materialize. The cost incurred is the cost of the risk-reducing action and the benefit gained is the reduction of risk exposure that results from the action. Cost/benefit decisions can be based on calculations of risk reduction leverage, where:

Risk Reduction Leverage = $(RE_{Before} - RE_{After})$/Risk Reduction Cost

$RE_{Before}$ is the risk exposure before initiating the risk reduction activity and $RE_{After}$ is the risk exposure afterwards.

In addition to providing a rationale for choosing among alternative courses of action, risk reduction leverage can be used to decide "How much is enough?" when an activity is seen to be good (such as reviews and tests at every stage of product development) but very expensive when carried to extremes. It is clear that difficult decisions will only be made early enough and firmly enough when the risk reduction leverage calculations have sufficient credibility to support those decisions.

## Risk Mitigation Planning

It is important to coordinate and reconcile the effects of various risk mitigation plans on the schedule and planned utilization of resources. This is typically done by developing the risk management plan and the risk abatement strategies and then comparing the initial risk exposure for the project to the adjusted risk exposure, taking into account the effect of the proposed risk reduction plans and their associated costs.

For example, on a project having a budget of $1M and a risk factor having an original risk exposure of $500K, implementing various risk mitigation strategies and plans, at a cost of $100K, might reduce the adjusted risk exposure to $50K. The project now has a budget/plan of, effectively, $900K with a risk exposure of $50K, which is a much less risky project. However, some other risk exposures may have increased due to the budget reduction for some of the tasks; they will have to be re-estimated or the lowest-priority requirements may have to be eliminated. Iterative reworking of all the action plans and contingency plans must be accomplished. Also note that real technical insight and real re-estimation is required, not just some playing around with risk exposure numbers.

| RISK ITEM | RISK REDUCTION TECHNIQUE |
|---|---|
| 1. Personnel shortfalls | Staffing with top talent; job matching; team building; training; prescheduling key people |
| 2. Unrealistic schedules and budgets | Multisource estimates; design to cost; software reuse; requirements scrubbing |
| 3. Wrong software functions | Mission analysis; Ops-Concept; user surveys; prototyping; early users' manual |
| 4. Wrong user interface | Operational scenarios; prototyping; task analysis; user characterization |
| 5. Gold plating | Requirements scrubbing; prototyping; cost/benefit analysis; design to cost |
| 6. Continuing changes in requirements | High change threshold; information hiding; incremental development (defer changes to later) |
| 7. Shortfalls in externally supplied components | Benchmarking; inspections; reference checking; compatibility analysis |
| 8. Shortfalls in externally performed tasks | Reference checking; preaward audits; award-fee contracts; competitive design or prototyping; teambuilding |
| 9. Real-time performance shortfalls | Simulation; benchmarking; modeling; prototyping; instrumentation; tuning |
| 10. Straining computer science capabilities | Technical analysis; cost/benefit analysis; prototyping; reference checking |

*Figure 4. A Checklist of Software Risk Items and Risk Reduction Techniques*

If systematic risk management is to be used to control risks to a project, then the estimates on which the project plan is based should not be padded for contingency. Estimates should be based on expected costs, with the assumptions clearly defined. This provides a baseline cost estimate for the project.

Each chance of an assumption being invalid is treated as a risk factor, with assessed probability and cost/schedule impact. For a high risk project, it is highly probable that the project cannot be completed within the baseline cost estimate; an extra budgetary reserve is necessary for successful project completion. The size of this reserve is usually more a matter for negotiation than true analysis based on risk exposure. Having been agreed to and allocated to the project manager's budget, this reserve is usually referred to as the "management reserve." The reserve is used by the project manager to support implementation of risk management plans and to cover unforeseen eventualities (the unknown unknowns) which require resource expenditure. A similar procedure can be applied for schedule contingency.

The management reserve can, in theory, be defined statistically to cover a reasonable percentage of the costs that would be required to deal with foreseeable project uncertainties—the 'known unknowns'. In practice, this reserve is usually negotiated downward, which creates an additional risk; that is, the risk of insufficient funds for the risk management plans. Also, having been allocated to the project, the reserve does not have the senior management's immediate attention. Major schedule delays may be introduced when the project manager has to finally go back and ask for more money or time.

An alternative approach is for the agreed-to reserve to be held outside the project (by the customer or senior management) even though inalienably committed to the project. When the project manager needs to call on the reserve, a case must be made that the perceived risk can be best mitigated by an action involving expenditure from the reserve. This encourages, in fact ensures, continuing communication between the project manager and the funding organization on the basis of management of risk.

In financial terms, the total unmitigated risk exposure for the project can be calculated from the sum of the risk exposures for all identified risk factors. The reduced risk exposure is calculated following the risk reduction activities, using the costs of those activities and the resulting risk exposure for each risk factor (calculated from the probability of occurrence and the cost impact). The resulting total risk exposure is compared with the project budget, profit margin, and commercial exposure for the organization. This can form the basis of effective communication with senior management, financial controllers, and the customer.

However, this approach treats total risk exposure in only its simplest form (a summation assumes that the cost and schedule impacts of each risk factor are independent; this may or may not be a valid assumption). More detailed analysis of interdependencies among risk factors may be required.

Decision makers also need information on the time element. The potential loss caused by a schedule delay may happen as a lump sum at a point in time, it may have a pattern of expenditure, or there may be a choice on the timing of actions, and there will be predictions of occurrence of external events. Similarly, the proposed courses of action to reduce or prevent the loss will have time-based costs and triggers for decisions which themselves will be timed (perhaps related to the reporting and decision-making processes). The combination of possibilities can be expressed as a time-based cash flow. Thus risk exposure may need to be shown as a time-based graph, or a series of graphs.

## Risk Mitigation

According to the taxonomy presented in Figure 1, risk mitigation includes risk monitoring, problem resolution, and risk reassessment. If adequate risk assessment and risk reduction are accomplished at the start of a project and on a continuing basis, then, as the project progresses, the action plans and contingency plans actions should, for the most part, have the intended effect of mitigating the risk factors.

Risk monitoring (and reporting) on a regular, continuing basis have the goals of identifying risks that are about to become, or have become, problems, determining whether risks and problems are being successfully resolved, and gaining insight to identify new risk factors as they arise.

Two useful techniques for risk monitoring and reporting are Risk Item Tracking Forms and Top-Ten Risk Lists. Figures 5 and 6 provide an example of a risk item tracking form. This form consists of two parts: the risk item registry and the risk mitigation progress report. As illustrated in Figure 5, the risk registry form provides fields for identifying a risk factor, describing it, assessing it, and developing a mitigation plan to control it. The risk status and date fields provide a mechanism for tracking the progress of risk resolution. As illustrated at the bottom of Figure 5, there are several possible Risk Status Values. Figure 6 illustrates a mechanism for tracking progress on working the mitigation plan identified in Figure 5 by date and the responsible party. As indicated in Figure 6, there are several possible status values for the mitigating action.

| RISK NO: | TITLE: | STATUS | DATE |
|---|---|---|---|
| Risk Item Description:<br><br>Author____________Date______ | | | |
| Assessment/Alternatives Considered:<br><br>Risk Owner____________Date______ | | | |
| Mitigation Plan:<br><br>Planned Manager's<br>Start Date____________Approval__________Date____________ | | | |

Possible Risk Status Values:

IDENTIFIED
ASSESSED
PLANNED
CONTINGENT
PROBLEM
CRISIS
RESOLVED
CLOSED

*Figure 5. Risk Item Tracking Form*

| DATE | MITIGATION STATUS | ACTIONS COMPLETED | NEXT ACTIONS TO BE TAKEN | BY WHOM |
|---|---|---|---|---|
| | | | | |
| | | | | |
| | | | | |
| | | | | |
| | | | | |
| | | | | |
| | | | | |
| | | | | |
| | | | | |
| | | | | |
| | | | | |

Possible Risk Mitigation Status Values:

PLANNED
CONTINGENT
AUTHORIZED
IN PROGRESS
LATE
FAILED
ALTERNATIVE PLAN
SUCCEEDED
UNNECESSARY
OVERTAKEN BY EVENTS
INCORPORATED IN PROJECT PLAN

*Figure 6. A Risk Mitigation Tracking Form*

Risk items to be included in the risk registry can be brought to the attention of lead engineers, project managers, and other decision makers using one or more "Top-Ten Risk Item Lists." A Top-Ten List is illustrated in Figure 7. In some organizations, Top-Ten lists are used at all levels, from the individual development team, to the subsystem manager, to the project manager, to the department manager, to the vice-president, to the customer/developer interface. Each group has a different list, depending on their responsibilities; for example, the project manager's list is a prioritized aggregation of top ten reports from the team leaders plus other risks at the project level; the department manager's list includes a prioritized aggregation of project managers' lists and other risks at the department level, and so forth. Reporting is upward through the management chain. If possible, a risk factor is mitigated within the group that identifies it, and reported to the next level. A risk that cannot be mitigated within the bounds of authority of the group that identifies it is promoted to the next level for mitigation.

Each item on a top-ten risk list should have a corresponding risk item tracking form, as illustrated in Figures 5 and 6. The top-ten list should be updated, and the status of risk tracking reviewed weekly at the team and project levels. In the absence of severe risks and problems, the lists at the department level and higher levels should be reviewed and updated monthly.

The term "Top-Ten" implies exactly ten risk items at each reporting level, but in fact, there is no particular best size for the reported list. If the true number of risk items is less than ten, then the report should concentrate on what is important without padding out the list. Ten serious risk items is about as many as a group can cope with, but if there are genuinely more, each should be reported, together with one further item that indicates there are so many risk factors that the project may be in serious trouble.

Communication at the senior management and customer levels using risk, including financial impact in terms of risk exposure, is much more effective than attempting to report progress against deterministic plans. Progress reporting against plans, and updates to plans, must still be done, but that should underpin the dominant theme of reporting in terms of risk. Attempting to communicate with senior management and the customer only on the basis of progress against plans is inadequate for high risk projects (which includes most software projects).

Risk Reassessment is a continuous process. The risk management control loop depends on risk monitoring which leads to corrective action, risk reassessment, and adjustments to risk management plans to stay in control of the evolving risk factors. Further iterations through full risk assessment will be needed on an ad-hoc basis as new risks arise, as well as at regularly scheduled intervals.

## Implementation of Risk Management at the Organizational Level

Organizations that deal with advanced technology are increasingly mandating risk management plans on their development projects—the key driver being the use of systematic risk management as a means of relating technical and team/process risks at the project level to company/consortium/customer/commercial/mission risk. Communications with senior management and the customer that are based on risk enables them to understand the financial and strategic implications of risky technical undertakings in a way that they could not before. Understanding risks in financial and strategic terms also provides a basis for risk sharing between the developer and the customer.

Organizations that successfully introduce risk management incorporate:

- Explicit definition of their development and management processes
- Communication based on risk
- Risk reporting to senior management
- A corporate policy for risk management on projects that includes:
    - risk management plans developed at the planning stage of a project and incorporated into the overall project plan
    - project-specific tailoring of the development process and the risk reduction and risk control techniques to be used
    - risks explicitly reviewed on a regular, on-going basis

Deming's principles teach us that improvements must be based on analyzing how the work is done (that is, the development and management processes) rather than merely analyzing the resulting products. This applies not only to quality and productivity, but also to successful risk management [Deming86].

Documenting the development process implies level three of the SEI process maturity model [Humphrey89] and an engineering infrastructure with codes of practice supported by standards, procedures, and training. SEI Level 3 is the first level at which tool support is introduced to support the process (as opposed to tool support for activities within the process). Without tool support, it is only rarely and with difficulty that there is much communication outside

| RANK THIS WEEK | RANK LAST WEEK | WEEKS ON LIST | RISK ITEM | POTENTIAL CONSEQUENCE | RISK RESOLUTION PROGRESS |
|---|---|---|---|---|---|
| 1 | 4 | 2 | Replacement for sensor-control software team leader | Delay in coding with lower quality - less reliable operation | Desired replacement unavailable |
| 2 | 6 | 2 | Requested changes in user interface | Will delay delivery date if not finished for demo next week | Two additional people assigned and working |
| 3 | 2 | 5 | Compiler problem | Delay in completing coding of hardware drivers | New release of compiler appears to solve most problems but must be fully checked out |
| 4 | 3 | 6 | Availability of work stations for system test | Delay in software system testing | Procurement delay being discussed with vendor |
| 5 | 5 | 3 | Hardware test-bed definition | Must be completed by end of month to avoid system integration delay | Work being completed; review meeting is scheduled |
| 6 | 1 | 3 | Fault tolerance requirements impact on performance | Performance problem could require major change to hw/sw architecture with severe impact on schedule and budget | Latest prototype demonstrates performance within specifications but fault tolerance still to be determined |
| 7 | - | 1 | Delay in specification of tele-comm interface | Could delay procurement of hardware subsystem for integration | Meeting scheduled to consider alternatives |
| 8 | 8 | 4 | Unavailability of technical editor | Insufficient time to produce high quality manuals | Staffing requirement placed with job agency |
| - | 7 | 4 | CM assistant needed | Inadequate support for increasing workload | Experienced CM assistant has joined team on full-time basis |
| - | 9 | 5 | Inability to reuse database software | Increase in planned development effort | Uncertainty resolved in latest prototype |

*Figure 7. Example of a Top-Ten Risk Item Report*

the various project teams on how the work is being done and the risks being identified and mitigated.

## Summary

The use of risk management as a common basis for communication at all levels throughout an organization provides for:

- identifying risks
- systematic risk analysis (putting numbers on probabilities and impacts)
- prioritizing risks and evaluating alternative courses of action for risk reduction
- developing risk abatement strategies
- developing action plans and contingency plans for accepted risks
- systematic monitoring and control of accepted risks
- on-going identification of new risk factors
- routine reporting of progress in terms of risk in addition to reporting progress against the project plan
- linkage from project level risks to company/customer/commercial/mission risks

Accepting risk-oriented reporting indicates new corporate attitudes about risk management. Our earlier discussion of the time-based effects of decisions and cash-flow in terms of risk penalty can also be portrayed in terms of probability of benefit as the result of decisions, actions, or expenditures (opportunity being the converse of risk).

In many organizations the effective application of risk management depends on highly motivated individuals who understand risk management and who hold key positions in the organization. It is our hope that, in the future, risk management will become a routine way of doing business at all levels and in all organizations rather than the special domain of a concerned few.

## Acknowledgment

The first draft of this paper was prepared by Paul Rook before his untimely death. He is missed as a friend and colleague.

## References

[Boehm89] B.W. Boehm, *Tutorial on Software Risk Management*, IEEE Computer Society Press, Los Alamitos, Calif., 1989.

[Boehm93] B.W. Boehm, *Tutorial on Software Process Models and Software Cost Models,* 8th Int'l COCOMO Meeting, Pittsburgh, Oct 1993.

[Charette89] R.N. Charette, *Software Engineering Risk Analysis and Management,* McGraw-Hill, New York, 1989.

[Charette90] R.N. Charette, *Application Strategies for Risk Analysis*, McGraw-Hill, New York, 1990.

[Deming86] W.E. Deming, *Out of the Crisis,* Cambridge, Mass., MIT Center for Advanced Engineering Study, 1986.

[Fairley91] R.E. Fairley, *Risk Management of Software Projects Tutorial,* at 13th ICSE Conference, Austin, 1991.

[Fairley93a] R.E. Fairley, "A Case Study in Managing Technical Risks for Software Projects," *Proc. 2nd SEI Risk Conf.,* 1993.

[Fairley93b] R.E. Fairley, "How Software Cost Models Deal with Risk," *Proc. 4th ESCOM Conf.,* 1993.

[Fairley94] R.E. Fairley, "Risk Management for Software Projects," *IEEE Software*, Vol. 11, No. 3, 1994.

[Humphrey89] W.S. Humphrey, *Managing the Software Process,* Addison Wesley, Reading, Mass., 1989.

# Chapter 11

# Software Development Process

## 1. Introduction to Chapter

A *life cycle model* is a model of the phases or activities that start when a software product is conceived and end when the product is no longer available for use. It depicts the relationships among the major milestones, baselines, reviews, and project deliverables that span the life of the system. The software life cycle typically includes a requirements phase, design phase, implementation (coding and unit testing) phase, integration and testing phase, installation and checkout phase, operation and maintenance phase, and, sometimes, retirement phase. Depending on the life cycle selected, these phases or activities may occur once in a prescribed sequence, or may occur several times in varying sequence.

The first software life cycle model was the "waterfall model," developed by Dr. Winston W. Royce. His original model is shown in Figure 11.1. This and other life cycle models are described in the papers in this chapter.

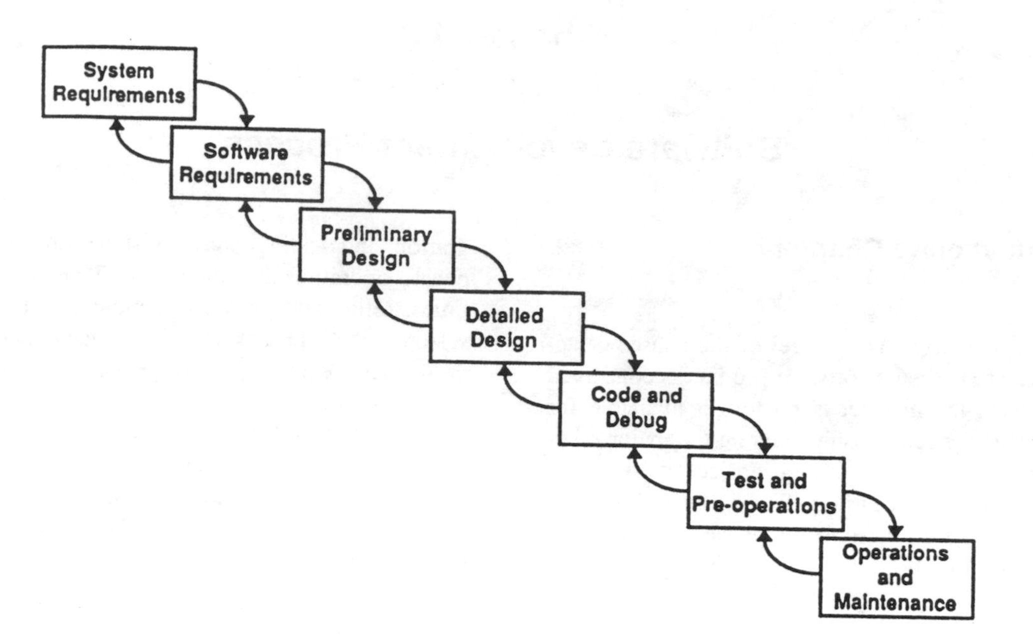


*Figure 11.1. Waterfall model*

A *process model* is a description of the sub-activities or tasks within a phase or activity, the dependencies among them, and the conditions that must exist before the tasks can begin or be considered complete. The process model may also include information about the performer(s) of a sub-activity or task. A process model can thus be considered as a more detailed statement of a life cycle model. Hence, any number of process models can be compatible with one life cycle model and, if the activities that make up two or more life cycle models are the same or similar, a process model may support more than one life cycle model.

## 2. Introduction to Papers

The first paper in this chapter is an overview of life cycle models by Edward Comer entitled "Alternative Life Cycle Models." The word alternative is used to separate the models discussed by Comer from the conventional or classical models based on Royce's Waterfall model. Comer describes the conventional life cycle models as well as the original Waterfall model. Because of the growing complexity of software systems, many practitioners feel the need to have different life cycle models available than the conventional requirements, design, implementation, and testing model.

These alternative models are radically different from the conventional model and include such approaches as rapid prototyping, incremental development, evolutionary prototyping, the reuse of previously developed software, and automated software synthesis. Comer points out that many of these alternative models are not yet standardized and are still being developed. (It should be noted that the current US Mil-Std 498, "Software Development and Documentation," recognizes, among others, three life cycle models: the conventional Waterfall, the incremental, and evolutionary development.) Comer's paper also discusses in summary form Barry Boehm's spiral model (see next paper).

The second paper, "A Spiral Model of Software Development and Enhancement," by Barry Boehm, was, when published, a revolutionary new look at the software development life cycle. An earlier version of this paper was presented by Boehm at a workshop on software requirements in early 1985. The spiral is a more general software development model than those typically in use today and treats as special cases the waterfall and other popular software development paradigms. (Boehm has referred to the spiral model as a "process model generator"—given the conditions and constraints of a particular software development project, the Spiral Model can be used to generate the correct process for that project.)

Whereas the waterfall is "documentation driven," the spiral model focuses on risk management. At the completion of each phase or major activity of software development, the spiral model prompts the developers to review objectives, alternatives, and constraints, to evaluate alternatives and risks, and to determine the nature of the next phase (prototyping, specification-driven, and so forth).

The third and final paper in this chapter is by Mark Paulk, Bill Curtis, and Mary Beth Chrissis of the Software Engineering Institute (SEI) and Charles Weber of Loral Federal Systems (formerly IBM Federal Systems and now part of Lockheed Martin). The paper is an update of a 1993 article [1] that introduced the SEI's Capability Maturity Model for Software (CMM), Version 1.1, and described its rationale and contents. During development of CMM Version 1.1, Weber was a resident affiliate at the SEI.

The CMM, and the process improvement efforts it fostered, represents perhaps the most important real change in the past 20 years in the way large-scale, mission-critical software is developed. Until the mid-1980s, efforts to improve the quality of software products and the cost and schedule of developing the products were focused almost entirely on technology (methods and tools) and people (hiring, educating, and training). A third aspect, the process by which software is developed and maintained, was neglected; its recognition as a factor of equal importance to the other two is largely due to the SEI.

The CMM is the result of about seven years of work on quantitative methods by which a software developer, or a potential customer of that developer, could determine the maturity of the developer's process. The US Department of Defense (DoD) sponsored the SEI's work; the SEI in turn convinced the DoD that process maturity should be a factor in the selection of contractors to develop software for DoD.

The CMM defines five levels of process maturity through which a software developer must move in order to become truly effective:

1. Initial (ad hoc, chaotic; process not defined and followed)
2. Repeatable (basic software management processes in place, defined and followed at the project level)
3. Defined (standard process defined at organization [company or division] level and tailored for use by projects)
4. Managed (measurements taken and used to improve product quality)
5. Optimizing (measurements used to improve process; error prevention)

The CMM has become a driving force in the US and elsewhere in the world for the improvement of software development processes. Many companies and US government agencies strive to improve their software engineering through the use of the goals and activities associated with this model. At the present time, achievement of Level 3 is the goal of many development organizations, although some have achieved Level 4 and a handful are reported to be at Level 5.

1. Paulk, Mark C., Bill Curtis, Mary Beth Chrissis, and Charles V. Weber, "Capability Maturity Model, Version 1.1," *IEEE Software*, Vol. 10, No. 4, July 1993, pp. 18–27.

# Alternative Software Life Cycle Models

Edward R. Comer
*Software Productivity Solutions, Melbourne, Florida*

*The classic waterfall model for the software life cycle (See Fig. 2.3.1) was defined as early as 1970 by Dr. Winston Royce [1] to help cope with the growing complexity of the aerospace software products being tackled. During the past 5–10 years, alternative, radically different life cycle models have been proposed, including rapid throwaway prototypes, incremental development, evolutionary prototypes, reusable software, and automated software synthesis. Although most of these alternatives are still maturing, many of their aspects have been integrated with the basic life cycle model to form hybrid life cycle models. In fact, the most recent life cycle models are actually hybrid models, including DoD-STD-2167A [2], the NASA Information System Life Cycle [3], and Barry Boehm's Spiral Model [4]. The following sections define a software life cycle model, introduce alternative life cycle models, and present an approach for contrasting and evaluating alternative life cycle models.*

## Introduction

Software development, for any application, is an expensive and risky endeavor. Critical software errors often remain in deployed software systems. Software maintenance is expensive and, too, error-prone. The software development process is often ad hoc and chaotic.

Aerospace systems offer special challenges for embedded software that make its development even more difficult, such as real-time, multi-mission, distributed, or autonomous.

The classic waterfall model for the software life cycle (see Figure 2.3.1) was defined as early as 1970 by Dr. Winston Royce [1] to help cope with the growing complexity of the aerospace software projects being tackled. With several years of experience with developing software for spacecraft mission planning, commanding and post-mission analysis, Dr. Royce had experienced different degrees of success with respect

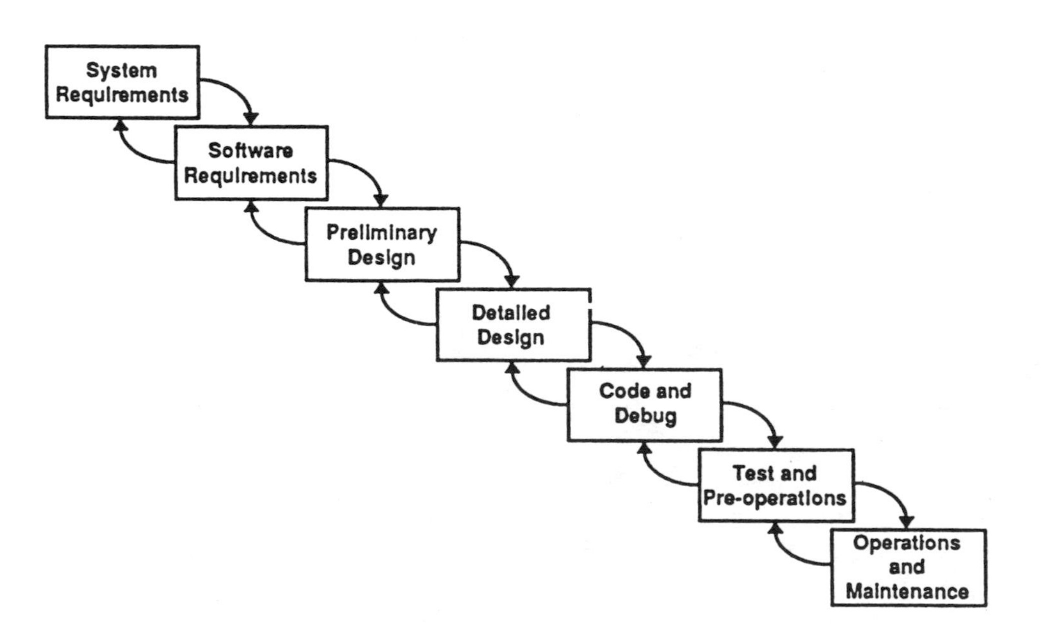


*Figure 2.3.1 Waterfall life cycle model of software development*

to "arriving at an operational state, on-time, and within costs" [1]. The resulting sequence of steps that he outlined, with various refinements and minor modifications, became the road map for the software development process for the last two decades.

During the past five to ten years, alternative, radically different life cycle models have been proposed, including rapid throwaway prototypes, incremental development, evolutionary prototypes, reusable software, and automated software synthesis. While most of these alternatives are still maturing, many of their aspects have been integrated with the basic life cycle model to form hybrid life cycle models. In fact, the most recent life cycle models are actually hybrid models, including DOD-STD2167A [2], the NASA Information System Life Cycle [3], and Barry Boehm's Spiral Model [4].

The following sections define a software life cycle model, introduce alternative life cycle models, and present an approach for contrasting and evaluating alternative life cycle models.

## Definition of a Life Cycle Model

While the concept of a life cycle of software development is well known in the aerospace community, there are numerous misconceptions about its intent and purpose. A life cycle model is not a definition of the process a software development organization follows; the actual process is typically far more complex and includes many activities not depicted in the life cycle model. A life cycle model is not a methodology; it does not provide rules or representations for development.

Instead, we define a software life cycle model to be a *reference model* for a software development process, in the same manner that the Open Systems Interconnection (OSI) model [5] is a reference model for protocols for computer system communication. Such a reference model:

1. provides a common basis for the definition and coordination of specific project and organization software process standards, allowing these standards to be placed into perspective within the overall life cycle reference model;
2. describes the major functions, or activities, involved in software development and the terms used to define those functions;
3. highlights important aspects or features that are deemed to be important for common understanding and focus.

While a life cycle model is insufficient to represent a definition of a software development process, or to describe the methodologies applied for software development, it does serve as a reference model for these processes and methodologies. Indeed, the intent of standard DoD [2] and NASA [3] life cycles is to provide a common framework for contractor-specific processes and methodologies.

## Alternative Life Cycle Models

### Waterfall Model

The waterfall model documented in 1970 by Royce [1] and later refined by Boehm [6] in 1976 is the most popular and proven of the alternative life cycles. Figure 2.3.1 illustrates a waterfall model, defining the major steps, or phases, and their approximate sequence. A *phase* consists of a set of activities to accomplish the goals of that phase [3]. Additional arrows are added to represent the inherent feedback that occurs between these phases.

Most software development processes in aerospace corporations or mandated by governmental agencies have followed some basic variation of the waterfall model, although there are a variety of different names for each of the phases. Thus, the requirements phase is often called user needs analysis, system analysis, or specification; the preliminary design phase is often called high-level design, top-level design, software architectural definition, or specification; the detailed design phase is often called program design, module design, lower-level design, algorithmic design, or just plain design, etc.

In 1984, McDermid and Ripkin [7] noted that waterfall life cycle models, such as depicted in Figure 2.3.1, are too simple and abstract to deal with an embedded software development project's problem of developing, adopting, or assembling a coherent methodology. Their variant of the waterfall model, shown in Figure 2.3.2, highlights several important issues:

1. The level and purpose of the various representations are identified.
2. Activities are viewed as transformations from high level representations to low level representations.
3. Verification within a representation and between representations is explicitly shown.
4. Iterations around representations occur, as errors are discovered and changes are identified; this includes both fine and coarse iterations.

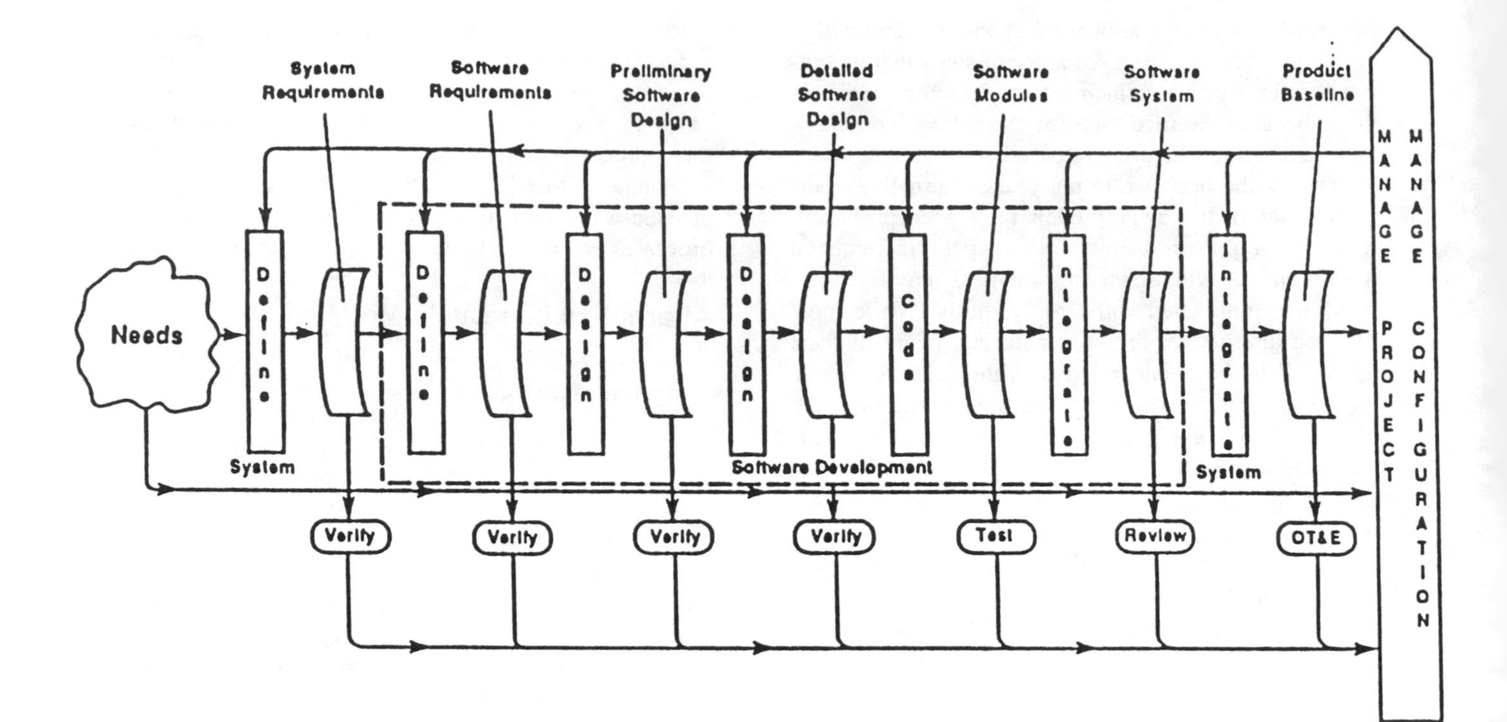


*Figure 2.3.2 Another view of the waterfall model [7]*

5. Project and configuration control is a special activity; this problem is compounded the presence of iteration.

Development processes based upon the waterfall model have been commonplace for aerospace software development. The use of a waterfall life cycle model:

1. encourages one to specify what the system is supposed to do (i.e., to define the requirements) before thinking about how to build the system (i.e., designing);
2. encourages one to plan how components are going to interact (i.e., designing) before building the components (i.e., coding);
3. enables project managers to track progress more accurately and to uncover possible slippages early;
4. demands that the development process generate a series of documents which can later be utilized to test and maintain the system;
5. enables the organization that will develop the system to be more structured and manageable.

Much of the motivation behind waterfall life cycle models was to provide structure to avoid the problems of the "undisciplined hacker" [6].

**Rapid, Throwaway Prototypes**

The rapid, throwaway prototype, made popular by Gomaa and Scott [8] in 1981, focuses on ensuring that the software product being proposed really meets the users' needs. Difficulties are often experienced using a waterfall model in the initial step of deriving a requirements specification:

1. Requirements specification documents have problems with correctness, completeness and ambiguity.
2. Errors in requirements specification are usually the last to be detected and the most costly to correct.
3. There is a communication gap between the software system developer and the user. This results in difficulties of the developer truly understanding the user's needs and difficulties of the user in understanding and approving a requirements specification.

Gomaa and Scott found that both the quality of the requirements specification and the communication of user needs can be improved by developing a prototype of the proposed system [8].

The approach is to construct a "quick and dirty" partial implementation of the system prior to (or during) the requirements phase. The potential users utilize this prototype for a period of time and supply feedback to the developers concerning its strengths and weaknesses. This feedback is then used to modify the software requirements specification to reflect the real user needs.

At this point, the developers can proceed with the actual system design and implementation with confidence that they are building the "right" system (except in those cases where the user needs evolve). An extension of this approach uses a series of throwaway prototypes [6], culminating in full-scale development.

**Incremental Development**

Incremental development [9] is the process for constructing a partial, but deployment-ready, implementation build of a system and incrementally adding increased functionality or performance. Two variants of this approach, shown in Figure 2.3.3, differ only in the level of requirements analysis accomplished at the start. One approach is only to define the requirements for the immediate next build, the other is to initially define and allocate the requirements for all builds.

Incremental development has received government recognition as an acceptable, or even desirable, alternative to the classic waterfall life cycle. Such an approach has been proposed in a 1987 Joint Logistics Commanders (JLC) guidebook for command and control systems [10] and discussed in the NASA Information System Life Cycle and Documentation Standards [3] for their aerospace applications.

An incremental development approach reduces the costs incurred before an initial capability is achieved and defines an approach for the "incremental definition, funding, development, fielding, support and operational testing of an operational capability to satisfy the evolving requirement" [10]. It also produces an operational system more quickly, and it thus reduces the possibility that the user needs will change during the development process.

Experience with the incremental development life cycle for aerospace applications has shown that the approach provides better visibility into the development to better assess progress and has been shown to decrease risk and to increase reliability and productivity in the development process [3]. The approach is compatible with the philosophy of "build a little, test a little" that is popular in the Ada community. Incremental development does require the use of a flexible system architecture to facilitate incremental enhancement and expansion [10] and increases the configuration management support required during the development process [3].

**Evolutionary Prototypes**

Evolutionary prototyping extends the concept of incremental development to its ultimate conclusion, viewing the software life cycle as a set of numerous prototypes that are evolved through successive experimentation and refinement to meet the user's needs. The approach, described by Giddings in 1984 [11], addresses the inherent problem of truly satisfying user needs and the problem of evolving a software system as the needs of the application domain change. This aspect can be important for many applications, including aerospace systems, that have a very long operational life time, often two or three decades.

In an evolutionary prototyping life cycle, shown in Figure 2.3.4, the developers construct a partial implementation of the system which meets known requirements. The prototype is then experimentally used by its users in order to understand the full requirements better. The usage observations are analyzed and used as the basis for the next evolution of the prototype. This cycle continues until a prototype is considered by the users to be acceptable for operational deployment. Future evolution of the application requirements can be addressed by continuing this evolutionary development process.

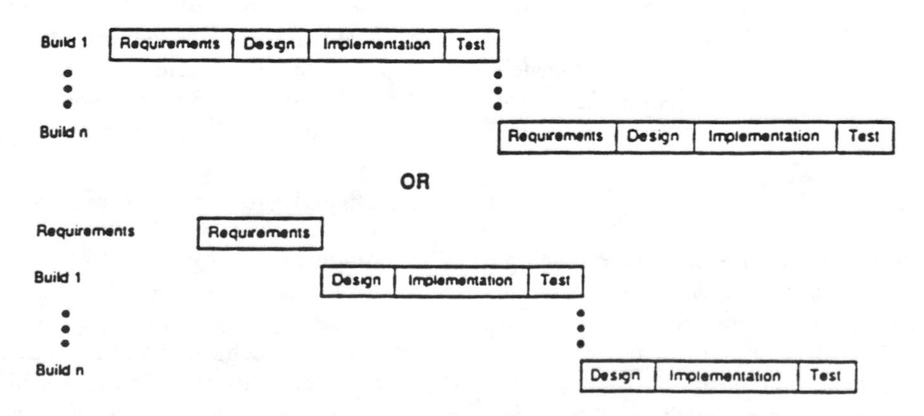


*Figure 2.3.3 Incremental development life cycle models*

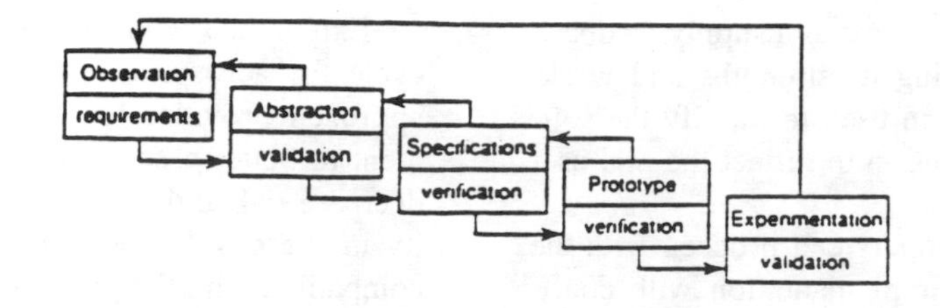


*Figure 2.3.4 Evolutionary prototyping life cycle [11]*

Whereas incremental development implies a high level of understanding of the requirements up front, implementing subsets of increasing capability, evolutionary prototyping implies that we do not know up front all of our requirements, but need to experiment with an operational system in order to learn them. Note that in the case of throwaway prototypes we are likely to implement only those aspects of the system that are poorly understood, but that in the case of evolutionary prototypes we are more likely to start with those system aspects that are best understood and thus build upon our strengths.

Evolutionary prototyping has challenges in scaling up to very large systems, ensuring process visibility and control, avoiding the negative effects of "information sclerosis," and avoiding the "'undisciplined hacker' approach that the waterfall and other models were trying to correct" [4]. Information sclerosis is a "syndrome familiar to operational information-based systems, in which temporary work-arounds for software deficiencies increasingly solidify into unchangeable constraints on evolution" [4].

For complex aerospace applications, it is not reasonable at this time to expect evolutionary application of prototypes to be particularly "rapid" because reliability, adaptability, maintainability, and performance (RAMP) are major forces behind making such system developments expensive and time-consuming. Since the technology is not yet available to *retrofit* RAMP requirements, they would have to be implemented up front, thus forcing software development costs high and schedules to their limit. Evolutionary prototypes will become more practical in the future as automated techniques for retrofitting RAMP requirements are developed [12].

**Reusable Software**

Whereas prototyping attempts to reduce development costs through partial implementations leading to a better understanding of requirements, reusable software is the discipline of attempting to reduce development costs by incorporating designs, programs, modules, and data into new software products [13]. Because the emphasis of reusable software is on a different approach for constructing software rather than specifying it, the approach is compatible with prototyping approaches.

The software industry is guilty of continuously reinventing the wheel. Reusability has achieved only limited application, mostly in business applications. There are few tools available to help reuse software designs or code from previous projects. Clearly, what is needed are techniques to analyze application domains for reusability potential, create reusable components, techniques, and tools to store and retrieve reusable components, and component specification and classification techniques to help catalog and locate relevant components. The net effect of reusing components would be shorter development schedules (by using wheels rather than reinventing them) and more reliable software (by using components that been previously "shaken down").

A life cycle incorporating reusable software is a major objective of the government's Ada initiative. Many of the features of the language supporting abstract data types and generics are designed to directly support the development and effective usage of reusable modules.

The most significant work in reusable software for aerospace applications is the Common Ada Missile Packages (CAMP) effort [14]. In a multi-phased Air Force program, McDonnell Douglas provided a comprehensive demonstration of a reusable software life cycle. The effort accomplished a domain analysis of missile software, identified commonalities of that application, specified and constructed a set of over 200 Ada "parts," developed tools to support reusability, and finally accomplished a missile software development using the developed reusable software parts.

**Automated Software Synthesis**

Automated software synthesis is a term used to describe the automated transformation of formal requirements specifications into operational code [15]. Such an approach, shown in Figure 2.3.5, relies heavily on automated tools. Formal specifications are created and maintained by users using specification tools. The formal specifications become prototypes for the

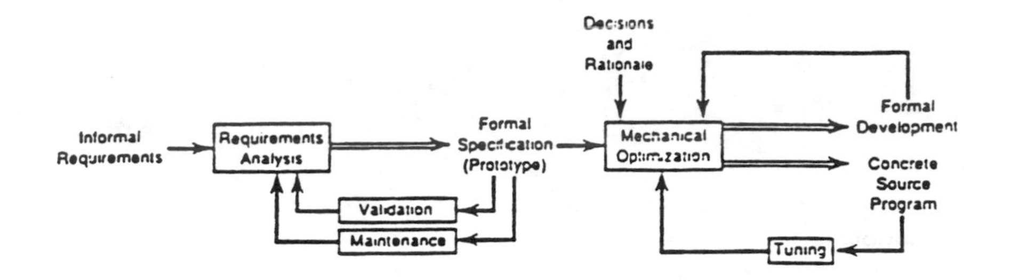


*Figure 2.3.5 Automated software synthesis life cycle [15]*

desired system that are used to refine the specification. Implementation of a production software system is accomplished using a highly automated transformational programming approach from the formal specification.

Transformational programming [16] is a methodology of program construction by successive application of transformation rules. The individual transitions between the various versions of the program are made by applying correctness-preserving transformation rules, stating with the formal specification. It is guaranteed that the final version of the program will satisfy the initial specification.

Fully automatic transformation clearly is best. Unfortunately, such a solution may not be feasible because of the wide gap between high-level specification languages and implementations. A partially automated solution is more feasible, in the form of an automated assistant. [15]

Automated software synthesis is an active research area [16]. To become practical for aerospace applications, there are two significant technologies that must be matured: tools for derivation of formal specifications using informal specifications and prototyping, and tools for automatic transformation of formal specifications into optimized code. Both are still highly experimental.

User derivation and maintenance of a specification, rather than code, has many advantages. The user as the systems analyst, with the aid of prototyping via an executable specification, can completely and accurately determine what the system will do and evolve the system as the application requirements change. Because implementations can be easily transformed from updated specifications, enhancement can be accomplished easier and more frequently; "it will stay 'soft' and modifiable rather than become ossified and brittle with age" [15].

## Evaluation of Alternative Life Cycle Models

It is difficult to compare and contrast these new models of software development because their disciples often use different terminology, and the models often have little in common except their beginnings (marked by a recognition that a problem exists) and ends (marked by the existence of a software solution). This section provides a framework originally described by Davis et al. in 1988 [12] which can serve 1) as a basis for analyzing the similarities and differences among alternative life cycle models; 2) as a tool for software engineering researchers to help describe the probable impacts of a new life cycle model; and 3) as a means to help software practitioners decide on an appropriate life cycle model to utilize on a particular project or in a particular application area.

### Life Cycle Model Evaluation Paradigm

For every application beyond the trivial, user needs are constantly evolving. Thus, the system being constructed is always aiming at a moving target. This is the primary reason for delayed schedules (caused by trying to make the software meet a new requirement it was not designed to meet) and software that fails to meet customer expectations (because the developers "froze" the requirements and failed to acknowledge the inevitable changes).

Figure 2.3.6 shows graphically how users' needs evolve over time. It is recognized that the function shown is neither linear nor continuous in reality. Please note that the scale on the X axis is not shown (the units can be either months or years), but could be assumed to be nonuniform, containing areas of compression and expansion. The units of the scale on the Y axis are also not shown, but are assumed to be some measure of the amount of functionality (such as DeMarco's "Bangs for the Buck" [17]). However, none of the observations made are dependent on either the uniformity of the axes or the linearity or continuity of the curve shown in Figure 2.3.6.

Figure 2.3.7 shows what happens during a conventional waterfall life cycle software development. At time $t_0$, a need for a software system is recognized and a development effort commences with relatively incomplete knowledge of the real user needs. At time

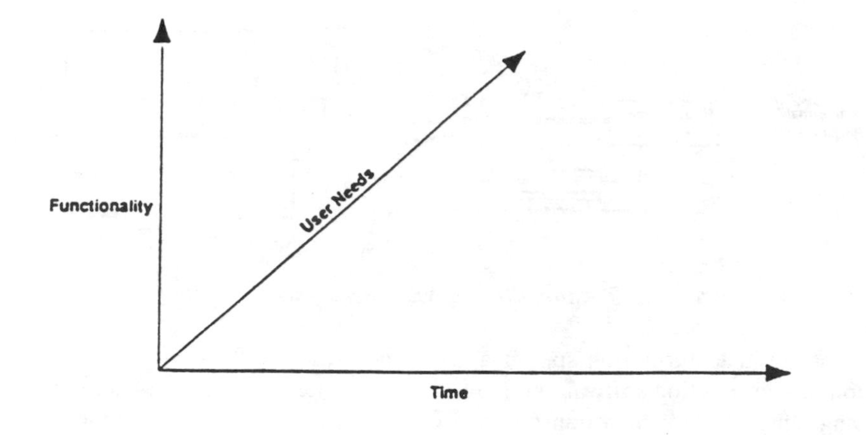


*Figure 2.3.6 Constantly evolving user needs [12]*

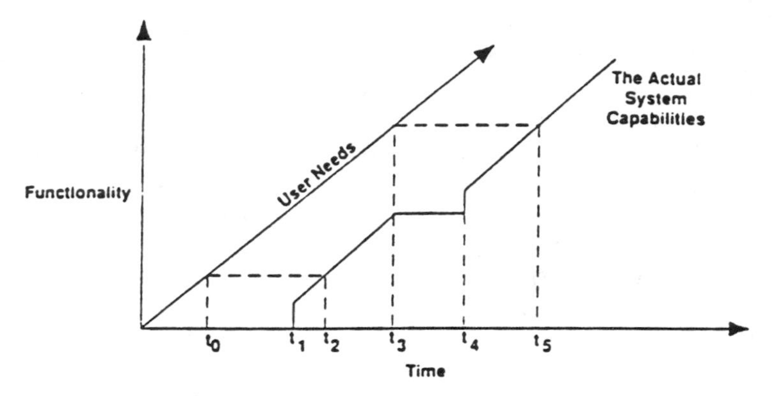


*Figure 2.3.7 Evaluation of waterfall model in satisfying evolving user needs [12]*

$t_1$, the development effort has produced an operational product, but not only does it not satisfy the current $t_1$ needs, it does not even satisfy the old $t_0$ needs because of a poor understanding of those needs in the first place. The product now undergoes a series of enhancements (between times $t_1$ and $t_3$), which eventually enable it to satisfy the original requirements (at $t_2$) and then some. At some later point in time $t_3$, the cost of enhancement is so great that the decision is made to build a new system (once again based on poorly understood requirements), development of the product is completed at time $t_4$, and the cycle repeats itself.

A number of useful metrics can now be defined based on the paradigm defined above. These metrics can later be used to compare and contrast sets of alternative life cycle approaches. These metrics are portrayed graphically in Figure 2.3.8 and are described below [12].

1. A *shortfall is* a measure of how far the operational system, at any time *t*, is from meeting the actual requirements at time *t*. This is the attribute that most people are referring to when they ask "Does this system meet my needs?"
2. *Lateness is* a measure of the time that elapses between the appearance of a new requirement and its satisfaction. Of course, recognizing that new requirements are not necessarily implemented in the order in which they appear, lateness actually measures the time delay associated with achievement of a level of functionality.
3. The *adaptability* is the rate at which the software solution can adapt to new requirements, as measured by the slope of the solution curve.
4. The *longevity* is the time a system solution is adaptable to change and remains viable, i.e., the time from system creation through the time it is replaced.
5. *Inappropriateness* is the shaded area between the user needs and the solution curves in Figure 2.3.8 and thus captures the behavior of

shortfall over time. The ultimately "appropriate" model would exhibit a zero area, meaning that new requirements are instantly satisfied.

Each of the alternative life cycle models defined earlier is now analyzed with respect to the paradigm described above.

### Rapid, Throwaway Prototypes

The use of a rapid throwaway prototype early in the development life cycle increases the likelihood that customers and developers will have a better understanding of the real user needs that existed at time $t_0$. Thus, its use does not radically affect the life cycle model per se, but does increase the impact of the resulting system. This is shown in Figure 2.3.9, where the vertical line (i.e., the increase in functionality provided by the system upon deployment) at time $t_1$ is longer than in the waterfall approach.

Figure 2.3.9 also shows the rapid prototype itself as a short vertical line providing limited and experimental capability soon after time $t_0$. There is no reason to believe that the length of time during which the product can be efficiently enhanced without replacement is any different than with the waterfall approach. Therefore, this period of time for the rapid prototype-based development (i.e., $t_3$ minus $t_1$) is shown in Figure 2.3.9 the same as for the waterfall developed product.

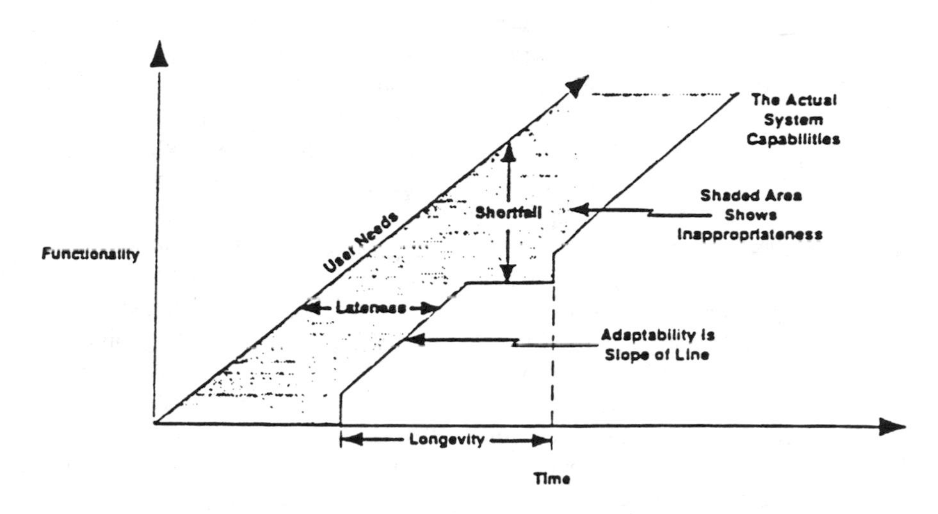


*Figure 2.3.8 Life cycle evaluation metrics [12]*

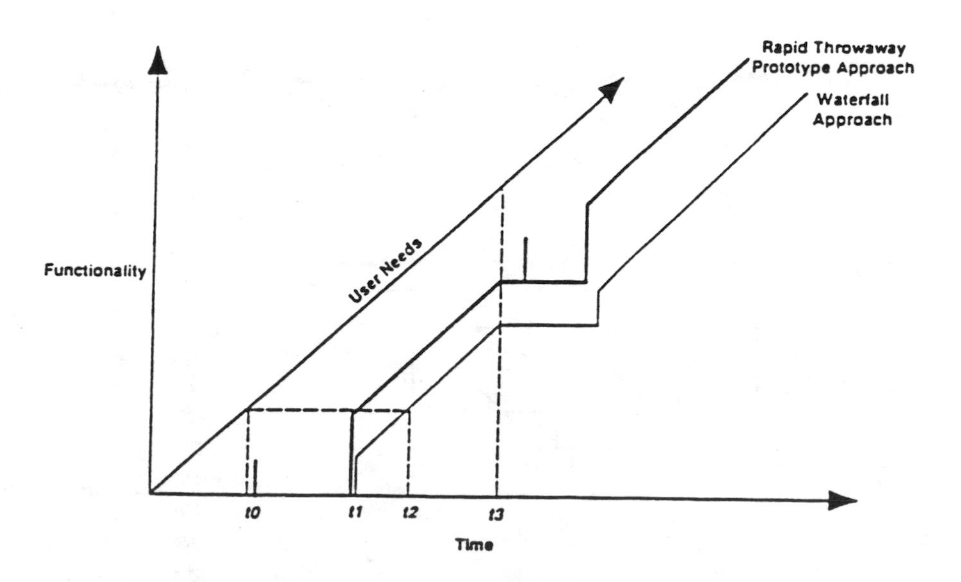


*Figure 2.3.9 Comparison of rapid prototyping vs waterfall life cycle [12]*

### Incremental Development

When using incremental development, software is deliberately built to satisfy fewer requirements initially, but is constructed in such a way as to facilitate the incorporation of new requirements and thus achieve higher adaptability. This approach has two effects: 1) the initial development time is reduced because of the reduced level of functionality, and 2) the software can be enhanced more easily and for a longer period of time.

Figure 2.3.10 shows how this approach compares to the waterfall life cycle. Note that the initial development time is less than for the waterfall approach, that the initial functionality (A) is less than for the waterfall approach (B), and that the increased adaptability is indicated by a higher slope of the curve A-C than that for the waterfall approach (line B-D). The stair-step aspect of the graph indicates a series of well-defined, planned, discrete builds of the system.

### Evolutionary Prototypes

This approach is an extension of the incremental development. Here, the number and frequency of operational prototypes increases. The emphasis is on evolving toward a solution in a more continuous fashion, instead of by a discrete number of system builds.

With such an approach, an initial prototype emerges rapidly, presumably demonstrating functionality where the requirements are well understood (in contrast to the throwaway prototypes, where one usually implements poorly understood aspects first) and providing an overall framework for the software. Each successive prototype explores a new area of user need, while refining the previous functions. As a result, the solution evolves closer and closer to the user needs (see Figure 2.3.11). In time, it too will have to be redone or undergo major restructuring in order to continue to evolve.

As with the incremental development approach, the slope (line A-C) is steeper than in the waterfall approach (line B-D) because the evolvable prototype was designed to be far more adaptable. Also, the line A-C in Figure 2.3.7 is not stepped like line A-C in Figure 2.3.6 because of the replacement of well-defined and well-planned system "builds" with a continuous influx of new, and perhaps experimental, functionality.

### Reusable Software

Reuse of existing software components has the potential to decrease the initial development time for software significantly. Figure 2.3.12 shows how this approach compares to conventional waterfall development. No parameters are changed, except for the development times.

### Automated Software Synthesis

In the ultimate application of this approach, as an engineer recognizes the requirements, these are specified in some type of formal specification and the system is automatically synthesized. This approach has two dramatic effects: 1) the development time is greatly reduced, and 2) the development costs are reduced so much that adapting "old" systems is rarely more meritorious than resynthesizing the entire system. Thus, the longevity of any version is low, and the

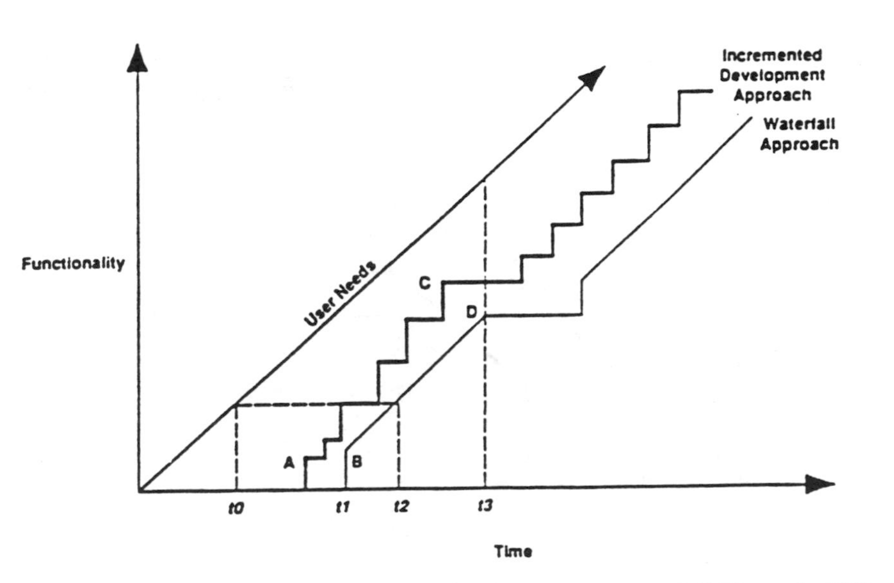


*Figure 2.3.10 Comparison of incremental development vs waterfall life cycle [12]*

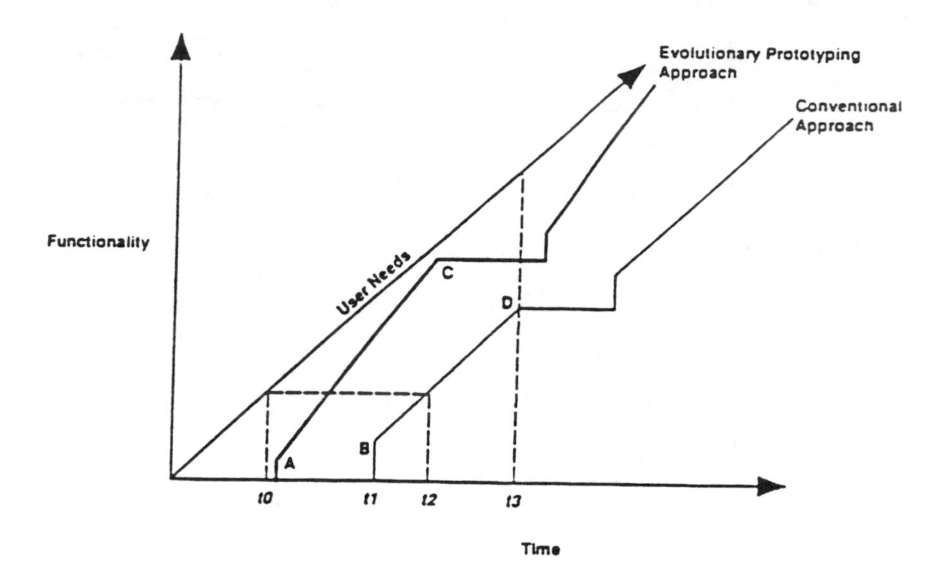


*Figure 2.3.11 Comparison of evolutionary prototyping vs waterfall life cycle [12]*

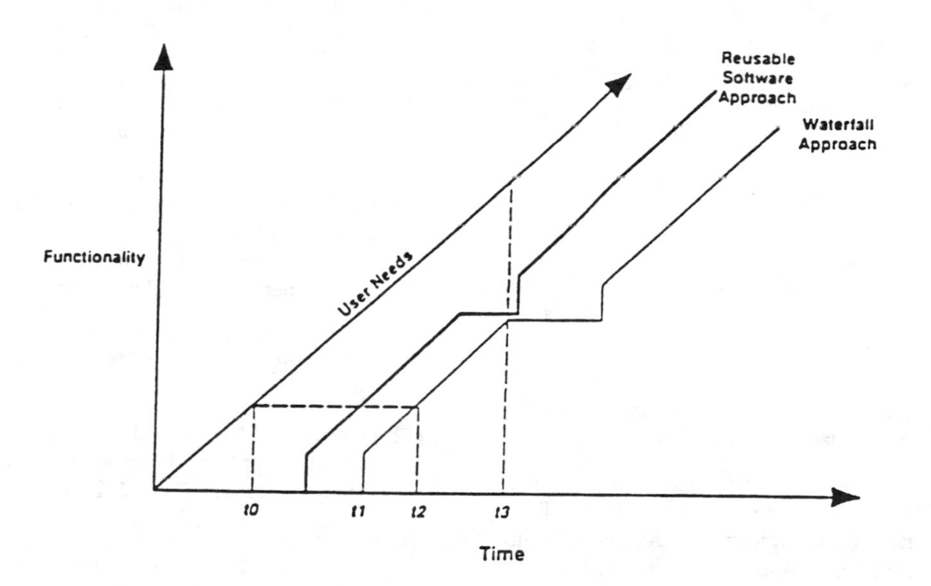


*Figure 2.3.12 Comparison of reusable software vs waterfall life cycle [12]*

result is a stair-step graph, as shown in Figure 2.3.13, where the horizontal segments represent the time the system is utilized and the time needed to upgrade the requirements. The vertical segments represent the additional functionality offered by each new generation.

## Defining, Selecting, or Adapting a Life Cycle Model

The various life cycle alternatives reflect different approaches for improving the software development process. The life cycle model evaluation paradigm [12] provides insight into how we might define, select or adapt a life cycle model to improve our process.

Currently, many project managers make this selection based on fuzzy perceptions and past experiences or blindly follow life cycle standards. The evaluation paradigm presented points to some application aspects that should affect selection of a life cycle approach:

1. requirements volatility (that is, the likelihood that the requirements will change);
2. the "shape" of requirements volatility (such as discrete leaps, based on brand new threats; or gradual changes, as with a need to do things faster);
3. the longevity of the application; and

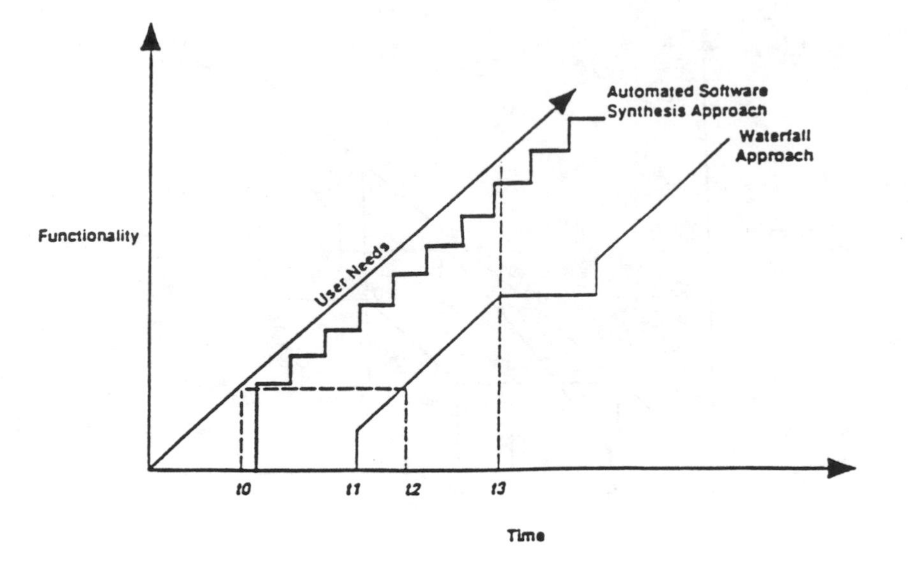


*Figure 2.3.13 Comparison of automated software vs waterfall life cycle [12]*

4. the availability of resources to develop or effect changes (i.e., it may be easier to get resources up front than to devote significant resources for enhancements).

## References

[1] Royce, W.W., "Managing the Development of Large Software Systems: Concepts and Techniques," *1970 WESCON Technical Papers,* Vol. 14, Western Electronic Show and Convention, 1970.

[2] *Defense System Software Development,* DOD-STD-2167A Military Standard, Feb. 29, 1988.

[3] *Information System Life Cycle and Documentation Standards,* Release 4.3, NASA Office of Safety, Reliability, Maintainability, and Quality Assurance, Software Management and Assurance Program (SMAP), Washington, D.C., Feb. 28, 1989.

[4] Boehm, B.W., "A Spiral Model of Software Development and Enhancement," *ACM SIGSOFT Software Eng. Notes,* Vol. 11, No. 4, Aug. 1986, pp. 14–24.

[5] Information Processing Systems—Open Systems Interconnection (OSI)--Basic Reference Model, International Standards Organization ISO-7498-1984, Oct. 15, 1984.

[6] Boehm, B.W., "Software Engineering," *IEEE Trans. Computers,* Vol. C-25, Dec. 1976, pp. 1226–1241.

[7] McDermid, J. and Ripken, K., *Life Cycle Support in the Ada Environment,* Cambridge University Press, Cambridge, UK, 1984.

[8] Gomaa, H. and Scott, D., "Prototyping as a Tool in the Specification of User Requirements," *Proc. 5th IEEE Int'l Conf. Software Eng.*, 1981, pp. 333–342.

[9] Hirsch, E., "Evolutionary Acquisition of Command and Control Systems," *Program Manager*, Nov-Dec 1985, pp. 18–22.

[10] Joint Logistics Commanders Guidance for the Use of an Evolutionary Acquisition (EA) Strategy in Acquiring Command and Control Systems, Defense Systems Management College, Fort Belvoir, VA, 1987.

[11] Giddings, R.V., "Accommodating Uncertainty in Software Design," *Comm. ACM*, Vol. 27, No. 5, May 1984, pp. 428–434.

[12] Davis, A.M., Bersoff, E.H., and Comer, E.R., "A Strategy for Comparing Alternative Software Development Life Cycle Models," *IEEE Trans. Software Eng.,* Vol. 14, No. 10, Oct. 1988, pp. 1453–1461.

[13] Jones, T.C., "Reusability in Programming: A Survey of the State of the Art," *IEEE Trans. Software Eng.,* Vol. SE-10, Sept. 1984, pp. 488–494.

[14] McNicholl, D.G., Palmer, C., and Cohen, S., *Common Ada Missile Packages (CAMP),* Vol. I and II, McDonnell Douglas, AFATL-TR-85-93, May 1986.

[15] Balzer, R., Cheatham, T.E., Jr., and Green, C., "Software Technology in the 1990's: Using a New Paradigm," *Computer,* Nov. 1983, pp. 39–45.

[16] Partsch, H. and Steinbruggen, R., "Program Transformation Systems," *ACM Computing Surveys,* Vol. 16, No. 3, Sept. 1983, pp. 199–236.

[17] DeMarco, T., *Controlling Software Projects,* Yourdon Press, New York, 1982.

# A Spiral Model of Software Development and Enhancement

**Barry W. Boehm, TRW Defense Systems Group**

*"Stop the life cycle—I want to get off!"*
*"Life-cycle Concept Considered Harmful."*
*"The waterfall model is dead."*
*"No, it isn't, but it should be."*

These statements exemplify the current debate about software life-cycle process models. The topic has recently received a great deal of attention.

*The Defense Science Board Task Force Report on Military Software*[1] issued in 1987 highlighted the concern that traditional software process models were discouraging more effective approaches to software development such as prototyping and software reuse. The Computer Society has sponsored tutorials and workshops on software process models that have helped clarify many of the issues and stimulated advances in the field (see "Further reading").

The spiral model presented in this article is one candidate for improving the software process model situation. The major distinguishing feature of the spiral model is that it creates a *risk-driven* approach to the software process rather than a primarily *document-driven* or *code-driven* process. It incorporates many of the strengths of other models and resolves many of their difficulties.

This article opens with a short description of software process models and the issues they address. Subsequent sections outline the process steps involved in the spiral model; illustrate the application of the spiral model to a software project, using the TRW Software Productivity Project as an example; summarize the primary advantages and implications involved in using the spiral model and the primary difficulties in using it at its current incomplete level of elaboration; and present resulting conclusions.

**This evolving risk-driven approach provides a new framework for guiding the software process.**

## Background on software process models

The primary functions of a software process model are to determine the *order of the stages* involved in software development and evolution and to establish the *transition criteria* for progressing from one stage to the next. These include completion criteria for the current stage plus choice criteria and entrance criteria for the next stage. Thus, a process model addresses the following software project questions:

(1) What shall we do next?
(2) How long shall we continue to do it?

Consequently, a process model differs from a software method (often called a methodology) in that a method's primary focus is on how to navigate through each phase (determining data, control, or "uses" hierarchies; partitioning functions; allocating requirements) and how to represent phase products (structure charts; stimulus-response threads; state transition diagrams).

Why are software process models important? Primarily because they provide guidance on the order (phases, increments, prototypes, validation tasks, etc.) in which a project should carry out its major tasks. Many software projects, as the next section shows, have come to grief because they pursued their various development and evolution phases in the wrong order.

**Evolution of process models.** Before concentrating in depth on the spiral model, we should take a look at a number of others: the code-and-fix model, the stagewise model and the waterfall model, the evolutionary development model, and the transform model.

*The code-and-fix model.* The basic model used in the earliest days of software

Reprinted from *Computer*, Vol. 21, No. 5, May 1988, pp. 61–72.

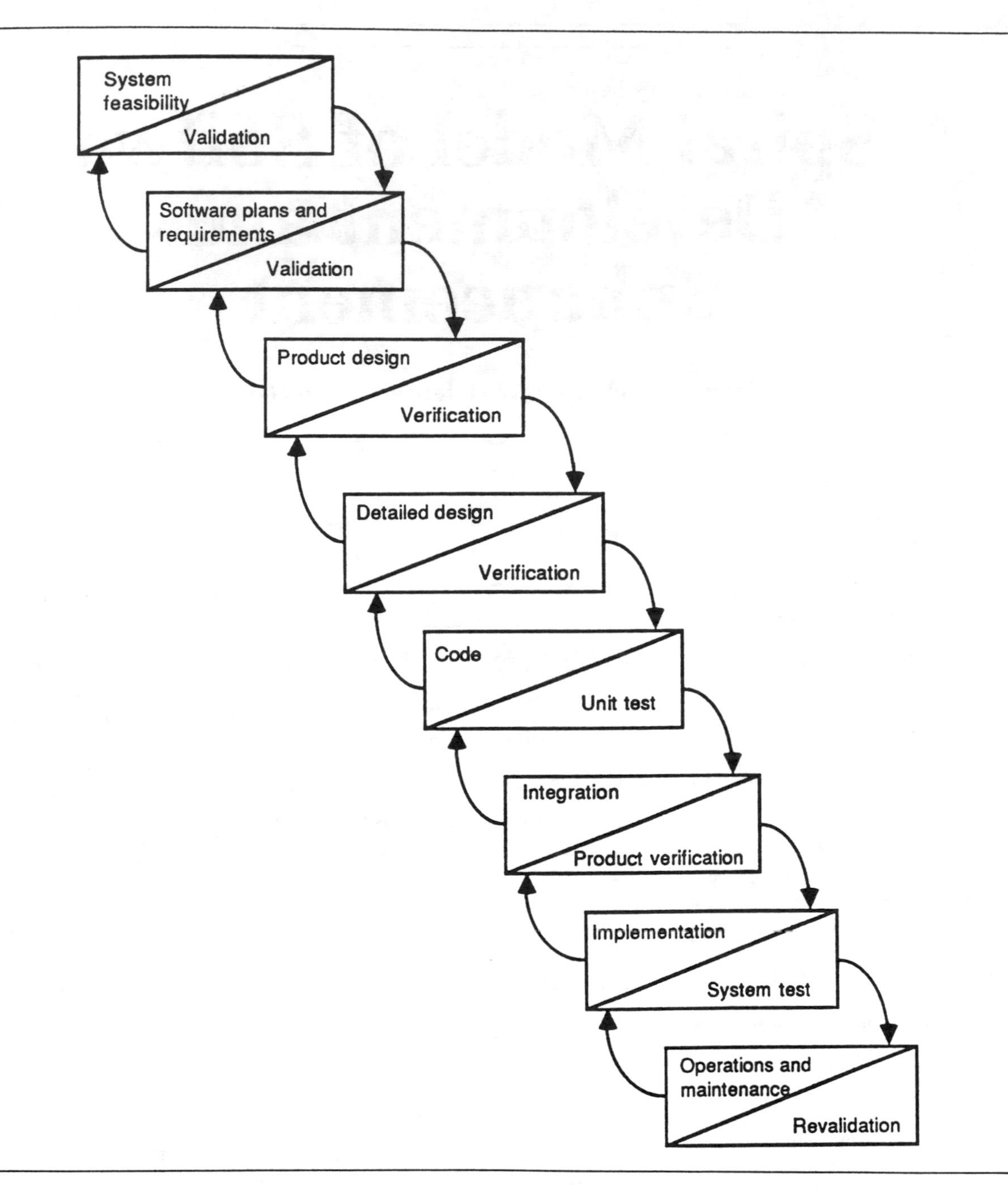


**Figure 1. The waterfall model of the software life cycle.**

development contained two steps:

(1) Write some code.

(2) Fix the problems in the code.

Thus, the order of the steps was to do some coding first and to think about the requirements, design, test, and maintenance later. This model has three primary difficulties:

(a) After a number of fixes, the code became so poorly structured that subsequent fixes were very expensive. This underscored the need for a design phase prior to coding.

(b) Frequently, even well-designed software was such a poor match to users' needs that it was either rejected outright or expensively redeveloped. This made the need for a requirements phase prior to design evident.

(c) Code was expensive to fix because of poor preparation for testing and modification. This made it clear that explicit recognition of these phases, as well as test-and-evolution planning and preparation tasks in the early phases, were needed.

*The stagewise and waterfall models.* As early as 1956, experience on large software systems such as the Semi-Automated Ground Environment (SAGE) had led to the recognition of these problems and to the development of a stagewise model[2] to address them. This model stipulated that software be developed in successive stages (operational plan, operational specifications, coding specifications, coding, parameter testing, assembly testing, shakedown, system evaluation).

The waterfall model,[3] illustrated in Figure 1, was a highly influential 1970 refinement of the stagewise model. It provided two primary enhancements to the stagewise model:

(1) Recognition of the feedback loops between stages, and a guideline to confine the feedback loops to successive stages to minimize the expensive rework involved in feedback across many stages.

(2) An initial incorporation of prototyping in the software life cycle, via a "build it twice" step running in parallel with requirements analysis and design.

The waterfall model's approach helped eliminate many difficulties previously encountered on software projects. The waterfall model has become the basis for most software acquisition standards in government and industry. Some of its initial difficulties have been addressed by adding extensions to cover incremental development, parallel developments, program families, accommodation of evolutionary changes, formal software development and verification, and stagewise validation and risk analysis.

However, even with extensive revisions and refinements, the waterfall model's basic scheme has encountered some more fundamental difficulties, and these have led to the formulation of alternative process models.

A primary source of difficulty with the waterfall model has been its emphasis on fully elaborated documents as completion criteria for early requirements and design phases. For some classes of software, such as compilers or secure operating systems, this is the most effective way to proceed. However, it does not work well for many classes of software, particularly interactive end-user applications. Document-driven standards have pushed many projects to write elaborate specifications of poorly understood user interfaces and decision-support functions, followed by the design and development of large quantities of unusable code.

**The waterfall model has become the basis for most software acquisition standards.**

These projects are examples of how waterfall-model projects have come to grief by pursuing stages in the wrong order. Furthermore, in areas supported by fourth-generation languages (spreadsheet or small business applications), it is clearly unnecessary to write elaborate specifications for one's application before implementing it.

*The evolutionary development model.* The above concerns led to the formulation of the *evolutionary development* model,[4] whose stages consist of expanding increments of an operational software product, with the directions of evolution being determined by operational experience.

The evolutionary development model is ideally matched to a fourth-generation language application and well matched to situations in which users say, "I can't tell you what I want, but I'll know it when I see it." It gives users a rapid initial operational capability and provides a realistic operational basis for determining subsequent product improvements.

Nonetheless, evolutionary development also has its difficulties. It is generally difficult to distinguish it from the old code-and-fix model, whose spaghetti code and lack of planning were the initial motivation for the waterfall model. It is also based on the often-unrealistic assumption that the user's operational system will be flexible enough to accommodate unplanned evolution paths. This assumption is unjustified in three primary circumstances:

(1) Circumstances in which several independently evolved applications must subsequently be closely integrated.

(2) "Information-sclerosis" cases, in which temporary work-arounds for software deficiencies increasingly solidify into unchangeable constraints on evolution. The following comment is a typical example: "It's nice that you could change those equipment codes to make them more intelligible for us, but the Codes Committee just met and established the current codes as company standards."

(3) Bridging situations, in which the new software is incrementally replacing a large existing system. If the existing system is poorly modularized, it is difficult to provide a good sequence of "bridges" between the old software and the expanding increments of new software.

Under such conditions, evolutionary development projects have come to grief by pursuing stages in the wrong order: evolving a lot of hard-to-change code before addressing long-range architectural and usage considerations.

*The transform model.* The "spaghetti code" difficulties of the evolutionary development and code-and-fix models can also become a difficulty in various classes of waterfall-model applications, in which code is optimized for performance and becomes increasingly hard to modify. The transform model[5] has been proposed as a solution to this dilemma.

The transform model assumes the existence of a capability to automatically convert a formal specification of a software product into a program satisfying the specification. The steps then prescribed by the transform model are

- a formal specification of the best initial understanding of the desired product;
- automatic transformation of the specification into code;
- an iterative loop, if necessary, to improve the performance of the resulting code by giving optimization guidance to the transformation system;
- exercise of the resulting product; and
- an outer iterative loop to adjust the specification based on the resulting operational experience, and to rederive, reoptimize, and exercise the adjusted software product.

The transform model thus bypasses the difficulty of having to modify code that has become poorly structured through repeated reoptimizations, since the modifications are made to the specification. It also avoids the extra time and expense involved in the intermediate design, code, and test activities.

Still, the transform model has various

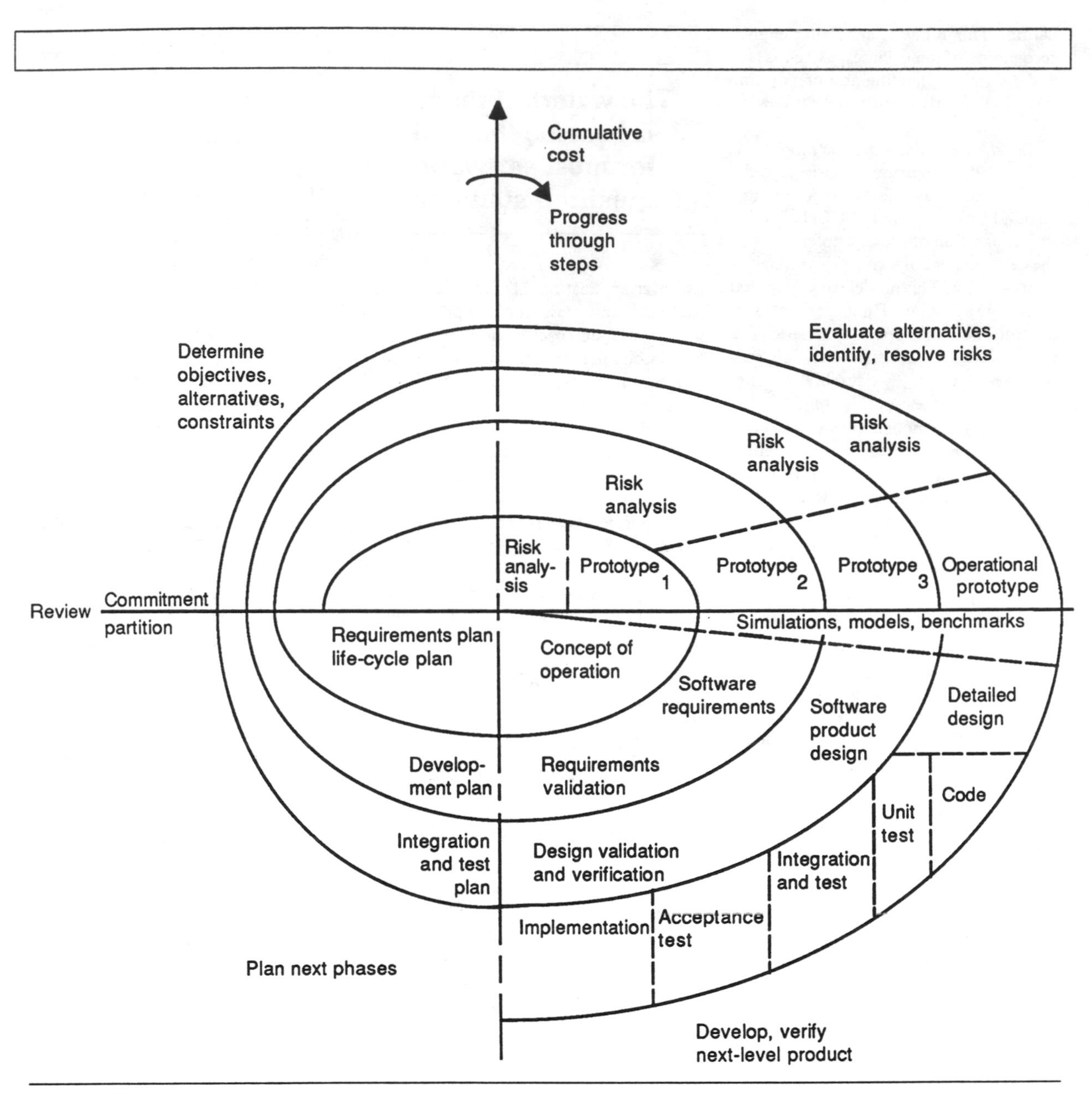


**Figure 2. Spiral model of the software process.**

difficulties. Automatic transformation capabilities are only available for small products in a few limited areas: spreadsheets, small fourth-generation language applications, and limited computer-science domains. The transform model also shares some of the difficulties of the evolutionary development model, such as the assumption that users' operational systems will always be flexible enough to support unplanned evolution paths. Additionally, it would face a formidable knowledge-base-maintenance problem in dealing with the rapidly increasing and evolving supply of reusable software components and commercial software products. (Simply consider the problem of tracking the costs, performance, and features of all commercial database management systems, and automatically choosing the best one to implement each new or changed specification.)

## The spiral model

The spiral model of the software process (see Figure 2) has been evolving for several years, based on experience with various refinements of the waterfall model as applied to large government software projects. As will be discussed, the spiral model can accommodate most previous models as special cases and further provides guidance as to which combination of previous models best fits a given software situation. Development of the TRW Software Productivity System (TRW-SPS), described in the next section, is its most complete application to date.

The radial dimension in Figure 2 represents the cumulative cost incurred in accomplishing the steps to date; the angular dimension represents the progress made in completing each cycle of the spiral. (The model reflects the underlying concept that each cycle involves a progression that addresses the same sequence of steps, for each portion of the product and for each of its levels of elaboration, from an overall concept of operation document down to the coding of each individual program.) Note that some artistic license has been taken with the increasing cumulative cost dimension to enhance legibility of the steps in Figure 2.

**A typical cycle of the spiral.** Each cycle of the spiral begins with the identification of

- the objectives of the portion of the product being elaborated (performance, functionality, ability to accommodate change, etc.);
- the alternative means of implementing this portion of the product (design A, design B, reuse, buy, etc.); and
- the constraints imposed on the application of the alternatives (cost, schedule, interface, etc.).

The next step is to evaluate the alternatives relative to the objectives and constraints. Frequently, this process will identify areas of uncertainty that are significant sources of project risk. If so, the next step should involve the formulation of a cost-effective strategy for resolving the sources of risk. This may involve prototyping, simulation, benchmarking, reference checking, administering user questionnaires, analytic modeling, or combinations of these and other risk-resolution techniques.

Once the risks are evaluated, the next step is determined by the relative remaining risks. If performance or user-interface risks strongly dominate program development or internal interface-control risks, the next step may be an evolutionary development one: a minimal effort to specify the overall nature of the product, a plan for the next level of prototyping, and the development of a more detailed prototype to continue to resolve the major risk issues.

If this prototype is operationally useful and robust enough to serve as a low-risk base for future product evolution, the subsequent risk-driven steps would be the evolving series of evolutionary prototypes going toward the right in Figure 2. In this case, the option of writing specifications would be addressed but not exercised. Thus, risk considerations can lead to a project implementing only a subset of all the potential steps in the model.

On the other hand, if previous prototyping efforts have already resolved all of the performance or user-interface risks, and program development or interface-control risks dominate, the next step follows the basic waterfall approach (concept of operation, software requirements, preliminary design, etc. in Figure 2), modified as appropriate to incorporate incremental development. Each level of software specification in the figure is then followed by a validation step and the preparation of plans for the succeeding cycle. In this case, the options to prototype, simulate, model, etc. are addressed but not exercised, leading to the use of a different subset of steps.

This risk-driven subsetting of the spiral model steps allows the model to accommodate any appropriate mixture of a specification-oriented, prototype-oriented, simulation-oriented, automatic transformation-oriented, or other approach to software development. In such cases, the appropriate mixed strategy is chosen by considering the relative magnitude of the program risks and the relative effectiveness of the various techniques in resolving the risks. In a similar way, risk-management considerations can determine the amount of time and effort that should be devoted to such other project activities as planning, configuration management, quality assurance, formal verification, and testing. In particular, risk-driven specifications (as discussed in the next section) can have varying degrees of completeness, formality, and granularity, depending on the relative risks of doing too little or too much specification.

An important feature of the spiral model, as with most other models, is that each cycle is completed by a review involving the primary people or organizations concerned with the product. This review covers all products developed during the previous cycle, including the plans for the next cycle and the resources required to carry them out. The review's major objective is to ensure that all concerned parties are mutually committed to the approach for the next phase.

The plans for succeeding phases may also include a partition of the product into increments for successive development or components to be developed by individual organizations or persons. For the latter case, visualize a series of parallel spiral cycles, one for each component, adding a third dimension to the concept presented in Figure 2. For example, separate spirals can be evolving for separate software components or increments. Thus, the review-and-commitment step may range from an individual walk-through of the design of a single programmer's component to a major requirements review involving developer, customer, user, and maintenance organizations.

**Initiating and terminating the spiral.** Four fundamental questions arise in considering this presentation of the spiral model:

(1) How does the spiral ever get started?
(2) How do you get off the spiral when it is appropriate to terminate a project early?
(3) Why does the spiral end so abruptly?
(4) What happens to software enhancement (or maintenance)?

The answer to these questions involves an observation that the spiral model applies equally well to development or enhancement efforts. In either case, the spiral gets started by a hypothesis that a particular operational mission (or set of missions) could be improved by a software effort. The spiral process then involves a test of this hypothesis: at any time, if the hypothesis fails the test (for example, if delays cause a software product to miss its market window, or if a superior commercial product becomes available), the spiral is terminated. Otherwise, it terminates with the installation of new or modified software, and the hypothesis is tested by observing the effect on the operational mission. Usually, experience with the operational mission leads to further hypotheses about software improvements, and a new maintenance spiral is initiated to test the hypothesis. Initiation, termination, and iteration of the tasks and products of previous cycles are thus implicitly defined in the spiral model (although they're not included in Figure 2 to simplify its presentation).

## Using the spiral model

The various rounds and activities involved in the spiral model are best understood through use of an example. The spiral model was used in the definition and development of the TRW Software Productivity System (TRW-SPS), an integrated software engineering environment.[6] The initial mission opportunity coincided with a corporate initiative to improve productivity in all appropriate corporate operations and an initial hypothesis that software engineering was an attractive area to investigate. This led to a small, extra "Round 0" circuit of the spiral to determine the feasibility of increasing software productivity at a reasonable corporate cost. (Very large or complex software projects will frequently precede the "concept of operation" round of the spiral with one or more smaller rounds to establish feasibility and to reduce the range of alternative solutions quickly and inexpensively.)

Tables 1, 2, and 3 summarize the application of the spiral model to the first three rounds of defining the SPS. The major features of each round are subsequently discussed and are followed by some examples from later rounds, such as preliminary and detailed design.

**Round 0: Feasibility study.** This study involved five part-time participants over a two- to three-month period. As indicated in Table 1, the objectives and constraints were expressed at a very high level and in qualitative terms like "significantly increase," "at reasonable cost," etc.

Some of the alternatives considered, primarily those in the "technology" area, could lead to development of a software product, but the possible attractiveness of a number of non-software alternatives in the management, personnel, and facilities areas could have led to a conclusion not to embark on a software development activity.

The primary risk areas involved possible situations in which the company would invest a good deal only to find that

- resulting productivity gains were not significant, or
- potentially high-leverage improvements were not compatible with some aspects of the "TRW culture."

The risk-resolution activities undertaken in Round 0 were primarily surveys and analyses, including structured interviews of software developers and managers, an initial analysis of productivity leverage factors identified by the constructive cost model (Cocomo)[7]; and an analysis of previous projects at TRW exhibiting high levels of productivity.

The risk analysis results indicated that significant productivity gains could be achieved at a reasonable cost by pursuing an integrated set of initiatives in the four major areas. However, some candidate solutions, such as a software support environment based on a single, corporate, maxicomputer-based time-sharing system, were found to be in conflict with TRW constraints requiring support of different levels of security-classified projects. Thus, even at a very high level of generality of objectives and constraints, Round 0 was able to answer basic feasibility questions and eliminate significant classes of candidate solutions.

The plan for Round 1 involved commitment of 12 man-months compared to the two man-months invested in Round 0 (during these rounds, all participants were part-time). Round 1 here corresponded fairly well to the initial round of the spiral model shown in Figure 2, in that its intent was to produce a concept of operation and a basic life-cycle plan for implementing whatever preferred alternative emerged.

**Table 1. Spiral model usage: TRW Software Productivity System, Round 0.**

| | |
|---|---|
| Objectives | Significantly increase software productivity |
| Constraints | At reasonable cost<br>Within context of TRW culture<br>• Government contracts, high tech., people oriented, security |
| Alternatives | Management: Project organization, policies, planning, control<br>Personnel: Staffing, incentives, training<br>Technology: Tools, workstations, methods, reuse<br>Facilities: Offices, communications |
| Risks | May be no high-leverage improvements<br>Improvements may violate constraints |
| Risk resolution | Internal surveys<br>Analyze cost model<br>Analyze exceptional projects<br>Literature search |
| Risk resolution results | Some alternatives infeasible<br>• Single time-sharing system: Security<br>Mix of alternatives can produce significant gains<br>• Factor of two in five years<br>Need further study to determine best mix |
| Plan for next phase | Six-person task force for six months<br>More extensive surveys and analysis<br>• Internal, external, economic<br>Develop concept of operation, economic rationale |
| Commitment | Fund next phase |

**Round 1: Concept of operations.** Table 2 summarizes Round 1 of the spiral along the lines given in Table 1 for Round 0. The features of Round 1 compare to those of Round 0 as follows:

- The level of investment was greater (12 versus 2 man-months).
- The objectives and constraints were more specific ("double software productivity in five years at a cost of $10,000 a person" versus "significantly increase productivity at a reasonable cost").
- Additional constraints surfaced, such as the preference for TRW products (particularly, a TRW-developed local area network (LAN) system).
- The alternatives were more detailed ("SREM, PSL/PSA or SADT, as requirements tools etc." versus "tools"; "private/shared" terminals, "smart/dumb" terminals versus "workstations").
- The risk areas identified were more specific ("TRW LAN price-performance

within a $10,000-per-person investment constraint" versus "improvements may violate reasonable-cost constraint").

• The risk-resolution activities were more extensive (including the benchmarking and analysis of a prototype TRW LAN being developed for another project).

• The result was a fairly specific operational concept document, involving private offices tailored to software work patterns and personal terminals connected to VAX superminis via the TRW LAN. Some choices were specifically deferred to the next round, such as the choice of operating system and specific tools.

• The life-cycle plan and the plan for the next phase involved a partitioning into separate activities to address management improvements, facilities development, and development of the first increment of a software development environment.

• The commitment step involved more than just an agreement with the plan. It committed to apply the environment to an upcoming 100-person testbed software project and to develop an environment focusing on the testbed project's needs. It also specified forming a representative steering group to ensure that the separate activities were well-coordinated and that the environment would not be overly optimized around the testbed project.

Although the plan recommended developing a prototype environment, it also recommended that the project employ requirements specifications and design specifications in a risk-driven way. Thus, the development of the environment followed the succeeding rounds of the spiral model.

**Round 2: Top-level requirements specification.** Table 3 shows the corresponding steps involved during Round 2 defining the software productivity system. Round 2 decisions and their rationale were covered in earlier work[6]; here, we will summarize the considerations dealing with risk management and the use of the spiral model:

• The initial risk-identification activities during Round 2 showed that several system requirements hinged on the decision between a host-target system or a fully portable tool set and the decision between VMS and Unix as the host operating system. These requirements included the functions needed to provide a user-friendly front-end, the operating system to be used by the workstations, and the functions necessary to support a host-target operation. To keep these requirements in synchronization with the others, a special minispiral was initiated to address and resolve these issues. The resulting review led to a commitment to a host-target operation using Unix on the host system, at a point early enough to work the OS-dependent requirements in a timely fashion.

• Addressing the risks of mismatches to the user-project's needs and priorities resulted in substantial participation of the user-project personnel in the requirements definition activity. This led to several significant redirections of the requirements, particularly toward supporting the early phases of the software life-cycle into which the user project was embarking, such as an adaptation of the software requirements engineering methodology (SREM) tools for requirements specification and analysis.

It is also interesting to note that the form of Tables 1, 2, and 3 was originally developed for presentation purposes, but subsequently became a standard "spiral model template" used on later projects. These templates are useful not only for organizing project activities, but also as a residual design-rationale record. Design rationale information is of paramount importance in assessing the potential reusability of software components on future projects. Another important point to note is that the use of the template was indeed uniform across the three cycles, showing that the spiral steps can be and were uniformly followed at successively detailed levels of product definition.

**Table 2. Spiral model usage: TRW Software Productivity System, Round 1.**

| | |
|---|---|
| Objectives | Double software productivity in five years |
| Constraints | $10,000 per person investment<br>Within context of TRW culture<br>• Government contracts, high tech., people oriented, security<br>Preference for TRW products |
| Alternatives | Office: Private/modular/. . .<br>Communication: LAN/star/concentrators/. . .<br>Terminals: Private/shared; smart/dumb<br>Tools: SREM/PSL-PSA/. . .; PDL/SADT/. . .<br>CPU: IBM/DEC/CDC/. . . |
| Risks | May miss high-leverage options<br>TRW LAN price/performance<br>Workstation cost |
| Risk resolution | Extensive external surveys, visits<br>TRW LAN benchmarking<br>Workstation price projections |
| Risk resolution results | Operations concept: Private offices, TRW LAN, personal terminals, VAX<br>Begin with primarily dumb terminals; experiment with smart workstations<br>Defer operating system, tools selection |
| Plan for next phase | Partition effort into software development environment (SDE), facilities, management<br>Develop first-cut, prototype SDE<br>• Design-to-cost: 15-person team for one year<br>Plan for external usage |
| Commitment | Develop prototype SDE<br>Commit an upcoming project to use SDE<br>Commit the SDE to support the project<br>Form representative steering group |

**Succeeding rounds.** It will be useful to illustrate some examples of how the spiral model is used to handle situations arising in the preliminary design and detailed design of components of the SPS: the preliminary design specification for the requirements traceability tool (RTT), and a detailed design rework or go-back on the unit development folder (UDF) tool.

*The RTT preliminary design specification.* The RTT establishes the traceability between itemized software requirements specifications, design elements, code elements, and test cases. It also supports various associated query, analysis, and report generation capabilities. The preliminary design specification for the RTT (and most of the other SPS tools) looks different from the usual preliminary design specification, which tends to show a uniform level of elaboration of all components of the design. Instead, the level of detail of the RTT specification is risk-driven.

In areas involving a high risk if the design turned out to be wrong, the design was carried down to the detailed design level, usually with the aid of rapid prototyping. These areas included working out the implications of "undo" options and dealing with the effects of control keys used to escape from various program levels.

In areas involving a moderate risk if the design was wrong, the design was carried down to a preliminary-design level. These areas included the basic command options for the tool and the schemata for the requirements traceability database. Here again, the ease of rapid prototyping with Unix shell scripts supported a good deal of user-interface prototyping.

In areas involving a low risk if the design was wrong, very little design elaboration was done. These areas included details of all the help message options and all the report-generation options, once the nature of these options was established in some example instances.

*A detailed design go-back.* The UDF tool collects into an electronic "folder" all artifacts involved in the development of a single-programmer software unit (typically 500 to 1,000 instructions): unit requirements, design, code, test cases, test results, and documentation. It also includes a management template for tracking the programmer's scheduled and actual completion of each artifact.

An alternative considered during detailed design of the UDF tool was reuse of portions of the RTT to provide pointers to the requirements and preliminary design specifications of the unit being developed. This turned out to be an extremely attractive alternative, not only for avoiding duplicate software development but also for bringing to the surface several issues involving many-to-many mappings between requirements, design, and code that had not been considered in designing the UDF tool. These led to a rethinking of the UDF tool requirements and preliminary design, which avoided a great deal of code rework that would have been necessary if the detailed design of the UDF tool had proceeded in a purely deductive, top-down fashion from the original UDF requirements specification. The resulting go-back led to a significantly different, less costly, and more capable UDF tool, incorporating the RTT in its "uses-hierarchy."

*Spiral model features.* These two examples illustrate several features of the spiral approach.

- It fosters the development of specifications that are not necessarily uniform, exhaustive, or formal, in that they defer detailed elaboration of low-risk software elements and avoid unnecessary breakage in their design until the high-risk elements of the design are stabilized.
- It incorporates prototyping as a risk-reduction option at any stage of development. In fact, prototyping and reuse risk analyses were often used in the process of going from detailed design into code.
- It accommodates reworks or go-backs to earlier stages as more attractive alternatives are identified or as new risk issues need resolution.

Overall, risk-driven documents, particularly specifications and plans, are important features of the spiral model. Great amounts of detail are not necessary unless the absence of such detail jeopardizes the

**Table 3. Spiral model usage: TRW Software Productivity System, Round 2.**

| | |
|---|---|
| Objectives | User-friendly system<br>Integrated software, office-automation tools<br>Support all project personnel<br>Support all life-cycle phases |
| Constraints | Customer-deliverable SDE ⇒ Portability<br>Stable, reliable service |
| Alternatives | OS: VMS/AT&T Unix/Berkeley Unix/ISC<br>Host-target/fully portable tool set<br>Workstations: Zenith/LSI-11/. . . |
| Risks | Mismatch to user-project needs, priorities<br>User-unfriendly system<br>• 12-language syndrome; experts-only<br>Unix performance, support<br>Workstation/mainframe compatibility |
| Risk resolution | User-project surveys, requirements participation<br>Survey of Unix-using organizations<br>Workstation study |
| Risk resolution results | Top-level requirements specification<br>Host-target with Unix host<br>Unix-based workstations<br>Build user-friendly front end for Unix<br>Initial focus on tools to support early phases |
| Plan for next phase | Overall development plan<br>• for tools: SREM, RTT, PDL, office automation tools<br>• for front end: Support tools<br>• for LAN: Equipment, facilities |
| Commitment | Proceed with plans |

project. In some cases, such as with a product whose functionality may be determined by a choice among commercial products, a set of weighted evaluation criteria for the products may be preferable to a detailed pre-statement of functional requirements.

**Results.** The Software Productivity System developed and supported using the spiral model avoided the identified risks and achieved most of the system's objectives. The SPS has grown to include over 300 tools and over 1,300,000 instructions; 93 percent of the instructions were reused from previous project-developed, TRW-developed, or external-software packages. Over 25 projects have used all or portions of the system. All of the projects fully using the system have increased their productivity at least 50 percent; indeed, most have doubled their productivity (when compared with cost-estimation model predictions of their productivity using traditional methods).

However, one risk area—that projects with non-Unix target systems would not accept a Unix-based host system—was underestimated. Some projects accepted the host-target approach, but for various reasons (such as customer constraints and zero-cost target machines) a good many did not. As a result, the system was less widely used on TRW projects than expected. This and other lessons learned have been incorporated into the spiral model approach to developing TRW's next-generation software development environment.

**All of the projects fully using the system have increased their productivity at least 50 percent.**

## Evaluation

**Advantages.** The primary advantage of the spiral model is that its range of options accommodates the good features of existing software process models, while its risk-driven approach avoids many of their difficulties. In appropriate situations, the spiral model becomes equivalent to one of the existing process models. In other situations, it provides guidance on the best mix of existing approaches to a given project; for example, its application to the TRW-SPS provided a risk-driven mix of specifying, prototyping, and evolutionary development.

The primary conditions under which the spiral model becomes equivalent to other main process models are summarized as follows:

- If a project has a low risk in such areas as getting the wrong user interface or not meeting stringent performance requirements, and if it has a high risk in budget and schedule predictability and control, then these risk considerations drive the spiral model into an equivalence to the waterfall model.
- If a software product's requirements are very stable (implying a low risk of expensive design and code breakage due to requirements changes during development), and if the presence of errors in the software product constitutes a high risk to the mission it serves, then these risk considerations drive the spiral model to resemble the two-leg model of precise specification and formal deductive program development.
- If a project has a low risk in such areas as losing budget and schedule predictability and control, encountering large-system integration problems, or coping with information sclerosis, and if it has a high risk in such areas as getting the wrong user interface or user decision support requirements, then these risk considerations drive the spiral model into an equivalence to the evolutionary development model.
- If automated software generation capabilities are available, then the spiral model accommodates them either as options for rapid prototyping or for application of the transform model, depending on the risk considerations involved.
- If the high-risk elements of a project involve a mix of the risk items listed above, then the spiral approach will reflect an appropriate mix of the process models above (as exemplified in the TRW-SPS application). In doing so, its risk-avoidance features will generally avoid the difficulties of the other models.

The spiral model has a number of additional advantages, summarized as follows:

*It focuses early attention on options involving the reuse of existing software.* The steps involving the identification and evaluation of alternatives encourage these options.

*It accommodates preparation for life-cycle evolution, growth, and changes of the software product.* The major sources of product change are included in the product's objectives, and information-hiding approaches are attractive architectural design alternatives in that they reduce the risk of not being able to accommodate the product-charge objectives.

*It provides a mechanism for incorporating software quality objectives into software product development.* This mechanism derives from the emphasis on identifying all types of objectives and constraints during each round of the spiral. For example, Table 3 shows user-friendliness, portability, and reliability as specific objectives and constraints to be addressed by the SPS. In Table 1, security constraints were identified as a key risk item for the SPS.

*It focuses on eliminating errors and unattractive alternatives early.* The risk-analysis, validation, and commitment steps cover these considerations.

*For each of the sources of project activity and resource expenditure, it answers the key question, "How much is enough?"* Stated another way, "How much of requirements analysis, planning, configuration management, quality assurance, testing, formal verification, etc. should a project do?" Using the risk-driven approach, one can see that the answer is not the same for all projects and that the appropriate level of effort is determined by the level of risk incurred by not doing enough.

*It does not involve separate approaches for software development and software enhancement (or maintenance).* This aspect helps avoid the "second-class citizen" status frequently associated with software maintenance. It also helps avoid many of the problems that currently ensue when high-risk enhancement efforts are approached in the same way as routine maintenance efforts.

*It provides a viable framework for integrated hardware-software system development.* The focus on risk-management and on eliminating unattractive alternatives early and inexpensively is equally applicable to hardware and software.

**Difficulties.** The full spiral model can be successfully applied in many situations, but some difficulties must be addressed before it can be called a mature, universally applicable model. The three primary challenges involve matching to contract software, relying on risk-assessment expertise, and the need for further elaboration of spiral model steps.

*Matching to contract software.* The spiral model currently works well on internal software developments like the TRW-SPS, but it needs further work to match it to the world of contract software acquisition.

Internal software developments have a great deal of flexibility and freedom to accommodate stage-by-stage commitments, to defer commitments to specific options, to establish minispirals to resolve critical-path items, to adjust levels of effort, or to accommodate such practices as prototyping, evolutionary development, or design-to-cost. The world of contract software acquisition has a harder time achieving these degrees of flexibility and freedom without losing accountability and control, and a harder time defining contracts whose deliverables are not well specified in advance.

Recently, a good deal of progress has been made in establishing more flexible contract mechanisms, such as the use of competitive front-end contracts for concept definition or prototype fly-offs, the use of level-of-effort and award-fee contracts for evolutionary development, and the use of design-to-cost contracts. Although these have been generally successful, the procedures for using them still need to be worked out to the point that acquisition managers feel fully comfortable using them.

**Table 4. A prioritized top-ten list of software risk items.**

| Risk item | Risk management techniques |
|---|---|
| 1. Personnel shortfalls | Staffing with top talent, job matching; teambuilding; morale building; cross-training; pre-scheduling key people |
| 2. Unrealistic schedules and budgets | Detailed, multisource cost and schedule estimation; design to cost; incremental development; software reuse; requirements scrubbing |
| 3. Developing the wrong software functions | Organization analysis; mission analysis; ops-concept formulation; user surveys; prototyping; early users' manuals |
| 4. Developing the wrong user interface | Task analysis; prototyping; scenarios; user characterization (functionality, style, workload) |
| 5. Gold plating | Requirements scrubbing; prototyping; cost-benefit analysis; design to cost |
| 6. Continuing stream of requirement changes | High change threshold; information hiding; incremental development (defer changes to later increments) |
| 7. Shortfalls in externally furnished components | Benchmarking; inspections; reference checking; compatibility analysis |
| 8. Shortfalls in externally performed tasks | Reference checking; pre-award audits; award-fee contracts; competitive design or prototyping; teambuilding |
| 9. Real-time performance shortfalls | Simulation; benchmarking; modeling; prototyping; instrumentation; tuning |
| 10. Straining computer-science capabilities | Technical analysis; cost-benefit analysis; prototyping; reference checking |

**Table 5. Software Risk Management Plan.**

1. Identify the project's top 10 risk items.
2. Present a plan for resolving each risk item.
3. Update list of top risk items, plan, and results monthly.
4. Highlight risk-item status in monthly project reviews.
   - Compare with previous month's rankings, status.
5. Initiate appropriate corrective actions.

*Relying on risk-assessment expertise.* The spiral model places a great deal of reliance on the ability of software developers to identify and manage sources of project risk.

A good example of this is the spiral model's risk-driven specification, which carries high-risk elements down to a great deal of detail and leaves low-risk elements to be elaborated in later stages; by this time, there is less risk of breakage.

However, a team of inexperienced or low-balling developers may also produce a specification with a different pattern of variation in levels of detail: a great elaboration of detail for the well-understood, low-risk elements, and little elaboration of the poorly understood, high-risk elements. Unless there is an insightful review of such a specification by experienced development or acquisition personnel, this type of project will give an illusion of progress during a period in which it is actually heading for disaster.

Another concern is that a risk-driven specification will also be people-dependent. For example, a design produced by an expert may be implemented by non-experts. In this case, the expert, who does not need a great deal of detailed documentation, must produce enough additional documentation to keep the non-experts from going astray. Reviewers of the specification must also be sensitive to these concerns.

With a conventional, document-driven approach, the requirement to carry all aspects of the specification to a uniform level of detail eliminates some potential problems and permits adequate review of some aspects by inexperienced reviewers. But it also creates a large drain on the time of the scarce experts, who must dig for the critical issues within a large mass of noncritical detail. Furthermore, if the high-risk elements have been glossed over by impressive-sounding references to poorly understood capabilities (such as a new synchronization concept or a commercial DBMS), there is an even greater risk that the conventional approach will give the illusion of progress in situations that are actually heading for disaster.

*Need for further elaboration of spiral model steps.* In general, the spiral model process steps need further elaboration to ensure that all software development participants are operating in a consistent context.

Some examples of this are the need for more detailed definitions of the nature of spiral model specifications and milestones, the nature and objectives of spiral model reviews, techniques for estimating and synchronizing schedules, and the nature of spiral model status indicators and cost-versus-progress tracking procedures. Another need is for guidelines and checklists to identify the most likely sources of project risk and the most effective risk-resolution techniques for each source of risk.

Highly experienced people can successfully use the spiral approach without these elaborations. However, for large-scale use in situations where people bring widely differing experience bases to the project, added levels of elaboration—such as have been accumulated over the years for document-driven approaches—are important in ensuring consistent interpretation and use of the spiral approach across the project.

Efforts to apply and refine the spiral model have focused on creating a discipline of software risk management, including techniques for risk identification, risk analysis, risk prioritization, risk-management planning, and risk-element tracking. The prioritized top-ten list of software risk items given in Table 4 is one result of this activity. Another example is the risk management plan discussed in the next section.

**Implications: The Risk Management Plan.** Even if an organization is not ready to adopt the entire spiral approach, one characteristic technique that can easily be adapted to any life-cycle model provides many of the benefits of the spiral approach. This is the Risk Management Plan summarized in Table 5. This plan basically ensures that each project makes an early identification of its top risk items (the number 10 is not an absolute requirement), develops a strategy for resolving the risk items, identifies and sets down an agenda to resolve new risk items as they surface, and highlights progress versus plans in monthly reviews.

The Risk Management Plan has been used successfully at TRW and other organizations. Its use has ensured appropriate focus on early prototyping, simulation, benchmarking, key-person staffing measures, and other early risk-resolution techniques that have helped avoid many potential project "show-stoppers." The recent US Department of Defense standard on software management, DoD-Std-2167, requires that developers produce and use risk management plans, as does its counterpart US Air Force regulation, AFR 800-14.

Overall, the Risk Management Plan and the maturing set of techniques for software risk management provide a foundation for tailoring spiral model concepts into the more established software acquisition and development procedures.

We can draw four conclusions from the data presented:

(1) The risk-driven nature of the spiral model is more adaptable to the full range of software project situations than are the primarily document-driven approaches such as the waterfall model or the primarily code-driven approaches such as evolutionary development. It is particularly applicable to very large, complex, ambitious software systems.

(2) The spiral model has been quite successful in its largest application to date: the development and enhancement of the TRW-SPS. Overall, it achieved a high level of software support environment capability in a very short time and provided the flexibility necessary to accommodate a high dynamic range of technical alternatives and user objectives.

(3) The spiral model is not yet as fully elaborated as the more established models. Therefore, the spiral model can be applied by experienced personnel, but it needs further elaboration in such areas as contracting, specifications, milestones, reviews, scheduling, status monitoring, and risk-area identification to be fully usable in all situations.

(4) Partial implementations of the spiral model, such as the Risk Management Plan, are compatible with most current process models and are very helpful in overcoming major sources of project risk. □

## Acknowledgments

I would like to thank Frank Belz, Lolo Penedo, George Spadaro, Bob Williams, Bob Balzer, Gillian Frewin, Peter Hamer, Manny Lehman, Lee Osterweil, Dave Parnas, Bill Riddle, Steve Squires, and Dick Thayer, along with the *Computer* reviewers of this article, for their stimulating and insightful comments and discussions of earlier versions of the article, and Nancy Donato for producing its several versions.

## References

1. F.P. Brooks et al., *Defense Science Board Task Force Report on Military Software*, Office of the Under Secretary of Defense for Acquisition, Washington, DC 20301, Sept. 1987.
2. H.D. Benington, "Production of Large Computer Programs," *Proc. ONR Symp. Advanced Programming Methods for Digital Computers*, June 1956, pp. 15-27. Also available in *Annals of the History of Computing*, Oct. 1983, pp. 350-361, and *Proc. Ninth Int'l Conf. Software Engineering*, Computer Society Press, 1987.
3. W.W. Royce, "Managing the Development of Large Software Systems: Concepts and Techniques," *Proc. Wescon*, Aug. 1970. Also available in *Proc. ICSE 9*, Computer Society Press, 1987.
4. D.D. McCracken and M.A. Jackson, "Life-Cycle Concept Considered Harmful," *ACM Software Engineering Notes*, Apr. 1982, pp. 29-32.
5. R. Balzer, T.E. Cheatham, and C. Green, "Software Technology in the 1990s: Using a New Paradigm," *Computer*, Nov. 1983, pp. 39-45.
6. B.W. Boehm et al., "A Software Development Environment for Improving Productivity," *Computer*, June 1984, pp. 30-44.
7. B.W. Boehm, *Software Engineering Economics*, Prentice-Hall, 1981, Chap. 33.

## Further reading

The software process model field has an interesting history, and a great deal of stimulating work has been produced recently in this specialized area. Besides the references that appear at the end of the accompanying article, here are some additional good sources of insight:

### Overall process model issues and results

Agresti's tutorial volume provides a good overview and set of key articles. The three recent *Software Process Workshop Proceedings* provide access to much of the recent work in the area.

Agresti, W.W., *New Paradigms for Software Development*, IEEE Catalog No. EH0245-1, 1986.

Dowson, M., ed., *Proc. Third Int'l Software Process Workshop*, IEEE Catalog No. TH0184-2, Nov. 1986.

Potts, C., ed., *Proc. Software Process Workshop*, IEEE Catalog No. 84CH2044-6, Feb. 1984.

Wileden, J.C., and M. Dowson, eds., Proc. Int'l Workshop Software Process and Software Environments, *ACM Software Engineering Notes*, Aug. 1986.

### Alternative process models

More detailed information on waterfall-type approaches is given in:

Evans, M.W., P. Piazza, and J.P. Dolkas, *Principles of Productive Software Management*, John Wiley & Sons, 1983.

Hice, G.F., W.J. Turner, and L.F. Cashwell, *System Development Methodology*, North Holland, 1974 (2nd ed., 1981).

More detailed information on evolutionary development is provided in:

Gilb, T., *Principles of Software Engineering Management,* Addison Wesley, 1988 (currently in publication).

Some additional process model approaches with useful features and insights may be found in:

Lehman, M.M., and L.A. Belady, *Program Evolution: Processes of Software Change*, Academic Press, 1985.

Osterweil, L., "Software Processes are Software, Too," *Proc. ICSE 9*, IEEE Catalog No. 87CH2432-3, Mar. 1987, pp. 2-13.

Radice, R.A., et al., "A Programming Process Architecture," *IBM Systems J.*, Vol. 24, No.2, 1985, pp. 79-90.

### Spiral and spiral-type models

Some further treatments of spiral model issues and practices are:

Belz, F.C., "Applying the Spiral Model: Observations on Developing System Software in Ada," *Proc. 1986 Annual Conf. on Ada Technology,* Atlanta, 1986, pp. 57-66.

Boehm, B.W., and F.C. Belz, "Applying Process Programming to the Spiral Model," *Proc. Fourth Software Process Workshop*, IEEE, May 1988.

Iivari, J., "A Hierarchical Spiral Model for the Software Process," *ACM Software Engineering Notes,* Jan. 1987, pp. 35-37.

Some similar cyclic spiral-type process models from other fields are described in:

Carlsson, B., P. Keane, and J.B. Martin, "R&D Organizations as Learning Systems," *Sloan Management Review,* Spring 1976, pp. 1-15.

Fisher, R., and W. Ury, *Getting to Yes*, Houghton Mifflin, 1981; Penguin Books, 1983, pp. 68-71.

Kolb, D.A., "On Management and the Learning Process," MIT Sloan School Working Article 652-73, Cambridge, Mass., 1973.

### Software risk management

The discipline of software risk management provides a bridge between spiral model concepts and currently established software acquisition and development procedures.

Boehm, B.W., "Software Risk Management Tutorial," Computer Society, Apr. 1988.

*Risk Assessment Techniques*, Defense Systems Management College, Ft. Belvoir, Va. 22060, July 1983.

# The Capability Maturity Model for Software

Mark C. Paulk
*Software Engineering Institute*
*Carnegie Mellon University*
*Pittsburgh, PA 15213-3890*

Bill Curtis
*TeraQuest Metrics, Inc.*
*P.O. Box 200490*
*Austin, TX 78720-0490*

Mary Beth Chrissis
*Software Engineering Institute*
*Carnegie Mellon University*
*Pittsburgh, PA 15213-3890*

Charles V. Weber
*Lockheed Martin Federal Systems Company*
*6304 Spine Road*
*Boulder, CO 80301*

## Abstract

*This paper provides an overview of the latest version of the Capability Maturity Model$^{SM}$ for Software, CMM$^{SM}$ v1.1. CMM v1.1 describes the software engineering and management practices that characterize organizations as they mature their processes for developing and maintaining software. This paper stresses the need for a process maturity framework to prioritize improvement actions, describes the five maturity levels, key process areas, and their common features, and discusses future directions for the CMM.*

**Keywords:** capability maturity model, CMM, software process improvement, process capability, maturity level, key process area, software process assessment, software capability evaluation.

## 1 Introduction

After decades of unfulfilled promises about productivity and quality gains from applying new software methodologies and technologies, organizations are realizing that their fundamental problem is the inability to manage the software process. In many organizations, projects are often excessively late and over budget, and the benefits of better methods and tools cannot be realized in the maelstrom of an undisciplined, chaotic project.

In November 1986, the Software Engineering Institute (SEI), with assistance from the Mitre Corporation, began developing a process maturity framework that would help organizations improve their software process. In September 1987, the SEI released a brief description of the process maturity framework, which was later expanded in Watts Humphrey's book, *Managing the Software Process* [Humphrey89]. Two methods, software process assessment[1] and software capability evaluation[2] were developed to appraise software process maturity.

After four years of experience with the software

---

[1] A software process assessment is an appraisal by a trained team of software professionals to determine the state of an organization's current software process, to determine the high-priority software process-related issues facing an organization, and to obtain the organizational support for software process improvement.

[2] A software capability evaluation is an appraisal by a trained team of professionals to identify contractors who are qualified to perform the software work or to monitor the state of the software process used on an existing software effort.

process maturity framework, the SEI evolved the maturity framework into the Capability Maturity Model for Software (CMM or SW-CMM[3]). The CMM presents sets of recommended practices in a number of key process areas that have been shown to enhance software process capability. The CMM is based on knowledge acquired from software process assessments and extensive feedback from both industry and government.

The CMM provides software organizations with guidance on how to gain control of their processes for developing and maintaining software and how to evolve toward a culture of software engineering and management excellence. The CMM was designed to guide software organizations in selecting process improvement strategies by determining current process maturity and identifying the most critical issues for software quality and process improvement. By focusing on a limited set of activities and working aggressively to achieve them, an organization can steadily improve its organization-wide software process to enable continuous and lasting gains in software process capability.

The initial release of the CMM, version 1.0, was reviewed and used by the software community during 1991 and 1992. The current version of the CMM, version 1.1, was released in 1993 [Paulk95a] and is the result of extensive feedback from the software community. The CMM has evolved significantly since 1986 [Paulk95b], and the SEI is currently working on version 2.

## 1.1 Immature Versus Mature Software Organizations

Setting sensible goals for process improvement requires an understanding of the difference between immature and mature software organizations. In an immature software organization, software processes are generally improvised by practitioners and their management during the course of the project. Even if a software process has been specified, it is not rigorously followed or enforced. The immature software organization is reactionary, and managers are usually focused on solving immediate crises (better known as fire fighting). Schedules and budgets are routinely exceeded because they are not based on realistic estimates. When hard deadlines are imposed, product functionality and quality are often compromised to meet the schedule.

In an immature organization, there is no objective basis for judging product quality or for solving product or process problems. Therefore, product quality is difficult to predict. Activities intended to enhance quality such as reviews and testing are often curtailed or eliminated when projects fall behind schedule.

On the other hand, a mature software organization possesses an organization-wide ability for managing software development and maintenance processes. The software process is accurately communicated to both existing staff and new employees, and work activities are carried out according to the planned process. The mandated processes are usable and consistent with the way the work actually gets done. These defined processes are updated when necessary, and improvements are developed through controlled pilot-tests and/or cost benefit analyses. Roles and responsibilities within the defined process are clear throughout the project and across the organization.

In a mature organization, managers monitor the quality of the software products and the process that produced them. There is an objective, quantitative basis for judging product quality and analyzing problems with the product and process. Schedules and budgets are based on historical performance and are realistic; the expected results for cost, schedule, functionality, and quality of the product are usually achieved. In general, a disciplined process is consistently followed because all of the participants understand the value of doing so, and the necessary infrastructure exists to support the process.

## 1.2 Fundamental Concepts Underlying Process Maturity

A *software process* can be defined as a set of activities, methods, practices, and transformations that people use to develop and maintain software and the associated products (for instance, project plans, design documents, code, test cases, and user manuals). As an organization matures, the software process becomes better defined and more consistently implemented throughout the organization.

*Software process capability* describes the range of expected results that can be achieved by following a software process. An organization's software process capability is one way of predicting the most likely outcome to expect from the next software project the organization undertakes.

*Software process performance* represents the actual results achieved by following a software process. Thus, software process performance focuses on

[3] A number of CMMs inspired by the CMM for Software have now been developed, including the Systems Engineering CMM [Bate95] and the People CMM [Curtis95]. Additional CMMs are being developed on software acquisition and integrated product development. To minimize confusion, we are starting to use SW-CMM to distinguish the original CMM for Software, but since this paper focuses on software engineering, we will use the CMM acronym.

the results achieved, while software process capability focuses on results expected.

*Software process maturity* is the extent to which a specific process is explicitly defined, managed, measured, controlled, and effective. Maturity implies a potential for growth in capability and indicates both the richness of an organization's software process and the consistency with which it is applied in projects throughout the organization.

As a software organization gains in software process maturity, it institutionalizes its software process via policies, standards, and organizational structures. Institutionalization entails building an infrastructure and a corporate culture that supports the methods, practices, and procedures of the business so that they endure after those who originally defined them have gone.

## 2 The Five Levels of Software Process Maturity

Continuous process improvement is based on many small, evolutionary steps rather than revolutionary innovations. The staged structure of the CMM is based on principles of product quality espoused by Walter Shewart, W. Edwards Deming, Joseph Juran, and Philip Crosby. The CMM provides a framework for organizing these evolutionary steps into five maturity levels that lay successive foundations for continuous process improvement. These five maturity levels define an ordinal scale for measuring the maturity of an organization's software process and for evaluating its software process capability. The levels also help an organization prioritize its improvement efforts.

A *maturity level* is a well-defined evolutionary plateau toward achieving a mature software process. Each maturity level comprises a set of process goals that, when satisfied, stabilize an important component of the software process. Achieving each level of the maturity framework establishes a higher level of process capability for the organization.

Organizing the CMM into the five levels shown in Figure 2.1 prioritizes improvement actions for increasing software process maturity. The labeled arrows in Figure 2.1 indicate the type of process capability being institutionalized by the organization at each step of the maturity framework.

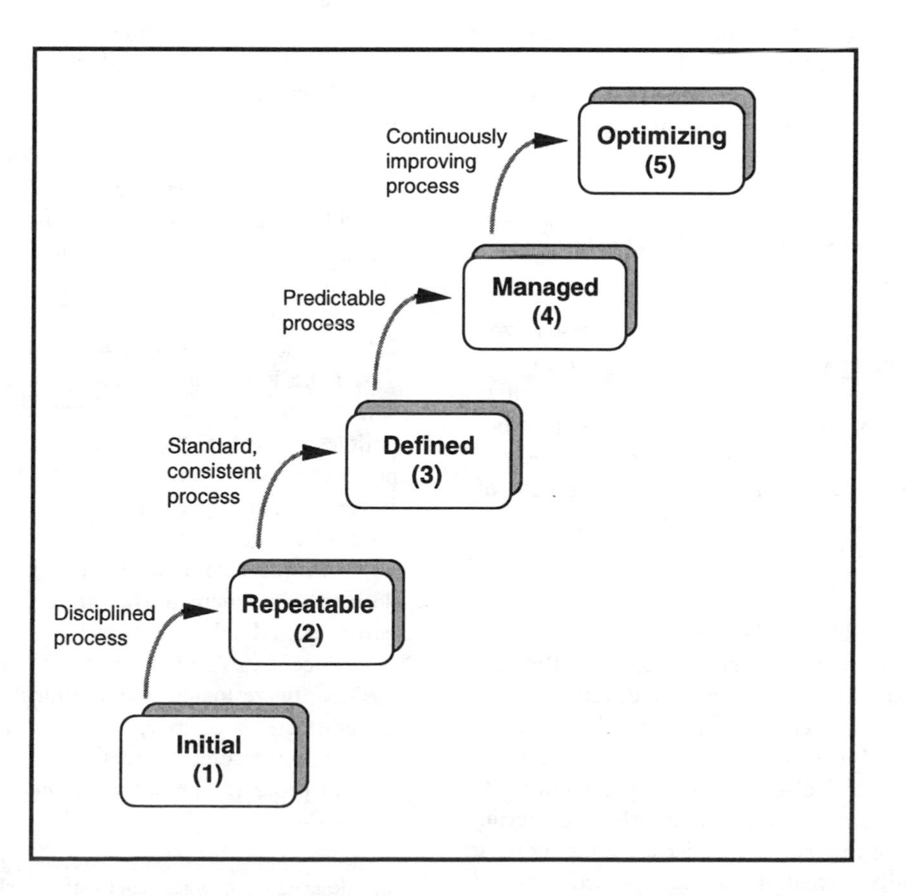


*Figure 2.1 The five levels of software process maturity*

The five levels can be briefly described as:

| | |
|---|---|
| *1) Initial* | The software process is characterized as ad hoc, and occasionally even chaotic. Few processes are defined, and success depends on individual effort and heroics. |
| *2) Repeatable* | Basic project management processes are established to track cost, schedule, and functionality. The necessary process discipline is in place to repeat earlier successes on projects with similar applications. |
| *3) Defined* | The software process for both management and engineering activities is documented, standardized, and integrated into a standard software process for the organization. All projects use an approved, tailored version of the organization's standard software process for developing and maintaining software. |
| *4) Managed* | Detailed measures of the software process and product quality are collected. Both the software process and products are quantitatively understood and controlled. |
| *5) Optimizing* | Continuous process improvement is enabled by quantitative feedback from the process and from piloting innovative ideas and technologies. |

These five levels reflect the fact that the CMM is a model for improving the capability of software organizations. The priorities in the CMM, as expressed by these levels, are not directed at individual projects. A project that is in trouble might well prioritize its problems differently than the taxonomy given by the CMM. Its solutions might be of limited value to the rest of the organization, because other projects might have different problems or because other projects could not take advantage of its solutions if they lack the necessary foundation to implement the solutions. The CMM focuses on processes that are of value across the organization.

## 2.1 Behavioral Characterization of the Maturity Levels

Maturity Levels 2 through 5 can be characterized through the activities performed by the organization to establish or improve the software process, by activities performed on each project, and by the resulting process capability across projects. A behavioral characterization of Level 1 is included to establish a base of comparison for process improvements at higher maturity levels.

### 2.1.1 Level 1—The Initial Level

At the Initial Level, the organization typically does not provide a stable environment for developing and maintaining software. Over-commitment is a characteristic of Level 1 organizations, and such organizations frequently have difficulty making commitments that the staff can meet with an orderly engineering process, resulting in a series of crises. During a crisis, projects typically abandon planned procedures and revert to coding and testing. Success depends on having an exceptional manager and a seasoned and effective software team. Occasionally, capable and forceful software managers can withstand the pressures to take shortcuts in the software process; but when they leave the project, their stabilizing influence leaves with them. Even a strong engineering process cannot overcome the instability created by the absence of sound management practices.

In spite of this ad hoc, even chaotic, process, Level 1 organizations frequently develop products that work, even though they may exceed the budget and schedule. Success in Level 1 organizations depends on the competence and heroics of the people in the organization[4] and cannot be repeated unless the same competent individuals are assigned to the next project. Thus, at Level 1, capability is a characteristic of the individuals, not of the organization.

### 2.1.2 Level 2—The Repeatable Level

At the Repeatable Level, policies for managing a software project and procedures to implement those policies are established. Planning and managing new projects is based on experience with similar projects. Process capability is enhanced by establishing basic process management discipline on a project by project basis. Projects implement effective processes that are defined, documented, practiced, trained, measured, enforced, and able to improve.

Projects in Level 2 organizations have installed basic software management controls. Realistic project commitments are made, based on the results observed on previous projects and on the requirements of the current project. The software managers for a project

[4] Selecting, hiring, developing, and retaining competent people are significant issues for organizations at all levels of maturity, but they are largely outside the scope of the CMM.

track software costs, schedules, and functionality; problems in meeting commitments are identified when they arise. Software requirements and the work products developed to satisfy them are baselined, and their integrity is controlled. Software project standards are defined, and the organization ensures they are faithfully followed. The software project works with its subcontractors, if any, to establish an effective customer-supplier relationship.

Processes may differ among projects in a Level 2 organization. The organizational requirement for achieving Level 2 is that there are policies that guide the projects in establishing the appropriate management processes.

The software process capability of Level 2 organizations can be summarized as disciplined because software project planning and tracking are stable and earlier successes can be repeated. The project's process is under the effective control of a project management system, following realistic plans based on the performance of previous projects.

### 2.1.3 Level 3—The Defined Level

At the Defined Level, a standard process (or processes) for developing and maintaining software is documented and used across the organization. This standard process includes both software engineering and management processes, which are integrated into a coherent whole. This standard process is referred to throughout the CMM as the *organization's standard software process*. Processes established at Level 3 are used (and changed, as appropriate) to help the software managers and technical staff perform more effectively. The organization exploits effective software engineering practices when standardizing its software processes. A group such as a software engineering process group or SEPG is responsible for the organization's software process activities. An organization-wide training program is implemented to ensure that the staff and managers have the knowledge and skills required to fulfill their assigned roles.

Projects tailor the organization's standard software process to develop their own defined software process, which accounts for the unique characteristics of the project. This tailored process is referred to in the CMM as the *project's defined software process*. It is the process used in performing the project's activities. A defined software process contains a coherent, integrated set of well-defined software engineering and management processes. A well-defined process includes readiness criteria, inputs, standards and procedures for performing the work, verification mechanisms (such as peer reviews), outputs, and completion criteria. Because the software process is well defined, management has good insight into technical progress on the project.

The software process capability of Level 3 organizations can be summarized as standard and consistent because both software engineering and management activities are stable and repeatable. Within established product lines, cost, schedule, and functionality are under control, and software quality is tracked. This process capability is based on a common, organization-wide understanding of the activities, roles, and responsibilities in a defined software process.

### 2.1.4 Level 4—The Managed Level

At the Managed Level, the organization sets quantitative quality goals for both software products and processes. Productivity and quality are measured for important software process activities across all projects as part of an organizational measurement program. An organization-wide software process database is used to collect and analyze the data available from the projects' defined software processes. Software processes are instrumented with well-defined and consistent measurements. These measurements establish the quantitative foundation for evaluating the projects' software processes and products.

Projects achieve control over their products and processes by narrowing the variation in their process performance to fall within acceptable quantitative boundaries. Meaningful variations in process performance can be distinguished from random variation (noise), particularly within established product lines. The risks involved in moving up the learning curve of a new application domain are known and carefully managed.

The software process capability of Level 4 organizations can be summarized as being quantified and predictable because the process is measured and operates within quantitative limits. This level of process capability allows an organization to predict trends in process and product quality within the quantitative bounds of these limits. Because the process is both stable and measured, when some exceptional circumstance occurs, the "special cause" of the variation can be identified and addressed. When the pre-defined limits are exceeded, actions are taken to understand and correct the situation. Software products are of predictably high quality.

### 2.1.5 Level 5—The Optimizing Level

At the Optimizing Level, the entire organization is focused on continuous process improvement. The organization has the means to identify weaknesses and strengthen the process proactively, with the goals of preventing defects and improving efficiency. Data on process effectiveness are used to perform cost/benefit analyses of new technologies and proposed changes to the organization's software process. Innovations that exploit the best software engineering practices are identified and transferred throughout the organization.

Software teams in Level 5 organizations analyze defects to determine their causes, evaluate software processes to prevent known types of defects from recurring, and disseminate lessons learned throughout the organization.

There is chronic waste, in the form of rework, in any system simply due to random variation. Organized efforts to remove waste result in changing the system by addressing "common causes" of inefficiency. While efforts to reduce waste occur at all maturity levels, it is the focus of Level 5.

The software process capability of Level 5 organizations can be characterized as continuously improving because Level 5 organizations are continuously striving to improve the range of their process capability, thereby improving the process performance of their projects. Improvements occur both by incremental advancements in the existing process and by innovations using new technologies and methods. Technology and process improvements are planned and managed as ordinary business activities.

## 2.2 Process Capability and the Prediction of Performance

An organization's software process maturity helps predict a project's ability to meet its goals. Projects in Level 1 organizations experience wide variations in achieving cost, schedule, functionality, and quality targets. Figure 2.2 illustrates the kinds of improvements expected in predictability, control, and effectiveness in the form of a probability density for the likely performance of a particular project with respect to targets, such as cycle time, cost, and quality.

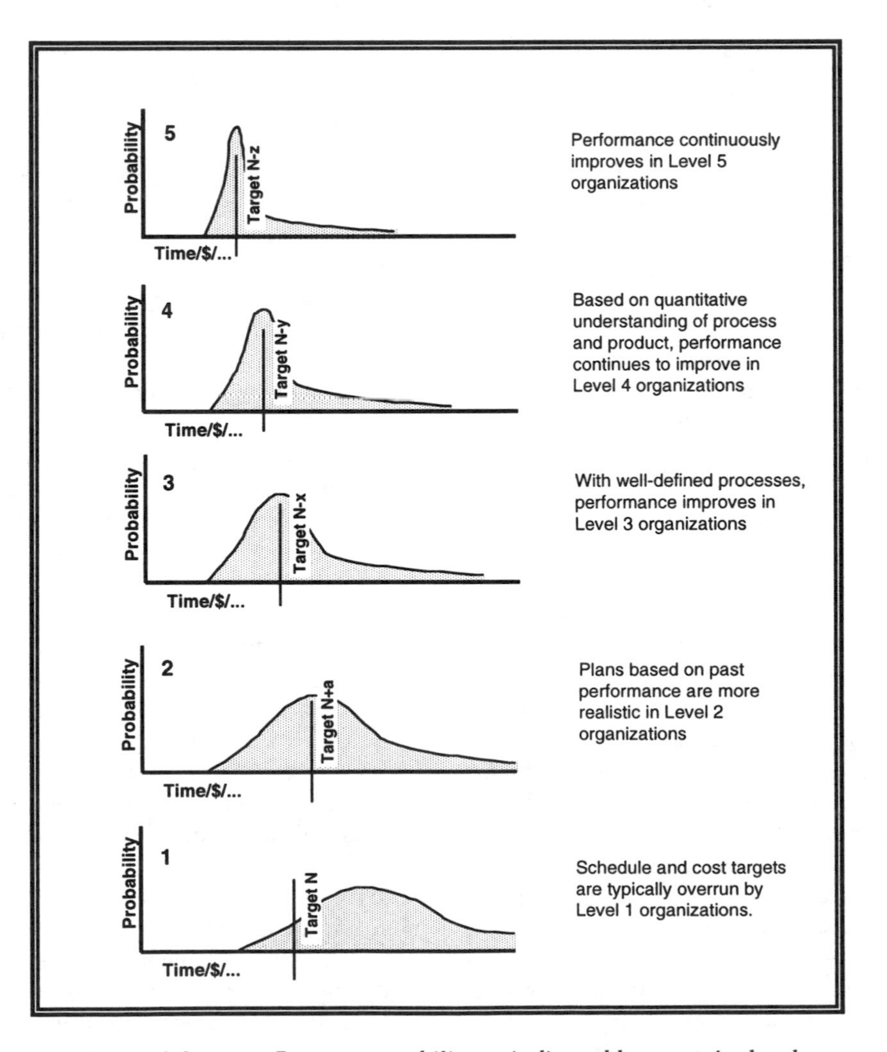


*Figure 2.2 Process capability as indicated by maturity level*

The first improvement expected as an organization matures is in predictability. As maturity increases, the difference between targeted results and actual results decreases across projects. For instance, Level 1 organizations often miss their originally scheduled delivery dates by a wide margin, whereas higher maturity level organizations should be able to meet targeted dates with increased accuracy.

The second improvement is in control. As maturity increases, the variability of actual results around targeted results decreases. For instance, in Level 1 organizations delivery dates for projects of similar size are unpredictable and vary widely. Similar projects in a higher maturity level organization, however, will be delivered within a smaller range.

The third improvement is in effectiveness. Targeted results improve as the maturity of the organization increases. That is, as a software organization matures, costs decrease, development time becomes shorter, and productivity and quality increase. In a Level 1 organization, development time can be quite long because of the amount of rework that must be performed to correct mistakes. In contrast, higher maturity level organizations have increased process effectiveness and reduced costly rework, allowing development time to be shortened.

The improvements in predicting a project's results represented in Figure 2.2 assume that the software project's outcomes become more predictable as noise, often in the form of rework, is removed from the software process. Unprecedented systems complicate the picture since new technologies and applications lower the process capability by increasing variability. Even in the case of unprecedented systems, the management and engineering practices characteristic of more mature organizations help identify and address problems earlier than for less mature organizations. In some cases a mature process means that "failed" projects are identified early in the software life cycle and investment in a lost cause is minimized.

The documented case studies of software process improvement indicate that there are significant improvements in both quality and productivity as a result of the improvement effort [Herbsleb94, Lawlis95, Goldenson95, Hayes95]. The return on investment seems to typically be in the 4:1 to 8:1 range for successful process improvement efforts, with increases in productivity ranging from 9-67 percent and decreases in cycle time ranging from 15-23 percent reported [Herbsleb94].

### 2.3 Skipping Maturity Levels

Trying to skip maturity levels may be counterproductive because each maturity level in the CMM forms a foundation from which to achieve the next level. The CMM identifies the levels through which an organization should evolve to establish a culture of software engineering excellence. Organizations can institute specific process improvements at any time they choose, even before they are prepared to advance to the level at which the specific practice is recommended. However, organizations should understand that the stability of these improvements is at greater risk since the foundation for their successful institutionalization has not been completed. Processes without the proper foundation fail at the very point they are needed most—under stress.

For instance, a well-defined software process that is characteristic of a Level 3 organization, can be placed at great risk if management makes a poorly planned schedule commitment or fails to control changes to the baselined requirements. Similarly, many organizations have collected the detailed data characteristic of Level 4, only to find that the data were uninterpretable because of inconsistent software processes.

At the same time, it must be recognized that process improvement efforts should focus on the needs of the organization in the context of its business environment, and higher-level practices may address the current needs of an organization or project. For example, when prescribing what steps an organization should take to move from Level 1 to Level 2, one frequent recommendation is to establish a software engineering process group (SEPG), which is an attribute of Level 3 organizations. While an SEPG is not a necessary characteristic of a Level 2 organization, they can be a useful part of the prescription for achieving Level 2.

## 3 Operational Definition of the Capability Maturity Model

The CMM is a framework representing a path of improvements recommended for software organizations that want to increase their software process capability. The intent is that the CMM is at a sufficient level of abstraction that it does not unduly constrain how the software process is implemented by an organization. The CMM describes what we would normally expect in a software process, regardless of how the process is implemented.

This operational elaboration of the CMM is designed to support the many ways it will be used. There are at least five uses of the CMM that are supported:

- Senior management will use the CMM to understand the activities necessary to launch a software process improvement program in their organization.

- Appraisal method developers will use the CMM to develop CMM-based appraisal methods that meet specific needs.
- Evaluation teams will use the CMM to identify the risks of selecting among different contractors for awarding business and to monitor contracts.
- Assessment teams will use the CMM to identify strengths and weaknesses in the organization.
- Technical staff and process improvement groups, such as an SEPG, will use the CMM as a guide to help them define and improve the software process in their organization.

Because of the diverse uses of the CMM, it must be decomposed in sufficient detail that actual process recommendations can be derived from the structure of the maturity levels. This decomposition also indicates the key processes and their structure that characterize software process maturity and software process capability.

## 3.1 Internal Structure of the Maturity Levels

Each maturity level, with the exception of Level 1, has been decomposed into constituent parts. The decomposition of each maturity level ranges from abstract summaries of each level down to their operational definition in the key practices, as shown in Figure 3.1. Each maturity level is composed of several key process areas. Each key process area is organized into five sections called common features. The common features specify the key practices that, when collectively addressed, accomplish the goals of the key process area.

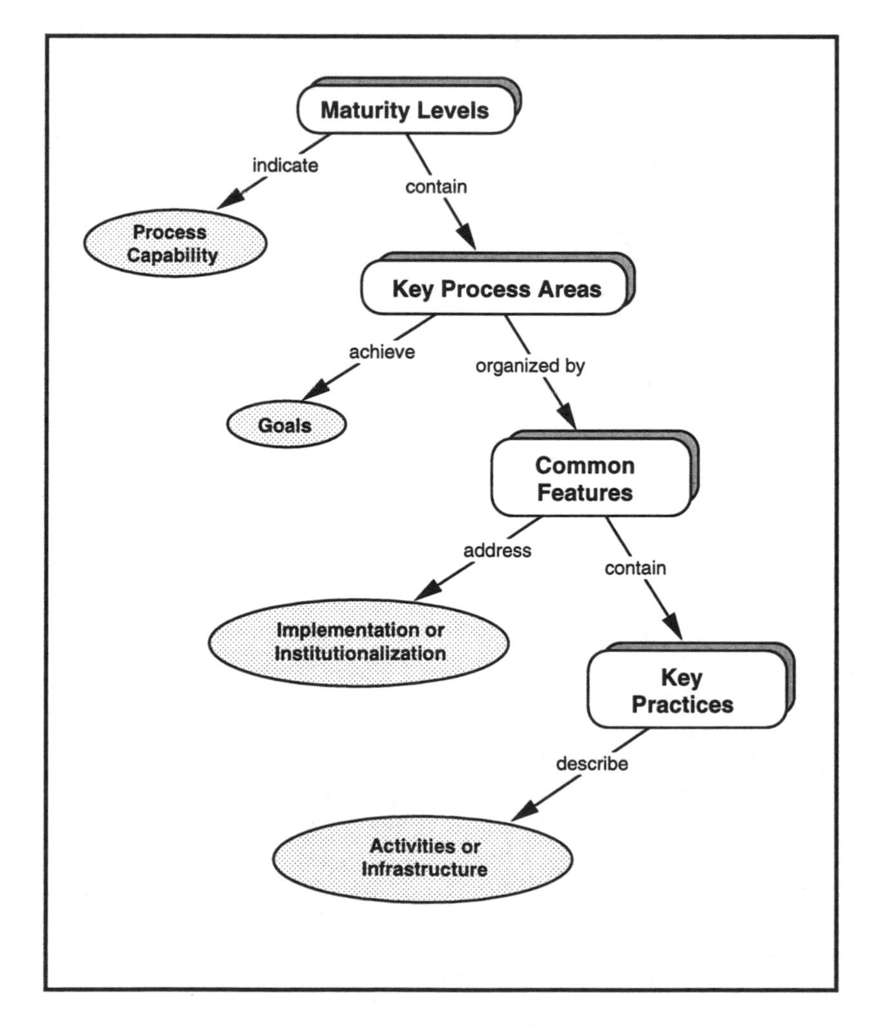


*Figure 3.1 The CMM structure*

## 3.2 Maturity Levels

A maturity level is a well-defined evolutionary plateau toward achieving a mature software process. Each maturity level indicates a level of process capability, as was illustrated in Figure 2.2. For instance, at Level 2 the process capability of an organization has been elevated from ad hoc to disciplined by establishing sound project management controls.

## 3.3 Key Process Areas

Except for Level 1, each maturity level is decomposed into several key process areas that indicate where an organization should focus on to improve its software process. Key process areas identify the issues that must be addressed to achieve a maturity level.

Each *key process area* identifies a cluster of related activities that, when performed collectively, achieve a set of goals considered important for enhancing process capability. The key process areas have been defined to reside at a single maturity level as shown in Figure 3.2. The path to achieving the goals of a key process area may differ across projects based on differences in application domains or environments. Nevertheless, all the goals of a key process area must be achieved for the organization to satisfy that key process area.

The adjective "key" implies that there are process areas (and processes) that are not key to achieving a maturity level. The CMM does not describe in detail all the process areas that are involved with developing and maintaining software. Certain process areas have been identified as key determiners of process capability, and these are the ones described in the CMM.

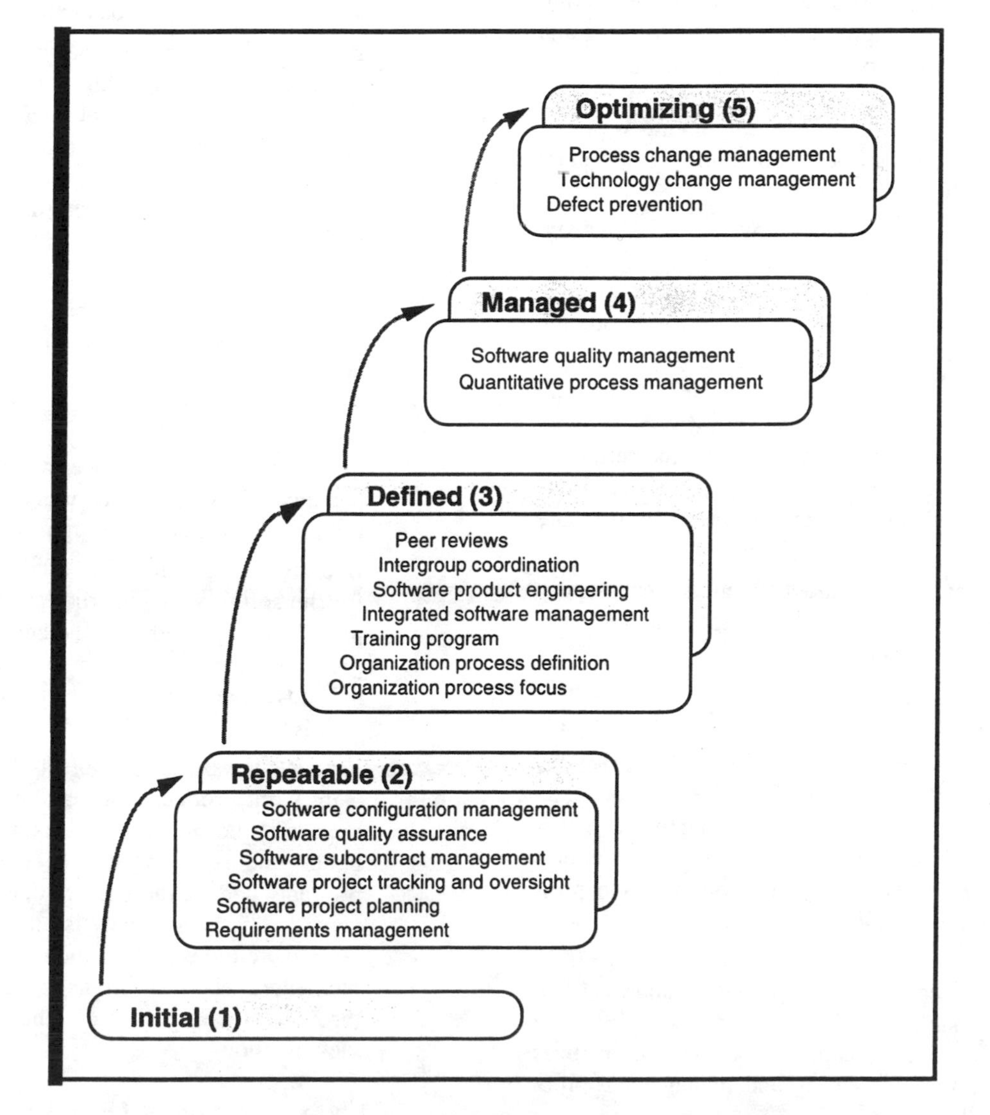


*Figure 3.2 The key process areas by maturity level*

The key process areas are the requirements for achieving a maturity level. To achieve a maturity level, the key process areas for that level and the lower levels must be satisfied (or not applicable, such as Software Subcontract Management when there are no subcontractors).

The specific practices to be executed in each key process area will evolve as the organization achieves higher levels of process maturity. For instance, many of the project estimating capabilities described in the Software Project Planning key process area at Level 2 must evolve to handle the additional project data available at Level 3, as described in Integrated Software Management.

The key process areas at Level 2 focus on the software project's concerns related to establishing basic project management controls.

- Requirements Management: establish a common understanding between the customer and the software project of the customer's requirements that will be addressed by the software project. This agreement with the customer is the basis for planning and managing the software project.
- Software Project Planning: establish reasonable plans for performing the software engineering and for managing the software project. These plans are the necessary foundation for managing the software project.
- Software Project Tracking and Oversight: establish adequate visibility into actual progress so that management can take effective actions when the software project's performance deviates significantly from the software plans.
- Software Subcontract Management: select qualified software subcontractors and manage them effectively.
- Software Quality Assurance: provide management with appropriate visibility into the process being used by the software project and of the products being built.
- Software Configuration Management: establish and maintain the integrity of the products of the software project throughout the project's software life cycle.

The key process areas at Level 3 address both project and organizational issues, as the organization establishes an infrastructure that institutionalizes effective software engineering and management processes across all projects.

- Organization Process Focus: establish the organizational responsibility for software process activities that improve the organization's overall software process capability.
- Organization Process Definition: develop and maintain a usable set of software process assets that improve process performance across the projects and provides a basis for defining meaningful data for quantitative process management. These assets provide a stable foundation that can be institutionalized via mechanisms such as training.
- Training Program: develop the skills and knowledge of individuals so they can perform their roles effectively and efficiently. Training is an organizational responsibility, but the software projects should identify their needed skills and provide the necessary training when the project's needs are unique.
- Integrated Software Management: integrate the software engineering and management activities into a coherent, defined software process that is tailored from the organization's standard software process and related process assets. This tailoring is based on the business environment and technical needs of the project.
- Software Product Engineering: consistently perform a well-defined engineering process that integrates all the software engineering activities to produce correct, consistent software products effectively and efficiently. Software Product Engineering describes the technical activities of the project, for instance requirements analysis, design, code, and test.
- Intergroup Coordination: establish a means for the software engineering group to participate actively with the other engineering groups so the project is better able to satisfy the customer's needs effectively and efficiently.
- Peer Reviews: remove defects from the software work products early and efficiently. An important corollary effect is to develop a better understanding of the software work products and of the defects that can be prevented. The peer review is an important and effective engineering method that can be implemented via inspections, structured walkthroughs, or a number of other collegial review methods.

The key process areas at Level 4 focus on establishing a quantitative understanding of both the software process and the software work products being built.

- Quantitative Process Management: control process performance of the software project quantitatively. Software process performance represents the actual results achieved from following a software process. The focus is on identifying special causes of variation within a measurably stable process and correcting, as appropriate, the circumstances that drove the transient variation to occur.
- Software Quality Management: develop a quantitative understanding of the quality of the project's software products and achieve specific quality goals.

The key process areas at Level 5 cover the issues that both the organization and the projects must address to implement continuous and measurable software process improvement.

- Defect Prevention: identify the causes of defects and prevent them from recurring. The software project analyzes defects, identifies their causes, and changes its defined software process.
- Technology Change Management: identify beneficial new technologies (such as tools, methods, and processes) and transfer them into the organization in an orderly manner. The focus of Technology Change Management is on performing innovation efficiently in an ever-changing world.
- Process Change Management: continually improve the software processes used in the organization with the intent of improving software quality, increasing productivity, and decreasing the cycle time for product development.

### 3.4 Goals and Key Practices

*Goals* summarize the key practices of a key process area and can be used to determine whether an organization or project has effectively implemented the key process area. The goals signify the scope, boundaries, and intent of each key process area. Satisfaction of a key process area is determined by achievement of the goals.

*Key practices* describe the activities and infrastructure that contribute most to the effective implementation and institutionalization of the key process area. Each key practice consists of a single sentence, often followed by a more detailed description, which may include examples and elaboration. These key practices, also referred to as the top-level key practices, state the fundamental policies, procedures, and activities for the key process area. The components of the detailed description are frequently referred to as subpractices. The key practices describe "what" is to be done, but they should not be interpreted as mandating "how" the goals should be achieved. Alternative practices may accomplish the goals of the key process area. The key practices should be interpreted rationally to judge whether the goals of the key process area are effectively, although perhaps differently, achieved.

## 4 Future Directions of the CMM

Achieving higher levels of software process maturity is incremental and requires a long-term commitment to continuous process improvement. Software organizations may take ten years or more to build the foundation for, and a culture oriented toward, continuous process improvement. Although a decade-long process improvement program is foreign to most U.S. companies, this level of effort is required to produce mature software organizations.

The CMM is not a silver bullet and does not address all of the issues that are important for successful projects. For example, it does not currently address expertise in particular application domains, advocate specific software technologies, or suggest how to select, hire, motivate, and retain competent people. Although these issues are crucial to a project's success, they have not been integrated into the CMM.

The CMM has evolved since 1986 [Paulk95b] and will continue to evolve. Feedback from the use of the CMM in software process assessments, software capability evaluations, and process improvement programs, the continuing evolution of the field of software engineering, and the changing business environment all contribute to the need for a "living CMM." To achieve a reasonable balance between the need for stability by organizations using the CMM in software process improvement and the need for continual improvement, we anticipate a 5-year cycle for major revisions of the CMM. Version 2 of the CMM is planned for the 1997 time frame.

The SEI is also working with the International Standards Organization (ISO) in its efforts to build international standards for software process assessment, improvement, and capability determination [Dorling93, Konrad95]. This effort will integrate concepts from many different process improvement methods. The development of the ISO standards (and the contributions of other methods) will influence CMM v2, even as the SEI's process work will influence the activities of the ISO.

## 5 Conclusion

The CMM represents a "common sense engineering" approach to software process improvement. The maturity levels, key process areas, common features, and key practices have been extensively discussed and reviewed within the software community. While the CMM is not perfect, it does represent a broad consensus of the software community and is a useful tool for guiding software process improvement efforts.

The CMM provides a conceptual structure for improving the management and development of software products in a disciplined and consistent way. It does not guarantee that software products will be successfully built or that all problems in software engineering will be adequately resolved. However, current reports from CMM-based improvement programs indicate that it can improve the likelihood with which a software organization can achieve its cost, quality, and productivity goals.

The CMM identifies practices for a mature software process and provides examples of the state-of-the-practice (and in some cases, the state-of-the-art), but it is not meant to be either exhaustive or dictatorial. The CMM identifies the characteristics of an effective software process, but the mature organization addresses all issues essential to a successful project, including people and technology, as well as process.

## 6 References


Bate95 Roger Bate, et al, "A Systems Engineering Capability Maturity Model, Version 1.1," Software Engineering Institute, CMU/SEI-95-MM-003, Nov. 1995.

Dorling93 Alec Dorling, "Software Process Improvement and Capability dEtermination," *Software Quality J.*, Vol. 2, No. 4, Dec. 1993, pp. 209–224.

Curtis95 Bill Curtis, William E. Hefley, and Sally Miller, "People Capability Maturity Model," Software Engineering Institute, CMU/SEI-95-MM-02, Sept. 1995.

Goldenson95 Dennis R. Goldenson and James D. Herbsleb, "After the Appraisal: A Systematic Survey of Process Improvement, Its Benefits, and Factors that Influence Success," Software Engineering Institute, CMU/SEI-95-TR-009, Aug. 1995.

Hayes95 Will Hayes and Dave Zubrow, "Moving On Up: Data and Experience Doing CMM-Based Process Improvement," Software Engineering Institute, CMU/SEI-95-TR-008, Aug. 1995.

Herbsleb94 James Herbsleb, et al., "Benefits of CMM-Based Software Process Improvement: Initial Results," Software Engineering Institute, CMU/SEI-94-TR-13, Aug. 1994.

Humphrey89 W.S. Humphrey, *Managing the Software Process*, Addison-Wesley, Reading, Mass., 1989.

Konrad95 Michael D. Konrad, Mark C. Paulk, and Allan W. Graydon, "An Overview of SPICE's Model for Process Management," *Proc. 5th Int'l Conf. Software Quality*, 1995.

Lawlis95 Patricia K. Lawlis, Robert M. Flowe, and James B. Thordahl, "A Correlational Study of the CMM and Software Development Performance," *Crosstalk: The Journal of Defense Software Engineering*, Vol. 8, No. 9, Sept. 1995, pp. 21–25.

Paulk95a Carnegie Mellon University, Software Engineering Institute (Principal Contributors and Editors: Mark C. Paulk, Charles V. Weber, Bill Curtis, and Mary Beth Chrissis), *The Capability Maturity Model: Guidelines for Improving the Software Process*, Addison-Wesley Publishing Company, Reading, Mass., 1995.

Paulk95b Mark C. Paulk, "The Evolution of the SEI's Capability Maturity Model for Software," *Software Process: Improvement and Practice*, Pilot Issue, Spring 1995.


## For Further Information

For further information regarding the CMM and its associated products, including training on the CMM and how to perform software process assessments and software capability evaluations, contact:

SEI Customer Relations
Software Engineering Institute
Carnegie Mellon University
Pittsburgh, PA 15213-3890
(412) 268-5800
Internet: customer-relations@sei.cmu.edu

# Chapter 12

# Software Technology

## 1. Introduction to Chapter

This chapter introduces a number of different and somewhat independent technologies that can be applied to many aspects of the software development process. It includes such topics as reverse engineering, re-engineering, reuse, prototyping, CASE tools, and metrics.

*Reverse engineering* is the process of reconstructing products developed earlier in the life cycle from products later in the life cycle, for example, deriving the program requirements or design from the code. It involves analyzing a subject system to: (1) identify the system's components and their interrelationships, and (2) create a representation of the system in another form or at a higher level of abstraction.

*Re-engineering* is the examination and alteration of a subject system to reconstitute it in a new form, and the subsequent implementation of the new form. Re-engineering generally includes some form of reverse engineering (to achieve a more abstract description) followed by some form of forward engineering or restructuring. For example, existing code is reverse engineered in order to obtain requirements and/or design, and new (better structured, designed, and documented) code is then generated. A re-engineered software system typically performs the same functions after the re-engineering as before.

*Reuse* is the act of using an existing software product in a new project. It is a software development strategy that attempts to reduce development costs and to improve software quality by incorporating previ-

SOFTWARE TECHNOLOGY

ously proven work products such as designs and code into a new software product. The net effect of reusing software work products would be shorter development schedules (because components do not have to be re-invented) and more reliable software (because the components have previously been used successfully).

In engineering, a *prototype* is a full-scale model and the functional form of a new system or subsystem. (A prototype does not have to be the complete system; only the part of interest.) A software prototype would be a computer program that implements some part of the system requirements. This prototype can be used to assist in defining requirements or evaluating alternatives. Examples of the use of prototypes include determining how to obtain the required accuracy in real-time performance, or evaluating user interface suitability. The process of building the prototype will also expose and eliminate a number of the ambiguities, inconsistencies, blind spots, and misunderstandings incorporated in the specifications, or the statement or concept of the project that exists when the prototyping takes place.

It has been argued that software people misuse the term prototype, which causes confusion particularly among people trained in some form of hardware engineering. The following short paper by Gregory explains the problem.

## On Prototypes vs. Mockups
## S.T. Gregory [1]

Over the last several years, an increasing amount of attention has been given to a subject commonly referred to as rapid prototyping. The discussions tend to refer to the creation of programs that have user interfaces similar to the desired final product, but that are incomplete or severely restricted functionally. I have always contended that the Computer Science jargon should contain true (as opposed to false) cognates from English or the general engineering jargon. Thus, I would like to point out that the term prototype in this context is inappropriate. A more accurate term would be mock-up.

In non-computer science usage, a prototype is a hand-crafted version of a final production model. It has all of the production model's functionality. Webster's New World Dictionary of the American Language, Second College Edition, defines a prototype as "a perfect example of a particular type."

A mock-up, on the other hand, resembles the final product only at a surface level. It has little of the eventual functionality, and is often used near the beginning of a project to ensure that the customer's requirements are understood. According to the same dictionary, a mock-up is a "scale model [...] of a structure or apparatus used for instructional or experimental purposes."

Perhaps, in the future, authors will think more carefully before choosing to use the word prototype, and will pay more attention to which words they appropriate to have specialized meanings in our field.

Samuel T. Gregory University of Virginia
Dept. Computer Science, Thornton Hall
Charlottesville, VA 22903

A *CASE* (Computer Aided Software Engineering) *tool* is an automated software engineering tool that can assist software engineers in analyzing, designing, coding, testing, and documenting a software system and managing a software project. John Manley of the University of Pittsburgh is apparently the first person to use the acronym "CASE" for computer-aided software engineering. [2,3]

A *metric* is a measure of the degree to which a process or product possesses a given attribute. Besides process and product metrics, other definitions of types of metrics are (adapted from IEEE Std 610.12-1990 [4]):

- *Software quality metric*—A quantitative measure of the degree to which software possesses a given attribute that affects its quality. Examples are: reliability, maintainability, portability
- *Software quantity metric*—A quantitative measure of some physical attribute of software. Examples are: lines of code, function points, pages of documentation
- *Management metric*—A management indicator that can be used to measure management activities such as budget spent, value earned, costs overrun, and schedule slippage

In the early 1980s, the US Air Force's Rome Air Development Center (now known as Rome Laboratories) developed a set of software metrics called quality factors that represent the product attributes most desired by customers [5]. These metrics have become part of our metrics environment and as such are used in many developments of software systems. These metrics are:

| | |
|---|---|
| correctness | reliability |
| efficiency | integrity |
| usability | survivability |
| maintainability | verifiability |
| flexibility | portability |
| reusability | interoperability |
| expandability | |

Perhaps the most important software quality attribute is software reliability. Software reliability measures the extent to which the software will perform without any failures within a specified time period [6].

Other important attributes not on the RADC list include safety, security, complexity, and user friendliness.

An important set of metrics for software management was developed by the MITRE Corporation for the US Air Force Electronic Systems Division (ESD; now Electronic Systems Center) [7]. These ten metrics are considered by many to be the best set of management metrics available today. They are:

- Software size metric
- Software personnel metric
- Software volatility metric
- Computer resources utilization metric
- Design complexity metric
- Schedule progress metric
- Design progress metric
- Computer software unit (CSU) development progress metric
- Testing progress metric
- Incremental release content metric

Another set of management metrics was published by the US Air Force Systems Command (now part of the Air Force Materiel Command) in 1986 [8]. This set included:

- Computer resource utilization
- Software development manpower
- Requirements definition and stability
- Software progress (development and test)
- Cost and schedule deviations
- Software development tools

Measurement has been an integral part of the Software Engineering Institute's process improvement project. The first set of guidelines published by this project [9] included 10 metrics at process maturity level 2:

- Planned versus actual staffing profiles
- Software size versus time
- Statistics on software code and test errors
- Actual versus planned units designed
- Actual versus planned units completing unit testing
- Actual versus planned units integrated
- Target computer memory utilization
- Target computer throughput utilization
- Target computer I/O channel utilization
- Software build/release content

With the publication in 1993 of the Software Engineering Institute's Capability Maturity Model for Software [10], measurement became one of the "common features" that are part of every Key Process Area at all maturity levels. The paper by Paulk, Curtis, Chrissis, and Weber in the preceding chapter provides an overview of the SEI's model of process maturity and the role of metrics in this model.

One of the major issues in applying any of the new technologies or methodologies is the technology transfer gap. The technology transfer gap is the time interval (measured in years) between the development of a new product, tool, or technique and its use by the consumers of that product, tool, or technique. Redwine and Riddle [11] have concluded that the technology transfer gap is in the range of 15 to 18 years.

## 2. Introduction to Papers

The first article, by Patrick Hall and Lingzi Jin, on the re-engineering and reuse of software, is an original paper that explores the current use of re-engineering, reuse, and, as a side issue, reverse engineering. Production of software is expensive, and the authors point out that, with the cost of hardware decreasing, we need to increase productivity in software development. Software re-engineering and reuse is a method of increasing software development productivity. This paper provides historical background behind reuse and re-engineering and discusses, as a necessity of re-engineering, the need for reverse engineering.

The second paper, "Prototyping: Alternative System Development Methodologies," by J.M. Carey, explains what prototyping is, as well as pointing out that it has become a popular alternative to traditional software development methodologies. The paper discusses the various definitions of prototyping, looks at the advantages and disadvantages of using a prototyping approach, and looks at one positive and one negative case study of prototyping in an industrial setting.

From Carey's point of view, prototyping is a process of quickly building a model of the final software system, used primarily as communication tool to assist in meeting the information needs of the user. Software prototyping became popular with the advent of Fourth Generation Languages (4GLs) (also called application generators). The author points out some of the advantages of prototyping, including faster development time, easier end use and learning, reduced cost of development, decreased backlogs, and enhanced user/analyst communications. Some of the disadvantages of prototyping are also discussed, including fostering of undue expectations on the part of the user.

The third paper in this section, by Alfonso Fuggetta, is on the classification of CASE technology. The purpose of this paper is to provide a survey and a classification system to help categorize CASE tools. Some of the tools looked at by the author are editing tools, programming tools, configuration management tools, verification/validation tools, project management tools, metrics and measurement tools, and some miscellaneous tools.

The fourth paper, written by Ronald Nusenoff and Dennis Bunde of Loral Corporation (now part of Lockheed Martin), describes how Loral's Software Productivity Laboratory (SPL) makes use of metrics to improve its software engineering process maturity. The SPL has developed a metrics guidebook to define a set of standards for software metrics and to specify procedures for collecting and analyzing metrics data. The SPL also developed a spreadsheet tool to provide automated support for metrics generation, collection, graphical representation, and analysis.

These Loral corporate metrics were defined to map to the corporate development methodology. Both were part of the program being developed to advance Loral Corporation to Levels 4 and 5 on the SEI's process maturity scale. The paper demonstrates Loral's commitment to process improvement, as defined by the SEI, and Loral's belief in the close relationship of process and metrics.

The Loral metrics were based on the MITRE software management metrics [12]. The paper compares the MITRE and Loral metrics to those defined in the SEI's 1987 software maturity questionnaire [13], the precursor to the CMM. Loral used the 1987 document as the basis for its process improvement efforts because most of the work was done before publication of the CMM in 1993.

The last very short paper in this section, by Barry Boehm, is entitled "Industrial Software Metrics Top Ten List." This is an interesting list of metrics developed by Dr. Boehm in the late 1980s. The value of this list is that these metrics are well established and each one of them affects our ability to deliver software on time and within budget. This very short list has been circulated around the industry for years and has proved to be useful to any software engineering practitioner. For the most part they still appear to be valid today.


1. Gregory, J.T., "On Prototypes vs. Mockups," ACM SIGSOFT, *Software Engineering Notes*, Vol. 9, No. 5., Oct. 1984, p. 13.

2. Manley, J.H., "Computer Aided Software Engineering (CASE): Foundation for Software Factories," *Proc. IEEE COMPCON '84 Fall Computer Conf. Small Computer (R)Evolution* IEEE Computer Society Press, Los Alamitos. Calif., 1984, pp. 84–91.

3. Manley, J.H., "Computer Aided Software Engineering," *Selected Conference Papers, 10th Ann. Federal DP Expo & Conf.,* Interface Control Group, Inc., Vienna, VA, 1984.

4. IEEE Standard 610.12-1990, *IEEE Standard Glossary of Software Engineering Terminology,* The Institute of Electrical and Electronics Engineers, Inc., Piscataway, NJ, 1990.

5. Software Quality Measures for Distributed Systems (Vol I), Software Quality Measures for Distributed Systems: Guide Book for Software Quality Measurements (Vol II), and Software Quality Measures for Distributed Systems: Impact on Software Quality (Vol III), TR RADC-TR-175, Rome Air Development Center, Griffiss AFB, NY, 1983.

6. Bowen, T.P., G.B. Wigle, and J.T. Tsai, Specification of Software Quality Attributes: Vol. 1, Final Technical Report; Vol. 2, Software Quality Specifications Guidebook; Vol. 3, Software Quality Evaluation Guidebook; RADC TR-85-37, prepared by Boeing Aerospace Company for Rome Air Development Center, Griffiss AFB, NY, Feb. 1985.

7. Schultz, H.P., *Software Management Metrics,* ESD TR-88-001, prepared by The MITRE Corporation for the U.S. Air Force, Electronic Systems Division, Hanscom AFB, MA, 1988.

8. "Air Force Systems Command Software Management Indicators: Management Insight," AFSC Pamphlet 800-43, 31 Jan. 1986

9. Humphrey, W.S., and W.L. Sweet, "A Method for Assessing the Software Development Capability of Contractors," CMU/SEI-87-TR-23, Sept. 1987.

10. Paulk, Mark C., et al., "Key Practices of the Capability Maturity Model, Version 1.1," CMU/SEI-93-TR-25, Feb. 1993.

11. Redwine, S. T., Jr., and W. E. Riddle, "Software Technology Maturation," *Proc. 8th Int'l Conf. Software Eng.*, IEEE Computer Society Press, Los Alamitos, Calif., 1985, pp. 189–200.

# The Re-engineering and Reuse of Software[1]

Patrick A.V. Hall[2] and Lingzi Jin[3]

## Abstract

*Since software re-engineering and reuse have matured and the major technical problems have been solved, the emphasis is now on introducing reuse and re-engineering into practice as a management activity. Re-engineering methods predominantly address the code level, but for full effect we should understand the main purpose for which software was built: the application domain. Reuse methods focus on library organization and on standards for component production, with much interest in object-oriented methods. Similarly, in order to reuse software effectively, we need to understand the application domain so that we can choose the appropriate parts, organize these effectively into libraries, and deploy the library components to solve new problems. This leads us to domain analysis. Although management, social, and economic issues remain to be solved, current developments suggest reuse and re-engineering will be re-absorbed into main-stream practice.*

## 1 Introduction

Software re-engineering and reuse are concerned with maximizing software usage for any given development effort. The production of software is expensive, and with the decrease in the cost of hardware and the increase in hardware capability, we have been led to ever more ambitious development projects, while qualified and experienced software development staff are in short supply. How can we keep up with this demand for more software? How can we maximize the usage we obtain from software? One response has been to re-engineer software for further use, to reuse the software, and to produce software for widespread reuse from the start.

Figure 1 illustrates the problem. During software development, many alternative ideas and designs are considered and rejected, and thrown away, even though they may have great use in other applications. Tools may be built and discarded, and test cases used and then set aside. At the end of its useful life, the

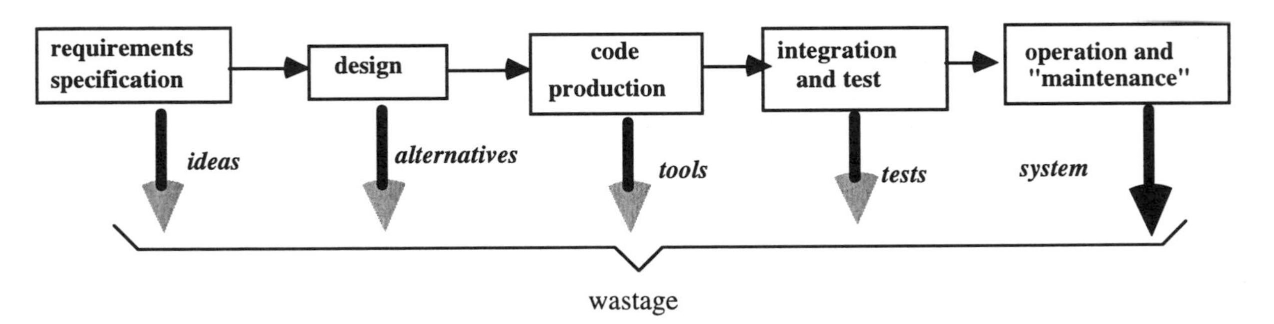


*Figure 1. Software development and the products wasted during and at the end of the process.*

[1] This review of the area is updated from many previous reviews of the area cited in the references.

[2] Department of Computing, Open University, Milton Keynes, England, MK7 6AA

[3] Now with Department of Computer Science, Nanjing University , Nanjing, PR China, 210093

complete system itself may be thrown away. It is the objective of software reverse engineering and reuse to recover some of this investment. We define the basic terms below, in preparation for the later fuller description of the areas in the body of the paper.

### 1.1 Re-engineering

Within the development of software, some 60 to 70 percent of total life-cycle costs are spent on "maintenance"—the activities undertaken after software is first delivered to remove bugs, change it to meet the real requirements, and enhance it to meet new or changing requirements (see Swanson and Beath, 1989). In order to make changes, we have to first understand the software, often involving 47 to 60 percent of the maintenance effort because of inadequate software documentation. Often, the maintenance effort is forced to rely on the code itself. This means that 30 to 35 percent of total life cycle costs are consumed in trying to understand the software after it has been delivered in order to make changes. Anything that we do to alleviate this situation will reduce costs. The tools and methods used to understand software are known generically as reverse engineering. Reverse engineering may be applied as required, or it may be applied in anticipation of changes as part of a preventative maintenance activity to reconstruct all the necessary documentation to support future maintenance and change.

Having reverse engineered a complete system, it may be necessary to clean up the software or restructure it to meet current standards. We may even re-implement the system by forward engineering it in a newer version of the programming language or some other language (for example in moving from C to C++), or onto new hardware and a new operating system (for example, moving to the latest version of Windows). This complete cycle of reverse engineering followed by forward engineering is called re-engineering.

### 1.2 Reuse

One method proposed for making a significant improvement in productivity and quality is software reuse: using a given piece of software to solve more than one problem. Frequently, this is taken to mean the reuse of program components like library subroutines in more than one application. However, reuse can also be applied much more broadly to include the redeployment of designs, ideas, or even the skills and experience of people. Re-engineering can be viewed as a form of reuse, because we take a complete system and improve it and then redeploy it. Reverse engineering and re-engineering are more important within reuse because of the help they give in creating components.

The creation of components is sometimes known as component engineering. Components can be extracted from existing software using reverse engineering techniques to describe the existing software and identify the modules within it. These modules would then be candidates for reuse. Of course, we would not simply use the modules as we find them, but re-engineer them to the quality standards that we would now expect. The alternative is to create new components from scratch, sometimes referred to as design-for-reuse.

We need to select components that will be useful in the application area concerned and need to know how to use these in meeting a user requirement. The activity of understanding an application area is known as domain analysis. Domain analysis is also important for reverse engineering because we need to know what we might expect to find before we analyze a system to understand what it actually contains.

Component collections are often surprisingly small, perhaps a few hundred, but they can be very large. While small collections can be remembered by the re-user or supported by paper catalogues, large collections of many thousands of components need to be organized within a component library using specially tailored library management methods.

We also need to have methods for using components effectively. This is often known as design-with-reuse. Here the most effective approach is the use of architectural components or frameworks, an approach which originated in a couple of European projects and has since become an integral part of object-oriented methods.

### 1.3 The organization of this paper

Reuse and re-engineering have been with us since the beginning of computing, but have only gained prominence over the past 10 years or so. The area has now matured, all major technical barriers have been solved, and the emphasis is almost universally on management making it happen. Some recent developments indicate that the area is turning full circle and is likely to dissipate into routine practice and other areas of computing.

In this article, we will start with a review of the history of the area and look at what the traditional practice has been before we review the two major strands of the area, Reverse Engineering and Re-engineering and Software Reuse. We then move to the more general consideration of domain modeling and how this fits in.

Next we consider the non-technical issues of management, economics, and social groups. While reuse programs depend upon the development of the technology as discussed above, they cannot succeed solely because of the technology. Software engineers, either as producers of software, or as managers, frequently resist ideas of reuse, because they cannot see the benefits of reuse. A number of issues are discussed.

Finally we look back at progress to date, and at two significant papers which indicate how things might develop from here.

## 2. Historical background

The reuse of software has been with us from the beginning through the publication of algorithms, the use of high level programming languages, and the use of packages, as has been pointed out by many people (see Standish 1984 and Hall 1987).

Reuse through the publication of algorithms and designs has been very important for the development of computing. Textbooks published on a certain area indicate its maturity and are an important vehicle for promoting reuse. Indeed, it is at this level of abstraction that ideas are most transferable and form the cornerstone of our educational systems. As will be seen later, recent work by Arango, Shoen, and Pettengill (1993) is returning us to these origins.

However, it is the consideration of high level programming languages as examples of reuse that is the most illuminating. In high level languages, many frequently used combinations of instructions at the assembly level (for example, for subroutine entry and exit with parameter passing) have been packaged into single constructs at the higher level. A high level language gives a notation for selecting these constructs and composing them to build software systems. Facilities are provided for user created components to be stored and reused, for example through subroutines and macros. This is not the usual way of viewing programming languages and compilers, which are usually seen as "tools" rather than as the engineering foundations of software production. This view of programming languages emphasizes the unique nature of software, the great diversity that its components might take, and the very flexible way they might be interconnected. This programming language orientation has continued through module interconnection languages (see section 4), and has reached its apotheosis with the introduction of domain specific languages and associated compilers in the work of Batory and O'Malley (1992).

Similarly, procuring standard packages is an important example of reuse, and the availability of a wide range of products is again an indicator of the maturity of an area of technology. Capers Jones (1984) made a thorough appraisal of this. Packages which are rigidly defined are seldom useful—some flexibility is essential. This flexibility is provided through a range of capabilities, from simple parameterization and configuration following some elaborate build script (as is usually done for operating systems), to the modification of the package at the source level. The interconnection of the packages during systems integration then becomes the important process of design with reuse, with standard patterns of interconnection being the frameworks that guide this.

Re-engineering and reverse engineering have also been with us since high level languages and compilers were invented. Very early on there were automatic flow-charting tools—a kind of reverse engineering—and with the need to keep software systems in operation with changing hardware, re-engineering appeared. Cross-reference listings of variables were provided with compilers to help understand the large pieces of software. Systems for converting from file based systems to database systems and between database systems also appeared.

The first part of traditional systems analysis describes the current system. That is reverse engineering, though what is different now is that the current system is a computer system and descriptions of it are available in machine readable form. We could in principle use computer tools to assist us in the conventional system analysis phase of describing the current system. The description involves abstractions that remove the detail and reveal the essential nature of the current system and the subsequent development of the new system, using conventional development processes, then makes the total process re-engineering.

When connecting one piece of software to another through an interface, we need to know in great detail the representation of the data that crosses the interface and what it means in terms of the functions that are performed on it. Frequently the supplier's documentation is inadequate, and so we examine the software by running critical test cases to probe the interface or, as a last resort, looking at the code itself. Again, this is reverse engineering.

However, none of these were addressed explicitly as reuse and re-engineering until relatively late. Reuse as a concept was introduced in 1968 in the celebrated paper by McIlroy (1976), but only took hold much later in the Draco research project in the late 1970's (see Neighbours 1984), and in the many projects that followed. Reverse engineering and re-engineering as concepts seem to have crept into software development in the early 1980's, driven by the commercial need to sustain COBOL "legacy" systems and with emerging products that facilitate the maintenance of COBOL.

## 3. Reverse Engineering and Re-engineering

Reverse Engineering is a general area that embraces several subtly different ideas. The January 1990 issue of *IEEE Software* is devoted to Software Maintenance and Reverse Engineering. Our use of terms is consistent with that given by Chikofsky (1990) in that special issue of *Software*, though other terms are in use, such as re-documentation, design recovery, or program understanding.

### 3.1 Current Solutions

At any exhibition of tools that support software development, you will discover many suppliers offering Reverse Engineering tools. Rock-Evans and Hales (1990) gave a very comprehensive survey of these tools. This survey happens to be a UK publication, but a survey report produced anywhere else in the world would be very similar. While many of these tools originate in the US, many also come from elsewhere within the increasingly global CASE tool market. What are the real capabilities of these tools?

Many tools are really very simple, having been in use for many decades, and it is surprising to see these being offered now as if they were new. Outlining tools would list the functions contained within the software, giving the function names, arguments and data types, and possibly the key data structures manipulated and leading comments. The internal operation of the procedures may also be condensed in the form of a flow diagram to show its essential structure. Cross-references between modules may also be extracted, perhaps showing which procedures call which other procedures and use which data structures and distinguishing defining occurrences from places where the data structures are used. All of this may be put together in some diagrammatic form exploiting the bit-map graphics technology of modern platforms and perhaps hypertext technology.

Method and CASE suppliers will commonly include tools to reverse the software to their own notations. Early tools here were for PSL/PSA, and more recently this has been done for dataflow diagrams (Excelerator) and data structures (Bachman).

All of these commercial offerings seem relatively conventional, and the really hard problems, like re-engineering assembly programs, are left aside as activities that require essential human interaction.

Because of these hard research problems, there has been much recent activity in exploring both formal transformations and less formal pattern matching methods. The formal approaches seem to have been mostly a European interest, while the informal approaches have been mostly in the US.

### 3.2 Formal transformations

Formal transformations have usually been viewed as tools of forward engineering, for example transforming a simple but inefficient algorithm into one that is equivalent but more efficient, such as replacing recursion by iteration. However, these transformations can be used in reverse to simplify a well engineered and efficient, but complex and obscure, algorithm. In the process of simplification, details of the software may be removed, such as the decisions that were taken to enhance efficiency. In doing these transformations, we then progress backwards along the software development lifecycle to produce design descriptions and specifications.

Extracting flow diagrams from code is an example of the reversing from code to design. A recent example of this is the paper by Cimitile and de Carlini (1991). However, the objective here is not to produce flow diagrams—after all that had been done 20 years earlier—but to establish an intermediate representation that would serve for transformations

Other projects seek to move from code, possibly Assembler, all the way to formal specifications, typically in Z (see Spivey 1989). One example of this is the work of Martin Ward (1988), who transforms the code into an intermediate "wide-spectrum-language" and then transforms the code into Z. Ward's system is not automatic, but an interactive system which provides the user with a selection of candidate transformations which the user then applies to progressively move towards an acceptable specification. Intermediate states are removed until a pure function mapping inputs to outputs has been abstracted.

A similar system using a different intermediate language has been developed by Lano and others as part of the REDO project (see Lano and Breuer 1989, Lano, Breuer and Haughton 1993, and van Zuylen 1993). The method proposed by Lano, Breuer and Haughton reverse engineers COBOL applications back to specifications. Under manual guidance, the process consists of three stages:

1. Translation from COBOL to their intermediate language Uniform to obtain a restricted subset of constructs.
2. Transform from Uniform to a functional description language. Dataflow diagrams are used to group variables together to create prototype objects (in the sense of object-

oriented approaches). Equational descriptions of the functionality are abstracted from the code. Some simplification to obtain the normal form of the representation may be necessary.

3. The functional descriptions are combined together with the outline objects to derive a specification in Z, or an object oriented version of this, Z++.

With the widescale availability of parallel hardware, there has been considerable activity at parallelising both FORTRAN and COBOL program (see Harrison, Gens, and Gifford 1993). This is a form of re-engineering recognized in this paper, though the community that undertakes this work seems seldom to appreciate this and takes a narrow compilation view of the problem. To parallelize effectively, it may be necessary to reverse the sequential code right back to its specification where parallelism may be natural.

### 3.3 The importance of informal information

The importance of other information in the Reverse Engineering of code was pointed out by Ted Biggerstaff in 1989. Figure 2(a) shows an example in which all the identifiers have been replaced by meaningless numbers and letters, and all the comments have been stripped out. What we get is the machine's-eye view of the code, but to us it is incomprehensible. Figure 2(b) shows the code with the identifiers re-inserted, making it much more understandable. From the chosen identifiers we can immediately see this has something to do with symbol tables and can guess about the structure of the code and the way it operates. What we are doing is using a higher level of understanding of the problem domain being addressed to understand the code. With the comments replaced we would find ourselves even more capable of understanding what is happening.

From this simple example we see that we are concerned with several dimensions of analysis. There is the traditional technical dimension of notations and their inter-relationship. There are layers of abstraction that go from the application, to a generic view of computing problems, to the methods we use for the architectural description and design of software, to the particular constructs we use in program code. And then there are the degrees of formality of representation, from the very formal descriptions associated with program code and the newly emerging formal description techniques to the other extreme of very informal representations of knowledge contained within peoples heads.

### 3.4 Recognizing higher level domain concepts

We have seen that the important part of the whole reverse engineering process is recognizing the known higher level domain concepts in the code.

One method for doing this is matching patterns (also called schemas, templates, cliches, or plans) against the code. The pattern could be the occurrence of a loop and some particular instructions somewhere inside. The whole process could be quite complicated, since in matching several things we could get overlapping matches and have to decide which match to accept. This is the approach taken in the programmers apprentice at MIT (see Rich and Wells, 1990), and that at Arthur Anderson and the University of Illinois (Kozaczynski and Ning 1989, Harandi and Ning 1990, Kozaczynski, Ning, and Engberts 1992). Figure 3 shows the general approach of Harandi and Ning.

A different approach has been the recognition of "objects" in the sense of object-oriented programming. Can particular data items and the functions that operate on them be identified? One method by Garnett and Mariani (1989) looks for data declarations in C and procedures where these appear as arguments, then groups these together. Lano and others on the REDO project (see section 3.2 above) have examined COBOL code and focused on the major files used, grouping these with associated variables and procedures. Both these approaches focus on the code, and the names of the objects would arise accidentally from the data-item names or file names in the code. If these are "meaningful," then the code will have been reversed into a domain model, though clearly the names and other informal information do guide the transformation into objects.

(a) Concepts or "plans" are looked for in the code. The rules show how a particular combination of constructs is taken as evidence that some larger concept is present, for example P52, where a particular combination of assignments indicates a swap.

(b) Sample of a description of software produced by their system. The collection of concepts recognized are displayed within a hierarchy. Note how verbose this description is, with its complete audit trail of how the Bubble sort was recognized.

Throughout this discussion we have had to assume that we knew what we might find in the code we were reverse engineering. Reverse engineering can only take place in the context of a particular domain. This

*(a) a machine-eye view of code*

```
var
    v001: array[1..v009] of record
            v002: char;
            v003: integer;
        end;
    v005, v006: integer;
function f002 (v004: char): integer;
    var
        v007, v008: integer;
begin
    v008 := 0;
    for v007 := 1 to v005 do
        if v001[v007].v002 = v004 then
            begin
                v008 := v001[v007].v003;
                leave;
            end;
    f002 := v008;
end;
```

*(b) the human-eye view of the code—meaningful identifiers added: comments would add yet more information*

```
var
    symboltable: array[1..tablesize] of record
            symbol: char;
            location: integer;
        end;
    lastsym, symmax: integer;
function STlookup (sym: char): integer;
    var
        i, loctn: integer;
begin
    loctn := 0;
    for i := 1 to lastsym do
        if symboltable[i].symbol = sym then
            begin
                loctn := symboltable[i].location;
                leave;
            end;
    STlookup := loctn;
end;
```

*Figure 2. The importance of informal information in the understanding of software. The example here is part of simple compiler used for teaching purposes*

(a) *Concepts or "plans" are looked for in the code. The rules show how a particular combination of constructs is taken as evidence that some larger concept is present, for example P52, where a particular combination of assignments indicates a swap.*

P50: If there exists a decremental FOR-LOOP event
then there exists a DEC-COUNTER event

P51: If there exists an incremental FOR-LOOP event
then there exists an INC-COUNTER event

P52: If there exists an ASSIGN event from ?V1 to ?T
which precedes an ASSIGN ?T to ?V2 event and
another ASSIGN ?V2 to ?V1 event on a control path
(c-precede)
then there eists a SIMPLE-SWAP(?V1,?V2) event

. . .

P57: If a FORWARD-MAP-ENUMERATOR event c-encloses
GUARDED-MAP-SWAP event
then there exists a FILTERED SEQUENTIAL-MAP-SW
event

P58: If a DEC_COUNTER event c-encloses an
FILTERED-SEQEUNTIAL-MAP-SWAP event
then there exists a BUBBLE-SORT-MAP event

(b) *Sample of a description of software produced by their system. The collection of concepts recognized are displayed within a hierarchy. Note how verbose this description is, with its complete audit trail of how the Bubble sort was recognized.*

This program implements a BUBBLE-SORT-MAP event at
lines ... which sorts the map A using a bubble sort
algorithm,
It consists of:

1: A DEC-COUNTER event at lines (203 245) which
decrementally changes the value in K from N-1 to 1.
It consists of:
1.1: A FOR-LOOP event at lines (230 245).

2. A FILTERED-SEQUENTIAL-MAP-SWAP-MAP even
lines ... which sequentially switches the adjacent
elements in a map A if A(J-1)>A(J), indexed by J
from 1 to K
It consists of:
2.1: *etcetera etcetera*

*Figure 3. Analysis approach of Harandi and Ning to understanding a bubble sort program.*

knowledge is captured within a domain model, but domain models have to be produced themselves. This is the subject of the later section on domain analysis.

## 4. Software Reuse

### 4.1 The reuse process

The general idea of software reuse is that it is a component repository from which reusable components may be extracted. Figure 4 shows the general idea. To be able to reuse software components, we need:

- a building-up phase when reusable software is identified and brought together into a library (shown on the left side of Figure 4), component engineering; and
- a design-with-reuse phase when reusable software is selected from the library on the basis of system requirements and reused in the construction of a new software system (shown on the right side of Figure 4). New components may be designed for this system and added into the library.

There is also a need to consider more general knowledge about the area or domain of application of the components, as shown at the bottom left of Figure 4. The knowledge helps us identify suitable components and to structure the component library to aid retrieval (for example with an index or a thesaurus). This domain analysis will be discussed in more detail later.

This overall process could be refined to show more internal details. We will see some of these details in the following sections. A formal process model could be created and enacted under the control of appropriate work-flow software; some Esprit projects, notably RECYCLE, are in the process of doing this.

Integrating reuse within any particular lifecycle of software development is required. In analyzing and designing new systems, the possibility of reuse needs to be considered and the appropriate library components incorporated; new elements of software that are needed should also be considered as candidates for the library and added to it. The REBOOT project has done this for a number of standard development methodologies, from the Clean Room to Structured Analysis and Design (Karlsson 1995).

### 4.2 Component models

The central ingredient for reuse is the component. Figure 5 gives a visualization of components and their points of connection. Note that in this general view of components, they have multiple interfaces. Components have to be interconnected; in Figure 5 this would take the form of "plugging" the components together as permitted by the type of plug and socket. The equivalent of plugging components together in software is procedure calling, possibly with the additional use of program code to convert data. The programming language used for this purpose is sometimes known as a module interconnection language, introduced by De Remer and Kron in 1976 (see Prieto-Diaz and Neighbors 1986 for a survey).

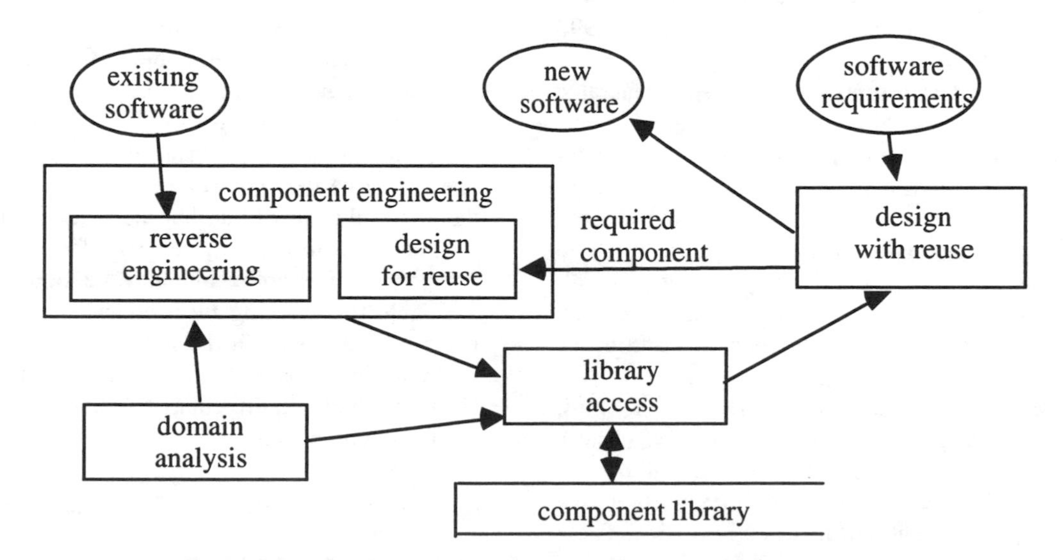


*Figure 4. The Reuse Process, built round a component library into which components are added after component engineering, and from which components are taken during design-with-reuse.*

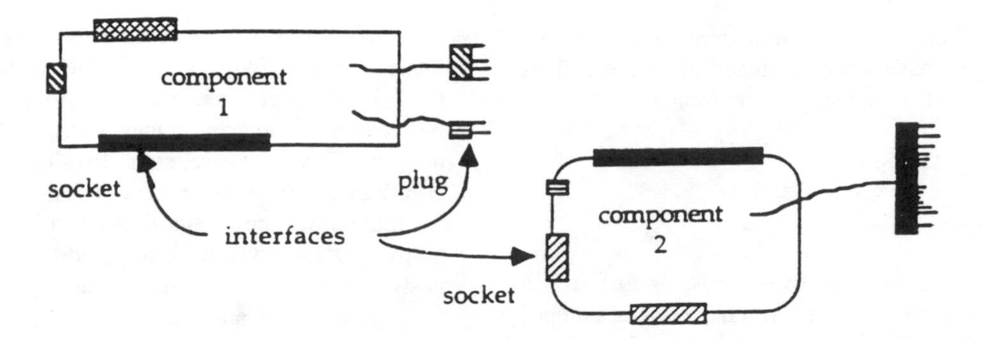


*Figure 5. Software components—a diagrammatic representation, showing their interfaces. Plugs show interfaces called (required), while sockets show interfaces offered (provided). Where the shading is the same, the interfaces are of the same type, and plugs can be connected to sockets of the same type.*

Deciding which components should be built is guided by domain analysis. When the component is extracted from existing software, reverse engineering is used to identify the component and to abstract the specification. Alternatively, as shown in figure 4, we could create useful software components when developing new software, a process called "design for reuse." We would focus extra effort on developing the new reusable parts to maximize the cost and quality benefits derived from the reuse of these parts within the domain.

Each reusable component should be given a clear specification and description of the principles and concepts underlying the component, independent of any particular implementation. Quality information should be recorded, for example the levels of inspection or proof undertaken, the level of testing carried out, and the results of various metrics. Other administrative information should also be recorded, such as who produced the component and when, its revision history, and a reference site (see Moineau et al. 1990 and Karlsson 1995).

In all cases it is essential to create as general a component as possible, while avoiding over-generalisation which could make specific uses difficult to specialize and inefficient in execution. This requires that generalizations and inductions are made over several more specific components, a process for which no general guidance is available as yet. The general-purpose component would be suitably parameterized, so that particular uses are easily specialized from the generic part.

Very formal models can be created; the most sophisticated are probably those of Goguen (1986), Cramer et al. (1991), and Tracz (1993), but all models have more or less equivalent capabilities for precisely defining the component interfaces and function. These definitions will identify a number of other external components. Interfaces as depicted in Figure 5 can also be viewed as components. Generic parameters will be components. Decomposition will be in terms of an implementation using other components, and in an object-oriented approach, there will be hierarchical subclass relationships to other component classes. It is clear that the particular external connections are interchangeable, and how a particular interconnection is articulated is an issue for the designer of the component.

Object-oriented methods are seen as important for reuse (see Booch 1987, 1991 and Cox 1986, 1990). The objects are the components, providing the encapsulation that is necessary, while inheritance structures provide the contexts for reuse to take place and one important method for actually effecting the reuse. Cox has called reusable parts "software integrated circuits," basing his proposals on object-oriented methods. OO methods are being applied industrially (see Harris 1991), and several ESPRIT projects are taking an object-oriented approach to reuse, for example, REBOOT (see Morel and Faget 1993), ITHACA-2 (Ader et al. 1990, Nierstrasz et al. 1991), and BUSINESS CLASS. This motivation continues with current developments in Object Oriented methods, frameworks, and patterns (see Gamma et al. 1993).

An important issue is the size or granularity of the components—are they small like scientific subroutines, or large like word-processing packages? Clearly there is a place for both, but the requirements for description and storage may be very different. With large components the collection may be quite small and amenable to searching by hand, while small components such as those in the NAG library of numerical routines or the Smalltalk library may lead to very large libraries which require computer support for finding a particular component.

### 4.3 Storing and Retrieving Reusable Software

Having identified software which is potentially reusable and described in such a way that anyone wishing to reuse it would be able to do so, the problem arises as to how to organize the total collection of all such software and related descriptions. Such a library can be structured by classifying the reusable software in various ways. A good system of classification not only provides the basis for cataloguing the software, but also provides a means for finding a particular piece of software held in the library. One could even view the classification system as a domain model.

Large collections of software present similar problems of classification to those of Information Retrieval (see Salton and McGill 1983). This has proved an attractive area for the research community, with many applications of library classification methods to software component libraries (see Frakes and Nejmeh 1985, Prieto-Diaz and Freeman 1987, Wood and Sommerville 1988, Prieto-Diaz 1991, and Maarek et al. 1991). The faceted classification method of Prieto-Diaz and Freeman (1987) is the current favorite. Albrechtson (1990) has also surveyed the field.

So far software libraries have been very small—typically only a few hundred components, though some special cases like Ada and Smalltalk have a few thousand. The Eiffel libraries have only 300 classes containing some 5,000 visible operations (Meyer 1990). With such small collections, the need for sophisticated library search facilities must be in doubt.

### 4.4 Designing Software using Reusable Parts

Given a statement of requirements or a detailed specification, or even a high level design, we will need to match this with the reusable software held in a library. We could find a single component that would fully, or almost fully, satisfy our requirement, but might only find a collection of components which, when suitably interconnected, would satisfy the requirement.

The first case is already a common problem in package selection, though this important part of commercial software practice is almost entirely ignored by system development methodologies. What we have to do here is match the requirements or specification against the specifications in the library, using the retrieval mechanisms described above. Exact matching of precise (formal) specifications will in general be undecidable (that is, impossible), and we therefore must necessarily reduce our descriptions for search purposes, accepting that we can only find near matches. Further, even if we could match precisely, we need to recognize that if we cannot find an exact match, we can always customize by adding extra software "shells," or even by modifying code (sometimes called white-box reuse and discussed later). Thus, we would be quite content to accept partial or approximate matches, with some further manual process required to select the most suitable of the retrieved components.

If some combination of several components could satisfy our requirements, we need to decompose our requirements in some way. One way is clearly an extension of the first, looking for some sub-match of library components to the requirements by searching strings for substrings or graphs for subgraphs. We know of no work in this area.

Alternatively, we could first decompose the requirements into parts, and then search for these in the library; that is, do a high level design. One way to do this would be to use stereotypical designs, often called frameworks, such as those used in some approaches to object oriented design (Wirfs-Brock and Johnson 1990) and described for the ESPRIT Practitioner project (Hall et al. 1990). Frameworks are now well established in object-oriented software development, and the Choices operating system (Campbell et al. 1987) is based on these principles. In OO approaches, a framework is a collection of interconnected objects (abstract classes) which defines the overall architecture of the system. The framework is instantiated by supplying concrete classes to match the abstract classes of the framework. These could be selections of classes that are already available, or they could be created specially in conformance to the abstract class.

Note that the use of a framework is equivalent to the reuse of a design, but it is still code! While many people claim code reuse is irrelevant and that higher level design and specification reuse carries the benefits, frameworks actually help these ideas become concrete and become a special form of code reuse.

The most recent development in the frameworks arena is the use of design patterns. These are small configurations of components which work together to achieve particular ends, but which could not themselves be encapsulated as a component. Rather, they show how to use components and how to build frameworks. The leading book in the field is that of Gamma, Helm, Johnson, and Vlissides (1993), though patterns have been the subject of many conferences and workshops, and many other books are now appearing.

Having selected a component (or set of components) for reuse, it is necessary to adapt the component for its intended use by composing it with other components and new software to achieve the desired results. Adaptation or specialization could vary from modification of sources to the provision of parameter values to a generic package to instantiate it for a particular use, as in Ada or in fully polymorphic languages such as ML. Modifying sources, sometimes known as white-box reuse, is done as a last resort, for this could compromise the quality of the component, and quality was one of the main motivations for software reuse.

To compose components we need a language for building systems. This could be the simple linkage mechanisms of the programming language being used, or the mechanisms available at the command language level, such as pipes in the UNIX shell. However, the language for system building could be developed specifically for module interconnection, either as part of a larger programming system such as Conic (Sloman et al. 1985) or C/MESA (Lauer et al. 1979), or could even be an independent language, such as INTERCOL (Tichy 1980). These module interconnection languages (MILs) enable the consistency of interconnection to be checked by strong typing: a good survey has been given by Prieto-Diaz and Neighbours (1986).

When specialized and connected together, the available code components will probably be insufficient to meet the full requirements and other original code may be necessary, perhaps to transform the outputs from one component to the required form of inputs to another, or perhaps to add other functions not available from the component library.

## 4. Domain Analysis

In both Reverse Engineering and in Reuse, we have seen that a proper understanding of the application domain is essential. We termed the process of obtaining this understanding domain analysis. To do this we need to identify the major concepts of the area and identify the relationships between these concepts. The importance of this was first identified in the DRACO project (Freeman 1987, Prieto-Diaz and Freeman 1987). The fruits of this analysis are a domain model or domain language.

There will be a number of domain models, ranging from application specific domains like steel rolling mills to generic applications like continuous process control systems, or from generic technology like real-time distributed systems and data base systems to programming domains of procedure call, variables, and assignments.

In Reverse Engineering possible components or concepts are determined by the higher level domain model and the software (code, design description, or whatever) is searched to identify parts which could be components. Having identified potential components, these will be transformed, generalized, and compared against a base of already discovered components until a candidate component has been demonstrated. We can then abstract to the higher level of description and replace the component discovered by the higher level concept. The demonstration that a component is present could be very formal, involving proof techniques or it could involve access to a human to obtain confirmation. It could also involve the execution of code against some critical test case which will confirm or refute the hypothesis. This continues by finding and confirming/discarding the components as the software is progressively understood in terms of the higher level domain language and moving up levels of language as the reverse engineering progresses.

In Software Reuse domain understanding is important in a number of ways. One way was to guide the production of components. These could be reverse engineered out of existing systems, as described above, or components could be produced from scratch. The important components in the domain are indicated by the domain model. These components then need to be organized in a way that is helpful to designers; again, domain understanding is important, typically being captured as a thesaurus. Components need to be assembled into particular systems—often these will be stereotypical solutions or frameworks-again manifesting domain understanding.

The notations used for domain analysis could be conceptual dependencies (Schank 1972) or, similarly, simply some form of data analysis using entity-relationship models (see Teory and Fry 1982 and Nijssen and Halpin 1989). They could even be thesauri (see Aitchison and Gilchrist 1971 and Townley and Gee, 1980). Object-oriented methods have also been proposed. The process of domain analysis has much in common with knowledge acquisition, but needs further development (see Simos 1988 and Prieto-Diaz 1990). In its most general form, domain analysis could be viewed as an attempt to formalize scientific method, an enterprise that is doomed to failure.

What constitutes an adequate domain model is the subject of much debate. We need compact and precise modeling methods that have an adequate expressive power, and a strong case against entity-relationship models has been made (Carasik et al. 1990) on the basis of its inadequacy for modeling natural language. However, this does seem to miss the issue of whether or not it is adequate for the required modeling task. Entity relationship models have been widely used and found adequate, particularly when extended with inheritance in what is sometimes called structurally object-oriented systems. Whether fully object-oriented methods will prove adequate remains to be seen, though clearly they are the premier candidates for use in domain models.

Domain models and design frameworks are converging in domain specific software architectures. A workshop was held by DARPA in 1990 and the idea of domain specific software architectures recurs from time to time as a means of leveraging specific applications and encapulating commercial assets (Tracz 1995).

## 5. Implementing software reuse and re-engineering

In order to promote reuse, it is not sufficient to establish the correct technical environment; we must also address other non-technical issues, such as managerial practices and the legal constraints of a particular community.

### 5.1 Reuse methods

A number of reuse methods have emerged and there is an increasing volume of literature describing the successful introduction of reuse into companies (see Matsumoto 1993 and Kruzela and Brorsson 1992). NATO has developed a reuse policy, and the US armed forces are mandating reuse similar to the way they earlier mandated the use of Ada.

Basili's approach (1990, 1991) is proving popular. This approach focuses on the comprehensive or full reuse of requirements, design, and code from any earlier versions and the reuse of processes and other knowledge. It includes a reuse model (Basili 1991), characterization schemes, and a supporting environment model. Each reuse candidate is characterized as a series of descriptors: name, function, use, type, granularity, representation, input/output, dependencies, application domain, solution domain, and object domain. Required objects are also described in the same way. Reuse consists of transforming existing reuse candidates into required objects and comprises four basic activities: identification, evaluation, modification, and integration. The categories for each reuse activity are name, function, type, mechanism, input/output, dependencies, experience transfer, and reuse quality. The important components of the supporting environment model are the project organization and the experience factory. Each project is carried out according to the quality improvement paradigm consisting of the following steps: plan, execute, and package. At each step, reuse requirements are identified and matches made against reuse candidates available in the experience base. In the final step, a decision is made as to which experiences are worth recording in the experience base.

A comprehensive methodology has been developed within the REBOOT project which will enable reuse to be added to any existing method. Pilot studies have been made of integrating reuse into the cleanroom method and object oriented methods. A reuse handbook has been published (Karlsson 1995).

### 5.2 Personnel issues

People who work in software production like producing software and will develop software rather than look for existing ideas, algorithms, or code. They use all sorts of personally persuasive arguments:

- "Reinventing software is fun!"
- "Why buy when you can build?"
- "Having seen the commercial product, I know I could build it better."
- "If somebody else built it, could you really trust it?"
- "In acquiring software from outside, there is always some compromise required; it never does exactly what is wanted."
- "If you build it yourself, you can control its future development; it will always do what you want."

The ability to build software yourself, be it by an individual software engineer, by a project, or by the organization as a whole, is an enormous barrier to reuse. Contrast this with electronic engineering, where the cost of designing and fabricating your own microprocessor is so enormous, and requires such specialized equipment, that it is only undertaken in very special circumstances—the margin between buying and building is very many orders of magnitude. The margins between buying and building software are not so great, except in the large volume micro-computer marketplace. In other cases, a first shot development could be as cheap as acquiring the software from elsewhere.

For the individual, the cost of acquisition consists of finding the requisite software, and we can address this through the various technical measures discussed above, as well as by the continued training and education of the individual so that more abstract entities will also be reused. The use of networks, with global information access mechanisms like Gopher, WWW, and Internet, has led to the wider dissemination of information, and the Esprit project EUROWARE has investigated the problems of offering a commercial service using these network technologies. A follow-on project, IECASE, has found that there was commercial potential here, particularly if associated with support services.

It is the ratio of cost to benefit that counts, and in addition to reducing the cost, we could also increase the benefit. If reuse does enhance productivity, then at least at the project and company levels there are payoffs. But what about the individual? What extra benefit does he/she get from reuse?

The Japanese practice of changing the monetary and status rewards for individuals is worth considering. Firstly, those who provide software for others to reuse could receive some form of royalty for this reuse, encouraging both the production of general purpose elements suitably proven and packaged for reuse, but also encouraging the promotion of the element's availability. The actual reuse should be encouraged, perhaps through piecework where the reward for the job was assessed without reuse in mind, or perhaps through a royalty on reuse for the reuser as well as the supplier. The status of people who succeed in reuse could be enhanced, possibly with the position of manager of the library of reusable components being made a highly rewarded and sought after post. This status and reward should be comparable with systems architects and database administrators which are highly sought after and respected jobs and are very similar in their intent. See for example the writings of Yoshiro Matsumoto (1981, 1992).

There is no doubt that for reuse to be successful, some form of cultural shift is necessary, with people's and institutional attitudes changing.

### 5.2 Economics of Reuse

The payoff for reuse occurs only after the item's initial production. Projects are usually established simply to look after the initial development of a software system, with their performance being judged solely by the costs and timescales of the project. Frequently there are quality problems resulting from this practice which become the responsibility of the maintenance team. This management practice does encourage reuse to reduce project costs, but does not encourage the production of reusable components for other projects because there are no benefits. Again, some form of royalty payable to the project might be appropriate as long as company accounting practices agreed. Alternatively, the Reusable Components Manager could be given a budget to invest in the production of components, either by subsidizing their production on projects or creating them speculatively.

A preliminary economic analysis appropriate to individual organizations has been given by Lubars (1986) and taken further by Gaffney and Durek (1989). Wolff (1990) and Barnes and Bollinger (1991) view this as an investment activity. Clearly commercial decisions concerning investment in components is very similar to investment in research and development, and company policies in these two areas could be usefully related. Accounting practices will often treat software as a consumable, and not as a capital asset, and this needs to be looked into.

Software reuse between organizations, both nationally and internationally, currently takes place through the production and sale of packages. The experience of the software packages industry is important in understanding how the reuse industry could be expanded to include reusable components.

If you build it in-house, you may be in total control of its development, but unaware of other costs. Maintenance of in-house software is likely to be more expensive since the software is likely to be less robust and it may be subject to uncontrolled voluntary "improvements" that are not required and add to cost.

Preparing software for reuse as a component does require extra effort and this extra effort needs to be rewarded. In the open market this reward would be some form of royalty or license fee. There may be problems in enforcing these payments, and disputes within the industry are frequent. However, libraries of mathematical routines have been marketed successfully for many years by the Numerical Algorithms Group in Oxford, and one person has produced a set of Ada components and is selling them (Booch 1987).

It is clear that to avoid some of these problems, a software components industry should be high-volume and low-cost, producing robust and stable products with low or zero maintenance costs. The margins between buying over building should be so great that one would never contemplate building when a component was available for purchase.

### 5.3 Legal issues

Illegal copying of software is a problem (see Suhler et al. 1986). Copyright protection of software is emerging, but clearly needs to be practiced internationally and improved. Many software producers appear to accept this situation and seek to earn revenue from their software in other ways, such as selling manuals or books about using it, or by selling training services. But the problem is more subtle than that.

The ability to reverse engineer software brings about conflicts concerning the market for software products. On the one hand the suppliers of software products should be protected against their products being illegally copied, not just at the level of software piracy, but at the level of rival products developed. Reverse engineering makes it possible to work back from executable code to design descriptions of exactly how the software works, and then to re-engineer the software with selected additions to form the rival product. In Europe the CEC has issued a directive making this illegal (see Lee 1992).

However, we also want an open market so that third party suppliers of software can provide products that connect to those of others, particularly the big suppliers. To do this, public interfaces need to be used and adequately documented, although in practice they often are not. All too frequently, when interfacing two pieces of software, some level of reverse engineering needs to be undertaken, and this seems to be a legitimate activity in the interests of open markets. This conflicts with the CEC directive which forbids any reverse engineering.

To maintain competitive advantage, some parts of a company's software may always be proprietary. The proprietary software may not even be sophisticated but comparable to the way application specific integrated circuits are used in hardware designs to make designs difficult to reproduce. We must always expect some level of non-reuse.

Software is not a commodity. It does not become an asset of a company that purchases it. Software may be written off in the first year after purchase, whereas hardware may be written off over 3 to 5 years or more. Software may not be allowed to be sold. For example, a computer manufacturer has required that purchasers of second-hand hardware relicense the software. There is no market in second-hand software; indeed, the very idea seems mildly ridiculous. Could this be changed? One could envisage some legal remedies to remove the restrictions and monopolistic practices. Could we get as far as enabling competitive third-party software maintenance? This whole area is receiving much more serious attention now that trading assets on the Internet is seen to have great potential, providing that intellectual assets can be suitably protected.

## 6 Conclusions

We have seen the development over the past 25 years of the practice of reverse engineering, re-engineering, and software reuse. Reuse is concerned with accumulating libraries of components, which could be designs and specifications, as well as code. Reverse engineering is the abstraction of design and specification descriptions of existing software to increase the life of the software. It is usually a prelude to restructuring and forward engineering, which together constitute re-engineering. Reverse engineering is also one method for obtaining components.

The technology for these is now well established, and while it is the focus of on-going research, there is really no technical barrier to reuse and re-engineering. We saw how the issue now is implementing the practices in this area.

Recently there have been two developments that point the way forward. The first is a research program by Batory and O'Malley (1992) who have separately developed sets of components for databases and communications respectively, together with a set of tools for composing particular configurations of their components to meet a particular need. They call their approach generative reuse. It can be seen as a domain specific language and compiler, and is a re-absorption of reuse into language technology, which we saw at the start of this paper as one of the origins of reuse.

The second is a program of reuse implementation at Schlumberger, reported by Arango et al. (1993). Here, instead of developing software components, they have written technology handbooks to document the corporation's expertise in their market areas. When this paper was presented at the international reuse workshop in Lucca, Italy in March 1993, it was awarded the prize for the best paper, so the program committee considered this a very important development for reuse. Recall the discussion at the start of this paper, that one of the conventional forms of reuse had been through the educational process? Here we see a further example of this conventional process, though the education is within company and proprietary.

In the implementation of reuse, existing methods are having reuse added into them. This is yet another example of the acceptance of reuse as part of the normal process of software development.

Does this mean that reuse, and reverse engineering and re-engineering, have now become established as part of the normal processes of software development? Should we now anticipate the demise of these areas as a separate branch of study?

## 7 Bibliography and References


Abbott, B., T. Bapty, C. Biegl, G. Karsai, and J. Sztipanovits, "Model-Based Software Synthesis," *IEEE Software,* May 1993, pp. 42–52.

Ader, M., O. Nierstrasz, S. McMahon, G. Mueller, and A.-K. Proefrock, "The ITHACA Technology: A Landscape for Object-Oriented Application Development," *ESPRIT '90 Conf. Proc.,* 1990.

Aitchison, J. and A. Gilchrist, *Thesaurus Construction: A practical Manual*, Aslib, 1971.

Albrechtson, H., "Software Information Systems: Information Retrieval Techniques," in *Software Reuse and Reverse Engineering in Practice,* Unicom seminar, Dec 1990.

AMICE ESPRIT Consortium, ed., *Open System Architecture for CIM*, Springer-Verlag, 1989.

Arango, G., E., Shoen, and R. Pettengill, "Design as Evolution and Reuse," *Advances in Software Reuse: Selected Papers from the 2nd Int'l Workshop on Software Reusability*, IEEE Computer Society Press, Los Alamitos, Calif., 1993, pp. 9–18.

Arnold, R.S., *Tutorial on Software Restructuring,* IEEE Computer Society Press, Los Alamitos, Calif., 1986.

Barnes, B.H and T.B. Bollinger, "Making Reuse Cost-Effective," *IEEE Software*, Jan. 1991, pp. 13–24.

Basili, V.R., "Viewing Maintenance as Reuse-Oriented Software Development," *IEEE Software*, Jan. 1990, pp. 19–25.

Basili, V.R. and H.D. Rombach, "Support for Comprehensive Reuse," *Software Eng. J.*, Sept. 1991, pp. 303–316.

Batory, D. and S. O'Malley, "The Design and Implementation of Hierarchical Software Systems with Reusable Components," *ACM Trans. Software Eng. and Methodology*. Vol. 1. No. 4, 1992, pp. 355–398.

BCS Displays Group, *Proc. Systems Integration and Data Exchange*, 1990.

Biggerstaff, T.J., "Design Recovery for Maintenance and Reuse, *Computer*, July 1989, pp. 36–49.

Bollinger T.B. and S.L. Pfleeger, "Economics of Reuse: Issues and Alternatives," *Information and Software Technology*, Dec. 1990.

Booch, G., *Software Components with Ada, Structures, Tools and Subsystems*, Benjamin/Cummings Publishing Company, 1987.

Booch, G., *Object Oriented Design with Applications*, Benjamin/Cummings Publishing Company, 1991.

Callis, F.W. and B.J. Cornelius, "Two Module Factoring Techniques," *Software Maintenance: Research and Practice*, Vol. 1, 1989, pp. 81–89.

Campbell, R, G. Johnston, and V. Russo, "Choices (Class Hierarchical Open Interface for Custom Embedded Systems)," *ACM Operating Systems Rev.*, Vol. 21, No. 3, July 1987, pp. 9–17.

Carasik, R.P., S.M. Johnson, D.A. Patterson, and G.A. Von Glahn, "Towards a Domain Description Grammar: An Application of Linguistic Semantics," *ACM SIGSOFT Software Eng. Notes*, Vol. 15, No. 5, Oct. 1990, pp. 28–43.

Chikofsky, E.J. and, J.H. Cross, II, "Reverse Engineering and Design Recovery: A Taxonomy," *IEEE Software*, Jan. 1990, pp. 13–17.

Cimitile, A. and U. Decarlini, "Reverse Engineering—Algorithms for Program Graph Production," *Software—Practice & Experience*, Vol. 21, No. 5, 1991, pp. 519–537.

Cox, B.J., *Object-Oriented Programming*, Addison-Wesley, Reading, Mass., 1986.

Cox, B.J., "There is a Silver Bullet," *Byte*, Vol. 15, No. 10, 1990, pp. 209–218.

Cramer, J., W. Fey, G. Michael, and M. Große-Rhode, "Towards a Formally Based Component Description Language—A Foundation for Reuse," *Structured Programming*, Vol. 12, No. 2, 1991, pp. 91–110.

DARPA. *Proc. 1990 Workshop on Domain-Specific Software Architectures*, available from the DSSA Program Manager, DARPA/ISTO, 1400 Wilson Blvd., Arlington, VA 22209.

De Remer, F. and H.H. Kron, "Programming in the Large versus Programming in the Small," *IEEE Trans. Software Eng.*, June 1976, pp. 312–327.

Dulay, N., J. Kramer, J. Magee, M. Sloman, and K. Twiddle, *The Conic Configuration Language*, Version 1.3, Imperial College London, Research Report DOC 84/20, Aug. 1985.

Fickas, S. and B.R. Helm, "Knowledge Representation and Reasoning in the Design of Composite Systems," *IEEE Trans. Software Eng.*, Vol. 18, No. 6, June 1992, pp. 470–482.

Frakes, W.B. and B.A. Nejmeh, "Software Reuse Through Information Retrieval," *SIGIR Forum*, Vol. 21, 1986–1987, pp. 1–2.

Freeman, P., "A Conceptual Analysis of the Draco Approach to Constructing Software Systems," *IEEE Trans. Software Eng.*, 1987 and included in *IEEE Tutorial: Software Reusability*, IEEE Computer Society Press, Los Alamitos, Calif., 1987.

Gaffney, J.E., Jr., and T.A. Durek, "Software Reuse—Key to Enhanced Productivity: Some Quantitative Models," *Information and Software Technology*. Vol. 31, No. 5, June 1989, pp. 258–267.

Gamma, E., R. Helm, R. Johnson, and J. Vlissides, *Design Patterns: Elements of Reusable Object-Oriented Software*, Addison Wesley, Reading, Mass., 1995.

Garnett, E.S. and J.A. Mariani, *Software Reclamation*, Dept of Computing, University of Lancaster, 1989.

Goguen, J.A., "Reusing and Interconnecting Software Components," *Computer*, Feb. 1986, pp. 16–28.

Goldberg, A. and D. Robson, *Smalltalk-80: The Language and Its Implementation*, Addison-Wesley, Reading, Mass., 1983.

Hall, P., "Software Reuse, Reverse Engineering, and Reengineering," *Unicom Seminar Software Reuse and Reverse Engineering in Practice*, 1990.

Hall, P., C. Boldyreff, P. Elzer, J. Keilmann, L. Olsen, and J. Witt, "PRACTITIONER: Pragmatic Support for the Reuse of Concepts in Existing Software," *ancillary papers at ESPRIT Week, 1990*

Hall, P.A.V., "SOFTWARE COMPONENTS Reuse—Getting More Out of Your Code," *Information and Software Technology*, Butterworths, Jan/Feb 1987. Reprinted in *Software Reuse: Emerging Technology*, Will Tracz, ed., IEEE Computer Society Press, Los Alamitos, Calif., 1988.

Harandi, M.T. and J.Q. Ning, "Knowledge-Based Program Analysis," *IEEE Software*, Jan. 1990, pp. 74–81.

Harris, K.R., "Using Object-Oriented Methods to Develop Reusable Software for Test and Measurement Systems: A Case Study," *Proc. 1st Int'l Workshop on Software Reusability*, 1991, pp. 71–78.

Harrison,W., C. Gens, and B. Gifford, "pRETS: a parallel Reverse-engineering ToolSet for FORTRAN," *J. Software Maintenance,* Vol. 5, 1993, pp. 37–57.

*IEEE Trans. Software Eng.*, Special Issue on Software Reusability. Vol. SE-10, No. 5, Sept. 1984.

Jones, T.C., "Reusability in Programming: A Survey of the State of the Art," in (IEEE 84), pp. 488–494.

Karlsson, E.-A., *Software Reuse—A Holistic Approach,* Wiley, New York, N.Y., 1995.

Katsoulakis, Takis, "An Overview of the Esprit project REDO, Maintenance Validation Documentation of Software Systems," *Proc. ESPRIT Conf.*, 1990.

Kozaczynski, W. and J.Q. Ning, "SRE: A Knowledge-based Environment for Large-Scale Software Re-engineering Activities," *Proc. Int'l Conf. Software Eng.,* IEEE Computer Society Press, Los Alamitos, Calif., 1989, pp. 113–122.

Kolodner, J.L. (ed.), *Proc. Case-based Reasoning Workshop*, Darpa 1989.

Kozaczynski, W., J. Ning,, and A. Engberts, "Program Concept Recognition and Transformation," *IEEE Trans. Software Eng.*, Vol. 18, No. 12, 1992, pp. 1065–1075.

Kramer, J. and J. Magee, "Dynamic Configuration for Distributed Systems," *IEEE Trans. Software Eng.,* Vol. SE-11, No. 4, Apr. 1985, pp. 424–436.

Kruzela, I and M. Brorsson, "Human Aspects and Organizational Issues of Software Reuse," in *Software Reuse and Reverse Engineering in Practice*, P.A.V. Hall, (ed.), Chapman & Hall, London, U.K., 1992, pp. 521–534.

Lanergan, R.G. and C.A. Grasso, *Software Engineering with Reusable Designs and Code*, in (IEEE 1984), pp. 498–501.

Lano, K. and P.T. Breuer, *From Programs to Z Specifications*, Z User's Meeting, Dec 1989.

Lano, K., P.T. Breuer, and H. Haughton, "Reverse-engineering COBOL via Formal Methods," *J. Software Maintenance,* Vol. 5, No. 1, Mar. 1993, pp. 13–35.

Lauer, H.C. and E.H. Satterthwaite, "The Impact of MESA on System Design," *Proc. 4th Int'l Conf. Software Eng.,* IEEE Computer Society Press, Los Alamitos, Calif., 1979, pp. 174–182.

Lee, M.K.O., "The Legal position of Reverse Software Engineering in the UK," *Unicom Seminar Software Reuse and Reverse Engineering in Practice*, Chapman & Hall, London, UK, 1992, pp. 559–572.

Lehman, M.M. and N.V. Stenning, "Concepts of an Integrated Project Support Environment," *Data Processing,* Vol. 27, No. 3, Apr. 1985.

Littlewood, B., "Software Reliability Model for Modular Program Structure," *IEEE Trans. Reliability,* Vol. R-28, 1979, pp. 241–246.

Lubars, M.D, "Affording Higher Software Reliability Through Software Reusability," *ACM SIGSOFT Software Eng. Notes,* Vol. 11, No. 5, Oct. 1986.

Lupton, P., "Promoting Forward Simulation," *Proc. 5th Ann. Z User meeting*, 1990. To be published in the BCS and Springer in their workshop series.

Maarek, Y.S., D.M. Berry, and G.E. Kaiser, "An Information Retrieval Approach for Automatically Constructing Software Libraries," *IEEE Trans. Software Eng.*, Vol. 17, No. 8, Aug. 1991, pp. 800–813.

Matsumoto, Y, *The Japanese Software Factory*, Academic Press, New York, N.Y., 1992.

Matsumoto, Y., "Experiences from Software Reuse in Industrial Process Control Applications. Advances in Software Reuse," *Proc. 2nd Int'l Workshop Software Reusability*, IEEE Computer Society Press, Los Alamitos, Calif., 1993, pp. 186–195.

Matsumoto, Y, O. Sasaki, S. Nakajima, K. Takezawa, S. Yamamoto, and T. Tanaka, "SWB System: a Software Factory," in *Software Engineering Environments,* Huenke, ed., North-Holland, Amsterdam, The Netherlands, 1981, pp. 305–318.

McIllroy, M.D., "Mass-Produced Software Components" in *Software Engineering Concepts and Techniques*, Petrocelli/Charter, Belgium, 1976, pp. 88–98.

McWilliams, G., "Users see a CASE Advance in Reverse Engineering Tools," *Datamation*, Feb. 1, 1988, pp. 30–36.

Meyer, B., "Lessons from the Design of the Eiffel Libraries," *Comm. ACM,* Vol. 33, No. 9, 1990, pp. 69–88.

Moineau, Th., J. Abadir, and E. Rames, "Towards a Generic and Extensible Reuse Environment," *Proc. SE '90 Conf.,* Cambridge University Press, 1990.

Morel, J. and J. Faget, "The REBOOT Environment," *Advances in Software Reuse: Selected Papers Proc. 2nd Int'l Workshop Software Reusability*, IEEE Computer Society Press, Los Alamitos, Calif., 1993, pp. 80–88.

Neighbors, J., *The Draco Approach to Constructing Software from Reusable Components*, in (IEEE 84).

Nierstrasz, O,. D. Tsichritzis, V. de May, and M. Stadelmann, "Objects + Scripts = Applications," *ESPRIT '91 Conf. Proc.*

Nijssen, G.M. and T.A. Halpin, *Conceptual Schema and Relational Database Design*, Prentice Hall, Englewood Cliffs, N.J., 1989.

Prieto-Diaz, R. and P. Freeman, "Classifying Software for Reusability," *IEEE Software,* Jan. 1987, pp. 6–16.

Prieto-Diaz, R., "Domain Analysis: an Introduction," *Software Engineering Notes*, Vol. 15, No. 2, Apr. 1990, pp. 47–54.

Prieto-Diaz, R. and J. Neighbors, "Module Interconnection Languages," *J. System Sciences*, Vol. 6, No. 4, Nov. 1986, pp. 307–334.

Prieto-Diaz, R., "Implementing Faceted Classification for Software Reuse," *Comm. ACM,* Vol. 34, No. 5, 1991, pp. 88–97.

Rich, C. and L.M. Wills, "Recognising a Program's Design: A Graph-Parsing Approach," *IEEE Software*, Jan. 1990, pp. 82–89.

Rock-Evans, R. and K. Hales, *Reverse Engineering: Markets, Methods and Tools*, Ovum 1990.

Salton and M. McGill, *Introduction to Modern Information Retrieval,* McGraw-Hill, New York, N.Y., 1983.

Simos, M.A., position paper for the *Proc. Workshop on Tools and Environments for Reuse,* 1988.

Sloman, M., J. Kramer, and J. Magee, "The Conic Toolkit for Building Distributed Systems," *Proc. 6th IFAC Distributed Computer Control Systems Workshop,* Pergamon Press, London, U.K., 1985.

Sneed, H. and G. Jandrasics, "Software Recycling," *Proc. Software Maintenance Conf.*, IEEE Computer Society Press, Los Alamitos, Calif., 1987.

Sneed, H.M. and G. Jandrasics, "Inverse Transformation from Code to Specification," *Proc. Software Tools '89,* Blenhiem Online, 1989, pp. 82–90.

Spivey, M., *The Z Notation,* Prentice-Hall, Englewood Cliffs, N.J., 1989.

Standish, T.A., *An Essay on Software Reuse*, in (IEEE 1984), pp. 494–497.

Suhler, P.A., N. Bagherzadeh, M. Malek, and N. Iscoe, "Software Authorisation Systems," *IEEE Software,* Jan. 1986, pp. 34 et seq.

Swanson, E.B. and C.M. Beath, *Maintaining Information Systems in Organisations,* Wiley, New York, N.Y., 1989.

Teory, T.J. and J.P. Fry, *Design of Database Structures,* Prentice Hall, Englewood Cliffs, N.J., 1982.

Tichy, W.F., "Software Development Control Based on Module Interconnection," *Proc. 4th Int'l Software Eng. Conf.,* IEEE Computer Society Press, Los Alamitos, Calif., 1979, pp. 29–41.

Tichy, W.F., *Software Development Control Based on Systems Structure Description*, PhD thesis, Carnegie-Mellon University, Computer Science Department, Jan. 1980.

Townley, H.M. and R.D. Gee,, *Thesaurus Making. Grow Your Own Word-Stock,* Andre Deutsch, 1980.

Tracz, W., "LILEANNA: A Parameterized Programming Language," *Advances in Software Reuse: Proc. Selected Papers 2nd Int'l Workshop Software Reusability,* IEEE Computer Society Press, Los Alamitos, Calif., 1993, pp. 66–70.

van Zuylen H.J., (ed.), *The REDO Compendium: Reverse Engineering for Software Maintenance,* Wiley, New York, N.Y., 1993.

Ward, M., *Transforming a Program into a Specification*, Computer Science Technical Report 88/1, University of Durham, Jan. 1988.

Waters, R.C., "Program Translation via Abstraction and Reimplementation," *IEEE Trans. Software Eng,* Vol. 14, No. 8, Aug. 1988, pp. 1207–1228.

Wegner, P., "Capital-Intensive Software Technology," *IEEE Software*, July 1984, pp. 7–45.

Wirfs-Brock, R.J. and R.E. Johnson, "Surveying Current Research into Object-Oriented Design," *Comm. ACM,* Vol. 33, No. 9, Sept. 1990, pp. 104–124.

Wolff, F., "Long-term Controlling of Software Reuse," PRACTITIONER working paper BrU-0100, Brunel University, Sept. 1990.

Wood, M. and I. Sommerville, "An information Retrieval System for Software Components," *Software Engineering J.,* Sept 1988, pp. 199–207.

Yau, S.S. and J.J. Tsai, "Knowledge Representation of Software Component Interconnection Information for Large-Scale Software Modifications," *IEEE Trans. Software Eng.,* Vol. 13, No. 3, Mar. 1987, pp. 355–361.

# Prototyping: alternative systems development methodology

J M Carey

*Prototyping has become a popular alternative to traditional systems development methodologies. The paper explores the various definitions of prototyping to determine its advantages and disadvantages and to present a systematic methodology for incorporating the prototyping process into the existing system development process within an organization. In addition, one negative and one positive case study of prototyping within industrial settings is included.*

*system development methodologies, prototyping, software life-cycle*

In recent years, use of prototyping has increased dramatically for both the requirements definition phase of the systems development life-cycle and rapid building of end-user systems[1]. The increase has been primarily due to the advent of fourth-generation language (4GL) application generators.

A study of Texas-based computer facilities showed that prototyping was more widely used than almost any offline, structured, software-development tools, such as dataflow diagrams and decision tables[1].

This paper explores the definition of prototyping, the advantages and disadvantages of using this technique, and how to determine when a prototyping approach is appropriate.

## CONSENSUS DEFINITION

If various analysts and programmers were asked to define prototyping, the responses would vary considerably, depending on experience and training. Prototyping has taken on a variety of meanings and uses and has been variously defined as follows:

> 'a strategy for determining requirements wherein user needs are extracted, presented, and defined by building a working model of the ultimate system – quickly and in context' (p 25)[2]

> 'Prototyping is based on building a model of the system to be developed. The initial model should include the major program modules, the data base, screens, reports and inputs and outputs that the system will use for communicating with other, interface systems' (p 69)[3]

> 'working models used to check accuracy of designs before committing to full-scale production' (p 79)[4]

> 'The idea behind prototyping is to include users in the development cycle' (p 93)[5]

What do these definitions have in common? First, prototyping is seen as a model of the final system, much like in the automobile industry where prototype or model cars are built and tested before full-scale production is attempted. In prototyping a software system, only parts of the system are developed, with a key emphasis on the user interfaces, such as menus, screens, reports, and source documents. The prototype is then a shell of the final system with no calculations and data behind the interfaces. The final system is either built from scratch using the prototype as a model or evolved from the prototype.

Second, the emphasis is on user involvement in the software development process. In the traditional software development life-cycle, communication between analysts and users occurs early in the cycle to determine information needs, then the analysts work, in isolation, to develop the system and seldom interact with the users until system delivery and production. As users have little input into the development process, the resultant system is often dissatisfactory and difficult to learn and use. Prototyping provides a 'hands-on' communication tool to allow the analyst to determine user needs and ensure ongoing communication throughout the development process, thus ensuring that the system is the 'right' one for the user.

Third, prototyping produces an information system faster than using the traditional life-cycle approach. When users are frustrated by the development backlog that exists in most organizations, speed of delivery can be a great selling point. This is often called 'rapid prototyping' by proponents and 'quick and dirty' by opponents.

Taking these three underlying ideas and incorporating them into one gives the following consensus definition:

> 'Prototyping' is the process of quickly building a model of the final software system, which is used

Arizona State University – West Campus, P.O. Box 37100, Phoenix, AZ 85069–7100, USA.

Paper submitted: 19 April 1989.
Revised version received: 12 September 1989.

primarily as a communication tool to assess and meet the information needs of the user.

## RATIONALE FOR PROTOTYPING

The traditional software development approach has several inherent problems, which prototyping attempts to address. These problems include the following[2,6]:

- Users seldom have clear, concise understanding of their informational needs. Therefore, they cannot prespecify the requirements. Once they begin to use a system, however, it is clear to them where the problems lie.
- The traditional function specification is a narrative description of an information system that is technical and time consuming to read. Static graphic techniques (such as dataflow diagrams, and data dictionary entries found in the structured approach) once thought to be the solution to communication cannot demonstrate the workings of a live dynamic system[7].
- The larger the development team, including user representatives, the more difficult communication becomes[8]. Semantic barriers and lack of physical proximity and time inhibit the ability of all members of the team to have a common understanding of the system being developed.
- Even if systems developed in the traditional manner function correctly, they may be difficult to learn and use.
- Both traditional and structured approaches emphasize documentation, which is time consuming and as the system changes may not be accurate[9].
- Systems being developed today are more complex, have a larger mission, and require many months to complete. The traditional approach has not served to shorten delivery time, in fact it may unduly lengthen the time required due to the emphasis on documentation[9].
- Because of the large number of people/months involved and time-consuming methods, traditional approaches not only seem to deliver late systems that do not please the user, they are also costly.
- Most large companies have a long backlog of projects awaiting initiation, while the users who requested them are frustrated, disillusioned, and ready to revolt.

All of these problems suggest that some revolutionary technique is needed. Prototyping is one technique that attempts to address these problems and provide possible solutions.

## PROTOTYPING ENVIRONMENTS

There are two major types of prototyping environments[5,10]. One is a complete and integrated application-generator environment or automated development environment (ADE), which can produce quick, integrated menus, reports, and screens and is tied to a database. Examples are R:base 5000 or System V for the microcomputer and NOMAD2 for the mainframe.

A prototyping toolkit comprises the other environment. The toolkit is a collection of unintegrated tools that aid the rapid building of the separate pieces of a system, such as screen painters, data dictionaries, and report generators. Together, these tools are often referred to as analysts' or programmers' 'workbench'.

The following 'workbench' tools can aid the prototyping process:

- text editors
- screen generators
- report generators
- relational databases
- fourth-generation languages (4GLs)
- spreadsheets
- data dictionaries coupled to database management systems
- *ad hoc* query languages
- security
- statistical packages
- back-up routines
- documentation generators
- online help
- interactive testing system

If purchased separately, these tools are initially expensive when compared with the traditional method of coding in a third-generation language (3GL) such as COBOL. Also, before jumping into prototyping, a training period for both development team and users is required.

Acquiring the tools or environment is just the first step. Once the environment for building a prototype has been created and staff and users thoroughly trained in the use of prototyping tools, a systematic methodology should be adopted that is tailored to the specific organization and then followed to ensure that the system that results from the prototyping technique is both usable and correct. All too often, companies purchase prototyping packages and jump into prototyping without trying to determine when and how to use the technique.

The following five steps are suggested by Klinger[6], manager of laboratory systems and programming at Ortho Pharmaceutical Corporation, as a successful approach to the use of prototyping:

- Assess each application individually. Would prototyping provide gains?
- Look at the environment and then develop and document a formal prototyping life-cycle that fits it.
- Acquire appropriate software tools and train the staff.
- Decide how the software development process will be managed and controlled.
- Train end-users in the procedures that will be followed during the prototyping life-cycle.

## ITERATIVE (TYPE I) VERSUS THROWAWAY (TYPE II) PROTOTYPING

One confusion in defining prototyping arises from the existence of two distinct types of prototyping that are used by various companies. These two basic approaches to prototyping are iterative and throwaway. The iterative approach (Type I) uses the prototype as the final system after a series of evolutionary changes based on user feedback. The throwaway approach (Type II) uses the prototype built in a 4GL as a model for the final system, with the final system coded in a 3GL.

In the Type I (iterative) approach, the life-cycle consists of the following stages[6]:

- training
- project planning
- rapid analysis
- database development
- prototype iteration
- modelling
- detailed design
- implementation
- maintenance

The inclusion of training and project planning is unique. These stages are seldom mentioned in the traditional life-cycle. The modelling stage is also unique and important. It is at this stage that the prototype system is tested through benchmarking to make sure it performs within acceptable standards. Possible replacement code may be needed at bottlenecks in the prototype. Sometimes 3GL code may be substituted for any original 4GL that has been determined as inefficient. Figure 1 shows the system development life-cycle incorporating Type I prototyping.

In the Type II (throwaway) approach, some iteration occurs and the steps of analysis, design, coding, testing, and modification may be repeated many times until all of the users' requirements are identified and met. Once the prototyping phase is complete, then the prototype serves as a model for final production system, but is discarded at the project delivery[6]. The throwaway prototyping approach generally adheres to the traditional life-cycle once the prototype has been developed. Figure 2 illustrates the system development life-cycle incorporating the Type II prototyping technique.

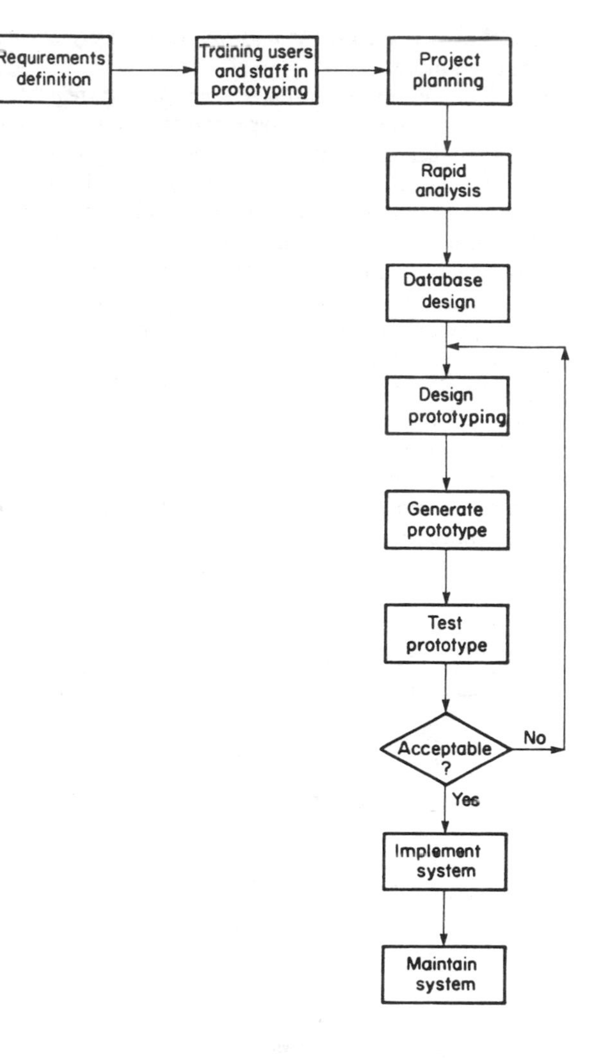


*Figure 1. System development life-cycle using Type I (iterative) prototyping*

## ADVANTAGES OF PROTOTYPING

Prototyping is being used in industry with varying degrees of success. Proponents of prototyping cite the following positive attributes:

- Systems can be developed much faster[11].
- Systems are easier for end-users to learn and use.
- Programming and analysis effort is much less (less humanpower needed).
- Development backlogs can be decreased[12].
- Prototyping facilitates end-user involvement.
- System implementation is easier because users know what to expect.
- Prototyping enhances user/analyst communication.
- User requirements are easier to determine.
- Development costs are reduced.
- The resultant system is the 'right' system and needs little changing.

All of these positive attributes make prototyping sound like the system development dream, like the answer to all analyst's and user's problems. Indeed, many organizations have adapted some use of prototyping within their development life-cycle. However, there is a downside to prototyping.

## DISADVANTAGES OF PROTOTYPING

*Undue user expectations*[13] The ability of the systems group to develop a prototype so quickly may raise undue expectations on the part of the user. They see the shell and may not understand that it is not the finished system. They may have been waiting for this system for months or even years and are so anxious to get something in place that being so close and yet so far may frustrate them even more.

*Inconsistencies between prototype and final system* If the prototype is a throwaway type, the end system may not be exactly like the prototype. In other words, what the user sees may not be what the user gets. It is up to the analyst to communicate any differences between the prototype and the end system; if the user is forewarned, the negative reaction may be ameliorated. It is advisable to ensure that the resultant system be as close to the prototype as possible to avoid this potential problem.

*Encouragement of end-user computing* The availability of prototyping software both in the organization and on the general market may encourage end-users to begin to develop their own systems when their needs are not being met by data-processing staff. While end-user involvement in system development is positive, end-user computing (development of systems by end-users) may have some negative ramifications for system integration and database integrity.

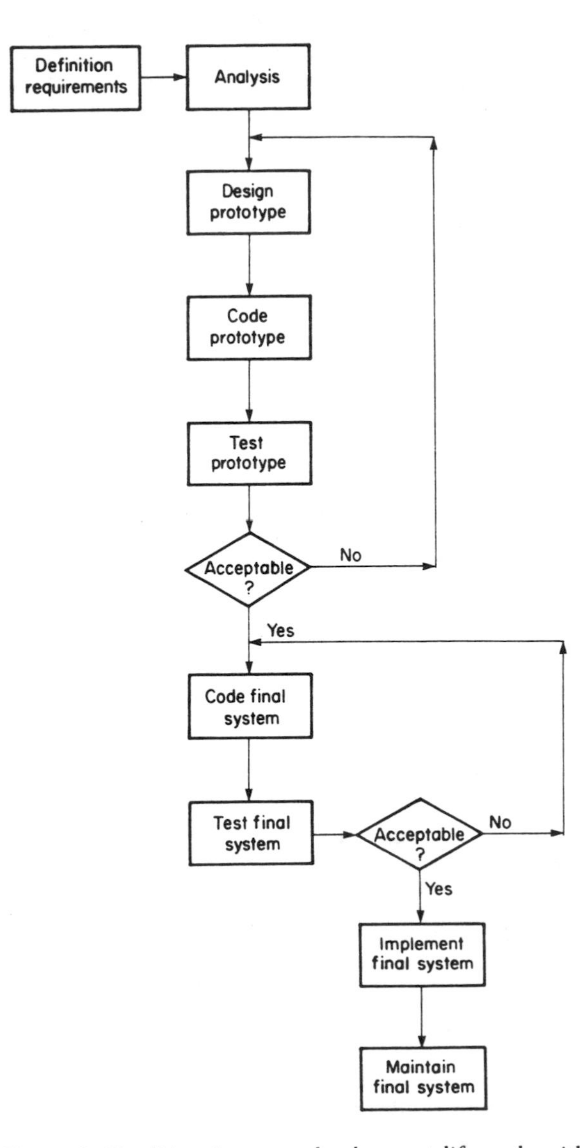


*Figure 2. Traditional system development life-cycle with Type II (throwaway) prototyping*

*Final system inefficiencies*[14] Large, complex systems that require voluminous numbers of transactions may not be good candidates for the iterative prototyping technique. 4GLs have a reputation for generating less than optimal code in terms of efficiency and throughput. Care must be taken to predetermine whether the new system should be written with an application generator/ prototyping tool or prototyped in a 4GL and then coded in a 3GL for maximum efficiency. A discussion of how to make these determinations is included in the next section.

*Lack of attention to good human factors*[5] The use of application generators as prototyping tools does not ensure that the resultant systems will adhere to human-factors guidelines. In fact, many application generators have rather inflexible screen and menu formats, which often inhibit the use of good human-factors techniques unless additional background code is written (defeating the purpose of the application generator).

*Inattention to proper analysis* Because prototyping application generators are relatively easy to use and produce quick results, analysts are tempted to plunge into prototyping before sufficient analysis has taken place. This may result in a system that looks good, with adequate user interfaces, but that is not truly functional. This is how the reputation of 'quick and dirty' prototypes came about. To avoid this pitfall, a well defined methodology that stipulates the stages of prototyping is necessary.

## DETERMINATION OF WHEN TO PROTOTYPE

Some form of prototyping may be used in the development of all systems from large and complex to small and simple. Determination of whether to use the iterative prototyping technique, which will evolve into the final system, or the throwaway type, which may be used primarily to model the user interfaces, however, is dependent on several variables.

If the system in question has the following characteristics, it may be a prime candidate for iterative prototyping[3,6]:

- is dynamic (always changing)
- is transaction-processing based
- contains extensive user dialogues
- is small versus large
- is well defined
- is online
- 'is' the business (i.e., billing, record management, transaction-driven, predetermined structure)

On the other hand, if the system exhibits the following characteristics, iterative prototyping is unlikely to enhance the final system[3,6]:

- is stable
- is decision-support based

- contains much *ad hoc* retrieval and reporting
- is of no predictable form
- is ill defined
- is batch
- makes little use of user dialogues
- is large and complex
- is real-time
- does extensive number crunching
- is 'about' the business rather than directly involved in transaction processing (i.e., decision support and expert systems)

## METHODOLOGY

Type I or Type II prototyping can be effectively used when developing information systems; the key to success is carefully determining which prototype type to use and then following a well defined methodology.

The methodology should include thorough requirements definition and design stages before any prototyping is attempted. The prototype should then be defined, coded, tested, and used to refine the requirements and design and put to use as a Type I or Type II prototype. During the refinement process, user comments and responses can be solicited and used to alter any unsatisfactory portions of the prototype. Once the user(s) and analyst are satisfied with the prototype, then the prototype can either be retained and expanded to become the final system or used as a model for the final system that is developed in a 3GL.

There are four phases that are inherent in the development and completion of a prototype[15].

**Determination of key aspects of system to be prototyped**
The three main areas that are often prototyped include the user interface, uncertain or vague system functions, and time and memory requirements. Any or all three of these aspects can be prototyped.
*User interface* The most common area to be prototyped. Many prototyping tools are specifically aimed at rapid development of menus, screens, and reports. This is the aspect that the user must understand and accept for the system to be successful.
*Uncertain system functions* Often, the development of a new system includes some functional processing that may not be well understood by any team members. This uncertain area is a probable candidate for prototyping. The development of a working model allows the team to make sure that the solution they are proposing will indeed satisfy the requirements and perform effectively. The involvement of the user will not be as heavy for this type of prototype as for the user interface. The user may not fully understand the calculations and output. The user may be able to provide both test input and output data, however, to verify the model.
*Time and memory requirements* The exercise of these aspects may be more appropriately termed a simulation instead of a prototype. Many systems may be characterized by huge volumes of transactions and data manipulations. Standards for interactive response times and memory use can be established, and the prototype/simulation is exercised to ensure that the system can accomplish the functional tasks within the standards range.

**Building the prototype**
Many tools are available for building prototypes, as already mentioned. The prototype is initially built quite rapidly using one or more of the prototyping tools.

**Testing the prototype**
The prototype is tested and debugged based on user and performance feedback.

**Using the prototype as a model**
The prototype is used as a model for the final system (Type II) or as the base for the final system (Type I).

Adherence to a strict methodology will help to ensure the success of the prototyping approach and will combat the 'quick and dirty' system development that sometimes results from prototyping in a haphazard manner.

## INCORPORATING HUMAN-FACTORS GUIDELINES INTO PROTOTYPING

Even though prototyping provides an excellent method of analyst/user communication, there is nothing inherent in the prototyping tools to ensure adherence to good human-factors guidelines. Therefore, analyst/programmers should have additional training in this critical area. Human factors in systems and the issue of 'user friendliness' or 'usability' has been recognised recently as a determinant of system success. Just because a system is technically sound does not mean that it will be easy to learn and use. The following human-factors guidelines[16] should be adhered to as part of the system design phase.
*Know your users* Users today range from novice to expert. There are many variables that can help profile users, including previous exposure to computers, the nature of the task they are attempting to perform on the system, level of training, how often they use the system in question, level in the organization, amount of dependency on the computer, etc. One of the first tasks of the analyst should be to profile the user population.
*Use selection not entry* Whenever possible, allow the user to select information from possible options on the screen rather than require the user to remember what to do next. Humans forget and have enough task variables in their short-term memory to worry about without having to memorize how to get the system to function. The only problem with selection not entry is that it may slow up the experienced user. In order not to frustrate this type of user, program selections to accept multiple keystrokes that will allow the experienced user to sidestep the selection process.
*Make the system behave predictably* Consistent design of function keys and options will lead to ease of learning and use. Switching and interchanging will lead to frustration and abandonment of the system.

*Make the system as unobtrusive as possible* The focus of any computer session should be on the work task rather than on the system itself. Some aspects of the interface, such as blinking, reverse video, colour use, and audibles can be distracting rather than meaningful, especially when the user is doing routine data entry and has to be involved with the system on an extended daily basis. These attention-getting devices may be helpful as 'training wheels' during the learning process, but probably should be removed once the user is 'up' on the system.
*Use display inertia when carrying out user requests* The display should change as little as possible. This helps to prevent user distraction.
*Conserve muscle power* A single keystroke or depression of a function key is usually faster and less cumbersome than multiple keystrokes, particularly for the intermittent user who is not a proficient typist.
*Use meaningful error messages* If the user makes a mistake, advise on what the mistake was and how to correct it. Avoid negative, patronizing messages. Simply state the problem and how to correct it.
*Allow for reversing of actions* Protect the users from the system and the system from the users. Create a suspense file that can be altered and verified before the database is altered; this will help to ensure database integrity. Allow failsafe exits from the system at any time.

This list is not all inclusive, of course. There are many other sources for user-interface design guidelines[17]. Incorporating these guidelines into interface designs and using prototypes to communicate user requirements will help to ensure system success.

## TWO CASE STUDIES WITH PROTOTYPING

### Case 1: New Jersey Division of Motor Vehicles[14]

From 1983 to 1985, the State of New Jersey Division of Motor Vehicles contracted Price Waterhouse and Company to build its primary information system. A new 4GL named Ideal from Applied Data Research (ADR) Inc. was used to develop the system. When the system was delivered, the response times were so slow that the backlogs generated from using the system resulted in thousands of motorists driving with invalid registrations or licences. Overtime pay to employees amounted to hundreds of thousands of dollars. In short, at delivery time, the system was declared a total disaster.

Why was Ideal chosen as the language for this development project? First, time pressures dictated speedy completion of the project and, second, the Systems and Communications (SAC) Division of the State of New Jersey had already acquired ADR's Datacom/DB, which supported Ideal as a 4GL. The decision was made by Price Waterhouse to use Ideal, against the recommendations of several members of the SAC.

Robert Moybohm, the SAC's deputy director, had earlier evaluated Ideal for possible use in other, smaller projects and determined:

- Ideal would not be able to handle the development of large, online systems. He ran some benchmark tests against COBOL programs and Ideal ran three times slower on simple processing.
- Ideal did not offer index processing, a performance-related feature that had been the initial reason that SAC purchased the Datacom/DB system in the first place.
- Ideal did not allow computer-to-computer interfacing. The large system would need to interface with 59 other computers. This fact alone should have precluded the selection of Ideal.

Why did Price Waterhouse choose Ideal? What went wrong? From the beginning, poor decisions were made about the system development process. Ideal was a brand-new product and was not well tested. The development staff had no experience using any 4GL and considerable time was spent learning and making mistakes. All along the development cycle, it became apparent that the system was not going to meet performance requirements, yet no one was able to stop the process and change to a 3GL or determine how to combat the performance problems. It seems that one of the driving forces was the fact that the development team was locked into a fixed-cost contract and delivery date and that every month after deadline would incur a stiff financial penalty. So a decision was made to deliver a nonperforming system within the deadline rather than a late, but functional, one.

After failed implementation of the new system and the resultant flurry of irate users died down, an attempt was made to rectify the problem. It was determined that only about 58 of the 800 program modules needed to be converted to COBOL to meet acceptable, response-time criteria. Eight modules were responsible for the nightly batch updates. The other 50 modules were online programs that were handling 85% of the system's transaction volume. It was not merely a simple line-by-line conversion; many modules had to be redesigned to achieve performance requirements.

The impact of a failed system on the motorists of New Jersey could have been avoided by running the old system in parallel with the new system until the problems were rectified. Instead, due primarily to costs and inadequate hardware resources, direct cutover implementation was used as a strategy. Consequently, the failure of the new system was evident to everyone in the state of New Jersey, not just to internal staff.

Was Type I (iterative) prototyping with a 4GL the wrong choice for the New Jersey Division of Motor Vehicles? Given the volume of transactions, and the development team's inexperience, the answer must be yes. A more effective approach would have been to use the Type II (throwaway) approach, using the 4GL to model the system, rather than use the Type I (iterative) approach to develop the end system.

## Case 2: Town and Country Credit Line (TCCL)

In early 1988, Town and Country Credit Line (TCCL) decided to develop a system to enhance their competitive advantage over other banking cards. TCCL has long seen itself as the leader in banking card technology. (The actual nature of the system is proprietary at this time and the name of the company has been changed.) TCCL decided to explore the costs and benefits of using CASE technology to enhance delivery time for new systems. They chose a service request system as an eight-week pilot project to accomplish this purpose. They hired outside programmer/consultants who had experience in the use of CASE technology and purchased IEF (Information Engineering Facility) from Texas Instruments.

The decision to develop the service request system as a pilot was based on the following:

- the estimated short time required to deliver this product to the user community (it was perceived to be a system with a fairly narrow scope)
- the time the user community had been promised the system with no delivery
- it was felt that this system would give the development team the 'biggest bang for the dollar' (quote from project manager)
- it was felt that this system would provide the user community with a system that would dramatically enhance productivity while simplifying complex choices

Why did they not just use traditional methods to develop this system? The system had features that they felt would be very difficult to design and produce using traditional methods. These features were interprocedure communication and linking of procedures.

Because CASE technology was new to the organization, the pilot project would additionally serve to provide a knowledge base within the team to make accurate estimates for projects that use the CASE tool, and give each team member an opportunity to gain 'hands-on' experience with all phases of the CASE tool, and in doing so provide understanding of the limitations and capabilities of the CASE tool.

Two consultants were hired to provide support during the pilot project as the team had no experience with IEF. One consultant provided guidance on the methodology and project management, the other on IEF itself.

Training of the resident staff members was limited. At the beginning of the pilot project, only two team members out of nine had any training beyond Business Area Analysis and Business System Design. No team members had any training or experience with IEF technical design and construction. One team member had no training in CASE and IEF at all.

The system was developed by breaking it into its logical business components and then distributing one task to each group. The system was developed within the eight-week deadline and performs the required tasks efficiently and effectively with user acceptance. Two problems were encountered during the development process. One was related to the CASE technology and the other to the nature of the system. As the CASE technology was new to the organization, a learning curve was encountered. The competence of the team and a willingness to work additional hours helped to overcome this problem. The other problem was a lack of communication between groups. The groups sometimes went off on inconsistent tangents and some work had to be redone. Once the product is familiar to the team, and less time is spent on learning IEF, scheduled full-team meetings could alleviate this problem.

IEF divides the development process into seven steps:

- ISP (Information Strategy Planning). Allows identification of areas of concern and establishment of direction.
- BAA (Business Area Analysis). Areas of concern are analysed for entity relationship and process dependency.
- BSD (Business System Design). The processes are packaged into procedures that are user interactive.
- TD (Technical Design). The conversion of BAA/BSD designs into specific database tables (such as DB2), CICS transactions, and COBOL II code.
- Construction. The generation of source and executable code and database definition and access statements.
- Transition. Loading data into the databases, determination of conversion strategies.
- Production. Actual implementation and ongoing use of the system.

Throughout these phases, testing also occurs. Unit or program testing is performed by individual team members. System testing occurs when the entire system is operational. User acceptance testing occurs at various points in the development process.

Some problems occurred with the interfaces between systems. Once these problems were solved, the end system performed adequately in terms of efficiency and effectiveness measures. The users were pleased with the system and it is currently functional.

Why was this prototyping effort successful, whereas the effort made by the New Jersey Division of Motor Vehicles unsuccessful? One of the main advantages is five years of advancement in prototyping tools. Ideal is less integrated and much less sophisticated than IEF. Also TCCL has had a chance to learn from other companies' mistakes. As prototyping software tools become more and more sophisticated, the inefficiencies will be reduced dramatically.

## SUMMARY

Prototyping is the process of quickly building a model of the final software system, which is used primarily as a communication tool to assess and meet the information needs of the user.

Prototyping came about with the advent of 4GLs, which enabled application or code generation. The reasons for the success of prototyping arise from the problems encountered in the use of the traditional development of software systems using 3GLs.

Prototyping environments are divided into two major types: complete application generator environments and toolkit or 'workbench' environments.

There are two major types of prototyping approaches: iterative (Type I) and throwaway (Type II). In the iterative approach, the prototype is changed and modified according to user requirements until the prototype evolves into the final system. In the throwaway approach, the prototype serves as a model for the final system, which is eventually coded in a 3GL or procedural language.

Some advantages of prototyping include: faster development time, easier end use and learning, less human-power to develop systems, decreased backlogs, and enhanced user/analyst communication. Some disadvantages of prototyping include: the fostering of undue expectations on the part of the user, what the user sees may not be what the user gets, and availability of application-generator software may encourage end-user computing.

Not all systems are good candidates for the prototyping approach. Care should be taken to determine whether the system in question exhibits characteristics that make prototyping a viable option.

No current prototyping tools ensure that good human-factors guidelines will be exhibited in the final system. Analysts should be aware of these guidelines and build systems that adhere to them, regardless of the use of prototyping tools.

Prototyping is a powerful and widely used approach to system development. Systems built with the use of prototyping can be highly successful if a strict methodology is adhered to and thorough analysis and requirements definition takes place before prototyping is attempted.

## REFERENCES


1 **Carey, J M and McLeod, Jr, R** 'Use of system development methodology and tools' *J. Syst. Manage.* Vol 39 No 3 (1987) pp 30–35

2 **Boar, B** 'Application prototyping: a life cycle perspective' *J. Syst. Manage.* Vol 37 (1986) pp 25–31

3 **Lantz, K** 'The prototyping methodology: designing right the first time' *Computerworld* Vol 20 (1986) pp 69–74

4 **Staff** 'The next generation' *Banker* Vol 136 (1986) pp 79–81

5 **Stahl, B** 'The trouble with application generators' *Datamation* Vol 32 (1986) pp 93–94

6 **Klinger, D E** 'Rapid prototyping revisited' *Datamation* Vol 32 (1986) pp 131–132

7 **Yourdon, E** *Managing the structured techniques* Yourdon Press, New York, NY, USA (1976)

8 **Brooks, F P** 'The mythical man-month' (chapter 2) in **Brooks, F P** (ed) *The mythical man-month essays on software engineering* Addison-Wesley, Reading, MA, USA (1979) pp 11–26

9 **Boehm, B W** 'Structured programming: problems, pitfalls, and payoffs' *TRW Software Series TRW-SS-76-06* TRW Defence Systems, Redondo Beach, CA, USA (1976)

10 **Sprague, R H and McNurlin, B C** *Information systems management in practice* Prentice Hall, Englewood Cliffs, NJ, USA (1986)

11 **Boehm, B W** *IEEE Trans. Soft. Eng.* (1984)

12 **Goyette, R** 'Fourth generation systems soothe end user unrest' *Data Manage.* Vol 24 (1986) pp 30–32

13 **Kull, D** 'Designs on development' *Computer Decisions* Vol 17 (1985) pp 86–88

14 **Kull, D** 'Anatomy of a 4GL disaster' *Computer Decisions* Vol 18 (1986) pp 58–65

15 **Harrison, T S** 'Techniques and issues in rapid prototyping' *J. Syst. Manage.* Vol 36 (1985) pp 8–13

16 **Sena, J A and Smith, M L** 'Applying software engineering principles to the user application interface' (chapter 6) in **Carey, J M (ed)** *Human factors in management information systems* Ablex, Norwood, NJ, USA (1988) pp 103–116

17 **Shneiderman, B** *Designing the user interface* Addison-Wesley, Reading, MA, USA (1986)


## BIBLIOGRAPHY


**Doke, E R and Myers, L A** 'The 4GL: on its way to becoming an industry standard?' *Data Manage.* Vol 25 (1987) pp 10–12

**Duncan, M** 'But what about quality?' *Datamation* Vol 32 (1986) pp 135–6

**Staff** 'Why software prototyping works' *Datamation* Vol 33 (1987) pp 97–103

# A Classification of CASE Technology

Alfonso Fuggetta, Politecnico di Milano and CEFRIEL

**The variety of CASE products available today is daunting. This survey provides a classification to help in assessing products ranging from tools and environments to enabling technology.**

The design, implementation, delivery, and maintenance of software are complex and expensive activities that need improvement and better control. Among the technologies proposed to achieve these goals is CASE (computer-aided software engineering): computerized applications supporting and partially automating software-production activities.[1] Hundreds of CASE products are commercially available, offering a wide spectrum of functionalities.

The evolution and proliferation of such tools has forced CASE researchers to address a new challenging topic: How can they develop more integrated and easier to use CASE tools? In response, they have conceived and introduced new products that extend traditional operating-system functionalities to provide more advanced services, such as sophisticated process-control mechanisms and enhanced database-management functionalities.

Another growing research area is the development of technologies to support formal definition and automation of the software process, the total set of activities, rules, methodologies, organizational structures, and tools used during software production. Developers generally agree it is not possible to identify an optimal, universal, and general-purpose process. Rather, each organization must design and evolve the process according to its own needs, market, and customers. To better manage and support software processes, researchers and practitioners need new means to describe and assess them. Moreover, the descriptions must be usable by a computerized tool to guide, control, and, whenever possible, automate software-process activities. This research has produced its first results, and several industrial products have appeared on the market.

The availability of a large number of products is contributing to the improvement and wide diffusion of software-engineering practice. However, this product proliferation is creating critical problems.

It is more difficult to assess the real capabilities and features of many products on the market, and to understand how they are related to each other functionally and technologically. The terminology is often confusing or misleading. For example, terms such as tool, workbench, toolset, and environment are given very different meanings and interpretations. It is difficult, therefore, to develop a clear and systematic classification of the available technology for effective assessment and acquisition.

Reprinted from *Computer*, Vol. 26, No. 12, Dec. 1993, pp. 25–38. 

## Critical issues in classification schemes

The basic choices and purpose of the classification scheme for CASE technology I propose in this article can be criticized in many ways. First, the acronym CASE is associated with many different definitions often less general than the one I use here.

Sodhi, for example, proposes the following definition: "Computer-Aided Software Engineering (CASE) encompasses a collection of automated tools and methods that assist software engineering in the phases of the software development life cycle."[1] This definition takes into account only the production-process technology.

Next, Pressman defines CASE as follows: "The workshop for software engineering is called an integrated project support environment, and the toolset that fills the workshop is CASE."[2] The author also includes what he calls framework tools: products supporting infrastructure development. This definition extends the scope of CASE.

And Forte and McCulley define CASE this way: "We take CASE literally, that is, CASE is software engineering enhanced by automated tools (i.e. computer-aided). . . To us, it's all part of a coordinated approach to the design and production of systems and products containing software."[3]

Finally, Sommerville proposes a CASE definition similar to the one I present in this article: "Computer-aided software engineering is the term for software tool support for the software engineering process."[4] These examples show that the term CASE is assuming a wider meaning and becoming associated with the computer-aided support offered to the entire software process.

A second criticism is that the goal of this type of classification and its approaches are shallow. It is not easy to agree on the levels of abstraction of the reference framework used to classify CASE products, or on the products' assignments to the identified classes. Moreover, it is difficult to find the right focus to technically profile the different classes of products.

Nonetheless, the need for a conceptual framework and a classification of available technology is increasing. Practitioners and researchers need to assess and compare existing technology. Customers (software-production organizations) need to have a clear overview of the available technology and its potential benefits. Educators and consultants need a solid conceptual basis for their presentations of the state of the art in the field.

Pressman makes a significant observation on this issue:[2] "A number of risks are inherent whenever we attempt to categorize CASE tools. . . Confusion (or antagonism) can be created by placing a specific tool within one category when others might believe it belongs in another category. Some readers may feel that an entire category has been omitted — thereby eliminating an entire set of tools for inclusions in the overall CASE environment. In addition, simple categorization tends to be flat. . . But even with these risks, it is necessary to create a taxonomy of CASE tools — to better understand the breadth of CASE and to better appreciate where such tools can be applied in the software engineering process."

Pressman's words point to a particularly important problem that deserves some additional comments. An ideal classification should define an equivalence relation on the considered domain. Then it becomes possible to partition the domain in equivalent classes and assign each element in the domain to just one class. An entity's class precisely and unambiguously characterizes it for easy comparison and assessment.

Often, however, it is not possible to find such an equivalence relation, and an entity might span different classes. This risk is particularly real with CASE products. Their functionalities and characteristics are not standardized, so it may be quite difficult to assign a given product to a unique class. Nevertheless, an effective classification should aim at limiting these situations to retain its overall soundness and usefulness.

#### References


1. J. Sodhi, *Software Eng.: Methods, Management, and CASE Tools*, McGraw-Hill, Blue Ridge Summit, Pa., 1991.
2. R.S. Pressman, *Software Eng. — A Practitioner's Approach*, McGraw-Hill, New York, 1992.
3. *CASE Outlook: Guide to Products and Services*, G. Forte and K. McCulley, eds., CASE Consulting Group, Lake Oswego, Ore., 1991.
4. I. Sommerville, *Software Eng.*, Addison-Wesley, Reading, Mass., 1992.


In this article, I propose a classification with more precise definitions for these terms. To avoid any misunderstanding, I use the term "product" to identify any object in the classification.

Even the development of a precise classification can introduce additional conceptual and practical problems that make such efforts useless or even dangerous. The criteria must clarify the rationale, purposes, and limitations of the proposed approach. The level of abstraction must strike a balance between analysis and synthesis, and avoid the introduction of useless details or vague concepts.

My classification of products supporting the software process is based on a general framework derived from the work of Conradi et al.[2] Figure 1 shows the framework. The software process is decomposed in two subprocesses: a *production process* and a *metaprocess*.

The production process includes all activities, rules, methodologies, organizational structures, and tools used to conceive, design, develop, deliver, and maintain a software product. A production process must be defined, assessed, and evolved through a systematic and continuing metaprocess.

The purpose of the metaprocess is the acquisition and exploitation of new products supporting software-production activities and, more generally, the improvement and innovation of the procedures, rules, and technologies used to deliver the organization's artifacts. In the last decade, efforts aimed at understanding the metaprocess include those of the Software Engineering Institute, whose well-known Capability Maturity Model[3] defines five levels of process maturity and provides guidelines to progressively improve it.

The production process can be supported and partially automated by the *production-process technology* — aids to software developers to specify, build, and maintain a software product. In an organization, the specific technology and related procedures and guidelines used to support the production process are called *production-process support.*

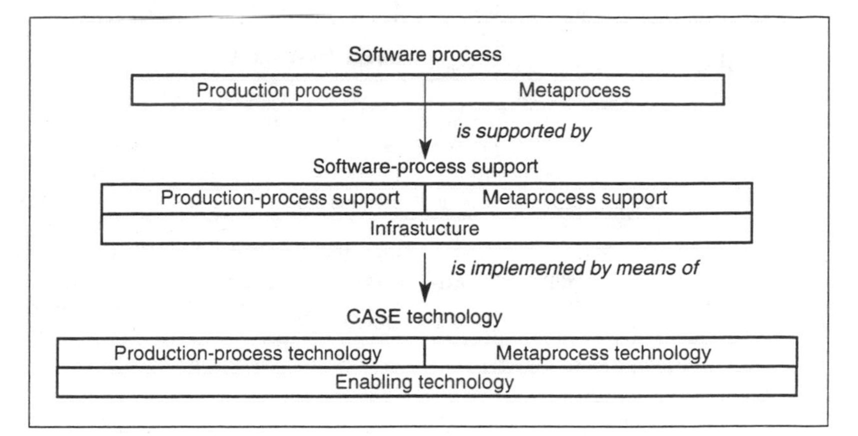


**Figure 1. The general framework.**

The metaprocess can be automated and supported as well with a *metaprocess technology* used to create the *metaprocess support* — the specific aids used in an organization's metaprocess to automate and guide metaprocess activities.

## Related work

One of the first and most important classification attempts was that of Dart et al.,[1] who presented a taxonomy of the trends that have produced state-of-the-art software-development environments. They defined a software-development environment as "an environment that augments or automates *all* the activities comprising the software development cycle." The aim of their classification was to understand the evolution of the principles on which environments have been built.

The taxonomy identified four basic categories:

- *Language-centered environments* built around one language (for example, Interlisp, Smalltalk, or Rational). They are highly interactive, but offer limited support for programming in the large.
- *Structure-centered environments* incorporating the idea of environment generation (for example, Mentor, Cornell Program Synthesizer, and Gandalf). These environments let users directly manipulate the grammar of a programming language to produce structure-oriented tools, such as syntax-directed editors.
- *Toolkit environments* consisting of small tools intended primarily to support the coding phase (for example, Unix PWB and VMS VAX Set). They do not offer any control of the way the tools are applied.
- *Method-based environments* centered around specific methodologies for software development, such as structured analysis and design techniques or object-oriented design (for example, Excelerator, TAGS, and Software Through Pictures).

This pioneering article has several merits, but its scope is limited. It does not offer any finer grained classification of existing products, nor does it take into account the metaprocess and enabling technologies. Moreover, it tends to consider at the same level of abstraction entities that are quite different (for example, complete environments like Interlisp and Smalltalk, and more specialized products like Excelerator).

Forte and McCulley's more recent classification[2] introduces a *tool taxonomy* on two levels. (The term "tool" identifies any product considered in the Forte and McCulley classification.) At the first level, the taxonomy proposes the following classification domains to characterize a tool: application areas targeted by the tool, tasks supported in the development cycle, methods and notations, hardware platforms, operating systems, databases and transaction processing subsystems supported by the tool, network and communication protocols, and programming languages supported by the tool.

At the second level, the authors specify attributes for each domain. Figure A shows the description of the development-tasks domain. This scheme partitions the total set of CASE tools in two main classes: vertical and horizontal tools.

Vertical tools are used in a specific life-cycle phase or activity (for example, testing), while horizontal tools are used throughout the entire software process. The merit of this classification lies in the richness of the domains to characterize tools. Moreover, it is implemented in a tool called Tool Finder, which lets users retrieve product descriptions from an electronic archive.

Unfortunately, the classification does not take into account the conceptual architecture of the software process (as I discuss in the main text). It is not easy to classify tools according to the breadth of support offered to the production process. For instance, Forte and McCulley classify a compiler under the construction task, along with other more complex and sophisticated products (workbenches supporting coding, debugging, and incremental linking). They classify tool integration and process modeling in different horizontal tasks, but provide no hints for understanding their mutual dependencies or their relationships with other classes of products. Moreover, the division between vertical and horizontal tasks becomes unclear if we consider unconventional life cycles not based on the waterfall model.

Production-process and metaprocess supports are based on a common *infrastructure* that provides services and functionalities for their operation in an integrated and homogeneous environment. The infrastructure can be implemented using operating-system services and more advanced and recent products for, say, process control and database management. The products supporting infrastructure implementation are globally identified under the term *enabling technology*. The infrastructure, production-process support, and metaprocess support constitute the *software-process support.*

The classification I propose in this article considers all products in the production-process technology, metaprocess technology, and enabling technology. Globally, these products represent CASE technology.

## Refining the reference framework

To refine the framework presented in the previous section, I further classify CASE products used in the production process according to the breadth of support they offer. A production process may be viewed as a set of elementary *tasks* to be accomplished to produce a software application. Examples of tasks are compiling, editing, and generating test cases from requirements specifications.

Tasks are grouped to form *activities*, sets of tasks supporting coarse-grained parts of the software-production process. For example, coding is an activity that includes editing, compiling, debugging, and so on. The activity concept is not to be confused with the phases of a waterfall life cycle. Activities are not necessarily carried out in strict sequence: They can be composed to form any type of life cycle.

According to these definitions, I classify CASE products in the production-process technology in three categories:

(1) *Tools* support only specific tasks in the software process.
(2) *Workbenches* support only one or a few activities.
(3) *Environments* support (a large part of) the software process.

Workbenches and environments are generally built as collections of tools. Tools can therefore be either standalone products or components of workbenches and environments. For exam-

---

Pressman's classification[3] is based on the identification of these different functions supported by CASE products: business systems planning, project management, support (documentation, database, configuration management, and so on), analysis and design, programming, integration and testing, prototyping, maintenance, and framework (support for environment development). Even in this case, however, little help is given for understanding the architecture of the software-process support. Moreover, Pressman does not take metaprocess technology into account.

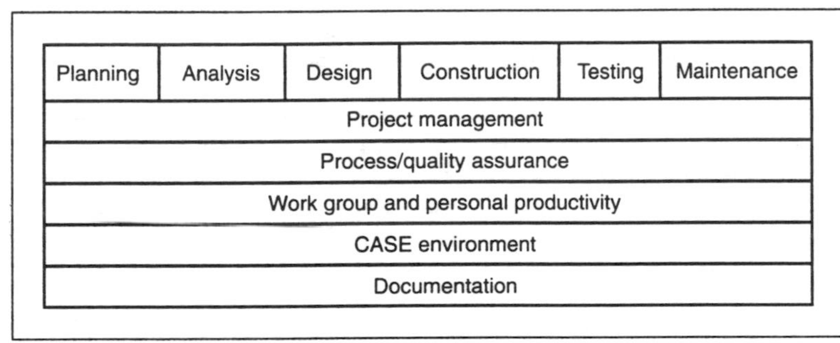

**Figure A. Development tasks in Forte and McCulley's classification.[2]**

In another important classification, Sommerville[4] defines CASE tools as the basic building blocks used to create a "software engineering environment." He classifies CASE tools according to the functions they offer and the process activities they support. CASE tools are integrated by an environment infrastructure. Integration can be achieved along four different dimensions: data integration (sharing of information), user-interface integration (common interface paradigms and mechanisms), control integration (mechanisms to control the invocation and execution of tools and applications), and process integration (integration in a defined process model). Environments are collections of tools classified in three different categories:

- *Programming environments* support programming activities, but provide limited support for software analysis and design.
- *CASE workbenches* provide support for analysis and design, but little support for coding and testing.
- *Software-engineering environments* comprise tools for all activities in the software process.

Sommerville proposes a reference framework with two levels of tool aggregations: *stand-alone tools* and *environments.* Moreover, he relates important concepts such as process integration and environment infrastructure. The classification I present in this article inherits several of these concepts and further refines the idea of a layered classification scheme.

A different type of effort is represented by the *Reference Model for Frameworks of Software Engineering Environments*, jointly developed by the European Computer Manufacturers Association (ECMA) and the National Institute of Standards and Technology.[5,6] This reference model "is a conceptual and functional basis for describing and comparing existing SEEs or SEE components."[6] (SEE stands for software-engineering environment.) Thus, it is not a classification of CASE technology, but it is important because it defines the framework for constructing, operating, and evolving a software-engineering environment. The framework is a set of interrelated services for object management, process management, user interfaces, communication, tools, policy enforcement, framework administration, and configuration.

A software-engineering environment in the ECMA model is similar to the software-process support presented in the main text. The ECMA model's goals and scope, however, are quite different: It is oriented more to the definition of the ideal func-

ple, most computer manufacturers sell tools such as compilers as stand-alone products.[1] They may also integrate compilers with other tools to support both coding and debugging. (In this section, I use "integrate" in its informal and intuitive sense.) In general, these products also include a debugger, an editor, and an incremental linker. Compilers are also very often marketed as standard components of environments (for example, the C compiler in the Unix PWB environment). Some kinds of tools are seldom available as stand-alone products. For example, graphical editors for dataflow or SADT (structured analysis and design technique) diagrams are usually embedded in products also offering other components to support analysis and design.

The distinction among tools, workbenches, and environments further extends Sommerville's classification,[4] which includes only two levels of granularity: tools and environments. Fernström, Närfelt, and Ohlsson[5] advocate a different approach based on four levels of granularity: service, tool, toolset, and environment. In their classification, the term "toolset" is equivalent to workbench, while "service" identifies an operation embedded in a tool.

Production-process support may be built by adopting and integrating one or more tools, workbenches, and environments. In general, it is composed of an environment, which acts as the "backbone." It can be further extended by introducing additional tools and workbenches to fully cover the production process. (All products mentioned in this article are examples. No evaluation is associated with their citation. Readers should refer to specialized publications[1] for a complete presentation of existing products.)

## Tools

A CASE tool is a software component supporting a specific task in the software-production process. Table 1 classifies such tools.

**Editing tools.** Editing tools (editors) can be classified in two subclasses: *textual editors* and *graphical editors*. The first subclass includes traditional text editors and word processors used to produce textual documents such as programs, textual specifications, and documentation. Editors in the second subclass are used to produce documents

tionalities to be offered by the infrastructure, so it does not discuss in much detail the characteristics of CASE technology. Also, it does not present a detailed classification of tools (in the ECMA terminology) and does not evaluate the different philosophies adopted by existing environments.

ECMA concepts can be easily recognized in the classification I propose in this article. My infrastructure takes into account all the ECMA services, except for process-management services, which I consider as a separate entity in the production-process and metaprocess supports.

Perry and Kaiser's more general approach[7] for analyzing software-development environments is based on a general model consisting of three components: structures, mechanisms, and policies. Structures are the objects on which mechanisms operate. Mechanisms are the basic functionalities offered by tools. Policies are the procedures, rules, and guidelines offered to and imposed on software developers by environments. An environment can be described by specifying these three components. Classes of environments can be identified by considering analogies and commonalities. For example, toolkit environments[1] can be described by the following model:

```
Toolkit environment =
  (
    {file system/object-management system},
    {assorted construction tools},
    {laissez-faire}
  )
```

To describe the problems of scale in software production, the authors introduce a metaphor that distinguishes four different classes of environments: individual, family, city, and state. Environments in the individual class emphasize software-construction activities and are dominated by mechanisms. Family-class environments address coordination and are dominated by structures. The city class emphasizes cooperation among software developers and is dominated by policies. Finally, environments in the state class address the commonality issue and are dominated by higher order policies.

This classification identifies the components useful in evaluating a software-development environment. Moreover, the metaphor characterizes the different problems that software-development projects must address when scaling up. The model is less useful when applied to classifying the large variety of commercial products, since it considers only environments and does not provide any categorizations for other types of products.

In conclusion, even if the classifications available so far have substantially contributed to the state of the art, they are still incomplete. Much work is needed to provide an effective and comprehensive reference framework and the related classification scheme.

**References**


1. S.A. Dart et al., "Software Development Environments," *Computer*, Vol. 20, No. 11, Nov. 1987, pp. 18-28.
2. *CASE Outlook: Guide to Products and Services*, G. Forte and K. McCulley, eds., CASE Consulting Group, Lake Oswego, Ore., 1991.
3. R.S. Pressman, *Software Eng. — A Practitioner's Approach*, McGraw-Hill, New York, 1992.
4. I. Sommerville, *Software Eng.*, Addison-Wesley, Reading, Mass., 1992.
5. "Reference Model for Frameworks of Software Engineering Environments," jointly published as ECMA Tech. Report TR/55, European Computer Manufacturers Assoc., Geneva, and NIST Special Publication 500-201, Nat'l Inst. of Standards and Technology, Gaithersburg, Md., 1991.
6. M. Chen and R.J. Norman, "A Framework for Integrated CASE," *IEEE Software*, Vol. 9, No. 2, Mar. 1992, pp. 18-22.
7. D.E. Perry and G.E. Kaiser, "Models of Software Development Environments," *IEEE Trans. Software Eng.*, Vol. 17, No. 3, Mar. 1991, pp. 283-295.

using graphical symbols. Typical examples are general drawing and painting tools (such as MacDraw), tools to enter graphical specifications (for example, those based on dataflow diagrams), and tools to paint the forms and layouts constituting an application's user interface.

Examples of textual and graphical editors are Pmate, a text editor for professional programmers running on MS-DOS personal computers; MacBubbles, a Macintosh-based editing tool for Yourdon-DeMarco diagrams; and DV Draw, an editor that creates several types of graphical output.

Syntax-directed editors are an important category of textual editor. Two examples are Keyone and DEC LSE — Language Sensitive Editor.

**Table 1. Classes of CASE tools.**

| Class | Subclass |
|---|---|
| Editing | Graphical editors<br>Textual editors |
| Programming | Coding and debugging<br>• Assemblers<br>• Compilers<br>• Cross-assemblers<br>• Cross-compilers<br>• Debuggers<br>• Interpreters<br>• Linkage editors<br>• Precompilers/preprocessors<br>Code generators<br>• Compiler generators<br>Code restructurers |
| Verification and validation | Static analyzers<br>• Cross-reference generators<br>• Flowcharters<br>• Standards enforcers<br>• Syntax checkers<br>Dynamic analyzers<br>• Program instrumentors<br>• Tracers/profilers<br>Comparators<br>Symbolic executors<br>Emulators/simulators<br>Correctness proof assistants<br>Test-case generators<br>Test-management tools |
| Configuration management | Configuration- and version-management tools<br>Configuration builders<br>Change-control monitors<br>Librarians |
| Metrics and measurement | Code analyzers<br>Execution monitors/timing analyzers |
| Project management | Cost-estimation tools<br>Project-planning tools<br>Conference desks<br>E-mail<br>Bulletin boards<br>Project agendas<br>Project notebooks |
| Miscellaneous tools | Hypertext systems<br>Spreadsheets |

**Programming tools.** These tools are used to support coding and code restructuring. The three main subclasses are *coding and debugging tools*, *code generators*, and *code restructurers*.

The first subclass includes traditional tools used to compile, run, and debug a program. Examples are the numerous traditional compilers and interpreters available on the market, interactive tester/debuggers such as Via/Smartest, and cross-compilers such as HP Cross Compilers, a family of Unix-based C cross-compilers.

The second class includes tools that generate code starting from a high-level description of the application. Typical examples are compiler generators and Cobol generators. Compiler generators (for example, yacc/lex) automatically build lexical analyzers and parsers starting from the formal description of the language syntax. Cobol generators produce Cobol starting from a high-level program description (for example, the VAX Cobol Generator).

The third subclass includes tools used to restructure existing programs. These tools can analyze, reformat, and in some cases improve existing source code by performing actions such as elimination of "gotos" and unreachable portions of code. Examples of such tools are AdaReformat and Via/Renaissance.

**Verification and validation tools.** This class includes tools that support program validation and verification. Validation aims at ensuring that the product's functions are what the customer really wants, while verification aims at ensuring that the product under construction meets the requirements definition. This class has many subclasses:[6]

- *Static and dynamic analyzers* analyze a computer program without executing the program (static) or by monitoring program execution (dynamic).
- *Comparators* equate two files to identify commonalities or differences. Typically, they are used to compare test results with the expected program outputs.
- *Symbolic executors* simulate program execution using symbols rather than actual values for input data and produce outputs expressed as symbolic expressions.
- *Emulators/simulators* imitate all or part of a computer system. They accept the same data, provide the same functionalities, and achieve the same results as the imitated system.
- *Correctness proof assistants* support formal techniques to prove mathematically that a program satisfies its specifications or that a specification satisfies given properties.
- *Test-case generators* take as input a computer program and a selection of test criteria, and generate test input data that meet these criteria.
- *Test-management tools* support testing by managing test results, test checklists, regression tests, test coverage metrics, and so on.

Examples of such tools are AdaXRef, a cross-reference generator; Q/Auditor, a standards enforcer; lint-Plus, a syntax checker; Instrumentation Tool, a program instrumentor; CICS Simulcast, an execution tracer; Playback, a test-result comparator; and HP Basic Branch Analyzer, a test-coverage tool. (See the detailed classification scheme in Table 1.)

**Configuration-management tools.** Configuration-management techniques coordinate and control the construction of a system composed of many parts.[7] Software development and management can greatly benefit from configuration management, which can be decomposed into the following tasks:

- *Version management.* During software development, more than one version of each software item is produced. Versions must be managed so subsequent work incorporates the correct version.
- *Item identification.* Each software item must be unambiguously identifiable. Software-process agents (all people working in the software process) must be able to retrieve specific software items to build and rebuild coherent configurations of the product under development.
- *Configuration building.* A software product is a complex collection of versioned software items. Building a product requires invocation of operations such as preprocessing, compiling, and linking on a possibly large set of software items.
- *Change control.* Changes to a software item may have an impact on other components. Moreover, if several programmers can access the same software items, control is necessary to synchronize their activity to prevent the creation of inconsistent or erroneous versions of software items.
- *Library management.* All the software items relevant in a software process must be subject to effective storage and retrieval policies.

Products that support specific configuration-management tasks — such as configuration building (for example, make, MMS, and Pmaker), version management (SCCS and CMS), and library management (Plib86) — do not offer comprehensive and integrated support to all tasks. Most configuration-management tools in this classification constitute the first generation. The second generation of configuration-management products offers much wider support by integrating into a single product most functionalities offered by the individual tools considered here.

**Metrics and measurement tools.** Tools that collect data on programs and program execution fall into two subclasses:

- tools to analyze the source code and compute several source-code metrics (for example, to evaluate code complexity according to Halstead's or McCabe's metrics), and
- tools to monitor the execution of programs and collect runtime statistics.

Examples of such tools are Performance Architek and HP Apollo DPAK.

**Project-management tools.** Several types of products support project management. A first subclass includes products used to estimate software-production costs. These tools typically implement techniques such as Cocomo (Constructive cost model) or function points, and provide user-friendly interfaces to specify project information and analyze estimation results.

A second subclass comprises tools supporting project planning — that is, project scheduling, resource assignment, and project tracking. These tools are based on well-known concepts and notations such as WBS (work breakdown structure), Gantt, and PERT (program evaluation and review technique) charts.

A third subclass includes tools to support communication and coordination among project team members. Some permit on-line and deferred interaction among people — for example, teleconferencing systems (also called conference desks), e-mail systems, and electronic bulletin boards. Other tools are project agendas used to coordinate activities and meetings.

Examples of these tools are CA-Estimacs (cost estimation), MacProject (project planning), VAX Notes (conference desk), and DateBook (distributed agenda).

**Miscellaneous tools.** Products difficult to classify include spreadsheets and hypertext systems.

A spreadsheet can be used as a project-management tool to perform what-if analysis or to develop models of the development process (for example, by implementing the Cocomo model). Spreadsheets can also be used for programming. Several applications have been developed using spreadsheet languages, particularly in business administration and marketing. These applications are marketed as add-ons to standard products such as Excel. For example, Computerized Classic Accounting is an integrated accounting system developed for the Macintosh version of Excel.

Hypertext systems can replace desktop publishing systems for authoring advanced documentation. They can also be used as programming tools to develop prototypes or even final applications. Many applications for the Macintosh have been developed using HyperCard — for example, Client, a personal data manager, and MindLink, an idea processor.

## Integration in CASE products

The need for integration in CASE technology is increasingly acknowledged by researchers and practitioners.[1] According to Thomas and Nejmeh, integration can be analyzed in four dimensions:[2]

- *Data integration* ensures that all the information in the environment is managed as a consistent whole, regardless of how parts of it are operated on and transformed.
- *Control integration* permits the flexible combination of an environment's functions according to project preferences and the underlying processes and environment supports.
- *Presentation integration* improves user interaction with the environment by reducing users' cognitive load.
- *Process integration* ensures that tools interact effectively in support of a defined process.

We can identify several levels of integration according to the degree of technology exploitation along these four dimensions. For example, Brown and McDermid define five levels of integration, focusing on functionalities and features that support data and control integration.[3]

**References**

1. *IEEE Software* special issue on integrated CASE, Vol. 9, No. 2, Mar. 1992.
2. I. Thomas and B.A. Nejmeh, "Definition of Tool Integration for Environments," *IEEE Software*, Vol. 9, No. 2, Mar. 1992, pp. 29-35.
3. A.W. Brown and J.A. McDermid, "Learning from IPSE's Mistakes," *IEEE Software*, Vol. 9, No. 2, Mar. 1992, pp. 23-28.

## Workbenches

Workbenches integrate in a single application several tools supporting specific software-process activities. Hence, they achieve

- a homogeneous and consistent interface (presentation integration),
- easy invocation of tools and tool chains (control integration), and
- access to a common data set, managed in a centralized way (data integration).

Some products can enforce predefined procedures and policies within the workbench (process integration).

Table 2 shows eight classes of workbenches.

**Business planning and modeling workbenches.** This class includes products to support the identification and description of a complex business. They are used to build high-level enterprise models to assess the general requirements and information flows, and identify priorities in the development of information systems.

The tools integrated in such products include graphical editors (to provide diagrams and structured charts), report generators, and cross-reference generators. For example, PC Prism integrates tools to create enterprise models and automatically generate documentation from the information stored in its repository.

The borderline between this class of products and analysis and design workbenches is often quite fuzzy.

**Analysis and design workbenches.** Products for analysis and design activities constitute an important class of workbenches. In fact, very often the term CASE is used to denote just this class of products. Since the term CASE has a wider meaning, "upper" CASE is more properly used to denote this class of tools, which are used in the early stages of the software process. Today's upper CASE workbenches automate most of the analysis and design methodologies developed in the past decades such as SA/SD (structured analysis/structured design), object-oriented analysis and design, and Jackson System Development.

An upper CASE workbench usually includes one or more editors to create and modify specifications, and other tools to analyze, simulate, and transform them. For example, Excelerator has editors to create dataflow diagrams, structure charts, and entity-relationship diagrams. It also includes an editor and a simulator to create and test mock-ups of system inputs and outputs (forms and reports), as well as a code generator to produce skeletal Cobol source code starting from structure charts. Software Through Pictures includes several graphical editors to support the creation, for example, of control-flow diagrams, process-activation tables, and state-transition diagrams. It also includes code- and documentation-generation facilities.

The functionalities these workbenches offer depend heavily on the notations on which they are centered: If the adopted notation is not formally defined, a workbench can provide only editing and document-production facilities. Using a formal notation permits a higher degree of automation.

Table 3 shows a further classification of this class of workbenches according to level of formality, supported application, and activities covered.

*Level of formality.* Analysis and design workbenches support notations at different levels of formality:

- *Informal.* Structured English and other informal, textual notations, whose syntax and semantics are not formally defined.
- *Semiformal.* Notations for which it is possible to build syntax checkers. Such notations still lack a precise semantics. Dataflow diagrams are a typical example.
- *Formal.* Notations whose syntax and semantics are formally defined. Finite-state machines, Petri nets, and Statecharts are examples.

*Supported applications.* No notation can universally support the specification of all types of applications. In each project, the software engineer must be allowed to choose the most suitable notation — or combination of notations.

For assessment and selection, notations fall in two main categories:

(1) notations for data-intensive applications, such as banking or accounting systems (for example, dataflow and entity-relationship diagrams), and

**Table 2. Classes of CASE workbenches.**

| Class | Sample Products |
|---|---|
| Business planning and modeling | PC Prism |
| Analysis and design | Excelerator<br>Statemate<br>Software Through Pictures |
| User-interface development | HP Interface Architect<br>DEC VUIT |
| Programming | CodeCenter |
| Verification and validation | Battlemap<br>Logiscope |
| Maintenance and reverse engineering | Recoder<br>Rigi<br>Hindsight<br>SmartSystem |
| Configuration management | PCMS<br>CCC<br>SCLM<br>DSEE |
| Project management | Coordinator<br>DEC Plan<br>Synchronize |

**Table 3. A sampling of "upper" CASE workbenches.**

| Sample Products | Examples of Notations Supported | Level of Formality | Class of Applications Supported | Activities Covered |
|---|---|---|---|---|
| Excelerator | Dataflow diagrams<br>Entity-relationship diagrams | Semiformal | General purpose | Both |
| Teamwork | Dataflow diagrams<br>Ward and Mellor | Semiformal | General purpose | Both |
| Statemate | Statecharts | Formal | Control intensive | Both |
| TAGS | Input/Output Requirements Language | Formal | Control intensive | Both |
| ASA | Integrated System Definition Language<br>Finite State Machine | Formal | Control intensive | Analysis |
| GEODE | Specification Description Language | Formal | Control intensive | Design |
| ER-Designer | Entity-relationship diagrams | Semiformal | Data intensive | Both |
| IEW | Dataflow diagrams<br>Entity-relationship diagrams | Semiformal | General purpose | Both |
| STP | Dataflow diagrams<br>Object-oriented structured design | Formal and semiformal | General purpose | Both |

(2) notations for control-intensive applications, such as avionics and control systems (for example, finite-state machines, Statecharts, and Petri nets).

According to this distinction, analysis and design workbenches can be grouped in three subclasses:

- workbenches for data-intensive applications (for example, Excelerator),
- workbenches for control-intensive applications (for example, Statemate), and
- general-purpose workbenches — products that support notations for both types of applications (for example. Teamwork).

*Activities covered.* I call these products analysis and design workbenches because most cover both activities. However, some cover only one. Thus, I classify analysis and design workbenches as analysis only, design only, or both.

**User-interface-development workbenches.** This class of CASE workbenches is distinct from the others already presented. Its products do not help with specific software-process activities but rather with user-interface design and development.

Many authors have suggested that the user interface is the most critical part of some programs. Kay has even argued that in many cases the user interface *is* the program.[8] Effective support for user-interface design and development is important.

The products in this class exploit the capabilities of modern workstations and graphical environments such as Motif or Windows. They let the developer easily create and test user-interface components and integrate them with the application program.

Typically, a user-interface workbench offers

- graphical editors to paint windows, dialog boxes, icons, and other user-interface components;
- simulators to test the developed interface before integrating it with the application;
- code generators to produce the code to be integrated with the application; and
- runtime libraries to support the generation of executable code.

Examples are DEC VUIT and HP Interface Architect, both developed for the Motif standard interface.

**Programming workbenches.** The workbenches in this class evolved from the basic programming tools and provide integrated facilities supporting programming:

- a text editor to create and modify the source code,
- a compiler and linker to create the executable code, and
- a debugger.

For effective user interaction with the different tools, programming workbenches provide an integrated and consistent interface, and manage all information created during work sessions (source-code files, intermediate files, object- and executable-code files, and so on). Often, the workbench integrates the compiler with an interpreter or an incremental linker to speed the transition from editing to testing.

Examples of programming workbenches are Turbo C++, Turbo Pascal, and CodeCenter.

**Verification and validation workbenches.** This class of workbenches includes products that help with module and system testing. Products in this class often integrate several tools from both the metrics and measurement class and the verification and validation class. The functionalities offered by both classes jointly analyze the quality of code and support actual verification and validation.

A typical verification and validation workbench includes

- static analyzers to evaluate complexity metrics and call and control graphs,
- cross-reference and report generators,
- a tool to instrument a program and a tracer to support dynamic analysis, and
- a test-case generator and a test-management tool to produce, store, and manage test data, test results, and checklists.

Act and Logiscope are typical products.

**Maintenance and reverse-engineering workbenches.** In the past, software engineers often assumed that maintenance had only to do with fixing bugs. This approach proved inadequate for evolving software according to changes in the supported business environment, changes in the available technology, and new requirements from the customer. Now maintenance must be a component of the "forward" development process.

For maintenance, software engineers use the same tools and workbenches they normally use for development. They have to modify requirement specifications, designs, and application source code. They have to repeat the testing procedure to verify that the new version of the application can be released into service. And, with appropriate configuration-management techniques, they have to manage the artifacts of the process (documents, source code, makefiles, and so on).

Even if most maintenance is performed with the same techniques and products used during software development, some more specific tasks must be approached with ad hoc techniques and tools — in particular, techniques identified as *reverse engineering*. Müller et al. describe this discipline as "the process of extracting system abstraction and design information out of existing software systems."[9]

This goal has not been completely fulfilled. Perhaps it will be impossible to fully achieve the automatic derivation of analysis and design information from code. Such an operation requires higher level information to be synthesized from low-level descriptions (the program statements), and it appears that this can be done only by humans with knowledge of the application.

Several available maintenance and reverse-engineering workbenches provide interesting and seemingly effective features. An example is Recoder, one of the first commercial reverse-engineering workbenches. It includes a code restructurer, a flowcharter, and a cross-reference generator. It analyzes unstructured and hard-to-read Cobol programs and produces new, more readable and modifiable versions. Rigi, another reverse-engineering workbench, can build a program's call graph and suggest possible clustering techniques to achieve strong cohesion and low coupling.

Other sample workbenches in this class are Ensemble and Hindsight.

**Configuration-management workbenches.** The workbenches in this class integrate tools supporting version control, configuration building, and change control. For example, the HP Apollo DSEE workbench integrates a history manager to store versions of source elements, a configuration manager to define and build configurations, and a task manager and monitor manager to control the process of changing a software item. Thus, the single product integrates and substantially extends most features offered by tools such as make, SCCS, and RCS.

A few products in this class also offer more advanced functionalities to support process modeling. For example, software-process managers can tailor PCMS according to policies and roles they specify. Policies and roles are described through the possible states of a software item and the operations applied to them to change their state.

Other examples of configuration-management workbenches are CCC and SCLM.

**Project-management workbenches.** There are very few products in this class. Most potential candidates address only specific project-management tasks, and it seems more appropriate to classify them as tools.

Coordinator integrates several project-management functionalities based on an extended theoretical study of how people operate in a structured and complex organization. It lets development team members create typed messages — that is, messages with a precise meaning, requiring a specific action of the addressee (for example, requests for information or submissions of a proposal for approval). Also, Coordinator keeps track of

- the activities a person has to complete,
- temporal relations among significant actions to be completed by the organization, and
- actions that must be scheduled periodically during the project lifetime.

Other examples of project-management workbenches are Synchronize and DEC Plan. Synchronize includes several tools such as a distributed agenda, memo-distribution facilities, distributed to-do lists, and a meeting scheduler. DEC Plan offers functionalities similar to Synchronize, and also addresses project-planning and task-assignment problems.

## Environments

An environment is a collection of tools and workbenches that support the software process. Some of the names I use to identify the different classes in Table 4 come from existing terminology — for example, "toolkit and "language-centered environments."[10]

**Toolkits.** Toolkits are loosely integrated collections of products easily extended by aggregating different tools

**Table 4. Classes of CASE environments.**

| Class | Sample Products |
|---|---|
| Toolkits | Unix Programmer's Work Bench |
| Language-centered | Interlisp<br>Smalltalk<br>Rational<br>KEE |
| Integrated | IBM AD/Cycle<br>DEC Cohesion |
| Fourth generation | Informix 4GL<br>Focus |
| Process-centered | East<br>Enterprise II<br>Process Wise<br>Process Weaver<br>Arcadia |

and workbenches. Unlike workbenches, toolkits support different activities in the software-production process, but their support is very often limited to programming, configuration management, and project management (and project-management support is generally limited to message handling). Typically, toolkits are environments extended from basic sets of operating-system tools; the Unix Programmer's Work Bench and the VMS VAX Set are two examples.

Toolkits' loose integration requires users to activate tools by explicit invocation or simple control mechanisms such as redirection and pipes in Unix. The shared files users access for data exchange are very often unstructured or in formats that need explicit conversion so different tools can access them (via import and export operations). Because the only constraint for adding a new component is the formats of the files read or created by other tools or workbenches, toolkits can be easily and incrementally extended.

Toolkits do not impose any particular constraint on the process that users follow. Users interact through a general-purpose interface (for example, the shell or the command-language interpreter) that leaves them free to decide which procedures or operations to activate.

**Language-centered environments.** Examples of environments centered around a specific language are Interlisp, Smalltalk, Rational, and KEE, developed respectively for Lisp, Smalltalk (the language and the environment have the same name), Ada, and Lisp again.[11]

The peculiarity of this class of products is that very often the environment itself is written in the language for which it was developed, thus letting users customize and extend the environment and reuse part of it in the applications under development. The main drawback is that integrating code in different languages may not be feasible. Smalltalk is an environment that suffers from this problem. These environments can hardly be extended to support different programming languages, and they are often concentrated on the edit-compile-debug cycle, with little or no support for large-scale software development.

Language-centered environments offer a good level of presentation and control integration: Users are presented with a consistent interface and are given several mechanisms supporting automatic tool invocation and switching among tools (for example, among the editor, compiler, and debugger). However, these environments suffer from a lack of process and data integration. They are based on structured internal representations (usually abstract trees), but these mechanisms are invisible or hard for users to access for extending or customizing the environment with other products.

**Integrated environments.** The environments in this class are called "integrated" because, with some limitations, they operate using standard mechanisms so users can integrate tools and workbenches. These environments achieve presentation integration by providing uniform, consistent, and coherent tool and workbench interfaces: All products in the environment are operated through a unique interface concept. They achieve data integration through the *repository* concept: They have a specialized database managing all information produced and accessed in the environment.

The database is structured according to a high-level model of the environment, so users can develop tools and workbenches that access and exchange structured information instead of pure byte streams. This greatly enhances the functionalities and level of integration offered to the user. Control integration is achieved through powerful mechanisms to invoke tools and workbenches from within other components of the environment.

Such mechanisms can also encapsulate[12] a tool not written to make use of any of the environment framework services. They surround the tool with software that acts as a layer between the tool and the framework. Integrated environments do not explicitly tackle process integration. This distinguishes them from the process-centered environments discussed later.

The infrastructure needed to create an integrated environment is generally more sophisticated than traditional operating-system services. Later, I discuss *integrating platforms* — extensions to operating-system services that provide the tool builder with advanced features.

The DEC Cohesion and IBM AD/Cycle integrated environments provide basic tools and workbenches, and an integrating platform that lets other companies enrich the environment with additional products. For example, DEC Cohesion is based on an integrating platform offering tool encapsulation, a repository, and user-interface-management and tool-integration facilities (ACA Services, CDD Repository, and DEC Fuse). It includes several tools and workbenches to support production-process activities (DEC Set, DEC VUIT, DEC Plan, and DEC Design), and it can be extended with third-party products.

**Fourth-generation environments.** Fourth-generation environments were precursors to and, in a sense, are a subclass of integrated environments. They are sets of tools and workbenches supporting the development of a specific class of program: electronic data processing and business-oriented applications. At least four characteristics distinguish these applications:

(1) The application's operations are usually quite simple, while the structure of the information to be manipulated is rather complex.

(2) The user interface is critical. Typically, it is composed of many forms and layouts used to input, display, and modify the information stored in the database.

(3) The application requirements are very often not clearly defined and can be

detailed only through the development of prototypes (very often, mock-ups of the user interface).

(4) The software process to produce such applications is generally evolutionary.

Fourth-generation environments were the first integrated environments. In general, they include an editor, an interpreter and/or a compiler for a specialized language, a debugger, database access facilities, a form editor, a simulator, simple configuration-management tools, document-handling facilities, and, in some cases, a code generator to produce programs in traditional languages such as Cobol. Often, these components are integrated through a consistent interface, data are stored in a central, proprietary repository, and built-in triggers activate tools when specific events occur in the environment.

However, fourth-generation environments provide a low degree of process integration, and ad hoc nonstandard mechanisms support the other dimensions of integration. In many cases, for example, programs and other application-related information are stored in proprietary databases. This makes it difficult (or even impossible) for other manufacturers to extend the environment with new products and components. To overcome this problem, most of these environments are migrating to standard platforms for evolution into true integrated environments.

I defined these products as "fourth-generation environments" instead of the more traditional "fourth-generation languages" to emphasize that they are more than compilers or interpreters for specific languages: They are collections of tools to manage the design, development, and maintenance of large electronic data processing applications.

Table 5 presents a more detailed division of fourth-generation environments into three classes. *Production systems* are oriented to the development of banking or accounting systems with strong performance requirements. These environments replace traditional Cobol-based environments and fall into two subclasses: *language-based systems* and *Cobol generators*. The former are based on a language that is directly compiled or interpreted. The latter are products that start with a high-level description of the application and generate Cobol source code for new applications to integrate with existing ones. Natural 2 is a language-based system; Pacbase is a Cobol generator.

**Table 5. Fourth-generation environments.**

| Class | Sample Products |
|---|---|
| Production systems | |
| • Language-based systems | Natural 2<br>Informix 4GL/OnLine |
| • Cobol generators | Pacbase<br>Transform |
| Infocenter systems | Focus<br>Ramis |
| End-user systems | Filemaker |

*Infocenter systems* support the infocenter department of an organization in extracting and manipulating the information managed by the main electronic data processing application. To ensure high performance, the main system is usually developed using a production system. Typically, infocenter systems do not provide the same level of performance, but offer more flexible facilities to produce, say, nonstandard reports for management, based on the information stored in the main database. A typical example in this class is Ramis.

*End-user systems* support end users in directly defining their database and access functionalities. They provide predefined functions and forms that users customize easily through interactive facilities, without writing traditional programs. Many products developed for the Macintosh and MS-DOS personal computers can be included in this class. A typical example is Filemaker Pro (running on the Macintosh).

**Process-centered environments.** A process-centered environment is based on a formal definition of the software process. A computerized application called a *process driver* or *process engine* uses this definition to guide development activities by automating process fragments, automatically invoking tools and workbenches, enforcing specific policies, and assisting programmers, analysts, and project managers in their work.[13] Thus, these environments focus on process integration. This does not mean they do not address other integration dimensions. Rather, other integration issues are the starting points for process integration.

A process engineer or process modeler (that is, someone who can analyze a process and describe it formally) produces the formal definition of the production process (called the *process model*), using specialized tools with functionalities to define, analyze, and manage it. Thus a process-centered environment operates by interpreting a process model created by specialized tools. Several research prototypes and even products on the market support both the creation and the execution of a process model. These products are therefore *environment generators*, since they can create different, customized environments that follow the procedures and policies enforced by the process model.

Process-centered environments are usually composed of parts to handle two functions:

- *Process-model execution.* The process driver interprets and executes a specific process model to operate the process-centered environment and make it available to software developers.
- *Process-model production.* Process modelers use tools to create or evolve process models.

Because of their process-model-execution function, I classify such products in Table 5 as process-centered environments, concerned with production-process technology. However, their process-model-production capabilities also qualify them as metaprocess technology.

Examples of products and research prototypes are East, Enterprise II, Process Weaver, Arcadia, Process Wise, EPOS, HPSF, Merlin, Marvel, and SPADE/S Lang (Software Process Analysis Design and Enactment/SPADE Language ), whose functionalities I discuss in the later section on metaprocess technology. (EPOS, a project at Norges Teckniske Hogskole (NTH) in Trondheim, Norway, is not to be confused with an existing CASE product with the same name.)

## Metaprocess and enabling technologies

The metaprocess and enabling technologies are important in developing effective software-process support. Metaprocess-technology products let a process manager create, operate, and improve production-process support. Enabling technology provides the basic mechanisms to integrate the different products in both the production-process and the metaprocess technologies.

**Metaprocess technology.** Toward the beginning of this article, I defined the metaprocess as the set of activities, procedures, roles, and computerized aids used to create, maintain, and further improve the production process. The metaprocess is similar to the software processes. Process managers must conceive, design, verify, use, assess, and maintain a production process (the output of the metaprocess).

To achieve these goals, process managers may be able to use traditional production-process technology — in particular, analysis and design workbenches. For instance, they can create and maintain a process model using Statecharts with the support of Statemate.[14] In this way, however, it is possible to achieve only a quite limited goal: A process model created through traditional CASE products such as Statemate can be used only as a vehicle to communicate process rules and procedures, or to document and assess the existing practice. It cannot automatically generate more advanced environments and production-process supports.

Researchers have tried to develop technologies and methodologies to provide these advanced process supports. The first results were the structure-centered environment generators[10] (for example, Gandalf and the Cornell Program Synthesizer). These meta-environments can produce a set of tools starting from a formal description of the grammar of the language to be supported. Their initial aim was to produce a syntax-directed editor, but their scope has been progressively augmented to support more production-process tasks. These products are therefore environment generators, classified as metaprocess technology.

Recent work on process-centered environments and process modeling (discussed previously) has produced many research prototypes and a few commercial products,[15,16] whose goals I summarize:

- *Process modeling.* The development of notations to describe rules, activities, organizational structures, procedures, deliverables, and CASE products that constitute (or are used in) a software process, and the development of tools to validate and simulate the resulting model.
- *Process instantiation and enactment.* The development of runtime monitors and interpreters to execute or enact a software-process model — that is, to provide guidance to the people, tools, and workbenches involved in the process — and, whenever possible, to automate software-process activities. The resulting support to the production process is called a process-centered environment.
- *Process evolution.* Development of tools to support process-model evolution during the process lifetime.

The results of this research are encouraging, but several problems such as the process-model evolution have not yet been effectively solved. Nevertheless, some commercial products are available and, most important, the industrial community is becoming increasingly aware of the relevance of metaprocess technology.

**Enabling technologies.** Developing the complex products described in the previous sections requires services more sophisticated than the basic file-system-management and process-control mechanisms traditionally provided by operating systems. CASE products need functionalities such as advanced database-management systems to create and manage the repository, and sophisticated user-interface-management systems to design and develop graphical, easy-to-learn user interfaces for tools and workbenches.

To tackle these problems systematically and effectively, several industries and computer manufacturers are developing a new class of products that provide standard extensions to traditional operating systems (especially Unix). Built on top of the operating system, these products provide the tool developer with runtime libraries implementing several advanced features. Typical examples of this class are the already-mentioned DEC Cohesion Platform, HP SoftBench, and Atherton Software Backplane. Another example is PCTE (Portable Common Tool Environment), which is actually a standard interface definition, not a product. Currently, several existing or forthcoming products comply with this standard: the initial implementation by Emeraude, the Oracle-based version by Verilog, and implementations by DEC and IBM.

A key feature of these *integrating platforms* is their support for the creation of logically integrated but physically distributed systems. The development of personal computers, workstations, and local area network technology has made distributed implementations particularly suitable for advanced software-development environments. Hence, platform designers conceive and implement all the services for a distributed architecture. Moreover, the same services are very often available on different operating systems (for example, Unix, OSF/1, NT, and MS-DOS) to make the creation of heterogeneous architectures possible.

*Standardization* is a key aspect for such products. CASE developers can embed most of the functionalities offered by a platform in an application by adopting ad hoc components and products already available on the market. However, to develop distributed, highly integrated, and heterogeneous systems, they must identify standard mechanisms that ensure the required degree of product interoperability. (Interoperability is "the ability of two or more systems or components to exchange information and to use the information that has been exchanged."[6])

Besides the repository- and user-interface-management mechanisms, integrating platforms offer (or soon will offer) other key functionalities:

- *Advanced process-control mechanisms.* These let CASE developers encapsulate tools and workbenches, and invoke and control them through standard methods and event-generation mechanisms. Examples are the HP Encapsulator and the ACA Services offered by the DEC Cohesion Platform.
- *Support for the creation of multimedia products.* These features extend the functionalities offered by

traditional user-interface workbenches and let designers create advanced multimedia tools such as video documentation facilities and visual e-mail systems. A product offering these functionalities is the Multimedia Development Kit for Microsoft Windows.

- *Support for the creation of cooperating CASE tools and workbenches.* Typical examples of such applications are on-line agendas and concurrent/distributed editing tools. For example, DEC Fuse, Sun ToolTalk, and HP BMS give the tool developer a message-handling facility to support the integration and cooperation of CASE products.

The total value of the CASE technology market has grown from an estimated $2 billion in 1990 to $5 billion in 1993. Despite the recession Western countries have experienced in recent years, the CASE tool growth rate for the next couple of years is expected to be between 20 and 30 percent.[1]

Such high rates are justified because the total cost for human resources in software production amounts to about $250 billion per year. Therefore, even a modest increase in productivity would significantly reduce costs.[1] For this reason, CASE technology will play a key role in the information technology market, and many new products will appear.

The availability of such a large number of products and the complexity of the technologies used in software-development organizations make a reference framework for market evaluation and technology transfer essential. Moreover, it is important to facilitate comparison and exchange of experiences with other information-technology areas, such as VLSI design, factory automation, and office automation, where there have been similar efforts.

I have proposed concepts to bring in focus the state of the art of CASE technology. Attempts to classify and organize according to complex concepts may lead to extreme simplifications or, conversely, useless details. Moreover, the rapid changes in this area will quickly make some observations obsolete. As a result, this work will need to be updated incrementally as the technology develops. My aim in this article is to provide a reference framework and an initial classification of existing technology as a solid starting point for such a continuous updating. ■

## Acknowledgments

I thank Carlo Ghezzi and the anonymous referees for their stimulating and helpful comments.

## References

1. *CASE Outlook: Guide to Products and Services*, G. Forte and K. McCulley, eds., CASE Consulting Group, Lake Oswego, Ore., 1991.

2. R. Conradi et al., "Towards a Reference Framework of Process Concepts," *Proc. Second European Workshop Software Process Technology*, Springer-Verlag, Berlin, 1992.

3. M.C. Paulk et al., "Capability Maturity Model for Software," Tech. Report CMU/SEI-91-TR-24, Software Eng. Inst., Carnegie Mellon Univ., Pittsburgh, 1991.

4. I. Sommerville, *Software Eng.*, Addison-Wesley, Reading, Mass., 1992.

5. C. Fernström, K.-H. Närfelt, and L. Ohlsson, "Software Factory Principles, Architectures, and Experiments," *IEEE Software*, Vol. 9, No. 2, Mar. 1992, pp. 36-44.

6. "Standard Glossary of Software Engineering Terminology," in *Software Eng. Standards*, IEEE, Spring 1991, pp. 7-38.

7. D. Whitgift, *Methods and Tools for Software Configuration Management*, John Wiley, New York, 1991.

8. A. Kay, invited address at the 11th Int'l Conf. Software Eng., 1989.

9. H.A. Müller et al., "A Reverse Engineering Environment Based on Spatial and Visual Software Interconnection Models," *Proc. Fifth ACM SIGSoft Symp. Software Development Environments*, ACM Press, New York, 1992, pp. 88-98.

10. S.A. Dart et al., "Software Development Environments," *Computer*, Vol. 20, No. 11, Nov. 1987, pp. 18-28.

11. *Integrated Programming Environments*, D.R. Barstow, H.E. Shrobe, and E. Sandewall, eds., McGraw-Hill, New York, 1984.

12. "Reference Model for Frameworks of Software Engineering Environments," jointly published as ECMA Tech. Report TR/55, European Computer Manufacturers Assoc., Geneva, and NIST Special Publication 500-201, Nat'l Inst. of Standards and Technology, Gaithersburg, Md., 1991.

13. M.M. Lehman, "Process Models, Process Programs, Programming Support," *Proc. Ninth Int'l Conf. Software Eng.*, IEEE CS Press, Los Alamitos, Calif., Order No. 767, 1987, pp. 14-16.

14. M.I. Kellner, "Software Process Modeling: Value and Experience," *SEI Tech. Rev.*, Software Eng. Inst., Carnegie Mellon Univ., Pittsburgh, 1989, pp. 23-54.

15. C. Liu and R. Conradi, "Process Modeling Paradigms: An Evaluation," *Proc. First European Workshop on Software Process Modeling*, Italian Nat'l Assoc. for Computer Science, Milan, Italy, 1991, pp. 39-52.

16. P. Armenise et al., "A Survey and Assessment of Software Process Representation Formalisms," to be published in *Int'l J. Software Eng. and Knowledge Eng.*

**Alfonso Fuggetta** is an associate professor of computer science at Politecnico di Milano and a senior researcher at CEFRIEL, the Italian acronym for the Center for Research and Education in Information Technology, established in 1988 by a consortium of universities, public administrations, and information-technology industries. His research interests are software-process modeling and management, CASE products, and executable specifications.

Fuggetta is chairman of the steering committee of the European Software Engineering Conference (ESEC) and a member of the steering committee of the European Workshop on Software Process Technology. He is a member of the board of directors of AICA, the Italian National Society for Computer Science, and of the Technical Committee on Software Quality Certification of Istituto Marchio Qualità. Fuggetta is also a member of IEEE and ACM.

Readers can contact Fuggetta at Dipartimento di Elettronica e Informazione, Politecnico di Milano, P.za Leonardo da Vinci, 32, 20133 Milano, Italy, e-mail fuggetta@IPMEL2.elet.polimi.it.

# A Guidebook and a Spreadsheet Tool for a Corporate Metrics Program

Ronald E. Nusenoff and Dennis C. Bunde
*Loral Software Productivity Laboratory, San Jose, California*

A metrics guidebook and a spreadsheet tool have been developed at the Loral Software Productivity Laboratory as a start–up kit to enable Loral divisions and projects to implement the Loral corporate metrics program. The metrics guidebook defines a standard set of software metrics and specifies procedures for collection and analysis of metrics data. Guidelines are provided for revising schedules, resource allocations, and project procedures in light of the analysis of metrics data. The corporate-, division-, and project-level roles and responsibilities for metrics activities are discussed. The spreadsheet tool provides automated support for metrics generation, collection, graphical representation, and analysis.

This article explains the guidelines that were followed in constructing a guidebook and a spreadsheet tool that would both motivate and enable divisions and projects to implement the corporate metrics program. Metrics use is motivated at the division level as a means of developing a metrics database which will improve the organization's development and bidding capabilities, while motivating individual projects requires more emphasis on the role of metrics in monitoring and controlling project progress. Corporate metrics were tied to previous software metrics collection activities and to other data already collected and used within the organization and were mapped to Software Engineering Institute (SEI) level 2 and 3 maturity level requirements.

Guidelines for division and project tailoring of corporate metrics were provided. The corporate metrics were defined to map to the corporate development methodology, and so tailoring of that methodology by divisions or projects requires corresponding tailoring of the corporate metrics. Automated support for metrics collection and analysis, which also must be tailorable, was found to be a critical factor in enabling division and project implementation of corporate metrics. Feedback from divisions and projects that implemented the corporate metrics program is being used to improve the current program and extend it to cover SEI level 4 and 5 maturity level requirements.

## 1. INTRODUCTION

In a corporate software metrics program, a set of metrics, collection procedures, and analysis procedures are defined and then implemented throughout the company. A corporate metrics program presupposes a corporate standard software development methodology. A software development methodology consists of a process model which specifies all of the activities involved in software development, plus the individual methods, practices, and procedures which instantiate the steps of the process model. When a standard methodology has been specified, software development can be a defined, repeatable process rather than an ad hoc activity reinvented for each new project. Projects that follow the methodology can be planned, monitored, and controlled through the use of metrics which will have been defined in terms of the components of the methodology.

Projects that adopt a corporate metrics program need a guidebook (*Webster's Ninth New Collegiate Dictionary* defines a guidebook as a "handbook; esp: a book of information for travelers") that tells them how to implement this program. This guidebook should be a user–oriented handbook containing metrics definitions, collection and analysis procedures and tools, and guidelines for corrective actions. Projects also need automated support for metrics collection and analysis. This article explains guidelines we have found useful in constructing a metrics guidebook and a spreadsheet tool for the Loral Corporation corporate metrics program. Section 2 of this paper provides background on our metrics program. Section 3 covers the issues of enabling and motivating company divisions and projects to use metrics. Section 4 covers guidelines for

*Address correspondence to Ronald E. Nusenoff, Octel Communication Corporation, 1001 Murphy Ranch Road, Milpitas, CA 95035*

Reprinted from *J. Systems and Software*, Vol. 23, R.E. Nusenoff and D.C. Bunde, "A Guidebook and a Spreadsheet Tool for a Corporate Metrics Program," pp. 245–255, 1993, with kind permission from Elsevier Science–NL, Sara Burgerhartstraat 25; 1055 KV Amsterdam, The Netherlands.

defining a set of metrics. Section 5 covers guidelines about providing automated support for metrics collection and analysis. Section 6 discusses guidelines we are following in getting the guidebook and spreadsheet tool adopted on projects at Loral divisions. Section 7 describes the next steps planned in our metrics program.

## 2. BACKGROUND

The Loral Software Productivity Laboratory (SPL) is a central organization responsible for the formulation of a corporate standard software development methodology employing modern software engineering disciplines and techniques and meeting the software development requirements of Loral customers [1]. The SPL is also responsible for developing a corporate computer-aided software environment (CORCASE), which supports and enforces this methodology, and a software total quality management (TQM) program.

We have chosen the Software Engineering Institute (SEI) capability maturity model and associated assessment methodology as a framework for our software TQM program [2]. The levels within the SEI model provide the specific measurable goals which have been missing from previous TQM initiatives. The SEI maturity level hierarchy is shown in Figure 1. The three lower levels of the SEI capability maturity model are based on empirical observations about the best current software engineering and management practices. These practices are organized into levels 1–3 in a manner that provides a road map for increasing software development process capability maturity. The SEI has been conducting process assessments since 1987 and has found 81% of organizations assessed to be at level 1, 12% at level 2, and 7% at level 3. No level 4 or 5 organizations have been identified. Levels 4 and 5, therefore, represent a view of what software organizations beyond the current state of the practice might look like.

A central activity of the TQM program is the definition and implementation of a corporate software development metrics program. The goal of this metrics program is to improve contract bidding, software project management, and software engineering practices by enabling software project managers to measure, monitor, predict, and control project progress, costs, and quality. The SPL metrics program currently addresses the metrics required to achieve SEI levels 2 and 3. What characterizes the advance from a level 1 to a level 2 capability is the introduction and enforcement of formal engineering management controls and procedures, which are prerequisites to the availability and validity of schedule and effort metrics data. All software project managers must control projects using well-defined procedures for scheduling, effort and size estimation, collection of schedule and effort metrics, configuration management of baselines, and quality assurance monitoring. The advance from level 2 to level 3 is characterized by the introduction of a defined software development process in which all software engineers are formally trained in the process and its associated engineering methods. The advance to level 3 does not introduce substantial metrics collection requirements beyond those of level

| Level | Characteristic | Key Challenges | Result |
|---|---|---|---|
| 5 Optimizing | Improvement fed back into process | Still human intensive process<br>Maintain organization at optimizing level | Productivity & Quality |
| 4 Managed | (Quantitative)<br>Measured process | Changing technology<br>Problem analysis<br>Problem prevention | |
| 3 Defined | (Qualitative)<br>Process defined and institutionalized | Process measurement<br>Process analysis<br>Quantitative quality plans | |
| 2 Repeatable | (Intuitive)<br>Process dependent on individuals | Training<br>Technical practices<br>• reviews, testing<br>Process focus<br>• standards, process groups | |
| 1 Initial | (Ad hoc/chaotic) | Project management<br>Project planning<br>Configuration management<br>Software quality assurance | Risk |

**Figure 1.** SEI maturity level hierarchy.

2, but the defined process provides a stable baseline of technical activities which can be measured.

We divide these SEI level 2 and 3 metrics (which we call management metrics) into two types: schedule and effort, and quality. Schedule and effort metrics are used to detect variance between planned and actual progress and labor costs. A software schedule represents the planned progress of a project. Schedule metrics summarize project progress information so that the software manager can detect and compensate for unplanned schedule trends. Effort is the labor portion of software cost; it does not take into account overhead, travel, and capital expenses. Effort metrics summarize effort information so that the software manager can detect adverse trends and control software costs.

Schedule and cost variance are signals that future completion dates and the overall project budget are at risk. Further analysis is required to determine the causes of schedule and cost variances so management can adjust plans and take actions to maintain control of the project. Significant analysis of schedule and effort metrics requires plotting of collected values together with project estimates on a regular basis. This enables the identification of trends in both the measured data and its variance from estimates. These trends can be extrapolated to provide more reasonable revised estimates. Comparison with data and trends from previous projects can be used to predict where a current project is going. Where metrics are known to correlate, i.e., changes in one metric cause changes in others, comparisons of data are used to isolate problems and identify corrective actions.

Quality metrics are quantitative measures available during the software development process. They are indicators of final product quality (e.g., correctness, reliability, maintainability) and allow managers to predict and influence final product quality. The quality of the final product can be predicted by measuring the quality of the process used to produce it and of the products generated along the way. Measuring the quality of the process and its products provides early warning signs that there will be cost and schedule problems before they actually occur. Once a quality metrics data base has been established, quality data expectations can be established by reference to data and trends observed on previous projects.

Quality metrics include errors detected, the stability of requirements/design/code, and the complexity of requirements/design/code. Number of errors detected is a measure of intermediate product quality and of the quality of the error detection process. Detected error data is a predictor of remaining errors, which is an indicator of system reliability and correctness. Design and code inspections, test reviews, and software problem/change reports are the primary sources of error data. Instability in intermediate products is measured by software problem/ change reports. Large numbers of reports against a baselined intermediate product are a signal that subsequent products based on it could be delayed. The complexity of system components is an indicator of system maintainability. Increases in measured complexity across the development phases indicate that additional effort will be required later.

## 3. ENABLING AND MOTIVATING METRICS USE

### Guideline 1: Produce and Publish a Metrics Guidebook

The first major step of the Loral metrics program has been the production of a metrics guidebook [3]. Individual projects have neither the time nor the resources to develop a metrics program. They need a start-up kit that enables them to implement a well-defined program. The metrics guidebook defines a standard set of software metrics and specifies procedures for collection and analysis of metrics data. Guidelines are provided for revising schedules, resource allocations, and project procedures in light of the analysis of metrics data. The corporate-, division-, and project-level roles and responsibilities for metrics activities are discussed. Automated support for metrics generation, collection, and analysis, which includes a spreadsheet tool for organizing and graphically representing metrics data, is explained.

### Guideline 2: Provide Motivation for Implementing Metrics

Metrics are still neither well understood nor widely applied within the software industry, despite extensive literature which provides a good case for the use of software metrics in terms of increases in quality and productivity [4–8]. Fear and/or loathing is a typical reaction to metrics from upper management ("the only thing metrics adds to a project is cost"), project management ("we couldn't pass data on up even if we believed it"), and engineers ("they're going to measure *us*"). Such reactions made us realize that the guidebook must do more than describe how company divisions and projects can implement metrics collection and analysis; it also must provide motivation for doing so.

At the division level, a motivating goal for metrics use can be the development of a division metrics data base. The data base provides an empirical foundation for future project estimations, analysis, and predictions. Historical data is used to analyze measurements of current projects to predict subsequent progress and suggest adjustments to current plans and schedules. Data collected from projects is used to validate and refine the metrics data base. Project data is also used to measure how well the division's version of the corporate methodology is working and the effect of either changing it or introducing new methods or technology.

SEI maturity level has also become a significant motivating factor at the company division level. The Department of Defense and other government agencies are phasing in use of SEI capability maturity levels as a criteria for contract awards. Government agencies have been using the SEI model to evaluate contractors during the contract bidding stage. The government's rule of thumb may soon be, try to find a level 3 contractor and do not deal with a level 1 contractor. The improvement of SEI maturity level was selected as the incentive for implementing a software TQM program at Loral. The SEI model was used to derive requirements for capability improvement and actions to meet those requirements. The metrics involved in advancing to SEI levels 2 and 3 are minimum requirements for the Loral management metrics program. Our interpretation of SEI level 2 and 3 metrics collection requirements is given in Figure 2. The SEI question numbers in parentheses are taken from the original SEI technical report [2].

Motivation at the project level is a different issue than motivation at the division level. Once a project has started, the main motivation for using metrics has to be that it will enable the project manager to monitor and control project progress, costs, and quality. In the early stages of the corporate metrics program, there will at best be disjoint historical data rather than a corporate metrics data base to use as an empirical basis for estimations and planning. The fact that a pioneer project's implementation of the corporate metrics plan will produce data to help future projects does nothing to help the pioneers in their current endeavors.

## 4. DEFINING A SET OF METRICS

### Guideline 3: Align Metrics with External Requirements

### Guideline 4: Relate Metrics Program to Previous Metrics Collection

The Loral management metrics were selected based on literature research and investigation into current metrics activities at Loral divisions. The 10 metrics presented in "Software Management Metrics" [9]

| SEI Level 2 Metrics Collection Requirements |
|---|
| Plot planned and actual staffing over time. (2.2.1) |
| Plot computer software configuration item (CSCI) size versus time. (2.2.2) |
| Record number and type of code and test errors. (2.2.4) |
| Plot planned and actual number of software units for which design reviews have been completed, versus time. (2.2.7) |
| Plot planned and actual computer software units (CSUs) for which unit testing has been completed, versus time. (2.2.8) |
| Plot planned and actual CSUs for which integration testing has been completed, versus time. (2.2.9) |
| Plot estimated and actual target computer memory utilization versus time. (2.2.10) |
| Plot estimated and actual target computer central processing unit (CPU) utilization versus time. (2.2.11) |
| Plot actual target computer input/output (I/O) channel utilization versus time. (2.2.12) |
| Plot planned and actual CSCI test progress versus time. (2.2.18) |
| Plot software build size versus time. (2.2.19) |
| **SEI Level 3 Metrics Collection Requirements** |
| Record number and type of software design errors. (2.2.3) |

**Figure 2.** SEI metrics collection requirements.

were selected as a primary model. The software management metrics were defined by The MITRE Corporation for the Electronic Systems Division of the Air Force Systems Command, based on three years of government and industry experiences in the collection and analysis of the 8 metrics presented in "Software Reporting Metrics" [10]. A comparison of the two sets of MITRE metrics is given in Figure 3. The MITRE metrics are collected and reported at monthly intervals. They are plotted in a format showing the past 12 months of planned and actual data and the next 5 months of planned data.

The MITRE metrics are a reasonable starting point for the Loral metrics program for several reasons. They cover all phases of the software development process as defined in Department of Defense standard 2167A, from which the Loral software development process model is derived. The SEI level 2 metrics were based on the first MITRE set of eight metrics. The only SEI level 2 and 3 metrics not covered by the MITRE metrics are the numbers and types of design, code, and test errors. These data are collected during design, code, and test case inspections. A metrics program which included all of the

| Metric Name | Status | Description |
|---|---|---|
| Software complexity | deleted | initially plotted complexity of the 10 percent most complex CSUs. Complexity was estimated on a scale from 1 to 6, as found in Boehm [13]. This metric was replaced by design complexity. |
| Software Size | same | plots new, modified, and reused SLOCs for each CSCI as well as for the total system. |
| Software Personnel | same | plots total and experienced numbers of personnel, planned and actual, plus unplanned personnel losses. |
| Software Volatility | modified | plots total number of software requirements, cumulative number of requirements changes, and numbers of new and open software requirements action items. Initially was a plot of the number of lines of code affected by ECPs. |
| Computer Resource Utilization | same | plots planned spare and estimated/actual percentages of utilization for target computer CPU timing, memory, and I/O channels. |
| Design Complexity | new | plots the average design complexity of the 10 percent most complex CSUs, CSCs, and CSCIs. It is based on McCabe's measure of complexity. |
| Schedule Progress | new | plots estimated schedule to completion based on the delivery of software work packages defined in the Work Breakdown Structure. |
| Design Progress | new | plots planned and actual numbers of software requirements from system design documents which been completely documented in software requirements documents, and in software design documents. |
| CSU Development Progress | same | plots planned and actual numbers of CSUs designed, tested, and integrated. |
| Testing Progress | same | plots planned and actual numbers of CSCI and system tests completed, numbers of new and open SPRs, and number of SPRs per 1000 SLOC. |
| Incremental Release Content | same | plots planned and actual estimates of release date and number of CSUs included in each software release. |

**Figure 3.** MITRE metrics comparison.

MITRE metrics, plus data from design, code, and test case inspections, would meet all of the SEI level 2 and 3 metrics collection requirements. Finally, the original MITRE metrics have been a model for much of the metrics collection currently practiced by Loral divisions and are required by several government customers.

Mapping of SEI metrics collection requirements and MITRE metrics to the Loral metrics is shown in Figure 4. Each of the SEI level 2 and 3 questions is mapped to a recommended Loral metric. Nine of the 10 MITRE software management metrics map at least partially to one or more Loral metrics.

### Guideline 5: Tailor Metrics to Fit the Activities and Methods of the Methodology

### Guideline 6: Specify Concrete Criteria for Applying Metrics

We needed to tailor several of the MITRE metrics to fit them to the Loral software development methodology. MITRE used software problem reports as part of the testing progress metric and software action items as part of the software volatility metric. Loral methodology includes a software problem change report (SP/CR) system which is used for all configuration-controlled software and documents starting with the software requirements documents. It therefore seemed appropriate to define an SP/CR metric that corresponds to this system.

A corollary of guideline 5 is that defining metrics may suggest simple yet useful modifications to the corporate methodology. It would be useful to know when errors are introduced into the process, but the current SP/CR forms do not contain an entry for when a problem was introduced. This information is already determined when an SP/CR is assigned for resolution, but is not recorded in a readily collectable manner. It has therefore been suggested that a problem introduction entry, defined relative to the earliest document needing changes, be added to the SP/CR form.

A general rule we followed in defining management metrics to fit the corporate software development methodology was to establish concrete binary

| Loral Metric | Mitre Metric | SEI Question |
|---|---|---|
| Schedule Progress | Schedule Progress | — |
| Software Cost | — | — |
| Software Size | Software Size (T) | 2.2.2 |
| Staffing Profile | Software Personnel | 2.2.1 |
| CSU Development Progress | CSU Development Progress (T)<br>Incremental Release Content(T) | 2.2.7, 2.2.8<br>2.2.9, 2.2.19 |
| CSCI Test Progress | Testing Progress | 2.2.18 |
| Requirements Volatility | Software Volatility (T) | — |
| SP/CR | Testing Progress<br>Software Volatility (T) | — |
| Computer Resource Utilization | Computer Resource Utilization | 2.2.10, 2.2.11, 2.2.12 |
| Inspection Defects/Hours | — | 2.2.4, 2.2.3 |
| Module Complexity | Design Complexity (T) | — |

(T) = significant tailoring

**Figure 4.** Mapping of MITRE and SEI to Loral metrics.

criteria for applying metrics. For example, the completion criterion for the design of a computer software unit (CSU) had to be an all-or-nothing affair, with no partial (e.g., 90%) criterion accepted. The criterion we found within the methodology was that CSU design is finished if the detailed design inspection has been completed. This is the point at which the design is placed under configuration control. On the other hand, the MITRE design progress metric, which tracks the allocation of software requirements from system design documents to software requirements documents to design documents, was not adopted because its units are neither precisely defined nor readily collectable. Before baselining a document, it is not obvious how to count incrementally the number of individual requirements allocated within that document.

When projects have acquired experience using CORCASE analysis and design tools, we intend to introduce metrics based on discrete units which can be counted directly by these tools. These metrics should provide measures of the progress between the analysis and design phases and a means of tracking the evolution of system complexity. Detailed ongoing measurement of system complexity has long been advocated by DeMarco [4]. Streamlined versions of this approach have been advanced by Card [11] and by the Software Productivity Consortium [12].

### Guideline 7: Relate Metrics to Other Data Already Collected and Used

The schedule progress metric calculates the estimated schedule to complete each month by multiplying the planned project schedule by the ratio of the budgeted cost of work scheduled (BCWS) to the budgeted cost of work performed (BCWP). BCWP and BCWS are based on an earned value assigned to each discrete task in a project, as described in Boehm's *Software Engineering Economics* [13]. The difference between BCWS and BWCP is the schedule variance for the entire project. What was needed to complement this overall schedule variance metric was an overall cost variance metric. We found that many Loral divisions use financial reporting systems that plot budget at completion (BAC), which is the budgeted cost to complete a project, along with a monthly estimate at completion (EAC). EAC is calculated by multiplying BAC by the ratio of the project's current expenditures to the earned value of the tasks actually completed (i.e., the ratio of actual cost of work performed (ACWP) to (BCWP). We adopted this as our cost metric because it uses data already collected and used throughout the company.

The software size metric uses counting rules for added, modified, reused, and removed source statements presented in the IEEE *Standard for Software Productivity Metrics* [14]. These rules had already been adopted by metrics working groups at the SEI, the Software Productivity Consortium, and by at least one Loral division. This same division also develops some code for reuse, and we have adopted their suggestion that such code be tracked separately from other newly developed code.

### Guideline 8: Provide Tailoring Guidelines for Metrics

No set of definitions will fit every project perfectly. Divisions and projects that tailor the corporate methodology according to customer requirements, division standards, or business area may also need to tailor their implementation of metrics. Where we were aware of established division procedures that implied changes to the metrics definitions or analysis guidelines, we included them in the guidebook as tailoring guidelines. One Loral division uses a series of quality point reviews during the development process rather than the corporate standard inspection process. Quality point reviews generate metrics which replace our inspection metric and supplement the SP/CR metric.

## 5. TOOL SUPPORT FOR A METRICS PROGRAM

### Guideline 9: Make Collection Nonintrusive—Automate if Possible

Much of the current resistance to metrics use on projects is based on the concern that the benefits to be gained from the analysis of metrics data will not compensate for the effort required to collect the data. The key to overcoming this resistance is to point out that most of the data that need to be collected for metrics purposes are already collected for other purposes. Most of the metrics data items recommended for collection in the guidebook are either generated automatically within CORCASE or are already being entered manually into the system independent of their use for metrics.

A detailed table was prepared listing each primitive (i.e., noncalculated) metrics data item along with the tool or other source that generates it and its location within the CORCASE data base. Most data used in estimating, planning, and tracking schedules, cost, and personnel resources is either generated by or manually entered through a Loral proprietary project management software package. Although this package does not currently handle data on actual labor hours worked, those data are available from the time card accounting system. Software size and complexity data are generated using language-dependent source code processing tools and are already recorded in electronic module software development files. Data related to numbers of and changes to requirements are already recorded in a requirements data base. Resource spare capability requirements would also be stored in the requirements data base. Data related to SP/CRs are generated and managed within an automated software problem reporting system, which also contains some data on requirements changes. Inspection data are already entered by the inspection moderators into a spreadsheet which generates statistics and graphs based on the collected data.

### Guideline 10: Provide Automated Analysis Templates and Tools

The problem with much metrics data collection is that the data are merely collected. Analysis of collected values, calculation of derived values, trend extrapolation, and graphical representation require a tool that can do the work and a template that provides a common format. A management metrics spreadsheet was developed which provides an organized format for recording collected metrics data together with automatic generation of metrics graphs. This spreadsheet was developed using Wingz, a commercial spreadsheet program which is included as a productivity tool in CORCASE. A spreadsheet template was set up to record and graph the metrics recommended in the guidebook. The spreadsheet template contains labels for all data to be entered, formulas that calculate derived values, and some explanatory text describing the contents of the data cells. When planned and actual data are entered in the appropriate cells, derived values are calculated and the accompanying graphs are automatically created and updated. An empty copy of this spreadsheet can be copied to create a spreadsheet for a project. A copy of the spreadsheet template with 18 months of data was also provided as part of a tutorial on how to use the spreadsheet. The layout of the spreadsheet template, along with brief descriptions of each labelled area, is given in Figure 5. A utility was added to the spreadsheet to provide printout of graphs without spreadsheet row and column headers. A sample of this printout is given in Figure 6.

Collection of metrics data for insertion into the metrics spreadsheet within CORCASE is presently a manual process performed by a project metrics coordinator. Metrics collection and insertion into the management metrics spreadsheet will be automated in later releases of CORCASE. A metrics collection utility will be written for use by the metrics coordinators which will collect all of the metrics data items, generate a report listing the collected items, and insert the collected data items into a specified spreadsheet upon request.

### Guideline 11: Make the Tools and Templates Tailorable and Portable

As with the metrics definitions, the analysis tool may need to be adjusted to fit the needs of divisions or individual projects. We included instructions for adding metrics definitions, calculations, and graphs to the spreadsheet template. We have converted the spreadsheet template from the SUNView version of Wingz on which it was developed to an X Window version. We have also successfully converted a metrics spreadsheet file into Lotus and Excel formats (even the graphs converted over), which makes it accessible to those divisions and projects that are already committed to using those packages. In the interest of portability, we avoided using any unique special features of the Wingz program.

## 6. ONGOING GUIDELINES IN TECHNOLOGY TRANSFER

### Guideline 12: Locate Metrics Technology Transfer Point Above the Project Level

The initial criterion of success for a corporate metrics program is that it be adopted by projects at different divisions of the company. (The second criterion is that it is subsequently adopted by other projects at those divisions.) Personnel in corporate-level organizations generally have limited access to personnel at the project level, and project personnel generally do not have the position and funding to sponsor the establishment of a metrics program (or generally, any new methods). We have so far found that implementation of the metrics program at the division level is best accomplished through a division software engineering process group (SEPG) [7]. As a corporate-level organization, the SPL tailors and integrates state-of-the-practice methods and tools into a corporate methodology. The division SEPG

| INTRODUCTION |
|---|
| General comments which describe the spreadsheet. |
| **RAW DATA** |
| Rows for entry of project data. The first cell (column A) of each row contains the text string naming the data. The first row of this area contains the project calendar in text strings. |
| **METRICS FORMULAS** |
| Formulas for calculating values to be graphed. Column A contains the text string naming the value to be calculated. Copies of the formula are contained in all remaining cells of the row, up to the column for the last month of the project calendar. |
| **GRAPH WINDOW DEFINITION** |
| Rows for entry of current project month and software start month, and a formula to calculate which 18 months of data to store in the Graph Data area. Data is stored for the current month, the 11 previous months, and the 6 subsequent months. |
| **GRAPH DATA** |
| Rows of 19 columns each for storage of pointers used to create graphs. All rows for a given graph must be consecutive. Column A of the first row for each graph contains a pointer to the graph title. Column A of the subsequent data rows contains a pointer to the name of the data for that row. Columns B..S of the first rows use an INDEX function to access the required 18 columns of the project calendar. Columns B..S of the data rows use the INDEX function to access either raw data from the Raw Data area, or calculated values from the Metrics Formulas area. |
| **GRAPH AXIS LABELS** |
| Rows for storage of text strings to be used as labels for the graph axes. A new label can be added to any empty cell in this area. |
| **GRAPHS** |
| Area in which graphs using rows from Graph Data area are located. |

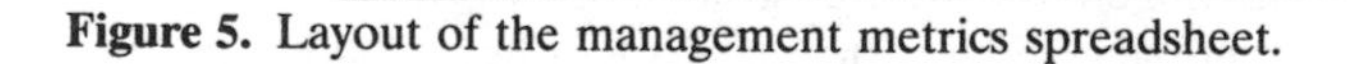

**Figure 5.** Layout of the management metrics spreadsheet.

then tailors this methodology to meet the requirements of the division customers and business area. In the case of a metrics program, the SEPG would tailor the corporate metrics definitions, procedures, and tools to keep metrics in alignment with the division version of the corporate software development methodology. The SEPG is also responsible for using metrics data and analysis from projects for developing and maintaining a division metrics data base and a division cost model, for passing data base information back to the corporate data base, and for implementing enhancements to the corporate metrics program.

Each project should have a metrics coordinator who consolidates project metrics data and prepares reports and analysis for the project manager to review. The position of metrics coordinator may not be a full-time position, but requires an experienced engineer who is well versed in the corporate or division methodology. This position might best be filled by a person from the SEPG who is matrixed into several projects as metrics coordinator. This person from the SEPG could be someone who works on the division metrics data base. Using SEPG personnel as metrics coordinators would be an instance of the collaborative technology transfer method [15], in which end users are involved in developing the technology, rather than the more traditional transfer-and-feedback mechanism which most corporate–level organizations use.

### Guideline 13: Find a Pilot Project

The best way to test a metrics guidebook and spreadsheet tool is to find a real development project on which to use them. Testing with a pilot

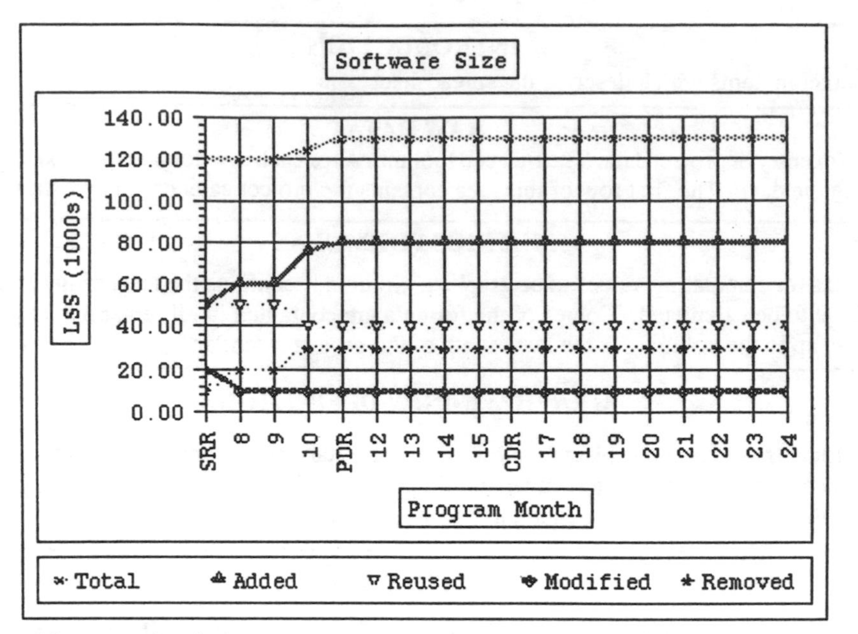


**Figure 6.** Sample spreadsheet graph printout.

project will uncover errors, omissions, and ambiguities more efficiently than one more review or simulation. It will also provide a practitioner's viewpoint as to what is useful, what is not, and what else is needed.

### Guideline 14: Be Ready to Train and Consult

Even with the existence of a division SEPG, the corporate-level organization's job is not done. Some SEPGs may be as small as two people or may be staffed by project personnel devoting personal time to the effort. Even with a well-funded SEPG, comments and questions on the guidebook and on how to use the tool should come back. No metrics guidebook can anticipate all of the questions and even have all of the answers to the expected questions. Few (if any) tools can be used effectively without some expert guidance. No comments, questions, or corrections coming back is a bad sign: it means that users did not read the guidebook and did not try the tool.

## 7. NEXT STEPS

The program defined in our metrics guidebook has been implemented at four Loral divisions. The corporate metrics guidebook was used as the basis for division metrics standards, and the spreadsheet template has been modified to accommodate division tailoring of the corporate metrics definitions and procedures. Two divisions are using the Wingz spreadsheet and two divisions are using Excel versions. Several other divisions have requested soft copies of the spreadsheet. Up to this point, the availability of personnel and resources to experiment with the spreadsheet tool has been a critical factor in getting the corporate program implemented at the division level.

Loral software projects that use the metrics, procedures, and tools defined and explained in the management metrics guidebook will provide us with feedback in the form of spreadsheets and commentary on their use of analysis guidelines and corrective actions. We plan to develop a corporate management metrics data base using the spreadsheet format and will validate and refine the metrics and procedures contained in the guidebook. Changes in the corporate software development methodology will be reflected in the corporate metrics program as required.

We also plan to develop a process improvement metrics guidebook, based on SEI levels 4 and 5, which will provide methods, guidelines, and tools for stabilizing and improving the methodology. SEI level 4 metrics address improvement of the implementation of the defined process which was established in advancing to SEI level 3. Process performance variations are measured and their causes identified. The metrics required to advance to SEI level 5 address improvement of the defined process itself. The effects of planned changes to the process are measured and compared with the predicted values of the unchanged process.

## REFERENCES


1. Loral Corporation Policy on the Development of Software, Policy Letter SW-01, San Jose, California, December 14, 1990.
2. W. S. Humphrey, and W. L. Sweet, A Method for Assessing the Software Engineering Capability of Contractors, Software Engineering Institute Technical Report CMU/SEI-87-TR-23, Pittsburgh, Pennsylvania, 1987.
3. D. Bunde and R. Nusenoff, Management Metrics Guidebook, Loral Software Productivity Laboratory Technical Report SPL_SEGB_9A-91008-M, San Jose, California, 1991.
4. T. DeMarco, *Controlling Software Projects*, Englewood Cliffs, New Jersey, Yourdon Press, 1982.
5. R. B. Grady and D. L. Caswell, *Software Metrics: Establishing a Company-Wide Program*, Prentice-Hall, Englewood Cliffs, New Jersey, 1987.
6. V. R. Basili and H. D. Rombach, The TAME Project: Towards Improvement-Oriented Software Environments, *IEEE Trans. Software Eng.* 14, 758–773 (1988).
7. W. S. Humphrey, *Managing the Software Process*, Addison-Wesley, Reading, Massachussetts, 1989.
8. F. McGarry et al., Experiences in the software engineering laboratory (SEL) applying software measurement, in *Proceedings of the Fourteenth Annual Software Engineering Workshop*, SEL-89-007, Goddard Space Flight Center, Greenbelt, Maryland, 1989.
9. H. P. Schultz, Software Management Metrics, MITRE Technical Report ESD-TR-88-001, Bedford, Massachusetts, 1988.
10. R. J. Coles et al., Software Reporting Metrics, MITRE Technical Report ESD-TR-85-145, Bedford, Massachusetts, 1985.
11. D. N. Card and R. L. Glass, *Measuring Software Design Quality*, Prentice-Hall, Englewood Cliffs, New Jersey, 1990.
12. J. E. Gaffney and R. Werling, Estimating Software Size from Counts of Externals, A Generalization of Function Points, Software Productivity Consortium Technical Report SPC_91094, Herndon, Virginia, 1991.
13. B. W. Boehm, *Software Engineering Economics*, Prentice-Hall, Englewood Cliffs, New Jersey, 1981.
14. Standard for Software Productivity Metrics, P1045/D4.0, Draft, IEEE, New York, New York, 1990.
15. J. D. Babcock, L. A. Belady, and N. C. Gore, The evolution of technology transfer at MCC's software technology program: From didactic to dialectic, *12th International Conference on Software Engineering*, IEEE Computer Society Press, Los Alamitos, California, 1990, pp. 290–299.

# Industrial software metrics top 10 list

*Barry Boehm, TRW, Inc.*

I am always fascinated by top 10 lists. So, when Vincent Shen asked me to write a piece for this department, I decided to present my candidate top 10 list of software metric relationships, in terms of their value in industrial situations. Here they are, in rough priority order:

1. *Finding and fixing a software problem after delivery is 100 times more expensive than finding and fixing it during the requirements and early design phases.*

This insight has been a major driver in focusing industrial software practice on thorough requirements analysis and design, on early verification and validation, and on up-front prototyping and simulation to avoid costly downstream fixes.

2. *You can compress a software development schedule up to 25 percent of nominal, but no more.*

There is a remarkably consistent cube-root relationship for the most effective schedule $T_{dev}$ for a single-increment, industrial-grade software development project: $T_{dev} = 2.5 \times MM^{1/3}$ where $T_{dev}$ is in months and $MM$ is the required development in man-months.

Equally remarkable is the fact that virtually no industrial-grade projects have been able to compress this schedule more than 25 percent. Thus, if your project is estimated to require 512*MM*, your best schedule is $2.5 \times 512^{1/3}$, or 20, months. If your boss or customer wants the product in 15 months, you will barely make it if you add some extra resources and plan well. If he wants it in 12 months, you should gracefully but firmly suggest reducing the scope or doing an incremental development.

3. *For every dollar you spend on software development you will spend two dollars on software maintenance.*

A lot of industry and government organizations created major maintenance embarrassments before they realized this and instituted thorough software life-cycle planning. This insight has also stimulated a healthy emphasis on developing high-quality software products to reduce maintenance costs.

4. *Software development and maintenance costs are primarily a function of the number of source instructions in the product.*

This was the major stimulus for migrating from assembly languages to higher order languages. It is now a major stimulus for developing and using very high-level languages and fourth-generation languages to reduce software costs.

5. *Variations between people account for the biggest differences in software productivity.*

Studies of large projects have shown that 90th-percentile teams of software people typically outproduce 15th-percentile teams by factors of four to five. Studies of individual programmers have shown productivity ranges of up to 26:1. The moral: Do everything you can to get the best people working on *your* project.

6. *The overall ratio of computer software to hardware costs has gone from 15:85 in 1955 to 85:15 in 1985, and it is still growing.*

This relationship has done more than anything else to focus management attention and resources on improving the software process.

7. *Only about 15 percent of software product-development effort is devoted to programming.*

In the early days, there was a 40-20-40 rule: 40 percent of the development effort for analysis and design, 20 percent for programming, and 40 percent for integration and test. Now, the best project practices achieve a 60-15-25 distribution. Overall, this relationship has been very effective in getting industrial practice to treat software product development as more than just programming.

8. *Software systems and software products each typically cost three times as much per instruction to fully develop as does an individual software program. Software-system products cost nine times as much.*

A software system contains many software modules written by different people. A software-system product is such a system that is released for external use. The discovery of this cost-tripling relationship has saved many people from unrealistically extrapolating their personal programming productivity experience into unachievable budgets and schedules for software-system products.

9. *Walkthroughs catch 60 percent of the errors.*

The structured walkthrough (software inspection) has been the most cost-effective technique to date for eliminating software errors. It also has significant side benefits in team building and in ensuring backup knowledge if a designer or programmer leaves the project.

I had a hard time picking number 10. I ended up with a composite choice:

10. *Many software phenomena follow a Pareto distribution: 80 percent of the contribution comes from 20 percent of the contributors.*

Knowing this can help a project focus on the 20 percent of the subset that provides 80 percent of the leverage for improvement. Some examples:

- 20 percent of the modules contribute 80 percent of the cost,
- 20 percent of the modules contribute 80 percent of the errors (not necessarily the same ones),
- 20 percent of the errors consume 80 percent of the cost to fix,
- 20 percent of the modules consume 80 percent of the execution time, and
- 20 percent of the tools experience 80 percent of the tool usage.

I think it has been a strong credit to the software metrics field that it has been able to determine and corroborate these and many other useful software metric relationships. And there are many useful new ones coming along. I look forward to reading about them in this department.

Reprinted from *IEEE Software*, Vol. 4, No. 5, Sept. 1987, pp. 84–85.

# Chapter 13

# Software Engineering Education

## 1. Introduction to Chapter

Efforts to establish a curriculum in software engineering began soon after the definition of software engineering as a separate discipline in 1968. A workshop organized in 1976 by Peter Freeman and Anthony Wasserman was a major influence in curriculum design [1]. The first published curriculum was a masters degree program authored by Richard Fairley under the auspices of the Association for Computing Machinery (ACM) and published in 1978 [2]. Since that time, the IEEE Computer Society and the ACM have published computer science curricula, including software engineering material [3].

In 1987, 1989, and 1991 the Software Engineering Institute (SEI) published model curricula for masters programs in software engineering [4, 5, 6] and has been working toward future undergraduate curricula. While software engineering is part of many undergraduate computer science curricula, and there are some undergraduate degrees or specializations in software engineering, most degree programs exist at the masters level. Continuing education for practicing professionals is also an area of emphasis.

As of this writing, software engineering education is an important part of an effort by IEEE and ACM to establish software engineering as a profession [7]. The Steering Committee for this effort has constituted three task forces, concerned with:

- the body of knowledge of software engineering
- ethics and professional practices
- curriculum

All three task forces have educational implications: the professional and ethical material that practitioners should know, and the approach for imparting that knowledge, at undergraduate, graduate, and professional levels.

## 2. Introduction to Paper

There is only one paper in this chapter on software engineering education. The paper, by the well-known computer scientist David Parnas, addresses a broader topic, "Education for Computer Professionals." Dr. Parnas developed the concept of information hiding and has a large number of other noteworthy achievements [8, 9, 10]

Parnas believes that present-day computer science education is inadequate. He says that computer science graduates are employed to produce useful artifacts, often software systems, and that their education must therefore emphasize classical engineering and other fundamentals such as mathematics and science, rather than programming languages and compiler theory (topics of interest when computer science first became an independent discipline) and the research interests of computer science faculty. Computer science graduates do not possess the fundamental knowledge needed to sustain them during their professional careers; the material they learn quickly becomes obsolete. He cites computer system researchers and implementers who would prefer to take graduates in engineering, mathematics, or even history and train them in programming rather than hire computer science graduates.

Based on the above assertions and beliefs, Parnas outlines a curriculum for computing professionals. It includes:

- Mathematics (calculus, discrete mathematics, logic, linear algebra, graph theory, differential equations, probability and statistics, optimization, and linear analysis)
- Science (physics and chemistry)
- Engineering (electricity and magnetism, circuit theory, mechanics, systems and control theory, information theory, digital systems and logic design, and signal processing)
- Computing science (programming, documentation, algorithms and data structures, process control, and system architecture and networks)

He also believes in the value of cooperative education, in which students spend time in industry developing "a real product and getting feedback from interested users."

While Parnas does not propose a course or courses called "Software Engineering" as part of an undergraduate program, many elementary aspects of the material in this Tutorial appear in the computing science courses he does recommend. Other topics, such as system engineering, requirements, configuration management, quality assurance, and management topics, are, in Parnas's view, not part of an undergraduate education in computer science.


1. Wasserman, Anthony L. and Peter Freeman, eds., *Software Engineering Education: Needs and Objectives*, Springer-Verlag, New York, N.Y., 1976.
2. Fairley, Richard E., "Toward Model Curricula in Software Engineering," *SIGSCE Bulletin*, Vol. 10, No. 3, Aug. 1978.
3. ACM/IEEE-CS Joint Curriculum Task Force, *Computing Curricula 1991*, ACM, New York, N.Y., 1991.
4. Ford, Gary A., Norman E. Gibbs, and James E. Tomayko, *Software Engineering Education: an Interim Report from the Software Engineering Institute*, CMU/SEI-TR-87-109, Carnegie Mellon University, Pittsburgh, Pa., 1987.
5. Ardis, Mark A., and Gary A. Ford, *1989 SEI Report on Graduate Software Engineering Education*, CMU/SEI-89-TR-2, Carnegie Mellon University, Pittsburgh, Pa., 1989
6. Ford, Gary A., *1991 SEI Report on Graduate Software Engineering Education*, CMU/SEI-91-TR-2, Carnegie Mellon University, Pittsburgh, Pa., 1991.
7. Barbacci, Mario, "Panel presents first four recommendations aimed at establishing software engineering as a profession," *Computer*, Feb. 1994, pp. 80–81. Since this report, ACM has joined the effort.
8. Parnas, D.L., and P.C. Clements, "A Rational Design Process: How and Why to Fake It," *IEEE Trans. Software Eng.*, Vol. SE-12, No. 2, Feb. 1986, pp. 251–257.
9. Parnas, D.L., "On the Criteria to be Used in Decomposing Systems into Modules," *Comm. ACM*, Vol. 15, No. 12, Dec. 1972, pp. 1053–1058.
10. Parnas, David L., "Software Aspects of Strategic Defense Systems," *American Scientist*, Vol. 73, Sept.-Oct. 1985, pp. 432–440.

# Education for Computing Professionals

David Lorge Parnas
Queen's University

Engineering is often defined as the use of scientific knowledge and principles for practical purposes. While the original usage restricted the word to the building of roads, bridges, and objects of military use, today's usage is more general and includes chemical, electronic, and even mathematical engineering. All use science and technology to solve practical problems, usually by designing useful products.

Most engineers today have a university-level education. Government and professional societies enforce standards by accrediting educational programs and examining those people who seek the title "Professional Engineer." Certification is intended to protect public safety by making certain that engineers have a solid grounding in fundamental science and mathematics, are aware of their professional responsibilities, and are trained to be thorough and complete in their analysis. In each of these aspects, engineers differ sharply from technicians, who are trained to follow established procedures but do not take responsibility for the correctness of those procedures.

Engineering education differs from traditional "liberal arts" education as well. Engineering students are much more restricted in their choice of courses; this ensures that all graduate engineers have had exposure to those fields that are fundamental to their profession. Engineering education also stresses finding good, as contrasted with workable, designs. Where a scientist may be happy with a device that validates his theory, an engineer is taught to make sure that the device is efficient, reliable, safe, easy to use, and robust. Finally, engineers learn that even the most intellectually challenging assignments require a great deal of boring "dog work."

**Computing science graduates are ending up in engineering jobs. CS programs must therefore return to a classical engineering approach that emphasizes fundamentals rather than the latest fads.**

It has been a quarter century since universities began to establish academic programs in computing science. Graduates of these programs are usually employed by industry and government to build useful objects, often computer programs. Their products control aircraft, automobile components, power plants, and telephone circuits. Their programs keep banking records and assist in the control of air traffic. Software helps engineers design buildings, bridges, trucks, etc. In other words, these nonengineering graduates of CS programs produce useful artifacts; their work is engineering. It is time to ask whether this back door to engineering is in the best interests of the students, their employers, and society.

I have written this article to discuss a trend, not to single out any particular department's curriculum or any particular committee report. Each new curriculum proposal includes more "new" computer science and, unavoidably, less "classical" material. In this article I reject that trend and propose a program whose starting point is programs that were in place when computing science began.

Reprinted from *Computer*, Vol. 23, No. 1, Jan. 1990, pp. 17–22.

## An historical debate

In the early 1960s, those of us who were interested in computing began to press for the establishment of computing science departments. Much to my surprise, there was strong opposition, based in part on the argument that graduates of a program specializing in such a new (and, consequently, shallow) field would not learn the fundamental mathematical and engineering principles that should form its basis. Both mathematicians and electrical engineers argued that computing science was an integral part of their own fields. They felt that students should major in one of those fields and take some computing courses near the end of their academic careers, rather than get an education in computing science as such. They predicted that graduates of CS programs would understand neither mathematics nor engineering; consequently, they would not be prepared to apply mathematical and engineering fundamentals to the design of computing systems.

My colleagues and I argued that computing science was rapidly gaining importance and that computing majors would be able to study the older fields with emphasis on those areas that were relevant to computing. Our intent was to build a program incorporating many mathematics and engineering courses along with a few CS courses. Unfortunately, most departments abandoned such approaches rather early. Both faculty and students were impatient to get to the "good stuff." The fundamentals were compressed into quick, shallow courses that taught only those results deemed immediately relevant to computing theory.

## The state of graduate CS education

Nearly 25 years later, I have reluctantly concluded that our opponents were right. As I look at CS departments around the world, I am appalled at what my younger colleagues — those with their education in computing science — don't know. Those who work in theoretical computing science seem to lack an appreciation for the simplicity and elegance of mature mathematics. They build complex models more reminiscent of programs written by bad programmers than the elegant models I saw in my mathematics courses. Computing scientists often invent new mathematics where old mathematics would suffice. They repeatedly patch their models rather than rethink them when new problems arise.

**As I look at computing science departments around the world, I am appalled at what my younger colleagues don't know.**

Further, many of those who work in the more practical areas of computing science seem to lack an appreciation for the routine systematic analysis that is essential to professional engineering. They are attracted to flashy topics that promise revolutionary changes and are impatient with evolutionary developments. They eschew engineering's systematic planning, documentation, and validation. In violation of the most fundamental precepts of engineering design, some "practical" computing scientists advocate that implementors begin programming before the problem is understood. Discussions of documentation and practical testing issues are considered inappropriate in most CS departments.

Traditional engineering fosters cooperation between theory and practice. The theory learned in mathematics and science classes is applied in engineering classes. In computing science, though, theory and practice have diverged. While classical mathematical topics, such as graph theory, continue to have applications in computing, most of the material in CS theory courses is not relevant in practice. Much theory concentrates on machines with infinite capacity, although such machines are not, and never will be, available. Academic departments and large conferences are often battlegrounds for the "theoretical" and "applied" groups. Such battles are a sure sign that something is wrong.

As the opponents of computing science predicted, most CS PhDs are not scientists; they neither understand nor apply the methods of experimental science. They are neither mathematicians nor engineers. There are exceptions, of course, but they stand out so clearly that they "prove the rule."

## The state of undergraduate CS education

The preparation of CS undergraduates is even worse than that of graduate students. CS graduates are very weak on fundamental science; their knowledge of technology is focused on the very narrow areas of programming, programming languages, compilers, and operating systems. Most importantly, they are never exposed to the discipline associated with engineering. They confuse existence proofs with products, toys with useful tools. They accept the bizarre inconsistencies and unpredictable behavior of current tools as normal. They build systems of great complexity without systematic analysis. They don't understand how to design a product to make such analysis possible. Whereas most engineers have had a course in engineering drawing (also known as engineering graphics), few CS graduates have had any introduction to design documentation.

Most CS graduates are involved in the construction of information and communications systems. These systems are highly dependent on information representation and transmission, but the graduates working on them are almost completely ignorant of information theory. For example, CS graduates are not conscious of the difference between the information unit "bit" and the storage unit, which is properly called a "binary digit." As a result, conversations on important practical issues, such as the design of data representations, proceed on an intuitive ad hoc level that engineers would consider unprofessional.

Although most CS graduates have been exposed to logic, the topic's treatment is usually quite shallow. The students are familiar with the symbol manipulation rules of predicate calculus but are usually unable to apply logic in practical circumstances. For example, most graduates cannot use quantifiers properly to "translate" informal statements into formal ones, perhaps because their instructors prefer inventing new logics to applying conventional ones. Mathematicians can successfully invent formalisms, but engineers usually succeed by finding new ways to use existing formalisms.

Because they lack knowledge of logic and communications concepts, CS graduates use fuzzy words like "knowledge" without the vaguest idea of how to define such a term or distinguish it from older concepts like "data" and "information." They talk of building "reasoning" systems without being able to distinguish reasoning from mechanical deduction or simple search techniques. The use of such fuzzy terms is not merely sloppy wording; it prevents the graduate from doing the systematic analyses made possible by precise definitions.

Reliability requirements are forcing the introduction of redundancy in computer systems. Unfortunately, current CS graduates are usually unfamiliar with all but the most naive approaches to redundancy. They often build systems that are needlessly expensive but allow common mode failures. Many CS graduates have not been taught the fundamentals needed to perform reliability analyses on the systems they design. Few of them understand concepts such as "single error correction/double error detection." Familiarity with such concepts is essential to the design of reliable computing systems.

Public safety is seriously affected by the fact that many CS graduates program parts of such control systems as those that run nuclear plants or adjust flight surfaces on aircraft. Unfortunately, I do not know of a single CS program that requires its students to take a course in control theory. The basic concepts of feedback and stability are understood only on an intuitive level at best. Neither the graduates nor most of their teachers know of the work in control theory that is applicable to the design of real-time systems.

Some graduates work in the production of signal processing systems. Unfortunately, signal processing is not offered in most CS programs; in fact, many departments will not allow a student to take such a course for CS credit. Signal processing deals with issues that are fundamental to the science and application of computing, but it is neglected in most programs.

Although many CS programs began with numerical analysis, most of our graduates have no understanding of the problems of arithmetic with finite representations of real numbers. Numerical analysis is, at best, an option in most CS programs.

## What went wrong?

Most CS departments were formed by multidisciplinary teams comprising mathematicians interested in computing, electrical engineers who had built or used computers, and physicists who had been computer users. Each had favorite topics for inclusion in the educational program, but not everything could be included. So, the set of topics was often the intersection of what the founders knew, not the union. Often, several topics were combined into a single course that forced shallow treatment of each.

**The manager of one safety-critical project stated with evident pride that his product was produced by engineers, "not just computer scientists."**

The research interests of the founding scientists distorted the educational programs. At the time computing became an academic discipline, researchers were preoccupied with language design, language definition, and compiler construction. One insightful paper speculated that the next 1,700 PhD theses would introduce the next 1,700 programming languages. It might have been more accurate to predict 700 languages, 500 theories of language semantics, and 500 compiler-compilers.

Soon, "artificial intelligence" became a popular term with American funding agencies, and the CS field expanded to include a variety of esoteric topics described by anthropomorphic buzzwords. Cut off from the departments of mathematics and electrical engineering by the usual university divisions, CS graduates came to view their field as consisting primarily of those topics that were research interests in their department. The breadth that would have come from being in one of the older, broader departments was missing.

Today, it is clear that CS departments were formed too soon. Computing science focuses too heavily on the narrow research interests of its founding fathers. Very little computing science is of such fundamental importance that it should be taught to undergraduates. Most CS programs have replaced fundamental engineering and mathematics with newer material that quickly becomes obsolete.

CS programs have become so inbred that the separation between academic computing science and the way computers are actually used has become too great. CS programs do not provide graduates with the fundamental knowledge needed for long-term professional growth.

## What is the result?

In recent years, I have talked to a number of top industry researchers and implementors who are reluctant to hire CS graduates at any level. They prefer to take engineers or mathematicians, even history majors, and teach them programming. The manager of one safety-critical programming project stated with evident pride that his product was produced by engineers, "not just computer scientists." The rapid growth of the industry assures that our graduates get jobs, but experienced managers are very doubtful about the usefulness of their education.

As engineers in other fields are becoming more dependent on computing devices in their own professional practice, they are also becoming more concerned about the lack of professionalism in the products they use. They would rather write their own programs than trust the programs of our graduates.

As awareness of the inadequacies of CS education grows, as people begin to realize that programming languages and compiler technology are not relevant background for the people they hire, our students may have trouble getting jobs. The main problem now is that their education has not prepared them for the work they actually do.

## A new program for computing professionals

While the critics of the original CS programs were quite accurate in their predictions, I still believe that a special educational program for computing professionals is needed. When we look at the programs produced by engineers and scientists who did not have such an education, we see that they are quite naive about many of the things we have learned in 25 years of computing science. For example, new programs in the defense industry are written in the same unsystematic style found in programs written in the 1950s and 1960s. Our graduates should be able to do better.

I believe the program proposed below would provide a good education for computing professionals. It is designed to draw heavily on the offerings of other departments, and it emphasizes mature fundamentals to prepare our graduates for a life of learning in a dynamic field. Wherever possible, the courses should be existing courses that can be shared with mathematicians and engineers. Students should meet the strict requirements of engineering schools, and the programs should be as rigid as those in other engineering disciplines.

**Very little computing science is of such fundamental importance that it should be taught to undergraduates.**

**Basic mathematics.** The products of most computing professionals are so abstract that the field could well be called "mathematical engineering." In fact, this is the title used at some Dutch universities. Computing professionals need to know how to use mathematics, although they rarely need to invent it. Some computer scientists have suggested that their students need only discrete mathematics, not the mathematics of continuous functions. However, while discrete mathematics is used in theoretical computing science, many practical applications use computers to approximate piecewise continuous functions. Computer professionals need a full introduction to mathematics; they should not be restricted to those items taught as theoretical computing science.

*Calculus*. All computing professionals should take the standard two- or four-semester calculus sequence taken by other engineers. This is the basic preparation for understanding how to deal with dynamic systems in the continuous domain. Many computer applications are best understood as approximations or improvements of dynamic analog systems. Computer professionals require the full sequence.

*Discrete mathematics*. CS students should join mathematics students in a course on such fundamentals as set theory, functions, relations, graphs, and combinatorics. In current computing courses, students view these topics as notations for describing computations and do not understand mathematics as an independent deductive system.

*Logic*. Logic is fundamental to many of the notations and concepts in computing science. Students should have a deeper understanding than that usually provided by CS logic courses or a few lectures on logic in some other course. I propose a two-semester sequence, taken with mathematics students, covering such advanced topics as decision procedures and higher order logics. The relationship between logic, set theory, lambda calculus, etc. should be thoroughly explored. Applications to computing should not be discussed.

*Linear algebra*. This should be covered in the standard one-semester course for engineers offered by the mathematics department.

*Graph theory*. Graphs offer useful representations of a wide variety of computing problems. Students who understand graph theoretic algorithms will find them useful in a variety of fields. An optional second course could deal with the application of this theory in computing practice.

*Differential equations*. This also should be covered in the usual one-semester course offered by mathematics departments for engineers. Many modern computer systems are approximations to analog circuits, for which this analysis is essential.

*Probability and applied statistics*. The reliability and adequacy of testing is a major concern in modern computing applications. Probability theory is also a fundamental tool in situations where random noise is present in communications. Everyone who works as an engineer should have at least a one-semester course on this topic; a two-semester sequence would be better for many.

*Optimization*. Linear and nonlinear programming are major applications for large computers. A course in this area would make students aware of the complexity of search spaces and the need to precisely define objective functions. One need not look very far into the class of programs known as "expert systems" to find areas where optimization concepts should have been applied.

*Numerical analysis*. This topic could be taught as either computing science or mathematics. (It is described below under "Computing science.")

**Basic science.** Computing professionals need the same knowledge of basic science as engineers. A basic course in chemistry and a two-semester sequence in physics should be the minimal requirement for all technical students.

**Engineering topics**. Computing professionals are engineers and should be educated as such. Computers and software are now replacing more conventional technologies, but the people who design the new systems need to understand fundamental engineering systems as well as did the engineers who designed those older systems.

*Engineering electricity and magnetism*. This topic should be covered in the standard one-semester course taken by electrical engineers.

*Electric circuits*. This also should be covered in the standard one-semester course for electrical engineers.

*Mechanics*. An understanding of mechanics is essential to a study of practical robotics, automated manufacturing, etc. This topic, too, should be covered in the standard, one-semester, electrical engineering course.

*Systems and control theory*. This standard two-semester sequence for electrical engineers should emphasize the use of differential equations, transforms, and complex analyses to predict the behavior of control systems. The course should also discuss the discrete analogues of methods for dealing with continuous functions.

*Information theory*. This is one of the most fundamental and important areas for computing professionals. In addition to the standard one-semester course for electrical engineers, a second course on applications in computer design would be useful as an elective.

*Digital system principles/logic design*. This topic could be covered under either computing science or electrical engineering. (It is described below under "Computing science.")

*Signal processing*. This area should be examined in a one-semester course introducing the concepts of noise, filters, signal recognition, frequency response, digital approximations, highly parallel algorithms, and specialized processors.

**Computing science**. Before the advent of CS departments, engineering and science students were expected to learn programming and programming languages on their own or through noncredit courses. Computers were compared to slide rules and calculators: tools that university students could learn to use. Engineering and science faculty felt that courses in programming and programming languages would not have the deep intellectual content of mathematics or physics courses. We responded that we would teach computing science, not programming or specific languages.

Unfortunately, many of today's courses prove the critics correct. The content of many courses would change dramatically if the programming language being used underwent a major change. The courses proposed below assume that students are capable programmers and avoid discussions of programming languages.

*Systematic programming.* This would be taught in a two-semester sequence covering finite-state machines, formal languages and their applications, program state spaces, the nature of programs, program structures, partitioning the state space, program composition, iteration, program organization, program design documentation, systematic verification, etc. Students should be competent programmers as a prerequisite to this course.

*Computer system documentation.* This one-semester course would teach formal methods to document computer system designs, with emphasis on methods that apply to both digital and integrated digital/analog systems.

*Design and analysis of algorithms and data structures.* This course would discuss comparative analysis of algorithms and data structures as well as theoretical models of problem complexity and computability. Students would learn to predict the performance of their programs and to chose algorithms and data structures that give optimal performance.

*Process control.* This integrated treatment of the theoretic hardware, software, and control problems of process control systems would include hardware characteristics, operating systems for real-time applications, the process concept, synchronization, and scheduling theory. Students would learn how to prove that their systems will meet deadlines and how to design for fail-safe behavior. A course in control theory should be a prerequisite.

*Computing systems architecture and networks.* This fairly standard course, now taught in both electrical engineering and CS departments, would cover the structure of a computer and multicomputer networks, communications bus design, network performance analysis, etc. A knowledge of assembly language should be assumed. Students should be taught to avoid buzzwords and discuss the quantitative characteristics of the systems they study.

**Inadequate analyses and unsystematic work are often rewarded and reinforced by high grades.**

*Numerical analysis.* This course, which could be taught as either computing science or mathematics, would cover the study of calculations using finite approximations to real numbers and would teach round-off, error propagation, conditioning of matrices, etc.

*Digital system principles/logic design.* This standard one-semester course for electrical engineers should cover the basics of combinational circuit design, memory design, error correction, error detection, and reliability analysis. The emphasis should be on systematic procedures. The course could be offered as either computing science or electrical engineering.

As in any academic program, the above program includes compromises. Many topics, such as databases, compilers, and operating systems, were considered and omitted because of time limitations. It is not that these areas are uninteresting, but rather that I have chosen the oldest, most mature, most fundamental topics over those that are relatively recent and likely to be invalidated by changes in technology. Some may find the program old-fashioned. I prefer to call it long-lasting.

One obvious exception to the "older is better" rule is the course on computer system documentation. I would like to think that its inclusion reflects its importance, but it may simply reflect my own research interests.

The program is rather full and far more closely resembles a heavily packed engineering program than the liberal arts program to which CS educators have become accustomed. The educational philosophy issues behind this traditional split are clearly outside the scope of this article. Personally, I would welcome a five-year undergraduate engineering degree to allow a broader education, but would find it irresponsible to make substantial reductions in the technical content of four-year programs.

## Projects versus cooperative education

CS students are burdened by many courses that require hours of struggle with computing systems. Programming assignments include small programs in introductory courses, larger programs in advanced courses, and still-larger projects that comprise the main content of entire courses. This "practical content" is both excessive and inadequate. Much effort is spent learning the language and fighting the system. A great deal of time is wasted correcting picayune errors while fundamental problems are ignored. "Practical details" consume time better spent on the theoretical or intellectual content of the course.

Also, the programs that students write are seldom used by others and rarely tested extensively. Students do not get the feedback that comes from having a product used, abused, rejected, and modified. This lack of feedback is very bad education. Students and faculty often believe they have done a very good job when they have not. Inadequate analyses and unsystematic work are often rewarded and reinforced by high grades.

There is no doubt that students cannot learn programming without writing programs, but we should not be teaching programming. Small assignments should have the same role as problems in a mathematics class and often should be graded the same way. The computer and the person grading the program both provide feedback, but the computer is often quite demanding about arbitrary details while ignoring substantial weaknesses in the program. The person who grades the program should be tolerant on matters of arbitrary conventions but should pay attention to the fundamental issues.

Properly run cooperative education programs provide the desired transition between academia and employment. Students produce a real product and get feedback from interested users. Review and guidance from faculty advisors is essential to integrate the work experience with the educational program. Project courses can and should be replaced by such a program. The use of the computer in academic courses can be greatly reduced.

## Student needs versus faculty interests

I do not expect these remarks and proposals to be popular with the faculty of CS departments. We all have considerable emotional investment in the things we have learned and intellectual investment in the things we teach. Many faculty want to teach courses in their research areas in the hope of finding students to work on their projects. Moreover, my criticism of the education we now provide is unavoidably a criticism of the preparation of my younger colleagues.

A university's primary responsibilities are to its students and society at large. It is unfortunate that they are often run for the comfort and happiness of the teachers and administrators. In this matter, the interests of our students and society coincide. It is not in the students' interest to make them perform engineering without being prepared for that responsibility. Nor is it in their interest to give them an education that prepares them only to be technicians. Too many graduates end up "maintaining" commercial software products, which is analogous to electrical engineers climbing poles to replace cables on microwave towers.

My industrial colleagues often complain that CS students are not prepared for the jobs they have to do. I must emphasize that my proposals will not produce graduates who can immediately take over the responsibilities of an employee who has left or been promoted. That is not the role of a university. Universities should not be concerned with teaching the latest network protocol, programming language, or operating system feature. Graduates need the fundamentals that will allow a lifetime of learning new developments; the program I have proposed provides those fundamentals better than most current CS programs.

CS departments should reconsider the trade-off in their courses between mature material and new developments. It is time for them to reconsider their role, to ask whether the education of computing professionals should not be the responsibility of engineering schools. ■

## Acknowledgments

I have developed these views through a great many conversations with engineers, mathematicians, and computer professionals around the world. The contributors are too numerous to mention. Selim Akl, David Lamb, and John van Schouwen made helpful suggestions about earlier drafts. The referees made several helpful comments.

# A Software Engineering Bibliography

David Budgen and Pearl Brereton

These pages list some of the source material that we use for classes that we teach on Software Engineering and also identify some papers and books that refer to particular topics in greater depth. The list does not purport to be comprehensive, but it does provide pointers to most of the key papers and texts. (For a comprehensive set of references, the list in Ian Sommerville's book is about as good a source as will be found anywhere.)

## 1. Know your Journals

While relevant papers are published in a wide range of journals, some are specifically targeted at Software Engineering themes. Key journals to be aware of are:

**ACM Software Engineering Notes.** Essentially a 'fast print' journal used for short and topical papers.

**Communications of the ACM**. (CACM) At one time this published some quite technical papers, but in recent years it has changed its slant somewhat and now tends to publish more review-style papers. These often provide a very readable introduction to a topic.

**IEEE Software.** Similar to the CACM, but almost entirely review-style papers.

**Computer**. More general than *IEEE Software*, the papers are more technical in nature while still being well presented and readable.

**IEEE Transactions on Software Engineering**. (TSE) Publishes fairly 'heavy' technical papers. Standards are generally high, but a bit uneven over the years.

**Information & Software Technology**. Publishes some quite readable and useful papers, including some that are tutorial in style. Papers on Software Engineering form a large part of its content.

**Journal of Systems & Software.** Another fairly 'heavy' journal that concentrates mostly on research papers. Again, the content is a bit uneven.

**Software Engineering Journal**. UK-based (published by the IEE in conjunction with the BCS). Quite technical in terms of the content of most of the papers.

**Software—Practice & Experience**. Papers tend to be quite long and technical. Widely read in industry, it seeks papers that report on experience with new ideas.

**Software Maintenance: Research & Practice**. Some useful papers that provide tutorial or survey introductions to aspects of maintenance.

Other, more specialist journals (for example, the *Journal of Object Oriented Programming Systems*) are also available, and so the above list is not meant to describe all of the journals that might usefully be consulted.

Many papers are published in conference proceedings. A particularly relevant series is the *Proceedings of the International Conferences on Software Engineering*, published jointly by IEEE/ACM. The IEEE also publishes a number of tutorials on particular topics that are essentially collections of the main reference papers for the given topic. Tutorials often provide a useful source for finding a paper without needing to locate a copy of (possibly) obscure journal issues.

## 2. General Textbooks

In the ideal, we suggest that *everyone* should read the following book at least once, in order to understand just what our courses are addressing:

*The Mythical Man-Month*, F.P. Brooks, Jr., Addison-Wesley, 1982

This is a collection of quite readable essays drawn on Professor Brooks' experiences with the earliest large-scale software development. A twentieth anniversary edition has recently been produced and an interesting excerpt from this is published as:

"The Mythical Man-Month After 20 Years," F.P. Brooks, Jr., *IEEE Software*, Sept. 1995, pp. 57–60.

Our current "preferred" overview books are:

1. *Software Engineering*, (5th ed.), I. Sommerville, Addison-Wesley, 1995.
2. *Software Engineering Principles and Practice*, Hans Van Vliet, Wiley, 1993.

Another good book is:

*Software Engineering: A Practitioner's Approach* (Third Ed.), R. Pressman, McGraw-Hill, 1987

and a book which takes a more business-oriented view of Software Engineering is:

*The New Software Engineering*, S. Conger, Wadsworth, 1994

## 3. The Software Problem

There are many papers and books that deal with the crises that have been occurring for the last twenty years or so in producing large software-based systems. The various papers (and the book) produced by Barry Boehm of TRW are particularly influential. A useful overview of some current trends in tackling the issues involved is provided in:

"Programming in the Large," C.V Ramamoorthy, V. Garg, and A. Prakash, *IEEE Trans. Software Eng.*, Vol. SE-12, July 1986, pp. 769–783.

**Operational lifetimes**—a survey by J.F. Green et al., "Dynamic Planning and Software Maintenance—A Fiscal Approach," Naval Postgraduate School, US Dept. of Commerce, NTIS, 1981, suggested that mean lifetimes for programs were climbing steeply. Over the period of a decade, the mean lifetime had climbed from three years to seven or eight years.

**Human capacity to process information**—the classical paper on this, frequently cited (and probably rarely read) is:

"The Magical Number Seven, Plus-or-minus Two: Some limits on our Capacity for Processing Information," J. Miller, *Psychological Rev.*, Vol. 63, 1956, pp. 81–97.

Later authors have pointed out that Miller's paper is really concerned with *events*, rather than with discrete items of information (such as the use of a variable), but the concept seems intuitively attractive nonetheless.

The following paper by Brooks contains some good points for debate:

"No Silver Bullet: Essence and Accidents of Software Engineering," F.P. Brooks, Jr., *Computer*, Vol. 20, No. 4, Apr. 1987, pp. 10–19.

and some of these are answered by David Harel in:

"Biting the Silver Bullet: Toward a Brighter Future for System Development," D. Harel, *Computer*, Vol. 25, No. 1, Jan. 1992, pp. 8–20.

Both papers are eminently readable.

## 4. The Software Lifecycle

The texts by Sommerville, Van Vliet, and Pressman, as well as most other introductory books, discuss this. The specific details of the phases may vary, but the overall flow usually doesn't. The life-cycle isn't necessarily an asset, and two papers that challenge its usefulness are:

1. "Life Cycle Concept Considered Harmful," D.D. McCracken and M.A. Jackson, *ACM Software Eng. Notes*, Vol. SE7, No. 2, 1982, pp. 29–32.
2. "Stop the Life-Cycle, I Want to Get Off," G.R. Gladden, *ACM Software Eng. Notes*, Vol. SE7, No. 2, 1982, pp. 35–39.

There are various other opinions expressed for and against in the issues of *Software Engineering Notes* immediately following the one containing these papers.

Barry Boehm has advocated the use of the *Spiral Model* for describing the software development process. A good description of this is in:

"A Spiral Model of Software Development and Enhancement," B.W. Boehm, *Computer*, Vol. 21, May 1988, pp. 61–72.

## 5. Configuration Management

A recent book giving good coverage is:

*Configuration Management,* W Tichy, Editor, Wiley, 1994

and a useful review paper is provided by:

"Concepts in Configuration Management Systems," S. Dart, *Proc.3rd Int'l Workshop in SCM*, ACM Press, New York, 1991.

## 6. The Design Problem

A book that (not surprisingly) covers much of the coursework in this area is:

*Software Design,* D. Budgen, Addison-Wesley, 1993

Three papers that describe studies conducted on software designers are:

1. "The Role of Domain Experience in Software Design," B. Adelson and E. Soloway, *IEEE Trans. Software Eng.*, Vol. SE-11, No. 11, Nov. 1985, pp. 1351–1360.
2. "A Field Study of the Software Design Process for Large Systems," B. Curtis, H. Krasner, and N. Iscoe, *Comm. ACM*, Vol. 31, No. 11, Nov. 1988, pp. 1268–1287.
3. "Requirements Specification: Learning Object, Process, and Data Methodologies," I. Vessey and S. Conger, *Comm. ACM*, Vol. 37, May 1994, pp. 102–113.

An interesting (and readable) paper that discusses the role of documentation and, in particular, whether we should document what was done or what should have been done is:

> "A Rational Design Process: How and Why to Fake It," D.L. Parnas and P.C. Clements, *IEEE Trans. Software Eng.*, Vol. SE-12, Feb. 1986, pp. 251–257.

## 7. Diagrammatical Forms for Design

A survey of diagrammatic forms and the roles they are used for in design, is in:

"Mapping the Design Information Representation Terrain," D.E. Webster, *Computer*, Dec. 1988, pp. 8–23.

## 8. Top-down Design Approach

The classical reference for this is:

"Program Development by Stepwise Refinement," N. Wirth, *Comm. ACM*, Vol. 14, 1971, pp. 221–227.

## 9. Structured Analysis and Structured Design

There are many good texts in the series of books published by Yourdon Inc., (most are now available from Prentice/Hall), although probably the best are:

1. *Structured Analysis and System Specification*, T. De Marco, Yourdon Inc, 1978.
2. *The Practical Guide to Structured Systems Design*, 2nd ed., Meilir Page-Jones, Prentice/Hall, 1988.
3. *Modern Structured Analysis*, E. Yourdon, Prentice/Hall, 1989.

## 10. Jackson Structured Programming (JSP)

The original (rather COBOL-flavored) reference for this is:

*Principles of Program Design*, M.A. Jackson, Academic Press, 1975.

There are several useful articles and examples given in:

*JSP & JSD: The Jackson Approach to Software Development,* 2nd ed.,

J.R. Cameron, IEEE Computer Society Press, Los Alamitos, Calif., 1988.

This is an excellent example of an IEEE tutorial.

Two good (and cheap!) introductory texts are:

1. *JSP—A Practical Method of Program Design,* L. Ingevaldsson, Chartwell-Bratt, 1986.
2. *Program Design Using JSP,* 2nd ed., M.J King and J.P. Pardoe, Macmillan, 1992

## 11. Jackson Structured Design (JSD)

The IEEE tutorial referenced for JSP also includes a section on JSD and the paper:

"An Overview of JSD," J.R Cameron, *IEEE Trans Software Eng.*, Vol. SE-12, Feb. 1986, pp. 222–240

provides precisely that. A good and concise book on JSD is:

*Jackson System Development,* A. Sutcliffe, Prentice/Hall, 1988.

## 12. Other Methods of Software Design

Two significant contenders here are SADT and SSADM. SADT has only recently been the subject of a book, although it has been in use for many years. This is:

*SADT: Structured Analysis and Design Technique,* D.A. Marca and C.L. McGowan, McGraw-Hill, 1988

For SSADM a good summary is available from:

*SSADM: Application and Context,* 2nd ed., E. Downs, P. Clare, and I. Coe, Prentice/Hall, 1992

## 13. Object-Oriented Development

A particular problem with this term is that there are different techniques describing themselves in this way! An early version of an OOD technique was outlined in the paper:

"Object-Oriented Development," G. Booch, *IEEE Trans. Software Eng.*, Vol. SE-12, Feb. 1986, pp. 211–221

although the approach described in this paper might now be more correctly described as being *object-based.* An earlier paper, on which some of Booch's work was based, is:

"Program Design by Informal English Descriptions," R.J. Abbott, *Comm. ACM,* Vol. 26, Nov. 1983, pp. 882–894.

A more recent work by Booch which gives lots of very good ideas about the object-oriented philosophy and provides an excellent framework is:

*Object-Oriented Analysis and Design With Applications,* G. Booch, Benjamin/Cummings, 1994.

A paper which gives a good summary of object properties and which tries to clarify the terminology is:

"The Essence of Objects: Concepts and Terms," A. Snyder, *IEEE Software,* Jan. 1993, pp. 31–42.

A recent and very good book that describes ideas about how to actually design with objects is:

*Object-Oriented Development: The Fusion Method,* D. Coleman et al., Prentice/Hall, 1994

For the really determined, the following paper provides details and abstracts of over 240 papers in this area:

"An Annotated Bibliography for Object-Oriented Analysis and Design," S. Webster, *Information & Software Technology*, Vol. 36, No. 9, Sept. 1994, pp. 569–582.

## 14. Information Hiding

The original (and much-cited) reference for this concept is:

"On the Criteria to be Used in Decomposing Systems into Modules," D.L. Parnas, *Comm. ACM*, Vol. 15, 1972, pp. 1053–1058.

To be honest, this paper is not easy reading by any means, but then the concept is not easily applied in any systematic manner either!

## 15. Comparison of Design Methods

There is surprisingly little literature of this form, and much of what there is can hardly be described as particularly complete. The later chapters of (Budgen, 1993) describe a number of design methods using a common framework. A much fuller comparison in a structured framework is provided in:

" 'Design Models' from Software Design Methods," D. Budgen, *Design Studies*, Vol. 16, No. 3, July 1995, pp. 293-325.

A fairly analytical look at the distinction between the object-oriented strategies and the longer-established forms is provided in:

"Object-Oriented and Conventional Analysis and Design Methodologies: Comparison and Critique," R.G. Fichman and C.F. Kemerer, *Computer*, Vol. 25, No. 10, Oct. 1992, pp. 22–39.

## 16. Formal Description Techniques

The study of FDTs (or less accurately, 'formal methods') is a major topic in itself. Their use is increasing, especially for 'critical' parts of systems, and everyone should really know something about their strengths and limitations. The most common need is probably to be able to *understand* a formal specification, rather than to be able to *create* one, and the following papers address that by providing some overview information as well as some simple examples.

1. "Seven Myths of Formal Methods" A. Hall, *IEEE Software*, Sept. 1990, pp. 11-19.

2. "A Specifier's Introduction to Formal Methods," J.M Wing, *Computer*, 1990, pp. 8–24.
3. "Notes on Algebraic Specifications," I.M. Bradley, *Information & Software Technology*, Vol. 31, No. 7, Sept. 1989, pp. 357–365.

## 17. Verification, Walkthroughs and Testing

A useful reference is:

"An Engineering Approach to Software Test Data Design," S.T. Redwine, *IEEE Trans. Software Eng.*, Vol. SE-9, 1983, pp. 191–200.

## 18. Programming Environments

There are plenty of research papers that cover plans for IPSE and APSE development, but these are mainly published in conference proceedings. A particular series of relevance is:

*Software Engineering Environments*, Ellis Horwood, 1988, 1989, 1991 (Vols 1–3)

*Software Engineering Environments*, IEEE Computer Society Press, Los Alamitos, Calif., 1993

with Volume 3 being particularly useful as an introduction to Process Modeling. There is also the book:

*Software Engineering Environments: Automated Support for Software Engineering*, Alan Brown, A.N. Earl, and J McDermid, McGraw-Hill, 1992

## 19. Software Maintenance

Two interesting papers covering this topic include:

1. "Problems in Application Software Maintenance," B.P. Lientz and E.B. Swanson, *Comm. ACM*, Vol. 24, No. 11, Nov. 1981, pp. 763–769.
2. "Mental Models and Software Maintenance," D.C. Littman et al., *J. Systems & Software*, Vol. 7, 1987, pp. 342–355.

Of course, there is also a specialist journal, as mentioned in the opening section.

## 20. Cost Modeling

A survey paper often cited is:

"Software Cost Estimation: Present and Future," S.N. Mohanty, *Software Practice & Experience*, Vol. 11, 1981, pp. 103-121

which gives a comparative review of a number of cost models. Boehm's COCOMO model is summarized in:

"Software Engineering Economics," B.W. Boehm, *IEEE Trans. Software Eng.*, Vol. SE-10, 1984, pp. 4–21

and also in the following book, although this chiefly describes the Putnam Model:

*Cost Estimation for Software Development*, B. Londeix, Addison-Wesley, 1987

## 21. Software Metrics

Recent years have produced a lot of papers on various aspects of metrics. A good survey of the field is given in:

*Software Metrics: A Rigorous Approach*, N.E. Fenton, Chapman & Hall, 1991.

Some papers covering important aspects are:

1. "Software Function, Source Lines of Code, and Development Effort Prediction: A Software Science Validation," A.J. Albrecht and J.E. Gaffney, *IEEE Trans. Software Eng.*, Vol. SE-9, No. 6, Nov. 1983, pp. 639–648.
2. "An Evaluation of Some Design Metrics," B. Kitchenham, L.M. Pickard, and S.J. Linkman, *Software Engineering J.*, Vol. 5, Jan. 1990, pp. 50–58.
3. "Evaluating Software Complexity Measures," E.J. Weyuker, *IEEE Trans. Software Eng.*, Vol. 14, No. 9, Sept. 1988, pp. 1357–1365.

Three recent papers which examine wider aspects about the meaning and use of metrics, and which discuss the whole question of how to measure software qualities, are:

1. "Software Measurement: A Necessary Scientific Basis," N. Fenton, *IEEE Trans. Software Eng.*, Vol. 20, No. 3, Mar. 1994, pp. 199-206.
2. "A Critique of Three Metrics," M. Shepperd and D.C. Ince, *J. Systems & Software*, Vol. 26, No. 3, Sept. 1994, pp. 197-210.

3. "Towards a Framework for Software Measurement Validation," B. Kirchenam, S.L. Pfleeger, and N. Fenton, *IEEE Trans. Software Eng.*, Vol. 21, No. 12, Dec. 1995, pp. 929–943.

# Software Engineering Standards

Richard H. Thayer

## Introduction

A *standard* is: (1) An approved, documented, and available set of criteria used to determine the adequacy of an action or object or (2) A document that sets forth the standards and procedures to be followed on a given project or by a given organization.

A *software engineering standard* is: (1) a set of procedures that define the processes for and/or (2) descriptions that define the quantity and quality of a product from a software engineering project.

This list of software engineering standards was compiled from numerous sources: The two primary sources were:

- *Survey of Existing and In-Progress Software Engineering Standards,* Business Planning Group, IEEE Software Engineering Standards Committee, Version 1.1, August 8, 1994.
- Thayer, R.H., and A.D. McGettrick, *Software Engineering: A European Perspective*, IEEE Computer Society Press, Los Alamitos, Calif., 1993.

This document lists the current and available national and international software engineering standards and also provides a list of the sources of these standards keyed to the individual standards. Note: many of the standards can be purchased from general standards organizations such as the American National Standards Institute and other distributor of technical documents

## Standards Development Organizations

Standards generally come from many different organizations and institutions:

- International standards are standards that are issued by organizations that are international in scope, for instance, IEC or ISO.
- National and multi-national standards are created under the direction of a national standards organization, for instance, NIST, CSA, U.S. DOD, or an organization representing a group of nations, for instance, CEN.
- Professional standards are standards created by professional organizations whose primary criteria for membership are individuals in a profession, such as EE, or a group of professions, such as IEEE Computer Society or ASTM.
- Other professional standards are created by organizations whose primary criteria for membership are organizations who are interested in promoting the welfare of a particular industry, for instance, EIA or ECMA.

## Acknowledgments

Thanks to my Scottish colleagues who helped me identify standards development organizations in the United Kingdom and Europe: Dr. Robin Hunter, University of Strathclyde, and Ms. Anne McCullock, University of Stirling.

## Standards Sources

The standards listed in this compendium come form:

**AECL**—Atomic Energy Canada Limited, c/o Ontario Hydro H12 D27, 700 University Avenue, Toronto, Ontario M5G 1X6 Canada

**AFNOR**—Association Française de Normalisation, Tour Europe - Cedex 7, F-92049, Paris La Defense, France

**AIAA**—American Institute Aeronautics and Astronauts, 370 l'Enfant Promenade, S.W., Washington, DC 20024-2518 USA

**ANS**—American Nuclear Society, 555 N. Kensington Avenue, La Grange Park, IL 60525 USA

**ANSI**—American National Standards Institute, 11 W. 42nd Street, 13th Floor, New York, NY 10036 USA

**ARINC**—Airlines Electronic Engineering Committee, 2551 Riva Road, Annapolis, MD 21401. USA

**AS**—Standards Association of Australia, Standards Australia, P.O. Box 1055, Strathfield NSW, Australia 2135

**ASME**—American Society of Mechanical Engineers, 345 East 47th Street, New York, NY 10017, USA

**ASQC**—American Society for Quality Control, 310 West Wisconsin Avenue, Milwaukee. WI 53203, USA

**ASTM**—American Society for Testing and Materials, 1916 Race Street, Philadelphia, PA 19103, USA

**ATA**—Air Transport Association of America, 1709 New York Avenue, N.W., Washington DC 20006, USA

**BCS**—British Computer Society, P.O. Box 1454, Station Road, Swindon SN1 1TG England, U.K.

**BS**—British Standards Institution, Linford Wood, Milton Keynes MK14 6LE England, UK

**CCITT**—International Telegraph and Telephone Consultative Committee (Comité Consultantif International de Télégraphique et Téléphonie.), 12, rue de Varembé, CH-1211 Genèva 20, Switzerland

**CEN**—European Committee for Standardization (Comité European de Normalisation), Rue de Stassart 36, B-1050 Brussels, Belgium

**CSA**—Canadian Standards Association, 178 Rexdale Boulevard, Rexdale, Ontario M9W IR9 Canada

**CSSC**—Canadian System Security Centre, Communications Security Establishment, P.O. Box 9703 Terminal, Ottawa, Canada K1G 3Z4

**DIA**—U.S. Drug Information Association, P.O. Box 3113, Maple Glen, PA 19002-8113, USA

**DIN**—Deutsches Institut für Nomrung e.V., Burggrafenstrasse 4-10, Postfach 1107, D-1000 Berlin 30, Germany

**DOD**—Department of Defense, Standardization Documents Order Desk, Building 4D, 700 Robins Avenue, Philadelphia, PA 19111-5094, USA

**ECMA**—European Computers Manufacturing Association, Rue de Rhône 114, CH-01204, Genèva, Switzerland

**EEA**—Electronic and Business Equipment Association, Russell Square House ,10-12, Russell Square, London, SC1B 5AE U.K.

**EIA**—Electronics Industry Association, 2001 Pennsylvania Avenue, NW, Washington, DC 20006, USA

**EPRI**—Electric Power Research Institute, 3412 Hillview, Palo Alto, CA 94304, USA

**ESA**—European Space Agency, European Space Research and Technology Centre (ESTEC), European Space Agency, Postbus 299, NL-2200 AG Noordwijk, The Netherlands

**FAA**—Federal Aviation Authority, Department of Transportation, 800 Independence Avenue, S.W., Washington DC 20591, USA

**FDA**—Federal Food and Drug Administration, Washington DC 20330, USA

**FIPS PUBS**—Federal Information Processing Standards Publication. *Published by NIST*

**GER GFMT**—German Federal Ministry of Transport, Bonn, Germany

**GER KBST**—Federal Ministry of Interior, (Budenesministerium des Innern), KBSt, Postfach 170290, D-53198 Bonn, Germany

**GER MOD**—German Ministry of Defense, Riit III, Einsteinstrasse 20, D-8012 Ottobrun, Germany

**GISA**—German Information Security Agency (Bundesamt für Sicherheit in der Infromationstechnik (BSI)), Bundesanzeiger Verlagsges. mbH, Postfach 10 05 34, D-50445 Koein, Germany

**GPA**—Gas Processors Association, 6526 East 60th Street, Tulsa, OK 74145, USA

**IAEA**—International Atomic Energy Agency, Wagramerstrasse 5, P.O. Box 1700, A-1400 Vienna, Austria

**IEC**—International Electrotechical Commission, 3, rue de Varembé, P.O. Box 131, CH- 1211 Genèva 20, Switzerland

**IEE**—Institute of Electrical Engineers, Michael Faraday House, Six Hills Way, Stevenage, Hertfordshire, SG1 2SD England, U.K.

**IEEE**—The Institute of Electrical and Electronic Engineers, 445 Hoes Lane, Piscataway, NJ 08854, USA

**ISA**—Instrument Society of America, 67 Alexander Drive, P.O. Box 12277 Research Triangle Park, NC 27709, U S A

**ISO**—International Standards Organisation (International Organization for Standardisation), Central Secretariat, 1, Rue de Varembé, CH-1211 Genèva 20, Switzerland

**JIS**—Japanese Industrial Standards, c/o Standards Department, Agency of Industrial Science and Technology, Ministry of International Trade and Industry, 1-3-1, Kasumigaseki, Chiyoda-Ku, Tokyo 100, Japan

**JPL**—Jet Propulsion Laboratory, California Institute of Technology, 4800 Oak Grove Drive, Pasadena, CA 91109, USA

**JTC1**—Joint Technical Committee 1, Joint committee from ISO and EC for information technology. *See IEEE for additional information on standards*

**NASA**—National Aeronautics and Space Administration, Technical Standards Division, Washington. DC 20546, USA

**NATO**—North Atlantic Treaty Organization, B-01110 Brussels, Belgium

**NATO DPC**—NATO Defence Planning Committee, c/o North Atlantic Treaty Organization (NATO), B-1110 Brussels, Belgium

**NISO**—National Information Standards Organization, P.O. Box 1056, Bethseda. MD 20827, USA

**NIST**—National Institute for Standards and Technology, Standards and Codes Information: Room A163, Bldg. 411, Gaithersberg, MD 20899, USA

**NMTBA**—Association for Manufacturing Technology, 7901 West Park Drive, McLean, VA 22102, USA

**NRC**—Nuclear Regulatory Commission, Washington DC, 20005 USA

**NSA**—National Security Agency, Fort George G. Meade, MD, USA

**NSAC**—Nuclear Safety Analysis Center, 3412 Hillview Avenue, Palo Alto, CA 98430, USA

**RTCA**—Requirements and Technical Concepts for Aviation, 1140 Connecticut Avenue, N.W.. Suite 1020, Washington DC 20036, USA

**SAE**—Society for Automotive Engineers, 400 Commonwealth Drive, Warrendale, PA 15096, USA

**SDA**—Scottish Enterprises, 120 Bothwell Street, Glasgow G2 7JP Scotland, U.K. (Formerly the Scottish Development Agency)

**SIS**—Standardiseringskommishion i Sverige, Box 3295, S-10366 Stockholm, Sweden

**SPAIN**—Asociación Española de Normalización y Certificación (AENOR), Calla Fernández de la Hoz, 52, E-28010 Madrid, Spain

**STRS**—Stennis Technical Reports Server, NASA Stennis Space Center Technical Reports, Stennis Space Center, MS 39529

**UK DOH**—United Kingdom Department of Health, Skipton House, 80 London Road, London SWE1 6WL England, U.K.

**UK DOTI**—United Kingdom Department of Trade and Industry, Information Technology Division, 151 Buckingham Palace Road, London SW1 9SS England, U.K.

**UK HSE**—United Kingdom Health and Safety Executive, HSE Books, P.O. Box 1999, Sudbury, Suffolk CO10 6FS England, U.K.

**UK MOD**—Ministry of Defence, Directorate of Standardization, Kentigern House, 65 Brown Street, Glasgow G2 8EX Scotland, U.K.

**UK NCC** United Kingdom National Computing Centre, The, Oxford House, Oxford Road, Manchester, M1 7ED England, U.K.

## Software Engineering Standards

The standards listed in the compendium arc divided into 21 parts and 17 are the process as defined in DIS 12207 [1]: acquisition, supply, development, operation, maintenance, documentation, configuration management, quality assurance, verification, validation, joint review, audit, management, infrastructure, improvement and training. There are also 4 additional parts that include safety, terminology, user support, and miscellaneous.

[1 ] DIS 12207, *Information Technology - Software Life-cycle Process*, DEC 1993

## *1. Acquisition Standards*

| | |
|---|---|
| AFNOR Z67-131-HOM | Manual Describing the Purchaser-Provider Relationship for the Purchasing of A Software Package |
| AIAA G-043-92 | Guide for the Preparation of Operational Concept Documents. 32 pp. |
| ASTM E 623-89 | Guide for Developing Functional Requirements for Computerized Laboratory Systems. 6 pp. |
| ASTM E 731-90 | Guide for Procurement of Commercially Available Computerized Systems. 7 pp. |
| ASTM E1283-89 | Guide for Procurement of Computer-Integrated Manufacturing systems. 13 pp. |
| BS 6719-86 | Guide to Specifying User Requirements for a Computer-based System. 16 pp. |
| DIN 66 271 | Information Processing: Software—Dealing with Failures in Contractual Situations |
| DOD AFSC 800-5 | Software Development Capability/Capacity Review, 1987. 62 pp. |
| DOD MIL-HDBK-782 | Military Handbook, Software Support Environment Acquisition. 75 pp. |
| DOD MIL-STD-498 | Software Development and Documentation, 5 Dec 1994. |
| DOD MIL STD-1521B | Technical Reviews and Audits for Systems, Equipment, and Computer Programs, 4 Jun 1985. 125 pp. |
| DOD SEI-87-TR-23 | Method for Assessing the Software Engineering Capability of a Contractor, Sep 1987. |
| DOD STD 2168 | Military Standard - Software Quality Assurance Requirements, 29 Feb. 1988. 12 pp. |
| ECMA-4 | Flowcharts, Dec 1966, 17 pp. |
| GER MOD GEN DR 220 | Framework Decree for the Development and Acquisition of Material |
| FIPS PUB 56 | Guidelines for Managing Multivendor Plug-Compatible ADP Systems |
| IEEE 1029-1088 | Standard for Software Reviews and Audits |
| IEEE 1062-1993 | Recommended Practice for Software Acquisition. 40 pp. |
| UK MOD DEF-STAN 05-21 | Guide to Contractor Assessment. Computer software QA systems, Book 4 |
| UK MOD NES 620 | Requirements for Software for Use with Digital Processors, Naval Engineering Standard, Issue 3, 1986. |
| JPL D-4000 | JPL Software Management Standards Package, Dec 1988. |
| NATO NAT-PRC-4 | Government Evaluation of Contractor Software Quality Assurance Program |
| NIST S.P. 500-180 | Guide to Software Acceptance |
| NIST S.P. 500-136 | An Overview of Computer Software Acceptance Testing |
| NIST S.P. 500-144 | Guidance on Software Package Selection |
| UK MOD DEFCON 143 | Software Development Questionnaire—for Inclusion with Invitations to Tender. 10 pp. |
| UK NCC-I | STARTS Purchaser's Handbook: Procuring Software-Based Systems |

## *2. Supply Standards*

| | |
|---|---|
| AFNOR Z67-131-HOM | Manual Describing the Purchaser-Provider Relationship for the Purchasing of A Software Package |
| DIN 66 271 | Information Processing: Software—Dealing with Failures in Contractual Situations |
| DOD AFSCP 800-14 | Software Quality Indicators, 20 Jan. 1987 40 pp. |
| DOD STD 2167A | Military Standard—Defense System Software Development, 29 Feb. 1988. 59 pp. |
| DOD TADSTAND E | Software Development, Documentation, and Testing Policy for Navy Mission Critical Systems. 16 pp. |

## *3. Development Standards*

| | |
|---|---|
| AFNOR Z67-103-1 FD | Analysis Engineering |
| AFNOR Z67-120-HOM | Minimal Packaging Identification |
| AFNOR Z67-121-HOM | Minimal Packaging Identification, Part 2 |
| AFNOR Z67-122-HOM | User Documentation for Consumer Software Packages |
| AIAA G 009-91 | Guide for Implementing Software Development Files Conforming to DOD-Std-2167A. 16 pp. |
| AIAA G 031-93 | Guide for Life-Cycle Development of Knowledge Based Systems with DOD-Std-2167A. 26 pp. |
| ANS 10.2-88 | Recommended Programming Practices to Facilitate the Portability of Scientific and Engineering Computer Programs. 12 pp. |
| ARINC 651 | Design Guidance for Integrated Modular Avionics |
| ASTM E 622-94 | Guide for Developing Computerized Systems 31 pp. |
| ASTM E 623-89 | Guide for Developing Functional Requirements for Computerized Laboratory Systems. 6 pp. |
| ASTM E 624-90 | Guide for Implementation Designs for Computerized Systems, Developing. 13 pp. |
| ASTM E 730-85 | Guide for Developing Functional Designs for Computerized Systems. 7 pp. |
| ASTM E1340-90 | Standard Guide for Rapid Prototyping of Computerized Systems. 11 pp. |
| BCS-90 | A Standard for Software Component Testing, ISS. 1.2. 69 pp. |
| BS 1646-84, Pt 4 | Specification for Basic Symbols for Process Computer, Interface and Shared Display/control Functions. 8 pp. |
| BS 4058-80 | DP Flowchart Symbols, Rules and Conventions. 32 pp. |
| BS 5487-82 | Specification of Single-hit Decision Tables. 20 pp. |
| BS 5887-80 | Code of Practice for Testing of Computer-Based Systems 8 pp. |
| BS 6078-81 | Guide to the Application of Digital Computers to Nuclear Reactor Instrumentation and Control. 20 pp. |
| BS 6224-87 | Design Structure Diagrams for use in Program Design and Other Logical Applications. 36 pp. |
| BS 6719-86 | Guide to Specifying User Requirements for a Computer-Based System. 16 pp. |
| BS 6976-90 | Program Constructs and Conventions for their Representations. 12 pp. |
| BS 7153-89 | Guide for Computer System Configuration Diagram (symbols and conventions). 18 pp. |
| BS 7738-94 | Specification for Information Systems Products Using Structured Systems Analysis and Design Method (SSADM) |
| BS DD 196-91 | Guide for Modular Approach to Software Construction, Operation and Test (MASCOT) |
| CCITT Z.100-104 84 | Functional Specification and Description Language (SDL) |
| DIN 66 001 | Information Processing: Graphical Symbols and Their Application: Layout of Graphical Symbols on a Template |
| DIN 66 241 | Information Interchange: Decision Tables Description Medium |
| DIN 66 261 | Information Processing: Nassi-Shneiderman Flowcharts Symbols |
| DIN 66 262 | Information Processing: Program Constructs and Conventions for Their Use |
| DIN 66 285 | Application Software: Principles of Testing |
| NATO DPC 85/60355 | Guide for Specifying Requirements for a Computer Based Systems |
| EIA CRB 1-89 | Managing the Development of Artificial Intelligence Software. 20 pp. |
| EPRI EL 3089 | Software Development and Maintenance Guidelines, Vols. 1–3. 1602 pp. |
| ESA PSS-05-0, Iss 2 | ESA Software Engineering Standards, Feb 1991. 133 pp. |

| | |
|---|---|
| ESA PSS-05-02 | Guide to the User Requirements Definition Phase, Issue 1, Oct 1991 |
| ESA PSS-05-03 | Guide to the Software Requirements Definition Phase, Issue 1, Oct 1991 |
| ESA PSS-05-04 | Guide to the Software Architectural Design Phase, Issue 1, January 1992 |
| ESA PSS-05-05 | Guide to the Software Detailed Design and Production Phase, Issue 1, May 1992 |
| FAA STD-026 | National Airspace System (NAS) Software Development. 15 pp. |
| FDA | Technical Reference on Software Development Activities. 42 pp. |
| GER MOD AU 253 | Handbook: Relations between GAM-T17(V2) and V-Model |
| GER MOD GEN DIR 253 | Handbook: Relations between GAM-T17(V2) and V-Model |
| GER GFMT BDLI | Testing, Documentation and Certification of Software-based Systems in Aircraft. 98 pp. |
| IEC 8631-89 | Information Technology—Program Constructs and Conventions for Their Representations, Second Edition. 12 pp. |
| IEE-2 | Guidelines for Assuring Testability, 1988. 88 pp. |
| IEEE 1008-1987 | Standard for Software Unit Testing. 25 pp. |
| IEEE 1016-1987 | Recommended Practice for Software Design Descriptions. 15 pp. |
| IEEE 1016.1-1993 | Guide to Software Design Descriptions. 26 pp. |
| IEEE 1074-1991 | Standard for Developing Software Life Cycle Processes. 111 pp. |
| IEEE 829-1991 | Standard for Software Test Documentation. 47 pp. |
| IEEE 830-1993 | Recommended Practice for Software Requirements Specifications. 32 pp. |
| IEEE 990-1992 | Recommended Practice for Ada as a Program Design Language. 15 pp. |
| ISA S5.3 | Graphic Symbols for Distributed Control/Shared Display Instrumentation, Logic, and Computer Systems. 14 pp. |
| JIS X 0121-86 | Documentation Symbols and Conventions for Data Program and System Flowcharts, Program Network Charts, and System Resource Charts. |
| JPL D-4001 | Overview and Philosophy, Dec 1988. 19 pp. |
| JPL D-4003 | [Sub]system Requirements Analysis Phase. Dec 1988. 26 pp. |
| JPL D-4004 | [Sub]system Functional Design Phase. Dec 1988. 21 pp. |
| JPL D-4005 | Software Requirements Analysis Phase. Dec 1988. 26 pp. |
| JPL D-4006 | Software Design Phase. Dec 1988. 36 pp. |
| JPL D-4007 | Software Implementation and Test Phase, Dec 1988. 42 pp. |
| JPL D-4008 | [Sub]system, Integration, Test, and Delivery Phase, DEC 1988. 33 pp. |
| JTC1 1028-79 | Information Processing—Flowchart Symbols |
| JTC1 2636-73 | Information Processing—Conventions for Incorporating Flowchart Symbols in Flowcharts. |
| JTC1 5806-84 | Information Processing—Specification of Single-Hit Decision Tables, First Edition. 16 pp. |
| JTC1 5807 | Documentation Symbols and Conventions for Data, Program and systems flowcharts, program network charts, and system resources charts. |
| JTC1 6593-85 | Information Processing—Program Flow for Processing Files in Terms of Record Groups, First Edition. 9 pp. |
| JTC1 8631-89 | Information Processing—Program Constructs and Conventions for Their Representation, Second Edition. 12 pp. |
| JTC1 8790 | Computer System Configuration Diagram Symbols and Conventions |
| NATO NAT-STAN-1 | Software Development Requirements |
| NATO NAT-STAN-6 | Software Testing Requirements |

| | |
|---|---|
| NATO NAT-STAN-8 | Software Specification Preparation Requirements |
| NIST S.P. 500-136 | An Overview of Computer Software Acceptance Testing |
| NIST S.P. 500-148 | Application Software Prototyping and Fourth Generation Languages |
| RTCA DO/178B-92 | Software Considerations in Airborne Systems and Equipment Certification. 100 pp. |
| SDA SDPG | Software Development Practice Guidelines |
| SIS TR 321 | System Development Reference Model |
| UK MOD NES 620 | Requirements for Software for Use with Digital Processors, Naval Engineering Standard, Issue 3, 1986. |

### *4. Operation Standards*

| | |
|---|---|
| ASTM E 626-90 | Guide for Evaluating Computerized Systems. 7 pp. |
| ASTM E1246-88 | Practice for Reporting Reliability of Clinical Laboratory Computer Systems. 6 pp. |
| BS 5760 | Reliability of Constructed or Manufactured Systems, Equipments, and Components |
| BS 6238-82 | Code of Practice for Performance Monitoring of Computer based Systems. 12 pp. |
| BS 6650-86 | Code of Practice for the Control of the Operation of a Computer. 12 pp. |
| BS DD 198-91 | Assessment of Reliability of Systems Containing Software. 82 pp. |
| DIN 66 273 | Measurement and Rating of Data Processing Performance |
| FIPS PUB 72 | Guidelines for the Measurement of Remote Batch Computer Service |
| FIPS PUB 96 | Guidelines for Developing and Implementing a Charging System for Data Processing Services |

### *5. Maintenance Standards*

| | |
|---|---|
| EPRI EL 3089 | Software Development and Maintenance Guidelines, Vols. 1-3. 1602 pp. |
| FIPS PUB 106-1984 | Guideline on Software Maintenance, Jul 1984 |
| IEEE 1219-1993 | Standard for Software Maintenance. 42 pp. |

### *6. Documentation Standards*

| | |
|---|---|
| AFNOR Z67-100-1FD | Computer Engineering Documentation Information Systems |
| AFNOR Z67-122-HOM | User Documentation for Consumer Software Packages |
| ANS 10.3-86 | Guidelines for the Documentation of Digital Computer Programs. 13 pp. |
| ANSI X3.88-81 | Computer Program Abstracts (R 1987). 14 pp. |
| ASME Y14-2-77 | Guidelines for Documenting of Computer Systems Used in Computer-Aided Preparation of Product Definition Data User Instructions. 9 pp. |
| ASME Y14-3-77 | Guideline for Documenting of Computer Systems Used in Computer-Aided Preparation of Product Definition Data Design Requirements. 9 pp. |
| ASTM E 627-88 | Guide for Documenting Computerized Systems. 6 pp. |
| ASTM E1029-84 | Guide for Documentation of Clinical Laboratory Computer Systems. 10 pp. |
| ASTM E919-90 | Specification for Software Documentation for a computerized System. 3 pp. |
| ATA 102 | Specification for Computer Software Manual |
| BS 4884 | Guidelines for Software Manuals |
| BS 5515-84 | Code of Practice for Documentation of Computer-Based Systems. 16 pp. |
| BS 7137-89 | Specification for User Documentation and Cover Information for Consumer Software Packages. 12 pp. |

| | |
|---|---|
| BS 7649-93 | The Design and Preparation of Documentation for Users of Application Software. 104 pp. |
| CSA Z243.15.1-79 | Basic Guidelines for the Structure of Documentation of Computer Based Systems. 16 pp. |
| CSA Z243.15.4-79 | Basic Guidelines for the Structure of Documentation of System Design Information. 18 pp. |
| CSA Z243.15.5-79 | Basic Guidelines for the Structure of Documentation of System Data. 15 pp. |
| DIN 66 230 | Information Processing: Software Documentation |
| DIN 66 231 | Information Processing: Documentation of Software Development |
| DIN 66 232 | Information Processing: Data Documentation |
| DOD ICAM-1 | ICAM Documentation Standards, IDS 150120000A, Air Force Materials Laboratory, 28 Dec 1981. 230 pp. |
| DOD ICAM-2-1980 | ICAM Software Documentation Standards, NBSIR 791940®, Air Force Materials Laboratory, Feb. 1980. 191 pp. |
| DOD MIL STD 490A | Specification Practices, 4 Jun 1985. 115 pp. |
| DOD STD 7935A | Automated Data Systems (ADS) Documentation, Oct 1988. 150 pp. |
| FIPS PUB 105-1984 | Guideline for Software Documentation Management, Jun 1984 |
| FIPS PUB 38-1976 | Guidelines for Documentation of Computer Programs, Federal Information Processing Standards Publication 38, 15 Feb 1976 |
| FIPS PUB 64-1979 | Guidelines for Documentation of Computer Programs and Automated Data Systems for the Initiation Phase, 1 Aug 1979 |
| GPA Std 9175-81 | Computer Program Documentation and Development Standards. 4 pp. |
| IEC TR9294-90 | Information Technology—Guidelines for the Management of Software Documentation, First Edition. 12 pp. |
| IEE-1 | Guidelines for the Documentation of Computer Software for Real-Time and Interactive Systems, 1990 2nd Edition. 116 pp. |
| IEEE 1063-1987 | Standard for Software User Documentation 17 pp. |
| JIS JX 0126-87 | Guidelines for the Documentation of Computer—Based Application Systems. 27 pp. |
| JTC1 6592-85 | Information Processing—Guidelines for the Documentation of Computer-Based Application Systems, First Edition. 20 pp. |
| JTC1 9127-88 | Information Processing—User Documentation and Cover Information for Consumer Software Packages, First Edition. 11 pp. |
| JTC1 9294-88 | Information Processing—Guidelines for the Management of Software Documentation, First Edition. 12 pp. |
| NASA-STD-2100-91 | NASA Software Documentation Standard, Jul 29, 1991. 172 pp. |
| NATO NAT-STAN-8 | Software Specification Preparation Requirements |
| NISO Z39.67 | Computer Software Description |
| SAE ARP 1623A-86 | Guide for Preparing an ECS Computer Program User's Manual. 5 pp. |
| UK MOD JSP 188 | Requirements for the Documentation of Software in Military Operational Real Time Computer Systems. |

### *7. Configuration Management Standards*

| | |
|---|---|
| BS 6488-84 | Code of Practice for Configuration Management of Computer-based Systems. 8 pp. |
| DOD ML STD 483A-1985 | Configuration Management Practices for Systems, Equipment, Munitions, and Computer Programs. 4 Jun 1985. |
| DOD ML-STD 973 | Configuration Management, 1990. 237 pp. |

| | |
|---|---|
| EIA CMB4-2-81 | Configuration Identification for Digital Computer Programs. 28 pp. |
| EIA CMB4-3-81 | Computer Software Libraries. 23 pp. |
| EIA CMB4-4-82 | Configuration Change Control for Digital Computer Programs. 47 pp. |
| EIA CMB4-lA-84 | Configuration Management Definitions for Digital Computer Programs. 46 pp. |
| EIA CMB5-A-86 | Configuration Management Requirements for Subcontractors/Vendors. 42 pp. |
| EIA CMB6-2-88 | Configuration and Data Management In-House Training Plan. 18 pp. |
| EIA CMB6-5-88 | Textbook for Configuration Status Accounting. 69 pp. |
| EIA CMB6-8-89 | Data Management In-House Training Course. 134 pp. |
| EIA CMB6-lB-90 | Configuration and Data Management References. 19 pp. |
| EIA CMB7-1 | Electronic Interchange of Configuration Management ]Data. 11 pp. |
| EIA CMB7-2 | Guideline for Transtioning Configuration Management to an Automated Environment. 17 pp. |
| ESA PSS-05-09 | Guide to Software Configuration Management, Issue 1, Nov 1992 |
| FAA-STD 021 | Software Configuration Management, FAA-STD-021, Federal Aviation Administration. 116 pp. |
| IEEE 1042-1987 | Guide to Software Configuration Management. 93 pp. |
| IEEE 828-1990 | Standard for Software Configuration Plans. 10 pp. |
| JPL D-4011 | Software Configuration Management Planning, Dec 1988. 21 pp. |
| UK MOD DEF-STAN 05-57/2 | Configuration Management Policy and Procedures for Defence Material (Standard) |
| NATO NAT-PRC-2 | Software Project Configuration Management Procedures |
| NATO STANAG 4159 | Configuration Management |
| NIST S.P. 500-161 | Software Configuration Management: An Overview |
| RTCA DO/178B-92 | Software Considerations in Airborne Systems and Equipment Certification. 100 pp. |

## *8. Quality Standards*

| | |
|---|---|
| AFNOR NF X50-162 | Customer-Supplier Relations—Guide to the Drawing up of the Quality Assurance Handbook |
| AFNOR NF X50-163 | Quality and Management—Typology and Use of the Documents Describing the Quality Systems |
| AFNOR NF X50-164 | Customer-Supplier Relations—Guide to the Drawing up of a Quality Assurance Plan |
| AFNOR Z67-123-HOM | Compliance Approach for An Application Package |
| AS 3563.1-1991 | Software Quality Management System, Part 1, Requirements. 10 pp. |
| AS 3563.2-1991 | Software Quality Management System, Part 2, Implementation Guide. 40 pp. |
| ASME N45.2.11 | Quality Assurance Requirements for the Design of Nuclear Power Plants |
| ASME NQA-2 1990 | Quality Assurance Program Requirements for Nuclear Power Plants. 101 pp. |
| ASME NQA-I 1989 | Quality Assurance Program Requirements for Nuclear Facilities. 69 pp. |
| ASQC Z-1.15 1979 | Generic Guidelines for Quality Systems |
| BS 4778-89 | Glossary of Terms used in Quality Assurance |
| BS 4891-72 | Guide to Quality Assurance. 28 pp. |
| BS 5750: Pt 1 | Specification for Design/Development, Production, Installation and Servicing |
| BS 5882-80 | Specification for a Total Quality Assurance Programrne for Nuclear Power Plants. 12 pp. |
| BS 7165-91 | Recommendations for Achievement of Quality in Software |
| CSA Q396.1.1-89 | Quality Assurance Program for the Development of Software Used in Critical Applications |
| CSA Q396.1.2-89 | Quality Assurance Program for Previously Developed Software Used in Critical Applications |

| | |
|---|---|
| CSA Q396.2.1-89 | Quality Assurance Program for the Development of Software Used in Non-Critical Applications |
| CSA Q396.2.2-89 | Quality Assurance Program for Previously Developed Software Used in Non-Critical Applications |
| DOD MIL-STD-1535B | Supplier Quality Assurance Program Requirements. 8 pp. |
| DOD ML-HDBK-286 | Military Handbook, A Tailoring Guide for DOD-STD-2168 (Defense System SQA Programs), 14 Dec 1990. 57 pp. |
| DOD STD 2168 | Military Standard—Software Quality Assurance Requirements, 29 Feb. 1988. 12 pp. |
| EEA-I | Guide to the Quality Assurance of Software |
| EIA CRR-2-89 | Computer Resources Discourse Quality Assurance Requirements for Software Processes. 9 pp. |
| ESA PSS-05-11 | Guide to Software Quality Assurance, Issue I, Jul 1993. |
| FAA STD 018a | Computer Software Quality Program Requirements, FAA-STD-018a, Federal Aviation Administration, Sep 1987. 11 pp. |
| FDA 90-4236 | Reproduction Quality Assurance Planning: Recommendations for Medical Device Manufacturers. 19 pp. |
| GER KBST V Model | Software Life Cycle Model (V-Model). 500+ pp. |
| IAEA-1987 | Quality Assurance for Computer Software |
| IEE-4 | Software Quality Assurance: Model Procedures 1990. 107 pp. |
| IEEE 1298-1993 | Software Quality Management System, Part 1: Requirements |
| IEEE 730-1989 | Standard for Software Quality Assurance Plans. 12 pp. |
| ISO 9000, Pt. 3 | Guidelines for the Application of ISO 9001 to the Development, Supply, and Maintenance of Software, 1991 |
| ISO 9000-87 | Quality Management and Quality Assurance Standards Guidelines for Selection and Use |
| ISO 9001-87 | Quality Systems—Model for Quality Assurance in Design/development, Production, Installation and Servicing. |
| ISO 9002-87 | Quality Systems—Model for Quality Assurance in Production and Installation |
| ISO 9003-87 | Quality Systems—Model for Quality Assurance in Final Inspection and Test |
| ISO 9004-87 | Quality Management and Quality Systems Elements Guidelines |
| UK MOD DEF STAN 05-95 | Quality System Requirements for The Development, Supply and Maintenance of Software. 16 pp. |
| UK MOD DEF-STAN 00-16/1 | Guide to the Achievement of Quality in Software. 57 pp. |
| UK MOD DEF-STAN 05-21 | Guide to Contractor Assessment. Computer software QA systems, Book 4 |
| NATO AQAP-13 | NATO Software Quality Control System Requirements, Aug 1981 |
| NATO AQAP-14 | Guide for the evaluation of a contractor's software quality control system for compliance with AQAP 13. |
| NRC BR-0617 | SQA Software Assurance Guidelines |
| NRC NUREG/CR-4640 | Handbook of Software Quality Assurance Techniques Applicable to the Nuclear Industry |
| RTCA DO/178B-92 | Software Considerations in Airborne Systems and Equipment Certification. 100 pp. |
| SPAIN UNE73-404 | Quality Assurance in the Nuclear Installations Information Systems (Spanish) 1990 |
| STRS STRITSE | Modeling a Software Quality Handbook (MSQH) |
| UK DOTI TickIT | Guide to Software Quality Management System Construction and Certification using EN29001, 30 Sep 1990. |

### *9. Verification Standards*

| | |
|---|---|
| ANS 10.4-87 | Guidelines for the Verification and Validation of Scientific and Engineering Computer Programs for the Nuclear Industry. 43 pp. |

| | |
|---|---|
| BCS-90 | A Standard for Software Component Testing, ISS. 1.2. 69 pp. |
| BS 5887-80 | Code of Practice for Testing of Computer-Based Systems. 8 pp. |
| DIN 66 285 | Application Software: Principles of Testing |
| DOD TADSTAND E | Software Development, Documentation, and Testing Policy for Navy Mission Critical Systems. 16 pp. |
| ESA PSS-05-10 | Guide to Software Verification and Validation, Issue 1, Feb 1994 |
| FIPS PUB 132-1987 | Guideline for Software Verification and Validation Plans, Nov. 1987 |
| FIPS PUB 101-1983 | Guidelines for Lifecycle Validation, Verification, and Testing of Computer Software, Jun 1983 |
| GER GFMT BDLI | Testing, Documentation and Certification of Software-based Systems in Aircraft. 98 pp. |
| GER KBST V Model | Software Life Cycle Model (V-Model). 500+ pp. |
| IEE-2 | Guidelines for Assuring Testability, 1988. 88 pp. |
| IEEE 1012-1992 | Standard for Software Verification and Validation. 26 pp. |
| IEEE 1059-1993 | Guide for Software Verification and Validation Plans. 121 pp. |
| NATO NAT-PRC-3 | Software Project Verification and Validation Procedure |
| NATO NAT-STAN-6 | Software Testing Requirements |
| NIST S.P. 500-165 | Software Verification and Validation: Its Roles in Computer Assurance and Its Relationships with Software |
| NSAC 38-1981 | Verification and Validation for Safety Parameter Display Systems, NSCAC-39, Nuclear Safety Analysis Center, Dec. 1981. |
| RTCA DO/178B-92 | Software Considerations in Airborne Systems and Equipment Certification. 100 pp. |

### *10. Validation Standards*

| | |
|---|---|
| ANS 10.4-87 | Guidelines for the Verification and Validation of Scientific and Engineering Computer Programs for the Nuclear Industry. 43 pp. |
| BCS-90 | A Standard for Software Component Testing, ISS. 1.2. 69 pp. |
| BS 5887-80 | Code of Practice for Testing of Computer-Based Systems. 8 pp. |
| DM 66 285 | Application Software: Principles of Testing |
| DOD TADSTAND E | Software Development, Documentation, and Testing Policy for Navy Mission Critical Systems. 16 pp. |
| ESA PSS-05-10 | Guide to Software Verification and Validation, Issue 1, Feb 1994 |
| FIPS PUB 101-1983 | Guidelines for Lifecycle Validation, Verification, and Testing of Computer Software, June 1983 |
| FIPS PUB 132-1987 | Guideline for Software Verification and Validation Plans, Nov. 1987 |
| GER KBST V Model | Software Life Cycle Model (V-Model). 500+ pp. |
| IEE-2 | Guidelines for Assuring Testability, 1988. 88 pp. |
| IEEE 1002-1992 | Standard Taxonomy for Software Engineering Standards. 26 pp. |
| IEEE 1059-1993 | Guide for Software Verification and Validation Plans. 120 pp. |
| NATO NAT-PRC-3 | Software Project Verification and Validation Procedure |
| NATO NAT-STAN-6 | Software Testing Requirements |
| NIST S.P. 500-165 | Software Verification and Validation: Its Roles in Computer Assurance and Its Relationships with Software |
| NSAC 38-1981 | Verification and Validation for Safety Parameter Display Systems, NSCAC-39, Nuclear Safety Analysis Center, Dec. 1981 |

### 4.11 Joint Review Standards

| | |
|---|---|
| DOD MIL STD 1521B | Technical Reviews and Audits for Systems, Equipment, and Computer Programs, 4 June 1985. 125 pp. |
| IEEE 1028-988 | Standard for Software Reviews and Audits. 35 pp. |
| JPL D-4014 | Work Implementation Planning |
| NATO NAT-STAN-5 | Software Design Review Requirements |

### 4.12 Audit Standards

| | |
|---|---|
| IEEE 1028-1988 | Standard for Software Reviews and Audits. 35 pp. |

### 4.13 Problem Resolution Standards

| | |
|---|---|
| IEEE 1044-1993 | Standard Classification for Software Anomalities. 20 pp. |

### 4.14 Management Standards

| | |
|---|---|
| AFNOR Z67-101-1FD | Recommendations for Conducting Computer Project |
| ASTM E 622-94 | Guide for Developing Computerized Systems. 31 pp. |
| ASTM E 792-87 | Guide for Computer Automation in the Clinical Laboratory. 44 pp. |
| ASTM E1113-86 | Guide for Project Definition of Computerized Systems. 6 pp. |
| DOD AFSCP 800-43 | Software Management Indicators, 31 Jan. 1986. 27 pp. |
| DOD AFSCP 800-45 | Software Risk Abatement, 30 September 1988. 31 pp. |
| DOD MIL STD 1521B | Technical Reviews and Audits for Systems, Equipment, and Computer Programs, 4 June 1985. 125 pp. |
| EIA CRB 1-89 | Managing the Development of Artificial Intelligence Software. 20 pp. |
| EIA DMG-1-86 | Data Management Implementation Guideline. 31 pp. |
| EIA DMG-2-89 | Automated Data Management Guideline. 31 pp. |
| ESA PSS-05-08 | Guide to Software Project Management Issue 1, July 1994 |
| GER MOD PROSIS | Project Control and Information Standard |
| IEEE 982.1-1988 | Standard Dictionary of Measures to Produce Reliable Software. 36 pp. |
| IEEE 982.2-1988 | Guide for the use of Standard Dictionary of Measures to Produce Reliable Software. 96 pp. |
| IEEE 1045-1992 | Standard for Software Productivity Metrics. 37 pp. |
| IEEE 1058.1 1987 | Standard for Software Project Management Plans. 16 pp. |
| IEEE 1061-1992 | Standard for a Software Quality Metrics Methodology. 88 pp. |
| IEEE 1209-1992 | Recommended Practice for Evaluation and Selection of CASE Tools. 35 pp. |
| IEEE 1220-1994 | Application and Management of the System Engineering Process |
| JPL D-4011 | Software Management Planning, Dec 1988. 21 pp. |
| NATO NAT-PRC-1 | Software Project Management Procedure |
| NATO NAT-STAN-7 | Software Metric Requirements |

### 15. Infrastructure Standards

| | |
|---|---|
| AIAA G-010-93 | Guide for Reusable Software: Assessment Criteria for Aerospace Applications. 22 pp. |
| DOD MIL-HDBK-59A | Computer-Aided Acquisition and Logistic Support (CALS) Program Implementation Guide. 216 pp. |

| | |
|---|---|
| DOD MIL-HDBK-347 | Mission Critical Computer Resources Software Support, May 1990. 77 pp. |
| DOD MIL-HDBK-782 | Military Handbook, Software Support Environment Acquisition. 75 pp. |
| ECMA 149 | PCTE: Portable Common Tool Interface |
| ECMA 158 | PCTE: C Programming Language Binding |
| ECMA 162 | PCTE: Ada Programming Language Binding |
| EIA IS-81 | CDIF—Framework for Modeling and Extensibility. 101 pp. |
| EIA IS-82 | CDIF—Transfer Format Definition |
| EIA IS-83 | CDIF—Standardized CASE Interchange Meta-Model |
| GER MOD GEN DIR 252 | Functional Tool Requirements (Standardized Criteria Catalogue) |
| GER MOD AU 252 | Functional Tool Requirements (Standardized Criteria Catalogue) |
| FIPS PUB 99-1983 | Guideline: A Framework for the Evaluation and Comparison of Software Development Tools, Mar 1983 |
| IEEE 1175 | Standard for Computing System Tool Interconnections |
| IEEE 1209-1992 | Recommended Practice for Evaluation and Selection of CASE Tools. 35 pp. |
| NIST S.P. 500-142 | A Management Overview of Software Reuse |
| NIST S.P. 500-155 | Management Guide to Software Reuse |
| UK MOD DEF STAN 00-17 | Modular Approach to Software Construction, Operation, and Test—MASCOT. 5 pp. |

### *16. Improvement Standards*

| | |
|---|---|
| DOD SEI-91-TR-24 | Capability Maturity Model for Software, Aug 1991. |
| DOD SEI-91-TR-25 | Key Practices of the Capability Maturity Model, Feb 1993. 404 pp. |
| IEEE 1044 1993 | Standard Classification for Software Anomalities. 20 pp. |
| SDA STD | Software Technology Diagnostic |

### *17. Training Standards*

| | |
|---|---|
| ASTM E 625-87 | Guide for Training Users of Computerized Systems 4 pp. |
| EIA CMB6-2-88 | Configuration and Data Management In-House Training Plan. 18 pp. |
| GER MOD GEN DIR 258 | Functional Requirements for Dp Education and Training |

### *18. Safety Standards*

| | |
|---|---|
| AECL STD-00-00902-001 | Standard for Software Engineering of Safety Critical Software |
| DIA-1 | Computerized Data Systems for Nonclinical Safety Assessment, 1988. |
| DIN V/VDE 0801 | Principles for Computers in Safety-Related System, 1989 (Preliminary Standard). 172 pp. |
| EIA SEB6-84 | A Method for Software Safety Analysis. 30 pp. |
| EIA SEB6-A-90 | System Safety Engineering in Software Development. 140 pp. |
| IAEA-1993 | State of the Art Report on Software Important to Safely in Nuclear Plants |
| IEC 880-86 | Software for Computers in the Safety Systems of Nuclear Power Stations, First Edition. 134 pp. |
| IEC 987-87 | Programmed Digital Computer Important to Safety for Nuclear Power Stations |
| IEE-5 | Software in Safety-Related Systems, Oct. 1989. |
| IEEE 1228-1993 | Standard for Software Safety Plans |
| NATO STANAG 4404 | Safety Design Requirements and Guidelines for Munition Related Safety Critical Computing Systems, Mar 1989 |

| | |
|---|---|
| UK DOTI SafeIT | A Framework for Safety Standards, May 1990. 56 pp. |
| UK HSE PSE Guidelines | Programmable Electronics Systems in Safety Related Applications, 1987. |

### *19. Terminology Standards*

| | |
|---|---|
| AFNOR X50-106-2 | Vocabularie Project Management |
| ASTM E1013-87a | Terminology Relating to Computerized Systems. 3 pp. |
| BS 4778-89 | Glossary of Terms used in Quality Assurance |
| CSA Z243.27 1-79 | Data Processing Vocabulary—Fundamental Terms. 35 pp. |
| CSA Z243.27 4-81 | Data Processing Vocabulary—Organization of Data. 38 pp. |
| CSA Z243.58-92 | Information Technology Vocabulary. 597 pp. |
| FIPS PUB 11-3 | Guidelines: American National Dictionary for Information Systems |
| IEEE 610.12-1990 | Glossary of Software Engineering Terminology. 85 pp. |
| JTC1 2382, Pt 20 | Information Processing—Vocabulary—System Development |
| NMTBA | Common Words as They Relate to NC Software |

### *20. User Support Standards*

| | |
|---|---|
| AFNOR Z67-110-1 FD | Ergonomics and Man-Computer Dialogue |
| AIAA R-023-92 | Recommended Practice for Human-Computer Interfaces for Space System Operations. 22 pp. |
| DIN 66 234 | VDU Work Station: Principles of Ergonomic Dialogue Design |
| ECMA TR 61 | User Interface Taxonomy |

### *21. Miscellaneous Standards*

| | |
|---|---|
| AFNOR X50-105 | Concepts |
| AFNOR Z67-102-1FD | Specification for Management Applications-Software |
| AIAA R-013-93 | Recommended Practice for Software Reliability. 70 pp. |
| ASTM E 792-87 | Guide for Computer Automation in the Clinical Laboratory. 44 pp. |
| ASTM E1206-87 | Guide for Computerization of Existing Equipment. 6 pp. |
| ASTM E1239 | Guide for Description of Reservation/Registration Admission, Discharge, Transfer (R-ADT) Systems for Automated Patient Care Information Systems. 10 pp. |
| ASTM E1246-88 | Practice for Reporting Reliability of Clinical Laboratory Computer Systems. 6 pp. |
| ASTM E1384 | Guide for Description for Content and Structure of an Automated Primary Record of Care. 11 pp. |
| BS 5760 | Reliability of Constructed or Manufactured Systems, Equipments, and Components |
| BS 6154-81 | Method for Defining Syntactic Metalanguage. 14 pp. |
| CEN ENV 40 003-90 | Computer Integrated Manufacturing (CIM): CIM Systems Architecture Framework for Modeling 26 pp. |
| CSSC-1 | The Canadian Trusted Computer Product Evaluation Criteria, Ver. 3, Jan. 1993. 208 pp. |
| ESA PSS-05-01 | Guide to the Software Engineering Standards, Issue 1, Oct 1991 |
| FDA CS-91-1.1 | Application of the Medical Device GMPS to Computerized Devices and Manufacturing Process. 24 pp. |
| FDA DS-9 | Reviewer Guidance for Computer-Controlled Medical |
| GER MOD AU 248 | Handbook DP—Security Requirements |

| | |
|---|---|
| GER MOD AU 251 | Methods Standards |
| GER MOD GEN DIR 248 | Handbook DP—Security Requirements |
| GER MOD GEN DIR 251 | Methods Standards |
| GER GFMT BDLI | Testing, Documentation and Certification of Software-based Systems in Aircraft. 98 pp. |
| GISA ITSEC 1.2 1991 | Information Technology Security Evaluation Criteria |
| IEC 643-79 | Application of Digital Computers to Nuclear Reactor Instrumentation and Control. 33 pp. |
| IEE-3 | The Software Inspection Handbook. 26 pp. |
| IEEE 1002-1992 | Standard Taxonomy for Software Engineering Standards. 26 pp. |
| NSA Spec. 86-16 | Security Guidelines for COMPSEC Software Development |
| SAE ARP 1570 | Flight Management Computer System |
| UK DOH GLP | Good Laboratory Practice—The application of GLP practices to computer systems, 1989. |
| UK MOD DEF 5169/11 | ImproveIT. 180 pp. |
| UK MOD DEF-STAN 00-41 | Practices and Procedures for Reliability and Maintainability, Parts 1-5. 171 pp. |
| UK MOD NES 620 | Requirements for Software for Use with Digital Processors, Naval Engineering Standard, Issue 3, 1986. |

# APPENDIX

## Software Engineering Survey Results

The Editors of this Tutorial have many years of experience in the practice and management of software engineering. Both of us attend conferences, subscribe to journals, visit libraries both here and abroad, access information available electronically, and try to read the current software engineering literature. We know, however, that we simply cannot be aware of, much less read or even scan, all sources of software engineering information. To overcome this "handicap," we determined that we should enlist the assistance of a large number of practitioners and researchers to help us identify the articles most suitable for inclusion in the Tutorial, and to identify those areas where there is a lack of suitable articles. We then identified over 200 software engineering professionals whose opinions we should solicit, and prepared a survey to send to them.

We also felt it was important to seek out software professionals outside the United States, since they would be likely to have access to journals, conferences, and other sources of material that would be less known in the United States. While most of the individuals surveyed resided in the US, there was also a significant number from other countries, including Canada, the UK, France, Germany, Spain, the Netherlands, Australia, and New Zealand.

Since the main objective of the Tutorial was to be useful in education and training, we particularly sought out software engineering educators from industry, government, and academia. Our primary sources for the mailing list were (1) the names of educators from a list provided by the Software Engineering Institute (SEI) and (2) the attendees at the SEI's Sixth Annual Conference on Software Engineering Education. To these lists we added software engineers whom we had meet at conferences and elsewhere as well as through correspondence.

Survey material included a cover letter, a list of papers under consideration at the time, and a response form. The cover letter is reproduced at the end of this Appendix. The list of papers was divided into 13 categories, matching the chapters of the book as envisioned at that time, and amounted to an overly-ambitious Table of Contents for the book in that it included 203 papers! The response form asked whether the recipient was familiar with each paper and, if so, to rate it on a scale of 1 ("marginal") to 5 ("must include"). Recipients were also asked to list any other papers worthy of inclusion and to identify possible authors for new papers for that category. Recipients were advised that they could nominate themselves to write new papers.

Space was also provided for recipients to make additional comments. Each recipient was asked if he/she wanted a complimentary copy of the Tutorial when it was published, and if we could use his/her name and affiliation in the Tutorial as a contributor.

The survey material was mailed in May, 1993, and responses were requested by June 30. Some addresses were determined to be incorrect and the forms had to be remailed. Some additional names were acquired. In these cases a later response date was permitted.

We received 70 responses that ranged from checking a few boxes to providing extensive comments and copies of recommended papers. Let us say at this point that the contributions were invaluable, and it would have been very difficult to compile the Tutorial without these responses. However, we were surprised to observe that

- Most responses agreed with us that there were very few papers in our list that really met the criteria
- There were very few usable suggestions for papers beyond those in the list
- There was not a large number of volunteers or ideas for authors of new papers.

We reluctantly concluded that there simply are not many good survey papers either on software engineering as a whole or on its subspecialties. (Indeed, some of the survey responses said this in so many words.) Apparently, as a field matures, papers are published on results of research and industrial practice and/or on ideas for further advances, but few are written to summarize the state of practice.

The range of opinions was surprising. It was not unusual for as many as five responses to describe a paper as a "must," while several others might specifically reject the same paper. The survey did provide a consensus on a few papers:

- Brooks, F.P., "No Silver Bullet: Essence and Accidents of Software Engineering," *Computer*. Vol. 20, No. 4, Apr. 1987, pp. 10–19.
- Parnas D.L., and P.C. Clements, "A Rational

Design Process: How and Why to Fake It," *IEEE Trans. Software Eng.*, Vol. SE 12, No. 2, Feb. 1986, pp. 251–257.

- Mills, H.D., M. Dyer, and R.C. Linger, "Cleanroom Software Engineering," *IEEE Software*, Vol. 4, No. 5, Sept. 1987, pp. 19–24.
- Fagan, M.E., "Design and Code Inspections to Reduce Errors in Program Development," *IBM Systems J.*, Vol. 15, No. 3, 1976, pp. 182–211.
- Leveson, N.G., "Software Safety: Why, What, and How," *ACM Computing Surveys*, June 1986.
- Brooks, F.P., Jr., "The Mythical Man-Month," *Datamation*, Dec. 1974, pp. 44–52
- Boehm, B.W., "Software Engineering Economics," *IEEE Trans. on Software Eng.*, Vol. SE-10, No. 1, Jan. 1984, pages 4–21.
- Boehm, B.W., "A Spiral Model of Software Development and Enhancement," *Computer*, Vol. 21, No. 5, May 1988, pp. 61–72.
- Humphrey, W.S., "Characterizing the Software Process: A Maturity Framework," *IEEE Software*, Vol. 5, No. 2, Mar. 1988, pp. 73–79.

The observant reader will note that we used less than half of these "consensus" articles. In the end the editors' judgment prevailed, particularly when we felt an article, though excellent when written, was obsolete or excessively long.

Based on the results of the survey, we reluctantly concluded that a Tutorial could not be compiled using a high percentage of existing papers and just a few new ones. The necessity of obtaining the new papers delayed publication by approximately a year, during which time we identified the areas where new papers were needed; solicited authors; and negotiated time in their busy schedules to write the papers. It goes without saying that we are grateful to these well-known and busy people for agreeing to write the papers.

The following individuals responded to the survey and agreed to allow us to acknowledge their contribution. The affiliations are those of June 1993, and may have changed since then.

Dr. A. Frank Ackerman
*Institute for Zero Defect Software*

Prof. Brent Auernheimer
*California State University, Fresno*

Dr. David Barstow
*Schlumberger Corp.*

Dr. Joan Bebb
*TRW, Inc.*

Mr. James Brownlee
*Center for Systems Management*

Mr. Fletcher Buckley
*Martin Marietta Corp.*

Prof. David Budgen
*University of Keele*

Capt. James Cardow
*Air Force Institute of Technology*

Mr. Peter Coad
*Object International, Inc.*

Dr. Ken Collier
*Northern Arizona University*

Prof. James Cross II
*Auburn University*

Dr. Darren Dalcher
*South Bank University*

Dr. Alan M. Davis
*University of Colorado at Colorado Springs*

Mr. Thomas Fouser
*Jet Propulsion Laboratory*

Dr. Lisa Friendly
*First Person, Inc.*

Ms. Suzanne Garcia
*Lockheed Missiles & Space Co.*

Mr. Robert Glass
*Computing Trends*

Prof. Donald Gotterbarn
*East Tennessee State University*

Ms. Martha Ann Griesel
*Jet Propulsion Laboratory*

Prof. David Gustafson
*Kansas State University*

Mr. Simon Harris
*Swinburne University of Technology*

Dr. Warren Harrison
*Portland State University*

Ms. Jennifer Harvey
*University of South Australia*

Dr. Sallie Henry
*Virginia Polytechnic Institute and State University*

Dr. William Howden
*University of California at San Diego*

Prof. Pei Hsia
*University of Texas at Arlington*

Dr. Robin Hunter
*University of Strathclyde*

Prof. Xiaoping Jia
*DePaul University*

Prof. Kemal Koymen
*Moorhead State University*

Dr. Arun Lakhotia
*University of Southwestern Louisiana*

Mr. Frank LaMonica
*US Air Force Rome Laboratory*

Mr. Pierre Y. Leduc
*Universite de Sherbrooke*

Prof. Michael Lutz
*Rochester Institute of Technology*

Mr. Jukka Marijarvi
*Nokia Telecommunications*

Chris D. Marlin
*Flinders University*

Dr. J. Luis Mate
*Polytechnic University of Madrid*

Dr. Ed Miller
*Software Research, Inc.*

Mr. John Musa
*AT&T Bell Laboratories*

Dr. Richard Nance
*Virginia Polytechnic Institute & State University*

Prof. Jeff Offutt
*George Mason University*

Dr. James Palmer
*George Mason University*

Prof. Ronald Peterson
*Weber State University*

Prof. Keith R. Pierce
*University of Minnesota, Duluth*

Dr. J.H. Poore
*University of Tennessee, Knoxville*

Mr. Robert Poston
*Interactive Development Environments*

Prof. Pierre N. Robillard
*Ecole Polytechnique—Montreal*

Mr. Paul Rook
*City University of London*

Mr. Walker Royce
*TRW, Inc.*

Mr. Terry Snyder
*Hughes Aircraft Co.*

Dr. Robert Steigerwald
*US Air Force Academy*

M.A. Stephens
*University of Wolverhampton*

Mr. Alan Sukert
*Martin Marietta Corp.*

Dr. Wim H. Walk
*Shell Research*

Dr. Anthony I. Wasserman
*Interactive Development Environments*

Prof. Timothy D. Wells
*Rochester Institute of Technology*

The editors also wish to acknowledge the assistance of Mr. Fernando Proaño, a graduate student at California State University, Sacramento, who helped reduce and analyze the survey results.

May 15, 1993

To: Instructors, practitioners, and researchers in software engineering

From: Richard Thayer and Merlin Dorfman

Subj: Survey of Software Engineering Papers

Richard Thayer and Merlin Dorfman, co-editors of two *IEEE Tutorials on Requirements Engineering,* are developing a new *Tutorial* volume on Software Engineering, containing papers describing the best current practices in the field of software engineering. The *Tutorial* will be approximately 500 pages in length, with about 400 pages consisting of new or reprinted papers, and the other 100 consisting of a glossary, references, chapter introductions, etc. The project has been approved by the IEEE Computer Society, with estimated dates of January 1994 for submission to the publisher and mid-1994 for publication.

The *Tutorial* is targeted for an upper-division or first- year graduate course in software engineering. This collection of reprints and original papers will enable instructors of software engineering to provide their students with the latest state-of-the-practice papers without the effort, inconvenience, and expense of obtaining numerous copyright clearances. This *Tutorial* can also be used in industry by organizations that are new to software development and/or wish to learn the current state of the practice. We believe this *Tutorial* will be a valuable contribution to the dissemination of software engineering knowledge.

We are asking professionals in the field of software engineering to help us select the best paper(s) in various topics, or to identify those areas where new papers are needed. This survey is being sent to approximately 400 software engineering instructors, practitioners, researchers, and authors, about two-thirds of them in the US and the remainder in Canada, Europe, and, in a few cases, the Far East. While no individual is expected to be an expert in all aspects of software engineering, we believe that the group contains sufficient expertise to make good selections in every topic.

Attached is a list of topics in software engineering, along with references to a few papers in each topic. The major purpose of listing these papers is to describe the intent of the topic subject rather than to dictate a choice of papers. May we ask you to indicate, on the *Survey Response Form*, each paper with which you are familiar by placing a check mark next to its number; and to rate with a number those papers that should be considered for inclusion in the *Tutorial.* A "1" would indicate a paper that is marginal for inclusion, while a "5" indicates a paper that should not be omitted under any circumstances. More than one paper may be recommended in a single topic. May we also ask you to add, in the indicated area after each topic, any papers that we have not listed that should be considered. We are looking for tutorial-type papers that describe the best current practice rather than unproven or speculative advances in the state of the art. The "ideal" paper is eight to ten pages in length, but it need not be from a well-known or refereed journal. Please cite a reference or, if convenient, mail us a copy. Finally, if you believe that there are no existing papers on a topic worthy of inclusion, please provide the name(s) of author(s) who are qualified to write a new paper. You may nominate yourself!

If you have a reading list for a software engineering course, we would appreciate a copy of that also.

IEEE has agreed that all participants in this survey will be provided, if they so request, a complimentary copy of the *Tutorial* when it is published. If you would like to receive a copy, please complete the enclosed request form and return it with the survey response. We have provided a postage- paid, pre-addressed envelope for return of the survey response and, if you wish, the request form. (For obvious reasons the return postage is not provided for non-U.S. participants.) Also, please keep this letter and notify us of any changes of address between now and the publication date. Finally please indicate if you wish your name and affiliation to be listed in the *Tutorial* as having contributed to the effort through participation in the Survey.

We have asked the IEEE Computer Society Press to send a copy of its current Publications Catalog to all survey recipients to ensure that you are familiar with the scope and contents of its tutorials, and we have enclosed a copy of the biographies from our *Requirements Engineering Tutorials* for those of you who are not familiar with our work.

To be sure that your inputs are available in time to be included, please return the survey by June 30, 1993. Thanks for your help.

Sincerely,

Richard H. Thayer, PhD
Professor in Computer Science
Sacramento State University, Sacramento
6540 Chiquita Way
Carmichael, CA 95608
Home tel: 916-481-5482
Home fax: 916-481-8778
Email: thayer@ecs.csus.edu

Merlin Dorfman, PhD
Technical Consultant
Lockheed Missiles & Space Co.
6072 Burnbank Place
San Jose, CA 95120
Home tel: 408-268-4219

Email: dorfman@netcom.com

## Biography of Merlin Dorfman

Merlin Dorfman, PhD, is a Technical Consultant in the Space Systems Product Center, Lockheed Martin Missiles and Space Company, Sunnyvale, Calif. He specializes in systems engineering for software-intensive systems (requirements analysis, top-level architecture, and performance evaluation), in software process improvement, and in algorithm development for data processing systems. He has performed concept exploration, system implementation, and operations and maintenance of data systems and has worked on proposal teams and company-funded technology projects as well as on development contracts. He was in charge of the development of the Automated Requirements Traceability System (ARTS). He was the first chairman of Space Systems Division's Software Engineering Process Group. He represented the Lockheed Corporation on the Embedded Computer Software Committee of the Aerospace Industries Association, and was Vice-Chairman of the Committee.

Dorfman wrote and taught a four-day course, "Software Requirements and Design Specifications," for Learning Tree International of Los Angeles, Calif. He co-teaches a two-week course in Software Project Management for the Center for Systems Management of Cupertino, Calif. He has been a guest lecturer on software systems engineering at the Defense Systems Management College. He is a Fellow of the American Institute of Aeronautics and Astronautics (AIAA), a member of its System Engineering Technical Committee, past chairman of the Software Systems Technical Committee, and past Chairman of the AIAA San Francisco Section, and is currently Assistant Director of Region 6 (West Coast). He is an affiliate member of the Institute of Electrical and Electronics Engineers (IEEE) Computer Society.

He has a BS and MS from the Massachusetts Institute of Technology and a PhD from Stanford University, all in Aeronautics and Astronautics. He is a registered Professional Engineer in the states of California and Colorado and is a member of the Tau Beta Pi and Sigma Gamma Tau honorary societies.

He is co-editor of two IEEE Tutorial volumes, *System and Software Requirements Engineering* and *Standards, Guidelines, and Examples for System and Software Requirements Engineering*, and co-editor of a volume, *Aerospace Software Engineering*, in the AIAA "Progress in Aeronautics and Astronautics" Series.

## Biography of Richard H. Thayer

Richard H. Thayer, PhD, is a Professor of Computer Science at California State University, Sacramento, California, United States of America. He travels widely where he consults and lectures on software requirements analysis, software engineering, project management, software engineering standards, and software quality assurance. He is a Visiting Researcher at the University of Strathclyde, Glasgow, Scotland. As an expert in software project management and requirements engineering, he is a consultant to many companies and government agencies.

Prior to this, he served over 20 years in the U.S. Air Force as a senior officer in a variety of positions associated with engineering, computer programming, research, teaching, and management in computer science and data processing. His numerous positions include six years as a supervisor and technical leader of scientific programming groups, four years directing the U.S. Air Force R&D program in computer science, and six years of managing large data processing organizations.

Thayer is a Senior Member of the IEEE Computer Society and the IEEE Software Engineering Standards Subcommittee. He is Chairperson for the Working Group for a Standard for a Concept of Operations (ConOps) document and past chairperson for the Working Group for a Standard for a Software Project Management Plans. He is a Distinguished Visitor for the IEEE Computer Society.

He is also an Associate Fellow of the American Institute of Aeronautics and Astronautics (AIAA) where he served on the AIAA Technical Committee on Computer Systems, and he is a member of the Association for Computing Machinery (ACM). He is also a registered professional engineer.

He has a BSEE and an MS degree from the University of Illinois at Urbana (1962) and a PhD from the University of California at Santa Barbara (1979) all in Electrical Engineering.

He has edited and/or co-edited numerous tutorials for the IEEE Computer Society Press: *Software Engineering Project Management* (1988), *System and Software Requirements Engineering* (1990), and *Software Engineering—A European Prospective* (1992). He is the author of over 40 technical papers and reports on software project management, software engineering, and software engineering standards and is an invited speaker at many national and international software engineering conferences and workshops.